CAPTAIN TOM DRAKE,

OR

ENGLAND'S HEARTS OF OAK,

BY

W. L. EMMETT, ESQ.

PROFUSELY ILLUSTRATED.

LONDON:

A. RITCHIE & Co., 6, RED LION COURT, FLEET STREET.

CONTENTS.

BOOK THE FIRST.

BOOK THE SECOND.

CONTENTS.

CONTENTS.

SEQUEL.—ADMIRAL TOM.

THE END.

CAPTAIN TOM DRAKE.

OR,

ENGLAND'S HEARTS OF OAK.

By W. L EMMETT.

CHAPTER L

OUR HERO.

"I TELL you, madam, the young scamp shall be packed off at once. Confound him! I won't put up with his tricks any longer; he's always at mischief. He shall go."

"But Gregory——"

"Don't Gregory me. He shall pack off to sea, I'm determined."

"He is so young."

"Young—fiddlesticks! he's old enough to be always in some confounded mess or other. He's a perfect torment—and I won't stand it any longer."

Mr. John Gregory—Old Gregory he was usually called—sat in his breakfast parlour; his head was swathed in bandages—his feet were rolled up in blankets—his nose was red and swollen like a large beetroot—his eyes were bunged up with neuralgia, and each foot was the size of two with the gout.

As he addressed these testy words to the lady who was seated at the table, a sudden wrench of his two continuous visitants—gout and lumbago—sent him back puffing and panting in his easy chair.

The lady, who was no other than Mrs. Drake, the mother of our hero, remained silent after he had spoken. She was evidently used to him, and knew how useless it would be to attempt to alter his determination.

Mrs. Drake was Gregory's own sister; he had a half-sister, who was also married, and, like Mrs. Drake, had a child, a boy, who was named Reuben.

Between the two half-sisters there had never been much affection.

Mrs. Drake was lady-like, generous, and gentle at heart.

Her half-sister was proud and designing; she had striven to obtain the best offer for herself when the two were unmarried, and now her jealous cares were bestowed upon her boy, whom she sought to advance in his uncle's favour by any unscrupulous means.

It was her continued complaints that helped to set old Gregory against our hero.

The two boys were so different in their natures that they were continually at variance, and seldom a day passed without some direful account of Tom's delinquency being poured into the ears of the old gentleman.

John Gregory was a bachelor, rich, and the guardian of an old friend's child—Minnie Atherton —a fair young girl, heiress to immense wealth.

Mrs. Harpy cherished the hope of not only getting Gregory to leave the bulk of his money to her son, but also of marrying him to Minnie Atherton, when he was of age, that he might come into possession of the Atherton estates.

It was easy enough for Reuben to assist his mother in her mercenary schemes; he was a cunning, vulgar-minded boy, capable of any meanness, while Tom was too high-spirited and noble to stoop to the sneaking hypocrisy his cousin practised in order to get into the good graces of his uncle.

There was a tragic portion of their family history with which both the boys were unacquainted, though it had been the means of depriving each of a father.

Both Tom's and Reuben's father were officers in the navy—on board the same ship, in fact.

Lieutenant Harpy had conceived a fatal passion for Mrs. Drake, but finding his insinuating addresses indignantly repelled, resolved upon basely gaining access to her chamber, disguised and masked, when Lieutenant Drake was, as he thought, away.

But at the moment of this attempted outrage, Tom's father returned.

He hurled the villain from the window, but not before he had recognised him.

He kept his secret to himself, not even informing his wife. Lieutenant Harpy never even suspected that his treachery was known.

But when the ship arrived at the station, it chanced that both officers were sent together.

Then Tom's father took the villain by the throat, and challenged him to mortal combat.

Foot to foot they stood on the brink of a jagged cliff. Simultaneous reports of their pistols and both fell lifeless into the sea beneath.

This was the way Tom's father avenged his honour, and that was how the two cousins were left fatherless.

After old Gregory had twisted about in his chair for a minute or two in the most agonising contortions, he broke out afresh,—

"Besides, isn't he always picking a quarrel with his cousin Reuben? It's time they were separated. I'll send him to sea."

Mrs. Drake had no time to reply before the door was forced open with a snap, and the subject of their conversation, our hero, stood before his relatives.

He was a well-formed youth, slight in figure, but with well-knit limbs and expanded chest. His face was delicate in feature, though his complexion was somewhat bronzed with exposure to the sun.

His eyes were calm in their expression, but penetrating and fearless beyond his years. His rich brown hair was clustered carelessly about his broad intelligent forehead.

Young as he was, there was something in his graceful form and careless defiance of bearing indicative of proud undaunted resolve and energy.

His whole *physique* was that of a delicately nurtured boy, sensitive in mind, high-spirited and generous, but unyielding and brave.

At a glance you could see that he was fitted for some high destiny, and that a word was enough to kindle the fiery nature that lay hidden beneath his frank boyish looks and symmetrical form.

The mother's heart filled with proud joy as she gazed on her handsome son, and even old John Gregory felt more gentle towards the boy whom he had been urged by Reuben's mother to repel and mistrust.

"Well, you young scamp," he exclaimed, "is that the way to come blundering into your uncle's room, like an elephant breaking through a jungle—confound you? What do you mean?"

"I did not know you were here, uncle."

"Didn't know, you plague! Where did you think I was, and what's that you've got there?"

"A bird's-nest, uncle; I got it from the tree on the peak. Minnie said she would like to have it, so I climbed up and got it, with the eggs."

"And risked breaking your neck, and putting me to the trouble of seeing after your funeral, besides breaking your mother's heart," bawled old Gregory. "Do you know, you plague, that the peak is three hundred feet above the precipice, and a slip would have dashed you to atoms—eh, sir?"

"I did not stop to think, sir; Minnie wanted it, and I got it."

"You did, you young rascal, as we see; but there, it's of no use talking to you. I've made up my mind what to do with you. I'll send you where you won't have a chance of half-killing poor Reuben again."

"Reuben's as big as me," Tom replied, boldly.

"He's not such a young tiger as you've turned out, you scamp! Pray, sir, what had he done to you that you should knock him over a fence, and send him in with a nose like—like—like a boiled tomato?" old Gregory added, lost for a simile.

"Because he insulted me, and said what was not true."

"Indeed!"

"He said my mother depended on your bounty; and he told me he was to marry Minnie Atherton, and that I shouldn't have anything to say to her when she grows up."

"No more you shall—nor he either, you brace of young schemers. Do you think I would allow my old friend General Atherton's child to be thought of by such scapegraces as you! Do you think, sir, I'd have people say I gave his child and her fortune to my own penniless relations? So that's your fine notion of the truth, is it? You first dare to say you have pretensions to Minnie, and then punch his head because he won't believe you; get out of my sight, sir—out, sir, this instant, or I'll kick you out!"

Considering the old fellow's disabled condition, this threat was, to say the least of it rather strong; but Tom did not take advantage of him, he stood quietly waiting for what was to come next.

"You—you dog!" exclaimed Mr. Gregory, presently; "I'll have you sent off somewhere where you won't plague me any more, and where they'll warm your jacket for you if you attempt any more of your tricks. You shall go, sir, and never expect to see Miss Minnie again."

"Then I won't go," Tom said, abruptly.

"What!" cried the old gentleman, furious with passion. "You impertinent jackanapes! you scamp! you rascal!—oh, my foot!—you villain! all through you I've this attack. Oh—whew—oh!"

"You must be good and obey your uncle," Mrs. Drake remarked; "he has been kind to you and to me, and you must not be ungrateful."

"I don't want to be ungrateful," Tom replied, his clear eye moistening, "and I don't want to do wrong; but everyone seems against me. Uncle Gregory always blames me, and takes Reuben's part. And where does he want to send me to now?"

"To sea, you dog!" roared the old fellow, convulsed with agony; "to sea, where you'll be properly salted, and made a man of—whew! Come here, you scoundrel, will you? Lift my foot on to the sofa carefully; you let it fall, and I'll kill you."

Tom, who in his heart deeply sympathised with his uncle's afflictions, hastened to him, and tenderly raised his foot to the required elevation.

John Gregory grunted out a surly "thankee," and waving Tom and his mother from the room, rolled on his back, and groaned himself into a profuse perspiration.

CHAPTER II.

THE CLIFF IN THE BAY.—REUBEN HARPY ATTEMPTS A WICKED DEED.

OUR hero went from his uncle's presence with his mind fired by the vision of the new life promised him.

The sea!

Often had he gazed from the windows of the comfortable old-fashioned home—gazed across the blue waters of the quiet bay it overlooked—watched the sails of distant vessels as they skimmed over the sea beyond, and thought how glorious a life it must be on board some gallant ship, sailing from end to end of the world, touching at distant climes, and now and then engaging in some desperate conflict with a pirate.

Often had he longed to be on board.

Many a longing, almost envious look, had he cast on the dashing uniforms of the officers or middies who at times came up from the beach, and wished that his lot was cast among them.

So full was his mind of this new idea that his eager questions troubled his loving mother, who could not bear the thought of parting with him.

She answered him quietly, trying to still his enthusiasm, and telling him of the hardships and perils of life at sea.

But the very means she took to check only newly enkindled his ardent expectations.

The recital of the terrors of a tempest, when the

wave ship rolled like a mere atom on the foaming waves—of the daring encounters with pirates, caused the boy's heart to yearn for a share in such enterprises.

And when his mother left him, she saw, with pain, that he was bent on his new and exciting career.

Truth to tell, old Gregory, when he decided on sending him to sea, did so in the full belief that the lad would soon distinguish himself, and rapidly gain promotion in the service.

He knew that, with all his faults, Tom was as brave as a young lion.

The only fear he had was lest his hot blood should lead him into serious quarrels with his companions.

If Tom had been his only nephew, the old gentleman would never have found fault with him; but the care Reuben's mother took to make her son a paragon of virtue, while she used every means of undermining his affection for Tom, with the fact that, in spite of every admonition, the headstrong boy was constantly in some reckless scrape, lessened his regard for him; and Tom, though of an affectionate disposition, was too proud to cringe before his uncle as his cousin Reuben did.

Tom left his mother, and scampered off to the woods to dream of future greatness as a naval commander, for, of course, he expected to rise, in a few weeks, to the highest grade.

Many a daring deed he planned and executed in his mind, and it was nearly evening before he thought of returning homewards.

He had nearly reached his uncle's home when he was aroused from his pleasant dreams and castle-building by hearing his name called in an eager childish voice.

The boy's heart leapt at the sound, and a hot rush of blood deepened the healthy glow on his cheeks.

He knew the voice belonged to his little sweetheart, Minnie Atherton.

She was standing on the brink of a running stream, preparing to cross the fording-stones, over which the clear water rippled.

As she stood there, with her golden hair fluttering in the breeze, and her light robes clinging to her fragile form, with her hand outstretched for him to help her across, and her pleasing blue eyes turned gladly towards him, she formed so pretty a picture that our youthful hero was, for the moment, only able to stand mutely gazing upon her.

And while he hesitated, spell-bound by her loveliness, a quick footstep sounded behind him, and his cousin, Reuben Harpy, hurried to Minnie to help her over the stream.

With the bound of a young deer, Tom sprang between him and Minnie, and the two boys stood confronting each other, each with a foot on the first stone of the ford.

They were nearly of the same age, but different in every aspect of form and feature.

Reuben was considerably shorter in stature than Tom, and though his frame was broad, and evidently possessed of great muscular power, his body had a crouching attitude when contrasted with the upright bearing of Tom.

Nor was the difference in features less marked and characteristic of their natures.

The boy Reuben had a sullen heavy cast of countenance; his eyes were deeply set, and leered maliciously from under their thick brows. His complexion was sallow, his lips were almost colourless.

Tom was the first to speak.

"Go back, Reuben," he said; "I will see Minnie home."

The boy's eyes sparkled maliciously.

"I wouldn't leave you with her," he replied. "Uncle told me not; you know he can't trust you."

"Don't say that again," Tom exclaimed, his eyes flashing, "or I'll knock you into the pond."

"Yes; you'd like to push me in there and drown me, if nobody saw you," replied the cowardly boy, "only you're afraid."

"Don't say I'm afraid," Tom cried, elbowing Reuben out of his path, "or I will."

"No, you'll not, you spiteful young vagabond," a voice exclaimed, and Reuben, with malicious satisfaction, stepped back as the new-comer approached.

He was a short, thick set man, in naval attire; he had an ugly cast of visage, coarse, repulsive, and exceedingly hairy.

He was well known to both the boys, from the fact of his being a frequent visitor at Mr. Gregory's, to whom he was known as Lieutenant Andrew Sanderson, officer in the King's service.

This man was the sole confidant and admirer of Reuben's mother.

An unholy tie existed between them, which, while it placed her in his power, rendered him useful as an ally.

As might have been expected, Sanderson hated Tom.

He feared the boy's penetration; besides, he stood in the way of a devilish design, by which he hoped to benefit himself.

A gleam of self-satisfied triumph shone in his steel-blue eyes as he came near Tom.

"A lucky thing for you," he said, "I'm here in time to prevent your murderous wickedness, you little villain. If I had my will I'd thrash all that out of you."

"You'd never thrash me," Tom answered, loftily; "try it if you dare."

Sanderson's face grew green with passion.

He dared not strike the fearless boy, much as he desired to stretch him at his feet.

"If I had you with me on board ship," he exclaimed, savagely, "I'd teach you what I dare do, mind that. I shall, perhaps, some day, and then I'll whip that tiger spirit out of you."

He turned to Reuben.

"Take Miss Minnie's hand, and we'll see her safe home. Away from there, young whelp."

Reuben took a step forward; but, swift as lightning, Tom was in front of him.

"Nobody takes Minnie home but me!" he cried; "and don't you call me that name again, or I'll CHOKE you."

The excited boy looked as if a word more would have made him leap at the man's brutish throat.

Perhaps Sanderson thought he might, for he did not attempt to interfere further with Tom, who, taking Minnie's hand, helped her across the stream, and escorted her home.

Sanderson and Reuben followed close behind, nursing the evil passions which they did not feel inclined to vent on the excitable boy.

Sanderson did not fail to enlarge upon this episode before Mr. Gregory.

He represented Tom's conduct in so murderous a light, that the old gentleman grew frightened, and determined on hurrying our hero's equipment for sea.

Tom did not fret about this anxiety to get him out of the way.

His only regret was that Minnie would be left behind with Reuben; but then, he thought, he would soon come back an officer, and renowned for exploits, when he could claim her as his bride, and challenge Reuben to mortal combat if he dared to seek her hand.

Tom noticed sometimes, that when his prospects as a middy were spoken of, a cunning grin curled the lips of Sanderson, and a meaning glance passed between him and Reuben's fallen mother; but he did not trouble himself about the cause.

He had reason enough afterwards to bitterly wish he had been warned by it.

Old John Gregory, since his last misconduct, had finally disgraced him, and would not allow him in his presence, but petted Reuben with every proof of affection, though often his heart reproached him when he happened to catch sight of the fearless boy going to or from the house, and he would growl out sullenly,—

"The scamp will be a man some day—come home with the gold epaulette on his shoulder—I'll forgive him then—not before—not before."

But the old gentleman's forgiveness was destined to come earlier.

Seated at his open window one calm summer evening, he saw his graceful little ward, pretty Minnie Atherton, run down to the little lake near his house, and enter a beautiful fairy-like boat he had built expressly for her.

It was an exquisitely-shaped vessel, chastely painted and gilt, and Minnie, who was quite an expert rower, looked very much like a fairy herself as she took the feather-shaped oars in her tiny hands and glided gently over the smooth water.

"Wrong of her to get in by herself with no one near," grunted the old gentleman, "wrong—very wrong."

With graceful movements the young child skilfully guided the boat up and down the lake.

Suddenly he saw her bend with the oars, and impel the boat straight from the bank.

His surprise was great when he saw that she had done this to get away from Reuben, who had advanced to the brink of the lake.

The swiftness of the movement brought the fragile vessel in contact with a cluster of water-lilies, and, to the old gentleman's dismay and horror, the boat, in a moment capsized, and the child sank.

John Gregory forgot gout, lumbago, neuralgia, and the other ills that afflicted him, as he sprung up, and leaning half out of the window, cried out, lustily,—

"In—in, boy!—save her!—rescue my child, my darling child!—she is drowning! Help—help!"

His cries, and the suddenness of the echo, seem to have startled away all the little nerve Reuben might have possessed—for, in place of leaping in to rescue Minnie, he turned away, and ran wildly towards the house, screaming, like a girl, for help.

"My God!" the old gentleman exclaimed, in palsied accents, "I shall lose her. The coward! Oh, that I could get there! Help, help—she will die! Ah, thank Heaven! he is there—he sees her; noble boy!—he leaps in—has gone down—now he comes up—her face is above the water—he swims to the bank—oh, God be praised!—God be praised!"

The old gentleman's voice sank to a tremulous whisper, and the tears coursed down his cheeks, as his head sank to the sill of the window.

Tom had seen the accident. He was far away—too far, he feared, to be in time—but, nimble as a young deer, he was soon at the edge of the lake—passing the craven-hearted Reuben on the way.

One swift plunge, and he had dived down to the bottom. A practised swimmer, he knew how to rise with Minnie encircled with one arm.

She was senseless when he brought her to the bank, and the boy, with a strength he had never before experienced, held her to his breast, and ran with her to his uncle's house.

John Gregory met him on the threshold.

"My boy—my brave boy," he murmured; "lay her down here. Alas, poor child!—now lift her head. She breathes. Kneel, boy—kneel—kneel, and thank God she is safe!"

Reverently did our hero go down upon his knees, and thank Heaven, when he saw Minnie open her fine blue eyes, and look fondly round.

A slight shiver ran through her gentle frame, and then she seemed herself again.

"Don't cry, pa, dear," she said to John Gregory, whose cheeks were saturated with tears; "I am safe now. I didn't see Tom, or I should not have been afraid. Wasn't he noble, pa, to save me, when Reuben ran away?"

"He is a brave, noble-hearted boy, whom I have wronged and treated harshly," exclaimed the old fellow, warmly clasping Tom's hands, and pressing them to his heart. "But he shall be recompensed for it—he shall. As for that coward—that Reuben—who left you to die, I shall never like him again."

Reuben sneaked in at that moment, blubbering like the chicken-hearted cur he was.

Old Gregory turned upon him fiercely.

"You let my Minnie drown," he said. "Why didn't you jump in to save her?"

"I couldn't swim," blubbered Reuben, ramming his knuckles into his watery eyes.

"Couldn't swim, you brute; you're not good for anything except cowardice and deceit. Don't stand snivelling there, you big baby—go and try to learn to swim, and be a man."

"Don't scold him, pa," Minnie said. "I didn't want him to save me."

She looked fondly at our hero.

Tom returned the glance with one of equal affection.

For the last few moments his brain had been in a whirl.

He had heard ringing in his brain those electric words of hers.

"I didn't see Tom, or I shouldn't have been afraid."

Minnie got over her immersion sooner than might have been expected; in a little while she laughed merrily at the adventure.

Reuben's designing mother and her associate, Sanderson, could have wrung Tom's neck when they heard of his heroic act, by which he had restored himself to his uncle's favour.

John Gregory had been brave as boy and man, and, from the bottom of his honest old heart, he despised a coward.

In proportion as he idolized our hero for his gallant courage, so did he dislike the craven-hearted Reuben.

The tables were turned. Reuben was in lasting disgrace, while Tom stood on the summit of his uncle's esteem.

Instead of being ashamed of his own cowardice, Reuben allowed his malignant mind to brood over his downfall until his feelings were full of bitterness against his high-spirited cousin, and in his heart he cherished a savage animosity which Tom's noble nature could never have dreamed of.

One evening, about a week after this occurrence, Tom had gone up to his usual resting-place at sunset, the brow of a cliff above the bay, where he could lie at full length, indulging in blissful visions of the future, and watching the vessels in the bay or out at sea.

Already, in his fancy, he had advanced through rapid stages of promotion, and had returned to claim Minnie for his wife, an officer's epaulette on his shoulder, and sword girded by his side, when he thought he heard a stealthy step creeping behind him.

At the moment he was seated on the very brink of the cliff, the view down to the clear blue waters fascinating him with its subtle sense of danger.

He knew that few people could sit there and not become dizzy, and it was more out of daring hardihood than anything else that he had taken up so perilous a position.

The sun was just setting in all its grand and glorious beauty across the sea.

The air was soft and cool.

For hours he could have gazed on the enchanted scene.

The footsteps disturbed the current of his thoughts, but he had not time to turn or rise before a shadow was thrown beside him, a shadow which he instinctively felt belonged to his cousin Reuben, and he could almost feel his ill-odoured breath as he heard a hoarse whispered cry of hate given at the same time that he received a push that thrust him over the top of the cliff.

His breath went from him in the giddy descent.

Not a gasp, not a cry escaped his lips.

He had made a vain wild clutch at the rock as he slipped down headlong.

There was a stunning and suffocating crash—and after that darkness.

And then the sullen, murderous visage of Reuben Harpy, which had peered over the edge as far as he dare venture, was withdrawn as the craven boy, trembling in every limb, shivering with fear at his own dastardly act, reeking with clammy sweat, but savagely exulting even in his quaking heart, made his way down the grassy slope.

CHAPTER III.

TWO JOLLY SALTS —TOM FINDS HIMSELF IN THE HANDS OF THE PRESS GANG.

THE cliff, from the brink of which Tom had made his abrupt descent—a descent that would have taken him to another world, and made this history unnecessary, had he not been providentially watched over, even as the sparrows are, which do not fall to the ground unobserved, though oftentimes mercilessly riddled with shots from the guns of cockney sportsmen—overhung the bay, its crest projecting considerably over its base, which was hollowed out in immense fissures, through which the waters sometimes penetrated, but which in calm weather were left secure and dry.

One or two of these hollows led underground, and were taken advantage of by certain enterprising gentlemen who were addicted to habits of a smuggling nature.

There was one passage, indeed, that had been delved into till its outlet ran directly under an old-fashioned inn of not very good repute, situate some distance inland, and much frequented by weather-beaten mariners whose characters were not of the best, and regarding whose health sundry gentlemen, known as Custom-house officers, were particularly and intrusively anxious.

It happened that on the eventful evening of Tom's unprepared-for header, that two gentlemen of the smuggling fraternity were snugly ensconced in this particular fissure, and were indulging, like two tried boon-companions, in long draughts of smuggled brandy, when the apparition of Tom, tumbling down with the speed of Vulcan's anvil, when its owner was kicked out of heaven, startled their vision, and caused the worthy who was then pulling at the flask to pause, after a hearty swig, and say to his messmate,—

"Jerry, did anything tumble before your top-lights?"

To which Jerry emphatically replied,—

"No; nothing didn't."

"Dash my timbers if I didn't see a summat a-tumbling all adrift overboard; and, as sure as my name's Bob Hauler, some blessed lubber's took a header off the cliff. I'll peep out and see."

"And be nabbed by some of them darned revenue sharks? Take the advice of a true tar, Bob, and stay where you are. 'Tain't no business of ours if any lubberly lout wants to go to Davy Jones's locker, or take dinner with old Neptune; so have another swig, and stick here as I do—like a limpet to a crag, or a barnacle to a ship's bottom."

The advice of the redoubtable Jerry was thrown away on Bob Hauler—a weather-beaten, brawny youngster, of devil-may-care rollicking aspect—who had already crept to the extremity of the fissure, and now startled his mate by singing out,—

"Avast there, mate! Here's a fellow-creature drowning in the water!"

Jerry Mizzen, such was his name, staggered to his feet.

"Where away, messmate?" he cried.

But Bob Hauler had already flung off his jacket, and leapt into the bay.

He re-appeared in a few minutes, holding the inanimate face of Tom above the water.

A few strokes of his brawny arms brought them both to a landing-place; and Jerry Mizzen relieving Bob Hauler of his boyish burthen, carried Tom in, and by the time his gallant preserver had clambered inside, was pouring copious draughts of brandy down our hero's throat, grumbling all the while, in true sailor style,—

"What the devil did he perch up there for, like a mouse on a peacock's tail? He might have took his davey that he'd go, like a plummet, stern over bows into the bay. Well, the dousing, perhaps, will do him good. Ah, that's bringing him too a bit, the lubber."

Bob Hauler was silent.

He had lifted our hero's head to his knee, and was as anxiously waiting for signs of returning consciousness as if Tom was his own son.

"Jerry," he said, presently.

"I'm all ears," Jerry replied, attempting a laugh.

"Well, they are long," Bob remarked, looking at the articles in question, which were as much like a pair of flappers as anything, "Jerry, I'd like to know who pushed him over."

"Pushed! why, in course he tumbled off his perch himself."

"I'll go short of grog for a week if he did; I know the lad; he's nephew of old Gregory, up yonder; a fine brave lad, too, with spirit enough in him for anything. I've seen him perched aloft, there, for hours; his brain wouldn't get dizzy with looking down here, mark my words! Someone thrust him over, and I should very much like to find out the gentleman that did."

Tom had by this time opened his eyes.

He was still giddy with his fall, but felt reassured when his gaze met the careless countenance of Bob Hauler.

"Well, my young skylark," Bob cried, "how d'ye feel? Any the worse for your dousing, eh?"

"Cheer up, my hearty," put in Jerry Mizzen, "and tell us how you felt when you came through the air like a corkscrew. Rouse up, lad; we'll take care of you. Drink, my lad, and tell us how you came to tumble off."

"I didn't tumble," Tom replied; "I was pushed into the bay by Reuben Harpy."

"Hang me if I didn't think so!" Bob Hauler cried. "But never mind, Master Tom, you're born for better things than to be drowned by such a lubberly skunk as Reuben Harpy, any way."

"Yes," chimed in Jerry Mizzen; "them as is born to be hanged will never die by drowning."

This speech on the part of Jerry was rewarded by a spanker between his eyes from a dead fish, which happened to be the most handy thing Bob Hauler could find.

A good-tempered scuffle ensued between the pair, who belaboured each other with such perfect good will, that, incensed as Tom was at Reuben's craven treachery, he could not forbear laughing heartily.

Ben Hauler gave a sailor's genuine cheer when he heard Tom laugh.

"That's a good sign," he said; "shows the right stuff. I'll wager a cask or two of the King's brandy that your sneaking snivelling cousin won't laugh like that after he claps eyes on you."

"Why don't you make a row?" Jerry exclaimed, sulkily. "Ain't we got all our work to do to elude them King's officers, and there you are, braying like a jackass."

"Hush!" Tom said; "I hear the sound of oars."

The trio lay still, but could presently discern a boat approaching.

Two custom officers were seated in its stern.

Jerry Mizzen's face wore the most ludicrous expression as the boat went by.

They had fourteen casks of smuggled brandy in the hole in the cliff, and under the very nose of the —nue officers.

He could have stood on his head when the boat pulled out of sight.

Then Bob Hauler respectfully took Tom's hand.

"Master Tom," he said, "you've shown the mettle of a man; you might have betrayed us, had you chosen. Don't think Bob Hauler ever forgets; should the day come when he can be of service to you, only ask, and all he can do shall be done."

"Clap a stopper on your jawing tackle," Jerry exclaimed, "and let this young gentleman go home; the smell of the brandy might get too strong for him if he stays here any longer."

Tom, who understood readily that they had some smuggling venture in progress, smiled good-naturedly, and thanking both for picking him out of the water, took his departure, much to the satisfaction of Jerry Mizzen, who never cared about having too many eyes upon him during his delicate operations of tricking the revenue officers.

Our hero encountered his treacherous relative almost on the threshold of their uncle's dwelling.

Had the cowardly boy suddenly met a spectre he could not have been more utterly awe-stricken.

His features went livid, his jaw hung, his eyes grew fixed in terror, his knees shook beneath him.

Tom did not deign him a word, but looked at him till the terrified wretch dropped cowering to the ground in a fit.

Then our hero passed in and left him.

Reuben gathered some courage after our hero had gone.

He managed to crawl away and tell his infamous mother and her paramour what had transpired.

They were in close consultation, when Reuben with his white face and knees knocking together came to tell his tale.

At first Mrs. Harpy was in high consternation; but the more calculating Sanderson quieted her fears.

"I wish your boy had more courage," he observed, after he had sent Reuben away; "he is scared by a look."

"Whatever courage he has," Mrs. Harpy replied, "remember he inherits from you."

Sanderson grinned coarsely, and after a few remarks at the expense of her husband's memory, the conversation turned upon the best means of arranging matters in connection with our hero.

"That cursed boy!" Sanderson began; "had the fool shown the least pluck, all would have been well. I know old Gregory's temper; he'll never forget his cowardice."

"What are we to do?" Mrs. Harpy rejoined, with ashy face. "Would it be better to put him out of the way?"

"Not yet, if you mean the old fool, he is useful—no, I have a plan; he has got this brat—his favourite Tom—a middy's berth in the navy. He won't do as much for Reuben, for fear he should prove a coward, and disgrace the profession. I propose, then, that we let him have his own way; but instead of this Tom flaunting it as a midshipman, I'll have him taken by the press-gang, and shipped as a sailor-boy. If hard work don't kill him, his gunpowder nature will soon get him into a scrape that will finish him."

"I hope it may soon do so," Mrs. Harpy exclaimed; "he has been a thorn in my side since he was born. I have felt that he would ever stand in my boy's way."

"He might not have done so had Reuben been different, but there is no help for it now. To make our plans complete, Reuben must enter himself in the name of Tom Drake."

"Is this necessary? Could not something speedier be done?"

"No. Do you think I would wait a day otherwise? John Gregory must not die yet; his consent alone disposes of Minnie Atherton and her property, and that cannot be touched till she is of age. I know enough of Reuben to be aware that in a short time he will bring disgrace enough on the name of Tom Drake to make Gregory repent, especially when he is dismissed the service and degraded—mind, as Tom Drake. We'll gull the old fool till he is sick of the name of his hopeful—get Reuben again in his favour—obtain his consent to his union with the girl—his ward—make certain that his will is signed in Reuben's favour—and then, into the *madhouse* or the *grave* with John Gregory."

Mrs. Harpy's eyes glittered as her base accomplice unfolded his vile plans.

"Is this plan sure of success?" she asked.

"Certain."

"When will you put it into execution?"

"At once—all my arrangements shall be made to-night—to-morrow this boy, whom we have such reason to dread, shall be removed from our path. The press-gang will have him safe, and if he should get put on my vessel, God help him! I've a long account to settle with him when once he is in my power."

Our youthful hero, little suspecting the vile plot maturing against him, was singularly happy the whole day.

His commission as a middy had arrived, and all arrangements were complete for him to enter on his new career.

The only sadness that clouded his joy was the thought of having to bid his mother and Minnie farewell.

His little sweetheart took matters more bravely than he had expected.

She felt proud of him in his new position, and her encouragements and girlish vows got over half the pangs of his separation from her.

Old John Gregory allowed them to ramble forth together that evening, as it was the last day of Tom's stay.

They wandered to the old place by the lake, where they had often plighted their childish vows, and which had been the scene of his prompt rescue of her.

"Don't you think, dear Minnie," Tom said, his earnest voice husky with emotion, "they will ever persuade you to be untrue to me?"

"They never shall," Minnie replied, gaily; "they may try, but I know you will come back in time to save me, as you did from the lake. You'll be a brave, handsome officer then, and so proud with your sword and your epaulettes, and your cocked hat."

Tom kissed the fair cheek of the coquettish little speaker, and in true lover fashion gallantly fastened round her neck a small gold chain, suspended to which was a gold ring.

"That shall be your love-token," he said. "No one shall take it from you till I ask you to give it back to me, and this shall be mine."

He kissed his own love-token.

It was a small minature, attached to a tress of Minnie's golden hair.

A proud look passed over the boy's handsome face as he replaced it in his breast.

"No one shall take that from me while I have life," he said, drawing Minnie closer to him, and looking lovingly in her fair young face.

"You are not afraid that I shall never come again?" he said, presently.

"I dreamed you came back again," Minnie said. "I'm sure you're born to be a great man, because when I saw you it was on the deck of such a beautiful ship, and you had stars and orders on your breast, and were dressed like a great admiral, and you looked so handsome," Minnie blushed as she said this, "a large black flag was over your head, but I thought it only meant that you were the king of every ship, and that none were so great as you."

Tom's fine eyes kindled as he listened; it was a picture congenial to his own mind, to stand supreme on the broad deck of some noble ship, with a willing crew ready to obey his slightest will.

He kissed Minnie for her prophecy, and when he bade her farewell, all that she had conjured up rose as vividly before his mind as if it had actually occurred.

Even to the black flag—but he had forgotten that the black banner was the insignia of piracy and death.

Our hero wandered through the seafaring town down by the bay, to take his farewell of scenes he was so soon to quit, for years, perhaps.

In front of a little tavern, of anything but inviting appearance, his attention was drawn to three or four ill-looking fellows, half crimp, half sailor in appearance, who were loitering in front of the tavern, and regarding him with sinister gaze as he went by.

He had got some distance on his way home when he again found himself confronted by these same men.

He might not have heeded them then, but he was in a dark deserted lane, with no human habitation near, and the men were, to say the least, suspicious in their regard of him.

But they passed him without molestation, and he was reproaching himself for his momentary apprehension, when he felt himself suddenly seized from behind.

Before he could utter a sound, a gag was forced before his mouth, and a coarse laugh behind him told him the meaning of his capture.

The press-gang.

With the fury of a young panther he bounded from the grasp of those who held him, and with flashing eye demanded how they dared attack a midshipman in the king's service.

The only reply was a mocking laugh, that he thought sounded familiar; then a swift blow was dealt him on the back of his head, and he fell to the earth unconscious.

CHAPTER IV.

OUT AT SEA.—TOM MEETS AN OLD ENEMY.

WHEN our hero came to his senses he was lying on a hard pallet, in a close suffocating pen, so dark that he could distinguish nothing but a number of prone objects lying about him, with the roof of the place so low that his uplifted hand touched it, and the floor heaving beneath him in a way that passed his comprehension.

By degrees, as his eyes became accustomed to the gloom, he perceived that the shadowy objects seen by him were human beings, and in a little while, as his faculties became clear, he could distinguish the low buzzing of their conversation.

Now and then a deep groan startled him, and then a bitter oath or a curse, whose blasphemy seemed to freeze his blood.

And now began the painful task of recalling the incidents that led to his presence there, wherever it was, that he was held prisoner.

That he was still a captive he was disagreeably made aware of by the fact that his wrists were bound together by rope.

The truth of his position soon dawned upon him.

His remembrance of the attack under which he had succumbed, and the oaths and converse of those who, like himself, were confined in that stifling hole, left no doubt upon his mind.

The oscillation beneath his feet was now no mystery to him.

He was penned up in the hold of a vessel moving out to sea.

Bitter were his feelings as he realized his fate.

Snatched away from his mother—from Minnie—without a word of adieu; his absence unexplained, and that at the moment when his prospects were so promising.

Brave as the boy was, he could not repress a cry of anguish and anger.

"Why—why am I trapped like this?" he cried, clenching his bandaged hands. "Why am I brought here?"

"To serve the King, my little man," a voice said close to him; that's why we're all brought here; not because it's our wish, but because we couldn't help ourselves; and a man don't have much chance when he's felled like a bullock."

A coarse laugh from the more careless prisoners, oaths and imprecations from others, followed this speech.

"But I already had a midshipman's berth," Tom cried.

"You'd better tell that to the marines," the same voice observed; "slack yarns don't run down here."

"What ship did you say?" another voice asked.

"The *Thunderer*—Captain Hyde."

"Oh, well, thunder or lightning, it's all one; you'll have enough of both if you're not knocked over at first."

Tom hazarded no further remark; he felt that no one there could help him. His only chance was when the captain inspected them the next morning, as he heard one of the prisoners say he was sure to do.

Besides, keenly as he felt his own misfortune, he was not the only sufferer.

Many of those present, as he could hear from what they said, had been torn from home and wives or sweethearts.

One young fellow was to have been married the next Sunday; another had only been married a week.

The latter suspected a discarded lover of being concerned in getting him pressed, and with many a deep curse he swore he would have his heart's blood should he live to return.

The weary hours of night passed slowly away.

At early bells, and when the light was struggling into the hold, the captain and two of his officers accompanied by two seamen, came to look at them.

He was a tall, hard-featured man, with iron resolve in every muscle of his stern face.

He listened coldly to their several complaints, and passed each by till he came to Tom.

"This boy is young," he observed, regarding our hero attentively.

This was the chance Tom wanted.

As briefly as possible he related the facts of his capture.

The captain listened unmoved.

It was impossible to gather from his features what impression the recital had made.

"Have you your midshipman's warrant with you?" he asked, when Tom had finished.

"It was in my breast-pocket, sir. But it is gone now."

"Humph! Mr. John Gregory, did you say?"

"Yes, sir."

"Then we will see to the truth of your story. We have an officer on board who comes from the bay. He shall see you."

Tom's heart leaped gladly within him.

His story would be corroborated, and that would release him from the hardships which otherwise were in store for him.

He never felt so impatient as while the officer was being sent for; but he came at length.

"There is a lad here who says he has been kidnapped," the captain said, "and bears a middy's rank, a nephew of Mr. Gregory's. Do you know him, Sanderson?"

Sanderson!

Tom's heart felt like lead.

He needed only to look up and see the brutal face of his old enemy, with the malignant eyes glaring in triumph over him, to know that all his hopes were dashed to the earth.

But he was not prepared for the consummate lie Sanderson now asserted.

"Yes, sir; that is Mr. Gregory's graceless nephew, a bad boy, the one he has had continual trouble with, I regret to say—his name is Reuben Harpy."

As Tom sprang angrily to his feet and looked the dastard in the face, the captain turned his cold glance upon him.

"Reuben Harpy—he told me his name was Drake."

"Falsehood is his besetting sin, sir. Tom Drake is a worthy lad, and was shipped as middy on board the *Thunderer*."

"Liar!" Tom cried hotly. "How dare you utter so atrocious a falsehood?"

"Enough," interrupted the captain, "the trick is palpable; by taking his cousin's name he hoped to get off. I have no wish to begin harshly with you," he continued, addressing Tom; "my name is Captain Parker, this ship is the *Arethusa* frigate. I am a strict officer, but you seem a likely lad, and I should like to see you get on—try and make a change for the better—but remember, if we have advancements and favours for those who do their duty, we have punishments, and severe ones, for the idle and disobedient."

With these words Captain Parker turned on his heel, and the door was shut upon Tom and his companions in misfortune.

So excited was the high-spirited boy by this undeserved treatment that he would have battered the panels in with his clenched hands, if he had not been pacified by the rest.

With cheeks crimson, and eyes flashing indignantly, the proud boy sat down, resolved to bear the worst rather than give his enemy a new chance over him.

"They shall see that I can bear hardships at least," he exclaimed, half aloud.

"That's right, my cheery lad," a familiar voice exclaimed, and looking round he saw the careless features of Bob Hauler, and the woe-begone visage of Jerry Mizzen.

Another hope sprang up in Tom's breast.

"You are my friends," he said, "you can testify that I have spoken the truth?"

"No use, Master Tom," Bob Hauler replied. "I'd have spoken before, only I knew it would not do any good—there's a dead set against you, and you must tide it over. I should not be believed, and might be a marked man, if I swore till I was blue—so, my cheery lad, pluck up your true mettle, and

do not give that yellow alligator we've got over us—your friend Sanderson—a scrape of a chance—he is waiting for it, and won't let it go by if you give it him—so show him your true stuff, and don't forget, if our mouths are tied as yet, that you've some friends on board this hulking boat, which, for aught I care, might sink to the bottom to-morrow."

Tom stretched out his hands.

It was something to be sure of a friend.

The manly grasp of the tar was balm to his wounded spirit—and he resolved at all hazards to do his duty.

When eight bells were struck, the boatswain came and set them free, ordering them at the same time to follow him on deck, that he might set them about the work of the ship.

Tom cast one wistful glance across the ocean.

The cliffs behind the bay were almost out of sight, and the freshening wind promised soon to take them far out to sea.

Indeed, more canvas would have been flying but that they were partially lying to, to allow a tender to overhaul them.

This she did about two o'clock, and then another batch of prisoners were helped on board the man-of-war.

The last one who was helped on deck was a powerful, muscular man, with a fine classical head and massive black beard.

He had been severely wounded, and was even now suffering from the effects of some stupifying drug, which, powerful as it was, had failed to prostrate his herculean frame.

He glanced round him like a captive panther when he stood on the frigate's deck, and fearlessly facing the captain, said hoarsely,—

"They've trapped me, Captain Parker, but I have marked my man, and as God is above us, so will I squeeze the life out of his throat the first time he comes within reach of my hands. I'll do a man's work while I am caged here, but let me have one chance of liberty, and I'll show you what use I can make of it."

His strong voice shook with passion.

Captain Parker betrayed no sign of having heard him, and he stepped back among the rest.

He was a singular man this.

He was called Ben Barnacle.

He went about his work with the skill of a practised seaman.

He was tireless, too; fatigue never seemed to touch his stalwart frame.

When the men sang at their work, his was the one grave, stolid face amongst them, conspicuous by its sullen look of deadly resolve.

He ate, too, and drank with his messmates, but in silence, never once exchanging a word with officer or man.

Thrice under most hazardous circumstances he made desperate attempts to escape.

Once he cast himself adrift on a plank.

Once he was taken up while clinging to the rudder.

On a third occasion he actually lowered a boat, and was almost in it when he was discovered.

Each time he heard with sullen silence his punishment, and returned to his duty as before.

Our hero felt a strange interest in this singular man, who, on his part, seemed less unfavourably disposed towards the young sailor.

Galling as Tom found his life on board the frigate, he was careful to give his enemy, Sanderson, no pretext for accusing him before the captain.

He was ever attentive and willing, and Sanderson, who watched eagerly for the least chance against him, ground his teeth in savage chagrin when he saw the gallant boy not only foiled him, but was gradually gaining favour with the captain.

With all his faults of discipline—and there were times when he made the frigate a floating hell—Captain Parker had a keen appreciation of the true qualities of a sailor; and these he instinctively recognised in Tom the first time he saw him go about his work.

"I am glad to see that lad striving to gain a better character," he observed once to Sanderson. "I have good hopes of him if he goes on as he has begun."

And Sanderson, who hated Tom more intensely every hour, was compelled to pretend acquiescence to the captain's words.

Off a reefy coast in the Mediterranean a violent storm suddenly came upon them, and though sails were taken in immediately, the fury of the tempest was so tremendous that the ship swung round leeward of the dangerous coast, and had not righted herself when an immense sea struck her between decks and washed the helmsman off his feet.

Captain Parker saw the imminent peril of his ship.

A moment, and she seemed about to plunge headlong amongst the boiling breakers.

The catastrophe was so sudden that he had not time to give the sharp order before Tom had taken the helmsman's place, and with his slim figure defying the fierce gale, guided the vessel from its dangerous course.

At the rate at which the ship was heeling to, with the seas sweeping her at every minute, Tom's intrepidity and daring were the more conspicuous.

The iron-hearted captain gave him an approving glance, and the men set up a cheer that almost drowned the deafening roars of the breakers.

As calm as if he was on the smoothest river, Tom steered the *Arethusa*, managing the wheel so cleverly that Bob Hauler could not restrain his enthusiasm, but cried lustily,—

"There he is, like a little captain, steering us as if the sea were a smooth lake instead of a boiling cauldron. Hurrah for our little captain! Three cheers for Captain TOM!"

The ringing cheer was taken up by every throat, and Lieutenant Sanderson, cowering in malice, secretly cursed the noble boy for his daring, even though it saved the ship.

And Tom never swerved from the helm till the ship was safely through the sea of rocks and foam, and then he gave up his post and allowed himself to be carried off in triumph to the shout of "Three cheers for Captain Tom."

And that was how he gained a name destined afterwards to be renowned far and wide as the name of the daring princely boy whom no power could capture or subdue, and whose flag bore the one motto—"Invincible."

All the next day Sanderson went about with the most demoniac passion seething in his breast.

He would have given much for a chance to vent his spleen upon our hero, but was baffled in every attempt.

Tom treated him with a contemptuous semblance of respect, that galled him to the quick.

He strove all in his power to insult the high-spirited boy.

It was marvellous how even Ben Barnacle endured the persecution of the low-minded tyrant.

The ship's crew had a severe time of it for the next few days; when it was Sanderson's watch they knew the treat in store for them.

"Anchors and jackstays are always dirty," he would cry. "Away you go, you lazy lubbers, with your hammers and knock the rust off!"

And the "lazy lubbers," looking fierce and sullen, but not daring to utter a word of complaint, would obey.

Sanderson had the Captain's orders to trim them

into able seamen; to get them "salted," as he termed it.

And he salted them; salted them in a way which was not at all to their taste!

Salt beef for breakfast, dinner, and supper; salt crackers, soaked in salt water! a bottle of salts for rheumatism; the same medicine for a broken leg.

"Aye! even for a broken neck!" howled one morning a poor devil who had fallen from the maintop.

The fifth day after Tom's exploit at the helm a terrific squall pounced upon the frigate, taking her unawares, and knocking her over on her beam ends.

Royals and top-gallant sails had been taken in, but the topsails, not having yet been stowed, were torn to tatters, and the rags sent to Neptune for a present.

The water poured over the lee bulwarks in torrents; the cook's galley was blown to pieces; three or four pigs running at large, slipped squealing to leeward, and finally rolled over the partially submerged bulwarks into the sea.

It was Sanderson's watch, and he stood howling out his orders in a voice like that of a caged tiger, while the "lazy lubbers" hopped to and fro like so many madmen, tugging first at one rope and then another.

Suddenly a little Sandwich Island boy, named Kanak, with an enormous head, appeared at the companion-way.

"Dinner is ready!" he shouted, with all the strength of his lungs.

Sanderson hated this boy—hated him because Tom had taken notice of him, and because he displayed a faithful affection towards our young hero in return.

In a moment he sprang upon him with a bound, and, seizing him by his shirt-collar, dragged him on deck.

"You miserable shark—you infernal little imp—you cannibal's whelp—do you dare speak of dinner at such a time as this?"

The "little imp," who was but thirteen years of age, clasped his hands, and howled for mercy.

"Aye, aye, I'll mercy you!" roared the tyrant; and pointing to the spanker-boom, which had been slushed only the day before, he ordered him to get a sharp knife and scrape it.

"Oh, no! no!" cried the poor lad, in piteous tones; "de ship roll, de wind blow, and s'pose me go up dere, me quick fall into de sea."

"So much the better!" cried Sanderson, "there will be one lubber the less in the world."

With these words, he drew a long sharp knife from a leathern belt about his waist, and put it in the hand of Kanak.

"Now then, away you go!" he cried, dealing the boy a kick, which almost knocked him into the sea. "Away you go, and scrape that boom."

Repressing his excitable feelings as well as he could, Tom came aft, and respectfully offered to do the task so brutally imposed upon the helpless lad.

His old enemy glared on him as if he thought he had at last got a chance of getting him in a snare.

"Who the furies called you to interfere, you mutinous young vagabond?" he cried, hoarse with fury. "Clamber up to the top fore-sails, and stop half-way if you dare."

Tom stayed a moment to speak encouragingly to little Kanak.

"Cling fast with your ankles and knees when you go up there," he said, "and don't look down—if you fall a murder will be done."

"D——n you, go up both of you, cursed hounds!" Sanderson roared, choking with fury.

Tom gave a light spring, and was quickly up the shrouds.

Little Kanak was not so fortunate.

He stood shivering with fear, and the tyrant, dealing him another violent blow, sent him reeling against the mizen-mast.

An indignant glance shot from Tom's eyes, but he continued his ascent—while a second menace from Sanderson sent the trembling boy up to his task.

Bruised and limping, he drew himself into the mizen-shrouds, and soon gained the boom.

Here he paused for a moment, and looked piteously down into the red upturned face of the tyrant, hoping that he would relent and call him back.

Sanderson cursed him, and bade him go on.

"Me know me fall," cried Kanak, still hesitating. "De boom so slippery, me no can stay dere long. Me fall, and p'raps break leg or neck; p'raps go into de sea."

With an oath Sanderson sprang through the companion-way, and soon reappeared with a pistol, which he aimed at Kanak's head.

"Go on, go on at once," he shrieked, "or you are a dead lad."

"Well, den," moaned the youngster, "me will go, but know me can nebber hold on dere. And, if me killed, me like you tell captain to take Kanak's Bible out of my trunk, missionary gib me, and let dis boy's mudder hab it when ship get to de Sandwich Island."

The lieutenant did not reply, but the click was heard as he cocked his piece, and with a groan the boy threw himself upon the boom.

Trembling in every limb, he began to crawl along the projecting spar.

His hands slipped several times, and it seemed as if he would fall; but, with a desperate effort, he contrived to regain his balance, and finally to reach the end of the boom.

"Now, then, scrape away!" roared the tyrant, springing upon the round-house, "and see that you do your work well."

He was now directly beneath the lad, looking up at him, with a gleam of malicious pleasure shining in his hard blue eyes.

Kanak was clinging desperately to the slippery boom with his hands and knees.

It was evident that the moment he should let go of it to grasp the knife which was between his teeth he would fall either upon the deck or into the sea.

The quivering of the spar almost caused him to lose his hold as it was, for there was no rope near enough to be grasped.

With starting eyeballs and chattering teeth, he glared upon the foaming hissing waves of the sea, upon the hard pitiless face of the lieutenant, upon the pistol still aimed at his head, and uttered a low groan.

"Come! come! lively with that knife. Go to work, you infernal imp of Satan—go to work, or whizz flies a bullet through your cussed brain."

Again the ominous click of the piece was heard, and Kanak, clutching the spar with his left hand, until his nails almost pierced the surface of it, let go of it with his right, and succeeded in grasping his knife.

At the same moment the ship made a furious plunge, and the boy uttered a loud shriek as his knees slipped from under him.

He was thus brought astride of the boom; but, as the bows lifted, he was hurled sideways from his position.

His wild cry pierced the ears of his shipmates, and made the blood leap back to their hearts.

They saw him fall, saw his body strike the lieutenant in the descent, and heard the report of the pistol.

Then, rushing aft, they witnessed a spectacle fearful to behold.

The lieutenant lay upon the round-house, with Kanak's knife buried to the hilt in his chest.

The boy was not badly hurt.

His fall had been broken by coming in contact with Sanderson.

He was somewhat bruised, however, and needed the assistance of one of the men to regain his feet.

"Me no do dis on purpose," he moaned, pointing to the wounded officer. "When me fall, me strike him, and de point of de knife go into his chest. Dey no hang me? You no t'ink dey hang me?" he continued, looking round with a terrified countenance.

Sanderson glared round him savagely.

"The other one as well," he said fiercely.

"He prompted him to do it. You heard him say if he fell there would be murder! Let both suffer —both die!"

Tom had reached the deck by this time.

Captain Parker gazed sternly in his face.

Sanderson's accusations had taken ground, and before Tom could repel the charge, he and little Kanak were manacled together and thrust into the frigate's darkest place of confinement.

CHAPTER V.

THE COURT-MARTIAL.

FOR five days our hero and poor little Kanak were kept in close confinement.

They took their food together and slept with the iron manacles on the wrists of each.

Little Kanak, at first gave way to excessive grief, but Tom's coolness and fortitude eventually quieted him.

On the sixth day they were brought before a naval court-martial, at which Sanderson, who had sufficiently recovered to give evidence, attended.

He was still pale and weak, and his bold features showed the amount of suffering he had endured.

He gave the two boys a look of murderous hate when they were brought in, and made his evidence as telling as he could against them.

If he had been well liked by the other officers, or death had resulted from his injury, it might have gone hard with Tom and the island boy; as it was, they did not hold the charge well proved, and the boys were set at liberty.

A cheer ran through the ship when the decision was made known.

The sailors were glad to see their tyrant discomfited.

Events of a stormy nature now occupied the minds of all.

The *Arethusa* had received orders to make for Algeria, and take part in attempts to destroy the fleet of terrible pirates whose merciless ravages made the civilised world shudder to hear.

The pirates had a numerous fleet of vessels which they adroitly managed, and though some hard knocks were exchanged with the *Arethusa*, they eluded all Captain Parker's attempts to take or sink any one of them.

At the first opening of the cannonade Tom felt in his proper element.

Amidst the smoke and din he stood upon a gun under a heavy fire, deliberately directing it to be pointed so as to disable an enemy.

And when the word ran round to prepare for boarders, the boy's bold heart dilated with joyous enthusiasm, and he longed for the exciting moment of hand-to-hand encounter.

As yet, however, the pirates had sense enough keep out of boarding distance.

Captain Parker, who was as brave a comma as ever trod a deck, galled at his non-success, de mined upon the bold attempt of attacking the pir under the guns of their forts; and early morning, in conjunction with several other ship opened fire, which was hotly returned.

In the midst of the fray an armed corvette, which had only recently come up with the English squadron, was observed to run under the fire of a masked battery, which instantly swept her decks.

She lay in such a position that none of the pirate vessels could come out to take her, on account of the fire of the rest of the English squadron, and every eye was anxiously turned towards her to see whether she would run in close to the guns and silence them.

So excited was Tom at the spectacle that, forgetful of his duty, he leapt into the shrouds to see what was going forward on her decks.

A group of officers were standing on her decks, and he saw a sudden discharge pour in amongst them, and instantly stretch them all bleeding or dead upon the deck.

A moment after a young midshipman crept to the mizenmast, and the flag was lowered as a token of surrender.

A derisive groan attended this act.

The vessel's escape would have been so easy had she been properly managed.

Shouts from the pirates proclaimed their pleasure at this first instalment of victory.

Then the corvette's boats were lowered on the side protected from the fort's cannon, and the whole of her crew tumbled hastily in.

They were coldly received on board the *Arethusa*, the nearest ship.

Captain Parker, with a dignified wave of the hand, ordered them below.

He would not allow them to share in the fighting on board his vessel.

Evening came on before anything decisive occurred on either side, and the British ships ceased firing and got out of range for the night.

Then Captain Parker sent his first lieutenant to summon the officers of the surrendered ship.

His lieutenant returned with the intelligence that all the superior officers had been killed by a fatal discharge from the fort, and that the next in command was midshipman Drake, who had ordered the flag to be struck and had then deserted the ship.

Our hero leaped as if he had received a bullet when he heard this statement.

A moment after his cowardly cousin stood on the same deck with him.

Captain Parker exchanged a few words only with Reuben Harpy.

He dismissed him in frigid silence and full of shame and mortification.

The craven-hearted dastard was turning away when his gaze met the piercing glance of his wronged relative.

He started back as if a serpent had stung him.

That look sufficed to excite the impetuous boy beyond control.

Regardless of the presence of his captain, forgetting that, spurious as was Reuben's claim, he was in the light of a superior officer, he seized him abruptly by the throat and cried—

"Coward! we meet at a fitting time. Lay down the rank you deprived me of! Confess your villainy, or, degraded as you are, I will strip your borrowed plumes from your base carcase."

As may easily be imagined, this fierce onset on the part of the hot-headed boy created amazement.

Reuben, whose cheeks had gone pale with deathly fear, now hardened his nerves to forced composure, and tried to outface his high-spirited cousin.

But he had only time to give him the direct lie, when the excited boy struck him a fierce blow in the face, and with one snatch stripped the gold lace from his jacket.

What further violence he would have proceeded to, is hard to say

He was stopped by finding himself suddenly seized and made prisoner, and then the consciousness of his position suddenly flashed full upon him.

His dauntless breast swelled with indignant rage as he was eagerly laid hold of.

"Captain Parker!" he cried, "I denounce this impostor who has stolen my name and rank, and disgraced me by his cowardice! Let me have justice, and I am content!"

For once in his life, the usually impassive features of Captain Parker were inflamed with passion.

Such an outrage on his quarter-deck, and in his presence, was the highest insult.

"You shall have justice!" he cried, hotly. "By six to-morrow a court-martial shall try you for this conduct, and if you cannot prove that he is not your superior officer you shall be shot without mercy two hours after!"

Tom struggled to get free, that he might have one more chance of dealing the treacherous dastard a deadly blow.

But in the grip of four stalwart men he was powerless, though he strained every sinew in his efforts to escape.

It was not till he was loaded with heavy irons that he desisted from his furious struggles to get free, and then, with the consciousness that all hope was over, he allowed himself to be thrust into the usual place of confinement.

A sentry was placed over him, and the general belief was that his hours were numbered.

Left to the loneliness of his imprisonment, our hero had leisure to reflect upon the serious position into which his own rashness had brought him.

Had he calmly prepared his statement against Reuben, and solicited inquiry, the facts might have come out, or even had they not he would have been simply reprimanded and sent back to his duty.

But an open attack on one who, rightly or wrongly, stood as his superior, was an offence for which Captain Parker would entertain no palliation.

Of course, the deliberate lie of Sanderson would destroy his assertions, and he might regard death as the certain punishment for his hasty act.

The brave boy's heart swelled in his breast—even now his fingers clenched eagerly, and his impetuous soul flashed from his eyes.

"If I could only get free," the boy muttered, straining at his manacles—"free for one half-hour —I would wring the lie from his throat."

His bitter reveries ended at last in sleep.

It was the still hour of night when he was gently aroused.

A hand was laid on his mouth, and a voice softly bid him be silent.

Tom looked up, and saw that his visitor was Ben Barnacle.

"Is it time?" he asked, sadly. "I did not think I had slept long."

"Speak softly, all is in readiness for you to escape."

"Escape!"

Tom raised his eyes half dreaming, and a wild hope shot through his heart.

But it died away instantly.

"No," he said, "I prefer to remain here till I am tried."

"Don't be foolish, boy. If you are here to-morrow you will as certainly be shot as you are now living."

"Let them shoot me then."

"And have your cousin enjoy the pleasure of seeing you riddled with bullets, while he lives to personate you and defame your name?"

A faint flush swept to the poor boy's features.

"No," he cried; "I will escape if only for that. Let them shoot me down in the attempt. I shall not die a felon's death."

REUBEN HARPY PUSHES TOM OVER THE CLIFF.

"You need not die at all Give me your hands. Good. They are small. and will slip through these irons easily. There. Now your legs. So. Can you stand? If so, follow me, but as stealthily as a cat."

Released from his irons, which his deliverer took off with adroit and noiseless celerity, Tom stood erect.

"Softly," Ben Barnacle whispered. " I have quieted the sentry for a time ; if he should wake I will wring his neck. A moment while I tell you our plans. The middies on this ship believe your statement; they are disgraced by the presence of your cousin, and, anxious to wipe off the stain of his cowardice, purpose taking the vessel he lost to-day ; it is still under the guns of the fort—we can cut her out. What say you? are you willing to share the danger?"

Tom replied by a nervous pressure of the speaker's hand.

"I owe you more than life," he said, fervently.

"No words—follow in silence."

It was quite dark.

They passed the sentry who lay outside the door, breathing heavily, and apparently in a fit.

Ben Barnacle led his young companion down to the lower hold, where he saw Bob Hauler, Jerry Mizzen. little Kanak, and the whole of the middies belonging to the ship.

Their looks told of their adventurous enterprise.

A silent pressure of hands, and then, one by one, crept out of the lower port-hole where two boats, had been noiselessly lowered

In silence they took their places, and before their daring attempt was discovered, their muffled oars had taken them out of sight of the ship.

2

A deafening roar of artillery startled the officers and men of the *Arethusa* from their slumber.

They looked towards the shore and saw the whole of the forts encircled in sheets of flame as the cannon belched forth their destruction, yells and cries of conflict rose on the air, and in the midst of the vivid flare of the guns Captain Parker distinguished the figure of our fearless hero leading on small band of followers to meet the onset of legions pirates who swarmed from every side.

Dumbfounded by the sight, he ordered the frigate to be brought up for action.

But as abruptly as it had commenced the conflict ceased, and the forts and ships were enveloped in darkness.

The two boats' crews reached the corvette unperceived, but at the same time a body of pirates arrived there with the same intent, and the two parties thus unexpectedly meeting, at once engaged in sharp and deadly fray.

Alarmed by the tumult, the batteries and ships began to open fire, and the daring adventurers would have been annihilated if Tom had not conceived the audacious plan of driving the ship boldly in shore and running the gauntlet of the pirate fleet.

Heading an impetuous charge, he drove the last of their assailants over the sides, and with guns hastily loaded, ran into the midst of the fleet, opening fire as the vessel cut through, and scattering the double broadside amongst the pirate barques, which were too closely packed to return the fire, without injury to each other, and, with scarcely a man wounded, Tom drew the ship they had so gallantly cut out away from all danger from fort or fleet.

This manœuvre placed the pirate fleet between them and the British ships, and when their loud hurrahs had somewhat subsided, Ben Barnacle called all hands together, and thus harangued them—

"Now, my lads, we've cut out this gallant craft, shall we take her to the fleet and be tried and sentenced for acting without orders, as well as for setting our brave comrade free and quitting the ship? I say, no! We have most of us been torn from our homes, and shall get little thanks for anything we do for the British flag. Therefore, let us salvage for ourselves. Let us scour the seas of these pirates, and repay ourselves with their treasures. Let us all be rovers free, and choose a leader who shall help us to defy any power to subdue or take us."

The loud and prolonged cheer that followed his speech caused Tom to suspect that the whole affair had been previously planned.

He remained silent, however, and Ben went on—

"Now that's settled, we must choose a leader. We want one who is brave as a lion, skilful in seamanship, able to command, daring and generous. That leader is here—Captain Tom Drake! We've helped him from unjust imprisonment, but we'll not let him go back to death. We've seen that he has the right stuff in him, and know that he'll never desert us, or yield while a bit of our flag holds together. Choose, then, with one voice for Captain Tom. Cheer to proclaim him our leader, then one shot to say farewell to the frigate, and let them follow and take us when they can."

The cheer that succeeded this harangue was so loud and prolonged that our hero was deafened by it.

He heard his name vociferated by every throat, and a daring pride rose in his heart.

Giving one glance in the direction of the frigate, he allowed himself to be carried away by the tumultuous enthusiasm of the crew.

And as Ben Barnacle fired the farewell salute at the frigate, the air rang with the name of CAPTAIN TOM DRAKE.

CHAPTER VI.

CAPTAIN TOM BRINGS DOWN THE FRIGATE'S FLAG.

THE acclamations of the crew, who had so staunchly proclaimed him their leader, had scarcely died away before Tom was called upon to exercise those qualities which were to prove him worthy of the dignity conferred upon him.

Captain Parker had watched his gallant cutting-out exploit with strange interest, and had got his ship hastily in trim for action, when a lurid light following the darkness which had hid Tom's course from him, revealed the plucky little corvette running through the very midst of the pirates, cannonading them as she passed.

"Mr. Burley!" Captain Parker cried, "we must follow and rescue that boy; his daring has taken him amongst the pirate fleet!"

"I don't think, sir, any ship would get out again from such a trap."

"Nonsense! an English ship can do anything. Ah! do you see that, Mr. Burley? he has got his ship through. By heaven, they're off! He's running away with his prize! Send up a light to bring them to, or, by God, we shall lose the corvette after all!"

Lieutenant Burley sprang to the quarter-deck, and an instant after a blue light went up from the ship.

Captain Parker, who was anxiously watching the result, rushed to the deck like a madman.

"They defy us!" he cried. "Pipe all hands to the guns—crowd all sail! By heaven, they shall not escape!"

Tom understood the meaning of the signal sent from the frigate.

It was a summons for him to heave to, and surrender his ship.

At first his intention might have been to do so, but since he had trodden its deck as its commander, a new spirit was infused into him—he felt himself a monarch where he trod, and a resolution to die rather than yield crept upon him.

The frigate had sailed round by the forts, and with all press of canvas was on his track.

He looked round and saw his daring crew gathered at the guns and awaiting his commands.

No sign of yielding was in their looks.

Captain Tom sprang to the top of the capstan.

"Run up a flag," he cried. "Let them see we will never yield; and bring a gun aft to reply to them if they creep too close."

A black flag, hastily put together by Ben Barnacle, was run up from the mast.

As its folds fluttered in the air a shot was fired from the frigate, and a stern voice came across the water calling on them to surrender.

Captain Tom was standing by the mainmast when the huge ball, hurled from the frigate's side, tore up the water in front of his ship.

He had the opportunity then of lying to and taking his chance of pardon, or of hurling defiance at his pursuers, and hazarding the risk of rebellion.

He chose the latter.

"Reply to them with a gun," he cried; "let them know that we defy their power. The ship we stand on we mean to keep, and so long as a timber holds together we will fight for the flag that waves over our head!"

A loud report followed his word, and the iron missile sped to the frigate's hull.

Ben Barnacle had aimed it.

It brought down the mizen-mast, and, for the time, crippled her in her pursuit.

As Tom spoke, he happened to look up.

The flash of the cannon showed him the sable flag floating at his mizen-peak.

He had not noticed it before; but now, as it fluttered above his head, the memory of Minnie's vision flashed to his mind, and his cheek went pale, and a creeping chill stole over his frame.

In a moment he recovered himself.

His crew were crowding all sail, and the corvette —a fast sailer—was rapidly travelling over the vast waters.

The frigate, thrown into confusion by the loss of her mast, hung behind, and a good chance was now given for the *Thunderer* to escape.

A grim smile curled the lips of Ben Barnacle as he stood resting on the rammer behind the gun he had aimed with such effect.

"We have crossed the Rubicon now," he said, with a defiant laugh. "If they take us now they will deal with us as pirates."

They had loaded and run out another gun.

The frigate, though brought to by the damage, was hastily preparing to give the runaways a broadside.

Her object was evidently to sink the corvette.

The eagle-eye of Tom Drake discerned their object as they manœuvred to take his vessel at a disadvantage.

Standing by the mast, he issued his commands with such cool precision, and displayed such consummate seamanship, that the hearts of his crew were won by his first effort.

The frigate had no chance of using her guns as she desired, and fired the broadside at last to such little purpose that the corvette swung round unharmed, and a derisive laugh rose from her crew.

Then Tom jumped down to the deck, a brilliant light shone in his eyes, a rich colour deepened his cheeks, his breast swelled with proud emotion.

Putting the speaking-trumpet to his lips he sang out boldly—

"Captain Parker, you have asked us to surrender, Captain Tom Drake sends you his reply."

Tom sprang to the gun his men had run out; taking deliberate aim, he applied the lighted tow to the touch-hole, and stood back to watch the effect.

The flash and report were succeeded by a crash, and the frigate's flag came tumbling down to her deck.

A cry of rage came from her officers, but the crew of Tom's ship set up an enthusiastic hurrah, and crowded joyfully round her skilful leader.

"Now," Tom said, "let them seek us if they dare; run up more canvas, they'll have a sharp chase before they can bring us to."

Every stitch of canvas was spread, and in less than two hours Tom had the satisfaction of being out in deep water, far from the guns of his Majesty's frigate.

By Tom's direction the ship was run into the nearest port, in order that the valuable cargo it had on board might be disposed of, and such necessaries purchased as were required for their desperate cruise.

The corvette was a splendidly-built vessel, and though it only carried twenty guns, was so fast a sailer, and so easily managed, that Tom had no wish to tread a better deck.

Her equipments, too, were in good condition, and it was marvellous how she could ever have been got into such a disaster as that which left her helpless under the guns of the pirate forts at Algiers.

Nothing but the rankest cowardice and incompetency could have brought about such a result, and Tom could not help feeling that had he been there, as he should have been instead of his cousin Reuben, he would have run his vessel from under the enemy's guns, or have had a hard fight for victory before he thought of surrender.

Still he could not find fault with the mischance that had placed him in so splendid a position.

The chief things he found himself in want of were provisions and costumes for his crew.

These were soon purchased, and Tom himself trod his own quarter-deck attired in a magnificent dress as a boy-captain—his first appearance being the signal for a succession of honest cheers that sent the hot blood gushing to his heart, and caused him to vow that nothing but death should destroy his prestige and power.

His boy crew he made some additions to.

They were all fantastically dressed, some as Greeks, others as Mediterranean pirates; all were well armed—all resolved to follow their chieftain to the death.

Ben Barnacle, though not less reserved and strangely silent than before, displayed the most devoted affection towards Tom, and little Kanak was never happy out of his sight.

As for Bob Hauler and Jerry Mizzen, they seemed happier even than when they were a brace of cunning smugglers; they were unscrupulous gentlemen, and cast many an eye across the sea in quest of any vessel which they hoped would turn out a rich prize.

Some time was occupied before Tom had got his ship in perfect trim for every emergency, and now that he was prepared for friend or foe, he resolved to run back and try to meet one of the Barbary or Algerine pirates, with whom the British vessels had had a most unlucky encounter, which had resulted in their being dispersed with great loss.

Tom's cheek burned when he heard of this.

He was ashamed.

For the honour of Old England he determined to do something, and his heart leaped gladly when on the fifteenth day of their cruise, at about daybreak, a sail was reported coming towards them.

Without pausing to consider the weight or probable superiority of his antagonist, Tom no sooner saw that it was a Barbary cruiser than he gave chase.

A spirited pursuit of three-quarters of an hour brought them within cannonading distance of the pirate.

She attempted no disguise or flight.

Confident in her own powers, she lay to for the attack, and then, broadside to broadside, the engagement began.

The fight was hot.

Shots flew about freely.

Even Bob Hauler and Jerry Mizzen seemed to think it anything but relishing as they dodged from the continuous peppering.

As for Ben Barnacle he was in his element.

His dark eyes burned with a wild light, and a fierce glad cry escaped him.

The guns of the corvette told upon her opponent.

In the heat of the fight Ben turned towards Tom, who was calmly directing the attack.

"They are getting ready to board us," he said. "Shall we fight them on our own deck?"

"No!" cried Tom, his dark eyes ablaze, "no! we will board them on their ship, and then bring down their flag over their heads!"

He gave the word, and his crew, gathering up pike, pistol, and cutlass, followed him to the shrouds.

First in the daring attack, Tom leaped to the enemy's deck, and instantly found himself encircled by a dozen fierce, turbaned pirates, cutting furiously at him with their tremendous scimitars.

Tom had hard work to defend himself, and stood a narrow chance of being cut down, when Ben Barnacle leaped down amongst them.

He had snatched up a heavy battle-axe.

With this he brained the pirate who menaced Tom; then, swinging it round, dealt swift havoc amongst them.

By this time Tom's crew had swarmed to the attack, and a hot conflict at close quarters ensued.

At first it seemed likely to go against our hero, the pirates so outnumbered his band; but his own cool heroism and the desperate character of his gallant crew repelled every onset of the corsairs, and drove them inch by inch back to the stern of their vessel.

Their leader, a fierce gigantic corsair, had anticipated an easy victory, and his fury knew no bounds as the tide of battle seemed to go against him.

He had an immense quantity of plunder on board, besides some very beautiful captives, whom he was anxious not to lose.

He had been so used to knocking British vessels about that he never expected any trouble from so small a craft as Tom's ship.

Looking savagely round for the leader of a crew of boys, who fought so well, his glaring eyes lighted on our hero, who, with his sword reddened from tip to hilt, was waving his crew on to victory.

Tom heard a fearful yell, then a faint cry from one of his boy crew, and the next instant the tall, bearded corsair chief stood before him, his blood-red scimitar describing a swift circle above his head, as he made a wild sweep at Tom, in hopes of cutting him down as easily as he had cut down the unhappy middy.

But he found better mettle here.

Captain Tom met his furious attack with undaunted coolness.

He found that he was confronted by the corsair chief, and with impetuous pride he waved back Ben Barnacle, who had tried to force a combat with the pirate.

The corsair was too incensed at the slaughter on his decks to heed Tom's gallant and staunch heroism.

He saw before him a mere stripling, and laughed at the idea of his contending against him.

There was a contempt in his angry eye as he cleft at Tom's skull.

The boy met him with a cool bravery that amazed him.

Had his sweeping cuts not been well parried, Tom's head would have rolled from his shoulders, but our hero was an adept in the art of swordsmanship, and parried the heavy cuts of the pirate with quick and scientific success.

Tom had not expected so desperate an encounter —the idea, too, of being chopped down was not at all pleasant.

Still, he felt glad of this chance of single conflict with a redoubted leader of pirates.

Should he vanquish him he would gain a prestige over his daring crew, and if he should fall—

Tom thought of Minnie and his mother, and as the pirate, with grating teeth, and eyes flaming from their sockets, tried to batter down his guard, he stepped swiftly aside, and parrying one of the many cuts made at his head, made a sudden leap and lunged his sword full at the corsair's throat.

Tom's sword reached the pirate in an undefended part, he felt the keen blade travelling swiftly into his throat, but the hilt had struck against his chin before he could realize that the fierce fray was ended so abruptly and so fatally.

He gave one wild gurgling cry, and as Tom drew his sharp weapon forth, tried to clutch it with his hand, and to cut at his slightly-built conqueror.

The hot blood followed the withdrawing of Tom's sword.

It gushed over him as he saw the huge pirate stagger; but bent on his own defence, Tom thrust at him again, and sent his deadly weapon home once more.

This time in the pirate's heart.

The corsair chief was possessed of immense strength, and wondrous power of life.

He had cut at Tom, and glared upon him with a deadly look of hate when the boy's sword was forcing its way through his throat.

Even with the point at his heart, his iron soul could not believe in being subdued, and he tried to grip his opponent with his hands and squeeze the life out of him.

But his strength was passed.

A sickly hue overspread his swarthy countenance, his eyes rolled in mad agony; his hands clenched, and with his huge chest labouring in one fearful throb, he dropped to the deck, and lay at Tom's feet—dead!

The death of their ruthless leader brought it to a close; the corsairs had laid down their weapons and craved quarter, and Tom bent over his dead adversary.

He could see that he had been a pitiless and a savage man of blood and passion; there were lines about his mouth and on his shaven brow that proved him to have had a will of iron and a soul hardened to the most merciless deeds.

Even in death a stern glare of ferocious cruelty shaped itself on his features.

Tom could not help feeling that he had ended the brutal career of a man who rejoiced in the most desperate iniquity; and yet, as he gazed upon him, stiffening in death, a strange feeling of interest stole over him, and he almost wished he had not slain him.

He was recalled from this reverie by the cheers of his gallant crew, who had hauled down the pirate's flag, and securely bound those who had surrendered, and were now busily engaged in ransacking the ship.

A scream from below warned Tom that there were ladies on board, and he was wondering whether they were captives or the willing slaves of the pirates, when Bob Hauler came aft, and respectfully touching his forelock, said—

"There's a lady in the cabin below, sir, we don't know what to do with; 'spect she's been belonging to that turbaned gen'lman you put out of his troubles. She only screams when we look at her. What shall we do?"

"Leave her to me," Tom replied; "I will see her; perhaps she may have been the mistress of this fearful man—in which case, ruthless though he may have been, she will merit our sympathy."

"Aye, aye," Bob Hauler said, "he's been a very devil by all account. I was half inclined to send a bullet through his hide when you were fighting, for he seemed savage enough to eat you, but Ben Barnacle stayed me; p'raps you like it better, for it's something to have conquered a devil like this."

He spurned the prone carcass with his foot.

"Let me take your sword, sir, and clean it," he said, "it's in a precious state. It's done its duty, as you have, sir—pardon my freedom; but if we wouldn't all go to the end of the world with you now we should be cowards—not fit to draw breath in these scenes of glory. She's a fine ship we've took; and I make bold to say, she'd never have been took if our admirable skipper—you, sir—had been her captain."

Tom felt grateful for the compliment, and handing Bob Hauler the red sword, descended to the pirate's cabin.

It was a most luxuriously furnished apartment.

The treasures of a world were heaped there.

Rich fabrics, costly treasures, gems of most wondrous beauty, were strewn in all directions.

The walls were hung with the richest silk—the ceiling was fringed with solid gold—the windows looking out on the sea were screened by the choicest lace.

Beautiful carpets sprang beneath the tread— brilliant mirrors reflected the thousand and one elegances of the apartment.

But our hero's attention was firstly drawn towards its occupant—a young maiden who could not have been more than fifteen summers.

She was of the fairest and most exquisite form, and her features dazzled the gaze by their superb loveliness.

Her dress was of the rarest materials, and in exquisite harmony with her Oriental style of beauty.

Her softly moulded limbs, and finely tinted bosom, were but half concealed by her robes.

Pearls and trinkets hung from her matchless hair, which fell in wild profusion over her neck and shoulders.

She raised her fine languishing eyes as Tom respectfully entered, and a faint flush stole to her alabaster cheeks.

Our hero had doffed his cap, and standing respectfully in the doorway, with the scarlet flush of battle in his handsome features, and its vivid light beaming from his eyes, looked, to the full, the brave during hero of a woman's love.

As Tom first put his foot upon the threshold of the luxurious cabin, the young girl drew back and gave a startled cry, putting up her roundly moulded arms in wild terror; a deathly pallor overspread her delicate cheeks, but her dark eyes, which were swimming in tears, flashed with a passionate fire as if she scorned the weakness of her nature which made her afraid.

But as he stepped before her, and bowed with princely politeness, she ventured to take a second look at him between her alabaster fingers, and finding he was not the desperate ruffian she had expected, suffered him to approach a little nearer.

Before, however, he could reach her, she uttered a second startled cry, and slipping from the velvet couch, ran to the farthermost end of the cabin.

As she glided hastily down, one beautiful limb, half hidden by her silken robes, was for a moment revealed; and now, as she stood panting at the end of the apartment, her white bosom was visible beneath her coquettish jacket as it rose and fell with her timid emotion, and Tom thought he had never seen such a little model of perfect loveliness.

Making a gesture that he intended her no harm, Tom again advanced.

But the young girl no sooner saw him lift his hand than she screamed wildly and plucking a miniature poniard from her embroidered vest, turned its point towards her fair bosom.

In another moment the sharp weapon would have pierced her flesh, but Tom was swift and sure in his movements.

With one bound he had leaped to her side, and while one hand seized her wrist, his other arm encircled her slender waist, and drew her heaving bosom to his, while with gentle force he took the jewelled weapon from between her slender fingers.

She made no resistance after he had seized her, but lay in his arms as passive as a captive bird—her large wondrous eyes dilating as she gazed into his frank countenance—her ripe lips apart—a faint flush stealing to her waxen features.

Tom did not know how to make her understand his intentions, as he was totally unacquainted with her language; so he did what he thought was the best thing to assure her.

Gallantly pressing her hand to his breast, he drew her closer to him, and kissed her with respectful gallantry.

Then smoothing back from her white forehead the rich masses of hair which had escaped from the circlet of opals and pearls, he allowed her to release herself, and gently led her back to her couch.

She understood by his manner that she was safe from molestation, and a look of grateful gladness settled on her face.

She seemed to comprehend, too, that he was master there, for she folded her arms meekly before her, and followed his movements with her large black eyes.

Tom was glad that he had got on so far with her, and he now proceeded to make an examination of the place.

His wildest dreams were realised as he gazed around.

Never could he have conceived of rarer treasures than were here displayed.

The wealth contained in that cabin alone was worth the ransom of a score of kings.

It was evident the maiden had not been alone. A table that literally sparkled with gems was heaped with delicious sweetmeats and fruits, piled on vessels of solid gold, and a goblet of massive gold, the brim gleaming with diamonds, was half filled with the richest wine.

Two smaller goblets of the same precious make were overturned, as if hastily left.

Tom turned from these to the young girl.

Was it possible that she was in any way connected with the ruthless pirate he had slain on deck?

Looking at her exquisitely moulded form, and contrasting her almost childish purity of countenance with the brutal visage of the corsair, it seemed out of all possibility; yet there were articles of male costume about the place, and by the couch was a splendid turban and a massive scimitar which must have belonged to the ruthless corsair.

Our hero did not want the turban, though the gold crescent in front of it was studded with diamonds of the first water; but the scimitar attracted him.

He stooped and picked it up from the floor.

The blade was of the finest Damascus steel—sharpened to the keenness of a razor, and so well tempered that at a touch it bent double and sprang back with a whizzing force.

Its belt was set with an immense emerald almost as large as an egg, and rounded off smooth. A gold guard protected the holder's hand.

"This is a prize, indeed," Tom cried, proudly balancing it in his hand. "It shall be mine, and no other hand shall wield it while I live."

He was so intently engaged in fastening the splendid weapon to his belt, that he did not observe the young girl glide from the couch, and, with a face colourless as marble, creep from the cabin.

He missed her the instant she was gone, and hurried after her as she fled like a fawn up the hatchway.

Quickly as he followed she was on deck before he had time to stay her.

He heard her swift inquiring cry as her wild glance swept round the scene of carnage, while she ran to and fro, seeking some one among the slain, till her gaze rested on the cruel visage of the giant corsair, when, giving a thrilling, horrifying shriek, she fell on the deck apparently senseless.

As Tom sprang forward to raise her, she leaped to her feet.

In a moment she had again fallen beside the pirate, and lifted his massive head, raising it higher and higher till it touched her bosom, and her tears fell to the lifeless face.

It was piteous to see her grief. How she raved in agony, screaming as the dead man gave no answer to her cries to call him back to life.

She loosened the dark masses of her hair, and wiped the blood-stains from his face, trying with her white fingers to close the horrid gash in his bearded throat; and when she found that he was past all hope—that there was no beating of the heart that had so lately throbbed in his powerful chest—her eyes swept round in search of him whose murderous hand had let forth the pirate's life.

Tom was standing near her, thinking remorsefully that he was the guilty one, when the young girl's sweeping glance rested upon him, piercing to his soul, and reading there all she sought to know.

Such a look of awful agony and horror settled in the maiden's eyes that Tom was touched to the heart; a chilly, rigid expression fixed her pallid features, and with a low moan of soul-wrung agony, she sank prone on the dead corsair's breast.

Tom stole softly towards her—she was insensible.

He took her hand; it was clammily, deathly cold.

He raised her beautiful face—it was like the face of a corpse.

He lifted her tenderly in his arms, and carried her away.

His heart smote him as he saw a slender stream of blood trickling from her mouth.

As he was descending the hatchway, a girl, attired as an Oriental slave, encountered him.

She was paralysed with fright, but had gathered strength enough to creep from her hiding-place and come forth to see after the young maiden, her mistress.

She followed him to the cabin, and with many ejaculations knelt down beside the inanimate form of her mistress; and our hero, leaving her to bring the hapless girl to consciousness, hurried again upon deck.

Considerable clearance had taken place under the directions of Ben Barnacle; the dead had been thrown overboard, with the exception of the corsair chief, whom they were now preparing to commit to the deep.

Tom came to the side as they lifted the pirate from the deck, and took his last look upon his formidable foe.

Even in death the corsair looked the ruthless man of blood and rapine.

His hands were tightly clenched, and a cruel, savage look had settled on his face.

As they raised him above the netting, the grim ferocity of the set features seemed to deepen in hate; and Tom almost started at the cold, relentless expression of the dull, glazed eyes, as their fixed stare seemed to meet him.

The sailors gave a hearty "ahoy," and the next instant dropped the pirate over.

The splash sent its cold dash into Tom's face.

For a second or so the transparent waves seethed over the rigid visage and huge frame, then with a cold gurgle plashed over him, and the pirate sank down.

Sank deeper and deeper, till pitiless face, and staring cruel eyes were out of sight, then our hero turned thoughtfully away, while his crew with one hearty cheer proclaimed the disappearance of the chief of the corsairs.

Anxious as he was to go below and look after the hapless maiden, whose association with and tender love of the pitiless pirate strangely interested him, Tom felt it his duty to stay upon deck, and direct the disposal of the vast booty.

Not one of the pirates had been spared, their crimes had been too notorious; but there were many on board the vessel who had taken no part in their deeds of violence, but had been hired or compelled to attend to the cooking and other work.

These were permitted to remain.

Several captive maidens were on board.

These were allotted a cabin till means could be found to put them on shore.

All that now remained was to decide respecting the booty and the vessel.

The Barbary cruiser was a heavier ship than Tom's; she carried more guns, was better equipped, and built for greater speed.

Had the corsairs not been certain of victory and hove to for the encounter, Tom would not have easily come up with them.

These facts, and the difficulty of removing the immense plunder stowed in her holds, and indeed, crammed wherever room could be found, induced Tom to entertain the idea of quitting the corvette, and risking his fortunes on the pirate ship.

So when the wounded were placed under surgical care, and the number and names of the killed had been taken, he called the remainder of his crew to the poop, and put the question.

The middies as well as the others were overjoyed at the idea.

It was more glorious to have a ship of their own, instead of the one they had ran away with.

Tom's propositions were consequently most cordially welcomed.

The only question was, what they should do with the corvette.

Ben Barnacle decided that.

"Let us send her back as a present for those who could neither take nor keep her."

Tom's eyes sparkled at the thought.

He gave the word, and in a short space of time the powder, shot, and all valuables were removed on board the Barbary cruiser.

"We'll send a message with her," Ben Barnacle said; and taking a paint-pot and brush, he wrote on the mast—

"We took this ship from under the guns of the pirate. Captain Tom, who wants her no longer, sends her back as a present for the frigate, in hopes they will be able to keep her when they catch her."

Tom smiled when Ben had finished.

Then the corvette's sails were trimmed, her helm secured, and the last of Tom's crew having quitted her, she went swiftly on her journey across the seas.

It was nearly dark when the wind carried her out of their sight, and then as Tom's crew gave her a farewell cheer, Ben Barnacle, who had run up our hero's flag in place of the pirate's pennon, hurled a bottle over the new vessel's bows, and christened her by her new name, the *Will-o'-the-Wisp*.

Captain Tom Drake and his boy crew had good reason to be satisfied with the success of their first enterprise.

There were treasures enough in the vessel's hold to have made each of them rich for life.

Any who desired to quit their companions could have gone away well satisfied, had gain alone been their object.

But the boys were animated by another influence.

They had been so basely treated under the stern discipline of Captain Parker, and the ferocious brutality of the malignant Sanderson, that their new life of liberty had a charm for them nothing could subdue.

Even the risk they ran of being taken and treated as pirates by any British ship sent out to pursue them, only enhanced the excitement of their career.

Besides, they were devotedly attached to their gallant young leader, and not one of them would have deserted him while he desired them to serve under his flag.

All thoughts, then, of returning to their duty on the frigate were ended, and Captain Parker, who was hotly chasing them, and imagined he had only to come up with them to surrender, was destined to find out his mistake when they should fall in with each other.

The corvette had not gone out of their sight before Tom Drake, having seen that nothing required his further presence on deck, descended to the cabin of the Eastern maiden.

Bob Hauler and Jerry Mizzen, who saw him go below, and pretty well guessed whither he was bound, indulged in sundry comicalities one with the other, giving vent to remarks that would have got them into pretty hot water had they been overheard by Tom, or even by Ben Barnacle, who was staunchly jealous of his young chieftan's fame.

The worthy pair of smuggling gentlemen, only waiting for the conclusion of the fight—for to do them justice, they were no cowards, and had that day given many a fierce pirate a chop on the skull or a dig in the ribs that had proved a settler—had sneaked down below to gloat over the accumulated heaps of treasure, and had stolen from the cabin while it was empty the large goblet containing the rich wine, and now, snugly ensconced under the boom sheets, were getting rather elevated—the wine being of such quality as they had never before had the felicity of tasting.

For the present we must leave them.

When our hero entered the cabin the corsair maiden was lying in a trance-like stupor, extended on the couch. The slave was bending over her.

On Tom's entrance she waved her hand as a gesture for him to tread silently, and gave him a look that told him as plainly as words that he was not wanted there, at least by them.

Having given a glance at the pale girl who lay breathing heavily, but apparently unconscious, our hero would have obeyed the slave girl's behests and withdrawn, if the corsair maiden herself had not, by a feeble movement of her arm, indicated that he was to approach.

Advancing hastily, but with noiseless, diffident step, he stood before her.

She lay with her eyes partially closed—the lids quivering, and steeped with tears—her cheeks were ashy pale, and wore a frozen woe-begone look that smote our hero to the soul.

Her bosom was heaving hard, as if she tried to repress her emotions; her lips were slightly apart, and had lost all their bright richness; her eyes were dull and strangely sad.

When Tom was near enough, she raised herself slightly, and outstretching her white arms, took both his hands in hers, and looked him full in the face with such a gaze—so plaintively reproachful, so sorrowfully accusing, that he was forced to avert his face, and hide his quivering lip.

After she had fixed him with her stare of stupor for some moments, she drew his hand closer to her bosom, and drooping her pale face, burst into a bitter flood of tears.

Tom tried to withdraw his right hand—the hand that had killed the corsair chief—but as if she guessed what was passing in his mind, she held it more tightly, letting her tears fall faster, as if to wash its stains of blood away.

For half-an-hour, at least, she sobbed as if her heart would break, the slave girl doing all in her power to assuage her grief—calling upon her as "Zeila," which Tom surmised to be her name.

She released his hand at last, and the noble boy, sinking to one knee, respectfully kissed her hand, and silently quitted the cabin and ascended to the deck

Meanwhile, Bob Hauler and his mate, the redoubtable Jerry Mizzen, had been pulling at the goblet, till, having drained its last dregs, they became quarrelsome, and some not over polite words were followed by a smart interchange of smacks—Bob Hauler getting a spank in the eye that made him see about twenty stars between him and Jerry, while the latter individual got such a smeller on his nose, that the nasal organ rose to the size of a young pudding.

The mélée was wound up by Jerry seizing the handsome goblet, and felling Bob by a knock which nearly crushed his skull, at which juncture Ben Barnacle sent two of the middies with buckets of water, with which they drenched them to the skin and drove them half sobered to their hammocks.

Jerry Mizzen sneaked off triumphantly with the valuable goblet, which he had, unperceived, concealed in the hinder part of his loose trousers; but which, forgetting all about as he was preparing to turn in, he let fall on the snout of a middy who slept beneath his hammock, awaking the youngster in such a state of alarm, that thinking the ship was boarded by pirates, he sprang to his feet and dealt Jerry a blow in the wind that knocked him off his feet like a thunderbolt, and stretched him on the boards, where he lay gasping.

A week of fine weather attended our young adventurers in their first cruise with their new ship, and a happy time of it they had under their boyish leader.

They had liberally helped themselves to the costly dresses and weapons of the corsairs, and proved a handsome crew when they assembled to hear the orders of their young captain.

Our hero had been rather sad of late—his girlish captive began to exercise a strange influence over him.

For the first few days she had kept to her apartment, during which time he had been continually by her side.

She seemed to be getting over her feelings on account of the corsair's death, and though she shivered slightly when her gaze rested on Tom, she was evidently pleased to have him in her presence.

And the gallant boy—whose whole thoughts were of his girlish love, Minnie Atherton, whose love-gift rested at his heart—felt grieved that the corsair maiden's forlorn condition forced him to occupy the dangerous position of her protector; for, boy as he was, he could not fail to see that her eyes lighted with gladness at his coming, and that her bosom swelled with passionate emotion when her soft arm reposed beside his.

True as he was to Minnie, he could not disguise from himself that his fair captive enthralled him by the fascinations of her beauty, and by one look could stir the depths of his impulsive soul.

Still he could not conquer the sympathy and interest he felt for the young girl.

He longed to learn her tongue—to learn what connection or relationship there was between her and the ruthless pirate leader whom he had sent to his long account.

On her part, Zeila—as her attendant called her—seemed as eager to converse with him.

She tried to make him understand her by signs, and talked to him in the Oriental tongue till Tom began to comprehend her words, and taught her their meaning in English.

It was astonishing how soon they picked up an idea of each other's language.

Zeila was a very assiduous teacher, and our hero proved himself so apt a pupil that in a surprisingly short space of time he was able to comprehend her when she told him her history.

She was an Arabian by birth, but at an early age, when she was quite a child, had been taken to Turkey, and promised in marriage to a wealthy young merchant.

A favourite attendant of a rich pasha—Seyd Ali—had, however, seen her, and resolved to get possession of her for his master.

The young merchant, however—whom she feared and disliked—heard of the plan, and fearing to openly claim her, entered her chamber one night and carried her off.

A corsair captain, Kaboo Rahi, who had previously made love to her and been repulsed by her father, heard her shrieks, and hastening to her rescue, encountered her abductor and slew him with her in his arms.

He was seized while his sword was yet red with the merchant's heart's blood, and thrust into prison, and the next day found her an unwilling inmate of the pasha's harem.

The treatment with him was more gentle than she had expected.

He refrained from entering her chamber, preferring to wait till he could join her alone.

But one stormy night the palace was in flames, and in the midst of the confusion, Kaboo Rahi burst in, followed by half-a-dozen desperate corsairs, slew the pasha on the threshold, hurled him into the flames, and bore away herself and half the women of the harem.

She was carried senseless on board the corsair's vessel.

He had been desperately wounded, and when she came to herself, she felt bound in gratitude to tend upon him.

He had scarcely recovered, when his merciless crew, who had severely treated and thrown overboard the pasha's captured wives, rose in mutiny, and demanded that she, too, should be cast into the sea, it being a law with them that no woman should be on board.

By becoming his wife she was saved from death, and, strange to say, her abhorrence of the desperate corsair changed into passionate love, and she chose to follow his fortunes till the fatal hour when he met his death at our hero's hands.

Captain Tom felt more a man of mettle when he heard what a redoubtable chieftain he had vanquished; for Zeila told him tales of his exploits that proved him to have been a desperate and daring adventurer, and a perfect demon when aroused, and one whose merciless instincts were only satiated in blood.

Having told him her history, Zeila was as eager to learn his.

She heard, with brightened colour, the recital of his escape from the *Arethusa*, but started as if she had been stricken by a bullet when he told her of his love for Minnie Atherton.

Then Tom knew what dangerous ground he stood upon.

The corsair maiden had transferred her affections from her dead lover to him.

The discovery was not unmixed with a pleasurable pride.

She was so beautiful, and seemed so pure, that it seemed no sin to permit her love.

And the corsair maiden, now that she had overcome her anguish at the pirate's fate, used all the endearments of her nature to chain our hero to her side.

Tom was seated with her one evening in the luxurious cabin, when word was brought him that a heavy frigate had been sighted in their track.

Our hero hurried to the deck.

A few minutes' careful survey through his telescope enabled him to make out the coming ship to be their old pursuer, the *Arethusa*.

She had evidently sighted them, for she began to crowd more canvas, and shaped her course directly after them.

Captain Tom handed his glass to his first officer, and looking round on the eager faces of his crew, said—

" The frigate is on our track. Up lads, we must take the wind out of her sails; for I mean to run to England, and get away again before she can overhaul us."

Ben Barnacle sang out his orders; all sails were set, and soon the *Will-o'-the-Wisp* flew like a bird before the wind as her bows were turned for her run to England.

.   .   .   .   .

We must return awhile to old Gregory and his ward, whom, with Tom's mother, we left at the old-fashioned mansion by the seaside.

Tom's abrupt departure had mystified them.

Old Gregory raved for three days like a madman, and frightened Mrs. Drake till she went about the house white as a ghost.

Her half-sister, Mrs. Harpy, made good the occasion to say all she could against Tom's character.

And Sanderson, before he departed, spread the report that Tom had fallen into dissipated company, and gone on board in a state of drunkenness.

A day after he had gone Reuben Harpy suddenly disappeared.

It was reported that he had been seized by the press-gang at Tom's instigation.

Old John Gregory hotly scouted the idea, and when Mrs. Harpy came before him in violent hysterics, he ordered her out of the room.

A change came over Minnie Atherton after Tom had gone.

Day by day she waited, expecting to hear from him; and day by day she grew paler and more sad as the expected letter failed to arrive.

She thought it cruel of him not to write; but her pure faith was placed in his honour, and she still believed the time would come when the mystery of his silence would be cleared away.

Very often she wandered to their old tryst-place by the pleasant little lake where her skiff lay idle now, for she had no heart to use it—she felt too lonely.

Tom's love there lay like a burning weight at her heart; and sometimes when she feared he might not return, she stole to some secluded hiding-place in the woods and gave way to her tears.

All this time Tom was enduring the galling yoke of his servitude on board the *Arethusa*,

How it would have stung his mettlesome spirit had he known how she suffered for his sake!

Many months had gone by.

Old Gregory was seated in his arm-chair by the bay window overlooking the bay—that window from which he had seen Tom's gallant rescue of his darling Minnie.

The honest-hearted old fellow was recalling the scene now.

He saw Tom in his youthful glow of beauty leaping again into the blue waters, and springing to the bank with Minnie in his arms; and a tear trickled down his cheek as he thought of the change that had taken place.

Minnie was sitting by his knee.

She was very fond of sitting with her guardian since Tom had gone.

The two understood each other's thoughts well, and though our hero's name was seldom mentioned, they knew that each still had faith in the proud-spirited boy.

It was sunset.

The evening chills were creeping over the glorious scene—the sun setting, like molten gold, behind the peak from which Tom had been tumbled into the sea.

A great alteration had taken place in John Gregory—he seemed breaking fast.

"Minnie, darling," he said, abruptly, " do you remember when that—that graceless scamp pulled you out of the lake ?"

Minnie sighed.

" I shall never forget, papa."

" Ah, he was a fine lad then. I'm afraid he's gone to the bad now."

" Oh, no!" Minnie cried; " I am sure he is true to us."

" Why don't he write to me, then ?" growled old Gregory.

" Perhaps he will come back soon and explain all."

" If he does—the rascal ! the scoundrel !—I'll turn him from the door. How dare he steal your heart and run away like this ?"

Minnie's eyes filled with tears.

" I wish he would only come back," she said, sadly.

"Yes, yes," John Gregory muttered, "I wish he would come back—I wish he would come back."

The silence that succeeded the old gentleman's words was abruptly broken by the door being suddenly burst open.

Minnie gave a slight scream and sprang to her feet.

For the moment she almost expected to see the graceful figure and handsome face of Tom Drake.

It was not our hero—he was far enough away—but Mrs. Harpy, who, with her face streaming with hypocritical tears, entered quickly, and cried hysterically—

"I knew it!—I knew it! My dear boy!—my poor dear boy! That wicked favourite of yours! Oh, my poor Reuben, I shall never see him again!"

Old John Gregory started up in anger.

"The devil take you, and Reuben, too," he cried; "a precious good job if you never see him again, the cowardly cur!—the—the—hypocritical vagabond!"

Mrs. Harpy forced a fresh flood of tears to her eyes.

"Yes," she exclaimed, "that's how you always are—always against my poor boy. But perhaps you'll believe now what this good man has to say about your favourite and my poor boy."

"Good man! What good man? Who the devil do you mean, woman?"

"This honest mariner," Mrs. Harpy replied, as a seafaring man advanced awkwardly into the room.

He had a weather-beaten, well-salted face, but his features did not bear the impression of an honest tar, as he stood in front of old Gregory, touching his forelock and scraping his restless feet.

His shifting gaze wandered uneasily about the room till it rested upon Mrs. Harpy's face, when it lit up with a momentary gleam of assurance.

"Well," roared old Gregory, "who the devil are you? And what do you want?"

"I'm Dan Cuttle, your honour," the fellow replied; "at your honour's service."

"Well, you swab—well?"

"This lady, please your honour, wanted me to come and tell your honour about Master Reuben and Master Tom."

"You, sir? And what the devil do you know about them, eh?"

"I served in the same ship as Tom Drake, sir! was under him before he got into disgrace, sir."

"Go on—you vagabond—go on."

"The man will tell you," Mrs. Harpy interrupted, "that this favourite Tom of yours, after disgracing himself in every possible way, finished his brilliant career by losing his ship, under circumstances of such rank cowardice that he was disgraced and dismissed."

Mrs. Harpy's cheeks coloured with some little shame as she remembered that it was her own boy to whom all this had happened.

Old John Gregory leaped round like a wounded panther.

"What!" he roared, "you brace of liars! Tom a coward! Lost his ship! It's a lie—a lie! and you know it—both of you."

Mrs. Harpy screamed and sank back in a pretended faint.

Minnie, whose face was of a waxen pallor, stepped up to the sailor, and asked him huskily if he spoke the truth.

"It's all true, miss," the fellow answered. "Moreover, when they took the middy's jacket off him he confessed as how he'd got his cousin Reuben took by the press-gang and sent to sea."

"Yes," screamed Mrs. Harpy, "the press-gang! My poor boy!"

"I wish the press-gang had you and all," John Gregory yelled. "It's a lie, I say, a lie!"

"'Taint no yarn, your honour. And a nice young devil—saving your presence, miss—he's turned out since——"

"How? Where is he now? Where, sir—where?"

"Running away from the frigate that's after him for the ship he took."

"Took—a ship?" Minnie said, breathlessly.

"Yes, miss; and got all the middies to leave their duty and join him. They've turned pirates, miss, and he calls himself Commodore Tom."

"This is a wicked calumny!" old Gregory vociferated, "a base invention—I never will believe it."

"'Tis as true as gospel, your honour, and if you don't believe me, here's a proclamation of his Majesty you can read."

John Gregory clutched the paper.

Hurriedly he read its contents, Minnie listening pale as a ghost, and scarcely breathing.

"PIRACY! PIRACY!!

"PROCLAMATION.

"£1,000 REWARD

"Will be given to any commander of our ships who shall either slay or take alive Captain Tom Drake, the Boy Buccaneer, now infesting our coasts and defying our power on the high seas.

"Moreover, all our Admirals, Captains, and other Officers of our Royal Navy, are commanded to take, sink, burn, or destroy his Pirate vessel, known as the *Will-o'-the-Wisp*, when and wherever found, and to execute as Pirates the rebellious Midshipmen serving under his flag.

"GOD SAVE THE KING."

When old Gregory had finished reading, he let the fatal paper fall from his hands, and sank back in a fit.

Minnie flew to his side and raised his head, and as she wiped the beady sweat from his clammy features, Mrs. Harpy, darting her a look of vicious hatred, left the apartment, followed by the sneaking ruffian who had brought the news.

The fellow was a myrmidon in the pay of Sanderson, who was on his way to the place, and had bribed the man to bring the intelligence to old Gregory.

He had Reuben with him.

The cowardly lad had been tried by court-martial for losing his ship, and dismissed with ignominy.

In furtherance of their crafty plan, he was tried under the name of Tom Drake, in order that the disgrace might fall upon our hero.

It nearly broke Mrs. Drake's heart when she heard about her son—the story seemed too well confirmed; yet she could not believe it possible for him to prove a coward.

As for John Gregory his faith was terribly shaken, and he went about the house in silent moodiness.

A week after, Lieutenant Sanderson arrived.

He brought with him the full particulars of the trial, and represented Tom in a hideous light.

When he thought he had sufficiently prepared the old gentleman's mind, he sent word to Reuben to present himself.

They had got him a forged commission as lieutenant in the navy, Sanderson swearing that Reuben had risen by his own merits.

It was thought that this would be enough to make him replace Tom in John Gregory's affections, but the result was a total failure.

The old gentleman received him coldly, and waved him from his presence.

Sanderson had brought with him a stranger who bore a captain's rank, and who corroborated the tale of Reuben's brave conduct.

His name was Captain Angel.

He was a slightly built man, with a pale parched visage; his eyes were of a cold vacant blue, and when he laughed his teeth glittered like the fangs of a wolf.

He had exceedingly small white hands, but the fingers were long and pointed.

Looking at them in their supple movements, for they were perpetually entwining restlessly—it was hard to repress the feeling that sharp talons were covered by the white skin.

Neither John Gregory nor Mrs. Drake liked the company of this Captain Angel.

He was very quiet in manner, but he had a stealthy kind of laugh that was strangely repulsive.

There was at times a steel-like glitter in his cold eyes when his gaze rested on the fair face of Minnie Atherton.

The young girl instinctively shrank from him.

She mistrusted his looks from the first moment his sleepy cruel eyes stared into hers.

Sanderson and his friend Captain Angel were constantly at the house.

John Gregory did not like their presence there; he hinted as much to his half-sister.

But she assured him that their stay would soon be at an end, as it would be time for them and Reuben to go again to sea.

"Very glad to hear it," the old fellow growled; "want them all to go away—all of them—every one."

Mrs. Harpy left him with her face livid with passion, and her half-brother, who caught the vicious look in her eyes as she went from the room, felt a strange misgiving creep to his heart.

"I wish Tom would come home," he muttered, as he went moodily about his house. "He's been a scamp—a scoundrel—a—but, hang him, I'd like to see his noble face once more."

The same wish was in Minnie's breast.

His mother, too, yearned for his return, and while the malignant plotters were scheming darkly against the three, Tom's coming was anxiously prayed for by those who were still his friends.

After Mrs. Harpy had left John Gregory she went to her room, where Captain Angel sat waiting.

"Is it time?" he asked, a cynical smile flitting over his bloodless features.

"His heart is still fixed on his favourite," Mrs. Harpy replied, spitefully; "he wishes Reuben away, and longs for the other's return."

"Ah!" Captain Angel smiled again, the same cold smile; "his health is giving way—it is time for his friends to look after him."

"Yes, and after her as well; my half-sister—tell me, cannot you kidnap her, Captain Angel? Get her on board your ship, treat her vilely till she wishes for death—you understand what I mean."

Mrs. Harpy's voice sank to a sharp whisper.

Her eyes blazed vindictively, and a slight colour stole to her cheeks, as Captain Angel's glance met hers.

"Oh, yes," he replied, carelessly, "I understand, perfectly; I can do that—but upon one condition—can you guess?"

The revengeful woman turned a shade paler.

Captain Angel crept stealthily to her, and fixing his cold eyes on her face, said—

"You must pay the price if I do this—I must be paid first, too. Do you consent?"

"What mean you?"

He drew closer to her till his colourless visage touched her.

Then he put his lips to her ear and whispered a few words that sent her blood back frozen in her veins.

"Must that be your price?" she asked, faintly, for evil as she was, his cold, deliberate proposal shamed her.

"It must. Is it too great for the task of ridding you of her?"

His voice was a deep, hoarse whisper, and the vindictive woman shivered, but said nothing.

The sinful woman stopped at nothing to secure her purpose.

Sanderson entered at this moment.

Like most men of his debased nature, he suspected the woman who had given herself up to him.

Whatever thoughts Sanderson entertained, he kept them to himself, and the trio sat down to their future plans.

John Gregory was to be got to sign a will in favour of Reuben, and disinheriting Tom, at the same time leaving his solemn injunctions to Minnie to marry Reuben Harpy.

Sanderson chuckled over the prospect.

His avaricious nature yearned for the rich estates, over which he longed to have control.

Besides, he entertained sinister intents towards Minnie—intents which, as yet, he concealed within his breast.

"It will be a difficult task to get the old curmudgeon to sign," Captain Angel said. "His is a tough nature, but I think I know of a way to ensure his compliance."

To look in his fairish face as he spoke these words, no one would have suspected the diabolical design lurking under his smooth aspect.

He smiled cynically when Minnie was spoken of as Reuben's bride.

"There is only one chance of our plan being knocked on the head," he observed, with his cold, quiet laugh; "it would be all over with our hopes if this Tom Drake should return."

Sanderson started to his feet.

"Curse him!" he cried fiercely; "should he return I would strangle him!"

His cynical smile played about Captain Angel's lips, but he said nothing, and Sanderson walked restlessly up and down the room.

A dark vision had disturbed his mind—the vision of our gallant hero, speeding across the seas, and putting foot on shore in time to hurl him to the earth, foiled and vanquished.

Captain Angel left soon after.

The next day, a peculiar circumstance was reported.

Mrs. Drake had disappeared from John Gregory's house.

No one knew why she had fled, or whither.

None had seen the previous night a prone, muffled, senseless form, in the rude grasp of four brutal ruffians, who, under the direction of Captain Angel got their victim down to the bay.

No one saw the vindictive visage of Mrs. Harpy as she watched from her concealment the abduction of Tom's mother.

This new incident disturbed John Gregory's mind.

At an early hour he wished Minnie good night, and retired to his chamber.

It was one of those old-fashioned, solid-built apartments, with thick doors and walls, and high massive windows.

Once shut in there, with the heavy shutters closed, no more sound entered from the outside than from a tomb.

John Gregory shut himself in, and crawled to his easy chair by the fireside.

A small table was placed within his reach with a tumbler of hot grog upon it.

It remained untasted and getting cold. John Gregory was deep in thought. A strange mystic foreboding was at his heart.

It seemed as if that hour was to bring about his doom.

"If the boy would only come back," he mused, "I should feel safer. I am not safe now. No, I can feel my danger, and I cannot help myself."

The old gentleman buried his face in his hands, and mused bitterly.

He started up suddenly as if a serpent had stung him.

His name had been pronounced in an icy, creeping whisper that crept through his veins, freezing his heart's blood.

Some one was in the room with him.

"My God," he exclaimed, his features bathed in sweat, "who is here?"

"A friendly visitor," a quiet voice exclaimed, and John Gregory's gaze rested on the bloodless visage of Captain Angel.

He had crept into the room unheard—the door was closed behind him—closed and fastened as old Gregory instinctively felt.

His features were set to a forced calmness, but the subtle look of a hidden devil peered from his hard blue eyes.

When old Gregory saw him he made a quick movement as if to seize the bell-rope and summon help, but Captain Angel stepped before him and cut it above his reach.

"You need not trouble yourself," he said; "I desire a few minutes' conversation with you."

"Not here—not now," John Gregory said, trembling violently as the lynx-eyes of the captain fascinated him.

"Here—and now," Captain Angel replied; "sit down and listen."

He forced John Gregory into his chair, and seated himself at the table.

"I have here," he began, taking a bundle of papers from his pocket, "certain documents which I require you to sign; we have pen and ink here. You have only to affix your name, I and my witnesses will do the rest."

"I sign no documents. What mean you? What papers are these?"

"One is your will, bequeathing the whole of your property to Reuben Harpy, and disinheriting your nephew, Tom Drake. The other is a paper rendering up to Lieutenant Sanderson the guardianship of your ward, Minnie Atherton, and enjoining her to bestow herself and property upon the aforesaid Reuben."

Captain Angel's tones were coldly deliberate.

He spread the papers before him as he spoke, and then, with a slight touch of his hand, pushed back John Gregory, who was rising in alarm from his chair.

"Scoundrel! villain!" John Gregory cried, "leave me before my cries summon help."

"Your cries will not be heard—sign."

"Never! I will not lend myself to this base plot. God help me! I see through it all now—all—all."

He fell back shaking in his chair.

"John Gregory, sign."

The tones were murderously calm.

"Never—so God help me! No—not even if you murder me."

"We shall not murder you; a dead man could not do our bidding. These papers, John Gregory, shall be signed by you. Sign freely, or we will find fearful means to compel you."

"Help, help! murder!" John Gregory cried, springing from his chair.

Captain Angel thrust both of his clenched hands on his throat and hurled him back. Then he stepped quietly to the door, which he unfastened and opened.

"Enter," he said softly; "he needs your persuasion."

John Gregory was rising again, breathless, when Sanderson and Mrs. Harpy glided in.

They had not brought Reuben with them.

They were afraid his cowardly nerves would be unstrung by the sight.

Mrs. Harpy stepped softly up to her half brother, who shrank from her as if she were a serpent ready to coil its loathsome folds about his body.

Sanderson fastened the door, and Captain Angel approached on tiptoe to his victim.

"My dear Gregory," Mrs. Harpy said, "you must sign these papers."

"Not if you murder me," repeated Gregory in a hoarse whisper.

"We are losing time," Captain Angel exclaimed, and flung his lithe arms round John Gregory.

The helpless old gentleman struggled to get free; but Mrs. Harpy treacherously held back his head, and kept one hand over his mouth to stifle his cries.

Sanderson assisted in the devilish work; and, amongst them, they got their victim to the ground and secured him.

They had gagged him effectually.

Only his hoarse whispers of agony could be heard.

He thought they were going to murder him.

Captain Angel had a more terrible intention: he removed John Gregory's boots and socks, and, sitting down quietly in front of him, coolly began his horrible process of tickling the old man's feet with feathers.

At first John Gregory writhed and shivered; but as the merciless torture proceeded, the reeking sweat rolled down his features, which were drawn up in frightful convulsions.

His eyes rolled wildly.

Foam gathered about his lips.

At a gesture from Captain Angel, Sanderson forced the pen into his hand.

But, despite the agony he endured, the stout-hearted old fellow seized the pen between his fingers, and snapped it into fragments.

Captain Angel laughed his cold-blooded laugh, and resumed his infernal work.

Hardened as Sanderson and Mrs. Harpy were, they could scarcely endure the awful spectacle.

Had quick murder been done they might have borne it better.

But this unnerved them.

The guilty woman turned away from John Gregory's eyes, which rolled upon her as they started from their sockets.

Every muscle of his broad chest—every fibre of his body worked up and down in horrible contortions.

And still Captain Angel went on with his horrible work—went on till a wild cry of anguish came from the victim's muffled lips, and his head rolled helplessly back.

"Sign," Captain Angel cried.

Old Gregory made no reply.

He had fainted.

Blood and foam frothed about his mouth.

His whole frame quivered with a deathly tremor.

The very muscles of his body seemed rolling about under his skin.

Hitherto their infernal work had been carried on in silence, but now Mrs. Harpy drew back as white as a sheet.

"I cannot witness more of this," she said, shaking from head to foot.

Even the callous Sanderson was sickened at the sight.

Captain Angel's well-defined lips curled in a disdainful smile.

"Faugh!" he exclaimed, "your nerves are as weak as a child's; take some of this, then help me to get some down his throat. We must not lose him yet."

Mrs. Harpy drank eagerly of the strong brandy, a flask of which he handed to her; then they poured some down John Gregory's throat, and brought him back to consciousness.

He gazed piteously upon them.

But Captain Angel replied by offering him a pen.

He refused to become the instrument of their villainy, and Captain Angel began anew his horrible task.

Human nature could endure no more.

The cruel device prevailed, and at last they got him to consent, and guided his shaking hand over the paper.

Even then he would not have yielded, but that he resolved to undo on the morrow the work of this night.

He had not calcu'ated on the brutality of his pitiless tormentors.

While he lay gasping and sti1 convulsed, Captain Angel with a demoniacal glitter in h's cold eyes, again picked up the feather instruments of torture.

Unable to speak, John Gregory's agonized face spoke his horror of this new barbarity.

Captain Angel answered him by a careless, mocking laugh, as he sat grimly down again to his fiendish work.

"Did you think we should let you off after this, you old fool?" he asked, cynically. "No, John Gregory, we are n)t going to kill you, because that is clumsy work; in fifteen minutes you will be mad —stark, raving mad. Aha! I thought that would make you writhe; a few more such touches, and then——"

The fifteen minutes had passed; the hellish deed was done; the guilty woman and her guiltier paramour, with ghastly looks, were bending over the prone babbling man who lay at their feet, bathed in reeking sweat, and clenching his convulsed hands in his palpitating flesh.

They had replaced his boots and unloosed his hands—he was too exhausted to do any injury yet, and now Captain Angel glided to the door.

"It is done," he exclaimed. "Do your part now."

Noiselessly he descended the stairs.

Not a pang of remorse was there in his hard cruel breast for the merciless deed he had done.

He and Sanderson were hiding in the shrubbery, when a succession of ringing shrieks from Mrs. Harpy aroused the house and brought the domestics to the chamber of old Gregory.

There they found their master with foaming lips and staring eyes—a raving madman.

They kept Minnie out of the way till he was secured, and the physician was sent for and informed of the sudden calamity.

The pitile-s conspirators had done their work cleverly; in one of old Gregory's clenched hands was found the proclamation offering a reward for Tom's capture.

Even the physician was deceived, and the belief went forth that the misconduct of his favourite nephew had turned the old gentleman's brain.

For a day or two he was cared for in the old house.

But after that he was carried off to a lunatic asylum.

Deprived of her last protector, and under such appalling circumstances, Minnie felt more lonely than before.

The papers relating to her disposal were read to her, and Mrs. Harpy put on a semblance of kindness towards the orphan girl.

Reuben persecuted her with his unwelcome attention.

The three plotters now took up their abode in Gregory's house, where they had it all their own way.

Mrs. Harpy set creatures of her own to watch Minnie, and the young girl found herself helpless in their hands and powerless to withstand their wishes.

The only point she would not yield in was in consenting to be untrue to Tom and become Reuben's bride.

She had vow'd to be faithful to her lover, and she resolved to prove herself so, though every device was tried to make her accede to what was represented as John Gregory's wish.

She was still so young that she might have been allowed a few months more liberty if her prosecutors had not been hurried in their work by a letter which was brought by a foreign ship.

It was boldly addressed, and Sanderson, who interpreted it, felt slightly uncomfortable when he found it was from the high-spirited boy, whom he greatly feared.

Tom had sent the letter to his girlish love, and this was what the evil plotters read:—

"Dearest Minnie,

"Have you forgotten me, or thought me untrue? I will come to England soon, and you shall hear my defence. If you do not reject me, then I will bear you away in my beautiful ship as my bride.　　　　"TOM."

For one week after they had received this letter —which was destroyed as soon as read—every means was tried to overcome Minnie's constancy.

Cruelly treated by Mrs. Harpy, confined day by day in her chamber, the friendless girl knew not where to look for help.

Her only consolation was to gaze from her window to the distant sea, and watch for a coming sail which might prove to be Tom's ship, for the brave little maiden would not believe that he had deserted her.

But no welcome sail hove in sight; and her persecutors, finding threats and entreaties alike useless, resolved to effect her espousal by force.

They gave her no chance of refusal, and a clergyman was bribed to perform the nuptials; and on the appointed day Mrs. Harpy had her attired as a bride, and carried, more dead than alive, to the carriage which was to convey her to the place where the marriage service was to be performed —a little, lonely chapel, within sound of the beating waves by the sea-shore.

Reuben Harpy gazed in malignant triumph upon the fair young creature as she was led half-fainting into the sacred edifice.

He had no love for her—his base nature was incapable f so pure a feeling, but she had despised him, and he longed for revenge, yearned to have her in his power that he might gratify his evil passions on her weakness, and make her repent in bitter sorrow for having preferred Tom to him

When the hapless girl was led into the chapel her agonized glance wandered from face to face in search of some one who would aid her.

There was no pity on the vindictive countenance of Mrs. Harpy, and the ill-visaged Sanderson gloated over the spectacle of her misery.

As for Captain Angel, his hardened stare of sinister cruelty was worse than the malignant triumph of Reuben.

Her gaze at length rested on the clergyman, and forgetting that he was the hired instrument of their will, she fell on her knees before him, and besought him to save her.

"Help me!" she exclaimed. "I am forced to this hate union."

"Be calm, child," the minister said. "The union is for your good. You will think ess unkindly of it by-and-bye."

With tears streaming down her fair cheeks, Minnie drew back from the man that disgraced his holy calling.

"Are you God's minister," she cried, "and

TOM TAKEN BY THE PRESS GANG.

suffer this cruel wrong? Oh, help—help—help—mercy! Is there no one to succour me?"

"To the devil with her cries!" Captain Angel exclaimed, as he pushed her violently from the door which h closed and fastened.

"Hasten the ceremony We shall have meddling witnesses here if h r screeching continues. Stifle h r screams, and drag her to the altar; and you, sir, quick with your mumbling."

Reuben caught the shrieking maiden as she tried to flee to the window and escape that way.

Roughly forcing her to her knees on the cold marble of the chancel, he dragged her towards the altar.

His mother and Sanderson assisted.

But even their efforts failed to keep her from shrieking for help.

Captain Angel, who, like the es', was armed with his dress sword, had a hard matter to keep the keen blade in its scabbard.

More than one he clutched the hilt as if about to draw the weapon an plunge it into her body.

Reube force the weeping girl to kneel before the altar, and gagged her mouth while the ceremony began.

The first part was briefly hurried over—Minnie Atherton shivering from head to foot—but when it came to the question whether she would have him for her wedded husband, she shrieked a wild, defiant "No," and springing to her feet fled from Reuben's grasp.

Captain Angel seized her by her hair as she flitted down the chancel.

"Take her, fool," he said to Reuben; "and hold her more securely."

"I will not be his victim!" Minnie cried. "Help! help! Will no one help a poor girl? Help, oh, help!"

Captain Angel stole swiftly up to her.

"Quiet, screech-owl!" he exclaimed, dealing her a violent blow on her fair throat that for the moment stupified her.

Reuben took advantage of this to seize her again.

"Mine—mine!" he shouted, as the clergyman went on with the service.

But the words had hardly left his lips when, with a wild shriek, more of joy than terror, Minnie leaped from his side.

"He comes!" she cried; "I hear his steps I feel his breath in the air! I am saved! saved! Help! I am here!"

"Minnie—Minnie!" it was a manly voice that answered her, "who dares to harm you? Open the doors here, or by heavens this sacred edifice shall be battered down—open, I say, or one stone shall not be left standing upon another."

There was a crash at the door as he spoke, then it was burst open, and a tall, finely-formed youth, enveloped in a long black cloak, and with his features concealed by a naval hat, sprang into the chapel.

He cast one glance at the group before the altar.

The trembling clergyman in his white robes, the bride with the torn orange blossom in her disordered hair, the three armed men standing in his path, with their hands on the hilts of their swords.

One glance he gave them, and with the bound of a young lion he dashed up the aisle, and hurling the three men aside, flung one arm round Minnie, and lifted her tenderly from the floor.

"Who dares to harm her now?" he cried loftily, his eyes ablaze with passion, his tones thrilling with their impetuous rage, as the weeping girl with a glad cry, clung trustingly to his breast. "Uplift a finger the bravest of you, stand a moment in my path, and this sword shall travel to the hilt in your blood. Look up, dear girl, a living host, armed to the teeth, dare not harm you now."

Captain Angel took a step forward, and at this signal the three swords were plucked from their sheaths.

The fact of the interrupter of the wedding being alone gave Reuben courage to advance.

"Stand back!" he cried; "she is my bride, I yield her to no man. Release her or you are a corpse."

"Release her!" the stranger's eyes flashed with a terrible light. "Release her! and to you. Move but one inch and I split you where you stand, take but one step and you step into your grave. I am here with an arm mightier than a thousand such as yours to save my bride—I, Captain Tom Drake, one of England's Hearts of Oak!"

Beating down Reuben's weapon as if it had been a reed, he threw aside his cloak and hat, and in his handsome uniform, with the glittering stars on his breast, revealed the gallant figure and noble features of Captain Tom Drake.

CHAPTER VII.

CAPTAIN ANGEL PUTS HIMSELF IN OUR HERO'S WAY, AND GETS MARKED FOR HIS PAINS.

THE utterance of our hero's name fell like an electric shock upon his hearers.

They fell back a pace as his unquailing eye swept from face to face—none dared uplift a weapon against him—none dared to meet the fierce challenge of the dauntless boy; and, though only one opposed to three, his defiant bearing kept them cowering at bay.

He looked very noble as he stood with one arm supporting Minnie as she lay upon his breast, the other extended as he held his sword a-tilt, ready to pierce the heart of the first who moved.

He was somewhat altered since they had last seen him.

Exposure to the sea-air and scorching sun had browned his noble features, which were stamped with the dauntless, devil-may-care expression of his rover's life.

His frame had grown more stalwart, his chest had expanded, his limbs were more finely developed, and though his figure was graceful as ever it was more indicative of his lion-like strength.

At the present moment his hot young blood mounting to his temples had crimsoned his countenance—and an angry light was leaping from his peerless brown eyes, and with his fine form set off by his rich uniform, he looked to the full the daring boy whose exploits had already made his name famous throughout the world.

Mrs. Harpy was the first to arouse them from their stupor.

"Are you all chicken-hearted?" she exclaimed. "Are you all afraid of a boy? Oh, that I were a man, that I might pluck his heart out. Pick up your sword, Reuben, and try if your coward arm can strike a blow for your wife and her rich lands."

Tom's glance swept proudly round.

"It was for that, then, this infamy was begun—to get her lands away. I am here only in time."

"In time to fall to the earth a corpse," Sanderson shouted, hoarsely, "unless you release that girl. Devil's brat! I thought I had seen the last of you."

"Not yet, ruffian; we have an account to settle first," Tom replied, setting his teeth firmly as he saw the three preparing to attack him.

Hitherto the minister had remained passive.

Tom's violent entry was so startling, that, fearful for his life, he had slunk behind the altar.

But now he came forward, hoping to interfere and save bloodshed.

"Young sir," he drawled, "let there be no bloody work done here. Remember, ere you raise your impious hand, this is the house of God."

"The house of God!"

Tom's voice quivered huskily.

"And yet this deed was to be committed under its roof—this unholy bartering of this dear girl."

"She was willing, sir."

"Liar!" thundered Tom. "Minnie, darling, you hear him? He would have me believe you had broken all your vows to me, and consented to wed yourself to this vile thing."

He raised his hands towards Reuben, who shrank from his angry gesture.

Minnie looked up into his excited face.

"I never proved faithless to you," she murmured through her tears. "They dressed me in these hateful robes, and dragged me here. Oh, Tom—dear Tom, they have cruelly used me."

"I know they have, dear dove. Don't weep and tremble now, rest securely on my breast. They must be of better mettle than these kites to tear you from me now."

"We will see that, braggart!" Sanderson cried, as he made a cowardly thrust at Tom's unguarded breast.

Minnie screamed when she saw her lover's danger; but Tom, with a reassuring word, bade her not fear.

He seemed to hold very lightly the peril he was in.

Swiftly parrying Sanderson's dastard thrust, he pricked him in the shoulder, and dashed at Reuben, who with Captain Angel, now confronted him.

With a wrist of steel, he forced down their weapons, striking Reuben's from his nerveless grasp, and dealing him a fearful blow with the flat of his sword across the forehead, bringing him to the ground stunned and bleeding.

"Now," he cried, "who stands in my way?"

Sanderson had crawled out of reach of his trusty sword; but Captain Angel, stealing behind him, made a murderous plunge at Minnie's side.

If Tom had not seen the treacherous movement, Minnie would have been transfixed to the heart.

As it was, the thin blade passed so close to her breast that she shrieked convulsively.

Captain Angel had no time to make a second thrust.

With a furious onset Tom battered down his sword.

His rage was terrible at the base attempt on Minnie's life.

"Pirate!" he cried, "had you but grazed her fair skin, this weapon's point should have been driven into your brain. I will not slay you now; we have to meet again; but I leave you my mark, that I may know you when next we meet."

Twice, with swift force he slashed at Captain Angel's cheek, cutting a frightful gash on each side; and as his treacherous opponent fell back, blinded with his own blood, he transfixed him through the neck, and held him up by his red blade.

"I have not touched a vital part," he exclaimed, as he held the writhing wretch in this agonized posture. "You will live, but these wounds will be like a canker in your breast till we meet again."

He withdrew the weapon sharply, and Captain Angel, with a horrible groan of agony, fell to the marble floor.

This swift bloodshed had paralysed Mrs. Harpy.

She had expected to see Minnie torn from Tom's arms, and our hero stretched bleeding at the altar steps.

And now the whole of his assailants had fallen beneath his prowess, while he stood unharmed, and with no one to oppose his departure.

She had only sufficient strength to fall beside her son, and lift his guilty head from the chapel floor, as Captain Tom sheathed his red sword, and flinging open the door, passed out with Minnie on his arm.

A moment after, she heard the roll of wheels, and knew that he had escaped.

Escaped with Minnie!

There was an end, then, to all their schemes, to say nothing of what they had to dread, should he discover what they had been guilty of with regard to his mother and John Gregory.

The wicked woman's tongue clove to the roof of her parched mouth.

She had seen enough of his hot nature to show that their lives would not be safe for a moment, should he learn their infamous secret.

He would be certain to make inquiries, and his penetration would lead him to suspect some deadly wrong; and then the terrible consequences of their crimes would overtake them.

There was only one chance—to have him taken.

A reward was offered for his capture, and, once taken he would be speedily tried and shot.

"Quick," she cried; "we have no time to lose. We must act instantly or we are destroyed. A thousand pounds are offered for his capture. Let us have him taken in his first moment of triumph, before he finds out what we have done."

"Aye," Sanderson replied, "once get him taken we are safe. Stay here till I send assistance—you, Reuben, come with me; the officers must be set on his track before another hour."

Meanwhile Tom had got Minnie safely inside the carriage outside the chapel.

His opportune arrival may be quickly explained.

After eluding the pursuit of the frigate, he made a rapid run to England, and, leaving his vessel, came ashore in a boat which was waiting for him by the beach.

He had brought the faithful Jerry Mizzen with him, and, having disguised himself, was making his way towards John Gregory's house in entire ignorance of what had occurred during his absence, when the redoutable Jerry, ever on the alert, perceived the carriage stop at the little chapel, and the helpless girl lifted out.

With no conception that she was Tom's plighted bride he called his young leader's attention to it, and proposed that they should rescue the lady, whoever she might be, as she was evidently being forced to an unwelcome marriage.

The dauntless boy was as ready as his faithful follower to hasten to the lady's deliverance.

He had no suspicion that it was Minnie until he was almost at the chapel, when he recognized her voice screaming for help.

It did not take him long to force his way in, and Jerry was utterly at a loss to account for his sudden movements, he disappeared so quickly.

He tried to follow him but was only in time to receive a tremendous blow on his head from the heavy door, as it swung back and knocked him out of the church.

As soon as he could recover himself, Jerry looked round and saw the driver of the coach in which Minnie had been conveyed, grinning at him, and significantly rubbing his head—two open insults which added to the force of the blow—already raising a big bump on his head—were not to be borne.

So he turned quickly on the offending coachman.

"What are you grinning at, you infernal landlubber?" he cried "d'ye want me to pull that wig off your chump?"

"You'd better go inside and help your master," the coachman rejoined; "he'll find it hot enough among them officer-chaps."

"Not he, you thick-headed swab; why he'd eat a dozen or two of them before breakfast, and pickle 'em in the bargain, that's what he'd do, you holler-faced mummy. Come down off that perch, will you, or see how soon I'll pull you off."

"What?"

The coachman put one finger delicately to the side of his nose.

This was a good deal more than Jerry Mizzen could stand.

Clambering up the side of the carriage like a cat, he collared the coachman by the nape of the neck, and swung him off his seat, giving him a kick to help him to the ground.

"Make a sight at me," he cried, pummelling the coachman till he bawled for mercy. "I'll teach you manners, you long-nosed shark. Belay there, make a clean run for it, or I'll thump you to a jelly."

The coachman was not valorous enough to strike even in self-defence.

He had already lost his wig, hat, and cloak, and leaving them in the hands of the exasperated Jerry, he scrambled to his feet, and ran nimbly out of sight.

"Curse him, I'll trundle the skunk," Jerry muttered, as he vented his rage on the hat and wig, "a pretty swab to wear these things and talk to a man."

Jerry paused suddenly in his work of battering in the cocked hat.

It had all at once occurred to him that his young chieftain, after rescuing the lady, would be glad of a conveyance to put her in.

Full of this bright idea, he stuffed his sailor's hat

23   CAPTAIN TOM DRAKE;

inside the coach, and putting on the wig, hat, and cloak, mounted to the box, and took the whip and the reins which had been dropped in his fright by the coachman.

"Shiver me, if I shan't make as good a Jarvey as any of th m longshore lubbers," Jerry muttered, as he gazed complacently around. "Now, then, my brave skipper, as soon as you like to bring that gal along, we'll start."

He never once doubted that Tom would succeed, nor did he think it worth while to go in and help him.

He had seen Tom victorious in too many sharp encounters to have any fear for him when opposed to any number less than a dozen or so.

A few minutes only had elapsed when the chapel door was flung open, and Tom Drake appeared with Minnie on his arm.

His sword was only half way in its sheath, and Jerry could see that it was steeped in blood.

"Ah!" he soliloquized, "I thought he'd get up to summat of that sort; he's as good as a doctor for drawing blood; a word and then a piff, whip goes his sword through your blessed carcase. It's a pleasure to serve under the flag of such a skipper."

Tom came quickly out and looked round for his sailor friend

He did not recognize him in his disguise.

Jerry chuckled when he saw his mystified look.

"He don't recognize his own man," he muttered, gleefully.

Our hero, prompt in action, stepped with Minnie to the coach, and had opened the door sharply, when Jerry sang out—

"Avast there, skipper; I'll be down the blessed gangway in a minit and hold the door for you to help the dear lady in."

Tom looked up in surprise at the metamorphosis of his faithful attendant.

"You there?" he said.

"Aye, aye, sir; here I is, perched up aloft like a little cherub. I thought you'd be wanting to get the lady away, so I tumbled the lubber off like a alligator, and here I is, ready to drive you where you like."

"Quick, then!" Tom said, when he had handed Minnie in. "Drive to the boat—no, to the coast; we must place this lady in safety before I seek my uncle and my mother."

"Aye, aye, sir," Jerry answered, as he whipped the horses into a smart gallop; "an' shiver me if I don't think we'd better sheer off while there's time, or there'll be such a hullabalo that we shan't be able to hear the tune of our own blessed voices."

Seated in the carriage with his arm round Minnie, her fair face upturned to his, her gentle bosom throbbing against his breast, Tom felt that hour the happiest one in his life.

They had many things to relate to each other, and our hero's cheeks burned when he heard how Minnie had been ill-treated.

He betrayed no surprise when he heard that she had not received his letter, though he could not restrain his pleasure at the proofs she gave of her faithful confidence.

His heart reproached him when he thought of his weakness with the corsair girl; still, even with her, his affection for Minnie had not faltered; it was still as deep and as true—aye, and as pure, for he would not have sullied the fair young creature beside him even by thought.

During the brief time since they had left the chapel he had made up his mind what to do respecting her.

He would not keep her on board his own ship, lest in future years any one should say words which would bring a blush to her cheek.

He resolved to hurry with her to London, where she had friends, and leave her in the charge of a distant relative—Lady Castlemaine.

"For one year," he said, when Minnie seemed loath to let him leave her. "I have a name to win, and my fame to clear. Then I will return to demand you for my wife."

And Minnie, though in her heart she would have gladly followed his fortunes, felt that he was right, and that for the present it was better for her to remain with her friends.

One year—at the expiration of which time he would return loaded with honours and dignity, and claim her before the world.

They little thought what that one year would bring forth.

Tom listened in alarm when Minnie informed him of his mother's disappearance, and of the dreadful calamity which had befallen his kind-hearted old uncle.

His face grew pale and stern, and, with knit brows, he determined on fathoming these unwelcome mysteries.

The young pair were aroused by Jerry Mizzen, who, leaning over the seat, put his head near the window, and sang out—

"Skipper, ahoy!"

"Aye, aye!" Tom said, emphatically.

"There's been a crew of lubbers a-bellowing like mad; and just now, shiver my beams, if I didn't rest my blessed top-lights on a pack of revenue hossifers and sogers a giving us chase!"

"Alas!" Minnie exclaimed, "they will take you."

"Will they, miss? Well, that's what I think they just won't do. Eh, sir?"

"Fear not, dear Minnie; I am well armed."

"Yes; but you might get hit."

Tom's face wore an heroic look.

"I should not regret death if I died defending you. But don't be afraid; I am not anxious to die. There is no danger to me in the pursuit of those rabble."

"Danger!" chimed in Jerry, "should say there wasn't, indeed; the pack of longshore lubbers! Shall I drive faster, sir? Take the young lady out of hearing, you know."

"Right," Tom said.

And Jerry, who had been driving the horses at a smart rate before, now lashed them into a furious gallop.

Jerry was not the most accomplished driver.

He handled the whip as if it were a ramrod, and tugged at the reins as if he were hauling the ropes of a ship.

The spirited horses, unused to having their mouths sawn right and left, as well as being lashed into the bargain, began to get restive, and plunged right and left, jolting the heavy carriage from one side to the other.

Our hero bore the bumping for some time; but at last his patience got exhausted, and he put his head out of the window.

"What are you doing?" he cried.

"All right, sir; get there presently. There's a shoal on my lee I'm steering clear of."

The shoal on his lee was a post set up as a landmark, for Jerry had long since got off the beaten track, and was floundering about in the deep ruts alongside the road.

In his anxiety to escape the post, he did not see an overthrown tree on the other side, nor was he aware of its being there till the fore-wheel came in violent contact and brought him to grief.

He was flourishing the whip at the time, when his heart was jerked into his mouth by the sudden jar, and before he could do more than make a frantic clutch at the reins he was shot clean over the horses' necks.

He was brought up with a heavy bump on the

hard ground, while the carriage, being then on the verge of an incline, rolled over, and fell up against the elevation on the other side.

The sudden shock extorted a little cry of fear from Minnie.

But Tom, cool and collected as ever, forced open the door, and assisted her out, seating her on the green sward while he went to seek their unfortunate coachman.

He found that worthy seated among the wreck.

He was rubbing his head in a confused way, as if not quite certain whether or not he had broken his neck.

Tom laid his hand sharply on his shoulder.

"How came this about?" he asked, angrily.

"That infernal, sunken bit of timber," Jerry said ruefully, as he struggled out of the mire. "The lady, sir—is she hurt?"

"Fortunately she is not. It is an unlucky event, but it cannot be helped now. We must set to work putting it to rights."

Putting it to rights proved altogether a different matter.

The carriage-pole was splintered, and one of the wheels so wrenched that it was impossible to proceed.

Jerry's visage wore a rueful expression when this discovery was made.

"It's no go." he exclaimed, "we're aground, and them darned lubbers will be forereaching upon us afore we can get clear of the wreck."

This reflection, too, aroused Tom.

He had seen that the horses, after being removed from the broken carriage, were comparatively uninjured.

He remembered that Minnie, when a child, had been famous as a horse-rider.

For himself, he would have ridden, bare-backed, the wildest steed of the Tartar steppes.

But whether Minnie could ride without a saddle was another matter.

He put the question, and was joyfully answered by her willing assent.

"There is a house, a few miles from here," he said to Jerry, when he had assisted Minnie on the back of one of the spirited animals. "Farmer Inglis used to dwell in it, a stanch old English gentleman; we will make our way there, and you can follow for orders. I am not decided whether to return to the boat or not."

"Better wait another day, sir; them cut-throat revenues are sure to be on the look-out."

"Why should they suspect me?"

Jerry put his lips close to his young chieftain's ear.

"One thousand pounds reward, sir."

"True—and that renders every moment of my stay perilous. No matter. I will run the hazard for this night—follow us at your leisure. Now, Minnie, for our ride."

The horses cantered off, side by side, and were soon out of sight.

"And now," soliloquized Jerry, "I can take this confounded head-gearing tackle off."

He alluded to the hat, and wig, which he threw contemptuously aside, and taking his hat from under the seat of the broken carriage, sauntered off after his dauntless chieftain.

All sounds of pursuit had died away, and Jerry, whose throat was becoming unpleasantly dry, thought that there would be no harm in making for a little hotel near the coast, with which he had been well acquainted in his smuggling days, and refreshing himself after his luckless tumble in the mire.

He had to go a little out of his way, to get to the place, but at last he had the satisfaction of seeing it in front of him

It was the old-fashioned inn where Tom had seen the men of the press-gang, by whom he had afterwards been captured.

The "Blue Lobster," it was called, and was kept by a low, ill-bred villain, named Simon Gagg.

Jerry had been one of the most constant frequenters, and had been well acquainted with most of the rough characters who associated there.

In his days its customers had comprised a ruffianly crew of crimps, smugglers, and runaway seamen.

Under its dilapidated roof many a villainous scheme had been planned, and its white washed parlour was the rendezvous of the officers and men of the press-gang.

Jerry did not enter without a qualm.

There was a good deal of uncertainty regarding the reception he might get.

None, however, seemed to recognize him.

The landlady, a tidy-looking little woman, whose pleasant face bore marks of coarse ill-usage, looked up as he crossed the threshold, but without appearing to recognize him.

A very old magpie in a wicker cage startled him by a familiar caw.

Jerry remembered the bird—it always had a habit of calling out, in a croaking tone, "Pie, pie!" when anyone entered it did not like, and its warning note was often the means of indicating the arrival of any of the revenue officers, against whom it had a mortal instinct of dislike, and many of whom would have been glad of the chance of wringing its talkative throat.

The parlour door was partially open, and the discordant hum of men's voices came from the room.

Some one was bawling out a seafaring song, and the hubbub of approval, stamping of feet, and knocking of mugs and measures on the table indicated its termination.

CHAPTER VIII.

A REVENUE OFFICER.

"You will be welcome inside," the landlady said, mistaking Jerry's hesitation; "it's only a pleasant party of our usual chaps."

Jerry thought he might as well hear a song for half an hour as stand at the bar and drink, so ordering a stiffish glass of grog, he pushed open the door and entered the room.

A dense cloud of smoke half hid the faces of the men seated drinking at the tables, but Jerry could see that they were of the usual stamp.

Simon Gagg, the landlord, was near the door.

He was a short, thick-set ruffian, with low repulsive features and big hairy hands.

He leered at Jerry from under his thick brows, and our wayfarer thought for the moment he was recognized.

If Simon knew him he did not betray his knowledge, and Jerry, bowing to the company, who greeted his entrance with a tumultuous welcome, tumbled into a seat in a more retired part of the room.

No sooner was his grog brought him than a tall lumbering sailor, with a massive sunbrowned countenance, and heavy black beard, came up to him, and bringing his huge hand down on Jerry's shoulder with a force that nearly bent him double, and jerked the sip of grog out of his mouth, sang out—

"What cheer, messmate—where d'ye hail from? ain't seen any of them lubbers of king's craft men, eh?"

"No," Jerry replied, "I ain't."

"Sing us a song, my hearty, then—and be hanged to all king's officers, I say."

"Sing," Jerry echoed. "Why, there ain't no more music in my voice than in the turn of a capstan; let some other gentleman of the company give us a song—I'll help him in the chorus."

"I'll be hanged if you shan't sing, you longshore lubber—heave to, or by thunder I'll sink you."

"Let the lad alone," Simon Gagg exclaimed. "Don't you see he's just off a cruise, and ain't took his bearings of the company yet?"

"Off a cruise?" hiccupped Jerry's persecutor, "and can't tip us a stave? I'll be hanged if he shan't sing. Heave ahead, you stopper-faced crocodile!—heave ahoy there, you lubber! That's to clear your toplights for you."

He deliberately took up Jerry's glass and dashed the hot contents in his face.

There was a general roar of laughter, and shouts of applause went round the room; but before they had subsided, Jerry, half blinded and smarting from the effects, was on his feet and facing his big antagonist.

"I've stood your cheek, you elephant," he exclaimed; "but if I stand that, my name ain't Jerry Mizzen."

To the surprise of the whole company, he administered such a straight one from the shoulder between the eyes of his opponent, that the brawny giant went sprawling over a table, and came heavily to the floor.

Cries of "bravo!" rewarded this unlooked-for act, and Simon Gagg stepped up to Jerry as the big sailor tumbled to his feet.

"Glad to see you back, Jerry," he said; "we've heard of your cruise. Where's your ship—and how's your boy-skipper, Captain Tom Drake?"

A buzz went round the room as the landlord spoke, and most of those who had known Jerry before soon crowded round him, looking with eager curiosity on the face of one of the daring band of the Boy Buccaneer.

But the big sailor struck his fist violently on the table.

"Off your cruise, are you?" he said; "then your skipper ain't far off. There's a thousand pounds reward for him, and blow me if I mayn't as well earn it as them revenue sharks that's sure to get wind of it."

Jerry Mizzen was plucky at heart.

He stood in front of the tall sailor and barred his way.

"You don't get out of here to sell my skipper," he said; "and if these will let you go, I won't."

"You—you swab! Who's to stop me?"

"We shall," Simon Gagg said. "We don't have any blood money brought here, Black Bill. It's enough for them revenue sharks to do that."

Black Bill would have made an attempt to pass, but catching Simon's significant look, he pretended to give in.

He knew that Simon had made up his mind to have a finger in the business, and wanted him to wait till the proper time.

"An' now," Simon exclaimed, "as we're glad to see you back again, Jerry, you shall drink a glass of grog at my expense."

"And one at mine," Black Bill chimed in, "tip us your fin, messmate, and don't mind if I've been a little free and easy."

Considering that his being "free and easy" had resulted in his getting a knock on the forehead that would have stunned a less hard-headed man, and, as it was, had raised an unsightly bump between his discoloured eyes, the concession on Jerry's part was not so great a matter.

He, however, bore no malice, and Black Bill, having drunk with him and sworn eternal friendship, staggered off to chat confidentially to Simon about their sinister intentions of betraying Tom.

They were arranging their plans in a low tone when the magpie cried out—

"Pie—pie!"

"A king's officer!" Simon muttered.

The door was opened, and a revenue officer appeared.

He was well known for his frequent visits there, and as he never minded taking a pipe and a glass in their company when his mission was not the arrest of any of their number, they did not so much mind him, though they took good care not to give him much opportunity of learning what they talked about.

He came in looking pleasant enough.

"Don't disturb yourselves," he said. "I've just dropped in in a friendly way, just to have a glass and a pipe."

"You're always welcome, Sam Andrews," exclaimed Simon Gagg, who would willingly have twisted his neck.

"I know it—I know it. A health to you, lads. Merry sports and good hauls to you, and when it comes to the last, may you take the halter gamely."

Having given utterance to this inspiriting speech, he sat down at the same table with Jerry, who wished him at the devil.

He tried to get up a conversation with our adventurer, but Jerry met him with the shortest replies.

He began to regret having come into the place.

It was a breach of duty, and he wished himself safe away again.

"Off a cruise?" Sam Andrews asked presently.

"Go to the devil, and find out," was Jerry's reply.

"Don't be uncivil, Jerry; we are old friends, you know."

Jerry started.

He had been in hopes that this cunning limb of the law, whom he had known before, and had often given him the slip after a hard chase, would not remember him.

The discovery was not pleasant.

"I'm very glad to see you here again, Jerry," Sam Andrews went on, in a low stealthy tone of voice, "because, you see, Jerry, we may make some money together; and money is what we all want, even if we've come off a rich cruise—eh, Jerry?"

Jerry gulped down his liquor, and stared speechlessly at the other.

He began to think he had been there long enough.

The place was getting disagreeably hot.

He made an attempt to leave his seat, but Andrews quietly put him back.

"Don't go yet, Jerry; we must have a little chat after this long separation. Ah, Jerry, you gave us the slip nicely, after you'd stowed them thirteen casks of brandy under our noses. It's a pity to see such a clever fellow swing; but you must—we've got enough against you to hang you, Jerry. You've been a long time wanted; but you've turned up at last."

"I wish I'd turned up in the middle of the Red Sea," thought Jerry. "What the devil did the skipper want to come here for at all? He might have been sure they'd try to nab us all."

Andrews, who had been watching Jerry's face with a satisfied leer, now placed his hand softly on his knee.

"Jerry," he said quietly, "now you must buy your neck out of the noose. We don't want you to swing, but we want the thousand pounds."

Jerry got uncomfortably hot.

"Ah, Jerry," Andrews continued, "what a fool he was to poke his head in the net!"

This was precisely what Jerry thought, but he did not say so.

"You see Jerry, he must be nabbed. We've got our fellows on the look-out all the way down the coast, so he can't get away; he ain't gone far off

BEN BARNACLE, SEIZING AN AXE, RUSHED TO THE RESCUE.

yet, so must be hid somewhere, and Jerry, I'm going to follow you with a few mates, wherever you go, till we find him."

"What!" Jerry cried. "Then I won't go anywhere."

"Hush! don't speak so loud, and don't be a fool, Jerry; he must be caught, and you may as well share with us. You needn't lead us there, we'll follow; and when we've nabbed him there'll be four hundred pounds out of the thousand for you and a free pardon; and if you don't—" he placed his lips close to Jerry's ear, and whispered, "you'll be squared up with a rope round your neck, Jerry, before you're three days elder."

Jerry listened with open mouth.

He was certainly in a fix.

He did not fear death.

He could do his share in the hot conflict where

shot and steel where doing their deadly work, but to be hanged by the neck and have the life squeezed out of him was an exceedingly unpleasant mode of letting out of the world.

He looked into the hard face of Andrews, and saw that he had no chance of escaping him.

As if to further convince him on that point, Andrews remarked, quietly—

"There's six of my fellows outside—make up your mind, Jerry; I'll smoke this pipe out while you think."

Jerry cursed him for his cool effrontery, but he was in a quandary, and he pondered how best to get out of it, sipping his grog desperately, while Andrews whiffed quietly at his pipe.

When he had smoked it out he knocked the ashes on the table, and swept them off with the palm of his hand, then looking at Jerry, he said,—

" Well !"

" I can't !" Jerry exclaimed; "I can't do it."

Andrews rose.

" Very well; we must first place you in safe custody, then see after him. But, mind, we're certain to take him."

" Stop," Jerry cried, looking round as if to see if any one of those present would help him. " Sit down again."

" Ha! I thought you'd come round. It ain't pleasant, after all, to have a rope tied about your throttle."

" It's ag'in' me to sell him," Jerry said, but there's no help out of it."

" Not a bit; you act wisely, Jerry, in deciding to share with us."

" I don't want the money—I couldn't touch it —but I don't want to swing."

" No, it must be uncomfortable. I never heard no one say anything after it—but they always look as if they didn't like it."

" It hurts me to do it."

" Oh, that's all right; you only go quietly out, we'll follow you to the house, then you can show us which room he's in ; we'll do the rest."

" Have you got arms ?"

" Yes, Jerry, we've got pistols and swords, and we know how to use them."

" Because he's a desperate hand at cutting his enemies down; besides, my life wouldn't be safe a moment if he thought I'd sold him; he'd wring my neck like a chicken's."

" No fear ; you leave it to us—you'll be all right."

Jerry still offered objections, but Andrews decisively overruled them; and finding no other means open, he presently got up and left, the officer following immediately after

In less than two minutes after they had gone, Simon Gagg and Black Bill sallied forth armed, and with a determined look on their ruffianly faces.

Andrews allowed Jerry to go on in advance of himself and party, but took care not to let him out of sight.

The redoubtable Jerry trudged ruefully along, as if overcome by the thoughts of what he had to do.

Once Andrews saw him wipe what he supposed was a tear from his eyes with his sleeve.

It was evident he took the matter sorely to heart.

Andrews had no sympathy with his compunction; he had made up his mind, not only to capture Tom, but to secure Jerry himself as well.

As for all he had said about pardon and share of the reward, that was pure moonshine.

When Jerry had got to the house where he had been told by Tom to seek him, he paused, and allowed the officers to come up with him.

" I shall have to go in first," he said. " If they see you, they'll shut us all out."

Andrews considered.

" Don't try to trick us."

" We'll go in all of a bunch, if you think they'll let us."

" No, we'll stay here, we'll wait ten minutes, but mind, at the expiration of that time, if you don't return, we shall force our way in."

" Ten minutes ain't no use. I want to tell him all I've heard, and get his orders, and that is how it'll have to be. He's sure to want to send me down with a message for them at the coast. I'll leave him writing that—come down and let you in—then you pops upstairs—opens the door—he thinks it's me, so doesn't turn round—of course you nabs him before he can move hand or foot—and then you has him. But mind—quietly; if he hears you it will be all up."

" Hum—can't you contrive to place his sword out of reach ?"

" I'll try. Now you stand back so as not to be seen; in fifteen minutes I'll make it right."

" Only mind, we shan't wait longer."

Jerry nodded, and the officer drew back from the house, while Jerry knocked for admission and was let in.

After the door had closed, Andrews repented having let his man go off so incautiously.

He had no check now against him, if he intended to prove treacherous; and it was not at all a pleasant idea to imagine a window suddenly opening and a shower of bullets whizzing about the heads of himself and his companions.

His only consolation was in the hope of Jerry being influenced by the bribe.

He judged men's natures by his own, and believed that, like him, they would barter honour and all else for a price.

To his great relief, at the lapse of the fifteen minutes the door creaked on its hinges, and the face and figure of Jerry appeared beckoning them in.

" Follow gently," Andrews said to his men, " and be prepared. Now," he continued, catching Jerry by the wrist, " is it all right ?"

" All right—come on quietly."

" Lead on ; but the least treachery, and I'll blow your brains out."

Jerry closed the door, and they were in almost total darkness.

Just light enough came in for them to see each other's creeping form as they went on tiptoe up the stairs, Andrews holding Jerry's wrist with one hand, while the other presented the cold muzzle of a pistol to his ear.

" He's in his room upstairs alone," Jerry whispered ; " he's got his sword on—you must take him quick—if he hears you he's sure to run the first through. I've put his chair so that his back's to the door. Knock twice before you go in—that's the signal —he'll think it's me."

They encountered none of the domestics on their way.

Lights were in several of the rooms they passed, and from one or two came the sound of voices.

" They'll have something to astonish them," Andrews thought, " when they see us here."

Jerry stopped at a door on the top of the third flight of stairs.

It was just ajar, and a faint light shone forth.

Holding Jerry's wrist with a grip of iron, and waving his men back as they pressed forward, Andrews stooped down and peeped through the key-hole.

A small lamp was burning in the room, its light enabling him to see all he wished.

There, at the table on which the light was burning, was the figure of the daring boy they came to capture.

There he sat, cocked hat and commander's coat and all, his dress sword in its scabbard by his side, the gold lace of his uniform glittering in the dull glare of the lamp.

He was leaning forward as if in deep thought, his head resting on his hands, his elbows on the table, a better posture for non-resistance could not have been devised.

Andrews released Jerry's wrist, which, till now he had gripped, and replaced the pistol in his vest.

His heart beat wildly at the prospect of his capture.

It was not alone the reward, large as it was, it was the glory of taking the Boy Cruiser.

This inflated his breast, and his voice was thick with excitement as he, in a low tone, said—

" Now burst in with me—seize him before he moves—one of you take this other—bind him while we do our work. Now in—aha! Captain Tom Drake, you are our prisoner."

With a swift, noiseless push, he burst open the door.

At the same time one of his men in obedience to his orders, made a clutch at Jerry.

Our worthy friend, however, was not in a mood to be trapped like that.

Sending out both of his awkward arms straight as an arrow, he sent the officer reeling with the blow, and kicking his feet from under him, by way of helping his descent, sent him tumbling down the stairs.

At the very same moment, Andrews and his men had sprang upon the sitting figure at the table.

Giving him no time to stir, he flung both his arms tightly round him, while his men fell upon their captive, putting pistols and sabres to his head.

"Our prisoner!" cried Andrews, "stir, and you die!"

"Aha!" laughed the voice of Jerry outside the door, "bind him fast—mind he don't burst from you—ah, ah!"

Andrews and his men started back—the figure they had so suddenly pounced upon fell over in their arms and dropped to the floor, and there lay, not the struggling figure of our daring hero—not the graceful form of the dauntless boy, whom they had thought to capture—but a capitally made up effigy stuffed with straw.

At the instant when the baffled officers made this unpleasant discovery, and were furiously gazing at one another, a voice, whose ringing defiant tones made them quail, cried—

"Stand where you are—the first who stirs a finger or moves a foot dies a sudden and unseen death!"

A defiant laugh followed these words, and then the heavy door swung too, and closed with a metallic snap.

The entrapped officers stared at each other aghast. They were prisoners.

Shut in that strong room with the windows securely barred from the outside, and the door fastened by a secret spring.

Shut in, foiled, and ensnared, and menaced by an unknown death.

CHAPTER IX.

AN INTERESTING ADVENTURE.

THE ruffianly landlord of the "Blue Lobster," and his rascally confidant, Black Bill, having followed the officers to Farmer Inglis's house, hastened off to give information to the authorities, and to claim the reward for our hero's capture.

Simon Gagg was too well acquainted with the astute cunning of Jerry Mizzen to imagine he would allow the officers to fall unawares upon his young master; he had no doubt they were being led into a sure trap, from which they would not be permitted to escape till their intended prey was out of their reach.

His own stratagem was to lie in wait for Tom somewhere between Farmer Inglis's house and the beach, with a sufficient party to take him when he was unsuspicious of danger.

The authorities were eager to capture one whose daring deeds had already made him so notorious, and as quickly as possible an armed body of men, under the guidance of the two rascally associates, made their way towards the place of ambush near the beach.

It fell out as they had surmised.

Tom was all ready for departure when his commanding tones appalled his would-be captors, whom he had so cleverly trapped; and while they were staring at each other in speechless dismay, he and Minnie, accompanied by the faithful Jerry

Mizzen, left the farmer's hospitable shelter, and proceeded coastward through the darkness of night.

Farmer Inglis would fain have persuaded our hero to remain till morning, but Tom did not deem a longer stay prudent.

For fear of pursuit they walked the whole way, leaving the horses to be found by the officers' party, when they succeeded in getting out.

Tom had dismissed all idea of further pursuit just now, and was joyously conversing with Minnie, while Jerry Mizzen trudged thoughtfully and silently behind them.

It was now the lightest hour of the night, the moon was up, and shone upon the cold leaden waters of the distant bay, lighting up the tangled gorse and clumps of shrubs and trees through which our adventurers had to force their way.

The part they had reached was dense enough to have concealed twenty men.

As it was, half-a-dozen were lying in wait, almost at their feet, lying so well concealed that their presence was not even dreamed of till they started up all of a sudden in Tom's path and challenged him to surrender.

Half-a-dozen officers, well armed, their weapons pointed at our hero's breast; behind them were Black Bill and Simon Gagg, instantly recognized by Jerry Mizzen, who was so confounded by the unexpected vision that he could only stand still in dumb amazement.

Minnie Atherton uttered a faint cry.

Her quick gaze was turned from the threatening men to our hero's face.

He had not uttered a sound, but she could see his fine eyes flashing, and could feel how his daring breast swelled with rising anger.

Jerry was the first to speak.

"Well, my kiddies," he said, "what does yer honours want?"

"Captain Tom Drake," one of the officers replied, "we call upon you to surrender. Resistance is useless, therefore don't put us to the trouble of shooting you down."

Our hero's lips curled in scornful contempt; but in no other way did he deign to notice their challenge.

Simon Gagg and Black Bill, who had kept at a respectful distance, now urged the officers forward.

"Take him," they said; "and mind, it's our reward."

"Your reward is here, ruffians!" a voice cried hotly.

And from the shelter of the thick gorse rose the form of bold Ben Barnacle.

A dozen of Tom's crew were at his heels.

They had their drawn cutlasses in their hands and their pistols ready for use.

Jerry Mizzen no sooner saw this welcome help out of their difficulty, than he indulged in a hearty burst of laughter, and, sidling up to the first of the officers, he coolly tweaked his official nose.

"There, you lubber!" he cried, "what d've think of that, eh, you ugly son of a sneak? What about surrender now?"

Ben Barnacle's first act was to salute his youthful leader; his next, to turn and face Black Bill.

The swarthy ruffian's face grew ghastly as he met Ben Barnacle's eye, his fierce eyes quailed, and his huge limbs trembled beneath him.

"We meet sooner than I expected, devil's spawn," Ben Barnacle hissed. "When we last parted I swore by the living God to mark you when we met. You have asked for your reward—here is an earnest of what you will get"

With the full force of his herculean frame he dashed out his tremendous arm, and struck Black Bill a terrible blow between the temples.

It seemed to crash in the burly ruffian's skull.

He uttered a sudden cry, and dropped to the earth as if his brains had been beaten out by the kick of a horse.

Ben Barnacle cast one look of deadly hate on the prone form, then he faced Simon Garg, and the officers, who shrank respectfully out of his reach.

"I have been lying in wait as long as you have," said. "I knew your purpose when I saw you hither by that cursed reptile. Did you think, ls, we should let our chieftain fall into your hands like that? Go, and be thankful for your lives. Let one of you remain after I count five, and we will show you what a dangerous game it is to meddle with the crew of Captain Tom Drake."

He had no occasion to trouble himself with counting.

At the first number the whole body of officers took to their heels, and in less than a minute were out of sight.

Ben Barnacle rested his foot on the broad chest of Black Bill, who lay breathing heavily and incapable of movement.

At first he seemed about to trample the ruffian's life out.

But a second thought prevailed, and, spurning him with his heel, he turned to our hero, who cordially held out his hand.

"Thanks, Ben," the brave boy said. "The fellows might have caused me some trouble, and, as you see, I have a lady here."

"We began to grow anxious, sir," Ben replied, when he had doffed his cap to Minnie, "so we landed, and were making our way inward when we saw them lie in wait for you, and crept up without being seen. We were not afraid of you being taken," Ben added, an admiring look on his manly features; "but they're as troublesome as vipers, these land sharks, and it's best to draw their sting."

Once more he spurned Black Bill's body.

"Lie there, hound!" he cried. "The time will come when I will stretch you at my feet never to rise again."

"Yes, lie there," Jerry Mizzen chimed, dancing delightedly round the prostrate giant, "and wait till we send your mammy to put a smelling bottle up your ugly nose."

Black Bill staggered helplessly to his feet as soon as they were out of sight.

His coarse repulsive features were set in ghastly hatred.

His bleared eyes were starting from their swollen sockets.

"Curse you," he hissed, as he ground his teeth savagely; "you've put a mark here; but I'll be even with you yet, and then, Ben Barnacle, I'll have revenge for this."

He struck his clenched hand against the bump on his swollen forehead, and steadying his shaking frame, staggered after the officers and his cowardly confederate.

No further adventure interfered with our hero and his party

They soon arrived at the beach where the boats were waiting.

The nearest one was manned by half-a-dozen of Tom's favourite middies, the leader of whom, respectfully saluting our hero, said—

"There's been a revenue boat on the look-out, sir; and they made such a stir up at the fort just now that we were getting ready to come and rescue you. They're keeping a sharp look-out. Some one's betrayed you, sir, that's quite certain."

"Let them do their best," Tom replied, "they'll not take us yet. Come, dearest Minnie, yonder lies my ship, like a white dove on the waters. A few leaps of the boat, and we shall be safely aboard, and your gentle fears will be at rest."

This was said with tender gallantry as he assisted her into the boat.

And the middies, who were heartily glad to see their loved commander back, pulled lustily away from the shore.

As soon as he and Minnie were seated, Ben Barnacle and Jerry followed in the wake of their chieftain, Jerry turning up the whites of his eyes and lolling his tongue out in his cheek, as he pictured the meeting of Zeila and Tom's bride.

"I always knowed him to be plucky," he soliloquized; "but he must have the audacity of the devil to cheek being on ship with them two women. Two women! if there ain't a mutiny and a scrimmage aboard with 'em both afore we're many days at sea, why I'll marry the first woman I tumble across next time I'm on shore; if I don't, shiver me."

The challenge was softly given when they were near the ship, and this having been quickly answered the two boats pulled alongside, and the whole party were soon on deck.

"Weigh anchor silently," was Tom's first order, as he mounted the ladder. "Not a sound till we are far out at sea."

Late as the hour was, Zeila, the corsair girl, had not yet retired to rest.

She had been anxiously awaiting his return, and ran lightly towards him when she heard his thrilling tones.

The glad light of joy went from her eyes when she saw Minnie leaning on his arm.

Her swift instinct told her that this was Tom's maiden love—the worshipped idol who alone had a place in his heart.

Yet there was more of sorrow than of passion in her looks, as she stood half trembling and pale, like the frail child of nature she was.

Captain Tom's voice startled her.

"Come hither, Zeila," he said.

And fleet as a young fawn the corsair girl ran to him.

"This is my boyhood's love," he continued. "I want you to welcome her, Zeila; Minnie, dearest, say a kind word to this Eastern pearl; she has a strange history. You will sympathize with her when you hear it."

As if by instinct those two young girls made a movement towards each other, and while our hero was speaking had taken each other by the hand.

The cold embrace did not satisfy the emotional Arab girl.

After she had quickly scanned Minnie's gentle face, and glanced from her to the handsome countenance of Captain Tom, an approving look beamed from her dazzling eyes, and folding Minnie to her breast, with her exquisitely-shaped arms entwined round her throbbing bosom, she imprinted fervid kisses on her lips and cheeks, and with fairy-like gentleness led her down to the cabin.

"Well," muttered Jerry Mizzen, who had been an observant spectator of this meeting, "she's been and took to her like that. Well, if that don't bang all! Ah! they means mischief though, I'll swear, or they're not two women. Two women! I'd as soon have two she-cats tied round my neck."

Busy hands had meanwhile got the sails aloft.

The anchor was noiselessly brought from the blue bed of the bay, and as the light breeze filled out her canvas the *Will-o'-the-Wisp*, swaying with a graceful motion on the surface of the waves, sped with her accustomed swiftness out to sea.

For hours after she had been conducted by Zeila to her cabin did Minnie lie in a dreamy kind of wakefulness, trying to realize the change in her destiny.

Less than twenty-four hours ago she was a captive in the power of her enemies, and doomed to a loathsome union.

Her lover's coming, and her swift deliverance, seemed more like a vision of enchantment than reality.

How grateful she felt for having been rescued from his base-minded cousin!

How joyous to be with him!

How much more joyous if she were his bride, sharing his adventurous career!

A little pang of regret shot through her heart as she thought of their speedy separation, and a little pang of jealousy when she thought of the corsair maiden, who would have the privilege, denied to her, of sharing his cruise.

But then she remembered how noble it was of him not to want her to stay with him till he had made himself respected and admired throughout the world.

Then she would be his bride, and no Zeila should stand between her and her hero lover.

Zeila had shown her the utmost kindness and delicacy, yet there was something in the wild, gazelle-like eyes of the corsair maiden that made her almost fear her presence there.

With the quick perception of love she scented a danger our hero would never have dreamed of—the danger of such an impulsive nature as Zeila's, should she really love Tom, and have that love changed into jealous hate and revenge.

The cabin in which she lay was most luxuriously fitted—it was more like a fairy boudoir than anything else.

Rich silken curtains, gauze-like festoons of snowy whiteness, lace-like drapery delicate as an insect's wing, floated around her; beauteous and rare-scented flowers were heaped in magnificent vases, and a subtle delicious perfume filled the air.

The couch on which she lay was almost too soft and buoyant even for repose—it yielded with every light movement, and rose again more buoyant than before.

The coverings were of the richest velvet or silk and the finest wool, and so many novelties of wonder met her gaze that daylight was faintly peeping into the apartment before our heroine's eyes, tired as they were, closed in slumber.

The sunbeams were stealing through the gossamer curtains when she awoke.

Her first languid movement as she sat dreamily up, was to ring a little bell, and before its silver tingle had died away, Zeila glided softly into the cabin.

She seemed to have constituted herself Minnie's attendant.

With playful grace she caressed her and then set about helping her with her toilette, arraying her with such taste that our heroine could not restrain a blush of pleasure when she caught sight of her own graceful figure in the many mirrors surrounding her.

Captain Tom greeted her proudly when Zeila led her from the cabin.

He had been awaiting her for hours, and felt supremely happy as he assisted her to the quarter-deck.

A seat had been already placed for her, and, with a giddy sensation, Minnie gazed around.

They were far out at sea.

The ship's white sails were fluttering like the wings of a beauteous bird as she went on her silent way

The decks were scrupulously cleaned, and every stitch of canvas was in its place.

The greater portion of the crew were grouped about the decks—a fine, handsome set of fellows—boys and men richly attired, and with the daring brand of their bold career stamped on their sun-browned faces.

But what most charmed Minnie was the devoted and admiring faithfulness with which they regarded their princely boy commander, when he appeared like a demigod amongst them.

It gladdened her to see that he could count on the love and heroism of so many stanch hearts, for she knew the secret of his hazardous career, and was well aware what evil the treachery even of one amongst them might work.

Land was out of sight.

The sun was dancing merrily on the blue waters.

The sky was almost cloudless.

A dreamy rapture stole to Minnie's heart.

All seemed so peaceful and happy.

It was almost with pain she observed the shining guns of brass and iron ready to be run out at the open ports, and the neat piles of round shot at hand for deadly service.

A glance, too, at the diversity of weapons in the sashes of the daring boy-voyagers told her plainly, too, how warlike were their intents, should opportunity call them to action.

Our hero watched with strange interest the varying emotions depicted on her fair face.

"So you like my ship?" he ventured to observe at length.

"It is a noble vessel," Minnie replied, ardently; "and your crew seem so daring and handsome."

"They are of true metal—staunch to the death. As for this brave craft we took her from the Barbary pirates. It was by slaying their fierce leader that I became, as it were, the protector of little Zeila. She has clung to me ever since, and I do not like to send her away."

Tom said this half as an excuse. He did not know how she would regard his guardianship of Zeila.

Minnie was, however, too guileless to be estranged on that account.

On the contrary, her interest in Zeila increased, while she looked upon our hero with even more idolatry of admiration when she heard of his desperate bravery in vanquishing the corsair.

Minnie seemed so delighted with her life at sea that Tom ran his ship to the Canary Islands, and round the coast of Spain, giving her a delicious pleasure trip before he took her back to England.

And during all this time Zeila attended upon Minnie with the assiduous fidelity of the most devoted slave; her chief pleasure being to gratify her every wish, even before expressed, and to array her with such grace that she stood more enchanting in Tom's eyes.

The joyous voyage was over at last, and Minnie grew sad at the idea of their speedy separation.

Often, indeed, was our hero tempted to take advantage of her love, and induce her to become his bride there and then, and remain with him for ever.

But the true nobility of his nature triumphed, and he adhered to his intention of placing her for one year under the care of Lady Castlemaine.

Having altered the trim of his ship—a practice he always adopted when making for an English port—Tom sailed to Gravesend, Lady Castlemaine being then at her mansion at Purfleet.

He had assumed the uniform of a captain, and quitting his ship at noon of the day of his arrival, took Minnie ashore, and no adventure befalling him on his way, announced himself to Minnie's relative.

She was a prim elderly dame.

She received Minnie coldly, and listened in silence to Tom's account of himself till he got as far as the carrying her from the church, when she interrupted him by saying—

"This was sacrilege; and however evil-intentioned your relatives may have been, there were other means of dealing with them without this unjustifiable outrage in God's house."

"I did not stop for justification," Tom said.   I rescued Minnie, and took her to my ship, and now I ask you to take charge of her till I return."

Lady Castlemaine inclined her head, and our hero drawing Minnie to his breast, took an affectionate farewell of her.

"One year," he said, tenderly, as he toyed with her glorious hair, "then I will come back, and you shall be my bride."

Minnie could not answer him.

She kissed him through her tears.

Her young heart was stricken, and Tom half repented he had brought her back, as he tore himself from her mbrace, and hurried out of the house.

Lady Castlemaine said nothing to Minnie about her future that day; but the next, after she knew that the young girl had watched the sails of Tom's ship fade from sight, she called her to her boudoir and addressed her gravely.

"You must make up your mind to forget this foolish romance," she observed, quietly. "A more fitting destiny awaits you than a life with this unscrupulous adventurer—you must maintain a discreet silence, too, about the past. Were it known that you had allowed him to carry you off on board his ship, the doors of society would be closed against you."

Minnie raised her sorrowful glance in surprise.

There was a world of meaning in the quiet inflexible look of her relation; that look troubled the young girl's heart, and made her wish herself again on board our hero's noble vessel.

When Tom returned to his boat, he was informed that a king's cutter had brought up alongside them, asking them a great many questions respecting the ship, her crew, and destination.

They were particularly anxious to know if she was commanded by a youthful captain.

"But I paid them out strong," Bob Hauler said. "I swore our skipper was at least seventy years old, and had gone ashore to give his great grandchild a birthday present, so they steered off then, the hulks; but hang me if I like the cut of their craft, and I make no doubt they'll be somewhere on our lee, trying to overhaul us."

Tom thought it would be very much like overhauling a tiger, but he said nothing.

Stepping on board when they reached the ship, he ordered the anchor to be weighed and descended to his cabin.

Zeila crept in noiselessly as he sat moodily at the table, and placed her soft arms round his brow.

It was almost with relief that she had seen Minnie depart.

The high-minded girl was passionately fond of adventure, and feared that Tom would forget the calls of his exciting career if Minnie remained on board.

Tom did not repel her—her sympathising presence soothed him, and almost unconsciously he suffered her caresses.

In a little while Bob Hauler came to the cabindoor and, respectfully saluting his boy-leader, inquired which way they were to steer the ship.

"To Portsmouth," Tom said, "the British fleet is there. I have business with some of them. We will run amongst them and afterwards hoist our own colours, and cruise for the pirates of the Mediterranean.

Bob Hauler saluted and withdrew, a grim look about his massive features.

Something seemed to please him in the idea of his youthful chieftain running the gauntlet of the British fleet.

Zeila clapped her hands with joy at the prospect of a more stirring life than they had been leading.

She longed, too, to be away from sight of England, whose cold cliffs were so uncongenial to her ardent mind.

Perhaps, too, she thought that the further Tom was from his lady-love the better would be her chance of engrossing his affections.

The news that they were about to start on an adventurous cruise ran like wildfire through the ship, and every daring heart was elate at the promise of a speedy encounter with some richly laden Barbary cruiser.

The British fleet was at this time lying off Spithead, awaiting orders to proceed against the French with whom hostilities had been opened.

As usual in time of war every vessel upon arrival was subjected to a severe examination, and the spruce vessel of our boy-adventurers was certain of a strict overhauling.

As far as possible, alterations had been made in her rig, a coat of paint had aided her disguise, and no trace of her notorious name appeared on her bows. There was written there in gold letters—

The Saucy Sea-Dove.

Care had been taken, too, not to make too great display of her armaments, whilst the boy-crew had laid aside their picturesque buccaneer costume, and were dressed in a fitting naval uniform.

Tom still wore his handsome dress as captain.

There was one thing more respecting which great care was exercised.

The immense quantity of riches they had on board was stowed out of sight.

As soon as they came in sight of the fleet they were signalled from the flag-ship, and full particulars demanded of them.

They were well prepared, and having eluded the viligance of their questioners, were soon lying quietly in the roadstead.

The business which had brought him there was to make an offer of undertaking certain hazardous missions against the French, with whose intended movements he had been made acquainted.

In pursuance of this he visited every admiral in the fleet, but his services were declined by one and all.

They were too jealous and greedy of fame to follow in the wake of Tom's stripling crew.

Our hero was much nettled at this cool reception, and he inwardly determined to make them regret the slight.

Indeed, he did not strive to conceal his feelings, and completely astounded the last admiral, a prim methodical old fellow, with whom he held conference, and whom he talked to, as Jerry Mizzen afterwards said, "like a Dutch uncle."

The redoubtable Jerry could scarcely repress his feelings as he helped to row his young leader ashore.

The idea of their lying under the very bows of a fleet of armed vessels, each one of which was under orders to take the saucy vessel, whenever they could lay hold of her, and clap irons on her desperate crew!

As for the brave boy-skipper, he scarcely gave the matter a moment's thought, but with the most consummate coolness trod the quarter-decks of the frigates, though he knew that the officers and admirals with whom he conversed had in their pockets the proclamation offering a thousand pounds for his capture.

Truth to say, the daring boy delighted in peril—it suited his mettlesome nature to walk amidst the most imminent danger.

As he had gleaned intelligence concerning his mother, which caused him to make inquiries amongst the shipping there, he was forced to stay some time in Portsmouth, so he thought he could do no better than improve the occasion by making friends of some of the authorities on shore.

THE MIDDY SPRANG UP AND DEALT JERRY A BLOW WHICH KNOCKED HIM OFF HIS FEET.

One evening an adventure befell him which was destined to bring him into the society he desired.

It was rather a dark night, and he was walking cloaked and armed towards the batteries on shore.

He was deep in thought, thinking of his mother whom he yearned to discover—thinking of his kind old uncle Gregory—thinking of Minnie, whose simple truth was so trustingly given to him—thinking of Zeila, whose love for him was growing deep as the passion of an Oriental mind could be.

Quick, heavy steps near him interrupted his reverie.

He heard a faint scream, evidently from a young girl's lips answered by rude oaths and coarse menaces.

Then the angered tones of an old gentleman struck upon his ears.

"You rascals! Stop a commodore in the king's service, you swabs? Sip your stern-sheets, or I'll send you to dock for repairs. Rob me, indeed, a commodore!"

"Come, old buffer, hand over all your valuables, or we shall hurt you and the lady, too," a rough voice answered.

"What, strike my colours to you, landsharks? Come on, and look out the first one that comes within arm's reach of me."

Tom was near enough by this time to see the speaker, a fine, stalwart old English gentleman, of unmistakable naval aspect.

He was wielding a heavily-knobbed stick, with which he kept at bay four ill-looking ruffians, whose purpose had evidently been to waylay and plunder him in that lonely place.

A young girl of about seventeen summers clung to his side, too terrified to do more than gaze in speechless dismay on the coarse scoundrels.

Brave and determined as the gentleman undoubtedly was, he must have experienced some rough handling, and, with his young charge, have been despoiled of his money and valuables, if our hero had not been near.

The place was lonely.

The few houses near gave shelter to a rapacious crew of evil-minded beings of both sexes, ready at any moment to resort to deeds of plunder and violence.

The ruffians did not for a moment anticipate any interruption, and were considerably astounded when our hero stalked into their midst, and with lion-like strength hurled two of them aside, and sent a third reeling with a blow from his fist.

The fourth would have showed fight with his youthful assailant, but seeing his hand on the hilt of his rapier, and not at all relishing his dauntless look, took to flight, followed by the others, who, with bitter curses at being disappointed of their prey, disappeared down a dark alley.

The old gentleman warmly thanked his young preserver.

"Just in time, young sir, to do me a service. Many thanks—many thanks. The scoundrels to attempt to rob me! I thank you, young sir, for ridding me of the impudent rascals! Hang me, sir, you managed them well—eh, Jenny? It was capital to see him send them to the right-about."

The young girl whom he addressed as Jenny had all this time kept her gaze on the symmetrical form of their youthful deliverer.

She blushed as the old gentleman spoke, and timidly joined in thanking our hero.

"In uniform, too," the old fellow exclaimed. "Glad of it, sir; like to see the honour of the cloth upheld. Your hand, young sir. Dine with us this evening, and listen to an old sailor's yarns over as good a bottle of port as you'll sip in a cruise. Come, let's hear where you hail from, and what you're called. I'm Commodore Ellis, of his Majesty's service. This is my niece—Jenny Ellis, my brother's child—as true-hearted a girl as ever had her cheeks kissed by the sun, though a little wayward. And now, sir, what may we have the pleasure of calling you?"

"I am called," our hero replied, "Captain Grey."

"Captain! Egad! and so young! Our navy, sir?"

"No, sir; I hold my commission from his Majesty the Emperor of the Brazils."

"Whew—humph!" the commodore whistled. Then, altering his tone, continued; "ah, well! a brave man is the same, whether he holds his commission under another flag or no—unless it were the Frenchmen yonder. While I serve my king, never would I touch hand of theirs."

Tom smiled.

"I am with you there, sir." he exclaimed. "I honour the flag of old England, and long may it triumphantly wave over every sea—aye, and every foeman's deck."

"Hurrah!" sang out the old commodore, grasping Tom by the hand; "there's the ring of the true metal. Jenny, my love, there's a hero for you; take his arm, and bring him on to our house. Remember, he's our prisoner for to-night, and I give the captive to your keeping."

The fair-faced Jenny timidly let her glance fall as our hero, with quiet gallantry, gave her his arm, while the hearty old commodore walked on by Tom's side, conversing with much gusto upon their approaching battle with the Frenchmen, whom they were about to sweep from every sea.

When they had got away from that part of the town, the commodore's stentorian lungs brought a coach to take them up.

The old seaman growled out the address, and after fifteen minutes' jolting over the stones, the ricketty vehicle brought up in front of a handsome residence standing in private grounds, and illuminated from attic to basement.

"Now, you lubber!" bawled the commodore "open the door and be hanged to you! What the devil do you mean by keeping a king's officer waiting like this?"

He did not give the driver time to descend, but bundled out, and gave a tremendously noisy summons at the gate.

Tom handed Jenny gracefully out, and the pair walked leisurely up the gravelled path while the commodore settled with the driver, whom he furiously abused, and afterwards made amends by over-paying him.

Our hero was surprised to see that preparations were made for dinner on a large scale.

Numerous guests were already arrived, and the commodore, having started Jenny off with her maid, conducted Tom to his own room to prepare for the reception below.

As soon as the officious valet—whose attentions were testily dispensed with by Commodore Ellis—had left them, the commodore faced Tom suddenly, and leaning his back against the door said, abruptly—

"Now, young sir, you're alone with me in my private room, and, hang me, I mean to speak my mind!"

Tom was somewhat surprised at this mode of address; the more so when the commodore brought his hand down heavily on his shoulder. He thought he was discovered, and a rather ludicrous look stole over his careless features.

"I know you, sir," continued the old gentleman——

"To be Captain Tom Drake," thought our hero. "I'm discovered, and have got into a fix."

To his relief, the commodore, however, said—

"I know you, sir, to be a noble and worthy youth—a-hem!—officer and gentleman. I can trust you, and you shall be let into our family secrets—secrets sir, that have stolen the blush from that young girl's cheek, and made her a prey to the most unhappy feelings. Yes, sir, you shall know all by-and-bye."

Tom was a little mystified at this, but the old gentleman left him without another word, and said no more on the subject when he appeared a few minutes afterwards to conduct him to the reception-room.

It was a grand old saloon, brilliantly lighted and tastefully furnished.

At the present moment it was crowded with guests, and the eyes of all were turned towards the handsome figure and fearless countenance of our hero as he entered with his noble friend.

He was attired in a rich uniform, and with his gold-hilted sword by his side, his bold chest expanded, with the glittering epaulettes on his tall shoulders, the scarlet glow on his cheeks, and the defiant light in his fine eyes, he looked, indeed, the beau ideal of a dashing and gallant sailor.

Many a lovely bosom throbbed as he passed gracefully by—many a bright eye flashed its bewitching glance upon him.

Even the guests who were chiefly officers, and wore their best uniforms, regarded him with some interest as he passed like a demigod amongst them.

Commodore Ellis introduced him in his bluff way to beautiful women and distinguished officers, as he passed towards the end of the saloon, where, seated on a small settee in one corner, was Admiral Ellis, the father of Jenny, and brother to the commodore.

He was a little, dry, spare man, small and slim of limb.

His face was dry and hard as leather, and of a deep sallow tint.

His small grey eyes shifted in a restless and piercing manner from beneath his scanty eyebrows.

His forehead was wrinkled into thin hard lines, his mouth was firm-set and inflexible, his lips almost colourless.

His feet were exceedingly small, as were his hands—the latter the colour and texture of parchment—the thin bony fingers nervously entwined whenever he spoke or seemed in thought.

At the first glance Tom could determine his character.

He knew that he stood before an iron man of discipline—a strict martinet; whose word was law, whose frown a terror; who stood the tyrant of his quarter-deck, his hundred seamen flying at the sound of his harsh dry voice.

There was nothing kindly in his aspect—as there was in the bluff countenance of the brother whom he was in every respect so unlike—but Tom could see that his was the eye for command, the mind for skilful arrangement of his forces, the heart, albeit almost shrivelled in his breast, that would beat its last throb for duty and the honour of old England.

He fixed upon Tom his penetrating gaze as the commodore introduced him, austerely waving him back, said—

"I've heard of you, sir—rescued my daughter from violence, my brother from robbery—sort of thing they write of in story-books; but come, I am a king's officer, as you see; before I regard you as officer or gentleman you will pardon my desire to see the credentials that establish your claim to the decorations I see on your shoulders."

He glanced at Tom's epaulettes.

"I have much pleasure, sir, in handing my commission for your inspection," our hero replied, with a polite bow, as he gave the little admiral the captain's commission he had secured in the Brazilian service.

A few moments' perusal satisfied the scruples of the punctilious admiral.

He saw that our hero's commission was marked with exploits of a daring nature, for Tom had actually rendered good service to the Brazilian Government.

Rising from his seat he held out his hand, and with more warmth than could have been expected, exclaimed—

"Pardon my scruples; allow me to say I'm well satisfied, and that these proofs accord with my own impressions. As my brother observed, a brave man is always a welcome friend, and though I am sorry so fine a young fellow is not in our service, I am proud to meet you under this roof."

Tom bowed courteously at this generous reception, and the little old admiral, giving him a swift glance as he turned away, reseated himself, and with a dignified wave of the hand indicated that the interview was at an end.

But after he had watched our hero led away by the commodore, he sat back in his chair with his thin hand clasped before his thoughtful brow.

As the commodore and our hero were sitting by one of the bay windows our hero's attention was drawn towards Jenny Ellis, who was seated almost opposite to him.

She was attired with the utmost simplicity, yet with such exquisite taste that many brilliant toilettes near her looked quite garish and vulgar beside her.

A few pearls dropped like mistletoe berries from amongst her light tresses, a necklet of the same,

with a splendid opal suspended like a cross, encircled her fair bosom.

Tom watched her fixedly, and saw that, in spite of the soft colour on her cheeks, she was affected by an uncontrollable emotion.

Her bosom heaved as if she sighed, very, very often, and there seemed teardrops glistening from her drooping eyelashes.

Near her, but apart from each other, were two young gentlemen, the very opposite of each other in look and behaviour.

They were each dressed in the uniform of naval lieutenants, the one to Jenny's right apparently being the senior of the two.

He was tall, well-formed, with broad shoulders and expansive—chest, handsome, too, but not the prepossessing beauty of honoured manhood.

There was the proud look of a fallen angel in his flashing eyes, and Lucifer himself could not have wreathed his lips in more withering scorn than were his, as he gazed from Jenny to the other—his rival.

The other, a little younger of the two, was slighter built, but well-knit of limb, his face fair, and of the Grecian mould; his eyes were singularly soft in their expression, but flashed with a wild light when his gaze encountered the scornful look of the other.

Whilst Tom was contrasting the appearance of the two, and getting considerably drawn in favour of the last described, the commodore touched him on the shoulder, and with a sigh observed—

"Ah, there is our sad secret. Those two young men were fast friends once, but see what bitter rivals time has made them."

"Rivals!" Tom echoed.

"Yes, they both love Jenny. He on the right is a young man of good estate, the Hon. Archibald Gaston. My brother has thought fit to select him as Jenny's future husband. The other is Lieutenant Henry Vere; he is of good family, but has nothing else except his commission in his Majesty's service to offer in his own behalf. He is aware that his pretensions are discountenanced by my brother, yet, strange to say, persists in being head over ears in love with our Jenny."

"And the lady——"

"Stranger still, leans towards the one whom her father disapproves. Ah, see how they regard each other! There will be bad blood between them some day."

As if conscious that he was the subject of remark, the Hon. Archibald Gaston presently moved away, and soon after, the dinner having been announced, the whole party proceeded to the room where the delicious banquet awaited them.

It was a feast that did credit to the generous giver.

Rich wines flowed, and the rarest dishes were placed in profusion before the guests.

Under the influence of such good cheer the spirits of the visitors rose.

Bright bewitching glances shone from lovely eyes; smiles were freely bestowed, and merry laughter rippled from the lips of beauty.

In the midst of the general enjoyment a privileged servant brought an official missive to the little old admiral, whose brows pursed up when he had read it.

"A strange thing," he observed, aloud; "I have received a despatch here, and as are all, I trust, in one cause, I will state its nature. This missive states that the daring boy-depredator, whose career is now so notorious—this Captain Tom—not satisfied with his practices at sea, has had the temerity, not to say the impudence, to run his ship to England and is believed to to at be at the present moment about our coast."

"Of course he his disguised; so doubtless, his

vessel," the admiral continued, when various comments had been made; "but, gentlemen, as you are all king's officers, and will soon be on your cruise, I trust a very short time will elapse before this boy-criminal is cut short in his desperate career, and brought ignominiously before his judges, who will know how to deal with him. I say we are all his Majesty's officers—our honoured guest will pardon the allusion; but I presume I must except him?"

He glanced at Captain Tom Drake.

Our hero had been sitting, feeling very much as if a score or so of thunderbolts were buzzing about his ears, but his countenance never changed, and the admiral, who had given him one of his hasty, piercing glances, bent his eyes again to the paper.

"What a very interesting creature this Captain Tom must be!" observed one bright-eyed maiden. "We hear so much of his daring, and no one seems able to take him."

"He must be very handsome and noble," another observed, "and so brave. We hear continually how he goes about in disguise; actually being sometimes on board the very ships sent to take him. He must be very clever."

"Clever or no," exclaimed the commodore, reddening, "I only hope it may be my fortune to take him under one of his disguises. The hospitality of my roof should not shelter him. I should not consider my duty done till I had handed him over to be punished for his crimes."

"Oh, commodore! and he is so young."

"And they say he carried off his bride when she was to be married to some one she did not like."

Jenny raised her blushing face at this remark, and a quick glance passed between her and Harry Vere.

Suddenly every one's attention was directed towards our hero.

"Oh, Captain Grey," exclaimed Lady Arbuthnot, a peerless woman of seven-and-twenty, "you have been all round the world, and you must have surely seen this paragon of perfection—this Will-o'-the-Wisp gentleman, whom our entire fleet cannot subdue or ensnare; do tell us—have you seen him —is he so handsome as they say?—is he really brave —is he—is he like you?"

This was a direct thrust; our hero thought it best to evade it.

Glancing carelessly at his arch questioner, he replied—

"Should it fall to my lot to meet this famous boy, rely upon it your curiosity shall be satisfied; indeed, I will pledge myself to capture him and bring him in fetters to your presence, to answer for himself."

"That will be too generous," Lady Arbuthnot replied, her splendid eyes flashing a look upon our hero that thrilled to his soul.

The little old admiral looked up at this moment.

"You had better deliver yourself in propria persona, Captain Grey," he said drily, "for, really the description given of him is marvellously like yourself."

"Indeed," Tom said, laughing gaily, "then I may deliver myself, already bound, to some one of these fair ladies, if one can be found ready to take charge of so humble a character."

The bluff old commodore laughed heartily.

The idea of Captain Grey being the notorious Boy Buccaneer was a most excellent joke.

Tom felt certain that he entertained no suspicions.

Of the admiral he was not quite sure—there was something he did not like in the little old officer's dry cough and dry laugh.

At this juncture matters were nearly brought to a crisis by an unforeseen circumstance that may be briefly explained.

The redoubtable Jerry Mizzen and his faithful messmate, Bob Hauler, had, like their chieftain, sallied forth that night in search of adventure.

It happened that while they were indulging in a convivial glass at an inn by the wayside, two gorgeous flunkeys entered, and by their conversation enabled our pair of worthies to hear that they were going out that evening to attend a grand party.

The mere description made Jerry's mouth water, but when it came to the mention of the pretty lasses below stairs, whom they were privileged to kiss, Jerry got frantic with excitement, and a whispered conference between the two, resulted in a hastily-formed plan to make the two flunkeys drunk, exchange clothes with them, and sally forth to supply their place.

"We might pick up summat you know," Jerry observed, with an eye to the stray forks and spoons.

It is not needful to relate how they succeeded in their subtle plan.

Suffice it that, in less than thirty minutes after, they were to be seen wending their way towards the house of Commodore Ellis.

They were a little bit taken aback at the scene before them, and their awkward attempts at waiting excited many animadversions, to which, however, copious draughts of wine had made them proof.

While the conversation was going on about Tom, Jerry, who had smuggled sundry articles of light value, amused himself by lolling out his tongue on his cheek, in a very significant manner at Bob Hauler, and was in the act when a majestic word of command from the head-serving man sent him to attend upon Tom.

Our hero was speaking, and Jerry was standing behind him when their eyes met.

The effect on Jerry Mizzen was electrical.

He started back a step, and, with a smothered ejaculation, stood staring open-mouthed, and with eyes fixed at his youthful captain, over whom, in his sudden fright, he had scattered the luscious jelly he had been sent round to serve.

Tom's features never changed a muscle.

Looking Jerry sternly in the face, he said, angrily—

"Have you no more care, fellow, than this? Fetch a napkin instantly, and remove this stain from my coat."

"Aye, aye, skip—, yes, sir, I mean—oh lor'——"

Commodore Ellis plucked Jerry by the shoulder as he was sidling away.

"You stupid clown!" he exclaimed, "who are you?"

"I'm Jerry—leastways—oh, lord—my——"

"Rogue! scoundrel! you are unfit to attend upon gentlemen! See that he leaves the house at once!"

The head waiter assisted Jerry out.

Glad enough was he to escape.

In his fright, he forgot to take out of his pocket a dozen or so of gold and silver spoons.

He did not feel safe till he and Bob Hauler were far away.

Then only did the frightened Jerry venture to speak.

"Blowed if I ain't skeared, Bob. Oh, lord, if it isn't a mercy I didn't shriek right out when I clapped my peepers on that happarition. To think of him doing the grand with all them nobs, and every one on 'em having in their blessed pockets a proclamation of a thousand pounds for his capture! Shiver me if he don't bang the devil!"

Tom's amazing coolness having got him so far through the evening, he was in high spirits when the dessert was ended and dancing commenced.

He found no lack of partners.

Many a fair bosom palpitated warmly against him under the slight pressure of his arm; many a wistful glance was cast after him as his handsome form disappeared amongst the crowd.

At an early hour he had claimed Jenny for his partner, and she was being subjected to the importunities of the Hon. Archibald Gaston when Tom gallantly led her off, to the evident mortification of her persecutor.

It struck Tom, as they waltzed joyfully round the room, that the slender supple form clung with something of a trusting confidence towards him, and that the face beamed a grateful look whenever his glance encountered hers.

After the fascinating dance was finished, he led her to a retired part of the room, where the rich perfume of flowers, and the soft music stole pleasantly upon them.

He had purposely led her there, that he might have a few moments' conversation with her, for he had already conceived a strong interest in her fortunes.

He saw that she loved Harry Vere, and that she regarded with abhorrence her proposed union with the suitor whom her father favoured.

By instinct they seemed to understand each other.

They conversed long and earnestly, and when they rose there was an excited flush of pleasure on Jenny's cheek, and a glad light beamed from her eyes.

She trembled slightly, and her hand rested in Tom's with more than sisterly affection.

As for our hero his cheeks beamed with a manly pride; he had formed a daring scheme, and now he set about effectually carrying it into execution.

That scheme was no less than getting Jenny and Harry to elope, and be married to each other before their flight could be stayed.

CHAPTER X.

TWO DRAWN SWORDS.

THE gardens belonging to the commodore's mansion were lighted up by myriads of lamps, and here, while the night was still young, a throng of guests promenaded.

Commodore Ellis had his grounds laid out with excellent taste; the fine statues and vases, the rare flowers, the velvety slopes of grass, all elicited admiration; and there were secluded fairy-like bowers and glades, where lovers might stray and breathe the very soul of romance.

Our hero, after his conference with Jenny Ellis, quitted the heated saloon, and, descending by the conservatory, passed out into the open air.

He was in search of one who was almost a stranger to him, but in whose welfare he was interested.

He sought him fruitlessly for some time, but as he was anxiously scanning every form, Lady Arbuthnot came hurriedly from one of the glades, and putting her small hand softly on his arm, said, huskily—

"The rivals have met. They stand at the end of this avenue, each with his sword raised to take the other's life! Follow them, while I bring the revellers upon them!"

She hurried away, before he could reply, and our hero walked quickly along the glade.

Stepping behind the trees he saw the glittering of steel, and was upon the combatants before they perceived him.

Archibald Gaston alone had his sword drawn.

His fine features were distorted with passion, foam coated his lips, and he stamped his feet in fury.

"If you are not a coward," Tom heard him say, his face livid with rage, "draw and defend your worthless life. Curses! I saw you dallying with

her hand; and I tell you, worthless beggar, I would sheathe this weapon in your heart and hers, before I would see her your prize."

These were hot words.

Henry Vere met them by words as fierce, and the next moment his sword crossed Gaston's.

They were standing almost foot to foot, regarding each other with deadly hatred; each eagerly seeking an opportunity to transfix his adversary's heart, when Tom stepped from behind the cluster of trees.

He had drawn his sword, and the lithe well-tempered steel beat down the two opposing blades as they were tilted for a murderous thrust.

Keeping them apart by a wave of his hand, Captain Tom Drake stood between them.

"No sword play here, gentlemen,' he said; "there is a fitting time and place for affairs of of this kind—this is neither."

Gaston glared savagely on the slender figure of the boy intruder.

"To the devil with your interference!" he cried, "My sword was at the reptile's throat."

"Liar!" Henry Vere exclaimed; "but for this interference your carcase would ere now have been carrion at my feet."

"Try, then, who can first carve carrion!" Gaston shrieked, hoarsely. "And you, headstrong fool keep back, before both our swords be in your breast."

"Leave us," Henry Vere said; "you cannot interfere; we have sworn to fight till one lies bleeding and slain."

Their swords crossed.

In a moment a purple flush swept to the noble brow of the boy cruiser.

Like lightning his keen sword circled through the air, and a second time battered down their weapons, knocking Henry Vere's from his grasp, shivered to the hilt.

"And I have sworn you shall not fight here," he cried, his angry breast expanding as he spoke. "Lift a hand again, and you shall learn what it is to be brained by a devil."

The impetuous boy's whole form rocked in his fierce passion; the thin veins were swollen on his temple, and his eyes literally blazed.

The graceful stripling was, in an eye's twinkling, transformed into a formidable foe.

For a second Gaston drew back daunted; but instantly his proud soul swelled with fury, and he would have met the attack of Tom, but the sound of excited voices and hasty feet told him that the guests were coming that way, and he sheathed his sword with a savage snap.

"I will not slay you unarmed," he exclaimed, casting a withering look of hate on Henry Vere. "This meeting is deferred, not relinquished. I shall know when and where to seek you. For you, sir," he turned upon Tom, "you will understand that the satisfaction I expect for this is your life."

Tom replied only by a haughty smile of disdain, and Gaston, choking with rage, left the spot.

"Come, sir," Tom said to Henry Vere, who stood half confounded, "pick up your broken sword, and accompany me. We shall have curious eyes upon us if we stay."

Tom led the young lieutenant aside as the guests came hurrying to the spot.

"I must ask pardon of Mr. Vere," he said sheathing his sword, when they had reached a more secluded avenue; "but I have reasons for my interruption—reasons which, I believe, will satisfy him when he hears them."

"Reasons!" the young officer exclaimed, hotly; "what reasons can satisfy me for taking my enemy from my sword's point?"

"Urgent ones. The cause of your angry meeting was your rivalry about Admiral Ellis's pretty daughter. Now, had I allowed you to fight, you might possibly have been killed, in which case your rival woull have been left to possess your lady-love; while even had you succeeded in killing him, either you must have been forced to fly, or have been arrested to answer the charge of slaying him; so that your chance with the admiral's daughter would have been quite as hopeless."

"I am not in the habit of giving explanations of my conduct," Tom continued, a flush mounting to his cheeks; "but I give you th se reasons because I am interested in your suit, and should like to see you successful by other means."

"What hope have I?" the young lieutenant exclaimed, bitterly. "Her father is against me, because I am not equal to my rival in position. Curse him! why did you give him a chance to depart? He will make the worst of this, and to-morrow I may endure the bitter humiliation of having to answer the charge of lifting my hand against him, for he his my superior officer; but let him beware!" Henry Vere continued, fiercely; "there is bad blood between us, and if he degrades me in her eyes, he shall answer with his life!"

Tom laid his hand gently on the excited youth's shoulder.

"Lieutenant Vere," he said; "the laly loves you. Bear her from your rival—marry her."

"Sir, do not madden me! she would not consent; and, if she would, could I take advantage of her love? Her father would never forgive her, and she would bitterly repent her love for me."

"She never would; her love is woman's love, and that means truth. As for her father—that withered martinet—what is her happiness to him? H would barter her away for a price, and would rather see her dead than disobedient and happy."

"True, true," murmured the young officer, feverishly.

"Why, then, hesitate? This Gaston is your senior lieutenant. If he should inform the admiral of this night's encounter, you would lose your commission, and be banished from his doors. Now, if you married Jenny, he might relent when he saw he could not undo the tie; if not, the world is before you; you could battle for your young wife, tnd in some distant land of enchantment could live a life of joy, if you shrink from a more stirring and brilliant career."

"No career would lie open to me, if I am degraded from the service."

"A career that I could offer you—rank on the deck of a rover ship, with a crew of daring noble young fellows like yourself, stung by the cursed treatment of the British authorities—a flag that never yields above your head—freedom before you—rich spoils—cruises in the sunny lands of romance—the golden islands of summer seas—these, and possession of your bride, I can offer to you; as for your rival, should you meet him at sea, when his ship and yours were hidden in the smoke of a glorious cannonade, why, then Lieutenant Vere would know how to humiliate his mortal enemy."

The young officer paused, and excitedly looked the young speaker in the face.

"Who are you, that tempts me with such hope?" he cried. "Are you a devil, sent in this fair guise to bid me sell my soul for such a dream of delicious ecstacy? Show me how I can gain all you have pictured before me, and I will follow you like a slave, through fire and death, to the end of the earth."

Tom put his face a little closer to Harry Vere's.

"I am known as Captain Tom Drake, King of the Boy Buccaneers!"

The young officer looked at him as if he could not believe his ears.

Then, taking both the young chieftain's hands in his, exclaimed—

"You make the earth reel beneath my feet. I have heard of you and have often yearned to be amongst a crew whose daring bids defiance to the world! It has been so bitter to feel the cold scorn of those whose position is above me."

"As it was mine," Tom answered. "I remember when the world had me at its feet—and now who dares to raise a hand in my presence? I have had my old persecutors crouching at my feet, and so can you."

"I will if dear Jenny will consent."

"She will consent—I have spoken to her."

"You—then you know of our unhappy love?"

"I won the story from her lips; I am glad I find you true. You must bear her away to-night."

"This hour—no time is to be lost!"

"Leave all to me. A few of my brave crew shall be in readiness at moonfall to-night. You must not see her again. I suspect Gaston's nature; he will report you to the admiral, who will forbid your speaking to his daughter while you are under suspicion. Be beneath her window when the moon wanes—it is a quiet hour; the grey morning will be struggling with departing night, the stars will not give light to betray us. When you see the casement open, be ready to throw a rope ladder up to the balcony and assist her down; we will be near, but wear your sword; your rival is watchful and suspicious, and may be on the alert. Now let us separate; you know your part, leave the rest to me."

The youthful lieutenant gripped Tom's hand warmly.

"You have indeed proved my friend," he said, his manly voice husky with generous emotion. "If I do not repay this kindness with a life's devotion, may the breath of a deadly pestilence blight me in the first hour when I hold my bride in my arms! Farewell for this hour. I have my part by heart; I will wear a sword, too, and if my accursed rival throws his evil visage in my path, I can be rid of him in the same hour that gives me my bride!"

The young officer's voice quivered, his eyes were moist; in the gush of his grateful enthusiasm he embraced Tom with almost womanly fervour, and hurried from the glade.

Our hero sauntered leisurely along the avenue after his new friend had left him.

Numerous thoughts were crowding in his mind.

How the times had changed since he was a fatherless and almost friendless boy.

What an alteration since he served on board the *Arethusa*, and had to bend his proud spirit before the brutal degradations Sanderson chose to heap upon him!

Then he was an oppressed, outraged boy.

Now what was he?

A king!—chieftain of a devoted crew, monarch on the deck of a noble ship, whose holds were crammed with the richest treasure; a flag above his head fluttering defiantly in the breeze—loud-mouthed cannon at his feet, ready to speak his defiance of his foes—his name renowned throughout the world— renowned for bravery and skill, that made him the hero of lovely women, and the feared amongst strong men.

A word from his lips as he stood amidst the brilliant throng of guests, in the admiral's saloon, and what a flutter of consternation there would have been! how people would have gazed at the princely boy, who, with a price set upon his head, anchored his vessel in the midst of a British fleet, and had the audacity to share the hospitality of a naval officer, and mingle in the society of the very Lords of the Admiralty who had issued the proclamation for his capture and execution.

The proud boy laughed in scorn at the thought, and instinctively touched the hilt of the thin rapier

As he did so he heard a rustling of the foliage behind him, and Bob Hauler, as if called there by that gesture, stood respectfully in his front.

"There's been a suspicious sarpent a dodging you about, sir," the honest smuggler said, touching his forelock, "I doubled on the varmint just now, but he slipped away like an eel, and I lost sight of the skunk—but I've come to tell you as I was afeard some lubber suspected summut."

"Thanks, Bob, for your warning, Tom replied; "it is welcome, though I am too much used to stalk in the heart of danger to be apprehensive when spies dodge at my heels. Where's Jerry Mizzen?'

"He is snug in the kitchen, sir, with the cooks, making love to the servant-women, and trying to catch what he can; for you know, sir, what is said upstairs oftentimes comes down to the kitchen."

"True. If anything transpires, come to me." Bob touched his hat.

"Where is Barnacle?"

"He's in the neighbourhood at hand, if wanted."

"Tell him to have the boat ready in three hours."

"Aye, aye, sir."

"And at moonset to be here with an armed party; he can lie in wait in the wood behind these grounds till the hour."

"Aye. aye, sir."

Bob Hauler respectfully drew back, and his young leader, sauntering past him, soon mingled amongst the festive revellers.

Before one of the elegant tables, spread with ices, champagne, and other refreshments, a group of young noblemen, with several of the Lords of the Admiralty were standing or seated when Tom came up.

The magnificent shrubs which embowered the splendid statues and fountains screened his approach sufficiently to hear their conversation without being seen, and the first words that caught his ear made him pause and listen.

"By the way, Claremont, who's that young fellow, Captain Grey? Precious young to be a captain: seems in good favour, though—the commodore's awfully wrapt up in him; and even old sky-dry, our parchment admiral, took lots of notice of him."

Lord Claremont, a handsome, careless-looking young nobleman, laughed lightly.

"It struck me he was much favoured by the fair sex; pretty little Jenny stuck close to him, and, by Jupiter, if I had been in love I should have been jealous of the way he watched all the belles of the evening round the room—Lady Arbuthnot, too. Jupiter Tonans, he's a lucky dog—he can make way with her."

"That's what no other fellow could do—eh, Walpole?" said a third, addressing the first speaker.

"Except Jinks; he's the Adonis for this modern Venus. We shall have the jealous Vulcan taking both in a net, and meshing in irons the stalwart form of our rash wooer."

Lord Augustus Vane—the noble whom they referred to as Jinks—did not seem disposed to bear these remarks good-humouredly.

He was a slim, dandified little man, with evidently as much stamina as a reed; but he tried to look nettled, and tapping the hilt of his sword pettishly, said—

"Look ahere, Moreton; by jinks, Lady Arbuthnot's name is—aw—sacred in my—aw—estimation; and any—aw—fellow that insults her—aw—shall—aw—answer to me, by jinks—aw."

The young noblemen laughed at this display of temper.

"Don Quixote in disguise," said Lord Moreton.

"No, Lord Lovel," laughed Lord Harry Walpole.

"Or Don Juan," exclaimed Claremont.

At each of these remarks little Lord Vane turned petulantly away, and uttered an impatient exclamation.

He was evidently used to be teased, and his reckless young companions knew how far they could go without ruffling him too greatly.

"But about this Captain Grey," observed Claremont. "I wonder how the fellow got his ship. He seems in capital case. The hilt of that sword he wears is of pure gold."

"What!" interrupted Lord Vane; "pure gold—aw—pure devils! I'll tell you what—aw—wager you two hundred guineas—aw—it's no such thing."

"Perhaps the blade is silver, and the point a diamond," put in Walpole, sarcastically.

"I shall take Lord Lovel's bet," replied Claremont. "With reference to the blade being silver, the point a diamond, such extravagances have been known; and as the captain is something of a rover prince, he may have picked up weapons as remarkable as any you have heard of."

"Bravo, Claremont!" said Lord Moreton, "you've been dipping into romance lately. Won't you wager that his ship is laden with the spoils of Greek corsairs, and that his cabin contains some dazzling houri, stolen from the harem of some old Pasha, to minister to his pleasures, and sing at his feet the plaintive airs of her native land?"

The laugh was turned against Claremont by Moreton's speech, but when they had ceased their merriment, he said, gravely—

"Romance or no, I'll warrant the weapon of our unknown friend is a tried and trusty one, and that his arm is clever in its use. I observed his build—his limbs are formed for supple strength, and his eyes are like an eagle's!"

"Ha, ha! Claremont grows eloquent," said Walpole.

"Perhaps he knows the strange guest."

"Some famous corsair possibly."

"Or the renowned Captain Tom Drake."

"Laugh on, gentlemen," Claremont exclaimed; "but I should not be surprised if even that were the case; at any rate, I'll take Jinks's wager for two hundred guineas."

"Aw—you shall; and—aw—I'll bet you another couple of hundred that my sword has a better blade than his."

"Done! And now how shall we prove it?" said Claremont.

"Aw—I'll ask him to let me try it, of course," lisped Vane.

"A very unlikely thing that he will consent."

"You'd have to fight him, Jinks."

"And might try whether the point's diamond made."

Lord Vane got very red in the face.

"Confound you all!" he cried, angrily, "aw—I'll fight him, too—aw—he shall show me his sword, or I'll make it cross mine."

"And lose your life as well as your wager," Walpole observed.

Lord Vane was about to make some excited reply, when the form of our hero was seen as he came through the shrubbery.

"By Jupiter, here he is. Now then, Jinks, look out!" cried Claremont, as Tom strode up to them.

Our hero was wearing his most careless air, and as if he had heard nothing that had passed, and was walking quietly by, when the young lords accosted him by wishing him good evening.

"Good evening, gentlemen," Tom replied, politely, and Lord Vane edged himself in his way.

"Aw—there's a good fellah," he began; "don't—aw—take offence, I'm Lord Augustus Vane; these are my friends—Claremont, a wine-drinking, quarrelsome, woman-hater; Walpole, a big-headed, obstinate, good sort of a baby; Moreton, the lady's man, and as touchy as gunpowder—we're all friends—we're just strolled out—aw—damme, will you drink with us?"

Lord Vane got a little closer to Tom while he made this long speech, and now he carelessly put his hand on our hero's sword.

The young chieftain gently stepped back so as to bring his sword-hilt from Lord Vane's reach.

"Upon some other occasion," he said, "I shall be happy to drink with such noble gentlemen; to-night I must beg to be excused."

Lord Vane again stepped purposely in his way.

"Aw—don't go like that—aw—don't, there's a good fellah; we—aw—want to see—aw—your sword; my friend here's made a—aw—statement, and—aw—I——"

Tom drew himself proudly up, and looked down upon the young lordling.

"My Lord Augustus Vane," he said, "I wear my sword for use, not as a toy for fools to wager upon."

Lord Vane got redder still in the face.

At any other time this answer would have been enough to excite his anger, but now he smothered his wrath, and said—

"Aw—don't be so deuce uncivil. Fact is, my friend here made an—aw— absurd wager about your—aw—sword having a gold—aw—hilt. Walpole, here—aw—hints the blade's made of—aw— silver, with an—aw—diamond point ; but I've——"

"Enough !" said Tom, "there is one way to decide your silly wagerings; you are armed, I perceive—the first of the four who can disable me can examine my sword at his leisure. For your personal affront, my Lord Vane, suffer me to say that when I have tried the mettle of men, there will be time to notice a jackanapes like you."

He thrust the young lordling quietly aside and stepping back a pace, stood with his hand on the hilt of his sword, waiting for the first to draw.

Lord Vane, excited to blind passion, plucked his sword from its sheath, and would have rushed hotly to attack Tom, but Lord Moreton put him back.

"He has insulted us as well as you," he cried, "and shall first give me satisfaction."

His sword flashed from its sheath.

"Not so, he shall answer first to me," Claremont cried, drawing likewise.

"While you are settling your dispute as to precedence," Walpole exclaimed, "this privateer can flesh his sword on me."

"Gentlemen," Tom said, quietly, as the four swords menaced him, "I await your pleasure."

"I am at your service first," Claremont exclaimed. "Gentlemen, you will give me precedence, seeing that I am concerned in the wager, and may decide that at the same time that I pluck the feather off this braggart bird."

"Claremont is right," Walpole said, drawing back, and the rest, following his example, sheathed their swords.

Then Tom coolly drew his sword.

Claremont put himself in a posture of easy defence, and their shining weapons crossed.

At the first glance it could be seen that they were careful swordsmen.

There were no desperate thrusts—no hazardous play.

The duel might have been a drawing-room passage of arms, instead of having a life for its stake, they fenced with such elegance and quiet ease.

The gay young noblemen watched every movement of the youthful combatants with intense excitement.

The two thin, bright swords seemed to play about each other like serpents.

A moment's thrust might stretch Captain Tom or his noble opponent lifeless on the green sward.

Their very breath seemed held as the movements of the pair became quicker.

At one instant, Claremont's blade was lunged direct at Tom's throat, the next, and the lordly duellist only saved himself by a parry swift as a gleam of lightning.

Their weapons hardly appeared to cross again, when Claremont was seen to start and turn pale, and his sword, with a dull ring, went whirling from his grasp, and fell at Lord Walpole's feet.

He made no effort to regain his rapier.

He knew he was at Tom's mercy; but he had the soul of a Spartan, and drawing himself proudly erect, he awaited his antagonist's thrust.

Lord Augustus Vane gave utterance to a cry of vexation, and Walpole stooped to pick up Claremont's sword, but as he touched the hilt our hero, stepping forward, quickly struck it from his hold, and taking the weapon, laid it across his own blade and presented it to Claremont.

Then the noble lookers-on saw that Tom's sword was reddened with his opponent's blood, and that there was a spreading crimson spot on Claremont's breast.

"Take your weapon, my lord," said Tom. "You are winged, sir ; and there are others eager to help you to pluck the feathers from the braggart bird."

With a dash of his hand Claremont hurled his sword to the earth.

"Strike !" he cried. "Taunt those who yield —life would be a curse accepted from your hands !"

A quiet smile curled our hero's lips, and he sheathed his sword.

"Bind up yor wound," he said. "I never strike a foeman twice."

He was turning to see who was the next claimant for the honour of disarming him, when Commodore Ellis came hurrying to the spot.

"How now, gentlemen ?" he cried. "What is the meaning of this—swords out and angry looks exchanged ? Captain Grey here, too ?"

He did not notice Claremont was wounded, as the young noble drew his sash over the hurt.

Lord Moreton answered him with affected gaiety—

"A little passage of arms, commodore. This gentleman and Claremont were trying the temper of their blades—a wager, you know. Young blood will have its excitements. Claremont is pale, you see—he did not hold his weapon well, and is mortified accordingly."

Saying this lightly, he passed the commodore, and stepped up to our hero.

"You escape this time, adventurer !" he said, in a low tone of deep passion, "but I will find the opportunity to chastise you like a dog before you leave these grounds !"

Tom's hands clenched ; a wild glitter shone in his eyes ; swift as lightning the veins rose like cords to his forehead.

For a moment he seemed about to strike the speaker to the earth, or pluck out his rapier and stab him to the heart; but in an instant he calmed himself, and with a quiet, disdainful smile on his lips turned away.

Moreton raved like a madman when our hero had left with the commodore.

"Before the night is over," he cried hotly, "he shall answer for this with his life, or I will lie dead at his feet !"

"Let us help Claremont in," Walpole said. "He is hurt deeper than he shows."

They gathered anxiously around the young noble.

He was pale as death, and scarcely able to stand.

"I know not if I am pricked to death, Claremont observed, faintly. "Confound my ill-luck ! The captain fenced like the very devil. I did not feel I was touched till he drew his sword out of my chest. It's only a little hole he's made, but all my heart's blood seems trickling out of it."

The young lords supported their wounded friend, gazing with tender solicitude into his ghastly face.

Claremont observed their anxiety, and forcing a smile on his features, he said—

"Don't give me over yet, gentlemen. Let me rest here, it is out of sight; and you, Walpole, fetch Vincent to stop this confounded bleeding ; and hark, as friends, whichever of you may have the next tilt with this captain, never let your eyelid wink, or you'll have his sword-hilt knocking at your ribs."

The commodore had meanwhile led our hero back to the saloon, and had hardly introduced him to some new guests, when a message came from Admiral Ellis, summoning his brother to his room.

When the commodore entered his brother's apartment he found that personage seated at a table, on which lay a number of open despatches, with some letters ready sealed for transmission.

The little old admiral's face was as grave and inscrutable as ever; but there was more than usual dryness in his throat when he said—

"Be seated, brother. I have excellent orders for you. Information has placed it in my power to secure this boy-freebooter, Captain Tom Drake, and to offer you the honour of taking his ship. Ask no questions. Here are your instructions, containing a full description of his ship and crew. You will sail in your own vessel at daybreak; by sunset I shall expect your return with the captured pirate. Their leader you will not trouble yourself about; he, probably, will not be on board."

Accompanying these words with a significant look, the withered old naval veteran handed his brother his letter of instructions, which the commodore, too much used to his relative's ways to offer any remarks, took in silence, only bowing as he received them from him; for the formal courtesies of their respective ranks were punctiliously kept up between them.

"And now," said the little admiral, "about your young friend, Captain Grey; he must remain here all night. Have you a room to offer him?"

"My own apartment shall be at the service of my brave young guest, if he will accept it."

A cynical look flitted across the sallow visage of the admiral.

"Press your hospitality upon him. Meanwhile let this revelry continue—it will aid us in our plans."

The latter part of his speech was spoken more to himself, and taking up a pen, he was soon busily engaged in writing despatches which he carefully folded and sealed.

When the door had closed after his brother, who left almost immediately, the little admiral leaned his withered cheeks upon his hand, and mused aloud—

"It is a pity I cannot trust my brother with this secret; he would spoil everything with that great baby good honest heart of his; and he might give this graceless dog a chance of escape because he played the gallant to my daughter. A fine young dare-devil scoundrel to set his Majesty's navy at defiance—hum—we shall teach him a different story when we get him in the net. The fellow must have nerve, too, or he would never have outfaced me at the dinner-table when I put him to that test. Almost a pity to stop such a career; ha! quite as well I had my spy on his track. His audacity in coming here is something above the usual run of such adventurers, who are not so anxious generally to put their necks inside the noose. Ah, we'll get him safely caged in my brother's apartment; we'll make no noisy capture—oh, no! At moonfall, when all is dark and quiet, an armed party shall break in upon his slumbers, and then, my dear Captain Grey, alias Captain Tom Drake, privateer and runaway, we shall enjoy the felicity of seeing how you will behave with a halter round your neck."

If the distinguished old naval veteran had turned round at that moment, he would have seen a face, with a very comical expression on it, peering from behind a huge, old-fashioned chair in one corner of the room.

The face belonged to our old friend, Jerry Mizzen.

He had sneaked upstairs after having accidentally, while prowling about the house, overheard the admiral tell a suspicious-looking seaman to follow him to his room.

He had stowed himself away amongst the lumber in time to hear the betrayal of Tom by the spy, who had brought the intelligence of his expected visit—and was the man Bob Hauler had seen dogging his footsteps—had heard Tom's capture planned, and was now in a vexatious sort of quandary, for, apart from the chances of his discovery, it was of little use for him to know the nature of the snare set for the young chieftain, if he could find no means of putting him on his guard.

Still Jerry was in high glee.

He could not help grinning behind the admiral's back as he heard the old fellow rubbing his hands in glee at the prospect of our hero's expected capture.

Indeed he could hardly resist the temptation of flinging something at the little old officer's head.

He began to get uncomfortable after awhile.

There was he, cramped up behind that chair, with no power of movement, and there sat the withered old fellow as busily engaged over his despatches as if he had no intention of quitting the apartment until morning.

Tom found, on his return to the saloon, that his estimate of the Hon. Archibald Gaston's nature was correct.

The story of his encounter with Harry Vere had been told with malicious exaggeration, and the young lieutenant had been forbidden entry again to the commodore's house.

The craft of Gaston had gone even further, and an order for Vere's arrest had already been signed by Admiral Ellis.

Our hero learned all this soon after he entered the room, and a glance at Jenny's tear-stained face showed him that she was informed of her lover's banishment and danger.

When her glance met Tom's a deep flush rose to her cheeks and her eyes brightened.

There was a world of inquiring eagerness in her looks, and our hero saw that her bosom palpitated violently when he seated himself gracefully beside her.

Although so many of the guests were in the gardens, the saloon was still crowded.

Jenny had chosen the most retired part of the room, but even then she was in the midst of a merry party of male and female guests, whose heedless converse fell unnoticed on her ear.

There was some interest excited when Tom strode up and quietly took his seat.

People wondered whether the youthful captain was a suitor of the admiral's daughter.

As for Jenny, her brain was swimming since Tom had inspired her with his scheme for her elopement.

She wondered how he had fared with her lover; whether Henry Vere had proved true, or if the daring flight was impracticable.

Our hero, who saw her eagerness to know, soon lit upon means of informing her.

He saw that it would be impossible to get her away even for a moment.

She was closely watched by order of her father.

It was not an easy matter to foil our adventurer when he had a purpose in view.

Adroitly guiding the conversation, he related the story of an exploit that had befallen one of his officers.

How he had loved a certain lady, whose guardians forbade their union, and how he had won her from a host of rivals.

The fairer portion of Tom's hearers were eager to learn how.

"You shall hear," Tom said. "The lady was gentle, but she loved her daring suitor. Her guardian shut her up in a secure chamber; but at night, just such a night as this, at moonset, precisely, a rope ladder is thrown up to the lady's balcony, her lover ascends, he bears her in his arms; a carriage waits, they flee, and when the pursuers overtake them at daybreak in a little chapel whither they have fled, she leans on the arm of her husband."

"A romantic love-chase," Lady Arbuthnot observed, coming up at that moment.

Other comments were offered.

None noticed that Jenny Ellis had gone pale as death, and that she took the opportunity of quitting the saloon.

None, except our hero, who caught her timid grateful look as she went, and knew that she understood his story, and would be prepared at the hour named.

Lady Arbuthnot arose immediately afterwards.

In passing our hero, a richly jewelled fan dropped from her grasp and fell at his feet.

Our hero picked it up, and was politely returning it to her, when it fell open a little way, and he saw pencilled on the smooth leaves in small round letters—

"You are discovered   Beware!"

His eyes met Lady Arbuthnot's at the moment; they seemed as brilliant as the priceless gem blazing on the costly fan.

She was evidently trying to gather from his looks whether he had seen her warning.

Captain Tom bowed as he placed the fan in her lily hands.

Lady Arbuthnot was evidently ill at ease.

She tried to smile with her accustomed ease as she thanked him.

"It is a curious article," she said, lightly lifting it to her cheek, "and gentle treasures are hidden among its leaves."

"I observe all," Tom replied quietly, and Lady Arbuthnot, now better assured, quitted the spot.

She encountered Tom shortly afterwards as he was making his way towards the gardens.

She was greatly agitated, and in a low tone said hurriedly—

"Rash boy, why have you ventured hither? The admiral suspects all; a word or an incautious look will be your death-warrant."

Tom doffed his hat gracefully, and the fearless woman, without another word, passed him by.

He understood the reason.

They were watched.

The same suspicious ruffian who had been dogging his steps the whole evening, was behind him now.

If there was one thing repugnant to our young adventurer's impulsive nature it was the idea of being tracked wherever he went by a treacherous spy, too cowardly to come before him and perform his dastard duty for greedy gain.

The princely boy's heart swelled with daring pride as dangers thickened about him; he was aware now that he was in peril.

The few simple words he had seen on Lady Arbuthnot's fan—words that thrilled upon his sight more than the clustered gems that sparkled there like fire, recalled him a little to a sense of the risk he ran.

"I may have occasion to thank the lady for her kind interest in me," he mused, "meanwhile I will be on my guard; firstly, however, I may as well give this houndling spy at my heels a lesson."

Walking on for a few moments in deep reverie, he turned suddenly, and springing upon the shadowy form behind him, dragged the spy from the shelter of the bushes.

The fellow's heart sank like lead—Tom's grasp throttled him.

A dangerous look was in our hero's eyes.

"Worm!" Tom said, "I have had you at my heels long enough, I will spare you any further trouble concerning my movements."

"Mercy, mercy!" gasped the man.

"I'll not take your worthless life, but I'll put you where you'll be safe," Tom replied, dragging the fellow out of sight.

There were several old trees about the grounds, trees with trunks hollowed by age.

Tom bound the shivering wretch hand and foot, and having securely gagged him, thrust him by bodily force through a narrow opening in one of the hollow trees, and left him to his fate.

Commodore Ellis, who had no suspicion of the truth, pressed Tom to remain all night when he encountered him, and our hero, who had his own reasons for wishing to be in the place, readily consented.

When the news was brought to the little old admiral that Captain Grey had retired to his apartment, he rubbed his shrivelled palms together and chuckled in unusual glee.

It was something to effect the capture of the notorious boy-cruiser, whose exploits had been as daring as they were audacious.

He went joyfully to his room to be in wait till the proper moment came, for the withered veteran was very precise, and wanted everything effected with noiseless dexterity, so as not to disturb the guests.

When he was gone, our old friend, Jerry Mizzen, whose long back ached with being doubled up so long, wriggled out of his cramped position, and crept out of the apartment.

The little admiral was punctilious in all his acts.

When all was ready for the taking of our adventurer he attired himself in full dress, and, with his cocked hat on his head, and his state sword by his side, headed the party who were told off to the eventful service.

On tiptoe they crept to the bedchamber whither Tom had been conducted.

The door was opened noiselessly, and one of the little admiral's band stationed the marines on each side of the doorway.

They had their muskets loaded.

Their order was to fire the instant Tom attempted to escape.

As yet they were in total darkness.

Now the old naval veteran gave the signal.

They heard a heavy breathing under the bed-clothes. Admiral Ellis fancied he detected them move as the light of a lantern was, in obedience to his command, turned on.

Scarcely had the lights flashed feebly through the apartment when he cried, in a voice whose hoarse stern notes had often been heard with effect on an English quarter-deck—

"Steady, marines—at the word 'fire,' shoot him dead; advance—halt—present. Now, my bold boy-corsair, awake and surrender—you hear my orders; resistance will be your death."

The muskets were turned towards the bed, from whence came a smothered cry, as of human fear and agony; a movement was perceptible beneath the bedclothes—it was the culprit's tremor.

Admiral Ellis smiled drily.

"In the King's name, Tom Drake, rise and surrender," he exclaimed.

The same cry and struggle as before.

The admiral drew his sword and stepped to the bed-side.

With a swift clutch he pulled down the coverings.

In a moment a dark form sprang from the bed and flung itself violently upon him and brought him to the ground before he could give the word to fire.

The marines, who had at first levelled their pieces, now ran forward in amazed dismay.

Admiral Ellis had rescued from the superincumbent weight of bed-clothes a huge mastiff belonging to the commodore, which had been securely muzzled and rolled up in the blankets to take the place in the bed of Captain Tom.

The little naval officer no sooner saw the trick that had been played upon him than he struggled angrily to his feet, and cried—

"Search the place, he must be here—unmuzzle the hound; dead or alive, I'll take this Pirate Boy."

Even while he spoke a sudden tumult rose from below, the cries of furious men—a woman's wailing cry—a shriek as of deadly agony.

Then a voice—the voice of the Hon. Archibald Gaston—cried, in startling tones—

"Help, help! Wake all of you! Admiral. I am slain! Your daughter is borne off by villains! Help, help! Murder!—oh, help!"

CHAPTER XI.

THE CHAPEL UNDER THE CLIFF.

OUR readers will have guessed that the stratagem by which the little old admiral was outwitted owned its invention to the fertile wit of Jerry Mizzen, who no sooner got out of the room in which he had been so long playing the part of eavesdropper, than he sneaked down to the kitchen to find out from one of the maids in what part of the house the commodore's chamber was placed.

He had been making desperate love to one of the servant maids—a spruce little country lass, new to her situation—and from her he gleaned the intelligence he desired.

His next proceeding was to arouse his boy-leader without creating any alarm.

This was done without difficulty.

Our hero was watchful, and on the alert.

At the first soft tap given by Jerry outside he opened the door.

He was dressed, and had his hand on the hilt of his sword.

When he recognized his faithful servant, he drew him inside, and noiselessly closed the door.

A few words explained his danger.

The story did not disturb him much.

A quiet smile played about his lips when Jerry proposed muzzling the dog, and putting it in the bed.

Jerry had a knack of getting on familiar terms with dogs, and had already made friends with the big mastiff.

Time was nearly up when Tom and he quitted the chamber, and softly descended the stairs.

The house was in perfect quiet.

The revellers had departed, the lamps in the garden had died out.

A strange calm and darkness had fallen upon the scene so lately full of life and brilliancy.

The armed party of marines were concealed in a lower room.

Admiral Ellis did not wish his brother to know of their presence.

He was afraid that the blunt-hearted fellow, with all his loyalty, would give the Boy Buccaneer one chance of escaping—preferring to take him at sea, rather than beneath the roof whose hospitality he had bestowed upon him.

So there was no interruptions to Jerry's doings.

A savoury bone brought the huge mastiff to his feet; the gag was adroitly slipped on, and, in spite of his struggles, the huge animal was carried upstairs, and secured beneath the blankets.

This ruse accomplished, our hero and his accomplice silently quitted the house.

It is time, now, for their night's adventure.

Jenny Ellis had extinguished her lamp, and in the stillness of her chamber awaited the waning of the moon.

Her heart was sad and ill at ease.

Spite of her love and sympathy for Harry Vere, she reproached herself for the disobedient step she was about to take.

At times, too, she was a prey to the acutest forebodings.

What if their attempt should be discovered, and her lover should be slain in her arms?

What if the daring boy-adventurer had deceived her, and had only planned this as a means of getting her into his power, and conveying her on board his ship?

What if her lover should, after all, betray her, and leave her deceived and deserted?

She stood by her half-open casement with these thoughts troubling her gentle mind, and her heart leaping at every sound.

Occasionally she listened for any footstep coming from her father's room.

She yearned to cross to his chamber, and give him one last parting kiss—shed one farewell tear on his silvery beard, but she dared not let him suspect her.

His stern kindliness had driven her from his love, and, whatever might be the consequences, her fate for the present was decided.

One by one she watched the bright lamps die out in the garden.

One by one the stars faded from the sky.

Stealthily, as it seemed, a stillness crept upon the scene—a solemn hush that came with the gathering darkness, and crept about her very heart, with its gloomy sense of fear and awe.

Now and again the moon shone in at the casement—shone on her pallid, tearful face and throbbing bosom, bared to the cool fresh air of night—for she still wore her light evening dress, and had only drawn a robe about her fair shoulders as the evening became more chill.

She was a pure-minded, simple-hearted, loving English girl.

She had been early left without a mother, and her father was too much absorbed with his profession to lavish affection on his only child.

Besides, the strict discipline of his quarter-deck had made him so hard and cold in manners that his word or look repelled his daughter's love, and made her sigh still more deeply for the mother, whose tender care she missed as the years crept on, that transformed her from the delicate child into the gentle maiden, whose whole soul thrilled with a longing for a love she had never known, till her young nature's affections were given to Harry Vere.

She sighed as she thought how, if her father had been different, she would not have stood there that night like a guilty thing, waiting for the still gloom of midnight to hide those who stole thither to steal her from his care.

By degrees her sorrowful reverie changed to a dreamy stupor—an oblivious lethargy that almost steeped her senses in a whirling forgetfulness, under the influence of which her thoughts wandered from the turmoils of the world, and a sweet calm fell upon her mind.

Hark! a rustling of the leaves beneath her window.

She started, her heart throbbing violently.

A step!

A light shriek escaped her lips.

Something fell softly against the balcony.

The rope ladder.

She aroused herself by an almost unconscious instinct.

She fastened back her sunny tresses, and passing her hands before her white forehead, opened the casement.

It was too dark to see below, but at her feet lay the coils of a silken ladder.

The moon had waned, the wind was whispering among the leaves—all was silence.

She listened on the brink of the balcony.

A tremulous voice breathed her name in a low, fervent whisper—

"Jenny, dearest!"

"OUR PRISONER," CRIED ANDREWS.

Her lover's voice.

The tones thrilled her gentle breast.

He was there to conduct her to freedom and love.

With trembling eagerness her slender fingers made fast the silken cords.

She had hardly stepped back, shivering guiltily at her own deed, when the ropes were drawn to their tightest tension, as a clinging form sprang up them, and her lover leaped softly into the chamber.

Her timid little breast gave a weird bound; she tried to speak—her tongue refused utterance—she shrank away from her lover's arm, but he had clasped her to his breast, and with gentle firmness held her beating bosom to his.

"My life—my love—my beautiful—my own—my dear, darling Jenny!" he murmured, "Oh, can I believe this delicious hour to be real? Come, gentle dove, give me one word—say that you for-

give me for tempting you to this step—one kiss, that I may be assured this is not a delusive dream!"

She struggled to free herself from his passionate embrace.

"Oh, Harry, this is so sinful," she whispered, faintly; "my brain reels—I am sinking in fear."

Her lover held her closer in his arms—his lips were pressed close to hers—he kissed her cold cheeks, and parted the silken locks from her fair brow.

"I could fain die now," he murmured, his deep tones thrilling with the ecstacy of his delirious joy, "but that life so sweetly promises a blissful future! Come, dear one, let me lead you hence; the hour is brief, and danger to our hopes comes with the morning light."

"Alas, I fear! An unknown dread creeps upon

my heart; the heavens are so black. Oh, Henry, is it too late to retract?"

"Late enough to give me to death if I quit this place without you," her lover cried, impulsively. "Come, dearest; fear nothing, there is no danger that can sunder our love. Lean on me, let me guide your steps. Once clear of these prison walls we shall be free."

He drew her cloak and hood round her trembling form.

She was powerless to resist or act for herself.

But she allowed herself to cling to him, and step by step—bearing her as if she were a child—the young lieutenant bore her down the ladder.

She recovered a little when her feet touched the grassy ground.

Her lover caressed her soothingly.

"Now, dearest, we must be swift. Thus far we are safe, but one moment's delay may end all."

He had led her a little way from the wall, when she paused abruptly, and, with a sudden cry, flung her arms about his neck.

"Oh, Henry, I can go no further. My mother's portrait—I cannot leave it behind me; this letter, too, I had forgotten to leave on the table. It is for my father and explains why I have deserted him."

She burst into tears.

The young lieutenant looked round anxiously.

"Delay may be fatal," he muttered; "but it must be done. Remain here, dearest. Give me the letter. As you love me, do not move. I will not waste a moment in bringing you the miniature."

Almost before she could comprehend his act he had taken the letter, and, leaving her beneath the shelter of the overhanging trees, sprang up the ladder and mounted the balcony.

He hardly seemed to have time to reach the chamber before she heard his quick step returning.

He had the miniature in his hand.

His face was deathly pale.

His eyes flashed wildly in the darkness.

Before he could reach her, she heard another step, and a choking sob of agony rose stifling to her throat as a second figure stepped between her and Henry Vere.

Her lover's rival—the Hon. Archibald Gaston.

Poor Jenny would have shrieked, but fear had made her mute.

Gaston had given her one withering, indignant look.

Now he turned, like a wild animal, upon her youthful lover.

"So," he said, hoarsely, his visage swollen with passion, "this is how you creep, like a thief in the night, to steal this girl from her home—an elopement! It is a pity to spoil your pretty plans; but even against the lady's will I must bar your dastard flight. Back, poltroon! this girl shall not share your infamy!"

Big beading drops of sweat gathered on the young lieutenant's brow.

He put himself in Gaston's path so as to keep him the admiral's daughter.

"Touch her not!" he cried, fiercely, "or by the brave, Gaston, there will be deadly work done. Stand from my way! I have set life, honour, tion, all on this; and as I am a man, with the of death in my hands, I will dare all to gain rpose!"

ston uttered a scornful exclamation.

pare your threats, hound! this lady is not s yet. One word of mine, and we shall have erry party to see the two runaways dragged ack; one like a truant girl, and the other like the knavish cur he is."

"And were that cry to leave your lips," the young lieutenant cried, "this sword's point should choke the other in your throat. I am in no mood for words; stand aside, or draw and defend your life!"

Gaston laughed as the excited speaker's sword flashed from its sheath.

"It is well I have a weapon too," he said, sneeringly, "or the would-be runaway might play the assassin too. Stand from between us, misguided girl. When I have stretched this dastard at my feet, I will assist you to your chamber before the world's tongue can wag at your disgrace and your father's shame."

The young lieutenant saw the pleading look in Jenny's eyes as Gaston almost thrust her aside.

But there was no time to heed her supplication—each moment's delay was full of perils; besides his blood was up.

Gaston's words and his act excited him to passionate madness.

He flew at him as their swords met.

There was a clash—one swift, murderous thrust, and his sword went nearly to the hilt in Gaston's breast.

The stricken officer staggered back as the transfixing weapon was drawn from the terrible wound.

His eyes rolled wildly, and he made an ineffectual effort to return the thrust.

Even then the red blade in Henry Vere's hand was poised for a second stab.

But Jenny, with a face pale as marble, clutched his wrist.

The young lieutenant was in a frenzy of rage.

Jenny's agonised shriek caused him to abstain from the second thrust.

But he pushed his reeling antagonist from his path, and cried, huskily—

"Now, stay me if you can; cry loudly for help; wake the sleeping household; bring armed soldiers in my path; ah! ah! Lieutenant Gaston, that thrust has settled our rivalry for ever; you will see me escape—escape with this priceless maiden—while your heart's blood is flowing drop by drop!"

Gaston had reeled against a tree.

Clinging to a withered branch with one hand, he rested the point of his sword upon the ground to support himself from falling, and getting all his strength into one vehement cry uttered the alarm that had roused the baffled admiral and warned him of this new outrage.

His cry was answered by the quick trampling of feet and rattling of arms, and a gleam of triumph settled over Gaston's deathly features.

"Flee as fast as you may," he cried, hoarsely. "Ha! ha! the lights flash forth. I am heard, and you, dastard, are baffled in your murderous flight!"

As the young lieutenant turned fiercely towards him, the strength which had lent his brief support to his wounded rival forsook him, an ashy pallor overspread his ghastly features, he gave a hoarse cry, and sank powerless to the earth.

Then Jenny Ellis, with a scream of intense agony, fell senseless in her lover's arms.

While Henry Vere stood almost paralysed, with his abducted bride supported on his breast, his other hand still grasping his ruddy sword, quick footsteps sounded behind him, and our hero stepped to his side.

"Escape!" he cried. "The house is alarmed; in a few moments you will be lost. Follow me; be swift, and bear her in your arms."

The young chieftain's words roused Vere from his stupor.

He lifted Jenny from the ground and followed Tom through the shrubbery.

Not an instant too early.

The admiral's voice was heard as he hurried to the parapet, leading half-a-dozen men with muskets and lighted lamps.

Alarm bells rang from all parts, and the commodore was already in the gardens, his drawn sword in his hand.

Henry Vere gave himself up for lost.

"We are surrounded," he said, huskily, to our hero; "hide while they take me; in the confusion you may escape; for me there is no chance."

"Never say yield," Tom replied quickly. "We are not seen yet; if we can reach the grotto, where my men are placed, we may bid defiance to a host."

Henry Vere was not reassured by the boy-cruiser's words. The baying of dogs in his rear seemed further to unnerve him.

The hounds were let loose.

"Further flight is hopeless," he exclaimed. "I will halt here, and sell my life as dearly as I can."

"Pause and be taken. Listen, Lieutenant Vere, if you halt for one moment, I will slay you as a white-livered poltroon, and bear your bride to my crew."

Tom's determined look convinced the young officer he meant what he said. He set his teeth together, and inspired with new energy, hurried onwards with his inanimate burden.

The glare of lights lit up the scene behind them, as now and then a musket was discharged in their track.

The baying of the hounds came nearer.

Dark as it was, their eyes becoming used to the gloom enabled them to see the place where our hero had left his men in ambush.

It was an artificial grotto formed in the natural rock, which here underran the estate. Innumerable fissures, through which the water travelled, furrowed its winding sides, and a ship's crew might have hidden there unperceived.

But the lieutenant did not know what our hero was informed of, that there was a subterranean way to the shore through the grotto, a way of peril and difficulty, but their only way of escape.

When they were almost there, the flare of a score of lamps and torches revealed them to their pursuers.

They were close upon them—the hounds in front; the admiral white as a sheet, following in the rear.

He saw the fugitives as Tom put his foot on the rock, and in a firm voice, he gave the word for the marines to present.

Before they could fire, Harry Vere had leaped upon the rocks, and faced them with Jenny in his arms.

"Fire," he cried, in a deep excited voice, "but remember, Admiral Ellis, the bullets that bring me down shall make a target of your daughter's breast. We die together, old man, thus, lip to lip, heart to heart. one bullet or a score—we are sworn and affianced now, and death—only death shall sunder us."

Jenny had partly recovered her consciousness, and now, as her lover drew his manly form erect, and she let her fair head nestle on his breast, she heard his words, and knew that a moment might decide their fate; but true to the death, she was content to die with him, with her face pressed to his, her fair bosom resting against the strong breast she could feel throbbing defiantly against her

Even with the certainty of sacrificing his only child, the admiral would have ordered them to fire, but while the fatal word was on his lips, a terrible stupor seized his heart, and he fell speechless and in a fit.

Jenny did not see her father fall, her lips were glued to her lover's in what she thought to be their last caress, and she was waiting for the deadly volley, when the commodore sang out—

"Let loose the hounds, let no man fire while that poor girl is in danger."

He elevated his voice, for Lieutenant Vere to hear.

"Put down my niece, villain, and you shall have five minutes' grace to escape; hold her, and these hounds shall tear you to pieces."

"Leap down here," Tom said, in a low tone to Vere, "I will answer the commodore."

As the dogs came leaping on, our hero, who was in the shadow of the rocks, gave the signal to his men.

There was a sudden flash.

The rattle of fire-arms filled the calmness of the hollow rocks, and the two hounds fell, riddled with bullets.

The suddenness of this unexpected volley threw the commodore and his men into confusion, but instantly the marines, believing they were attacked by their unseen foes, levelled their muskets and fired.

The blinding flash was succeeded by a shriek of agony.

It came from Jenny's lips.

The commodore, stricken as if by a bullet staggered back.

"My God!" he cried; "she is killed."

Then, with the marines, he rushed forward, but the rocks were vacant.

The whole party had disappeared in the gloom.

Jenny Ellis was not hit.

The flash of the musketry had shown her her father being raised from the earth, apparently lifeless, and it was that sight which extorted the scream from her lips.

Harry Vere, who at first thought she was struck, leapt down the rocks with her, in obedience to a word from Captain Tom.

They were in almost total darkness, but he could see the dusky forms of a party of men, who, he judged, were some of Tom's crew.

Our hero took him by the wrist, and in silence they traversed a narrow winding passage, Jenny again lying senseless in his arms.

The passage became more cramped as they followed its intricacies, and seemed to burrow more and more under the earth.

It was total darkness now; not even the hand of Tom could he see; but he heard the trickling of water.

A pause of a few seconds presently occurred, then the young chieftain said, in a low voice—

"Step carefully, and give your burden to me."

The young lieutenant allowed Tom to take the inanimate form of the young girl, and to guide his feet, as he made the step into what he discovered, to his surprise, was a boat.

"We are safe now," he heard Tom whisper, when he was seated, with Jenny again in his arms. "This is a secret way to the sea—dangerous, and not particularly comfortable—but in an emergency we must dare all risks."

Lieutenant Vere soon experienced the discomfort Tom alluded to.

The air became close and stifling; the heavy moisture beaded their faces.

It seemed as if they were buried alive in a tomb, only that the boat was gliding along slowly, with a sluggish heaving motion, as if it were sinking deeper into the bowels of the earth.

After a few weary minutes of this progress, the air became so suffocating that Harry Vere experienced the greatest difficulty in getting breath.

He bent down in alarm to Jenny Ellis, who had been breathing heavily, but now lay as still as if she was in the sleep of death.

As he stooped down, Tom grasped his hand.

"We have risked blocking up the inlet," he whispered, his voice ringing strangely through the echoing cavern; "it is a hazardous resource, but it makes all pursuit by this channel impossible; until that stone is removed even those who know the path would never discover the way."

"How fares it with the lady?" he asked presently.

"She is in a stupor like death," Harry Vere replied, his voice husky with emotion. "If I lose her now, I can only turn on my foes and die. How long must we endure this torture tomb? I cannot wonder if her tender life has sunk under its horrors, The air chokes me—my heart seems bursting—my blood is bursting my veins—my eyes are starting from their sockets—it would be a relief if I could plunge a knife in my veins!"

"It will be less painful to bear presently," Tom replied, "and you are not the only traveller by this unearthly passage of the tomb; as for your bride, her stupor is her salvation; a breath of fresh air will bring her to; were she to revive in here, the first breath would choke her lungs and kill her."

Tom said no more after this.

Folding his arms, he awaited the termination of the subterranean passage.

It had already told its tale upon some.

Two of the crew lay in the bottom of the boat in a convulsed stupor.

The young lieutenant's eyes were getting accustomed to the gloom; he could distinguish the figures of Tom's crew, as they sat like dusky statues—none moving except those who were guiding the boat in its tortuous passage.

Lieutenant Vere had ceased to feel the painful effects of the close air.

On the contrary, a dreamy stupor was stealing upon him—a stupor that he well understood.

His lungs were ceasing their action, his heart its beatings.

Death, in the form of a subtle lethargy, was creeping upon him.

He had but dimly begun to realize this when a puff of fresh air gave his lungs play, and enabled him to breathe.

Tom, who had been seated immovable, now bent towards him.

"Raise her head," he said, softly; "the danger is over; in a few seconds we shall be on firm land."

This was joyful intelligence to Lieutenant Vere—joyful, too, to Tom's faithful followers.

And now the cool breeze blew freshly against their clammy brows, and a faint gleam of light penetrated the cave—a gleam anxiously watched till it grew broader and broader, and became at last comparatively light.

The crew of adventurers were able to see each other's faces; dimly, but they could see what an effect their underground journey had exercised upon them.

Their faces were haggard and beaded with sweat, their eyes projected, their cheeks were sunken, their lips shrivelled; each man looked years older than when he entered that secret way.

Before the struggling light grew much stronger, the boat grated on a ledge of rock, and was fastened by Ben Barnacle to a staple in the solid wall.

And now flasks of powerful brandy were produced, and the men revived by strong draughts of it.

A little was applied to Jenny's lips, and her anxious lover had the joy of seeing her unclose her eyes.

She was still deathly pale, and shivered when her lover spoke to her.

She lay upon his breast for some time after she had revived, during which Tom, with the delicacy of his nature, signalled his men to quit the boat, and leave the young couple to themselves.

When Tom came back Jenny was evidently much the better of her fears.

She gratefully pressed our hero's hand, and forced a faint smile to her colourless lips.

Tom gallantly assisted Vere to lift her out of the boat.

"We are now," he said, "directly beneath the ruined chapel, near the old monastery by the beach My ship's chaplain is waiting. Are you strong enough to take your part in the ceremony that w put it out of the power of mortal man to sunder y hereafter?"

A faint blush stole to Jenny's cheeks.

Henry Vere looked diffidently in her fair face

"Dare I dream that you will consent to be min to follow my fortunes whatever may be my future Can you forget all I have done, dearest Jenny?"

He paused at the remembrance of the deadly stab she had seen him deal his rival—he looked in mortified shame at his hand, stained with his rival's blood.

Jenny saw the direction of his gaze, and, with true woman's instinct, crept closer to him, and said gently—

"Can I forget that all you have done has been for my sake? No, Henry, I am yours—yours heart and soul till death shall close my eyes."

The young lieutenant strained her passionately to his breast, while Tom looked approvingly on, and then the three ascended by a passage, roughly hewn in the structure of stone, to the ruined chapel, where in the presence of his crew, Captain Tom saw the truant pair made man and wife.

When the chaplain had pronounced his blessing, Henry Vere led Jenny to our hero, and said—

"Dearest, we must not forget how much we owe to our preserver. He has given me more than life. You must love him for my sake as a sister."

The fair young girl ran lightly towards Tom, and uplifted her maiden's face for him to kiss.

And our hero, not backward in claiming this virgin offering, drew her to his breast, and, tenderly caressing her, gave her back to her husband.

As he did this, the irrepressible Jerry Mizzen, who could control his feelings no longer, flung his cap up to the roof of the ruined chapel, and cried—

"A cheer, mates, for the bold lieutenant and his plucky bride."

Before Tom could stay the incautious act, such a hearty cheer came from the throats of the men that the antique structure seemed to shake with its echoes.

Three genuine British seamen's cheers they gave them, while Jenny stood blushing like the timid, gentle little bride she was, and Henry Vere looked as proud and happy as the lucky possessor of such a treasure ought to have looked.

A strange stillness succeeded the prolonged hurrah.

The daylight came stealing into the grand old place, making its ruins more solemn in the subdued hush of dawn.

Ben Barnacle, who had given a quick anxious glance round, now leaped up to one of the broken windows, and Tom, following his swift survey, instinctively knew that foes were near.

It was so—the commodore and his men. They had heard the cheers.

Every one in the chapel knew that a danger was brought upon them by that unguarded call.

Jenny went a shade paler, but looked more assured when Tom spoke.

"Our friend, the commodore, is coming this way. Ben Barnacle you will lead the way to the boat. Lieutenant Vere, you will follow with the chaplain and your bride, steadily, but quickly. We have not much time to spare."

The descent from the chapel was by means of a stone trap behind one of the massive crypts of the grand old structure. It was closed by hidden machinery, and was too narrow to admit of more than one at a time.

The commodore and the party with him would have made an entry before Jenny could have been got out of the way, if the stout old door, which they had hastily fastened, had not shown some strength in resisting their efforts to break it down.

It gave way at last, when the lot of Tom's crew had gone down, and our hero alone stood in the ancient crypt.

The commodore, who had growled out a hasty summons to them, bidding them surrender, stopped short on seeing the place deserted by all except the gallant boy, whose handsome features beamed with amusement at the old officer's mystified looks.

"You here, Captain Grey!" he exclaimed, recognising our hero at once. "Have you, sir, had a hand in this night's work? Tell me, sir, where is that rascal, and where is my brother's child?"

"Your brother's child, commodore, is safe with her husband—safe beyond the power of that disciplinarian her father—safe beyond any pursuit you may be disposed to institute after them. Had you arrived a few minutes earlier you might have been present at the ceremony performed under this sacred roof, which made them man and wife. As you were not, you must be content to let me bear your well wishes to the happy couple."

The features of the commodore underwent a complete transformation as he listened—surprise, anger, incredulity, successively stamped themselves on his blunt countenance.

"Are you aware, young sir," he cried, hotly, stepping closer to our hero, "that this dastard whom you have, as I see, aided, had stolen my niece from my roof, and added the murder of his rival to his heinous crimes?"

"Perfectly. Seeing that I advised him to steal her from your roof, that I prompted him to wear a sword in case he was waylaid by his rival, that I planned the elopement, won the fair Jenny to his suit, and with a trusty party of my crew, kept pursuit at bay till they were safely married, as I have informed you, here, not fifteen minutes since."

A proud, joyous light sparkled in the dark eyes of the daring boy.

Confronted as he was by so many armed men, he stood the model of princely grace and gallant bearing, his left hand lightly resting on the gold hilt of his rapier, while the commodore, perfectly aghast at his audacity, could only stare upon him as if he could not believe that he was awake.

At length he roared out—

"Are you the devil himself? Confound you, to do all this! Can a boy's head be set on such a demon body? Am I to believe this villainous betrayal of yourself! Answer me, sir; and then, if you have done masquerading, show us where that scoundrel and my misguided niece are hiding."

"I have told you, commodore, they are safe from your pursuit. I am not the devil, I hope; but you may be less mystified when you know who I am."

"Who are you—who the devil are you?"

"I am Captain Tom Drake," replied our hero, quietly; and now, commodore, I wish you farewell. In 'our-and-twenty hours I shall be out at sea, with your niece and her husband aboard my ship. Should it please you, I shall be happy to exchange a challenge with you there."

For the first moment after Tom had spoken the old sea-dog was thunderstricken. He looked at the graceful figure and careless features of the princely boy, and his words seemed choking in his throat.

It was an instant or so before he could blurt out his angry speech.

"Then if you were the devil himself, you shall not escape again. In the king's name I command you to surrender. Cover him, and shoot him where he stands if he attempts to move."

"In the king's name—ha, ha!" Tom laughed; "no, no, commodore, Captain Tom Drake never surrenders for fifty kings, or twenty commodores."

The old sea-dog's rage was fairly roused; he raised his hand as a signal to his men, and himself made a spring at Tom's collar.

But his youthful opponent anticipated his act; there was a click—the stone swung heavily round, and as Tom's laugh rang through the chapel he vanished from their view.

The commodore who had found himself clutching at the air, looked at the ponderous stone which had closed above our hero's head as if he thought he was the victim of some wizard's enchantment.

When he found that he was fairly outwitted his rage was like the fury of a baited lion.

Every effort was made to remove the trap, but the stone was closed securely in its place, and all the king's horses with all the king's men, would never have got it up again, unless some one knew the secret of the hidden spring.

The rampant old fellow was keen enough to understand that either Tom and his party were concealed under the church, or exploring some subterranean passage leading them to the shore.

So dividing his party, he made a thorough search all round the chapel, and finally finding all attempts fruitless, then left one-half of the men to watch by the chapel, while with the rest he hurried shorewards, having first despatched a messenger to inform his brother, the admiral, of what had occurred, and relating his intention of at once repairing to his vessel in order to catch Tom's ship the moment it attempted to make for sea.

Admiral Ellis had recovered from his swooning fit long before they reached the house with him, and when he found himself being led from the scene of action his small muscular frame stiffened itself like iron, and before his servants could divine his intention, he broke from their hold, and with a frantic outburst of rage ordered them all in pursuit of the fugitives.

By the time all had left him his iron composure had returned, whilst his thin lips were set to a cruel firmness, and a harsh look gleamed from his piercing eyes.

He was determined to make Lieutenant Vere suffer the severest penalty of his offences.

Court-martial and execution.

He had made up his mind to have his daughter present when her lover's death took place.

Of course he did not anticipate for one moment that the abductor of his daughter would escape.

On our hero, too, he resolved to wreak his vengeance.

He repented now that he had not trusted his brother with the secret of Tom's identity, or at least have made an open capture of the daring boy.

Still he consoled himself with the idea that both would be speedily taken, and he retired to his room to await their being brought before him as bondaged prisoners.

The Hon. Archibald Gaston had been carried into the commodore's house, and a surgeon was attending him.

He had been stricken deep, and the loss of blood had weakened him to the lowest ebb.

Many of the young noblemen, informed of the tragic occurrence, had returned, and watched anxiously the features of the surgeon, to judge of Gaston's hope of life.

Claremont had been taken to his home.

Gaston suffered the man of science to dress his wound in silence.

When it was finished he fixed his dark eyes upon the doctor's face, and said, huskily—

"Doctor, one word. Am I a dead man?"

"You are hurt seriously," was the reply, "but not mortally, unless circumstances should——"

Gaston waited to hear no more.

"Enough," he muttered, a wild light blazing from his eyes. "I can bear all the rest, so that I have life enough left to follow that accursed reptile, whose life I swear to choke in his throat whenever we meet!"

Admiral Ellis was growing nervously impatient when his brother's messenger arrived.

When he had delivered his news, the little admiral sprang from his chair.

"What!" he cried, "escape? Impossible—my brother is mad! Away, for your life—have signals run up—alarm the fleet! By heavens, if he were ten times the devil they report him he shall not escape! Away, dolt—turn out the shore batteries —challenge every ship, and let the first that attempts to leave be blown into pieces by our guns."

The eyes of the excited officer blindly blazed with fury.

A hectic flush glowed on his sallow cheeks.

With an impetuous wave of the hand he peremptorily dismissed the messenger, then sitting down to his desk hastily wrote despatches to the commander of the fleet.

When he had sent these off he paced his room in nervous excitement.

"Curse him!" he muttered, "outwit an admiral, and my brother, too—foiled like this—my child, too—oh, she shall suffer for this when she is once more in my power; as for these adventurers, they shall hang in her sight!"

So prompt and effective were the measures adopted in obedience to the admiral's command that our hero, and the party in his charge, would never have left the shore, even, if he had not been previously prepared for the hazards he expected to incur.

When he emerged from the narrow underground passage, he saw the shore batteries, and every part of the coast swarming with men.

Guns were run out, signals and lights of different colours were sent up from every point, and answered by the fleet, amongst whom the greatest activity prevailed, as they answered the danger signals, and got ready to weigh anchor, and stop the passage of any runaway vessel.

Admiral Ellis was determined not to be baffled this time.

Our hero's practised eye rapidly scanned the movements made for his reception should he venture in sight of those who were eager now to capture him alive or dead.

His daring breast thrilled with the imminence of his danger, and with flushed cheek and flashing eye, he turned to Ben Barnacle and remarked—

"They mean to take effectual measures this time."

Ben Barnacle smiled grimly.

"Never saw them so active, sir. To look at their preparations, one would think a rat could not escape them."

Tom's eyes roamed from the heavy fleet of armed ships to his own graceful vessel, lying almost under the bows of one of the largest frigates.

"There lies our little craft," he observed, "and we must reach her. Ah, she knows her book—she answers their signals—that will divert suspicion from her. And now, as no boat will pass unchallenged, we must lie close in this broken ground till we have made some alterations in our rig."

"Shall I signal the boat, sir?"

"No; send Bob Hauler down to tell them to send up some fishing disguises for us all."

"Aye, aye, sir," Ben replied, and going back to his party, he sent Bob Hauler on his mission.

The place whence they had emerged was almost under the level of the sea.

It was a broken, ragged fissure, but so tortuously formed that it afforded them a good screen from observation, either from sea or land.

Of course, so soon as they emerged on to the beach they would have become instantly visible.

This was not Tom's plan.

He lay low till the men from the boat brought the necessary disguises.

A few moments effected a complete transformation in their appearance.

A big hood and a cloak, with the assistance of a bushy wig, and the application of a dark wash to her face, rendered Jenny Ellis a capital old fish-wife.

Tom sported a fishing-jacket, and a grizzly wig of stiff grey hairs, assisted by a wash of a deep colour, to which Ben Barnacle added a few finishing touches with a bit of burnt cork.

Ben Barnacle, himself, and Bob Hauler, with Jerry Mizzen, were turned into capital fishermen, while Harry Vere appeared as a most dissipated trawler's wife.

When all was complete, Tom had the boat hugged in under the shore; and the boat's crew having disembarked, Tom, with Ben Barnacle, Jerry Mizzen, Bob Hauler, and Harry Vere—Jenny Ellis lumbering after them in a pair of wooden shoes—got into the boat.

"What name did you give our ship," Tom asked of Ben Barnacle, "as we rounded the point?"

"The *Fair Fanny*," was Ben's reply.

"Good; an English name will excite less attention than a foreign one. Give the signal to make all right aboard. I see they've got the British flag up; there's a Swedish vessel in the offing they're crowding round, innocent enough, no doubt, while the real cruiser is under their bows. Ha! you lads must stay behind till you've changed the cut of your trimmings, and made yourselves respectable seamen belonging to the *Fair Fanny*, which ship will send a boat to fetch you from shore as soon as her papers are cleared. Be alert, lads; spend your next hour in the nearest grog-shop, and be ready when you hear the bosun's call."

The middies gave a responsive "aye, aye, sir," to their beloved leader's words, and were seen on their way to the grog-shop, while the boat, considerably altered in its trim was sluggishly pulled from shore.

Tom himself had taken an oar.

Jenny, with a firmness not to have been expected from her under such a trying exigency, was tugging at the rope which loosened the ragged bit of coarse sail they had set up to their one mast, while Henry Vere, as cool as if he had been accustomed to the business all his life, squatted in the bottom of the boat, busily overhauling tangled fishing-nets.

In this manner they passed under the British flag-ship, the officers and men of which were crowded at the sides, scanning every object that came near.

Presently the expected summons came.

"Ahoy, there, boat! heave to, here, and let's have a look at you!"

Tom stole a quick glance at Jenny.

A tremour had made her start when the officer spoke; but now she quietly seated herself beside Henry Vere, and looked up at the ship under whose figure-head they were passing.

"Lay to, you daft swab!" Jerry Mizzen shouted to our hero, who was pulling his one oar with such force that he purposely swung the boat against the war-ship's side. "See where you're a swinging the blessed boat to! Strike me daft if you ain't as deaf as a sign-post!"

TOM KNEW THAT HE STOOD BEFORE A MAN OF IRON DISCIPLINE.

"I'll knock you over the gun'al with the oar, you wishy-washy skunk!" growled Tom savagely, imitating the tones of a Cornish fisherman. "Who's to know when you're going to stop, you jelly-faced shore-monkey——"

"Stop," roared Jerry; "didn't you hear them hossifers a bawling to you to lay to?"

Tom uplifted his glance with the most perfect air of disbelief on his face.

"What the devil do them want wi' us? we ain't smuggled nothing out of the king's cutter. We are——"

"We don't know that," the officer sang out from the topsail; "you might have a good deal there we'd like to overhaul. Here, sentry, keep your piece pointed at that fellow in the stern, and give him an ounce of lead in his ribs if the boat attempts to leave."

The "fellow in the stern," was no other than Ben Barnacle, who made a capital wince and rolled over into the boat.

"Don't shoot, mate!" he yelled; "damme, I'm not starting the boat."

"You'd better not," the officer replied, drily. "Now, young fellows, have you any objection to coming on board?"

"We ain't got the least, your honour," replied Jerry Mizzen, readily; "and maybe we'll get treated to a stiff sip of grog, just to take the salt out of our throats."

"You're more likely to get a cat over your ugly back. Steady, there. you whelp! who the devil do you think wants lubbers like you aboard? Clap on to them chains there, and answer me—where are you cruising to in that wooden dish?"

"We're bound for the *Fair Fanny*—there she is,

leeside of the *Triton*—and a clean craft she be, only her skipper hasn't settled for a cargo of fish he had yesterday," Tom answered, keeping to his assumed voice.

"We've got fish here, we'll give you presently," exclaimed the officer. "Keep your piece cocked, sentry. Now you snail-catching crawlers, have you seen any people making from the shore—a party of officers disguised, and a lady with 'em?"

"Ain't seen no hossifer, except a drunken buff being cleared out by the shore women," sang out Jerry Mizzen, in reply; "he was as ugly as cussed sin—guess you must be a brother of his'n. Say, buffy, got that gal aboard I seen you tawsling with abaft the bittens, last time you wene ashore?"

"You scoundrel! I'll sink your ugly craft if you give me any impertinence—answer me—did you see the party described?"

"No, we didn't."

"You are sure of that?"

"Don't you think we could trust our toplights if we had? Tell you we ain't seen nothing of any disguised buffs with a gal in tow—nor don't want to neither."

"Pass on then—but first give us the password."

"The what?"

Jerry's tones were not so confident, but he cheeked it as was his wont.

"Summut good to eat, eh?" he asked.

The officer laughed.

"All right," he cried, "the password's 'Nelson;' get your wooden clog of a boat out of our way; ahoy, got any fish there?"

"No, we ain't."

"There's one for you, then—you won't catch such another heavy one between this and France."

Tom and Bob Hauler glad of the opportunity to get away, were clumsily backing from the ship's side, when the "fish," in the shape of a heavy cannon ball, was pitched into their boat.

It came so suddenly, that nothing but the heap of tarred sacking prevented the bottom being stove in.

As it was, the boat careened with such abruptness, that Jenny Ellis, unused to such rough progress, leaped from where she sat.

Luckily, the ever ready Jerry Mizzen caught her in his arms, and stopped her mouth with his rough sleeve, at the same time addressing her so coarsely, that she shuddered as she heard him.

But she felt grateful, nevertheless; for, but for his promptness, she must certainly have shrieked, and then all would have been discovered.

Ben Barnacle hastily picked up the ponderous missile and stowed it away.

"I say," he sang out to the officers, who were laughing at them from the deck, "going to meet Boney's ships, ain't you? You'll get more fish there than your long stomachs will care for, you half-starved horse marines; and I'd like to be there and see the licking you'll get."

This was hardly official language, but the boat was now comparatively out of danger, and the officers were too much amused with their freak to be angry with the speaker.

Every moment was like an age.

Yet, eager as they were, they dared not quicken their progress, for fear of exciting suspicion.

The distance between them and their ship was at length got over, and with a glad feeling at his heart Tom heard the boat grate at the side.

The deception had still to be carried out.

One by one they lumbered up the companion-way, Tom staying to see all on board before he followed.

When he stood upon the deck a joyous pride dilated his breast.

"Now let them take us if they can," he said, as he looked proudly round and saw what excellent order the ship was in. "Get all ready, lads; we shall be boarded before we start, and it won't do to let them suspect our true character by anything they see on deck."

He descended to his cabin to change his dress.

Zeila came gladly forth to welcome his return.

She had been very anxious on his account.

"I knew, when I saw the excitement among the fleet and on shore, that you were discovered, and in danger," she said, tearfully regarding our hero.

"We have had a risky run," Tom replied, "and are not yet safe; but I think it will try their mettle to take us."

He returned to his own cabin, and speedily changed his attire.

Six of his crew were disguised in the fishermen's costume, and sent back in the boat, which they were to afterwards leave, and join the other party at the grog shop.

Tom never neglected any means of secrecy; and he knew they would still be watched from the ships.

Jenny Ellis and Henry Vere having been furnished with more suitable raiment, were secreted in one of the hiding-places of the vessel.

Ben Barnacle dressed himself as its skipper, and Tom walked the deck by his side dressed as a young officer.

They were not mistaken in their expectations.

Morning was not far advanced before a party of the authorities came on board to examine the ship and her papers.

They were very suspicious, and eyed the crew and equipments of the vessel narrowly.

"I see you have a gun here for defence," the officer in charge of the inspecting party observed.

"Yes," Ben replied, "it's as well to be prepared; the sea privateers don't make many mouthfuls of an unarmed trader."

Some other observations were exchanged, and the officers, partially satisfied, retired to the companion-way.

Here the one who had before spoken paused.

"Are you not very low in the water for your build?" he asked, abruptly.

They were.

Ben could have told him the reason was that they had secret parts of the vessel crowded with treasure.

But he didn't.

He merely observed that it was a grave fault in her construction, and bowed the officer over the side.

As they were descending, a second boat pulled alongside, and our hero recognized the bluff old commodore.

"Have you well searched this?" he asked. The officers replied that they had.

"Hang me, if I know what to think," replied the commodore, "there's no vessel here at all corresponding to that infernal cruiser, except that Swedish barque, which we've overhauled. I'll have her papers looked to again; it would be a lasting disgrace, if, after this, that confounded devil of a boy-cruiser got clear away from the eyes of the British fleet."

They heard him grumbling in a more furious style as the boats rowed away.

Ben stood with arms folded, scanning the exciting scene as if it did not interest him a bit, while Tom perched himself on the taffrail and watched the movements on sea and shore.

Presently a cry of delight broke from Tom's lips.

He had seen the boats approach the suspected Swede, which, Tom had no doubt whatever, was a disguised privateer, and now he saw her sails set with a precision and suddenness that confirmed his suspicions.

She was evidently unwilling to be overhauled a second time, and was standing out to sea in the twinkling of an eye.

As might have been expected, the utmost commotion was caused by this act.

A gun was fired from the fort, but did not reach, and signals of pursuit being made, a light-armed schooner got away from the heavy frigates, and went after the Swede.

Tom's eyes sparkled merrily at this sight.

"Now is our chance," he said to Ben; "while they are after that privateer, and she'll give them a smart run for it, we will gently get away, hoist the blue-peter, and send a boat ashore to pick up our men."

Firing was heard seaward as these orders were being executed, and by the time all hands were on board the schooner was brought in disabled by one of the pursuing frigates.

The Swedish vessel had shown her teeth and given the schooner a taste of her fighting powers.

It was the general belief that the frigates were in chase of the real rover ship, and so our hero, after his men had been brought on board, was allowed to go quietly out from among his grim neighbours.

As he passed the flag-ship he saw her yards covered with seamen and officers, who were watching the chase of the Swedish privateer.

Tom had his vessel brought alongside the flag-ship.

He had hastily written a letter, which he now held in his hand as the two vessels almost touched.

"Is there a Commodore Ellis on board you?" he asked, innocently.

"No," sang out an officer, "his ship is after that cursed runaway cruiser."

"I'm sorry for that," Tom replied, "I've a letter here for him."

"You can drop it with us," the officer replied, "we'll give it him when he comes in with the prisoner."

"Thanks," said Tom, dexterously throwing the letter to the other's deck. "Is she a pirate?"

"Pirate—yes; it's that infernal *Will-o'-the-Wisp*, with that boy-cruiser, Tem Drake, on board."

"I hope they'll take him," Tom said; "don't forget to give the letter to the commodore."

"All right; a good voyage to you."

"Hurrah!" came from the throats of Tom's daring crew as the breeze filled their sails and bore them from the liner's bows.

Little by little they left the ships in the rear, the Needles came in sight, were safely passed, then the last of the British ships went out of sight, even from the masthead, and the *Will-o'-the-Wisp* stood out to sea.

Then as Tom leaped joyously to the deck, and Harry Vere with his young bride came from their concealment, such a ringing cheer went from stem to stern of the saucy vessel that proclaimed the joy of the crew at their clever escape.

With sparkling eye and flushed cheek the princely boy-cruiser cried—

"Hurl down those colours, knock this lubberly trim off our ship, run up our flag; the *Will-o'-the-Wisp* is at sea again, let her enemies catch her when they dare."

The commodore returned with his ship late that night.

The Swedish brigantine had, after a smart chase, escaped them.

Foiled and angry he sent intelligence to his brother, the admiral, at the same time stating that he would follow anew on their track, and vowing never to return until he had fallen in with Tom's ship.

Having sent off this news he was standing on the deck letting off his superfluous steam when a boat pulled alongside and a middy clambered on board, and respectfully saluted the old naval veteran.

"Well, sir," the old sea-dog exclaimed, "who the devil are you? and what the devil do you want?"

"I'm Midshipman Herley, sir, of the flag-ship *Victory*."

"Well, you young whelp, well."

"This letter, sir, for you, sir."

He handed him the letter Tom had dropped on the flag-ship's deck.

The commodore hastily tore it open.

What a change came over him as he read!

His bluff visage purpled, his eyes literally glared, his teeth champed at his grey moustache, and, stamping his foot passionately on the deck he cried hoarsely—

"Confusion!—who sent you with this? Answer me, you jackanapes, or I'll wring your infernal neck; who gave it you?"

"An officer of the *Fair Fanny*, sir," answered the middy, aghast at the commodore's rage.

"An offi—cer—of—the—*Fair—Fanny!*" reiterated the commodore, hoarse with rage. "And where, sir, is this *Fair Fanny*—or *Betsey*—or *Jane*——"

"Went away this morning, sir, while you were chasing the Swede."

The commodore's face was the colour of a fine pickling cabbage.

"Went away this morning, confound you!" he bellowed, "then, sir, go back to your officer, sir, and tell him that the *Fair Fanny*, that he let slip out of his hands, was the ship of the boy-cruiser, and that the officer who gave him the letter was Captain Tom Drake. There, go back, sir, and tell him to put that in his pipe and smoke it, and see how much promotion he can see in the smoke, sir—confound you!"

The commodore uttered a savage laugh, and giving the young middy a cuff under the ear, yelled him off the deck, and then turned to his first officer.

"Look at this, Mr. Fennel; read this—read it, sir, and tell me how you feel afterwards."

Lieutenant Fennel, a tall, austere officer, took the letter and read—

"Dear Commodore,—I hope you may catch the Swede—she has a clean pair of heels; your niece is on board my ship with her husband. Farewell till we meet again. "TOM."

"Yes," roared the commodore—"what after that, eh? Runs through His Majesty's fleet, sir—and got away, sir, while we've been chasing that infernal confederate! Crowd up our canvass—double shot all our guns—by Heaven, I'll not taste food or drink till I am even with that boy-devil!"

Without waiting to do more than signal with the authorities on shore, the commodore sailed.

The start Tom had got was against him, but he fell in with a vessel that had been to the same port and was informed of the whereabouts of the famous boy-cruiser.

For the first time since he started the commodore seemed subdued; and, standing on deck with glass in hand, he surveyed the horizon patiently for a sight of our hero's vessel.

Captain Tom, after a spirited cruise of a week and more, ran his vessel into a snug little bay off the coast of Africa, and lay there for the night.

It was early dawn when word was brought him that another and bigger vessel had anchored alongside them in the night.

Tom hurried on deck, a strange surmise floating in his brain.

The strange ship lay quietly rocking on the billows, her tall masts almost overhanging his; at a glance Tom could see that she was armed and well manned, and while he was looking at her the voice of his old acquaintance, the commodore, singing out from her quarter-deck, almost lifted him off his feet.

"So you've woke up, you young sea-devil, eh? Surrender, sir! The *Amazon* is up with you, and won't leave you till we've taken the devil out of you!"

"Glad to see you, commodore," Tom laughed in reply. "Have you come to take me back to England?"

"I'll—I'll string you up to my yard-arm," bellowed the old officer, "when I catch you."

"Which will not be yet," Tom answered. "Come, commodore, you wish to take me—if you can bring your ship one mile from the shore you shall try your hand at taking my ship."

While Tom spoke he had given his men the word of command.

In an instant the canvas was outspread, and the *Will-o'-the-Wisp* stood out to sea.

The commodore was furious at the attempt, as he supposed, to escape.

"Heave to," he cried, "you ragamuffin, or I'll sink you."

Tom was near enough to him to reply—

"I'm not running away, commodore. I mean to fight you and take your flag."

The commodore had ordered a gun to be hastily run out.

But he did not fire, determined not to be out-manœuvred by his youthful antagonist.

He was out at sea almost as soon as our hero was.

Tom kept his vessel saucily in the way, not getting more than fighting distance from the commodore, who was chafing like a baited panther all the while.

The two ships were fairly out at sea at last, and the commodore sang out through his speaking-trumpet a summons for our hero to surrender.

Tom sent him back a defiant reply.

Then, turning to Henry Vere, said—

"Now, sir, you have a chance of fighting for your bride. I make you first officer. Let me see how you direct your attack."

Jenny Ellis, who had been standing on deck during this colloquy, raised her pale timid face to her husband.

But Tom who understood what she meant by that look, took her gently by the hand and leading her away said—

"Do not fear for your husband; we have mettle enough here for any of His Majesty's ships; and now as we shall have it pretty warm on deck, will you wait below till all is over?"

"May I not stay here with my husband?"

"Our rules will not permit it," Tom answered. "Zeila will take charge of you while the engagement lasts."

Zeila herself came on deck and took Jenny below.

By this time the commodore had got a little closer, and again he summoned Tom to surrender.

The idea of his engaging an armed frigate seemed to him preposterous.

"Save yourselves by surrender," he roared, "before we shatter you to pieces."

"We never surrender," Tom replied; "you have seen us run—you shall see how we can fight."

The commodore growled savagely the word for his men to commence the engagement, and the only language now exchanged was the roar of the cannonading, which soon began to get pretty sharp on both sides.

Commodore Ellis had often had a hot brush with a desperate enemy; but he had never such a one who so skilfully evaded his broadsides and so well peppered him in the bargain.

Usually with the toughest it was shot for shot, broadside for broadside—the superior weight of metal deciding the fight.

But here was a little vessel, ridiculously inferior to his own in size and weight, literally leaping round his huge ship, and pouring a well-aimed fire into him from all quarters.

And he was getting as furious as a muzzled bear, when a loud cry from his men called his attention to Tom's flag, which had hitherto floated defiantly in the breeze.

A well-directed shot had struck it, and now it came fluttering to the deck.

The commodore pretended to regard this as a token from the boy's ship that they were yielding.

By this time the two vessels were hauled to such close quarters that the stern of the *Amazon* was athwart the bulwarks of Tom's ship, and the old commodore from his quarter-deck was within easy hail of our hero himself as he stood amongst his officers calmly directing the fight.

The fearless old commodore's heart, in spite of himself, warmed towards the intrepid boy—he could not but admire his style of getting his ship into action, as well as the cool pluck with which he maintained the battle.

"Tell that harum-scarum boy to surrender," he bawled out to his first lieutenant, "or we'll blow every timber out of his ship."

Captain Tom received the summons with his usual quiet firmness.

"Tell the commodore," he replied, boldly, "that Tom Drake does not know how to yield—you have shot away my colours, but in twenty minutes I promise to stand on your deck and haul your flag down under my feet!"

When this audacious answer was delivered to the commodore, he gave vent to a genuine British growl, and waved his hand for the cannonade to re-commence.

The crew of the *Amazon* fought well, and served their guns as only British seamen can do.

But their system was the old style of heavy pounding; the style of maritime warfare had not been yet changed by the brisk exploits of immortal Nelson—Trafalgar's deathless hero—and the commodore, brave as a lion, and cool in the hottest cannonade, was baffled by the quick manœuvring of our hero's light vessel, whose guns, loaded with cannister and grape, swept the decks and scattered destruction around.

There was another circumstance he could not comprehend.

He had given the gunners orders to fire at the hull of their opponent, in order that he might get the boy-cruiser to yield when he found the vessel sinking.

The guns had been well served, and a terrible weight of iron had been hurled against the *Will-o'-the-Wisp*.

But the deadly missiles, in place of making her a complete wreck, though they swung her quite round with the concussion, seemed to do her no damage whatever.

At the same time her rapid discharges struck his ship at every turn.

The sailors, true-hearted as they were, began to lose nerve.

They seemed contending against no mortal foe.

All the superstitious stories they had heard of Tom and his crew seemed confirmed.

And the commodore's cheeks grew pale, though not with fear, when he saw the influence on his men.

The cannonading was sharp enough on Tom's deck.

Ponderous chain-shot came swinging from stem to stern.

The quarter-deck where Tom stood with Henry Vere, ready to board the *Amazon*, was almost untenable.

"They make it warm for us, Vere—no seamen except British tars could fight so manfully."

"They are the real bull-dogs of war," Henry Vere replied, as a huge cannon-ball struck their mizen-mast, and shivered it in splinters.

"We must make it hotter for them," Tom said, as a number of his crew sprang forward to repair the damage. "Boarders ready! Time is nearly up—in two minutes we must take their ship."

A ready cheer replied—and the boy-adventurers plied the port-holes and deck of the enemy with such rapidty and precision, that the gunners were driven from the guns and the quarter-deck cleared of the commodore and his officers.

There was hardly standing place clear of the fierce iron hail, and the commodore's brave spirit sank when with a sudden crash his mainmast came tumbling down to the deck.

Ben Barnacle had fired the shot.

As if to add to their discomfiture, a moment after Tom jumped upon a gun, and pointing it at their Union Jack brought it down.

The cheer which followed this sudden crippling and humiliation of the commodore's ship had barely died away, when Henry Vere, burning to distinguish himself, cried to the boarders under his command—

"They waver—follow me—death or victory!"

The boy-adventurers, answering him with a loud burst of enthusiasm, leaped to the quarter-deck of the *Amazon*.

A brief but determined conflict ensued as the boys sprang through the smoke.

Captain Tom, who had watched this swift onset with pleasurable pride, uttered an exultant laugh, and, unable to keep out of the fray, bounded after his ardent lieutenant.

Ben Barnacle's fingers itched to lay about him with a pike or cutlass on the frigate's deck; but his own place was at the guns, and these he served so well that a few minutes' desperate encounter on the *Amazon's* deck resulted in the surrender of the vessel to the princely boy hero.

The commodore himself would never have yielded.

So mortified was he at his discomfiture that he would have blown up his ship rather than have given in.

But with his flag shot away, his vessel crippled by the loss of her mast, and the terrible boy-devils swarming on his decks and taking possession of his guns, there was no resource left.

Tom had judged the old fellow's mettle, and when the commodore's first officer proposed blowing up the ship, it was found that Harry Vere and a select party had taken possession of the powder magazine.

The ship was, in fact, in the possession of the boy-buccaneers, and the conflict at an end.

A dull haze of smoke still rose from the frigate's deck.

Here and there rang the sharp crack of musketry, as one of the marines fired his final shot, but the deep sullen roar of cannonading had died away.

The *Amazon's* crew, such as were the survivors of as desperate a fray as they had ever been engaged in, were aft in moody submission—while the boy-buccaneers, leaning on their blood-red pikes and cutlasses, gathered round their idolized leader, and awaited the final surrender of the ship.

Commodore Ellis looked round his vessel in despair.

His first officer, a proud haughty, and brave man, stood at his elbow goading him to a last effort.

"It is useless," the commodore replied; "with our magazine in possession of these boy pirates, and our decks swept by their guns, we can do nothing. I would rather die than yield; but we have not even the chance of blowing up the frigate, or else friends and foes should be hurled in the air."

His lieutenant took his sword out of its scabbard and flung it into the sea.

"That, at least," he exclaimed, "I will never surrender."

The commodore sighed, and, followed by his officers, walked aft to surrender his sword.

Our hero stood on the quarter-deck, looking as jauntily as if he had just gone through a pleasant pageant instead of a deadly conflict.

Henry Vere, trying to look as if he was not awfully delighted at the scene, stood by Tom's side while the redoubtable Jerry Mizzen, leaning upon a gun, broadly grinned at the commodore's woeful plight.

"Young man," the commodore said, stooping low in his humiliation, "you have conquered us. I know not by what means; for myself, I would rather the first shot had slain me than have given in to your pirate gang; but I have my men to consider, and on that account, finding further fighting useless, I make a formal surrender of my ship. Take my sword; it has served me well, but after this disgrace I could never wish to wear it again."

He handed up his sword to our hero.

Our hero's saucy feelings left him as the brave old commodore, bowing low, almost touched him with his grey beard.

Daring as the noble boy was he was high-spirited enough to admire courage in a foe, and be magnanimous in the hour of victory.

Besides, he saw that, as the commodore stooped, a tear fell to the deck.

"Commodore," he said, "the fortune of war has given your ship into my hands. I accept your surrender. You were sent out to capture me—to treat me as a pirate; may I ask what was to have been my fate had I been taken?"

"My orders, young sir, were to hang you from my yard-arm."

Tom's face flushed.

"Then," said he, "return to those who gave you that order, tell them you met me at sea—that I took your ship, as I will any other ship sent out to take me. Keep your sword—I give you that; take your ship, but tell the Admiralty that if they dare to send another war vessel after me to capture me as a pirate, I will take the ship they send and blow it into the air."

He handed back the commodore his sword, and an admiring murmur ran along the ranks of his boy crew.

The commodore reeled as if he had been stricken by a bullet.

"Receive back my ship!" he cried. "Give me an hour to repair, and I will renew the fight——"

He paused—his own ingratitude struck him to the heart.

Dropping his sword to the deck, he suddenly seized both hands of the impetuous boy, and cried aloud—

"Forgive me, noble boy—I thank you for your gift; I will return, and lay your message before the Admiralty. I know they have proclaimed you pirate; but I may have influence enough to alter their decree; if so, you might serve our country instead of being its foe; if not, should they repel me, I know how to act according to that honour which I have never sacrificed yet—I can blow out my brains."

"And deprive England of a good officer," Tom said, in reply. "No, commodore, a brave man should bear his defeat."

nd I will bear mine," Commodore Ellis cried. ne more request—my niece, my brother's child —can I speak with her? I will not ask her rash abductor," he exclaimed, glancing hotly at Harry Vere. "I ask it of you, as the commander of your ship."

"I will not deny you," Tom answered, "come with us to my ship. You shall see the lady, and if she wishes to return you shall take her back to England."

"And me with her if she consents to go," Harry Vere cried.

"We should not take you so far," the commodore's first officer exclaimed, "we should string you up there like a dog, before you saw old England."

Harry Vere laughed in reply, and leaving the discomfited officer on that shattered deck, Tom, with the commodore and his boy crew, returned to the *Will-o'-the-Wisp*, from which their movements, since the surrender, had been anxiously watched.

"Let Lieutenant Vere's wife be requested aft," Tom said to one of his crew.

Little Kanak ran down to the cabin, and soon Zeila appeared, leading Jenny by the hand.

The young wife was anxiously awaiting the permission to see her husband, into whose arms she rushed, before she even remarked the presence of the old commodore.

When she saw her uncle she drew back bashfully, but an instant after, running forward, threw her arms about his neck.

"Uncle, dear uncle," she cried, tears filling her eyes, "do not chide me, I—I am so happy!"

"Chide you!" cried the commodore, huskily. "You—you—baggage, to run away from your father, and cause this havoc, and desert your foolish, fond old uncle—I—I—I go—no—hussey—I won't say a word to you ever again."

In spite of all his furies the old salt's sternness gave way.

He turned aside to hide his tears, and Jenny, her own tears mingling with his, flung her arms round his neck and tenderly kissed him.

CHAPTER XII.

JERRY MIZZEN OPENS THE TREASURE CHEST.

WHAT Jenny said to the commodore, as she lay dutifully nestling to his breast, was sufficient to make him think less harshly of her conduct in running away from her father; and had Harry Vere's only offence been marrying his pretty niece, the gallant old sea-dog might have overlooked that offence too, but the young lieutenant had sinned deeply in his sight.

His attack on his superior officer, Gaston, and his defection from his duty, were crimes too heinous to go unpunished, and though the old fellow would have grieved to deprive Jenny of a husband, he would have considered it his duty to carry out even the sentence of death against Harry Vere.

Jenny, simple-minded as she was, could not understand that her husband had erred so deeply; she tried to lead the commodore to him, and putting on her sweetest look, said pleadingly—

"You have forgiven me; you must forgive my husband, too."

"I will forgive him, and even intercede for him—scoundrel as he is—on one condition."

"And that is," Harry Vere said, stepping forward.

"That you surrender yourself a prisoner, and accompany me back to England to answer for your crimes before a court-martial."

Harry Vere lovingly took the hand of his fair young wife, as he replied—

"Surrender myself! yes, commodore, but it shall be when I am weary of life—weary, too, of this dear being whom I now proudly call my wife."

"Reflect, sir," the commodore exclaimed. "If you surrender, I might have power to save you; if you are taken—and taken you will assuredly be, be your career long or short—expect no mercy from us."

"Commodore," Harry Vere said, "I expect none; there is no such thing as mercy for me at the hands of British authorities. When I am taken I shall prepare to die an ignominious death."

He put his arm lovingly round Jenny's waist as he spoke, and fondly looked into her tender blue eyes; and the commodore, finding he could exercise no influence over Harry Vere or his niece, took a brief farewell, and departed for his ship.

The two vessels parted company, and in an hour's time were almost out of sight—Tom steering for a fresh cruise, the commodore making for the white cliffs of England, to tell the story of his defeat and the failure of his enterprise.

When the old fellow went back to his vessel, he fancied that he was regarded coldly by the officers and middies who were gathered on the *Amazon's* deck.

He was not deceived.

Lieutenant Fennel, a strict martinet, a man moulded to a stern iron sense of duty, could not conceive it possible that a British officer, after suffering such a defeat, could make a friendly visit to those from whom he had met with such disgrace.

His looks plainly told his feelings, and though he served the commodore with the respect due to him as a superior officer, he exchanged no words with him beyond what he was actually compelled to do.

During the whole of his passage home, too, he wore no sword; once he appeared without his epaulettes, but Commodore Ellis ordered him to resume them.

The same cold studied respect met the commodore from all hands on board the frigate. Men, officers, and boys, seemed to feel their commodore's humiliation, and in silence they did their duty.

Commodore Ellis understood all this.

He heard, too, that it was Lieutenant Fennel's intention to ask leave to change from his ship as soon as they reached England.

All this amounted to an imputation of cowardice on the part of the commodore, but the brave old salt, though keenly galled and stung to the soul by the humiliation of that homeward journey, bore all in moody silence.

He might have made the frigate a floating torture-room, but he remembered the time when those same officers and crew had followed him into the deadly peril of victorious battles, and how noisy had been their cheers as they gathered round him after the fight was over, and like the brave old sea-dog he was, he forgave them their importation on his courage.

But very often as he sat in the privacy of his own cabin did he examine, with stern but quiet resolve, his handsomely mounted pistols.

When the time came, and he had to meet the brow-beating accusations of the Admiralty, he knew how to vindicate his honour as became a British officer.

Very different was it on board Tom's ship.

The boy-crew were delighted with their victory over the vessel sent to take them and execute their leader, and while the frigate sailed sullenly homeward, fresh breeze filled the sails of the *Will-o'-th Wisp* as she crossed the seas on her new cruise adventure and daring.

On the day after their parting company with the

"GENTLEMEN, I AM AT YOUR SERVICE," SAID TOM.

commodore, Tom summoned his crew aft to the quarter-deck, and gathered them round him under their defiant flag, which now floated ominously in the wind.

Zeila, the corsair maiden, reclined at the feet of the princely boy-hero, Jenny sat by the vessel's side, gazing lovingly upon her husband as he stood by Tom's side.

Ben Barnacle—his manly features stamped with a noble devotion—was, as usual close to his daring leader, for whom he would have cheerfully laid down his life.

"I have called you aft," Tom said, "to tell you that as we have now been some time engaged in our buccaneering career—in which we have been, as I hope we ever shall be, brilliantly successful—it is as well we divide our immense spoils. You know that we are all agreed to share alike, and the share

of each of you already amounts to the value of a thousand pounds. Now, if there are any of you who would like to relinquish this career, he shall be given his share in money, and put ashore at the nearest port; the rest who agree to remain under our victorious flag will cruise with me from sea to sea, gaining fresh booty; but, of course, with the hazard of the dangers we must incur while engaged in these enterprises."

The first and concluding parts of our hero's speech were received with loud and prolonged cheering; but loud cries of "No," responded to his question if any were ready to leave the ship.

None were disposed to retire from their freebooting career, and when Tom had assured himself of this, he continued his address, his fine features beaming with enthusiasm, for reckless as he was, the devoted daring of his crew pleased him.

G

"We sail, then," he said, "on our new cruise in quest of adventure. It has pleased the authorities at home to proc'aim us pirates, to set a price on our heads, and to menace us when taken with an ignominious death. They forget that they have driven us from the service, that our bitter wrongs made us take up arms against them. We have defied them, and take us they never shall. You must swear all of you to abide with me, to follow my orders in all things, and, if the time comes, to die with me, for we will never surrender. When no hope is left, I swear to blow this ship into the air."

A noble look of enthusiasm was on Tom's face.

The boy-cruisers took up his words, and a cry of "Never surrender!" ran along the breadth of the noble ship.

Then Tom continued—

"Though they have branded us pirates, we have never been pirates yet, and never mean to be. Of course we mean to fight for our ship, and, if necessary, to take or sink any vessel sent to pursue us; but our mission is not to fight against our country. The career I have fixed upon—the career in which I hope we shall distinguish ourselves, and make a name to be remembered—aye, and revered throughout our dear native land—for, proscribed outcasts that we are, we love our country still—is the career that first crowned us with laurels, and gave us this noble ship. We will scour the seas, attacking all privateers and pirates, destroying the hordes of assassins who plunder unarmed ships, and murder our helpless fellow-creatures—we will pursue them from sea to sea. They have treasure caves, and islands gorged with plunder—we will take these from them, release their captives, and clear these waters of them—their spoils shall be our reward, and we will discover some fair island where we can make ourselves a home, and own no allegiance except to our own defiant flag, which shall be, as it has been, invincible."

All through this inspiring speech the boy-leader had been accompanied by a succession of ringing cheers.

At its close, the enthusiasm of the brave boy-crew rose to such a pitch that they crowded round their beloved leader, and frantically kissing his hands, as if he had been a demigod, took oath to follow his daring leadership even to death.

And Ben Barnacle, lifting his deep voice amongst them, exclaimed—

"We will follow to the death—our leader shall be our king, and our island home shall be our kingdom, where we will defy the power of the world,"

Wild visions flashed dazzlingly before the eyes of our hero as his name rang aloft above the cheers of his staunch followers.

The noble grace of a youthful monarch beamed upon his frank countenance, and his devoted boy-crew, carried away by their enthusiasm, raised him on their shoulders and thrice bore him round the deck, amid such tumultuous cheers as were never before heard sounding across the mighty sea.

And it was under these thrilling circumstances that our boy-adventurers began a career of exploits so dashing and brilliant that even England's cold officialism yielded before the fame of their daring deeds.

But before chronicling the succession of incidents that proved Captain Tom to be the foremost among the most skilful and plucky sea-rovers, we must pause to relate the sad predicament into which his irrepressible propensities led the reader's redoubtable acquaintance, Jerry Mizzen.

The *Will-o'-the-Wisp* was speeding across the blue waters of the sunlit sea.

Evening was drawing on, and the boy-cruisers were gathered idly about the decks conversing to-gether, as the rippling wavelets murmur ceaseless broken plash against the vessel's bows.

Our youthful readers who have not as yet the pleasure of an evening at sea, when land from sight, and nothing is to be seen but the br expanse of blue-grey sky and breadth of ocean, rocking peacefully beneath the glare of the sinking sun, except the distant sails of some unknown ship, no bigger than the white-winged birds that now and then soar skimming above the masts, can hardly realize the listless quietude and dreamy beauty of such a scene.

On this occasion its sublimity of grandeur had its influence on those noble-hearted boys, whose fearless breasts panted for the coming hour of desperate peril and encounter.

Their looks were more subdued, and many a straying thought wandered to some little brother, a loving sister, some boyish sweetheart, or perhaps a mother, yet revered, and whom they longed to see; for, in spite of their wild career, Tom's crew were true-hearted English boys.

The sun went down, and with it the breeze fell; the white sails began to hang idly against the raking masts, and the ship's pace slackened.

As the sun went suddenly from view, and was succeeded by the grey gloom of night, the irrepressible Jerry Mizzen stole quietly from the "cat-head" —that part of the ship's prow where he had hitherto been on watch—and, securing a moment when he was unobserved, slipped stealthily down the gangway.

He was bent on a buccaneering expedition on his own account.

Jerry had a curious mind, and a purloining one also, even though, as in the case of the magnificent goblet, not yet disposed of, and hanging guiltily on his conscience with the chances of detection, his depredations were not always successful.

He had a knack, which he could not overcome, of fingering property that did not rightfully belong to him.

It had chanced that twice when sent on some service to one particular part of the vessel, a kind of cabin never used except for storage purposes, he had observed a ponderous box amongst the lumber.

There was nothing peculiar about the box.

It was a squarish, plain, ugly piece of furniture, with large iron handles.

But it was securely locked, and though only bound together by nails roughly driven in the sides, resisted all his efforts to open it—a feat which, on each of the two visits, he had tried unseen to accomplish.

Jerry had inquired respecting the contents of the box, but no one knew anything of it, except that it was in Zeila's cabin when the Barbary vessel was taken, and that Captain Tom, in obedience to her wish, had given orders that it should be left untouched.

He was as eager to penetrate to the mysteries of the box as Blue Beard's unlucky wives were to get at the secrets of the dreaded chamber of death.

At his duties during the day the big ugly box stood prominently before his eyes—at night, when on the watch, he found himself speculating wonderingly on the nature of its contents—asleep, he dreamed of hideous terrors shut in beneath its lid.

Human nature, such as Jerry's, could endure it no longer, and now he had sneaked there to try his skill at forcing it open by means of some useful curiosities in the way of keys—articles he was never without, owing to their handiness in cases where any captured booty chanced to be enclosed in strong boxes, the keys of which might not happen to be in the way.

No one observed his descent.

No one was in the cabin when he, falteringly, pushed open its door, which he cautiously, though not without some trepidation, fastened, in order to be safe from interruption.

So far he was successful.

He had got there unperceived, and there stood the big wooden chest before him, looking more than ever solemn and curious in the faint light stealing in from the small glazed apertures on the outward side

Jerry's heart was bumping against his ribs as he picked his way across the bales of lumber and knelt down in front of the closed box.

He found it necessary to recruit his courage with a long draught from a flask of strong rum, which he habitually carried concealed about him.

Even this sustaining dram hardly dispelled his fears, and with something of nervous anxiousness he looked round the sombre cabin as if he expected to see the spectral shape of the former owner of the vessel rising from amid the scattered plunder, to scathe him for his temerity in intruding there alone.

The very silence of the place was oppressive.

He was shut in from every sound.

He seemed inclosed in a tomb.

He almost began to repent having come there.

But, desperate at length, he tried his keys, and had the satisfaction of fitting one in the rusty lock.

With his fingers closed on the keys, he paused suddenly.

He fancied he heard a sound behind him—a strange ominous sound.

His heart quaked, and a moisture gathered on his brow.

What if that uncouth box was a tomb?

What if some bearded corsair, clothed in terrible attire, and grasping his scimetar, lay there in a trance, only awaiting that moment of release to rise and slay.

Jerry thought of the big corsair chief as he had seen him when they cast him from the vessel's deck, whose boards reeked with his life's blood—thought of his terrible, glaring, glazed eye and swarthy visage, even in death fierce in its implacability of hate.

What if his apparition should creep behind him, and twisting his fingers in the roots of his hair, drag him to his feet?

These were real terrors that Jerry endured.

But they were brought about by his own fears of conscience, and with trembling hand he at last summoned nerve enough to turn the key.

Noiselessly the lock slid back, noiselessly and steadily the lid opened of itself, and Jerry's hair stood on end as it rose slowly up and up till it fixed itself perfectly straight.

Then Jerry, half rising to his feet, looked in.

What a glittering sight!

What rubies, emeralds, and opals! but all set in such uncouth shapes that they startled him.

With bounding heart and panting breast, he was gazing on the fascinating display, when, with a flash as it were, a red light shone across the jewelled heap.

A low unearthly noise that froze the marrow in Jerry's bones succeeded, and the glittering treasures tumbled in as it were from his gaze.

A white something shook itself before his eyes, and, with a hollow rattle, a grizzly skeleton sprang bolt upright!

A winding sheet, damp and musty, fell horribly about its bony frame.

Its ribs were hideously bare.

The eyeless sockets gleamed from the polished bone.

The big discoloured teeth shook and chattered frightfully together.

One fleshless arm lifted the shroud above the skull; the other, outstretched and rigid, almost touched Jerry's cheek.

With a paralyzed cry of fear, Jerry fell shivering back, his knees knocked together, his jaw fell, his hand clutched convulsively in his hair, as he propped his shaking form against a box.

And then, horror of horrors, before he could move or utter another cry, the fearful spectre made a swoop towards him.

In an instant it locked him in its bony grip, and he was held firmly against its skeleton ribs—his face almost touching the cadaverous jowl—pinned immovably in the embrace of a moving skeleton!

CHAPTER XIII.

DUTCH PAUL, THE CAPTAIN OF THE " VULTURE."

"SAIL-HO!" sang out the look-out man from the masthead.

It was the evening of the succeeding day.

Our hero sprang to the binnacle.

"Where away?" he asked.

"Off our starboard quarter, sir."

Tom adjusted his telescope, and took a survey of the horizon.

Far, very far away, was the faint indication of a vessel.

She was coming in their track, a minute's examination proved, and our hero, with a satisfied smile, handed the glass to the first lieutenant, while the officers and middy crew, with curious interest on their faces, gathered about the quarter-deck.

" Sail-ho!" again sang out the look-out.

" Where away?"

" Off the stranger's lee."

Henry Vere gave our hero the glass.

The two vessels were coming plainly in sight.

They seemed close together, but the one they had last seen was the bigger of the two, and, by the manner in which she gained upon the other, evidently the swifter sailer.

As Tom gazed across the sea an excited look crossed his features.

" I could have sworn," he observed to Ben Barnacle, "that I saw smoke about the stranger's bows."

"Not at all unlikely," was Ben's reply. " There's plenty of warm work in these seas; and the looks of that big craft don't please me at all."

A few moments of anxious suspense ensued.

All was silence on board.

Presently everyone started.

Boom came the sound of a gun across the sea.

Another—then a quicker succession of shots.

There could be no uncertainty now—the two vessels were engaged.

Captain Tom cast an anxious look around at the lowering sky.

"Have all sail spread," he shouted; " we may come up with her before darkness sets in. Clear the decks and run out the guns; and boarders, look to your pikes and cutlasses!"

A score of willing hands sped about the ship.

Sheet after sheet was unfurled, till the masts bent like reeds beneath the pressure of the gale.

The wind was blowing swiftly, and the *Will-o'-the-Wisp* leapt fleetly over the intervening space.

In a little while could be seen an occasional sheet of light leaving the sides of the two vessels, over whose hulls the smoke hung in dense clouds.

The booming of the guns was more startling, but less frequent.

The weaker vessel was yielding to the superior force of her enemy.

"The little one is beaten," Tom said.

"Yes," Harry Vere, replied; "they have taken her. I hope we may be in time to do the same for them."

"See," cried Ben Barnacle, "they have fired the ship."

As if it had been flooded by instantaneous liquid fire, the smaller vessel, all in a moment, was ablaze from stem to stern; but her big opponent did not even then cease firing into her, and half-a-dozen shots brought her so low in the water, that her speedy destruction by fire and leakage was certain.

Whether her crew and passengers had been removed, or were left to their terrible fate, it was impossible to conjecture; but a determined look settled on the faces of the excited boys as their ship began to forereach upon the victorious cruiser.

Having accomplished her swift ruthless work, the strange vessel, deigning her pursuer no notice, now spread her sails, and shaped her course in another direction; but she went at an easy speed, as if glutted with the plunder of her prey, and at every leap of the ship the distance between them was lessened.

Now that they got closer, the appearance and build of the enemy they were so soon to encounter were the subjects of curious observations.

She was a rather ungainly craft, heavily laden, and carrying an enormous weight of sail.

Her hull was low, and so oddly shaped, that had her masts been cut down she would have looked like a huge tortoise upon the waters.

Her prow was sharp, and like a beak in shape, and her figure-head was a monstrous vulture, painted yellow, and with its talons extended on deck, as if to seize its prey.

Her decks were crowded with men, and the long lines of dark muzzles protruding from the portholes revealed how deadly was her armament.

The unfortunate vessel she had captured, and which was now blazing to the water's edge, had no more chance in an encounter with so formidable a foe than a dove had in contending with a vulture.

"Give her a gun," Tom said to Ben Barnacle; "she shows no colours; but that will bring her to."

The gun was fired.

Scarcely had the sullen roar died away than, as if by magic, the stranger's yards were stripped, and she lay to under bare poles, her motion as abruptly arrested as if a giant had held her in her course.

"The pirate means to fight," Harry Vere remarked. "I should like to send her a shot that would sink her. Hullo! that's in reply to ours, I suppose. Not badly aimed, either! By Jove! I thought my head was carried away in splinters."

A puff of smoke had come from the stranger's hull, and, as Vere spoke, a big cannon-ball came tearing up the beams of the quarter-deck and knocked its way out at the other side.

Before Tom could reply, the ship's doctor, a gaunt, thin, cadaverous-faced vampire, with a sort of blood-letter face, crawled aft.

He had a case of instruments in his hand, and quietly squatting down on the splintered deck, he said, drily—

"Ha! you've got a tough devil there, my young bloods. I shall have all my work cut out to stop all the holes they open before you are two minutes older. Here, Jacob, bring a basket for the legs and arms; we shall have plenty kicking about here presently."

Jacob, an ungainly, blubber-faced lout, with a hideous grin about his meaningless face, sidled up to his master, and began unrolling bandages as he sat beside him, and peering at the points of murderous-looking surgical instruments.

"Come, doctor," Tom said, quietly, "we can't have you on deck; you must do your work below."

"Aye, aye, my fine young skipper; they'll do work enough for me first up here," said the doctor, as he sidled away, followed by his assistant.

Doctor Shrike and his assistant, though so unprepossessing in their appearance were very clever in their art.

Our hero knew their worth when the battle was over, and so he overlooked the peculiarities of the pair.

The stranger vessel had as yet shown no colours, and in silence her gun had been fired.

The men who had swarmed upon her decks were nowhere visible; but now a little ball was run up her halyards, and her flag unrolled.

A blood-red banner, with the device of a monstrous yellow vulture in the centre.

Tom's own death banner had already been run up.

No sooner was the flag of the stranger seen than Zeila, who stood beside our hero, uttered a startled cry, and exclaimed—

"The Red Pirate! He fights with living fire. Keep your vessels apart, or we are all lost."

As if in reply to Zeila's warning words, a deep hoarse laugh came from the stranger's deck, and a voice cried—

"Now, devils, give them their salute."

A swift, sudden, and deadly broadside answered this command, and a fearful weight of metal pounded against the hull of the Will-o'-the-Wisp.

It was well that her sides were protected by a secret defence, or that well-directed volley would have sent her foundering to the bottom of the sea.

As it was, it did some damage, and our boy-adventurer's deck was strewn with the wounded before they well understood the sudden attack.

"Salute them in return," Tom cried. "Zeila, your place is below. Ben Barnacle, be ready with your boarders. Fire or no fire, we will not shirk the guns."

Zeila descended with a warning look on her beautiful face, and then began the swift and deadly cannonading for which the boy-cruisers were already so famous; while their light vessel, under a heavy press of canvas, flew like a bird, as she obeyed the manoeuvres of her skilful commander.

Their telling fire, and the skill with which they evaded his deadliest volleys, evidently baffled the leader of the stranger pirates, whose deck was almost untenable.

In the hottest of the fight his deep voice resounded amid the din, as he gave some orders to his crew.

A moment after, a blinding flash shot like lightning from his bows, and the Will-o'-the-Wisp was visited with a perfect hail of what seemed living fire.

For the moment, as the scathing balls of fire ran from stem to stern, and made a mimic hell of their decks, the boy-adventurers fled stricken from their guns, as they strove to escape from the ravaging flames, but the angry tones of their dauntless leader recalled them to their duty.

"Back to your guns?" he cried, leaping amidst the fiercest raging fire. "See, I am unharmed! Fear not this harmless flame. Keep up your fire—deluge their decks with iron hail! Boarders, prepare; I alone will stay here while you take their ship!"

The flaming missiles, blazing furiously at our hero's feet, cast a lurid glow on his excited features.

He seemed more than mortal as he stood unscathed amidst the terrible element; and his followers, with a ready cheer, served their guns with deadly effect.

The pirate captain was paralysed at receiving this

storm of shot and grape from the vessel he had encircled with fire.

His fierce voice again rang out its commands, and with sudden swiftness his canvas fell, and his vessel drew away.

Tom, standing dauntless in his perilous position, looked through the smoke, and saw a burly-formed stalwart man, with a massive head set on immense shoulders, looking at him from his shattered decks.

He was dressed in rover's costume, a black bushy beard encircled his chin, and his belt was crammed with huge pistols and short cutlasses.

"Ahoy, there!" he cried, to Tom; "are you the *Will-o'-the-Wisp* and Captain Tom Drake?"

"We are," our hero replied, "and defy you still."

"Then I fight you no longer. I'm sorry I've encountered. Look to your holds, or the fire we've given you will blow your ship to pieces. I can give you no help—I've too much powder on board. We shan't fight if we meet again. You'll know me—I'm Dutch Paul, the captain of the *Yellow Vulture!*"

He waved his hand and stepped down from the carronade on which he had been standing, and as his vessel answered her helm, and sheered off from the scene of action, the boy cruisers saw, to their consternation, that the liquid fire, running like mercury about their decks, had set the holds in a blaze.

The position of our hero and his boy crew was critical in the extreme.

The burning ingredient, whatever it was, seemed harmless so far as its flame was concerned, for Tom had thrust his hand into it without even being scorched; but it dropped a glowing mass, like red-hot mercury, and this ate its way through every beam and plank, and was lodged in all the crevices of the ship.

Prompt and collected in the deadliest peril, Tom sprang from his dangerous position, and issued his swift orders, himself aiding in the efforts to put out the fire.

In this they could succeed so far as the material of the ship was affected; but the blazing liquid proved to be inextinguishable, and burned as vividly under water as on the deck.

Our hero's officers and our hero himself looked blankly in each other's faces.

The fire was travelling to the powder magazine.

One spark there, and the noble vessel with its daring crew would be blown to pieces.

Now that the last echoes of the cannonade had died away, a strange silence reigned.

Noiselessly the fearless boys kept at their dangerous task of putting down the fire, while our hero, with a select party, saw to the powder magazine.

Their only chance of safety lay in keeping the blazing element from this place, and a direct approach of the flames was prevented by a barricade of iron plates, with which they shut off the place where the powder was stored.

The worst danger, however, lay in the fact that the insidious ingredient, working its way through the beams, might at any instant fall over their heads, and instantly compass their destruction.

With this peril before them, our hero and his chosen band set to work.

Their resolve was a desperate one.

Every barrel of the explosive material was hauled from the storing-place, and thrown singly into the sea.

The powder in bulk was well saturated by means of a hose kept playing upon it, and after an hour's imminent peril, any moment of which might have hurled every living soul into eternity, the last barrel of powder was—amidst a cheer that proclaimed the salvation of the ship—hoisted out at the lower portholes.

The task of quelling the fire was comparatively trifling when this was accomplished and the adventurous boys worked less quietly now that the fearful imminence of their danger was past.

It took them a long time to extinguish every trace of the fire, and when this was effected the boy crew gathered round their idolised leader to thank him for preserving their lives.

He was paler than he had ever been before.

He had fully realised their jeopardy, and though danger was his proper element, and defiance of death his kindred nature, the threatened destruction of his ship and crew had quelled the usual fervour of his dauntless breast.

Every inch as brave and staunch a hero as ever, he looked sadly on the havoc around him, and his beautiful vessel, charred, riddled, and splintered in all directions, seemed a perfect wreck.

And now, even though they had saved themselves from their threatened fate, their position was critical still.

At any moment they might meet one of their old enemies, and they had not an ounce of powder to serve their guns.

Tom looked somewhat ruefully on the begrimed and excited countenances of his devoted crew.

"We have been taught a lesson," he said; "one that we shall profit by. Our lamentable experience has left us in a sadly crippled state; but we must not despair. Our best plan will be to disguise the condition of our vessel, and, under the flag of a trader, run into a safe port, where we can lay in a stock of powder and repair our serious damage. Till then we must not show fight. Let our bows be turned towards Barbadoes. Israel Shawm, our Jew dealer, will get us all we want when we arrive there, and we can take advantage of the occasion to convert some of our valuables into specie."

Repressing his feelings at the crippled condition of his graceful vessel, our hero saw all his directions carried out, and then went to visit the wounded, while the ship's prow was shaped towards Barbadoes, the residence of their Jewish confederate, Israel Shawm, an individual to whom we must introduce our readers, as he plays no unimportant part in the fortunes of our boy-adventurers.

CHAPTER XIV.

ISRAEL SHAWM.—THE CHASE.

ISRAEL SHAWM was a wealthy Jew trader, who carried on an extensive business with the merchants and shippers.

His dwelling was situate close to the coast, where he had several wharves crammed with every description of merchandise.

He was not of the usual style of parchment-skinned, decrepit money-grubbers—on the contrary, he was tall, and well-fed, and affected some style in his attire and appearance.

His office was open to all comers, and here he sat, day after day, amidst piles of ledgers, papers, and samples of some of the things in which he traded.

He always had, too, large sums of money on the table before him, for he bought as well as sold; and then many shippers who parted with their wares to him were exceedingly anxious to get to sea again with their money.

It was reported that the merchant Jew's business was not only a mixed one, but one that would not bear too much investigation, and such was the case, though few suspected the extent to which he carried his nefarious dealings.

Israel Shawm asked no questions when shiploads of valuable property were brought to his wharves, not even when the costly fabrics he purchased, in bales upon bales, were darkly stained—the stain blood.

46 CAPTAIN TOM DRAKE;

His dwelling-place was attached to his office premises.

Here he dwelt with his only daughter, Hester, a peerless girl, not yet eighteen, but of as perfect a mould of beauty as any of the famed dark-eyed Jewish maidens.

Another unusual trait in the character of the Jew trader was, that he lavished, with no niggard hand, the costliest gifts on his daughter.

She had the most superb jewels of anyone in the island, and when she went out into society, the rich dresses which set off her matchless form were the envy of the wives and daughters of the wealthiest.

Israel Shawm did not often go out, but he allowed his daughter to go to balls and parties of the island's aristocracy.

Sometimes, when he did accompany her, his eyes gleamed with satisfied pride as he saw the homage her magnificent loveliness commanded from the noblest.

She had an unusually impulsive disposition, and at times her eyes flashed with a light which was as dangerous as fascinating.

To her father she was all obedience, but to all others whom she met, even such as knelt at her feet, worshipping her as an idol, she treated with the most supreme and scornful pride.

Many a dazzling offer had been made; but she laughed her suitors from her presence, and her avaricious father did not as yet interfere.

He was waiting till an offer was made worthy of her position; then he had no doubt she would obey his behest.

The window of the office in which he usually sat commanded an uninterrupted view of the bay, and his high chair was so placed that he could see the vessels entering or leaving the harbour.

Here he sat early one morning awaiting his visitors.

His daughter was seated on a magnificent couch, silently employed in some delicate tapestry work, when old Israel, who had been muttering repeated ejaculations to himself, twisted suddenly round in his chair, and exclaimed—

"Hester, my child, take te glass, and tell me what you make of that ship coming in—my eyes may deceive me; but it looks much like that ship of my fine young friend Captain Tom Drake."

Hester paused abruptly in her work, the rich materials fell from her snow-white fingers, and her cheeks became as crimson as the roses she was deftly embroidering.

She made her father no reply; but taking from its case a sliding telescope set in gold, scanned the distant view.

"'Tis he, father," she cried, eagerly. "I can make out the trim of his vessel, and he floats the pale blue flag with the silver cross in the centre—the one he told us his corsair captive worked for him."

"Ah, he ish a fin lad—a brave one. He and I hash done good business together, and doubt not he comes with more heavy cargoes, for which we shall give him te monish. Ah, he is a phenturesome poy.'

"His career is indeed a dangerous one."

"Dansheroush! why, mine Got, ish it not one tousand pounds rewardsh on hish head? Dansherous! why, my girl, ish there one of those ships, vit te English flag flying, that wouldt not blow down this place about our earsh to get at him and te rewardsh?"

"Surely, father, no one would betray him for that?"

"Eh, what?—what you say, my childsh?"

The old Jew looked at his daughter as if he could not credit his ears.

"Not petray him for the rewardsh? Why, my poor childsh? I shoodsh meself pe glad to have te monish, and might shell this shentleman, but he ish so goodt a customer of mine."

The dark eyes of the Jewish maiden flashed vividly when she heard the first part of her father's speech, and she seemed about to answer him angrily, but at its conclusion she drooped her eyelids over her brilliant orbs, and seated herself beside her father to await the coming of their expected visitor.

Our hero's ship came gallantly into the bay, and cast anchor in the offing outside the bar.

Her sails were trimmed, and the blue banner with its silver cross floated from her peak.

Besides this, he displayed the Brazilian colours, and had the name of the *Santa Anna* in gilt letters over the true name of his ship.

Israel Shwam's face puckered up in many villainous wrinkles when he saw the boat manned and rowed ashore.

He could distinguish Tom's figure seated at the stern long before the boat reached the landing-place, and an avaricious leer sparkled in his bleared sunken eyes.

Hester, with eyes unusually brilliant, and crimsoned cheeks, saw our hero step ashore alone, and wend his way to their house, while the boat was rowed back to the ship.

"Alone," muttered the Jew, as if speaking his thoughts aloud. "Ah, how eashy it woodt pe to take him now! Te shentlemansh is prave, but he ish not discreetsh; if it was a tousand poundsh on my head, I woodt not come alone—no, no—I woodt not, on my shoul."

The lustrous eyes of his peerless daughter were fixed upon him with a strange stealthy look when he uplifted his gaze.

For the first time in his life the rapacious Israelite felt a sinister thrill as he encountered his daughter's fascinating glance.

He looked more keenly at her, but the moment her eyes met his, hers were veiled by their snowy lids, and he could glean nothing of what was passing in her mind.

In a few minutes a coloured domestic announced the expected arrival, and immediately afterwards our hero entered the room, and formally greeting the old Jew, gallantly bowed to the Jewish maiden.

"Ah, captainsh, glad to see you!" the old Jew cried. "Hester, my child, place a chair, and some wine—our famous wine—for the captainsh—he, he, he!—eh?"

Captain Tom, with an easy grace, reached a chair for himself, and with a light compliment to Hester, seated himself at the table with the Jew.

"Well, my tear young friendsh," began the hypocritical old trader, "you have had fine voyages—been cruising round te world mit all te men-of-war at your heels. Ha! we've heard of your pranksh, captainsh. Mine Got, but you are a gallant shentlemansh! But how do you give them te sli, eh? You must have te nine lives, eh, my tear captainsh? he, he!—eh?"

Tom merely bowed to this speech, and the bright-eyed Jewess, stealing a quick glance at his handsome bronzed face, placed the wine and glasses before them.

It was a choice wine, and as she poured it from the richly-cut crystal decanter into the veined Venetian glasses, the ruby liquid sparkled lusciously, and seemed to excite a keener gleam in the Israelite's eyes.

"We have two glasses only," Tom said, as the soft white arm of the Jewish maiden almost touched his shoulder; "has our fair Hebe forgotten herself?"

"She dush not drink te wine," the Jew began,

HE RESTED THE POINT OF HIS SWORD ON THE GROUND TO KEEP HIMSELF FROM FALLING.

"She ish a goodt girl, and has not te taste for strong liquors."

"Then must I instruct this houri in the forbidden drink. N protests, Israel Shawm—I insist; a glass for herself, if she only moistens her lips 'By heaven! it would be sacrilege to drink in such presence and forget the peerless enchantress of your abode."

The Jew's thin lips mumbled dryly—he did not relish our hero's freedom, but he thought it best to disguise his real feelings, and, at a nod from him, Hester brought herself a glass.

"You will have your way, captainsh; yesh, you musht alwaysh have your way. Te poor Jew can say nothing while you make free in hish home."

"Pardon me. I pledge your daughter's health. May her eyes never be less bright, her cheeks less red, her heart more sad, than I would make them."

He rose and drained his glass.

Hester scarcely sipped hers, but her large eyes shone lustrously as she drank in his words, and it was almost with a sigh, as she placed the wine down, that she obeyed her father's gesture and left the room.

"And now, my tear poy, let us to bishness," the Jew exclaimed; "but I hope it ish not much monish you want. I am not so rich as I wash—heavy losses, my tear captainsh."

"Save your breath, old huckster," Tom replied, refilling his glass. "I shall not take your cash. The goods I wish you to have I can exchange f r an article I require, and that is some of the excellent powder you are in the habit of supplying the French ships with, without the permission of our Government."

The Jew's face went ashy pale, and his lips dried like withered sticks.

He did not think his infamous traffickings with the enemies of the English government were known.

His teeth chattered as he thought of his certain fate should he be betrayed.

"Py te Got of Abraham, captainsh," he mumbled, "I am not able to guess what you mean. I have not sell——"

Tom interrupted him.

"Like all your race, you have a ready habit of lying; the devil, who is at your elbow in your hucktstering dealings, is always prepared, I suppose, to help you when you want him. Don't be afraid, Israel, I am not going to betray you, but I want a full quantity of powder. By the way, this wine is excellent; 'tis rare enough to intoxicate the soul of a prophet."

The Jew trader had, by this time, recovered a little from the effects of his fright, and forcing a smile to his shrivelled lips, he said—

"It ish rare wine—rare as te wine you had from te corsair cruiser. Ash much ash you like you shall have of it for your ship; you will not mind te price—it ish high, but te wine ish goot; and te powder, you shall have it—it ish for your ship?"

"Well, yes, I want it sent aboard."

"Smuggled aboard you must have it. Te authorities here are phery sharp, and te risk makes te bargain dearer."

"Very sharp, indeed," laughed Tom, "when half-a-dozen French ships are supplied with powder from your wharves. No, no, Israel, you must get it aboard free of risk, and then you can take seven bales of this to repay you."

He placed a sample of rich silk before the Jew.

Avaricious and greedy as the lying old huckster was, he could not cavil at the liberal offer of repayment.

His cunning eyes glistened as he saw the quality of the silk, and pawing it with his withered hands, he said—

"All like thish, captainsh, the sheven pales?"

"All—are you satisfied?"

"You are generoush, captainsh, phery generoush; but then te risk ish great. Te silk ish goodt. Have you many more pales besides?"

"I have seven bales for you, Israel Shawm, and the rest of my cargo you may guess at as much as you please."

A sinister gleam shone in the Jew trader's eye as he put the question.

Tom's ready reply baffled his curiosity, however, and the gleam died away again.

"And now, captainsh," he exclaimed, after the arrangement of their bargain had been concluded, "I have a proposition to make, and if you will agree you shall make monish enough to fill your ship."

"A rich venture—what is its nature?"

"Te plack man, captainsh—te nigger. I have a treaty with a king on the coast of Africa. He shall give you te placks, and you shall take them where it will be safe, and I will give you a mint of money for te run. You can do it well, captainsh; you have a fine ship, and she ish swift as a pird, and you can fight——"

A deep flush had suffused our hero's bronzed features as the rascally Jew began his infamous offer; now he rose, and bringing his clenched hand heavily down on the table, faced the cringing speaker.

"No more!" he cried. "Think you I would sully my ship with such traffic? Think you I could tread her white deck, if her holds were crammed with a suffocating mass of humanity, brutally torn from their homes, crowded, bruised, and bleeding, with irons festering into their gashed bodies, and

the iron of slavery doomed to eat into their souls? You mistake me, grey old blood-sucker. Single out another for your infamous traffic in the blood and flesh of your fellow-man; but let me cross the track of one such ship, and I will send crew, vessel, and all, with its load of suffering wretches, to the depths of the sea."

Tom looked very noble as he stood erect, facing the shivering Jew trader, who was staring half-scared at him.

The force of Tom's hand striking the table had hurled one of the glasses, with its measure of luscious wine, into Israel's lap, and he seemed anticipating to be himself hurled to the ground.

"Got of Abraham!" he cried, aghast. "I thought you wash a pirate, captainsh, and wouldt not mindsh——"

"I am called pirate, drivelling old huckster, because I fight for my independence. It is true, too, that I take spoils at sea, but I plunder only those who have stolen amid bloodshed their costly gains. I know it is no legal crime, this traffic in helpless humanity; but to me it is an abhorrent trade of infamy, and that act is merciful which does as I would do—free the penned wretches from their misery by sending them to a swift watery grave. Therefore, Israel Shawm, look out. I have a keen scent, and if one of these blood-traffickers crosses my track—a shot from my ship straight through her hull—the rest you understand. And now, farewell! I shall not visit you again this voyage. Fulfil your compact—I will not fail in mine."

Saying this, our hero took up his gold-laced hat, and, bowing stiffly, left the apartment.

Hester encountered him as he left the threshold.

Her face was blanched, and a wild look shone in her dark eyes.

"You have angered my father," she said, in a low whisper; "be on your guard."

"Ha!" Tom cried, catching her wrist.

Hester released her hand quickly, and stepped back.

Her quick hearing had detected her father's footstep, and she retreated as the door opened and the knavish face of the merchant peered forth.

But the warning look was still in her bright eyes.

"Captainsh," Israel Shawm came forth, his voice whining, his frame obsequiously bowed, "I have repented that I made the offer. I shall not deal in thish trade, and I shall still call you mine goodt friend h."

Tom's frank eyes revealed his discredit of the Jew's assertion.

He waved his hand, and passed from the house.

At the doorway he paused, and bowed gracefully to the dark-eyed Jewess.

Then sticking his cocked hat jauntily on his head, he gave the Jew trader an incredulous look, and, with a mocking laugh, departed.

No sooner had the door closed behind him than Israel Shawm, whose visage was ashy pale and clammy, struggled up to it, and shaking his palsied hand after our hero, cried, huskily—

"My curses wither you, dog of a pirate! Ah, I will stop your fine career. So you will sink my ships. Ah, captainsh, that was a bad threat, a phery bad threat, with a thousand poundsh reward on your headsh."

"Father, father!" Hester cried, moving towards him, "you would not betray him?"

"My curses on you, too, child of mine, if you have a word to say for him! Persh'nsh! did he not take you by the handsh? What had he to do vit te colour of your cheeks, and te prightness of your eyes? A curse on his blood and flesh, I say!"

The Jew's whole frame quivered with passion.

He tottered back to his room, and still mumbling

his poisted curses on our hero's head, closed the door behind him.

An hour afterwards his bell summoned his daughter.

Israel Shawm held a sealed letter in his shaking hand.

"Shend Diego here. I want him to go to te commandantsh vit this letter."

Hester sighed as she obeyed his orders.

She guessed at the purport of that missive; but nothing was to be gained by intercepting her father's messenger.

Half an hour had not elapsed when the British commandant arrived, and was ushered into the presence of the Jew, by whom he was directed to take a seat.

The commandant was a quiet-featured elderly Englishman.

He was on slightly intimate terms with Israel Shawm, who found it his best policy to keep up good acquaintances on the island, that his nefarious practices might be less likely to be suspected.

The commandant, after he had formally greeted him, began the conversation.

"I duly received your note, Mr. Shawm, and am here, all eagerness, as you may guess, to learn what important communication you have to lay before me."

"My good friendsh, you shall hear quickly. You sha'l have heard of one pirate poy, Captainsh Tom Drake?"

"Of course I have. You do not mean to say you know anything of him?"

"Suppose I do, my good friendsh? Suppose I know where you can send a shipsh to take him?"

"Where—where, my dear Mr. Shawm? This is really important. I will take instant measures——"

"No, no; you will alarmsh te island, and thish pirate captainsh ish like te tevil himshelf in getting away. No, no—suppose this poy captainsh come to me, and say I must shend him a cargo of powdersh; suppose I sand in te parrels, and suppose your shipsh go after his shipsh, and when he gets ready to fight, he findsh the powdersh no powdersh at all, and shall not be able to load his guns, while you blow his shipsh up, and take him your prishoner?"

The commandant did not quite understand the Jew trader's words; but a more precise explanation sharpened his wits, and in high glee he took his departure, having warmly thanked the Jew for putting the chance of promotion in his way.

"You will have the shipsh ready by nightfall?" the Israelite said, bowing him to the door.

"Ready, and armed to the teeth."

"And te tousand poundsh?"

"Shall be yours. The honour of his capture will be enough for me."

Hester heard those last words as she sat, pale and motionless as a statue, in her own room, the door of which being open, allowed her to overhear what the commandant said.

Her father did not even give her a thought. He shuffled back to his office, and seating himself by the window, peered through his spectacles at Tom's graceful ship.

"I could have her taken now," he mumbled; "but then I shoodt not get my pales of silk, and is will be more bettersh to be played the tricksh I will play him. Ah, py my shoul, he shall pay wit his life."

His skinny fingers entwined themselves restlessly, and presently his thoughts took another turn.

"If it shoodt fail," he mumbled; "but no, that ish imposhible—imposhible."

An uneasy feeling, nevertheless, marred his gleeful anticipations; an unpleasant vision rose before his eyes—the vision of the fiery boy-cruiser, escaped from the snare, and confronting him in hot fury—eager to crush his life out.

He shook off the feeling, and persuaded himself that his treachery could not fail.

It was dark when a lighter, laden to the edge with what seemed barrels of pork, lay at Israel's wharf ready to depart.

The old trader himself stood peering from his window, chuckling as he saw the cargo embarked.

The lighter was just about to move off, when a cloaked female—a lady evidently, though disguised—walked hastily up to the quay, and, stepping into a boat, was rowed from the wharf.

The gathering gloom had hidden the lighter from the Jew trader's sight when a boat was brought alongside it, and the lady, leaning towards the nearest man, addressed him in a low tone by name.

The man started, and bowed respectfully.

The lady's gloved hand was extended; a little note was held between her fingers.

A few words in a low tone—the man took the letter—the lady drew her veil closer about her form—the lighter again went on its way, and the boat was rowed back to the quay.

Softly as the lady had spoken another man on board the lighter had heard the words and recognized the voice.

He knew that it was his master's daughter, and overheard when she charged her messenger to deliver the letter without fail.

He was a fellow of an evil and suspicious mind: he watched where his companion put the letter, and before they were much further on their way had dexterously purloined it.

Bending low down, so as to be unseen, and to get the reflected light of the waters, he read the superscription of the letter.

It was simply addressed to "The Captain."

The man's active fingers noiselessly opened it, and he read the words intended for our hero—words which the peerless Jewess had hastily penned to put him on his guard.

"Fly, you are sold! the blood-money has caused your betrayal. At nightfall you will be pursued. Beware! you are taking an enemy on board instead of a friend!"

The letter was written on a double sheet of paper, and the man who had deciphered its message tore off the written half and concealed it inside his shirt; the other half he folded neatly as it had been before, and restored it to the open pocket whence he had abstracted it.

Five bells had just struck on board our hero's ship when the lighter grated its side.

The work of unloading the barrels was soon accomplished, and the bales of silk transferred to their place.

Just as the lighter was leaving, the man, in obedience to the instructions of his young mistress, handed the letter to one of Tom's boy-crew.

Little Kanak, who was at the gangway, snatched the missive and ran with it to his youthful master, who was superintending the stowage of the powder.

Admiral Tom opened the letter, and looked curiously at the blank sheet of paper.

He was accustomed to cyphers and secret writing of all kinds; but every device was tried in vain to bring any traces of ink or pencil marks on the unsoiled sheet.

"Strange!" he mused; "it is a female's hand—the writing, I could almost swear, of the Jew trader's daughter. Something is wrong. Stop that lighter, we will question the men."

The lighter paid no heed to the summons to return, and the darkness rendered the lowering of a boat useless.

So our hero, who regarded the blank sheet as a warning, ordered the anchor to be quietly weighed, and stood out to sea.

They sailed under easy pressure of canvas till daybreak, when two large war-vessels were discovered full on their track, hoisting signals for them to lay to—signals of which the boy-buccaneers took no notice, until a gun was fired from the nearest war-ship, and the spread of canvas told them they were hotly pursued.

Our hero was standing on the deck with Ben Barnacle and his boy officers when the shot was hurled across his bows, and reddening to the temples, he ordered the decks to be cleared for action, intending to give his pursuers a sample of his mettle before taking leave of them.

A sudden cry from Bob Hauler, who came rushing hurriedly from the magazine, was the first means of discovering to him how he had been tricked by the Jew.

Bob Hauler's honest face was agbast with mingled dismay and chagrin.

"We're cheated, sir," he cried to his young chieftain; "the powder's a trick; you can fire a red-hot shot into it without doing any mischief."

"Eh!" Tom exclaimed, angrily, as he walked down to the magazine. "If he has tricked me, he shall pay dearly."

"It's true enough, sir; he's dusted a cargo of charcoal dust with gunpowder, and put powder on the top, but there ain't enough in the whole batch to charge a broadside."

A hasty inspection revealed to our hero the Jew's knavish trick. He had filled the barrels with finely powdered charcoal, with which a little gunpowder was intermixed.

The brow of Captain Tom grew dark; his eyes blazed with fierce anger.

"Knock in every cask-head!" he exclaimed "Perhaps we can find enough powder for a broadside."

Ben Barnacle respectfully saluted his youthful leader as he remarked—

"It would be hazardous, sir, engaging them, if we even found so much as that."

"Do not fear me, Ben; I am not so reckless of the lives of my gallant band. No, I do not wish to fight these vessels; but I should like to double on them, and, with one broadside, blow that knavish Jew-trickster's house about his ears."

"We ain't enough for a couple of guns," Bob Hauler said, ruefully. "The rubbish is only fit to pitch overboard, except one cask, which I should like to cram down that thievish Jew's throat—staves, charcoal-dust, and all—and I'd make him swallow every grain, if it took him a week to make the meal."

Bob Hauler viciously rammed his brawny arm into the worthless mass, and clenched a handful as if it were the old Jew's windpipe.

"We must make a couple of fools of these ships," Tom observed, as he ascended to the deck. "They are evidently aware of our predicament, and are doubtless enjoying the anticipation of an easy capture. They shall have a morning's amusement for their pains."

On deck they had not been idle. More sails had been crowded aloft, in order to increase the distance between them and their pursuers.

As Captain Tom reached the quarter-deck, a simultaneous report came from the two vessels, which were now close alongside, and had given this imperative summons for the boy-buccaneers to yield.

Our hero quietly issued his orders to his crew.

The decks were cleared, their sails trimmed, and every appearance of preparation for battle made—manœuvres which easily misled the pursuing ships, whose commanders, aware of the empty state of Tom's magazine—for they had rightly divined that they had no powder on board, and from the reports of the charred state of the decks and some of the masts, guessed the cause—imagined that this was only an empty demonstration before their surrender—and took in nearly all their canvas, in order to show how well they were prepared for a desperate conflict.

The instant this movement checked their speed, they had the mortification of seeing the *Will-o'-the-Wisp* spread all her sails with magical celerity, and begin one of the daring runs for which she was already famous.

Determined not to be baffled, the commanders gave a hurried order to fire their broadsides at the hull of the saucy runaway.

The word "fire" rang over the billows—the men flew to their quarters—the guns were thrust out—and, amid the deafening roar, the iron missiles sped across the sea.

Everyone paused after the discharge, and looked to see the cruiser ship annihilated; but when the smoke cleared away, it showed them, to their surprise and chagrin, the *Will-o'-the-Wisp* unharmed, and literally dancing over the sparkling waves.

"Now," Tom cried, his dark-brown eyes sparkling with excitement, "shake out a reef or two more. If they pursue us we'll lead them such a dance that they will as lief think of chasing the churchyard will-o'-the-wisp as of tracking us again."

More sails were spread, and the speed of the ship increased. The British vessels, too, got up an extra display of canvas; but our hero's ship soon began perceptibly to recede, and though the chase was hot, and they did their best by an occasional gun to bring them to, the *Will-o'-the-Wisp* sped slowly out of sight, and by nightfall all pursuit of her was hopeless.

Tom remained on deck all that night.

Their position was critical. Powerless to fire shot, they had no chance except by boarding, and their vessel, securely as it was protected, might be crippled and themselves shot down before they could get a chance of using their cutlasses and pikes.

And as if a persistent fate menaced him with extra perils, now that he was less able to meet them, the grey daylight showed him another vessel hanging on his track.

She was some leagues in the rear, and it was a long time since he had seen her; but a careful survey through his glass convinced him that she was their old pursuer, the *Arethusa*, the ship upon whose deck he had first taken his lessons in sea life, under Captain Parker and his old enemy, Sanderson.

On board the frigate they were not able to make out the character of the ship they pursued; but from her manner of keeping before the wind, their suspicions were aroused, and at the risk of suffering some serious casualty, Captain Parker had every stitch of canvas crowded that the vessel would bear, and with her powerful masts straining like reeds, the frigate made such good way that the ship of our boy-adventurers was never out of sight until towards dusk, when she began imperceptibly to grow less, and at last only her hull, like a small speck, could be discovered.

Captain Parker strained his eyesight till the glass was of no further use to him, when with a vexatious exclamation, he handed the telescope to his lieutenant, and wiped the moisture from his aching eyes.

"Can you make her out now, Mr. Burly?"

"No, sir, she has disappeared, masts and all."

"Curse her!—after a whole day's chase"

"I think, sir, it must have been that spectre ship,

the *Will-o'-the-Wisp*. If it was, and they've that boy-devil aboard, Tom Drake, we may whistle our ears off before we take her."

"I'll take her, by Heaven! Crowd all sail! Up, up, lads! we're in chase of that young devil, Captain Tom!"

CHAPTER XV.

POWDER BARRELS AND THEIR LIVING CONTENTS.

THE result of this determination on the part of Captain Parker was, that our hero, who had slackened sail during the night, found his old acquaintance still on his track, when, after snatching a few hours of repose, he came upon deck.

A stiff breeze was blowing, and would soon have taken them clear of their pursuers, but the efforts they made to get quickly away proved disastrous to their attempts.

One of the masts had been so severely charred during the time the fire raged on board, that, although every means had been used to strengthen it, the weight of canvas suddenly brought it down with a crash about the ears of the boy-buccaneers, who would almost as soon have expected the frigate's boarders to have dropped upon them from their own shrouds.

Bob Hauler, who, with the others, was soon busily at work repairing the damage, went thoughtfully about his task.

Ever since the disappearance of Jerry Mizzen—and the ship had been vainly searched for that hapless individual—they had experienced a run of ill-luck, which, somehow, Bob Hauler could only associate with the loss of his former messmate.

"My poor mate's been and tumbled overboard," Bob mused, "and my word for it, he's a travelling after us on the wide ocean, and we shan't have nothing but bad luck till we pick him up and give him decent burial, like a true tar; and the sooner we falls in with him, the better, for if we arn't going all adrift here, I arn't a Christian."

Tom, who was growing more defiant of danger as the difficulties thickened, hit upon a daring device to save him from the frigate, which, since his mishap, had been steadily gaining upon them.

He had amongst his crew men of all nations, and picking out a few Swedes, Danes, and Norwegians, he had the flag of Norway run up, and altering the trim of his vessel, determined to run into the nearest French harbour.

He had descried the French coast long before his arrangements were complete, but just as all was ready, he came in sight of a portion of the French fleet, standing out to sea.

An accomplished linguist—for he had a remarkable facility of acquiring languages—Captain Tom, dressed as a Norwegian coasting captain, answered the questions of the French commanders and had the satisfaction of seeing the *Arethusa* turn tail as soon as she saw the company he was in.

The French commanders were very civil; they afforded Tom all the information he desired, and when he informed them that he had been boarded and fired by the English ships, directed him, with many expressions of sympathy, where to go in order to repair.

In its altered trim, no one would have suspected the real nature of Tom's vessel, so well were her crew and armaments concealed, while the fact of her being chased by the British frigate added confirmation to our hero's story, and the Frenchmen, on parting company, expressed their hope that they might fall in with his pursuer; a hope which made some of Tom's crew, when they heard it, stick their tongues in their cheeks in a way anything but complimentary to the Frenchmen, who had no sooner turned their backs

if such a term may be used in a nautical signification, then our hero, summoning Ben Barnacle and Harry Vere to accompany him, descended to his cabin.

"Now Ben," he said, when Zeila had placed choice wines before them—for our hero affected little formality with his trusty officers—they were his friends, and as such he valued them—"now, Ben, we have a capital opportunity, not only of storing our magazines with powder of the right sort, but also of performing a little exploit, which, though British obstinacy and red-tapeism may preclude from being of lasting service to our country, will be of some use at the moment, and will teach these braggart Frenchmen that England can produce a few good and daring sailors—I mean the capture of the Fortress Renauf."

Ben Barnacle looked thoughtfully in his leader's face.

"To capture the fortress, although they brag so much about it," he observed gravely, "might not be so difficult after we have enough powder to serve our guns; but in our present crippled state, could we attempt it with any hope of success?"

"We could land and attack its gates; carry it by boarding, as we would a ship," Harry Vere cried, ready, with his usual impulsive recklessness, to head even so hazardous an attack.

Our hero smiled.

"Strange as it may appear," he observed quietly, "I propose taking the fortress without the expenditure of an ounce of powder and shot—without calling on my rash lieutenant here to lead his boarders against an impregnable wall. I purpose effecting its capture by the new art—Diplomacy."

Ben Barnacle looked grave as before.

Harry Vere whistled.

Zeila, who had taken her usual resting-place on a cushion at our hero's feet, gazed wonderingly up in his handsome countenance.

"You shall hear my plans," Tom said. "Our friend, the admiral of that portion of the French fleet we have just parted from, was kind enough not only to impart much useful information, but to direct me where we could repair, and even gave me a letter of introduction to certain individuals living within shelter of this famous fort. It happened that when he gave me his letters, a packet lying open on his table, and which I had before noticed, happened to slip into my pocket; it is from the French Minister; here is his signature—a signature which I have faithfully copied and attached to a document empowering the commandant of this fortress to deliver up such stores as I, Admiral Duquesne, of the glorious navy of France, may require. Armed with this document, I shall enter the fortress alone, and state my mission to the commandant, and await its result."

Ben Barnacle looked with admiring pride in the fearless countenance of his daring chief, while Harry Vere uttered an excited cry of delight.

Zeila was silent and sadly thoughtful.

"It is possible," our hero continued, "that the commandant may refuse to believe in the genuineness of the orders, and decline to deliver up the stores, in which case I shall simply, in the Republic's name, order his own men to place him under arrest, as an enemy to his country; the superior command would be vested in me, then"—the boy's eyes blazed with enthusiasm—"old England's banner, with our own free flag, shall float above the walls of this fortress."

Harry Vere sprang from his seat.

"Magnificent!" he cried. "Sir, I envy you the glory of such an enterprise. You will succeed, too, I feel assured. By Jove! how dearly I should like to be behind you when you are ordering the commandant's own men to arrest him; but of cour-

that cannot be, success depends upon your being alone."

"Entirely," Tom answered. "Ben Barnacle, the ship will be in your charge from now. I shall not attempt the affair until we have refitted, which will be in about five days. But I must not be seen on board. To you, Vere, I leave the task of superintending the expedition to land and take the stores. Zeila I leave in the care of all my faithful band. I shall enter the fortress precisely at eleven on the fifth day from this; in less than two hours either ou will receive the signal to land, or I shall have sailed. Should that last occur, Ben, forget not that the ship is yours."

Ben sprang up—a tear glistened in his fine dark eye.

"Mine!" he cried in a husky voice. "I would make it my tomb—my funeral pyre! No, no—Ben Barnacle takes no command when he loses his leader—he will avenge him and die."

The gallant-hearted fellow seized Tom's hands in his grasp, and pressed them convulsively to his heart.

"God, who alone reads our hearts," he cried, "knows the great love I bear you; He knows too, I could not survive if you were lost to me."

Our hero was touched by this emotion.

Harry Vere turned away to hide a tear.

Little Zeila, springing to her feet, actually took Ben Barnacle's hands in both her own fair palms, and bravely kissed him.

. . . .

Our adventurers found no difficulty in getting the requisites for their repairs—which were chiefly carried out by themselves; they had no wish for prying eyes on board their vessel.

Within the five days their refitting was complete, and all arrangements were made.

Our hero had quitted the vessel and gone ashore the previous day.

His farewell of Zeila had been tender and affectionate.

The corsair maiden, usually so daring, was on this occasion a prey to the weakest forebodings, and it was with a sad heart that she saw the last of his gallant figure in the boat that carried him ashore.

His leave of his daring boy-crew had been scarcely less affectionate.

In silence, but with the deep fervour of faithful loving hearts, they had taken their farewell, and many an eye was moist as they looked their last on their idolised leader.

Even their jaunty hardihood and reckless defiance of danger could not ignore the fact that his enterprise was beset with peril.

The slightest error, and the roll of musketry in the churchyard of the fortress would be the speedy record of his execution, unless a worse fate—incarceration in its deepest dungeon—awaited him.

Very naturally, then, they awaited with anxious hearts and eager eyes the events of the next day.

There was one expressed intent in the mind of every one of that devoted band.

Should calamity befall their leader, they were sworn—as soon as they could supply themselves with ammunition—to make an attack on the fortress, and take it, or perish in the attempt.

And now, leaving our adventurers to their uncertain conjectures on deck, we must follow our hero in his daring but dangerous exploit.

At precisely eleven o'clock he presented himself before the gates of the fortress, and demanded admittance.

He was attired in the uniform of an admiral of the Republic—the tricolour was in his hat, the democratic sash round his waist, and his dress-sword at his side.

He wore big boots, as if he had come a journey; a wig of long hair and a curling moustache further Frenchified his appearance, and for the rest he trusted to his proficiency in the French language, his coolness, and the bold intrepidity which he knew would not desert him.

The diligence in which he had been driven up to the fortress was conspicuously dusty; the two men outside were the perfection of official menials.

The gates were opened in obedience to our hero's summons; he passed in, and was ushered into the fortress.

Then the heavy gates closed, and he stood alone in the stronghold of the enemy—perhaps never to go forth from its walls alive.

Still, so constitutionally brave was he that not even a thrill quickened his pulsation.

With genial but decided dignity he stalked across the courtyard, and was received at the entrance by the sergeant on duty, who, deferentially recognising his rank, conducted him inside.

"Usher me into the presence of Monsieur le Commandant," said Captain Tom, "or state to him that Admiral Duquesne, with letters from the Chief of our great Republic, desires audience of him."

The sergeant bowed and left him.

He returned almost immediately, and led the way to the commandant's room.

The commandant, however, had come forth to receive his visitor.

He was a quiet-looking undignified man, wearing a pair of spectacles, which he seemed to require more from some defect in his sight than from his age.

He was dressed in the Republican garb, and had the appearance of a placid but shrewd and obstinate man—not over venturesome, not particularly active, but one who might be safely entrusted with any responsibility.

"I have the honour," our hero said, in capital French, when he and the commandant had saluted each other, "of addressing Monsieur Citizen le Maitre, commandant of the fortress Renauf?"

The commandant bowed.

"It is the will of the chief of our great Republic," Tom continued, following the commandant, into his apartment, "that I should lay before Monsieur le Commandant, firstly, this packet, which I have now the honour to hand to him; and afterwards this other, which I detain until he shall have acknowledged the first."

He handed a packet, which the commandant, after respectfully saluting the seal of the great Republic (which Tom had capitally forged), broke open, as he observed—

"Monsieur the Admiral will please be seated."

"With due thanks, Monsieur, I would prefer to be allowed to stand."

The commandant carefully read the document.

Every word he examined, cautiously scrutinizing the various signatures.

Without a movement of his countenance, our hero waited in an attitude of dignified composure.

The forged document was an order for him to answer, without reserve, all questions of his visitor, to conduct Tom whithersoever he desired within the fortress, and to attend reverently to the instructions contained in the other package.

The commandant perused the paper twice before he spoke.

"Monsieur the Admiral will understand that I am at his service and that of the great Republic."

Our hero bowed, and without altering his position, put a series of questions, which the commandant politely answered.

Tom then desired to be conducted to the storerooms and magazine.

"I SEE YOU HAVE A GUN HERE FOR DEFENCE," THE OFFICER REMARKED.

7

If the commandant felt any hesitation he did not betray it.

Silently he led the way to the store-rooms, offering no remark until addressed by his visitor.

At the entrance of the magazine he paused.

"Monsieur the Admiral will pardon me, but one injunction of our great Republic directs that only the commandant shall enter the magazine of a fortress armed."

"Monsieur must pardon my neglect of the orders," our hero observed, taking off his sword and placing it on the stores outside.

The commandant seemed better satisfied at this, but it was plainly evident that, like all good servants of the Republic, he was suspicious and exacting.

Still entertaining his reserve, he unlocked the heavy door, and they entered the magazine.

A good deal of powder was stored here; there were weapons and munitions of war of all descriptions besides.

The place was beneath the fortress, and admitted no light.

The covered lantern which the commandant had brought only barely lighted up the place, but it enabled our hero to see that all he required was within his reach.

The commandant spoke.

"Monsieur the Admiral is satisfied with his inspection?"

"Perfectly. It will be my pleasing duty to report favourably of what I have seen. The Republic may be satisfied that it has a good servant in Monsieur le Maitre."

The commandant bowed, and our hero took the second packet from his breast.

His most difficult part was now to come.

"I have now the honour to convey my second instructions, to which I am charged to add verbal explanations. Monsieur will please read."

He handed him the second packet—the commandant saluted the seal and superscription as before, and began slowly to read.

Before he had finished, he started and turned pale, then looked up at his visitor's face.

Our hero remained immovable.

"Monsieur is aware of the nature of this despatch?"

"To the letter."

"Is Monsieur prepared to explain the reason of these extraordinary instructions?"

"The great Republic, of which we are humble citizens," Tom replied, impressively, "issues not explanations, but orders."

The commandant mused.

"This despatch commands me to give up my stores and ammunition. My fort would be defenceless."

Our hero shrugged his shoulders.

"Monsieur has seen a vessel lying outside?" he asked.

The commandant bowed.

"She has seemed a Norwegian sloop. She is not. Her nationality is French. She is armed to the teeth, but ill-supplied with powder. It is the order of the chief of the Republic that this magazine furnish her. Monsieur will not forget that the fortress he commands has the repute of being impregnable. For eight-and-forty-hours it will be defenceless. But who will learn the secret? Monsieur has his instructions. It is my duty to see to the requirements of this vessel, for the destination of which I have secret instructions. If monsieur hesitates, it will be my duty to command."

The features of the commandant flushed.

"Monsieur," he said, angrily, "when the Republic honoured me with the command of this fortress, it instructed me to surrender to no one its

stores or defence. Monsieur talks of command. Does he not see that with a touch I could blow up the stores from beneath his feet—the walls about his ears?"

"Citizen le Maitre," Tom said, "the instructions I have handed you authorise no such waste of useful munitions of war."

The commandant looked at the speaker.

Our hero's cool way of speaking of being blown up in the air surprised him.

He could not fairly suspect him, and yet he could not reconcile himself to the idea of stripping the fortress.

"Monsieur will not forget," he exclaimed, "that a Frenchman's honour is sacred. The insult he has offered me must receive satisfaction. Monsieur has no weapon. I spare him a sword—let him use it."

He placed the packets in his breast, the lantern on a barrel of powder, and kicked a sword towards Tom's feet, at the same time drawing his own weapon from its scabbard.

Our hero did not stir.

"Monsieur forgets," he said, quietly, "that my instructions have to be carried out before I can engage in any private matters."

"Are you a coward?"

"Monsieur speaks like a traitor, and not like a soldier of the Republic, whose duty is to sink his private wishes and serve his country."

The commandant's face was white with passion.

"Monsieur can fight," he cried. "Should he kill me, he can satisfy the garrison of the genuine nature of his instructions; should I kill him, I shall act up to my first orders. Monsieur forgets that his despatches have omitted to cancel my first instructions, and that one document he has brought commands me to conduct him within the fort, but does not specify that he is to leave it again. Monsieur forgets, too, that under his feet are deep dungeons, where I could place him by the uplifting of a finger. He had better, then, take up a sword."

The critical moment had arrived—the moment on which his fate depended.

All rested now on the result of his abrupt appeal to the garrison.

He had failed with the commandant, whose staunch and dogged devotion to his cause made him prefer death rather than even run the risk of betraying the charge entrusted to him.

Our hero was not without admiration for the determined pluck of the eccentric commandant, but the emergency of his position demanded prompt and effective action.

He might have chosen the course then offered him, of running the devoted Republican through the body.

Alone as they were, he could easily have done so, but apart from his unwillingness to shed the blood of a brave and true man, such a proceeding might only have increased his difficulties.

"Citizen le Maitre," he said, "I do not pick up that sword because I am not a traitor to my cause as you are."

He stepped back quickly and thrust open the door.

"Ho! there! Soldiers of the Republic, enter! Treachery is in your midst! Advance, before your magazine is given to the enemy, and your country betrayed. Advance! I hold the traitor here, and only over my body shall he pass!"

The commandant made a rush at Tom as his loud tones rang along the corridor, but our hero, by a gesture that awed him with its dignity, caused him to pause, amazed and dumbfounded, and while he hesitated, the soldiers—who had hastily snatched up their muskets—rushed into the magazine.

"Citizen soldiers," cried Tom Drake, "in the name

of the Republic. I denounce this traitor! Arrest him. Let the officer of the guard be called, that this traitor be searched, and all treasonable papers taken from him."

The commandant was so dumbfounded that he could not speak.

The soldiers, looking from the erect, dignified figure of Captain Tom, to the scared, half-paralysed attitude of the commandant, had no doubt that he was detected in some traitorous intrigue, and in a trice he was seized and disarmed.

When the officer of the guard came, our hero placed in his hands the papers he had taken from the commandant's breast.

"Citizen soldiers," he exclaimed, "these are the despatches of our glorious Republic, which he has dared to repudiate, and, besides, he has long been amongst the suspected and denounced. Convey him to the dungeon beneath the magazine, he will there await the trial of a traitorous conspirator."

If the men had been at all inclined to hesitate, our hero's commanding bearing would have decided them.

As it was, appearances were so against their late commandant, and the rank of our hero appeared to be so great, that the unfortunate commandant, was not allowed to speak, the breath was jerked out of him as he was rudely dragged along.

He was loaded with chains, and conveyed to the dark, noisome dungeons underground, where he was left in darkness and solitude, to ponder upon the unexpected fate that had converted him from a trusted and honoured citizen and officer into a denounced, manacled captive, awaiting an ignominious doom.

The high-handed manner in which Captain Tom had carried matters left him so far successful in his daring scheme—he had passed through his most imminent moment, for it was the hazard of a die whether the commandant might not have had sufficient nerve to denounce him as a traitor, and order him to be shot where he stood.

Now he stood master of the fortress, and though a hundred perils yet menaced him, he trusted to his consummate hardihood to get him safely through the remainder of his enterprise.

When the commandant had been safely got out of the way, he told the officer to lock up the magazine and accompany him to the casemate of the fort, from which, with proudly beating heart he signalled his sloop to send the boat ashore.

How gladly was the signal received by those on board!

A wild, thrilling cheer ran along the vessel's decks, and the boy-buccaneers, burning with enthusiasm to share the fortunes of their leader, got ready their boat while Ben Barnacle had the French tricolour run up at the mast-head.

When the boat's crew, who were dressed as French sailors, landed, and Harry Vere, attired in the costume of a young officer of the Republic, stood in the presence of his brave leader, he could scarcely repress his enthusiastic looks of admiration.

Our hero, coldly recognising his respectful salute, stiffly directed the sergeant to see to the embarkation of the munitions of war, while he himself proceeded to seal up the commandant's papers.

The whole of that day was occupied in passing to and fro the ship to shore.

By evening the fortress was stripped of its stores.

To deceive the eyes of any who might be observing their proceedings, as Tom pretended, he had as many barrels conveyed back to the fort as he took from it; these were placed in the magazine.

Their contents were of a very suspicious nature, each barrel containing two of the boy cruisers, who lay patiently doubled up and half-suffocated till the

time came for their release, which took place at nightfall, when our hero adroitly removed the cask heads, and in silent determination his devoted followers gathered around him.

Not a word was spoken.

The boy-adventurers were locked up in darkness, while their chieftain proceeded to the crowning part of his audacious stratagem.

He went back to the commandant's room, and seating himself at the table, rang the bell for the officer to appear, and began leisurely writing what seemed to be a despatch.

"Citizen officer," he said, when the officer had stood uncovered in his presence some few minutes, "you will be good enough to despatch ten soldiers and a corporal to the *Victoire*; they will be required to attest that they have seen the powder disposed in the war-sloop's magazine; they will make their observations and return."

The officer saluted and retired, and Tom continued his writing.

The officer had got about half-way along the stone corridor, when he abruptly paused; a sudden suspicion had flashed to his brain.

What if, after all, he was being betrayed, and was helping to lay the fortress defenceless and open to a traitorous attack!

He reeled under the vague misgiving.

A few moments' deep meditation, and on tiptoe he stole back to the commandant's room, and stooping down peered through the keyhole.

Our hero was still seated at the table, the commandant's papers in sealed packets lay before him; he was slowly writing; a hard inscrutable look was on his face, but not a muscle quivered.

The officer watched his hand travel across the paper—it never faltered or shook as it guided the obedient pen.

There was not the least sign of nervous haste or trepidation; one by one the words were firmly formed.

The suspicious Frenchman watched him finish and sign the document which he addressed to the President of the Republic, and after a moment's calm thought begin another.

"He is very young," thought the officer; "but these are times when a man's advancement rests on his exploits, not his age; his looks might decide the fate of a nation. I never saw so commanding an eye; his must be a will of iron. But what can he want of ten men to assist the stowage of our stores? Parbleu! He may, after all, be one whom our Republic has rightly trusted, and my suspicions are ungenerous."

Apparently satisfied, the man dismissed the suspicion from his grim visage and went softly on his way.

But he acted with caution, nevertheless.

Selecting ten picked men, he called the corporal aside, and, without communicating his suspicion said, after he had given him his instructions—

"Citizen Corporal, make use of your eyes and ears while on board, and inform me of all you see and hear."

The corporal touched his cap, the soldiers rammed the bullets down the barrels of their muskets, and in single file passed out of the fort.

The garrison numbered forty-five men, and this proceeding of Captain Tom was a device to get ten men out of his way, as well as to bring ten more of his crew to his side.

The corporal, alarmed by the hints of his superior officer, determined to be on his guard.

When the boat touched the ship, he ordered the soldiers to fix bayonets and ascend, he himself following last.

Nothing in the appearance of the vessel was otherwise than he might have expected from a war sloop, which, after being so long disguised, was bringing out its concealed armaments.

The brotherhood greeting, usual to the citizen soldiers of the Republic when they met, passed between him and Harry Vere; the latter led the way, and one by one the soldiers descended to the magazine.

This was the trap laid for them.

The entry was so dark and narrow that they could only enter singly.

The boy-adventurers were in ready ambush.

One by one the soldiers were seized, muffled, and disarmed; and when the corporal entered last, and found himself all of a sudden pounced upon and gagged, he beheld, to his consternation the whole of his detachment prisoners like himself.

A torrent of the most abusive oaths and curses saluted the boy-buccaneers as soon as the mouths of their captives were unfettered, but the daring boys, without ceremony, despoiled them of their uniforms, and bundled them neck and crop into a place of close confinement, where they might fume and chafe, and nibble their ragged moustaches off, in their rage at being trapped on board the jaunty vessel whose true character they recognised when too late.

A very short space of time sufficed for Harry Vere and ten of Tom's crew to disguise themselves in the costumes of their prisoners, and complete their make up with moustaches of the shaggiest and most fierce aspect.

Then they descended into the boat, and were silently rowed ashore.

Our hero had contrived to have the officer in his presence, under pretence of placing under his care the commandant's papers.

But the soldier's ear detected the unclosing of the fortress gate, and he listened uneasily as the tramp, tramp of heavy feet passed along the corridor.

Eleven men.

He counted their steps as they passed the door.

Eleven men with bayonets fixed walking in the direction of the magazine.

Presently they halted and grounded arms.

Captain Tom finished putting his signature to the document.

He, too, had listened, and the ring of steel, as the bayonets went past, was grateful to his ear.

He looked up at the officer's face and saw the darkly gathering doubts and suspicions the soldier could not conceal.

But his own features were stolid and inscrutable, as he said, coldly—

"These documents and treasonable papers, then, you will have in your charge, until orders from the Republic relieve you of the care of the fortress."

The officer touched his cap.

He was eager to get away.

"And now, citizen officer," observed our hero, rising, "you will be good enough to parade your men under arms with the exception of those on sentry, in the corridor leading to the magazine, that they may hear the orders of the glorious Republic."

Tom walked to the door, and the officer not daring to go towards the magazine, and satisfy his suspicions, hurriedly saluted and went to assemble the garrison.

There was little light in the corridor; but the ten bayonets gleamed in the darkness, and our hero, approaching the dusky figures, recognized his own boy-followers.

Harry Vere, who had assumed the corporal's post, respectfully saluted him, and said, in a low tone—

"We have no time to lose. A French vessel has been descried; if she enters here we shall be taken like mice in a trap."

"We shall be speedy now," Tom replied; "the officer suspects something wrong—be alert."

He retired to his room.

Tramp—tramp—tramp, came the steps of the soldiery, their fixed bayonets glittering in the gloom —two abreast they advanced, the officer grim and watchful in front.

"Halt! salute!" he cried, as they neared our hero.

Tom acknowledged the salute, and the soldiery passed by.

Hardly had the officer given the word to halt and ground arms, on arrival in front of the magazine, before our hero, with measured tread, came up.

He was in time to prevent the communication the officer was eager to hold with him he supposed to be his corporal.

It was rather a curious scene, this assemblage of armed soldiers in that gloomy corridor of the fortress; their officer, stern and motionless at their head; the ten disguised adventurers, with Harry Vere, in rank by themselves, against the darkest wall; while between them and the rifled magazine stood the graceful figure of the boy-rover—the intrepid princely commander—whose audacious pluck had brought him and his devoted few into the very heart of one of the strongest fortresses of the Republic.

He wore his sword and belt, and his hat with the tricoloured cockade; a bundle of papers was thrust in his Republican coat, and amidst breathless silence he took them forth and spoke in the cold stern tone he knew so well how to adopt—

"Citizen, your Republic charged you with a sacred duty when it left you here with strict orders to guard the stores, which you have suffered to be taken from under your care. Traitor, I denounce you! Yield your scarf and arms to those who are no longer your comrades, and await the sentence of your unworthy negligence. Citizen corporal, arrest him!"

For a moment the officer stood thunder-stricken, but, as Harry Vere took a step forward, he sprang back amongst his men, and drawing his sword, cried—

"Treachery! Soldiers, we are betrayed! These are not our comrades. Present—ready—fire! Shoot down these daring robbers, or the fortress will be in the hands of our accursed enemies!"

A subdued growl of sullen rage ran along the corridor, as the soldiery, stern and solemn, raised their bright weapons, and levelled them at our hero's breast.

Nine-and-twenty glittering bayonets pointed at his body—nine-and-twenty bullets ready to leap from the long dull barrels and riddle his heart, at the next movement of the roused officer.

Death, sharp and certain, seemed looking, then, into the handsome face of the dauntless boy.

Yet in that moment, before foe could fire or friend could interpose before him, the daring boy, with one sweep of his arm, thrust open the door of the magazine, and cried, loudly, elate as by twos and fours his desperate band, with glittering pike, cutlass, and pistol, poured like a torrent to his side—

"Back, all of you! Who lifts a finger, dies! We outnumber you, with a desperate, daring band, inured to danger—sworn to death! Surrender! your fortress is betrayed! Our guns are at your gates! Resistance is madness! These are my boy-rovers, and I am Captain Tom Drake!"

Even as his words were ringing in the ears of the French soldiery, the sullen boom of a gun came across the waters.

Our hero knew the signal to be one of danger.

He sprang to the casemate, and pulling down the iron screen, showed the astonished garrison the ship which they had imagined to belong to their Republic lying close under the fort, with her black banner with its silver cross flying, her boy-crew at their quarters, and every preparation made for an engagement.

The grim visage of the French officer fell as he saw this, but with an angry cry he urged his men to the conflict.

"Defend the fortress with your lives!" he roared. "Let us die gloriously in the cause of our Republic."

Like lightning the sword of our hero flashed from its sheath.

"You shall have your fill of fighting if you will!" he exclaimed; "but mark me, if a weapon is fired, or a bayonet tinged with blood, not one of you shall receive quarter. I will pile your bodies in a heap, and level the fortress with the ground."

He turned fiercely on the officer.

"Madman, sacrifice your own life, not the lives of your men!" he said, as he struck the officer's sword from his grasp, and made him prisoner.

The soldiery wavered—fighting was hopeless—and on Tom's next order to his crew to cut them down if they made any resistance, signified their surrender; and almost before the reverberations of the gun had died away, the fortress was in the hands of our rover and his crew, its colours torn down, and the English banner streaming from the highest tower.

The whole of the prisoners, having been disarmed, were marched outside the walls and bidden to disperse.

The officer was confined in a cell.

The soldiers' muskets were then placed in the boat.

The band of the boy adventurers struck up, from the ship, an inspiriting tune, and our heroes embarked, taking with them the keys of the captured fortress.

One or two trading vessels were lying under the supposed protection of the fort.

These, when the French tricolour had floated from our hero's ship, had hoisted their gayest flags in honour of their fighting acquaintance.

The echo of that gun startled them from their peaceful dream, and looking up they saw the flag torn down, and the English colours fixed in their stead.

But a more rueful moment awaited them when the supposed *Victoire*, with the piratical flag, hove alongside them in succession, and they were boarded by a reckless, dare-devil set of young fellows, who lightened them of their cargo and possessions, and gave them fifteen minutes to clear out to sea.

When he had stripped every barque, Captain Tom turned the prow of his vessel seaward; and as the twilight deepened, they sailed out of sight of the fortress they had so gallantly taken.

Three days after, some commotion was created amongst the British fleet by the rumour that one of their ships had been visited by a strange barque, the skipper of which handed them a letter which ran as follows:—

"The fortress of Renauf is defenceless, and left without a garrison. Its munitions I have captured. If you enter you will find its commandant and officers in the dungeon beneath the magazine. My flag, and the flag of my country, have replaced the tricolour.

"Signed,   CAPTAIN TOM DRAKE."

The commander to whom this letter was delivered sneered incredulously at the idea of the impregnable fortress being taken; and it was not until confirmatory rumours of the flag being seen flying over the empty fortress arrived, that the British autho-rities bestirred themselves, and sent three ships of war to ascertain.

But the story of the daring act had already run like wildfire throughout the French frontier.

The day before the British ships arrived, the French, burning with shame at their humiliation, took swift measures.

The fortress was occupied by a strong force and a French fleet protected it from the sea.

And thus was this important fortress—the capture of which forms one of the most daring exploits in history—lost by the stupidity and delay of the English commanders.

CHAPTER XVI.

FROM ONE PREDICAMENT TO ANOTHER.

THE commodore returned to England to relate the story of his humiliation and discomfiture.

His reception was as cold as he anticipated.

Naval men could not believe it possible for a British ship of war to fail in taking the vessel of the boy-cruisers.

As for Admiral Ellis, the unexpected tidings of his daughter's escape and dishonour, as he deemed her connection with Harry Vere, drove him to frenzy, and he bitterly reproached his brother.

"Had I stood upon his deck," he cried, angrily, "I would have run him through where he stood! A brave officer should have done so. Curses! had you seen my child lying dead at your feet, I should have been better satisfied. By Heaven! they shall be overtaken! I will myself set sail, and see whether they can overcome me!"

Commodore Ellis made no reply to his brother's vituperations. He bowed and withdrew; and the little old admiral, shrivelled up with passion, got his vessel equipped and prepared to set sail.

The Hon. Archibald Gaston had recovered from his severe wound, and was in company with Claremont, Moreton, and Lord Vane, when the commodore, his head bowed with shame, came from his brother's antechamber.

The old naval veteran could see that they were conversing of him; but he took no notice until, as he passed Gaston, the word "coward," breathed in a low tone of hatred, escaped that officer's lips.

Commodore Ellis stopped instantly, and drawing his stalwart form erect, looked calmly upon the young officers and noblemen.

They expected a stormy outburst, but the old fellow was tamed, and though his unquailing eyes glittered, his voice was calm and passionless, as he said—

"Lieutenant Gaston, I heard that word. There was a time when, as you all know, I should have struck you to the earth on such a provocation. To-day I pass it by unheeded."

"Pardon me, sir," Gaston observed, his lips scornfully curling, "I have no desire to escape the consequences. The word I have used I am prepared to use again."

Something of the aroused nature of a lion gleamed from the old fellow's eyes.

Stepping up to Gaston, he cried fiercely—

"And were you to breathe that word again I would stretch you senseless at my feet with one blow of this hand! Do not mistake me, young sir. If I return here disgraced, I am not disposed to bear the impertinence of untried boys."

A deadly glare shone in Gaston's eyes.

He seemed about to make some goading reply when Claremont spoke—

"Gentlemen, no bear-baiting here. Until the commodore proves himself dishonoured, I am his friend. Gaston, be good enough to select your second. Let him name the time and place to me. I will answer for my friend as a brave officer."

"Not so, Claremont," cried the old fellow huskily. "I will not consent to this duel."

"Not fight? Is it the lion-hearted commodore I hear refuse a challenge?" Claremont exclaimed, stepping back in surprise and mortification.

"Distinctly I refuse. I will not fight against my conscience. At a fitting time I will prove to you how a man may be brave when he declines a challenge."

"Why, then, commodore, we must needs believe that your brush with the cruiser-boy has shaken your nerves. Pardon my intrusive services. I withdraw them. Au revoir, sir, till your proper mettle has returned."

Claremont waved his womanish hand; Walpole drew out his cambric handkerchief, and shook it under his nostrils; Lord Vane laughed, and took a pinch of snuff, while Moreton, setting his arms akimbo, stuck his dress sword between his legs, and laughed derisively.

And thus—amidst the humiliating contempt of those whom he could have scattered like leaves had he been so minded—did the old commodore slowly depart.

In one hour Admiral Ellis received a missive from his brother requiring him to appoint Gaston to a command on board the ship in which he purposed sailing after the boy-adventurers.

The letter concluded by stating that the writer was going a journey, and wishing him a brief farewell.

The little admiral felt more warmth towards his stubborn-hearted brother when he read his letter.

He surmised that he had decided on cruising after Captain Tom Drake, determining to fight and take him prisoner.

Such was not the commodore's intention.

He had resolved upon another means of wiping out his dishonour.

For one hour he was shut up in his own room writing documents, which he carefully sealed and addressed.

When all was complete, he arose from the table, and taking a handsomely-mounted pistol out of a drawer, he examined the priming, and slowly walked to the window.

A quiet thoughtful survey he took of the peaceful country beyond, then drawing back a step, he placed the loaded weapon to his temples.

"It is time," he mused. "This act will clear my honour. Now to teach those lordlings that a man may refuse to fight in an unjust duel, and yet not be afraid of death."

A calm, heroic look settled on the brave old veteran's features.

The cold tube touched his brow.

Another moment and the leaden bullet would have traversed his brain, but even as his finger was on the trigger a hand struck up his arm, and the ball went with a crash through the ceiling.

It was Claremont who had saved him.

He had come to see if he could not persuade him to accept the challenge, and had noiselessly entered the room while the old sea-dog was absorbed in his silent reverie.

"Not yet, commodore," he exclaimed, his features flushed as he held down the would-be suicide's wrist. "I understand you now; and by heaven! any one who whispers a suspicion of your bravery shall find an enemy in me quick to avenge an insult offered to a friend. Give me the weapon, sir. There is a law against self-murder, and you shall not break it."

"Claremont," the commodore said, huskily, "I am sorry you have come. When you stayed my hand I had taken leave of the world, and was at peace with God and man."

Claremont led the staunch old fellow to a seat.

He remained with him some time, and only left when he extracted a promise that he would not again attempt his own life.

Claremont's reappearance amongst his young friends was waited for anxiously; but their surprise was great when he announced his intention of championing the cause of the commodore.

His known quickness in resenting an affront convinced them he meant what he said, and as not even Gaston wished to pick a quarrel with him, he was not called upon to take up arms in defence of the commodore's honour.

The little admiral gained a new insight into his brother's character when he heard of his suicidal intentions, and his austere severity relented so far that he prevailed upon the commodore to accompany him in his cruise after Tom.

He had a deeper motive than this.

He knew his brother's unsuspicious nature, and fearful lest our hero might, after all, baffle him, as he had all others who were sent to capture him, resolved to make the commodore the innocent means of luring the boy-adventurers into his power, and bringing Harry Vere to the doom he had sworn he should suffer.

The commodore had formally relinquished his command of the *Amazon*, and on a well-equipped frigate he and Gaston, with the admiral, shipped on the third day after the latter had completed his arrangement for his departure in quest of the boy-rovers and their daring leader.

A well-armed and swift schooner accompanied the frigate, to act as her consort, and receive Tom as soon as he should be taken.

Leaving them to get clear of old Albion's shores, we will again repair to our boy-cruisers, against whom such desperate expeditions were continually fitted out.

There is one among them whose fate it is time to clear up.

Jerry Mizzen.

Our redoubtable and irrepressible friend was left, as the reader will remember, locked in the grim embrace of a grisly skeleton.

How long he remained in that awful grip—whether many nights or days—Jerry never knew; but he seemed to have been locked to that bony frame through hours and hours of horror and darkness before his senses mercifully gave way, and left him unconscious of the terrors of his situation.

An age of torture seemed to have passed when he came back to his senses.

A cold clammy sweat beaded his face and limbs.

The hard cold bones of the skeleton touched him, the dank jowl chilling his shivering cheek.

He was sinking again into a horrible stupor when a mighty hand of iron plucked him by the hair of his head, and drew him by main force from the skeleton's hold.

He heard the clanking bones close together with a snap.

There was a rattle, as if the appalling remains were sinking again to their place of concealment, and, as he sank half-swooning to the boards, a cold awful voice whispered in his ear—

"Rash fool! you escape this time—be warned! Should you again dare to gaze within that chest, you shall be lashed inside alive within the arms of that skeleton occupant."

Jerry was too much benumbed with fear even to try to look up.

His teeth chattered, and his hair seemed rising out by the roots, when he felt himself being lifted out into the darkness, whirled through the air, and sent down a dizzy depth, he knew not where.

When he recovered he was lying amongst the bales and packages of the deep hold.

The air was close and suffocating, and the gloom

THE COMMODORE SURRENDERS HIS SWORD TO CAPTAIN TOM DRAKE.

was so dense he could see nothing about him; but he realised where he was.

He was entombed in the deepest hold of the ship!

Entombed alive! for even if starvation did not kill him, there was no chance of any one descending to that part of the vessel until she put into some safe port to discharge her stores.

For hours Jerry lay in a semi-prostrate condition, pondering upon the fate that stared him in the face.

He tried to conjure up hope, but in vain; there was no chance of release. It might be months ere anyone ventured down there; and then—Jerry shuddered at the thought—his grizzly remains would be found lying amongst the bales.

The weary hours passed away, and the pangs of hunger began to urge their claims.

Jerry had always been carefully solicitous about his stomach, and now he crawled on his hands and feet in the hope of finding some store of food which

might sustain him while he lingered out the few brief days of his existence.

A keen and unerring instinct guided him to some bags of biscuit, and as his reasoning faculties grew less confused he remembered that there was a water tank below him.

It was not difficult to reach, and he soon had an abundant supply of the precious liquid.

So far, then, he was safe from the torments of hunger and thirst, and while he could manage to breathe, the torments of his living tomb were less dreadful.

At all events it was better than being shut up above in the embrace of the horrible skeleton.

Bearing his fate as calmly as he could, after he had vainly tried every means of making his position known aloft, Jerry remained in his durance vile all through the cruise of the ship up to the time of her encounter with Dutch Paul, the captain of the *Yellow Vulture*, when he was sent shaking in his shoes by the liquid fire that came dropping suddenly down his back.

He was in a good position to extinguish the fiery mass; but his natural conclusion was that the ship was in flames, and the prospect of being roasted alive or blown up into atoms through the air was the reverse of comfortable. But at length this danger passed away.

Day and night went by, each alike to him. He slept but little, and could he have seen the haggard ghastly wretch he was, he would have been scared at the sight.

He could tell when the vessel lay at anchor, and it was tormenting in the extreme to wait hour by hour in the hope of a deliverance that never came.

He gnashed his teeth and tore his hair—reason seemed leaving him—and at last he gave way, and lay down to die.

It was after the daring capture of the French fortress, that Bob Hauler, having certain stores to look after, descended with a few mates to the hold where Jerry was confined.

They brought lanterns with them, and the first seaman who entered was scared out of his wits by beholding an unkempt, spectral figure crouched against some immense packages in the gloomiest corner of the hold.

"How—ow—oo!" bellowed the man, starting back in fear, as he saw the uncouth object; "wha—wha—what's that?"

"Where away?" cried Bob Hauler.

"There—there!" echoed the man, pointing towards the figure.

Bob Hauler started forward.

"Halloa!" he exclaimed; "douse my toplights if it ain't Jerry's ghost!"

The sailors stepped back with wondrous celerity. Their proximity to a ghost was not pleasant, and Jerry might again have been left to his fate if he had not suddenly bundled forward all of a heap, and with chattering teeth and palsied jaw cried—

"Save me—I ain't no ghost—I'm Jerry—been starved—locked up here—caught in the arms of a skeleton—ow—oo—ow!"

Bob Hauler took a step forward.

"You, Jerry?—this ghost of a scarecrow my old messmate, Jerry Mizzen?—you? Why, shiver me if it ain't! Jerry, Jerry, old mate, come to my arms—come to your own Bob's arms."

With a wild, hysterical cry, Jerry flung himself into Bob Hauler's arms, and wept convulsively on his stalwart breast.

"Yes, Bob," he answered, "it's your Jerry—been shut up here till his very marrow bones has got shrunk up to a mummy. Oh, lor! ain't it been awful!!"

"Here, take a pull at this," the generous Bob exclaimed. "It's grog, Jerry—grog."

"Grog!" Jerry almost shrieked for joy.

He hugged the bottle to his lips, and took such a long strong pull that his true-hearted messmate thought he would never have relinquished it.

"There," Jerry said, "I'm better for that. Help me aloft, Bob, and I'll tell you all I have endured. Another swig. Hoorah! Jerry's himself again."

The appearance of Jerry on deck drew an eager group around him, curious to learn the cause of his captivity and to hear what sights he had seen.

Jerry did not satisfy them then.

The restoration to light and companionship was too much for him; but in a day or so he was able to be with them on the watch, when he lied to them to his heart's content, and told such strange stories that the oldest salts were outdone in the length of their yarns.

As a sample of Jerry's inventive powers the following account of his adventures may prove interesting.

"You see, mates," said Jerry Mizzen, "I was sent down to the storage for something the captain wanted; and when I got down there I smelt something like brimstone.

"Thinks I to myself there's summat wrong here, I must see into this.

"So I moved to the door of the little cabin where the big box was put, that came off the Barbary vessel."

"Well when I got to the door I was suddenly knocked down by something—though what it was I don't know.

"When I got up and could scrape my wits together enough to see what was going on, I saw a sight that nearly knocked me over again.

"Seated on the floor round the box were five figures playing with dice.

"Four of the figures were skeletons, and the fifth was a very tall, thin man, very much like a Lascar in colour, with a long pointed moustache."

"'Hullo, Jerry,' says he, 'come and have a hand with the dice.'

"I then saw that he was acting like the fellow with the rake you see at the gambling shops.

"I was so frightened that I could not reply, when he took hold of me again, and made me sit on the floor by one of the skeletons.

"As I sat down I saw that his boots were odd ones—very odd ones; and looking up I saw he had something like a pigtail hanging from under his coat.

"I saw it at a glance then; this must be the old 'un himself—though what his little game was I could not guess at all.

"However, when he sat down, he said—

"'Come Jerry—take a hand, seven's the main.'

"'But, skipper,' says I, 'I ain't got no coin.'

"'Never mind coin,' says he, 'I'll trust yer.'

"Then I knew what his little game was; so I thought a little, and then I said—

"'I can't say as I know what game you're playing, show us what seven's the main is.'

With that the skeletons began playing, fast and furiously—my long friend keeping account.

"Bymebye, he says, 'come now, you've seen enough, take your place.'

"So as I didn't know how he might take it I thought I had better begin, so I said—

"'Well skipper, I told you I ain't got no money—what's the stakes.'

"'Well,' he says, pulling a box from somewhere under his cloak—'I'll stake this against your word.'

"As he said this he opened the box, and I saw it was full of diamonds and jewels that glittered and shone as if they was worth millions.

"'But,' says I, 'what's the meaning of "my word," as you call it?'

"'Ho! ho!' says he, 'I'll tell you afterwards.'

"So I looks at the box and thinks what a lot of rum and bacca I could get for it, and at last I consents—feeling very queer over it all the time.

"Well, when I consented, all the skeletons begins a-waggin' of their jaws and a rattlin' of their bones together in such a way that I nearly lost my senses altogether.

"However, I looks one of them full in the face—that is full in where his face ought to have been, and said—

"'Well, mate, enjoy yourself while you're young, but let those laugh that win,' for you see I had just hit upon a plan to circumbendibus the old naygur.

"They then gave a tremendous rattle, and then all became as still as death, while the old 'un moves up to the table and says—

"It will be my throw against yours—not seven's the main this time—and I'll throw first.

"As he said this he took up the dice-box and shook it

"But as he threw the dice on the box I made the sign of the Cross unseen by him, and the dice came up three aces.

"He scowled fearfully, and I thought he was going to tear me limb from limb; but he checked his rage and motioned to me to throw.

"I did so, and threw a two, a four, and an ace.

"When I saw what I had thrown I begins to feel as bold as brass, cos I knew the Cross had licked him.

"So, with that I says—

"'I'll thank you for that box, skipper, if you don't mind.'

"He took out the box and regularly threw it at me.

"'Come, don't be cross,' says I, 'better luck next time.'

"He catches me up at this and proposes that we should throw again for something else, but I puts my finger to my nose and says—

"'Not to-day, skipper, some other time. I'll be after wishing you a good day, now.'

"At this he signs to the four skeletons and they comes up to me and catches hold of me, and were going to carry me off somewhere or other when I suddenly sees the old 'un stand in front of me wery tempting like, so I ups with my foot and makes a cross on his latter end.

"Immediately the cabin filled with smoke and I was thrown heavily to the ground from where I did not dare stir till you came and saved me, mates; and now let's have a drop of rum."

Whether it was that the recital of the awful things he had witnessed below made him continually dry, or whether the horror of the time he had passed in his solitary imprisonment had afflicted him with an insatiate yearning for strong rum, certain it is that Jerry, who had ever been known as a thirsty soul, was now never happy unless in a half-seas-over state.

The grog bottle was rarely out of his hands, and many a stolen visit did he make to the rum puncheons at night, when he could take in a supply with impunity.

This predilection was the cause of his falling into a worse predicament than even his adventure with the skeleton who guarded the treasure-chest, for it helped to put him in the power of a very old enemy.

Tom had run his vessel into port at Rio Janeiro, and Jerry, with a number of others, obtained leave to go ashore.

Jerry, giving his party the slip, popped into one of the liveliest taverns, where he was soon joined by a merry party of sailors, with whom, as was his custom, he made so free that the night was far advanced before he remembered that his time was up, and that he ought to be on board.

With some difficulty he got away from his boon companions, and made his way alone towards the shore.

His gait was exceedingly unsteady—the result of the excessive potations he had taken—and his ideas concerning the number of ships at anchor or the stars over his head were not particularly clear.

Jerry was aware that he had been playing truant, and that the boat having been sent to pick up the men would not be likely to return for his especial benefit.

Besides a punishment in the shape of short grog and extra night watches awaited his truancy. So Jerry thought that if he could get into one of the boats, noiselessly push it off, and row himself to the ship, he might clamber up the bows unseen by any but his mates, who were certain not to betray him.

Nearly all the boats were covered by a tarred sheet of canvas, and the first one towards which he staggered presented an obstacle in the form of a large uncouth boatman, with a massive beard and white glistening teeth, who on being disturbed growled out a furious curse, and as if about to spring to his feet, clutched his stiletto in a murderous sort of way, extremely uncomfortable to Jerry's feelings, who quickly covered him up again and left him to his repose.

He was more careful in peeping into the others, but so many of them had an occupant ensconced inside, like a periwinkle in its shell, or a kernel inside its nut, that Jerry began to despair of getting off at all.

To arouse one of the boatmen and get him to row to the ship was out of the question, as the fellows were such unmitigated thieves that he would have been certainly betrayed in the dispute about the fare.

Jerry found one at last tenantless, and adroitly unfastening it from its moorings he slipped into it and noiselessly pushed off from the beach.

Stealthily as he moved, he disturbed a fellow lying near, who sprang to his feet, and grasping the boat by the prow, in a stentorian voice cursed Jerry for a thief. Jerry had no time to lose; the fellow's brawny throat expanded to such good tune, that he momentarily expected to have the whole body of savage boatmen roused from their slumbers and falling tooth and nail upon him.

Raising the oar with which he had been shoving off the boat, he lunged it straight at the boatman's chest, and sent him flying to the beach with all the breath knocked out of his body. At the same time, the impetus of the awkward thrust tumbled Jerry head over heels into the water as the boat shot out from the shore.

The unexpected sousing sobered Jerry a little; he made a few clumsy strokes, and reaching the boat clambered over the side and seated himself at the bottom, where he sat shivering with the effects of his cold bath, afraid to use the oars lest he should be heard, and expecting every moment to hear the boatmen, alarmed by their mate, come furiously in pursuit.

That worthy, however, had been dealt such an effective coup de grace that he had not once moved since the blade of the oar sent him sprawling on the shingle, and Jerry, beginning to wonder whether that stroke had finished him, peered over the bows and saw that he was far enough away to ply his oars stealthily.

All remained quiet on land, and soon Jerry passed under the bows of the nearest ships. It was still very dark, the stars had faded from view, and the blackness that precedes the dawn of day enshrouded the scene.

It took him a long time to make out his own ship, and when at length he discovered her she was lying so close under the lee of a heavy frigate, that he fervently wished the darkness might continue until he was safely aboard.

Arrived near her quarter, he rested on his oars and took a good view to ensure himself she was the right vessel.

Apparently she was lying in exactly the same position, with her stern facing the town, the roofs and spires of which he could see dimly in the distance; the only change was in the fact of the frigate being so close to her, and Jerry tried hard to come to a correct conclusion as to why the frigate was there now; but tried in vain, his ideas being extremely cloudy and vague.

No one was stirring on board, as Jerry, using only one oar, propelled his boat from the ship's quarter to her bows.

It was as he anticipated. All he had now to do was to get out of the boat and allow it to drift away while he climbed the chain. This feat he accomplished without any further mishap than slipping one leg into the water; but, as no shark was near to make an early mouthful off that member, and he was already too well soused to mind a little more wet, he did not look upon this as any disaster; but, steadying himself on the buoy began to clamber up the iron cable.

The anchor-chain had been so excessively loaded with grease, that Jerry found the operation of mounting it less easy than he had expected; and when, by dint of extraordinary perseverance and agility, he got half up the chain he found himself in the unpleasant predicament of being unable to get any further.

Perched monkey-fashion across the heavy links, suspended, as it were, Mahomet-tomb-fashion, between heaven and ocean, Jerry wishing hearty curses on the zealous hands that had so well greased the cable, gazed up to the bulwarks above him with the conscious feeling that the effort to get so high was beyond his powers, gazed downwards with the equally disagreeable certainty that if he slipped—and to descend by any other means was an absolute impossibility—he must inevitably be maimed and stunned against the wooden buoy, and either quickly drowned or snapped up as a tasty morning meal by some foraging shark.

As if to add to his dilemma, the clouds of night were clearing away, and the light of daybreak—a light that would speedily betray him in his uncomfortable perch—approaching.

How long he might have remained clinging with hands and feet to the slippery chain is uncertain.

He was delivered from his quandary by a sudden inspiration, which induced him to take off his saturated necktie, and by passing it through the links get a purchase by which he was, after an exertion that, cold as the morning was, bathed his face in sweat, enabled to get within reach of the coveted bulwarks.

As he was pausing for the final spring, he heard a sound that sent all his blood, like an electric flame, to his heart and arrested him where he clung.

A horrible misgiving, merging to a fearful certainty, broke suddenly upon his mind, and in his fright he was preparing for a descent at all hazards, when a fiery grip clutched him by the hair—a second heavy hand seized him by the collar, and as a howl of fright broke from his parched lips he was lifted bodily over the bows and brought to his feet, not on the deck of his piratical vessel, but on the forecastle of what he at once saw was an English armed schooner.

CHAPTER XVII.
AN UNCOMFORTABLE LODGING.

To say that Jerry Mizzen's feet went from under him, and that all the breath left his body with the sudden shock, will only express the anticipations of our readers.

Never in his whole life had he been so completely staggered.

The sloop was the very counterpart of the pirate cruiser. Her size was the same, she occupied exactly the position taken up by the *Will-o'-the-Wisp*, and so minutely resembled her that he was not certain he would not have picked her out in broad daylight as the buccaneer's vessel, to whose deck he imagined he was climbing.

Had a half-spent cannon-ball struck him in the small of his back he could not have been more completely knocked all of a heap.

Very roughly he was skulldragged to his feet and enabled to look about him. A broad grin was on every face, and he could plainly perceive that his perilous ascent had been watched the whole time by those who had kept themselves concealed, waiting to pounce upon him so soon as his unfortunate head neared the bulwarks.

If he had experienced no uneasiness at his awkward mistake, the sight of a familiar face which he immediately discovered amongst the seamen would have been enough to make him wish himself on board again.

Andrews, his old enemy, the custom officer, whom he had served such a trick when leading him to the pretended capture of Tom, stood calmly and maliciously enjoying his discomfiture.

Jerry's face grew ruefully long.

The deck of that vessel was too hot a place for him.

He made a sudden bound to the side, with the intention of leaping neck or nothing overboard, but a half-a-dozen brawny tars pounced upon him, and in a trice he was securely bound.

Andrews, who had lent active assistance in binding him, grinned savagely in his face.

"Don't run away from us, Jerry," he said. "You've been on a long cruise, and must want a change. You've tumbled into good hands, Jerry. I'll put in a good word for you if I can. I've been waiting a long time to pay you for that trick of the straw dummy."

Jerry wished devoutly he had burnt his fingers off before he had gone on shore, for then he would not have been in his present plight.

His rueful-looking visage lengthened as his captors dragged him the whole length of the ship, and brought him before the officer commanding the sloop, a young, good-looking fellow, who scanned Jerry attentively, and after a few questions, ordered him to be taken below.

In ten minutes' time the boatswain came to tell Jerry that he would be taken on board the frigate as soon as the admiral had finished his breakfast.

"Admiral who?" Jerry asked, "and what's the frigate?"

"The frigate is the *Thunderer*, Captain Hyde, and the name of the admiral is Ellis," replied the bo'sen, grimacing at Jerry's eagerness.

"Admiral Ellis!—the devil! Then I hope he may choke before his breakfast is over."

The boatswain laughed at Jerry's vehemence.

"I ought to report you," he said, "but you'll have enough without me against you, and you'll get enough without my help."

"Shall I!" gasped Jerry. "You couldn't tell a fellow, now, what he's likely to get, could you?"

"Well, my hearty, you'll get a sound catting as a beginning, and you'll certainly be either hanged or shot directly afterwards. So make yourself easy, Jerry, and all I can say is, that if I've the stopping of the number of your mess I'll do it quick and comfortable for you."

"Will you?" thought Jerry, as the grinning boatswain left him; "you're a kind sort, you are. I hope I shan't want to trouble you, I'm sure. A precious pickle I've got in, all through that infernal carousal on shore. I know'd how they bring a fellow into trouble, they allers do; it's that skeleton gemman that done it as well. Jerry Mizzen ain't been hisself since that night—ugh!"

Jerry was not long left to his reflections.

The boatswain and three jolly tars presently descended to his place of confinement, and escorted him on deck.

Without being allowed to say a word he was bundled into a boat, and taken to the frigate.

Here he was bidden a derisive adieu by those who had brought him, and handed over to the charge of a squad of marines.

Jerry shook himself as a discontented dog might do at this new transfer.

To be skulldragged to his fate by his brother tars was not so repulsive, but to be marched off by a squad of stiff-necked, red-coated "jollies," was extremely repugnant to his feelings, and he eyed them with distasteful and supreme contempt when they placed him in their midst.

They had their bayonets fixed, which was another matter disagreeable to Jerry's nerves.

The little old admiral had descended from the quarter-deck, and with the commodore, Gaston, Captain Hyde, and an Irish peer by his side, stood by the mizen-mast. He was dressed with punctilious care, and his face was savage, sharp, and stern.

When his small, grey, ferret-like eyes rested on Jerry, they seemed to run him through, and our adventurer's knees began to shake unsteadily.

The commodore looked bluff and glum—Captain Hyde was gentlemanly and at ease as usual—Gaston's features were bleared with hate; he looked as if it would give him some satisfaction to be able to revenge himself even on one of Tom's crew.

The corporal of marines gave the word, and Jerry was halted in front of the admiral, whose keen dry visage never changed its set expression as his eyes met Jerry's rueful gaze.

"Corporal, bring your prisoner here," he said, in his harsh, dry tone, "and bind him to the mast."

Jerry was bumped with his back against the mast, and the marines not being able, on account of their stiff stocks and pipeclay, to tie him there, a couple of sailors ran a stout cord round his arms and waist, and bound him fast and taut.

As soon as Jerry was tied to the mast Admiral Ellis stepped forward to question him.

As he did so he was interrupted by the Irish peer—Admiral Lord Killcrew, who said—

"Don't be hard on the spalpeen, Ellis: faith and its meself that likes a good swimmer."

"But," said Admiral Ellis, "this man did not swim out here—he came in yonder boat."

"Yes, but if he hadn't a boat he must have swum," said Lord Killcrew.

At this those surrounding the two admirals were seized with a simultaneous fit of choking, which, anywhere else would have deepened into a hearty laugh.

"Faith, and it's meself that ought to like a good swimmer; wasn't my ancestor, Colonel James Roch, the finest swimmer that ever breathed. And if ye like I'll tell ye what he did."

And to Jerry's discomfiture he began the following story—poor Jerry being fit to drop with cold and exhaustion, and in fact only being held up by the cord round his waist.

You must know (said Lord Killcrew), whose narrative we will divest of its numerous Irishisms, that my ancestor was promised a speedy restoration to his forfeited estates if he would throw in his lot against James the Second.

Well he agreed, and was sent out with the expedition under Kirke, for the relief of Derry, in 1689.

Now by the time Kirke's expedition arrived at the mouth of Lough Foyle, the gallant defenders of the beleaguered city were dropping into their graves by scores.

One day, however, a watcher who had climbed a tall pinnacle, announced a forest of shipping at the mouth of Lough Foyle.

This was the expedition under Kirke.

To the horror of the inhabitants, days passed and the reinforcements did not come any nearer.

What did it mean?

Why it meant that Kirke, being a turncoat was only a lukewarm friend; and he was soon daunted by the heavy guns of Charles's Fort, and the endless lines of musketeers on either shore.

Signals were made by the town expressive of the extremity of its condition, and still Kirke wavered.

He responded to their entreaties by hanging out certain flags, expressive of his kind wishes to the garrison, but he gave no command to his fleet to carry out these views.

At length he decided that he would postpone any attempt at relief until he received further reinforcements.

Fancy this! Thirty ships stored with food and ammunition lying useless within sight of the starving city!

The feeling of disgust which this conduct inspired in the men at length found vent in words, and taunts loud and bitter were hurled at the head of Kirke.

He saw at last that he must do something or his life would not be worth a day's pay.

So he offered a promise of three thousand guineas to the soldier who was willing to convey a letter to the governor of Derry.

There was one who heard this offer; he listened with disdain to the golden hopes held forth for a venturesome envoy.

But as he thought of the brave men and helpless women and children mewed up in the city and about to be sacrificed to helpless imbecility, a bitter smile curled his scornful lips as he said to a brother officer, "Can nothing be done to save them?"

"Nothing," was the reply.

"Then I go myself."

And as he spoke Colonel Roch, for it was he, strode into the general's presence and a few words which thrilled every heart except Kirke's with emotion, announced his determination to swim from the fleet to Derry with the necessary despatches.

Kirke heard him graciously and at once prepared the various documents; addressed them to the heroic General Walker, and handed them to Roch.

The Colonel folded the despatches in a piece of bladder to preserve them from the water, and attached a piece of lead to the packet—so as to sink it if he was taken.

Then, after bidding adieu to his comrades, he was rowed in a small skiff down the lough, in the direction most remote from the city, and far beyond the farthest sentinel of the enemy.

He stepped ashore with his life in his hand, but willing to lay it down for those he had undertaken to succour.

He had marked well the position of the town, and thought if he could move along under the shelter of the trees, he might pass the enemy's sentinels unseen, and arriving at the point of the shore nearest Derry, make a bold plunge into the water, and so reach the beleaguered city in safety.

Two days and a night he beat about in the woods on the shore; now passing close to a sentry, now hearing no noise save the hum of insects.

At the close of the second day heavy clouds began to gather; the wind moaned sadly, and gradually increased to a tempest. The sun went down in anger.

Thick drops of rain began to fall. They thickened, and at last fell in torrents.

The sentry tightened his jerkin around him and ceased his round.

His fellows drove their tent pins more tightly, and then, running beneath the canvas, closed in the flapping drapery.

And now, denuding himself of his heavy upper garments, bareheaded and unbooted, Roch creeps forth from his hiding-place.

He traverses the encampment without observation.

He passes unchallenged one guard after another.

He reaches the water-side. The war of the elements forbids any watching ear to detect a splash.

The swimmer is strong for his purpose, although three miles of the river must now be got over.

The tide rushing up from the lough bears him onward; and long before the sun has glittered on the thin spire of the cathedral—long before his rays have lighted up the enclosure of the Diamond, a band of the 'Prentices have admitted, through the ferry gate, Kirke's wearied envoy, and the tidings he brought are circulated far and wide through the town.

And now one day to be with them.

One day to meet their leaders, and take counsel together.

One day to go among the burghers and confirm them in their resolution.

One day to see with his own eyes the state of the town that he may report it on his return.

One day, and the same day, to refresh himself, and he will leave them.

On the evening after his arrival, at nightfall, Roch is again breasting the waters, and bears with him General Walker's reply.

Again he swims the long three miles in safety.

Again he reaches his lair in the forest unharmed.

But the foeman has been there in the interval, and the clothes he had hidden are removed.

Another messenger, despatched by Kirke, soon after himself, had been taken prisoner, and immediately afterwards gibbeted, and the whole wood is alive with the enemy's scouts.

It is not long ere the pursuers are on his track.

Like a hunted deer he flies away before them, his only hope being the thick underwood.

Into this he dives deeper and deeper.

The briars tear gashes in his uncovered limbs, and send streams of gore down his person.

He has escaped!

He has left his pursuers far behind.

Hark! their voices grow fainter and fainter as they rush away to a wholly different quarter of the forest.

For nearly an hour the weary one remains in his covert, hardly daring to breathe for fear he should betray his hiding-place.

Now he comes forth that he may retrace his steps.

For three miles he passes through the forest and comes again to the water-side.

But, alas, he has lost his way.

Ere he can plunge into the river he is in the midst of a party of the enemy's dragoons.

To their cry of "Rendez-vous" he makes a motion for escape, whereupon one burly trooper lifts a halbert and inflicts a ghastly wound on his head, breaking his jawbone.

The rest grasp at him to make him a prisoner; but his want of clothes saves him, and he slips from their hold.

One effort more for dear life.

Bloody and disfigured Roch leaps into the river; and none are courageous enough to follow him, battered and bleeding as he is.

But pistols are plucked from holsters, and instantaneously a score of bullets plash in the water.

Three hit him in the arm, breast, and shoulder; and his whole frame is convulsed with agony.

Still he strikes out, for he will drown rather than yield.

Offers come to him, across the water, of life, liberty, and rich reward, if he will only deliver up his despatches, but all in vain.

He still persists in his effort. Shots are again discharged at him, but this time happily without effect.

He grows faint from loss of blood, and thinks all is over.

Suddenly he sees that he is being borne near the town.

He makes one more gallant effort, and it is successful.

He reaches land and is taken up by grateful burghers, to faint and fall down before them almost a lifeless corpse.

How long he lay in the swoon he could not tell, but he recovered to find himself in bed surrounded by Walker and Baker and other gallant souls, who were kneeling in his chamber praying for his recovery.

How he recovered and how Derry was relieved after losing 9,000 men in the sallies of the gallant garrison, I need not tell; but ever after my kinsman, Colonel James Roch, was known by the title of "The Swimmer," and now you know why I always like to see a good swimmer.

"Thanks for your story, Killcrew," said Admiral Ellis, "but as the boarder there did not swim, I trust you will not stand between me and my wrath from any sentimental grounds."

"Bedad, no," said Lord Killcrew, "serve him as you please."

The admiral coughed drily.

"Prisoner," he said, "what were your orders when you attempted to play the spy on the deck of the sloop?"

"Yes, you spalpeen, tell us what you'd like to be after there?" chimed in Admiral Lord Killcrew. "Stealing up the anchor-chain, at that early hour."

"Me a-spying you out?" Jerry exclaimed, "why if I'd thought it hadn't been my ship, I'd sooner have dropped to the bottom of the sea, then have tried to get aboard."

"And it's a fine meal for the genteel sharks ye'd have made, if you'd done that same," said the Irish Admiral, with a look at Jerry's full limbs.

"Oh," Admiral Ellis muttered, "then it was by a mistake you climbed the Mercury's anchor-chain. You were left ashore then?'

"I went ashore yesterday, sir, and I wish I'd never had leave, for then this trouble wouldn't have nabbed me."

"Ah! indeed; well, now, sir, look round, and tell me if you see your pirate ship?"

"It's not likely yer honour," Jerry replied, straining at his cords as he looked about him, "that he'd stay here when he smelt a frigate so close."

"No; the fellow has a wholesome fear of us," put in Captain Hyde, "Captain Parker, and myself have chased him repeatedly in vain."

"It's like an eel the way he slips through your fingers," remarked Lord Killcrew.

Admiral Ellis bit his lips.

"Tell me, fellow; for what purpose did he put into this port? My daughter, sir, was she on board of his ship?"

Aye aye, sir, she was; she wanted laying over on her side, and being brushed up a bit."

"Who do you mean, you scoundrel?" cried the excited admiral, "my daughter, fellow?"

"Oh, lord, no your honour—the ship I meant."

"Hum—and who has charge of my child?"

Jerry was about to answer, her husband, but he did not relish the look of the old naval veteran's eye, so he invented a lie for the occasion.

"There's a nice young nigger she always has with her—sleeps with her—keep her out of harm."

"A negro sleep with my daughter!" vociferated the admiral. "Prick him with your bayonet, corporal, and if I lift my hand run the scoundrel through."

"Oh, murder!" bawled Jerry, wriggling from the sharp weapon, "it's a nigger woman I meant."

"Ah, by St. Patrick, that same makes all the difference," cried Killcrew, laughing.

"Yes, yer honour, and very careful she is to look after her well and keep her to her cabin; for you know, sir, she's a devil to

JERRY MIZZEN IN AN AWFUL FIX.

comp with the sailors, and a nice girl she'd be for a cruise if she had not such a shiny skin."

"Oh, by the powers," roared Killcrew; "Admiral, I always thought your delightful daughter had more propriety as well as beauty."

"His daughter," cried Jerry, aghast, as the little old officer's eyes literally blazed upon him; "I meant the nigger girl—oh, lord! marder."

"Hound!" hissed Gaston, who had leapt forward and seized him by the throat; "answer like this again, and I will beat your brains out against this mast."

"Take him away, take him away," ca Killcrew; "its the hanging, and the pink, and the other deaths that's been too mue for him.'

Gaston shook Jerry till his vehemence le very little breath in his body.

The little admiral looked viciously up to the yardarm, and our adventurer expected nothing less than being strung up there and then; yet in spite of all, the effects of his blundering speech were so absurd that he could scarcely repress a chuckle.

The old admiral pounced upon him instantly.

PUBLISHER'S NOTE

PP.86-97 ARE MISSING.

" You are laughing, fellow," he cried ; " laughing at us."

The way the admiral yelped at him nearly took him off his feet, and before he knew where he was he was under arrest and dragged off to bear his punishment for laughing at the admiral.

Jerry was now subjected to a continued cross-questioning respecting the probable movements of his ship, every endeavour being made to frighten him into betraying all he knew. His brief survey of the harbour had convinced him that, under whatever guise he had effected his flight, captain Tom had quitted the place, either the preceding evening or under cover of the night's darkness. He was, therefore, able to answer more readily questions which, had there been any danger to his daring chieftain in them, he would have been slowly pricked to death before he would have replied.

Even as it was he lied most plentifully, and the description he gave of the altered trim of the Boy Cruiser's ship was so striking that Ellis walked to the quarter-deck to see if he could make out through his telescope the runaway Will-o'-the-Wisp.

A long and careful survey afforded him no clue, and with deeper vexation on his withered visage he was stepping down the ladder, when his sword got between his legs, his foot slipped, and he fell with a bump to the cleanly scrubbed boards.

It was a tremendous fall ; all his dignity was lost in it ; his cocked-hat flew one way, his telescope another ; his boots stuck out ; his arms were outstretched, and his whole posture so ludicrous that Jerry Mizzen, forgetful of his position, laughed outright.

The old fellow leapt to his feet before any one could pick him up.

He fixed his wrathful eyes on Jerry, and in a voice which made that individual shake in his shoes, cried—

" Take down that fellow, make a spread eagle of him, give him four dozen with the lash, and place him in the dark hole till day-break, when he shall be hanged at the yard-arm."

CHAPTER XVIII.

A RAFT ASTRAY.

LEAVING the unlucky Jerry Mizzen for the present in his disagreeable pickle, we will follow anew the adventures of our hero, who, having seen the frigate bear into port, had rapidly altered his vessel's trim, and got out of port almost under her very bows.

It was the hour of noon a day or two after their departure from Rio Janeiro.

Our hero, with Zelie reclining at his feet— Harry Vere, Jenny, and Ben Barnacle at his side—sat under a canopy on the quarter-deck, watching the glorious expanse of wave and sky.

The breeze had fallen, and they were lying almost idle on the glistening waters—a few of the white sails fluttered listlessly in the calm, the boy crew stood in groups by the vessel's sides—the guns were tompioned, and a peaceful quiet reigned on board the notorious cruiser—a quiet, that like the tiger's glossy skin, only concealed her deadly powers —the least alarm and her warlike character would have been displayed, and the gentle

looking middies, armed to the teeth, have stood by the loaded guns ready to do battle to the death.

At present her aspect was, as I have said, peaceful enough, and the same quiet seemed to reign in the hearts of the daring boy chieftain and his friends.

Our hero and Ben Barnacle were in earnest conversation, Zelie's face upturned as she listened to her boy lover's words, when Bob Hauler came aft and respectfully saluted his chief.

" Well, Hauler," our hero said, adopting this pleasant manner that helped to gain him the hearts of the men, " you wish to speak to me ?"

Bob touched his forelock.

" Ax pardon, sir, but thought I'd tell you, Jerry Mizzen went on shore just before we made our run from port, and he ain't been seen nor heard of since."

" Left ashore, a most unfortunate fellow— well, Hauler, we shall be back there in a day or two, and then we may find your mate—he'll lie snug enough when he finds we're gone, I'll warrant, especially when he sees the frigate that came to take us."

" Ay, ay, that he will, sir," replied Bob, and again saluting he withdrew, little thinking of the plight the luckless Jerry had got himself into.

The cry of the man at the mast-head presently rang out,—

" Aloft, sir."

" Ay, ay," Tom said. " What now ?"

" Something ahead, sir."

" Where away ?"

" Off the starboard quarter. A good two leagues, I should say."

" What do you make it out ?"

" Looks like a raft, sir, as near as I can make out ; but it goes out of sight every moment."

Tom leaped to his feet, and springing lightly to the rigging, looked in the direction whence the strange object came.

It was some time before he could discern the small speck floating flat upon the water ; but he had no doubt of its being a raft—perhaps with some living occupant on board, whom they might yet save from a lingering death.

He jumped down to the deck, and handing the glass to Ben Barnacle, had fresh canvas adjusted to catch the slight breeze, and saw that the prow of the Will-o'-the-Wisp was guided towards the distant speck.

Zelie, standing beside Ben Barnacle, watched his features anxiously.

" Is it a raft ?" she said, at length.

Ben Barnacle replied in the affirmative as he gallantly gave her the telescope, and turning to our hero said,—

" There's something aboard that looks like a human being, only it does not move, and our course is so slow we scarcely seem even to creep near enough to see."

" There isn't a capful of wind," Tom replied, " but we are catching all we can."

The middies had crowded to the vessel's bulwarks, and were looking eagerly in the distance, while Bob Hauler, and a few of the older sailors, who had a strong belief in sea superstitions, were whistling assiduously for the wind to come.

An exclamation from Zelie caused all eyes to strain in the distance.

"It is a woman," she said. "She is lying as if dead. Something I cannot make out is beside her."

This intelligence increased the excitement on board, and the raft was never lost sight of as it floated nearer.

It was close enough now for the telescope to reveal it distinctly.

Ben Barnacle surveyed it curiously.

"Well," Tom said, "is Zelie correct?"

"She is," Ben answered. "A woman is lying across the raft. She is bound to a spar, and is either sleeping or dead."

"Can you make out the object beside her?"

"The headless trunk of a man," Ben replied, in a tone that made his listeners shudder.

The progress of the ship was tortuously slow, and an hour or more passed away before the raft, with its motionless burden came within bullet range.

It could be seen that it was a roughly formed raft of broken spars and masts.

Lying right across it, bound hand and foot, was a young and delicate-looking female, pale and ghastly as the dead.

Her eyes were closed, her colourless hands corded together, were clasped upon her fair bosom.

The sea gushed over her at every wave, and she gave no sign of life.

Bound to her side was the headless trunk of a man in naval attire.

The head was tied between his hands, but was so slashed and disfigured that the features could not be traced.

Strong excitement was depicted on the faces of the daring boys, and they looked anxiously towards their youthful leader, who now cried, in a ringing voice—

"Lower a boat. Jump in her, Ben, and bring the raft alongside. We may unravel this terrible mystery."

Willing hands promptly lowered the boat.

Ben Barnacle, and half a dozen of the boy crew sprang in.

A few strokes brought them to the raft, which was quickly taken in tow and brought to the vessel.

The order was given to lay to, and then Ben Barnacle, with reverential tenderness, proceeded to unfasten the thongs that bound the pallid girl to the spar.

Death seemed to have done its work, as he bent over her; her soft white throat was marble cold, and her fair fingers pressed into her wasted arms by the hard cords, were blue and corpse-like.

Her eyes were closed; her lips were slightly apart, and as Ben lifted her in his strong arms her head fell heavily back.

She had been rudely and cruelly bound.

A cord was passed round her waist so tightly as almost to cause suffocation, another bound her feet to the spar, its coils deeply imbedded in her soft skin.

Her wrists and arms were bruised, swollen, and bleeding.

With deep fierceness in his heart against the inhuman monsters who had perpetrated such deliberate cruelty, Ben Barnacle swiftly cut the galling thongs and released her.

She was light as a child in his arms, as he sprang up the vessel's side and leaped with her on deck.

Captain Tom and the others met him there.

"Is all hope past?" Tom asked.

"I fear so," Ben replied. "Her heart does not beat; poor hapless victim. I would give my heart's blood to meet the fiends who have so mercilessly used her."

Ben said this with a husky fury in his tone, and a passionate gleam in his dark eyes.

"Bear her to Zeilie's cabin," Tom said; "there may yet be a spark of life. Go with her, Zelie, Doctor Shrike will accompany you, and then, Ben, let us examine the remainder of this mysterious traverser of the sea."

He was over the side and on the raft before Ben Barnacle, who had placed the pallid girl on a soft couch in Zelie's cabin, could return.

There was little to be gathered from the appearance of the raft, excepting the huddled form of the headless man, and the cords which had bound the young girl, nothing was there.

The corpse was evidently that of a merchantman's captain, but nothing was left on him to lead to his identity, but on raising him they saw that his breast had been gashed open, and the ghastly shape of a death's head and crossbones slashed upon it.

The spars and broken masts had been cut down with hatches.

Some bits of cordage still clung to them, in places they were marked with bullet holes, and one was splintered at the end as if shattered by a cannon ball.

Beyond this the mysterious raft gave no clue—no clue as to name or destination, but enough for our adventurers to surmise that those broken spars were the remnants of a merchant vessel, whose crew and passengers had met their fate at the hands of merciless pirates.

"We can do nothing more here, Ben," Tom said, "except commit this dismembered body to the deep; it has drifted to sailors' hands, and shall have a sailor's burial."

Ben Barnacle inclined his head; a hasty shroud was made, and the ill-fated skipper committed to an ocean grave, when the raft was cut adrift and Tom and his followers returned on board.

The only chance of learning the sad details of the story rested with the maiden whom they had conveyed apparently lifeless below.

Doctor Shrike was still with her, but on Tom sending to ask if he might descend, he received word to come.

The faces of Zelie and Jenny were almost as pale as that of the young girl over whom they were tenderly bending, but from their looks Captain Tom saw at once that he was not in the presence of the dead.

Doctor Shrike's skill had brought back a faint pulsation of life to the poor girl's heart; her stained and sea-steeped garments had been exchanged for some of Zelie's softest robes, and while the doctor was administering his restoratives, Jenny and the corsair maiden had dried her rich dark tresses which were before matted with seaweeds and the salt of the spray, and smoothed them over her pale placid brow.

When Tom drew softly near she was lying feebly breathing; her lips parting as if in pain; her eyes half closed, but she evidently neither saw nor heard anything that was passing round her.

Tom took her hand—it was wan and wasted, but even in its pallor, was the well-shaped hand of a lady. Her features were saint-like in their chastened beauty. Tom's heart swelled as he saw the blue swollen marks where the thongs had bound her fair flesh, and his hand instinctively clenched.

Doctor Shrike sidled up to his side, and spoke.

"She has been in a swooning state some days; to that she owes her existence. She is in a semi-stupor now, but her return to life is certain. The medicaments I have used are potent, and for my skill, the fact that she breathes will answer. She is an interesting case to add to the Book of Medicines," the gaunt, vulture-faced doctor continued, gazing with professional pride on his unconscious patient; "but it is questionable whether it would not, after all, have been better to have let her sink into the sleep of death."

"It is our duty to save life," Tom remarked, quietly.

Doctor Shrike gave vent to an amused chuckle.

"To save life," he cried, rubbing his claw-like hands, "he, he! Why, I've seen you slice away at a dozen lives, as if for mere sport. To save life, and the limbs I've seen you hack!—ho, ho!—he, he!—a capital joke! Why, I shall die wheezing at the very idea."

He shuffled off to a corner of the cabin, where he sat chuckling and sniggering audibly.

He had not got over the idea by the time our hero quitted the cabin; and even the calm rebuke his boy chief gave him did not restrain his glee.

Too accustomed to treat with life and death to reveal any interest in the case of a patient, beyond the professional pride on which he piqued himself, he had no sympathy for the hapless girl who had been wafted to them across the deep. But he was nevertheless assiduous in his intentions and skill, and before he left the sufferer's bedside that evening, she was in a conscious state.

He gave strict injunctions that she should not be be asked to speak, and the cabin having been darkened in accordance with his wish, he left his pallid charge to the care of Jenny and the corsair girl.

"Jacob!" he bellowed, as soon as he got clear of the cabin, "bring me the man with his head chopped off, and I will see if he can be brought to life again—he, he!"

He chuckled drily as the long, slim form of Jacob appeared.

"There ain't any man with his head off here," that worthy said.

"The man that came in the raft with his head in his hands—ho, ho!"

"Ho, ho, and he, he," mimicked Jacob; "they threw that fellow overboard."

"What!" screeched the doctor, "threw him overboard! and you let them do that, when I had not even looked at the cut, to see if his head was cleanly cut off or haggled! Get out of my sight, you poison spawn—get out of my sight! To lose such a subject! Get out of my sight, or I'll flay you with this scalpel!"

He made an excited rush at his faithful man, who had only time to dodge back as the ugly-looking instrument shot past him.

The impetus with which the irate doctor flew at his man made him lose his balance, and he went head over heels down the gangway.

Jacob very philosophically looked after his angered master, and having seen him pick himself up, slunk away out of further danger. While doctor Shrike, jumping to his feet, rush furiously to his berth and vehemently cursed every one on board the ship losing him so fine a subject.

CHAPTER XIX.

THE STORY OF THE SEA EMERALD.

JENNY ELLIS, or as we must henceforth call her Jenny Vere, and Zelie proved themselves excellent nurses, and before a week had elapsed the castaway of the ocean was able to sit up and converse with them freely.

One quiet evening, doctor Shrike having granted his permission, she told them the story all were anxious to learn.

Almost her first inquiry had been concerning the headless man who was found at her feet; but though she had shuddered at the recollection of the horrible contact, she did not display that emotion which had been anticipated.

The simple truth was, he was no friend or relative of hers.

The story she told was a singular one. She had been sent to India a few years previous to join her father, a gentleman of property much persecuted by the English authorities, who, under the pretence of his disloyalty, were striving to confiscate his property.

Fearful that they might accomplish at his death what they could not in his lifetime, he sold off the whole of his property and purchased with the proceeds a large emerald of rare size and beauty and valued at many thousands of pounds.

It was a jewel with a history. Its first possessor had, it was said, brought it from the depths of the sea, where it had been embedded.

But its possession led to his being cruelly assassinated by an Indian prince, who coveted the precious gem. He, in turn, was murdered by his own sister, she falling by the hands of her son.

Princes had warred for it, and its last owner a needy potentate, sold it to Andrew Melville —such was her father's name—with strict injunctions to secrecy.

Her father, afraid of the perils he incurred, determined to send his daughter to England with the jewel; arrived there she was to convert it into money, be wedded to a young officer to whom she was engaged, and send for her father, he having an imitation of the emerald made, which he carried about him as if it were the real gem.

His fancied possession of the fatal jewel proved as dangerous to him as the rest.

On the very night before his daughter's departure for Europe he was waylaid, and so brutally hacked with knives that he only lived long enough to enjoin his child to flee the country before his murderers discovered they had only stolen the imitation.

Thus, without being able to see her father's remains interred, she was forced to flee.

But the curse of blood still hung over the fatal emerald.

The captain of the vessel in which she had hastily embarked proved to be a notorious slaver and pirate.

He plundered his passengers of all their valuables, and, in spite of Miss Melville's efforts to conceal possession of the emerald, he dragged it from her bosom.

This was at daybreak.

At nightfall, while the slaver captain strode up and down his deck, cursing the idle breeze, which kept him almost motionless, a large vessel, propelled by double rows of sweeps, came down upon him, and without giving him even the warning of hoisting a black flag, deluged his decks with broadsides of grape and hail, and before he could recover from the shock, he was boarded by a crew of ruthless Barbary pirates, who butchered all they came near.

Their leader, a hideous being, with the head of a skeleton in the place of a human face, seemed literally to glut himself in blood.

He spared none—neither man, woman, nor child—herself and the slave captain excepted, the latter saving his life at the time by dazzling the Death Pirate's eyes with the lustrous emerald, but which the horrible monster no sooner grasped, than, with a fiendish laugh, he flung him to the deck, and gashed his breast open in the terrible manner they had seen.

Expecting every instant her own doom, she had barely consciousness enough to know what happened to her till she found herself bandaged on the broken raft with the slaver captain by her side.

He was not dead then, though covered in blood, but was still hoping to escape with life, when the Death Pirate, amidst the mocking laughter of his atrocious followers, hacked his face about till it was indistinguishable, and swept his head from his shoulders.

It was bound then to the hands of the bleeding corpse, and with her senses swooning, she felt herself drifting over the sea in the grim company of the dead slaver captain, the mocking scoff of the merciless pirates grating on her ears as her senses died away, and she thought she had closed her eyes for ever.

How long she was upon the water she could not tell. It must have been many days—ages it appeared to her; but she was mercifully nearly the whole time in continued swoons, and thus, she believed, escaped the terrible results of her fearful situation.

When Helen Melville had finished her interesting recital, she sighed, and said,—

"That fatal sea emerald has had, indeed, a curse of blood upon it, and not only have I lost a father, but now I am penniless and without a friend."

"Not without friends," Jenny Vere observed.

"Nor penniless," Tom cried, excitedly. "We have wealth and to spare, and you shall share with me; and as for this sea emerald, we will see whether its curse of blood still clings to it. I have heard of this Death Pirate—a grisly being, whom no power can subdue. To seek him shall be our next cruise, and when we meet, by force or stratagem, I will wrest the precious jewel from his grasp."

Singular to relate, no sooner had this resolve been communicated by Tom to his crew, and the ship's prow was turned towards the Barbary coast. than, as if the celebrated jewel had the power of drawing those who sought it into danger, tidings of the Death Pirate began to meet our adventurers at every turn.

But everywhere the story was the same dire tale of merciless bloodshed and plunder.

Every report mentioned a hideous unhuman object, with the form of a man and the head of a skeleton, as the grisly leader of as brutal a horde of ravagers as ever left their task of bloodshed on the ocean's breast.

Tom kept pretty well in his wake.

The pirate was as swift in his movements as our hero, and had the same knack of running from place to place, turning up when least expected, and far from where last heard of.

He brought up with him at last, and, of all places the least unexpected, at Rio Janeiro.

The trim of the Barbary ship had been altered, and she now appeared as a respectable Indian trader.

Her warlike armament was well concealed, and a brace of Parsee merchants—a pair of astute vagabonds and cut-throats, prepared to swear to any villanous lie—were on board to attest the ship's respectability, and render any other service as needs might be.

If they deceived everyone else, they were not so successful with our hero.

The keen perception of the roving boy taught him how to penetrate her disguise, and without exciting suspicion by anchoring beside her, he lay close enough to overlook her decks, and see his suspicions confirmed a score of ways.

He saw many villanous-looking, yellow-faced old scoundrels dressed as merchants, but who, he felt pretty certain, were disguised pirates,

Of their grisly leader he saw nothing, except one night, when, from his place of concealment, his telescope enabled him to discern an uncouth figure concealed by a cloak, hiding even his face from view, stalk along the deck and survey the shipping in port.

And once as he turned, our hero caught sight of a hideously protruding piece of ghastly bone where the face should have been, and then he had no doubt that he gazed upon the fearful being known as the Death Pirate.

When he had assured himself of this, Tom Drake addressed himself to Ben Barnacle, and informed him that he had made up his mind to get on board the corsair ship alone, and on that very night.

"Now it is a favourable moment," he added. "Half their crew is on shore; a great number lie concealed under the hatchways. I shall assume to be an officer of this port, and once in the cabin of this Death Pirate, be he man or demon, he shall yield to me. If I should come to grief, Ben," he observed in conclusion, "attack him without mercy—even here, under the guns of Rio Janeiro."

Half an hour later our hero was rowed ashore.

He had changed his intention, and instead of assuming the disguise of a Rio Janeiro officer, took with him an oriental costume, in which he arrayed himself after leaving the boat, and then, after instituting the necessary inquiries, had himself taken to the disguised ship of the Death Pirate.

He learned all he required to know—the name of the vessel and its supposed captain.

Arrived at the corsair's sides, he was challenged from the deck.

To this he replied in Algerian, stating he had private business with the captain, and was at once desired to ascend.

The person to whom he was introduced as the captain was a knavish half-cast African—certainly not the being whom he sought for.

Tom disposed of him in a few whispered words, giving him to understand that he had a secret warning to convey to their leader, and without waiting for further leave, stepped quietly down to the principal cabin.

His abrupt entry disturbed its only occupant—a being fearful to behold.

A figure attired in eastern costume, armed with scimitar, yataghan, and pistol—the hands horribly long and clawlike—the face, not the face of a man, but the grisly mask of a death's head, behind which glistened two demoniac eyes.

Daring as our hero was, the sudden vision of the hideous being gave him a start; but he instantly recovered himself, and standing between the cabin door and Death Pirate, as the disfigured being leapt to his feet, and grasped the hilt of his scimitar, said in excellent Algerian—

"Pirate, you are discovered—I am Captain Tom Drake! My ship is at hand with orders to attack you and reveal your real character if I do not return within fifteen minutes. Before I return, I require from you the Sea Emerald, now in your possession—I also intend to *see your face.*"

The demoniacal eyes of the Death Pirate glared horribly, and, striding towards our hero, he clapped his hands, and with a hoarse voice cried,—

"You are in a cage, brave bird, and had you a hundred lives you could not escape. The signal I have given will spread our sails—I defy all the ships in this port to stop my course; and as for your crew, we will show them your gory head stuck like a scarecrow above our banner as we pass like the wind."

The Death Pirate's laugh had hardly died away when a tramping of feet and sound of hurried voices convinced Tom how well he had been obeyed.

Like lightning his sword flew from its scabbard, and closing the door, which shut with a spring, he leapt upon his grim antagonist.

There was no need of further words—each knew by instinct the mettle of the other.

Our hero had worn a huge turban and long robe, these he threw off and cast at Death Pirate as he drew a pistol out from his belt and fired.

The folds of the garment diverted his aim, and before he could do more than draw his yataghan, Tom had dashed the pistol from his grasp, and seized him by the throat.

Forcing him back over a gilded piece of furniture, he thrust his knee in his chest and held him powerless, while, with eager haste, he felt for the sea emerald.

His hand touched the jewel at last—it was in a bag over the pirate's heart—but in the act of drawing it forth he paused to snatch at the mask of death which hid his antagonist's features.

This act seemed more to excite the Death Pirate than the expected loss of the priceless emerald; he uttered a cry more like a fiend's than a man's, and with a sudden exercise of strength, broke from our hero's hold.

At the same moment the cabin door was noiselessly opened and the African, who acted as captain's servant, stole behind the daring boy.

Unseen by Tom he raised his deadly stiletto, when the youthful chieftain's attention was attracted by the noise of armed men descending to the cabin, and he sprang back in time to escape the assassin's stab.

It was well that he did so. The stiletto was poisoned, and a scratch would have been his death.

The movement allowed Death Pirate to spring again to the attack, at the same time that a score or more of his armed followers broke into the cabin with matchlocks, swords, and daggers, prepared for a deadly onset on their victim.

Tom Drake felt the cabin floor giving beneath his tread, and he knew that the pirate vessel was moving out to sea.

His danger was certainly as imminent as it had ever yet been; but, furious as a young leopard brought to bay by the hunters, he turned upon his assailants.

One swinging cut of his heavy sword stretched the treacherous black bleeding at his feet; a second struck the helmet from Death Pirate's head; then, with bounding heart, he leapt to the cabin window, and facing the herd of savage pirates cried,—

"Take me who can! Pirate, I am beaten now; but, mark me, Captain Tom Drake will return to wrest that jewel from your grasp, and rend the mask from your face."

Captain Tom Drake!

The merciless corsairs had heard the dreadful name, and, awed by the imposing attitude of the undaunted boy rover, they let the moment slip by in which they might have easily brought him down.

Death Pirate, with a bitter imprecation, sprang to the window.

A stab—swift, sharp, and true, sent from our hero's hand, struck the grisly death's head across the bony brow, and sent him reeling back.

Then arose a fearful crash and tumult—a dozen matchlocks flashed. There was the crashing of shivered glass; the intrepid boy, bleeding and confused, stood reeling in their sight; and as the corsairs bounded forth to slay him, if yet he lived, a cry, whether of defiance or his last death agony, sounded in their ears, and Tom fell backward into the sea.

CHAPTER XX.

OUR HERO HAS ANOTHER CHASE FOR THE BIG EMERALD.

THIS sudden tumult and activity was observed not only by the watchful crew on board our hero's ship, but by the authorities on shore, and all the other vessels in the port.

The noise of firearms, and the sudden movement of the Barbary ship, excited suspicion, and two frigates immediately left to stop her departure, while the cannon from the forts played with a sudden roar.

But the corsair turned suddenly upon them,

and left the marks of her teeth upon the two frigates.

Then she turned her broadside toward the *Will-o'-the-Wisp*, and, as if in sheer wanton devilry, swept her deck with a shower of deadly grape.

The boy adventurers would have tackled her instantly, if Ben Barnacle had not at that juncture discerned his beloved young chieftain struggling, faint and bleeding, in the water.

Restraining the excitement of his impetuous crew, who were burning to cast themselves on the brutal corsairs, he sprang over the ship's side, and swam to Tom.

The dauntless boy was exhausted with loss of blood, and, in spite of his indomitable energy, was sinking when Ben Barnacle flung one arm round him, and buoyed him on the surface.

This timely rescue—which was greeted with loud cheers from the ships in harbour—was the occasion of a dastardly attack from the unfeeling corsairs, who levelled a gun at Ben Barnacle, and fired with such deadly aim, that the huge cannon-ball tore up the water beside the gallant-hearted fellow, and literally blinded him with spray.

Smarting as were the boy adventurers under this new affront—which had so nearly cost them the lives of their idolized leader and the faithful Ben Barnacle—their attention was given to his rescue; boats were lowered, and the *Will-o'-the-Wisp* swung round to intercept the corsair's guns, if she should renew her dastard fire.

She contented herself, however, with merely sheering off, and Tom, in an exhausted state was carried on deck.

He had been hit in three places, and the blood was oozing from his vest as well as down his clear forehead as he lay tenderly supported on Ben Barnacle's arm.

Stricken as he was, his strong young brain could not give way, and bounding erect, he cried, angrily,—

"The corsair—she will escape—attack her; she has baffled me, and I will still have my revenge."

He clutched at his empty scabbard—his sword had gone to the bottom of the bay—but his momentary strength forsook him—a sickly smile flitted across his lips, his cheeks paled, and in a low tone he asked for drink.

Harry Vere brought him a goblet filled with luscious wine, and he drank it to the dregs.

It gave him fresh strength, and gasping wildly for air, he ordered swift pursuit and attack on the Barbary pirates.

Ben Barnacle was still supporting him.

Then one of the frigates ranged alongside.

"Ship ahoy, there!" hailed the captain, in French. "We saw you attacked; if you are much hurt, we can give you help."

Captain Tom Drake hurled the goblet he still held in his hand to the deck.

"Give help to those who cannot help themselves," he cried, hoarsely, "and not to Captain Tom Drake."

The impulsive boy's rash words were ringing in the air as the frigate dropped astern, her commander petrified at what he had heard.

Then our hero's head sank again on Ben Barnacle's shoulder.

"Let me help you below," the faithful fellow urged. "You are seriously wounded. Have your hurts bound up, or this drain of blood will kill you."

"No, no," cried the heroic boy, a hectic flush burning on his cheek; "lay me on deck, where I can see how we gain on our foe. Let my wounds be bound up here; they are deep, but I will deal deeper ones to avenge them yet."

Zelie, who had hovered near her boy hero, fearingly shrinking from his violence of manner, hurried to her cabin and brought two of her softest cushions. These were placed in a raised position on the quarter-deck, and then Tom suffered himself to be laid down and have his hurts examined.

Two of the bullets had gone deep into his flesh, and their extraction was a slow and tedious process, but the headstrong boy never flinched during the operation.

Zelie, sighing as she saw them taken from his fair flesh, took the bits of murderous lead from the doctor's hand, and stamped them under her feet.

"Would that Zelie could lodge them in the Death Pirate's heart!" she cried, her cheeks crimson with excitement and passion.

Our hero took her hand.

"We shall meet him yet," he said, faintly, "and then he shall pay for this."

Helen Melville, who had stood weeping apart, sobbed bitterly on Jacob's bosom.

"It is the curse of blood on that fatal jewel!" she sighed. "Would that I had never told him the story."

Softly as she spoke, Tom heard her, and he clenched his hands in impotent rage. Dr. Shrike, who was afraid he would spoil all his pains-taking in the way of applying bandages, and make his wounds break out afresh, heartily cursed the Sea Emerald, and wished it, with its history, Helen Melville and all, at the bottom of the sea.

Having relieved himself next by breaking a bowl over the thick head of his faithful Jacob, he proceeded to another part of the vessel, where those who had been swept down by the corsair's sudden broadside lay wounded and requiring his care.

The corsair vessel had the advantage of a start, and the peculiar arrangement of tiers upon tiers of sweeps, working like so many powerful oars, greatly accelerated her speed, and night came on before she could be overtaken.

A sharp look-out was kept for daybreak, but the morning light showed no vestige of the pirate.

All that day and the next they cruised, meeting with no fresh adventure, except encountering their old friend the *Arethusa*, whom they eluded as before, without the trouble of firing a gun.

A week was spent in the fruitless cruise.

By that time Tom's wounds were healing, and the fierceness of his mortification at his defeat was partly subdued.

But there was no change in the deep-settled purpose of his heart.

He had sworn to hunt the Death Pirate to the furthermost corners of the earth, and he was of a right nature to keep his word.

Meanwhile Death Pirate sailed on his murderous cruise.

Never a sun set but had witnessed some atrocious deed commited by his merciless crew.

Many a defenceless ship was boarded and taken; many a brave husband died bleeding in his wife's arms; many an innocent child was slaughtered on its mother's bosom.

Such tragic deeds could not escape being known, and the Death Pirate was chased by English ships.

But the terrible corsairs were too powerful to be taken, and each vessel sent out to destroy them was driven from the conflict shattered and beaten.

Running the gauntlet of a whole squadron, the Death Pirate made for the shores of the Dardanelles, and cast anchor at Constantinople.

A merchant lived there to whom he usually disposed of his blood-stained spoils, and having effected a sale of every valuable—including the precious emerald—he re-embarked, and steered for the Mediterranean.

Captain Tom, following in his wake, arrived at the city of the East immediately afterwards, and learnt that the corsair had been, and was gone.

It was the first time our hero had seen the famed city of domes and minarets, and quelling his impatience to overtake the Death Pirate, he determined to pay a visit on shore.

At that time it was death for any stranger to be found within the city gates, and Zelie, who had taught Tom perfectly the Eastern language, cautioned him that it was death to enter a Turk's house unbidden; death to speak to a female; death to even gaze at the face of a lady of any rank.

A massive beard and turban and a sweeping robe transformed the graceful young chieftain into a ferocious Turk, and chiding Zelie for her fears, he proceeded to the shore.

Everything he now saw delighted and interested him. He walked amidst whole lines of shops heaped with the rarest silks and velvets, the costliest arms, and most priceless jewels.

So much wealth was displayed temptingly around him, that he could not help thinking what a splendid booty it would make for his middies to carry off.

He saw many oriental ladies, but their faces were hidden by the thick veil universally worn, and he longed to tear aside the hideous mufflers, and gaze on the fair features of the lovely damsels.

Tired at last with his rambles, he seated himself by a fountain beneath a cypress tree, and, deep in meditation, did not notice that his Musulman garb had fallen aside, disclosing his richly embroidered corsair vest and jacket, or that he had been for some time the object of the gaze of a pair of large lustrous eyes, belonging to a girlish maiden, who had been some time blushingly regarding him, having, almost at the first glance, penetrated his disguise.

When our hero raised his eyes and saw the dark-eyed damsel, he sprang to his feet, and, forgetful of the penalty of his act, suddenly seized her by the hands and addressed her softly in her own language.

Startled by his abrupt behaviour, the girl uttered a slight cry of alarm, and would have fled if Tom had not slid his arm round her supple waist, and with gentle force held her beating bosom to his heart.

"Struggle not, fair one," he cried, ardently "I know it is death to hold you in my arms and gaze on your sweet face. But I am a stranger seeking rest and shelter. Will you betray me?"

The girl tried to withdraw herself from his grasp, and to turn away from his pleading, earnest gaze.

She knew the sin and peril of his act, but his thrilling tones enthralled her heart, and she remained entranced while he drew her fair face towards him, and, putting aside her veil, permissively kissed her ripe lips.

"Oh! sir, are you mad!" she said, in a low musical voice. "If we are seen, the men would kill me and you without mercy. Leave me; and if you are a dreaded corsair, escape before your disguise is discovered."

"Nay," our hero cried, gallantly; "I am too fearless a corsair to flee from the delicious bliss of this sweet embrace. I would not flinch were twenty spears being driven into my breast. Let me hold you thus, and I could endure death a thousand times."

Captain Tom was certainly a most persuasive wooer; the very audacity of his daring gallantry more than won the peerless maiden's heart.

She could see by the symmetry of his elegant form that he was young and noble; and, as he spoke he removed his beard, and she saw how handsome and fearless his features were. She trembled like a captive bird at the thought of the deadly danger there was in that stolen meeting, but his rich, earnest tones charmed her, and she suffered him to lead her unresistingly into the shadow of the tall cypress trees.

"And now, fair angel," Tom said, still holding her to his heart, and gently caressing her, "tell me your name, that I may remember you when far from this enchanted Paradise, for I must soon depart. My vessel lies on the blue Bosphorus, her white sails set, like the wings of a bird, ready for flight."

"Lena is my name," whispered the blushing girl. "I live with uncle, Imaun Bey, a rich merchant, but a bad man. He has dealings with the terrible Barbary pirates, and I fear will some day sell me to those inhuman wretches, if, indeed, his base passions do not doom me to a worse fate."

The maiden's cheeks grew paler as she spoke, and she made no resistance when our hero tenderly pressed his lips to hers in an assuring kiss

His adventure was growing interesting.

Here was a case for interference. A young and beauteous damsel, left to the brutal disposal of a sordid knave, whose vicious passions might carry him to any excess.

"And where does your relative dwell?" he asked, eagerly.

"Not far from where we are; he has a shop in the bazaar stored with rich jewels—he buys them of the pirates," she added in a whisper, as if fearful of being heard.

Our hero picked up his ears.

"Indeed! Do you know the name of any of those pirates!"

"No, I have never heard them named, but I have peeped through the lattice, and once I saw one of them—a dreadful being"—she shuddered and nestled closer to Tom as she spoke—"hideous man, with a horrible skull where his face should have been!"

Our hero uttered an incautious cry.

"The Death Pirate!" he exclaimed. plays into my hands. When—when, was he last here?"

"But two days since. Hush! not so loud, we shall be heard!"

"Forgive my rashness. Tell me, has your uncle, think you, purchased any gems of value of him lately—one in particular, a large emerald of rich lustre and beauty?"

"He has—I saw it in his hands. He caressed it as if it were a gem from heaven—lavished hi; kisses on it—and wears it near his heart!"

"The Sea Emerald," Tom cried, "with its curse of blood! Over his heart! by heavens, he shall sleep to-night with my dagger's point driven to its very core! Lena, dearest, enter your uncle's house. You must admit me to-night by your latticed window, or I will come battering at the door. Your uncle must lose this jewel, or guard it with his lite! Fear not danger. You, too, I will bear hence! Nay, deny me not; I cannot brook control. There is hot blood in my veins, and when it surges like this to my temples I should not hesitate had I to step to death! Haste—I will follow your steps! My disguise will hide my real character. I will be in waiting by your window, and when all is still you must admit me. Oppose me not—flee quickly—do my bidding, or beware of more desperate deeds!"

White with fear, she turned to flee, and our hero, readjusting his disguise, stepped quickly after her.

Once or twice the scared maiden looked over her shoulder to see if he followed, but she never paused in her hurried flight. Passing through a richly perfumed olive-grove, she flew towards the quaint doorway of a house standing embowered amidst the trees, and had only gained a hasty admittance and slammed the door, when our hero was abruptly stopped by coming face to face with half-a-dozen fierce bearded men, their sashes bristling with deadly weapons, and their shaggy brows wrathfully bent, as they glared upon the daring stranger who had the insolent hardihood to follow in the steps of the dark-eyed daughter of their race.

The first glance at the fierce countenances of the armed Turks convinced Captain Tom that they had detected his disguise.

He laid his hand on the hilt of his sword, as the foremost one, levelling a huge dirk at his breast, rushed at him, crying,—

"Dog of an infidel, die!"

"Not by that thrust," our hero replied, as he quickly drew his weapon, and skilfully turned the dirk aside, and with the rapidity of lightning, stabbed his powerful assailant to the heart.

The fall of their comrade was the signal for a furious and simultaneous attack on the part of the others.

With cries, giving vent to their rage, they pressed upon the youthful corsair so determinedly, that it required all his skill and swiftness to keep their thirsty blades at bay, as, step by step, they forced him backwards.

He had no time for thrusting in return.

His furious opponents crowded round him with unsparing ferocity, and though he managed to despatch a second foe, he was already pricked in three places, his disguise was torn off, and bareheaded and exhausted, he was falling back from their continued attacks, when a tremendous blow, dealt him by his foremost antagonist, struck his guard down, and brought him to earth.

In that moment he was defenceless, and at the mercy of the Moslems, for, though he still grasped his sword, the revengeful blow had so benumbed his arm that he could no longer use it.

But his eyes glanced boldly at his assailants.

The thirsty scimitars were raised, and came swooping in the air—a murderous blade was within an inch of his heart—and the exultant shouts of his conquerors already proclaimed his doom—when the swift reports of two pistols rang from behind him, and before he could realize how he was saved, two of his fiercest foes were bleeding at his feet.

While he struggled to rise, a light form passed him—a slender arm was outstretched to grasp the deadly scimitar, which had fallen from the fierce Turk's hand, and as he stood on his feet, he saw the excited features and graceful figure of the corsair maiden, as she nobly threw herself between him and his remaining opponents.

Zelie's sudden appearance, and the fall of their two comrades, was quite enough for these two worthies, and contenting themselves with a howl of discordant rage, they rapidly took to flight.

"Zelie," our hero murmured, grasping the delicate arm of the devoted girl, "I owe you my life! How can I thank you?"

"By hastening from this place," the corsair maiden cried. "We are discovered and betrayed. Signal lights have been sent up from the shore, and already our vessel must be surrounded by the fleet. Every moment is one of danger.

Our hero's thoughts went to the old Moslem and the Sea Emerald.

"Are we alone on shore, then?" he asked.

"A part of your crew have landed. I ran here first—but if the enemy gets between us and our ship we cannot hope to leave the place alive."

"Then for the present, old Imaun Bey, that precious jewel must be left in your care; but when I come again I will rid you of its burthen."

He slashed the nearest trees with his sword, that he might know the spot again, and suffered Zelie to lead him away.

Ben Barnacle, leading a portion of his disguised crew, met him as he left the cypress trees.

"Thank God I see you safe," he cried, a tear glistening in his honest eye, "this noble girl outstripped us all. Her coming was only in time," he added, glancing at the bodies of the dead Turks.

"What news from shore?" interrupted Tom.

"All depends on our speed; the alarm is given. But if we reach our ship we shall not fear to run the gauntlet of the dreaded Dardanelles."

The straits of the Dardanelles are lined with forts, so placed that their artillery is calculated to destroy any passing ships. Many war vessels have been battered to pieces in attempting to pass without permission.

Captain Tom put himself at the head of his men, and at a quick pace they descended to the shore.

It was just getting dusk, and the sentinel from the nearest tower challenged them as they went by.

Our hero answered him in the name of the prophet, and they were allowed to pass to their boat unmolested.

No time was lost in embarking, and pulling away from the numerous *caiques*, or small boats of the Turks, they gained the side of the ship, on whose deck the rest of the boy-rovers were gathered, anxiously awaiting their leader's return.

A wave of the hand enjoined them to receive him in silence, and Tom, handing Ben his sword, gave the word for instant sail.

A fleet of small armed vessels were creeping out from shore, and it was with contemptuous defiance of their power to interfere with him that our hero ordered his own far-famed banner to be run from the masthead.

As its folds fluttered in the air, the boom of a gun rolled across the smooth waters of the Bosphorus, and a puff of smoke came from one of the advancing ships.

Just then a long, bony hand was laid on Tom's shoulder, and the snuffling tones of Doctor Shrike muttered in his ear,—

"I'm ready to attend you, sir. I see they've taken a little of that hot blood out of you. My fine young captain, you'll get a scratch some of these days that'll let a little too much out of your active body."

"To the devil with your croaking!" cried the boy chieftain. "I need none of your help. Zelie can bind my scratches in her cabin."

"So, so," muttered the old blood-letter, with a chuckle; "and there'll be some scratches for me to bind up presently, or I've mistaken the mettle of the fleet that's creeping up to us. Ha!—there goes another gun. Jacob! Jacob! Get the sawdust spread in the cockpit, and set up a skewer for the first head these corsairs cut off!"

CHAPTER XXI.

CAPTAIN ANGEL AND SANDERSON MAKE AN ARRANGEMENT FOR MUTUAL BENEFIT.

FOR awhile we must shift the scene to the home of our adventurer's boyhood.

Honest old John Gregory, our hero's eccentric uncle, is still in the madhouse, to be slowly driven mad by the brutality of his keepers.

Tom's mother had been destined for a more fearful fate.

Captain Angel, in accordance with the dastardly compact made between him and Mrs. Harpy, had her and a faithful servant named Joseph carried off by a tribe of gipsies, with whom the heart-broken woman, ignorant of her boy's fate, was travelling the country, an unwilling prisoner.

Sanderson took possession of the property.

Captain Angel and Reuben Harpy had recovered from the wounds inflicted by Tom, but they were doomed to bear for life the disfiguring scars.

And now that they were freed from the presence of their youthful enemy, the dastardly confederates began to quarrel over the spoil they had so infamously obtained.

It had been Sanderson's hope that Captain Angel would put to sea as soon as he got the ...arts.

Sanderson sat alone at breakfast; delicious viands were spread before him, but they remained untasted.

His meditations were that morning very bitter.

Suspicious of the intimacy between Mrs. Harpy and Captain Angel—whom, now that he was, as he believed, secure in the possession of John Gregory's property, he loathed and hated—and haunted by the demon fear that he would remain and share his wealth, he was pondering how he could contrive to rid himself of his dreaded *confidante*, when the door of his room opened, and Captain Angel, with stealthy, cat-like steps, glided into the apartment.

At that moment, so intense were his feelings, he could have stabbed his comrade in guilt to the heart; but he checked his emotion, and greeted him with attempted composure.

Captain Angel seated himself at the breakfast-table in silence, and began his meal.

The whitelivered rage and chagrin he had experienced at his defeat by Tom had left a demon-like expression on his sinister visage—disfigured as it was by the branding scars on each cheek, where our hero's sword had slashed him.

There was a vicious gleam in his small restless eyes.

He looked up presently in Sanderson's bloodless face.

"My dear friend," he said, "you are dull this morning; one would suppose you were troubled in conscience."

"I am well enough," Sanderson replied, sulkily.

"And Mrs. Harpy—I beg pardon, your wife—she is not with us this morning—we miss her. *Our wife*, eh, Sanderson?"

A choking sensation rose in Sanderson's throat.

"What mean you? Dare you hint——"

"Oh, nothing. Some chocolate, if you please. Thank you! This ham looks inviting. What have we here? Ah, potted shrimps. A favourite delicacy of mine. Don't trouble, I'll help myself."

Sanderson with a murderous look on his bloodshot eyes, had snatched at a knife lying by his plate.

He felt as if nothing could keep him from the other's throat.

Captain Angel, with his usual cold smile, leisurely helped himself, but his keen restless eyes watched Sanderson furtively.

"After all, my dear friend," he said, after a while, during which he had breakfasted heartily, "why should there be any false delicacy between us? Dear Mrs. Harpy is a charming woman——"

Sanderson leapt from his chair.

"Scoundrel! villain! miscreant! if I thought she was your victim, I would plunge my knife into your heart!" he gasped, passionately.

Captain Angel poured himself out another cup of chocolate, and having added sugar and cream thereto, replied, quietly,—

"Sanderson, my dear fellow, you are not yourself this morning. Those terms are not fit language to use towards your dearest friend, and as for that carving-knife, its purpose is to carve ham, and would not be a very useful weapon of attack. So come, sit down again, and be cool."

Sanderson mechanically seated himself.

"Captain Angel," he said, "you have had your price for your aid in getting John Gregory out of the way. I will not begrudge you more gold, if you desire it, before you go away, but——"

Captain Angel paused in his meal, and looked up in Sanderson's face, with an air of the most supercilious wonderment.

"Before I go! Why, surely you do not suppose I intend leaving these comfortable quarters for life at sea? No, no; I'm quite satisfied, and shall remain."

"Remain—with me?" gasped Sanderson.

"Ay, with you, my dear friend; we will have equal shares in old Gregory's property! but, as I am the best hand at arranging matters, I shall take possession of all cash, and manage the estate in the fittest manner."

"And I——"

"Will be my most happy confederate—sharing my wealth, riding in my carriages, hunting in my preserves; in plain terms, Sanderson, I am to be master here, and you must make over to me *all* your possessions."

Sanderson listened like one in a dream.

This was what he had never expected when he began his infamous plans against old John Gregory and the mother of Tom.

"Captain Angel!" he gasped, "are you mad? Do you think I would listen to this monstrous proposition?"

"I do; and more, against your will you shall consent; more still—if I have further opposition, I will drive you forth to be the beggar you are."

Sanderson glanced at his self-possessed accomplice.

He had pistols at his hand; and a demoniac impulse urged him to shatter his taunting confederate's skull, and risk the consequences.

But in the same moment, a new idea occurred to him: he would employ stratagem, outwit his triumphant associate, pretend to yield, lull his suspicions, and have him removed from his path secretly, and for ever.

Captain Angel, pretending not to regard him, but watching him furtively, seemed to read all his thoughts, for a smile flitted across his thin visage, and a diabolical light gleamed in his eyes.

Sanderson raised his glance suddenly.

"I have been hasty," he said, "let us not quarrel, we can doubtless amicably arrange matters."

"Of course we can, give me your hand."

Their hands met, each grasped the other's, as if their friendship were newly patched up, but deadly hate was in their hearts, and a deadlier purpose settled in the mind of each, a resolve to be rid of the other's hateful presence.

They had no quarrels after this. Captain Angel did as he pleased, and Sanderson offered no opposition.

He was too much afraid of his sinister confederate in villainy.

Reubin Harpy had no part in their plans; his mother's guilt could not be concealed from his penetration, and a bitter quarrel ended by his rushing off again to sea, after cursing his mother for her infamy.

The dastardly spoilers of old John Gregory, were thus early disappointed in their hopes of enjoying their basely acquired wealth, and the issue now lay between Sanderson and the cold-blooded Captain Angel, each striving to dispose of the other, but concealing his perfidious treachery under the guise of assumed friendship.

Sanderson was uneasily revolving in his mind the probabilities of his being able to rid himself of the presence of this spectre of evil, when a visitor was announced in the person of Simon Gagg, the landlord of the Blue Lobster.

Simon Gagg entered with a sluggish gait, and bowing awkwardly, stood with his rough fez in his hand awaiting the order to speak.

"Well, Simon," began Sanderson, somewhat testily.

"Oh, if you please, guv'nor, I've jist come to see if you had any orders for I; biziness is werry dull, and the missus is in want of money."

Mr. Sanderson frowned.

Here was another man who knew too much and suspected more.

"Already!" he exclaimed. "Can you have expended that sum I gave you so recently."

"Every blessed screw."

Sanderson knew this to be a lie.

He resolved to test the man and see if his suspicions concerning him were correct.

"I cannot keep supplying you with money," he replied, "for what services you have done, you have been well paid; what more can you want?"

Simon brushed his shaggy hair off his low brow, as he rejoined,—

"Captain Angel told I that I should never want a few shiners if I did what he wished."

Sanderson moved towards the speaker.

"Scoundrel!" he exclaimed, "what do y mean?"

"Oh, it be all right," replied the imperturbable Simon; "I beant gwine to peach, so long as you pays I well. I be up to snuff, though, and knows all about that biziness; 'sides if I hadn't fust found out as how Tom's mammy had eloped with old Joe, nobody would a believed it."

There was a cunning gleam in Simon's eyes.

Sanderson sat down to think.

While rushing headlong into crimes for the attainment of his object, the cares of the future had not troubled him; but now that he had succeeded in his projects, he saw how dangerous a precipice he reposed upon.

Either those who knew so much that he would fain keep concealed, and who hovered like vampires about him, must be satisfied in their inordinate demands, or his life would be harrassed by continual torments and danger.

A bright thought arose in his mind.

"You do not make much of a fortune at the 'Blue Lobster,'" he observed.

"A werry small one," said Simon, showing the whites of his eyes.

"You would not then object to relinquish it, if you were well provided for?"

The man's eyes glistened.

"Lord bless you, no. Missus and I often thought of retiring from biziness as soon as we were well up in cash; but somehow, we never could get it.'

"I will aid you, then. But it will be necessary for you to quit the country."

A cunning smile distorted the villanous countenance of Simon.

"No, thank yer honour," he replied. "I loves the place too well to think of going to any furrin part. Leastways, I shan't go till I am perwided for at his Majesty's expense and sent to Botany gratis. Perhaps, howsumdever, Captain Angel wouldn't mind going?"

The eyes of the two met.

The polished rogue read a hint from the untutored ruffian.

"Simon," he said, "let me understand you. Sit down and speak freely."

"Oh, it's nothink," returned Simon, seating himself in one of the velvet-cushioned chairs. "I wor only thinking that maybe Captain Angel wor fond of travelling, and wouldn't object to going over the briny."

"Would it were so!" muttered Sanderson, "It's as yer honour likes."

Sanderson looked at the man, who had drawn closer to where he was sitting.

"It's as yer honour likes," again said Simon; "and there's a werry good opportunity now. A capt'n, pertikler friend of mine, is up at my house. He's got a ship what's going to Barberry, and mayhap, for a consideration, wouldn't object to taking the gemman as a passenger."

Sanderson looked the cunning rascal hard in the face.

"Accomplish this," he said, "rid me of this incubus, and I will not fail to reward you. Let us understand one another fully. When does your friend's ship start?"

"Two or three days."

"To Barbary, said you?"

"Barberry—fever coast of Africa, where they drop off like leaves. P'raps yer honour would like to see the capt'n?"

"As speedily as possible. Here."

He took from his pocket-book several banknotes, and handed them to Simon, who clutched them eagerly.

"Take these in earnest of what I will do if you serve me in this."

"I'll sarve yer honour all right enough."

"Do, and you will not repent. Return as quickly as possible with your friend; I would confer with him at once."

Simon bowed and withdrew, and Sanderson, flushed and excited, paced up and down the room.

"Let me but once be freed, for ever freed from this haunted spectre—this mirror of my crimes, and I breathe freely. Something tells me I shall know no peace while I am tortured by his presence. Dispose of him, and I will easily settle with this cunning clown."

Chuckling upon the good fortune that awaited him, Simon returned to his house of happiness, and leaving the grey mare to graze in a neighbouring field, entered his habitation.

Simon was not a jealous man; his nature was too coarse for that, and the captain was, as he said, a particular friend of his.

Nevertheless, he felt a slightly disagreeable rising in the throat when his vision took in the view of his domestic hearth.

For there, in the snug bar-parlour, before a cosy fire, and with glasses and punch before them, sat the bold captain and his (Simon's) wife.

The captain had one arm round the waist of the fair Nancy, and with his heels on the hob, and a long pipe in his hand, was laughing immoderately.

Nancy was also highly amused, and her merry laugh sounded in shrill contrast to the gutteral ha! ha! of the captain.

Captain Yates was a thin-faced, sprucewhiskered salt, a fellow apparently of unscrupulous morals, and whose mind was evidently tutored to the maxim that all was fair in love and war.

Simon looked somewhat malignantly on the unconscious pair.

They appeared to have forgotten that there was such a being as himself in existence, and he felt as the unhappy spirits are supposed to have felt, who, leaving the quiet seclusion of their graves, returned to find their loving partners as joyous as though they (the dead) had never had existence.

"It was a capital joke," said the merry sailor, was it not? Ha, ha!"

"Ha, ha!" laughed Mrs. Simon, in reply.

"Ha, ha!" disagreeably attempted Simon to laugh.

The surprised pair turned round.

"Ha, Simon!" said the self-possessed captain, "back so soon, eh!"

"Sooner than you expected," growled Simon, glancing at his wife in a manner that she well understood, and which took the happy colour from her cheeks and the merry brilliancy from her eyes.

"Well, I didn't expect you back just yet. I was just telling your missus of a most laughable affair that occurred in our last voyage. You see, one of our mates fell splash over head and ears in love with a pretty young woman, who had the misfortune to have a husband."

"Oh! said Simon, gruffly.

"Yes, but Jeremy Dindle was not the fellow to be daunted at that. He carried off his prize, and had just got safe out of port, when a lubberly craft ran alongside of us, and who should get on board but this very 'coon of a husband. He'd come to look after his wife; and you may guess what happened. Wal, somehow they got the tar all over him, and stuck wings to his shoulders—made a reg'lar Cupid of him—and dropped him into the sea. I was mentioning how he floundered about in the water, and the pictur' he cut when they hauled him up into the boat. Guess he didn't come after his wife again. But what's the matter? Shatter my beam! there's the pair of you ogling at one another as if you were going daft! Sit down, Simon, and spin us a yarn, or else troll out a song."

"I have something better than either," returned Simon.

"Ah! what's that?"

"Bisness to arrange. Nan, you may go."

Nancy, thus adjured, departed.

"Now, what's up?" inquired the captain, puffing a huge cloud of smoke in the face of the worthy landlord.

"Put that eternal pipe down, and come with me. I will tell you as we go."

"Go where?"

"Up to Sanderson's."

"Oh! What's in the wind?—what we were talking about?"

"The werry same thing."

The captain rose from his seat, knocked the ashes out of his pipe, and drained the last glass of punch.

ZEILA SAVES TOM'S LIFE.

"I'm ready," he said, and the two sallied forth.

Sanderson endured an age of expectancy in the interval that elapsed before the return of the worthy Simon and his coadjutor, and it was a relief to him when the illustrious pair were announced.

A long consultation the trio held; when it was ended, Simon and the captain sallied forth, big with success and importance, while Sanderson, albeit still somewhat perturbed, awaited with less anxious dread, the return of his absent friend, Captain Angel.

That night a jovial party assembled at the

"Blue Lobster;" they were principally sailors, and their convivial jollity, over the freely dispensed liquor, was such that the walls of the old house rang with their merry shouts and boisterous singing, while the very signboard swung too and fro as if in glee.

CHAPTER XXII.

CIRCUMVENTED.

"READ this 'ere *billy-do*," exclaimed Simon Gagg to his friend, the gallant captain, as he handed him a note just brought in by his shock-headed nephew, Tim, a stupid-looking lad, whom he kept, as he said, out of charity to his dead sister, the boy's mother.

"Where's it come from?" inquired the captain, as he took the note.

"From Mr. Sanderson."

The captain opened it and read,—

"Slacken not in your vigilance, night or day. Watch well if he leaves the house at evening, but be on your guard; you have a dangerous man to deal with. I warn you that he always carries a loaded pistol in his pocket; but that you need not fear if your measures are well planned. Remember, I double the promised reward if he is safely secured and away before three days."

"I reckon that's bisness," said the captain, when he had finished the perusal of Sanderson's note; "perhaps we *won't* be cautious. Here, Tim, you young kid, send Black Jones and Long Jerry to me, and come back yourself, I want you."

The shock-headed boy departed, and, in a short time, returned with the two worthies in question, who formed part of the crew of Captain Yates' vessel, the *Civet Cat.*

A short conference was held in that little room at the "Blue Lobster," and, when it was ended, Black Jones and Long Jerry (and their names aptly designated them), took their departure, each proceeding in a different direction.

"And now," said Captain Yates, addressing Tim, "I'll jest trim you to what I want. Look here; take this note, and go up to the hall with it, and when you sees (which your sure to do) that thin hulk which they call Angel sneaking about, put on a look as if the devil had scared you, and make pretend as if to hide this note. In course the slim sarpent 'll want to twig the note, which you musn't let him do, leastways, not then; but jest say, sez you, 'Oh, if yer please, I want to see Mr. Sanderson, 'cos I've got a note here which I musn't let nobody have 'cept hisself. Then, if the old coon *perticklerly* wants to see it, and won't be denied, why I guess you must let him, 'specially if he tips some shiners. which, if he does, you may keep for yourself, I guess you understand now what you've got to do?"

"Yes, I knows," said the boy, grinning from ear to ear.

"That's right. Now go; and hark'ee, young fiery-head, jest give it to anyone else, 'cept that long customer Angel, and p'raps I *won't* break your blessed back."

The boy gave another significant grin, and departed.

"A cute chap, that nephey of yourn," said the captain to Simon. "Guess I'd train him to something if I had him aboard the *Civet Cat.*"

"You're welcome to take him," said Simon, "and a good riddance he'd be."

"Well, that's settled, then. Guess that note 'll do the bizness, or else I'm out o' my reckoning with the slimy varmint."

And congratulating himself upon his sharp-witted scheme, the captain filled his mouth with tobacco, and entertained the host of the "Blue Lobster," and his little wife Nancy, with sundry accounts of his wonderful personal exploits in far off seas.

Let us now see how his *'cute* project prospered.

The estimable Captain Angel was walking leisurely round the ornamental grounds in front and around poor old John Gregory's house.

He was complacently gazing upon the splendid property so soon, by his consummate *finesse*, to be his own.

His mind was calm and unperturbed, for all his plans had been successfully achieved, and there seemed nothing likely to disturb him for the future.

To be sure, he knew that his very affectionate friend Sanderson *did* harbour some scheme menacing his personal welfare, but of what nature he had not yet been able to acertain, and he despised his confederate in guilt too much to let that thought disturb his accustomed serenity.

Only he resolved to watch cautiously and vigilantly.

He presently discerned a stupid-looking boy, looking nervously around him.

He was evidently charged with some mission, the execution of which occasioned him considerable anxiety and trepidation; for, on observing Captain Angel, he became very red in the face, and attempted to sneak off unperceived.

On the *qui vive,* Angel followed stealthily, and waiting till the boy reached a narrow avenue, where they were screened from observation, touched him on the shoulder.

In great confusion the lad turned round, in his fright dropping a letter, which, however, he hastily scrambled after, and regained.

"Oh, oh!" thought the astute Angel; "something is going forward that I must pry into. A secret of Sanderson's, perhaps. Well, boy," he exclaimed, aloud, "what are you doing here?"

"Nothing, zur," stammered the lad.

"Nothing! Well, what had you in your hand; nothing, too?"

"Yes, zur."

"Let me see this 'nothing' which you seem to guard so preciously."

"Musn't, zur; I be told to gie it to Mr. Sanderson, and I munnot gie it to anybody else."

"Indeed, do you know who I am?"

"Noa, zur."

"I am Mr. Sanderson."

"Be 'ee! 'Ee bean't who I woant to see, then."

"Give me the letter, and I will take it to him."

The boy put on a knowing look, half serious, half comic, and placing his finger along the side of his nose, shook his head in a very cunning manner.

"I beant to give the note to ony one but hisself."

Captain Angel drew out his purse, and drew thence a guinea.

"Do you know what this is?" he asked.

"Oh! ay! it be 't guinea."

"I will give it to you if you will give r that letter."

The rustic's face brightened.

"Ha!" said Captain Angel, "I thought I could bring you to reason. Give me the note."

But the boy drew back.

"I'll let 'ee look at 't note, if 'ee gie I the money."

A slight smile flitted over the thin lips of the man of cunning.

"That will do, my boy. Open the note, and here is the money."

In great apparent trepidation, Tim opened the letter, and spread it out, at the same time Captain Angel dropped the guinea into his extended palm.

Hardly however had Tim's fingers closed with a greedy snap over the wondrous treasure, when Captain Angel made a sudden snatch at the letter, and took it from his hand.

Had the captain been there, he would have bestowed another guinea upon Tim for the supremely excellent manner in which he acted his part.

He burst into tears.

He knelt at Captain Angel's feet, and implored him to give back the note.

"Feyther," he said, "'ull beat I to death if I go home wi'out gieing letter to t' Mr. Sanderson."

Captain Angel smiled scornfully.

"Go, Red-headed whelp," he replied; "depart at once, or I will have you whipped as a vagrant for prowling on these grounds."

Poor Tim made a great outcry, and disappeared.

The smile of ineffable triumph which played about the lips of the astute Captain Angel would have been dispelled had he seen the antics of Tim, when he was safely out of distance.

First he rolled over head and heels in a field; then he stood on his head, at the same time indulging in merriment of the most boisterous kind.

Finally, he sat upon a stile, and having long and fervently worshipped the bright coin in his hand, carefully secreted it, and, glancing in the direction in which he had left Captain Angel, placed his thumb against his nose, having his fingers extended, and the thumb of the left hand, with the fingers likewise extended, resting against the little finger of his right.

Having indulged in this elegant salute, he cried out, in the exuberance of his joy, something which sounded like,—

"Oh! my hies, mo-r-i-ow!"

And turning a hasty somersault over the stile, returned to the "Blue Lobster," where, with many grimaces, he poured into the ear of the delighted captain the tale of his prosperous and most consummate success.

"You jolly young kiddy!" exclaimed the captain, as he in his joy bestowed two kicks upon the boy, giving him a dollar to heal the bruises, "you're a stunner, and blow me sky high but you shall come along with me."

The face of Tim lengthened as he heard the captain's concluding words, and he lost no time in making his exit.

Meanwhile the subtle captain remained standing where the boy had left him.

The open note was in his hand.

His features were lighted up with a malignant expression of sardonic triumph.

Again he read the note, which was as follows,—

"MISTER SANDERSON.—If zo be as how 'ee wants to git rid o' tall captain as 'ee sent aboot, cum to neet, at ten, to old yoak, neer middle o' t' wood. I will be there.
"B. YOYLER."

"Yoylar—Yoylar!" muttered the man of schemes. "I know of no such name in the neighbourhood. It matters not, I will meet him instead of Sanderson. Perhaps he does not know Sanderson personally; if so, I will gain some information before he discovers his mistake. It will be hard, too, if he is not bought, and then, dear Sanderson, you shall receive the note, and go there only to fall into the power of those to whose considerate tenderness you would have committed your faithful servant. Get rid of me! Humph! This is, indeed, kind. Ha! my dear, loving Sanderson, you shall find what a gentle lamb you have to deal with. 'The old oak in the middle of the wood.' A lengthy journey. No matter, I will be there."

He carefully refolded and concealed the note.

Then, turning back, bent his steps towards the entrance of the house.

All that day he went about the house as calm and unmoved as if nothing had occurred, appearing to take no notice of Sanderson's evident uneasiness.

He conversed lightly upon ordinary topics, and seemed to avoid those subjects which lay nearest the heart of his friend.

"He suspects nothing," thought Sanderson, as he watched his thin, undisturbed visage. "I trust they are well on the lookout. Would that I could persuade him to go forth this evening."

His persuasion was not requisite.

The polite Angel had an impulse in his breast, which tended to that consummation his dear friend so devoutly desired.

CHAPTER XXIII.

IN THE TOILS.

THE spruce captain of the Civet Cat, which lay at anchor some dozen miles distant, went jauntily about the arrangements necessary for that evening's performance.

He was well aware of the dangerous and subtle disposition of the foe against whom he had to contend.

"Howsomever," he observed to Simon, "I've served my 'prenticeship to trapping wild animals, from a sarpint to a whale, or a tiger's cub to a heliphant, and jist kalkerlate I knows how to kidnap this kiddy, notwithstanding that I reckon him more 'cute nor a sarpint, and a good deal more venomous, and more determined nor a tigress robbed of her young 'uns."

"Pray be careful," said the affectionate Nancy. "You know he carries pistols, and is sure to aim at you, and if he does you'll be killed."

"To a dead sartainty But never mind, my beauty, I'll jist give him a clear spell. We'll have his fangs drawn afore he has time to squint."

"Oh, I hope you won't get hurt; but he's such a dreadful man, I'm so afraid of what he'll do."

Simon glanced fiercely at his wife.

It was not pleasant to hear her express such anxiety for the gallant captain.

But he said nothing, though Nancy coloured to the temples beneath his ferocious look.

"Ah," thought the captain, "I guess I know what he means by that loving look. But p'raps he won't find his claws clipped when he goes to maul her."

Long Jerry here entered.

He was a curious-looking customer.

He was as straight and as thin as a poplar, and his face was long and narrow proportionately to his body.

As for his legs, it was painful to see them when bent in sitting; it seemed that no earthly power would enable him to straighten them sufficiently to rise.

But he was a tough fellow, though seemingly all bone.

He was lithe and muscular, and had arms lank and skinny, which looked as if they would writhe round their victim like the coils of a snake.

The captain rose, and inserting another "chaw," prepared to depart.

"Where's Tim," he exclaimed. "Fetch him here."

But Tim was nowhere to be found; he had not been seen since he had disappeared after receiving the captain's intimation that he was to accompany him on his cruise.

It was plain he had no relish for salt water, and had declined the honour conferred upon him.

"Well," said the gallant cruiser, "I guess we must get in sort o' motion without him."

They left the house, and leaving Nancy to attend upon the customers, departed in the direction of the old oak in the forest.

Arrived there, the captain whistled low, and was instantly surrounded by his rough-looking crew; yet, so well had they been concealed, that not a sign of their presence was to be seen a moment before they had issued forth.

"That's right, my kiddies," said Yates, "be on the look-out for anything in the shape of a squall, and take care when you get hold of the dear gentleman to hold him fast; he's as slippery as a' eel, and if he once gets his fin to that horse-pistol of his, some on you, I guess, will go to sleep without brains. Avast! my luckies, run in for shelter."

The men again disappeared; not the rustling of a leaf betokening their proximity.

Captain Yates walked leisurely round the tree, which he closely examined; it was very ancient, the boughs were withered, and the roots decayed; the trunk was hollow like a shell.

"This 'll do," said he, as he twisted some straw round his right leg, and pulled his lank hair over his eyes, "I guess I'll make a fustrate rustic. Now then, my blind alligator, I'll wait while you walks as innocent as a newborn babby into this nice little trap we've planned for your special comfort."

He seated himself behind a projecting part of the decayed tree, and wrapped himself in his cloak, only allowing his straw-cased leg to intrude forth.

Unconscious of the preparations made for his reception, Captain Angel proceeded to his room as the clock on the staircase chimed in its loud tones the half hour after nine.

He put on a great coat, and arrayed himself in an immense pair of whiskers, and pulling his hat forward, so as to enshroud his face, placed a large scarf round his neck further to disguise himself.

Then he took forth his constant and trusty companions, two long-barrelled pistols, and having ascertained that the priming was all right, replaced them in the breast of his coat and left the house.

It will be seen by these precautions that the wary schemer had not overlooked the possibility of there being danger attendant upon his expedition.

He was on his guard against any emergency which might arise; but it was not that he had any suspicion that he was the victim of a cunning plot.

The boy's fright and acting throughout had been so thoroughly natural, that a suspicion of the real nature of the communication never for a moment glimmered in his mind.

Indeed, he would have smiled in disdain had the thought presented itself that he, the man whose whole existence was a tissue of subtle scheming, and who prided himself upon his faculty of reading through a trick as through glass, could have been outwitted by a simple and awkward plough-boy.

And thus, while his mind was teeming with fresh schemes, and he was congratulating himself upon his success in having intercepted the letter intended for Sanderson, he was actually walking blindly into a snare, of whose existence he would never have dreamed.

Guided by the light of the evening star, he made his way towards the ancient oak.

The starlight fell softly upon its aged trunk, whitening the boughs which spread leafless above it.

He cautiously surveyed the spot.

Not a vestige of a human being was to be seen.

"An excellent spot," thought he, "for an ambuscade. An army might hide here unseen. Ah! Sanderson, when you come hither on a like scent, methinks the path will not be smoothed for your return. But where is this fellow. Ha! there he is," he continued, catching sight of the straw-bound leg protruding along the ground. "A cunning dog, he wishes to scan the enemy before he is himself seen. I must walk round to get a better view of him."

He placed his hand upon the butt of a pistol, and cautiously lifting the boughs, crept round so as to face the sitting man.

So intent was he upon getting round unperceived, that he did not discern a figure, half-hidden by a projecting bush, which, in the deep shade, looked like the projecting branch of a huge tree.

He did not see this, but passed on, and the concealed man breathed freely.

The cautious Angel was now directly opposite the sitter.

"How easily I could take him," muttered Angel. "From my concealment I could pick him off without any trouble; but that is not my object. He sees me not. Would I could discern the fellow's face."

Ah! cautious man of plots and crime, there was much that you did not see at this time.

There were a dozen stout fellows around you, lying beneath your feet, leaning against trunks, which they seemed to form portions of, stretched out along the limbs of leafy trees, and all awaiting the slightest suspicious movement on your part to spring upon you.

There were also two lynx eyes peeping at you from beneath the brim of that countryman's clumsy hat.

More, there was, pressing against the inside of his cloak, the muzzle of a pistol, and there was a finger upon the trigger, which, had you drawn forth your weapon, would have sent you at once to concoct plans in eternity.

Unaware of this, Captain Angel advanced clear of the bushes, and stood in the open space. The man, crouching by the foot of the tree, rose awkwardly, and touched his forelock humbly.

It was as well he did so.

Had he risen swiftly to his feet, it is more than probable that Captain Angel's pistols would have been first to speak.

"Got up remarkably well," thought the captain, as he stood awkwardly before Captain Angel.

"Hope I'm got up better nor that."

Captain Angel spoke,—

"Your name is Yoylar?"

"That be it, zur," said the quondam countryman.

"And you are aware who I am?"

"Oy; 'ee be Squire Sanderson."

"All is well," thought Captain Angel, "then," added he, aloud,—

"As we understand each other so far, it is unnecessary to be beating about the bush. There is a man whom I wish quietly looked after; you understand me?"

"Sit 'ee down, an' talk a bit. Thee sees zum bargain must be made."

"I will well satisfy your avarice!"

"Noa, doant! But what would 'ee like I to do wi' him?"

"With Captain Angel?"

"Oy."

"Remove him from my sight, from my path for ever! Let him be where I shall see him no more, and where his carcase may never be stumbled upon!"

"This be a foine pleace, captain."

"To slay him, yes. Think you that I should require your aid for that when I could put death in the wine he drinks, in the flowers whose odour perfumes his chamber, in the very gloves he wears, in the air he breathes. You are acquainted with men who, if well paid, will aid you to drag him hence. Tear him from this spot, from wealth and luxury, to toil and penury; let him labour—aye, even as a slave, dragging on his weary existence beneath a burning sun, that should blister his aching body—aye, even from head to foot, while his conscience, guilty and damned, should wear his heart out! That is what I would have done! If you can do this, money shall be yours: if not, let us end this meeting."

He spoke with apparent calmness, but in tones that revealed the concentrated fury of his black heart.

All that time those lynx eyes were watching their opportunity, and the word was trembling on his listener's tongue, which should bring from their place of concealment the ambushed crew.

"Well," thought the disguised captain, "how mighty fine he lays out what will be his natteral doom. I be able to do it though."

"Stay! Are you particular as to its being this Angel? Should you hesitate if it were any other?"

He stooped closely to the disguised Yankee.

"De'll a bit, zur."

"Then know that I am Captain Angel, and he whose future I wish looked after as I have said, is no other than Sanderson."

"Hilloa!" exclaimed the supposed rustic, as if in surprise, but in reality uttering the signal agreed upon with his men, "Then, in that case you're just the identical critter we wants."

As he spoke the first word, he placed his hand heavily and adroitly upon the breast of the astounded schemer, grasping the pistol, upon the butt of which that worthy's fingers were closed.

In a moment, ere Captain Angel had time to strive to draw the weapon from the close grip of his assailant, he was seized from behind.

In vain he writhed upwards and downwards and strove to wriggle his slim frame out of his captors' grasp.

He was held by the shoulders, by the arms and legs, and by the head, while the lank, sinewy arms of Long Jerry were entwined completely round his body.

At the instant of the change in the captain's voice, the whole truth flashed upon the mind of Captain Angel; he saw with bitterness, that he was outwitted, foiled, and a captive.

His struggles were futile, for he was held firm as in a vice, while his arms and legs were quickly bound.

He knew it was useless to cry out for assistance—no help was to be obtained in that lonely spot.

So he stood, silent and unflinching, his deadly eyes and ghastly visage only expressing the hate which was welling within him.

He was not the man to indulge in vain regrets; he saw his position at a glance, and the only thing that remained for him to do, was to watch for the opportunity of bettering his condition.

"And now," said the captain, as he unrolled the band of straw from his leg, "let us have a kinder look at you; and here, jest let's take them pretty jewels that's resting agin your heart. Darned pretty things!" he continued, as he presented one of the pistols at the head of his captive, whose false whiskers &c., he proceeded to pull off.

CHAPTER XXIV.

A LONG FAREWELL.

"Now, old sarpent, you're in your natteral skin at last; and now jest say your prayers, for I'm going to pelt yer brains out with this here popgun."

He held the cold muzzle of the shining barrel against the head of Angel as he spoke; the latter neither flinched nor moved.

"Well, don't yer feel squeamish like?"

Captain Angel laughed derisively.

"Fool!" he said, "you are not playing with a child. Do you think I don't know that if you had wanted my life you would have got your fellows to shoot me down without entering into any parley? Put down that toy, and let us depart towards our destination, wherever that may be."

The captain seemed slightly staggered.

"Well!" he exclaimed, "darn'd if yer ain't a cool bird. I like yer, I do; and shall be tarnation happy in yer company; for ye see ye are just going a journey, and that's what we want yer for. What a blessed pair of chums yon and that fellow up at the Hall must be. He's just been and planned out for you what you so nicely sketched out for him. It's a pity to part yer."

Captain Angel looked up.

"It is. Secure him, even in his triumph; let me see revenge on him, and I care not what ensues."

"Won't do, guv'nor. It's all very well, but who's to pay us? No, no; you must part company."

Yates turned to his men.

"Bring him along to where his carriage is awaiting. And you, Long Jerry, jest start on that *other* biziness; and make sartin d'ye hear?"

"Aye, aye," responded Long Jerry, as he disappeared.

No sooner had Angel left the Hall, than Simon entered, and requested to see Sanderson.

Being shown into the presence of the master of the house, he hastily explained what was going forward.

Sanderson rose, trembling with agitation.

"I will accompany you, Simon," he said, as he took from a drawer a brace of shining barrelled pistols. "He must never return alive. I should not live in safety for an hour should he escape them."

"No fear of that," returned Simon, with his peculiar smile. "There be too many of them to let him go. He's walked into the trap with his eyes wide open, like a new-born innercent babe."

Sanderson hastily completed his arrangements, and, leaving the house, followed Simon, who had preceded him.

Simon conducted him to a spot where a shut-up vehicle was waiting.

This was the carriage destined for the cautious Angel when he should be trapped.

Here Sanderson waited, enduring an age of suspense, until he was relieved from his anxiety by the approach of the indomitable captain and his band, bearing in their midst the outwitted captive.

Sanderson slunk aside, that he might not be perceived; but the quick eye of his foe discerned him at a distance, his penetration enabling him to pierce the disguise of the cloak and muffler in which Sanderson was enveloped.

"Farewell for awhile, Sanderson," Captain Angel said, calmly, as he was bundled into the vehicle; "farewell, my good friend. I shall come back again, believe me, when we will settle this little matter."

His steel-blue eyes glared terribly.

Sanderson shrank back in very dismay.

He feared that man, bound and imprisoned as he was, and only the welcome click of the door of the conveyance, as it was locked, roused him from his dread.

He placed a roll of notes in the hands of the captain, and did the like to Simon.

"You will soon sail?" he inquired of the former.

"Within an hour. Sails are flying, and she's only waiting us to be aboard afore she shoots over the seas. Forward, my men!"

The closed carriage started, the men following quickly, and the whole party with their prisoner, were soon out of sight.

Then Sanderson breathed freely.

"So, I am freed of that ceaseless torture.

He has gone. Would that the angry sea might engulf the whole crew, ship and all, within her bosom."

He turned and proceeded homewards, little deeming how nearly a prophecy was his charitable wish.

And Simon returned to his home.

He was gloating over his success.

He held the money, and the captain was gone.

He would now, previous to leaving the inn, settle a few matters with his wife.

He swaggered in, and looked round for Nancy.

She was not to be seen!

The house was empty; and after searching every room, he rushed to the yard, a terrible suspicion flashing to his mind.

His fears were realised by the ostler's replies to his eager inquiries.

Nancy had gone off with the jaunty captain.

CHAPTER XXV.

HOMEWARD BOUND.

THE ships which drew near to engage our hero's vessel, were manned by a piratical set of rascals from all countries, whose practices were to lie in wait for single ships, and plunder and destroy them.

When they opened the ball with Captain Tom, they imagined they would have an easy capture of a very fine craft; and as a portion of their spoil was always paid to the perfidious Turks on shore, no interference was likely to stop them in their murderous designs.

But, to their astonishment and dismay, no sooner had the first volley rattled harmlessly against the iron-cased sides of the daring *Will-o'-the-Wisp*, than they were greeted with a storm of grape and canister, that soon sent the foremost ships reeling back, crippled and beaten.

Tom's crew were in the humour to make quick work of it; and a deadly broadside was poured into the retreating ships.

Then, with a loud hurrah, the canvas was set, and the saucy ship made a clean run from the harbour.

The Turkish corsairs, ruthless enough when they encountered but little resistance, made no attempt to follow their hard-fighting enemy.

Had they done so, it would have been glorious sport to the boy adventurers, as Tom had given orders for them to draw off each ship singly, and sink it by a close broadside.

It was a disappointment to them when they found the corsairs too faint-hearted to give them this pleasure; and they looked eagerly in their young chief's face, hoping he would give the order to run in amongst the pirates.

But the forts were already making a threatening demonstration; and one or two big ships of the Turkish navy were lumbering heavily towards the scene.

Our hero was anxious to make the run of the Dardanelles before it grew too late.

Reluctantly, then, he gave directions to continue their course.

Doctor Shrike, or the vampyre, as he was called on board, grunted out his discontent, as he slunk down to his operating room.

Only one subject had been given him—a fair-faced boy—formerly middy in the *Arethusa*.

He had been stricken to the deck by a spiked shot, and the cadaverous Jacob had already pounced upon him, and borne him below.

"We should have scattered their feathers," Ben Barnacle observed, as he leapt down from the big gun he had been securing.

"Yes," Tom replied, "had they followed us, we could have blown them to pieces one by one."

"I hate craven-hearted foes," cried the hot-headed Harry Vere; "can't we do something to lure them on in a body. I had only begun to smell the fight."

"We must wait for another day," our hero replied. We shall come here again. I must have that jewel," he added, mentally, "though I tear it from the heart of Imaun Bey."

A change in their rig was necessary before they neared the eagle eyes of the Dardanelles forts.

Their disguise having been skilfully assumed, Tom went below to await, with the utmost composure, their passage of a channel fraught with so many dangers as to have been named the "Straits of Death."

The flush of excitement still burned on the young adventurer's fair brow.

His daring soul could not brook defeat in any degree, and he had set his heart upon the acquisition of the priceless jewel, with its history of blood.

His destiny, as he believed, had put him upon its scent, and he felt certain it was his destiny to be the possessor of the famous gem.

Come what might, he had sworn to wrest it from the grasp of Imaun Bey.

For once Zelie did not encourage his desperate purpose.

The Legend of the Sea Emerald had sunk deep in her heart.

She feared that its curse of blood would cling to her idolised boy hero, and with the gentle tenderness of her nature, she strove to turn him him from an enterprise that had so nearly proved fatal.

"There are other treasures as rare and priceless to be sought in the holds of corsair ships," she said, as she bandaged Tom's wounds, "treasures that have not this crime of blood upon them. Surely for one jewel you will not madly risk your life."

There were tears in the bright eyes of the corsair maiden as she softly pleaded.

Tom kissed her tenderly.

"You are growing weak, my Zelie," he said, with a smile.

The proud eyes of the Oriental maiden flashed.

"Was I weak," she exclaimed, in a tone of subdued reproach, "when my hands wrenched the scimitar from your bloodthirsty enemy, and kept them at bay with its point at their hearts?"

"Forgive me, Zelie," Tom cried, "you are a brave girl, but you must not make me a coward. Is not danger a part of my career? Must I not dare death in some form each hour of my existance? Do not dissuade me, Zelie. This jewel has no ordinary attractions for me. I feel that its history is in some mysterious way linked with mine—that it must exercise some talismanic, perhaps terrible influence on my destiny. Though I have never seen it, I feel that I should know it at a glance. It flashes on my sight now, and I seem to see within its brightness a blood-red glare, that has a meaning for me alone, and which I must fathom."

"And it is because I fear so, too," Zelie replied, mournfully, "that I would counsel you to shun it as you would the coils of a serpent, beautiful to look upon, but deadly to touch."

"If it were death," Captain Tom exclaimed, "I would clutch it—if it lured me to the depths of hell, I would follow in the chase, nor pause till my soul snatched it from the infernal fires!"

The corsair maiden, with her cheeks blanched and her eyes streaming, uttered a faint cry, came and placed her finger on our hero's lips.

"Hush," she cried, "you chill my heart with fear—the demon of fate is gleaming from your eyes, and as you speak the wild laughter of fiends ring in my ears!"

The door of the cabin opened, and Doctor Shrike put his hideously grinning face in the doorway.

"Just come to tell you about that boy who was hit with the spike shot," he mumbled, wrapping a cloth close round something his skiny hands held to his vest. "I've got his heart here. He wanted some message sent to his mammy, when he found he was done for, so I thought——"

"Vampyre!" Zelie cried, springing to her feet, and rushing towards the callous-hearted old fellow. "Can you dare make sport of the tenderest feelings of that poor boy? Shame on you, coward! Give me this sad relic, it is not fit your foul hands should pollute it. Begone!"

Impetuously she tore the gory parcel from his claw-like fingers, and before he could mumble out a word, thrust him from the cabin, and shut the door.

Our hero's face grew graver as Zelie, with a sigh, came beside him.

"I feared his wound was mortal when I saw him struck," he said. "Poor boy, he was the gentlest of my crew, as devoted and brave as the most desperate man on board. am sorry we have lost him, Zelie. I will go on deck. He shall have all we can give him now—a sailor's funeral!"

"His noble heart shall not lie under the sea," Zelie cried. "I will embalm it. I have heard him talk to his messmates of his sisters and his mother. He had run away to sea against their will; they shall have this relic, all that is left of him, returned to them."

Our hero made no reply.

His heart was full.

Desperately daring as he was, the softer part of his nature was almost womanish in its tenderness.

He could look on unmoved when some stalwart and bloodthirsty foeman fell, bathed in his gore, but he never looked without remorse on the pale cold face of any one of his devoted boy crew as they lay still in death.

Nor could he repress the feeling, that if he had not led them on their wild career, they would not have run the hazard of such an untimely death.

The quiet form of the stricken boy was brought from below, and placed in its last shrouding robe.

The spike shot had torn part of his fair chest away, but the most terrible-looking gash was that made by the Vampyre in removing the heart.

The boys, who had dearly loved their gentle messmate, gathered around to take a last look at his placid features, so calm and peaceful in their expression, that he seemed only sleeping, and when, amid mournful silence, he was consigned to the blue waves, their sorrowful glance followed his sinking form till it went from their sight, and sank to its lonely grave.

Doctor Shrike, with scalpel in hand, stood cynically watching the proceedings.

But the boys, incensed at his callous behaviour, set upon him in a body, and amidst general execrations so worried him and his cadaverous assistant, that the pair were heartily glad when they could retreat to their cabin, and lock the door upon their youthful tormenters.

Tom slept uneasily that night. He fancied himself in continual chase of the sea emerald.

At times it was tantalizingly near, but as often it eluded his clutch.

He went strange weird journeys, with it dancing in front of him, urging him on like a demon hand.

And at last it was within his grasp, but even as he touched it its green glitter changed to a cluster of red fire, out of which a legion of dancing demons lept.

Then again, it became bubbling blood in his hands, and seemed to deluge him.

And while he looked, the pale boyish face of him they had that day given to his ocean grave, rose before him pleading and white.

Then this too changed, and he looked upon the fierce blood-stained visage and glaring eyes of the huge corsair, whom he had slain when he took the Barbary ship, with Zelie on board.

As it had sank then, so it now sank beneath the dark waters, but, deep as it went, he could plainly see the murdered lineaments, and when it rested at the bottom, the awfully staring eyes were still fixed upon him.

Strange monsters of the deep with shining scales and eyes of fire, swam round the swarthy head, and a thrill went through Tom's heart, when the dead clammy hand of the giant pirate rose as if to brush them away.

This vision faded, too, and one, more awfully thrilling, replaced it.

The scene was the same—the deep bed of ocean, with its caves of coral and floor of gems; but instead of the pirate's features, he saw the pale wan face of his mother.

Minnie Atherton was there, too.

Her arm was outstretched, pointing to his mother's bosom, where he could see a horrid gash—red and widening, with the slender stream of crimson bubbling forth, and tinging the waters around, till they became of a ruddy hue.

Cold beading sweats stood on our youthful hero's brow—in his sleep he groaned and tried to rise.

Presently, the warning look in Minnie's eyes changed to one of terror, and as he struggled to break from the stupor which held him, the red waters changed to leaping flames, and the faces of Reuben Harpey, Sanderson, Captain Angel, and Reuben's mother, rose distorted and malignant.

A wild shriek of agony smote upon his ears—his mother's face sank from his sight—a fearful crash succeeded, and the whole scene vanished.

He gazed on a black, rugged coast.

The sea was beating fitfully against a blackened rock, at whose base lay, cold in death, the form of his beloved Minnie, and bending over her, with her once beautiful features distorted to a fiendish expression, was Zelie, the corsair maiden—her right hand grasping a keen dagger, from which the red drops fell on Minnie's lifeless breast.

Tom saw his own ship next—he was standing on her deck, directing her course towards the fearful coast.

Suddenly, the air grew hot—the boards quivered under his feet—the masts came toppling about his ears—a frightful explosion succeeded, and the ship seemed to strike upon the rock.

He stood alone on his blazing deck, in the midst of raging flames.

With a sudden and mighty effort Tom broke the bonds of slumber, and sprang from his couch.

Standing erect in the middle of the cabin, he gazed wildly around, expecting to see some part of his dream realized before him.

But he was alone and safe.

His lamp was dimly burning, and he could see that everything in his cabin was as he had left it.

His scimitar hung within his reach—his rich apparel lay carelessly flung over a couch.

A goblet, still containing a draught of wine, stood untasted as he had left it on the table.

The ship was in gentle motion.

The waves rippled past the glazed portholes of the cabin, and only their sullen murmur broke the silence of the ship.

All he had seen, then, was but a dream.

Yet why?

A warning!

He could not but feel it so.

Wiping the cold sweat from his forehead, he sat down to think.

His mother's face, so strangely cold and wan!

What could that mean?

Was it that he had so long neglected her?

Minnie—his promised bride—lying pale and bleeding on that ominous shore—the assassin, Zelie, his corsair attendant, bending over her!

Was that, then, to be the tragic end of her fatal love for him?

The bold heart of the daring boy was strangely troubled.

A cold thrill crept over it, and seemed to still its beatings.

Musingly he rose from his couch and attired himself, buckling his sword by his side, and still pondering on his dream.

One face he had missed from all those familiar ones.

Honest old John Gregory.

His kindly countenance was not amongst them.

This thought had barely crossed our hero's mind, when a peculiar sensation stole over his frame, and involuntarily his gaze was drawn to the furthest end of the cabin, there to be rivetted on a vision that made him uncertain whether he was still dreaming.

A greyish mist pervaded that part of the cabin, and out of that mist distinctly seemed to rise the form and features of his uncle, John Gregory.

He only saw it for a moment, but its reproachful look went like an electric shock to his heart.

The vision, too, was so palpable, that the youthful rover uttered his uncle's name and sprang forward as if to greet the worthy old fellow by the hand.

But even the grey mist was gone, and only a cold, damp air played about over our hero's brow.

There was something in all this.

Our hero was not superstitious—he was no coward.

Still there was an unaccountable tremour at his heart, not the quake of guilt or fear, but the thrill of a soul, whose faith was firm in the after world.

He wandered up and down the cabin, trying to find some solution of the mystery; and then, with slow, thoughtful steps, he ascended to the deck.

His crew and officers, whose watch was on, were at their posts.

The ship was making good way through the waters—a clear, star-light sky was over head.

Nothing appeared more distant than any idea of danger; yet it was with gloomy brow and oppressed mind that our hero walked the deck till morning light.

With the first flush of daybreak, Zelie, fresh and charming from her luxurious bath, came from her chamber.

She looked very lovely as she tripped gracefully towards the young chief; but the memory of his dream was vivid on his mind.

He saw in her not the brave-hearted maiden who had risked her life to rescue him, and would gladly have died for him, but the revengeful murderess, steeped in the blood of his betrothed bride; and when she came to welcome him, with the glad light of love in her lustrous eyes, and a soft greeting on her lips, he thrust her coldly from him, and passed her sternly by.

If the corsair maiden had been stung by a venomous serpent, hidden in that hand she had striven to kiss, she could not have sprung more suddenly aside.

All the gay look went from her face; her cheeks grew white and cold; a tremour chilled her bounding form, and with a startled moan she shrank shivering away.

A timid, startled glance she gave him, and then, with her dark orbs swimming in tears, silently and sorrowfully went to her cabin, to weep unseen.

All that day she remained out of sight, but towards evening Jenny Vere, who had tried to soothe her grief, took her by the hand, and led her to Tom's cabin.

Our hero's heart was thrilled with remorse at the sight of Zelie's sad face.

He outstretched his arms, and, with a joyous cry, the corsair girl flung herself on his breast.

She did not move after she had nestled there.

He raised her head.

She was in a deep swoon.

After he had kissed her back to consciousness he told her of his dream.

A strange look settled on her face as she listened, and she entwined her supple arm round his dauntless breast, as if to shield him from some subtle peril.

But when he told her of his vision of her as the murderess of Minnie, the strange look deepened, and a peculiar frozen look settled on her damask cheek.

Tom saw that an icy shiver convulsed her delicate frame.

The next day came, and saw them far from any danger of meeting with their Oriental foes.

As day after day took them nearer England the boys began to wonder wistfully whether they were to make a run to the land of their birth—the land whose flag they had defied, but where they had left friends whom they dearly longed to see.

It was, therefore, amidst ringing cheers that the news was received they were homeward bound.

Our hero's dream had worked its influence upon him, and, regardless of danger, he was determined to visit England once more.

CHAPTER XXVI.

A FEARFUL DOOM.

ARRIVING near Algiers, they were becalmed for a day; but as soon as the wind freshened they fell in with a raft, which had been tossing about for days on the sea.

So its sole occupant, a brawny English sailor, with anything but an honest face to recommend him, stated when he was hauled on board, in a very hungry and exhausted state.

Plied with biscuit and rum by the good-natured boys, he became furiously attached to them, swore he hated the service, and vowed he was willing to incur death in any shape, if he could only be suffered to remain in such comfortable quarters.

Ben Barnacle, who trusted none till he was assured of their honesty, would not allow him to be sworn in as one of their band.

He allowed him to work as an able seaman, so the real character of their vessel was thus concealed.

With this, the castaway, who called himself Noll Garner, and said he had run away from his ship, seemed content.

He proved an easy-going mariner, never straining himself by overwork; in fact, the boys made his incapacity for the true work of the ship a laughing-stock; he was in no ways bad-tempered, and allowed himself to be made the butt of their jokes, and to be kicked and cuffed for his laziness, without manifesting any displeasure.

He had a curious turn of mind had this Noll Garner, and often he might have been seen prowling quietly about, inspecting the different appurtenances of the ship with apathetic interest.

And one day, when the ship was off Malta, this curious turn of mind led him to sneak unseen down the gangway, and explore the passage leading to the powder magazine.

Not content with this, he, in the same spirit of investigation, managed to open the door with a skeleton key, and snugly ensconce himself amongst the barrels, where, seated at his ease, he loosened one of the staves and strewed a quantity of the powder around.

Then, but with a little more trepidation in his manner, he untwisted a piece of prepared rope, well steeped in inflammable matter, and boring holes in the nearest barrels, inserted a strand of the rope in each. Creeping on tiptoe, and anxiously listening for any sound of danger, the skulking villain, whose design was to blow up the ship and its boy crew, took a slow match from his vest pocket, lighted it at one end, blew the spark carefully—very carefully, shielding it with his hand from the scattered gunpowder, and laid it down so that the unlighted end came in contact with the prepared rope.

All was nicely done so far, the train was beautifully laid, the prepared rope was in contact with the barrels, the slow match was lighted, it would burn one hour, and then there would be a bang, and ship, spars, masts, beams, cannons, and cargo, and all, with its bold crew of adventurers, and their dashing leader, would go up with the explosion into the air, and come down again in pieces that could not be put together.

The traitor paused to rub his hands gleefully, and chuckle at his success.

He had been well paid for his dastardly deed—well paid by the old Jew, Israel Shawm, who, hearing with dismay that Captain Tom Drake had escaped his treacherous snare, and apprehensive of the boy's vengeance, bribed this unscrupulous ally with a handsome reward, to effect the destruction of the ship and all on board.

Noll Garner's uncouth visage puckered up in delight as he stepped to the doorway.

Now to ascend quietly.

They were near the harbour of Malta. A plank thrown overboard, he could leap upon it, and in safety witness the blowing up of the vessel and her unsuspecting crew.

Not so fast, Noll Garner.

Watchful eyes are on board the *Will-o'-the-Wisp*—watchful eyes and active hearts.

Such movements were not likely to be unseen by those whose duty it was to protect the vessel against a hundred such dangers.

No. Noll Garner had been watched, suspected, followed, and now, at his heels, were half-a-dozen of the boy-adventurers, who with their youthful chief, informed of all, sprang down the ladder, and, sword in hand, burst into the magazine, as the traitor was in the act of opening the door.

The entry was so sudden, that Noll Garner had barely time to give vent to a startled "Oh!" and open his wide jaws to their fullest extent, before Tom had borne him to the floor, and while his heel crushed out the lighted match, forced his sword point an inch into the ruffian's throat.

He yelled in the wildest terror as Tom pricked him again and again.

Then the boys rushed into the magazine, and the shaking wretch was in a trice bound and dragged from the place.

The discomfitted traitor shook in every limb. His eyes rolled wildly on his captors, as they carried him on deck.

His tongue, parched and swollen with fear, protruded from his mouth.

In feeble palsied tones he mumbled for mercy—implored him to stop the bleeding from his coward throat.

Of course a deaf ear was turned to his pleadings, and quaking at the prospect of his dreadful fate, he was flung to his knees on the forecastle.

He had heard terrible rumours of the boy-cruiser's ruthlessness—of the tortures they inflicted on their prisoners.

What could he expect but the worst as his fate?

It was not without coercive persuasions that the Jew had induced him to attempt the hazardous enterprise—and now his most horrible anticipations were realised.

The carrying out of his sentence alone remained.

Would he be shot?

Would he be slowly hanged!

Would he be cast into boiling tar?

His eyes glared frenziedly around.

No sign of Captain Tom.

One man approached him—the vampire, Doctor Shrike.

He came with the steady step of the executioner, and after him came his gaunt attendant, Jacob.

Noll Garner howled in agony.

The vampire's eyes, piercing like red-hot gimlets, were fixed upon him.

He strode up beside the culprit, and took forth a case of instruments.

"So, so," he began, "this is the fine young man who wanted to blow us all up into the air. Soul of Galen! what hot brains he must have—Jacob!"

As his assistant approached, the vampire pulled off Noll Garner's cap.

His claw-like fingers fastened themselves in the fellow's shaggy hair, and Noll Garner gave a howl of agony.

"Take this nightcap, Jacob," said the imperturbable doctor; "they'll bring him a warmer one directly. Ho, ho, ho, he, he!—blow up the ship, oho, he, he!"

The vampire chuckled.

He still had his fingers on the traitor's hair Slowly he began to clip.

Clip, clip, clip.

The shaggy hair began to fall to the deck. Good God! was he to be scalped alive?

He tried to escape the torturing scissors.

They seemed red hot.

But the middies held him firmly, and, in a short time, his hair was cropped close.

Then the vampire began a process of scraping, which seemed to tear off his scalp at every draw.

It was horribly torturing.

Huge drops of sweat poured down his quivering cheeks.

"Mercy, mercy!" he bellowed. "I am not tried yet."

"Bring the nightcap, Jacob. We shall have him tried. Ho, ho, oho!—blow up the ship—ho, ho, ho!"

The vampire chuckled, and laid down his scraping-iron.

The scalp of his victim was smooth as a shell.

But every pore was open and full of agony.

He tried to surmise what the "nightcap" could be.

Some fearful torture, he did not doubt, to which the vampire so jocularly alluded.

He was not long in doubt.

Jacob appeared, taking from the hands of a sailor a metal pan full of steaming hot tar.

That was the nightcap.

The craven wretch shrieked for mercy when he saw it.

His knees sank under him.

Terror convulsed his livid cheeks.

The vampire enjoyed the terror of his victim.

Slowly and remorselessly he went on with the punishment.

Slowly he poured the hot tar on the sensitive scalp of the ruffian, paying no heed to his cries and struggles, till the punishment was complete, and Noll Garner lay senseless, huddled, and convulsed.

Then the vampire said, drily, and with a low chuckle,—

"Put the smelling-bottle to his nose, Jacob.'"

No one saw what it was the second of those callous tormentors applied.

But its effect was thrilling.

It no sooner touched the ruffian's nostrils, than he broke from his swoon of agony, and leapt bolt upright.

His eyes were starting from their sockets, his teeth chattered audibly, his bondaged hands clenched till the nails pierced the flesh, his whole body quivered in a fearful tremor.

The vampire coughed and chuckled as he sidled away.

His chosen part of the punishment was accomplished.

All that remained now was speedily done.

Four of Tom's crew bound the shaking wretch to a plank, and he was dropped over the side.

They heard a horrible cry, as the cool waters hissed over the scalding tar; then the plank righted itself, and the convulsed visage, with its starting eyeballs, rose above the waves.

Slowly it went towards the harbour with its tortured burthen, and the gallant bark of the boy-adventurers, escaped from the treacherous peril, sailed gracefully on her way.

The punishment of the traitor was a terrible one, but his meditated crime sent out mercy from every heart.

CHAPTER XXVII.

SHRIKE AND JACOB.

It was the vampire Shrike who had devised the punishment for the traitor.

He had begged permission to be his judge, and carry out the sentence, and our hero, merely stipulating that he should not take the wretch's life, gave him over to his tender mercies.

When the tortured rascal had been hurled overboard, Doctor Shrike and his lank assistant went down to their cabin, chuckling gleefully over the torments they had made their prisoner endure, and little thinking that the boys had determined to serve them out, and were already devising a plan to be revenged on the pair for their callous conduct towards the poor middy, killed by the Turkish corsairs.

A favourable opportunity did not present itself to the brave-hearted boys till the ship's arrival at Gibraltar, at which our hero touched

to get, from a trusted agent there, all letters and information from England.

There were a great many communications awaiting him—letters informing him of the intentions of the authorities to take him at any risk, and warning him of the plans by which they hoped to effect their object.

These Tom put aside with contemptuous indifference.

He had defied the authorities too often to regard their attempt to capture him.

Several letters from Minnie Atherton were there; letters couched in the tenderest language, and breathing the warmest love for him.

The last one he took up, in her fair handwriting, and which bore the latest date, made his cheeks flush hot with anger, and caused his hand to instinctively clutch his sword.

It ran as follows:—

"My dear darling Tom, I know not whether you will receive this letter, for Lady Castlemaine has openly turned against me because I have refused to forsake you; has shut me up in this lonely place by myself, and set so close a watch upon my actions, that I fear the discovery of my attempt to send you this may result in my being removed to some place where you will never find me.

"She wishes me to marry an Irish nobleman, called Lord Killcrew, and has made him promise that he will have you taken and tried, and executed, unless I become his wife.

"And that dreadful man Sanderson, and your cousin, Reuben Harpy, have been here. I overheard their interview. Dear Tom, you cannot think what wicked things they have done.

"They have shut up poor uncle Gregory in a madhouse, and all they want now is to find his will, in which I have discovered he has made you his heir. They have tried to make him confess where he has put it, so that you may never come into the property, and I am fearful they will kill him if he does not tell.

"Dear Tom, if you could come and rescue me from this dreadful place, I think I could describe where the madhouse is, and then you and your brave people could get in and help your poor old uncle out before they cruelly beat him to death.

"But you must disguise yourself, for so many persons are ready to betray you, and get the reward. Besides all these enemies—but you are so brave I should not mind your coming here—although Lady Castlemaine did try to persuade me to get you to come here, that she might have soldiers in ambush to capture you.

"She has cruelly used me for refusing such a wicked plot, and has told me that I shall be made to marry Lord Killcrew, whether I consent or no. So, dearest Tom, if you can come and help me away from their power I shall be safe, but if I am left much longer here, you may never find me, and I would sooner die than have you forsake me or love another.'"

The letter concluded with a fervent appeal to him to hasten to her deliverance; there was a postscript, too, which told him she had just been visited by Lady Castlemaine, who had striven, by every species of threats and ill-usage, to get her consent to the hated marriage.

This part of the missive was blotted and steeped in tears, and a fierce light gleamed in our hero's eyes as the thought of his darling Minnie, imprisoned, and at the mercy of such inhuman relations.

Giving his agents hasty instructions, he abruptly took his departure and repaired to his ship, to give immediate orders for all sails to be spread for a speedy run to England.

But on setting his foot on deck he found himself amidst a scene of wild confusion, a scene which had its origin in the tricks the boys had in his absence played upon the vampire and his cadaverous-faced assistant, and the nature of which we will now explain.

Our adventurers had little affection for the blood-letting old vampire who was doctor on board their vessel.

Fearless, as brave-hearted English boys ever are, they regarded with a shrinking repugnance the hour that might place them, either through sickness or wounds, under the hands of Dr. Shrike.

True, the old fellow was possessed of wondrous skill, and had brought many of them from the jaws of death, but it was the cynical sinister way he had of going about his business, and his chuckling manner of boasting they would yet need his services, that made the devil-may-care middies of Tom's crew loathe both him and his cadaverous assistant.

Ready and ripe for mischief at any time, they neglected no opportunity of making the pair the butt of their wilful pranks—pranks, to do the boys justice, played good naturedly hitherto; but his conduct in respect of their poor-stricken messmate had been so revolting, that one and all had made up their minds to play a trick upon him he should remember for many a day.

Our hero had no sooner gone on shore, than half-a-dozen middies slipped below to the doctor's quarters, and having busied themselves, there unseen, stole cautiously on deck, where their messmates were doing their portion of the programme, by surrounding the vampire and Jacob, and pelting them from deck to deck.

Old Dr. Shrike's thin hard visage was screwed up into very evil puckers, as he tried to shake off his numerous assailants, while poor Jacob, whose long limbs and body ached with the merciless way in which he was pulled about, implored the boys to desist, and finding prayers of no avail, threatened them with what he and the doctor would do for them when they came under his hands.

This only made the boys worse, and the gaunt-faced confederates were at length driven below.

Here the boys made no attempt to follow them.

It was no part of their plan that they should do so.

Dr. Shrike went down the steps in a very stealthy and malignant way.

Jacob followed him, rubbing his long back, bruised and shaken by his young tormentors.

The vampire was half-way down, when the step on which he was softly placing his foot gave way with a bang, and before he could clutch at anything to save himself, he went sprawling neck and crop to his own door.

At the same moment a singular phenomenon occurred to Jacob.

A mysterious hand grasped him by his lank hair, lifting him completely off his feet, and hurling him headlong on the top of the doctor.

Both were equally astounded—both equally savage.

The vampire made a clutch at something which proved to be Jacob's nose.

Jacob frantically swung his arms right and left, and made his master's eyes water and smart before either knew what he was doing.

By this time they were on their feet, and were shaking each other fiercely, when a chorus of merry laughs sounded from above.

Their look up was incautious.

A sack of flour was just then in the act of being emptied on their heads, and eyes, nose, and mouth were filled with the white mass, which covered them from head to foot.

Then spank came a dead rat in the doctor's eye.

A second, equally well-aimed, went into Jacob's open mouth, and half-way down his throat.

"Jacob, Jacob!" squealed the vampire; "catch one of those cursed boys, and I'll tear his skin off in strips."

Jacob, who had just extricated the rat from his mouth, made a dart, but not towards the deck, where the boys were heard scampering away.

Jacob had not a delicate stomach, but the stinking rat was too much for him.

A strange sensation was in his throat, and feeling dreadfully sick, he made a rush for the cabin, and bundled hastily in.

Dr. Shrike cleared his eyes and mouth, and glared viciously up the ladder.

But no one was to be seen.

The boys, content with what they had done, had fled out of sight; and muttering very vindictive oaths, the vampire entered, after his faithful Jacob, whom he found leaning over a basin, and very sick indeed.

The vampire gave his serving man a thump in the back, and kicked him savagely into a corner, while he set himself to work to remove the uncomfortable mess which half-suffocated him.

Jacob got up awkwardly; but no sooner saw the woeful plight his master was in, than he set to violently laughing.

"Ho, ho! master," he cried, "if you're not a sight! Oho, here's a pickle! Why, you're like an Egyptian mummy shook out of a miller's sack."

"D—— you, for a long-backed ill-looking hound," was the doctor's reply, "and d—— those young cusses above! I'll make them smart! Oho! let me get them under my thumb, I'll make them smart! D—— you! brush this muck off me, will you! and don't stand there grinning, like an ass on its hind legs."

Jacob, who was still in convulsions, groomed his master down, and, in the course of time, the pair presented a more respectable appearance.

But the vampire was still in a dreadful rage; and happening to look round and see the grin still on Jacob's face, he pulled off one of his boots, and hurled it smack between his eyes.

"Hoo—oo—ow!" bellowed Jacob, as he rolled over.

"Hoo—oo—ow!" mocked the vampire. "Sit down on that box, and howl there, and be cursed to you! and let any mosquitoes

THE ISHMAELITE IN TROUBLE.

come to my hammock, and I'll flay your long back with my scalpel."

Jacob perched himself in the corner, and the vampire clambered to his hammock, which was already slung close to the ceiling of his cabin.

The doctor had a habit of lying full length in his hammock, and thoughtfully swinging to and fro.

For hours at a time would he remain there, and never, during the whole of that time, would his vulture-like face change its expression.

Silently and slowly, without moving a limb,

would he swing backwards and forwards, and Jacob, who knew his habits, prepared for a comfortable snooze, till such time as his master should arouse him, by putting a bit of lighted tow in his ear, or stuffing his mouth with some nauseous compound.

In either case it was a sight that tickled the doctor to see his cadaverous-faced assistant leap up as if he were shot—a sight that made him chuckle gleefully for an hour after.

The doctor began to swing slowly to and fro, his hook nose, sticking out of the hammock, being the only part of him visible to Jacob, who, as soon as he saw it comfortably swinging to and fro, coiled his long form up like an earwig, and began to snooze.

The vampire, with half-closed eyes, lay still, devising schemes by which to wreak his vengeance on the boys.

He was lying as quiet as death, when he heard a peculiar rustling sound beneath him.

It was not human.

It seemed the sullen rustling of two immense wings.

A low buzzing noise accompanied it, and slowly it rose and rose, till it came behind his head.

Dr. Shrike stopped his hammock from swinging, preparatory to lifting his head.

But at that moment a horrible slimy something swept suddenly across his face, half-blinding and nearly suffocating him.

With a start the vampire leapt up, and hit his head such a violent bump against the roof that he went down again.

The slimy buzzing thing came over his face a second time, and, hardened as he was, a strange thrill crept over him.

He twisted his head over the side of the hammock, and saw—

A something in all his life he had never before seen.

A peculiar slimy-looking thing, with a round, shapeless body, from which distended an immense pair of quivering wings, and a head so horribly hideous that he stared at it aghast.

Head, body, and wings seemed alike shapeless as he gazed.

Now a dozen snakes seemed writhing within the skin—then wings and body worked themselves into hard palpitating lumps, while the head gaped and gurgled in a way that terrified even his shrivelled old heart.

"Jacob, Jacob!" he cried, as the hideous monster came tumbling in a peculiar motion towards him; "Jacob, Jacob! what the devil's this? Get up, get up! Hi, ho! Curse it! it's the devil in a new skin."

Hearing his master's croaking voice, Jacob uncoiled his lank body, and looked sleepily about him.

But no sooner did he see the hideous object rolling like a living ball about the cabin, and making its wild flight towards him, than he uttered an awful howl of fright, and rolled in terror to the floor.

Dr. Shrike at the same moment became aware of two disagreeable facts.

Firstly, the monster was fluttering towards him again; secondly, as he turned to beat it off with his hands, his hammock was, by some means, slipping away from under him.

Letting down one another's hammocks when the victim is in it, is a very common practice with our lads at sea.

And there are three methods of doing the trick.

The first by letting the victim down by his feet, the second by his head, and the third by head and feet together, when he comes down all in a heap by his middle.

The vampire came down by the second way.

He was frantically trying to beat off the winged monster, when the fastenings at his head slipped, as if by magic, and head foremost he came down with a thud, not to the hard floor, but into a concealed tub of bilge water, artfully covered over by his boy tor-

mentors, who, knowing his custom, had prepared this fragrant bath for him.

The splash and the doctor's howl made Jacob again look up.

The vampire was struggling in the tub, spluttering the filthy water from his mouth, and keeping his shiny pate out of the reach of the hideous thing, which, at the instant of his downfall, swooped towards his head.

"Jacob, Jacob!" yelled the doctor. "Curse you! where the devil are you?"

"Here, here! Oh, mercy! Keep off! It is—it is—the devil himself! He's come to take you for your sins. Take him off!—take him off!"

Jacob's cries of terror were caused by the approach of the mysterious object, which now began to buzz round and round the cabin, swooping alternately at the vampire and at him.

The former, who had crawled out of the tub, began to feel less fear of their unknown enemy, and once, as it pounced at him, he clutched it with his arms.

Horror!

It folded up, as it were, into a skin of living bodies, a dozen dagger-points struck at him, and wherever his flesh touched, he was stung as if by a venomous insect.

This was too much for the vampire to endure without an effort to determine the nature of his mysterious enemy.

He called out to Jacob, who believed they were attacked by the devil in disguise, and howled and shook with fear, for his "belly skewer," which was at the back of that worthy.

With trembling hands Jacob held it out to him, dropping on his knees the instant the winged horror came upon him.

The vampire, by this time, was maliciously cool.

He took the "belly skewer," a long, rusty, straight-bladed sword, and standing in the middle of the cabin, waited till the thing came within arm's length, when he thrust viciously at the slimy body.

The weapon passed completely through, and the doctor, with a dry hollow chuckle, drew the blade upwards, nearly severing the thing in two.

But no sooner had he done this, than a score of winged animals, with a cloud of buzzing insects, crowded forth, and encircled his head and that of Jacob, who vociferously bawled "murder, fire, and devils," as he fled round the cabin, trying vainly to escape this new attack of what he looked upon as a legion of devils let loose.

To the vampire it was all clear—clear as the consequences of what he had done.

The mischievous boys had strained a bladder to that peculiar shape, and imprisoned inside it a number of bats and mosquitoes.

They, in their efforts to escape, set the strange body rolling through the air, and being now at liberty, attacked the vampire and his howling assistant.

The doctor, blinded and stung, clapped vainly at his venomous assailants, while Jacob, with both hands over his ears, fled howling for shelter.

It was at this juncture that the daring boys, listening for the success of their plans, and unable to contain themselves any longer, burst out into uncontrollable laughter.

Doctor Shrike leapt erect as he heard them.

His visage seemed changed in a twinkling to the deadliest passions.

With a volley of the most malicious oaths, he burst open the door, and sprang up the ladder.

But the boys were waiting to receive him, and he and Jacob, who wildly followed him, were immediately drenched by a shower of bilge water, which drove them back, while the boys fled for their lives.

The vampire, breathing the deadliest fury, was after them in a second.

His vulture-shaped features were set to demoniac rage, his ferret eyes blazed with fury, the most fearful oaths left his quivering lips, and with the rusty old sword in hand, he flew along the deck, the boys scampering in all directions at his approach, some springing aloft, some to the chains, others dodging from deck to deck, while not a few sought safety in the yards above his head.

Things were at this crisis, when our hero, almost unnoticed in the general confusion, set his foot on board.

His arrival was most opportune.

Some serious consequences must have ensued, for the old blood-letter was warily pursuing an intended victim, when our hero's stern command, bidding him go below, recalled him to the fact that his leader was on deck.

As soon as he saw that he was baulked of his revenge, the old fellow, glaring viciously round him, shook his shrivelled fingers at the boys, who now gathered round him.

"You shall have milk and honey for this," he cried; "ho, ho, ho! all of you. Let fever scorch you, plague writhe you, wounds fester you! I will not stretch out a hand to help you—you shall rot—rot—rot and die—like rats—like rats!"

Glaring round like a savage panther, thirsting for their hearts' blood, the venomous old fellow spat at the daring boys, and still muttering his furious curses, tottered from the deck.

And Jacob, who saw him coming, slunk out of his way, for there was a look in his master's eye he had never seen before, save on one occasion, and that was such an hour as he had no wish to ever see again.

CHAPTER XXVIII.

A LETTER OF MARQUE.

NEWS that the notorious cruiser had been seen homeward bound reached Admiral Ellis as he was scouring the Indian seas, and, putting his ship about immediately, he made for the British shores, arriving there two days after our adventurers had cast anchor under the white cliffs of old England.

Aware of the dangers that menaced him at every step, when once he came within hail of his native land, Tom laid aside his cocked hat and well-known uniform, and in the undress of a young lieutenant, went ashore, and having bidden adieu to Ben Barnacle and Harry Vere, who accompanied him so far, set off with the faithful Bob Hauler on his perilous mission.

Scarcely four-and-twenty hours had succeeded his departure, when a boat put off from the jetty, and rowed towards the ship.

The rowers were naval officials, and two elderly gentlemen, in gold-laced uniforms and cocked hats, sat in the stern.

As soon as this was seen by the look-out, their mission was at once suspected, and word was passed that the authorities had sent to examine the vessel.

As usual, when in port, more than half the boy cruisers were concealed below, and the principal guns, &c., were carefully placed out of sight.

The remaining middies were idling about the decks, or listlessly looking over the ship's sides.

Not the least sign of tumult or consternation was visible on board, nor would any one have suspected they had reason to be confused by the official visit.

That is to say, by the appearances on deck.

Below it was somewhat different.

The middies were providing themselves with a double set of weapons in case of need, and old Doctor Shrike lingered wistfully about with a red-hot scalpel in his claw-like hand.

He was waiting for any spy, who in the interests of his country might sneak below.

The boat grated alongside, and after a few words with the officer on deck, the gold-laced gentlemen ascended the side, and were conducted aft, where Harry Vere and Ben Barnacle awaited them.

Both saluted Harry Vere coldly, and requested a private interview with Ben Barnacle.

Ben eyed them narrowly.

He could see they were sent on some mission connected with the character of the ship, but reasoning that they would do less mischief below than on deck, he bade them follow to his cabin.

Seated here, the elder of the two opened the conversation.

"We have the honour," he said, "of sitting in the second cabin of the *Will-o'-the-Wisp*, commanded by Captain Tom Drake. This statement of that fact, Ben Barnacle, will be sufficient for you to understand that you are discovered. We perceive your leader is not aboard, and as our mission here is to capture him, my friend will take charge of the ship on deck, while I await here the return of Captain Tom."

Having delivered himself thus, the elderly officer leaned back in his chair, and awaited the effect of his speech upon Ben Barnacle.

The honest-hearted Ben looked from one to the other with great surprise, which changed to a comical expression of merriment as he replied,—

"Gentlemen, whoever has been at the pains to give you this information has succeeded in making a precious pair of fools of you. Excuse my freedom, but I am an independent sailor, and have a knack of speaking plainly. As far as I am concerned, you are at liberty to stay on my deck or in my cabin till the ship sails, and if you like to imagine this a pirate ship, and think you are likely to catch your fish on board, why, that's your look-out, not mine."

"Come, come, Ben," said the second of the two officers, "this is all stuff, you know. Come, let us play into each other's hands—it will pay us—it will pay you. Now we know this is the ship we named, and that your leader is the fellow we want; but as we wish to do this business on our own account, and not have the whole place up in arms and sharing his capture, we will make terms with you—for you must understand we have come here of our own accord, and without communicating our suspicions to our brother officers, who, with their usual greed, would claim a share of the reward if they knew we had come."

"Ah,' Ben said, drily. "Then the authorities do not know you have come on board."

"Certainly not. There would have been a hue and cry all over the place if we had. No, no; we've waited this month past expecting you to put in, and now you've come, we've got you."

"Have you?" observed Ben.

"Yes; but we want everything managed quietly. Listen, leave us to arrest him, and the price of your assistance shall be this noble ship. We have come prepared. My friend has in his pocket a letter of marque, with a blank for the ship and captain. It is signed by King George's own hand, and shall be yours, with this ship and her crew, as the price of your assisting us to capture Tom Drake."

Ben Barnacle mused.

"You see," observed the other speaker, "the offer is tempting, and not likely to be made again. We will deal plainly with you—of course it would be easy for any one of those ships of war lying within musket-shot of this vessel to take you and all on board; but you understand our motive. We wish to get the reward, which we should not get if others divide the honour of his capture."

"I do not like to consent to this," Ben said.

"Your scruples are foolish. Sooner or later you must all be taken, and then you know what they will do with you. They will hang you as pirates."

"When they catch us."

"Pooh, pooh! They must take you sooner or later. Some one is certain to betray you."

"Any one guilty of treachery on board here," Ben remarked significantly, "would be dealt with in a proper manner. Not one of these boys but would tear him to pieces; and let me tell you, also, if they suspected the object of your visit to me, they would rend your bowels out before you reached the ship's side."

The elderly gentleman turned pale, and began to feel uncomfortable.

"Still," Ben said, musingly, "protected by that letter of marque they would no longer be in dread of being treated as pirates."

"Certainly not. The change would be this, whereas you are now hunted felons, with blood money on your heads, you could still pursue your practices, but with this difference, that not one of our fleet could meddle with you."

"True. May I examine this said letter of marque?"

"In our hands, yes. We dare not relinquish it till we have made our capture."

They spread open the document on the table and Ben closely examined it.

Everything about it was correct, except the filling in of the names.

"You see all is satisfactory there," remarked one of the officers.

"I perceive," Ben replied, "that were I to betray my commander for that, it would be perfectly useless to me."

"Useless—how?"

"It would not be valid, unless the filling in of my n me was attested by a British official."

"Oh, that will soon be remedied if you will give us a pen. There, Captain Ben Barnacle, of the ship—what ship shall we say?"

"The *Judas* were the fittest name," Ben remarked, bitterly.

"A good name. Of the ship *Judas*—signed Daniel Drummond, officer of His Majesty's customs. There, it is perfect now."

"It is," Ben said, drily. "Gentlemen, I mistrust you no longer. I agree to surrender the captain."

"Excellent—and wise."

"But mind—no treachery. I must have that document on the instant of his capture."

"On the instant."

"Are you prepared to capture him yourselves?"

"The devil—no."

"And you might as well try to capture the devil himself."

"We must have our boat's crew on board, they are officers disguised."

"I thought so, from the way I saw them pull."

"They are better hands at making a capture than at rowing a boat. You can conceal them in Captain Tom's cabin."

"His own cabin is too well watched by his corsair girl. No, they must be secreted here, and to make matters safe on both sides that letter of marque must be hung upon this hook, within my reach, to take when he is captured."

The officers exchanged a significant look, but readily acquiesced, pretending nothing would give them greater joy than to see him captain of the vessel under a letter of marque.

"I must leave you now, gentlemen," said Ben, "give me the signal to bring your men on board."

"A wave of your left hand. Stay, one moment while we are about it, you would perhaps be glad to be warned that the authorities have, in conjunction with Admiral Ellis, arranged a plot for the capture of Henry Vere. He is to be lured on board their ship and shot."

"The letter of marque will protect him."

"Not if he leaves your ship. Don't forget, we have fairly warned you."

Ben nodded and left the cabin.

"Well, Bob," said Daniel, "we've managed that well."

"Yes, he's evidently taken with the idea of the letter of marque."

"Ha, ha, and he'll get it, won't he?"

"For my part, I should not care if he did."

"Nonsense! we want it for the other pirate fellow."

"But you've put his name to it."

"The pirate must change his."

"Of the two I would rather this Ben Barnacle escaped, he is tolerably honest, the other we know is a demon steeped in innocent blood."

"But, man, look at the price he has offered for the letter of marque. We must consult our purse, not our feelings."

"Well, I am with you, what will these fellows get?"

"The leader and officers are sure of being hanged, and a good many of the others will share their fate; they have been represented to the king as a venomous band of pirates, and he has given orders to have them all flogged, shot, or hanged."

"Just like his sapient majesty, why, two or three of these dashing boy devils would gain more victories than all his cat-'o-nine tailed fleet."

"Yes, but that's no business of ours. We've only to look after what we can get out of it all."

"Hallo, what's that?"

Officer Drummond peered out at the porthole.

He had heard a suspicious sound.

"It's all right," he said, presently, "they're gone on deck."

Directly after he had spoken, Ben Barnacle appeared.

The disguised officers followed him, and were ushered into the cabin.

"Keep silence, gentlemen, as you value your lives, Ben said, when he had placed sundry bottles of wine on the table. "No one will enter till I come to conduct the skipper in. Be ready with your weapons, but remember, no noise of firearms, or I cannot answer for your leaving the ship alive."

Ben might have added that the mere suspicion of the officers being concealed there for such a purpose, would have been enough for the daring boys, had they known it, to have dragged them forth, and almost torn them limb from limb, but he didn't; he merely gave them another caution to remain quiet, and left.

As soon as he had gone, the two elderly gentlemen in gold lace and cocked hats, the would-be pirate-takers, placed their fingers knowingly alongside of their nose, a significant gesture which was imitated by their men, and then the whole party sat at the table to discuss in silence the excellent liquor Ben Barnacle had placed before them.

CHAPTER XXIX.

THE YELLOW ALLIGATOR.

WHILE this ambuscade had been, with the connivance of his trusted follower, prepared for our hero, he had been engaged on a perilous series of adventures, none more treacherous than the snare by which he was to be captured, when, escaped from all dangers, he should set foot on his noble vessel.

Tom's purpose in hazarding a visit on shore was to discover the whereabouts of Admiral Lord Killcrew, for he naturally reasoned that if he were still at sea, Lady Castlemaine could not force Minnie to become his bride.

He was also in quest of intelligence concerning his uncle, poor old John Gregory.

How he succeeded in both matters, will be by-and-bye related.

For the present we must leave him, and repair to the "Yellow Alligator," an old-fashioned inn situated a few miles from Portsmouth.

It was a queer, dilapidated old house.

The Cavaliers and Puritans had alternately lodged there in King Charles's time, and rumour reported it to have, upon one occasion, given shelter and concealment to the Young Pretender, when his merciless foes were pursuing him to the death.

During the troublous beginning of the war then raging against Napoleon, it had been the resort of all sorts of characters.

Here the press-gang inveigled their victims, and officers of justice waited to waylay highwaymen and pirates, who were expected, and on whose heads blood-money was placed.

As might have been expected its landlord, Zachariah Magpie, was a queer old stick.

He had been a Kentuckian, and fought in the first war of independence.

Six foot two he stood in his boots.

His body was lank and slim; his limbs seemed too long even for his body—he had a game eye, which rolled quaintly in its socket, and his hands hung down like the paws of a gorilla.

But for all that, Zachariah Magpie was a dangerous customer to meddle with.

One way or the other he had been of use to the authorities, and so they overlooked the playful knack he had of pitching any man who offended him out of window, or spitting him against the gate with a pitch-fork.

Mrs. Zachariah Magpie was a worthy partner of such a man.

She weighed at least seventeen stone, and had a fist like a leg of mutton.

It was getting towards evening, and the old man was behind his primitive bar, dispensing liquors to his customers, when two well-known thief-takers and officers of justice walked in.

Old Zachariah knew that they never came his way unless they had some business in hand.

They had once walked off a particular favourite of his, and he never saw their ill-looking mugs without feeling an inclination to smother them in the cask out of which he drew his beer.

But prudence compelled him to be outwardly civil.

"Good day, Jonas," he said to the ugliest one. "I kalkerlate it's a gone day since you turned up here, and you, too, Master Matthews; still I'm glad to see yer. Come, what'll yer take?"

The fellow whom he had addressed as Jonas gave his confederate a significant leer.

"We'll take the bloke as we're looking after, won't we, Bill, eh?"

"Like to," quoth the other, as Zachariah handed them the jug of beer.

Zachariah leaned his brawny elbows on the bar.

"Well, my kiddies. and who's the unlucky coon you're kinder after now?"

"Oh, we don't tell you all our business," replied Matthews, "you ain't one of the right sort for us to do that with."

"May I go slick down an alligator's throat if I ever ask you a civil question again," growled the landlord as he mixed a mint julep and drank.

"Oh, Zachariah won't peach on us," said

onas. "Beside, I don't suppose he's seen or heard of our bird."

"Is it a land-crab or a water-shark?" asked Zachariah.

"Both, 1 think. Some devil of a son of a pop-gun. Leastways, he's always popping out of the way when he's wanted to be nabbed. But I think we'll have him this time, eh, Matthews?"

Matthews grunted out some hopeful reply, and went on with his beer.

"Yes," continued Jonas, "he's got the cheek of the old 'un to come here at all, when there's such a mob on the look out for him. But we've had the straight tip, and he'll be nabbed before night, as sure as his name is Captain Tom Drake."

Zachariah turned up his eyes in the least expressible manner.

"Guess I've heard of that coon before to-day, I have," he observed. "Seems a slippery kind of a greasy eel, that you can't get by the tail."

"Oho, we shall get him, I'll bet; and then he may make up his mind that it's good-night with him."

"Why, stranger?" asked Zachariah, "what'll they do with him?"

Jonas made a motion of passing his fingers round his throat, ending with a jerk, typical of hanging.

"That's what they'll do with him," he said; "but guess it ain't no businesses of ourn, so long as we swags the ready, eh, Matthews?"

"No odds at all; come on, drink up. We're wasting time when we ought to be on his track."

The worthy pair of blood-hunters drank up and departed.

Zachariah watched them swagger out of sight.

His face puckered up in a peculiar expression of coarse jocularity and strong contempt.

"Yes, toddle off, yer varmint coons," he soliloquized; "but if ever he's took by the likes of you, I'll eat my own head off without any salt. You take him! yes, yer tarnal pair of blowpipes. I gue s if yer don't find you've cotched a sarpint, when yer do get paws on him, I ain't never knowed the habits of the critter—not at all—oh, no—not at all."

Old Zachariah drained off his mint julep with a chuckle.

One of the thief-takers at that instant returned.

"Hallo, scorpion!" was on the old fellow's lips, but he checked himself, and merely looked up as he said,—

"Turned in again, Jonas."

"Yes. Come back to leave this here; it's his description, and cautions against any of His Majesty's subjects, not to harbour him under a penalty of imprisonment for life."

"Harbour 'em," bellowed Zachariah, "me harbour such riptiles?"

"Oh, I don't suppose you'd do that, but it's a caution, and so I'll just stick it up against this wall."

"Jest stick it up wherever yer please!" exclaimed the landlord, "and put another outside, may be it'll bring me customers. Have some o' this paste."

"Thanks; there, anyone can read it now, I say Zach, you see what the reward is.

If he should give us the slip, and come down here, there's only us three, we can divide the swag, you understand."

"Tarnation well. Say, Jonas, going any-where's special to nab him?"

Jonas placed the thumb of his right hand against his nose, and extending the fingers towards Zachariah, made a significant grimace, and departed.

He had evidently made up his mind not to be caught napping.

An hour or so after, while Zachariah was thoughtfully sipping another mint julep, his wife came bouncing like a young avalanche into the bar.

Her first act was to hit him a tremendous blow in the pit of the stomach with her fat hand, and dislodge the grateful draught he had just imbibed.

Her next was to clutch the glass from his hand, and drain the contents.

"Guzzling again," she cried. "guzzle, guzzle, guzzle! I should like to know when you mean to leave off guzzling all the profits, and intend to take to your business like an honest man, instead of a big-bellied, blown-out whale—you guzzling sponge, you."

"Tarnation devils!" gasped Zachariah, "say, missus, don't come that again with this chi d, or there'll be mischief."

"Mischief, there'll be mischief enough if I let you have your own way, you idling, guzzling sneak of a thief, spending all your days over the bar, lolloping with your fine companions, who'd drink the place out at elbows, drink me out of house and home, and you'd not care a straw."

Zachariah might have added that the quantity he guzzled in improving the trade, was nothing to what she put away upstairs, but he didn't, and Mrs. Magpie's fiery eye happening to alight on the proclamation, which the officer had pasted up, her indignation took a new turn.

"Ha! another of them skulking reprobates hiding from the law, and I suppose you'd shelter him, and give him meat and drink, as you did that vile highwayman you put in my room last time the officer came here, but let me tell you this viper—this whatever his name is—oh, Tom. A pretty name for such a villain. I'll betray him. I'll shriek out that he's here if he dares to put one foot inside my house—I swear I will, as I'm an honest woman."

Two strangers sauntered in at that moment.

They were both cloaked, and appeared to have come some distance.

One, the younger of the two, who was attired in the undress of a young naval lieutenant, was evidently of authority, for the other kept at a respectful distance, and once or twice seemed about to make him some salutation, when a glance from the other checked him.

While they were being served with liquor, the younger sauntered up to the proclamation, and leisurely read it.

He was a good-looking young fellow, almost a youth, though with bigger whisker and moustachios than might have been expected from his age.

After having perused the whole announcement, he turned to the landlady, and said, with a smile,—

"Some desperate marauder. Not expected here, I trust."

"Expected here?" Mother Magpie almost shrieked, "no, sir—bless you, no, sir. I should say not indeed—the terrible ruffian!"

"He appears to be a most deadly desperado —an unmitigated villain, judging by the announcement."

"He is, sir, a bloodthirsty wretch. Heaven grant he may never darken my threshold."

Just the faintest vestige of a smile puckered up old Zachariah's long visage.

"Well, stranger," he remarked. "Seems as how we mightn't know the varmint, even if he did come here."

Mother Magpie almost shrieked.

"Not know him, Zachariah—how can you. I am sure I should know him the instant he set his foot on the doorstep. Don't you think I should, sir, with my instincts of bad people?"

That quiet smile again flitted round Zachariah's lips.

"Well, well," he said, gruffly, "don't let's bother the gentleman. Perhaps he'd like to sit down."

"My best room is at your service," cried the politely-smirking landlady. "walk this way, sir, if you please. It's a pleasure to offer such a gentleman my humble shelter—a pleasure to see you, sir, when such bloodthirsty marauders are about. Walk in, sir, who knows, but even now the villain might be lingering within ear-shot."

"Ah!" Zachariah exclaimed gravely. "Who knows, indeed."

A close observer might have detected a knowing kind of wink in the corner of Zachariah's eye.

But Mother Magpie was already leading the way to their own snug little room, and the youthful wayfarer, gaining the noisy-tongued woman's good opinion, by his gentle acquiescence in all that she said, followed her, his companion walking in company with Zachariah.

A bright fire was burning in the room, and the hostess, taking down glasses and decanters, bade her guests be seated, and ordered her husband to get some of his best wine.

Zachariah soon returned, with a cobwebbed bottle in each hand.

"Be merry, strangers," he said, placing the bottles on the table. "You'll find the wine tasty, and there's no fear of that desperate pirate, Captain Tom Drake, getting in here, any way."

He winked knowingly at the young stranger whose handsome features flushed as the landlord spoke.

"Zachariah," cried his worthy partner, "if you mention his very name, I shall have spasms."

The youthful guest smiled.

"Come," he said, filling his glass, "let me pledge our kind hostess in a bumper. Madame, your sweetest health, and may all robbers and pirates be kept from your door."

The landlady made the best curtsey her seventeen stone of flesh would permit.

She was flushed and pleased.

"Was ever such a well-spoken gentlemen?" she cried. "Zachariah, how ill-mannered you are. Fill your glass, and drink the gentleman's health."

Very quaintly did Zachariah fill his glass.

Very quaintly did he, with his one game eye, cocked to a curious expression, glance over the rich ruby fluid at his young guest.

"Strangers," he said, "old Zachariah drinks your health, and may you never need a more snug shelter than he can give you."

The younger of the new comers gave him a quick glance.

But old Zachariah's face was half hidden as he let the grateful juice gurgle down his capacious throat.

Hardly had he set the glass down, when a noisy scuffling of feet was heard outside.

Mother Magpie gave a spasmodic start.

Old Zachariah looked gravely round.

"Now then, you old yellow alligator," exclaimed a voice outside, "come out, will you, or we'll precious quick come in, I can tell you."

"Dame," said the landlord, "somebody calls you."

Mother Magpie's full round face flushed the colour of a raw beefsteak.

"Well, if ever I heard the like, to be insulted under my own roof, and you to stand there and tamely hear that—there, don't go; I'll soon see whether I keep open house for this or no."

The excited landlady pushed past her husband, and was presently heard in high altercation with some one outside.

"Oh, no good," a man's voice exclaimed, "tell yer he's been tracked here. We're officers of justice, and we means to search."

"And if you try to search here," screamed the landlady, in reply, "I'll claw the scalp off your beastly skulls."

"What do you mean, woman?" was the reply. "I'll tell you a-harbouring pirates and setting the officers of justice at defiance won't do them nor you any good."

"Strangers," observed Zachariah, gently, as his better half's voice was heard screechin reply; "them's officers on the look-out. They're unwelcome varmints at all times, and if you'd like not to see 'em, why, there's a corner in my house where they may stare their eyes out of their heads and not smell a scrap of yer skin."

He looked meaningly at the younger traveller as he spoke.

"Oh, no, thank you," replied the other, carelessly, "they will not interfere with our comforts I assure you."

Old Zachariah looked surprised, but said no more.

Mother Magpie came bounding heavily into the room, her eyes blazing, her voice thick.

"You Zachariah!" she shrieked, "there is a thief of a sneak—officer of justice he calls himself—I'll justice him with a warming-pan about his ugly ears—says we're a-harbouring that Captain Tom Drake, the pirate, and says he'll search the house—my house, Zachariah. But let him attempt it—let the insignificant puppy, the snivelling sneak, the pitiful cur, attempt it, and I'll show him what's what, I will."

"Well, my dear," put in Zachariah, "if them officer coons like to be darned jackasses, and want to search our house, why, tarnation pippins, let 'em; we'll give 'em leave to eat all they find, and much good may it do their skins, the tarnation cusses."

"Oh, indeed, a pretty thing; and so you will allow your house to be turned upside down, and your wife too, perhaps, you'll allow to be turned upside down—I said upside down, did you hear, Zachariah. Rummaged all over, with their beastly noses prying into every corner."

"Snakes and crocodiles!" exclaimed Zachariah, who evidently misunderstood his better half, "I shouldn't think any critters would want to do that."

"Oh, and that's all you have to say; a pretty landlord you, and these gentlemen disturbed in this way."

"I assure you, madam, they will not disturb us in the least," observed the younger traveller; "I should let them search the place if they wish to do so."

"Of course," chimed in Zachariah, "don't want 'em to think you won't let 'em in because you are harbouring malefactors—do you, eh?"

"Me harbour malefactors? Here, you spy, you pitiful imitation, you sneaking Paul Pry, walk in. Begin your search; there's some gentlemen here—perhaps they're the pirates. Pray come in, and pray see if you can discover your beautiful Tom, your precious Tommy. I said Tommy, you thieves, I did!"

The last words were a perfect squeal of fury.

"Yes," chimed Zachariah, who, for some reasons of his own, was only making believe to be at ease, "walk in, you young snakes and alligators. Here you'll find the spotted jackass eating his tarnal toes off, and the big baboon a-cutting of his blessed corns."

Whether he alluded to himself. his worthy partner, or his two guests, was not clear.

The officers entered; two low-looking, ill-bred blood-hunters; their faces stamped by cunning greed. Neither of them were Jonas or Matthews. Others there were on our hero's track.

"Look sharp in there," cried a surly voice, "no use your hiding him away. Dead or alive, we mean to have him!"

The officers looked cautiously round.

"Don't want to put you out of the way, Zachariah," said the foremost, "but bizness is bizness, and dooty is dooty; we've been on the trail of Captain Tom Drake, and he's expected here; so, if he ain't here now, he's on the road, but in case he should be here we means to make all safe—Don't we, Jem?"

"No mistake," retorted Jem.

"I'll break your ill-looking jaws, I will!" screamed Mrs. Magpie, seizing a heavy decanter.

"Better patch up your own ill-looking mug first, ma'am."

"You villain—take that! I'll teach you to insult me here, you white-livered sneak, that I will!"

With a fearful crash she hurled the decanter at the officer's head.

Had it struck him it must have knocked his brains out; but he ducked in time to let it shiver in atoms against the wall.

Mrs. Magpie took up another with the same intent, but old Zachariah got between her and the object of her rage.

"Look here, critters," he said to the officers, "you've come to look after a pirate, so you are, some—jest do that, and go your tarnation ways; but as to speakin' ag'in' my missis, do it, an', snakes an' kangaroos! I'll pitch yer by the scurf of the neck out of window!"

Zachariah stretched himself up till his six feet odd looked more than their full measure.

He looked dangerous to tamper with.

The officer was cowed, and said no more to the infuriated landlady.

"These gentlemen will excuse us," one said, "but we must ax their names, and where they come from."

"Yes," squealed Mrs. Magpie; "and their mammy's names, and their grandmothers' names, you sneaks, you."

"My dear madam," observed the younger of the travellers, "these men are only obeying their orders; as an officer myself, bearing His Majesty's commission, it is part of my duty to assist them in their search; and, much as I should regret joining in any disturbance under your hospitable roof, I should be compelled, were this boy-pirate to show himself, to help take him prisoner. I am sure these good men will only do their duty, and no more."

He drew a small packet from his breast, and displayed it open to the officers.

"You will see by this that I am Lieutenant Clifford, of the *Neptune*. This gentleman has been my travelling companion—he ships with me; and now, having satisfied you about ourselves, I hope you will excuse me from accompanying you on your search. Should I be fortunate enough to help you capture him, we shall travel together; if not, I may see you at Portsmouth, when I hope to use my influence to increase your reward, should you take him."

The officers touched their caps.

"We beg pardon for intruding," they began.

"Don't name it. Nay, we are all comrades under the king—drink to his health."

He filled out their glasses, and refilling his to the brim, drank to the dregs.

"There," exclaimed the irascible landlady, "perhaps now you will come bundling in upon people, looking for your pirate; perhaps you'll say again that one of these gentlemen might be him."

"Don't never know, ma'am; he's like the devil, and takes a good many shapes. don't he, sir? And besides, here's his description, and it is a little like this young gentleman."

"Pooh!" cried the landlord, knocking the document from his hand, "you're a fool."

The young lieutenant smiled, displaying a handsome set of teeth.

"I hope I am not too much like him," he said, gaily; "but I had heard he was a ferocious monster, with fangs besmeared with blood."

"Oh, no, sir; he is, so they say, a perfect chick to look at; but, chick or no chick, there's a good many been a long while on the look-out for him, and now he's put his foot in it by comin' on shore; if me and Jem don't nab him others will—there ain't no fear of his dodging off again."

"Well,"—the young officer poured out more wine—"I hope, my worthy fellows, you may get him; but I'm afraid you won't find him here—drink!"

"Much obliged to you, kind sir, but we mustn't take no more; afeard we shan't know him when we see him. It'll be a tough job when we nabs him; howsomdever, we'll give a look round, like. Pr'aps, ma'am, you'll show us round."

"Show you!" screeched Mrs. Magpie. "Me show you, indeed!—catch me!"

Zachariah chuckled, the young traveller laughed, and the officers left the room.

Then, and not till then, did old Zachariah seem more at ease.

To observe him closely, one would have thought that our hero was indeed somewhere under his roof.

The irascible hostess could not content herself with staying behind.

She followed after the officers, giving them the length of her tongue till they had been all over the place, and had reluctantly determined to depart, when, with derisive satisfaction, she hissed them off her doorway, calling all the grinning yokels from the taproom to hoot the discomfited officers till they were out of distance.

Mrs. Magpie came back to the snug parlour with a face like pickling cabbage.

"There!" she exclaimed, as she triumphantly squatted down in the only chair that would bear her weight, "that's the last of them."

Old Zachariah cocked his game eye to a comical expression, and a genial smile flitted about his lips.

When an hour or so had passed, the lieutenant's companion, taking advantage of the landlady's absence to serve customers, hinted that they had better be gone.

"Strangers," said Zachariah, "if you'll take a trapper's advice, you'll lie tarnal quiet where yer are, for thar's them about as is more dangerous than scotched rattlesnakes, and a tarnal sight more cunning than vipers. I guess yer are in comfortable quarters, like, and if I was yer, I'd stay till daylight afore I went further."

The same significant look beamed a moment from the old fellow's eyes, and he did not seem surprised when the travellers decided to stay.

The discussion of another bottle brought them to the hour of retiring, and after they had wished their hostess good night, old Zachariah conducted them to their rooms.

The sleeping apartment to which he led the younger traveller was a large, rumbling square-cornered chamber of very antique construction.

A monstrous wooden bedstead stood at one end.

A large chest of drawers at the other end; and all the other furniture was of the most primitive and massive construction.

A big, uncouth-looking window, with bars across the thick shutters outside, took up nearly half the wall on one side, an immense fireplace was on the other.

"'Tain't the best looking corner in the shed," the landlord observed, as if by way of apology, "but its tarnation convenient, and you may make up your mind to sleep comfortable *till I calls you.*"

"Thanks," said the young stranger, divesting himself of his cloak and naval jacket, "I shall rise with cock crow."

The landlord lingered as if he wanted to say more.

He stood opposite the noble form of his youthful guest, and looked him keenly, though respectfully, in the face.

"Stranger," he said, "'tain't in me to pry into your secrets, or to offer my council like, but if yer should hear a tarnal row in the night, and shouldn't want to be seen here,

yer have only to touch that knob at the back of yer head, and you'll go out of sight; only *jump off the bedstead,* arter it's done it's tarnation wal through the floor."

With these words, the old fellow was about to retire, but the young sailor, by a quiet, graceful movement, indicated him to stay.

"Zachariah," he said, in an altered, pleasing voice that fell like magic music on the staunch old Kentuckian's ears, "I have not mistrusted your fidelity, nor forgotten when I was last *here;* look at me as I am."

He removed his disguise of whiskers eyebrows, &c., and revealed the handsome boyish features of Captain Tom Drake.

Old Zachariah did not seem a whit surprised, if anything he was a little affected.

"Stranger," he said, "you're jest a brave kinder coon, and that's what yer are. I knowed ye the fust time I heard yer voice: for I haven't all forgot when I used my ears on the trail of the Injuns. Wall, I reckon you've the stomach of an alligator; tip us your fin, and cuss me, I'm glad to see yer."

Tom grasped his hand warmly.

"I was sure of a welcome here," he said; "poor madam did not even suspect me."

"She—why, she ain't no more scent of a human critter than a walrus with its blowing hole stuffed up; and if she had, with all her ways, she d let her flesh get tored off her back afore she'd betray you, and that's saying a tarnal good deal, it are."

"It is, indeed; and now, my worthy friend, leave me. I need not conceal from you that I am pursued, and expect to be tracked here by more keen-scented blood-hunters than the precious pair who have just left."

"And if you are, when you hear 'em battering ag'in the door, you'll know where to go. I shan't be in a hurry to let 'em in, and maybe they'll kinder knock ag'in summut on their way; and I shan't nary come to wake yer, anyways, for I know yer have as quick ear as a hunted Injun, and the spring of a young lion when you're roused. So stranger, good night, and a tough 'un yer are, as I allers said you d be."

Once more he gripped Tom's hand.

"A moment," our hero said, "has anything further transpired about my mother?"

"Nothing since that infernal yarn of her having bolted."

Tom's cheeks flushed.

"I will force that lie down their throats yet. My uncle, has anything been heard of him?"

"Wall—yaas—they've got cheeky, and it's said he's in a sort of Bedlam."

"By heavens, I will rescue him from his cowardly keepers, if I have to thrust my sword down their brutal throats."

"I kalkerlate yer will; but just take an old sarpint's advice. When yer are going there, don't let 'em smell yer comin, or yer may find when yer gits him out, that he's mad enough to all etarnity."

Cheerily bidding the bold boy good night, the landlord of the "Yellow Alligator" quitted the apartment, and our hero threw himself on the bed, to snatch a few hours repose, and was almost instantly in a sound slumber.

CHAPTER XXX.

ONE THOUSAND POUNDS REWARD.

Two o'clock had just struck from the neighbouring church clock—the solemn hour when the ghosts, who have been flitting about the damp church-yard since midnight's chimes, are warned to go back to their damp winding sheets and damper graves.

Two o'clock, the cocks, waiting in doubt between the moonlight and the faint peep of day, began to crow.

Old Zachariah turned his lank frame over in his bed; Mrs. Magpie grunted thrice, and once more began to snore.

The church chimes died into stillness; the latest cock crowed his last faint hoarse crow, and sleepily settled himself down again on his perch.

A deeper quiet than before seemed to reign—not even a cricket chirped or frog croaked.

Amidst the peaceful hush of this silent hour, old Zachariah was suddenly startled from his sleep by such a battering at his door, as had not made the echoes of the neighbourhood resound since the time when iron-handed Roundheads banged at the stubborn door in quest of hated Royalists.

The worthy landlord drowsily awoke, and he pricked up his ears, and turned his game eye towards the ruddy face of his better half, which till now had lain half smothered amongst the pillows, but now bounced up as sharply as if a shell had exploded in each fiery ear—alarm, rage, dismay, in every lineament.

A moment she listened; the very frills of her nightcap standing on end with fright, then, with both hands, she seized on her husband, and shook him to and fro.

"Zachariah! *Zachariah!* ZACHARIAH! do you hear that?"

The passive Zachariah drowsily kicked out one lanky leg, and sniffled out as he turned over again,—

"Hush! it's the tarnal rats."

"The rats! Are you mad? and is this Bedlam! Wake, wake, and listen! There, you hear now. The house is being knocked down about our ears."

Bang! bang! bang! came violently against the door.

A giant's hand seemed to be making a plaything of the knocker.

And an excited voice bawled out,—

"Open, open, I say—open, in the king's name. Oh—within—ostlers—landlord—all—open the door!"

"There," screeched Mrs. Magpie, in a suppressed whisper. "It's the rats, eh? The rats, you old crocodile-headed ass."

Old Zachariah slid quietly out of bed, and thrust his long legs into his trousers.

Creeping softly to the window, which swung open inwards, he noiselessly pulled it back and peered out.

He was a bit "skeared" at what he saw.

A party of officers were in front of his house.

These were battering lustily at the door.

Apart from them, their steel bayonets glittering in the uncertain light, were a party of marines.

Old Zachariah knew very well what this meant.

They had been put on the right scent now, and had come to capture Tom.

Very softly he slid the window to, and crept back to bed.

"It's them tarnation fools of officers again," he said to his better half, as he slipped gently under the bed-clothes.

"The officers!" gasped the lady, "and you come in to bed again with them trying to knock the house in!"

"Sartin'; let 'em knock, and be cussed to 'em; they'll get tired afore I'm tired of listening I guess—some."

At a loss what to do, the infuriated dame punched into her husband right and left.

"They'll break the house in—the house in! Do you hear?"

"Sarpints seize yer, woman; ain't the door stouter than a Californy tree? Let 'em knock, I say, and blazes to 'em!"

Bang, bang, bang! Clatter, clatter, clatter! Crash!

All the bolts seemed to be flying out of the ponderous door.

Smash went in a portion of the strongly-barred window.

It is possible, that even then, the landlord of the "Yellow Alligator" might have quietly dozed off again, so confident was he in the superior strength of his door, if his excited better half had not seized him by the hair of his head, and literally jerked him out of bed.

"Say, old girl," exclaimed the easy-going Kentuckian, "them roots ain't clenched tother side, and wool don't grow again at my time of day."

"You beast, you!" squealed his partner. "Go to them—speak to them, or I'll speak to them for you!"

"I guess, if I'd my tarnal will, I'd ram that old knocker down their cussed throats, and this long arm and fist in the bargain; if I wouldn't, snakes-hides and sugar!" grunted the old fellow, as he returned to the window. One of the officers was just then performing a vigorous flourish on the knocker; two others were battering it with immense beams.

As Zachariah put his head out, the summons for him to open the door became louder and fiercer from the perspiring officers.

One voice he could detect; it was that of Matthews, prominent amongst the others.

"Open house!" he bawled. "We are king's officers, come for pirates and robbers! Open, I say, or the door shall be battered in, and the house pulled beam from beam."

"Say, strangers," said a quiet voice above them

Looking up, they saw the nightcapped head of Zachariah.

"Say, strangers, you're kicking up a precious shindy down there among yourselves."

"You rascally hound!" cried an officer, "you are giving our prisoner a chance of escape. Come down at once, before we put a bullet through your skull."

"Tell you what, ole hoss," Zachariah said, coolly, "if I'm to be made a mark for your tarnal bullets, I'll pull in my old wool again; and as for letting yer prisoner escape, whoever that coon may be, strikes me you're making row enough outside to let any cuss know yer game, and send him out of yer way."

"Come down, I say!" roared another voice

"the house is surrounded by soldiers; no one can escape—open to law and justice!"

The head of old Zachariah went in with a jerk, and the inflamed visage of his better half popped out in its place.

"And if he stirs a step to let you in, the chicken-hearted stick," she shrieked, "I'll break his bony back in half, that's what I'll do! Open the door to you, indeed—a pretty set of ruffians to come banging at a peaceful woman's door at this hour of the night!"

"Come, come, Mother Magpie," you've tried this game before, you know. Open the door or it will be worse for you in the morning."

"Mother Magpie!" screamed the virago, "call me names. too, and to my face! There, that's for your precious impudence!"

Her head went in, her arm came out; something else came out also.

It was not the wash basin.

Nor were its contents harmless soapsuds.

And so the officer felt, as, before he could dodge out of the way, they came down in his chops, cannoning, as it were, from his face to those of his comrades.

As they howled with rage, the head of Mrs. Magpie went in, and the window closed with a sharp snap.

"This will never do!" exclaimed the sergeant of marines, now coming forward, "idling our time here; give them another challenge, and if that is not answered, my men shall beat in the door with their muskets."

The officer did give one more challenge; such a one it was—right and left the echoes rolled in a startling clamour.

It brought the scared heads of chambermaid, ostler, and travellers out of their respective windows, and shook the stoutly-built old habitation from basement to its topmost tile.

Whether this had its desired effect, or that old Zachariah had overheard the determination of the sergeant, there was no longer any delay.

In a half-clothed state he shuffled down the stairs, and after a tedious delay, during which his unwelcome visitors battered impatiently outside, the last bolt was withdrawn.

Two or three officers were pressing heavily against the door, and Zachariah, like the cunning old fox he was, drew it back with a jerk.

As a natural consequence, the said officers tumbled in, and rolled sprawling about his legs.

"Say there," growled mine host, "ain't yer got no manners, bundling in neck and crop like that, cuss yer, yer sarpints."

The pimpled countenance of his better half peered over the bannisters as the officers rolled in.

She was only half attired, had a monstrous bed-post under arm, and looked at the sprawling disturbers as if she would much have liked to single out a head for a drive.

And a tap of that bed-post, lunged with the force of her big, powerful arms, would have produced an uncomfortable crash on any skull it happened to hit.

"Now, lads,' said the sergeant, briskly, "search the place well while I and my men remain outside."

"Are you all loaded, men?"

A responsive reply came from the rank.

"Then keep your weapons cocked, and bring down, dead or maimed, any man you see attempting to escape from the house."

"You infernal old scamp," cried Matthews who was one of the tumbled officers, "you shall pay for this."

"Don't ruffle your wool, my 'tarnal lamb," replied Zachariah, quietly.

His more irascible wife bawled over the banisters,—

"Hit him, Zachariah—knock him down if he attempts to come this way."

"Sergeant," Matthews exclaimed, "let your men make that dangerous woman prisoner."

"Make me prisoner!" shrieked she, "let them try it! let them try it, I say!"

She flourished the bed-post as if it had been a toy.

"We don't want to annoy you, my good woman," Jonas said, "we've come for our man, and there's no occasion for you to be put out of the way. You needn't stay in your room when we come to search it."

"Say, stranger," exclaimed Zachariah, holding the flaring candle above his head, "guess I'll come and see yer scotch this critter."

Matthews snatched the light from his hand.

"Take care," he said, and grinding his teeth, led the way.

The officers were bent on a search, and a search they made in earnest.

They rummaged room after room, from kitchen to attic.

They scoured the cellars, and even ventured out of the lofts on to the tiles.

They peeped into cupboards, and under beds; dragged out musty old furniture, which had not been disturbed for years; tapped ceilings and walls, and sounded floors.

They hunted between the chambermaid's mattrasses, and banged her pillows, to see if they contained a huddled form.

The sleepy ostler was dragged from his straw; night tramps and wayfarers were roused from their drowsy rest.

But no sign of the culprit could they discover.

The only thing they started was a huge Tom cat, which howled and grimaced awfully as it scudded away.

During the whole of their search, the imperturbable Zachariah was at their elbows, stinging them to madness by his goading suggestions and sarcastic sneers.

In one room they found a weather-beaten tar, soundly asleep amidst all their din.

He was roughly awakened, and bidden to give an account of himself, which, albeit, in a very sleepy manner, he did to their satisfaction, and was left to his repose.

We need hardly say that the weather-beaten tar was our friend Bob Hauler.

The officers must have felt very hot indeed when they crept into the big desolate room where stood the veritable bed on which the object of their search had been sleeping less than half-an-hour before.

They found it, as Zachariah had expected, empty, and presenting no appearance of having been tenanted.

Our hero had heard the first of the disturbance, and touching the spring, had gone down to the secret hiding-place, between the floor of that room, and the ceiling of the next.

Here he was lying in silence and darkness,

when the hubbub over his head announced that the officers of justice were searching that room.

In his present concealment he was comparatively safe, but there was just a chance of the spring of the moveable bedstead being discovered, and so, listening for every sound, he waited with hand on his sword-hilt, ready to spring forth, or stand at bay for liberty or life.

Matthews, who directed the search, evidently had his suspicions about that room, not unreasonably, for, in spite of its bareness, it looked a likely place to hide in.

With a knowing look on his ill-bred face, the thief-taker stalked across the room, stamping heavily with his feet.

"Sounds hollow here," he said, stopping in the centre of the room, and looking cunning Zachariah.

The old fellow grinned.

"He ain't hiding in one of them cracks, is he?" he asked, sarcastically.

Matthews scowled.

"He's hiding here somewhere," he exclaimed, fiercely, "and we mean to find him, or we'll pull this place down level with the ground."

Old Zachariah grinned from ear to ear.

"Hearn tell of them sort o' tarnal places; but tell yer what, ole hoss, this here ain't one of 'em. When the lease is out I'll let you know."

"Men," shouted Matthews, beside himself with passion, "I am convinced he is skulking here somewhere. Follow me round the rooms; knock against the walls; we'll soon find out if he's behind them."

"Is that him behind you?" asked Zachariah.

Matthews sprang round, nearly knocking over a confederate.

"Look out!" bawled Zachariah.

Matthews leaped back again.

"Mind he don't get out at the window."

Matthews made a run towards that part of the room.

"Perhaps he's behind those curtains."

Matthews tore the moth-eaten old hangings open.

Nothing was there but an immense cloud of dust.

"Hallo, there he goes!" cried Zachariah.

There was a scuffle under the curtains.

All the officers rushed there at once.

But the disturber was only a monstrous rat.

"You're getting *hot*," said Old Zack, as they passed by the bedstead.

"Men," yelled Matthews, "this old scoundrel is only laughing at us—follow me."

They followed him in a body round the room, tapping at the walls with the butts of their pistols.

But everywhere it gave back the same dull sound.

One of those old-fashioned staircase clocks stood in a corner by itself, covered with dust, and looking a likely place for a pirate to hide in.

"Colder, colder, colder," Zachariah said, as Matthews cautiously tapped the case.

"I want the key of this!" Matthews exclaimed.

"Guess you'll want, seeing as how he put it in his pocket before he looked himself inside."

This was not very probable, considering that the door only locked from the outside, and Matthews, with a savage curse, took out a broad-bladed knife, and forced back the lock without further preamble.

The inside was vacant enough.

There hung the long pendulum, quiet enough, and crowded with cobwebs.

The two heavy weights were drawn up to the top.

Matthews put his head in.

"Plenty of dust and cobwebs inside—nothing more."

"Hallo! stop him!" bawled Zachariah.

Matthews sprung back in such a hurry that his thick skull came against the iron weights with a concussion that sounded all over the room.

The blow was so sudden that he thought he had been felled by the concealed boy buccaneer.

"Murder! seize him!" he cried.

Old Zachariah's laugh recalled him to his senses.

And with a malicious gleam in his evil eyes he kicked to the door of the clock.

Without deigning the old fellow a word, he walked straight to the big bedstead.

"Darned warm," cried Zachariah.

Matthews rapped against the post.

"Hotter! hotter!" the landlord sang out.

Matthews tried to understand what he meant.

Very cunningly he examined the affair.

"Curious kind of bedstead, that," Zachariah said.

"Yes," Matthews replied.

He had been stooping down to examine the wooden posts, and now he cried, quickly,—

"Here, men; two of you stand by the door, and keep an eye on that old thief; the others come here. We'll have these boards up."

"Snakes and alligators!" sang out Zachariah; "if it don't get darned hot—some!"

The officers had no doubt that their leader had stumbled upon a clue to Tom's hiding-place.

They got their pistols ready.

Some of them went rather pale, as Matthews began to rip the boards apart.

They had heard of the prowess of the daring boy hero, and at every sound expected to see him spring, like an angry panther, in the midst of them.

All their pistols were on full cock, and they meant to fire all together when he did show himself.

The old boards were well laid down, and it was some time before one could be lifted from its place.

No sound came from beneath.

Another plank was removed, and Matthews looked in.

"Just as I thought; room enough to hide a dozen."

"Say, ole hoss," Zachariah said, "shouldn't put my head in too far."

To do him justice, the thieftaker was no coward.

Taking no notice of the Kentuckian, he lit a closed lantern, and, pistol in hand, thrust his body half way in.

"Captain Tom Drake," he exclaimed, "surrender! I shall fire in each direction, so you'd better give in."

His voice sounded strangely hollow under the floor.

THE DOCTOR STRUCK VAINLY AT HIS ASSAILANTS.

There was no other sound.

Matthews spoke again.

"I warn you. When I have counted three I shall fire."

No answer.

Matthews counted slowly,—

"One, two, three."

A moment's silence.

Then the sharp crack, as he fired his pistol.

All was silent again.

No cry, no movement.

He took another pistol and fired again, this time in another direction, but with the same result.

When he had discharged a bullet in every direction, he took another loaded one from the hands of one of his comrades.

"If I raise a cry" he said, "rip open the boards. You will find me with the pirate, dead or alive."

He slipped his body under the musty boards, and crawled out of their sight.

So dense was the darkness that his lantern enabled him only faintly to look about.

The place was dark and close to suffocation.

It seemed to go the whole way under the floor, and he had just room to lie flat and crawl along.

He certainly had courage, to venture there.

To any one concealed in the misty hole, he must have been a visible mark, and the first token of the boy adventurer's presence might have been the passage of a sword through his prostrate body.

Crawling slowly over the heavy joists, he tried, by the light of his lantern, to look for the bleeding form of Captain Tom.

At almost every moment he had to stop, and clear the thick cobwebs from his face, while the thick mouldy dust rose in blinding clouds every time he raised his arm.

He had been under about five minutes, when the officers kneeling by the open gap were startled by a sudden agonized cry.

It was the voice of Matthews, convulsed and horrible in its shaken tones.

The officers sprang back, expecting to see the dreaded boy cruiser leap forth, his hands red with the blood of their comrade.

Even old Zachariah gave a start.

For a moment all stood still, then, remembering their leader's instructions, the officers tore up another of the worm-eaten planks, making an opening wide enough for them to see the struggling feet of their hardy comrade.

Half a dozen stood ready with loaded pistols, while two seized Matthews by his heels, and with a jerk dragged him forth.

He held no deadly pirate in his grasp.

No deed of blood had been committed under those mouldy boards.

The cause of this outcry was explained by the sight of a huge black rat, which had fastened on to his cheek, and still clung by its sharp fangs.

"Tarnation devils!" Zachariah cried, with a laugh, "I calkerlate yer make a better rat-catcher nor a trapper of pirates."

With his fingers and thumb he nipped the body of the ferocious animal.

The huge rat gave one writhe, and relinquishing his hold of Matthews' face, lay in Zachariah's grasp, its life squeezed out of its body.

"There, ole hoss," said the landlord, "that's done his business, and next time I want more on 'em caught, I'll send for you, cuss me if I don't."

Matthews wiped the blood from his lacerated cheek.

"We are foiled," he said; "I've been over every inch under there—a cat could not have escaped me."

"Nary rat either, I guess."

"Silence, you old scoundrel! We may have him yet, and then you shall answer for all."

A quiet grin passed over the old fellow's face.

He thrust his tongue significantly in his cheek as Matthews and his party left the room, and when the last had crossed the threshold, hummed, loud enough for them to hear,—

"Opossums and snakes, boiled beans and butter,
Sartain, I guess, you won't get any supper."

CHAPTER XXXI.

DEATH.

A FEW words are necessary to explain how it was that, after getting under the boards, the officer did not discover Tom.

The bedstead was so constructed that on pressing the spring, the lower part, with the bed, sank right through the floor, going beneath the parted floor, on the top of which Matthews had crawled.

As soon as it stopped, our hero slid off, when the bedstead rose to its place, and the ceiling of the lower room, which descended with the bedstead, resumed its proper position, leaving Tom ensconced in a narrow compartment under the wall, behind the bedstead.

A heavy beam was between him and the under floor, so that when Matthews discharged his pistol, the bullets flattened against the massive wood, leaving our hero unharmed.

The irascible hostess was waiting for them on the landing.

She had put down the formidable bedpost, but was evidently in no humour to put up with much more of their annoyance.

"Well," she exclaimed, "you've been having a pretty amusement, firing your pistols about every one's ears; but I hope you are satisfied, I'm sure I do. But where's the pirate?—haven't you got him yet?"

"No," gruffly replied Jonas; "but we mean to have him."

"Oh, you mean to; and pray where next are you going to turn topsy turvy?"

"We're going in here," responded Jonas.

And, suiting the action to the word, he walked into the landlady's own room, followed by the others.

Mrs. Magpie went in at their heels.

Every place they ransacked, amidst the biting sarcasm of the lady's tongue.

Jonas gave the landlady a furious look.

But her menacing attitude did not invite an attack; so, amidst the merriment of his brother officers, he bestowed a cursory examination upon a chest of drawers, but finding there not even the ghost of a pirate, was fain to confess himself beaten.

"Say, ole coons," said Zachariah, as the discomfited officers were looking blankly in each other's faces, "guess I might have saved yer a world of trouble."

"How?" was the angry inquiry.

"Wal, yer see; when these two hosses, Jem and his pal, comed here before, thar was a young cuss here, as says he was a liftenant in the navy."

"What of him?" asked Jem, hastily.

"Wal, yer see, sarpints, when you'd gone, he ups, and sez, sez he, 'Stranger, in case yer should want to know me when yer sees me agin, my name's Captain Tom Drake!'"

The landlady gave a squeal, and clung to the bedpost.

The officers surrounded Zachariah, and with angry cries demanded why he did not detain the pirate.

"Wal, yer daft critters, don't yer see, he didn't wait for this child to grab him. I was strick all of a heap, like, an' when I comed to, he'd gone slick clear, like a flash of greased lightning."

"You villain!" Jonas exclaimed, shaking the imperturbable landlord roughly, "why didn't you tell us this before?"

"Cos yer never asked me," replied the old fellow, quietly wriggling out of his grasp.

"Curses!" Matthews cried; "this infernal scoundrel has tricked us after all; separate, scour the place singly; and then to the rendezvous, to lay our plans for his capture."

Pell mell, they rushed down stairs, and tumultuously hurried out of the house; a brief consultation below, then, with slow steps, the soldiers tramped away, and the inn was left to its former silence.

Old Zachariah, who had walked to the window, waited till the last of the thieftakers were out of sight, when the broad grin left his face, and with a grave look he turned towards his wife.

A few words he spoke softly in her ear—words that seemed to deprive her of all power of speech or movement, for she stood gazing, open-mouthed, until he had quitted the room and closed the door, when she sank heavily on the bedside, and with her fat arms akimbo, appeared to be awaiting some unexpected and dreaded sound.

The gaunt Kentuckian stealthily descended to the apartment, where stood the big bedstead; thoughtfully, and as if scarcely conscious of what he was doing, he pressed the spring.

Slowly the bedstead went down—stopped—the machinery clicked—the bed re-appeared, and our hero scarcely waiting for it to stop, leapt gladly to the door.

"Thanks for that deliverance," he cried, "my limbs are stiff with their long confinement, and my eyes ache with the darkness. A snug hiding-place, Zach! but anything but a comfortable place to breathe in."

"Is all safe?" he asked presently.

"Wal, the varmints is gone for the present; but yer'll have to get out by underground, lest the sarpints 'll spot yer off as yer leave."

"Any way, old honest heart," our hero replied, "so that I depart unseen, and many thanks for your vigilance."

"Here," said the old man, slowly, "take this lantern, and go down stairs—fust door to the right. Count seven planks, go straight along the seventh; yer'll see a nail in the wall, pull it, a tarnal trap 'll open, go down, an' wait for me."

Tom threw his cloak over his shoulders, and taking the lantern, departed.

It struck him there was something peculiar in the old fellow's manner, but he asked no questions then.

When he was gone, the landlord of the "Yellow Alligator" walked slowly towards the room where Bob Hauler lay anxiously awaiting the result of the night's commotion.

He sprang eagerly up when Zachariah entered; but the old man beckoned him to be still.

"The skipper?" Bob asked, breathlessly.

"Guess his skin's whole, and likely to be, yer can make yer mind easy. I'll come for yer when all's clear."

"One an' eight," mumbled Zachariah, as he descended after Tom, "one an' eight make nine, I guess that's clear as day. Ah, nine in, eight out! eight out, one in. Wal, yes, I reckon. Sarpints, *whar's the one!*"

He walked straight along the plank, and opened the trap.

A ray of light came from below.

Tom was there awaiting him.

An iron ring enabled him to pull the trap down. A ladder reached to the floor. An instant or so he waited, *listening*, and a strange expression settled on his face.

And he was mumbling "one and eight," when he stood beside our hero.

They were in what appeared to be a series of dark cellars; that they were sometimes used was apparent from the fact that barrels and hogsheads were in most of them, and in one a store of bottles that had not been disturbed for years.

All the cellars communicated by small apertures, in some of which iron doors had been.

Time had been when the place was put to a different use than the storage of beer and wine.

There was another entry to the cellars—the way by which he had led the officers who had well searched the place at first, suspecting it to be the most likely hiding hole.

Zachariah, who had taken the lantern, led the way, and our hero following in silence. The old man was still muttering to himself. He was listening, too, intently, as if he were keeping his watch amid the subtle perils of the Indian's hunting ground.

Tom stopped abruptly while they were traversing the fifth cellar.

Quietly he laid his hand on Zachariah's arm, and looked meaningly in his face.

Zachariah started.

A cold moisture was on his iron features.

"Wal, I guess you've got ears," he said, scarcely above a breath, "and you've not made any tarnal mistake."

As if to himself, he muttered,—

"It's the *one.*"

All this occurred in a moment. Hardly had they paused when the sound that had arrested our hero's attention was repeated; this time plain enough to hear.

A man's footstep.

A tumult of conjectures were flashing through our hero's mind.

Was he betrayed?

Had the landlord inveigled him there, unarmed as he supposed him, to fall an easy prey to his assailants?

He had barely time to clutch a concealed pistol, when a shadow sprang from one of the dark apertures, and the form of the thieftaker, Matthews, stood revealed.

"Stand there!" he cried, huskily. "Life or death. I have you now. Move a finger, and I send this bullet through your skull. Ah, Captain Tom, you are trapped. Down on your knees and surrender, before I count two, or your brains will be scattered where you stand."

The thieftaker was shaking with excitement; his face was ghastly pale; the blood on his cheeks where the rat's fangs had torn the flesh, was horribly congealed; his lips were dry, his eyes stared wildly. He knew the hazard he run in seeking that single-handed capture; but there was triumph in his hoarse tones, as he stood, with his pistol held point blank at our hero, holding him for the moment at his mercy.

"Back, fool!" Tom cried, "you seek your death."

"Death, then; but for you!" Matthews cried, as, pressing his finger on the trigger, he sprang forward.

Old Zachariah had been keenly watching his movements.

A peculiar glitter was in his game eye; the glitter of mischief.

When he saw him take that bound, a strange exultant cry escaped his lips, and he dashed his hand fiercely against the wall where he stood

"Sarpints and squalls," he cried, "capture him thar."

What followed was almost too rapid for the eye.

Matthews' finger sharply pressed on the trigger—discharged the pistol as he moved forward—but simultaneously with that fatal step, the floor went from beneath his feet, and as the bullet sped harmlessly to the roof, he rolled heavily down the yawning gulf.

"Help! help! help!"

His cry was too late.

Old Zachariah had decoyed him to a trap.

The instinctive consciousness of his fate seemed in that moment to flash upon the thief-taker's mind, and the dull glare of the lantern, held in the landlord's trembling hands showed his haggard face and its deadly and convulsed agony, as the pistol dropped from his hold, and he went tumbling down.

One moment's wild tumultuous work.

The next, a strange awful stillness.

Then our hero followed Zachariah to the brink of the trap.

They looked down the blackness of the yawning gap.

The lantern flashed to its depths; flashed on a slimy, oozy, trickling mass—flashed on a haggard, bleeding face, a clenched, disabled hand, a prone, huddled form.

Not a cry; not a sound; not a quiver, even, of death's agony.

The work was done.

CHAPTER, XXXII.

MADE CERTAIN.

"Is it all over?" Tom asked, mournfully; for the man was brave, and though he knew he would have taken his life for the blood price set on his head, he pitied his fate.

"He won't feel the rats finish him," Zachariah replied; "it's his own tarnal fault, and now we'll close the hole; guess it's kinder unpleasant work, anyways; but 'twas him or you for a dead coon——"

"Hark!"

Our hero interrupted him with a sudden cry—

"He stirs! he speaks!"

Old Zachariah put out his brawny arms, and thrust Tom aside. He held a large horse pistol in his hand.

"It's a tarnal rat—a rat!" he cried, hoarsely. "See, I'll bring him down. Aha—thar, thar, thar!"

A sudden sharp report; a flash that lighted up the murderous cavern; something like a gurgling cry from below.

Then the trap door closed with a clang; the lantern fell from old Zachariah's hand, and the darkness and silence of a tomb reigned in the vault.

"Zachariah," Tom said, "was this necessary?"

The old man trembled like a leaf.

He turned his gastly face from the fearless boy hero's gaze.

"Stranger," he exclaimed, "it was him or you. I knowed the sarpint was tracking you, an' he's got the scent of human blood as would'nt disgrace a Cuba hound—it's jest his fate; but tell yer what, I've had many a fit with the Injuns; but nary day's work I've had with them critters has shook me like this

tarnal bisness. It's like murder—jest—an' that's how I feel it; but it war him or you—and I'd sarve a hundred more the same before I'd have you trapped by the varmints; an' now let me shew you the way out,"

"Let me first see if this man lives."

"Sarpints, no! I'll come agin, when you are safe from their hands, an' if his tumble down thar, an' the rats, ain't done his business, I'll let him out."

He forced Tom from the trap, and led the way from the cellar.

"You'll find your man thar," he said, pointing to Bob Hauler's room. "Thar's time for yer to clar out, and that's all. Them varmints is in ambush, or I'm no judge of human dealings, an' they'll come agin for their mate, sartin.

Without waiting for a word from our hero, he hurried from the landing.

Bob Hauler was ready dressed.

He saluted his brave leader warmly and respectfully, and in silence followed him down stairs.

Zachariah was at the door.

He seemed inclined to avoid his young guest, but Tom went straight up to the stanch old fellow, and gripped him by the hand.

"Farewell, Zach," he said, "I shall not forget the service you have rendered me. I owe to you my safety, perhaps my life—thanks. The time may soon come when I shall see you again."

Old Zachariah turned his head away.

A tear was in his eye.

"God bless yer," he cried, as he wrung the boy chieftain's hand. "I shall see yer a king yet among yer fellows—an' it'll cheer this old heart to know yer don't think harshly of Zachariah."

Tom's foot was on the threshold.

He was in the act of stepping forth, when his old friend was pushed sharply aside, and two big, soft arms wound themselves round our hero's graceful form.

He felt himself drawn towards a huge mass of flesh, and as soon as he could look up he found that he was in the embrace of Mother Magpie.

"I know you," she cried. "You desperate, determined, good-looking, blood-thirsty, merciless, noble young man! You wicked fellow, you! I ought to betray you, I ought—you are so bad. But I can't forget the times I've nursed you when you was a boy. There, good-bye, you bad boy."

She gave our hero a regular hug, and bestowing two hearty smacks upon his round cheeks, in the way of kisses, released him from her fat arms and pushed him from the door.

In spite of his feelings, Tom could not help smiling.

He waved his hand gallantly, and bade the pair adieu—but not until he was out of sight was the door closed upon him by old Zachariah and Mother Magpie.

The human blood-hunters seemed off the scent.

Tom and his faithful attendant walked on in silence, and unmolested.

Each was busy with his own thoughts—our hero thinking of the tragic fate of the thief-taker and Bob Hauler mentally wishing himself and his beloved leader safe on board ship, and far out on the sea away from the dangers of shore.

Once or twice the brave-hearted fellow stole a glance at his chieftain's youthful face.

Seldom had he seen so grave a look on Tom's handsome countenance

Bob Hauler had no need to ask questions.

He *felt* that his young commander's life had been jeopardised, and that some fearful tragedy had taken place within the walls of the ancient inn.

A walk of a few miles across country brought them to a rambling old tavern, bigger, but more secure than the one they had left behind them.

Bob Hauler, having wistfully regarded the hospitable-looking tavern, raised his inquiring glance to his chieftain's face.

"We will enter," said Tom, replying to Bob's look. "We have need of refreshments before proceeding on our way."

"Ay, ay, sir," Bob replied; "and if I might be so bold, an hour's sleep wouldn't do you no kind of harm, for I'll warrant you've had little sleep since we came ashore."

"I have not had too much sleep, Bob," our hero remarked with a smile, "but we will make sure of the character of the house before we think of taking rest under its roof."

"As for me, sir, I've slept enough; it's for you I speak, and the house seems quiet like; I shouldn't think you'd be disturbed."

"No, they don't seem to have pirates and such marauders here."

"Nor them fierce blood-hunters," rejoined Bob, "that's a sight worse than even a pirate or the highwayman they runs down to death"

A summons at the door brought forth a sleepy ostler, who speedily, however, admitted them to the house, and conducted them to a cozy room, where he begged them to sit while he called the landlord to do honour to the gentlemen.

Mine host, a stout, jolly-faced, hale old man, soon made his appearance, and having learned his guests' demands, quickly had them attended to.

He took a hard look at Tom as he put wine and viands on the table, and in reply to the question whether they could rest there till the day advanced, protested that his best chamber was at their service.

A spruce, clean housemaid appeared by the time our travellers had partaken of refreshment, and with respectful courtesies conducted them to their room—a large, old-fashioned chamber, so big that the two huge four-post bedsteads were lost in its corners.

Our hero hastily divested himself of his outer clothing, and threw himself upon one of the beds, motioning Bob Hauler to follow his example.

But the faithful fellow, though worn out from want of sleep, refused to go to bed.

"I'll keep watch while you sleep, sir," he said. "I don't half like the cut of this caboose; besides them big bedsteads ain't within hail of each other. So, by your leave, I'll keep watch in this chair."

Captain Tom did not press his follower, but resolving to snatch an hour's repose while he had the chance, closed his eyes, and was almost instantly asleep.

Bob Hauler seated himself in a big arm chair, and edging close to the fire, with his back to the wall, watched the boyish face of his youthful leader.

"Sleeps as quiet as a babe," Bob Hauler soliloquised; "who'd think, to look at that quiet gentle face of his, that he could be such a devil when he's roused. Ah! nobody would believe what he's gone through since me and poor Jerry saw him tumble off the cliff into the Smuggler's Bay. I could'nt never have dreamed he'd have come to be what he is. It don't seem hardly likely, much less true."

"Don't like his giving himself up to these long shore trips," he presently resumed; "'taint to his good—there's such a many trying to nab him for the blood-money, and he'd never be taken if he'd stay aboard, for there ain't one of us would'nt be chopped to bits rather than see him took."

BOOK II.

CHAPTER I.

TOM'S DREAM.

MUSING in his way, and alternately gazing into the flickering fire and his young chief's features, Bob Hauler trying to keep off his growing drowsiness, unconsciously dropped into a reverie, under the influence of which combined with the lonely desolation of the big room, he fell into a slight doze.

He hardly seemed to have slept two seconds when he awoke with a sudden start, and leapt to his feet.

A strange conviction of treachery flashing to his mind.

The fire had nearly burnt out, the candle gave only a faint glimmer, lighting a few yards around, and leaving the rest of the room in utter darkness.

His first glance was towards the bed.

It was empty.

But between him and the ponderous bedstead stood the graceful form of the Boy Rover.

He was gliding towards Bob Hauler—his face was deadly pale—his eyes were fixed and staring, and there was something in his look that made Bob Hauler's flesh creep, as Tom got nearer to him.

Evidently he did not see him.

He had leapt from his bed in a state of stupor, and was still under its influence.

Bob Hauler put himself right in our hero's way, and seizing his hands uttered his name.

The sound of his voice aroused Tom.

He leapt as if he had been shot.

Then instantly recognising his follower, spoke—

"I have alarmed you—it was a dream—it could have been nothing else. No, no; I could never believe it to be real!"

He passed his hand before his eyes.

"I dreamed," he presently said, "that my dearest wishes were all accomplished. My country no longer ungrateful for the services I had rendered, recognized and honoured me, and I stood on the quarter-deck of my gallant ship, an English admiral, all my brave crew surrounding me—faithful hearts, their honest cheers were yet ringing in my ears, when the dream changed. I dreamed my darling bride, my Minnie, forswore me, and became the

tribe of another. I saw her by her husband's
side, and it was to get at his throat that I
leapt from the bed."

Bob Hauler saw that his youthful chieftain
shivered slightly.

His hand was cold as death.

With tender respect, he counselled him to
forget his dream, and again seek repose.

"No, no," Tom replied, "I cannot sleep
again; it is your turn now. I will sit here
while you sleep."

Bob Hauler would have held out, but Tom
was peremptory; and the bold hearted tar
took his turn in, while our hero sat still and
thoughtful by the flickering embers.

The day was far advanced before he aroused
from his reverie, and bestirred himself to
action.

The fire was dead in the grate, and a feeble
gleam of light shone in at the darkened windows.

He removed the heavy shutters to let in the
daylight, and aroused Bob Hauler.

The hardy fellow sprang to his feet, and together they descended the stairs.

Our hero ate but sparingly of his breakfast.

His mind was troubled by his dream, and
in spite of his efforts he could not dismiss it
from his mind.

The meal despatched and the reckoning
paid, they departed from the house, the landlord thoughtfully gazing after them until
they were out of sight.

When they were a little way on their road,
Bob Hauler ventured to inquire whether they
were bound for their ship.

"I shall not yet return," was the chieftain's
reply. "When we reach Smuggler's Point,
make the best of your way on board, and say
I shall follow you in a few hours. Tell Ben
Barnacle to be on the look out for shore, and
to have all ready for instant departure."

Bob did not much relish the idea of leaving
his beloved leader, but he knew he must perforce obey orders.

Our hero, meanwhile, repaired to the residence of Lady Arbuthnot.

He wished to see her respecting Minnie,
whom she had visited at Lady Castlemaine's.

Her ladyship was not at home the first time
he called, and it was getting dark when he
again presented himself.

Knowing that old Lord Henry, her ladyship's husband, was of an awfully jealous
temperament, it struck him that he might
have seen him approaching and have denied
him a audience, a trick that he had been
known to serve other gallants, who he feared
might make too free with his lovely wife.

Our hero resolved to enter by the side
gate, and make his way through the shrubbery.

The old lodge-keeper, who saw him go in,
smiled quaintly.

Not fifteen minutes earlier, the antique gate
had creaked on its hinges to admit another
visitor.

The lodge-keeper had been in the family a
generation; his master was young when he
himself was a boy, and he had never liked
his taking to himself Lady Arbuthnot for a
wife.

She was too young and beautiful to suit
the decrepit old servitor's taste.

Besides, her time was given to ceaseless
balls and parties, in place of being spent with

her venerable husband in the old rookery
known as Castle Rock.

So he smiled knowingly when he saw Tom
go in.

He who had entered before was one whom
Tom might have had reason to avoid had he
known of his presence there.

The Hon. Archibald Gaston.

He had come ashore the previous day from
Admiral Ellis's ship and had stole into the
shrubbery in the hope of meeting Lady
Arbuthnot, whose ravishing beauty, as she
danced with him the previous night, had
excited his hot passions, and made him dare
all in the hope of gaining her smiles.

Very like a thief in the fold did he look
as he crept along the concealment of the
shrubbery to her ladyship's favourite bower
—a charming, secluded spot, begirt with rarest
flowers, and surrounded by cool fountains,
making the air soft and fresh.

He was uncertain whether Lady Arbuthnot
might be out of doors, and his heart beat
with fervid excitement when he came upon a
full view of the fairy-like bower, and beheld
the beautiful mistress of Castle Rock.

She was standing within the shadow of a
marble temple, round whose slender columns
roses and eglantines climbed.

She was attired in a robe of purest white;
its soft folds falling ravishingly about her
voluptuous form.

Her beautiful arms were bare, and a
gossamer-like scarf was drawn across her
shoulders, whose dazzling loveliness were
only half hidden by the transparent drapery.

Gaston was transfixed for the moment by
this vision of her superb loveliness.

She looked so purely beautiful, that if his
brain had not been fired by his blind passion,
he must have retreated, ashamed of his vile
intents.

But her charms only gave new fervour to
his wild hopes, and, advancing softly, he
placed himself in her sight.

Lady Arbuthnot started when her glance
fell upon him.

He seemed to her like some noisome thing,
obtruded suddenly from amidst her favourite
flowers.

She inclined her head coldly, as he bowed
almost to the ground.

This did not content him.

He advanced to the marble pillars, and
stood between her and her way of egress.

The picturesque little temple could be seen
some distance off, and our hero had just caught
sight of Lady Arbuthnot, standing like a
priestess beneath its fane, when Lieutenant
Gaston came upon the scene.

He did not at first recognize Gaston, and,
not knowing that he might not be intruding
on some assignation, held aloof.

"Some favoured cavalier, bidden to meet
his mistress in that bower of love," he mused;
"yet it seems strange she should yield; had
any man hinted this to me I should have felt
inclined to drive the lie at the top of my
sword down his throat. The old, old story
though—youth and age—a withered imbecile
plucks some such blooming flower for his own,
and thinks to revel in its sweetness. Vain
delusion—oh! they meet—not a very warm
greeting for a lover that—perhaps I do the
lady wrong, I'll watch."

He did watch, and was considerably interested at what he saw.

Gaston got closer to Lady Arbuthnot.

He was warmly pleading his sinister suit—pleading in words and manner which brought the rich flush of anger and shame to her ladyship's brow, as she bade him leave her presence, at the same time asking him why he chose that occasion for so base an insult.

Tom, who had quickened his steps, was near enough to overhear the audacious answer.

"I have sought you alone, Lady Arbuthnot, because I was resolved no one should interrupt the pleading of my cause—blame not my rashness, your loveliness has driven me mad. I love you madly, devotedly. Oh! do not spurn—smile on me, and I will give you a love more dear and devoted than the cold fancy of your aged husband. Be mine! our love can be in secret. On my knees I implore you to let me love you, and call you mine!"

Lady Arbuthnot's cheeks crimsoned.

"Rise sir," she cried. "Linger here an instant and my husband's servants shall lash you from these grounds. Dare to repeat your infamous proposals, and I myself will strike you where you kneel."

Gaston leaped impetuously to his feet.

"If I meet a madman's punishment," he cried, hoarsely. "I will have a madman's bliss. You shall be mine—I swear it, by heaven and hell, and this kiss shall seal our passion."

His arm entwined her supple waist, his hand fastened on her wrist.

The insult rendered her speechless with rage, and he was drawing her so close to him, that in another instant his hot lips would have polluted hers with his burning caress.

This was the moment our hero resolved upon for interference.

Quickly stepping from his concealment, he took Gaston by the nape of the neck, and, dexterously planting his foot, hurled the would-be libertine down the marble steps on to the gravel path beneath.

Now to be taken aback at such a moment, when, heated with excited passion, his lips were almost touching the ripe lips of the beautiful woman with whom he fancied himself alone, and whose soft, enticing limbs and exquisite form were in blissful contract with his own—to be taken by the nape of the neck in a rude grasp, twisted helplessly off his feet, and sent ignominiously reeling on all fours down a flight of steps, was enough, in all conscience, to sting to frenzy any cavalier of such vicious impulses, and spur him to the fiercest revenge.

But when Gaston leapt to his feet, ghastly in feature, his eyes wild, a foam of fury about his lips, he no sooner caught sight of the graceful form confronting him, in all the resolute beauty of its slim strength—than he reeled again, ghastlier than before, and in place of springing wildly upon him, fell back, thunder-stricken.

He seemed paralyzed for a moment; but then a change came over him.

He did not attempt to pit his fury against the known prowess of our hero; but, with a deadly glare of hate on his features, he cried hoarsely—

"Pirate, I know you! Run for your worthless life! You will not escape! You shall swing this time on a gallows tree!"

Tom took a step towards Harry Vere's old foe, but Gaston did not wait for him to reach him.

He hastened from the spot to summon a trusty party, who would satiate his venomous hate by the capture of Tom, and our hero was left in the interesting position of being alone with the lovely lady whom he had rescued from a libertine.

———

CHAPTER II.

THE LANDLORD OF THE "BLUE LOBSTER" STARTS ON THE TRACK OF HIS WIFE AND THE GALLANT CAPTAIN.

SIMON GAGG swore a dreadful oath when it became too evident that little Nancy had departed with the spruce captain of the *Civet Cat*.

He cursed the folly which had led him, after what he had seen, to leave his wife the opportunity of quitting the house during his absence.

But it was the very last thing he would have expected to occur, for Nancy, notwithstanding he treated her most brutally, was docile and obedient, and had, he imagined, too great a dread of him ever to oppose or act against his wishes.

The truth was, that very dread induced Nancy to listen to the ardent solicitations of the gay captain, and leave for ever the husband whose cruelty and violence she knew she would be subjected to after the captain had taken his departure.

So, with many qualms and misgivings, she had consented to trust herself on board the *Civet Cat*, and seek in the society of her admirer that happiness which she knew was not to be attained in the company of her husband.

Nancy was a notable instance of what a really true-hearted woman might become under the harsh usage of the man who was bound to be her protector and guide.

Despite his rough aspect and coarse manners, she entertained an affection for Simon, which it had been in his power to render abiding and strong.

But he drove her love from him by ill-usage, and thus smoothed the way for the advances of the gallant and more attentive captain.

But Simon stayed not to consider this.

He heaped curses upon her, and as he stood at the door of the inn, now so desolate in her absence, he took, as I have said, a dreadful vow of retaliation.

"I will cross 'em," he said, his passion gaining complete mastery over him. "Curse 'em! I'll reach 'em yet, and then let 'em look out, for when I do strike they shall feel the blow!"

Muttering thus, he took his way towards Willesdale Hall, where, fattening on his ill-gotten gains, the brutal Sanderson lived in state with poor old Gregory's money.

He had pampered menials to wait upon him, and one of these was Rupert Jeames, a flunkey of the very first water, who was standing at the hall-door, absorbed in admiring contemplation of his own calves, when Simon Gagg arrived.

The landlord's ill-humour was at its height when he encountered this exquisite menial, gorgeous in plush and powder, and striding up the steps he pushed him roughly out of the way.

"Where's yer master, booby?" he said, "I wants him."

"Fellow!" replied the astounded flunkey—"aw—keep off. Aw—Mr Sanderson is—aw—engaged."

"Tell him as Simon Gagg wants to see him, jackanapes," exclaimed the irate landlord, "he'll see me, I knows."

"Fellah! what do you mean? Get out, before I call my fellows to turn you out."

"Look here, you monkey in plush; jest go and give my message, or it'll be worse for you."

"You're drunk, you idle vagabond!" rejoined Rupert, now thoroughly aroused. "Get out at once, or I will turn you out."

Rupert looked ineffably grand at that moment.

Simon regarded him with a curious look.

"Well!" he ejaculated, that is a good 'un! Turn I out! Well, you'd better try that on,' an' squared up to the refined Rupert.

Now, to the sensitive and polished mind there is something most disgusting in the sight of a rough bully squaring and sparring his blackguard arms before a gentleman, more especially if he of the refined and polished mind be the gentleman so menaced.

It is not, therefore, surprising that the polite Rupert on beholding the coarse Simon Gagg advancing in the most scientific and pugnacious manner, instinctively retreated a pace or two.

Whether it was that his retrograde movement, which, it is said, inspires even a coward with valour, influenced Simon, or whether it was that his wrath was thoroughly aroused, cannot be vouched for, but certain it is that as Rupert Jeames retreated, Simon angrily advanced, and before his astonished opponent could divine his intention, struck him two such scientific blows in the face that the blood poured in jets from his delicate nose, and a discolouration commenced immediately around his eye.

There have been brave men who have fainted at the sight of a cat's back being rubbed the wrong way; or when the scratch of a knife on a plate has jarred upon their ears.

Rupert Jeames was not without his particular antipathy, and when he received those stinging blows, and saw the stain oozing down his immaculate shirt-frill he was completely overcome.

His courage left him, and he fled hastily to the kitchen stairs, followed by the wrathful Simon.

He had just placed his toe upon the top stair, when the upraised foot of his vengeful foe lodged in the small of his back, increasing the velocity of his descent to such a degree, that his head reached the stone flooring of the passage before his feet.

While he lay rubbing the bump on the back of his wounded head, a door was opened quickly, and Sanderson appeared upon the scene.

"What is the meaning of this?" he said, angrily. "You here, Simon!"

"I be wanting to see 'ee Squire."

"Come this way then. Now what is it?" he said when they had entered his sitting room.

"I be going to do what 'ee said; I be going a furren journey.

Sanderson stared at him in surprise; but Simon briefly explained matters, and ended by a demand for money,

"It'll be some time afore I troubles you agin, 'cos it's werry likely I shan't coame back jest yet."

Sanderson seemed, by the glance he bestowed upon him, to wish he might never come back; but he wrote out the order for the sum demanded, and handed it to Simon.

"'Ee be glad I be going," said that worthy, as he placed the cheque in his pocket. "'Ee be loikely to have a quiet time if we doan't coame back agin."

"Are you going far, Simon?"

"Werry far."

"What have you done with the inn?"

"Left it. You can gie it to Tim when yer sees him"

So saying Simon shuffled out of the room, and out of the house; and that same day he departed on his distant expedition.

He had sworn not to rest till he had tracked the pair, and made his wife, and the man whom she had eloped with, feel the sting of his revenge.

CHAPTER III.

ON BOARD THE "CIVET CAT."—CAPTAIN ANGEL TAKES SERVICE WITH HIS CAPTORS.

BOUND hand and foot, Captain Angel was brought by his captors on board the *Civet Cat*, then lying off Morecambe Bay.

He was placed securely in the hold, nor was he suffered to come upon deck until the schooner was standing out to sea.

The *Civet Cat* was a somewhat suspicious-looking craft.

She bore her canvas heavily, and seemed clumsy in her gear, but her length of beam, and the sharpness of her bows, with the motley crew that manned her decks, were less suited to a peaceful mercantile vessel than to one of a more questionable nature.

Her crew consisted of a rough, dissolute set of men of all nations, and apparently the pick of the worst class; but the discipline on board was perfect, and Captain Yates strode the quarter-deck like a monarch.

Nancy, who had cast in her fortunes with the captain, remained much below.

Her conscience reproved her for the step she had taken, and more than once her mind was troubled with strange fears respecting the character of Captain Yates and his determined-looking crew.

Had she known the actual truth, not all her husband's cruelty, nor the captain's persuasions and assurances of love, had induced her to tread the deck of that ship, for the *Civet Cat* was nothing less than a slaver and a *pirate*.

They were sailing in the Bay of Biscay before Angel was allowed to come on deck.

Since his forced embarkation, he had been moody and sullen, neither replying to the familiar overtures of the men, nor noticing their derisive scoffs.

There was an alteration in him already.

His cheeks had become somewhat sunken and sallow, and he kept his lips closed as though they were sealed together; but it was in his small, deadly eyes that his inward fury was revealed.

In these few days since his capture he had endured an age of torture.

To have been foiled, outwitted, and entrapped, was wormwood to his soul, but to be swept from the path of his dupe at the moment of triumph, when all he had so long and so cunningly plotted for appeared within his grasp, was indeed torture.

He fancied he could see the exultant Sanderson, hear his laugh as he rejoiced over the discomfiture of the man he dreaded, and whom he had out-Heroded in cunning.

Prominent in his mind was the desire of escape.

At one time he thought of leaping into the sea, and trusting to the chance of being picked up; reflection convinced him that the scheme would be worse than madness.

Then he thought of watching his opportunity to murder the captain and his officers, but this he abandoned, the chance being that he would swing from the yard-arm in the attempt.

He would have fired the ship, and destroyed himself and his captors, but that the idea of vengeance upon Sanderson was uppermost, and he would not throw away his life without the acquisition of his revenge.

"No," he muttered, "to do that were to play into Sanderson's hands. How he would rejoice in my death! Curse him! he is successful now, but I shall yet return to mar his felicity, and spoil his dearest schemes. Aye, aye, his hour of triumph shall be brief. Fool that I was to suffer myself to be decoyed into the trap! Out-witted by a boy! Out-manœuvred by the shallow Sanderson! Oh! the hour shall come for my revenge."

"Stranger," said Yates, approaching, "yer don't seem to find yer voyage kinder pleasant. You're oneasy at the thought of the friends you've left behind yer."

Angel turned fiercely upon him.

Had they stood there alone, it is more than probable that he would have hurled his mocking foe into the sea, but there were some of the seamen near, and he restrained himself, though with difficulty keeping his fingers from the captain's throat.

"Come, stranger, don't be onsociable; if yer wants gentlemanly treatment ye'll have to be mighty civil here, I can tell yer, an' no mistake."

Angel glanced along the expanse of waters, as he replied—

"Words are not needed to convince me into whose hands I have fallen."

"Well, it's jest your own look-out how yer find the voyage."

"Is your destination far?"

"I guess yourn is," the American replied with a laugh.

That deadly gleam in those snake-like orbs grew deadlier.

"Fool! whither are you bound?"

"Fool! I kalkerlate that style of language won't do here; so I recommend yer jest to guard that tongue o' yourn."

"Pshaw! these are idle threats; you have taken an enemy into your keeping more deadly than the venomous snake of the jungle—beware of its fangs!"

Captain Yates ejected his quid of tobacco from his mouth, and inserted another "plug," ere he replied.

"Look here, stranger, you see that 'ere yard-arm? Well, I guess, fangs or no fangs, you'd look darned queer dangling there in the blessed sunshine. I know yer—I knew afore I had yer in my keeping what a blessed chicken yer wor; and I've looked after you like a mother. Don't put yourself out o' the way, we've taken your measure entirely."

The thin lips of Captain Angel quivered a little as he listened.

"Do you fear to tell me," he exclaimed, "whither we are bound?"

"Well, yer going a pleasant voyage, passage paid by a very pertioler friend up at the old Hall. We're going to the land of niggers and guineas, and I guess we'll have plenty o' both before we return."

"Then we shall return?"

The captain looked cunningly at him.

"Well, we've got to leave yer with the natives; ye'll be happy enough, I dessay; might teach the blacks an' be their king, who knows?"

Captain Angel had now regained his wonted collected and composed manner.

He had found at length a man worthy of trying his powers with.

He had failed once, but then he did not know whom he had to cope with.

He knew now, and doubted not of the result.

"That it was the wish of my friend Sanderson that my bones should lie on African soil I do not doubt, but that is not your intention I am equally sure."

"Well, you're a 'cute chap. What makes yer think I've took sich a fancy to ye?"

"The trouble you have taken to bring me here, which you would not have taken with a doomed man, whose burial fees you were paid. You see I am not quite loose-witted. And now, my friend, what is it you want me for?"

He laid his hand familiarly upon the captain's shoulder as he concluded.

"Well, darn me! I likes yer, snakes if I don't. I knew you'd be useful when I saw yer cool nerve up yonder in the wood. And now I'll tell yer what I want yer for. This lubberly-looking craft that I've seen yer admiring so—and I guess you've took her build entirely, does a little business whar we re going to? She'll be smarter in her out when we get out o' these seas; and you'll find the Civet Cat can show her teeth when the time comes. And yer see, guv'nor, I've read you; I know you've trod a quarter-deck afore, and by the seaman-like out o' yer cat-head, I see yer could steer the Puss through a shoal, whether of rocks or enemies; and so, if yer like, yer shall be my liftenant, and darn me if I shan't be proud o' yer?"

Angel manifested neither surprise nor impatience at this lengthy address, but when it was finished he coolly surveyed the ship and crew, and then replied,—

"I accept your offer."

"Well, so I guess; yes, rather; so tip us yer fin."

"It is unnecessary! when the time for action comes, you will find me in my place. I keep my hand and arm for my enemies; my friends need not desire either."

"Well, you're a queer customer; but never mind, only just remember this, that there's only one master aboard this precious kitten, and I'm that coon."

"Your authority will not be questioned, at least by me."

"Wal, that's all right; only look out that yer don't try any sneaking off bizness. I want yer here, an' I tell yer, just try to bilk us by slipping away, and darn me yer'll find how well ye'er looked after."

"Enough," said Captain Angel, as he turned away, and leant over the taffrail. "I shall not fail in my part of the compact."

Who shall tell what was passing in his mind as he gazed across the interminable sea?

There was more trace of emotion in his looks than was usually to be seen there; his thin lips quivered and quivered, and even his sullen eyes seemed moist.

Was he thinking over some devilish plan to rid himself of the man who, instead of sending him to death in the ocean's depths, or leaving him to die on the fever-bound coast of Africa, as Sanderson had paid him to do, had made him his associate, and given him command on the vessel which had been his prison?

Was he thinking of that in order to turn the schooner's prow towards Albion's white cliffs, that he might return, and, with his deadly venom swelling in his breast, fling himself upon Sanderson's sight, to dash the cup of triumph from his lips, and shrivel his very heart with the horrible terrors of his hate—of his revenge.

Perhaps so, for as he gazed, the murderous gleam deepened in his eyes, and his lips curled and wreathed with a Satanic sneer.

No one came near him to disturb his thought, and he stood yet moodily glancing across the sea, when the gloomy vapour of night varied the colour of the moaning waters.

*   *   *   *   *

Out on the broad expanse of the North Atlantic Ocean the aspect of the *Civet Cat* underwent a change.

The heavy lumbering sails and yards were cleared away.

The masts were lengthened, and the vessel was rigged smart and trim.

The decks were cleared, and four long brass guns hauled from their secret stowage.

The *Civet Cat* was in her proper latitude, and had begun to sharpen her claws and display her teeth.

Under the impetus of a freshening breeze, she rode swiftly through the waters, and Captain Angel saw that she excelled in those qualities essential to fit her for the work she had to engage in.

The crew were ever on the alert, and a good look-out was kept from the maintop; the *Civet Cat* was in quest of her prey.

Angel was pacing the quarter-deck with Captain Yates, when the man in the maintop sung out that there was a sail ahead, and the captain, taking a glass, surveyed the horizon; but he discerned nothing save the sky and the waves.

"Where away?" he asked.

"On the larboard quarter."

Captain Yates again raised his glass, and after a long survey, distinguished a small speck in the distance.

"I can't make her out," he said, turning to Angel.

The latter took the glass.

"A merchantman by her rig," he said, presently.

"Ready, my lads, there's a prize in view!"

exclaimed the captain, and he was answered by shouts of "Ay, ay, sir," as the crew hurried away in all directions, and busied themselves in deadly preparations.

The captain again sung out,—

"Run up the Spaniard."

Up went the flag of Spain.

The preparations were brief, but deadly; the guns were loaded, and the men arming themselves with muskets, pistols, pikes, and cutlasses, lay down on the deck, and awaited the approach of the unsuspecting merchantman, gradually becoming more distinct.

She was a rather large sailing vessel, and now, as she neared them, bounded over the billows with a graceful sweep; her direction, unless changed, would bring her right across the bows of the *Civet Cat*.

Captain Yates prepared to bring his vessel to.

"Make ready, boarders; here with the grappling-irons and boarding-pikes."

"Ay, ay, sir," was the ready response.

"I will lead them," said Angel, to which proposal the captain assented.

Steadily careering over the bosom of the wide ocean, the strange vessel approached; the British flag swayed from the mizen peak, and every sail seemed spread to accelerate her speed.

And Now the two vessels neared one another; all was silent on board the *Civet Cat*; the captain, with his speaking-trumpet in his hand, stood by his new associate, and a few of the crew were about the bulwarks, the rest were crouched on the deck preparing for the deadly spring.

Captain Yates's voice was now heard as the vessels came within speaking distance.

"Ship ahoy!"

"Hilloa!" rang out from the other's deck.

"What ship, and where from, and where bound?"

"The *Josephine*; from Cape Town to Belfast. What ship is that?"

No answer was returned, but, in an instant, the Spanish flag was hauled down, and from the mast floated the ominous banner of doom—the pirates' black flag.

At the same moment the loud tones of Captain Yates were heard as he gave the order—

"Fire!"

The decks of the *Josephine* were crowded with people; the passengers, who were gathered to greet an outspeeding vessel, and the crew, who stood to cheer her as she passed.

When that flag of death streamed before them, they retreated in horror and dismay, and the ship bore away.

But the murderous discharge poured into their midst, and the deck was strewn with the wounded and slain.

"About ship!" shouted the astonished captain of the *Josephine*.

But he was too late, the grappling irons of the *Civet Cat* held her fast.

Another discharge swept her decks, and the ruffianly pirates swarmed up her sides.

Then arose the din of musketry, and the clash of steel, mingled with the shrieks of women and the groans and prayers of men.

The crew of the *Josephine*, taken by surprise, made what defence they could, but the pirates dealt death with unsparing ferocity nd the deck of the ill-fated ship was heaped with the slain.

Foremost in the conflict was Captain Angel, his slim form towering above his men; calm, cool, and collected, armed only with a light cut and thrust, he slew all that came before him.

His was no arm unused to strike; the slender blade fenced off every blow that threatened him, and dealt death indiscriminately around.

In the midst of this deadly strife, he found himself confronted by one of the passengers of the *Josephine*

He was an elderly, distinguished-looking man, and stopped suddenly on beholding Angel.

"Good heavens, Angel!" he exclaimed, "you here in this sanguinary business? For God's sake stop this horrible massacre."

"I will," said Angel, as he ran his thin blade through the other's body, and passed on to fresh slaughter.

Quarter was asked, but none was given.

Not until the last of their antagonists sank beneath his numerous wounds that the carnage was stayed.

Then the pirates rushed *en masse* down the gangways, and into the cabins, and, having ransacked the vessel for its valuables, soon appeared on deck laden with rich spoils, for the *Josephine* was freighted with silks and specie, and had amongst her passengers many who had brought much wealth on board; she had besides a number of casks of wine, and these were hauled upon deck.

Captain Yates stepped on board from the *Civet Cat*, and proceeded to superintend the carrying away and secreting of the booty thus lawlessly gained.

"What do you intend doing with these?" asked Angel, pointing with his blood-stained rapier to the unhappy women whom the pirate-crew held prisoners.

"Prizes," was the laconic reply.

"A pretty arrangement, truly; but see, they are shipping the wine on board the *Civet*. You will not burden yourself with that at the outset, will you?"

"The lads will look for a swimming carousal."

"Then while I'm first lieutenant of the *Civet Cat*," Captain Angel said, "they do not have it. What! at the very commencement of our cruise, ere we can have the vessel trimmed to avoid suspicion, you take on board two such dangerous articles as wine and women—the very ingredients of discord. The ship will be in a mutiny in a week, and remember, British men-of-war are always fishing in these waters."

Captain Yates wrinkled up his features with a puzzled air.

His lieutenant's coolness surprised him.

"What are yer driving at?" he said. "I should have a mutiny if I were to deprive them of their prizes."

"Leave them to me; see, even now their passions are aroused. Heated with wine, and slaves to their captives, they would not be safe for a day. Have you done with the prize?"

"Wal, I reckon yes."

"Then if you will return I will manage the crew."

Captain Yates went back to his vessel, and Angel walked aft to the men.

"Now, men, get ready to ship off. Leave those barrels, we have wine enough on board. Fire the ship and leave her."

The ruffians murmured at being deprived of their intended carousal; but their lieutenant was not a man to be questioned, and in a few minutes all was completed, and smoke issued in various directions from the ship.

"Now, men, get on board your own vessel at once. On board with you. Leave those ladies here. Away with you," he continued, as the crew began to remonstrate.

They sullenly obeyed, and leapt on to the deck of the *Civet Cat*.

"Ladies," said Captain Angel, "I have rescued you from a fate which, as Englishwomen, you would, I know, have thought worse than death. You may thank me for that. I must leave you, as the flames are rising round us. Farewell! you will without doubt meet your fate with becoming firmness."

He spoke in a tone of quiet irony, and, pointing to the water, followed his men on board his vessel.

The grappling irons were unfixed, and the two vessels parted company—the *Civet Cat* bearing away on her course, and leaving the ill-fated *Josephine* to her doom.

And now from the deck of the *Josephine* rose a succession of wailing shrieks, as the wretched women, conscious of the fearful fate to which they were left, clustered to the bows of the vessel, and beseeched for mercy.

But they appealed to hearts that exulted in destruction.

The pirate-crew laughed at their entreaties, and scoffed at their terror.

The smoke of the burning vessel became more dense, and the forked tongues of flames shot up around them, and their screams of agony and despair died in the distance as the *Civet Cat* bore away from her stricken foe.

A fire at sea!

How terribly thrilling, when even the first dread rumour spreads from tongue to tongue, and while there is yet a chance that the exertions of the crew will subdue the flames.

But, oh God! how frightful to those poor doomed creatures who had seen their defenders, their kindred, slaughtered before their eyes—who had knelt by the gashed, disfigured body of some loved one, and tried to kiss him back to life!

How they huddled together and flew from the maddening tongues of fire, and shrieked for mercy, till it seemed strangely hard that Heaven could see their distress and turn a deaf ear to their plea for succour.

The devils in human guise had too well fired the ship, and circling flames narrowed the scanty spot upon which these despairing women clustered, until the frenzy of their agony made them leap into the bosom of the sea, seeking there release from the torments of that floating hell.

And farther and farther away sailed the destroying vessel—fading at last in the distant gloom, passing out of view like a vanishing spectre of ill, but not losing sight of the burning wreck, whose place was revealed by the red glare, diminishing as the wind bore them away, but growing more vivid even as it became less to view.

CHAPTER IV.

ISRAEL SHAWM LOSES HIS GOLD AND FALLS INTO A TRAP.

THE day was slowly drawing to a close, and the sun sent forth its dazzling golden rays, ere it sank from view behind the vast expanse of water, through which the *Civet Cat* was gently gliding towards the Barbadoes Islands.

Israel Shawm, the money scrivener, was seated at the window of his office after a long day's toil of going through his ledgers and accounts, reckoning the amount of his gains and speculations.

An enjoyment most of the sons of Abraham indulge in when they have a spare hour.

"Hester, my child," said the Jew, suddenly to his beautiful daughter, on perceiving the sails of a ship through the dim of the evening. "Can you make that ship out? my eyes are not so british as they used to pe."

The lovely Jewess took the jewelled telescope from her father's hand, and scanned the surface of the water, until her gaze fell upon the advancing barque.

"Vel, my tear, what have you made out of her?" asked the Jew, anxiously, as his daughter laid the glass down.

"It looks like Captain Yates' ship," she answered, "It is rather too dark to discern her properly, but they are making for us with all sail spread, to catch what little breeze there is."

"My old friendsh te captainsh," he said leaning back in his chair, much relieved at the intelligence. "Thank Got it ish no one elsh."

The old Jew money scrivener always felt uneasy when he saw a sail in view, especially when making for his port.

He had a great objection to strange visitors, more so, when they felt a particular desire to inspect his merchandise storage, which he kept securely closed from any inquisitive eye.

If anyone did feel particularly anxious to know what the warehouses contained, and get in unobserved, they were never observed to come out again, therefore they were unable to make any observation on the knowledge they had gained.

What became of the intruders is best known to the Jew, who kept the knowledge to himself, as he did the contents of the stores.

"I calculate we'll pay the old blood-sucker a trick to-night," said Captain Yates to Lieutenant Angel, as the boat was lowered and rowed ashore, when the *Civet Cat* had anchored, and gone under a complete disguise

"What is the nature of this trick?" asked Angel, quietly.

"I guess the tarnation old cuss will find out when he is doing a slick dance of death at the end of the rope."

His Lieutenant gave a quiet grin at the idea of the joke.

"Tarnation blazes men," cried Captain Yates furiously, after extricating his head from under a seat, where he had been suddenly shot by the boat, as it grated up the beach, "why the furies don't you pull more steady?"

He jumped out of the boat, amid the tittering of his crew, uttering some of the most elegant ejaculations in the Yankee phrase.

He soon reached the residence of the Jew, his lieutenant accompanying him.

"Ah, my tear captainsh, glad to see you," cried the Jew, as the pirate captain entered.

"This is an unexpected visit from my old friendsh. Who is that shentlemansh with you?" he asked, anxiously, indicating Lieutenant Angel.

"I guess he is one of the right sort," replied the American captain, smacking the Jew on the back with all the force of his huge rough palm, making the old huckster wince and writhe, with the breath knocked out of his body.

"Dat wash too bad, to hitch me like that by the son of Moses, you captainsh make too freesh," the Jew said, sulkily, scowling maliciously beneath his shaggy brows.

"To blazes with yer, for a tarnation old sneak," cried Yates. "Welcome my friend, and bring some wine, then to business."

"You ish alwaysh phelcome to the housh of Israel Shawm, my tear pot,' said the Jew, addressing Angel. "Phenever you are cruishing tish way, and want to runnish into this port."

"I thank you for your cordial welcome," replied Lieutenant Angel, ironically, "but we should never encroach upon your generosity by running into your port were a fleet of war frigates on our track. However, get the wine, my throat is parched. We have no time for gabbling here all night."

"Hester, my child," cried the Jew at the door, for his daughter.

His face puckered up with a cynical expression, and his eyes, sunken back in their sockets, glistening like the eyes of a demon with a dangerous gleam of treachery.

His callous heart was stung to the very core by the other's words.

The change of his countenance was wonderful as he turned to face his guests.

The villanous expression that a minute before had drawn every muscle of his face into a hideous shape, had now vanished for a time, hidden beneath a sickly smile, that played in mockery about his visage.

He was dissembling his rage until an opportunity would occur when he could reek his vengeance on the offender to the utmost power.

Lieutenant Angel stared at the beautiful Jewess as she entered.

Never had he beheld such rare loveliness before.

"Bring some of our famous wine for the captainsh," said the Jew, addressing his child.

"Get it yourself, and be ——" Angel would have finished the sentence, but he caught the gaze of the peerless Jewess fixed upon him, so he cut it short and said,—

"You, my pretty queen, will sit with me."

Her cheeks flushed at his words.

She was rather taken by his fascinating manner, and would have readily accepted the offer; but she met a withering frown from her father that made her shrink away.

The lieutenant saw the look, and his lips curled scornfully.

"Away with you, for a vicious old brute," he said, sternly, waving his hand impatiently, "and make haste about it, and if I see you look like that again, I'll kick you downstairs."

"You will have your way, my gay shentleman," mumbled the discomfitted Jew, as he left the room. "It will be my turn soon to be mashter, then, my fine poys——"

His conversation was abruptly stopped by

the voice of Y___ , that sounded like a clap of thunder, as he ord red him to hurry with the wine.

"You should not have spoken to my father like that," sai Hest r, as she seated herself beside Angel, whose arm had gently stolen round her white sh ulders. "You have angered him, and he is very dangerous when angered."

Lieutenant Angel laughed satirically at the remark of his fair compa ion.

"I fear no ti a ar or treachery," said Angel, "but I ug t hat you should be left here with him shut away from society and the world. Would you like to take a cruise with us," he continued, speaking in a lower tone, "yes, you must, we shall return here again very soon, then you shall join us as our fair queen."

"Oh, minsh Got!" shrieked Israel Shawm, entering with the wine, just in time to hear the last part of the tempter's speech, "wouldst you take my child from me—no—no, cap tainsh."

"Peace," shouted the lieutenant.

The Jew mumbled maliciously, poured out the wine, and handed it round with tremblin hand.

"Tarnation seize it, Angel," said Captain Yates, "I guess yer is almighty struck with that pretty gal. but we ain't agoin' to drop anchor for the night, so I guess we had better settle the bizness and cl'ar out afore squalls."

His lieutenant took the hint, and imprinting a kiss on the fair face of the Jewess, released her from his embrace, greatly to the comfort of her worthy sire.

"You can go to your own room, my tear," he said availing himself of the opportunity of getting her away from Lieutenant Angel, "te shentleman hash got some private bizness to talk wid me."

"Now my tear captinsh," he said, when his daughter had quitted the room, "what ish you got for me tish time?"

"I reckon it is one of the finest cargoes an Indian merchantman ship was ever laden with," said Yates, blowing the smoke of a very fine cigar across the table, and spitting over the head of the Jew, who sat opposite him. "I guess I'll want ten thousand dollars more for this freight than I got for the other. Old hoss, what der think of that?"

"Minsh Got! I hash not got so much monish in te banksh."

"I reckon yer'll go to tarnation blazes for a darned old liar," said Yates, helping himself to a bumper of the sparkling liquid, which he tossed off at a gulp. "Send me twelve dozen of this wine on board, d'ye hear."

"Yesh, my tear boy, it shall pe done, and I will give you the same amount of monish ash I did for te other."

"I kalkerlate yer had better bring the money with yer to the 'Flying Dutchman to-morrow. We will settle tizness there."

Old Israel, who preferred having them anywhere else than in his house, mumbled his willingness, and the American captain and his lieutenant departed, leaving the money scrivener to his mutterings and threatening menaces.

"Yesh, my fine shentleman, you shall have te winsh he—he—he! but it will not pe so goot as tish," he said, draining a glass that stood on the table, "no—no—no, it will pe weakish, he—he—he, ah—ah!"

While the Jew was planning revenge, and gabbling and grinning like a gorilla, the pirate captain and his subordinate had reached the "Flying Dutchman," a suspicious, dingy-looking inn, much frequented by a set of mysterious-looking men, who were making a boisterous noise in a mysterious parlour at the back of a mysterious bar, behind which stood a stout, bloated, round-faced, red-nosed, long, straight-haired individual, with his hands thrust to the depths of his pockets.

He started forward as Captain Yates and Angel entered, extending his short, chubby hand across the bar to the former. He looked mysteriously at the latter.

The American captain was evidently well-known to the red-nosed host of the mysterious inn, by the familiar way in which they addressed each other, and it was not long before Angel was introduced to the landlord of the "Flying Dutchman."

The loud shouts that were ringing through the quaint old building ceased on the instant the captain of the *Civet Cat* entered the room; and the mysterious-looking individuals clutched very formidable, jagged and bloodstained weapons, that lay by their sides, and stood in very threatingly picturesque attitudes.

Yates laughed derisively, as he pushed two burly fellows from his path, and swaggered in with his lieutenant

"Darn me, you are a blustering lot of kiddies," he said, catching hold of a huge tankard and drinking part of its contents; "sit down, mates, and put down them juggler swords."

"How ere yer?" asked a brawny big fellow, with broad shoulders and a massive black beard.

"I kalculate yer may soon find out, if yer has any pertikler wish," replied the intruder, tapping the butt of a finely chased revolver that stuck in his belt.

"Shiver my mizzen-mast, mates, are we to be overhauled in our own cabin by these lubbers?" asked the same brawny fellow, addressing the gang of ruffians, that still held their cutlasses.

"No," shouted a chorus of hoarse voices.

The same bearded man who had before addressed the crew of ill-looking fellows made a sign.

A shout, more like the growl of so many enraged lions, and the men ran forward with their weapons upraised, ready to strike the strangers to the earth."

"Back fools," said Lieutenant Angel, confronting the ruffians coolly, holding a revolver in each hand; "do you think we are babies, to be frightened by such as you?"

"Tarnation blazes, I kalculate we'll riddle them ugly carcasses of yer, if yer don't sit down."

"Suppose we do stop," said one of the men, who having no particular wish for his carcase to be riddled, had got behind his messmates, out of the way of the muzzle presented straight at his nose.

"I kalculate you'll be quiet."

"Curses, are you frightened of two men, mates?" shouted the leader.

"No, no," shouted the men again, "death —death to them!"

Several of the men rushed at the intruders, who were quietly awaiting the attack.

One struck furiously at Lieutenant Angel, who guarded the blow off with the muzzle of his firearm, and as the man was retreating, he fired.

The smuggler, for they were a crew of the most desperate and lawless smugglers in existence, fell back among his comrades, lifeless, his skull shattered to pieces.

"That's one of your brave men," said Angel, with provoking quietude to the leader, "and you, my bearded friend, will have the next shot, unless you teach your gang the wisdom of not interfering with us again."

His quiet voice controlled their angry passions, and the pirate captain and his confederate strode over the bleeding body of the smuggler, and passed to an inner room.

Israel Shawm kept his appointment, and on the following day he arrived with two huge bags of money, to buy the cargo of the plundered merchantman.

"Mine Got," said the Jew, entering the room where the American pirate sat with Angel, contemplating a plan by which they could play their visitor a trick, and rob him of his money, "ish you there, my dear friendsh?"

"Come in, younker," shouted Yates, "and hold your tarnation row."

Israel Shawm shuffled into the room, looking very suspiciously about him.

"Clare yer throat with this glass of wine," said Yates, pushing a huge goblet towards him.

"Thish ish not like te wine I have sent you on board," remarked the Jew, with a chuckle, as he sipped the liquor.

"Did yer get it all shipped?"

"Yesh captainsh," replied the villainous Jew merchant, a cunning leer lurking in his small eyes.

Captain Yates detected the insidious look.

"I kalculate," he said, looking the Jew sternly in the face, "If yer have been at any of yer tarnation tricks, I guess I'll give yer such a souwestering clout, that I'll knock the head off yer shoulders."

"Py te son of Moshesh I hash done nothing, captainsh."

"I guess I saw you give a tarnation cunning grin when yer spoke of the wine."

Israel made no answer, but looked at the speaker in surprise.

"I reckon yer saw the cargo, old hoss," Yates said.

"Yesh, my poy, I jushed looked; it ish pery goot," said the Jew. "I will alwaysh give you a good price for your cargo."

"Have you brought the amount agreed upon?" asked Angel.

"Yesh, my tear friendsh, and given you te wine for nothing."

"Hand it over," said Captain Yates.

"Here it ish," said Israel Shawm, holding the two bags up, one in each hand, "phen you gve me te receiptsh, I will give you te monish My Got captainsh, you will soon retire from the bishness, if you ish so fortunate, eh, captainish?"

Captain Yates had risen from his chair at a sign from his lieutenant, and unperceived by Israel Shawm, whom Angel kept in conversation, he carefully contrived to throw a rope across a beam that ran across the room.

"Holy Moshes!" shrieked the Jew, turning sharply round, and seeing the noose dangling over his head, "woot yer mur—mur—mur—mur—ter m—e?"

The American captain dexterously slipped the noose under the chin of the terror-stricken trader with a snap that put an end to his cries of terror.

His cheeks turned ashy pale, his lips had shrivelled up to two thin streaks, and his eyes glared wildly about him with sinister expression.

He fought desperately to free himself from the cord.

The pirate captain had secured the rope so that it could not slip.

"I guess, old blood sucker," said the American, tauntingly, "yer'll go to tarnal destruction now."

His voice, deep and hoarse with terror, the miserable wretch tried to call for help.

A cruel sneer writhed the lips of his tormentors.

With a sinister grin that meant unutterable mischief, Captain Yates approached the trembling Jew, and whispered some taunting words to him, that made his cheeks flush, and then turn white and haggard again by turns, and his whole frame shake convulsively.

He stamped on the floor, and a trap slowly opened.

The chair gradually slid from under their victim.

Lieutenant Angel clutched the bags of money from the convulsive grasp of Israel Shawm.

"Down among the dead men, down you go," said Yates, in a rejoicing, brutal voice, pricking the plunging legs of the Jew with the point of his sword.

The victim of their sport kicked and plunged about like a hanging cat that battles desperately for a spark of its ninth life.

"Put a stop to that kicking," said Lieutenant Angel, pitilesly.

The Jew closed his eyes as the captain advanced towards him, sword in hand.

A cold chill ran from the roots of his hair to the tips of his toes.

His time had certainly now come.

Horror, horror!

Every second he expected to feel the point of that cold steel in his flesh, and slowly drive through until it should pierce his heart's core.

Then he would be a hanging corpse, murdered by the two pirates.

He shuddered visibly as these thoughts coursed through his distracted frame.

A faint gasp for mercy came from his palsied jaws, as Lieutenant Angel laughed in his face, while the brutal Yates, in wanton cruelty, slapped his cheeks with his open palm.

"Mine God! son of Moshesh!" he cried; "mershy, mershy! you will not kileh me."

"I kalkerlate ye'd better say yer prayers," the American replied, as he drew his sword.

Old Israel Shawm kicked and shrieked fearfully.

His eyes seemed bolting from their sockets —his tongue lolled from his mouth.

One swift circle—the keen edge of the sword touched his skinny neck.

The old Israelite shrieked as if it had been red hot.

He expected to feel the cold weapon cut through his quivering flesh.

But, instead, the American captain, by a skilful blow, severed the rope above his neck, and Israel Shawm, senseless from mortal terror, fell through the open trap.

"I guess we'l leave him thar," said Yates, as he and Angel gathered up the moneybags. "Good-bye, ole hoss," he shouted down the trap, "yer can send for the cargo when we come again."

CHAPTER V.

BETRAYED.

WE left our hero and the lady whom he had rescued from Gaston's coarse insults, alone in the quiet beauty of her charming bower.

Strange to say, Lady Arbuthnot did not manifest much surprise at her unexpected deliverance.

She looked gratefully into our hero's face.

Thanking him as warmly with those bright eyes of hers as if she had spoken with her tongue.

Very warmly she held out her arms to him, and did not seem offended when, in the impulse

of the moment, he drew her slightly towards him.

A little embarrassment ensued immediately afterwards.

All things taken into consideration, their meeting certainly was interesting.

She had been rescued from an attempted outrage, so plainly intended, that our hero must have been conscious of the fact.

Her deliverer was a young and handsome fellow, and at any moment her jealous husband might find them there alone.

Then there was a price upon Tom's head, and at any instant the flash of weapons might fatally speak his capture.

She had not forgotten, too, when last they met, how his tender gallantries had made her bosom swell with emotions that might not have been strictly agreeable to her aged lord.

Gratitude again compelled her to thank him for saving her from Gaston's rudeness.

And so, though she knew how dangerous it was for them to linger there, she was not sorry that our hero did not force himself away.

"I thought I had disguised myself from all but the eyes of love," our hero said; "but I see the eyes of hate are as keen. Gaston recognized me."

"He did, and will betray you. You must escape before he has time to effect your capture."

"You would not have me taken then, pirate as I am? Have you then an interest in my fate?"

Her ladyship's eyes were downcast, as she replied,—

"You are daring, and bravery always commands a woman's—" "love," she was going to say, but substituted instead the word "esteem."

"Your husband would not like you the better for such sentiments," Tom said, playfully.

"He would have you taken, if he suspected you were with me. Flee, I entreat you; accept my thanks for saving me from that ruffian, and let us say farewell. Some other time I may see you, when there is less risk in our meeting."

Tom gallantly drew her a little closer.

"I will pray, then, for that happy time to be speedy. A moment—have you intelligence of Minnie?"

Lady Arbuthnot gave a start.

"I have a letter," she began.

"A letter from her dear hand; let me possess the precious treasure."

"Not now; you might be taken; the letter is in my desk. We have no time. I will contrive to send it you by a trusty messenger."

"Now, now!" Tom cried, excitedly. "There is time enough, if ten thousand soldiers surrounded me. Fly to the house; I will wait here. No words. I must and will have her letter of love."

"Stay here, then; do not stir. I will be fleet. But if you are captured, rash boy, your fate will be death."

She was gone in an instant; a rustling among the leaves, and he stood alone.

It was growing darker; everything around him was strangely silent.

If Gaston had given the alarm, there was no noisy effort to intercept him.

Worse, by far, if they crept stealthily in his track.

Still, the brave boy's fearless heart never failed him.

Scarcely a minute seemed to have elapsed, when he heard the quick tread of a light footstep, and Lady Arbuthnot, breathless and excited, stood before him.

"Read it when you have escaped," she whispered; "the house is alarmed, and as I came I caught the glitter of soldiers' weapons.

As if he had not heard her, Tom kissed the missive, and broke the seal.

Lady Arbuthnot, with her hand on his arm, urging him to go, felt the sudden start he gave as he read the letter.

The glad excited look left his face, and in its stead came an ashy pallor.

Turning almost fiercely upon Lady Arbuthnot, he cried hoarsely—

"Is this friendship to me—had you this from her own hands?"

"I had, indeed; with the request that I should convey it to you by a trusty messenger; her own lips kissed the missive as she gave it to me."

"Kisses, and on such perfidy as this! False to me—false to our vows—dismiss our loves! Oh, Minnie, Minnie! God of heaven, if this be true, I care no more for life, no more for liberty. Let mine enemies come now. This perjured note has slain me more cruelly than their steel, and thus I rend its cursed characters!"

He tore the note into shreds, and threw them to the ground.

Lady Arbuthnot, whose beautiful face was blanched like marble, clutched him by the wrist.

She was listening, anxiously listening to the tramp of armed men.

"They come!" she whispered. "Save yourself."

"Let them come. Ho! there, ye who seek Captain Tom Drake. He is here."

Forth from the brushwood came the glittering bayonets, borne in the hands of stalwart soldiers.

A tall, hard-featured man, with drawn sword, directed their weapons to be levelled at our hero's breast.

He thought the fearless boy meditated a fierce resistance.

"Captain Tom Drake," he cried, "resistance will be vain. Surrender, or we fire—you are our prisoner."

Our hero made no offer at resistance.

A strange, hard look was on his fearless face.

His lips curled to almost cruel indifference, and, calmly folding his arms, he allowed himself to be surrounded by the soldiers.

They put him in their midst, turning their bayonets towards his breast.

The tramp of their feet echoed through the garden.

The officer marched triumphantly in front, and Lady Arbuthnot, white as a sheet, stood alone, with the fatal shreds of paper lying at her feet.

CHAPTER VI.

A PASSAGE TO LIBERTY

SEATED on a stone bench in a close, unwhole-some dungeon, heavily ironed from his wrists to his ankles, our hero had leisure to reflect upon the position to which his own rashness had brought him.

Had he escaped before the soldiery came upon him, he might now have been on his own deck again, a monarch, defying the power of his enemies to take him.

Now what was he?

A doomed captive!

Immured within those four bare walls, from which he would only be taken to be led to a bitter trial, and ignominious death.

There was no uncertainty of the fate await-ing him.

As a pirate he would be tried, and as a pirate sentenced and executed.

Outside the harbour, his noble ship, with its gallant crew, awaited his return, and here he had, by his tame surrender of himself, placed his life in the hands of those who had gone so far as to send ships of war to effect his capture.

And this he had done because of one decep-tion.

Minnie had proved false to him.

The blow had fallen with terrible swiftness on his ardent heart.

He had deemed his fair young bride the soul of truth and purity.

She had forgiven him when she knew the nature of his career, and had bound herself to him by sad, softly-spoken vows, that he could not realise the blackness of her treachery.

And so he sat, in moody, bitter reverie in the solitude of his cell, never heeding his approaching fate, but only thinking of the faithlessness of his idolized, promised bride.

He had her miniature still resting against his breast—resting there with the soft tresses of her golden hair wound about it.

It had never been taken from his bosom since she gave it him on that still summer's evening when they had plighted their troths, except when he had taken it forth to shower caresses on her beautiful, innocent face.

Now it rested over his breast like a leaden weight—crushing his heart's fervent beat with the oppressive sense of her treachery.

The shadows had deepened in his lonely cell, when he was aroused by hearing the harsh creaking of the key in the ponderous lock.

He heard the rusty bolts pulled back, then the door swung heavily on its hinges, and the glare of a lantern shone upon his face.

Two figures stood in the doorway—a lady, and the jailor who was ushering her in.

One glance was sufficient to assure him that his visitor was Lady Arbuthnot.

The jailor closed the door when they had entered, and turned the light more fully upon their prisoner.

"There he be, my lady," he said, with a coarse grin on his low-looking visage, "trap-ped at last. We've been a long while a-try-ing to nab him, but we've got him now, and will keep him safe enough, I warrant, like the pretty bird he is."

Our hero's face flushed, and his kindling eyes flashed angrily as the jailor spoke, but her ladyship, stepping in advance of the man, raised her gloved hand for him to pay no heed to the fellow's words.

She was very pale, and looked sorrowfully at the heavy irons on our hero's wrists.

Tom understood what was passing in her mind.

He smiled bitterly, and said,—

"They have chained me down, as you see. I am like a caged beast. I wonder whether I shall be made a show of before I am led out."

Lady Arbuthnot's eyes filled with tears.

"Rash boy," she exclaimed, "what have you done? Do you know the merciless nature of those to whom you have surrendered your-self?"

"Oh, yes," replied our hero, carelessly; "they will cage me here till they take me out to try me as a pirate; they will sentence me for being what they made me, and, after that, a very brief affair—just one sharp volley, and they'll have no more to fear from Captain Tom Drake."

Lady Arbuthnot wrung her hands as if in pain.

"And can you so calmly regard your cer-tain fate?" she cried. "Foolish, hot-headed boy, you have indeed, taken a fatal step. All your enemies could not have been so treacherous to you, as you have been to your-self in this fatal step that will lead to —"

"To the grave," our hero replied, calmly, but with sparkling eyes. "I have tamely rushed into their hands, but, let them know, had I not been shackled by the base faithless-ness of my heart's love, not all their power could have brought me here. No, I had still defied them all, and laughed to scorn their efforts to make me captive! Even now," the fearless boy arose, and shook his clanking irons as he straightened his limbs, "I would not answer that their triumph should not be dashed to the earth in the last hour, and all their strength defied. It has been before—no, no, it is not their iron links that bow me to my fate, but the cold, cruel iron that has entered my soul, and chained me like a coward, with-out an atom of manly strength or ardent fire to lift myself against my foes, and beat my life out in a last fight for liberty!"

Lady Arbuthnot sighed as the graceful form of the boy hero stood erect before her.

It seemed so cruel that he should be im-prisoned there, caged like a snared beast of prey.

So hard that he should be led forth to die in the very freshness of his youthful strength and beauty.

He was so young, too, a stripling in years; such a youth in looks, so princely noble in spite of his fierce, heroic deeds—deeds that had amazed the world, but for which he must surely die, unless he baffled the vigilance of his foes, and escaped their vengeance.

"Oh! why were you so hasty?" she cried. "There is no hope of mercy; the news has gone forth that you are taken, and no influence will avail to obtain clemency."

"And if it would!" Tom exclaimed, "it should not be granted for me. I disdain to except my country's clemency; its pardon for crimes of which I am guiltless. They have raised my hand against their laws, and for what I have done I will suffer, but never ask mercy. Besides," his head dropped mournfully, "if Minnie had not betrayed me I should not have been here, and when I gave up life and liberty, it was because both had lost their charms in the bitterness of her falsity."

He sat himself moodily down as he continued,—

"We were sworn to each other; if I had not seen the proof in her own words I should never have believed it. I could not think she would ever deceive me."

"Nor could I. Think well—are you sure you have not been deceived by others, and not by your bride?"

Tom leapt to his feet.

"If it were so, and I could but get my fingers to the throat of any one that wronged her and betrayed me, I would wring his heart's gall into his venomous throat, and crush his life out like an adder's! But no, no; it is she only who has deceived me."

"She may have been coerced—forced to write this note against her consent."

"And if she were so weak she would be quite unworthy to be mine. No, when I rescued her in the old church, whither she had been dragged an unwilling bride, she was a helpless victim—led like a lamb to the slaughter, menaced with cruel force; but, even then, her lips refused to utter the unwilling lie that gave her to another, and when at my sword's red tip I kept her foes at bay, and drew her to my breast, her looks of love and joy belied their infamy, and told me she was mine. I was mad to leave her after that. I might have known a woman's constancy could not endure in absence."

"You wrong her, sir. I am convinced she is true as steel, and loves you with the steadfastness of a woman's love. This letter—I have gathered the pieces and joined them—had she written it, must have been blotted with her tears—faltering with the trembling of her nervous hand; but here the letters are written with the greatest care—the blistering words in which she renounces you, and bids you never seek her again, stand out bold in their infamy—like the lie they are. Look at the missive—read it again, not with half-blind jealousy and passion, and tell me if these are such words as her gentle soul would prompt."

Our hero drew back.

"I will not look on the hateful lines again; another prompted the accursed words, but she alone penned them."

"I will not believe it. When I saw her at Lady Castlemaine's, her eyes were filled with tears, as she spoke your name; her words were gentle and full of love, and when she gave me the letter, she took your love token from her bosom, and kissed it before she tenderly replaced it. This was not faithlessness. I tell you her words were all innocence, truth, and constancy. If there was a serpent, it was her lady protector, who met me on the threshhold, smiling in triumph when she saw me conceal the letter."

Our hero's features were swarthy with excitement.

He gazed as one in a dream in his fair visitor's countenance.

"What would you have me believe?" he asked, wildly.

"That she as well as you has been deceived—that this letter was written before I came—that some one stole to her desk, took out the note she had written, and replaced it with these forged lines, written to convince you she was false; and, who knows, that same hand may have intercepted your letters to her, and given her others, so cunningly worded, as to wring her gentle heart with the pangs of your unfaithfulness."

Our hero reeled.

A dim idea of the possibility of what she suggested was creeping with awful import on his misgiving mind.

"Give me the letter—let me look at it again," he cried, stepping towards her.

She held it out to him.

He took the missive in his fettered hands.

Line by line, and word by word, he followed it, and as he read, he seemed comparing the characters with those she had before written to him.

Before he had half read it through, a cry of fierce anguish escaped him, and he crushed the letter in his palm.

"It is too true," he cried, fiercely. "I have been betrayed and snared. It is a forgery!"

"And serve you right," the jailor exclaimed, fiercely. "Such as you deserves all you gets."

The sudden spring Tom made at the fellow sent him cowering back in fear to the ironed door.

As it was, he would have suffered from the excited fury of his manacled prisoner, if Lady Arbuthnot had not placed herself between them.

"Calm yourself," she said; "this base hireling is unworthy of your notice. Besides, you have need of all your energies to meet this fatal calamity."

"Be calm! God of Heaven! with this foul treachery selling me to death. Oh, what a mad fool have I been, to be hoodwinked and cajoled like this. Deceived by so base a lie—caged here to meet my doom while she, stricken bird, believes me false! Oh, for an hour of liberty, to battle for my life! God! that I had twenty of my faithful followers to batter down these walls, and fight the myriads of hired foes! One brief day's life, and I would leave a bloody mark behind me that should wipe from earth those whose accursed treachery has come between me and my bride, to sunder us for ever."

The excited boy strode fiercely across his cell, his fetters clanking at each step.

"Give me the air of freedom," cried Tom. "Give me life—life! I shall go mad! A word to my staunch crew, to bring them here! I should not despair if only twenty came. But to be here alone—alone! let me forth, I say! set my limbs free of these manacles, or I shall crush your brains out with my rage."

The jailor retreated in alarm.

Such a look of mad fury was in the daring hero's inflamed face, the veins on his forehead were purple, and swollen, and his chest expanded in its lion-like-strength, as he tried to snap his chains.

Lady Arbuthnot laid her hand softly on his heated brow.

"Listen to me," she said, "you have brought yourself here. It is useless beating your wings against your cage. You have no faith in a woman's constancy, try and have a little in a woman's wit to help you out of your difficulty."

Our hero looked wildly in her face, but said nothing.

Lady Arbuthnot continued—

"The inexplicable hand of fate is visible in every incident of your strange career You had no sooner been led from my garden a prisoner, than I received intelligence that Lady Castlemaine had arrived here with her young charge, Minnie."

"Minnie here, and I a prisoner?"

"She is brought here that she may be thrown into Lord Kilcrew's society, her future husband, if Lady Castlemaine's plans succeed. She will meet him to night at a masquerade, to which I have tickets of invitation."

"To-night! By heavens, I would give my life for one hour at that masquerade—one hour with my sword in my grasp!"

"It shall be so. You shall see your bride to-night."

Our hero looked wistfully at her, then his glance fell on his fetters.

"To-night! How? All you tell me seems like a dream; but have you the wand of an enchantress to wave, that these walls may open and reveal my path to liberty?"

"Ah," put in the jailor, "it'll want a fairy's wand to set him at liberty again."

"My man,"—Lady Arbuthnot's voice was strangely cold and calm—"I have resolved at all hazards, he shall be set at liberty, and I have taken every precaution to ensure his freedom."

"You'll have to get the right side of some high person, for it ain't to be supposed they'll let him off if they can help it, now that they have cotched him."

Her ladyship stepped nearer to the man.

Her face was frigid and pale, her tones as deep and calm as before.

"I am aware that you have charge of this prisoner, and will have to answer for his safety; therefore, in the event of his escape, you will need a handsome reward to repay you for any punishment you may receive."

"Oh, you needn't trouble, ma'am. If you was to fill this place with gold it wouldn't bribe me to let him off. I'd sooner a sight see him turned off with a rope round his neck."

"I shall not bribe you, my man; but you will be well paid as the price of his liberty. At the present moment your wife is in possession of a sum of money which will make you both independent for life She understands all, and knows the risk you run, but I have assured her that whatever may be your sentence, I will secure your pardon."

The jailor drew back.

"'Taint no use, my lady, you don't bribe me at no price."

"It is unnecessary."

The words were spoken in a strangely thrilling tone.

Her ladyship's gloved hand had gone to the pocket of her richly embroidered dress.

Now she drew forth her lace edged handkerchief.

She was standing face to face with the jailor, at less than arm's distance.

When she spoke these few significant words, the fellow, with an instinct of the subtle sinister danger, was retreating to the door.

Lady Arbuthnot's fascinating eyes were looking into his.

They warned him of his danger, and a sudden cry came to his lips.

Too late.

The small gloved hand was raised swiftly to his mouth; the elegant embroidered handkerchief was pressed to his nostrils—a subtle odour arose from the folds of lace, and the jailor, with ghastly face and set staring eyes, sank heavily against the door.

Still the fatal cambric and lace was held firmly to his nostrils—held till the ghastliness of his visage settled to a look like death; his arms hung powerless to his side, and the large keys, dropping from his nerveless hand to the floor of the cell, falling with a rattle and ring that seemed to strike to the very soul of our hero, as he watched this brief and sudden tragedy.

Pale as the man himself, Lady Arbuthnot drew her hand away.

The jailor sank heavily to the stones, and lay as if dead.

"Now," Lady Arbuthnot cried in a hoarse whisper—"quick, before it is too late."

She stooped over the prostrate man, her nimble fingers searched his pockets, and plucked forth a small bunch of keys.

"Your fetters, quick," she cried.

Tom held forth his hands.

The key turned in the lock, and the irons fell heavily to his feet.

All this had passed so quickly, that our hero could scarcely comprehend what was going forward, before he found himself released from his fetters, and standing free of limb, with the keys that would unlock his way to liberty lying within his grasp.

In the excitement of the moment, he drew Lady Arbuthnot towards him, and fervently kissed her.

The beautiful woman blushed, and gently released herself.

"We must not delay," she said; "discovery will be fatal."

She drew a folded parcel from beneath her skirt.

Their position was too critical for her to affect any false delicacy, but there was a deep tinge on her beauteous cheeks, as she turned towards Tom.

"I have come prepared!" she exclaimed. "Put on this dress, and let us go forth."

The dress was that of a lady, and our hero instinctively drew back.

Her ladyship understood him.

He did not want people to say that he ran away in woman's clothes.

She spoke quickly.

"You will bring me in danger if you hesitate. Consider—what would my husband—the authorities say, if they discovered what I had done for you?"

Tom hesitated no longer.

In a few seconds he was arrayed in the costume of a lady of fashion.

Nothing was wanting in the disguise, even the head-dress was perfect.

He looked rather a tall young lady, it must be confessed, but a touch of rouge put a more effeminate bloom on his cheeks, and made him fit to pass muster.

"Now," his fair deliverer said, "I need not caution you to be calm, whatever happens."

Tom smiled in reply.

"This man, here," he said, "is he——"

"Not dead—he will be insensible for an hour, that is all."

"Enough!" Tom said, and they went forth.

They locked the door, and bolted it.

The keys our hero put into his pocket.

They were heavy, and might make a serviceable weapon if needed.

All was silent in the stone corridor.

They descended the stairs, and arrived unchallenged at the outer gate.

A jailor and the porter were there.

They rose respectfully, and opened the portal.

Lady Arbuthnot drew forth her purse.

"Something for yourself and comrade," she said as she gave them a couple of guineas each.

Captain Tom passed out.

The gate was held open a second or so; then it closed as they entered the carriage which waited by the door.

"Didn't know as two on 'em comed in," said the porter, as he put the shining coins into his waistcoat-pocket.

"I only seed one," replied his companion; "suppose t'other comed arter."

"Likely; 'spose you ain't going to share with the others, eh?"

"Not if I knows it. Keeps all I gets to myself."

Meanwhile, our hero and his lady liberator had entered the coach.

Lady Arbuthnot, anxious to see him safely seated, would have made him enter first; but, with his natural gallantry, the brave boy insisted upon handing her inside.

As soon as he had taken his place beside her the coach rolled away.

Before it had proceeded far, it stopped in front of a deserted-looking house.

The footman came to the carriage door, and respectfully touched his hat.

"Go with this man," her ladyship hastily whispered; "he is my confidential servant; he will procure you costumes. Farewell for the present. We shall meet at the masquerade."

Tom squeezed the fair hand held out to him.

"Stay," her ladyship said. "If you wish to communicate with me, you can entrust your commands to my messenger."

"A thousand grateful thanks," our hero exclaimed, kissing her ladyship's hand; "and now farewell for the hour."

"Farewell, rash boy; and for the future, think better of woman's steadfastness, where the object of her love is worthy of her devotion."

It struck Tom that her ladyship's voice quivered strangely as she spoke these words.

Had it not been too dark, he would have seen that her ladyship's eyes were filled with tears.

The truth must have been plain to him had he stopped to inquire.

Hers was no ordinary interest in his welfare.

She loved him with a deeper fervency than she could give her mistrustful dotard of a husband—loved him devotedly, and, as yet, purely.

Whether that love would be tarnished by passion's indiscreet warmth remained to be determined by the incidents of the future.

Lady Arbuthnot drove off, and the footman led the way round the back of the house.

He admitted our hero and himself by a side door.

The interior was dark and silent, but the footman seemed to know every inch of the way.

He conducted our hero to a commodious apartment, and lighted some candles which were placed on the table.

Our hero took a good look at his new adherent.

He was a quick-witted looking fellow, of about thirty.

At first sight, perhaps, he looked younger, but there were deep-set lines about his face, and a firm contraction of the muscles about the mouth, which showed he had served some apprenticeship in the world's ways.

He gathered up the feminine attire which Tom hastily threw off, and then said, respectfully,—

"I am to take your orders, sir, if you please."

"You know me?" Tom asked, steadfastly eyeing the man.

"I do, sir; my lady——"

"Enough! Can you find your way to the coast?"

"I know every step from here, sir."

"Good! You will find by the beach a fisherman's hut, supposed to be——'

"Bill, the Smuggler's; I know the place, sir."

"Go there. When the door is opened, say merely, 'Three green lights,' and return. I want my crew ashore; that will bring them. And now about our costumes."

"How many, sir?"

"Thirty, and my own."

"Her ladyship has one prepared for you, sir."

"What character?"

"A Greek corsair."

"Excellent! I think the character will suit me to-night. And my men's costumes—they must not be suspiciously disguised—no. Ah, I have it!"

He pencilled a few words on a slip of paper, and handed it to the servitor.

The man bowed.

"You will please stay here till I come back," he said; "no one will disturb you; the house is tenantless, and belongs to my lady; I will execute your commission, and bring your costume."

"How shall I know whether to admit you?"

"I shall not enter by the door, nor in the same garb that I now wear."

Bowing again, he went out by the door, and our hero was alone.

What excited emotions were swelling within his breast!

An hour since a manacled captive in a strong prison cell.

Now he was free.

Free to dare his foes to their worst—free to carry out any audacious venture, and strike one blow at his foes before he embarked on board his gallant vessel.

How he longed for the coming hour!

Impatiently he strode up and down the barely furnished room.

Lady Arbuthnot had evidently made up her mind that he would be able to escape, for wine had been placed on the table for his refreshment, and he thanked her thoughtful care, as he drank deeply of the generous fluid.

Thinking of his unexpected escape—of the

lady who had so daringly delivered him—of Minnie, and of their coming meeting, kept his mind pretty well occupied till a footstep outside warned him that Lady Arbuthnot's messenger had returned.

He entered immediately after.

He was no longer dressed in footman's garb, but in an attire that gave him a distinguished appearance, and convinced Tom that his position was greater in life than he had pretended.

He bowed as usual.

"Her ladyship has sent by me this costume, and this weapon," he said, unrolling a rather bulky parcel. "This letter is from her. Your message has been conveyed to your ship, three white lights answered the signal."

Our hero opened the note and read :—

"DARING BOY,
    "The costume I have chosen, I think, will be most congenial to your wishes; the sword is a trusty one, and not a toy; the pistols are loaded.

"I hear that you have ordered your men ashore.

"Let me entreat caution in whatever plans you have formed.

"The garden will be thronged with naval and military officers, and an alarm given must result in your capture.

"A word more of news.

"Your Minnie will be in the costume of a vestal virgin. Lord Kilcrew will appear as an Indian chief. Gaston takes the part of a freebooter. Admiral Ellis will be there in the wig of a lord chancellor.

"All this I have discovered from the costumiers.

"Adieu! Be on your guard!
                    "CLARY."

"The news is welcome," Tom exclaimed, filling himself another goblet of wine. "Ha! that puts some fire in my creeping blood. By the heavens! my blood shall not run sluggish to-night. Now, friend, the costume; first let me try this blade, I may have need of it."

He bent the blade nearly double, and as it flew back with a swift spring, he laughed lightly, and returned it to the richly ornamented scabbard.

"The blade will do; the pistols are well primed. Commend me to the lady's thoughtful care. Now for the dress. Hurrah for the masquerade!"

CHAPTER VII.

AN UNREAL MASQUERADE.

THE night was yet young when our hero sallied forth to the scene of the masquerade. His corsair suit was a matchless fit, and was well set off by his graceful form and bearing.

Lady Arbuthnot had displayed exceeding taste and judgment in the selection of such a dress.

"Nothing could be more picturesque and daring than its effect.

The material of which it was composed was of the choicest texture and colour, and from the elegance of its golden embroidery, it must have been the handiwork of some of those Eastern ladies, who, shut up within their luxurious chambers, amuse those hours of loneliness, while awaiting the coming of their lord, by fashioning and adorning raiments of the richest workmanship.

Captain Tom gave no thought to the fair fingers that might have braided his gay costume—nor to the lonely state of so many beauteous women, condemned to be the slaves of one husband.

He was thinking of the events that night might bring forth, if he should burst like a thunderbolt upon the gay revellers, declaring his name and character.

A long blue cloak shrouded his slim figure, partially hiding his masquerade attire, as he stepped into the coach his lady deliverer had placed at his disposal; but on arriving at the scene of the revels, he threw aside his mantle, and appeared in his gorgeous costume.

The masquerade was given by the young and fashionable Countess St. Albans, whose magnificent mansion and splendid grounds were one brilliant array of light and colour when our hero arrived.

As it was one of the conditions of the masquerade that the names of the guests should not be known until the hour of the banquet, when, at a signal from their hostess, all should unmask,—our hero had only to present his card of invitation, and was then ushered into the splendid reception room.

A great many of the guests were there, all, of course, masked, and each in some costume the beauty and effect of which tried to outvie all others.

The young and lovely Countess was there.

She gave Tom a curious glance when her eyes rested on his graceful form, and seemed striving to penetrate his mask, to discover who so youthful and handsome a stranger could be.

The Countess was unknown to our hero, but he could see she was a mask of high rank, and bowing gallantly as he passed her, he joined the throng hurrying to the fairy-like gardens.

Out in the charming grounds the scene was one bright festival.

Wierd-like music floated from every grove, and myriads of coloured lamps of chaste construction showed their light upon the brilliant company.

Tom smiled as he thought what a tumult amongst them the mere mention of his presence would create.

What a scene there would be when he unmasked!

It made his hot blood thrill in his veins with an ecstacy of delight.

He had come there on an adventurous mission—come to seek his lady-love, and learn from her own lips the truth or falsity of her broken vows.

Come with a sword by his side, and a trusty crew at his back, to carry his dear prize off from the midst of the armed revellers should her love remain unchanged.

There was something highly congenial to the roving boy's daring mind in this romantic way of coming for his bride.

Something of the adventurous spirit of the old buccaneers—the old corsairs, who were wont to descend upon a coast, and carry off their maidens amidst sword and flame.

His joyous escape from captivity, too, helped to inspire him with wild audacity, and as he strode amongst the gay throng, his step was elastic, and his bearing full of graceful ease and conscious dauntless power.

He passed among people whom he recognised; an instinct of detecting other people's disguises was one of the traits for which he was remarkable; but, as yet, he had seen neither Gaston, Admiral Ellis, or Lord Kilcrew.

Amongst a group of young nobles he recognised his former acquaintances, Lords Claremont, Moreton, Walpole, and Vane.

His adversary in the duel he had fought in the bluff old commodore's grounds — the handsome, gentlemanly Claremont was, as ever, courteous and at ease; Walpole, carelessly merry.

Moreton seemed more touchy and quarrelsome; the fact was, he had been jilted where he imagined he had made a conquest, and was very troublesome in consequence.

Little Lord Augustus Vane was the *beau ideal* of perfection.

His costume was resplendently faultless, and he looked at least an inch higher in his own opinion.

It was a freak of our hero's wayward nature that a very little occasion sufficed to make him put himself in harm's way, and he no sooner saw little Lord Augustus Vane, decked out like a popinjay, than, with the old love of mischief beaming from his bright brown eyes, he stalked into the midst of the young nobles, pressing so close to Vane that the little lordling was forced to step back to avoid having his toes trodden upon.

"My dear Lord Vane," Tom said, bringing his gloved hand heavily on the young fop's satin doublet, "I am glad to see that your costumier and valet have done for you that which nature forgot to do—given grace and elegance to your lordship's figure; your dress is superb, I congratulate you."

Lord Vane stepped back.

"Aw—fact—aw—is, this is an—aw—insult!" he cried, tapping the hilt of his sword.

Tom laughed heartily.

"Oh, not at all; no, no, my lord. I am pleased to see so young a fledgling turned out so much like a modern Apollo."

"Sir," the young lord exclaimed, angrily, "this is—aw—beyond—aw—bearing! If you —aw—desire a quarrel—aw—"

"Save your anger, my lord; I will not trouble you to flesh your weapon, it were a pity to see so pretty a toy soiled with the nasty stain of blood—what say you, my lords?"

"That your interference with our friend is cursed impertinence!" cried Lord Moreton. "I don't know you, sir, but if you are seeking a change from the peaceful programme of this night's amusement you can take your choice of us."

The daring boy hero's eyes brightened.

He was in the mood to pick a quarrel with anyone for the mere fun of the thing.

A bout of fencing, he thought, would be a good thing to get his hand in for the more serious business of the evening.

So, tapping his sword lightly, he said—

"You are right, my lord; the amusement here is slow. A little blood-letting will be an agreeable diversion; so, if it suits your purpose, I will take your challenge."

"Return with me, then—this way!" Lord Moreton cried, furiously passionate in a moment, "unless you would wish all gaping eyes to witness our brawl."

"Gentlemen," interposed Claremont, "pray stay this foolish quarrel. On such a night as this even language has a little licence."

"But an insult is not to be brooked," Moreton cried. "Come, sir, follow me."

He led the way to a retired cluster of shrubs, and Tom, lightly humming a Greek corsair song, followed him.

The young nobles accompanied them.

Lord Claremont, stalking gravely in rear, watched anxiously every movement of our hero's graceful figure.

He was trying to recollect where he had before encountered that well-knit frame, with its conscious arrogance of careless strength.

Lord Moreton laid his light cloak on the green sward, and drew his rapier.

"I presume we need not unmask."

"Unless the physician unmasks us," Tom replied, drawing his heavier blade.

The swords crossed.

Moreton, impetuous and skilful, attempted to make short work of his antagonist; but our hero, throwing himself into a careless attitude of defence, quietly baffled his adversary's rapid attack.

"My lord, you thrust wildly," he said, presently; "you have twice been open to my stroke."

"Strike, then," Lord Moreton cried, watching keenly for an opening.

The slur upon his swordsmanship stung him more keenly than if he had been stung by his opponent's weapon.

Standing easily upon the defensive, Tom gave the excited nobleman his fancied opportunity for a thrust.

It was delivered well; but almost before he had lunged at our hero's breast, a hand of iron seemed to twist his wrist, and his sword span from his grasp and lay at Tom's feet.

"My lord, I have disarmed you," Tom said. "Pick up your sword, and let us not be worse friends."

He sheathed his sword.

"Spoken like a gentleman," Walpole exclaimed. "Come, Moreton, shake hands with your opponent, and let us be glad that no blood is shed."

But Moreton, stung by his defeat, turned away with a mortified air.

A strain of such ravishing music at that moment stole on their ears, that Walpole, picking up his mortified friend's weapon, exclaimed—

"Fie, gentlemen, we insult the witchery of this scene. Come, let us have no more illblood; join hands, and think no more of this passage of ill-humour."

He turned to Tom.

"You will drink wine with us; see, a page approaches with the juicy drink."

"Not now, gentlemen; we shall meet again at the banquet, till then I drink with none."

He waved his hand, and, forcing his way through the shrubbery, was gone.

The young noblemen looked at each other.

Then Lord Walpole broke out —

"Now who the devil can he be?"

"Aw, that's a puzzler," Lord Vane observed; "he fences like—aw—the dence! He must have studied that trick of disarming."

"I never saw but one man fence like that," Claremont remarked, thoughtfully; "only one man with that wrist of steel, and quick ease with his rapier hilt——"

"And he?"

"Was my opponent once—Captain Tom Drake."

"I'll unmask him at the supper," Moreton said savagely.

"Better not, he may have the face of a demon under his mask."

The young nobles laughed at their companion's mortified vexation, and having drunk of the generous wine, strolled to another part of the illuminated gardens.

Meanwhile our hero sauntered on his way.

The little passage of arms had stirred his blood, and his heart was all aglow as he proceeded in the direction whence came the sounds of soft melodious music.

An instinct told him that Minnie Atherton was most likely to be in some secluded nook apart from the revellers, and near to the concealed musicians.

The path led him to a spot of such extraordinary quietude and beauty, that he sat down entranced, and listened to the splashing of the cool fountains over the marble at his feet.

He wondered so few of the guests were drawn to such a retired nook of loveliness, and while he sat musing and wondering, he became conscious of the fact that he was not alone.

They were two female masks who came towards him.

One, in the character of Diana, he knew at the first glance.

It was Lady Arbuthnot.

The other, a vestal virgin.

How his heart bounded as he recognized his boyhood's dream—Minnie Atherton!

He could not mistake her.

There was the same beauteous form of grace; the same white rounded arms—how often he had wished to have them entwined about his neck, as they had been softly entwined in days gone by.

There were the same sweet blue eyes, slightly mournful now, and timid, but gentle and tender as ever; the same ripe chiselled lips he had so sacredly kissed; the same abundance of golden hair—one tress of which yet lay in its purity and grace against his heart.

It was very hard to restrain himself from leaping towards her, and folding her to his breast.

But the time was not yet come, and so he remained where he had stood on rising, while Lady Arbuthnot advanced with her girlish charge.

She surveyed our hero's appearance with admiration.

He certainly did justice to her care.

He looked incomparably noble, as he drew his elegant form erect; his costly costume according so well with his careless, defiant bearing.

Lady Arbuthnot, smiling pleasantly on Minnie, now spoke,—

"A corsair here; tell me, sir mask, are you awaiting your mistress fair, or bring you tidings to lovely maidens from across the sea?"

Tom disguised his voice very much indeed, as he replied gallantly,—

"Fair lady, if I sought my mistress, I should go no further; this sweet nymph's eyes would chain me here captive to their brightness."

"Fie, fie, you rovers of the sea are fickle lovers; but there, the nymph shall judge your worth. But remember, no oft-told vows of love—I shall be listening."

Before Minnie had time to retreat she had quickly retired, and the timid girl found herself alone with the dashing corsair.

Alone with his boyhood's love!

Tom's heart beat wildly.

He had not seen Minnie since the day when he had given her into the care of Lady Castlemaine.

Since then, what an eventful career had been his!

A proscribed pirate, with a price upon his head! Now, escaped all dangers, he stood in the midst of pitiless foes, who would beat him down without mercy, there amid that revelry.

He thanked Lady Arbuthnot in his heart for choosing his corsair costume.

It was pleasing to meet Minnie there, dressed as he would have had her see him, if he had taken her on his daring voyages—dressed as he would have those who sought his life see him when he unmasked his face at the banquet that night.

Sorrowful as were her thoughts, she could not help feeling a strange interest awaken in her heart, as she gazed on his handsome figure; but timid at being left there, she would have retreated after her companion, if Tom had not quietly stepped to her side.

"Do not leave me, fair mask," he said; "I am very sad—sad as any corsair can be who has lost his lady-love; hear my story, and you will pity me."

Tom's voice was excellently disguised.

He was standing in the shadow, too, so that Minnie might not see his eyes.

He feared she would discover him if once their glances met.

"It is a corsair's fate to be sad," Minnie replied, softly; "sad, because of the dangers of their career; sad, because they are fickle in their loves, and can break a maiden's heart without remorse."

"A corsair loved a maiden once," our hero said, with some difficulty mastering his emotion, "but she was false to him."

"She did not break his heart. He took another bride—corsairs always do," Minnie said, dropping her fair head, for she was thinking of the boy-lover who had stolen her heart away.

"He took no other bride. He came amid danger—jeopardised his life, that he might seek his false-hearted bride, and demand why she had forsaken him."

"That was very brave. He should have given his love to a more worthy maiden. What did he say to her—was he very angry?"

"Not angry. He talked with her of his childhood; the days they had spent together wandering side by side, and vowing eternal love; he talked to her of the exciting dangers of his career, how he had been nearly stricken to the death; told her how he had been saved by his love-token, which, lying over his heart, received the bullet, and asked her, if she no longer loved him, to give him back the pledge of love he gave her when they parted."

Minnie uttered a little cry of alarm and suspicion.

Her hand went swiftly to her fair bosom, and clutched at some relic treasured there—clutched as though to feel that it was safe.

"Speak," she cried, in a strangely anguished whisper, "who are you? If you know my story, oh, tell me, is it true that he sent me that cruel letter, renouncing our loves for ever?"

Before our hero could reply, a harsh female voice was heard, saying,—

"Left her with a corsair? Gracious me! Poor child, the worst thing you could have done—excite her mind; set her thinking of that worthless pirate! Why, she may run away!"

"By St. Patrick, and well she might" cried the voice of Admiral Lord Kilcrew, "if I may judge of the man by the figure he cuts in his dress. See, there she is, and it's an elegant boy that same corsair is."

Lady Castlemaine, Lord Kilcrew, Lieutenant Gaston, and Lady Arbuthnot came forward.

"Lady," our hero said, quickly, in Minnie's ear, "believe not that he was false until he returns your love token, which still guards his heart."

Stepping quietly back, he bowed gallantly to the new comers.

"My child," Lady Castlemaine cried, with affected gaiety, "I am glad to see this young corsair has not run off with you. Come, you shall listen to him in the dance. It is indiscreet to stay *alone* with a strange mask—gentlemen, *au revoir*."

Minnie gave our hero a wistful lingering glance, as Lady Catlemaine took her by the arm and led her away.

Lady Arbuthnot went with them, but Lord Kilcrew and Gaston stayed behind.

When she was gone, Tom stepped from the shadows that had hid him from the penetrating gaze of love.

Bowing slightly to Lord Kilcrew and to Gaston, whom he recognized by his sinister looking eyes, he was about to leave the spot, when Lord Kilcrew stayed him.

"St. Patrick's honour," he exclaimed, "I am pleased to meet so comely a gentleman. Come, sir, let us take wine, and drink the health of the fair guests of the revels—ho, there, boy! bring the wine."

A page in the countess's livery ran forward with wine and goblets.

Filling the goblets he handed one to each.

Lord Claremont came sauntering up the marble steps as the wine was passed round.

"I will join you, gentlemen," he said laughing.

"And it's welcome you are, my bonny highwayman!" Lord Kilcrew cried. "Fill another bumper, you spalpeen; and here's to good company, you highwaymen and pirates."

This was in allusion to Tom's corsair garb, and to Claremont, who was dressed as Claude Du Val.

Hitherto, Gaston had said nothing. Now he came forward with a sneer upon his lips.

It was impossible that he could have even suspected that the man whom he had surrounded by soldiers and marched off to a secure cell, was standing defiantly before him; but at the first glance, when his and Tom's eyes met, he felt an antipathy towards him, that brought all his ill-humour in full play.

Perhaps, too, his temper was further roused by his meeting with Lady Arbuthnot, who had passed him with contempt that cut him to the soul.

Something in his evil nature prompted him to speak and act maliciously.

Glancing towards Claremont, he said, in a sneering tone,—

"Not over respectable society; for highwaymen and pirates, I believe, are robbers alike; but our friend here steals only our friendship; this strange mask may have worse designs."

Tom's fingers clenched on the richly chased goblet, as he replied, quickly.—

"My friend, be wise; wearing a mask on a carnival like this may not always keep you out of a quarrel."

Gaston laughed savagely.

"A mettlesome corsair!" he cried. "Sir, I will drink your health, coupling therewith the health of the fair virgin with whom we found you practising virtue."

Something in the glitter of our hero's eyes must have warned Claremont of his rousing anger, for he said, aside to Gaston,—

"Beware, Gaston, you know not with whom you tamper."

"If he were the devil I would make him join in drinking the lady's health," he said. "In what terms shall we toast?"

"In silence, if you are wise," Tom replied, angrily.

"St. Patrick, man," cried Lord Kilcrew, "and it's myself that will have a word to say to the scoundrel that vilifies that lady's name; so be civil, and drink to the gentleman with fair words, or, by the devil that's in my veins, you may find my sword with just the hilt knocking your teeth down your throat."

Gaston had drunk just enough to make him quarrelsome.

The sneer deepened on his well-defined lip, as he exclaimed,—

"Two champions to one such lady! Gentlemen, I drink you joy in the possession of her charms; but don't forget that the pirate, who is in jail now, had her on his ship for some days and nights, and so had the first picking of her maiden charms."

"Liar!" Tom cried. "Let this choke the cursed lie in your throat!"

He dashed his goblet of wine full in Gaston's face.

Such a cry as an enraged panther might have given, came from Gaston's lips as the red juice splashed over him, for the moment actually choking his utterance.

He reeled in the intensity of his fury—a deadly gleam shot from his dark malicious eyes, and instantly his rapier left its sheath.

"Stand between them, men," cried Lord Kilcrew. "There'll be bloodshed presently, and though I take it a little of this hot blood being drawn, wouldn't be bad for either at all, it isn't decency to go sword-scratching here."

Gaston put Lord Claremont aside.

"I will have his heart's blood," he hissed, "if to strike him I have to pierce the hearts of my friends."

"St. Patrick, then, let them have their way. Draw your blade, man, and have your fill of it, and good luck to the pair of you."

THE DUEL AT THE MASQUERADE.

Gaston was too excited to stay for any fighting preliminaries, and as Kilcrew got from before Tom, he rushed fiercely upon him.

Our hero had only just drawn his sword in time to ward off the treacherous thrust, and eyeing Gaston with a look that plainly spoke mischief, he kept him at bay, waiting till he saw a fatal opening.

Lord Kilcrew watched the sudden duel with intense interest.

A perfect fire-eater himself, he was always ready for a little sword-play on his own account, and liked to see two gentlemen dis-

port themselves properly, when fencing for each other's life.

Their first rapid passes convinced him that Gaston had no chance with his better skilled adversary, unless he allowed himself to be pricked in Gaston's impetuous attack, and he was admirably regarding Tom's style of handling his weapon, when he saw Gaston leap wildly forward, and make a furious lunge at our hero's heart.

But Drake was simply standing on his defence.

Without shifting his posture, or seeming to move a muscle of his body, with no more than a slight play of the wrist, he turned Gaston's blade aside.

His own sword was held out at full length, and on its sharp murderous point Gaston came with the force of his own impetus.

Tom stood immovable—his lips not [even quivering; his eyes were set in a cold, hard stare; his arm seemed formed of stone.

Coldly, pitilessly, he looked his adversary in the face, as he paused in his headlong rush, with the deadly weapon transfixing him, passing completely through his side, not an inch from the recently healed wound, where the sword of Harry Vere had gashed its frightful path on the night of the abduction of the commodore's niece.

It was a strangely terrible scene.

The four men, in their quaint attire, apart by themselves, with the revelry so near—the Indian chief, with his tall plumes—the highwayman, with his brilliant scarlet and gold—the corsair, with his red blade dipped in gore.

Not a moan from the wounded man.

His arm fell.

His hand relaxed the hold of his sword.

Then Tom plucked his sword from his bleeding breast!

With a gurgling cry Gaston fell to the ground.

Resting his bloody sword on the marble terrace, now deeply stained with his opponent's blood, our hero took off his mask.

The effect on Gaston was electrical, a convulsion passed through his entire frame.

He tried to raise himself, but fell back helpless in the attempt.

"Demon—fiend!" he whispered, hoarsely, "you here! Hell's power is on your side! Devil—d—d——"

His utterance died away in a gurgling whisper, but his eyes gleamed their unspeakable hatred on his opponent.

Then Claremont spoke.

"Fly," he said, waving Tom to be begone, "this is a bloody night's work—begone, while you have time."

A cruel smile curled the lips of Captain Tom.

Coldly he bent towards the wounded man.

"Close your eyes, Gaston," he said, "the masquerade is over for you for ever."

CHAPTER VIII.

THE BRIDAL STAYED.

OUR hero sheathed his sword.

"Gentlemen," he said, "I leave you to your wounded friend; you will testify there has been fair play in this encounter; if you think otherwise, I shall be ready to answer you."

"I' faith, man," said Kilcrew, "and it's myself would like the honour of crossing swords with you; but helter-skelter fighting is no man's price, so I'll not press the point just now; but when you've an idle five minutes on your hands, it's proud I shall be to have a tilt with you."

"My Lord Kilcrew," Tom replied, "you may have that pleasure earlier than you expect.

Gentlemen, for the present, adieu—you will find me at the banquet."

He bowed, and left them.

Admiral Lord Kilcrew looked after him in some surprise.

"St. Patrick!" he exclaimed, "but he seems to know the whole of us. The devil's own son must he be!"

While this colloquy was going forward Claremont had kneeled beside Gaston, whose head he was supporting as he tried to stanch the wound.

"How goes it with you, friend?" Lord Kilcrew asked. "Is the hurt too deep for a brave man to bear?"

"He is bleeding to death," Claremont answered, quietly.

"Faith, man, then let me be his doctor; for it's many the gaping wound I've bound before to-night. Your handkerchief—tenderly now; there, raise him gently. Ah, that stops the running tide, which, hark ye, no man can safely let have its course. He'll do now; let us lift him out of sight, and we'll take off his mask, that we may see who he is, and send him home."

A very different scene was taking place at another part of the gardens.

There all was festivity, mirth, and gay pleasure.

A magnificent band was stationed in an oriental pavilion, outside which a hundred cavaliers and fair ladies were gaily joining in the dance. In another part, a crowd of guests were hurrying to the supper-hall.

Captain Tom mingled in the general throng, and allowed himself to be taken towards the brilliant room where the banquet was spread.

At the hour fixed for the banquet, the guests began to make their way from the gardens.

Our hero, standing by one of the spacious doorways, had a good view of all who entered.

He saw the young and lovely Countess St. Albans, the giver of the fete, escorted in.

Admiral Ellis followed.

Then came the commodore, amidst a crowd of male and female masks, who were unknown to our hero.

Lady Arbuthnot, with Minnie and Lady Castlemaine, entered late, and took their seats.

Lord Kilcrew accompanied them.

He seated himself beside Minnie, to whom he was very anxious to pay his attentions.

Tom was pleased to see that the fair young girl gave him no encouragement.

When nearly all were seated, Lords Claremont, Walpole, Moreton, and Vane, who seemed inseparable, sauntered in at the doorway where Tom stood.

Claremont gave our hero a quick, inquiring glance, and lingering behind his companions, said in a low tone,—

"Are you prepared to convert this brilliant scene into one of bloodshed and terror? You are known—all must unmask after the supper—one word of warning, the grounds are filled with armed soldiery."

Our hero bowed gallantly.

"My lord," he said, "we were once foes, I thank you for your warning."

"I'll not betray you," Claremont exclaimed; "retire while you are undiscovered."

Our hero's lips curled scornfully.

"My lord," he said, "I shall not turn my back upon my foes till the mission that brought me here is accomplished."

Lord Claremont said no more, but passed in with his friends.

A couple of monks, dressed as Capucin friars, pushed their way in at the same time.

A number of masks, similarly dressed, were already in the hall.

Lord Walpole stepped aside, as one of them brushed close to him.

"Who the devil are those fellows?" he said to Moreton. "All the evening I've been pushing past them.

"Haven't any idea; fact is, I'm sick of trying to find out. Everywhere I've knocked against them—there must be a score or two, at least, of them in the grounds."

Claremont rejoined them at that instant, and they went out of our hero's hearing.

Nine-and-twenty Capucin friars had entered; their faces hidden by their silk masks, their grey cloaks bound gracefully about their forms.

Each of the nine-and-twenty, as he passed our hero, made a sign which was answered by the young hero chief.

The thirtieth, a tall, graceful young fellow, stayed a moment to speak in a low tone to Tom.

Then he went in, and our hero, quitting his post, took a seat near Admiral Ellis and Lord Kilcrew.

Tom's young acquaintances, the four youthful noblemen, were each seated beside a lady, whom they escorted to the hall.

Each, of course, thought he was playing the gallant to the most peerless and beautiful, and anxiously awaited the moment for removing their masks, that they might see who their fair companions were.

When they were carefully posted at the table, they looked up, and were considerably struck to see our hero seated opposite to them.

"Aw—by jinks," said Lord Vane, nudging Moreton in his side, "there's that confounded corsair!"

Moreton, who was just then whispering soft nothings in the ear of the lady who sat beside him, frowned, and giving Tom a fierce glance, went on with the converse.

Rebuffed in this quarter, the young foppish noble drew Walpole's attention to Tom's presence.

"And I say, Walpole, he said he'd drink wine for supper—aw—let's try him."

"With all my heart," Walpole said, laughing.

Lord Vane filled his glass.

"Aw—you corsair fellar—aw—we want you to—aw—take wine with us."

Our hero called a page to fill his glass.

"Gentlemen," he said, "the ladies of the masquerade."

"Hurrah," lisped Lord Vane; "aw—capital fellow after all."

Each of the young noblemen raised his glass, and drank to Tom.

Moreton alone left his goblet untasted.

Lord Vane might have attempted to get Tom into further conversation, but the lovely being to whom he was paying his addresses, rebuked him for his want of attention to her, and the vain young lordling had neither eyes or voice after that for anyone else.

Our hero was not sorry to see him thus enchained, for he was in no mood to join in the young nobleman's frivolous conversation.

He was jealously watching Minnie, now the object of Lord Kilcrew's attention.

The banquet that now ensued was a perfect feast for gods and godesses.

Had there been any there, they would undoubtedly have done justice to its rare delicacies.

In their absence, the mortals who were present did their best to show their appreciation of the good things set before them.

Rich ruby wine sparkled in choice crystal glasses—bright eyes twinkled merrily—pearly teeth glistened, and many a fair bosom throbbed under the thrilling words of the enamoured cavaliers.

None seemed to give a thought to Lieutenant Gaston, even if they knew he had been carried bleeding and unconscious to his home.

The feast was nearly over, when Admiral Ellis arose at the right hand of the beautiful countess.

A messenger had just handed him a private communication.

The little old officer did not seem to believe his eyes as he read, and when he rose sharply, his dry, husky cough betokened his ill-concealed satisfaction.

But before speaking aloud to the guests, he spoke a few words in the messenger's ears, who instantly departed.

"Lady revellers, and you gentlemen," said the admiral, "I ask your grace for interrupting your festivity, but I have just received the glad tidings that the notorious Boy Pirate —Tom Drake, has been taken prisoner, and is now confined in the town jail. This is the more satisfactory, for not an hour since I was secretly informed that the audacious pirate had determined to attend this masquerade, with his ferocious crew, and convert this fair carnival to a scene of rapine and bloodshed."

The admiral's words were succeeded by a thrilling shriek, and Minnie Atherton, starting from her seat, fell back fainting into the arms of Lady Castlemaine.

Lord Claremont was watching our hero, for he expected to see him leap to Minnie's side and support her as she fell; but the Boy Corsair remained calm, and, apparently, unmoved.

"By jinks, Moreton, d'ye hear that?" cried Lord Vane, "that pirate, Captain Tom Drake, the—aw—fellow Claremont fought with, you know."

"Hush," Walpole said, "there's a lady ill, and, if I suspect right, she's the corsair's bride."

Minnie came to herself without the assistance of the ladies, who crowded round her.

Very few were acquainted with her name and history, and it was generally believed that she had been frightened by the mention of the pirate's name.

Admiral Ellis waited until silence was completely restored, when he spoke,—

"Before the revellers unmask, it is the wish of our fair hostess, that they close the night's festivity by attending at the nuptials of a bride and bridegroom, who are this night to be king and queen of the masquerade."

Captain Tom started, and clutched his dagger-hilt.

Minnie Atherton sat pale as a statue of stone.

A good deal of clattering of glasses followed the admiral's speech.

The approval of men, and the merry laughter of the ladies.

The idea of such a bridal was a fitting climax to the masked ball, and cries arose for the name of the bridegroom and bride.

"The bridegroom," exclaimed the little old admiral, in his dry tone, "is a gallant officer in our service, the bride is a fair ward, whom the King, our gracious majesty, as guardian elect, has been pleased to give him in marriage. It is the King's wish this marriage takes place to-night. Our hostess has fitted up her chapel for the purpose—a clergyman waits with the royal licence, and now, unmask all. There stands the bridegroom, Admiral Lord Kilcrew, and his bride is by his side."

His out-stretched arm pointed to where Minnie sat, shivering and in tears.

Lady Castlemaine had just bidden her prepare for her hated bridal.

There was a general removal of masks, amidst loud hurrahs, and the revellers gazed on the silent bride.

She did not offer to remove her veil, but Lady Castlemaine did so for her, and revealed her pale, beautiful features.

Then it was noticed that the corsair and the thirty Capucin friars were still masked. Before the buzz of common excitement had died away, our hero stood erect.

Every eye was fixed on his graceful form.

"My Lord Admiral," he said, "I forbid these nuptials; no forced bridal shall take place to-night."

"And who are you, who dare speak against the King's decree?" cried the admiral, hoarse with rage. "Unmask the fellow—let us see the intruder's face!"

Cries of "Unmask! unmask!" came from all sides.

Captain Tom Drake's bright eyes flashed dangerously.

He had not yet assumed his natural voice, but his tones were tremulous with anger.

"I dare to speak against the King's decree," he cried. "This maiden is the betrothed bride of Captain Tom Drake, and till he surrenders her love for him she shall wed no other!"

The Admiral coughed drily.

"We shall see," he said; "in anticipation of some interruption, I have ordered a guard of marines, who will assist the ceremony. As for that pirate, whom we have at last, he will certainly be executed before another sunset."

"The lady shall give her consent; or, were these gardens teeming with armed soldiery, no bridal should take place. Answer, Minnie Atherton, will you be his bride?"

"No, no—help me!" Minnie cried.

Lady Castlemaine tried to stop Minnie's voice, by placing her hand on her lips, and the hapless young girl sank again to her seat.

The thirty Capucin monks, still masked, and in their cloaks of grey, had left their seats, and were now in rear of Captain Tom.

As our hero cast his angry eyes around, the little old admiral observed their suspicious movements, and in a loud voice—as loud as it had often rung on the quarter-deck in the heat of battle, cried,—

"Lord Kilcrew, look to your bride! Sound the alarm—beat the drums—there is treachery in our midst!"

Admiral Lord Kilcrew tenderly put his arm round Minnie's waist; but, in an instant, his arm was torn from its hold, and the masked corsair, hurling him aside, lifted Minnie from amidst her friends.

"Away," he cried. "Stay every hand! She is my bride, and thus do I snatch her from you. Stand forth, my gallant band—let them see the glitter of your steel! Aha! Behold, these are my Boy Rovers, and I am Captain Tom Drake!"

He plucked his mask aside, and stood revealed.

Such a scene of confusion, alarm, and dismay followed his action and speech.

Ladies shrieked and fainted; gentlemen sprang forward, their swords flashing from their sheaths; glasses and decanters crashed to earth.

Admiral Ellis reeled, thunder-stricken.

Lord Kilcrew, for the moment, stood dumb and motionless.

And then, as Minnie crept, with a glad cry to her daring lover's breast, his gallant crew, armed to the teeth, with their masks and friars' cloaks thrown off, gathered around their dauntless leader, whose sword, already out of its scabbard, kept Lord Kilcrew at bay.

A strange hush followed, the momentary hubbub of alarm.

Then the deep rattle of drums, as the alarm was beat in the distance.

———

CHAPTER IX.

CAPTAIN ANGEL TRIES A LITTLE STRATAGEM.

"I GUESS that's the last of her," said Captain Yates, as he turned to Angel.

A flare had shone a moment on the horizon, and then passed away, leaving blackness where the ship had been.

Angel made no reply; his mind was absorbed in a reverie, and he heeded not the words of his superior.

A dark purpose was floating across his wily brain, and he required undisturbed silence to mature it.

Since he had assumed the position of lieutenant he had beheld with joy that his installation into that rank had created a vindictive feeling in the breast of worthy Jeremy Dindle, whom he had thus displaced from the chance of being first lieutenant.

He had been pleased to see this, because it gave him a hope of creating a division amongst the lawless crew, and thus perchance affording him the opportunity of becoming master of the vessel, in which case he proposed running her into the nearest port, and returning to England by the quickest route.

He was most anxious to return; his absence, and the knowledge of Sanderson's triumph, were a festering gangrene at his heart's core, and each day that kept him confined was a day of torment.

It was in furtherance of his purpose that he had interfered and prevented the men bringing to the vessel the unfortunate captives and the wine; he reasoned rightly when he conjectured that this would lead some of the men to league and conspire to break the bonds of discipline.

They had hitherto, in their evil career, been permitted to have their own way when they took any craft; they had been deprived of this privilege by Angel, and, being further incited by Dindle, many of them became sullen and discontented, and showed signs of a gathering mutiny.

When the crafty plotter perceived that matters were brought to this verge, he ingratiated himself into Dindle's confidence by proposing that the ship should be seized, and the captain, with such as sided with him, overpowered. Dindle was then to take charge of the ship, and Angel to be his lieutenant.

The gullible victim fell into the trap, and, having organised a rising of the discontented, they rose one morning in open mutiny.

But he had overlooked the penetration of the redoubtable Captain Yates.

That worthy, having got scent of the projected rising, had taken his measures well, and when Dindle, with his party, appeared on deck, he found himself confronted by the captain and the greater portion of the crew, each of whom presented his musket at Jeremy's breast.

Angel, too, was arrayed on the side of the captain.

"Wall," said Yates, as he looked upon the discontented faces, "what's up now? Are yer gathered here for sport or bizness? Blazes seize yer! Put down yer weapons as soon as yer can, and jist remember that the last man swings from the yard-arm!"

The dismayed mutineers laid down their arms with alacrity, and Dindle stood unsupported and alone.

"So," said the captain, "yer ill-looking skunk, yer want to lead the ship, do yer? Wal, yer shall, my hearty. Clap hands on him, yer ragamuffins, and bring him for'ard."

The would-be rebel was seized in a trice, and securely bound.

Yates turned to the others.

"And now, my lads, jist don't try this on again. Yer'll have plenty o' carousing when we get to the island; but any more rising, and I'll blow the brains out o' the lot o' yer."

He turned to Angel.

"You've had a hand in this mess; don't come it again. I reckon yer wanted to get him out o' yer way; but, by the living jingo, if I thought yer were trying to cheat me, I'd have yer neck wrung!"

"Pshaw!" returned Angel. "Swear by dead gods; they will hear you as soon, and your oath will be as strong."

Captain Yates glanced fiercely at him, and then turned to the captive Dindle.

"And now, yer cussed scarecrow, I'll show yer how to lead the ship. Bring him on, my lads."

A few instructions were given to the men, and the wretched culprit was conveyed to the bows, where some of the crew lowered themselves down, and bound him fast with ropes and chains to the figure-head.

"There, yer beauty," said Yates, "I told yer I'd let yer lead the ship, and, furies, so you shall. Let any man go to him, speak to him, or give him a morsel to eat or a drop to drink—especially to drink—an' I'll crucify him! Farewell, my beauty; you'll be thirsty by-and-by, but there'll be plenty of water round yer—more'n yer'll drink, I'll swear."

He turned away, and left the doomed man to his fate.

And Captain Angel, though only partly successful, had gained a point, for he had learned now who were, and who were not, to be depended upon.

CHAPTER X.
DINDLE'S FATE.

THE figure-head of the Civet Cat rose high above the water, and the doomed wretch, bound fast, condemned to that lingering, dreadful death, saw nothing but the broad expanse of the billows around him, heard no sound but their surging roar as they gurgled in his ears.

The sun went down, and the shades of night gathered slowly; the foaming black waters bubbled in the frothy stream as they fled from the vessel's keel; still Dindle, wakeful and agonised, piloted the vessel on her speeding career.

He had cried to his captain for mercy; he had appealed to his comrades for aid, but the frothing billows had drowned his tones, and only the wind answered him.

And so through that terrible night, on through the blackened gloom—the waters around him, the waters beneath him, the waters above him, as the vessel dipped in the waves, the wretched culprit hung helpless beneath the bows.

A fearful pain crept over his joints, a dreadful terror preyed upon his heart, and as the wild waves dashed in his face and sounded their ceaseless hum in his ears, he raved aloud in his agony, and cursed the God that suffered him to endure such torment.

And all through that dark night there rose before him the faces of the many helpless victims who had perished before his lawless violence in his career of evil.

A ghastly troop! They hemmed him in and floated before him on the crested waves; their stony eyes were fixed, and their fingers were raised towards their murderer.

And the winds howled over the sea, and the water rose with a stupendous roar, and dashed the gathered cold sweat from his clammy brow.

The night passed away—how he had counted the minutes!

The morning dawned—how grateful to him was its welcome light!

His face was ghastly and distorted with horror; his teeth chattered, and his limbs were benumbed, though where the cords pressed the agony was unendurable.

His eyes were bloodshot and staring, and his matted hair, stiff and clotted with the saline waters, hung in a dishevelled mass.

But he looked on the dawn with fresh hope.

He had suffered much; surely the captain would relent, would reprieve him, and overlook his offence.

Alas, no!

The morning passed; he counted the chimes as the bells were sounded.

Hour after hour dragged by, still no cessation from his trusting in rescue from his fate.

Nor food nor drink was given him, and he was left to his despair.

And now his sense of hearing became terribly acute.

He could hear the voices on the deck above him, could distinguish their tones—aye, he could even detect the hasty step of the captain, and the slow, stealthy footfall of Angel.

Some one approaches the bow—they are coming to release him; his punishment is over!

How his heart leaps—how he strains at the bonds which confine him!

They come nearer; how, with palpitating heart, he counts each step! Alas, there is no hope!

They have returned, and have left him there to perish.

How he groaned in agony as the ship dipped into the sea, and the waves dashed over him!

His blood was hot, and his brow fevered; and the cold touch of the foaming billows was torture immeasurable.

The sunshine played upon the waters; big fishes rose to the surface; they swam around him, before, and by his side, marvelling why he of the living was there amongst them; and they gambolled in glee, and darting to the ocean's depth, rose again to torment him by their presence.

The sky was fair and cloudless, and the wavelets in the distance rippled in joy.

And he was perishing!

Dying of hunger and thirst—dying in torment—dying unheeded.

Thirst inwardly consumed him; his parched tongue lolled from his mouth, and he drank eagerly of the salt spray and foam as it rippled over him.

And a huge tenant of the deep arose, and turned its deadly eyes upon him.

It was terrible, and he struggled to free himself, until his bonds entered like burning shackles into his flesh.

And that day passed; the sun blistering his features and the waves chafing him to madness, while the salt water burned like molten lead within him, and hunger gnawed him like the sharp beak of a raven.

And the night came with its gloom and its terrors, its darkness and its pain.

Still the ship plunged through the waters, and the rushing of the foaming waves poured wildly to his brain.

Again those faces of the murdered were before him; they danced around him, and seemed to shout in glee as they leapt high on the crested waves.

And he called aloud on Heaven, and prayed that he might die.

An age of darkness had passed—the light of day streaks the sky—his head droops upon his breast, and his arms hang idly by his sides.

But he has not found release.

The sun darts down its fiery rays upon his brow, searing like the brands of doom, and he arouses from his stupor of exhaustion ;arouses to fight with the elements around him; arouses to do terrible battle with slowly-conquering death.

His lips are swollen and black—an unearthly gleam in his eye; it is the wild spark of madness, for his brain is on fire and his reason has left him.

And he raves unheard to the winds and to the waters.

Down deep into the foaming trough plunged the speeding ship.

The waters gurgled over him, surged in his ears, and roared their death-song in his brain.

Then the vessel rose high above the seething mass, and the frothy ripples bubbled, foaming beneath him.

And his raving cry was, "Water, water!"

Far in rippling circlets spread the blue waves.

How tempting and cool they looked! yet he, in their midst, was fevered and agonised.

He would have given worlds, could he have possessed them, for one plunge in the heaving sea.

But this was denied him—his ligatures resisted even the fury of his madness.

Hark!

There is a roaring in his ears; it sounds like the falling of a mighty torrent, and he pauses to listen.

The waves seem to rear in mighty masses before him, towering their crests into the sky; and from their boiling tops rise dense masses of spray, which, ascending to the clouds, fall in distilled jets on his parched lips and burning brow.

And the waves as they rise, seem to have each on their front a face, huge, terrible, and grim—and eyes that glitter in varied hues, peer upon him from the seething billows.

But he fears them not—heeds not the howling of myriads of strange beings dancing before him, for his lips, his tongue, his mouth, dried as the walls of a furnace, have received no blessed quenching drops.

He heeds them not, but laughs aloud.

The waves rise higher and higher; the roar becomes louder and more terrific.

Now the ocean, now the sky, whirls swiftly round him.

Swifter and swifter!

All is one stupifying whirl and deafening roar.

Strange forms, strange faces encompass him.

Anon the faces change.

These are the forms of his friends.

He sees his mother, his aged father, his sister, and she whom he loved—they whirl away—their place is supplied by jeering devils, and hollow-eyed spectres.

The waves tower above him—they fall upon him—still those loathsome objects whirl near him.

Now he is dragged into the terrible vortex—he clings, but in vain; he shrieks, but mocking laughter only answers his wild cry.

The falling drops descend like boiling lead; his tongue is fixed, he can no longer cry; the whirling waves, the mighty roar increases to one dreadful pitch; a cry that seems to rend his heart asunder breaks from his soul; the waves subside, the deafening roar is hushed, and all is dark and still.

The ghastly mortal form, all that is left now of the deeply sinning ruffian, hangs in its bonds, and guides the pirate ship on her guilty course.

CHAPTER XI.

ANOTHER RAFT.

It was a fearful hour for Nancy when she first became aware of the real occupation of the man for whom she had forsaken her husband.

She prayed to be put on shore, but the miscreant captain was deaf to her entreaties, and disregarded her remorse.

When the conflict of death was going on she was kept imprisoned in the cabin, where she could hear the terrible tumult, but not see the fearful occurrences.

But from the cabin window she saw the burning ship, with its helpless victims, and her blood froze within her at the appalling sight.

And, when Dindle was left to his terrible death, her implorings were ceaseless that he might be pardoned.

Her misery was increased by the presence of Angel, who, with his cold, cutting sarcasms, contrived to set her sin before her in its very worst light.

ATTACKED IN REAR.

He it was who informed her of the lawless nature of the captain and his crew, and he took a savage delight in contemplating her anguish and remorse.

She paid in full the penalty of her crime, but the worst was yet to come.

Arrived at a slaving depot on the slave coast, Captain Yates disposed of his spoils and shipped a cargo of captive blacks.

Then, again altering the trim of his vessel to the cut of a rough merchantman, and having obtained false papers, he hoisted the British flag, and shaped her course for the coast of America.

Off the coast of Africa they were overtaken by a terrific storm, and the vessel, with her human cargo, rolled fearfully amidst the boiling waters.

But she was a seaworthy craft, and in practised hands; and, though much damaged at the onset of the gale, she scudded along under bare poles, and survived the tempest's wrath.

During the rest of the night the hurricane raged with terrible wrath; but towards dawn the breeze subsided, and the thick heavy clouds began to disperse.

But the sea laboured tremendously, the waves rising in mountainous masses, and bearing aloft the rolling vessel.

And the groans of the helpless living freight, crowded in the suffocating hold, were terrible; packed closely together, breathing a contaminated and pestilential air, the sick and dying huddled with the strong in one steaming heap, their sufferings were truly horrible; whilst at each pitch of the vessel their iron links were jammed burning into their quivering flesh.

And the roar of the waves in vain attempted to drown their cries and moans.

As the day passed the sea became more calm, though the breeze was fitful and uncertain, the ship making but little way.

The sun went down gloomy and red upon the heaving waters; the breeze had drooped almost to a dead calm, and the vessel, with her sails flapping against the masts, drifted on with the ocean's flow.

As the last streaks crimsoned the west, the man at the cat-head detected a dark speck in the distance.

The captain turned his glass in that direction, and Angel, with his eagle glance, strove to make out what it was.

"Tarnation seize me!" said Yates, "it looks mighty like a boat, or a raft."

"It is a raft," exclaimed Angel.

As it floated nearer it became apparent that it was a raft, and the Civet Cat bore down upon it.

A dark object lay across it: it seemed like a human form, but whether living or no it was impossible to discern.

Just as the ship's bows neared the raft, its occupant sat up, and gazed wildly around.

On observing the approaching ship, he feebly waved his hand, and clutched tightly a heavy-looking bag.

"Lower the boat, and haul him up here," said Yates.

A boat was lowered, and the ship being brought to, several of the crew stayed the raft, and took the man and his leather bag, to which he clung most tenaciously, into the boat.

They then brought him on deck, a matter of some difficulty, as he appeared so faint and exhausted as to be unable to stand on his feet.

He was a short middle-aged man, with a profusion of beard and whiskers; his lank hair, straight and stiff, stuck out from beneath a battered hat, and he had on a rough sea-jacket.

But there was a peculiar shifting gleam of his eyes that chiefly attracted attention.

"Well, shipmate," said Yates, when he had taken a quiet survey of him, "yer seem kinder done up."

"I am," muttered the man; "I've been drifting about for the last four days, with nought to eat but a biscuit."

"Was yer wrecked?"

"Yes."

"An' what's yer name?"

"Samuel Warr," replied the man, after a pause.

"Wal, whar d'ye want to cruise to?"

"Home—to England. If you will give me a passage as far as you go I will pay you well."

"I guess so, too, stranger. What yer got in that 'ere bag—shiners?"

"It is my own property," replied the man, curtly.

"Wal, yer needn't be so 'cute, shipmate; however, yer may jine us if yer like, an' ain't pertikler."

"I am not particular."

"You'll do; and as yer seem faint, yer'd better git some o' these lads to take yer to the purser, where yer can have a chaw."

The man growled out his thanks, and having had some refreshment was shown to his berth.

"Guess I'll overhaul that bag of his'n," mentally exclaimed Captain Yates, as he stood on the quarter-deck. "He's a 'cute coon; but he'd better have left those 'ere shiners on shore when he came on board the Civet."

Soon a breeze sprang up; the sails were set, the masts strained with the weight of canvas, and the Civet Cat leapt over the wild ocean.

The shipwrecked man had sufficiently recovered to be on deck the following day. He was moody and uncivil, scarcely heeding what might be going on around him, nor deigning to enter into converse with any one on board.

That evening, as Nancy was descending the gangway, she observed his eyes fixed upon her with a peculiar glance; her heart leapt wildly: too well she recognised those savage orbs.

She turned deadly pale, and her head became so giddy that it was with difficulty she kept herself from falling.

A smile of triumph settled upon the man's coarse features; then he turned and walked away.

He saw not that the sharp eye of the captain was fixed upon him, watching his every movement.

Poor Nancy descended to her cabin, and gave way to her grief.

A dreadful presentiment was at her heart. She knew that it was not for a purposeless object that he had tracked her across the broad waters, and she augured the worst from his presence in the ship.

And even Captain Yates's self-confidence would have been dissipated, could he have known the exact purpose that caused the man to place himself in his power, or have watched his work at night.

When the watch were on deck, and the rest of the crew snug in their hammocks, he, sleepless and indefatigable, laboured in the deepest hold, among the heavy ballast. For there, when there were none to witness his toil, nor to impede his progress, he worked secretly and noiselessly; he drilled holes in the vessel's side, and removed tack and plank till he came to the outer coating.

This he loosened and undermined, and then lightly fastening thin planks before the gaps he had made, he stole to his berth and chuckled in secret delight.

He had placed the ship at the mercy of the waves; a rude buffet, a sudden surge, and the thin protection would be washed away, and the waves rise in an overwhelming mass.

And he would be avenged!

He would hear their cries, scoff at her shrieks, and laugh at their consternation and dismay.

Well might he chuckle and rejoice; he had gained the end for which he had risked that long journey; his was now the triumph—for, as sure as the fixed decree of Fate herself, was the vessel doomed.

CHAPTER XII.
HUSBAND AND WIFE.

OVER the leaping waters of the surging sea sped the pirate barque, the doom of certain destruction unseen but slowly encompassing her.

The pirates caroused and made merry.

They thought of their gains and exulted in their deeds of violence, and they scoffed at the power of the wind and the waves, though but a few yielding planks were between them and eternity.

And the pent-up living freight, a compact mass of suffering and pollution, was stived in the loathsome hold, in sickness and pain.

And they called on the God of the white man to soften the hearts of His people.

They knew not that their release was coming, and that their miseries would be ended in speedy death.

On, with her human load of misery and sin, flew the Civet Cat—on, dancing in pride above the ocean, while the wedge of Fate was driving to her very heart, and the waters were beating away the frail bulwarks beneath her decks.

Sombre and threatening the black clouds piled to the sky; around her, above her, lowering and dense, they gathered, like the harbingers of doom.

And night, with its sable wings, was creeping fast upon her, but the pall that hid the sky, tinged by the fiery lustre of the setting sun, was not the shroud of night, but the wings of the gathering storm.

The wind swept by with an angry roar, and the canvas beat with a sullen flap against the creaking masts; and, as the red sun dipped in the frothing sea, a hollow rumbling sound pealed over the horizon.

"Close reef, and get the storm-sails set," cried Captain Yates to his men. "The storm-claps boomed, but we must make what way we can."

Willing hands raised the flying sails, and rigged the ship taut and trim.

Then the last ray faded from the sky, and nothing was seen but the blackened clouds, and the inky, foam-tipped waters.

And with a mighty surge, the billows bore against the speeding vessel.

A broad, whitened flash passed like a sheet of flame beneath the heavens. Then all again was darkness.

But far in the distance boomed the low, muttering voice of the echoing thunder.

The scene was ominously grand.

The horizon was now hid by the murky masses of gloom, and the fretted waters, cold and dark, spread their vast expanse.

The wind had dropped, and through the pitchy darkness the doomed ship rode silent and stately, like a phantom vessel.

The air was hot and close, and those who stood upon the deck knew how fearful was the storm that was coming on.

But they knew not that the sun had gone down which they would never behold rise again.

Yes, there was one who looked out upon the night, and knew that the dawn would never come to them.

That one was the shipwrecked stranger whom they had taken aboard; he knew how surely their fate was fixed, and the knowledge gave him joy.

CHAPTER XIII.

THE GALE.

YET he knew that he must perish with them. But he was a dogged, perverse man, moody and resolute, and he waited in exultation for the hour of his vengeance and his triumph.

The breeze sprang up, the ocean swept on its heaving course, and the Civet Cat scudded over the waves; she rolled heavily, dipping her bows and then her spars in the foaming billows.

And the gale increased; sheeted lightning lit up the labouring sea, and the thunder spoke loud and deep.

Soon the storm raged in its utmost violence, and as the vessel rolled in the surging troughs of the sea, every wild clap of thunder rang to the hearts of those who heard it.

The captain walked the deck fearless and confident; he had weathered before the severe gales of those latitudes, and had no doubt of the ship's security.

For he knew not that the cry of his slaughtered victims had reached to heaven, and that a guilty mortal was made the instrument of doom.

It is a terrible thing a tempest on the sea, when the helpless barque stands alone on the whirling waters—when sheeted and forked lightnings sweep circling around, and the thunder speaks in its awful tones, like the terrible voice of an angry God.

The mariners feel their helplessness and danger, and even the hardened pray to heaven for the help it is not in the power of man to bestow.

An hour passed.

The Civet Cat was borne by the wrath of the waves high on their frothy crests.

Down, whirling in the whitened vortex, as the waters, breaking, recede, she swiftly sinks; the waves leap high against her sides, and wash with a sudden plunge over the decks, and the tempest-blast, shrieking shrilly by, lashes the sea into mountains of spray and foam.

And all this time, with a trickling splash, the water was oozing through the shattered planks, creeping steadily and stealthily into the lower hold; but the men of the ship knew it not.

Suddenly there is a call from below, and the hardiest becomes blanched as he hears that ominous cry—

"The ship has sprung a leak—three feet of water in the hold!"

A terrible curse broke from the captain's lips, and Angel, turning slowly round, scanned the faces of the crew.

"All hands to the pumps," cried Yates, and the men hastened to grapple with the mighty enemy creeping upon them unawares.

But the surging water proved a formidable foe to cope with.

All the pumps were kept in full play, and the crew laboured with vigorous energy, but half an hour brought the unwelcome intelligence that the water was still rapidly gaining upon them.

And the efforts and skill of the captain and Angel were vainly called into requisition, for they failed to subdue the danger.

Slowly but surely, right into the heart of the ship, crept the gurgling waters, and their onward approach was the certain advent of death.

And now a man was sent down to dive beneath the rising water in the hold, and report upon the state of the terrible leak.

A short time he remained there, and when he again came up his words carried consternation to every heart.

"The water is oozing in from several gaps on either side of the lower hold!"

"Then there has been foul play somewhere," said the stern voice of Angel.

"Tarnation, yes," exclaimed Yates; "it's that snake we picked up. Take anything you can get to plug up the leaks, while I look arter him."

And with a look of mischief in his eyes he proceeded in quest of the stranger.

While the storm was raging, and the ship heaving to and fro, Nancy, on her knees in the cabin, was imploring the mercy of her Maker.

She deemed the tempest as a righteous retribution sent to overtake her for her sins, and the pirate gang for their many crimes.

Thus, while weeping bitterly, and regarding her fate as just, she prayed for those helpless beings cooped and bound between decks.

In the midst of her prayers a hand was laid roughly upon her shoulder, and a voice, whose tones shot through her brain, saluted her ears—

"Come, don't 'ee know me?"

She turned slowly, and confronted Simon Gagg, her husband.

The false whiskers and beard were gone, and the old brutal grin played upon his ruffianly visage.

"Come, doan't 'ee weep; here's yer husband, yer see, come to comfort yer."

Nancy made no reply; her whole frame quivered, and her tongue clave to her mouth.

The looks of her husband convinced her that her last hour had come.

"So yer thought yer'd given I the slip, with yer loving cap'n, did yer? Never thought, I dessay, that I should come across yer; but I have though, you see, and I bean't come for nought, naythur."

The shuddering woman needed not to be told that; she read his intentions in his scowling visage and his murderous glance.

"Noa, I be come to put a stop to your billing and cooing! Look at me, wife that was, and see if yer can guess what I am here to do!"

He grasped her slender arm rudely as he spoke. She replied faintly—

"Yes, Simon, you have come, I know, to kill me, but I do not fear to die. I have no wish to live longer in this terrible world; you may kill me, and I will not cry, even when your knife is at my throat. But I pray that heaven will forgive both you and me. Yet reflect, Simon, in this, our last meeting, that you alone are to blame that I have sinned. I bore patiently your harsh treatment, and endured without complaint your wicked temper; but you tried me too far at last. If you had treated me even with a trace of kindness I should never have left you, but you treated me worse than a dog, and I was driven to leave you."

The ruffian grated his teeth savagely, and hissed in her ear—

"Do you prate of heaven, and then of the past, in my teeth? How would you have been treated? Did you want I to worship yer? But never mind, I didn't come here for that. I come to tell you that this ship and all that's aboard on her's doomed. Not one'll see the morning!"

"I know it," said his wife.

"Do you? Well, let me tell you that it's my work. I've been pretty busy since I came here, working down below The hold's nigh full o' water, an' it's my doing, that it be so."

"It's the hand of the Almighty!"

"Hold yer prate, an' listen will you? I've been a long time follerin you about, but I made sure who'd pick me up afore I went adrift. Dang yer, I'll settle yer fust, and then I'll go above and see how they're getting on. But I'll finish you fust, I will."

As he spoke he drew a large clasp-knife from his pocket, and, holding Nancy firmly by one hand, drew open the blade with his teeth.

Nancy did not flinch, though her face became a shade more ghastly, and her eyes were fixed in horror.

"Look at me!" exclaimed the brutal wretch. "Look at me, while the knife is at yer throat. Take yer last look. I swore to have revenge, and I've kept my oath. Now say your prayers; quick! here goes the knife into yer gullet."

"Not yet, yer ugly sarpint!" said a well-known voice behind him, at the same moment that a swinging blow sent him reeling to the floor.

The captain and several of his men were in the cabin.

Nancy continued kneeling, her eyes still fixed in that stony glance.

Simon was seized, and the murderous-looking knife taken from his grasp.

He glared vindictively at his captors, and then fixed his savage glance on the wretched Nancy.

"Darn ye all," he said, "yer can't balk me of my revenge; she shall die, and ye all shall die this night."

He turned to the captain.

"You know me, doan't ye? You see I wasn't bilked so easily."

"Yer hugly animal," returned Yates, "I knowed yer from the first; but I thought I watched yer too closely for yer to do any mischief."

Simon laughed coarsely.

"I've drowned yer all!" he said, in tones of triumph.

"Five feet of water in the hold!" sang out some one from above.

A gleam of satisfaction flitted over Simon's features.

"It'll soon be six feet!" he exclaimed.

"Yaas," said Yates; "and when it's six feet you'll swing at the yard-arm, which I guess 'll stop yer crowing."

Simon changed countenance.

"I doan't care," he rejoined, the moment after "'Ee can't escape; you maun all die too."

"Bear him on deck," said the captain. "Sling a rope round his neck, and when the time's up we'll run him up to the yard-arm."

Here Nancy threw herself at the captain's feet.

"Spare him," she cried. "Oh! if it is as he has said, and we are all to die, let us die peacefully together. Think of the great Judge whom we must presently meet, and do not anger Him by further deeds of vengeance!"

"Wal, that's kinder considerate of yer, seeing he was jest about finishing you when we came down."

"He is my husband."

"Sorry I can't oblige yer, Nan; but I allers pays off as I go; I reckon it's the best way, an' we mightn't get another opportunity. Don't ask any more. Lead him up, my men; his time's up when there's six feet of water in the hold."

They passed up to the deck, leading the scowl ing culprit between them, and the wretched Nancy followed after to beseech mercy for her worthless husband.

The tempest was raging furiously; in the dark vortex of the black waters the reeling vessel seemed but a mere speck.

The ocean still surged with its frightful roar, and the rude wind, shrieking past, drowned the words of command given on board the ship; it stifled, too, the groans of the wretched blacks, who, conscious of impending doom, raised an appealing outcry for help.

Nancy shuddered as she gazed around upon the terrible scene, and moaned in anguish as she beheld the dreadful preparations for the execution of her husband.

He, hardened and brutal, beheld undismayed his approaching death, and the kneeling woman prayed for him, as she heard his coarse oaths.

"Ye are all doomed!" he shouted, as he struggled to get to his hapless wife. "Ye will all go down; there is no escape, ye must die."

And the hearts of the ruffians around him quaked as they heard his confident boast.

But new hope was suddenly enkindled; it was reported that the pumps were telling upon the water, and the men worked with redoubled energy when they heard that pleasing intelligence.

"Work away, my hearties!" shouted the captain. "Stuff all yer can into the holes; stop the leak an' we shall be safe."

He turned to Simon, who, with the rope round his neck, was held by the vessel's side.

"Don't think yer'll get off, yer sallow-faced wretch; yer shall swing when yer see we have got the best of yer handiwork."

"Four feet of water in the hold!" was now the welcome cry.

"D'ye hear that?" exclaimed Yates, thrusting his finger in Simon's face.

A look of chagrin flitted over Simon's features, but it presently passed, and was succeeded by his accustomed grin of brutal ferocity.

"Doan't 'ee fear," he said. "There be one plank as haven't gone yet; yer'll soon fill when it does."

Yates looked fixedly at him; there was no misunderstanding the look of coarse satisfaction on Simon's countenance.

"Fiends and fury seize yer!" he exclaimed, as he struck him full in the face with a belaying pin. "Sarpint, if there was time I'd crucify yer!"

He rushed hurriedly to the men at the pumps.

"Look out sharp down thar!" he shouted to those who were below. "Plug up the leaky parts with stout timber, or yer'll have another bilge in 'minnit."

Even as he spoke, a huge wave struck the vessel full; she swayed and shivered from stem to stern, then there came a wild rush as of surging water and a sudden cry from those who were engaged in plugging the leaks.

The vessel righted, but rocked from side to side; a gurgling cry arose from the hold, and then nothing was heard but the sound of the rushing water.

And the men at the pumps were aghast, for they knew that the water was rapidly filling the hold.

Captain Yates came on deck white and haggard, but there was the glance of a demon in his piercing eyes.

"Ha, ha!" laughed Simon. "It's all up wi' yer now; I knowed it would be."

"Darn ye," said the captain, bestowing on him a look of deadly rage. "If we go you shall choke fust."

"Oh, no!" exclaimed Nancy, rushing forward, "spare him, I implore you."

She clung to her husband's knees; but the brute cursed her bitterly, and kicked her wan, white face, as she besought mercy for him.

"Get away from him," exclaimed Yates, "his time's up when there's six feet of water in the hold."

"Sound the lead," he said to Long Jerry.

"Five feet and a quarter," returned that worthy.

The shuddering wife heard, and shrieked loudly.

"Five feet and a half!"

The noose was tightened round the culprit's neck.

"Five feet and three-quarters!"

Nancy sprang forward.

"Oh, spare him; spare him!"

A few inches more of the rapidly rising water and the shivering wretch would take his last leap.

"Six feet!"

Above the wildness of the loudly raging storm, unhushed by the surging of the terrible waters, rang forth that cry of doom.

And as the hapless Nancy threw herself forward to cling to her husband's feet, that they might not slay him, the stout cord leapt through the creaking pulley, and Simon Gagg hung from the yard-arm.

The shrieking woman fell prone on her face on the vessel's deck; insensibility saved her the agony of that dreadful scene.

CHAPTER XIV.

THE LAST OF THE DOOMED SHIP.

NOT so quickly now did the Civet Cat scud through the billows; the weight of water in her hold retarded her progress, and forced her down into the angry ocean.

She had drifted far since the storm commenced, and now, as the struggling light glimmered occasionally through the dark heavens, it showed, stretching out before her, a low, rocky coast, on which the water beat in a frothing mass.

Heavily water-logged, her progress became slower, and she sank down deeper in the fretful sea, till her black hull was near the water's edge.

And the surging billows sweeping her decks hurled some ill-fated pirates into the sea.

A boat was lowered, and a score of eager men leapt into her.

Pale but determined, like the hardened but courageous criminal that, standing beneath the fatal beam, looks calmly round, resolute to meet his fate if the end has come, yet unwilling to take his leave of dearly-loved life while the slightest chance remains, stood Angel by the wave-washed bulwarks, looking into the leaping sea.

His last hour seemed come, and he shrank not from it; yet, while prepared to meet his death, he eagerly scanned the prospects of life.

When these anxious men entered the boat a disdainful smile curled his lips.

"Wal," said the captain, who was watching him, "d'ye think she'll live in such a sea?"

"No," replied Angel.

"Yer don't try to keep 'em from their fate?"

"For the same reason that you do not. The fewer there are left the more chance they will have when the final moment comes."

Yates looked at him with some degree of pride.

"It'll be a pity if we has to part," he said, "with so cool a hand as yer to help me, I could ha' swept the world."

"See," said Angel, "they're off."

The boat passed from the ship's side, and rose high on the crest of a huge wave.

It was but for a moment; even as they looked the mighty waters hurled it back against the vessel.

A cry broke from the men; the boat was crushed to atoms, and the crew left to contend against the fury of the raging element.

A rope might have saved them, but it was withheld; and the rocking ship, ploughing on its retarded course, left them in the midst of the foaming breakers.

And one by one the pirates sank to rise no more.

Those who remained on deck secured themselves to broken beams and shattered masts and spars, that the waves might wash them off and carry them to land.

But the imprisoned blacks, the closely-packed living freight, for them there was no hope. They were heavily shackled in pairs, and when the ship sank, must go down with her.

The timbers, creaking with the terrible strain, were bilging apart; the masts and spars were carried away with a fearful crash, and the decks stove in.

The dismasted ship, with her groaning load, was drifting helplessly on, and the waters breaking over her bulwarks mingled with the fast-rising waters in the hold.

Suddenly there was a frightful crash. The Civet Cat reeled for a moment with the violence of the shock, then the groaning timbers were riven apart, the foaming waters broke over her, and every living soul was washed from her deck.

The broken masts and rigging went over her side, then she fixed firmly, with the gurgling waters pouring into her.

She had struck upon a low reef of rocks.

From the distant shore to where she lay, surging breakers formed one boiling mass of beating surf.

The white foam leapt to the sky, and the salt spray fell into the roaring billows.

Spars, beams, cargo, and human beings were all whirled round in the frothy cauldron, and those who were in the midst of those angry waters saw with dismay that a new and fearful danger cut short their slender chance of existence.

Leaping and sporting in the tempest was a shoal of sharks.

Angel and Yates floated near each other, their eyes fixed eagerly upon the distant strand.

The boiling surf blinded them, and the roaring billows dashed them fiercly against the floating pieces of wreck

The ill-fated Nancy was not to be seen.

Presently they saw, with horror, the dark body of a shark approaching.

A whirling wave dashed them apart, and Angel, half stunned, heard the cry of death uttered by the captain.

The shark had snapped at his lower limbs as he clung to the supporting spar, and the waves were washing to shore his severed trunk.

The kidnapped blacks, huddled together, beheld the water rising slowly to them. Cooped up as they were in that stifling hold, they knew that their end was near.

Some, at the last stage of sickness, turned their rolling eyes upon their helpless comrades; and some, who had passed all pain, lay cold and stiffening, yet linked to the living doomed.

Higher rose the water, ebbing above their knees, washing their shivering limbs and surging in their eyes—higher and higher till the sick and dying gurgled forth their life.

Then, with a leaping roar, the mighty waves rose against the vessel, and bore her from the rock.

Her bows pitched foremost, her side gave way, there was a sudden whirl, and the frothing billows formed like a wall around her.

In the eddying whirl the fated ship went down, and the surf rushed over her place.

Down, whirling to the ocean's mighty depths, she sank with her helpless load, and the doomed blacks, ironed and confined, were overwhelmed by the rushing sea.

But, even as she sank, there arose from the ocean's midst an agonising cry, the awful wail of helpless drowning men.

High above the raging roar of the wild ocean, ioad above the blast of the fearful gale, it arose—the wail of agony and despair, the quivering cry of death.

It rose prolonged and deep, and pierced the darkened sky—it rose, a cry of horror and vengeance, reaching to the very throne of heaven.

. . . .

The waters have swept over the place where the vessel went down, and the doomed crew have perished in their guilt.

The storm-clouds have swept from the sky, and the rage of the sea is hushed.

But the whitened breakers, leaping over the low-lying rocks, yet beat against the jagged edges the ghastly corpses of some of that pirate crew. And the shattered remnants of the wreck are floating to the rugged shore.

Still over the chafing deep the sea-winds blow with a shrill, wild cry.

And the thunder speaks its dreadful tale.

The cry of those who have perished at the hands of that ruthless crew has been answered, and a swift retribution has overtaken the lawless band and their evil leader.

And has the guilty wife atoned for her sin?

But see, far in the breakers' midst floats a heavy spar, and the pale form of a man is resting upon it.

The rude waves buffet him; they bear him aloft on their bosom, they hurl him down to their whirling depths.

And the white foam breaks over his whiter brow.

Now he sinks from view; he is lost, sucked down by the hungry waters. No, he rises amidst the foam, and the waves carry him nearer the shore.

It is Captain Angel.

Is he living, or is he dead?

If dead, the waves may cease to buffet him; living, his chance of escape is small.

The surging breakers have cast him from the midst, and hurled him on the rugged shore.

And he lies pallid and motionless as the dead.

CHAPTER XV.
AFTER A MERMAID.

WE will return to our old friend, Jerry Mizzen, who, it will be remembered, had by mistake clambered up the cable of the Thunderer, and to his consternation, found himself on his enemy's deck, after being hauled up by the hair of his head.

After his examination before the little Admiral Ellis, Lord Kilcrew, and several other commanding officers, he was placed in irons for further inspection.

"Prisoner, if you wish to save your life, you will tell me all you know of that pirate, Tom Drake," said the little admiral sternly, fixing his small grey eyes on Jerry Mizzen, as he was led on deck by a body of marines.

"Yes, yer honour," said Jerry, trying to look serious.

"Where does he generally run to?"

"He don't run yer honour, the Will-o'-the-Wisp takes him anywhere."

"If he answers like that again," said Admiral Ellis to the marines, "put your bayonets into his ugly carcase."

"It's as good as his shrivelled-up piece of parchment," muttered Jerry, meaning the little admiral's carcase.

"What ports or harbours does he put into?" asked Admiral Ellis, frowning.

"Well, yer see, yer honour," he said, "there ain't many ports that'll harbour a pirate, so he's obliged to cruise about anywhere."

The little admiral foamed with rage, and he commanded the marines to bayonet their prisoner. Jerry saw the formidable weapons approaching his broad breast.

A cold perspiration ran down his back as his legs gave way, and he fell to the deck doubled up.

"He, he, he, he—oh, oh, oh—he, he, he—oh, oh, oh!" he grinned, the water streaming down his face.

And the officious marines put the points of their bayonets through the shoulders of Jerry's shirt, and picked him up.

Boom!

The little admiral jumped up about three feet, and Jerry poked his head aside, as a ball came whizzing past his ear, from a small vessel to the leeward.

"Take the prisoner below while we capture his leader, then we'll hang both together," shouted the admiral of the Thunderer, in great excitement.

The Union Jack was run up, but before Admiral Ellis had time to give chase, the saucy little vessel had disappeared.

Again Jerry Mizzen was brought up, this time with a smile of triumph on his swarthy features.

A young officer, who had taken a great liking to him for his peculiarities, and disliked his commander, Admiral Ellis, unfastened his manacles, so that Jerry could throw them off at any moment.

"Prisoner," said the little admiral, "this is your last chance; reveal anything you know of your notorious pirate leader and you shall be set at liberty."

"Yes, your honour, I shall be set at liberty

JERRY AND THE MERMAID.

when I turns pilot for you to catch him," replied Jerry firmly. "I'd rather have two shots spliced round my legs and be sent down to Davy Jones's locker than betray a messmate."

"You are determined not to give me any information?" thundered Admiral Ellis in a terrible passion.

"I am," replied Jerry, defiantly.

"Give him forty lashes, and then hang the villain to the yard arm!" shouted the irritated little commander.

"Thank you," said Jerry, striking Admiral Ellis, stunned and bleeding to the deck.

Shaking the irons from his wrists, he sprang over the bulwarks, amid a volley of bullets from the marines' muskets.

A heavy splash, a gurgling sound, then all was quiet.

Admiral Ellis was taken to his cabin quite insensible.

In a few minutes a boat was manned and lowered.

Gaston was sitting in the stern sheets swearing.

A search was made for the escaped prisoner, but in vain, and after pulling about for two hours to no avail they returned to their ship.

The sailors had to keep from the path of Gaston, who had now taken command, and would use his authority to the utmost extent.

By this time the unfortunate Jerry Mizzen had drifted some distance with the current on the crests of foaming spray.

When he had made that bold stroke for life, and sank deeply into the water, he swam under the keel of the Thunderer, and came up on the other side.

14

All his energetic powers he put into that useful art, swimming, and soon left his prison some distance behind.

On, on he kept.

Fighting desperately for life with raging elements, that tossed him about like a cork.

He could not pursue this fearful course much longer.

His strength began to fail him.

Each stroke he took got weaker.

He looked around him with hopeless despair at the vast expanse of water, without a speck on its surface to which he might swim for rescue from the boundless watery grave that stared him in the face.

A fearful dread took possession of him as he thought of the fate that now awaited him, after escaping from one to fall into another.

"Never mind," he soliloquised, "I shall die like a true British tar, and not by them cussed marines! I should like to see poor old Bob Hauler before I go to Davy Jones's locker," he muttered, as his limbs relaxed and his eyes closed.

Fortunately, he turned on his back when he felt his strength leaving him, or otherwise we should have lost a very amusing character.

Like a floating raft Jerry was being carried along with the tide, quite unconscious as to where he was drifting.

As though guided by an unseen Providence, he was suddenly thrown upon a small island by a huge billow.

The sudden shock as he fell recalled him to his senses.

For some minutes he lay on his back staring vacantly about, totally unable to realise his position.

Presently the truth flashed to his mind, when he felt his nose blistering by the rays of the burning sun that were pouring down on his face.

Springing to his feet, he exclaimed—

"Saved, saved!"

Then his face lengthened to a most ridiculous shape, and he heaved a despairing sigh on beholding his helpless state.

What was he to do?

Cast upon a small desert island, surrounded by the roaring sea.

Stay there and be starved to a mere skeleton, then to be eaten by the monstrous birds of prey that were flying over his head howling and shrieking in a fearful manner; or plunge into the water, and so put an end to his miserable life.

Such distracting thoughts rushed through his wandering brain, and, uttering a melancholy cry, he dropped his head on his hands despairingly.

Thus he stood for some time, until he was roused from his reverie by a horrible shriek in his ear.

His hair bristled up like wire, and his eyes almost darted from their sockets.

Before he could ascertain from whence it came he was felled to the earth by an unexpected smack in the face.

Burying his face in the sand he gave vent to a series of miserable groans, kicking and plunging about on all fours, and driving his nose deeper into the sand.

Regardless of the pain caused by the blisters, he strove to bury his head.

So strong were his apprehensions of being clutched by the hair, and carried away by some hideous monster, which he imagined was hovering over him.

"Oh, lor, boo-oo-oo," he howled, wriggling about, trying to get his leg out of some painful grasp that had hold of his calf.

"... saved me! I aren't deserted it! it ain't me ... Bob was ..."

He received no answer.

His leg was released, and a painful grip tightened on his seat of honour.

Springing to his feet he beheld his mysterious assailant.

A monstrous bird!

That was the horrible creature that had caused the redoubtable Jerry such awful fright, and knocked him down with its wing.

Jerry felt inspired with some of his old pluck, and thought he could easily rid himself of such an opponent.

But his courage failed him when he beheld at least a score more sailing down towards him.

Their cries and shrieks were frightful, as they clustered round their victim.

Jerry saw his danger, and, again gathering his shattered courage he drew a long clasp-knife and tried to defend himself.

The birds fought bravely.

So did Jerry.

Had he been on the deck of the Will-o'-the-Wisp, defending his beloved commander from an attack of the murderous pirates, he could not have fought with more determination.

He soon laid several hors de combat, and catching hold of the ringleader by the throat, he drove his knife into his breast, and threw him into the sea.

The rest then gave a shriek, and picking up their dead companions, flew away to have a sumptuous meal.

Again left alone, Jerry looked across the boundless surf, in the vain hope of seeing a distant sail.

What is it he sees?

His gaze is fixed upon something not far from him.

A look of surprised pleasure suffuses his face.

'Tis a form.

The form of a beautiful female, gradually rising from the water to her waist.

She has a face angelic and smiling, with beautiful tresses falling around her alabaster shoulders.

A mermaid.

Jerry seemed transfixed.

In a tremulous voice he cried—

"Swim ashore and live with me; I ain't got any one to speak to. I love yer to madness, as I heard the skipper say. If yer—"

The mermaid shook her head, and glided through the water.

"May I be fed on chunk and sea-brine for a month," Jerry exclaimed, "if I don't give chase, and clap my grappling irons on her, and then—let me see," he considered for a minute, "if she won't come with me, I'll go with her. Where she lives, I can live."

With this resolution he plunged into the water, and boldly struck out in the direction she was going.

"Hi!" he shouted "I am coming. Lay to a minute I shall ... alongside yer."

The mermaid looked ... her shoulder, but still glided onwards.

Jerry Mizzen ... every way in swimming he knew to overtake her.

By degrees he got nearer.

His heart began to beat like a drum against his hollow side (hollow because he had had very little food since he had been a captive).

A few more good strokes, and he would overtake her.

Kicking out desperately, he cut through the water like a dart.

Three more yards, and he would reach her.

At that moment, when crowned with success as he thought, she glided round some breakers.

Jerry looked disappointed, but thinking she had gone into a cave in the rocks, he followed.

Reaching the corner she had turned, he uttered a most awful howl of fear, and came to a dead stop.

Confronting him was a terrible sea monster, with open jaws ready to receive him.

CHAPTER XVI.

JERRY MIZZEN'S ENCOUNTER WITH A SEA MONSTER.

JERRY MIZZEN'S ruddy face had beamed with gleeful anticipation, and his heart beat wildly with hope of overtaking the fabulous sea beauty by whom he was so smitten, as he swam around the grotto rock where she had so suddenly disappeared.

His gleeful hope fled, and he gave vent to a dismal groan, as a huge sea monster rose up through the water, and confronted him with threatening open jaws.

Jerry had heard something about Jonah living inside a whale, and did not doubt the truth of it when he compared the size of his assailant to himself, but not liking the idea of close confinement, he wisely backed out.

His monstrous assailant followed him, flapping a pair of huge fins most vigorously, almost blinding the unfortunate tar with the spray.

Jerry's terror grew intense.

The more he receded the quicker his opponent followed him, and kept him within reach.

Jerry would have resigned himself to the fate he felt was certain to befall him, but the vision of the beautiful mermaid seemed to flash before his eyes.

He could not die without a struggle for life when he thought of her.

Mustering his remaining courage and strength together, he resolved to turn his back towards his brutal enemy and swim away.

He was about to put this resolution into execution when the fins of his assailant were put in motion, and one caught him such a stinging smack on the cheek it knocked him under water.

He had hardly disappeared from the surface, when the hideous-looking head, with open jaws, dived after him.

At the same moment Jerry re-appeared, looking very rueful and much terrified.

His huge assailant dashed at him with a sudden snap.

Jerry Mizzen clutched his long clasp knife that hung at his side, and plunged it into the brute's belly.

An exciting encounter then took place between the sea monster and Jerry Mizzen, which several times nearly resulted in the tar losing his head.

By dexterous digs and quick movements he avoided that calamity, and succeeded in bleeding his huge opponent, and thus rendered it harmless.

Not wishing for a second opponent of the same description, he scrambled to the top of the rock, where he triumphantly watched it go down.

Walking to the end of the rock, he threw himself down, and sipped of the clear and sparkling rivulet to test it.

The next instant half his face was buried in the water, and he was drinking greedily.

When Jerry had appeased his thirst he rose, very grateful for the providential draught.

"If I can only get something to eat," he muttered, "I shall be able to live a little longer, and perhaps hail a ship."

By this time the sun was hidden behind the rising clouds, and evening was fast advancing.

Jerry was suddenly startled by hearing a flock of birds flying about him.

They were not like the monsters that had previously attacked him, but small and tame.

Pulling off his shirt, Jerry made a rush at the birds, and knocked down four.

Bounding upon them like a savage Indian, he twisted their necks, and, laying them down, got off the rock.

The tide being low, he collected together a heap of weed that had been thrown upon a sand-bank with the waves, and dried by the sun.

Rolling it in a tight bundle, he put it under his arm, and ascended the rock.

The next idea was to kindle a light.

How was this to be done?

That is what our adventurer thought.

He was not at a loss long.

Piling a heap of the driest weed under a projecting crag, he furiously struck the blade of his knife against the corner.

A spark flashed presently, and soon the weed began to smoke.

Jerry Mizen was delighted by his success, and commenced puffing with his mouth like a pair of forge bellows.

The sea herbs began to crack, and soon a flame rewarded him for his ingenuity.

We cannot venture to describe his gratification, but let it suffice to say, he cheerfully set to work to cook the birds, and had a sumptuous meal.

Never in his life before did he eat anything with such a relish as he did those small birds.

Smacking his lips, and rubbing his long stomach, he piled up the fire, and seemed quite contented with his position.

Stretching himself full length before the fire, he resolved to sleep until the morning, when he intended to renew his search for the mermaid.

It was barely daybreak, when he was aroused by a stinging sensation in his back.

"Shiver my timbers? what's that?" he said.

Whiz, whiz, whiz, came a dozen arrows, flying past his ears.

Paddling towards the rocks was a canoe, manned with a crew of savage-looking red Indians.

They shouted in a most horrible manner as they caught sight of his rough head.

"Ship ahoy!" he shouted, standing erect, and trying to appear bold, while his knees knocked together with fright, and he nearly fell backwards on the fire.

Threatening menaces, and another awful yell responded to his call.

"Where from?" he shouted again.

More yells, and much more threatening menaces came from the savages.

The canoe stopped under the rocks, and three of its occupants got out and clambered up the side like monkeys.

The Indians reached the summit of the rock, and pointed to him to get down.

Jerry did not see it, and tried to make them understand that he was quite safe and contented to be where he was.

The redskins grew exasperated.

Jerry got frightened.

He retreated from them.

They followed him.

The next instant he was hurled over the rocks.

Another instant, and there was a loud splash, and he sank under the water.

A third instant he was lugged out by the hair with rough hands, and pulled into the canoe.

He was then bound hand and foot, and his captors paddled their canoe away in triumph.

CHAPTER XVII.

A CAVE OF TREASURE.

IT is scarcely necessary to dwell upon the utter consternation into which Admiral ——— is and his party were thrown by the apparition of Captain Tom and his crew.

The suspicious movements of the cloaked friars had given Admiral Ellis an inkling of treachery, but even he was not prepared for what occurred.

Our hero's audacity, coupled with his mysterious escape from prison, staggered him.

He had heard of the supernatural attributes by means of which the Boy Cruiser eluded all his foes, and for the moment the idea stole upon his mind that Captain Tom was indeed in league with the Evil One.

As for the commodore, he was petrified, and could scarcely believe his eyes.

Admiral Lord Kilcrew was the first to break the spell Tom's presence had caused.

"And it's yourself, my young pirate captain, I see, at last," he cried. "St. Patrick, but I've been half round the world, trying to meet you; but I tell you, man, to leave that lady's side, or it's amidst your own roystering crew will I cut you down!"

His bright sword flashed in the air.

"And, by jinks!" little Lord Vane cried, "here's—aw—aw—devil—friend, Captain Tom, again!—aw—I wonder if he's got his sword of silver with him now?"

"You can test the blade, my lord," our hero said.

Lord Augustus Vane did not seem to relish the challenge.

He shrank back as the boy chieftain's bright eye flashed angrily upon the assembly.

Lords Moreton and Claremont, with Walpole, got near Tom.

"There'll be warm work presently," said Walpole. "I vote we take care of his bride."

Tom heard the young lord's remark, and his fingers angrily clutched his sword.

Admiral Ellis had by this time recovered his presence of mind.

His parchment visage was of a leaden hue.

His gray, piercing eyes were almost hidden by the wrinkles of his face.

"So, pirate," he exclaimed, "the devil has helped you to break out of your prison, but you will need a thousand devils to save you now. It is fortunate that I have been prepared for any interference here, and much as I regret the bloodshed that must ensue, I will take care that this is the last of your escapades."

"Indeed!" (Tom's lips curled scornfully.) "Admiral Ellis, you have hunted me from sea to sea. Had you met me there, I would have shown you what a task my capture would have been. You boast of taking me. Bring forth your hidden soldiery; but let me tell you that, as I came here unseen, I will so depart. Lift your hand for bloodshed—you shall have your fill of it. Not all your country's power shall capture me!"

Commodore Ellis here intervened.

"Pirate boy," he cried, "release that maiden. Take one hour's grace, and you may escape."

Our hero's bright scimetar glistened in the air.

"When I release this dear girl," he cried, "it shall be when my hand can no longer grasp my sword-hilt. When I am subdued it shall be when I lie still and prone at your feet."

He clasped Minnie affectionately to his breast.

Admiral Ellis drew his dress-sword from its scabbard.

With an angry cry he dashed his hand on the table.

"To arms," he cried. "Guard the way men. Shoot down all who attempt to pass. A thousand pounds to those who take this buccaneer!"

The rattle of steel was heard as the soldiery fixed their bayonets.

The boy cruisers, armed with sword, pistol and pike, gathered round their beloved leader.

One moment more, and Admiral Ellis would have given the signal for the attack on the daring intruders.

But at this juncture the young and lovely giver of the banquet, the Countess St. Albans, laid her soft hand upon his arm.

"Let us have no bloodshed here," she exclaimed. "Oh, sir," she added, addressing our hero, "release that lady and depart. I promise that no one shall molest you."

Very gracefully Tom Drake bowed to the beautiful young countess.

"Madam," he said, "I shall not begin the work; but I have claimed my bride; more—I swear that this night's ceremony shall proceed. You shall witness the marriage—but I will be bridegroom to this bride!"

Minnie gave him a grateful look.

In their danger it pleased her to hear him say she should be his bride.

"There'll be two to have a word in that," exclaimed Lord Kilcrew, "besides the lady."

"I will hear the lady; if she consents, I want no other voice. Tell me, Minnie, are you willing to be my bride—will you wed me this night? Say that you will, and I will carry you to my ship—you shall be queen, and no power of earth shall come between us. Answer, Minnie, will you be mine?"

"For ever," Minnie answered, softly.

"God bless you for that promise! Thus I seal our vows!"

He drew her to his breast, and fervently kissed her.

"Now, my lord, he cried to Kilcrew, "this quarrel is between us."

Admiral Ellis, livid with rage, sprang from where he stood at the head of the table.

"Give the pirate no chance of mercy!" he yelled. "Take the lady while we make him prisoner."

"That is much sooner said than done, exclaimed Tom, stepping back, and standing on his defence. "My gallant crew will deal with you. Now, my Lord Kilcrew, if you have any claims to make for my bride, follow to the chapel and contest it with your sword. If you can slay me, I yield her; if I am victor, I promise to leave you a corpse on the altar steps."

Admiral Ellis sprang upon our hero.

"Pirate, you shall never leave the hall alive except a prisoner!" he shouted.

Captain Tom put Minnie aside.

Very quietly he took the angry officer by the throat, and before any one could divine his intent, drew him amidst his boy followers.

"Now, he said, laughing lightly, "you are my prisoner; lift a finger to your men, and I will brain you where you stand!

Tom's sudden seizure of him had prevented all resistance, and he was a helpless captive before he had time to retreat.

Still, he would have ordered his soldiers, at any hazard, to shoot down his daring captors, but Lord Kilcrew stayed him.

"It shall be tried by me; if I fail I leave you to effect his capture."

"My Lord Kilcrew," said Tom, "I am about to fight you; our duel should be to the death; you are a brave man, but I shall conquer you. I will not take your life; you shall be spared to witness my marriage with my bride; my old friend, the commodore, shall give her away, and Admiral Ellis shall drink the happiness of the Rover's Queen

Very daring he looked as he faced the excited assemblage.

The rays of the many lamps shone on his glittering mail, beneath which his bold heart throbbed with proud joy at the prospect of making Minnie his wife.

Lord Kilcrew looked at him as if he could not believe his ears.

Here was a proscribed pirate, betrayed and surrounded by armed soldiers, comparatively alone in the midst of his foes; doomed to certain death unless he could fight his way to the shore, and embark on his own vessel unharmed; yet who dared to speak to them in the terms of a conqueror.

Lord Walpole could not help admiring our hero's coolness.

As for the commodore his rage knew no bounds.

Admiral Ellis had all the true characteristics of a thorough sea-going old martinet, and, under the influence of his chagrin at being taken prisoner, he would not have hesitated in giving the order for his soldiery to attack Tom's crew, even though his first word of command resulted—as it probably would—in his brains being blown out without further ceremony.

Our hero, who knew his distinguished hardihood and iron strength of nerve, had well arranged his programme beforehand, and the signal he now gave saved Admiral Ellis from all risks.

Two of the cruisers, seeing the admiral's mouth about to move, and having no doubt he was about to precipitate matters by ordering an immediate and murderous attack, kindly spared him the trouble by slipping a gag over his mouth, and adroitly blindfolding him at the same moment.

Then Harry Vere, who was at the head of the shore party, placed the muzzle of a pistol against the little admiral's ear while Tom spoke.

"Commodore," he said, "your brother is in our power. Let there be a single drop of blood spilled, or a hand raised to obstruct our path, and his brains shall be scattered before your eyes. You are a brave man, commodore, but you know well Captain Tom Drake will keep his word!"

The staunch old commodore looked as if he would rather have eaten his own sword, scabbard and hilt in the bargain, than have been there at all.

He felt something like a muzzled bull-dog, and glanced at our hero as if he thought he must be the very devil himself sent to torment him.

Ever since he had encountered our hero he had been in the very thick of failures and mortifications.

First there was Harry Vere's duel with Gaston—then his elopement with his fair niece, both at Tom's instigation.

After that came his mysterious disappearance from the chapel where they had had the consummate impudence to marry the runaway pair.

Then came his encounter with our hero, in which he had not only been worsted, but had to sink his ship, and now, when he fervently hoped his youthful opponent was miles and miles away, here was he turning up again.

First of all, to get clapped into prison, and then, after escaping by magical or mysterious means, to intrude in that masquerade, and act with all the effrontery of a young conqueror.

"Well, commodore," our hero, who saw his puzzled look, said, "is it peace or war?"

"You young scoundrel set my brother at liberty—let me take his place."

"No, commodore, were I to do that, he would not hesitate to sacrifice you."

"You dog, what new violence do you purpose now?"

"None, unless driven to it in self-defence. We shall proceed to her ladyship's chapel, where you shall witness the ceremony of marriage between me and this dear girl. After that——"

"Well, after that, you young devil, what then?"

"Why, then," Tom answered, proudly, "as I have won my wife at the point of my sword, so with my sword's point I will maintain her."

He waved his hand, and his boy crew took the route to the chapel.

The soldiery dared not obstruct their progress, because of the jeopardy in which Admiral Ellis was placed.

The guests crowded after the daring adventurers eager to see the result of so singular an interruption to the masquerade.

Lords Walpole, Claremont, Moreton, and Vane, kept close to our hero and his bride.

They were curious to witness the end of the adventure.

Admiral Lord Kilcrew stalked moodily in the rear.

He was waiting for an opportunity of crossing swords with the youthful sailor, who had defiantly dared him to single combat.

Almost in solemn silence they entered the picturesque chapel.

Minnie was very pale.

She realised the danger in which her young lover was placed, and, though willing to share his fate, she shivered at the thought that another half-hour might see him lying cold and lifeless on the altar steps.

With our hero the matter was simple enough.

He meant to fight Lord Kilcrew, and then carry the little admiral with him on board his own vessel, there to keep him prisoner till he could depart safely.

Our hero was in advance with Minnie, who clung, half-fainting, to his protecting arm.

At the door of the chapel he encountered Lady Arbuthnot, her face pale as a sheet, her looks wild and aghast.

Clutching Tom's hand, she whispered hurriedly—

"You must fly. The soldiers are secreted outside the chapel, to shoot you as you come forth. There is no time for this rash ceremony. Bid only your boy crew enter, then shut the door and follow me—I will lead you to safety."

Captain Tom looked in the agitated face of his fair admonitress.

There was no mistaking the anxiety depicted on her face.

He did not like the idea of abandoning his enterprise.

There was something congenial to his daring nature in the thought of marrying Minnie in the midst of them all.

At the same time he felt that, hemmed in as he was by unseen dangers, it was scarcely advisable to risk all for the sake of being wedded to Minnie in that place, especially as the ceremony could be performed equally as well on board his own ship.

He resolved to follow his lady friend's advice.

A few words passed to Harry Vere explained his intent.

Lady Arbuthnot glided into the chapel first, then Tom and Minnie.

His boy crew followed two by two.

Admiral Lord Kilcrew was the first of those who came after.

He was stalking jauntily on, his hand on the hilt of his sword, when the chapel door, as his foot was on the very threshold, swung to, and closed in his face.

This act was so sudden, so little what he expected from our hero, that the Irish nobleman tapped softly for admittance.

When he found he had been purposely shut out, his excited feelings knew no bounds.

In the most insulting terms he called upon Tom to turn and fight him.

Our hero heard his insulting challenge, but Lady Arbuthnot would not suffer him to stay ; she took his hand, and led him on in darkness, his boy crew following.

In the centre of the chapel she paused—a grating noise—a rush of cold air—then they descended one by one into pitch darkness.

Hardly was the last of the boy cruisers out of sight, when the door was burst violently open, and Admiral Lord Kilcrew, followed by the enraged soldiers, burst into the chapel.

They found no trace of the adventurers, but stumbled over the prone form of Admiral Ellis, who lay gagged and blindfolded in one corner of the chapel.

Lady Arbuthnot led our hero along what seemed to be a labyrinth of passages, until they discovered a faint streak of light in the distance, when she paused, and tenderly kissing Tom's hand, said—

"Follow the windings of this chamber till it leads you out by the sea. Be silent, as you value your lives. God speed you."

The pressure of her hand was gone.

Our hero peered through the darkness, but her sylph-like form had vanished.

Keeping on in the direction indicated, he wandered for some considerable time, without finding the expected outlet.

He had, in fact, lost the glimpse of moonlight which at first promised to guide them.

"We are out of our course," he whispered to Harry Vere.

"There is a light yonder," his young lieutenant said.

Tom looked.

There was a light—a peculiar glittering light.

It shone as if from a sullen cavern some distance before them.

It was an unearthly, spectral light.

Not like the gleam of the moon, but a cold, dull glisten of many colours enshrined in inky darkness.

Continuing their way onward for some few minutes, brought them to the explanation of the mystic light.

The spectacle they beheld was so startling that one and all forgot their danger, and gave vent to exclamations of amazement at the scene before them.

It was a narrow, oblong cave.

The walls were reeking with the moisture of ages, but the trickling stones were lit up by a row of curious-looking lamps, in each of which burned a blue flame, that seemed to have burned for ages undimmed.

These were the first cause of the lights, but on the damp slimy floor, where lizards, newts, and horrible snakes crawled and coiled, were heaped in wild profusion the rarest and most wonderful jewels.

Emeralds of large size, uncut rubies, pearls, diamonds, lying in odd-looking piles, each costly heap emitting its dull, sickly glare of coloured light.

Here and there a snake crawled in and out of a whitened skull, of which there were many, but otherwise the cave showed no relics of the presence of human beings.

The Boy Rovers gazed in breathless surprise at their new Aladdin's cave.

Some stepped forward to admire the costly gems.

Even Minnie raised herself to look around at the strange sight, while Harry Vere, with a cry of delight, scooped up a handful of the finest emeralds, and gave them to his youthful leader.

And then, by one accord, they commenced to load themselves with the shining gems.

CHAPTER XVIII.

THE DEATH GRASP.

THE sudden way in which Jerry Mizzen was conveyed from his rocky couch, the unexpected plunge into the water, and the rough way he was pulled out and dragged into the canoe amid low mutterings and dusky forms moving about, quite stupefied him.

Jerry was not certain whether he was lying at the bottom of the ocean with the graceful forms of beautiful mermaids hovering about him, or whether he had been bolted by a friend of his late opponent, and was confined in a living tomb, where he would have to remain until the monster went to sleep, when he might crawl out of its mouth, and so escape.

A miserable groan escaped his lips as the last idea passed through his mind.

He soon discovered the real character of his position.

His captors, not liking the musical strain of their prisoner's miserable groan, awarded him a vicious smack on the prominent part of his corporation with one of the paddles.

Jerry turned blue in the face, gasped for breath, and sent up his feet with a velocity quite surprising, lodging them in the back of one of his red-skinned captors.

The savage went flying over the bow of the canoe, taking a companion who stood in front of him, with him.

Two successive yells, and two loud splashes made Jerry start.

Opening his eyes, that had previously been closed, he discovered where he was, and fought desperately to free his limbs.

His hands being free, he soon made good use of his liberty by cutting the band that bound his feet together, despite the many brutal blows he received while accomplishing this feat.

Springing to his feet, Jerry wrenched a paddle from one of his assailants.

He struck him on the head with it, and sent him reeling over the side of the canoe.

Clutching another by the throat, he sent him to follow his companion.

Seizing another in the same way, he tried to force him into the water.

But Jerry found his antagonist a much tougher one than those preceding.

A desperate struggle took place.

While they were swaying to and fro, and in a close, deadly grip, the canoe rocking from side to side, which several times nearly terminated the fight by precipitating both into the sea, Jerry was pulled down by two of his enemies from behind.

The savage redskin kept a firm hold on his opponent as they fell.

Jerry fell to the bottom of the canoe.

The redskin having the superior power, drove his huge knee into the tar's chest.

He grasped his throat, putting all his lion strength into the grip, and drove his nails into his assailant's flesh.

The unfortunate tar fought desperately to free himself from the iron grip of his huge, brawny assailant, who was crushing his very life out.

Jerry now really thought that his time had come.

His brutal enemy seemed to delight in watching the painful agonies his victim exhibited, by the horrible working of his distorted features, as he increased the tightness of his grip.

JERRY RECEIVES ANOTHER VISIT FROM AN OLD FRIEND.

He only thought of revenge and thirsted for his prisoner's blood.

Which he was not destined to have.

With an involuntary thought Jerry Mizzen clutched the knife that hung by his side.

Using the remaining strength which had not been squeezed out of him, he drove the knife into the redskin's side.

The islander roared like a stricken tiger, as the sharp blade entered.

His savage-looking eyes rolled frightfully, and his fingers fastened deeper into his opponent's flesh, as the last pangs of death made his body quiver, and he rolled over on his side, dead.

Jerry, thinking he had had quite enough knocking about, sprang to his feet.

The sudden jerk upsetting the canoe, the contents disappeared under the water.

The indefatigable Jerry was the first to re-appear.

Getting into the canoe again, he commenced to propel it along by using one of the paddles at her stern.

Owing to its peculiar shape, he was not able to make much way, when his enemies came following in his track, yelling and shouting in a manner that Jerry knew meant unmistakeable mischief.

While gazing at his pursuers, and working desperately to keep ahead of them, the canoe, with a jerk that sent Jerry Mizzen flying over the stern head first, grated on a small sand bank.

The next minute the savages had overtaken the poor ill-fated tar, and binding him more securely than before, he was tied across the seats and made a cushion of.

The unfortunate adventurer was again in the power of his enemies, and helpless.

He closed his eyes to shut out the imaginary torturing visions that passed before him, as a warning of what he might expect.

The canoe cut through the water with the velocity of a dart, and before Jerry had any time for surmising as to where he was, or where they were going to take him, the canoe again grated upon a bank, and he was roughly pulled out by his hair.

A long thong was fastened on each of his arms, and he was pulled along by two of the savages who walked in front, while the others followed behind.

After a half-hour's travelling through a dense forest, the glare of a large fire broke through the thickly-studded trees.

The party, with their prisoner, turned sharply off to the right, and pressed their way through a narrow winding path made by the trees, only wide enough to admit one person to pass through at the time, forming a file, with Jerry in the middle.

Quickly passing through this narrow lane, they came to a small plain, where a large fire burned.

The tribe of men, who were lying round the fire in different attitudes, immediately rose to greet their companions, as they entered with their captive.

Jerry Mizzen's mouth watered, as a savoury odour arose from the huge joints that were roasting by the blazing fire, and tantalisingly tickled his nostrils by their delicious fragrance.

Satisfactory nods and gratulations were passed by the savages, alluding to their prize, but no notice was taken of our hungry adventurer's longing looks.

When he had been well examined by the whole tribe, Jerry was thrust into a rudely-constructed hut.

He perfectly understood, by their looks and antics, they were content with their repast for the night, and would reserve him for the time when he would be pulled out of the hut like a pig from its sty, and share the same fate as the joints he so longed to help them to eat.

Every minute seemed an hour to poor Jerry, especially while the meal was going on, and he, hungry, was watching through a crack in the hut, when he saw a ravenous mouth open, and a piece of the most coveted meat disappear.

After their sumptuous repast, which Jerry wished would choke every one of them, the fire was piled up, and the redskins, lying around in groups, were soon snoring like so many roaring lions.

Jerry, who had watched the whole of the proceeding, thought he would follow their example, and sleep while he could, muttering as he lay down—

"I thinks the greedy, dirty-looking swabs might have axed me to mess with them, especially as they is going to have me for breakfast."

He had not been asleep long when a door at the back of the hut opened, and a female Indian quietly entered, and gently shook the sleeper by the shoulder.

Light as was the touch of her hand, Jerry arose in a moment, and sprang to his feet.

The half-caste woman put her finger on her lip to quiet the outburst of Jerry's surprise she saw by his looks was about to follow.

The astonished tar stared at the intruder in amazement.

A flush of anticipated pleasure suffused his swarthy features, as his gaze rested on the disrobed form.

"I have come to save de white man," said she, in very bad English. "If de white man wants to escape, he must come along with me."

"Escape with you," shouted Jerry with delight, thrusting his bound hands before her; "draw my cutlass (meaning his knife that dangled at his side) through these cussed cords, and I'll cruise about with you anywhere."

"My broder should not make a noise, because

he will wake my people, and they will scalp you and kill me."

"The cussed, dirty swabs," said Jerry, with great vehemence, "I'd eat all of them before eating breakfast. Bless yer pretty figure-head," added Jerry, altering the tone of his voice to almost a whisper, "such pretty top-lights I never clapped my glimmers on afore."

The female, being greatly flattered with Jerry's expressive remarks, instantly cut the thongs which bound his wrists.

As soon as he found himself free, he threw his arms round his liberator's neck, and kissed her.

"Oh, yer hangel," he began, but his companion placed her hand before his mouth, and stopped his further remarks.

"My broder should hold his tongue, his noise has aroused the people."

"Oh, gor, let us get out of here. You can steer the way," muttered Jerry, trembling at the news.

"Follow me," said the woman.

Woman she was, being over thirty years of age, and not one of the most attractive beauties to be found in a forest.

She stood about four feet eight inches in height, of a fat and squatty build, and not at all an amiable countenance.

Nevertheless, that did not alter our adventurer's opinion why she should not be an angel, sent to save him from the barbarous fate for which he was intended.

Proudly taking the proffered plump arm, Jerry followed his guide in silence.

Through a dense thicket, where the hissing of reptiles rustling through the fallen dried leaves made the superstitious sailor's blood run through his veins like frozen water.

So closely packed were the huge towering trees, with their clustering leafy branches, that they kept out all light, save for a fierce streak of the shining moon, that fought and struggled to penetrate the mass of clustering leaves as the wind blew them apart.

Several times Jerry had been addressed by his companion, but had not answered.

He was too much terrified by the strange humming and various other strange noises, and much stronger visions, that the rays of the moon presented, as its glimmering rays kept dancing around the massive stems of the trees, and seemed to make imaginary objects flickering about.

His terror grew into a long melancholy growl as something clutched his hair.

"Oh, lor, leave go," whined Jerry Mizzen dismally, "I ain't done nothing."

"What is my broder making a noise about?" asked his companion, in surprise.

"Oh, dear, I don't know, only I think some swab tried to scalp me."

"I see no one," remarked the half-breed, looking round.

"Oh, lor', I can feel some one now, though."

A peculiar grinning and muttering told Jerry from where the strange grasp came.

"Cast them pretty eyes of yours up to the sky-scrapers."

His companion, comprehending what he meant more by his movements than by the order, looked over his head, and discovered the cause of our adventurer's sudden outcry.

Swinging by its tail from an overhanging branch, was a mischievous little ludicrous ape, tugging away at Jerry Mizzen's flowing locks with all its strength.

The saucy little ape let go Jerry's hair, and sprang from one branch to another, chattering in high glee.

The exasperated tar stood with his face upturned

giving vent to his spleen by shaking his fist at the retreating monkey.

"Ugly little thief, I'll make you eat your own tail if I catch hold of you! I——Oh!"

A large cocoa-nut came down with great force, and struck the unfortunate Jerry just between his eyes, knocking him on his back as flat as a flounder.

A few soothing words from his coloured companion soon made the unlucky tar get up, and they resumed their journey without any more misfortunes.

"I say, my hangel," can you see all them stars jumping about ahead of us?"

"No."

"I can," said Jerry.

"Where are they?"

"Right afore my glimmers."

"My broder am much mistaken, his eyes are closed."

"Oh, lor, are they, my hangel? Then I suppose it is caused through that cussed little jackanapes throwing that nut on my figure-head."

He was not sorry when they emerged from their dangerous path into an open plain.

He felt safe then, and removed his hand, which he had hitherto held beside his head, in order to guard it from the flying missiles.

He breathed a deep sigh of relief, and looked inquiringly at his dark companion.

To stop any inquiry she motioned him to be silent, and pointed to some forms crouched beneath the shade of the trees.

In a moment all the terror of Jerry Mizzen returned. His knees began to knock together in a very uncomfortable manner.

"They are scouts of my people; and if they see us they will scalp you."

A very uncomfortable feeling took possession of our adventurer at the idea of feeling the point of a sharp knife as it was being driven into his head.

He passed his hand to the back of his cranium as a horrid presentiment flashed to his mind.

What if one of these dusky brutes were behind him, and with uplifted weapon within an inch of his skull?

Appalled by that fearful foreboding, poor Jerry's physical powers began to desert him, and he would have fallen to the ground had it not been for his guide, who told him they were safe so long as they were quiet.

She pulled him after her down a slope, at the bottom of which was a stream.

On reaching the other side, some twenty minutes' walk through a circuitous path brought them to a high bank surrounded by clusters of trees.

To Jerry Mizzen's surprise, his companion removed, as it were, a piece of bark from the trunk of one of the largest trees, which presented, to his astonishment, a large cave.

This she invited him to enter, which he did willingly.

When inside, she carefully closed the aperture, and the exterior of the tree looked as though it had never been touched; so neatly had that piece of ingenuity been executed, that it would have defied the nearest inspection to detect any traces of the secret entrance.

Our adventurer took a minute inspection of the interior of the cave, and appeared much gratified by what he saw.

In one corner was a rudely-constructed couch, made of bars of wood, and covered with dry foliage.

His eyes first rested on this, and then his gaze ran over the form of his partner

A look of satisfaction suffused his swarthy features as he finished his inspection of her, and he assumed an air of the most perfect self-confidence.

In another corner was a heap of dried skins of various wild animals.

In the middle of the cave was a huge table, with a varied description of eatables.

The whole place was lighted by several glimmering oil lamps.

"My brother is hungry," remarked the female, after watching her companion's eyes wander from one thing to another.

"Yes, my angel, I is," replied Jerry, hugging her affectionately.

"Then I will get him something to eat."

Sliding a piece of wood aside in the side of the cave, she soon kindled a fire in the gap, where some embers were still smouldering, and ere her guest had time to imagine what she was doing, she had cooked some wild birds, which she placed before him.

After putting away sufficient for a giant, Jerry turned away from the table and looked longingly at the couch.

"My brother is tired, and would go to rest."

"He is, and would go to rest," said Jerry.

Fatigue and excitement, however, prevented him from sleeping for some time after he had lain down, and when at length he fell asleep it was only to continue in his dreams the incidents of the last four-and-twenty hours.

When our adventurer awoke in the morning, to his surprise his rescuer had gone, and the cave was deserted.

Jerry rushed about frantic to find the entrance, when suddenly it flew open, and his companion returned heavily laden with spoil.

She had been out hunting.

Breakfast being prepared was very soon demolished. Having secured the entrance, Jerry, getting rather weary of the unmistakable advances of his dusky companion, started forth on a hunting expedition, armed with a gun, tomahawk, and a long broad knife, leaving his loving mistress in the cave.

The unfortunate sailor had not proceeded far on his journey when he encountered three of his old savage enemies. On perceiving their escaped prisoner, they each gave a yelling whoop, leaped in the air, and then pursued him.

Jerry threw the gun over his shoulder as he ran, and pulled the trigger.

A roar of pain informed the adventurer that the shot had taken effect.

The foremost of the foe was stricken to the ground; the next fell over his prostrate form, and so allowed the sailor sufficient time to make good his escape. Which he did.

CHAPTER XIX.

THE LETTER OF MARQUE.

WITH all haste he sped back to the cave, which he reached, distinctly hearing the whilst the yells of his pursuers.

Removing the secret door, the tar bounded breathless into the cave.

Scarcely had the secret entrance closed when a monstrous black sprang from a corner in the cave, and Jerry Mizzen was held in his powerful embrace.

The unhappy tar gave a searching look round for his angel, and gave himself up for lost as the breath was being crushed out of him.

. . . .

Leaving the boy cruisers to cram their pouches with the spoils of the treasure cave, and to find their way as best they could to the shore, we will return to our hero's vessel, where it will be remembered we left the two cunning old officers snugly ensconsed in Ben's cabin, waiting the moment when they could pounce upon Tom, and make him prisoner.

So secure were they in their own cunning that it never occurred to them that Ben Barnacle was fooling them to the top of their bent.

They imagined him got over to their schemes by their offer of making him captain of the ship, which, as the reader knows, they had no intention of keeping.

Had they been able, while they were comfortably draining their wine, to see the preparations going on in different parts of the ship, they would not have taken things so easy.

We hope the reader has never done the faithful Ben Barnacle the injustice to believe that he would listen to any schemes for the betrayal of his beloved chieftain.

The staunch-hearted Ben was too devotedly attached to Tom, and his demeanour during his interview with the officers was a capital piece of acting to disarm their suspicions.

He knew the jeopardy his leader, through his rash visit on land, would incur. Shut in as they were by so many heavy war vessels, and commanded by the batteries of the shore, their ship stood a good chance of being blown to pieces on the first alarm, and when the officer produced the letter of marque he saw a way to ensure Captain Tom's safety.

That letter of marque would be a protection to the whole ship.

So Ben meant to have it.

As soon as he had seen the worthy pair of officials and their disguised comrades quietly toping, he repaired to the deck, where Zeila was anxiously expecting him.

The middies had seen that something was wrong, and now they gathered round him as he explained the true state of affairs.

Some laughed lightly at the idea of the officers expecting Tom's capture.

Zeila looked anxious.

She was, like Ben Barnacle, thinking of the letter of marque.

"You see," said Ben, "if we let them suspect anything, they will destroy the letter of marque. We must, therefore, proceed cautiously."

Dr. Shrike sidled up at that moment.

He had seen the officers concealed, and was gloating over the anticipated pleasure of having them given up to his tender mercies.

He overheard Ben's remark, and his parchment visage puckered up in knowing wrinkles.

As noiselessly as he had come he had sidled off again.

Presently he was heard calling down the gangway.

"Jacob! Jacob!"

The lank form and cadaverous face of Jacob appeared.

"Jacob, there's some gentlemen on board would like some of our wine—a leetle of our wine, Jacob, bring up half a dozen bottles of the richest, Jacob, for these merry gentlemen—oho—oho—he—he," he chuckled in his gleeful way, and Jacob dived down again.

In a few minutes he returned bringing half a dozen bottles of apparently fine old crusted wine.

The Vampire fingered them with his lank, skinny fingers.

"Th—ere," he drawled, a malicious grin wreathing his parched visage, "there, let the gentlemen drink of this, it will do their hearts good—oho—and then, Jacob, we shall know how to find them a soft pillow for their heads—ho—ho!"

Jacob grinned from ear to ear.

He had a keen remembrance of their last victim's agonies.

The doctor having thus found the means of drugging the would-be captors, the next question was what to do with them.

Jacob was for letting them down by their heels into the sea until they were half drowned and then dropping them bodily under water by way of a finish.

But the Vampire, who felt as little compunction in tormenting spies as he would in spitting a beetle, was not inclined to let them off so easily.

As a beginning, he proposed waking them up by pouring molten lead down the nape of their necks, and was proceeding to describe other equally agreeable processes, but Ben Barnacle opposed his subtle cruelty.

"Let me at least have the two officers," the Vampire pleaded, stretching out his shrivelled, claw-like hand; "I must have them."

"Very well," Ben said; "tease them as you will, but do them no harm."

The Vampire's face was a study.

Any one to have seen him would have fervently wished to be spared falling into his hands.

Not harm them! Oh, no. He only meant to be a little playful with them.

To give them something by which they might remember their visit to the ship.

Quite unconscious of the preparations made for their personal comfort, the over-zealous officers continued their carousal.

In imagination they already divided the immense rewards they would receive.

The two elderly gentlemen were especially anxious to get the biggest share.

Had they expected what their reward was to be, they would have been less desirous of sharing in it.

Bottles were nearly out, when Ben Barnacle tapped softly at the door and entered.

The officers winked in a knowing and familiar manner.

"All is safe as yet," Ben Barnacle said, "but no signal yet of his return."

"Oh, we're in no hurry; we can make ourselves comfortable another hour or so. You'll give us warning when he comes?"

"You shall be warned in time."

"Right! take a glass with us."

Ben took the glass—it was only half filled.

"Are you sitting over dead marines?" he asked, indicating the bottles.

"Yes, they're all out. Our fellows have thirsty throats."

"You shall have another bottle or two; but don't drink too freely."

"No fear of that; we've got our eyes open, ain't we, Bob?"

"Yes, and our ears too," growled that worthy.

"You're a precious pair of blind jackasses," was Ben's thought, but he kept it to himself, and raised his glass.

"Gentlemen," he said, "here's to a speedy and safe capture."

He drained the bumper.

The courteous Daniel Drummond tapped him jovially on the arm.

"Right," he said, "here's to the same, and I say, Ben, you'll have a glorious time of it, won't you, when you've got the letter of marque, and can call this vessel your own—eh?"

"I shall when I get it from you," Ben thought, but he laughed in reply, and got outside the door.

"So they think they could trick me," he mused, as he went to fetch the wine; "well, they're welcome to the belief."

The officers were in close consultation when he came back with the new supply of liquor.

"All going well?" was the query.

Ben set the bottles on the table.

"I fancy some of them suspect all is not right," he answered. "I must disarm their suspicions. If anything threatens you, I will give you the alarm—then look to your weapons."

Some of the officers turned very pale.

They had heard a good deal of the ferocious doings c. the boy pirates, as they termed them, and they did not altogether relish being in their midst.

They were very likely to find themselves in a hornets' nest.

The officers looked at their leaders. The two leaders, who themselves were very pale, looked at Ben.

"There's no danger, we hope," they said.

"Not at present; but the boys are watchful."

"The young fiends—can't you drug them with grog?"

Ben shook his head.

"I'd like to string up a dozen of them."

Ben looked serious.

"I don't mean that, but you must keep them quiet."

"I will," Ben replied, "till the time comes," he added to himself.

"Yes, Ben, Captain Ben, as you're to be," observed Drummond, familiarly holding him by the sleeve, "it all rests with you. Now see us safe, and you know what to hope for."

"I do," Ben replied, pithily.

The officers looked at him to see if his words implied suspicion of their intended faithlessness, but Ben's face was the mirror of trusting confidence.

"Hush," he said, as they were about to speak again, "I hear the young devils astir, I'll creep up to them. Lock yourselves in, gentlemen, and drink in silence."

He closed the door; a half-amused, half-grave look was on his face.

It pleased him to see men so easily deluded.

The would-be pirate-catchers lost no time in obeying Ben's artful injunction, and locking themselves in, one of them even went so far as to put the key into his pocket, a precaution he would not have taken if he had known that the middies had another mode of entrance to the cabin, and that by pocketing the key he was embarrassing their chance of getting out.

For some time after Ben had left them the party listened anxiously.

All remained as usual on board the roving vessel.

Nothing occurred to give them alarm, and, with their minds more at ease, they began operations on the full bottles.

These were soon uncorked.

The wine was good.

Its flavour exquisite.

They were born guzzlers.

Besides, they had nothing else to do but to drink and keep quiet.

So one by one the bottles were emptied, and the racy liquor gurgled down their throats.

The Vampire, who, accompanied by his long-visaged assistant, had crept on tiptoe to the door, chuckled as he saw the wine disappear.

He knew its fascinating flavour would seduce them so long as there was a drop left to drink, and nudging his faithful Jacob, he bade him peep in and see how well they took to the bounteous liquor.

Jacob surveyed their mugs with intense amusement.

"They takes it like mother's milk," he said, subsiding in a whispered giggle.

The doctor indulged in a dry grimace, and then precious pair, linked arm-in arm, sidled up the

gangway, to complete their preparations for the reception of their victims.

"Bob," observed the worthy Drummond, suddenly, "how do you find the wine?"

Bob stuck his heels on to the cabin table, and thrust his hands into his breeches' pockets.

"Fine," he answered. "Wonder if they've got any more of it."

"Never tasted finer," Daniel remarked, holding up his half-emptied glass.

Bob kicked over the last emptied bottle

"Gone," he said, ruefully eyeing the luscious draught that yet remained, to his comrade. "Dan, when we take the ship——"

"Yes, Bob, when we take the ship."

"Why, we'll smuggle a few bottles of the right sort, eh?"

"Won't we; I believe you. Say, Bob."

"Yes."

"Their mugs'll be a picter when they finds we don't mean to let 'em have the letter of marque, eh?"

Bob indulged in sundry antics expressive of his delight at the manner in which they had tricked the "greenhorn," Ben Barnacle.

All of a sudden Bob felt himself taken with a sudden fit of laughing.

He rolled from side to side, indulging in an hysterical outburst, till the tears rolled down his cheeks, and the breath seemed to leave his body.

"Bob, Bob, don't go on like that," Daniel cried.

He himself was feeling very queer.

"Can't—he—he—help it," giggled Bob; "I've—he, he—a he, he—a he, he—!laughing fit."

One of the men began to yawn.

Another got up shaking all over as if he had the palsy.

"Captain, captain," he muttered, "something's wrong with me; I don't know if I'm standing on my feet or my head."

A good many others felt in precisely the same predicament.

The worthy Daniel did not know what to make of his own peculiar symptoms.

"He, he, he." Bob giggled again. "It's the wine—he, he—the wine."

"He, he he!" echoed a sepulchral voice outside.

"It's the wine—he, he—and it's all over with you, my fine gentlemen."

It was the voice of Doctor Shrike.

The least affected of the party sprang to their feet.

Hastily they tried to seize their weapons.

They had a very vague idea that something was wrong.

"He, he!" cried Bob again. "Look, the cabin's opening."

All stared aghast at the end of the cabin.

Slowly it opened, and the black lid of a coffin fell in their midst.

The fall of this ominous article was followed by a frightful crash—as if a mine had exploded under their feet.

Something rattled on the table.

A ghastly death's head lay there staring them in the face.

Petrified with fear, the officers reeled back, and frightful noises succeeded each other.

The room filled with blue sulphurous smoke.

The table in the centre of the cabin tumbled in

The bottles rolled in all directions.

And bolt upright, in the midst of the scared officers, rose a grisly skeleton.

As well as they were able, the officers staggered back one upon the other.

The skeleton darted out its arm:

Its fingers seized in Drummond's hair, and now him in an awful grip.

"Murder, mur-der," he gasped.

The skeleton's jaws opened and shut with a snap.

Another rose amidst the cowering officers.

Both arms outstretched and seized a victim.

A third and then a fourth.

The palsied wretches were powerless to escape.

Each was seized and held by the roots of the hair.

Then the end of the cabin opened again, and armed with pike, cutlass, and dagger, the middies rushed in.

The officers' limbs shook under them.

They believed they were surrounded by a legion of devils.

But for the bony grip in their hair, they would have tumbled helplessly at the feet of their captors.

Ben Barnacle stepped from amongst his band.

"Gentlemen," he said, "we have snared you well. We shall get the letter of marque, and you'll not get Captain Tom."

The officers groaned.

"As a memento of your visit here, our doctor will mark with a hot iron on your breasts, or some other part of your person, the words, 'Visited the ship of the boy cruisers, but did not take Captain Tom!' Your leaders will then walk the plank, and the rest of you will be otherwise fittingly rewarded."

The teeth of the hapless officers chattered.

Cold sweats stood thickly on their brows.

Ben Barnacle clapped his hands.

"Grisly beings from the grave," he said, in mocking solemnity, "begone!"

The skeletons unloosed their horrid fingers.

There was a rattle of bones in the sockets and as the officers fell to the floor, the skeletons vanished.

Then the Vampire, a malicious grin on his parchment visage, put his hand outside the door, and cried—

"Jacop, make the pincers red hot, and get ready the bath of molten lead."

CHAPTER XX.

JERRY MIZZEN'S ESCAPE.

THE many perilous adventures and narrow escapes Jerry Mizzen had had to encounter since he made that unfortunate blunder by getting on the deck of the little admiral's vessel, had strengthened his constitutional malady.

Thus it was some time before he recovered from the unexpected attack of the wolf that sprang upon him as he entered the cave, after eluding his pursuers.

To be embraced round the waist with the paws of such a savage wild animal as a wolf, and drawn vis-a-vis with its hideous jaws, is not at all consoling to a stronger nerved man than our adventurer.

Finding he could breathe freely, and life not being squeezed out, as he fully expected it would be, Jerry began to wriggle about to free himself from the hairy clutches.

Jerry had a suspicion that there was something peculiar about the monster that held him so affectionately.

Such savage animals as his assailant make as short work as possible of their victims.

This beast did not appear at all in a hurry to shorten Jerry's career.

It stood quite still.

Its eyes never moved, nor did its jaws open in the threatening manner that animals of that kind generally do.

"Yer cussed ugly lubber, if I could only get hold of my knife I'd scuttle yer infernal carcase," said Jerry.

The supposed wolf gave a furious yell, and sprang back.

Jerry twisted round, broke from the monster's grasp, ran forward, and struck the brute in the belly with his head, and sent it rolling into a corner.

"That's yer skunking game, is it? I'll put a stopper on yer now," muttered Jerry, vehemently.

Jerry Mizzen quickly discovered the nature of his assailant when he heard it yell.

He knew wolves did not yell.

He came to the sensible conclusion that it was a redskin in wolf's clothing.

Which it was.

Rushing to where the panting savage lay, the enraged tar was about to drive his knife into its hide when the supposed wolf sprang up, gave vent to a piercing whoop, and bounded over Jerry's head.

Ere he had time to turn he was dragged to the ground by the weight of the skin, as it fell from the islander's carcase and enveloped him. When he rose, his enemy was gone.

Where?

Jerry made a search.

He had not heard the slide open or shut.

He rushed to the secret entrance and looked out.

An exclamation of disappointment escaped the tar's lips.

Flying across the hill like a bloodhound was a redskin.

Jerry Mizzen concluded at once that was his enemy.

How could he stop his flight?

Going back into the cave, he saw in a corner a bow and arrows.

Fixing one of the arrows, he pulled the string.

He dropped the bow with a howl, and rammed his knuckles in his mouth, as the fugitive echoed his howl, and fell on his face, with the arrow sticking in the back of his neck.

The reader can easily imagine the cause of Jerry's howl, when the bowstring went back with a twang on his fingers.

It was not owing to his good marksmanship that he brought his retreating enemy to the ground.

Had he been three or four minutes fixing the arrow, and taking a steady aim, probably he would have missed, but when things are done in a hurry they are more likely to take effect than they would otherwise.

"I am always being knocked about through some lubber," whined Jerry, squeezing his hand under his left arm to subdue the pain. "I wish I could get out of this cussed place."

He sallied out and made his way across the forest towards the sea.

Instinct guided him to the water-side, and here to his joy he discovered one of the island canoes, into which he unhesitatingly sprang.

The sun glanced brightly on the rippling water, as Jerry propelled the canoe lightly along.

He still kept labouring on, vainly hoping and gazing about, for the glimpse of some distant sail.

Day had far advanced, and sun had sunk to rest behind the vapours of rising clouds, when fatigued and weary, Jerry laid his head down to quiet, peaceful repose, that he might awake at dawn, to find the long, dragging hours passed, and again paddle about the vast ocean with the never-fading hope of being picked up, and restored to his own vessel.

He had barely closed his eyes, and shut out the visionary torments of the coming morrow, when the reverberation of a cannon echoed across the water, and made the would-be sleeper jump up with his heart beating with excitement.

JERRY MIZZEN TO THE RESCUE.

Another single shot, and then whole broadsides boomed over the deep.

The sight that met Jerry's eyes fairly astounded him, for he beheld two pirate vessels battling over a merchantman, which one of the pirates had already taken as a prize.

Jerry paddled to the nearest vessel—the one without the prize—and clambered on deck unperceived.

He selected one of the dead pirates' broadswords for his weapon, and then mixed with the boarders, who were standing ready to spring on to the other ship immediately the two vessels came together.

When the crash came Jerry was among the first on board. He sought out the captain. killed him, and the crew then surrendered. They were placed under hatches, the merchantman was sacked of its valuables and burnt, and the pirate was taken in tow as a prize.

Jerry still remained undiscovered.

Whilst the combat was raging below, the elements were preparing for a grand struggle aloft, and the decks had not been cleared of the dead and wounded when the thunder pealed forth and the vivid lightning flashed.

At last an awful peal, that suddenly

15

made every man start from his post, rent the air with a deafening report.

The lightning darted forth again, and lighted up the agitated water, and then all was dark, and a death-like silence reigned.

"Hard ⸺ weather, hard up, hard up, for your life!" shouted the captain hoarsely to the helmsman.

The next instant he had sprung at the helm, as the tempest burst forth, ploughed up the sea, and ran the line of white foam across the horizon, caught the furious winds, whirled the cataract into the air with an awful roaring noise.

The storm was at its fullest height.

Now the huge mountains of water dashed over the pirate's deck.

The spars and mizzen mast were cut down by the fierce flashing lightning that leapt through the air like electric fire, and felled everything the scorching thing touched.

Peal followed peal of the loud clapping thunder that went reverberating along the skies, and away in loud and distant murmurs across the horizon.

"Now," muttered Jerry, the raging storm carrying his voice away in a whisper, "it's my time to go. If I stay aboard here any longer, I shall go with the rest to Davy Jones's locker."

He walked to the stern, got aboard of the prize unobserved, and then cut her moorings.

"I now stand on board the ship, where I killed the leader," continued Jerry, speaking in a low tone. "I wonder how them lubbers below 'll like me for their skipper."

He stopped, as though meditating what to do.

"I must try 'em," he suddenly broke out, "and trust to my sword to be a friend in case of need—then I have my pistols."

He approached the hatchways, and tapped upon them with the hilt of his sword, and was answered by the savage cries of the suffocating men below.

"Well, here goes," he said, throwing open the hatchway, for the imprisoned men to escape the suffocating death that would probably soon have overtaken them, had they not been so timely released, though they did not appreciate his kindness by the way they dashed upon him.

"I am yer captain!" shouted Jerry, trying to keep a respectful distance from the dangerous pointed weapons.

"No, I'm hanged if you are!" shouted one.

"That's the swab that killed the skipper!" said another.

"That's him—give him a dig!" cried another, as the whole crew rushed upon the unfortunate and ambitious adventurer.

His life was in peril.

He was lying on his back, imploring mercy from those men who had no heart, or, if they had, the thick coat of crime that covered it was impenetrable.

Jerry was dragged from the deck by his hair, and tied to the mizzen-mast, while twenty of the stoutest and biggest pirates were sharpening their swords for an attack on their would-be captain.

CHAPTER XXI.

THREE CHEERS FOR THE NEW CAPTAIN.

JERRY MIZZEN was rather astounded by the ungrateful way the imprisoned captives assailed him for his kindness in liberating them.

"Hi, hi!" he shouted—"keep off. Do you know who I am?"

"No, yer swab, nor we don't want to," replied one of the bearded pirates, revengefully, preparing to thrust a dagger into Jerry's heart. "We saw you kill the skipper, and we mean to kill you!"

"Thank you," said Jerry, tremblingly.

The pirates grinned maliciously, and brandished their knives over his prostrate form.

Jerry trembled like an aspen leaf, rolling over to escape the points of the blood-stained blades that looked so cold and sharp.

A long marlingspike was put under his left jaw; a sudden twitch creaked his neck.

Jerry howled with the painful sensation.

A clout with the before-mentioned implement induced another yell.

A bump about the size of a turnip quickly rose on the back of his head, and his eyes streamed with water, caused by the aching pain, and a clout on the nose made him sneeze.

His tormentors got a respectful distance from him, looking much scared at the distorted features of their liberator.

"I say, Jack!" exclaimed one of the pirates, turning a sickly hue.

"Well?" said another, changing colour to the same tint.

"Cuss me if that lubber hain't swallowed a magazine: let's chuck him over, we don't want the ship blown up."

His mate agreed to the proposition for their own safety, and having unbound him, they took hold of Jerry by his arms and legs.

They were going to drop him over the side of the ship, when he sneezed so loud the pirates let go with fright.

In another moment Jerry sprang to his feet and confronted the superstitious crew with a pistol in each hand, and the scimitar held firmly between his teeth.

"Now, friends," he said, "is this the thanks I get for letting yer have yer liberty?"

The men murmured savagely, like so many tigers.

Jerry felt very uncomfortable, and trying to look brave, he threw off the cloak that concealed his costly dress.

Drawing himself up to his full height, he tried to look consequential, but his dignity fell when he slipped backwards and rolled over and over.

He slowly rose from the greasy deck, looking very sheepish, and kicked a huge piece of fat along, that had been the cause of his sudden downfall, thinking that he looked large by assuming an air of disgust and indifference.

"Look here," he began, drawing himself erect, but being very careful not to overbalance himself, "it ain't any use of you to mutiny against me, as the fust one as does has a slug. I've freed yer from them as is now either in Davy Jones's locker, or looking out for us; and I've saved yer ship. So if yer like to have me as yer captain, why we'll start on a fresh cruise, and share the plunder equally."

The pirates looked surprised at the nerve of the lubber.

"You can see I've been a captain afore,"

remarked Jerry, by way of inducing them to accept his liberal offer. "Look sharp. Speak, or else one of these will speak for me."

"Will they?" exclaimed one of the men, springing up.

"Yes," said Jerry, firing.

The bullet took effect.

The next instant the stricken pirate took a leap over the bulwarks, and disappeared under the foaming sea.

"One gone," he said, coolly.

The perspiration rolled down his cheeks through fright, for fear he should be made mincemeat of.

"Two going," repeated another pirate, firing likewise.

Jerry saw the act, and moved aside.

The ball whistled past his ear, went in the open mouth of a pirate who stood grinning beside him, passed through the back of his head, and stuck between the eyes of another grinning brute.

The two rolled over together.

Jerry was secured, fastened to a rope, and hauled to the top of the mizzen-mast to be laughed at.

The storm that had raged so furiously when Jerry did his quiet bit of smuggling, had now abated to almost a calm.

Still the black, overhanging clouds looked very gloomy, and indicated a fresh outbreak of the tempest.

The poor discomfited Jerry had not been hanging to the mast-head long before the wind went howling through the rigging, and sent him swinging about like a pendulum, while the ship rose and sank on the breast of the leaping waves.

Every pore in his body streamed with perspiration.

His tongue hung out of his mouth.

And his eyes stared wildly from their sockets, from exhaustion.

What would he give if he could drop!

He would rather chance the consequences of falling, than to be swung about up there.

He groaned miserably.

A gust of wind blew him round and round like a windmill.

The wind ceased as he was flying round with his heels over his head.

The rope relaxed and he came down with a jerk that nearly dislocated his neck, and shook all the breath out of him.

The rope snapped, and he came flying through the air, falling on a pirate, who stood beneath, grinning like a baboon in a fit.

Jerry gave a sigh of relief as he rolled off the man's broken neck.

The pirate howled with pain as he rolled over the deck with his dislodged head swinging about loosely.

Jerry had barely regained his feet when he received a kick from a big foot that sent him flying head first down a hatchway.

Exasperated beyond bounds through the tortures of his tormentors, he rushed upon deck frantically, with a huge sword raised menacingly above his head.

Three men guarded the companion-way, as he bounded up the steps three at a time. Driving his head forward, he sent them spinning across the deck, they settled down passively, forming, as they lay, a triangle.

Springing towards a group who were preparing for an attack, the redoubtable Jerry clutched the foremost by the throat, and threw him amongst his companions, and, shouting like a demon, he fired the pair of pistols over their heads.

The lawless men looked scared, and huddled themselves in a heap, while our adventurer looked down upon them like a towering monarch, and, in a voice of quivering thunder, said—

"The first one of you that rises his arm against me I'll make a dinner for the sharks."

He shivered as he pronounced the last word; the recollection of his late assailant, with its open mouth and savage eyes, seemed to flash vividly to his memory.

"Well, we must have a leader, mates," said one of the gang, rising.

"Ay, ay," responded several.

"He looks the right sort o' chap," said another.

"Get up," said Jerry, waving his hand.

They rose instantly.

"What do you say? Am I to be your skipper?"

"What do you say, messmates?" inquired the one Jerry Mizzen had nearly choked, addressing his scowling companions.

"Ay, he looks the right sort," said another, clutching Jerry roughly by the shoulder, and twisting him round for inspection.

"I should say I am the right sort, only you can keep your hands off."

"Ay, ay, we'll have you," shouted the whole crew in a chorus.

"What name, cap'en?" asked one of the crew.

"Cap'en Mizzen," replied Jerry proudly.

"Hurrah! hurrah! hurrah! for Cap'en Mizzen."

"Fetch the grog up," said Jerry, "and drink success to our next cruise."

A cask of rum was brought upon deck, and each man took a bumper.

"Hurrah for our new cap'en of the *Flying Vulture*," responded the pirates, enthusiastically, holding their brimming goblets above their heads; "may we sail long and have a wealthy cruise."

Jerry gave a toast which was received with thunders of applause, and then ordered the men to get to their posts. His orders were willingly obeyed; the ship was soon under weigh, and the men were anxiously looking out for a ship to plunder.

The new captain of the pirate brig felt uncomfortable in his smuggled costly suit, and went into the cabin to change it for a more common outfit. When he again came on deck he had on a loose white guernsey, a pair of well-bottomed trousers, a large silk neck-tie, and a broad-brimmed serviceable hat.

The pirates, that two hours before were knocking him about as they liked, now hailed him with the greatest marked respect.

Slowly pacing the deck, with all the dignity of a rear-admiral of a man-of-war, while the vessel made good headway before the strong wind that every now and then blew him along the deck, he thought of his late encounter, and wondered at his own courage.

A heavy rain began to fall and again he went below to the state cabin, where he enjoyed a bottle of fine old crusted wine, and smoked the fragrant weed.

One, two, and the third bottle was emptied. He began to feel very heavy, in fact, when he tried to stand h,? body seemed to over-balance him, and he felt he could not resist the temptation of another bottle of the delicious juice.

Drawing the cork of the fourth bottle, he thrust the neck into his mouth, and began to take a long draught, supporting himself by leaning over the table.

A panel slid aside at the end of the cabin, and a beautiful creole girl glided through and stood at the table facing the unbelieving Jerry; the bottle dropped from his mouth, and uttering a yell he fell back upon a luxurious cushion.

The maiden looked surprised at the stranger, and turned away, her large bright eyes brimming with tears.

"Stay," shouted Jerry, jumping up.

The girl gave a timid scream and disappeared the same way as she came.

In his hurry to catch her, his foot caught against an iron bar that stood in the cabin, and he fell forward, his head going through the aperture.

The consequence was, as the panel slid back it jammed his neck and nearly strangled him. The creole seeing what had happened, and hearing his gurgling cry for help, released him from the vice, and gently laid him in the cabin, where he lay, blue in the face, working his eyelids up and down like a Dutch doll's.

How long he lay like that he knew not, but when one of the men came to inform him that there was a sail in view, he had not moved an inch. Restoratives were given him, and he soon recovered from his dumbness.

"Sail in sight, cap'en," said the man.

"Wait till yer see the vessel, then come and tell me."

The man left him and went on deck.

"She is in view now, sir," said the man returning.

"Who?"

"The vessel."

"Where?"

"On the leeward."

"Wait till she is on the larboard."

The messenger again went on deck.

Jerry Mizzen had not recovered from the effects of his strong wine and strangulation, and preferred being in the cabin to on the deck fighting, besides, he did not feel comfortable, and he had a presentiment that if he went in an engagement that evening he would not come out of it again, and forty winks in the cabin was a much better idea than one long wink, that would close his eyes for ever, and leave him dabbled in blood on the deck.

He had just stretched himself full length along a kind of couch, and throwing out his long arms he was giving vent to a long yawn, when the man entered, but fell back at the sight of the opened mouth, and waited until it closed before he spoke.

"She is on our larboard quarter."

"Wait till she gets ahead of us, and be d—— to yer."

"But, yer hon——"

"No buts, do as I tell yer."

The man reluctantly went on deck to wait until the vessel worked round.

Jerry had just dozed off when the messenger again returned.

"Beg pardon, yer honer, but she is going out of sight."

"Wait till she has gone right out of sight."

"Go on."

He did go, but soon returned.

"She is out of sight, now," the man said savagely.

"Wait till she comes in sight again."

Jerry aimed an empty bottle at the man's head.

It missed.

Jerry threw a pistol next.

That did not miss.

It struck him on the nose, and made him blink.

The man rushed away howling, and another appeared.

"She has come in sight again," he said.

"I wish she had sunk, and you with her," replied Jerry, getting up from the couch, very much annoyed; "let her have a piece of iron, that'll bring her to."

A gun was fired, and they had a piece of iron.

The pirate vessel shook beneath the report, and Jerry Mizzen, who had got to the top of the companion-ladder, slid down again backwards.

"Boarders ready," he said, rubbing his long back.

"Aye, aye, sir."

Boom!

A shot from the supposed merchantman came whirling through the air, and carried away the bowsprit of the pirate.

This exasperated the crew, and they poured a broadside into them.

As the smoke cleared away, to the surprise of Jerry Mizzen and his crew the ship was standing steadily on the water.

Jerry Mizzen shouted frantically for the gunners to re-load.

He had barely given his orders when a second shot bounded over the side of their ship; passing within an inch of his ears, and carried away their mizzen-mast.

This was more than the buccaneer could stand, to see the ship carried away a bit at a time, while his crew were wasting shot.

Ordering the men away, he sprang to a gun, and taking aim, fired.

His shot proved effectual, carrying away their opponent's bowsprit.

A second proved equally successful, by clearing their mizzen-mast from their deck.

This gallant firing brought shouts from his crew, and raised him much higher in their esteem.

Heated by the excitement of the engagement, Jerry wheeled round another gun, and was taking a steady aim, when a third shot from the other vessel whizzed over the water, and went straight into the mouth of the one he stood by.

Too excited to notice what had taken place, though the shock made him reel, he levelled the gun for their stern, and firing their own shot, with one from the pirate, raked their deck, and carried away tiller and helm.

Both vessels were disabled, though the pirate had the advantage, and steered towards their victim.

They had got within a hundred yards, when a huge man-of-war suddenly appeared in front of them, from an inlet, where it had been waiting to see the result of their decoy, the supposed merchantman.

"We can't turn tail now," said Jerry, despairingly. "Shall we strike colours or fight for our liberty?"

"Fight," shrieked the men, savagely.

"There ain't any quarter from them when we begin."

"We'll fight for it," the pirates said resolutely.

A shot from the man-of-war made their craft jump out of water.

But the men were resolved to fight until there was not one left before they would submit to be captured.

A shout of laughter rang from the deck of the war ship, as the pirates poured broadside after broadside against them.

Boats were lowered and manned by true British tars.

They were armed for a desperate fight with desperate pirates.

The pirates tried to keep them back by continually firing into the advancing boats.

Still the sailors kept onwards.

Though their comrades were falling dead and stricken at every stroke they took nearer towards the pirates.

A shout rends the air as they pull alongside and clamber up the side of the *Flying Vulture*.

Jerry Mizzen, with his crew standing around him, await their advance.

CHAPTER XXII.

CAPTAIN TOM'S MIDDIES PREPARE TO RECEIVE A SPY.

It was not to be expected that the boy buccaneers, who so curiously found themselves in the cave of glittering treasures, would leave behind them anything they could conveniently carry.

On the contrary, making the most of their opportunity, they crammed pouches, pockets, and the insides of their capacious vests with its most costly jewels—using great expedition, for time was precious, considering the enemies waiting for them to appear.

The next thing was to find a way out from their Tom Tiddler's ground. Their youthful leader took that task upon himself, and went on in front.

Some of the middies yet lingering behind to secure some tempting spoil.

The party thus profitably employed numbered half a dozen of our hero's most dare-devil boys. They had been middies on board the ship on which Tom was taken, after being kidnapped, and were always at some rollicking mischief or other.

The eldest, who usually constituted himself leader in their harum scarum pranks, was a merry youngster named Harry Martin. He it was who had urged them to stay behind, in the hope of gathering up a few more treasures, and all six were now on their hands and knees, groping in every corner for jewels, and laying hold occasionally of a slimy toad or lizard, which invariably went spank into the nearest middy's eye.

Harry Martin heard, or fancied he heard, a suspicious sound.

Captain Tom, and those who followed him, were some distance ahead, and the other five middies were silently feeling for treasures—but the sound Harry Martin heard was distinctly like a man taking a long breath.

"Boys," Harry whispered, "here's a lark, some one's getting in; keep quiet, and I'll give you a nudge when he shows himself—it's very likely a spy—I hope it is."

The middies relinquished their scramble for wealth, and got huddled up in the darkest corner, hushing their very breathing, and peering anxiously in the direction in which Harry Martin's glance was fixed.

That young gentleman having speedily made up his mind that some one had breathed, or rather snorted, and that somebody must be somewhere near, crawled along the floor of the cave on his hands and knees and peered round the winding corners of the cavern.

He kept his head close to the ground, and so escaped bringing it with a bump against another head, which at that moment protruded stealthily from a hole in the shining wall.

It was a big, ugly head, surmounted by a big fur cap, and belonged to a burly, hairy ruffian, who was crouched up like a ball as he dragged his body a little at a time out of the hole, through which he had barely room to squeeze.

Harry Martin's first impulse, when he saw the head, was to pick up one of the big stones lying about, and give it a topper, to send it in again.

Next was to seize the big ugly ears, and drag the spy from his concealment.

But refraining from the temptation, he slid nimbly back to the middies, and gave them a warning nudge.

"He's coming—he's coming!" he whispered, smiling with delight. "Won't we warm him, that's all!"

The middies, overjoyed at the prospect, and utterly regardless of any danger, got up from their crouching position in the corner, and silently followed Harry Martin to the corner. Each in turn took a peep at the spy.

Each got out sword, dirk, or pike, in readiness to receive their visitor. The unconscious gentleman for whom so warm a reception was prepared had evidently endured an uncomfortable time of it during his tortuous progress along the winding passage, for previous to emerging forth he rested himself on his hands and knees, and drew another of those awful long breaths, the first of which had betrayed his presence.

Harry Martin nudged Neddy Winn, a fair-haired slim lad at his side.

"A snout like an elephant," he said in a whisper.

"More like a whale. Let's prick his nose with my sword, and make his eyes water."

"No, keep back—he'll be out presently."

Unaware of the proximity of the dare-devil younkers, the spy—if such he was—now began to pull himself out of the hole somewhat after the fashion of a crab crawling out of his shell.

He had squeezed half-way out, when he thought he would take a cautious survey of the subterranean chamber.

If he had taken that careful peep a moment or so before, he would not have ventured so far out.

For that first look discovered to him the middies, drawn up in single file, each one ready to spit him through if he stirred an inch.

To say that he was taken aback would but faintly convey an idea of his utter dismay and amazement.

A look of the most ludicrous perplexity settled on his face; his hands seemed stuck

fast where they sprawled over the ground;
and with eyes and mouth wide open, he stared
dumbfounded at the boys.

Having apparently satisfied himself that his
eyes had not deceived him, but that he was
indeed confronted by half a dozen armed and
piratical middies, he would very hurriedly
have retired from such unwelcome presence,
and was making quick tracks to get back into
his shell, when young Harry Marvel frustrated
his intended movement by driving a long pike
through the hinder part of his apparel, in
uncomfortable closeness to the same portion
of his person, while Neddy Winn dexterously
ran his sword point through his necktie, and
assisted to hold him immoveable.

"No you don't!" Neddy cried; "we want
you first, so tumble out, you spy!"

The polite invitation was backed by several
lusty arms, which unceremoniously laid hold
of him by collar, cuff, and frizzly hair, and
pulled him bodily into the cavern.

"Stand up, you spy!" said Harry, shaking
him.

"I—ain't—a spy!" cried the man, looking
ruefully on his boy captors. "I'm smuggler
Joe! I am—I am!"

"Don't tell lies! What did you come here
for?"

"I—I came for summut I wanted."

"And you'll get summut you don't want—
won't he, Ned?"

"I believe you, my boy!" was Neddy's
quick reply.

Harry Martin administered another shake,
then sang out—

"Stand up! What are you shaking for?"

"Don't—shake—me—to—bits!" gasped the
man. "Let me go!—I say!"

"We're sure to do that, ain't we, Ned?"

"Like niggers!"

"No, you'll have to come before our chief,
Captain Tom."

The brawny fellow started.

"Captain Tom! He—he here?"

"Yes, he—he!" Neddy cried, mimicking
his rueful voice; "and that's what you came
for—to betray him!"

"On my soul I didn't know as you was
here! No, I've seen a lot of pirate folks—a
set of rascally lubbers——"

"Silence, you scamp!"

"Mercy! I didn't mean you, but some big
pirates, as I knowed hid their spoils somewhere hereabouts, and I was creeping in when
I seed you!"

"Gammon!" Neddy said.

"It's true as the Gospel, and if you're going
to get out, you'd better all of you come this
way."

"And be taken like rats in a hole?"

"No, no, Master Smuggler Joseph, you'll
have to come with us."

"I—I comed to find the pirates' walley-
ables."

"There's nothing worth picking, Joe; we've
got the lot."

The worthy Joe lifted up his eyes.

"What, all the blessed swag?"

"Every jot."

"Then I'm a ruined coon."

He said no more, but with downcast eyes
and very woebegone visage allowed himself to
be dragged along the passage by the middies,
who, to make all things safe, previously
crammed the averture out of which he had

crawled in so effectual a manner that no one
else could come that way.

They soon overtook their youthful chieftain, who, having heard their story, narrowly
scanned the smuggler's face.

He made no comment beyond simply telling
them to keep him a prisoner.

Smuggler Joe set up a howl. "Don't take
me away," he cried out; "I've got a wife and
eleven young babes, all depending on me for
their support! Let me go, please!"

Tom fixed his glance sternly upon him.

"You will go with us on board our ship,"
he said, "and if you attempt the least
treachery, or to so much as utter a sound,
you shall die on the instant.

"Hold him secure," he exclaimed to his
middy, "and pay him if he attempts to breathe
a single word."

Admonished no less by Tom's speech than
by the rough shaking the middy gave him,
Smuggler Joe thought fit to resign himself to
his fate, and leave his wife and eleven young
babes to take care of themselves.

But fervently he wished the young rovers,
ere they reached the shore, would be set upon
by the officers of justice—whom if he had not
understood what fate would befall him, he
would have summoned to the capture of
Captain Tom.

We will not follow our heroes through the
windings of that underground passage, nor
accompany them in the hazardous incidents of
their flight to the shore.

Enough that the young rovers knew that
their lives depended on their speedily reaching
their vessel, and that their daring chieftain,
with this accustomed dauntless energy and
fearlessness of design, got them by stratagem
and audacity through every peril, and that
daybreak saw them pulling manfully in two
open boats towards the *Will-o'-the-Wisp.*

Here they were gladly received, Zelie joyously greeting her beloved boy adventurer,
though a sad look clouded her fair brow as she
took Minnie into her care.

The young rovers had been hotly pursued,
but they had time to signal their coming as
they left the shore, and those on board had
lost no time in making all ready for immediate
departure so soon as they got their idolised
chieftain on board, and with wild enthusiasm
they heard the order given in his firm, commanding tone to unfurl every sail and stand
out for sea.

The orders were being carried out with
alacrity, and every heart was bounding at the
prospect of a fresh cruise, for they had been
long enough in those coasts, when a red light
shot up from shore, and boom came the roar of
a gun from the port.

An instant after a score of warning lights
blazed in different directions, and the ships at
anchor were signalled by the authorities as
follows:—

"Pirates—escape—visit every barque—pour
a broadside into any vessel making for sea."

"Oh," said Tom, as his crew gathered
blankly round him on reading these signals,
which were rapidly transmitted from ship to
ship, "they mean to stop us at last."

"Let me see, if we remain here we shall be
visited and taken; if we attempt to run out we
must stand the risk of being blown in the air."

He happened at this juncture to catch sight
of Smuggler Joe.

That worthy, having no wish to take a journey in the pirate barque, or be on board while she was made the target of the frigates' guns, was trying his hand at communicating with the shore by innocently leaning over the vessel's side and waving to and fro a small lanthorn, which he had managed to purloin unseen.

He was so deeply engaged in this interesting occupation that he did not hear the quick tread of Captain Tom as he stepped angrily towards him, and was only made aware of his little game being discovered by receiving a blow under the ear from the fiery young chieftain's hand, which lifted him off his feet and sent him rolling head over heels, uncertain whether he was hurled down the hold or tumbling overboard to Davy Jones's locker.

His trickery had, however, succeeded.

The light had been seen and understood.

Not from shore, but by a big ship.

One of their warlike neighbours, which now bore down upon the graceful vessel, her decks swarming with armed men.

Her guns run out at the portholes and bristling, ready to belch forth a thundering broadside.

Captain Tom Drake took his speaking trumpet and walked aft, as the heavy man-of-war sidled up to him.

Day was just breaking, and in the hazy light he could see that several other vessels of like armament were standing under easy sail to block his passage.

There was no chance of running the gauntlet, and he waited till the quarter-deck of the big liner came towering above his.

A tall young officer stood on the poop.

Several junior officers were congregated round him.

A party of marines were drawn up in the rear, their bayonets glistening in the creeping light.

Short as the warning had been, every preparation had been made for the combat.

The sailors were at their posts, some by the guns, others on the yards and crosstrees ready to reef sails, or assist in other duties of working the ship.

And our hero, though inwardly wishing his huge blockader seven leagues away, could not but admire the precision and celerity with which all was made taut and trim.

"Ahoy, there," presently rung out from the young officer's trumpet.

"Ahoy, ho," Tom said in reply.

"There's a party coming from shore to board you, we're to keep you under our guns till they arrive."

"Thank you," Tom said, with a light laugh.

It crossed his daring brain, even then, to whisk suddenly from under their bows, and give them a run for it, armed as they were.

The officer seemed chagrined.

"You can take that as notice," he sang out, "and if you stir a ship's length I'll fire into you!"

Tom's face flushed excitedly.

"For a wager," he cried, "I would, even now, you 'longshore lubbers, run my ship from under your nose! and, as for firing into us, we've guns aboard."

A sensation was observable on the liner's quarter-deck, but the officer who had spoken, replied—

"I never wager with pirates, but if you want to try our mettle, run your ship a length from us, and you can have your fill."

The angry light deepened in the dark eyes of the proud boy cruiser.

His breast throbbed with fierce excitement.

It made his blood course hotly through his veins to endure that taunting challenge.

Stamping his foot upon the deck, he turned haughtily away.

For a moment his fierce glance ran along the daring faces of his crew, and he seemed about to give the word to light up the scene with the red flash of a broadside, and dash from the liner's side.

But he conquered his stubborn pride, and kept his rage to himself.

There was light enough now for them to see a boat push off from shore.

Lusty strokes propelled it towards the ship, and they recognised, seated in the stern, their old enemy, Admiral Ellis, and his bluff brother, the commodore.

A party of marines, with bayonets fixed, sat behind the rowers.

Little Jenny turned pale as she saw the deadly look on her father's ashy face.

Minnie crept close to Tom.

Zelie stood close to the bulwarks, gazing moodily at the advancing boat.

The least careworn face among the crew was Harry Vero's.

He seemed to relish the idea of a visit from his irate father-in-law, and there was a rollicking look in his eyes as he looked from the thin cadaverous visage of the admiral, to the glum countenance of the old commodore.

Admiral Ellis was ghastly with passion and triumph.

He glared at the boy cruisers, whom he now deemed doomed, and, as soon as he came near enough, his iron tones rang out—

"Keep a sharp eye on the pirates. If they resist my going on board, fire at their leader."

He shook his arm at our hero, who was listlessly leaning by the mast.

"We have you," he cried, "and will see if a rope can't take a little of your bravado out of you."

Tom smiled, but made no movement, though his dauntless followers eagerly watched for a signal from him to begin the desperate conflict.

Jenny Vero shivered, and shrieked slightly, when she heard her father's agitated voice.

But Harry Vere slid his arm round her slender waist, and whispered, lovingly—

"Do not fear your father's rage, Jenny. We are protected against all that he can do."

The boat grated against the vessel's side.

Two of the boy rovers, who were at the side armed, and prepared to dispute the passage, looked inquiringly at their leader.

Tom Drake walked to the vessel's side as the foremost marines touched the ropes to ascend by.

"Admiral Ellis," he said, quietly, "do you wish to come on board?"

"Do I wish, you lawless ruffian! I'll let you see. Mount, men—present—be ready to fire!"

Minnie Atherton ran towards Tom, screaming at his danger.

But the young chieftain put her gently aside.

"Not so fast, Admiral Ellis," Tom said, "I

am commander here. A word from me, and not only you, but all that sit in the boat with you, would have a bullet through your hearts—ay, though we are under the guns of your ships. But you are welcome to come aboard. Stand aside, lads, and let them pass."

Admiral Ellis grinned savagely.

He was the first of the party who mounted the ladder.

The commodore followed.

Then, two by two, the marines stepped on deck.

Jenny, as full as ever of filial love, broke from her youthful husband's arm, and ran towards her father, but the angry old officer moved her away.

"Back, unworthy girl," he cried; "when your unholy union with that pirate is severed by death, then only will I receive you as my daughter."

Harry Vere's face flushed, as Jenny fell sobbing in his arms.

"Admiral Ellis," he cried, "you are a surly old bear, and thus I snap my fingers at you."

The admiral's parchment-like face was livid with fury.

"And this," he cried, "do I end for ever your career of infamy. Cover the two pirate leaders, men. Present—make ready. Aha! Now—now. One word from me, pirates—one word—"

"Shall never be given," the deep tones of Ben Barnacle exclaimed, as Minnie Atherton ran to her boyish lover, to shield his breast from the dreaded volley, while Jenny stood between her husband and the marines, whose loaded muskets were levelled at his heart, "for all that you do here, vindictive old man, your country's laws, and the king's authority shall make you answer for. Smother your hate, Admiral Ellis. See—here is the protection to this ship, and her crew. Behold! The king's royal hand. Your prey escapes you. In the teeth of your armed soldiery—in the teeth of those bristling men-of-war creeping to destroy us, I wave their shield and safeguard—the Royal Letter of Marque, against which not even you dare raise a finger!"

A thrill rang along the deck.

Admiral Ellis, stricken to the heart, staggered dizzily back.

Minnie, with a glad cry, nestled to Tom's heart, while those on board the man-of-war looked curiously on the scene they could only imperfectly understand.

Recovering himself a little, the admiral, trembling in his baffled rage at the very thought of his victim's escape, with a husky cry of fury, dashed the hated parchment from Ben Barnacle's hold, and as it fell to the deck, where Harry Vere carefully put his foot before it, exclaimed to the young lieutenant—

"Coward, trickster, craven, white-livered boy! have you the baseness to take refuge under this miserable subterfuge. Stand from my daughter. Draw your sword, and here, on your pirate captain's deck, meet me like a man, if you have the heart to face an angered father's rage."

He ground out the words savagely.

His gray eyes blazed with frightful fury.

Jenny Vere turned her sad, imploring countenance up to her husband, who seemed to enjoy immensely the old fellow's rage.

"Why, you savage old bear," he cried, "if it were not for your daughter's sake, I should be tempted to forget your gray hairs."

Admiral Ellis stamped his foot on the deck. His mouth was covered with foam.

He would have leapt upon the young lieutenant, whose galling words stung him to the soul, if Captain Tom had not stepped between them, as Ben Barnacle picked up the letter of marque.

"Sir," he said, "no duels while I am commander here."

In an instant the little old admiral's fury was turned upon him.

"Another beardless trickster," he cried. "Pirate, if there is a trace of manliness in the scum of your accursed nature, give me satisfaction—give me satisfaction."

Our hero smiled quietly.

"You're in a precious hurry to eat fire with somebody," he said.

"No quibbling, cur. Are you a coward too?"

"You are at liberty to find out," Tom said, "whenever you please."

"Now, now," yelled the excited old officer, unsheathing his sword.

"Not so. When I fight you, Admiral Ellis, it shall be when I am on my quarter-deck, and you on yours—the smoke and flame of battle raging between us. So, when you are disposed, take out a rival letter of marque, and come across the sea to fight us."

Admiral Ellis snapped his sword asunder, as if it had been of glass, and hurled the pieces to the deck, stamping them under foot in the mad paroxysm of his ungovernable rage.

"Oh, that I could drag the chicken hearts out of your coward breasts!" he cried huskily. "Oh, that you had one amongst you man enough to let me wreak my rage upon. Devils—death—seize you—fooled—curses—hell!"

He fell back, reeling and ghastly.

Two of the marines caught him in their arms.

Timidly and tearfully, Jenny ran towards her father.

It wrung her gentle breast to see him so overcome with hate and baffled vengeance.

"Father, dear father," she cried, falling on her knees at his feet, "forgive me. Oh, uncle, intercede with him for pardon for his child."

The commodore's eyes filled with tears.

He turned his head away to hide his emotion.

The wrathful admiral, bounding from those who held him, spurned his daughter with his foot.

"Hence!" he cried. "Shrink from a father's rage—cringe in your miscreant pirate's arms—live with him in infamy and unforgiveness."

"Oh, father, father! spare me!" shrieked the sobbing girl.

"Live with him, I say, unforgiven—live with him accursed. Die with my bitter curses heaped upon your head—die spurned—forsaken—accursed."

He reeled again in his mad excitement.

Jenny fell back, weeping as if her heart would break, and trying, with her fingers thrust in her ears, to shut out her father's curse.

Harry Vere's eyes flashed furiously as he held her to his breast.

The purple veins stood swollen upon his temple.

One hand clutched his sword-hilt.

Had it been any other but her father, his

sword would have drunk the blood of the man who cursed and spurned his gentle wife.

Admiral Ellis threw his arms up wildly in the air, and raving like a madman, sprang to the vessel's side.

"Withdraw!" he shouted to the man-of-war. "We are cheated—tricked by the pirates! Withdraw—wrap your guns in lavender! The king's decree, curse them, is their shield—we are baffled of our revenge!"

"Yes," Ben Barnacle said, "you can't hurt us much now—so good bye, admiral. Up, my bold lads, paint out our pirate name; stretch every stitch of sail; run up our new flag, and give a ringing cheer in honour of our new cruise—a cheer for the king, a cheer for our new flag, and a cheer for Captain Tom!"

CHAPTER XXIV.

DUTCH PAUL APPEARS UPON THE SCENE OF ACTION.

JERRY MIZZEN felt anything but comfortable when boat's crew after boat's crew of the true tars began to scramble up the side of his vessel.

Not that he was frightened, but he did not like the idea of fighting against his majesty's ships.

He knew that if he did not fight, he and his crew would be taken and hanged without the least remorse or hesitation, therefore he had no alternative but to fight.

The pirates rushed desperately at the sailors as they reached the bulwarks, with marling spikes and cutlasses, and thrust them into the sea, awfully cut and mutilated.

Three, four, and sometimes more of the poor fellows were sent to an untimely watery grave, and so far the buccaneers kept their deck clear.

Driven to desperation by seeing the havoc amongst their faithful messmates, another boat's crew, headed by a young dare-devil officer, made a frantic attempt to gain the pirate's deck.

They were met by the pirates, and after a fearful struggle, about a third managed to board, while the others, who had been driven back and hurled into the water, were fighting despairingly with the raging tempest for their lives.

The young officer with his little band kept the bloodthirsty wretches from the vessel's side, while reinforcements of their own companions swarmed on the deck.

A desperate and bloody combat then ensued.

Men fell stricken on both sides, and amidst the terrible meleé Jerry Mizzen stalked like a spectre, quietly putting the nearest of the enemy hors-de-combat, while volley after volley of the dead missiles showered about him.

He seemed to bear a charmed life, and many of the astonished sailors, who left off fighting to watch his movements, got an ugly dig that sent them rolling to the deck howling.

The crew of the Flying Vulture were getting dreadfully thinned.

Still they fought bravely.

A superstitious feeling crept over Jerry, and he fancied he could see himself dangling from the yard-arm of the man-of-war.

"Into the lubbers—let them have it," said the young naval officer.

Another boat-load of sailors clambered up the side of the Flying Vulture, and added to the fearful odds Jerry Mizzen and his crew had to contend against.

One of the pirates, a Spaniard, plainly seeing they had no chance against these fighting sailor devils, went below to fire the magazine, and blow themselves and the ship into the air, in preference to being vanquished and taken prisoners.

He had got a lighted torch in his hand, and stood a moment meditating before he blew the freight of living beings into eternity.

Another moment, and there would have been a terrific explosion, and the accursed ship would have been blown into a thousand pieces.

But that instant saved it.

Instead of a terrific explosion, there was a frantic shouting on deck.

They were shouts of welcome, and from his own companions.

Treading the burning torch under his foot, he rushed upon deck.

The fighting had subsided.

A look of terror settled upon the face of every man pirate exclusive.

What had been the cause of this sudden change?

The sudden appearance of Dutch Paul, the flaming pirate, as he was termed.

The very mention of that name struck terror to the bravest men's hearts.

Every one belonging to the war frigate stood panic-stricken.

Even Jerry Mizzen was as much scared as any one, although his crew were delighted by the appearance of Dutch Paul, and tried to hail him.

The illustrious adventurer had not forgotten the visit his beloved leader had from him when he set the decks of the Will-o'-the-Wisp on fire.

A deafening report made every one start, as though suddenly awakening from some horrible nightmare.

A ball shot from Dutch Paul's deck, and flew through the air with a flaming tail of fire.

With an explosion it fell on the British war ship, and spread its destructive liquid fire in every crevice.

Then did their energetic life return to the terror-stricken men.

The deck of their vessel was in one mass of flame.

Amid the torturing element stood their noble commander, with their officers around him, frantically imploring his men to leave their would-be prize, and return to their ill-fated vessel.

"Away with yer; clear out of this, yer swabs," shouted Jerry, as the sailors scaled over the side of the pirate barque, and dropped into their boats.

The true naval sailors took no notice of his remonstrances, but pulled with a will towards their burning ship, as each boat was manned.

The pirates shouted like a lot of demons when the last of their enemies had left their deck.

Shout after shout of welcome rose from the Flying Vulture, and rent the air, as Dutch Paul bore down upon them.

Jerry looked bewildered at the strange enthusiasm of his wild crew.

With one accord they all raised their firearms and gave a *feu-de-joie* as the terrible pirate came alongside them.

"Ha, ha!" laughed Dutch Paul, as he stepped on the other's deck, "you have had some ugly work here."

"Yes," said Jerry, "them cussed men-o'-war's men can bite when they like."

"Who the devil are you?"

"Don't yer know?"

"No, yer lubber, I don't," said Dutch Paul.

"Then I pity your ignorance."

"Clear out, yer swab," said the pirate, administering a kick on Jerry's prominent person that sent him sliding across the deck.

"Where is your captain?" asked Paul, turning to Jerry's lieutenant.

"Davy Jones's, by this time."

"Is he dead?"

"Yes."

"The devil!"

"No, yer honour, our captain."

"How did it happen?"

"In a scrimmage."

"My favourite friend, too," he added, in a low, reverential tone. "My curses on the accursed hound that slew him."

A demoniac look overspread his swarthy features.

Then turning to the man he had before addressed—

"Can you tell me the name of the ship or the commander?" he asked.

"You mean the one we had the engagement with?"

"Yes."

"I can't," answered the lieutenant. "When she came across us, the night was dark, and a fearful storm raged."

"Furies!" then I am thwarted."

The men stared uneasily at the change of his brutal face.

Not that they feared him.

He was always kind to his friends, and would have fired his last shot in their defence, were there a fleet of war ships standing round, ready to pounce upon him, when he was helpless to defend himself.

The loss of the pirate chief had touched his hardened nature, and a look of deep anguish and regret settled on his face.

So earnest was his sorrow, that it brought a look of pitying sympathy from the hardened crew of the *Flying Vulture*.

"Who is that lubber?" he said, sharply, pointing to Jerry Mizzen, as though he did not wish the men to see his grief.

"That's our captain."

"Where did you get him from?"

"When they killed our captain," he commenced, "they fastened us down in the hold, and took our ship as a prize."

He paused here, as though thinking what to say.

"Well," said Dutch Paul, "and what then?"

"Well, yer honour," he went on, "as I said afore, there was a fearful storm, and the night was black with thick clouds——"

"Yes, yes; yer told me that afore—I want the story."

"Our cap'n, as is now," he continued, "had been picked up by them, and he was aboard when we were fighting; not liking the cap'n of that ship, he watched for an opportunity to get away; so when they were all up

fo'castle-way, he went astern and cut our bark free; so, being a good sort of a fellow, we made him cap'n."

"Oh," said Dutch Paul, at the conclusion of the man's recital.

Jerry Mizzen had been leaning over the bulwarks, attentively listening to every word that was exchanged between them.

His knees trembled violently, and every pore in his body was dripping with perspiration, fearing every moment that the man would denounce him as the assassin of their captain.

The long breath of relief he drew as the man finished was like a gust of wind.

How he blessed that man for his noble faithfulness.

He felt that he could have hugged him to his breast.

"I'll promote him, that I will. Yes, I'll promote him—make him cap'n under me," he muttered to himself.

"What is the name of your new captain?" Dutch Paul asked.

"Captain Mizzen."

"Captain Mizzen!" shouted Paul.

"Aye, aye," responded Jerry, confronting the Dutch captain.

Jerry stood trembling beneath the stern inquiring gaze of the other's eyes.

"Are you the lubber they call captain?" was Dutch Paul's polite query.

Jerry made no answer, but looked indignant.

"A nice-looking shark you are, to be commander of the *Flying Vulture*."

Jerry felt insulted, and walked away.

His interlocutor pulled him back sharply by the collar.

"Where are you going?" he asked.

"If yer want to get at any one," said Jerry, "get at the marines."

"Oh, that is it, is it?"

"It is."

Jerry's lieutenant, seeing there would be a row, came to his relief, and said to the Dutch captain—

"It's all right, yer honour; the cap'n is a good sort, and we all likes him; and our motto is ' All for one, and one for all.'"

The hint was given with a significant look; but the Dutch captain wished to appear as though he did not see it, though he altered his manner in addressing Jerry, and said—

"Your lieutenant told me that you were on board the ship that took this barque for a prize?"

"Yes," said Jerry, "they picked me up."

"Would you know the ship again?"

"Yes."

"You know the captain."

"By sight."

"That is well. You saw the fatal blow given that killed the late commander of this ship?"

"I did," stuttered Jerry, turning white and trembling. "I ought to, mine was the hand that dealt it," he thought, but did not say.

"What are you trembling about?"

"The way he was killed."

"Curses on the slayer, were he near me now I would hack him in a thousand pieces."

The remark was not at all refreshing to Jerry; he stepped aside as Paul drew from its scabbard a long scimitar.

"I would bleed the hound's very heart's core with this," he said, holding the formidable-looking weapon above his head.

"Would you?" thought Jerry, "it's dangerous for me to stay here, if that's yer game." He would have retired to his cabin, but his visitor again spoke—

"If ever you run across him, sink his infernal ship, and take care of him until we next meet. I will settle accounts with him."

"I won't forget," said Jerry, taking his leave of him. He felt much safer when the terrible pirate stood upon his own deck.

"Glad they put the fire out," muttered Jerry, leaning over the bulwarks and watching the bustle on the frigate, where the carpenters were repairing the damage done. "I like them English war ships, only I don't like 'em to come too near. All very well in their place, but they can keep at a respectful distance from me."

Turning to his crew, he gave orders for repairs of damages done to them by the decoy ship.

The men readily set to work, and soon their vessel was ready to be put under weigh.

A consultation was then held between Jerry Mizzen and his lieutenant, concerning the nature of a new expedition.

"Well, cap'en," said the lieutenant addressing Jerry with much respect, "we must bear off leeward now, then we can suddenly tuck her round and run into land."

"Yes," said Jerry, "that is a good notion, but what's the name of the part where this cave or grotto is?"

"Well, cap'en, I can't tell yer the name of the place, but I can take yer to it."

"Very well, that will do as well; but what is there there?"

"Why, cap'en, it's a cave where some smugglers hid their valuable treasures, and I heard say they had all been caught."

"The treasures?"

"No, cap'en, the smugglers."

"Their treasures haven't been found by anyone else do you think?"

"No, cap'en, because nobody else didn't know anything about it."

"Then how did you know anything of it?"

"Because the cap'n used to do a little business with 'em."

"Ah!" exclaimed Jerry, satisfied with his officer's answers.

Orders were given to the men to carry out the manœuvre to elude the vigilance of the war ship, that was rapidly progressing in repairs, and would soon be on the track of the *Flying Vulture*, that had flown with the wind straight ahead of them, and was out of sight before they could get ready to pursue them.

The pirates had managed thus far successfully, then turning off seaward, they ran back.

So far they were safe.

Every stitch of canvas was then set, and the pirate vessel made good headway towards the smuggler's cave.

"Land ahead."

Jerry Mizzen sprang up the rattlings with the glass at the sound, and scanned the mountains of rocks that every minute became visible.

"What can you make it out?" said Jerry, handing the telescope to his lieutenant.

"That's the very place."

Part of the sail was taken in, and the ship was slowly taken through a winding inlet, between a mass of towering rocky crags, towards the secret cave.

Many people could hardly imagine that such a place existed.

The Garrote, as it was called, was a mass of huge rocks, that seemed to bury their tops in the clouds.

In many places the huge stones projected out, and looked as though they would topple over, and crush the very earth beneath.

At about the middle of this majestic pile, it precipitated forward in a massive bulk, and formed a kind of terrace.

In the middle of this terrace the rocks went back, forming a deep arch.

Over this hung large drooping trees, and different coloured foliage, making a kind of portico.

Jerry looked bewildered at this strange structure of Nature, and seeing no way of entrance, enquired of his officers.

Having a dozen of the most trustworthy and stalwart men with them, well armed in case of an emergency, they started forward, and arrived at the bottom of the rocks.

"I don't see how we are to get in," said Jerry.

"You see that water running down those steps to the left?" asked the lieutenant.

"Yes."

"Well, we have got to get up there."

Jerry nodded, and letting the officer lead the way, he followed him in the ascent, the men following in the rear.

The steps, as the lieutenant termed it, was a sort of spiral slope, walled in on either side by huge pieces of rock.

A clear, silvery stream flowed rapidly down the rude steps.

To look at it, any one would have said that the work was artificial, but a close inspector could plainly see that had a stone been moved, the whole would come crushing down.

Thus it could have been seen that nothing but the mighty and wonderful hand of Nature had worked this massive, extraordinary, and beautiful piece of art.

Reaching the top of the spiral steps, they found themselves on the terrace.

The leader, Jerry's lieutenant, made his way through the long recess, then he turned sharply off to the right, and had to descend a steep of jagged rocks.

At the bottom was a large sort of room.

In every corner were stowed heaps of the most costly articles of every description.

This could be seen by a small glimmer of light that broke through a crevice in the side of the wall.

An exclamation of surprise and joy broke from the lips of all who beheld the valuable heaps.

Jerry was in ecstacies, and could do nothing but dance about with delight, while the others were loading themselves with the costly treasures.

Boom!

Then a sharper report followed this unexpected interruption.

Jerry leapt off his feet with fright, and turned a somersault in the air.

"Don't any of you move," he said, "I'll see what's the matter."

And so he did.

Like a maniac he rushed on to the terrace, and ere he had time to look round, another shot seemed as though fired close to his head.

ring they had been discovered, and not

thinking of the consequence, he gave a sudden spring, and bounded over the parapet.

His blood chilled in his veins as he flew through the air, at the horrible spectacle beneath him.

He knew he must fall upon these hideous-looking rocks, and be dashed to pieces.

He closed his eyes as he fell with a despairing cry.

CHAPTER XXV.

DON PARDO GETS THE WORST OF A BARGAIN.

IF it had not been for the respect the boy buccaneers had for Jenny's feelings, the old admiral, her father, would have been made the subject of their free frolics.

As it was, he got off comparatively unmolested, but with a farewell salute that in no way tended to lessen his chagrin or his discomfiture.

The boat in which he was returning to the shore had not time to leave the ship's side before several of Tom's middies hurried to the bulwarks, bearing in their midst some immense sacks.

Doctor Shrike, and his satellite, Jacob, accompanied them.

Arrived at the companion-way, the middies challenged the little admiral.

"Boat ahoy!"

"To the devil with you!" grunted the old commodore.

The boys laughed.

"Here's a present for you," Harry Martin sang out.

Amidst the giggling of the ship's crew, a well-filled sack was dropped over the side.

"Here's another," young Neddy Winn cried; "take it ashore, you lubbers."

A second sack dropped over.

A strange phenomenon accompanied these descents.

Each sack seemed animated as it went down.

Not only did it draw up in convulsive contortions, but a peculiar cry, resembling a howl, came from the puffy folds.

Perhaps the dig each sack received before it went over the side, from a keen scalpel plied by the vampire fingers of Doctor Shrike, had something to do with the wriggling and howling.

As the second sack went over, the boat left the vessel's side.

The party in the boat, suspecting the truth, hastily undid the fastenings of the sacks, and enabled the cadaverous, woe-begone visages of Drummond and his companion, the two officers who had gone on board to capture Captain Tom, to peer ruefully forth.

How they had been maltreated since that fatal hour when, under the influence of the drugged wine, they had been made helpless captives, will be discovered hereafter.

Suffice it, that after enduring untold tortures, to which the vampire and his assistant subjected them, they were crammed, more dead than alive, into the sacks, and thrust over the vessel's side.

The frolicsome young middies lined the bulwarks as the second load tumbled into the boat.

"Good-bye, admiral," they cried to Ellis, who sat in the stern, looking like a living corpse; "you'll hear of us at sea."

They waved their caps and cheered lustily, until the boat was out of hail.

The big war ship which had at first blocked our hero's flight, still held its position alongside.

There had been a minute's conversation going on at the quarter-deck, and Captain Tom thought they were going to risk all by attacking him.

But they evidently thought better of the idea.

They expected, however, that the boy buccaneers would make good their escape.

Such was not our hero's intention.

With the audacity peculiar to his headstrong nature, he resolved to remain in harbour a little longer.

A resolve that was near being fatal to them.

The little English admiral reached the shore in a state bordering on madness.

If he had dared, he would have given orders forthwith to have Tom's ship blown into the air.

But the letter of marque, so cunningly obtained by Ben Barnacle, and signed by the royal hand of King George himself, restrained him.

Brave as he was, he dared not lift his hand against the king's decree.

But he closed with the first opportunity of having the boy buccaneers attacked, and their leader slain.

Officer Drummond, as soon as he got safe out of reach of the boy devils, at whose hands he had received such frightful treatment, recalled to Admiral Ellis the purpose that had taken him on board.

The irate veteran pricked up his ears at the mention of the pirate for whom the letter of marque had been originally intended.

"We cannot get it from them now the blank is filled up," he said, bitterly; "it is most unfortunate that you should have allowed yourself to be so tricked."

The precious pair of pirate catchers looked as if they thought the result had been deucedly unfortunate for themselves, seeing that they had not only lost their chance of reward, but had been mercilessly ill-used in the bargain.

"Now, if this man," hissed the admiral, "could be induced to attack their ship, we would grant him an indemnity."

"That is to say," observed Drummond, "if he can beat them at sea, he may have the letter of marque."

"Ay," the little admiral cried, "and such a reward as you never dreamed of shall be yours, if this boy pirate is taken, with his lawless crew."

"Hum," growled the commodore, "those boys can fight. If this pirate captain has not a good stomach for fighting, he had better leave them alone."

"What sort of a man is he?" inquired the admiral.

The officers gave a description of their man.

He was one of the most merciless pirates who had ever infested the seas.

Every clime he had visited, he left a track of blood, and the ocean dotted with burning wrecks.

Don Pardo was his name, and such was his prowess in combat, that few cared to dare him to a personal encounter.

Added to this, he was a most consummate hand at eluding pursuit and avoiding suspicion, by assuming new devices where-ever he went.

THE PIRATE DISCOVERS THE MISER'S HOARD.

The vindictive little admiral listened with pleasure to these details.

"Where is your man to be found?" he asked.

"At the Paddy's Goose," replied Drummond.

"Humph!" growled the commodore, "a den of thieves."

"Silence, brother," Admiral Ellis exclaimed. "Remember this boy pirate has, with impunity, cast defiance in our teeth, and we must not be particular, so long as we take him in the end."

"Humph!" growled the old fellow, "I don't think he'll be taken yet."

"We shall see," was the little old admiral's response. "At all events, I'll see this Da Pardo to-night, at the Paddy's Goose."

One of the rowers at that moment seemed so absorbed in listening to the arrangements, that he missed his stroke, and, as a result, landed a beautiful "crab," which not only sent him over on his back, but regularly deluged the boat with water.

Any one might have supposed that he was more interested in listening to what was going forward than in rowing the little admiral ashore.

Such was the fact.

He was one of Tom's numerous spies, and his purpose there was to hear what was likely to go forward, and report accordingly to his young chieftain.

Perhaps it was owing to this interesting individual being amongst the rowers, that early the same evening, a tall well-formed young fellow might have been seen sauntering leisurely towards the rendezvous known as the Paddy's Goose.

His bearing was unmistakably nautical.

His dress was a sort of half-naval undress, over which he wore a long blue cloak, beneath the folds of which hung a very serviceable sword.

Any one peering beneath that same cloak, could have got a glimpse of a pair of finely-mounted pistols, and a short dirk.

He evidently knew the nature of the men he was about to meet that night.

The Paddy's Goose was a big shantling building, in a densely populated part of the town, the Alsatia of the place, for in it were congregated some of the worst type of humanity—men who had fled thither red-handed from their crimes—men who defied the law's control, and banded together in a desperate league within the sanctuary of this ill-omened quarter.

The narrow streets and alleys along which the stranger took his way were thronged with women of the notorious class—some showily dressed and outwardly fair to look upon, others huddled in rags, filth, and bestial drunkenness.

These put out their coarse tawny arms towards our young traveller, and followed him with howls, when he openly displayed his disgust at their clamouring obscenity.

Lots of ill-looking ruffians, their brutal visages stamped with the haggard traces of disease and crime, got in our adventurer's way, but he invariably walked straight through their midst, putting them aside without the least discomposure, and a look of his unqualing glance sufficed to convince the cowed rascals he would be dangerous to meddle with further.

Arrived at the Paddy's Goose, the door of which swung wide open, he sauntered in.

The landlord, a wolfish-looking scoundrel, with bare brawny arms, took a swift survey of his person as he entered, and glanced after him with a sinister leer as he strode past the groups at the bar—men and women steeped in gin and squalor, and who were bandying the most indecent jests their foul lips could utter.

As our readers may imagine, the Paddy's Goose did not bear a very good repute.

There were rumours of deeds done within its reeking walls that made the heart shudder, and if there was a place where the worst characters were to be found in plenty—fellows ready to do any bad deed, this establishment was the one.

Indeed, such were the ferocious instincts of the brutes who took shelter there, that the bravest officers of justice shrank from crossing its fatal threshold.

Yet, strange to say, it was the nightly rendezvous of the young bloods and nobles who were " doing life " thereabouts.

True, their visits were not always purely to study what they saw there.

If there was an enemy to be stabbed in the dark, or a fair woman to be carried off, it was

at this haunt they found the ready instruments of their will.

The room into which our adventurer now strode was of huge dimensions, and more than one hundred lamps lighted its dim corners.

Tables innumerable were placed before rudely constructed seats, and at those tables were sitting or standing groups of the most curiously mixed characters it would be possible to describe.

Rough seafaring men—fellows of undoubted piratical habits; slim youths, sickly with dissipation; men, who by their bearing, if not by their disguised costumes, could be seen at a moment's glance to belong to the higher walks of life; women, some young and handsome—blooming girls, who, out of that fearful place, might have been deemed a worthy prize to be sought for in holy marriage; others, whose charms might have compared with the famous courtezans of ancient Greece—the houris who won philosophers from their gloomy studies, and made them lie dallying in their arms; others, again, who were past their attractive years, and seemed only there to lure their unsuspecting victims to murder and foul death.

The fumes of liquors and tobacco pervaded the atmosphere of that rendezvous of vice and infamy.

Glasses clattered, tables shook, dice rattled; women shrieked or laughed, and, ever and anon, there arose above the eternal hum, the heated clamour of voices, in deadly dispute, to be followed, perhaps, by some deadly fray, in which weapons were freely dabbled in blood.

Our youthful adventurer had scarcely taken in this scene with his eagle glance, when a tall, powerful bully of a man, in seafaring attire, walked up to him, and said, with a curse—

" Now, my young blood. Body of me, d'ye think you're going to pass unchallenged, eh? Damme, what's your name, and who are ye? Let's look under that cloak, and see what you've got there. You don't pass without my taking toll, I can tell you."

The young stranger put aside the fellow's swinging arm.

" I've a capital sword under that cloak," he said, quietly, " but as I do not think you are a good judge, I shall not let you see it. As for toll, if you stand in my way, you'll get it."

The fellow stared at his youthful opponent.

" Body o' me," he said, planting himself in the stranger's way, " hark ye, young blood, you don't know yer way here, I can see, and you'll have to give toll afore yer finds out."

" There it is, then," was the quick reply, and the left arm of the stranger shot out like an arm of steel.

The bully, happening to stand just within beautiful mark, got a fine one between the two eyes.

It was so fine that he could not see it, but shutting both peepers, and emitting a howl of pain, he staggered back, and fell over a table.

When he got up, half a dozen worthies of a like feather surrounded him and the young stranger.

They looked very big at first, and talked awful big things, but there was something about the youthful intruder, as he stood facing them, in an attitude of easy indifference, they did not exactly seem to relish, and as none

...de an effort to tackle him, our adventurer sauntered up to a table, and took his seat.

The big bully whom he had floored here sidled up to him.

"Body o' me," he bellowed, blinking with his injured eye. "Darn yer, I never take a blow."

"You took one then," replied the stranger, with a laugh.

"Curses!—I'll have revenge!—blood, blood!"

He clutched the handle of a clumsy sword.

Our adventurer gently took a thin, bright sword from its sheath.

"Look here, my friend," he said, "I have no wish to quarrel with you, but if you stand there, grinning like a baboon, I'll put this blade in your ugly carcase."

He set the point atilt against the other's breast.

The fellow backed from the keen weapon.

The unconcern of the stranger cowed him.

"Body o' me, I didn't mean no offence," he growled, "but it's our rules not to let any new customers in till we see what stuff they're made of."

"I hope you are satisfied with mine, if you are not you can have a stronger taste, if you have had enough, why, as I never bear malice, you and your friends can drink a bottle at my expense."

"Body o' me," cried the bully, "but I like yer pluck. You can hit out straight, and I daresay can use that thrasher of yours well. I'd have a bout with yer, for I bean't feared of mortal man, but as you've said we're to be friends, it's friends we'll be; so give us your fin, and I'll drink yer health in a full bumper."

He held out his huge fist.

The stranger smiled and took the proffered grip.

His opponent then introduced him to a few villains who came shambling up, and soon all memory of the little *fracas* was drowned in wine.

The stranger did not drink with them.

He sat at a table apart from where they were.

He had ordered a bottle of canary, and was drinking by himself, when a blue-eyed little girl, about sixteen, seated herself uninvited before him.

"I'm glad you made up your quarrel with Ben Bault," she said, "he isn't so bad himself, but there's a lot of his followers that would waylay you as you went out."

"Would they indeed? Well, these gentlemen may find out that I carry a sword, and know how to use it. Besides, I knew the character of the place and its frequenters before I came here."

"Who are you, then—you're not an officer of justice? You wouldn't get out alive if you were."

"Do I look like one?"

The young girl smiled.

"No, you're too handsome and young, but what have you come for?"

"You are very inquisitive—are you the spy of the place?"

"No, I'm blue-eyed Loo—that's what they call me here, but I like your looks, and so I wish to know all about you."

"I am flattered. You said just now no officer of justice could leave here alive, now I happen to know there will be one here this night."

"Here?—he must be well disguised then, or you'll see."

"I don't think he'll be well disguised, but he'll be well protected."

"How—is the place to be attacked?—they'd never take it."

"Don't be curious. You'll see strange things to-night. Tell me, do you know a Spanish pirate called Don Pardo?"

"The Spanish captain—yes."

"Is he here now?"

"No, it's too early for him."

"When he comes, point him out to me."

"Oh, you'll soon find out. He's a big, ugly, black-whiskered brute. I hate him. He never comes without picking a quarrel with some one, and he's sure to set on you, if he sees you are strange."

"As I said before, I wear a sword."

"Yes, but he has learned how to fence. I have seen him kill three good men. The last was a young captain in the navy, and we thought he would have been taken for that."

"I shall impatiently expect this fire-eater."

"Yes, but do not fight unless he insults you, and then——"

"Well, and then?"

"I hope you will kill him—run him through the heart, as he did the poor middy, the other day."

"What—did the coward fight a middy?"

"Yes, and killed him with his big sword."

"And these cowards allowed the murder?"

"They allow anything here. They would see you killed without leaving their seats."

"Would they?"

"Yes. Hush! there is the captain. I must run away, for if he sees me with you, he will pick a quarrel directly."

She was running away, in an evident state of fright, but the young stranger pulled her back.

"Sit down again, my little friend," he said. "If you are to be the cause of the quarrel, you shall see it."

The young girl trembled, and her pretty face blanched.

She had that moment caught the ruffianly gaze of the Spanish pirate, Don Pardo, fixed on her and her companion with a significant glare.

———

CHAPTER XXVI.

THE LAST OF THE PIRATES.

As cleverly as they thought they had eluded their late antagonist, little did they think that the decoy ship was following in their track.

But such was the case.

It had received instructions from the commander of the man-of-war, and had followed the Flying Vulture until it had cleverly worked its way through the rocky crags.

Then it returned to the disabled war ship, which by this time had repaired the damage done by the liquid fire ball from Dutch Paul, and giving information as to where the pirates were, they started to capture the daring outlaws.

On their course they fell in with another war vessel, evidently on a searching cruise for some sea rover.

A communication was held between the two

commanders, and they followed the decoy-ship to the rocky mountain.

Making their way through a different inlet to that taken by the pirate barque, the large war vessel blocked the Flying Vulture in.

Before the few men left in her could give an alarm, their late opponent fired into them.

This was the shot that poor Jerry heard while in the treasure cave, and caused him to take that dangerous leap.

The pirates, driven almost mad by the unexpected attack, worked like demons, and looked worse.

Shot after shot they fired in rapidly at their opponent.

The commander of the war ship, seeing that by the desperation they worked, that it would be useless to ask them to surrender, had a broadside poured unto them.

With a fearful explosion, the destructive missiles crashed on the daring pirate barque, spreading destruction and scattering the fighting devils in all directions.

A shout from a troup of sailors, that rushed upon the now helpless ship, rent the air, and went echoing through the lofty tops of the towering rocks.

A shout of daring defiance of a more discordant nature, followed that of the British tars, as the bloodthirsty crew met them with a desperate onset.

A regular hand-to-hand combat then ensued, and parties on both sides fell hideously slaughtered, and strewed the deck with their writhing forms, dabbled in the swamp of steaming gore.

So determined they were not to surrender, that they appeared almost inmortal, and fought while blood was pouring from the many deep gashes they had received.

Every sense of feeling must have deserted them, and artificial strength had taken possession of their brawny frames.

As bad as they were, they were devoted to one another, and fought only to save their ship.

The captain of the man-of-war, seeing the horrible slaughter going on, ordered a second party of sailors to aid their companions.

Hardly had he given the order, before a complete troup rushed amongst the combatants, and thrust the pirates in every direction.

The fight was soon ended then.

The pirates were overpowered, but made a desperate effort to retain their liberty.

But no avail.

The sailors firmly secured them, and they were taken aboard the man-of-war, prisoners.

The remainder of the pirates had remained in the treasure cave, in deep suspense, expecting Jerry Mizzen to return as he had arranged.

His lieutenant, fearing that something had happened, had resolved not to wait any longer, but ascertain the cause of that sudden uproar that had so recently taken place.

He had barely ascended to slope that led to the terrace, when a rush of feet, coming in his direction, made him start and fall backwards.

Then he heard a loud, merry voice singing out—

"Come on, my men, this way; we'll ferret the lubbers out, and make weathercocks of them! This way, men; move your stumps."

"We are discovered, mates," gasped the lieutenant.

The men sprang to their feet.

"We will fight to the death before we yield!"

"Here, here!" shouted the men.

"Here we are," said a dashing young naval officer, sliding into the cave.

With revengeful oaths the pirates rushed upon him.

Ere they had time to put their intent into execution, at least fifty hardy-looking sailors jumped into the cave, and saved their young officer from the threatening weapons that were raised in a menacing manner over him.

"Don't be in a hurry to spit a fellow," he said, when free from their grasp.

"Ready, men? let the braggarts have it!"

The sailors dashed at their opponents, but they were met by the pirates with a determined resistance.

Urged on by their young leader, who was highly enraged by their dogged stubbornness, the English tars gave no quarter.

It was a sickening sight to see those miserable, outcast men, fighting desperately for their wretched existence.

Like unchained fiends did they dash upon their opponents, thrusting and cutting on every side, striking to the ground every one that came in their reach.

Driven to desperation, by seeing the unnecessary slaughter among their companions, the sailors rushed upon the maddened wretches.

Hitherto they had avoided as much bloodshed as possible, but seeing the brutal pirates took advantage of them for their kindness, they were enraged, and drove the bloodstained vampires back.

Horribly they shrieked and yelled when they were driven into a corner, vanquished, and seven out of the dozen slain.

Even then they would have resisted, but the sailors fell upon them, and they were quickly secured.

"I am a good mind to finish the lot here," said the young officer. "I would, too, but they will add to the number already on board to take their last leap over the bulwarks."

"A fine mess, too," he added, looking around; "five of my fine men, and seven out of twelve of these infernal lubbers. Bring them along, men!"

"Aye, aye, yer honour."

The men then followed their leader, with the pirates swearing the most vile oaths, though they knew they were so soon to depart from this world for their journey to the next.

The treasure cave was then deserted, and the costly articles strewn about, soaked in the crimson gore of the still writhing bodies.

What a tale many of those things could have told had they been but possessed of the faculties of speech—of fearful murder and bloody combats that had been enacted by different persons to possess themselves of the valuable property that now lay useless and hidden from the world, with a dozen of its victims lying around it.

"Is this the remainder of the scamps?" asked the captain, as the pirates were taken aboard the frigate.

"All but seven," said the officer.

"And why did you leave seven behind, sir?"

"Because we settled accounts with them in the cave."

"Oh, indeed; rather a stiff affray. Many of our men left behind?"

"Five, sir."

"Furies!" said the old captain, in a terrible passion, "send the captain of the marines to me."

"Ay, ay, sir," replied the young officer, going on his commission.

The captain of marines came forward, and saluted the commander of the ship.

The enraged commander ordered his prisoners to be shot overboard without delay.

His commands were readily obeyed.

The miserable wretches were placed in a line on a level with the bulwarks, and the marines, with some considerable amount of pleasure at the idea of being the executioners of these lawless men, formed a double line, and anxiously waited the word of command.

"Present!"

With a slight clicking noise the muskets were raised to their shoulders; the barrels were pointing in a line with the unflinching men, who in another minute would be hurled into a depthless watery grave.

"Fire."

A deafening report followed the word of command.

Not a sound escaped the unfortunate men's lips as the leaden missiles carried them from the ship's side.

The only sign that told they were gone before the smoke cleared away were the heavy splashes that followed in quick succession, as their quivering bodies sank into the deep waters.

As the white, vapoury smoke curled upwards from the vessel's side to the fleeting clouds, so their blood-stained bodies sank deep, deep into the bosom of the ocean with their heavy burdens of sin.

There were none to mourn their loss—no one to shed an affectionate tear for them.

They were alone in the world, and with all their life's sin and wickedness stamped upon their dark souls, they lay at the bottom of the mystic ocean, hidden from the surface of the earth for evermore.

Then another scene took place that would not leave a trace or sign to show that such a band of lawless men existed.

Their barque was towed some distance out to sea, and fired.

As the frigate slowly retreated from the ill-fated ship the roaring flames rose mountains high, and illumined the elements for miles round.

The war vessel sailed away as their victim slowly burnt out.

They had gained one victory and cleared the seas of one band of lawless men, and were now on the track of another.

*　　*　　*　　*

The many miraculous escapes Jerry Mizzen had gone through during his adventurous career, had hardened his nature and made him careless to a certain degree.

He beheld with horror the hideous-looking cragged rocks, he felt that his time had come; he knew that no earthly power could save him; he offered up a silent prayer and put his hands over his ears to shut out the crashing noise of his own body he expected would follow as he reached the bottom.

His breath was held, and every pulse seemed as though stopped, as his huge body was spinning through the air.

A loud splash followed the heavy fall of his huge body, then a long dismal howl escaped the unfortunate buccaneer's lips.

He had not fallen on the crags beneath as he thought.

Certainly no earthly power could have saved him, but the power of Providence did.

Jerry had fallen in a pool of water; he thought he had fallen on the rocks and was smashed, so lay in the water perfectly still, and fancied he was dead, though not in the least hurt.

No, Jerry Mizzen's career was not yet ended.

He was to go through more yet, his name, as was his young commander's, was to ring through generation after generation, with the startling incidents of their strange adventurous lives.

The loud shrieks and firing of guns made Jerry spring to his feet.

"Where is my body?" he said, looking wildly about. "I ain't Jerry Mizzen—no, I am his ghost."

Springing out of the water on to a rock, and looking up to the terrace, he said—

"Didn't I fall down from there? Yes, I did, on these rocks, and got smashed—where is my body then—some one has taken it away?"

Poor Jerry really thought he was not himself.

"I look like Jerry Mizzen used to look," he suddenly broke out, "I wonder if I am him after all?"

Looking at himself up and down, he said again—

"I'll try."

He tried, and made himself shout.

"I suppose I must be Jerry, then," he said.

"Ah, what's that," he exclaimed, as the shouts of men broke upon his ears. "Can it be—yes, the lubbers have taken my ship, and all my men, too."

A sudden report of musketry made him start.

"There they go," he said, meaning his men.

Then he saw his ship towed out to sea, and fired.

The tide had run up to a considerable height, and before he had time to scramble out of the water, he heard a loud sniffing and snorting close to his heels.

Turning sharply round, he beheld an old acquaintance, the huge sea monster, glaring at him savagely.

Jerry's blood ran cold at the sight of the huge tusks and hungry-looking mouth.

Darting forward, he caught hold of a branch of a tree, that hung over the rocks; but ere he had time to drag his long legs out of the water, his old enemy grabbed hold of the stern of his trousers, and a piece of the flesh, that caused him to howl.

Jerry broke out in one of his old maladies at this unexpected meeting with an old acquaintance, whom he thought he had settled in the last encounter. But the monster had recovered the slight injuries which Jerry had inflicted, and again came to torment him.

Jerry Mizzen pulled with all his strength to break away, and his old acquaintance pulled with all his strength to shake him away from his hold.

The unfortunate tar felt with horror the branch he held giving way.

The perspiration rolled off him in big drops, as he made a frantic effort to clutch a branch that hung over his head.

The sea monster saw the act, and giving a sudden jerk, Jerry went flying about a yard over its head.

No time was to be lost.

Jerry, knew this, and struck out furiously to keep ahead of his enemy.

The enemy was as quick as Jerry, and swam after him with a savage glare in its huge round eyes.

Then an exciting chase ensued.

Jerry Mizzen swam between the rocks.

His enemy swam after him.

The chase lasted more than twenty minutes, Jerrry swimming through all the crevices he came near.

His huge assailant dodged after him.

Jerry at last won the victory by squeezing himself through such a narrow opening between two large pieces of rock, that he gasped for breath, and turned blue in the face.

His enemy snorted, and bellowed violently, because he could not follow.

Jerry then scrambled up a rock, and looked down upon his enemy triumphantly.

His enemy sat beneath, and looked up at him savagely, with his huge mouth wide open.

Jerry did not like the look of that open mouth.

It looked dangerous, and made him feel uncomfortable.

"Suppose I fall?" he soliloquised, "why, I should go down that ugly great throat."

Pulling down a huge piece of rock that nearly toppled him over, he said—

"How do you do, old fellow, will yer have a pill?"

Jerry received no answer, so he thought he would try.

The huge monster looked knowingly at the upraised piece of rock in Jerry's hand, and understood his thoughts evidently, and not having any particular wish for indigestible pills, he shut his mouth as the rock fell.

The heavy piece of stone fell with a hollow sound on the monster's mouth.

The huge monster ducked his head under the water, shook its head spitefully at Jerry, and vanished.

A faint wailing came faintly across the water.

Jerry started at the sound.

He attentively listened, his heart beating against his side like a drum.

Again that faint distressing cry was borne to Jerry's ears by the gentle breeze.

Again Jerry started, and strained his eyes across the rippling water.

Again that cry came.

The dark clouds had cleared away, and the pale streaks of morn threw a subdued light on the water.

Jerry shaded his eyes with his hands, and scanned the sea.

His heart fairly leapt in his mouth as his gaze fell upon a form—a form of a female struggling to save her life!

Without another thought, or another look, Jerry sprang from the rock into the sea. The huge waves overwhelmed him, and for the moment he thought he should never rise to the surface again.

A bold swimmer, however, he soon rose above the surging waters, and striking out gallantly, he soon reached the sinking girl.

He recognised her as the one he had seen in the cabin of his late vessel.

Holding her to his breast, he with great difficulty struck out for land.

CHAPTER XXVII.
DON PARDO RECEIVES A CHALLENGE.

THE make-up of the Spanish pirate was truly formidable.

He was dressed in a sea rover's costume; big boots encased his burly legs, his sash was stuck full of heavy pistols and daggers.

His looks were of the fiercest, his whiskers black and bristly, and as if to increase the terror of his appearance, he wore on his capacious chest the grisly device of a skull and crossbones.

That he was prepared to make light work of the youthful intruder was apparent, for he twisted his moustache angrily, and regarding him with a savage glare, clutched his hand on his ponderous sword-hilt.

Whatever truculent intentions he entertained, were, however, for the moment cut short by the entry of two new-comers, who at once engaged his attentions.

The youthful intruder there looked up quickly as he saw them enter.

"Two very old friends," he muttered, "in spite of their disguise—Admiral Ellis and Officer Drummond—pirate catchers."

Smiling at his own thoughts, he yawned at his fair companion, and stretching himself out at full length along the bench, seemed to fall presently asleep.

An introduction had in the meantime taken place between Don Pardo and the new-comers.

The trio, after a few whispered words, came and sat at the table behind which our adventurer was lying.

And then the conference began.

"Don Pardo," Admiral Ellis observed, taking the measure of his man at a glance, "the authorities here have a very awkward case against you."

"Well, admiral, I can't always pick my way."

"So it appears ; but this last little affair threatens to bring your neck into a noose, unless you can work out of it."

"Trust me, senor. If any man can give the noose the slip, its Don Pardo."

"We'll say no more about that. Let us to business. Drummond has told you how that cursed Boy Pirate tricked him out of the letter of marque?"

Don Pardo swore a deep oath.

"They wouldn't have tricked me," he observed, gruffly.

"As you are aware, this letter of marque protects the bearer : it was to have given you immunity for your crimes; it now protects those pirate boys."

"S'death, senor," cried the pirate, grinding his teeth, "if this haggler had not tried to drive a bad bargain he might have put my name to it first."

"He did not; and the consequence is, you will have to take it from its present owner."

"Trust me senor. By the Virgin, I'll take it from them!"

"We should not ask you to do our work," the admiral continued, drily, "only you see, our hands are tied. We dare not attack him, but we can give you full liberty to do so."

"I understand, senor."

"Take him, and his ship as well, and the letter of marque is yours ; but, understand, if you fail, if you let him escape, if you suffer defeat, I will have you and your whole crew hanged on shore."

"Oh! don't fear, senor, I'm not likely to be beaten by these boys. Aha! I promise you, admiral, I will run out to sea, and take this boy buccaneer's ship before twenty-four hours has passed. As for the leader, I shall slice his carcass with this good blade! And now, senor, have you any more to say?"

"None, except that you may reward yourself with the treasure you'll find on board his ship."

"All right, senor, shake hands over the bargain."

Admiral Ellis drew back—

"Well, drink with me—drink success."

"You will succeed without my drinking with you, or not at all."

"S'death, senor, I drink his heart's blood! Shall I spare any of his crew?"

"Those you spare we shall hang."

The ruffian grinned, and pouring himself out a larger bumper of wine, drained it leisurely, while Admiral Ellis, accompanied by Drummond, left the place.

"Aha!" soliloquised the pirate captain; "this is a good stroke. Those dare-devil boy cruisers have a rare stowage of spoils; things could not have fallen out better. Take them! S'death, I fancy I'm the man to settle this business."

"Hallo!" he bawled, his bloodshot eyeballs resting on the sleeping stranger as he lay against the wall. "Wake up, you prying whipper-snapper. Wake, curse you, or I'll douse your baby face with this!"

He raised a full glass of wine.

The sleeper did not move.

Don Pardo eyed him savagely for a moment, but changing his mind about the wine, sent it at a gulp down his own throat.

"I'll slit your ugly weasand, curse me if I don't," he growled, stretching his huge arm towards the sleeping youth, who seemed to have specially aroused his quarrelsome spirit.

Just as he grasped him rudely by the collar, with the intention of shaking him off the bench, and forcing him to fight, a hand was laid gently on his shoulder.

Looking round, he saw a tall, cloaked individual standing by his side.

"S'death, senor, how now?" growled the pirate.

"St. Patrick, I thought I hadn't mistaken my man at all. It's Don Pardo himself I've the special honour of speaking to."

"Yes, that's me, at your and anybody's service; and now, senor, who the devil are you?"

"Faith, man, not the devil's own, or his polite self either; it's Admiral Lord Kilcrew I am, and your servant."

"Admiral — S'death, they're all sailors: Admiral you, Admiral Ellis, and the Captain Tom."

"'Tis of that same last captain I've come to speak with you. Sit here, man, and let us talk. What wine is there? It's meself will drink with you."

"So do—s'death, I like free people; and now, senor, the business?"

"Oh, 'tis easy enough; it's that same boy captain of a devil's son you're going out to fight, and harkye, man, he's the devil's own hand at a fence, and will spit you as neatly as a lark before you can wink if you cross swords with him."

"How—spit me?—to the devil with you. I'd carve a dozen such."

"Faith, 'tis not so easy; and his boy crew are the devil's own fighters, too."

"What, do you think I'm to be made afraid?"

"Not at all, at all. Hearken! It's meself that would like to tilt swords with him, and it's just a little arrangement we'll make between us. You'll let me wear your dress, and I'll fight him as captain of your ship."

"S'death, senor, no. What! Am I to be bullied off my own deck? No. I'll hash his carcass myself, but as you're eager to be in at the death, you shall come on board my vessel, and take a share in the fight. There!"

"St. Patrick keep you. It's glad am I of even that indulgence."

"But, mark me, no one else carves his hide but me."

"Unless you fail——"

"Fail? How, senor—would you insult me?"

"Faith, no; but it's a private quarrel I'm anxious to settle myself."

"So you shall, after me. Let's have more wine, senor. Prime our blood ere we go aboard."

His bellowing call brought the landlord with fresh bottles of wine, and while ruby liquor was gurgling down the braggart ruffian's throat the youthful stranger rose sleepily from the bench, and drawing his cloak tightly round his frame, sauntered behind Don Pardo.

"Hallo, there," bawled the bully, suddenly. "Silence, dog, and drink with me. Here's destruction to the ship we're going to take, destruction to her crew, and death to her leader."

Filling his flagon to the brim, he raised it to his lips, but had barely moistened his heavy mouth when the hand of the youthful stranger, laid suddenly on his shoulder, made him start, and with a curse set down his glass, and clutch his ponderous sword-hilt.

"Hold, Don Pardo," the stranger cried, "before you drink that toast, I challenge you to a wager on the result."

"Challenge the devil's imps," roared the pirate captain.

"Softly, I shall wager you, or any one of the company, my sword, which, as you see, is ruby-hilted, against yours or theirs, that you'll not conquer this Captain Tom, but that he beats you on your deck, and takes your flag."

"Dogs and devils, am I to be bearded by an unshaven boy? Draw, ere I despatch you. S'death, but I'll chastise this insolence in blood—blood!"

"Spare your rage, we'll draw blood presently. What say you to the wager?"

"Faith, man," Lord Kilcrew cried, "it's myself will be even with you there. I'll take you at your bet."

"Agreed. With Don Pardo I will settle my next wager at the time I make it."

"Stay. How shall we decide our stakes?"

"On Don Pardo's deck, where I shall be when either his flag or Captain Tom's is beneath our feet."

Lord Kilcrew leapt up.

Something in the speaker's careless tones excited his suspicions.

"Hold, man! St. Patrick, I could swear I knew you. If it's right, I and you'll not leave here till your blade has fenced with mine."

"Sheathe your sword, Lord Admiral Kilcrew; I shall take up your gauntlet on Don Pardo's deck."

"Furies!" bawled the Spanish pirate, banging his fist heavily on the table, and springing to his feet. "S'death, I'll have your name or your heart's blood before you pass."

"Back, pirate! Stand in my path, and you fall as dead as carrion!"

The daring tone thrilled every hearer's heart.

The boyish intruder stood erect.

His graceful form thrown in an attitude of easy defence, his chest expanded, his bright sword balanced for a deadly thrust.

The pirate bully was cowed.

But, still clenching his hands on his sword-hilt, with the broad blade half drawn from its scabbard, he crept nearer to his boy antagonist, and cried—

"No man ever beards Don Pardo and lives. Speak—what devil are you to challenge him? Remember, it is to the death!"

"See!"

The stranger threw aside his cloak.

Lord Kilcrew uttered a cry of surprise.

The pirate captain stared aghast.

A graceful stripling, in the costume of the King of the Boy Rovers—a chain mail of solid gold glittering on his breast—the well-known death's head and crossbones on the sleeve of his gold-braided corsair jacket.

A rich sash of crimson silk, with its jewel-hilted weapons, girding his slender waist.

There was a commotion amongst those present as they gazed on this unexpected vision.

"I am the fittest to make this wager," the boy chieftain said, with a laugh that was almost musical in its careless undauntedness; "my name is Captain Tom. Don Pardo, I challenge you to the death, and as I stand here I swear to bring your flag down, and tread as conqueror on your deck in sight of the forts on shore. Lord Kilcrew, when next we meet we will cross swords at your pleasure. For you, coward and braggart bully, as I spill this red wine in your face, so will I dabble my sword-hilt in your heart's gore when we meet on your blood-stained deck."

As the daring boy concluded, he took the goblet full of wine from the table, and hurled it in the pirate captain's brutal face.

Blinded and stung to the quick, Don Pardo, with a yell of rage and shame, cried loudly—

"The door—stab him to the heart. The reward's a thousand pouds—a thousand pounds for the death of Crptain Tom Drake!"

A fearful tumult succeeded the pirate's outcry.

Weapons flashed from their sheaths, and men crowded to the doors, to bar the passage of the dauntless boy buccaneer.

But not enough to stay him.

With his fine face flashed, his eyes brightly kindling, the princely boy leaped swiftly from their midst, his thin gleaming blade stabbing at them as they came near.

Lord Kilcrow had no time to reach him.

The pirate captain made a vain clutch at his cloak.

Captain Tom was at the door.

Here he paused, with a score of thirsty weapons pressing at his back.

Darting his sword at the first of the clamour-ing gang, transfixing the fellow through the throat, he flung his cloak on the points of their blades, and sprang into the passage.

The sudden hubbub — men's cries, the pirate's warning, the clash of steel, and the firing of pistols mingled with the death shrieks of agony from those who fell stricken to the earth by the swift strokes of death our hero dealt them as he passed.

The brutal landlord heard the confusion, and rushed forward to bar Tom's exit, by bolting the heavy door.

Doing this, he turned his back towards Tom, and got for his pains two sharp digs in the seat of honour.

Howling with the sudden pain, he dropped to the floor, and the bold-hearted boy chieftain, kicking him out of the way, opened the door and passed out.

There were several rough-looking fellows hanging about the bar, but they did not make any demonstration against his flight.

The sight of his thin long sword was enough for them.

It was crimsoned from point to hilt.

The Spanish captain, followed by a yelling crew, came furiously from the scene of tumult.

With fierce curses, Don Pardo hurled open the door, and, sword in hand, dashed into the street.

He fell back with a howling cry of rage and disappointment.

Captain Tom was gone.

CHAPTER XXVIII.

FOREST ADVENTURES.

THE unfortunate Jerry heaved an immense sigh of relief, when he found himself safely on *terra firma.*

He placed his unconscious burden upon the hard rocky ground, and shaking the spray from his garments, glanced wearily around.

But his first thought was to endeavour to bring the unconscious girl to her senses.

He wiped her face with the already soaking handkerchief, and wrung the salt water from her raven tresses.

He was well aware that people who swoon can be brought to by the aid of fresh water.

Where was he to procure any.

Was there such a thing upon the deserted place? was his next thought.

He glanced at the rocks, there was his only hope.

Hastening to the large mass of stone, he commenced searching for the precious liquid.

In a hollow in the rock he saw water—not much, true, but enough for his purpose, and he was not long in scooping it up with his hands and placing it in his hat.

It was now with a feeling of delight that he approached the inanimate form of the creole maiden, and in a few minutes he brought her to consciousness.

She gazed round with a vacant stare for some minutes; but as the dreadful scenes of the last few hours came vividly before her, she shuddered, and hid her face in her hands and wept.

But not for long did she remain thus.

Dashing away her tears, she leapt to her feet, and gazed steadily at the bashful countenance of her gallant preserver.

She seemed to comprehend the true state of affairs, for with a mournful smile she approached Jerry Mizzen, and took his great rough hand in her own tiny bronzed palm.

The scenery for miles around was beautiful.

Fruits and nuts were to be seen in abundance, which Jerry no sooner saw than his natural gallantry returned.

He picked some of the most choice fruits, and, before tasting them himself, proffered them to the handsome creole.

She took them with a faint smile, and thanked Jerry for his kindness.

At that moment his eye alighted upon a cocoanut tree, upon which hung many of the milky nuts.

"Shiver my timbers, I'll have one of them," he muttered, placing his load upon the sod, and ascended the slender tree with the agility of a cat, and after some little difficulty, returned with a couple of huge nuts, which he broke, and handed one to his companion, that she might drink the milk, the other he retained himself.

"I don't know how you feel, lady, but I feel as though I should like to cast my anchor, and lay to until I have taken a cargo of this blessed stuff. I saw while I was up that blessed spar, a stream not far off, 'spose we take our moorings thereabout.

Evidently his companion understood him, for she replied with a smile which was quite sufficient for Jerry, and he trotted on in front to find a pleasant spot for their encampment.

They seated themselves upon the bank of the stream beneath the shade of a huge tree, and made their scanty meal.

Jerry thought it advisable to rest for a short time, his late experience had taught him the value of his strength.

When the burning rays of the sun began to draw in, Jerry and his companion rose and renewed their hopeless journey.

They proceeded along the banks of the stream, but nothing met their gaze to denote the existence of any human being.

Still Jerry trudged along, always on the alert, but each moment becoming more miserable. An exclamation of surprise from the creole maiden caused him to turn quickly round.

His dusky companion stood motionless, her eyes intently fixed upon something in the distance.

Jerry Mizzen naturally followed the direction of her gaze, and apparently he too saw something rather remarkable, for he suspended his breath, his mouth wide open, and his eyes staring, as he stood in silent amazement, watching a thin black column of smoke rise from behind a thicket, and slowly ascend towards the clouds.

Each seemed equally astonished.

Neither spoke.

What could it mean?

Yet there was but one cause for such a phenonemon.

Perhaps a whole tribe of savage Indians, Jerry thought, and the supposition made him anything but comfortable.

"You must be cautious," said the creole maiden, speaking in a low voice, "this island is infested with some of the wild tribes of the south."

"Only wish I had a cutlass, and my old barkers here, then I wouldn't care for the black lubbers."

"Still it is useless to shrink from danger. Our safety depends upon how we meet it. Come."

The resolute tone in which she delivered the last words, and her firm step and determined flashing eye, caused Jerry to follow almost mechanically, and his old courage returned under her haughty tone of command.

Jerry could scarce restrain his admiration for the courageous girl, now cautiously approaching the nest of savage foes.

They were partly approaching a thicket, and now each step she took she became more cautious.

They could hear nothing.

He could see nothing but the dense column of smoke, each moment growing more dense.

They arrived at a slight declivity, that brought them in full view of the town.

Jerry Mizzen's hair began to stand on end, and his face lengthened awfully.

From the position they held they were enabled to reconnoitre the scene below.

The ground from where they stood sloped down to a hollow, thickly lined with brushwood and undergrowth.

But in the centre was a clear plot of ground, in the middle of which burnt a large fire of shrubs, dry leaves, moss, &c., and from which the column of smoke now issued.

It was not the fire, or the little valley that so astonished our adventurer and his dark companion.

Round the fire squatted five or six Indians half naked, and covered with paint, and a frightful-looking group they made.

They had evidently just ended a long journey, each one having the appearance of being very much fatigued.

So much so that they kept a continual silence, broken at intervals by a deep grunt, or the word "Waugh," from one of the eldest warriors, who sat impatiently watching two young men of his tribe preparing their meal.

"They have just returned from the hunt," exclaimed the creole girl, in a whisper.

"I shouldn't mind sharing the mess," replied Jerry, licking his mouth as he watched the cooking of savoury buffalo meat.

"They are on the war path, too, and if we are seen we shall be scalped."

"Oh, lor," murmured Jerry, his blood running cold.

The words had barely left Jerry's mouth, when a low, suppressed, guttural kind of laugh, sounded behind him.

His blood seemed to freeze in his veins, and his hair stood on end.

He turned round, and came face to face with a tall furious savage.

Jerry Mizzen stood rooted to the spot, so unexpected was the sight.

He was dumb and helpless with horror.

He felt he was lost, entirely lost.

With nothing to defend himself with from the powerful red-skin, who clutched a huge tomahawk in his hand.

He gave a diabolical grin as he stepped back and raised the murderous hatchet on high.

It whizzed through the air, and the next instant Jerry lay flat on his back upon the sward.

But not with the hatchet in his brain, as he

had imagined, though it was some seconds before he could make himself believe such was the case.

He had been saved by a miracle, or rather by the quick, determined courage of his companion.

She too had been unable to move, through the unexpected sight, but when the savage raised his hatchet she leapt forward, and as the terrible instrument cleaved through the air, she pulled Jerry down in time for the tomahawk to fly over his head and bury itself in the trunk of a tree just behind him.

"Up, up, and defend yourself!" exclaimed his brave partner, wildly.

The act had already roused all Jerry's blood, and he sprang to his feet just as his foe, with an exclamation of rage, had fitted a shaft to his bow, which he levelled in a line with Jerry's head.

Whizz.

Away went the arrow.

Jerry dropped again to the ground.

Before the red-skin could place another shaft to his bow, Jerry was upon him like a tiger.

The furious and unexpected attack caused the Indian to drop his bow and close in with Jerry.

Even now, Jerry Mizzen stood a very poor chance.

He had nothing but his fists, for he had not time to draw his clasp-knife, but his antagonist had drawn his long hunting-knife.

Jerry Mizzen seemed to have supernatural power as he struggled frantically for the possession of the murderous knife.

They swayed to and fro, now twisting and turning about, now they rolled over and over upon the ground.

Still the savage red-skin retained the knife. Jerry Mizzen fought desperately, but it is not to be wondered at, considering his weakened condition, that the Indian would be the victor, unless some unexpected event occurred to save the unfortunate seaman.

Now he flagged dreadfully, and it was with the extremest difficulty Jerry could keep the knife from entering his heart.

Indeed that was all he could do.

Now came the climax.

With a desperate effort the red-skin broke away from Jerry, and leapt to his feet, his face marked horribly with passion, and he thirsted for the blood of his foe.

A fiendish laugh escaped his lips as he brandished the knife in the air, and bounded forward to bury it in the heart of Jerry Mizzen.

Then came a whizz, followed by a death cry.

An agonising sob, and the savage lay a corpse by the side of his intended victim, an arrow still quivering through his dusky breast.

CHAPTER XXIX.

BOB HAULER GOES OUT ON A DISCOVERY.

WE will bring the faithful Bob Hauler forward, and carry him through a devoted enterprise he had undertaken to perform for his beloved young commander.

The honest tar had not been himself since the sudden disappearance of the adventurous Jerry Mizzen.

With all their peculiar ways to each other, the rough-hearted fellows were devotedly attached to one another.

Bob Hauler had been sulky and cross with every one.

He actually gave up his place at the wheel to one of his mates, and at last resolved to fathom out the hiding-place where the villanous Sanderson had put Captain Tom's uncle, John Gregory.

He could not rest aboard.

The deserted berth brought back reflections of the past, and reminded him of the many jovial hours he and his bosom companion had spent there together.

Getting leave to go ashore, he provided himself with provisions and a flask of rum. He started forth on his adventure of discovery, determined not to return until he had performed his undertaking.

Every building he came near he carefully examined, and listened for any sound that might induce him to enter.

On, on, he travelled, until nightfall, when his feet having got sore, and his legs refused to go any further, he sat down beneath a cluster of trees that hung over and shaded a pretty picturesque spot, where Nature's art had erected one of those fairy-like waterfalls, from which the silver stream gently rolled down, amid clusters of fragrant wild flowers, that perfumed the ebby flow, and dazzled the eye with their many-coloured blossoms.

It was a place such as the young love to dream of—a dell of beauty and romance surrounded by sloping hills that charmed the heart of the gazer.

Bob Hauler, who had no eyes for rural beauties, took a long draught of his rum from his flask, and prepared to go off to sleep.

At that moment the clouds were swept from the moon, and a soft blue light poured down from the heavens, and illumined the whole scene to his drowsy gaze.

In wonderment and admiration he stared about him.

Could he have been dreaming, and was that scene of loveliness the passing away shadows of his slumbers?

He rubbed his eyes with his rough hands as these thoughts passed through his mind, thinking that it must be a delusion.

But no.

It was real.

A shriek, uttered in a sweet, frightened voice, made the astonished Bob start to his feet, straining his eyes almost out of their sockets in the direction of the rippling stream, from whence he fancied the sound proceeded.

At that moment the silvery rays of the moon fell upon the form of a female, cloaked in a white robe.

The worthy tar's first impulse was to rush forward, to ascertain whether the fairy-like intruder was a mermaid or a water-spirit, but his resolution failed him, and he stood still, as the figure lightly stepped from each protruding crag, the water flowing over her tiny feet.

Had he been suddenly seized and gagged by a dozen of ruffians he would have realised his position, but to have to stand there (he could not move, he appeared as though spellbound) while a white-clothed figure, or a ghost (for he could not tell which) approached him, was more than his nerves could endure.

Uttering a miserable groan, he fell to the earth, his hair gradually rising on his head, and his eyes still fixed upon the mysterious stranger.

Presently he heard another shriek.

The being of mystery darted across the waterfall, and disappeared among a cluster of trees.

The disturbed leaves had barely subsided, when Bob was aroused from his fallen position.

He looked in the direction from which he heard very gruff voices, swearing in a most ungentlemanly manner.

He saw two men come from the same direction as did the white stranger.

The truth now flashed across his mind as he watched the two ill-looking brutal men pursue the track taken by the fair creature that had frightened him.

She was no phantom.

A mermaid?

Mermaids don't dress in white, and phantoms don't have beautiful hair like that which hung round her white shoulders like golden thread.

She must be some young lady trying to escape from their vile clutches.

Coming to this sensible conclusion, he started after them, calling himself all the lubbers imaginable.

He first caught sight of the two men who were running after their victim.

She had got ahead of her pursuers, and was speeding along with the swiftness of a frightened deer.

Like a trained Indian, Bob followed the ruffians, keeping well out of sight.

On, on they went, one running after the other, for more than a mile.

Bob Hauler was in high glee.

He had hastened his speed, and was rapidly gaining on those in front.

But, unexpectedly, his high glee was brought to a sudden termination by his striking his foot against a stubble.

He stumbled over it, his face coming in very close contact with the wild vegetation, such as stinging-nettles, thorny bushes, and heather, that did not add to the comfort and beauty of his face.

He was soon on his feet again, looking all the disgust he felt at his undignified position.

A shriek, that ran through the air like electricity, and went echoing along the valley that he had not long since quitted, made him jump up at least three feet from the earth, as though he had suddenly been shot in the spine of the back.

The men had vanished; and while glaring about, considering the best course to take, the piercing cries, in quick succession, again rang through the night air, each time growing fainter, until they died away in a gurgling, suffocated sound.

He waited to hear no more.

Dashing forward, he broke through a thicket.

There he saw the helpless girl being dragged along between her assailants.

The honest tar continued his chase with indefatigable energy.

Again he lost sight of them as they hastily turned down a long narrow lane to the left, dragging their victim with them.

Bob arrived at the top of the lane in time to see their retreating forms; he soon got close to them, but not near enough to rescue the unfortunate girl.

Fortune appeared as though turned against Bob Hauler that night.

Each time he neared the caitiffs he met with some misfortune.

He was not more than fifty yards behind them now when his foot slipped, and he sprained his ankle.

This time he began to despair, but determined not to lose sight of them, he hopped along as best he could.

It was, as fate would have it, that he was not to rescue that gentle captive, but to follow her captors, which led him to a much greater enterprise.

Gradually they were fading from his vision in the gloom, each minute taking them further from him.

He could not follow much further; the acute pain of his foot increased at every step.

He was much crestfallen and disappointed at having been thus prevented from doing an act of humanity, by liberating that fair, gentle creature from two brutal ruffians; he was about to give up the chase, when the men halted with their captive before a pair of high iron gates that enclosed a large piece of ground, in the middle of which stood a miserable, gloomy building. One of the men opened the gates with a key, and the trio entered.

"Shiver my timbers, if this ain't the werry place I'm looking for," mused the worthy Bob, as he limped up to the gates. "I suppose them lubberly gulls have captured that pretty little craft for a prize, to be mauled over. Hang me if they do, though! If I can only get alongside of 'em, I'll pour in such a broadsider that'll spoil the look of their figureheads."

Carefully examining the construction of the building as he walked round, he came to the back. Here he stopped.

"May I be dipped in a tar-barrel," he said, "and spliced at the fo'top-tail, to be laughed at, if I don't settle accounts with them swabs! "Let's see," he continued, "how am I to board 'em? If I can only get over this cussed high wall, I shall be all right."

The wall surrounding the mad-house stood ten feet high, with nothing near it by which he might aid his ascent.

A huge tree stood some distance off.

This he clambered up with the agility of a monkey.

Reaching a long, outspreading branch, he crawled along it on all fours, with the confidence of the before-mentioned chattering individual, until he reached the extreme end that overhung the wall.

To this he hung by his hands, the branch gradually lowering.

Imagine his terror when he looked down, and there beheld a shed covered with glass.

He could not get back again, because the branch was cracking; the least jerk the branch would break, and then——

He shuddered to think of the consequences.

He fancied he could hear the crash as he disappeared; then the vision of himself appeared before his eyes in a most deplorable condition, still grasping the treacherous branch in his hand.

He groaned loudly; he could feel himself going.

Making one desperate effort to save himself, he made a clutch at a few leaves above his head. He caught them, but they gave way. So did he.

A dismal howl was succeeded by a fearful crash, as his legs made way for his body through the glass; then there came a splash, a loud shout of many voices from below, and a loud scampering of feet.

The unfortunate Bob was pulled out of a cistern of water, amid the shouting and cuffs of his rescuers.

Fortunately for him he fell into the water, otherwise he would have broken his neck on the flagstones beneath.

"Hallo!" said one of the men, "how did you come here?"

"Ain't he one of 'em escaped?" asked a second man.

"No," said a third; "'cos he fell through the top."

"How did you get here?" demanded the first speaker, digging his knuckles in Bob's neck. "Answer me, you ill-looking vagabond."

"All right, yer honour," said Bob Hauler. "If you'll take them 'ere grappling-irons out of my neck, I'll tell you."

"Make haste about it," said a voice behind him.

"Look sharp," repeated another, slashing him across the legs with a whip.

Bob jumped up to avoid it.

In doing so he bent forward, striking a man in the wind with his head, that sent him rolling over and over like a ball.

For that act he received such a terrific clout between the shoulders that he could not speak for several minutes.

"If you don't say what you came here for in another minute," exclaimed one of the whip-holders authoritatively, "we'll give you a hundred lashes; that will soon make you speak."

"Clear the decks," shouted Bob in a terrible passion, dashing amongst them, "yer ugly-looking cowards! Do you think you will do as you like with a British tar."

"Secure him!" shouted the men in confusion, at one another.

"Put a stopper on yer jaw," shouted Bob, flooring a fellow with a tremendous blow in the mouth.

The fight was growing desperate.

Every minute added to poor Bob's assailants.

He could not contend much longer against such fearful odds.

He was receiving kicks and lashes on all sides.

Catching two men by the throat, he hurled them forward.

He made his escape in a terrible plight through a side door.

He had scarcely got on the threshold when, with a yell, his assailants dashed after him.

Bob, not liking the idea of fighting against a dozen men armed with gutta-percha thonged whips, took to his heels.

Being very fleet on his feet, he sped along at a rate that would have done credit to an Indian, and soon left his pursuers a considerable distance behind.

Seeing it would be fruitless to continue the chase, they returned to their cheerful asylum.

Each to torture some innocent and sane person to madness by their systematic cruelty.

Bob was not aware that his pursuers had retired.

On he kept.

Never once turning his head.

Every minute he expected to feel a hand grasp his shoulder.

So fearful was he of being re-captured, that he did not notice a treacherous pond, covered with long wavy grass, until it was too late to avoid it.

He made a sudden stop.

But his foot slipped.

In he went.

Head first, under the thick, slimy water, and came up the other side covered with the green filth.

Grasping hold of some short stubbles, he drew himself out, and again started off at the speed of the antelope.

Never slackening his pace, until he reached a small and dimly-lighted beer-shop.

A house where he knew he could find some of his messmates.

A loud shout of laughter greeted him as he entered.

"Bear a hand, mates, to unfurl my sails," cried Bob, holding out his arms for his men to pull his jacket off.

"Where have you been steering to, Bob?" asked one of the crew, laughing loudly at the deplorable state of his messmate. "I should say you ran into the Black Sea."

"Hand over the grog basin, mate, then I'll tell yer."

"I say, Bob," said another, "you wouldn't look worse if you had been keelhauled?"

"Avast, yer lubbers," cried Bob, greatly disgusted at the comparisons passed on him by his shipmates; "where is Lieutenant Harold?"

"Well, Bob," replied the young officer, coming forward, "where the deuce have you been to get into that mess?"

The slimy Bob looked at his nauseous condition with a long rueful face, and related how it occurred.

"Why were the men pursuing you?" asked the young officer, laughing.

"Well, yer honour, I'll tell you how it happened."

"Do," he said, "but you had better change your things."

"It ain't the first time I have slipped overboard."

"Proceed then."

"Well, you know I had leave to go ashore," he began. "I thought to myself the captain wants to find out where Mr. Gregory is, so I started off. I had been walking all day, when I was obliged to drop anchor. I hadn't been there long, when I heard a scream. I looked up, and saw one of the most pretty crafts that ever set sail. At first I thought she was a ghost or a water spirit, but she gave another signal of distress, and darted through some trees.

"Then I saw two ugly-looking sharks running after her.

"I jumped up and followed.

"They captured their prize just when I was going to grab 'em, but I slipped.

"They got ahead of me again, and I saw 'em enter a large iron gate, and lock it after 'em. I got over the wall and fell throw

"CAPTAIN TOM DRAKE, I ARREST YOU."

some glass. Then the lubbers captured me, and that was how it was I fell into the pond when I escaped."

"You did not continue your search for the mad-house."

"No, yer 'onner, 'cos that was the werry identical place."

"How know you this?" asked the young officer, in surprise.

"'Cos, yer 'onner, them lubbers that laid their whips about me was the keepers, and I heard screaming and loud groans from inside."

"Are you certain?"

"Yes, yer 'onner."

17

Another young buccaneer, who had heard the last part of Bob's recital, stepped forward and grasped his shoulder.

By this time the crew had clustered round, looking on in amazement at the strange scene.

Bob, who was held in a grip like a vice, began to feel uncomfortable, and thinking that he might have done wrong, stammered out—

"I—I—h-o-o-pe, yer 'on-on-er, I ain't done wrong?"

"No, no," cried the young officer, clasping his rough hand warmly.

With the aid of the two young officers, the

honest tar concocted a plan by which they could gain admittance to the mad-house.

One of the officers, being a better scholar than Bob Hauler, wrote a letter to the keeper of the asylum, stating that he wished to put under his care a friend who was in a very unsound state of mind, and dangerous to be at large, offering a large sum of money by way of temptation.

The following morning they received an answer from the master, stating that he would be most happy to receive their friend, vowing that he should have every care and indulgence.

Bob Hauler, who was to act the lunatic, was attired in a most quaint fashion, and taken to the mad-house by the two officers, who were dressed as private gentlemen.

They were admitted by one of the keepers— to speak the truth, one of the tormentors.

"Who do you want, sir?" asked the man.

"The master," replied Harold.

"He is engaged, and cannot see any one this evening," returned the man.

"He will see me," said the officer; "tell him Sir Harold Oswald is here, by appointment."

The man disappeared and the master appeared.

"Good evening, sir," said the new comer, bowing and scraping, "I presume this is my new patient. I trust, sir, you have not had much trouble in bringing him here."

"Oh, no," replied Harold. "I brought him in my brougham (one he had borrowed for the occasion). He was a considerable deal quieter than he usually is. Probably he thought by being quiet he would be indulged in the luxury of a drive through the country every day."

"Not at all unlikely; they are very artful," replied the master. "I had better take him to his chambers. I will see that he shall have the best of everything."

"You needn't trouble yourself," thought Bob, "I'll look out for myself."

"Yes, yes," he said aloud, "you will take me to see her—ha, ha, ha! Behold!" he shouted, sending his arms out suddenly, catching the master a smack on the face that made him reel round—"behold her. There she goes. 'Tis my Cassandra. Look, look. She is dressed in white. Two men are running after her. Stop them. Ha, ha, ha! A sailor has rescued her—he brings her to me—she is saved, saved! Cassandra, Cassandra, Cassandra!"

Uttering the last words in a whisper, he collapsed, and fell back, sending the master sprawling, falling on him with his whole weight, that shook the breath out of the unfortunate man.

Harold and his companion tried to keep a serious face, but the excellent manner in which Bob took the part made the two laugh outright.

"Laugh," said Bob, getting up and making a peculiar grimace to his superior officers, which they understood, and returned by a wink. "Laugh, fools, laugh!"

"Come, come," said the master, trying to speak kindly, all the time feeling as though he would like to tickle his feet with a feather until he went into laughing convulsions; but saving his vengeance for a more favourable opportunity, he continued persuasively, "I will take you to the Lady Cassandra."

"He, he, he, he!" laughed Bob. "You take me to Cassandra? She is in my state cabin. Away, sir. Take yer hand off a captain of his majesty's navy, or by the sweet breeze that is blowing the golden ringlets of Cassandra, I will have you swung to the yard-arm before to-morrow. Lead on, man," he continued, "I will follow thee."

The master led the way to a chamber prepared for the supposed lunatic.

Bob followed him, cutting some most ridiculous antics behind him.

The young buccaneer officers then took their leave, promising Bob that they would keep the secret to themselves.

Bob Hauler had not been there long, before he discovered where John Gregory was kept, and paid the old gentleman a visit.

The old gentleman was not so mad as had been reported, and Bob Hauler was sane on the instant, though an awful lunatic when any of the community belonging to the establishment were near him.

"I beg pardon, yer honour, for intruding," he said, entering.

John Gregory started to his feet, and looked inquiringly.

Then his countenance changed with a look of recognition, and stepping forward, he said—

"I know you."

"You ought to," muttered Bob.

He did.

He had not forgotten a pair of smugglers who occupied a certain portion of the bay near to his estate, which Sanderson was enjoying.

"Who are you?" asked the old gentleman.

"You just now said you knew."

"You were a smuggler, and saved my dear nephew."

"Now I am a buccaneer, and serve under his flag."

"Are you one of his brave men?"

"Yes, your honour."

"Why are you here?"

Bob told him.

The old gentleman listened with much excitement and interest to the sailor's story, when their conversation was brought to a sudden climax by a timid tapping at the door.

Bob instantly threw himself into a wild and ludicrous attitude.

John Gregory knew the sound, and told him to compose himself.

"Douse my toplights," muttered Bob, as a most pretty girl of about eighteen entered, "if that ain't the werry one I tried to save the other night, and——"

"That is one of my nephew's brave men," said the old fellow, introducing Bob Hauler.

The worthy tar pulled his forelock, and saluted her as he would a superior officer.

The young lady laughed sweetly though sadly at his peculiar way.

"She can't be mad," thought Bob.

His conjecture was correct.

Then why was she confined in that asylum?

She had told John Gregory why, and her history had corresponded with his own; she had been placed there by a relation who coveted her property.

She was an heiress to an immense fortune, which she came into at her father's death.

Since then she lived with an uncle, a greedy, avaricious man, who knew she had no relations near but herself, and taking advantage of her unprotected position, he placed her in the asylum, and took possession of her property.

CHAPTER XXX.

THE BOY ROVERS' FIGHT WITH THE PIRATES.

THE news of Captain Tom's audacious visit to the pirates' haunt ran like wildfire through the town.

His disappearance was more than a mystery.

People did not hesitate to own he had dealings with the Evil One, and bore a charmed life.

They shook their heads when they heard of Don Pardo's intended enterprise, for it got rumoured that he was engaged to fight the boy buccaneer and bring down his flag.

The sensation was not lessened when, with the morning light, Captain Tom's ship was seen riding gracefully at anchor, her banner of death floating ominously in the freshening breeze.

When, at a later hour, Don Pardo's vessel was seen making signs of departing on its desperate mission, the excitement grew more intense.

Some thought the chances were in favour of the Spanish pirate and its swarthy crew of blood-thirsty ruffians.

But others believed that the boy crew of Captain Tom were protected by the fell agency of the Evil One, whose dusky arm, invisible, but not less potent, they declared held aloft his flag, while his fearful breath sent a death blast into her sails, to lift her from the line of the enemy's fire.

By the time the pirate's sails were set to the wind, and the deadly preparations were made for the coming fight, the shore was lined with the thousands who awaited with the keenest excitement the result.

The men-of-war and vessels in the harbour had their flags flying.

Boats were ready to be lowered in case of need, and guns were shotted and run out in hope that some turn of the battle might give them a chance of joining in.

The sun was shining brightly on the clear waters when the pirate's sails took the wind, and the heavy vessel made her way slowly to sea.

She was a bigger vessel than that of the young sailors, and her armament appeared more deadly.

Hitherto it had been disguised, but now every gun was run out, and along her hull and stern the gaping muzzles yawned like mouths of hell.

Her fierce marauding crew were armed to the teeth and clustered on her decks, where, moody and savage, her bloodthirsty captain stalked in a furious state of rage.

A more graceful and well-proportioned figure paced moodily aft.

Admiral Lord Kilcrew.

Not a sign of preparation for the conflict was made as yet by the boy sailors.

The graceful sea cruiser lay idly on the smooth waters.

Not a gun destroyed her peaceful guise.

Quietly, placidly she lay in the sight of all, with scarcely a soul visible on her decks, and only her black banner flaunting from her mizzen peak, indicated the desperate character she could without warning assume.

As Don Pardo's mission was to intercept her departure, his manoeuvre was to get past her without exchanging any challenge, so as to stand between her and the sea.

Amidst breathless suspense the Spanish pirate executed this movement, and his success was rewarded by a loud cheer from the ships and shore.

Still no token of defiance or defence from the ship of the Boy Cruisers.

People began to think those on board were awed by the superior weight and metal of their big adversary, and were showing the white feather.

There would be no fight after all.

She was afraid to venture out.

The big pirate, standing off about a mile from shore, tacked suddenly, and stood still.

She was right in their track now.

To get past they must take the edge from her bristling teeth.

A minute's ominous pause.

The pirate had taken up her position.

No sign yet from the Boy Cruisers.

The pirate was evidently chagrined at her silence.

Suddenly a puff of white smoke left her side.

She had thrown out her challenge, and the iron missile came hurtling over the sea.

Up to this moment there had been, as we have said, scarcely a sign of life on board the cruiser ship.

Now the change was magical.

As if the discharge of that gun had acted like a wizard's wand, her white sails dropped instantly from her yards.

She rocked on the smooth waves — took motion, and with a graceful sweep glided out to sea.

An ominous silence still reigned on her decks —her motion through the water was slow, but was full of defiant grace as she moved direct towards her savage antagonist.

Within hail of the big pirate, she stood suddenly motionless.

A small red ball ran up her halyards.

It fell.

A red flag, with the insignia of death, streamed in the wind.

The pirates received this with a derisive cheer.

Then a fierce voice gave the word to fire.

Almost before the command left the pirate's lips, the whole hull of the cruiser ship was enveloped in white smoke and sheeted flame.

Her every timber seemed to strain as she reeled under the rebound of her own guns, the roar of which rocked the very air, as with a thundering crash her deadly broadside poured full against the pirate's hull, and swept her decks.

This sudden beginning of the fight seemed to take half the sound out of the pirate's broadside as it came in answer.

The cruiser ship, rebounding from the shock, tacked swiftly, and fired again.

And now from both ships came intermittent jets of flame, and thunder of guns, till the clouds of smoke hid both vessels from the spectators' gaze, and only the concussion of their volleys told of the work of destruction hotly raging between them.

The commodore, Admiral Ellis, and a host of others to whom Tom was known, stood on the deck of a war frigate watching the uncertain fray.

Till the smoke hid both ships, they followed eagerly the movements of the pirate, but now they could only judge of what was going forward by the difference in the sharp ring of Tom's guns and the sullen roar of the pirate's.

For fifteen minutes this frightful cannonade echoed along the shore, and then, as the sharp rattle of firearms mingled with the clashing of steel, and the ruthless cries of the fierce combatants, the sulphurous haze cleared slowly away, and the two ships were seen locked together in a deadly grip.

It was hard to say which had the advantage now.

The big pirate rolled heavily and labouring, her sails were riddled and torn, her ropes severed, her masts shivered, her spars splintered to pieces.

Half of her bulwarks were shot away, and the sea rushed in at some ugly holes in her hull.

But still, though riddled and rent, her flag floated defiantly overhead.

The cruisers' ship lay close in to her big antagonist.

She had sustained, like her terrible foe, damage above board, but her graceful hull seemed yet intact, and her prow, with its sweeping lines, rode more lightly on the rocking waters.

Her banner, too, flaunted in defiance from her peak. She moved proudly through the waters in spite of her condition, and the men on board uttered yells of rage and defiance.

Black ominous clouds were rising on the horizon, the wind moaned through the torn rigging, and the angry waves lashed the side of the disabled vessel in fury.

The men worked at the pumps until they were black in the face, but the water gained upon them.

Admiral Ellis took a swift survey of their situation through his glass.

CHAPTER XXXI.
THE BRIDGE ACROSS THE STREAM.

For the instant Jerry was not aware that he had not got an arrow quivering in his breast, when his would-be murderer collapsed, and suddenly fell in a heap at his feet, but his gentle preserver bounded to his side with the fleetness of a fawn, and reassured him that he was safe.

Jerry breathed again.

"Was that you that settled that black lubber?" he asked of the Creole girl who had so bravely preserved him.

"Yes," she said, "but hush, we shall disturb the tribe."

"Shall we?" he said, looking scared. "I don't want the cowardly lubbers to give chase now."

"Why?" asked his companion, with a smile.

"Because I can't run till I have had a dish of their mess, then I could settle the lot by myself."

"We will hide; they are very tired, and will soon fall asleep."

"And I don't care how soon they do," said Jerry, as they crept noiselessly through a cluster of thick foliage close behind the feeding savages. "I feel as though I have got a shark in me. I should think you feel fearfully hungry, don't you, what shall I call you?"

"My name is Creula. I don't remember any other—that's what the captain used to call me."

"A pretty name."

Creula smiled, but did not reply.

"Where do you intend to go now?" asked Jerry.

"With you."

"Well, o' course you will until we gets out of this blessed port where there's no straight steering; for we are sartain to run foul o' something, but, missus, ain't you got any parents—I think the land lubbers calls 'em father and mother—I means."

A shade came over the bronzed face of his companion, and heaving a deep sigh, she said, sorrowfully—

"I have been alone since I was very young, with no one to care for me, until the captain took me. I have often wished I might die."

Jerry drew the cuff of his sleeve across his eye, and a large lump stuck in his throat.

"Never mind, my dear, cheer up. Lord love them pretty eyes. When I sees 'em dim, mine is sure to spring a leak. But bless yer pooty little 'art, there's them yet that'll care for you, and what's better than a honest sailor's wife?" said Jerry, taking her dusky little hand.

He had great difficulty in getting out the word honest, for at the moment he was about to utter the word, his old smuggling career passed vividly before his mind, and he fancied he could see the casks of contraband brandy snugly ensconced in the recess of the old cave.

Creula thanked him with a smile.

"Could yer iver love sich an old skunk as me, d'ye think?" he asked.

"Why not? You are a gallant, good-hearted sailor, brave as a warrior, and have you not saved my life? Then what more does a woman want? Yes, Jerry, I love you."

"Yer do? Lord love yer—yer shall never be sorry for them words! Love an old hulk like me—strike my toplights!" exclaimed Jerry, bringing his hand down with a loud slap on his thigh, and rolling his tongue round his cheek, forgetting in his present bliss, he had no quid there. "And yer will stay with me?"

"Hush!" she said, placing her finger on her lip for silence.

"Ah!" she continued, in a whisper, "as One is keeping sentry over his sleeping companions."

"Can we not get some of their provisions?"

"If we are careful it can be managed."

"How?"

"I must think."

While Creula was planning their course of action, Jerry peeped over in the direction of the fire, round which the Indians were sleeping.

He saw his preserver had spoken too true.

Standing with his back towards the fire was a red-skin of great stature, his right hand resting upon his spear, evidently keeping a strict watch over the others.

This was unfortunate.

He turned, and looked at Creula for advice. She appeared troubled and perplexed.

"We have only one chance," she said.

"And that?" asked Jerry.

"Is to kill him."

"Well, self-preservation is the first law of nature," said Jerry, appealing to a very old piece of divine philosophy, "and besides, it don't matter so much, seeing as how he is a savage—perhaps a kannybile." (He meant a cannibal.)

"Come, then," said Creula, speaking in a whisper, and creeping stealthily forth.

Jerry followed, clutching the knife in one hand and the hatchet in the other, both of which he had taken from the dead Indian.

As soon as they got in a clear space, Creula took an arrow and fitted it to the bow.

She glanced from the barb of the arrow to the fearful savage, for the space of a few seconds.

Then came the twang of the bow-string, and the arrow sped on its journey of death.

Whizz.

Jerry tried to watch its progress, but could not. He saw its effect.

So sure had been the aim taken by the brave girl, it entered the Indian's breast, went through his very heart's core, and passed through his back.

Without a cry or a groan he threw up his arms, and fell upon his face—dead.

Jerry could not restrain his admiration for the brave girl.

"She beats all I ever come a-nigh," was Jerry Mizzen's mental observation.

"Now," said Creula, "we must be cautious, or all is lost! Hide while I——"

"If I do may I be hanged!" said Jerry. "What, me skunk away, while you go among that set of murdering villains! No, Jerry ain't quite sich a lubber as that, neither."

"I didn't ask you to stay because I feared your courage, Jerry dear; but courage will not save us from those bloodthirsty wretches."

"Perhaps not, but I ain't a going to let you go into danger."

"Then what we have done is useless. We must stay here and starve," she said sorrowfully.

"Why, ain't it better for me to go than you?" asked Jerry, softening down.

"No. I know their customs. I was brought up in the woods, and I could walk among them a dozen times without disturbing one, so if you will keep watch, but do not move from where I leave you, I will go and take what we require without waking any, then we can be far away by sunrise."

But, however, it was not without a deal of persuasion that Jerry Mizzen could be induced to hide, in case of a surprise.

Creula then cautiously started off on her enterprise, and Jerry was left alone.

He stood for some minutes in a state of great anxiety.

A wild unearthly whoop rent the air.

His blood ran cold.

He was about to rush forward, thinking his lady love was in danger, when he was struck back into the thicket, and he fell amongst the brushwood.

At first he thought he was being attacked by the whole troop of savages, until the gentle voice of Creula bade him keep the strictest silence.

"Take this," she said, handing a piece of something like buffalo meat to Jerry.

He took it without replying.

"Can you creep along on your face?" she asked.

"I'll try," replied Jerry.

"Quick, then." As Creula spoke, she threw herself down, and crept away, by a peculiar motion of the body.

They had not proceeded far when another yell sounded close behind them.

Jerry's hair began to stand on end.

Still each kept on in the same silent manner.

The savage redskins were beating about in all directions for the slayer of their companion.

Several passed so close to Jerry as to touch the handle of his knife; the savage looked down, could see nothing, so proceeded with his search.

A few seconds after that narrow escape another came and stepped upon the loose dress of Creula, but being so excited, he thought of nothing but uttering wild yells and brandishing a huge tomahawk.

Perhaps there were never before two such miraculous escapes from the redskins as those just recorded.

Jerry lay, hardly daring to breathe for fear an Indian should be near.

For quite twenty minutes they remained thus, neither daring to move or speak.

The suspense was horrible.

More than once did Jerry think of springing up and taking his chance with Creula.

But greatly to his joy, she told him they were safe for a time at least.

"I ain't sorry, but we had better keep our weather eye open; I don't want to be run down in the fog by them pirates."

"They won't return for many hours; now let us have our meal."

Jerry did not wait for a second invitation for that.

He sat upright and glanced, or rather tried to see, what it was he had been holding in his hand, but the darkness was intense and the attempt was a failure.

Still Jerry would not—using his own phraseology—"be done," so he placed his nose to the article, and found it to be a delicious piece of buffalo meat.

Jerry thought he had never smelt anything so beautiful; he therefore took another long sniff in consequence.

The savoury odour caused his mouth to water; chancing the quality of the meat, he took a big bite, and ate it with much relish.

The taste was delicious, and the rich gravy that ran from it set his ravishing pangs of hunger in motion, and caused him impulsively to ram the remainder in his mouth.

The greasy meat slipped down his throat with a gulp, and nearly choked him, as a thought suggested itself to him.

He had forgotten his companion.

"Cuss me, if I ain't a glutinous lubberly son of a shark," said Jerry, vehemently.

"Why are you calling yourself these curious names?" asked Creula, surprised at her gallant lover's sudden outbreak.

"Ain't I been an' eat all the meat and never gave you none."

"Never mind, Jerry, there is plenty more," said the pretty brunette, looking at him fondly.

"Shiver my timbers if I ever knowed such a darling as you," remarked the buccaneer, kissing her with an ardent affection. "Do you think we can get any more stuff like that?—it was fine."

"Plenty more," she said; "come with me."

Jerry followed her as stealthily as a cat to where the dusky Indians had not long since been doing a sumptuous meal.

Jerry, with his courageous companion, seated himself beside the still kindling fire and soon diminished the quantity of buffalo meat left there.

"I feel like Jerry Mizzen used to feel," remarked the quaint fellow.

"Why?"

"The reason I feel like Jerry Mizzen used to feel is, because I have had a good meal," he said, throwing his arms out and stretching himself full length on the sward; "but I feel better than Jerry used to feel, and the reason I feel better than Jerry used to feel when he felt his best is because I have got you to love me."

"You are a funny fellow," said his companion, patting his weather-beaten cheek.

"Do you like funny fellas?" asked Jerry, curiously.

"I like you," was her frank reply.

"Will you always like me as much as you do now?"

"Always."

Jerry got sentimental, and passing his arm round her slender waist, laid her pretty brown cheek on his shoulder, and toyed with her rich black tresses.

"Oh! lor!" murmured Jerry, heaving a deep sigh, "ain't she beautiful! I wish I was in England. I would get spliced, so as no one couldn't take her from me."

His head lowered until his lips reached hers.

Thus they sat for some time until the fire had nearly burned out; then Jerry raised his companion's head from his breast.

She was asleep.

They slept until nearly dawn, when by instinct they both awoke.

They finished the remainder of the meat and fruit for their breakfast.

"Oh! yes, I dare say; but I never wait for that, I always provide for myself."

"Hush, Jerry; it is very wicked of you to talk like that," she said, angrily, "the hand of Providence guides everything to be done."

"Does it? I am very sorry, only you know what I meant. Why, I meant to say that I'd cruise about to-day for a port."

"You should explain more explicitly."

"Who's he?"

Creula smiled, and playfully smacked his face.

"Well, do you think I could let you live in this place? Not for Jerry."

"I am happy anywhere with you, dear Jerry."

"So am I with you, only I should be happier anywhere else."

"You are a dear, kind fellow, Jerry, and I know not how to express my gratitude."

"Don't say that—say that you love me."

"Fondly."

"Now," said Jerry, "we will go in search of a home."

"Come, then," said Creula, springing to her feet, and taking her companion's hand.

The honest tar took her little hand, and they started off.

They had been traversing for nearly two hours, when they saw a clear rippling stream that ran through the forest.

A rudely-constructed bridge had been erected across, evidently made by the savage tribe that infested those parts.

Jerry laid on his face and took a long draught of the silvery stream; his companion drank by the same means; and barely had they appeased their thirst, when long, savage whoops and yells made them start to their feet.

Jerry sprang on to the bridge, clasping Creula securely by his side, then a savage shout rent the air.

Our adventurer looked scared by this unexpected outburst.

The exulting yells rose as though from the earth, rending the air as they rose, echoing through the lofty trees, and dying away in dismal hisses.

Creula gave an involuntary shudder.

"Jerry," she said, "we have left all our arms."

"So we have," said Jerry, his face lengthening as he thought of their helpless position; "even my knife. We can't go back, because them sneaking lubbers would jump on us."

"Where do you think they are concealed?"

"I don't know," said Jerry.

A shower of arrows flew from a thicket, and whizzed over the wanderers' heads.

This was followed by a deafening shout, as the dusky tribe rushed from their place of concealment and gathered in a group round the foot of the bridge.

"What do you want?" asked Jerry.

The Indians threw up their arms in violent gesticulations.

"What do you mean?"

They hurled very formidable-looking bludgeons at the bold speaker, jabbering away savagely in a language incomprehensible to Jerry's conception.

Creula understood their tongue, and translated what they said into English.

She told Jerry the savages wanted the white man's scalp.

"Come on," said Jerry, rolling up his sleeves; "you want my scalp, do you, you lubbers?"

Two of the brawny brutes pulled themselves up on to the narrow bridge. Jerry stood in their path as they rushed at him; sending out his clenched fist from the shoulder, he struck the foremost one a terrible blow between the eyes.

Uttering a fierce yell, he fell backwards, rolled off the bridge, and floated down with the stream, stunned. His companion's foot slipped, and he fell into the water, following the other, on his back.

"Two of 'em gone without much trouble," remarked Jerry satisfactorily.

"And a dozen more coming," said Creula.

A dozen more came for revenge.

They got it.

Crowding on the narrow plank which Jerry took possession of, they commenced a furious attack upon the unfortunate buccaneer and his bride.

Creula, like her companion, fought bravely, and sent several flying into the water.

Jerry's strength began to flag, the many uncouth blows he had received from his opponents' heavy cudgels had rendered him almost powerless, and he knew it would be useless to attempt to contend against such fearful odds, and taking a quick survey of his position, and rushing at his foremost assailants, he sent them sprawling, then catching Creula up under his left arm, he sprang into the water.

At that instant there came a fearful crash, succeeded by horrible shrieks and groans, then the bridge, with its dusky burden, came crashing into the water.

A voice from the shore warned Jerry of his danger.

The brave girl struggled to break away from his arms, but Jerry, despite all her struggles, held her securely, and saved her by swimming gallantly to the shore as the mass fell in.

A kindly voice cheered him for his gallant bravery, and a helping hand took Creula from the exhausted Jerry's arms as he reached the water's edge.

The brave adventurer dragged himself out of the stream and grasped the hand of a fatherly person who stood with the Creole girl leaning on his breast for support.

Jerry, through the labour and excitement of the struggle, was faint and exhausted.

The old fellow who had rendered him so much timely assistance poured a little brandy down the throat of the fainting girl, and then handed the flask to Jerry.

Jerry took it with a greedy but grateful look, and nearly drained the contents down his throat.

"There, my son, I guess you are better after that," said the kind old fellow.

"Yes, thank you," said Jerry, "that's something like a drop of grog."

"The lady will be all right presently; get a little water in your hat."

The tender-hearted sailor looked at his companion with tears in his eyes; it touched him to see her so inanimate and helpless; he was in doubt whether she would return to consciousness.

Kneeling by her side he tenderly bathed her temples.

The old gentleman, noticing Jerry's sorrow, reasoned with him that his Creula would soon be better.

"Do you think she will ever come to life again?"

"Oh! yes; it ain't the fust time Ben Hunter has seen a pretty girl faint."

"I wish she would open her eyes and speak to me," murmured Jerry.

She opened her eyes and faintly smiled at him, then she took Ben Hunter's rough hand in hers, and gratefully thanked him for his kindness.

"Don't thank me, my dear; it's no more 'an one critter ought to do for another," replied the old fellow, warmly.

"How did you manage to knock them black lubbers overboard?" broke in Jerry, suddenly.

"Oh," said Ben Hunter, smiling, while he handled a huge hatchet, "tarnation blazes to their dirty souls, I knocked the props down with this."

"The staves I suppose you mean," said Jerry, using his nautical terms.

"Wal, the foundation, if yer like; it don't make a tarnation bit o' difference to me so long as I stopped their cussed game."

"I don't know how to thank you, but—"

"Never mind about that, so come down to the settlement with me and see the missus, if you ain't got anywhere else to go."

"No, I ain't got anywhere to go, because I was just looking for a place."

"Does yer mean to say that you are walking about the forest?"

"I does."

"How did yer get down here?"

"I was 'recked."

"Then how long have you been here?"

"So long that I forget."

"Then you shan't remain here any longer; it shall never be said that Ben Hunter ever refused a fellow critter a part of his caboose. come, my son, and bring yer pretty little wife; the missus will make a great fuss with her, and my son George will be happy to have a companion; come on."

Jerry and his companion readily accepted the kind offer, and went with the old fellow some two miles, when they came to a small settlement.

The old fellow introduced his new acquaintances to his wife and son, and ordered a sumptuous meal to be got ready for them, which they did not refuse.

Jerry and George Hunter soon became bosom companions, and so day after day passed happily.

Until at last a cloud came to throw a blight on the happy home, and tear the loving friends asunder, and leave the old people desolate and miserable.

Great excitement prevailed the whole of one day amongst the small congregation. They had received news that a ship had run into a small port not far from the settlement.

Such a thing was so uncommon that they were all ready to receive the sailors in their open arms, to gain what news they could from abroad.

The sailors flocked into the little settlement the following day, and the captain, a half Frenchman, distributed various articles amongst the inhabitants. The half of the crew were French, and the other half was a mixture of Spanish and English.

The hunters pressed the captain to stay with them, as they had the most room and more convenience than their neighbours.

The captain accepted their hospitality with many thanks, and stayed.

It would have been better had he not.

But he did, and there was no preventing it.

Seeing by Jerry's appearance that he was a sailor, the captain got into conversation with him.

Thus Captain Debuscan, learning that Jerry Mizzen was a very clever sailor, and understood more about navigation than he did himself, persuaded him, under false pretences, to sign ship's articles, which the unsuspecting sailor did.

The ship was to start on the third day from the engagement for England, as arranged.

On the second day Jerry was to take leave of his friends, to ship.

A very touching scene ensued when he parted from his brunette bride, and not without a desperate struggle was it that he tore himself away reluctantly and made his way to the ship.

The kind old people with whom he left his bride promised faithfully to look after her and protect her from every evil.

Jerry believed them, and went happily to his ship, though feeling very miserable at having to part from his future bride.

He took a minute inspection of the ship and her crew when on borrd.

She ship presented a suspicious appearance to his searching gaze. The crew he noticed in particular; they were of various nations, most of them being French, and showing very much the appearance of pirates to Jerry's suspicious imagination.

Night wore on, and Jerry paced up and down on his watch, deeply absorbed in thought.

"I don't like the look of her," he muttered; "I wish I hadn't left Creula now."

Tramp, tramp, and he paced along the deck.

Heavy clouds hung around the vessel like sombrous black palls. Not a star or a streak of light broke through the heavy vapours that shrouded the face of the heavens, and everything tended to give a gloomy appearance to his distracting thoughts.

"I wish I had not come on board," he continued. "I know these lubbers are pirates by the cut of their figger 'eds."

"Creula," he murmured, "Creula, I wish I could come back to you; something seems to say that you are not safe there."

His cogitations were interrupted by the sound of the captain's gig approaching. Jerry hid himself as the boat came alongside. A scuffle ensued with the crew of the boat and some captives they were bringing along.

"Let me go!" he heard some one implore.

"Curse you, I'll brain you if you don't stop yer jaw."

"Why should you take us from our homes?" said another.

"Put a stopper on the lubber's jawing-tackle, mate," suggested one of the sailors.

His mate put a stopper on his mouth.

Or rather a dirty hand, which is all the same.

It stopped the man's talking, and nearly made him sick.

That was all they wanted.

Captain Debuscan clambered up the side of the vessel, sprang on deck, and in a terrible passion commanded the men to bring along their captives.

The men had a very tough job to manage their prisoners, and not until they had struck them such fearful, cowardly blows that rendered them insensible, did they succeed.

They were then lowered down the hold, and the captain, looking cautiously round, said—

"Now, my men, bring the ladies up, and treat them carefully."

"Ay, ay, sir."

And the men brought upon deck two young and beautiful girls, but of different complexions.

The half-insensible girls struggled desperately to break from their captors.

The captain seized one by the arm and savagely dragged her from the men. In so doing the gag slipped from her mouth, and she shrieked for Jerry. That worthy recognised the voice, and, springing from his place of concealment, dashed upon the captain like a fiend.

CHAPTER XXXII.

BOB HAULER PLAYS A SHORT ACT, AND ESCAPES FROM THE ASYLUM.

BOB HAULER gazed upon the fairy-like beauty. Enthralled by her matchless loveliness, his every sense seemed in a whirl, and, forgetting where he was, he began to murmur aloud about her beauty, and how he would like to serve her persecutors.

"Hauler!" called old John Gregory.

"Yes—I beg pardon, yer honour."

"What were you talking about?"

"I was thinking."

"Then don't think so loud."

"No, yer honour; I'll go."

"No, you need not; you can stay."

Bob stayed.

Twiddling his fingers one over the other, with his head bent almost to his knees, because he was too bashful to look a pretty woman in the face, though when he thought she was not looking at him he would steal a sly side glance, and encounter her soft blue eyes watching him closely, Bob felt uneasy, and tried to look another way, but some fascinating charm seemed to draw his gaze in the direction of her sweet, plaintive face.

"Mr. Hauler," said old Gregory.

"Yes, yer honour," answered Bob, glad of an opportunity to draw his attention from the lady's sorrowful countenance.

"When do you intend to leave me?"

"To-night, yer honour."

"That is capital."

"And to-morrow we shall come down with our gallant buccaneers, force an entry, and save you and—and—the lady."

"What lady, you blackguard?"

"This lady."

"How did you know the lady wants to escape?"

Bob looked at the delicate creature rather crest-fallen.

The lady returned his look with a sweet smile that reassured the buccaneer that his surmise was correct.

She did want to escape, he could see it plainly written in the soft eloquence of her large bright eyes.

"Well, yer honour," said the boatswain in answer to John Gregory, "if I ain't made a mistake, this is the very lady I followed and tried to save."

"Yes, sir, you are correct," said the old gentleman; "and if you return safely to-morrow and save us, you shall have a thousand pounds."

"I will give him five thousand," said the lady, softly.

"I don't want any reward," said Bob, proudly, and looking at both the speakers. "I have quite as much money as I shall ever use, only, if I can serve you, dear lady, in any other way, Bob Hauler's services are at your command."

"You are a noble fellow," she said, sweetly; "and your kind, generous offer shall not be forgotten, please God we escape."

"Can I do anything for you, my lady, to-morrow?"

"I thank you, not to-morrow; but if we escape, your faithful services will be invaluable."

Bob's face brightened at the gentle words.

The heavy tread of a keeper approaching made the trio start.

In an instant Bob Hauler assumed his disguise, and looked as great a lunatic as ever.

"You had better go back to your den," said John Gregory.

"Yes, yer honour; and to-morrow you will see me again," said the brave buccaneer, taking the old gentleman's proffered hand and shaking it heartily.

Bob pulled his forelock and "hoisted his slacks," by way of salute to the young lady.

She put out her tiny white hand to him, and said—

"Good night, Mr. Hauler. I hope you will succeed in your faithful undertaking."

The honest tar looked at the little delicate hand, then at his own, and taking the tips of her fingers, raised them to his lips, and departed.

Closing himself in his chamber, he anxiously awaited for the noise and bustle to subside.

At last the place became wrapped in sombre quietness, with its many unhappy inmates.

Then Bob commenced the preparations for his escape.

His way of escape was finite, and that by the window of his chamber.

He knew this, and prepared accordingly.

Firstly, he tore a sheet from his bed in strips and plaited them together like a rope; then he took a survey of the yard beneath his window. Pulling a leg off one of the chairs, he put it across the open casement inside, then throwing the rope across it, with the two ends hanging out of the window, he commenced his descent.

Getting out of the window, he twisted his legs round the rope, and reached the ground in safety.

So far he was successful.

Was he to continue his escape as successfully?

The same idea struck him at that moment.

And pulling the rope down, he looked cautiously around.

He started suddenly, with a wild light kindling in his eye and an awful look on his face.

What caused that sudden alarm and those horrible looks?

We will enlighten the reader on the subject by explaining.

Bob Hauler's searching gaze fell upon a form—yes, and that of a man crouched in a corner on a heap of dirty sacks.

Awfully bloodthirsty and revengeful thoughts suggested themselves to his racking brain.

He thought of the helplessness of the beautiful heiress—of the barbarous cruelty his beloved young commander's uncle had been treated with, and then of his own jeopardy.

Which would be the greatest sin—to leave those two helpless beings to be tortured to death—and perhaps lose his own life besides—or slay that one man and save them?

Would it not be a just retribution to kill him if he was one of the tormentors?

The honest tar thought it would.

And like a second professional robber at one shilling and sixpence per night in a gory tragedy at a minor theatre, he drew a long knife, and approached the sneaking Judas on tip-toe with the gleaming weapon clutched in his hand at arm's length.

A deadly intent kindled in his sparkling eyes, and a noble act of revenge was his only thought at the time.

The crouching individual lay perfectly still and breathless.

The buccaneer approached him, and, holding his breath, he stooped over the form with the gleaming blade raised above his head.

He sleeps.

Ah! ah! here's triumph.

Murder him in cold blood while in that unconscious state? He can't resist, and would know nothing about it. That's the thing.

No, no; although a buccaneer, he was not so bad as that.

He did not take mean advantages like the second robbers at one and six per night, when they stab a pillow twenty-seven times, and then escape by jumping through a broken second-floor window and fall on a scene-shifter's head, or roll down an open trap and spifflicate their necks.

Bob Hauler did nothing of the sort.

He looked carefully at the sleeper, whom he found to be a watchman sleeping off the essence of very strong brandy he had been indulging in rather too freely.

The sailor was perfectly satisfied by his appearance, and proceeded on his adventure.

Fastening a huge stone to an end of the rope he threw it over the wall and fastened it in a crevice.

Scrambling up the rope like a monkey, he had barely got half way up when a huge mastiff came dashing at him, making a terrible noise.

Then came several two-legged bloodhounds, rushing after him with long gutta-percha whips in their hands.

Bob gave a defiant shout, and fell over the wall.

Ere he had time to gain his footing the men came rushing upon him.

Bob Hauler did not intend to be caught, and dashing at his pursuers he sent them sprawling, and then flew with the swiftness of an antelope.

His would-be captors were soon on his track, and followed him like a lot of unchained demons.

Bob kept well ahead of them, but it was not to last for long.

Unfortunately for him, he suddenly dived down a narrow turning.

He had not proceeded far when he was suddenly confronted by a gang of ill-looking sea-faring men, who emerged from a dirty-looking beer-house.

"Don't be in a hurry, my pippin!" exclaims one, clapping his hands on Bob's shoulders.

"Clear the way, mates," said Bob, trying to force his way through the rough gang, "there is a lot of lubbers giving chase."

"All right, my young shark, don't be in a hurry, you are the very fellow we were looking for!" said another.

Bob looked surprised.

"What for?" he asked.

"All right."

Here his pursuers came rushing up breathless, but came to a sudden halt.

"That's our man," said one.

"Is he?" remarked a dirty-looking seafarer.

"Yes; he has just escaped!"

"You look as though you have escaped too."

"Never mind what I look like. Give him to me."

"Clear out, yer lubber," and the keeper received a kick that sent him reeling.

The keepers' companions rushed at their opponents with their whips.

The seafarers could not stand that, and in a very short time they settled accounts with the keepers by keeping them off their captive, and knocking them down as soon as they came up

They soon commenced to shout for quarter.

Which they did not get.

They had commenced the row, and the sea rovers finished it with a *coup de grace* that made the keepers slink away howling as though they were hurt.

Bob Hauler had a vague idea that the men had only rendered their assistance out of kindness, and when he saw his pursuers vanquished he looked at the men who held him as though he expected they were going to let him go.

Which they were not.

"Thank ye, mates," said Bob; "you can let me go now."

"Can we, though!" replied one of the men.

"If yer want any grog for lending a helping hand, why I can pay for it."

"Well, we don't mind having some grog, but we shall take care of you at the same time."

"What do you want me for?" asked Bob Hauler, surprised.

"Ah, you are just the boy we do want; there ain't many like you hanging about!"

That was complimentary. The buccaneer would rather have had his liberty than their compliments.

Nevertheless, it was true there were not many men like Bob. He was a thorough sailor, any one could see at the first glance; he was hearty and jovial, knew every inch of the sea, could take a ship to any port, run her within an inch of the breakers, guide her through a heavy storm, run her into a nook or inlet safely, and without a compass.

He was bewildered for the moment; he had not dreamed that such an unfortunate end would happen to spoil all his generous arrangements.

"What do you want of me?" he asked again.

"Oh! we just want you to go for a cruise."

"But I am going for a cruise in my own ship."

"You will come on ours for a change."

"Do you know what ship I belong to?"

"No! nor don't care."

"Do you think I am going with you?"

"We think so."

"Then you are mistaken, for I ain't," said Bob Hauler, emphatically, growing enraged.

"That's your caper, is it?"

"Yes, and I can tell you, you ain't going to kidnap me."

"Dry up, cuss yer."

"I'll see yer blowed fust."

"Clap a stopper on his jawing tackle."

"Try i-t."

A gag being suddenly put over his mouth from behind, cut his last word in two, and made its pronunciation sound very peculiar.

Bob fought desperately to free himself. His captors were too many in number and of a nature too powerful for him to slip through their fingers.

The ruffianly gang rather unceremoniously dragged him through many long lanes; when they stopped, they roughly threw him into the boat.

He was rowed out to sea, and taken on board, the gag was taken from his mouth, and the cords cut that bound him.

CHAPTER XXXIII.
CAPTAIN TOM DRAKE VANQUISHES THE PIRATES.

"THE pirate wins!" Admiral Ellis exclaimed; "the boy buccaneers are beaten from their deck."

"They are fighting like so many devils," growled the commander. "See, the flag falls!"

"Where—where?" the little old admiral said, scarcely daring to turn his face that way.

"The pirates—and serve the lubbers right, curse them!" was the commander's reply.

Admiral Ellis, sick at heart, let his glass fall to the deck, and turned away.

Now let us see how the combatants fare.

Leaning upon his jewelled scimitar, Captain Tom watched with eagle eye the preparations of his huge adversary.

A smile flitted across his handsome features when he saw Pardo execute that movement which caused that ringing cheer from the shore and the vessels.

"Don Pardo," he said to those near, "has many friends; let us change that shout. Up with the signal."

"Now, my boys," he continued, as the whip-like canvas floated above his head, "to your guns. My hands shall fire the first shot."

Then the roar of artillery began. Tom's well-aimed shot telling with marvellous effect upon the huge hull of the pirate ship.

Amid a heavy cloud of gray opaque smoke the vessels closed, and like a lion bounding on his prey, the gallant boy sprang upon the enemy's deck, followed closely by his band.

There was a momentary pause in his career as the swarthy crew rushed to meet the boy buccaneers, a pause that was broken as the youthful band, like an avalanche, broke through the living wall, and plied their blades until, from hilt to point, the glowing steel was red with the foemen's blood.

Time after time were the boys driven back by the pirate crew; each time they strewed the deck of the huge vessel with Spanish blood.

Pausing for a moment in the grim work, Captain Tom glanced hastily over the red scene of slaughter, then high above the clash of steel and the fire of small arms, his clear voice rang out—

"Forward! follow me."

His blade was fleshed in the foremost of his foes, then, with a mighty cheer, the youthful rovers hurled back the pirates, and spreading out like a fan, they swept all before them from the quarter-deck.

The red stream ran like a deluge from the lee scuppers, and the ocean for many fathoms beyond the locked vessels was tinged with a crimson hue.

Led onward by the towering form of Don Pardo the boarded pirates fought with demon-like frenzy.

The hand of the boy king of the buccaneers was upon the flag, and a hundred blades threatened to slay him.

"Santa Maria!" roared the pirate, "cut them down, hurl them into the sea—the flag, the flag!"

Like maddened beasts they strove to reach the gallant boy.

As well might the caged lion try to break the strong bars of his prison as the yelling crew to pierce that line of steel that surrounded Captain Tom.

"Stand by me," he said, "hurl them back until I drag this emblem of rapine from the mast."

They obeyed him.

Built high, piled one above the other, lay the quivering forms of the Spanish crew.

A rampart of gashed and mangled flesh that became higher every fresh attack the pirates made to reach the boy chief of the buccaneers.

At last there came a yell of rage from the swarthy crew.

A yell that was answered by a cheer of fresh young voices as Don Pardo's banner was torn down by the small white hands of Captain Tom.

Trampling the banner beneath his feet, he again strode to the front of his fearless band.

Don Pardo, the white foam gathering thickly upon his lips and his face blanched with passion, at that moment threw his colossal form upon two of the middies.

He sought to bear them down by brute force, and, disregarding their blows, bore the gallant boys to the deck.

There was a snapping of steel as the middies' swords shivered upon his coat of mail.

Springing forward with the lightness and determination of a jaguar, Captain Tom arrested the Spaniard's progress.

"Lubber!" roared Pardo, raising his huge blade; "how dare you touch my flag? Ha!"

With a force that seemed marvellous for one so young, the daring boy dashed the golden pommel of his sword in the pirate's face.

The sharp top struck the ruffian full upon the forehead, and like a stricken bear he fell to the deck.

In the swaying to and fro of the hand-to-hand fight, the pirate chieftain's fall was unnoticed, save by two persons who were closely following him to avenge the loss of their flag.

These two were the lieutenant of the Spanish ship and Lord Kilcrew.

The first, with a savage oath, lunged at our young hero's breast.

Like the lightning's swift flash, Captain Tom's well-tried blade turned the Spaniard's long Toledo aside.

Then, before his hand could be withdrawn, he was spitted upon the boy's weapon.

A convulsive shiver passed over his frame as he madly struggled to push back the hand that had delivered the death-thrust. Then he fell to the deck—dead!

With the red blade, reeking with the lieutenant's warm blood, Captain Tom met Lord Kilcrew's weapon.

"By Saint Patrick!" said the nobleman, as he ran forward to cleave our hero's skull in twain, "the time has come for the sword of an Irish gentleman to do its duty!"

The boy's handsome face was flushed with the combat he had just passed through, and throwing his handsome head back, he met Kilcrew's blade, and said—

"I have not forgotten my promise, Lord Kilcrew; "when I have taken this vessel we can settle our affair."

"Settle! By Saint Patrick! you go not past me, my young fire-eater. Kilcrew has sworn to run you through the body, and he will do it."

There was a calm, defiant smile upon the young rover's lips, as, disdaining further parley, he attacked the admiral.

Kilcrew was a splendid swordsman, but for once his skill availed him but little.

The light, supple blade wielded by Captain Tom played like a serpent round Kilcrew's weapon, and at last, when by a skilful feint the gallant boy caused Kilcrew's sword-point to be raised, he ran the thin blade inside his opponent's hilt.

Kilcrew felt the sharp point upon his knuckles, and sought to shake it off.

The effort was useless.

Captain Tom, with a light laugh falling from his lips, marked the nobleman's struggle to relieve his blade, and wrenching his arm, Lord Kilcrew felt his weapon torn from his hand.

He stood for a moment as though expecting a death stroke.

Looking up, he beheld Captain Tom leaning upon his weapon and regarding his vanquished foe with a look of quiet irony.

"My lord," said the graceful boy, "keep your life. Remember he who idly boasts of checking Captain Tom places his life in jeopardy."

Lord Kilcrew, pale with baffled rage, listened to the merciful boy, who forbore to strike his most inveterate foe, although that foe was at his mercy.

Admiral Lord Kilcrew's passion blinded his reason, and instead of quietly accepting the life Tom had foreborne to take, sprang a few paces back, and seizing a cutlass from a seaman who was passing, turned upon his chivalrous foe, and hissed savagely—

"Admiral Kilcrew never accepts favour at the hands of a robber. Guard, or by Saint Patrick, I'll cleave your skull."

The red-blooded scimitar was again raised, and as the boy's eyes blazed with passion, he said—

"Be it so, my lord. Have at you! Remember, I shall again disarm you, and expect but scant mercy for your base ingratitude."

"Vile braggart, this weapon shall drink your blood unto death. I will stand before you."

"Unto death be it."

Quick of eye and sure of hand, Tom met his adversary. Twice their blades were locked; each time the nobleman wrenched his wrist away.

"That trick of fence," he said, with a savage bitterness, "shall not disarm Kilcrew again."

Tom's reply was a smile.

Vainly Kilcrew put in practice every point to throw his young adversary off his guard.

Vainly he left his wrists exposed for Tom to strike.

The feint was detected by the young and brilliant swordsman, who, watching his chance, pressed upon his adversary with such determination that Kilcrew was compelled to fall back.

At the second step his foot slipped, and threw him for a moment aside.

Before he could recover his balance, the heavy cutlass was shivered to the hilt, and Captain Tom's sword point touched his throat.

Undismayed, the gallant Irishman looked steadily at the weapon.

"Strike," he said. "Kilcrew will not ask for quarter."

Captain Tom's brave heart was touched by such an utter fearlessness of death.

He could not but admire his fierce, lion-like demeanour, and turning the point of his sword, he said—

"For the second time I will spare you; beware of the third—that will be death. Captain Tom never breaks his word."

Kilcrew could have wept with rage.

"Strike!" he said. "I tell you, boy, I will not have my life at your giving."

Captain Tom turned from this frenzied nobleman.

One scarcely perceptible gesture served to nave Lord Kilcrew bound and placed out of the reach of the combatants.

Reckless of the flying bullets and the thrust of pike and cutlass, Captain Tom mingled in the thickest of the fray.

Oft in that long struggle his Damascus blade acted as a buckler, and saved his young life from the savage determination of his foes.

Splitting tough pike-staffs as though they were fancy reeds, the boy passed onwards through the fiercely contending crowd.

His tall, lithe, handsome form set off to advantage by his rich dress, passed scathless the many weapons raised to bar his passage.

Like an avenging Nemesis he cut his way through his foes, his course marked by a trail of blood and fallen bodies of fierce desperadoes.

The stories in circulation respecting his wondrous powers, which defied mortal weapons to do him harm, rushed to the pirates' minds.

And many who had sworn to take his life, turned away in affright from his calm, handsome face, and the red weapon which ran with the blood of all who sought to stop his path.

Lead and steel fell harmless upon him.

Pistol after pistol was fired at his heart, and the bullets, with a dull, heavy thud, fell flattened to the deck.

Then the boy, with murder glaring from his dark eyes, would slay those whose weapons yet smoked from the discharge of the well-aimed shot.

Suddenly there was a cry from the pirate horde, and they fled in wild dismay to the forecastle of the huge ship.

"The devil! the devil! See, he is invulnerable."

A scornful smile played upon Captain Tom's lips, and, calling upon his crew, he bore down upon the huddled mass of dark-bearded men.

There was one among them who heard the cries of his affrighted companions, and, with an evil glitter in his eyes, he tore a silver button from his jacket, and placed it in the muzzle of his pistol.

"Lead will not kill him," said the pirate; "the power of hell cannot withstand bullets of this kind."

He fired point blank at the boy's breast, and to his dismay the charmed bullet fell upon the deck.

It rebounded from the sheet of golden mail as though it were an india-rubber ball.

Captain Tom cut down a huge pirate who stood in his path : then stooping, he picked up the silver button.

"Now, my lads," he said, "Captain Tom and victory! Forward—drive them into the sea."

They rushed upon the pirates with an impetuosity which cleared all before them.

There was a long, fierce struggle—bright swords flashed in the air.

Then fell, and rose again, dimmed with the sickening work of slaughter.

Then a shout of victory from a hundred youthful voices as the last of Don Pardo's band threw down their weapons and begged for quarter.

The might of the Spanish rovers was broken, and Captain Tom and his buccaneers were masters of the ship.

The mighty vessel that one short hour before rode so defiantly upon the blue waste of waters now lay with her huge bulwarks shot away, her foremast gone by the board, and the sails flapping in ribbons against the spars.

"Hoist our banner," said the young leader, proudly. "Let those whose cheers goaded these men to risk a fight with Captain Tom behold their fall."

He spoke, and the buccaneers' flag streamed out defiantly in the sun glow.

There was a rich hue upon the boy's handsome face, and a proud look in his dark eyes as he gazed upon the banner of victory.

From this joyous emblem his glance wandered among the group of crest-fallen pirates, and his eagle eye detected the jacket from which the silver button had been torn, a stern, pitiless expression came over his face.

"Bring that fellow here," he said to his middies, as his extended hand pointed in the direction of the shining jacket.

Many rushed forward to fulfil their young leader's order, and, half dead with fear, the Spaniard was dragged from the forecastle.

He read his doom in the face of his stern conqueror, and, falling at our hero's feet, whined for mercy.

"Mercy!" repeated Captain Tom. "Yes, the same mercy as you would have shown me."

"Senor, by the Vir—"

"Silence! Here, one of you take that pistol from his belt."

A midshipman plucked the weapon from the Spaniard's waist, and handed it to Captain Tom.

He took the pistol, and for the second time the silver button was dropped into the barrel.

The Spaniard's teeth chattered with agony, and the big drops, of cold clammy sweat stood thickly upon his brow.

"Pirate," said the boy, "twice have you sought my life; twice has this weapon sped a ball against my breast—"

"Mercy! Oh! holy—"

"Silence! Go upon yonder bulwark."

The pirate cried upon the Virgin to aid him in his hour of peril.

Again the stern, pitiless words fell upon his ears—

"Stand upon the bulwarks."

The hapless wretch looked up at the unyielding face above him, and with a cry of terror arose.

His limbs could scarcely lead the shaking body to the side, and, like the culprit mounting a scaffold, the swarthy Spaniard crawled upon a gun, thence to the side; then clinging to the spikes, he waited the boy's next words.

There had fallen upon the deck of the vessel a chilling, terrible silence.

The fierce blaze of passion that had been called up by the conflict had begun to subside, and victor and vanquished were again human.

Spell-bound, they stood and watched the first act in this strange scene.

ADMIRAL POMP ASTONISHES THE INDIAN CHIEF.

When the doomed wretch stood upon the vessel's side, the boy chief raised the pistol in a line with his heart, and in cold, measured accents that grated upon the ears of his devoted crew, said—

"So perish the enemies of Captain Tom. Listen, pirate. I shall count three; as the last word leaves my lips the silver bullet will pierce your breast, unless you are beneath the wave."

"Mercy! signor, mercy!"

"One—two—three!"

Mingled with the report of the pistol, came the death-cry of the pirate as he fell back-

wards from the bulwarks, and went whirli down, his heart cleft by the silver button wit which he had intended to have slain Captain Tom.

A weight seem lifted from the boy cruiser's heart as the stricken wretch disappeared beneath the blue wave; and the deed lost its cold-blooded character when the youthful leader turned to his crew and said—

"That wretch, whose life has just vanished, my hand once saved from a fearful death. Base, black-hearted treachery was the way in which he requited me for perilling my life. He is gone, and had ....en at the altar, or guarded by a thousand soldiers, I would have slain him."

Anxious, glowing faces changed to looks of admiration and love. Had Captain Tom sullied his brilliant career by one foul act, no matter upon whom his vengeance had fallen, his brave and devoted crew would have lost their love and respect for their idolized leader.

Bloodshed, when useless in self-defence, was looked upon as murder, and the hand that could deal a coward's stroke would always have the red stain of blood in their eyes.

"Now, my boys," said the chieftain, "on board with you, and hang out a cable to take this shattered hulk in tow."

With her white canvass bellying out to the wind, the stately ship of the buccaneers, with their prize in tow, sailed towards the frigate.

When within hailing distance the boy captain sprang upon a gun and shouted—

"Admiral Ellis, when next you bribe a band of cut-throats to sink Captain Tom and his ship, I promise to bring them to you as I do this hulk. You will find your friends on board. Adieu! When next we meet you can thank Captain Tom for his gift. Cut the cable, my boys."

The shot-torn vessel, like a stricken beast when hit by the hunter seeks refuge with the herd, drifted towards the frigate and became entangled with her bows.

Then, like magic, the buccaneers' yards were manned by the daring boys, and as the vessel turned her prow seaward, a ringing cheer rang out that echoed far away among the distant hills.

Then the thousands who had stood spellbound during the terrible fight gave back the cheer, and many hearts thrilled quicker than their wont as they watched the stately vessel and her daring crew glide out upon the mighty, trackless waste of waters.

CHAPTER XXXIII.

DESTRUCTION OF A SETTLEMENT BY PRIVATEERS—JERRY MIZZEN'S SUSPICIONS CONFIRMED — STRUGGLE WITH A CAPTAIN— PLACED IN A BLACK HOLE—CREULA DEFENDS HER HONOUR.

THE night following Jerry Mizzen's departure from the settlement for the ship saw an awful tragedy enacted in the midst of the peaceful little dwellings.

At the same time on that dark night when Jerry was leaning over the bulwarks of the strange ship, thinking of his brunette love whom he had left with the kindly old hunters, the villanous Captain Debriscan, with his brawny crew, crept like so many evil spirits into the sleeping village and commenced their devilish work.

How innocent were those generous people of the sorrow and unhappiness they were bringing on their own heads when they so gladly accepted the strange captain and his men into their humble houses, and offered them the best of their hospitality.

Little did they think of the base ingratitude and cruelty they would receive in return for their honest offering.

Had the planters suspected the base designs of the half-caste captain who daily sat at their table and partook of their humble meals, it is probable he would never have returned to his ship.

But the honest settlers were blind and unsuspecting, though a close observer would have read his treacherous thoughts as his savage eyes rested on the beautiful form of Creula with an evil glare.

But having no close observers in the happy family, the captain was not detected in his dark plot.

He left the settlement with a frank face and extended hand, hiding his evil purpose behind a veil he assumed, and in the middle of the night returned to carry his villanous purpose out.

The little village was wrapped in quiet tranquillity, when he returned like a fiend from hell, with his vile crew, to spread destruction in every house.

He glared round with a look of triumph and satisfaction at the helplessness of his intended victims.

Dividing his men into several bodies, he picked a dozen of the most hardy and brutal to accompany him.

He was short of men, and seeing several hearty, robust fellows there, he intended to take them from their homes when they were unprepared to defend themselves.

He pointed out the dwellings to which they belonged, for his men to attack, while he, with his dozen picked ruffians, seized the hunters.

Fearful banging and crashing plainly told that their work had commenced.

In an instant their noise had awoke the slumbering peasants.

The alarmed people at first thought they were attacked by a tribe of savages who infested the forest, but to their surprise they soon discovered who their assailants were.

Their shrieks and shouts rent the air, echoing to the boundless forest, and were answered by the growling of the disturbed beasts.

The settlers seized their guns and hatchets to meet the enemy and defend their families.

But the savage sailors heeded them not; they burst into the dwellings, pillaged them of any valuable relic, tore the helpless girls from their beds, and brutally struck down all who stood in their way.

The French privateer, Captain Mons. Debuscan, had forced an entry into the planter's hut, and was met by the two powerful men, old Ben, and his son George, who stood determined and dangerous in their path.

"Out of this, old man," said the captain, trying to push Ben aside.

Ben stood resolute and immoveable.

"Tarnation blazes to your cussed sneaking soul!" said the old fellow. "I guess old Ben'll give you a twister if you don't clear out!"

"Sacre!" exclaimed the Frenchman.

"Treacherous hound!" said George Hunter, his large bright eyes looking dangerous; "is this the gratitude you return for the kindness you have received, base wretch?"

"Ah! ah!" laughed the privateer; "my friend seems surprised."

The young settler, without uttering another word, aimed a fearful blow at the captain's head with a hatchet.

The Frenchman stepped aside in time to save his worthless life. A man who stood behind him fell to the earth howling, with the weapon buried in his shoulder.

The captain grunted like an enraged tiger, and sprang upon his opponent, griping him by the throat. The young man was prepared for the attack, and catching the privateer in his arms, rolled to the ground with his assailant beneath him.

The privateers saw their leader's danger, and ran to his rescue.

George Hunter had got him by the throat, squeezing his despicable life out.

The men seized the daring fellow savagely, and would have torn him to pieces, but old Ben hurled them back with a strength super-human, and thus kept them off his son, until at last he was felled to the ground with a cowardly blow from a man who crept behind him.

George heard his father groan as he fell, and springing to his feet, leaving his opponent, dashed furiously at the cowardly men.

The captain staggered to his feet, weak and exhausted, but soon recovered his brute strength.

"Curses on ye!" he shouted to his men, who had got the young fellow down and were brutally treating him. "Secure your prisoner! Confound it. I don't want him killed."

"He has killed two of our mates," answered one of the men, sullenly.

"Curse your mates! he is worth a half dozen of you."

The man muttered some dogged reply, and placed his sword at George Hunter's throat.

"Hell's furies!" yelled the privateer, passionately, striking the man full in the face with his clenched fist. "Am I to be obeyed?"

The man reeled round and fell to the earth stunned and bleeding.

"Go and bind him," said Captain Debuscan, "and then some of you follow me."

"Ay, ay, sir," answered the privateers.

The young settler was bound hand and foot by three privateers, who took possession of him, while the remainder followed their captain to the chamber of Creula.

But to the Frenchman's surprise he found that the brave girl had securely fastened and barricaded her door.

"Come, open the door, my pretty brunette," he said, persuasively.

He received no answer, but heard low sobs within.

Again he called for the Creole girl to open the door, but, as before, received no answer.

This enraged his passionate nature, and he ordered his men to force an entry.

The ruffianly crew dashed at the door with a force that would have shaken a house down. The door shook and trembled.

Another rush, and it fell, shattered and crashing over the barricade.

Creula ran to the window, and was about to leap out, when the French captain sprang forward, caught her round the waist, and hurled her back.

The girl struggled desperately to break away from her brutal captor, but he held her to his breast in a vice-like grip, and bounded out as a shout rose from his men.

What fearful devastation met his gaze! Women and children on their knees, piteously imploring the pitiless wretches to release their husbands and brothers.

In other directions were lying in pools of blood, dead and wounded men, fainted women, and slaughtered children.

A red glare suddenly burst forth and lighted up the horrid spectacle.

Several of the huts were on fire.

Captain Debuscan's countenance changed to a deathly hue.

"Whose infernal work is this?" he inquired in a voice of thunder.

Several of the privateers slunk away as he spoke.

Their leader was one of the most cruel and determined men that ever sailed on the ocean, and they well knew the penalty of doing anything against his will.

Hardened as his inflexible nature was, the sorrowful desolation, that fell work of setting the homes of the poor unhappy people in flames, touched a hidden chord of his nature, and for the moment made him regret the foul work.

"It is done, but not by my wish," he said, as though speaking to himself. "Now, my men," he said, aloud, "bring along your prisoners."

He carried Creula to the boat, followed by his men bringing their prisoners.

A tussle ensued between the settlers and their captors when they were taken on board.

The faint cry for Jerry was that of Creula, as the reader already knows, when she struggled with the captain and the gag slipped from her mouth.

So sudden was Jerry's furious attack upon the false captain, that he had not time to defend himself. When the buccaneer bore him to the deck with such fearful force, it shook the life nearly out of him.

Gripping each other in a lion-like grasp, they rolled over and over, the Frenchman trying to free himself from his unknown assailant, while Jerry fought fiercely for revenge.

M. Debuscan had got him on the ship under false pretences, and then committed an outrage on Creula, the brave old tar's only thought and care.

Jerry could have pardoned him for the first crime, but the latter he could not look over, and meant to take just retribution at his own hands for the deed.

The night was so intensely dark that an object could not be distinguished a yard off, and thus it was that the privateer captain discerned his opponent.

The fight was long and terrible.

Each man fought with wild desperation.

But the captain had the advantage, and Jerry was at length overpowered and safely placed in the hold.

Such was the awful fate of the brave Jerry, who had fought so gallantly but vainly to rescue his beautiful mistress.

Captain Debuscan, foaming at the mouth with passion, after seeing the safe imprisonment of Jerry Mizzen, descended to the cabin and placed the senseless form of Creula upon a couch.

His eyes blazed like burning coals, and his face was purple with the black, evil passions that raged in his breast.

He glanced gloatingly upon the dusky form of his inanimate captive, who lay still as death, scantily robed, and the greater portion of her nether limbs displayed to his sensual gaze.

A savage smile played round his firm-set mouth, that boded no good to his intended victim.

"Mine at last! Ha! ha! Now let them save you who can," he muttered, striding towards the door and securely locking it.

Again he stood and gazed upon his captive. His base intentions could be seen by the look upon his swarthy face.

"Ha!" he exclaimed, "she awakes."

Creula moved at that moment and seemed to partly recover her senses.

The low, almost silent, savage chuckle of the captain seemed to have an electric effect upon her.

She unclosed her eyes, and gazed for an instant vacantly around, until her dark orbs rested upon the bearded face of her ruffianly captor.

She shuddered, and shrank back with a cry.

"Oh! Jerry, Jerry, where are you?" she murmured, trying to cover her heaving bust with her tiny dark hand.

"You need not fret about that precious skunk, who is now food for the rats?" said the brutal privateer, with a coarse laugh; "because I am going to keep you company until I get tired of you; and you ought to be proud of the honour, my young darkie. Any other nigger would—"

Creula sprang from the couch, her eyes flashing dangerously and her lips compressed like a vice.

"Beware, inhuman monster, how you treat me, for, by Him above you, you will find you have no child to play with!" she exclaimed, indignantly.

A loud laugh of derision came from the captain.

He seemed to admire her more since she had risen and stood before him in her bold defiance.

"See, girl," he said, striding towards her, "see! I told you you should be mine—sacre! and you shall!"

He caught her by the wrist, and attempted to draw her towards him.

She sprang back to the farthest recess of the cabin, and stood with a look of wild determination in her flashing eye.

But Captain Debuscan only smiled a grim kind of satisfaction.

He did not alter his purpose.

But only increased his desire to slay her.

Again he clutched her by the wrist.

Creula struck him upon the cheek with her hand.

The act for a moment staggered him, but he gradually recovered, and his fury came to a pitch of madness.

With a savage cry, he bounded forward, and before Creula was aware of her situation, she found herself powerless in the arms of the villanous privateer.

She struggled madly to break from the ruffian's grasp, but to no purpose—he held her like a vice.

She screamed wildly for help, but the coarse hand of her captor stifled her cries.

She kicked furiously, but he only gave a savage grin at that; and Creula very soon ceased kicking, as the unpleasant conviction came upon her that in doing so she was depriving herself of the power to resist the murderous pirate who strove to force her hands behind that he might draw his knife.

It was impossible for her to hold out much longer.

Her strength was gradually failing her, each moment she became more exhausted, and the feeling that she was thoroughly helpless, and at the mercy of her captor, stole upon her.

Creula had fought bravely until her strength failed, and when she could not hold out against his brute power any longer, she wept bitterly.

"Ha! ha! Cry, my beauty. Who has conquered?" said the captain, in a hoarse, impassioned voice, removing his hand from the fainting girl's mouth, and placing her struggling form upon the couch.

She seemed now entirely lost, to be sacrificed to his ruthless fury.

Another minute, and Creula would have fallen a victim to the privateer captain.

But unknown deliverance was at hand.

At the very instant Captain Debuscan imagined his triumph was complete there came a loud crash at the cabin door.

He leaped round, and a vile oath escaped his lips, and drawing a revolver he shouted—

"Who's there?"

"I, captain," replied a youthful voice from the outside.

"What the —— do you want?"

"A sail, captain—right in our wake."

"Well?"

"The lieutenant is waiting for orders."

CHAPTER XXXIV.

THE CURSE ATTENDING THE POSSESSION OF THE SEA EMERALD FALLS UPON IMAUN BEY.

FROM the towers of the lofty minarets the muezzin's monotonous voice could be heard calling the faithful to prayer.

The followers of Mahomet obeyed the call, and, leaving their slippers at the door of the mosque, entered the sacred building, and were soon prostrate before the believers' shrine.

There was one among the faithful in that vast city upon whom the sacred call fell unheeded.

It was Imaun Bey, the possessor of the sea emerald.

He sat cross-legged upon a pile of cushions, hugging the priceless gem to his heart.

Fondling and speaking to the inanimate stone as though it were a thing of life.

He had heard of its fell properties, but, secure in his chamber, a keen scimitar and a loaded pistol within his reach, he scoffed at the mystically fearful legend.

The merchant's heart thrilled with wild tumultuous joy as he feasted his eyes upon the lambent fire which glittered from the gem and lit up his face with a pale, sickly light.

"Mine! mine!" he said, as he pressed his lips to the fatal gem. "Imaun Bey, the Prophet has given thee that which the whole wealth of the empire cannot buy."

The rustling of the silken curtains caused him to start and hide the jewel in his breast. The other hand was stretched forward menacingly towards the naked scimitar, which lay near.

Lena entered as his finger touched the hilt.

"Fear not, uncle," she said, "it is I."

"Fear! Oh! daughter, why should I fear?"

"Your hasty clutch at the scimitar."

"It was but—but——"

"I can fathom its cause. Oh! my uncle, that gem with its fearful curse!"

Her uncle pressed the sea emerald closer to his heart.

"Hush! girl, by the Prophet. Think you

I am to be frightened from its possession by the lying stories of those cut-throat pirates?"

Lena stepped softly to the merchant's side, and sinking her voice, whispered—

"Uncle, the cadi——"

Imaun Bey sprang up as though he had been shot.

"The cadi!" he repeated, turning pale. "What of him, girl?"

"His messenger is below, and seeks an audience. Be careful, uncle; the report of that accursed jewel has reached his ears."

"Allah be merciful!" gasped the merchant. "He will seek to wrest it from me. Run, girl, to the small box in my safe, and bring me an old leather case you will find inside."

Lena was quitting the chamber when her trembling uncle added——

"When you have brought the case, then let the cadi's messenger be admitted. Not till then—not till then."

The girl left the chamber, and Imaun Bey fell back upon the soft cushions half stupid with despair.

"The cadi," he murmured. "Allah is great. Ten rose-coloured diamonds I gave the cadi but a week since to close his eyes, when the pirate ships came into the harbour."

Lena re-appeared and gave her uncle the case, and as he emptied the glittering contents into his open palm, the look of fear was superseded by an expression of dry cunning.

A small shower of glittering gems fell into his hand. From among them he selected an emerald not one-third the size of the priceless gem which had been fished from the bottom of the sea.

To exchange them was the work of a moment, and giving Lena the leather case, he said—

"Hide it—hide it. The sea emerald is inside. "Yes, that will do—under the cushion, now admit the cadi's messenger."

Imaun Bey, secretly chuckling over his scheming, awaited the coming of the avaricious functionary's servant.

"If," he murmured, "the cadi wants the jewel, may Allah blind his eyes, and enable this to pass for it."

He placed the small gem 'in a fold of his turban, just as Lena appeared on the threshold.

Behind came the messenger, a short, thick-set Moslem, whose dark eyes glanced furtively round the chamber, and Imaun's heart leapt when he found that his glance rested upon the very spot where the sea emerald was hidden.

Wiping the cold drops of fear from his brow, the merchant bowed his head, saying—

"What does our master, the most happy of the faithful, require of his servant, Imaun Bey?"

"Know, O Imaun," said the messenger, "a report has gone about that you have among your jewels a stone of such monstrous size that its value cannot be calculated by golden pieces."

"And does," Imaun asked trembling, "our master give heed to such idle stories? Imaun's very poor, and the best jewel he possesses the mighty cadi would not ornament his chiboque with."

The messenger thought of the rose-coloured diamonds, and answered drily—

"The cadi would see this jewel, O Imaun, that he may judge if report speaks truly."

"We are all the cadi's and Allah's servants, and their will must be done. Here, take this—be careful. Imaun's poor, and can ill afford

to lose even this stone that lying tongues have magnified into such wondrous value."

He placed the emerald in the messenger's hand. Then, as the man left the chamber, a cunning leer came over his face, and he muttered—

"Thou art great, O cadi, in thy cunning, but Imaun is greater. Allah be praised!"

Had the merchant known the messenger's thoughts, as he went slowly back to the cadi's house, he would not have been so confident in his powers.

"Son of a jackass!" thought the messenger, "and does he try to throw dust in our eyes? May his beard grow white with the lies he utters. By Allah! it was good that I followed that dark-eyed houri, or else had I not seen the dog change the jewels."

He reached the awful presence of the gray-bearded rapacious old cadi, and bowed with slavish humility.

The old tyrant gave a growl when his messenger appeared, and blurted out—

"Well, dog, have you the sea emerald?"

"Thy slave has a jewel of that name."

He held the stone to the cadi as he spoke.

"By the beard of the holy prophet!" the cadi growled, "the lying tongue of the black slave shall be torn from his mouth."

The cadi alluded to Imaun Bey's servant whom he had placed in the house as a spy.

"Wherefore, O prince," asked the bearer of the emerald, "this anger?"

The keen little restless gray eyes were fixed upon the speaker as the cadi roared—

"Wherefore do you mock me, slave? Is this stone of a size with a black fowl's egg? Does its lustre send a sheen over my face?"

"It doth not, my prince?"

"Ussof!" said the cadi, viciously, "the cunning twinkle in thine eyes tells me there is another stone; is it so?"

"Thy slave has eyes."

"Yes."

"Thy slave has feet."

"Yes—yes."

"Thy slave used his feet."

"Yes—well."

"And followed the miser Imaun to his chamber."

"Ha! go on, good Ussof."

"His eyes looked through the curtains."

"Ussof, thou art in our favour—go on."

"And he saw Imaun Bey place the sea emerald in a bag instead of this."

"Ussof, there will be a post for thee to fulfil. Good Ussof, thou shalt be our pipe-bearer —go on."

"Thy servant saw it hidden and marked the spot."

"Mark this day, Ussof, with a white stone in thy life. Good Ussof, go on with thy story, our ears are pleased with it."

"When thy servant left the house of Imaun Bey—that dog! May a jackass defile his grave!"

"And," added the cadi, "may the curse of Allah freeze his heart, may his food be pebbles, and his bed thorns."

"Allah listen to thy words, O cadi!"

"Thy story, good Ussof."

"When thy slave brought with him the small stone, he came to thy presence with a joy hung upon his soul."

"Why thus, good Ussof?"

"O my prince, Ussof is not fit to eat dirt in

hy presence, or he would have plunged his yataghan in Imaun's heart, and brought thee the mystic jewel of the ocean's bed."

The cadi's eyes began to twinkle, and his heart fill with a greedy avarice for the priceless gem.

Ussof's words suggested a safe means of being the happy possessor, and beckoning his servant towards him, he said—

"Remember thou those words which Imaun's slave overheard the pirate who sold the jewel say when he gave it to yonder dog?"

"Yes, my prince; he spoke thus—

"'IMAUN, GUARD WELL THY TREASURE, LET NOT ITS LUSTRE BE SEEN BY MAN, OR THY LIFE WILL PAY FOR ITS POSSESSION.'"

"Was that all, Ussof?"

Again the messenger was silent.

"He told him, O cadi, that it might be death to all who held it; told him that when the time was near for it to pass from his hands, the effulgent light would fade for a time and a film of blood will appear to warn him of death."

"Ussof, my soul longs for this wondrous jewel. Go seek Nuline-Geni; but if the film of blood has passed over the stone, is it as——"

He whispered the remainder of his sentence, and Ussof, with a dark smile, touched the silver hilt of his yataghan, and backed out of the house.

"So, dog that thou art," the cadi muttered, "thou would pass this upon us for the wondrous stone whose mystic powers foretell the time of death. By the soul of my father, the wondrous gem once mine, I'll——I'll——"

The cadi paused.

He had suddenly recalled to his mind the fearful curse which came with the possession of the coveted treasure.

"By the tomb of the Prophet," he mused; "but it tells only of the death of its possessor. Even so, it is but little to live for such a mean treasure, and a cadi, surrounded by guards, cannot be bound. Speed back with thy gift, Ussof. Once mine, I'll defy its curse."

He clapped his hands for his pipe-bearer, and under the soothing influence of the opium-drugged Narghile he indulged in the prospective ownership of the famous mystic gem.

Ussof reached the merchant's house as the twinkling stars began to glimmer from the blue canopy above. Ussof knocked softly at the door, and waited for Nuline, the merchant's slave, to admit him.

The brain of the cadi's servant was ripe with a new purpose. The wish to obtain the emerald had crept over him as he walked slowly from the palace.

"The cadi," he thought, "shall possess this treasure; but may Allah turn Ussof from the gates of paradise if he does not yet become master of the priceless gem."

Many schemes were ripe in his brain.

He knew he should have the gem in his keeping that night unless his arm failed in slaying the merchant; but to keep it he knew would be impossible.

The cadi would discover him, no matter where he hid, then the bowstring would be his portion.

"No," he mused, "the cadi shall have the stone. When I have made every preparation for flight, the same weapon can obtain for me what it has to obtain for the cadi."

Revolving this matter in his mind, he forgot the length of time that had elapsed since he applied for admission.

Again the summons was repeated.

The same result followed. The door remained secure, and not a sound or sign was heard in the diamond merchant's house.

"The curse of the prophet be upon Nuline," he muttered, angrily; "has he forgotten my summons?"

Again and again he tried, until tired of waiting. He growled out an angry curse upon the black slave, and gliding to the back of the house, noiselessly scaled the wall.

*   *   *   *   *   *

When Ussof left the merchant's house, Imaun Bey took the sea emerald from the leather case, and, chuckling with glee, bestowed fond endearments upon his treasure.

"Ha! ha!" he laughed, "the cadi will treasure the worthless imitation of this wonderful prize, while I shall be no more troubled by his accursed greedy demands."

He held the shining gem at arm's length, and gazed with silent admiration at the sparkling light that gleamed from the wondrous jewel.

As his greedy eyes devoured the beautiful gem, an exclamation of astonishment, not unmixed with dread, came from his lips.

A crimson mist had suddenly risen over the stone, eclipsing the myriad sparks of fire, and throwing a blood-coloured hue over his face and form.

Imaun Bey saw his reflection in a long mirror opposite, and shuddering with deadly fear, he sat in speechless terror.

"The death warning!" he gasped at length. "No, no! I cannot die and leave—"

The crimsoned hue, so blood-like, faded as quickly as it came, and Imaun, with a cry of joy clutched the jewel to his heart, and jumped to his feet.

"It is the flicker of the lamp," he cried; "I am growing dull with the lying stories of the death omen."

He clapped his hands, and Nuline came noiselessly inside the chamber.

Had not the merchant's nerves been so unstrung by his late fear, he would have noticed that Nuline must have been behind the silken hangings by the instant answer to his summons.

He pointed to the lamp which hung by massive chains of wrought silver from the centre of the apartment, and said—

"Dog, why is this?"

The black made no reply, but glancing furtively round the chamber, he came swiftly towards his master.

The merchant's hand was in his breast, clutching the mystic jewel to his heart, and Nuline, when he came within a few paces from where his master stood, drew a bright-bladed knife from his waist, and with one bound sprang upon Imaun Bey.

Totally unprepared for this attack, Imaun was unable to grasp the drawn scimitar which lay upon the cushions, and the black, with murder in his dark eyes, drove the keen blade into his master's heart.

The bey fell without a murmur, his warm blood bedabbling the silken cushions.

"Mine! mine!" said the black, tearing open the fingers which had closed upon the fatal gem; "mine, and I am rich—rich, and can buy slaves and keep a harem of beautiful women."

He sat upon a cushion and gazed with joyous rapture at his prize.

He held it so that the light fell upon the ocean's treasure, and laughing aloud in his glee, the murderer pressed the fatal gem to his lips.

"Bags of gold," thought Nuline, "yonder dead man gave for you—heaps of yellow, shining treasure—and I have got thee for one blow. Ha! ha! ha! Rich, rich, rich!"

He held the sparkling emerald at arm's length, and watched the thousand lights as they sparkled in his trembling palm.

And as he watched, the green light suddenly faded, and the forerunner of death rose like a misty vapour before him.

Like the late possessor, the dead Imaun Bey, the black glanced upward at the lamp, imagining that the flickering light from the untrimmed cotton had caused the sudden change, for the wondrous brilliancy returned to the sea emerald, and Nuline, with a cry of joy, arose to fly from the house before the murder should be discovered.

His foot was upon the silken drapery and his hand stretched forward to draw the curtains aside. Before he could touch the heavy folds he fell back with a half-smothered cry of terror falling from his lips.

Ussof, with naked weapons and set teeth, stood before him.

The black was unarmed, and at the mercy of the cadi's servant; but he thought not of his safety.

His only thought was for the blood-bought treasure, and retreating from Ussof he placed the gem in his bosom.

The fellow's quick eye told him all that had passed, and closely following Nuline he said in his fierce accents—

"Murderer! where is the emerald you have stolen from your victim?"

"By the sacred tomb of the Prophet!" said Nuline, "I know not of what you speak."

"Liar! yonder dead body tells its story. Give it up to me or you die."

Nuline saw that parley or denial would be useless with his accuser, so, with a cry like a caged panther, he sprang upon Ussof.

The latter was thrown off his guard for a moment by the sudden attack.

Already had the slave's sinewy fingers begun to tighten round his neck.

Another moment and he would have been placed beside the stiffening form upon the pale silken cushions.

With a mighty effort he shook his sword arm free, and dropping the blade he plucked a curved dagger from his sash.

The act was seen by the black, and he strove with all the force of his giant strength to hurl his opponent to the ground.

Before he could do so the long blade of Ussof's dagger was plunged in his back, severing the vertebræ, and with the withdrawal of the weapon Nuline fell upon the soft Persian carpet a corpse.

Then Ussof sought and found the sea emerald, and hiding it in the folds of his turban, he placed the dead body of the slave beside his master, and left the house as he came, unheard and unnoticed.

So quiet had the double tragedy taken place, that Lena, although sleeping in the next chamber, heard not a sound.

The sea emerald was fulfilling its terrible mission, and bearing out the mystic skill of its terrible finder whose hand had plucked it from the ocean's depths.

CHAPTER XXXV

ADMIRAL ELLIS DISGRACES HIS COMMISSION AND HIS MANHOOD.

THE heart of the little admiral was torn with rage, and his brain felt as though being dried by a scorching heat, when he beheld the vessel of the Spanish pirate captured by the Boy Buccaneer.

For some time he could not believe the truth. It seemed impossible that Don Pardo's huge ship and savage crew could have been overmatched.

When the galling reality with terrible force came upon him, he reeled as though the lightning's scathing power had struck him to the earth.

Such emotions, so terrible to the revengeful spirit, that had caused the fierce corsair to go forth and crush the brave boys, were multiplied when the Will-o'-the-Wisp glided through the waters with her huge adversary in her wake.

Admiral Ellis gave one long, bitter look at the sight.

It was too much for his overcharged brain. The hope he had cherished to be thus plucked away, and the man whom he waited to greet as a conqueror to be delivered into his hands half dead from the stroke of the brave, handsome Captain Tom.

Then the taunting words rang upon his ears, and with a convulsive cry he sank down upon the frigate's deck.

The gallant old commander knelt beside the fallen form.

He pitied the man whose revengeful passions could reduce body and mind to this pitiable condition, but in his heart he rejoiced at the indomitable pluck which the lads had displayed in crushing the might of the terrible Spaniard.

With returning consciousness, the insatiable wish for revenge came with redoubled force to the admiral's heart.

He was weak and powerless in body, and had to be conveyed to his cabin, but, while prostrated, his mind dwelt upon a black scheme to avenge what he called his daughter's dishonourable union.

The commander, with his kindly heart, saw not the hidden treachery beneath his brother's words when he called for his child.

"The Will-o'-the-Wisp," he said, "is yet in sight; it is not yet too late to bring Jenny on board."

The admiral turned his pale face from the speaker's open countenance, and answered—

"I am ill, brother, very ill; but let me see my child."

The commodore pressed his hand, then rushed on deck to signal the graceful Will-o'-the-Wisp, which had hove to, while the crew repaired the damage sustained in the terrible encounter.

While the various coloured signals were floating from the frigate's masthead, and being returned from the Will-o'-the-Wisp, the admiral dragged himself from the couch, and, opening his desk, began to write.

There was a steel-like glitter in his eyes,

and a most pitiless expression upon his compressed lips as the pen flew rapidly over the paper.

The last word was written; the paper folded; then the large official seal, bearing the arms of England, pressed upon the document.

Admiral Ellis extinguished the taper which he had used to melt the sealing-wax, and as the white coil of smoke rose from the wick, he muttered with savage earnestness—

"So shall his life be extinguished, low, grovelling hound. May his soul be cursed hereafter, as I curse him in life."

The commodore's firm steps were heard descending.

Admiral Ellis clutched the sealed document, and, creeping back to his bed, placed it under the pillow.

"I have signalled," said the old commodore, "and it has been answered."

"How?"

"Favourably; a boat is now being lowered from the Will-o'-the-Wisp, and Jenny will soon be here—poor girl."

Admiral Ellis looked up.

"Brother," he said, "you feel that I have been harsh to her?"

The admiral inclined his head.

"I have," the admiral continued, "but it is not too late to make reparation."

The admiral's face beamed with joy as he asked—

"You intend to forgive her?"

"I do."

"And her husband?"

The admiral's face reddened with savage hate.

"I will consider about that," he said, as calm as the pallor of passion would permit him to speak.

Commodore Ellis was about to venture upon a gentle remonstrance for his brother's bitter animosity to Harry Vere, when a strange noise caused him to start.

Above his head he heard the hurried tramp of feet, and a confused cry of alarm mingled with the harsh voices of the officers giving orders.

Then the clatter of ropes, and the swift falling of a boat past the cabin windows.

A sense of dread came over the commander's heart, and springing across the cabin, he exclaimed—

"What can be the matter?"

"A lubber fallen overboard," said the admiral, "and serve him right. Why—"

The cabin door was hastily opened, and a midshipman rushed in, pale and frightened, saying—

"The admiral's daughter is drowned!"

A sob of agony came from the commodore's lips, and, rushing past the boy, he dashed on deck.

The admiral spoke not. The sudden entrance of the boy and the fearful words he uttered fell with crushing force upon his heart.

His face paled, and, clutching at the coverlit, he lay back in speechless agony.

The vengeful man, with his brain filled with black and treacherous thoughts, felt that the avenging hand of heaven had brought about this sudden and terrible calamity.

The words he had but a few moments since penned in the paper that lay beneath his head were dancing in flaming letters before his eyes, and a thousand furies seemed to fill the cabin

and laughed with diabolical joy at the wretched man.

He lay in this stupor until a hearty cheer from the men who crowded the vessel's side caused him to spring up.

He felt his child was safe, and the revulsion of feeling was more than his agonized spirit could bear.

A cry of mingled joy and fear came from his dried lips; then clutching wildly at the empty space, he fell back as ghastly and rigid as a corpse.

When the signal to speak with the Will-o'-the-Wisp fluttered from the frigate, Captain Tom was standing upon the quarter-deck, surrounded by his officers.

Doctor Shrike and his assistant were in their element. Arms and legs were taken off by the dozen, much to the vampire's glee; and when the ghastly work was finished, and the table in the cockpit was encumbered with a heap of grisly relics, the vampire went on deck.

He saw the signal flying from the frigate, and, rushing down below, he gave Jacob a dig with the scalpel, and cried out gleefully—

"Throw these limbs into the sea; there will be more work presently, Jacop—more glorious work for us."

"More work?"

"Yes, you mummy, more work. The frigate has signalled, and that means fighting, don't it—eh, you scarecrow?"

"S'pose it does. Bear a hand here to chuck these things to the sharks. Hallo!"

"What—what's the matter?"

"Listen."

The vampire did so, and he heard a moan of agony from one of the wounded sufferers.

"Jacop," he said, grinning from ear to ear, "there's a fellow grumbling at the way in which I have treated him."

"I hear him; he ought to be glad he has fallen into such skilful hands."

"He ought, Jacop; so off with you and stick a pitch plaister over his mouth—that'll stop his jaw."

Jacob hurried off to obey his master.

Taking a huge pitch plaister in his long claw-like hands, he went to the hammock from which he fancied the wail of suffering had proceeded.

Unfortunately for the operator, it happened to be the hammock of one who had passed through the conflict unharmed.

The youngster was fast asleep until the plaister was suddenly clapped over his mouth.

Jacob stood for a moment pressing the filthy mass into the lad's mouth and nostrils—a proceeding that did not please the recipient; and before Jacob knew well what had happened, a clenched fist came from the hammock and lodged fair upon his nose.

The blow was well and forcibly aimed, and the long Jacob tumbled to the floor as though he had been shot.

Much astonished at such treatment, he arose, and fearing the legs that belonged to so strong a fist would soon appear over the side of the hammock, he sneaked back to his master, a double stream of blood flowing from his nose.

When the vampire beheld his assistant's face, he clutched his dissecting knife and ran forward, shouting—

"Jacop, I must operate upon you."

The long mummy retreated in dismay, the

vampire, flourishing the knife, followed, shouting—

"Come here, you fool; I'll whip your nose off, and cure it at once."

Jacob only ran the faster.

"D—d cur! he's suffering from *epestaxis hematemesis*: bust cure is to cut it off."

Jacob, with one hand clutching his long nose, continued his flight, but had not a friendly hand dropped a round-shot upon the vampire's bald head, as he ran under the open hatchway, he would to a certainty have lost his nasal ornament.

The round-shot knocked the vampire to a sitting posture, and glaring around, he rubbed the newly-raised bump, and muttered—

"Just as there's more work coming in—plenty of arms and legs and heads to be taken off; he won't be cured, the cussed long effigy!"

For once Doctor Shrike was mistaken. The signal was far from being a harbinger of coming strife.

Harry Vere was the first to discern the signal, and turning to his young leader, he asked—

"Shall I answer it, sir?"

"Yes," said Captain Tom; "it is an insulting message, I expect."

"Sure to be from that quarter," said Ben Barnacle. "I should not care about being on board that frigate just now. The hell we read about would be child's work to life on board under old Ellis."

Ben's sentiment was echoed by all who stood upon the quiet deck of the Will-o'-the-Wisp.

Strange emotions, not unmixed with fear for his beloved wife, passed through the young officer's mind, as he made out the captain's request.

"Admiral Ellis is ill, and wishes his daughter to come aboard. Will you send a boat?"

"Yes," said Tom, when Harry had spoken; "gladly, and I hope this may be a forerunner of peace between the angry sire and his child."

"I hope so too," said Harry. "But the—"

Jenny crept to her husband's side, her tearful face upturned, and such a pleading, wistful look was there, that Harry felt the injustice of his suspicions.

He drew her to his breast, and kissing her pale face said—

"You shall go, Jenny. I will take you on board."

"No—no," she answered quickly; "stay where you are, Harry. My father is ill. Let me see him, I will plead for your forgiveness. If he relents, you shall come to me, if not, I—"

"Well, Jenny."

"I will not stay."

"Noble girl!" Then to Captain Tom, "Have I your permission to pipe a boat away?"

"Yes," said the buccaneer king; "but you had better stay with us."

"It has been so arranged, sir."

The shrill whistle was followed by the cry of—

"First cutter's crew away!"

A few minutes after Jenny Vere, with a yearning heart, was being rowed to the flagship by the young buccaneers.

Harry Vere stood upon the vessel's bows, watching his wife as the boat danced upon the tops of the white-crested waves.

Watched her until the distance and the heavy sea that was running caused the frail craft to be hidden from his view. Then he turned sadly towards the quarter-deck, and his thoughts found utterance in words.

"Would," he said, "that I could look upon this as a harbinger of good! Alas! I cannot. There seems a dark cloud behind this momentary happiness for poor Jenny."

An unerring instinct but dimly warned the young officer of coming evil. It assumed no tangible shape, so left him cheerless and melancholy until the boat should return with his bride.

He little imagined as he stood with our gallant young hero conversing upon the last fight, and planning out great achievements for the future, the dark cloud which was gathering above his head.

The boat sped merrily forward until the huge hull of the admiral's ship rose tower-like above.

At every stroke of the long oars, Jenny's excitement increased, and when they shot past the bows she stood upright, her small fingers opening and closing in her anxiety to clutch the main ropes and ascend the side.

The midshipman in charge saw the dangerous position, and observing a large wave rolling towards them, called out—

"Sit down! You will be capsized. Great heavens! she has fallen overboard. Haste, haste, all of you!"

His warning came too late. A lesser wave than he had been watching struck the side of the boat, and Jenny, thrown off her balance, fell over the side.

One scream of fear—one wild clutch at the boat, and calling out in piteous accents—

"Harry—father—save me!"

She disappeared below the treacherous ocean's surface. The accident was seen by many on the frigate's deck, hence arose the confusion and quick lowering of the boat which had startled the veteran brothers in the cabin.

Then came the confused cries.

"Lower down the boats! Where's the crew?"

Then a rush of good-hearted men and busy hands began casting off the gripes.

The cry of the young buccaneers when the sad misfortune took place, showed how deeply Harry Vere's gentle wife was loved by the gallant lads.

Frantically they pulled to the spot where Jenny's light form had divided the wave, and their cry of horror was repeated by a shriek from the old commodore upon the frigate's deck.

Jenny had disappeared.

Who shall attempt to portray the terrible agony of her uncle's mind when he saw his niece's form carried upon the crest of a huge billow?

How his face flushed, and his eyes appeared ready to burst from their sockets, when he saw the wave break into feathery foam, and amid the whirl of waters his brother's child disappear beneath the hissing element!

A mingled shriek and cry came from his lips as he saw this—saw the white arms raised for succour—saw the boat dash into the surge, and, as though stricken by a bullet, the strong man who had faced death in a hundred forms, reeled backward, and moaned—

"Great heavens! she is lost!"

The boat from the frigate was by this time aiding the cutter from the Will-o'-the-Wisp.

and despite their frantic search, nothing of the hapless girl could be seen.

Awed by the sudden calamity that had befallen them, the boy buccaneers rested for a moment upon their oars, and, as the boat rose upon the summit of a foaming billow, they looked fearfully around for Jenny Vere.

Then as the latter was carried down into the trough of the sea, a shout came from the crowded deck of the admiral's ship.

They saw the hapless girl being carried upon a mighty wave towards the shore, and the seamen's faces blanched and their breaths were suspended as the knowledge of the fearful fate that awaited the now senseless girl broke upon their minds.

Should the wave reach the rock-bound shore, no earthly power could save Admiral Ellis's child from being dashed to pieces.

Madly the boats, guided by the cries of those on board the frigate, dashed forward to rescue the poor girl from such a dreadful death; and many closed their eyes in silent horror as they saw the distance was too great for the boats, well as they were worked, to reach her in time.

During this awful moment a circumstance occurred that called forth a mighty shout from the seamen, whose eyes, with a strange and horrible fascination, were riveted upon the helpless form as it was borne to destruction.

Springing from the jutting point of a rock, a light figure cleft the air and dived into the waters.

In a second he arose to the surface, and every eye became fixed on his movements.

Buffeting the foam and regardless of the blinding spray, he swam towards Jenny; and almost before the anxious watchers could believe the fact, the daring swimmer had clutched the admiral's daughter from a fearful fate.

One determined struggle with the baffled waves, and he was safe; and carrying Jenny up the rocks, he stood, one hand clutching the close vegetation, the other hand round her waist, awaiting the arrival of the first boat.

Placing his senseless burden in the cutter's bows, the gallant fellow would have retreated without a word had not the middy, in grateful but firm terms, compelled him to accompany them to the ship.

He yielded to the boy's solicitude, and entered the boat amid a ringing hurrah from the frigate's crew.

The excitement, the blended joy and fear of the commodore, resembled the ravings of a lunatic; and while Jenny was being taken below to her father's cabin, the commodore, grasping the stranger's hands, poured forth his gratitude for the noble act.

The brave fellow's face tinged with a modest blush as he heard the commodore's words. He seemed to consider the act as undeserving of so much gratitude.

Jenny's preserver was a noble-looking fellow, and his dress—which consisted only of a pair of high boots and white leather riding trousers, and a shirt—showed his form to advantage.

The remaining garments he had evidently thrown off as he prepared to leap into the sea. Except for a scarlet velvet cap with a golden tassel, he might have been taken for a gentleman of birth and position.

The old commodore pressed the brave fe

to wait and receive Jenny's thanks, but to no purpose, nor would he give his name.

The only favour he asked was to be allowed to go ashore at once.

A favour that was granted; and as the boat neared the shore, and the commodore stood with swelling heart watching the preserver of his brother's child, and wondering to what grade in life he belonged, he heard one sailor in conversation with another say—

"I'm certain of it—that is Hugh Baldrick, the Smuggler Prince."

The commodore started. Twice had his niece, if this was true, been rescued from danger by outlaws.

The first time by Captain Tom, when the commodore and Jenny had been saved from the attack of footpads.

The second was the recent escape from being dashed to pieces on the rocks.

Marvelling much that such bravery should seem inherent in those who set the laws of their country at defiance, the bluff, good-hearted old fellow stole softly down to his brother's cabin.

He paused at the threshold.

Once glance showed him father and daughter locked in a fond embrace.

He knew not that beneath this semblance of love there lurked a serpent's sting in his brother's heart.

So while tears of joy welled from his heart, he stood silent and happy, gazing upon those he loved so well.

Could Commodore Ellis have read the thought uppermost to his brother's mind as he strained his daughter to his heart, the honest-hearted old man would have recoiled with horror at the fell iniquity of the admiral's nature.

And his kind, genial nature would have revolted at the degradation the truth would have made apparent.

CHAPTER XXXVI.

SEALED ORDERS—THE FATE OF HARRY VERE.

FATHER and daughter remained for some time locked in each other's arms.

"God bless you both," said the old commodore, huskily, "I have longed for this hour to come."

Jenny left her father and came to the speaker's side.

"So," he said, drawing her to his breast, "you were nearly killing your poor old uncle, you puss."

"I——"

"Yes, you miss. Do you call falling into the water before my eyes nothing, eh!"

"I was much to blame, uncle; but my eagerness to see my father must palliate my carelessness."

"Oh! you were eager to come aboard, were you?"

"Yes."

"And that ras—I mean your husband—what did he say to it?"

Jenny looked up at her uncle's face and replied—

"Harry would not have uttered a word to deter me from coming here, although it might have separated us for years."

"Hem! ha! there's some good in the fellow. I suppose you love him very much, Jenny?"

The roseate tinge that came upon her cheeks.

glad sparkle in her eyes, assured him eloquently than words.

I see you do," the old fellow said; then aking his voice, he added, "we must see what can be done for him."

Jenny looked up interrogatively.

" I mean to get your father's forgiveness."

"Oh!" she said, "what a happy time that would be for us all!"

With a lighter heart than he had possessed for some time, the commodore went on deck.

"Hang it!" he mused, "my brother ought to forgive Harry Vere; the mischief is done now, and it's no use fretting about it; it is what I should do were it my case. Well, what do you want?"

This was to a middy who had come to the old sailor's side.

"The boat, sir," said the boy; "is it to wait?"

"Boat—which boat?"

"From the Will-o'-the-Wisp."

"Captain Tom, be d—d! No; I mean that young villain out there."

"Yes, sir."

"Ha! wait! No; tell them to go and be d—d to them."

The middy saluted, did a grin, and danced down the steps.

The commodore's voice stopped his grinning and dancing instantly, as he called out—

"Come here."

The boy came.

What message did I give you, sir?"

"You told me to tell them to go and be d—d. I don't like to say it, sir."

"Say what! d—d, eh!"

"Yes, sir."

"Well, I'll say it for you; d—d!—there."

"That was the message, sir."

"Was it? Well, tell them we will signal for the boat to return, and give Commodore Ellis's compliments to the commander of the Will-o'-the-Wisp, and tell him to keep within sight for a short time."

"Yes, sir."

The middy made a bolt.

"Come here, you young jackanapes."

"Also tell him that Admiral Ellis is very ill, and his daughter will remain with him for a short time."

"Yes sir; is that all?"

"All. Now, be off with you."

The boy gave the message to Captain Tom's young officer, and the boat glided swiftly away.

"A pity to see those brave young fellows going to the devil," thought the commodore, as he watched the boat cleave the water. "Curse the rascal, I say, that caused them to mutiny. Were I King George I'd give them all a free pardon, and hang the fellow to the yard-arm that deprived the navy of so many gallant fellows."

He turned angrily upon his heel, and went below to his brother's cabin.

Admiral Ellis lay back in his cot; his face the hue of Parian marble, save where a small bright spot shone on either cheek.

The commodore stepped to his brother's side, and gazing intently at the pale face and restless eyes of the sick man, said—

"Brother, you are ill, very ill."

The admiral pulled up the coverlet sharply and answered testily—

"I know it; get well some day, I suppose, or die."

It was some time before the admiral was able to leave his cot, and during that time Jenny had scarcely left her father's side.

During his illness the good-hearted old commodore had forborne any mention of the subject uppermost in his mind.

But now the admiral had recovered, and they were standing side by side on the quarter-deck, the commodore began to reason with the irascible father.

"Brother," he said, "is Jenny to return to her husband?"

Admiral Ellis started.

"Return to her—her—"

"Husband," said the commodore. "It's no use, brother, beating about the bush, I see."

A peculiar look passed over the admiral's face.

"No," he said, "it is not. What do you advise in this matter?"

"My sentiments are the same."

"That I should freely forgive him?"

"Exactly."

The admiral pondered for a minute.

"I dare not," he said at length.

"Then," began the commodore, hotly, "you have no gratitude. Did he not, without murmuring, send Jenny to you when the signal was sent that you were ill?"

"Well?"

"Well! It is not well, brother. Come, throw aside this pride, and acknowledge the boy. Curse it, he is a brave——"

"I do not," said the admiral, coldly, "wish to hear his praise sung by you. I have heard enough of that already."

"From whom?"

"Jenny."

"I am glad to hear it. I imagined from her happy face that you had given her some promise of extending your forgiveness to her husband."

"Husband!" hissed the admiral, turning his head away so that his brother could not behold the expression of malice upon his features; "husband—curse that word! It scorches my brain."

"What are you muttering about?"

"Nothing."

"Hem! Well, have you done so?"

"What?"

"Given Jenny any promise?"

"Nothing definite yet."

"Brother," said the commodore, "plain sailing is the best."

"Another homily?"

"No; but if you have given that poor girl any hope——"

A harsh grating laugh came from the admiral's lips as he said—

"I have held out no promise but one, and that I shall be able to fulfil."

"And that affects Jenny's husband?"

"It does."

"And I hope——"

"Hope for nothing." said the admiral; "it will all rest with the fellow."

"I do not understand you."

"I suppose not," said the admiral, drily; "shall I explain?"

"Do."

"I am about to try the fellow," the admiral began. "If he acquits himself as I expect he will, Jenny shall be forgiven."

"Try him. What, by court-martial?"

"No; I propose sending him for a cruise on board the Lapwing. If my plan does not succeed, why I will wash my hands of the pair."

"Send him for a cruise!" said the puzzled commodore; "and if he does not acquit himself, you—— Curse me if I can make head or tail of it!"

"You will know all very soon," said the little admiral, with a sinister smile.

He walked away, and put an end to the conversation by ordering all hands on deck to exercise at the big guns.

The blue-jackets having acquitted themselves to the little martinet's satisfaction, he went below.

Jenny was sitting upon a locker when he entered, and, jumping from her seat, she ran towards him with a glad cry.

"Have you sent for Harry, father?" she asked.

"I have not."

"Then you have not altered your mind. Oh! father, do not——"

"Peace, girl! I find that I cannot have an outlaw upon my ship but if he will go at once on board the Lapwing, I will ascertain at the end of the cruise how he has conducted himself. Should it be satisfactory, perhaps I may forgive the crime he has committed."

"I am sure, father, he will acquit himself to your satisfaction."

"We shall see. The cruise will be a long one, and he will have every opportunity of becoming all I wish."

There was something in her father's manner that sent a chill to Jenny's heart. Strong in her love for her husband, she said, quickly—

"Father, I must accompany Harry on this cruise."

The admiral pondered.

"Well, be it so," he said, "you shall. It may be better for both. Now, girl, the Lapwing's boat will be here directly—so get ready."

"I am quite ready, father."

They went on deck, and the admiral signalled a sloop of war that lay at anchor near the frigate.

The signal was answered, and soon after the captain of the sloop came on board, and saluted the admiral.

"Come below with me," said the little officer. "I wish to speak to you, Captain Clark."

The captain of the Lapwing followed his superior to the state-room.

From his desk the admiral took a sealed packet, and gave it to the young officer with the words—

"You will have Lieutenant Vere and his lady on board your vessel."

The captain bowed.

"When you reach the latitude marked on this cover, open the seal and act as the instructions dictate."

"I will, sir."

"You will take Lieutenant Vere on board from that vessel with the high topmasts that lies out in the bay."

"The 'Will-o'-the-Wisp'?"

"Yes. When he is on board your vessel, lose no time in reaching the latitude marked on the cover of the sealed orders."

Captain Clark bowed assent, and, following his superior, they went on deck.

Jenny was standing by the gangway, waiting eagerly for the captain.

Her parting from the admiral was marked by that cold hauteur which characterised every action of the stern little officer.

While from the good-hearted old commodore she had a rough but kindly salute.

The admiral had walked to the mast, and, glass in hand, was keenly watching the sloop's boat as it sped to Captain Tom Drake's graceful vessel.

He saw the boat range under the quarter of the Will-o'-the-Wisp, and a laugh of more than ordinary meaning came from his lips.

Presently he beheld, by the aid of his powerful glass, a form, which he conjectured to be Harry Vere's, leave the buccaneer's vessel, and step into the boat.

"So!" he chuckled savagely; "he has fallen into the trap, and my daughter's disgraceful union will be soon cancelled."

"Muttering again," said a cheery voice at his elbow.

The admiral turned, and beheld his brother standing close beside him.

"I see the Will-o'-the-Wisp," said the commodore, "is making sail."

"Curse her! yes. I should be happy could I see every timber of that infernal ship blown up in the air."

"Not a charitable wish."

"No, but a sincere one."

The commodore made no reply.

That night the commodore went below to take leave of his brother, previous to going on board his own vessel.

He was much surprised at beholding the slim, elegant figure of Admiral Lord Kilcrew sitting in the cabin."

"Where, in fortune's name," he said brusquely, "did you come from, my lord?"

"From the Spanish ship, commodore."

"You were in the fight?"

"By St. Patrick! you speak the truth, and a hot fight it was."

"So I should think. But what the devil brought Lord Kilcrew in the doubtful company of Don Pardo?"

"A little business, commodore—fact I wanted to cross swords with this fire-eating devil, Captain Tom Drake."

"You got your wish, I suppose?"

A WARM RECEPTION.

"By St. Patrick! I did, for once; but I mean to have another try."

"Take care, my lord. He is a matchless swordsman, this Captain Tom."

"Faith! commodore, he is; and for that same reason it behoves Kilcrew to meet him again."

"As you will, my lord," said the commodore, "you are the best judge of your own safety."

"Is it the harm that slip of a boy can do me? By St. Patrick! the next time Kilcrew gets forninst him, he will be sorry for the day."

"Perhaps," thought the commodore, "the case may be reversed, and Lord Kilcrew will be the one to be sorry."

"Bedad!" said Admiral Lord Kilcrew, suddenly, "is it true that the boy buccaneer's ship has gone?"

"Run up and make sure," said the commodore, briskly.

"By Saint Patrick! and my bride on board among those devils!"

"She is as safe there," said the commodore, "as safe as though she were under the protection of her relatives."

"May be. But still it's not the most pleasant thing in the world to know. Anyhow, I'll go and look. Perhaps, after all, it may be the 'Lapwing' you are thinking of, commodore?"

"Not at all, my lord. The 'Lapwing' and the 'Will-o'-the-Wisp' went in quite contrary directions."

"Bedad! May the old jintleman fly away with him! Anyhow, I'll go and see."

The Irish nobleman went on deck, but it was little he discerned of the gallant ship of the boy adventurers.

"Brother," said the commodore, when Kilcrew had left the cabin, "you seem merry to-night."

"I am," replied the admiral; "quite overjoyed."

"May I ask the cause?"

"Undoubtedly—and learn it. How is the wind?"

The commodore stared at this speech, but, being used to his brother's peculiarities, he said—

"It was blowing hard a minute since."

"May it keep so till morning."

"What has the wind to do with your log?"

"Everything."

"Everything? What, in fortune's name, do you mean?"

"This," said the admiral, with cold, pitiless emphasis on every word. "Should the wind keep up until to-morrow the disgraceful tie my daughter has contracted will be broken."

"What?"

"You are dull of comprehension."

"I am not!" said the commodore, excitedly. "Speak, for Heaven's sake! I do not understand your ambiguous words."

The admiral laughed—such a cold, satanic laugh, that it froze the blood in his brother's veins.

"Divesting my speech of the ambiguity you complain about, in plain English, the matter amounts to this—"

He leaned on his hand, and watched his brother's expectant face.

"Should the wind," he said, "carry the 'Lapwing' to the latitude I have marked on the sealed orders now in Captain Clark's possession, by to-morrow's sunset Harry Vere will be shot, that's all."

The commodore reeled backward at the fell iniquity of his brother's mind.

"All!" he said, when the first feeling of horror had passed away. "All! Are you man to thus calmly murder a fellow-creature, and the husband of your daughter, above all others?"

"The family honour demands the sacrifice."

"Curse the family honour, and you, too! Look here, brother—I tell you this foul murder shall not take place."

"Indeed!" was the sneering answer; "who is to prevent it?"

"I!" shouted the commodore. "I'll prevent it—a—a wicked, pitiless—ugh! I—I—"

He rushed from the cabin, followed by the admiral, shouting-

"Here! Come back! I was but joking. Come back!"

The commodore was on deck before his brother could reach half-way up the hatch, and ordered the sleepy watch to be quick and lower a boat.

The admiral followed closely, and rushed to the side, just as the boat fell upon the waters.

"Stay!" he shouted. "The first man that puts his oar in the water shall receive three dozen to-morrow morning."

"Give way, my lads," said the commodore. "Curse the three dozen! Take me to my vessel, and remain there. I am short of hands, and the frigate has several supernumeraries."

"Mutiny, by the Lord!" yelled the little admiral, dancing about on deck. "Here, you fellows, drop a cold shot in that boat; and you, Commodore Ellis, I arrest you for inciting my men to mutinise against me, their superior officer."

The men on deck were a long time finding the best shot to stave the boat in, and, to the admiral's rage,

he beheld the commodore being taken swiftly from the frigate's side.

A few words from the commodore had been sufficient to cause the men to use every effort to get clear of the frigate.

"You hear that order," he said, when the admiral ordered the shot to be hurled into the boat. "Stay here, and be fished up by boat-hooks, or come with me and be safe."

"But, sir," said the coxswain, "we shall be tried for mutiny"

"Nonsense; how many supernumeraries are there on board the frigate?"

"About twenty, sir."

"Very well; ten are for my ship. I have eight volunteers in this boat. Your place can be supplied from the extra hands."

"But our kits, sir?"

"Curse them! I'll buy your new rig out, and give you five guineas each in the bargain."

"Pull, you lubbers," said the coxswain; "pull off, or we get cold iron among us."

The men pulled with a will. They were going to a good ship, and to have five guineas to spend, and a frolic ashore.

The little admiral's anger cooled upon reflection.

"He can't overtake them," he muttered; "long before the old tub he commands can sight the sloop that beggarly lieutenant will be food for sharks. As for those men who have gone with him, I'll disrate the petty officers, and not one of them shall place his foot upon the frigate's deck while I have command."

Dressed in her snowy canvas, the commodore's vessel started in pursuit of the "Lapwing."

The commodore passed the whole of that night upon deck, his mind torn by racking thoughts.

He could not at times realise the terrible truth. So foul a deed—a cold-blooded, deliberate murder—to be planned by his brother, seemed such a monstrosity that his blood curdled at the very thought.

Morning came, with its glad sunshine falling upon the trackless waters; and its warm glow fell upon the grey-headed veteran, whose anxious eyes were fixed upon the distant horizon.

Still no sign of the "Lapwing."

On, on, through that long day, until the twilight shadows began to creep over them, the good ship held on her course.

And twilight deepened into night, and still the hoped-for sail was invisible.

To and fro the narrow limits of the deck the veteran passed. Neither food nor rest had he taken since he rushed from the frigate, the horrible story of fell murder ringing in his ears.

There, with compressed lips and straining eyes, he stood, the noble vessel, the mighty waters, the vaulted canopy of Heaven, all unnoticed.

He saw but the bleeding corpse of Harry Vere as he fell, riddled by bullets; he heard, in fancy, the long shriek of agony from Jenny's lips, and saw her fall to the deck lifeless.

And as these images of an excited mind grew stronger upon him, he felt as though his brain was being scorched with molten lead.

Several times his hand was pressed to his brow, and he murmured, in accents of acute mental agony—

"Great Heavens! save me, or I shall go mad!"

Still, with the hope strong within him that he should be in time to prevent the foul deed taking place, he kept his station.

At last the man at the mast-head sang out the welcome news that a sail was in sight.

And soon after the commodore beheld the lights of a vessel far ahead.

He looked up at the white mountain of canvas and cried out—

"Clap on more sail there, my lads. We must be up with that vessel before morning."

His orders were obeyed, and all through the long interval between darkness and dawn he watched the blazing lights of the distant ship.

Once the terrible thought crossed his mind that, after all, the vessel he was following might not be the "Lapwing."

But that thought was banished; it was too horrible to think upon.

Sometimes invisible, at others gleaming out afar like twin stars, the lights guided the commodore upon the track of mercy; at other times his heart would sink as they disappeared with the rolling of the ship.

Disappeared, to rise again with greater brilliancy, and bring the glad light to his eyes and the glow of hope to his face.

When the early day loomed through the hazy clouds the outlines of the chase were seen by all on board.

Then every doubt vanished from the commodore's mind, there could be no mistake now.

It was the "Lapwing;" and he was in time to save his brother's soul from the stain of murder.

"Quick, there!" he shouted; cast loose a gun and fire a shot over the sloop's bows."

While the men were casting loose the gun the commodore's eyes were fixed upon the vessel.

Was he dreaming, or had some fiend conjured up the horrible vision?

As he gazed upon the shadowy outlines of the sloop of war, and before the gun could be fired, a bright flash, followed by a quick rattle, was seen upon the vessel's stern.

The commodore gave one mighty cry of heartfelt agony, and fell to the deck as though the bullets of the distant muskets had cleft his heart in twain.

He guessed but too well the meaning of that bright sheet of flame, and the quick report that followed. It was a mercy his senses forsook him, or he would have become a raving maniac.

CHAPTER XXXVII.

HARRY VERE'S HEROISM.—THE CAPTAIN OF THE "LAPWING" BREAKS HIS SWORD AND RESIGNS HIS COMMISSION.

BETWEEN the captain of the "Lapwing" and Harry Vere a feeling of sincere friendship soon sprung up.

The gallant officer, like most of the commanders of the navy, was well acquainted with the young bride's story, and when he gazed upon Jenny, he felt that, had he been placed in Harry's position, he would have risked everything for such a gentle wife.

They were upon deck one calm eve, and Captain Clark was conversing with Harry about the romantic marriage that had taken place in the chapel.

"I'm afraid, Harry," he said, "that, had the case been mine, I should not have been as fortunate as you have."

"Fortunate—how?"

"The sudden assistance Captain Tom Drake gave you I consider a piece of extraordinary good luck."

"It was. By the way, have you ever seen the gallant young buccaneer?"

"Never; that is a pleasure to come."

"You will like him," said Harry, enthusiastically, "a splendid fellow."

"So I have heard."

"The report, for once, does not lie."

"Report," said Captain Clark, "speaks truth in one instance."

"Which is that?"

"Respecting your amiable father-in-law."

"Yes."

"Well," said Harry, "perhaps, after all, we wrong him; you know the pride of birth is strong in many of the old families, and it must gall the old fellow when he thinks of a moneyless fellow like myself marrying his daughter."

"He be hanged, and his pride of birth, too; you are a fit husband for any girl, no matter had she a pedigree as long as the Monument."

"You flatter me."

"No, I do not—I admire. A fellow with an untarnished name and a good sword by his side, ought to brave his way through the world, and any woman he may condescend to smile upon, ought—"

"Stop—stop! you are laying it on too thick!"

"No, I'm not."

"I'll tell you what," said Harry, laughingly, "I shall depute you, when we return, to soften down the old fellow."

"Will you? Thanks; but I'd sooner go upon the previous station, and have a fit of yellow jack, than face that happy old rascal."

"You are not friends, I see."

"Far from it; I dislike him—a fact that is mutual."

"I wonder that he chooses you to take me on this service."

"So do I; but, truth to tell, I was the first he could come at; so no thanks for that."

"What can be his motive for this freak?"

A shade came over the captain's face, as he answered—

"I do not know, and do not care to surmise."

"Why?"

"That I can't tell you; but his bitter look of hatred when he gave me the sealed packet, and mentioned your name, I shall never forget."

"Sealed packet?"

"Yes."

"I cannot say, but, strange to tell, I seem to dread the breaking of that seal."

"I'll do it for you," he said; "surely you do not think it is a death-warrant?"

"I do not care about thinking—it only tends to confirm a conviction I have formed of the packet."

"That conviction is," said Harry, "that I am to be forgiven."

Jenny came to her husband's side at this moment, and led him away.

The captain of the "Lapwing" looked after the young pair, and muttered—

"I cannot help it, but I feel that accursed packet has some reference to Harry. Yet—no he would not dare carry out such a pitiless deed."

The time came at length for the sealed orders to be read, and Harry laughingly said—

"Don't look so glum, I'll read them for you."

"Be it so," said the captain. "I do not seem to like even the sight of the oblong official envelope, and its huge seal."

Harry made a jesting reply, and broke the coat of arms that was stamped upon the seal.

He read the contents, and his face became the hue of scarlet.

Beyond that momentary change of colour, he exhibited no outward emotion.

Captain Clark read the confirmation of his suspicions in the expression of mute agony that came over Harry's face, as he passed the document to its owner.

When Captain Clark read the fearful words that were written inside the large sheet, an agonising cry came from his lips.

"The cold-blooded, pitiless villain," he said, furiously. "By hea——"

"Hush!" said Harry, "the sentence must be carried out."

"The—the—do you think I can?"

"As long," said Harry Vere, "as you wear the King's uniform, you must do as you are ordered."

"Must? Hark you, Harry Vere——"

"I will hear nothing. Read that paper. You see I am to be executed ten hours after you get the orders. When will that be?"

"Never, I swear!"

"You forget you are compelled, by your oath, to obey all orders you may receive from your admiral."

"I care not. Think you that I will have the sin of killing your gentle wife upon my head?"

Harry Vere's frame shook when the captain of the "Lapwing" mentioned his beloved wife's name.

"She will hold you blameless," he said, as well as his quivering lips would permit. "It is your duty to obey this merciless order, and——"

"Do not madden me, Harry Vere," exclaimed Captain Clark: "think you that I would stand by and behold the man with whom I have lived in the bonds of friendship murdered before my eyes?"

Harry Vere was silent, he felt for the gallant young officer. And with the heroism worthy of a martyr, he determined that his friend should not blast his prospects in the service through a refusal to carry out the vindictive old admiral's orders.

"You are aware," Harry Vere said, "of the punishment for disobedience of orders?"

"I am. It is death."

"Such would be your fate. Now listen."

The captain of the "Lapwing" clasped his clenched hands to his forehead, and murmured——

"God help me! I know not what to do."

"There is but one course—your duty."

"And you?"

"I must die."

"This is horrible. Your wife, Harry, think you her reason will survive the terrible sight?"

Harry Vere was for a moment a prey to the most conflicting emotions.

He saw the platoon of marines as they levelled their pieces at his heart—heard the report, and Jenny's cry of heart-broken desolation, as he fell upon the deck!

It required a Spartan fortitude for the gallant fellow to endure these terrible thoughts without wishing, at any sacrifice, to live. Hard as it was to die, his noble nature could not accept life at the expense of his friend's death.

Closing his eyes, as though to shut out the horrible vision, he said—

"I have but one favour to ask you before I leave this world."

"A favour at the hands of your murderer, Harry?"

"Dismiss that idea from your mind."

"I cannot."

"Does the hangman," said Harry Vere, "when he carries the law's dread sentence into execution, feel that he is a murderer?"

"No; he has no cause."

"I do not see the difference in the——"

"It is plain," said Captain Clark; "the wretch who can strangle his fellow-man for a paltry fee must be so thoroughly brutish by nature that he can have no feeling in common with his fellow-res; besides——"

"Besides what?"

"Were he capable of feeling, he would have the satisfaction of knowing that he rids the world of a crime-stained wretch. With you it is impossible to draw a parallel case. You are innocent of all crime.

"In your eyes, perhaps; but not to him who has so craftily lured me to destruction. Would to Heaven I had been warned by my gallant young leader!"

"Did he suspect the admiral's sincerity?"

"He did, and was loth for me to leave the protection of the buccaneer flag."

"Would to Heaven you had been guided by him!"

"Regret is useless now. I must die! Let me die as a man should die! When is the execution to take place?"

Captain Clark was silent.

"I need not have asked," said Harry; "the time has already passed. You can extend it until daybreak to-morrow?"

"For ever, were my inclinations consulted."

"You will grant me entire the time I have asked?"

"I will; and —"

"Thanks. Now for the second," here Harry's voice faltered; "do not let my wife know anything of this until all is over."

"Harry, you —"

"It is my wish; do not try to dissuade me from it. I have but a few hours to pass with her in this world, and I would have that brief space pass in joy, and not in sorrow."

His wish was granted.

The brief time that stood between the gallant fellow and eternity was passed with his beloved wife.

With wondrous nerve, Harry shut out from his mind the terrible knowledge of his impending fate, and amused his young wife with various stories of his boyish freaks.

Unconscious of coming evil, she sank into a soft slumber, her lips sweetened with a happy smile.

As she lay thus, the doomed husband stood by the couch, and breathed a prayer for the hapless girl, who was so soon to be left desolate.

As he stood watching the slumberer's sweet face, his gallant heart for the time felt the full force of the coming bitterness that awaited her.

"Can it be true," he thought, "that in so few hours I shall be a lifeless corpse, the blood that now tingles through my veins become cold and stagnant, and my limbs food for the hungry sharks? No, no; it cannot be true; I am dreaming; Jenny, my sweet wife. Oh, God! am I to leave thee without one word of farewell; leave thee with that happy smile upon your lips, and your heart filled with joy? Can you, sweet girl, live when I am gone, live with the fearful knowledge preying upon you that your father has been my murderer?"

He turned away from the bedside, his heart filled with poignant misery, and his brain scorched by the force of his anguished thoughts.

Upon a table in the small cabin writing materials were placed ready for use.

To these Harry Vere turned, and seating himself, wrote a long and impassioned letter to his gentle wife.

"Forgive thy father, my darling Lucy," he wrote at the conclusion of the final farewell; "forgive him as I do. We shall meet, dear one, in a place far happier than this world, a bright land where sorrow and suffering can never reach us."

The last word was penned as the first thin line that heralded the coming day broke through the sky.

As he folded the paper, a tramping overhead, and

he rattle of firearms, told him that his hour was come.

Clasping his burning forehead with both his hands, he listened to the dread sounds; then creeping gently to the bedside, he stooped and pressed his lips to the sleeping girl's.

Slight as the caress was, it partly awoke Lucy, and, half opening her eyes, she stretched forth her hands and passed them around his neck.

"Come to bed, Harry," she murmured; "it must be late."

He made no reply, and then the white arms relaxed their hold.

The heroic victim of the admiral's savage hate stood for a few seconds upon the topmost step of the hatchway, and gazed at the preparation for his doom.

The ship's company were at their stations, and, facing a raised platform on the quarter-deck, a party of marines were drawn up.

Every eye was turned towards Harry as he stepped proudly upon the deck, and many a hard, horny hand was drawn across a weather-beaten face.

The marines, too—those steel-nerved warriors, whose indomitable pluck had shone so conspicuously in our mightiest battles—shook for a moment in their serried line.

They were men, and brave men; and the emotion that thrilled through their frames and sent the blood rushing like a torrent to their hearts did honour to their manhood.

Placed before England's fiercest foes, this phalanx of men would have stood until the last had been mowed down by shot or shell—stood without a muscle relaxing, or their iron nerve for one moment giving way.

But now, standing with loaded weapons under the first blush of the early morn, to calmly slay a brave fellow, whom one and all loved—no wonder that they felt as men, not as bloodthirsty hirelings.

Captain Clark came forward to meet the principal actor in this dread spectacle, and, taking his hand, said—

"Good-bye, Harry; God bless you! I can—"

His voice broke under the fearful strain upon his nerves, and he could do no more than stand clutching the young lieutenant's hands, holding them with a grasp that seemed as though he never would relax.

Harry Vere was resigned.

"Good-bye," he replied. "Give my dying love to Jenny, and tell her, as the bullets tear out my life, her image will fade from my heart, not till then. In the cabin there is a letter. I have spent the last hours of my life writing it. Give—give it to her when I—I am no more."

"Harry—" Captain Clark began, passionately.

"Do not unman me," said Captain Tom's lieutenant. "Farewell; I will give the signal for the men to fire."

Before Captain Clark could utter a word of remonstrance or entreaty, Harry Vere had broken from his grasp, and walked swiftly to the quarter-deck.

With one bound he stood upon the platform, and, turning to the firing party, said, in clear, ringing tones—

"Make ready, men, and, when I drop my hand, fire!"

He then surveyed the rippling waters, gave one anguished look in the direction of Jenny's cabin, and, dropping the hand that had been elevated above his head, cried out—

"Heaven receive my soul! Jenny, good-bye. Fire!"

A bright sheet of flame ran from muzzle to muzzle, and, mingled with the sharp report, there came a scream of piercing agony that caused every man upon the crowded deck to spring up as though the bullets which had left the yet smoking muskets had cleft their hearts.

Then, with hair dishevelled, and in her night-dress, Jenny rushed upon the deck.

Like an enraged lioness she sprang towards the marines, and wresting a musket from one of them, she screamed—

"Wretches! Murderers! My husband! my husband!"

And, before a hand could be put forth to save her, she sprang upon the quarter-deck.

One wild, affrighted look she gave at the spot where Harry had stood, and, dashing the musket to the deck, she uttered a shrill, maniacal scream and plunged into the water.

Noble, devoted woman, strong in her love for her husband, she had determined to perish with him.

The first feeling of stupefied amazement over, the horrified crew rushed to the side, and began to cast down the boats.

As the light crafts fell upon the water, there came a cry—

"Too late! too late! She has gone!"

"Quick—quick, men!" shouted Captain Clark, as he seized a rope which hung over the side, and slid into the largest boat; "oars out and pull, the ship cannot have drifted far."

They put back into the corvette's track, and sought eagerly for the hapless, hidden girl.

Sought with untiring perseverance, until every hope had died out; then, as a last resource, life-buoys, hen-coops, and spars were thrown upon the water, and the men, with downcast heads, and heavy, sorrowful hearts, pulled slowly back to the ship.

So great had been the excitement caused by the morning's dread work, that the crew of the corvette had not noticed a large vessel dash down upon them, and before they could pass it the corvette's yards were grappled to the stranger, and an old officer, shaking with passion, sprang upon the "Lapwing's" deck.

It was Commodore Ellis.

"Scoundrels!" he roared, dashing in amongst the startled seamen; "where is your villainous captain?"

As the commodore came over one side of the vessel, Captain Clark ascended the other.

He overheard the commodore's words, and, stepping upon the deck, said—

"I am here, sir."

"Here!" roared the old fellow, "and a scoundrel you are!"

Captain Clark came forward, his handsome face scarlet with indignation and shame.

"Keep off—keep off!" said the commodore gripping the hilt of his sword. "Where is Harry Vere?"

There was a dead silence.

A chill hush that damped the spirits of all who stood within hearing, and made them curse the day that they had left their homes to serve under the flag of England.

At length Captain Clark told the angry old commodore, and in his tone there was such a touching sadness, that the old fellow began to feel that he had wronged the gallant captain of the "Lapwing."

"Harry Vere," he said, "is now in that Heaven above, where your brother's pitiless hate cannot reach him."

The old commodore tried to reply, but the words stuck in his throat, and with difficulty he gasped—

"Where—where is my niece?"

"She," said Captain Clark, "has followed her husband—sought a Lethe for her desolation under the waters that engulped all she loved in this world."

A tear stood in the honest seaman's eyes as he uttered these words, and, turning round, he walked slowly to the open hatch.

The commodore was so stricken by these words that he receded backwards, one hand clutching the hilt of his sword, the other placed upon his throbbing brow.

"Jenny—Jenny—gone!" he gasped. "Merciful Heaven! can this be true?"

Captain Clark turned.

"Too true," he said, "too true, for lasting shame and dishonour of your brother's name."

"It is a judgment, captain," said the old commodore, big tears of bitter anguish rolling down his furrowed cheeks. "A judgment upon the merciless monster who sought to slay his child's husband. I swear, brother though he is, to make him repent this foul deed."

The captain of the "Lapwing" came to the sorrow-stricken old officer's side, and said—

"Commodore, a brother's hand should not be raised against a brother."

"What? to die—"

"Hear me out, commodore. That brave fellow who fell this morning was a friend of mine, and my hand shall avenge his death."

"Yours! You—you—forget that it is your superior officer you threaten."

"I have forgotten nothing, sir. Behold!"

Captain Clark drew his sword, and snapped the blade across his knees, then threw the broken parts overboard.

Then, taking from his breast a leather pocketbook, he took out his commission, and deliberately tore it into shreds, and threw the fragments after his sword.

The commodore gazed at the young officer in breathless surprise, and would have remonstrated, had not the noble fellow stopped him by saying—

"Thus I free myself of the service; now, as man to man, I can meet this cold-blooded villain. All I ask of you, commodore, is a passage back in your vessel."

"You shall have it," said the commodore, bluntly. "You are a fine fellow, and I ask you to forgive me for the unjust words I used when I first came on board your—at least, the corvette."

"Forgiven and forgotten," said Captain Clark, extending his hand. "I knew my old commander too well to mind the words he used when under the influence of such terrible excitement."

The commodore grasped the extended hand with a warmth that told of the genuineness of his heart.

The two vessels soon after parted company.

The "Lapwing" to continue her course, the frigate to return from whence she came, carrying the avenger of Harry Vere's murder and Jenny's suicide upon her decks.

When the last ripple caused by the passage of the ships through the water had died away, the tiny wavelets glittering under the glowing sun, the sea rolled on as peacefully as though nothing had happened to mar the coming of the new-born day.

CHAPTER XXXVIII.

HOW THE BULLETS DID THEIR WORK.

IN that dread moment when the marines had the deadly muzzles of their muskets levelled at Harry Vere's heart, the corvette, struck by a wave, lurched over and caused the firing party to stagger backward.

At the same moment Harry's voice rang out the command for them to fire.

High above his head flew the bullets, save one, and that grazed his temple with sufficient force to hurl him from the raised platform into the sea.

Partly conscious of what had happened, Harry Vere, when he came to the surface, struck out madly for the vessel.

A breeze filled the corvette's sails, and sent her onward at a swift pace.

So swift that the desperate swimmer was soon left far astern.

One wild look of agony he gave at the fast-receding hull, and raised his voice to attract the attention of those on board.

While the frantic yell was yet borne on the winds, he heard his wife's shriek of agony; then beheld her leap into the sea.

The numbing effect of the bullet passed away when he saw Jenny's danger, and, setting his teeth firmly, the resolute swimmer struck out for the spot where the form he loved so well had cleft the waters.

From the crest of a wave he had seen Jenny disappear, and his heart sank within him when he perceived the distance that intervened between him and the wretched, desolate girl.

Impelled forward by the gentle gale, the vessel soon left husband and wife far behind, and when she was hove to, and the boats were seeking for Jenny, the waves caused by the vessel's passage through the water carried both far away.

Maddened with despair, the agonised husband beat the waters, and swam to where he had seen her disappear.

Like a maniac he shrieked when he found that she had not risen again to the surface.

Harry Vere was an expert swimmer, and in his hour of dire calamity he thanked Heaven for this skill.

With a resolve to save his heart's idol, or die with her in the ocean's mystic depths, he dived beneath the surface.

And, while he remained below, the boats from the corvette, impelled by their strong-armed rowers, passed and re-passed the spot.

When Harry at length rose to the surface, the senseless form of his devoted wife clasped fondly to his heart, the boats had struck off in another direction, and he was left to perish.

Too much weakened by his exertions in rescuing Jenny, he could not call loud enough to attract the rowers' attention.

Thus, while he beat the waters with one hand, the other clasped Jenny, and, his eyes fixed in mute despair upon the receding boats and the corvette's dark hull, he gave himself up for lost.

There was even in this mournful conviction a sweetness that robbed death of its sting.

He would die with the form of her he loved so well pressed against his breast.

A moment after his feelings changed.

He looked at the pale, sweet face which rested upon his shoulder, and the wish became strong within him to live.

Live for the sake of one who ever proved her love and devotion to him.

Much as he prayed for his life to be spared, the crushing truth was too palpable for the faintest hope.

He was upon the boundless tract of waters, and those who were here served him when far away.

The remarkable look of silent despair which he gave his wife was a truthful reflex of the heart-agony he suffered.

"Jenny, Jenny," he cried, wildly, "are we to perish after all; is there no hope?"

He looked, and the boats were being hauled up the vessel's side. He saw there was none.

For the first time he beheld the frigate grapple with the vessel from which he had fallen, and he cried aloud for help.

None came.

And the horrible sensation came with redoubled force to his mind.

He must die.

Die, after escaping the flight of bullets which a merciful Providence had turned aside—death to claim him just as he was united to his bride, whom he thought never to behold again.

No wonder, with these thoughts coursing through his brain, that the gallant fellow's heart sank, and he cried in his agony.

He felt the end drawing nigh—his strength was rapidly failing him, and the strong arm that had so long buffetted with the waves was growing feeble.

"Help!—help! Ship ahoy!"

The wind carried the faint sounds far away, until they became blended with the ripple of the waves.

Help!—help! Save us—save us!"

As well might he have been entombed in the bowels of the earth as within sight of those vessels; there, his voice would have failed to penetrate the vast prison; here, the wind wafted the sounds away from the ships, and his agony was increased by the knowledge that he should pass away from the world and help so near.

Every motion of his arm now became weaker, and at last the wearied limb fell to his side powerless.

The dying man pressed his lips fondly to the cold, white face of his senseless burden, and, with a silent prayer to Heaven for mercy, he began to sink.

The wavelets had already began to ripple against his brow, and his eyes were closed upon the world.

Before the noble fellow had altogether disappeared, a hard substance came floating towards him, and the little hat that was left on his head stopped the welcome mass on its way.

When he felt the slight concussion which ensued, a giant's strength seemed to become inspired in his youthful frame.

With a mighty effort Harry threw back his head, and raised his right hand.

And his fingers came in contact with the thin line that was attached to a life-belt.

Madly, eagerly he clutched the unexpected hope of salvation; and as tears of gratitude welled up from his heart, he uttered a silent but fervent prayer of deep gratitude for his miraculous preservation.

"Saved! saved! darling!"

He said to his senseless burden; but she heard him not. The terrible shock she had sustained had so utterly prostrated her faculties, that she seemed like one who had passed into the land of shades.

With one arm passed through the life-belt, Harry floated easily upon the waters.

When the first reeling of joy had passed away, he looked around the sunlit ocean, and sought for an explanation of the unlooked-for appearance of the life-belt.

One glance explained the mystery.

Within two fathoms of the spot where he now floated, he saw another belt, two spars, and an empty barrel.

Though within this distance of the hapless pair, the floating objects were far apart from each other.

"The boats," thought Harry, "must have thrown out these things when they were about to return to the ship. Kind, thoughtful fellows—may Heaven reward them for it!"

He saw, too—when the frail structure which supported him had turned his face to the westward—the two vessels now separated, and sailing away in opposite directions.

In vain Harry puzzled himself for an explanation of the assistance.

The strange appearance of the frigate so soon after his supposed death was an enigma which he failed to solve.

"Perhaps," he bitterly moaned, "it is the admiral's ship, and he has come, thinking to behold the fulfilment of his wish."

How far Harry Vere was right in his conjecture the reader may judge from the perusal of the preceding chapter.

When the noble proportions of the frigate became a mere speck in the distant blue horizon, the hapless girl awoke from her death-like stupor.

The first feelings upon finding herself leaning upon her husband's arm were of strange admixture.

The wretched girl believed for some time that she had passed the portals of death, and entered upon a new sphere of existence.

Then, when she gazed around at the expanse of waters, a strange feeling took possession of her brain.

Was she suffering a penance in the unknown world for faults committed before death?

Her husband's voice broke the chaos of feeling that filled her brain.

"Jenny, my darling," he muttered, "you are at length restored to me."

She looked at him for a moment, then said—

"What has happened? Where am I?"

He told her, in gentle, soothing tones, how he had escaped from death; then asked her, in return, for the cause of her strange appearance in the water.

"Something awoke me," she said, "soon after you left the cabin. I saw the letter you had written upon the table, and, impelled by a strange curiosity, I left my cot to read it. I had already concluded, when your voice upon deck caused me to rush to your side. I was too late to reach you—the deed was, to all appearance, done. What followed I know not. I can only remember rushing to the vessel's side and jumping into the sea. I could not live without you, Harry."

He drew her closer to him, and murmured—

"My poor darling!"

There, upon the wide ocean, no help near them, did the young pair pass a few moments of blissful love.

Soon after this a squall arose, and the water, sweeping over the helpless pair, again separated them.

Harry was driven upon a rock, and lay as dead.

The vultures swooped above, uttering their horrible cries; and the gallant young fellow would have fallen a victim to the dreadful birds, but a magnificent dog, which had been cast from some wreck, dashed to his rescue, and bade the vultures defiance.

Harry soon returned to consciousness, and his first thought was of his darling wife, whom he saw lying senseless beneath him.

To rush to her assistance, and bathe her pale face with water, was but the work of a moment; and soon he had the satisfaction of seeing her lovely eyes open, and felt her arms once more round his neck.

They were re-united, and the manifold dangers that beset them were for the time forgotten.

When the first delicious feeling of ecstatic joy had passed away, Jenny looked fearfully around, and asked—

"How are we to escape from this fearful fate which threatens us?"

"That, my own Jenny," he said, with touching sadness in his tones, "is a question which is unanswerable by me. The same hand that has been our guide through our past dangers, will, if He so wills it, save us now."

As he spoke, hope filled his handsome face, and a certainty of being saved gave back the glad smile to his lips.

Far away—as far as the eye could reach—he saw an object which, from their position in the water, seemed no more than a white dot against the expanse of blue horizon which rose heavenward behind it.

This dot, he knew, would soon become enlarged to a ship—a ship that he hoped and prayed would save them from perishing.

Drawing an imaginary line from the small distant object, he found that a few hours would, should the wind keep up, bring the coming vessel within a fathom or two of where he pointed.

The skilful sailor's reckoning turned out correct.

When the mid-day sun rose high in the heavens, the distant ship was within two cable-lengths of the helpless pair.

As though husbanding his resources to the last moment, Harry had not spoken to his suffering, anxious wife until the vessel was within hailing distance.

Then, high above the rippling of the waves, as they rolled back from the vessel's bows and cutwater, came the cry of—

"Ship, ahoy—ahoy!"

The poor fellow's heart sank within him as he beheld the vessel rush onward—onward, until his aching eyes beheld her gilded stern, upon the fantastic carvings of which the sun glittered with glaring effulgence.

It is hard for thee to die, and help so near.

Though neither of them spoke of this sad thought, the same feelings were in the breasts of each.

So close was the ship to them, that they could perceive a tall figure upon the quarter-deck.

Under any other circumstances, Harry Vere would have hesitated before placing his young wife upon that vessel which he had so frantically called upon for aid.

The dress and strange apparel of the figure which stood upon the deck would have warned him of the terrible danger he incurred to his lovely bride.

There was something terribly grave in the appearance of that solitary form, which, instead of being garbed as men garb themselves who sail upon the seas, his head and breast was covered in a glittering panoply of burnished steel.

A cuirass and helmet, upon which the sun shone, gave the figure an aspect as weird as it was terrible.

The maddened husband saw not this. Before him was the form of his wife perishing by slow degrees for the want of even a drop of water to moisten her lips.

He forgot, when this fearful picture arose before him, that the steel-clad figure which stood upon the quarter-deck of the passing ship was the terrible Skeleton Face, or Death Pirate, as he was more commonly called.

Forgot that the being before him, and to whom he now called, had sworn to destroy the gallant Captain Tom Drake and his brave crew.

At last he was heard, and the leader of the terrible gang turned sharply and looked over the vessel's side.

Like magic, the sails were seen to hang motionless upon the yards, and the mystic being, whose name was a terror to all who crossed his path, made an impatient gesture with his hand.

A boat fell upon the waters, and the men, grim and silent, dragged the exhausted pair into the boat.

Both swooned from excessive joy, and had to be carried upon the pirate's deck.

Saved from one death to find another and worse fate.

CHAPTER XXXIX.

AN INTERRUPTION TO THE DEATH PIRATE'S FEAST OF BLOOD—CAPTAIN TOM TO THE RESCUE.

UPON the deck of the "San Josef," the Death Pirate's ship, a strange scene was taking place.

Near the capstan stood Harry Vere, his arms bound behind him, and the grim figure of the Skeleton fiend mocking his agony, and the frantic cries of Jenny, who knelt at the Death Pirate's feet, sounded like sweetest music to his ears.

Bound to the main-mast was another form. It was one of the crew, who had dared, in a moment of compassion, to commiserate the hapless lieutenant of the "Will-o'-the-Wisp" and his lovely bride.

In front of the capstan stood a gigantic African, whose white tunic and golden ornaments contrasted strangely with his inky skin.

This terrible being was the Death Pirate's executioner. Leaning upon his spear, Skeleton Face ordered Captain Tom's lieutenant to place his head upon the capstan.

When the harsh, grating voice came upon the dusky executioner's ears, he bared his arm, and prepared for the fell work.

"Spare him! spare him!" pleaded Jenny; "he has given thee no cause for offence."

"Ha! ha! ha!" mocked Skeleton Face. "Spare him. Ha! Has he not done me any harm? Ha! ha! Does he not belong to a nest of devils who have defied me? Ha! ha! I'll spare him!"

"Have mercy, dreadful man," cried the pleading girl, as she raised her clasped hands to her merciless persecutor—"oh! do not slay him."

"Slay?—as he repeated the word he laughed like a demon—"I'll not slay him, no! Ha! ha! Captain Tom's lieutenant—the second in command of the Buccaneers. I'll not slay him, certainly."

She felt an age of care taken from her bosom as the pirate leader spoke.

Poor girl, she knew but little of the fiend who gloated over her agony.

"I will pray for you," she said softly, "if he is spared. Kill him, and you will kill me."

"Ha! ha! ha!—shall I kill you? Not yet, my beauty."

"Monster!" she shrieked, springing to her feet. "Cruel, merciless monster, let your executioner do his work, we will die thus."

She threw herself upon her husband's breast, and clung to him with frantic energy.

The Death Pirate glanced satanically upon the pair.

"You will die with him, will you?" he said, "ha! ha! my little one—ha! ha! Alma!"

The slave bowed when called by name.

"Go, Alma," said the monster, "and fetch the pincers! Make them hot, Alma!"

The fiendish purpose manifested by these

words sent a thrill of horror through Harry Vere's frame.

He had, until now, stood firm and resolute before the ruthless pirate. Now, as his imagination pictured Jenny being torn by the fearful instruments for which the slave had been sent, he said—

"Let her die with me, I—"

"What!" yelled the pirate, "let her die! Not yet, you first."

"Would to Heaven I had a blade in my hand," said Harry frantically, as he struggled with his bonds; "I would cut that foul carcase of yours into pieces!"

"Oh, for Captain Tom and his gallant boys!" whispered Harry to his shrinking wife. "Could I but behold our flag we should be safe."

Speed on, gallant ship. Sharpen your blades, and look to your priming, young rovers. There is one of your bravest and best companions in such dire peril that nothing but your hands can free him from.

Zephyr-like blew the winds, and the gallant fellow, with his helpless bride clinging to his breast, felt there was no hope of the graceful "Will-o'-the-Wisp" and her peerless leader coming to the rescue.

With a malignant leer upon his visage, the executioner came to the pirate leader's side.

His ebony hands grasped a pair of long-handled pincers, the tops of which were white with heat.

So fierce had been the fire that had heated the infernal instrument of torture that the very iron seemed molten and soft.

"Try them, Alma. We'll see whether she will die with him or not. That's it, Alma. I think going to my temple of love with me will be much better than that."

While he was speaking, the miscreant slave applied the seething iron to her delicate shoulder.

Without a murmur, without a muscle of her fair face contracting, the heroic girl endured the horrible torture.

The fiendish pirate was staggered by her fortitude, and bade the grim executioner tear away part of her flesh.

Still with the same result.

The white arms that were entwined round her husband's neck did not relax their grasp, nor did the faintest cry escape her.

Poor Harry Vere was mad. The white foam gathered on his lips, and he shrieked aloud for the merciless wretches to slay them both.

To his wild cry the pirate's mocking laugh was given in reply. He told Alma to apply the torture to a more susceptible part of her quivering frame.

With such a look of calm fortitude she turned and gazed upon the heartless wretch, that, had he been less brutal, he would have desisted from the diabolical work.

Plainer than words could speak, the expression upon Jenny's face told of the determination at her heart.

Between the points of the pincers a piece of her flesh was twisted away.

Mingled with her cry of more than human agony came the Death Pirate's horrible voice.

"Now," he said, "will you take your arms from his neck?"

"Never! monster!" she said, "shall these arms relax their hold until all power of life has passed away."

"We shall see," said the pirate. "Alma!"

"Your slave, oh, master, hears."

"Try one of her cheeks, Alma; we'll spoil her beauty."

The wretch, exulting in the task assigned him,

placed the burning iron upon the heroic girl's face.

She felt the flesh hiss as the hot metal almost touched her, and, as the torturing agony drew up her form as though she had been in a convulsion, she cried out piteously—

"Is there no justice in Heaven? Oh, Father above, help us and punish these wretches."

The Death Pirate's laugh came upon her ears, and, as the mocking accents floated away, a cry was heard from the forepart of the vessel.

A single cry of fear, despair, and surprise, and, before Harry Vere or his young bride knew what had occured, there came a noise like the rushing wind, and, to their blended joy and surprise, a tall-masted ship dashed alongside, and grappled with the "San Josef."

As though the symmetrical vessel had risen from the ocean's depths, she had come upon the pirates, who, dismayed at what they imagined was a shadow or resemblance, a harbinger of coming doom, bore hastily back, and many let their weapons fall from their grasp as they cowered from the dread spectacle.

If the mystic vessel was a shadow, it soon became evident that her daring crew were mortal, and fought with carnal weapons.

Like young tigers they rushed upon the pirates, and cut them down like sheep; and, as many fled from the avenging swords, their pale lips gave utterance to the words—

"Help! help! it is the Death Avengers and the Spectre Ship of the Sea!"

Borne in the van of the stream of boarders was the sable banner with the word "Death" in white letters upon the centre.

Harry Vere's face shone with joy as he watched the dismayed host fall back before the resistless onslaught of the Death Avengers.

"Saved! saved!" he murmured. "Jenny, my darling, your prayer has been heard and answered."

His words fell upon ears that heard him not.

Sudden joy and pain had deprived Lucy of her senses.

Harry struggled madly with his bonds, and called aloud to be released.

None were near to heed him.

The Death Pirate and his sable executioner were at the head of the pirate horde, engaged hand to hand with the foe.

CHAPTER XL.

BOARDING THE PIRATES.

HER white sails spread to woo the flickle winds, the "Will-o'-the-Wisp" proudly rode the waters.

Her gallant young commander stood with Ben Barnacle upon the quarter-deck, conversing in low tones.

Tom's mind was troubled, and he sought the society of Ben to pass the slow hours away.

"I know not," said the young leader, "what to think of Harry Vere."

"Why?"

"I doubt the admiral's sincerity. This cruise of the 'Lapwing' is but a cover for some sinister purpose."

Ben Barnacle's dark eyes flashed angrily.

"By Heaven!" he said, "you may be right."

"An inward conviction," said Captain Tom, "which has been long at work—haunts me with a shadow of coming evil for poor Harry."

"Let us rescue him, then."

"We cannot."

"Why?"

"The 'Lapwing' has seven hours' start, and I know not which direction she has taken."

Ben Barnacle left the buccaneer ship's side for some minutes.

When he returned, he said—

"She has gone westward. We can but follow. In an hour the wind will be in our favour, and, unless the 'Will-o'-the-Wisp' has gone to the bottom, we shall overhaul the corvette before morning."

Ben Barnacle's prophecy was correct. Within the hour the wind had risen, and the swift vessel, under a press of sail, swept through the waters.

Zelie, the corsair maiden, stood by the young chief's side, and, as her dark, swimming eyes were fixed with mournful sadness upon his face, she asked, plaintively—

"Your vessel cuts the waters like an arrow. Are you again upon the eve of danger?"

Captain Tom laughed at her maiden fears.

"Danger, Zelie!" he said. "When did Captain Tom evade peril?"

"Alas!" she replied, "never! The fire and smoke of battle seem your natural element."

"It is, Zelie. Without the clash of foemen's steel, and the roar of guns, life would be but a sorry burden to bear."

He looked so grand, so noble, as he spoke that the young maiden for a time forgot her fears for the young hero.

"I ought," she said, "did I love you less, to worship you as one too noble for one so humble as myself to claim a thought; but my fear for your safety in these terrible encounters makes me tremble with dread."

He took her hand kindly.

"Zelie," said the youth, "one and all of us have our fate marked out from the beginning. Mine is to come like a shadow upon the evil-doer, and wreak a fitting vengeance for his crimes."

She looked at him interrogatively.

"You do not understand me, Zelie?"

"I do not."

"Have you," he asked, "ever heard of the Shadow Avengers?"

Zelie started.

"I have, she said, "but the story is so full of strangeness, that I cannot credit such beings' existence."

"Why?"

"The mystery of their sudden appearance. Do they not rise from the depths of the sea?"

"Such is the story."

"Is it not true, then?"

"No; the Avengers and the Spectre Ship are as substantial as my crew and the vessel upon which you stand."

Zelie cast a quick look, and said—

"Are you speaking the truth?"

"I am, Zelie. Nay, more; you shall yet behold the Avenging Band and their mystic vessel."

To the mind of the Eastern girl, a mind filled with strangely-fraught fancies, the idea of the supernatural has every comprehension.

"You," she said, anxiously, "will not meet this dread ship?"

"I shall not," said Captain Tom, smiling; "for I am the chief of the terrible league, and this is the Spectre Ship of the Sea."

Zelie uttered a quick cry, and recoiled from the young chief.

"Be not alarmed," he said; "the strange, weird character of the Sea Avengers has been sustained without the help of magic."

"But—but—" she began, "can you bid the vessel go beneath the waves, and appear beside a foe?"

"Not to such an extent does my power extend," he said. "Be not alarmed, Zelie· it is but a lever application of mechanism which causes the sudden appearance of—"

"Sail ho!"

Captain Tom took the glass from the deck, and asked the look-out the direction of the vessel.

"On the larboard quarter, sir."

"Can you make her out?"

"Partly, sir; it is a man-of-war."

"The 'Lapwing,'" thought Captain Tom, as he levelled his glass. "If so, all will be well."

When the vessels came within hail, the stranger turned out to be the frigate commanded by the old commodore.

He acknowledged the young buccaneer's salute, and went on his way without one word of the terrible truth being imparted to Captain Tom Drake.

Truth to tell, the old seaman's mind was too much bowed down by the sudden grief which had fallen upon him to be very communicative.

The day mingled with night, and the night gave place to another day, before the man at the mast-head gave the welcome signal that a sail was in sight.

Impelled by a strange feeling, Captain Tom ascended the mainmast, and, placing his glass to bear upon the stranger, he took a long and careful survey.

It was not the "Lapwing;" but, to judge from the expression upon Captain Tom's handsome face, it was evident that the coming vessel was known to him.

"Ready, there below!" he suddenly shouted. "The Spectre Ship is upon her path of vengeance."

His strange words were well understood by those on deck, and in less time than the words can be written, the white pyramid of sail fell from the hull, and the ship's yards to the deck.

She was under bare poles.

And, another word from the young leader, a strange rolling noise came from beneath the vessel—a noise that resembled hidden machinery being set in motion.

Then from the open hatches there arose a white vapour, which, instead of being blown away as it ascended, clung to the vessel's hull and spars, and gave her the appearance of a white cloud floating on the waters.

Though thus deprived of her sails, the "Will-o'-the-Wisp" continued her onward course.

Captain Tom's words were fufilled.

The Spectre Ship of the Sea was upon her path of vengeance.

While the "Will-o'-the-Wisp" crept, unseen, towards the strange vessel, Captain Tom Drake, from the masthead, beheld a sight that sent the hot blood from his cheeks, and caused every fibre in his frame to thrill with excitement.

Ben Barnacle, who stood with folded arms at the foot of the mainmast, watched the varying hues of his young leader's face.

"Something," he thought, "of more than ordinary import is going forward upon that vessel."

Suddenly a cry of rage fell from the young buccaneer's lips, and, dashing the glass to the deck, he glided down a rope, and stood beside Ben Barnacle.

"You are strangely morose," said Ben. "What has happened?"

"Enough Ben," said the buccaneer leader, "to pierce a stronger brain than mine."

"Its nature?"

"The vessel," said Captain Tom, "that we are gliding invisibly towards is that of the Death Pirate."

Ben Barnacle uttered a short cry, and his dark eyes shone with fury.

"The fiend," he hissed through his clenched teeth, "who under that ghastly mask hides his face from the world—curse him! There will yet come the time when I shall rend that covering from his face, and—"

Captain Tom had never beheld Ben's features so expressive as they were in this instance.

"Ben," he said, interrupting his companion, "you know this fellow?"

"I do. Did you know how much of that ruffian's early career has blended with your path—but—I—"

"Go on, Ben."

"Some other time—I have said too much already."

"You have not; you spoke of my father. Tell me—do you know him?"

There was a strange quivering motion perceptible upon Ben's lips as he answered hastily—

"I did."

Captain Tom's heart beat strangely as he gazed into the speaker's dark eyes.

"Ben," he said, "you are not what you seemed when you were brought upon the roaming ship by the press-gang."

"Another time," said Ben Barnacle, hastily, "you shall know all. Do not ask any more questions now, but tell me what you beheld on the deck of that vessel?"

There was such an entreaty in the voice that uttered these words that Captain Tom Drake, much as he wished to learn the strange history of his father, was compelled to refrain for the present.

"Be it so," he said; "but, remember, when this engagement is over, and Harry Vere rescued, I must learn the mystery that surrounded my early days."

"You shall, at a fitting time, know all," said Ben Barnacle. "Should I fall, there is a packet in my breast that is for you. It —"

"For me?"

"Yes; then you will learn the cause of your — Ha! what is that? A woman's voice in distress!"

"It is Jenny Vere's."

"Jenny Vere's!" said Ben, in astonishment, "and on board that vessel?"

"She is there with her husband."

"What fearful mystery is this?" said Ben; "should that fiend harm her, the measure of his sins will be filled to overflowing."

"You speak strangely, Ben."

"Perhaps so to you. The strangeness may pass away when I tell you that between Jenny Vere and the Death Pirate, as he is called, there exists a close tie of blood."

"Does he know it?"

"No! Neither must you know more until the fitting hour comes. Now, tell me what you beheld upon the deck of the 'San Josef.'"

"A strange and horrible scene," said Captain Tom; "Harry Vere was bound with cords, and his wife was clinging to his neck."

"Ha! male— But proceed."

"That black devil Alma was standing near them, and, from what I could make out, he seemed to be torturing the unhappy girl."

"For mercy's sake drive the ship on faster, we may be too late to save them."

"We are moving as quickly as the strong wind that is full against us will permit—behold, we are within musket-shot."

Peering through the white cloud of vapour, Ben Barnacle beheld the huge hull of the pirate ship close upon them.

At the moment his eyes discerned the deck of the pirate ship the inhuman wretch was calmly standing by and watching his myrmidons torturing Jenny Vere.

Ben Barnacle gnashed his teeth with rage, and his dark face became convulsed with the terrible conflict of harrowing feelings in his heart.

"Fierce monster!" he shouted, as his hand sought the hilt of a heavy blade that hung by his side, "all the devils in Satan's gang shall not save you from my hand when we meet."

A hand was placed upon the angry seaman's shoulder; he turned, and beheld Captain Tom Drake.

The gallant boy, though appalled at the horrible brutality taking place on the pirate's deck, was singularly calm.

"When I have crossed blades with the devil in human form," he said, with great quietude, "it will be time for you, Ben Barnacle, to take your weapon in your hand."

Ben's brow became as black as night, and in his sudden anger he uttered words that he would have given worlds to have recalled.

"My quarrel," he said, angrily, "dates from a time before you came into the world; therefore, I have a prior right in this matter."

An angry flush came to Captain Tom Drake's handsome face.

"I am master here," he said, proudly, "and all who serve under my flag must obey. I tell you that my hand, and no other, shall punish this miscreant."

Ben Barnacle stamped his foot upon the deck as he said, passionately—

"Boy, you know not to whom you speak!"

"I do," was the quiet reply; "I speak to Ben Barnacle, a man in whom, it appears, I have placed too much trust; one, of all others, who should be the last to use mutinous language to Captain Tom."

The angry young chief turned away from Ben, and placed himself in front of a number of gallant lads, who, with drawn weapons, were awaiting the moment to throw themselves upon the pirate's deck.

Ben looked after the latter's graceful form as he muttered—

"This is fearful to endure; it wants but another scene like this, and I shall be compelled to proclaim myself, and be master here."

Strange and mystic words were these for Captain Tom's followers to hear, and Ben Barnacle was a man that never made an idle boast or threat against the true leader of the brave spirits who thronged the decks of the splendid ship.

It was a position that a prince might give his birthright to attain.

Yet this man, a subordinate officer under the fiery young captain's command, talked of leading on the terrible band.

Unless some dark secret lay beneath the usually calm demeanour of Ben Barnacle, his words were but the effect of sudden passion. Time will solve the truth, and raise the supposed obscure seaman to the position for which his kingly mien and bright intellect so eminently suited him.

In grim silence, and enveloped by the mystic cloud of invisibility, the Death Avengers rushed upon their foes.

Like an avalanche, the gallant lads swept the broad decks of the pirate ship—thrusting their bright steel in the pirates' bodies, and driving the fear-stricken crew like a herd of sheep towards the fore part of their huge vessel.

Foremost in the death struggle could be seen the splendid form of the gallant young captain; and close beside him was Ben Barnacle, his dark eyes watching for every blade that was levelled at the fearless boy's heart.

Like an Apollo of old, Ben Barnacle swept down all before him, his strong arm wielding a carved scimitar, and ere the fray was scarce began it ran with blood from point to hilt.

Mighty were the efforts made by Captain Tom

Drake and Ben Barnacle to reach the steel-clad form of the Death Pirate.

Efforts that were for a time unavailing.

The grim leader of the pirate horde rallied his band and led them onward to repel the daring attack of Captain Tom's gallant crew.

Wielding his scimitar high in the air, he shouted—

"Follow me, pirates of death—hurl back those striplings into the sea—were they demons we could out-number them. Follow! follow!"

Animated by the tone and example of their mystic leader, the Corsairs bore down in overwhelming numbers upon the small band of heroes.

There was a short but sickening scene of strife.

The middies fought and fell without yielding one inch of vantage ground.

Returned stab for stab and shot for shot with a silent attention that showed their foes there would be no victory unless the second band of English boys were decimated.

Now, amid the dreadful strife, did Ben Barnacle and his young leader perform such prodigies of valour that the fierce-headed foemen who fell beneath their mighty arms formed a rampart of quivering flesh before the gallant pair.

Captain Tom, though so fiercely engaged with the terrible odds before him, watched with eagle eye every movement of the pirate gang.

Four young midshipmen who acted as his aide-de-camps stood within earshot, and to them he from time to time gave his orders for the disposition of his forces.

He saw with mingled feelings of bitterness and pain that the enemy's best marksmen, who filled the tops, were pouring down a shower of bullets from their long matchlocks upon his brave, unyielding boys.

Others, he saw, were crowding the open hatches and with their long-barrelled weapons were taking sure and deliberate aim at his crew.

"Go," he said to one of the middies, "and lead a party to the quarter-deck—tell them to pick off their enemies in the top."

The boy hastened to obey the order, a proud smile upon his lips at the honour thus bestowed upon him.

He had not taken more than three paces from his leader when a ball from one of the very men he was sent to dislodge, cleft his heart in 'twain.

He fell at our hero's feet, the proud smile still upon his lips.

A smothered cry of rage came from Captain Tom's lips at the sight, and his handsome face became convulsed with passion.

"That ball," he said to Ben, "was intended for me; keep them in check here, Ben, I'll go myself and dislodge those fiends."

He cut his way through the savage horde, and, leaving a trail of blood in his path, reached the quarter-deck.

"Quick!" he said to those who followed him, "hand me a rifle. Now to make them clear the tops."

With a deadly, unerring aim he began the work. At every flash of his rifle a turbaned pirate came whirling through the air, stricken to death by the angry youth.

As long as there remained a foe along the rigging did the gallant young captain and his companions keep up a stream of fire, and when the pirates' life-stream ran along the masts, and fell drop by drop upon the hands and faces of the gallant crowd below, a terrible cry from Ben Barnacle caused our hero to hurl his rifle into the sea and spring with one bound from the quarter-deck.

The cause of Ben's sudden cry and our hero's swift movement was as unexpected as it was terrible.

Minnie Atherton—his darling Minnie—whom he had left in safety upon the "Will-o'-the-Wisp," was in the grasp of the Death Pirate.

Captain Tom's brain was in a whirl at the sight. He for a few moments could scarcely believe his senses, and, as he rushed madly along the deck—bringing down all who stood in his path—he beheld the grim monster throw Minnie's light form to a dark-bearded Arab who stood near, and like an enraged wolf turn and meet the angry Ben Barnacle.

Captain Tom paused hesitatingly as the two crossed blades—he saw the hate that gleamed in Ben's dark eyes, and heard the strange words that fell from his lips as his weapon clashed upon that of the Death Pirate.

"So," mused Ben, "we have met at last, Henri —oh! heavens!"

His falchion shivered to the hilt as he dealt a powerful stroke at the Death Pirate's head.

He heavy blade fell upon the miscreant's steel corselet, rebounded, and broke like a reed.

The next moment Captain Tom beheld Ben's kingly form stretched prone upon the deck, and heard the Death Pirate's mocking laugh of triumph.

Then the youth, with eyes ablaze with passion, strode forward and faced the hideous monster, who, raising his scimitar, rushed forward and shrieked—

"Now for the cub, the wolf is gone."

Levelling a pistol straight at the Death Pirate's head, the brave youth said—

"Thus will I avenge his fall!"

He pulled the trigger.

Horror! the treacherous pistol flashed in the pan.

Then the Death Pirate, with a yell of joy, sprang towards his young antagonist to cut him to the deck.

But as his flashing blade descended it was caught by the Damascus blade wielded by Captain Tom.

The hideous pirate foamed at the mouth with rage.

Every feint, every cut, every slash he made was met by the splendid swordsmanship of the graceful youth.

Had the pirate not been defended by entire mail steel, Tom's sword would have passed through and through his body.

Nerved by the fate of Ben Barnacle, the young leader, with matchless skill, probed the pirate through the interstices of his corselet.

The Death Pirate yelled with baffled rage to be thus slowly slain, and attacked him like an angry panther.

In vain he sought to crash down on his guard. His blade was turned aside, and before he could recover it Tom's keen point had found an entry to his flank, and he felt a stream of fresh, strong blood ooze out between his armour.

Captain Tom marked his baffled rage, and with lightning swiftness caused the angry monster to yell with pain.

"My blade is good," he would say, when he made a terrible lunge. "Ha! there is ample place for its point to enter. You felt that."

"Hell's lad—devil's imp!" yelled the pirate, "thus do I cut on you."

"And thus," said Tom, driving his sword point in the pirate's shoulder as far as the small space between the steel plates would permit, "do I bleed you little by little until your strength fails you— then," added Tom smiling-ly, "I'll tear that mask off, saw the head from your body, and place it on the masthead for vultures to feed upon."

The Death Pirate began to feel himself getting weaker, and a foreboding that his brave, skilful, lithe adversary's words would come to pass came to his mind.

MY HAND SHALL FIRE THE FIRST SHOT.

There was but one course for him to take.

Humiliating as it was, he must call assistance to aid him to beat off his foe.

The words were upon his lips that would have brought a score of his own men to his side, when Harry Vere, with his scimitar reeking with slaughter, rushed to Captain Tom's side.

"Let me," he said to Tom, "take this fiend out your hands."

Captain Tom smiled.

"Not yet, Harry," he said; "see, he is falling. We shall yet have his head for vultures' food. I must finish what I have begun."

"Not yet. This blood is that of his fiendish executioner, the black. Let me have his to mingle with it, and I care not though I die the next moment."

"I will rid the world of this wretch. Go, Harry, as you love me, and rescue Minnie. See, they are taking her below."

Harry Vere dashed after the pirates, who were bearing Minnie away, and the combat between the young buccaneer and his foe was continued.

They were almost close. The gallant middies had driven the pirates to the forecastle, and none but the dead and dying were left upon the deck, save our hero and the pirate chief.

The Death Pirate saw this, and, to add to his bitterness, he beheld Harry Vere, after cutting down the Arab who had endeavoured to carry Minnie below, supporting the senseless form of the beautiful Minnie Atherton.

"My revenge for the barbarity to my—"

"Seems," said Tom, "to judge by your weapon, to have been pretty well accomplished."

Foiled at every point, his gigantic power broken by the Death Avengers, and his life-blood ebbing away in spite of his steel panoply—no wonder that the miscreant fell back, and sought to evade the avenging blade of the young buccaneer.

Step by step Captain Tom followed, and, had not the pirate gang, in a moment of frenzy, broke away from the little band of resolute boys, the Death Pirate's hour would have come.

In this mad flight, the surging crowd separated our hero and his steel-clad foe, and, calling upon Allah for aid, they rushed to the quarter-deck, followed by the middies, shouting—

"Hurrah! hurrah! Victory—they fly! they fly! Hurrah!"

A gesture from Captain Tom stayed the pursuit.

"They are beaten," he said; "let there be no unnecessary bloodshed. Gather your dead and wounded, and let the 'Will-o'-the-Wisp' appear."

Every word and look of their leader was law to the brave band, and, flushed as they were with their great victory, they without a murmur began to collect the fallen forms of their companions.

As they bore them to the side, the white cloud which had enveloped the "Will-o'-the-Wisp" rolled away, and the stately vessel's beautiful outlines stood out in bold relief against the blue sky.

As the vapour rolled upward, the grinning, expectant faces of Doctor Shrike and his factotum, Jacop, could be seen waiting for their subjects.

The Death Pirate stood motionless on the spot where his flying crew had posted him.

Through the holes in his ghastly mask his eyes could be seen glaring with a fierce, maniacal stare.

The wish was strong within his heart to spring upon his gallant young foe, but he felt that the first movement of his hands or feet would be the signal for Captain Tom's sword to finish the work he had so well begun.

While standing thus, gazing with savage bitterness at his young adversary's movements, a subtle, daring scheme came to his brain.

Minnie Atherton, whose love for Tom had caused her in a moment of frenzy to rush on board the pirate ship, to be near him should the foeman's steel destroy his young life, no sooner placed her feet upon the "San Josef" than she was clutched in the arms of the terrible Death Pirate.

The ghastly visage, which Minnie, in her terror, did not think was a mask to hide his features, caused her to swoon, and from that state of insensibility she had not recovered until the shout of victory from the young middies' throats told that the fight was over.

Now she stood timidly near her lover, waiting for him to conduct her back to the ship.

The Death Pirate's eyes were fixed savagely upon her beauteous face, and he determined to yet kill her, and be revenged upon his foe.

It was a bold stroke to play with Captain Tom, but the mystic pirate felt the prize worth the risk.

When the young buccaneers had removed their dead and wounded companions to their own vessel, they drew up in two lines at a respectful distance from their young chief.

Captain Tom waved them back and addressed the leader of the Moorish corsair.

"Pirate," he said, "if the blood of your miscreant crew has flowed to-day, and the barbarity with which you inflicted such torture upon the helpless maiden who fell into your paws has been atoned for, I will not slay you, though by so doing I should rid the world of a monster whose very breath pollutes the air that streams in sunny wafts to every living thing—take the remnant of your breath. Keep your vessel, and learn from this act to be more merciful. Beware! night and day the shadow stranger will be near you, and you would get less mercy from the forest king than from Captain Tom!"

With bowed head, and seeming contrition of spirit, the Death Pirate listened to the young chieftain's words, and, when he had concluded, the pirate held his sword by the point and offered the hilt to his conqueror.

Captain Tom Drake pushed the weapon aside with his hand.

"Take it, noble youth," said the Death Pirate; "you have, by your valour, broken a band of men that I deemed invincible. I have nothing now to live for."

"You have repented for your crimes?"

"Tut! I will; the life you give me shall be devoted to that purpose. Thus do I begin."

He broke the blade of his scimitar upon the bulwarks, and tossed the pieces from him.

"I have but one wish now," he said; "will you grant it?"

Captain Tom Drake looked the surprise he felt.

"It is, perhaps, a strange one," said the Death Pirate. "Give me a passage to the nearest port we meet, and my name shall disappear with me for ever."

"Are you sincere?"

"I am, by the sa—"

"Do not profane the name of the Deity which you have so often outraged by calling him to witness your oath. You shall have the boon you ask; but remember, if you intend treachery, far better had you cast yourself into a burning cauldron of oil than ventured on board the 'Will-o'-the-Wisp,' and on that vessel every action known to you will be watched and rewarded; and the faintest suspicion of your sincerity will be the signal for a death so horrible that, refined in cruelty as you are, the bare mention of it will make you shudder."

"I will take the risk."

"Be it so. As a proof of your sincerity, begin by unmasking your face."

The Death Pirate started.

"Not here," he said. "Alone with you the wish shall be gratified; here I would sooner die than unmask."

Captain Tom reflected for some moments.

"It shall be as you wish," he said. "Are you ready to come on board?"

"Before you have cast off the grappling-irons I will follow. I wish to tell those who have served me so long and faithfully of my intentions."

Had Ben Barnacle been by our hero's side, he would have warned his leader of the danger he incurred; but poor Ben was at that moment under the treatment of Dr. Shrike and his assistant, Jacop the Maory.

The young buccaneer went back to his ship, Captain Tom and Minnie closely following them.

And the Death Pirate, striding towards the point where his desperate crew were huddled, addressed them in a sharp, savage tone.

"Desperadoes," he said, "man the lower-deck guns to bear upon the spars of that infernal vessel when I give the word to fire; I am going on board. It may cripple her so that she can't follow us. Ha! ha! ha! I'll whine like a beaten cur to this brat, until I—"

"We are casting off," sang out Captain Tom.

"Quick! or the vessels will be parted."

The Death Pirate, with bowed head, walked to the side and clambered over the bulwarks—the next moment he stood upon the side of the ship.

He stood for a moment as though sorrowfully contemplating his vessel, as the Moors were busy shaking out the sails.

Then, with a sudden bound, he sprang past Cap-ain Tom Drake, and, swinging Minnie in his powerful grasp, he sprang upon the bulwarks, and from them to his own ship.

"Fire!" he yelled, as his feet touched the planks. "Fire!"

The iron storm tore through the lower rigging of the buccaneer's vessel—crashing through the spars, and tearing the white sails into ribbons; and in a moment the graceful ship was rendered useless to pursue the "San Josef," which shot quickly ahead of her crippled adversary.

With such swiftness had this daring act taken place, that the buccaneers were not aware of what had happened until their vessel reeled like a stricken steed under the concentrated fire of the "San Josef's" heavy guns.

Dashing through the thick white smoke, Captain Tom Drake, sword in hand, followed the daring abductor of his love.

He reached the pirate vessel a moment after the wily villain had given the order to fire.

With a cry of rage he sprang forward to where the Death Pirate stood, his sword upraised to cleave him to the deck.

The weapon cleft the air, and, as the mocking voice of his subtle foe ran out with devilish glee, Captain Tom Drake beheld Minnie and her abductor sinking through the deck.

She was being taken to the "San Josef's" stateroom by means of a trap-door, which worked by hidden machinery.

Captain Tom would have hurled himself after her, but the trap rose swiftly, and a number of his foes, armed with spears and yataghans, rushed from all parts of the vessel to slay the gallant boy.

He was alone upon the pirate ship, surrounded by his foes. Minnie in the room of this ruthless leader, and his own vessel disabled by the close broadside, was soon left far behind.

It was a moment of such dire peril, that, brave as he was, he felt appalled.

CHAPTER XLI.

IN WHICH TWO OLD FRIENDS BECOME UNITED IN A MOST UNEXPECTED MANNER.

WISHING the strange sail at the warmest place imaginable, Captain Debuscan, the French privateer, gave a longing look at Creula, and muttered—

"I'll settle this fellow—then for your turn, my dusky beauty."

The stranger who followed in the privateer's wake was a long, rakish-looking craft, far inferior in size to the "Tourterelle," Captain Debuscan's vessel.

The privateer's lieutenant was closely examining the stranger, when the dissipated captain came on deck.

"Well," asked Debuscan, "what do you make of her?"

The lieutenant handed him the glass.

"I cannot," he answered, "make her out."

"Why not?"

"You see," said the officer, "she has been in sight for some time, and I have tried her powers of sailing, yet, no matter whether we increase or decrease our speed, she keeps the same distance from us."

"Your fancy leads you to this conclusion. See! she is coming down every minute."

The lieutenant uttered an exclamation of surprise.

The strange vessel, without having made the least alteration in her sails, was gliding onward at a pace that threw the white foam up in showers before her sharp bows.

Captain Debuscan did not like the appearance of the short boat.

"I'll drop that gentleman's crew," he muttered "Henri Debuscan is not to be caught asleep."

"What do you make of her, sir?" asked the second in command.

"A rascally forebooter, by her looks," was the answer. "He is trying to overhaul us. Cast loose a gun astern. him."

A gun was cast loose, and double shotted by the captain's orders.

"Blaze away!" he cried. "Give it him right in the teeth; perhaps that will make him show a flag.'

The twin shots sped from the gun, and the stranger, as though aware of the salute they intended for him, let off a couple of shots, and the shots went hissing some yards wide of the mark.

"Missed, by all that's infernal," exclaimed Debuscan. "Try again, you lubber."

The black lubber tried again.

This time with better success, for the captain saw part of the stranger's bulwarks staved in."

As the last splinter fell to the deck, the pirate captain uttered an angry cry.

"To quarter! to quarter!' he shouted; "by all that's good, it is Dutch Paul, the pirate."

A black banner streamed out from the stranger's stern—a flag once seen, was never to be forgotten.

Unlike most freebooters, Dutch Paul eschewed the black flag, and its grinning, ghastly emblem of death.

The colours that floated out in the bright sunshine were of the richest and softest silk.

The ground-work was virgin white, and emblazoned in the centre were embroidered in gold thread the words—

"I conquer."

A strange story was often told by seamen, when beguiling the time away, about this immense flag and its golden letters.

Dutch Paul (so ran the story) once entered the convent with his freebooters at his back, and would have carried off the youngest nuns had not the lady superior bribed him with a heavy sum of gold.

The freebooter pocketed the ransom, then swore he would attack the convent and carry off the women, unless in four hours a flag was made from the newest silk, and embroidered with the words he wished in letters of gold.

With such a fate before them as he threatened, there was nothing left but compliance with his wishes.

And while his ruffianly crew made merry with the convent wine cellar, the frightened nuns made his banner from the choicest silk.

Such was the story.

The privateer's crew had scarcely cast loose the guns, when Dutch Paul's vessel swept alongside.

Seated upon the breech of a gun was the famous freebooter.

Between his lips a fragrant cigar emitted a perfumed odour, as he leisurely glanced at the privateer between each puff of smoke.

His crew, stripped to the waist, stood by their guns—those fearful engines of destruction which vomited liquid fire.

Captain Debuscan's swarthy face blanched as he thought of the terrible flame which, at a word from the pirate, would stream upon his vessel, and consume her stout timbers to the water's edge.

Discretion was the better part of valour in this instance, and the Frenchman, jumping upon the bulwarks, hailed the pirate.

"To what," he asked, "am I indebted for the honour of this visit, Captain Paul?"

"You know me, then?"

"I do now," was the guarded reply "I did not when I fired the shot."

Dutch Paul's eyes twinkled mischievously.

"If Monsieur Debuscan," he said, "wishes to try

his strength with me he had but to give the word
We are both at quarters, and I know my men are
willing."

The privateer prefaced his answer by a graceful
bow.

"The renown," he said, "which Captain Paul has
achieved would not gain any additional lustre by
crushing such a poor vessel as mine."

"Politic," thought Dutch Paul, "and polite;"
then, aloud, he added—

"You wished to know why I visited you?"

"I did."

"You shall. I want a few men; have you any to
spare?"

The Frenchman thought of the hapless Jerry Mizzen, and answered—

"I have one—a thorough English seaman."

"Good!" said Dutch Paul. "He is worth a dozen
others. Send him here."

The Frenchman winced at the uncomplimentary
manner in which Dutch Paul alluded to foreigners
in general.

Jerry was soon brought from his place of confinement, and landed on board the pirate vessel.

Dutch Paul started slightly when he saw Jerry,
and muttered—

"Another: this must be more than chance."

"Belay there, you lubbers," said Jerry, as the privateers now threw him neck and crop over the side.
"I ain't agoing on this ere craft unless the gal goes
with me."

"We want no women here," said a voice close
behind Jerry. "Turn round, my fine fellow; let
me have a look at you."

The first sound of Dutch Paul's voice caused
Jerry to rub his eyes, as though he had just arisen
from a slumber. As the pirate captain continued
to speak. Jerry's mouth assumed the shape of the
letter O, and giving a low whistle, he said—

"May I be tarred, feathered, roasted, boiled, fried,
if it be not Re—"

"Here!" shouted Dutch Paul, "turn your face
this way."

Jerry turned, and they regarded each other for a
few seconds, then the pirate leader beckoned Jerry
forward.

"Look here, my fine fellow," said the pirate, in a
voice only audible to the startled Jerry, "you are
in a grand berth on this ship, unless you spoil yourself."

"Spoil myself!" replied Jerry; "I ain't the sort
of chap to do that."

"I hope not; but I may as well tell you that
any talking about a certain spot close to a certain
cave used by two respectable smugglers, will be
followed by a quick turn up to the yard-arm."

Dutch Paul looked just the man to keep his word,
and Jerry, whose brain was a little deranged by the
sudden change in his affairs, stood silently gazing
on the yard-arm.

"You can go forward to your duties," said
Dutch Paul. "You will find someone there with
whom you are acquainted."

Jerry moved mechanically to the place indicated,
but before he reached the foremast he stood still,
then turned, and walking back to the captain,
said—

"Look here, cap'n, I has a girl on that there ship;
and if so be—"

"Go to the devil, let him keep her."

"But, cap'n, she is—"

"A black, I shouldn't wonder," said Dutch Paul,
with a laugh. "Go forward, man, you shall have
plenty of women."

Jerry wiped his eyes with the cuff of his jacket,
he did not feel happy at the prospect before him.

"Well, cap'n," he began, "may be she ain't as
white as some gals, but—"

"Jerry—Jerry Mizzen!"

Jerry jumped round as though a red-hot poker
had been suddenly put to the small of his back,
and when he beheld the speaker, he rushed forward,
and cried—

"Bob—Bob Hauler!"

The old attached messmates rushed into each
other's arms, and, like a couple of young bears, embraced before the whole of the ship's company.

While they remained thus, Dutch Paul signalled
to the privateer to make sail.

A signal that Henri Debuscan gladly obeyed.

Dutch Paul's acquaintance was more agreeable at
a distance.

To do the privateer justice, he made every
effort to get as far away as possible.

Jerry Mizzen was now far away from the dusky
Indian girl, and the impassioned Frenchman went
below, his brain on fire, to communicate this intelligence to Creula.

He found the Indian girl much changed since he
had been on deck.

Her tears and supplications were changed to a
quiet look of stern defiance.

The French privateer was for a moment staggered
by this alteration.

"So, my little beauty," he said, as he trod upon
the carpeted floor; "you have thought better of me
now—eh, my angel?"

He advanced towards her as he spoke, his hands
outstretched, and the lurking devil in his dark eyes
growing fiercer every step.

When within ten paces of the Indian girl, Monsieur Debuscan leaped back, a cry of rage yelling
from his lips.

Creula had, during his absence, possessed herself
of a keen yataghan which hung over the captain's
cot, and as the privateer advanced towards her, she
drew the shining blade from its scabbard, and
levelled the point at her persecutor's breast.

"Stand where you are, captain," said the girl,
"or, by the Great Spirit that dwells in the happy
hunting grounds, I'll slay you like a dog."

Monsieur Debuscan listened to the girl's cold
words. Then glanced at her lithe figure, and calm,
determined face.

He saw she fully meant all she had uttered; and,
not wishing to become spitted upon the blade of the
sharp yataghan, he stood perfectly still.

"Wretch!" said the brave girl, contemptuously.
"Cowardly man! Behold! I have found a weapon
that will keep you at bay."

Captain Debuscan shrugged his shoulders.

"True, ma belle," he said; "you have a weapon,
but you will put it down soon."

Creula clutched the silver hilt fiercely, and said—

"Never!"

"You will, mademoiselle; if you do not, I will
hang your friends cleverly to the yard-arm, and by
the heels, too. You won't like that, my beauty."

A scornful laugh came from the girl's lips.

"You threaten," she said, "what you cannot
perform."

"Parbleu! you dusky little Venus; sacré mon
Dieu!"

Captain Debuscan was getting angry.

"You knew when you made that threat," she
said, "that they were safely on board a vessel we
lost sight of, which made you turn pale."

This stung the Frenchman to the quick.

"Sacré!" he hissed. "Then you saw that boat
taken aboard?"

"I did," was her cutting answer; "and I saw
the great Captain Debuscan stretching himself
humbly before the strange-looking commander of
the pirate vessel."

The Frenchman stamped impatiently upon the
deck, and made an angry stride towards Creula.

The light blade flashed before his eyes, and her voice, full of menace, sounded upon his ears.

"Keep off!" she said. "Remember, I have warned you."

The captain of the " Tourterelle " became motionless.

The yataghan's point was within two inches of his throat.

"Diable!" he muttered. "I must alter this."

"Never!" she cried.

"I am sorry," he said, to be rude to a lady, "but, by all the little devils below, you shall be mine."

Creula laughed in his face.

"When Captain Debuscan," she said "meditates wrong towards a helpless woman, he should be careful to keep sharp weapons out of her reach."

"Fine menaces!" he said. "The fault is mine. I must atone for it."

As the last word came from his lips, his thin rapier flashed from its scabbard, and before Creula knew what had happened, the yataghan was knocked from her grasp.

She made an effort to pick it up.

Too late!

The Frenchman's foot was placed upon the blade. With a cry of despair, the Indian girl rushed to the farthest corner of the cabin, and cowed before the blazing eyes of the miscreant privateer captain.

.   .   .   .

In the first transport of joy at meeting his old companions, Jerry Mizzen forgot his dusky Indian bride, and not until the privateer had gone some fathoms ahead did he realise the truth.

Creula, the companion of his past adventures, was taken from him.

Bob Hauler heard the frantic cry that came from Jerry's lips, and asked, in astonishment—

"What's the matter, Jerry?"

"She!—she!" half blubbered the bewildered lover, "are gone!"

"She!" repeated Bob, in surprise, "what she?"

"Cruela, my—my wife."

"Your wife, Jerry; when was you married?"

Jerry looked upon his friend with such a solemn expression upon his face, that Bob burst into a hearth laugh.

"It won't do long," he said; "you is best without her now."

"I ain't—oh, Lord! and to think I shall never see her again."

"Don't take on so, Jerry. Tell us all about her."

Bob led him forward, and the two perched upon a coil of rope.

Jerry gave a huge sigh, then a couple of groans, and, casting a glance at the privateer's white sails, told his messmate how he had become acquainted with the Indian girl—their adventures together, and the clever manner in which Captain Debuscan trapped her on board.

Bob paid great attention to every word Jerry uttered, and when a succession of sighs wound up the story, he said—

"And so, Jerry, she were a black lass after all?"

"Not black, Bob—a little too much colour—but she were awfully pretty."

Two sighs and a groan wound up this speech.

"Maybe she were," said Bob; "but, arter all, you is best without her."

"Eh?"

"Best without her, Jerry; 'cos some day she might fall in with our plucky young captain, and, you know, he will not have any wemmin on board the 'Will-o'-the-Whisp.'"

"He has one hisself," said Jerry. "Ain't I as much right as him?"

"No, Jerry, you haven't; he is a captain, and

you is a — a — I means you is only Jerry Mizzen, don't you see?"

"Jerry did not see," he calmly replied.

"Eh?"

"Besides," continued Bob, sentimentally, "if she wor as well as you says, why the cap'n here might take a fancy to her, and that would be worser than better."

Bob was making an impression upon Jerry, for that brave individual said—

"Perhaps, arter all, you is right, Bob."

"Course I is, Jerry. Here, have a swig."

Jerry had a swig, and smacked his lips, approvingly.

"He ain't werry bad," thought Bob Hauler. "Have another, Jerry."

Jerry had another. He began to see better, and asked—

"Where did you get this, Bob, it's fine?"

"It are," said Bob, and there's plenty more below. Finish this, and I'll get it filled again."

"Not for me, Bob—poor Creu—"

"Go on, Jerry, there's only a little drop."

Jerry took the little drop to oblige his messmate, although the act of placing the bottle to his lips cut the beloved name in two.

Bob was not gone long to refil the black bottle, and when he returned, Jerry, with a doleful shake of the head stretched forth his hand, saying—

"I is bad, Bob. I shall never get over this. Oh! my poor Creu—"

Bob came to the rescue again, and stayed the completion of the Indian girl's appellation.

He placed the mouth of the bottle to Jerry's lips, and said—

"Take a little drop, old messmate—you is getting worse."

"I is, Bob. Oh! my poor Cre—guggle—guggle—guggle."

Within two hours from the time that Bob Hauler so unexpectedly found his old companion, the love-lorn Jerry was fast asleep upon the forecastle, the ring of a spare anchor for a pillow, and several coils of rope for a bed.

Bob's face had a truly satisfied look when Jerry began to snore.

"I've cured him," thought Bob. "There couldn't a' been much the matter, or he wouldn't have left off blubbering about her, and taken so kindly to his medicine."

Bob was pretty well right in his remarks, and, like a careful doctor, he took measures to prevent a relapse, by placing a full bottle of Jerry's medicine by his side.

When Jerry awoke, his senses were a little settled by late events. A few moments' reflection put his recollection right, and he began—

"It's all true, then? Oh! my poor Creu—"

He caught sight of the bottle Bob had brought, and left his damsel's name to be finished another time. Now the neck of the bottle and Jerry's lips were kissing together in a manner that did Bob Hauler's heart good to behold.

The careful Bob was behind a gun-carriage, watching Jerry.

"Feel all right now?" he asked, leaning to Jerry Mizzen's side. "You looks better."

"Very bad, Bob—very bad."

"Have another pull—go on."

"Think I will, Bob; it will do me good perhaps. I feel very bad. Oh! my poor C—"

Up went the bottle, and the heart-stricken Jerry took it from his lips empty.

Bob assisted his messmate to rise, and propping him to a sitting position by the aid of sundry sacks, pieces of rope, and other soft articles, including a couple of capstan-bars, he asked—

"Feel better, don't you, Jerry?"

"A little, Bob; I feels weak—don't think I could walk if I was to try."

Bob Hauler thought of the tar's emptied bottle, grimaced, and cried sympathetically—

'Don't think you could, Jerry. Don't try to walk, sit down."

"Yes, I must, Bob. Losing that gal as made me feel werry weak, and my head ache—oh, my poor—"

"Jerry, have a little drop more."

"Eh?"

"Just another taste, to make you strong."

"Perhaps it will do me good, Bob; just a little drop. Not too much; I can't take much, Bob."

"I know that, Jerry; you can't get over it yet."

"No, Bob, nor never shall. Oh my poor—"

"I shall be back in a minute, Jerry; don't get bad till I come."

Jerry promised not to faint from weakness if he could help it, and Bob, grinning all over his face, went below.

"Well," he muttered, as he went down the hatchway, "for a chap as says he's a-going to die about a gal, I thinks three pints of rum not a bad dose."

Bob Hauler indulged in a hearty laugh at the recollection of Jerry Mizzen's woe-begone face. But when he approached the disconsolate swain Bob's face would have been a fortune to any of our local expounders.

The pair sat for some time discussing the merits of the last small drop which had appeared, and to Bob's joy the Indian girl's name was soon forgotten by Jerry, and he so far recovered that he asked his friend how he came on board Dutch Paul's ship.

Bob told him of his mission to find old Gregory, Captain Tom's uncle, and his capture by the press-gang.

"I didn't stop long with him," said Bob, alluding to the man-of-war before which he was taken by the press-gang; "there was too much of the cat-o'-nine-tails, Jerry, for me, and too little grog."

"I expect there was, Bob."

"I gave them the slip," Bob Hauler continued, "when we were sent for water; but I hadn't been long ashore afore I was picked up by this craft."

"You was lucky," said Jerry. "Some people is—I wasn't"

Bob, thinking his friend was about to indulge in another moan, promptly applied the bottle.

Jerry took it like a lamb, and, after a hearty pull, said—

"Well, Bob, have you noticed anything in this craft?"

"Lots of things, Jerry."

"You have?"

"Yes; but most awfullest, then, is the liquid fire he uses."

"Liquid fire," replied Jerry. "What, the same sort of stuff as he used when he had a brush with our young commander?"

"The very same,' said Bob. "Do you know what I've been thinking, Jerry?"

"No, Bob."

"Well, I've been thinking this. Suppose now, I finds out how this stuff is made, and when we gets back to our old ship I tell Captain Tom all about it."

"What for?"

"What for, Jerry?" Don't you see he'd be able to use it, and there wouldn't be a ship afloat as could touch us."

"They wouldn't, Bob. How are we to find it out?"

"That's it, you see. The stuff is put in holler shot, and when it breaks against another ship it all runs out and sets fire to 'em."

"Ugh!" Jerry shivered, he's a perfect devil, this cap'n of ours."

"He is," said Bob; then lowering his voice to a whisper, "do you think, Jerry, you ever saw him before?"

"Didn't I know him directly?" said Jerry. "I'd have known him if he had twice as big a beard."

"Did he seem to know you?"

"Yes; and he told me if I talked too much the would be something swinging at the yard arm."

"That something was yourself, Jerry."

"Yes; so I'll put a stopper on my jawing-tac but I say, Bob?"

"Well?"

"If he's alive, where's the other? There two of 'em—don't you remember?"

"I do," said Bob Hauler, slowly, "unless t other died. I haven't seen a man more like him than—"

He whispered a name in Jerry's ear, which caused the latter to exclaim—

"May I be made into a suet pudding for the lollie's dinner if you ain't right. I thought I knew his face the first time he came aboard the 'Will-o'.the Wisp.'"

"I knew him at first," said Bob, "but did not like to say anything, because I thought he'd be sure to make himself known to our captain."

Jerry scratched his head reflectively.

"Well, Bob," he said, "our young captain don't remember anything about it, he was too young at the time; but it strikes me there will be a row if ever them two meet."

"Perhaps, Jerry."

"Perhaps?"

"Yes; I'll tell you why; it's this way. The report came that they stood upon a rock, and blew each other's brains out."

"Yes."

"You see they couldn't do that, or else they wouldn't be here."

There was no contradicting this so Jerry assented.

"If it is him," he remarked, and the other is the other, I can't see why—"

"The yard is for fools," said a deep, stern voice, which made the two buccaneers spring to their feet, and, to their astonishment, they beheld the tall form of Dutch Paul, the pirate, sitting upon the breech of a gun.

Neither Bob nor Jerry could speak; and as they looked into each others faces they seemed to ask—

"Has he heard all our conversation?"

Their minds were much relieved when the pirate leader said—

"Keep the grog bottle a little less in use, and your tongues quieter, or both will be stopped. Go below. And do not forget my warning."

The pair quickly decamped, and the pirate chief, when they had gone, clasped his forehead and muttered—"So he lives, then. My hand failed me, and my disguise is discovered."

Little did Dutch Paul imagine that the subject of his thoughts was at that moment in a state of delirium on board a swift vessel, and raving about the terrible encounter that took place between them.

Shouting with maniacal glee at the thought of having slain his hated antagonist.

Much less did he think that they had both been made the victims of a base deception, and that the demon lived, though his face was hidden from mankind by a mask.

CHAPTER XLII.

THE SEA EMERALD PASSES INTO STRANGE KEEPING.

WHEN Usof reached the cadi's house he found his master in a state of excitement.

"Good Usof," he said, when his servant entered the chamber, "thy face tells me that the wondrous gem is mine."

Usof took the gem from his turban, and, prostrating himself, said—

" Thy servant was but in time, or the wondrous treasure would have been far away."

The cadi eagerly clutched the blood-bought emerald, and concealing it beneath his robe, said—

" Far away, good Usof ? Did the dog know that we had discovered his trickery ?"

" That, my master, he was beyond the power of divining."

" Ha! speak, Usof There is blood upon the hilt of thy weapon. Did the dog resist our wishes?"

" No, my master; he was dead before I reached the place."

" Dead !"

As the cadi repeated the word, a cold shudder passed over his frame. He thought of the emerald jewel he now possessed, and its mystic curse.

" Yes, dead, my master—slain by the hand of his slave."

" The black, Usof ?"

" Yes, O my master! He aspired to the possession of the wondrous jewel."

" By my soul, Usof !" continued the cadi, " the dog deserved death."

" He received his deserts, O my master! Thy slave's rapier became red with his base blood."

" You did well. Here, Usof, good Usof, take this as the forerunner of our goodness to thee."

He gave Usof the small emerald that the unfortunate merchant had sent as a bribe.

Usof, with deep reverence, received the gift. Kissing the hem of the cadi's robe (a general mode of expressing gratitude among the Easterns), he poured forth a long speech, in which the cadi, according to Usof's opinion, was the most generous of men, and ought to sit upon a sultan's throne, instead of being but a humble servant of the Ottoman dynasty.

The cadi smiled. Flattery was to him a sweet and grateful ear-tickler.

" We will not forget thee, Usof." He lowered his voice as he added, " Much may be done towards putting us in positions we both should occupy."

" O my master, I am unworthy of a thought."

" You are excessively good Usof," said the cadi, complimentarily. " We have now much wealth and money, and my friend will do much with the vizier."

" Thy servant begins to see thy meaning."

" I will tell thee, Usof. Come nearer."

Usof came to the edge of the divan upon which the cadi was seated.

" Now, hearken," said the aspiring Mussulman. " The time may come, Usof, when thou shalt become cadi of this town."

" O my master, my soul is filled with gratitude. What wilt thou be?"

" I," said the cadi, stroking his beard complacently, " will be the governor of this province."

Usof started. The cadi's aspiration was not impossible to attain. That the cringing servitor knew.

Money, judiciously employed, would, at the time of which we write, attain for the lowest positions of trust and emolument.

Usof, soon after, took his leave of the doomed possessor of the sea emerald.

Already had the shadow of evil fallen upon the possessor of the mystic jewel.

The cadi, as he hugged his treasure to his heart, little imagined that a pair of fiend-like eyes were peering out from a pair of curtains, beholding every sparkle of the mystic gem.

When Usof came to the cadi's chamber upon his return from the merchant's house, the seraskeer (general) of the troops which garrisoned the town was on his way to seek an interview with the magistrate.

He was not one of the cadi's best friends, and seeing the favourite servant hurrying up the marble passage, the seraskeer hid himself near the chamber door, with the comment—

" There is much meaning in yonder dog's look. I will listen."

If there was one passion stronger than another in the heart of Rachet Bey, the seraskeer, it was avarice. Gold he loved; not as misers love the tempting metal—Rachet Bey loved it for the honour it brought to its happy possessor.

The seraskeer's next passion was power—the command of some two thousand wild Moslems did not (to him) come within the meaning of the word.

He had grown grey beneath the star and crescent banner, and in spite of his long service, he had remained poor.

The seraskeer had often wondered why others who had but little claim to the country's gratitude should receive high distinction from the Sublime Porte.

He thought the matter over, until by chance he discovered that worth was not the key to the mystery. A handsome present to the chief vizier was, he found, of more utility than a hundred scars received beneath the sacred flag.

The seraskeer's limited means had prevented him from greasing the chief minister's helm; but now, as he listened to the conversation between the cadi and his servant, his eyes shone with joy.

Here, at last, was an opportunity for him to become rich, and perhaps, after all, he should become a governor of one of the provinces.

Once in that position, the seraskeer knew he could dispense justice at a certain price—i.e those who sent the heaviest bribe would have the decision in their favour.

With roseate visions of future greatness floating before his eyes, the seraskeer crept away from the cadi's chamber

" So," he thought, " the cadi has wealth—that wealth a wonderful jewel—and the dog would become governor. Oh, Allah ! thy servant seest how great thou hast been in directing his steps to yon presumptuous dog's chamber. By the Prophet's sacred beard, it was well."

He paced to and fro in the silent courtyard, and many cunning schemes came to his brain.

Once he had made up his mind to have the cadi slain, and possess himself of the jewel.

But mature reflection dismissed that idea.

He had a better and surer mode by exciting the cupidity of others.

He wanted not the jewel; but he knew the power it would bring.

" There is but one God," he murmured, " and that is Allah, and Mahomet is his prophet. Yes, this is the plan of Allah's servant First I will tell the governor of this gem. He will take it from the cadi. Then I will tell the vizier, when the governor has it, and he, Allah be praised! will, perhaps, have the governor bowstrung. Then I will ask the vizier for the governor's place If he does not give it to me, then—then I will let the Sultan know the wonderful gem is in his vizier's possession. Yes, Rachet Bey, Allah is good to thee, and thou art, I hope, thankful.

*   *   *   *   *   *

With the jewelled amber mouthpiece of his narghili between his lips, the cadi reclined upon a heap of silken cushions.

There was a glow of happiness upon his face, and a feeling of joy in his heart.

Between each puff of the perfumed herb he would mutter parts of the Koran, and his professed sense of Allah's goodness.

"Am I not," he said, "the richest cadi in the land of the faithful? Have I not a gem in a leathern bag, inside my breast, worth all the gold in Byzantium? Allah be praised, I have, good Allah—good cadi—good Maho—"

A Nubian entered the chamber.

"Dog!" roared the magistrate, "darest thou appear before me—before the richest cadi of all the cadies? Dog, I will have thy neck twisted, thy head chopped off, thy feet blistered. So go, jackass, go!"

The possession of so much wealth was turning the cadi's brain.

Had he taken the jewel from its case while speaking, he would have beheld its wondrous colour changed to the crimson hue—the sure harbinger of coming death.

He saw not this.

He felt the mystic stone against his flesh, and was happy.

The cowering slave waited until his arrogant master had ceased his abuse, then, meekly folding his arms across his breast bowed his head, and said—

"Gracious lord, thy servant dare not dis obey. He who now stands at thy gates —"

"Dare not, eh! By Allah! am I a dog, that every fool shall come to my house and swear he will see the cadi? Who is below, son of a burnt father?"

There was a malicious twinkle in the Nubian's eyes, as he slowly answered—

"The bearer of the b owstring!"

The jewelled pipe-stem fell from the cadi's lips. His hands clutched the cushions; his face became of a greenish hue, and, falling back, he moaned, in terror-stricken tones—

"The bearer of the bowstring!"

There was no hope for him now. Not all the fabulous wealth of the Indies could save him from strangulation.

Death had come upon him at a moment when his senses were steeped in bliss. The joys of the Moslem's paradise were faint in comparison to his happy state until the fearful, fatal, blighting words fell from the Nubian's lips—words that fell like the shadow of the tomb over the hapless possessor of the sea-emerald—that mystic stone, whose trail of blood would continue until the world should end, and all things should become chaos.

A few words of explanation is due to the readers of these pages—explanations of the hapless cadi's terror when the dread announcement fell from the Nubian's lips.

The bearer of the bowstring was the public executioner.

A dread being, whom the Governor or the Prime Minister had at his command, one whose mission was never resisted. In his person was blended the Sultan's power, and when a dignitary, either from a real or fancied crime, became obnoxious to the Government, the executioner was sent to strangle the hapless wretch.

No questions were ever asked by the doomed. The fatal messenger had but to appear, and, without a murmur, the cord would be wound round the neck of the victim.

The work over, the dread being went on his way, shunned, feared, yet unmolested. So great was the people's dread that they dared not, either by word or look, express their distaste for the wretch's power.

Such was the state of Turkey, under the rule of the merciless potentates half a century since.

Civilisation has done more of late years to alter this fearful state of things.

Without moving from that position in which he had fallen, the cadi awaited the coming of the executioner.

Had the wealth of the universe been offered him, he could not have moved.

The terrible words had scorched him like a sheet of vivid lightning, and he lay helpless and motionless.

One thought alone came across his mind.

How, and in what manner, had he excited the displeasure of his superiors?

The question would never be solved in this world. Had the cadi bestowed one thought upon the blood-bought jewel which lay next his heart, perhaps he would have known why the laws of the country came like the angel of death.

Clad from head to foot in spotless white, the messenger of death glides into the apartment.

The Nubian shivered as the softly-treading figure passed him, and crept cautiously from the chamber.

Without looking to the right or the left, the executioner went straight to his victim.

From beneath his white, flowing robe he took the fatal cord, and passed it round his neck.

The cadi gave a low cry, as he felt the cord tighten.

That cry was his last.

The judicial murderer placed one knee upon the cadi's quivering chest, then united all the power of his brute strength to tighten the noose.

Was it only chance that the wretch's knee should press upon the fatal gem, or but a working out of its mystic destiny?

As the life was crushed out from the cadi's body, he felt the blood-stained treasure breaking through his skin, and adding an additional pang to his last moment.

The dread scene was soon over, and the man who but a few minutes before had imagined he had attained the zenith of his wishes, lay a hideous, ghastly, huddled heap of stiffening flesh upon the very divan where he had so often sentenced poor trembling wretches to be bastinadoed.

When the last convulsive throe told the practised dispenser of death that the cadi was no more, he loosened the bowstring, and arose from his kneeling posture, and awaited the coming of an officer who had accompanied him upon his ghastly errand.

This functionary's duties consisted in proving that the execution had taken place, and from long practice he knew the precise moment when to enter the chamber.

He came in as the executioner stepped back from the dead body, and looked at the cadi's distorted, horrible face.

He saw that life had quitted the senseless clay, and walking to the gong, which hung from the ceiling, gave the brazen drum three distinct blows with the butt of his pistol.

This was the signal for the slain official's servants to assemble and hear the mandates of the Sultan.

The household, with Usof at their head, came trembling and silent in obedience to the well-known and dreaded summons.

One and all as they entered cast a startled, fearful look towards their late master, then fell back awed by the terrible frown of the Sultan's messenger.

The officer held a small square of parchment open in his hand, and, when the servants were all present, he read in a slow, audible voice the cause for which the late magistrate had suffered death.

"There is but one Allah," he read, "and our sovereign lord is his favourite on earth. May his shadow never grow less."

The awed listeners bent in lowly, reverential homage, and responded—

"May his shadow never grow less."

"Your master," the officer resumed, "is now dead. Look upon him and be warned. He broke the trust our gracious Sultan placed in him, and has been punished; such is the justice of the glorious Light of the Universe, our gracious Sultan. Speak, is it justice?"

As though fearful of hearing their own voices, the servants responded—

"It is justice; he deserved his fate. May Allah be merciful to him."

"Usof!" said the messenger, "Where is he called Usof?" Usof stepped forward.

"I am he," he cried; "what would my gracious master with his slave?"

Though he spoke calmly, the wily Usof knew the honour that awaited him.

The cadi's words were fulfilled, but not as he had anticipated.

The Judas servant had betrayed his master to the plotting seraskeer, and the latter had given him the honour he promised as a reward for his treachery.

The officer then read the Sultan's order which appointed Usof in his master's place, and even as the cold form lay huddled upon the cushions, Usof took his seat and received the homage of his late companions.

The officer's mission was accomplished, and he left, accompanied by the gaunt form of the executioner.

When Usof was alone, he detached the leathern bag, which held the mystic treasure, from the dead man's neck.

"It has worked out the prophecy of its finder," thought Usof "Allah be praised. I am rewarded by its aid, and covet not its possession."

The seraskeer's plot had prospered well.

The governor's cupidity was excited by the seraskeer's story of the wondrous emerald, and, with Usof's aid, they soon found a mode of bringing a charge against the cadi.

The charge was laid before the vizier, and by him to the Sultan, and the result was the departure of the bearer of the bowstring.

A swift messenger, while the body of the cadi was yet warm, spurred onward with the sea-emerald to the governor of the province.

"Allah is great!" said Rachet Bey, the seraskeer, as he beheld the messenger bearing away the treasure of the deep. "The first step is taken. Now, O governor, is thy turn!"

.   .   .   .

Ali Serap, the governor of the province, sat in his harem, surrounded by a bevy of beautiful women.

There were black-eyed beauties from the isles of Greece, whose Juno-like forms would have tempted the good Saint Antony to sin had he been there.

Fair Circassians, delicate and graceful as fawns, sought to gain a smile from their master.

Reclining upon divans, where golden embroidery shone beneath the blaze of twenty pensile silvery lamps, were a number of Turkish women, who vied with their companions in driving Ali Serap from his melancholy.

To all their smiles and blandishments the Pasha took no notice, and might have been a statue for all the impression their soft, seductive smiles made upon him.

The great man was ill at ease.

Two long hours had passed since the time he had expected his messenger to return with the sea's mystic treasure.

Twenty times the thought crossed his mind that the cadi had fled with the wondrous emerald.

And, as the hours wore on, the Pasha could have torn his beard with anger and suspense.

A fair Georgian whose pensive eyes at other times fired the Pasha's soul, timidly approached her lord.

"My lord," she murmured, "is angered with me to-day; shall I tune my lute to please him?"

The Pasha turned and roared—

"To the —— with thy lute; the curse of Allah fall upon the whole of them."

The girl shrank back, a frightened scream escaping her lips.

This seemed the culminating-point of Ali Serap's misery.

One of his slaves to scream when his mind was ill at ease, threw him into such a towering passion, that the vituperative abuse that had here followed, nearly choked him.

He could not speak for passion; his favourite Sultana, seeing her lord black in the face, ran forward to give him aid.

The whole troop followed her example, and while every nerve was strained listening for the sound of the horse's hoof that announced his messenger, a dozen little hands were patting him on the back.

As he could not speak, the Pasha could raise his hands, and good use he made of them.

Striking out right and left, he floored seven of his tormentors, then, yelling out a volley of curses, he rushed from the harem, leaving the frightened fair ones to condole with each other.

This tyrannical old sinner had once a narrow escape of his life.

He had ordered the bowstring to be sent out for the especial benefit of a certain young officer, when one of the ladies at his feet turned ghastly pale, and, falling on her knees, pleaded that the young man's life might be saved.

Ali Serap, foaming with rage, struck the unhappy girl, when she sprung to her feet, and, drawing a gleaming dagger from her girdle, rushed at the tyrant.

It would have gone hard with him, for in another moment the knife would have been in his heart, but a Nubian slave caught the enraged girl's wrist and held her fast.

The officer died by the bowstring, and the girl was sewn in a sack and flung that night into the river.

Stalking savagely down the vaulted passage that led from the women's apartments, he reached the audience-chamber.

Here an unhappy slave had fallen asleep upon one of the divans.

The Pasha could have howled with delight. Here was something, at least, to vent his spleen upon—something to atone for the mauling he had received in the harem.

Rushing from the chamber, the Pasha called for his guards.

A dozen grim Moslems came running towards him.

"There—there!" he cried. "Behold the son of a jackass! Take him up—take him up! Does he dare sleep in the face of Ali Serap, protector and governor? Bastinado him; bastinado the hound!"

The happy sleeper awoke in the grasp of the palace guards.

And, before he well knew what had happened, he was thrown upon the ground, and the soles of his feet warmed with a smart application of a bamboo rod.

The poor slave's howl of agony was music to Ali Serap, and running about the chamber like a madman, he yelled—

"Harder! harder! by my soul, I'll have you all bastinadoed—every one. The curse of Allah be upon you all!"

The culprit roared louder at every fresh stroke of the bamboo.

Suddenly Ali's hand was held up, and he cried—

"Stop! stop! It is, it is!"

To the amazement of his guards, he re-entered the chamber. repeating—

"It is it is!"

The welcome clatter of horses' hoofs, ringing upon the paved courtyard, saved the unfortunate slave's feet from being skinned.

The Pasha could, in the fullness of his joy, have hugged the dust-covered messenger.

He forgot his previous anxiety as the man handed him a small packet and a letter from the seraskeer.

The letter he placed in his girdle, and, readjusting the packet, walked quickly back to the audience-chamber.

The effulgent rays of the vertical sun streamed through a large window as he viewed the priceless gem.

Much as he had been prepared for the splendour of the mystic emerald, he could not repress a cry of admiration as the sun's rays fell upon the sparkling stone.

A million flashes of glittering light played over the lustrous jewel, and the Pasha, putting it back in its leather case, passed the thong round his neck.

Seid Ali Serap, think of the last neck that thong had entwined! Had the thought come to his brain, he would, perhaps, have been less exuberant in his joy.

Around the very spot where that thong had been wont to rest when the gem was in the cadi's possession. the blue mark left by the bowstring formed a deep indentation.

"A true friend thou art, O Rachet Bey," said the Pasha. "Such a gift as this is worth a dozen cades—a dozen, aye, a thousand."

He pressed the precious but fatal gift to his lips, then opened the wily seraskeer's letter.

Divesting the epistle of its flowery terms, it ran thus—

"This wondrous jewel, my friend, was taken by an infidel from the depths of the ocean. It has rare and curious properties. Watch it well, and should harm threaten thee, its colour will change, and give thee warning. May thy shadow never grow less, and thy possession of the sea-emerald never bring thee harm'"

"A generous friend at last; Allah be praised!" muttered the Pasha, as he folded the letter.

"Well shalt thou be rewarded, O seraskeer; our bounty shall be great for thy kindness."

The cunning in the old fellow's eyes belied his words.

Ali Serap now possessed the jewel, and his brain was busy finding a mode by which he could rid himself of the seraskeer.

He felt none should possess the secret of its existence, and at once commenced planning the seraskeer's destruction.

Three days passed before he could find a safe method of repaying his good friend.

Then he sent a messenger to the grand vizier, impeaching the seraskeer's loyalty.

Quick as he had been, the old seraskeer was before him, and, at the time his messenger arrived, the vizier was racking his brain to find an excuse for getting rid of the Pasha.

The seraskeer had sent a detailed and glowing account of the jewel, and the vizier, longing to possess the wonderful stone, could scarcely brook an instant's delay.

The Pasha's destruction was at once resolved upon.

But how was it to be effected?

The visit of Ali Serap's messenger solved the question, and, with the latter's report against the seraskeer, the vizier sought an audience with the Sultan.

The effeminate monarch left the government of his kingdom to his vizier, and when he heard the cunning lies with which the Pasha sought to belie the faithful old general, his answer was—

"Send the bowstring to the dog, and make Rachet Bey governor in his stead."

The vizier's heart leapt for joy. He should have the gem, and the seraskeer the post he coveted.

When Ali Serap was in hourly expectation of his messenger's return, he was appalled by the sudden appearance of the bearer of the bowstring and his attendant officer.

The trembling Pasha's guilty mind recalled a hundred crimes which he had committed; each one, he knew, was punishable by death.

Which particular crime had been discovered, and brought his doom, he endeavoured to learn, but his inquiries were cut short by the tightening of the cord.

The scene that took place was a repetition of the cadi's death; but this time the slain cadi was represented by the seraskeer.

Thus had the fearful gem brought death upon five of its possessors, and yet in its onward course two men had been benefitted.

True, neither had coveted the mystic, fearful stone and the words of part of the legend were being carried out.

"Those who covet me not shall be rewarded; those who possess me shall die."

.   .   .   .   .   .

Plunging forward like a maddened steed, a small vessel was striving to ride out the fearful storm.

Such a storm! One of those sudden changes from bright, glorious sunshine and cerulean clouds to fierce, howling winds, and heaven's canopy, like a thick, murky fog, hanging over the ocean.

Here and there, as the storm-clouds were lifted by a sudden gust of wind, light blue glimpses of the hidden day would appear.

And when the storm-clouds closed the gap, a sombre hue fell upon the troubled face of the great watery world.

The storm had burst so suddenly upon the affrighted seamen that they had not time to take in a single reef of their flowing canvas before the vessel swung round, and dashed onward like a stricken steed.

Afar could be heard the dull roar of the surge as it broke upon the rocky shore.

A storm so portentous of evil to the cowering crew that they bent their heads to the deck, and prayed to their Deity for help.

It was an Eastern bark, of light construction, and manned by a crew of Moslems.

They heard not the wild shrieks of their captain, as he called on them—some to take the helm, and others to let fall the sails that were hurrying them to destruction.

It was their fate, they thought, to be cast upon the rapidly-nearing breakers, and human agency could not save them.

Their last hours must be devoted to supplications to Allah and his prophet.

Aiding the captain, by fierce and frantic promises of fabulous wealth, was a tall, big-bearded Moslem.

His dress was such as worn only by the highest and most favoured in the East.

He promised them wealth in abundance—gold that would enable them to create a paradise on earth, but his words fell unheeded.

It was their kismet (fate), and none but Allah could save them now.

So the captain and the richly-dressed Pagan seized

the wheel, and sought, by their heavy weight, to jam it down.

When their hands grasped the spokes, a mighty wave came leaping over the vessel's stern. The wheel was wrenched from their grasp, and the two feeble men were hurled against the vessel's side.

One fell to rise no more.

It was the captain. His skull came in contact with an iron bolt, and he died where he fell.

Then on——on through the heaving billows, went the light craft; on——until the dull roar of the breakers sent a chill of their coming doom to the abject crew.

Suddenly the vessel stopped, and quivered as though a shudder was passing through her timbers.

Then the huge waves leapt around her—there was a stifled shriek—a long, despairing cry—and where, a moment before, a ship stood, reeling to and fro, nothing was left but a confused medley of spars, sails, and struggling seamen.

Then the waves, as though rejoicing at the fell havoc, rose higher, and all that were left of the crew were hurled against the jagged reef, and crushed into indistinguishable shapes.

But one of those who had trod the deck of the storm-riven vessel reached the shore alive.

He, only with the energy that desperation alone can give, clung to a spar—then, torn and bleeding, was cast out of the reach of the angry waves.

When the new-born joy arose in his breast of renewed life, the castaway struggled to his feet, and staggered towards a clump of dark-jutting trees.

Here he paused for a moment, and, taking a small, dark-looking object from his breast, muttered—

"All is gone—save this. Allah be praised! Allah be praised!"

The speaker held in his grasp the sea-emerald—that fatal jewel which carried death to all who held it.

Yes, he alone escaped the fearful wreck.

Death by drowning was too easy for those who possessed the precious gem.

The mystic ritual of blood must fall upon its possessor.

Now, torn, bleeding, and weary, was the Grand Vizier to the Sultan of the great and powerful Ottoman empire!

The man who had become possessed of the sea-treasure, and its curse.

From the time the leathern bag had first been placed upon his neck, peace and happiness had fled from his mind. In daily, hourly fear of losing the inestimable gem, his life became a living torture.

There was little of the crafty statesman left in his failing brain.

All his thoughts became centered upon this one, this fatal object.

And one morning his royal master missed his great minister.

He had gone, none knew whither; left during the night, so stealthily that none could give a clue of his whereabouts

The ship which had just been shattered upon the sunken reef was chartered by the vizier to bear him to a secluded spot, where, alone, he could exist in the enjoyment of his wealth.

In the haunts of his fellow-men he felt his life was not worth an hour's purchase.

But the storm had turned his cherishing hope, and he was now alone, and panting for food, upon a strange and uninhabited shore.

The full horror of his position burst upon him when he had regarded the mystic treasure; he burst into tears, and, staggering a few paces forward, fell to the earth prone and powerless.

The glad sunshine came again, while the stricken man lay in his death-like torpor—came; and, as the first ray shot upon the earth, a figure, wild-looking and attenuated, came out from the thick underwood.

He beheld the fallen form of the wretched vizier, and a cry of surprise fell from his lips

A cry that was turned to joy, when, in placing his hand inside the vizier's robe to feel if life yet beat within his breast, his fingers touched the bag containing the sea-emerald.

The wild denizen of that strange land paused in his act of mercy to examine the contents of that strangely-fashioned case.

Then, as the glittering fire from the dire jewel came before his eyes, a grim and demoniacal expression came over his pale, thin face.

"He must die," he muttered. "Were ten lives in the way, I would take them all to possess this."

He raised a huge jagged piece of rock, and poised it for a second above the vizier's head.

It fell with a dull, sickening crash; the vizier gave one convulsive shudder, and his spirit fled.

Another had gone—another had paid the forfeit of the sea-emerald's possession.

Then the madman, with a greedy look in his swollen eyes, left the stiffening form, and sat upon the trunk of a fallen tree.

In his hand he held the fatal gem, and, like a demon, he exulted over its possession.

The strange, wild figure was that of Captain Angel, the only survivor of the "Civet Cat."

The waters which had engulphed his companions had refused to claim him for its own.

CHAPTER XLIII.

CAPTAIN TOM DRAKE SAVED FROM DEATH BY THE AVENGER, IRON ARM

THE fierce cry of rage which came from the boy buccaneers, when they beheld their leader alone on the Death Pirate's deck, was followed by a rush of excited men, as the crew began to cast loose the boats.

Harry Vere, by voice and example, cheered the buccaneers, as they grasped their arms and hurried into the boats.

"There is not much chance of saving him," he said, sternly; "but I swear never to place my foot on this deck again unless I bring back Captain Tom Drake."

"We will follow you to the death," was the cry of the brave lads. "Lead us on, we are ready."

Though trembling for the safety of his gallant young leader, Harry Vere had sufficient forethought to set a number of hands at work to repair the spars shattered by the Death Pirate's tremendous broadside.

"You can follow us," he said to those who were engaged in this duty, "should we soon come up with the pirate-ship; he will lead us back again. Now, my lads, pull with a will. Remember, Captain Tom Drake is in peril."

The oars fell with a plash upon the waters, but before a stroke had been taken a pale face appeared over the bulwarks.

It was Ben Barnacle; his wounds yet bleeding, and though Doctor Shrike and his assistant tried to force him back to his berth, he clung to the shrouds, and called out—

"Stern all—stern all!"

Harry Vere and his followers looked up. The voice arrested them. There was such a stern air of grim resolution upon the wounded man's face that Harry felt, if he refused to take him on board, Ben would, in the excitement of the moment, have jumped overboard.

All on board the buccaneers' vessel knew the great love which Ben Barnacle had for their young leader, but not in their wildest dreams had they the least knowledge of the cause. None would, had the truth spoken, have credited that Ben Barnacle was other than he seemed.

The kingly, dark-eyed man kept a close guard upon his tongue, and such a restraint upon his every act, that he would have misled the most skilful.

The attentions of Doctor Shrike and his follower were distasteful to the wounded seaman.

Turning upon them, with a glitter in his dark eyes that spoke of the volcano rising in his breast, he said, fiercely—

"Back, cursed vampire! or I will hurl you both into the sea."

The doctor and Jacop retreated precipitately.

Ben, though severely wounded in his encounter with the Death Pirate, still had sufficient strength left to have crushed both the vampire and his assistant.

"Come below, Jacop," said the doctor, leading the way. "He will find it worse for him by-and-by—eh, Jacop?"

To which the mummy replied—

"Much worse! much worse! He is bleeding from his wounds now."

"You are too much hurt, Ben," said Harry Vere, "to accompany us."

Ben made no reply.

Taking a heavy cutlass from the rack, he buckled it round his waist, and, scrambling over the side, seized a rope, and dropped lightly into the cutter.

The word was now given to "give way," and the light crafts rushed with terrific speed through the water.

Fixed upon the longboat's bows was a small brass howitzer, and, with this single small piece of ordnance, the gallant lads kept up a brisk fire upon the Death Pirate's vessel.

Not a sound, save the sharp report, broke the stillness.

Silent, deadly, and determined, all who went to Captain Tom Drake's rescue continued, until they beheld from the huge vessel's deck a white puff of smoke curl upwards. It needed no explanation to the silent avengers.

This small spiral cloud they knew came from a weapon that had been fired at the gallant Captain Tom Drake.

Then, as though the Death Pirate was within hearing, the deep, stern voice of Harry Vere called out—

"Harm but a hair of his head, touch but the hem of his lady's garment, and, by my hopes of mercy hereafter, I swear that such a fate shall be yours that the bare detail of your sufferings will cause the cheeks of the hearers to blanch with horror."

As he ceased speaking, a deep response was made by the gallant buccaneers.

The words were but few, but of such import that the Death Pirate would have been safer in a den of hungry lions than at the mercy of Tom's crew.

Many anxious eyes were turned towards their own distant vessel, as the thought would unbidden rise, that after all their exertions the pirate would escape them.

Such an unfortunate end to their enterprise was present to the minds of all.

There would be no hope for their young leader were such a dire calamity to occur. The spars of the ship were too much damaged to take up the pursuit for some time yet, and this small brass gun seemed to inflict but little damage upon their huge opponent.

While these conflicting thoughts passed through their anxious brains, a second puff of smoke was seen to curl among the shrouds of the pirate vessel.

Then, in the glowing sunlight, bright blades were seen to flash upward. A moment after, and a form, which they pronounced to be that of their brave leader, toppled over the bulwarks into the sea.

As their mingled cry of rage and grief went floating away, a second figure fell from the ship's side. Then upon the breeze a chorus of hellish mocking laughter came wafted to their ears.

The excitement in the boats beggars all description. Some were on their knees praying to their Maker to stop the miscreant pirate's career.

Others, whose home recollections of early piety had passed away, sat gripping their blades, and cursing the boats for not flying quicker through the water.

To add to their fierce feelings there came a cry of—

"Pull! pull! it is our chief who has been hurled over."

There was no necessity for the injunction to the rowers. They needed no words to encourage them in the task.

They pulled with a vigour that brought the flesh up in hard lumps upon their arms, and caused the veins on their brows to stand up like whipcords.

Every eye, every nerve was strained, the latter to reach the spot where the form of their beloved leader had disappeared.

As they neared the goal, the pirate fired his stern guns full at the bows of the advancing boats.

The iron hail came whistling among the devoted crew, and, though many fell stricken to death, not a murmur emerged from their lips.

Another and another discharge followed, and brought death with it, still the undaunted fellows went onward.

One of the boats soon filled.

Her bows were riddled like a sieve, and all who sat in her would have gone to the bottom without a murmur.

There must have been a wondrous depth of love in the undaunted crew for their young leader, for when the cutter backed to take them on board, the gallant fellows cried out—

"Never mind us; forward, and be revenged for the death of our chief."

"We will save you first," said Ben Barnacle, quietly; "should Captain Tom Drake have fallen, not the bowels of the earth or the depths of the ocean will save his slayer from my vengeance."

The fierce glitter of the speaker's eyes, and the clenched hands and throbbing breast, showed that, though he spoke quietly, there was a conflict of passion within.

While the lads continue their search for their gallant leader, we will see what befel Captain Tom Drake when he found himself alone on the pirate's deck.

As the grisly-headed leader of the Moorish horde disappeared with Minnie Atherton's senseless form upon his arm, Captain Tom Drake bounded forward—his weapon, meteor-like, flashing from its sheath.

Vainly he tried to discover the spring that opened the hidden trap.

Vainly he called upon the Pirate of Death to come upon deck and face his young foe.

From the open skylight which gave light and air to the cabin, the miscreant's voice rang out a mocking reply.

"Trapped! trapped!" he shouted, gleefully. "Trapped! Your ship dismasted, and your mistress here in my power!"

Captain Tom Drake placed his hand to his throbbing brow.

THE FATE OF THE SPANISH PIRATE.

"Vile, treacherous miscreant!" he said, "though a hundred blades stood between us, you shall die!"

He dashed to the after-hatch as he spoke, and would have sought out his foe, had not twenty fierce-bearded Moors barred his passage.

Scimitars, pikes, yataghans, and knives were levelled at his breast, but he saw them not.

Before his victim was the prone form of his lovely bride, as she lay helpless, senseless, and powerless, at the mercy of the pirate fiend.

Many a sharp weapon's point rang against his golden mail, as he hurled himself against the bristling line of steel.

Many a death-cry followed the swift downward stroke of his scimitar, as a Moslem fell headlong down the steps, his skull cloven in.

While he fought, like an enraged tiger, with the crowd who stood between him and his boyhood's love, another party came in rear, and would have decimated the gallant boy, had not aid suddenly come.

Help so sudden and powerful that Tom, for the first few moments, could scarcely believe the truth.

He felt a towering, muscular man place his back against his shoulders—heard the cries of rage and astonishment that fell from the lips of those who sought to creep upon him.

He knew, too, that a massive weapon was wielded by his unknown friend, and at every stroke the crowd counted one less.

Still the odds were fearful.

Although the gallant fellow who had come to Tom's aid was a Colossus in stature, and Tom's bravery and skill was worth a dozen ordinary men, both must soon have fallen, for the Moors gained strength every moment.

While the fight was at its highest, the voice of the unknown whispered to Tom—

"Be of good heart; your boats are coming to the rescue."

"They will never reach us."

As they spoke, both were bravely plying the work of death

Neither could turn their heads—eyes and hands were wanted to repel the forest of weapons that were opposed to their single arms.

"They will not," was the answer. "Keep close to me; we must swim for it."

"Never," said Tom, firmly. "I will die; but leave this vessel without my bride—never!"

An exclamation of disappointment came from the unknown, and, as he plied his massive weapon, he said—

"It is certain death for us to stay. I will force my way through this crowd of devils. Keep close, and follow."

"Death first!"

"Be it so," was the answer. "I care not; yet, were I in your place, I would live to be avenged for the miscreant's treachery."

Captain Tom remained silent for a few seconds. He felt that his adviser was right; yet the stubborn, bull-dog nature would not let him yield until the last moment.

"What is your plan?" he asked.

The reply did not come immediately.

Captain Tom's colossal friend was fiercely engaged with three of his late companions—three who seemed, more than all who opposed him, to seek his death.

When the steel-spiked mace had settled the trio, he answered—

"Swim for the boats, regain your ship—then rescue your bride. There is no other plan."

"Be it so," said the exasperated boy, jamming the point of his sword between the teeth of a powerful pirate. "I will follow you."

The herculean fellow swung his mace around with both hands with such terrible swiftness that the foremost rank of his adversaries were mowed down as though the swift lightning's flash had stricken them.

He followed the momentary pause that ensued by stepping forward.

Captain Tom stepping back at the same time.

Thus, back to back, they fought a lane to the bulwarks.

Another moment and the deadly mace would have crushed the last who stood between them and liberty.

Before the mighty arm could accomplish this last stroke, the Death Pirate, foaming at the mouth with passion, came upon deck.

Until now he had been kept below by the surging crowd that barred Captain Tom's descent into the cabin.

But as the gallant pair clove their way to the vessel's side, the pirates gradually left the blood-stained hatchway, and enabled their savage leader to ascend.

He saw at a glance what had taken place, and his eyes blazed like living coals.

He saw the strongest and bravest man among his followers fighting like a demon for his bitterest foe.

He beheld the giant frame towering high above his men, wielding that terrible steel mace, the very weight of which was as much as any two men of the vessel could lift.

Yet the colossal owner of this mighty hand could raise it with as much ease as another could handle a pike or cutlass.

Iron Arm, so was the giant termed.

He had received the soubriquet from his companions for the wondrous strength he possessed—not strength alone, but such untiring energy was in his powerful limbs, that it seemed as though they were moulded from the tough metal, the name of which he bore.

If he had another name, none on board the pirate vessel knew it.

His nationality was as little known as his name.

Though his skin was dark enough to have proclaimed him of African descent, his massive features possessed that frank, handsome outline only to be seen among the Saxons.

His language was pure English, though it was well known he was familiar with several tongues.

Some among the pirate horde thought he had sprung from an English father and African mother. Others, judging by his tanned skin, inclined to the belief that he was an Indian.

Many of the keenest among the Moorish gang had noticed that Iron Arm's hands and face at times seemed of a darker hue than usual.

Those who beheld this came to the conclusion that his skin was stained by some sable dye, which concealed his nationality, and required renewing from time to time.

Whatever opinions were entertained by his fellows, none dared to openly question him.

His marvellous strength and fiery nature stopped prying curiosity, and his reticence, for he rarely exchanged a word with those with whom fate had placed him.

He seemed like a lion in the company of wolves and, like the noble forest monarch, he was more dreaded than liked.

Had the pirate horde been less engaged when the spectre-ship of the sea so suddenly fell upon them, they would have noticed that the tremendous weapon wielded by Iron Arm was the only one that was idle during the fray.

Both the mace and its gigantic owner were absent from the fight.

And, had they sought the giant they would have found him leaning leisurely against the foremast, his large, dark, expressive eyes following the graceful form of Captain Tom with more of love in them than hate.

They would have seen, too, that when danger of more than an ordinary kind menaced the gallant, graceful boy, as he, like the God of battle, moved among the combatants, the massive mace clutched by its owner, and his attitude changed from calm repose to that of the jaguar about to spring.

Then, as the boy extricated himself from peril, a proud look swept over his features, and he became a passive spectator of the fight.

A cynical look that settled upon his face when the Moors were driven back by the young buccaneers showed that his sympathy was not with his companions.

Such was the being who had come to Tom's rescue when he was pressed hard by the Moslem pirates.

So great was the terror in which his mighty arm was held, that unless a score of Moors crowded upon him by the mere force of numbers, none would have faced him.

The pirate would have sooner beheld two-thirds of his crew pass over and aid the young buccaneer, than the redoubtable Iron Arm, the man whose single weapon was a host in itself.

"So!" he hissed, when he came within a few paces of the young chief and Iron Arm, "thus you heard me? Die, recreant dog!"

He levelled a pistol point blank at the head of his late follower.

Iron Arm felt the ball tear a furrow across his cheek as it sped forward, and, with a deep cry of rage surging up from his broad chest, he bore down his Moslem foes, and sprang towards the pirate.

The latter knew the fearful weight of the uplifted mace—knew that, despite his steel breast-plate and chain mail, he would be (to use a homely simile) but as a fly beneath the terrible weapon.

He dared not stay for the onset of the angered giant, but, with a curse of baffled rage, ran among his Moors, and yelled—

"Where are your pistols and matchlocks? Shoot the renegade; shoot him!"

A matchlock ball whizzed past Iron Arm's head, and, knowing that his giant strength would not save him from a bullet, he strode towards the spot where the gallant young buccaneer stood, with his back against the bulwarks, battling fiercely with his foes, and cried, as he swung his mace around—

"Now, leap for it; away! I will prevent yon treacherous scoundrel from having your bride."

Tom thanked him with a look, and, cutting a Moslem's pikestaff in two, he sprang upon a gun, from thence to the bulwarks.

He stood and turned to see whether his gallant friend, the Hercules, could force his way through the crowd, and beheld, to his joy, Iron Arm spring upon the same gun from which his foot had just alighted.

The Colossus paused for a moment, and, with a swing of his iron mace, awed back those who would have stayed his leap into the sea.

One withering look of hate he bestowed upon the Death Pirate, then, with unerring aim, he sent his ponderous weapon flying through the air.

"This," he said, "until we meet again; that is the first mark from Iron Arm, the Avenger."

The spiked missile struck the miscreant pirate upon his steel corslet, hurling him to the deck, and crushing through the glittering metal as though it had been but a sheet of glass.

He waited until he saw the Death Pirate's mouth and nostrils streaming with blood, then turned to Captain Tom, and curtly remarked—

"Some of his ribs are broken, I expect. Now, jump; they are loading a dozen weapons for our benefit. Away! he will be safe from mischief until we meet him again."

Captain Tom plunged into the ocean, followed by his mysterious friend.

As their bodies cleft the waves, the sharp ring of a dozen matchlocks told what their fate would have been had they stayed another second.

When they came to the surface, the pirate vessel had passed on ahead.

"It will be some time before we are picked up," remarked Iron Arm to his companion. "Should those devils see us, our friends will come in vain."

Before Tom could speak, Iron Arm called out, suddenly—

"Sink! sink! We are seen!"

Twenty long barrels blazed out from the pirate's side, and the water, where the gallant pair had been floating, was dotted with minute sprays of foam by the well-aimed bullets.

CHAPTER XLIV.

ADMIRAL ELLIS RECEIVES A CHALLENGE.

THE little admiral whose name adorns the heading of this chapter, had not the remotest idea that his victim could escape him.

He calculated, within an hour of the time, that "Lapwing" would reach the latitude which he fixed on the corner of the sealed orders.

Pacing to and fro on the quarter-deck, he thought, with gleeful feelings, of the clever stroke he had made in getting rid of his hated son-in-law

"Jenny," he muttered, "will make a fuss at first about what she will be pleased to term my cruelty but a season in London will soon cause her to forget him; and, by a little policy, I can manage to make her the Honourable Mrs. Archibald Gaston—a connection, by the way, that will be of some moment to me just now."

A shore boat came alongside with a letter for the admiral.

The missive was opened by the martinet, and he read its contents.

An angry flush came over his sallow features, and he muttered—

"Of course. Fool that I must have been, not to have known that letter of marque was surreptitiously obtained! Well, regret will not alter the state of affairs. I must go ashore, and talk it over with his lordship."

He went ashore, and then hastened to the house of Lord Collingford, the Lord High Admiral of the British Navy.

There was a frown, portentious of coming evil to the little admiral, upon his lordship's face, as he pointed to a chair, and said, tersely—

"Be seated, Admiral Ellis."

The admiral seated himself, and calmly awaited the storm he saw impending.

Lord Collingford turned over a mass of papers which lay upon a table before him, and fishing out a formidable-looking document, with a large seal dangling at the corner, spread it open.

"I have," he began, "been honoured with a communication from the Home Government respecting your conduct upon a late occasion, Admiral Ellis."

The admiral smiled blandly, and said—

"Indeed, my lord?"

"The matter to which it refers is of serious import to you, and, I may say, to the country at large."

Admiral Ellis began to fidget about in his chair; things wore a more startling aspect than he had imagined.

"What I mean by a serious—hem!—I suppose I had better let you know the worst at once, Admiral Ellis."

The admiral's bland smile had passed away, and his face wore a troubled look.

He made no answer to his lordship's suggestion about knowing the worst.

Much as he was prepared for a startling piece of intelligence by his superior's strange manner, he was scarcely able to credit his senses when his lordship said—

"You are charged, under one section of this document, with aiding and abetting the piracies of one Thomas Nelson, better known as Captain Tom Drake, the Buccaneer."

The little admiral sprang at least two feet from the chair upon which he was seated, and spluttered out—

"I aid him? I, my lord? You really must be jesting?"

"I never jest, Admiral Ellis," was the freezing response, "never."

"But this charge against me—against one who would string the whole of them up to the yard-arm."

"Yet," said Lord Collingford, "you were on board this vessel, and allowed this audacious young pirate to escape."

"I—I—my lord, there is some mistake."

"None whatever; the matter is plain enough. You went on board, came away, and soon after his vessel sailed."

" Perfectly true."

" Yet you say there must be some mistake."

" Decidedly ; a great error in accusing me of being an accomplice. My lord, the Government must be his accomplice, if any."

" Indeed. How ?"

" Have they not furnished him with a letter of marque ?"

" Certainly not," said his lordship, placing the forefinger of his right hand upon a marked passage in the paper. " It is stated here that you suffered him to escape by the production of a letter of marque, which you well knew, at the time, he had no right to possess."

" It is false, my lord !"

" Be careful, sir. Remember to whom you speak."

The admiral was, by this time, in a high state of excitement. Above all men in the world, he was the last man to expect such a charge.

His sallow visage grew white, and his dry, mummy-like fingers worked with a convulsive motion.

" I do not forget to whom I speak," he answered, and, excitedly pacing the room, he sought to cool his rising anger, " but hope, my lord, you will allow for my outraged feelings."

" Hem !" coughed his lordship.

Private feeling had but little weight with him when public duty stood in the way.

" I should have sooner expected a reprimand," the admiral resumed, " from the Government, for my severity, than such a charge as this. My lord, I would feel indebted to you for ever if you could cause inquiries to be made. You—"

" There will be a court of inquiry upon your conduct," said his lordship, coldly. " I should deem it necessary. I have full instructions from the Home Government how to act."

Admiral Ellis fully understood the meaning of this official speech.

As plainly as possible his lordship implied that he had it in his power to try the little admiral, by court-martial, for the charge specified in his official communication.

Admiral Ellis grew red to the roots of his hair.

He knew, should he be placed before a jury of his brother officers, so great was their dislike to him, they would seize the opportunity to pass off many an old grudge they had stored up against him.

He saw himself stripped of his rank, disgraced, and beggared.

As coolly as his excitement would permit, he told his lordship the scene that had taken place on board Tom's vessel.

" In the face of such a document, he said, " I was baffled and outwitted. My men had the pirates' hearts covered by their weapons, yet I dared not fire."

" You examined the letter of marque ?"

" I did, my lord, and found it perfectly legal."

" I must let the affair stand over until I write to the Home Government."

" Do, my lord, and tell them that I took upon myself, in spite of the Royal seal which I then supposed to be genuine, to punish one of the pirate leaders."

Lord Collingford looked up, and said—

" You committed a breach of orders, then, Admiral Ellis."

The little officer was nearly driven mad by this.

" Breach of orders, my lord ? And yet I am to be arraigned before a court-martial for not destroying the pirate gang !"

" But you tell me that, at the time, you imagined the sign manual to be that of your Royal master."

The little admiral ground his teeth with fury.

" I should have stood the risk, my lord !" he said. " As it is, I have but done my duty !"

" True, as matters have transpired, you are safe ; but I question if the Government will not look at the action as an implied insult to their letter of marque—which you believed to be correct at the time."

Admiral Ellis bit his lips until the blood oozed through.

" If you will detail the affair of which you speak," Lord Collingford said, " I will lay the statement before the Admiralty. In the meantime you must surrender your sword, and deliver yourself up as prisoner."

" My lord, I—"

" I am but following out my instructions, Admiral Ellis," the Lord High Admiral said. " You shall be released on parole until I hear from England.

His face scarlet at such humiliation, the proud officer unsheathed his sword, and placed it upon the table.

" Now," said Lord Collingford, " I will take down your statement in writing."

With quivering lips and difficult articulation, old Ellis detailed the mode by which he had entrapped Harry Vere.

When he had finished speaking, his superior said—

" By the time that has elapsed since the ' Lapwing' sailed, this pirate will have suffered death."

Admiral Ellis inclined his head in token of assent.

He found a solace in the midst of the misfortune which had so unexpectedly fallen upon him.

It was the thought of Harry Vere's fate.

Witholding from Lord Collingford the secret source of his antipathy to Harry Vere, he endeavoured to show that his sense of public duty, and that alone, caused him to have Harry Vere destroyed.

Lord Collingford's keen grey eyes watched the admiral's face as he detailed the plan for ensnaring the young lieutenant.

And he saw by the malignant hate that shone in the narrator's eyes that other motives than the high sense of duty he owed his country had been the primary cause.

He said nothing to the admiral of his suspicions, but when the humiliated officer was taken back a prisoner to his ship, Lord Collingford rang a small bell which stood on the desk.

The summons was answered by a skulking form, garbed as a seaman in the Royal Navy.

There was a hang-dog look about the fellow's face, and a furtive expression in his eyes, that bespoke a mean and petty soul.

He has once before figured in these pages, as a fitting agent for Lieutenant Sanderson's lying report to poor old Gregory, about Captain Tom.

It was Dan Cuttle, crimp, spy, and informer, who slunk into his lordship's presence.

" Cuttle," said the nobleman, " who is this Lieutenant Vere ?"

" Captain Tom's officer, my lord."

" Yes, I know that. But what do you know of his former history ? To be brief, had he ever anything to do with Admiral Ellis ?"

" Yes. my lord," he said ; " the lieutenant you speak about ran away with the old admiral's daughter, and married her in spite of her father's wish."

Lord Collingford made a note of this.

" That will do, Dan ; you can go."

Dan Cuttle shuffled out of the room.

" This is his high sense of duty," mused the stern old naval commander-in-chief " He makes use of the power which our Royal master entrusts him with for the settlement of private affairs."

Lord Collingford did not forget to describe this in his report respecting the admiral.

And under his able pen the crime was not glossed over.

It bore a strong resemblance to a charge of murder.

Admiral Ellis was spared the torture of knowing the storm that was gathering above him.

Two days after the admiral delivered his sword, the commodore's vessel came into port, bringing Captain Clark to seek satisfaction for his friend's death.

The young commander's first act was to send a challenge to the admiral—a firmly-worded epistle, in which he stigmatised Jenny's father as a cowardly murderer.

This missive despatched, he went ashore to wait upon Lord Collingford, to formally resign the command of the " Lapwing."

His lordship received the young sailor very graciously.

Captain Clark had been a midshipman on board his lordship's vessel, and he felt an interest in the brave fellow.

" So you have come to see your old captain ?" his lordship said, extending his hand. " Good boy ; I am pleased with this mark of your attention."

" I have come, my lord," said Captain Clark, with quivering lips, " upon an errand which I know will grieve you as much as it — "

The old nobleman saw by the mournful expression upon the young officer's face that something of more than ordinary import had taken place.

" Grieve me ?" he said. " What is the matter, my boy ?"

" I am compelled, my lord, to resign the command of the ' Lapwing,' and — "

" What ! what ! Are you mad ? Is this the return for the unremitting interest I have always taken in your advancement, is it ? How absurd ! Your brain is disordered ! You cannot be sane to speak thus !"

Captain Clark remained silent for some minutes.

He knew he should pain his father's dearest friend by the course he had taken ; yet with the murdered form of Harry Vere before his vision, he felt he could not serve under a flag where such cruelties were permitted.

" My lord," he answered, " I do not take this step from a mere caprice. Give me your attention for a few minutes, and I will convince you that I could not do otherwise."

" Proceed," said Lord Collingford, angrily.

Captain Clark related the execution of Harry Vere, and Jenny's suicidal leap into the sea.

" I feel," he said, in conclusion, " that I have been the executioner of an innocent man · and while the recollection of that tragic scene lives within me, I shall never know one moment's peace."

" Your resolution is unalterable ?"

" It is, my lord."

" Be advised by me, and take a few days to consider the matter over."

" I shall feel the same then as I now feel."

" You do not know. At any rate, I will not accept your resignation until then."

Captain Clark bowed.

" Under those circumstances," he said, " I have no other course but to wait."

He left his angry old patron, and went towards the boat which had brought him ashore.

" It's a pity," mused Lord Collingford, thoughtfully. " that the service should lose such a promising officer. Perhaps, when he finds the Government

takes Harry Vere's cold-blooded assassination in hand, he'll alter his mind."

His lordship added another postscript to the paper he was about to send to the Home Government respecting Admiral Ellis.

When Captain Clark reached the boat, he walked moodily to the stern-sheets, and said—

" Row to Admiral Ellis's ship. Give way."

He reached the frigate, and was ushered into the admiral's presence by a midshipman.

The sudden change in old Ellis's position had not improved his temper, and, when Captain Clark entered the cabin, he looked up angrily, and said—

" Who the devil are you, sir, that you intrude upon my privacy in this manner ?"

The young officer turned, and closed the cabin door, then, taking a brace of loaded pistols from beneath his boat-cloak, he held the butts towards the admiral, and said—

" I am an avenger, Admiral Ellis. I have come to wash out my murdered friend's blood by slaying his murderer. Take your choice of these weapons, for but one of us leaves this cabin alive. If you do not take the weapon, I shall brand you as a coward as well as a murderer."

The little admiral, though at first startled by his visitor's strange manner, soon comprehended the cause of his visit, and, with an angry oath escaping from his pale lips, he sprang to his feet, and snatched one of the pistols from his challenger's hands.

" But one of us," he said, savagely, " shall leave this place alive. Stand where you are, sir—the length of this table is quite sufficient for our purpose."

" Quite !" said Captain Clark. " We have but to settle the signal for firing."

" That is soon done. Hark !"

The ship's bell began to strike slowly.

" That is seven bells," said the admiral ; " at the last stroke we will fire."

Captain Clark bowed assent, and raising his murderous weapon in a line with the admiral's heart, he mentally repeated the stroke of 1 mellow-toned bell.

Admiral Ellis followed his example, and brought the muzzle of his piece to bear upon his challenger's head.

Thus, in grim, breathless silence, the duellists stood foot to foot, within six paces of each other.

Their weapons raised—both silently waiting the chimes of the ship's bell, each knowing that the last stroke would be the signal of death to one, perhaps both.

Standing thus upon the brink of eternity, what thoughts must have hurried through their minds !

Perhaps they both thought of that noble form, but with different feelings—that gallant fellow who had fallen from the " Lapwing's " bulwarks into the restless waters.

It was a strange and awful moment of suspense, one that the survivor would never forget, no matter ... time and change should alter his life.

... ment in which the dark hours of a life floated ... before the man who had taken the ... whose only crime was to love one ... at with a responsive passion.

Un... the volley of musketry from the baffled pira... ain Tom and Iron Arm soon rose to the surfa... oth, with one accord, struck out towards the a... g boats.

" We were onl... n time," resumed the strange being who swam by Captain Tom's side. " Another moment, and our bodies would have been riddled like an old sieve."

"An undeniable fact," said the gallant leader, "which we live to recount; and, unless a shark favours us with his presence, we shall soon, I hope, come up with that vessel."

"Your lady-love will be safe for a time," said Iron Arm. "My goodly weapon will stop that scoundrel's villany until he renews our acquaintance."

With calm and unruffled demeanour, although they both knew that at any moment their limbs might be seized by a triple row of shark's teeth, the brave-hearted pair swam swiftly onwards.

The leading boat from Captain Tom's vessel was within half a mile of the young leader and his mystic guide.

Harry Vere, when in the act of levelling the howitzer, caught sight of the two dark objects that floated upon the ocean's surface.

Pausing in the act of discharging the piece, he called out—

"Safe—safe! Give way, my lads! Our chief is swimming towards us."

A loud hurrah followed this announcement, and the rowers exerted every muscle to urge the boats forward.

Ben Barnacle, when he heard the welcome news, rose from his seat, and looked vaguely about.

A lowly-uttered prayer came from his lips, and a gladsome sparkle shone in his dark eyes.

"The time has not yet come!" he muttered, as he reseated himself. "It would be a strange fatality that could save him, had the blood of Tom Nelson been spilt to-day."

Soon the kingly head drooped on the massive chest, as Ben Barnacle became absorbed in a strange reverie.

The man of mystery seemed for a moment to forget the peril of his gallant leader.

When Captain Tom Drake and Iron Arm heard the shout which came from the buccaneers' lips, they knew, unless the pirate vessel put about, their danger would soon be over.

With scarcely any perceptible motion of the arms, they supported their bodies upon the bosom of the deep.

Iron Arm, conversing with his companion in a careless, happy strain, and as easy as though they had been seated in the state-room of a stout ship, rather than immersed up to their neck in water, and liable at any moment to have their lower limbs gnawed off by the teeth of the hungry monsters who infest the deep.

"So you think my sudden aid a strange proceeding," said Iron Arm, replying to a question from Captain Tom. "You would think it stranger did you know me."

Captain Tom gazed earnestly at the handsome face before him.

"It seems," he said, "when you speak, as though your voice recalled some forgotten event in my life. Tell me, have we met before?"

Iron Arm smiled.

"We have," he said; "but it was when you were a curly-haired, ruddy-cheeked child."

"I thought so."

"Why?"

"The sound of your voice is familiar, and strikes upon my ears like the half-forgotten tones of one I knew in childhood."

"You were too young at the time to know me, therefore do not seek to penetrate the mystery that caused my action of to-day."

"But," said the young captain, "your conduct is so inexplicable—one hour defending the very men that you struck down to save me, the next coming to my side when I —"

Iron Arm interrupted the speaker.

"There you are wrong," he said. "When your crew boarded the 'San Josef' I was a passive spectator of the fight."

Tom looked the astonishment he felt.

"You are a strange being," he said; "and to you I owe my life, and I would give much to know the cause of your sudden friendship."

"Not sudden, Captain Tom. From the first hour you have become famous I have been your friend. Your daring encounter with the pirates caused me to come many, many miles of sea and land to behold you. I came. I saw one that had more than a common interest to me."

"More than a common interest?"

"Yes. I departed as I came—unseen; and chance brought me in contact with that scoundrel who hides his face beneath that hideous mask."

"The Death Pirate?"

"Yes, and from him I heard of his vengeful desire to slay you. It was enough. I agreed to serve under his banner, and waited for the time when I should be wanted."

"To save me?"

"Yes."

"May I ask why you took this step?"

"My destiny bade me."

"Your destiny? I do not understand."

"When the time comes you will know all. But of this much I may tell you, that our lives are strangely interwoven, and there are many yet to thwart who seek your life."

Captain Tom, surprised at what he heard, remained for some time silent, during which time his mystic companion recapitulated many of the past events of our young hero's life.

He spoke of poor old Gregory, and his lips quivered.

He spoke of Tom's mother, and a vengeful gleam shone in his eyes.

"There is one," he said, in conclusion, "who will yet work you evil, unless a watchful eye and sure hand thwarts his purpose."

"That one?"

"Reuben Harpy."

"Reuben Harpy, my cowardly, treacherous cousin, whose accursed villany first drove me from the service?"

"Yes, Reuben Harpy. Disgraced for cowardice, and dismissed with ignominy from the navy, now, under another name, and claiming the protection of a foreign Government, commands a vessel carrying the Brazilian flag."

"In their service?"

"No. A letter of marque from that Government to enable him to attack defenceless merchantmen, and act the pirate, without incurring a pirate's risk of the law," Iron Arm added. "I would prefer yonder miscreant, from whose clutches we have just escaped, than the slimy, subtle, cowardly Reuben."

This unexpected intelligence somewhat astonished our hero.

"Well," he said, after a pause, "about the best thing among the many discoveries I make, is this. How, in the name of all that's wonderful, did he obtain a letter of marque?"

"Not by his bravery, you may be sure. His good friend, Sanderson, I believe, gave Reuben a false set of papers; thus he has been enabled to pass himself as an English officer of tried courage."

"But will they not discover the cheat?"

"Not yet; the base Reuben takes especial care to keep clear of the Chilian men-of-war; the capture of a rich trader now and then quite satisfies his Brazilian Majesty."

"I cannot see what I have to fear from him."

"Nothing by open hostility. Remember, the assassin's knife is a sure weapon."

Tom's eyes flashed.

"Would the cowardly dog dare ?"

"He will, when the opportunity offers; brave as you are, and surrounded by those who would gladly die in your defence, I would not give an old copper coin for your life were any of his cut-throats put upon your trail."

Tom's lips curled with a smile of disdain.

"I would," he said, "crush the viper under my heel."

"Had you the viper there to crush. No, he will take care to keep out of your reach."

"I have faced the grim tyrant too often," said Tom, "to fear harm from the puny efforts of Reuben Harpy."

"Raise your feet," said Iron Arm. "Let us float on our backs until the boats arrive. We are not making much head against the wind."

The young chief acted upon the suggestion.

"You underrate your enemy," said Iron Arm, as they floated side by side. "I knew one," a dark shadow come over the speaker's face as he spoke, "who, like yourself, laughed at the cowardly poltroon, whose hate he had incurred."

"How ?"

"Much the same cause as produces this feeling all over the world."

"A woman, I expect, by your cynical smile ?"

"You are right—a woman." Iron Arm raised his head for a moment. "We have a few minutes yet to spare. Shall I tell you the story ?"

"Do."

"I will be as brief as possible. When Reuben first went to the Brazils he became enamoured of a dark-eyed beauty, the daughter of an old officer. She was affianced to a young naval lieutenant at the time, and gave Reuben but scant encouragement to his passion. Her betrothed not being near, your gallant cousin—pardon for naming the relationship—insulted the young girl, and soon after her lover returned. What think you he did ?"

"Challenged the scoundrel, perhaps ?"

"No; his hot Southern blood could not wait for the preliminaries of a duel. He lashed the precious Reuben in the public square, spat in his face, then sent him a challenge."

"Which was not taken up ?"

"No; the perfidious villain crept on board his ship, and, by the aid of his ruffianly lieutenant, concocted such a fiendish plan of revenge that, even cold as I am now, my blood is on fire at the recollection."

"What was it ?"

"There is not time to tell you the details; sufficient only to bring you to the climax. The pair were united, and they started upon a cruise in a small yacht belonging to the young husband. Scarcely had the land faded from sight, when Reuben, who had been like a tiger waiting for his prey, bore down upon them. The fond young wife clung to her husband when she saw into whose hands she was likely to fall. 'Be brave,' he said, folding her to his heart; 'we cannot die but once—God help us!' Gold had bought Reuben's ruffianly crew to commit the atrocious deed, and, like a swarm of devils, they boarded the hapless yacht. Her scanty crew were cut down in a few moments, and the bridal pair were tied back to back to the mast. I—I—can scarcely tell you. The vessel was fired by the cold-blooded miscreants."

"Surely they did not die ?"

Captain Tom's frame trembled with excitement as he asked this question.

"They did," was the answer. "The cowardly villain stood by the blazing vessel until nothing remained but a blackened smouldering line upon the waters."

The brave youth's voice quivered as he asked—

"Has the deed not been avenged ?"

His companion raised his powerful muscular arm from the water, and said, fiercely—

"Not yet! Unless this hand loses its power, I will crush the life out of that craven carcase ere many suns have set."

"I will aid you," said the buccaneer. "My life, my ship, are at your service, to avenge the death of that hapless pair."

Before Iron Arm could reply, the boats shot alongside, and they were taken on board.

A few words from the young leader explained the presence of the coloured stranger, and he received a warm greeting from the crew.

There was but one who held aloof from him, and that one was Ben Barnacle.

He started when the huge form entered the boat, and his face became the hue of death.

"Can the grave," he muttered, "have given up its dead ?"

The sight of Ben Barnacle sitting in the stern-sheets of the cutter had a strange effect upon the mystic being who had that day saved Captain Tom's life.

He was in the act of speaking to our hero, when he beheld the dark eyes of the pale and wounded man fixed upon him.

The words were checked upon his lips, and his hand went mechanically to his side.

Luckily it was without a weapon.

A visible tremor passed over his powerful frame, and as his eyes kindled with sudden passion, he crouched as though about to spring.

Ben Barnacle half rose from his seat, and clutched the hilt of his cutlass.

Then, as though yielding to better feelings, Iron Arm stepped across the thwarts, the evil light fading from his eyes, and his lips relaxed from their stern compression to a half smile.

Ben reseated himself, and gazed strangely at the muscular form of the man whose sudden presence had so powerfully excited him.

Iron Arm stooped over Ben's form, and, in a voice so low that it reached only the ears of him whose strange, wondering look showed the fearful conflict within, said, as he extended his hand—

"For his sake, let the past remain in oblivion."

"Be it so," was the reply, spoken in the same low tone. "Let us meet as strangers—the bitter memories of the past for a time forgotten."

A grave inclination of the head gave token of acquiescence, and Iron Arm went back to the bow of the boat.

Here Captain Tom, Harry Vere, and others of the band, were grouped, watching with deep interest the movements of the "San Josef."

Until the moment when the young leader and his companions were picked up by the boats, the pirate vessel had been rapidly sailing before the wind.

While the boats were lying to, the "San Josef's" courses were hauled up, and, to the surprise of all, the huge vessel was seen describing a circle.

"They have found out," he said, "how their bullets failed to stop us."

"Curse him, yes!" said Iron Arm. "He will be down upon us in less than an hour."

"Let him come," said the young leader. "With true, gallant fellows at my back, I will rescue Minnie, or die in the attempt."

"We have no chance," said Iron Arm. "Once on the deck we could hold our ground; but we shall never be able, I am afraid, to board the 'San Josef.'"

"I will make the attempt."

" We shall not get near enough."

"That scoundrel's heavy guns will smash these light boats before we can get within two fathoms of his vessel."

Captain Tom knew the terrible disadvantage under which he stood, and, looking around at his followers, said—

"My lads, in that ship is all I hold dear. I know it is almost asking you to walk into the cold embrace of death. I want but one boat; who will volunteer?"

With one voice the reply came—

" I will—I will!"

"Think again," said the young leader. "We shall soon be at the mercy of his guns. There is time to get back to the 'Will-o'-the-Wisp' for those who value their lives."

How proudly the gallant leader's heart beat beneath the golden coat of mail as his followers repeated their cry.

"You will all come with me?"

"We will. Lead us on! We will rescue the lady or die."

"Thanks, my brave fellows. There is but one chance for us—a bold dash, when we are near enough. Now, spread yourselves out, and keep as clear of the shot as possible."

"Aye, aye, sir!"

Captain Tom Drake's dispositions for the fight were soon made.

Harry Vere, with the barge, was to operate on the starboard bow, Ben and the pinnace on the larboard bow, while the young leader, in the cutter, would make for the "San Josef's" stern.

There was no dissenting voice to this arrangement, and, as a white puff of smoke came from the ship's bows, the boats dispersed.

The shot fell short of its mark, and Ben Barnacle, who had watched the iron messenger of destruction bound from wave to wave, muttered, angrily—

"They will get the range directly. Would to Heaven the 'Will-o'-the-Wisp' were here."

There was a long interval before another gun was fired.

The pirates were for a moment baffled by the sudden dispersion of the boats.

Each of the light craft pulled in a zig-zag direction, thus rendering the aim of the pirate's gunners more difficult.

Three white jets proceeded simultaneously from the vessel. This time one of the balls came so near their boat that the oar was taken from the cutter's bow-oarsman, and riven into splinters.

"Are you hurt, Maxwell?" asked Tom, as the man fell back over the thwart.

"No, sir."

"That is fortunate. Starboard your helm, there."

"Starboard it is, sir."

" Keep it so, and the nose of the boat in a line with that fellow's bowsprit."

"Aye, aye, sir!"

There was another long interval, then the pirate ship swung round, and, as though determined to crush their audacious pursuers, a lurid sheet of flame ran along the vessel's side.

"Here comes his larboard battery. Down, every man, for his life!"

The crew threw themselves forward, and the iron storm came hurling over their heads.

"I thought so," was Tom's cool comment. "They fired when we were in the trough of the sea. What did you say, Mr. Vere?"

"The barge is struck, sir."

"Serious?"

"I fear so. There is a hole just between wind and water."

"Stuff a jacket in. Now, my lads, a good pull before he can reload. Down with the helm!"

"Aye, aye, sir."

The dark hull of the "San Josef" rose above the water like a huge beast of prey, and her forecastle could be seen crowded with turbaned heads.

"She can sail well," was Captain Tom's remark, as his fearless eyes were fixed upon the coming vessel. "Mr. Vere."

"Aye, aye, sir."

"Use that howitzer of yours; cram it with musket-balls for the benefit of that mob on the bows."

The tiny gun was loaded nearly to the muzzle with the deadly ammunition, and Harry Vere, waiting until the boat rose to the top of a wave, fired.

The work of the closely-packed charge was plainly audible as it rattled upon the huge ship, and closely following the sound of splintering wood, a confused yell of pain was borne upon the breeze.

"That has cleared the forecastle," said Captain Tom. "Try again, Mr. Vere."

The barge had fallen far behind the other boats, and, as the cutter dashed onward, Harry Vere called out—

"We are done for, sir. A plank has started."

Captain Tom uttered a cry of anger.

"Are you filling?"

"We are."

"Back water, my lads. We must take them on board."

"No, sir, go on; we shall be safe until the—"

Harry Vere's last words were drowned by a deafening report in the rear.

That report was the roar of the "Will-o'-the-Wisp's" guns.

The smart crew had rigged jury-masts, and, under the mystic cloud of smoke, had glided within gun-shot of the pirate vessel.

A shout from the boats greeted the arrival of the gallant ship, and many who had felt death so near, now breathed freely.

Even the steel-nerved young leader gave a cry of joy as the ship dashed on to grapple with the huge vessel, which, reeling under the unexpected broadside, was endeavouring to go about and escape.

"Grapple with them," shouted Captain Tom; "we shall soon join you."

"Hurrah!" came from the middies, as they sent another close shower of shot into the Death Pirate's timbers. "Hurrah for Captain Tom!"

Under the excitement of the moment, the young leader took off his cap, and cheered in return.

"We have them now," said Iron Arm, as he quickly broke the blade off a long oar; "there will be a short reckoning this time."

He balanced the heavy weapon in his hand, and the gleam in his dark eyes boded ill for the pirate horde.

The cutter and pinnace followed closely in the wake of the "Will-o'-the-Wisp," and the barge, not to be left behind in the coming fight, had an extra jacket in her shot hole, and made every effort to keep up.

"Pull!" cried Captain Tom, waving his light sword. "Let the ship attack them on the larboard; we will pay our respects on the other side."

As he spoke, the "Will-o'-the-Wisp" ranged up alongside the "San Josef," and cast the grappling-irons on board.

The pirates fought with that desperation which despair alone can give.

Too well they knew the fate that would befall them should the Boy Buccaneers once gain a footing upon the deck.

Maimed and bleeding by the terrible blow he had received from Iron Arm's mace, the pirate leader lay upon a pile of cushions, giving directions to his crew.

By his orders the grappling-irons were cast overboard before they could get entangled, and the sides of the "San Josef" were thronged with her fierce dark crew.

"Keep them off! keep them off!" shouted the Death Pirate, in a voice in which rage and pain were strangely mingled; "beat them back, tars! Sheathe your blades in their bodies!"

The pirates answered with a fierce yell, and pressed to the side in dark swarms.

From every part of the "San Josef" that offered a chance of reaching the "Will-o'-the-Wisp" they sprang, and, cutlass in hand, leaped on board.

Many fell into the sea, others catching desperately at the shrouds, or whatever offered, sought to board the buccaneers.

Those who clung to the rigging had their hands severed from the wrist, and, uttering the most diabolical cries, fell into the ocean, or were jammed between the hulls of the vessels as they grated together.

Some of the Moorish horde reached the deck of the "Will-o'-the-Wisp" only to be hurled back by her gallant defenders.

Everywhere in this first daring attempt to board, the hated Moslems were met with equal determination; and of the number of those who gained the forecastle, not one escaped the shot or steel of the young buccaneers.

Vainly did the Death Pirate yell to his crew to cut down the small band that defended their ship, and the crowds of yelling demons were met at every point.

Again a dark mass of bearded Moors made a rush to board the buccaneers. This time such a hurricane of slaughter swept amongst them that they recoiled, with the most horrible curses and imprecations upon their lips.

Well for Harry Martin, who was in charge of the "Will-o'-the-Wisp," that he had made this last attempt, or his small band of middies would have been swept from the deck by the mere force of numbers.

The boy, with a skill that would have done credit to many an older hand, prepared for the onslaught.

He saw the boats were yet too far to give him any potent aid, and knew that his attempt to board the pirate would be but a waste of life against such fearful odds.

While the greater portion of his followers defended the bulwarks with such firm resolution, he took three men and loaded one of the larboard guns to the muzzle with grape.

He waited until the dense mass rallied, and prepared to rush over the side; then his voice, loud and clear, rang out above the yell of the pirates.

"Now—now! pour in your fire!"

The gun belched forth its flight of destruction, and the howling demons were driven back with terrific slaughter.

Mingled with the oaths of the buccaneers and the screams of the dying, came the hearty hurrahs of Captain Tom's comrades, as they followed their young leader up the side of the huge ship.

Like devils incarnate the Moorish horde fought against the sudden attack.

But vainly.

The irresistible torrent was not to be stopped or turned aside.

Iron Arm fought like a lion beside his new leader.

Wielding the novel weapon he had prepared in the boat, he swept down all who came within reach of his arm.

Maddened by the sight, the Death Pirate yelled out—

"Receive them on your pikes! A thousand dollars for the man who slays that renegade, Iron Arm!"

A scornful laugh came from the giant's lips, and scattering his foes right and left, he hewed a passage for those in his rear.

Captain Tom, Ben Barnacle, Harry Vere, and others of the "Will-o'-the-Wisp," seconded the efforts of the terrible being who had placed himsel in the van of the fight.

Their sharp blades struck the stout spikes straight in twain, for the Moors, packed in a dense mass, levelled the bristling points of their dangerous weapons to stay the advance of the leaders.

The fight was now close and deadly, and at times doubtful of success.

In spite of the recent carnage among the pirates, they still outnumbered by far Captain Tom's crew.

Yet numbers were of but little avail against the determined phalanx who fought so stubbornly for the foothold they had gained.

Every sweep of Tom's sword was fatal; every circle of his bright blade left a gashed face or headless trunk. He fought to rescue one who was dear to him, and whose honour was at stake.

So back, step by step, the pirate horde were forced, until the living mass were grouped across the hatchway.

Through this crowd Captain Tom, Iron Arm, and Ben tried to cleave a passage.

For the living wall stood between them and Minnie Atherton.

The Death Pirate saw their motive, and gnashing his teeth with impotent rage, called out—

"Below there, one of you, and cut that girl's throat!"

The order was heard and understood by Iron Arm, as he stooped to pick up his terrible steel mace, which lay where he had hurled it at the Death Pirate.

The massive weapon once more in his grasp, he felt able to contend with a host, and, as he dashed like a thunderbolt among the Moslems, he sang out to Captain Tom—

"Quick! as you value your lady's life!"

Right and left, like ninepins, the pirates fell before the sweep of his terrible weapon; and, as he reached the top of the hatch, his mace fell upon the skull of the miscreant who had begun to descend to slay the beauteous Minnie.

As the man fell, prone and lifeless, his skull crushed and undistinguishable, the light form of the young buccaneer sprang down the steps.

He had comprehended Iron Arm's meaning, and, fearful that another might creep down by the forehatch and slay his love, he slew all who came before him, and flew past Iron Arm, his blade raised on high.

The Death Pirate saw himself baffled, and the white foam gathered thickly on his lips as the buccaneer cut down his crew.

"Both friend and foe," he howled, "shall die."

Amidships stood a mortar, crammed to the muzzle with shells, and from this fearful engine of slaughter the merciless wretch fired terrible missiles among the combatants.

The sparks flying from the blazing fuse, the shells soared upward, then fell to the deck, rebounded, then broke into fragments, and slew both Moors and Christians.

Where the storm of iron fragments and blazing shells fell thickest, Captain Tom dashed through, the senseless form of Minnie upon his arm.

CHAPTER XLV.

THE HONOURABLE ARCHIBALD GASTON AND LORD KILCREW PLAN ADMIRAL TOM'S CAPTURE—THE STRANGER WHO WORE A CLOAK OF RUBY-COLOURED VELVET.

BENEATH the quiet starlight, a thousand gay-coloured lamps swung pendulous to the gentle breeze; sweet strains of music filled the air with melody; and from fragrant arbours where the jasmine and rose grew in rich luxuriance, came peals of joyous laughter.

Broad walks, whose mazy windings led to glistening fountains and sparkling grottoes; smooth grassy lawns, looking like velvet beneath the soft light; parterres of choice flowers, whose perfume filled the air with sweetness.

It was Vauxhall. The grand old gardens were in their zenith. Vauxhall, where the courtly dames and richly-dressed cavaliers were wont to gather, and pass their evenings in revelry.

Within hearing of a murmuring cascade, and partly hidden from the gay throng by the flower-covered trellis-work of the arbour, six gaily-attired cavaliers were leisurely sipping the generous juice of the grape.

To judge from the noisy peals of laughter that came from the sequestered corner, the young nobles were in high spirits.

The noisy revellers were Lords Walpole, Vane, Kilcrew, Moreton, and Claremont, and, sitting a little apart, in sullen silence, was the Honourable Archibald Gaston.

The butt of the party was, as usual, little Lord Augustus Vane.

For, to be more at their ease, the noble party had taken their sheathed swords from the richly-embroidered belts, and laid them upon the table.

"Look here, Vane!" cried Lord Walpole, suddenly; "I shall wager my black Arab against your grey, that I find out that dark-eyed damsel you were dancing with this evening."

"Take him, Vane," roared the remainder of the party, except the moody Gaston: "you are sure to win."

The little lordling bit his lips angrily. Of all men, he wished to know the damsel in question; Walpole was the last.

"I won't take his wager," Vane said. "I don't want his beastly, kicking black : and I wouldn't like to lose my grey."

"Bravo, Vane!" said Lord Moreton, "bravo!"

"By St. Patrick!" said Kilcrew, "it's my belafe ye are afraid of losing the lady, Vane."

Lord Augustus looked mischievously in the Irish nobleman's face, and retorted—

"Lord Kilcrew speaks feelingly. He knows by experience how—aw—unpleasant—aw—it is to lose a lady; although," added Vane, "I am not upon the point of marrying the dark-eyed beauty that my Lord Walpole is so anxious about."

This allusion to Captain Tom's daring abduction of Minnie, when she was about to be wedded to Lord Kilcrew, drew a burst of merriment from the thoughtless gallants.

'Well done, Gus," said Claremont, slapping the little lord on the back; "you gave him a Roland for his Oliver."

"Well aimed, Vane, that thrust," said Moreton. "Gentlemen, Gus is getting sarcastic."

Lord Kilcrew's brow became as black as night, and turning fiercely upon Vane, he said—

"By St. Patrick, my lord, were you a little more of a man, and less of a fool, I should make you answer for that!"

Lord Augustus jumped from his seat, and making a clutch at his sword, said angrily—

"Fool! aw, demme! He shall see! I—aw—d——d Irishman! Pick up your sword! He shall see! Fool—aw—get up!"

"Sit down, Vane—sit down," said Moreton, pulling the little fellow back into his seat, and holding him there. "He'll spit you like a lark is spitted for roasting."

Lord Vane kicked and plunged to release himself from his friend's strong grasp—much to the detriment of his silken doublet.

"Let me go, Moreton," he spluttered. "I—aw—demme—won't be called a fool. Let me go!"

Thanks to the delicate material which composed the lordling's outer garment, he broke away from Moreton, minus his collar.

Before his hand could grasp one of the weapons that lay on the table, he was seized by Lord Claremont and jerked back to his seat.

"Be quiet, you little ass!" said the young noble. "Kilcrew meant no insult!"

"He did—demme! I'll have satisfaction! You, too, called me an ass! I won't stand it! If I do—I—I challenge the whole lot! Yes—aw—demme every one! I'll fight you all!"

This wholesale challenge produced such a roar of laughter from all, save Kilcrew and Gaston, that the whole place rang with the sound of their voices.

Lord Augustus looked around with silent rage. That was too much, thus to be made an object of ridicule after the insults he had received.

"You—you grinning monkey-faced—demme—set of—hounds—I tell you, I'll fight the lot! I—I—"

Walpole dexterously stopped the little fellow's mouth by inserting a champagne cork between his teeth.

During this scene, Admiral Lord Kilcrew had sat with folded arms and downcast eyes, his usual frank open brow contracted, and his fingers working convulsively.

It was not the little nobleman's hectoring that affected his lordship.

His thoughts were away from the gay scene around.

He had been recalled, by Lord Vane's taunt, to the loss of his bride, the gentle Minnie.

Bitter were the reflections that passed through the fiery noble's mind, and his heart filled with pitiless, remorseless, undying hate against the gallant boy who, at the sword's point, had borne Minnie away at the very moment of his fancied triumph.

A deeper intensity was given to the fierce hate that raged in his heart, when his mind reverted to signal defeat he had sustained when crossing blades with Admiral Tom.

Raising his eyes, as the fight between the "Will-o'-the-Wisp" and Don Pardo's vessel floated by his vision, his gaze met Gaston's.

Their eyes were fixed upon each other for a few seconds, then the Honourable Archibald said, just loud enough for Kilcrew to hear—

"Leave that shallow-brained fool! I have something to impart to your lordship!"

Kilcrew arose to comply, the more readily, perhaps, as he remembered that Gaston was Captain Tom's implacable foe.

Before he could leave the group who were trying to pacify young Vane, Claremont placed his hand upon Kilcrew's shoulder, saying—

"Come, Kilcrew, pacify this poor little devil. You should be more careful—curse it—all the fun is gone when Vane will not sit quiet and be bad-gered by us."

A fierce answer rose to Kilcrew's lips; but, at the sight of the angry little lord, who was struggling in Moreton's arm, a smile flitted over his manly countenance, and he replied—

"With pleasure, my friend; by St. Patrick, I had almost forgotten the little privateer."

"Give it him strong," suggested Claremont, "or we shall never get him in good humour again to-night."

Kilcrew walked within a pace of Lord Vane, and, doffing his plumed hat, he said, with mock gravity—

"Lord Augustus Vane, by St. Patrick, I would not wish to quarrel with a gentleman like yourself; and if an apology will make us friends again, Admiral Kilcrew is ready to give it."

Little Vane ceased kicking, and somewhat of his warlike look passed away.

"I should be sorry," he said, drawing his little figure up, "to kill you, my lord, but I call these gentlemen to witness how great has been the pro-vocation I have received."

"You hear Vane, don't accept it," chorused the noblemen, their fun reviving at the joke. "Fight, Lord Augustus! Fight! remember the honour of your family is at stake."

"I will be generous," said the little lord, extend-ing his hand to Kilcrew. "My Lord Kilcrew, your apology will be ample satisfaction."

Much as the Irish nobleman's mind was troubled, he could scarcely forbear laughing outright as he tendered the necessary apology.

That concluded, he turned upon his heel, and went to Gaston's side.

"You wish to speak to me," said Kilcrew; "I am at your service."

"I do; the words that empty-headed fool has spoken has recalled a circumstance far from pleasant to your mind.

"By St. Patrick, it has!"

"We have both," Gaston continued, "cause to hate the very name of that fellow, Captain Tom, as he styles himself."

Kilcrew's eyes flashed angrily.

"We have," he said, "and destruction is the only boon I would ask Fortune to bestow upon me."

"Think you," said Gaston, "the attainment of that wish is impossible?"

The Honourable Archibald Gaston's eyes glim-mered like a snake's as he put this question to his companion.

"I do," Kilcrew said, savagely. "If mortal hands could destroy him, I should have done so when my good sword was opposed to his. Curse him! I was but as a child when foot to foot we stood upon the enemy's deck."

"A mere trick of fence," said Gaston. "The most skilful, my lord, are often deceived by a lout whose hand has never before gripped a blade."

"Have you," Kilcrew asked, "crossed swords with that devils's-limb?"

"Once; but this is irrelevant. Will you aid me in my plan to capture that fellow?"

"By my soul, I will. To the last drop of my blood—to the last penny in my purse."

"Enough! Move farther this way, and I will unfold a plan. Open warfare seems to fail: per-haps stratagem may be more successful."

They moved farther from the noisy group, and Gaston was about to speak, when a rustling among the leafy screen behind them caused him to pause.

"What was that?" he asked.

"Some lady's dress," said Kilcrew. "Never

mind. Now for the plan; I'm all expectation; re-have it."

In a low, subdued voice, Gaston began to unfold his plan for capturing Captain Tom, the noise and laughter from the group close by drowning his voice.

When Kilcrew left Lord Vane, the little noble mollified, and, swelling with pride at this public apology from the renowned swordsman, turned fiercely to his companions, and said—

"Lord Kilcrew has escaped my sword; but re-member, Moreton, Claremont, and the rest, I expect instant satisfaction, or I shall brand you all as cowards."

The young nobles, with serious faces, came in a body to the little lord, and one by one tendered a most abject apology for their past conduct.

The vain little fellow was equally pleased to tender his hand as a token of amity, and the for-givers began afresh to torment him.

"Pass the bottle round," said Walpole, giving his companions a significant look. "Here's your health, Vane, and may your courage never grow less."

"It never will," was the answer, "while this heart beats beneath this breast."

"Bravo!" said Claremont, roaring with laughter; "hear, and tremble."

The gay young lords, not deigning to notice the plotting twain, re-seated themselves, and again the mirth became general.

"By the way, Vane," said Lord Moreton, "you hit Kilcrew too hard about that pirate fellow carrying off his bride."

Lord Augustus Vane twisted his straw-coloured moustache.

"Did I?" he asked. "Well, you see, Moreton, he called me a—— I will not repeat the word for fear my hot blood will again rise."

"Don't," said Moreton, "we can't afford to lose Kilcrew, and you are such a fire-eater that he would stand but a poor chance."

"A very poor one, indeed," said Vane, signifi-cantly tapping the hilt of his sword; "still, I only told the truth."

"Respecting Kilcrew?"

"Yes; he had the lady on the way to the a— when this smug—no, pir—no, free—demme— mean buccaneer, took her away," continued Lord Vane.

"I'll wager a dozen of the sparkling," said Wal-pole to Lord Claremont, "at this moment, that Vane cannot tell us the difference between a smuggler, a pirate, and a buccaneer."

"You hear that, Vane?" said Claremont.

"Yes—aw, demme—of course I do."

"Shall I take his wager?"

"That I don't know the difference between a pirate, a smuggler, a free-booter, and a buccaneer?"

"That's the wager, Gus; do you?"

"Of course, any fool knows that."

"Then," whispered Walpole, "you should know, for you are the king of fools."

Luckily Lord Vane did not overhear this, or his valour would, after the recent scene, have risen and boiled over.

"Very well," said Claremont, with a smile; "I shall accept Lord Walpole's wager."

"Done," said Walpole, "I shall win."

"Not so fast," Claremont said. "Before we pro-ceed any further, who is to be umpire? I do not know the difference between these fellows; the question is, who can decide the wager?"

"As I am the only disinterested party in this affair," said Lord Moreton, "I should act as umpire."

"Do," Claremont said; "the very man."

"I am content," said Walpole.

"Stay," Moreton said; "I cannot give an impartial opinion."

"Why?" Claremont jerked out.

"Why?" Walpole asked.

"Simply this: I do not understand the difference between the estimable gentlemen who follow their avocations under the names before mentioned."

"If you will allow me, gentlemen——"

The young nobles turned their heads suddenly towards the entrance of the arbour, and observed an elegantly attired gentleman advancing towards them.

When he raised his plumed hat, a shower of dark luxuriant curls fell around his well-set neck; a pale classical, but somewhat feminine face, destitute of hair, save on the upper lip, which was shaded by a long silky moustache.

From the long riding boots and the heavy jingling spurs which graced his heels, the princely-looking stranger had evidently ridden to the old gardens.

The young nobles had no opportunity of judging much of the handsome horseman's figure, as a long cloak hung in graceful folds from his shoulders.

Such a cloak!—it made Lord Augustus Vane's heart beat, and he determined to make friends with the intruder to more closely examine the garment.

It was fit for a king to wear; and little Vane, whose whole thought was centered in the adornment of his person, felt convinced that none but a prince could wear so rich a garment.

Made from the richest velvet, ruby coloured, and trimmed with heavy gold embroidery, the materials alone were worth a sum of money that proclaimed the riches of its owner.

As though velvet and gold were but a secondary consideration, the splendid garment was clasped at the neck by a golden ornament, profusely studded with small brilliants.

The soft light falling upon the precious stones caused them to sparkle, and emit a thousand flashes, as the stranger gracefully inclined his handsome head to the admiring party.

"To decide this wager," the stranger continued, "I can only say my judgment shall be impartial."

Claremont threw out a hint respecting the knowledge the well-learned gentleman knew of the matter.

"That," said the stranger, "I am qualified to answer, by telling you that few men are better able than myself to explain the difference between the names and avocations of these outlaws," he added, with a smile that disclosed his white, faultless teeth, "for I am thoroughly conversant with the subject."

Though apparently occupied by his conversation with the young noblemen, he darted from time to time a keen, searching glance at the lowered brows of Archibald Gaston and Lord Kilcrew, who were so absorbed in their revengeful plans that they had not noticed the new arrival.

There was a savage expression in his dark eyes as they rested upon the pair, and a smile of deep meaning passed over his pale, handsome face when Gaston, carried away by excitement, said to Vane—

"With such aid, my lord, the plan must succeed; failure is utterly impossible."

Lord Claremont turned to Vane, and said—

"Well, what do you say to this offer? Will you accept this gentleman as umpire?"

Lord Augustus was devouring the handsome cloak with his eyes, and, longing to touch the rich gems, he quickly replied—

"Accept?—demme—yes. Very kind of our new friend—aw, demme—wonder how he knew we wanted some one to decide the wager."

The stranger smiled placidly, and answered—.

"Tired of the noise and excitement of dancing, I wandered past this secluded arbour, and overheard the wager and the various comments respecting the difficulty of coming to a decision. If I have intruded, I will retire."

"No—aw—demme!" said Lord Augustus Vane; "it's very kind of you. Aw—shall be glad to make your acquaintance. Aw—come and take wine with us."

"I feel honoured by your kind invitation, and if agreeable to your friends I will make one of the party."

Walpole, Claremont, and Moreton joined in the invitation; his courtly grace and handsome form had already won their goodwill.

The stranger seated himself as near the plotting pair as possible, without exciting suspicion.

Lord Augustus did the honours of the table, and, filling the stranger's glass from a long-necked bottle, said—

"Aw—demme—very kind—aw—of you, but—aw—I am Lord Vane—Augustus Vane. Aw—what shall I call you—aw?"

"My name?" the stranger said; "by all means. We will introduce ourselves to each other."

"Yes—demme—that's it. I am Lord Vane."

"And I," said the stranger, "am called Sir Baldwin of Baldwin."

The name, like the person of Sir Baldwin, was unknown to the young nobles until the present moment.

Now the lost time was made up, and Sir Baldwin's gay companions felt as though they had known him for years.

"Now, my lords," said Walpole, "order, for Vane's explanation."

"Order!" shouted Moreton, dashing a glass down upon the table to enforce silence; "order, you noisy chatterers!"

"Now, Gus," said Claremont, "stagger them with your knowledge, as," he added, mentally, "you staggered me with your courage."

The little lordling smiled confidently, and whispered to Moreton, who sat next to him—

"Aw—demme—you will observe how my—aw—knowledge will win Claremont the wine."

"Come, Vane," said Walpole, "the bottles are empty. Decide this wager, there's a good fellow."

"Yes—aw—demme—I will. Now, Sir Baldwin of Baldwin, can you give ear to this? My friend Walpole has wagered a dozen of the sparkling Moselle with Claremont that I—aw—could not tell the difference between a smuggler, a pirate, and a buccaneer. If I do, Walpole loses—demme, I hope he will."

"I quite understand," said Sir Baldwin. "I intend to let the wager be left to your explanation. But understand, one mistake on your part will cause Lord Claremont to become a loser."

"Yes—aw—quite right—demme—I'll begin. A smuggler is a fellow — aw — that — aw —demme—gets lots of things without paying the—the—duty—duty—to the King."

This was prodigious for Vane, and the company cried—

"Bravo!"

"So far," said Sir Baldwin, "you are correct in your explanation. A smuggler is one who imports and exports goods without paying the Customs."

Lord Augustus gave Walpole a triumphant look, and resumed—

"A—pirate—is—is—demme—is a fellow—that robs—on the sea—and cuts people's throats some-

CLINGING TO THE ROCK HE SUPPORTED HER WITH HIS ARMS

times. if they—aw—won't let them have the cargo and—aw—things quietly."

Again the company rattled their glasses, and ied—

"Bravo."

Lord Augustus was making a name for valour and intellect.

"Quite right, in the second instance," said Sir Baldwin. "I'm afraid, Lord Walpole, you have but little chance of winning."

Walpole laughed.

"I care not," he said. "My only fear is that Gussy Vane will have the brain fever should he answer the third time correct."

"That's spiteful," said Moreton, mischievously.

"A fellow would think you meant an offence to Vane."

"An offence, how?" queried Walpole.

"The brain fever which you imply will be the result of this sudden emptying of Vane's head."

"Demme—aw—I," began Vane, bristling up.

"I recall my words," said Walpole. "Sit down, Gus, and finish your erudite explanation."

"Well, a—buccaneer—is—aw—demme—a—aw —buccaneer—is—aw—"

"Go on, Gus, go on."

Lord Vane began to feel confused; the buccaneer was too much for him.

Yielding to the promptings of his friends, he again stammered out—

"A buccaneer is—aw—demme—is—a—a—buc-caneer."

A roar of laughter followed this, and poor little Lord Augustus became red with shame.

Sir Baldwin came to his relief, and said—

"Though I am compelled to adjudge Lord Walpole the winner, yet Lord Vane has, in my opinion, acquitted himself very well."

"He has," shouted the noisy Moreton.

"The terms, pirate, freebooter. and buccaneer, have, since the first organisation of the buccaneers, become blended into one, and have much the same signification."

"By that," said Claremont, " Walpole is the loser, instead of the winner."

"No, my lord; your wager was made respecting the distinctive classes—pirate, freebooter, and buccaneer."

"But you say that the three terms have but one signification."

"Now they have become, by long usage, to express but one meaning; formerly the class was as distinctive as the name."

Claremont yielded to Sir Baldwin of Baldwin's knowledge of the matter; but, as though a lurking suspicion yet existed in his mind, he asked—

"Should I be deemed impertinent were I to ask you to explain the term in its original state?"

"The buccaneer or freebooter, my lord?"

"The buccaneer."

"With pleasure."

The young gallants ceased their noisy laughter for a few moments, and drew close to the ung stranger, to listen to his words.

"The buccaneer," he ——n, —— so called from the boucan places of rest, in the island of St. Domingo. When the brotherhood were first established, they consisted of adventurers from all parts of Europe."

"Bravo!" shouted Moreton. "What do you think of that, Vane?"

"Aw!—demme! be quiet: I am listening. Next time I shall know."

"So far," continued Sir Baldwin, smiling at little Lord Vane's eagerness to learn the definition of the word, "from this having anything to do with the sea, they lived exclusively on land, and subsisted by hunting wild cattle."

"Yet," Claremont began, " the bucc—"

"One moment, my lord. The Spaniards, to drive these men from the island, contrived to destroy all the cattle; consequently these men were without subsistence."

"Aw, demme—how instructing."

"Severed from their peaceful pursuits, the boucans, or buccaneers, were obliged to take to another mode of living. Being long inured to the dangers and excitement of the chase, they united themselves with the freebooters."

"These fellows, then, were the dangerous foes to the peaceful traders?" said Claremont.

"They were, my lord, a desperate band, composed of the scum of Europe. Lured by the prospect of plunder, they frequented the coasts of New Spain and Cuba, and fell upon every vessel that came from the then little-known continent of America."

"Why America?"

"Because, at the time of which I speak, gold and silver, in its pure state, were brought in large quantities from the great continent."

"I suppose," said Claremont, "that the blending of these two bands of adventurers, caused them to be designated by either name?"

"Exactly. But the word buccaneer now is usually applied to brave spirits, who too noble to descend to bloodthirsty piracy, take from the vessels of every country without using unmanly bloodshed."

"Thanks, Sir Baldwin," said Claremont, "for your courtesy. The information you have imparted has cleared a difficulty that I have been long trying to solve."

"Your informant," said Gaston, coming forth and fixing his eyes upon the stranger, "should be worthy of belief, my lord."

"Worthy of belief, Gaston?"

"Yes; his intimate connection with the outlaws of society makes him a good authority upon these matters."

The young stranger's cheek slightly flushed, and his hand went mechanically to the hilt of his sword.

"His connections?" repeated Claremont; "what mean you, Gaston?"

"This," said the naval officer, his eyes glaring snake-like with anger—"your boon companion is Hugh Baldrick, the smuggler!"

Little Augustus Vane jumped back and repeated—

"Hugh—aw, demme—smuggler—Baldrick—aw, I'll ask him to sell his cloak; he can get another."

"Yes, by St. Patrick," said Kilcrew, "it's the very man; he saved the admiral's daughter, for which you ought to be grateful, Gaston; but, by the good saint, as there is a thousand pounds reward offered for him, dead or alive, we may as well have the money.

CHAPTER XLVII.

HUGH BALDRICK, THE SMUGGLER PRINCE, ATTACKED BY THE OFFICERS.

ADMIRAL KILCREW, as he spoke, picked his weapon from the table, and advanced towards the young smuggler, saying—

"Before such good company, my fine fellow, you had better quietly surrender, before I pin you to the stump of that tree."

A scornful smile was the answer, and, without betraying the least alarm, Hugh Baldrick threw back his cloak, and drew a heavy, serviceable sabre from its sheath.

"These gentlemen," he said, "are neither spies nor informers. My quarrel is with you, Lord Kilcrew, and your worthy friend Archibald Gaston. We have met before, and I warn you, should one cry escape your lips to cause my detection, I will sheathe this blade in your body; and you, Lieutenant Gas— "

He found the Honourable Archibald Gaston had left the arbour.

The reddening cheeks and kindling eyes showed the anger within the young outlaw's breast.

"So," he said, his proud lips curling with scorn, "he has gone to set the bloodhounds upon me. I will wait his return."

The appeal the gallant smuggler had made to the chivalry of his noble entertainers was not without its effect.

Claremont, obeying the impulse of his generous nature, snatched his sheathed sword from the table, and, buckling the weapon round his waist, stood beside Hugh Baldrick, and, fixing his fiery eyes upon Admiral Lord Kilcrew, he said, sternly—

"Hearken, my Lord Admiral. It may be consistent with the position you hold to capture this gentleman."

"Gentleman!" repeated Kilcrew, sarcastically.

"Yes, gentleman—I repeat the word," said the young noble, hotly. "He is our guest, and by Heaven! I will stand by him were a hundred of the law's myrmidons to bar my passage."

He drew his sword as he spoke, and with the

point of the bright weapon resting upon the ground, he glanced fiercely, defiantly towards the baffled admiral.

Walpole bared his weapon, and came beside his friend.

"I am with you, Claremont; our guest shall be safe while with us."

"Bravo!" shouted Moreton, also drawing his sword, "give me your hand, Hugh Baldrick, I would that you had devoted your brilliant intellect to another mode of life, but, like my friend, I will defend you to the last."

Lord Augustus Vane, after the recent display of valour, could not withhold his assistance; he, too, drew the slender blade that hung at his hip.

"Aw—demme!" he said, "you are a good fellow, Hugh—our smuggler, Baldrick—and Vane will help you—demme, that he will!"

Hugh Baldrick's quick ear caught the sound of advancing footsteps, and, unsheathing his heavy sabre, he said—

"Thanks, gentlemen, for your assistance; but I would not that you risked your lives in my defence. Sheath your blades. Leave me to settle with the rabble that Gaston will bring at his heels."

Claremont's reply was more emphatic that polite.

"I'll be hanged if I do!" he said. "We all owe those runners a debt! What say, you, gentlemen; shall we settle old scores with them? Mine is for being taken to the watch-house for pinking a fellow in the Mall."

"Mine," said Mortimer, "is for having my skull broken by one of their staves. May the gods send the fellow here that did it."

"There is a little matter on my side," said Walpole, "an assignation, in fact, with a citizen's pretty daughter, which was spoilt by these pimping rascals. May the fellow who raised the alarm of thieves, while I was climbing to the window, come here."

"Aw—demme!" said Vane, "two of them; and one knocked me down, and spoilt my new doublet."

"That," said Claremont, laughing, "deserves your strongest blow, Gus."

Kilcrew's face was pale with rage.

"Cease this nonsense," he said, advancing towards the group; "this fellow is my prisoner, and, by the good St. Patrick! I'll have him."

Hugh Baldrick's eyes flashed fire as he stepped out from his friends.

"My lord Kilcrew," he said, "when I yield myself a prisoner, it will be when this arm can no longer use a blade. Come, my lord, forestall this affair—if you can."

"Kilcrew's light sword soon leapt from its scabbard, and, lunging forcibly forward, the enraged admiral said, fiercely—

"Thus do I rob the gallows of its due."

The long, thin blade, played for a moment upon the Smuggler Chief's sabre.

The next, Kilcrew fell back, the blood streaming from his face, and grasping only the hilt of his weapon.

The blade was shivered into twenty pieces, and lay at his feet.

"Bravo!" shouted Moreton, "that trick is worth knowing. Come, gentlemen, rally! Out with your blades! Here comes the pack in full cry!"

The leafy screen of the arbour was dashed aside, and Archibald Gaston, with a dozen officers at his back, rushed in.

"There is your prisoner," he shouted. "Upon him. Remember, half the reward is yours."

This sudden onset was checked by the bristling line of swords that were suddenly raised.

Gaston uttered a cry of rage.

"What is this, my lords?" he said. "Do I find you aiding a common outlaw, and defying the King's authority?"

"You do not," said Claremont. "This gentleman is our guest—a baronet, and a member of one of the oldest families in England. As such, we will defend him from this gang of low-looking ruffians, who, like curs beneath the whip, cower before us."

"We are hossifers," cried one of the pack. "We knows you, Lord Claremont."

"The recognition is mutual," said the young noble. "You are the fellow that helped to take me to the watch-house."

"Yes, I is; and if you don't mind I'll take you there again. Oh! oh! oh!"

Lord Augustus stopped the fellow's insolence by suddenly digging the point of his sword in a spot that would render sitting an unpleasant posture for some time to come.

"Aw—demme—take that—aw—speak to a lord like that, you rascal!"

"Lieutenant Gaston," said the smuggler, "your motive in thus trying to hunt me down disgraces your manhood, shallow-brained fool that you are. Even should I be taken, the lady, who shall be nameless, will be safe from your sinister designs, and by this she will know that Hugh Baldrick has marked his foe."

A swift pass of his broad-bladed weapon followed these words, and Archibald Gaston fell back, with a cut across his brow.

Blinded with the blood that fell in a stream down into his eyes, he yelled—

"Curse him! Upon him, you cowards—shoot him—cut him down! A thousand pounds for the man who takes him, dead or alive!"

The six blades that menaced the officers were gripped tighter, as their owners saw a strong disposition upon the others' part to begin the attack.

The tempting reward, coupled with their superiority in numbers, urged them forward.

"Back," shouted Hugh, his heavy blade describing a swift circle. "Back, fools, unless you are tired of existence."

They cowered shrinkingly from the flashing eyes and sharp weapon, until the voice of Gaston again urged them forward.

There was a mingling of excited men, the clash of weapons, and five shots, followed by cries of pain, as the officers were forced back to the open space in front of the arbour.

Four of their number had fallen bleeding to the earth, and the smuggler and his friends pressed closely upon them, every moment diminishing their numbers.

"Bravo!" shouted Moreton; "I've pinked that fellow. Stand—charge—hurra!"

The reckless fellow plunged forward, followed by his companions.

A moment the combatants surged to and fro, then the yet unwounded officers, now reduced to five in number, broke away, and fled madly across the parterres of choice flowers.

"Hurra!" shouted Claremont, dashing after them. "Hurra!—come on—pursue them!"

The young noblemen took up the pursuit with as much zest as they would have run a fox to earth.

There was not much good feeling existing between the young bloods of the period and the law officers. Perhaps our modern swells and the policemen who spoil their midnight freaks will serve to render the idea easier of comprehension

It was with much the same feeling that half a dozen

"Magnificent bricks,
Who had made up their minds for a spree,"

would cry "Here we are again," and chase a policeman, who, with that meekness only to be found in the force, had very gently advised the half dozen "magnificents" to quietly desist from their pranks, that the young nobles gave chase to the officers.

Claremont, closely followed by Walpole and Moreton, chased the runners out of the gardens. Little Augustus Vane would have joined in the sport, but his sword scabbard getting between his legs, pitched him head foremost into a small basin, which received the minute spray of an illuminated fountain.

Saturated to the skin, his silken doublet and velvet hose completely spoilt, the little lord sat upon the edge of the marble basin the image of despair.

"Aw—demme," he muttered, "that stranger—aw—catch cold—have red nose — aw—demme—shall go home. Demme, smugglers—aw — who's that?"

Grinning and smirking, his lordship's valet came towards the marble fountain.

"Been looking for you, me lud. Lud Claremont told me you were in trouble; are you, me lud."

'Aw—demme—yes—where's the carriage? Let us go home, Mirks, I'm—aw—cold."

"Yes, me lud, carriage at gate. Lean on me arm, me lud—you look like a drowned—ra—I mean a—"

"Aw—demme, you villain, I'll discharge you, I will—demme."

"Now, me lud. Very well, I'll go. Here, me lud, comes the lady. Had better get behind me—if she sees you, she will laugh."

"Yes—demme—hide me, Mirks."

"Will you discharge me, me lud?"

"Aw—aw—demme—here, quick! quick!—here she comes."

"Get behind me, me lud."

Hidden by his valet, the little fellow crept from the gardens, his rueful face expressing the agony within his vain heart.

When the young patricians gave a view-hallo, and started in pursuit of the officers, Hugh Baldrick turned and faced Kilcrew and Gaston.

"Harkee! lieutenant," he said, clutching Gaston's shoulder in his sinewy grasp, "the mark I have set upon you is for the daring presumption that caused you to molest Lady Arbuthnot. Had mine been the hand to have chastised your insolence that night, I would have slain you on the spot. Remember, Hugh Baldrick never forgives a foe; he knows both you and your companion, or many suns would not rise and find you in the world."

He drew Gaston towards him as he spoke, then with a sudden extension of his strong arm, hurled the lieutenant against Kilcrew's light form.

The admiral was struck to the ground, his mouth and nostrils crimsoned with the stream of life.

Gaston, stunned by his head coming in contact with a beam that crossed the arbour, fell prone and inert beside his friend.

Hugh Baldrick stood for a moment gazing at their fallen forms, his hand tightening upon his sword-hilt, and the expression in his dark eyes showing how strong the wish was within him to slay his foes.

"Not now," he muttered; "I will have a bitter vengeance. Captain Tom rescued my sister from that fellow. The good deed shall be rewarded by my marring their devilish plot to destroy the gallant fellow."

Hugh Baldrick had, through the leafy screen, overhead their loudly-spoken plot to capture Captain Tom.

A plot laid with such consummate skill that even the gay Buccaneer must have fallen into his enemies' clutches, had not the gallant outlaw overheard the baffled pair as they combined to have revenge for the loss of Minnie Atherton and Jenny Vere.

Sheating his sword, and drawing the ruby-coloured velvet cloak around his form, Hugh Baldrick strode by a quiet path from the scene of revelry.

Once he turned aside.

It was to avoid the young nobles, who, pleased and excited by their chase, had now returned to hold high revel over the revenge they had obtained over the runners.

"I would meet them," thought Hugh, "and return my thanks for the service they have rendered me, did not this vile plot threaten the life of the noble fellow who had saved all I hold dear from a miscreant. Every moment of my time, every energy, henceforth will be called into service to crush their design, and catch them in their own toils; then my Lord Admiral and his worthy colleague shall learn more of Hugh Baldrick, the smuggler."

He found his horse ready without the gates, and giving the man a handsome reward for taking charge of the animal, he leapt into the saddle.

The horse, a splendid black, broad of chest and long of limb, curvetted and pranced when it felt its master on its back.

Hugh stroked the arched glossy neck, and said—

"So-ho, my beauty. You must carry me beyond the boundary of noisy London to-night."

He pressed his legs to the superb animal's side, and cantered away, the jingle of his steel scabbard, as it beat against his armed heel, keeping time to the hoof-strokes on the hard road.

After the late scene of excitement through which he had passed, the quiet beauty of the starlight night, and the exhilarating pace of his mettled steed, produced a calm state of feeling in the outlaw's mind.

Along the quiet green lanes (now a maze of close, stifling streets) his steed bore him past clean white-washed cottages, past large homesteads, where the bay of the watch-dog rang out and broke night's quietude, as the iron-hoofed steed awoke the noisy guardians of the night.

The outlaw saw not the peaceful dwellings, nor heard the baying of the watchful dogs—his head was drooped as though in deep thought.

And, as the silver moonbeams fell upon his face and form, he looked so singularly handsome, it was little marvel the peerless Lady Arbuthnot loved, and deeply loved, the gallant fellow.

The hands that held the bridle gleamed out soft, white, and slim as those of a lady; his pale classical face, with its chiselled features and well-defined silken moustache, added to his beauty, and gave him that appearance which carries a charm to the female heart—a bold, daring, adventurer's charming recklessness of manner that was inevitably fascinating.

A slight stumble made by his Arab steed broke the train of thought, and, pulling the animal up by a slight feeling of the slender bit, he mused—

"The marring of this plot will tax my resources. Had I but the schooner back from France the matter would be easier; but, this visit to her I love, and then to work.

He turned down a narrow lane, and rode towards a large house, which loomed out dark, massive, and sombre against the starry skies.

A slight flush tinged his cheek when he beheld a light gleaming from one of the lower chambers, and, touching his steed with the spur, he pressed forward at a quicker pace.

An avenue of tall, dark trees led to the gates the noble mansion, and, still keeping his gaze the light, which, like the mariner's star, led him onward, he turned up the narrow drive.

Suddenly an exclamation of rage fell from his lips, and, pulling the animal up so sharply that it reared upon its haunches, he drew a pistol from his holster.

"Betrayed!" he muttered, fiercely. "Would that I had slain that caitiff ere I left."

From behind the trees a half dozen men sprung out and barred his passage.

Hugh saw, as they neared him, they were of the tribe Gaston had brought to the gardens to capture or slay him.

"Caught!" said a powerfully-built fellow, springing forward, and catching the bridle with one hand, while the other levelled a sword at the horseman's breast.

A sharp report, a bright flame from the barrel of the long pistol, and the speaker rolled upon the earth, a bullet in his lungs.

With a savage cry the remainder rushed towards the undaunted fellow, but ere a hand could be placed upon the horse or rider, or a weapon raised against him, the outlaw drove both spurs into his steed's glossy flanks.

A scream of pain came from the startled animal, and like a deer he bounded clean over the officers' heads.

They stood for a moment, dumb with astonishment, gazing after the daring fellow.

The leader of the law's myrmidons raised himself upon his elbow, and, in a voice of pain, strangely blended with hate, said—

"Follow him to the house; see old Lord Henry, and tell him how his young wife—wi—f—e di—s—g—"

A rush of blood choked his utterance, and the message that Archibald Gaston would have paid this man to convey to Lord Henry was never finished in this world.

Baffled as he had been upon the night when Captain Tom hurled him down the marble steps, Gaston had, when assured of the young buccaneer's absence, repeated his visit to the beauteous lady.

His malignant passions were aroused to a pitch of frenzy when he beheld her strained to the breast of the handsome outlaw, Hugh Baldrick.

The destruction of his second rival was at once determined upon; that failing, unless the lovely creature listened to his suit, he determined to tell her aged husband, and be revenged by her disgrace.

Then, when he brought the officers to the gardens, he had told their leader, in the event of not effecting a capture, to lay in ambush near the residence of Lord Henry; should he again escape, to reveal all to the jealous old nobleman.

Death had fallen upon his messenger, and the bold devil-may-care smuggler had escaped, and was now within that chamber where the glowing lamp had shed its pale light.

Thither the officers followed, their heroism awed by the death of their chief.

Another ten minutes, and the fate of Hugh Baldrick and Captain Tom would be decided. Should the smuggler chief fall by a stray bullet, Kilcrew's plot would end the career of our young hero.

CHAPTER XLVIII.

THE MISER AND THE PIRATE.—WHAT BEFEL JERRY MIZZEN AND BOB HAULER WHEN THEY WENT TO DISCOVER HOW DUTCH PAUL MADE THE LIQUID FLAME.

WHATEVER the secret was that connected Dutch Paul's former life with that of our two adventurers,

Jerry Mizzen and Bob Hauler, they had sufficient discretion to keep the matter to themselves.

Dutch Paul was not the sort of man to utter a threat without fulfilling it, and as neither Jerry nor his companion wished to figure on the yard-arm, they acted accordingly.

As far as comfort was concerned, the pair were as well off as they would have been on board the "Will-o'-the-Wisp."

But, as Jerry expressed it—

"If the cap'n was to stick his 'air full o' diamonds, and make him second in command, he would sooner be a loblolly-boy with his young cap'n."

A sentiment that Bob fully shared, for he, too, loved the dashing young adventurer with a rugged affection, none the less true because he lacked that refinement which is necessary to give an eloquence to his language.

Though doing seamen's duty upon the freebooter's vessel, both Bob and Jerry flatly told Dutch Paul that the first chance they obtained of getting back to the "Will-o'-the-Wisp" they would use it.

The freebooter's answer was, as usual, not remarkable for its length.

"Very well," he said "When you have a chance, take it, but, until then, remember that you belong to my crew."

The two old companions found rumour, as usual, had belied their new leader.

So far from his nature being cruel or bloodthirsty, he never used a weapon in plundering a ship, but in the event of being overhauled by a Moorish or Algerian pirate he became a perfect fiend.

The Moslems had no compunction in their mode of ravaging the seas; in fact, often a stronger vessel of the same class would fall upon the weaker—slay the crew, pillage the ship, then burn or blow her up.

If death could render their deeds secret, they were safe from the vengeance of their own countrymen.

In fact, it was dog rob dog—if I may use the expression, dog murder dog.

Against these gentry Dutch Paul seemed to have a most inveterate hatred.

With closed ports, and two-thirds of his crew below, he would lure them on.

Once within range, open would fly the ports, and the subtle liquid fire, blazing from the long guns, would soon run over the decks, and annihilate the Moslem ships.

True to his purpose, Bob Hauler used every endeavour to find out the secret of the subtle fluid.

In vain he crept about the state-room when he knew Dutch Paul was engaged in its manufacture; he could not glean the least insight into the mystic work.

Jerry, his hair on end with fright, would stand behind his companion as he peeped through the keyhole; but beyond the gleam of a fiery furnace and their leader at work, stripped to the waist, they saw nothing that would reveal the secret.

Baffled, but not dispirited, Bob Hauler ceased for a time to pry about when the ship's lights were extinguished and the crew below in their hammocks

"Let's turn in," he said one night to the shivering Jerry; "it's our next turn for watch. We must try again another time."

"I wouldn't, Bob," was Jerry's advice. "If he catches us at it, Lord! what shall we do then?"

"Swing at the yard-arm, Jerry."

"Oh, don't talk about it."

Jerry crept into his hammock, and soon fell asleep.

The recollection of the liquid fire, and the probable fate that would follow their discovery, rendered his dreams anything but pleasing.

He dreamt, and his brow was damp with fear as the vision passed, that Dutch Paul had cast him into a large cauldron of seething liquid.

He felt the flame boiling the flesh from his bones, and, in fancy, the effluvia rose thick and hot into his nostrils.

So great was his terror that he sat bolt upright, and flinging his long arms out right and left, as though struggling to escape from the hissing cauldron, he brought the weight of his right hand plump down upon Bob Hauler's nose, which was at the time performing a snoring fantasia.

The blow awoke Bob, and without staying to seek for the cause, he struck out at random, and gave Jerry such a punch in the mouth that caused his teeth to rattle.

The yell Jerry gave awoke all within hearing, and a volley of curses came from their lips.

Jerry lay perfectly quiet.

"I ain't being boiled arter all," he thought. "It was a dream arter all. I'll go to sleep again."

He did, only to be roused by the boatswain's shrill whistle calling him up to relieve the watch on deck.

Jerry thrust his fingers in his ears, and secretly wished that watching was unknown upon shipboard.

It was no use trying to shut out the hateful sound.

Much against his will he had to turn out from his comfortable hammock, and go upon deck.

It was not pleasant.

The morning was raw cold, and a drizzling rain made everything as wet and uncomfortable as can be imagined.

"I say, Bob," Jerry said, savagely, "I wish there wasn't any watches, don't you?"

"Tumble up there, you lubbers," said the boatswain, "or I'll come down and help you with a taste of rope's end."

"Cuss!" said Jerry, angrily. "I've lost my sou'-wester."

"Take mine," said Bob, quickly.

"What'll you do, Bob?"

"I've got yours, Jerry. It's a better one than mine."

Jerry made a grab at the better one, but, missing it by an inch, tumbled forward, and did not stop until his nose tried to make a hole through the planks.

When he scrambled to his feet, Bob had gone on deck, and left his battered sou'-wester for Jerry.

"Cuss!" commented Jerry, ruefully. "Some people is born to bad luck, and I's one of 'em."

Jerry's station was on the bows, and to his discomfort the rain beat against his face; and, finding the leak in Bob's sou'-wester trickled down his back, it caused him to invoke blessings upon his worthy comrade's eyes and limbs.

When the morning light broke upon the ocean, Jerry beheld the hazy outline of land ahead.

A fact which he lost no time in making known to the officer of the watch, who went below and communicated the intelligence to Dutch Paul.

The freebooter was soon upon deck, and as soon as the shore became visible, he gave orders for the vessel to enter a little harbour, where a small forest of masts could be seen looming out against the leaden sky.

"Don't forget," Dutch Paul said, "that we are the 'Myrtle,' from Lisbon, while we stay in port, quarter-master."

"Aye, aye, sir!"

"Have the guns lowered, and fish up a few hogsheads from below!"

"Aye, aye, sir!"

"Ready there, sail-trimmers!"

"Ready—all ready, sir!"

"Stand by to let fall! Quick there—up to the maintop, one of you, and take out that hitch in the rope!"

Everything was soon ready, and the cloud of white canvas, at a word from this strange captain, came down with a run to the deck.

In place of the snowy sails, a set of discoloured, patched old canvas was soon run up, and the freebooter's ship, looking as clumsy as hands could make her, sailed slowly into the port of Baraces, and, with consummate daring, anchored right under the guns of a British line-of-battle ship.

When the sails were furled—a proceeding which took up some time, and was done as clumsily as possible—much to the merriment of the officers and crew of the line-of-battle ship—Dutch Paul called one of the men to his side, and ordered the cutter to be piped away.

The man whom Dutch Paul had selected to accompany him in his dangerous expedition was of Titan build and wondrous strength.

His height was over six feet, and his limbs were powerfully made, and in proportion to his huge, bull-like neck and shoulders.

"Do you think, Vargas," Dutch Paul asked, "you could remember the spot?"

"Well—every stone."

"Accompany me ashore, and let me but see the place where the old rascal keeps his gold, and I'll clean him out as clean as a Portsmouth doll cleans out a homeward bound man-o'-war's man."

Vargas laughed grimly.

"What are you distorting that not too handsome face of yours about, Infant?" Dutch Paul asked.

"A passing thought, cap'n."

"What was it on—eh, my Infant?"

"I was thinking of Israel Shawm."

"What about the old villain?"

"He is the proprietor of the hidden money-bags."

"The devil!"

"Mr. Cap'n—old hound—late Jew—now a clean-shaved Christian."

"What! has he parted with his beard?"

"Every single hair, cap'n; and had it not been for a chance sight I obtained of his daughter, I should never have known the old rascal."

"His daughter — what Hester, that dark-eyed beauty?"

"The same, cap'n."

"I am much inclined, Vargas, to first help myself to his gold, then carry off the girl. She would be better among the others on the treasure-island than with that old mummy."

"Much better, cap'n."

The boat was rapidly nearing the shore, and Dutch Paul, pointing to the liner's massive hull and triple battery, said—

"What would this fellow think, did he know the 'Yellow Vulture' lay beneath his guns?"

"I don't know what he'd think, cap'n, but I do know what he'd do."

"What's that, Infant?"

"Sink the 'Yellow Vulture.'"

Dutch Paul took a leisurely puff at his cigar, and answered, coolly—

"Perhaps he would, Vargas—perhaps he would."

His captain's coolness somewhat staggered Vargas.

"Well, cap'n," said the giant, "you are about the most devil-may-care fellow I have ever seen."

Dutch Paul leisurely ignited a fresh cigar as he asked—

"Devil-may-care? How's that, Infant?"

"Well, cap'n, ain't I seen you defy a ship load o' reg'lar old salts to attack your cave when you haven't had more than a handful of men, and haven't they been afraid to come 'cause Dutch Paul called 'em? and, considering our little craft is right under the teeth of that liner, your question is—is—what do you call it?"

"Irrelevant, eh?"

"That's it, I think, cap'n; only it's too much of a word for me."

"Your mouth is big enough to give it utterance."

As he spoke the keel grated on the beach, and the pair, drawing the light craft above high-water mark, went towards the town.

Israel Shawm, the Jew, since the privateer captain let him down with a hempen collar round his neck, had been haunted with a continual fear of losing his ill-gotten wealth.

In this out-of-the-way port he had purchased an old house, and under another name carried on his nefarious transactions.

Beneath the antiquated building, which formed part of a long-disused convent, the old miser found a good hiding-place for his gold.

The vaults were large, and supported by massive granite pillars, and it was asserted that each pillar contained the dust of a frail member of the sisterhood who had once dwelt in the sombre pile.

Beneath this vault there were several large stone chambers, accessible only by raising a square stone. Legend had a ghostly use for these noisome places, by asserting that, when the pillars were all filled with their living occupants, small holes were dug wherein to place those who erred in spite of the horrible death their sins brought upon them.

Here, in this silent vault, where every gleam of the lamp seemed to reveal a spectre, Israel Shawm was wont to gloat over his bags of gold.

"My monish," he would mutter, insensible to the vague horrors that the solitary charnel-house would have filled other minds. "By the shoul of my father, I shall not loshe it here!"

Here, when night set in, he would carry the heavy bags from their hiding place, and piling them in a heap, caress and fondle the golden coin. Then with his pale, hard face aglow with exultation, he would replace them, close the trap, and ascend to his room.

"This is the house," said Vargas, as the came opposite the gloomy building. "Keep back, cap'n, while I get inside."

"Then?" asked Dutch Paul.

"Wait, cap'n, until I let you in."

"Good; don't keep me long, or I will shatter the old lock with a pistol-ball."

"If you do, cap'n, the old man's money will not touch our fingers to-night."

"Well, have your own way. I will stand in the shadow of the door and finish my cigar."

In answer to Varga's summons, Hester, the dark-eyed daughter of Israel, made her appearance.

Faithful to her father's orders, she only opened the massive door as far as a strong chain would admit.

"What would you?" she asked.

"I would see your father, girl," said Vargas. "Hurry! tell him the cargo of a Barbary cruiser is awiting to be cleared."

"My father," said Hester, timidly, "will not see any one after nightfall. Come in the morning."

"Too late for our business, girl There's a British ship in the port—you understand—we can't stay."

Poor girl, she did understand but too well.

Her father's traffic with the lawless desperadoes was breaking her young heart.

She stood with one white, slender hand upon the door and said—

"I know not what to do. My father would not open this door until to-morrow, yet, as your time will not admit of such delay—I—I—"

"You had better seek him, my girl. I want not to enter the house; he can converse with me as you and I converse."

"I will tell him. Wait a few moments, I will return and tell you my father's—"

"Quick, my good girl; we lose time."

Hester moved back, and was about to close the door, when Vargas placed his foot in such a manner that she was obliged to leave it fastened by the chain.

"Pretty, but rather pale," was Dutch Paul's comment, as he watched Hester up the wide, passage; gloomy "she is too good to live in this rat-hole. Vargas!"

"Cap'n."

"What the devil are we to do now?"

"Get inside."

"Humph, easier said than done. He will not let us in to-night."

"I know it."

"The devil you do?"

"So," Vargas continued, "I must be door-keeper."

Dutch Paul looked curiously in his companion's face.

"Door-keeper?" he repeated; "what do you mean?"

"All right, cap'n. You see, the girl won't be back for some time."

"How do you know that, my Infant, eh?" asked Dutch Paul.

"Because old Israel is now in the vaults—it's about his time."

"Well."

"While the girl is tickling his ears with the story of the Barbary cruiser, we must get inside."

"Through the keyhole?"

"No, cap'n, this way."

Vargas took a pair of pincers from his pocket, and with as much ease as he would have broken a reed, twisted one of the iron links asunder.

"Now, cap'n, inside with you."

Dutch Paul cautiously entered the high marble passage, and throwing the fragment of his cigar into the street, remarked—

"Don't like smoking here. I suppose, Vargas?"

"Can't say, cap'n; it's better not to leave the smell inside, or she'll know we've got in."

"The broken chain will tell her that."

"Now, cap'n—oh, no; I'll mend that."

He closed the severed link as he spoke, and Israel Shawm's visitors, chuckling with glee, walked softly towards the sombre-looking stairs.

They had not gone far when the gleam of a lamp could be seen ascending the spiral steps which led from the vaults.

"Step in the doorway, cap'n," whispered Vargas, it's the girl."

They had barely time to withdraw within the open door of a chamber which stood on the right when Hester appeared at the end of the passage.

There was a sad, troubled look upon the poor girl's face, and as she came near the hiding-place of her father's unwelcome visitors, she murmured, loud enough for them to hear—

"Abraham protect my poor father, and cure him of this accursed love for gold! Day or night, sleeping or waking, his thoughts are with the hidden dross. Accursed money! Its possession has driven him to become a dweller in this dreary place. Would the earth would open and swallow it, then peace would again come to us."

Dutch Paul chuckled, and whispered to Vargas—

"Lucky you came to-night."

"Why, cap'n?"

"You can bring peace to the house of Israel Shawm. Ha! ha! ha!"

"Yes, cap'n, I'll cure him. Ha! ha! ha!"

"Away with you, I'll secure the girl."

"Hist! she is returning."

The oil lamp drearily lit the old place as Hester, thinking that the stranger had gone, came slowly back to tell her father.

Dutch Paul slipped off his heavy boots, and as she passed the door, threw his cap at the light.

The lamp fell from her hand, and the girl uttered a slight cry.

"How foolish," she murmured. "It was a bat, disturbed by the light, flew against the—"

She was groping in the darkness for the lamp, when a hand was placed over her mouth, and before she could give utterance to the scream that came to her lips, she felt herself thrown over the shoulder of her unseen assailant.

Vargas followed his leader's example, by drawing off his long boots and replacing them by a pair of soft shoes.

With a stealthy, noiseless tread, he hurried down the spiral staircase and stood for a moment at the small iron door which led to the subterraneous stone chamber. The scene was well calculated to gladden the robber's heart, and cause his eyes to gleam with greedy exultation.

The grim, damp walls and massive pillars, but partially lighted by a flickering lamp, the stone pavement covered with green fungus, except at one part where a trap was open and revealed a square, black chasm.

Near one of the pillars was a heap of canvas bags tied at the neck; on the outside black figures told the respective value of each.

Between the open trap and the pile of wealth was Israel Shawm, his white hair and pale, bloodless face giving him an unnatural expression, as his slippered feet shuffled on the damp stones.

Each of the Jew's claw-like hands clutched a bag of treasure; his cracked voice came upon the pirate's ear as Israel, in terms of endearment, addressed the yellow ore.

He had been, since sundown, in this fœtid place, carrying his wealth from the darksome cavity to the light, and, after gloating over the canvas bags, he was reluctantly replacing them.

One bag had evidently fallen from his nerveless grasp, for it lay near the hole, the string broken and its shining contents scattered temptingly around.

With the wary gait and noiseless tread of a beast of prey, the pirate glided towards the gold-loving Jew.

Israel was in the act of stooping over the open trap when the pirate's heavy breathing caused him to start and turn pale.

"The ratsh," he mumbled, "Mine Got, I taught it was a man."

A mocking, low, devilish laugh sent a thrill of agony through the Jew's frame; and half turning his head, he gave a scream of sudden terror.

His startled gaze met the long shining barrel of a pistol, and, standing in bold relief against the murky light, was the huge form of Vargas the pirate.

Israel Shawm stood as though suddenly turned to stone—neither eye, hand, nor limb moved, and from his forehead big drops of cold, clammy fear fell upon his white, shrunken hands.

The pirate mocked Israel's terror.

"Ratsh!" he repeated. "Yours, Israel, is a huge rat, a water-rat—ha! ha! I've burrowed into your hole—ha! ha!"

The Jew's cold lips moved as though in prayer, then springing across the dungeon, he threw himself upon his treasure-heap, and cried—

"Robber! Oh, Got of my fathers, I will not be robbed!"

Vargas, like a huge tiger about to spring upon its meek and defenceless prey, stood over the feeble old man, who, with wild despair upon his face, was trying with his attenuated form to screen the ill-gotten heap.

Replacing the pistol in his belt, the pirate stood for a moment contemplating the miserable Jew.

"You came many miles, Israel Shawm," said Vargas, and the cold, pitiless tones fell upon the doomed man's ears, and he felt that all hope of eluding the pirate's vengeance had passed away—"many miles to elude the fulfilment of the oath I made when you delivered me into the hands of my foes."

"Mercy! here is one bag of monish for you!"

"One bag!"—he laughed such a devilish laugh that it stayed Israel's blood—"I have come for every bag!—every coin! Israel, and your life as well!"

"Oh, Got! Mr. Vargash, have mercy! I was obliged to tell the captain of the man-of-war you were in my house!"

"Liar! You betrayed me for the reward! Ha! ha! Israel, when the money was paid to you, did you think I should come and claim it?"

"Mercy!"

"Yes, Israel, the same mercy you showed me when I was taken! The same mercy you thought I should receive when they sentenced the pirate to be hung to the yard-arm!"

Israel Shawm shrieked with terror.

He saw the pirate's eyes ablaze with a dusky glow—saw his hand clutch the hilt of a long knife that hung from his belt.

The blade shimmered for a moment as it left its sheath, and Israel, dropping the money-bags he had hitherto clutched, placed his hands over his eyes, and yelled piteously to be spared.

Vargas stood with uplifted knife, Israel at his feet writhing with agony.

The pirate waited but for the moment when a vital part should come beneath his knife.

He was in no haste to strike, the mind's agony Israel Shawm was suffering was part of Vargas' revenge.

The Jew did suffer—suffered as no pen can describe or words portray; his mind wrought to a fearful pitch of anguished dread; his body feeling every moment as though the gleaming weapon had found its sheath in the cold, quivering flesh.

It was keen enjoyment to the vengeful pirate.

A moment he had long waited for—one that had been before his mind for many years.

At last it had come. The man who had first taken his cargo of mercers' stuffs, then betrayed him to the captain of an English war-brig, now lay quivering with terror at his feet.

The bodily struggles were becoming feebler, then ceased, and Israel, with such a look of mute entreaty and horrible expectation upon his face, crouched before the pirate.

Such a look—though the old miscreant had so vilely betrayed his guest—would have turned a man of less nerve than Vargas from his purpose.

It found no echo in the heart of him who came

to slay. Mercy and forgiveness had long been strangers to Vargas the pirate.

"Grovelling worm!" he hissed, and his face bore such an expression as Satan's when he fell, and became a curse to mankind, "where is your mocking laugh of triumph now? where are your gibing words such as you used when I was dragged from beneath your roof—do you remember them?"

Israel bowed his head in silent anguish.

"I will repeat them, thou craven hound; listen."

Israel Shawm turned his head aside to escape the glare of the pirate's dark vengeful eyes.

"Good-bye, Misther Vargas," continued the pirate, mimicking the Jew's voice; "good-bye, you'll soon swing at the yard-arm, good Mr. Vargas, and I shall have the reward, and the fine cargo of your ship."

Israel Shawm groaned feebly.

"I did not swing at the yard-arm," Vargas resumed; "I have come back, Israel, to scorch your brain with these words, which, from the hour I saw your villainous face mocking my efforts to escape, I have treasured them in my memory until the hour —this hour, Israel—the hour of my vengence, and your death."

The knife glittered high above the speaker's head as he ceased speaking, and Israel closed his eyes to shut out the sight of the descending weapon.

In the very act of striking his direst foe, the pirate paused.

A faint aroma came, wafted upon the damp air of the vault, a fragrant perfume that he knew was the herald of Dutch Paul's appearance

It had the odour of the choice cigars that Dutch Paul's lips, except in sleep, were never without.

As Vargas, with the blade on high, paused, the door opened, and the captain of the "Yellow Vulture" entered.

His quick glance comprehended the scene at once; and, looking from Vargas to the Jew's prostrate form, he puffed a cloud of smoke upwards and said—

"Quite a tableau; go on, Infant, with " next posture."

Until Dutch Paul's manly voice told of his presence, Israel Shawm was in ignorance of a third party being in the treasure-vault

As the last words fell from the pirate's lips, Israel, with a sudden bound that belied his wasted limbs and fallen strength, threw himself at Dutch Paul's feet, and shrieked—

"Save me; save me; oh, good Misther Paul, save me!"

Vargas dropped his arm at a gesture from his leader.

"Save you from what? honest Israel!"

"Death—death! Don't you see it in his eye, in his face, and the long knife? Oh, Mi—"

"Jew knave!—you howling old devil!—you deserve your fate. Yes; don't clasp your hands and look like a Methodist at a tea-drinking. I say you deserve it. You infernal old traitor! you know you'd sell us both. Eh, wouldn't you?"

"Misther Paul, by the—"

"Hold your lying tongue, and listen to what I have to say."

"Yes; oh, Mi—"

"By all the imps in—the place were you will go, Israel—if you commence whining again, I will ram the butt of this pistol down your throat."

Although the captain of the "Yellow Vulture" had such a pleasant manner, Israel knew he would keep his word to the very letter.

Knowing this kept him silent.

"What," asked Dutch Paul, "do you value your life at, Israel?"

"Very much. Oh! good Mi—"

"Plain sailing, Israel, or you'll have this mahogany pill to swallow. How much?"

"Very much. I must have time to repent all that I have donsh in the way of trade, captain."

"Not forgetting, Israel, the many good fellows you have been the cause of getting a rope."

This was touching upon dangerous ground.

Israel made no answer.

"Well, Israel," said Dutch Paul, giving Vargas a significant look, "is your life worth all these bags of money?"

"Monish. Oh, captain! by the soul of my fathers, it ish not mine—only one little bag—you may have it—dat is every farthing. The rest is—is—"

Dutch Paul jerked his toe against that part of the Jew's anatomy commonly termed the wind, and sent him gasping on his back.

"Quite enough for one, Israel," said Dutch Paul. "I do not believe you, and, not caring for your money, I must have something else, if I save you from the knife."

"Anything, captain, any—"

"This heap of gold?"

"S'help me—may—I never—"

"Very well. Your daughter for my wife, then; will that do?"

Israel sat bolt upright. First he glanced at his money-bags, then at the knife, which Vargas still held.

The old miscreant's mind soon came to a decision. His gold was dearer than his daughter.

"Yesh, good Mr. Captain Paul, you shall have Hester; she will be a goot girl—yesh, she shall be your wife to save her poor old father."

A faint cry came from the direction of the cavern door.

It was Hester, who had crept down, and overheard all that passed.

Dutch Paul's face became overcast with anger, and stamping his feet impatiently upon the stone floor, he seized Israel by the collar, and dragged him upon his knees.

"Worm!" said the captain of the "Vulture." "Dog! you would barter your own flesh and blood —sell your only child to any ruffian rather than lost this vile dross!"

He spurned a bag of gold with such violence as to cause it to burst, and the glittering coins strewed the floor.

Israel Shawm—although in the hands of a man who valued his life less than he would have valued a dog's—though crouching in deadly fear from the naked blade and fierce eyes of Vargas—forgot not his ruling passion.

The words which came from Dutch Paul's lips were unheeded. When the canvas bag scattered its contents at his feet, he heard the chink so grateful to his sordid ears, as the metal rung out upon the stones—saw his beloved wealth scattered broadcast —and, forgetful of everything save this sight, he strove to wrench himself from the pirate leader's iron grasp.

The sunken eyes greedily followed several pieces as they rolled away, and his claw-like fingers looked as though eager to restore them to their receptacle.

The sight was too much for the little that remained of Dutch Paul's equanimity.

"You vile old reptile!" he roared. "Curse you! sordid, gold-worshipping old hermit! Here, Vargas, he shall have a resting place with the yellow metal, whose chink is more music to him than his daughter's voice."

Vargas came forward and gripped Israel by the windpipe with one hand; the other uplifted the threatening blade.

Dutch Paul stayed the upraised arm, and, pointing to the open trap, said—

"Not that way, Vargas; it is too good a death. There, let him sleep with all he loves."

And, before Israel's white, quivering lips could utter one word, he was seized and hauled into the excavation where he had been wont to keep his hoard.

Then the pirates, without a thought of appropriating the treasure to themselves, cut bag after bag open, and poured the contents over Israel.

The golden shower lasted until every bag was empty; then the two demons threw them in, and the helpless old wretch, too terror-stricken to attempt rising from his tomb, gave one wild scream as the heavy slab was dropped in its place, and the miser was immured alive with his gold.

When the work was done, the pirates looked into each other's faces.

Neither spoke, but the expression each saw was—

"The sentence is just!"

From beneath the massive stone came first piteous cries for help, then the jingling of money, as Israel Shawm madly strove to force his way out.

Hardened as the pirates were to scenes of violence and bloodshed, this fearful scene blanched their bronzed cheeks, and neither spoke until the heavy door had closed upon the first unearthly shrieks and the clinking of golden pieces.

"Well, cap'n," said Vargas, as they reached the entrance-hall; "it goes agin the grain to leave so much good coin here."

Dutch Paul had by this time regained his cool nonchalance.

"Curse it, my Infant!" he said, lighting a fresh cigar; "it would go against mine were it other money than that."

"It's good coin, cap'n, and all full weight, or that old limb of the devil would not have it."

"It's blood money, Vargas!—blood money!—let it lie with him; there would be a curse upon him who touched it."

"Perhaps there would, cap'n. What's the next tack to go upon?"

"Find the girl. I must not leave her here to die."

They searched every grim-looking chamber in the sombre old dwelling, but to no purpose.

Hester had escaped, and the open door showed the mode of her departure.

"Gone, by the eternal!" said Dutch Paul.

"Gone—clean gone!" said Vargas, in the same breath.

"We'll go!" said the captain of the "Yellow Vulture," "it will not do to stay too long ashore."

"Right, cap'n! that liner is too close to the 'Vulture.'"

"Much too close, my Infant—let's aboard?"

The boat's stern was in the water when they returned, and quickly pushing her off, Vargas pulled silently and swiftly towards the ship.

Unnoticed by all, save the officer on watch, the pair got safely aboard. Dutch Paul, with Vargas, descended the hatchway.

Outside the cabin door he came to a standstill, and, holding up his hand to enjoin silence, he peered through the keyhole, through which a light was gleaming.

A low laugh came from his lips as he beheld Bob Hauler and Jerry Mizzen busy with a chemical apparatus, which stood upon a locker.

He arose, and silently walked from the small orifice.

Vargas stooped and gazed quietly through the door. When he arose he whispered—

"They are on a voyage of discovery, cap'n."

"Yes," said Dutch Paul, "and instead of finding fire they shall have something cooler."

Vargas replied with a grim smile.

CHAPTER XLIX.

AN UNEXPECTED BATH.

WHEN Dutch Paul and Vargas left the "Vulture" to visit Israel Shawm, Jerry Mizzen Bob Hauler were standing by the mainmast.

"He's going ashore, Bob," remarked Jerry, "only taking one hand with him."

Bob Hauler watched the light gig, as it was propelled by the powerful Vargas, skimming through the water.

"Yes, Jerry," he replied; "now is our time."

"Time, Bob! What for?"

"To find out how he makes the fire."

Jerry's face became elongated.

"Bob," he said, "in course, if yer goes I goes too; but I wouldn't if I was yer."

"Why not?"

"Why not, Bob! I'll tell yer why not. If he comes back and catches us, that's where we shall be."

Jerry pointed to the yard-arm.

Bob Hauler laughed.

"Why, Jerry," he said, "anyone would think yer was afraid."

"I aint afraid, Bob; but still, yer see, when I think of it, it makes me feel a bit queer like."

"Nothing venture nothing have."

"That's all very well, messmate; I remember saying that once when I was a boy."

"It had nothing to do with this, Jerry."

"No, Bob; but it was something like it. Yer see, I wanted some pears that growed in a garden which didn't belong to my old man."

"Your father?"

"Yes, Bob; but we allers used to call him the old man."

"All right—go on."

"Well, as I was saying, I wanted some of the pears, and when I used to go past every morning to school, I used to feel the water a running down each side of my mouth."

"It's a wonder, Jerry, you was not drowned."

"Drowned? Why?"

"With the water—considering the size of your mouth."

"Eh! you are a funny chap, Bob. Well, as I was a say—"

"Don't say it again, Jerry. Tell the yarn straight off."

For Jerry to tell a yarn, as Bob Hauler termed it, straight off, was more likely to lead to more than the usual roundabout manner.

Fortunately for Bob, and the reader's patience, Jerry went straight to the point.

"In course," he resumed, "looking at em' did not get 'em. One morning the schoolmaster writes out in my copy-book, 'nothing venture nothing have.' Well, somehow, Bob, I keeps on all day thinking about that I'd been writing, and, when I comes home, I passes the garden, and there was the pears a grinning at me."

"Wonderful fruit," Bob interrupted.

"They was, Bob; such a size, and so juicy. Well, I stands looking at 'em, and was going away, when I thinks of what I'd been writing, and says to myself, 'Now, Jerry, if yer don't venture to take some, you won't have any.'"

"Exactly," said Bob. "Go on."

"So with that I puts down my bag and creeps through the hedge into the garden—didn't I wish I hadn't, that's all!"

"Why, Jerry?"

"Because no sooner had I got to the biggest tree, and was just a going to climb, when snap goes something, and I feels two rows of teeth catch hold of me by the leg."

"What was it, Jerry?"

"A trap, and I had trod on the spring."

"Well, what did you do?"

"Do, Bob? Why I hollered, and hollering brought the old gardener out, and he brought a stick, and if he didn't lay on to my back with it, it's a caution."

"Is that all, Jerry?"

"All! I should think it's enough. You would if you had had the walloping I did."

"P'raps I should, Jerry. But what has your pears to do with this affair?"

"Everything, Bob. If I had not ventured, I shouldn't have got such a licking as that; if we ventures below, p'raps the skipper has a trap to catch us, then, instead of being walloped, we shall dance on nothing."

"Well, perhaps, Jerry, there is something in what you says; but if he had forty traps, and the 'Yellow Vulture' had as many yard-arms as she has guns, I'd have a try."

"Don't see what you want to try at all for—we is both very comfortable on board this craft."

"Don't you? Well, I'll tell you, Jerry, I want to find out the secret of that liquid fire for our young chief."

"I'd do anything for Captain Tom," said Jerry; "you know that, Bob; but, somehow, I don't think we shall find it out."

"Nothing venture, nothing have, Jerry."

"Yes, that's all very well. I've told you how I tried that."

"Well, Jerry," said his companion, "you are a great calf. I don't ask you to come with me any more, so here's off."

Jerry caught his messmate by the sleeve.

"Bob," he said, "where you goes, I goes. If yer was to walk into a fire, I'd follow yer—if you have to swing for this, damme, I'll swing too!"

The quaint pair shook hands, as men who were about to lead a forlorn hope.

A vague sense of danger filled their minds—danger of a subtle, unseen nature—that caused their hearts to beat faster as they neared the state-cabin of the "Yellow Vulture."

Creeping stealthily below, pausing and listening at every sound that came from the deck above.

The cabin-door yielded to Bob Hauler's hand, the well-oiled hinges allowing it to swing back without the slightest noise.

Another step, and they were in the luxurious cabin, their feet pressing rich carpets from the famed looms of Persia.

It was a strange place, this state-cabin of the "Yellow Vulture," and Bob and his companion, the latter a little scared at finding himself inside Dutch Paul's sanctum, stared for a few seconds in mute admiration at the dazzling splendour which surrounded them.

No portion of the woodwork was visible—floor, ceiling, walls, were hidden by the most cunning and elaborate skill.

There were eight panels of glass in the cabin, in each of which the spies saw their forms reflected from head to toe.

Around the glass, looped up in elegant festoons, was a network of silver lace; outside this, rich curtains, fringed and looped up with heavy golden cords and tassels.

The ceiling was, perhaps, the most striking feature in the place, the heavy timbers being painted to represent the canopy of Heaven.

There were but few articles of furniture—a soft yielding couch, an easy chair, an inlaid table, and a stand of arms.

Bob Hauler, when he had sufficiently admired this strange display of Barbaric splendour, turned to Jerry with a puzzled look upon his face.

"It can't be here, Jerry," he said, "yet when I peeped through the keyhole I saw our skipper at work at a furnace, here—yes, this was about the very spot."

He pointed to a handsome porcelain stove as he spoke.

"I could have sworn it, too, Bob," replied his companion; "but somehow this cabin don't seem to be as big as—"

"Right, Jerry; the mystery is explained. Of course—"

"Of course what, Bob?"

"The stern windows—where are they?"

Jerry peered round quickly.

"There must," he said, "be another one."

"Another cabin?"

"Yes."

"That's my opinion."

"Belay there, Bob; it was mine first."

"The opinion?"

"Yes."

"You are welcome to it, Jerry; but the discovery is mine."

A knob upon the framework of the glass panel that formed the door had attracted his attention whilst Jerry was speaking.

To seize and turn it was the work of a moment, and, as the door swung back, he beheld the place he sought.

The mystery was now explained.

The second portion of the state-room was fitted as a laboratory, and when Bob Hauler saw Dutch Paul at work, the door of communication must have been open.

Bob's eyes dilated with joy when he beheld the various articles used by the captain of the "Vulture" in manufacturing the subtle liquid flame.

In one corner was a small forge, and upon this several crucibles.

A shelf near the forge was filled with large bottles containing various acids, and upon a table was a large heap of gold-dust.

While Jerry stood scared and trembling, his companion was filling a small bottle with a minute portion of the contents of the large vessels that stood upon the shelves.

Jerry watched his proceedings with frightened interest, and when Bob completed his arrangements by taking a pinch of gold-dust and dropping it into the bottle, he burst out—

"What's that for, Bob—that ain't the fire?"

"He puts it in," was the reply, "or it would not be here."

"Ugh!" Jerry shivered. "Don't shake it, it might go off."

"I'm afraid not, Jerry. I shall try to-night whether I have the secret."

"How, Bob?"

"By putting this in a hollow shot, then pitching the shot ashore."

"Yes; but—"

"Don't you see, you great lubber, if I've got it right the flames will run over the water."

"If not, Bob?"

"I shall come here again and have another try."

"Never!" said a voice. "You have gone on your last cruise, Bob Hauler."

Before either could speak, the boards opened at their feet, and both fell through.

A splashing of water followed, and as Jerry's voice came upward for help, Dutch Paul, followed by Vargas, entered the cabin.

Both for a moment peered over the open trap, and Dutch Paul said—

"Eight have gone this way, Vargas. Think you we shall have nine seek to learn the secret?"

"Can't say, cap'n; hope not. Don't like to know so many good fellows have gone to Davy Jones for prying into our secret."

"Shut the trap. Infant, and leave off moralising. Death is the only plan to keep it to ourselves."

The trap, worked by a lever, glided into its place, and, as Dutch Paul said, if death could keep the hidden mystery of the liquid flame from his fellow-men, it had always been resorted to.

As the captain of the "Yellow Vulture" and his companion closed the door that held the strange elements of the deadly fire, a faint sound of men struggling for life came upon their ears.

There was a stern battle going forward with the Grim Destroyer in the polluted waters of the secret well, and both, callous as they were, paled slightly as the subdued sound came upon their ears.

CHAPTER L.

CAPTAIN TOM ON THE DESTROYER'S TRAIL.

SAFELY on board his own vessel, Captain Tom placed the senseless form of Minnie under the care of Zelie.

"Guard her," he said to the corsair maiden, "as you would your life."

His foot was upon the bottom step as he spoke —another moment and he would have been on deck had not the voice of Zelie arrested him."

"Whither go you?" she asked. "Has your red, thirsty blade not drunk enough blood for one day?"

Captain Tom turned his angry face towards the speaker.

"It has not, Zelie," he replied, "nor would it, were the lives of my foes as many as the sands by the shore, and I had them all within my grasp."

"Be careful," she said, pleadingly. "The mystic Death Pirate has a terrible engine of destruction when he finds himself in dire peril—one," she added, "that will send both his friends and foes into eternity."

"What mean you, Zelie?"

"Be warned," she said. "Zelie has never yet spoken falsely."

There was something in the girl's voice and manner that caused the impetuous boy to pause.

"You warn me, Zelie," he said. "Give the object of your words some tangible shape, that I may know where to meet the danger."

"Go not on board the Death Pirate's ship; you have worked him enough misery for one day."

"Zelie, this is madness. Think you that the treacherous trick by which he gained possession of that poor girl can be requited by less than his life?"

"If you value your own, or value those about you, hearken to my words—go not on board that vessel again!"

"Were a thousand—"

"A million of brave men could not save you from certain death! Listen—"

Admiral Tom beat the deck impatiently with his foot.

"From the magazine of the 'San Josef,'" Zelie resumed, "her commander has wires leading to his cabin. A golden tassel, that hangs above his cot, would fire the train that would blow you and your ship into atoms!"

"Enough, Zelie; he shall never reach his cabin to pull that tas—"

A terrible roar at that moment, followed by the recoil of the "Will-o'-the-Wisp," caused the young chieftain to rush upon deck.

It seemed as though Zelie's words were proved, and the pirate ship blown into the air.

Zelie fell upon her knees when the terrible sound burst upon them, and, hiding her face with her hands, prayed for the life of him she loved to be spared.

When Captain Tom rushed on deck, he found the main and foremast hanging over the side, and a number of cannons hurled from their carriages.

A score of his crew were also struck down, and everywhere men were running hurriedly towards the yet undamaged guns.

He looked towards the "San Josef," and an angry exclamation fell from his lips as he beheld the pirate vessel, her yards dressed from deck to truck, sailing swiftly away.

He turned towards his officers to ask an explanation of this sudden change in affairs.

Both Ben Barnacle and Harry Vere were being conveyed below to the care of Dr. Shrike and his man Jacop.

From this sad sight he turned his eyes sorrowfully, and met those of young Harry Martin, who was hastening towards his young chief.

The boy touched his cap respectfully, and said—

"It was not our fault, sir. We followed you closely, but by some misfortune the vessels became separated before Lieutenant Vere, Ben Barnacle, and that brave fellow, Iron Arm, could get aboard."

Captain Tom looked around for the giant form of Iron Arm, and not seeing him, his heart anticipated fatal news.

"We saw them fighting hard with these copper-coloured devils, and made a run to their assistance. We were too late, sir. Mr. Vere and Ben Barnacle had time to jump on board."

"Iron Arm? What of him?" was the anxious query.

"He was struck down, sir, as he leapt on the bulwarks, and either fell overboard, or on the 'San Josef's' deck."

"Curses! I would not have had harm happen to that gallant fellow for the sea's worth."

"We knew that, sir, and made an attempt to board the pirate—this is the result."

He pointed to the broken masts and the torn bulwarks.

The last broadside had done more mischief to the hull of the ship than any engagement the dashing vessel had ever been in previously.

It was the last and only blow the pirates were capable of striking—one that had enabled them to get clear of their determined little foe; and to the Death Pirate's joy, Iron Arm was in his power.

Regret for what had occurred was useless, and the young leader, for the time striving to banish the thought of Iron Arm's probable fate from his mind, set to work to rig jury-masts, and bring the shattered vessel into sailing condition again.

His crew, longing to avenge the loss of those who had fallen, worked with a will, and in three hours the gallant little vessel was cleaving the waters.

The "San Josef" had long since disappeared in the distant horizon, and Admiral Tom, with his dark eyes fixed upon the spot where the last white speck of his foe's sails had sunk into invisibility, stood moodily upon the quarter-deck.

His soul was filled with bitterness as he thought of the fate that his gallant friend would have to meet.

The young buccaneer knew enough of the Death Pirate's pitiless nature to assure him that a sharp and sure death would be the result of Iron Arm's captivity.

Other thoughts added to the intensity of his agony, and he felt as though the mystic voice of Nature whispered strange words respecting Iron Arm to his ears.

The young leader's heart, which, in the hottest

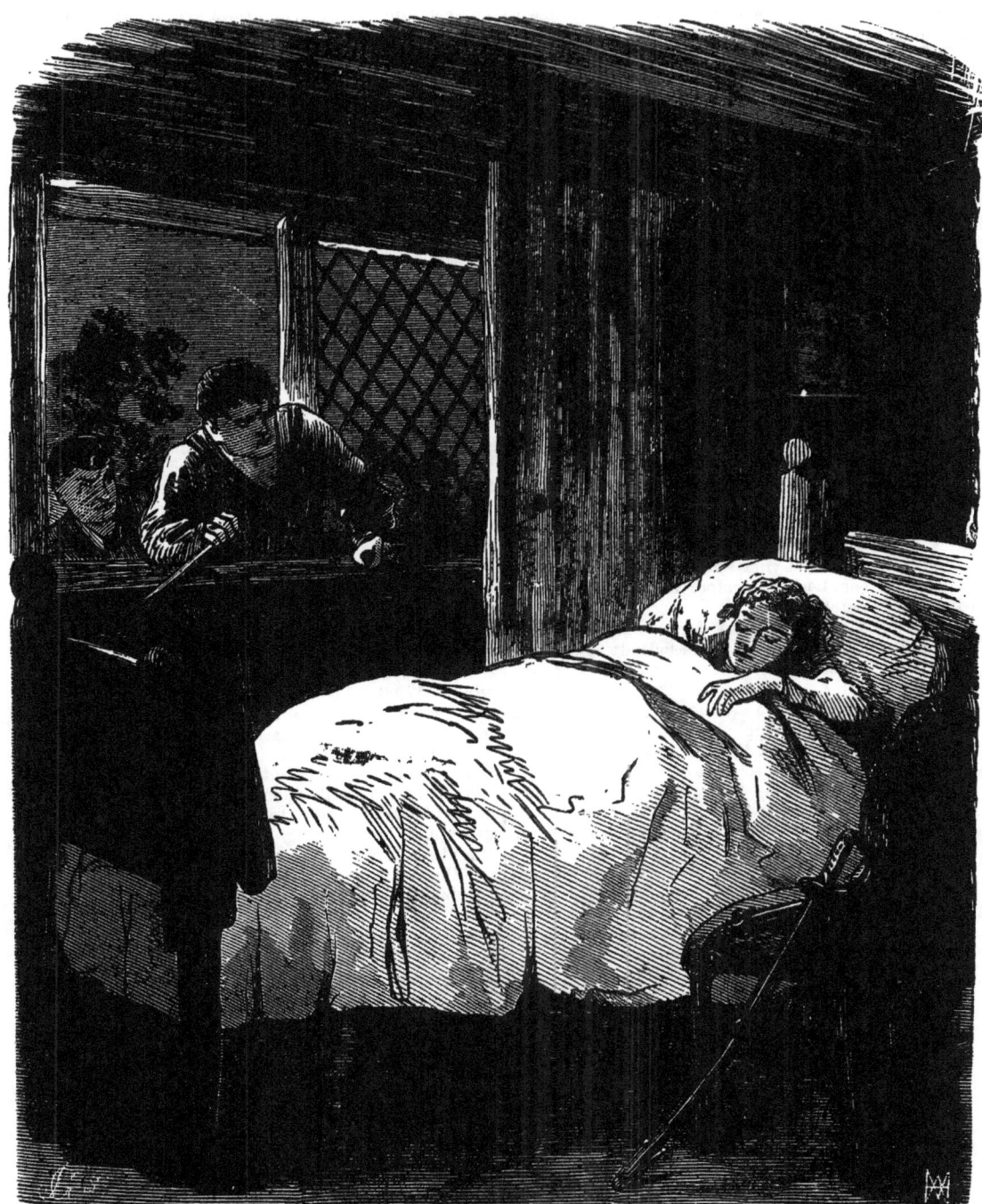

THE ASSASSINS OPENED THE WINDOW AND PEERED INTO THE ROOM.

fire never quickened its pulsation, now beat fast and audible.

The boy's mind had gone back to the time when he knelt at his mother's knees, and uttered a simple prayer for one for whom his little limbs were clothed in solemn garb of mourning.

He remembered once, when borne down by the weight of his childish sorrow, he had strayed from his mother's side, and sought the green fields.

He remembered, while sitting there, and, child-like, wondering why his mother's sweet, sad face should so often be bathed in tears, a tall, handsome stranger who came to his side, and in cheerful tones told him not to weep, for his father would on day return, not from the grave, but from a far-off land, where he was held in bondage.

He remembered, too, the stranger going to their cottage, and, when he followed soon after, seeing his mother clasped to the stranger's breast.

Then came her joyful tones as she bid him kneel and receive a father's blessing.

Then came a chasm in the chain of long-forgotten events.

Then a sad, hideous story of two men dying by each other's hands—one, his father.

The mental torture he suffered when he fancied he recognised the tones of Iron Arm's voice resembled those of his parent, maddened him; and half frenzied with excitement, he involuntarily said—

"No, no! it is too horrible. It is a mere fancied resemblance—"

"To whom?" asked a voice at his side.

Captain Tom turned suddenly, his hand upon the hilt of his sword.

It was withdrawn when he recognised the speaker, and, extending his hand, he said—

"I am glad to see you here. Ben. I fear this day's work has upset me a little."

"Little wonder," said Ben, taking the proffered hand. "It has done the same to us all."

"Are you badly hurt Ben?"

"No. I fell against a gun-carriage and lost my senses. It was lucky I remained there, or I should have received on board this ship what my enemies failed to give me."

"What is that. Ben?"

"My death. That cussed doctor of yours and his phantom were making preparations to take a piece out of my skull."

"They wanted a subject, perhaps."

"They have he now—at least, the doctor has."

"How?"

"I doubled up his mummy, and left the old villain about to bleed his precious Jacop. But, by the way, what were you raving about when I came on deck? It must have been something more than usual to have stirred your nature."

Captain Tom hesitated before he answered Ben's direct interrogation.

The boy's rapid, brilliant career since he had spurned the hateful yoke of servitude under his worst foes had shut him off from the companionship of men.

As commander of the vessel which now bore him so swiftly over the rippling waters, he could not freely associate with his officers, could not maintain discipline by a free interchange of thought.

When Ben spoke, he felt the need of a companion—such a companion that could calm his perturbed spirit, and drive away the melancholy which hung over his soul.

"I was much disturbed," Tom said, at length. "The excitement caused by the loss of the man who so nobly saved me from death, brought a long-forgotten episode of my life before me."

"You allude to Iron Arm?"

"I do."

Ben's features changed slightly, but his dark, earnest gaze was fixed upon his young leader's face.

"From what I could gather," Ben said, "from your disjointed words, this Iron Arm bore a resemblance to one whose memory is fraught with pain?"

"You are correct in your supposition, Ben; but, after all, I must be wrong—he perished years ago."

"Of whom do you speak?"

"My father."

Ben Barnacle's face changed, and for a moment his breast rose and fell under an intensity of feeling that was unusual to him.

"Your father?" he repeated, and his lips quivered strangely as he spoke; "did you associate this being with your father's memory?"

"I did. What is the matter, Ben? You are pale."

"Nothing—the effect of my fall," he said, with a sickly smile; "I find I must go below—I am yet too weak to stay on deck."

Captain Tom gazed earnestly into Ben's face.

"Ben Barnacle," the young chief said, "you are acquainted with my past life."

"Ha! I? No—you are mistaken."

"I am not. More than once words have fallen from your lips that have proved the truth of this.

Tell me, I implore you, am I right in my conjecture?"

"I will. You are not; I swear by the sacred canopy above us, you are not."

"Is he of my blood? Have we met before?"

"You have met. More I cannot—dare not tell you now."

"Sail ho!"

The voice of the look-out stopped any further conversation, and as the young chief seized his glass, Ben Barnacle, pale with ill-suppressed emotion, left the quarter-deck.

"Sail ho!" came from the maintop again, and the cry was taken up by the man on the forecastle.

"Where away?" asked the young captain.

"On the weather-quarter, sir."

"Can you make her out, Stevens?"

"Not distinctly, sir. There's a mist over the sea which partially hides her hull and lower rigging."

By the aid of his powerful glass the young chief saw the strange sail beating up to windward.

It was not the "San Josef" he knew by the difference in size, and glad of anything to break the heavy weight upon his spirits, he had the crew beat to quarters and everything made ready to give the stranger a warm reception if necessary.

There was something in the appearance of the stranger that puzzled Captain Tom.

One moment she would seem as though about to bear down upon him, the next she would start off upon a directly opposite course.

Watching the ship closely, the young chief said to Harry Martin—

"She seems as though she were drifting before the wind. What do you think?"

"I have thought so for some time, sir, but did not like to make the remark."

"Strange," mused the youthful leader; "there have been no storms lately. Surely the vessel cannot have been abandoned."

He placed his glass to bear upon the stranger's decks, her hull having by this time become distinguishable by the naked eye.

What he saw sent a red spot to his cheeks, and turning to Harry Martin, he said—

"Pipe all hands below. This is an empty vessel."

The crew, relieved from their stations, crowded to the side to gaze upon and wonder at the strange behaviour of the coming vessel.

It was near evening when the "Will-o'-the-Wisp" ranged alongside.

Captain Tom's words were verified. The brig was deserted, and at the mercy of wind and waves.

The "Will-o'-the-Wisp" was brought round to the wind. The sails for a moment flapped against the masts.

The young chief, though watching the coming vessel, turned his eagle glance upon the sail-trimmers and asked, sternly—

"Do you wish that vessel to run into us?"

The men were silent, and hung down their heads.

In their eagerness to execute the order that would bring them alongside the stranger, they had allowed the wind to be forced out of their sails.

Captain Tom turned to the helmsman, and said—

"This is partly your fault."

"I put the helm down, sir," was the reply, "as ordered by the officer of the watch."

Captain Tom walked quickly to the wheel, and, seizing the spokes, said—

"Yes, you did! A landsman could have done it as well. Look, here, sir."

The man's face coloured at his young leader's rebuke.

"Bear in mind," he continued, suiting the action to the word, "put the helm down spoke by spoke, not suddenly, by doing so the ship loses her way; do it slowly, and she keeps her velocity in coming to the wind."

He resigned the wheel as he spoke, and the helmsman, looking after his light form, muttered—

"I'd sooner have three dozen any time than one of his quiet looks."

The young chief went back to his station on the quarter-deck, and, in a voice that could be heard all over the ship, said—

"Mainsail haul."

There was a whistling noise as the after-braces and bowlines were let go, and the yards hauled up on the other tack.

Then followed the order—

"Head braces—fore tack—head bowlines."

"Mr. Martin!"

"Aye, aye, sir!"

"Take a turn with the weather topsail braces, or we shall have the yards flying fore and aft!"

With a promptitude and exactness that would have done credit to the smartest man-of-war, these orders were carried out, and the vessel was soon brought alongside the stranger.

It was not the work of a minute to throw the grappling-irons; the next, the young chief, followed by Ben Barnacle and several of the crew, went on board.

To the strongest-nerved men there is always a strange felling of awe comes over their minds when boarding a deserted vessel upon the wide ocean.

The quietude of the decks, the sails set, perhaps, for the very reverse weather in which the desolate bark is found.

The mystery that attaches to her being in this lone state tends to augment this strange sensation, and make the flesh creep as the thought of some fearful fate having come upon the crew will force itself upon the mind.

The buccaneers paused for some minutes upon the deck, and gazed with saddened feelings upon a crimson stain near the step of the main-mast.

"There has been foul work here," said Captain Tom. "Follow me! we shall, perhaps, find the solution of that red trail!"

He went quickly down the after-hatch, followed by his men, Ben Barnacle muttering—

"The Death Pirate's work, or I'm much at fault."

They were soon clustered at the open door of the state-room—clustered in a silent, horrified group at the terrible sight within.

Some of the bodies were yet warm, and the blood slowly oozing from deep and ghastly wounds.

A group of slain men and women, some of the latter scarcely in the first bloom of womanhood, lay upon the ensanguined carpet.

To fill the horrible picture, two infants were pinned by long knives to the panels of the cabin.

Not a word was spoken by the buccaneers until their young leader, plucking one of the weapons that had drunk the innocent babe's life from the little corpse, took it to the light, and said, in a hushed voice—

"It is a Moorish weapon. Here is the clue to the foul deed."

A whisper began among the men, until it rose, and was taken from lip to lip, and the words, swelling into a chorus, proclaimed the miscreant who had suffered this deed to be committed.

"The Death Pirate!"

"You are right, my lads, it is his fell work, and he cannot be far away from us."

The boy lowered his knee, and, raising his right arm on high, said, vehemently—

"Hear, and aid me, kind Heaven, in my vow to sweep this demon from the sea!"

The buccaneers bowed their knees as their young leader spoke, and many silently prayed that the vow might be registered above.

Ben Barnacle, who had turned away from the sad sight, and gone down the fore-hatch, soon returned.

"The crew," he said, "some eighteen hands, are lying butchered in the fore-cabin."

A groan burst from the buccaneers, and, with reverential tread, they left the scene of slaughter.

Upon a closer examination of the vessel, it was found that her hold was filled with rich merchandise, and the buccaneers, returning to the deck, gathered round their young leader.

"They must," he said, alluding to the slain passengers and crew, "have been murdered as they slept."

"Such is my opinion," said Ben; "unless from the fact of their all being dressed, the pirate took them by surprise, and, driving them below, carried out his hellish work."

"It is useless," said Captain Tom, "to waste time in idle conjecture. They are all barbarously slain, and we must avenge them!"

"One word!" said Ben, suddenly. "The object of this slaughter was plunder, yet not a cask or bale of goods has been touched!"

There was a dead silence for several minutes; this mystery caused many conjectures, but none spoke until the young chief.

"There is," he said, "but one hypothesis for this—the bloodthirsty gang must have been disturbed either by a fresh victim or a man-of-war."

"Look there!" suddenly shouted one of the seamen. "Here's something alive!"

He looked aft as he spoke, and the eyes of the party following his movement, saw just above the hatch a black, shining face, and a set of white, gleaming teeth.

The buccaneer soon returned to the astonished party with the owner of the shining ebony face and white teeth, the latter chattering with the quick convulsive movement of the lower jaw.

The poor wretch was evidently in a state of the most abject terror, for no sooner did he behold the glittering form of Captain Tom than he threw himself upon his knees, and, lifting the whites of his large eyes, he said—

"Gorramity; massa! listen to a poor ole Coromante! For de Lord sake do, massa, an now let 'em kill me!"

While the poor fellow was speaking, the young chief had time to scan the general appearance of the kneeling supplicant.

He was a true negro in every sense of the word. Black as night, a skull large, and crowned with crisp, woolly hair; his ears, large and broad, stood out prominently from the sides of his head, and at any other time would have given him a ludicrous appearance.

His purple lips were of great thickness, and extended almost from ear to ear; but for the horrified expression of his eyes, the negro's facial outlines would have been irresistably comic.

"You have nothing to fear," said Captain Tom, kindly; "there is no one here that will kill you."

Somewhat reassured by the young chieftain's voice, and the pitying faces of those around, the black arose, and leaning against the mainmast, gave vent to a burst of grief.

When he had become sufficiently calmed to answer, the young chief asked—

Can you give me any information respecting this fearful massacre ?"

" Tell you, massa, how de crew am killed ?" asked the black, with a shudder.

" Yes."

" Just dis, sar. We lying on de water like a log ob 'hogany, when up come big ship, an' a lot ob debbils come aboard shrieking, an' drive us all below ; den, massa—oh, gorramity !"

The black covered his face with his hands, and his whole frame shook violently with emotion.

" The crew and passengess were all killed," said the young chief, finishing the sentence for the trembling black. " Is it so ?"

" It am, sar ; ebery one die, ebery one."

" You, how did you escape ?"

" I was feard, massa, an' hid behind de locker until dey go."

" Did you see any of the men who boarded your vessel ?"

" Ebery one, sar."

" Did you notice anything particular about them ?"

" I did, massa. Dey look jes like dibbils, an' one ob dem had him face all bone."

" A skeleton face ?"

" Jes so, sar, dat it."

" The Death Pirate, to a certainty," said Ben. " How is it, I wonder, they did not touch the cargo ?"

" Hem hab no chance, sar."

" How was that ?"

" 'Cos a man-ob-war come up an' fire gun, den de debbils ran from hyar, an' de man-ob-war follow, fire guns all de time."

A flush spread over the young chief's face as he said—

" There is not a vessel in the navy that can overtake the ' San Josef ;' we shall be in time, my lads, to grapple with the miscreants."

" What are we to do with this vessel ?" Ben Barnacle asked.

" I should like, had we time," said Captain Tom, " to unship her masts, but it cannot be done ; we must trust to our broken spars holding together until we overtake the ' San Josef,' then to port and refit. Go below, some of you, and scuttle this hapless bark."

The men hurried away, and the young chief, turning to the black, said—

" If you have anything on board you wish to save get it, for we shall soon be on the track of the villains who did this foul deed."

" I hab nothing, sar ; me only de cook ob dis vessel ; if 'em had woudn't take 'em, dey look always like blood."

Large holes were soon made in the vessel's bottom, and the buccaneers went on board their ship.

As fast as the damaged rigging and imperfect mast would permit, the " Will-o'-the-Wisp " sped through the water.

When the evening shadows began to fall upon the restless face of the deep, the scuttled bark, with her ghastly freight, went to the bottom.

Many eyes watched the ill-fated ship as she sank, and all felt a cold weight lifted from their hearts when the waters closed over her.

The Coromante, much to his joy, was placed in the caboose of the buccaneers's ship ; and, after the terrible scenes he had witnessed passed from his mind, he became an endless source (as will be seen hereafter) of amusement to the fun-loving middies of Captain Tom's vessel.

Not a man left the " Will-o'-the-Wisp's " deck that night.

The story of the heartless massacre had been told by those who went on board the silent ship of death.

Long and wearily the darkness passed away, and morning came without bringing any tidings of the " San Josef " or her pursuer.

Had the miscreant band escaped the man-of-war, or had the latter, by an unlucky shot from the pirate, been blown into atoms ?

Again, had the " San Josef " been destroyed by the war-ship ?—if so, what had become of Iron Arm ?

These and other equally perplexing thoughts passed through the young leader's mind, and left him as anxious and perplexed as when he first started in pursuit of the destroyer.

As the evening wore on, the wind freshened, and Captain Tom, to his annoyance, found his shot-torn spars were incapable of standing long against the elements.

CHAPTER LI.

ADMIRAL TOM IN DANGER.

In that out-of-the-way port, where the " Yellow Vulture " lay at anchor beneath the guns of a British line-of-battle ship, the " Will-o'-the-Wisp " glided gracefully towards the inner harbour.

The splendid vessel was much altered ; a violent storm had carried away her foremast and her maintop, and it had tried the skill of her young commander to make this offing in safety.

The crew had changed as much as the vessel. Ben Barnacle now wore the undress uniform of captain.

Captain Tom that of a second lieutenant.

The crew were also dressed in seamen's usual neat costume, and wore round their glazed hats in golden letters—

The " Sea Hawk."

Under the very bows of the huge three-decker, the " Sea Hawk," in spite of her battle with the Moors and the angry elements, glided swan-like towards her anchorage.

Her officers for the time were grouped upon the quarter-deck, Ben Barnacle looking every inch a captain ; Harry Vere his first lieutenant, and Captain Tom his second.

Under the formidable triple row of gun-muzzles the buccaneers passed in safety, and were upon the point of rounding the entrance to the inner basin, when Ben said, in a low voice—

" Dutch Paul's vessel under the liner's bows !"

Too well trained to turn suddenly towards the object of Ben's exclamation, Captain Tom left the quarter-deck as though upon a matter of duty, and, leaning over the side, pretended to be examining the main-chains with a proper zeal for a young officer.

When he rejoined his companions, there was a smile upon his face that betrayed some new and daring project at work within.

" You are quite correct, Ben," he said ; " it is Dutch Paul."

" Did you see him ?"

" Yes ; he was seated upon a gun, smoking his cigar as quietly as though that line-of-battle ship were a hundred miles away."

Ben laughed as he said—

" The admiral on board his Britannic Majesty's ship would not believe that a freebooter could dare such a close proximity to his effulgent self."

" Why ?"

" The very fact of the ' Yellow Vulture ' being here is her safeguard."

" I do not quite see it."

" No ? Well, for argument's sake, suppose this vessel was commanded by a post-captain ; suppose, also, this vessel carried the British flag."

" Well ?"

" And her commander knew Dutch Paul, and as

he came into this port he ranged alongside and ordered her to surrender."

"Yes. Well?"

"What do you think would be the consequence?'

"A fight, perhaps, for Dutch Paul is not the man to yield without a blow."

"Nothing of the sort."

Captain Tom looked astonished, and asked—

"Have you taken leave of your senses, Ben?"

"No; the explanation is easy. If Dutch Paul refused to surrender, the post-captain would not dare to fire a shot in port without the admiral's permission."

"Which he would soon give."

"Wrong again. He would order the captain to take his vessel into the inner harbour, and give Dutch Paul a hint."

"A hint?"

"Yes. For instance, if he did not make his way out of port in a given time there would be a possibility of the three-decker opening fire upon him."

"Why all this?" asked Captain Tom. "Surely the liner could capture the 'Yellow Vulture.'"

"Wrong again. Do you think his admiralship—if I may use the word—would allow such a report to reach the Home Government?"

"What report?"

"That he was quietly at anchor with a notorious pirate under his bows without knowing it until a junior officer came in and wanted to grapple with the light-heeled gentleman."

"I begin to understand," said Captain Tom, laughingly; "such a proceeding would not add to the admiral's vigilance."

"Precisely. You see we have passed him without questioning, simply because, in self-conceit, he imagines the very sight of his ship would be enough to terrify any roving gentleman, and prevent him from entering the harbour."

"In which his self-conceit much misleads him. Hallo! what is this? This corvette is making direct for us. Be on the alert, men! One false move, and we shall be blown out of the water. Now, Ben, ready for that fellow; he is about to hail."

Closely following the "Will-o'-the-Wisp" was a heavily-armed corvette, the red cross of England fluttering at her peak.

In spite of the buccaneers' hardihood, many intuitively turned away from the swiftly-coming vessel; even the dauntless young leader paled a little.

It was the uncertainty of the subject that brought the corvette so closely upon them which caused this state of feeling on board the "Will-o'-the-Wisp."

The suspense was soon over, and the buccaneers breathed freely again.

When the corvette became abeam of the "Will-o'-the-Wisp," an officer, holding on by the shrouds, called out—

"Lay to—we want to speak with you!"

The vessel's progress had been arrested, and, the corvette drifting closely alongside, the following conversation took place between Ben and the officer who had first hailed—

"You came in," said the latter, "by the rocky headland?"

"We did."

"Did you see any boats creeping close in-shore?"

"None," answered Ben; "have you lost any?"

"No," was the reply; "we have chased a rascally pirate until he run aground, and before we could and with our boats the gang escaped."

Ben and his young leader exchanged a look as the same thought came to their minds, that beside them was the vessel which had driven the Death Pirate from his stricken prey.

To make sure, Ben asked, carelessly—

"Was it a Moorish vessel?"

"It was. Do you know her?"

"Our spars," said Ben, "are the mark of our acquaintance."

The officer's eyes brightened.

"Then you have had a brush with the devils?"

"Yes," said Ben. "Had not their cursed shot crippled us, that little bark would not have fallen into their hands."

"You came in with the merchant ship, then?"

"We did."

"Any left alive?"

"One, a black. He told us you were upon the pirate's heels."

"Poor devils. I wish we had been in time to have saved that crew. I have ordered a party to pursue them, should they go ashore. What is the name of your ship?"

"The 'Sea Hawk,' letter of marque."

"Mine is the 'Venus.' Shall I see you ashore this evening? I must go and report to old Blueblazes, or shall get a wigging."

"Blueblazes!"

"The admiral on board that liner. Good-bye—get refitted. Want any help?"

"None, thank you, we are pretty strong handed. By the way, where will you be this evening?"

"At the hotel. I had forgotten to tell you, we captured one of the pirate's gang, though he stands out that he was a prisoner on board, and belonged to a privateer."

Captain Tom and Ben Barnacle started. They would have made inquiries respecting the prisoner, but were saved the trouble by the loquacious officer.

"He is a splendid fellow," he went on. "You will see him, I dare say, when he is taken to the prison, ashore. Good-bye."

"Good-bye," said Ben. "Make your report; I see the admiral is on the forecastle watching us."

The officer jumped down, and soon after the corvette put about, and ranged under the frowning hull of the line-of-battle ship.

Not a shadow of doubt existed as to the identity of the prisoner on board the "Venus;" "it could be no other," argued Captain Tom, mentally, "than Iron Arm."

Why he yet lived was easy of explanation—the Death Pirate probably intended to wreak a terrible vengeance upon his late follower, but waited until a more favourable time, there being the dauntless "Will-o'-the-Wisp" in his wake.

The young chief, carried away by his mental argument, and allowing for no possibility of mistake, turned to Ben Barnacle and seized his arm.

"Ben," he said, passionately, "he is a prisoner. Come what may, I will rescue him."

"From the corvette? It would be madness."

"I will make the attempt—twice he saved my life. Think you I would see him perish?"

"You would belie your nature, did you do so. This matter requires a cooler brain than yours is at the present moment."

"Ben—"

"Now spare your anger, and listen calmly to me. The attempt must not be made while he is on board the corvette."

"There is no other chance."

"There is; you forget that he will soon be taken ashore."

"I did," said the impetuous boy. "I will way-lay the boat."

"And draw the fire from these men-of-war upon you!"

"How, then? What is your plan?"

"To wait until he is in the prison, find out where he is confined; then, if we have to burrow like rats beneath the old building, we will release him or fall in the attempt."

Captain Tom's reply was stopped by the report of a gun from the direction of the inner harbour.

Turning quickly, he beheld a long, rakish-looking craft, carrying the Brazilian colours, saluting the line-of-battle ship.

Under the influence of some strange feeling, the young chief could not withdraw his eyes from the Brazilian ship.

It seemed to fascinate him, and putting the glass to his eye, he scanned the deck.

Upon the poop he beheld a young officer in the splendid uniform of the Brazilian Navy.

Though the face was turned away from him, there was something in the officer's appearance that seemed familiar.

Many minutes passed before he could take the glass away.

When he did, he mentioned his suspicions to Ben Barnacle.

"Your mind is disturbed by the events of the past two days," Ben said. "Go below, and calm yourself. We have much to do, and coolness, with promptitude, will be required."

Had Captain Tom remembered the conversation he held with Iron Arm when they were upon the ocean, he would have known why the Brazilian ship and its commander so forcibly arrested his attention.

Too much absorbed by the capture of his favourite, the warning had not recurred to his mind.

When in the act of stepping below, the voice of Ben Barnacle arrested him.

"Here is the Brazilian," he said; "you can have a closer view of your fancied acquaintance."

Captain Tom sprang lightly to his side, and his dark, earnest eyes were fixed upon the stout Brazilian vessel.

She glided gracefully past the "Will-o'-the-Wisp," so close that the features of the swarthy crew became plainly visible.

The officer with the heavy golden epaulettes was not upon the poop.

His place was filled by a tall, bearded officer, evidently of inferior grade to the gold-bedizened youth who had so powerfully attracted Captain Tom's attention.

Though Ben Barnacle and his young leader anxiously scanned every face as the vessel glided onward, they failed to discover him they sought.

Had they by chance directed their gaze towards one of the after-ports, they would have seen the face of the Brazilian commander peering up at them from behind a gun.

Had they looked a little further, they would also have seen a second face, not so young or so fair-skinned as the first, upturned towards the place where Captain Tom stood.

From the Brazilian commander's gestures, and the movement of his companion's eyes, it was evident that the former was pointing our hero out to his swarthy companion.

They saw not this, and the smart-looking vessel passed round and anchored close under the shore batteries.

Not long after this occurrence a boat left the "Venus."

The crew of the "Will-o'-the-Wisp" had got, by some unaccountable means, the knowledge that Iron Arm was in the corvette's boat, and, anxious to have a glance at the man who had so imperilled his life for their beloved young leader, they stood in groups, waiting for the boat to pass.

The glittering of bayonets in the stern of the coming boat showed that a prisoner was there, and closely guarded.

When it passed close under the buccaneer's quarter, officers and men beheld the colossal form of Iron Arm, heavily manacled, and surrounded by marines.

The strange being looked up, and his eyes met Captain Tom's.

Beyond a meaning look and a slight inclination of his head towards the shore, he betrayed no knowledge of the "Will-o'-the-Wisp."

"What does he mean," asked the young leader, "by that meaning look and gesture?"

"Perhaps," said Ben Barnacle, "it was to imply silence on your part."

"No," said Captain Tom, "that could not have been his meaning, there was something of deeper import in it than that—he knows well that we shall not betray our knowledge of him."

"I can form no conception of the warning—we shall, perhaps, know more when we see him to-night."

"That," said the young buccaneer, "is too great an uncertainty; the walls of the old castle are strong."

"True," said Ben, "but our teeth are stronger. Now, go below for an hour, it will be sundown then, and dark in a few minutes."

Ben was right, there is no twilight in the tropics.

Counting the minutes as they passed, the young chief kept on deck.

Ben's advice was kindly meant, but the excitement under which our hero was suffering was too great to admit of any repose.

The last gleam of the setting sun had barely died away when Captain Tom stepped into the gig, and gave the word for his men to row him ashore.

No definite plan had yet been agreed upon between Ben Barnacle and his young leader, and the fiery boy, not deigning to listen to Ben's cooler advice, determined to go ashore alone, and reconnoitre the prison.

Both Harry Vere and Ben Barnacle offered to accompany him—an offer which he refused.

While the boat was being lowered, Ben whispered in young Harry Martin's ear—

"Follow your chief when he gets ashore, and see that he does not want assistance. Take this rocket, and should anything go amiss, we will soon come to the rescue. Be careful he does not see you."

Harry Martin nodded a reply, and putting the rocket beneath his vest, he stepped into the boat.

That precaution saved Captain Tom's life.

When the keel of the boat grated upon the bank our hero stepped ashore, and wrapping his cloak around him, he strode towards the old castle, which was used as a prison by the authorities.

Almost at the same instant that our hero's feet touched the ground, a light skiff shot from under the bows of the Brazilian vessel.

A few strokes brought the light craft ashore, and a man (the same who had been watching Captain Tom from the gun-port) jumped out, and followed the young buccaneer.

Harry Martin waited until his chieftain had gone some distance, then, seizing a thick club, he followed.

The boy was not long on the track of his youthful leader before he became aware that a second man was dogging Tom's form.

He saw, too—and his heart leaped to his throat —that the stranger had a long, gleaming blade in his hand.

There could be no mistaking his motive for this, and Harry, creeping warily upon the would-be assassin, waited until the moment came for him to strike.

The action came.

Captain Tom turned the angle of the old castle, and, keeping his eyes towards the massive gates, as though debating whether the tough old house was capable of standing a siege, strode moodily on.

The assassin chose this moment to put his fell project into execution, and, gliding towards the unsuspecting boy, raised the keen blade on high.

Another second, and it would have been planted in the young chief's back.

But, before the blow could be struck, the assassin was felled to the ground by a blow from Harry Martin's club.

Captain Tom turned at the sound, and his sword leapt from its scabbard.

He saw at a glance what had occurred, and, thanking young Harry, he placed his foot upon the fellow's breast and prevented him from rising.

"Mercy!" cried the wretch. "Mercy! I will tell you who bribed me to do this deed."

The keen point of Captain Tom's sword was at the fellow's throat, and his dark eyes, flashing with anger, boded but scant mercy for the hired assassin.

He looked from the trembling wretch to Harry Martin's face, and withdrew his hand to strike; then, as though yielding to the wish to know who had sent this fellow forth to slay him, he lowered the point of his weapon.

CHAPTER LII.

CAPTAIN TOM OFFERS HIS SERVICES TO DUTCH PAUL.

"What mercy," said the young leader, "would you have shown me, had not my faithful follower stayed your murderous hand?"

The assassin made no reply.

Harry Martin whispered a few words in his young leader's ear, and Captain Tom, putting his sword-point at the fellow's throat, said, sternly—

"You plead for your life; I will grant it upon one condition."

The assassin's lips unclosed, and he uttered a joyful cry.

"Anything, senor," he said, "anything I will agree to."

"Very well. Now tell me, and beware how you answer, who sent you upon this errand?"

"Captain Gompertz, senor."

"Captain Gompertz," repeated the young chief. "I do not even know the name. Is he a Spaniard?"

"No, senor; English, like yourself. I know not his proper name; this is the name by which he is known in the Brazilian service."

"The Brazilian service! Now, by Heaven! a light breaks in upon me; it is Reuben Harpy."

The conversation he had held with Iron Arm when they sprang from the bulwarks of the Moorish vessel came to the young buccaneer's mind.

Bitterly lamenting the evil fortune that had placed his friend within the walls of the old citadel, Captain Tom turned to Harry Martin, saying—

"Guard that fellow while I reconnoitre this place. I must save Iron Arm; his services are of more value now than ever."

Reuben Harpy's emissary was deprived of his weapons, and young Martin, standing over him with the massive club, awaited his leader's return.

It was a stronghold of grim and sombre aspect, the old castle of San Lois.

As our hero approached the gates, his mind misgave him at the prospect of gaining admittance.

In his chequered life he had found that a bold stroke had often served his purpose better than diplomacy, and in this instance, though despairing of success, he walked to the massive gates, and applied the hilt of his sabre smartly to the old woodwork.

His imperious summons brought a grim-visaged official to a small grating in the gate, who roughly demanded the young chief's motive for being there.

Captain Tom looked at the Cerberus, and knowing that men were pretty much of the same stamp when in office—as far as fees are concerned—adroitly passing a golden doubloon through the grating, which shining coin, much to our hero's gratification, was grabbed by a very dirty hand, he said—

"I have called to see the governor of San Lois; he is within the castle, I presume?"

The gatekeeper's fingers were closing upon the piece of gold, and in a less surly tone than before, he answered—

"He is, senor; but unless you are a friend you will not be admitted."

A second golden piece passed through the small iron bars.

"I am not a personal friend of the worthy governor's," said Captain Tom, blandly; "but having important business with him, I shall be glad if you will convey a message."

The pair of golden coins jingled musically in the gatekeeper's ears, and under its influence, he said—

"I will bear your message, senor."

"Thanks! Tell his Excellency that an officer of the Spanish Navy would speak with him upon affairs of State."

"I will, senor."

The wicket closed, and the daring boy heard the man's heavy footsteps as he passed towards the governor's apartments.

"Now," thought Captain Tom, "for a story to tickle his Excellency's ears—if," he added aloud, "I get inside."

The man returned after a few minutes' absence and said, through the grating—

"His Excellency desires you will forward your name."

Captain Tom had not thought of one sufficiently impressive. In order to gain time to hit upon a title that would aid his design, the young captain opened his tablets, and said—

"This is very unusual—very; but I must comply as the matter in hand will admit of no delay. Take his Excellency this."

He gave the man a leaf bearing the words—

DON VINCENT VELASCO.
A.D.C. to His Majesty Ferdinand II.

The man caught sight of the second line, and bowed nearly double. The presence of one of the King's aides-de-camp was not of daily occurrence.

Carrying the white tablet as though it was a thing too sacred for his dusky fingers, he hurried away.

Captain Tom looked after him and muttered—

"Should his Excellency be acquainted with the gentleman whose name I have taken the liberty to borrow, I shall most certainly not sleep on board the 'Will-o'-the-Wisp' to-night."

The messenger soon came back, and, after a few minutes spent in withdrawing the rusty bolts, the doors were thrown open.

Our hero strode inside, and followed a man who had come to conduct him to his Excellency's presence.

When the daring boy entered the large stone chamber, where sat the great man, his pulse beat a little quicker than its wont.

It was a moment of peril for him. One false move would be the precursor of a long and hopeless incarceration—the end, death!

He would be treated as a spy and possibly hung at the eastern gate.

The Governor of San Lois was a small, wiry man, whose snow-like hair and beard told of long years passed in the service of the State.

His eyes, deep set, dark, and penetrating, were fixed upon our hero as he entered the room.

The thought uppermost in Captain Tom's mind was that of being discovered; an event that seemed not unlikely to happen, as the governor, when the first greetings were over, said—

"How time does change us, Don Vincent; it seems but a few years since that I danced you upon my knee. I suppose you scarcely remember that?"

Captain Tom, with good reason, replied in the negative.

"Ah, well," said the old gentleman, "you young gallants soon forget your early friends. I hope your good old father has a better memory for his old companion-in-arms."

Captain Tom took the cue immediately, and acted upon it.

"He has," he said; "for it was only upon the previous night to my departure from Madrid that he spoke of you."

"Did he? Did he?" The governor rubbed his hands gleefully. "Yes, and what, Don Vincent, did he speak of—our campaign in Morocco, or the great siege of Arras?"

While the governor was speaking, the young chief felt he would have given much to have known the old gentleman's name. Perhaps fortune would favour him, he thought.

"Arras," Tom said—the governor had placed the word "great" before it, and this acted as a second cue—"in fact, your Excellency, I believe that great siege will live for ever in my venerated father's mind;" then, as a feeler, he added, "I think, not without good reason, if report speaks true of the deeds performed by two officers, who shall be nameless."

"What, do they speak of it now?"—the small eyes sparkled with delight as he spoke—"one would think the country would forget it. You see, I am so much out of the world here, that I know nothing, really nothing. So they really speak of the great siege, and tell how your father and myself led the assault."

"Such deeds," said Captain Tom, readily, "live for ever."

The old soldier's eyes glistened with pride.

"It is our only reward, Don Vincent," he said. "The fame, but little else, has fallen to my lot; your father is different, he has much to be grateful for."

"Very much."

"By the way, my dear boy, you have not told me how fares your sister Beatrice; she gave promise of great beauty."

"She is, indeed, beautiful."

The old soldier was rapidly drifting into an embarrassing topic for our hero; he began to regret having chosen the name of the young Spanish aide-de-camp.

He would soon have more cause for regret.

"And Isolina, your eldest sister," the old fellow asked, "is she still with—"

A servant entered at this moment, and gave the governor a letter.

"Still with," thought Captain Tom, "with what, or whom, I wonder?"

The old veteran, after scanning the first lines of the letter he had received, looked in our hero's face, and burst into a fit of laughter.

Captain Tom, wondering at the cause of this cachinnation, waited until it was over in no very amiable state of mind.

"You young rascal," the old fellow said, "not to tell me about this—just like you—even when a boy you were full of tricks."

Captain Tom, at a loss to understand the affinity of the letter with his visit, knew not what to say, so laughed also.

"You must have outstripped your messenger," said the governor. "Here is your father's letter, apprising me of your coming, and the handsome present he has sent his old friend."

"The devil!" was Tom's mental ejaculation. "This is getting warm."

"I expect your young blood would not keep pace with the bearer of this," said his Excellency "Eh, Vincent?"

Captain Tom admitted the truth of the old gentleman's surmise, and evidently wondered how this was all to end.

"Your father," said the constable of San Lois "tells me here that you are wonderfully altered. So you are. He does not mention anything about the State affairs that brought you here. Had you not told me, I should have thought your visit was, as he describes it, one of a private, friendly nature."

Our hero felt himself getting rapidly into a dilemma—in other words, a fix.

Not a muscle of his face moved as he drew his chair closer to the governor, and said, in a confidential tone—

"State secrets are never trusted to more than is necessary."

"True, Vincent, true!"

"The King and myself only know the object of my visit here; you will be the third and only confidant."

The governor began to feel important, and said—

"A wise precaution, perhaps."

"A necessary one," said the young adventurer. "You see, he knew so little of my movements that he could not tell you when I should arrive."

"True, Vincent; he says, to-morrow at daybreak."

The young chief felt grateful for this intelligence, he already had a plan for preventing the real Don Vincent Velasco from visiting the castle until Iron Arm should be rescued.

"He was not far out in the time," said Captain Tom; "but I hope before then to have explained my mission; we will enter into family details afterwards."

"Spoken like a true servant of the State, Vincent. Suppose we go into that now."

"Perhaps it will be as well," said our hero; "so I will explain our Royal master's wishes at once."

The old Castilian put on a proper majesty of mien to receive the commands or wishes of his Royal master.

"State reasons," began Captain Tom, "render it imperative that a certain number of political prisoners should be placed in a remote part of our possessions."

"Yes, yes; exactly."

"Therefore his Majesty, in selecting the old castle of San Lois, in Baracoa, does so with a full knowledge of the capabilities of its governor."

The old fellow's face shone with pleasure.

"Does his Majesty know me?" he asked. "Do you really say that he knows me?"

"Perfectly," was the cool answer. "There's little but comes to the ears of his Majesty."

"But in this out-of-the-way spot?"

"You are," said Captain Tom, "as well known as though you had charge of the arsenal at Madrid."

"As well known, how?"

"There are secret agents at all times in the State service."

"I understand. Yes. Well, you were saying—"

"That it may be necessary to make this place a

political prison, and for that purpose I have come to examine every chamber and dungeon."

"A prudent measure on his Majesty's part When will you commence the investigation, to-night?"

"Not to-night," said our hero. "To-morrow morning at sunrise you may expect me."

"Surely you are not going away to-night?"

"I must."

"Must! how is that?"

"I may tell you in confidence, I suppose?"

"I am as silent as the tomb."

"Well, the fact is I have to watch the movements of a certain vessel in the harbour. That done, we can go over the castle."

"To-morrow morning?"

"Yes. Then I will bring the present from Madrid."

"A glass of wine before you go."

Captain Tom, while speaking, had risen from his chair, preparatory to leaving.

"No, thank you," he said; "I must keep my head clear to-night."

The old soldier arose, and accompanied him to the gate. As they were parting, he whispered—

"A safe issue from your mission."

"Thanks; good night."

"Good night."

"Well so far," muttered our hero. "By what happy chance or luck did I pitch upon young Velasco's name? Who would have supposed that he had an acquaintance in this place?"

He walked quickly towards the spot where he had left Harry Martin guarding the captive.

To his surprise he found them both gone. Standing for a moment to look round, he beheld a close huddled heap near the base of the castle wall.

The young chief's heart misgave him, and, going towards the dark object, he found his fears realised.

It was the senseless form of Harry Martin, his face pale and blood-stained, and his clothes torn, as though a struggle had taken place.

Stooping over the stricken boy, Captain Tom raised his pale face, and bent his stately knee, to listen for a token of life.

A slight respiration relieved the young chief's anxiety, and, chafing his stricken follower's temples, he sought to restore his faculties.

With a start, Harry Martin opened his eyes, and, gazing wildly at his leader, he said—

"Kill me, sir; kill me!"

"What is the matter, Harry?"

"My prisoner has escaped. Kill me, sir; I no longer deserve to belong to your band."

"Be calm. Now, come, tell me how it occurred."

Harry Martin raised himself upon his elbow, and answered—

"When you left me, sir, a number of men came on shore, and one, when he saw the fellow I had in charge, said something to him in a language I did not understand."

"Can you describe him?"

"The officer who spoke to the prisoner?"

"Yes."

"He was about your age, sir, and nearly as tall."

"Was there the mark of a sabre-cut on his face?"

"Across the left cheek?"

"Yes."

"There was, sir."

"It is Reuben Harpy," thought the young chief; then said aloud, "Go on."

When they had exchanged a few words, Harry Martin said, "The whole gang suddenly drew their cutlasses, and surrounded me."

"The cowardly hounds!"

"I fought as long as I could with them, but what could my club do against ten cutlasses?"

"Nothing, Harry. Under the circumstances there was no means of preventing the fellow's escape."

"None, sir; for I was cut down by the cowardly officer from behind."

"Like his nature," thought the young leader; "he would not, though a dozen men were at his back, face this stripling"

Captain Tom assisted his follower to rise, and they went towards the beach.

Suddenly the young buccaneer halted, and gazed attentively out upon the waters, and from his lips fell the words—

"We are betrayed!"

With startling abruptness the expression came upon Harry Martin's ears, and, gazing at his leader, he said—

"Betrayed, sir!"

"Yes! Look! See the danger lights!"

Harry followed the direction of Captain Tom's outstretched finger, and beheld the red lights gleaming from the "Will-o'-the-Wisp's" bow.

"Who can have done this?" he asked.

"The fellow that gave you that coward's stroke, Harry. It matters little. I will fire upon him, though the next broadside sent us to the bottom! Quick! Where is the boat?"

They ran swiftly to the place where they had left the gig.

It was gone.

With a blank, hopeless look their eyes met, and Captain Tom said—

"More of his work!"

"What can we do now, sir?"

The young chief was standing upon the edge of the jetty, his hand shading his eyes.

He made no reply to Harry Martin's query, but, as though conning his thoughts, he muttered—

"The line-of-battle ship is at quarters. Ah! the 'Will-o'-the-Wisp' has opened her ports! Be careful, Ben, or you'll draw the three-decker's fire upon you!"

It was a moment of anxious suspense to the daring boy, as he beheld his stately craft glide towards the huge liner.

A moment passed, and he thought his fearless crew were about to engage with the three-decker. The next he saw the "Will-o'-the-Wisp's" ports close, and the two red lights suddenly change to white.

It was the private signal to their chief, should he be near—one that told him all was safe at present.

In a state of feverish excitement he strode to and fro the jetty.

The glaring lights of the distant ships now and then revealing the forms of men passing hurriedly to and fro.

Nearly an hour passed, and from the evident signs passing before him, the young buccaneer had no difficulty in understanding that a dispute was taking place between the three vessels which lay so closely together.

Three vessels he conjectured (and rightly) to be the line-of-battle ship, "Will-o'-the-Wisp," and the Brazilian privateer, commanded by Reuben Harpy.

The nature of the dispute he could not imagine, but from the faint sounds he knew that words were being loud and hotly spoken.

"What would be the result of this angry conference?"

This was the question he mentally asked upwards of a dozen times.

The brave boy felt nervous and excited. He

feared that Reuben Harpy would yet bring the "Will-o'-the-Wisp" under the liner's guns.

Had he been on board his mind would have been at rest.

But the taunting thought that his gallant band would yet be engaged in a desperate conflict to escape maddened him.

Striking his brow with his hand, he suddenly exclaimed—

"I would give a thousand pounds to be again upon my ship!"

"Listen, sir," said young Martin, "there is a boat coming."

The regular stroke of a disciplined boat's crew came upon their ears.

Not knowing whether it might not be a boat from the English war-vessel, the young buccaneer drew back in the gloom, and waited until the keel should strike upon the beach.

The young leader listened intently to the jerk of the oars, and when he fully expected the boat to run aground he heard the orders given for the men to back water, and then one of the crew said—

"This is the place, sir."

"How do you know?" said an angry, gruff voice.

"The cap'n told us, sir, as the boat was being piped away—that was afore you come on deck."

"Told you what—eh?—you—"

"Told us we should see a young chap at the jetty as would pilot us out of the straits."

"The captain was wrong, for there is no one here."

Captain Tom had recognised the officer in the boat as one of the group he had seen on the deck of Dutch Paul's ship.

Obeying a sudden impulse, he quickly drew off his long boots, and gave them to Harry Martin.

"Give me your shoes," he said, "and cap, also your jacket. This is an opportunity I have long wanted."

The midshipman, while complying with his chief's orders, looked at him in silent surprise.

"You do not understand my motive."

"No, sir."

"This boat," said Captain Tom, "is from Dutch Paul's ship, the 'Yellow Vulture.'"

"Yes, sir."

"I have long wished," our hero continued, "to board that vessel. Fate has granted my desire. Ere long, Harry, I hope to become acquainted with the secret mode of preparing the wondrous liquid flame."

While speaking, the daring boy had assumed Harry's jacket, hat, and shoes.

"May you have a safe issue," said Harry, "from your adventure. What shall I do, sir—remain here or go on board?"

"Return to the ship the first opportunity, and tell them I am on board the 'Yellow Vulture;' that is," he added, "should the little 'Will-o'-the-Wisp' yet be free to dance upon the waters."

"What do you apprehend, sir?"

"I scarcely know, Harry. That our vessel is or has been in peril, I am assured."

"Taken, sir?"

"No; there are those on board who would never yield without firing a shot."

"None has been fired."

"Not yet. Now away with you, and mind you are, if captured, Captain Tom."

"I shall not forget, sir."

The boat had, during the time necessary for the exchange of dresses, been rowing slowly backwards and forwards, while waiting for the pilot.

Captain Tom now came forward, and called out—"Boat ahoy!"

"Ahoy!" was the answer.

"The pilot."

"Come aboard, then, we have been a waiting for you."

The young buccaneer stepped on board; the order was given to give way, and in less than five minutes the daring boy stood face to face with Dutch Paul.

The pirate leader was seated upon a cask, a cigar as usual, alternately between his lips and his fingers.

"So," he said, eyeing the young chief from head to foot, "you are the pilot?"

"I am," was the calm reply.

Dutch Paul's eyes twinkled mischievously as he asked—

"What do you know about the Rocky Straits?"

"Sufficient," said Captain Tom, "to take your vessel through."

"If I let you."

Our hero looked up in surprise.

"What," he asked, "do you want me for, if not to pilot your ship?"

Dutch Paul laughed in a peculiar manner.

"You are," he said, "a tarnal cool one."

Captain Tom felt all was not right; but, determined to carry out his assumed character, he said—

"Coolness is one of the requisites for a good pilot."

"Right," said the pirate; "but it strikes me there's a pilot wanted a little way off from here."

"I do not understand you."

"Perhaps you will when I say I mean the 'Will-o'-the-Wisp.'"

The young chief started.

"You know what I mean—eh?"

"Scarcely."

"Well," said Dutch Paul, "I'll be plain. The pilot that is wanted there is her captain. Do you understand me now, young fellow?"

"I do not. What have I to do with her captain?"

"Well, by all the snakes in the earth! I suppose you will tell me I am not Dutch Paul!"

"Why should I do so?"

"Why! Why, you young cuss, you have as much cause to do that as I have to tell you that you are not the captain of the 'Will-o'-the-Wisp'—eh? Are you Captain Tom?"

The young buccaneer's hand went to his side Dutch Paul laughed long and loudly.

"There is no blade there," he said; "if there was, what would you do?"

"That," said our hero, "would depend upon circumstances."

"Fight?"

"Possibly."

"A cool one. Well, you are a fine young cuss. Give me your hand—why should we not be friends?"

The boy frankly extended his soft, white hand and said—

"Why not? I accept the friendship."

"Here is mine, Tom, and by Jove! I'll strike good blow for you when you may require it. B what, in the name of the great serpent, brought y on board?"

"Tell me first," said our hero, "how you easily found me out?"

"I knew you," Dutch Paul answered, laughing "the moment you came over the side."

"Knew me?—how?"

"Your tread; the haughty manner in which you answered my second officer."

"Anything else?"

"Yes, your hands. Pilots do not, as a rule, have the softest hands in creation."

Tom smiled.

"Well, Captain Paul," he said, "I will now answer your question."

"Speak the truth, Tom."

A slight flush mantled the young chief's handsome face as he answered—

"I would not lie to save my life."

"Off you are, like a powder magazine when struck by a red-hot shot."

"I am cooler, now."

"Right—I meant no offence."

"The reason I came on board your ship was to find out a little about the liquid fire your crew poured into my vessel."

Dutch Paul's brow darkened for a moment, then cleared as he said—

"Well, I ought not to feel savage—I should do the same myself; but, take my advice, although we are friends, don't try to find it out."

"Why not?"

"Because the secret will die with me."

"A bold assertion."

"Yes; but as many a good fellow has been on the same tack as you came on, I do not fear discovery."

"Did none find a clue?"

"None; they found something else."

"What?"

"The great secret."

"Died?"

"Yes. We will change the subject. Were you on board when your vessel was claimed by the Brazilians?"

"I was not."

"The devil! Where were you?"

"Ashore, reconnoitring the castle."

"Your purpose?"

"To release one of my hands."

"Lost time. You will never get inside."

Captain Tom smiled.

"Why not?" he asked.

"The old Spaniard who governs the citadel would not permit a rat to enter."

"I had just left there when the signal-light gleamed from my vessel."

Dutch Paul elevated his eyebrows as he said—

"The devil you had! How, in the name of Fortune, did you manage it?"

Our hero told him.

"Well," said Dutch Paul, "you are about the coolest one I ever knew. What are your intentions respecting the real Don Vincent?"

Captain Tom's answer was very laconic.

"Capture him," he said; "take the present he has away, and return to the castle."

Dutch Paul slapped his leg, and cried out—

"Bravo, my young game-cock! But why, in the name of Fortune, did you use that fellow's name?"

"For a very simple reason—I knew the name was well known among the Spanish officers."

"Why so well known?"

"The old Don Vincent is Secretary of State."

"Capital! but were you not afraid the old fellow would discover you?"

"I was—especially when he touched upon family matters."

"You had a narrow escape. It was strange this fellow's letter should arrive while you were there."

"A mere chance. That was not the worst of the affair."

"No?"

"I did not know the old fellow's name, neither do I now."

"Don Alvarez Resperto."

"Thanks; I shall not forget to use it when I next see him. For the present, I must say adieu. Will you send me aboard?"

"I will. Vargas!"

The giant came sidling up beside his chief.

"Get a boat ready, Infant."

"Yes, cap'n."

"Now," said Dutch Paul, "as we have at last met, we will keep company for some time, if you are willing."

"Quite."

Our hero's thoughts were still upon the liquid flame.

"Very well," Dutch Paul said; if you want my help, up with two blue lights, and I'll give them a light they won't put out in a hurry."

"Many thanks for the offer. With you for an ally, I should not fear even that grim-looking liner."

"You need not. Another word—will you accompany me to the Treasure Island when we leave here?"

Captain Tom's eyes sparkled. He had often heard of the wondrous island, and longed to behold it.

"I will," he said, "and gladly."

"You shall. Come below with me for a moment; I wish to show you something."

They descended to the luxurious state-room, and from there to the laboratory.

"Stand a little aside," said Dutch Paul, "I want to open that part of the deck."

The young chief obeyed, and to his surprise a portion of the flooring opened.

His wonder increased when a huge piece of perforated copper rose through the opening; as it did so the water rushed out through the holes.

"The sea runs through this," said Captain Tom.

Dutch Paul made no reply.

He was standing with mouth agape and eyes distended.

The copper well was empty.

"By the tarnal," he said at length, "two fellows went down in this net four hours since. Where the devil are they now?"

"Gone," said Captain Tom, seriously.

"Yes, but how?"

"Through that hole, I expect."

"Hole!"

Dutch Paul yelled out the word, and jumped forward.

"By the tarnal, you are right. Well, I never knew a shark's teeth to tear away the copper casing like that. Ugh! Poor devils!"

Captain Tom could not repress a shiver at this explanation of the fate that had befallen the hapless wretches.

He little thought the captives were two of his old friends.

The well sunk again, and the boards moved slowly to their places before he asked Dutch Paul why two human beings had met such a fearful death.

"They came," was the pirate's answer, "to find out the secret of the liquid flame."

Captain Tom was silent.

The warning, he felt, was given; yet he felt from that moment a deeper yearning to learn the terrible mystery.

No words were exchanged until they reached the deck, and our hero was about to descend to the boat which awaited him.

"Don't forget the signal," said Dutch Paul, "I shall be on the alert."

"I will not."

"Right; good-bye. You have your hands pretty full of business."

"I have my vessel to clear from that three-decker, to capture Don Vincent Velasco, and release Iron Arm, also a little difference to settle with that Brazilian gentleman."

"When do you expect to get through it all?"

"By to-morrow night. I hope."

He seated himself in the boat, and Dutch Paul, leaning over the side, muttered—

"Well, he's about the cutest, coolest young lad I ever knew. I'm glad we are friends, for he is a fine, plucky fellow."

Vargas came up at this moment.

"Cap'n," he said, "there are sharks in these waters."

"Yes, Infant, plenty."

"Yes; and they have crushed in the side of the well."

"I know it."

"All right, cap'n; didn't think you did."

"Have the hole repaired; we may want it again some day."

Vargas evidently looked upon that as a certainty, for, as he walked away, he muttered—

"Of course we shall. I must have a double sheeting on the sides. What teeth that shark must have had !"

"Very strong teeth, indeed, Vargas."

CHAPTER LIII.

FROM BAD TO WORSE.—REUBEN HARPY FOILED.— CAPTURE OF THE BUCCANEER KING.

WHEN Jerry Mizzen and his inseparable friend, Bob, suddenly descended into the copper well beneath the Yellow Vulture, they gave a simultaneous cry of horror.

The inky darkness of their watery tomb for some moments prevented them from knowing exactly the extent of the horrible fate that had befallen them.

The first impression was that the shaft they had so swiftly descended led into the open sea.

This impression was but of short duration, for Bob Hauler, as he rose to the surface, struck out madly to swim away from the vessel's keel.

A cry of pain came from his lips as his fingers grated upon the jagged holes of the well.

At the same moment Jerry gave a long howl, as his hand came in violent collision with a grating which fitted as a cover to the skilfully-contrived receptacle for those who sought to pry into the pirate captain's secret.

A few moments passed—both silent with horror, as the fearful truth flashed before their minds.

Bob Hauler, the last to give way to despair, groped about for some mode whereby he could escape the fearful doom.

There was no hope.

Upon every side his hands, now torn and bleeding, came in contact with the sides of the well.

Above, so close that his cap touched it, was the cover of the infernal contrivance.

Both men were above the average height, or they would have been instantaneously stifled by the water.

The rippling waves, as they flowed under the vessel and through the open well, were upon a level with their lower lips.

"It's all over, I s'pose," Jerry groaned. "Well, a man can die but once, and there's one comfort, I've done my dooty."

"Never say die, messmate," Bob joined in. "I'm goin' to make a voyage round the premises. Hullo! what's this?"

"What's the matter?" Jerry asked.

"I've got hold of something."

"What is it?"

"It feels like a handle," Bob said, "somethin' like the crank of a barrel-horgan."

"Turn away," said Jerry, "it's a poor crank that et no turn in it."

did turn with all his might, and presently

there was a grating sound, and a plate of copper flew back, and daylight streamed in.

"Hurrah!" Jerry cried, "we ain't dead men yet."

As Jerry spoke there came a sound, borne upon the wind like the booming of a cannon, then a hurrying of feet and clattering of arms above.

"It's the 'Will-o'-the-Wisp,'" Bob cried. "I'd take my oath on it."

"Then let us get out of this infernal hole," Jerry said. "I 'spect we can give them the slip easy."

The two men crept through the aperture, and in a few seconds had entered one of the deserted cabins, and were making for the port hole, when one of the buccaneers entered.

He started back for an instant, but, recovering his presence of mind, drew from his belt a silver-hilted pistol, and called upon the men to surrender.

"We don't know what that means, you ugly swab," Bob said, as he dashed up the pirate's arm, and with his right brawny fist floored the man. "Stand out of the way, and let an Englishman pass."

The blow stunned the pirate, and Bob and Jerry threw themselves into the sea.

They were perceived by the buccaneers on deck, and several shots were fired, which fell short, and splashed up the water in their faces, but neither Bob nor his friend were touched.

And before a second volley could be fired, they had grasped the ropes of the "Will-o'-the-Wisp," and amid the cheers of their comrades were hauled on board.

Shaking the salt spray from his clothes, Bob Hauler touched his cap to his chieftain, and said—

"Thankee, sir ! thankee for the rope. Can I have my old place at the swivel-gun amidships ?"

"You can, Bob," was the smiling reply, "and take Jerry with you."

Bob Hauler collared Jerry Mizzen by the hair of his head, and dragging him towards the long brass gun said, gleefully—

"Hear that, you swab ?"

"Yes !" yelled Jerry, dancing with pain; "I does, and feels it too ; leave go, you ugly cuss, can't you !"

Bob released his messmate's hair when they reached the gun, and slapping the polished breech with the palm of his right hand, he said—

"Back again, old girl; if you don't drop a lump of iron in that ship's hull, I'll never polish you again ; do you hear that ? Hallo, Jerry ! what's up?"

The illustrious Jerry was standing, a shoe in each hand, looking the very picture of woe.

"Baling out my shoes, Bob," he said, ruefully; "they is full of—"

Bang !

Jerry hopped round, and took refuge behind his friend.

"Cuss 'em !" he muttered; "they might have waited until I got my shoes—Oh, murder !"

The last word was jerked out as Jerry rolled upon the deck, his long body doubled up, and his two hands pressed convulsively to his stomach.

Jerry's first thought had been that the ball from the gun, which had just been discharged, had taken up its quarters beneath the spot he so tightly pressed.

But Bob Hauler's grinning face and his words to the fallen Jerry assured him that matters were not quite so bad as he anticipated.

"If you had kept that ugly karkiss of yours out of the way," Bob said, "you wouldn't have got that shove in the bread-basket from my rammer. Get up, do; don't lie there rolling your eyes about like a stranded cod-fish; get up, and serve my gun with shot. Now, look here, Jerry, if you don't look sharp, I'll shove the end of this rammer down your throat."

The cause of Jerry's sudden collapse was the

CHASING THE PIRATES.

energetic manner in which his friend had just rammed home a 32-pound shot.

Unluckily, Jerry had hopped behind Bob at the very moment the latter sharply withdrew the rammer.

The top, as a matter of course, caught Jerry, and, as he called it, capsized him.

He had to grin and bear the pain, and got up to escape having the large end of the rammer pushed down his throat.

When the muskets were levelled over the privateer's sides a second time, our hero sprung upon the bulwarks of his vessel. and grasping the shrouds with his left hand he presented a pistol at Reuben Harpy, and sang out in a voice that was heard by the baffled coward as plainly as though the young chief had stood by his side—

" Hold, or you shall have this bullet through your skull."

The threat was sufficient. Reuben knew the deadly accuracy of his cousin's aim, and he ordered his men to throw up the muzzles of their pieces.

" Now, treacherous miscreant," said the young chief, " the time has arrived for me to repay the disgrace you brought upon my name—to repay you for the base attempt that you made to betray me to the admiral in command of the line-of-battle ship—yet I will spare you even now if you will solemnly swear never to attempt to cross my path again."

Reuben listened to his cousin's words, and the

......of the well known voice roused all the black passion in his heart.

He looked at his crowded decks, the formidable array of guns, the bristling weapons, and the eager impatience of his men to begin the fight.

His vessel was the larger, and carried more guns than the buccaneer; added to this was the voice of his first officer prompting him to shoot the young chief who had so recklessly exposed himself.

"If I shirk this fight," Reuben thought, "I shall lose all prestige with my crew, and possibly be shot for dishonouring the flag under which I stand. No, sink or swim, I will fight him."

He gave his first officer an order in a low, tremulous voice, and, as the Portuguese left the quarter-deck, he said, in reply to our hero's words—

"Boasting beggar, you talk of punishing a man who stands upon the deck of a ship better manned and better armed than your own. It is I that should make conditions, not you."

"Is that your answer?"

"No."

"Quick with it, then—I am in no mood for trifling."

Reuben raised his right hand, and said—

"That is my answer."

As the last word left his lips, a gun belched forth flame and smoke, and the ball whizzed past our hero's head.

A cry of rage came from the buccaneers, and the length and breadth of their vessel was lit up by the sudden discharge of their starboard battery.

Every ball did its work among the spars of the Portuguese ship.

The foremast was cut in two near the yard, and for a moment or two the broken part, held by the thin cordage, swayed to and fro.

Then, as the wind filled the topsails, the cordage snapped with a loud noise, and the topmast fell with a crash to the deck.

Fore and aft the splinters from the shivered wood dealt out ugly wounds among the crew.

And almost the first who fell bleeding to the deck was Reuben Harpy.

The boom, upon which the studding-sail was yet spread, was snapped in two, and a large splinter from the heavy pole struck Reuben's head, and felled him as though he had been stricken with a sledge hammer.

Guzman, the first officer, saw his leader fall, and ordered him to be conveyed below.

"Now," said the fiery Portuguese, "the men shall have what they have long wanted. That coward has never tried their mettle. Pour in your fire, men. Huzza! give it them. In ten minutes I will haul their flag down, and the prize will be ours."

The seamen answered by a loud shout, and, stripped to the waist, they poured in a close and deadly fire upon the "Will-o'-the-Wisp."

There were many besides Lieutenant Guzman who would have died at their guns rather than yield.

Many had anxiously longed to hear the roar of battle going on around them.

But, like the first officer, their wishes had never been gratified since the hour Reuben took command of the well-equipped privateer.

Now, like hounds suddenly released from the leash, they rushed eager to the fight, and so close was their fire that both ships became enveloped in a cloud of white, opaque smoke.

The Portuguese lieutenant suddenly bellowed forth from his speaking-trumpet—

"Cease firing—cease firing—they have struck."

A few shots only were fired after this order reached the forepart of the ship.

As the smoke rolled away before the wind, the graceful buccaneer's ship, to the surprise of the Portuguese, was seen to have shifted her position, and now lay right across their bows.

A white flag fluttered from her main peak, but beyond this there was no appearance of surrender on the buccaneer's part.

A burst of sunshine showed the young captain standing on the quarter-deck, surrounded by his officers.

The guns were still run out, and the men at quarters.

What could it mean?

Guzman went quickly forward, speaking-trumpet in hand, to ascertain the cause.

By the time he reached the forecastle the young buccaneer chief had advanced to the side of his vessel, and when he beheld the Portuguese officer, he said—

"I saw your leader fall, and would spare useless bloodshed, if possible. Deliver him up to me, and your vessel can make sail in safety."

Lieutenant Guzman's cheek paled with anger at this speech, and he answered, in a voice husky with rage—

"This is the cause, then, of your flag of truce, vile trickster; or was it a ruse to gain time to execute this manoeuvre which has placed your vessel across our bows?"

"My purpose, lieutenant," said the proud youth, with dignity, "is to save your crew from slaughter. Give up your captain, and you are free to depart."

"Never!" was the fierce reply, "never, while a plank of this ship remains; and, harkee, pirate, by the Madonna I swear to pull that flag from the yard with my own hands, and hang you in its place. To your guns, men! Ready, sail-trimmers, to wear ship!"

He sprang down with a loud cry of defiance; and, as the vessel swung round, and brought her broadside to broadside with the "Will-o'-the-Wisp," our hero said, in a low, stern tone—

"Be it so. I would have saved this slaughter, but it is not to be. Ready there, larboard battery."

"Ready—aye, ready, sir!"

"Fire!"

The guns belched forth their murderous contents, and were answered by the Portuguese broadside.

So the cannonade continued for upwards of twenty minutes, the young chief and his officers, regardless of the iron-storm which came whistling around their heads, stood quietly conversing on the quarter-deck.

Iron Arm, leaning upon his ponderous mace, watched with keen interest the progress of the fight.

"They serve the guns well," was the remark. "That daring lieutenant is a more worthy foe than Reuben."

"He is," said Harry Vere. "My surprise is that, with such a ship, Reuben has not made more havoc among the merchantmen and small war vessels."

Iron Arm laughed.

"Reuben," he said, "has taken every possible precaution to keep out of the way of any vessel that carried only a couple of guns. He has a constitutional dislike to cannon-balls."

"So it would appear. Ho! boarders, follow me!"

Harry Vere dashed towards the larboard bow, swinging his bright sword above his head, closely followed by his boarding party.

Captain Tom's voice rang out clear above the din of battle as he said—

"Stand by, boarders, to repel boarders."

"The devil!" growled Iron Arm; "they have not tried to board us."

"They have," was the answer. "There is the result."

He looked towards the larboard bow, and beheld

Harry Vere and his men   t close deadly work with the Portuguese privateers.

Covered by a thick smoke, Guzman had led a resolute party to carry the buccaneer's ship by boarding.

They were met by the long, murderous pikes, wielded by strong arms, a d were compelled to retire.

The conflict raged fiercely 'or some time.

The Portuguese lieutenant tried to animate his men to leap upon the enemy's deck by holding out hopes of rich reward.

"Leap upon them," he yelle '. "There is not only riches enough for us all on board, but there are lovely women. These shall be given to the men who first place their feet upon the deck. '

Iron Arm, who was famili r with the language, gripped his mace, and, striding forward to the combat, said, grimly—

"I will give them something else besides the women and riches—just a taste of this little club, to add a sweetness to the prize in store. '

Our hero smiled as he saw the business-like manner in which Iron Arm went to put his project into execution.

He had no misgivings as to the result. The boy knew his power was quite equ l to repel the fierce attack; his place was on the quarter-deck, not only to give various commands to the crew, but to prevent a surprise from the boarders, who were clustered near the privateer's aft-hatch, waiting for an opportunity to aid their companions forward.

With one foot planted firmly on the breech of a carronade, and the other on the   ulwark, Iron Arm stood with uplifted weapon, mo ing down all who were rash enough to force their   ay upon deck.

Their minds inflamed by Gu man's words, the privateers swarmed towards the bulwarks.

Springing from the muzzles of he guns, dropping from the lower spars and rigging of the ship, they sought to effect a lodgment where so great a reward awaited them.

Those who reached the decks were met upon the long pikes so well handled by Har y Vere's men.

Others, as they took a flying leap from the shrouds, were received by a blow from the steel-piked mace, which hurled them to the other side of the vessel, every bone broken, and he flesh smashed into an undistinguishable, horrible mass.

They were like so many shuttle-cocks being struck by a bat—the bat Iron A m's tremendous weapon.

The white foam gathered upon Guzman's lips when he saw the slaughter whi h followed his attempt to carry this part of the ship by boarding.

Beaten back upon every point—foiled in every stratagem, he was compelled to call away his men, and retire again to the quarter-dec' .

Here he encouraged the gunners to keep up their fire, and to use grape instead of round shot.

The close discharge of grape was returned by the buccaneers with fatal effect, and Guzman, instead of endeavouring to board the enemy, found all his energies taxed in keeping the men t the guns.

Time after time they were compelled to rush from their pieces, and seek refuge from the storm of shot.

Lieutenant Guzman, though much weakened by the slaughter which ensued during his attempt to board the "Will-o'-the-Wisp," still had a crew which numbered more than twice the buccaneers.

Fearful that the boy buccaneer ould retaliate and board his vessel, he had the tops filled with the best marksmen in his ship.

These men kept up a continual fire   on the "Will-o'-the-Wisp's" boarders, who were massed in different parts of the vessel, waiting their chieftain's orders to rush over the bulwarks.

Captain Tom saw the well-aimed shots from the Portuguese main-tops were doing much mischief among his men, and he ordered them to retire from the line of fire.

An order which was not obeyed with half the readiness one to move forward would have been.

The cannonade from the Portuguese ship was delivered with a resolution that had been totally unlooked for by the boy buccaneer.

Although he had not yet placed himself at the head of his invincible band, and carried the enemy's ship by that irresistible mode of attack which had made his name famous, it was not because he feared the result.

Far otherwise; he did it to save as many of his men as possible, and when urged to end the fray by the fiery Iron Arm, he answered—

"We are but little touched among the spars, and the hull can never be injured by their guns. I do not see the policy of wasting life upon a foe so much beneath us."

"The devil!" growled the giant. "They make it pretty hot for the men at the guns."

"There is a place of shelter for them."

"True; but the bulldogs would sooner be shot down than driven away from the battery."

"That is their fault. The boarders shall not suffer through an ill-judged move on my part."

"Why ill-judged? One rush, and the ship is ours."

"One rush," said Captain Tom, pointing to the dark forms which lined the enemy's tops, "and two-thirds of our men go down before their fire. Remember, a bullet does its work upon the cowardly as well as the brave."

"There goes the mainmast; and as I live that fellow is endeavouring to persuade his men to try another attempt at boarding."

"He is. Ready there, forward, to repel boarders. Now—well done, Bob Hauler."

Iron Arm looked towards the long gun, and beheld Bob Hauler and Jerry Mizzen stripped to the waist, and so begrimed with smoke that their features were undistinguishable.

They were, at the moment Iron Arm's notice was attracted towards them, throwing buckets of water over the breech of their gun.

The imprisonment on board Reuben's ship was being repaid by Bob and his companion with interest.

Every heavy spar that had fallen had been the work of the long brass gun—loaded by Jerry, elevated and fired by Bob.

They were now compelled to desist, for their gun had become so heated by the quick firing that it was dangerous to put a charge of dry powder near the hot metal.

Bob Hauler was heaping abuse upon his companion for not making more haste with the water to cool the gun.

"You crawling alligator," roared Bob; "clap on more sail, or the fun will be over before I can send another message."

"Wish it was," said Jerry. "My arms ache awful with ramming home the balls. Why don't they make 'em smaller ?—then they wouldn't want shoving in so hard."

"I'll shove your head in for a charge. Quick, Jerry, with the powder. Hurrah!—that's it, you long-backed, yellow-belly, you've spilt half."

Jerry dived out of the way only in time.

Bob Hauler made a blow at his messmate with the blazing port-fire he held.

It missed Jerry, and the end swung back and struck Bob between the eyes.

He gave a yell of pain, and although the balls from the Portuguese privateer were flying thickly across the deck, he left his gun, and began to pommel Jerry.

A scuffle ensued, which ended by a hearty laugh, and the queer pair went to work again at the delightful occupation of smashing the enemy, as Bob said, into nothing.

Captain Tom, tired of the long conflict between the guns, yielded to Iron Arm's advice, and called his boarders together.

Another moment, and they would have poured over the enemy's side.

Before the young chief, swift as he was, could jump before a gun, a strange scene took place, which, for the time, put a different aspect on affairs.

They had, until the present moment, been closely engaged with the larboard battery of this vessel.

But, as the vessel was under the wind, a heavy broadside was poured in on the starboard side.

For a moment the buccaneers were thrown into confusion by this unexpected attack, and, leaving their guns, they looked over the vessel to ascertain the cause of that close broadside.

The terrible truth soon became apparent.

They were between two vessels, both doing their utmost to annihilate the gallant band.

Outward objects hidden by the thick smoke, had enabled the pirates, from whose clutches our hero had saved Hester the Jewess, to creep upon the "Will-o'-the-Wisp" unnoticed.

When close enough, he soon made his presence known by a rapid succession of broadsides, which would have sunk the buccaneers had not their vessel been invulnerable.

Iron Arm was the first to make out the foe who had sought to cripple or sink them, and, dropping his mace, he soon cast loose a gun, and began to return the close fire.

Bob Hauler speedily joined him with the long gun, and in a few minutes both sides of the vessel were vomiting forth death and destruction.

Guzman, the Portuguese, took advantage of the momentary surprise which this unexpected evil had caused, and springing unobserved upon the "Will-o'-the-Wisp," he began to ascend the rigging.

The young chief had just succeeded in manning all the guns, and placing men at different parts of the vessel to prevent boarding from either side, when Jack Langton, who was in charge of one of of the parties near the quarter-deck, called out—

"The flag!—the flag!"

Captain Tom looked upward, and through the dense cloud of smoke he beheld the dark outlines of a human form.

Calling upon his men, many of whom had already raised their pieces to bring down this daring intruder, to withold their fire, he sprang upon the bulwarks, and regardless of the iron-storm which whistled over his head, began the perilous ascent.

"So," he muttered, "this fellow means to keep his word—his the task to tear down my colours, mine to defend them."

Like a meteor—so swift, so sudden was our hero's appearance—the gallant boy came face to face with the Portuguese.

Guzman released his grip upon the colours, and then drew his sword.

Before he had time to make any cut at the buccaneer chief he was hurled from the lofty mast by a blow from the butt end of Captain Tom's pistol.

CHAPTER LIV.

DUTCH PAUL KINDLES A FIRE NOT EASILY PUT OUT.

SLIDING quickly to the deck by descending a single rope, Captain Tom was just in time to behold the quivering disfigured remnant of humanity flung overboard by Iron Arm.

"Quite dead," said the giant, in answer to Tom's look of interrogation; "and he came down within two inches of my head."

"He was a brave fellow," said our hero, "and I would have saved him had there been a possibility."

"No doubt," said the giant, ironically; "but, as there was no possibility, you sent him down quicker than he went up. Now, my chief, take my advice, and move ahead."

"Why?"

"You ask why, and the ship is in range of their broadsides! Forge ahead is the idea, and leave them to fight it out."

"Can it be done?"

"Yes; the smoke is thick enough to suffocate a nigger, and as boarding is out of the question, I do not see why we should stay here for a target."

The young chief pondered for a moment.

He looked sadly at the fallen forms which strewed his deck, and calculated the chance of sinking one or both of his foes by boarding.

There seemed no possible chance of doing this without a fearful loss, and as nothing on board either vessel would compensate for the wholesale slaughter of his men, he thought Iron Arm's advice was the best under the circumstances.

Then Reuben Harpy yet remained in his cabin, and our hero knew if the cowardly fellow had recovered from his wound sufficiently to enable him to walk he would be stowed away out of sight, and possibly, while seeking for him, the pirate crew would take advantage of his absence and swarm over the side.

The immense wealth reported to be in the "Will-o'-the-Wisp's" hold was a sufficient inducement for them to brave any danger.

Rumour had also magnified the beautiful corsair maiden into a bevy of Eastern beauties.

Together with the fabulous wealth the boy buccaneer had acquired, the report was current and implicitly believed that Captain Tom had a harem on board, in which was to be found the most beautiful women in the world.

Some put down the number at twenty, others (and they were not the minority of the believers) calculated that one hundred and twenty would be nearer the truth.

Captain Tom knew how rife these reports were among the lawless rovers, and he had no doubt that the rascals who had captured Hester for the purpose of gaining the hiding-place of her father's riches would be well satisfied with the contents of his ship instead of the old Jew's coffers.

Acting upon the train of thought suggested by the pirate's manner, he said to Iron Arm—

"I think your plan admirable; pass the word for the gunners to use smaller charges of powder in their guns."

"If that," said Iron Arm, "does not choke them, they have but little—Hallo!"

He faced round, with his weapon raised—a figure sprang over the taffrail.

The young chief followed his movement, and uttered an exclamation of surprise.

Dutch Paul, with a light laugh at his astonishment, jumped to the deck, saying—

"Very careless to leave a rope dangling at the stern; a foe could have as easily ascended as a friend."

"True," said our hero; "where is your ship?"

"Her bowsprit is within a yard of your stern. Did you not see us approach?"

"No, the smoke is so thick I can barely discern the men at their stations."

"So I perceive. Can you move ahead?"

"Yes; I was about to do so when you appeared. Why do you ask?"

"Because I think you are in a nice position to be pretty well mangled by your friends on either side."

"You saw that fellow come upon me?"

"I did, and weighed anchor as soon as possible, but not soon enough to prevent him from giving you a broadside or two. What have you done to bring the pirate gang so close?"

Captain Tom told him.

"So that is it? Well, my boy, you have brought a pretty wasp's nest about your ears. That fellow your pistol ball knocked over is Rafael of the Gulf."

"Rafael of the Gulf!"

The name was well known to the buccaneer chief.

Rafael of the Gulf, as he was termed, was a renegade Spaniard, whose lawless deeds and bloodthirsty nature made him a terror to the whole seaboard of Spain.

"Yes," Dutch Paul said, "Rafael, the pirate. I see he is trying on his favourite mode of attack with you."

"What is that?"

"Were your ship not shot-proof, you would have found out before. He believes that a good pounding from his heavy forty-twos a necessary prelude to boarding, and by the quickness of their fire that will soon follow."

"They will find Captain Tom on his deck."

"No doubt, my boy; but as he can show four men to your one, the sooner Captain Tom and his deck are out of the way the better; especially as you have Captain Pellam doing all he can to aid Rafael."

The young chief turned to Iron Arm, and said—

"I am more disposed to stop, and meet those fellows."

"It would be madness," said the giant; "we can do all that mortal men can, but against the combined crews of those vessels we should, at the best, gain a victory, and lose ten out of every dozen men on board."

"Be it so; were time saved—"

"Are you mad?" Dutch Paul said. "Listen to me. Draw ahead, and I will come into your place."

"For what purpose? To bear that danger which I am af—"

"Don't be alarmed, you obstinate young fire-eater; I shall come to no harm."

"Your men are not invulnerable."

"No; but if I do not give them enough work to put out a fire I will kindle—more than enough to let me pass without a shot being fired."

These and other arguments were used until the young chief was compelled, though reluctantly, to consent to Dutch Paul's wish.

"Very well," Dutch Paul said, "I'll go back the same way I came, meanwhile push a— Ah! the devil! are you alive?"

This strange interruption to Dutch Paul's words was caused by the sudden appearance of Bob Hauler.

"Yes," said Bob, "but we ain't got much to thank you for."

"The other as well?"

"Yes, both of us."

"Well," Dutch Paul said, "you are the first that have made their escape from the well. I thought it; but, there, I'm glad you got away. Good-bye, captain—go forward—I will soon be with you!"

The double charges of powder aided the young buccaneer's plan, and, amid a terrible roar from his guns, the vessel was set in motion, and the "Will-o'-the-Wisp" glided slowly forward.

Her stately hull had barely passed the bows of her foes, when the "Yellow Vulture" filled the gap.

The buccaneers, now relieved from their deadly work, crowded aft to behold the issue of the strange proceeding.

Both ships were still sending in their fiercest broadsides, when from the "Yellow Vulture's" open ports a stream of liquid flame darted forth.

Instantly the cannonade ceased.

Shrieks and yells succeeded the noise of the guns, and like magic the Portuguese privateer and the Spanish pirate vessels became one sheet of lurid fire.

As the forked, flickering light sped upwards, and the sails and rigging caught fire, the "Yellow Vulture" shot forward, and, as she passed the buccaneers, Dutch Paul, cooly puffing his cigar, said to our hero—

"That will amuse them for some time to come—that may help to repair damages."

The gallant boy could not answer; he was standing spellbound and horrified at the fearful spectacle of a mass of human beings being burnt alive.

CHAPTER LV.

THE DUEL BETWEEN BOB HAULER AND JACOP.

THE Portuguese vessel was soon beyond all hope of being saved, and our hero, fearing every moment that an explosion would take place, moved further from the blazing ship.

On board the Spanish pirate there seemed less confusion than had been aboard with her companion in misfortune.

The blazing masts and sails were cut down, and hurled into the sea, and by the time Rueben Harpy had succeeded in lowering his boats the Spaniards had hastily subdued the fire upon their hull.

The crowded boats from the Portuguese privateer pulled swiftly towards the blackened remains of the Spanish pirate.

They had barely ascended the side when their own vessel blew up, and the air became darkened with the charred fragments of wood, and the scorched bodies of those who had fallen during the fierce fight.

Iron Arm stood calmly watching their proceedings, and, as the boats left the ill-fated ship, he said to the young chief—

"There is yet time to overhaul that villain."

"Reuben Harpy?"

"Yes. Remember I have an old debt to settle with the cowardly murderer of my friend."

"Another time," the young chief said. "This is punishment enough for once."

The "Yellow Vulture" came within hailing distance of the buccaneers, and Dutch Paul said—

"Well, captain; are you ready to accompany me?"

"Quite."

"Spread your wings, and keep near the 'Vulture.' Hallo! the liner, as I live!"

Looking to the westward, they beheld the massive hull and huge pyramid of canvas of the line-of-battle ship.

"The firing," Dutch Paul said, "has brought her back. What is it to be, a fight or a run?"

Our hero, who made it a point never, if possible, to raise his hand against the ships of his nation unless hard pressed, promptly replied—

"Neither."

"Neither!" repeated Dutch Paul, his astonishment causing him to put the lighted end of his cigar in his mouth. "Are we to be captured, then?"

"No; we will sail quietly away."

"If he follows?"

"Put on more sail."

"Well," Dutch Paul said, "if that is not a run,

blest if I know the meaning of the word. Shake out your canvas, lads. That fellow is bearing along at seven knots."

The "Yellow Vulture," under the impulse of her huge sails, shot swiftly ahead of the buccaneers.

The "Will-o'-the-Wisp" was not far behind.

Propelled by her large, fan-like wheels beneath the stern, she was more than a match for the "Yellow Vulture."

As she glided gracefully onward, her shot-torn spars without a vestige of canvas upon them, she had the appearance of a vessel lying immovable upon the waters.

An appearance which often puzzled those who were sent in pursuit of the daring craft.

Many a sharp-eyed officer had seen the "Will-o'-the-Wisp" lying like a log, not a sail set, or a man visible upon her deck, and chuckling at the prospect of taking the buccaneers by surprise, they had come within hailing distance.

But to their astonishment the seemingly deserted ship would suddenly glide forward, without a sail being loosened, and the trick would not become apparent until a mocking laugh came from the young rover's deck.

Possibly the line-of-battle ship was under the same delusion, for as our hero glided onwards, a puff of white smoke came from her bows, and a shot fell within a dozen fathoms of the "Will-o'-the-Wisp."

Among the wounded buccaneers was Bob Hauler.

He had received a flesh-wound in the arm as the vessel moved from between her foes.

Doctor Shrike and his vampire Jacop saw the blood trickling down Bob's arm, and at once dragged him below.

Bob Hauler had a constitutional horror of doctors, but in this instance he suffered himself to be taken to the cockpit.

A flesh wound in a colder climate would not have been a serious affair.

But beneath the burning tropical sun a neglected wound would soon mortify.

This Bob knew, and consoling himself with the reflection that—

"They were going to clap a piece of plaister on," he consigned the limb to the doctor and his shadow, Jacop.

Doctor Shrike had an inquiring mind.

When Jacop had washed the red stain from Bob's arm, he armed himself with a long probe, and adjusted his spectacles.

Bob Hauler watched the proceedings with great interest until the doctor began to probe the wound.

Then Bob gave a yell, and, dancing about the place with pain, shouted—

"Belay, you old blood-letter. What's that for?"

"Collar him, Jacop," said the doctor. "This is a wonderful case. There is an inch of plank between the wound and the bone. Collar him, until I find out whether the bone is all right."

Jacop danced after the victim with praiseworthy eagerness, and Bob, retreating to the corner of the cockpit, said—

"Look here, doctor, clap a bit of stuff on it, and I shall be all right."

"Collar him," said Doctor Shrike, "we must open the wound—eh, Jacop?—that will make him dance."

Bob Hauler brought up his horny fists in a pugilistic attitude, and said—

"Shorten sail, you mummy, or I'll give you a broadside."

Jacop stopped short.

First he looked at the double fists, then at the doctor.

"Go on," said his master; "we must have a subject, Jacop."

"Can't, sir; he's got his fists up, and might hit me to the effusion of blood."

"Blood, eh? Collar him, or I'll bleed you."

The doctor dropped the probe, and snatched up a dissecting knife."

"Go on, Jacop," he said, flashing the keen blade "or I'll make a subject of you."

Between two evils, always choose the least. So says adage; so thought Jacop.

A punch, whether it be received on the nose or in the mouth, would be better than the doctor's knife.

Accordingly, Jacop made a rush at their refractory patient, with the intention of putting his long arms round Bob's body.

"Shear off," cried Bob, "or I'll drop you one."

"Go on, Jacop—collar him," said the doctor, coming close behind his man, "or I'll tuck you up with this."

Jacop gave a howl as the doctor made a stab at his back.

Bob Hauler gave Jacop all he had promised him.

The right hand came out like a young sledge-hammer, and, coming in contact with the vampire's nose, caused the effusion of blood he so much dreaded, and sent him sprawling on his back.

Jacop's yell was answered by one from Bob Hauler.

The doctor had avenged the fall of his assistant by giving Bob a dig in that part of his body which would render sitting an unpleasant position for some time.

Bob did not wait for a second touch from the sharp instrument, but, with one hand to the wounded part, and the other striking wildly at the doctor, he rushed on deck.

Jerry Mizzen was seated upon a coil of rope, quietly discussing his own and Bob Hauler's share of the double allowance of grog which had been served out since the action.

Jerry took the can from his mouth when his messmate scrambled through the hatchway, and said—

"Thought you was on the sick list, Bob?"

"Sick list!—no, not me!" Bob answered. "Look here."

He showed his hand, wet with a crimson stain.

"How did you get that, Bob?"

Bob told him.

Jerry burst into a fit of laughter, and rolled off the coil of rope.

"Well," he said, as the tears rolled down his cheeks, "that—ha! ha! ha!—don't, Bob; I can't help it—ha! ha! ha!—sit down—ha! ha!—and have some—ha! ha! Oh!"

This last exclamation was caused by Bob Hauler bringing his fist down with no gentle weight.

"Curse you," he said, "can't you find something else to laugh at?"

"Ha! ha! ha!" cried Jerry, "fancy the doctor striking you there—ha! ha! ha!"

Bob made another strike at Jerry, and missed.

The impetus of the blow, and the slippery deck, brought him from the perpendicular to the horizontal, and upon that very spot Doctor Shrike's sharp instrument had so recently operated upon.

He scrambled to his feet, his recently jovial face the picture of woe.

While he stood debating whether to pulverise Jerry or go below and smash Jacop, Jack Langton came to him, and said—

"The chief wants you, Bob."

He obeyed the summons, and went aft, much to Jerry's delight, who finished the grog, then went below and hid himself, to escape his messmate's wrath.

"Can you tell me," the young chief said, "anything respecting Mr. Martin?"

"Yes, sir," Bob answered; "the last time I saw him—"

"You saw him!"

"Yes, sir."

"Where?"

"On board that very craft with Mr. Harpy."

"Yes; well?"

"Jerry and I, sir was giving them a stave—"

"Never mind that; keep to Mr. Martin."

"Yes, sir. Leastways, I wish I had; but I couldn't."

Captain Tom smiled. There was no means of hearing young Martin's fate unless he allowed Bob to tell the story in his own way.

"You could not," he said, "see through that, Bob?"

"Well, you see, sir, Mr. Harpy sends for him on deck, and when he comes back agin, that was the last time I see him."

"Yes; proceed."

"So he says to me, 'Bob,' says he, 'if I'm taken away'—at least, he didn't say that, exactly, but—"

"Words to that effect, I suppose, Bob?"

"Yes, sir; it meant that."

"I understand."

"'If I'm taken away,' he says, 'tell the chief that I shall be taken to a place with a double O on the top.'"

"Double O, Bob?"

"Yes, double O, or couple O."

"Cupola?" suggested Iron Arm.

"That's it," said Bob, much relieved. "Cuppelo—yes, that's what he said."

"Well."

"On the top," Bob continued, "close agin the clock; and he was taken away, sir. That's all I knew."

"He did not return?"

"No, sir."

"Certain?"

"Yes; as certain as I am that that beast of a Jerry Mizzen is drinking my grog at this very minnit."

"That is a certainty," said the young chief, laughing. "Never mind, you shall not lose your share."

"Thankee, sir."

"Go to the purser, and tell him to give you all that you require."

"As much as I like, sir?"

"Yes."

"Hoo—no, I mean thankee, sir. Hoora—y!"

Bob finished the shout of triumph as he made all haste from the quarter-deck.

"Not a drop," he muttered, "shall that beast taste. I'll have six allowances and get as drunk as a—Oh, you swine!"

Lord he would have said, but catching sight of the vampire's form, he gave a howl and started in pursuit.

Jacop dodged out of the way, and Bob went to the purser.

It is not right to pry into any gentleman's private affairs, so I will not state here how many times a tin cup Bob carried with him was filled and emptied.

Suffice it to say that Bob's head caused him, after his visit to the purser, to stagger to and fro, and declare with remarkable warmth, that the something ship was rolling about like a washing-tub.

Indeed, he went so far as to say that the masts were dancing about the deck. The last that was seen of Bob for many hours was his heels, as he went head foremost down the hatchway.

"A peculiar pair," Iron Arm said, as Bob hurried from the quarter-deck.

"They are," our hero answered; "they love each other with more depth than you would think their nature capable of feeling. Yet, when together, they are, to all appearance, continually disagreeing; part them, and you rob them of half the pleasures of life."

"I can fully understand that feeling," the man said, rather sadly. "I once loved a man with a mother's love, yet he blighted my existence."

The young chief looked up, and said—

"That man was my—"

"We are losing the man-of-war, sir."

Captain Tom turned angrily to the midshipman who brought this intelligence, and said—

"Very well; send the carpenter aft to report damages."

The boy touched his cap and went upon his errand; and our hero turned to resume the conversation with Iron Arm.

He was disappointed.

The giant was leaning moodily against the taffrail, gazing at the shadowy outline of the line-of-battle ship.

Captain Tom knew his follower had one of those deep fits of melancholy upon him—moods which had such an effect upon the giant's mind that he would repair to his berth and remain for days, shunning and shunned by his fellow-men.

The young chief touched his arm lightly.

Iron Arm turned at the touch, and his face slightly flushed, as though savage at being disturbed.

The angry look passed away when his eyes met the handsome young chief's, and he said—

"I am glad you awoke me."

"Indeed; why so?"

"I was rapidly drifting into a sea of disagreeable recollections, when your touch awoke me to the world."

"I am glad I did so. I want your counsel."

"You can command my life."

"Not that yet, I hope. Now, what is to be done about poor Harry Martin?"

"Ah! I had forgotten."

He passed his hand over his forehead as though to collect his thoughts, and said, slowly—

"From the description Hauler gave of the place, the poor boy must be in the power of those real fanatics in the House of Exercise."

"House of Exercise!"

"Yes; a place where they purify the soul from sin for so many dollars, and give you a passport to Heaven."

"A strange place to take young Martin."

"Not strange; the dungeons hold many a victim whose presence is undesirable in this world."

"Yet I cannot see the utility of taking him there."

"Did not Reuben wish to betray you to the line-of-battle ship?"

"He did."

"Would not a confession wrung from one of your followers answer the same purpose?"

"Possibly; but Harry is as true as steel."

"The rack and thumbscrews may draw; they will make the most stubborn speak."

"They would not dare—"

"They would dare anything for gold. He must be released, if living; if dead, avenged!"

"He shall; but how is that to be effected?"

"There is but one way—we must keep on our course until nightfall, then double back."

"In the harbour of San Lois?"

"No; to a small creek a few miles below the harbour."

"It seems our only plan. I will signal to Dutch Paul."

The "Yellow Vulture" answered the signal by going alongside.

"What, in the name of all the snakes, is the matter now?" Dutch Paul asked. "Sprung a leak?"

"No; one of my followers has been left behind."

"Serve him right—he should have come aboard in time."

"He was unable to do so."

"Unable? How is that?"

"He has been taken prisoner."

"That alters the case. Well, what are we to do?"

"You had better keep on your course. I will follow when I have rescued him."

"You may want a little help."

"No."

"Don't be too sure. The whole story of your impertinence in anchoring within gunshot of the English ship will be known by this time, and a fishing-boat will be searched upon its entrance to the harbour."

"I shall not go there."

"The devil you won't. Where will you go?"

"To a small inlet below the town."

"That will do; but I shall cruise within sight of land until you appear again. It may be useful."

"Yes; to bring the enraged old admiral upon you."

Dutch Paul laughed, and said—

"He would soon be glad to let me go again. I would give him enough of the 'Yellow Vulture's' claws that would satisfy him for a month."

"Be it so—do as you will."

About two hours after the "Yellow Vulture" had spoken with the buccaneer's ship, Captain Tom ordered the drummer to beat to quarters.

Though every freedom was permitted to the men on board the "Will-o'-the-Wisp," our hero maintained a strict discipline that would have done credit to a man-o'-war.

There was one particular he never neglected.

That was, the cleaning of the arms.

No matter how fierce the engagement had been, the roll of the drums called every man from his berth just two hours after the fight had concluded.

The crew, when he first established this regulation, were much dissatisfied at being turned out from their snug sleeping-places, and gave vent to their annoyance in strong language.

Our hero, who chanced to pass a group that were lazily polishing their pistols, overheard words that brought the hot blood to his cheeks.

"We might as well," one said, "be on board a man-of-war. I don't see doing this when we have put our necks in the halter."

"Neither do I, Jem," said a man near the first speaker. "I'd make one to go to the chief, and tell him we won't do it."

Captain Tom passed on unnoticed, but there was a deepening gleam in his eyes that showed how much this little incident had angered him.

When he reached the poop, he beckoned Harry Vere to his side.

"Lieutenant Vere," he said sternly, "take a party of armed men, and bring those fellows here that are seated near the mainmast."

The astonished grumblers suddenly found themselves in the centre of an armed party, and, much to their annoyance, they were marched to the quarter-deck.

The young chief turned angrily towards them, and said—

"I have a few words to say to you."

Every man dropped his eyes and endeavoured to look as though they were innocent of any attempt at mutinous language.

"When you elected me as your leader," Captain Tom went on. "I explained to you then that every law which has passed should be as rigidly obeyed as though we sailed under the King's flag. Many among you are not content with the duties I have thought fit to impose upon you. Any man that does not like the discipline on board is at full liberty to leave; remember, as long as I command here my order shall be implicitly carried out, and without grumbling. You can go; release them, Mr. Vere."

From the day of this occurrence up to the time when the crew went out after the terrible battle, not a murmur was heard at any order the young chief issued.

His was not a semblance of power; he ruled absolute monarch of that stout ship, and grey-bearded men came to him for counsel.

The summons aroused the worthy Jerry and the illustrious Bob from their nests, and, much against their will, they were compelled to turn out and take their share of the work on deck.

Bob Hauler's allowance was a heap of cutlasses which had to be cleaned from the tell-tale marks of the fray.

Jerry was near him with a small pile of muskets, which had to be cleaned before putting away for use.

If there was one regret Bob Hauler had when he set about his work, it was that he had not left his splitting headache below.

He had just grumbled out something to Jerry, when Jacob's long body was seen above the hatchway.

"There he is, Bob," said the mischievous Jerry; "wait till he comes past us, then dig a cutlass point in his foot."

Bob looked quite savage enough to follow this advice, and when Jacob came daintily along the deck, he received a blow upon the toes from the heavy hilt of a cutlass.

The vampire sprang upward with pain, then, catching up a naked sword, he turned upon Bob and yelled—

"Get up, you thing, and defend yourself."

"That's it, is it?" said Bob, jumping to his feet, cutlass in hand. "Curse you, I'll make mincemeat of your ugly carcase."

Jacob's appearance, as he hopped about flourishing the long rapier, was so grotesque that it drew the men from their work to ascertain the cause of his antics.

One look was sufficient to explain the affair, and the mirth-loving jolly tars, seeing a prospect of some fun, began to take sides with the combatants.

Ned Hartley, a grey-headed old tar, proffered his services as second to Jacob, and, by artful whispers, kept up the vampire's courage.

"Now, Jacob," he said, "let's have everything right and proper; you must fight a duel."

"A duel, ugh!"

"Don't shiver, Jacob; you can easily win. Come, off with your coat, and I'll put you in proper trim."

The coat was taken off, shirt-sleeves rolled up, and Jacob's three-cornered hat stuck firmly on his head.

Ned Hartley arranged this by giving his principal a bonnetting.

Jerry Mizzen was second to the grinning Bob, and, nearly choking himself with laughter, Jerry came forward and said as gravely as he could—

"Now, Ned, is your man ready?"

"Quite, Mr. Mizzen, and willing to have satisfaction for the blow he received from your principal."

"My principal," Jerry said, "won't apologise; he means to let the wind through that ugly one—no, no—I mean—he means to have a go in. What are you grinning at, Ned? Ain't I pitching the right palaver, when two 'longshore lubbers fight a duel, and two more pay out the slack?"

A roar of laughter came from the men and boys who had congregated around.

Jerry had most signally failed in his part as mediator.

"Yes, Jerry," Ned said, "it's all right. My principal won't 'cept any 'pologies; he wants satis—"

"Yes, I will," Jacop said, kindly; "I'll accept any—"

"You hear," Ned shouted, loud enough to drown Jacop's voice, "my principal says he will fight till every 'air of his 'ed turns to a hicicle, and the hicicle grows as big as the North Pole."

"I hear," Jerry said, "therefore they must fight till one on 'em gives in."

Ned Hartley bowed in what he thought the proper style for such occasions, then whispered to Jacop—

"Keep up your pecker—lunge straight out every time you have a chance—don't forget."

Jacop had seen the boy buccaneers drilled and exercised with their swords by their young leader, and calling to his aid the various modes of attack and defence he had seen, screwed up his courage, and advanced to meet his foe.

He found Bob Hauler quite ready, and, amid a confused cry of—

"Give it him, Bob!"

"Go it, vampire—make him a subject for the old blu 'letter!" the fight began by Jacop making a wild lunge at his grinning adversary's heart.

The vampire assumed what he thought was the proper and most scientific attitude, but his sword was caught by Bob's ready guard.

There was no attempt on Bob's part to use any trick of fence.

Every fierce lunge from his adversary was well met, and, to Jacop's annoyance, Bob kept jumping from side to side, thus keeping his adversary continually on the move.

"Why don't you stand quiet?" gasped Jacop, out of breath with following his adversary about. "You don't know how to fight."

"Don't I, lantern-jaws? Come on—ha! that's one to me."

He gave Jacop a smart blow with the flat of the cutlass just above the right ear.

The vampire yelled, and jumped quickly backwards, followed by Bob, who managed to catch Jacop upon the collar.

This was the climax. The vampire felt a sensation like pins and needles pass through his arm, and making a wild but unsuccessful attempt to throw his opponent, his foot slipped, and he fell.

Bob aided the downward inclination of his body by a heavy slap from the cutlass.

Just as Jacop sprawled forward, the tar struck an attitude, and called out—

"Yield, traitor, or cuss me if I don't make a hole in your karkiss."

"I yield," said Jacop, in a smothered voice. "Don't make a hole in me."

Doctor Shrike came upon the scene at the moment of his assistant's discomfiture, and, rushing forward, he chuckled—

"Where's the wound—where's the wound? I'll soon put him to rights."

Jacop dreaded his master's approach more than the uplifted sword of his adversary, and, scrambling to his feet, he made a rush to the hatch.

The doctor was close upon him, and behind the doctor a posse of mischievous boys, ready for any fun.

"He'll bleed to death," said Doctor Shrike. "Watch him, my lads. We must shave his head, and blister his feet; nothing better than that remedy for wounds when they bleed inside."

Jacop had practised the doctor's remedy too often not to know the pain it caused, so, with a sudden yell of terror coming from his lips, he made a bound down the hatchway.

He missed the first step, and, as a natural consequence, his back scraped the edge of the ladder as he tumbled to the bottom.

"Fracture of the spine," said Dr. Shrike, gleefully. "I shall have to saw him in half, and stick him together again."

Jacop was too much shaken by his fall to escape from the doctor's clutches, and, in spite of the ingenious manner in which he raised his long, bony legs, he was carried to the cockpit, and laid upon the table placed there for the doctor's use.

"Hold him, hold him tight!" said his master. "Stick to him, lads; we'll soon shave his head and blister his feet."

The lads, nothing loth, held Jacop tightly by the arms and legs until Doctor Shrike returned with a case of razors, and a large shaving-brush.

"That's it," the doctor said, maliciously glancing at the vampire's white face; "that's the position. Now, boys, which shall we do first—saw him in a half, or shave him?"

"Shave him! shave him!"

"Very well; perhaps that will be best."

A pair of thick, ragged moustaches had hitherto graced Jacop's upper lip—said moustaches being a terrible eyesore to Captain Tom's middies.

They had often tried to cut off this appendage to Jacop's cadaverous face, but the vampire, who prized his ragged moustaches too highly to suffer them to be shorn off, always defeated the boys' object at the moment they were about to use the scissors.

Now the youngsters saw a chance of having their wishes gratified, and, in spite of Jacop's yells, they did their best to keep him still during the time Doctor Shrike plied the scissors and razors.

The deed was done.

Jacop's vampire-like appearance was not diminished by the loss of every hair upon his head and face.

They released him when all was over, and, almost suffocated by suppressing their laughter, the boys rushed on deck, and left Jacop and the doctor to fight it out.

They paused upon the top of the hatch, and looking down, beheld Jacop's long fingers grasping the doctor's nose.

A bucket of dirty water stood near.

"This," said Jack Langton, "will do for a shower—hoo!"

The leathern vessel was emptied, and the contents were equally distributed between the doctor and his man.

They were about to disperse, when the shrill whistle summoned all hands to shorten sail.

The gallant vessel gradually slackened her speed, and as the darkness began to fall upon the waters, the "Will-o'-the-Wisp" sped to the rescue of the gallant Harry Martin.

The spot our hero had selected for a landing-place was a small rocky inlet between five and six miles from the town.

The surf seethed and bubbled above the sunken rocks as the young buccaneer stood at the wheel, his eyes and hands taxed to their utmost skill to guide his vessel through the dangerous passage.

Iron Arm, Harry Vere, and Ben Barnacle were anxiously looking out ahead, and the crew, awed and silent, stood in scattered groups watching every look upon their young leader's face.

They knew his daring nature would prompt him to run the vessel into the most dire peril to rescue their young companion, and as the ship came nearer the foaming, bubbling waters, they knew the slightest deviation from the intricate passage would dash her stout timbers to fragments.

So assured were they of their leader's skill, that none uttered a word apprehensive of a mischance overtaking their splendid ship.

The young baccaneer's eagle eyes kept upon an old tree which stood a few yards from the shore, and slowly brought the vessel's bows in line with its dark trunk.

And from time to time the death'y stillness was broken by his orders to the sail-trimmers to keep the ship from falling off.

"If we get through this," said Iron Arm to Harry Vere, "the captain can take the ship through the eye of a needle."

"If large enough," said Harry. "Yes; we shall be safely at anchor upon that broad piece of water in ten minutes' time."

"I hope so."

Looking over the bulwarks, they beheld in many places sharp points of the sunken reef.

"This," Iron Arm said, pointing to the shallow water, "would not be credited."

"The sunken rocks?"

"No; the fact of our vessel passing safely through."

"Such ventures as these are our safeguards."

"I question if the commander of that liner would allow a boat from his vessel to pass up here."

"He would not. Ah! she's struck!"

A dull, scraping noise startled all on board, and there was a rush to the side to ascertain the cause.

They were safe.

It w s but the sharp point of a stone, larger than any t s ve l had yet passed, that scraped harshly against the copper sheathing.

"Let go the maintop," the young commander said; "quick about it, my lads, or we shall be drilled through and through."

The sail flapped for a moment against the mast, then, as the wind came whistling among the cordage, the canvas bellied out, and the ship dashed forward.

"Hurra!—hurra!"

This cry came from the men's throats as the vessel glided into deep water.

They were safe for a time—safe until the rocky passage had to be repassed.

Many shuddered at the thought; the passage would have to be made at night, with nothing to guide their daring leader save the remembrance of the peril he had so lately passed through.

That was sufficient for one whose eye never forgot the bearings of the most intricate creek, and whose hand was never firmer than when driving his vessel through the greatest peril.

The sails were now hanging in the brails, the watch set, and our hero preparing to go ashore.

In silence the boat was lowered, and, with muffled oars, the light craft glided shoreward.

Captain Tom, Iron Arm, Bob Hauler, Jerry Mizzen, and two of the crew, quietly left the boat, and went towards the town.

———

CHAPTER LVI.

A TREACHEROUS MESSMATE.

IRON ARM and the young chief were a few paces in advance of the men; had it been otherwise, the giant would soon have noticed the suspicious manner in which a half-caste, who formed one of the party, watched our hero.

Though the giant's vigilance was not over the fellow's movements, there was another who felt that all was not right with their companion.

Bob Hauler, Jerry, and Ned were walking abreast, and between them and their young leader was the

suspicious, slimy, treacherous-looking Anglo-Indian, who had given the name of Iljure when he entered the ship.

He was no other than Sanderson's murderous enemy—the villainous Skopey.

None of the men liked the fellow.

His was the only voice that ever uttered a word against their young leader—his the only lip to curl with affected scorn when Captain Tom's deeds were spoken about by the faithful crew.

Once he had attempted to excite a mutiny among the men, but the rope's-ending he had received so cured him of his seditious designs that he ever after affected to be one of our hero's most faithful followers.

Captain Tom knew nothing of this.

The crew had taken the case in their own hands, and from that moment the half-caste became an object of suspicion.

Though he knew it not, there was always a close watch upon his actions.

The petty officers, in stationing the men, were careful not to put Skopey upon any part of the vessel where he could work any mischief.

They were waiting and watching for a confirmation of their suspicions.

Their suspicions, had they known all, would soon have brought Skopey to the yard-arm.

Surrounded by so many foes, whenever an addition was made to the crew, the old and faithful band who had first raised the banner of revolt always narrowly watched the new comers, to ascertain, if possible, whether they were true friends, or traitors sent by their young leader's foes.

As the three seamen followed their chieftain, Ned told his companions of their suspicions respecting Skopey.

And, as the traitor walked in front of them, he became the subject of conversation.

"Well," Bob said, "if he's always up to these games, why don't you tell the chief?"

"Yes," said Jerry, "that's what I think."

"Because," Ned answered, "we are not sure that he is a traitor yet."

"Not sure?"

"No."

"If trying to get up a mutiny ain't enough, what is?"

"Well, any man might do that, you know, Jerry."

"Might he?—not if he was all right."

"P'raps not; but you see we all had a palaver over it, and it was settled that we was to wait till we got a chance of nailing him; then a rope would do the rest."

"Up to the yard-arm?"

"Yes."

"Look at him now," Jerry said; "he's a looking at the chief as though he'd like to knife him."

"He'd better try it on," Bob said; "I've a little cutlass here that would soon let daylight through his ugly karkiss."

"So have I."

"And I have, too."

Skopey suddenly turned, and, seeing his messmates intently regarding him, he came towards them, and said—

"Well, messmates, what do you think of this expedition?"

"We never thinks," said the sturdy Bob; "the chief does that, and we does all he tells us."

"Yes," Jerry said; "that's just what we does, and if he was to tell us to hang you to that tree, we'd do it."

The half-caste's face wore a sullen look, and as he fell behind the buccaneers he muttered—

"There may be a chance yet. They are talking

about staying all night at a farm-house; once asleep, and away from his men, my knife shall prevent his awakening."

He had followed Captain Tom and Iron Arm close enough to hear their conversation, and to plan a mode of carrying out his employer's wish.

Sanderson had chosen a fitting instrument for his murderous design—one who, it was said, had the bloodhound's pertinacity and the serpent's cunning.

When the bucaneers left the boat, our hero and Iron Arm were for some time at a loss how to make the attempt to rescue Harry Martin.

"It will be no use," the giant said, "to attempt an entrance by the front of the building."

"So I thought, yet we could force the door."

"Yes, and bring the old Don and his friends upon our heels—perhaps the crew of the man-of-war."

"True. What is to be done?"

"Harry Martin," Iron Arm said, "must be rescued; the plan I have not yet decided upon."

"You know the place?"

"Well."

"That is something, should we ever get inside."

"Yes, the knowledge may be useful; but how to get there?"

"Can you not suggest a—"

"Yes, decidedly I can. Why did I not think of it before?"

The young chief saw, by the expression of his follower's face, that there existed a probability of penetrating the interior of the gloomy building.

"Yes," Iron Arm continued, "the task will not be so difficult, but it will involve time."

"How long?"

"Until to-morrow morning—daybreak, at the earliest."

"How is this?"

"I will explain. There is an old house at the back of the building which formerly did duty as a chapel."

"What is it now?"

"A wine-shop and place of entertainment for man and beast."

"A change, certainly."

"It is, if it serves our purpose, we need thank the change."

"Yes. Continue your explanation."

"Well, that old hostel was reached by a long underground passage."

"Was. The passage does not exist now—"

"It does; the entrance only has been blocked up, and, if I mistake not, there is an aperture now of sufficient width to allow sundry bottles of the forbidden liquid to pass through."

"For the use of the holy brotherhood?"

"Yes; the saintly rascals were afflicted with the same thirst that tickles the throats of less godly men."

The young chief laughed lightly at his follower's words, and said—

"So far I cannot understand why we should have to pass the night at the hostel before making an attempt to rescue poor Martin."

"The house," Iron Arm said, "is kept open all night for the convenience of travellers, and during the time the attendants are about it will not be possible to put our project into execution."

"True. Is that the place?"

"There?"

"Yes."

"That is it. Leave the arrangements to me. I understand the ways of these innkeepers better than you do, captain."

CHAPTER LVII.
CAPTAIN TOM'S ADVENTURE WITH THE SPANISH GIRL.

WHEN they reached the hostel, the party had drawn their caps over their faces and hidden their weapons with their heavy boat-cloaks.

Mine host stood at the doorway, and greeted his guests with a profound bow.

Captain Tom's princely bearing was not without its effect upon the landlord, and he muttered—

"A nobleman and his suite; I must charge well for their accommodation. It is not often the saints send us good customers now-a-days."

He crossed himself at the saints' goodness, and bowed our hero and his men inside the building.

"Your excellenza," he said to the young chief, "has selected the best and only respectable house of entertainment in Barracoa; for this honour I thank your excellenza, and await, with profound respect, your commands."

Captain Tom felt much inclined to kick the obsequious innkeeper for his servility, but, controlling his inclination, he said—

"My attendant will explain."

He referred to Iron Arm by a gesture, then passed the cringing landlord, and seated himself by a bright wood fire that was burning in the grate.

"His Highness," the landlord said to Iron Arm, "has been pleased to refer me to you, and—"

"That will do," the giant cried; "spare your breath, and answer my questions."

"I am dumb."

"Can we be accommodated here until morning?"

"For a month, if you require to stay so long, sir."

"Until the morning will do. See the beds are prepared, and bring a dozen of your choicest wine."

"A dozen, your excellenza?"

"A dozen."

"Does your highness know that the wine you ask for is four silver dollars the bottle?"

"Bring them, no matter if they are forty dollars."

The innkeeper bustled away, muttering—

"They must all be princes; I wish I had said six dollars each bottle. Yes, they must all be princes."

So thoroughly convinced of the exalted rank of the visitors was Boniface, that he drank a bottle to his own good health before he left the cellar, and resolved to charge for it in the bill.

Our hero and Iron Arm sat at a table together, Jerry Mizzen, Bob Hauler, and their companions at another; and when the wine was placed before them, and the rich juice gurgled from the neck of the bottle to their glasses, the ex-smugglers' mouths began to water at the sight.

"Bob," whispered Jerry, nudging his companion, "this stuff looks fine, don't it?"

"Sooner have a pint of the good old rum we used to get, Jerry."

"Would you, Bob?"

"Yes."

"I'll drink your share, then; this might not agree with you, as you don't fancy it."

Bob Hauler declined Jerry's generosity, and from the oft-repeated filling of his glass, he seemed to manage it pretty well, considering he did not care for it.

The room in which the bucaneers were seated was the general resort of the idlers of Barracoa.

When they first entered the place was empty, but by degrees the seats became occupied by the frequenters of the tavern, and two swaggering Spaniards seated themselves opposite the young chief and his companions.

Captain Tom and Iron Arm carried on their conversation in English, and the Spaniards, as the wine began to warm their blood, indulged in sundry personalities, which caused the hot blood to redden the boy's cheeks.

"Who are these fellows, Pedro?" asked the Spaniard who sat opposite our hero, of his companion. "They seem to have money; shall we challenge to a game at cards?"

"A parcel of rough sailors, I think. Yes, we empty their pockets; the money is better in our than in theirs."

"Carrambo, you speak the truth;" then pushing glass towards Captain Tom, he added, "Drink, comorado."

The young chief moved his head, as though not understanding the Spaniard's words.

The don twisted his moustache fiercely, and said—

"Drink, comorado, or, by the blood of old Spain, you will insult us."

Iron Arm looked quietly at the speaker, and said—

"We wish to drink our own wine in peace; yours is not wanted."

There was something in the Hercules' look that for the moment somewhat cooled the Spaniard's prating.

"We meant not to offend," said the don; "it is our custom to drink with a stranger here."

"Keep your customs and your card-tricks for those who need them, we do not."

The Spaniard's swarthy face paled with rage, and he whispered to his companion—

"By the saints we will pick a quarrel with these fellows; there are but two."

"We will pass the word to Jacques for assistance."

The Spaniard rose, and went to a table at the extremity of the room.

Here a dozen of villainous-looking fellows were drinking and lazily puffing their cigarettes.

Iron Arm watched him, and said to our hero—

"Those fellows are what we should term blacklegs in England. Those with whom he is speaking are part of the gang, ready, should these rascals' roguery be discovered by a victim, to aid, either by word or the knife, in silencing any dupe bold enough to proclaim their rascality."

"A pleasant set. How did you become acquainted with them?"

"During my stay at the pirate lair."

"They do you credit."

"They make up the measure of the strange beings one meets during his life."

"True; he is returning. I expect we shall have something to pass away our time."

"No doubt they would try and quarrel with us for the opportunity of plundering our persons."

The young chief smiled.

"The dons," he said, "will presently find that we shall be more trouble than profit."

"The knowledge, captain, will be imparted through their broken skulls."

The don, looking fiercer than ever, came to his companion's side, and seating himself, said, in a quiet voice—

"The young one is a rich nobleman, his companion a servant; we shall probably do a good stroke of business by drawing our blades upon him."

"How is it to be done?"

"We must wait for an opportunity."

The landlord, with a possible and profitable bill bating before his mind, had given the don a description of the buccaneers.

"Rich," he said, "decidedly rich. Why they drink wine at four dollars the bottle."

He made no mention of the men who sat near the young chief, and the Spaniards not having the least idea that the two parties were in any way connected, thought their plan easy of accomplishment.

The wished-for opportunity of insulting the young stranger soon occurred.

A pretty, dark-eyed girl entered the room, and standing near Captain Tom's chair, she began to sing a love-song, accompanying herself upon a guitar.

When the song was finished, our hero gave her a small golden coin.

"Here, pretty one," he said; "it is not often such sweet notes sound upon my ear."

The girl cast down her eyes upon our hero's admiring gaze, and said—

"My song has pleased you, noble sir. Shall I sing you another?"

"Do, and I will give you another piece of money."

"I do not require it, excellenza. You have spoken kindly—that is more to Ninetta than gold."

"Kindly, my pretty one! Does an unkind word ever repay you for your sweet song?"

The girl looked cautiously around, and said, just loud enough for the chief to hear—

"You are a stranger, senor. Yes; worse than unkind words—insults often—for I am poor and friendless, and the roystering young gallants think I should sell my beauty to their caprice."

The girl's face tingled as she spoke, and a tear came into her eyes as she added—

"They think, senor, that a poor girl should not be as virtuous as her richer sisters. It is hard, but I must bear it, for I have a poor lame mother, who would starve but for the little I glean by singing."

"Such ruffianism does no credit to your countrymen, Ninetta," said the impulsive young chief. "Here, pretty one, take this purse of gold, it will be a good dower for you. Yes, take it, and become the wife of him you love best."

The girl's eyes sparkled at the shining coins visible through the network of the purse, and she said—

"This is too much, senor; I cannot, dare not take it."

"Why?"

"Beppo would cast me off for ever."

"Beppo! Who is Beppo, pray?"

The rosy blush became deeper upon the girl's face and neck as she answered—

"My affianced husband, senor."

"Yes; why would he cast you off?"

"He would say, senor, that I came by this wrongfully; for, though but a poor muleteer, Beppo is honest."

"He is an ass," said Iron Arm; "such a girl as this is fit for a noble. What think you, captain, to making her an addition to your state-room—she is beautiful enough?"

Captain Tom did not answer. He was too much engaged with the pretty ballad-singer.

"Tell Beppo," he said, "that a friend gave you this as a dowry."

A little hesitation on the girl's part, then she took the purse and placed it in her breast.

"May the saints," she said, taking our hero's hand and kissing it, "watch over and protect you. Tell me your name, senor, that we may pray for you."

The young chief was at a loss to reply; but his inventive brain did not long fail him.

He wished the gift to benefit the girl, and, at the same time, not to excite the jealousy of the too susceptible muleteer.

'NOTHER MOMENT AND THE KNIFE WOULD HAVE PIERCED HIS HEART.

"Tell Beppo," he said, "the present is from a nobleman; but stay, did he tell you that he acted as guide to a travellernot long since?"

"Yes, yes," the girl said, eagerly; but, suddenly changing her gladsome tone, she added, "yes, senor; but that takes place so often—almost every week. He shows the safest paths over the mountains to those who travel the same way."

"Quite right, Ninetta; tell him this present is from one as a reward for his good nature and civility; tell him, also, that he is to be kind to you, and you are only to sing within your own cottage."

"He will be kind, sir: this is all we wanted, a little sum to buy a place to live in; now we can be happy, and I shall never be compelled to seek a livelihood again; and," she added, "all this

through your kindness, senor. May the Virgin shield you from harm!"

She pressed her warm lips to her benefactor's hand, and, taking the broad ribbon which suspended the guitar around her neck from the instrument, was about to leave the room, when the baffled gamester, who sat opposite our hero, called out harshly—

"Stay, girl; come here and sing to us."

The young creature gave a wild, startled glance at the speaker, and said—

"No, no, senor; I shall not sing any more."

The ruffian muttered a coarse oath, and shouted out to the man who sat near the door—

"Stop the girl, Cervante; she shall sing."

A tall, burly fellow, garbed in a shabby

velvet, and armed with a long Spanish rapier, jumped from his seat and caught Ninetta by the skirt.

A slight scream came from her lips as she was forcibly drawn back, and, with a pleading look at our hero, she said—

"Save me, senor—save me!"

Prudence was not a leading trait in our hero's temperament, or possibly he would not have acted as he did upon this occasion.

Before the girl could speak he was upon his feet.

One bound brought him beside the ruffian who held the girl, and, in spite of their disparity in size, the chivalrous boy seized the fellow by the throat, and hurled him headlong to the floor.

He fell beneath the table where his companions sat.

A fierce cry came from the Spaniards who had been seated opposite our hero, and with their hands upon the hilts of their weapons, they arose.

Before they could leave the table, Irom Arm jumped to his feet, and said, in a determined tone—

"Keep your seats!"

The Spaniard who had offered our hero a glass of wine twirled his moustache proudly, and said—

"Keep our seats! Who the devil are you to make that request?"

The giant vouchsafed no answer.

One stride brought him beside the swaggering pair. and seizing them by the shoulders, he forced them to a sitting posture with the greatest ease.

There was no help for it, in spite of their resistance, they were compelled to yield to the mighty hands.

"Move from there." Iron Arm said, "and I will hurl you both through the window."

The Spaniards sat for some moments half stupified with surprise.

They were both tall, powerful men, but in the hands of the gigantic buccaneer they had seemed like infants.

In all probability they would have remained as Iron Arm had placed them, had not the giant been compelled to look to his young chief's rescue.

The party who were seated near the door consisted of about a dozen men.

When they beheld their companion so unceremoniously hurled at their feet, they drew their blades, and gathered round our hero.

Flinging open his cloak, the chief unsheathed his sabre. and stood ready for the first who had grown tired of existence.

There was such a devil-may-care fearless look in the young chief's eyes—such a perfect mastery displayed in the use of the weapon he held—by that graceful attitude that caused the Spaniards to pause for a moment to contemplate the daring young stranger.

"Have a care, my friends," he said, "the point of this blade is sharp, and my eyes sure."

He stood thus, and, with a happy, careless laugh falling from his lips, he beheld the Spaniards pause in evident astonishment at his daring.

With sundry oaths, more or less fierce, they were about to rush forward, when a voice yelled out—

"Avast there, you lubbers! Eleven to one! Come on. Jerry; give them a bottle first."

Jerry followed Bob's advice by hurling an empty bottle among his leader's foes, then, whipping out his cutlass, he cleared the table at a spring, and stood beside his chief.

Ned and Skopey followed their companion's feat—the latter, not from any good will he felt towards the young buccaneer, but because he could not do otherwise.

The time had not come to show the serpent's folds.

The unexpected aid—four strong seamen, each grasping a bright cutlass—was as unexpected as it was unwelcome to the Spaniards, and their sudden eagerness for the fray decreased most wonderfully.

The forms of the young chief and his followers were hidden from Iron Arm by the circle of Spaniards.

The giant, thinking his leader was in danger, when he had thrust the men who sat opposite him to their seats, strode across the room, and placed himself by the buccaneer chief's side.

No sooner had he left the table than the Spaniards jumped to their feet, and joined their companions.

The fellow who had been hurled to the ground by Captain Tom scrambled up at the same moment.

This addition gave the Spaniards courage, and, seeing but six opposed to their fourteen, the ruffian Captain Tom had floored roared out—

"At them, my friends! Wash out the insult we have received with their blood."

Iron Arm's mace described a swift circle as the foe began to press forward, and the giant said, sternly—

"Back, fools! are you tired of life?"

They drew back as the heavy weapon flashed before them.

But only for a moment.

Then, levelling their swords, they commenced the attack.

The landlord, with pale face and frightened gestures, stood in the centre of the room, crying—

"Gentlemen, gentlemen, do not bring discredit upon my house. Go outside and fight."

No one paid the least attention to his appeal, and the clash of opposing steel soon drowned every other sound.

The needy Spanish adventurers, when our hero threw open his cloak, saw the massive golden chain that hung around his neck, and, actuated by a desire to obtain possession of the beautiful ornament, as well as to be revenged for the insult to their companions, they sought to beat down the young chief.

The task was more difficult than they had imagined. Although the best and strongest swordsmen of their party sought to overcome the youthful leader, they found themselves compelled to look well to their own safety.

Jerry Mizzen and Bob Hauler laid about them with their cutlasses.

Disregarding all the studied rules of fence, they kept up such a succession of cuts and thrusts that the Spaniards soon appeared to find it warm work to keep a whole skin.

Ninetta, the cause of the affray, had disappeared when the combatants first drew their swords.

Well for our hero she had done so.

Iron Arm, as though the puny efforts of the Spaniards were too much beneath his strength, stood aloof from the fray.

Leaning upon the handle of his fell weapon, he kept his eyes warily upon the young chief, ready at a moment to crush any who should threaten the life of the boy he loved so well.

It soon became evident that the Spaniards were using every effort to drive the buccaneers from the room.

Finding they could not accomplish this so easily as their overwhelming numbers justified, they changed their mode of attack.

A few thuds had been given and received on both sides, and the illustrious Jerry had received a prod in the left arm.

This so exasperated him that he followed his antagonist with such vigour and determination that the Spaniard retreated to a corner.

A retreat that Jerry took especial care he did not move from.

Several had essayed their prowess with the gallant youth, who laughed at their efforts, and caused all who opposed him to retreat with a mark that would em'nd them of the combat for some time to come.

... cing they could not gain their end by attacking ...m by twos, six of the most valiant made a ...dden onslaught.

It was then Iron Arm, like an angry lion, rushed the encounter, and while fiercely egaged with this erwhelming gang, two of their number slipped eacherously behind our hero.

The buccaneers were too much occupied with the Spaniards' long blades to notice this; and one of the would-be assassins had already withdrawn his hand for the fatal stroke.

Another moment and our hero's blood would have strewed the floor, and his young life would have been forfeited in a tavern brawl.

But, before the stroke could be given, a dark, handsome youth bounded into the room.

He saw our hero's danger, and with the butt-end of a long whip he carried he felled the villain to the ground.

The other turned with a savage oath upon the intruder.

Turned just in time to receive a stinging, blinding cut from the new-comer's whip.

The thin lash cut like a knife, and the ruffian, dropping his sword, placed his hands to his eyes and rushed about the room blinded and maddened with pain.

"Thanks, friend," said Captain Tom; "your assistance is most welcome."

"I deserve no thanks, senor," said the youth, modestly. "Brave senor, that point was well given!"

His expression of admiration was caused by observing the young chief pink a fellow who had endeavoured to get under his guard.

The stranger was not idle; he plied his long whip-thong about the loins of the Spaniards until two or three of the gang ran howling from the fight.

"Keep together," said the young chief. "Bear down upon them; one good charge and the room will be cleared."

Back, step by step, the Spaniards were forced until they reached the door.

Here they made an attempt to rally; but, Iron Arm making a savage rush at them, they broke and fled.

The invincible Jerry still held his man in the corner; and when the Spaniard beheld his companions make their escape, he threw down his sword in token of submission.

"Let him go, Jerry," said the young chief; "no bloodshed is necessary."

"All right, your honour; only one prod at ..s ugly karkiss."

The Spaniard did not wait for the one prod.

He took advantage of the opportunity, when Jerry turned his head to answer his young leader, and made a move towards the door.

He was greatly assisted by the youthful stranger giving him a sharp cut ac... the legs with his whip.

The sharp sensation of pain caused the Spaniard to howl and swear most energetically.

"Now," the buccaneer chief said, "we may perhaps be allowed to finish our wine in peace."

"Yes," Iron Arm answered, laughing, "and with additional relish."

"Why additional relish?"

"The fight, or scramble rather, has made me thirsty."

They resumed their seats as though nothing had occurred to interrupt them.

Bob Hauler and Jerry Mizzen, to judge from the copious draughts of wine they swallowed, required a great quantity of the juice of the grape to restore their nerves.

The young stranger sat at the same table with Iron Arm and Captain Tom.

"Had it not been," the youthful leader said, "for your opportune arrival that fellow would certainly have made an ugly hole in my body."

"He would, senor; but Ninetta told me to return thanks for her. I came in time."

"Ninetta?"

"Yes, senor."

"You are Beppo, then?"

"Yes, senor; Beppo, the muleteer."

"Ninetta has told you of the present I—"

"She has, senor; I came to thank you for the gift, and to warn one so generous of danger."

"Danger?"

"Yes, senor; do not sleep here to-night."

"Not sleep here! Why, my friend?"

The muleteer lowered his voice to a whisper, and said—

"More than one rich traveller has stayed at this hostel and never been heard or seen again."

"You tell me this, and yet the man is allowed to keep the house open."

"Ah! senor, there has been inquiries made, but nothing has been found to criminate the scoundrel."

"This is pleasant," the chief said to Iron Arm. "Shall we stay?"

"By all means," was the answer. "If there is any villainy we shall be most likely to find it out, better than a solitary traveller."

"True."

The muleteer looked anxiously at our hero as he spoke with his companion.

The words were spoken in English, therefore incomprehensible to the Spaniard.

When they had finished, he said—

"You will not stay, senor?"

"Yes," Captain Tom said, "we are too many, and too well armed, to fear any attempt upon our lives or purses."

The young Spaniard shook his head regretfully, and said—

"I am grieved to hear it, senor, for there is more than one man connected with the murders and robberies that have taken place here."

"You suspect more than the innkeeper?"

"I do, senor—the saints forgive me!—but there can be none other than the holy brotherhood who assist this villain."

"The brotherhood!—what of the House of Exercise?"

"The same, senor."

"Do you think the saintly men would aid in this bad work?"

"Heaven knows; there are dark stories about these holy men."

"Idle rumours, perhaps."

"Perhaps so, senor; yet many believe them to be true."

"The monks do not seem to be in favour, then?"

The Spaniard shrugged his shoulders, and said—

"Not with me, senor—my faith has been shaken in them, and not without cause."

"Have you ever delivered yourself over to their tender mercies?"

"No, senor—the saints forbid! Why I mistrust them is from quite a different cause to the rumours of their debauchery and profligate habits."

"Is that their character?"

"It is; but true or false I cannot say. But I will tell you, senor, why I dislike the very name of the monkish breed, if you like."

"Do, Beppo."

"About two months past," the muleteer said, "I was asked by the superior of the order to bring a large box from Santa Fé, that is about twenty leagues from here.'

" Yes."

" Well, senor, I harnessed my mules to a cart, and brought the box to the House of Exercise. What think you occurred soon after ?"

" I cannot imagine."

" The heir to a large estate disappeared most mysteriously, and has not been heard of since."

" What has this to do with the box ?"

" Everything, senor. That box contained a man."

" Alive ?"

" Yes ; but drugged, I expect."

" How do you know this ?"

" Coming down a steep hill, senor, I thought I heard a groan from the inside of the cart. I thought nothing of it until the news of the young don's disappearance was made known."

" I cannot yet see the connection between the box and the missing heir."

" This is how I connect the affair, senor. The box had a number of holes pierced through the upper part, and from one of these holes this dropped out."

He held up his hand and showed a magnificent diamond ring upon the little finger.

" This jewel, senor, has the family arms engraved inside. You see, senor, the connection ?"

" I do ; but this is barbarous. Why do you not state this affair to the missing youth's friends ?"

" He has none, senor, except the man who has succeeded him to the title and estate."

" Well, why not expose the brethren of the House of Exercise ?"

The muleteer smiled.

" Three men, senor," he said, " were known to speak ill of the monks ; in less than a week they were found by the roadside, each with a cross-hilted dagger in his breast."

" Horrible ! and this state of things is allowed to exist in a civilised place ?"

" Yes, senor, and will exist until some conclusive proof can be brought to the evil-doers."

Iron Arm, who had listened with a quiet smile to his conversation, now said—

" You seem surprised, captain ?"

" Surprised ! I am horrified, and can scarcely believe these—"

" You have heard nothing yet," said the giant, cooly ; "nothing in comparison to the real state of society here."

" I have heard sufficient. I shall not have much compunction, I fear, in ridding the world of any cowled rascal who crosses my path."

" When we get inside," said Iron Arm ; " we are not there yet. Here comes the landlord with candles, as a hint for us to retire."

" I am not sorry, for I feel fatigued."

" You do not fear the dangers our friend Beppo points out ?"

" No," said the young chief, laughing. " I do not think I shall sleep unsound for the warning. How are we to manage about waking in time ?"

" I shall not sleep," said the giant. " In any case a sentry will be at your door."

Beppo, the muleteer, left the young chief, with a hope that he should behold him alive in the morning.

CHAPTER LVIII.

CAPTAIN TOM NARROWLY ESCAPES ASSASSINATION.

THE upper chamber of the quaint old hostel was the chapel gallery, partitioned off by thin boards.

In one of these our hero slept ; but outside the door stood Skopey, leaning upon the muzzle of a musket.

It was his turn for sentry, and a look of malignant triumph passed over his features as he thought—

" So they have put me here to watch over the very life I have sworn to take. So the opportunity has come at last."

The deed was not easy of accomplishment.

So the hired assassin found upon reflection ; his only chance was to trust to the chapter of accidents

Opposite the young chief's chamber was a small room, the door of which was open, and by the ruddy glare of a wood fire Iron Arm's giant form was visible.

Our hero's faithful friend was seated near the doorway, his head resting upon his hand, and his face full of deep thought, as he watched the flickering light rise from the red embers.

Beyond this room was another, and to gain admittance to the interior it was necessary to pass through Iron Arm's chamber.

Here Bob Hauler, Jerry Mizzen, and Ned were sleeping.

And soundly, if the trio of noses were a proof of the drowsy god's presence.

Skopey, as he gazed at the giant's figure, felt that unless he could creep inside our hero's chamber, and slay him without making the least noise, the attempt would be fatal to himself.

He knew that the mere turning of the door-handle would arouse Iron Arm from his reverie, and cause him to visit the young buccaneer chief's chamber.

" I would as soon, sooner have a sleeping lion to pass than have to elude that giant's vigilance."

So thought the half-caste as he stood upon his post.

He would have received as much mercy from the forest monarch as he would from the man who thus acted as a check upon his design.

There was another difficulty.

He knew well that the young chief was a very light sleeper, knew that the stealthiest footfall would arouse him

Once aroused, Skopey felt he would be no match for the lithe, muscular boy.

His thoughts changed.

Supposing the deed consummated, and Captain Tom's faithful guardians in ignorance of the deed how was he to escape ?

True, the passage was open to him.

But how was he to leave his post ? The very act of descending the stairs would cause Iron Arm to leave his seat.

Then, should he not escape—and it would be no easy matter for a stranger to unfasten the heavy bolts and bars—his life would be crushed out before he had gone a dozen yards.

Yet, in the face of these dangers, the opportunity was not to be lost.

" Now," he thought, " I have the first and only chance that has ever presented itself since I became a member of their band Yes ; the attempt must be made to-night."

The solemn bell of the adjacent monastery chimed the hour of midnight.

" Twelve," muttered the half-caste ; " I shall be relieved at two—two hours. Much may be done during that time."

So he stood watching and waiting for the opportunity to execute Sanderson's fiendish mission.

The deep-toned bell had chimed one when Skopey crept on tiptoe to the entrance to Iron Arm's chamber.

The wood fire had subsided to a few smouldering embers, and the room was in complete darkness.

The half-caste listened intently for a few seconds, then, as the giant's deep, regular breathing came upon his ears, he muttered—

" He sleeps. Now for the blow that will make me wealthy and independent of the world's frowns.

He crept back to his post, and placed the musket against the wall, then drawing his knife, he began to gently and noiselessly turn the handle of the door.

. . . . .

When the landlord of the hostel had shown his guests to their room, he went to a small chamber which opened close to the foot of the staircase.

Closing the door carefully, he placed the lamp upon the table, then rubbing his hands, muttered—

"It is a risk, a great risk, but they are too rich to slip through my fingers. I will confer with—"

A soft tap was heard outside the door, and the villainous host, rising, muttered—

"Talk of the devil, he is here in this instance."

He admitted a dark-skinned Mexican.

The new comer was a true type of ruffianly idle adventurers, who are ever ready to supply their wants with the knife rather than toil for a livelihood.

The man cast his sombrero upon the table, and pushing back his dark matted hair from his forehead, said—

"We are in luck's way to-night, Miguel."

The landlord shuffled about in his seat, and answered—

"I am afraid to risk it, Andrea."

Andrea helped himself to a flagon of wine and repeated—

"Afraid! What is the matter, Miguel?"

Miguel did not reply directly to the question.

"Could we not manage," he asked, "to rob these travellers without using the knife?"

"Would it be safe, Miguel?"

"That is the very question I have been trying to solve."

"What danger do you fear?"

"They are strong men, and well armed."

"Tush! A giant asleep is as harmless as a child."

"True, but among the number one may be awake, and these English, so like bulldogs, they do not flinch from a drawn knife, and cry out like a Spaniard to the Madonna for aid."

"It is so, Miguel; but the young traveller, you say, is rich."

"Very."

"The question amounts to this: shall he depart in the morning with his gold, or shall that gold be shared between us?"

"The latter arrangement would be most to my liking, Andrea, but I cannot shut my eyes to the danger. It is very great."

"Peste! What matter? The risk is only in proportion to the gain. Drink, comarado, and get some courage. I suppose you used your eyes last night among them."

"How used my eyes?"

"Did you notice which carried the money?"

"I did."

"That is something. Was it the young one?"

"It was."

"Good! Of course you put him in the proper chamber?"

"I did, but—"

"No buts, Miguel; the thing is easily done."

"I know it, but how are we to account for the young traveller's disappearance?"

"Account?"

"Yes, to his servants."

"I had not thought of that. Well, the old way, I think."

"Tell them their master left early?"

"Yes, that will do, and I think we will so manage matters that the keenest lawyer in Madrid would be baffled to bring the young traveller's death to our door."

"We have baffled them hitherto."

"Yes; but not without exciting suspicious rumours respecting the house, Miguel."

"That's true. Now, what is your plan, Andrea?"

"I think you said the rich traveller was in the west chamber?"

"Yes."

"Well, I shall go by the old way."

"From the passage in the rocks?"

"Yes. You would not have me go by the stairs?"

"No, certainly not. That would betray us at once."

"Just my opinion. Well, I will leave the door open as I pass, and when the blow settles the young fellow, I can carry the body down the secret staircase, and leave him on the rocks."

The innkeeper rubbed his hands gleefully.

"Well thought of," he said, "well thought of."

"Yes, I think it will do, Miguel."

"Do; such a plan would—But there, Andrea, we will not talk about it; somehow, these affairs always send a chill through my body."

"Your nerves are out of order," Andrea said. "Drink; come, fill up. Here's a health to our master."

"Our master?"

"Yes, the devil."

"Bravo! here's to Satan and his imps."

"Imps, Miguel?"

"Yes, the brethren of the House of Exercise."

"Ha! ha! Well done, Miguel; that old wine is giving you wit."

"And you, Andrea—"

"Well?"

"Courage, Andrea; for you always drink deeply before arranging this kind of business."

"A bad habit, that's all, Miguel. Now for our arrangements."

"There is nothing to arrange."

"The wine," said Miguel, "is getting to your head. Courage; do you think I am fool enough to take the plunder with me."

"Put it where you put the last."

"Carrambo! you are certainly in a hurry to have the noose round your neck."

"How; what mean you, Andrea?"

"Do you remember when the last little affair came off?"

"Yes."

"Also the narrow escape we had from the gendarmes going to that very cupboard and finding the dead man's money?"

"The saints protect us! Yes, I had forgotten that."

"I thought so. Now pay attention to me for a moment; but first pass that flagon."

Andrea refreshed himself, then resumed—

"When I go to the room, you stand beneath the window and receive the plunder."

"Yes."

"Bury it; and be on the alert for the alarm when the servants find their master gone."

"I shall be there, and ready to swear he left before daybreak."

"You will see, his body will be found among the rocks. Your statement that he left to view the scenery around Barracoa will disarm suspicion "

"Yes, but should the body be found?"

"The very thing."

"How?"

"The opinion will be that he has fallen by the hand of robbers."

"Good, so far. There is one thing we have forgotten."

"What is that, Miguel?"

"The stains upon the bed."

"Peste! did you not put double bed-clothing on?"

"I forgot it."

"You deserve to—Never mind, I will take a change of bedding, and carry the others away."

"That will do. Now what hour was that struck?"

"One."

"One hour past midnight; it is time I prepared."

The ruffian took off his garments, and, save for a piece of linen round his waist, he was naked.

The villainous innkeeper then smeared Andrea's dusky skin over with oil; this precaution being taken to prevent the victim from seizing his murderer.

The strongest grasp could not retain its hold upon any part of the ruffian's body, thus anointed.

Thus prepared for any emergency, the assassin armed himself with a broad-bladed knife, and said—

"Another draught, Miguel, to keep the cold out."

He drank deeply from the silver flagon, then left the apartment, followed by the innkeeper carrying his faded habiliments.

Like twin shadows they left the hostel, and keeping close beneath the shade of the quaint old building, they reached the door directly beneath our hero's window.

Under the twinkling starlight, the open rocky shore wore a wild appearance, and the pale moon, as though ashamed to light the villain's path to murder, hid herself beneath a heavy dark cluster of clouds.

After hiding Andrea's clothes beneath a heavy stone, the innkeeper went to assist his companion in opening the secret entrance to the old chapel.

The contrivance did credit to the monkish originator's skill.

Two square blocks of stone, so placed that the keenest scrutinizer would fail to have detected they were more than they seemed—a portion of the fallen cliff—formed the entrance.

Miguel had brought with him a short iron crowbar.

The point of this instrument was forced between the stones, and in a few seconds they fell asunder.

The aperture that now became plainly visible was not more than a foot in width and breadth, and, as Andrea glided through, a faint click was heard, and the stones, without any aid, closed above his head.

Miguel Ramos crept away, and with the large drops of cold clammy sweat standing upon his forehead, he stood beneath the young buccaneer's window.

The minutes seemed to lengthen into hours as he crouched awaiting for the plunder.

Could it be fancy?

A deadly tremor came over Miguel's frame as he saw, or fancied that he saw, the outlines of a man's form.

He closed his eyes with the hope of reopening them and finding the sombre-looking figure gone.

Now, between the crescent-moon's pale light and the place where he stood, he beheld a dark form; it seemed, to his guilty mind, as though the stranger was keenly watching the young chief's window.

Miguel's breath came short and quick.

Fain would he have called out to his accomplice, and bid him keep the spoil.

Too late.

Andrea had passed beneath the secret opening, and must now be in the very chamber.

The innkeeper's teeth chattered with fear.

He pictured his accomplice in the chamber, the deadly blow given, the victim rising, then falling back with his slayer's murderous grasp upon his throat.

Then followed the vision of Andrea getting the spoil; then—and his terror increased with the thought— the window opening, a falling parcel, and that dread figure standing before him.

Miguel's mental tortures during the few seconds that those thoughts passed through his mind were as horrible as they are indescribable.

Suddenly he looked towards the jagged piece of rock where he had beheld the dusky cloaked figure.

Joy! he had departed.

No, no; he would be discovered—discovered in the very act of assisting in a fell murder.

The strange form was walking slowly over the rocks towards the very spot where he cowered.

Another moment and it would be too late to save himself.

The window, he knew, might open, the tell-tale booty might drop at his feet, and no earthly power could save him from the hangman's grasp.

This terrible state of suspense was too much to bear.

He was unarmed, and by the pale light he saw a gleaming weapon in the stranger's hand.

Had it been otherwise, he would have sprung upon the advancing figure, and risked the result.

As it was, there was, or seemed to be, no means of saving himself.

Stay! A sudden thought came to Miguel's brain: The thought was parent to the act.

As the figure came near him he flattened himself against the wall, and, scarcely daring to breathe, crept towards the door of the hostel.

His trembling hand was upon the latch, another moment and he would have been inside.

But before he could push open the door, the stillness was broken by a loud report of fire-arms.

Miguel Ramos reeled forward and gasped—

"*Madre di Dios!* (Mother of God) he has failed."

The shot was followed by hasty trampling and men's voices; and the innkeeper, to keep up a semblance of innocence, hastily threw off his clothes, and seizing a candle, was about to hurry upstairs, when the door was burst violently open, and a cloaked figure rushed inside.

Miguel Ramos recognised the figure at a glance, and his heart sank within him.

It was Beppo, the muleteer.

"What has occurred?" asked the youth, fixing his dark eyes upon Miguel. "*Madre di Dios!* what has happened?"

"I know not," said the shivering wretch; "something strange must have taken place."

"Very strange," was the curt answer; and Beppo rushed past the host, and went towards the broad staircase.

Miguel followed him, the gallows and the grim executioner standing out vividly before his eyes.

CHAPTER LIX.

THE WOULD-BE ASSASSINS.—THE TREACHEROUS SKOPEY SAVES CAPTAIN TOM'S LIFE.

WORN out in mind and body, the young chief slept soundly—slept while two bloodthirsty wretches were creeping upon him to rob him of life.

One his own follower, the traitor Skopey.

The other Andrea, the assassin.

When the half-caste began to quietly turn the handle of our hero's chamber-door, every nerve was strained to catch the faintest sound.

Iron arm slept. The remainder of the young chief's devoted followers were far away from the gallant boy they loved so well.

Inch by inch he opened the door, and holding the handle of the lock in his hand, the half-caste listened for the boy's deep breathing.

A fiendish smile came over his face, and he muttered—

"He sleeps, and heavily. Now, or never! Ah!"

He stepped swiftly and noiselessly back, and gripped the barrel of his musket.

Gradually the piece was brought to his hip, the hammer drawn back, and Skopey's eyes dilating with superstitious fear, stood spell-bound, watching a portion of the wall open, and a weird, dusky figure step noiselessly into the chamber.

The half-caste thought of the many rumours he had heard about our hero having a compact with the Evil One.

And as he watched the strange, stealthy figure creep towards the young chief's bed, his hair bristled with fear, and his tongue clave to the roof of his mouth.

The half-caste, for the moment, thought his intended victim had received aid from the terrible quarter idle rumour among the ignorant attributed our hero's dashing success.

He had no idea that another, bent upon the same villainous errand as he had been, had crept towards the young chief's bedside.

Had this suspicious truth flashed to his mind, he would have stood calmly by and witnessed the deed.

Fear magnified the nude assassin's form into a prodigious size, and the most unearthly shape.

Under this influence his grasp relaxed upon the door-handle, and the bolt shot forward with a faint click.

The noise did not disturb the assassin, who, knife in hand, was creeping towards the sleeping chief.

But the ever-watchful Iron Arm was aroused from his sleep by the light sound, and jumping from his seat he called out—

"Sentry, what noise is that?"

Skopey could not reply.

That voice caused him to feel the danger he was in, and scarcely knowing what he did at the moment, he brought his piece to the shoulder, and fired.

The crack of the rifle was followed by a scream of agony, and as Iron Arm dashed to the door he beheld the midnight assassin upon his face.

His blood welled sluggishly from a wound between the shoulders, and the stream oozing out from beneath his breast told the ball had passed completely through his body.

It was a strange scene.

A scene full of melo-dramatic effect, the more natural because of the players' unstudied attitudes.

Bending over Andrea's lifeless form was Iron Arm; a few paces from the bleeding object was the young chief, his ever-ready hand grasping his naked sabre

At the door, leaning upon his musket, stood the bewildered Skopey.

The scene had been so strange and sudden that the half-caste knew not for the moment whether all that had passed was a dream or a reality.

Bob Hauler was the first to reach the scene, and, with drawn cutlass in hand, he rushed upon Skopey, and would have cleft the half-caste's skull in twain, had not Iron Arm sprung forward and received the blow upon his wrist.

The sharp weapon cut through to the bone, and the giant, closing the wound with his right hand, said—

"What would you do, fool? that man has saved your chief!"

Bob, wonder-stricken, looked from the speaker to the lifeless body, now becoming rigid and cold, and mechanically repeated—

"Saved your chief! Skopey saved the chief! Am I dreaming?"

Beppo, the muleteer, and Miguel Ramos came to the door.

The latter was as whit⋅ ⋯hrouded corpse, and his hand trembled so viole⋯ ⋯at he could scarcely hold the candle.

Jerry Mizzen and Ned came also; both were undressed, but with that instinct which seems peculiar to men who live by the sword, both had a naked weapon in their hands.

Iron Arm was the first to speak.

"Now, Skopey," he said, "explain the meaning of this strange affair."

The half-caste saw the opportunity. and determined to profit by it.

"You remember calling out to me when I opened 'eftain's door?"

"I do; the noise of the handle awoke me."

"I heard, or fancied that I heard, something moving inside the chamber," said the cunning half-caste, "and when you spoke I was in the act of opening the door. I saw a man's form creeping towards the chieftain's bed, saw the knife in his hand, and shot him."

Captain Tom came forward, and taking the half-caste by the hand, said—

"I have to thank you for my life; tell me, friend, how can I reward you?"

"I did but my duty, sir," was the subtle reply, "did only what you would have done had my life been in danger."

"Still your watchfulness demands a fitting recompense; I shall not forget it."

Bob Hauler came forward.

There was a glow of shame upon his face as he said—

"Skopey, shipmate, I nearly cut you down; do you forgive me for it?"

"I do, Bob, but should like to know why you were about to slay me."

"You shall; plain-sailing, shipmate, is the best. We suspected you."

"Suspected me?"

"Yes, shipmate; not I alone, but all on board the ship. That's why I made that chop at you."

"You were very hasty, Bob."

"Yes, shipmate; I thought something had gone wrong with the chief, and thinking you did not like him, I made sure you had shot him. But give us your hand, if any man says a word agin you in future, he will have to answer Bob Hauler for it."

The half-caste grasped the honest tar's hand, and they were, to all appearance, friends.

Bob next made his peace with Iron Arm, and expressed the sorrow he felt for inflicting the wound upon the giant's hand.

Iron Arm laughed good-humouredly, and said—

"Never mind, Bob, the cut will soon heal; think no more about it; possibly, had I suspected Skopey, I should have slain him when the shot was fired."

While they had been speaking the young chief's attention had been directed to the shivering innkeeper by a significant gesture from Beppo, the muleteer.

"Now, landlord," he said, "what do you know of this?"

"Nothing, senor; nothing, I swear."

"Are you sure?"

"Senor, by my hopes of life hereafter, I swear I do not."

"Strange," said the boy, smiling; "this is not the first affair of the kind that has occurred beneath your roof."

"Senor, you wrong me."

"His Excellency speaks the truth," Beppo said; "several travellers have disappeared."

"Yes, yes; true, most excellent Beppo; I had quite forgotten."

"Stranger still, they were all known to have slept in this room."

"My poor memory fails me. Were they missed from this room, are you sure, most estimable young man?"

"As sure, Miguel Ramos, as I am that you are a party to this vile work."

The candle fell from Miguel's hand as he uttered a frightful cry.

"It is false!—it is false!"

"We shall soon prove that," the young chief said. "Let us first discover how the miscreant came into the room unseen by the sentry."

The sliding panel was open, and Beppo said—

"It was through there the villain came, and with yonder trembling caitiff's knowledge."

"Have you any proof of this, Beppo?" the young chief asked, "or is it merely supposition."

"Your Excellenza shall hear. You remember the warning I gave you before I left?"

"I do."

"I went home, senor, but could not rest. I know not how it was, but I feared something would happen to you."

"Such interest is rather unusual for a stranger, Beppo."

"To you it may seem so, senor. You had been kind to my betrothed, and I felt that if danger threatened you I ought to repay that kindness by keeping watch over your safety.

"I left my cottage, senor, and came to the rocks to be within sight of your window. Perhaps two hours had passed while I stood there, and as I was upon the point of retiring I saw the door open."

A startled expression came upon the listeners' faces, and they involuntarily looked towards Miguel Ramos.

"Two men came out," the muleteer continued. "One was naked, or nearly so; the other was Miguel Ramos."

The innkeeper gave a spasmodic cry, and would have fled from the spot had not Bob Hauler clutched him.

"Stay here, shipmate," he said, "until the palaver is over; and harkee, if you attempt to make sail you shall have six inches of cold steel in your hull."

Ramos did not understand his captor's words.

The movement of his weapon was significant enough, and with all hope of escape dying from his mind, he stood, pale and trembling, while Beppo spoke.

"I watched them, senor," continued the muleteer, "until they reached a peculiar-looking piece of rock. Here they stood for some minutes. Miguel Ramos placed a bundle beneath some loose stones—"

"No, no!" shrieked the wretch. "It is a mistake."

"Silence!" said the young chief, sternly. "It is for others to judge of the truth. Be silent, and remember that strict justice shall be meted out to you."

"Senor, senor, pray, for the love of—"

Bob Hauler placed his hand over Miguel's mouth, and silenced him for a time.

The young muleteer then resumed his narration.

"When Miguel had hidden the bundle," he said, "both men applied some instrument to the strangely-shaped stones.

"I saw them open—open, senor, as near as I can describe it, like a box.

"The naked figure then passed through, and the strange opening then closed over his head.

"I was spell-bound with unknown-to-me sensations, or I should have rushed forward, and followed Miguel's companion.

"As it was, I kept to my hiding-place, and watched Miguel's movements.

"He left the place I have described, and placed himself beneath your window.

"Then, senor, the terrible truth flashed to my mind. I felt sure they were about to kill you, and this ruffian had placed himself beneath the window, either to receive whatever valuables you had, or to take your murdered body.

"So strong was my excitement that I forgot for the moment that my form was visible to the villain, Miguel, and, as a matter of course, when I reached the place where he crouched he had disappeared.

"I followed stealthily, and reached the door just as the report of a rifle came from this room."

"Where," the young chief asked, "was this man at the time?"

"A few paces inside the door, senor."

"Was he dressed?"

"Yes, senor; when I pushed open the door he was hurriedly divesting himself of his clothing."

"I understand the motive," said Iron Arm. "He wished to appear before us as though he had just left his bed."

"Do you know where his sleeping-chamber is?" asked the young leader. "I should like to visit it."

"Yes, senor."

"Will you show me the place?"

"Willingly, senor."

"Keep that man here until I return. Come, Beppo, we will soon find out whether this fellow is guilty or innocent."

They went to the chamber, and found the bed had not been disturbed.

"The first part of your story is substantiated," said Captain Tom. "Now let us descend to the door."

In the long passage, and within four paces of the door, the young chief beheld Miguel's clothes, where the miscreant had hurriedly thrown them.

The boy's face wore an anxious look.

"I must," he thought, "tell my followers what has occurred, and then in all probability they will, unless I can restrain them, fall upon the scoundrel, and cut him to pieces."

When they returned to the chamber, the wretched innkeeper looked wistfully at our hero.

He saw by the boy's face that his villainy was discovered, and falling upon his knees, shrieked out—

"Mercy, senor, mercy! and I will confess all. Do not slay me! Let me live to repent my crimes."

Captain Tom, Iron Arm, and Beppo conversed together in Spanish.

"I know not what to do," the young chief said. "The fellow justly merits death, but I do not feel that I should be his judge."

"Give him over to the men," suggested Iron Arm; "they will be judge, jury, and executioners."

"Better still," Beppo said. "Let me take down his statement in writing; then give him one hour to quit the town, if he has not gone by that time, I will place the confession in the chief officer's hands."

"Yes," our hero said; "I think your plan the best, Beppo. But, by-the-way, what would become of his property?"

"It will go the State, senor, if they learn the truth."

"The State has sufficient," said Captain Tom; "I think it would be a fitting reward were the place given to you and Ninetta. She would make a charming hostess."

"Senor, you are too good to us."

"Not much goodness, Beppo, in giving away that which does not belong to me. The property rests between you and the State, and I think you want it more than his Majesty does."

"Your Excellenza forgets that I cannot take the ——— unless it is given me by the consent, in writing, of ——— ——— ——."

"We ——— what can be done with our prisoner. Come let us put him out of his misery."

Groveling at our hero's feet, the cowering wretch told the young chief of the plan he had entered into with the slain Mexican to rob and murder his guest.

The youth listened without comment until Miguel Ramos had concluded.

CHAPTER LX.

BEARDING THE LION IN HIS DEN.

"WERE I to do my duty," he said, "I should have you drawn up to that beam above your head."

"Mercy, senor, mercy! I was tempted by Andrea. He it was who first made me tread the wrong path."

"Your accomplice," our hero said, "is not able to answer for himself. Tell me, caitiff, what would you do were I to spare your life?"

"Spare my life, senor! spare my life! Are you in earnest?"

"It depends entirely upon yourself."

"If so, senor," said the Spaniard, eagerly, "I am ready to become your slave, anything, rather than die with my soul steeped in sin."

"We shall see how far you will carry out your words. But first tell me how many guests have you sent to their last home?"

"None, by my hand, senor."

"By your consent and aid—it is all the same. Now, how many? Quick with your answer."

"Three, senor."

"Three. And what profit have you reaped from this cold-blooded work?"

"Not much, senor. The whole amount put together—that is, my share—did not not reach one hundred crowns."

"One hundred crowns! So for this paltry sum you have slain three of your fellow-creatures."

"Not my hand, senor; Andrea—"

"Silence, miscreant! or I shall be tempted to avenge them with my own hand. Where are the bodies?"

"Burned, senor."

"Burned?"

"Yes, senor. Andrea cut them up, and threw the pieces upon a large fire."

Captain Tom shuddered with horror at these words.

"Vile wretch!" said the boy; "your very presence pollutes the air."

"Senor," whined Miguel, "I have suffered more to-night than twenty years' penance could make me suffer. Let me live; let me go from here, and I will retire into a monastery, and, by scourging and fasting, try to atone for my ill-spent life."

"You shall have the opportunity. I will give you one hour to leave Barracoa; if in that time you are within the town I will have you handed over to the gendarmes."

"Senor, I will go—go now; I do not require ten minutes."

"The sooner the better; but before you leave here I want you to dispose of your house. Have you any relatives?"

"None, senor."

"So much the better. Here is pen and paper, sit there, and make over the contents of this den of infamy to Beppo."

"Beppo! the man who ha—"

"Decide at once; your life is in the balance. Do as I wish you and you are safe; refuse, and you shall be within the prison walls in less than the time I have given you to escape."

There was no help for it, and in spite of the deadly feeling of hate that raged in his heart against the young muleteer, he was compelled to yield to our hero's will.

When the arrangements were concluded, and the overjoyed Beppo held the precious paper which made him comparatively rich, Captain Tom desired his followers to prepare for the invasion of the sombre monastery.

Beppo overheard our hero and Iron arm speaking of the intended rescue of Harry Martin, and said—

"Your pardon, senor. Do I mistake when I say that you wish to enter the House of Exercise unseen?"

"You do not, Beppo; such is our wish."

"Had I known sooner that you came here for the purpose, I could have prevented your risking your life."

"You could! How?"

"There is a secret way, senor, to the lower cells—a passage that I do not think, with the exception of the monks, is known to any but myself."

"This is fortunate. We had thought of entering the cloisters by taking out the stones that block up the passage to this house."

"You would never pass through, senor."

"Why?"

"Because the passage is so low that only one could creep forward upon his hands and knees."

"That would not render the passage impossible."

"Perhaps not; but there is another reason."

"What is that?"

"At every ten paces there is a wire placed upon the ground, connected with a bell in the superior's room. The first sound would alarm them, and I would rather be in a den of wild beasts than at the mercy of the Black Monks."

"You seem pretty well versed in their secrets, Beppo."

"I am, senor; I had a relative who was for some-time a servitor to the brethren; he used his eyes and ears pretty well during the short time he was in their service."

"For what purpose is the passage you spoke of used?"

"It is not used by the brethren now, and it is but one of the many that exist among the rocks. The monastery is a strange old place, senor—very strange."

"So I should imagine. Come, Beppo, time presses Can we go at once to this place?"

"I cannot find it until daybreak."

"Very well; we must wait. Now, Beppo, begin your duties as host by bringing us some wine."

The muleteer gladly obeyed, and our hero and his followers passed the short time before dawn in sipping their wine and commenting upon the late strange and terrible affair.

With the first grey streak of the coming day they left the hostel, and Beppo, acting as guide, led them to a small hollow.

"Here, senor," he said, "we must disperse."

"Why?"

"It is necessary, senor, in consequence of the upper windows of the monastery overlooking this place."

"Very well: my men shall conceal themselves."

"A better plan would be," the muleteer said, "to post the men at different parts of the place while I seek for the mark I placed near the secret opening."

"For what purpose are the men to be placed thus?"

"To prevent a surprise from the Black Monks."

"We have nothing to fear from them."

"I know not, senor. Even now some of them may be watching us from the grated windows."

"In that case your measure will be a prudent course to adopt."

"Such is my opinion, senor. If you will post the men in such a manner among the rocks that they are concealed, yet able to see all who may approach, I will await your return."

"What is to be done in the event of any one approaching?"

"All who approach, senor, treat them as enemies; they will be either the monks or some of the ruffians in their pay. Above all, keep them from coming near this place, for should they suspect our intention, not one of us would leave this place alive."

"These monks of yours are dangerous people, Beppo."

"They are, senor; these precautions I have taken may not be useless."

Our hero, to humour Beppo, placed the buccaneers among the rocks, and telling them to keep a wary look-out, he rejoined the young Spaniard.

"If you will stay here, senor, between these pieces of rock, I shall be able to find you when I succeed in discovering the opening," Beppo said. As he began to descend the narrow pathway, he turned and added, "Remember, senor, do not permit any one to pass you."

"I shall not, rest assured of that."

Some time passed, and no sign of the young Spaniard or of the dreaded Black Monks appearing, our hero sat upon a huge stone, and soon became lost in a deep reverie.

From this half-wakeful state he was aroused by the falling of loose stones, and the sound of feet, behind where he sat.

Beppo's instructions came to his recollection, and starting to his feet he drew a pistol from his belt, and facing round quickly, said, with dangerous calmness—

"Not this way."

The intruder raised his hand, and said, hurriedly—"Do not fire, senor."

"Beppo," said our hero, replacing the weapon in his belt, "I did not expect you to return this way."

The muleteer had a long knife between his teeth as he descended the rocks, and to the young chief's interrogative look he said—

"I have been using it, senor, to cut away the thick vegetation that grew before the entrance to the secret passage."

"You succeeded in finding the place?"

"I did. Now, senor, call the men together, and we will go before the bell rings to summon the brethren to prayer."

A low, peculiar cry brought the buccaneers to their chieftain's side, and in silence they descended the rocks.

CHAPTER LXI

JERRY MIZZEN'S WEAKNESS FOR WINE, AND ITS RESULT.

THE opening to the old passage was situated among a confused heap of fallen masonry.

And from the remains of a few pillars, and the stone framework of several small windows, it was evident that the passage had, at one time, communicated with a small shrine that had been erected apart from the main building when the structure was first raised.

The gradual changes that had taken place, and the lapse of years, had caused the small structure to fall into disuse, then into decay.

Our adventurers did not pause to admire the remains of the quaint grotesque carving yet visible upon the mossy stones, but passed at once inside the dim, gloomy place.

The passage was vaulted, and of sufficient height to allow Iron Arm to stand erect.

For some distance they went onward in silence, but, the place being so intensely dark that the buccaneers kept falling over each other, our hero called a halt.

"Stay here," be said to his men. "I will go forward and reconnoitre."

Iron Arm and Beppo accompanied him.

They had not gone many paces before the cause of the sudden darkness became apparent.

The passage terminated abruptly, then branched off to the right.

This turn was not many feet in length, and when

our hero and his companions had turned it they found themselves in a large, square chamber.

Wooden shelves, well stocked with provisions, and various casks and bottles told them that they were in the larder, and Captain Tom said—

"The saintly men, if others fast, do not believe in practising that mode of penance themselves."

"No," said Iron Arm. "The contents of this place would satisfy the greatest gourmand."

"It would. Will you call the men? We may want them soon."

Iron Arm went back for the remainder of the party, and when Jerry Mizzen saw the portly casks he smacked his lips, and whispered to Bob Hauler—

"I wish the chief would heave-to here for a little time."

"Why, Jerry?"

"You ask why, and see the casks grinning at you."

"They are full of holy water, Jerry."

"Is they, Bob? I'll have a drop."

He lingered a few paces behind the party, and discerning a tin can upon one of the shelves, took it down, and hastily placed it under the nearest tap.

The red, juicy wine gushed out when Jerry turned the tap, and soon filled the tin vessel.

From pure mischief Jerry kept the tap turned on, and swigging his wine, hastened after his companions.

They had turned into a long corridor, and upon each side were a number of small doors.

When Jerry was within a few paces of his shipmates, he placed the huge vessel to his mouth and drank as he walked on.

If the colour was good, Jerry thought the taste better, and so absorbed was he in the delightful sensation—that of feeling the wine trickle down his own thirsty throat—that he ran against Bob Hauler, whose back was towards him.

The bottom of the tin can came with no gentle force against the back of Bob's head, and brought Jerry's enjoyment to a premature end.

The edge of the can being between his teeth when he came into collision with Bob Hauler, the shock nearly drove the unfortunate Jerry's teeth down his throat.

The contents, too, in place of flowing down his windpipe, were jerked all over his face, and Jerry, uttering a loud cry, let the can fall.

"What are you doing?" he said, savagely, to Bob. "Cuss you, you nearly cut my mouth open as wide as the fore-hatch of a ship."

"Serve you right, you guzzling swine."

"Does it? Take that!"

Bob ducked to escape Jerry's fist, and the latter, losing his balance, fell forward and grazed the skin off his nose and chin.

The rattle of Jerry's cutlass as he fell caused the young chief to turn hastily, and he said—

"Steady men—be careful;" then seeing Jerry Mizzen's face covered with the red wine, he added—"You are bleeding, Jerry. Where are you hurt?"

"It's wine, sir," Bob Hauler said. "He stole it coming along, and while he was guzzling he ran foul of me."

The young chief turned his head aside to hide a smile.

"Sneak!" whispered Jerry, savagely; "well, you is a sneak, Bob."

"How's that, Jerry?"

"Why, to go and tell the chief about that."

"It's true."

"Never mind, you needn't have told him."

Bob Hauler grinned at Jerry's woeful-looking face, much to the latter's disgust.

The adventurers came to a standstill, and the young chief, accompanied by Iron Arm, went to one of the doors in the long corridor.

Without making the slightest sound, they lifted the latch and entered the cell.

It was the sleeping-place of one of the monks, and he was awakened by feeling a hand upon his shoulder.

The sight of the armed men standing by his bedside for a moment deprived him of speech.

When the faculty did return he said—

"In the name of the Virgin, what do you here?"

"We want you," Iron Arm said. "Awake, and answer our questions."

The member of the Black Monks sat bolt upright and gazed at the intruders.

"Want me!" he said. "For what?"

"To answer," the giant said, "any questions I may put to you."

"If I refuse?"

The tapping of the knife-handle was the reply he received.

The monk quite understood its significance, and folding his arms sullenly, he asked—

"What would you have me answer?"

"There is a youth," Iron Arm said, "incarcerated in this place. Where is the dungeon?"

"I know not."

Iron Arm held the point of his knife to the monk' throat, and said—

"Perhaps this will assist your memory."

The man shrank back from the keen-pointed weapon, and said—

"Senor, I speak the truth. I am but a novice in this establishment yet, and know nothing of any transaction that takes place."

Iron Arm looked at the young chief, and said in English—

What is to be done, captain?

Do you think this fellow speaks the truth?"

I cannot do otherwise."

"There is but one way, then, to attain our end."

"Which is that, captain?'

"We must search every cell in this old place, unless—"

"Unless—go on."

"Unless we compel this fellow to show us the superior's chamber."

"A good thought, captain. It shall be done."

He changed the language into that understood by the monk, and said—

"Very well, my friend; as you know nothing of the prisoner we come to liberate, perhaps you will show me the superior's chamber."

"I dare not, senor."

"Dare not! Why?"

"The rules of our order forbid me leaving my cell until the bell rings for morning prayer."

"Tush, man! you must do as I wish, or you will never leave this place again."

"Senor, my vow!"

"Never mind your vow. I will absolve you from both vow and life if you do not comply."

"My life, senor," the man said, doggedly, "I value less than my oath. Strike, if you will, but I never will comply."

Iron Arm raised the gleaming knife as though about to strike, and the fanatic bared his chest to receive the blow.

"Stay!" Captain Tom said, "do not slay the madman."

The knife paused in its descent, and Iron Arm asked—

"What is to be done?"

"Leave him to me;" then, addressing the monk, he added, "I will save your life upon one condition."

"I will comply, senor," was the answer, "to anything that does not bear upon the fearful oath I have taken to respect the rules of the brotherhood."

"Very well; all I wish you to do is to point out the chamber where the superior sleeps."

"Do you meditate violence towards him?"

"We do not."

"I will do it, senor. Keep on until you reach the end of this passage, then turn to the right, and you will see an archway; pass through the curtains, and you will be opposite the superior's door."

"You are not playing us false?"

"By my hopes of eternal life, I am not!"

"I will trust you. Should one falsehood have left your lips, no earthly power shall save you from death."

"Senor, I have spoken truly, I swear!"

The buccaneer chief and his followers were about to leave the chamber, when Beppo whispered to our hero—

"Do not trust him, senor. Place one of your men in this cell."

"He can do no harm."

"You mistake, senor; once rid of our presence, he will ring the alarm-bell."

"Then?"

"Then, senor, you will have to face two hundred determined men; and, believe me, they would do all in their power to prevent your return to the outer world."

"Perhaps it would be as well to do as you propose. Here, Jerry Mizzen!"

"Aye, aye, sir."

"Draw your cutlass, and remain here. Remember, you do not permit this man to leave the cell."

Jerry whipped out his blade, and said—

"If he does, sir, it will be when Jerry has gone to Davy Jones."

"Should you," the young chief said, "hear any unusual noise soon after we leave, come to us at once."

"Aye, aye, sir."

The buccaneers left the cell, and went towards the superior's chamber.

Jerry, with his cutlass resting on his shoulder, walked slowly to and fro, his eyes fixed upon the monk. The latter seemed to take no notice of his presence, but lay back with his hands folded across his breast, and his eyes closed as though in deep thought.

"Saying his prayers to hisself," thought Jerry. "Wonder if he'll go to sleep?"

The monk remained immovable for some time, and Jerry Mizzen's thoughts went back to the large vault where the huge barrels of fine old wine were standing.

The more he thought of them the thirstier he became, and once he muttered—

"It ain't far to go. If I was sure that beggar wouldn't move, I'd slip away and have another taste."

This soon resolved itself into a determination to go back into the wine-cellar, and Jerry, finding the monk was to all appearance asleep, quietly stole from the cell.

He went half way down the passage, then, fearing all was not right, came back again.

A peep inside the dim chamber showed the monk's form in the same position as when he left.

"It's all right," thought Jerry; "he's off like a porpoise."

This time the whole length of the passage was traversed, and Jerry, with his mouth watering, stood before the huge barrels.

The wine was still running as he had left it, and Jerry, stooping down, placed his mouth under the tap.

The ex-smuggler found no difficulty in drinking in this uncomfortable posture.

Quite the reverse—he rather liked it.

When Jerry had imbibed sufficiently of the rich wine he raised his head and muttered—

"This beats drinking grog out of a tub; yes, it's fine, only got to put your head down, and it rolls down your thoat—like—like—anything. I think Ill have just another taste."

He did have another—then another.

When Jerry Mizzen began to walk back to the cell, he found the position he had used caused his legs to form the letter X.

Jerry swayed from side to side, and, as he sought to walk erect, he thus soliloquised—

"I ain't drunk—that's impossible; but I'm blessed if I know what's the—hic—the—hic—the matter with my legs; and—hic—the walls is a-dancin' like —hic—mad, or I'm—hic—not—hic—right about —hic—the toplights. It's funny, but—hic—I'll take my solemn davy I ain't—hic—"

Clang! clang! clang!

Jerry stopped short, and listened, as a deep-toned bell rang furiously.

This summons was succeeded by a rush of feet.

Then sharp, angry cries, mingled with the clash of steel.

"A fight!" Jerry thought, and the thought partly sobered him. "I wonder where it is?"

He drew his cutlass and staggered forward.

He had not taken more than six paces when he received a blow upon the back of his head, which sent him face foremost upon the ground.

Jerry made an attempt to get upon his feet, but before he could accomplish this a heavy cloak was thrown over his head and he was dragged away.

"Cuss," Jerry said, "I's in for it again. Let me out, you swabs, and I'll slit yer ugly wizzens."

His captors, not understanding a word that came from beneath the cloak, hurried him forward.

Whatever befell Jerry in this dilemma he most richly merited.

Had he remained upon his post, and not yielded so readily to his tickling throat, all would have been well.

When Jerry left the cell, the monk lay for some time perfectly quiet; then finding his guardian did not return, he crept quietly out of bed, and hurried up the passage.

At the end a rope was suspended, this he eagerly seized with both hands, and rang out that peal which brought the monks from their cells.

"Arm! arm!" he cried; "the Father Superior is in danger. There are heretics within the walls."

Seizing whatever weapons they could grasp in the haste necessary to save their superior's life, the monks hurried towards the saintly prior's chamber.

Here they were met by the buccaneers' bristling steel, and the giant's deep voice rang out as he said—

"Back all of you, or there will be bloodshed; back I say!"

They paused, awed by the determined-looking buccaneers, and held a whispered parley.

CHAPTER LXII.

TRAPPED.

OUR hero, Iron Arm, and their companions had found their way to the superior's chamber.

The saintly man was asleep when the buccaneer chief crept to his bedside.

Captain Tom placed his hand upon the prior's shoulder, and said, softly—

"Awake!"

The superior started, and, looking strangely at the group, yelled—

"Help! help! Ambrose—Giuseppe—help! Sound the ala—"

"Quiet, you old rascal!" said Iron Arm, placing his hand over the superior's mouth—"quiet, or I'll drive the butt of my dagger down your throat."

Half suffocated by the pressure upon his mouth, the superior lay back upon his pillow, and by signs expressed his desire to speak with his captors.

Iron Arm removed his hand, and the prior—his hard, sallow face convulsed with rage—said—

"What is the meaning of this outrage? How did you gain admittance here?"

"One question at a time," said Captain Tom. "In the first place, we come for a youth belonging to my ship, who has been placed here by a scoundrel whose throat I should like to grasp, as I will grasp yours if you do not give up your prisoner to our keeping. In answer to your second query, I do not think it prudent to tell you how we came here, in case we may have to visit you again."

"Dogs!—English hounds!—how dare you address the superior of the Casa des Exercios thus!"

"We would do the same were you a king, instead of what you are."

"What I am! Villain! I am—"

"You are not unknown," said the young chief; "you are at the head of a nest of rascally hypocrites who flog and torture their victims—or fools, I should say—who place themselves in your power. Don't grind your teeth. I repeat, you torture the brainless fanatics for your own gain, not for the good of their souls or the Church you profess to serve."

The prior writhed with passion, as the boy continued speaking.

Our hero saw the effect his words had upon the superior, and fixing him with those dark, handsome, inscrutable eyes, he continued—

"As I am so well acquainted with you, I think you will see the folly of not at once yielding to my request."

"Yield! yield!" the superior gasped. "I'll—But who are you that dare beard me thus?"

"I am Captain Tom."

The superior looked contemptuously at the slight, graceful boy, and said, sarcastically—

"Commissions must be plentiful when beardless boys hold such rank. Well, Captain Tom, this is my answer."

The prior sat up and made a clutch at a silken tassel that hung close to his head.

Our hero was too quick for him.

One blow of the keen-edged sabre severed the bell-rope just above the prior's fingers.

"Curse you!" said the saintly man. "So far you have the best of our position; but, be you captain, king, or devil, you shall not have the boy you came for, neither shall one of you leave this place alive."

"Now, good, but very hot-headed father of rascality, 'captain, king, or devil,' perhaps you will find me—chiefly the latter—unless you alter your tone."

"Alter, fool! and surrounded as I am by men who would tear you piecemeal at a word. Begone before I—"

"Shut up!" said Bob Hauler, striking the pommel of his cutlass against the superior's white, pig-like teeth. "I don't understand your lingo, but I knows it ain't the sort of slack to pay out to our captain. Shall I skewer him to the bed-post, sir?"

"No, Bob," answered our hero; "we have not done with him yet."

The prior tumbled back from the effect of Bob's blow, and yelled out—

"Help! help! Sound the alarm!"

"Pull him out of bed," said our hero to Bob and his companions; "we are losing time."

Much to the superior's humiliation and consternation, he was seized by the ankles and whisked from the bed.

The indignity did not end here.

Bob Hauler, with the spirit of mischief which

"BE BRAVE," HE SAID, "WE CAN DIE BUT ONCE."

seems inherent in the British seaman, knocked the prior's skull with no gentle force upon the stone floor.

This was too much.

The godly man wriggled himself from Bob's grasp, and, to that worthy's surprise, the enraged prior clenched his fist, and gave Bob a blow in the mouth that caused his teeth to rattle.

Bob jumped nimbly back, amid shouts of laughter from his companions—merriment in which the gloomy Iron Arm, and the more light-hearted young chief, lustily joined.

Bob tenderly rubbed his mouth, and, throwing off his jacket and cap, growled—

"That's it, is it? My toplights, if you shan't have enough."

The superior came up with a rush, his clenched hands striking out wildly right and left.

Bob had by this time prepared for his antagonist, and meeting him in the true and most approved style usual in these cases, warded off the superior's blow with the right hand, and with the left gave the holy father a "clout" that sent his holiness on his back.

Unable to speak for passion, the superior scrambled to his feet and attempted to make a rush from the chamber.

Iron Arm caught him before he had taken a dozen steps.

"Stay," the giant said, "this farce has gone f enough."

"Sacrilege. heretic

Iron Arm shook him violently as he said—

"Your answer; show us the cell, or by Heaven! I—"

The great bell rang out sharply, and the superior, breaking away from his captors, cried, joyfully—

"Saved—saved! Ha! ha! the Black Brotherhood to the rescue!"

He heard the monks come thronging towards the chamber and redoubled his cries.

"Curses!" said Iron Arm, "that is the alarm-bell, we shall be surrounded by this gang."

Captain Tom drew his sword.

"Bar the door," he said; "we will rescue our companion or die in the attempt."

"Senor," Beppo whispered, "have the superior bound and gagged. It will be better. I will assist if you give your consent."

"Thanks, do; it may be better."

The superior was seized in the midst of his rejoicings by the active muleteer, and the severed bell-pull tied across his mouth."

Then Beppo, despite his struggles, bound the enraged prior to the bed-post.

The monkish brotherhood, awed back by the sight of the determined buccaneers, held a long parley.

Every moment their numbers increased, and when they again advanced there could not have been less than one hundred savage, sullen men bearing upon the gallant fellows who stood shoulder to shoulder across the door.

Iron Arm stood with his mace poised upon his shoulder, and in a voice that echoed along the vaulted passages, said—

"Are you so tired of life that you attempt to oppose men whose lives are passed with their blades ever in their hands?"

One of the brotherhood, an old man, whose beard swept his chest, said—

"Men of wickedness and sin, you have sought the secret passages of the holy house of San Juan; your deaths rest upon yourselves."

A mocking laugh came from the fiery young chief.

He surveyed his opponents, and laughing to scorn the crowd that faced him, said—

"Old man, you must have much faith in your power of using temporal weapons, to imagine that your staves can oppose our passage."

"We rely upon mightier aid, rash youth. There is yet a chance of saving your sinful lives; take it, and leave us in peace."

"We will depart, upon one condition."

"Foolish boy; does it become the lamb, when beneath the lion's claws, to ask for conditions?"

"I do not see the force of your simile, old man; but this much I can tell you—we came here for a purpose, and until that is accomplished our sword-blades will protect our lives."

"Your purpose, blind and sinful youth? Came you here to plunder the monastery?"

"No, old man; we came to rescue a companion who has been delivered into your infernal power. Release him, and we depart as we came: oppose our wish, and by the new-born day I swear that the walls of this place shall be levelled to the ground, and your order broken and dispersed."

"Your threats are idle. All that are within our walls are secure from your touch. Begone, I say!"

"You refuse to give up your prisoner?"

"We have no prisoners. All who are within this holy place came to seek refuge from the outer world, and while one stone stands upon another, or one of the mighty brotherhood exists, they will remain in their cells as securely as though in the bowels of the earth."

"Enough," Captain Tom said; "your blood be upon your own heads. Form, men! Drive them

from the door! By Heaven! we will teach these monks what it is to defy our power!"

Foremost in the fight Iron Arm strode, swinging his weapon from right to left, and dashing to the ground all who opposed him.

The young chief, Bob Hauler, Ned, and Skopey beat back the forest of staves which opposed them, and in less time than had been consumed between the young leader and the old monk's conversation, there was a clear space around the door.

"Back, all of you!" said Captain Tom. "Close the door. We must compel the superior to tell us where Harry Martin is confined."

The men stepped quickly backward, and before the monks could prevent it the heavy door was closed in their faces.

They heard the bolts shot into the sockets, and a yell came from them at the danger that menaced their superior.

While the baffled brotherhood were trying to burst in the door, the superior was surrounded by the grim and determined buccaneers.

The gag was taken from his mouth, and our hero said—

"If you would save bloodshed, tell me where the young seaman's cell is situate."

"Never! You shall die for your insolence."

"Captain," Iron Arm said, "have I your consent to compel him to speak?"

The boy knew the terrible, pitiless man would fearfully torture the obstinate prior, and, before he gave his sanction to the deed, he again spoke to the superior.

"Old man," he said, "do not compel us to do that which, as Englishmen, we abhor. Give the desired information at once. Save yourself from having the words wrung from you by torture, for our position is desperate, and our acts will be in proportion to our danger."

"You may tear me piecemeal," was the stubborn reply, "then I will repeat what I have before told you—never!"

"Reflect. This is your last chance."

"I have. Do your worst."

A regretful look accompanied our hero's words to Iron Arm.

"You have my consent," he said. "There is no other way."

The giant inclined his head, then placing his mace upon the ground, drew his long knife and approached the superior.

He severed the cords that bound the angry priest, and said—

"It is not too late to save yourself. Give us the information we require, and all will yet be well."

"Do your worst," was the answer. "The door will soon yield, then I will have a deep revenge for the indignity I have suffered."

Affixed to the ceiling was a large iron ring, which had evidently been placed there to hold a lamp.

Iron Arm tested the strength of the ring with his hand, then turning to Bob Hauler, said—

"Pass a cord through this."

Bob stood upon Ned Hartley's shoulders and passed a strong cord through the ring.

The prior had a dire foreboding of what was to happen, and he cast many an anxious look towards the door, upon which the brethren still continued to use their efforts to beat open.

Captain Tom placed his hand upon Iron Arm's shoulder, and looking at the formidable cord, asked—

"Is there no other way?"

"None," was the grim answer.

Our hero walked towards the door to escape the sight of the prior's torture.

The three seamen, by Iron Arm's direction, set one end of the cord.

The other was fastened to the obdurate superior's ankle.

He looked on undismayed at their preparations, evidently hoping that the crowd of men who clamoured at the door would yet be in time to save him.

He was mistaken.

At a signal from the giant the cord was tightened until the prior felt the pressure upon his ankle.

A gesture caused the men to stop, and Iron Arm said—

"Answer, or I will have you strung up."

"You have had my answer."

Then, perceiving his peril, he yelled—

"Quick! Batter the door in, or you will be too late!"

"Were the door to yield now, they would be too late," said the grim giant. "Haul up, men!"

There was a hasty trampling of feet—a sudden suppressed cry of pain as the prior was jerked off his feet.

The next moment he hung by the leg from the ceiling.

The blood rushed to the prior's head and face—although the agony was intense, he uttered no sound.

Iron Arm stood beneath the suspended form, his face dark, stern, and pitiless.

The monks outside, driven to desperation by the cry of their superior, did all that men could do to force the door.

Heavy axes were brought and plied by strong arms.

Yet the massive oaken frame seemed to defy their efforts.

Large drops of agony stood upon the tortured man's forehead, and he bit his lips, until the blood came, to crush back the cry of agony caused by his sufferings.

The buccaneers pitied the man, and fain would have cut him down; but the uncertain fate of their young companion, and the prior's obstinacy, soon changed this feeling into a deep and stern resolve to continue the dread ordeal until they learnt where Harry Martin was incarcerated.

Suddenly there came a cry of joy from the monks, and the buccaneers, turning sharply, beheld the glittering edge of an axe through one of the upper panels of the door.

"Pistol them, captain," said Iron Arm. "This fellow cannot hold out much longer."

The prior heard the cry from without, and, straining his starting eyeballs in the direction of the sound, awaited for the door to yield.

Crash! crash!

The panel gave way, and the interior of the chamber became revealed to those without.

They yelled with rage when they beheld the horrible position their chief was in, and the axes went to work with a vigour that promised soon to beat in the door.

The young chief looked to the priming of his pistols.

Then levelling them at the crowd of eager faces without, said, sternly—

"The next that strikes a blow upon the door dies."

He was answered by a defiant cry, and the axe gleamed through the air and came crashing through the framework.

Bang!

Then a sharp cry of pain, as the man who had wielded the axe left it buried in the panel, and fell backward, shot through the head.

"I have warned you," said the boy. "The next that is tired of his life can follow that fellow to eternity."

The sudden death of their companion struck an awful chill upon the black brotherhood, and they fell back from the gap in the door, the levelled pistol, and the boy's dark, determined, flashing eyes.

The superior had, until the moment the fatal shot was fired, hoped that his release was at hand.

He heard the young chieftain's words, and from the sudden hush that fell upon the brotherhood thought that they were awed by the determined boy.

His bodily torture was now terrible, and when the hope of his release crumbled away, he gave such a heart-rending cry of agony that it pierced the buccaneer's heart.

"I cannot endure this," the young chief said, in English; "lower him at once."

"He will yield in a moment," said the imperturbable Iron Arm. "It is weakness to give in."

"But his torture?"

"He brought it on himself."

Captain Tom made no answer. He saw, by the hasty, excited movements of the attacking party, that his attention was required to defend his post.

After that cry of more than mortal agony came from the prior's lips, a chill hush came upon all who stood near.

Those outside were also silent.

That cry had, for a time, numbed their faculties, and they stood pale, sullen, and awe-struck.

The quietude was broken by another horrible scream from the prior's lips, and, as his hands grasped wildly at the empty air, and the crimson stream rushed from his mouth and nostrils, he exclaimed—

"Release me! release me! Are you human to torture a fellow-creature in this horrible manner?"

"Where is he whom we seek?"

The prior turned his distorted face towards Iron Arm, and answered—

"Seek him; the knowledge will never come from my lips."

"It will," Iron Arm said, calmly, "or your life shall depart under the most horrible torture."

"I will die before! Oh, for the love of Heaven take me down, or bury your knife in my heart!"

"Madman," said Iron Arm, "speak—tell us where we may find our countryman, and end this horrible scene."

"Never!"

The giant's massive brow grew black with passion as he seized the prior by the wrists, and said—

"You suffer now—do not defy us longer, or I will add my weight to that which is already upon your ankle."

"Mercy!"

"Answer at once."

He gave the wretched man a slight jerk as he spoke, and a terrible, piercing cry came from the suffering wretch.

The agony was more than he could endure.

The young chief's face paled as the dreadful cry came from the prior's lips.

"Release him," he said; "this is unendurable."

"Captain," was Iron Arm's reply, "the torture this miscreant suffers is child's play compared to that which he has inflicted upon many who have died beneath this roof."

"Ah! Is this true?"

"It is. You shall see the torture-chamber before we leave, and judge for yourself. In all probability poor Harry Martin may be there yet, spread upon the excruciating instrument of torture."

"If so," the young chief said, "I will wreak a terrible revenge upon the whole— Ah! he speaks!"

The prior was fast sinking beneath the agony he endured, and in a voice so still that Iron Arm was compelled to place his ear close to the wretched sufferer's mouth, he said—

"Take me down—I will tell you."

One cut from Iron Arm's knife severed the cord, and the giant, catching the falling body in his arms, walked towards the bed.

He placed the almost senseless superior upon his back, and said—

"Come—quick with your words."

The superior turned his fast-closing eyes towards the speaker, and there was such a deadly gleam of hate in them that the stout-hearted buccaneer for a moment felt awed by the fearful look.

"In the chamber—be—beneath the dome you will find him."

Was there any hidden meaning in that peculiar smile that passed over the prior's face, or was it but the working of his distended lips?

"Is the place easy to find?" Iron Arm asked.

The reply was in the negative.

"If I admit one of your order, will you command him to lead the way?"

"I will."

"Admit one," Iron Arm said. "Keep the rest at bay, captain."

Our hero unfastened the door, and called upon one of the monks to appear.

There was a movement among them as though they intended making a rush at the open door.

The young chief saw it, and said—

"Keep back. You know the result if you disobey. Let one of you approach, and one only."

A dark-bearded, sinister-looking monk came cautiously forward.

"There is nothing to fear," said our hero; "the superior wishes your presence."

The man glided softly to the bedside, and, with bowed head and folded arms, awaited the communication.

Again that faint smile flickered across the superior's face, as he said, faintly—

"Conduct these men to the chamber beneath the dome. Let them have the youth they came for."

When he mentioned the chamber beneath the dome, the monk's eyes shone with a triumphant light, and he made a sign to the superior.

The sign was merely the extension of one finger.

It was answered in the same manner. Then the monk said—

"Am I to dismiss the brethren, holy father?"

"Yes. Let these men of violence pass free. Their punishment will follow this sacrilege."

The monk bowed his head to hide a flush of triumph that came over his face, and turned to leave the chamber.

The buccaneers silently, but with their daggers drawn, followed him to the corridor that led to the fatal chamber.

CHAPTER LXIII.

THE CHAMBER BENEATH THE DOME.

The monks, with lowering brows and vengeful eyes, made a lane for the buccaneers to pass through.

They would, but for the naked blades that were so firmly gripped by the little band, have sought to avenge their companion's death.

One glance at the silent, determined men who strode through them three abreast and shoulder to shoulder, showed they were yet prepared to battle, and battle firmly, for their lives.

Not a hand was raised as they passed through the long line of dark, sullen forms.

Yet each man breathed more freely when they emerged from the long corridor into a brilliantly-lighted chapel, rich with golden trimmings and ornaments studded with precious stones.

Bob Hauler's fingers itched to pilfer a massive candlestick, or a small statue of the Virgin, of which there were many in the chapel.

Near the altar was a small door covered with crimson cloth.

Through this the monk passed and waited for the buccaneers.

Bob Hauler was the last to leave the chapel—there was a fascination about the golden images he could not resist.

Giving a hasty glance around, he passed his hand over the rails that divided the altar from the open space, and quickly transferred a golden jewelled cup to his pocket.

"Got something," thought Bob. "My eyes, if Jerry was here, wouldn't his fingers itch to take something from that little lot."

Grinning with joy at the possession of the richly-engraved cup, Bob rejoined his companions.

Their guide stopped before a huge iron door, and drawing back the bolt, said—

"The chamber beneath the dome."

Our hero uttered an exclamation of anger as soon as the door was opened, and the remainder, forgetting their usual caution, hastily followed to learn the cause of his sudden outcry.

They had barely passed inside when the door closed, and, to their amazement the monk's mocking laugh and triumphant voice sounded upon their ears as he said—

"Trapped—ha! ha!—trapped!"

Iron Arm turned quickly, and swung his mace against the ponderous door.

The weapon caused a loud clanging sound, and one of the sharp steel spikes snapped off.

The door was of wrought iron.

"Yes, my friend," said the giant, "we are trapped, but if I once get out, I will wring your neck."

To judge from present appearances, there did not seem much chance of the giant's threat being executed.

Turning savagely from the door, Iron Arm went to the end of the chamber, where the young chief was stooping over a huddled heap of something which, in the dim light, seemed more like a bundle of clothes than a human form. When Iron Arm came near enough to distinguish the object of Captain Tom's solicitude, a cry of hope escaped his lips.

The cry was repeated by the buccaneers as they stood by, gazing at the mangled form of young Harry Martin.

He lay upon a heap of straw, and near him was the hellish instrument of torture which had so cruelly and fearfully maimed his young limbs.

True to his leader, he had borne the most terrible agony when under the remorseless hands of the monks.

His frame had been torn almost asunder by the rack. Pieces of his flesh had been twisted out by red-hot pincers, and a long steel nail had been driven slowly through the right foot.

Yet, powerless, and only prevented from succumbing by the strong elixir given by one of his torturers, the brave boy refused to fill in the paper left by Reuben Harpy.

They desisted when every horrible mode of increasing his agony had been resorted to.

Then, when every limb was powerless, every joint wrenched from its place, and that which had been a youth full of life and vigour was reduced to a limp, shapeless mass, they left him upon the straw pallet.

Left him, in order that his dislocated frame should become stiffened, while the joints were out of their place.

Left him, with swollen tongue and parched mouth, to endure the most horrible agony from thirst.

And with a fiendish desire to increase his pangs, a crystal jug filled with bright clear water was placed within a dozen inches of his burning mouth.

They well knew his nerveless hands were incapable of reaching the tempting, maddening draught.

From time to time one of the monks entered the torture chamber, and hissed in the sufferer's ears—

"Consent to our wish, or the torture will be renewed."

The boy had suffered all it was possible for mortal to suffer, and he knew that death must soon place him beyond the reach of his merciless persecutors.

Death in the most hideous and protracted form was preferable to betraying his companions.

The young chief could have wept over the sufferer, and, as he held the crystal jug to Harry's parched lips, he said, fiercely—

"Better had they fallen into a den of wild beasts than committed this outrage, Harry. Are you better?"

"A little, sir," he answered, in a faint voice; "that delicious draught of water has put new life in my veins."

The giant form of Captain Tom's faithful follower stooped over the young prisoner, and, as a fierce light shone in his dark eyes, he asked—

"Was the superior present when this hellish work took place?"

"He was, and when they would have unbound me he ordered fresh tortures to be applied."

Iron Arm gave his leader a glance which was rightly interpreted.

"He deserved the torture," our hero said, alluding to the superior. "Had I known this I would have had his sufferings increased."

"I thought this had happened," Iron Arm said, "or I would not have been so severe with the miscreant."

"Curse him!" our hero said; "he shall answer yet for this atrocity."

The men who stood near gripped their weapons in a manner that bespoke but scant mercy for any of the brotherhood who should cross their paths.

"Now," said our hero, "to begin our work of retaliation. Commence by destroying these accursed instruments."

With as much zest as though it were the monks they were punishing, the buccaneers began to destroy the hideous racks.

Iron Arm's heavy mace splintered the hellish machine into a hundred pieces.

The same fate befel every strange-looking article they found in the chamber, and when the floor was strewed with fragments of wood and iron, the young chief said—

"Bind some of the longest pieces, and make a litter to carry away this poor sufferer."

The men quickly executed their chieftain's order, and over the frame a boat-cloak was placed.

Beppo, Bob Hauler, Skopey, and Ned constructed a hurdle, and were about to raise the improvised litter from the floor, when Iron Arm said—

"Stay; we must first find a way to get out."

The young leader looked at his follower, and repeated—

"A way to get out?"

"Yes; we are stopped by that slimy monk who brought us here."

An exclaimation of rage and astonishment came from our hero's lips.

He had been so engrossed by young Harry Martin that, until this moment, he was in ignorance of their imprisonment.

The precarious condition in which Harry Martin was rendered the young chief still more anxious to reach the vessel.

"Is there no way of escape?" he asked.

"None," Iron Arm said, "unless we can walk through the wall."

"The door?"

"That is of wrought iron."

"The windows?"

"I have not yet—Ah!—look!"

The buccaneers followed the direction of Iron Arm's outstretched finger, and a cry of dismay came from their lips.

One side of the chamber was silently closing towards them.

They gazed at the strange sight, spell-bound with horror.

Two large windows which admitted the light were being rapidly hidden by the moving walls.

There was something so terrible in this sight that even our hero's lion heart felt cold.

There could be no doubt of the terrible fate they were doomed to suffer.

The walls each side were coming towards them already. Part of each window was hidden.

"Captain," the giant said, "in another hour, unless we can escape, these walls will close and crush us."

There seemed no hope of escape—no means of averting a death which approached with such sure and fatal strides.

"Are we to die thus?" said our hero, pointedly, "use your mace Iron Arm. Batter the door down."

"It would be as easy to batter the cliffs of our native land."

"There is no hope, then?"

A small slit—so small that it only revealed a portion of the face that appeared—was suddenly opened in the centre of one wall.

The buccaneers saw a pair of eyes gleaming through, and a mocking laugh at their agony; then the panel closed as quickly as it had opened.

"Captain," the giant whispered, "there is hope.

"Hope? Can we escape?"

"If that panel opens again, we may."

"How? Explain."

"Draw a pistol. Should that face appear again, send a bullet through it."

"Then?"

"Wait until that is accomplished; I must have time to ponder over it."

With his finger on the trigger, our hero stood in a line with the door where the grinning face had appeared.

The walls had not yet ceased to move. Slowly, surely, they were closing upon them, and, to render their situation the more horrible, the chamber was becoming dark.

He looked towards the window, and beheld the cause of the coming darkness.

But a small portion of the stained glass was visible; a few seconds more, and they would be in darkness and waiting for death.

The first thrill of horror over, Iron Arm stood with folded arms, calmly calculating the possibility of escape.

He found there was none until the monk appeared at the small opening above the panel.

"That panel," he thought, "must be set in a wooden frame. Could I but have it opened, it would not be a hard matter to enlarge the space."

On either side the massive walls had closed to within six feet of the buccaneers.

They had been compelled to move to the centre of the chamber, forced forward by the terrible stone wall.

Now they stood silent, yet powerless, waiting the approach of the grim monarch whose power they had so often defied.

Every hope had died away; every eye was watching the narrow strip of light yet visible, and when by chance one caught a glimpse of a companion's face, he saw it was pale, yet without fear

They were doomed to die, but, like brave men, each determined to meet their fate unmoved.

It was hard for any in that silent chamber to die thus; but upon Beppo, the muleteer, death seemed more cruel.

He thought of the handsome Ninetta—thought of the sudden change in his fortune—and little wonder that he was most moved of that silent group.

Our hero could just discern the muleteer's dusky face, and in a voice of heartfelt sorrow, he said—

"I am sad for your sake, my brave fellow; death could not have chosen a moment more unwelcome."

"True, senor, but it must be borne. Poor Ninetta, she is all I love in the world; but, thanks to you, she will not want."

"Ha! ha! ha!"

The buccaneers started. There were the sinister eyes, at the narrow opening, watching with fiendish delight the close approach of the grim tyrant.

The laugh of mocking triumph changed quickly to a scream of despair, as the loud detonation of our hero's pistol rang out.

The monk's form was heard to fall with a dull thud upon the stones, then all became still.

"Well aimed," said Iron Arm; "that fellow has gone to Hades beforeus. Ah! by—yes, yes; the walls have stopped!"

It was the truth.

Eager eyes scanned the massive-looking stones, then turned to the thin strips of light which gleamed at the far end of the chamber.

They see, and their hearts beat with renewed hopes of life, that the two shreds of pale light remain stationary.

Not, as heretofore, diminishing by slow, yet perceptible degrees.

The buccaneers felt as much joy as though a sudden reprieve had rescued them from the hangman's fingers, and gazed in each other's faces as though doubting the reality of their sudden escape from a fearful death.

Iron Arm was the first to speak, and his words explained the cause of this sudden change.

"That fellow, captain," he said, "had charge of the machinery that put these walls in motion; your timely bullet has done us a service."

"It was just in time; we are not safe yet."

"No, there is not a moment to be lost; there may be some of the saintly gang near us waiting to hear our death shrieks when being crushed by those walls."

"What is to be done?"

"We must reconnoitre. Bob Hauler, jump upon my shoulders, and look through the hole."

Bob scrambled upon Iron Arm's shoulders, and standing erect, his face was level with the slit in the wall.

There was a moment's pause, then our hero asked—

"What can you see, Bob?"

"All clear, sir; the monk you shot lies on his face, as dead, I should say, as a herring."

"Can you see the place he stood upon?"

Bob squeezed his face into the narrow slit, and answered—

"I can."

"What is it?"

"A sort of platform, sir."

"How is it reached?"

"By an iron ladder."

"Anything else?"

There was a pause.

Then Bob cried out—

"Yes, sir, just about two feet below my face—there is a handle standing out."

"I thought so," remarked Iron Arm. "That is the means of working the machinery that puts these walls in motion."

"We are—"

A cry of alarm from Bob stayed our hero's speech; then he said, hurriedly—

"There is a lot of 'em coming. Hand me up the whole of the pistols. While our ammunition lasts they shall never get to the ladder"

Bob commenced by loading his own weapons, and as each man carried a brace of pistols and twenty ball cartridges, a good shot could keep the brethren at bay for an indefinite time.

"Can they see you?" Captain Tom asked, as he stood upon a table with a pair of loaded pistols in his hands.

"I think not, sir; they are looking at the fellow you dropped. Now one of them is making a run this way."

Bob Hauler's companions listened anxiously to his words, and watched with keen interest his slightest movement.

They saw him withdraw his face from the narrow slit, then insert the muzzle of a pistol in its place.

Bob Hauler knew his own and his companion's lives depended upon his skill and coolness.

He waited until one of the brethren had mounted the narrow platform; when the shaven crown came level with the slit, his finger tightened upon the trigger of his ready weapon.

The exterior of the chamber beneath the dome was flooded with bright sunlight.

This accounted for Bob's face not being seen by the astonished fraternity as they stood around their fallen brother.

When the monk who stood within such dangerous proximity of Bob's piece placed his hands upon the handle, the buccaneer fired.

There was no occasion to take aim; their would-be destroyer's neck was level with the pistol muzzle, as it rested upon the bottom of the small opening.

The bullet passed clean through the monk's neck, and he fell backward, then lay upon the stones close beside his dead companion.

There was a move among the black brethren as the monk fell dead at their feet, then a cry of rage when they beheld the smoke curl upwards from the muzzle of Bob's pistol.

"Do not spare the shot, Bob," our hero said, "we have nearly ninety rounds between us."

"All right, sir; shall I blaze away among these beggars?"

"You can try the effect of a few rounds."

Taking the best aim he could, Bob fired among the cluster of dark robes.

A scream of pain, and the welcome sight of a black-robed figure limping away upon one leg caused Bob to raise a cheer.

His bullet had broken the fellow's ankle.

Six shots were fired with such rapidity and accuracy of aim that those of the brotherhood who were not hit made the best of their way out of the line of fire.

"They are going, sir," Bob said, "there is four on the ground, and three went away as though a lump of lead wasn't nice."

Bob descended from his pedestal quite satisfied that, for the present, neither the superior nor any of his saintly miscreants would attempt to touch the handles of the hidden machinery.

A council was held as to the best mode of proceeding.

They were safe while the commotion lasted, unless there was another subtle plan to crush them to death.

"Had we thought of this before," said Iron Arm, "we should have had more space; however, it is as well we have this much."

"It is," our hero said; "the question is, how long shall we be left to the enjoyment of our chamber."

"They will not attempt to crush us yet," the giant said; "but there is a mode of destroying our lives worse than being put out of the way by these walls."

"A worse way? How?"

"Starvation!"

This word fell like a thunder-bolt among the buccaneers.

"Yes," Captain Tom said, "that will be our fate, unless we can widen that small hole and escape."

"Escape!" Iron Arm said, fiercely; "once outside this chamber, there will be a heavy retaliation upon these miscreants; I will not leave one alive."

"We will get out of this chamber first," our hero said, "seek revenge afterwards."

"Perhaps that would be the best plan, captain. Now to begin."

The table was placed beneath the hole which had served Bob Hauler for a battery. Upon the table a short, three-legged stool.

Iron Arm measured the distance as he stood with one hand resting upon the handle of his mace.

"It will do," he said. "Be ready, captain, to hand me a pistol should any of our foes appear."

The young chief stood near, his dark eyes watching his follower; in his hand was a brace of richly-mounted pistols.

———

CHAPTER LXIV.

JERRY MIZEN AMONG THE MONKS. — A GAP MADE IN THE STONE WALL.—THE BUCCANEERS' REVENGE.

THE illustrious Jerry Mizen, when he found himself in the power of the Black Monks, did his best to regain his liberty.

Fortunately for that luckless individual, his captors had been in such haste to throw their heavy cloak over his head, that the fact of their prisoner being in possession of a cutlass and pair of pistols was unnoticed.

When Jerry came to the conclusion that kicking and struggling would not avail him, he lay quiet.

"Collared!" he thought. "Cuss 'em! What is they going to do with me, I wonder?"

He was quite sobered by this time, and feeling the butts of his pistols pressing against his chest suggested an idea which gave the inestimable but not over-careful Jerry great glee.

"I feels yer," he muttered, taking the pistols from his belt. "In case they might want to borrow 'em, I'll put 'em out of sight."

As quietly as possible he placed the weapons in his breast, and buttoned his jacket over them.

He felt outside his trousers pocket, and found the cartridges he had placed there were still safe.

"I'll give 'em something," Jerry thought, "when they puts me down."

His cutlass still remained in its scabbard, and Jerry, but for its length, would have placed it with his pistols.

The monks seemed to the captive to traverse a great distance before stopping.

When they did so, Jerry heard a door unlocked, then opened—the next moment he was pitched, most unceremoniously, inside.

Luckily, a heap of straw intervened between Jerry and the stone floor, or he would have been a trifle shaken by the fall.

As it was, beyond having his breath jerked out of his body for a few seconds, he was none the worse.

Jerry did not attempt to move. He was so thoroughly exasperated by his capture that he determined to wreak summary vengeance upon the monks.

For this purpose he waited until they should uncover him, then he would make a bold attack for vengeance and freedom.

He waited for some time for the cloak to be taken from his head and body, but finding that no one came near, he thought it would be as well to free himself.

Jerry did this with his left hand, the right, meanwhile, grasping the hilt of his cutlass.

By degrees he removed the many folds of the suffocating garment, and at length put his head through, the long folds of the cloak hanging most gracefully from his shoulders.

Jerry looked about for a few seconds, then scrambling to his feet, ejaculated—

"Well, I'm blessed if they ain't gone!"

The monks, when they pitched their prisoner inside the cell, closed the door softly, and hurried away to answer the sudden summons from the alarm-bell.

Jerry tried the door, but that, he found, was securely fastened.

He next looked towards the window as a means of exit; here again he was foiled.

The long, narrow slit which admitted light to the cell was securely guarded with iron bars.

"Well," Jerry thought, "I'm in a blessed fix this time. I can't get out. Cuss that wine, I says; if it hadn't been for that I shouldn't have been here."

Jerry gave another revengeful look around his prison, then crossed to a small stone bench, the only seat in this grim dungeon.

Upon this he seated himself, and began to ponder over the probable result of his capture.

"I shall be made into a monk," muttered Jerry, dolefully, "and have my head shaved."

This thought was not pleasant to a gentleman of Jerry's roving disposition.

The bare idea of being shut up in the gloomy cloisters gave him, as he expressed it—

"A turn."

No; it would not bear reflection, therefore Jerry did not remain long on the cold seat.

As a last resource, he seized a pistol by the muzzle and began to hammer against the door.

"Hi! hi!" he shouted. "Let me out, you long-shore, bare-pole, black-souled lubbers! Hi! hi! hi!"

When Jerry's arm was tired he desisted, and listened for the expected sound of footsteps.

None came; the place was as silent as the tomb.

"They won't," he said, "and I shall have to be a priest, and sail under bare poles. Cuss 'em, I say cuss the wine—cuss the chief for sending me to keep watch over that long-shore ugly thief."

Jerry, after this explosion, took several rapid turns to and fro his cell.

"I is," said Jerry, mentally, "the unluckiest cuss as ever was born, that I is. Hallo!"

He stopped abruptly in his walk, and faced towards the door.

This aperture was guarded by four small iron bars, and, to Jerry's rage, he saw a dark, sinister face close to the small rails.

"Well, you monkey-chops—you ugly long-shore swine—who are you grinning at?"

Jerry, when he delivered this polite speech, was somewhat surprised to receive an answer in English.

"At you," was the reply. "How do you like your quarters?"

"Come inside, you ugly cuss, and I'll tell you."

The monk placed the forefinger of his right hand against his nose as he said—

"I shall come in when you are dead."

"Dead!" Jerry repeated, his hair beginning to bristle with dread. "Dead, you be hanged!"

"You will," said the monk "be both soon.

The speaker was the renegade Englishman, formerly a pirate, now one of the Black Brothers.

"Shall I?" Jerry said. "It ain't three like you that will kill me."

"Perhaps not; but as you will have nothing to eat or drink while you are in there, and you'll not come out again, it is most likely starvation will do something for you."

"Swine!" said Jerry. "I shall get out when my cap'n finds me here."

"You think so."

"I knows it."

The monk laughed derisively, and said—

"Your captain and his men are now in the torture-chamber, and, like yourself, would be glad to get out again."

Jerry's faith was so strong in the good fortune and bravery of his young leader that he laughed outright.

"A lot of ugly, miserable wretches like you kill Captain Tom. Go away, you cuss, or I'll send a pill down your throat that won't want swallowing."

"In less than one hour from this," the monk said, calmly, "your companions will be crushed by the walls of the torture-chamber."

Jerry had been quietly cocking a pistol during the time the monk was speaking; then suddenly drawing the weapon from his breast, he said—

"That's a lie, and this is the pill I promised you."

He fired, and to his satisfaction the monk gave a yell of pain.

Jerry went to the grating, and beheld his tormentor leaning against the opposite wall, with both hands pressed to the side of his head.

Jerry's bullet had cut away part of the man's ear as clean as though it had been done by a knife.

"Like it?" Jerry asked. "I've got a pocket full of 'em; you can have another, if you like."

Jerry thrust the muzzle of his dread pistol through the grating as he spoke, and the monk, catching sight of the dark tube, uttered a savage oath, and retreated out of sight.

"Give him something, anyhow," Jerry chuckled, as he reloaded; "and if any more on 'em comes grinning at me, I'll do just the same." After a pause, he added, "I wish the chief would make haste and come here, cos, per'aps, arter all, these beggars might keep me without grub till I kicked up my toes."

With this pleasant reflection uppermost in his mind, Jerry took up a position opposite the grating, ready to dispense another pill.

CHAPTER LXV.

IRON ARM AT WORK.—FREEDOM.

LIFE and liberty were at stake, and Iron Arm, throwing the whole force of his giant strength into the task before him, began to widen the gap in the stone wall.

The small door which had served for the executioner to mock or intimidate those in the terrible chamber was set in a thick wooden frame.

This Iron Arm, with one blow of his mighty weapon, dashed from its place, and the splinters fell among the monkish crowd who were savagely watching every movement of the man they had destined to destroy.

For once the superior had met with men who, despite the terrible appliances in that dread place, were not to be easily subdued.

Had the prior used some artifice to prevail upon them to lay aside their weapons, he would have triumphed.

Several times one of the brotherhood, with more hardihood than his companions, walked towards the iron ladder to finish the work his dead companion had left undone.

The long, dark-barrelled pistol was quickly protruded, and sent the fellow, cursing, back.

The pair of dark eyes, which shone with such a dusky, vengeful light through the opening in the wall told them that but little mercy was in their vicious hearts.

The mighty blows of the giant's weapon reverberated along the crooked passage.

Long and arduous was the task to dislodge a stone, and even Iron Arm's muscular powers began to tire ere the least impression seemed to be made upon the massive masonry.

"I shall be compelled to give in," he said to the young chief; "this stone is too firm to be removed."

"No, no," Captain Tom said, eagerly. "See, it yields—it yields!"

The boy's words spurred him on to continue his task, and, when he felt the stone begin to sway to and fro, a joyful cry came from his lips.

A crash followed the cry, and the stone fell to the ground.

Without waiting to call upon his companions to follow, Iron Arm passed through the opening, and began to descend the steps.

There was an expression upon his dark, kingly face that told how deeply the passion for revenge was in his heart, and the crowd of monks, falling back step by step as he descended, at last broke into a run, and disappeared from view.

"I shall track you to the very bowels of the earth," Iron Arm muttered, fiercely, "and not one, by my consent, shall escape the death you would have meted to us."

He was about to start in pursuit, when the young chief came through the opening, and said—

"Are you mad, to pursue them alone?"

"Not mad, captain, but fiercely bent upon revenge, and intend to wreak it upon these miscreants before I leave this building."

"You shall have the opportunity, my friend, but stay until we can accompany you."

"Yes, stay, and give them time to burrow in some hidden vault."

"Would you leave this poor boy here to be again tortured?"

"I would not. What do you propose?"

"Let us take him to the beach, and send him on board, then return, and repay these miscreants for their villainy."

"Be it so."

He retraced his steps in obedience to his young chief's wish, the fierce passion in his heart gaining strength every moment he waited for the consummation of his revenge.

"I will unfasten the door," Iron Arm said; "it will be easier than passing through that hole with poor Harry."

The young chief went inside again, and the giant drew back the massive bolts.

The rude litter they had constructed was now brought into use, and the limp, mangled form, covered with a cloak, was borne from the horrible chamber beneath the dome.

The least movement gave the poor boy the most exquisite suffering, and, in spite of the slow pace and the careful manner with which he was carried, a groan of agony ever and anon came from his white lips.

Captain Tom's kindly voice sought to cheer the poor fellow, but the bodily anguish he endured was too excruciating for him to bear.

He would have thanked his young leader, but his utterance was gone, and the only sign of life visible was the half-suppressed cry, and the nervous twitching of the pale youthful face.

Whatever mercy our hero would have shown the miscreant gang was banished from his mind by this terrible sight, and, as he walked beside the litter, he pondered over a plan for punishing the pitiless gang of villains who sought, under the garb of religion, to hide their evil deeds from the outward world.

Iron Arm walked moodily in rear of the party, his eyes and ears strained to catch the slightest sound

He had thought it scarcely possible that the incensed monks would permit them to depart unmolested.

He was watching and waiting for the first signal of their attack, and his fingers worked nervously upon the handle of his mighty mace.

The silence was suddenly broken by Bob Hauler.

He had not, until the present moment, thought of his old messmate. the redoubtable Jerry.

So quickly had their peril and escape been brought about, that it left no time to think of other matters.

But now, as they were passing a number of doors which seemed to correspond with the place where our hero had posted Jerry as sentry over the monk, Bob suddenly remembered that his old friend had accompanied them upon this expedition.

"Captain," he said, " poor Jerry has gone."

Our hero started.

"Jerry Mizzen?" he said. " It was here we left him."

"This," Iron Arm said, pushing open one of the doors, "is the very cell."

He passed inside, but nothing was there, except the low truckle-bed, a crucifix, and a wooden seat.

"He is not here," said the giant, " and I fear we have seen the last of him."

Bob Hauler's face looked the picture of woe as he said, sorrowfully—

"Poor Jerry! These accursed scoundrels have murdered him by this, captain."

"Well, Bob?"

"We are to return when we have taken Mr. Martin aboard?"

"Yes."

Bob looked perfectly savage, as he said—

"Woe be to them—woe be to them if my poor old messmate is not found uninjured!"

"I fear he has gone, Bob, to the place we have so narrowly escaped."

"If so, sir," Bob Hauler answered, "I shall never die content unless I revenge his death. Come, then, I will—"

"Ship ahoy! Bob ahoy! Captain ahoy!

The voice seemed strange and unnatural that gave utterance to these words, yet so much like the illustrious Jerry's well-known cry that the party came to a standstill, and looked eagerly around.

"It's his ghost," said Bob. " Jerry, my hearty, appear to your old messmate, and point out where you are buried."

"I wish I could appear, Bob."

"You are not dead?"

"Dead! No, curse you. Let me out—I'm here. '

"Where, Jerry? I can't see you."

"Here—nearly opposite. Don't you see a door?"

"Yes."

"Look in the middle, and then you'll see my face.

Guided by the sound, Bob Hauler found the door, and soon drew back the belts.

"I thought you were done for, Jerry, that I did," said Bob, when he came to his companion's side. " I never expected to see you any more."

"I'm as right as anything, old messmate," said

Jerry; " but I might have been turned into a monk hadn't I took a piece of a long-shore swab's ear off with a bullet."

"What did you do that for, Jerry?"

"'Cos he told me that you, and the chief, and all on you was going to be smashed up."

"We had a narrow squeak for it, Jerry. But heave ahead; we have to go, and then come back and settle our shot with these beggars."

Jerry went ahead; at heart very thankful for the timely deliverance.

He gave the huge cask of wine a sidelong look as they passed, and seemed, in spite of the recent danger he had been drawn into through its aid, much inclined to have another taste.

The party passed through so quickly that Jerry had not an opportunity, and he had had quite sufficient of the monks to dread being left behind.

The brotherhood had evidently not had time to search for the means of ingress used by the buccaneers.

For when they returned to the secret opening everything was precisely as it had been left.

"Had they stopped this place," Iron Arm said, "we should have had some trouble in getting out again."

"We must have gone by the first entrance," our hero said, " had we been compelled to have cut our way through the whole band of rascals."

"That," said the giant, with energy, " would have pleased me better than leaving as we do now."

They passed through, and were soon beneath the sunlight, and breathing the sweet air again.

They found the boat where they had left it, and poor Harry was soon on the way to his ship.

That beautiful vessel he had despaired of ever seeing again.

When they went on board, Ben Barnacle came forward and said—

"I am glad you have returned."

"Is anything amiss?"

"No; but we have had the pleasure of seeing the line-of-battle ship's tall masts pass and repass the end of this creek."

"We are safe from her," our hero said; " this rocky strait would fix her huge hull before she had advanced a fathom."

"None but the boats could make the passage."

"Should they do so, two guns would keep a fleet of boats at bay."

A sudden uproar at the gangway caused our hero to turn sharply, and to his surprise he beheld Doctor Shrike eyeing Bob Hauler, a large dissecting-knife in his hand.

"What is the meaning of this?" our hero asked.

"Meaning—meaning?" the doctor said. " This villain, this low-born ugly thief, threw a wet swab at me; that's the meaning of it."

"Did you?"

"Yes, sir," Bob said. " The doctor wouldn't come, so I woke him up with a wet swab."

"Go to your patient, doctor, he needs your care; and you. Bob Hauler, bring ten men to aid us in punishing the monks."

Bob went to collect the men, and Doctor Shrike was soon busy with poor Harry. Whatever the doctor's faults were, he was a clever surgeon. and when he saw the exhausted state the young midshipman was in, he lost no time in rubbing the boy's limbs with a powerful lotion, which soon allayed the pain, and caused the over-strained muscles to resume their place.

The doctor spared no exertions; he rubbed the sufferer's limbs for nearly two hours, and rubbed with such assiduity that the perspiration rolled in big drops from his bald, shining head.

When the young chief first came aboard, he despatched Bob for Doctor Shrike.

When that party went to the doctor's cabin, he heard a peculiar noise, and the doctor's voice from time to time singing portions of various drinking-songs.

Somewhat astonished at these strange sounds, Bob Hauler pushed the door open a few inches, and peeped inside.

He beheld the floor strewed with empty wine-bottles, a chair upset, and the doctor and his lank assistant indulging in a war-dance over the bottles.

Doctor Shrike brandished a bottle above his head with his right hand, and with the left he kept time to his singing by smartly tapping the bottle.

Jacop, divested of his coat, was hopping about with an energy that gave him the appearance of being suspended by wires.

"Well," Bob muttered, "old fools is the worst of fools, they say; here's one, anyhow."

He put his head inside the door, and said—

"Doctor, the captain wants you."

Doctor Shrike stopped short in the midst of a series of leaps that would have done credit to a Red Indian, and looked towards the direction of the voice.

He caught sight of Bob's grinning face, and without a word flung the bottle at it.

Bob ducked and escaped the missile, and repeated—

"The captain wants you."

"What, what, you monkey-faced grinning ape? Wants me? Tell him to go to the—"

"All right," said Bob; "I'll tell him what you say, and I'll also—"

"You villain!" yelled the doctor; "go, or I'll amputate you."

Bob went as far as the deck, then fixing a line to a large swab, dropped it into the sea.

"I'll sober him," he said, "the old cuss; and if his skeleton—the long Jacop—comes anigh me, I'll black his eye."

Armed with this watery weapon, he went below, and pushed open the door of the doctor's sanctum, and shouted—

"Are you coming, Old Pillbox?"

The doctor, annoyed at this second interruption to his jollifications, snatched a dissecting-knife from the table, and made a rush at Bob.

Splash!

The wet swab caught the doctor fair in the face, and caused him to stagger backward, his mouth and eyes filled with the dirty water from the mass of wetted rope.

Jacop, in spite of the fear in which he stood of his amiable master, was so tickled with the doctor's woeful plight that he stopped dancing, and burst into a roar of laughter.

Spluttering and swearing at the indignity he suffered, Doctor Shrike turned savagely upon his assistant, and roared—

"You, you sneaking anatomy—you bag of bones—to laugh at me! Curse you! I—I—Take that!"

"Oh! oh! oh!"

He disentangled the wet ends of the swab which had entwined themselves affectionately around his neck, then rushing upon Jacop, he beat him about the head and face until the vampire roared for mercy.

Doctor Shrike was in no mood to listen to the long Jacop's appeal, so he continued the punishment until Jacop rolled underneath the table.

Bob Hauler was nearly black in the face with laughter, and rolled from side to side with glee at the edifying spectacle.

The doctor, foaming at the mouth with passion, flung the swab at Bob's head, then made a charge at him with the dissecting-knife.

Bob scrambled up the ladder with the agility of a monkey.

The doctor, in imitating his plan of taking two steps at once, came to grief.

He had nearly reached the top when he missed a step, and went down considerably quicker than he came up.

Bob heard him bumping from step to step, and, turning round, said—

"All the skin off your back, doctor?"

Old Shrike had sustained a severe shaking, and, more incensed than ever, he scrambled to his feet.

"Curse you!" he said; "you grinning hound, I'll skin you alive."

"When you can catch me, doctor."

They had a smart chase amidships, the doctor striking out right and left until he caught his foot in a coil of rope, and went sprawling, face downwards.

While in this position one of the impudent middies threw the contents of a water-bucket over him.

Insulted, enraged, and hot, the doctor arose and ran after Bob, who by this time had reached the quarter-deck.

Here a stop was put to the fracas by the young chief ordering him to attend upon poor Harry Martin.

CHAPTER LXVI.

REVENGE.—THE ATTACK.—A NARROW ESCAPE.—DUTCH PAUL AND THE LIQUID FIRE TO THE RESCUE.

THE "Will-o'-the-Wisp's" jolly-boat and crew were about to push off from the ship, when Harry Vere ran to the side and called out—

"There is a boat coming towards us—see!"

Our hero uttered an impatient exclamation; to be delayed thus in the execution of his vengeance brought an angry flush to the boy's face.

"We had better wait the arrival of this boat," said Iron Arm. "It may be from the 'Yellow Vulture' with news of importance."

He waited, and Iron Arm's surmise turned out correct.

It was from the "Yellow Vulture," and in it sat an old weather-beaten seaman, a perfect stranger to our hero.

"You have a message from your chief?" the boy asked. "Be quick with it."

"I guess I have," the old fellow cried. "But what the deuce—"

"Dutch Paul!" said Captain Tom, astonished at the pirate chief's make-up.

"Yes, captain! the same old coon."

"What, in the name of all that's good, caused this transformation?"

"Not much, my young friend—not much."

"Something of importance, or you would not be here."

"No, no. Only a three-decker and a corvette lying-to about a mile from here."

"Have they the scent?"

"Well, yes; pretty strong, I guess."

"Ah!"

"Don't be alarmed."

"Alarmed!"

The gallant fellow repeated this word with a proud, scornful smile.

"Yes," Dutch Paul said, lighting a cigar; "alarmed was the last word."

"Come, quick with your intelligence, Paul; I—"

"Yes, yes; you, of course, are in a violent hurry; but take things cool, my young friend, it—"

"Cool the devil!"

"Well, yes, that would not be a bad plan; the old gentleman must be pretty warm, if all accounts are true."

Our hero beat his foot impatiently upon the bottom of the boat, and said—

"You will drive me mad!"

The pirate leader coolly emitted a puff of smoke from his lips, and, to our hero's annoyance, watched the fleecy cloud until the last trace had disappeared then he said—

"If you go mad, captain, there—"

"For Heaven's sake cease this trifling. I am—"

"Yes, you are, as usual, just ready to—"

"Give way, men!" said the young chief. "Give way!"

"Here!" said Dutch Paul, "come back; I have something of importance to communicate."

At a gesture from the chief of the buccaneers the men ceased rowing.

"Now," our hero said, "I am waiting your communication."

"That's right. In the first place, I must tell you—"

"With as few words as possible, please."

"Snakes and serpents! you are in a hurry, as the lawyer said when the devil came to take him below."

Captain Tom found there was no means of stopping Dutch Paul's provoking manner of speech, so with a sigh he threw himself back in the boat, and affected an indifference he did not feel.

"That's right," Dutch Paul said; "nothing like being cool. Now for my yarn. Let me see, I believe I told you about the three-decker and the corvette being on the look-out?"

"You did."

"That's all right, that little matter will not need repeating."

"Do, for—"

"Yes, decidedly. Well, you must know I have been cruising about, and for a long time could not make out where you had hidden."

"I thought you had decided to steer for the Treasure Island."

"Such was the arrangement; but knowing the faculty you possess, and to an eminent degree, of getting into peculiar scrapes, I thought it better to return."

"Well?"

"Don't be impatient."

"I have a matter of importance on hand."

"No doubt. To resume—while dodging about after you, the two gentlemen outside—"

"The liner and corvette?"

"Exactly. What a devil of a hurry you are in."

"You would be, had you endured all—"

"You shall tell me about it when I have finished."

"At this rate you will be until night."

"You should not interrupt. Now, where did I break off?"

"You saw the two vessels coming."

"Ah! exactly; yes, and pretty soon the smaller one sent a shot across my bows."

"They were in a hurry."

"Yes; and had it not been for you I should have shown my heels pretty quickly."

"You are very kind."

"Sometimes. Well, I lay to, and they boarded me. Ha! ha! ha!"

"What are you laughing about?"

"I will tell you. I suspected they were after you, and as I looked over the side I recognised the officer in charge of the boat."

"An old enemy?"

"Yes; but luckily, as the deaf old captain of the merchant ship the 'Myrtle,' I bamboozled the fellow completely."

"You were not long in effecting a disguise."

"No; we do that sort of thing pretty smart on board the 'Yellow Vulture.' Now shall I edify you with the scene that took place?"

The young chief consented to be edified. He knew a refusal would only make the yarn longer.

Dutch Paul, with a little facial change and alteration of manner, went through the scene that took place on board the "Yellow Vulture," and Captain Tom, in spite of his anger, could not refrain, in common with the boat's crew, from indulging in a hearty fit of laughter at his friend's mimicry.

We will give the particulars of the scene as told by Dutch Paul—the pirate personating the naval officer, who commenced by asking—

"What ship is this?"

Dutch Paul placed his open hand against his ear, and shouted—

"The 'Myrtle.'"

"Is he deaf?" the officer asked one of the crew.

"Awful deaf, sir; can't understand only when we shout through the trumpet."

The lieutenant raised his voice, and yelled—

"Where are you from?"

"The 'Myrtle.'"

"You old fool! Where are you from?"

"Eh? Ah! Yes. Hamburg."

"Curse the old ass! An English ship from Hamburg! How long have you been in these waters?"

"Water? Yes—plenty aboard."

"No, no. How long have you been here?"

"Here? No; below, in tanks. Do you carry yours on deck?"

The officer looked the picture of despair.

"Here," he said to one of the men, who could scarcely restrain the inclination to laugh outright, "give me the trumpet; perhaps that will make him hear."

"Yes, sir; here it is."

The officer placed it to his mouth, and in a tone that nearly broke the drum of Dutch Paul's ear shouted—

"How long have you been in these waters?"

"Oh! how long have I been here?"

"Yes."

"Three days."

"Ah! the old fool must have seen one, perhaps both vessels. Seen any ships down here lately?"

"Eh?"

The officer yelled the words over again.

"Ships? Ah! Yes—two."

"Two?"

"Yes; that's it."

"Did you notice anything suspicious about them?"

"Suspicious, eh? No. Why do you ask?"

"Both pirates."

"Pirates? Oh, Lord! but are you sure?"

"Yes; we had the information from the governor of San Lois."

"San Luis, eh? Bless me, pirates! Oh, but—eh?—might be a mistake, eh?"

"No, old man; no mistake."

"Oh Lord! and they both spoke to us."

"Ah! Did they? Ah! and what did they say?"

"Say? Oh, yes. Told me not tell you."

"Tell me?"

"No; I swore not to tell anybody they had spoken with me. Ugh! Oh, Lord—pirates! Going to hang 'em?"

"Yes; when we catch them."

"So I thought," Dutch Paul said, laughing; "but I did not tell the poor devil who shouted himself hoarse."

"I cannot imagine," our hero said, "how you kept your countenance."

"Easy enough. My face was turned away from the fellow the greater part of the time, and while he shouted his queries two or three times over I had time to have a good laugh."

"So I should think. Well, how did it end?"

"I told him the pirates were coming back at nightfall to sack the town."

"The devil you did."

"I did.   Why not?"

"That is the only time I can make a run for it."

"Exactly; therefore, while they are watching the entrance to the harbour we can make our way out to sea from this point."

"A good idea."

"Yes, pretty well.   So, there they are waiting for our appearance?"

"Yes; a letter was given to one of the man-o'-war's men, when they overhauled your vessel, and were so cleverly baffled by Ben Barnacle."

Captain Tom's eyes blazed fiercely.

"If so," he said, "there is a traitor on board my vessel."

"That's a fixed fact, and the sooner you find him the better."

Skopey, who had taken the bow-oar of the boat in which our hero sat, turned pale at these words.

He had given the letter, and faithfully described the "Yellow Vulture" as well as the "Will-o'-the Wisp."

Bob Hauler saw the half-caste's face change colour, and mentally resolved not to slacken his vigilance, in spite of the manner in which Skopey had saved his young leader's life.

The change was unnoticed save by Bob Hauler, and he was too prudent to mention his suspicions to the chief or any of the officers until he had better grounds for his mistrust than the mere change in the fellow's countenance.

"Should I find the knave," our hero said, "his will be a short shrift, and quick death."

"That's the thing, and find him you must."

"I shall.   Did you obtain the letter?"

"No; I could not gammon the fellow out of that, although I tried pretty hard."

"I wish you had.   Now, about this affair. Will it not look suspicious for you to be seen about here?"

"Not at all."

"How so?"

"I am waiting until they catch the pirates before I venture out to sea."

Captain Tom laughed at Dutch Paul's coolness, and asked—

"What do you propose respecting this unlooked-for arrival?"

"The best plan is that suggested by yourself."

"To remain here until dark?"

"Exactly."

"Then?"

"Make the best of your way out of this place, join me, and away we go."

"Wind permitting you."

"If it does not, you must take me in tow."

"Very well. No; you had better return and look after the 'Myrtle.'"

"Where are you going?"

"To settle a little account ashore."

"Be careful; they are on the watch at the castle."

"I care not.   I could pursue these miscreants I am about to punish to the quarter-deck of the line-'-battle ship."

"Bravo!   Plucky; but rather dangerous."

"That would add a zest to my vengeance."

"Who has changed your usually amiable temper into this form?"

"A set of devils, who deserve the worst death uman ingenuity could devise."

"A pleasant party!   Have I the honour of their acquaintance?"

"I know not."

"Name them."

"The monks at the Casa des Exercios."

"Whew!   The devil!   Have you fallen of them?   Well, my young friend, a nest of scorpions would be safer to handle than fall in their power."

"So I found it."

"And have escaped?"

"Yes."

"Prodigious!   Pray enlighten me upon the affair."

Our hero told him all that had taken place from the time of their arrival at the inn.

The quarrel upon pretty Ninetta's account, the attempted murder, and the perilous adventure in the chamber beneath the dome.

When he had concluded, Dutch Paul said—

"Upon my word, my young friend, you must be protected by a good or evil spirit. A perfect string of adventures, and all within a few hours. Well, I think, as you have got so far safely, you had better let the brotherhood alone."

Captain Tom looked up in surprise.

"Allow them," he said, "to go unpunished?"

"Well, ye—yes.   I think so."

"Would you do so, were the matter in your hands?"

Dutch Paul smiled grimly, and answered—

"No, I don't think I should."

"Yet you advise me to do so."

"It's as a friend, my dear boy.   It is dangerous, believe me, to return.   They have had time to prepare for you."

"I care not."

"I am quite prepared to hear that.   Well, you must go, I suppose, and, as I have nothing better to do, I will accompany you, if you have no particular objection."

"None; but I have no right to lead you into danger."

"That is quite a secondary consideration, my dear boy; besides, I owe these fellows a little, and I think the present time will do for us both. By the way, I have something here that will be useful in this affair."

He pulled up a loose board that covered the bottom of the boat, and, to our hero's joy, revealed several bottles of the subtle fluid which Dutch Paul alone possessed the secret of its manufacture.

"The very thing," our hero said; "if we cannot gain admittance, we shall be able to set the abominable building on fire."

"I am of opinion," Dutch Paul said, "that a better plan would be to gain admittance, then drive the shaven crowns into one room and burn them up with a little of this warm elixir."

Much as the young chief felt incensed against the villainous brotherhood, this cold-blooded proposal caused him to shudder.

Dutch Paul's quick eye noted this, and, half sarcastically, he said—

"Is their death so repugnant to you that you shudder?"

"No."

"Yet you looked not unlike a landsman first time at sea when I proposed exterminating the scoundrels."

"I did."

"Why?   What reason had you?   Give way, lads, and pull like devils."

The boats began to move slowly through the water, until the rowers had space to bend to their work, then the light boats bounded from wave to wave with wondrous swiftness.

Captain Tom and Dutch Paul were side by side as their boats skimmed the white-topped waves.

"You ask me," the boy said, "why I shivered."

"Such was the nature of my query."

THE SMUGGLERS' ESCAPE.

"I will tell you frankly."

"Do."

"Your project seemed so pitiless."

There was something much like a sneer upon the pirate's handsome face as he said—

"Well, Tom, I hate humbug, or cant of any kind, and I will be frank with you. That shudder, though involuntary on your part, was either one or the other."

"I cannot agree with you."

"Why, my dear boy, the thing is as plain as possible."

"To you perhaps."

"Is it not to you?"

"Far from it."

"I will render my meaning clear. You are upon your way to the monastery, are you not?"

"To a certainty."

"What is your object in going there?"

"Captain Tom began to see his friends meaning, and said—

"My object? Revenge for the brutal treatment one of my followers has experienced from the miscreant gang."

"Very well; how do you intend to revenge yourself upon them?"

"That must be left to circumstances."

"Bah! you are evading my questions."

"No; far from it, I am endeavouring to answer them as clearly as possible."

"Well, you will leave the mode of revenge to circumstances."

"Yes; I shall endeavour to find the men who tortured the poor boy."

"Should you do so?"

"They shall die."

"By the sword or bullet?"

"Exactly; should the gang resist your entrance to the monastery?"

"I will fight my way inside."

"And, as a matter of course, not stand particular who may fall by your shot or steel."

"No; all who bar our passage will run the risk of being shot or cut down."

'That will be killing them, will it not?"

"It will."

"That is the point I wished to come at. You go to this place, your hand grasping a weapon, your heart filled with anger against a set of murderous rascals who were nearly cutting you off from the world, do you not?"

"I do."

"Well, you do not certainly go to shake your blade at them and cry out, 'Don't do this again, or I will hurt you.'"

"That would scarcely repay the trouble."

"Exactly; you go to slay all who may have been concerned in the attempt upon your life, and the ill-treatment of your followers."

"Yes."

"Well, tell me the difference between your mode of killing and mine."

"A vast difference."

"True, yours perhaps is, of the two, the simpler mode of death; still the end will be the same."

"Precisely; but there will be less torture with my plan."

"Granted; but not sufficient to cause you to shudder at the bare idea of killing a number of rascals who have too long encumbered the earth."

The boats grounded at this moment, and put an end to the conversation.

When the men were all landed, a long consultation was held between our hero, Iron Arm, and Dutch Paul.

It was resolved to seek the secret entrance to the monastery; should that have been closed during the time our hero had been away, the pirate agreed to demand admission upon some pretence, and open the gate for his companions.

When the party passed the hostel where our hero's life had been so nearly sacrificed, the boy called Beppo to his side.

"Beppo," he said, "it will soon be the hour for the hostel to open. Leave us, my good friend, and begin your new duties."

"Senor," said the muleteer, "I will leave you, if you wish it; but if my arm is of any service to you, command it. I shall but too gladly obey."

"I know that, my friend. Your gallant behaviour has already proved that the old blood of Spain runs in your veins."

"Senor, you are too flattering."

"No, Beppo; I owe you much, and would repay the debt by keeping you from danger."

"Yet you seek—"

"Remember, Beppo, the bright day now reveals our forms. Should you be seen among a band of men attacking the convent, it will be unsafe for you to reside in Barracoa."

"I can follow your fortune, senor."

"And leave your pretty Ninetta to the gay gallants who openly insult her?"

The young chief had touched the right cord. He could not leave the poor friendless girl.

"Senor," he said, taking our hero's hand and pressing it to his lips, "I will obey your wishes without a murmur."

"Take possession of your good fortune, Beppo, and be kind to the poor girl who loves you so well."

"I will, senor."

The muleteer could say no more. He felt a choking huskiness at his throat, and could not give utterance to the gratitude which welled up from his heart.

The young chief saw the moving lips, and instinct told him all the grateful muleteer would have said.

"Farewell, Beppo," he said; "we shall meet again, perhaps. Until then, may you prosper and be happy."

"Farewell, senor. The Virgin keep you from harm."

So they parted.

The handsome chivalrous boy had, in his strange career, made two young hearts as happy as though they had been visited by a white-robed angel.

He passed on to danger, perhaps death, and the young muleteer stood by the door of his new home sad, yet joyous.

Sad, when he knew that his friend, his benefactor was about to place his young life in jeopardy; joyous, when he looked forward to the grand fortune that had so suddenly befallen him and his pretty Ninetta.

The buccaneer found the secret entrance to the monastery closed.

So effectually that Iron Arm's wondrous strength and mighty weapon failed to remove the obstruction.

"I must try the front gate," said Dutch Paul. "I will go in advance. Don't forget, captain, to have the men within call of each other, for fear of an accident."

"Everything shall be arranged for the best."

Dutch Paul gave his handsome sabre to our hero's care, and, assuming a crooked posture and limping gait, went slowly towards the huge door of the monastery.

His boat's crew and the buccaneers followed two by two, and by keeping close to the wall escaped observation.

The pirate's summons at the gate was answered by a monk whose duty it was to officiate as porter.

He surveyed the humble-looking form through a hole in the strong door, and gruffly demanded his business.

"It is with the superior, holy father."

"He cannot be seen, old man. He is ill, and confined to his chamber."

Dutch Paul gave a groan.

"This," he said, "is bad news. I have travelled the whole length of Spain to see his holiness, and cannot linger but an hour here."

"Is your business of importance?"

"It is, holy father."

"Tell me its nature, and I will go to the superior. He may see you if this visit is needful."

"It is. Tell him one Rialto of Seville desires to speak with him."

The monk closed the wicket, and went to the superior.

Dutch Paul had heard the name of one of the terrible chiefs of the Inquisition who was known to go from place to place for the purpose of visiting the different ecclesiastical establishments.

The name acted like a charm.

The monk returned, and throwing open the door, bent his head lowly to receive the great man's blessing.

He was somewhat astonished when he felt the aged stranger suddenly seize him by the throat, and before he could utter a cry he found the cold rim of a pistol-barrel pressed against his forehead.

"Not a word!" Dutch Paul said, firmly, "or I will scatter your brains out."

To the monk's horror these words were f[...]

by the appearance of Captain Tom and about twenty armed men.

They came swiftly through the gateway, and, led by the young buccaneer, went straight towards the superior's chamber.

Dutch Paul signalled to three of his men, and in a second the monk was gagged, and then thrown upon the cold stones that paved the court-yard.

The superior, waiting to receive the visit of the great chief of the dread Inquisition, was amazed at the entrance of Captain Tom and his hardy followers.

The sight of Banquo's ghost had not a more terrible effect upon Macbeth than the appearance of our hero and his men had upon the miscreant chief of the Black Monks.

He lay back in his chair, his face as white as the sheeted dead, and his eyes rolling wildly from side to side.

"We have met again!" the boy said, in stern accents; "this time not to part until I have had a just and fitting vengeance for all that has been perpetrated at your instigation."

The prior's lips moved convulsively, but no sound came from them.

He could not speak. Terror held him so completely in her power that he was literally bereft of speech or movement.

The buccaneers stood in two lines behind the young chief. Upon his left the giant stood silent, sullen, and with a deadly light gleaming in his dark eye.

Dutch Paul stood near the young buccaneer's right, a cigar between his lips, and a mischievous smile upon his face, as he watched the monks glide silently into the chamber, and form in semi-circle near the prior's chair.

"There will be a row," thought Dutch Paul. "Unless I am very much mistaken, the holy brotherhood have concealed weapons beneath their long black gowns."

The pirate's surmise was correct. The monks were armed, and by the determined expression upon their sallow features it was evident they were resolved to stand by the prior.

When the latter found himself in the midst of his miscreant gang his terror partly left him, and fixing his eyes upon our hero, he said, fiercely—

"What has brought you again within these holy walls? Are you not content with the violence and bloodshed that has already desecrated the sacred edifice?"

"Vengeance has brought me," the boy said, and the hot blood mounted to his cheeks. "Deliver up the accursed wretches who tortured the poor boy I rescued from the chamber of death, or, by Heaven! I will exterminate the whole brotherhood."

"Dare you bandy words with me, sacrilegious youth? Are you not afraid that the mighty wrath of the Great Being in whose temple you stand will descend and curse you?"

A scornful laugh came from the young buccaneer's lips.

"Do not," he said, "outrage the name of the Deity by your false words. Deliver up the men I require, or dread the result."

The prior made a signal to the men who stood near him, as he said—

"The brotherhood are not responsible for their acts to any here below; they serve a higher power. Learn, rash boy, that even these saintly men are ready to resist carnal weapons with carnal weapons, and drive from beneath this roof those who have come with violence in their hearts."

"Wretch!"

Captain Tom gave utterance to this exclamation as he sprang upon the prior, and seized him by the

He gave a yell of terror as the boy's fingers tightened—a yell which was answered by his villainous gang as they each drew a weapon from beneath their robes, and rushed to their superior's assistance.

It would have gone hard with the impetuous boy had not Dutch Paul and Iron Arm rushed forward in time to check the sudden onslaught that was made

The mighty mace beat down a line of glittering swords, and Dutch Paul drove his weapon through a monk's body who had crept behind the young chief.

For a moment the brotherhood swayed to and fro, then, with the cry of—

"Saint Joseph to the rescue!" they rushed forward upon the gallant pair.

The buccaneers had stood passive until this moment. The thought of attacking a body of unarmed men had not been sufficient to arouse the fierce desire for fighting that slumbered in their hearts.

Now, when they saw a hundred dark-robed forms, each grasping a blade, they gave a cry, and drawing their weapons, dashed to the fight.

Our hero had nearly strangled the prior; then casting the miscreant's form from him, he drew his sabre, and called out—

"Upon them, men! Show no mercy; remember the torture chamber! Let every blow tell!"

They came like a torrent upon the black brotherhood, beating up their weapons as though they had been tiny reeds.

Then followed the quick stab, the death-cry, and the sound of falling bodies.

Here and there a hand-to-hand struggle, as a stalwart buccaneer or pirate grappled with his foe.

Then arose the sickening reek of blood, as the chamber was strewn with gashed and bleeding bodies

Amid this terrible scene the voice of the pirate leader could be heard as he cheered his men on.

"Strike!" he said; "strike well home, Yellow Vultures! Victory first, then to plunder this fat monastery!"

The buccaneers needed no cry, no urging on. They fought for revenge, and did their work with silent determination. Twenty of the black brothers lay upon the stone floor, their lives ebbing fast.

Twice that number, wounded, and sick from the loss of blood, were leaning upon their weapons and watching the combat with a savage, devilish expression of countenance.

They had thought, from overwhelming numbers, to have gained an easy victory, but they knew not the men who that day came upon the path of vengeance, or they would not have sought the fight.

Inch by inch they were beaten back, and at length, seized with a sudden panic, they made a rush towards the door.

A fierce "Hurra!" came from the seaman's throats as they flourished their red blades and dashed after the fleeing crowd.

In the great hall the monks made another stand. It was but for a moment.

Like an avalanche their pursuers came upon them.

There was no resisting the impetuosity of this charge, and the craven monks, with a cry of despair, turned and fled.

Fled beyond the reach of the fierce men who would, in their passion, have sacrificed the whole brotherhood to the sword.

In one of the secret vaults they found a hiding-place, and, mingling the most terrible curses with their prayers, they invoked vengeance upon the heads of their foes.

"Gone to their rat-holes," said Dutch Paul. "Now, men, to the chapel; there may be something there to recompense us for this little affair."

Bob Hauler knew the road to the chapel, and acted as guide to the party.

Our hero offered no opposition to the plunder of the place. He knew that the massive ornaments had been procured by force and cruelty, and looked upon this as a just retribution.

Jerry Mizzen, who had been one of the foremost in the fight, now suggested a visit to the wine-cellars, as he felt sure they must feel thirsty.

"We'll go there afterwards, Jerry," said Dutch Paul. "Gold before wine."

Jerry thought the reverse, but, as he did not wish to be out of the general scramble, he accompanied the party.

Our hero and Iron Arm stayed in the large vaulted passage to await the return of the plunderers, and scarcely had the last man passed inside the chapel-door, when the sharp roll of a drum caused them both to start, and Iron Arm exclaimed—

"Curses!"

"What is the meaning of that din?"

"We are surrounded by troops. That accursed monk must have escaped from his bonds and alarmed the soldiery."

It was so. The monk they had left bound at the gate had struggled out of his bonds and brought Don Resparto's company of soldiers to the scene.

It was the work of a moment to alarm the men, and, ready for the fight, they emerged from the chapel loaded with plunder.

"Take care of the cargo," said Dutch Paul. "Bring forward the bottles."

Half a dozen men came to the front rank, each carrying a bottle of the subtle liquid fire.

The troops led by Don Resparto came at a swift pace down the long passage, and when the Don caught sight of our hero he called out—

"Shoot them down—shoot them! Fifty dollars for the man who brings down that boy with the star on his breast."

"I'll stop that noisy lubber," Dutch Paul said, levelling a pistol at the Don. "Take that!"

He fired, and the Don fell with a bullet in his shoulder.

"Now," the pirate leader said, "cast the fire!"

The six men raised the bottles above their heads. There was a crash. The soldiers attempted to run from the body of flame that rose before them.

Too late. The subtle liquid caught their clothes as it spread around, then ran up the wall, setting fire to the woodwork.

"Now," Dutch Paul said, "to the boats!"

They passed swiftly through the gate as a bright sheet of flame shot upward.

They saw the soldiers rush suddenly towards the water to extinguish their burning clothes, and as they passed the angle of the old grey pile a mighty roar told them that the House of Exercise was in flames, and the miscreant brotherhood had no chance of escape from an awful death.

CHAPTER LXVII.
ZELIE'S REVENGE.

In that narrow creek the "Will-o'-the-Wisp's" yards projected some distance over the shore. A plank placed from the low bulwarks was sufficient to form a bridge from the deck to the rich green sward and the tempting shade of the fragrant orange grove.

While our hero was absent with Dutch Paul upon his mission of vengeance, Zelie, the corsair maiden, and Minnie Atherton came on deck.

There was nothing in the Arab girl's pale, classical face to betray the dark thoughts at work within her heart.

She was all gentleness to the fair English maiden, and as they sauntered to and fro, inhaling the sweet aroma from the scented groves, th as loving as the fondest sisters.

"It is indeed inviting,' said Zelie, in reply to a remark Minnie had made respecting the delicious perfume which the breeze wafted over the ship, "and I would give much to wander beneath those shady groves."

Minnie sighed.

She, too, would have liked to have left the vessel, if but for a few moments, but the fear that her young lover would be angry with her for leaving the vessel caused her to turn from the tempting sight.

"You sighed," said Zelie. "Is your heart sad at the sight of the fresh green sward?"

"No, Zelie," answered the fair girl; "I do not covet the cooling breeze which sighs among those sweet groves; I could not be happy in wandering there when all I love has gone upon a mission that may end in death."

The Arab girl's face became darkened, and her heart felt every word uttered by Minnie in reference to the young chief like the repeated thrust of a keen dagger.

She clenched her hands until the nails cut deeply in the flesh, and her brilliant eyes shot forth glances of mingled hate and pity.

She hated the gentle girl because her presence on board the vessel robbed her of the society of the young chief.

She pitied, because she loved her too much to slay her by the knife or a poisoned drink, yet her passion for the handsome young buccaneer urged her onward to put her gentle, unsuspicious rival from her path.

"He would be angered," Zelie said, "were you not to accept the offer that presents itself. The roses have faded from your cheeks, and a ramble among those trees would restore them."

Minnie shook her head.

"He would be angered," she said, "were I to leave the vessel. Perhaps I should not return when he wished to depart, and there is too much danger to the brave men he commands to waste the precious moments lingering here for me."

Lieutenant Vere came towards the handsome girls, his wife leaning upon his arm.

"A charming prospect, ladies," he said, "and one that would bid me almost forget my duty and run ashore, if only to exchange for one moment the hard deck for the soft yielding turf."

"I have been trying to persuade Miss Atherton," said Zelie, "to go ashore for a short time. Do you think we could venture to walk as far as the end of the orange grove before the chieftain returns?"

"I think so," was the reply. "The boats will have to pass round the bend of the inlet, and there would be ample time to return on board before they could reach the ship. Shall I have the accommodation-ladder rigged?"

A few words from Harry Vere caused Minnie's wavering resolution to yield, and, with a sweet smile, she thanked the gallant officer for his kindness.

While the ladder was being lowered, a black attendant ran below and brought the young girl's hats and scarves, and Zelie, a strange light burning in her dark eyes, led the way.

Once ashore, there was so much to admire—the birds, the insects, the brilliant flowers—that Zelie soon led the remonstrating girl far beyond the orange grove, and when the boats rounded the inlet, Zelie came swiftly towards the vessel alone.

. . . .

The boats were abreast of each other, and the two commanders were conversing as they passed swiftly towards the ship.

"I think," Dutch Paul said, calmly puffing his

, that the Yellow Vultures made a profitable visit out of this monk-roasting business."

He pointed to the bottom of the boat, which was covered with the spoils from the chapel.

Images of the Virgin in pure gold, cups, large silver candlesticks, and richly-embroidered vestments lay at his feet in a confused heap.

Bob Hauler and Jerry Mizzen were the only two of the buccaneers that had been able to secure anything worth having from the chapel, and they grinned, as the young chief said—

"I am glad that my men have none of the booty."

"Why?" asked Dutch Paul; "have you become Covenanters?"

"No; but a curse would attend the possession of any article from the shrine."

Dutch Paul laughed.

"The Yellow Vultures," he said, "take the blessings and curses together. Ugh! I wonder how the monks feel by this time, captain?"

The young chief shuddered.

He was not cruel by nature, and he could not calmly reflect upon the monks' probable fate without a chill passing over his frame.

"Poor wretches!" he said; "theirs is a fearful fate."

"A warm one," he said; "but it serves them right."

Captain Tom did not reply.

He was sorry for the wholesale destruction of life that he had supposed had taken place. He did not for a moment imagine that the whole of the brotherhood had passed safely from the blazing building, and were at that very moment grouped upon a rock, watching the progress of the fire; had he known this, his mind would have been less troubled.

Dutch Paul rallied him smartly upon his tender feelings, as he termed them, and by the time our hero reached his ship, the pirate was lying back in the stern of his boat convulsed with laughter.

"Good-bye, captain," he said, as the young chief ascended the "Will-o'-the-Wisp's" side. "You will find the 'Myrtle' outside waiting for you. Shall I tow you out of this sweet spot?"

"Go to the—"

"Perhaps I shall. There's no knowing. At any rate, if I do, I shall not want company. What say you, captain, eh? Monk-roasting will be a serious affair against you. He's gone, and pretty considerably riled, I think. Give way, lads, and get to the ship before we are overhauled, and lose our booty."

The "Yellow Vulture's" boat was soon out of sight; so, likewise, were our friends Jerry and Bob.

They were in the orlop-deck hiding the spoil they had gleaned from the chapel.

When our hero stepped upon the quarter-deck Ben Barnacle came forward, and passing Iron Arm as though the Hercules and himself had never met, he went straight to our hero, and said—

"A most extraordinary circumstance has taken place since you left the vessel."

The young chief saw by his follower's manner that the matter was serious, and, looking round the vessel to see if any accident had happened to her spars or rigging, said—

"Do not keep me in suspense."

"I will not. Your bride, Minnie Atherton, has disappeared."

"Disappeared! How?"

"That is the mystery."

"I do not understand you."

The boy spoke wildly; his senses were dazed by the suddenness of this misfortune, and he glared upon his faithful follower as though the wish was strong within him to spring at Ben's throat.

"Zelie," said Ben, looking compassionately at the wild eyes and haggard face, "went ashore with Minnie during your absence, and when they reached the end of the orange grove a number of men sprang forward and rushed away with her."

Our hero waited to hear no more. With a frantic cry he dashed down the aft-hatch and sought Zelie.

He found the Arab girl with her head buried in the soft cushions of one of the couches, and weeping as though her heart would break.

She raised her tearful face when he entered, and in a remorseful voice cried out—

"Kill me! Kill me! It was my fault."

Captain Tom raised her from the floor, and said, in a sad voice—

"Your fault, Zelie—your fault? You that loved the gentle girl so well! Arise, and tell me how she was lost, and you returned."

Zelie brushed back her long sable tresses, and in a wild, incoherent manner, answered—

"I will. Though you slay me for telling you the truth, Zelie will speak."

He thought she was distracted by the loss of her fair and beautiful companion, and, as he drew her throbbing form to his breast, he kissed her burning forehead, and said—

"Fear not, Zelie. The blow is heavy, but I can bear it with sufficient calmness to listen to your words. Come, speak; time presses, and I would fain be in pursuit of those who have robbed me of one that was too guiltless to do harm."

Zelie nerved herself for the task.

She could not, now that Minnie had been torn from them, help feeling that her wicked deception upon the poor girl had been the cause of the desolation that had fallen upon the youth she loved so well.

"Better," she thought, as she gazed upon his altered features, "for me to behold them together, though the sight wounds my heart, than to see him thus."

"Speak, Zelie!" said Captain Tom, "my blood seems to be drying up within me, and my brain is on fire!"

The Arab girl lowered her head, and, in a low, subdued voice, began—

"I went from the vessel, and my heart was full of black thoughts against the fair English maiden."

The young chief started, and with difficulty repressed the cry of rage that rose to his lips.

Zelie bowed before him as he thrust her hands away, and, putting them across her breast, resumed—

"We wandered hand in hand amid the sunshine and flowers, and my brain was busy how to dispose of the maiden who stood between us—"

"Traitress!" he hissed, his self-control rapidly leaving him.

"We reached the end of the grove," Zelie went on, "and still I could not bring my mind to commit the deed I had so long planned."

Captain Tom looked as though he would have slain the beautiful speaker, and his hand wandered mechanically to the jewelled hilt of his long yataghan.

Zelie moved not, nor cowed before his fierce glance; she was innocent of the poor girl's disappearance, and in telling the young chief her motives for wishing to destroy the young girl she was but expiating the contemplated sin, a peculiar absolution, she thought, would clear her soul should harm befall the poor hapless girl.

"When the time came," she said, "I could not look upon her fair face and commit evil, and as the barbarous thoughts left me, I drew her to a fallen tree, and, as we sat side by side, began to tell her how evil had been my thoughts, and to ask her forgiveness."

"Quick, Zelie!" said the frenzied boy.

She bowed her head and resumed.

"I had barely finished, when a rustling of the fallen leaves caused us both to start and look around."

Captain Tom's chest rose and fell with the excitement he felt.

"We saw," Zelie said, "the forms of three Spanish officers emerge from the forest; they had guns in their hands. and were evidently in search of the wild animals of the chase.

"When they saw us they gave a cry of surprise, and one who was in advance said—

"'Here is a prize! What say you, commander, shall we carry them off to Fort St. Joachim?'

"The others laughingly assented, and made a quick movement towards us. Minnie fled towards the forest, and the officer who first spoke went in pursuit; the others came close upon me, and had I not been fleet of foot I should have been also captured.

"They gave up the pursuit when they saw me rush towards the vessel, and went after their companion. I reached the ship when your boat reached the point, and Minnie has not yet returned."

Captain Tom gave her a look expressive of the agony he suffered, then replacing the pistols he had taken from his belt, drew a pair capable of carrying twice the distance of those he had used upon his expedition against the monks, turned and swiftly ran upon deck.

Without a word to his followers, he sprang from the bulwarks to the shore, and made his way rapidly towards the orange grove.

"Fort St. Joachim!" he muttered. "If she once reaches the interior of those walls I shall never see her more."

Iron Arm saw him leave the ship, and calling upon the men around him to follow, he sprang ashore.

The men were not far behind; as he heard their voices he turned. Seeing that more than one-half the crew were following his footsteps, he selected but three, and sent the remainder back to the ship.

The three were—

Bob Hauler, Jerry Mizzen, and the traitor, Skopey.

Iron Arm had seen what he believed to be a proof of the half-caste's devotion to the gallant boy, or he would not have chosen him from among the many good and true men who would have followed their chief to the death.

CHAPTER LXVIII.

A CLOSE PURSUIT.

THROUGH the orange grove, where the trees, laden with their fragrant blossoms, gave the woodland the aspect of a giant flower garden.

Out beyond this delightful spot to the adjacent forest, where the tangled brushwood tore the stout leather of his long boots, and laid bare in many places the fair skin, passed the young chief of the buccaneers.

His brain was in a whirl, and his eyes, wild and bloodshot, gave him the appearance of one who had beheld a terrible apparition, and as he strode forward, without selecting a pathway that promised an easier passage than the thick undergrowth, he seemed as though he was flying from a dreaded and terrible pursuer.

Oft he came to a sudden halt as he toiled onward, and, smiting his forehead with his clenched hands, he would murmur, in heart-broken accents, the name of his soul's idol.

Iron Arm, and those who followed the young chieftain, held back. They were touched by his grief, and, rough-hearted as they were, felt saddened by the sight of their lion-hearted leader's sufferings.

The boy knew not that he was followed by this small but trustworthy band, until he was compelled to seek a few moments' rest from the long and arduous walk through the forest. As he sat beneath the shelter of a large tree, he discovered the giant's towering form as he advanced through the brushwood.

The boy was by this time sufficiently calm to know that any attempt he could make alone would be attended with more danger and less result, than by the co-operation of the cool brains and strong arms of his faithful followers.

He smiled faintly as the Hercules came to where he sat, and said—

"I am glad you have come. This blow had so unnerved me that I started, like Don Quixote, to attack a castle single-handed."

"I saw you leave the ship," said Iron Arm, "and brought these men; they will be useful should we come up with the poor girl's captors."

"They are beyond the reach of pursuit before this."

The giant started with surprise.

"Yet," he said, "you know this and follow the trail. Where have they taken Minnie?"

"To Fort St. Joachim."

"Fort St. Joachim? One of the strongest places on the frontier."

"I care not. I will have her, or die in the attempt."

"Any open effort," said Iron Arm, "will be the forerunner of your death. We have some distance to go. Perhaps before we sight the fortress I may think of a plan."

The party again moved forward. Our hero silent and wretched, Iron Arm's brow clouded with anxiety and deep thoughts.

When the night began to draw in upon them, Iron Arm drew closer to his chief, and said—

"A thousand and one plans to gain an entrance to the fort have presented themselves and been dismissed from my mind. One only promises the least success, and there is so great a danger attending it that I almost fear it will also be impracticable.

"Danger!" Captain Tom said, "and Minnie a captive! I would face the cannon's mouth in the attempt to release her"

"A useless attempt," said Iron Arm, "which would result in your own death, and not benefit the gentle girl."

"Your plan?" said the young chief. "Let me know it. If it can be carried out I will make the attempt."

"Fort St. Joachim," said the giant, "is built upon a scarped rock on the western side; the lower rampart is formed from the foundation."

"You mean that the embrasures for the guns are cut out of the rock."

"I do."

"Proceed."

"This portion of the fort is defended by a wide ditch, at the very least thirty yards across."

"I have often swam treble the distance."

"Possibly. But beneath the surface of this water sharp-pointed stakes have been driven in the bottom; once impaled upon them, no earthly power could save you from being shot by the sentinels on the ramparts."

"I will make the attempt."

Iron Arm bit his lips. He regretted having told the impetuous boy this much of the dangerous approach.

"This is not all," he said. "After the moat has been crossed, and the base of the rock reached, the danger becomes tenfold."

"How?"

"The face of the rock has been hewn as smooth as human hands can make it, and, to increase the peril a besieging force would have to encounter in any attempt at storming, it is nearly perpendicular in form."

These were mighty perils, but not sufficient to damp the boy.

"I would make the attempt," he said, resolutely, "were every inch of the rock covered with the most deadly scorpions. There must be patches of rock-plants sufficient to give my hands a purchase; if so, I shall succeed."

"I fear not. There is no crevice large enough for the tiniest seed to vegetate."

The giant did all in his power to deter the wayward young chief; but had the danger been, if possible, greater, he would have answered with the same words—

"I will make the attempt."

They left the forest as the darkness increased, and came upon a wide roadway, evidently, by the peculiar marks left by numerous wheels, a military road.

"Artillery," said Iron Arm, "must have passed here lately."

"Such was the thought the marks suggested to my mind."

The giant reflected for some minutes before he again spoke.

"If so," he said, at length, "the garrison has been reinforced, and that would not be done unless there is a fear of the Republicans contemplating an attack upon the fortress, which," he added, "will increase the danger of an attempt. They will be more watchful than ever."

The boy smiled. He thought this was but a ruse of his friend to deter him from making his rash attempt to gain admittance to the fort.

Soon after Iron Arm had spoken, they were startled by the clatter of horses' hoofs, and turning their heads in the direction of the sound, they beheld three horsemen in the glittering uniform of the Spanish army emerge from a cross-road.

One of them had a girl before him, and our hero's heart stood still at the sight.

The white dress worn by Minnie flashed to his mind, and he sprang forward at the thought that his bride and the white-veiled form before him were the same.

The horsemen were going at a swift pace, and the buccaneers, though fleet of foot, were left far behind their young chief as he started in pursuit.

Mile after mile was passed, and still he seemed not to tire, and his followers were compelled, Iron Arm excepted, to pause and regain their breath.

Iron Arm and the boy ran side by side. The road was straight as an arrow, and they could discern the outlines of the horsemen's forms, though so great a distance intervened between them.

The mystery attending the appearance of the young girl's abductors was soon cleared up by Iron Arm.

"We have," he said, in answer to our hero, "by crossing the forest, come direct upon the road that leads to the fort, while Miss Atherton's abductors have had to come by the road."

They kept up the headlong race until the dark towers of Fort St. Joachim could be seen standing out in bold relief against the pale moonlight, and then the young chief, thoroughly exhausted, fell to the ground with a despairing cry.

Iron Arm raised the fallen head upon his knees, and as he chaffed the forehead he murmured—

"Poor boy! he suffers even more than I do, upon her account. Will the time ever come when I may tell him how dear poor Minnie's safety is to me?"

These strange words were brought to an abrupt conclusion, as the boy opened his eyes and looked wildly around.

"Minnie," he murmured; "my own, my beautiful girl—lost, lost, lost!"

"There is hope yet," said the giant; but his quivering, hushed voice seemed to belie the words.

"We are close upon them; come, my chief, shake off this feeling, and let us resume the pursuit."

The boy arose, and placed his hand to his brow like one who had received a blow. Then, with a wild cry, he dashed forward, and soon outstripped Iron Arm.

Jerry Mizzen, Bob Hauler, and Skopey came up as he sprang forward; and though they were somewhat refreshed by the pause they made, they did not overtake their chief until he stood beneath the dark walls of the massive stronghold of Fort St. Joachim, the impregnable frontier town of the monarchy of old Spain.

CHAPTER LXIX.
JOHN GREGORY RECEIVES A VISIT.

A MISERABLE wreck of the once hale old man sat in the narrow chamber in Doctor Burchenall's private establishment.

His clothes hung in shreds from his worn and attenuated frame, and the iron-grey hair had changed to the purest white.

John Gregory sat upon the side of his little pallet, his head bowed in his hands, and the tears coursing each other down his sad, pinched face; and as his frame shook with the weight of affliction upon his mind, he moaned—

"Why am I suffered to live? Oh, Death! thy cold hand upon my heart would be bliss to the existence I am compelled to endure."

He raised his eyes and saw the sunbeams struggling through the closely-barred windows.

This sight, at all times saddening to the captive mind, increased his agony, and, as he watched the motes dancing in the glorious light, he said, in heart-piercing accents—

"The blessed sun comes to cheer my lonely lot, and I, instead of being grateful, endure the most terrible pangs at the sight. It brings before me the green fields, the sweet breezes, and the wish for freedom that I never more shall feel. Freedom!" he continued. "How oft have I read of the sufferings of those who, like myself, have been captive; but never has the most graphic pen realised one-twentieth part of my sufferings. Death is all I ask for, why does it not come?"

He threw himself back upon his pallet, and strove to hide the faint sun-gleam—a sight that brought with it the wish for freedom.

While lying thus, his hands tightly compressed over his brow, he thought how different would have been his fate had he not sent his bold, handsome nephew, the gallant Captain Tom, to sea.

"I am the cause of all I have suffered," he thought. "Had he been here, I should have had a champion who would have defied my subtle enemies, and protected my poor old body against these inhuman monsters."

He thought of his sister, Tom's mother, and wondered what had been her fate.

He knew she had disappeared, and he felt that the cunning villain, Sanderson, had been at the bottom of the vile work.

He thought, also, of his ward, the peerless Minnie, and a feeling of relief came to his aching heart at the knowledge that she was with her handsome lover. He knew she was safe with him; not even the devilish machinations of his foes could be brought to bear upon her while the noble boy trod the deck of his powerful vessel.

His mind wandered from her to the woman who was allied to him by marriage.

"Surely," the old man moaned, "Jane Harpy is not a party to this diabolical work. No; the influence that scoundrel holds over the wretched being compels her to hold aloof from any attempt to help me in this great hour of need. Would it were otherwise! Then there would be a chance of my once more beholding the outer world."

So ran his musings, and he wondered whether his boy would visit the shores of his native land again. He knew the price that was set upon his head, and he knew also that there were many who would, for the sake of the reward, betray the noble fellow to the men who thirsted for his blood.

No, there was no hope for him; he must bear his misery yet longer, his only hope of release being death, and the grim tyrant's approach would be to him bliss.

The door of his cell was opened by one of the keepers, and a rough, brutal voice called out—

"Get up! Here is a lady wants to see you!"

The old man arose—he knew a refusal to comply with the man's words would be followed by a blow from the thick, heavy stick he carried.

A female form entered the cell, and, the face being hidden by a thick veil, old Gregory's heart beat hopefully at the thought which came to his mind.

"My sister!"

The keeper withdrew, locking the door after him, but, before he left, he gave the poor old man a malicious look, and said—

"If he is violent, madam, you have only to ring that bell, and I will soon come and keep him in order."

The veiled woman bowed coldly, and the hand that held the folds of the thick lace that hid her face shook slightly.

She must have been less of a woman had she beheld the wreck that old John Gregory presented.

The hope was still strong within him that Mrs. Drake had, by a heavy bribe, penetrated the private asylum, and, as he was upon the point of enfolding her in his arms, she drew the veil aside.

John Gregory recoiled, and from his parted lips came the words—

"Jane Harpy!"

"Yes, John Gregory, and, like yourself, but a wreck."

He extended his hand, and, as the woman felt the contact against hers, his wasted fingers seemed to scratch her flesh.

"We are both strangely altered, Jane," he said, as he looked into her pinched white face; "you must have suffered much."

"I have," she answered, her voice scarcely able to articulate a word; "but it has been the mind, John, which has caused this frame to waste, and my eyes to lose their lustre."

Old John Gregory needed no telling this; he could read the impress left by the searching finger of remorse, and wondered whether the same hand had brought them mutual misery.

He was not long left in doubt.

"The day may come," she said, "when we may both be avenged for all this. Even now the white sails of Tom Drake's ship may be spread to bring him to England."

"Tom Drake—Tom, my gallant boy! Is he coming to save his poor old uncle from worse torments than were ever inflicted by the Evil One upon those whom he had caused to sin, and then claimed their spirits as his own?"

This subtle manœuvre had thrown the old man off his guard, and the woman, though her heart revolted at the task before her, was compelled to carry out the vile scheme hatched by the scoundrel Sanderson.

She was compelled to do this for two reasons—weighty reasons for a woman.

She hoped and believed that the guilty partner of her sins would, at last, make her his wife, and take from her the shame she felt when facing her fellow-creatures.

This powerful incentive was sufficient to steel her heart against all emotion of a womanly nature, and she set about the tempter's work with a cunning that would have met the approval of him who had set her upon the task.

To John Gregory's outburst she held down her head—she could not look her victim in the face while she said—

"I only draw this inference from Sanderson's sudden wish to cast the blame of your incarceration upon other shoulders. He knew that Tom Drake would as soon carry him off and hurl him in the sea when he discovers how you have been treated, as he would drown a rabid dog."

"There is hope," said the old man, joyfully. "Oh! that he would come! Oh! that I could see his vessel in the bay! There would be a heavy reckoning with the fiends who inhabit this accursed place."

"Heaven send him hither, to prevent worse misfortunes than have already befallen you and yours."

"More misfortunes, Jane?"

"Yes, tenfold more. What, think you, is my errand here?"

"I know not; can form no conception."

"Sanderson has sent me to you. Oh, John! did you know how I have been beaten by that fiend before I would consent to come, you would believe with me that Heaven will soon send an avenger to redress our wrongs."

"Beaten, Jane?"

"Aye; worse than he would have lashed one of his hounds."

John Gregory groaned; he believed the woman, and sympathised with her well-got-up misery.

"What reason did you give," he asked, "to be thus brutally treated?"

"You shall hear," she answered, sobbingly. "A few days since this man, who has been like a demon to me, received a letter from abroad."

"Ah! from my boy, or one who has been set to give notice of Tom Drake's arrival."

"I knew not its contents, or the writer," she craftily answered; "but when Sanderson read it, his face became as white as that of a corpse, and I overheard him mutter words that led me to the belief that Tom Drake's ship will soon be here."

John Gregory's wan face glowed with joy at the prospect the cunning woman held, and clasping his hands, he exclaimed fervently—

"Thank God my prayers will soon be answered! Oh, Jane, you know not how I have supplicated the great Omnipotent to send the brave boy home. I could weep for joy at the thoughts which this blissful picture brings to my mind."

The woman turned her head away—she feared the deceived man would read her thoughts and discover how terribly he was being deceived by the false hopes she held out to him.

"I have prayed and wept," she said, "and now the joyful time approaches, my heart smites me for my former wickedness to the boy, and at times I fear he will withhold the bud of success from one who has been his foe."

"He is a noble fellow," said old Gregory, enthusiastically, "a noble, high-spirited boy; and he will be ready to forgive and forget all that has passed."

"I fear not."

"I know him better than you, Jane, and even should he be disposed to remember the past, a word from me will make him your friend."

"Thanks, John, for the prospect you hold out."

The hypocrite pretended to weep, and poor old

Gregory soothed her with words of comfort—soothed the serpent who was about to sting him.

When the fit of emotion had lasted long enough, Tom's good-hearted old uncle said—

"Now, Jane, tell me the purpose that rascal has in forcing you to come here. Speak plainly; hide nothing. I can see that you are an unwilling instrument in his hands, and perhaps we can yet thwart him by seeming to accede to his wishes."

Mrs. Harpy's eyes shone with the exultation which filled her heart. She saw the old man was falling easily into the very trap she had laid.

"We can," she said, "do this by a seeming compliance on your part to come to his proposal. I need hardly tell you that a refusal will be followed by a bribe from him to the ruffians in the pay of the doctor. You know the result."

Old Gregory's frame quivered.

Too well he knew the brutalities of the ruffian gang to willingly place himself in their power. He knew also that gold from the brutal Sanderson would not be spared to carry out any plan his subtle brain had concocted.

With such reflections as these in his mind, he speedily became an easy prey to the artful woman.

"You tell me," he said, "that by a seeming compliance with his request I can, with your assistance, yet thwart him?"

"You shall hear and judge for yourself."

She took a folded paper from her pocket, then, seating herself beside her visitor, resumed—

"When Sanderson received the letter of which I have spoken, he seemed at first as though a spectre had risen in his path. After he had muttered for some time about the return of young Tom—"

"God bless the noble fellow!"

John Gregory's eyes glistened as he uttered these words.

"He broke out some strange expressions," she resumed, "of the danger which menaced him. After a time he became calm, and told me there was but one way to avert the boy's anger from falling upon his head."

Old Gregory smiled. His mind was filled with the joyful prospect of our hero's return, and rubbing his hands he said—

"Yes, yes—go on."

"I asked him how it could be averted, and he told me that he would have a deed drawn up for you to sign."

"Ah! Its purport?"

"To make over the Atherton estates to his keeping until Minnie returns with her lover."

Old Gregory started.

"Never!" he said; "never will I place such an instrument in his hands."

"You forget," she said, "our mutual contract, by which we can lull him into a sense of false security."

"True. go on."

"He imagines with this deed he can meet the young heir, and—"

"Enough; I never will consent."

"You forget."

"I forget nothing. I accepted that trust, and was bound to keep it sacred. I have done so, and sooner than betray it I will suffer the most infernal torments."

There was a savage gleam in Mrs. Harpy's eyes as he spoke, and her white lips trembled at the thought of losing her coveted prize.

She knew that, John Gregory's mind once resolved, the most diabolical torture could not cause him to swerve.

"You are excited," she said, "and will not let me finish all I have to say."

"Speak! Go on! I can listen, but consent I never—"

"You have not heard me out."

He lowered his hand, and signed for her to finish her explanation.

"When I heard his plan," she said. "I saw at once that he would play a high stroke to make himself master of the Atherton estates, and as I listened to his plan the memory of the wrongs I have suffered at his hands came upon me, and I determined to be avenged."

"How?"

"Thus. I resolved to outwardly aid him, and consented to bring the deed to you which makes him master of the poor girl's property."

"Well, be quick!"

She was not hurried by his nervous, excited manner. She saw too well that he must become her prey.

"He gave me this deed, told me that a refusal to sign on your part would be followed by torments. The sufferings which you have undergone will be child's play in comparison to them."

"Curse him!"

"I listened to all he wished me to impart to you, and when the deed was in my possession I, too, had a plan to checkmate the evil-doer."

Old Gregory glared so savagely at the folded paper Mrs. Harpy held that she placed it beneath her mantle. The paper seemed to have the same effect upon the poor fellow as a red mantle upon a goaded bull.

"My plan is this," she continued; "Tom Drake, expect, will be here within a few days, by that time. I hope, that Sanderson takes possession of the Atherton es—"

Old Gregory sprang to his feet, and gave vent to an expletive, forcible and condemnatory to the soul of John Sanderson, Esquire.

"Hear me out," said Mrs. Harpy. "We can have a brilliant revenge if you agree to sign the paper."

"Never!"

"Well; my plan will crumble away—without that, revenge will lose its sweetness. There is no risk. He will have the deed, and imagine he is in absolute possession of the estate. and when the sweet child arrives he will be driven like a dog from the doors of the place he so fondly believed his own."

"How will you manage this?"

Old Gregory tried to speak calmly, but his intense passion gave a fierceness to his face that was unnatural to his usual placidness.

"Very easily," she said, scarcely able to collect her thoughts; "I have prepared a bottle of ink which has the peculiar property of fading when used, and leaving the paper blank."

John Gregory looked at the woman, and said—

"Are you speaking truly?"

"I am. To prove it, I will leave the ink in your possession."

"That," old Gregory said, "will not alter the signature, should the fluid not act as you expect."

She took a small bottle from her pocket, a pen, and a blank sheet of paper.

"Here," she said, "are the proofs. Write on this paper. I will leave the pen and ink with you, and in two days you will find the paper as spotless as it is now. I will then return, and give you the deed to sign."

This seemed fair enough, and he was satisfied. He filled the half side of the paper with close writing, then put it, with the pen and ink-bottle, under his pallet.

Mrs. Harpy soon after left. Had he heard her triumphant mutterings as she left the madhouse, he would have known that a strong acid diluted with water would, by being poured over the writing, make it indelible—it would have lasted until the paper rotted with age. Poor old John! his nature was too simple and frank to suspect aught of this.

CHAPTER LXX.
INSIDE FORT ST. JOACHIM.

One chamber in the grim fortress was ablaze with the concentrated lights of a hundred waxen tapers.

The officers of the garrison had not degenerated from that love of luxury so inherent in the Spanish nature, and the chamber where they were wont to assemble was fitted out with a voluptuousness which a Sybarite would have envied.

Young nobles, dark-skinned, but eminently handsome, their graceful forms set off to advantage by the glittering uniform of the Imperial army, reclined upon the soft couches, sipping the rich wines from golden goblets, and leisurely puffing blue wreaths of smoke from their choice and fragrant cigars.

"I wonder," one of them asked, lazily, "what has befallen Juan and his companions? They went out to the chase soon after daybreak."

"Lost their way," suggested another, "or—"

"Or what?" asked the first speaker.

"Found the bright eyes of some forest girls too enticing to leave."

"Most likely. Well, I envy them."

"Why?"

"You ask why with as much indifference as though we were at the Court of Madrid, where pretty girls are as plentiful as they are scarce here."

"But a peasant?" said the second speaker.

"A peasant! If she has a pretty face she will do for the time; for my part, I am quite content to open a flirtation with the first lovely girl I meet."

"So am I," said another. "I would, were I commander-in-chief, have a company of handsome girls attached to a fort like this, so that we all could make love."

There was a good laugh at this.

"The discipline of the army," said a burly major of artillery, "would soon go to the devil had we a company of petticoats attached to our brigade."

"Curse the discipline!" said a young officer; "enjoyment is the thing. I say, with Rafael, this is a beastly place, and unless we keep up a flirting and soft talk with the peasant girls, we shall be like savages when we return to the capital."

The old major gulped down a goblet of wine and grumbled out—

"A good campaign would suit me better than fooling with a parcel of women. Confound them, I say."

"Yes," said Captain Rafael, "the major always says that since the dark-eyed widow of old Don Mendoz eloped, and left him to serenade the moon."

A burst of laughter from the thoughtless young officers caused the old fellow's cheeks to redden with anger, and calling them a set of empty-headed fools, he jumped from his seat and rushed from the chamber, his heavy sabre clanking upon the stone passage.

He was annoyed, but knowing how useless it would be to show this feeling to the reckless young officers, he went to the western rampart to smoke his cigar in peace.

Had he not been so much occupied thinking savagely of the fickle, buxom widow who had made him the butt of the whole regiment, he would have seen a dark form hanging by the tips of his fingers to a small crevice in the scarped rock.

The major did not see this; the vision was strong upon him of the night he stood strumming an old guitar beneath the widow's chamber while she was seated in a carriage beside her lover.

The young officers, when the major left the chamber, began once more to speculate upon the absence of their companions.

Their speculations were suddenly brought to a close by the clatter of horses' hoofs in the narrow courtyard, and their absent companions soon after entered the room, one of them bearing Minnie's senseless form upon his shoulder.

He placed the fair girl upon a cushion, and as the officers gathered round, they were loud in their expressions at her marvellous beauty.

"Who does she belong to?" Rafael said. "By Heaven! he is a lucky dog."

"That," Pedro said, "remains to be decided. We all lay claim to her; therefore we must settle the dispute by cards."

"Bravo!" said Rafael. "But while you are playing would it not be as well to send the poor girl to a room, under the care of one of the men's wives. She will have time to recover, and greet her lover. My faith! I would mine were the happy chance."

The advice was attended to, and Minnie was carried away in the strong arms of an artilleryman's wife, and placed in a small chamber near the western tower, there to await the issue of the fickle goddess of fortune.

There were three aspirants for her possession, and the contest occasioned the liveliest interest among their companions.

The game proposed was a long one. The pack of cards was divided in three parts, and each player laid a card alternately upon the table, the highest, as a matter of course, taking the trick.

The game ended by the exhaustion of the cards. Then the player who had the greatest number of spots was declared the victor.

While the game progressed, the fair girl recovered her senses, and when she found herself in that strange chamber she called aloud upon our hero to save her, then swooned again.

. . . .

Looking upward, from the base of the rock which terminated in the western rampart, the attempt to scale the perpendicular face seemed hopeless.

Even our hero was staggered by the dizzy height, and the smooth, almost polished, surface.

"There is not," he said, "a footing for a goat upon this ascent, yet it must be done."

"The attempt," Iron Arm said, "can have but one ending."

"That?"

"Death!" was the terse reply.

"Think you," the boy asked, "that I can stand outside these walls and know that all I love on earth, save my mother, is a captive, and at the mercy of these lawless men?"

Iron Arm was silent for some time, and, leaning upon his mace, he seemed to ponder over a plan to enter the fort.

"Captain," he said, at length, and placing his hand upon the boy's shoulder as he spoke, "you know not how dear the gentle Minnie is to me, and were the attempt likely to avail us anything, I would batter the gate in and drag her from those men; it would not aid us. We should be shot down like vermin, and she—I tremble to think what would be her fate."

Captain Tom knew not the import of his words when he said how dear Minnie was to him. He knew that one and all of the "Will-o'-the-Wisp's" crew were devoted to the gentle girl, and the inference he drew was that Iron Arm spoke as any of the crew under his command would have spoken of the lovely Minnie Atherton.

How much his judgment was at fault will be seen in the astounding sequel to his narrative.

"You, whom no danger ever daunts," our hero said, "admit there is but one plan to save her, and that is by scaling the face of the rock; yet you would dissuade me from the attempt."

"I would. Think you that I could see your form dashed to a shapeless mass, and know that my words were the cause?"

The boy took his hand.

"That you love me," he said, "I know; I feel that yours is a love free from worldly motives. Could I think that you would wish me dead? I am light of foot, and have climbed the grassy slopes of the cliffs, often three hundred feet above the sea, merely to rob a bird of her young. I have done this with nothing but a few blades of grass to clutch, think you I would not do more for my heart's idol?"

"Go, boy," said the giant; "may Heaven bring you safe out of your peril."

Their dispositions were soon made.

Iron Arm and his men were to stay beneath the rampart, and be ready to aid the young chief by covering his advance or retreat with the fire of their pistols.

Leaving his sabre with Iron Arm, the young chief began his perilous ascent.

His short Eastern knife stood him in good stead as he climbed up the frightful acclivity.

The keen point was capable of entering the smallest crevices, places too small for his beautifully-shaped white hand to grasp.

It was a toilsome, arduous task. Many times his life depended upon the strength of a small tuft of grass.

Many times, again, was he without the least support from his hands, and his safety only consisted in pressing his chest against the surface of the rock, and keeping his toe firmly fixed in the small crevices. He spread his hands out, and felt cautiously for a jagged point or a tuft of vegetation.

In such moments as these a strong gust of wind would have been sufficient to have caused his death, and hurled him to the foot of the rock, every bone crushed, and his lithe body a disfigured, ghastly heap.

His followers watched him with beating hearts as he ascended, inch by inch, the frightful place.

They saw him at times when he flattened his body against the rock, and their hearts stood still when his hands were seen to pass cautiously about in search of the smallest possible crevice to aid his ascent.

He reached half way, and a new danger stood in his path.

It was the form of the major of artillery, as he bent over the ramparts, thinking how the widow had befooled him. The soldier knew not that four pistol muzzles were in deadly line with his head.

The buccaneers breathed freely when the officer left the rampart, and soon after they beheld their young chief entering one of the embrasures.

Standing for a moment upon a gun, the boy waved his cap to those below as a signal of his success in overcoming the deadly, perilous ascent.

They would fain have answered with a cheer, had not Iron Arm's stern voice bade them remain silent.

Crouching for a few moments in the shadow of a buttress, the boy listened intently for the slightest sound.

He heard the clanking of sabres as the officers passed along the wide stone galleries, but beyond this all was for some time silent.

Quitting the ramparts, he passed through a small door, and entered the corridor.

The place was in darkness, and as silent as the tomb.

Bewildered by the magnitude of the place, our hero went cautiously forward, the hope of finding his beloved Minnie every moment growing less.

Between a narrow loop-hole the pale moonbeams stole softly through, and shed a spectral halo around.

Captain Tom beheld a heap, in shape not unlike a human form.

He drew a deep breath, and, cocking one of his pistols, stood ready to fire upon the slightest movement of what he believed was a sentinel crouching ready to spring upon him as he passed.

He could have laughed at his fears when he came near the object, which turned out to be a coil of rope.

Our hero's heart bounded with joy; he saw at once that he should, by the aid of this, be able to leave the fort.

Replacing the pistol in his belt, he lifted the rope, and retraced his way to the rampart.

By ascending a small flight of steps, he reached one of the highest towers, and making one end fast to a heavy gun-carriage, he cast the remainder over, and, to his joy, he felt it being pulled by his followers beneath.

He answered this signal, then descended, and again entered the corridors.

He had not gone more than twenty yards when he saw a light gleaming beneath the bottom of a door.

With a noiseless tread he crept towards it, and placed his ear to the key-hole.

Did he hear aright, or was a demon mocking him? No, it was the voice of the gentle girl whom he loved.

To lift the latch was the work of a moment, the next he stood in the chamber.

Minnie gave a joyful cry, and would have run towards him had not the woman held her back.

Like a panther she sprang upon the soldier's wife, and, before she could make an outcry, she was bound and gagged.

One soul-thrilling embrace, then the young pair started from the chamber and shot swiftly towards the tower.

In the bewilderment of the moment, Captain Tom missed his way, and found he was traversing a passage formed by Nature in the solid rock which supported one of the heavy towers.

Faint streaks of light struggled through the crevices, and showed him sufficient to judge that it led to the magazine of the fortress.

"I would like to blow them up," he muttered, in his momentary excitement.

Minnie started in horror.

"For Heaven's sake—for our own sake—be no so rash!" she pleaded.

Captain Tom, in his hasty view around, had discovered a barrel of powder, so placed that it would blow up the tower above them, and a slow match placed ready for igniting.

Minnie uttered a low cry.

Tom had fired the match and was examining the priming of the barrel.

One spark from the smouldering match would have sent them all into eternity.

Tom did not think of this under the momentary impulse, he wanted to be revenged, until Minnie's voice awoke him to his senses.

"Bah! what a fool I have been," he said, as he dashed the match on the stone floor and trampled it under his feet.

Then taking Minnie by the hand he led her gently onwards.

A few seconds served to put him in the right way, and he eagerly examined the rope to see that it was quite safe.

Minnie wound her arms around his neck, and he had begun to descend the rope when the sound of the Spanish woman's voice sent a thrill of horror through him.

"She has broken her bonds," he said, fiercely. "God help us!"

The girl clung to him, and they descended the rope. Midway between the tower and the trusty friends beneath, a man's form appeared at one of the embrasures—an arm protruded—a flash, and a bullet whistled past our hero's head.

Minnie uttered no cry, though she knew that they had escaped by a miracle. She heard her lover's deep breathing as he went swiftly down the rope, and when they reached the ground the ramparts became alive with armed men. They were seen, and the Spaniards dashed to the gate to slay or recapture them.

CHAPTER LXXI.
THE SIGNING OF THE DEED.

FAITHFUL to her time, Mrs. Harpy returned on the morning of the third day after she had left the paper and writing materials with John Gregory.

Whatever suspicions he had entertained, they passed away when he beheld the paper, one side of which he had filled so closely, perfectly blank within twenty hours from the time he used the peculiar ink.

Not the faintest trace of the writing could be discovered, and had he not retained the paper in his possession he could not have credited the extraordinary occurrence.

He met the treacherous woman with a smiling face and friendly grasp of the hand.

"You have not deceived me," he said. "The fluid has done all you described."

"Did you," she asked, "think I came with that intent?"

"I know not. The cruelty I have endured, and that villain's baseness have made me suspicious of all who approach me."

Mrs. Harpy sighed, and her face wore a compassionate look.

"You have, indeed," she said, "suffered; but, thank Heaven, the hour fast approaches when you will be avenged tenfold."

"I care not for revenge," said John Gregory. "Even now I could forgive that scoundrel were he to restore me to liberty."

"That," she said, "he never will do. He fears the past too much to feel safe should you be at large."

She immediately corrected herself by adding—

"That is, unless the deed which I have brought you to sign were in his possession."

Old Gregory did not clearly see his way, although he believed that the signature he was required to affix would fade in a few days.

"How," he asked, "will the possession of the deed of transfer affect the matter when my gallant boy returns, and liberates his poor old uncle?"

"As far as I can learn," she said, "Sanderson, when the deed is signed, and in his keeping, will come to you upon Tom Drake's return, and offer you the transfer upon condition that you will not implicate him in your ill-treatment."

"He, of course, imagines that I shall be only too glad to obtain possession of the document, and will consent."

"Such is the motive."

For the first time for many long days poor old John indulged in the luxury of a hearty fit of laughter.

"The scoundrel!" he said. "Ha! ha! How I will astonish him when I tell him to keep the deed, and threaten him with punishment for his villainy. Ha! ha! The rogue will defy me, secure in the thought that he has Minnie's property. Imagine his dismay, dear Jane, when I disclaim any knowledge of the signature. Ha! ha! He will bring forth the document in triumph, and behold the place where my name should be as vacant, as white, as spotless as when the paper left the mill."

She laughed too, and entered into the spirit of the affair that quite won upon the victim.

"It will, indeed, be a triumph for us," she said "and when, like a baffled demon, he stands glaring at the paper, my wrongs will be avenged."

Old Gregory became as eager to sign the deed of transfer as though it were an order for his liberation from Doctor Burchenall's private asylum.

"Where is the document?" he asked, "you have brought it, I suppose?"

"I have," was the answer.

She placed it in his hand, and old Gregory, without reading more than the first six lines, spread it upon the table, and with a firm hand affixed his signature.

She watched him closely, and had to compress her lips to prevent a cry of joy escaping them, and as the scratches of the pen sounded upon her ears her heart beat violently, so much so that its throbbings became distinctly audible.

"There," he said, "it is done; now I shall count the hours until I behold the white sails of the gallant boy's ship as she sweeps into the bay."

She took the deed, and her heart thrilled with joy at the success which had attended her vile plot.

"May you," Mrs. Harpy answered, "soon behold the joyful sight. I, too, though I do not expect to be forgiven by your nephew, shall watch for his vessel, and when she appears will I mock the villain who imagines he has us so completely in his power."

"It will be a joyful hour when you can openly defy him," said old Gregory, "an hour that will recompense the long days of suffering you have endured."

She extended her hand to the poor old dupe, and while they exchanged a friendly parting grasp she said—

"It will—it will. Good bye. I must now return to the man whom my sins have made my master. Good-bye, and be of good heart."

She left the cell, and poor old Gregory, stripped of the last penny he possessed, sat on the edge of the pallet, conjuring up pleasant visions of the hour when he should again breathe the free air which Heaven's mercy wafts to rich and poor alike.

Mrs. Harpy met John Sanderson in the doctor's private room. He had been long closeted with the head of the private asylum, and when he arose to join his companion he shook the doctor's hand, saying, in a low voice—

"Remember, the sum will be trebled when your patient dies."

The doctor was too cautious even to commit himself with his villainous visitor.

He bowed him out, and said, blandly—

"Your poor friend shall have every attention my skilful assistants and I can bestow. We cannot do more."

Doctor Burchenall rubbed his spotless hands as he watched Sanderson and the woman leave the outer gate, and muttered softly—

"Well, my friend, you are the quintessence of scoundrelism. So I am, to use plain words, to murder old Gregory for a paltry sum. Yes, I will do it, as far as you are concerned, my loving friend. A coffin, filled with stones, and a plate, with the old man's name, will not cost much; and when you have possession of his wealth I think I can draw a little sum from you which will be useful. If you do not consent, then, my friend, I shall release the old man, after making terms that will repay the trouble I am taking in this affair."

Mrs. Harpy and her companion, elated with the success by which they had become possessed of the Atherton estates, went joyfully homeward.

Laughing at the manner in which John Gregory had been duped, and talking over plans for the future, they saw not a tall figure, draped from head to foot in a boat-cloak, coming towards them.

DUTCH PAUL, THE SMUGGLER.

The stranger paused when he beheld the vile pair, and, breaking through the hedge, concealed himself until they passed.

He watched them until they reached the hall—watched them with an evil glance in his sunken eyes, and a red spot upon his sallow cheeks—and when the door closed upon their forms the stranger drew his cloak closer round him, and strode slowly down the quiet, dusty road.

The Blue Lobster seemed to arrest his attention, and catching sight of Mrs. Magpie, who was standing at the door, with her arms a-kimbo, he turned suddenly towards the house of entertainment, and entered.

Mrs. Magpie gave him a searching glance as he entered the quiet little room behind the bar, then,

rubbing her forehead, she went in quest of her spouse.

Old Zachariah had changed but little since the night he aided our hero's escape from the officers.

His game eye was, if possible, "gamer" than ever, and his portly frame had lost none of its rotundity.

When Mrs. Magpie popped into the room, old Zach was quietly smoking his pipe, in company with a few of his select customers.

Men who would have passed for fishermen or smugglers, they had a smack of either following in their persons and appearances. Possibly, as old Zachariah was able to bring forth a glass of stronger and purer spirits than any landlord on that part of the coast, there may have been some truth in the report that he took more than an ordinary interest in the successful landing of a contraband cargo, and helping the smugglers to escape from the active revenue men.

When he saw the fiery face of his better half, he turned his eyes towards her, and, taking his pipe from his mouth, grunted out—

"Well, what do you want?"

She placed her finger on her lips, and with the other hand pointed towards the door inside of which the cloaked stranger was sitting.

Old Zachariah had on the previous evening assisted in the disembarkation of the freight from a suspicious-looking lugger, and, thinking that a revenue officer was in the small room, he arose, and, making a gesture to his companions, left the room.

Mother Magpie placed her hand upon old Zachariah's shoulders, and whispered—

"It's him!"

"Him!" repeated the landlord of the Blue Lobster. "Who the devil's him?"

"Hush!"

"Hush be blowed! What's the matter with the old fool?"

Mother Magpie looked much inclined to draw her nails down her better half's face.

"Old fool!" she repeated. "I certainly must have been a fool to have had anything to do with such an ugly, ill-shaped wretch as you are, considering the chances I had before having you for—"

"That's enough," growled old Zachariah; "I've heard that before. Now, who is it in there?"

She placed her mouth close to his ear, and whispered two words.

"The devil!" muttered Zachariah. "There will be some warm work soon."

"Serve 'em right," Mrs. Magpie said, "serve 'em right."

"You need not say it twice, old woman. Go to the bar—there's a customer waiting."

When the landlord of the Blue Lobster entered the small room the stranger looked up, and fixed his eyes upon old Zachariah's countenance.

"Bring me some brandy," he said, tersely, "and quickly."

"Yes, sir. Hot or cold?"

"Hot."

Old Zach vanished.

"He means mischief," he thought; "those eyes of his mean it, they do."

"Unrecognised," muttered the stranger; "this fellow, had he remembered me, would have shown it by his face. No, he thinks me dead." He laughed, it was not a pleasant laugh. "So be it, I shall come upon them like a phantom. This report of my death has no doubt reached him, and in the midst of his fancied security."

Old Zachariah returned with a steaming tumbler of the desired liquor, and placing it upon the table, said—

"Anything else, sir?"

"Nothing."

"Thank'ee, sir."

Before he reached the door, the stranger called him back.

"Stay," he said, "I want you."

Old Zachariah rolled his game eye upward, and turned towards his guest, saying—

"Yes, sir; at your service."

"I want," the stern stranger said, "to ask you a few questions."

"Any number you—"

An imperious wave of the hand stayed the landlord's garrulity. He was brought up, as he afterwards expressed it, with a "round turn" by the stranger's abrupt question

"Does John Sanderson still live at the hall?"

"Yes, sir."

"Any one else?"

"Mrs. Harpy."

The snake-like eyes glistened at the words.

"Mrs. Harpy," he repeated. "Both are well I presume?"

"Both well, sir—eh? Mrs.—I don't—"

"You don't understand me, eh?"

"Not exactly, sir."

"Are they in good health—happy, enjoying themselves, and that sort of thing?"

Old Zachariah scratched his head.

"I don't know much about 'em," he said, "but from what I hear, I don't think they are particularly happy, sir."

"Indeed! Pray what do you hear about them?"

"They do say, sir—"

"They. Who are they?"

"The people at the hall."

"The servants?"

"Yes."

"Well, let me hear what they say."

"They don't speak, sir—"

"Confound your 'theys'! Who the devil do you mean?—the people, or Sanderson and the woman?"

The landlord's game eye was cast towards the door.

His visitor looked so savagely at him that he fully expected to have the tumbler hurled at his head.

To prevent this, he blurted out—

"Squire Sanderson and Mrs. Harpy."

"Proceed."

"They do say, sir, that she leads a most awful life."

"Ha!"

The pale, sinister face flushed with joy.

"And," old Zachariah continued, "Mrs. Harpy used to tell the housekeeper that the squire beat her awful."

"Ah, indeed! Dear me, poor thing! Pray go on."

It struck the landlord of the Blue Lobster that his strange guest rather liked this intelligence than otherwise.

"But somehow," old Zachariah continued, "they have got mighty good friends lately."

The stranger looked evidently surprised, in spite of his great power of self-command.

"Good friends," he repeated, "and lately. Do not your gossips assign a motive for this?"

"They say all sorts of things, sir."

"Can you remember any of the many reasons they give for this sudden change?"

"That isn't all, sir."

"What do you mean?"

"Why, there is something else besides their being such friends."

"Indeed. What may that be?"

"They are going to be married."

"What?"

This ejaculation was accompanied by a sudden leap, which brought the stranger to his feet.

He seemed to remember that it would appear peculiar in the landlord's eyes, this display of astonishment, so, quietly reseating himself, he asked—

"When does this take place?"

"It ain't quite settled yet, sir."

"The day is not fixed. Ha! ha! I suppose the blushing bride has to prepare her *trousseau*."

Old Zachariah opened his eye (he had but one) at the last word.

"Perhaps she have," he said; then, mentally, "I wonder what he means by saying tross-hoo!"

I suppose it's a foreign word for something—the cake, perhaps."

The stranger sipped his now cold brandy and water as he pondered over the news.

"Marry her!" he repeated, mentally. "There must be a cause for this. What is it?"

Old Zachariah brought the truth of the affair at once to his mind by saying—

"Poor old Squire Gregory, sir. I don't think he will live much longer. He is very bad, sir—so bad that Mrs. Harpy has been twice to see him in three days."

The stranger knitted his brows and compressed his lips, as he muttered—

"The clue. I have no time to lose."

"It's my opinion," Zachariah went on, "that the poor old gentleman was not half so mad as they made out; leastways, the man who attends upon him in the madhouse says—"

The stranger gulped the remainder of the contents of his glass, and jumped to his feet.

"Here," he said, "this is in payment for your drink; keep the change."

He hurried past the astounded landlord, who stood gazing at a bright guinea in his open palm.

Zachariah soon recovered from his surprise, and pocketed the cause.

"I wouldn't," he thought, as he watched the stranger's tall form as he crossed the roadway, "be in either of their shoes. No, not for a cargo of these yellow-boys."

A loud summons from the tap-room caused Zachariah to leave the door and wait upon his customers.

He would have given much to have followed the late occupant of the small room—very much, could he have done so unseen.

* * * * *

When Sanderson and Mrs. Harpy reached the hall, the subtle villain lavished the tenderest caresses upon his companion.

"Commend me to a woman," he said, gleefully, "for invention; had it not been for you, my dear Jane, I should never have been in possession of this deed. It was a lucky thought, that dodge about the ink."

"I did my best," she answered. "The reward you held out would have tempted me to have done more had it been necessary."

"A reward you shall receive. First let us make the signature fast, then we will arrange about our nuptials. Where is the deed?"

She drew the paper from her breast, and placed it in his hands.

"You will not," she said, "play me false, John?"

"Play you false? What! and with such evidence of your usefulness as this in my possession? I must indeed have fallen low for you to have such a thought in your head."

"You have not fallen low," she said; "but I am almost bewildered by the prospect of such happiness. Oh, John! believe me, it was the hope of becoming your wife that made me so cruelly deceive the poor old man."

"A prospect," he said, "that will soon be realised. Hang it!" he added, "I have forgotten the bottle of fluid to finish this document; it is in my room. Will you fetch it for me?"

She went gladly upon the errand, and when her hand left the door-handle he went to one of the ornaments which stood over the fireplace, and took therefrom a small packet of powder.

Two decanters of wine stood upon the table.

Taking the stopper from one, he quickly dropped the white powder inside; then, giving the wine a shake to disseminate the powder, he sat in the same position as when she left.

He had only time to take up the deed; and, to all appearance, he was deeply engrossed with its contents, when she opened the door.

She placed a phial upon the table, then took a seat opposite.

"Before we begin," he said, "we will drink success to our nuptials. Here, Jane, hold your glass."

She held it towards him, and from the decanter he had poured the powder in he filled the wine-glass.

Pausing in the act of filling a second glass for himself, he said—

"This is port; I think I will have brandy. Push the bottle this way."

She did so, and, when both glasses were filled, he said, raising the one he had filled for himself—

"Success to our wedding! Drink with me, Jane."

She raised the glass, and it was within an inch of her lips.

Another moment, and she would have swallowed a deadly poison; but, in the act of drinking, the door opened suddenly, and the cloaked stranger entered the room.

Sanderson's glass fell from his fingers when he beheld the dreaded form, and a yell of more than mortal agony came from his lips, as he shrieked, in terrified accents—

"Captain Angel!"

CHAPTER LXXII.

SKOPEY'S TREACHERY.

THE five buccaneers turned and faced the Spaniards, as the latter, headed by the officer who had brought Minnie from the orange grove, rushed from the gate of Fort St. Joachim.

Iron Arm, who always seemed cooler when in the greatest peril, placed himself before his followers, saying—

"Madness! Back, Bob Hauler; and you, Jerry Mizzen, sheathe your cutlass. Do you think we can contend with the whole garrison?"

Our hero, who was supporting Minnie's trembling form, looked towards the gate of the Spanish fort and asked—

"What are we to do?"

"Swim," the giant said, coolly. "See, there is a broad river near! Quick! Plunge in—we shall escape the first volley!"

They saw the soldiers' weapons cocked, and, turning quickly, ran towards the river.

"Fear not, darling!" our hero said to the trembling girl; "it is better to be wet than shot down by these fellows."

She clung closer to him, and the next moment the waters closed over their heads.

Just in time was the leap taken.

The bullets cut the water some ten yards in advance of the spot beneath which they had disappeared.

When they rose to the surface the soldiers gave a yell, and again brought their muskets to their shoulders.

Iron Arm saw the act and cried out—

"Dive!"

Instantly the buccaneers disappeared, and, as before, the bullets flew harmlessly over them.

Until they reached a bend in the river, where a cluster of drooping plants hung some distance over the water, this system was kept up.

The buccaneers and the now senseless Minnie reappearing every time the soldiers' weapons were emptied, and diving when they were reloaded.

The trees grew thickly for upwards of a hundred yards from the bank.

Among these the fugitives took refuge, and to their joy they beheld the soldiers pause on the opposite bank, and after firing a harmless volley among the branches gathered around their officers and seemed to hold a council.

Bob Hauler danced the first part of a hornpipe with delight.

"Look at 'em !" he said, giving Jerry a drive in the ribs; "not one of the beggars can swim."

The drive in the ribs had deprived the illustrious Jerry of breath, therefore he was unable to make any reply for some time.

When he did, it was a striking reply for Bob.

Jerry picked up the limb of a tree, and, slinging it round his head, knocked his messmate clean off his feet.

Upon a smooth flower-clad bank Captain Tom laid his fair mistress, and bending over her with tender solicitude, he chafed her cold hands in the endeavour to restore her faculties, which the long struggle in the water had for the time subdued.

Iron Arm, with more than ordinary emotion depicted upon his handsome face, stood leaning upon his terrible weapon, watching our hero and the pale, beautiful, statuesque girl.

Once or twice his lips moved, as though he was about to give vent in words to the powerful emotion which struggled in his breast.

But ere he could utter a sound a nervous twitching contraction of the lips showed that he had obtained a mastery over the flood of unusual passion.

He turned away, a mighty sob of agony welling up from his surcharged heart, and a moisture about his dark eyes which looked strangely out of place in that stern, warlike man.

Our hero heard the evidence of Iron Arm's emotion, and, looking up for a moment from his efforts to restore Minnie, he asked—

"What is the matter ?"

"Nothing," was the stern, terse reply.

"You are strangely moved at nothing."

"A passing thought, that is all."

The young chief again resumed his task, and as he bent his head an exclamation of surprise came from his lips.

"This," he thought, "is more than a chance resemblance—yet is cannot be.   I will speak to him upon the subject, and by watching his face, perhaps, may detect a confirmation of my suspicions."

Iron Arm, when our hero first spoke, was standing with his face half turned, and as the boy looked from him to the beautiful girl he was startled by the close resemblance of their features.

Ever obeying the first impulse his mind suggested, the boy said—

"Look here, my friend."

Iron Arm turned and gazed at the girl's face.

"Can you," Tom continued, "account for the close resemblance in features and general expression of countenance between yourself and Minnie ?"

Iron Arm's fingers tightened their grasp upon his mace. and turning away to hide his working features he said, in a broken voice—

"Too well."

Captain Tom placed Minnie's head upon the ground, and sprang to his friend's side.

"My suspicions," he said, "are correct."

There was no answer.

"Speak," the impetuous boy said, "and relieve my mind of this terrible load."

"I dare not."

"Dare not !   These are strange words."

"Aye, boy : they are, perhaps, incomprehensible to you."

"They are, indeed."

Captain Tom drew his friend aside from the group, who were keenly watching the baffled soldiers, and beneath one of the spreading trees he wrung, bit by bit, word by word, the giant's secret from his hitherto closed lips.

"My breast alone," Iron Arm said, "has held this secret.   I need not tell you that it must not be known beyond ourselves."

"It shall not, until you bid me speak."

"That," his companion said, sadly, "will never be."

"A rash resolve."

"Possibly, but one that will be kept."

"There may," said Captain Tom, "be changes which we can neither prevent nor foresee in this life, changes that may cause you to resume your name, and again mix in that society which has lost an ornament, and the country a faithful servant, since you forswore wealth, rank, and honour to become a wanderer upon the ocean."

"Country !" Iron Arm said, bitterly.   "What affection can I have for the land that has been so ungrateful to one that has fought and bled for the honour of the old flag ?   Have they not disowned my very existence, published lying reports that I was taken prisoner by a fault of my own, and basely hinting at cowardice to injure my spotless frame, and damn my reputation ?"

"They were unjust."

"Unjust!   That is scarcely the word to use. Curse them! I say.   They have made me what I am, branded me as a traitor, and, by Heaven! they have felt the weight of my vengeance, and shall feel it more yet—aye, a thousandfold more !"

The young chief placed his hand upon the giant's shoulder.

"Forget the wrongs you have suffered," he said; "time will clear your name of the vile calumnies your foes have cast upon it."

Iron Arm ground his teeth savagely.

"Remember," the boy continued, "there is one that needs a—"

His speech was brought to an abrupt termination by Minnie suddenly opening her eyes, and exclaiming, in frightened accents—

"Save me, save me !"

Iron Arm would have sprung forward, but some spell seemed to root him to the ground.

Our hero passed him, and was soon beside the lovely girl.

"You are safe, Minnie," he said ; "safe, and with those who will protect you while life remains in their bodies."

She raised herself upon one arm, and as a pleasing smile played upon her lips, she murmured—

"It must have been a dream."

"A dream, darling ?"

"Yes ; I thought the rope had broken by which we descended from the fort, and that we were falling through the air.   Oh ! it was a most horrible sensation !"

"It must have been, darling.   Do you feel better now ?"

"Much better," she said ; "and safe, now that you are with me."

"There is another here, sweet one, that deserves your thanks."

He pointed to Iron Arm as he spoke, and the girl's eyes shone with joy.

"I should like to thank him," she said, "but he is so cold and reserved I fear to speak."

"You fear him, Minnie ?"

"No ; that is not the feeling exactly.   Will you be jealous if I tell you what I feel towards that strange, gloomy man ?"

A peculiar expression came upon Captain Tom's face at these words.

"Jealous!" he said. "No, Minnie; I wish you to like him."

"I do," she said, "although he has never spoken to me; but I have often caught his large eyes upon me. And, do you know, Tom—"

"What, darling?"

"That—that—I don't like to tell you."

"Do."

"You will not be angry?"

"No."

"Sure?"

"Quite sure."

"I will tell you, then. Often when I have seen him looking at me, I have felt a peculiar sensation creep over my frame."

"Can you describe the feeling?"

"No; but can try."

"Do, darling."

"Well, I have felt that I could have jumped from my seat and thrown my arms around his neck. You are not cross with me for telling you?'

"I am not; far from it, my dear girl. Had you done so, you would but have obeyed the—"

He paused abruptly.

Iron Arm's warning gesture stayed his words.

"What should I have obeyed, Tom?"

The young chief was rather staggered.

"Obeyed?" he said; "you would have obeyed—a—hang it!"—this mentally—"obeyed a passing whim, that is all."

"But that would have been very wrong, would it not, Tom?"

"Well, rather; yes, of course it would. Oh, most undoubtedly it—"

Much to his relief, Bob Hauler came running towards him, and when he came within speaking distance, Bob said, most joyfully—

"We have found a boat, sir."

"A boat, Bob?"

"Yes, sir; Jerry and I came across it while we were creeping among the long grass on the river's bank, a-lookin' arter the soldiers."

Iron Arm came forward at this juncture.

"A boat," he said; "it is large enough to hold us?"

"It's as large," Bob said, "as our jolly-boat, sir, and there is sail, oars, seats, and everything in it for use."

"This is fortunate. I had begun to despair of leaving the river. By the aid of this boat we shall be enabled to reach the ship without any trouble."

"Glad we found it," said Bob, "for it strikes me the soldiers are gone for a boat to cross over to us."

"We have no time to lose. Is the boat ready?"

"Quite, sir; I left Jerry stepping the mast."

Overjoyed at this fortunate discovery, the buccaneers were soon seated in the boat, and, the oars once more in their sinewy hands, it would have taken better oarsmen than any in the Spanish service to have overhauled them.

The distance, by pulling through the serpentine river, was more than double the distance by land.

But, under the circumstances, the fortunate possession of the boat would enable them to reach the ship without having to swim the river, or expose themselves to the muskets of the Spanish soldiery.

Jerry Mizzen and Bob Hauler were at the oars, Skopey in the bow with his musket cocked, ready to fire upon the first blue-coated soldier who presented himself upon the banks.

In the stern sat Minnie.

Iron Arm upon her right; our hero upon her left.

The soft, gliding motion of the boat, the regular dip of the oars, and the charming scenery through which they passed soon restored the young girl's spirits, and forgetful of the past danger, and her wet clothes, she clasped her hands and said, enthusiastically—

"What a lovely spot! How grand, how noble those old ruins appear amid the wild, luxuriant foliage of this beautiful place."

"Those ruins," said Iron Arm, "are the remains of one of the most beautiful cities in the world. In my younger days I remember being one of a boat's crew that routed a nest of pirates at this Iery river."

Our hero knew that his strange and mystic follower possessed a marvellous knowledge of most parts of the known world.

Oft had they paced the deck together, the giant speaking of strange climes and scenes in which he had mingled, bringing before our hero's mind places and circumstances, by his fanciful imagery and glowing words, with as much truthfulness as though a well-painted picture of the sights and scenes had been placed before him.

To beguile the time, and, if possible, efface all recollection from Minnie's mind of the dangers she had so providentially escaped, the boy said—

"From the fragments that remain, I should imagine the city had been a splendid place."

"It was," said Iron Arm. "There once stood the city of Baza, built and enriched by the Moors; taken and destroyed by the Spaniards."

"A brief and comprehensive history," said the young chief. "Could you not tell us more of the city whose remains fill the beholders with such rapture?"

Iron Arm closed his eyes — a habit with him when he wished to collect his thoughts—and after a moment's pause, he said—

'I remember sufficient of the first attempt which was made by the Spaniards to capture Baza. Shall I tell it?"

"Do," Minnie said. "I should much like to hear some legend connected with those grand solitary mementoes of bygone days."

Iron Arm bowed his stately head, and, without any prefacing, began—

"The Moorish city of Baza was situated in one of the most luxuriant and lovely of earthly valleys, about twenty-four miles long and nine miles wide. Two crystal streams, sparkling down from the mountains of Granada on the north, flowed through the valley, their waters in a thousand canals embroidering the whole surface.

"In the midst of this smooth and verdant plain there was spread out what was called the 'orchard' of Baza, embellished according to the highest teachings of landscape gardening then known.

"The 'orchard,' or garden, was three miles in length. It contained walks and drives in labyrinthine intricacy, mimic lakes, and dense groves, and many ornamented villas reared as pleasure haunts by the wealthy citizens.

"The menaces of war had converted the whole of this once smiling expanse, where young lovers had been wont to meet, and where all the voices of joy had been heard, into a series of gloomy fortresses frowning with the enginery of death. It was enclosed by a rampart of massive fortifications.

"The city was garrisoned by 20,000 Moorish troops, under the command of one of their most distinguished leaders. The town was provisioned for a fifteen months' siege, and the veterans were commanded to defend it to the last possible extremity.

"The first effort of the Spanish sovereigns was to get possession of the garden. Without this the city could not be perfectly invested. The broken surface of the ground, the intricate paths, the thorny hedgerows, the rivulets, the edifices of stone, and the dense groves rendered the place admirably adapted to the wild and desultory military tactics of the Moors.

"The splendid Spanish cavalry effected a passage into the garden, but here they were brought to a stand. Their horses could scarcely move a rod in line of battle.

"The cavaliers dismounted, and were led to the charge on foot; but the narrow, serpentine paths led in all directions. Obstructions headed them everywhere. The men were soon scattered far from their banners and their leaders.

"Ferdinand, who, from an elevated position, endeavoured to overlook the field, and to guide the currents of assault, soon became bewildered as he lost sight of his columns, as they straggled through the ravines, or were buried in the thick masses of foliage which everywhere intercepted his view.

"There was no possibility of a well-ordered battle, or of any tactical movements of the troops. It became simply a hand-to-hand fight, like the surging of infuriated mobs. For twelve long hours Spaniard and Moor thus desperately struggled; but Castilian discipline gradually gained the ascendency.

"The Moors were driven back over a small portion of the garden, and the Spaniards, constructing hurriedly a defence of palisades, established themselves on the field of battle. The ground won was, however, much too limited for a general encampment of the Spanish army. The small force Ferdinand could maintain there would be exposed to destruction.

"Retreat became necessary. Skilfully, Ferdinand withdrew his victorious division away from the garden to the open plain. The Spanish troops could not bear reverses. This repulse disheartened them. Rumours came that a strong Moorish army was at Guadix, but twenty miles distant, prepared to march for the relief of Baza.

"It became manifest that the siege must be long and severe. Frightful stories were told of the winter rains descending from the mountains in foaming torrents, and inundating the whole plain of their encampment.

"A council of war was held. Many of the boldest cavaliers urged that it was not prudent to continue the siege until some of the neighbouring formidable fortresses were reduced.

"Ferdinand, in all cases of great perplexity, always took counsel of the Queen. He at once applied to her for counsel. A packet of despatches was transmitted to her at her station at Jaen by a fleet courier. She read them with chagrin, alarmed lest all the vast preparations she had made should result in nothing.

"Very sagaciously, without assuming to condemn the manifest judgment of the King and his generals, she besought them not to distrust God, who had so often given them the victory.

"She reminded them that the Moors were never before so weak and despondent as now; and she urged that they probably could not again raise an army so large, so well equipped, and so inspired with hope.

"In conclusion, she urged that, should they judge it best to continue the siege, they might rely upon her for all the requisite supplies.

"This letter of the heroic Queen produced an instantaneous effect in silencing the murmurs of the timid, and in inspiring the bold with new confidence.

"Its contents became known to the army, and the heart of every soldier throbbed with new enthusiasm. Seldom has there been witnessed such an example of the power of a single heroic mind to sway the will of a vast multitude.

"The army was immediately divided into two encampments, one on each side of the garden. All the energies of the army were devoted to get possession of this contested ground, to clear it of its timber, and of all its other obstructions.

"Seven thousand picked troops were stationed to guard the pioneers against the sallies of the Moors. Four thousand pioneers, with axes, bars, and spades, were employed in the work of devastation.

"Still, the Moors made such desperate opposition, that with all their efforts they could not advance more than seven paces a day. But in seven weeks, even at that slow rate, much ground may be passed over.

"By the close of that time the ancient groves, which had for so long been the pride of the city, had disappeared.

"A widend deep trench, through which a mountain stream was caused to flow, connected the two Spanish camps. Strong towers rose at regular intervals, connected by palisades and earthworks; the garden was won.

"At another point where the line of communication was open, two stone walls were constructed, with a deep trench between, and thus Baza became thoroughly invested.

"In constructing these lines of circumvallation, ten thousand men were incessantly occupied for two months.

"The Moors were now almost in despair. Their little kingdom was divided by hostile claimants for the Throne.

"Abdallah had ignobly become the feudal servant of Ferdinand and Isabella. He held the city of Granada and several other important fortresses, thus palsying the energies of Moorish defence.

"El Zagel, in his extremity, sent to the Sultan of Egypt for help. The Sultan sent despatches by an embassy of two Franciscan friars, from his dominions.

"In these despatches the Sultan very temperately, but with great dignity and earnestness, remonstrated against the persecution of the Moors by the Spanish sovereigns. He contrasted their illiberal spirit with the protection the Sultan had ever extended to all the Christians within his dominions.

"The communication concluded with the following menace:—

"'If your Majesties persist in your hostile action towards the Moors of Granada, I will retaliate, by visiting similar severities upon all the Christians within my realms.'

"Ferdinand, upon receiving these despatches, immediately forwarded them, by the two ambassaders, to Jaen.

"But the menace did not shake the purpose of the King and Isabella. They returned the answer 'that all loyal subjects, whether Christian or Mahommedan, were treated alike; but they could not submit to see their ancient inheritance in the hands of strangers; that if the Moors of Spain would live under their rule as faithful subjects, they should enjoy every indulgence conferred upon the Christians.'

"With this answer, and loaded with presents, the ambassadors returned to the Holy Land.

"And Ferdinand of Spain continued the siege until the Spanish banner waved over the town of Baza, and the Moors, defeated, but not subdued, retired to the hills to carry on a harrassing warfare against their conquerors."

He ceased, and his listeners, looking back at the fallen monuments of Moorish grandeur, pictured the fair city as she stood when her dark-skinned children so manfully held the splendid army Ferdinand and Isabella so long at bay.

They saw their infantry retreat step by step before the old chivalry of Spain—the cresent humbled, and the cross waving triumphantly from battlement and tower.

From these fancies they were recalled to their position by a shout of joy from Bob Hauler.

There was not much poetry in this rough seaman's nature; he cared not for fallen splendour, neither did he love to dwell upon the past.

He had been silent during the time Iron Arm was speaking.

But the silence was kept from a feeling of respect to his officer, not from any wish to listen to what he termed a long-shore yarn.

He was glad when it was over; more so, when the boat, suddenly gliding round a bend in the river, showed the tapering masts of the "Will-o'-the-Wisp" above the tree-tops.

"There she is!" he shouted; "the little beauty!"

Ten minutes brought them within view of the vessel, but though her masts had been so plainly visible, they found that a narrow strip of land had to be crossed before they could reach the arm of the sea wherein this gallant ship lay.

The order had passed the young chief's lips for the rowers to pull for the shore, when they were startled by the whizzing of a dozen bullets above their heads.

White puffs of smoke curling upwards from the trees showed where the assailants were posted, and a loud word of command given in their native tongue caused their hearts to leap.

Admiral Tom drew a pistol from his belt, and would have fired, had not Iron Arm spoken.

"It is a party of marines from the man-of-war of which Dutch Paul spoke," he said; "see you not their red coats among the foliage?"

"Poor Minnie!" our hero said, "a chance bullet may slay her."

"Stern all!" said the giant, "steady, now pull for those drooping trees."

The men obeyed, and when the boat came in contact with the soft bank, the giant said—

"There is but one chance for us to escape those fellows."

"That?" our hero asked.

"We must send Minnie across this neck of land, the trees will hide her form, and throw them off the scent; we must back out, and pull for the middle of the stream."

Our hero knew that, in point of cunning warfare, no red-skin could compete with his gigantic follower, so bidding Bob Hauler and Jerry Mizzen escort his bride to the ship, he took the bow-oar when the trio had landed.

"One moment," Iron Arm said; "while those fellows are dodging us up the creek, I think the best plan will be for the ship to slip her cable, and when the darkness comes on we can cross to the inlet, and drag the boat with us, then join her outside."

"A good plan," our hero said, "and the only one."

He took an ivory tablet from his pocket, and wrote—

"Take the vessel out from the rocky pass, and get into deep water. We will join you at nightfall. Meanwhile, act as circumstances may transpire."

"Give this," he said, handing the tablet to Bob, "to Ben Barnacle, and tell him to join Dutch Paul, if possible; also tell him not to engage the man-of-war, if it can be avoided. Should he be compelled to make sail, he is not to wait for us; we will join him hereafter."

Bob touched his cap, took the tablet, and then, drawing back the hammer of his piece, took his place beside Minnie, proud and elated at the honour of being her guide and defender.

When the boat emerged from the concealment of the drooping branches, our hero and Skopey pulled for the middle of the river.

A point they reached without hearing the unpleasant ping of a rifle bullet.

Iron Arm laughed grimly at the success of this plan, and said—

"They are baffled by our sudden disappearance and evidently think we have made off on the opposite bank."

"But Minnie? How—"

"She will be safe; they have gone to the point to intercept us."

Admiral Tom looked up in astonishment, as he repeated—

"Gone to the point to intercept? She will fall into their power."

"If we allow them to remain there."

"How is it to be prevented?"

"This way."

He fired a pistol in the air, and soon after the shouts of the marines came upon their ears.

The ruse was successful.

The marines had, as the giant surmised, gone to the point between the drooping tree and the ship, and had another two minutes passed, Minnie would have been in their hands.

The report of Iron Arm's pistol brought them to the bank, when to their chagrin they beheld the boat far up the river out of musket-shot, and leisurely gliding through the water.

The distance was too far for them to distinguish the occupants of the light craft, and much to our hero's joy they began to run towards the bend of the river, round which the boat was now passing.

A few smart strokes kept the boat far ahead, and the sea soldiers, finding that pursuit was useless, fired a couple of shots, then retired to the clump of trees which had sheltered them from our hero, before he landed Minnie and her two rough but staunch guardians.

Waiting with impatience for night to throw her dark and welcome veil over the earth, the adventurers kept rowing to and fro.

About an hour before sundown they were suddenly alarmed by the sound of a distant heavy cannonade.

The young chief bit his lips and muttered, angrily—

"Confound him; he has engaged the man-of-war."

"I fear so," Iron Arm said; "unless it is Dutch Paul's guns."

"I trust it may be. To be stuck here like a hunted water-rat while the ship is in action would drive me mad."

"It is not pleasant, I must confess, but under the circumstances we can do nothing."

"True. But do you not think we may now venture ashore?"

"Judge for yourself."

Iron Arm pointed to the trees which lined the bank, and our hero beheld the sun's rays gleaming upon the tops of the marines' bayonets.

"Come, then," he said, firmly, "we shall be compelled to stay here until the night sets in."

"I never expected anything else."

"Is there no means of landing without drawing their fire upon us?"

"None."

Our hero's eyes blazed with anger, and, throwing himself back in the boat, he crossed his arms, and strove to keep down the fiery impatience which raged in his breast.

The cannonade still continued, and, as the night began to fall, the reports were heavier, as though the ships had come broadside to broadside.

Our hero was almost mad with excitement, when Iron Arm said—

"I think it is now dark enough to venture. Pull to the same place, Skopey, that was before touched at."

The half-caste obeyed.

When they reached the deep shadow of the drooping tree, Iron Arm placed his fingers upon his lips, to imply silence.

All would have been well had the impetuous buccaneer chief been guided by his friend.

Unfortunately, he disregarded the silent warning, and sprang hastily ashore.

"You are running into danger," whispered the giant, as he followed his chief. "Those fellows are in the bend yet, depend upon it."

"I care not. Better face their levelled bayonets than remain here."

"A matter of taste," said Iron Arm. "Lend me a hand, captain, to bring the boat to land."

They drew the boat upon the bank, and Iron Arm and Skopey were about to hoist it upon their shoulders.

Before they could do so they were startled by the hurried tramp of feet, and turning in the direction of the sound, they beheld a dozen of the frigate's marines, headed by a young midshipman, coming towards them.

"Here is the pirate," shouted the middy; "take him alive, boys!"

Captain Tom's sabre flew from the scabbard, and with an angry cry he turned and met the gallant little middy.

The youngster, true to his colours, and scanning the pirate leader as one to be despised, not feared, drew his dirk, and came boldly forward to the attack.

One swift pass of our hero's weapon knocked the dirk from the boy's fingers.

Another moment, and he would have been cut down, had not Iron Arm caught the young chief's descending blade upon his mace.

"Find a foe more worthy of your steel."

He said these words somewhat sternly, and there was an angry expression upon his face as he turned towards our hero.

Somewhat abashed at the rebuke, Captain Tom lowered the point of his weapon.

The middy, quick as thought, picked up his dirk, and made a clever cut at the buccaneer chief.

Iron Arm caught the boy by the collar and swung him round.

Releasing his grip, the middy spun like a top for several yards, then came in contact with the trunk of a tree.

The blow caused him to recoil stunned, and he fell face downwards upon the green sward.

The marines had by this time come upon the scene, and believing the boy had been killed by the buccaneers, they hurriedly raised their muskets and fired.

The haste they used spoilt their aim, and by the time they had reloaded the buccaneers had disappeared.

Iron Arm had seized the boat as though it were a single plank, and, throwing it across his shoulder, he called upon his companions, and fled from the spot.

They followed.

To have stayed would have been madness, for the men, rendered furious by the supposed fall of the young midshipman, would have shot them down like dogs.

To cross the narrow neck of land was but a few minutes' work.

And while the pursuers were hunting about among the bushes the boat was quietly launched.

Iron Arm's silken sash was used to muffle the oars, and like a shadow the light craft glided from the shore.

Pulling swiftly but noiselessly, they reached the rocky inlet where the "Will-o'-the-Wisp" had been moored.

They passed the orange groves, and the sweet perfume came upon the zephyr breezes, bringing with it, to our hero's mind, fond yet anxious thoughts of the beautiful bride he so fondly loved.

It was a long pull to reach the mouth of that inlet. There was danger on every side.

The darkness hid the points of the reefs from their eyes, and every movement they knew might cause the frail craft to be shattered like a fragile vessel of glass.

Everything had been quiet for some time, the firing had lulled until only a single gun came from either the victors' or the vanquished ship.

When this ceased the fugitives bent every nerve to listen for the faintest sound.

While every head was turned towards the sea, the boat struck upon the point of a dangerous reef.

There was a crash, a cry of fear from Skopey, then all became chaos.

The boat was riven in twain, and her crew were struggling for life in the inky waters.

CHAPTER LXXIII.
A TERRIBLE ADVENTURE.

THE struggle that followed the immersion of the gallant chief and his followers was brief but desperate. A strong swell was rising, and as they tried to strike out for the land, their flesh was brought in violent contact with the sharp jagged rocks.

Their clothes were rent and tattered, and their bodies were torn and sadly bruised. Skopey, who was a good swimmer, was not long in gaining the shore; but Iron Arm and the gallant captain were not so fortunate.

Captain Tom, owing to his heavy boots, and the weight of his weapons, had gone down and got entangled with the fragments of the shattered boat.

Iron Arm felt his heart sink within him as he vainly sought for the reappearance of his young chieftain through the deepening gloom.

Once or twice he pronounced his name, but received no answer.

He could make out the form of Skopey as he stood on a projecting point of rock, and muttered a bitter curse at the black's cowardly action of seeking his own safety before that of the daring boy.

As he supported himself on the blade of a broken oar, his hand wandered instinctively to his belt.

Had his powder not have been wet there was every probability of his trying a shot at Skopey, and punishing him for his ungenerous conduct.

It was fortunate for them all it was so.

The report of a pistol would have brought their pursuers upon them, and in their present unfortunate position they would doubtless have been made captives.

But Iron Arm in that moment of unutterable anguish and suspense did not think of this.

His breast was torn with the conflicting emotions of sorrow and revenge.

Every black rugged projection of the sunken reef, as it was laid bare by a receding wave, and showed its head above the snowy foam, he took for the head of his beloved chief.

Then, as it disappeared, the cry of joy that was about to escape his lips was replaced by one of bitter disappointment. Suddenly his eye rested on a portion of the wrecked boat that had floated unobserved towards him.

Grasping it in his sinewy hand with the intention of converting it into a float, for he was firmly resolved not to leave the spot until all hopes of recovering either the gallant boy or his lifeless body were passed, he was startled by a cold, clammy substance coming in contact with his flesh.

A cold shudder went through his frame.

His blood seemed suddenly frozen in his veins.

A sickening sensation seized upon him, and caused him almost to faint.

The cold substance, he was sure, felt not unlike a dead body, and he doubted not that it was the lifeless form of the gallant boy.

The daring captain, after braving the wrath of both storm and man, had fallen a victim to the treacherous wave.

As this conviction flashed to his mind it drove him almost to madness.

The sudden qualm then passed away, and on opening his eyes, which had been involuntarily closed, his gaze rested on the pale, wan face of the youthful captain.

To clear his neckerchief of the splintered keel that had thus held him prisoner was but the work of a moment, and then the devoted fellow put out his giant strength and made for the shore.

To gain it was a task of both difficulty and danger.

With perseverance, however, this was overcome, and Iron Arm once more got foothold on terra firma.

Carrying the unconscious boy in his stalwart arms with as much ease and no less care than if he were a babe, the giant bore him towards a cluster of bushes, and laid him on the grass beneath them.

The night air was now blowing raw and chill, and the first sign of life he discovered in the half-drowned boy was a slightly preceptible shiver.

Iron Arm well knew that one of the most requisite things wanted now was a fire.

There was plenty of wood at hand, but, owing to his pistols being wet, he had no means of procuring a light.

Even if he had, it would have been dangerous.

The fire would point out their position to the marines, who, he felt certain, were not far away.

By this time he was joined by Skopey.

After reprimanding him severely for his selfish behaviour, he set him to work in rubbing the limbs of the inanimate boy, whilst he went in search of some fitting place to suit their purpose and the means of procuring a light.

It was some time before he found either.

When he did so he was well rewarded for his pains.

A cave sheltered from seaward by a wall of rock, and evidently not long deserted by its late occupants, he by accident discovered, and in groping about he found that it was by no means destitute of the requisites needed by them.

A small piece of dry rag was the first treasure he took possession of, and by means of a stone and his sword-blade he soon ignited it, and then made a fire with some dry wood.

This accomplished, he conveyed the captain to their new abode, and by means of a little brandy, a small keg of which they found concealed in one corner, our hero was soon sufficiently recovered to speak.

The sound of the captain's voice afforded Iron Arm no little relief.

He first despatched Skopey in search of some dry leaves to make a bed, and then commenced a stricter examination of their new and, under present circumstances, gorgeous abode.

The first impression from what he saw was that the cave had been occupied by some shipwrecked mariner.

In a rudely-constructed box he found a saw, a hammer, and several wooden pegs.

Some pieces of old sails, too, he found, a coil of rope, a bag of biscuit, and several casks.

One of the casks contained a small quantity of beef in pickle, and the others had evidently been used for water.

In a niche which had been used as a cupboard he found a wooden pipe and tobacco, and several little articles, such as sail-needles, a tinder-box, a ship's hour-glass, and a small boat compass tied up in a bundle.

The giant's heart leapt with joy on making this discovery, but his brow became clouded on pursuing his search further.

The cause of this was the discovery of a chain with a large ring attached, on which was branded, in Spanish—Madonna, J. G., No. 20.

This, Iron Arm well knew, had once graced the ankle or wrist of a galley slave, and he shuddered.

Had some poor wretch escaped from his terrible exile and made his way to some more Christian land, or had he been pursued and re-taken when preparing for his voyage?

These thoughts haunted Iron Arm all that night.

In the morning he was astir long before the others awoke.

Climbing to the highest point, he scanned the horizon, but could see nothing in the form of a ship.

The ocean was as smooth as glass.

The very air seemed hushed into stillness.

Save the splash of a porpoise, as it rose and disappeared, not a sound could be heard.

Iron Arm sat down and viewed the charming scenery, and after a while retraced his way to the cave.

On his return, Iron Arm took a different route, a path that led him to the back of the cave.

Here he met with an adventure of which he little dreamed.

The path was narrow and rugged, and on either side a wall of rocks reared its head to a considerable height.

To turn to right or left was impossible.

Forward, forward, was the word, but this also was an impossibility, for a quantity of heavy boulders had been rolled from the giddy height, and completely barred the way.

Annoyed at this, Iron Arm stood for a moment eyeing the barrier in silence.

To turn and walk calmly back was contrary to the giant's nature.

Go forward he could not.

He felt half inclined to climb the rugged sides of the rock.

Gradually the desire increased, for it occurred to him that the stones could not have fallen there of themselves, and he felt certain no one would have taken the pains to place them there without sufficient cause.

Having come to this conclusion, he commenced the difficult ascent.

Arrived at the top, he paused, only sufficient to recover his breath, and then crawled along the narrow ridge.

On the opposite side of the stones the path still continued, and Iron Arm passed along the ridge far as he considered it safe, and then descended.

This he did at the risk of breaking his neck.

Wrapped in silent meditation, and wonder within himself how his adventure would end, walked on until he reached a small open space.

Here he paused awhile to look around.

The sight he saw astonished him.

Lying on rollers on the ground were several large bulks of timber, and so placed as to leave no doubt that they had been intended to form a raft.

Pieces of old rope, and a broken mast, together with several other useful and necessary appendages.

On seeing these, Iron Arm naturally surmised that there was some other way of communication, with the outer world besides that by which he had come, and he set about at once to find it.

At this spot all traces of the passage disappeared, but on closely examining the further wall, he found that an artfully-contrived door of wood had led him to believe it was solid stone.

This he was not long in opening.

A few strides brought him on the beach, and when he entered the cave he found Captain Tom and the black in the same positions he had left them; at least, he could see no difference, but on stooping down he could see that the brave boy's cheek had grown paler, and then—oh, horror!—he found himself kneeling in a pool of blood.

To account for this he knew not how, until, raising the gallant captain in his brawny arms, and rousing the black with a smart application of his boot, he found the blood was flowing from a wound in the captain's arm.

A wound so small as to leave an idea that a needle had been pierced deeply into the flesh.

Such really was the case.

Skopey, the treacherous black, on finding that his endeavours to betray, and also his ruse of swamping the boat and drowning the captain, had not succeeded, determined to watch the first opportunity of putting his villainous project into execution.

The sharp words that Iron Arm had reproved him with were not forgotten, and he lay all night brooding over his supposed wrongs.

The fear in which Iron Arm held him would not permit him, either by sign or gesture, to betray himself in his presence, but as soon as he rose and departed, the subtle wretch crept from the dark corner in which he had lain, and approached the sleeping captain.

Stooping down, he listened to his breathing to make sure that he slept.

Having satisfied himself that he would require something more than ordinary to awaken him, he drew a small case from his breast, and took from it a small steel instrument.

A dark, malicious gleam shot from his eye as he examined its point and rubbed upon it the juice of a certain leaf.

This enabled him to plunge it into his victim's flesh without producing much pain.

This done, he stooped down and selected a spot where, he supposed, one of the principal veins ran, and plunged the sharp, deadly instrument into the unconscious boy's flesh.

A convulsive shudder passed through the frame of Captain Tom as the deadly wound was inflicted, but, with the exception of this, he never stirred.

A gleam of satisfaction and malicious cunning stole over the black's face as he completed his deadly work, and then, noiseless as a cat, he stole back to his bed.

There he lay counting each moment of Iron Arm's absence, and caculating in his mind how long his victim would be ere he breathed his last.

He had intended to bleed him to death, and with this humane intention he laid down and shammed sleep until Iron Arm disturbed him.

Never for a moment did Iron Arm, though the wound of itself was certainly sufficient to warrant his doing so, suspect the treacherous black of foul play.

He had saved the captain's life once, and he little deemed he would meditate mischief towards him. To stop the life-stream that was ebbing with slow but certain effect was his first act, and then, raising the captain on his arm, he revived him with a little spirits.

Skopey chafed inwardly at being thus foiled in his fiendish purpose, but he secretly vowed not to let the next opportunity slip.

As yet he was ignorant of the discovery Iron Arm had made.

He was somewhat surprised when he heard the giant inform Captain Tom and propose leaving the place.

The youthful captain, weak as he was, could not help smiling, and he readily assented to Iron Arm's proposal.

The mind of the young chief was far from easy concerning the safety of his crew. The cannonading on the previous evening had filled him with a presentiment that all was not right.

Having breakfasted, and the captain feeling stronger, Iron Arm led him to the little dock-yard —for such it was to them—and the giant, aided by Skopey, set to work at once preparing for their voyage. The massive timbers were dragged down to the beach and firmly lashed together. A mast was stepped, and a sail constructed of the old pieces of canvas.

Whilst Captain Tom and his faithful companion were busied in this, Skopey prepared them another meal. After partaking of which, they collected all their provisions and launched the raft.

The day had far advanced by the time their little ark was afloat, and the captain, worn out with fatigue and loss of blood, gladly sought the rude bed Iron Arm had made for him.

Even the lion strength of the giant had been over-taxed, but the faithful fellow would not give way to it, though Captain Tom tried to persuade him to seek a little repose and leave Skopey to look after the raft.

Of the three, Skopey was the most wakeful and attentive.

Not but what he had worked hard; but the sullen and silent manner in which he preformed his task told that something more than duty to his chief had strengthened his powers of endurance.

The demon of revenge was working in his breast.

He saw a chance now of accomplishing his devilish design.

Anxiously he watched his sleepy companions, and longed for the time when languor should overpower them.

Iron Arm had made a kind of rudder out of a piece of wood, so that they might guide the raft, and, aided by the compass, they had little to fear, unless a storm should suddenly rise, or a man-of-war run down upon them.

Captain Tom raised himself on his elbow and scanned the distant horizon in the hope of seeing a sail.

"Where can they be?" he ejaculated, mentally.

Then turning to Iron Arm, he added—

"I hope nothing wrong has befallen them; if they have fallen into the clutches of—"

"No fear of that," Iron Arm replied. "Dutch Paul is too cunning to be trapped."

"But the man-of-war might have sighted them as they left the rocky pass."

"And if so," said Iron Arm, with a meaning smile, "she has felt them too."

Captain Tom felt the truth of this remark, and it increased his uneasiness.

He did not like his ship being engaged during his absence.

"Curse the fate that has placed us here like a pair of caged eagles!" he burst out. "I shall not feel comfortable till we get on board again."

"I hope that will not be long first," said Iron Arm. "If this wind favours us a few hours more, and our timbers hold together, we shall soon round the point."

A long point of land could be dimly seen stretching out before them, and towards this Skopey was steering the raft.

It made but slow progress through the water,

owing to its rude construction; but as darkness set in the wind increased.

"Think you we shall meet them there?" asked Iron Arm.

"I do."

"I hope you will not be disappointed."

"How so?"

"Simply because I think they are hunting about for us. You promised to join them last night."

"I did, and they will certainly feel anxious for our safety, they doubtless think we are captured, and poor Minnie, what an agony of suspense she will endure."

The giant gave a convulsive start; the mention of Minnie's name seemed to bring to his mind some bitter memories.

Whilst the foregoing conversation was going on, Skopey continued eyeing the speakers with tiger-like ferocity.

A faint smile beamed on his dusky features, a kind of demoniac grin, when he saw Captain Tom stretch himself upon the bed of canvas, and Iron Arm take up his position to watch.

The exhausted faculties of the youthful leader soon gave way.

His eyes closed, and he fell into a deep slumber.

Iron Arm soon followed his example.

He strove hard to bear against it, but could not.

No sooner were they asleep than Skopey stole from his post, and glancing cautiously round, drew his huge knife.

His first act was to sever the rope that held the raft together.

Two of the timbers he separated from the rest, and then lashed them firmly together.

These he intended for his own use.

His next object was to transfer the provisions from the main raft to his own.

To do this, he must disturb the captain or Iron Arm, so he contented himself with cutting away the sail and loosening the mast.

Having possessed himself of all he could, he cut the remainder of the ropes, then leapt on board his own raft and pushed off.

Scarcely had he done so, when the unsuspecting sleepers were aroused by the timbers separating and the mast coming down by the run.

It fell in the direction of the captain's head, and would have crushed it had not a cask miraculously intervened.

At the first crash, Iron Arm sprang to his feet, but the timbers opened, and he was suddenly immersed.

Captain Tom, more fortunate, happened to be lying crossways, and so he had several to support him, and, drawing them together with his feet and hands, kept the raft from separating altogether.

Iron Arm, on rising, found himself beneath the logs, and he was compelled to dive again to get clear of them.

Captain Tom, on missing Iron Arm and Skopey so suddenly, and under such strange circumstances, was at a loss to account for the cause of the calamity.

A half-stifled cry from Iron Arm caused him to turn his head, and, to his surprise, he beheld the giant clutching at one of the logs, which necessarily rolled over and over at each attempt of his to grasp it.

At any other time it would have brought a smile to the captain's lips.

As it was, he felt vexed, for Iron Arm could not save him, even if he were drowning

The gallant captain was for once beaten; he could devise no means of succouring his friend.

Suddenly his eye rested on a dark object to lee— and it was some time before he could make

He did so eventually, and an exclamation of surprise escaped him as the thought occurred to him that Skopey had proved treacherous.

CHAPTER LXXIV.
THE STRANGE SAIL.

IT was night, dark and gloomy, when a vessel crept out of one of the narrow inlets, and stood out to seaward.

Grouped upon her deck were many officers and men, who, as soon as the sails were spread and the ropes coiled down, seated themselves upon the guns to enjoy the evening breeze.

"A yarn! a yarn!" clamoured a noisy personage in one of the groups.

"Aye, aye, my hearty!" was the cheerful response of a bluff old salt; "and a tough 'un you shall have, too."

He thrust a huge plug of tobacco in his cheek, gave his pants a South-Sea hitch, and then began—

"Well, mates, it's no use spinning the old yarns over again, so I've stowed them down in the orlop-deck, and now I'll begin a fresh one.

"It's some time since I heard my brother spin the yarn, but I think I can remember it, so here goes.

"Our regiment was laying in the West Indies, and deuced hot it was (I mean the weather), I can assure you.

"So hot, indeed, that, what with it and the mosquitoes, we could get but little, if any, sleep.

"There was a light air stirring, and leaving the window open, I resumed my place in the hammock, and, while viewing the prospect before me, and inhaling the fragrance of my cigar, sweet and pleasing ideas of country and of home rose gradually within my mind.

"The landscape slowly faded from my view; the thoughts of kindred, of friends, and of the green banks of the Shannon, continued to mingle undefinedly with lofty palm trees, smoking mountains, cigars, swizzle, sentries, grand rounds, rum, and prisoners of war; in a word, I was fast asleep, and so might have continued till morning, had I not been awakened by an unusual commotion in the men's guard-room, separated from mine by a thin wooden partition only.

"The confusion of tongues at Babel was order and regularity compared with the uproar I now heard; but at intervals I thought I could distinguish the low moanings of one in pain.

"To snatch my sabre from the table and run into the adjoining room was the thought and work but of a minute; and if the confusion of noises only was astounding, the scene that met my eyes, on crossing the threshold, was perfectly alarming.

"A huge wood fire, that incongruous but invariable appurtenance of a West-Indian guard-room, threw its fitful beams on the rough and marked features of the whole assembled guard, who were congregated round a black soldier of my regiment, nay, of my own company, who lay on the hearth, agitated almost convulsively.

"His face, as the fire-light gleamed on it, was deadly pale. Yes, my friend, a black man can look pale; and nothing can be more horrible than the colour which at such a time the negro assumes. The blood forsakes the countenance; the lips become a dull, yellow white; a circle of bluish tinge surrounds the eyes, the red veins in which, being swollen and filled with blood, seem of the hue of fire; while the ivory whiteness of the teeth imparts to the whole face a character almost demoniacal.

"I elbowed my way with difficulty through the circle, for authority seemed lost; I shouted, stamped, swore, and at last was heard.

"'That black spalpeen has run away from his post, and never stopped to look behind him,' says the sergeant.

"'Where was he stationed?'

"'In the archway by the prisoners' quarters.'

"'Turn out the relief, then, and post another sentinel.'

"I, at length, by dint of shaking, kicking, roaring, and thumping drew an answer from Blackie himself, who gasped out, as his mouth opened and shut like a dying dog-fish—

"'Oh, Massa Coptin! Oh, Massa Coptin! me savee—sartin me safe—sure me go da *kicke raboo*—me die—me go da Guinea—me see da Jumbee!"

"I was but a new-comer in the colonies, and did not understand him. I demanded an explanation from the sergeant.

"'Sure, and plase your honour, he says he saw the "*White Gentleman*," that is the devil, yer honour.'

"'The superstitious scoundrel! the prisoners have been endeavouring to terrify him,' exclaimed I; 'turn out the relief this instant; take off his accoutrements; make a prisoner of him, and follow me to his post.'

"This was soon arranged. The sergeant and three men were selected; the word was given—'With ball-cartridge prime and load!' and off we went towards the massive archway dividing the lower from the upper compartment of the fortress, where the sentry had been posted, and where the French prisoners were locked up during the night-time.

"We reached the spot. I advanced alone under the archway, but saw nothing; and at last slowly and pensively returned to the soldiers I had left beyond the arch. All there continued still, and remained so for upwards of half an hour; at the end of which time, weary of inactivity, I placed one of the men on the duty which his fellow had abandoned, and proposed returning to the guard-house with the others.

"Scarcely had I turned my back for this purpose, when shrieks of terror burst from the newly-placed sentinel, who, after about a second, presenting his musket down the archway, flung it violently from him, and fled precipitately, as also did the sergeant and his comrades.

"My eyes followed the direction of the levelled musket, and I do not fear being accused of cowardice when I say I followed the example set me, and also ran away, for never did a more fear-inspiring object meet the human vision than that on which my terror-stricken gaze was now riveted.

"The moon, as it shone brightly into the avenue, showed me, near to the summit of the arch, and almost on a level with my head, floating towards me, a human form self-sustained in air, the arms of which were stretched out, as if to enfold me within their grasp.

"It was clad in a short tunic, of transparent white, which showed more pure in contrast with the pitchy darkness behind it; the head was not quite severed from the body, but hung upon the breast, attached to the breast by a slight portion of the skin on one side.

"The legs were tossed to and fro in such a manner as clearly showed that the bones had been broken in many places, and from the severed neck a stream of crimson blood gushed over the white raiment even to its feet.

"Covering my eyes with my hand, I fled towards the guard-room, and had nearly reached it, when the sound of distant laughter from the vessels moored below the fort struck on my ear, as if a ray of sun-light had pierced through the thickest darkness.

"The consequences of my conduct flashed at once upon my mind. I halted—my breast heaved—my knees trembled—and a profuse perspiration rushed from every pore.

"Mustering every energy that fear had left me, I slowly retraced my steps. The feelings of the condemned criminal, as he paces between his cell and the fatal gibbet, would be a state of bliss compared with what I suffered, as I endeavoured to muster in my mind every motive that could stimulate me to exertion.

"At last I stood, trembling and breathless, on the spot I had quitted. Slowly I raised my eyes, and shuddering, closed them in terror, though nothing met my view within the dreary void before me.

"The heavy-toned bell of the fort tolled the hour of one. Reassured, I gazed more earnestly towards the summit of the arch, and beheld, while the deep note of the bell yet sounded in my ear, the same frightful object emerging, as it were, from the solid masonry of the roof.

"It now hovered over my head in a horizontal position, which, as it floated nearer and lower, was changed for an upright one; the breast dilated and swelled, as when one draws a heavy suspiration; no sound accompanied the motion.

"Despair gave me courage. At my feet lay the loaded musket of the sentinel; I seized and cocked it, viewing the object of my dread more earnestly. The suspirations were continued, and I now saw that the head was but one unshapen, battered mass of red, raw flesh.

"Assuming as military a tone as terror would permit, I shouted—

"'Who goes there?'

"No answer.

"Again and again I shouted the soldier's challenge, though each time fainter and fainter. I now fancied I could almost touch it. Bringing the gun to my shoulder, I took aim—I fired.

"The loud echo was repeated a hundred-fold, reverberating hollowly from the arch before me, and more sharply from the graveyard beyond.

"Thick smoke filled and obscured the passage.

"I could not have missed—my courage was the nerve of despair.

"Slowly the breeze dissipated the dense smoke; and there, fluttering wildly, like an eagle over its prey, and certainly now not more than two feet from my head, was this 'thing of fear and dread.'

"I sprang upwards, and clasped it in my arms. I felt a slight resistance. Something snapped loudly; and a cloth—cold, dark, and damp as the covering of the dead—enveloped my head and shoulders!

"'Twas no 'unreal shade'—I felt 'twas substance.

"Terror vanished, and I became on the sudden strangely valiant. Sounds of human life were around and about me; the prisoners were alarmed, and talked loudly in their quarters. Lights moved towards me from the guard-house, with the sound of measured footsteps. It was the sergeant and the entire guard.

"They moved in line, steadily, and with ported arms, ready for the charge; and low at my feet lay the object of this warlike preparation.

"And what was it?

"A shirt of white linen! which had been pinned by the sleeves to a drying-line, reaching from a window of the casement to the opposite one; to the collar were pinned a red night-cap and a pair of red garters (the seeming stream of blood), and to the bottom was attached a pair of stockings (the joint legs of my ghost!).

"The line being rather slack, it had been wafted backwards and forwards in the breeze that blew down the passage, causing it to advance and recede; and as it bellied with the wind, it seemed to di——

CAPTAIN TOM AND MINNIE IN THE MAGAZINE OF THE FORTRESS.

and diminish in form, causing the before so evident suspiration, and giving it the appearance of supernatural animation."

When the old salt had finished his yarn he was cheered lustily, and after taking a pull at the lee-braces, and a swig at the grog can, Ben Bobstay, another old salt, was called upon to spin them one of his old twisters.

Ben was a noted hand at yarning, but the long cruise had completely exhausted them all, so he had recourse to an old thumbed book that he carried in his jacket-pocket.

By the light of a lantern he then commenced to read.

The night was black, and the awful thunder

rolled, while the forked lightning's vivid flashes flitted round the ill-fated brig. 'Achilles.'

"She drove before the wind; her sails were torn to ribbons; her mainmast, rocking in the gale, snapped and went by the board; her rudder was unshipped, and she was left to the mercy of the raging waves.

"At length she drove upon the rocks and went to pieces.

"Day broke on the wreck, but the hazy atmosphere and the drizzling rain added to the dreary aspect of the surrounding cliffs.

"The cabin boy was one of the few survivors, he had lashed himself to a frail yard, which snapped asunder as it went overboard. The furious billows dashed him to and fro; one wave would wash him on shore, while the succeeding one would take him out to sea again; but, fortunately, the tide was ebbing, and, at length, a friendly wave cast him so far on shore that the next failed to reach him.

"Here he lay some time insensible; at length returning reason showed him his forlorn situation. He disengaged himself from the fragment of the mast to which he was attached, and crawling into a crevice of the rock, sought a temporary shelter from the pouring rain.

"Here he pondered on his hopeless condition, without food, without shelter, and scantily clad, even hope seemed to desert him; and reclining his drooping head on his trembling hand, he gave way to despair.

"The boisterous weather gradually moderated; the clouds divided, and a gleam of sunshine lighted up the rocky eminence.

"More dead than alive, he crawled from the crevice; the sunny ray cheered his heart; he knelt in prayer, and returned thanks for his deliverance from death.

"He gazed upon the wreck which lay within a quarter of a mile of the main land, but not a living soul was to be seen.

"He thought he heard a sound besides that of the murmuring waves— he listened—he was not deceived. The distant chiming of church bells struck upon his ear—he sprang on his feet—hope and joy at once took possession of his breast; he was near the habitation of man. He ascended the cliff in order to ascertain his situation, and, to his great joy, discovered he was within a mile of a village; thither he bent his way, weak and fainting from fatigue and hunger.

"He arrived at the door of a fisher's hut; he paused, and feared to knock, lest he should meet a refusal; at length he mustered sufficient resolution, and tapped gently at the door.

"'Who's there?' inquired Jane, as she opened the latticed window.

"'A poor shipwrecked sailor boy,' replied Richard, 'who craves both food and shelter.'

"'Wait awhile, and I'll tell my father,' said the gentle girl, as she disappeared from the window.

"A few moments elapsed, the door flew open, and little Jane, followed by her father, appeared.

"'What did he say?—food and shelter?' ejaculated the old fisherman, as he approached. 'He shall have both, poor boy.' As he concluded, he bent an eye of compassion on Richard. 'But tell me, boy,' continued he, 'where does the wreck lie?'

"Richard pointed in the direction, and added it was within a mile of the village.

"'Here, dame!' cried the fisherman, 'take this poor lad, and give him some dry clothes and something to eat, while I go down to the sea-shore and see if anything can be saved from the wreck, before our land-sharks hear of it and go down to plunder.'

"'I'll take in the poor boy, and get him some breakfast,' said Jane. 'Come, poor sailor boy,' continued she, 'lean on my shoulder, and I'll lead you in.' He did so, and the affectionate girl conveyed him into the cottage.

"Old Bowman, the fisherman, took his oars, called up his boy, and bent his way to the sea-shore. Here he beheld the hulk of the vessel jammed between the rocks, she was now lying high and dry; he approached her, but not a living soul was visible. He went on board, and descended into the cabin. Heavens! what a sight was there; the lifeless bodies of the many who had been unable to escape from the wreck

"He found two chests uninjured; with difficulty he got these on deck. The tide was now rapidly rising, and his boat being brought alongside, he lowered them into it, and made the best of his way homeward.

"On his way he was observed by Will Sterner and some other wreckers, who immediately guessed what had happened, and without delay spread the news through the village.

"The wreckers were soon on the alert, and, hastening down to the strand, commenced the work of plunder.

"When Bowman reached the cottage, he found the boy much recovered; he opened the broken chest, and supplied him with clothing.

"Richard was anxious to go to the wreck, in case there should be any living person on board. Bowman knew it was useless, but, not wishing to check the good feelings of the youth, he agreed to accompany him.

"They went by a bye-path, not wishing to meet any of the plunderers. The boat was therefore sent afloat from a small creek which runs alongside of the cliff. They could observe the wreckers busily engaged in plundering the vessel. They turned from the scene with disgust, and ascending part of the cliff, intended to watch their departure.

"Richard made a sudden pause. Bowman looked at him with surprise, and inquired the cause.

"'I am not quite sure,' said Richard, 'but I could almost swear I saw a hand raised above yon low crag.'

"They looked towards the spot. Richard was not mistaken—a hand was seen raised for a moment.

"'I am right! I am right!' exclaimed Richard; and, hastening towards the spot, he descended quickly, followed by Bowman.

"'Gracious Heaven! it is my captain!' exclaimed Richard. 'Thanks to Providence, he lives! he lives!'

"He threw himself by his side and raised him. Bowman applied the brandy bottle to his lips; then lifting him in their arms, they carrried him to the boat, and shortly after brought him safely to the cottage.

"By strict attention and the supply of every needful comfort, he soon partially recovered from the many bruises with which his body had been wounded, and was sufficiently restored to be able to travel.

"One of the chests which Bowman had rescued from the wreck belonged to the captain, and contained money and valuables to a large amount.

"A chaise was procured from a neighbouring town, and the captain, after thanking and rewarding the old fisherman, took his departure, accompanied by the cabin boy, who declared himself resolved never to leave him as long as he would accept his services.

"They travelled swiftly, and soon reached London.

"The family of the captain were mourning his loss, because the news that had reached them was, that every soul had perished with the wreck.

"When he entered the room, a burst of joy broke from the anxious family, which was increased to admiration on the captain taking Richard by the hand, and saying—

"'Now, let me introduce my preserver.'

"Richard felt abashed, and returned their compliments with such modest and retiring manners as strongly prepossessed them all in his favour; and his continued good behaviour so charmed the captain that he failed not to use his interest in his behalf.

"One morning he called Richard into his private room.

"'Richard,' said he, 'you will be obliged to quit us soon.'

"'Sir!' exclaimed Richard; 'do I hear aright? Leave you, sir! In what have I offended?'

"'In nothing,' replied the captain. 'It is in consequence of your exemplary conduct that I have used my interest at the Admiralty, and have procured for you a midshipman's berth on board the "Defiance," as trim a ship as ever floated on the ocean's bosom; and her commander as bold a sailor as ever stepped on shipboard.'

"Richard felt the obligation, and testified his gratitude for the captain's solicitude, but candidly confessed he would rather have remained under his present master's command, though even in a more subordinate situation.

"The captain assured him that he would most willingly retain him; but he was not then in commission, and he told Richard it might be six or eight months before he was appointed to a ship; but he promised, whenever opportunity offered, that he would certainly take him on board.

"They parted. Richard waited on the captain of the 'Defiance,' and in consequence of his excellent character, was most cordially received on board.

"Yet his ardent mind was not satisfied with his only being employed as an officer of the navy; he sought to understand the full management of a ship, and the method of steering by the compass.

"He availed himself of every opportunity of getting into the company of the ship's master and his mate, and, by degrees, acquired so much knowledge, that, in the course of two years, he was considered one of the best steersmen in the service.

"The first opportunity which offered itself to display his seamanship was during an action off Toulon, when the master, and his first and second mates were successively marked out and killed, while at the wheel, by the enemy's marines.

"Richard immediately tendered his services to supply their loss, which were accepted, and he displayed such ability and precision in his new station that he received the approbation of his captain and officers immediately after the engagement.

"One thing that weighed greatly in his favour was the discovery of the treachery of the pilot, who had engaged, for a certain sum, to pilot the vessel into the harbour, and land a boatful of armed men where they could easily capture the fort.

"Richard, who had now reached his twentieth year, volunteered on board the 'Monmouth,' which was about to sail on a six months' cruise in the Straits of Gibraltar. They touched at St. Just, in order to take in water, and Richard went ashore with part of the crew.

"He was now within two miles of the cottage inhabited by the fisherman who had saved him from perishing by shipwreck, and he felt a strong inclination to visit him. He named it to his lieutenant, who informed the captain of the circumstance, who granted him leave of absence till next morning.

"He then returned on shore, and immediately bent his way towards the fisherman's dwelling. Here, indeed, was a wide alteration; the poor, tattered-looking cottage was now neatly and comfortably fitted up, and gave ample evidence that the owner had improved in circumstances.

"A handsome-looking girl was sitting at the door, feeding poultry.

"Hearing an approaching footstep, she looked up and beheld the form of Richard.

"Each gazed at the other, and seemed uncertain of the recognition.

"At length Richard, looking steadfastly in her face, said—

"'Jane, don't you know me?'

"'Know you?' replied she. 'You are grown so tall, and look so smart in your uniform, that I could hardly suppose you are that same poor little cabin-boy who, but a few years since, sought food and shelter at our cottage; but I suppose you have forgot all that, since you have become a great man?'"

"'You are mistaken there, Jane,' replied Richard. 'The kindness which I experienced from yourself and your father is so deeply impressed on my heart that time can never efface it.'

"Jane invited him into the cottage, while she ran to seek her father, but Richard preferred accompanying her, because, not having been ashore for some time, he had not been in such pleasant company, and as his time was short, he determined to make the most of it.

"There was a charm about this beautiful but artless girl which had evidently begun to work on the heart of Richard; and the tie of gratitude was probably quickly emerging into that feeling which poets call 'love!'

"He took Jane's arm under his own arm, and merrily they trudged along to the haven, to meet Jane's father.

"William Stamford had long observed the growing beauties of Jane Bowman, and had meditated the girl's ruin; he had bought over to his interests one Black Donald, a fellow who possessed not a spark of generous feeling.

"It was arranged between these two desperadoes that, as she was in the habit of going to the beach every evening to meet her father, they would intercept her, and bear her off.

"This was the very evening they had pitched upon; and they lay in wait for that purpose: they were secreted in a small cavern, but were restrained on observing that she was accompanied by Richard. Black Donald was for darting out upon him at once.

"'We are two to one,' he exclaimed, 'and it's hard if we can't master him.'

"'True,' said Stamford, 'but perhaps he carries pistols; and if so—'

"'Pshaw, nonsense!' replied Black Donald. 'A sailor never carries pistols on shore unless he is on duty. I have been on board a man-of-war, and I know their regulations pretty well, although I seldom stuck to them. Somehow I think there is a little of the smattering of the coward about you.'

"'Coward!' retorted Stamford, 'there is no cowardice in me, but I exercise more caution. Follow me down this bye-path, and we'll seize her at once.'

"Richard had now proceeded nearly half way, when it was proposed between them that Richard should go a little in advance, and meet her father alone, in order to ascertain if he would recognise him.

"He agreed to do so, and had just turned out of the path which hid him from Jane, when a violent scream struck upon his ear.

"He returned instantly, and beheld her in the clutches of the desperadoes, who were armed with bludgeons.

"He rushed towards them, and, seizing Stamford by the throat, hurled him on one side, and, drawing his hanger, parried the blow which Black Donald had aimed at him, and vowed that he would cut down the first who approached.

"This gave Jane an opportunity of darting from the ruffians. She rushed towards the beach, loudly calling for aid. Her father heard her cries, and ran quickly from the beach, followed by his son David carrying the oars.

"They hastened to the spot, where Richard, nearly exhausted, was contesting with Black Donald, for he had succeeded in wounding Stamford.

"Fierce was their struggle when Bowman rushed forward, and by a well-aimed blow brought Black Donald to the earth, exclaiming—

"'Lie there, scoundrel!'

"Meanwhile, Stamford had crawled towards the spot where the bludgeon lay, and having seized it, had raised it, intending to give a murderous blow to Richard, but young David had watched his motions, and gave him such a severe stroke over the arm with his oar that the villain roared with pain.

"'Oh, Richard!' exclaimed Jane, 'are you hurt?'

"'Richard!' exclaimed Bowman, 'what Richard? This can never be the poor ship-wrecked cabin-boy?'

"'It is the same indeed,' replied Richard. 'The same whom your benevolent heart saved from perishing; the same which your good Jane attended and nursed during his sickness; and it has pleased Providence to ordain that I should arrive in time to save her from the fangs of these vile monsters, and thus enable me in some degree to requite the obligations I owe.'

"'If these are your sentiments,' replied Bowman, 'if this is the tack you have been sailing upon since I saw you last, I don't at all wonder at your advancement in life. You are a brave lad, and one after my own heart, and if the hand of an honest but poor fisherman will not disgrace—'

"'Disgrace? It is an honour, friend,' said Richard, as he grasped the hand of the good fisherman. 'But what's to be done with these desperadoes?'

"'Oh, we'll soon settle their account!' said Bowman; 'here are some of my brother fishermen coming, and the best thing we can do for them is to give them a jaunt before the magistrate, and see what he will say to them.

"At this moment several fishermen approached, who took charge of the two desperadoes, and conveyed them to the town, where they were examined, and Donald, being discovered to be a deserter from the navy, was turned over to the captain of the 'Monmouth.'

"The old fisherman gave Richard a hearty welcome at his cottage, and the best fare which it afforded.

"Bowman explained that his rise of fortune was through the means of the captain whom he had saved from the wreck; he had not only given him the means of providing better for his wife and family, but had provided for Jane as soon as she was old enough to quit home.

"That time had now arrived, and the following week she was to go to her situation in the captain's family.

"Richard was rejoiced to hear it, and only regretted that duty prevented him from accompanying her, and seeing her safe to her destination.

"The morning came, and with it brought its regrets—the hour of parting.

"Richard felt much sorrow in separating from Jane, and when he took her hand for the last time a tear glistened in her eye.

"'Good-bye, my friend Bowman. Good-bye, my dear, dear Jane,' said he, as he pressed her hand to his lips, and hastily departed, not daring to look back.

"Richard soon reached the ship, and was welcomed by his messmates. But he had left his heart on shore. He could not drive Jane from his mind, sleeping or waking.

"The next day, the wind proving favourable, the anchor was weighed, and they put to sea.

"Jane rose early and ascended the cliff, from which she perceived the 'Monmouth.' Blue Peter was flying at the mast-head, and soon after the sails bent to the wind, while the distant 'yeo ho!' of the men at the windlass faintly reached her ear; it sounded to her like 'Farewell, farewell for ever.'

"She kept her eye fixed on the ship, which gradually receded from the shore until it was lost in distance.

"The following morning Jane rose early, took farewell of her father and mother, and, accompanied by her brother David, departed for London, to join the captain's establishment.

"It was about this period that the defeat of one of our great admirals caused some commotion, and Captain Grafton had in some measure shared the disgrace; but, being an officer of prodigious bravery and tact, was extremely anxious to find an opportunity of wiping off the stain, and vowed, if he should ever meet with the 'Foudroyant' again, nothing but death should prevent his taking her.

"The opportunity at length offered; for, being amongst those appointed to intercept the French admiral on the North American station, he got sight of the very ship which had out-manœuvred him on a former occasion.

"He gave chase. The Frenchman was far ahead, nevertheless, he was determined to persevere. He knew the 'Monmouth' was one of the best sailers in the navy; every stitch of canvas was spread, and in two hours she was within gunshot.

"'Master,' said Captain Grafton, 'lay me alongside the 'Foudroyant'.'

"'Yes, captain,' replied the master. 'Let her sail as fast as she will, I'll be close on her stern in less than an hour, or my name's not what it is.'

"'And when we meet,' rejoined the captain, 'Heaven alone knows who will outlive the action—for I have sworn to take her, or perish in the attempt.'

"'Hurrah for our brave captain!' cried the men, as the fire of his words took possession of their souls.

"'We'll fight while a seam of our good ship will hold together,' cried the first lieutenant.

"''Tis bravely said,' replied Captain Grafton, 'we are gaining fast upon her, and we shall soon try her metal.'

"A shot whizzed across the trisail.

"'Ah! there's the stern-chaser, by way of a compliment, from the Frenchman,' said Captain Grafton. 'It is, however, a piece of politeness which shall be returned with interest.'

"The 'Monmouth' wore, and gave her a tier of guns which rattled among her rigging; she tacked and gave her a return. The 'Monmouth' was quickly laid on her quarter; at this moment Jones received a shot in the arm, but he did not quit his post.

"The action was now maintained with unabated fury.

"At length the mizen-mast of the 'Monmouth' went by the board; the Frenchmen gave three hearty cheers, and one of the British sailors, who went by the cognomen of 'Witty Jack,' half in dudgeon, cried out—

"'Aye, cheer away, Misther Mounseer. It's well you've got something to brag about, but depend upon it we'll be even with you by-and-bye.'

"Jack was a true prophet, for, in a few minutes down went the mizen-mast of the 'Foudroyant.'

"'There, I told you so!' roared Jack, in ecstasy. 'Three cheers for old England!'

"An incessant fire from the 'Monmouth' drove the Frenchmen from their guns.

"At this moment, while encouraging his men to persevere, Captain Grafton received a second shot, in the forehead. Feeling it was his death-blow, he immediately sent for the first lieutenant, a brave fellow, named Jones.

"'Jones, my dear friend,' said the dying Grafton,

'do not quit the enemy, or strike the ship, if you outlive the action.'

"'Never,' said Jones, ' as long as a timber of the 'Monmouth' will hold together, I will not quit the enemy, and, as an earnest that I will not strike my flag, look what will be done.'

"So saying, he nailed the flag to the staff, and taking a pistol in each hand, vowed he would shoot the first man who attempted to strike the colours.

"'Thanks, thanks!' exclaimed Grafton, and, as he grasped Jones's hand, he fell back in a state of insensibility, and was carried down below, in the agonies of death.

"The action was continued with redoubled fury, and Jones nobly kept his promise. He fought the ship with such resolute bravery that the enemy's decks were nearly deserted, and her fire almost silenced.

"It was in this action that Richard had covered himself with glory, for he had alternately served at the wheel, the guns, and the waist.

"Roberts, the master, had received a musket-ball in the thigh, which rendered him unable to continue at the wheel. Richard instantly replaced him.

"The gunner on the main-deck had been killed. Richard took his station until his place was otherwise filled up. And last, not least, he rigged out jury-masts for the crippled vessel. He escaped with a wound in the left shoulder, and remained by the side of Lieutenant Jones during the progress of the action, until the enemy surrendered.

"Lieutenant Jones towed his prize into Gibraltar, where he was received with every honourable testimony by the garrison.

"Richard, being the slightest wounded of the junior officers, was appointed to bear the tidings of the victory to England, and, as soon as he was sufficiently recovered, set sail for that purpose.

"Jane had, without adventure, reached the captain's residence. Her reception was most flattering. She was neither received nor treated as a servant or dependant, but rather as a person to whom the family conceived they owed some obligations.

"Indeed, the captain's wife and daughters looked upon her as the protector, the saviour of the captain.

"Jane did not expect such marked kindness, and her heart bounded at the prospect of her good fortune.

"Her education was, of course, but moderate—the daughter of a fisherman could not be expected to possess many accomplishments—yet, being now placed in a family of higher grade, it was no matter of surprise if her manners became more polished.

"Jane gained so rapidly on the affections of her master and mistress that, in the course of time, she was almost considered as one of the family.

"Her father often visited her, and she had every prospect of happiness before her; but still she occasionally appeared to be sorrowful.

"Her heart was not her own, and he that possessed it was far from England's shore, fighting the enemies of his country.

"Richard, during this time, had returned in safety, and despatched one of his men (Jack Gasket) with a note to his captain.

"Jack was big with importance in being the messenger, and as he approached the house he began to turn in his mind how much grog he could stow away.

"Once arrived, he was not long in making known the object of his visit, and he was no little surprised when the white-headed son of a sea-cook, as he denominated the powdered lacquey, handed him into the drawing-room.

"The luxury of a carpeted floor was one with which Jack was little acquainted, and having trans-ferred a huge quid from his mouth to the crown of his tarpaulin, he returned the hearty grip with which the captain received him, and then uncoiled his yarn.

"He narrated their adventure with the Frenchmen, and how nobly they had defeated them, and when he had done, the captain said—

"'Jack! here's a guinea for you. You are a good seaman, and an honour to the navy, and while you continue to do your duty as you have done, you shall never want a friend while I can aid you."

"'God bless your honour,' cried Jack, ' and may you live long; aye, till the English navy gets beat by the French, and that will be a jolly long time, I'll swear.'

"So saying, Jack made his best bow, rolled out of the drawing-room, hitched up his pants, and, replacing his quid, descended the stairs, and made the best of his way to the Admiralty, to meet Richard.

"Captain Dempster was resolved to receive his preserver with every honourable testimony, and invited a few nautical friends to meet him.

"A chaise drove up to the door, a crowd was instantly collected round it, and the cheers of the assembled persons gave token that it was one of the naval heroes.

"The chaise-door opened, and a young man in a naval uniform, with his arm in a sling, alighted from it.

"Jane was at the window, and beheld him. She flew to the stairs; her feet refused to move forward. Richard flew up the stairs.

"'Jane, my dear Jane!' exclaimed he, as he caught her in his arms, 'do I again behold thee?'

"The captain, who had left the room to meet him, was surprised at what he saw, but a moment's reflection told him the whole secret. He read the real cause at once, but he did not betray the least suspicion.

"Richard and Jane immediately recollected themselves, and followed the captain to the room where the company had assembled.

"Here Captain Dempster took him by the hand, and introduced him as the man who had so honourably acquitted himself on board the ' Monmouth.'

"Richard then informed him that he had had the good fortune to give full satisfaction to his officers, and, at the recommendation of the admiral, was put on the list for immediate promotion, and was not to return to the ship until he was rated as a lieutenant, which would shortly be the case.

"Captain Dempster was rejoiced to hear that his conduct was properly noticed, and pledged himself to forward his interests by every means in his power.

"Richard had, however, a stronger point of attraction at the captain's house than the splendid company to which he had been introduced; he watched for an opportunity to have a stolen interview with Jane.

"This soon occurred, and reciprocal vows of constancy passed between them.

"Among the party who had assembled at the captain's house, was the son of a deceased officer, named Aston.

"Through interest of powerful friends, he was rated on board a ship-of-war, but as yet had not seen any service, but he was descended from a family who possessed great interest with those at the head of the Government; therefore, notwithstanding the praises and honours which had been heaped upon Richard, he looked upon him with contempt, and scorned him on account of his low origin, for he knew that he gradually rose from a cabin-boy.

"This Aston was of a dissolute and unprincipled

character, and associated with the most dissipated boxcombs who lounged about the town.

"He had noticed the growing charms of Jane and had marked her as one of his intended victims.

"The sudden return, however, of Richard, promised to mar his plans for the present; but some space of time elapsed before he discovered that Jane and Richard were acknowledged lovers.

"One morning he was riding through the park when he observed a person in naval costume, having his arm in a sling, walking with a lady.

"It immediately struck him that it was Richard, and being anxious to ascertain the fact, he took a circuitous route in order to meet them in close quarters; he did so, thinking to catch Richard with some favoured *chere amie*, and chuckling to think what a fine tale he could make of it to the captain.

"But when he drove up to them, to his utter surprise he discovered the female to be no other than Jane Bowman, the inmate at Captain Dempster's.

"A kind of envious feeling circled round his heart, and he determined from that moment to accomplish their ruin.

"The ruffian from whose vile attempt Jane had been rescued by her lover, as we have before observed, proved to be a deserter, and was consequently turned over from the 'Monmouth' to the flag-ship.

"He had then the option of receiving one hundred lashes and being discharged the service, or serving before the mast on a foreign station for seven years; he according availed himself of the latter offer.

"The naturally ferocious temper of this fellow was rendered more so by vexation, and it was therefore no matter of surprise if all his energies were exerted to ruin the future prospects of Richard and Jane.

"It so occurred that this fellow had been shifted into the same ship to which Aston was appointed, and by a train of circumstances fell in his way at the very moment when he required the aid of a ruffian of his description.

"He soon ascertained that Richard and Jane had left London for Jane's father's residence, and immediately laid his plans to circumvent the lovers.

"At this time men were wanted to recruit the fleet, and the press-gangs were busily engaged at every out-port.

"Black Donald was attached to one of these gangs, and was therefore often on shore.

"Aston engaged this fellow to assist; he found him apt, and a couple of gold coins dropped into his hand, settled the business, and they left London together.

"Richard and Jane soon arrived in the neighbourhood of Bowman's cottage. It was agreed between them that Richard should enter the cottage alone. He arrived at the door and knocked; the latch was raised by a lad about fifteen.

"Richard instantly guessed it was Jane's brother David. He stared at Richard in surprise, but he did not appear to recollect him until he inquired for Bowman.

"David instantly recognised the voice.

"'Well, I declare, it is Mr. Richard!' said David. 'Oh, dear! who'd have thought it was you, with your arm slung up in that fashion. Come in, father and mother will be glad to see you; and if our Jane was at home wouldn't she be the same. Oh, she'd jump out of her skin for joy.'

"Richard entered the cottage.

"Bowman and his wife were rejoiced to see him, and he failed not to inquire how matters went with them. Bowman informed him that he had now become the owner of two good fishing-boats.

"Richard congratulated him on his cheering prospects.

"'And now, friend Bowman,' said he, 'I have a

matter to state to you on which I wish to ask your advice and assistance. I have seen much service since last we parted, and, thanks to Providence, have hitherto been successful far beyond my best hopes. Preferment has followed so quickly that I am now placed on the list to be promoted to a lieutenancy. You are aware that a sailor is not much on shore, but even the little time he is he requires a home. I feel the want of it. When, after hard service, I come on shore, I find myself alone. I have no relatives, neither father, mother, brother, nor sister. I have therefore made up my mind to take a wife.'

"'And a very sensible resolution, too,' exclaimed Dame Bowman.

"'Hold your tongue, Alice,' said old Bowman. 'What do you know about the matter? Go on, Mr. Richard.'

"'I say I intend to take a wife. I have searched for one; I have found one.'

"'Aye!' exclaimed the dame, 'some great man's daughter, I'll be bound. Is she very handsome?'

"'You shall shortly see her, and form your own judgment,' added Richard. 'And to convince you of the esteem I hold you in, I will not wed the lady unless you approve of my choice.'

"'Well, to be sure,' exclaimed the dame. 'who'd ha' thought that a lieutenant in His Majesty's navy would condescend to ask the advice of a poor fisherman and his wife on a matter of such consequence. But when shall we see the lady?'

"'This moment,' replied Richard. 'Keep your seat, and I will introduce her.' So saying, he quitted the cottage.

"Bowman and his wife looked at each other with inquiring glances.

"'I wonder who she can be?' ejaculated the dame.

"'Heaven knows,' replied Bowman. 'Some fine lady out of London, I suppose. Well, I'm glad to see the boy get on so well; he's a worthy soul, and no doubt will be a great commander ere he dies He has no pride. He is all gratitude and affection and never forgets that he was once a poor cabin-boy.'

"'Nor will he ever forget it,' echoed Richard, as he threw open the cottage door. 'Here is my intended bride. Look upon her, and say if you approve of my choice.'

"Jane rushed in, and flew to embrace her father and mother.

"'What!' exclaimed the dame. 'Our Jane going to marry a lieutenant in the navy?'

"'Am I to be brother-in-law to such a brave lad!' said David.

"'It is indeed so,' responded Jane.

"Much congratulation took place, and it was arranged that the ceremony should be performed before Richard returned to his ship, and that Jane should remain with her father and mother until the wedding-day.

"Richard, however, was obliged to return to London, in order to attend the Admiralty, and as he intended to send some presents to Jane's family, it was agreed that David should accompany him, and return with the packages.

"All matters being settled, Richard took leave of Jane and her parents, and, accompanied by David, jumped into the chaise, and were soon on their way to London.

"Aston had watched their departure, and considered this a good opportunity for putting his plan into execution; he, therefore, provided a chaise, which was kept in waiting at a sequestered spot, in order that he might quickly convey her away, as soon as he had seized upon her.

"Bowman had not been out with his boat for

three days; and, as the market-day was fast approaching, he determined to put to sea with the next retiring tide.

"Jane accompanied him to the beach, and watched the sporting of the trim little bark as it receded from the shore.

"She was returning home to the cottage, when, in an instant, a cloak was thrown over her face, which prevented her calling for help—she felt herself lifted from the ground and carried some distance, and, shortly afterwards, was placed in a chaise.

"The cloak was now removed, and she beheld, to her dismay, the villain Aston seated by her side, and on the bar in front of the chaise the diabolical Black Donald.

"Tears and entreaties were in vain, and ruin, inevitable ruin, seemed to be Jane's wretched fate. The chaise at length stopped to change horses, when another chaise was seen coming towards them from the London side.

"Jane instantly recognised David sitting in the front, and, at the moment she had an opportunity, uttered a loud shriek, and called on David to save her.

"In an instant David jumped down, and, opening the chaise door, quickly roused a person who was sleeping inside.

"A stentorian voice was heard exclaiming— 'What's the matter, boy? Is the enemy coming aboard of us? I'm ready; pipe all hands to quarters.' And the brave seaman, Jack Gasket, jumped out of the chaise.

"Aston and his accomplice were striving all in their power to get the horses put to the chaise, in order to get away with their prize.

"But in this they were foiled, for Jack Gasket was not a man to be easily circumvented.

"With a well-aimed blow he brought Aston to the ground, and, seizing Black Donald by the throat with his iron grip, exclaimed, 'Now, what ship, my hearty?'

"David, in the interim, had taken Jane from the chaise, and Aston, fearing the disgrace which would fall on him if discovered, took advantage of the confusion, and, mounting the horse that was ready saddled for the postilion, galloped off, leaving his colleague to get out of the hobble how he could.

"'Let's see what sort of an animal you are,' said Jack, as he looked in the face of Donald. 'Oh! I've seen you before, my hearty. You're the swab what was sent aboard to serve seven years as a punishment, and a pretty disgrace you are to the navy. Why, a crew such as you would make a ship of war more like a gaol of Newgate. I tell you what, my fine fellow, if I was a boatswain's mate, I should like to have you on board of the ship—the rope's-end shouldn't be idle. How came you ashore without leave?'

"'I have a press warrant,' growled Donald.

"'Oh, well,' said Jack; 'that's a service that no good seaman likes to meddle with; and, as it's but a dirty job, why it just suits you. But, answer me this—Does your press warrant authorise you to take women? Give me hold of that pistol, you 'long-shore lubber?'

"Jack snatched the pistol from his girdle.

"'Now mount that chaise-bar, and, if you offer to stir an inch, by the honour of a sailor, I'll blow your brains out; for I'm resolved not to part company with you till I've lodged you safe in limbo. Your commander seems to have sheered off. Well, that shows he's ashamed of the colours he has hoisted. Now, young lady, only just get aboard the chaise, and we'll pilot you into harbour safe enough, be assured.'

"Jane did as she was requested, and placed in safety under her father's roof.

"Richard, having learnt what had occu was anxious to ascertain who was the principal this nefarious transaction, in order to call him to account.

"In this he immediately succeeded; for Jack Gasket having observed Aston's cloak (the same which had been thrown over Jane), thought it would be a snug thing to travel in, and, therefore, did not hesitate to use it for that purpose.

"The cloak was immediately recognised, and Richard forthwith challenged Aston.

"But he was not fond of powder and shot, and therefore declined to meet him, his excuse being that a gentleman could not condescend to put himself on an equality with a man who had sprung from the station of a cabin-boy.

"Richard, in the heat of passion, threatened to post him as a coward; and Aston, driven to extremity, had no alternative but that of applying to his powerful friends to relieve him from this dilemma.

"They therefore called upon Captain Dempster to interpose his authority; but the brave captain felt that Richard was right, and could only reply that he would speak to Richard on the subject, and accordingly sent to him for that purpose.

"In the interval, the captain was visited by one Admiral Broadside—a brave old veteran, who had been in no less than thirty actions, and had been covered with wounds received in the service of his country.

"He had heard something of the matter, and came down to Captain Dempster to know particulars.

"The brave old veteran was soon made acquainted with all the particulars, and from what he learnt he concluded that Richard's conduct was perfectly justifiable on moral grounds, but not in accordance with the rules of the service.

"He was, therefore, charged with insolence to a superior officer—for Richard was not yet rated lieutenant—and tried by court-martial.

"The trial was long and tedious, for the captains assembled, though conscious that Richard was in the right, could not give a verdict in favour of the accused, who had sprung up, as it were, from oblivion, and condemn the pampered son of the aristocrat.

"Richard was, therefore, pronounced guilty, and dismissed from the service, but, in consideration of the good character he had hitherto borne, he was allowed the privilege of entering again before the mast.

"But this the brave fellow disdainfully refused.

"The injustice stung him to the soul, and he secretly vowed to wreak a bitter vengeance on those who had so foully wronged him.

"Seeking his friends, of whom he had but few, he made known his intention of marrying the object of his love—alas! that love that had wrought him so much bitterness—at once.

"This done, with the prize-money he had amassed, he purchased a small vessel, secretly manned and fitted her out, and, in company with his faithful Jane, he sailed away on his perilous adventure promising his friends they should hear of him soon.

"He kept his word.

"Some few months after his departure, intelligence reached England of the sudden appearance of a pirate in the Caribbean Sea, whose bold daring had absolutely set the authorities at defiance, and baffled all their efforts to capture him.

"Reports of the doings of this unknown desperado at length became such as to throw the Admiralty into the greatest alarm, insomuch as the men-of-war had been attacked, and one of them severely mauled, even under cover of a fort.

"The next report was the total defeat of the vessel in which Aston was lieutenant.

"Her commander had been wounded in the neck with a bullet, and Aston, who was next in command, replaced him.

"His unskilful management gave the pirates an opportunity of boarding—a privilege of which they quickly availed themselves—and as the British seamen were disheartened by the tactics of their untutored officer, they fought less vigorously than they would otherwise have done.

"Amongst the foremost to board was the pirate chief himself, and his sword made a path to where Aston stood half bewildered.

"Their eyes met, their swords clashed, and the pirate's steel found a sheath in Aston's breast.

"The life-blood gushed from the wound as he fell, and raising his eyes, which were already filmed with death, he recognised the features of Richard.

"With a moan of agony he rolled over, and closed his eyes to hide the fearful vision from his view, then as his last breath was departing, a voice whispered hoarsely in his ear—

"'Tis I, Roland the Rover. 'Twas you that made me as I am, and this is my revenge.'

"The pirate chief then turned to his men and cried—

"'Cease fighting, all of you, and retreat—my work is accomplished, I am satisfied.'

"An angry growl was the reply to this.

"The lawless horde did not care to give up what they already considered their well-earned prize.

"They obeyed him, however, with lowering looks, the pirate chief being the last to leave the deck of the man-of-war.

"Aston's bewilderment and sudden death had so disastrous an effect on the seaman that they could not raise a weapon against their foes, but stood looking on in dreamy silence.

"The rover chief was the last to ascend the side of his own vessel.

"Dark looks and murmurs of dissatisfaction greeted his return and nervous hands clutched the glittering steel.

"But the chief's stern, unquailing glance curbed the mutiny at once, and order was quickly restored."

The boom of a gun sounding over the water put an end to Ben's yarn, and dousing the light, he thrust the book into his pocket and sprang to his feet.

Every soul on board the schooner were immediately on the alert.

The sailors sprang into the nettings or crowded to the ports; but the captain coolly took his glass and approached the vessel's side.

With steady glance he surveyed the horizon, and then addressed the mate—

"Ha! ha! they are at it, and pretty tight work it seems to be. Can you make out either of them?"

"At present I cannot. What with the darkness and the smoke they are completely hidden."

"So much the better; we can crawl down upon them unobserved. Let every man stand to his post."

"Aye, aye, sir," cried the boatswain, who was within hearing; and muffling his voice he passed the word fore and aft.

Some of the men, eager to catch the least glimpse of the combating vessels—for such evidently they were—did not obey immediately, and then the captain's voice rang out—

"Down, every one of you! The last man who obeys shall pay with his life!"

The captain's voice had scarcely ceased when every man was crouching at his gun.

A death-like silence now prevailed.

The captain only breaking it at intervals as he gave an order to the helmsman or guided him in his movements with his hand.

At first sight, any who had glanced upon that vessel's deck would have taken her for a trader but an experienced eye might have detected something in her rake and build, and the construction of her decks, that would lead them to believe otherwise.

She was a fast sailer, too, for though the wind was but light, she made good progress towards where the vessels were enveloped in smoke.

Boom, boom! crash, crash! sounded at intervals, and now and then a bright red flame would shoot out from the misty vapour.

That both vessels were fighting with equal desperation there could be no doubt, as they answered each other's fire so rapidly, and as the schooner drew upon them, the shouts of the combatants were plainly audible.

A cheer or a shout of defiance succeeded each broadside.

Then the firing suddenly ceased.

The thick vapours of smoke rolled away, and disclosed the shot-torn hulls and riddled sails of two vessels.

The larger of the two was a man-of-war, and from her quarter-deck a bright streak of flame was gradually rising, making its way like a serpent up the mizzen-mast.

All her guns were hushed and ports lowered, and her men were doing all in their power to extinguish the devouring element.

Their dark forms could be seen gliding hither and thither, and the shouts of the officers, as they directed their movements, rang out on the night air.

Whilst the captain of the schooner was looking at them, and wondering in his mind how it had come to pass, the other vessel crept quietly under the schooner's stern, and placed her guns in such a position as to rake her fore and aft.

The captain of the schooner, on seeing this, wore round, and laid his ship on the other tack.

The movement was only in time.

The broadside that would have swept his deck, and mowed down the greater part of his men, flew harmlessly by.

"Sharp work, that," he said to his mate, who was eyeing the stranger's movements. "He is a bold one, whoever he is; his vessel is but small, but a regular spitfire."

"And so we should have found had we kept in her line of fire."

"No doubt," answered the captain, thoughtfully.

"Shall we engage her, sir?" asked the mate.

"Not yet, unless she throws us another challenge. By my soul she has played sad havoc with the French man-of-war."

A sudden noise caused the captain to turn his head.

The flames had now gained complete mastery over the French man-of-war.

The colours were hanging carelessly over the taffrail, and her crew were rushing wildly to and fro.

The captain was trying to rally his officers, and he shouted loudly to the gunners to flood the magazine.

This done, they prepared to launch the boats.

The pinnace was lowered successfully, but the cutters, owing to the crowding of the excited men, were swamped alongside.

It was with difficulty the barge was got clear of the ship, for the marines had taken possession of her.

They raised their loaded muskets, and swore with bitter oaths to shoot the first of their drowning com-

canoes who offered to clutch at the gunwale to save their lives.

In this they kept their words.

Many a brave fellow who tried to escape a watery grave fell a victim to the murderous bullet or the deadly knife.

Many a white face disappeared beneath the tinted waves never more to be seen.

Horrified at the sight, the captain of the schooner and his crew stood watching the deadly strife, and for a time forgot their own position.

The mate was the first to arouse from the dreamy stupor into which they had been thrown.

"Look! look!" he cried, pointing with his glass. "See, they have gone to the rescue!"

The cause of this exclamation was the strange vessel making her way to the burning ship. In a moment her boats were lowered, and a young officer, followed by half a dozen stout fellows, leapt into the foremost one, and pulled amongst the drowning men.

The other boats soon followed.

The hardy old captain was rather taken aback at this.

To see the gallant fellows stripped to the waist, as they had left their guns, risking their lives to save the lives of those with whom they had been engaged in deadly conflict.

The crew of the man-of-war had evidently been very numerous, for though a great many had escaped in the boats, and a great many were drowned, there was still a considerable quantity clinging to broken spars, hen-coops, and pieces of planking.

It was a sight of awful grandeur to see the gallant fellows making their way through the floating _debris_, and picking up the half-dead seamen from their frail supports.

To stand tamely by and look on was against the grain of the rough, but honest-hearted captain, and he intimated as much to his mate.

The mate took the hint.

The order was given to lower the boats.

The sailors sprang lightly into them.

Then the word was given to shove off.

"Avast, there!" cried the captain, as the oars dropped in the water. Then to the nearest boat he shouted "Astern all, I cannot stay behind—ah!"

This last exclamation was uttered with mingled terror and surprise.

With a bound he leapt into the boat, and at the pitch of his voice shouted—

"Give way, my lads, give way!"

The mate's boat was some fathoms from the ship by this time, and the mate was urging his men to their utmost, whilst he himself steered the boat with one hand, and with the other assisted in working the after oar.

The cause of this sudden commotion was known to all.

One of the boats, the one with the young officer in, having taken in all it could hold with safety, put round to return to the ship, to disgorge its freight, when the frantic cries of a poor little boy, who was clinging to a grating, smote their ears.

Instantly they put round and pulled towards him, but in taking him in the boat heeled, gunwale under, and they were all immersed.

The scene that followed was truly heartrending.

Piercing cries and shouts for help came from the poor exhausted wretches.

The strongest clung to the upturned boat, and those who were already exhausted were soon overpowered.

When the schooner's boats dashed alongside, only a dozen remained, and the majority of these were the boat's crew.

Willing hands soon set to work in pulling them in, and the captain, whose brawny hand had seized the young officer by the collar, gave a startled cry.

"What, Harry Vere, is it you?" he exclaimed. "Who the devil would have thought of seeing you here?"

Harry Vere—for it was he—could not reply having swallowed a bucketful of salt water.

Having received all that came to hand, the boat was pulled towards the strange vessel, and the half-drowned men hoisted up the side.

Amongst these was the redoubtable Jerry Mizzen.

Doctor Shrike was at the gangway, ready to meet them.

Jacop, his faithful attendant, was there also, ready to assist.

A malicious smile played on his lips as he beheld Jerry.

"I'll bleed him this time, blowed if I don't," thought Jacop.

Jerry could not hear what he said, but he could read his intentions in his looks.

"Blowed if yer do," thought Jerry; "if yer does, I'll have blood for blood."

Jacop made a move towards him.

Jerry tried to make a move also, but in an opposite direction.

Weakness prevented him doing this.

The vampire drew closer to him.

Jerry shuddered, and could scarcely suppress a howl.

He saw the case of instruments under Jacop's arm, and it made his very blood run cold.

The grin on the vampire's face was perfectly demoniacal as he bent over Jerry's prostrate form and brandished a lance.

"Ho-o! ho-o!" cried Jerry, wincing and doubling himself up like a ball, as the instrument flashed before his eyes; "ho-o! ho-o!"

"Ah! it's no use, it's no good. You won't get off this time," said Jacop, sarcastically. "I thought I'd have you."

"Cuss yer!" muttered Jerry, making a kick at his tormentor.

Had it not been for Jerry's weakness the kick would have taken effect to some tune; as it was, Jacop escaped.

The unfortunate Jerry had now no other alternative but to quietly submit to the operation, which by-the-bye, was greatly repulsive to his feelings.

Already he fancied he could feel the knife piercing his flesh, and he cast a despairing look around, in the hope of seeing Bob Hauler.

"Oh, Bob! Bob! where are you?" roared the terrified Jerry.

"Not far off," muttered a voice.

Jerry did not hear it, though.

Neither did he see the grinning face peering from behind one of the guns.

Jacop did not see this either.

With a fiendish grin he set about his work of mercy, first rolling up his sleeves to the elbow and then going through a little pantomimic performance preparatory to starting.

This finished, he knelt down and seized Jerry's arm.

Jerry fairly howled with terror.

This cry was echoed by the vampire, who went sprawling over his patient, and landed all of a heap in the lee-scuppers.

"Take that, you lubberly swab!" cried Bob Hauler, stepping forward and glaring fiercely at him; "and mark me," he added. "when next my shoemaker comes in close quarters with your tailor, there'll be such a score to pay as you'll never forget."

Jacop was some time before he thoroughly recovered from his surprise, and lay rubbing himself as though he were in doubt as to whether his pants would require a new seat or not.

A second application of Bob's sea-boot, however, brought him to his senses and his feet at the same time, and he slunk away aft.

"The bloodthirsty vampire!" cried Bob, as he glanced after him, and shook his huge fist threateningly. "If he comes athwart hawse of me again, I'll give him such a keel-hauling as he never dreamed of."

The appearance of Bob wrought a sudden change on Jerry.

He seemed to recover almost immediately, and when Bob gave him a nip of rum, he scrambled to his feet.

Bob lent him a hand down the forecastle hatchway, and assisted him in changing his wet clothes.

Harry Vere, on gaining the deck, divided his men into parties, some of whom he left to look after the Frenchmen; others set to work in repairing the rigging, and the rest cleared the decks and put the gear in order.

"Will you step down below, Captain Baldrick?" said Harry; "we can talk better there."

"Now," he added, as they entered the cabin, "let me hear what news you have."

"Nothing very pleasant," replied Hugh Baldrick. "Do you know I hold a warrant for your capture?" he asked.

"I have heard as much," said Harry, "and, of course, believe it."

"Certainly."

Hugh Baldrick burst into a hearty laugh.

"What would Admiral Ellis say if he knew I had boarded you so easily? But come; where have you stowed Captain Tom—eh, Harry?"

Harry's brow grew thoughtful.

"I cannot say where he is stowed," he answered. "I am afraid he has fallen into no good hands. This is the last I have heard of him."

He handed the tablet to Hugh Baldrick.

"Ah!" cried the gruff sailor, as he ran his eye over the words, "we must seek for him at once. There are no less than five vessels beside my own waiting for him."

"Five!" echoed Harry.

"Yes," said Hugh Baldrick, "and they reckon the 'Owl' as six. You, of course, have not forgotten that my name is now Captain Moore?"

"Forgotten? Ha! ha!" Harry laughed. "Who could forget?—though, certainly it would be hard to remember all the changes that occur through life."

"But," he added, suddenly recollecting himself, "I must seek for the captain. I feel anxious for his safety."

"Not more anxious than I, my boy; but how are you going to dispose of these infernal frog-eaters?"

"Treat them as prisoners of war."

"Prisoners of war? Ha! ha!"

"Certainly; the clumsy fool threw himself in my way, and you see I have beat him."

"You have, and bravely, too. I suppose you will string them up now?"

"Not so harsh, Captain Baldrick, not so harsh," said Harry Vere, with a touch of feeling in his tone. "I must land them somewhere."

There was something in Harry's tone that made the captain regret what he had said.

"Take no notice of me, boy," he said, "it was but a joke, but whatever you intend doing, I would advise you to do at once; remember, there is no time to be lost."

There was truth in the remark, and Harry well knew it, and after consulting their plans, Hugh Baldrick repaired to his own ship, and Harry steered in for the land.

The place where the Frenchmen were put ashore happened to be the very spot where Captain Tom and Iron Arm had launched their raft on the previous evening; therefore, with the provisions Harry had given them, and the few articles of clothing he could spare, they soon made themselves comfortable.

CHAPTER LXXV.
THE FATE OF SKOPEY.

HAD Iron Arm been alone, he might have remained in the water till now, for his strength was fast leaving him, and the log still baffled all his endeavours to get upon it.

Tom saw the imminent danger of his friend, and, though still weak, he made a desperate effort to save him.

All his attempts failed, till at length he hit upon a scheme.

Laying flat on his belly, to keep the logs from parting, he clutched the fallen mast and laid it crosswise on the logs.

Then Iron Arm swam into an opening between two of the timbers, and, aided by the mast and the assistance of the captain, drew himself on to the raft.

By this time all traces of Skopey had disappeared in the darkness, and the two unfortunate adventurers lashed their raft together as best they could, and let it drift as it liked.

Fortunately the current set towards the point, and they soon had the satisfaction of hearing the raft grind on the beach.

Iron Arm was the first to land, and, supporting the captain on his arm, led him into a gulley formed between two rocks.

There was plenty of wood at hand, and, having lit a fire, so as to dry their saturated garments, Iron Arm seated himself on a crag and relapsed into a dreamy state of thought.

Captain Tom looked serious and thoughtful, but observing Iron Arm settle into his wonted gloom, he tried to cheer him.

"What, Iron Arm," he said, "in the doldrums again?"

The sound of his voice caused Iron Arm to start suddenly.

He sprang to his feet and clutched at his pistol.

"Treacherous miscreant!" he hissed between his clenched teeth, "the death of a traitor shall—"

He paused suddenly as his eye rested on Captain Tom.

"Pardon me," he said, "I was dreaming."

"So I should think," Tom replied.

"Yes, my heated fancy pictured the form of that black monster. Would to God it had been a reality!"

Captain Tom remained silent for a moment.

He was evidently struggling with his feelings.

Never till this night did he have occasion to doubt the black's fidelity.

Even now he could scarce believe in the reality of the fact.

"Iron Arm," he said, "be seated. I must have a word with you on this subject."

"Aye, as many as you like," replied the giant, huskily.

"Know you any reason for this deed of Skopey's?"

"None at all."

"'Tis strange."

"True; and our escape is stranger. But the villain shall not go unpunished. I have sworn it, and will not break my vow."

He started again to his feet, and paced the ground nervously.

Then turned his eye in the direction of the sea, on which the first grey streaks of morning began to throw its tints.

As he glanced around, a sudden exclamation burst from him.

Before Captain Tom could fully comprehend the cause, he bounded up the rocks and gained the summit of the cliff.

Captain Tom watched him, and when he saw him drop on all fours, and crawl along like a cat, he was lost in wonderment.

Presently he caught sight of a dark figure on the verge of the cliff.

That this was Skopey he had not the least doubt.

He saw Iron Arm approach him cautiously, and then rise suddenly and pounce upon him.

The treacherous villain cowered beneath the pair of fierce eyes that glared upon him, and winced with pain beneath the iron grasp.

For a moment, and only for a moment, did the giant give him time to think of his fate.

Raising him in his giant arms, he held him above his head, and, deaf to heartrending appeals for mercy, he hurled him from the terrible height into the frothy sea.

One wild shriek rang on the morning air—a dull splash was heard—and Skopey disappeared beneath the waves.

Iron Arm, with a look of grim triumph upon his massive face, still remained watching the spot where the treacherous black had disappeared.

"The bloodthirsty wretch will rise again," he muttered, and so he did.

Half suffocated from the dizzy height he fell, the black sank deep into the turbid waters.

It seemed an age before he arose to the surface, and when he did the cool sea air came refreshingly upon his brow.

He cast his bloodshot eyes upwards with a glance of wild supplicating agony to Iron Arm, whom he thought might relent and save him.

But no.

The gigantic follower of the gallant boy captain was lost to all feelings of compassion for one who had attempted the destruction of his beloved young chieftain.

Even had he wished to save the unhappy wretch he could not, and unable to look upon Skopey's distorted face, he turned and retraced his steps down the dangerous cliffs.

Skopey saw him go.

His heart sank within him—he was lost.

His coward heart could not stand the fearful reality that death stared him in the face.

He gave one wild shriek, and battled madly for his life against his mighty foe.

The water mocked his efforts; the gentle breeze seemed to howl past his ears like the screeching of so many fiends, and the water dashing against the reefs caused a confused noise terrible to his heated brain.

Vainly he strove to get upon the rocks.

He swam against them.

Grabbed at the jagged points.

Placed his feet upon the slimy surface of a hidden crag—stuck his knees upon other parts—but only to be hurled away—his limbs cut and bleeding, his hands torn to pieces, and his strength nearly exhausted.

His cry of terror became fainter — ever and anon stifled by his sinking beneath the waves—a gurgling yell being all that told of his whereabouts.

Terrible and appalling was his struggle for life. He was a strong man, and the fear of death lent him supernatural power.

Again and again he rose—each time he fought madly to get upon the reefs—once his hand grasped a projecting point.

How he clung to it! He uttered a quivering cry of joy.

"Saved!" flashed through his mind, as with distending nostrils, dilating eyes, and palpitating heart he drew himself out of the water.

Higher and higher he came.

His sore and bleeding feet rested upon a slippery stone beneath the ocean.

For a moment he paused; bad—heartless as he was, he could have wept with joy.

Wept—aye, bathed the rocks in tears—kissed its slimy surface, and worshipped the place that first gave him the means of escape.

Higher he went.

A long, projecting, pointed piece of the cliff, just above his head, attracted his attention; if he could get there it would be a resting-place for a few minutes, and then he might begin his difficult ascent.

The peak in question was very sharp and thin; evidently it had gradually crumbled away from its frequent soakings from salt water and exposure to the sun.

It was within the black's reach, and he had very little trouble in getting upon it.

Several pieces crumbled away and fell from his touch, but he at length sat across it with his face to the cliff, holding himself steady by clutching a little piece above it, that was only large enough for his two fingers and thumb.

He saw the fearful danger attending his ascent any higher; he had gone through the easiest part.

As he sat there, as he thought, free and saved, his good feelings quickly vanished, and his evil passions were welling up in his breast.

Already was he meditating the bitterest revenge against Iron Arm, and the destruction of Captain Tom.

Something like a smile of deep ferocity came upon his dusky face, and his white teeth gleamed like fangs.

He almost forgot his acute agony as he sat thus dreaming of his vengeance—the revenge to come.

"Dey shall suffer," he muttered. "Goramighty! dey shall all! all! Sanderson, too! Ha! ha! Cuss dem! I will hab a cupful of blood for every pang of agony I suffered. Cuss dem! How I would dabble in dere blood! Me could drink—suck it from the throat like um vampire. Ha! ha! No vampire shall equal Skopey when he hab him toes under his knife. Ah!"

He gave an exclamation of surprise, and a look of deadly terror came upon his blood-covered features.

Something crashed beneath him.

The slim fragment of stone had loosened.

How his blood froze when this thought came upon him. His hair rose, and his frame quivered.

The rocky point was giving way.

He glared upwards, and his fingers tightened upon the small bit he held.

Just as he had been thinking over his fiendish designs he was being hurled to destruction.

Making a frantic effort to save himself, he placed his toe in a little ridge, and raised himself from the breaking-point.

A yell of wild terror broke from his lips.

His foot slipped.

He came with a jerk upon the decayed crag.

Then came a crash.

The noise of the stones as they rattled down the cliff.

He clutched madly at the piece his hand held.

But in vain.

His fingers lost their hold.

A loud, deafening shriek, and he was again whirling through the air.

He fell upon a projecting point that nearly broke his legs.

His yells of agony were fearful, until he sank beneath the water, to rise once, and once only.

But how long those few seconds of submersion seemed to the dying wretch.

At one moment he clutched at what he thought was a floating spar, at another he fancied he was being rescued by a boat, and that he could feel the soft grasp of a gentle female sitting in the stern.

In imagination he could see the pitying eye and fancy conjured the features into those of Minnie.

But this delusion was not to last.

He came to the surface.

He could only keep his chin above water, and that for a few seconds.

His fate was obvious.

For the last minute he kept his eyes turned upwards, and his lips moved.

But not in prayer.

He breathed a bitter oath against the young captain and his slayer—Iron Arm—madly he called for vengeance, and his last sigh was a curse upon Sanderson, who had brought this upon him.

Thus he died.

Wicked to the end, and the expression of his dark form as it sank for the last time was such that if seen would never have been forgotten.

His life had been one of crime. He had been a heartless monster, living on without remorse or compassion, and his death had been fearful—without pity, without hope for life hereafter.

. . . .

Captain Tom rose painfully to his feet, as Iron Arm returned, and he glared inquiringly at his follower.

"What have you done?" he asked.

"A deed of justice," replied Iron Arm, firmly; "I have ridded the world of a cold-blooded wretch, to whom life was worthless."

The young chief turned moodily away.

"Come," said Iron Arm, "we cannot remain here to die, let us see what can be done."

"What hope have we?" asked the captain, gloomily.

"We have life," remarked Iron Arm, philosophically.

"Which, in the present circumstances, we may lose at any moment."

"Let us hope for the best. Hallo! what's this? Come, help me."

Iron Arm went to the edge of the reef, which was nearly level with the sea, and glanced curiously at two dark objects floating upon the foam-tipped water.

"A couple of the casks from our raft," he said. "We will haul them up."

And, without waiting for the assistance of the chief, he pulled them on shore.

"They will make seats, at least," he said, rolling them towards our hero, who was looking gloomily on.

"Now, captain," said the giant, taking a seat upon the cask nearest him, "can you advise any plan that would help us out of this?"

"None," replied the boy, sadly.

"I feared so."

"Can you?"

"Unhappily, no."

"Our position gets worse every hour."

"It does here."

"We cannot get away."

"Nor travel shoreward. I am certain we could not travel for half an hour over these rocky cliffs."

"I would not attempt it."

"Shall we venture on these casks, captain?"

"Useless, quite."

"Then we can do nothing."

"But remain here to die, or be rescued."

"We have got out of worse scrapes than this one," replied Iron Arm, "and Providence will, perhaps, get us out of this one."

"What will Ben Barnacle think? He must suppose we are dead."

"Perhaps they are looking for us now."

"Perhaps—aye, perhaps!"

"Why do you speak thus despondingly?"

"How can we tell what has occurred? The vessel went to action without my being there, and I dare say did not come out again."

"You have not a very good opinion of your lieutenant," said Iron Arm, with a slight touch of irony in his voice.

Captain Tom's face flushed. He thought his friend's words were a reproach for his unjust speech.

"I would give half my wealth to see 'Will-the-o'-the-Wisp' bearing down upon us."

"I would give all mine," replied Iron Arm.

"Fate has been against us lately."

"Nay—"

He did not finish the sentence, but set his eyes fixed on a star upon the horizon.

Captain Tom followed his gaze, and faintly sprang up with a cry.

He saw a distant speck, so small that it would have escaped the eye of any but a practised seaman.

"Hope!" he involuntarily murmured.

"It's a strange sail," remarked Iron Arm.

"Thank God!" murmured the gallant boy.

He stood watching it as it grew larger and larger, until the speck took the shape of a fine frigate.

He shouted lustily, and made every effort in his power to attract attention, but as yet the ship was too far off.

Iron Arm sat unmoved and apparently indifferent to the appearance of the sail, and he shook his head when the young chief uttered his useless cry.

The vessel came on, and at last Captain Tom, determined it should not go another way for the want of signalling, took a long silk tie, and starting forward, waved it in the breeze.

Iron Arm still watching intently how the huge sails flap in the breeze.

The ship's head turns.

She veered a little.

The sails refilled and she darted forward.

He leapt up with a cry of joy.

"Saved!" he cried; "we are seen—we are saved!"

CHAPTER LXXVL

HOW SANDERSON TRIED TO RID HIMSELF OF CAPTAIN ANGEL.

THE ruffian, Sanderson, and his guilty paramour stood in speechless horror, glaring upon the dreaded figure and rigid form of Captain Angel, who seemed to have come from the grave.

Jane Harpy went white as a corpse, and Sanderson's heart quaked in fear.

Of all he most dreaded, Captain Angel was the one.

He never faced that little, cold, determined man without a shudder, and the glitter in Angel's eye at this moment was enough to awe a bolder man than Sanderson.

"You've returned!" said Mrs. Harpy, mustering sufficient strength to speak.

"I have returned. You do not look happy for such a loving pair."

And Captain Angel indulged in his cold, mirthless laugh, which chilled the blood in his listener's veins.

"You did it, Charley Sanderson."

THE BEGINNING OF THE END.

The ruffian shuddered.

"Did what?" he asked, pretending not to understand.

"Don't understand, eh?"

"Not exactly."

"Ah!" Captain Angel took a few steps forward and stood in the centre of the room.

Sanderson and his vile associate retreated.

Angel smiled.

It was a pleasure to him to see his enemies thus fear him.

"It was a neat trick, that sending me on the Civet Cat, very; but I am not dead, you see."

"I—I—"

"Don't lie."

"But—I—I say—"

"Look you, Sanderson, don't lie. I've come back, which you didn't expect. You have been enjoying my property, while I have had to live on air and salt water; but, cuss you, you won't get off; no—there's a heavy reckoning to pay, Sanderson, and, by God! you shall pay it to the full. You can go, Jane, to your room until I come," he continued, to Mrs. Harpy, whose cheeks crimsoned with shame. "It's a long time since I've seen a charming woman but yourself, Jane, and will come and enjoy your pleasant company when I have settled with friend Sanderson."

Mrs. Harpy left the room, and Sanderson's face was flushed with anger at the words and look that accompanied them.

Sanderson was nerving himself a little, and

endeavouring to muster up sufficient courage to meet the attack of his dreaded foe, whatever it might be.

At first he had expected Angel to leap at his throat and strangle his life out, but now he was quite at a loss to understand his rescued associate.

Captain Angel was not a man who would let his intentions be known. His scheming brain had been work, and he was careful how he played his cards.

His thirst for revenge was quenchless—but rottling a man or putting a knife into him was not Angel's idea of revenge.

Moving towards the door with his stealthy, cat-like tread, he went to the door, fastened it, and taking a big chair, motioned Sanderson to do the same.

"Our wife, Sanderson, doesn't look well under your treatment. I don't think you love her very much. Eh?"

Sanderson winced, and his eye involuntarily wandered to the glass that held the fatal draught.

Slight as was the movement, Angel saw it, and could read it as plain as if the words had been written on the ruffian's forehead.

Not one eye-lash quivered, nor did he let his glance rest upon Sanderson or the glass.

"You are not hospitable, Sanderson," he said. "I am weary; a little wine would be refreshing."

Sanderson rose with averted face. In that instant a dark thought came to his mind.

He gave Captain Angel a glass of wine, filled from the decanter he had dropped the powder in.

Angel took it, held it up to the light, and then placed it to his lips.

Sanderson could scarcely keep his seat, and a perspiration oozed out upon his brow.

At the very moment he thought Angel would drink it, that individual put it down, and fixing his cold grey eye upon Sanderson, said—

"What is in the decanter you are drinking from?"

"Brandy."

"Then I'll have brandy."

Sanderson gave him brandy.

"You do not seem happy at seeing a friend return," he said.

"I never expected to see you again," replied Sanderson.

"Of course not. Pity that nice little trick failed, eh?" he said, tauntingly. "Pity, too, I didn't drink that glass of wine."

Sanderson went a ghastly hue. He was boiling with rage and fear, which at length got the better of his prudence, and jumping up, he cried, hoarsely—

"Look ye, Captain Angel, you have worked me enough. Don't go on with it, now I warn you. I did no more to you than you would have done to me, but I outwitted you—that you know."

"Very true," replied Angel, with provoking coolness. "Quite true; therefore, make your mind easy. I was merely caught in my own trap. Ha! ha! Capital! But now I've returned, you know, and want a little talk to arrange affairs, and so on What have you been doing lately? How do things go on? Come; sit down. Take your hand from that pistol-butt, and answer my questions. Hang it, man! you can't expect, after my miraculous escape, that I can want less than a little of my own."

The baffled villain took a seat, and glaring his confederate in the face, said—

"Let us understand each other, Captain Angel."

"Certainly."

"Let there be no underhanded work."

"Decidedly not. You would not be capable of it."

"Let me know your intentions. Do you mean treachery, or not?"

"Treachery! No."

"Well, if you do, say so. Let me know what I am to expect. If your spleen is up against me, and you intend driving a knife into me on the first occasion, say it, and do it openly; in fact, Captain Angel, let me know what your intentions are. Is it shares, or foes to the death?"

Angel was a little taken aback at this.

"Candid," he said, at length. "So will I be, I don't know about friends or foes. Your own judgment ought to tell you that. But I want, as you say, no treachery. You came back, and, much as you may dislike it, I want to know how things have been going on, and how we stand. Mind you don't try to cheat me, for if I find you have deceived me in one thing I will bring you to the gallows. Now, mark me."

Seeing it would be safest to comply with Angel's demands, Sanderson reluctantly told him what had taken place between Mrs. Harpy and poor old John Gregory, and mentioned the document which placed everything in Sanderson's power.

Once or twice the villain thought he could defy Captain Angel with it, but he knew that gentleman would very soon walk off on being opposed, and divulge the whole base plot to the law.

Angel chuckled with glee.

"Let me see that document, Sanderson."

Sanderson produced it.

"Very good. Pity he didn't know I was coming back. It would have saved me the trouble of erasing your name to put mine there."

Sanderson stood open-mouthed.

"You need not be afraid," continued Angel, tauntingly. "I shall serve you very fairly. For instance, you shall have the left wing of the hall to yourself, and a thousand a year. About Jane—well, I think you may take her; her charms are not so many."

Sanderson felt inclined to leap upon his mocking foe. It was with difficulty he restrained himself, and said—

"What mean you, Captain Angel? Think you I will put up with this? Never!"

"Well, my dear Sanderson, I do not ask you to. Don't take any. I won't press you."

"Curse you!" muttered Sanderson.

"And I am sure you need not remain here."

"I tell you, Angel, I will never submit to this."

"Don't."

"Do you think I will let the whole of these estates be taken from me thus—this that I have toiled for so long—this I have gone to my neck in sin for. Ha! ha!—you must be mad; do you think I will agree to have the paltry sum?"

"Can you get more?"

Sanderson ground his teeth in suppressed fury, and his nails were dug into his flesh.

He turned his face, which was a livid hue, upon Angel, and cried, hoarsely—

"If it comes to that I would sooner we should end the dispute—now—now, and let it be none or all—"

"For the conqueror?"

"Yes, taunting devil, yes."

"Very well."

Angel drew a long, slender-barrelled pistol from his belt, and rose from his chair.

"Where shall we go, there is plenty of ground outside?"

Sanderson gazed upon him frantically.

He had not courage to face him with the deadly weapons.

"This man is a fiend in human form," he muttered, "sent against me to drive me on to destruction."

And he paced the chamber excitedly. Angel watched him with a cruel smile.

"Ah!" he muttered, "I will make you shed tears of blood before I have done, and curse the hour you were born."

Aloud he said—

"I am weary, 'tis long since I have enjoyed the luxury of a good bed and a hearty meal; I will take the rest first, my strength is nearly gone ; you can think over what I have said, friend Sanderson, and give me your answer in the morning." He strode towards the door, folding the document and placing it in his breast. "Don't forget—a thousand a year and the left wing, or a trial and the gallows ; good-night."

With a mocking laugh he closed the door and was gone. Sanderson had watched him in a state of frenzy. He knew it would be like extricating the talons of a wild cat to attempt to get the document from Angel.

The captain prowled along the corridor until a faint light gleamed through the crack of a door ajar ; he peeped in.

It was Mrs. Harpy who sat within.

Her head resting upon her breast, her arms folded, and her whole appearance told she was completely lost in a reverie.

With his familiar noiseless tread, Angel entered, and stood beside her.

Then she was not aware of his presence.

"Jane !"

She started with a cry of fright. His voice had gone like a cold chill through her heart. She rose hastily, and made a stride towards the door.

. . . .

For hours did Sanderson pace the room after the departure of Angel. He was deep in thought.

He saw all his hopes about to be blasted, his wealth scattered to the wind.

Dark thoughts flashed through his brain, but they were useless. He feared Angel too much to attempt treachery.

He would give half what he possessed to have seen Captain Angel's lifeless corpse at his feet.

He thought once of poisoning all the food, but then the servants, and perhaps himself, might fall victims to it.

Captain Angel, too, would notice the slightest alteration in him, and his suspicions were easily aroused.

Suddenly he thought of Mrs. Harpy.

Where was she all this time ?

He glanced at the clock.

He was surprised to see that it was some hours since Angel had departed.

"Does she not know he has gone ?" he thought, then another idea flashed through his brain, and he clenched his hands until the nails entered his flesh. He wanted the crafty woman's council.

Unable to bear the suspense of his terrible thoughts, he was about to go in search of her, when she came quickly along the hall, and in at the door.

Her eyes were fierce in the cold glitter, and her hands were clenched tightly. At that moment she made a very fine Lady Macbeth.

"Why are you here, Jane ?"

"John !" she replied, with a visible shudder ; "do you intend to let him in peaceably, then ?" she said, and stretching her hand in the direction of the room in which Captain Angel slept, "are we to be turned out of this ?"

"Never, Jane ; but what is to be done ?"

"Done !" she replied, waving the candle she held about until it nearly went out, "done ! ask yourself."

"I have been doing so, Jane ; but can find no way of ridding myself of him."

"Are you a coward, then, that you speak thus .

"I am not."

"Would you throw away an opportunity ?"

"No !"

Then she replied in a hoarse whisper, and her ey perfectly blazing, as she held before his eyes a long dagger—

"Go—take this—he sleeps—he is overcome and exhausted ; it would take much to wake him. I stole from the room—the door is open—go !"

Sanderson stood deathly pale, and trembling in every limb.

"But—"

"Art thou a craven ?" she said, again. "That's the way, the door is open, and his heart is unshielded. Can you want more ? Make sure with this, the blade is long ; take your aim that he may not cry out."

"You know not, Jane, the fiend he is ; he would wake before I could accomplish the deed, and—"

"You fear a sleeping man," she cried, in scorn.

"I fear Captain Angel asleep more than two other men awake."

"You will not do it, craven ? Let this opportunity slip by, and this time next week all that you now possess will be wrested from you, and he will end by stretching your neck on the gallows. Go ! I say ; 'tis but a stroke of this knife. Mark me, if you do not, he will to you some time."

Partly from shame, and partly from a desire for revenge, Sanderson took the knife.

Mrs. Harpy's words of scorn stung him to the quick, and gripping the murderous weapon with one vicious grasp, he stole up the corridor and ascended a flight of stairs.

Mrs. Harpy followed, carrying the light.

Never had a look so truly demoniacal been upon her face before, and Sanderson felt slightly awed in her presence.

He paused outside Captain Angel's sleeping-room door.

Mrs. Harpy brushed past him, and throwing it wide open, pointed to the sleeping form.

Then she said to him in a low whisper, "There lies the man that holds you in his grasp, and your life oo."

Goaded on by these words, and by the sight of his sleeping foe, Sanderson stole in and stared on his slumbering enemy.

Even in sleep there was something menacing in the look of Angel's face to Sanderson as he paused in the fell act.

But the voice of Jane Harpy again roused him—for a second time the knife was raised.

Captain Angel made a slight movement, and his form became perfectly rigid.

"I can't," said Sanderson, stepping back. The coward even feared to strike his enemy in his sleep.

With a look of deep scorn, Jane Harpy said—

"Miserable craven—back !"

Snatching the dagger from his hand, she gave him the light.

Her fingers tightened upon the hilt of the murderous weapon, and turning up the sleeve of her robe to the shoulder she stared on Angel.

It is impossible to describe the fiendish look upon her face.

"Now," she muttered, "will I avenge my shame !"

The long, glittering blade gleamed in the air and swiftly descended.

There was a deep groan of mortal agony !

A cry !

And Jane Harpy retired with a smile of fiendish triumph.

CHAPTER LXXVII.

A FATAL DISCOVERY.

THE strange sail sighted by Iron Arm and the young captain bore down for the rocky point with all possible speed.

They had evidently been seen, and to keep them on the right track Iron Arm rose too, and waved his sash on high.

Every minute seemed an hour to them, until the vessel was near enough for them to discover the figures on deck.

A gun was fired as a signal to tell the castaways they were seen.

"I wish he would hoist his flag," said Iron Arm.

"I, too."

"She's a first-class frigate."

"Yes."

"And, if I am not mistaken, an Englishman."

"I fancy so, too. Still, we must get off here, whether friend or foe."

"Truly—ah! I thought so."

This exclamation from the giant was caused by seeing the flag of Great Britain run up to the masthead.

"As I thought," said Captain Tom.

"We shall have to be careful."

"Why?"

"Are they not our most dreaded foes?"

"True, but how are they to know us?"

Iron Arm pointed with a grim smile to the young captain's handsome dress, and glanced at his own picturesque costume.

"Shall we cast them off?" said the captain.

"I would, if it was any use; but it will avail us nothing."

"How?"

"The questions we shall have to answer will tell the tale."

"Still, I think it would be as well to go on board without our coats until we have recovered our strength. At the present moment I could not hold out ten minutes if they meant mischief."

Iron Arm saw what the young chief said was perfectly true, and therefore did as Captain Tom did—

Divested himself of coat and sash, which they made up into a bundle and placed near their feet.

By this time a boat had been put off, and was rapidly approaching the rocky shore.

The officer in command tried all he could to come within reach of the shipwrecked men.

But in vain.

Seeing all attempts to touch the shore, or go within forty yards of it, were useless, he stood up in the stern-sheets, and taking a speaking-trumpet shouted out—

"Are you right?"

"Yes," replied Iron Arm, in his stentorian voice.

"The sound of that voice is quite enough to prove that," smiled the lieutenant to himself.

"I cannot get any closer, unless you know any safe creek."

"Do not trust it, lieutenant," shouted Iron Arm again.

"What will you do, then?"

"Jump for it."

"Bravely said," muttered the officer. "All right —we will look after you. Make haste."

"We must swim for it," said Iron Arm.

"We can do that," replied the bold young chieftain.

Iron Arm hurled the bundle of clothes to the sailors in the boat. The man-of-war's men gave a slight cheer.

"That were a good chuck, mate," said one.

"Aye, aye, and a strong arm that sent it this distance."

"Silence!" said the officer, who was earnestly watching Captain Tom and his gigantic follower.

The young chief had gone on the most projecting peak, and taken a terrific leap into the sea.

Iron Arm followed.

In less than ten minutes they were hauled into the boat, and the sailors, with their characteristic willingness, rowed back with all possible speed.

The lieutenant eyed the handsome young chief curiously, and felt he was no common individual but, seeing the men were fatigued, he refrained from asking any questions.

On board, that day, there had been a serious disaster. Two of the seamen had quarrelled up aloft, and one, in a fury of passion, hurled the other to the deck.

Nevertheless, all the ship's crew were grouped at the vessel's side to get a glimpse of the castaways as they were hauled on board.

The captain, a fine old fellow, who had grown grey in the service, stood on the quarter-deck, and regarded the young chief, whom he took for a handsome youthful passenger, with a look of paternal kindness.

"Pretend to be faint," whispered Iron Arm, "we will not answer any questions yet."

"Very well."

"Have you been there long?" asked the captain, mildly.

"'Tis nearly a week since we were cast upon the island," replied Iron Arm, with feigned faintness.

"Poor fellows," mentally observed the kind old commander; "you are not common sailors?"

"Not exactly," replied Iron Arm, with a faint smile.

"I thought so. Well, go below, take rest and refreshment, and when you are strong enough I will take your statements."

"A thousand thanks, sir," replied Iron Arm, and they went below to a spare berth which was allotted to them.

Refreshments were brought them, and then they were left to themselves.

Captain Tom scarcely tasted his food, but, throwing himself on the bed, soon fell fast asleep.

Iron Arm, knowing the necessity for rest, did the same, but not until he had fastened the door.

"I do not want to be taken in our sleep," he thought.

His was a wise precaution, as the reader will see.

Among the boat's crew who went to get the shipwrecked buccaneers was a midshipman, who took great care of the bundle thrown into the boat by Iron Arm.

He was a good-hearted boy, and no sooner got on board than he ran below to his berth.

"I'll undo this," he said to himself; "the poor fellows may want the things, and they feel awfully wet."

He was in the act of untying the bundle when he was summoned on deck to his duty.

Muttering something about being bored at that moment, he hastened on deck, and, to his chagrin, was kept there for some hours.

When at last he was allowed to leave the deck, he again darted below, and very busily pulled the parcel to pieces, and shook out the wet and creased clothes of the young captain.

Suddenly he paused, with a look of blank astonishment on his face.

"I say, Sam!" he called, to a brother mid.

"Hallo!" replied a voice from a hammock.

"Come here."

"What's up?"

"Come and see," yelled the youngster, holding the loose jacket of Captain Tom by the shoulders, and staring at a device upon the sleeve.

"Well," said Sam, coming up yawning, "what were you bawling about?"

"Look here."

"Where?"

"On this sleeve."

"What's the matter with it?"

"Look, you blockhead, and see," replied the mid, getting in what he termed "a wax."

"Well, what of it?"

"What of it?"

"Yes."

"Don't you see that device on the sleeve?"

"Of course I do," responded Sam, scratching his head.

"If you were not so sleepy, you would see what I mean. Does it not strike you there is something peculiar about this jacket altogether?"

"It hasn't struck me at all yet."

"You are a fool, Sam."

"That's through keeping your company, Ned."

Ned felt inclined to give his companion a wipe across the mouth with the wet jacket.

"It's a pity you can't come up like a rational being when one calls you."

"Who's he?"

"Who?"

"The rattling being?"

Ned turned up his nose in extreme disgust, and put down the jacket.

"You are an ass, Sam, to go on like this, when I have made a discovery."

"Eh, what? Discovery—when?" asked Sam, eagerly.

"Don't you know those two fellows we picked up?"

"I think I heard something about it."

"Dare say you were asleep, as usual, and I got called up to do your duty."

"Never mind about that—go on about the fellows."

"Why, this is a bundle belonging to them, and look at those jackets—I'll swear they belong to some corsair, pirate, or smuggler."

Sam took up the coats, and examined them.

"So they do," he said; "but I thought one was a young gentleman."

"So he is, but I'll vow that's his jacket; and if so, there is but one person with such a face and form as his."

"And he—"

"Is Captain Tom."

Sam emitted a wry whistle, dropped the coat, put his hands in his pockets, and with a serio-comic look at his companion, said—

"Ah! so help me never! Who'd a thought it? What are you going to do?"

"Tell the luff."

"Hurrah! Of course; here's a spree!" and with that he darted up the gangway.

The lieutenant came down instantly upon hearing the boy's story, and examined the clothes.

For a few minutes the lower deck was crowded with the officers, the news had gone through the vessel like wildfire, and every man on board was anxious to catch a glimpse of the famous buccaneer's clothes.

The lieutenant ordered them to be taken before the captain.

"We shall have some fun," yelled Sam, leaping over a gun-carriage.

"So it appears," replied Ned, as the other's heel slipped, and he rolled on his back.

"I've broken my spine, I verily believe."

"I'm sure it would be a blessing."

"Spiteful brute."

"But I say, Sam, supposing they ain't the buccaneers after all, and only just the clothes?"

"If they ain't, they must be other pirates, or thieves."

"Thieves!"

"Yes. What business have they with other people's clothes? I suppose you expect promotion for this discovery, should it be Captain Tom?"

"I don't expect anything, nor do I wish to be the cause of a fellow-creature's death, whether he be a buccaneer or not," and with that the boy went on deck.

Had he looked at the door of the berth in which Iron Arm and the young chief slept, he would have seen the former's brilliant eye glaring out upon them.

Unable to sleep, the giant had remained in a drowsy state, when he heard the communication caused by the unfortunate discovery.

He cursed the boy's meddling fingers most bitterly, but when, by the little fellow's talk, he found it was done out of sheer kindness, he could but curse his own forgetfulness for having left them.

He awoke the sleeping captain.

At the first touch of his fingers the boy leaped to his feet.

"Danger?" he said, half asleep.

"Aye, captain, danger caused by my neglect."

"What is it?" asked Captain Tom, perfectly awake now.

Iron Arm told him all that had taken place.

"Unfortunate occurrence," he replied.

"Very! I wish we had left the clothes on shore."

"And I, too."

"But what is to be done? You may rely upon it, we shall be summoned before the commander presently."

"That is certain."

"Shall we disown the clothes?"

"I do not like the idea," replied Captain Tom.

"What can be done, then?"

"Wait the course of events, and act as circumstances may dictate."

"I think that is our only plan."

It was now evening, and the ship was being shrouded in darkness.

They were interrupted in their conversation by the entrance of the lieutenant.

He put a few questions to them respecting the morning, and so on, and asked them if they thought their strength would have sufficiently returned to be examined in the morning.

Iron Arm answered in the affirmative.

The lieutenant retired.

The night drew on, and the two adventurers sat ruminating over their dangerous situation.

"If it comes to the worst, we can but fight," said the brave boy, glancing round upon a pair of officers' swords that were hung upon the cabin wall.

"We—"

"Hush!" said Iron Arm, as a light step was heard outside the door.

Then came a quiet rap.

Iron Arm stepped forward and opened the door a little way.

"Let me in," said a boyish voice.

The door opened a little wider.

A small form darted into the cabin.

Iron Arm recognised the young middy who had made the discovery.

"Your business?" said Iron Arm, sturdily.

The boy raised his finger for silence.

"I don't know," he replied, in a calm voice, "who you are; but if you are he whom the commander suspects you are, your lives are not worth much."

"Is that all you have come to tell us?" Captain Tom said, angrily.

"No, sir. I came to warn you. It was through an indiscreet act of mine—though, goodness knows, I meant only kindness—that your clothes were seen;

and now, seeing the mischief I have done in endangering a fellow-creature's life, I came to put you on your guard. You will be examined at daybreak, and if you cannot clear yourselves from this, you both will be put in irons. Promise me that if the worst should happen, and I give you arms, you will not use them against the commander, who is one of the kindest men on earth, or the officers. Do you promise?"

"I promise not to use arms until our lives are actually menaced, and then they will only be in defence."

"Take them, then."

From underneath his coat he took two pairs of pistols, which he gave to Iron Arm.

"Keep your promise," he said, "and forget my indiscretion." With that the brave boy opened the door, and slipped out.

"Noble lad!" said Captain Tom.

* * * * * * *

As the first morning watch was set, an officer came and summoned Captain Tom to go before the commander of the frigate.

The grey-haired captain was in the state-cabin with his chief officers around him.

Captain Tom's quick eyes detected a company of marines near the entrance.

The commander bowed lowly in answer to their salute.

"It is necessary," he said, "I should have your statement."

Captain Tom bowed.

"Firstly. What are you? Naval gentlemen?"

"Captain and officer," replied Iron Arm, readily.

"How long is it since you were wrecked?"

"A week."

"The name of your vessel?"

Iron Arm started, and, for an instant, could not reply. At length he said—

"The Ocean Witch."

"And your name?"

"Captain Atherten."

"I have no wish to doubt you," replied the old commander, kindly, "but your dress is that of men not in his Majesty's navy. Perhaps you can explain this?"

He waved his hand.

An officer displayed the jackets.

"You know them?"

"They are ours," replied Captain Tom, with a flush of pride.

The officers exchanged looks.

"Ah! you admit the clothes are yours?"

"Yes."

"Then you are not in his Majesty's navy?"

"No."

"And, of course, not in the merchant service."

"No."

"Then, who are you?"

"Captain Tom!" cried the young chief, folding his arms proudly.

"Rash boy!" muttered Iron Arm.

There was a slight commotion among the officers, and the commander looked surprised.

"You are bold," he said.

"I am Captain Tom," was the reply.

"You must be put under arrest, and I hope you will surrender quietly, as I should be very sorry to have recourse to extreme measures."

"I surrender!—to be put in chains!" cried the young chief, hotly. "I?—never! He who wants me must take me!" And, with a spring, he was upon one of the officers, and snatched his sword from its scabbard.

Iron Arm drew his pistols.

The officers drew their arms, and crowded round the gallant pair.

"Back!" said the commander. "Marines—ahoy!"

He struck the table with his sword hilt, and the next instant a party of marines rushed in with loaded muskets and bayonets fixed.

"Surrender!" cried the commander.

"Never!" shouted Captain Tom, leaping amongst them.

Iron Arm was with him.

The giant hurled the foes away on all sides, and cleared a path for his young chief.

"Form in front!" cried the officer of marines, seeing the buccaneers would get on deck.

"Give in."

Captain Tom's only answer was to cut right and left, and Iron Arm took the nearest man in his powerful arms to hurl at the officer, when the commander said—

"'Tis their fault. We must take them dead or alive. Fire!"

CHAPTER LXXVIII.

THE FATAL DOSE.

THE doctor of the private asylum in which poor old John Gregory was confined, sat thoughtfully in his chair after the departure of Sanderson and his accuser.

Long did this man of science remain absorbed in deep thought, with an ever-changing look upon his countenance.

"If he dies," he muttered, at length. "Ha! ha! Yes, my fine pair, if he dies; he shall, if it's only to please you."

He indulged in a momentary chuckle, but it passed instantly, and he became grave as before.

"I have a drug of my own discovery," he went on cogitating, "that might do what I want. Yes, it shall be done, by Heaven!"

Pausing, he unlocked a small cupboard, from which he took several small bottles, all labelled in Latin. With great care he examined all the inscriptions on them, and, after some few minutes, selected a long thin phial.

"This will do," he mentally observed, re-locking the cupboard and returning to his chair.

"I must see him," he went on; "my measures must be well taken."

Putting the phial in his pocket, he proceeded to the prison of old Gregory.

The poor old fellow saluted him with a bow.

He was thinking of his estates being in the power of that villain Sanderson. In spite of himself, a dread feeling of impending evil came over him, and he felt all was not safe concerning that document, and he blamed himself for being gulled into signing it

But regret was now too late.

Supposing, after all, Mrs. Harpy had led him into a snare? The thought made him groan aloud.

The doctor, who entered as he gave thus evident signs of his mental anguish, glared at him pityingly, and said just loud enough for Gregory to hear—

"Poor old fellow; he is much worse."

"Worse! Yes, I am worse!" said John Gregory, excitedly, "and who made me so?"

Doctor Burchenell kept his unflinching gaze upon the poor old fellow, and his look went from pity to sorrow.

"It's too bad," he again muttered, "to think a fine old fellow like this should be so dreadfully insane."

Gregory seemed as though he would leap at the doctor's throat.

"Go!" he cried, vehemently, "go! I am not mad, and you know it. Go! I say. If I am to stand this fearful torture, let me be alone. Do not come to mock me."

Burchenell put on a look of extreme astonishment. He was playing his part well.

"Good heavens! those words were spoken like anyone sane."

Like the rest, the doctor said this part loud enough for John Gregory to hear.

The poor old fellow's heart leaped with joy.

He could at that moment have thrown himself upon the doctor's neck, and implored him to listen to his story.

"Doctor, for God's sake, believe what I say—I am sane—aye! my faculties are as clear as your own, though, God knows how long I shall remain so under this torture."

"Come, come, you must not excite yourself," said Doctor Burchenell, kindly.

"'Tis you who excite me."

"Hush!"

"If you want to quiet me, listen to what I have to say. For Heaven's sake, take pity on me."

"Would that I dared believe you," said the doctor, half aloud.

John Gregory glared at him beseechingly, his eyes filled with tears that were welling up from his own stout heart.

One step he took forward, and then fell upon his knees before the doctor. His pleading look and two dimmed eyes touched Burchenell's heart, and his lips quivered slightly as the old man said, in a grief-stricken tone—

"Doctor, I pray you listen to me. If I was ever a little mad, my senses were driven from me by the dreadful tortures I have had to suffer. Look upon me now, and see if I am anything like the John Gregory of late. Listen, doctor. I am not insane—these are not madly spoken words. Give me a book. I will read you a page. Ask me anything, and I will answer."

"My God!" cried Burchenell. "Can it be possible that you are sane, and have been duped? God pardon the doers of this evil, if such be the case," he cried, with well-feigned surprise and rage.

John Gregory leaped to his feet.

"God in Heaven bless you, doctor! Then you, at least, believe me?"

"Yes—yes," said the doctor, evidently much touched.

Gregory clasped his hands with a passionate burst of joy.

Fixing his eyes upon him for a minute, Dr. Burchenell became absorbed in thought.

Suddenly, breaking from his reverie, he put several questions to Gregory, who replied to them in that quiet manner none but a sane man could.

At length the doctor took his hand, and said—

"God be praised that I have discovered the way in which I have been duped. You shall no longer suffer, Mr. Gregory. Tell—how long have you been thus?"

"How long?—always."

"And to think I have been duped—"

"You will let me go?"

"Mr. Gregory, you certainly must be insane to speak thus. Your life would not be safe an hour, were you to go amongst those bloodthirsty pack of wolves. No, no—we must deal with them differently. I will do all I can to make you comfortable; but, firstly, do you want anything?"

"No, sir."

Poor old fellow, he was too overjoyed to eat or drink.

"Then tell me what has passed between you and your visitors. Do you know the last who came?"

"Yes. Jane Harpy."

"Her mission?"

"To get me to sign a document that would put my estates in the power of Sanderson."

"And did you comply with the demands?"

"I did."

"You did?"

"Yes."

"Impossible!"

"I did, but under very ~~strange circumstances~~."

"Explain."

"I will."

He then related to the doctor why he signed the document brought by Mrs. Harpy. Burchenell listened attentively to the old fellow.

"I fear, Mr. Gregory, you have been the victim of some base scheme."

"God of Heaven, I hope not!"

"I fear such is the case."

John Gregory placed his hand to his heated brow, striving vainly to still its violent throbbings.

"Come!" said the doctor, kindly. "We must thwart the villains somehow; but you are excited. Retire to your bed. I will have sent up whatever you may wish, and you must remain calm, as I have a great deal to say."

Gregory felt weakened from his late excitement, and, yielding to the doctor's advice, he retired.

Burchenell left him for a few minutes. When he returned, Gregory was in bed, looking pale and exhausted.

"I think we had better postpone our interview until to-morrow," the doctor said.

"No! no! for God's sake, speak! Ease my mind at once," faintly answered John Gregory.

The doctor took a seat by the bedside, and after a few minutes' reflection, began—

"When the scoundrel Sanderson, with his other accomplice, left me to-day—"

"Who? Sanderson!" cried Gregory, jumping up nearly out of his bed.

"Yes, Sanderson."

"Then Heaven help me!" murmured the old man, falling back upon his pillow. "I am lost. I have been duped."

"As I thought," replied the doctor; "but listen to me."

"Proceed!" gasped Gregory, faintly.

"Before they departed," continued Burchenell, "they threw out many dark hints to me concerning your deplorable state, and how much better it would be were you to leave this world of troubles altogether."

"Curse them! I daresay."

"Well, the scoundrel went so far as to offer me a heavy amount of money to—in plain words—murder you."

Old Gregory ground his teeth, and glared at the doctor savagely.

"You may be sure I did not reply, but simply bowed them out. When they were gone, I sat and thought over the cold-blooded proposal, and naturally my thoughts—"

The doctor paused, and glared at John Gregory in amazement.

The old fellow seemed nearly choking, his face was purple, his eyes starting, and a foam round his mouth, he wriggled about in his bed, and made several attempts to speak.

"What is the matter, my dear sir?"

"The—the matter?" yelled Gregory, at last mastering his stifling fury enough to speak. "Matter, curse you—curse them—curse you all! Let me out, let me wreak my vengeance upon the scoundrel. Will you let me out?"

And he leaped from his bed.

"I see it all; ha! ha! Verily I have been duped by that snake in woman's form—you are a lot of plotters, and want to murder me. Why don't you do it at once; but you shan't, no—it is through you my estates are gone, all—all—taken from me—then you, with a sneaking face, come, offering some base proposals! But I know you—curse you all!"

"He has really gone mad."

"Has he?—let me out, I say!"

"Return to your bed, Mr. Gregory."

"Let me out!"

"Do not compel me to use force."

"Force!" howled John Gregory, dancing about like a madman. "Will you let me out?"

"No!"

Gregory gave a yell, and sprang at the doctor's throat.

Burchenell expected this, and was prepared, but in spite of his preparations he found Gregory's fingers were clenching him pretty tight round the throat.

Doctor Burchenell struggled fiercely to release himself; it was wonderful to see the strength he had, but John Gregory had as much from his almost mad frenzy.

The struggle lasted for some minutes; and in all probability Burchenell would have suffered had not the old fellow fainted from sheer exhaustion.

The doctor, finding himself released shook himself a little, and then glanced with a pale, stern face at his fallen assailant.

"That was unexpected and dangerous," he muttered, leaving the room to summon assistance, and, returning with one of his men, he had old Gregory placed on his bed, and then left the room to return to his own private apartment, where he could remain undisturbed.

There was a strange calmness about him since the struggle he had with John Gregory, and his lips moved constantly, as though he was carrying on a mental conversation.

He, ever and anon, fell into deep fits of abstraction, and he was evidently planning some great undertaking; at length he arrived at what he wished, and, then rising, he again took the phial from his pocket; after holding it up to the light for some minutes, he entered his laboratory, and was soon at work over his chemicals.

Night drew on, and still he was at his work, in which his whole mind was completely absorbed.

When at length the huge clock in the private asylum struck eleven he started.

"So late!" he muttered. "I must begin, or my plans will fail." Depositing the phial he had kept in his pocket all day in his breast, he left his study, and went to the room in which John Gregory lay asleep.

Softly as a cat he trod, until he stood by the invalid's bedside. Bending his ear that he might the better hear the breathings of the old man; he placed a tiny scent-bottle to Gregory's nostrils.

A slight convulsive shudder passed through his frame, and the poor old fellow slept more soundly than ever.

"That is well," the doctor muttered. "He will not wake under my operations."

With such care that he rarely used, the doctor examined John Gregory; felt his pulse, listened to his breathings, counted the pulsations of his heart, sounded his chest, and performed several other medical practices to discover the state of his patient.

He paused at length, and in silence regarded the pale, pain-distorted face of John Gregory.

His own was particularly pale, and his lips firmly closed; his eyes were strangely brilliant, which added to his look of cool firmness.

The phial he had taken such infinite care of was again produced, and he stood over Gregory with it in one hand, and the other upon his brow.

"It must be done," he muttered; "now is the time."

With a silver spoon he gently opened Gregory's shut teeth, and poured into his mouth several drops of the contents of the phial.

Then he stood watching the effect.

Not a muscle of his face moved.

His hand was firm and steady, his face calm and rigid.

While he stood thus, a rapid change came over John Gregory. The slight feverish flush left his cheeks; his lips went pale, and his hands worked nervously; indeed so did his whole frame, as though he was vainly striving to master some terrible form that was standing over him.

Each moment his struggles became worse, until he shook the bed in his violent movements.

Eventually he tried to speak, but no sound, save a slight gurgling left his throat.

So terrible in his struggles he became that at length Dr. Burchenell was compelled to hold him down.

He did so, still unmoved, though the scene would have unnerved many men.

Long this fearful scene lasted, and once Dr. Burchenell turned away his head, sick at heart.

As the clock struck twelve, Gregory's struggles ended, and he lay back pale and ghastly as the dead.

His eyes were fixed in a glassy stare upon the wall, and the doctor took his thumb and gently closed the eyelids.

"At last," he muttered, with a sigh. "I will go now, and say the deed is done."

Giving one last glance at the pale, deathly form, he left the room, securely locking the door, and taking the key with him.

When he reached his sitting-room he paused for a few minutes.

"I cannot go to-night," he cogitated. "Past midnight!"

He seemed vexed at this, but, knowing regret was useless, he determined to go the first thing in the morning.

"Ha! ha!" he continued, cogitating, "I wonder what Sanderson will say. He did not expect the work done so quickly. I must be careful, and be on my guard. So he has the document! Well, well! I must get that. Ha! ha! Sanderson, we will go shares. But I must not say it is done; no, I will promise to show Gregory's body, cold and stiff, in twenty-four hours, if he will come to my terms. Ah! I had forgotten; the undertaker must be consulted at once."

Doctor Burchenell instantly donned his cloak and hat, and putting a pair of pistols in his pockets, he quietly left the asylum.

He had to go across a nasty, dreary country; but he did not mind that—the darkness was the only thing that caused him any trouble, as he could not get along.

Iron-nerved as he was, a slight feeling of uneasiness came upon him, and every minute he thought he saw something.

Presently he started—drew back—and hid behind the trunk of a tree.

He could have sworn he saw a dark shadow before him, and that someone was near.

He knew very well that none but desperadoes would be out at that time of night, and his life was in danger.

He started, suddenly, with a cry.

Something touched his leg.

"Ah!" he muttered. "Someone creeping upon me from the ground! Leave go—leave go! I say, sir!"

He drew a pistol as he said this.

All was silent.

"I shall not challenge you again. Who is it?"

No answer.

Another twitch at his leg.

"Leave go! Your blood be upon your own head, then!"

He pointed his pistol upon the ground, and fired.

The loud report awoke the stillness of the night, and the lurid flash showed a huddled mass at his feet.

CHAPTER LXXIX.

THE PHANTOM.

Mrs. Harpy's cry was more like the screech of a maniac than anything else, as she stepped back after plunging the knife in Captain Angel.

Sanderson shrank back with a gasp of horror at the fearful appearance of Captain Angel, who drew the reeking blade from his body, and, by a mighty effort, slipped from his bed.

The deathly, but cruel, revengeful gleam in his eyes was appalling. His teeth were firmly locked, and the blood poured from the wound in his side.

"Fiend!" he cried, "you have done it. But even in my last death-throes I will have revenge!"

Mrs. Harpy laughed wildly, and while he madly thrust at Sanderson she flew upon him like a wild cat.

The knife was wrested from his grasp.

Again it was driven into his side.

With a scream of mortal agony, he fell backwards upon his bed. Mrs. Harpy glared triumphantly upon him, while her fingers played with the gory handle of the murderous blade.

Three times did Captain Angel's eyes open and close, but each time cast a glance upon his murderess that sent her blood like ice through her veins.

He gave a gurgling sob, and, by a great effort, spoke.

"My curses be upon you! Remember! Living or dead, I will be the curse to your lives! Remember!"

His eyes closed, and the blood gushed forth. Then his eye-lids re-opened, his look of inveterate hate was fixed upon them, and he was lifeless.

"'Tis done!" said Mrs. Harpy, in a hoarse whisper.

Sanderson could not reply, but stood shaking from head to foot.

"Art thou still craven-hearted?" cried Jane Harpy, clutching his shoulder with her blood-stained hand, and gazing into his face with her horrible, starting eyes. "He must be removed. Now, would you have us discovered?"

"What can we do?"

"The north wing has chambers that no one ever enters. Shall it be there?"

"It must," said Sanderson, nerving himself a little, and lingering to exult over the thought of being ridded of his foe for ever.

"To work, idler—nor fear not!" said the hoarse voice of Mrs. Harpy.

They shut themselves in while they commenced operations, which consisted of stripping a sheet from the bed, and wrapping the bloody form of Captain Angel in it.

"Those stains?" said Sanderson, pointing to the blood-stains on the floor.

"I will remove myself," replied Mrs. Harpy.

For fear of being seen, they left the light in the room, and conveyed the form of Captain Angel in the dark to a suite of apartments which had long since been disused.

They stole away, neither daring to breathe for fear of being heard.

Sanderson's flesh crept at every little sound he heard, and more than once he felt inclined to remain in fear.

At length they reached the apartment, and passing into a dark, inner room, more like a closet than anything else, they placed Angel's body on the floor.

"Get a light," said Sanderson, hoarsely.

"One is here," was the reply, in a smothered whisper.

Sanderson's hair stood on end as he closed the door, while Mrs. Harpy ignited the tinder to get a light.

At length, a faint glimmer thrown out by the flickering light of a candle displayed the sweat-bedewed faces of the guilty pair.

"The cupboard?" asked Sanderson.

"Yes."

Sanderson walked round the room, appearing to be looking for something. Whatever it was, he soon found it, for, pausing, he said—

"Drag him here, Jane, I've got it."

His thumb pressed some shining knob as he spoke.

Then came a click.

The grating of disused hinges.

Then a door that had seemed part of the wall flew open, displaying a dark, cavernous-looking apartment.

The body of Captain Angel was dragged into this gloomy chamber.

Far into the cell-like closet they pulled him, and when at length they had gone to the extremity of the place, Sanderson and his vile accomplice paused, and turned their bloodshot eyes upon each other.

"It will be better, Jane," he said, in answer to a meaning look from her.

"Yes," she replied, with a fiendish smile.

Wiping the perspiration from his brow, Sanderson and Jane Harpy left the chamber, and closed the door.

"Where's the spring, Jane?" he said, groping about the floor.

"It must be near your fingers," replied the blood-stained woman.

They intended to make sure of Angel this time. The spring Sanderson was now in search of would let down a trap on which the form of Angel was lying, and he would be hurled to the bottom of a fearful dungeon, where he would remain a shapeless mass, that, even if found, would be unrecognisable.

"There, there," said Mrs. Harpy, "I see it!"

"Ah! yes. Curses!"

This last exclamation was caused by the light, by some mysterious means, going out, and they were left in total darkness.

Sanderson's blood crept in his veins like ice.

"Did you do that, Jane?" he asked, in a whisper.

"I?—n—no," was the shaky reply, showing she was in nearly the same state.

"I could have sworn I saw a form."

"So could I."

"Let us leave this place—he will be safe."

"Yes—yes."

Each were in a standing posture. The guilty wretches, in fear, clung to each other, and began to grope their way to the door.

"Ah!—what's that?" gasped Sanderson. "Did you—"

"I saw a shadow pass! My God! let us leave or my brain will burst!"

As she finished speaking, both gave an appalling cry.

With a loud snap the door of the closet in which they had put Angel was dashed open, and as it flew back they recoiled speechless in their horror.

They clung to each other madly. Neither could speak, nor utter a cry, but remained shrinking back at what they saw.

Captain Angel—erect—his eyes open and fixed

upon them in a glaring stare—his blood-stained form showed plainly, and the life stream was still, as they fancied, slowly ebbing from the world.

His fearful words—the last he uttered—flashed through their brain.

"Living or dead, I will be your curse!"

The sound echoed now in their ears as the phantom slowly raised his hand—his forefinger pointing in a line with Mrs. Harpy's face.

It was too dark to see the lips move, but they heard these words spoken in a loud, warning voice.

"Remember, living or dead—aye, destroy my body—crush every bone to powder, and cast it to the winds—obliterate every stain from the floor—destroy everything belonging to me—then, even then, I will be your fate—your living terror—and when the day does come, beware!—tremble wretches!—you shall live in sin—well in blood—crave for each other's life—and die a death of hell's torture! Beware! the third visitation of the Death Phantom will be your last hour of existence!"

The voice ceased—they saw the phantom move.

"He is coming upon us," Mrs. Harpy shrieked, in a hoarse kind of whisper.

It was more than they could stand.

Each broke from their lethargy. One loud, piercing shriek broke from them, and they fell huddled all of a heap to the floor in a dead swoon.

An unearthly, mocking laugh followed this. The form of Captain Angel vanished, and a tall, shadowy figure with gleaming eyes passed across the entrance, as the door of the closet shut with a crash.

The tall, shadowy form came to where the guilty, unconscious pair lay. It was enveloped in a long cloak from head to foot, only a portion of the face and long, claw-like hands were visible.

The gleaming, basilisk-like eyes were fixed upon the inanimate pair, and a low chuckle escaped the mystic being's lips.

"Ha! ha! ha!—my beautiful pair. This is nothing to what you shall suffer. Ha! ha!"

Low as the laugh was, it would have chilled the blood in a listener's veins.

Not long did the weird figure remain, but, cautiously opening the door, she went forth to search over the house, and unravel the dreaded haunts of those guilty beings.

They had an enemy they had little dreamed of—one that would surely work their destruction.

Even now, while they lay insensible, was this mysterious being unravelling the mysteries they would have kept in their own breasts.

It evidently knew the house very well, and every apartment in it, as, without any apparent embarassment, it wended its way to the chamber from which Captain Angel had been dragged, and began, with an amount of curiosity surprising, to search about the room.

Not being successful, it descended to the room lately occupied by Sanderson and his victim.

There was a light there—the glimmer of an oil lamp, the dull, red flame of which showed the weird figure up in all its ghastliness.

As we have before said, it was tall, and enshrouded in the folds of a long sable cloak, which was thrust aside, and displayed the features of a horrid-looking old hag.

I know not whether her appearance at this moment would have impressed a beholder with more dread than would the sight of a supernatural being.

The face was the colour of parchment, wrinkled from chin to brow. A few long elf-locks straggled down from beneath her hood; her eyes twinkled with an unearthly lustre, and the two long fang-like teeth made her appearance as horrible as it could possibly be with any resemblance to humanity.

Still giving vent to her mirthless chuckle, she approached the light, and glared upon something she held clutched in her claw-like hand.

It was a blood-stained document—the one taken from John Gregory.

"Ha! ha! ha! My fine birds, take care—take care! Danger you little dream of hovers over you. Fly! aye, fly at once! But even wings would fail to carry you from the reach of their claws!"

And she worked her bony hands nervously.

"The night wanes," she continued, but in a much lower strain, as though merely giving vent to her thoughts. "I must be gone. There is him to restore, and the other to see."

Folding the document with the wet stains of gore upon it in her breast, she left the room to return to the apartment in which Sanderson now lay.

She found him there without deigning a look, and went into the closet where Angel's bleeding form lay.

Long was she shut up there; but at length she came forth, and with her ghost-like tread left the house altogether by a secret way.

She glanced up at the black clouds which rolled overhead, and her croaking voice sounded hollow and unreal as she wended her way slowly, and leaning upon a long stick for support.

"Yes," she muttered in reply to a passing thought, "I have it—ha! ha! Yes, there has been enough crime, enough blood spilt, too; but there will be more—ha! ha! Yes, more; but not among the innocent, no! Ah!" she exclaimed, starting, "it lightens, that was a flash! There, too, is thunder in the clouds, a storm is brewing with a will; the fiercest tempest that ever blew has no terror for me, I am alike shunned and disliked by Heaven, as by earth and all upon it."

She spoke true, a storm was fast approaching—long, forked darts of the electric light shot through the heavens.

The distant roar of thunder awoke the dead stillness and echoed over the distant country—the deep boom of Heaven's artillery—and large drops of rain began to fall.

As the old hag had said, the storm had no terror for her, she went on muttering as was her usual habit upon all she intended doing.

The tempest increased in its fury each minute, until the very earth shook from the continual and loud claps of thunder.

The lightning illumined the scene for miles around.

Raising her head, she glared out, and by aid of the flashes of light, could see some yards before her.

She started—

"Ah!" she muttered, and quickened her steps to such a degree that it was truly wonderful to see how that bent, time-worn form could move along.

The cause of this acceleration in her speed was two figures, which she had caught sight of, crossing a lonely, wide part of the country.

It was impossible to have recognised either of them from the momentary glimpse she caught, yet some strange fancy urged her on, and ere long she had nearly reached the man nearest her.

A little distance before him was another, who ran hurrying along to get out of the storm, but the first-mentioned was evidently only following for a motive best known to himself.

A bright gleam of light showed his form plainly. He was broad built, and in the costume of a fisherman or smuggler.

He increased his speed as the traveller did, who had just crossed a rising piece of ground.

For fear of losing him altogether, the smuggler or fisherman went at almost a running pace.

Once or twice something gleamed in his hand. It bore greatly the resemblance of a long-bladed knife.

He did not know the old hag was following close at his heels.

Ignorant of a third party being observable, he reached the little hillock which had hidden the person he was following from view.

He paused, and muttered an inward curse.

He could not see him anywhere.

Suddenly a vivid flash of the electric fire revealed the form he was in search of crossing a little valley.

He made a sudden spring, and would have darted off had not something caught his hand.

With a half kind of yell he turned, as the knife was snatched from his grasp.

He recoiled with a cry of horror.

The lightning played in long forked tongues round himself, and a tall, weird figure before him.

The thunder rattled louder than ever, nearly drowning the voice of his pursuer.

"Where go you?" cried the hag. "Where go you, such a night?"

Seeing his assailant was real, and not a spectre, the ruffian replied—

"I go where I choose, old woman."

"You are out for no good. Who were you following?"

"Look'ee, hag, begone! and stand from my path. My actions are nothing to you."

"They are. You go to murder. I can see it in your eyes."

"'Tis a lie!"

"Is it? Ha! ha! What was this grasped for?" —and she brandished the knife before his gaze. Ha! ha!—you can't defy me—take my advice, Red Hugh, return—return—but beware! I have warned you twice before! Let your hand be raised against him again, and, by all that's real, I will bring your death quick and terrible! Go!—take your knife— but depart!"

The ruffian started back in horror. He was awed by the voice and manner of the strange woman, and she seemed perfectly enshrouded with light. Stretching forth her bony hand, she muttered, "Don't defy me!" Something gleamed before his eyes, and the lightning illumined the wild scene, as she gave him the knife.

CHAPTER LXXX.

IRON ARM SAVES CAPTAIN TOM FROM CAPTURE.

THE order to fire upon our gallant hero and his gigantic follower would instantly have been carried out, and they would have been unmercifully slain, had not Iron Arm hurled the man he had grasped in his iron grip at his foes, and clutched at the captain of marines, who, in his zeal, came within the giant's long arm.

The Hercules saw his opportunity—saw his young chieftain's life was at stake—that was sufficient to urge him on to anything; and, quick as thought, he snatched the valiant captain up and held him before Captain Tom and his own huge person, of which very little was hidden by the captain's diminutive form.

He laughed mockingly at the soldiers, and cried—

"Yes. Ha! ha! Fire!"

Never was the aged commander in such a rage as now. To be thus defied, made the old fellow's blood boil.

He could not have his captain shot, and he liked not being bearded in his own ship.

Iron Arm spoke.

He had placed the struggling captain on his feet, and drew a pistol, which he placed in the unfortunate individual's ear.

"Captain," he said, and his stentorian voice rang through the ship's cabin in the tones of a bell, "pirates as you term us, we are averse to bloodshed.

Do not drive us to it. I would be sorry to harm yourself or officers; but, by Heaven! we will never surrender without a struggle, in which our capture will cost dearly. I have one request to make."

He paused.

The captain was too embarrassed to reply.

Iron Arm saw this, and saved him the trouble of doing anything unpleasant.

"You wish us to surrender, to be put in the hold in chains. My reply is—never! while we have strength or life left; but, to save bloodshed, we will give in quietly, providing you promise to let us remain unmolested prisoners, if you like, on parole."

"What!" cried the commander, "let two pirates have the range of my ship?"

"Such is what I mean."

"Then I decline."

"Your answer is prompted by a groundless fear," Iron Arm answered. "I am certain your chivalrous nature would not let you reply thus had you not a misgiving that we should attempt treachery. I swear that we will neither speak to man or officer, unless you wish it. That we will keep in any part of the ship you choose to name, and give up our arms."

"If I decline?"

Iron Arm cocked his pistol, and the captain of marines turned pale.

"Then," was the giant's reply, "I will blow this man's brains out."

"And I," said Captain Tom, "will fight to the last."

It required but one look to show they would keep their words.

The commander was by no means a cruel man, nor did he wish to resort to extreme measures.

For the moment, he scarcely knew how to act, and he turned towards his officers.

They exchanged glances, and a few whispered words passed between them.

The captain turned, and addressed Iron Arm.

"I will agree to your proposal," he said "on one condition."

"That?" asked the giant.

"You neither mingle or converse with the men; that you will be unarmed, and keep to the berth given you, at the door of which will be placed a sentry at night, and when you come on deck you go right aft or amidships."

He ceased speaking, and waited for a reply.

"Go on," said Iron Arm.

"That is all; beyond that I warn you, if either attempt to leave the cabin at night, the sentry has orders to shoot you down. If you attempt to pass amidships, to go to the men on the forecastle, you will be instantly shot. If you are seen to touch arms of any description, the same result will be the consequence. To interfere in any way with the officers in their duty will be instant death. That is all."

"Oh, you call that programme a condition, do you?" smiled Iron Arm. "Well, captain, you are rather severe, but all we want is our liberty. Of course, we neither expect the whole range of the ship; and your conditions—though many are reasonable— should either of us break from the rules you have laid out, why—"

The giant shrugged his shoulders by way of a finish.

"Only," put in Captain Tom, "we hope you will not break faith, as we never do."

"I," replied the old man, proudly, "have said, and never break my word. There is one thing more I would say."

"Ah!" muttered Iron Arm, firmly gripping his captive by the shoulder, just as the unlucky captain thought he was going to be set free.

"It is to this effect," continued the commander

" Should we meet a homeward-bound vessel you will be put on board; if not, when within hailing distance of port, you will be handcuffed."

Iron Arm saw his young chieftain's face flush, and, fearing his hot blood would rise and spoil their present chance, he replied, quickly—

" Be it so."

The commander made a sign to the marines, who beat a retreat, and Iron Arm released the captain.

An officer came forward, and took the arms from our hero and his follower.

An instant later and they were alone.

" We will retire," said Iron Arm, moodily.

They did so, to converse upon the present situation.

" Have you any plan?" asked Captain Tom.

" None yet."

" We are caged."

" Without doubt."

" But we have got out of a stranger cage than this."

" And will again," replied the giant, with a grim smile.

" I almost wish," said the impetuous boy, " we had not agreed to his terms."

" What else could we do?"

" Fight."

" Bah! I'm sick of it; it gets a mania with you. Be advised, my boy; use more caution, and fight less; you will do just as much, and with less danger to yourself."

Captain Tom frowned. He liked not being thus addressed.

" Perform, then," he said. " Do not preach."

An angry flash darted from the giant's eyes, but it passed instantly, and a smile wreathed his lips as he replied—

" We must preach without performing for some time before we shall leave this prison."

The young chief ground his teeth.

" I would, however, it had been a fight to the death, than this captivity."

" Supposing we had fought, and held out, were beaten on our way to the deck, or right through the ship, what could we have done after—jumped into the sea?"

Iron Arm laughed.

Captain Tom beat his foot impatiently on the floor. He was worried at being thus long parted from his ship. He knew not what had become of her, or his gallant crew.

" It is useless to worry about what cannot be helped," said Iron Arm, in reply to a remark made by his young chieftain. " No doubt the ship is safe, and all on board."

" Yes; and we might be hanged, and hunted to the masthead, for gulls to peck at, while they are cruising about."

" That's very likely."

" Iron Arm!" exclaimed the boy, vehemently, " for God's sake! try and help me in some plan to escape from this, or I shall go mad!"

" Well," replied the giant, " I know not what to say, beyond that our only hope lays in waiting for a passing ship, and, providing it should not be English, we will get on board, however far we have to swim for it."

" Vain hope!" muttered the noble boy, despairingly.

The day was a long, weary one to the two adventurers, and when at last the shadows of evening were coming on, they felt weary, and lay down to sleep.

They knew not how long they had been slumbering, when a boyish voice awoke them, saying—

" Awake! Hush! hush!—don't make a noise!"

Iron Arm recognised the voice, and jumped up.

Captain Tom did the same.

They saw Neddy—the mid—with his hand, standing before them.

" It's late," Tom said.

" Yes, sir," replied the youngster

" Do you want us?"

" Hush!—speak low!" said the boy. " A sail has been in our wake a long time, and nearly up with us. She comes at an awful rate, somehow, I think it's a free trader. If so, and could get on board, you might be safe."

" Get on board? How?"

" Well, sir, by some means get on deck, and make a leap for it. I will be near at hand, and drop a life-buoy overboard. I dare not do more, or I would."

" Generous boy!" muttered Iron Arm.

" Ah! They are challenging," cried Captain Tom, making a leap for the door.

" Quick, sir!" said the boy, hearing the commotion on deck.

" But our sentry?" said Iron Arm.

" Is gone," replied the middy, with a grin.

" Then, we will go, too," replied the young chief.

" Wait, sir, for Heaven's sake! Give me time to get clear of the cabin, and if I should whistle twice, return."

The boy darted away, and Captain Tom, with his trusty follower, stole forth.

Not having heard any whistle, they went on deck, just as the commander had layed-to, that he might question the stranger.

" She does not answer," said the captain, " or show any colours. Fire a gun."

The blank cartridge was fired, and the vivid flash lit up the vessel for an instant, giving all on board the man-of-war a momentary glance.

Iron Arm gave a cry as the vessel layed-to, and Captain Tom shouted incautiously—

" It's the 'Will-o'-the-Wisp'!"

In his excitement he gave a shout.

" Ahoy! ahoy! I am here, your chief! Lay-to, Ben!"

" We are lost," muttered Iron Arm, as the captain of the frigate jumped round.

" Ah!" he said. " Sentry, do your duty!"

The marine on deck brought his musket on a level with his shoulder, as the officers and men rushed forward to capture the daring buccaneers.

" Now," cried Iron Arm, " life or death!" and he made a leap for the bulwark.

Captain Tom followed.

Too late!

The marine fired.

The loud report was followed by a cry, and the gallant Captain Tom staggered back, swayed to and fro, and then fell to the deck.

Iron Arm gave a howl like that of a panther, and before any could clutch the fallen young captain, he snatched him up, and, with a whoop, leaped the bulwark, as several other shots were fired.

The loud splash was succeeded by a yell from the sailors, who were amazed at the daring feat.

The strange sail hauled up the instant Captain Tom's voice hailed those on board, and lights were flashing about all over the vessel.

When Iron Arm rose to the surface with the stricken form of the young chief on his arm, he saw the vessels were some distance apart, and the weight of his burden would make it difficult for him to reach the barque he had taken for the " Will-o'-the-Wisp."

Presently something fell with a splash in the water by his side.

He turned, and, to his joy, saw something floating near his elbow.

His face gleamed with joy. It was a life-buoy!

The brave little middy had kept his word.

Several shots had been fired in the water, but all without any fatal result to our hero,

ATTACKING THE PIRATES' STRONGHOLD.

The commander of the frigate was in a boiling passion.

"Beat to quarters!" he shouted. "I will blow that ship out of the water if they do not reply."

The rattle of drums followed this, and the frigate was instantly put in fighting trim.

Clearly did Iron Arm hear all this from the ocean, and he strove madly to get through the water quicker.

At length he came beneath the dark hull of the rakish craft, and he looked up.

He saw the ship's side was lined with forms.

"Throw a rope!"

His words were heard, and twenty men ran to obey.

But some one else was before them.

Long ere a rope could be thrown out, one was seen dangling from out of the lower ports, and the head and shoulders of Bob Hauler appeared.

"Hold on, you lubber, or this weight will pull me through!"

The lubber evidently meant Jerry Mizzen, who was tugging away at the rope from the inside. Iron Arm linked the rope round his wrist, and supporting his chief on the left arm, said—

"Hold tight!"

"Aye, aye, sir."

"It's all right, Bob," shouted a voice from between decks, "I've fastened the rope to a gun."

Upon hearing this Bob Hauler stretched forth his hands to assist the giant, who had just firmly

31

fixed his feet against the ship's side, and began to ascend.

A few minutes later they were safe on board, surrounded by Ben Barnacle and Harry Vere.

"The chief!" cried Ben, hoarsely.   "He lives!"

"I hope so," replied Iron Arm, faintly.

"My G—"

His speech was cut short by a terrible report, and the "Will-o'-the-Wisp" shook in every part.

"We are fired at!" cried Ben.

"Beat to quarters!—ready at the guns!—or we shall be smashed!" shouted Harry Vere, rushing on deck, as the frigate prepared to send another broadside into them.

CHAPTER LXXXI.

CAPTAIN TOM LEARNS THE PLOT, AND DETERMINES TO MEET THE PLOTTERS.

BEN BARNACLE, seeing the danger of the "Will-o'-the-Wisp," veered her round and tacked out of range, or at least a safer distance from the man-of-war's guns.

Not that he feared the frigate or her immense crew, but because his chief would not allow the guns to be turned against his own country.

The man-of-war captain hailed for them to lay-to, but the buccaneers took no notice of it.

A proceeding that slightly enraged the captain, who ordered a broadside to be poured into her.

The order was immediately executed, but with little effect.

"Another like that, and we will return," said Harry Vere.

"We will," put in Ben Barnacle, grimly.

The brave old captain of the frigate could not stand quietly on his deck and see the vessel carry away his escaped prisoners, especially when that vessel was the well-known "Will-o'-the-Wisp." He therefore gave orders for the frigate to give chase, and to keep up a counter-fire from the gun amidships.

The instant his vessel was put in motion, the "Will-o'-the-Wisp" increased her speed, until the English sailors were completely amazed.

"Dash my eyes, mate—she seems to fly!" said one.

"Don't know where her wings are, then. For blow my toplights if I've seen a stitch of canvas hoisted since she came alongside."

"Sink me, you're right," replied the first speaker, rubbing his eyes to assure himself they were not deceiving him.

"Well, arter a ship walking through the water without any sails—why—"

The ejection of the stale quid over the ship's side, and replacing another piece of tobacco in the cheek, finished the sailor's sentence.

The aged commander was more surprised than any.

"Strange!" he muttered.

"Very!" replied his first luff.

"Well, I've heard of the Flying Dutchman," said the midshipman Ned to his friend Sam, "but this fellow beats him into fits."

"Strikes me they deal with the Old One!"

"Pooh! haven't you heard of the 'Will-o'-the-Wisp'?"

"Yes."

"Well, that's it. The ship that can go without sails faster than our revenue cutters, and, when it likes, the craft disappears from view altogether."

"You don't say so?" replied Sam, in amazement.

"I do! and that young fellow we had on board is the commander of that gang of roughs."

"Why did our skipper let him go, then?"

"Because he was not able to keep him."

"But look!"

"Look where?" cried Ned.

"At the buccaneer!"

The "Will-o'-the-Wisp" was cleaving through the water, though she had not hoisted one sail extra, yet her speed increased each minute.

The captain of the frigate had every stitch of sail hoisted, and tried to give chase.

A few minutes showed him how inferior was the sailing of his vessel to that of the buccaneers; and, fearing that in a few minutes they would be out of range, he ordered a broadside to be fired into them.

Much against their expectations, they had a reply —a pretty stiff one, too.

The frigate quivered from stem to stern under the volley, and when, at length, the smoke cleared away, the hair began to stand on the sailors' heads, and the captain's cheek paled.

Not a sign of the daring barque could be seen— nothing but a thick mist could be observed floating slowly on the ocean's surface.

They little knew that floating cloud enveloped the gallant "Will-o'-the-Wisp," which very soon was safely away, and careering over the broad xpanse of waters.

Long ere morn broke another ship came up to the frigate, and, to the commander's surprise, his interrogator was no other than Admiral Ellis.

"Have you," he shouted, "seen anything of the pirate vessel?"

"We chased one last night."

"Did you know her?"

"Yes—the 'Will-o'-the-Wisp.'"

Admiral Ellis jumped round, and had his vessel brought to.

"I will come on board," he shouted, a boat as was being lowered.

The aged commander had the sailors and marines drawn up to receive the little admiral with proper pomp.

But he very prudently made his officers keep secret the escape of Captain Tom.

He well knew the vindictive little admiral's motive, and that Ellis had it in his power to work any junior officer harm.

The admiral, however, came on board, and, returning the salute of the captain with a stiff bow, said—

"Will you minutely detail the whole occurrence?"

"Certainly, admiral."

"You are sure it was the 'Will-o'-the-Wisp'?"

"My officers assured me of it."

"Good. We will go below."

"Certainly, admiral."

They went to the state-cabin of the frigate, and then the captain told the admiral how they had given chase, but suddenly lost sight of the buccaneer's ship all at once.

Admiral Ellis ground his teeth furiously.

"So, he is still able to impose upon his enemies by that cursed jugglery," he muttered, aloud.

"Jugglery, admiral?"

"Yes, captain. He deceived you as he has done others, by some hellish machinery he has. But he shall be caught yet. There are six vessels in search of him, and before two months have gone he will be driven in a corner, and caught like a rat in a trap."

"I am glad to hear this, admiral."

"Yes. Ha! ha! ha! Nicely he'll be caught. By the way, Captain Stanly, you had better make one of the party."

"Willingly."

Ellis then very slowly, but briefly, made Stanly acquainted with the plot, and gave him instructions how to act.

Too glad to render his country a service, Captain Stanly immediately acquiesced.

Admiral Ellis left in high glee, and returned to his ship to continue his search for Captain Tom.

Not for a moment did the passion-blinded old man imagine that the scent had got to the ears of Captain Tom, and, nourishing his vengeful passions, he strolled his quarter-deck all day, in the hope of coming up with the gallant buccaneers.

During the time Iron Arm and Captain Tom were safe on the deck of the "Will-o'-the-Wisp," and Harry Vere, the instant he saw his young chief was only insensible, had Doctor Shrike sent for, and when Captain Tom had recovered, communicated to him all that had occurred.

"Why," asked Tom, as he was seated round the table with his officers, "did you leave the deck?"

"We were compelled to," replied Ben Barnacle.

"For why?"

"It was dangerous to remain."

"Can you explain the cannonading I heard?"

"Yes. As we expected, the frigate, finding she could not come over the ropes, sent boats, which we received with a hearty welcome."

Captain Tom smiled.

"After our engagement with the Frenchman," continued Ben Barnacle, "we were joined by Hugh Baldrick, the smuggler, who, under the name of Captain Moore, commands a ship in the fleet that has come out to hunt you down."

Ben smiled grimly as he said this.

"Let him come," was the noble boy's reply, as his hand gripped the hilt of his sword.

"But you need not fear Captain Moore."

"I fear him?" asked Captain Tom, in surprise.

He laughed derisively.

"Even could he work you harm you need not."

"I do not understand."

"I will explain then."

"Do—briefly, and as explicitly as possible."

"You have not a great amount of patience," smiled Ben.

"I have less when what little I have is tried too much."

Ben laughed good-humouredly at the words, which would have made anyone else feel that they warned him not to go too far.

"Come, come!" said the boy.

"Well, it is this," replied Ben. "Your friends, Archibald Gaston and Kilcrew, have been making a nice little plot to whop you."

Captain Tom laughed again.

"And they evidently intend putting all their powers into execution to carry it out."

"Let them."

"They will. And it would have been a more serious matter than you think."

"Why?"

"Well, I think that had half a dozen of the best-manned and best-sailing ships the navy could produce been sent after us, without our knowing it, we should have been on dangerous ground."

"We are free now?"

"I think not."

Captain Tom looked up in surprise.

"You, see," replied Barnacle, by way of explanation, "we have gone through dangers that seemed almost impossible for one to escape from; but none save the cool, scheming, cowardly subterfuge that this one has."

"It must be something wonderful."

"You shall hear. Six ships," Ben Barnacle went on, "were to start from this point—"

He placed his finger on a certain part of the map.

"And, by following their instructions, they would, in time, scour the seas, and meet here."

"Well?"

"Why, they naturally calculated that you would

be driven there, too; and it being a rocky point with more sunken reefs than all the other places put together, they have the idea you will have to fight or surrender."

"It would be the former."

"Just so; but as six well-armed men-of-war ships are not a light foe, we should have stood a poor chance. But, fortunately, the tables were turned."

"Dame Fortune seems ever to hover over us," smiled the daring boy.

"True," replied Ben. "Hugh Baldrick was in the gardens of Vauxhall, and overheard the plans being concocted by the two friends, and before they could communicate it to the Lords of the Admiralty, he went and disguised himself, staff and crew, and offered his services, as a personal enemy to you, hunt you down."

The boy captain's eyes flashed brightly.

It made his heart swell with pride to hear of subordination from men who might make themselves his enemies.

"By showing off the swift-sailing qualities of his vessel, and the way in which his men could handle their guns, he was admitted, and let into the secret; and then he lost no time in finding us and making known the whole plot."

"Then what do you propose?"

"That we find them."

"How?"

"Easily."

"I should like to hear."

"Well, Dutch Paul is near us, and so is Hugh, who is compelled to keep up his character as yet; but long before the time arrives he will be ready to appear upon the astonished crusade by your side, as the Smuggler Prim, instead of Captain Moore."

"I see, then."

"'Tis simple. With his aid and Dutch Paul's, we could defy a dozen ships, especially as we are warned, and knew exactly when and how to be prepared."

"Firstly, I should say, we will not let them drive us to this point."

"Quite the reverse."

"For why?"

"It would be the best."

"Certainly our ideas differ."

"They will not for long."

"They will, unless you can give me good proof for what you assert."

"I can. We have not held council, as I left that until you came, but I think I have a plan which I will submit to the consideration of yourself and officers."

"Let us hear it."

"Firstly, you fully understand all I have told you about our present situation?"

"Quite."

"Well, the result of some hours' careful thought and calculation on my part is this, that we can be sure that Ellis, as well as the others, will hail every British ship as it passes, and give instructions to do all they can towards driving you to the point mentioned, and thus we shall find it very difficult to give them the slip."

"Very true."

"Instead of which, supposing we were to go quietly on, as though quite innocent of their plan, and let them get us to this rocky point."

Ben smiled, as he regarded the excited face of his young chief.

"Well," continued the faithful follower, with a twinkle in his eye, "imagine yourself, then, with Dutch Paul and Hugh by your side, all piped, and waiting for the enemy, which would then only be five ships. Even if more—what then? I question whether two of them will go in such shallow water as we can. Ha! ha!—fancy how they would be on in when they found they had three ships to combat with, one of which will give them enough liquid fire to destroy a fleet."

Ben laughed loudly.

"By Heaven!" he went on. "I fancy I can see Admiral Ellis, when he sees his ships beaten and his squadron conquered, and himself put back like a beaten cur, without sword or epaulette!"

"That is your plan?"

"Yes."

"I think it a brilliant one," said Harry Vere.

Which was the general opinion.

Captain Tom rose and paced the state-room excitedly.

His face was flushed, and his eyes burned like living coals.

The anticipated triumph made the blood run through his veins like fire.

One hand was thrust in his breast, the other rested upon the hilt of his sword.

"It shall be so," he muttered. "And, then, Kilcrew and Gaston look to it."

"Well, my chief, what is the reply?"

"It shall be as you say."

He again seated himself, and discussed his plans, as well as gave directions for the future. After which, he related his adventures, and the death of Skopey.

There were two persons on board the "Will-o'-the-Wisp" who particularly rejoiced over the death of the black.

They were our friends Jerry Mizzen and Bob Hauler.

Jerry, always on the alert, contrived, by a trivial excuse, to be engaged with some little job near his chief whilst he was relating his adventures and the death of Skopey, and he had hardly concluded before Jerry had finished his work and run off in search of Bob Hauler. Seizing Bob by the arm, he said—

"I say, Bob."

"Well, Jerry?"

"What d'ye think?"

"Can't say."

"Well, it's good news."

"Let's hear it, messmate."

"Why, that black lubber, Skopey, has gone to his last account."

"Serve him right."

"D'ye know who sent him there?"

"No."

"Iron Arm."

"Well, then, he had been up to summut."

"Of course he had."

"What?"

"Tried to kill the chief."

Bob Hauler leaped to his feet.

"The black thief!" he said.

"So I say, Bob."

"Yes, Jerry."

"I feels so bad, Bob, at the werry idea of his trying to kill the chief, that if I don't have a drop o' grog, why blow me I'll—I'll—"

"So shall I, Jerry. I feel worse; it gave me quite a turn."

"You want some rum, too, Bob?"

"Yes, Jerry."

"We'll get some."

They did, and sneaking behind a coil of rope near the forecastle, they began to discuss it with such gusto that their momentary indisposition had soon passed away.

"Jerry!"

"Yes, Bob."

"Let's drink the chief's health, 'cos he ain't been here for a long time."

"All right, Bob. Give us a swig."

A few "swigs" managed to place them in a blissful state of unconsciousness, each snoring loudly, and lying one across the other.

Jerry was on his back clutching an empty bottle, his mouth was wide open, into which Bob had, in his last struggle, thrust the neck of his bottle, where he held it securely.

It was evident neither had the slightest grain of sense left, or they would have seen three or four grinning faces, the owners of which sneaked from behind the guns, and came towards the unconscious pair.

They were four of the youngest mids on board and who were ever in mischief.

"Gus," whispered one.

"Hallo!"

"We'll serve them out, eh?"

"Yes, they're always tight."

"What shall we do?"

"I'll tell you."

The four heads might have been seen together, as the young tormentors held a whispered consultation.

For a few minutes they parted, laughing gaily and dived below, but quickly returned, and then began operations.

They first removed Bob Hauler from Jerry, and placing each of them on their side, but back to back, one of the mids produced a long sail-maker's needle, and some thin twine.

Ramming their handkerchiefs in their mouths to stifle their laughter, they began to sew the precious pair of ex-smugglers together by the waist-band of their trousers.

A feat which was soon performed. The mischievous young monkeys quietly slipped the bottle from Bob Hauler's hand, and filling it full of bilge water, replaced it. One was thrust in the huge fist of Jerry.

Then the boys drew a safe distance off.

"It will be rare fun," said one.

"Won't it? The first thing they will do on waking will be to take a pull at the rum-bottle. Ugh!" said the youngster, as he imagined the filthy water going down their throats.

They waited with untiring patience for the two victims to wake; but finding at length they could not throw off the effects of the rum, one of the mids proposed waking them.

"How?" cried one.

"I'll show you," replied the boy who held the long sail-maker's needle.

Walking towards Jerry, he inserted it in a part of his body that shall be nameless.

A groan was all the notice Jerry took of it.

But when the sharp steel point had been inserted several times, the agony became too much, and Jerry awoke.

"Bob," he growled, sleepily; "Bob! Oh, lor'!"

"Yaw! blow it!" howled Bob, with a twitch of agony. "Jerry, you swab!"

"Yes, Bob."

"Don't do that again!"

"What, Bob? I didn't do nothing."

"You liar! You lubber! don't do it, that's all!"

"My throat is parched, Bob."

"So is mine."

"Ah! I've got some left," said Jerry, feeling neck of the bottle in his grasp.

Raising it to his mouth, he took a tremendous draught.

Gugle—guggle—guggle—gugg—g—

A few seconds' silence.

Then a start.

"Yah!—hoo!—ugh!—Oh, Lor'! I'm poisoned" he cried, dashing the bottle to the deck, and spluttering as though he had taken something nasty.

"What's the matter, Jerry?" asked Bob laughing.

"You be blowed!"

Bob replied by thrusting the neck of the bottle in

...t in his mouth, and taking, if possible, a longer ... than Jerry.

...ry forgot his own torture in the delight of the ...

He heard his friend stop suddenly.

The bottle was put down.

"Ugh! the dirty thief!" gasped Bob, nearly ...ed, and vainly trying to close his mouth.

"W—w—wh—a-t's—the—m—at—ter, Bob?" asked Jerry, laughing until his sides ached.

"Matter! Curse you—you long-faced thief, I'll —I'll—oh, Lor'! I shall heave my heart up."

This part of his speech was very low and dismal.

But Jerry and the mids heard it, and howled with delight.

Bob made an attempt to rise, just as Jerry was trying to roll over.

"Jerry, curse you! let go!"

"I ain't touching you."

"You lying swab, let go!"

"I ain't holding you."

"Will you let me get up?"

"'Cos yer I can't help it."

Bob began to get furious.

He made a vicious kick at Jerry, but could not do much damage.

Each tried to get up, and pulled each other over.

Bob's rage was great.

At last he sprang to his feet, by the aid of the bulwarks; and the cord with which they were fastened together being more on one side than the other, Jerry was taken off his feet, and lost his balance.

Bob made a rush, carrying Jerry, who was swinging crossways on Bob's back; and the luckless Mizzen had his head knocked against everything in the way.

His howls were pitiful, he felt the string giving way, and madly clutched at something to save himself; but no good, Bob rushed on. Just as he passed the hatchway the ship gave a lurch, Jerry shot forward, the string gave way, there was a yell, and Jerry went head-first down the hatch, as Bob was hurled to the deck.

CHAPTER LXXXII.

THE BODY OF JOHN GREGORY.

It was long before the ruffian Sanderson and his guilty accomplice came to their senses.

Morning had long since thrown its pale light over the earth, and a ray found its way into the room where they lay.

Mrs. Harpy seemed bereft of reason, and Sanderson was pale and haggard, with bloodshot eyes and ashy lips.

Staggering to his feet, he called upon Mrs. Harpy "Jane!"

No reply.

"Jane!"

She raised her head, and with a wild stare regarded him.

"Jane! For God's sake, get up!"

"Yes, yes—I know."

"Are you mad?"

Mad! Ha! ha! Mad, say you?—No! not mad! I remember—remember!"

Her voice sank into a whisper, and she sat bolt upright.

"The deed! Yes! Look—look upon this hand! The stain is there still and yet—ha! ha! ha!"

The laugh was wild and maniacal.

"He," she continued, "came back—held out his hand to me."

"Jane!"

"Ah! Who speaks?"

"I do, Jane. Don't be a fool. Get up!"

Fearing that the servants were about, and would hear him, Sanderson lifted her from the floor, and with a suspicious look at the door of the closet, hastened from the apartment.

He placed Mrs. Harpy in her room, and went to his library, and had to resort to some strong brandy to give him nerve, he was fearfully shaken.

Those few hours had worked the change of years in that brutal man's frame, he sat thinking over the night's fearful work.

Presently an evil light came in his eyes, and he smiled in a way that meant no good.

"Ah!—good!" he muttered. "She can be removed without trouble."

He was thinking of Mrs. Harpy, he wanted her removed, and nothing seemed easier than to place her in Dr. Burchenell's private asylum.

"I will do it," he muttered, starting up.

Suddenly he started back, as though shot.

"Very good," he murmured. "The will!"

He remembered, for the first time, the papers which Angel had thrust in his breast.

His first impulse was to rush up to the closet in which he had locked the victim of his passion, but the coward quailed. He could not.

While he sat thinking, a knock came at the door.

"Enter!" he called.

"Doctor Burchenell wishes to see you, sir," said a servant, entering.

"Show him up."

The footman bowed, then retired.

A moment later, Dr. Burchenell was shown up.

"Good morning, Mr. Sanderson."

"Good morning, doctor."

"You do not look well."

"I am not," replied the ruffian, with a ghastly smile.

"Indeed! What ails you?"

"I know not, nor do I care. If you will go to Mrs. Harpy's room, she wants your assistance."

Burchenell went. He started when he saw the woman in a deathly kind of stupor.

"My God! how altered!" the doctor said. "How long has she been like this?"

He asked this of Sanderson, who had come with him into the room.

"Only this morning."

"Indeed!"

The doctor began to examine her.

"Her nerves have received a severe shock," he said.

"Perhaps so," was Sanderson's evasive reply.

Presently she began to rave in the same mad way as she had done before.

They listened intently.

"She has been raving in that mad way ever since the night," Sanderson said.

"Indeed!" was the only reply.

Sanderson began to get warm, but, much to his relief, Burchenell turned, and gave his directions as to the treatment of Mrs. Harpy.

"I will send medicine soon," he said. "I can do no more now. If you will give directions now to her maid, we will go to the room below. I have something important to say."

Sanderson did as instructed, and then went with the doctor to the library.

"You have something to impart?"

"I have—it is this," replied the doctor, taking a seat and going at once into business. "I came to see you this morning on a very important matter."

"Well, friend?"

"You were saying something about doubling a certain price if you could see John Gregory dead."

"I did."

"Well, I've been thinking. What would you give if I could produce to public inspection, and announce the death of John Gregory, who, of course, has died from natural causes, and thus you would be safe in all your plans?"

"What would I give?" cried Sanderson; "any-thing! Do as you say. Show me the dead body of Gregory, and name your terms."

"Very well."

"Do you mistrust?"

"Oh, no! If I do you have only just to write on this, that you will pay me the sum of so-and-so. Do you understand?"

"Perfectly."

"Will you do it?"

"Now?"

"When you like."

"Let me rightly understand."

"Well, you can do it when you like; only you will have to bring it with you when you come to see the body of John Gregory."

"I agree."

"Good! come two nights hence, and you shall have your wishes gratified."

"Without fail?"

"I never break a promise."

They parted, and the doctor left with a peculiar gleam in his eyes, and he muttered things to himself as he went on.

So—so," he muttered. "They have been at foul work! Well—well—it's fearful!—horrible!"

When he returned home, he found a visitor waiting for him. It was the horrid old hag who had left the hall just before the storm came on.

"Well, Elza?"

"Ah!—'tis you, doctor!"

"Yes."

"I have waited long."

"Have you?"

"I have been out all night."

"And I, too, Elza."

"Must be strange things to take you out, doctor."

"They are, Elza—but you want to see me?"

"I do—I have kept watch, and find it time to come to you. There has been fearful doings at the Hall."

"As I thought."

"You, doctor! Why?"

"I have been there."

"Ah! and—"

"Found Sanderson looking as though he had been through some dreadful illness, and his accomplice, horrible—she was raving—half mad—and her hair, in that night, has grown nearly grey."

"Crime, doctor, is bringing its own punishment."

"True—but go on."

"The other returned yesterday."

"Ah!—say you so?"

"Yes—he put them in deadly fear before retiring to rest—got all he wanted—and the papers that made Sanderson the possessor of all. But, while asleep, Mrs. Harpy strove to make her accomplice remove him from their path. Ha! ha!—poor fool!—she would steep herself to the neck in blood to get what he will never give her—a name that will enable her to look other women in the face.

"But the craven would not—he feared his enemy in his sleep—and, in the despair of the moment, she took the knife and thrust it in the breast of Angel—ha! ha!—they little knew I was watching them; and when the deed was done, they removed the body, forgetting the very thing they did the deed for."

"The paper?"

"Yes, doctor. Here!"

"Good! Ha! ha! Now—now they are in my power!" and the doctor tore open the document, and glanced at the signature of John Gregory.

"Have they quite succeeded with their foe?" he asked, suddenly breaking from his reverie.

"I think not, doctor. I administered some of the potion you gave me, and dressed the wounds, and shouldn't wonder if he comes to."

"So much the better!"

"Yes; all the better—all the better!" muttered the old witch to herself.

"Well, they will be here soon. Keep watch; but be careful, and we shall have them wholly in our power."

"Yes, doctor. I go now; but give me a little more of that elixir, it is good that he should not die."

The doctor gave the old woman a phial containing some powerful liquid, and then she left to return to her abode.

Dr. Burchenell pondered long on the bloodstained document. He was maturing something against the pair of wretches who were outwitted at every turn.

Mrs. Harpy, on the second day after the visit of the doctor, returned to consciousness, but there was still an appearance of a shaken mind. She was melancholy quiet.

"Jane," said Sanderson, "I have something to tell you."

She looked up, and stared vacantly in his face.

"Do you understand?" he went on, with almost a feeling of pity for the wretched woman.

"Yes, John, I hear."

Her reply was faint, and she seemed thinking of other things.

"Will you prepare to accompany me?"

"You?" she said, starting.

"Yes! Then why start?"

"Did I start, John? Well, go on."

"You wish to see Mr. John Gregory dead! I have received a letter to say he is. You will see him?"

A cold shudder passed through the frame of Mrs. Harpy.

"Let us go."

"I am willing."

She rose, and busied herself to go out with her brutal companion, whose mind was still racked by the missing document. He did not want to mention it yet, as, in her present state, Mrs. Harpy would very likely swoon. They were soon on the way to the doctor's house. He met them with a bland smile at the door.

"I am sorry, sir," he said, blandly, "to give you the melancholy tidings that your poor relation is lost to you."

Mrs. Harpy shuddered again.

"Are you better?" he asked.

"Yes," she replied, in her cold tone.

"You are," he thought. "The torture you will suffer will be worse than death. Poor, misled woman, not long will you have the blessing of reason."

He glanced at her, as he muttered these things to himself. Her dull, glaring eye, and sunken cheek was enough to turn a heart of stone to pity. Her gaze for ever wandered from point to point, and the doctor noticed, with a feeling of remorse, that her hair was quite grey.

"Now, doctor, your promise."

"Is faithfully kept. Follow me."

He led the way to the room in which old Gregory was kept, and, opening the door, went towards the bed.

Removing a long, white sheet, Sanderson and Mrs. Harpy paused. There lay John Gregory, cold and rigid.

His face wore a calm, placid look, that shewed he had not gone through much pain in his last moments of consciousness.

John Sanderson approached the cold brow, placed his hand upon the breast, and a sickly smile for an instant played round his mouth. He thought himself full possessor of the old man's property, and triumph drove all feelings of sorrow from his heart.

Mrs Harpy stood cold and quiet, her unsteady gaze fixed on the rigid form. Not a word escaped her, nor did she seem to pay attention to what was going on around her.

"I have saved you trouble, sir," said the doctor, breaking the silence, "in the way of burial. The coffin is ordered, and will be here shortly. Would you like to see the body again?"

"No; it unnerves Jane. I think you had better have him screwed down, and the last rites performed, as soon as possible."

"It shall be done."

The doctor escorted them to the door. As they were about to leave the asylum, something was brought in on the shoulders of four men. It was the last receptacle for poor old John Gregory.

Sanderson caught sight of the plate on the lid, and on which was engraved the name of John Gregory, who died such-and-such a date.

"Screwed down," muttered the doctor, as he watched Sanderson's retreating form, "yes, it shall be done at once."

CHAPTER LXXXIII.

CAPTAIN TOM BEGINS THE DESTRUCTION OF THE ALGERIAN PIRATES.

TRUE to his colours, Captain Tom had his ship put in trim, and he sailed in the course he knew would place him at the point so wished for by his foes. The day was not far advanced when Harry Vere sighted a sail.

"What is it like?" said Tom. taking his glass.

"I think it's the 'Yellow Vulture.'"

"It is—ah!"

"What's the matter, captain?" asked Ben.

"I see a regular fleet of sails."

"Where away?"

"Westward."

Ben took out his glass, but all endeavours to make out the strangers was impossible. A strict watch was kept, and the "Will-o'-the-Wisp" was turned to meet Dutch Paul.

When they came alongside, the gentleman pirate jumped on board.

Captain Tom did not for the moment recognise his old friend. Dutch Paul had so disguised himself and the whole of his crew, that it took a shrewd glance to recognise the captain and officers of the "Yellow Vulture."

"How do, captain?" he said, "I'm not sorry to see you back. Where the deuce have you been, eh? —campaigning among the Hottentots?"

"Before you ask questions, tell me if you can make out that swarm of sails?"

"Of course I can."

"Have you any idea what they are?"

"Yes, our friends."

"Friends!"

"Yes, friends is the word. You see our friends in the freebooting way. The fleet of Algerian pirates. Now do you understand?"

"Confound them! I should like to pepper some of the rascals. I have disguised my fellows, as you see, so that I might give them a surprise."

"Why don't you, captain? There is only about seven sail in all."

"At that rate about ten men to my one."

"Say fourteen, captain."

"As you will."

The young chief again raised his glass to watch the movements of the pirates.

"They are parting company," he said.

"Yes," replied Dutch Paul, "they are going to part company and go in twos to scour the seas."

"Are they?"

"They are, unless you are going to stop them."

"I have a score to settle with that nest of devils."

"Pay it, then—I half guess there's a fine haul to be had from them."

"Hark!" cried Tom, "is not that the sound of guns?"

"Of course it is."

"They are attacking some one."

"Probably."

"A merchantman."

"That's more likely still."

"Top-men, away!" shouted Captain Tom. "Ready to shake out every reef!"

"Aye, aye, sir!"

"Down with the helm!"

"Aye, down it is, sir."

"Ben, have the decks prepared to repel boarders, and prepare the men for a fight."

"You never—" began Ben.

"I intend taking or destroying as many as I can of that horde of ruffianly cut-throats," said the boy, proudly, pointing towards the distant ships with his glass.

"So be it."

"Then I'll jump on board, and follow in your wake," said Dutch Paul.

The devil-may-care fellow leaped over the bulwarks to the deck of his ship, and, giving orders, she was put in trim to follow the "Will-o'-the-Wisp."

"Captain!" he shouted through his trumpet.

"Well?"

"If you are going to walk through the water, like this, you will have to take me behind."

"Very well."

The chase was begun. The "Will-o'-the-Wisp" seemed to fly through the water, and the "Yellow Vulture" kept pretty well in her wake. Before they had gone far, the distant cannonading had ceased, and shortly after the pirate fleet separated.

Captain Tom went on, he noticed a speck on the waters where the pirates had just been, his heart leaped and his face flushed, well he knew what that speck was; the fated victim who had followed in their wake, and he expected—and rightly—that all on board were murdered.

"If so," he muttered, "I will hunt down every one of the accursed murderers!"

They were some two hours or more before they came up to the spot. When they did, every cheek burned with rage.

"Lower a boat!" was the first order.

It was done, and in a few minutes after they were on board. The sight they beheld made the blood freeze in their veins. The ship was battered almost to pieces and fast sinking; her crew lay strewn over the decks, cut and hacked in a most fearful manner. Captain Tom went below, and similar sights met his view.

On the floor of the state-cabin lay an aged man with silvery hair; his hand grasped the butt of an exploded pistol, near him was the form of a dead pirate. The poor old fellow evidently fought to the last moment, but was at last struck down. Captain Tom turned moodily away—as he did so, a faint groan came on his ears.

He turned quickly.

"It is from the old man," he said.

"Yes," replied Ben. "Thank God!—he lives, I think."

"Hauler and Mizzen," called the chief.

"Aye, aye, sir," replied the two sailors.

"Go quickly on board and bring Doctor Shrike here."

"Aye, aye, sir."

With a rush they left the cabin. Nothing gave them greater delight than to fetch the vampire. They scrambled on board and scampered to his cabin.

"Doctor," shouted Bob, opening the door.

"Yes."

"You've got to go aboard the craft where the chief is. You is wanted."

"Ho! ho!—wanted. Jacop! Jacop! you lazy, smoking effigy, come here."

"Yes. What d'ye want?"

"Come, sir, Jacop, or I'll amputate you."

Jacop sneaked towards his master, and the two sailors went on deck. They waited a few minutes, but finding the vampire and his assistant were quarrelling below, Bob stooped over the hatchway, and just as Doctor Shrike passed, he caught him by the collar.

"Curse you!"

"Yaw!"

The second howl came from Jacop as Jerry whirled him to the deck. Bob Hauler did not release the doctor, but dragged him to the bulwarks, and dropped him over into the boat.

"There, you swab!"

"There, you lubber!"

Jerry dropped Jacop on the head of his master, who expressed his rage by a howl, and taking a long dissecting knife made several vicious plunges at his assistant, and while they were having a nice little battle, Bob and Jerry rowed them to the ship.

Before the chief they were quiet, and the doctor set about restoring the old man. It was a tedious task, and nothing but the great skill of Dr. Shrike brought him round at all.

"That will do. I will have him conveyed on board when he has answered a few questions," said the chief.

Jacop and his master left the cabin. Presently the vampire's eyes fell upon the form of a finely-built young man.

"Jacop! Jacop!—there's a fine subject. We will take him on board."

They did, much to Jerry's disgust. When the old gentleman was able to look round, he gazed upon the handsome face of Captain Tom, and his first feeling of fear passed away.

"Where are they?" he murmured.

"Where are who?" asked the young chief, kindly.

"Who—who—ah! you know nothing of it. I remember all now. My God! my God!—my daughters and my niece! Where—where are they?"

"Come, tell me, what has occurred?"

"Oh, heavens!" groaned the old fellow.

"Speak, for God's sake! I came too late to save, but will dearly avenge this cold-blooded massacre. Tell me, are those ladies you speak of carried away?"

"Yes."

"Tell me."

"We were boarded by the pirates, after they had fired into the ship until they saw she could not float any longer; then they boarded, and, without the least provocation, began to cut and hack at the defenceless women and children and the crew, who fought bravely while they lasted.

"The ruffians rushed below, and took my darling girls from the cabin. One I slew when he put his hand on my daughter, but before I could do more in their defence I was struck down.

"I suppose they ransacked the ship, and carried off the girls, whose fate will be worse than death."

"Come, then, sir, on board my ship. You will find a comfortable resting-place; and, be assured that, ere the morning dawns, I shall be upon the doers of this fell work."

The old man, with a look of surprise at the bold speaker, and wondering who he was, went on board the "Will-o'-the-Wisp," where he was greeted with kind and pitying looks from all on board.

He was taken below, and attended by the vampire,

while the "Will-o'-the-Wisp" continued her path of vengeance.

Captain Tom, in his heart, swore a fearful curse that he would exterminate the whole fleet of pirates from the sea.

The "Yellow Vulture" was far ahead.

Dutch Paul knew his assistance was not wanted at the wreck, and, knowing the swiftness of the "Will-o'-the-Wisp," thought it wise to be a little ahead.

"That young fire-eater will catch it pretty sharp," he said, puffing away at his cigar.

Ben smiled when he saw the way Dutch Paul was driving before the wind.

"He does not like being behind," he said.

"He wants to keep the pirates in sight. Now, Ben, put wings to the 'Will-o'-the-Wisp.' I must come up with the miscreants before morning."

The splendid vessel went at a fearful pace through the waters.

Every man was on deck.

Armed to the teeth, and excited to an unusual extent.

Captain Tom was pacing the quarter-deck.

"We are going twice the pace of the pirate barque," he said to Iron Arm.

"Quite."

"So much the better."

It was not long before they came up to Dutch Paul, who yelled out—

"Go it!—you'll catch them presently at that rate."

Each minute now they appeared nearer to the pirates, who did all they could to get away.

Strong as they were in numbers, they did not like the look of the swift vessel that was coming upon them with such lightning-like rapidity.

The chase was long and exciting.

Towards evening Tom tried a gun.

They were not close enough yet.

The pirates, seeing how useless it was to attempt to fly, double-shotted their guns, and tried to keep their pursuer off by a few balls.

They, like that from the "Will-o'-the-Wisp," fell short of their mark.

"Don't fire any more," said the young captain. "It stops the vessel."

The pirates had the advantage there.

They could fire from the stern, and, instead of being any impediment, it increased the velocity of the ship.

"Ah! That's near."

A ball came so close as to dash the water over the bows.

Crash!

Captain Tom leaped round.

The martingale was cut from under the bowsprit, and the ball dashed against the prow, bounded away, and then fell into the water.

They were coming dangerously near.

Still the brave boy kept on.

He had sworn to conquer them, or die, and such was his determination.

"Signal to Dutch Paul," he cried. "We are getting close. Fire a shot for them to lay to. If they send another ball here, hoist the flag, and let them see who we are."

The men answered with a cheer.

The signal was hoisted for Dutch Paul, and the invincible flag run up to the mast-head.

A yell from the pirates announced they saw and knew it.

"Send them a challenge, Ben," cried Tom.

Ben sent them one.

It was not from bravery that the pirates accepted it.

They saw the utter uselessness in trying to get

away, and they knew that fighting was their only chance.

Then, again, their numbers made them bol—

They could number more than three to one against the boy buccaneers.

When Captain Tom saw they were slackening speed, he shortened sail, to await the coming of Dutch Paul, who was not far behind.

The gentleman pirate was as cool as ever.

A long cigar was between his teeth, and he came along quite indifferent, saying, carelessly, to his men—

"Prepare to warm them, my lads."

They replied with a shout, and went to the guns.

By this time Captain Tom was making every preparation for the conflict.

The two huge pirate ships brought their broadsides to bear on the "Will-o'-the-Wisp," thinking they might sink her long before Dutch Paul could arrive.

They little knew what it was to engage with the brave Captain Tom.

They hoisted private signals to Dutch Paul, who readily understood them, and prepared to obey their meaning.

The gallant young captain intended to run his ship in between the two huge pirate barques, and, while Dutch Paul was coming, he would keep them both engaged.

"Ben."

"Yes, captain."

"Is all ready?"

"Quite."

"Fire, then, and we will run in under cover of the smoke."

A terrific roar answered this, and the "Will-o'-the-Wisp's" side was a mass of flame.

With a yell the pirates returned the fire.

Then the terrible fight began.

"Keep it up," cried Captain Tom, to the gunners, who, stripped to the waist, were plying the guns in a most approved style.

The "Will-o'-the-Wisp" cut through the water at a great pace while the firing was kept up. She was completely hidden by the smoke, and when the pirates fired, their guns were ranged for the distance at which they first engaged the "Will-o'-the-Wisp."

Suddenly, both the pirate vessels felt an awful shock, and beheld a vivid blaze within a few yards of them. They gave a yell that was something like the roar of wild beasts. Another volley was poured into their sides and on their decks before they had time to recover from their surprise.

The idea of seeing the "Will-o'-the-Wisp" right between them was more than the blood-thirsty crew could stand. They yelled like demons, and plied their guns. The vessel on the starboard side of the "Will-o'-the-Wisp" manoeuvred to get closer, that they might board Captain Tom, while he was engaged with the other.

Captain Tom had prepared for all this. His signals had brought Dutch Paul on the pirates that were preparing to board, and, just as the vessel began to near Tom's, Dutch Paul opened fire.

The fearful screams, yells, and curses, told Captain Tom what had occurred, and, exchanging a succession of volleys with the enemy, he prepared for another manoeuvre.

The smoke completely hid his vessel again, and, while the firing was at its hottest, he shipped the "Will-o'-the-Wisp" through, and the pirate poured his shot into the sides of his own crippled companion, which was already in a blaze from the liquid fire of Dutch Paul.

The careless, indifferent freebooter, with his usual indifference, did not move from his seat, but with lighted cigar, he, in his usual sitting place, gave orders to keep up the horrible work.

He smiled cruelly when he saw the horror of the pirates, and he watched them clamber up the rigging to get away from the flames that run all over the deck like fiery serpents.

"Ha! ha!" he chuckled, watching the pirates clinging to the shrouds. "I'll bring you down. Elevate a gun."

This he cried to an officer. It was done.

"Bring those devils down!"

The long streak of flame went forth. What a yell came from the pirates' throats! They saw it run over the rigging consuming every rope and spar in its career, and the masts were in a blaze from the top to the deck.

The crew ran howling and screeching from one part of the ship to another, and yet could not escape. Several leaped into the sea; others tried to lower a boat.

Through all this Dutch Paul did not move. He had no pity for them, and, knowing the captives taken from the merchantman were on the ship engaged by Captain Tom, he cared little whether any of the ruffianly horde were saved. One thing was certain. He would not let any escape, even if they should get a boat out.

"Lower the boats," he cried, at length.

Nor was it too soon; in a few minutes the vessel would blow up, and now the water was perfectly alive with human forms. Some yelled piteously for help, others struck out bravely for Dutch Paul.

The boats were soon lowered and filled. Had not the officer in command threatened to shoot those who did not wait their turn, the boats would have been swamped.

As the boats returned, and the suffering wretches were taken on board, the bowsprit of the "Falcon" —such was the pirate ship named—fell into the sea, with its burden of human beings.

"Quick!" cried Dutch Paul. "We have no time."

The prisoners were brought on deck, the boats hoisted, and the "Yellow Vulture" began to move out of the way.

Well for them they did so. They had not gone far when there came a mighty roar.

The "Yellow Vulture" was nearly lifted out of the water, and Dutch Paul was thrown from his seat under the bulwarks, where he lay for a few seconds, not knowing what had happened.

Several of his crew ran forward to see if he was hurt, and to assist him to his feet.

"Sheer out, will you?" he yelled, jumping up, in a furious rage. "Curse the ship, I hope that has sent them all to their last account!"

He glanced anxiously towards the spot where floated only a few spars of the late pirate vessel—the "Falcon."

CHAPTER LXXXIV.

THE BLACK PANTHER.

THE pirate ship engaged by Captain Tom was much larger than the one so quickly destroyed.

Captain Tom knew this; he knew also that the vessel contained the chief of their fleet; that was the reason he engaged her.

The name of the pirate ship was the "Panther." The crew outnumbered the gallant boy buccaneers by fearful odds.

Nevertheless, he was determined to take the host of ruffians, and, had the ship been twice as large, or the crew ten times the number, he would have made an attempt.

The pirates were named after the ship, and called the "Panthers." They did not discover that Captain Tom had slipped from between the ships, until the awful cries and the blazing vessel showed them what had occurred.

With a horror-stricken cry, the Panthers left their

guns, and many began to turn the ship to get her away, while others rushed below appalled.

In vain did their chief, the Black Panther, try to rally them back. He swore and jumped about the deck like a madman.

"To your guns!" he howled.

One or two of the most courageous returned, but the rest would not. All the tales they had heard concerning Captain Tom and his band came to their minds, and they swore it was useless to fight against demons, who were aided by supernatural power.

With a howl of rage the Black Panther drew his pistol, and, pointing it at the captain of the larboard battery, who was about to spring into the rigging, ruffian fired, and the man fell, with a groan, dead.

Without caring who the next person was, the brutal commander fired a second pistol; another man fell. Then he drew his sword.

"Now then!" he yelled, "to your guns, every man, or I'll cut you down!"

He stood in amongst them; they cowed back, and the unlucky pirate who could not get out of his way was cut down.

This awed them. They returned to their guns, and the rest came to their various duties, just as the last volley from the "Yellow Vulture" put the "Falcon" in flames from stem to stern.

The "Panther" would have gone to his assistance, but a yell from the crew told the commander his dreaded foe—Captain Tom—was on their weather side.

The Black Panther was made aware of this by a terrific volley that was poured in.

He leaped round and saw the boy buccaneers were preparing to board them.

He returned their fire with all his power, but he howled like a wild cat when he saw the shots rolled off the "Will-o'-the-Wisp."

"Aim at her spars," he yelled.

"You won't have much time for that," said Captain Tom, who heard the order.

He glanced down the sides of his noble vessel, which was lined with his gallant band, armed to the teeth and ready for the fray.

At length the "Will-o'-the-Wisp" touched, and the brave buccaneers rushed upon their swarthy foes.

Dutch Paul's vessel was seen to move.

This slight movement had made the Black Panther quite unprepared for this attack on her, and was powerless to prevent the boarders gaining the ship.

He saw Captain Tom leading the whole party, and Harry Vere, Iron Arm, and Ben Barnacle were at his back.

When the pirates saw their danger, then they swarmed up.

Then came a sudden stoppage.

The deck was crowded.

The buccaneers began to cut their way through them.

Iron Arm's huge sword did deadly execution, as did Captain Tom's mighty blade, which, in a few minutes, was reeking from point to hilt.

He wanted to get at the Black Panther.

His wish was soon granted.

The pirate leader eyed him contemptuously, then swung his huge sword round.

It was met by Captain Tom's blade, and they began.

They fought for some time.

The Panther was beaten at every point.

He felt his arm tiring.

Then it was impossible to hold out much longer. He wanted to get from his fiery young antagonist. Captain Tom saw this by the look in his eyes.

He made a terrible onslaught upon the pirate,

and, just as he thought he could cut him down, the mass of men engaged in deadly conflict at his back opened, and the pirate-leader disappeared in their midst.

The brave young chieftain would have sprung after him, but a cry from behind warned him his assistance was wanted.

His gallant band had been beaten back by overpowering numbers.

Another and fiercer onslaught they made on the pirates, who could not keep the barque again.

Inch by inch the ruffianly horde gave way.

Presently there was a cry, and a cheer from the buccaneers.

Harry Vere had fought his way to the mast-head and hauled down the flag.

The Black Panther saw this.

He yelled like a madman, and rushed at the head of his band.

But it was useless.

It was like fighting against so many demons.

Another shout from the young mids proclaimed something had occurred.

Dutch Paul, with his crew at his back, made his appearance on the other side.

The pirates were driven to desperation when they saw it would be hot work with them.

They were perfectly hewn down, and in less than ten minutes after Dutch Paul boarded they surrendered.

Seeing he was beaten, and in their power, Black Panther dashed below.

He was determined to blow the ship up sooner than let his riches fall into their hands.

"Hold, captain!" cried one of the pirate crew, as he endeavoured to guard the hatchway that led to the powder magazine. "There may yet be hope for us."

"None! none!" hissed the pirate chief, bitterly. "Stand from my path, or—take that!"

The man groaned and rolled over mortally wounded; and the pirate chief, throwing away the empty pistol, took another from his waist-sash and raised the magazine hatch.

At that moment Captain Tom Drake, who had seen the pirate captain go below, entered the gun-room.

The young chief was not a minute too soon.

The ruffian would have fired a quick match, had not Captain Tom leaped upon him.

"Back!" he cried, dashing the pistol from his grasp, and forcing the burly ruffian upon his back.

The Black Panther's eyes glared savagely; but he was for a moment quite passive.

Yet the instant Captain Tom's follower approached to tie him down he leaped up.

So sudden, and with such power did he do it, that he broke entirely from the young chief's grasp, and the next minute was gone.

Dashing up the hold, he went against the door of a cabin with all his force and burst it open.

He peeped in.

A scream came from someone within.

Captain Tom with his gallant followers heard it, but when they came to the door they found it fast.

"Break it open!" he said.

Faint sobs came from within, which so goaded the men that they battered the door in instantly.

With a leap Captain Tom was inside.

He gave a cry of disappointment.

The Black Panther had disappeared.

Not a soul inhabited the cabin.

"Search every corner of the ship through," he cried.

The search was continued. But in vain.

Evening now was coming on.

Captain Tom could not account for the disappearance of the pirate chief.

"He must have escaped," he muttered, and again he went to the cabin.

The window was closed as it had been.

Not a sign could be traced of the desperate villain.

It was not his escape that troubled the brave young chief, but the sounds he had heard of a female voice.

He felt sure that if the ruffian had gone by any cunning contrivance, the poor captive maiden had gone too.

He little knew how much his surmise was correct.

The brutal pirate had a captive girl in that cabin, and he went there, it being his safest means of escape.

But even in that moment of danger he would not go without a victim.

He clutched the terrified girl in his arms, and gagged her.

Then he opened the window, which was astern, and floating, with everything prepared, was a small boat.

He clutched his now senseless burden and dropped into the tiny vessel, taking care to close the window after him, and thus throw his enemies off the scent.

Noiselessly he pushed the boat off, knowing that the crews of the vessels were too much occupied to notice anything.

One man, however, saw him, and was about to shout, when a blow from a marlin-spike stretched him senseless on the deck.

The one who dealt the cowardly blow was one of the pirate horde.

The instant he had done the deed, he crept over the ship's side, and into the water, to follow his captain.

The Black Panther thought it advisable to take him in the boat, after having done him such a service.

"That was well done," smiled the ruffian.

"I saw yer danger, cap'n."

"Can you see any of them about?"

"They are about to break the cabin door in, cap'n."

"Good. Ha! ha!"

"They won't overtake us."

"No, darkness will aid us soon."

And the ruffian chuckled at his success.

Meantime, the buccaneers had conveyed the captive maidens from the pirate barques to the "Will-o'-the-Wisp."

Dutch Paul and his crew were chiefly employed in taking the booty from her hold and stocking the lockers of his own vessel with it.

When everything was removed from the deck of the "Panther," and the wounded attended to, Dutch Paul came to the young chief, who stood with his officers on the quarter-deck.

"Well, captain, I guess we had a shindy."

"We certainly did."

"What do you intend doing with this old barque?"

"It is a splendid ship," replied Tom, eyeing the pirate barque with a look of admiration.

"Perhaps so," replied Dutch Paul, with a sidelong glance at the rigging.

"What do you think of her?"

"Capital, captain. But what are your intentions?" "It's mighty clear you had better hold a council of war."

"I will."

Captain Tom called his officers, and asked what they should do with the prize.

"Make one majesty a present of it," smiled Ben.

"Capital! Why don't you?" said Dutch Paul.

"Can't spare the men," said Tom.

"Men be blowed!" put in Dutch Paul. "Make the prisoners do it."

Captain Tom considered He certainly would have liked to send it to the King. But how was it to be done without periling his own men?

"Gentlemen," he said, at length, "I propose we settle it at the dinner-table. We have certainly earned our dinner nobly, and I propose we have a good one in consequence."

"Quite right," said Dutch Paul.

The others seemed to think the same, and they went on board the "Will-o'-the-Wisp."

Captain Tom gave orders for the prize to be towed behind, and the prisoners confined below.

An hour later, and Dutch Paul, with the officers of the "Will-o'-the-Wisp," were seated round the table over a very sumptuous repast, when a shout made them all leap up, and dash from the cabin.

CHAPTER LXXXV.

THE VAMPIRE'S SUBJECT.

It will be remembered that from among the massacred crew of the merchantman, Doctor Shrike and his assistant took a fine young fellow, to gratify some strange whim.

When the body had been conveyed to the doctor's berth, Doctor Shrike called Jacop.

"Jacop."

"Yes."

"Come here, you lantern."

"I am coming."

"Coming, you scarecrow," cried the doctor, musingly, and clutching a long, murderous instrument. "I'll wake you up, you effigy."

Jacop sneaked in at the door.

"Come here," cried the doctor.

Jacop drew near to him.

"Look! this is a subject for you, Jacop," said Shrike, with a grin, and pointing to the fine form of the young fellow who lay upon the table.

Certainly it would be difficult to find a more splendid form than this man. The limbs were magnificent and well-knit, and the body and chest would have done honour to Hercules.

For a few minutes Doctor Shrike eyed the inanimate body in silence.

"A pity—great pity," he muttered, at length, "fine young man, very."

The doctor seemed to regret the young fellow being past recovery.

"If there was a spark of life," he continued, "I would save him."

"But there ain't," put in Jacop.

"Hold your tongue."

"Can't I speak?"

"No."

"I shall, then."

"Leave the cabin, you whining thief."

"Who's a thief?"

"You."

"What did I ever thieve from you, you porpus?" cried Jacop, evidently hurt.

"What, you lantern-jawed ass! Didn't you come, like the thief you are, and steal my last bottle of port?"

"No, you old bloodsucker!"

"Am I?" yelled the doctor, making a rush at his assailant with a long knife.

For once in his life Jacop took courage, and snatched up a lancet, and dared his master with a look as furious as he could summon to his aid.

The doctor was so struck with his first act of bravery that he stood still and only glared upon him.

"Jacop," he said, "put down the knife."

"I won't."

" Don't be a fool, Jacop."

" I takes after you, them."

" Ha! ha! We'll see."

" Yes, we will."

" Jacop, put down that knife."

" I'll see you blowed first."

" Very well."

The doctor looked round the cabin for something larger to make a hit at Jacop.

But a new thought came to his aid—to let Jacop off now, and pay him another time.

" Jacop," he said. " Come, strip and help me with this subject, we shan't have any time soon—there's going to be a fight, Jacop—lots of arms—legs—heads—trunks—and so on."

" How do you know ?" asked Jacop, in the most friendly tone of voice.

" How do I know ?"

" Yes."

" Ha! ha! ha!" chuckled the doctor. " I know. Yes. Shall I tell you, Jacop, how I know ?"

" Yes, if you like."

" Well, my hand always itches, and my fingers tingle at the tips, as though the blood had gone from them."

" Well, then, if we are going to have such a lot of subjects, we don't want this one."

" Ah, yes, Jacop! this is a fine one—never saw one in my life like this !"

And the doctor began to tuck up his shirt sleeves before commencing his operations.

Jacop did the same.

Then the doctor began to feel if any bones were broken.

" Hope not," he thought.

At length he discovered they were not.

" Hold the basin, Jacop."

Jacop came forward with a huge bowl.

The doctor then opened the chief vein in the arm of his subject.

A small jet of blood started out.

Jacop gave a yell ; it went in his face.

" Ha! ha! ha!" laughed the doctor. " Ah! hallo !" he roared.

This sudden exclamation brought Jacop round to his senses, and he stared at the doctor, who stood, lancet in hand, his head over his subject, and his ear upon the throbless heart.

" He lives ?" asked Jacop. " Oh !"

The doctor answered him by striking the lancet in his thigh, for making a noise.

" Jacop! bandages—bandages, Jacop. He lives —what a pity so fine a subject as this should live ! What a pity !"

" Why, you said it was a pity when you saw him dead, now you say it's a pity 'cause he's alive !"

" Get the bandages, Jacop."

This was said in a persuasive tone that Jacop well knew meant mischief. Jacop obeyed.

The doctor was a strange man.

He saw there was a spark of life in the young man's body—he became serious instantly ; nor did he even speak until all that lay in his power was done for the sufferer.

He had little hopes of him recovering, and could not spare any more time at present, as the engagement began between the " Will-o'-the-Wisp " and the pirates.

As usual, Doctor Shrike was engaged for some hours with the wounded.

It was evening before he could return to his patient, whom he had taken for dead.

He saw with delight there was great hope of his recovery. When the crew learnt this, they gave a shout of joy.

Ben Barnacle, Harry Vere, and one or two officers were on deck at the time, breathing consolation to the late captive ladies, and when they heard the gladsome news Harry Vere brought up some wine and toasted the health of the young man, and " a fair wind and prosperous voyage."

This was the shout that brought Captain Tom from the cabin.

" What is this ?" asked Captain Tom of a mid.

" The young man who was brought from that merchantman. sir, lives."

" Ah! this is the first I heard of it."

The mid explained why he had been brought by the doctor on board.

" Can I see him ?"

" No," said a voice behind.

It was Doctor Shrike.

" You can't," he continued. " He ain't sensible ; you must wait. What a pity I've lost such a fine subject."

Captain Tom turned away, saying—

" Let me see him the instant he is well enough, doctor."

" Oh yes, captain," replied the doctor.

" Jacop is his nurse."

" Very good."

But the doctor had not gone from the cabin many minutes when Jacop, who thought the sick man would not wake yet, stole away for some purpose best known to himself.

A few minutes after his departure his patient awoke, and looked dreamily around.

He could not make out where he was.

He was not so badly wounded as had been supposed.

His face and eyes, as he gazed round, shewed he was quite absent of mind.

" What is this?" he murmured, raising himself up on one arm.

He remained perfectly still, and in a listening attitude.

His face wore a look of extreme agony, and he seemed striving to recall something to his memory.

Suddenly he gave a cry.

Glared upon his bandaged arm, and he underwent a great change.

His face became diabolical in its expression.

" My sister !" he groaned, " my sister ! Curse them ! I will save or avenge her !"

He stole from his cot, and glanced round the cabin.

An approaching footstep made his bosom heave, with a madman's light in his eyes.

He waited a minute in breathless silence.

Jacop appeared.

His eyes extended to a wonderful size when he saw the bed was empty.

Before he had time to turn he was clutched by the throat.

He gave a shriek when he saw the blazing orbs and distorted face of his patient, and he shivered when the gleaming blade was before his sight.

" My sister!—where is she ?" cried his assailant, in a fierce whisper.

" Don't !" gasped Jacop.

" Tell me ! Don't utter a cry, or I'll hack you to pieces !"

" Oh! pray don't! Mercy!—I saved your life !" gasped Jacop, in a disjointed manner.

" You will not tell ?"

" I—I do—not—know."

" Silence, fiend !"

The hands tightened their grasp.

Jacop felt himself whirled through the air. He thought the sword had gone through his body.

One long howl he gave.

A gurgling sob for mercy.

Then he lay all of a heap in one corner of the cabin.

His foe was gone.

Jacop howled most piteously.

THE TREACHEROUS PILOT CONFRONTED BY THE MAN-OF-WAR CAPTAIN.

He could not comprehend what had occurred.

He thought he was certainly killed.

"Oh!" he gasped, "I wish he had been made a subject of."

Then he lay still, trying to get breath.

Meantime, his "subject" had dashed on towards the hatchway.

He was about to ascend the companion-ladder, when the sound of many voices from the cabin arrested him.

With one tiger-like spring he was against the door, and it giving way with a crash, he went into the cabin.

With a wild cry, he leaped at the throat of Captain Tom, and, raising his sword, yelled—

"My sister—my sister, pirate and murderer! Where is she?"

"Release me!" said Captain Tom, with flashing eyes.

His captor laughed like a madman.

"It's my subject!" howled Doctor Shrike, who was there.

The young fellow placed the point of his sword against Captain Tom's white neck, and cried—

"My sister! Answer me, or I'll drive this sword in you."

Ben Barnacle, who could now understand what was the cause of this, sheathed his sword, and, going behind the apparently mad man, held him securely.

Captain Tom broke away, his face scarlet.

His sword leapt out.

But one glance at that fine, classic face, made him feel pity.

Ben held his prisoner firmly, though his struggles were fearful to behold.

"My sister—my sister!" was all he screamed, and it was as much as Ben could do to hold him.

"Poor fellow!" said Captain Tom, feelingly.

Ben had tried to make him understand they had saved him, but he evidently had lost his reason.

It was an appalling sight to see him struggling to get from the powerful arms of his captor, and at length Harry Vere and his chief had to go to Ben's assistance.

They hurled him down on a couch.

Then his struggles increased.

He foamed at the mouth.

His eyes were starting from their sockets.

His face was convulsed.

At length, with a scream, he went into a strong fit.

Doctor Shrike came forward then, and he was carried away.

The skilful doctor did all he could to restore him, but as yet all was useless.

"My God! what a sight!" said Ben.

"Dreadful!" said Vere.

"Poor fellow! do you think he will ever get his reason again?"

"'Tis hard to say."

"I don't think we have his sister amongst the ladies?"

"Why?"

"Because I think we should have found it out."

"What could have become of her, then?"

"We can discover."

"How?"

"By going and asking the ladies."

"Very true. I will go at once."

Captain Tom went to the cabin in which the ladies were.

Those who were well and sitting up, drew back at his approach.

"Do not fear, ladies. I have come to ask if any of you had a brother—or rather had one with you?"

Many of them replied by bursting into tears, and saying they had.

"Come," he said, "you shall see if this gentleman is."

One at a time he took the captives, but none recognised the stranger.

With a heavy heart, Captain Tom watched the last one, a fair young creature.

She shook her head mournfully.

"No, 'tis not he."

"Do you know him at all?"

"Yes, sir," she replied, tearfully.

"Do say what you know."

"He was on board with us, and had a very lovely sister with him, who was taken by the pirate chief into a separate cabin. I have not seen or heard of her since."

"The villain!" muttered the young chief, passing his hand over his brow, "it was her scream, then, I heard, when the pirate dashed into the cabin."

Captain Tom Drake led the young lady back to the cabin, and then went on deck.

He then thought he would question the men, which he did.

One man came forward with his head in a bandage—

"Excuse me, yer honour."

"Well, you want to speak with me?"

"Yes, yer honour."

"Go on."

"I was going to say that, after the fight, I was standing near the quarter-deck of the pirate barque, when you were trying to overhaul the skipper. I looked over the ship's side, and saw the black lubber just about to sheer off in a boat. He had a beautiful young lady with him. I was going to shout, when one of his cut-throat crew knocked me on the head with a marlin-spike, and stopped my jawing tackle—that's all, yer honour."

"All!" cried Tom Drake, stamping his feet on the deck with rage. "Gone!—escaped!—while we were losing time."

"Do you think, sir, he is still on the water?" asked Harry Vere.

"God knows!" and a faint groan came from the brave young chieftain's lips.

"God help her!" muttered Ben.

"I tell you, Ben," cried Captain Tom, with startling vehemence, "she shall be saved. I swear it! God of Heaven! look at the sufferings of that young fellow, and what she may have to go through! I shall go mad, if I think of it. Put the ship back, and we will go on the track of the scoundrel; and let him beware of the Shadow Avengers, for, by Heaven! this revenge shall be dreadful!"

CHAPTER LXXXVI.

A BROTHER'S OATH.

THE vessels were put back, and Tom was on the track of the Black Panther.

A good look-out was kept, and not a vessel allowed to pass until well scrutinised.

Nothing was decided about the prize, in the excitement of the moment.

Two days passed.

No sign of the boat and its burden.

Dr. Shrike came on deck.

"Well?" asked Tom.

"Yes," replied Shrike.

"Yes what?" asked Tom, impatiently.

"He's all right."

"Who?"

"The fellow that nearly choked you. Ha! ha! ha!"

Doctor Shrike laughed unpleasantly.

Tom's hand went to his sword.

"Be careful!" he muttered.

"Some of your hot blood rising again?"

"Dr. Shrike, go below."

"Very well."

"Begone!"

Captain Tom stamped his foot.

"Do you want to come down to see him?" asked Shrike, ironically.

"I shall suit myself."

"Very well. You have ordered me from the quarter-deck; and if you come to my berth, I'll have you kicked out."

And Doctor Shrike turned on his heel to walk away.

Captain Tom bit his lip.

"Doctor!" he called.

The doctor went back.

"Is he in his senses?"

"Yes."

"And will comprehend?"

"Yes."

Tom stepped into the cabin.

The young fellow glared at his handsome appearance eagerly.

The young chief, with a quiet smile, took his hand, and said—

"I am very glad you have so far recovered. I thought you were mad, when you attempted to choke me."

"You! God forbid!"

"Well," smiled Tom, "I won't speak of it."

"But, sir—"

"Nay, nay."

"But I must speak, sir," persisted the invalid.

"my conduct requires an explanation and an apology."

"Nonsense."

"Brave sir, you cannot imagine what I have suffered since the meeting with those pirates—"

"Who are now at the bottom of the sea."

"Is this true?"

"Aye, I hunted them down after I saw what had occurred—overtook their handsome vessel, and captured the other. Several lady pirates are on board."

"My sister, she—"

He paused during the sorrowful look that came over the young chief's handsome face.

"I am grieved to say that the ladies on board are all strangers to you."

"Oh, God! but how do you know?"

"By bringing them down to see if they knew you."

"Well?"

"They did not."

"This is torture!"

And the poor fellow hid his face in his hands and wept.

"Do not give way," said the young buccaneer, soothingly, "we are on his track now. I have learnt how the villain escaped with your sister."

"My poor sister; oh, God pity her!"

"Bear up, it will not be long ere we are up with her ruffianly captor."

"Then," said the young man with blazing eye and startling vehemence, "then, God have mercy on the murderer, for I won't. I swear to track the ruffian horde, if it be to the end of the world. If dead, my sister shall be fearfully avenged; if living, I will save her."

He was sane, now.

Calm, too.

This was no rash vow, but one he would carry out.

"I," said Captain Tom, "will assist you in it; my ship and crew are at your service, and if we do not come up with the Black Panther, why I will sink the 'Will-o'-the-Wisp' as useless."

"The 'Will-o'-the-Wisp!' You are, then—"

"Captain Tom Drake."

"I thought so."

"May I know what name we can call you by?"

"Yes; Gerald."

"Very well, Mr. Gerald."

"Captain Gerald."

"Captain!" echoed Tom, in surprise.

"Yes, captain in the Dragoons."

"You have seen a little service, then?"

"I have."

Tom saw the young soldier was in a moody fit, and saw he would like to be alone.

"You shall be waited on," he said; "summon a servant when you want anything. If you should not be well enough to come on deck, I will come down and see you again."

"Very well, sir."

Tom went on deck, and the young soldier was left to himself.

The young chief signalled for Dutch Paul, who was in sight.

It was answered; and shortly afterwards the "Yellow Vulture" made for the buccaneers' ship, and they were soon in hailing distance.

"Dutch Paul!"

"Hallo!"

"Can you come on board?"

"Yes."

"Very well, I'll lay to."

Dutch Paul ordered a boat to be prepared for him to go aboard Drake's ship.

Shortly after, he stood on the deck of the "Will-o'-the-Wisp."

"Dutch Paul," said our hero, "you can do me a great service, if you have a mind."

"Name what you want, captain."

"You have not heard what has occurred?"

"No."

"I will tell you, then."

Tom then related the incident of Captain Gerald.

Dutch Paul's eyes blazed for an instant, but seeing the young chieftain looked surprised, he gave a careless laugh, and said—

"Poor wretch!"

"His sister is in the hands of the Black Panther," continued Tom.

"That's bad."

"We are on his track."

"That's good," and Dutch Paul took a long whiff at his cigar. "Do you smoke?"

"Not when I have anything better to do. I—"

"Pardon, captain. Don't give a lecture on it, don't—tell me what you want."

"I want you to sail in a more easterly direction. I will keep on the same tack, and I think, by that means, one of us will overhaul the Black Panther."

"Why, where is he?"

"In a boat."

"Any one with him?"

"I know not, beyond Captain Gerald's sister."

"On my soul, that's too bad."

"Well, we have no time to waste here. We must name a point to meet at."

"True again."

Captain Drake considered for a few minutes, then arranged with Dutch Paul, who quickly departed to his own vessel, and was on the track of the pirate.

Nothing was seen during the night, but early the next morning Ben Barnacle, who was on deck, heard a little excitement among the men.

"What is it?"

"The look-out has reported something floating on the water."

Ben took his glass.

Long and earnestly he scanned a distant spec that floated on the mighty deep.

"'Tis small," he muttered, "and sometimes perfectly hidden by the waves. Can you make her out, Mr. Vere?"

"I am trying," Harry replied.

"It must be merely a spar—some wreck perhaps—or rather the remains of one."

"Very likely, Mr. Barnacle."

Still wondering what it could be, Ben smothered his impatience until the vessel got nearer.

When almost within view of the strange object, Captain Tom came on deck.

"What causes this excitement?" he asked, glancing round and raising his glass.

"Can you make out what it is, floating yonder."

"Just what we are trying to do, sir."

"I have it," said Ben.

"What?"

"It's a boat."

"As I thought," replied Harry Vere.

"Are we nearing it?" asked Tom.

"Rapidly."

And so they were. In a few minutes the boat was alongside.

Grapnels were thrown out, and she was hauled up.

She was empty, with the exception of a few biscuits, a little water, an old hatchet, and a few pieces of rope.

"'Tis the very boat," cried Tom.

"Which boat?"

"The one that ruffian escaped in."

"Then he has been picked up."

"That is obvious."

"It is better so, the poor girl may be saved."

"Yes," replied Tom, "and we know he must be on board some ship. Every one we pass shall be overhauled, and by that means we shall find them or a clue. Haul down the flag; put her in trim, and let the 'Will-o'-the Wisp' show its speed."

'Tis a dull, bleak morning. A small, drizzly rain is falling, covering the ground and every habitation, and soaking through the very roofs of the miserable huts.

The only bell in the quaint old church of the village is dismally tolling forth a solemn peal, at short intervals.

The church doors are open, and many poor, ill-clad peasants standing round, waiting for the arrival of the deceased person, for whom the before mentioned bell was tolling so dismally.

Many expressed surprise at not seeing either grave or grave-diggers.

One farm labourer suggested it was "the party up at the hall, and graves warn't good enou' for such folks—they must have a vault."

This seemed to be the general opinion.

Presently, every voice was hushed.

The approach of the solemn procession caused a calm.

Those near recognised the first two persons that alighted from the sable carriage, and followed a handsome (if we can use such a term for the ghastly article) coffin into the church.

They were John Sanderson and Mrs. Harpy.

The coffin rested upon two tressels while the service was read.

The name of the deathly occupant could be seen, engraved in large letters on a silver plate.

That name was—"John Gregory."

Doctor Burchenell was there, too.

He was paler than usual, and gloomy.

Not one word had he exchanged with his base employers.

He watched the sullen face of Sanderson, which, in spite of the solemnity of the occasion, was aglow with a fiendish look of triumph he strove, in vain, to conceal.

Mrs. Harpy was certainly the centre of attraction there.

Not one beheld that pale, worn face—those grey, straggling locks—the wrinkled brow, and those glaring, expressionless eyes, without a pang of pity shooting through their heart.

What a warning that woman taught to other crime-stained people!

Sin had brought its own affliction upon her.

The iron hand of sorrow had its grasp round her heart, slowly crushing out her reason, and her life.

When the funeral rites were all over, and the last office performed, the mourners returned to the carriages, and the people to their homes, away from the gloomy place, and out of the stormy weather.

Sanderson took Burchenell back with him to the hall!

They kept sullen silence all the way.

Mrs. Harpy was continually muttering to herself in a low, incoherent manner.

Sanderson now directed his gaze towards her, with a cruel smile instead of pity for the woman he had sent to perdition.

When at length they were in the hall, and alone, Sanderson spoke—

"Now, doctor," he said.

"Well."

"We will settle our business."

"With pleasure."

Doctor Burchenell took a document from his pocket, and spread it out upon the table, but he kept his hand on it the whole time.

For a moment, Sanderson's face lighted up with a dangerous look, but it passed instantly.

"'Tis a heavy sum, doctor," he said.

"Not for the work, Sanderson."

"It's nearly half the property."

"Ah, yes; but then there is Miss Atherton's, you know." The doctor smiled faintly, and continued. "And then you must remember you are safe now."

"Well—well. We won't quarrel."

Sanderson wrote a cheque for a very large sum of money. The doctor tendered a receipt, and shortly after left the house.

"Ah!" he muttered, "you shan't enjoy much— no, my friend, my greedy friend, you have not Miss Atherton's yet, and not likely to get it."

Sanderson, the outwitted villain—the man who thought himself the most cunning of all, who thought he had the game wholly in his hands, was a dupe— the dupe of one who would make him work his own destruction, drag himself to death; and then the scheming John Sanderson will learn that however good, clever, or villainous a man may be, there is always one to be found better, cleverer, and a greater villain.

But Sanderson thought himself safe; quite. With nothing to fear, all his enemies gone, he glared upon Mr. Harpy as this thought crossed his brain.

"Miserable wretch," he muttered, "she shall soon fill the chamber left vacant by the absence of John Gregory at the private asylum, and thence she shall go to the churchyard."

He had great faith in Doctor Burchenell. Strange it is; Burchenell was that man's most deadly enemy, and yet he could not see it.

He was blinded with success. Wait until all he could wish is fulfilled. Even when the cup is filled to the brim with all he could desire, it would never reach his lips.

"That document," he thought, "has put the Atherton estates in my power and the doctor— Bah! I don't fear him; he has had all he shall get from me, the next shall be a last draught. Then —then, the document. Ah! document. Have I been such a fool as to forget it? The document—is gone!"

Suddenly he gave an exclamation.

"I remember," he muttered. "He thrust it in his breast when he went, and now it must be there."

He turned a livid hue.

"I can't go there," he muttered. "Again to face him, would drive me mad."

Again he mused. Again he glared at Mrs. Harpy, who sat like one in a dream.

"Jane!"

She started.

"Jane!"

She looked up with a vacant stare.

"Come, Jane."

"'Tis you," she mused.

"Well, Jane, you know where we went this morning?"

"Aye, too well. I could stand all the other; but his death is on my head."

She murmured this in a low, solemn voice.

"We have nothing to fear now, Jane."

"Yes we have."

"What?" asked he, in surprise.

"Our conscience."

Such was the reply in a sepulchral tone. He saw that unless he dealt with her very carefully, her senses would be beyond comprehension.

"Jane," he said, "can you listen quietly to what I have to say?"

"Yes."

"To-morrow you shall be my wife. We will then leave the hall and live abroad—away from a place that has such unpleasant associations, our happiness will then be complete. But we want one thing."

"Yes, John, that document."

"The one signed by John Gregory and taken by—"

"Hush!"

Mrs. Harpy jumped up. Sanderson saw his mistake; he dared not mention that man's name; her reason would flee. This was her mad point.

The coward feared to go again in those apartments; he feared to look upon the dead. He could trust no one but himself or his guilty partner.

"Jane, we must have that!"

"Dare you ask me to return there?"

"We must."

"Look!"

She made a spring forward. Catching him by the wrists, she wheeled him round, his face to the door.

"Look!" she said again, raising her finger and pointing at the vacant space in front of her.

"Do you see that form?—that form—blood! blood! Oh, see!—look!"

Her hand tightened, her cheek almost touched his. Her eyes were starting from their sockets.

"Look! he moves!" she went on.

"Mad fool, let go!"

"Watch his eyes!—and the lips! Ah! he speaks! —he speaks our doom!"

A shudder went through her frame, but she did not move. Sanderson gave a cold shiver; the fearful incoherent ravings of Mrs. Harpy were more than he could stand. He was being worked up into a fit of desperation.

"Jane, let go."

"Do you say all this?" she almost screamed.

"By Heaven! unless you leave go, I will knock you down."

He tried to break away. Her hold was too fast. He swung her round, and, her feet slipping, she knocked her head against the door. She gave a scream.

"Hold your tongue, woman, the servants will be alarmed."

"Would you kill me?" screamed Mrs. Harpy.

"Silence, fool!"

"I dare not be silent."

"Jane!"

"Ah! you fear—you fear! Craven, stand still! See! he moves—he m—"

Sanderson could stand no more; the perspiration rolled off him in large drops. One powerful wrench he made, and Mrs. Harpy was knocked off her feet.

There was a low scream; a crash as she went against the door; a cry, followed by a fall. Then all was quiet.

"It was all her fault," and Sanderson ground his teeth in suppressed fury. "Curse her!"

Dragging Mrs. Harpy across the room, he placed her on a couch. She was insensible.

Pacing the room with hasty strides, he thought of the document.

"I'll go," he muttered, "what is there to fear? Ha! ha! it will be triumph to look upon his face —to gloat on it. Ha! ha!"

And, chuckling to himself, he left the room. He ascended the stairs and made his way to the apartments which had long since been closed.

"Ha! ha!"

He laughed triumphantly.

"Fancy his face for ever removed from my gaze. No—no longer will I fear him. I go and spurn her with my foot. Curse her!"

Sanderson was wound up; he could do anything at that moment. Without any seeming repugnance, he opened the door and entered the gloomy chamber.

Inside he did not feel so brave. The smile went from his lips, he glared fearfully round; the scampering of a rat made him jump.

The place seemed full of horrors, still he would not retire, to accomplish his object he was determined.

With shaking limbs and chattering teeth he went to the closet. The fatal closet wherein was hid the body of Captain Angel.

How the door seemed to creak; what a long time it was opening, too. He peeped in, all was dark, and a nasty odour saluted his nostrils.

"It must be done."

He took one step forward; upon the threshold he paused. Vainly he strove to pierce the gloom, nothing met his gaze; he went further in, still nothing but the bloodstained floor could he see.

Now he could see all the chamber.

"Ah!"

He leaped back with a loud cry. Written upon the floor, in large letters, and with human blood, were the words—

"Beware! Blood for blood!"

"Gone!" he cried, "gone!" and staggering out, he reeled and fell across the entrance, his hand in a line, and as though pointing to the blood-written words.

CHAPTER LXXXVIII.

THE CAPTURE OF CAPTAIN TOM DRAKE.

THE Black Panther, as the pirate leader was called, was as cunning as he was brutal. He valued his life very much.

He did all he could to save it. In the boat with his accomplice, and at a safe distance from the "Will-o-the-Wisp," he felt safe.

The tiny sail was hoisted, and the little barque shot through the water. The poor girl was insensible, and at the bottom of the boat. The pirate leader did not notice her.

He was absorbed in deep thought. He saw one of his fine ships, gorged with plunder, being burnt to the water's edge, and the other in the hands of the dashing Captain Tom.

It was a maddening sight to him. Long he fixed his eyes upon the spectacle, until it was hidden from his view. Then he turned his sullen brow upon his follower.

"What's to be done, cap'n?"

"Done!"

He ground his teeth, and clenched his hands furiously.

"Yes, cap'n, this boat won't last in a storm."

"Get out of her, then."

"Rather not."

"Then cease your prating, and steer her more eastward."

"Aye! aye!"

The pirate chief's eye rested for a moment upon the inanimate form at the bottom of the boat. A strange light shot from them, only for a minute.

It passed, and his dark face wore a kinder look, if we can term it a kind look at all. With the things he had in the boat, there was some brandy.

He poured some between the clenched teeth of the senseless girl. He noticed her violent struggles to get her breath, and he knew that the brandy was too strong.

He tried some clear, fresh water; this had its effect. A few minutes saw the poor girl restored to consciousness.

She glared wildly round, and, when the truth of her position flashed to her mind, she hid her face in her hands and wept.

The pirate leader turned away, without heeding her tears. The night wore on; it was a long, dreary night to those ocean waifs.

When at length morning came, a sail was seen in the distance. The pirate gave a grim smile.

"She may be a King's ship, cap'n."

"What then?"

"We should be nabbed."

"Should we?"

"With her, cap'n," the ruffian pointed to the trembling girl. "She would blab."

"Would she?"

Something was revolving in that man's mind. He had determined to go on board the approaching vessel, whether she be friend or foe. It was a rash thing, but he was equal to it.

Turning towards Captain Gerald's sister, he said, in his hoarse voice—

"Hark'ee girl!"

She shrank from the firm gaze.

"Don't shrink, but listen. We are going on that vessel, and mind you do what I tell you, or I'll hurl you overboard.

"I'm the captain of a trader. We have been overhauled by Captain Tom; you are the only surviving passenger. Do you understand?"

She made no reply.

"Well, remain obstinate, if you like. I don't want you to reply; but do anything but what I have said, and the first bullet I fire shall be in your skull."

He spoke quietly, but the ruffian meant it. The ship hove in sight, and, by the flag that was flying, the pirate saw it was a Britisher.

They saw, too, it was a trim little corvette. Ere long they were in hailing distance, and a signal was fired from the man-of-war.

The vessel lay to, the Black Panther steered his little barque towards it. The pirate had taken great care that his dress should not betray him. He wore nothing but a plain shirt and blue knee-breeches, with shoes.

The officer on deck, seeing a lady in the boat, lowered a ladder for her to ascend by. Much to his surprise, she was insensible.

The pirate leader carried her on board. When she was taken below, a hundred questions were put to the supposed merchant captain.

"How long have you been on the water in tha boat?" asked the captain.

"A day and night, captain."

"What is your name?"

"Captain Wilmot."

"Of what ship?"

"The 'Sunflower.'"

"Ah! That's the one we expected to have found before this."

"We were overhauled yesterday."

"By whom?"

"By that young pirate, Captain Tom."

"The scoundrel!" cried the captain, indignantly. "Do you mean to say he has robbed and destroyed an unarmed merchantman."

"Not only robbed, but murdered the crew in cold blood, after having their word that they would not oppose him."

"The rascal!" muttered the lieutenant.

Every one on board the corvette heard of this, and there was not an eye but what burnt indignantly against the perpetrator.

"How did you escape?" asked the captain of the corvette.

"From the window of the chief cabin into this boat; and while they were pillaging my vessel. The young lady I brought is the only one I could save from their clutches, and she was entrusted to my care by her guardians."

"Can you tell me what direction the pirates took?"

"I think they are chasing us."

"Then they will cross our track?"

"I fancy so, captain."

"Good! let them!"

"Should they do so, of course you will engage them?"

"This is a King's ship, sir," replied the captain, proudly.

"Pardon, I know it· but I was going to say that while I have an arm to use, I will have revenge for the ruin they have brought upon me."

"Do."

"Can I go below, now? I—"

"Certainly, Captain Wilmot."

"Thanks. You keep a good look-out, and the Will-o-the-Wisp' will soon be seen."

With that the Black Panther went below.

"Mr. Ashton."

"Sir," replied the lieutenant.

"Keep a double watch, and be well on the look-out. The murderers are not far off. This is rather fortunate, now, that we saw that boat."

"Why, sir?"

"Why, ain't we on the track of that young pirate, the very person we are hunting after? By Jove! if it were not for going against orders, I would put on all sail, and try to meet them."

"What will you do, sir?"

"The instant you sight the buccaneers, hoist all the canvas to attract attention, keep the ports closed and the flag down. When they see us veer the ship, and pretend to be running from them, they are sure to follow on your track; and while they are running us down, we can sight the admiral's ship, and signal to him to say we have the bird he has so long hunted for."

"But I might not know the ship, sir."

"Captain Wilmot will."

"Very good, sir."

The captain went below, and the lieutenant kept a good look-out for the "Will-o'-the-Wisp."

The day had nearly passed before anything was seen in the shape of a sail. When, at length, one was seen, great excitement prevailed on board the corvette. Captain Wilmot, alias the Black Panther, was called up.

"Would you know the 'Will-o'-the-Wisp'?"

"Yes, sir."

"Is that her?"

The pirate took a glass; after a few minutes' quiet scrutiny, he closed the telescope, saying—

"Yes, captain, that's her."

"Beat to quarters, Mr. Ashton."

"Aye, aye, sir!"

"Are we seen?"

"I think so, sir."

"Let us be sure."

"Aloft! aloft!" shouted the officer.

"Ahoy, sir!" replied the man on the foretop.

"Can you make anything out?"

"Very little, sir, it's getting so dark."

"Are we seen?"

"Yes, sir."

"Sure?"

"Yes, sir. They have just turned their prow in a line with us, and are coming straight upon us."

"Good."

"Veer the ship, Ashton."

"Aye, aye, sir!"

"Have a good look-out kept."

"Aye, aye, sir!"

The corvette was put back, and scudded away from the enemy at a rapid pace. But the "Will-o'-the-Wisp" came upon them like a racehorse.

The chase was a short and swift one. The captain of the corvette saw it was useless to continue it.

"We shall not come up with the admiral before they are down upon us."

"I fear not, sir."

"Then we must have him by subterfuge."

"True."

"Do not let him come alongside. We will get him on board with just a boat's crew."

"I see."

"Ashton."

"Sir."

"Station a company of marines behind the bulworks, and conceal the guns. We must get him on board, and then surround his party with the marines. Everything must be done quietly; and, covered by the darkness, we can sail away from their ship and deliver our troublesome bird into the hands of the admiral."

"Very good, sir."

"Do you understand?"

"Perfectly. I think the idea charming."

At that moment they were hailed.

"Ship, ahoy!"

"Ahoy!" replied Ashton.

"Lay-to. We want to speak with you."

"Aye, aye."

The sails were put back, and each vessel lay motionless on the water. The captain stood, speaking-trumpet in hand, by his side stood the pirate.

"That is Captain Tom's voice," added the commander.

"Yes, captain."

"Are you ready?" came across the waters.

"Yes."

"Have you seen anything of a small boat, with two or more occupants, one a lady?"

"Yes."

"Where are they?"

"Below."

"Do you know who the man is?"

"No."

"Wait. I'll come on board and tell you."

A boat was lowered from the "Will-o'-the-Wisp," and a few minutes later Tom was on board the King's ship; Captain Gerald was with him, and a dozen stout sailors.

"Will you come below, sir?" said the captain, after the customary salutes.

"With pleasure."

Tom Drake and Captain Gerald followed the captain of the corvette and his lieutenant below. Tom's followers remained on the deck, answering the questions put to them by the petty officers.

"Do you know who you have on board?" said the young chief.

"No—at least, Captain Wilmot."

"Wilmot!"

"Yes."

Tom laughed.

"You have the Black Panther, the leader of a pirate horde."

The captain started.

"Is it so? I will see to this."

"Pardon me, sir," said Captain Gerald, "but, for God's sake, conduct me to my poor sister, the lady that came in the boat."

"Why—why she—"

"I assure you, sir, she's my only sister."

"Then I have been deceived."

"Of course you have," replied Captain Tom, and he made the captain acquainted with the fearful work of the pirate barque.

"Pardon me a few minutes, gentlemen," said the captain, and he left the cabin.

He saw his lieutenant, and told him what he had heard.

"Then what is to be done?"

"Put the scoundrel under arrest. I don't like the work in hand, but it must be done. The boy is as brave as a lion. Are his men still on deck?"

"Yes, sir."

"Go, then. Have the ship towed silently away, until quite hidden from the 'Will-o'-the-Wisp' by the darkness; then hoist her sails, and make as much headway as possible."

"I will, sir."

"Then arrest that pirate ship."

The captain went to the cabin in which Captain Gerald's sister was.

He saw her reclining on the couch.

"Pardon, lady," he said "I only come to ask you one or two questions."

Receiving no reply, he continued—

"What is your name?"

"Gerald."

"Have you a brother?"

"One."

"Who was that who came on board with you?"

She glanced round in a terrified manner, without replying.

"What do you fear?"

"He is the leader of a horde of pirates."

"Ah!" he exclaimed. "Many thanks, miss."

He bowed and went out.

Rejoining Captain Tom, he told young Gerald to go to his sister.

The young chief and captain of the man-of-war then got into conversation.

Suddenly Captain Tom started.

He heard a loud scuffle on deck.

"The men are hunting for that pirate leader," said the captain, by way of explanation.

Which was not the truth.

It was a short, silent struggle with Tom's gallant followers, who, overpowered by numbers, were soon made captives.

The vessel was turned from the "Will-o'-the-Wisp," and put in full sail.

Just as they did so, a voice hailed them.

The lieutenant leaped up with a cry of delight. A slight bustle was heard on board.

Meantime, Captain Tom was below, in earnest conversation with the captain.

Suddenly an officer entered.

"The pirate has escaped, sir."

"Escaped!—how?"

"I know not, sir, but he has."

He then gave his captain a slip of paper, and departed.

The paper contained these words—

"The admiral will board in a few minutes."

The captain's face flushed.

Captain Tom had a strange misgiving all was not right.

"Escaped!" he said, jumping up. "Ah! Treachery!"

This he cried, finding the vessel was in motion. Crash!

The vessel came in violent contact with something, and Tom was hurled off his feet.

Leaping up, he drew his sword, and cried—

"Traitor! if you have dared to harm one of my men beware of the vengeance of Captain Tom!"

He leaped towards the door, which flew open, and a voice that made his blood curdle cried—

"Hold! Captain Tom, pirate and murderer! we have you at last."

Tom started back, and a mocking laugh came upon his ears.

He was confronted by Admiral Ellis, who, with a party of marines, stood in the doorway.

The admiral's face was fiendish in its look. Drawing his sword, he rushed forward, crying to the marines—

"Seamen!—your bayonets! Charge!"

CHAPTER LXXXIX.
A FIGHT IN THE SEA.

THE disappearance of the Black Panther can be easily accounted for.

He saw that he was discovered.

Beyond doubt, his fate would be to dangle at the yard-arm in the morning.

That was not pleasant.

He had heard all that passed between the commander of the frigate and Captain Tom.

He called his ruffianly companion.

" We must get away."

"Aye, aye, cap'n!"

" Hold your jaw, or we shan't get off."

" Don't see how it is to be done, as it is."

" Don't you?"

"No."

" Then I'll show you. Ain't there a boat along-side?"

"Aye, cap'n."

" Then there's our chance."

Quietly they made their way upon deck, and, after some difficulty, managed to get to the bulwarks.

While they were debating how they should get into the boat without being seen by the crew of the "Will-o'-the-Wisp," there was a sudden disturbance.

A short struggle.

A brief and bloodless contest.

And the gallant fellows from the "Will-o'-the-Wisp" were bound, and hurled below.

"Now's our time!" said the pirate, as he leaped the ship's side.

His man followed.

A minute later they were in the boat.

The rope was cut.

Then they shoved off.

Not a moment to spare.

Already they heard the sound of voices and the tramp of feet.

By the few words they overheard, it was evident they were being searched for.

"Pull!" he cried to his follower.

"Which way, cap'n?"

" Straight ahead."

"Then we shall pull on to that young devil's ship."

" Pull straight out, then, away from them both."

The boat shot forward just as the bulwarks were lined with men.

They would have been seen, and slain instantly, had not the captain of the frigate given express orders that no light should be used on deck, as they did not want to be seen by the "Will-o'-the-Wisp."

Another command was that no fire-arms were to be used.

Well for the pirate it was so.

The Black Panther and his companion pulled with great vigour.

They were on a fair way to freedom.

So much so, they were soon out of sight of the vessel.

The night seemed to have become much darker, the waves rolled high, and a heavy wind was blowing.

They were ignorant of the fact that the ship's prow was turned, and, instead of sailing from them, it was coming full upon their track.

Captain Gerald was frantic when he heard the miscreant had escaped.

He gnashed his teeth in wild fury, and he felt inclined to cut down those who stood around him.

He was too excited, under the circumstances of the moment, to notice that anything strange had occurred.

He knew nothing of Captain Tom's arrest.

He did not observe the vessel was sailing swiftly onward.

Even when his anger cooled, and he had returned to his sister, the joy at finding her safe and unsullied kept every other idea from his head.

He sat with his sister's hands locked in his own. The cabin window was open to admit the refreshing sea breeze.

He loved his sister dearly—and she was ten times more precious now he had nearly lost her.

He cast his eyes out upon the dark, troubled waters of the deep, while listening to her gentle voice.

With a cry, he leaped up.

She gave a slight scream.

" Albert, what is the matter?"

" 'Tis he!"

Seizing a loaded musket, he fired it from the cabin window, then, dashing the weapon to the floor, he leaped through the smoke and rushed upon deck.

" There's the boat!" he cried to the officers of the watch.

" Where, sir?"

" There—there!"

" So there is. All hands up!"

There was a scuffle of feet as the sailors rushed upon deck to see what had occurred.

" Put the ship back, and lower a boat," cried the officer.

"Aye, aye, sir!"

" They will escape!" cried Captain Gerald, excitedly.

" No, they won't."

" My God! let me get near the villain!"

The ship was put back, and a boat lowered.

" I can't see them," said Captain Gerald, in a voice of anguish.

Unable to control himself, he dashed below, clutching a loaded gun from the hand of a marine on his way. Rushing to the cabin, he put his head out of the window.

He could see nothing, but waited there for some few minutes; then he heard the splash of oars, and knew the boat had gone.

He was in the act of dashing on deck, and leaping into the water to join those in the boat, when a dark object attracted his attention. With an inward cry, he raised his gun. Then came a bright flash, a report, the bullet sped on, and he heard a low cry of mortal agony. He was unerring in his aim, and one of the figures in the boat fell back—dead. Then he rushed on deck.

" Stop for me!" he cried to the officer who had charge of the pinnace.

Without waiting to see whether they heard him, he leaped into the sea. Luckily, they heard him, and also saw him leap into the water.

" Lay on!" said the officer.

The men ceased rowing.

" Steady! back water!"

Ere long, Captain Gerald was in the boat, and urging on the men. He saw the little craft they were in search of for an instant; then it faded from view.

" He will escape!" he again cried.

" I think your shot took effect," said the officer, " I saw one fall."

" I do not know which, but I have sworn none shall live that come within my reach."

" Well, and you are right, too."

" Ah!"

" What's the matter, sir?"

" Is not that another boat putting off from the ship?"

" Yes."

" Good! They had better take another direction."

" They will."

The second boat was manned with eight stout rowers, and they soon came up to them.

" Is that you, Morris?" cried the first lieutenant.

" Yes, sir," replied Morris, the second officer, who had charge of the second boat.

" Keep more to the left, he has slipped us."

" Aye, aye!"

Long and earnestly they searched for the escaped pirate. Without success, he had evidently given them the slip. At length, a distant small light attracted the lieutenant's attention.

" Bo'sun."

"Aye, sir !"

"Signal for Mr. Morris."

The signal was given, and Mr. Morris soon came alongside.

"We cannot find him, Morris, and that light in the distance shows the ship must not remain here. We must return."

"Very well, lieutenant."

She put back for the ship. Not many hundred yards had they gone, when Captain Gerald gave a cry—

"The boat !" he said.

The sailors pulled with a will when they heard what was in sight.

"Bend your backs, my lads," said the officer.

My lads did bend their backs, and those who did not received a blow in the spine from the end of the oar in the hands of the sailors behind them.

It was but a few minutes' chase, and they were by the side of the pirate's frail barque. Gerald leaped up and raised his sword.

"Malediction !" he muttered.

Then, leaning over the boat, he examined a huddled heap at the bottom ; it was the form of the pirate's follower, who lay dabbled in his gore—dead —with the bullet from Captain Gerald's gun in his heart.

The Black Panther had gone. Where he could have escaped to was a mystery more than he was prepared to solve. Save the corpse, the boat was empty ; Captain Gerald muttered an oath.

"Have you any pikes in the boat ?"

"Yes, sir," replied the boatswain.

"Sink that little craft then."

A crash followed his words, the pikes made huge holes in the frail barque, and in a few minutes it had gone to the bottom with its bloody freight.

Enraged and disappointed, they returned to the ship. The men in the gig were the first to board and haul up the boat, then the lieutenant and crew went on.

Captain Gerald was the last in the boat. Just as he made a step forward, he felt the boat rock—he turned, a dark form was behind him.

An arm was raised from the water, and a knife gleamed in the air. Before he had time to move hand or foot, he felt a keen pain run through him.

A dimness came over his eyes, he reeled, a sickening sensation came over him, and with a groan he fell to the bottom of the boat.

The blood gushed from a wound in his back. The sailor who held the rope affixed to the prow of the tiny vessel, gave a cry and dropped it. He saw the deed, and the whole crew gave a howl.

They beheld a dark form trying to steal into the little barque—a dozen muskets were raised, a dozen bullets would have gone through the brain of him who had struck Captain Gerald, had not the lieutenant put up his hand.

"Hold !" he cried, "you dare not fire ! You would not only endanger Captain Gerald, but bring the 'Will-o'-the-Wisp' down upon us."

The men reluctantly put down their guns, many made a spring for the boat, one jumped in it. A powerful blow from some hard instrument upon his head felled him.

Another took his place, he was a fine, and powerfully-built young sailor, bold as a lion, and with the strength of Hercules.

He caught the form in the boat by the throat, he caught a glimpse of the face, it was the Black Panther.

The pinnace had now drifted some slight distance from the ship. The Black Panther grappled his foe as the young sailor drew his knife, and a short struggle ensued, the boat rocked to and fro whilst the men wrestled wildly.

Each were powerful men, and were enraged beyond control. They wanted each other's blood. It was

a fearful fight, once they swayed over more than ever ; the pinnace tilted, and each lost his balance and fell into the sea.

They released their hold upon each other, and the young sailor glanced around.

He saw some of his companions lowering another boat to came to his assistance. He saw the Black Panther swimming towards him with an upraised knife.

Bravely he met him ; with his left hand he kept himself afloat and in motion—his right grasped his knife.

He swam round the Black Panther, who had made several slashes at him, they both had received a slight wound.

The young sailor was determined to end the fight, so he dived beneath the water, when the Black Panther tried to swim away, fearing the result. One minute of awful suspense, then the pirate gave a groan of agony—the sailor's knife had gone into his ribs.

The young man-of-war's man came to the now blood-stained surface. And with pain and fury the Black Panther leaped almost out of the water and gripped him by the throat.

His dagger elevated, and was buried within the young sailor's shoulder. He uttered no cry, he caught the Black Panther by the throat, and his grip was like iron.

He could not use his right arm, that being the wounded one. Still his left had closed tighter each minute upon the pirate's throat, who could not strike a blow.

He was being strangled, the loss of blood and suffocation was too much. His eyes started, his jaw dropped, a foam came upon his lips, and the young sailor felt him go a dead weight beneath the water.

"I've conquered !" he muttered. "Help me, I shall sink !"

CHAPTER XC.

MRS. HARPY BECOMES A WIFE AND A LUNATIC. SANDERSON was now in a perpetual state of fear. The body of Angel had gone, and the document, too. What mystery could this be ? He stood upon dangerous ground.

He would have given much for the council of Mrs. Harpy now, he found he was lost in his villainy without her.

He did not mention his terrible discovery to her, as her mind would certainly give way under it. He returned to her, and found she had recovered, and was sitting in the same despairing attitude as ever.

She was enough to touch a heart of stone, and even he felt pity for the woman he had made to sin. Each day now she became worse.

Her hair was nearly white, and she could scarcely understand a word, and one point she was for ever harping on, that was marriage.

She, at times, declared herself the wife of Sanderson ; at others wailed and wept that she was not.

He knew not how to act, it was fearful to behold the woman thus.

He could not reside in the house where she was. Brute as he was, he could not look upon her without a pang of sorrow.

He was ever concocting schemes in his mind, he wanted to rid himself of the woman, but how could he was the point.

She was not outwardly mad yet, at least not enough to be put in the asylum. Still, he knew anything that would cause a revulsion of feeling, a sudden shock, would send her now beyond cure.

It was a melancholy madness upon her now, and that was worse than anything. One morning Sanderson, unable to endure it any longer, said, in his quiet, oily way—

"Jane !"

"Yes, John."

"Can you converse this morning? Are you well enough?"

The cunning villain was very careful how he addressed her.

"Yes, John. What would you say?"

"Simply, Jane, I can't bear to see you so unhappy. What can I do for you?"

"Don't you know, John?"

"No."

"I have but one wish."

"And that?"

"Is to become a wife."

"Well, Jane, you have longed for that, and I have promised. At last, I will keep my word. Get your clothes ready by the day after to-morrow, and we will be married."

"You mean it, John?"

"Solemnly—I swear it!"

He watched her as he spoke, and he saw the changes she underwent. Her face was flushed. Her eyes flashed, and she endeavoured to speak.

She could not, a flood of tears came in place of words, and she wept long and bitterly. Sanderson left the room, his callous heart was touched, and the scoundrel could not remain in her presence.

He was going to perform his promise, but the ruffian had a motive in it. His hope was that her mind would never remain sound under the ceremony.

He ordered his carriage, and went to the town, seven miles distant. That night packages came to the house for Mrs. Harpy.

She called her maid, and locked herself in her room that she might unpack these unexpected parcels.

How her eyes dilated!

Her face flushed, and her whole frame trembled From the interior of the package she took a long veil, a bridal wreath, and several handsome presents from her betrayer.

An elegant wedding dress came, too. It, of course wanted a little alteration, and that was all. Her mind seemed to revive under the excitement.

At times, though, she was very flighty, and frightened her maid by her strange conduct. One minute she would weep like a child, the next she would sing in the most melancholy strain.

Her maid used to be touched to her heart's core, and she would weep, too. She knew not of Mrs. Harpy's crimes, and thus could pity an unfortunate sufferer of her own sex.

During the time she was preparing for the wedding, she had seen little of Sanderson.

At length the morning arrived, the morning on which she was to be married. All was bustle at the hall.

Sanderson had sent up word to say he was prepared and waiting.

Two lady friends were called upon to act as bridesmaids. Mrs. Harpy seemed to possess all her faculties as she dressed.

She was robed in white from head to foot, and her wreath was lilies of the valley. She wore very little jewellery.

She looked at herself, when finished, in the glass, with a sad smile. Then, sending a message to say she was prepared, she went below.

On entering the drawing-room, she found Sanderson there waiting for her. He started. Her appearance struck him with a chill.

Robed as she was in white from head to foot, with her pale, wan cheeks, her glaring eyes, and ashy lips, she was suggestive of something that flashed through Sanderson's mind at that moment—the bride of death. Such she appeared.

"It is time we started, Jane."

"I am ready, John, dear."

"Come, then, the carriage is waiting."

The wedding party entered the carriages, and drove off to the church. Mrs. Harpy changed during the journey.

Her melancholy returned, and she talked in an incoherent manner. At length they were at the church. Again Mrs. Harpy changed for the better. Perfectly she understood all that was going on. The ceremony commenced. The usual forms were gone through.

Now it came when the bride was to reply—those words that made her his, for ever—the simple phrase—"I will."

Sanderson felt her tremble upon his arm. Her whole frame shook. The wedding ring was placed on her finger. It had closed like a vice.

She listened with a vacant stare to what was going on. At length there came a silence. She felt Sanderson trying to lead her away. His voice uttered the word—

"Wife!"

What a wild laugh she gave! "Wife!—ha! ha! Yes—I'm a wife!"

With a moan, she sank on the floor, in a deadly swoon. The bridesmaids screamed. The parson looked round.

"Water!" said Sanderson.

The warden brought some.

"Jane!"

Sanderson thought she was dead. No, he detected a movement, the pulse beat. Still, he saw it was useless to try and restore her then.

She was in a deadly swoon. She was carried to the carriage.

"Drive home," cried Sanderson.

The coachman started off.

"Quick!" called out Sanderson, who thought it would be policy to show a little distress.

The vehicles rolled along, and they were soon at the hall. A doctor was sent for. It was some time ere Mrs. Harpy—now Sanderson—recovered. When she did, Doctor Burchenell shook his head.

"Quite gone!" he said.

"What mean you?" asked Sanderson.

Burchenell tapped his forehead.

"She is beyond recovery."

A quick flash left Sanderson's eyes.

Burchenell saw it.

"What can be done, doctor?"

"Nothing yet."

"But—"

"'Tis no use contradicting. You can only treat her kindly, and let her do as she likes."

"See how far her mind has gone. If nothing can be done, why—"

He paused.

"I will put her under your charge," said John Sanderson, by way of a finish.

"Do."

"Am I to wait long before she is removed?"

"How do you mean?"

"Why, it is very uncomfortable for me to see her in that dreadful state. It makes me feel as though I could not stay in the house."

"I dare say. Well, two days will be sufficient. If she does not alter for the better, why, send for me."

"I will."

"I can do nothing for her until then."

"Very good."

"Remember, have her treated kindly."

"Most assuredly."

"Good day, Mr. Sanderson."

"Good day, doctor."

They parted.

"What a melancholy sight!" muttered Burchenell, as he went home; "and thus comes the punishment of crime."

As he had said, it was a melancholy sight. Mrs. Sanderson's reason was quite gone. She sang and laughed worse than ever, she would place herself before the glass, and remain there for an hour at a time, arranging her hair, and continually repeating the word—

"Wife!"

She had kept on her bridal clothing, and would not allow them to be removed, not even touched. At times she would regard the ring on her finger with a fixed stare.

When she met Sanderson she betrayed no sign of recognition. A cold shudder would pass over her form, that was all.

All the servants were unhappy, and pitied, in their own terms, "the poor, suffering lady."

Sanderson could not bear to look upon her.

"By God! I can stand it no longer!"

He rode down to Burchenell; he found the doctor at home.

"Doctor!"

"Well, she is not better?"

"Better! I shall go mad, too, if she stays there any longer."

"Then you want her brought here."

"At once."

"Would you like her to follow her brother?"

"I—"

He paused, he did not wish to let out too much.

"Poor woman," he said. "Perhaps it would be a relief to her; though, of course, I would sooner have her well."

"Liar," thought Burchenell.

Aloud, he said—

"Of course, Mr. Sanderson."

"You will send for her, then?"

"To-night."

"That will do."

"We will arrange matters at the hall?"

"Yes."

"That will do."

"Very well. Until then, adieu."

Sanderson returned home with a smile of triumph upon his face.

"At last!" he muttered. "Now I am freed from them all. Nothing is in my path. Ah! all mine. Atherton shall be mine. The estates, too, and then all will be accomplished."

He arrived at the hall and closeted himself in his room.

He was brooding on the future, laying his plans. But the disappearance of Captain Angel and the document still haunted him.

He would discover what had become of them. A loud summons at the door made him start, he knew what it was; the carriage for the removal of Mrs. Harpy.

Doctor Burchenell came in, they made arrangements; and then the doctor departed. Sanderson kept in his room—of course, because he could not bear to look upon his poor wife being removed.

He sat there listening to every sound, at length he heard the rattle of wheels; the vehicle was going, and all was over.

He heaved a sigh of relief.

"At last!" he muttered, and rose from his chair.

He started back with a cry; his hair rose up on end; his face went bloodless; his tongue clove to the roof of his mouth.

His eyes started from their sockets, and he looked on in deadly fear at what he saw. It was a face, white, ghastly, and horrible at the window.

The dark, gleaming eyes glared upon him through the glass. The teeth glistened like the fangs of a tiger.

Sanderson shrank back, he could have screamed, but his tongue refused its office. Well he knew that face, too well he understood that fearful look; it seemed like a forewarning of his doom.

The fearful words he had heard before came upon his memory; the words spoken by Captain Angel.

And now—now—that face at the window, which looked upon him with such demoniac hatred.

"Captain Angel!" he gasped, and staggered back, with both hands placed upon his heated brow, and the face disappeared from the window.

CHAPTER XCI.

CAPTAIN TOM IS TO BE EXECUTED.

CAPTAIN TOM was not easily captured. He fought with his usual lion-like courage.

Admiral Ellis, with all the hatred he felt in his heart written on his face, rushed forward before the marines, and he would have cut the brave young chief down, but Captain Tom was too good for him.

Ellis found his sword shivered in his hand ere a minute had elapsed. He gave a howl; it fully expressed his hate and rage.

"Fire!" he said, hoarsely.

Tom turned to attack the marines, he saw his trusty blade was of little use against their weapons, but he fought to the last.

Two of his would-be captors lay bleeding on the floor of the cabin, a third retired wounded.

With a rush the whole company swept upon him, and though he received the points of their bayonets in his breast, he did not give in until his senses forsook him.

The vindictive Admiral Ellis ran forward, and stood over him with a laugh of vicious triumph.

"At last!" he muttered.

The captain of the frigate left his cabin; he could not look upon the pale, motionless form of that brave boy without a pang of remorse shooting through his heart.

He had been the cause of the young chief's arrest; now he repented the act most bitterly.

"Load him with irons," said the admiral, "and secure him in some place that he won't have the slightest chance of escape. Let the marines guard the door, and if he should escape, I'll flog every man that was ordered to prevent it."

The sailors knew he would keep his word. Much against their inclination, the brave tars manacled our hero, and he was thrust into the loathsome hole.

Admiral Ellis rubbed his hands with glee, and went on deck, the captain was there.

"What headway are we making?" asked the admiral.

"About twelve knots, admiral."

"Good."

His dry, grating laugh came unpleasantly upon the ears of the captain.

"We have outstripped the 'Will-o'-the-Wisp'?"

"Yes, admiral."

"Ha! ha! I thought so, captain. Keep alongside me until the first streak of day."

"Very good, sir. Any more orders?"

"No. I simply want to carry out what I thus have failed in."

"May I presume to inquire, admiral?"

Ellis laughed drily.

"Decidedly. I mean to wait until that confounded young pirate's vessel is in sight, and hang him to the yard-arm before the eyes of his whole crew. And hark you, captain, if by any means that young cut-throat escapes, not one on board this vessel shall escape punishment—not one."

The admiral placed great stress on the word "one," and the captain understood it as a hint to him.

"Very good, admiral."

Ellis went on board his own ship, and just as she was about to cast off, he called out—

"Captain!"

"Sir."

"Send the prisoner on board at the first streak of daylight."

"He could come now, admiral."

"Ha! ha! Yes; let him out now—he will be under safe keeping."

The spiteful little fellow's order was instantly carried out, and Captain Tom, senseless, and bleeding profusely from his wounds—his hands and feet strongly bound—was conveyed on board the frigate.

The doctor, who saw him, addressed the admiral—

"Pardon, Admiral Ellis; but unless he is attended to, he will not live to take his trial."

The admiral would have given some angry reply, but on second thoughts he consented to allow the doctor to dress the young buccaneer's wounds.

Admiral Ellis was afraid of losing his revenge; that he could not stand. The doctor went instantly and bound up the three gaping wounds in our hero's breast.

Then the bold, lion-hearted chief was hurled below into the filthy hold, there to await his doom. The words spoken by Admiral Ellis were no idle boast; he meant it.

Nearly two hours elapsed ere Captain Tom recovered his senses. Bitterly at a loss to know what had occurred, or where he was, the young chief tried to rise.

The clink of his chains, the pain of his wounds, the agony of the manacles round his wrists and ankles, in an instant told him his fearful position.

It wanted no second thought for him to know he was in the hold of a ship, and instinct told him that ship was commanded by Admiral Ellis.

It was dark and loathsome down in his prison. He could tell by the sound of the water he was much below the water-line. He felt and heard the rats all about him.

His was a fearful position. A less brave heart than the one that beat in the breast of Captain Tom would have quailed; his did not.

"I can meet my fate," he muttered, "whatever it may be. Would my hands were free! With my liberty, I would defy them, and should not die without a struggle!"

He ground his teeth savagely.

"Anything were better than to have that fiendish little admiral to exult over me."

He rose to a standing posture, the rats were becoming too familiar. He did not want them or their company, as they made too free.

So far so that one crawled up and bit his hand. Quick as lightning he caught it by the middle of the back.

Then he placed his fingers on its throat; the horrid little animal gave a spasmodic struggle, and then ceased to live.

Captain Tom hurled it among the rest, and then stood waiting another attack. He found a little relief in having these little reptiles to vent his rage upon.

For a moment the rats seemed scared at finding one of their companions hurled among them in a lifeless state.

But they regained courage, and returned in a body.

Captain Tom could tell they were coming.

He dashed forward, swinging his heavy chains round right and left.

Several little squeaks of agony, and a dull thud told the effect.

His terrific onslaught quite frightened them, and at length he was left in peace.

He wanted a little sleep, he felt faint and exhausted.

Yet he dared not lay down in that loathsome den.

How much longer was he to stay there? How many days had passed already?

These were his thoughts as he leaned against the side of his narrow, gloomy dungeon.

It seemed an age since he was thrust there.

"I shall go mad if they do not let me out."

And such would be the case; but he knew not that he would soon be taken out—taken out to death—an ignominious death.

As he had said, he was prepared to meet his fate, for he knew full well who was his enemy.

Time wore on, and faint voices came upon his ears.

They were the preparations for his reception on deck.

.   .   .   .

Morn had just broke.

The sombre mass of drifting clouds rolled away, and the first streak of the coming morn made its appearance, throwing its faint, grey light upon the vast ocean.

Admiral Ellis's frigate was motionless upon the waters.

Her sails were furled, the decks cleared, and the crew were bustling about.

Admiral Ellis soon appeared on deck.

He summoned his lieutenant.

"Where's Captain M——'s frigate?"

"Can't say, sir. She has lost her reckoning, no doubt, and taken another direction."

The admiral gnashed his teeth.

The captain of the frigate had purposely sailed away from the presence of the detestable little admiral.

He (Ellis) scanned the horizon with his glass.

Nothing could be seen. Ellis turned to his first officer.

"Run a noose up to the yard-arm."

"Aye, sir!"

"Bring all the men on deck—prisoners too."

The lieutenant went forward to see the orders carried out.

Admiral Ellis paced the quarter-deck, a smile of cruel satisfaction upon his sallow, dried-up visage. He was wishing the "Will-o'-the-Wisp" would come in sight, that he might hang the leader before the eyes of the daring crew.

But through the absence of the frigate, he was not so sorry the buccaneers were not there. Admiral Ellis did not wish to engage them alone, he found it would be a losing game.

Ever and anon as he gazed up towards the yard-arm of the frigate, the smile would deepen on his lips. At length everything was prepared, the crew lined the deck on either side.

From the yard-arm hung a long rope, a ghastly-looking noose at the end.

"Bring up the pirate!" said Admiral Ellis, putting great stress on the word pirate.

His order was obeyed.

Captain Tom—pale and weak from loss of blood, and haggard for want of rest—was brought on deck. Calmly, proudly he looked upon the scene. His lips wreathed with a smile of scorn, as his eyes caught the noose dangling in front of him.

"Bring up the rest."

Admiral Ellis said this with a chuckle, and loud enough for Captain Tom to hear.

In a few minutes the boat's crew of gallant fellows who had accompanied the young chief was brought up under arms.

A file of marines stood before them, with their fingers on the triggers of their guns.

"If one should move hand or foot, shoot him!" cried the old admiral.

"Fix the noose," was the next command.

It was done.

Captain Tom, bound firmly with strong cord, was led forward, and the rope placed round his neck; the men with the other end of the coil in their hands stood ready to take the fatal run.

It was a fearful moment for him.

Admiral Ellis took out his watch, at eight o'clock

STAND FROM MY PATH.

Captain Tom was to die, it only wanted twenty minutes to the hour.

"Sail oh!" came from aloft.

"Where away?"

"Straight on our lee!"

Ellis took his glass.

"The frigate," he muttered.

Captain Tom caught his gaze fixed upon the approaching sail, which seemed to have emerged from a cloud.

His eyes gleamed and his face flushed.

"Hope!" he muttered. "It may be there."

The vessel seemed to possess wings, as on she sped towards the admiral's ship.

"That's not the frigate, sir," said the lieutenant, when it had come close.

"An! so I thought."

Ellis again raised his glass. He gave his peculiar dry laugh, and turned his glance towards our hero.

"See!" he said. "Ha! ha! that's your vessel, with your crew of cut-throats on board, and I will wait, yes—ha! ha!—wait until they are close enough for them to see you dangle aloft."

Captain Tom deigned no reply to this taunt. The ship came nearer, all faces were turned towards it.

"Every man at his post! Double-shot the guns!" cried Admiral Ellis. "We will hang the leader and capture the crew!"

The guns were run out, and the men prepared for a conflict. All this delay was worse than death to our hero.

He stood, his breast heaving with emotion. J 5

himself he cared not, but should his gallant crew get into danger, through any rash act, he would be sorry.

The stranger sped on, she was now within speaking distance. The banner of death was run up—the invincible flag of Captain Tom.

"Ship, ahoy!" cried Ellis.

"Ahoy!"

"Lay-to!"

"Why?" cried a powerful voice.

"Come another hundred yards, and you shall know!"

Captain Tom saw a figure mount the distant ship, and stand glass in hand. It was Ben Barnacle.

"My God!" he said, and then leaped down.

He had seen all. What a yell came from the crew when they knew what was going on! Every man dashed to his post, and the guns were run out.

"Admiral Ellis!" shouted Ben, "for the sake of all on board your ship, don't attempt it!"

The admiral laughed.

"When I cry 'Fire!' haul him up!" he cried.

The "Will-o'-the-Wisp" came on. Admiral Ellis waited, watch in hand—he had delayed the execution until nine. He waited patiently until the hand was nearly on the hour.

One minute more—sixty short, fleeting seconds—and Captain Tom would be dangling in the air. The "Will-o'-the-Wisp" was so close that every man on deck could be plainly seen.

Now came the crisis. Nine! Admiral Ellis looked around.

"Near enough," he thought.

Aloud, he shouted—

"Save him if you can! Ha! ha! Fire!"

There came a report, a vivid flash, the rush of feet, and a mighty crash. Fearful, bloody work was going on.

"Avengers away!" cried the voice of Ben Barnacle, and they were hidden in a cloud of smoke.

CHAPTER XCII.

STILL ALIVE.

THE dusky tint of the setting sun streams its golden rays through the tiny lattice window of a private and secluded room in the asylum of Doctor Burchenell.

The chamber was one of many in that building known only to the occupant and the doctor. Indeed it would puzzle the inmate, if he got out, to find his way there again.

It was a small, square room, lighted by one small, diamond-shaped window, round which was a border of coloured glass, through which the fading sun-glow pierced, and cast a number of lovely tints over the room, which was neatly furnished, and had an occupant.

He sat in a large, comfortable chair near the window. A book lay open in his lap, he had been reading it.

Now he seemed lost in a reverie; several times he would pass his thin, white hand across his aged temples and aching eyes, or smooth back the silvery locks from his fevered brow.

"There are many wonders in this world that, if revealed to its people, would not be credited," he murmured, giving vent to his thoughts in words. "Men," he continued, "are strange creatures. Those you may shun and look upon as your enemies are often one's friends. May God reward him for all he has done for me! He whom I thought my most deadly foe has become a brother—a salvator!"

He paused in his mutterings, and glanced towards the casement.

"I never thought to see this evening's setting sun," he went on, "or myself in this room. I can bear this imprisonment now—yes, now I know that

villain is in my power. Ha! ha! he followed my funeral, did he? Well, I rather think I shall have the felicity of wearing mourning for him, unless he is hanged like a dog."

The old fellow rose up and strode the room. A smile was upon his face, and happiness beamed in his eye.

"How lovely the earth looks!" he cogitated, glancing through the glass. "And I alive to enjoy its beauty."

The aged form was drawn erect, the eyes sparkled, and the once stout frame seemed to regain some of its lost vigour.

It was a pity Sanderson could not have seen through the walls into that room, he would have felt less secure.

It would be more than he ever dreamt of to see his victim—poor old John Gregory—standing there with apparent health and strength.

John Gregory had found a friend—a valuable one—and it was the last person the poor old fellow would have asked aid of, Doctor Burchenell, the master of that private asylum.

The doctor had from the first pitied the victim of the ruffian Sanderson. He watched well their work, played the game well into his own hands, then he began to act.

But not for himself. He wanted not the vile dross, gold, and he reasoned with himself that a thousand pounds given him by a man whose life he had saved would be attended with a blessing, and that ten times the sum bought by blood would bring him to the grave.

He swore within himself he would save John Gregory, and he kept his word. Doctor Burchenell was a cautious man; he was inscrutable.

Neither by word, action, or look did he ever betray his intention to befriend the poor old fellow. It was a desperate plan of his, but it succeeded.

The draught he gave Gregory was simply a powerful drug which put him in a death-like stupor for three days.

Thus was Sanderson deceived, and a coffin filled with a block of wood was buried, and John Gregory came to life.

It was some time ere he awoke to fully understand what had occurred, when at length he could comprehend, Doctor Burchenell sat by his side and told him all that had occurred.

John Gregory wept for joy. He poured out his heart-felt blessings upon his preserver.

"I do not want this praise," said the doctor.

"May God in Heaven bless you, I cannot," and Gregory wept like a child.

"Stay in this room," said the doctor. "Everything you wish for shall be brought, and I will do all to promote your comfort; besides spending an hour or so every day with you, you can go to the window as often as you like—no one can see you from there. I have a private garden, in which you can walk in safety."

Gregory grasped his hand, and, unable to speak, he held it until the doctor left the room. Burchenell kept his word. He attended John Gregory like a son, and went every day to the lonely little room.

John Gregory was now awaiting the arrival of the doctor, he had not to wait long; a little rap at the door was heard, a moment later, and the doctor entered.

"Welcome, doctor."

"How are you, Mr. Gregory?"

"I am improving, doctor, thank God and your kindness, as well as skill."

"You are not lonely?"

"No, doctor, I am happy," he replied, grasping Burchenell's hand in both his own.

"You can bear the solitude?"

"I can, doctor, while it is necessary."

"I have news for you."

"Indeed! What?"

"You know Sanderson married the vile woman, Mrs. Harpy?"

"Yes—yes."

"She is now in my care, a raving maniac!"

"Good God!"

"Do you pity her?"

"Can I help it?"

"You ought to curse her. She has been a devil in woman's form towards you."

"And is punished severely."

"But I have not told you she assassinated Captain Angel."

"Good heavens!"

"Yes. He came and took the document from Sanderson, who could not get it back, and, therefore, went to extreme measures. He was too much the coward to do the deed himself, but tempted her."

"What vile crimes!"

"Retribution will come."

"Have you heard anything of him?"

"Your nephew?"

"Yes."

"There are a few flying reports."

"Concerning him?"

"Yes."

"Let me hear."

"Well, the King has some vain notion that his fleet will at length capture the young spitfire."

"Does it seem likely?"

"I think not."

Burchenell laughed.

"I hope Providence will protect the gallant boy."

"It has done so hitherto."

"True. Would he would come home."

"He will not be long ere he does."

"Doctor, I have been thinking of a plan—or, perhaps, more properly speaking, have a whim."

"I should be most happy to hear it."

"Firstly, do you think a trustworthy crew could be heard of?"

"I could obtain one."

"Good!"

"But first, Mr. Gregory, I want to do something which I cannot without you."

"What is it, doctor?"

"You want to know where Mrs. Drake is?"

"I would give all I possess to discover."

"I think there is an opportunity."

"How?"

"With Mrs. Harpy."

"You say she is mad?"

"She is; but I know what would have an effect upon her, especially as she is always raving."

"About what?"

"Her crimes."

"Have you tried to get anything from her?"

"Yes; but failed."

"Then what is it you wish?"

"To act upon her imagination and superstitious fears by letting her see you, but in such a manner we must contrive it that it will be impossible for her to discover you are earthly."

"Well?"

"Depend upon it—in fact, I am sure of it—Mr. Gregory, that if you will aid me in this, we shall discover where Mrs. Drake is."

"I cannot doubt you; but it will be painful work."

"Nay; think of the agony they have caused you."

"I have forgiven her, doctor."

"When it is necessary, I say it is right; but if you do not think of your own wrongs, think of what Mrs. Drake may be suffering; of what your nephew has gone through; and remember those who did it."

Gregory paced the room.

"As you will, doctor."

"'Tis for your sake I ask it."

"True. I know it."

"Will you do what I require?"

"Yes."

"Very well. I shall return to-night."

The doctor left, and went to a chamber below Gregory's. On entering the room he paused; seated in one corner was a woman. It was Mrs. Sanderson.

She still wore her wedding dress and bridal wreath. She was playing with her long hair.

She did not appear to notice the doctor when he entered, but went on talking to herself in a low tone.

"Mrs. Harpy!"

She looked sharply up.

"Mrs. Harpy!" the doctor repeated.

Her eyes flashed, and she clenched her hands.

"Who dares call Mrs. Harpy?" she screamed. "There is no such person. Ha! ha! Know you not I am Mrs. John Sanderson? Ah!—see! see! I've only just been married."

And she glared upon the doctor in an awful manner.

"Captain Angel is coming here," he said.

She started, and a shudder passed through her frame. Suddenly, with startling vehemence, she cried—

"Liar! he can't—he won't. Ha! ha! No, he sleeps the sleep of death!"

The last few words were spoken in a whisper

"He is," continued Burchenell. "Mrs. Drake is coming, too."

She leaped around. Then a cunning look came over her face.

"Let them come," she muttered.

"Are you prepared to receive them?" continued the doctor, in his cold tones.

"Them!"

"Your friends. John Gregory is amongst them!"

Mrs. Harpy placed her hand to her brow.

"John Gregory!" she muttered.

Then her eyes were fixed upon Burchenell with their vacant stare; she burst into a wild laugh.

"Begone, fiend!" she howled. "Leave me, fool! Think you to mock me? Ah! I know where John Gregory is."

"Do you, though?" thought the doctor.

"Begone!" she cried.

"Very well. Be prepared for your visitors."

He left the room.

"What devil can that be?" muttered Mrs. Harpy. "He is not like the one that comes at night. Ah, no! he is my devil. He is kind—he is obliged to be. Ha! ha! I am the ruler of all in that fearful, burning pit; but it does not hurt me."

She laughed again. This was one of the points she was most mad upon; so much so, that she would often leap at her jailor when he brought a light, and, in a most frightful voice, would declare he should go to the lower regions, of which unpleasant place she thought herself the ruler.

She was powerfully violent after the visit of the doctor. The brutal jailor dared not approach, she was like a wild cat, so he went to Burchenell.

"If yer please, we must put her in the jacket."

"Who?" asked Burchenell.

"That 'ere woman in the wedding gown."

"No, Thompson; not yet."

The man retired grumbling. Towards the latter part of the night Mrs. Harpy became more composed. She sang songs, and laughed, and cried at other times.

Once or twice a glimpse of intelligence seemed to return.

The night was calm, the stars peeped forth, and everyone had gone to rest except some of the inmates of the asylum.

A distant church clock chimed the three-quarters past eleven. Mrs. Harpy started, and the wild glare in her eyes returned.

"He will come," she murmured.

Silently she paced the chamber. Twelve! The last stroke of the hammer ceased, and the echoes rolled away in the silent night air.

Mrs. Harpy stood rooted to the spot. Her eyes started, her hands were clasped to her brow, and her whole appearance showed she was horror-stricken.

Not a sound had been heard since the clock had struck, yet a few feet from where she stood there rose, as though through the boards, a tall, aged form.

It stood erect, and the eyes were turned upon her. A finger of the right hand was raised, and pointed ominously towards the shrinking woman.

"Behold!" came in a low, solemn voice. "You know me not."

Mrs. Harpy seemed appalled. She gave a loud scream.

"John Gregory!" she cried.

The eyes of the spectre seemed to flash like lurid lights.

"Aye, John Gregory from the grave. Listen, woman! Reveal at once, to save your soul from perdition, reveal where is Mrs. Drake!"

CHAPTER XCIII.

TWO DEADLY SHOTS.

BEN BARNACLE soon missed the frigate on board which Captain Tom had gone in search of the pirate. By the aid of his night-glass, Ben soon discovered the ship had silently slipped away.

"Treachery!" he muttered. "Mr. Vere!"

"Sir."

"There is some sly work going on."

"Ah!"

"Yes, the frigate has gone."

Harry Vere jumped round.

"Impossible!" he exclaimed.

"Look for yourself."

He did, and saw nothing but the black, rolling waves.

"Gone!" he muttered.

"Set sail!" cried Ben. "We will overtake them ere the morning dawns."

"'Tis to be hoped so."

The "Will-o'-the-Wisp" was put in full sail; she almost flew through the water. Every man was on deck and at his post; none slept while their leader was in danger. The night went by and nothing was to be seen. Ben paced the deck like a madman.

"Fools," he muttered, "we were, to allow such a thing to take place under our very noses. A nice laugh they will have at us."

His brow was lowering. He meant mischief.

"I'll blow the cursed frigate out of the water, and send all on board with her."

"I cannot account for it," said Harry Vere.

"That little brute of an admiral has warned every ship afloat."

"He is a vindictive man."

"If ever I come across him, let him beware. He shall suffer."

Ben meant it, too. He had a rather strong wish to see Admiral Ellis dangling at the yard-arm of the "Will-o'-the-Wisp."

Daylight dawned, and still the gallant buccaneer's craft was sailing on with her crew and officers grouped upon the deck.

"Sail oh!" came from aloft.

Ben raised his glass, and there was a general commotion.

"It's the frigate!" shouted Ben.

The "Will-o'-the-Wisp" sped on. When near enough for Ben Barnacle to discern what was going on on board the other, he gave a howl.

"What is the matter?" asked Harry Vere.

Ben handed him the glass, he saw the frigate, and uttered a cry of rage.

He saw the preparations; saw Captain Tom with a noose round his neck.

"Load the long gun!" cried Ben. "Boarders ready, fore and aft."

His surprise was great to see Admiral Ellis on board.

"Strange!" he muttered. "Never mind, I will give him something for this."

Ben watched every motion of the admiral's, and when he saw by a movement of the men that they had the order to run the gallant young chieftain up to the mast-head, he shouted to the marines—

"Pick off the men!"

There was a blinding flash—a crash—and yells and curses.

"Fire!" shouted Ben, to the men at the guns.

A fearful broadside was poured into the frigate. Both ships were covered in a cloud of smoke. Then came a loud yell.

"Hoist the flag!" cried Harry Vere.

The hour of death was now up, and Ben, at the head of his men, poured over the ship's sides upon Admiral Ellis's ship, when they were met by a strong body of Britishers.

But they were nothing against the enraged buccaneers, who made a fearful onslaught to get at their leader.

He had been thrown upon the deck by the sudden jerk he experienced when lifted several feet from the ground, and then let down with a run.

The gallant buccaneers were met with a strong opposing party. Admiral Ellis howled with rage.

"Six of you haul that pirate up!" he yelled.

Six tried and failed signally. They were shot down while their hands grasped the rope. Admiral Ellis drew a pistol and stood forward.

He was determined to end the career of our gallant young hero. Captain Tom could not rise, as he was bound hand and foot.

Bravely Admiral Ellis's crew fought, but failed to beat the buccaneers off. Ellis ordered every man to aid the others in the attempt.

There was an immense barrier of human forms between Captain Tom and his gallant crew. Admiral Ellis chuckled with fiendish triumph.

"Let them fight," he muttered, "and when they are hurled back upon their ship, they shall have the pleasure of seeing you dangling at the yard-arm."

He was calculating victory, but one glance at the combatants made him wonder whether he would be the conqueror.

The gallant buccaneers were fighting like demons, as, inch by inch, they fought back the English crew. Admiral Ellis stood, a foam gathering upon his mouth, and a deadly light in his eyes.

The buccaneers made a terrible onslaught, with Ben Barnacle and Iron Arm at their head. The crew of the frigate gave way, and, with an awful yell, the young middies made a rush towards their young leader.

"Back!" cried Ellis, to his men. "Make way! Bring forward the guns, and mow them down with grape!"

His order was easier given than obeyed. With an oath he approached Captain Tom. Levelling his pistol at the young chief's head, he said—

"And now, young viper, at last I will settle my account with you."

Captain Tom did not reply, but turned his eyes with a look of calm defiance upon the little old admiral, who stood gazing upon his victim with such a look as a wolf would give a lamb.

"Fire!" said Captain Tom. "Fire, Admiral Ellis, and you will never live to report your own dastardly act!"

"You dare defy me now?"

"I have just done so."

Admiral Ellis laughed, but it was like the growl

of a wild cat. He saw his crew were falling in every direction. and the buccaneers were coming to save their leader.

The tube of his pistol was in a line with Captain Tom's forehead. A cruel glitter came into Admiral Ellis's eyes.

"Viper!" he muttered, in a hissing whisper, "at last you are out of my path!"

His finger found the trigger of his deadly weapon. There was a blinding flash, and a loud report. A deep groan of mortal agony, and a form lay a huddled heap upon the blood-covered deck.

Ben Barnacle, with a cry of rage, rushed forward. His sword mowed a path for him. Iron Arm followed in his track, and the giant laughed at all efforts of the sailors to stop him.

Each gave an inward exclamation of delight; they saw their beloved leader, helpless and bound, dabbled in the blood of the gallant young mid who had thrown himself before Ellis's pistol in time to receive the bullet instead of Captain Tom.

Ellis stood dumbfounded. In all probability, he would have tried another shot at the brave young chief, but a hand was laid upon his shoulder. It was the hand of Ben Barnacle.

"Admiral Ellis," he said, "call off your men—let them cease this carnage."

He replied by grinding his teeth savagely, and made a vain attempt to get away. Ben smiled grimly.

"Miserable little rat!" he said; "call upon your men to surrender, or I'll crush you!"

Admiral Ellis was nearly mad with rage, and vainly he tried to draw his sword. Ben Barnacle saw it was useless to think the little admiral would give in while he had life.

He was debating with himself how to act, when he caught sight of one of the admiral's hirelings making his way behind Captain Tom, who was fighting bravely with his crew.

It was the man's intent to send his cutlass through the young chief's back. Ben Barnacle released Ellis, and made a bound forward. His sword made a mighty sweep, and the man lay headless upon the deck.

"Thanks, Ben," said Captain Tom, who saw how he had been saved. "Ben, how can we end this carnage? I do not want the blood of these brave men—they are our countrymen. Ah! that was near!"

A bullet flew past Captain Tom's ear, and it was followed by another, quite as close, only at the other side of his head.

They came in succession, and at such short intervals that Captain Tom began to wonder where they came from; but Ben, who stood by his side, looked up.

"Curse him!" he muttered.

He saw the admiral perched upon the cross-trees, a gun in his hand, which he fired as quick as a man who was with him could load.

Ben drew his pistol. and, at the very moment the admiral was going to fire, Ben pulled the trigger. The bullet took effect, and Admiral Ellis fell, head first, upon his men, the blood streaming from a wound in the shoulder.

His men recoiled with a yell of rage and horror. Consternation reigned throughout the ship. Crack! It was the report of a single rifle, and a bullet whistled through the rigging.

The next instant Captain Tom reeled and fell without a cry or groan by the side of Admiral Ellis, who, with a smile of joy upon his face, turned over, closed his eyes, and lay motionless upon the deck.

This was the crisis. The frigate's men carried Admiral Ellis below, and Iron Arm took Captain Tom on board his ship.

Then the gallant buccaneers, with Ben, Iron Arm, and Harry Vere at their head, prepared themselves to finish the fight.

The captain under Ellis saw the terrible array. There had been blood enough shed, yet he cared not to surrender.

"Surrender!" said Ben. "We shall not touch either ship or crew, or a thing on board."

"Then I give in," said the captain. "Lay down your arms, my men."

They did so.

"No," said Ben, pushing away the swords given him by the lieutenants, "I want them not. Deliver to me Admiral Ellis."

The first officer hesitated, so Ben did not ask again. Turning to his own men, he said—

"Go below, and bring Admiral Ellis on deck."

They obeyed with readiness.

The searching gazes of the "Will-o'-the-Wisp's" crew followed the admiral's form as he was conveyed on board the buccaneer's vessel.

His crew would have protested, and in very strong terms, too, but Iron Arm had placed a very strong guard over all the arms, and they were defenceless.

"Haul down the flag!" was the next command given by Ben.

The emblem of England came rattling down to the deck.

Ben took it.

"Return to your ship," he said to his crew.

He was the last to return on board, and when the vessel was cast loose, he jumped on the bulwark, and called to the officers of the frigate—

"Return to England, and tell them how Admiral Ellis was beaten. Tell them also he will be fairly tried and hung by this time to-morrow. Do not fear for him. I have taken the flag that he may be tried with naval honours."

With a taunting laugh he jumped down, and the "Will-o'-the-Wisp" sped on.

There was a loud clamour when Ben returned.

The brave young mids were clamouring for the man who slayed their gallant young companion in his attempt to save Captain Tom.

"My gallant friends," said Ben Barnacle, "Admiral Ellis shall be tried."

"No! no!" they cried. "Blood for blood! Hang him!"

"There is no help," muttered Ben, as he turned away. "He must be hanged to-morrow morning!"

Murmurs of dissent broke from the crew.

"No! no! Let us kill him at once," they all cried, in a breath.

They followed Ben Barnacle into the cabin, armed with all sorts of weapons.

Harry Vere, seeing their threatening attitude, rushed to the assistance of Ben, who, pointing the muzzle of a small cannon down the hatchway, stood ready to fire it.

Harry Vere then held up his hand, and harangued the angry seamen.

"Back! back!" he cried, waving his hand, "if you value your lives. One step forward, and the ship and all on board shall go to the bottom!"

CHAPTER XCIV.

THE SMUGGLERS.

IT was night—dark cheerless, and cold; for a storm, that threatened destruction to the huge white cliffs, and lashed the angry waves into snowy hillocks of foam, had come on with the setting of the sun.

How many a smuggler's wife, while listening to the dashing of the rough waves on the shore of her home, and the loud winds blowing harmlessly over the roof of her dwelling, has breathed a prayer that the same storm may be landing her husband's cargo

... upon some unguarded beach, or filling the ... of his good ship in eluding the pursuit of a revenue cutter.

The night was far advanced, and the flower of the young men of Folkstone were out on a smuggling cruise, when four women were seated around a sea-coal fire, listening to the heavy rain falling in the street, and the scolding wind, as it rumbled in the chimney of the warm fire-place.

One of the party—from her occupying the low-seated, patch-work-covered chair, and the peculiar attention paid to her by an indolent cat, who stretched, and purred, and quivered her nervous tail, while peering sleepily in her protector's face—appeared to be the mistress of the house.

She was a young woman, about five-and-twenty, with all the happy prettiness of a country beauty—albeit, an indulged grief had thrown a pale tinge over the clear red that still shone in her cheek, as if struggling for mastery with an intruding enemy.

Her features, though somewhat irregular, if but carelessly viewed, failed not to secure the beholder's steadfast observance, from the peculiar interest which a full, blue eye, and light, arched brow, lent to the contour.

She was resting her face upon her hand, and looking at the red coals in the stove before her.

"There," said the young woman, "in that very hollow of the fire, I can almost fancy I see my James on the deck of the 'Mary,' looking through his glass to catch a glimpse of some distant sail. Ah! now it has fallen in, and all looks like a rough sea. Poor fellow!"

This was spoken in that abstracted tone of voice—that monotonous sound of melancholy—where every word is given in one note, as if the speaker had not the spirit, or even wish, to vary the sound.

"That's what I so repeatedly tell you of," said a fat old woman of the group; "you will have no other thought; morning and night hear but the same cry from you.

"Might I not sit here and watch the fire, and think of the time when my darling boy, Jack, was adrift day and night in a little open boat, with no other companion than a helpless girl, and they was day after day without water even to drink, or food to eat? Couldn't I look in that fire, and see him faint and ill, with his hands clasped over his aching eyes, and she looking on, half dead, and quite help-less? But it's over now. Providence rescued him and her too, which is more than it did for my poor husband."

"Look at me—isn't it fifteen years ago since my William, rest his soul, was shot dead while running his boat ashore on Romney Marsh? And am I any the worse for it?

"I loved him dearly, and when I was told of the bad news, I did nothing but cry for whole days; but then it was soon over.

"I knew fretting wouldn't set him on his legs again, so I made the best of a bad berth, and thought, if I should have another husband, all well and good; if not, why I must live and die Widow Major, and there was an end of it."

"Ah! neighbour," replied the young woman, "you knew the fate of your husband—you were acquainted with the worst—you had not to live in the cruel suspense I endure; but if I knew that he was dead," and here her voice grew louder, while the blood rushed into her fair cheeks, "I should think as much of him as I do now, and would think and think, and try to bring thoughts every day heavier on my heart, till it sunk into the grave."

"How fast it rains!" ejaculated a shrivelled old woman, who had hitherto remained silent. "How fast it rains!"

And she drew her chair closer to the fire.

"It was just such a night as this when—what's ...

that—the wind? Ah! it's a rough night; I suppose it must be near eleven o'clock. Now, I'll tell you a story that shall make you as cold as stones, though you crowd ever so close to this blazing fire.

"It was just such a night as this—"

"Gracious Heaven!" cried Susan, "I hear a footfall coming down the street, so like that which I knew so well."

"Listen! No, all is silent."

"Well, Margery, what were you going to tell us?"

"Eh! bless us!" replied Margery, "you tremble terrible bad, surely. What's the matter?"

"Nothing—nothing, dame. Go on."

"Well," said the old woman, "it was just such a night as this—"

"Susan!" cried a voice at the door, in that tone which implies haste, and a fear of being heard. "Susan, open the door!"

"Good God!" shrieked Susan, "that voice!"

And all the women rose at one moment, and stood staring at the door, which Susan was unlocking.

"The key won't turn the lock—it's rusty. Who's there?" she breathlessly exclaimed, as, in the agony of suspense, she tried to turn the key, while the big drops stood quivering on her brow.

She trembled from head to foot. Her companions stood like statues. The lock flew back, and the door opened.

Nothing was seen but the black night, and the large drops of rain which sparkled in the beams of the candle on the table.

"There is no one," said she, panting for breath. "But, as I stand here a living woman, it was his voice."

"James! James!" she cried, and put out her head to listen.

She heard quick, heavy footsteps hastily advancing at the end of the street.

Presently a party of six or seven blockade men rushed by the door, dashing the wet from the pavement in Susan's face.

They passed with no other sound than that made by their feet, and were quickly out of hearing.

"I wish I may die," said old Margery, "but the blockade men are chasing some poor fellow who has been obliged to drop his tubs; for I saw the blade of a cutlass flash in my eyes, though I couldn't see the hand that held it."

"My bonnet! my bonnet!" cried Susan; "there has more befallen this night than any here can tell. It was his voice—stay in the house till I come back—it was his voice!" and she ran out through the still driving rain, in the direction of the party that had just passed.

Susan reached the cliffs; the wind blew fresh and strong off the sea, and the rain appeared abating.

She thought she saw figures descend the heights; and, quickening her pace, stood on the edge, straining her sight to distinguish the objects flitting to and fro on the beach.

She heard a faint "Hallo!"—the sound thrilled through every nerve—it was the voice she had heard at the door.

She returned the salute; but the buffeting of the wind choked her timid cry. The hallo was repeated; Susan listened with her very eyes.

Her distended fingers seemed grasping to catch at sound. A sound did rise above the roar of the breakers and the rushing of the wind; it was the report of a volley of carbines fired on the beach.

Susan screamed, and sunk on the edge of the cliff, overpowered with terror and anxiety. Quickly there was seen a flashing of lights along the coast, and men running from the Martello Towers to the beach in disorder.

Then was heard the curse for curse, the clashing of cutlasses and the discharge of arms, and the hoarse shout of some of the smugglers, who had succeeded in putting their boat off from the shore with part of her cargo, which it appeared they had been attempting to work.

Susan well understood the import of these dreadful sounds, and, recovering from her fright, was striving to ascertain from her station the position of the parties.

When the hard breathing of some one, apparently exhausted, arrested her attention. It seemed to issue from beneath, and, looking over the summit of a cliff, she perceived the shadow of a man cautiously ascending.

He had almost accomplished his task, and was grasping a jutting fragment of stone, to enable him to rest a moment from the fatigue of his attempt.

Susan heard him panting for breath, and, in endeavouring to discover whether he wore the jacket or the smock-frock—the latter being the usual working attire of the smugglers—heard him sigh heavily.

She thought it was a form she knew. She bent over the edge, and held her breath in the very agony of hope and fear.

The figure stood with his back to the cliff, and, looking down on the beach, ejaculated—

"Oh, God!"

It was in one of those moans which betray the most acute suffering of mind, which thrill through the hearer, and create that kindred overflowing of the heart's tears which makes the sorrow of the afflicted more than our own.

Susan heard the sound, and breathlessly cried—

"Who is it?"

The figure sprang upwards at the response, and exclaimed—

"Susan!"

"James! James!" she cried.

He caught hold of a large tuft of grass, to assist him in darting into her extended arms, when the weed broke by the roots from the light sand in which it had grown.

A faint cry and the fall of a body, with the rattling of earth and stones, down the steep, were the sounds that struck terror and dismay through the brain of poor Susan.

She attempted to call for assistance, but her voice obeyed not the effort, and, in the delirium of the moment, she sprang down the cliff.

But fortunately alighting on a projection, and at the same time instinctively catching the long weeds, was saved from the danger her perilous situation had threatened.

But still she continued her perilous descent, stepping from tuft to stone, reckless whether she found a footing, or was precipitated to the base, which the darkness concealing all below, looked like a black abyss.

Susan alighted in safety on the beach. An indistinct form lying on the shingle met her view.

"James! James!" she cried, "speak! Let me hear your voice. For mercy's sake tell me are you hurt?"

No answer was returned; she grasped his hand, and felt his brow, but, on the instant, started from the form in horror.

The hand was stiff, and the brow was deadly cold. And then, as if all her powers of utterance had become suddenly re-organised, she broke forth into such a cry of anguish that it pierced through the noises of the night like the scream of a wounded eagle.

A pistol shot was heard, and the ball whizzed past the ear of Susan, and harmlessly buried itself in the sand of the cliff.

A party of the blockade men rushed towards the spot, and, by the light of a torch, discovered the poor girl stretched on the body of a smuggler.

They raised her in their arms—she was quite senseless—and, holding the light in the face of the man, they saw that he was dead.

"She's a pretty creature!" said one of the men; "it's a pity she could not let her sweetheart come to the beach alone, for she seems almost as far gone as he is. What shall we do with her, sir?"

This was addressed to a young man of the group wearing the uniform of a midshipman, and whose flushed and disordered countenance proved that he had taken a considerable share in the late desperate encounter.

"Take her to the Tower, Thomas," said he; "she may assist, with her evidence, the investigation of this affair.

"The body of the man must also be carried to our station, for I daresay we shall grapple some of the rascals before the night's work is over.

"Our lieutenant has ordered the boat to be pursued that put off in the scuffle; and, as some of the cargo is now lying about the rocks here, we must look out for another squall."

One of the sailors sustained the still senseless Susan in his arms, while the corpse followed, borne by four others on their carbines.

"This fun was not expected, Infant Joe," said one of the men, to the gigantic figure who carried Susan in one of his arms, with as much ease as he would have conveyed a child, and who, in mockery of his immense bulk, had been so nicknamed.

"No," was the laconic reply.

"I think," continued the other, "'twas your pistol settled that poor fellow, for he lay in the very point of the woman's scream when you fired."

"Yes," said Joe, with a grin, "mayhap it was; and I wish each of my bullets could reach twenty of 'em at once as surely and as quickly."

CHAPTER XCV.
THE TRIAL OF ADMIRAL ELLIS.

THE captain of the frigate attempted to pour a broadside into the "Will-o'-the-Wisp," but failed most signally.

The gallant buccaneer craft was out of sight ere he could call his men to quarters. His consternation was great, and he felt he was wrong in surrendering.

"Should they hang the admiral," he thought, "why, the court-martial will hang me."

It was not a pleasant thought, nor did he feel comfortable under such a position. He thought so, and he felt he would much sooner have had a sword through him than the disgrace that would come.

He called his officers up.

"What can we do?" he asked.

"Follow and fight!"

"Follow and fight!" echoed the second officer. "How can we follow the 'Will-o'-the-Wisp?' She would wait until we were in gun range, and then laugh at our attempts."

"Still something must be done," said the captain.

"Of course, sir."

"Hoist all sail. We can debate upon what shall be done."

The frigate was put in trim, a man sent to keep a sharp look-out aloft, which he did, for, in spite of the blinding rain, he shaded his eyes with his hand, and kept his glance fixed steadily on the horizon. The poor fellows who had fallen in the unfortunate affray were buried, or rather interred in their watery grave. The captain saw nothing of the "Will-o'-the-Wisp."

"Sail, oh!" sang out the man aloft.

"Where away?"

"Straight on our bows."

"Then it is not the buccaneer," remarked the captain.

Which was the case, and when the vessels hailed each other he found it to be the frigate which had first captured Captain Tom.

"Is the admiral on board?" asked Captain M—.

"No."

"Where is he?"

"We had a brush with the 'Will-o'-the-Wisp,' which came up just as we were about to hang Captain Tom."

"How did it end?"

"We were beaten, and they have carried off Ellis."

"Good God!"

"That is not all; they intend to hang him."

"What direction did they take?"

"A southerly."

"We will give chase then. You are on their track?"

"Yes."

The vessel's head was put towards point, and they started off on a wild-goose chase. The "Will-o'-the-Wisp" was not likely to be overtaken, as she was already far off.

Ben Barnacle saw with regret they were bent upon revenge. Admiral Ellis was put under the care of Dr. Shrike, who extracted the bullet with great facility.

Captain Tom's wound seemed dangerous. He lay long in a state of insensibility. Dr. Shrike would give no opinion. Ben Barnacle knitted his brows.

"If," he said, "the chief does not recover to-day, Admiral Ellis shall grace the yard-arm to-morrow."

Ben meant it. The day went on, and Admiral Ellis had recovered, though his wound was still very painful.

He kept a sullen silence, neither asking nor replying to any questions. He ate but little, and did not attempt to leave the cabin; he quite expected to be hanged upon the first opportunity.

He was perfectly careless of his fate; but it galled him to know his young foe still lived, and Harry Vere was walking the deck, full of health and manly pride.

Admiral Ellis ground his teeth when he thought of this.

"My daughter, too," he muttered. "Curse her! I could die in peace—laugh at this triumph—if I could but see my two hated foes prone before me."

Nothing on earth would ever quell the fearful hatred that rankled in the heart of the little admiral towards the gallant young buccaneer and his officers.

It was a fire burning to the very heart's core of Ellis—a fire that nothing but the blood of his foes could quench.

As yet he knew nothing of the fate of his vessel and he would not deign to ask. He could scarcely control his fearful rage. To think that the buccaneers dared capture him, was almost too much for Admiral Ellis.

When he thought of it he felt he could have annihilated the whole crew. If ever anyone wished for the strength of Samson, Ellis did, that he might break from his prison, and slay all his hated foes.

But, fortunately for the gallant buccaneers, he was not likely to have the power of Samson, and, therefore he was perfectly helpless.

At the time he was ruminating over his present position, Ben Barnacle and Harry Vere were conversing upon his fate.

"I request, Harry," said Ben, "that you will keep your wife in ignorance of the admiral's position."

"I will."

"Does she know it?"

"Not yet."

"Good! Does the chief get better?"

"Very slowly, I think."

"Well, we will hold a court-martial in the state cabin for our vindictive little foe."

"When?"

"Now."

Harry Vere looked sorrowful; he wanted a little time given that his chief might recover, for he well knew that the iron-willed Ben Barnacle would not show mercy to the man who had so repeatedly attempted the life of their leader.

But Harry Vere thought of his wife. He remembered she was the admiral's daughter, and he pictured to himself her grief and sorrow for her father.

She would look upon her husband as one of his murderers. All this passed through Harry's mind with lightning rapidity. He knew it was useless to remonstrate with Ben Barnacle.

"Then you really mean to carry out your intent?"

"Yes," Ben replied.

"Then what is the use of this trial?"

Ben smiled grimly.

"I will give him a chance."

Harry Vere's face brightened up.

"Then you are going to hold the court-martial now?"

"At once."

"Very well."

The state-cabin was cleared, and prepared for the trial. Ben Barnacle sat at the head of the tribunal, and the officers, with Iron Arm and Harry Vere, were seated around.

Ben touched a silver bell, and an officer of marines entered.

"Bring in Admiral Ellis."

The man bowed and retired. A scornful smile played round Ellis's mouth, as he glared round upon the assembled company.

"What," he said, "means this?"

"That you are to be tried," replied Ben, in his cold, ringing tones.

Admiral Ellis curled his lip in contempt.

"Mockery!" he said, "a set of pirates daring to talk of trying an admiral of his Majesty's navy!"

Ben's face flushed.

"We," he said, "have every right to try and execute you for the crime of murder."

Ellis did not reply.

"You attempted to have an officer—Mr. Vere—assassinated, and you have several times sought the life of Captain Tom."

"Would to God I had succeeded!"

"Silence!" cried Iron Arm.

"We," continued Ben, "have now to carry out what you may term a mock trial, but this is what I wish to say. You would have hanged our chief without a trial, but fortunately we were in time to save him. Still, on one condition we will give you your life."

Ellis remained silent.

"If you will swear to henceforth discontinue all attempts upon Captain Tom, and swear that you will forgive your daughter, then you shall be set at liberty."

For a moment Ellis could not reply. He seemed choking with passion. He was fearful to look at.

"Curse her! curse you! curse you all!" he cried, in a thick, choking voice.

"We want your reply."

"You have it, infernal pirates, you have it here! I defy you—I laugh at your power! I swear to slay your boy chief when or wherever I can, and his officers, too, and I invoke the bitterest curses upon the head of my ch—"

"Hold!" cried Vere.

"I will not! Curse you!"

With a spring like that of a wild cat, Ellis leaped upon the throat of Harry Vere. Every one jumped up, and the marines raised their muskets.

"Ground arms!" cried Harry Vere, as he shook the admiral off, and held him until two marines took him into their keeping.

Ellis was nearly suffocating.

"Will you do what I ask?" said Ben.

"Curse you, no!"

"That is sufficient. Gentlemen, you have heard. Now decide."

"Death!" came as though in one voice.

"Death!" cried a dozen young middies who were there. "Let him die as did our companion, with a bullet."

Harry Vere did not speak, but sat minutely watching the proceedings.

"Admiral Ellis," said Ben Barnacle, "you will be shot at seven bells to-morrow morning. If you have anything to say, be quick."

Ellis replied only by a stare.

"Take him away."

The marines removed him from the court, and he was put back in his prison. Harry Vere pleaded in vain for a respite.

"No!" was the stern reply. "Admiral Ellis shall die as he would have killed you."

The officers left the cabin. None felt any pity for the vindictive little sailor, excepting Harry Vere, and he did on account of Jenny.

The day passed, and Captain Tom still lay in a dangerous state under the care of his beloved Minnie and Zelie.

Admiral Ellis bore his fate bravely. He thought of nothing but how he could possibly wreak his vengeance upon one of his foes before he died.

He could find nothing, and he saw everything was hopeless. With a groan he threw himself upon his pallet, and rocked himself to and fro until sleep relieved him from his agony of mind.

. . . .

Morning broke on the waters of the vast ocean. Not a vessel, save the gallant "Will-o'-the-Wisp," could be seen.

The buccaneers' craft was almost motionless upon the water, and the men were up and busy about her deck.

Preparations were being made for the execution of Admiral Ellis. Ben Barnacle, the lieutenant, was impatiently pacing the quarter-deck.

It would not be long ere seven bells would strike, and the execution of Admiral Ellis would then take place.

At last the tattoo of the drum brought sailors and marines on deck. The sailors were ranged round the vessel's side.

The marines were stationed on the quarter deck, and a file of ten stood with loaded muskets facing the wheel.

"Bring up the prisoner!" said Ben.

Admiral Ellis was brought on deck. He was pale, his lips were ashy, and his eyes unnatural in their lustre; still he betrayed no sign of fear.

"Admiral Ellis," said Ben Barnacle, "there is still time to relent, will you consent to the conditions named yesterday?"

"Do your work."

He was led to the end of the quarter-deck, an ominous silence reigning over the ship. It wanted but three or four minutes to the time, as the word was given to the marines.

The muskets were raised, and the loud click of the triggers came upon the admiral's ears. Seven bells.

"Ready!" cried Ben.

Steady as a rock stood that line of men, with the cold, glittering weapons raised so that each bullet would find a resting-place in the admiral's heart.

"Present! —"

A loud, piercing scream stopped the finish of the word. There was a murmur from the men, as a light form broke in amongst them.

It was Jenny Vere. She threw herself at her father's feet.

"Oh, no!—no!" she cried. "Mercy! mercy!—for my sake!"

She clung to her father in wild terror.

"Mr. Vere," said Ben, "remove your wife. Men, keep your muskets levelled. When Mrs. Vere is removed, fire."

There was no mistaking those deliberately-spoken words.

"Never!—oh, no!" cried Jenny Vere, clinging in wild terror to her father.

"Away, girl!" he cried, "away! You have my curse, and may the—the—"

The pealing shriek from Jenny, as they tried to drag her away, touched his heart, and he motioned to break his bonds—to save him.

———

CHAPTER XCVI.

ISRAEL SHAWM SEES THE LAST OF HIS GOLD.

HESTER, the lovely Jewess, had fled, when freed from the clutches of Captain Paul, and she fled in wild terror, though not from the house.

She was a brave girl, and, when she found he had not pursued her, she regained a part of her self-possession; and, taking a jewelled pistol from a box, put a cap on it, and returned to the dingy chamber in which she had left Dutch Paul and her father.

The gloomy cell was empty, and the freebooter was gone when she arrived on the spot. She heard a low moan, proceeding as from beneath the floor.

She knew the voice; it was her father's.

"Father! father!" she cried.

Nothing but a faint moan came in reply.

"Where can he be?" she murmured.

Then, remaining still, she listened attentively, and at length with a cry bounded to the corner of the vault.

That frail, beautiful girl seemed gifted with the strength of Samson when she knew the position of her father.

Bad as he was, she could not let him die thus.

Dislodging the stone that covered the entrance of the pit, down which he had been hurled, she held a lamp over the dark gap, and called upon her father; but no answer came.

"Father! father!" she cried, in accents of anguish.

Still no reply.

"My father!"

A faint moan came in response.

Lowering the lamp as far as her arm would let her, she endeavoured to throw sufficient light into the dark pit.

The glittering coins, scattered in countless numbers on the bottom of the hole, she could plainly discern.

"Accursed dross!" she muttered. "How many lives have been taken for it! How many men have been driven to crime to gain it!—how many women to abstraction, and children to prison! And for what?—those yellow, glittering coins!"

She clenched her tiny hand, and again called her father.

"My taughter!" came in a faint voice.

Hester gave a low cry.

Her father lived.

She lowered the light, that she might see his withered form.

She beheld him, crouched in a huddled heap among the strewn gold.

"Father!"

"Mine Got! My taughter—my peautiful Hester, save me!"

"How can I, father? I cannot come down."

"Lower a rope, Hester."

"Stay."

Trembling from head to foot, Hester left the gloomy vault, and went in search of a rope.

She was not long in finding one; and, with a gladdened feeling at her heart, returned.

With her tiny hands she knotted the thick, coarse hempen cord, and lowered it down the pit

"My prave—my peautiful Hester !" murmured the old Jew. "You shall havsh anything you vantch when I get out. Holy Mosesh! my curse upon the captain for hurling me down here! Mine Got! Mine gold! mine gold!"

And the old sinner gave a groan. His daughter was standing trembling at the top of the hole.

"Father!" she cried. "Come, I beseech you. I cannot stay longer in this place of horrors."

"Yesh, yesh! I'sh coming."

Clutching the rope with his feeble hands, he made an attempt to clench it. Had not Hester thoughtfully tied the knots in it, he would never have come from that horrid hole alive.

As it was, he had extreme difficulty in doing so. He clung to the cord like grim death, and fixed the toes of his shoes like a vice upon each knot.

Faint and exhausted he at length appeared above the opening, and Hester, with all her gentle strength and energies thrown into the one effort, caught his long, bony arms, and drew his shrivelled form out.

"Mine Got !" he gasped.

Then he sank upon the floor thoroughly exhausted.

Hester, with a woman's forethought, had brought a small flask of brandy.

She gave her senseless sire a small draught, and heaving a sigh of intense relief, he sat upright, and glared, with his blood-shot eyes, which had not lost their look of terror, round the vault.

"Come, father," said Hester, as she saw his gaze wander to the black, gaping aperture, down which had been hurled his precious dross.

"Leave that," she cried, almost fiercely, "you have plenty without that ill-gotten hoard. Is your life of less consequence than your gold? Come, father, from this place of horrors."

"Eh?—mine Got !—mine gold—gold ! Oh, no !"

"Father!" cried Hester, rising, "father I saved you! God help me for being the flesh and blood of such a—a—Heaven help me! what am I going to say? Rise, if thou art a man, and I am your daughter; rise, leave this vault—leave that blood-stained gold. Conquer your quenchless thirst for the glittering dross—the curse of man—ere it drags us both to destruction! Come, I say! Live like one of God's beings, or from this moment I withdraw myself from the roof and protection of a father. I mean it, so help me Heaven !"

Somewhat surprised, the Jew rose, and casting a look at the gaping mouth of the pit, and then at his daughter, muttered—

"Hester, my tarling !"

"Come !"

"But—but—my g—"

"Father! father! Is that heap of coins more to you than my happiness—my life? Decide at once —leave those lawless gains, and be happy with what you have and me; or keep your vile blood-money, and you lose your daughter !"

Somewhat staggered at this assault from such an unexpected quarter, the old villain allowed himself to be led away.

Once in his room, and Hester out of his presence, he began to whine about his gold, and began devising means to get it again in his possession.

At length this wish became so strong upon him, he was compelled to relinquish all ideas of sleep, though he felt exhausted, and, preparing to retire to the vault, he took a lantern, and stole forth.

Quietly he went to his daughter's room.

She was not there.

Where could she be?

"Mine Got! Holy Mosesh!" he muttered, "where cansh she be—my taughter! Ah! vell—vell, she must go."

And mumbling to himself, he shuffled off to his— his what?

To his gold, he thought.

Alas! far better would it have been had he remained in bed, and obeyed the supplications of his daughter.

He was going to his death and to his grave.

What a curse money must be to some! How, instead of it bringing happiness, and one's earthly wants, it brought death and destruction.

Ignorant of his approaching doom, Israel Shawm traversed the long dingy halls and corridors of the huge old house; and ere long he stood in the vault that had well-nigh been his tomb.

Something like a cold chill crept upon him as he stood, with eager, glaring eyes, looking at the gap, down which his cherished hoard had been hurled.

He wavered at this moment.

Something seemed to whisper in his ear—

"Return !"

His withered frame shook from weakness and some strange emotion. He thought of his daughter's words— thought of his narrow escape from death.

The many attempts upon his life, and all for the gold he hoarded up.

"I vill return to-morrowsh," he thought, "ten I come down in te taylight."

Clink!

That sound was music to the attenuated old miser's ears.

He heard the clink of his worshipped coins as some of them rolled off a pile to the hard, stony floor.

He took a few steps forward.

He was at the brink of the pit.

The lantern threw its dull glare down the dark chasm.

He saw the bright glitter of the shining heap of gold.

He could not move his eyes.

Some strange power riveted him to the spot.

"My gold !" he muttered, in a thick, shaky voice. "Holy Mosesh, I can't leave you tere !"

And he could not.

Going to one corner of the vault, he took from a pile of lumber a very long ladder, to which he bound a small one with the rope that had been the means of his escape.

With some slight exertion, he managed to get it down the hole.

Then he gave a sigh.

It was a sigh of heartfelt satisfaction.

Pausing a moment to take breath, he wiped the perspiration from his brow, and then prepared to descend.

With faltering steps he went down the long ladder, and in less than a minute he was among his cherished heap.

"My gold !" he muttered. "My peautiful gold !"

Thrusting his hands among the loose coins, he took up a double handful and let them slowly drop among the rest.

What music it was to him!

How he gloried in the sound !

When he had satisfied himself by playing with his gold, he began to refill the bags, and as each one was filled, so did he crawl up the ladder and place them safely on the floor.

It was tiring work, but he continued it without a murmur.

Time after time he ascended those number of steps—each time he placed a huge bag gorged with money on the stone floor of the vault.

The perspiration rolled in big drops from his brow.

His limbs ached from fatigue.

But he would sooner have sunk under the task than have left a coin there.

The last bag but one was filled.

It was placed amongst the rest.

Now, for the last time, he descended the la—

Carefully he scraped together, with his long bony hands, the few remaining coins, and they were deposited in the bag.

It was not filled to such an excess as the rest.

He thought there were some missing.

On his hands and knees he groped round the pit.

Every corner and crevice was searched, and the dust raked over to see that not one coin remained hidden.

It was not until he was properly satisfied that not one was left he discontinued his search.

Taking the lantern in one hand, and the gold in the other he slowly ascended from the pit.

It was hard work for him to get up, both hands engaged as they were.

Still he accomplished it.

The last bag of his ill-gotten gains was placed with the others.

Then he paused to get his breath.

"My gold!" he muttered again, and casting his eyes with a look of love to the canvas sacks. "Safe—all safe!"

He took one step nigher, then paused. His hair stood on end. His blood ran like ice in his veins.

A scream, loud and shrill, came upon his ears.

"Holy Mosesh!" he cried. "My taughter! Ah! my gold—my gold! Murder!"

The last exclamation was called forth by a coarse, brutal laugh that came upon his ears.

Looking up, he beheld three swarthy-faced men. Seamen, he could see. They wanted his gold. He knew that.

With a cry he leaped among his blood-stained money, and covered it with his body and his long, wasted limbs.

"Spare me, holy Mosesh! My gold!" he gasped.

A cold, cruel laugh was the reply—their long, glittering blades shone before his eyes.

"Your gold, old huckster!" cried one.

"And your blood to christen it!" cried another.

CHAPTER XCVII.

THE FACE BENEATH THE VIZOR.

WHEN the "Yellow Vulture" sailed away from the bay, carrying Dutch Paul and his companion, after their visit to the old miser, another ship might have been seen coming in under the cover of night.

Whatever might have been its mission, those on board evidently wanted to have everything conducted in a silent manner.

Whether they had seen the "Yellow Vulture" depart it was hard to say.

But they took infinite care in not anchoring until the gentleman pirate was far out of the harbour. A few dark forms might have been seen skulking about the deck.

"Are you sure we are right?" asked a tall man on the quarter-deck, in the uniform of a captain or an officer.

"Quite, sir."

"This is the spot?"

"Yes, cap'n. I can see the old skunk's dusty old den from here."

"Very well. Have a boat lowered; put a stout crew on board, and come with me."

"Aye, aye."

The man went forward. He was something above the common sailor. He gave the necessary instructions, and then returned to his captain.

"Is all ready?"

"Yes."

"Come on."

They strode towards the boat.

For an instant a ship's-lantern threw its light upon the captain's face.

That moment was enough. It revealed the cunning features of Reuben Harpy.

His companion was a lawless, brutal ruffian, and one well adapted for his work; for his master had often proposed the most atrocious villainies to get wealth.

He knew of Israel Shawm, and mentioned Reuben Harpy.

It so happened the dastardly cousin of Cap. Tom knew the Jew's lovely daughter.

"Ah!" he said; "if I only knew where to find the old rascal and his lovely dark-eyed daughter, I would pay them a visit."

His eyes spoke plainly his thoughts. His companion smiled grimly.

"I can put you on the scent, cap'n."

"You can?"

"Aye, and will."

"When?"

"At once."

"Do so, and if I get that girl in my power, you shall have a fair half of all the wealth that is found in the old man's place."

"Agreed, cap'n."

The ship's head was turned, and thus they visited the old Jew. The boat was rowed silently ashore, and four figures alighted.

"Be on the alert," said Harpy to the officer in command of the boat.

"Aye, aye, sir."

With stealthy steps the four ruffians wended their way to the miser's house. At the door they paused.

"Ah!" said Reuben, as his fingers touched the door, "we have no trouble to get in."

With a slight push it opened, and the villains, bent on plunder and murder, entered the dark, dusty hall.

"Hist!" said Reuben.

They halted.

Reuben Harpy had been attracted by the gleam of a light, and the sound of a footfall.

Then the men took a step forward, and concealed themselves in the darkness of a doorway opposite the huge flight of stairs.

Then came a slight click, and one of the ruffians nearly lost his balance.

A door against which he had been leaning opened, and had he not clung to his companions for support, he would have fallen on his back in a manner more forcible than elegant.

"Come, we shall be discovered," hissed Harpy. "See, someone approaches."

Instinctively they shrank back into the gloomy chamber.

Reuben Harpy was light of foot in comparison to his men, and he stole stealthily away as soon as he found the approaching person with a light was the old Jew.

Thinking the suite of apartments would by chance lead him into the one containing the lovely Jewess, he went on, leaving his bad companions to follow the Jew, and plunder the house of its hoarded wealth.

He heard them slowly steal forth, and he knew they were on the trail of the Jew.

"Good!" muttered the villain, and he groped his way about in the dark.

The rooms through which he passed were more or less empty; those that did contain anything were merely contraband goods.

In a small ante-chamber Reuben Harpy paused.

At first he could not find any means of exit, but by the door he had entered.

He had no light.

Everything was shrouded in a deep gloom.

Placing his hands against the wall, he began very slowly to take a voyage round the room.

At first he could not feel anything in the shape of an entrance.

When within a few feet of the point from which he started, his hand clutched something that he knew to be tapestry.

"Ah!" he thought, "these long curtains cover some secret door. Now for it."

They were pulled aside, and carefully feeling about, he at length found a handle.

He turned it noiselessly, and a small door opened.

He paused, and peeped forth.

All was black—inky darkness.

Closing the door, he stole on tip-toe into what he thought to be another apartment.

With a sudden start he stopped.

A window, a little to his right, through which the twinkling stars sent a ray of light, fell upon something bearing the form of a gigantic man.

The blood ran cold in Reuben's body.

He gasped for breath.

Only for a minute did his terror last.

A second look revealed to him that the subject of his fear was only a mailed figure.

His eyes had become partially accustomed to the gloom, and he could discern several similar grim-looking monsters.

He was in the armoury.

"This has been a grand old hall in its time," he thought. "How that old bloodsucker became possessor of it is a mystery."

While he stood thus conversing with himself, he was startled by the sound of footsteps, and the distant gleam of a light.

Crouching behind the huge steel figure, he watched the approach of the light, and saw the bearer was the lovely Jewess.

She came slowly on.

Her face was pale and sorrowful.

Her large, luminous eyes were humid, and her dark silky tresses hung about her lovely shoulders.

Something like a shudder passed through her frame as she passed down the huge hall, with that row of grim figures looking upon her.

She paused before the figure of mail that had startled Reuben Harpy.

She glanced up at a dust-covered oil-painting that hung above the huge steel helmet.

Placing the lamp on one of the portals, she knelt before the grim figure, and clasping her hands, raised her eyes towards Heaven.

A sudden and unexpected change came over her.

Her face went bloodless.

Her eyes nearly started from their sockets, and she seemed like one frozen into an immovable block.

The cause of this sudden turn was a face, dark and sinister, that peeped from beneath the vizor, which closed in an instant.

Then the figure seemed to shake to and fro.

The arms moved.

The hands relaxed, and the fingers became straight.

Hester gave a loud, piercing shriek.

She felt herself grasped by some unknown hand.

"Silence!" said a voice that proved the arm to belong to one of earth's mortals.

She screamed again, and struggled to get up.

Useless—she was held in a firm grip.

She looked her captor in the face and shuddered.

She knew him, and recognised the Brazilian uniform.

"Another cry like that," he said, "and I'll strangle you!"

The Jewess was not wanting in bravery.

"Release me!" she said, and endeavoured to get away.

Poor child! What was her frail strength to the impassioned ruffian who held her in his grasp?

The cloak he had thrown on the floor he picked up, and while she was struggling, he perfectly enveloped her in its folds.

With a stifled cry she strove to get out, but in vain.

He held her with brute force, and winding the cloak round her head, he held her.

With one choking gasp, and a faint cry for help, she discontinued her struggles, and swooned in his arms.

He gave a laugh of exultation.

Uncovering her face, that she might not suffocate, he placed a silver whistle to his mouth, and blew a long, shrill note.

It was the signal to his companions.

Without waiting to see whether he was heard, he took the girl in his arms and strode away.

His ruffian accomplices had heard the call.

But they were engaged.

They had followed the Jew.

Tracked him to the underground vault where he went to remove his gold.

With fierce, bloodshot eyes, they watched him bring up bag after bag.

None spoke, lest they might disturb him.

The man Reuben Harpy had addressed on the quarter-deck seemed the leader of his companions, and, by his appearance and language, was English, though he spoke Brazilian.

When the last bag of gold was hauled up, and the Jew prepared to follow, they stole quietly upon him.

It was this laugh that gave the miser such intense fear.

He struggled wildly to regain his gold.

But they only laughed the more.

"Now," cried Rufus the Englishman, "your gold, old sinner, and no trouble, or—"

He drew his knife.

At that instant the whistle of their chief roused them.

"No more parley," said the ruffian. "Drag him off!"

The last part of his speech was spoken in a tongue quite strange to the Jew.

Israel Shawm soon understood its purport. Four rough hands grasped him by the shoulders, and dragged him from his money.

But the Jew was obstinate.

Love for his gold gave him supernatural strength. Though they pulled him off the ground, he clung like grim death to his hoarded dross.

He had a bag of glittering coins under each arm, and one in his mouth.

At first Rufus felt inclined to laugh, but a second distant call of the captain's whistle drew the smile from his face.

"No more fooling," he said.

They had prepared themselves with a sack.

Into this they thrust the ill-gotten wealth.

Then one of the ruffians, with brutal force, and a loud laugh, tore the bag of gold from the Jew's mouth.

He uttered a howl of pain.

It was not without a struggle they took the other two bags from him.

He was thrown upon his knees, and one of the men would have thrust a knife in him.

Rufus stayed his hand.

The Jew's coat and vest were torn off in the struggle, and with a howl he put his hand to his heart as his last bag of coins was taken from him.

The two sailors, with a smile of satisfaction, picked up their wealth, and said—

"What shall we do with him?"

"Leave him to me," was the reply of Rufus, who had a peculiar look in his eye.

A FAIR WIND AND PROSPEROUS WEATHER.

"Israel Shawm," he said, in English, "what have you got under your hand?"

Israel Shawm trembled from head to foot.

"Noting. Noting. So help me Mosesh!"

"Ah, liar! Remove your hand."

"No! no!" he screamed. "Go! go!—you have all I got. I am a beggar. Leave me."

"Remove your hand!"

"Vat for, good Mister—"

The ruffian tore the bony hand aside, and Rufus gave a cry.

He saw a small leather bag in which something round was hidden.

He made a clutch at it.

The miser placed both hands upon it.

He cried most piteously for help.

"Leave go!" cried the ruffian, hoarsely.

A danger signal from the chief came down the gloomy vault.

With such a cry as a panther might give, Rufus threw Israel Shawm down upon the brink of the pit.

His sword flashed from its sheath.

Not a word did the ruffian utter, for he had spoken enough. The leather bag, with its mysterious contents, was hung round the Jew's neck with a gold chain.

The ruffian, Rufus, in his brutal, savage temper would not ask again for it, nor spend the time to take it by a struggle.

"Curse yer!" he said. "I'll take the chain from your neck by removing your head."

The Jew turned a livid hue when he saw the other meant it. The sword whirled in the air, as round it went like a gleam of light.

One loud, appalling cry as the sword descended; a thud, and a sickening crash, and the Jew's head, with the eyes rolling horribly, and the jaws gibing at his murderer, rolled along the brink of the pit, and then, with a crash, fell below.

Rufus, with a cry, tore the chain from the reeking neck, and, laughing like a fiend, he kicked the body after the head.

"Keep each other company," he said.

Then the stone trap was placed on the entrance. With his blood-stained sword in his hand, he took the lantern, and said—

"Come on."

His companions, appalled at what they had seen, strode on in front.

Rufus, behind, fixed his bloodshot eyes upon the leather bag, which was crimson with the gory dye. He opened it a little way. How his eyes blazed!

"Ha! ha! ha! This was worth twenty such lives," he muttered, gazing, with a fascinated stare, upon the blood-red spot that shone like a light in the centre of a huge stone he held in his hand.

It was the fatal Sea Emerald!

CHAPTER XCVIII.

BREATHINGS OF MUTINY.

ADMIRAL ELLIS glared upon his daughter with a look that showed the hatred in his heart. He hurled her from him.

"Away with you," he cried. "Hear me, vile girl. Though they murder me the next instant, my last, dying words shall be a curse!"

"Gag him!" cried Ben Barnacle, in a voice of thunder.

It was done. Harry Vere's wife threw herself at his feet, and, clasping her hands upon his knees, cried, imploringly—

"Spare him! spare him!—for my sake! Would you murder my father?"

"Murder?" replied Ben, haughtily. "We don't murder, but require justice. He would have murdered our commander; he would, and tried to murder your husband. He has cursed you, and shall such a man live? I am sorry for your sake; but go below. He is not worthy the title of father from you. Justice must be done. Look around you—on those faces—do they look like mercy?"

"But," pleaded the poor girl, the tears streaming down her cheeks, "you command here. Pause, ere it is too late."

"Go below. I am sorry, Mrs. Vere, to cause you so much pain—but, unless you depart, I must have you taken below"

"For God's sake, delay this!" said Harry Vere, coming on the other side of Ben.

"Never!"

"For my sake?"

"Do not ask."

"For her sake—my God, in killing him, you will make me a widower! Spare him, I beg. Think of that dear girl's mind. Remember, whatever he may be, he is her father."

"Lieutenant Vere, go below, and take your wife with you."

"But, sir, for God's sake, I—"

"No more. It is your duty.'

"Listen. I—"

"Marines! conduct Mrs. Vere to her cabin, and place Lieutenant Vere under arrest."

Harry's poor little wife gave a scream. Harry Vere, with a face like one carved in marble, approached his wife.

"Come, dearest," he said; "let me conduct you below, to save you from the touch of those men."

The marines came forward very reluctantly, for Harry Vere was a favourite, and they could scarcely believe the command they heard.

"No—no, Harry dear; if you are to be confined in prison, I will share your captivity."

"Noble girl! But it would give me pain. I can bear my own punishment—but—but not with you, my darling—not with you in that loathsome place."

The marines went to Harry's side, they scarcely knew how to act.

"'Tis best to come, sir," the corporal said.

Harry Vere turned towards them.

"I can at least conduct my wife below," he said.

Ben waved his hand.

"Marines, do your duty!"

At the second word of command, they brought their bayonets down.

"Mr. Vere, surrender your sword!" cried the officer.

"Conduct them below!" Ben said, his bell-like voice ringing through the ship.

"Hold! What means this?" cried a low, clear, commanding voice.

All eyes were turned towards the gangway, where Captain Tom, pale and weak, stood, leaning upon his scimitar.

He was scarcely dressed, but looked as though he had just jumped from his couch, and thrown a loose jacket on him.

Still, he looked the fine, princely fellow he was.

His eagle glance swept round, and he could understand all.

"What means your arrest, Lieutenant Vere?"

"I know not, captain."

"Marines, go forward!"

With a look of pleasure upon their faces, the marines obeyed. Ellis's daughter threw herself at Captain Tom's feet.

"Save him! for my sake—for his!" she cried, pointing to Harry; "for your own, spare my father!"

Minnie Atherton came on deck, having raised her lover from his couch. She comprehended instantly what was going on, and lent her pleading voice to the admiral's aid.

Harry Vere went to his young chieftain's side, and said, in a voice only heard by Captain Tom—

"For God's sake, sir, think of my wife—think of me. She will lose her mind, should this be carried out before her. I do not ask you to give him his life; but spare him for a short time, I implore you."

Captain Tom turned to the two girls, who stood clinging to each other.

"Go below," he said.

They knew resistance was useless.

So they obeyed.

Captain Tom strode to where the admiral stood.

"Remove the gag."

It was done.

The click of several musket-locks made the young chieftain turn.

He saw a file of marines standing with levelled muskets.

The deadly tubes were in a line with Admiral Ellis's heart.

They had done so at a sign from Ben.

"Ground arms!" said the chief.

Ben Barnacle's eyes were ablaze.

He had watched his leader countermand every order he had given.

"Is he to be let at large again?" cried Ben Barnacle. "Boy, you know not what you do."

"I command here!" thundered Captain Tom, "and who dares dispute my right? Ben Barnacle, you have infringed upon the laws of the ship in trying and condemning a man without my sanction and presence. Under what charge dared you arrest Harry Vere?"

"For disobedience."

"Mr. Barnacle, go to your cabin. Men, conduct the prisoner below."

Admiral Ellis, in a state of bewilderment, was taken from the deck.

He could not speak or move.

Ben Barnacle's rage was fearful to behold.

"Boy!" he cried, "you illuse your power. Look round upon those faces—what do you see there? Discontent. In giving that man time, you not only endanger your life, but the whole crew's. Remember the terms—all for one, and one for all. Does it seem like it? You ought to hang your nearest relative if the lives of your crew are endangered by his existence."

"Ben Barnacle, I am master here."

"Take care, or perhaps you may lose your power."

"Enough!" cried Captain Tom. "Leave me, ere you provoke me to do what I may afterwards regret. I brook dictation from no man."

"And, like most who have power and abuse it, you will bring your own destruction. Am I here to command or not? By Heaven! are my words to be gainsayed?—my orders countermanded? Ellis shall die—I have sworn!"

"Ellis shall not."

"We shall see."

"Our brother mutiny! What means this? What ho! Here, marines, arrest Lieutenant Barnacle!"

The officers and crew had not moved from their respective places, though Admiral Ellis had long been removed from the deck.

The crew were not bloodthirsty, but they did not approve of Admiral Ellis having his liberty.

They watched the angry words exchanged between Ben Barnacle and his young chief.

When they received the order to come forward and arrest the man they loved, they were staggered.

Ben's face was a study.

When he heard the command, his eyes blazed, his lips were compressed, and he looked the magnificent fellow he was.

"By Heaven!" he cried, "this shall not be!"

"Surrender your sword!" cried the chief.

"Never!"

His massive sword was whirled round as he said this.

Captain Tom's scimitar flashed from its sheath, and he seemed as though he would have cut Ben to the deck.

Barnacle, with his eagle-eye upon him, kept his sword raised, and the marines, fearing a deadly conflict, rushed forward.

"Back!" cried Ben, as his sword whirled round, and came full upon Captain Tom's steel.

Then both paused. Something seemed to pass through Ben's mind as he looked into the flushed face of his young chief.

He wheeled suddenly round and hurled his sword to the deck.

"Do your duty," he said to the marines.

Then remained passive while he was hand-cuffed and taken below. Harry Vere and his brother officers, as did the middies, looked pained. Their hearts were blackened against Admiral Ellis—the cause of all this.

"That man," said one of the officers, "is our curse."

"He is," assented another.

"I hope he will die."

"He shall!" said one of the middies, sternly.

"To your duty!" cried Captain Tom.

Every man dispersed at the sound of that voice—the mids, and some of the best hands, going in groups

"I don't like this day's work," said one.

"Nor I."

"I propose we send in a deputation to the captain," said one of the elder middies.

"How?"

"Why, a paper signed by all the crew."

"For what?"

"To say Admiral Ellis shall only have his life on conditions."

"Yes, yes—go on!"

"Those conditions are, that he will henceforth cease to hurt, or seek, directly or indirectly, the lives of our chieftain, officers, or any of the crew."

"Hear! hear!" Loud applause succeeded this.

The matter was then put under consideration, and old tars were brought into the gun-room, and they had a cool and deliberate council.

It was the first time ever such a thing had occurred on board the "Will-o'-the-Wisp."

The first time either man or officer had ever raised a whisper in opposition to the young chieftain's commands.

It was dangerous ground, and they knew not how it would be received. Seeing their hesitation, the middy who had started it said—

"Remember, shipmates, we, the crew, and every one on board, has individually a right to protection and consideration. What has been done does not suit us, and we are only asking, not demanding. Have we no voice in the matter? Are we slaves? No, this is a free ship. We are all free men, and acknowledge no tyrants!"

A low murmur went round, and that murmur was a warning to the bold speaker.

"Harkee, Jasper," said an old tar, "none o' them words on board here, yer know; no disrespect to the chief."

"I do not wish to say aught against our gallant leader," replied Jasper Drew.

"Well, well; go on!"

"As I have said," continued the bold youth, "we are only asking for what is right, and I am sure the chief won't gainsay it. While we are about it, let us add another request to the bill."

"What for?"

"The abolition of women on board the 'Will-o'-the-Wisp.' Our chief has not been the same since the cursed petticoats have been on board. I volunteered here, risked my life, lost my name and character, outlawed from my nation, and cast out of my family circle, for a bold, jolly life, such a life as we had at first. when there were no women but Zelie; she can stay, she was here before we were. Not that alone; she revels in the din of battle, and danger, she excites the chief on, and, like one of the Furies, makes herself, and all who follow her, a terror."

A pause, in which not an answer, a murmur, look, or movement, betrayed what his hearers thought.

Great excitement was working among them, but they waited breathlessly for the bold young speaker to finish. He continued; but that he might be heard the better, he stood on a gun.

The door of the gun-room was closed, and he went on—

" Let us, at once, do this. Only think, comrades. no women! That old fiend out of our way, the chief would be like the lion he was ; then we could defy the world. If not—if he will not put the women on shore—why, then, it shall be a general licence—we will all have women."

A low murmur of approval followed this.

" Good! yes, yes; go on !"

" That is all. He can but refuse, then he must comply with our wish on the other hand. Let it be done.

" We will take it to the chief in a body. I will hand it to him, and, in the name of the Shadow Avengers, demand the boon which is just to one and all."

A cheer would have broken from the crew, had not a voice said—

" And take care how you work, or the head that has concocted so much may roll at the chieftain's feet !"

All eyes were turned towards the end of the gun-room.

All gave an exclamation of surprise.

Zelie, the lovely corsair maiden, stood before them, —bold, defiant, and unflinching.

CHAPTER XCIX.

A LUCKY SHOT.

INFANT JOE, as he was termed, made his way towards the fort with his insensible burthen with all possible speed.

In consequence of the darkness, he had to be very cautious. and, therefore, it was some time ere they turned the point leading from the beach.

" Halt !" cried the officer who was conducting the party.

" If I mistake not, I perceive a body of men, creeping on their hands and knees, at the foot of the cliff. Out with your torches, or we may be fair marks for a bullet."

The men instantly obeyed. and. at the same moment, discovered their progress was interrupted by a gang of armed smugglers, who instantly commenced a practical argument for the right of way by furiously attacking the blockade men.

At the first fire, the ponderous bulk bearing the light form of Susan reeled and fell with its burthen on the earth, and a smuggler was seen to rush wildly through the chaos of contending beings, hewing his passage with a short, broad cutlass, and apparently having but one object in view.

A retreat of the smugglers, and a consequent advance of their antagonists, brought him to the place where Susan. still senseless. lay wounded in the sinewy arms of the prostrate man-of-war's man.

He endeavoured to disengage her from his grasp, and, on placing his hand on her neck. he felt that his fingers were straying in warm and still oozing blood.

He trembled, and gasped for breath.

There were two beings senseless before him. one must be seriously wounded, perhaps dying or dead. He dragged Susan from her thrall.

The action was followed by a groan from the man. who faintly rose upon his knees. and made a grasp towards the female with one hand, and drawing a pistol from his belt with the other, discharged it at random, and again fell exhausted.

The report was heard by some of the still contending party, and forms were seen hastening to the spot.

At first he could discover no pulsation. He pressed his hand firmer against her side, and, with a cry of joy, sprang to his feet.

He again clasped her in his arms. and, with the speed of a hound, ran across the fields leading from the verge of the cliffs, darted through the church-

yard there, till his quick step was heard on the stones of the paved street.

The inhabitants were at their doors and windows, anxious to catch the slightest word that might give them some intelligence of the conflict ; for the reports of the fire-arms had been heard in the town, and all there was anxiety and agitation.

But the quick questions were unanswered—the salutes were unnoticed.

The form that rushed by them was heard to gasp hardly for breath, and they were satisfied that something desperate had taken place.

The smuggler gained 'he street that Susan had set out from.

The women, and others who had joined them, were gathered round the door of the house, waiting with breathless impatience her return, and various were the conjectures of the night's events ; when a voice, whose tones all knew, was heard to exclaim—

" Stand on one side there; a chair ! a chair !"

They made way for him in an instant.

He darted into the house, placed Susan in the arm-chair, and dropped on the floor, with his forehead resting on his arm.

" James !" the women cried, " are you hurt ?"

They received no reply, so they raised him from the ground, while one of the women lighted a candle.

At that moment a scream of dismay escaped from all.

Those who had stood listening at the door rushed in, and were horror-struck on beholding poor Susan lying apparently lifeless in the chair ; her face and neck dabbled with blood.

But she breathed.

Restoratives were applied to both, the blood was cleansed from Susan, and, to the joy of all, not a wound could be perceived.

James had now sufficiently recovered to stand and bathe her temples, and he kissed her cold and quivering lips.

She slowly opened her eyes. The first object they rested upon was her husband!

She started from the chair, and gazed at him with a mingled expression of terror and delight.

James, seeing the effect his appearance produced, pressed her in his arms, where she lay laughing and crying, and clasping him round the neck, till the shock had subsided. when she sat like a quiet child on his knee, reposing her head upon his shoulder.

None had as yet ventured to ask a question, but all impatiently waited till Susan should break the silence that had now followed the confusion of cries, tears, and wonder.

But she seemed to have no other wish on earth. She was in her husband's arms—beneath her own roof, and that was question, and answer, and everything to her.

James appeared restless, and attempted to rise. but the motion was followed by the close winding of Susan's arms round his neck.

Then, as if suddenly resolved, and chiding himself for some neglect, he started from his seat.

" Susan," said he, " you are better now : keep yourself still till I return—I shall be but a few minutes."

" No, no." cried Susan, grasping his arm with both her hands, " not again—go not again I shall be able to speak to you presently. Don't leave me now. James."

" You mustn't persuade me to stay." replied he ; " I left the crew fighting with the blockade men when I saw you in that fellow's arms; but I must go back again. for life and death are in this night's business. One of us has been shot, poor Peter Cullen drowned. He would drink in spite of our orders, and fell overboard. I tried to save him ; but I am afraid he lies dead under the cliff, just where I first saw you, Susan, when I lost my footing. But I must go back, and see the end of it—now, don't grip me so hard, Susan—I must go. I daresay all's lost —but I must go."

He struggled to release himself from Susan, when a smuggler rushed into the house, pale and exhausted.

He flung himself into a chair, and, throwing a brace of pistols on the ground, exclaimed—

"The boat's taken—the tubs we had worked to the foot of the cliffs are seized too. We fought hard for it, but it was of no use;" and then he breathed a bitter curse, in that low, withering tone which seems to recoil upon the head of the curser, and clings only to him that utters it.

"Well, it can't be helped," said James, calmly seating himself; "it's no use repining now. Words and sighs won't better it, though it is somewhat hard, after cruising about for three months, to lose our cargo at sea, and when we thought ourselves lucky that we escaped Cork gaol, and got back to Holland, with an empty hold, and tried to do a little business at home, to make such a finish to all as we have done to-night. Poor Peter's drowned too, Tom—d'ye know that?"

"Ah!" said the other, "I thought it was all over with him when I saw him go. But how did you manage with him?"

"Now it's all over," said James, "I'll tell you the affair.

"When I plunged in after him, I popped a tub under my arm, thinking we were opposite a point where there was no watch; for, thinks I, if I can work a tub and save a man's life at the same time, I shall do a clever thing; but it was some seconds before I could find Peter, it being so pitch dark.

"At last I saw something bob up to the top of the water, close to me.

"It was him, sure enough.

"I made a grasp, and caught him by the hair, kept his head above the water, and got ashore with him.

"At that moment a blockade man spied me, and fired a pistol.

"I heard some of them coming towards me, so I dragged Peter under the cliff, and made for the town; but the man-o'-war's-men followed me up so closely that I was obliged to drop my tub and crowd all sail.

"I got near home, and thought I could manage to drop in without being seen; but they had so gained upon me that I was obliged to run again right through the town, where I dodged them, till I found myself back again at the place where I had left Peter.

"I felt him, but he was stiff and dead, poor fellow.

"I then thought I'd try if I could hail you; but the only answer I got was a report of firearms on the beach, then I knew that you must be working the boat slap in the teeth of the blockade men.

"I listened a minute or two, and all was silent; so, thinks I, they have either put out to sea again, or have succeeded in working the cargo."

"Yes," interrupted Tom, "we had worked part of it, and had hid the tubs under the cliff, when we were discovered, and attacked; and three or four suddenly put off the boat, while we who were left had to fight it out, and get away as we could."

"Well," continued James, "I thought I'd mount the cliff, and look out, and had got near the top; but, what with wondering how you had managed, and thinking about poor Peter and our unlucky cruise, I felt very melancholy, and was pulling up to take fresh wind, when what should I hear but my Susan's voice! That so astonished me that I

lost my footing, and was capsized plump down again on the shingle. There were no bones broken, however; and I was just about to hail Susan on the cliff, when I thought I saw some of the blockade men coming; and, says I to myself, 'you mustn't see me, masters!' so I crept close under the cliff, and passed them safe enough.

"'Then,' thinks I, 'I may as well find out where the lads are;' and thinking Susan would be up to the rig, and wait where she was, or go home again, I contrived to run along the bottom of the cliff, till I found myself tumbling among a lot of tubs.

"'Oh!' thinks I, 'all's right yet; and, while looking about, I perceived all of you creeping down the cliffs.

"You recognised me, if you recollect; and we were just preparing to clear the tubs snugly away when the enemy's lanterns issued from a projecting part of the cliff.

"Douse they went in one moment, and, in the other, there we were with the blockade men, yard arm and yard-arm.

"But, when I first saw the light from their torches, what should I see but my Susan stowed in the arms of Infant Joe!

"In the surprise, I opened fire upon him, but took a good aim, notwithstanding.

"I saw him fall, and, laying about me right manfully, I seized upon my little brig, carried her away from the grappling-irons of the huge pirate, and towed her right into harbour; and here she is, safe and sound—there's some comfort in that, arn't there, my girl?"

And a hearty kiss, with a murmured blessing, escaped from the lips of the rough young smuggler, as he again pressed the now happy Susan in his arms.

Two of his companions now entered the house, and were cordially received by their acquaintances and neighbours assembled.

But the hanging of their heads, the ill-stifled sigh, and the languid manner of taking the hands outstretched to welcome them, proved how severely their bold hearts felt their chilling disappointment, and unrewarded toil.

A dead silence followed their entrance—for what could be said? The journal of their cruise and misfortunes was recorded in every line of their brows.

It was a sad meeting, and sadness and silence love to be together. At length, one of them, looking at James, said—

"We heard that you had brought down Infant Joe, but just as we came into the town we were told that he was only wounded, and had been carried to the tower, with a pistol bullet in his right shoulder."

"In his right shoulder, eh?" said James, as he gave a loud whistle, and looked at Susan. "It was a close chance for you, my girl.

"Well, I've no wish for his death; but if we ever should meet again, I am just as likely to snap my trigger, and perhaps with better success.

"But, Susan, my lass, I've been waiting all along to know how you came on the cliff at such a time; and I'm somewhat jealous, too, at that same Infant Joe, and the manner he was convoying you so snugly."

Susan smiled, and related her share in the events of the night, and concluded by entreating James to relinquish his desperate and unprofitable pursuit— to forego all thoughts of again embarking in a smuggling cruise.

And, when the employment of the coast failed to procure them a quiet subsistence, to remove to some happier land, where industry may reap its reward, and the strong arm and sweating brow know their hours of comfort and repose.

For a moment the smuggler's face grew thoughtful, and his sunburnt brow contracted.

"Susan," he said, "I have been thinking how foolish I was not to have joined the vessel that went in search of Captain Tom."

"What!" cried Susan, with a start, then added; "no, no, James, you would have repented more had you done so."

"What makes you think so?"

"Do not ask me, James. Is he not a brave and gallant youth—would you raise your hand against him? No, no, I know you better."

"Well, perhaps you are right," said the smuggler, moodily, "but we cannot starve, you know."

"Neither will we."

"Ah! what is that?"

The report of pistols at no great distance was the cause of this exclamation. In a moment the air was filled with the shouts and oaths of the combatants.

Some half-a-dozen or more smugglers had contrived to haul a few kegs of brandy to the top of the cliff, and the men-of-war's men had accidentally fallen across them.

The smugglers fought bravely for what they deemed their rights, and their opponents struggled with them desperately.

At the first sound, James and Tom were upon their feet, and, before Susan could remonstrate, they rushed wildly from the house.

CHAPTER C.
THE PETITION.

THE bold, unflinching gaze of Zelie swept round upon the excited faces of the crew, but none could read the look of the corsair maiden.

She looked the perfect goddess of beauty, as she stood there, her fearless eyes flashing brilliantly, more with a gleam of fierce joy than anger.

"'Tis well," she said; "fear not, I am not a spy. I have heard what has been said, and have come to aid you."

Those who had risen in an attitude of menace, sank back abashed, and involuntarily bowed their heads with a feeling of reverence for so much beauty, and all remained in quiet respect before their queen.

"You," she said, her voice sounding sweet and musical, the more so because she spoke with a strong accent, alluding to the young mid who had started the affair, "you have spoken wisely. Your chief is not the hero of yore; the pale-faced English girl makes his arm weak, and his heart childish; she unmans him; he listens to her, and his daring soul is subdued. The hand that never failed now grows weak, the heart that was never touched, the iron will that could never be broken, has what?—fallen under the control of a weak girl. And you, my brave hearts—you, whom he swore to lead on to wealth and glory—do what?—sit here, eat biscuits, and clean the rust from your arms.

"Your bitterest enemies are allowed to live, but only to again take up arms against you, and, in the end, the very man you gave up to-day will put a halter round all your necks, and thus will end the career of the Shadow Avengers!"

There was a lurking devil behind the sneer that accompanied the last two words, and scorn in the lovely smile that drove those brave hearts to desperation.

"Hush!" she said; "remember your oath. You have one and all sworn to die for your leader, and you must keep your vow. Raise not hand or voice against him you have sworn to defend. He rules here. He rules where none other could; but you have a right—it says so in the laws laid down by you all—to have a voice; you are allowed to speak your discontent, if you have any. You can abolish that which is in any way against the rules of the ship, or a detriment to your career. I have long since lost all power over your king, and so it will be while that pale, timid girl remains here. Do,

then, as you said; get pen and paper, state upon it what is required, and go forward to demand it. Lose no time!"

The mid jumped up.

Pen and paper were brought, and he, being looked upon as the leader, wrote down all that had been proposed, and read it, word for word, to see if it met the approval of all the crew.

It did.

He was helped by Zelie, and there were one or two little additions.

When it was finished, the middy mounted on a gun, by the side of which stood Zelie, and, for the last time, read the petition aloud. It was prefaced with a few words to the chief, and then briefly stated the wishes of the men.

It is necessary that the reader should know, and we therefore will give it as it was read. The first demand was this—

"1. We, the undersigned, as free men, who have thrown off the yoke of an ungrateful and tyrannical Government, to serve under a free flag and chosen leader, ask, under the name of the cause they serve, for justice. We demand justice, as being consistent with our laws and rules, which state that every life is valued the same—the smallest boy on board demands the protection of the leader, as the leader demands the protection of his crew; and for the sake of every individual life—for the sake of our safety —for the life of our chosen chief—we demand the death of Admiral Ellis; not because he is an enemy to the cause, but because he is a foe—a personal antagonist to all on board the 'Will-o'-the-Wisp.' To prove that we—the Shadow Avengers—wish to be lenient, if Admiral Ellis will draw up and sign with his own hand a document in which he swears to relinquish all further attempts upon the lives of Captain Tom, or his officers, or his crew, or on any single individual on board the ship; under such conditions do we, with the sanction of our chief, give him his liberty.

"2. When we turned against our flag to fight under the banner of Death—to be ruled by a chosen chief—to succumb to such laws as should be made by the mutual consent of the whole crew, we did so as men who had set aside the ruling power of tyrants, that we might live as free men and brothers—where we are all equals, obeying only the one ruler, under whom we had placed ourselves, to be led into danger, or even death—or glory. We are no longer under the yoke of servitude, but under free laws, where each man shall be allowed to put forth his vote in anything that may be for the comfort of us all. We acknowledge only one flag. The laws laid down by ourselves and our leader are the ship's rules. Women were strictly prohibited; yet he who should have been the first to uphold this law was the first to break it. Our motto is 'All for one, and one for all.' We find that a great many disadvantages have arisen through the presence of females on board; and, for the general benefit of all, we ask, in the name of the crew, fairness in all things, and that the women shall be put ashore on the first opportunity.

"3. That if this request is not granted, we one and all demand, by our rights, as stated in the rules, the privilege of having women on board; and that every man shall have one female companion.

"This petition is put forth merely as a request, stating the wishes of the men, and asking what is only fair. Never have we raised a murmur of discontent, or a voice of opposition to the doings of one we all feel proud to serve under, every man's most heartfelt wish is to see the invincible flag of Captain Tom for ever flaunting in the breeze; and one and all are willing to shed our blood at the feet of our beloved leader in defending the flag we raised above his head.

"Long life and prosperity to the Shadow Avengers! God bless our chosen chief—our lion-hearted king, Captain Tom!"

A faint cheer broke from the men's lips at the last words, so beloved was the very name of the gallant Captain Tom.

A few things were added to this; and when at length everything was finished, Zelie stole from the cabin, after having arranged with the crew that, upon a given signal from her, the whole crew were to come on deck.

The middy who had thus made himself conspicuous, amused himself by making a few corrections in the petition, and thus kept himself employed until the time should arrive.

Captain Tom strode the deck with quick and angry strides.

For once in his life he regretted a hasty action, and that was the imprisonment of Ben Barnacle.

Every man had either gone to his duty or his berth.

Harry Vere brought his chief's coat and hat. Hastily donning them, he, with scarcely a word of thanks, continued his uneasy walk.

Once Zelie passed him, but he did not even lift his head.

She cast one hasty and angry glance around, her eyes were fixed upon a man standing near the main-mast.

A silken handkerchief fluttered from her hand to the deck, and the sailor saw it.

Whether from surprise or intention we cannot say, but he let fall a huge steel marling-spike he held in his hand.

Then all was as silent as before. The officers kept conversing in a low tone near the taffrail.

The chief, with gloomy brow and compressed lips, continued his hasty strides on the weather side.

With head bent and arms akimbo, he seemed lost to all that was going on around him, until the tramp of many feet made him look up.

He started.

"What means this?" he demanded of Harry Vere, as his eagle glance swept along the faces of his crew, who stood in a group in front of the poop.

Harry Vere, with as much surprise as himself marked upon his face, could not reply.

The officers stood dumbfounded.

Iron Arm came forward with a vivid flash in his eyes.

"What is this?" cried Captain Tom, angrily.

One or two low murmurs were heard, but none spoke.

"Speak, some of you, or—"

He checked himself with an angry gesture.

Every eye was upon the bold young mid as he stood forth, cap in hand.

"Captain," he said with great courtesy, "I am compelled, at the request of all present here, to act as spokesman in this affair."

"For what?"

"A request they would make to their chief."

"What, discontent, or—"

"No, captain. They merely do what the laws permit; they have a boon to ask."

"Say rather some demand."

"No, sir."

"Go on."

"Firstly, they wish for the release of Ben Barnacle."

There was a pause.

"Oh!" came at length from Captain Tom. "And so now I am to be dictated in all I do—is that it?"

"No, captain, but the men have a right to petition for anything consistent."

"True. Proceed," said Captain Tom, with a sneer.

"I am commanded, in the name of the crew, to present this with all due respect and deference to your decision."

With a smile that brooded no good, Captain Tom took the documents, wondering what they were.

The first demanded the release of Ben Barnacle.

He read it, and then he crumpled it up in his hand.

The young captain fixed his brilliant eyes upon the sea of upturned faces.

"Did I hear aright?" he said, slowly. "What means that murmur? Is this merely a pretext to open mutiny? God of Heaven! who rules here? I or you? Am I not free to act?"

"Captain," said the bold young mid, "that paper was presented to you by men—not as mutineers but those who serve under a free flag, and have a right to vote for that which they think may be for the public good—presented also with every mark of respect for our ruler, and you hurled it in our faces. Was that not an insult?"

"Silence! I will do as I choose—enough to say that when I feel disposed I will release him, and not before."

Swiftly his eyes scanned the larger document. Every glance was fixed upon him. All watched his ever-changing face as a flush mounted his cheek and a lurid light burned in his eyes. When he had finished, he raised his head.

None knew what effect the reading of that had upon him.

He was now surrounded by a body of marines and young mids, his own boat's crew and body-guard, who came up under arms when they saw what was afloat.

Apparently not noticing the armed force behind him, he said—

"Who wrote this?"

"'Twas I, captain," replied the mid, fearlessly. "By the request of the crew."

"Good."

He waved the middy back, and with his eyes sweeping from face to face he continued—

"When I was elected chief, with the power to rule all here, I was given absolute control—it was for me to command and you obey. I trod the deck of the ship I won—won for myself and for you all. And is my power so limited that I am to ask the consent of you all whether I shall bring anyone on board? Are you the brave hearts I thought you were to thus wish to deny my protection to an innocent girl who is without a friend or relation on earth? Shame on you! Have you so soon forgotten one of our rules—'to release the oppressed, and defend the weak?' My brave hearts, you have been misled. I will find the leader. Return, my gallant men, to your duty, and think of this."

He paused, and whispered a word to Harry Vere. Without any confusion, he brought Minnie on deck. She looked pale and beautiful, as she glanced wonderingly upon our hero's face.

Captain Tom took her hand, and leading her forward said—

"Men!—hearts of oak!—the invincible Shadow Avengers! Look! behold the frail creature you have all rose up against! Can it be possible that I am addressing the gallant band I have led on to so much glory? Can I be before those who risked their lives for her and for me so many times? Look, Minnie, my bride! You see that body once true-hearted men. They refuse you protection they would have you thrust

side, and the safety of this vessel. What say you to this?"

Minnie, trembling from head to foot, and with cheek paler than usual, said, in low, faltering accents—

"If my presence be irksome, I would be put ashore; willingly would I sacrifice my happiness to promote yours or that of the noble men who have so long supported your flag."

"What can you say to that, my lads? Do you not feel yourselves degraded? Go to your duty, and forget that which makes you less men than I thought you. Go! I will consider, and in two days will reply; till then, to your duty!"

They gave a slight cheer.

Every head was hung in shame, and in a body the men returned forward and dispersed.

Captain Tom had used the most effectual means to subdue them when he had promised to release Ben Barnacle.

On going to the prison of his faithful follower he found him seated, his face buried in his hands and his whole frame shaking from great emotion.

Ben started when the chief entered.

"Forgive me, my trusty Ben. I am come to give you liberty, and ask your forgiveness."

"Boy," said Ben, strangely excited, "what would you say to a son if he drew a weapon upon his sire, and had him cast into a dungeon, manacled and fettered in irons?"

"I would call down my bitterest curse upon the son's head, and the hand that could be raised against a father's!" replied Captain Tom, in surprise.

"Then," replied Ben, in a low voice, "thou art a *rsing thyself!*"

CHAPTER CI.
THE COUNCIL.

IRON ARM had been a silent, though not a disinterested spectator of what went on.

"They are faint but sure symptoms of mutiny," he said to Harry Vere, when the men had retired, and Captain Tom had gone below.

"I fear so, too."

"Yet nothing is easier than to rule such men; you can sway them whichever way you like, providing they do not get too tight a hold upon you."

"I should like to know the contents of their petition."

"So should I."

"I fear it would not have ended so well had not the captain consented to release Ben."

"True, Mr. Vere."

While they were still conversing, Captain Tom came on deck.

Order was now perfectly restored, and the gallant "Will-o'-the-Wisp" sailed on.

"Gentlemen," said the young chieftain, addressing his officers, "will you come below?"

They instantly consented, and followed him to the state-cabin.

Captain Tom was seated at the head of the table, and when all his officers had entered he rose, and very briefly addressed them.

"The reason, gentlemen, I have summoned you all together is because I wish to hold a council, and have at once decided measures taken concerning this new—or I may say this first eruption among the men."

The document was read slowly by Captain Tom, and its nature was discussed with due deliberation.

"The men have left you no loophole to escape," said Ben, with a grim smile.

"How do you mean?"

"They do not demand that women shall not be on board, but they say if you keep them it must be a public privilege."

"Do you think I would grant it?"

"No."

"Well then—"

"Still you cannot retreat from the thing, you must give the men an answer. You have a crew of the most faithful hearts that ever stood beneath a rover's flag, and they must foretell or fear something happening to thus dictate.

"Again, they only wish that which the rulers of the ship grant the prisoners. They speak in every way reasonable. They are free men under a free flag, owning no Government, and no King but yourself. Therefore, to one extent, you must grant their request."

"I think it would be wisest," put in Harry Vere.

"The fact is," said Iron Arm, "the men get dissatisfied unless you continue to glut them with excitement, wealth, and glory, as you did at first.

"I can see through it. They imagine that Ellis was let off to-day, and many a wild adventure has been set aside through the pleadings of a woman. Pardon, captain, but if you would wish to hold sway as you have done, to rule a horde of daring outlaws, you must be dead to all such feelings as the person of one so dear as Miss Atherton makes you."

"There is truth in that," put in Ben.

And the young chieftain saw it. He knew that the ruler of his wild crew must be a man bolder, wilder, and more daring than themselves.

A long and steady deliberation was held, and it was hours ere the council broke up.

They were all of a mind that Captain Tom should grant the requests, but in such a manner that it would seem more as though he did it from his own free will, and in showing example to those who followed him, than because the crew had demanded it.

With that boldness so characteristic of Captain Tom, he was sailing on to the very point the six ships thought they were driving him.

How he would laugh in their faces when they perceived Admiral Ellis on his vessel!

The night-watch was set.

The steady tramp of the sentinel might have been heard, as he walked to and from the hour-glass, anxiously awaiting the time he would be relieved.

Suddenly the sentry paused, and brought his firelock down. He fancied he saw a stealthy, creeping shadow.

"Who goes there?"

"'Tis I."

The marine drew back with an obsequious salute. He was confronted by Zelie, the corsair maiden.

"All's well," he said.

She passed on.

Though he followed her with his eyes, she was soon lost in the gloom, and amidst the many gun-carriages that were upon deck.

With noiseless tread she made her way to the gun-room. A sentry stood at the door, and he seemed aware of her approach. In silence he drew himself up, saluted, and quietly admitted her to the gun-room.

The dim glare of a couple of oil-lamps threw their dull light upon the scene, and Zelie glanced round as she entered.

Making a sign to the sentinel, he closed the door, and resumed his regular tread.

"I am here," said Zelie, in a low tone, as though speaking to herself.

In an instant, from behind gun-carriages, off lockers, out of hammocks, and every dark corner, came the gallant buccaneers.

"'Tis well," she said, when they stood respectfully before her. "Speak—what are your resolutions?"

"As before," replied the young middy, coming forward.

"And those?"

"Not to yield our cause without a struggle."

"Good. Do so. You will see to-morrow how the petition is received. Be careful, and you will gain your point; but remember, the least sign of insubordination or opposition will end fatally. Do as I bid you, and all will be well.

"Keep firm, and have what you ask for, or resign. Nothing more can be done until we have heard the chief's decision. Keep all quiet, and be on the alert."

Gentle as she had come, she went away again. The crew returned to their hammocks.

When the morning came, Captain Tom went alone to the prison of Admiral Ellis.

The admiral's eyes lit up with a look of fire when the young chief entered, and his teeth could be heard to grate harshly together, and so intense was his passion that he buried his nails deep into his palms.

"Admiral Ellis," said Tom, calmly, and feigning not to notice his captive's frenzy, "I have come to offer you means of freedom and life."

Ellis did not reply.

"'Tis not I," continued Tom, "but my crew who put down these conditions. I intended to have given you your freedom and life, though you pursue me with such inveterate hatred, but now it is wholly out of my power and rule; but I cannot conquer the will or passions of my crew—read this."

Admiral Ellis took it, and read the contents slowly.

"Here is my reply."

Admiral Ellis tore the paper into shreds, as he spoke thus, and then hurled the fragments to the floor.

Without a muscle of his face moving, Tom replied—

"Very well, admiral. The crew are waiting on deck for your reply. I will send it to them."

He struck his heel twice upon the floor.

A marine entered.

"Pick up those," Captain Tom said, pointing to the bits of paper, "and take them to your companions as an answer from Admiral Ellis."

The marine did as desired, and left the cabin.

"Admiral, your life is no longer in my hands. I cannot help you." Captain Tom turned, and strode haughtily away.

The marine reached the deck, and going on the poop cried—

"Messmates, I am commissioned to give you the reply of Admiral Ellis. 'Tis here!"

He hurled the remnants of the document among them.

They gave a howl of rage as the wind bore the pieces of written paper away.

The murmur of a few voices was taken up. From mouth to mouth it went until it sounded like a deep roar, and it formed into one terrible word as the breeze bore it away—

"Death!"

With fearful distinctness it penetrated the cabin of Admiral Ellis, and his cheeks paled.

He felt how little hope there was for him, when a horde of ruthless men were thus awfully proclaiming his death.

"Death! death!" came again in the same mighty voice.

"Death to the foe!" and then came the rush of feet.

Ellis thought his last moments had come.

Harry Vere was on deck, and he glared with a troubled look from one to the other, and lastly upon Captain Tom.

"You are not going to let them butcher him, are you?" he asked, in a voice tremulous from emotion.

In an instant Captain Tom became the haughty being of yore.

With eyes that flashed fire, and a voice that could be heard by any one of that swaying mass, he thundered—

"Hold! Silence, every one!"

Something of the old devil-may-care aspect returned. He looked the sea king he was; and that sound of his voice—the angry eye—had quelled those rough hearts.

They stood silent and subdued.

"Are you men?" he cried. "What is this ship—what are we? Are you all fiends, and this ship a floating hell? Enough! To your duty! I am he who gives life or death to friend or foe. When you are men, and not savages, return and ask what you wish. Now go; begone!"

With bowed heads and cowed looks, the gallant fellows returned to their posts, with the exception of about twenty.

They were new hands; rough-bearded and fine-looking men.

They raised a hum.

"To your duty!" cried Captain Tom, sternly; but they did not move.

"If," he said, "you are not at your posts in three minutes, you shall be put in irons, every one."

"We ain't slaves," said one—a man who had been made captain of the forecastle.

He was rather young, and bore that rakish, careless air of vagabondage acquired by men whose whole life has been spent in wild lawlessness.

He was dressed in an elegant, fantastic costume, and his not unhandsome form looked picturesque and fierce.

"Nor do we serve in a King's ship," he continued.

"No words; to your duty—there is only two minutes and a half left."

"We are free men," the man continued, sullenly, "and you have no more right to rule than any of us. We can have who we like, and do the same—ain't that it, mates?"

"Aye, aye."

"We wants that old skunk hung."

"Yes, yes."

"D'ye hear?" he said, as he looked up in an insolent manner to the captain, "and we ain't going without."

"Mutiny!" cried Tom, drawing his scimitar. "Marines! what ho! arrest those men!"

The whole crew, who had stood looking on in the distance with wonder, now made a rush forward.

Captain Tom's body-guard, and all his officers, came on the quarter-deck.

Ben Barnacle and Tom thought the whole crew had mutinied. So did the twenty mutineers.

"Down with the boy!" they shouted, and they made a leap at Captain Tom.

"Death to the mutineers!" he said.

His body-guard would have poured a volley of bullets into the whole crew, had not Iron Arm stopped them.

"Hold!" he said. "Look!"

The instant the twenty, with the captain of the forecastle at their head, made a rush, the whole of the gallant buccaneers threw themselves upon them.

In a moment six were hacked to pieces, and the rest would have shared the same fate, had not the powerful voice of Ben Barnacle saved them.

"Hold!" he cried. "Put them in irons, my lads."

But so enraged were the gallant followers of Captain Tom, that, had not Ben leaped amongst them, they would have torn the daring mutineers limb from limb.

"Fool!" cried Captain Tom, to the man that had beset him. "See what you have brought on yourself and companions. There is mercy for them, and here is death for you."

His sword dashed round, and, before the other

could guard the thrust, the sword of his chief went through his heart.

With a gasp, and a low groan, he fell back on the quarter-deck, his sword falling from his grasp, and his face rigid in death.

At the same moment one of his companions, who had stole behind Captain Tom, fell, with a middy's knife in his heart.

CHAPTER CII.

THE FATE OF ADMIRAL ELLIS.

THE fate of the mutineers was a most terrible warning to the rest.

More than half of the mutineers had been slain instantly, and the rest were only saved from a cruel fate by Captain Tom.

It was a test by which he found that, whatever might be their demand, his crew never thought of mutiny.

The remaining mutineers were bound, and placed below in irons to await their fate. Another day's life was given Admiral Ellis, as the unexpected occurrence had settled the affairs for the day.

The gallant young chief was surprised to find his men so rigid and determined. They still demanded the death of Ellis. Once or twice Captain Tom had a suspicion that some one was exciting the men.

Who could it be? He thought of all the men likely to attempt it. Then, again, he knew none on board had the power over his men.

Not for an instant did the real truth flash to his mind, and Harry Vere did all he could to save Admiral Ellis for the sake of Jenny, but all his efforts were in vain.

"I will do all in my power,' said the chief, " but my men will have their way in this case."

"Then," replied Harry Vere, with a look of sorrow upon his face, " I must resign my sword. I can no longer serve under your flag, and should take it as an extreme favour if you would delay what measures you are going to take until I and my wife are put on shore or on the first prize you can take."

Captain Tom was staggered.

"Nonsense." he said.

Vere did not reply, but handed his sword to the young chief.

"Put it back, Harry," said Tom, pushing it away with his hand

"Captain, I mean what I have said. I am very sorry. You know I would have died, and will, if it be necessary, for you, but in this I am earnest.'

"Wait at least the issue of to-morrow before you take such steps."

The morrow came.

Things were changing. The gallant crew of the "Will-o'-the-Wisp" were bent upon their purpose—bent on opposing the chief.

Times had altered existence on board.

Peace had left the ship.

The leader feared his officers—the officers feared the subordinates—the subordinates feared the men, and the men feared each other.

Discontent had been breathed among them, and a critical moment had arrived.

Captain Tom came upon deck—calm, bold, lion-hearted, and defiant—prepared to assert his power and hold sway.

His officers were with him. His body-guard at his back. The noble boy is seen to turn, and his lips move. An order is given in a low voice.

The loud tattoo of the drum brings the men to the deck, and mustered aft.

And all hands are on deck, excepting a few that are kept to guard the prisoners.

Captain Tom strides haughty the quarter-deck. One hand grasps a roll of parchment, the other is thrust in the unfastened breast of his glittering corselet.

His heart is brave, his hand steady, his eye bold and defiant, his whole mien commanding.

Like a monarch he appeared before that sea of upturned faces. As he spoke, his voice, loud and thrilling, rang through the ship, and found an echo in every man's breast.

"Shadow Avengers!—defenders of that flag, the invincible banner. You are mustered here to learn the decision of your chief."

A silence.

"By the laws laid down by our free consent, it is against the rules to have women on board under any other circumstances than as passengers," he continues. "Long before I decided upon putting my bride and Mrs. Vere on shore ; but hitherto we have been prevented making a port by unforeseen circumstances. Are you answered?"

A murmur went round.

"Speak."

"Aye, aye, captain."

"Another rule in our laws is, that no life shall be given or taken : no quarter given or asked ; no prisoner put in irons without the consent of your chief—is it not?"

"Aye, aye."

"By the same rule, and the same power, I protect Admiral Ellis. His punishment shall be—"

"Death!" came as though in one mighty voice from that group of men.

"Silence!" the dark eye kindled like a lurid ball of flame, as this word was thundered. "Another shout like that, and I silence the shouters. Rule the twentieth of our laws—to approve whatever may be decided by the committee or your chief—to openly show opposition or dissatisfaction is mutiny ; and mutiny is death."

Another silence.

"I have sworn Admiral Ellis shall have life and liberty, and to seek his life will be seeking mine—to seek mine, is death!"

Another pause.

"Admiral Ellis will be cast upon the sea in a boat, with provisions enough for three days—and water for the same period—he shall leave the ' Will-o'-the-Wisp ' unhurt, and Fate shall decide what may become of him ; but should he, by attempting (if he survives) our destruction, fall into my power, then do I freely consent to his execution—to be shot, or the plank. Let this be the first and last eruption. To your duties, my men, I give three minutes for the deck to be cleared of all idlers, and twenty minutes for the boat to be prepared. Now go—not a word—to your duty!"

Then came a murmur. But only from one man. Like a tiger did Captain Tom leap from the quarter-deck in their midst.

He had picked the sailor out who had dared to raise his voice. The captain—quiet, firm, and terrible—strode to the man.

His white, delicate hands caught him by the throat, with giant strength he dragged him from the crew, and took the shrinking wretch from the midst of his companions.

He was hurled down—Captain Tom's foot was on his neck, and his scimitar gleamed in the air.

"Mercy!" gasped the shrinking wretch. "Mercy, my chief, upon me, for God's sake!" and he clasped his hands in supplication.

"If, in two minutes, every man is not at his post, you lose your head!"

First one—two—then three ; and, lastly, in a troop, the whole ship's company moved away.

Captain Tom released his prisoner.

"Go," he said " and let this be a warning."

The man rose, and tremblingly departed.

He was thankful for his life.

Captain Tom returned to his officers.

"Prepare the boat," he said.

The gig was launched, and water and provender put into it. A small sail: no compass, arms, or ammunition was allowed. Admiral Ellis was brought on deck.

"Admiral Ellis," said the young chief, "you see your fate. We give you life and liberty. There is the boat, with provisions enough for three days. Depart, and think yourself fortunate. May the ocean have as much compassion for you, and be as merciful, as we have. Go—but remember, this is the last time you may expect life at my hands. Should you get into our power again, immediate death—death, swift and terrible—will follow."

Admiral Ellis did not reply, but he descended to the boat.

He glanced upon his scanty allowance, his frail support, and then cast his eyes across the sea. Not a sail was visible.

He looked up at the line of dark faces that were along the bulwarks, and his heart filled with fierce passions.

"Curse you!" he cried, to Captain Tom. "Should I survive, beware!"

An angry yell came from the men at these madly-spoken words.

"Cast off!" called the chief.

The painter was cut, the boat dropped astern, and the "Will-o'-the-Wisp" shot ahead.

Ben Barnacle, Iron Arm, Harry Vere, and the chief stood on the quarter-deck, watching the tiny barque until it vanished from view.

CHAPTER CIII.

ANOTHER LIVES.

A TERRIBLE excitement prevailed throughout all the sea-ports of England, and indeed of many other countries.

The last homeward-bound mail had brought dreadful news concerning a blood-thirsty pirate—a new terror.

None knew anything of the leader, beyond that he was evidently English.

The reports circulated were many, and, of course, of very different natures, all varying more or less from the truth, and making this new pirate leader nothing less than a fiend. His crimes were few and appalling.

The account that reached England was to this effect. A fine merchant vessel had been discovered on the sea, with her two masts cut down, her bulwarks staved in, and she a complete wreck.

Not one of her crew had been spared. Passengers—men, women, and children—had shared the same fate

Perhaps the death, though fearful, was more merciful than taking the helpless young creatures on board a pirate barque where the men were like demons let loose.

Was it out of compassion that the leader of that pirate horde put the women to the sword instead of taking them on board?

No—undoubtedly no. Compassion was a stranger to him; compassion he never knew; compassion was a feeling worthy of man—he was a man in shape, a demon in soul—his heart was a stone, on which there could be made no impression, and if broken, an adder in venom would be found within.

He thirsted for blood—he could wade in blood. He drank blood—so it was said—human blood was his mania. Blood was everything—blood was everywhere—the sea might have been blood.

He left a bloody track behind him, and he saw a bloody track before him.

His ship was a large, fully-manned frigate—rigged and equipped.

It was named "The Furies," and certainly her crew were fiends.

The chief was tall and slim, with small, piercing eyes, a cold, rigid face, ashy lips—in fact it was more like a stone face carved over some pillar than aught else.

He was never known to laugh—never heard to give an order twice.

He always kept to himself and his own council—had no restriction beyond that the man who brought a woman on board would be tied to her with cords and cast into the sea.

The terrible horde of ruffians were carousing on and below deck. They were dressed in every kind of dress.

All suited their own tastes, and studied their nations. Some looked as though they were attired for a costume ball, others looked like stone-breakers, begrimed with dust, blood, and perspiration—others had nothing on beyond breeches and shoes.

Some were at their duty, others drunk—a few sober, and many playing cards.

But all drinking, more or less, and all looked more or less ferocious, blood-thirsty, grimy, and brutal.

The officers walked or gambled on the quarter-deck.

Their leader strode distractedly to and fro on the weather-side, and a look-out was kept.

The chief, with folded arms, and gloomy brow, kept his weary walk.

"Sail oh!"

The cry from aloft had an electric effect upon some. An officer looked up.

"Where away?" he called.

"On our beam," came in reply.

The chief still walked on.

"A sail, sir," said the first lieutenant.

"Sail?" echoed the leader, abstractedly.

"Aye! shall we give chase?"

"Yes."

"Top-men, away!"

Then came a rush of feet, and men, drunk and sober, stumbled up the shrouds. The ropes squeaked through the blocks, and the sails fluttered in the breeze.

The vessel veered round several points, received a momentary check, and then sped on.

The grim commander looked up, and glanced at the distant sail; the next moment his eyes were cast upon the deck, and his attitude was the same as before.

"Blood for blood!" he muttered, bitterly. "Yes, I can wait—wait for revenge on him. He is now enjoying all my wealth. The old man is out of the way. Yes. I saw his funeral, his coffin, and his grave."

Then he fell into his former moody silence, and continued his walk.

The breeze stiffened, and the ship increased her speed.

Many of the loitering sailors came to the side, and leaned upon the bulwarks, and, while lazily smoking their pipes, waited the vessel's progress.

Every officer was on the poop.

The men came up from below.

Others left their cards or dice and eagerly watched the stranger.

It was a wild, picturesque scene.

That ship's deck crowded with those lawless men in their half-savage garbs.

The men were always armed.

There was very little discipline, so long as the necessary orders were executed when given.

The moody chief cast his glance up towards the mast-head. He saw the banner of death flying, and he gave an impatient wave of the hand.

"Haul that down," he said.

The ships rapidly neared each other.

The stranger was a fast sailer, and a splendid specimen of naval architecture.

Whether she suspected the pirate barque, it is impossible to say, as she did not fear or avoid it.

She was a low-built schooner, and, as yet, none of the freebooters could tell whether she was armed.

However moody or mad the pirate leader seemed, he was always wonderfully exact in his orders and conduct when business was on hand.

He displayed an amount of wisdom that not only got him the name of a fine sailor, but a leader to be relied on, and prized as one on whom they could depend in danger.

He was dressed less fantastically than the men. He wore a long, dark blue coat, with huge pockets below the hips, and immense cuffs. His breeches were blue, and he wore high sea-boots of a fine leather. A long, silk cravat adorned his neck, and a fur cap completed his costume.

He did not indulge in a large amount of arms. A long, thin cut-and-thrust being his usual weapon, only on some occasions wearing pistels in his belt, though he always had a long-barrelled weapon in his breast pocket.

In every fight he led the men on—his was the first foot to touch the enemy's deck. His was the first arm to smite the unfortunate seamen down.

He would cut down all who opposed him, and stride on to more, without a muscle moving, or his pulse quickening.

His face would wear the same rigid look, save for a cold, cruel smile that would lurk at the corners of the mouth, and his eyes would be awful in their deadly glitter.

Lifting his piercing eyes across the waters, he could see the flag flying from the stranger's mast-head. She was English.

Whatever might have been the effect of this discovery, he did not change in the least.

It would not be long ere the ships met, and the officer gave the sign for the men to stand by their guns.

The men did so. Drunk and sober, together they took their stations. They were always sober enough for plunder.

A voice from the English schooner hailed them. No reply.

Again the voice came across the water.

The pirate barque sped on.

"Ship, ahoy! Answer, or we fire!"

Up went the black flag.

The ports flew open, and, with a yell, the men ran out their guns, and a volley was poured into the British ship, which it immediately returned with a cheer.

The vessels knocked together, and the pirates poured over the side. The moody chief was at their head.

The first he came across was a fierce old man with white hair, who stood sword in hand.

The pirate leader's eye swept along from face to face, and all over the schooner.

He saw she was fitted out for some particular purpose, and that the old fellow before him was owner or commander.

Again he looked at the aged face. Their eyes met. Each had his sword raised, and each paused. The pirate started. His face went white.

"Ah!" he muttered. "How comes this? I know him—John Drake!"

Then turning to his men, who were already in the fray, he yelled—

"Back to your ship, every one!"

Then he darted in amongst them.

The first he spoke to went on fighting, and the pirate then cut and thrust through the man's heart like a flash of light.

The man rolled to the deck a corpse.

The others took warning, and, howling like demons, they returned to their ship, as their leader turned towards the white-headed man.

"John Drake, if this ship is yours, be careful in whose claws you put her," and then he followed his men, waving his blood-reeking rapier in the air.

The crew of the British schooner were astonished by the attack and sudden flight of the ruffians, it was a mystery they could not solve.

The old fellow addressed as John Drake—who was no less a personage than the late inmate of Dr. Burchenell's asylum, John Gregory, and whom we shall in future know as John Drake—stood dumb-founded.

"I have seen that face," he muttered.

Then he fell into a fit of deep abstraction.

Long he paced the quarter-deck in deep medi-tation.

The face, the eyes, were not to be mistaken.

They brought to his mind several old associa-tions, but he could not help muttering to him-self—

"Yes, it must be Captain Angel!"

Why the pirate thus left him, he could not tell. It was a matter of wonder to all on board.

Once the thought had entered the pirate chief's head that they were too well matched in their crew, and well-fitted English ship.

A loss of men and no gain was a thing always attended with discontent.

The schooner went on its way. The pirate on its bloody course, and the crew went back to their games with sullen looks and lowered brows.

The leader watched them with a look of scornful indifference.

Dice, cards, and dominoes were brought out, and drinking began again, and this was the usual picture presented by the deck of that pirate barque, before and after the taking of a prize.

The officers, with the exception of one on watch, were below, regaling themselves. The leader still walked the deck.

Night was drawing on, and the din continued. Louder laughter than ever, drunken songs and brawls. Amidst which came the look-out's voice.

"Sail oh!"

Drunken sailors glared sleepily around. Some tried to stagger to their feet, while many left their play, took a look at the not far distant sail, and then returned to their companions.

"She won't be here yet," said one.

"Where away?" asked a burly ruffian.

"We are going straight upon her."

"S'blood! Good!"

"We shall be alongside by-and-bye."

"Good!" growled the other, again. "Have a toast. A good haul and a stiff fight. Long live the devil!" and he drank off a glass of pure rum.

A loud laugh accompanied this.

The floating hell went on like a fell destroyer as it coursed on in the dark, the lights on the unsus-pecting trader showing its destination.

The spray flies high above the vessel's bulwarks. Two fast, fleeting shadows can be seen, a dull glare seems floating on the crest of a huge wave, now going up high in the air, and then sinking from view.

The shrill call of a voice, calling demons on to carnage, is borne upon the breeze. A yell mingles with the deep roaring waters. Crash!

Suddenly there arises a dim, black column, as though from the ocean it soars high above, and bursts into a flashing streak of light.

A dusky red glare which follows the dense black line, displays a rocking vessel.

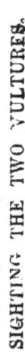

SIGHTING THE TWO VULTURES.

her deck streaming with gore, and covered with the maimed and lifeless bodies of men, women, and children.

Heads and trunks lie here and there; hands, arms, and legs are in other parts. The vessel has been ransacked, and stripped of every valuable, and now labours on with its bloody freight.

The dusky glow brightens into a lurid red. The deep black column's density is broken by a yellow glare, which starts up in its midst like a fiery tongue, while thousands of lower jets and sparks sport in the murky air.

The lurid red becomes larger and brighter; the black, dense column is dying away, and a blood-red glow takes its place.

A flaming mass descends through the air, and falls hissing into the sea.

Then comes several terrible sounds—a combination of crackling, hissing, and crash after crash—followed by black clouds of smoke.

The gloom was made glaring by the vivid illumination.

The giant waves are tinted with the brilliant glory.

The spray is made transparent by the light.

The heaving mass rises in the air, then sinks, as it were, into a depthless chasm, only to be hurled again on high, until the last scene is at hand.

The sea is lit up for miles round. The air is dotted with bright sparks, and a thick, rolling mass soars up, becomes suddenly rent asunder with a myriad of splinters, and all is over. Darkness, and gloom and charred fragments are where, a moment before, the good ship was blazing its life away.

CHAPTER CIV.

MORE OF THE BLACK PANTHER'S BAND.

ALL the former discipline and order was soon restored on the "Will-o'-the-Wisp."

There was one thing that troubled the young chief much. Where could he put Minnie and Jenny Vere. He dared not enter any English port.

"I will take my chance," he thought.

On the evening of the same day as Ellis was cast adrift, a sail was reported.

"Give chase!" cried the chief.

The gallant buccaneers obeyed with cheerfulness.

The strangers no sooner saw that Captain Tom was bearing down upon them, than they turned and cut away with all possible speed.

They knew not how useless it was to attempt to run from the "Will-o'-the-Wisp."

It went steadily, but surely, upon their track.

"I shall question her before dark," said Tom, as he strode the quarter-deck, with a glass under his arm.

"She is not English," said Ben.

"That is obvious," said Harry Vere.

"She is trying to show us a pair of heels," smiled Captain Tom.

Ben laughed.

"She flies no colours."

"Not yet."

Their glasses were raised, and the stranger scanned.

No flag could be seen, nor could they detect what nation she belonged to.

Patiently Captain Tom waited, until he was near enough to get his glass to bear upon her hull.

He gave an exclamation of surprise.

"She belongs to that fleet of pirates," he said.

"Which?" asked Ben.

"Those under the Black Panther."

Captain Tom called for one of the crew to come forward. He was a man who knew the whole pirate fleet well, and could tell instantly.

"Is not that one of the Panther's fleet?"

The man took a glass, and scanned the stranger.

"Yes, captain."

"You are sure?"

"Quite, captain. 'Tis the 'Two Vultures.'"

"Good! you can go."

He saluted and went.

"Beat to quarters! Prepare everything, but don't let them see we are prepared to board them."

"Aye, aye," said Harry Vere.

The "Will-o'-the-Wisp" increased her speed.

Another half-hour, and Tom ordered a gun to be fired. No heed was taken of the challenge.

"Fire another shot!"

Another was fired; still the stranger kept on.

"Hoist the flag, load the long gun, and put the 'Will-o'-the Wisp' at full speed!"

It was done.

"Signal for them to lay-to," he said; "if they don't stop or reply, fire!"

"Aye, aye, sir!"

"Now, I'll give them two minutes."

He waited, watch in hand, and when the two minutes passed, he fired again.

No reply, and still the ship went on.

"Ready there! Wait for the ship to rise. Fire!"

The match was applied. The ball sped on its course, the enemy's bulwarks were torn up, and the splinters flew in all directions.

Before they could reply, the "Will-o'-the-Wisp" hailed them.

"Ship, ahoy!" cried Ben.

"Ahoy!" came back.

"Surrender, or we will sink you!"

"Try," was the reply, and the black flag was run up. "Who are you?"

"Look, and see."

The invincible banner of death was hauled up to the main-mast, and Captain Tom's daring crew showed themselves.

"Will you surrender?" he cried.

"No!"

"Then we will take you!"

Each vessel was being divested of its sails, and they were in fighting trim.

Captain Tom had his broadside ready, and the instant he got the position he desired, he fired an awful volley into the "Two Vultures."

It was returned, and the firing became hot on either side.

Captain Tom was sure he was attacking the pirates now, and he determined to give them a warming.

"We will waste as little time as possible over cannonading," he said to them. "Get the 'Will-o'-the-Wisp' worked round, and we will board in the smoke."

Ben went forward, and the "Will-o'-the-Wisp" began to move slowly through the water, and walk round the enemy.

When the pirates fired the broadside, the "Will-o'-the-Wisp" had just moved out of range, and poured an effective volley into them.

It was useless the pirates trying to manœuvre.

If they fired the larboard battery, the buccaneers were at her stern.

If they fired the starboard broadside, the "Will-o'-the-Wisp" would rake her decks from the forecastle to the quarter-deck.

Each time the "Will-o'-the-Wisp" sailed round, she drew nearer the "Two Vultures," and the pirates began to get in a consternation.

They felt it was useless to combat with the mystic ship that moved round them without a sail set.

But their leader kept them at their work, and they fought with all the desperation of men used to such work, and knowing they had no other resource left them.

The ships were hidden in a cloud of smoke, and the pirates had to work entirely at guess.

They were surprised to find that Captain Tom did not do any considerable damage to their ship, but constantly swept the deck of the men.

The reason was, Captain Tom wanted the ship for a purpose, and he contented himself with sweeping her decks, and leaving her hull and rigging sound.

Very carefully had Captain Tom watched his opportunity, and just as the pirates had poured out a volley from the starboard side, Captain Tom closed in on their weather beam.

The vessels crashed together, the "Will-o'-the-Wisp" swung round as the grapnels were thrown, and the Shadow Avengers poured over the side, while the pirates were still at their guns.

Captain Tom's was the first foot on the pirate's deck.

His was the first sword that flashed out, and the first foeman fell by his mighty hand.

With ringing cheers the buccaneers poured over the bulwarks in a living stream.

With a yell that echoed far across the sea, the pirates turned from their guns.

The men, black with passion, grimy and horrible, clutched up tomahawks, knives, spikes, clubs, in short any kind of weapon, and rushed upon the daring buccaneers.

Though they came upon them with such impetus, they failed in gaining an inch of the deck already occupied by the Shadow Avengers.

The leader, a gigantic ruffian, a man whose

appearance would have struck terror to the heart of many—came forward, weilding a huge battle-axe, and he mowed down all who came in his path, until his terrible instrument of death came in contact with the mace of Iron Arm.

For once the axe was checked; and the pirate leader had his match.

Every onslaught made by his crew ended in a fearful slaughter, and they would retire, leaving the " Will-o'-the-Wisp " the same as ever.

Captain Tom fought like a fiend.

He strode on in front, and everywhere he went his gallant band followed.

By the sounds that came from below, it was easy for him to see, or rather hear, that captive women were below.

"To the cabin!" he cried.

"To the cabin!" echoed the gallant mids.

And they fought on with renewed vigour.

"Hunt every man upon deck that you find there, or slay them!" was the order.

And the boy buccaneers intended to comply with it. The pirates, though they were in such large numbers, and blood-thirsty as panthers, could not withstand the onslaught, and all who stood aft, near the gangway, fled—some below, others aloft.

Tom smiled.

"You will have to come up from there," he said.

And he led the way below with his own body-guard of gallant young mids.

He dashed into the state-cabin

As he had imagined, it was filled with captive maidens.

They stood in one corner, clinging to each other, and rending the air with their wild screams, as many of the cowardly ruffians sought protection behind them, or amongst them.

"Rout every pirate out of the cabin!" called Captain Tom.

The mids dispersed.

Every berth, locker, and cupboard were searched, and every skulking pirate was driven on deck.

Those who were mad enough to oppose the young buccaneers, paid the penalty with their lives.

When this part of the lower deck had been cleared, Captain Tom addressed the captives, saying—

"Ladies, have no fear. You are in safe hands now, and shall be returned to your native countries."

He said this in three languages, seeing there were women from several different nations.

A guard was then placed over the captives, at the foot of the hatchway, to prevent any of the pirates from getting below.

Another company of buccaneers were stationed on deck, to guard the companion-ladder, with orders to let no one pass but their own officers.

Then Captain Tom strode over the dead and dying—his foot slipping on the gory deck—to where the fight still raged.

The pirates fought desperately.

They gave way only inch by inch, though they saw how useless it was.

Captain Tom cut his way through the combatants to the mast, and taking the halyard in his hand, hauled down the banner of death.

It fell full upon the pirate leader, enshrouding his head and shoulders in its grisly folds.

He gave an inward shudder, feeling the ghastly thing about his face.

One effort he made to remove it, when the mace of Iron Arm sent him crushed to the deck.

He fell in his last death agonies, with the flag still upon him.

His blood stained the ghastly emblem, and, in his last throe, his teeth bit the sable cloth through, and he died.

"Hurrah!" shouted the mids.

"Quarter!" cried the pirates.

Captain Tom raised his blood-reeking blade on high, and called out—

"Hold!"

Quarter was given.

The pirates were called upon to put down their arms, which they did readily, and then were ordered below.

At that moment a loud clamour rose from the hold.

Cries, yells, and shouts, and Captain Tom started as a fearful cry sounded through the ship.

Though it only reached the upper deck faintly, he could detect the words—

"The women! Look out! Save them—save them!"

"What can it mean?" he muttered.

"The magazine! the magazine!" came a fearful answering cry. "It's blowing up!"

Captain Tom dropped his sword, and sped down the hatchway, to court death, swift and terrible, or save his gallant crew.

CHAPTER CV.
A RISING POWER.

THE pirate, seeing defeat staring him in the face, had boldly set light to a slow match connected with the magazine.

It had been set by the wily pirate to burn for a certain time, so that, should he be hanged, the match would not be discovered, and the victorious would, when they thought everything in their power, be blown into the air.

Fortunately for all on board, one of the young mids discovered the match.

The alarm was given.

Captain Tom rushed down below.

The dangerous light was soon extinguished, and all was safe.

Order was soon now restored.

"Confine the prisoners in the fore hold!"

This order was quickly carried out.

The arms that were not conveyed on the " Will-o'-the-Wisp " were put into a large arm-chest.

The decks were sluiced down with water, the dead dropped overboard, and the barque put into trim.

The captives were then brought up.

Captain Tom addressed them—

"Ladies," he said, "fortune has favoured me by putting this horde of ruffians in my power. You have nothing more to fear. The victory is mine, and the ship my prize, which, however, shall be the means of carrying you home, or at least to some port from whence you can take a passage. I request that each lady will follow one of my midshipmen, and that a general search shall take place, that each of you may reclaim the property that has been taken from you."

The noble generosity of the young chieftain brought tears to the eyes of them all.

Some poured out their heartfelt thanks and blessings upon him.

He waved his hand.

Half-a-dozen of his favourite mids came forward and received their instructions.

With a gallantry that perhaps was a little out of place under such circumstances, the brave young buccaneers conducted the fair captives below.

While the search is going on, and each fair damsel reclaiming her property, we will adjourn to the state-cabin of the " Will-o'-the-Wisp."

A council was being held.

Ben Barnacle had been propounding some bold project to his chief.

Now that they were going to decide about what should be done with the prize, Captain Tom thought it a good opportunity to acquaint his officers of what they intended.

Captain Tom made a sign.

Ben Barnacle rose to address the company.

"It has become necessary," he began, "for us to look more to our safety. The 'Will-o'-the-Wisp,' with its gallant crew and commander, would, we all know, defy one or two enemies, let them be what they may, but unfortunately the Government has discontinued that mode of hunting us down.

"They have now begun to track us in fleets, and where we had tens to contend against, we now have hundreds; we can fight tens with tens, but we must have hundreds to contend against hundreds."

Ben paused.

A loud hum of approbation went round.

Bowing his head in acknowledgment of the applause, he continued—

"We must have a fleet to fight a fleet. As we no doubt shall henceforth have to contend, not only against fleets but nations combined, we must defy such powers with power. How is it to be done?"

Another pause.

"We have all set out upon a course that we must keep to. Those who wish to retire may, and their share of the wealth would enable them to; but you cannot—it cannot be, unless we have a power to protect those. Then I propose to our chief, that instead of doing away with the prizes, or sending them to an ungrateful Government, we keep them—man and arm them—hoist the invincible banner of Captain Tom, and thus raise a fleet."

The loud, ringing cheers that followed this rang through the ship.

It was some minutes ere Ben could continue.

The wild enthusiasm with which this was received could not be quelled.

The daring, reckless fellows conjured up in an instant, in their mind's eye, a power that would defy the whole world.

They saw themselves the beginners of a community.

They saw themselves erecting their standard on some island, putting forth their own rules, building a town and peopling it; adjusting their own laws, trading with other nations, and acknowledged as a power.

No wonder their wild applause could not be stopped.

When at length Ben continued, they became more excited than ever.

"The treasure island is large," continued Ben, "and would afford us a good shelter, were it properly fortified. Can that not be done? We have riches enough. We can get men and ships. All that I want is the general consent of our faithful subjects."

Another round of cheers.

Ben smiled, and Captain Tom raised his hand for silence.

"Good!" Ben said, as he concluded. "Nothing more is necessary. It is, I see, an earnest wish of you all. Let it be so. We can now make a beginning. Commands will be given in the name of our own chief, and his commands executed under the laws established by us. Treachery or mutiny is death. Insubordination will be punished by disrating."

"Hear! hear!"

"Hurrah for the Shadow Avengers!"

"Long live Captain Tom! Long live our chief!"

These, and similar cries rent the air, and when at length quietness was restored, Captain Tom rose, and, addressing his gallant officers, said—

"I will decide who shall take command of the prize, and prepare the orders."

When Captain Tom went to his private cabin, he, for a few minutes, was lost in deep meditation.

He was troubled slightly.

He had great affection for all the gallant fellows who had so long stood by his side, and it was with pain that he parted from any of them.

He had long since seen and watched the terrible coldness existing between Iron Arm and Ben Barnacle.

He saw neither was happy while in the presence of the other.

He determined to part them.

Taking a pen, he wrote several long despatches, and when he at length finished, he sealed them up again, and fell into a deep fit of abstraction, from which he suddenly aroused, and returned to the cabin.

Many anxious glances were cast upon the young chieftain.

Each was wondering which would be the favoured individual.

Captain Tom ran his eyes along the faces of his officers, and, after a short pause, said—

"Much of our future prosperity will depend on our first measures, which must be taken with caution, and obedience to the orders given is in every way indispensable to our success. Therefore, the first step taken towards it must be taken with caution; and the officer I select will be one in whom I could safely place the responsibility of my life. He is—Iron Arm."

The giant's face flushed.

"I shall do my duty, my chief," he said.

"You will, I know."

"But, captain," said Iron Arm, with a tinge of huskiness in his voice, "think ere you decide. Is there no one you think more worthy of this signal favour?"

Tom smiled, and glancing upon his officers, he asked—

"What say you? Have I chosen rightly?"

"Yes, yes."

"Good," replied Captain Tom. "To you, then, my trusty follower, I give the command of the prize. Take as many men as the 'Will-o'-the-Wisp' can spare. Should they not be sufficient, work some of the prisoners until you can get a supply of men. I need not caution you to keep well under disguise until you have done with the English ports; then hoist the banner of death. Here are your sealed orders which you will open when the captives are put ashore, or on some vessel; and when you stand out to sea, with everything ready for your enemies, open your orders, and follow, to the best of your abilities, the instructions."

"To the letter," said Iron Arm, bowing, as he took the proffered packet.

"Sufficient. I trust on you, and depend on you. This is the first part of our bold attempt. On you will most part of our future success depend."

"Death alone will prevent me doing my duty to my chief and brethren."

"Good. You are at liberty to go on board when you like."

Iron Arm bowed, and left the cabin.

It did not take long to get the men from the "Will-o'-the-Wisp," or to have his own effects conveyed on board the prize, which was christened the "Black Prince."

When Iron Arm was ready to start, every sailor and officer came upon deck.

Three loud cheers were given as the ships parted company.

A salute was fired, and bottles of wine were hurled over the vessel's bows.

When the "Black Prince" was nearly out of sight, Captain Tom moved away.

"Now," he said to Ben Barnacle, "keep the

vessel in good trim. We must sail along on our course. I long to meet the fleet at the meeting point."

"We shall," replied Ben, smiling.

A weight seemed taken off his heart since Iron Arm had departed in the prize.

. . . .

Towards the close of the day, the look-out reported a sail to leeward. As yet all endeavours to discover what or who the stranger was had failed.

Another sail was reported on the larboard quarter.

"Enemies, no doubt," said Captain Tom.

"By the direction, I should think so too," replied Ben.

"Sail, oh!" sang out the man, again.

"Confound it!" cried the young chieftain, "how many more?"

Aloud he called—

"Where away?"

"Right away on our stern."

"Hum, that's bad, I don't like the appearances."

"Nor I," said Ben.

"We are all right while we have our bows clear."

"Yes, though there is no knowing how long it will be so."

"We have no doubt but they are enemies."

"None whatever."

"Shall we get in trim?"

Tom smiled at the question.

"There is no danger," he said.

"Well, I don't know about there being no danger."

"As yet there is none. We can find out what nation they belong to, and then show them how the 'Will-o'-the-Wisp' can walk through the water. We must have as little fighting as possible, because we want our men, and the ship's best qualities for the coming emergency."

"Which will be a great one, and one that will have a great effect upon our future, one way or the other," put in Ben.

"True."

And the young chieftain strode the quarter-deck moodily.

Great excitement prevailed through the ship.

Every glass was raised, and every officer scanned the coming strangers.

"They may be friends," remarked one of the officers to Harry Vere.

"They may," replied he. "But I think it unlikely —oh, no—you may depend they are those of our hunters."

"The chase will be a long one," said Ben.

"And the game hard to trap," put in an officer.

"And much harder to catch," laughed Harry Vere.

And they all laughed.

"They will have some other fiery vapour to contend with besides the 'Will-o'-the-Wisp,'" said Ben, with a grim smile, as he again raised his glass to scan some of the strangers.

The "Will-o'-the-Wisp" had been sailing at a slow rate, so that the strange sails might get near.

Ben Barnacle, who had his glass fixed upon the arm in the stern, smiled strangely.

"An English frigate," he said.

"I thought so," replied Vere.

"Look! they alter their course!"

"By Jove! yes."

"That manoeuvre is not for nothing."

"You are right. We shall see."

They did, and long before they expected.

The strangers were good sailors, and they had, to all appearance, sighted each other.

"Their actions would remove all doubts from our minds as to their intentions," Ben Barnacle said. "It is plain they have sighted each other, and their meeting is a premeditated one. Mark me—"

He paused and scanned them.

They were so near now that the buccaneers could see with the naked eye that signals were being exchanged.

"Those of an enemy," said the calm voice of the young chief. "That is obvious—look!"

The interchange of signals now ceased, and the three men-of-war came down like racehorses, full upon the track of the "Will-o'-the-Wisp."

"Be prepared," said the young chief. "Ready fore and aft for any emergency. Hoist the banner, and let them see that the 'Will-o'-the-Wisp' throws defiance in their teeth!"

A ringing cheer seconded this, and every order was carried out.

No notice was taken of this defiance by the frigates, but they came on slowly and surely, like huge birds of prey, with a grim determination that marked destruction itself.

CHAPTER CVI.

LIFE'S LAST THREAD.

FEW imaginations can realise the position of Admiral Ellis when, after many days' privation and suffering, he had, from sheer exhaustion, fallen asleep, and suddenly awoke from a dream to find himself in the water, with the keel of his boat floating upwards.

Half senseless, and bewildered by the shock he received from the sudden immersion, he knew not what had occurred.

His iron nerve and strong instinct to cling to life made him strike out madly, and thus he came to the surface of the sea.

Dashing the spray from his eyes, he glared with a look of horror and despair on the capsized boat.

In an instant a full sense of horror of his position came upon him.

He could have groaned in anguish, but at present all his energies were brought into play to save himself from the deep.

The frail barque, on which his life depended, was not many feet from him, and a few powerful strokes took him to the wreck of all that stood between him and death's door.

Frantically his thin, cramped fingers clutched at the slippery keel, and he held on with a resolution that nothing but death should make him relinquish his hold.

Saved thus from the grim destroyer, and gaining a few minutes of comparative safety, he recovered his breath and presence of mind—a thing that many stronger men than Ellis would have entirely lost under similar circumstances.

He glanced with his bloodshot eyes round the dreary waste of waters, on which the darkening shadows of night were fast throwing their sombre gloom.

It was easy to account for the terrible circumstance.

He had unwittingly relinquished his hold upon the tiller in his trance-like stupor.

The little vessel had gone on its own course, and a stiff breeze arising suddenly, had whirled the frail barque round like a cork, and as it heeled over, a heavy sea struck it under the gunnel and capsized it.

Having rested and recovered a little strength, Ellis thought of turning the boat over—a feat that might have been easily accomplished had not the large square sail been fixed to the tiny vessel.

All his attempts were in vain.

It baffled all his efforts, and he desisted with a sigh that resembled a stifled groan.

Though the day was so hot, the evening was cool and he felt a chill from being so long in the water.

Nothing else was left for him to do than to drag his cramped and shaking limbs over the boat's keel, and sit astride it like a horse.

A performance that was not accomplished without some little danger.

Bad as was the vindictive little admiral, his bitterest enemy would have felt pity for him under his present trying position.

He remained with his legs astride the boat's keel —holding on with his hands.

The boat was thrown high in the air ever and anon, and he was constantly immersed nearly to his arm-pits.

Every muscle and sinew in his body seemed petrified.

His blood seemed to have turned to water, and his whole form shook as though he was convulsed.

His face was rigid, his teeth were closely locked, and his eyes, round which was a black ring, looked vivid with an internal light, that brought them out with a grim, deathly effect on his shrivelled parchment-like face.

A face that, despite the terrible danger, still showed signs of bitter hate, and a burning desire for revenge, and while life remained to animate that cruel face those feelings would exist.

The most dire peril would fail to remove them. Death alone would crush out those poisons which were rooted in that man's very heart's core.

Night drew near. The black veil was gradually shrouding the earth. The sea ran high, and the wind was brisk. Still that solitary cast-away clung with grim desperation to the slight thread on which his life depended.

The pangs of hunger were almost unbearable, and his parched throat seemed dried up, and the root of his tongue shrivelled for the want of a little water to abate his thirst.

Not many hours before, he had at least a scanty share of the munities to keep his life and body together.

It had been snatched from him by one unforeseen —nay, never-dreamt-of—circumstance.

Day passed away.

An impenetrable blackness reigned over the turbulent deep. An inky darkness that no human eye could penetrate. The sea was like a boundless waste of ink. Over Ellis's head, around him, beneath, all was darkness—black, cheerless, and desolate.

It seemed to him as though the glorious orb of day would never more illumine the earth.

Vainly he strove to tell what latitude he was in, by the one solitary star he could see.

All in vain.

His imagination conjured up every kind of horrible and fantastic beings.

Creatures that belonged neither to heaven nor earth.

He felt like one in a dark, desolate universe, of which he was the only mortal—a world on which lived creatures of every horrible and hideous form.

Some bore a ghastly resemblance to humanity by a head only, the other part of the body, or rather shadowy form, being in the shape of a large fish.

He was in a world of terrible horrors, in which shapeless things mingled with half-human beings— half animals.

Some were high in the air—the murky clouds seemed their home; others round him, swam beneath him, yet they mixed with each other. They had no respective sphere—all was one hideous assembly of ghastly, grimy creatures, making shadows of reptiles, demons, and animals of every kind, known and unknown, that lived in this unbroken darkness.

The sufferer passes his hand over his brow— he tries to look round, to penetrate that dark, amphibious world.

How the hand clasps tightly that wrinkled brow, as though it would hold back his very reason, which seemed to be fast going.

The hand slowly seeks the aching brow, and that lonely being starts.

Starts at hearing a voice—his own. Starts at finding himself speaking—

"Is there a God—is there a Supreme Being, that can suffer this? May Heaven spare my reason—remove these horrors! What is life thus —would death not be preferable? Yes!—far! far! But—"

The voice ceases—the words are borne upon the breeze, and vanish alike in the darkness and the distance.

The weary, aching eyes are fixed upon the inky space, crowded with the floating shadows, and when the last word died away he thought he saw, standing out in misty, grey letters, the word—

"Revenge!"

"Revenge!" He echoed it. Again his voice mingled with the moaning of the sea and sighing breeze.

The wind floats away—all is again darkness, but that word lives in his memory—there it is, a flaming brand.

It eats into his heart, forms upon his brain, it plants in his mind's eye, and he utters—

"Revenge!"

Life is sweet while that thought is in the brain— the desire in the heart.

"God spare my life, and give me strength!"

The icy lips of that shrivelled-up being move again, and his whispered words pass upon the murky air—

"Life! life! Aye, I would cling to you for that —for revenge! Shall not this suffering be returned, this agony repaid? Aye, by blood—blood for all— a life for every pang! I will live!"

Strange mortal! Has he the power to rule—to keep or take life—the power to live?

The low moan of the wind continues.

The dark masses above roll round, but slowly pass away.

The fantastic shadows sport wantonly, in grim mockery to that frail mortal's sufferings, and they pass away.

The sombre clouds ascend, whirling upwards—the moving waters are calm, and a grey streak bursts through the fearful gloom.

Light appears upon the darkened universe. It is a world again—the raging main.

With the light comes day, with the day comes sun, with the sun comes life and animation.

With the new day comes new hopes and new fears.

With new fears, fresh desires—with the desires, fresh terrors—hunger, thirst, sleep.

Unbearable as had been the terrible darkness, the intense heat is still worse to bear.

The fierce rays of the sun appear to fall upon that ocean waif, burning his flesh and drying up the very blood in his veins.

The past night seemed long; the day seemed longer; the form is more bowed.

The face is more wrinkled and haggard; the eyes are more unearthly in their glare, and the lips more colourless.

The skinny fingers release their hold upon the boat's keel, which is like a piece of heated iron, and find a comfort in the cool waters around.

The sea is calm.

The little boat floats smoothly on its course, as though sporting with the frail life that depended upon its uncertain existence.

The day is only half gone, and already does that form give way under the terrible sufferings of heat and fatigue—the want of food, water, and rest.

The head droops on the bosom; the heart ceases

its organised throbbings; the tongue lolls from the parched mouth and cracking lips, as the eyes roll, dull and bloodshot in their sockets, and at last the bent form is motionless.

The hands still cling, with the clutch of fast-approaching death, to the tiny fabric—the thread on which hangs that almost extinct life.

Perhaps it is in pity that those sunbeams pass from that abject figure and alight upon the white sails and polished carronades of a graceful sailing ship—like balls of fire, reflecting their golden hue on the clear blue sea.

With an expressionless stare, the dull eyes of the ocean waif glances across the sunlit deep.

No sign or movement by him betrays any knowledge of the distant sail.

Once the bloodshot eyes flashed with a sudden gleam of joy.

Peering out, the overstrained eyes sought relief under the heavy burning lids.

The crooked became more bent, and the limbs more listless, for animation was almost gone.

Once a convulsive shiver passed over the weakened frame—a kind of mental struggle to master the coming stupor—to crush out the cold hand of the relentless destroyer—Death.

Then the body falls forward.

The hollow, furrowed cheek rests upon the burning keel of the boat. The bloodless fingers dabble in the sunny ripples as they sport past the frail support of that dead or insensible being.

The vessel's white sails float in the lurid light.

The huge barque alters its course, and bears swiftly away. The day passes.

The sun sinks with a dusky, fiery glow behind the vast expanse of waters.

Darkness draws on. The cool, refreshing evening breeze arises.

Between the crimson-tinted waves and the dark blue line of coming night floats a tiny speck.

A speck that bore an awful resemblance to a huddled human form floating upon a boat's keel.

Behind this speck—and not far distant—is a black mass that moves onward with life-like rapidity.

Ever and anon the sea is beaten into a foam.

A huge, shapeless head appears with a gaping mouth and a double row of glistening teeth, that are occasionally gnashed together in a manner terribly suggestive of what would likely follow.

The speck is closely followed up by a huge hungry monster of the deep—a shark—hungry for human prey.

The end is coming.

CHAPTER CVII.

MORE ON THE TRACK.

As the three English men-of-war came thundering on, Captain Tom had the "Will-o'-the-Wisp" put in sailing trim, and the Britishers had the mortification of seeing what they had looked upon as their prey slip from their grasp.

It was galling to them to see how they were despised, and their power laughed at by the gallant buccaneers, who had waited until they were so near, and now sailed away without any apparent effort.

Captain M——, or Morris, as we shall in future know him, was commander of the frigate to leeward, and his blood boiled at being thus foiled.

He was sorry for his share in the late capture of Captain Tom.

He would not have brought his ship against the gallant young chieftain had not Ellis been carried off in such an audacious manner.

He felt it his duty to follow and secure, if possible, Admiral Ellis.

Admiral Ellis's frigate, under the command of his first subordinate, was another of the three.

"I feel sure that is Captain Tom," Captain Morris said, addressing his first lieutenant.

"I would almost stake my life on it, sir."

This conversation was carried on before Captain Tom pretended to notice them.

"There must be something the matter with the vessel, or we are getting fast sailers. 'Tis the first time I knew the fastest sailing ship to come up with Captain Tom."

"Perhaps he is doing it on purpose, sir."

"Nonsense! How?"

"To fool us, and when we get near, like a will-o'-the-wisp, he will vanish."

"Pooh!" exclaimed Captain Morris, contemptuously. "Do you think that boy would wittingly keep thus within our reach?—not he."

"He has done more than that, if all accounts be true."

"Pooh! half of it is romance. Signal to the other frigate; say, Captain Tom is that sail across our bow."

The interchange of signals took place.

Captain Morris walked the quarter-deck excitedly, his glass was constantly raised to scan the daring buccaneer ship.

"I am sure 'tis he!" he cried, when joined by his first in command.

"It is to be hoped we shall save the admiral."

"We shall, or avenge him. You see, there is no mistake. We have hemmed the pirates in, and they can't get away. They will have to fight for it—which they won't do against three."

The lieutenant smiled without replying.

Captain Morris looked cross.

"You seem to doubt me, or have great faith in that young cut-throat."

Captain Morris was getting warm, and even used epithets he would otherwise never have thought of.

"Sir," replied the lieutenant, gravely, "Captain Tom would fight six rather than give in, I know it. And, mark my words, he'll have a laugh at us in a few minutes. Look!"

The old seaman pointed with his finger to the distant ship.

"There's defiance," he said.

Captain Morris's face flushed.

The banner of death—the well-known and dreaded emblem of Captain Tom—was run up to the masthead, and, as the folds were blown out by the breeze, the "Will-o'-the-Wisp" began to cut through the water at a rate that left no doubt as to its abilities.

"I am right, Captain Morris; in less than two hours not a speck of her will be seen."

Captain Morris looked very much inclined to swear.

"Signal to the others to give chase! We will hoist every bit of canvas, and keep on their track!"

"So you may," muttered the lieutenant, going forward; "but he who catches Captain Tom ought to be knighted."

"Topmen, aloft!" shouted Captain Morris. "Shake out the sails! We must come up with the pirate some way or other."

Many rough, weather-beaten faces wore a smile as they heard the orders.

"It's like trying to catch a sunbeam," muttered an old tar to his messmates.

"Aye, worse than that," replied one.

"Well, anyhow, the sunbeam would dissolve, and so will that 'ere pirate barque soon as we gets near."

"She be a wonder."

"She are, messmate."

"And, atween you and me, mates, I don't think as how they ought to call 'em pirates."

"Nor I, Bill—nor I."

"Reefers, aloft!" sang out a voice, and the old tars had to scamper off like monkeys.

The masts of Captain Morris's frigate creaked and

groaned under the strain of canvas; and, though the vessel was a good sailer, Captain Morris saw with chagrin that the "Will-o'-the-Wisp" could keep exactly the same distance off, whatever the speed of the frigate might be.

He felt this was derision—being laughed at, and his blood boiled.

Never had he such a strong desire to be aboard the gallant craft of the more gallant Captain Tom.

It was, of course, galling to the brave old officer to be thus laughed at, and he was determined not to rest while on the track of the daring outlaw.

Captain Tom was aware of the annoyance he was causing.

"Do not let the 'Will-o'-the-Wisp' get entirely out of their sight," he said.

"That," replied the more cautious Ben Barnacle, "is all very well, we can keep those gentlemen in full chase; but you must remember we shall have them coming upon us from every point of the compass, shortly."

"Perhaps."

"Perhaps! S'death! it's certain, unless anything happens to them. We shall have them from here—here—and here."

He held a small chart out in his hand, and pointed with his forefinger to the parts from whence the other ships on the track of Captain Tom would start.

"Well?"

Tom asked this haughtily.

"Nothing more than if you feel inclined to engage two or three that will try and intercept us, while we have these frigates right in our wake, why, you had better take and blow the ship up with all hands on board, as death would be quite as certain either way."

"True," replied Tom; "still, I hate being thus hunted."

"Wait until the time comes."

"The time?"

"Aye! the time when we have got them in their own net."

Captain Tom smiled.

"Then," he replied, "we will teach them a lesson."

"And show them what a rising power can do."

Then the King's ships began to get smaller each moment.

The "Will-o'-the-Wisp" sailed gallantly away, and ere long darkness had hid the Britishers from view.

Captain Tom and his officers went below, and Harry Vere to his wife.

He found her, looking pale and sad, awaiting his coming.

"My Jenny!" he said, folding her in his arms. "What ails you? Why this pale cheek? Come, tell me!"

"Ah, Harry!" she replied, tearfully, "I have had such a dreadful dream about—my—father!"

"Nay, you must not give way to such nonsense. Your father, ere this, is safe. His fate was a misfortune after all, although, God knows, I would have given him liberty and life; but it was out of my power, Jenny."

"I know it. Ah! but that fearful dream. It came upon me like a presentiment, and has left an impression I cannot shake off."

"But you may depend, dearest, it is nothing but a disturbed dream. The weather has been fine; your father had food and drink, so there was no fear."

"I wish I could think so, Harry," she replied, somewhat mournfully.

"Well," replied Harry, with feigned light-heartedness, "you must tell me your terrible dream, as I am sure that will relieve your mind."

"I know, dear Harry, you will only laugh at me, but still I cannot help my feelings. I saw my poor father, alone in the dream—not a soul near—not a crumb of bread—not a drink of water. He was laying at the bottom of a boat, around which were a number of sharks, waiting the moment that the boat would capsize with its burden. Oh! could you have seen that aged form as I did—the eyes that once opened and looked upon me—you would feel as I do, Harry, you would, indeed."

And she burst into tears.

Before Harry could say a few soothing words, the distant boom of a gun made him start.

The next instant a middy came down to summon the chief.

He hastened on deck instantly.

"What is it?" he asked.

"Lights are detected yonder, and the distant roar of cannonading has been heard. Look, sir! Elevate your glass; see the lights yonder!"

Captain Tom raised his glass.

"I see," he said. "You did well to apprise me of this."

Ben Barnacle and Harry now came up at that moment.

"Danger?" they asked.

"No."

"What are those lights?"

"I am trying to make them out."

In the distance could be discerned lights from the battle-lanterns of some distant ships.

"We are in dangerous waters," muttered Ben. "It is best we should be prepared."

"Have the men quietly brought upon deck," said Captain Tom, and this was done.

In silent expectation, all waited to see what would occur.

The firing had ceased, and the lights disappeared, with the exception of one, which ever and anon sent a bright yellow ray across the waters.

The "Will-o'-the-Wisp's" deck was crowded with the gallant buccaneers, who stood silently and anxiously waiting to discover the cause of the lights they saw, and the booming of the guns heard a few minutes before.

The streak of well-polished arms gleamed coldly under the twinkling light of the galaxy above.

The "Will-o'-the-Wisp" sped on, and suddenly the dusky sails of a huge ship could be seen, quite near.

Strangely enough, she seemed quite becalmed on the waters.

On her lee-quarter were two boats—a barge and a jolly-boat—both under a lug-sail, both carrying a long brass gun at the bow, and manned by an armed crew.

Whether they mistook the character of the big ship or not no one knew.

They were attacking her as if they thought of taking her by boarding.

But suddenly the vessel changed.

Her sails were spread, her ports opened, a deadly broadside was poured into the boats, and then she sped on.

Her terrible fire had been effective. The boats were destroyed, their crews left to battle with death, and the vessel approached the "Will-o'-the-Wisp."

"Ah!" cried Captain Tom, "she will run athwart our bows."

"She is a fast sailer," remarked Ben.

"And well handled," said Harry Vere.

"Have the men ready, fore and aft," said the young chief, in a low voice.

The order was given in a whisper.

A moment later, a dull, dusky glow was thrown

_ss_ "Will-o'-the-Wisp's" deck, from the half-concealed ports.

So near was the stranger, they could hear the water rushing past her, and the howling of the breeze through the ropes and blocks.

As Tom had said, she came right across the buccaneer's bows.

Boom!

A ball whistled over the "Will-o'-the-Wisp's" deck.

Captain Tom gave a cry of rage.

"Ship-ahoy! Don't try to run! Surrender, or we'll sink you!"

"Who the devil are you?" yelled Ben. "Curse you!"

"Who? None of your jokes. Haven't I been chasing you all day."

"We did not know it. What ship?"

"The "Owl"—Britisher."

"Confound you for a blockhead, you are firing upon the wrong ship!"

"Who are you?" cried another voice—a fine, manly, deep one.

Ben recognised it.

"Who am I? Curse you!" he replied, with well-feigned anger. "Who the devil do you take me to be—sending your confounded unwelcome messengers here?"

"I think I know that voice."

"You ought to—Captain Moore!"

This was said with a laugh.

"Am I not addressing Mr. Barnacle?"

"Yes."

A loud, merry laugh followed this.

The stranger ran alongside, and a tall, handsome figure jumped on board.

It was Hugh Baldrick.

"No damage done, I hope?" he said, grasping Captain Tom by the hand.

"None."

"Good. It was my stupid officer, who must have mistaken you for some infernal pirate fellow who has been leading me a chase all day long."

"It was fortunate for you," replied Tom, "that I did not give the order to fire. Every man was at his gun, and I could have raked you fore and aft."

"Glad you did not," laughed the dashing smuggler prince. "Now to business. I have been cruising at a break-neck pace this last fortnight to find you. I have a despatch for you."

"Come below."

"With pleasure."

Captain Tom, followed by Baldrick and his officers, descended to the cabin.

CHAPTER CVIII.

THE PILOT.

"Well," said Hugh Baldrick, stretching his legs out under the table in careless indifference, "we shall be in a charming fix if you still persist in letting the plot get you in that trap."

"Trap! By my faith! it is the best thing that could happen."

"Why?" asked Hugh, raising his eyebrows.

"Why? Because it would. Unless I go there, I shall not meet them."

"Truly."

"And unless I meet them, they will be sailing all over the seas until I have the whole British naval power on my track. I shall some day be trapped when not aware of it."

"True."

"On the other hand, if I know they are coming, I shall be prepared, and, unless fortune is against me, I shall beat them. And then I am sure of power, for a few months at least; as, after a defeat, they will be too enraged to make another attempt unless they

are sure of success; and fitting out a squadron for that purpose will take time."

"So far, so good. But let me inform you that you will have twice the number you think upon you."

"The devil!" said Ben.

Harry Vere whistled.

Tom simply said—

"How comes this?"

"Why, that the admiral and senior captains have orders to detain any homeward-bound English ship and add them to the crusade. They have added four to the number already. You will have a strong fleet against you."

Ben Barnacle became grave.

"Matters are becoming serious."

"We cannot retreat," said Tom.

"No. 'Tis too late now," said Hugh Baldrick. "You have come too far to go back, especially as to return would be attended with greater danger than going on."

"That is true. But, nevertheless, from that we must work with great caution. One foolish, rash step would bring destruction."

Ben spoke like one who had well weighed matters, and thoroughly understood the business in hand. All became grave, too.

Ben was the ruling point round which all worked. His judgment and advice kept everything in order, and without his council and guidance the whole power would have long since been crushed.

He hailed the news in a different light to the hot-headed Captain Tom, who looked upon the circumstance simply as so many more to contend with, and so many extra heads to be cut off.

On the other hand, Ben saw it in another light.

He looked upon it as power—unity is strength—and strength combined with numbers make it serious.

He saw a fleet of ships coming together that had on more than one occasion caused terror to the world.

He saw this power being brought out against a small, and, in comparison to some vessels, an insignificant power, made weaker by its being simply a confederacy of outlaws.

He had seen a whole navy destroyed, and a nation reduced to a colony by the very power that was coming to crush them.

Captain Tom watched his troubled look, and remained silently awaiting for him to speak.

At length Ben broke the silence—

"We are going unavoidably into danger that none here knows how it will end. We have to war with a power that has crushed nations, and what hope have we? What help have we, should any of our allies fail? Unless we combine ourselves, unite under one standard, there will be a fall; on the other hand, we could raise a power that should defy the world."

"That," replied Tom, "must be an after consideration. We want now some one who can communicate with our allies."

"Do not despair," said Hugh Baldrick, "you have friends; fortune has put a great deal in my power, since, having the confidence of the whole fleet, I can work them harm when they least expect it. Dutch Paul will be there, and he will give a few of them a little trouble in putting out the fire he will light."

A laugh followed this.

"I shall be near you," continued the smuggler prince, "and when I can no longer come on board or speak, I will hoist signals which I will arrange now."

"That is wise," said Ben.

Hugh Baldrick then drew out of his pocket a paper, on which he had drawn and written a code of signals.

"Now," he said, when Ben had listened to the

explanation, "let me give you a hint. Keep two points more towards the north, and enter the Strait from a more southerly direction. Thus you will have more scope in case of a surprise. I have also on board an old fellow who is acquainted with this rocky point, and will, to the best of his abilities, pilot you through. He may be necessary."

"Then we will have him on board."

"Secondly, you will be constantly meeting some of the ships. Let them come after you but do not alter your bearings, or you will get in a mess."

"I don't intend to."

"Good. Well, now I don't think there is anything more to say, beyond that if you pay attention to my signals, ere you are caged, as they call it, I will let you know how many ships there will be against you."

"That will be a consolation, at least," laughed Captain Tom.

"Now for the pilot, then away."

Hugh Baldrick rose, and ascended the companion ladder.

"How long will it be ere we arrive?"

"You will be driven in that course in about eight days, should nothing occur," replied Hugh. "Let me advise you upon no account to engage any of the enemy until the time comes."

"Why?"

"Because great danger is attached to it. In the first instance, they are not to engage you; and, again, they are not alone."

"Very well."

Hugh Baldrick took leave of the buccaneers. The old pilot was sent on board, and the ships parted.

The old fellow stood on the quarter-deck, cap in hand, his eyes glistened, and he glanced proudly at the young chief.

He had long wished to see the gallant Captain Tom. His wish was at length gratified.

The man was below the medium height, and slightly built, with a small head, which was covered with curly hair, once a nut brown, but now an iron grey.

His eyes were small, but strangely brilliant, and when fixed upon anyone he seemed to see into their soul.

His voice was, when in conversation, low, and calm, but any word spoken, ever so inwardly, came upon the air with great distinctness; and though he was easy and respectful in his manner towards Captain Tom, the young chief could see he was before a man who could command, and had been more used to that than obeying.

Something impressed him with the idea that he was looking upon a man with a superior mind, and a brilliant intellect.

The pilot looked about sixty. He was not more than fifty. His hands were small and sunburnt, and they were never at rest.

He answered all Captain Tom's questions with a truthful readiness not to be doubted, and in a few minutes he had won the confidence of the young chief and officers.

"Do you think, sir, you are capable of piloting me through that to me unknown Strait?"

"I am not well acquainted with it. I have been there. I took a ship through, and I would do my best in doing so with this."

"Friend, you may be necessary."

"That is more than likely, sir," he replied, in a tone of voice more confident than a mere assertion.

He began to ask questions concerning the "Will-o'-the-Wisp," and his face beamed as he heard an account of all her qualities.

His was no unpractised eye, and that could be seen as he took in at a glance every rope, and spar.

"You wish to volunteer as pilot?"

"If you wish it."

"Well, sir, I, of course, do not know anything of your abilities. You were recommended to me by one who is also ignorant of your powers; still I have great confidence in you, and hope I shall not be disappointed. You shall display your skill on the first opportunity, and should you do as I think you will, I shall be most happy to reckon you amongst my staff of gallant men, though I have no other post to offer you than that of pilot, and—well, we shall see."

The pilot's unchangeable face did not betray his feelings, but a quick flash of the eye told he was pleased with his reception.

"You will, of course, agree to our terms and rules?"

"If I become one of you, I shall do as you do."

The reply was satisfactory.

Captain Tom retired to his cabin to snatch a few hours' repose.

The pilot, not being yet placed in his position, went to the berth allotted him, and he was soon in a sound slumber.

He awoke at seven bells, and went on deck. He found Harry Vere on duty.

"Morning, lieutenant," he said, saluting.

"Good morning, sir. You are up early."

"I am a light sleeper," replied the pilot, with a smile that showed a double row of teeth like ivory.

"Are you a judge of the weather?" asked Harry.

"Slightly."

"What do you think of this morning?"

"We shall have a change shortly."

"You think so?"

"I am sure. Do you know the latitude?"

"Never here in this before."

The pilot smiled.

"Then you will know something ere long," he replied.

"It is fortunate we have one so experienced, and perhaps I may add, skilled as yourself on board."

"Don't pay compliments so early in the morning," replied the pilot, without a smile.

Harry Vere shrugged his shoulders.

"I'faith I did not mean it as such."

"So much the better. I don't like compliments."

"I suppose, sir, you are aware of the dangerous mission we are on?"

"I am used to danger."

"Very likely; but I don't know that you would willingly thrust your head into this if you knew its purport."

"Allow me to remove that impression. I do know the mission, and the danger attending it."

The appearance of Captain Tom cut this conversation short, and Harry Vere passed over to the starboard side of the quarter-deck—for discipline was as well carried out there as on board a man-of-war, and every officer gave up the weather-side of the quarter-deck to the chief, unless recalled to his side.

"How go we?" cried Tom, waving his hand for Harry Vere to return to the weather-side.

"Pretty well, sir."

"Do you know the latitude, pilot?"

"Well, captain."

"Good. I do not."

"The weather is very uncertain here."

"Indeed."

"Yes, pardon me, captain, for speaking before I assume my office, but I should like those topsails taken in."

Tom looked at him curiously.

He was absorbed in contemplating the sails and the fleeting clouds.

The peculiar way of expressing himself struck

the young chief, as it did Harry Vere, who had noticed the pilot never gave any long or explicit orders for anything, but expressed himself by— "don't"—"should"—and "do."

"I *don't* like the look of the sky," said he, half aloud.

Tom smiled.

"I am ignorant of these waters," he said; "and, as I am anxious to get a proof of your skill, I will leave the sailing of the ship to you."

"I am to begin office?"

"As a trial—yes."

The pilot saluted, and went aft. He assumed a calm, dignified air. His face was composed, and looked almost rigid when not in play.

The look of his face would not prepossess anyone under his command in his favour, but he had a most winning smile, though he never laughed; his lips merely parted, and displayed his beautiful teeth.

"Put the helm down," he said, in a voice not any louder than he would have used in conversation, yet it went distinctly to the helmsman.

"Down it is, sir."

Next was heard the order to take in the topsails. The topman obeyed with wonderful alacrity.

He seemed to command attention and respect everywhere, and the sailors obeyed him with a cheerfulness that they usually show when directed by one far superior to themselves in the movements.

The pilot now exchanged a word with Tom and his officers.

While he was putting the vessel in trim, Tom watched him with a feeling of great interest.

In a few minutes everything was made taut, and the sailors were on deck.

The pilot went forward, and minutely examined every rope and cord in the ship. Now and then he gave some orders in his low, clear tones, and they were immediately obeyed.

Old ropes and halyards were removed, and replaced by new ones. Slight alterations took place, and a few additions.

Captain Tom gave an exclamation of admiration.

Never had he seen the "Will-o'-the-Wisp" in such perfect order, and though she was not carrying half the quantity of sail, she went faster, if anything, than she had done half an hour before.

Then he retired to the quarter-deck.

"Admirable!" said the young chieftain, with enthusiasm.

"Splendid!" said Harry Vere.

The pilot bowed very slightly, and gave a faint smile in acknowledgment of the praise.

"You certainly displayed such skill in your seamanship as I never before witnessed," said Captain Tom, "though I think some of it was a little unnecessary."

"We shall see; but I should like the hatch amidships and forward to be closed."

"Give your own orders. Though I cannot understand why these preparations are being made, still I leave the command to you."

Another slight bow, and without giving any explanation that was so delicately asked for, the pilot issued his orders.

The "Will-o'-the-Wisp" looked in the most compact and perfect state than she had ever been seen.

And so Ben said, when he came on deck—

"We look as though prepared for a storm—I do not see any signs."

This was addressed as much to the pilot as to the chief.

The former either did not, or would not hear it; he was deeply engaged in watching a dusky mist that seemed to float midway sky and water.

Tom noticed now that the sea was very high, and the water was of a much darker hue than it had been.

The "Will-o'-the-Wisp" went through the roaring ocean without the least labour.

"What is that black cloud coming upon us?" asked Harry Vere.

"That is nothing," replied Ben; "it will pass in a few minutes."

The pilot smiled, but did not reply.

Captain Tom gave a cry of surprise.

Beneath the floating cloud the sea seemed to rise mountains high.

A perfect gale seemed blowing.

The "Will-o'-the-Wisp" kept on at an increased speed. Now the pending mist was almost over head.

The vessel rode high upon the crest of a wave— then sunk into a deep chasm—rose again—leaped on—again was hurled high on the crest of a wave amid the deep roar of the waters.

Then came a loud whirling sound, a low moan, the vessel shivered in every timber, and those on deck were hurled off their feet.

"Down, every one, and hold on!" cried the pilot, through his speaking-trumpet.

The clouds burst over head, a large sea swept over the vessel, and she heeled over; for an instant she tore along, her bulwarks level with the water; then she righted, her sails flapped, filled out, and she careered on as before.

"Marvellous!" cried Captain Tom, releasing his hold upon the ropes, and going to the pilot's side. His (the pilot's) face wore the same quiet smile—half of pride and self-satisfaction.

"Have I succeeded?" he said, and placed down his speaking-trumpet, as though to say—

"I now resign my command!"

"Keep your post, sir! You have outdone my most sanguine expectations—you knew your duty, and your place!" replied Captain Tom. "Henceforth you command as pilot!"

The pilot turned, picked up his speaking-trumpet, and walked to the taffrail.

CHAPTER CIX.
RESCUED AT LAST.

"MR. SKUNKER!"

"Here, sir."

"Just remove those spars and carry them for'ard!"

"Aye, aye," growled Skunker.

He was an indolent youth, who cared more for skylark; than aught else.

He lazily picked up the indicated spars, and moved at something less than a snail's pace from the quarter-deck of the frigate.

The "Phœnix" was a frigate of thirty guns, well manned and armed.

It was commanded by a Captain Leak

He was a man not celebrated for his good looks, or refined appearance.

He was, nevertheless, a good, rough, honest, fellow —a thorough sailor, and a good captain.

His lieutenant was another from the same school. Though he quite believed in mast-heading the saucy middies two or three times a day, he was kind and temperate in serious matters.

Lieutenant Filham strictly adhered to an old adage, which says—

"An idle brain is the Devil's workshop."

He never allowed boys to be idle during his turn on deck.

Therefore, when Mr. Skunker was skunking (this is unavoidable) about the deck, whistling for want of thought, and his hands in his pockets for the want of employment, Mr. Filham ordered him to carry the lumber from the poop to the forecastle it was a very hot day, and Mr. Skunker objected to manual labour.

"Can't be upon deck a minute before the grumbler is down on a feller," muttered the intelligent Skunker.

"Come, move sharp!"

"Perhaps you'd move sharp," said the mid, insolently.

"What did you say?" blustered the luff.

"Aye, aye, sir!"

"Aye! you lazy monkey! Come back, and remove these!"

Mr. Filham kicked with his foot a pile of rope's-ends. The hot and perspiring mid crawled back, stooped lazily on the ropes, and picked up a few pieces.

He was about to walk away, when the lieutenant, out of patience, kicked the scattered pieces together, and shouted to the mid—

"Take it all, you lazy lubber!"

The lazy lubber put down what he had picked up, and made a heap of the whole lot.

He very cleverly managed to place one short end (to which was attached a small block) on the rest, that it might fall on the lieutenant's pet corn.

Mr. Skunker calculated the distance well. When passing very unnecessarily near the officer, his face wore something like a malicious smile.

The ropes and the block fell, and there was a howl. Lieutenant Filham might have been seen dancing about the quarter-deck with his foot held in his hand.

Mr. Skunker hurled his load amidships, and, holding his sides to keep from convulsions, said—

"I beg your pardon, sir, but—"

"But—but—curse you, sir! Get out, you clumsy skunk! Curse you, you jackanapes!—you elephant! —you—you— Up the mast-head you go, and stay there until I call you down."

"But, sir, I—"

"No answer! Up you go!"

And Mr. Filham made a clutch at a rope's-end. Mr. Skunker made a bolt up the rattlings. The lieutenant made a cut at him with the rope.

Skunker shook his shoe off in the officer's face, and then gained the foretop. The heel of the shoe caught Mr. Filham on the nose, and made him blink.

"Curse him! He shan't come down until the middle watch!"

Anything but delighted at the prospect before him, the mid got to his prison, and sat up there with one shoe on.

"By Jove! I verily believe I shall get roasted here. If ever there was such an awfully hot day, why, blow me!"

Mr. Skunker took his handkerchief and tied it round his head. He let the ends hang down behind to prevent the sun from blistering his back.

"I've got nothing for you, old fellow," he muttered, looking at his shoeless foot.

Mr. Skunker sat up there in silent meditation. Mr. Skunker was like most lazy people—always wondering, and endeavouring to make discoveries.

"Wish I had a glass up here. Never saw such a peculiar look as the sea has yonder—never!"

Mr. Skunker took firm hold upon the halyards, and hung on the yard in a manner that enabled him to obtain a good view of the deck.

He saw a brother mid skulking about there. The officer had gone below.

"Charley!" shouted Skunker.

"Hallo!" replied Charley, looking up to his friend. "Where are you?"

"Here."

"Where? The sun is in my eyes, and I can't see you."

"Here, in the foretop."

Charley grinned.

"What d'ye want?"

"Bring me my shoe, and a glass."

"Which shoe?"

"The one that fell off by accident."

"Right; shut up—here comes the luff!"

"Blow the luff for shoving me here!" muttered Mr. Skunker.

He had to wait a long time before Charley could get an opportunity to get up to his friend. At length one offered itself.

Charley bolted up the rattlings, and took his friend his shoe, a ship's glass, and some biscuits out of the joint-stock locker.

Mr. Skunker hailed the things with delight.

"You are a good fellow, Charley."

"More than I can say of you; for you left me four hours t'other day, and I was so thundering thirsty I had to lick the dew-drops off the sail."

"Now, on my word, Charley, that's too bad. How could I come? You know I was below, and the luff kept me there."

"Yes, you could, you liar!"

"By my faith, 'tis true, Charley."

"All right, Skunk, I know; but never mind, I won't bear malice. Here you are. I must cut down."

Leaving his smuggled goods for his friend, Charley hurried down the rattlings in case the first lieutenant should be on deck ere he got there.

"All right," he thought, as his foot touched the bulwarks.

He was nearly petrified by hearing the dreaded voice say, very coolly—

"Go up again, go on, and keep the other company, until I call you down."

Charley put on a very injured look, but all remonstrance was vain, so he mounted up again.

"Glad you've come back, Charley."

"Spiteful thief, I'm mast-headed."

"Capital."

"Is it? I shan't come up again to you to get punished for doing you good."

"I am going to take observations."

"I wish you would take me down."

"Well, now, I'm always trying to take you down a peg or two, when you are confoundedly impudent. Ain't I now?"

"You?"

Charley turned up his nose in extreme disgust. Mr. Skunker raised the glass, and began to scan the horizon.

"The ship's course has been altered," he cried.

"Yes."

"I thought so. What a glorious sunset. But I say, Charley, don't you think that dark, shadowy kind of light over there rather strange?"

"No."

"I do. The ocean, too, has the same deep blue reflection. Hallo!"

"What's up?"

"Could have sworn I saw something floating along there."

"Where?"

Charley jumped up, anything to break the monotony of a sea-faring life was hailed with joy.

Without taking the trouble to ask for the glass, Mr. Charley made a grab at it, and took a cool survey of the ocean.

"By Jove! I verily believe I can see something too."

"Well, so could I, but you would not let me have my look out."

"Wait."

Charley took another, and a longer survey.

"It's something, I'll swear."

Skunker took the glass, and a few minutes after he gave a yell.

"It is!"

"What?"

BLACK JOE MOUNTED ASTRIDE THE SHARK.

"I don't know; something though, I'll swear."

The glass went from one to the other until there was no doubt as to the reality of the object on the water.

"Deck ahoy!" sang out Skuuker.

"Ahoy!" replied the officer.

"There's something floating away yonder, sir. Can't exactly see what it is. Looks like a boat."

"Where away?"

"Right off on our stern."

The officer took a glass.

His practised eye was quicker at taking it.

"I see something," he muttered, and calling the captain's steward said—

"Announce to the skipper that something is on the sea that we can't make out, and can I have the ship put back?"

A few minutes later the captain came on the deck.

"What is it?"

"Can't make out, sir. Looks wonderfully like a raft."

The captain scrutinised it well.

"Why, it must have passed us."

"So I think, sir."

"Put the ship back."

"Aye, aye, sir."

The orders were instantly given, and the frigate was put back.

"Who discovered it?" asked Captain Leak, when the vessel was sailing swiftly on the track of the unknown object. "One of the boys up aloft, sir."

"Humph!"

All hands were on deck.

The ship being put back, coupled with the news that something had been seen floating on the ocean, brought every man from his berth.

"I fancy it's a raft," the captain said.

Lieutenant Filham shook his head.

"Half-an-hour will show."

The half-hour soon passed.

He could see a dark object with the naked eye.

Captain Leak raised his glass.

"Ah!" he cried. "It's a shoal of sharks."

A laugh followed this announcement.

The captain was about to order the ship to be put in its former course, when the voice of one of the mids was heard.

"Deck ahoy!"

"Ahoy!"

The youngster put a hand on each side of his mouth, and halloed—

"There's a shoal of sharks. They are following something that looks like a form—a man floating on a spar."

The first lieutenant jumped round.

"Very likely," said the captain. "Can you see, Mr. Filham?"

Filham had mounted the mizzen-chains, and had taken a long survey.

"The boys are right, sir."

"Then hoist every stitch of canvas, or we shall be in time to see the poor wretch swallowed. Load the gun amidships. Be quick there, bring it to bear upon that dark speck there. Wait till I tell you to fire."

The frigate sailed on.

The huge sea monsters could be seen perfectly now with the naked eye.

The object in front was not clearly visible.

In range at length.

The captain kept remarkably cool.

"Ready?" he cried.

"Aye, aye, sir."

"Fire!"

The gun was well aimed.

The ball sped on, and darted among the sharks, dreadfully crushing one's head, and sending the others to flight.

"Get the boat ready."

It was done.

"By heavens! the boy is right," cried the captain, lowering his glass. "It is the form of a man on a spar."

Five minutes later, the ship lay-to.

A boat was lowered, and rowed off to the castaway.

One of the sharks, more daring than the rest, came up very near its anticipated prey, but a mulatto, one of the boat's crew, no sooner saw the danger of the castaway, than he leapt into the sea with a knife between his teeth, followed closely by two gallant sailors.

They snatched the apparently lifeless form from the object to which it clung, and with it between them, swam towards the pinnace.

The boat approached.

The lieutenant gave an exclamation of surprise.

"Why, the fellow's on a boat upside down, and he's got the uniform of our navy, too?"

The men pulled with a will.

"Steady, steady."

Pulling with less vigour, sturdy arms lifted the inanimate form from their mates into the boat.

"Dead, I think," said the lieutenant. "Anyhow, we will take it back, the uniform must be respected, and we can then at least bury it."

"The uniform?" muttered the coxswain.

"Pull away!" shouted the lieutenant, who had overheard the remark, but pretended he had not. "Back to the ship."

In a few minutes a score of willing hands placed the burden on deck.

The doctor was already there.

Captain Leak came forward.

He gave a cry.

"Why, it's one of our navy—our admiral! My God! it's Admiral Ellis!"

"Why, he is half eaten up by the sharks!" muttered Skunker, who had sneaked down from his prison, hoping in the excitement he would be forgotten.

While the two gallant sailors had swam back with Ellis, the indomitable mulatto had dived beneath the shark, and three times plunged his knife into the brute's belly.

Finding the beast wounded, Black Jack mounted astride the shark, and with his terribly long knife, finished the work he had so well and so bravely began.

CHAPTER CX.
A DESTRUCTIVE SHOT

PREPARATIONS for the coming terrible crisis in Captain Tom's career were being rapidly made.

Captain Tom had every one of the guns on board brought out and cleaned, and those that were out of order were repaired.

Ben Barnacle meantime worked the men at their guns until they could send a shot with startling precision.

The marines were drilled for four hours a day at least.

While they were all thus engaged in their various pursuits, the pilot was not idle.

He had the sail-makers and riggers up on deck. He had every bit of spare rope, chain, and cordage he could get brought upon deck.

He ordered boarding nettings to be made. He had an old cable brought on deck, and, with the armourer's aid, he had it manufactured in a manner, after his own invention, to make a kind of armour to shield the men at the guns.

Both Ben and Captain Tom looked on with surprise. They saw the great advantage the improvement made by the pilot would make.

The "Will-o'-the-Wisp" was not wanting in any defence the ingenuity of man could devise for her protection.

The strange pilot, who had as yet given no name, or, if he had, none knew it but the chief, was the wonder of the whole ship.

Every man looked upon him as a superior being.

There is nothing that goes so far with seamen as anyone whose great skill and splendid seamanship can suggest anything for their safety and comfort; or if he can excell all others in the profession alone, he is considered a wonderful being.

The pilot was either indifferent or appeared not to notice the warmly-expressed feelings of admiration from the crew.

He did his duty—more than his duty. Had he been commander, he could not have shown a greater interest in the affairs than he did now.

He was never idle, nor were the men that could be made useful in any way beyond their simple sea duties.

Each time the pilot came on deck he saw something wanting repair, or deficiency in this or that, or an improvement here or there.

He would immediately apprise the young chief of his discovery, and await orders.

"Do not wait to consult me. Your judgment and skill are sufficient guarantee for anything you may wish to do, and I am sure there's none on board the 'Will-o'-the-Wisp' more capable of dictating or so experienced as you."

The pilot bowed.

"A compliment," he replied, "perhaps not merited. My experience is not very good of commanders as a rule, regarding their seamanship; but allow me to observe, I know one to whom I would come to for advice."

"Indeed! And he?" smiled Tom.

"Is Captain Tom."

And the pilot walked forward, without giving the young chief time to reply. Captain Tom was astonished at this unlooked-for compliment.

"That pilot is worth his weight in gold," remarked the young chief to Ben.

"He is a prize."

Captain Tom made a particular confidant of the strange pilot, who, however, was anything but communicative; very laconic; could say sarcastic things sometimes, and when a faint smile wreathed at the corners of his mouth there was a scoffing sneer at times, and at times a lurking devil in his eye.

At noon a sail was reported some two points off the bow.

"Another friend," muttered Tom.

The pilot was there, glass in hand.

"Can you make her out?" asked the chief.

"English," replied the pilot.

"Oh, then is this another?"

"Shall we alter her course?" asked Harry Vere.

"Sail, oh!"

"Where away?"

"Coming straight on our beam."

"Then it would be useless."

"Quite," put in Ben. "Wherever we turn we shall meet them sooner or later, and at length we should only be caught in their midst, and, without any help, we should stand a very small chance."

"You need not alter your course," said the pilot, "and get from this Britisher."

"We could, I daresay," replied Tom.

"And without a fight. Hoist English colours. Let some one not known stand out as captain. Get fairly alongside, cripple her, and go on. She will then be one the less."

"True—we will."

The buccaneers were dressed in sailor's garb. The pilot was to be captain. English colours were flying. The "Will-o'-the-Wisp" sailed on.

The strange sail, on seeing them coming up, put themselves right in the buccaneers' way.

The pilot displayed a great deal of anxiety to see the stranger's name, which he could not discern on account of their respective positions.

"Get a red-hot shot ready," said the pilot.

It was done. The man-of-war was a two-decker, and would be a terrible enemy in itself.

It was not with the most pleasant feelings in the world that the men worked that double line of deadly instruments, and knew they were going near enough to get blown out of the water.

At length, they were in hailing distance.

"Ship ahoy!" cried the pilot.

"Ahoy!"

"What ship?" rang out in his clear, ringing tones.

"'St. George.' What's yours?"

"The 'Two Sisters.'"

There was a silence.

The pilot stood, trumpet in hand, ready to speak again, or sign to the buccaneers to fire.

A short, but unbroken silence.

"Where from?"

"The Cape."

"Liar! You are Captain Tom. Lay-to, or we'll sink you."

Up went the double row of port-holes.

Out shot the muzzles of the guns.

"Quiet!" said the pilot, in a low, steady voice. "Quiet, for your lives!"

Then, aloud, he howled—

"You mistake, Captain Seymour. Be careful you might do injury."

A slight commotion was visible on the quarter-deck. Then the commander of the line-of-battle stood out.

"Who is that who calls? I know the voice."

"You ought to," muttered the pilot, with a sudden gleam of his small eyes. "Do you not remember me, captain?"

"I can't make you out from here. Who are you?"

"Captain," called the pilot, without heeding the other's question, "have you forgotten this line— 'Still in existence?'"

The lurking smile of triumph was at the corner of the pilot's mouth, as he watched the effect of his words.

The captain of the line-of-battle reeled back, but recovering himself instantly, he replied—

"I remember you now. Where go you?"

"To blood and glory. Captain Seymour, good day. You now see me on board the 'Will-o'-the-Wisp.'"

A mortar, with a red-hot ball in it, was at his feet.

With a laugh, he stepped back, and as he said the last word, he fired the terrible instrument.

A moment or two after, a whizzing sound was heard.

"Fly if you can!" the pilot cried to Captain Tom, as a round, lurid mass was seen to descend and fall with a crash through the deck of the line-of-battle ship.

It rolled on to the lower deck from the cabin, setting on fire everything in its way, and causing no small consternation.

At length it went with a crash through the ship's side below the water-line.

"They will enjoy that!" sneered the pilot.

"But it will not do much harm," said Captain Tom.

"Won't it? It is through the ship's side below the water-line long before this."

"Why they did not fire mystified me!" said Harry Vere.

The pilot smiled again.

"Captain Seymour has respect for me," he said.

Captain Tom was struck with the strange scene, as were all on board.

"You will want help," said the pilot, "if such ships as that one are coming on you."

"We shall, indeed."

"And you will get it, ere long."

"How?"

"Wait," said the pilot, "and I will show you that help comes from where you least expect it."

"That is news, indeed; for I rarely get help from anyone whom I do not know."

"We shall see; the time is not very far distant. It won't be long ere the great battle will take place—the conflict that is to decide whether Captain Tom will be crushed, or rule as monarch yet."

Captain Tom started.

"Or rule as monarch yet"—those words flashed through his brain as though they were still spoken by the inexplicable pilot.

"Women are in the way, or will be," said the pilot.

"It cannot be helped."

"You must not keep them in such a dangerous position."

"What can be done?"

"Ah! truly. Still—wait till the time comes."

Everything must wait till the time comes—the man was a mystery. He promised everything—he seemed to have the power to do anything.

Perhaps such a man might be dangerous.

Captain Tom started at the thought.

"This man is strange. I must know more of him."

Turning upon his heel, he went below, leaving the pilot with the officers of the watch.

The pilot, after a few remarks to the officer, began very comfortably to take the ship's bearings, he then took a chart, found out the latitude, and so on.

He then seemed to be making calculations. Looked long at the sky above, and then went below.

He sought the young chief.

"Well?" asked Captain Tom.

"Can I address a few words to you?"

"Certainly."

"Well, then, captain, you must be careful. Have a double watch set. Keep it night and day. Have the ship in constant fighting order, and every man in a fit state for any emergency."

"Why this?"

"We are nearly upon the point where the King's ships so cunningly contrived to drive us. This part is dangerous, the weather uncertain, and the sea in some parts is very shallow."

"I will do it at once."

Captain Tom went on deck. As yet, nothing could be seen but a few strange sails, which appeared nothing more than specks.

Captain Tom was surprised with the way in which he had been followed up on every side by the squadron.

They were not a day behind him, and he knew to return in any one direction he must meet some of his enemies.

But when he sailed on, another sail was reported.

Captain Tom beheld with pleasure the swift-sailing vessel of Dutch Paul.

He hailed the gentleman pirate.

"Hallo!" came in response.

"All well on board?"

"Yes, captain. Are you?"

"Aye, aye."

"I want to run alongside."

"Do."

Twenty minutes later the "Yellow Vulture" was alongside the "Will-o'-the-Wisp," and Dutch Paul was on board.

After greeting the young captain in his usually careless manner, he glanced curiously at the new pilot.

"What, a new man?" he asked, in a whisper.

"A man whose powers are simply wonderful in navigation—he is my pilot."

Dutch Paul whistled.

"I've seen that face somewhere!"

"Indeed!"

"Yes."

"Well, never mind. Do you know we are very near our destination?"

"The devil we are!" said Dutch Paul, pulling a wry face. "By St. George! there will be some hot work! I have been manufacturing fire this last week—ha! ha! ha! We'll give them a roasting. But I came on board simply to learn what direction I am to keep—I have quite lost my reckoning. It seems to me that we are going to the devil rapidly."

Captain Tom laughed.

"Why?" he asked.

"Why? S'death! I was never in this part before."

"Nor I."

"Well, then, how the deuce can you know?"

"Firstly, we have been very carefully driven here. The commanders of the ships on our track have displayed more gumption than I ever witnessed; and, secondly, that the pilot must be perfectly acquainted with every corner of the universe."

"A devilish clever fellow, then."

"He is."

"Perhaps he'll give you a plan of the course I'm to take, because I can't keep up with your 'Will-o'-the-Wisp'?"

"Of course he will."

"Good! I'll go and cultivate his acquaintance."

Dutch Paul approached the pilot.

All his light, indifferent carelessness vanished before the cool brow and cutting sneer that lurked at the corners of the pilot's mouth.

"Captain Paul," said Captain Tom, "has promised us aid in the coming crisis. He is a total stranger to these parts, and wants a chart of the course he is to pursue to come up with us."

"I suppose you can furnish me with sufficient information to keep me on the right track?" asked Dutch Paul.

"Well, yes."

"That is all I require."

"Very good; but your voyage will depend more upon the navigation of your vessel than anything else."

"Humph! I'd take a ship through the toughest gale that ever blew."

The pilot smiled.

"You need nothing, then, but the direction?"

"Even so."

"Good! Follow me."

Dutch Paul followed the pilot to his berth, and received his instructions, with a plan which the pilot had drawn.

Dutch Paul could not conceal his admiration for the man who displayed such knowledge.

"Thanks," he said. "I've seen navigators before, but, hang me, if ever I knew one to come up with you! On my soul, with you for a pilot, I'd scour every inch of the sea, and laugh at the whole nation of ships!"

"And why?"

"Why!"

"Yes. I am not able to avert danger more than you or anyone else."

"If we agree, then—never mind—this will do."

Dutch Paul joined Captain Tom on deck, and said—

"Now, you can go. I'll follow. There is no fear of my not finding you. Good-bye. Brace yourself up for the whopping."

"I am perfectly prepared."

"So am I. Good-bye, captain! Now, then, clear away! Starboard your helm there! Shake out her reefs! Hurrah!"

And the ships parted.

CHAPTER CXI.

REUBEN HARPY CAPTURED BY IRON ARM.

IRON ARM strode the deck of the ship he now commanded with a feeling of pride.

He felt the full sense of the duty imposed upon him, and he was pleased at being the first chosen captain of Captain Tom's staff.

He longed to break the seal of his orders.

As yet he could not, for he had a scanty crew, so he made, with all possible speed, for the English port.

But the second day a sail hove in sight, which turned out to be an homeward-bound ship.

Iron Arm hailed it.

Being answered in English, he went on board, and asked the commander whether he would undertake the passage of some lady captives that he had saved from the pirates.

The English commander readily agreed, and the

news being conveyed to the captives that a ship was going direct to an English port, they were upon deck immediately, and were transferred, with all their effects, from one ship to the other.

Thus he was soon ridded of his burden.

"Did you have much loss?" asked the commander.

"Yes. I have scarcely enough men to work my ship."

"How fortunate! I have fifteen spare hands, if you are short."

"I will accept them with pleasure."

The men were called up, and drafted on board the vessel commanded by Iron Arm, under the arrangement that they were only to work the ship to its destination and home.

Iron Arm soon parted company with the Britisher, and sailed away.

The fifteen new hands were fine, tough specimens of Englishmen.

He mustered them on the quarter-deck, and, calling his officers, addressed the new hands.

"My lads," began the giant, "I have called you to address a few words to you that you may perfectly understand who and what I am. This ship is not one of his Majesty's, nor is it a trader; but one that sails under the flag of him you will be proud to serve."

The men glanced uneasily about.

"It is neither a pirate's nor a smuggler's craft, though under a free flag. Answer, one and all, would you serve under the flag of Captain Tom?"

"Captain Tom!" exclaimed some of the men, in amazement.

"Even so. What say you?"

There was a pause, the men whispered one with the other.

"What's the rules?" asked one.

"Read the ship's articles."

Some one pointed to the rules and regulations, which were printed on a large sheet of paper, and framed.

Those who could read told those who could not, and Iron Arm waited anxiously; but the men still wavered.

They at length went over, and said—

"We'll jein."

"Good!" smiled Iron Arm. "Come," he said to the others, "the conditions are good, the prize-money plenty, food and drink plenty, and no cat-o'-nine-tails."

"What say you, mates? It's not piracy," said one.

"No," said another; "but our necks will be in the same danger."

"There's danger everywhere, mate," put in a third.

"Maybe," growled a fourth. "Still, we are just as liable to get strung up on board one of his Majesty's frigates as here."

"So say I, mate."

"And if it's a short life, it'll be a merry one."

"True, sir. I am one then."

"So am I." "And I." "Me, too."

And so they went on, until the whole fifteen went willingly over to the buccaneers.

"I am delighted with you, my brave fellows," said Iron Arm. "Join your companions, and be merry."

They gave a cheer, and hurried off to the forecastle.

At the moment Iron Arm was going below, a middy approached, and, touching his cap, said—

"I've been down to look after the prisoners, cap'n, and some of them are English, and a few French, who say they hope you will not give them up, as they are not pirates, and were forced into the service. Perhaps some of them would join us."

Iron Arm began to consider.

"Do you think they spoke truthfully?"

"I do, sir."

"Have you any proof?"

"None more than what their manner furnished me with, and a circumstance I noticed in the conflict with them."

"What was that?"

"I noticed seven or eight who stood apart with arms in their hands, but took no part in the fray, but to save their own lives."

"Are you sure?"

"Positive, sir."

"Good! Bring them on deck."

"All?"

"No; only those who had been forced. Take a party of men with you, with arms."

"Aye, aye, sir."

And the mid hurried off.

He soon reappeared, with nearly, if not quite, a score of men.

He brought them up in a line before Iron Arm, who addressed them—

"Have any of you proofs to assure me you were not willing hands on the pirate ship?"

"I have, cap'n," said one.

"I have not, your honour, beyond my word."

Iron Arm began a very close and tedious examination of the men.

One by one he cross-questioned them, and they all gave, more or less, a good account of themselves; and he was convinced they were not willing cut-throats under the Black Panther.

"Still," he said, "I cannot do aught else than give you up."

"Not as pirates, I hopes, yer honour," said one.

"What am I to do?"

"Well, I can quite understand your position," continued the old sailor; "but I axes you, for the sake of men—as men appealing to men—not to give us up as allies of that pirate, as we should suffer worse nor death on the pirate's deck—Government ain't very particular as to stringing up a few."

The rest joined in with a few touching appeals.

Ben strode to and fro for a few minutes, the men watching him with beating hearts and hopeful looks.

"There is," he said, pausing, "a course open to you, under which I could offer you protection."

"Name it, your honour," cried the old sailor, joyfully.

"You may not or may be aware that this ship sails under a free flag. I am its commander, but its commission comes from one higher than myself. I give you the opening to sail under me in our cause, and you shall have the protection that all get who stand under the flag of Captain Tom."

Some of the men were too delighted to wait a minute to make inquiries, and, in a short time, Iron Arm had the pleasure of receiving twenty more gallant fellows under his flag.

"Join your new messmates," he said, and, giving some orders to the officers of the watch, went below.

"Things work well," he muttered. "Now for my orders."

Seated alone in his cabin, Iron Arm quietly perused the contents of his sealed orders.

"Good," he muttered. "You have placed your confidence in a fitting person. You have a most sanguine ambition, boy. You want to become a power; I am to be the first stepping-stone. 'Tis well; I will do all I can, but I intend to join you at the meeting point."

Muttering thus, he folded his papers, and fell into a fit of deep abstraction, from which he awoke to find himself confronted by a midshipman.

"A sail, sir."

"Near?"

"Yes, captain. She is not English."

"I will come on deck."

The middy departed, followed by Iron Arm, who ascended to the quarter-deck, and carefully surveyed the stranger through his glass.

For a moment a deep flush mounted his cheeks, and he muttered—

"I have seen that ship before."

Turning to the officer, he said—

"Give chase."

"Aye, aye, sir!"

It was not long ere the buccaneers' vessel was in hailing distance of the stranger.

Iron Arm had kept his gaze fixed upon the vessel ever since he had come on deck.

"I know her, I think," he cogitated. "I'll see. Ship ahoy!" he yelled through his trumpet.

He was answered in a strange tongue.

"As I thought," he muttered. "If that is not the voice of Reuben Harpy, I never heard it."

He was in act of calling again to the foreigner, when a startled exclamation from the mid made him turn.

"There is something up, sir. Look! Someone is making signs from that port-hole to us."

Iron Arm glanced in the direction.

He saw a female's tiny hand and arm waving frantically about to attract their attention.

The hand and arm was drawn in. For an instant, he saw a face. It was pale, tearful, and beautiful, and the large, dark eyes spoke volumes.

While Iron Arm was wondering how to act, the tiny hand of the female was again extended, and something dropped from it into the sea.

The middy, who was watching with startled gaze all this, saw that what the captive had hurled into the water was a bottle.

From the neck fluttered a piece of paper.

"She has thrown out a bottle, sir. Perhaps that contains some tidings. How shall I get it?"

"How?" answered Iron Arm, readily. "By taking a boat. Something is wrong. That female is in danger; she must be saved. I must have that bottle, and you must get it."

"And I will, too, sir."

"But how?"

"By taking a boat," replied the mid, using Iron Arm's own words.

"Wait a minute."

Iron Arm hailed the stranger again.

"Lay-to," he cried. "I want to send a boat on board."

"Be quick," was the reply. "We have no time to waste."

"All right."

The vessel, which had now run up the Brazilian flag, lay-to.

A boat was lowered from the buccaneers' ship.

The mid took charge of the mission, with instructions to board with an excuse.

He rowed off to the stranger, and he boarded her.

One of his men, unseen by anyone, save his companions, picked up the bottle.

After exchanging a few words with the captain, he rowed back to Iron-Arm, who had all this time brought his crew up to quarters.

He eagerly took the bottle from the young mid's hand, and tore the slip of paper from its neck.

"Save me, for mercy's sake! I am in the hands of monsters worse than pirates, who have murdered my father for his wealth, and seek to disgrace and torture me. There is no time to lose.

"HESTER SHAWM."

So ran the scrap of paper.

"Good," said Iron Arm. "I will save you. I wanted something of this to give me an excuse."

Putting his speaking-trumpet to his mouth, he called—

"Captain, have you not a young lady on board your ship?"

"No."

"Are you sure?"

"I have answered."

"One Hester, by name?"

"Don't know her."

"Liar!" thundered Iron Arm. "I know you, Reuben Harpy. Lay-to, and give her up to me, or I'll blow your ship out of the water!"

"Curses!" muttered Reuben, jumping up on the bulwarks. "Who, in the fiend's name! could have told them this?"

He raised his glass to see who his denouncer was. His cheek paled as he beheld the gigantic form of Iron Arm.

"You are labouring under some mistake!" he cried.

"Reuben Harpy, unless you deliver up that girl in ten minutes—unharmed, mind you—I will sink your ship."

"Try it."

"Do you intend to give her up?"

"No!"

"Beware! lest I have to force you."

"Ha! ha! ha! I know you, Iron Arm, but you will not intimidate me, not even if you had the 'Will-o'-the-Wisp,' and Captain Tom on its deck!"

"I shall not ask again!"

"Don't! It's waste of breath! Good day!"

The yards whirled round, the ropes creaked through the blocks, and then the ship was in motion.

Up flew the ports of the buccaneer's ship, and the loud voice of Iron Arm was heard to yell—

"Fire!"

A flash and a crash followed. Cries and groans and a yell of fear as the mainmast fell. Reuben Harpy uttered a cry like a wild cat.

"To quarters!" he yelled. "Load with grape and canister!"

Quick as his men were in trying to execute his order, Iron Arm poured in another volley of grape and chain-shot, that cleared the deck of half the men, and two-thirds of the guns on the upper deck were struck down.

Reuben Harpy quailed at this havoc. He saw the terror caused among his men. He would willingly have surrendered now, but he could not.

A sharp and rapid fire of musketry was poured into him.

Ere his second broadside could be fired, the buccaneers' ship touched his.

The grapnels were thrown. The ships were beam to beam.

With a yell, the buccaneers strode over in a terrible force upon the deck of the Brazilian privateer.

Iron Arm was at their head, and his sword was raised high in the air. All fell who stood in his path. Reuben Harpy shrank away. But Iron Arm singled him out.

Disdaining to use such a weapon as his fearful mace, Iron Arm merely shattered his foe's sword to the hilt, and catching him by the collar with the other hand, hurled him among the combatants.

Reuben Harpy fell among the assailants.

He was dreadfully cut and maimed, and lay stunned and bleeding on the gory deck.

"Quarter! quarter!"

Such was the cry from every part of the vessel.

Men threw down their arms and fled below. Others fled aloft, fled anywhere from those men who fought like fiends.

"Hold!" thundered Iron Arm.

Every weapon was stayed, and the conquerors paused.

"Do you surrender?"

"We do."

"Enough!" cried the giant. "Put down your arms, every one. Stand off there, in a row, with your hands behind you. Hawl down that flag, and hoist the invincible banner of Captain Tom."

This was done.

Iron Arm turned to the motionless Reuben Harpy.

"Put that hound in irons, and confine him in our fore-hold. Ha! ha! Reuben Harpy, you did not expect to fall into my power!"

Reuben Harpy was carried from the blood-stained deck, and placed in irons on the buccaneers' ship to await his fate at the hands of his gallant cousin, Captain Tom.

CHAPTER CXII.

THE STORM.—PASSING THE REEFS.

A storm at sea!

The dark, shifting clouds of night float on the ocean's misty surface, and whirl along as though borne by some mighty power beyond the limits of the universe.

The wind howls in wild fury. The rain falls in one perpetual torrent. The sea rolls high, and is beaten into a thick foam.

The black, angry waves sweep onward, while wave after wave bears upon its crest an argosy.

The vessel braves the storm well. Everything is taut. Her hatches are battened down. The crew are on deck, and she scuds along under bare poles.

A partly-reefed storm-sail is the only canvas displayed.

Every light is extinguished, and this gallant ship dashes on through the tempest and darkness, indifferent alike to the wind and the angry sea.

On the poop, one hand grasping a rope to help him to keep his feet, and the other a speaking-trumpet, stands a commander or pilot.

High above the howling blast can be heard that one man's voice, in clear, ringing tones, as each order is given and obeyed.

"Rig the pumps!" rang out through the speaking-trumpet.

"Does she leak?"

"No, captain."

"How, then?"

"She has just shipped a sea."

"I thought the 'Will-o'-the-Wisp' would not leak so soon."

"Are the lookers-out at their post?" asked the pilot.

"Yes."

"Good! Now then, hold on at the helm! Jam her down! Jam her down!"

"Down she is, sir."

"Steady at the pumps! Lash those larboard guns up! Square her yards off the for'ard! Look out! Hold on every one of you!"

The warning came only in time.

A tremendous sea caught the "Will-o'-the-Wisp" right in her beam.

She heeled over, and her bulwarks went under water. Her yards cut the waves, and the wind whistled through her ropes and blocks as high in the air she was borne.

Then she descended, quavering from stem to stern, and all her ropes groaning and straining. One great effort—she seemed to look like a thing of life—and she righted herself.

The sailors with difficulty regained their equilibrium—many of them were dreadfully torn and bruised. Some were lamed, others stunned, and one or two went overboard for all their companions could tell.

The pilot stood up, calm as ever.

"To the pumps!" he cried again.

Then came a crash, a snap, a rushing whirr, and the storm-sail was torn from its spar, the spars broke from the mast, the mast bent and crushed, until relieved of its terrible burden, which was hurled away by the breeze.

"Slacken out her jib!"

With difficulty, but, nevertheless, with willingness, the sailors executed this order, and the ship sped on.

It was an awful fatiguing time for the sailors. No rest could be obtained, as there was no going below, and all hands were constantly at work.

The pilot issued his orders with such rapidity that it was a wonder he had any breath.

This continued the whole of the following day, which was very little lighter than the night had been.

Signs of fear were visible in the faces of many of the men, who dreaded numerous dangers from being in a part of the world's wide waste of waters as yet unknown to them.

Two or three false reports were given out about sunken reefs, but they were soon discovered to be groundless, and the men were quieted.

The second night came. The storm abated a little, and, when morn broke, the heavy masses of sombre clouds rolled away, and left a grey mist on the ocean.

The "Will-o'-the-Wisp" rode safely through the rough sea, which had greatly abated in its fury, but still a most terrible roaring of waters could be heard ahead.

Captain Tom's acute ear caught the uncommon sound, and asked the pilot what it could be.

"We are," he replied, "more than two miles from the entrance of the rocky strait, but yet you hear the waters dashing against the reefs.

"Good heavens! you are not going into it with such a sea as this?"

"There is nothing else left for us to do."

"But the vessel will never do it"

"Yes, she will. Station a line of midshipmen from the helm right for'ard. I'm going to take the wheel."

It was done, and the pilot, calm as ever, took the wheel. His small, piercing eyes were fixed straight ahead, and the mids stood ready to give his orders.

The "Will-o'-the-Wisp" bounded on, and the mighty roar became louder and more terrible each minute.

The grey mass of clouds slowly ascended, and a streak of sunlight forced its way through the mist, displaying a tempestuous sea being hurled mountains high, and breaking with a terrible rush and roar over a double line of gigantic reefs, the white bleached points of which glittered ominously through the sunlit spray as it dashed on through the rocky points

"Breakers ahead! Breakers ahead!"

Such was the cry from the men on the look-out, as a huge wave took the ship high in the air, and revealed to view an appalling line of reefs that not only bounded on either side but right in front of them.

The men were appalled.

In an instant they thought the pilot had betrayed them.

"He is taking us on the rocks!"

"He wants to wreck us!"

"Down with the traitor!"

These and similar cries were heard, and the men made a rush to the pilot to wrench the wheel from his hands.

"Back!" thundered Tom.

The pilot merely gave them a smiling look—half scorn and contempt—and, fixing his eyes on the breakers in front, veered the ship two points off.

The buccaneers became furious.

"Unless you all retire," said the pilot, calmly,

"I will relinquish the wheel, and you will find yourselves upon the reefs long ere you expect it."

Tom drew his sword, and ordered every man back to his post.

"And," he cried, "should any order be given twice, there will be bloodshed."

Turning to the pilot, he said—

"Are you aware of this danger?"

"Perfectly."

"Be careful. The lives of my crew are in your hands, and to risk them would be death."

"I could take this vessel through, with twenty men to man her, were the weather calmer."

"Do you intend to enter that slit?"

"Yes."

"Why not veer the ship round?"

"Because we are going before the wind, and would be driven on to the rocks."

Captain Tom stood calm, as did his officers, upon the quarter-deck, watching the progress of the ship.

The men looked on, silent and gloomy.

They doubted the man they had before placed so much confidence in, and awaited in silence their fate.

Far away, on either side, was a long line of reefs, against which the water dashed with a terrible whirl, the rocks sloped off until the double line nearly met, leaving merely a slit, through which two ships could not pass, and here the reefs came up into a high, frowning cliff, with jagged points and towering peaks. Beyond this terrible barrier, the sea ran with a swift current into a channel, which became narrower for nearly a quarter of a mile, and the reefs nearly met, making a long, white line, forming a semi-circle.

Towards the first opening the "Will-o'-the-Wisp" sped. The pilot still steered and issued his orders.

The wind lulled, and the mist rolled away, but the sea still ran high. There were a few moments of terrible anxiety now, and all eyes were turned in horrible fascination upon the terrible line of rocks.

"Two hands aft!" cried the pilot.

Two sailors came by his side to assist at the wheel.

"Shake out her jib and foretopsail!"

It was done. The "Will-o'-the-Wisp" seemed lifted almost out of the water, and the loud rush and whirl was almost deafening.

Sea after sea broke upon the vessel, and hurled its spray into the ship.

One more moment's wild expectation, and they were within a few yards of the rocky mouth!

The "Will-o'-the-Wisp" was carried high upon the crest of the waves. The sea roared and raved round them.

There was a slight crash, then a grating sound; she shivered from stem to stern, received a momentary check, a shock, then a loud cheer rang across the waters, for she had passed the reefs, and was being rapidly borne along with the current.

All was safe. The pilot left the wheel, and, ordering the stern-sails to be furled, strode forward.

"Safe!" he said.

Another loud cheer told the joy of the men, and that the danger was past.

. . . . . .

The morning came, bright, clear, and beautiful. All traces of the storm having vanished, the sea was calm, and the breeze steady.

The "Will-o'-the-Wisp" lay calmly on the surface of the waters, surrounded by the terrible reefs, for which the men evinced no fear, for the pilot was on deck.

Captain Tom came up and approached the pilot.

"You brought us in here in a storm. Can you not take us out again?"

"Yes. But I came here to serve you."

"How?"

"You spoke of the ladies. It is dangerous to leave them here."

"True. But where can we put them?"

"On shore."

"Where?" asked Captain Tom, glancing round upon the line of rocks.

"Through there," said the pilot, pointing to a narrow sheet of water.

"Through there! What is this, then?"

"Land—an island."

"But there is great danger in passing those rocks."

"Take my advice—make good use of your time; the enemy will be down here by this time to-morrow. The ladies on board must be put somewhere for safety, and you must be out in open sea to receive the rest."

"That is obvious."

"Have a boat lowered, and put the articles required to erect a tent into it; send provisions, water, and take an armed boat's crew with you."

"I see now your design. To put the girls upon this island under the care of some of my crew."

"Yes. Can you do better?"

Tom did not reply.

He strode to Ben Barnacle, and made him acquainted with the pilot's proposition.

"Take my advice, captain," said the herculean officer, "and do it at once."

Tom was more disposed to listen to the proposal now, and, when Harry Vere strongly put forth his vote for it, he consented.

A crew of volunteers was called up for the service, and two boats were lowered. One with materials and provisions for the expedition, and the other with the girls, Tom, Harry Vere, and the pilot, who sat in the stern-sheets.

So particular was the pilot as to the second boat keeping in an exact line with his, he had a line fixed to them, and thus the two boats were inseparable.

It was with some trepidation that the men approached the more narrow inlet, but the pilot steered them through the double line of rocks, which inclined as they went on, and sloped off to the right and left.

Here the cliffs became less terrible in their appearance, and broken at many places by the land

The water was clear and still.

Not more than three hundred yards from them rose a high point of land, where the breakers were so few that only points could be detected starting, as it were, from beneath the earth.

It was not long ere the point of land was gained, and the party on terra-firma.

CHAPTER CXIII.

MEETING AT THE ROCKY PASS.

LATE that evening the long-boat returned, with Captain Tom, Harry Vere, and the pilot, and four men.

The rest stayed to guard the little encampment, which contained all that was dear, in this world, to Captain Tom and his officers.

Zelie remained with them on the "Will-o'-the-Wisp." She was at home in the din of battle, and she stayed to fight.

Ere long, she would see enough blood and death, carnage, desolation, and horror.

. . . . . .

The uncertainty of Admiral Ellis's recovery was very great, which Captain Leak soon learned from his physician.

Captain Leak evinced great concern about the little admiral. How he had got in that position was a mystery far beyond his power of solving.

The rest of the day passed in great suspense, and it was night ere the doctor announced that there was life, but very little.

The news was hailed with joy. Even young Skunker was delighted, as the discovery of Admiral

Ellis had released him from his painful confinement aloft long ere his time had expired.

Admiral Ellis was dangerously ill. Three days passed. He was in a raving fever, in which he was so terrible he had to be held down in his bed.

He lingered long in a state of unconsciousness, but when his senses returned he lay only in a state of bodily weakness that took every bit of power from his limbs.

The first words he spoke were to inquire on what ship he was.

"The 'Phœnix,'" answered the attendant.

"Send the captain."

The captain came. Admiral Ellis looked upon him with a cold stare.

"You do not recognise me, Admiral Ellis?"

"No."

"I am Captain Leak."

"Did you pick me up?"

"Yes."

"Where are we sailing?"

The captain told him.

"Bring me a chart."

It was brought, and Admiral Ellis endeavoured to sit up in bed, and trace out some direction, but he found his strength was as yet not equal to it, and he sank back.

Still, with that iron will so characteristic of him, he would be propped up, and then, tracing with his finger the ship's point, soon he informed Captain Leak of the point to which he wanted to go.

The captain could not conceal his surprise.

"Why, admiral, that point is dangerous to a degree."

"I go there."

The captain thought he was mad.

"'Tis to capture Captain Tom. Put the ship on that course, steer for that direction, I order it."

He sank down exhausted, and unable to speak another word.

Captain Leak knew he had nothing else to do but to obey, so the ship's course was put to that marked out on the chart by Admiral Ellis, and Leak retired.

The doctor, however, assured him that Ellis must not be in any way excited, so the admiral was left to himself.

The "Phœnix" sailed on, without anything occurring worth mentioning. Ellis at length recovered enough to be brought on deck, and he made the b   of his time.

Firstly he informed Captain Leak of the plot to capture Captain Tom, and explained in his own way how he had been cast upon the sea.

He could not sleep, so great was his excitement at knowing he was near the object of his soul's desire—the extermination of Captain Tom and his gallant band.

The chart was ever before him, and he calculated not only the days and hours it would be ere he was before his foe, but the minutes.

"Two days more," he muttered, "and I shall be there. Ha! ha!—he will not think to see me there."

So great were his revengeful feelings, he could not remain idle. The men were called up, and drilled. The ship was put in fighting trim, and the guns were kept loaded and prepared. He had the sails hoisted, too, until the masts nearly gave way under the load.

What was the ship—the lives of all on board—to his revenge? Nothing—nothing to what he had suffered so much to obtain.

It was no longer a desire to meet Captain Tom and have revenge. It was a mania—a life's purpose—a purpose that death alone could keep him from accomplishing.

The time was drawing near.

Admiral Ellis never thought that when the dark, stately clouds of night he was looking upon moved far away, the masts of the ships already joined to destroy the buccaneers would be displayed to his view.

.   .   .   .   .   .

Morn at the rocky creek.

The sun, bright and hot, fell full upon the bleached cones of the long line of cliffs, which were reflected upon the shiny surface of the deep.

Some hundreds of yards from this terrible inlet is a small squadron of ships, all of which have the British flag flying.

Just outside the rocky mouth of the channel two ships lie calmly upon the water. They displayed no ensign whatever.

One was a rakish vessel, very low in the water. No particular signs of life could be seen on board any of the vessels as yet.

Still, it was anything but difficult to see that war was declared between the squadron and the two ships lying so peaceful, upon the waters.

From the two-decker, that showed the commodore's flag, rang out the chief notes of the ship's bell, that seemed a signal for life and animation.

Signals were exchanged, and the ships got in motion. Boats were lowered and filled with men, then rowed towards the commodore's ship.

The commodore was Ellis, the vindictive little admiral's brother. From one of the boats that came alongside the bluff old commodore's ship, came Captain Morris.

"We have a favourable morning, commodore."

"Yes, Captain Morris; the young rascal hangs off there pretty boldly."

Commodore Ellis could not quite conceal a look of admiration for the young buccaneer, who could remain so passive almost within gunshot of the enemy.

"He is bold enough for anything, commodore; but I think he will find it rather dangerous, hugging the shore, or rather the rocks, in that manner."

Ellis shrugged his shoulders.

"We shall see," he said.

At that moment Captain Moore joined them.

"Our bird looks pretty defiant," he said, after having saluted the commodore.

"Ah! we will soon clip his wings, Captain Moore."

"Will we?" thought Captain Moore. Aloud, he said, "Yes, if he thinks to slip through that slit in the breakers he will be mistaken, and soon find that I have a vessel that will follow him even there."

"Bravely said!" cried the commodore.

Moore bowed.

"Sail oh!" reported the look-out.

Ellis jumped round. Owing to the fineness of the weather and the clear atmosphere, the distant ship could soon be made out.

"She seems to be bearing down for this spot," remarked the commodore.

"She does."

The council of war that was to have been held was postponed until the stranger came up.

"Can you see the name yet?" asked the commodore.

"Yes," replied Captain Morris, "the 'Phœnix.'"

"Good."

The stranger hauled-to. A boat was lowered, and they put off towards Commodore Ellis.

"I suppose you will demand Admiral Ellis from the power of the buccaneers?" observed Captain Morris.

"Dead or alive, I will have him. And should any harm have come to my poor brother, let them who did it beware!" and the commodore looked literally fierce.

"Don't trouble yourself," said a quiet, dry voice. "I am here"

The commodore gave a cry, and leaped round

Admiral Ellis stood on the ship's deck. Commodore Ellis rushed forward with open arms.

"You are safe!" he cried. "How comes this?"

"We have no time to fool away now. There is work to be done."

And he glared with a tiger-like glance towards the "Will-o'-the-Wisp," which he knew at first sight.

The kind-hearted old commodore saw that his brother had suffered. Admiral Ellis's usually meagre form had wasted away to a mere skeleton.

His face was pale to an unearthly degree. His eyes were sunken, and his lips dry and cracked. He certainly looked more fit for his bed than the deck of a war ship.

In an instant he feasted his eyes upon the "Will-o'-the-Wisp." Then he could see his foe in imagination, and anticipated the coming carnage.

From the buccaneer's craft his gaze wandered over the squadron, until his eye caught the name of his own ship.

He gave a cry of joy, and, turning to his brother, he said—

"Signal for my ship to come alongside. We have no time for any explanations now."

The commodore, not heeding the harshness of their meeting, had Admiral Ellis's frigate brought alongside, and the admiral went on board, followed by all the commanders.

Admiral Ellis ran his eyes, with a cold, stern look, along the faces of those assembled there, and for an instant his eyes rested on his lieutenant.

"Send a company of marines aft."

He addressed these words to a middy who stood by the door. The boy started off, and in a few minutes after an officer came with a company of marines.

All in the cabin had waited with beating hearts and abated breath, wondering what he intended. Giving no explanation whatever, Admiral Ellis pointed sternly to his lieutenant, and said—

"Arrest that man—put him in irons until I order his release."

Dumbfounded at this outrage, the brave fellow stood speechless. Resistance was useless, and he was disarmed, ironed, and confined in the hold in five minutes.

Taking no apparent notice of the surprise and indignation of the captains present, Ellis began his plans for the attack.

"What ship is that in company with the pirate?" he asked.

"The 'Yellow Vulture,' admiral," replied Captain Moore.

"Commanded by whom?"

"Dutch Paul."

Ellis frowned; he knew by repute the terrible enemy he would have to contend with in Dutch Paul. He had heard of the destructive liquid fire, and he felt anything but pleasure.

"I command you all," he went on, "to arrange yourselves in a line from my ship, so as to perfectly block the pass, that the pirate, under his cunning means—cover of smoke—shall not escape us or anyone come to his assistance. Not a shot shall be fired until I give the signal, which I shall not do until I have his refusal to surrender. I want someone to go and tell him to haul down his flag."

Captain Moore smiled.

"I should be most happy to volunteer my services for that," he said.

"Very good—you shall."

Moore bowed.

"Should he be obstinate, say that, unless he surrenders, I shall blow his ship out of the water, and give no quarter."

Captain Moore bowed, and departed on his mission.

The other commanders took their instructions and their leave.

The two brothers were left to themselves.

"Brother," said Commodore Ellis, when they were alone, "remember, in giving no quarter, you subject your daughter to death."

"So be it."

"Great heavens! would you have your own daughter slain?"

"Better that than she should be with a pirate."

"But think, brother, would it not be as well to, at least, let her know? She might either persuade him to surrender without bloodshed, or come over to you before the fight."

Admiral Ellis ground his teeth. Bloodshed was what he wanted. He knew that the gallant Captain Tom would not surrender, and only sent the message for show.

"Go to your ship, Commodore Ellis," he said, with all the haughty authority of his cold nature. "You have instructions how to act; do not lack in them. I will send a message to that minion who has disgraced my name."

"Surely, you are not going to make us all attack two miserable ships?"

"If necessary."

The commodore curled his lip in scorn.

"Not much like English courage, that," he said, and strode out to join his ship.

He saw the whole squadron drawn up in battle array—a squadron to capture Captain Tom. It was fearful odds.

The number of ships there were as follows—The "Falcon," Commodore Ellis; the "Phœnix," Captain Leak; the "Jason," Captain Morris; the "Golden Eagle," Captain Teddington; the "Owl," Captain Moore; the "Goldfinch," Captain Hanwell; and the two-decker commanded by Admiral Ellis.

Such was the number of war ships now under his command, and all to destroy a vessel smaller than any of them.

Captain Tom had not expected so many, and he counted upon more help. Where was that help? We shall see, but now the fight begins.

CHAPTER CXIV.

BEGINNING OF THE CONTEST.

CAPTAIN TOM had watched with careless indifference the war ships in their manœuvres after the arrival of the "Phœnix."

It was not hard to see that something strange had occurred; but what it was none as yet could tell. His bold eye glanced upon the seven men-of-war with actual indifference, and his thoughts were—

"I wonder when they intend to begin?"

He looked upon the beginning as simply a conflict not to be feared or sought.

Ben Barnacle, the pilot, and officers, were on the quarter-deck, and all differed, more or less, in their opinions and inward feelings concerning the coming fray.

Preparations had long since been made, and the "Will-o'-the-Wisp" presented a truly formidable appearance.

From the bulwarks to the fore-main and mizzen-tops she was covered with boarding-nettings, which rendered access to her decks difficult.

The chain-armour, made under the directions of the pilot, was fixed in a manner to guard the stern-battery and masts.

Every part of the deck was covered with arms. The guns were loaded—double-shotted—and the men were waiting eagerly.

Dutch Paul lay off within speaking distance, and he constantly carried on a conversation with the buccaneers, while his preparations were being finished.

He was as careless and indifferent as ever, enjoying his cigars and making bad jokes.

When he saw the "Yellow Vulture" was, as he said "Fit to fight a nation," he took his speaking-trumpet and called out to Tom—

"Are you ready, captain?"

"Quite."

"So am I."

"Did you see the new arrivals?"

"Yes. I wonder when they are going to begin?"

"Presently. The 'Owl' is coming towards us now."

"Good!" cried Dutch Paul. "We shall have other howls shortly."

"They are heavy odds—six to three."

It must be remembered that Hugh Baldrick only stayed with the squadron to learn their plans, and would join the buccaneers as soon as the fight began.

He was now coming forward with his vessel, and all on board the "Will-e'-the-Wisp" waited with some impatience to know what proposal the commander of the squadron would make.

When the "Owl" had gone as near as policy would allow her to the "Will-o'-the-Wisp," a boat was lowered, and Hugh got into her, and was rapidly rowed to the "Will-o'-the-Wisp."

His seaman-like eye took in at a glance the brilliant preparations on the "Will-o'-the-Wisp." He smiled.

Knowing every commander in the squadron had their glasses raised and upon them, the smuggler prince had to go through the usual forms with Captain Tom, who, too, played his part well, though his first impulse was to grasp Hugh Baldrick by the hand.

"Can you come below?"

"Yes."

"Let us go."

Followed by the smuggler, Captain Tom went to his cabin.

"What news?"

"Lots. Admiral Ellis came up in that ship you just saw arrive."

"Ah!"

"Yes; he looks almost supernatural, and though he hadn't seen his brother for such a long time, he did not exchange a word beyond what duty necessitated."

"Then he commands the squadron?"

"Yes."

"Then we shall have work."

"That you will find when you hear the conditions." Captain Tom smiled.

"Let me hear them."

"That unless you surrender, and come on board Ellis's ship, he will fire upon you with the whole squadron; and he particularly requests me to inform you that there will be no quarter given to you or your crew or any accomplices."

"Let it be so. Say his daughter is not on board, and that I will never surrender. I ask not for quarter, nor will I comply with any conditions whatever. They have driven me here to fight—and we will fight."

"I expected that before I came," laughed Baldrick. "Well, now as to my joining you. I suppose I had better do it the instant they began firing, though I could have rendered you assistance in another way."

"By remaining?"

"For a few hours, yes."

"I cannot conceive how."

"We must, if possible, delay the fight for a short time, as it will soon be dark. I could then play the devil among them without coming here, until I had succeeded in what I want. I suppose it is your intention to run them in among the rocks later?"

"Yes."

"Just what the cunning old parchment-face feared, and so intends following you on my ship, and his boats. He would have nearly all the commanders with him. What a fine idea it would be to let them come. Capture the lot, and then walk out, and, before their eyes, destroy or conquer their ships."

Captain Tom's face flushed at the bare idea of this.

"We shall see," he said. "You know the signals?"

"Yes."

"Be well on the alert, then. Act as circumstances dictate about joining me. I can trust you, I know, my faithful friend, and I leave you to your own judgment and good-will, knowing that you will do your best under any circumstances in my cause."

"I shall, and with renewed vigour, after such confidence as you have placed in me."

They grasped each other by the hands, and soon parted.

It was a moment of suspense on both sides now—on that of the buccaneers to begin the fight, on that of the fleet to know the daring boy's answer.

They had not to wait for the arrival of Captain Moore, for the banner of death was hauled up to the mast-head of the "Will-o'-the-Wisp," as the strange flag of Dutch Paul was hauled up.

The ports flew open, and this said plainly—

"Come on, we're waiting for you."

Admiral Ellis bit his lips at such defiance, though a light of unmistakable joy come into his shining orbs.

He instantly signalled for the fleet to make a move towards the enemy, going on himself in front, his eagerness to begin the battle being beyond control.

He met the "Owl" on its way back, and the reply of Captain Tom went from ship to ship.

It was rumoured among the fleet that from the boldness of Captain Tom he expected more aid, which was the truth, though it had not yet come.

Admiral Ellis, too, expected the addition of a brig and sloop to his already strong force.

The ships presented a terrible line as they went moving anxiously forward to the enemy.

Admiral Ellis could not conceal his vexation as he occasionally glanced up at the slowly-darkening sky. He wanted to begin the fight ere it was dark.

Captain Moore, he noticed, had dropped astern a little, and Ellis, thinking that some of the sea rovers might come to Captain Tom's aid in the dark, ordered the "Falcon," his brother's ship, to also drop astern, and thus keep up a defence in the rear.

As yet not a shot had been fired, partly because they were not near enough to do so with any effect, and partly because they feared failure from any imprudent step.

Ellis signalled to the fleet to keep near him, and draw in a close line. They were now on dangerous waters, and sunken reefs were all about them.

"Try the range," said Ellis to the officer he had made first in command.

The long gun was fired, but, owing to its being badly aimed, the shot fell short.

Another was tried. This time it fell just astern of the "Will-o'-the-Wisp."

"You cannot go any nearer," the pilot on board Admiral Ellis's ship said. "You draw too much water, admiral, and to run on the rocks would put us entirely in the power of the pirate."

The pilot was a loyal man, and followed the precept of his commander in using the word "pirate" whenever he spoke of their gallant foe.

Admiral Ellis saw fully the truth of what he said, and brought his ship to instantly, so as to bring his larboard-battery to bear full upon the 'Will-o'-the-Wisp."

He then ordered the "Phœnix" and the "Goldfinch" (Captain Hanwell) to proceed as far as it was safe for them to go.

The "Goldfinch" drew less water than any ship among them, with the exception of Hugh Baldrick's.

Captain Hanwell was ordered to get as near to Dutch Paul as it was possible, and engage him. Unable to wait until they opened fire, Admiral Ellis began.

The loud boom of his guns echoed far over the waters, and reached the ears of the two timid girls who were encamped on the island, and then they knew the war had began.

The first half-hour's firing was useless, and did no damage, at least to Captain Tom, who had sent one shell exploding among Admiral Ellis's crew.

The little old admiral watched every shot, and gave an angry exclamation every time they missed; but his face changed to a look of pleasure when he saw his men were getting the range better.

Captain Tom also saw it, and began to manœuvre, a circumstance that threw all their practice away, for now they had to alter the range.

Admiral Ellis bit his lips till they bled.

He was about to angrily command the two ships to begin action, when the "Goldfinch" sent a shot that caught Dutch Paul astern, and carried away some of his bulwarks.

"You deserve something for that," said Dutch Paul, viciously. "Blaze away, men!"

They blazed away, and every kind of shot and deadly missile was hurled at the "Goldfinch." Dutch Paul, as yet, would not have recourse to his fire, as a little went a great way.

Still, he fired red-hot shot—chain and grape—which came in showers upon the enemy. At the din of battle, and smell of powder and smoke, his gaiety revived.

Lighting a big cigar, he had a bottle of wine and a glass placed by his side on the deck, that he might keep the powder from his throat, which would prevent him from giving orders—so he said.

Captain Tom laughed at the attempts of Ellis to get at him; but when there came the addition of the "Phœnix," he thought the work was getting warm, and said so.

"We will silence that gentleman," smiled Ben Barnacle, grimly.

"We will."

Owing to the mysteriously-informed pilot, Captain Tom could work his ship with every manœuvre.

Turning her boldly towards the enemy's vessel, he came out, and, sending a chain-shot from her bow-chaser, hauled up in the wind, jammed down her helm, and sent a terrific broadside into the "Phœnix."

Then she backed water by means of her hidden machinery, and the shots that were aimed at her missed their mark, or fell harmlessly upon her armour.

The chain-shot sped over Ellis's ship, and, whizzing past his head, struck the third officer in the waist, carrying him, in a mutilated mass, along in its terrible fury.

It sloped upwards, cut the pinnace from the davits, scattering splinters all over the ship, some of which did such damage that two men in the mizzen-top fell, killed by them.

The poor, unfortunate officer was hurled to pieces, and his fragments went with the shot into the sea.

The broadside did equal execution on board the "Phœnix."

Four men were killed at their guns, and one of the cannons was rendered useless.

Admiral Ellis could see the confusion caused on the "Phœnix." He foamed at the mouth with fury. He ordered the guns to be loaded to their muzzles and fired, and it was done.

The men, rendered desperate at the fate of their officer, carried out their commander's instructions to the full.

Waiting until the cloud of smoke cleared away that was created by a volley from the "Phœnix," they saw the "Will-o'-the-Wisp's" clear broadside, and the word was given to fire.

There was a deafening boom, a loud crash, which seemed like an earthquake, and all on board were deafened for the moment.

That moment seemed a deathless silence, and the ship quivered from stem to stern. The smoke whirled up, and carried with it the souls of a heap of slain men, who lay around the fragments of a broken gun.

Yells and curses could be heard on board where many lay writhing in the last death-throes, while others were fearfully maimed or wounded.

Admiral Ellis had been carried off his feet, and hurled against the bulwark, where he lay, half-stunned and bleeding.

Two of the unfortunate gunners had been blown to pieces in the air, and the fragments fell on the deck and into the sea.

The rigging was injured, the maintop cut away, the hatches of the state-cabin burst in, and consternation reigned throughout the ship.

Commodore Ellis heard the unusual sounds, and feared something terrible had occurred.

Not being able to leave his station, he signalled for Captain Morris to go to the assistance of the admiral.

He ran alongside, and soon saw what had occurred.

"Where's the admiral?" demanded he.

"In the cockpit, wounded."

He darted down, and inquired of the doctor whether he thought there was any danger.

"None," replied the doctor.

Captain Morris returned to his ship.

He had seen and learnt enough to fire his blood, and many of the men saw the havoc also.

The news spread like wildfire among them.

One incited the other on to a pitch of madness, until they loudly clamoured for an immediate onslaught upon the buccaneers.

Captain Morris hoisted the signals that the admiral was safe, and required no assistance as yet.

Then, without waiting orders, he sailed boldly on towards the buccaneers, until he was far ahead of either the "Phœnix" or the "Goldfinch."

"Ready, fore and aft!" cried Captain Morris. "Fire!"

The boom of the guns was answered by Captain Tom.

He was ready as ever.

He had sustained some injury from the terrible fire of Admiral Ellis, though the damage was only in his nettings and chain armour.

But still, as the pilot said, that opening would give the enemy all they wanted.

If their balls came on their planks or amongst them, it would be serious.

Men were instantly put to repair it, when the "Jason" came upon them.

"The work is hot!" cried Ben Barnacle.

"Very!" replied Captain Tom. "Hoist the private signal to Hugh for him to still keep off, as we do not want his assistance yet."

Night wore on, the sun set with a blood-red glare. Dark, sombre shadows overhung the sea, giving a dreary aspect to that scene of wild horror and desolation, and which was to last long.

Blood would flow ere long. Not in sprinkles, nor in streams, but in rivers!

CHAPTER CXV.

DEFEATED.

Darkness had now set in, huge masses of vapour floated in the air, and the stars seemed to conceal

A CLEAN SHOT,

them.slves in their unknown regions from the sight of blood and slaughter.

This unexpected blackness put a momentary check to the fray.

Neither Dutch Paul nor Captain Tom displayed any lights beyond what they required below decks and at the wheel.

Captain Morris hauled up short in his course, not caring to risk his ship and men in waters so dangerous, and entirely unknown to him.

The "Phœnix" still fired at long intervals, so did the "Goldfinch."

She had got over her mark, and could drop a shot into Dutch Paul, which so angered that gentleman he replied.

the chain-shot cut away the man at the wheel and damaged the latter also.

"Curse you!" cried Dutch Paul. "You want light; you shall have it."

He went to a long brass gun, elevated it, laid the match, and fired.

Then came a long hiss, followed by a lurid stream of flame, which fell with a liquid-sounding rush upon the "Goldfinch."

It poured like streaks of lightning over the deck, and ran along the bulwarks like the huge tongues of fiery serpents.

The yellow gleam soon became a dusky glow, and a black, suffocating smoke mingled with the white vapour from the guns.

All hands were piped to the pumps and buckets

37

The firing was for the moment done with, and every thought now was how to save the ship, and in the meantime Ellis had recovered.

He came upon deck.

By the aid of his glass, and the lights displayed on her deck, he could discern Captain Morris's vessel.

Soon the glare of the "Goldfinch" showed visibly the "Phœnix," which still fired random shots at the buccaneers.

Admiral Ellis flattered himself with the idea that he had hemmed Captain Tom in, and that he could not get any further away.

"He must surrender or die," he thought, and he smiled viciously. "I have him in my power at last."

Still, with all these notions of certainty, he thought it advisable to call his ships off, and not let them remain fighting blindly and with danger around them.

One thing mortified him greatly.

That was that neither Dutch Paul nor Captain Tom showed any lights, nor would they fire a gun to betray themselves.

The signal was hoisted, the ships withdrew to a longer range, and Captain Morris and Captain Leak still kept up a slow fire.

Admiral Ellis threw several shells among the buccaneers.

He bit his lips with chagrin when he beheld the "Goldfinch" on fire.

To have one of his best ships thus destroyed before he had done any damage to the foe was galling in the extreme.

To those on board the other ship the fire seemed more dangerous than it really was.

Dutch Paul had only given what he called "a streak" to keep them from being idle.

And it most effectually did so.

Captain Hanwell had taken great pains in keeping the destructive flames from getting below, and succeeded, with great skill, in doing so.

The men worked with a will.

The fire was soon extinguished without material damage.

Admiral Ellis paced his quarter-deck angrily.

He was forming a plan in his head by which he would blow both ships to pieces.

Bright as had been the idea in driving his foe to that pass, it prevented him from wreaking his vengeance so swiftly as he had wished.

His sanguine expectations had been that he would, in less than half an hour, have annihilated the whole crew.

None of the ships could move with safety a hundred yards without the possibility of there being great destruction.

After due consideration, he determined that, while his men kept up a continual fire from the long-gun and mortar, he would, with his own boats and those of the "Phœnix" and "Jason," cut out the "Will-o'-the-Wisp" and "Yellow Vulture."

His fury was none the less terrible for being delayed a little time.

In fact, he mercilessly ordered that no quarter should be given to man, woman, or child.

The captains then gave their directions quietly—had their boats lowered, and manned with picked men, armed to the teeth.

The cutter containing the pilot was to proceed.

Admiral Ellis and the rest would follow in line.

He still feared that Captain Tom Drake would get assistance from some quarter, and ordered the rest of the fleet to keep on the look-out.

Hugh Baldrick, seeing his services were not as yet wanted, dropped off behind, to intercept any newcomers.

Every oar was muffled, not a light was displayed, and the men were ordered not to speak, while the commands were given in a whisper, and the boats glided noiselessly along, like so many evil spirits.

Admiral Ellis was like a fiend burning for revenge.

It suited well his vicious, vengeful nature to be able thus to steal upon his foe in the dark, and massacre the whole gang.

They were entirely ignorant of his coming, and would not know, he thought.

Certainly they would not, under ordinary circumstances, as there was not a star shining forth its light.

With his eager eyes fixed upon the impenetrable darkness, Ellis went on.

But as yet he could see nothing beyond shapeless shadows, that seemed to float in the air and on the water.

Suddenly a blue light was seen to dart up, as though from the ocean's depth.

From whence it came was a mystery, and again all was darkness. A few moments more, and the boats glided on. The blackness thickened around them, when there was a flash.

Up went a pale yellow streak, not far in front of the boats.

Twice a lantern gleamed in the distance.

Then all was as before—black, misty, silent, and ominous.

"Show our signals," muttered one of the captains.

"Our death-warrant—a messenger to prepare the way for our souls above," muttered a grey-haired tar.

"We are betrayed!" hissed Ellis.

"The light ought to have been red," thought another in the long-boat.

Red would follow soon enough, though not in lights.

The "Will-o'-the-Wisp" and her gallant crew might have been at the bottom of the sea.

So might the "Yellow Vulture," for all that could be heard or seen.

So vivid and rapid had been the lights that had been displayed, they only dazzled before the eyes of the men for a few seconds, and left no trace, or even gave an idea of the actual direction they had been in.

Slower and more silently go the boats.

The pilot has to feel his way.

Once a slight grating sound denoted the presence of sunken reefs.

A moment's delay. A few whispered orders, and a little management, and all was safe again.

Suddenly there arose a whisper, as though from the ocean depths. That whisper was—

"We are on them!"

Looming out in the inky mist could be seen three white straight lines towering up into the very clouds.

Those white lines were the enemy's masts.

They had not been discovered, was the thought that flashed through every brain, and with renewed hope and vigour they propelled the boats forward.

The men were crouching down ready to leap upon the black mass before them, and hurl themselves upon the enemy's weapons.

Captain Hanwell, burning for revenge at suffering as he did from the fire of Dutch Paul, most readily volunteered to undertake to cut him out, and while he crept on for that purpose, Admiral Ellis, with his fleet of boats, crept towards the "Will-o'-the-Wisp."

Even now no signs of life were displayed, and the buccaneers seemed an easy prey.

Arms were grasped with tiger-like eagerness, and some of the men rose up in the boats.

"Steady—disperse!" was the whispered command.

The boats were to surround the "Will-o'-the-Wisp," and they started off for that purpose.

There had been silence long enough. Darkness had continued long enough.

A light was seen like a floating ball in the misty darkness, and a voice thundered—

"Fire!"

Very rapidly the scene changed!

There was a light and noise now. Life and death as well as blood and carnage was rife. All in an instant one long line of livid fire shot up, and a deafening crash, that echoed for miles away, startled the silent crews.

Then came the weakened cries and moans of men as they were hurled from this world into the next.

Masts were reduced to a mass of useless splinters, and the wailing of the drowning and dying could be heard.

But only for a moment, for those noises were drowned in the fearful din of war.

Men were transformed into fiends.

They gave a yell showing their intense ferocity, and hurled themselves forward. They went through water, fire, shot, shell, and steel, and fearful carnage went on.

There came a groan for every pistol-shot, and a cry for every sabre-cut, and the men passed from the great universe like reeds or blades of grass before the scythe. The crews of two of the boats gained the bulwarks of the "Will-o'-the-Wisp." But that was all.

Could they have even survived the terrible fire that was poured into them then, they could not have broken their way through the terrible defence erected by the pilot.

One bold onslaught had gained the attackers a slight advantage, by the nettings being cut away from the forecastle.

First among the assailants was Admiral Ellis. Flourishing his sword over his head, he dashed forward, calling upon his men to follow.

Who could withstand such courage?

Everyone of his followers, with a yell, rushed on behind him

But they were met with the gigantic form of Ben Barnacle, who wielded a huge scimitar that would have taken both hands of any ordinary man to lift.

By his side was the lion-hearted chief, Captain Tom, who stood conspicuous among his crew of heroes.

His silver mail reposed on a breast calm even in this fearful scene of blood and woe. He saw his vindictive foe, but he had mercy in him still.

"The man who kills Admiral Ellis shall die!" he thundered.

His sword cut down the foes who stood in his path, and he strode on. Nothing was more obvious than their instant destruction.

Nor would anything have prevented it had not Captain Morris, followed by Captain Leak and the remainder of his crew, appeared on the forecastle.

Captain Leak had not twenty men left alive out of his three boats' crew, so fearful had been the havoc made among them by the first discharges.

It was Captain Tom's wish to capture the admiral, and he would have done so, had not the enemy poured on the deck, and entered between him and his aged foe.

The gallant buccaneers saw they must use effective means.

Guns, terrible in their close proximity to the assailants, and loaded to the muzzle with grape, were fired, followed by a volley of musketry.

It was a brief but hand-to-hand encounter, and Admiral Ellis would have fallen, had not Captain Leak thrown himself before him and received the thirsty blade in his heart.

"...d and my country!" he cried. "Long live

With that, and a wild wave of his sword, he fell dead upon the deck. Admiral Ellis was struck by the back of tomahawk, and fell at the same instant

The sailors were being beaten off the vessel's deck, and defeat was everywhere visible.

Captain Morris ordered a retreat, and, while his men covered his departure, he had Ellis taken from the bloody deck, and conveyed to the boat under the prow.

The Shadow Avengers would have gone over the side and captured all who would not surrender, but Captain Tom was cautious, and withheld his heated men.

He knew not whether other foes might not be at the vessel's side, and it would require all the fortitude of his men to withstand repeated attacks from so many; and, naturally, the buccaneers would tire when their assailants would be gaining strength.

Meantime, Dutch Paul had, by the same means as Admiral Tom, learnt the very close proximity of his foes, and he prepared to ruin them.

He had not one half the foes to combat with that Captain Tom had, and, therefore, kept himself cool in consequence.

He sat carelessly on a cask, with his legs crossed, a cigar in his mouth, and the bottle and glass by his side.

"Are they near?" he asked of an officer.

"Yes, cap'n."

"Get a cold shot ready to salute them with."

"Aye, aye."

"Don't show a speck of light, any of you. D'ye hear?"

"Aye, aye, cap'n."

"Not even a lucifer or glow of a pipe. Tell those skunks to get under the bulwarks, and not make targets of themselves for the bulldogs when they get on the bulwarks."

The skunks were a body of gallant fellows, complete fire-eaters, who had no motto but "Fight to the death." They never surrendered, and never would.

They now stood ready to repel boarders, but the words of Dutch Paul reminded them of their exposed position, and they crept beneath the vessel's side, and waited, eager to spring upon their prey.

Vultures, indeed, they looked at that moment; with half-naked forms, powder and blood-besmeared, their lank arms clutching any kind of weapon, and their blood-shot eyes rolling about with a fierceness that showed their characters.

"A nice-looking lot of cusses, certainly," muttered Dutch Paul.

It is possible that had the British tars known the reception in store for them they would have thought twice ere they put themselves under the claws of the "Vulture."

Cold shot was waiting on one side, fire and steel on the other. A slight creak was heard, and Dutch Paul grinned and paused in taking a gulp of wine.

"Drop the shot," he said.

The shot was dropped; there was a crash, a splash, and a tremendous yell of rage and fear, that was more like a howl.

The howl was echoed on the other side of the ship by a party of boarders, and a body of men streamed on the side.

Out flew the "Yellow Vulture's" guns, and a volley that sent many to kingdom come was poured into them.

"Bravo!" muttered Dutch Paul, rising lazily, and putting the glass of wine to his lips.

A bullet, fired point-blank at him, caught the glass, shattered it to pieces in his hand, and glanced over his shoulder.

"May I be cursed!" he muttered, and, in his haste to get at the fellow, he thrust the wrong end of his lighted cigar into his mouth.

"Curses!" he said, spitting out the burning ash, and rushing with his drawn scimitar upon his foes.

He singled out the man who had shot at him, and brought him to the deck with one cut.

"That's for spoiling my draught!" he said, and strode on.

The "Yellow Vultures" resisted the attack stoutly, and soon had the enemy over the side.

CHAPTER CXVI.
THE THREE BLUE LIGHTS.

CAPTAIN HANWELL would have continued while a man stood, but seeing the signals that told of the admiral's defeat, he drew off with his men only with the determination of getting a reinforcement and coming back.

"This is only a beginning," Dutch Paul said, with a smile. "If so, what will the end be?"

. . . .

During the terrible conflict, Hugh Baldrick had kept off and as far away from the ships as possible.

He happened to be in full confidence of all plans and actions, and he knew that two light war-ships were expected to join the fleet.

Should they come, the position of Captain Tom would be critical.

Scarcely had the sounds of the conflict ceased, and the booming of the guns commenced, as the officers in command of the ships did their best to cover the escape of their crew and commander, than a man on the look-out reported to Hugh Baldrick that a ship was close upon them.

"Ship ahoy!" he hailed, softly, though he knew not why.

He had no reply.

"Ahoy!" he called again.

"What ship?" came in a voice, powerful and stern.

"'The Owl'—Captain More."

"Are the rest of the ships in earshot?" asked the same voice, only in a more friendly tone.

"No."

"Good, my friend Hugh. I was about to fire into you then, had you not spoken your name."

"Who are you?"

"Iron Arm—commanding one of Captain Tom's ships."

"You have come to his assistance?"

"I have."

"Good. He needs it, but you cannot pass the fleet."

"We can."

"I have another ship in company, one I captured and manned. She is not many yards behind. I think, with your assistance, we would certainly make way through the fleet."

"Still, would it not be wiser to join Captain Tom, if you can, by slipping through. You may want your men and ammunition."

"Truly."

"You must know the signals, too, in approaching the captain. Hoist the blue lights, lower them, and then keep them up, or he will fire upon you for one of the fleet."

"Good."

"Also take the name of Captain Boyd. Your vessel will be the 'Hawk' for the time being, the other is supposed to be the 'Dolphin,' commanded by Captain Ertfort."

Iron Arm made a note of these instructions, and then sailed on boldly, going to the fleet as boldly as if he really had been the captain's reinforcement.

The moment he was signalled to from the flag-ship he answered promptly.

"Captain Boyd, the 'Hawk,' in company with the 'Dolphin.'"

But even while Iron Arm was thinking over the imposture, three blue lights appeared in another quarter, and in a moment it flashed across his mind that the ships he had counterfeited had arrived. The commodore was evidently puzzled, so he suddenly yelled through the speaking-trumpet—

"Mr. Boyd, come aboard!"

"See you blowed first!" muttered Iron Arm; and, signalling to his men, they opened the sails, and got the vessel rapidly under weigh.

"There is something wrong," he heard Commodore Ellis say. "Either one or the other must be an impostor."

In an instant Iron Arm comprehended what had occurred.

The two ships he was to assume the command of had arrived before him, without the knowledge of Hugh Baldrick.

Coming to this rather unpleasant conclusion, Iron Arm determined upon trying a running fight.

He had long since put his men at their posts, and they only wanted the word to begin the fight they were all prepared and waiting for.

The booming of the guns in the other quarter acted like the bugle upon an old war-horse.

Admiral Ellis had received only a slight hurt, and soon recovered, though for a minute he was a little wild.

"Where is the pirate?" he demanded. "Have you put him in irons?"

"No, admiral," replied the lieutenant, bitterly; "and it was only God's mercy that prevented us from being in his clutches and irons, too."

This signal of defeat touched old Ellis home, bad as he was, and his greatest faults were pride and malice. He was brave—brave to the core.

The instant he regained his ship, he ordered all his men upon deck, and had grog distributed. Then the fight continued.

He had heard of the death of the unfortunate Captain Leak.

By the lights that were displayed, and the signals exchanged, it was easy for Captain Tom and Dutch Paul to see the contest would be recommenced, and without any concealment.

At the moment he expected to be cannonaded by nearly all the fleet, a terrible firing was heard off where Commodore Ellis lay.

Flash after flash lit up the murky darkness, and the crash of the guns reverberated far and near.

"What is that?" Tom asked, involuntarily.

"Hugh," suggested Ben.

"He would never be so mad-brained as to attack the whole fleet out there."

"Ah! look!"

Up went a blue light in the air, sparkled, and then vanished.

A minute more, and another appeared, but this remained stationary—hung in the mast. Up went light number three—that, too, was at the mast head of a ship. A moment more, and then came another blue light.

"Friends," said Ben.

"Who can they be?" inquired the young chief.

"By heavens! the fleet will have to fight now, they will either get to us or we to them."

"Undoubtedly."

Admiral Ellis had given orders to renew the attack, at the same time signalling for one of the other ships to come up.

Many of the officers asserted that there were more than two ships fighting against them.

An idea readily taken up by the vanquished, as they scarcely relished being beaten by two ships smaller than themselves and with less men.

"Why," said Ellis, as his men renewed the conflict, "does not one of the ships come to our assistance?"

As he spoke these words, he saw a rapid interchange of signals.

Then the sound of voices was borne across the water.

The quick roll of a drum, the clank of arms, and commands were given in a voice he knew to be his brother's, which were taken up and re-echoed in loud, hoarse tones.

"What can it mean?" cried Ellis, but no one could tell him, and he glared at his officer for an explanation.

The men stood, lighted match in hand, glaring across the water at the terrific conflict until the passionate voice of Ellis cried—

"Fire! Continue firing until I order you to stop! Every man to his duty!"

The juniors rushed forward.

The whole sea, for miles around, was at intervals lit up with a vivid glare.

The ships, like huge things of life, moved about towards each other, each portending the other's destruction.

The terrible guns came with their grinning muzzles through the port-holes and glared blindly at their foes.

Then bellowed forth their fearful messengers of wrath.

Yet the three blue lights still shone bright and prominent, and seemed to raise a reflection.

For at the spots where the "Will-'o-the-Wisp" and "Yellow Vulture" lay could be seen two more blue lights, most likely inviting the companionship of the first three.

There were no idle ships nor idle hands now.

Everywhere could be heard the loud, thunder-like report, everywhere could be seen huge dark masses floating about, ever and anon lighted by the flames that would issue from their sides.

The shrieks of men, dying and wounded, sounded everywhere.

The hoarse commands of the captains, who were choked with powder and smoke, could be heard everywhere.

Everywhere was the same din, the same lights—noise—death—and destruction. There was plenty of the grim giant's work of Death—but little Glory.

The blue lights were always seen. Strange power had those blue lights; they were a language in themselves, and they spoke to each other with terrible significance.

They called upon each other in the dumb language to deal death—here or there—now in this quarter, now in that.

And, as the blood flowed, they became brighter—much brighter—and they, at last, seemed to take its sanguinary reflection.

Each blue light showed a dark crimson spot in the centre, and these blue lights, with their blood-red spots, glaring upon the opposite two blue lights, seemed to say, in their own way (could anyone have understood it)—

"We will join you."

Whether it was from surprise, fear, or that there was some more dreadful meaning in those three blue and red lights, the two blue ones turned green; perhaps with fright; but they did, and fearful was the effect.

From below the farthest off green light there no longer came the loud reports and momentary flashes; but a long, loud hissing.

Such a sound as molten lead would make when poured, boiling-hot, into the sea.

And a long streak of fire—liquid fire—went in a stream across the dark waters, and mingled with the lesser flashes of light from opposite.

Darkness, it seems, will never roll away. The stars hide their faces from view. The clouds roll heavier than before, and the light has left the earth.

Perhaps it would not mingle with that already made by the unholy war going on.

All the ships were in a heap now. There was no longer any order, for they went anywhere, following their foe in every movement, and fought on without ceasing; and when they lost their enemy they pitched into each other.

But all that was nothing.

Trivial circumstances those, so long as they continued to fight and to kill.

The air, and animals of the air, got used to firing—to flames and bullets—to splinters and shells—to the cries and groans and curses of men.

Even the sailors would lie unheeded, maimed, or dying, by the side of their companions of a minute ago.

And the three blue lights struggled on.

On, through this sea of fire—this world of death—to join the two green lights.

The half-destroyed and battered fleet followed up the blue lights, and did terrible execution in trying to prevent them getting to the green.

But they could not.

One of the late arrivals went to the help of Admiral Ellis, and turned their guns upon the farthest green light.

The farthest green light saw it coming, and it was instantly communicated by the other green light turning white.

The white light evidently objected to this addition of cannon-balls and shot.

More arms, heads, and legs were sent flying about on the deck below the white lights than was thought consistent, and the deck beneath the white light sent forth another streak of liquid fire.

And it did not die out, it enlarged in its flight, and became brighter. It turned into a number of forked tongues of flame, and brought out, in strong relief against the darkness around, the picture of a ship on fire.

The sight was wonderfully grand, and wonderfully dreadful.

The blue and green lights thought so, for they all turned white.

The huge mass of black clouds rolled away. As the mountains of flame shot up into the air, myriads of sparks followed in huge columns of smoke.

Men were seen, like so many little black specks—smoke-begrimed, blood bespattered, and fiend-like—rushing about the burning ship.

"To the boats!"

The men precipitated themselves over the ship's side, and found refuge in the sea.

Then in the boats, and then on board a vessel, or at the ocean's depth.

The flames shot higher and higher.

The sea was lit up for miles round, and a light thrown upon the ships, which showed that their sails were torn and tattered, their masts and spars were gone, their sides were torn open, and their guns were protruding from the deck and damaged port-holes.

The light only lasted a minute more, then came a sudden burst of flame, followed by a report and roar like an earthquake, then, as every ship trembled, the air was again darkened by a cloud of smoke that hid from view the disjointed limbs of men, and the last few splinters of the ill-fated ship which had blown up.

For an instant only darkness remained, then shone the pale grey light of morn, making the late wild scene more dreary and desolate—showing up the destruction in its most pitiable light, and also a gallant vessel, that had been fighting for four hours, stuck fast upon the treacherous breakers.

CHAPTER CXVII.

THE VAMPIRE'S COLLECTION.

THROUGH all this fearful strife, there was one who displayed a levity that, but for its realness, would have been out of place.

Not only a levity did this person—fiend in human form is a more appropriate term—display, but a gusto, a demoniac relish for the sickening scenes that went on around him.

He was Doctor Shrike.

Few of the most trivial or terrible incidents escaped him.

He, too, was stripped to the waist.

All his instruments were out upon the floor of the cockpit, which was lighted up with a ghastly kind of light from two oil lamps that swung with a sepulchral, ominous sound, from a beam in the roof of the cabin.

Jacop, the quaint attendant, was in his element, too—a fit assistant for the vampire. They were a useful, but a horrible pair.

At the first part of the conflict, Shrike had not many subjects.

It was not until night, and when the attempt at boarding was made, that he had any, then they came fast and numerous.

"We have no sick berths," muttered Shrike.

"No," whispered Jacop, with a ghastly grin, "none. There is only room for good 'uns."

Strange to say, after these observations, all that were brought to Doctor Shrike either had the full use of their limbs and were on the list of recovery, or the list of dead.

Not one man was found armless or legless, but many headless.

"Jacop!" cried the vampire, while going on with the work truly of "Kill or cure."

"Yes," whined Jacop, in a ghostly voice.

"Go on deck, Jacop, and bring down my subjects, Jacop; yes—wait, you long thief, till I have finished talking. Yes, that's it, Jacop. Oh, you know yourself—a brilliant idea struck me."

"What a wonder!" thought Jacop.

"Yes, Jacop, I am going to turn philosopher-physiognomist. I am going to make a collection of heads—yes, heads, Jacop—to see the difference—and no doubt it will be great—in the expression of the faces of the trunkless heads; then I will examine their bumps, and discover what merits they had. Go on, Jacop, bring me every head you see Don't forget. If you leave one behind, I will take yours to make it up!"

"Horrid old wretch!" muttered Jacop, rushing off; but the threat had its effect, and he did as desired.

He found heads rather plentiful, and, collecting them in a basket, conveyed them to Doctor Shrike, who began to range them round the cockpit, and in such a manner that any one who entered could not help greeting those ghastly emblems of destroyed humanity.

In one corner of the cockpit was a basket of limbs.

In another a heap of poor fellows who died from their wounds, and, in more cases than one, were assisted on their journey to the next world by some unseen influence of Doctor Shrike.

The vampire got but little time to rest, as subjects were being brought to him every minute.

"Jacop," he said, still at his work, and glancing round at the row of gory heads, "go on deck, Jacop, and look for more heads—only got eight—want more. I say, Jacop, listen, Jacop, look out for the pilot; his would make a fine head—what a study for a philosopher! What bumps he must have! Jacop, go and ask the pilot for his head."

Jacop went, but not to ask for anything so unreasonable.

He, also, had a great antipathy to the pilot.

He knew not why, but, using his own words, "Needles' eyes were ever so much too sharp for him."

Jacop, however, went on a round of discovery for heads.

In doing so, he went very close to Bob Hauler and Jerry Mizzen, who caught sight of the long vampire, and also saw the nature of the errand he was on.

"Jerry."

"Yes, Bob."

"See that long-boned thief?"

A vigorous thrust of the ram down the long gun followed this.

"Yes, Bob," softly from beneath the gun-carriage, as Jerry struggled up with a cannon-ball.

"Do yer see what he is doing, Jerry?"

"Course I do, Bob."

"We'll give him a pill; I owes him one."

"So does I."

"The bloodsucking, vampiring, lank-jawed, ugly thief!—curse him!"

The wad was rammed home, and the gun was run out during this colloquy.

The two inseparables fired their terrible charge.

"The gun's too hot, Jerry, let it cool."

Bob had fixed his eye on the form of the vampire.

"Jerry, we'll get him."

"How?"

"Why, you go and lay down under the larboard-gun there, then I'll cover you with a cloak, and smear your face with blood. He won't see your body. Shut your eyes, and, when he's a-going to touch you, bite his finger."

"Ha! ha! ha!" Jerry attempted to grin, but the idea of being smeared with blood was not pleasant, and he did not relish it.

Still, to pay off Jacop, and please his friend, he consented, and was very soon doing the "dead 'un."

Jacop, with his hungry eyes glaring upon every gory face and clotted hair, soon saw the ghastly-looking face of Jerry Mizzen.

"That head's worth the whole lot!" he grinned.

With more pleasure than reluctance he stooped down to clutch the bead by the nose.

His finger already touched the warm and quivering nostrils, when he gave a howl, or yell, of fear and agony.

The mouth, which had been firmly closed, opened, the fine double row of tobacco-stained teeth closed upon his finger, and were only stopped by meeting with the bone.

Jacop's howls were pitiful. He dropped in fright, struggling madly to get his finger out, but all such attempts were useless, and he would, perhaps, have fainted had not the pain been so great.

He opened his eyes, and beheld, to his horror, three heads closing round him.

His finger was released, when a head came upon his face—he felt the warm life stream running down his neck.

One more yell he gave, and, turning over, he crawled swiftly away on his hands and knees.

He thought all the heads were coming after him, and could have sworn one pitched him down the hatchway.

Whether or no, it is true he was discovered rolled up like a ball at the bottom of the companion-ladder, a spot he had reached without the aid of one step.

Had it not been so dark, someone might have seen that Bob Hauler's naked foot had something to do with his speedy exit from the deck.

Jacop shuddered when he entered the cockpit.

There was an addition to the heads. Instead of eight, there were thirteen.

Jacop shivered at his own thoughts.

The vampire was in the act of questioning his assistant, when Bob Hauler came in, leading his loved comrade by the arm.

"Hold up, Jerry, old mate. Don't be down-hearted. It's nothing much "

"I ain't afeard, Bob, only it makes me faint. Ugh!" shivered Jerry, as his eyes caught the row of dreadful reeking heads.

"Never mind, Jerry. Don't look at 'em," said Bob, consolingly.

"Ha! ha! ha!" chuckled the vampire, "it's you, is it, Jerry? What's the matter, Jerry, eh? Don't like the heads? Ha! ha! ha! Don't they look elegant? I'm turning physiognomist, Jerry. Yes, how many heads—let me see. One—two—thirteen. Oh! how much I should like yours, Jerry, to make even number! Your head would look well among them, eh? Don't you think so?"

"Look here, you blood-sucking swab, if you don't 'tend to Jerry's wound, I'll soon add your head to the number!"

Bob Hauler drew a huge cutlass, seeing which, Doctor Shrike got out of the way.

"Ha! ha! ha!" he chuckled. "You would not do that, Mr. Hauler. You are only in play."

"Maybe I am only in play—maybe I am not, but I do rum things in play, you blood-sucking swab, and, unless you dress Jerry's wound, I shall be apt to make a big mistake that you would not put right in your lifetime."

Doctor Shrike neither liked the look of our friend, or the tone of his voice, and, being at the same time aware of what he would do in behalf of his friend, Jerry, the vampire complied with his request.

"Haul up, then, a minute, you bloodsucker. Don't you give Jerry any extra pain, and if he ain't cured without any injury to his limbs—any one on 'em, mind ye, why, douse my toplights! I'll make yer suffer in that very same part."

Bob Hauler little thought that every threat he uttered was carefully noted down in the doctor's wonderful mind, and, though he complied with seeming humility and sympathy, he was chuckling to himself at the revenge in store.

He did not let Bob have everything his own way, as it was.

Much against Jerry's inclination, and greatly to his disgust, he was placed with his face towards the ghastly trophies, all of which looked more or less hideous under the dusky light.

Jerry closed his eyes to shut out the sight, but he still fancied the staring eyes of one was searching his very soul, and that the heads were walking towards him.

Remembering one of his own mottoes—" There's nothing like facing the enemy "—he opened his eyes, and faced the enemy accordingly.

Doctor Shrike kept him there as long as he thought it advisable for his own sake, and then said—

"You can go."

Jerry almost forgot the pain of his wound in his joy at being able to leave the cockpit, and, giving a wild stare, he rushed on deck.

Though the fight was going on with renewed fury the vampire had a short respite.

After surveying the heads with a complacent smile, he gave some instructions, and then went on deck.

Shrike glanced anxiously around, and it was with a feeling of joy that he could not see the pilot.

"I'll have his head," he thought.

At that very instant the inexplicable man appeared on the companion-way.

"What a head!" muttered the vampire, unconsciously giving vent to his thoughts in words. "With the last I have twenty. How I should like his to make twenty-one!"

At that moment his eye caught sight of Zelie, the Corsair maiden, who stood proud and beautiful in the handsome costume of her race by the side of Captain Tom.

She was armed to the teeth, and a veil of silver mail fell from her turban over her lovely neck and shoulders.

"I'd give up ten of my best subjects, and cut Jacop into mincemeat for that head!" said the doctor. "Lovely! sublime! what bumps it must have!"

His cogitations were cut short by a ball striking the ship near where he stood, then, careering across, struck an Arab at the bottom of the neck, severing his trunk from the head.

"Another head!" cried the vampire, and catching the reeking trophy in his hands, he hurried below to escape from any spent bullets.

"Twenty-one!"

Such was the number of human heads the doctor had ranged round the cockpit, to please his own morbid fancy.

It was a strange, wild, and unearthly spectacle were those twenty-one faces.

All different.

Each showing the individual passions of the human mind.

Doctor Shrike seemed struck with it, for he lost his levity, and paused. It made him reflective, though not remorseful.

He was lost in his own profound reverie, and he muttered unconsciously—

"I should like his to make twenty-two."

A hand, firm, though small, had grasped him by the shoulder, and he turned and saw the pilot.

"Dress the wound in my side," he said.

His cold, glittering eye went from the vampire's visage to those rigid, gory faces in front, and a look of ill-concealed disgust passed over his face, passed truly, for in a second it was as calm and placid as ever.

"Ha! ha! ha!—do you admire my collection, pilot?" said the vampire, bringing the necessary articles immediately to attend the wound in the strong man's side, and, without waiting for a reply, he continued, "I have turned physiognomist. I am going to study the bumps, organs, both exterior and interior of these heads. How widely different they are, are they not? See, for instance." Doctor Shrike left off his work, and pointed with his lancet to two of the heads, "the great difference in those two faces, so unlike the rest, and so unlike each other."

In spite of himself, the pilot became morbidly interested as he gazed upon the exhibition so ghastly and horrible, as the flickering light of the lamps played distinctly upon their faces, throwing many and various shades upon them.

"How different are they in life than in death!" continued Shrike, giving way to the weird fascination of the scene. "Those two"—pointing to two aged heads—"are the heads of men—ignorant, uneducated, with fine talents and instincts, perhaps, but which, like the grains in unpolished marble, were hidden. They were rugged, those men; and, in spite of their ways in life, had high notions and noble instincts, that only wanted bringing out. The look upon their faces is sublime in death—in the contraction of their nostrils, the drawing down of their mouths, you can detect the mortal agony that their captive feelings vainly strove to master. They died in glory; 'tis written on their brows—furrowed with the world's cares. They died as men doing their duty—as men, you can see it—whose last thoughts were 'I have done my duty, and die for him I swore to serve.'"

The vampire continued for a length of time describing the faces, and he unconsciously became eloquent, and opened to the pilot an hitherto unseen spring in his intellect, that both surprised and fascinated the hearer.

The pilot seemed lost in contemplation of their faces.

"A wonderful piece of machinery is the human mind," he thought.

Twenty-one faces, all cold in death, and yet everyone showed the workings of the brain when in life.

Some had an expression of awe and agony—not the fear of death, but fear of the next world—of after life.

On others could be traced a smile full of bold defiance.

Others had died in agony, with teeth locked and lips closed, battling against death to the last.

The Arab's face was a study. The expression was one of savage hate—brute ferocity—that remained even in death.

"All dead alike," muttered the pilot; "all the same stony lumps of clay and bone. All were God's creatures, yet how different! Every mind is a machine, with it own secret and intricate workings, all built upon the same base—love, aversion, hate, and fear, yet all so unlike. Ugh! have you finished? Let me go."

"And remove those from the cockpit!" said a quiet, stern voice.

It was Captain Tom, who had entered to have a cut in his shoulder dressed, and stood, like the pilot, facinated.

"Yes, captain," replied the doctor; and, in a low tone said, "*Twenty-one.*"

CHAPTER CXVIII.
PROGRESS OF THE BATTLE.

THERE would be plenty of opportunity yet for adding another score of crimson faces to the twenty-one.

The fearful strife had not yet finished, though a second day had broke, and threw its grey light on the scene of blood, death, and destruction.

Things looked more threatening than before.

Men—despite their firm instincts—were like all other animals in this one respect—it took them some time to begin the fell work, but when they began they knew not when to stop.

When blood had once flowed, they kept it running.

One of their great fabrics—one that had done much with its great powers—had been removed from the face of the earth—blown to atoms in the air.

Another—the "Golden Eagle"—lay pinned upon the jagged points of the sunken reefs. Another—one of the late comers—was rapidly sinking.

The whole fleet showed the same signs of desolation—such as torn sails, shattered spars and masts, splintered hulls, and blood-stained sides.

The three ships that had displayed the blue lights where in company with Captain Tom.

They were more equally matched now—five to six.

Iron Arm had gallantly brought his two ships through the whole fleet.

Hugh Baldrick had followed.

A ringing cheer followed this, and a broadside that made the "Owl" quiver from stem to stern, and cause Hugh Baldrick to utter a fearful oath.

"Six feet of water in the hold!" cried the man from below.

"The ship is foundering!" came from another quarter.

"To the boats! To the boats!"

"Silence!" thundered the smuggler prince. "Silence fore and aft!"

The men were quiet. Then he ordered a red-hot shot to be brought to him, and, with his own hands, he loaded the gun amidships.

Taking a steady aim, he sent the blazing ball crashing through the enemy's ship's side.

It was aimed for the magazine, but missed its mark, and it fell into the hold among the ship's stores.

A yell and loud cries followed this, which told Hugh Baldrick that it had done some mischief. Then, seeing his vessel was sinking, he signalled distress.

Iron Arm had already seen the panic among his men and his dangerous state. So did Dutch Paul, who was in hearing distance of Iron Arm.

"Save the men," he cried, "while I give the gentleman over there something to amuse him."

The gentleman over there was Captain Hanwell's officer who had sunk the "Owl."

Dutch Paul, puffing away at a huge cigar he had just lighted, gave the order to fire.

"Give them blazes!" he cried

Blazes was the destructive liquid fire, and his men gave them plenty of it.

At the very moment he fired, a cry, loud and appalling, came from the hold of the "Goldfinch."

"A fire has broken out in the hold!" was the cry.

Before the officer could give directions, the terrible liquid stream came pouring on the deck, driving the men away in terrible fear.

Everywhere was confusion, terror, and panic.

The guns of the "Goldfinch" were silenced as the fire poured over her deck

While the crew of the "Owl" was being safely hauled on board, the vessel sank.

As it did so—causing a whirlpool—the "Goldfinch" was shrouded in flames.

"She wanted to see the destruction of her enemy," said Hugh, taking a last fond look at his vessel.

Meantime, every other vessel had been doing all they could, and Seaward found himself hotly engaged. The fire from the "Will-o'-the-Wisp" was terrible. His men fell like blades of grass, but still he held out.

Captain Tom saw the condition of his faithful friends, and, wishing to save them, he quickly proposed a plan.

"Pilot!" he called.

"Captain!"

"Take us through that rocky mouth."

The "Will-o'-the-Wisp" was put in motion.

Though the clouds of smoke were thick, like a fog upon the water, the pilot took the vessel out.

Captain Tom had hoped this would have called one or two of the enemy off to follow him.

But to his chagrin and rage they did not, for none attempted to follow. Seaward fell upon Iron Arm just as the "Owl" sank.

Captain Tom was about to sail into their midst when the cry of—

"A ship is running into us!" was heard. He jumped round, but he could only just make out in the smoke the dark outline of a vessel.

"Ahoy!" he called.

No answer.

"Fire!"

A heavy volley was poured into the new-comer, and while the smoke clung round the "Will-o'-the-Wisp," there came a shock.

The buccaneer's ship shook from her keel to her mast-head.

Then came a loud yell, a British hurrah, and Captain Tom saw the form of his foe, Admiral Ellis, with a perfect legion of men at his back boarding his ship.

"Death or glory!" he cried, leaping forward

"Death or glory!" echoed the men.

"Death or glory!" the clear voice of the pilot rang out.

And "death or glory!" was heard across the blood-coloured sea.

The fight was coming to its end.

CHAPTER CXIX.

LAST OF THE BATTLE.

THE bloody work at the creek was coming to its climax now.

Captain Tom was compelled to set aside all feelings of remorse, and give full vent to his men.

Outnumbered as he was, with the enemy pouring upon his vessel from all sides, he was compelled to fight without mercy.

The well-devised means of keeping off the boarders by the chains and scuttlings succeeded in doing so in both the first and second attacks, during which attempts Captain Tom had a terrible fire poured into them, and for a second the vast numbers of the enemy were driven back.

But the frail handiwork could no longer hold out; cutlass and tomahawk did their work, and brought the barricades down.

With like success the English sailors poured in upon the blood-covered decks of the "Will-o'-the-Wisp."

Admiral Ellis bore a charmed life through it all. He was now here, now there, now at the head of one party, then at the head of another, and now striving hard to get at Tom.

The pilot, who was fighting and still watching affairs, called Jerry Mizzen and Bob Hauler.

"Load that gun with grape and small shot, and get the machinery in motion."

This was done.

"Now," he said, "look out for the opening, and, when you see none but the enemy, give them fire."

Captain Tom had just called off his men to make another desperate attack to beat the boarders off.

During this time, Bob Hauler took the opportunity to run the gun right in front of the advancing enemy, then he fired. The report was immediately followed up by a rush from the Shadow Avengers; and what with their terrible onslaught and the destruction done by the gun, the enemy was driven back, and more than half their number hurled on to their own boat or into the sea.

The instant the pilot saw that, he had the machinery put in motion.

He himself took the wheel, and, just as the captain —who was on the "Will-o'-the-Wisp"—called to the men, the vessel shot away, and those who had made another leap to board fell short and into the sea.

The fearful roar and din of the carnage drowned the noise, and none noticed that the "Will-o'-the-Wisp" had cut through the rocky ruck of land and was safe from the schooner.

The mad-brained sailors tried to follow, and, before they went a hundred yards, they were firmly poised upon a rock.

Admiral Ellis, his captains, and the men who were with them, were at the mercy of Captain Tom and his gallant band.

The schooner's boats were lowered, and they attempted to join their commander.

One of the boats succeeded in passing the breakers; but it never reached the "Will-o'-the-Wisp."

A well-directed shot crashed it to pieces, and the men were left battling for their lives in the water.

The "Goldfinch" would have followed, but the men—seeing the fate of the schooner, that did not draw half so much water as they did—refused to go, declaring they would not throw away their lives upon the rocks with the enemy in front of them.

Lieutenant Seaward saw how useless it was to try and induce them to do so; and, seeing that his assistance was wanted where he was, ordered them to their guns and went on fighting.

The day was drawing to a close, and the sun was sinking fast. The dreadful strife continued, and shadows were thrown upon the water long ere night came.

Dutch Paul was still in the midst of all. He had lost his masts and nearly all his spars. He had got a jury-rudder, and yet he fought on.

He glanced, with his usual carelessness, towards the setting sun, and remarked, drily—

"I'll add a paler glow to your blood-red tint presently."

Then, lighting a cigar, he went on with his work of destruction.

The vessel Iron Arm had captured from Reuben Harpy was also awfully disfigured, though it was able to fight on.

Commodore Ellis ordered the last attack to be made, and himself to board the ship commanded by Iron Arm; but he felt it was almost useless.

The vessel that had sunk the "Owl" was burnt to the water's edge, and they were thus rendered almost inferior in form to their gallant foe; but still the attack was made.

Commodore Ellis, aided by Lieutenant Seaward bore down, attacked, and boarded Iron Arm's vessel.

The other ship attacked Dutch Paul and Iron Arm's escort, which was also boarded.

Dutch Paul was the only one who continued commanding.

The sun sank lower still, and threw its dingy glow upon the already crimson-tinted waters.

Iron Arm beat off the enemy with a tremendous loss on his side. Dutch Paul kept them off his ship altogether.

He saw the boats approaching from the creek, those who had vainly strove to follow the "Will-o'-the-Wisp," and he stopped them on their way; then he turned to the ship that was attacking him.

"The sun is going, and I promised to light its departure. Let's see which will be the brightest light."

The fatal charge was fired, and the light of the sun was nearly eclipsed.

Dusk drew closer to its end. Captain Tom had been fighting all this time like a fiend.

The instant the buccaneers discovered that they had the enemy in their power they rushed forward. Such a yell they gave as would disturb the dead at the bottom of the deep.

"A hundred guineas for the man who will bring the commanders to me alive!"

The cry sounded through the ship, and the brave buccaneers, not so much for the bribe as to please their leader, made one mighty rush, drove back the men, and the captains—Teddington, Hanwell, and Morris—were captured.

Ellis was battling madly with Captain Tom, who, with one swift stroke of his sabre, shattered the admiral's sword to pieces.

Then he sprang forward, caught Ellis in his strong arms, and gave him over to his gallant mids, with instructions to secure him safely.

The men, seeing all their commanders in captivity, cried for quarter.

"Hold, fore and aft!" cried Tom, and every weapon was lowered.

The enemy surrendered their arms, and stood on the blood-streaming deck, with their blood-besmeared forms and faces displayed in the now sinking sun with a lurid glow.

Dusk swept past, and the shades of night were falling fast, when a bright, vivid glare lit up the scene of slaughter.

The noise, din, and terrible war-cry was increasing as the "Will-o'-the-Wisp" moved out with the flag of triumph flying at the mast-head.

The rest of the admiral's fleet were faint-hearted, and, giving way to despair, succumbed.

The "Will-o'-the-Wisp" ran alongside of Iron Arm just as the men gave up their arms, and the aged leader was seen to stagger, and would have fallen heavily to the deck, had not one of his men ran forward and caught him in his arms.

The excitement had proved too much for him, and he was seized with a fit.

Laying him gently on some canvas close at hand, some of the men applied restoratives, and after a while had the satisfaction of seeing their aged commodore open his eyes and gaze vacantly around him.

CHAPTER CXX.

THE SCORPION'S STING.

"Sail oh!"

How glorious the sound to the sea-tossed mariner that has looked upon nothing but the sky and water for weeks, save the spars and sails of his own gallant ship.

So it was with the crew of the "Emperor," as fine an Indiaman for its day as ever ploughed the foam, and the passengers, whose faces had grown long and wry, once more came on deck with a smile.

"News from home," whispered one to the other; and even the captain shared in the belief, for the vessel looked smart and trim, and had the appearance of not having been many weeks from port.

"As I thought, a Britisher!" exclaimed the captain, as the English flag was run up in answer to his own.

The captain, in his eagerness to gain any intelligence, leapt upon a gun-carriage, for they were well armed.

"What ship, and how long are you from port?" he cried.

"The 'Lightning,' one month from London."

This answer was given in a slightly foreign accent.

"Have you the mail on board?"

"Yes," was the ready reply; "and I have a small packet for the ship 'Emperor.'"

The crafty captain had caught sight of the name on the quarter.

Had Captain Johnson seen the fiendish smile on the half-turned face as this reply was given, he would not have felt so easy.

The mail bag was brought on deck, a packet of letters taken therefrom, and then a boat was lowered from the opposite quarter.

Captain Johnson, as did also his crew, gleefully watched the four sturdy fellows that pulled alongside, and the officer muffled in a boat cloak, as he stepped to the deck.

"Letters for the 'Emperor,'" he said, in a voice that sounded strangely harsh for one of such gentlemanly mien.

"Thanks; 'tis fortunate we met," said Captain Johnson, as his eye ran over the direction.

"Yes, captain—rather."

He laid peculiar stress on the last word, and his keen eye wandered restlessly from one end of the ship to the other.

The female passengers grouped about in whispers, each eyeing his noble form, and trying all in their power to catch a glimpse of his face.

No wonder—accustomed, as they were, to see the same faces each day, and especially as the stranger was so handsome.

As yet, the captain had not opened the packet, which was well tied and sealed; the mate had gone forward to give some orders.

Several of the sailors gathered round the boats' crew, asking questions, and greedily devouring the ready answers.

A slight cough from he in the cloak disturbed them.

The women gave a screech of horror.

The seamen gave a shout of alarm.

"Treachery! pirates!" thundered the boatswain, seizing the marlinspike with which he was working.

The cause of this was the appearance of eight sturdy ruffians, that had lain concealed in the boat.

The cloaked figure had thrown off his disguise, and discovered a corsair's dress, thickly studded with pistols and dirks.

The rest were equally well armed, and, without waiting for any further orders, commenced a fearful onslaught on the defenceless crew.

Seeing how matters stood, the mate rushed aft.

"Hold, villain!" he yelled, as he beheld the pirate leader, pistol in hand, threatening to blow out the brains of the captain if he did not at once disclose where the specie was hidden.

"Fool!" was the reply, and another pistol was levelled at the mate's head. "Back, hound!"

A swift blow from a handspike, which the mate had hastily seized, dashed the pistol from the pirate's hand, and the mate seized it.

"Now we stand level!" he shouted, "you bloodeater! This is the friendly packet you bring! Now, take this as your reward!"

The pistol was raised, but as the mate was about to fire, one of the pirate's crew buried a bowie knife in his shoulder.

For a moment he staggered as though about to fall, but, being a powerful man, he clutched a rope, and held himself erect.

The pistol was still in his hand, and the eyes of both the pirates were now fixed upon him with a deadly glare.

"Down with him, Sancho! Hew him to pieces!" yelled the infuriated chief.

He was afraid to move himself, for fear of the captain slipping from him.

Sancho was one of those bloodthirsty wretches who revel in torturing others, but have a great aversion to placing themselves in too much jeopardy.

He did not like the look of the pistol; it was too dangerous for him to offer to close; so, with crafty dexterity, he measured his mark, and sent his knife whizzing through the air into the breast of the already wounded mate.

The pistol, being cocked, went off, and the bullet severed the halliards of the black flag that had been hoisted to the peak in lieu of the British ensign.

Forward the fight was raging furiously.

The sailors, having armed themselves from the chest, struggled desperately with their assailants.

Yells and execrations burst from the inhuman fiends, as the boatswain urged the sailors to defend their lives.

The sailors, armed with a few rusty cutlasses, disputed every inch of the ship, and in a very short time would have gained the mastery; but a fresh levy of pirates poured on the decks.

Seeing their comrades lying bleeding around, they were excited to madness, and with horrid yells, made for the forecastle.

Here their impetuous course was checked.

Two of the seamen had cast loose the bow gun, and having loaded it with grape, swore to sweep down every pirate that advanced.

This they little expected.

Suddenly they came to a stand, and held a whispered consultation.

The leader, in the meantime, assisted by Sancho, had ransacked the cabin, and locked the ladies in one of the state rooms.

"Now, sir," the pirate chief hissed, savagely, "since you have shown us the contents of the cabin, you will, perhaps, be kind enough to lead us to where the treasures are stowed."

"And if I refuse?"

"Why, then, Captain Johnson, I must use force."

"Force! Have you not done so already?"

"No matter, I am in no humour to parley. You may call it what you like, but the treasure I must and will have."

The captain groaned.

He cast his eyes on a pistol that hung near, and was preparing to make a grab at it; once in his grasp, he might have one more chance of his life.

Still, there were two against him, but he feared not Sancho; he was only armed with a knife, and of that he might get possession.

"Well," he said, "I see it is no use reasoning with you; I will show you the specie, which, without my aid, you may never find; there are twenty thousand rupees, besides bars of gold—what conditions do you offer me?'

"Your life?"

"Nothing else?"

"Your life."

"Good, I agree; but stay, my men, what of them, and the ladies?"

"The women must be mine, the men shall be yours."

"Good heavens! What want you with the women?"

The pirate chief turned.

A fierce glare was in his eyes.

"Your questions are impertinent!" he hissed, a sardonic grin on his lips. "Have I not promised you enough? See you not that I am an Algerian pirate, and my ship, the 'Scorpion,' is one of a fleet sent forth to scour the seas?—and were it known that I had broken my oath by promising you life, I should meet my reward at the yard-arm of the first of our fleet I came across."

"Indeed, your laws are strict."

"And my commands also Quick, show me this hidden treasure, or I may forget my promise, and seek it myself."

The captain, during this conversation, had managed to shift towards the pistol, but the pirate chief, guessing his intention, snatched it from its bracket, and holding it threateningly towards the captain, said—

"This, perhaps, will decide the point. Two minutes I give you to show me the hidden store, and if in that time it is not in my possession, I send this through your stubborn skull!"

Snatching the captain's watch from his neck, he timed him by it.

Seeing that all further delay was useless, and believing that the pirate, having satisfied himself with plunder, and taken aboard the women, would keep his word, led the way by a secret entrance to the lower hold.

Little did he know that most of his crew had been butchered, for the fight had been carried on forward, or he would not have felt so confident in the company of the two pirates.

It was a rough road, over bales and cases, and through narrow holes, and the lantern showed but a faint glimmer in the inky darkness, yet on they went, the pirate chief's eye watching his every movement.

Keeping his pistol on the full cock, and motioning Sancho to keep his knife in readiness, the pirate followed his guide, his quick eye and ear ready to detect the least treachery.

At length they reached the end of the hold, and crawling on his hands and knees between two bales, the captain ordered them to follow.

They did, and then he said, pointing to what appeared a large iron tank, "There is the treasure, I have brought it thus far safe, but take it, 'tis valueless to me without life."

The chief gave another fiendish grin.

"What use is it to me thus? I cannot remove it. Show me the opening."

The captain knelt down, and after turning various screws, he with some difficulty slid back the lid.

The pirate glared in and held down the light, but though he could see several of the bars shining, and could count a great number of the bags, he was not satisfied, he forced the captain to enter and hand them to him.

This was most galling, humiliating for the captain, yet he obeyed.

One by one he handed up the bags, and as the sordid wretch leant over him and kept count, he muttered many a bitter curse.

The last at length came, but even then the pirate was not satisfied, he made him assist Sancho in removing them to the cabin.

When all were safe, the pirate chief made a sign to Sancho.

He disappeared, and returned soon after with a half-dozen burly fellows, who, having rolled their fiendish eyes round the cabin, seized upon the treasure, and bore it from the cabin.

"Now, sir," said the captain, with assumed boldness, "I hope you are satisfied, and that you will allow me to pursue my course."

The pirate gave a hoarse laugh.

"Have you forgotten," he said, "how reluctantly you yielded to my proposals, the time you wasted to no purpose? You are my prisoner, and must remain so till I free you."

Captain Johnson went livid with rage, his lips were colourless, and his whole frame trembled with excitement.

"Perfidious wretch!" he ejaculated, half choking. "Is it thus—"

"Hold! Enough of this!" yelled the pirate "Sancho, place him in safety."

Sancho stepped forward to obey, but ere his hand touched the captain, he seized him by the throat, and flinging him back across the table, held him in a grasp like iron.

"Confounded reptile!" he hissed, between his clenched teeth; "thus I repay the debt I owe you."

Sancho was a powerful fellow, but taken by surprise, and held in the manner he was, he was rendered powerless.

The pirate chief looked on aghast, and was unable to assist him.

The sudden change in the captain, his tiger-like gaze, and rage-distorted visage awed him.

At length, recovering his self-possession, he made a blow at the captain, rendering him senseless, and, then commenced to disengage the iron grasp; but too late, Sancho was dead.

With an angry frown he strode from the cabin, and went on deck.

The sight he witnessed seemed to please him.

Strewed about the gory deck were the lifeless bodies of the once gallant crew, some headless, others hacked and hewed in the most frightful manner.

The lieutenant, a Malay, stepped up to him.

"All silenced, sir," he said; "but they fought like devils. They turned the bow gun on us, but a bucket of water from aloft rendered it useless."

"Well done. Now cut away all the ropes and cordage, send some hands down the forehold to scuttle the water casks, pour a few buckets of salt water into the bread lockers, and file the wheel chains."

Having given these orders he walked hastily to and fro the deck, as though in deep commune with his thoughts.

Presently he broke out—

"Yes, I will keep my word with him, he shall have his life, his ship, and his men."

Then he walked up and down again like a fiend until the lieutenant reported all done.

"Now hand the women on board. Gently with them, or, mind you, I shall not look over it, as I did when last we captured a prize. 'Twas your rough handling that caused those two women to cut their throats. These I must take safely to the Pasha, or he will bring me to a terrible account."

The pirate's stern look was sufficient to assure the lieutenant that he must be careful.

So, selecting two of the others who were less blood-stained than the rest, he went below.

At the door of the cabin the captain met him.

He had just recovered, and seeing that he was ready to offer resistance, the lieutenant felled him like an ox with his pistol butt.

Drawing him under the table out of sight, he went to the state-room.

The ladies were clinging frantically together weeping, and uttering the most fearful moans; but the lieutenant, dead to all pity, tore two of them away, and consigned them to the arms of his ruffianly myrmidons.

The others fainted, and were easily removed, and the lieutenant desired to know what was to be done with the captain.

"Let him live as long as he can," was the fiendish reply. "I promised him his life, his ship, and his men. He can have all; let him enjoy them."

So saying, he beckoned his men to leave the ship; and as they shoved off, the pale face of the terrified captain appeared at the gangway.

He had only partially discovered the horrors of his position.

His cry of horror rang loudly over the waters, and was echoed back by the mocking laugh of the pirates as the "Scorpion" filled her sails, and sped away in search of further plunder.

CHAPTER CXXI.
THE MEETING WITH THE PIRATES

A WEEK had nearly passed since gallant Tom's glorious victory.

The crew were lying listless about the deck, when they were suddenly aroused to action.

"Sail-ho!" sang out the look-out man from the masthead.

Captain Tom sprang to the binnacle.

"Where away?" he asked.

"Off our starboard quarter, sir."

Tom Drake adjusted his telescope, and took a survey of the horizon.

Far, very far away, was the faint indication of a vessel.

She was coming in their track, a minute's examination proved; and our hero, with a satisfied smile, handed the glass to his mate, while the crew, with curious interest on their faces, gathered about the quarter-deck.

"Sail-oh!" again sang out the look-out.

"Where away?"

"Off the stranger's lee."

He gave our hero the glass.

The two vessels were coming plainly in sight.

They seemed close together, but the one they had last seen was the bigger of the two, and by the manner in which she gained upon the other, evidently was the swiftest sailer.

As Captain Tom gazed across the sea, an excited look crossed his features.

"I could have sworn," he observed, "that I saw smoke about the stranger's bows."

"Not at all unlikely," was Luff's reply. "There's plenty of warm work in these seas, and the looks of that big craft don't please me at all."

A few moments of anxious suspense ensued.

All was silence on board.

Presently everyone started.

Boom came the sound of a gun across the sea.

Another—then a quicker succession of shots.

There could be no uncertainty now—the two vessels were engaged.

Tom Drake cast an anxious look around at the lowering sky.

"Have all sail spread," he shouted; "we may come up with her before darkness sets in. Clear the decks and run out the guns; and boarders, look to your pikes and cutlasses."

"Besides," he added, "who knows but this may be the fellow we want."

A score of willing hands sped about the ship—sheet after sheet was unfurled, till the masts bent like reeds beneath the pressure of the gale.

The wind was blowing stiff, and the brig leapt swiftly across the intervening space.

In a little while could be seen an occasional sheet of light leaving the sides of the two vessels, over whose hulls the smoke hung in dense clouds.

The booming of the guns was more startling, but less frequent. The weaker vessel was yielding to the superior force of the enemy.

"The little one is beaten," said Tom.

"Yes; they have taken her. I hope we may be in time to do the same for them."

"See," he cried, "they have fired the ship!"

As if it had been flooded by instantaneous liquid fire, the smaller vessel, all in a moment, was ablaze from stem to stern; but her big opponent did not even then cease firing into her, and half a dozen shots brought her so low in the water that her speedy destruction by fire and leakage was certain.

Whether her crew and passengers had been removed, or were left to their terrible fate, it was impossible to conjecture; but a determined look settled on the faces of Captain Tom's crew as their ship began to forereach upon the victorious cruiser.

Having accomplished her swift, ruthless work, the strange vessel, deigning her pursuer no notice, now spread her sails, and shaped her course in another direction; but she went at an easy speed, as if glutted with the plunder of her prey, and at every leap of the ship the distance between them was lessened.

Now that they got closer, the appearance and build of the enemy they were so soon to encounter were the subjects of curious observations.

She was a rather ungainly craft, heavily laden, and carrying an enormous weight of sail; her hull was low, and so oddly shapen, that had her masts been cut down she would have looked like a huge tortoise upon the waters; her prow was sharp and like a beak in shape, and her figure-head was a monstrous vulture painted red, and with its talons extended on deck as if to seize its prey; her decks were crowded with men, and the long lines of dark muzzles protruding from the portholes revealed how deadly was her armament.

The unfortunate vessel she had captured, and which was now blazing to the water's edge, had no more chance in an encounter with so formidable a foe than a dove had in contending with a vulture.

"Give her a gun," cried Captain Tom, "she shows no colours, but that will bring her to."

A gun was fired.

Scarcely had the sullen roar died away than, as if by magic, the stranger's yards were stripped, and she lay to under bare poles, her motion as abruptly arrested as if a giant hand held her in her course.

"The pirate means to fight," remarked Bob. "I should like to send her a shot that would sink her. Hullo! that's in reply to ours, I suppose. Not badly aimed, either; by Jove! I thought my head was carried away in splinters."

A puff of smoke had come from the stranger's sullen hull, and, as Bob spoke, a big cannon-ball came tearing up the beams of the quarter-deck, and knocked its way out at the other side.

THE UNFORTUNATE YOUTH CONVULSIVELY CLUTCHED THE FLOATING SPAR.

The stranger vessel had as yet shown no colours, and in silence her gun had been fired.

The men who had swarmed upon her decks were nowhere visible; but now a little ball was run up to her halyards and her flag unrolled.

A black banner, with the device of a monstrous scorpion in the centre.

Tom's own banner had already been run up.

A deep, hoarse laugh came from the stranger's deck, and a voice cried—

"Now, devils, give them their salute!"

A swift, sudden, and deadly broadside answered this command, and the weight of metal pounded against the hull of the brig.

It was well that her sides were protected by a coat of sheathing, or that well-directed volley would have sent her foundering to the bottom of the sea.

As it was, it did some damage, and our hero's deck was strewn with the wounded before he well understood the sudden attack.

"Salute them in return!" Tom cried; "be ready with your boarders. Fire or no fire, we will not shirk the guns!"

Then began the swift and deadly cannonading, for which the buccaneers were so famous.

While their light vessel, under a heavy press of canvas, flew like a bird, as she obeyed the manœuvres of her skilful commander.

Their telling fire, and the skill with which she evaded his deadliest volley, evidently baffled the pirates' leader, whose deck was almost untenable.

In the hottest of the fight his deep voice resounded amid the din, as he gave some order to his crew.

A moment after, a blinding flash shot like lightning from his bows, and the brig was visited with a perfect hail of what seemed living fire.

For the moment, the seething balls of fire ran from stem to stern, and made a mimic hell of their deck.

The buccaneers fled from their guns, as they strove to escape from the ravaging flames, but the angry tones of their dauntless leader recalled them to their duty.

"Back to your guns!" he cried, leaping amidst the fiercest raging fire. "See, I am unharmed! Fear not this harmless flame. Keep up your fire—deluge their deck with iron hail! Boarders, prepare! I, alone, will stay here while you take their ship!"

The flaming missiles, blazing furiously at our hero's feet, cast a lurid glow on his excited features.

He seemed more than mortal as he stood unscathed amidst the terrible element, and his followers, with a ready cheer, served their guns with deadly effect.

The pirate captain was paralysed at receiving this storm of shot and grape from the vessel he had encircled with fire.

His fierce voice again rang out its commands, and with sudden swiftness his canvas fell, and his vessel drew away.

Captain Tom, standing dauntless in his perilous position, looked through the smoke, and saw a burly, stalwart man, with a massive head set on immense shoulders, looking at him from his shattered decks.

He was dressed in a rover's costume, a black, bushy beard encircled his chin, and his belt was crammed with huge pistols and short cutlasses.

"Ahoy, there!" he cried; "are you the buccaneer, and Captain Tom Drake?"

"We are," our hero replied, "and defy you."

"Then I fight you no longer. I'm sorry I've encountered you. Look to your holds, or the fire we've given you will blow your ship to pieces. I can give you no help—I've too much powder on board. We shan't fight if we meet again. You'll know me—i'm the captain of the 'Scorpion.'"

He waved his hand, and stepped down from the carronade on which he had been standing, and as his vessel answered her helm, and sheered off from the scene of action, the buccaneers saw, with consternation, that the liquid fire, running like mercury about their decks, had set the hold in a blaze.

The position of our hero and his crew was critical in the extreme.

The burning ingredient, whatever it was, seemed harmless so far as its flame was concerned, for Captain Tom had thrust his hand into it without being even scorched; but it dropped a glowing mass like red-hot mercury, and this ate its way through every beam and plank, and was lodged in all the crevices of the ship.

Prompt and collected in the deadliest peril, Tom Drake sprang from his dangerous position, and issued his swift orders, himself aiding in the efforts to put out the fire.

In this they could succeed, so far as the material of the ship was affected; but the blazing liquid proved to be inextinguishable, and burned as vividly under water as on the deck.

Our hero's crew, and our hero himself, looked blankly in each other's faces.

The fire was travelling to the powder magazine.

One spark there, and the noble vessel, with its daring crew, would be blown to pieces.

Now that the last echoes of the cannonade had died away, a strange silence reigned.

Noiselessly the buccaneers kept at their dangerous task of putting down the fire, while our hero, with a select party, saw to the powder magazine.

Their only chance of safety lay in keeping the blazing element from this place, and a direct approach of the flames was prevented by a barricade of iron plates, with which they shut off the place where the powder was stored.

The worst danger, however, lay in the fact that the insidious ingredient, working its way through the beams, might at any instant fall from over their heads, and instantly compass their destruction.

With this peril before them, our hero and his chosen band set to work.

Their resolve was a desperate one.

Every barrel of the explosive material was hauled from the storing place, and thrown singly into the sea.

The power in bulk was well saturated by means of a hose kept playing upon it, and after an hour's imminent peril—any moment of which might have hurled every living soul into eternity—the last barrel of powder was, amidst a cheer that proclaimed the salvation of the ship, hoisted out at the lower porthole.

The talk of quelling the fire was comparatively trifling when this was accomplished, and the buccaneers worked less quietly now that the fearful imminence of their danger was past.

It took them a long time to extinguish every trace of the fire, and when this was effected, the crew gathered round their leader, to thank him for preserving their lives.

He was paler than he had ever been before.

He had fully realised their jeopardy, and though danger was his proper element, and defiance of death his kindred nature, the threatened destruction of his ship and crew had quelled the usual fervour of his dauntless nature.

He gazed after the pirates' ship, fast receding from sight, and roused to sudden action by an exultant shout of triumph, which came across the waters from the pirates, he swore to hunt them down, and gave orders to put the ship under full sail.

CHAPTER CXXII.

CAPTAIN TOM DRAKE GIVES THE PIRATES A CHASE.

AT TOM's command the crew flew about the decks, headed by Harry Vere, who inspired them with fresh vigour.

The stunsail booms were quickly rigged out and tucks and halyards hove, and in a very short time, the little brig flew through the water with lightning speed, and her long, black hull appeared almost buried beneath the towering clouds of canvas, now spread to the wind.

The buccaneers' blood, red flag, embellished with the ghastly emblems of the skull and cross bones, now fluttered in the breeze, and on sped the villainous craft on her errand of destruction.

The "Scorpion" could not have been better adapted to the wishes of the pirate, being built for speed, and provided with six brass guns, of rather heavy calibre for vessels in those days.

With her crew of thirty well-armed and resolute fellows, she proved a formidable opponent to any vessel who might dare to cross her path.

The Pirate captain, and his chief officer, were standing on the poop, holding a short conference as to the best mode of proceeding, doubting their ability to escape the "Will-o-the-Wisp," when darkness hid the ships from each other.

As the pirate captain stood behind his companion

and the pale grey dawn of morning irradiated his swarthy features, clearly defined there was an unmistakable character of malignant treachery in the deep set glaring eyes, of unmitigated, cruel, tigerish ferocity, in the thin, scornful, glaring lips and large white, glittering, teeth, that remained, while heavy masses of damp black hair fell in clustering elf locks on his ample shoulders.

"Forward there; pass the word for the second officer; let him come aft for orders!" cried the pirate, in a clear but subdued voice, at the close of their short but evidently decisive consultation.

"Dick," he resumed, as that individual made his appearance on the poop, "let all the men be mustered aft."

"Aye, aye," he replied, as he hurried forward to obey the order.

In another moment the deck was crowded with a group of stalwart, fiend-like forms, whilst the resolute expression of their weather-beaten and sun-tanned features, added to their terror-inspiring garb, shirts, and skull caps of crimson serge, gave them a formidable appearance.

"Now, lads," he said, in an assuming tone, "we attack, plunder, and destroy. You all know the meaning which these words convey, therefore you require no further explanation; but hark ye," he cried, fiercely, "the first man among you who betrays the least signs of treachery, I'll send a bullet crashing through his brain!"

This fearful threat, uttered in such an impressive manner, seemed to have the desired effect, and a smile of satisfaction played on the lips of the pirate, as he gazed silently on their awe-stricken visages.

"Sail, oh!" now sounded from the mast head.

With an impulsive movement, the pirate sprang to the side, and scanned the horizon with his glass.

"In stunsails," he thundered, "and clear away for action. She appears to be an Indiaman," he said, turning to Dick, who stood at his elbow; "I dare say it's the 'Lady Sue.'"

The day had set in with thick and foggy weather, and a vessel could be only indistinctly seen at the distance of a mile.

Looming like a gigantic mass through the haze, might be seen a vessel of no small dimensions, braced sharp up on the wind, as though she were steering for the English Channel.

And it was apparent to all that she would cross the bows of the "Scorpion," and that shortly.

Speculation was rife as to the probable extent and costliness of her coffers, and the rapacious hearts of the pirates beat high in the anticipation of an easy capture and a glorious prize.

The pirate, who had been anxiously watching the "Lady Sue," as he termed her, for he felt certain it was her, now hailed her in the usual way.

But received no answer.

The vessel now crossed the bows of the "Scorpion," and appeared to be indifferent to the movements of the brig, as she hauled her wind, and proceeded in the direction of the stranger.

The brig soon overhauled her, for she appeared to be a sluggish sailer, and, in a very few minutes, ranged alongside.

"Ship ahoy!" thundered the pirate, for the second time.

And waited impatiently for the answer.

But no answer came.

"Ship ahoy!" he almost shrieke d, in a frenzy of rage.

At that moment a blue ensign was run up to the peak, and two rows of ports, each presenting the black muzzle of a gun, appeared to his astonished gaze.

What a change came over the features of the pirate as he saw the guns, with their dark, yawning chasms, ready to deal forth death and destruction.

For a moment he stood as though rooted to the spot, but, hastily recovering himself, he flew to the wheel, and, by a dexterous movement of the helm, he bore down on the breeze at the same moment the men squared the yards.

"The 'Will-o'-the-Wisp,'" he thundered, "by heavens she will knock us to pieces; we are no match for Captain Tom Drake!"

"Loose the royals, run up the stunsails!" he roared.

At that moment a deafening roar rent the air, and a shower of shot flew harmlessly by the brig.

Whilst the vessels, having changed places, the pursuer now being the pursued, flew rapidly before the wind.

The "Scorpion" was evidently increasing the distance between her and the pursuing ship, when a shot from the bow carried away the port topmast stunsail boom of the pirate's barque.

The sails were now dragging in the water, thus causing an impediment to their progress.

"Cut away the hamper," roared the pirate, "and drag two of the guns aft."

The order was quickly obeyed.

The "Will-o'-the-Wisp" had gained considerably on the brig, and it was apparent to all on board both vessels that the frigate would soon be alongside of her, whilst the sailors were already in the nettings, waiting to board her as soon as she should draw sufficiently close for them to do so.

"Try your hand at that gun," cried the pirate captain, "and mind, dread the consequences if you miss your mark."

"Drop down," cried Dick, "or them buccaneers won't miss their mark."

They had scarcely time to fall to the deck, when a shower of bullets from the muskets of a body of mids mustered in the bow, shot over their heads, lodging in the spars and different articles on the deck.

"They say a starn chase is a long 'un," said Dick, as his eye glanced along the barrel of the gun, "but, curse me, I would sooner have a short 'un, for it's growing rather hot!"

A bright flash at that moment, followed by a loud, crashing sound, told how truly Dick had directed his aim.

And now the foretopmast of the "Will-o'-the-Wisp" came tumbling down, causing those assembled on the forecastle to rush aft.

A smile of satisfaction lighted the swarthy visage of the pirate, as he patted Dick familiarly on the shoulder, and bade him try his hand upon the other gun, which, in the meantime, had been loaded by several of the crew, and now stood ready for him.

"Aye, aye," was the rejoinder, as he sprang lightly to the other gun, and leaned forward in a stooping attitude to insure his aim.

"Try the maintopmast," ejaculated the pirate.

But Dick only threw himself down flat on the deck at the rear of the gun.

For as he looked through the port he saw the barrel of a musket pointing in a direct line for his head, and scarcely had he fallen down when a bullet whizzed through the port and ploughed up the deck a few feet in his rear.

Like lightning he sprang to his feet again, and took his station at the gun.

A loud report followed.

The maintopmast swayed to and fro, and, in another moment, fell down before the mainsail, bringing its mass of sails and cordage down with it.

A yell of defiance now rose from the brig as she dashed away from the buccaneer.

At the same instant the "Will-o'-the-Wisp" made a yaw to one side, and delivered a broadside from her main-deck guns.

Another yell arose from the brig, as the iron shower flew past the vessel, tearing up her decks and killing and wounding many of the crew, and cutting the mainmast to its centre.

With a rending noise the shattered spar, with all it's entanglement of sails and cordage, heeled over, hissing like red hot embers, into the foaming sea.

Just then a startling cry of mortal agony, unearthly and appalling in its intensity of blended fury and despair, aroused the pirates from the trance-like stupor into which they had momentarily been thrown, and turning their eyes in the direction whence the sound had proceeded, they were horrified at beholding the mutilated body of Dick, whose legs had been shot off at the knees, and now he was clinging to the capstan for support, as he tried to walk upon the stumps.

A ghastly expression on his countenance, and a death-like pallor on his brow, he gazed with a wild, fixed stare of vacant horror, at the huge, black mass, almost obscured by the fog.

"Shipmates," he said, in a tone of agony, "I must have one shot at this cursed ship. Load her with grape."

The spectators listened in wonder to the words of the wounded man, and appeared like men who had awakened from a fearful scene.

"Do you hear me," he gasped, as he fixed his unearthly glare upon their awe-stricken features, "will you load that gun, that I may be revenged for the loss of two spars?"

A thrill of horror ran through the crew as he pointed to the now severed limbs as they lay near the stump of the fallen mainmast.

Scarcely knowing what they were doing, several of the crew moved aft and loaded the gun.

Dick's eyes lit with a lurid glow as he impatiently watched their every movement.

And while they were yet running out the gun, with an Herculean and final effort of his fast ebbing strength, he hobbled along the deck.

The crew started in horror, as the clump, clump, caused by the bone striking on the deck, fell upon their ears.

At length, faint and exhausted, he reached the breech of the gun, on which he placed his hands and leaned for support, whilst, with eyes dilating, he gazed through the porthole.

And now he stood erect, defiant, unsubdued, his right hand resolutely grasping the match.

For a few moments he regarded the dim outlines of the distant vessel with a frightful glare, then, dropping his head to a level with the gun, he gave the word to elevate.

A blinding flash, a deafening roar.

Followed by a crash.

The shot struck the bulwarks.

With a roar of disappointed rage, the maimed wretch let the match fall from his grasp, and, staggering, with a convulsive heaving of the throat, he fell heavily to the deck, uttering a hollow, wailing groan.

His shipmates, who, up to the present moment, appeared dumbfoundered, rushed to his assistance, and raising him from the deck, bore him, apparently lifeless, to the hold below.

The surgeon was already busily engaged in amputating and binding up the shattered limbs of those who had been wounded by the raking broadside of the "Will-o'-the-Wisp."

Both vessels were now obscured from each other by the dense fog that suddenly fell upon them.

And the pirates, having by this time recovered from the confusion, were busily rigging a jury mast, and having cleared away the wreck, they proceeded on their course.

Towards evening the fog cleared away, and the heavy mists disappeared as the sun sank below the horizon.

A gentle breeze blew from the westward, and the ship ploughed the rippling water.

The pirate chief, accompanied by his first officer, paced the quarter-deck, deeply engaged in conversation, whilst the crew were gathered in a group on the forecastle, and appeared to be conversing in low and evidently discontented tones.

"Shipmates," said a brawny, black-muzzled Cyclop, who evidently arrogated to himself the position and privileges of a forecastle oracle, "I told you last night I meant to give you a bit of my mind about this new gim-crack skipper of ours. I believe him to be a reg'lar coward."

"You ain't got the pluck to tell him so!"

"Why, you don't mean to say you'd go and blow on a feller 'cos he speaks his mind to his mates?"

"No, no," answered a dozen voices; "go on, Peter."

"Well, I say he's a coward, and for the matter of that, I wouldn't mind telling him so, if he'd give me fair play, but I never had a fancy for any hanimals, and I know he keeps a cat in the cabin, and werry likely he might lay it on my back."

Here he made a significant gesture to his mates, which implied, "You know what I mean."

A nod of assent was the only reply.

"Now, do you mean to tell me, messmates, that if the captain had been aboard last night, he would have cut away from these 'ere lubbers? Why, there wasn't a good handful of 'em."

"Well, I should think not," answered one of the group, as he folded his arms across his broad chest in dogged resolution; "now I arn't a mutinising chap nohow, but what I axes ye is this, what business has he to bring that 'ere Ralph aboard, and make him leftenant of this 'ere craft, when poor Dick, that's had a reef taken out in his lowermasts, ought to have had the first chance, for he's bin aboard on her ever since she was launched. Eh, brothers?"

"Right you are; go on."

Having thus relieved his outraged feelings, he drew forth a monstrous pouch of tobacco, thrust a consoling quid into his cheek, and took his seat on a coil of rope.

"Ah! I know the consequences, and have seen it proved in my time, and do you mind me, shipmates, bad luck is sure to foller."

The cry of, "Sail, oh!" brought them to their feet.

And every eye was now fixed in the direction of the ship's head.

"I hope it arn't another Johnny haul taut," ejaculated one of the pirates."

"No fear o' that, Bill; her spars aren't lofty enough."

"I lay it's some Yankee liner!"

"That won't be much of a haul, then," growled the others.

"It won't pay us for our dunnage," he said, holding up the breast of his shirt, and displaying two large holes made by a musket ball.

The shades of evening now spread her mantle over the wide expanse of waters, and the approaching vessel could not be clearly made out by the naked eye.

Ever and anon the men would cast an anxious eye towards the poop, where the captain was intently peering through his glass.

Every ear was on the alert to catch the least sound.

And the men listened intently for some order.

"What do you make her out to be?" inquired the new mate, who had been trying to pierce the gloom.

"Look for yourself," was the rejoinder, as the captain handed him the glass.

"I should think she's an Indiaman."

"I am sure she is, or I never saw one, and if I have not seen her before it's strange to me."

"Where do you suppose you've seen her?"

"Don't ask so many questions. Go forward, and do what I told you. If this is the vessel I take her to be, she is well manned and armed, and also freighted with a valuable cargo."

On came the doomed ship.

The crew and passengers had all come on deck at the sound of—

"Sail, oh!"

And were now anxiously peering at the vessel they supposed was an outward-bound merchant-man.

Darkness now reigned around, as the two vessels rapidly neared each other, for the moon had not yet risen, so that the unsuspecting crew could not see the deadly instruments of war that projected from the bulwarks of the brig.

They had now neared to within hailing distance.

"What ship is yours?" cried the captain, in a clear voice.

"The 'Lady Sue.'"

The captain smiled inwardly.

"Where are you from?"

"Calcutta."

"Whither are you bound?"

"London."

"You'll never get there, then," muttered the captain.

"What ship is yours?"

"The 'Vivid.'"

"Where are you bound to?"

"Malta."

"Are you from London?"

"No."

"Where, then?"

"Cardiff."

"Oh, indeed!"

"You have had rough weather?"

"No, pretty fair. We lost our mainmast in a fog—a vessel ran into us."

"Just so. Ah! some careless fellow, I presume?"

"I have a letter I should like to send by you, if you have no objection, and if you have any spare rope, as you are so near home, I should be much obliged if you could let me have it."

"With pleasure."

"I'll sent a boat."

Both vessels by this time had hove too, and they were laying almost motionless.

In the twinkling of an eye a boat was dropped from the quarter davits of the brig, and half a dozen resolute fellows having been secreted in the bottom, she shot rapidly under the quarter of the brig, pulled by six of the crew, who had doffed their terror-inspiring garb, and now assumed the appearance of merchant seamen.

A few rapid strokes brought them alongside the "Lady Sue," which was a fine East Indiaman of fifteen hundred tons, and was loaded with costly merchandise.

The pirate skipper seized the rope ladder that had been placed for his accommodation, and with a spring gained the deck, where the captain stood ready to welcome him.

"Step down in the cabin, if you please," said the captain, addressing the pirate chieftain.

On gaining the cabin an exclamation burst from the lips of the captain.

"What, is it really you?"

"It is, Mr. Thompson," was the cool reply of the pirate.

"Has the 'Sultan' arrived all safe and sound?"

"Yes."

"How is it you have left her? You have been two or three voyages in her, have you not?"

"I should have gone in her again, only her bottom wanted repairing, and her copper has to be renewed. It will take a considerable time to get her ready for sea again."

"Drink," said the captain, handing him a tumbler of pale brandy.

"Here's towards your good health, Captain Thompson."

"And here's towards your success. I suppose it's the first voyage you have been, captain?"

"It is," answered the pirate.

"I suppose you have not a very valuable cargo for the first voyage?" inquired the captain.

"No, not so valuable as yours, if I conjecture rightly."

"Well, you see, we are freighted well this voyage, and under the lazarete," he whispered, "are diamonds and precious stones to the value of half a million."

A smile passed over the features of the pirate, unobserved by the captain.

"Yes, valued at half a million," he repeated, emphatically, "but I am obliged to keep it a secret from the crew, or I fear they would murder me to get possession of it."

Another smile passed over the features of the pirate.

"Have you anything else valuable on board?" inquired the pirate, indifferently.

"Yes, down the after hold, are elephant's tusks, valued at two thousand, and under my bed," he said, in a tone of confidence, "there is specie to the value of five thousand pounds."

"They must put great confidence in you, captain, to place you in charge of so valuable a cargo."

"And have you no supercargo on board?"

"None."

"You have ladies on board. If I am not mistaken, I saw two as I came down the companion."

"Yes, an elderly lady and her daughter. They are on their return to England, after having amassed a large fortune in India."

"Indeed."

"Yes," he said, familiarly. "If you or I had only one half the riches this ship contains, we might lay up in dock for the remainder of our lives, instead of washing about the stormy seas."

A fearful look of avarice rested on the features of the pirate, as the captain entered one of the state-rooms, and his hand clutched a dagger concealed beneath his clothes.

He was about to follow him, when the captain returned, bearing a heavy box in his hand.

"This is their treasure," he said; "and if the crew only knew what the cabin contained, my life would not be worth a straw."

The pirate moved uneasily on his seat, and his hand clutched firmer the hilt of the dagger.

At length, resuming his former coolness, he inquired—

"I suppose you carry arms for fear of a surprise?"

"Yes; we have eight carronades on deck, and in yonder locker there is a plentiful supply of small arms."

"What, do you mean to say you don't keep them handier than that?" exclaimed the pirate, with feigned surprise.

"I have them there in case those pirates that infest this part should attack us, but I dare not trust them to the men under any other circumstances." He had placed his mouth close to the ear of his treacherous friend to utter the last few words.

The pirate chuckled inwardly, and he felt that he could not contain himself any longer.

The captain now returned to the state-room to replace the box.

The eyes of the pirate flashed fire.

He rose cautiously from his seat. A dagger gleamed in his right hand. And with a spring, he bounded forward.

In his impetuosity he had capsized the decanter, and the captain turned his head on hearing the sound.

The face of the captain assumed a look of terror as he saw the bright weapon in the hand of the pirate.

And ere he had time to recover himself, the dagger of the pirate was buried in his breast.

With a horrible groan he fell to the floor and rolled at the feet of the pirate, who now stood brandishing the blood-stained weapon over the head of his victim.

"Murderer," gasped the wounded man.

"Fool!" cried the pirate, "if you had not tempted me by showing me the gold, I should not have resorted to these means of obtaining it."

Footsteps were now heard on the companion ladder.

The pirate started, and was about to leave the cabin to see who it could be, when the wounded man, anticipating his intentions, clung to his leg.

The pirate tried to shake off his grasp. But his efforts were in vain, and with a cry of rage he buried the weapon in the breast of the wounded man a second time.

Still he could not shake him off. The wounded man only clung tighter.

The footsteps were fast approaching—they were at the door, and in another moment the mate entered the cabin.

His countenance changed to a corpse-like hue, and he staggered back a pace, as he gazed upon the scene before him.

There lay the captain weltering in his gore, while he clung tenaciously to the legs of his bloodthirsty murderer.

Before the mate could interpose to arrest him, the pirate chief tore himself away from the grasp of his victim, and flew from the scene of his bloody treachery.

On gaining the deck, he took one glance around the horizon.

The pirate crew had been busily engaged in conversation with the crew of the vessel during the captain's absence, and were not at all sorry on seeing their chieftain make his appearance on deck.

Taking a silver call from his pocket, he blew three distinct notes.

The men who were concealed in the boats now mounted to the deck.

At the same moment another boat, well loaded with men, pushed off from the brig.

The boat's crew, who had now gained the deck, commenced a fearful slaughter, whilst the crew of the doomed ship, being taken by surprise, were unable to offer the least resistance.

Seeing that they would receive no quarter by surrendering, they seized handspikes, capstan bars, marlingspikes, or any implement that lay about the ship's decks, with which they defended themselves as long as they were able.

At length all the gallant crew and passengers, save the two ladies, had been ruthlessly slain, and the pirates, with remorseless greed, searched every portion of the ship for the desired booty.

Boat-load after boat-load was conveyed from the blood-stained deck of the doomed ship, to that of the 'Scorpion," and a radiant smile played on the swarthy visage of the pirate, as he watched with intense interest and avaricious greed, the progress of the boats.

The ladies, who had fainted at the onset, were now seized by the rough fellows, and amidst their rude jests, and coarse rivalry, they were placed in the stern of one of the boats.

Having secured all that they possibly could, they first scuttled, and then set fire to the vessel.

A bright light simultaneously seemed to issue from all parts of the ship at once, and wound its serpentine folds round the masts and rigging of the doomed vessel.

Up, up, they creeped, licking the sails with their fiery tongues.

A shout of triumph rose from the deck of the brig, and by a blaze of lambent radiance might be seen the stalwart forms of the pirate crew as they clustered to the gangway, and now stood out in bold relief, as they waved their long, gaunt arms derisively, and again sent forth a yell of triumph.

For a moment it seemed as though the fire had suddenly died out, and yet another moment and a terrific explosion shook the "Scorpion" from truck to keel, and caused the waters around to heave and swell convulsively.

And now the few blackened spars that floated on the surface of the moonlit waters were all that remained of the ill-fated vessel.

The pirate brig now set her sails to the wind, and sailed away in triumph with the rich booty gained by dreadful murder.

Not long had they been on their course before a ship was sighted bearing down upon them.

"The 'Will-o'-the-Wisp!' " exclaimed the pirate, with a change of countenance, that told his fear of the bold buccaneers.

He had good cause to be afraid, too.

When Captain Tom Drake made up his mind to a purpose, it was not easy to escape him. He had made up his mind to punish the pirates for their audacity, and the hearts of oak who surrounded him made his cause their cause, and were as eager to have a brush with the bloodthirsty ravishers as their noble young chieftain.

Every man on board worked his hardest to increase the speed of their gallant ship, and every knot it gained more precipitately on the piratical craft.

There was no hope for the "Scorpion;" the pirates saw it; and, like the brutal cowards they were, they armed themselves to make a desperate resistance.

They did not want to fight the buccaneers if they could avoid it, and they strove their best to escape, but the "Will-o'-the-Wisp" bore down upon them like an avenger, ploughing grandly through the surging billows with the brave crew gathered on her deck armed and eager for the approaching battle.

Captain Tom stood amongst them like a young prince giving his orders, which were obeyed with an alacrity that proved how much he was loved by his crew.

The pirates watched them; they saw they had no chance to elude the "Will-o'-the-Wisp," and in wild desperation they fired the stern chaser.

The shot fell broad of its mark. It was replied to almost before the boom had died away with a volley that did terrible damage, tearing away the rigging, splintering masts, and dealing death amongst the pirates.

The consternation which now took place on board the "Scorpion" gave the buccaneers an advantage which they made the best of, and sent forth another volley of destructive missiles.

Tom thundered forth a crashing broadside that made a perfect wreck of the " Scorpion's " deck, felling masts and spars, and mutilating the savage crew.

The pirates, yelling like fiends in their fury, gave battle in sheer desperation.

The bold buccaneers went off in boats to board the pirate craft, amidst the shower of shot and shell that flew from ship to ship.

" They have rich store aboard," Ben Barnacle roared. " The wealth of an Emperor."

But Captain Tom forbade his crew to touch it. He would not take wealth aboard his ship—which had never yet been dishonoured—gained by savage murder, and there was not one voice to gainsay his wish.

The buccaneers gained the deck of the " Scorpion " with but a slight opposition. Then they fell upon the pirates with terrible fury, giving no quarter and asking none.

They fought with the most insatiable of all feelings, the feeling of revenge, and they fought to kill.

The buccaneers held together in a compact body, opposing all opposition, cutting their way through the savage horde step by step, leaving a dark stain of blood in their course, and strewing the deck with the pirates they hacked down.

The fight was nearly over, but six of the pirates remained, when a shriek of wild terror sent a chill to the hearts of the buccaneers, a cry that resounded from lip to lip of the panic-stricken women, who rushed upon deck, and was answered exultingly by the savage captain, the cry of—

" Fire ! The ship's on fire !"

There was not a moment to be lost.

The wretch, finding he was conquered, set fire to the ship, willing to perish in it rather than the buccaneers should profit by his plunder.

The flames had already burst through the upper deck, and by the direction whence they came it was known that the fire was raging near the powder magazine.

The confusion created by the terrified women caused a dangerous delay.

The buccaneers knew their peril.

At any moment they might be blown into eternity, yet they were too brave to leave the women behind, though they themselves might perish in the attempt to save them.

" Ha ! ha !" laughed the brutal pirate chief, with fiendish exultation ; " two minutes more and the ship will be blown up !"

With a cry like a young tiger one of Captain Tom's mids rushed at the ruthless villain, and plunged his sword through him.

A warning cry from one of the buccaneers, who was sliding over the burning ship's side, bade the brave boy lose not a moment.

But too late.

There came a mighty explosion, that burst the ship, and blew the inside into fragments.

When the clouds of white smoke cleared away nothing of the pirate craft remained but the shell— a raging mass of fire, which threw a lurid glare over the turbulent waters.

Amongst the charred and shattered timber the buccaneers saw a form clinging to a broken spar— the form of the brave mid who had been blown up with the ship.

Burnt and bruised, he clung to the spar with the tenacity of a dying man.

His strength was giving way, when his shipmates put off to pick him up, and he felt that it was the last moments of his life.

He uttered a despairing cry as his strength gave way—a cry that found a response in the hearts of his shipmates who saw him sink.

Bending well over their oars they reached the spot with a few mighty pulls, only in time to catch him as he rose to the surface apparently lifeless.

It was nearly dark now, and a storm was gathering. Captain Tom observed this with some uneasiness.

In the late battle, the " Will-o'-the-Wisp " had received sufficient damage to unfit her to weather a severe storm, so he gave directions for the ship to hug the shore, that they could seek a place of refuge in case of danger.

The darkness had increased to a thick blackness, and the storm was gathering in fury as it travelled across the water, when it was ascertained the " Will-o'-the-Wisp " was near land.

Through the sombre gloom Captain Tom Drake saw a strange light on the rugged cliffs.

" Is that a lighthouse beacon ?" he asked.

" We are near the haunt of a desperate band of wreckers," replied Ben Barnacle. " That light is a false beacon, to lure some homeward-bound ship to destruction."

" By Heaven ! then, such dastard villainy shall not be," cried Tom. " We will run the ship in here."

" What would you do ?"

" Extinguish that light, and hurl the ruffians into the sea."

" Do not be rash, boy ; I tell you that not one will escape with life you lead into this lair of wreckers ; they are desperate men, and dare much."

" Bah ! you would frighten me. The career of Captain Tom Drake is not ended yet."

CHAPTER CXXIII.

THE DEATH LIGHT ON THE CLIFFS.

" LAND HO !" sang out the man aloft, and the welcome cry went gladly to the hearts of those who, from the deck of the " Sultan," watched eagerly for the shore.

The " Sultan," an East Indiaman, heavily freighted with a rich cargo, sailed gallantly before the wind.

Like a race-horse with the goal in sight, she seemed to understand and answer the wishes of the passengers, and each plunge took her onwards to the dim gray line, the first glimpse of which had elicited the welcome cry from the man up aloft.

" We have had a pleasant voyage, sir," said a handsome young officer, approaching a fine old gentleman who, with his daughter, stood near the taffrail watching the gray and green blended in the distant lines of sea and land.

" The ship does her duty yet."

" As does her captain," said the gentleman, responding with a kindly bow to the respectful familiarity of the young commander's address. " I have made this voyage many times, but never before so pleasantly as on this occasion."

" Your praise is the more grateful to me since I owe so much to you," said Michael Rayner, bowing low, and as he bowed stealing a glance at the maiden. " It was a proud and precious trust, the command of this vessel, freighted as it is with so much that is beautiful and costly ; we shall run in before night comes on, I think."

" I think so, too," said Mr. Brocton, " and then my last voyage will be over, and—Captain Rayner—"

" Sir !" said Michael, approaching.

Mr. Brocton laid his hand on the handsome sailor's shoulder, and said—

" We are not very old friends ; but such an acquaintance as ours is better than a long one, for we know each other. I have found you a man brave, true, and devoted."

"You give me too much praise."

"Michael," Brocton proceeded, with much emotion, "had not you risked your life to save my daughter, I should now be a childless man, heart-broken, and worse than poor, for the wealth I have would be nothing without her. I said then that I never could repay so deep a debt of gratitude."

"I did not want a recompense, Mr. Brocton; any man on board would have done as I did. Every sailor in my command would die for Miss Brocton; and," he added, lowly, "so would I."

"You hear that, Susie," said Brocton, caressing his daughter; "see what it is to have a pretty face. Now, had I fallen, I do not think there are many who would have been willing to risk their life for me."

"Father," she said, deprecatingly, "I am sure Captain Rayner would have done the same."

"Then," rejoined Brocton, smiling, "you have found the way into my daughter's good graces, Michael."

Rayner coloured with pleasure.

"I was speaking of my gratitude." continued the merchant, "but words are not much"

"You have already done more than enough."

"In giving you the command of this vessel, you would say; but with your sailor-like qualities, you must have won as high a place eventually. Now I have been thinking of a plan which, I think, will please you. This, as I have said, will be my last voyage. The cargo I have on board is worth a million. I have another million coming from my India agents, and I have a third safely invested in England, so I shall not be a poor man, shall I?"

"It is regal wealth."

"Why, yes," smiled Brocton, "and more, for all monarchs are not rich; some of them would be very glad of the freight my other ship, the 'Bluebell,' will bring. She will leave Calcutta in about four months. I should have waited for her, but I wanted to come back to the old land."

"That is natural," said Michael; "I, too, long to see the white cliffs once more. Not that there are many friends to welcome me," he added, with a sigh.

"Have you no parents?"

"I have not," was the sorrowful reply; "both were lost at sea. The only one of kindred I have is my brother Gus."

"And he is your twin brother?"

"He is so."

"And an officer in the coast guards?"

"A lieutenant. He will be very proud to see me come home captain of a merchantman!"

"Doubtless, when you tell him what this will tell you," said Mr. Brocton, taking a packet of papers from his breast, "it will show, I think, my best recognition of my obligation. When shall we reach land, Captain Rayner?"

He spoke the last words as he put the packet into Michael's hand, and so that Michael might retain his self-possession.

"In less than four hours, sir," replied Rayner, wondering what were the contents of the packet, "with the fair wind and weather we have now."

"There is no fear of a change—a storm?"

"None," said the captain, looking up to the calm, unbroken beauty of the sky.

"Thank Heaven! we shall meet again at dinner, captain; and mind, no thanks then for that."

Rayner drew back, and raised his hat as Mr. Brocton and his daughter passed to the state-room.

"What can this be?" he thought, opening the document when the giver had disappeared with Susan; "some generous gift!"

He began to read, then started, his face beaming and his eyes glowing with glad surprise.

"The ship mine!" he exclaimed; "given to me, and with it a thousand pounds. It is too much—it is incredible!"

It was true, nevertheless; the papers were ten bank notes, each for £100, and a deed of gift making Michael Rayner sole owner of the "Sultan."

"What can I say to him?" he said; "how tell my gratitude for a deed so noble? And Gus, how pleased Gus will be; and Jessie, darling Jessie. Her words were prophetic, for she said I should not return a common sailor."

And he was thinking gladly of the beautiful maiden who, whether he went back poor or rich, had promised to be his bride, when a deep, sonorous voice at his side startled him.

He turned to face Bentley, the second mate of the "Sultan."

"We shall have a storm," Bentley said, and knowing the unerring judgment of his second mate, Rayner started.

"Why do you think so, Bentley?"

"Look!"

The mate pointed to the horizon, westward, and following his finger, Michael only saw the crimson sun deepening in hue.

"Nothing there to foretell a storm," said Rayner, "but you are an older sailor than I, and should know best. Do you think it will be soon?"

"Before we reach the land," replied Bentley, with a deep intonation that gave his words peculiar effect, "and when it breaks let Christians pray for those at sea."

"We have weathered many a tempest, Bentley!"

"I have fought in many a battle, captain, when the elements were like hell at war; when the lightning's gleams have mingled with the flash of steel; the crash of thunder with the roll of cannon."

He paused. His impressive words, and more impressive manner, sent a chill to Rayner's heart.

"I have been nearer home than we are now, but many a goodly ship has gone down within sight of land and sound of those on shore. This is the seventh voyage of the 'Sultan.'"

"What of that?"

"We have a tradition, which tells us that the ocean demon fights for every vessel riding for the seventh time on his breast. The storm is gathering."

"Where?"

"That white mist rising under the sun's rays is the spirit coming forth in quest of prey."

"A superstition, Bentley."

"A truth, captain; see how the sky darkens, even now."

And, as he spoke, the sun sank back, giving place to a funeral gloom.

A strange foreboding seized the youthful captain.

"We, too, have a tradition," he said, forcing a smile, "better than that of yours—the ocean demon; ours tells us there is a spirit of good aloft, ever on the watch to protect his children from the perils of sea and land."

"Yet we have storms that sacrifice human lives in myriads."

Rayner did not reply; he was watching the white mist rise, and spread.

It might have been fancy, but it seemed to take the shape of a shroud and come direct towards the "Sultan."

There was no wind yet; the sea kept calm, and but for the dense whiteness of the shroud-like mist fronting the more dense and darker gloom there was no token of a tempest.

"Steady there with the helm," said Captain Rayner; "stretch every sail, rope, and mast that will bear, and set in hard for shore."

The last word had hardly left his lips when a flash of lightning, blue and vivid, struck the flag from the mast. It fluttered to the captain's feet.

He was not superstitious; but the incident seemed ominous, and made him pale.

"The demon of the storm is at work," muttered Bentley, who now stood apart with a strange look upon his face; "is it then destined that tempest or wreck shall rob me of that on which my soul is set?"

His eyes burned with a sinister fire, and he glared towards the state-room.

Then he went on muttering; but nothing tangible could be gleaned from his incoherent, broken soliloquy.

The ship sailed on.

Two hours passed, and except for an occasional peal of thunder, preceeded by a vivid flash, there were no signs of the impending danger.

Michael began to hope he should make shore before the tempest attained its height.

It was not so to be!

Large whitened gleams swept through the clouds, and the thunder's heavy crash broke with a force that seemed to make the vessel rock.

Large drops of rain fell slowly first, then fast and furious; so swift and terrible the battle now raged in the sky, that the hardy sailors grew appalled, and did their work in dumb obedience to their captain's voice.

He was quite collected, as self-possessed and full of nerve as though calmly floating on a river.

He felt his peril, but did not fear it.

He did his duty like a man, thinking more of those in his care than of himself, but thinking too, of blue-eyed Jessie, the maiden whom he loved so well, and never more might see.

Mr. Brocton and his daughter came from the cabin.

She was very pale, and clung close for refuge to her father's arm.

The awful echo of the thunder, and the lightning's fire, made her shrink with dread, but no word of terror escaped her. For her father's sake she wished to know the worst at once.

"There is hope," said Rayner, as he took the helm. "I know the coast, every rock, and crag. Be calm, dear lady, put your trust in Heaven, we have a good ship, and a crew who will not flinch."

"Breakers ahead!" suddenly rang out from the powerful voice of Bentley. "Beware of the false beacon, beware of the wreckers' fire, and beware of the death light on the cliff!"

The storm was at its loudest then, yet every word was heard.

On the next instant, a rocket sent from Bentley's hand went like a meteor through the gloom.

While it was yet in the air, another rocket went up from the shore.

"A signal from the coastguard!" exclaimed Bentley. "Captain, let me take the helm, you are steering us upon the breakers!"

"Merciful powers! I could have sworn I had the vessel right! Stand back, Bentley, that may be the false beacon!"

"No!" thundered the man. "You would sacrifice our lives—get from the helm! That is the true light there."

The captain turned to look.

A crash of thunder drowned the cry, but a gleam of lightning revealed the wild and devilish expression of Bentley's face, as he stood like a demon at the wheel.

Another flash gleaming out upon the waters lit the pallid face of Michael Rayner, and on the pallor of his brow there was a broad red gush of blood.

None saw the deed—none saw the white face sink, nor saw the glittering blade in Bentley's hand.

"Mine!" he said, below his breath. "The ship with its glorious cargo, beautiful Susan Brocton—mine—for if we outlive the storm, Bentley is master here. Bentley, the second mate! Ha! ha! ha!"

His devilish laugh was loud, as with a giant's strength he wrenched the wheel round so as to steer the vessel for the place of safety indicated by the beacon.

"And then the 'Bluebell,'" he said, "she sails from India in four months hence. I can wait for her. The pirate—the tiger of the seas—can wait and watch."

Again that devilish laugh, but this time it did not last.

The "Sultan" leaped high up on a wave, and went down with a hideous crash, turning the brave crew sick and faint at soul.

"On the breakers!" thundered Bentley, like a baffled fiend. "Close reef the sails. Strip every mast. Let hell itself rise in the tempest, the 'Sultan' shall ride out to sea again."

And seeking to avert the catastrophe, he turned the massive wheel hard back, but useless quite his hope.

The ship drove resistlessly onwards, and struck on the breakers.

Shattered! Her huge side broken in like an eggshell, the "Sultan" lay impaled. The mate's defiant blasphemy had met a terrible reward.

"Doomed!" he said. "Lost. Lured to distruction by the wreckers' beacon. The death light on the cliff!"

CHAPTER CXXIV.

THE WRECKERS.

No boat could live in such a sea. The sailors dared not launch one. They knew that at the best it would be but to escape death on the ocean to meet a fate more cruel.

The wreckers had done their work surely. When the storm began, a horde of ruthless wretches stood on the cliff, waiting for the doomed ship to come.

"The harvest will be rich," said one who stood by a pile of torches unkindled yet. "The coming craft is an East Indiaman, crowded from stem to stern with gold and costly merchandise. See how the storm gathers, there will be darkness soon. Then—then for the rocket and the death beacon."

"Be careful, Ralph," said a dark-browed fellow, "Captain Tom has set his face against this work."

"Death! What is he, that we should fear him? Let him stand in my way if he dares. What is he? A smuggler who sickens at the sight of blood."

"He would not fear Satan's self—you know that, Ralph."

"Curse him! I hate him! I hated him from the time he came, and but for Black Bill he should have found a grave long ago. But leave me, Jones, if you are afraid."

"Afraid?"

"Well, you should not be; I have seen you knock out an old man's brains, and strangle a dying child."

"Enough of that."

"Why prate, then? Ha! they see the storm now. Look! The rocket. Now for an answer."

He took a lighted torch from Jones, and, setting fire to a rocket, sent it whizzing upward. Then he kindled the pile of torches.

"Now," he said, savagely, "let them come. The death light is near, and they must strike the rock. How gallantly she sails."

The desperate crew shrunk from the more desperate man, who, with the fiery torch above his head, watched the lurid death pyre glow.

Not a word was spoken.

Ralph threw fresh torches on the beacon as ever and anon it sunk.

All were listening for the crash they knew must come.

It came at last, and with the awful sound came Bentley's voice as he shrieked out his baffled rage. Ralph, the wrecker, laughed when he heard that.

Unmoved and pitiless, in spite of the despairing cries of anguish from the wreck. Ralph kept the beacon burning that he might see his victims die.

The storm lulled down.

The thunder rolled away.

The last gleam of lightning flashed out faintly in the spectral dimness. The gloom dispersed, and over the sky soft clouds began to drift.

The moon rode out in silvery majesty, and twinkling stars came out in glistening myriads to light the sorrowful night.

There lay the ship fast on the rock.

The water gushing through its broken side, and the poor sailors clinging to the spars. Their fruitless cries for aid met only mockery, and clinging until strength was gone, they were washed away, one by one, till of the many souls who some hours before were full of hopeful life, only three were left.

Bentley, Mr. Brocton, and his daughter Susan.

The wreckers saw all this, yet not one went forth in aid, though more than one staunch life-boat was at hand.

They wanted no witnesses to their dark work. No claimants for the cargo on the wreck.

Bentley had twined a rope round his arm, and bound himself securely to the helm.

Mr. Brocton had lashed his daughter and himself to the main-mast, but the rope was giving way, and he dared not move, lest it broke and launched them both into the ocean.

The "Sultan" had gradually turned over till it lay almost on its side, and a boat swinging by the chains rested within a yard of the water.

The merchant could not relieve himself without perilling the life of Susan.

He had hoped to be helped by those on shore, but now he saw the nature of the men, that hope perished.

"Bentley," he said, "have mercy on a father—save my child. Half the wealth that is here, my all, shall be yours, if you will save her."

"You forget the wreckers," said Bentley, grimly, "they look upon the prize as theirs already."

"Bentley, in the state-room there is a casket of diamonds worth a quarter of a million, you could hide it in your breast and the wretches on shore would not see it. Take it, then, and assist me to get the best and save Susan."

"We dare not venture to land."

"Why?"

"The wreckers would murder us."

"We could live in the boat till Heaven sent us aid."

"Could we," muttered the mate. "We will try, however; in the state room, say you?"

"A small morocco casket."

"Filled with diamonds worth a quarter of a million," said Bentley, in the same low, sinister tone. "Come, that is something; we will have this casket, and the boat."

He uncoiled the rope from his arm, and crept cautiously along the deck to the state room.

The luxurious furniture was piled in a confused heap, and some water had found its way in, but Bentley saw the casket.

"This, the boat, and Susan," he said, "and Bentley can begin life anew. The tiger of the sea

has not been heard of lately. Let us see if he can make up for lost time."

Creeping back as cautiously as he had descended, he reached the deck with the casket safe in his breast.

He had not forgotten other things—a small keg of wine and a case of delicate eatables, both of which he fastened to his waist by a belt.

Dropping keg and case into the boat, he got the oars ready, lowered the boat itself, and arranged the chain so that it could be cast off in an instant.

This done, he went to the mainmast.

Susan lay senseless, supported by her father's arm.

"How beautiful she is," said Bentley, gazing at the white, full breast displayed by the disordered dress her father had torn aside when he clutched it to save her from falling. "Limbs, too, such as would tempt a man to dare perdition, as I would, to possess her If I save her life, old man, will you give her to me?"

"My child to you!"

"Oh, you recoil because my skin is dusky; hers is fair, very fair. Would you rather see her die than in my arms?"

"A thousand deaths!" the merchant said, in horror.

"Then you shall not see it," said Bentley, as he deliberately cut the rope and hurled the old man overboard. "Adieu, Mr. Brocton; a pleasant voyage to eternity."

His mocking laugh was the last sound the merchant heard as the water gurgled in his ears, and he strove wildly to fight for life.

At that moment Susan recovered consciousness; she saw her father fall, and found herself in Benton's arms.

"Help!" she shrieked, "save him, Bentley!"

Without a word he threw her into the bottom of the boat, and leaping in after her, he set his foot on her breast to keep her down, then raised the oars and rode away.

"I shall be gentler soon," he said, his eyes lighting with a wolfish glow as, in her struggle to get free, she dashed the raiment from her limbs and left them bare; "but I cannot let you destroy yourself."

"My father, Bentley—do not let him die!"

"He can swim."

"Mercy! Why are you taking me from shore?"

"Wreckers are there," he said, "they would not spare you; they would not spare me."

In his face she saw the dark purpose of his soul.

The pirate had been her dread all the time they were at sea, for women are quick of instinct, and she knew how deep his passion was for her.

Rendered desperate by the thought, she made a plunge that freed her from the foot upon her panting breast.

Before he could drop his oar or stay her, she had jumped into the sea.

"Death with my father," she said, "not dishonour!"

The rapid element bore her away before Bentley could prepare to follow her.

When he turned he saw her father swimming by her side.

"Had I known the old man could swim," Bentley thought, "he should have gone into the sea with my knife in his heart."

"But I have not lost her yet," he added, drawing a pistol, and taking aim at Brocton; "he will not swim so well with a bullet through his head."

"Heaven preserve us!" the merchant prayed, seeing Bentley aim; "an assassin in the water, wreckers on land, we have not much hope."

Susan was too brave and true to endanger her one's life by losing courage; he told her to remain quite quiet, and to keep her hands beneath the water, trusting all to him; she did so.

And succour came.

The first part of this incident had not been seen by the wreckers on the cliff. The position of the wreck hid the boat and its occupants from view.

But as the boat veered round the wreckers saw it. They saw Bentley, and they saw the merchant and his child.

"They must not live!" said Ralph, the wrecker, levelling a gun; "one witness would be fatal to us all."

He fired at the merchant, but missing him, the ball struck the pistol from Bentley's hand.

"They must not live!" echoed a stern voice behind him. "Pitiless hound—brutal, cowardly ruffian!"

Ralph faced round like a wolf.

"S'death!" he said, "this business is mine; on your life, do not interfere with me!"

"On my life! Why, were you a thousand men in one, did your wretched crew outnumber the stars, Tom Drake would face them and defy them all!"

"I have said," he exclaimed, his clear voice ringing over the water, "that this foul, murderous sacrifice of life should not be. Hark! every one; stand by me those who will, and down with all who keep to the wreckers!"

"Down with Tom Drake!" shouted Ralph, "the buccaneer and the spy!"

"Liar," said Captain Tom, "I am a buccaneer, but no spy or wrecker—stand by me you who know me!"

Nearly half the wreckers withdrew from the rock; their hearts were not in the brutal work to which Ralph had tempted them, and now, rallying round the gallant buccaneer, they cried—

"Hurrah for Captain Tom!"

"Hurrah for Ralph, the wrecker!" cried the rest, and, encouraged by the cry, Ralph dashed at his antagonist.

Their swords were out; it took Tom but an instant to beat his foeman back and strike him down; then he leaped into the sea to rescue the merchant and his daughter.

Red Ralph rose. He saw how the appearance of Tom Drake had divided his band, and, smothering his hate, he said—

"Let him have the old man and the girl, we will have the plunder of the wreck. To the boats, then, before we have the coast-guard down upon us!"

His comrades rushed to the boats, and rowed towards the wreck.

Captain Tom swam bravely for the merchant, who was growing faint by this time, and had hardly strength to keep himself and child afloat.

Bentley was already out of sight—he did not care to trust himself with the wreckers.

Some of the men who had declared themselves in favour of Tom Drake moored a boat and followed, with some of Captain Tom's crew, as he swam, to render assistance in the rescue. The aid was timely; Mr. Brocton and his daughter sank when he was about ten yards from them.

He saw Susan throw up her arms, and, following their gleam, dived.

Had he been a minute later, they must have drowned; as it was, he brought Susan to the surface; her father, when he found he could no longer swim, had forced her hold away.

Otherwise she would have clung to him and both been lost.

"Captain Tom is a brave fellow," said one of the men who had followed him.

"He wants to save them, and he has saved one; here goes for the other."

The speaker threw himself headlong into the deep; he could dive well, and caught the merchant, who was rising then for the last time.

They were picked up by the boat—Captain Tom with Susan, the wrecker with her father.

Bentley, the mate, saw this while out at sea, and from the bottom of his soul cursed the men who had saved and won what he had lost.

"I wonder what the wreckers would say if I were to go back and ask for my share," he thought. "The shot that saved the old man came from Red Ralph, I think. I shall thank Red Ralph some day."

Bentley rested on his oars, smiling his dark demoniac smile; he was thinking, but though he smiled, his thoughts were deadly.

"These men—these wreckers, are cowards," he scliloquised. "They are brave only when together; but singly, have no courage. They are greedy, too; and not one would stay on the wreck while the others went ashore with the plunder. Now, I know the vessel better than they do. It has a secret hold, in which there is much rare storage. It would, I think, be worth my while to wait. There would, perhaps, be something left for me."

While Captain Tom went on shore with the maiden and her father, and while the wreckers were seeking out their plunder, Bentley rowed leisurely back. The sea was calm, and Bentley was smiling. He did not smile for nothing; he was thinking of the future, not the past. He gave no single thought to the brave young captain who had gone overboard with such a deep red gash on his brow.

CHAPTER CXXIV.
THE BATTLE IN THE CAVE.

WHEN Susan Brocton came to herself, she was lying on a locker in a cave-like chamber.

A tender hand had spread for her a couch of strange materials—rich furs and silken shawls having been placed for her tired, delicate form, and for her head a delicate roll of tawny sable.

The cave had no inhabitant, save herself.

A silver lamp hung from the roof, burning low.

The lamp was of antique shape, and quaintly fashioned.

The sides being fretted with innumerable perforations, through which the mellow light softened with beautiful effect.

Susan rested her arm upon the pillow, and looked around.

She felt no fear.

There was in her heart the memory of a fine young face.

Some such a one as in her love-dreams she had seen.

There was in her heart the music of a voice which had told her not to fear, and he who said this had saved her from the deep, and he had saved her father, too.

But the face.

She could shut her eyes, and conjure it back.

Its every noble lineament a charm; the deep and gentle hazel eyes; the rich crest of dark curls, like a coronet upon a kingly brow; the full red lips just shadowed by a silky line of jet; and all the countenance subdued.

It was pleasant to think that he, the owner of this face, had saved her, and placed her where she was now.

So pleasant, that the thinking of it tranquillised her troubled spirit, and she went to sleep again.

The door was softly opened, and the figure of a man crept in stealthily on tiptoe.

He did not come with cruel or unholy purpose, or her guardian angel would have warned her and awakened her.

He came to look upon the lovely being he had rescued, and, as he gazed, the hushed, mute softness of his eyes told an admiration almost wonderment.

"How beautiful she is," thought Captain Tom. "So pure, so trusting, and so tranquil in her childlike loveliness. How I could love her if I dared! how cherish her if the happiness were mine!"

She was beautiful indeed, and more than beautiful in the unconscious graces of her repose.

The Indian sun had given a warm glow to her cheek, and developed to the full her figure.

Its richness of outline and length could be seen through her closely-clinging garments.

She looked like the living statue of a slumbering Venus, draped like a Vestal with such drapery as did not hide her form.

Captain Tom had taken her father to the outer cave, having, with delicate forethought, considered it necessary that Susan should have a female attendant, and be alone while she changed her clinging garments.

There was a girl among the smuggler crew, a pretty, bright-eyed maiden, who had been saved from a wreck years ago, and having no friends or kindred in the world, she chose to stay with the rough set who had rescued her.

They called her Sweetheart Loo.

Loo was the pet of all, but especially of him who had brought her to land.

This was a Titanic fellow, by name Black Bill, a great, kind-hearted smuggler, who was the terror of the revenue men.

So terrible he was when roused, but so generous and peaceable by nature that he could not harm a child.

But for him, Sweetheart Loo would not have lived in safety with the crew of desperados. Her pretty face and supple form were more than they could resist, but the fate of one man who insulted her had been a caution to the rest.

The smugglers were away on an expedition once, and a wretch, who had sworn that Loo should be his, stayed behind that he might consummate his dastard purpose.

He found the girl alone, helpless, and she must have been his victim had not Black Bill returned.

Black Bill dashed him down, bound him hand and foot, and waited for the others to come back.

When they came, he said:

"Wreckers! if one of you had a treasure—something for which you had risked your life—something that you saved—and one of your comrades turned traitor, what would you do?"

"Turned traitor!"

"Sought to destroy your treasure—rob it of its beauty—render it worthless!"

"Kill him!"

"Well, see yon shrinking coward, who let us go to win a prize in which he would share, while he stayed behind to rob me of my treasure. You know what I mean. Sweetheart Loo; our pet—who loves us all, and whom I love dearer than aught else in the world."

"Kill him! kill him!"

And Black Bill dragged the traitor from his corner.

"Kneel," he said; "pray!"

The wretch shrieked for mercy.

"Pray!" said the stern, pitiless voice, and the smuggler's keen sword gleamed above his head. "You have one minute more to live!"

The traitor could not pray; he only shrieked

for mercy till the time was up, when Black Bill's sword, descending, swept his head off at a blow.

They cast trunk and head into the sea; from that time no man dared molest Sweetheart Loo.

This was the girl whom Captain Tom went to call, but, pausing ere he went, returned to Susan.

She lay so still that, but for the gentle heaving of her breast, he might have thought her dead.

Her lips were slightly parted, showing a pearly line of teeth, and Captain Tom bent low to listen for her breath.

Drawn irresistibly towards her, his lips sought and clung to hers in a long, passionate kiss; his heart thrilled, for, beyond a doubt, her lips gave back his caress.

She had been dreaming that he came into the cave, that he kissed her as he did—and waking, found her dream was true.

"Where am I?" she murmured.

"Safe, dear lady."

"I remember now. The wreck. Bentley. You saved us."

"I did, thank Heaven."

"Surely you are not one of the evil men who set the death light on the cliff, and wrecked my father's ship?"

"Lady," he said, gravely, "I am not a wrecker. Had I come in time, the evil would not have been done?"

"My father. Where is he?"

"Quite safe. You shall see him soon; but your dress is wet, and must be changed. I will send a girl to you with fresh apparel. When you are ready, I will take you to your father."

"Generous friend! How can I thank you?"

"Give me your faith; trust in me."

"Is there any danger, then?"

"The worst; but none so bad that I cannot save you. We will not say more now. When you are attired, I will come again."

He opened another locker, and took from it some garments such as an Eastern queen might have worn with pride.

"Wear these," he said. "I will send Loo to you. Should anything occur, call for me—Tom Drake."

He pressed his lips to her head, and left the cave to go in quest of Sweetheart Loo.

Susan watched him go, and sat in meditation long after he was gone.

Had she been dreaming, or was that caress real?

Did he—her rescuer and her champion—love her?

How noble he was, with that handsome face and gallant form.

The fine, tender voice, and gentle eye.

He was no common one amid the horde of desperadoes.

There was command in every gesture; he had the aspect of a chieftain.

Wondering what would be the end of the strange adventure, she rose, and prepared to lay aside her wet attire, when she heard voices in the adjoining cave.

"They must not live!" said one, in deep, savage tones. "They know too much, for the old man saw the beacon, and it seems the ship belongs to him. What say you, mates, are we to be ruled by Captain Tom?"

There was a silence.

"Recollect what he has said—that he will have no wrecking, no plunder taken, no women touched. He means to give the old man back all we have saved of the cargo, and keep the girl for himself. Shall it be so?"

"No! Hurrah for Ralph, the wrecker!"

"Hurrah for plunder and beauty. Join shares for the booty, and a lottery for the girl."

HAVING SECURED THE ROPE, CAPTAIN TOM BEGAN HIS PERILOUS DESCENT.

Faint and sick with terror, Susan rushed back to the locker, and threw herself upon it. She closed her eyes as the door opened, and Red Ralph the wrecker entered, followed by his band.

The poor girl shuddered, as the ruffian approached her. She gave a thrilling cry, as he put his arm round her waist, to drag her from the locker.

"Help!" she said. "Save me! Tom! Tom Drake!"

"Shriek your heart out. He dares not come. Call again if you like. You are mine."

"Help!" she shrieked again. "Save me! Tom! Tom Drake!"

Red Ralph the wrecker laughed.

"Keep the door, mates," he said, "he dares not come."

"Liar!" thundered the gallant buccaneer, as leaping into the cave, he smote down the foremost one who stood in his way, and, with his red sword reeking, confronted the savage horde.

"Look!" he said, setting his foot upon the body of the man through whom his sword had gone. "Mark me, Red Ralph! Touch this girl with but a finger, sully her with but a glance, and by the spirit of the storm, I send a bullet crashing through your brains!"

His face was not gentle now. There was a set resolution on his lip. A death-fire in his eye. The sword he held was dropping blood upon the fallen man. His left hand held a pistol levelled in a steady line for Red Ralph the wrecker's head.

He stood quite motionless.

Every muscle and fibre of his form strung into a stillness, statuesque.

Half crouching.

But erect he was. But like a panther ready to bound amidst, and rend his hunters.

The wreckers knew this man, they had heard of his daring deeds and bold exploits on the high seas long before he came amongst them.

They knew that when stung by a coward act—when his fiery blood was up, and thrilling in electric power through his veins, he was a very demigod of death.

No mercy then for the foes.

A word, a motion, would set him at work, and then woe to any who dared stand before him!

He had the strength and courage of a lion, and when he was as he was now, he had all a lion's thirst for blood.

His dark eye naturally burned, as it ran down the red glitter of his sword, and thence to the faces of the foe.

"This cave is mine," he said, "all here is sacred, and she is sacred, most of all. I have sworn she shall be unmolested, and she shall—listen to me. Let what I say now suffice to tell what I mean."

Not a breath broke the silence as he spoke. Not a man moved a step forward.

His pistol kept its deadly line with Red Ralph's brow; and Ralph knew that to make a hostile motion would be to die.

Susan lay upon the locker, watching with intense interest the scene going on between her champion and the wrecker.

Her heart beat high for his sake; but it did not beat with fear.

He stood like a monarch, before whom brave men shrunk and quailed.

"You know me, one and all," he said; "have heard of me in the battle and the storm. Is there one who can say I ever shrunk when outnumbered or in peril?"

No one spoke.

"As I have been true to my men, as I have fought by their side, been ever faithful to my comrades' welfare, suffered captivity, lain long in dungeons, and sworn to die, rather than betray my mates—as I have been just, never taking an atom more than my share, never being cruel, cowardly, or treacherous. So I ask you to use me now, if I am to be your captain. We are outlaws, desperate men, linked together in the common cause that has set the world against us, and us against the world; but should we be miscreants to shed innocent blood, monsters to outrage helpless women, assassins to destroy the ocean traveller, when by fighting as smugglers and buccaneers, we can grow rich!"

A faint cheer answered this.

"Make it a question of death, the jeopardy of tempest, and if we face them as smugglers, I am with you; make it a question of brutal cowardice, be with Red Ralph in the wreckers' cruel iniquity, and I am your foeman to the death.

"I hate the law, as you do. I see no crime in trading with the world's produce. What we gain is ours. The wealth of the world is ours. We owe no duty to the Government; and I will fight against their oppression to the death."

"Hurrah for Tom Drake! A cheer for Captain Tom!"

"Hurrah!"

"Smugglers or wreckers, then—what is it to be henceforth?"

"Smugglers, not wreckers. Hurrah!"

"Thanks. I knew my comrades were brave and true. I know Red Ralph has tempted you to his dirty work. He calls himself your captain; yet I was chosen. Choose between us now."

"Captain Tom! Hurrah for Captain Tom!"

"Thanks again, my friends. But stay. Make no rash choice, but have good cause why I, and not he, should be your chieftain. Where there are two claimants for leadership, the question should be decided by the two. Let us try which is the better man—foot to foot, sword to sword."

The challenge suited well the lawless men.

"A duel!" they said, and drew back to make room as the gallant buccaneer put his pistol in his belt and stepped forward to meet Red Ralph, the wrecker.

"A fight," Ralph said, his dark brows knitted close, and in his scowl a desperate desire to kill. "No quarter! no mercy!—a battle to the death!"

"Come on!" Tom said; "a battle to the death!" Their weapons crossed.

Red Ralph could use his blade, as he had shown in many a fray; but Captain Tom was matchless.

The wrecker's powerful form towered above his young antagonist's head; he bared his brawny arm to the shoulder, and his huge blade, sweeping round, seemed as though it must cleave his opponent down.

But Captain Tom did not give way an inch. He, too, had bared his arm, and, though he had not such muscle as had Red Ralph, his wrist was supple, and his sinews were of steel.

He met, and turned aside the mighty blow, then, cool and fearless, began his own brilliant sword play; his weapon clung like a glittering serpent to the other, and Red Ralph, with all his strength, could not beat it down.

His eyes shot fire, and his breath came hot, yet Captain Tom set a steady glance upon him, and used his sword with a skill next to instinct.

"Count twenty," he said, quietly, to one of the men, "and as you speak the last word, I will break his sword."

He never moved his foot from where he placed it first—never sought to avoid the other's deadly lunges by stepping back; but with his supple body, and incomparable skill, defended his life; he did not speak again after asking the man to count, only watched Red Ralph's fiery eye, and smiled to see that what he had said excited Red Ralph the more.

Wondering whether he could do so much, one of the men began to count.

He reached number fifteen, and as yet Tom Drake had not a mark, while the wrecker had two wounds, each of which might have been his death, had the young buccaneer chosen to send his weapon in.

Then, as the man spoke fifteen, Red Ralph bounded backwards and forwards, with his sword-hilt grasped in both hands.

"Die!" he said, with a savage cry.

Down came the weapon; the keen edge descending like a flash of lightning direct for the smuggler's head.

The spectators held their breath.

The man stopped counting at seventeen, expecting to see Captain Tom stretched bleeding at their feet.

The terrific descent was guarded with only a faint clash, and as Red Ralph recoiled from the force of his own blow, Tom Drake said—

"Count."

CHAPTER CXXV.

THE PHANTOM OF THE WRECK.

THE wrecker came at him again! Savage—mad, at being baffled with such careless, fearless grace. Eighteen! a fearful lunge from Red Ralph. Nineteen! and it was parried; a sudden quickening of Captain Tom's eye, then a cling of sword to sword—a gleam—a clash—and as the men said twenty, the wrecker's blade fell shivered to the hilt, broken like a strip of glass.

Captain Tom was master of the smugglers now; he had proved his right to the title beyond all dispute.

Red Ralph, vanquished, and at the mercy of his antagonist, crossed his arms upon his breast, and sullenly awaited the expected blow; disarmed and helpless, he said a savage oath, and exclaimed—

"Strike!"

The crew thought then to see the victor's weapon buried in the wrecker's heart; but gallant Tom Drake was not the man to slay a fallen enemy.

Taking the sword in his left hand, he held out his right, and said—

"No. I like living friends better than dead foes; if you had beaten me, and let me live, I should have accepted the defeat, and acknowledged you my captain; can you do the same?"

"Curse you, no! Strike, if you like. I hate you!"

"Shame!" said the men; "Captain Tom speaks fairly—take his hand!"

"May my own wither if I do! He can kill me if he likes. The humiliation of this defeat will eat my very vitals out till I have had revenge."

Tom Drake, the new captain of the smugglers, pointed sternly to the entrance of the cave.

"Go," he said; "be my foe if it so please you; but remember, I shall not spare you twice."

With another savage oath, Red Ralph was about to depart, when Captain Tom said—

"Stay!"

The wrecker turned.

"Go," said Captain Tom, "it is your choice, and take it; from this time hence you are not one of us. Go your own dark way, like the selfish, sullen dog you are. You would betray us if you dared. I believe there is no danger of that, or I would kill you. Go! it is by your own act you forfeit all right to participate in our peril and our gain; it is by your own act I send you forth an outcast. No treachery with me; no mutiny or wrecker's work. I can be merciful, but as surely as you give me cause you shall die."

Red Ralph left the cave.

"Devils and tempests!" he said, fiercely, "you shall not triumph long, Ralph the wrecker is not known yet. There is a demon raging in my breast for revenge, and though I devote my lifetime to it, and send my own soul to perdition, that revenge shall come!"

Captain Tom watched him out with a stern, deep smile of scorn.

"That man will die a dog's death," he said, "and so will all who follow him. Some of you would be in for it already, if it were told how the 'Sultan' was lured on to the rock."

"Hush, captain!" said one of the men; "the lady!"

"She knows it; but, for my sake, will say nothing. Neither will her father, whose ship it was. So now, lads, to the boats, and save what you can. Do all you can in atonement for the cruel massacre of life."

"Mind," he added, as the men went out, "let everything be brought in honestly. You caused the wreck. Do not rob the merchant of his cargo. We shall find him generous in reward; and a guinea given is better than a sackful stolen. The man who holds back a single article shall die as a mutineer!"

Captain Tom knew the men he had to deal with. They went forth as obedient as children.

"Strike me, Joe!" said Jem Chivery, with a solemn face, "that was a rattling fight, warn't it?"

"It were. Did you cotch what Red Ralph, the long-shore lubber, the blood-red vampire, said, when he got the licking?"

"Didn't I? He said as how the humili— something would eat his vittles out. I didn't see it go down his throat!"

"See what?" asked Joe Chiggler.

"The humili— What was it?"

"Hation," said Joe, who thought he knew. "Don't you see what he meant by that?"

"No. Do you?"

Joe scratched his head.

"Why—don't you see?—it means as how, when he gets a licking, it sticks in his gizzard, like."

"Then he ought to bolt it," said Jem Chivery, "like I did the pigtail baccy when the coastguard collared me. About a pound and a half there was; full flavoured. Measured over a yard."

"And you swallowed it?"

"Every inch, and bit off the last little bit for a quid."

"What a thundering cram!" said Joe.

"Do you mean to say it ain't true?"

"Get out, you big liar! How could you get it out again?"

"Why," said Jem Chivery, "I swallowed a pipe, and smoked it."

Joe was so exasperated by the wilful falsehood, that he stroked Jem down the long nose.

Jem, who was about to shift his quid, sacrificed a chew or so, for the pleasure of sending the whole lot into Joe's eye.

Then they had a fight, and kicked each other.

It was singular to mark the different influence exercised by Tom Drake, to the influence exercised by Red Ralph the wrecker.

The latter had made his men a set of savages, furious and untamed as breath of fury.

Now they quite changed.

Red Ralph had invited them to lure a vessel to destruction, for the sake of plunder.

Yet, at Tom Drake's command, they were going quietly to save the cargo, and were reconciled to the idea of seeing it given up to the lawful owner.

"It seems rather hard," said Jem, chewing, "to give up the swoop, as we goes to get it."

"Better let Tom Drake hear you say so," suggested Joe Chiggler, dryly.

"Did you ever notice those pistols of his'n?"

"Them handsome ones with the gold mountings. I knows."

"Well. They never misses. Do you mind when he shot the executioner."

"Not one of us ever forgot it," said Bob Hauler. "Tom Drake is the best and bravest man as ever trod a quarter-deck, and I should like to see the one as would say he wasn't. See what a glorious deed it was for him to run his brig right into the fort as he did. They were going to hang me over the sea, the warmints was, when I was captured by the King's men, and the rope was round my neck, I felt gone when the hangman went to drop the rope over my head, swinging me off, and when just as he got his foot to the board, a bullet went right through his head."

"Leap," I heard a voice say, "right into the sea! I am here!"

"And there, sure enough, he was. Tom Drake with his beautiful little brig. So I took the leap into the sea. The boat was waiting. They picked me up, and were away before a single gun could be brought to bear on us."

"We all liked him when we heard of his brave acts," said one of the smugglers. "I don't know how it was that Red Ralph turned our heads. He promised such a lot somehow, and was such a demon, that he had it all his own way. There ain't one of us but what would have gone with Cap'n Tom Drake afore, if we'd only had the chance."

"I'm glad he got a licking," said Jem, meaning Red Ralph. "We know who is captain now."

"And we've got the best one. Something like a captain, too. Why, Captain Tom would run his little brig right through the revenue fleet."

"He has done so. See how he brought that cargo of silk from France, and a Government schooner waiting for him all the while."

"And didn't he bilk the skipper of the schooner? He went on board as a French Customs' officer, Captain Tom did, and told the skipper to keep a sharp look-out, because Tom Drake, the buccaneer, was expected to run a cargo in that night.

"'Trust me,' says the skipper. 'He won't escape this time.' And he tells Captain Tom just what they are going to do to make sure of him.

"'Dine on my yacht,' says Captain Tom.

"'Thank you, no,' says the skipper; 'he might run by, meanwhile.'

"Captain Tom didn't press it. He had the brig trimmed yacht-fashion then, and away he sails, leaving the skipper looking out for him."

A dozen such anecdotes were related by Jerry and Bob, with pride, all more or less true, by the time the smugglers reached the shore.

The sea was almost calm again. The stars were out, but the sky had once more darkened, and a second storm seemed threatening.

The smugglers consulted before they put out; some were afraid, but the bolder overruled their fears; yet the most desperate shrank from the thought of going to the wreck, lest the spirits of the many they had slain should haunt it still.

No rough jokes were made, no stories told. Every tongue was silent, for the wind began to howl, and to their guilty ears its howling sounded like the death cries of their victims.

"It's an awful night," said one, shuddering as he spoke. "I wish we had not joined Red Ralph in his work. We've got nothing by it, and many a poor fellow's curse will come to us from his ocean grave."

A pale corpse floated past the boat just then. Its pallid face and staring eyes seemed to look reproachfully at the crew.

Every swarthy face went pale.

"Well, mates," said one of the smugglers, "we must not go back like cowards, empty-handed, to be laughed at; but this job over, you won't catch me at wrecker's work again. Smuggling I don't mind. There's some excitement in the moonlight run, and perhaps a fight with the revenue men. We seem to earn what we get then; but wrecking—not for me."

"Nor for me," said the rest, one after the other. "It's Red Ralph's fault. I should not have been sorry if Captain Tom had killed him."

"Nor should I."

"Nor I."

"Nor I," echoed the rest; and then no more was said till they were near the wreck.

The "Sultan" had struck in such a manner that the wash of the sea only fixed her more firmly on the rock.

When they were near, a faint blue light, glimmering through the darkness, startled all. Each looked awe-stricken at the other.

The light faded, reappeared again, and faded.

"It's a death light!" whispered one. "Let us go back!"

"See," said another; "now it comes again on the wreck. Let us go back."

"Death light or not, I don't go back," said Joe Chiggles. "I've seen such lights many a time."

"What makes it?"

"Don't know; but I ain't afraid of it."

His courage shamed the others from their cowardice. He was first to climb the wreck, and the rest followed him.

One then lit a torch.

The ship was very dark, and its deadened silence was oppressive.

Joe Chiggles had to lead the way, or none would have ventured into the hold where the valuable cargo was stored.

Part of the hold was full of water.

They had to go round to the side that lay uppermost on the rock.

Suddenly the torch went out, and a loud cry of terror went from lip to lip.

The man who had carried the light crept close among his comrades, and said it had been snatched from his hand.

"Kindle another," said Joe Chiggles. "You dropped it in your fright. Kindle another, and give it to Jack."

He was obeyed.

A second torch was lit. At that moment a hollow, horrible laugh sounded near.

"Who was that?" asked Joe.

"Not me, I swear!" said each, and a sweat of terror started on every brow.

"Forward with the torch, Jack!" exclaimed Joe. "This is some trickery to frighten us."

Jack went forward to the further and darker end of the hold.

The cargo lay piled there in heaps.

The horrible laugh was heard again.

It was no human voice, and the men retreated, not daring to go further.

In vain Joe urged them on. The second torch went out as suddenly as the other, and the wreckers heard an awful cry from Jack.

"The phantom!" he shrieked. "The black phantom! Take the water! Mercy! mercy!"

"Another light!" shouted Joe. "Let us seek out this devilish mystery."

He lit a third torch, but, before this could be done, the cries and shrieks of Jack became so awful that the weaker fled.

Joe Chiggles and his mate, Jem Chivers, alone had courage to stay, but the gloom was so intense they could see nothing.

Jack's cries grew faint. He seemed to be battling in desperate terror with some terrible foe.

Shriek after shriek, but low and muffled, now rang through the hold, and as they crossed, a heavy form was hurled at the buccaneer's feet.

Again that awful laugh, and Joe, throwing the glare of his torch upon the object at his foot, saw a sight whose horror haunted him to his dying day.

It was Jack, dead—strangled; his neck wrung, and his head wrenched round as by a demon's hand.

Nothing less than some demoniac thing could have left those blue and livid marks so deeply in his twisted throat.

CHAPTER CXXVI.

CAPTAIN TOM'S PERIL.

The defeat of Red Ralph at the hands of the bold buccaneer had raised a demon in the wrecker's breast.

The man had a vindictive and passionate nature.

He hated all who were better and more successful than himself.

The bitterest part of his mortification was that in so brief a time he had lost command of the buccaneers, his anticipated share of his plunder from the wreck, and Susan, the merchant's daughter.

"An outcast from the band," he muttered

savagely; "kicked out like a beaten one, and all through him, a stranger, who stole amongst us like a spy. A hundred curses blight him. My soul will gnaw itself in agony until I have revenge!"

A light footfall sounding behind him caused him to turn, and he beheld a slight form, that seemed at first a boy.

His eyes sparkled with malignant satisfaction.

He hated the buccaneers everyone now, and he knew that by no act of malice could he touch them so keenly as by doing harm to the figure before him, Sweetheart Loo.

Red Ralph stole a cautious look around.

He was near the sea shore now, and in a lonely place close by his own dwelling.

His voice vibrated huskily with an evil thought, as he said—

"Whither away, Loo?"

"Homeward, Ralph."

"Stay awhile for me."

"Are you going my way?'

"Yes."

"Then I will take another road," she said laughing, as she stepped lightly out of his path. "You look too full of mischief, Ralph; and I feel safer in my own company."

Her act exasperated him, while her musical tone fired his blood.

She was a pretty-faced creature, agile and graceful as a tigress, and her beauty lost nothing of its charm by her picturesque attire.

She wore a smuggler's frock with a sash, showing at once the fullness of her bust and her slender waist.

Her form, though slim, was powerful, her lips round and large, as were her legs, which her dress did not hide.

A dashing pair of boots fitting closely to her little feet and reaching nearly to the knee, threw out in striking relief the beauty of her limbs to where the frock concealed them.

Her frock itself was not low in the skirt, and kept her neck bare to the swell of her white breast.

She wore her hair in short black curls, and a Greek cap set on her fine brow like a coronet.

"So you think I mean mischief, do you?" he asked, trying to speak gently, and trying also to keep his fiery eyes from the lithe form he longed to clasp. "Why is that, Loo?"

"Why, I see it in your face."

"Do I look fierce?"

"Very."

"Kiss me, then, and that will charm the demon out."

"Will it?" she said, with a saucy laugh. "If the demon waits till I charm it out that way—"

"Well!"

"He will wait long enough."

"He will not, exclaimed Ralph, catching her by the arm, as she was about to slip past him. "You don't suppose a man can be a saint, with such a pretty little wench as you continually before him. Come with me."

Loo gave a low cry of terror.

He had picked her up in his arms like a child, and was taking her to his cottage.

"Look here," he said, setting her down, and placing his strong arm on her shoulder. "I've got the devil in me, Loo; and it all depends on how you answer me how I serve you. I have borne a good deal to-day—more than I shall forget or bear again. Now, I like you, and don't want to hurt you."

Sweetheart Loo was accustomed to some rough play from the buccaneers now and then, but they never went so far as to kiss her, or to lay a hand upon her against her will.

Clearly, then, Red Ralph was going too far.

He meant mischief.

She saw it in the burning fire of his eye, heard it in the husky thickness of his voice; and her position was one of no ordinary peril.

She was with him quite alone in his solitary cabin, where nothing could be heard save the hoarse roar of the ocean, and there was no other human habitation within sight.

Loo was so used to wander about by herself, that she never thought of fear.

The buccaneers, to a man, would as soon have thought of plunging headlong into the sea as of hurting her.

Ralph was the one exception; and her instinct had always warned her to be careful of him.

He was the last person she expected to meet at the present time, for she thought he was away at the wreck; but here she was, and in his power.

It needed all her nerve and wit to keep her out of danger.

But Sweetheart Loo was equal to most emergencies.

She saw that he needed some sort of provocation before he became absolutely dangerous.

Bad as he was, he was not bad enough to take advantage of her in cold blood.

A little thought prompted her how to act.

The most essential thing was that she must not seem to be afraid, or to suspect his real intention.

"I think you are very rude," she said, looking into his dark face; "and if you ever do it again, I shall tell Captain Tom."

That was the worst thing she could have said.

"Curse Captain Tom!" he said, with a bitter oath. "Don't say his name to me, girl, or it will be worse for you."

"Ralph!"

"Sit down. By all the furies, I hear of nothing but him! His name is on every tongue, and you all worship him as much as you hate me."

"I do not hate you, Ralph."

"So much the better."

"What has Captain Tom done to you?"

"That for which I should like to cut his heart out. That for which I should like to set my foot upon his throat and crush him. That which will rob me of sleep and rest till I have had such revenge as will not leave much left of him!"

"Ralph, what has he done?"

"Baffled me, despised me, beaten and disgraced me before my comrades, hunted me from the crew, made me an outcast, left the mark of his sword in my body, and the shame of it severing my soul. S'death! the thought of it is torture!"

"Did you quarrel with him?"

"I did," Ralph answered, with a savage laugh; "he contested my claim—my right, to be obeyed as chief. S'death! why, it was I who made the crew what they are."

"And he would make them different?"

"He prates like a chaplain about honour and mercy. Tells the men there is sin in assisting the tempest in its work. I hate him."

Sweetheart Loo knew that.

"Did you fight?"

"We did."

"Fairly."

"Fairly—he is a demon at it. I have held my arm against better men; but he treated me as though I were an angry boy, and he a Colossus."

"Do you hate him because he conquered you?"

"Take care, girl; do not mock me."

He strode to and fro on the floor like a hungry beast of prey waiting to spring upon and destroy his victim. Loo put her hands into the pockets of her frock.

"I don't mock you," she said, "and it is getting late, Red Ralph. I am going."

Stay."

"No."

In each pocket she had a pistol, pretty ornamental things, both; but each carried a tolerable charge of powder and a quarter of an ounce of lead.

When she said "No," she stood erect and faced him.

"No!" he echoed, fiercely. "Do you defy me, too?"

"I am not your slave, Red Ralph, because you are brute and coward enough to keep me here alone. I am not afraid of you."

"Take care, girl."

"Of what?"

"If you make me angry, it will be your own fault. All have turned against me, even the comrades I thought cared for me; and I am going away."

"Where?"

"Where there is wealth to be won, a wild life to be led, daring adventure, and rich reward. People who have spurned Red Ralph the wrecker shall dread the buccaneer. What say you, Loo? You have a fearless heart. Wilt come with me?"

He had stepped over and faced her.

"By the saints of perdition, so I am. Listen, Loo, I have a glorious idea."

She listened, thinking it might be something which to hear would be to benefit Captain Tom. She, like the rest, had taken a desperate fancy to the youth, and would have done anything to serve him.

"I am an outcast, and I shall not stay in a place where I am not wanted; but I will not go empty-handed."

Loo cocked her pistols in case she might want them suddenly.

"I have some few friends who will not desert me; they will accompany my expedition. There is the treasure of the wreck yet to come. There is a ship at leeward."

"A ship?"

"The 'Will-o'-the-Wisp.'"

"Captain Tom's vessel!" cried Loo, grasping her pistols tight.

"His if he can keep it; mine if I can get it, and I shall. With that, and a chosen crew, a few trusty hearts, and what may be left of the cargo of the wreck, we sail away—Red Ralph, the buccaneer, and you his bride. What say you?"

"I would not, if I dared," she answered, steadily, "and I dare not if I would."

"Dare not! Why?"

"Because of Black Bill, and every one. If you were to force me hence, they would follow; if you were to harm me, they would rend you limb from limb."

"If I were to force you hence, they would not find us. If I were to harm you, as you say, you would not tell them."

"Would I not?" she said, quietly; "I would, indeed; so now let me go, Red Ralph, and forget the nonsense you have been telling me."

She tried to pass him, but he held her back.

"It is not nonsense," he said. "I am going, and you with me."

"Keep your hands from me, Red Ralph, or I call for help."

"S'death, what care I! Let come who may, I have that which will stop him. You shall stay with me. If in the morning you are found here, it will be thought you stayed willingly."

A red flush mounted to her cheek.

The girl was pure of heart, though she had lived so long with lawless men.

"Red Ralph," she exclaimed, "you are a coward and a brute. Stand aside!"

And, much to his astonishment, a glittering pistol barrel flashed within an inch of his eye.

"S'death!" he said, savagely.

And then he said no more, but sprung forward to clutch her by the arm.

Her little finger tightened on the trigger; her eyes lit with a deadly flame.

"Red Ralph," she said, "for the sake of both of us stand back! I would not willingly do a desperate deed; but so surely as you move a step to touch me, so surely I send a bullet through your head."

In his fury, the wrecker would not pause, though he saw she was resolved; he tried to beat her arm down.

Then came a sharp report, an oath, a howl of fury, a blinding flash, and he staggered to the wall as she leaped out.

He was not wounded. Her pistol had no bullet in it, but the flash of powder had scorched his eyesight. Dashing away the tears that maddened him with pain, he too drew a pistol and followed Sweetheart Loo.

She was out of sight.

For nearly an hour the savage wrecker sought her on crag and beach, with murder, and worse than murder in his heart.

He saw her at last.

She was standing on a rock above the sea with Captain Tom; and when he saw them thus, Red Ralph the wrecker grasped his pistol by the barrel, and stole towards them like a stealthy tiger creeping to his prey.

CHAPTER CXXVII

A GALLANT RESCUE.

HAD not the shadow thrown by Red Ralph now caught his eye, the wrecker's pistol butt would have sunk buried in the gallant buccaneer's head.

The shriek startled Will.

Turning round he caught the traitor's descending arm.

"Coward!" he said, twisting the wrecker's wrist with giant's force. "Did I spare your life for this?"

"For this end I shall do it," returned Red Ralph, grimly; "your life or mine, Tom Drake! you will not leave the roof alive."

Sweetheart Loo gave a low cry of terror; the position of the two men was one of imminent peril.

They stood on a high precipice, within a yard of the edge, and a hideous depth beneath the wild sea roared; both were strong men, and each had the other gripped by the throat.

The pistol was useless; the grasp of Captain Tom had almost crushed the wrecker.

He held the weapon but could not use it; Sweetheart Loo dared not move to aid the brave young chieftain.

Unthinking of her own danger, she went back in expectant fear until her heel went over the rock.

Another inch, and she must have gone to eternity!

Her startled exclamation well nigh proved fatal to Tom Drake.

"Look!" said Red Ralph, with a demoniac smile, "she is falling."

Thrown off his guard by the remark, which Loo's exclamation made seem true, Tom Drake looked behind him.

On that instant the wrecker gave him a violent jerk, and one of the young buccaneer's feet went over the cliff.

"Die!" yelled Red Ralph, savagely.

"Not without you," replied Captain Tom, maintaining his hold. "We go together, Red Ralph, or you go alone."

The savage wrecker tried to get his teeth in Tom's arm.

Tom stopped him at that.

He raised his elbow, and made Red Ralph's teeth rattle by a blow under the chin.

The wrecker bit his lip with the pain, and backed a little.

That motion enabled Captain Tom to change the aspect of affairs.

He had the strength of a young gladiator, though Red Ralph was his superior in height and weight.

He was brave, and could forgive an enemy; but the dastardly attempt to assassinate him roused all the devil in his nature.

Loo had told him, too, of the wrecker's intended treachery towards her, and that made Tom more indignant than did the murderous attack upon himself.

Loo was safe.

She had recovered her footing, and moved from her dangerous proximity to the cliffs, where she watched with intense and terrified interest the progress of the struggle.

The combatants had changed places. It was Red Ralph now who stood with his back to the sea.

It was Red Ralph who was slowly yielding before the untiring strength that lasted longer and was greater than his own.

"Let go," Red Ralph said, hoarsely, and still striving, like a rabid dog, to bite the arm that held his throat. "Let go, or by the pit of darkness I will throw myself over with you!"

"Wait a bit!" said Tom Drake quietly. "I prefer to see you take the journey without my company—and you shall, too!"

"Never!"

Tom Drake said no more; speaking caused a waste of breath, and while he wasted breath he lost strength.

He wanted all his power to do what he intended.

His blood was up.

No mercy for the coward who would have struck him from behind.

Nothing but the utmost confidence and care could keep him from tumbling into the sea if Red Ralph went down.

Life was very precious to Tom Drake just now.

But Red Ralph fought like a warrior.

Reckless of his own existence, in his mad desire to gratify his hate, he only strove to drag his rival down that appalling way to eternity, caring nothing whether he himself went with him.

So, literally for his own safety, Tom Drake had to keep his face from death.

An awful struggle this in such a place.

The great veins on the wrecker's brow stood out like cords.

His breath came hot and quick.

There was a savage fire in his eyes.

The buccaneer's pressure on his throat was like a vice, but so was his upon the wrecker's.

And Tom Drake forced Red Ralph to his knee, hoping, by so doing, to break away.

He did not succeed.

Red Ralph clung to him like grim destruction.

"The bull-dog holds tight," he said, fiercely.

"But cannot bite," said Tom.

He had hardly spoken, when Red Ralph, who had risen, threw himself down again.

This time Captain Tom went with him.

Loo shrieked again with terror.

It was only by a miracle that both did not go headlong over, and had they gone they must, in falling, have struck her over, too.

The wrecker had the best of the fall.

Captain Tom's leg was bent under him, and the sharp, sudden pain forced him to release the wrecker's wrist.

Before he could rise, Red Ralph gave a savage shout, and struck heavily at the buccaneer's temple.

Tom saved himself from the full force of a blow that must have killed him had he received its weight.

As it was, the shock made him reel.

Red Ralph wrenched his throat from the hand upon it.

He was quite free now, and his foe was down, helpless for the moment.

"Now, who dies?" he said, setting the muzzle of his pistol right against the buccaneer's forehead. "Now!"

It seemed that the buccaneer's time had come.

There was the pistol at his brow.

The finger of his foe on the trigger.

Scarcely six inches between the iron of the muzzle and his brain.

"Now," laughed the wrecker, with brutal joy, "who conquers? Pant in your death agony, Tom Drake, for your time has come!"

"Liar!"

Sweetheart Loo spoke.

It was wonderful how her small fist could strike so hard, but it went with terrific force against the wrecker's ear, then both her little hands grasped his throat.

Red Ralph pulled the trigger. The barrel being jerked upward as he was dragged backward, sent the ball over, and not into the captain's skull.

Loo was in danger now.

More savage than ever at being baffled, the wrecker turned upon her. Threw her from him, then seized her by the neck and belt, and raised her in his powerful arms.

Raised above his head, he held her. Now to hurl her girlish form into the ocean.

Quite forgetting that Captain Tom was not dead, though the bullet going so near his head had stunned him for a minute.

The jeopardy of Sweetheart Loo roused him into action.

Leaping like a tiger upon Red Ralph, Captain Tom tore the trembling girl from him.

"Down," he said, "inhuman devil. Down."

A wild cry of hopeless agony rang out as hurled away by Captain Tom's hand, the wrecker rolled over the cliff.

Clutching madly as he went, shrieking as his hands vainly grasped the air, Red Ralph leapt through the night like a thunderbolt.

Headlong, and with a sudden plunge, he sank. The sea closed over its victim. Captain Tom stood triumphant on the rock above.

He had no just cause to feel sorry for what he had done, yet he felt regret when he saw a fellow creature go to what he thought must be certain death.

"It is horrible," said Sweetheart Loo with a shudder.

"His blood be upon his own head," said Captain Tom; "he, and not I, sought this."

The next instant, overcome by the tragic scene she had just witnessed, Loo fell fainting at the young buccaneer's feet.

The wild cry of the savage wrecker, as he was hurled over the precipice, brought a horde of his ruthless companions to the scene—men as savage as their ruffianly leader, thirsting to reek their vengeance upon the gallant buccaneer, who, by his own prowess, had made himself their chieftain, and frustrated their devilish work.

Captain Tom saw them coming at him with murder in their looks.

There was nearly a score of them, and he saw that he would have no chance of life to stand against them.

With the girl fainting at his feet, the savage wretches coming at him like a pack of wolves, Tom Drake saw no chance of escape but the foaming sea, and that was certain death.

Like a lion driven up into a corner, the brave buccaneer cast a wild look at his ferocious pursuers.

His life was in imminent jeopardy; he was meditating a leap into the sea, when he saw a coil of rope.

In a moment he made one end fast to the stump of an old tree; then, throwing the rest over the cliffs, he caught the girl up in his arms, and swung himself over the precipice.

He heard the savage voices of his pursuers as he slid down the rope, and he feared that they would cut it, and let him into the sea, before he reached the bottom.

He cared more for the brave girl who had saved his life than for himself, and, in his anxiety to protect her, he lost his hold, and slipped within an inch of the bottom of the rope.

As if Providence was watching over his welfare, raft from the late wreck glided over the water beneath him.

With a glad cry, he dropped upon it, as the wreckers above cut the rope.

Amongst the smugglers who stood, in breathless anxiety, watching his perilous descent, was Jerry Mizzen, who at once put off in a boat to render him assistance.

Several shots were fired at him from the wreckers above; but Captain Tom Drake was landed in safety with his fair burden, and a mighty shout from his bold buccaneers rent the air as he was led in triumph to his own abode in the cavern in the rocks.

When Red Ralph, the wrecker, went into the sea, he did not die.

Satan is kind to his own, and saved Red Ralph to do more devilry yet.

There were pieces of the wreck yet floating about.

One of these Red Ralph felt, and caught it as he rose.

It was a narrow chance; the height of the fall, and the shock with which his body met the water, nearly deprived him of breath. But he could dive and swim well.

When he found himself going, he had the presence of mind, even in that swift descent, to lock his hands together, and so he sank as though he had only taken a heavy leap into the waves.

He rose.

Blind with the spray, and bewildered by the fall, yet with sense enough to strike out like a swimmer.

The tide was with him—a slow, sluggish wash of wave that impelled him forward without drowning him.

He could not have sustained himself for any length of time, his heavy boots and clothing so encumbered him. But brave, with the desperate courage of an evil man, he kept himself calm, and made no more exertion than was absolutely wanted to keep him afloat.

Gradually as his clothes soaked, and his boots filled, he knew he must go down.

It was just when this conviction forced itself upon him, that he felt a broken spar.

To clutch this and put it fairly against his chest was an instant's work.

"Safe for a time," he thought, and still the sea washed him onward; "I can scarcely keep alive till I am picked up."

He shouted for help.

Only the echo of his voice went through the gloom.

Only the sea-gulls' shriek, and the dull murmur of the ocean answered him.

The night grew dark, and dense, and pitchy, and he in the gloom was drifting over the sea alone.

Whither?

He dared hardly ask; dared hardly think; but the reply was too terrible for his callous, savage soul.

To death; unless his iron frame would bear the inevitable fatigue of the night.

To death!

He tried to think which way he might be going; the thinking made him recoil shuddering from thought.

Judging by the way he had swam from the rock whence he had fallen, he must be going towards the wreck.

The wreck!

The shattered scene of the horrible catastrophe he had caused, the deserted hulk of the gallant ship out of which every human life had gone through his demoniac work.

The wrecker was not superstitious.

Yet the idea of being washed alongside the broken ship, caused a faint, strange emotion to creep through his brain.

What if some phantom of the many slain were to come from the slimy depths, and with its cold arm twined round his neck, take him down to perdition.

Horrible!

Was it fancy, or was there a pale, white form ahead, as in the shroud, gliding by his side.

He strained his sight to pierce the darkness, tried to see if there was ought besides the white froth of the waves.

There was.

Something near him.

A something in which he dared not look, with the murky moonlight showing the ghastly pallor of its brow.

A human form, dead, rigid, and with its garments clinging shroud-like to it, floating in the foam crests.

Lifting itself full length, rising and falling on the waves in sickening unison to his own motion as he swam.

His hair rose in terror.

He tried to swim away, but the motion of his body made a current that drew the dead thing after him.

Onward yet, still the spectral form by his side, or in his wake.

Sometimes it came against him, sullen and cold; and, driven to mad effort by the appalling haunting, he plunged forward, and got in advance.

Should he escape it?

For an instant it seemed likely.

In the next moment the clammy weight was on his legs, as though trying to bear him down.

In spite of even his desperate nerve, the horror was gradually overcoming him.

"Help!" he shrieked, despairingly. "Is it to be such a death for me? Help!"

No answer—only the echo floating far over the sea, waking the ocean birds from their sleep; only the dull murmur and the spectral form by his side.

He closed his eyes and swam blindly, pushing himself forward by using the broken spar like a paddle.

Suddenly it struck against a heavy, motionless object.

Red Ralph opened his eyes.

The dread companion of his midnight journey had disappeared.

But it had guided him to the wreck.

Faint, exhausted, and overcome, Red Ralph clung to a dangling rope his hand caught, when he struck out to catch at anything for safety.

The wreck, in spite of its horror, was a place of refuge.

Even had it unearthly inhabitants, it could not be more dangerous than the shore.

So he clung to the rope.

His eyes were half closed again, when he could have sworn he saw a faint light glimmering through the chinks of the shattered planks.

It was no fancy; the light was there, moving as though carried.

"Haunted or not," thought the daring wrecker, "demons or men, the night demon shall speak to me."

"Help!" he shouted.

The light flashed brilliantly, and a wild laugh answered him.

"Who asks help at the tiger's den?"

"I, a poor wretch dying for want of succour. If you be no phantom, help me, and I will help you to a glorious reward. I know where there are treasures hidden—thousands upon thousands in value; oh, help me!"

The same wild, devilish laugh was his reply; but the rope to which he clung was seized, and he drawn on to the wreck.

Staggering, he fell upon the deck, suspicion, wonderment, and joy, all blended in his face as he looked up.

Over him stood a figure with a blazing torch—a tall, powerful form, and the torch gleam lighting a swarthy face, magnificent in its beauty and devilry.

"The mate of the 'Sultan!'" shrieked Ralph, the wrecker. "The phantom! I slew him, and now he comes to haunt me!"

He sank back powerless.

"The mate of the 'Sultan,'" said the figure with the torch; "John Bentley, but not a phantom; the Tiger of the Sea is not killed so easily, he must work out his destiny before he dies."

His destiny!

CHAPTER CXXVIII.

THE MIDNIGHT BURIAL.

JOHN BENTLEY picked the huge form of the wrecker up as though it was a child's.

He carried it to the after cabin.

The position of this cabin was singularly altered.

The wreck lay upon its side, therefore, the cabin-side formed its floor, and the ceiling did service for a wall.

The floor and ceiling formed the walls, in fact, and the walls formed the floor and ceiling.

"One towards the many I shall want," said John Bentley, laying the wrecker on a couch, and pouring some brandy down his throat. "He shall have his choice—to serve me or die!"

The mate lit a handsome pipe—it had been the merchant's favourite hookah—and meditated while waiting for Red Ralph to recover.

It was strange he could sit calmly in the cabin of the vessel from whose deck he had hurled his gallant captain.

He was thinking how the world would be startled when it should be known the Tiger of the Sea was out again, destroying the fleets of every nation, giving once more his wild cry of bloodshed and destruction.

"I should have had the 'Sultan,'" he mused. "That, and beautiful Susan Brocton; but the crew were faithful to their captain, and dared not say too much, as they would have betrayed me.

"And now, here lies the 'Sultan,' a wreck, and I have not a single comrade. No matter, there is glorious treasure in the world—the wide world; but I dare not go on shore.

"I have prowled along, and gained intelligence, and the merchant and Susan were both saved by a young buccaneer, Captain Tom Drake, my most hated foe.

"They would recognise me; let us see what can be done with my friend Ralph, the wrecker."

He touched Red Ralph with his foot.

The wrecker, recovering consciousness, saw John Bentley smoking quietly.

Spectres do not smoke.

"Not dead!" said Ralph, in surprise.

"Not dead!" laughed John Bentley, "you are not a good shot, Red Ralph. Look here."

He swept the black hair from his brow. The ball had left its mark in a faint blue line on the temple.

"I bear no malice," the mate said, taking the wrecker's hand, with a peculiar sign; "it is against our creed, Red Ralph. Drink, there is brandy, and tell me what brought you here."

"You forgive me, then?"

"On one condition."

"And that?"

"Is that we are comrades henceforth."

"To the death!" said Red Ralph, returning the peculiar sign. "It is sworn!"

"It is by the silent oath we dare not break."

"I am your comrade, John Bentley, and you are mine. I will be by your side in death's peril, as you will be by my side; my life shall be risked for your life—your life risked for my life. In hate, in revenge, in woe, in joy, in future—we are one.

"It is sworn!"

"It is sworn!"

Each filled a glass and drank at the same moment; a second sign made, then completed an oath more terrible and binding than the oath of the Death Brotherhood of Ancient Rome.

"There are, or I should think there might be, some curious tales narrated since we parted at sea," said John Bentley.

"And such a parting," said Red Ralph, the wrecker, recovering, under the influence of brandy and such companionship, something of his grim hardihood. "When I was sent like a rocket to the sky amid a roar of fire. There was never such a total demolition as resulted from the blowing up of our ship."

It will be seen by this remark that Red Ralph and John Bentley were old acquaintances. Red Ralph had been lieutenant to John Bentley, the pirate.

"We were both nearer to Heaven than it is possible we shall ever be again," said John Bentley, with sardonic mockery. "I never thought we should meet here."

"Nor did I, or we might have arranged matters more satisfactorily."

"So we might; especially in reference to the shot. But let that pass; it did no harm, and we were faithful comrades before; besides, you owe me your life on the present occasion, and I do not think you are cur enough to forget that."

"Were I the veriest cur that ever existed, dare I break my oath?"

"Why, no; and so we are friends; two men who have done much, and may do much more."

"You want to know how I came here?"

"I do."

Red Ralph told him briefly the tale of the wreck; his quarrel with Captain Tom. His defeat, and subsequent attempt on Sweetheart Loo.

Then the scene and the struggle on the rocks

ending in his being hurled into the ocean, and his awful drifting over the waters, followed and accompanied by the dead form.

" So you hate this brave young buccaneer," said the mate.

" I would track him to death inch by inch, and watch each pant of agony with joy."

" He saved Susan Brockt—?"

" Curse him, yes!"

" And he loves her ?"

" He does—that is, he seems to; but, as you know, he has another lady aboard his ship."

" And he has a ship—a glorious little craft—as I hear ?"

" A splendid thing—a very bird upon the water; not a ship in the world could match it."

" But it is small," said John Bentley, reflectively. " Still, it would do for a beginning; you would be revenged, Red Ralph ?"

" Would I ?—aye! though getting the revenge took me to perdition."

" You have done enough to have earned a home there already, if there is such a place," said John Bentley, with his deep, sardonic laugh. " What say you to take this ship and the two girls? Susan for me, Sweetheart Loo for you—would that be revenge ?"

" The very thought I had; but how to get the vessel. Is it possible ?"

" There is no such thing as impossibility. How to get the buccaneer's vessel is a plan to be devised. Where is it now ?"

" There is a schooner chartered to watch and wait for it."

" Go on. The schooner's name ?"

" The 'Thunderer,' commanded by Commodore Ellis, who has sworn to have a terrible revenge for the defeat he sustained."

" Good. You know this ?"

" For a certainty."

" Anything else ?"

" A lieutenant of the coastguard will be down to-morrow to see whether the wreckers were at work, and what they did."

" Good. The name of the lieutenant ?"

" Augustus Rayner."

" Rayner ?"

" Twin brother to him that was captain of the 'Sultan.'"

John Bentley heard this with a strange thrill of soul.

" The twin brother of Michael Rayner," he said, " coming to see what has been done. Good, have you any other information ?"

" Tom Drake is to go on board the ' Thunderer' as pilot, and turn it out of the way, while the 'Will-o'-the-Wisp' runs the cargo in."

" Good! It's something to know this, Ralph. Now for my plan."

The wrecker listened eagerly.

" We meet that Augustus in disguise, take him to the smugglers' haunt, and kill him there."

" Kill him ?"

" So that it may seem Captain Tom has done it. Is the idea good ?"

" Worthy of Bentley; but how to reach the haunt in safety ?"

" Is there not a secret way ?"

" There is; you know that too ?"

" Few things are unknown to me," smiled the mate. " Then—"

" Then ?"

" Then to visit the 'Thunderer,' and tell them that the coastguard officer has been slain by Captain Tom Drake."

" And betray him ? Say that he is on board—a false pilot ?"

" No."

" Why ?"

" I will tell you anon; you shall see. Have you any comrades on shore who were faithful to you ?"

" I have. More like myself who hate the daring boy who has become a pet chief."

" Good again. Tell me their names."

Ralph told him.

John Bentley set them down on his tablets.

His fertile brain was at work.

" To have the coastguard officer killed, to have Captain Tom arrested for the murder; to tell the smugglers that their chieftain is arrested on the ' Thunderer,' and to have them go to succour him while we, with your faithful comrades, seize the 'Will-o'-the-Wisp,' and, with Susan Brocton and Sweetheart Loo, sail away. Would this be revenge ?"

" Such as would drive my rival mad."

" You shall see it done. Trust all to me. Act as I direct, and in two nights hence the 'Will-o'-the-Wisp' with its cargo and the owner is ours."

" Would it were to-night."

" Patience. It is not slow work to do so much in eight-and-forty hours. In the meantime seek rest. We can do nothing till to-morrow. Rest. Get both your strength of limb and nerve. You will want both."

" Do not fear for me."

" I do not, Red Ralph. You know John Bentley by this time, and are aware that when he fears or doubts, he does not caution."

" I know," thought the wrecker. " It is a dagger's point, or pistol's shot. But we are sworn. The contract cannot be broken."

The next evening, the mate and his companion, both disguised, visited the shore.

Ralph, under instructions from John Bentley, went to the quarters of the coastguard. He had a plausible tale prepared

" I want to see Lieutenant Rayner," he said to the sentry.

" What for ?"

" Mind your own business, my man. Let him know I want to see him, and say that I can tell him something about the light that wrecked the 'Sultan.'"

For it had already got rumoured abroad that the " Sultan " was lured to destruction by means of a false beacon.

The sentry asked no further questions, but passed the word to his comrades. A few minutes elapsed, and Red Ralph was desired to enter.

Obeying the order, he went in, and stood before a handsome young officer in uniform.

Looking at the brave fellow, with his noble head and gallant form, Red Ralph felt a thrill of remorse, when he thought of the job to which the devil, John Bentley, had devoted him.

" So you know something about the wreck, my man," said Gus Rayner, eyeing his savage visitor keenly. " What are you ?"

" Perhaps the less I say about myself, the better compliment; but, I know all you want to find out. The beacon on the cliff, and who put it there."

" My poor brother," answered Gus. " That treacherous light was the cause of his death. But we shall know the names of those monsters now, and you will be rewarded."

" Perhaps, lieutenant, I had better tell you first why I came. The fact is, I didn't like the work. I've been a smuggler since I was a boy, though I am going to cut it now; but when it came to wrecking, says I, not for me. So we quarrelled, and they cast me out."

" Who did ?"

" The captain, Tom Drake, and the rest of them."

" Tom Drake! What! the daring buccaneer

who has only lately joined the smugglers? Did he do the hideous work?"

"Piled the beacon, and fired it with his own hand, lieutenant."

"By Heaven! I will hunt him through the world!—hound him over sea and land, till I have retribution for my brother's death! You were one of his band?"

"I was. But, seeing as I've come to give evidence, I thought you might forget that."

"Fear not. Your repentance shall be rewarded. What become of the cargo saved from the wreck?"

"It was taken to the smugglers' cave, lieutenant, the secret one, where they meet to-night to share the plunder."

"I will be there, too," said Rayner, rising; "but, mark me, man! if this is a tale invented for some treacherous purpose, beware! Let me see a look or sign of betrayal, and you die!"

Red Ralph swore it.

"Heaven! Then I can meet him face to face, and let my sword seek vengeance for Michael's death. I can confront him in my brother's likeness, and kill him without having any remorse. I, too, will go alone."

Fatal resolve.

"That would be unwise, lieutenant," said Red Ralph, suppressing every sign of his pleasure at the young officer's valour. "Better have some of the crew near.

"I don't wish you to trust me, lieutenant; but I wanted revenge. It is natural you should doubt me; but I can't do more than offer to go with you, lieutenant, and show you the way in. The smugglers meet to-night. Captain Tom will be in the cave waiting for them."

"Alone?"

"Quite alone, lieutenant. I should like to see him captured, curse him!"

"Look you!" said Gus, gripping the wrecker tightly by the wrist, "you say that to-night my brother's murderer will be alone. Is it true?"

"Yes. But you had better take some of your men with you."

"What! To rob me of my revenge!—share with me the bliss of stilling the murderer's heart that had no pity for Michael! No! My revenge taken first, then my men will do their duty."

"Better have them near in case of danger," persisted Red Ralph, with seeming frankness, "in some place where a signal will bring them to you."

"A good thought. They shall wait in a galley beneath the rocks; my signal could be heard from there."

So it was arranged.

A galley was lowered with a strong party of the revenue men, all armed to the teeth. Red Ralph and the young officer went with them to the rock, and then disembarked.

"Remain here till you have my signal," said Rayner, "then come quickly to where its sound shall find you. I expect there will be some work to do."

"Lead on," he said to Ralph.

Climbing cautiously up the rocks, they reached an opening through which both passed, through narrow crevices and dark caverns oftentimes they went.

Rayner had explored the crags many a time, but never suspected these passes formed an entrance way to the smugglers' cave.

He followed without fear, never thinking that his guide was leading him to his fate.

Rayner was well on the alert in case of treachery, but the quiet manner of Red Ralph almost disarmed suspicion.

At length the wrecker stopped.

"Hish!" he said, in a whisper, with his finger on his lip. "Caution now. I hear him!"

Rayner's hand went to his sword.

He could barely resist the impulse that urged him to leap forward to confront the supposed assassin.

They had reached the cavern. A dim glimmering of light left visible the dark form of a man sitting by a rude table in front of a jutting crag.

"That is he," whispered Red Ralph.

Out flashed Rayner's sword, and he stepped forward, when a blow from Red Ralph staggered him.

"Ha!" he said, forcing round upon the wrecker; "is it treachery?"

"It is death!" said a sonorous voice, and the figure at the table, John Bentley, rose with a dagger in his hand.

Thus beset between two foes, the gallant young coastguardsman did not lose courage.

He went at Red Ralph sword in hand, and beat the wrecker back, when he felt John Bentley's powerful grip on the back of his throat.

"I am sorry for you," said the man, "but it must be done."

And, without another word or pause, he drew Rayner's head back.

Then a gleam like lightning, and a dull, quick plunge.

John Bentley's dagger quivered to the hilt in Rayner's breast.

"I killed your brother," he said, as Rayner fell weltering in blood, "I, John Bentley, the second mate of the 'Sultan.' Take the knowledge with you to the next world, and do not blame the wrong man."

He knelt to wipe his dagger on the victim's coat —listened to the bubbling as of agony, and felt the last, faint throbbing of Rayner's heart.

"Dead!" he said. "Now to give the signal for his men, and another for the smugglers, if you know it."

Taking the silver call from Rayner's neck, he went up the way, but keeping out of sight, and blew a prolonged signal.

"I know Captain Tom's own token," said Red Ralph.

"So, after some time of seeking the smuggler and the coastguard they meet here?"

"When the coastguard will think the smugglers have murdered their officer," said John Bentley, "and then there will be a turn-out battle. Hide back; the men are coming."

Both crouched in a crevice as the guard came through the passage in the rocks in single file. They were so near the assassins, that had one stumbled he must have fallen on them.

The men were in haste, for they thought their officer was in danger.

Some went in one direction, others in another, and left the galley to itself.

Creeping from their concealment when the men were out of sight, John Bentley and Red Ralph went to the galley.

In fierce, wanton deviltry, Bentley fired a shot through, and left it to sink.

The noise of the pistol alarmed the men again, and they rushed back to the rock where it floundered.

Red Ralph and Bentley were out of sight by this time.

Tired of their fruitless search, at length, the coastguardsmen returned to the galley.

It was gone.

"There is some treachery at work," said the next in command, who, in Lieutenant Rayner's absence, was obeyed. "We are in a nest of devils, mates; but we will watch them closely. Arrest every stranger you find. They shall take us to the cave, or we will send them to eternity!"

He was a resolute man, this person, and meant to keep his word.

He planted his men all round the rock in which he supposed the cavern to be situated, but the cavern was so strangely formed that it was impossible to conjecture its exact position.

It was late in the evening when Captain Tom Drake, having left Susan and her father, returned to the cave.

An awful sight met his gaze.

The body of Gus Rayner lying on his face in a pool of blood.

"Who has done this?" he exclaimed. "Who has dared?"

"Who has dared?"

His crying signal brought the buccaneers to him instantly.

He had moved the body, and his hands were stained.

"Whose work is that?" he asked, in a voice of thunder. "What cowardly ruffian has been so brutal as to hew the poor fellow's head, and murder him?"

The men looked at each other, at the still form, and at their chieftain's crimson hand.

Each one protested his innocence so solemnly that the captain could not doubt them.

They doubted him.

What else would it seem but that he had found the officer there and killed him to prevent discovery?

Now, afraid of his own act, he wished to affect innocence.

In spite of the fact that he was found there alone.

In spite of his crimson hand.

"It's a bad business," said Bob Hauler, gravely, "and the sooner we put it out of sight the better. No one knows who's done it, but if it were found here, we should all get in for it."

"And the coastguard prowling about," added Jerry Mizzen. "We must get him out quietly, and put him in a hole in the sand. Poor fellow! He was the best of the lot. Even I wouldn't have done that deed for all the gold in this here cave."

"Nor I," said Captain Tom, solemnly. "Comrades mine, I see by your looks you doubt me in this, but I swear most sacredly that as you see him so I found him."

"We believe you, captain," said the men, confirmed by his earnestness.

"I agree with you that, for all our sakes, it is better we should bury him quietly. A grave in the sands will be best."

"A grave in the sands; no one will find him there."

"Nor must we be seen, or it would seem that we were hiding our own crime. Bear him gently, comrades; he was a noble fellow."

And, covered with a cloak, he was placed on a rude litter formed of two planks lashed together.

First, with kindly thought, the smugglers cleansed the blood from his face, and arranged his hair upon his pallid brow.

There was sympathy in every rough face when they saw him lying so still and cold before them. These were men who could meet foes in battle and fight to the death, reckless whether they killed others or were killed themselves.

But this cold-blooded deed was quite out of their

tain Tom pressed the icy hand, and breathed that was not, perhaps, the worse received ?? from a buccaneer's tongue.

This concluded, placed upon a litter, the body was borne upon the shoulders of four men, while others carried torches to light them to the beach.

The scene was strange.

The swarthy, bearded features of the buccaneers, the covered form, and the torchlights' glare.

Captain Tom stood by while the grave was made —a deep hole in the sand.

A resting-place that left no token of its haunt.

The sand dug from the grave was thrown into the sea.

It might have been fancy, but the torchlight falling on Rayner's face gave it an aspect that was not that of death.

There was a faint colour in the cheeks, perhaps the reflection of the ruddy light.

There was no pulsation of the heart, not a motion in the wrist—he was dead.

So they thought—so it seemed.

Yet had they but waited!

Had not the necessity to hide his form impelled them to such haste, what a world of horror they might have saved Bentley's victim!

But he was buried, and the sand thrown in upon him; he was buried by the murmuring sea, and shut from the world, its delight and scenery.

One pale witness there was who, frozen into stone by the sight, stood like a statue, unable to move, and unable to repress her cry of terror.

Susan Brocton!

She saw Captain Tom superintend the midnight burial of Michael Rayner's brother.

What could she think but that Captain Tom was his murderer?

Or why this secrecy?

So she stood and watched until her shriek alarmed the buccaneers, who, turning round, beheld her fall.

One anxious thought spoke in every eye.

She had seen too much.

None liked to speak this thought, but it was expressed, and Captain Tom saw it plainly, as though it was spoken.

"Leave this to me," he said, quietly, but sternly. "I know my duty to my comrades, all that is necessary for our safety shall be done."

"Even to death," added they.

"Even to the sacrifice of this beautiful innocent. I know our motto. I will keep it, though with my own hand I do the deed that breaks my heart."

He took the slight form of Susan in his arms and sorrowfully led the way.

The men followed him in silence. They sympathised with, but could not relieve him of his stern responsibilities.

Susan Brocton was doomed.

"Leave her to me for awhile," Captain Tom said, for they were following as though to have the tragedy done then. "I will tell you when to come."

And so the midnight burial had this sad result, but there was one more sad and horrible.

In that grave by the sands on the sea shore, there lay a living human being, for Gus Rayner was not dead.

He was buried alive, buried in a trance, sleeping, and would wake to find himself there.

Horror!

Fancy dares not picture the awakening, and then the despairing battle for escape; was their hope? Only one.

THE VILLAIN GAVE VENT TO A HIDEOUS YELL AS CAPTAIN TOM SPRANG UPON HIM

CHAPTER CXXIX.

THE TRIAL

LATER by some hours than the midnight time when Susan saw the last of the sanguinary tragedy, the poor girl woke to find herself in the smuggler's cave.

Alone!

Her father was not near.

The place seemed very strange, but she could remember it as the scene of the duel between Captain Tom and Red Ralph the wrecker.

Captain Tom, the brave buccaneer who had seemed so chivalric and so handsome, what a bitter disappointment, when she had dreamed of him as her lover, to see him a wretch stained with brutal crime.

Susan knew Augustus Rayner by repute, she had heard his brother Michael speak of him in terms of the fondest admiration.

She had heard of the remarkable likeness existing between the two—so startling this resemblance that one might be taken for the phantom of the other.

So there could be no doubt as to his identity.

The man she had seen buried in the sand was brother to the captain of the 'Sultan.'

And Captain Tom was his slayer.

This she could not doubt.

The proof was incontestible.

There was no hope that the smugglers might not be guilty, or why the secret burial at midnight by the sea?

Susan could have wept alike in sadness for Rayner's death, and that the young buccaneer was the cause of it.

Her head was resting on her little hand, and hot tears were falling through her fingers, when a gentle touch upon her brow caused her to raise her face.

Captain Tom stood before her.

"Why do you weep?" he asked, tenderly.

She shuddered, and drew from his touch.

"Is it that you fear me?" he asked again. "Yet no. It cannot be that, for I would die for you."

"Such a fearful deed," she sobbed; "and you whom I thought so generous and brave."

He saw her suspicion in an instant.

"Lady," he said, sadly, as he knelt before her, "look upon me as I bend before the Great Judge above, and before you. Is mine the brow of an assassin? Is this a murderous hand?"

His whole manner, so full of conscious innocence, impressed her with a conviction that he was not the guilty thing she had thought him. That frank and manly brow bore not the red stain of crime. That steady hand, waiting for the clasp of hers, had never done a coward deed.

"Who did it, then?" she asked, taking his hand. "I cannot doubt your innocence."

"Who did it I would give much to know. I am linked with lawless men—such daring spirits as defy their King and country's laws; but I would stake my life there is not one in my command who would do such a deed as that."

"Why was he buried in such secrecy, then?"

"For common safety. He was an officer of the coastguard, sent especially to watch the smugglers, and ascertain particulars of the wreck. His body lay in my secret cave, and had he been found there, I and my comrades would have suffered. We seem guilty to you; how much more guilty should we seem to the Government men?"

"You are in danger, then?" she said, forgetting her suspicion of his crime in her fear for his safety.

"I have chosen a perilous life," he said, with a half-defiant laugh, "and one day with another my risk of danger is much about the same."

"Do you not fear sometimes?"

"Fear!—it is to me a word without a meaning; I have seen men in battle shiver, and go pale. That must be fear; but the sight of peril brings the blood to my cheek, the fire to my heart and eye—give me my gallant barque, with its trusty crew, and Captain Tom would not change place with a monarch."

Susan glanced at him with undisguised admiration; he had risen now, and as he stood erect, she could not resist an involuntary thought to share the destiny of such a man would be to be happy.

He, catching her glance, and seeming to read her thoughts, changed colour, with a glow of pleasure; then, at thought of the danger threatening, he went pale again.

His quick ear had caught the distant tramp of a party of men—the buccaneers coming to the cave to judge what should be done with the girl who had seen too much.

"What is it?" she asked, quickly, and with instinctive alarm. "These men are coming here."

"They are," he said, moodily, but encircling her by instinct with his arm. "Let them come; they shall not harm you."

"Would they?"

"Susan—Miss Brocton," he said, gravely, "it were wrong to hide your danger. You saw the midnight burial, and the men fear lest a word of yours should bring discovery, and they be punished for a deed they have not done."

She clung closely to him.

"You would not let them touch me?"

"Not while I live. But our bond of unity is such that were it put to judgment and decreed, a man would have to sacrifice his brother or his sire without a murmur."

"This is terrible! Yet you say they shall not harm me?"

"They shall not while I live."

"Leave them."

"If you must die, I will die, too."

He drew her trembling form to his breast, and nestled her head upon his shoulder as the tramp of footsteps was heard at the cave entrance.

"Let me live," she said. "Think of my father; I would never speak of what I saw."

"The power is not all mine," he replied, sadly, "but I will do my best. Be calm, and show no dread."

A signal, demanding admission, was given from outside.

"Enter!" said Captain Tom.

And the buccaneers entered.

Every face was resolute and calm.

The men seemed to fully understand the responsibility of the task before them; and just as fully they were determined for the worst.

An old buccaneer, a grey-haired man, with an iron face, had been selected as spokesman; he knew what his comrades wanted, and he said it in as few words as possible.

Not a man was entirely unmoved when they saw the poor girl clinging to the captain for protection.

"Captain," said the spokesman, "you know what we have come for—it's no use making a bad story worse by making it longer—we have considered the matter among ourselves, and, seeing as the gal has seen more than is good for us, why, you know the law."

"My men," said Captain Tom, with quiet dignity, "you are speaking out of place. When you considered the mattter among yourselves, did you forget that it is customary for the captain to have a voice in such things?"

The old buccaneer rubbed his shaggy head.

"But—" he began.

Tom stopped him.

"Keep back, and keep silent; the lady shall have a fair trial, and I will defend her."

Bob Hauler led a murmur of applause.

"I have only this to say," said the young buccaneer and smuggler chief, "she is satisfied that I nor any of my men did this deed—she has promised never to speak of it. Will you take her promise?"

"No," said the men, with few exceptions. "We cannot trust the safety of many lives to the discretion of a woman's tongue."

"Let her rejoin her father, and go."

"Her father is already gone," said the old buccaneer. "The coastguard found him and took him away, and there's a lot out looking for the girl. If they find her, it's all up with us."

Susan gave a low cry of anguish at hearing of her parent's departure.

"We must not break our law," said the old buccaneer; "you know it, Captain Tom, and have a double right to keep it, since, if you fail in example, you cannot blame the men. I don't want to speak out of place, captain, but I know it is a hard thing for you to do: you are young, and the lady is pretty, and naturally enough she clings to you, and naturally enough you feel like fighting for her, if need be, but duty must be done."

A cold perspiration broke out on Captain Tom's brow.

"Duty shall be done," he said, calmly. "Mine as a chief to you, and as a man to the lady."

Another murmur of approval.

"But," he added, resolutely, "she shall not die!"

"Not?"

"I do not think," he said, his brilliant eye glittering. "that any one here will wish to kill her, if I say him nay?"

There was a dubious pause.

Captain Tom Drake was a peculiar fellow to deal with at times, and when he said he did not wish a thing done, and his fingers were playing with a pistol-butt not the boldest of his band dared to raise an objection.

Very quick of hand, and sure of eye, was Captain Tom.

So the pause lengthened, and grew into a deep silence.

"Our law," said the young buccaneer, "based on an oath that binds each to the other till death, is one that must not be broken. My word, my promise given to the helpless maiden whom I rescued from the deep, is one that must not be broken. I have said that while I live she shall not die."

The silence was profound.

"I ask my comrades to give me her life."

No answer.

"Or I must cease to be your chief, or one of you must kill me."

"No! no!" exclaimed several. "No!"

"Well, then," he said, "decide."

He placed them in a serious dilemma.

They could not let the girl live.

And not one of them would have seen another raise his hand against their brave captain.

The bold buccaneer rubbed his head.

The rest looked at each other in much perplexity.

Bob Hauler stood forward.

"I've got a way, captain," he said, "if so be as you are agreeable, and the lady's agreeable."

"Speak out, Bob," said the rest.

"Well then, it's this; we must keep to our law. The captain says she shall not die while he lives—"

Susan, thinking Bob Hauler's words threatened death to her champion, turned quickly and faced the crew.

"Not for my sake," she said, artlessly, "shall he be injured; he saved my father, he saved me, he would have died for me, let me die for him."

And with her own little hand she bared her own white breast ready for the death blow.

Struck by the noble act of devotion, struck, too, by the beauty of the superb breast they saw, the men shrank back, as shrinking from the thought of killing her.

Bob Hauler's face lit with pleasure as he said.

"Captain and mates, what the lady has said tells me I was about to say the right thing; she need not die, and show me the man who would like to strike Captain Tom?"

He looked round as though it would not be a good thing for the man who might have a fancy that way.

"There's none, I know there ain't. So Captain Tom asked us to give him her life. Let him have it, mates. Let him take her on board his own ship. She is a noble girl, and if she cares as much for the captain as I think she does, she will make a brave queen for us; ask her, Captain Tom, ask her if she will be our chieftain's bride and queen of the buccaneers?"

"Hurrah for the Buccaneer Queen," said the crew. "Ask her, captain."

And Captain Tom, his fine face troubled with a cloud of perplexity at the decision of his crew, said—

"Shall I keep the precious life I saved? Will you share my fortune and peril?"

What a shout rang through the cave as Susan buried her blushing face in the buccaneer's breast, and with her arm round his neck, said—

"I will!"

"So be it," said Captain Tom, kissing her fair brow; but his heart was sad for all that, for he thought of his own beauteous bride for whom he had fought and dared so much.

What would gentle Minnie think of his promises.

He had no time to think.

The smugglers decided for him.

And the roof echoed with the echo of many voices shouting—

"Hurrah for Captain Tom! Hurrah for the Queen of the Buccaneers!"

CHAPTER CXXX.
NIGHT IN THE CAVERN.

WHEN the smugglers had retired, and Susan was alone with Captain Tom, she felt to the full the strangeness of her position.

She had saved his life, but by accepting a destiny, the very thought of which would even have shocked her to the soul.

A smuggler's bride! the companion of a lawless man—queen of a desperate horde—would she be happy?

The maiden asked herself this question a hundred times, and as often, in spite of her fear, her heart seemed to answer, yes.

One could not doubt the man upon whose breast her face was resting yet, she had seen him generous and brave.

Surely he loved her, or he could not with such resolution have chosen to die rather than see her sacrificed to his men.

He spoke.

"Susan."

She raised her swimming eyes.

"There was no other way to save you; but fear not."

"Fear you! my champion—my preserver!"

"Understand me," he said, quietly, "our relationship must henceforth be singular; had some kind fairy given me a chance of many gifts I would have chosen you before all others; but then I should have wished you had chosen someone more worthy of your love."

A pause.

Her eyes were downcast.

The colour came and went in her cheeks.

Her fair breast heaved and fell.

"Nothing but the fear of death," he said, in a tone that pained him deeply, "could have made you yield to such a fate."

"Tom."

There was an involuntary murmur, low, and reproachful—it thrilled him; he dared not give way to the tender feelings with which his heart thrilled for the gentle girl, when he thought of Minnie.

"It is not possible," he said, "that you, a gentle lady, delicately nurtured, and proud of birth, would willingly link your fate with one who, in the world's sight, is a malefactor."

"A malefactor!"

"A smuggler and baccaneer, and so, though you have consented to be mine, I should be worse than coward were I to seek fulfilment of a promise made at such a time."

Grateful as Susan felt for his delicate forethought, she had a faint idea that he was carrying it too far.

"I shall keep you as a sacred charge," he said, "a trust confided to my honour, something to reverence—but never fear."

"Never fear?"

"See what bitter pain it would be to have you, and feel that you would not care for me; and is it not possible that you would?"

She did not reply.

"So as I would guard a sister or a child, I will cherish you," he said. "Your place of rest shall be a sanctuary, and you the queen of a brave band to whom your word shall be law; then, when a chance shall occur, I will put you on board some ship, and you can return to your father."

"And you?" she asked, looking at him in a way that made the blood throb in his veins.

"I—I can live as I have lived before, and will forget you if I can."

His lip quivered at the thought.

It would be hard to part with her when each day spent in her society would make her doubly dear.

But, buccaneer though he was, Tom Drake had the soul of a prince.

He would not take advantage of the singular fate that threw the beautiful girl so entirely upon his mercy.

"And you," Susan said, "who are so noble—so delicate and kind. Think I cannot be grateful? To whom do I owe more than I do to you? What might have been my end, but for you?"

"Dear lady," he began.

She interrupted.

"Death. And worse than death. Thrice have you perilled your life for mine. And now you will not let me give you what poor reward is in my power."

"Why?" he said, eagerly, "could you love me? Would you go with me willingly as my bride?"

"Could I not? Could I do less?"

He strained her passionately to his breast, and for the moment he almost forgot his own dear girl.

"Dearest Susan. You know not what your choice is. The jeopardy and constant changes of such a wild career as mine."

"I should have no fear so that you were with me ever. I have seen the ocean in its fury, and felt no terror, and love would make me stronger."

"But we have battles sometimes, fierce, bloody strife, with flashing steel and crashing shot. That would be terrible to you."

"Terrible," she said; "but I could pray, you would not see my cheek grow pale, dear Tom, nor hear a cry of fear."

"Brave girl, and now the task be mine to make you happy, to shield you in purity and honour; will you trust me?"

"I am yours," she said putting both her hands in his.

He kissed her gently.

"The hour is late," he said, "and you must need rest. Sleep here where you rested when first I brought you from the wreck. You shall be sacred, as though by your mother's side. The cavern is secure, men dare not intrude, and I shall be near to watch over you."

He caressed her again, and said—

"To-morrow night I set sail for France, where a rich cargo awaits me; over on a foreign shore the nuptial rite can be performed, and you will be mine. Good-night."

His lawless men had so willed it, and by the oath which bound them together he would have to marry the merchant's daughter if he wished to save her life.

It was a terrible task to be compelled to forsake the gentle Minnie Atherton in favour of a strange lady, but there was no help for it now.

He climbed some rugged steps in the rock, and ascended to a cave over the one in which a couch was arranged for Susan.

Her reflections were strange, as, with full confidence in his promise, she removed her outer garments, and sank upon the couch he had spread for her repose.

It was a curious situation for a maiden to be in.

Alone in a cavern with the chief of a lawless crew who already looked upon her as their captain's bride.

She was trusting much to his honour, and perhaps trespassing upon man's virtue when, only in instinctive faith in him, she prepared for rest as though in the seclusion of her own boudoir.

Braiding the rich masses of her hair, and contemplating her own sweet face, she did not notice how the time sped on.

Thinking of Captain Tom still, she remained in front of the mirror, not seeing the hungry glare of those dark, fiery eyes piercing through the gloom, watching her every motion.

The eyes were the eyes of Red Ralph, the wrecker, who had entered by the secret way.

He expected to find Captain Tom and Susan together; he imagined that the buccaneer had taken the fair girl for his own long before this, and hoping to find them sleeping, Ralph had crept in to drive a dagger to his foe's heart, and take the girl away.

But there she was alone, and in such dress as filled the wrecker's heart with resistless desire; he crouched in the shadow of the cave, hardly daring to move or breathe, lest he should lose sight for an instant of the glowing figure, whose every new attitude was more beautiful than the last.

The man envied with a savage envy the gallant buccaneer, who, he thought, already possessed the girl.

And he thought with savage joy of the revenge now in his grasp.

He could have no better spite on Captain Tom.

But then there was John Bentley.

The mate had chosen Susan for himself.

Woe to Red Ralph, the wrecker, if he robbed the tiger of his prey.

The thought detained him for a moment.

Only for a moment.

She should be his.

He would sate his brutal passion.

Then leave her with his dagger in her heart for Captain Tom.

He laughed silently at the thought.

Laughed while creeping forward like a serpent, and thinking how she would tremble in speechless terror, when his huge hand grasped her soft white shoulders, and he threw her down.

So, creeping inch by inch, and gazing on her all the while, till desire grew to madness, he got so near that she was almost in his grasp.

Then, in his eager haste, he rose, and, clutching at her dress, missed and caught her leg instead.

A jerk and she was thrown to the floor.

"A word—a whisper, and you die!" in a savage undertone, and keeping her down by the weight of his heavy hand upon her breast.

The dagger flashed before her sight, threatening instant death; but honour was dearer far than life, and with a desperate swing of both her feet into his face, she dashed him back and rose.

Then, with a shriek for help, she snatched her dress and fled, attiring herself as she ran, she knew not whither.

The wrecker followed.

Out of the cavern where he had seen her first the way was dark, and she was blindly seeking a passage from his presence, and he as blindly groping after her.

And she felt his hot breath on her cheek.

She did not know he was so near.

Holding her breath in terror, checking the wild cry on her tongue, she crouched back.

Slipped, and fell into a recess.

He heard her.

Stooping low, and with his feet wide apart, he tried to find her.

Susan crouched out on her hands and knees, slid between his legs, and fled again.

At last a gleam of light.

A curse from him, an oath of exultation.

She could go no further, for the range of caverns ended in the hole where she had taken refuge.

"Help!" she shrieked, wildly. "Tom! Dear Tom!"

"Call again," said the wrecker. "Another cry, and this—"

His dagger gleamed again.

"And this," said a stern voice, immediately above his head. "I thought you were dead, Red Ralph. Now I will make sure of it."

Tom Drake was leaning over the crag above, with a pistol pointed at the wrecker's head.

Quick as lightning, Red Ralph saw his peril, and how to avoid it.

He sprang upon Susan, seized her in his arms, and put her before him.

"Fire!" he said, defiantly. "Kill her! Menace me, and I drive my dagger through her back; you shall see its point at her breast!"

The awful threat made Captain Tom's blood run cold.

"Put her down," he said, "and I will not fire."

"The devil doubt you; it strikes me you have not got all the best of it yet; had you been five minutes later, you would have been too late. I meant to make her mine, then kill her; and will kill her, if I like, as it is; and perhaps I shall like."

"And if you injure a single hair of her head," said the buccaneer, made desperately calm by Susan's danger, "no torture of the horrible hell shall be equal in a millioneth part to the death you shall die. You cannot escape; my hand is steady, my eye is sure. Put her down, or, a minute more, and at the risk of killing her, I fire and maim you; then you shall see how I can torture while I slay."

Something in his manner, and deadly ferocity of his voice, awed the wrecker, and he said—

"If I set her down, will you fire?"

"If you set her down unharmed, you may escape now; but I shall not have forgotten you by the time we meet again."

"I don't suppose you will," thought Ralph, as he let Susan go.

"Farewell, Captain Tom; if you do not take good care of such a bride, you will not have her long."

Susan fell to the ground.

Captain Tom, stooping down, raised her in his arms.

The wrecker disappeared.

Susan had not fainted, but was powerless with terror.

"Do not leave me again," she murmured.

"Never," he said, bringing the blood to her cheek with a tender caress.

"I shall not leave you to danger again."

And vigilant as a lioness keeping guard over its young, he watched her till the morning broke, and Sweetheart Loo came to the cavern.

CHAPTER CXXXI.

THE MAN AT THE WHEEL.

Tom left Susan to the care of Loo, having first explored the cave to see there was no stranger or traitors hidden.

Then he said farewell to Susan.

"To-night," he said, "Bob Hauler and his trusty comrades will fetch you in a boat to bring you to my ship. Loo will accompany you."

"You are going to danger," Susan said.

He laughed.

"I have been many times."

"But this is unusual danger."

"Fear not, Susan, I shall come back."

He had assumed the dress of a pilot; but wore a sword, and in his pockets two brace of pistols were secreted.

His expedition was one of great hazard.

It had been arranged between himself and Ben Barnacle that Tom should go on board the "Thunderer" as pilot.

The "Thunderer" was on special service.

Her mission was to effect the capture of the "Will-'o-the-Wisp," the vessel of the daring buccaneer who had for so long successfully eluded pursuit.

Captain Hall, her brave commander, had sworn to accomplish this since the defeat of Admiral Ellis.

He had taken every precaution.

Spies had been at work to ascertain every particular concerning the contraband craft.

Captain Hall thought himself sure this time.

He heard that the "Will-'o-the-Wisp" would make for the rocky bay at evening.

He heard that she was laden with a valuable cargo.

He heard also that to make certain of a capture he must follow till the "Will-'o-the-Wisp" was safe in harbour, when he would pounce upon her and take the lawless crew as well.

His informant promised to send a pilot who would take the "Thunderer" to a place where she could lie in wait in safety.

Otherwise, its purpose would be suspected.

Then the rocks would swarm with foemen, who, safely sheltered, would keep up a deadly fire on the Government schooner, and the sailors would be sacrificed without being able to return a blow.

His informant was an innocent-looking smuggler, who already introduced himself as a Government man on secret service.

The pilot he sent was Tom Drake.

So the buccaneer chief went to where a boat from the "Thunderer" awaited him.

He was taken on board.

The captain surveyed him searchingly.

Captain Tom's face did not change a muscle.

"Do you think we are sure this time?" said the commander. "You know when and where you are to wait for the rascally buccaneers."

"I do, Captain Hall; she will wear her sail brig fashion, and have her hull painted yellow, and call herself the 'Eaglet.'"

"Will the buccaneer himself be on board?"

"Which one?"

"That prince of daring contrabandists, Captain Tom."

"I think it very likely," said the pilot, with a smile. "He is sure not to be far away."

"That fellow, sir," said Captain Hall, "has the impudence of the very deuce."

"So I have heard."

"I should like to catch him, sir. By Jove! the audacity he has, sir, is wonderful."

"Really!"

"Why, I followed him right to the Spanish coast once, and saw the cargo put in the ship."

"Indeed!"

"And, thinks I, by Jove! if he gets away now, really Hall is a donkey; that's what I thought, sir."

"I daresay."

"And, by Jove!—I wonder I don't swear when I think of it—I kept her in sight as I thought, and the men were thinking about the prize money, when we got lost in a fog, and, by Jove, sir! when the fog was gone, the buccaneer had gone, too."

"Quite out of sight?"

"Clean. Not a speck was visible, so I put into Lisbon to make inquiries, and a young fellow comes on deck to me.

"'Captain Hall?' says he.

"'That's me,' says I.

"'Of his Britannic Majesty's schooner, the "Thunderer?"' says he.

"'The same,' says I.

"'Then,' says he 'I have a valuable cargo with which I want to reach England; but I've heard that there's a buccaneer on the look-out for me.'

"'A buccaneer?' says I.

"'Tom Drake,' says he.

"'We'll catch the beggar,' says I.

"'I hope so,' says he. 'You would perhaps be kind enough to take him in your company.'

"'Certainly,' says I.

"Well sir, the blackguard brought out papers, making himself out the supercargo, his charge of merchandise for somebody and something, and I took care of him, looking out for the buccaneer all the while.

"By Jove, sir! The blackguard of a pretended supercargo spent his time with me; a nice civil fellow he was, told capital stories, drank my wine, brought splendid cigars, and sang like a nightingale.

"Well, sir, we sailed in company till a dead calm came on, and the blackguard invited me to dine on his ship. By Jove, sir! I went.

"We had dinner, sir. The finest dinner I ever had, and all the time we were dining, he had some infernal machinery at work, and his ship was moving while the 'Thunderer' sat the water like an elephant."

"Yet she is a quick sailer," remarked the pilot.

"Magnificent. But what was the use of that? When dinner was over, I went on deck, and there we were, with the 'Thunderer' about six miles away.

"'Hello!' says I.

"'Captain Hall,' says he, 'we part company here.'

"'What for?' says I.

"'And allow me to thank you very gratefully,' says he, 'for having been kind enough to see me so far in safety, and,' says he, 'if I could do anything for you I would.'

"'I should like to see the buccaneer's ship,' said I, 'and its rascal of a captain.'

"The blackguard began to laugh, and, says he 'you're on board the buccaneer's ship now, and the rascal of a captain is before you.'

"By Jove, sir! what do you think of that, he put me in a boat with my officers, and captain, and my own six men, and left us to row six miles across the sea, while he sailed away in the calm, like the Flying Dutchman."

"Very exasperating," said the pilot, "very. So you are naturally anxious to make sure of him this time?"

"By Jove, sir! May I be a powder monkey if I don't."

The pilot smiled again, and turned to the wheel.

"I see you wear a sword," observed Captain Hall, after a pause.

"Captain Tom Drake may show fight, sir. I am a sailor, and would not be idle while a fight went on."

"Right," said Captain Hall, approvingly, and he thought the pilot a brave fellow.

"You know the place well?" he said.

"Every inch, captain. We shall want good steering as the night comes on. There will be low tide, and a pilot who did not know the way would be sure to run on the black sand."

"By Jove, sir! don't do that, we should stick there for a month, and the vessel might unload under our very nose."

"So he might," thought the pilot, "and perhaps he will."

Night came. The pilot stood like a statue at the wheel, as over the starlit sea a beautiful little brig came like a bird on the wing.

"Sail oh!" cried the man on the look-out.

"Up with the Union Jack," said Captain Hall, "the buccaneer is coming."

Up went the Union Jack, and on came the little craft with the English flag flying in the wind.

Captain Hall paced the deck of the "Thunderer," rubbing his hands in satisfactory joy at the capture he felt sure of making.

"By Jove!" he said, turning to join the pilot, to whom he seemed to have taken an immense liking, "how she comes! Seems anxious to run into the trap."

"Her captain seems determined to bear out his reputation," observed the pilot.

"By Jove, sir! I believe the daring vessel would come down in the same style if he knew we were here waiting for him."

"I believe so, too, sir."

"By-the-way, I thought you said the captain. Captain! a cowardly leader of rascals to call himself a captain. I thought you said he would not be on board."

"Your pardon, Captain Hall, I said he would not be far away."

"Humph! don't know how the dickens you fellows get all the information, though I heard the same from a fellow who came not long before you arrived."

"Indeed!"

"Yes, an ill-looking scamp, sir; said he had been a buccaneer, and repented. The Lord help his repentance, he looked as big a sinner as ever frightened a figure-head."

"And he gave you similar information?" asked the pilot, curiously.

"Nearly word for word. He told me a little more, though."

"Ah!"

"He said that this Captain Tom, sir—the felonious ruffian should swing at the yard-arm—had murdered a coastguard officer."

The pilot started.

He almost let the wheel slip from his grasp.

"He said that Captain Tom did so?" he began, in a voice of thunder, but recollecting himself, cooled down.

"Hallo, Mr. Pilot, sir."

"Pardon me, Captain Hall, but did not it strike you your informer spoke before his time? There had been no discovery of a murder when I left th village not an hour before I came on deck."

"By Jove! the fellow said he saw it done."

"A buccaneer, you say?"

"No, sir, a coastguardsman."

"But a buccaneer gave you the intelligence?"

"Yes; a big fellow, with black whiskers, and ugly slash across his left cheek."

"Red Ralph," said the pilot to himself. "No the mystery is over. He is the murderer of poor Rayner."

"You should have detained that man," he said, gravely.

"Why?"

"His eagerness to charge another with having perpetrated a horrible crime did not look well."

"By Jove, sir! it did not when you think of it."

"Did he tell you anything further?"

"A lot—where the deed was done. He promised to conduct us to the place and show us the body."

"Where?"

"In a secret cave or some such den."

"His knowledge, unless he was hoaxing you, is suspicious," said the pilot. "That little vessel is a splendid sailer. Look at her."

Captain Hall did

The coming vessel was within speaking distance now.

"Ship ahoy!" he yelled through his trumpet.

"Aboy, ahoy!" echoed a mighty voice in reply.

"Ben Barnacle's music," smiled the pilot. "We shall have sport directly."

He felt the pistols under his coat, to see if they were safe for sudden use.

"What ship?" asked Captain Hall.

"The 'Eaglet.'"

"Where from?"

"Marseilles."

"Where bound?"

"To Jericho, with moonshine!" was the startling answer given in defiance.

"Oh! that's your little game," said Captain Hall. The same voice asked—

"What ship is yours?"

"The 'Thunderer,' and be something to you. His Britannic Majesty's ship, the 'Thunderer,' Captain Hall, twenty-one guns, come out to catch the rascally buccaneer and his ship, the 'Will-o'-the-Wisp.'"

A ringing, laughing cheer came from the little vessel, as, with the velocity of a swallow, she shot across the ocean.

"All hands on deck!" shouted Hall. "Crowd all sail, give her a shot to bring her to, man the boats, swivel guns and cutlass! Quick, there!"

"Aye, aye, sir!"

"Man at the wheel, what the thunder are you doing?"

The man at the wheel did not reply.

But deliberately did he turn the helm, till the ship, under its crowd of all sail, veered completely round, and run upon the black sands, where she stuck fast, like an elephant in a bog.

Captain Hall sprang at the pilot with his eyes flashing fire.

"Curse me, sir! the black sand!"

"Entirely your own fault, Captain Hall. While the vessel was in my charge, you had no right to speak. If any damage is done, you will certainly be blamed for it, and the buccaneers will get away."

The captain stamped in wild fury.

"Out with the boats! Give chase! By Jove! the buccaneers are unloading and taking to the boats, too."

"Then he will land his cargo," said the man at the wheel.

"Who says that?"

"I do," said the pilot, letting go the helm, and taking a pistol in each hand. "I do, Tom Drake, the Captain of the Buccaneers!"

Nothing but the fearless devilry of his nature, roused by seeing his men unloading their cargo in the very teeth of the Government schooner, made Captain Tom say who he was at the peril of his life.

But having said it, there he stood with death in either hand confronting the captain, who was startled by the daring words, that after saying—

"Curse you, sir!"

He stood with his mouth open staring at the gallant figure at the wheel.

At last he found voice.

"Two marines!" he shouted. "Forward men! Here's the devil of a buccaneer at the wheel."

There was a general shout in reply, and it seemed to the pilot that they all rushed at him at once.

Then they stopped all of a heap.

Tom Drake had coolly faced them. His right hand grasped the cutlass that hung by his side, whilst his left clutched the butt of a pistol, and with a look of stern defiance on his pale, but handsome brow, he stood ready to meet the attack of his fierce assailants.

"The devil take you!" roared Captain Hall, on seeing the confusion into which his men had been thrown. "Secure him, you lubbers!"

But the lubbers, as he termed them, found they had a difficult task to perform; and having heard of the daring achievements of the young buccaneer, they did not care to be the first to tackle him.

Captain Hall was now placed in rather an awkward position. Every moment he was delayed, and the delay was giving time to the buccaneers; and as his eye glanced over the quarter, and he saw the boats conveying the valuable cargo towards the shore, he bit his lips with rage.

"Down with him!" he yelled. "But take him alive if possible! The yard-arm is the fittest place for him!"

So saying, he rushed towards the spot where Captain Tom now stood motionless, his ear drinking in every sound, and his eye ranging from one to the other of the many eager foes that were about to rush upon him.

"Murderer," said the captain of the schooner, "there is no chance of escape, you must now settle the great debt you owe to your country."

"Surrender, I never will," at once said Tom Drake, as he brandished his cutlass above his head.

Captain Hall was a brave man, and had never flinched from shot or steel, and believing Tom Drake completely in his power, and galled at the daring of the buccaneer, sprang upon him with a fearful yell.

The clash of weapons now rang on the night air, and the marines and blue-jackets could not suppress a murmur of admiration as they watched the rapid movements of Tom Drake, who appeared but a stripling compared to the herculean form of Captain Hall.

Captain Hall fought with the fury of a tiger, as he tried to beat his youthful opponent to the deck, whilst Tom Drake, who had never for a moment lost his temper, guarded the furious blows of his assailant with the coolness for which he was so renowned.

And, at length, by a dexterous movement, dashed the cutlass from the hand of Captain Hall, who was now at his mercy.

But Tom, though pressed as he was by his assailants, and with death almost staring him in the face, could not take the life of the now defenceless captain, though menaced by a score of muskets and pistols which were now pointed towards him.

"I do not wish to stain my hands in the blood of a fallen foe," said Tom, as he lowered his weapon; "I am no pirate, I fight for my own ends with the strong, and protect the weak."

As he spoke, he pointed towards the brig, the crew of which were toiling vigorously in landing the precious articles with which she was freighted.

All eyes were now directed towards the "Will-o'-the-Wisp," and a dark scowl rested on the brow of the captain, as he saw the loaded boats passing between the shore and the brig, and in that moment Tom Drake saw his chance.

When, foaming with rage, Captain Hall turned towards the spot where the pilot had stood but an instant before, he had disappeared.

"Where has he gone?" he shouted, turning to a marine who stood nearest to him. "Do you hear me, you villain?" he roared, seizing him by the throat, whilst the marine, who, like the rest of the crew, had been watching the buccaneers, stood paralysed. "If you don't answer me, I'll give you four dozen in the morning!"

"I don't know where he is, captain," said the man, recovering his breath. "He was there just now."

"Well, go and find him!" thundered Captain Hall, "or I'll find you at the grating in the morning!"

Everyone was now searching the vessel.

Every corner had been examined, but in vain.

"Search the hold!" roared the captain, at the top of his voice, "and lay aloft there, some of you lubbers; search the mastheads!"

A dozen of the sailors sprang aloft, but their search only proved fruitless; and they now descended to the deck to be loaded with abuse, for the captain, enraged at losing his prisoner in so mysterious a manner, looked suspiciously at every one who approached him.

"Lower the boats there!" he shouted, in a thick voice.

And as quick as thought the boats were lowered, and the marines seated in the stern sheets of each, whilst the sailors manned the oars, and pulled with a long, rapid stroke towards the brig.

As they neared the "Will-o'-the-Wisp," the forms of the buccaneers were plainly to be seen moving hurriedly about the decks, and now the clear ringing of the windlass pawls plainly told their work was accomplished, and that they were about heaving up the anchor.

"Give way, my sons," said the captain, in a husky voice. "We must not lose the vessel. Perhaps he swam on board of her, for I believe the fellow is endowed with power to do anything. Give way together!" he cried, through his clenched teeth. "They will give us a run for it now, if you don't bend your lazy backs."

On flew the boats, whilst the perspiration poured from the reeking brows of the sailors, and the oars bent like bows under their united efforts.

The sails of the brig were now hoisted to the breeze, and she began to skim lightly through the water, when all three of the boats dashed alongside.

But the buccaneers were prepared for them, and as they came on deck they were met with a stout resistance.

Ben Barnacle, who had charge of the vessel, had armed all the crew, and they had sworn to a man not to be taken alive.

A fearful contest raged on board the brig, and many of the man-of-war's men had lost their lives in trying to gain the deck.

And the voices of the combatants, mingled with the report of pistols and clashing of swords, sounded far over the rippling water.

The tall form of Captain Hall could be seen, as he tried desperately to cleave his way through the struggling throng of human beings towards the place where Ben Barnacle was rallying his band of bold and desperate men.

"Ha, ha!" shouted the captain, in an exulting tone, "I have met you at last, face to face, Ben Barnacle—eh!"

The recognition was mutual, and the two desperate men now closed in deadly combat.

Meanwhile, Captain Tom, who had purposely directed their attention to the brig, made his way with stealthy step to the fore-hatch, and instantly disappeared, and in a few minutes made his appearance on deck clothed in the uniform of the ship, having procured a suit of clothes from the bag of one of the sailors, and, before they were aware of his absence had mingled with the crew, who were all mustered on the quarter-deck.

Willingly he assisted in searching the vessel, and having ascertained when down in the hold that she made but little water, and well knowing that the tide was rising, he quickly formed a daring project.

When the order was given to lower and man the boats, he was the first to obey the order.

Having watched the whole of the crew into the boats, he crouched down below the bulwarks, and listened in breathless anxiety for the order to shove off.

Could Captain Hall have seen the smiling face peering out of one of the ports as he gave the order to give way, it might have changed his projects.

But his mind was so engrossed on the one object, that it had quite slipped his notice even that the vessel was beginning to float.

They had not left the ship many minutes when Tom commenced operations.

Having hauled the schooner's fore-yard aback, which he did in a very short time, the "Thunderer" began to slide off the sandbank on which she had been so firmly fixed but a short time before.

For, the tide having risen, and the wind blowing the sails aback, she had gently slided off into deep water, and was now steering in the same direction.

The boats had gone but a few minutes before Captain Hall and Ben Barnacle were fiercely contending for each other's life, when the schooner came sailing past the brig.

"Brig ahoy!" roared Captain Tom, as he stood at the helm.

Every one on board the brig seemed as though they were entranced, each one had paused as though by mutual consent, and hostilities ceased at the sound of that voice.

As Captain Hall gazed on the snowy canvas of the schooner, the beating of his heart for a moment seemed to have ceased; his features assumed an ashy paleness, while his herculean frame trembled like an aspen leaf.

Picking up the sword which had dropped from his grasp, he shouted—

"To the boats! By Heavens, that fellow is running away with our ship!"

The crew of the schooner dashed to the bulwarks, and tried to retreat to their boats, but the buccaneers pressed hard upon them, and only a few of the brave fellows who left the schooner were able to gain the boats alive, and those few had not escaped without wounds.

A boat well armed now shot from under the quarter of the brig, and hotly pursued the schooner.

A change in the aspect of affairs came at this juncture.

A dark shadowy mass was seen creeping upon the waters towards them.

It bore down upon the combatants, and, when it was near, a vivid flash came from its sides, revealing the crowded decks of a British man-of-war.

A cheer rose from Captain Hall's crew, and told the buccaneers of their new danger. A danger sharp and terrible; for the British frigate was bearing swiftly down, the guns were out at the port-holes, and now sheeted flames were vomited from her, and the ponderous iron missiles of death were hurled across the waves to annihilate the bold buccaneers, whose daring audacity had, as it seemed, brought them to imminent destruction.

A dead silence reigned after the first discharge of the frigate's guns, and in the dense darkness none knew what execution had been done.

But in an instant a blueish flash swept across the tossing waves, a loud report shook the air, and then all was again dark and still.

Then a loud hurrah broke from the men of the

frigate, and even the admiral joined in the shout that proclaimed that they had blown the buccaneer's ship to pieces in the air.

CHAPTER CXXXII.

PURSUIT OF THE DARING BUCCANEER — CAPTAIN TOM AND ADMIRAL ELLIS MEET AGAIN.

THE sea was still wildly tossed, but a strange silence had succeeded the terrible discord that had marked the conflict for life or death.

The night was still dark as pitch, but a light gleamed on the frigate's bows, and on shore, amongst the rocks, where the wreckers and smugglers had watched the action, lanterns flashed from point to point, and occasionally a blue light went up in the air.

Admiral Ellis, who was more inveterate than ever against Tom Drake, had received information of his enemy's whereabouts, swore a terrible revenge.

He had a sharp look-out kept for any drowning men or floating pieces of wreck from the vessel he believed he had shivered into atoms.

His first lieutenant stood by his elbow.

"We've done their business," the admiral observed.

"We have, sir."

"Knocked them into pieces, eh?"

"Aye, sir. We shall not hear much more of Tom Drake."

"Nor of his desperate crew either. The scoundrel fought well, too."

"And had evidently deceived the 'Thunderer.'"

"Deceived—I could have sworn at one time he had the vessel under his command, and if any one else besides my old friend Captain Hall had been on board, I should have believed he had, too."

"He was daring enough, sir."

"A brave rascal. He might have been an ornament to his Majesty's service if he had not been used to the rascally profession of a buccaneer, and then to take up with the smugglers, too. He is incomparable!"

The lieutenant was about to reply, when the little admiral suddenly cried—

"By Heavens! there is something wrong—the 'Thunderer' is on fire!"

The lieutenant looked in the direction of the vessel. Till now it had been only indistinctly visible, but as if by magic a subtile breathing light crept round its hull, and sped swiftly up its masts, then it was seen to roll and pitch in the waves.

While they looked, a lurid light shot from stem to stern, and the crew of the frigate suspended operations to gaze in dismayed horror at what they saw.

The deck of the "Thunderer" was one mass of lurid light, and in the midst of the flames could be seen the figure of a human being who sped quickly to and fro, thrusting with a cutlass at the sailors who were endeavouring to cut him down.

He had a lighted torch in his other hand, and wherever he went a blaze of light marked his track

Whatever he touched broke out into instantaneous flame.

Admiral Ellis was the first to rouse from the lethargy into which this spectacle had thrown them.

"Crowd all sail, lads," he cried, "and keep your guns ready to fire at my command!"

The canvas fluttered in the breeze, and the huge frigate swung round upon the burning ship.

A defiant laugh came from the deck of the ill-fated vessel, and Admiral Ellis almost leapt from where he stood.

"Point your guns, men," he roared "it is the buccaneer fiend, Tom Drake; he must be the very devil to escape so many deaths; make sure of him this time. Ready—fire!"

The loud crash of the broadside followed his words; the heavy iron swept through the air and struck the side of the "Thunderer," but almost before that flash died away, that defiant laugh came again from its deck, and the human figure was seen to leap headlong into the sea.

An instant after, with a fearful explosion, "Thunderer," blew up.

And by its vivid light the men on the deck of the frigate, saw a little boat flit along the surface the waves.

A solitary rower plied the oars, and the light of a burning torch gleamed upon his features.

"If a man could escape such certain destruction," said the admiral, "I should believe the rower to be Tom Drake. The devil must be at his elbow; it is the infernal robber! Bring your guns to bear, lads! Fire a broadside; sink him, boat and all!"

A wild laugh came back from the distance, then the frigate's guns belched forth flame and death.

The iron missiles ploughed up the water, but the solitary rower sat in his boat unharmed.

The little admiral was furious.

"Boats out!" he cried. "He is making for the shore. Follow, and bring him, dead or alive!"

Not content with waiting for the boats to be lowered, Admiral Ellis, in his bitter hate to rid himself of so daring a foe, who had humiliated his naval honours, pointed again at Tom Drake; but the huge ball only tossed up the waves yards from the boat.

The daring buccaneer could be seen making steadily for the shore, the glare of his torch, still burning at the prow of his frail vessel, revealing his track.

He might, by extinguishing this, have effected an escape under cover of the darkness, but, with the known devilry of his nature, he suffered them to see the course he took.

As for their guns, he laughed at the idea of any ball touching the boat he was in.

With the frigate so near, it would have been madness to have made for the shore, and yet there appeared no other chance of eluding his pursuers.

The buccaneers who were on shore flashed lights from point to point of the rocks, guiding him if he wished to make for land, but he kept away from the rocks. The frigate's boats were pulling steadily after him, towards the shore, to intercept and make sure of him.

The chase now became intensely exciting, and was watched with great interest both by those on board the frigate, and those on shore.

It was a hazardous run for life, and there did not seem much hope for the pursued.

The admiral watched Tom Drake round a rocky point, and, as he believed, draw into the shore.

He was afraid his own boats would not come across him in time, and so he pointed another gun at him, this time with perfect aim—so true, indeed, that the ball struck the flaming torch from the buccaneer's boat, and left him in total darkness.

The admiral foamed in fury at his own folly.

He had given Tom Drake his only chance of safety.

Running up lanterns from the yards of his vessel, he endeavoured, by continual discharges of unshotted guns, to throw a light on the receding boat, but Tom Drake, by skilful rowing, baffled his attempts.

Straining hard at the oars, he pulled vigorously out to sea, scarcely a splash betraying which way he went.

He was calmer now, and knew what a terrible risk he incurred.

He was far from the shore when he heard the

regular dripping of water, and knew that one of the pursu' boats was near.

It was too dark to see, but he drew steadily away, and then rested on his oars to allow the boat to come by.

The men were rowing cautiously, and he heard them conversing about the certainty of his capture.

"He's a devil to fight," he heard one say, "and we'd better settle him with a bullet as soon as we catch sight of him."

Captain Tom was so close to the speaker that he might have pulled him from his seat.

Another man spoke.

"We shall have a reward for catching him—sure to get something, I suppose."

He did get something.

Captain Tom sat still as a statute. As the boat glided by, carefully balancing himself, he leaned over and caught the blade of the oar the man was in the act of dipping into the sea.

Giving it a sudden wrench, he twisted it out of the man's hand so violently, that the fellow went sprawling on his back, while the boat lurched half over.

"The devil—I've caught a crab!" spluttered the man.

He caught something else, too.

Captain Tom gave him a drive in the ribs with the oar that sent him back again as he was trying to rise, and nearly knocked all the breath out of his body.

While he was lying prone he caught sight of a pair of eyes flashing upon him from the darkness.

With a sudden yell of affright, he clutched at the oar, crying—

"Here he is—Captain Tom—catch the devil—here he is!"

The sudden warning caused the boat's crew to start up quickly, and Captain Tom, by an adroit movement, capsized them all into the sea.

This accomplished, he thought it time to pull into shore.

With long, steady strokes he made for land, while the crew struggled to regain their capsized boat.

He had chosen a place some distance from where the frigate lay; it was where a little creek ran into shore.

There were no lights here, and he had a better chance of escape.

If he did not run foul upon the officers of the customs or the coastguard, who were always on the look-out at such points.

Peering through the darkness, he saw a favourable landing-place, and, as his boat grated on the sand, stepped to the beach.

At this moment a vivid flash went up from the frigate—a light so bright that it revealed the scene for miles round, and betrayed the spot where he had landed.

With a loud hurrah, the men in the other boats, who had been lying in close, made for the shore, and Captain Tom knew that unless he could speedily elude their vigilance, the most gallant defence would not avail to save his life.

A few rude habitations were scattered here and there about the rugged coast, but a little way inland were some mansions of large dimensions.

Many of these were familiar to our hero, and it was his object to keep as far away from them as possible.

He took care, too, to be as much in shelter as he possibly could.

Blue lights and rockets still went up from the frigate, which was signalling to those on shore to intercept the buccaneer, and Tom Drake had now to be cautious to keep in the shadow of the rocks,

in order not to be seen by the revenue officers who were turned out to capture him.

The commotion behind him assured him that his pursuers had landed, but he did not fear those in his rear.

He feared more the foes who were in front.

All of a sudden, as he was creeping by the rocks, a light flashed upon him, and he found himself confronted by a party of custom officers.

A cry from them, uttering his name, a rush, a swift report, followed by another, a gleam of steel, and he had forced through their midst—how he knew not.

Scathed but untaken.

He heard their shouts of rage and pain as he went like a meteor through them, and bounded fleetly away.

A short run brought him to the edge of a little stream, widening inland from the creek, here and there was a heavy boat, in which a roughish-looking man was seated, leisurely listening to the sounds of pursuit and strife.

When he saw Tom Drake he divined how matters stood, and standing up in the boat stretched out his long, gaunt hands to take the daring buccaneer.

"You've just dropped in the right spot," he said, with a grin; "make up your mind to stay till they come. I'm the boy to take care of you."

He laid his hand on Tom's shoulder.

The young buccaneer shook him quickly off.

"Fool!" he said, "a word, and I send a bullet through your brain."

He thrust a pistol against the fellow's temple.

The man looked at him in open-mouthed dismay. He had not seen that he was armed, and so made sure of an easy capture.

He was careful of what brains he had, and hesitated what he should do.

Gallant Tom, ever prompt in action, very speedily took him by the throat, and, having forced him to the bottom of the boat, leapt in, and knelt upon his chest while he gagged and bound him.

Then, with giant strength, he hurled him on to the water's edge and taking his seat in the boat, rowed away as his pursuers came upon the scene.

He was out of their reach long before they could get another boat ready to follow him, and he made the best of the advantage he had gained to keep out of their reach.

He was pulling for the open sea, when, to his dismay, he heard the other boats approaching, and not caring to run the gauntlet of them, he once more rowed for land, where, abandoning the boat, he sought safety in a speedy flight.

Owing to the darkness of the night he thought he had missed his way, and feeling fatigued from his recent exertions, he stopped for a moment.

It was not long, however, before he heard the voices of the revenue men close behind him.

There was not a moment to be lost.

They were coming after him in full cry, bounding over crag and rock like a pack of bloodhounds.

Fortunately for Tom Drake, it was too dark for his pursuers to see him, or they would have brought him to earth with a volley of bullets

As it was, they seemed more acquainted with the locality than he did.

He kept stumbling at every few steps, while his pursuers fairly bounded along the rugged way.

Matters were growing serious—Tom Drake was tiring, and the revenue men were every moment gaining upon him.

Dashing he knew not whither or cared, so that he escaped his pursuers for the time, he found himself in a deep and narrow ravine.

On he went, trusting to Providence to guide him to a goal of safety; and as he groped his way along, he had the joy of hearing the officers pass the mouth of the ravine.

Having ascended a steep aclivity, he paused to breathe and survey his position.

Not very far ahead of him, he saw a glimmer of light amongst a forest of trees, and thither he made his way, in the hope of finding a place of refuge.

Having neared the lights, he found himself in the vicinity of a splendid mansion, but driven now to desperation, he would not turn back, and sprang lightly up the rocks.

He held a pistol in one hand, and a sword gleamed in the other.

Suddenly he came upon a young and beautiful girl, who shuddered, for she saw that the sword was red.

The young buccaneer had only got a little way up the rocks when two of his pursuers advanced upon him.

The lady saw how his graceful figure was drawn erect, and how his kindling eyes flashed as his keen sword circled above his head.

She saw his assailants lunge at him with their weapons, and she suppressed a shriek, as it seemed that he was run through the head, but while she looked he had whirled the cutlass from the grasp of one and hurled the other headlong to the earth.

A loud shout now rose on the air, and as the young buccaneer sprang higher up the rocks a party of custom-house officers, armed with cutlasses and pistols, covered him with their weapons.

Her heart seemed stilled as she heard them summon him to surrender.

His undaunted reply answered them.

Then there was a blinding flash, and she saw him stagger and fall.

He rose again instantly but seemed faint and overcome.

He was bleeding and half stunned, but as if nerved to exertion by the approach of his foes, he drew himself erect, and seizing the first who came, thrust him down upon the remainder.

A moment more, and he had vanished from her sight.

The guests were pouring from the house with her father; the tumult had brought them forth, and she, horror-stricken by what she had witnessed, withdrew from observation.

She knew not why, but the youth had interested her; and she was sadly hoping that he might not be killed, when, with a single leap, he came from behind the rocks that formed a wall round the house, and stood suddenly before her.

Too startled to speak, she gazed upon him, with her large eyes dilating, and her fair bosom heaving in pity as well as alarm.

The brave Tom Drake stopped in surprise at seeing her, and then stepped towards her and said—

"Lady, I am hunted to death! Will you betray me to my foes?"

"Alas! what have you done?"

"Enough to make my life valueless. They come, and I must defend myself to the last drop of blood!"

The beautiful girl looked at the noble figure before her, wounded and blood-stained, faint and almost overcome; he yet seemed so noble and gentle that she could not bear the idea of his being slain.

"Alas!" she cried, wringing her hands, "they will kill you! Can you not escape?"

"This is impossible, lady. I thank you for taking an interest in my fate, but I am doomed, and can only sell my life dearly."

His hand clenched on his reeking cutlass.

She stepped towards him timidly.

"Oh, no, no!" she cried. "Don't sacrifice your life. Escape!"

"Lady, there is no way."

"There is! Hide in this house—in there—it is my chamber—enter by the balcony—quick! They are coming! Oh, Heavens! you are lost!"

He had stayed to fall on one knee, and take her hand in grateful respect.

Now he saw his pursuers advancing, and with one light bound he leapt to the balcony.

The folding windows were open, and he noiselessly stepped to the carpeted floor.

He was hardly out of sight, when the officers came up the rocks; at the same time her father, accompanied by his guests, came rushing to the spot.

"Seek your chamber, my child!" he cried, as they went past. "A noted smuggler and pirate is concealed about the place. His hands are red with blood, and he would murder you, should you fall in his way."

They went past her, little dreaming that her trembling, fragile form almost secured from their sight the young buccaneer whom they were seeking. They went, and left her standing there, mute with fear and horror at what she had done.

The words of the lady's father fell like a thunderbolt upon the ears of his daughter, and trembling in every limb she stood as though transfixed with horror.

Her tongue clove to the roof of her mouth, and the scream that arose to her lips died away unuttered.

It was well for our hero it did so, for that cry of alarm would have brought his pursuers, who, like a pack of wolves, were panting for his blood, to the place of his concealment.

And in his exhausted state he would, no doubt, have fallen an easy victim to their vengeance although he would have sold his life as dearly possible, yet eventually he must have succumb to the overwhelming number of his enemies.

The young lady, alarmed at the thought having sheltered so black a villain, who, if h father spoke true, had added murder to his crime and fearful for her safety—for she was now alone with him—her fear overcame her strength, and she swooned away.

She would have fallen to the floor, had not Tom Drake, who, seeing her stagger, flown to her assistance and caught her in his arms.

Having gently laid her upon a couch, he procured some water and gently bathed her pallid brow, and moistened the compressed and colourless lips of the apparently lifeless young lady.

The approaching voices of his pursuers now awoke him to a sense of his danger, and the awkward predicament in which he stood.

They had searched every place in the vicinity of the mansion where it was likely a man could conceal himself.

The voices of the men sounded as though they were now under the balcony by which he had entered, and now, from his position, he could hear their conversation.

"It's no use us of us searching in that direction," said a gruff voice under the balcony. "I believe he is in the mansion, for the last time I saw him he stood somewhere about this spot."

"Then search the house, by all means," said the owner, who had assisted in the search from roof to cellar, "for I shall not be easy till I am certain he is not in the neighbourhood."

A strong guard being posted round the mansion to prevent the escape of the buccaneer, they commenced a rigid search of the interior.

The young lady was now slowly returning to consciousness, and when at length her eyes opened, their pale blue orbs rested on the pale but handsome features of the hunted youth.

A thrill of horror ran through her frame.

A faint cry of alarm arose to her lips, and again she relapsed into a swoon.

Although only a few minutes had elapsed since the young buccaneer had entered the apartment, it appeared to him as though it were an age.

The sound of approaching footsteps in the corridor leading to the chamber aroused him into action, but he had scarcely time to conceal himself beneath the bed when the door opened, and a dozen man-of-war's men, armed with swords and pistols, headed by the lieutenant, entered the room.

The nobleman, on seeing the position of his daughter, as she lay on the couch, her small and delicate hands clasped as though in great agony, placed his hand upon his heated brow.

As he glanced towards the open window, his face assumed an ashy paleness, and his corpulent frame was seized with a violent trembling.

"Great Heavens!" he cried. "Has the villain dared to pollute the chamber of my daughter with his unholy presence?"

"And, oh!" he exclaimed, his voice hoarse with intense emotion, "has he dared to insult my daughter? If so, I'll hunt him like a beast of the forest; even were he to assume the form of a worm that burrows in the earth, I would find him."

"It's evident some one has been here, Sir Henry," said the lieutenant, "for see, here is a basin of water; it is probable he may have escaped by the window."

So saying, he rushed to the balcony.

"Below, there!" he shouted.

"Aye, aye, sir!"

"Have you seen anybody pass out this window?"

"No! no! no!" answered several voices.

"Keep a good look-out, then, for the villain is not far off."

Sir Henry had been so deeply engrossed in the thought of his daughter, that he was not aware of the presence of so many of the sailors.

Now, seeing them gazing on her inanimate, but lovely form, he turned angrily towards them, and ordered them to leave the room.

"A lady's chamber," he said, "is no fit place for a host of armed men."

Having closed the door, Sir Henry, by the aid of stimulants, proceeded to restore his lovely daughter to consciousness.

Having procured a small bottle from one of the drawers in the apartment, he placed it to the nostrils of his dearly-beloved daughter, and a burning tear coursed down the old man's face as he imprinted a kiss upon her marble brow.

In a few seconds she opened her eyes, and in as many more was able to speak.

The first question he asked her was, whether or no the buccaneer had entered her apartment, and being answered in the affirmative, a groan of agony burst from his lips, for he feared his worst doubts were confirmed, and springing to the middle of the chamber, he swore, with a bitter oath, to find the buccaneer that night.

The daring buccaneer, who, during this time, had been concealed under the bed, had listened with intense interest to their conversation, and a flush of indignation mantled his brow.

Creeping noiselessly from his place of concealment, he stepped sharply to the centre of the room, and with a look of defiance, faced Sir Henry.

Had his Satanic majesty appeared before them, they could not have been more astounded; but, afore they could recover from their surprise, the light barrel of a pistol was presented at Sir Henry's head.

"If you raise any alarm," said he, in a tone of "it will be the signal for the death of both

The young lady, on seeing the supposed pirate threatening her father with death, uttered a piercing scream.

Captain Tom was the first to speak.

"Hear me!" he cried, vehemently, "hear me, Sir Henry. I have heard you pronounce me a murderer and pirate. I deny the accusation; what I have done has been done in self-defence."

"And, again," he continued, "I have heard you accuse me of insulting your daughter. Of this charge, too, I swear I am innocent, and declare it in her presence."

At this instant a crash sounded in the casement behind him; a bullet whizzed past him, grazing his boot, and entering the leg of Sir Henry, who fell to the ground, uttering a deep groan.

"Treachery!" roared the lieutenant, springing to the window, and the lady flew to the assistance of her father, and raising his head, supported it on her snowy arm.

In the confusion caused by the shot, Captain Tom saw his only chance of escape.

Bending on one knee, and imprinting a kiss upon the delicate hand of the young lady, he said—

"I will go and fetch a doctor."

The lieutenant was engaged in loud altercation on the balcony, and the young buccaneer, well knowing there was no time to be lost, hastily left the room.

He threaded the various corridors without meeting with a single person, for the guests, who had been waiting in great anxiety, and eager to ascertain the result of their search, were getting uneasy at their long absence, and, on hearing the report of fire-arms, had rushed to the garden to ascertain the cause.

Having arrived in the hall without interruption, he speedily attired himself in the great coat and hat of one of the guests, and, thus disguised, emerged into the garden.

He had not proceeded far, when his progress was arrested by the stalwart form of one of the man-of-war's men, who threw himself into his path.

"Where are you steering to?" said the sailor, placing his brawny hand upon the shoulder of the young buccaneer.

Captain Tom grasped the butt of a pistol he had concealed in the breast of his coat, and affecting surprise at the conduct of the sailor, thus threw him off his guard.

"What! have you not heard that Sir Henry has been badly wounded, in attempting to capture Tom Drake?"

"What?" said the sailor, in amazement. "The genelman that lives in this big house?"

"Certainly; he was shot, when standing face to face with the buccaneer."

"Well, shiver my timbers!" said the sailor, taking an extra nip at the huge quid of tobacco, that caused his cheek to protrude, as though he was suffering greatly from the toothache. "Only to think of him shooting the genelman, arter us chasing him about all night."

"And was the buccaneer in the house?" he inquired.

"Yes; he was in yonder room a few minutes since."

"Are you quite sure it was him?" said the sailor, who could scarcely believe it to be true.

"I am positive. I was in the room at the time."

"And where are you going now?" inquired the sailor, eyeing him narrowly. "Our orders are to arrest anyone that offers to leave the mansion."

"Oh, indeed," rejoined Captain Tom Drake, affecting to be surprised; "but you will not dare to detain me. I am going to seek a doctor for the gentleman, who, I fear, is dangerously wounded."

TOM DRAKE DISARMS THE CAPTAIN OF THE GUARD.

"Oh! then you are under sailing orders. I am sorry I detained you so long, but duty is duty, and we must attend to it."

"You are quite right, my good man," said Captain Tom, "and though this delay may prove dangerous to the wounded gentleman, the fault will not lay at your door."

"But before you go," said the sailor, "tell me which room you saw this covey in, for I would not mind giving a month's grog, much as I like it, to have a fair look at his figure-head."

"Have you not seen him, then?" said Captain Tom, affecting surprise, which would certainly have allayed any suspicion that might have been lurking in his breast.

"No; but I will to-night if there is the least

chance. for he must be a devil in human form to escape us as he has done. I have to thank him for this," he said, raising his tarpaulin hat. and showing a ghastly wound in his forehead, from which the blood was oozing.

Captain Tom gazed at the wound, which assumed an ugly appearance, and feeling sorry for the poor fellow, resolved to make him the only recompense then in his power.

That was to obtain him an interview with the buccaneer, so that he might form his own opinion whether he was flesh and blood.

"Well, my friend," said Tom Drake, "you want to see Captain Tom?"

"I do."

"Then you shall see him, but, mind, only on on.

41

condition—that is, you must promise me that when you see him you will keep silent."

"Rather queer conditions, old fellow," said the sailor, turning his quid, "but, nevertheless, I will comply with them."

"Come this way, then," said the daring boy, taking a path that led towards the back of the mansion.

Then, stopping abruptly, he said—

"You see yonder casement?"

"I do."

It was plainly to be seen, for, from the window indicated by Captain Tom, streamed forth a bright light, and beneath the window might be seen the figures of many men, moving rapidly to and fro.

"That is the room in which I saw the buccaneer."

The sailor's eyes were now turned in the direction of the window, and Captain Tom, in the meantime, having divested himself of his disguise, said—

"And here is Captain Tom Drake!"

The sailor turned, and beheld with astonishment the young buccaneer, with his arms folded.

At first the thought crossed his mind that he would pounce upon him, who appeared but a boy compared with the herculean form of the stalwart sailor, but, catching a glimpse of a couple of pistols protruding from his elbows, it altered his views, and he was about to raise an alarm.

"Is that the way you keep your promise?" interrogated Tom, whilst a smile of contempt played upon his lips, for he had anticipated the intention of the sailor.

For a moment the sailor stood abashed, and as he gazed on the stern features of the buccaneer, a feeling almost amounting to fear seemed to take possession of him.

"See what is that yonder?" said Captain Tom, pointing with a pistol to something in the rear of him.

CHAPTER CXXXII.

THE SEARCH FOR TOM DRAKE.

THE sailor, alarmed at the tone in which these words were spoken, turned his head, and at that moment Tom Drake disappeared.

In the confusion occasioned by the firing of the shot, it was no wonder the absence of the bold buccaneer had not been noticed.

But they had captured the man who had shot Sir Henry by mistake, instead of Tom Drake.

On learning from the young lady that the buccaneer had gone for a surgeon, the lieutenant indulged in a loud laugh, although it ill accorded with his present feelings, and he dispersed the men in different directions to search for him.

These men it was who had attracted Captain Tom's attention when revealing himself to the sailor.

They came on, increasing their speed at every step, for they felt certain he was within their reach.

The men had seen him.

And with a cheer they dashed upon the sailor, just as Tom made his escape, and, before he could utter a word, he was gagged and bound, and borne to the mansion.

Imagine their surprise when, having procured a light, they discovered they had taken one of their own men, who did not forget to give them a specimen of his vocal abilities, or abstain in free use of his jawing-tackle.

Meanwhile, Captain Tom pursued his road without meeting with any obstacle, and soon gained the rocks in which the cavern was formed.

How his heart beat as he wound his way up a narrow and dangerous pass.

On one side lay a dark, yawning chasm; on the other the towering cliffs hung their dark heads over the path of the weary buccaneer, as he dragged his bruised and wounded limbs up the craggy rocks.

He had now reached a portion of the cliffs which formed a flat shelf, and he was about to make his way through a crevice in the rocks, which formed a passage just wide enough for one man to pass at a time, when two dark forms emerged from behind a projecting portion of the rocks, and, ere he was aware of the presence of anyone, he was thrown heavily to the ground, the pistols were snatched from his belt, and a heavy foot pressed firmly on his breast, a demoniac laugh echoed through the crevice, and died away among the rocks.

It was John Bentley, and his companion in treachery, Red Ralph, the wrecker.

"I told you we should met again," said Bentley, with a scornful curl of the lip.

"And what would you do with me now we have met?" said Tom Drake, casting a look of defiance at his cowardly assailants.

"We might deliver you into the hands of justice," said Red Ralph, "for the murder of Lieutenant Rayner, but it will be easier to drop you over the cliff."

"Liar!" cried Tom Drake, as he tried to disengage himself from the pressure of the foot of Bentley. "Let me but gain my feet, and then dare to tell me that to my face!"

He struggled frantically to release himself, but without success, for Bentley knew full well he would be a tough customer to serve if he once gained his feet, even though it were two to one.

The cowardly ruffian now seized him, and bore him, more dead than alive, to the edge of the yawning chasm, and, as they held him to the ground, knowing he had no power to hurt them, they began to taunt him.

"Now, my fine fellow," said Red Ralph, in a mocking tone, "you have forgotten throwing me over the cliff, have you? I have not."

"Neither have I forgotten the little debt I owe you," said Bentley, with a sneer. "We have made up our minds to throw you down the precipice; we can then take both of the girls just to amuse us, and to-morrow we shall sail away. We have made it all right with some of your men, who believe you have fallen in a skirmish, and they will be all ready by sunset. Ben Barnacle is to be drugged, and that will remove our only obstacle."

As the gallant buccaneer listened to the galling taunts of his enemies, the perspiration rolled in large drops from his heated brow, and, with a violent effort, he tried to wrest himself from the iron grasp of his cruel torturers.

But all his efforts were in vain.

He was sadly fatigued with the trials he had passed through already.

His opponents were two powerful and desperate men.

They tried to hurl him over the cliff, but he clung to them with death-like tenacity.

They had forced him over the edge of the cliff, and he was hanging amid air, the dark chasm yawning beneath him.

Still he clung to his would-be murderers, and it would seem they were all going over together.

In vain they tried to loose his hold of their garments.

He seemed to clutch more firmly at every attempt to shake him off.

A piercing shriek rose from among the rocks, and a dark form was seen hurriedly making its way towards the spot where the three men were engaged in deadly struggle.

CHAPTER CXXXIII.

THE DISINTERMENT OF GUS RAYNER.

WHEN Bentley buried his weapon in the breast of his victim, Gus Rayner, little did he think a pair of eyes were watching his every movement.

But there was one, Daft Watty, as he was called by those who knew him, he had narrowly watched the wrecker in all his movements.

He had seen John Bentley deal the fatal blow, and he had also seen the burial of the young officer.

They called him daft, or foolish, but there were certain times when his intellect was as clear as those who call themselves wise.

When the coastguard men were searching for the body of their lieutenant, he it was who led them to the grave, where his mortal remains had been buried.

Having provided a couple of spades, the body of Gus Rayner was dug out of the sand in which the buccaneers had so recently buried him.

As they gazed upon the calm, yet rigid features of the young officer, who was deeply respected by all who knew him, a silent tear rolled down the weather-beaten cheek of many of the coastguard men.

Silently they bore his body from the scene of bloodshed, and he was placed in a splendid apartment in one of the mansions in the neighbourhood.

Many of the nobility visited the mansion to view the last remains of the gallant young lieutenant, among whom were Sir Henry and his daughter.

She had met the young lieutenant, and had fallen in love with the bold and handsome countenance of the young officer.

As she gazed upon the marble features of the young man, she could not subdue the emotion that arose in her heart.

Her large dark eyes appeared as though starting from their sockets, and her heaving breast rose and fell like the gentle undulations of the waves, a faint scream burst from her lips, and she fell senseless upon the inanimate form of her lover.

At that moment a loud peal of thunder rent the air, and a blue flash of lightning illuminated the room.

Every eye was fixed towards where the body lay, and it seemed as though the dead man moved.

A small patch of blood appeared on the winding-sheet above the breast of the young man.

Another peal of thunder burst on their ears, even louder than the first, shaking the mansion to its very base.

Another flash of lightning illuminated the apartment.

Again they fancied they saw the murdered man move.

The red patch had grown larger, a low, unearthly moan sounded through the apartment.

Everybody stood awe-stricken, while the storm in mighty fury, raged without, the occasional flashes of lightning darting across the pallid face of the dead man.

Another sepulchral sound broke the stillness, and the guests, panic-stricken, rushed from the apartment.

Sir Henry was the first to recover from the stupor into which he had been thrown by sudden fright, and, seizing a lamp from the table, he was hurrying towards the chamber of death, for he feared for the safety of his daughter.

When the affrighted guests, fearing to be again left alone, clung to him tenaciously, and would not allow him to leave the apartment to which they had flown in their dismay.

After some trouble he broke from them, but his courage returned, and, with trembling steps proceeded to the chamber of death.

Here a horrible sight met his gaze.

His pulse beat violently, and his hair seemed to stand up straight on his head.

His knees trembled, and he would have fallen to the floor, had he not grasped one of the stout oaken chairs.

For there sat the ghastly figure bolt upright on the bed, a purple stream oozing from his breast, his white hand clasping the small, delicate hand of Sir Henry's daughter.

She stood motionless as a statue, a livid hue overspreading her beautiful countenance, whilst her left hand rested upon the shoulder of the young officer.

For a few moments Sir Henry stood as though spellbound, then his horror found vent in a cry that escaped his colourless lips.

A few of the guests more bold than the rest, on hearing the cry, rushed to the chamber to ascertain the cause.

The foremost of the party on entering the door, and seeing the ghastly apparition before him, stopped suddenly, whilst those in the rear, not having time to arrest their headlong course, knocked him down, and the others fell over him.

In the confusion Sir Henry was thrown to the door, the lamp dashed from his hand, and they were left in total darkness.

Frantically they struggled to gain their feet; each one in his eagerness to rise only impeded another's progress, and, as they clung tenaciously to each other, fearful of being left alone, they rolled over one another to reach the door.

Every instant they expected some goblin to appear before them, and everything they touched sent a death-like chill to their hearts.

At length one of the guests in falling staggered against the young lady, who reeled to the floor, dragging the young officer with her, who rolled upon the unfortunate guest who had been unwittingly the cause of the disaster.

On feeling the cold, damp flesh of the supposed corpse, and as the garment wet with blood now daubed against his cheek, a succession of shrieks burst from his affrighted lips, and seemed to rend the darkness of the chamber.

No pen can describe the horrible feelings of the guests who had ventured to the chamber of death, as these piercing shrieks fell on their ears.

They had gained the door which, in the confusion, had unfortunately been closed, and now they were pressing so furiously against the foremost ones, who were trying to pull the door open, that their efforts were rendered fruitless.

Whilst those who had remained in the adjoining apartment, on hearing the clamour and the dreadful shrieks that issued from the dreaded chamber, stood petrified with terror, and dared not venture forth for fear some horrid vision might meet their gaze.

A change in the aspect of affairs came at this juncture.

The lady, who by this time had recovered her self-possession, in a clear, calm voice, bade them not be alarmed.

On hearing her voice they began to feel more assured, and the clamouring guests now giving way, the door was opened and a light once more brought into the apartment.

What a sight that light revealed; there lay the young officer in his blood-stained winding-sheet.

His dark blue eyes staring wildly at the assembled guests, a death-like pallor on his handsome brow, whilst the lily hand of the lovely girl supported his head.

The mystery was soon explained; the gallant young officer had only been wounded by the deadly weapon of his would-be murderer, and he had been buried alive.

For, in the confusion into which the buccaneers had been thrown on discovering the body of the young officer weltering in his blood, the probability of his recovering never crossed their mind, or the gallant Tom Drake would never have consigned his body to the sea-washed grave he had chosen for the young officer's last resting-place.

But being quickly disinterred and laid out in his winding-sheet, he lay in a trance.

And when the lady embraced his cold form, it imparted a genial warmth to his heart, and caused the stagnant blood to flow through his veins.

This caused the crimson stream to ooze from his wounded breast, and the crashing peals of thunder had awakened the spirit that hitherto lay dormant in the almost lifeless clay.

Surgical aid having been procured as soon as possible, and the young man having been placed upon the bed from which he had been so violently drawn but a few moments before, his wounds were speedily dressed.

He was now slowly recovering under the tender care of his watchful attendants.

Thus was Gus Rayner, almost by a miracle, as it were, restored from life to death.

Only a few weeks had elapsed since the startling events recorded in the beginning of this chapter.

Many of the guests of Sir Henry had witnessed the strange scenes of that eventful night, and, on hearing that the fugitive was Captain Tom, and believing him to be the perpetrator of that horrible deed, their excitement was at its highest pitch.

Sir Henry, believing him to be a villain of the blackest dye, his hands red with the blood of his victim, afforded every facility in his power to capture the gallant buccaneer, Captain Tom.

Who can imagine the dismay of Sir Henry on hearing the buccaneer had escaped, but a great weight was removed from his bewildered brain when he heard from his daughter's lips that she had not been molested by the fugitive.

But when she informed him that it was she who concealed the brave buccaneer in her own apartment, and that it was at her own instigation, she believing him to be the injured party, he had entered by the window.

The appalled look that came over his face at these words was indescribable; he sank back into his chair, glaring like a wild wolf at his dismayed daughter.

She trembled like a leaf; her eye dropped beneath her father's savage glare.

"What have I done, dear father, thus to incur your anger?"

"What have you done?" he shouted, in a frenzy of rage, grasping her arm. "You have sheltered a polluted villain from the hands of justice! If it had not been for your folly, ere this he would have been safely lodged in gaol."

"Do not chide me, father," she cried, clasping her hands in despair. "When I saw the young man hunted to death almost, pale but noble, he appeared too good and young to be thus ruthlessly slain."

"Ah!" he said, tightening his grasp upon the maiden's arm. "It was love that prompted you to shield the villain, and you, having invited him to your chamber, have played the harlot beneath your father's roof."

She shook off his grasp, and suddenly stepped back a pace, her sweet face glowing with virtuous indignation, and her glorious eyes flashed as she said—

"Father, dare you accuse me? Do you doubt my chastity? What proofs have you to warrant such an accusation?"

"What further proofs are required," thundered Sir Henry, "but your own words? Your own instigation prompted him to enter your bed-chamber; you concealed him from our view with your person; and when, having searched the house, we enter your chamber and find you laying prostrate on the bed, your hair dishevelled, your clothes disordered, and the villain concealed beneath the bed."

The countenance of the girl assumed an ashy paleness, and her fortitude gave way.

"Father, father!" she cried, imploringly, dropping on her knees and clasping her hands, "spare my feelings I implore you."

He was about to spurn her from him, but she clasped his knees and clung frantically to him.

Then, with an inarticulate murmur on her lips, she fell to the floor in a swoon.

Her father gazed upon her death-like features, and wiped the cold dews from her brow, and a pang of remorse shot through his soul.

"Can she be guilty?" he murmured, half aloud; "no, I cannot believe it. My over-heated brain has conjured up imaginations too horrible to dwell upon."

"Oh! that I could be assured of her innocence," he thought. "But everything appears so suspicious, and her own words only confirm those suspicions."

He was aroused from his meditations by a loud knock at the door, and one of the domestics entered, followed by the surgeon, who had been sent for to dress the wound in Sir Henry's leg.

On seeing Sir Henry leaning over the prostrate form of his daughter they looked at each other in amazement.

Which, being noticed by Sir Henry, a flush of embarrassment mantled in his cheeks.

The young lady, having been placed in bed, her maids were summoned to attend upon her.

While the above scene was being enacted between the lady and her father, a scene of a different nature was taking place in the grounds surrounding the mansion.

Lights flashed in all directions, and the lieutenant, boiling with rage, followed by a body of men, rushed wildly about the grounds.

In vain they searched every rock, and every spot for a mile round, where it was at all likely a man might be concealed.

At length, one of the men caught sight of a dark figure as it stood in bold relief on the summit of a neighbouring rock.

He drew the attention of the lieutenant towards it.

With a yell of triumph, he bounded forward, closely followed by his men.

Nothing impeded their progress.

Onward they dashed like a pack of wolves.

Through bushes and brambles their way lay, but, nothing daunted, they dashed through them, tearing their clothes and flesh in the excitement of the chase.

They now ascended the steep and rugged side of the rocks.

And, above them they could see the object of their search, only a few yards more had they to ascend ere he would be within their grasp.

Another moment and the dark object had disappeared.

With an angry gesture, the lieutenant scrambled to the summit of the rock, and through the piercing darkness he could see the dim outlines of the same dark figure on another projection not far distant.

"Onward," he cried, "he cannot hold out much longer; he is almost winded."

Onward they flew again, reckless of danger.

Every moment brought them nearer to the dark

form, and they had now neared it within a few yards.

They were dashing along at headlong speed, when the lieutenant who was foremost of the pursuing host, stumbled and fell, whilst the others following closely upon him, ere they could check their head-long speed, followed suit.

It was well for them it was so for a few yards in advance, a dark chasm stood ready to receive them with extended jaws.

With a fearful malediction the lieutenant sprang to his feet.

On the other side of the gulf stood the object of their pursuit.

"Do either of you know how we can cross this yawning chasm?" he interrogated, fiercely.

"I do, your honour," answered one of the sea-men, drawing a plug of the favourite weed from his mouth, about the size of an ordinary egg.

"Lead the way, then," he cried, imperatively.

"All right, yer honour, but you must keep your lamps trimmed, for it's rather an awkward gang-way."

"Hold on a bit, old son," he said, shaking his fist at the motionless figure, as it stood like a statue on the edge of the chasm; "we'll soon have our grapline aboard of yer!"

He now led the way along the edge of the chasm, and, dropping down on all fours, like a cat, bade them follow him.

Which they did reluctantly.

He now proceeded along a narrow bridge, formed by the trunk of a tree, thrown across the gulf; they followed him cautiously, for the night was pitchy dark, and below them yawned the chasm.

One false step, and they must be dashed to pieces.

The seaman who had undertaken to guide them, had by this time crossed to the other side, and when he turned in the direction where the figure had last been seen, it had disappeared.

"Curse this Captain Tom!" roared the lieutenant. "They ought to have named him Will-o'-the-Wisp, for he beats all I ever came nigh. I think it would puzzle the devil himself to catch him."

"That's the name of his ship, yer honner," said the seaman. "They say a starn chase is a long 'un, and I think he has led us a good chase to-night, and we arn't had a toothful of grog over it, either."

"You're right, Bill," said another of the seamen, replenishing his quid, and giving it an extra nip, as he thrust it into his cheek; "I think it's time to splice the main-brace. I know if I wore braces they would have to be spliced long before this, for see here, mates, I'm flying signals of distress; they hang about me like Irish pennants, as old Pipes calls 'em."

As he spoke, he held up his arm, and displayed a number of ribbons, for they were nothing else; his jacket and trousers were one mass of tattered rags, torn by the rocks and bushes.

Meanwhile, the lieutenant had been trying to pierce the gloomy darkness that reigned around; at length his eye rested on an object, on a promi-nent rock, as though it were in a reclining posi-tion.

He pointed it out to his men, and they darted off like a pack of hounds in full cry.

The ground over which they were now almost flying, was of so rugged a nature, that they had great difficulty in keeping their feet.

Still onward they flew, feeling certain of obtain-ing some reward if they could only capture the daring buccaneer, who had, up to this time, eluded all pursuit, and escaped from the many snares that had been laid for him.

They were now closing fast upon the object of their pursuit, but owing to the rocky nature of the ground they were obliged to slacken speed, and proceed more cautiously.

"He's off again, yer honour," said one of the sailors.

True enough, the dark form now stood erect, and was rapidly moving away.

When the lieutenant, who was almost exhausted, and burning with vexation, levelled his pistol, the report followed, a blinding flash, and the retreating form dropped to the earth.

With an exultant cheer they now dashed forward, each eager to be the first to capture the daring young buccaneer.

A few moments brought them to the spot, the lieutenant, who believing his foe to be harmless, having previously shot him claimed the right to capture, and ordered his men to stand back.

Brandishing his cutlass above his head, he stepped boldly up to the crouching victim and was about to order him to surrender and lay down his arms—for his bullying propensities far exceeded his bravery—when his wounded victim, who had allowed him to approach to within a few feet, charged him in the stomach with his head.

And the lieutenant went sprawling on the ground, gasping for breath.

A hearty roar of laughter burst from the stentorian lungs of the sailors, as they saw the lieutenant panting on the ground, for the figure they had been chasing for the last two hours turned out to be an old goat.

The shot had entered his flank, and being, in great agony when the lieutenant came to make a capture, butted him in the stomach.

One of the seamen, in order to put an end to the torture of the poor beast, drew a pistol from his belt, and, a bullet went crashing into his skull.

The report of the pistol so near his head caused the lieutenant to spring to his feet.

"Blood and thunder!" he roared. "What is the meaning of all this?"

Another deafening laugh was the only response.

Burning with indignation, and stamping his feet with rage, he looked round at the men in fierce anger.

"I'll teach you to laugh the other side of your mouths, my beauties!" he cried, fiercely. "Black list and six water grog shall be your portion, when I get you on board the frigate." And turning to one of the petty officers, who gloried in the rate of captain of the afterguard, he said, "I'll be the means of taking the stripes from your arm, and placing them on your back."

The laugh had now subsided, but a kind of titter-ing seemed to have taken hold of the group, and the more they tried to look serious, the louder grew the tittering.

Mortified at being thus defeated, and indignant at the behaviour of his men, the lieutenant now led the way back to the mansion.

CHAPTER CXXXIV.

THE DEATH STRUGGLE ON THE CLIFFS

THE lovely Susan Brockton had watched the conflict between the "Meteor" and the "Thunderer," and her heart beat wildly as she saw the frigate belching forth flame and smoke from her dark sides.

She had watched with breathless anxiety the solitary boatman, with the flaming torch, in the bow of his little craft.

Even at that great distance she could discover the handsome figure of the sailor, for love is not easily deceived.

Then, when the light disappeared, she feared his

little boat had been dashed to pieces by the ponderous missiles that flew from the frigate.

Yet something whispered in her ear that it was not so; and long and anxiously she watched through the dark hours of the night in fear and dread.

She feared her lover had been slain, and dreaded to hear the tidings of his fearful doom.

Sleep had completely forsaken her, and she paced the craggy steeps and dangerous passes in hope of meeting the gallant Captain Tom, whose image had been so deeply engraven on her heart.

On climbing the giddy heights, she had seen the dark forms of the men as they swayed to and fro, and, ere she could suppress it, a piercing scream burst from her lips.

Something whispered inwardly that treachery was at work.

Had she been able to see through the gloom, she would have seen the gallant buccaneer hanging over the dreadful abyss.

A small drum hung suspended from her waist by a silken cord, and she beat a sharp tattoo, that sounded among the rocks.

Ere the sound had died away, the dark forms of the smugglers and buccaneers darted out from the dark recesses in the rocks.

Every moment swelled their number, as they pounced from over jutting crag or crevice.

Captain Tom's heart beat high as the sharp rattle of the drum broke on his ear, and died away in the dark depths of the yawning chasm, over which he was hanging.

His assailants struggled frantically to beat him off, but he only clung the firmer.

Mad with rage, John Bentley drew a pistol from his belt, and dealt Captain Tom a powerful blow on the head.

Approaching footsteps were now plainly audible.

Delay being dangerous, Bentley shook Tom, and with Ralph disappeared down a craggy steep.

Captain Tom, stunned by the force of the blow, staggered to a shelving rock, and awhile he struggled.

A dozen of the buccaneers appeared upon the scene.

"Whose devilish work is this?" said Jerry Mizzen, who was the first to discover their wounded captain. "Whoever it may be, I swear he shall pay dearly for it, or my name's not Jerry Mizzen."

A dreadful melancholy overspread the features of the buccaneers as they gazed upon the bleeding features of their beloved captain.

Two stalwart fellows lifted him to their shoulders, and bore him to the cave.

When they saw his pale face, and the red gash on his pallid brow, a cloud of sadness overspread their sorrow-stricken features.

Loudly they clamoured for vengeance.

Every man took an oath, on the hilt of his cutlass, to be revenged for the outrage to which their captain had been subjected.

One of the smugglers stepped forward from the background, and proposed that Tom Drake should now retire to the inner cavern, which proposition was seconded by the rest of the smugglers and buccaneers who were there.

And, forthwith, he was conveyed to the inner cavern, and placed upon a bed of furs.

Weary and exhausted he lay, and, at length, overcome by fatigue, he closed his eyes in slumber.

In the meantime, John Bentley and Red Ralph, the wrecker, pursued their way down the crag, until they arrived at the mouth of a gloomy cavern.

"Now for the girls; you understand?" said Bentley, turning to Red Ralph.

"I should rather think I do," said Red Ralph, his eyes flashing fiercely, "and then for the brig; but we have no time to lose, so farewell for the present."

John Bentley darted up a narrow and dangerous pass, as Red Ralph disappeared in the dark recesses of the cavern.

John Bentley rapidly ascended the ragged path.

So profound was his meditation that he did not observe the dark figure of a man that emerged from the shadow of a projecting crag, and stood directly in his way.

And before he was aware of the presence of any one, he had run full butt against him, causing himself to recoil a few paces backwards.

Bentley drew his tall figure to its full height as he glared furiously at the stalwart figure of the man who had thus thrown himself in his path.

"Ah!" ejaculated Bentley, in surprise.

"Is that you, you black-muzzled rascal?" was the rejoinder.

"It is the Tiger of the Sea!" was the fierce reply. "And now we have met, I may as well settle the little score I owe you."

"Right you are, my boy," said Bob Hauler, as he waved a glittering battle-axe defiantly above his head.

Bentley snatched a pistol from his belt, and presented it at the head of the buccaneer; but Bentley had not noticed that when he dealt the blow at the head of Tom Drake he had shaken the charge out of the barrel, so that it was useless.

In a frenzy of rage, he dashed the pistol to the ground.

His cutlass flew from its sheath, and, with a savage yell, he sprang on to his assailant, who warded off the blow with the axe he held in his hand.

With admirable coolness, Bob Hauler warded off the savage attack of his enraged adversary.

A rustling sound then fell on their ears.

Each drew back instinctively.

Bob Hauler had turned his head a little to the right to see who came, and in that movement Bentley saw his chance.

With the fury of a tiger, he dashed at the buccaneer, and hurled him to the earth, his head coming violently in contact with the hard ground. He lay half stunned, and dropped the axe, which was quickly seized by Bentley.

Bentley now stood over his fallen foe; both hands clutched the glittering weapon, as he held it high above his head, in order that it might descend with greater violence.

His eyes lit with a lurid glow, his features assumed a hideous expression, while his white teeth appeared like the fangs of a tiger, as he stood ready to bury the deadly weapon in the skull of the prostrate man.

The weapon was about to descend, when the same rustling sound he had heard but a few minutes before arrested his hand.

He turned to look in the direction from whence the sound proceeded, and there before him stood the lovely form of Sweetheart Loo, to obtain possession of whom was the sole object that led him that way.

A pistol gleamed in her right hand, as she stood firmly on the rock, her large eyes dilating, and her rosy lips compressed.

"Bloodthirsty villain!" at length she cried, "is it thus you treat a fallen foe? It is well you paused in your devilish design, or I would have sent this bullet crashing through your skull!"

Bentley bit his lips with rage, and a dark scowl rested on his lowering brows.

Too well he knew the daring spirit of the brave girl before him.

He knew full well, too, that to trifle with her would be death to him.

Bob Hauler, who had been partly stunned by the fall, now scrambled to his feet; his brain reeled, and he staggered to the rocky cliff for support.

A few moments and he had recovered himself, and drawing a few paces towards Bentley, he said—

"You piratical-looking rascal, if it wasn't for hurting yer feelin's, I'd damage the beauty of yer black-looking figure-'ed with this 'ere thirty-two-pounder!"

As he spoke, he held his huge fist unpleasantly close to the figure-head of Bentley, who appeared to grow uneasy.

Both men were unarmed, and as Bentley's dark eye glanced from the brawny hand of the buccaneer, which almost touched his nose, to the silver-mounted pistol in the delicate hand of Sweetheart Loo, his lips quivered with rage.

Bob, who, by-the-bye, was clever with his fists, and prided himself in his pugilistic talents, resolved to have a bit of fun, as he termed it, with the enraged John Bentley.

And he challenged him to fight, in John Bull fashion, which challenge John Bentley did not care to accept.

But Sweetheart Loo, who gloried in a bit of fun, volunteered her services as seconds to both, and promised to see fair play; he could not very well refuse.

The place where they now stood was not very well adapted for a pugilistic encounter.

It was a narrow shelf of rock not more than ten feet in its widest part, whilst on one side reared a wall of stone formed by the flat side of the cliff, and on the other side lay a fearful precipice of considerable depth.

When John Bentley accepted the challenge, a thought flitted across his mind: he hoped that he should eventually, by a stratagem he had formed, be able to dispose of his man by way of the precipice.

Sweetheart Loo now gave the signal for the engagement, and John Bentley, with a fearful yell, dashed at his opponent, and his nose coming in violent contact with the fist of Bob Hauler, checked his impetuosity for the moment, and causing a stream of blood to flow from his distended nostrils.

"That's one to you!" he ejaculated, fiercely, as he endeavoured once more to close with his wary opponent; but he met with no better success, for the quick eye of Bob detected his movements, and each time he rushed towards him Bob lunged out, and caught him in the face.

Bentley roared with fury.

Not one blow had he dealt the buccaneer, who appeared as calm and collected as though he were playing with a child, instead of warding off the furious attacks of an enraged savage, and could not refrain from smiling as he gazed on the battered features of the savage pirate, who by this time had been compelled, though much against his will, to swallow four of his teeth.

"I should advise you, old feller, to have yer biscuits soaked a little afore you attempts to eat 'em—that is, if you goes to sea agen," said Bob, in a mocking tone.

"Maybe I will!" growled the pirate, fiercely, as he wiped his blood-stained face.

Again he dashed at the buccaneer, but met with the same resistance; and, burning with rage, he glared at his adversary, who now stood with his back to the precipice, and only a few feet from its edge.

A hideous smile now rested on the damaged figurehead of Bentley, and in that moment he saw his only chance.

With lightning speed, he dashed at the buccaneer with the intention of forcing him over the precipice.

But the buccaneer, anticipating his design,

stepped nimbly on one side, and he dashed headlong over the rocks, thus falling a victim to his own evil design.

Sweetheart Loo, seeing his danger, sprang to his aid, and caught his garment just as he went over, and she would have been drawn over after him had not his clothing given way, leaving a portion of his garment in her hand.

Breathless they listened, as they heard the dull sound, as they supposed, caused by the body of the self-murderer as it bounded from crag to crag.

"Well, if he ain't gone to Old Nick," said Bob Hauler, turning from the spot, "it ain't no fault of his'n."

"No, they cannot blame him for neglect. I believe he has done all in his power, and now I daresay his majesty will claim him for his own."

"Do you know, Loo," said the buccaneer, taking her hand affectionately in his own, for he dearly loved her, and she beloved him in return, "that I have often thought he was some way related to his dark highness, for, accordin' to the description I've heard on him, there's a strikin' likeness; but let that be howsomdever it will, there's one thing sartin, he'll make a capital stoker for the old gentleman, 'cos the coal-dust and smoke won't spile his complexion."

By this time they had reached one of the secret entrances to the cavern, and imprinting a kiss upon her cheek, he bade her go rest herself awhile, whilst he proceeded towards the interior of the cavern.

The buccaneers were all assembled, and were engaged in deep conference, for Captain Tom Drake had informed them of the intentions of Red Ralph and John Bentley.

Captain Tom now stepped into the centre of the cavernous chamber in which they were assembled, and the light from the silver lamp falling on his pale features, revealed the look of determination seated on his brow.

Every eye was turned towards him, as though they would search the inmost recesses of his heart.

Waving his hand, as though to enjoin silence, his keen eye ran along the line of buccaneers to see if they were all mustered.

Folding his arms across his breast, he thus addressed them—

"Comrades, you are all aware that we are bound together by the most solemn ties, and that we cannot separate without breaking the oath we have taken of eternal friendship and union. You may think it strange of me in addressing you thus, but I have reason to suspect that one or more of our number are dissatisfied with the strict discipline I am obliged to maintain to carry on our lawless traffic. If there are any of you present who feel aggrieved at my conduct, I am now willing to release you from your oath of allegiance."

He paused and looked around at the wondering faces of the buccaneers.

"Is there any among you who wish to be released from your bond?"

All were silent.

"Are you all willing to own me as your chief, and obey my commands? That is, according to our own laws, for we recognise no other."

"Yes! yes!" they all exclaimed, in a voice.

"Then let each man, kneeling, kiss the hilt of my sword, as a token of his submission."

Each man walked to the centre of the cavern, and having knelt on one knee, kissed the handle of the cutlass he held in his hand.

As each man walked towards him, he narrowly watched their countenances, to see if there appeared any reluctance to obey his stern mandate.

"Where is Rufus?" he inquired, in an angry tone.

No one answered.

"Mark me, comrades, there is a traitor in our band. and he must be rooted out. Rufus is the only one absent. We must have him watched, and that narrowly, too, for I have reasons to suspect him."

So saying, he hurriedly paced the floor of the cavern, as though meditating; then, stopping suddenly, he said—

"See well to your pistols, for we must not let the brig slip through our fingers. Take each separate tracks, so as not to arouse the suspicion of the coast-guards, for they are prowling about like hungry wolves. And, hark ye, comrades, in one half hour from this we meet at the Black Rock."

The men now separated to prepare their firearms, and Captain Tom, in a gloomy mood, hastened from the chamber.

While strolling through the caverns, thinking of the strange events which had befallen him of late, and wishing himself away from the lawless crew of smugglers with whom he had become so strangely connected, he saw the shadow of a man flit across his path.

In an instant, Captain Tom was roused into action, and drawing his sword, he cautiously followed the shadow.

It was very dark, the shadow had disappeared in a moment. and the man was strange to him, but as Captain Tom knew that shadows were not caused without substance, he knew the shadow he had seen must have a substance lurking about for some evil purpose, and he went in quest of it.

The noise of something falling attracted him to a cave where the gunpowder was stored, while his ship was under repairs.

Peering through a crevice in the rocks, he saw Red Ralph with a lighted torch in his hand.

Watching him carefully, Tom saw that he had emptied several barrels of powder, and was about to light a train he had laid, with the intention of blowing the buccaneers into eternity.

Leaping into the cave, Captain Tom knocked the torch from his hand, and hurled him to the ground.

The villain gave vent to a hideous yell, as Captain Tom sprang upon him.

"Traitor!" cried the young buccaneer, fiercely. "Did I spare your life for this? Let this be your reward."

And he drove his dagger into the wrecker's breast.

The wounded wretch shrieked horribly, and implored for mercy.

Tom hated cowards, and could have slain the cruel wretch without remorse, but it went against his noble nature to take the life of an unarmed man, even though that man would have stabbed him in the back, the next minute.

"Go!" he said, dragging the red-bearded ruffian to his feet. "Go, and do not let me see you here again, or, by heaven I will show you as little mercy as you would show me, if you could get the opportunity to kill me."

Glad to escape, the ruffian fled with murder in his heart, and mentally vowing to have a terrible revenge for the wound Captain Tom had inflicted.

CHAPTER CXXXV.
GOING INTO BATTLE.

WHEN John Bentley fell headlong over the brink of the precipice, he did not fall to the bottom.

If he had he would have been dashed to atoms; but Sweetheart Loo, in her endeavour to save him, checked his impetuous flight, and he only fell a few feet, ere he grasped a tuft of herbage, that grew between the rocks, to which he clung tenaciously,

and in his endeavour to obtain a foothold he displaced a large piece of stone, which, bounding from rock to rock, led them to believe it was the mangled body of John Bentley.

They had scarce disappeared round a projecting point, when John Bentley dragged his wounded limbs to the surface of the rock.

Had Bob Hauler seen him at that moment, he would certainly have believed it was Old Nick himself, as he stood with clenched hands, his face smeared with blood and dust, whilst his features were distorted with rage, as he poured forth a volley of curses on the head of Bob and his fair deliverer.

Thus he stood for several moments, gazing in the direction they had gone but a few moments before.

Ah! something has caught his eye.

With one bound he clutches it.

It is his own cutlass.

A smile of triumph now lights his ghastly visage, and, like a tiger, he darted away, and was soon lost among the rocks.

"Is that Bentley?" interrogated a gruff voice.

At the same instant a dark form emerged from the shadow of the cliffs.

"Yes," was the brief rejoinder.

"Have you got the gals?"

"Got the devil, you mean."

"What have you been up to? Have you been using paint to try to make your phizog look handsome?"

"If you don't want a foot of this cold steel through your ugly carcase, I would advise you to keep your flattery to yourself, for I want none of it."

"Oh! oh! that's how the wind blows, is it? Well, I s'pose I must take in a reef. But, hang me, I don't much admire your style of beauty, old fellow. You looks more like one of those Injians."

"Mind, I have cautioned you. Do not play with my feelings too much, for I am desperate."

His eyes flashed fire as he spoke, and Red Ralph, who well knew it was dangerous to play with the Tiger of the Sea, contented himself with overhauling his "figur' 'ed," as he termed it.

The wound Captain Tom Drake had inflicted did not make his iron frame feel much the worse.

He had washed off the stains of blood, and knowing that Bentley would only have laughed at him for being worsted by Captain Tom Drake, he did not speak of being discovered in his treacherous work.

A boat lay on the beach, and. without another word, they stepped into it. and seizing an oar each, pulled vigorously in the direction where a vessel lay at anchor.

Another moment, and Tom Drake, leading his men, appeared on the beach.

A scornful laugh rang over the dark, rippling waters of the bay; and the rowers plied their oars more vigorously.

"Too late, too late!" said the gallant buccaneer, as he gazed mournfully at the fast-receding boat.

A dozen men were now busily engaged in launching a boat that had lain concealed in a cave hard by; and as the men sprang in and bent to their oars, it flew swiftly through the water, and sent the spray seething from her bows.

Eight pairs of sturdy arms plied vigorously at the oars; but though she shot like a dolphin through the water, yet the boat which they pursued had nearly reached the vessel, and it was evident they could not overhaul her before she drew alongside.

Yet still they exerted all their energies.

Each one strained to the utmost on his bending oar, and like a shooting star she sped through the dark waters of the bay, leaving a streak of white behind.

The pursued boat now dashed alongside the vessel,

which was no other than the "Will-o'-the-Wisp," Tom Drake's only pride.

And if a shot had pierced the breast of the brave buccaneer, he could not have felt acuter pain, nor his cheek have turned paler than it did, when he saw the snowy canvas drop from her yards, and heard the rattling of the gear and cordage as they sheeted home the sails and hoisted the yards.

When he saw the sails belly out to the breeze in the grey dawn of morning, an involuntary sigh escaped his lips, for his crew, having heard of his recent danger, had left the ship to rescue him, and his enemy, knowing this, had lost no time in taking possession of her, with such of the wreckers as he could get to join him in the enterprise.

Then, with a bitter oath, he swore to be revenged.

"Aye," he said, bitterly, "if they sail to the uttermost parts of the earth I will find them, and woe be to them when I do."

Three ringing cheers rose from the brig as she laid over to the breeze.

And, as they fell on the ear of the gallant buccaneer, he thought his heart would burst.

In a few moments he recovered his wonted coolness, and the boat pulled towards the shore.

A smile played on his lips, and not a sign betrayed the emotions that were working in his breast.

The boat grated on the beach.

In a few moments she was hauled up into her place of concealment.

The gallant Captain Tom, followed by his little band, were hurrying back to the smuggler's stronghold, when a shrill whistle broke the stillness that reigned around.

And, ere they were aware, a strong body of the coastguard fell upon them.

Fiercely they attacked the gallant band.

And fiercely they struggled against the overwhelming numbers of the coastguards, who, armed to the teeth, had taken them by surprise.

Shots flew about in all directions, mingled with the clang of arms, whilst the clamour of war rang on the still morning air.

Right gallantly did the little band of buccaneers defend themselves against the savage assaults of their antagonists, and had they been opposed to more equal numbers, would certainly have gained the victory.

As it was, they were now three to one, and gradually they gave way before the desperate attack of their formidable opponents.

A little apart from the rest, might be seen three men standing back to back, their bright blades whizzing through the air, with which they formed a circle, within which circle, the dozen coastguardsmen who surrounded them, dared not venture.

At length they draw back a few paces, and formed themselves into three separate bodies.

And simultaneously, at a given signal they charged the three brave fellows, who, unable to resist the furious charge, broke, and being thus separated, although they fought courageously, eventually succumbed to the overwhelming numbers that attacked them on all sides.

Although not until they had wounded several of their adversaries, the noble fellows were beaten down and were led away prisoners, having previously been deprived of their weapons of defence.

This gallant few were no others than Captain Tom and two of his daring band, Jerry Mizzen and Bob Hauler.

They were speedily conveyed to the gaol, and cast into a dark and dreary dungeon.

Being of a desperate class of men who had eluded the vigilance of the officers of the law, great care was taken for their safe custody, and the governor on hearing they had captured the redoubtable buccaneer, Tom Drake, ordered them to be heavily ironed.

And to render them more secure, he had ordered a strong guard to be placed at the door of their cell, and likewise around the walls.

Having thus arranged matters, he felt confident that they could not escape unless they had communication with the Evil One.

So thought the rest of the officials, for one man was placed at the door of the cell with strict orders to examine the bolts and bars that secured the massive iron door of their dungeon.

Whilst three men, well armed, were ordered to keep on walking round the building and on no account to speak to each other, nor to approach within a dozen yards of each other, on pain of arrest.

No wonder the governor thought them secure, for, besides these precautions, their hands were manacled, whilst a chain came from each ancle and connected with a heavy iron ring, which ring was firmly chained to the wall of the dungeon, with only length enough to allow the weary prisoners to lie down on the straw that supplied the place of a bed.

"This is rather a queer billet, Bob," said Jerry, addressing his companion. "It's wusser nor I thought it was."

"Oh, I 'spects it's the first time you've been aboard the stone frigit, eh, old cock? Why, I've bin in all on 'em about this quarter o' the globe, and I don't care who knows on it, either."

"Well, what do you reckon they'll do with us arter all?"

"Why, it's very likely they'll run you up to the masthe'd for a signal."

"What masthe'd? What do you mean?"

"Why, I means that aboard o' this ere' craft, instead of saving their money till they get enuff to buy a yard of bunting. Why, they hangs the poor devils, same as you and me, up there."

"What for?" inquired Jerry Mizzen, who began to grow more anxious.

"For a signal, to be sure."

"But what's the signal for?"

"Why, to guard the poor devils who are lucky enuff to be outside from going on the rocks."

"What rocks do you mean, Bob?" inquired Jerry, whose visage appeared to have grown a yard long.

"Why, the chaplain, as they calls him, used to tell me that we was all steering our vessels on the oshun of life, which oshun was full of rocks, shoals, and quicksands, and if we don't mind how we boxes our compass, and doesn't keep our weather eye open and pay great attention to the wheel, which, by-the-bye, he called the wheel of fortin,' why we shall go ashore on the rocks and become a total wreck, and he said that if I was to keep on smuggling, and drinking grog and smoking baccy without paying the King a good deal of money to let me drink it, I should get wrecked upon such a dangerous rock that no lifeboat would ever put off to try to save my life; and now you see we have got on to the rocks to-night just the same way."

"And a devilish hard rock it is, too."

"You're right, and I'm afraid we shan't have any lifeboat to come off to us either."

"Then I 'spose we shall be run up to the masthe'd?"

During the time the previous dialogue was going on, the daring buccaneer had not been idle.

He had been amusing himself with the handsome bracelets around his wrists, and had contrived at length to slip them off his hands

When the first rays of morning were peeping through the bars of the cell, Bob Hauler, by the indistinct light, fancied he saw the captain up to some of his tricks, and in a low tone he said—

"Well, captain, do they hurt your harm?"

"Not much."

"I dare say it makes you feel lighter."

"I dare say it does."

"Just come and take mine off for me, and let me see what it's like."

"How can I get them off?"

"Come here and I'll tell you."

"All right."

"Feel down in my boot."

He did so, and after some difficulty he brought out a couple of files.

"Well you see, captain, I've been in chokey so many times," he said, which wasn't true. "and have got out so many times, that I always carries the tools with me."

In a very few moments Bob's hands were free.

And now Bob and the captain set to work in right good earnest, and in less than half an hour they had rid themselves of all their encumbrance.

Bob now set to work to liberate Jerry Mizzen, who had all the while been listening in breathless anxiety to the grating of the files, and had given them warning as he was nearest to the door, whenever he heard the approaching footsteps of the gaoler, as he came to try the bolts and fastenings of the cell door, and as soon as he departed they commenced again vigorously.

Meantime the captain was not idle.

He was working away at the iron bars; already he had cut through two of the bars, and they were just barely holding in their places, for he had to be very cautious, as it was now getting light.

Whenever the footsteps of the sentry sounded on his ear, he had to suspend operations till they were gone by, and were out of the hearing of the grating of the file.

Rapidly, but cautiously, they proceeded with their arduous task.

At length the third bar was almost sawn through, and as luck would have it, the daring youth having caught sight of something in the distance, had for a moment ceased filing, and was gazing intently at the object in the distance, when a shadow on the grass caught his eye, and he drew back.

Breathless he listened; for the man had evidently stopped beneath the grating.

The captain, in his hurry to withdraw from observation, had dropped the file, and it fell with a ringing sound upon the stone floor of the cell.

Almost fearing to breathe, he listened to hear when he should move on again.

For each successive round, until this one the men had walked upon the gravel a few yards from the wall, but this time they had taken a fancy to walk on the grass, therefore the captain was not aware of his approach until he saw the shadow.

The sound of the other men's footsteps, were now plainly audible to all. And the man who had stopped under the grating, fearful of getting in closer proximity to his comrade than their orders allowed them, now continued his round.

Meantime Jerry Mizzen had been unburthened of his fetters, and as the bars were already loosened, he listened attentively till the last sentry had passed; then, with a violent jerk, he displaced them.

After ascertaining that the coast was all clear, each of them, armed with one of the bars, dropped in succession on to the grass beneath, and secreting themselves behind a projecting abutment, they lay waiting anxiously for the foremost sentry to make his appearance.

At length he came with measured step.

The captain lay in a crouching attitude behind the abutment, and as soon as he approached to

where he lay, he sprang upon him like a cat, and seizing him by the throat, dragged him on to the grass, and flung him down behind the abutment.

Seizing the woollen cap from the head of Jerry Mizzen, he thrust it into the sentry's mouth, so that he could not raise an alarm, and, with admirable coolness, the gallant captain transferred the pistols from the belt of the sentry to that of his own.

In less time than pen can describe it, daring Captain Tom had divested the sentry of his belt and muffler; and with these he securely bound and gagged the captive.

Then, raising him on their shoulders, they forced him through the grating of the cell, and lowered him gently to the floor beneath.

Not many minutes had elapsed since they had left the cell; and now the gallant buccaneer lay crouching ready to spring upon the next victim.

On came the unsuspecting victim, his regular footsteps sounding on the gravel; on he came, little suspecting that gallant Tom Drake, who not quite two hours before they had left heavily ironed in the gloomy dungeon, was waiting, ready to pounce upon him.

He was a stout, powerful fellow, of burly frame, and appeared to be endowed with giant strength; but the young buccaneer, though not above half his size or weight, was as nimble as a cat, and could twist himself about like an eel, so supple was he.

When the sentry approached to where the buccaneer lay in ambush, he sprang upon his back, and placing his hand upon his mouth, the two others seized him, and he was disarmed, bound, and gagged, and thrown down behind the abutment.

In like manner was his other companion served.

They were all three well armed now, and a good match for any six who might chance to stumble in their path.

The daring buccaneer, not content with having escaped from an ignominious death, fearless of danger, and resolved to finish the work he had commenced, now proposed to place the other two sentries in the cell.

It was no sooner proposed than seconded by Bob Hanler, who was always good for a joke.

Without further parley, the helpless captives were squeezed through the aperture, and being both of a burly frame, it required a great deal of pushing to get them through.

No sooner were they in than Captain Tom was in after them, and placed them each in one of the places they had vacated but a short time before.

He stood for a moment in silent satisfaction as he gazed upon the ridiculous expression of their features as they were lying, bound and helpless, on the handful of straw that constituted the beds of the prisoners

The rusty bolts of the ponderous door now grated in their sockets, and the daring buccaneer had scarcely time to escape by the grating ere the gaoler entered the cell with the morning meal.

On beholding the new prisoners, the gaoler stared stared in open-mouthed dismay.

For the moment he could not conjecture what really was the state of affairs.

But on closer inspection he soon found out that they had changed places.

The governor, on being informed of the escape of the buccaneers, stamped and swore and cursed them for their folly.

In his frenzy he tore the silvery locks from his head, and ordered the unfortunate men to be arrested on the charge of conspiracy.

Even the gaoler did not escape his wrath, for he was charged as an accessory.

Forthwith they were heavily ironed and thrown

nto a noisome dungeon, underneath the gaol, there to await their trial.

Then the governor started for the garrison, where he had authority, in such emergencies, to order out the soldiers to recapture the escaped prisoners.

Meanwhile the buccaneers had made the best of their way to a small wood, and edging along its border, they could have concealed themselves easily, if there were the least signs of alarm.

They pushed their way onward as speedily as possible, and were about to enter upon a road that led to the beach, when a party of preventive men, with their lieutenant, met them boldly in the front.

The lieutenant for a moment appeared thunderstruck, for he had not many hours since seen Tom Drake snugly moored in goal, and his two friends to keep him company.

Ere they could recover from the consternation into which they had been thrown by the appearance of the buccaneers, who, they believed, were endowed with supernatural power, the buccaneers dashed among them, and tried to cut their way through them, but they were repulsed.

A serious conflict now ensued, and, after a severe contest, Captain Tom and Bob Hauler managed to cut their way through the infuriated mass, and darting into the wood, with the agility of a cat the daring buccaneer, closely followed by Bob, ascended a tree, and lay concealed in the thick foliage of its branches.

From their position they could watch the movements of their pursuers, who searched every tree and bush in the vicinity, for they felt certain they could not be far away without they took wing, for not a moment had elapsed since they saw them.

At length, after a fruitless search, they reluctantly withdrew from the spot, searching every bush as they went by, and thrusting their bright cutlasses into the thick foliage.

Two of the party had not departed so soon as the others, and were holding a conference as to whether it were probable they would ever effect the capture of the brave and daring buccaneer.

Captain Tom, from his place of concealment, could overhear their conversation, from which he learned something to his advantage, as we shall afterwards find out.

They were now about to depart, when the gallant captain, making a significant gesture to Bob, crept slowly along the bough, and slid gently down before them.

A pistol was presented at the head of each, and before they could utter an exclamation, Bob, seizing one from behind, forced him to the earth and bound him.

In like manner Tom Drake served the other, and having supplied themselves with the ammunition of their captives, they cautiously proceeded through the wood, and emerged into the road.

Not far down the road they could see Jerry Mizzen, his tall, lank figure rearing above the heads of his captors.

With stealthy footsteps they crept along the border of the forest, and gained rapidly upon the retreating party.

Captain Tom and his brave follower glided onward with a cat-like motion, and as the two last men were about to turn the corner of the road, they pounced upon them and having thrust a twig across the mouth of each, and tied it firmly behind their heads, before they could offer resistance, the cold barrel of a pistol chilled their nerves.

Paralysed with fear the two men stood, whilst their assailants divested them of their pistols, and before they could recover from the astonishment into which they had been thrown, they were flung to the ground, and their arms pinioned behind them.

In this manner they were led into the forest, and firmly bound to the tree.

So speedily had they accomplished this daring feat, that before the two men could be missed by their companions, the bold buccaneers were at their heels again.

Only six of the party now remained, and Tom Drake, dealing one of them a blow with his pistol, dashed into their midst.

He quickly severed the cords that bound poor Jerry, and turned to defend himself from the fierce attacks of the furious coastguards.

He fiercely contended with four of their number, who fought with such desperation as is only known to those who have been engaged in the fearful struggle of life or death.

The clash of weapons rung through the wood that skirted the road, mingled with the firing of pistols, and the cries of anger from the fiercely contending parties.

When a cry of alarm broke from the lips of Jerry Mizzen, who had but just dispatched his man, and was now coming to the assistance of the captain.

For a moment only Tom Drake drew his eye from that of the remaining coastguard, and in that moment he had almost lost his life, for his assailant taking advantage of the indiscreet action of the brave buccaneer was about to cleave his skull in twain with his glittering weapon. But with an impulsive movement the gallant captain stepped to one side, which movement caused his adversary to stagger forward. And at that instant Jerry Mizzen buried his blood-stained sword in his breast.

With a groan of agony the wounded man fell to the earth and expired.

For a moment Tom Drake paused to look at the object that drew the exclamation from Jerry's lips.

A peculiar grin rested on the happy countenance of Bob Hauler, as he stayed the deadly blow which was about to descend upon the head of his foe, whom he had beaten to his knees, for far along the road he saw a body of soldiers.

Their bright bayonets glittered in the rays of the morning sun, while the heavy tramp of feet upon the hard road was plainly audible, and fell with a dull sound upon the ears of the reckless buccaneers.

The troop and their pace, which gradually increased, as they came galloping down the road, followed by the foot soldiers, who came on in double quick time.

By this time the buccaneers had disappeared in the intricacies of the forest.

The troop of cavalry on arriving at the spot on which the desperate men had but a few minutes before been engaged in deadly strife, dismounted from their horses; the foremost of them were quickly engaged in assisting the wounded men, and in binding up their ghastly wounds, whilst the wounds of the others were of so serious a nature that but little hopes were entertained of their recovery.

The remainder of the troops leaving their horses in charge of two of their number, dashed into the wood and were soon lost to view in the thick foliage.

There was no chance for the buccaneers to escape their pursuers.

The soldiers manœuvered under the direction of an officer who knew his duty, and at every point the fugitives saw the red-coats approaching with glistening bayonets.

"There is no hope for us if we keep together," said Captain Tom, quietly.

Jerry's face lengthened dolefully, and Bob Hauler would have been thankful had the earth opened at that moment and swallowed him.

"Our only chance is to disperse quickly," said Tom.

"I ain't going to desert you now, cap'n," said Jerry.

"No more am I," put in Bob. "And I ain't going to leave Jerry, that's more."

"And I ain't going to leave you old, mate, though you don't deserve me to stand by yer, and we ain't going to leave the skipper, are we, Bob?"

"That we ain't. We'll live or fall together."

Tom admired the sentiment of the true hearts of oak, and although he was reluctant to leave the brave fellows to look after themselves, he acted now, as he thought, for the best.

"You will obey orders," he said.

"Aye, aye, cap'n!" responded the redoubtable pair, touching their forelocks respectfully.

"Then I command you to separate, and take opposite directions, to throw our pursuers off our track."

"Ask me, cap'n, to stand before you and receive the bayonets through me, and I'll do it," said Jerry Mizzen. "But shiver my timbers, I can't run away and leave you to fight those long-shore lubbers alone. Maybe, cap'n, you think I'm mutinying by disobeying orders, but it's out of love for you it is, cap'n."

And the staunch-hearted fellow dashed a tear from his eye.

"Them's just my sentiments," said Bob Hauler "We've stood by yer, cap'n, in many a hard-fought battle on the sea, and we ain't going to desert yer now; it ain't in us, cap'n, cuss me if it is. I know why you want us to go—'cos you think we might save ourselves. Now don't say it ain't—axing your honor's pardon—'cos I know it is, and I can tell yer, cap'n, we don't try to save ourselves till we've seen you safe."

Having delivered himself of this, Bob Hauler hooked a stale quid of tobacco out of his cheek, and dashed it to the ground with a defiance that shewed he did not intend to move without the cap'n.

Tom Drake saw it would be useless to try and persuade them to leave him; used as he was to the marks of affection displayed by members of his gallant crew, the depth of rugged love and self-sacrifice which he now received moved him more than he cared to show.

He took each by the hand, and thanked them for their noble conduct.

"With such true hearts of oak to stand by me I could face a thousand dangers," he said. "But where there is no chance of life, let us be valorous by being discreet, and act up to the maxim which tells us to run away, that we may fight another day."

"I don't mind running away, cap'n, if you'll run with us," said Bob Hauler.

"Just like him, cap'n," said Jerry, contemptuously. "He's been wanting to run away all along, only he's been ashamed to."

Bob looked remarkably hurt at this unjust remark from his inseparable companion.

"I've stood by you, Jerry, when you've been in a scrape," he said.

"When you ain't been able to get out of it," was Jerry's reply.

Captain Tom saw that an argument was about to ensue, and interrupted it.

"Look!" he said; "the soldiers are coming at us. There is not a moment to be lost. If we keep together we shall be the easier found. Let us separate for a short time, and then get up the trees."

This was agreed to, and the trio started off in opposite directions; for sailors they ran remarkably well, and soon lost themselves in the depths of the forest.

Before the soldiers were again in sight, they were comfortably ensconced in the thick foliage of three fine old trees, where they obtained a good survey of the surroundings, and watched the bewildered soldiers making a diligent search for them amongst the entangled underwood.

One man, more cunning than the rest, went on the trail of the fugitives alone, and examined the ground for footmarks with the care of an Indian.

It happened that he worked his way to the tree in which Captain Tom lay concealed, and his features assumed a more cunning expression than before, which made our hero rather uneasy, for he could see the fellow had discovered the scent.

Fearing an alarm, which would bring all the other soldiers to the spot, and being struck with an idea at the same moment, Captain Tom suddenly dropped upon the cunning soldier.

The weight of our hero bore the fellow to the earth, and before he could ascertain whether he had been felled by a thunderbolt, or whether a tree had fallen upon him, felt a strong hand over his mouth, and another at his throat.

For safety, to prevent the soldier crying out, Tom Drake had to nearly strangle him; then he gave him a blow under the ear, to keep him quiet while he stripped him of his uniform, which, being big, easily slid on over his own.

The next thing was to keep the fellow out of sight.

This was no easy matter, as every inch of ground was likely to be searched over again.

Tom Drake was never long lost for an idea, and in a minute he had conceived a plan to overcome the present difficulty.

The soldier had not recovered his senses sufficiently to make any resistance when Captain Tom threw him across his shoulders, and mounted the tree.

Having secured him to the stout stem of the tree with his own belt, Tom watched the fellow's comrades working their way back, searching very cautiously and diligently every bush and covert they came across.

CHAPTER CXXXVI.
CAPTAIN TOM ASSUMES A DISGUISE.

THE soldiers advanced towards the forest, and beat down the twigs and boughs, that impeded their progress.

Their progress became more and more difficult as the exuberance of the foliage increased.

Still on they went cutting their way through.

While the perspiration from their reeking brows rolled down their swarthy features, in hot streams.

The daring captain of the buccaneers, who was never more happy than when surrounded by danger, now emerged from his concealment, and having possessed himself of a sword, he sprang lightly to the saddle of one of the beautiful coursers.

With stentorian lungs he made the woods resound to his calls, and at length some of the soldiers, on nearing the sound of his voice, appeared from various parts of the wood.

"Come on comrades," cried Tom Drake, "those murdering rascals are higher up the road."

"How do you know they are?" cried one of the soldiers, sullenly, for he did not appear to care about the game they were having, and as his eye scanned his mud-stained attire, terribly torn, and damaged by bushes, a malediction escaped his lips.

"I wish these fellows had stayed at home, and gone to bed," said the soldier, addressing Tom Drake who was so effectually disguised, that they could not detect him, and as his tall form stood erect he well became the handsome military uniform.

Even his comrades would have had a difficulty to recognise him if they happened to lose sight of him for a moment.

THE BEAUTIFUL GIRL UTTERED A STARTLED CRY AS SHE CAUGHT SIGHT OF CAPTAIN TOM.

Most of the soldiers had emerged from the wood into which they had so recently gone clamouring for vengeance, whilst the foot soldiers in the meantime crossed the fields that skirted the road on the opposite side, and were now lost in wonderment as to which direction they had best take.

Tom soon guessed the cause of their halt, and with the quickness of thought, he rode down the road towards them.

With an impatient gesture he advised them to hurry up the road where the cavalry were now engaged in consultation.

"I tell you, colonel, they are higher up the road. We must retrace our steps, and hunt them up."

"It's very evident we must do something. I shall be called to an account for the loss of these brave men, and what can I answer? I am almost ashamed to own that I have only seen three of the desperate band who must be concealed somewhere close here."

"Well, had we not better search the wood higher up, for I am sure I saw two of those rascals only a few minutes since?" said Tom, in an earnest tone.

"Where were they then?" thundered the colonel. "Why did you not follow them? I'll report you, if I live to return to quarters. Whereabouts did you see them?"

The colonel had by this time grown enraged at the wild goose chase the buccaneers led him, and now bestowed his ire on the supposed soldier, for he feared to return to his superior officer without having captured one of the consummated villains, as he termed them.

"Lead the way to where you saw them last," said the colonel, scowling fiercely at Tom. "If they have escaped, mind, it will be owing to your neglect of duty."

"How so?" inquired Tom, with apparent alarm.

"You ought to have informed me directly you saw them," he answered, fiercely, whilst the expression of his face indicated he would make the soldier suffer for his indiscretion.

Had he known who it was that strode the saddle before him, he would not have dared to talk so bold, for the soldiers had heard of the daring achievements of the gallant buccaneer, and there was not one among that troop of stalwart men who dare attack him single-handed.

Tom Drake had resolved to have his revenge on the colonel for his haughty insolence, and giving rein to his steed, he retraced his way up the road, followed closely by the rest of the mounted soldiers.

Tom Drake carefully eyed the various trees as he proceeded along, and having arrived at a part of the road where an aged oak spread its broad branches over the path, he alighted, and with an impatient wave of his hand, which implied that something had attracted his attention, he dashed boldly into the wood.

In a few moments the cry of Help!" echoed through the wood, and the soldiers, alarmed, made their way, with as much speed as they were able, for the wood was so thick and the path was so overgrown with the tangled bushes that it rendered their progress but slow, even at the best.

The colonel, who was the first to arrive at the spot from whence the sound proceeded, uttered an exclamation on beholding the soldier whom Captain Tom had robbed of his clothes crouching under a tree, the picture of abject misery.

Before the officer could understand the meaning of his man in that peculiar condition, several of the soldiers appeared on the scene, and quickly surrounded the unfortunate wretch, whom they dragged with remorseless fury through the entangled forest.

Not a word could he utter, for he was already gagged and bound.

In the meantime, Tom had disappeared, and was making his way as fast as possible to the place where he had left Bob and Jerry safely perched in one of the trees.

"Come down, lads," cried Tom, as he began to divest himself of his military array.

"Why, I thought you was one of the sodjers," cried Bob. "You looks mighty well in that fine coat."

Tom now began to recount his adventures to them, and they all indulged in a hearty laugh when they heard how he had tricked the soldiers; but the soldiers, having discovered their mistake, were after him again.

CHAPTER CXXXVII.

A SURPRISE.

WISHING to get back to the cavern as soon as possible, to allay the apprehensions of his followers, whom, he had no doubt, would feel uneasy at his long absence, he struck into a beaten path that diverged from the road and led by half a mile nearer to the beach.

His way lay through a thick wood, and he hurried on as fast as circumstances would permit, lost in deep meditation. He had proceeded some distance into the wood, when the report of a gun aroused him from his reverie

He stopped suddenly and listened, and was utterly at a loss to conjecture the cause, or for what purpose the gun had been fired.

"Surely," he thought, "they have not discovered my escape; if so, that sound, perhaps, emanates from the soldiers they have sent in pursuit of me."

While thus musing, he was startled by the sound of hasty footsteps and the crackling of branches, and two men with wild and disordered dress, torn to rags by the violent wrenching of the briars, burst through the thick foliage.

In their violent hurry, gallant Tom, who stood directly in their way, was thrown heavily to the ground, and again they disappeared into the bushes.

Scarcely had he recovered from the shock caused by the violence with which he had been thrown down, when the bushes again opened to admit the passage of a man followed close by two others.

"Here you are, Bill," cried the first of the trio. "Here's one of the covies."

"Right you are, Harry," rejoined the man addressed, "I thort he couldn't hold out much longer."

"Nor I either," cried the third party, panting, "but what a hansum plumage he's got We don't often cotch such fine birds about this part."

"Well, to tell you my mind about this 'ere cove, mates, I should think he ain't much of a poacher."

"What do you think he is, Jerry," inquired one of the party leaning his chin on the barrel of his gun, and eyeing our hero with a keen, scrutinising glance, "if you don't think he's a poacher?"

"Well, I should think he's a highwayman; p'raps it's Dick Turpin, p'raps it's Jack Sheppard, and p'raps it's—let me see who is the other covey there's so much talk about."

"Jack Ketch,' interposed Bill, with a knowing look.

"How can he be a highwayman, you donkey? Ain't he the cove that hangs all the thieves and robbers?"

' In course he is, and don't he rob 'em of their breath, and never axes 'em if it's agreeable; ain't that as bad as highway robbery?"

"I should think it was, mate, and a good deal worsser," said the third speaker, "'cos he don't give 'em half a chance to save their life."

"Now, I say, old cove, don't you call me by that name any more, 'cos I don't like it," said Bill, deeply affected.

"What name was that?" cried Harry, who appeared to be surprised.

"Why, you called me a donkey, and I take it as a great hinsult."

' Oh, you do, do you? Well, I can't help it, I'll call you a jackass next time."

"Oh, you will, will you?" growled Bill. "Well, only mind I don't kick at it, that's all."

At this juncture both parties had become enraged, and there is no doubt they would have got to blows, had not the other reminded them that they had a desperate character of some sort to deal with.

"Well, my tulip," said Harry, "what have you got to say for yourself? That's a fine coat of yours to go a-poaching in."

Tom Drake's proud spirit would not permit him to answer the taunts of his rude interrogators, and he still stood with his back to a tree, and his arms carelessly folded across his breast.

Tom had been hitherto so deeply wrapped in thought, that he had forgotten that he still wore the soldier's uniform, and was not aware of it till it had called forth the strange remarks from the the three men.

"Now, my beauty," cried Bill, "you'll have to go along with us, and then, p'raps, we may find out who you are, and what your little game is."

A look of scorn was the only reply.

"Come along, my hearty," said Harry, approaching Tom Drake, as though he were going to lead him by the collar.

But the daring buccaneer frustrated his intentions by delivering a well-aimed blow with his left hand under the fellow's right ear, that sent him reeling into a bush, and there he now lay stunned.

For a moment the gallant buccaneer stood irresolute how to act; he knew full well that if they once overpowered him and lodged him in the gaol, his life would not be worth the snuff of a candle.

These thoughts passed rapidly through his mind, and as quickly did he for n his projects.

Although he had for the present rid himself of one of his opponents, yet still had he two stout resolute fellows to contend with, each armed with a gun; whilst the only weapon of defence he had with him was a pistol, and even that he had not examined to see if it were loaded.

At a single glance he took the dimensions of the two burly gamekeepers, and saw plainly that he must make a bold and decisive stroke.

Scarcely allowing the astonished keepers to recover from their surprise, he drew the pistol from his breast, and with a true and deliberate aim he felled the one who stood nearest to him to the earth.

Then with surprising dexterity he flew at the other, and grappled fiercely with him.

Fearful were the exertions that the struggle called forth.

The perspiration burst out in beads upon the foreheads of both the desperate men.

It was evident the gallant buccaneer could not hold out much longer against his more powerful opponent; he felt he must at last succumb to the unequal contest; his hands were slipping from their hold.

His strength seemed deserting him.

The men whom he had knocked down were slowly returning to consciousness, and one had already risen to a sitting posture.

The man had now fixed a deadly grip upon the throat of the gallant Tom Drake, whose foot slipping on the muddy soil, caused him to fall heavily to the ground.

The burly keeper fell heavily upon him.

The daring captain now lay almost breathless on the ground, the knee of his more fortunate adversary pressing heavily on his breast.

By this time the other two men had risen to their feet, and, swearing deadly vengeance, they seized upon the exhausted Captain Tom, whom they dragged unmercifully and savagely through the intricacies of the wood.

"Where had we best take him to, mate?" enquired Bill.

"Oh, we'll just pop him in the cage till morning, then we can take him to the gaol, and get the reward all to our own cheek," replied Bill.

"Right you are, my boy; but how about the key?"

"Ou, I knows where to get that, never fear, leave me alone for a clean trick; dirty ones I knows a plenty on."

"Right you are—ha! ha! ha!"

Here they all burst into a fit of boisterous laughter, and even our hero could not suppress a smile.

In a short time they had arrived at the cage.

It was a kind of round-house, strongly built of stone, and a massive door, studded with nails, appeared the only entrance.

The buccaneer eyed the place closely in the hope of finding a grating, for he still had one of the files concealed about him, with which he had effected his escape from the gaol.

"Now, mates," said Bill, assuming a tone of dignity, "you stick to him like wax, while I go for the key."

"All right, my boy," answered another, casting a threatening look at the captain, which implied, "if you stir, or offer to stir, I'll blow your brains out."

In a few minutes Bill returned, bearing a huge key, and in a very short time had inserted it into the no small key-hole, and opened the massive door.

The gallant Tom Drake was now led into the building unresistingly, and without uttering a word.

"Here you are, my boy," said Bill, drawing a pair of handcuffs from his pocket, "you see I knows my book. When we gets such a purty bird as this, you know, mates, we must look arter 'em well; he's got a fine cage to flutter his wings in, and he'll just have three hours to shake his feathers afore we comes to 'scort him to his last domicile."

During the time he was delivering this speech, his comrades had seized upon the unfortunate Captain Tom, who, without resisting in the least, had allowed them to place the handcuffs on his wrists, carefully eyeing where the key had been placed.

They now proceeded to place the irons round his legs, attached to which was a massive chain, firmly secured in the stone flags which composed the floor.

The undaunted captain took a close survey of the place which was to be his temporary abode.

It was a room of a circular shape, and only about fourteen feet across its widest part; huge blocks of stones formed the wall, there being no corners, and was surmounted by a dome-shaped roof, in the centre of which, about twelve feet from the ground, was a small aperture, protected by two stout iron bars.

All this Tom could see by the feeble light of the lamp which Bill had provided, and he quickly set down his plans of escape.

"Why, you arn't brought the key to fasten these 'ere things, Bill. It won't do to leave this coon 'ere without summut fast to him," said Jem, in a business sort of way.

"I should rather think not, Jem. I'll go and get 'em; it won't take me long."

So saying, he disappeared.

"Am I to lay on the bare flags?" asked Tom, carelessly.

"In course not. Harry," he said, turning to his colleague, "go and tell Bill to bring a handfull of straw. The poor devil must have summut to lay on; it won't cost us anything, and I daresay we shall get a good round sum for our trouble."

"All serene, Jem," answered the man, as he hastened to obey the injunction of his companion.

Tom now saw his chance; only one of the men remained, and during the time they had been talking, he had, unobserved by either, slipped the irons off his wrists, and now stood ready to struggle for his liberty.

Mustering all his remaining strength, he sprang upon the gaoler with the agility of a wild cat, and seizing him by the throat, threw him prostrate on the flags.

In an instant he was upon him, and, ere the man could recover from the sudden attack, Captain Tom had placed the handcuffs on his wrists, and, taking the key from the pocket of the now prostrate man, he locked them.

Seizing a piece of rope that lay near at hand, he quickly bound his legs, and by the time the man had recovered from his surprise, he found himself a prisoner, bound hand and foot.

A bitter malediction burst from the lips of the baffled gamekeeper, who began to curse his own folly for having sent his comrade for the straw.

"Never grumble, my man," said the fearless buccaneer. "You have lost nothing, but have gained a great deal."

"What have I gained?" growled the discomfited man.

"In the first place you have gained knowledge," was the captain's cool reply; "in the next place, you shall gain information."

"I wish you would speak a little plainer," cried the gamekeeper, who was in hopes that if he softened down a little, he might keep his unsuspecting victim in conversation till the others should return.

"Very well, then, listen," said the captain, as though about to impress something of great importance on his mind; "the knowledge you have gained is this, the next bird you catch, be sure to tie a string to his leg before you clip his wings, for though you clip his wings, he may fly out of your reach."

"The information that you are about to gain, is this," Tom went on, "that the bird you caught was neither a poacher nor highwayman, but Tom Drake, the buccaneer."

As he spoke, he divested himself of his disguise, and stood gazing defiantly at the astonished keeper, who was about to shout out lustily for help.

But Tom, anticipating his intention, drew the cap from his head, thrust it into the fellow's mouth, and tied it behind his head.

"Good morning, friend," cried Tom, holding out his hand towards him, as though wishing to part friendly.

The gamekeeper appeared to understand him, but could not return the compliment.

The gallant buccaneer could not suppress a smile at the ridiculous figure before him, and expressing a hope that the unfortunate ex-gaoler might not be long before he should receive a visit from his friends, he bade him farewell.

The morning air blew cold and chilly, and the gallant captain walked rather sharp, for the twofold purpose of getting out of the reach of his enemies, and keeping himself warm.

He had taken one of the guns with him for fear of an accident, and it was well for him he did so.

He had proceeded some distance down the road, when he fancied he heard a rustling noise in the hedge that lined the road, but, on looking round, nothing was to be seen.

He proceeded on his way, not thinking more about it, until he was startled by the pressure of a heavy hand on each shoulder, and, before he could turn, a knee was thrust into his back, and he was rendered powerless.

The cowardly villain endeavoured to thrown him on his back, but Tom kept his body so fixed that he baffled all the attempts of his unknown enemy, and thus did they struggle for several seconds, until the undaunted buccaneer, who had not for one moment lost his wonted coolness, seizing the gun tightly in his grasp, jerked the butt sharply over his shoulder, striking his cowardly assailant on the head, causing him to relax his hold and stagger back.

Like a streak of lightning, Captain Tom was upon him, and seizing him in his arms, threw him heavily on the pathway, where he now lay moaning.

Turning to see who assailed him, Captain Tom was astonished to find himself confronted by one of the soldiers whom he had left in the forest.

The man, recovering his footing in an instant, dashed at our hero, and seized him by the throat.

Taken at a disadvantage, by a man much more powerful than himself, Tom Drake stood little chance in a struggle, but though exhausted with his late exertion, he did not intend to give in while he had strength to raise an arm.

The soldier gave a curious sort of whistle, and, having pinned Tom's arms down to his sides, held him almost powerless.

The signal was answered by a tramp of feet, and a body of guards made their appearance at no great distance.

"Trapped," Tom muttered, between his teeth.

Then, with a sudden wrench, he broke from the soldier's embrace and fled.

The guards dashed after him at the double, but being fleet of foot, our hero kept well in advance, and made towards an old ruined chapel, where he thought to elude his pursuers.

When near the chapel, another body of soldiers marched out from behind a wall, and drew in line across his path, with fixed bayonets.

Menaced with death before and behind, Captain Tom turned like a lion at bay, and, throwing the gun aside, drew his sword, determined to sell his life dearly.

The soldiers closed around him, and Tom, with a bitter smile of scorn, looked from one officer to the other in defiance.

"There are scarcely enough to capture me," he said, with a laugh of contempt. "Yet, with all your boasted valour as soldiers, there is not one amongst you who would meet me in single battle and defeat me."

"By heaven! I never yet refused a challenge to single combat!" exclaimed the captain of the guards, who was a brave man, and chafed under the taunt of the young buccaneer, "and, pirate though you are, I will fight you where we stand."

His fellow-officers tried to dissuade him, but he commanded them to stand back, and drew his sword.

Captain Tom admired the man for his courage, and met him with a smile of friendly gratitude.

Their swords met with a clash, and they fought with the easy grace of accomplished swordsmen. For some time neither gained a point more than the other, foot, hand, and eye, marked in perfect unison, and the captain of the guards, who had thought to gain an easy victory, bit his lip with chagrin to find himself met at every pass.

Tom smiled the whole time, and maintained that wonderful coolness which distinguished him throughout his whole career.

The soldier began to lose his self-possession with his temper, and fought with more fury and less care than he began.

Captain Tom had to use his sword with more dexterity, now that his opponent cut and thrust at him with savage recklessness, and wishing to end the combat to save the officer less annoyance he watched his opportunity.

It came sooner than he expected. The captain of the guards made a feint, and a furious lunge, throwing his whole weight forward.

Captain Tom caught the blade on his own, and, with a peculiar twist of his wrist, which seemed to wind his sword like a snake round that of his combatant, turned aside the murderous thrust, and at the same time disarmed the captain of the guard.

Our hero lowered his sword, and bowed to his opponent, who, purple with rage and shame at being defeated before his men, felt ready to plunge the sword through his own heart.

"For the first time I am defeated, and acknowledge it," he said, gnawing his moustache, "but I must do my duty in spite of that. Tom Drake, you are a prisoner. Men, arrest him!"

Without a word, Captain Tom burst like a thunderbolt through the opposing ranks, and vaulting on to the captain of the guards' steed, sped away before a man could stop him.

He had to go a long way round in order to find a path accessible to a horse, and, when at length he arrived at the mouth of the cavern, he was met by the band, one of whom held the horse's head, whilst another of the crew assisted him to dismount.

On reciting his adventures to the gallant crew, they made the cavern ring with their mirth.

Right willingly did they toast his health.

Whilst deafening cheers and boisterous merriment resounded through the vaults and subterranean passages, that formed the stronghold of the smugglers and buccaneers.

CHAPTER CXXXVIII.

THE MASQUERADE.

In the noble mansion of Sir Henry Wharncliffe, a masquerade ball was about to be held.

Great preparations had been made, and many of the nobility and fashionables were invited.

The guests were already thronging the splendid saloons and beautiful gardens, the terraces and avenues, which were splendidly illuminated with myriads of lamps.

Whilst the fairy-like conservatories were lit up, and the windows thrown open, and a flood of rich music burst forth upon the night air.

It was arranged that the guests were to remain unmasked until the hour of the banquet, up to which time they could wander whither they pleased.

Until this moment, the beautiful daughters of Sir Henry Wharncliffe had been the sole admiration of the assembled throng.

But when the arrival of Colonel Hawkins and his lovely wife and beautiful daughter was announced, a slight murmur of approbation ran through the astonished throng of spectators, who gazed upon them, the ladies with envious eyes, the gentlemen with looks of surprise and admiration.

At length it was announced that their long-expected guest, the noble lord, had arrived, and as he made his appearance among the guests already assembled, his presence caused the greatest excitement.

From head to foot he was one mass of brilliants and precious stones, and one of the chief occupations of the guests was to give rough estimates of the value of his gorgeous attire.

As all the guests were deemed of an equality, the utmost freedom of association was permitted, and the noble lord, with a free and easy gait, strolled among, and mingled with, the throng of fair admirers.

Each one tried to outvie the other in their attentions, whilst the many anxious mothers, eager to dispose of their daughters' hands as advantageously as possible, almost thrust their daughters in his way, and bestowed their utmost flattery upon the honoured guest.

At length this illustrious personage who had caused so much commotion, advanced to where the lovely daughters of Sir Henry Wharncliffe stood engaged in earnest conversation; his quick eye, in spite of their singular costume and masked faces, could easily detect who they were.

Bowing politely to both, he presented them each with a splendid bouquet, which they received with a graceful curtsey; and as they caught the piercing glance of his dark, black eyes, they seemed as though they would have given worlds to raise the cruel mask, if only for one moment, that concealed the handsome features they felt certain must lay hidden beneath.

There was one who noticed his attentions to the beautiful sisters, and in whose heart an unquenchable fire was ignited as he saw the wealthy stranger present the sisters with the bouquet, she could scarcely restrain from giving vent to her outraged feelings.

This was no other than the beautiful and coquettish wife of the colonel, for up to this time the wealthy nobleman had not bestowed the slightest attention upon her daughter, whose beauty everyone allowed to be matchless.

Nor did her daughter feel less piqued as she watched his handsome figure and graceful movements.

Had the mask been removed from her beautiful face, it would have revealed the features which but a few moments before were radiant with joy, now overshadowed by the clouds of disappointment.

At length he approaches towards her, and tenderly asks her to accompany him in the next dance.

What a load those few words removed from her gentle breast, and how the sweet music of his voice rang in her ears!

She felt as light as any fairy, and could dance and smile with any in that large assembly.

Her mother was elated with joy as she saw them gaily trip the floor; so changed were her feelings now that she felt her heart leap with emotion as though it were about to bound from her bosom.

But who can describe her feelings, when, having returned with her daughter, he begged the mother would favour him with her company for the next dance.

Her joy knew no bounds, she felt as though her feet scarcely touched the floor, scarcely deigning a look at her husband, she yielded to the gentle pressure of his hand, and allowed him to lead her to the further end of the hall.

The colonel, with a party of his friends, were sipping their wine and conversing freely, and when they saw his daughter led away by the illustrious personage, they congratulated him rather warmly on his great success, but when they saw the colonel's lady leaning on his arm as he led her away, and when they saw them mingling in the busy throng of gay and lithesome dancers, they formed a little plot among themselves, to which the colonel, who, having imbibed a considerable quantity of wine, soon fell an easy and unsuspecting victim.

Eagerly did he watch the movements of his wife, and what scenes did he conjecture in his heated brain, whilst the constant hints of his friends easily awakened the green-eyed monster in his breast.

The dance ended, the noble lord appears, leading the lovely coquette to where her daughter stands absorbed in deep meditation, and returns the gentle pressure of his hand.

He presses her to his breast, and imprints a fervent kiss upon the ruby lips that appear below her mask, and whispers softly in her ear.

"Oh, heaven! it is more than I can bear," muttered the colonel, painfully.

There is no doubt he would have flown at the young nobleman with the fury of a maniac, had he not been restrained by his friends, who had so far succeeded in their plot as to have already worked upon his feelings, and awakened a fiery jealousy in his mind; he felt as though a hundred snakes were crawling in his breast, and darting their forked tongues into his heart.

His eye darted fiery looks of hate at the apparently unsuspecting victim, whose dark eyes appeared to penetrate the masks of the ladies.

"I will bear this no longer," gasped the enraged colonel. "Though he were the King, I would not allow him thus to trifle with me."

"Be calm, my friend," cried one of his tormentors. "This is no place to decide such matters; besides, you know he is wealthy, and who knows but what he might ask the favour of your daughter's hand?"

"That is quite a different subject altogether," he answered, hastily.

Then, raising his voice to a pitch of anger, he exclaimed—

"Has he not dared to kiss my wife before my face? Have I not seen it with my own eyes? Does that look like courting my daughter? No. I will demand an apology or satisfaction!"

"Now you talk more rational, friend. I should advise you to have an interview with this sprig of nobility, and then you can form your own opinion of his intentions."

The ball had been kept up till a late hour in the morning, and daylight had broken in on the wearied guests, many of whom were prepared to depart.

Amongst those of the carriages that had been ordered was that of the magnificently-dressed nobleman, who had formed the theme of the various gossip and scandal of the evening, and who had been the source of great annoyance and the discomfiture of many of the young noblemen assembled, whose presence were no longer required by the fair coquettes.

So great was the excitement created by his presence that many would rather incur the displeasure of their betrothed than forego the honour of dancing with him, and those who had once danced with him were rendered unhappy the rest of the evening, and so graceful were his motions, and so lightly did he trip among the dancers, that his rivals were completely eclipsed, and the smiling fair one who was fortunate enough to be his partner sighed deeply as he withdrew his arm that encircled her delicate form, and relaxed the gentle pressure of her hand.

The handsome young lady-killer was about to depart, and leave the many aching hearts and sighing maidens, and, with a graceful bow to the ladies, he withdrew from the busy throng.

On gaining the hall, his progress was arrested by the pressure of a heavy hand upon his shoulder, which caused him to turn, and he stood face to face with the colonel.

"May I trouble you for your card, sir?" said the colonel, assuming a tone of calmness, and battling fiercely with the passions awakened in his breast.

"Most certainly," was the cool rejoinder, as he drew a jewelled case from his breast, and presented a card gracefully to the colonel, who was almost burning with rage at the coolness of the stranger. "Here is my card, and here is my present address," he continued, drawing another card from the case.

"And this is mine," rejoined the colonel, staggering.

He had imbibed so freely of the wine that two of his friends were obliged to support him.

"Don't forget the name—Captain Tom Drake," said our hero, whose clever disguise baffled the acute detectives who were present.

The coachman was seated on the box, and appeared as though he were rocking an infant to sleep, but in reality he had partaken so freely of the good things with which the mansion abounded that he could scarcely keep his perpendicular, whilst the footman, who held the door, was holding it more to support himself than for any other purpose.

The footman led the horses a little way down the road, until they could not be observed by any one in the mansion, and Tom Drake, who had been seated inside as though the cushions were stuffed with needles, mounted the box, and giving the horses several sharp cracks, they dashed down the road at a pretty good pace.

They now left the road, and turned down a green lane, when, at a given signal, five or six of the band made their appearance from among the bushes.

The buccaneers had a grand nobleman and his two flunkies with them, from whom Captain Tom had taken forcible possession of the carriage and the gentleman's clothes to attend at the masquerade; and having satisfied his freak, he restored everything to their owners, saving the two cards he had borrowed from the nobleman's case.

The carriage-horses were led back, and after thanking the enraged nobleman for his equipage, and apologising for their abrupt intrusion, they were about to depart; but the nobleman, whose anger was at its height, and burning with indignation, was not so easily satisfied, and was determined that some of them should pay for their temerity with their lives.

Snatching one of the double-barrelled pistols from the pocket in the coach (for Tom had replaced them), he presented it at the head of the reckless and daring buccaneer, who replied to his threat with a defiant laugh, for he had already taken the precaution to draw the charges.

With an angry growl, like a baffled tiger, he threw himself back in his seat, and ordered the coachman to drive on, which order the coachman willingly obeyed.

Whilst the footman, with despair in every feature, mournfully surveyed his soiled livery, and shook his fist menacingly at Bob Hauler, who had been the supposed footman, Bob Hauler and his comrade, while waiting for the captain, not feeling at home in the company of the other servants, withdrew from the hall, and at last found themselves in the kitchen.

There they made themselves as comfortable as possible, and having at last made themselves merry with the good wine, they commenced larking with the cooks, and eventually got so bold as to kiss them.

This the cooks took all in good part until they commenced further proceedings, when the two fat cooks retaliated, and having locked one of the offenders in the coal cellar, they both seized hold of Bob Hauler and carried him between them to where a barrel stood, which was half full of flour, and having by dint of great exertion, forced him into it, they rolled him about the floor.

Not satisfied with this, they wrapped the wet dishclout round his neck. And when, having extricated himself from his unenviable position, he came to examine his clothes, which but a few moments before were as gaudy as the plumage of the gaudy peacock, he found himself encased in flour and dough, which adhered firmly to his borrowed livery, and gave him the appearance of a sausage roll of rather large dimensions.

At this juncture of affairs, it was announced that his master was ready and waiting for the carriage, and he made a precipitate retreat from the kitchen amid roars of laughter; many others of the female domestics had been invited to see the sausage roll.

CHAPTER CXXXIX.
AFTER THE MASQUERADE.

On arriving home, Colonel Hawkins, boiling with indignation and panting for revenge, shut himself up in his own private chamber.

The green-eyed monster, jealousy, was busy at its work, and had now claimed him for his victim.

His wife and daughter proceeded to bed, but there he sat, wrapped in gloomy thought; he had written a hasty letter and was now waiting, anxiously hour after hour, for the arrival of the messenger with the answer.

At length it came, but it only served to add fuel to the flame.

"The scoundrel, the base villain!" he cried. "And is he not satisfied with kissing my wife in my presence, but now he must add to his villainy by denying all knowledge of the transaction, and declares he is the injured party, and that it is my duty to apologise instead of him?"

Here he raved and swore, and clutched his fingers in his hair as though he were going to pull it out by the roots, and seizing the pen, he sat down with the full determination of challenging the innocent man who he supposed had caused him so much unhappiness, to single combat with sword or pistol.

He was about to commence the all-important epistle, when a loud knock at the door of the apartment brought him on his legs.

"Who's there?" he inquired, having recovered from his momentary surprise.

"It's me, dear."

"Who's me?"

"Your wife, dear."

"I'm engaged, dear," retorted the injured husband, with a sneer.

"Oh, do let me in, dear, if only for one moment," she said, imploringly.

Having reflected for two or three moments, he opened the door, and, having admitted her, closed and locked the door behind her.

"Madam," said he, fixing his eyes sternly upon her, "you are aware of what took place last night?"

"I am sure I do not know what that was," replied the lady, coolly, "except that you were very tipsy."

"Granted, madam; you took advantage of it, and your conduct—"

"My conduct, Mr. Hawkins?" replied his wife, kindling with anger.

"Yes, Mrs. Hawkins, your conduct as a married woman, madam, who allow gentlemen—"

"Gentlemen! Mr. Hawkins, I allow no gentleman but yourself. Are you sure you are quite sober?"

"Yes, madam, I am; but this affected coolness will not avail you. Deny, if you can, that that sprig of nobility—I can't think of his name—did not last night—"

"Well, then, I do deny it. Neither Lord What's-his-name nor any other man ever did—"

"Did what, madam?" interrupted the husband, in a rage.

"I was going to observe that no one was wanting in proper respect towards me," replied the lady, who grew more cool as her husband increased in choler. "Pray, Mr. Hawkins, may I inquire who is the author of this slander?"

"The author, madam! Look at me to your confusion! Look at me!"

"Well, I'm looking."

"I saw it myself."

"Saw what yourself?"

"Do you wish me to repeat it, madam?"

"I don't know what you mean. Repeat what?"

"What I saw."

"I am sure you could not have seen much, for you were blind drunk. That's the word in English, Mr. Hawkins; and we did not do anything—"

"In the ball-room," he muttered, fiercely. "I know you did not; but you went on the promenade, and viewed the grounds."

"I did."

"That confirms my suspicion, Mrs. Hawkins," he said, sternly.

"Mr. Hawkins, I'm afraid your head is not right this morning."

"Indeed, madam! I only wish that your heart was as sound," replied the husband, with a sneer. "But, madam, I am not quite blind. An honest woman, a virtuous woman, would have acquainted her husband with the circumstances at once, if she were not a consenting party, not have concealed it; still less have the effrontery to deny it, after acknowledging you had deviated from the right path."

"Right path! If ever I deviated from the right path, as you call it, it was when I married such a wretch as you."

"Yes, sir," continued the lady, bursting into tears, "I tell you now—my life has been a torment to me ever since I married—(sobbing)—always suspected for nothing—(sob)—jealous—(sob)—detestable temper—(sob)—go to my friends—(sob)—may hereafter repent—(sob)—then know what you've lost—(sob, sob, sob)"

"And, madam," replied the colonel, "so may you also know what you have lost before a few hours have passed away; then, madam, the time may come when the veil of folly will be rent from your eyes, and your conduct appear in all its deformity—farewell, madam, perhaps for ever!"

The lady made no reply, but quitted the room.

Then the colonel, believing his wife to be guilty, and that he was a deeply injured man, sat himself down and wrote a challenge to the nobleman, who he now believed to be a thorough-bred villain and a bare-faced scoundrel.

When her tears had subsided, Mrs. Hawkins for some time continued in her chair, awaiting, with predetermined dignity, the appearance and apology of her husband.

Dinner was announced, and she certainly expected to meet him there, but he did not come. She then presumed that he was still in the sulks and had sat down to table without her, and therefore, as he would not come, she went—but he was not at the table!

Every minute she expected him.

"Had he been told dinner was waiting? Where was he?"

"In his own private room, was the reply."

Mrs. Hawkins swallowed a few mouthfuls, and then hurried upstairs.

Hour after hour passed away, yet she had neither seen nor heard anything of the colonel; at length, tired and worn out, she went to bed.

There she lay in agony of suspense, as hour after hour passed away, every minute listening for the slightest sound of his footstep.

At length she could bear up against her suspense and agitation no longer, and she rose from her bed and descended the stairs.

As she neared the door, she perceived a light gleaming through the key-hole.

Whether to peep or speak first she did not know. "Perhaps he might be asleep," she thought; "and, perhaps,"—oh, horror!—her blood curdled at the thought, and she drew her thin garment around her, for now she could feel the cold air on her delicate limbs, "he may have committed suicide!"

She feared to look through the keyhole, for even now he may lay weltering in his gore, a ghastly corpse.

Oh! what would she now have given to recall the last few hours.

Oh! what agony now rent her breast.

But remorse was useless; she should have thought of all this before, and even the last words he uttered seemed ringing in her ear.

"Oh, Heaven!" she murmured, and clung to the handle of the door for support.

Her limbs trembled violently, and her knees knocked convulsively together, and she dared not look through the keyhole, for she felt as though it would turn her brain should she gaze upon the dead form of her husband, who, through her own indiscretion, had been driven to so violent an act.

Cold drops of perspiration stood upon her pallid brow, and her face assumed the livid hue of a pale and ghastly corpse, and, as she stood in her white dress, with a snowy white handkerchief over her head, she looked like one just risen from the grave.

Again she starts convulsively; she hears the same sound.

This time it seems more hollow and sepulchral.

Her hold tightens on the handle of the door, her

limbs became rigid and motionless; her eyes become fixed in the direction whence the rumbling sounds proceed.

Ah! it seems to be drawing nearer; now she fancies she sees an unearthly light; a thousand thoughts flash across her bewildered brain.

Can it be the troubled spirit of her husband come to seek vengeance on the heartless destroyer of his happiness?

"Oh, Heaven!" she murmured, "I feel I am going. I shall faint."

Dazzling sparks flit before her eyes, and obscure her vision, and an unearthly and appalling shriek bursts upon her ear, followed by an unearthly and terrific noise, which seems to shake the house to its very base, as though a thousand demons had broken from their chains, and were now dancing frantically around her.

Petrified with terror and trembling with fear, she fell heavily on the floor in a swoon.

Colonel Hawkins having finished writing to his different friends, had been busily engaged through the long weary hours of night in settling his accounts, and had made all his property over to his daughter, scarcely leaving his wife enough to subsist on, and having finished his mournful task, he threw down the pen, pressed his forehead, and groaned deeply.

How long he had remained there he knew not, when he was startled from his reverie by a fearful noise, as though some one were falling downstairs, at the same moment something fell with a dull thud near his door.

Alarmed at these strange sounds he rushed to the door, and judge his surprise and consternation on beholding his wife in deshabille and senseless.

"What can be the meaning of all this?" he muttered, and placing his wife upon the couch, he seized the candle from the table, and descended the stairs.

Arriving at the bottom he was surprised to see the form of a man rolled up in the shape of a hedgehog, and by his side an extinguished candle.

"Burglars," he muttered, fiercely.

But on closer survey he discovered the supposed burglar to be no other than his own valet.

"By heavens!" he thundered, "is it possible. Ah, I see it all now, she has watched my movements, and thinking I should soon be no more, has selected my valet for her paramour.

"Ah!" he continued," thrusting his clenched fingers into his dishevelled locks, as though a sudden thought had struck him, "they have come to listen at my door, perhaps to see if I were asleep, and in his flurry the villain has slipped his foot, and she, terrified at thus being discovered, has fallen in a swoon.

So saying, he dealt the unlucky valet a tremendous kick with his heavy riding-boot. But the unconscious man could only reply by a deep groan.

Maddened with rage, and trembling with fury, he ascended the stairs, and by the time he reached his room Mrs. Hawkins had recovered from her swoon.

"Now, madam, I have found you out!" he roared, as he fixed his gaze upon her with a wolfish glare; "and if I had done right, I ought to have killed you both as you lay."

A low murmur, accompanied by a deep sigh, was the only response.

"Wretched, abandoned woman," he said, in a tone of intense bitterness. "When you draw as near to your end as I am at the present moment, perhaps your conscience may smite you, and you may then think of your past and dissolute life, and then"—here his voice faltered—"you may, perhaps, think of the misery and disgrace you have brought upon your much-injured husband, who has only erred in loving you too well."

Here the cheek of the lady grew paler, and she could not keep a limb still, while a flood of tears flowed down her marble cheeks.

The husband, blind with rage, believed this only a confirmation of her guilt, and he now gazed upon the lovely features he once so much admired, with a look of scorn and loathing hatred.

A loud knock was now heard at the door; it was the valet. And no sooner did his head protrude through the open doorway, and he saw the withering look of hate with which his master eyed him, than he disappeared, and with one bound, reckless of the consequences, he cleared the flight of stairs.

Another knock was now heard at the door, and upon it being opened, three gentlemen entered, but immediately withdrew on seeing the lady as she lay.

At length they were again ushered in, and now it was evident that business of very great import was about to be proceeded with.

"There is my card, sir," said one of the visitors. "I think you kept us waiting a long time in the hall. We sent your valet up twice to announce our arrival. The first time he came down with a lame story—something about seeing a ghost and falling down stairs; the next time he came down as though he had been scared out of his wits, and said you were a raving maniac. Nothing in the world could induce him to come on the third occasion, so, you see, we were obliged to walk up of our own accord."

The colonel, who had been listening with breathless anxiety to the above words, now for the first time ventured to draw his eyes from the speaker and turn them upon the card.

"Lord Dumbleton," he cried, as though waking from a horrid dream, "the wronger of my wife!"

All the visitors save one stared with astonishment, whilst the lord was so abashed, he knew not which way to look.

For I must explain that the gentleman who had paid so untimely a visit to the colonel, were no others than one of the most intimate friends of the colonel's, and Lord Dumbleton, and one of his friends who had unwillingly promised, in the event of a duel, to fill the unpleasant office of second.

The colonel's friend, who was one of the party had led him into the scrape, seeing matters assume so threatening an aspect, had gone to the young nobleman to offer an apology for the colonel, with the view of preventing the duel, but, of course, as there was a great mystery attached to the whole proceedings, the young nobleman could not honourably accede to the proposals, without first having an interview with the colonel, and as the duel was to come off at an early hour, it was thought expedient to visit him as early as possible.

At length the lord recovered from his confusion, and said, indignantly,

"Explain yourself, if you please, sirrah?"

"It requires no explanation," said the colonel, angrily, "your own conscience is sufficient."

The young lord and his friend looked astounded.

"The man must be mad," they exclaimed in a voice.

"I was sane enough to notice your actions at the ball."

The nobleman and his friend exchanged significant glances.

"I think," said the lord, "there must be some great mistake somewhere, I have not been to any ball."

"This is your card, I believe?"

"It is."

"And here is its counterpart," said the colonel, drawing another from his breast, "you gave me that on the night of the masquerade."

"I gave it you, could you swear to that?" inquired the lord, laughing, in which his companion also joined.

"Do not mock me, I am desperate!" roared the colonel, his eye lighting with a lurid glow.

"Be seated, friend," cried the nobleman, "and I will explain, as near as I can, how this mistake has occurred."

He now began to recount his adventures on that eventful night, and when he came to the description of the supposed highwayman, a heavy mist seemed to roll away from the eyes of the colonel—a heavy weight seemed to have dropped from his shoulder, and, drawing himself to his full height, he struck his fist heavily on the table.

"That was no other," he cried, vehemently, "than Tom Drake, the daring buccaneer; he has played me several tricks, and if ever I get once more in close quarters with him, I lay he won't forget it."

Thus ended the duel, and, peace having been once more proclaimed, the colonel ordered wine and refreshment.

His wife, who had lain listening to the whole of the conversation, could not restrain her feelings any longer, and, with an impulsive movement, she flew to her husband, and hung imploringly round his neck, begging forgiveness.

CHAPTER CXL.

PERIL OF THE TIGER OF THE SEA.

It was a dull, cloudy morning when John Bentley, the Tiger of the Sea, and his companion in crime, stood upon the deck of the "Will-o'-the-Wisp" they had so cleverly seized. Their faces seemed to be rather paler than usual, and presented a haggard appearance.

They watched with anxious eyes the dark clouds rising from the distant horizon, and could not help feeling that some dreadful calamity awaited them.

The wind, which now blew in anything but a favourable direction, seemed to increase, in fitful gusts as it howled mournfully through the cordage which clattered against the masts, and died away in low monotonous sounds.

Every one was wrapped in deep thought as they gazed in the direction of the gathering storm, which ere long they felt certain would burst upon them in its fury.

With an impetuous motion, Bentley seized the speaking trumpet.

"Boatswain, call all hands!" he cried, fiercely.

The heavy tramp of eager feet rushing up the forward hatchway, told how prompt the pirate captain's injunction had been obeyed. And in the space of a very few minutes the gallant ship lay beating to the wind under double-reefed topsails.

Each moment increased the fury of the gale, while the rain in large heavy drops came down like a deluge, and seemed as though in its fury it was striving to beat them to the deck.

The pirate crew looked at each other in superstitious dread, and an awful presentiment of some approaching evil took possession of them.

"Close reef the topsails," thundered Bentley; "go you, Red Ralph, see they haul up the earings well on the yard, for I fear we are going to have another fearful night of it."

Red Ralph hastened to obey the injunction, leaving the Tiger of the Sea buried in gloom and abject thought.

"Curses on that fellow!" he muttered, half aloud; "he seems to haunt me night and day, and now even I can feel his withering grasp upon my leg; he says I shall not be freed from his infernal machinations until I land the cussed girl and her mother in England—that I cannot do."

"It would be madness to venture into the English Channel; no, no, those waters swarm with danger too much now, like a sugar cask, with wasps and hornets, and what with King's cruisers on our weather bow, and landsharks under our lee, I might soon find myself dangling under the brace block at the fore-yard arm of a line-of-battle ship."

His soliloquy was abruptly broken by the appearance of Red Ralph.

"They are snugly reefed, John," he said, wiping the rain from his grimy face; "the earings are well hauled out, and the lugs well up on the yard, and I have examined every point, and find them securely tied; I think we can stand against a good blow now."

"I am not afraid of the storm, Red Ralph, but you know that devilish captain hangs on to us like grim death to a nigger, and so he will as long as we have them women aboard; I was in hopes the wind would have held favourable a few hours longer, and then we should have been able to run through the gut, but now the wind blows right dead in our teeth."

"Are you going to run through the Straits of Gibralter, then?" inquired Red Ralph, in surprise.

"I am, Red Ralph."

"Then the sooner this wind changes the better, for I don't much like beating about this part; what do you intend doing when we get through the Straits?"

"I thought of running along the coast of Barbary, and leaving her in charge of one of the many friends I am acquainted with there."

"Oh, indeed," said Red Ralph, "then you don't mean to ask my permission whether you may thus dispose of them."

"Why should I?" inquired John Bentley, coolly.

The eye of Red Ralph lit with a lurid glow, and he glared at the captain sternly as he listened to these words.

"Oh, I see it all now," he said, fiercely, "you want to have all the game to yourself. Ah, ah," he laughed savagely, "but you'll not do with me as you please, you shall find Red Ralph, the Wrecker, a match for the Tiger of the Seas."

"Is there not two of them?" inquired Bentley, mockingly.

"What!" cried the wrecker in a frenzy of rage, "do you think I will submit to salt junk and mouldy biscuits while you enjoy jugged hare and soft tack?"

"I don't clearly understand you," was the cool rejoinder.

"You very soon will, then," said Ralph, hoarsely.

"Let's have it at once," said Bentley, tauntingly, as he placed his arms across his broad chest, and leaned against the companion.

"Then listen," growled Red Ralph, through his clenched teeth. "I am not going to make love to that wizzened, grey-headed, old hag whilst you indulge in the smiles of her lovely daughter."

"Oh, indeed! we shall see. But this is no time to bandy words; we have sworn to stick to each other through thick and thin, fire and water, calm or storm, and now I think we had better make it up over a glass, for I feel as though I want something to warm me. I am drenched to the skin."

"I am not much better," rejoined Red Ralph, eyeing his dripping clothes.

"Boatswain!" cried Bentley.

As that individual promptly appeared he cried—

"Just keep an eye to the vessel for a few minutes, and see that she is kept cleverly full and by, and if she should break off, if only one point, or there is the least change in the weather, let me know directly."

"Aye, aye, sir," replied that worthy functionary, as he dashed the rain from his sou'-wester; "I s'pose if I see any signs of a strange craft or anything of that sort I am to give you a hail, your honour."

"Certainly," said Bentley, as he disappeared down the companion ladder.

The storm still raged with unabated fury, and the little brig made but slow progress through the water, as she lay under double-reefed topsails, labouring heavily she breasted the billows defiantly, while the sea assumed the form of one vast plain thickly intersected with high and lofty snow-capped peaks.

When Bentley got to the bottom of the ladder the cold sweat stood in thick beads on his haggard lineaments, and he was compelled to clutch the steps of the ladder for support.

A feeling that he could not overcome crept over him, and he almost feared to enter the cabin.

At length mustering courage he stepped into the cabin, and started back as he beheld the scene that that was presented to his gaze on entering the cabin.

There stood Red Ralph, near the after lockers, his left arm encircling the small waist of the lovely girl whom they had forcibly brought aboard, whilst with his right hand he was endeavouring to wrench the dagger from her grasp, which she held in her delicate little hand.

Without waiting for a moment's reflection Bentley sprang upon him, and having seized him by the collar, bore him to the deck, and held a pistol closely to his head.

"Would you murder me?" cried Red Ralph, in terror.

"I will if you offer to touch that girl again," growled Bentley, fiercely, his eyes aglow with the fierceness of a hungry wolf, "and if you dare touch her again I'll blow out your senseless brains."

"Let me rise," said Red Ralph, seeing him lag in his purpose.

"Not till you have sworn—"

Here he was abruptly stopped by the loud bang of a door, for the Wrecker, on entering the cabin, and finding the girl seated on the lockers, while her mother was in the state-room, pulled the state-room door to and fastened it, thus leaving the girl, as he thought, powerless and at his mercy, but as soon as she became aware of his presence she drew her dagger to defend herself, and was struggling fiercely against the superior strength of her enamoured assailant, when Bentley entered.

Upon being freed from his embrace, she flew to the state-room door and slammed the door to; thus causing Bentley for a moment to look round.

In that moment Red Ralph saw his chance; with a violent jerk he disengaged himself from the knee of his confederate, and mustering all his strength, he grappled with Bentley, threw him to the floor, and placed his knee upon his chest.

"What have you got to say for yourself, now?" inquired Red Ralph, in an exulting tone; "suppose I send a bullet through your brainless skull, eh? do you think it will be more than just?"

The enraged captain could only reply with a scowl.

Red Ralph could have easily settled his score with Bentley, but he knew full well it would not be to his advantage to do so, for one without the other would be powerless; besides, the crew, at the sight of their murdered captain might create a mutiny, especially after the strange incidents they had witnessed.

The voice of the boatswain caused him to start.

"It's coming on to blow great guns, captain," cried the boatswain down the companion, "we must take more canvas off her or else the sticks will soon go over the side."

Red Ralph sprang to his feet and rushed upon deck, and the captain followed as quickly as he was able, for he had been so fixed under the table by Red Ralph that it took him some few moments to extricate himself.

At first they could not see anything, for a pitchy darkness reigned around, and they had to wait a few seconds until their eyes became a little used to the darkness.

On either side of the tempest-tossed vessel the angry billows rose majestically, and threatened to crush the little brig with the fury with which they dashed against her sides.

All around presented a black mass of roaring billows, their tops crested with white seething foam as each angry wave rose, and then rolled away with a hissing sound.

Whilst the threatening aspect of the sky added to the dismal scene, for the masses of sable clouds overspread the canopy of the heavens.

Every sail was furled save the main topsail, and that was taken in to close reef.

The little vessel lay to, in the furious gale, while many anxious eyes watched eagerly the least sign indicating the abatement of the storm.

Most of the crew were crouching under the lee of the long boat, or in other parts of the vessel where shelter might be obtained from the heavy showers of spray that blew furiously over her bows and weather bulwarks.

"Now, shipmate," cried one, "just finish spinning that yarn of yourn. It may help to pass away a dull half hour, for we have no fear of being disturbed now till the watch is called."

"Aye, aye, watchmates, that I will, and that right cheerfully. How far did I get?"

"How can we tell how far you got? You only told us you was diving down his hatchway."

"Ah! you're right. Well, as I was saying, they just caught sight of my stern as I dived down the hatchway; and, thinks I to myself, I have been a good many years washing about in the lee-scuppers, and I have always been afore the mast, now, says I, I means to be captain, and I makes a bolt right into his after cabin.

"Well, messmates, it would have done your hearts good to have been there."

Several of them shrugged their shoulders, as much as to say—

"You are just about as wrong as ever you were right, old cock."

"There was gold watches, diamond rings, charts, chronometers, and a whole locker full of jewellery, and gold buckles, and what I wanted the most I found there."

"What was that, shipmate?" anxiously inquired one, whose face had stretched to within a very few inches of a yard long.

"Why, a chest of clothes, a breaker of rum, two bags of cabin biscuits, and a whole host of tins of soup and boulli, preserved lobsters, pickled salmon, and about a half hundred weight of the best cavendish baccy."

At this juncture, the listeners drew back a pace, and would, most likely, have called him by an improper name, had they not been arrested by the solemn tone of his voice, as he continued—

"Well, you see, mates, I was well provisioned for a long cruise, and time passed on merrily, and me and the cockatoo was the best of chums, and I learnt him to talk four different languages, and I also learnt him what I never ought to."

"What was that?" inquired several anxious voices.

"Why, to read and write."

"How could that be bad?" asked one, who, more successful than the rest, had been able to suppress the tittering that rose to his lips.

"Well, mates, I'll tell you. After me sticking to him through thick and thin, he sold me a dog, as the saying is, for, don't you see, arter I arrived in Portsmouth, I was walking along with him under my arm, and by chance I happened to look into a shop window, and when I was going to sail on again, he sings out—

"'Vast heaving there, shipmate.'

"'What's in the wind, now?' says I.

"'Do you see that paper?' says he.

"'In course I does,' says I.

"'Then read it,' says he.

"And taking his advice, I did so."

"What's that to do with the yarn, shipmate?"

"Why, it's all to do with it, in course. Well, I reads the paper; it said something about a cockatoo, with bansum figure-'ed, a white streak round its side, and could set so many feet of snowy canvas to the breeze, if required, and could talk English flewantly. Had been lost, stolen, or strayed from Lord Thin-a-my-jigs, and if any one was to find it and take it home, they would get six pounds for their trouble."

"Well, I reads it, and says the same as our mate there, what's that to do with me."

"'Oh! don't you know,' says the rascal, looking very innocently in my face, 'supposing you was to find the parrot, and take it home, what would you get?'

"Six pounds, in course,' says I.

"'And if you was to keep it instead?' said he 'what would you get then?'

"'Why, six months aboard the stone frigate, oakum,' says I.

"'Very well,' says he, 'you can have your choice, six pounds or six months.'

"Well, shipmates, these words took my head-sails aback, and I should certainly have gone down, starn first, if an old woman's apple stall had not brought me up all standin'; and I nearly got into limbo for that job, for coming athwart hawse of the old woman's stall it capsized, and every soul aboard went down, old woman and all."

A cold shudder ran through the attentive listners on hearing the recital of this fatal collision, delivered in so impressive a tone.

At length, one more bold than the rest ventured to ask, "Where they went down to?"

"Why, into the gutter, in course," answered the orator, not a muscle of his face moving.

At this juncture a peculiar restless movement was observant among them, whilst a noise something similar to a number of persons being choked emanated from the group, and a constant motion of their eyes, as they looked towards each other, would have impressed a casual observer with the idea that it was caused by the spray that still continued to fly over the bows.

After a pause of a few moments, he continued.

"Well, mates, as soon as I was righted again, I says, 'What do you mean?'"

"'Why,' says he, 'I'm getting tired of a sea life, and as there's a good chance of a berth for me ashore, you must take me there, for you see it answers my description, and I talks English flewently.'

"This I couldn't deny, for I found that out when he flew up into the cross trees, so I says, 'Do you mean to leave your old chum, after being ship-mates together for twelve months on board the Shark?'"

"'Yes,' said he, as bold as a seventy-four, 'or' if you don't give me up, I'll swear you stole me.'

"If a line-of-battle ship had opened her three tiers of guns at me I could not have been more astonished. Why he started every treenail and bolt in my hull; my heads— —vered in the wind, and I drifted away to —rward, ane — would have

gone ashore upon a reef of eggs and became a total wreck if I hadn't brought myself up with a round turn of my arm round a lamp-post."

"Well, brothers, as I got under weigh, again, I says, 'If you still sticks to this I'll choke you,' and he knowed too much for me. He swore by all the oaths in the four different languages I'd learnt him, he'd cry murder.

"So, thinks I, it's time for me to clue up now. You're too much of a clipper for me to beat against the wind with, and so let him go, and you may believe me, brothers, I never got a farthing more than the six pounds for the edication I'd given him, that was, learnt him to talk four different languages, reading, writing, and 'rithmetic, and included smoking and chewing into the bargain."

"Ware ship," now sounded on the gale, and caused them to scatter in all directions.

As soon as the vessel's head had been turned in the opposite direction they all mustered under the lee of the longboat, many of them lit their pipes, and others took a fresh nip of the fragrant weed.

"Now, brothers, for the yarn," cried several voices.

Forthwith, with arms akimbo, he continued his yarn.

"Well brothers, I seats myself down on the chest, pulls out my pipe, and begins to smoke, and all of a sudden I felt the vessel give a fearful lurch, and then it rolled right over and over, and then it rightened. 'Oh! lord,' says I, 'I'll lay a guinea we are dismasted,' and I looks at the cockatoo, as much as to ask him, but he was too artful then to talk, so I turns to look out of the cabin winders, but they was closed, so I keeps on smoking; by-and-bye, the vessel gave such a fearful bump, and knocks me off my perch."

"Well, thinks I, this is a rum'un, and I could feel the bottom of the vessel bend as though she was on a rock, and I was afraid the deck was going to fall in atop of me, for it come down and touched my head."

"Well, of a sudden I looks towards the bows and I could see the forehatch way open, and I makes my way there and pokes my head out.

"It was a beautiful moonlight night, the sea was as smooth as glass, and so I does my rum and water, and sits there above an hour smoking my pipe; all this time the shark lay as still as an alligator, catching flies, and when I was tired of sitting there, I goes back and sits on the chest, when the vessel began to pitch about with violence.

"'So,' says I, scratching my head, "captain what's in the wind?'

"And at last, thinks I—

"'P'raps he's not been used to company, an' don't like baccy smoke, and p'raps it gets down his throat,' so I lays down at that, for the rocking, rolling, and tossing of the vessel completely put my pipe out.

"So I stops there till all the grub was nearly done.

"So thinks I—

"'I must get another ship, somehow;' and one day, as I was sitting in the bows I pretends to slip, and falls over—ard

"But he grabs hold of me like a Newfoundland dog, and in I goes again."

"What was you going to do, then?"

"Swim ashore, to be sure; we wasn't more than a hundred miles from land."

"What, swim a hundred miles?"

"To be sure; why, I once swum from Jamaica to New York for a bottle of grog, and then walked ten miles afore I rested."

"Well, how did you get away at last?"

"Oh! easy enough. Grub got so short at last that we had to go on short allowance, and it almost come to casting lots, so I gets desperate.

"And one day, as I sat smoking, I sees an island.

"'By golly!' says I. 'Old codger, I trick you now,' so I makes a slip, and dives under his bottom.

"He tried to follow me, but, afore he was aware of it, I lays hold of his tail; the tighter I held him, the more he kicked and worked his tail, and the more he kicked and floundered, the faster he neared the shore. At last, he runs aground for'ard between two rocks.

"Directly he grounded, I drags myself on to his back, and runs along till I was able to jump ashore; then takes the cockatoo under my arm, and puts my shoulder to the muzzle of the shark, and shoves him off into deep waters."

"Did you ever have any visitors aboard, mate?" asked one of them.

"Yes, plenty. Among whom I can mention his glorious Majesty Neptune, who stayed aboard a week, while they were splicing the line, that had been broken through getting foul of some vessel's keel.

"And another one I could mention was the Flying Dutchman; he came aboard of my craft for a month, while it was bad weather, 'cos he suffered so with the skenmatics, and the doctor ordered him a change of air."

The motley crew, who had listened with the greatest attention up to this time, now indulged in loud roars of laughter, and many were the jokes cracked on the strength of it.

Meanwhile, Red Ralph and John Bentley had paced the deck in sullen silence.

Each felt as though he would have given half the riches the ship contained to see the other fall overboard, and yet, if such was the case, each would have been powerless without the other, for it was only by firm adherence to each other that they could accomplish their ambitious designs.

Yet a jealousy, strong and unquenchable, reigned within their breasts, and that jealousy was a protection to their captives.

As morning dawned, the gale gradually diminished, and once more the pale rays of the sun shone forth over the troubled waters.

A sail was reported to leeward, and the captain, with the agility of a monkey, sprang into the rigging.

Orders were given to loose and make sail, and, for a few moments, Bentley and his companion held a short but decisive consultation.

"Boatswain!" he roared.

"You know our motto," he resumed, as that personage made his appearance on the quarter-deck, "we attack, plunder, and destroy. Clear for action and bear down."

What an electrical and appalling effect did that shrill cry "Sail, oh!" produce upon the lawless crew.

In an instant all signs of idle lassitude, and careless abandonment had vanished.

Then came the tramp of eager feet rushing over the deck.

Crowding the lee bulwarks with savage, glittering eyes, and wolfish countenances, they glared upon the distant outlines of their anticipated prey, for, with the robber crew, to sight a merchant vessel was almost tantamount to her capture and destruction.

The brig's head now turned in the direction of appeared to be a ship of large dimensions, though only a sluggish sailor.

Every inch of canvas that could be spread was set, and right gallantly did she bear down before the breeze.

The heavy and cumbersome merchantman appeared to labour heavily in her endeavours to breast the surging waves, and it would have been

an easy task for the little brig to have overhauled her had she not been in so disabled a condition, for as yet the weather had not permitted them to refit top-gallant and royal masts, and repair other damages she had received in the storm.

All that day did the pirate captain and his bloodthirsty colleague pace the deck, watching the progress of the vessels, and towards evening they had neared within a mile of each other, when, to their astonishment, the strange vessel shortened sail.

A smile of satisfaction overspread the brutal visage of Bentley, and the deep gleaming eyes, and scornfully curling lips, proclaimed an unmitigated and tigerish ferocity, whilst Red Ralph, with his right hand grasping one of the shrouds of the main rigging, eyed the doomed vessel, which he already believed to be within their grasp.

The sun had now sank below the horizon, and evening began to throw her shades around, when the unwieldly and apparently indifferent merchantman hauled to the wind, and appeared to the astonished pirates, whose gloating eyes had never for one moment lost sight of her since morning, as though about to cross their bows.

They watched her movements, and various conjectures were made as to her probable intentions.

The starboard side of the strange vessel, up till now, had been the only one visible to those on board the pirate vessel, but now the stranger stood boldly across their bows.

Suddenly, even whilst Bentley was considering the best mode of attack, she squared away again, thus exposing her port side to the view of the astonished crew, as the vessels ranged alongside each other, their heads both pointing in the same direction.

Picture their dismay, as the strange vessel exposed to their view her port side, from which bristled a tier of guns, their black muzzles pointing directly towards them, and before they could recover from their astonishment, a black flag, with skull and crossbones, showing them to belong to the same class of blood-thirsty ocean ravagers as themselves, was run up to the masthead.

For a moment Bentley and Red Ralph stood astounded at this sudden change in the aspect of affairs, as the apparently inoffensive merchant vessel was changed into a death-dealing Nemesis.

It was evident all their combined energies would be required to beat off their superior antagonist, for a tier of eight bristling guns protruded from her dark sides, and her hitherto apparently deserted decks presented a scene of life, as the bloodthirsty crew thrust their heads above the bulwarks, and presented a stern front, so bold and formidable, that for an instant the Tiger of the Sea and his companion, Red Ralph, paused irresolute.

Bitterly did they curse their fate that had allowed them thus to be drawn into the trap of their formidable enemy.

Concealment was no longer necessary, and the crew of the "Will-o'-the-Wisp" who had hitherto lain crouched at their quarters, taking cursory glances at the strange vessel through the open ports, were now glaring at her with eyes dilated and knitted brows.

"Prepare for action!" roared the Tiger of the Sea.

But the crew paused a moment to take one more look at the strange sail, and to calculate what chance they were likely to have against so desperate an opponent.

Their indecision was but momentary.

They knew full well that in such lawless warfare as each waged against their fellow men, no mercy no quarter would be shown or granted by their implacable foes.

Through the force of sheer necessity, their battle

THE SOLDIERS POURED A DEADLY VOLLEY INTO THE BODY OF THE HAPLESS YOUTH.

cry must be, " Victory or death," and, goaded on by the three-fold incentives of, deadly vengeance, reckless desperation, and hopeless despair, the outwitted ruffians rushed like raving demons to the fray.

Red Ralph, assisted by a party of the pirates, was busily engaged in bringing round the three brass guns from the port side, and, by the aid of skilfully applied slings and levers, they were quickly placed in position, and now protruded their bright muzzles through the ingeniously contrived portholes, which until now, had remained unobserved by their astonished assailants, for so ingeniously and skilfully were they contrived, that it appeared as though they were thrust through the solid bulwarks.

Their blood-red flag, with the ghastly emblems of their profession was ran up to the masthead, as a token of defiance.

A yell of defiance from the decks of the stranger, and a volley of murderous shot and shell, responded to the challenge of Bentley.

Broadside for broadside was sent from the opposing vessels with all the deadly fury of their bloodthirsty nature

Bentley rushed about the ship heedless of the iron shower and shattered spars that fell around him, cheering on his men with words of promise, and an unlimited supply of rum.

"Stand to your guns, my brave tars !" he cried working amongst them, and so giving them courage to continue the battle, which every minute brought their messmates to the deck maimed and mutilated.

As the battle continued, raging with greater fury every moment, the ships drew nearer to each other.

On both sides parties of the crews stood ready to board, and when the vessels grated side by side, the men from the stranger, with a dash like a legion of unchained demons, fell upon the crew of the " Will-o'-the-Wisp " with fire and sword.

Taken so suddenly by surprise, Bentley's crew retreated before the invaders, but, recalled by the stern voice of their savage captain, they rallied, and, in a compact body, charged the invaders with deadly fury and half-drunken stubbornness

Step by step the boarders were driven back to the bulwarks, and many of them hurled into the sea.

"Stand by your guns!" cried John Bentley; "they shall not forget the Tiger of the Sea. Give them a broadside, lads!"

A boisterous cheer responded, and a mighty roar of artillery, that echoed far across the water above the din of battle, shook each vessel from stem to stern, and did fearful damage to the stranger.

The crew of the stranger fled in dismay to their own vessel, leaving their chieftain alone on the deck of the victors battling furiously for his life to escape.

Bentley and Ralph had fought side by side through the whole of the fearful fray.

The voice of Bentley, who, accompanied by Red Ralph, summoned the pirate captain to surrender, who had fallen badly wounded almost the same instant that his disheartened crew had deserted him.

Struggling with difficulty into an erect posture, he faced his surrounding foes like a wounded tiger at bay.

For a moment he regarded them with a frightful glare of scorn and hate.

Then vainly essaying to brandish the cutlass he still grasped in his hand, he shouted—

"Come on, dogs, I defy you yet. Come on. The rover chieftain yields to no man but death.'

With a savage, wolf-like cry, Bentley dashed upon his rival, and tried to bury a poignard in his breast, but the Rover, astounded and half-bewildered as he was, threw up his arm and warded off the deadly stroke, then closed with his murderous assailant, and concentrating all his strength into one mighty effort, strove to hurl him on the deck.

In making the attempt, however, his foot slipped in a pool of blood, and both fell with crashing violence against a shattered portion of the bulwarks.

There was a rending crash, a heavy plunge. and the grasping combatants were battling madly in the sea.

A rush was made to the boats by those on board, but to their great dismay they were found to be so seriously injured by the shots from the Rover, that for the time being they were totally unfit for service.

Meanwhile the Tiger of the Sea and his foe, still grappled with the tenacity and fierceness of infuriated bloodhounds.

Now lost to view beneath an overwhelming wave, now struggling to the surface, were fast drifting away from the vessels.

At this critical, and painfully exciting juncture, the voice of Red Ralph was heard.

"Bear a-hand, here, my hearties," he shouted, raising a large coil of rope, and nimbly bending one end thereof round his waist, "stand by, my lads, and when I give yer the signal, haul away cheer-'ily."

So saying, he dashed his tarpaulin hat on the

deck, and leaped gallantly overboard to the rescue but scarcely had he struck the water ere a skiff shot into view, out of the deep shadow of the Rover's stern, and pulled swiftly away towards the now dimly visible antagonists.

The boat ran along-side, and Ralph, dripping like a Triton, assisted by the brawny arms of one of the crew sprang up the gangway supporting the exhausted and almost senseless form of Bentley.

Having deposited his burden on the quarter-deck, he now commenced to shake the salt ooze from his shaggy sides.

The contest was now at an end; a few well-directed strokes of a hatchet sufficed to clear them from the detaining grapnels, and the " Will-o'-the-Wisp " drifted away to leeward.

CHAPTER CXLI.

THE BRIDE OF NANT GWRTHEYRN.

GALLANT Tom Drake now lay in the inner cavern on a couch made of the softest furs, so dangerous, indeed, were the wounds he had received, that for several days his life was despaired of, and even now it was feared the least excitement would extinguish the vital spark, and thus deprive them of their beloved captain.

To soothe Tom, and prevent him from thinking of any subject that might excite him, Susan Brockton bethought herself of an old story she had once heard ; and, seating herself at Tom Drake's feet, she commenced as follows—

" On the northern side of that narrow part of Carnarvonshire jutting into the Irish Channel, which is called the promontory of Llyn, is a grand, green, mountain dingle, known by the name of Nant Gwrtheyrn, Vortigern's hollow or valley (nant signifying a brook, also a hollow), from a tradition that the British king of that name there retired to die.

" In a mound of sod, called Bedd Gwrtheyrn, the grave of Vortigern (the site of some now fallen edifice), a stone coffin, enclosing a gigantic skeleton, was discovered in the last century; and its ' solitary state' (no other tumuli being found near) sanctioned the belief that those bones were not vulgar bones, but of royal dignity.

" This glen, containing but two or three houses, is open to the ocean, and green to its margin, while on every other side the descent is so frightfully precipitous that it secludes the valley from approach almost as effectually as that sea which rolls across its front.

" The country above is very wild and solitary, the poor fisher's town of Nevin being the only place to which the winding road conducts the traveller on that narrow projection of North Wales.

" Down the midst of this pastoral hollow runs, foaming, a strong torrent, dividing it into two banks, only united by that sort of natural bridge the poverty of such districts allows to their dwellers—huge stepping-stones of rock, with a mountain ash or two, to assist the timid in their leap or swing over the roaring water.

" On each side of this ravine stood opposite to, but at some distance from, each other, two cottages, so old and grey, and so much the colour of the russet sod and rock, that each appeared more like a bare projecting part of the rock itself than a good, warm, human dwelling such as it really was within.

" In one of these lived Rhys (Rees) Meredith ; in the other, his cousin, Margaret Meredith, with her infirm father.

" Except two sisters of Rhys, these were the only survivors of two families, who had long possessed that little glen, with its patches of green corn, small meadows, and stacks of black peat round about, as a patriarchal domain from generation to generation.

"Their situation rendered this young pair a sort of hermits by necessity; and, as he was handsome and sensible, though as shy as a child, and she a soft, sensitive, fair girl, it was not to be wondered at that an attachment almost romantic had grown up between them.

"The sea solitude of Nant Gwrtheyrn; the eternal measured dash of the waves on the beach; the vast shadow of the stupendous Craig y Llam stretching quite across the valley; her only companions her two female cousins, who were suffering from ill health; all these produced on the gentle spirit of the girl almost the effect of a convent amongst the mountains, with its solemn music and its pale sisterhood.

"A deeper solitude could hardly be imagined than brooded, even at noonday, over Nant Gwrtheyrn, with its few sheep bleating, its many waterfalls moaning, and the expanse of desert ocean in its front, where the only living motion was that silent, solemn, beautiful one of some white-sailed vessel gliding across the mountain opening, too distant for any voice or token of life to reach the land, from the many human beings it was bearing by on their silent and unknown course.

"But now an unwonted stir, and voices calling, and figures whose various-coloured woollen dresses shone in the sun as they straggled down the declivities, winding between clumps of flowering furze and points of ivied rock, all tending towards the cottages, proclaimed some highly festive occasion at hand.

"Rhys and his cousin are to be married to-morrow, Saturday, the favourite wedding-day of the Welsh, and these were the friends of the parties, who, having been bidden, were now congregating to present the gifts usual on these occasions, which custom is called 'Pwrs a Gwregys'—that is pulse and girdle.

"Every person invited brings, according to his or her ability, some gift for the young beginners in housekeeping—an important benefit to them in the aggregate, though a light tax on individual generosity.

"The present of everybody is recorded in a book by a person who takes upon him this office, and the same, in commodity or value, is expected to be returned at the future wedding of the giver; it is even recoverable by law.

"It was a pleasant sight, on so fine a day, to see these kind visitants thus wending their way, the young helping the old wherever the path was too steep for their stiffened limbs, all traversing the slopes in little groups, one above another, down the zigzag paths, and old and young, and richer and poorer, all in their best.

"Pinners and coifs, newly plaited, and burying the good women's chins and half (frequently) of a very pretty mouth, to the no small disfigurement of youth; small hats, glossy as jet, with large silver buckles, whose brightness shone in the broad sunshine from a distance—all these, with now and then a stumble and outcry of the old, and the loud laugh of the thoughtless young, joined to the wild beauty of the scene; the blossoming furze gold, the purple heath, and white spars all about, and the little fairy pastoral view round the farms below, almost overhung by mountains, and all basking in the full blaze of noonday summer blue, presenting a sort of moving panorama, not undelightful to eyes contented with rustic and grotesque beauty.

"Here an old body, who could just carry her own weight by the help of a crutch-stick, contrived, nevertheless, to grapple a cheese under her spare arm, or a basket of chickens suspended over the wrist of the same, to her imminent peril of a fall.

"Little ones carried bags of various seeds, others larger ones full of oatmeal; oatmeal cakes were even brought ready baked; eggs, poultry, stores of every kind necessary in so isolated a residence; and abundance of all products of the sheep and loom, conducive to warm sleeping, and warm walking in the snow season.

"A still busier spectacle appeared down at the two cottages.

"The goods were being removed across the ravine, from one house to the other, by such friends of the bridegroom as had already arrived; for it is a point of courtesy to perform this labour without troubling him, and in this instance the labour was not light, to transport heavy utensils over the tumbling waters of the ravine by the bridge of rocks.

"A huge coffer of antique oak, black as ebony; the crochon, or iron pot with three feet, inseparable from Welsh chimnies; pewter dishes of large size, wooden platters and trenchers, bowls and spoons made of beech or birch, formed a few of the articles of housewifery comprised under the general name of Ystavell, signifying a chamber, thence the furniture of it.

"Meanwhile, the bride of to-morrow, was quietly kneeling to buckle the shoe of a fine, ruddy-cheeked old man, with silver hair, seated in his chair at the antique low porch of his house, and whom she had just finished dressing, he being rheumatic.

"She had brought out his chair, and set it facing the wide sea-sky and dazzling ocean, for him to enjoy the fineness of the day, and the sweetness of his own new-mown fields, where the grasshoppers chirped among the clover flowers, not yet dead in the fresh swath, though the scythe was unheard to-day, all being busied in one absorbing occasion.

"Pretty Margaret looked up in his face, and thought he seemed sorrowful; for this was the last day of her living on this side the great gully.

"Early in the afternoon, the business of the presents being over, the rural economy of the hermits of that wild nook resumed its wild course.

"But when Rhys had made hay, and set it in cocks, in his own and uncle's two little fields; and Peggy (who had hid herself during all the turmoil) had helped her lover and cousins with the hay, and milked the ewes, and fetched home two lambs from the hill, the lovers snatched half an hour to watch the sun go down, round, red, cloudless, on the verge of the wide and glittering sea, lighting up gloriously all the bays, promontories, and noble headlands along the shore of the bay of Carnarvon, while their own barrier mountains, the Eryri, or Rivals, seemed to lift their two towering heads, as ramparts equally against the world and the waves beyond.

"On one lofty bank above the sea, where sheep had nibbled the sod into the smoothness of a grass-plot, there stood an ancient chestnut tree, quite out of the usual track of the few shepherds in that district, and the favourite haunt of our lovers, for its deep seclusion.

"Here, as they stood, and the sun shot full on the interlaced fretwork of the old tree's bark, she saw a part which her lover had planed smooth, and inscribed, with her name, under which he had carved, 'Married, June, 5,' in anticipation of that day on which all his thoughts were fixed.

"But Margaret had imbibed, from the loneliness and wildness of her birthplace, a strong taint of superstition, and, far from smiling at the handiwork of Rhys, she regarded it as a 'tempting of Providence,' according to the phraseology of the rural 'religious word;' that is, presuming on the future for the blessings that may not be within its dispensation.

"'Oh, but if we never should be married, Rhys, dear! I do not like that writing on the tree, indeed, indeed!'

"'Not married! and it's only to-morrow we are to be, my girl!' said Rhys, laughing.

"'Ah, there are so many things do happen when we do promise ourselves so much. Did na my father promise we would all go to Nevin wake the next Sunday, when he was struck o' the rheumatism the very Saturday, and could na turn in bed?'

"'But we live so safe here, my sweet; not like folk in great cities, among fires and murders, that we've less to fear from accidents.'

"'Not like folks in those great flying houses either, where you wanted to go riding once, and leave me to cry myself blind, and die before you got back again,' said Margaret, reproachfully. 'But you'll never, never think to go to sea now, will you now—will you, Rhys, my dear?'

"'Oh, poor wench!' said he, laughing. 'Didst believe I was half in earnest? Shall I tell thee why I thought of it? Sailors, and all travelled men, do find such favour with you womankind. I did dread the days, indeed, when that bold, wild man, Evan the smuggler, did come to sell his tea down here, and would tell you such stories—lies or what not—about parts and people abroad—I did fear my Peggy would despise poor cousin Rhys, who had seen nothing but Nant Gwrtheyrn all his life.

"'And were you so cruel to keep me in a long, long fright, that I could na eat nor sleep, though I never told a soul for that? I hated that lying fool, with his hat all aside. Oh! you did not know how I did use to cry, in a wild, roaring, frightful morning, after a storm all night, the wind bellowing down the chimney, the sea thundering, the high oaks creaking, the very rocks quaking, and I saw bits of wreck lie all about our beach, and I was feared to walk along it on the seaweed, for expecting to see a dead corpse thrown up, all bloated and horrid! For why? I thought soon you would be out all night o' such a nights, and how shall I bear it then?'

"Then followed the tender look, the sweet assurance of each other's health and safety, and the embrace, to render that assurance, if possible, more sure; the mutual grasp of hands, warm with life, temperate with the coolness of health, all those ensurings (fallacious often, alas!) against the perils of life, which renders the mere presence of a beloved object a soul-soothing happiness, the mere absence a real misery, absence, with all its doubts and dark conjecturings.

"It is reported that, before they left their tree, with that innocent coquetry which loves to dally with the fond fears of a lover, she erased the presumptuous word 'married,' and substituted buried, 'June 15;' lingering behind her lover for that purpose, intending it as a sort of mournful surprise for his next visit to their haunt.

"The 'day of days' is come, in beauty and in glory.

"The wedding of Rhys and his cousin was a very fine morning.

"There she stands in health and safety, and redoubled beauty, and again by her father's chair.

"The party of the bridegroom's friends which is to fetch or force her from that father's to a husband's arms, is momentarily expected, as may be seen in her smiling, blushing, yet anxious and palish face, ever turning to the heights of that valley's barrier hills, where they will be espied descending far off, as well as in her restless person, evidently stirred by an excited mind, and seeming to hold by the old man's hand and chair by turns, like one already being torn away.

"They come!

"The late blush yielded her whole features to an extreme paleness the moment that party became visible, though the timid girl had concerted with Rhys how to evade her pursuers.

"The sham flight and pursuit, as is well known, are usually enacted on horseback, but, besides that, the nature of the declivities rendered this almost a perilous feat; equestrian doings were as repugnant to her habits as her retiring nature, and it was only in obedience to her old-fashioned parent, who could not brook a wedding without some shadow, at least, of its concomitant revelry, that she submitted to the boisterousness of the rites of a rustic Welsh wedding.

"These young men (whose party is called 'Gwyr o wisgi oed'), the men of the age of vivacity, soon reached the little cultivated bottom, but the bird was flown.

"The small barn, with its outside of many-coloured mosses; the black peat stack, the last year's barley rick, the corners of an upright rock (on a ledge of which stood three beehives, overhung by a tree growing out of a crevice, and grassy lodgment above) all these, and a green bramble-pit full of foxgloves behind that rock—all had been searched in vain, when the peeping of a very pretty ankle and foot, and a bit of a long, pink sash, worn by our bride, adorning a white frock (never worn by a Welsh maiden but on such occasions), betrayed her hiding-place under one of the huge hay-cocks into which the small field of hay had been piled, despite a tempting day for haymaking, in anticipation of that morrow when no man should work—at least, in the valley of Nant Gwrtheyrn.

"A shout from her pursuers told her she was betrayed.

"Up sprung grasses, and buttercups, and clover flowers; and the the fair apparition of some wood nymph, or such Arcadian phantasy, stood dropping flowers; stood a moment, half fearful, half wishful to be caught, darted back a smile like a sun flash at her pursuers, then bounded away towards an obscure path along the breasts of two mountains, by which she had promised to join her cousin-lover, who now expected her at the church, instead of encountering the gaze of all the village in the procession of the Gwyr o wisgi oed.

"All is expectation, as the old lean over the tombstones, the young try to read them, and the youngest play upon them, or peep through the chinks of the massy nail-studded oaken door of Eglwas Beuno, whe he is said to have been buried, till the hour having arrived, some impatience began to be visible, young and old moving a little way on the road by which the expected bride was to be brought, the priest himself pulling forth his watch, and looking up that way.

"The little children, too, with faces rosy, and shining as the morning, with hats stuck with flowers, and flowers in every hand, ready to strew the way before the young couple, even they began to sigh and grow pensive with the delay, and eyed, sorrowfully, those wild flowers almost dead with carrying in their hot hands.

"Then those below called to them in the trees, 'Are they coming?'

"They could see a mile of road, but still they were not coming.

"During this suspense, Rhys had been long at his secret appointed stand behind the church, watching the bowered mouth of a mountain-forest's path, where he expected every instant the beautiful, breathless fugitive to appear and sink upon his bosom, and be secretly led by him at once up to the communion table, while the baffled pursuers were retracing their steps up the valley precipices.

"But when he saw how high the sun had mounted, and that the hour drew near, he quitted his stand with some slight alarm, concluding that she had been caught, and he hurried towards the expected party.

"What was his surprise to meet them not far from the church, yet Margaret not in their midst.

"'Name of Heaven, is she not with *you?*'

"'Is she not with *you*, Rhys?' was the mutual exclamation.

"'Back, lads, back!' he cried; 'she meant to play you all a trick,* and she has played me one, too, I think. She's sure to be at home. Good Heavens! how high the sun is! The parson will be there just now! Run! run!'

"'What run for, man alive?' they exclaimed; 'we've been already there, and her father's never seen her since she leaped up from the haycock. There's not a soul but the old man in the dingle.'

"Rhys stood pondering a minute, his eyes rolled, and drops of sweat stood upon his brow.

"Then, laughing (a hollow sort of self-cheating laughter) 'she's at the church-back by this time, my life on't,' said he. 'Run! run! run!'

"'Where, Rhys, where?

"'To ask pardon of the parson, sure! you'll find her about this end of the blind path, through the wood of the steep pitch, not in front of the church; there she's waiting me—my wife is expecting me, but I'll run home the while, and be back—tell her you!—instantly.'

"'Lord! Lord! the parson will be sure gone away! silly wench.'

"They hurried towards the church, he to the valley; there he found the almost bedridden father hobbled forth, and seated on a haycock (he who had not walked for years), such the effect of sudden excitement, under the alarm of his child's disappearance.

"Poor Rhys, who in his distraction had equally assured himself of two things, impossible to be both facts, that she was already at their meeting place, and that he should find her at home, stood unable to speak a word before the father, so shocked was he at thus finding him alone, and thus one of his only hopes annihilated.

"'Then she must be at the church.' he said at last, yet sat down by his uncle on the hay.

"Yet what possible danger awaited her in such a little journey?

"It was brilliant daylight, neither pit or precipice in her way; that way was not open to the sea, none could have seized her thence.—nor was such an occurence ever thought of, much less had known, in a country where not a highway robbery been known in man's memory; he had already nearly trod, in his impatience, the whole path she was to tread, that which her father had seen her make for; had she fallen ill he must have found her; if offered violence to, he must have heard her; in short, peace, security, and open day, seemed to insure his heart against every fatality, and he composed himself by such reflections into a sort of calm.

"Presently he started up.

"'Merciful God! What do I sit here for?' he said, as the mystery rushed back upon his thoughts, and he remembered that the hour was past, the parson doubtless gone. He who should have been a husband this hour past, sitting there exchanging strange looks with her parent, and she, who could tell where?

"'My heart flutters, and my limbs fail me, so

that I can hardly walk more than thou can'st, father!' said he.

"'Father, indeed, poor boy! God knows whether—'

"The young bridegroom struck his forehead, and stared in the old man's face like a madman.

"'Ha!' said he. 'I know what you would say—God knows if you will ever *be* my father, if I shall ever *be* your son—if I shall ever—ever be that blessed husband I fancied myself already! I shall go mad this day!'

"And away he scoured once more to mount the declivities, regain the church, and test the truth of that almost only possibility left of an issue out of this most astonishing kind of disappointment.

"He had not advanced far, when he saw descending the heights the party which had already ascertained the fact before him.

"His voice failed him for utter terror of the reply, when he would have shouted his inquiry to them.

"Peace and sunshine, and all beauty and all quietness, was around him, forming a dreadful contrast to the inward state of the tormented young man.

"He did cry to them at last, with all his might; but when, over all that calm deliciousness of nature, over golden furze flowers, snowy spars and lambs, bees, and thymy turf, and borne on the softest southern wind, smelling of early summer—when over all those came (like a death bell for some beloved friend heard booming across a moonlight summer lake), the repeated tremendous agitating "'No!'

"He stopped, looked wildly about, as one looking round for some escape from death, who can nowhere find a crevice or covert by which to hide or fly; then he seemed to himself waking into a night of storm—he sunk to the ground, and lay in a profound fainting fit as they approached, in which state they conveyed him to his (bridal) home.

"All that night lights were seen moving in every direction, and voices heard calling her name, re echoed by the hills, and only answered by the owl or some fishers lying off the land's edge, who thought themselves called to from the shore; all possible and impossible places were explored in vain; every brambled hollow below, and every natural quarry in the fractured rocks above—all in vain.

"Margaret never came again to tend her father's wants, or bless her wretched lover's arms, being no more seen or heard of from that day than if she had died a natural death and been buried; according to the strangely mournful tenor of her own sportiveness the previous day, which now seemed indeed to have been impelled by a dark spirit of prophecy.

"While the day-search proceeded, poor Rhys lay still insensible, under the effects of an over excited mind, and violent agitation under a burning sun, which threatened a fever of the brain.

"When he revived and came to his senses, his eyes rolled, searching her long before he spoke. He saw around him all the bridal preparations of their little decorated apartment, and all rushed back to memory. But what shocked him most was the sight of the sun visible through the leaf-curtained casement, now sinking in the sea, and yellowing the pretty rustic chamber with a rich placidity of effect — how delightfully in unison with the peace-breathing, peace-loving mood of a modest country bridegroom!—how discordant of his own.

"It told him that the sun had travelled its complete course, evening had fallen, the blessed hour of shade and deep silence was at hand; and

* Alluding to the Welsh custom of the bride trying to hide herself from the bridegroom on the wedding morn.

there he lay, feverish, wild-brained on his bed, the bridal bed! — alone — no bride had crossed his threshhold!

"Supernatural assistance to their search was, of course, to be procured. While one sister watched the bed of the sufferer, the other hurried away to the *gwraig hysbys* (cunning woman), who lived, high up the breast of one of the loftiest mountains, in a hut among the black mawn-pits—the world of human haunts in soundless depth below, above her only the cloud, the crag, the kite—a melancholy woman, whose strange lonely life, and partial insanity, made her the sybil of the country.

"Her answer, like all oracles, was a riddle, yet a consolatory one.

"'Will she be found?'

"'Yes.'

"'Who shall find her? And how and where shall we search?'

"She shook her head.

"'Will the bridegroom find his bride again?'

"'Yes.'

"'On earth, or in heaven?'

"'On earth.'

"'Thank God!' sobbed the fond, credulous sister, bursting into tears of joy and gratitude to God. 'But when? oh, when?'

"'When a light from Heaven shall show her to him: search no more; Heaven itself shall find her out, and face to face they shall stand by its light.'

"'How long shall she be away from him—from us?'

"'She is not away!'

"This was the last word the hideous-featured hermitess would vouchsafe.

"Smugglers occasionally would run their cargoes on that coast, in a hollow cove near the valley.

"Three days did Rhys try the oblivion of deep intoxication, from draughts of spirits supplied to him by desperate men, in the cruelty of their sport; but to him it brought no oblivion, only a sadder sense of life-weariness, and more courage to die, his mind remaining clear as ever, as he lay, seemingly senseless, under a rock, and though all was dizzy-dimness round him, as if the hour of death was indeed come.

"It was on the fourth day that he informed his sisters of his design to turn smuggler.

"On the third day, however, when they believed him far at sea, he stood among them at nightfall; his heart had failed him again before he could embark; the novelty of a new life, on a new element, had become old, even before he could realise the idea.

"'Never! never!' said he, as they drew him within the door; and he kneeled out on the bare rock, stretching up his thin arms to the lurid sky; 'never roof more but that for his head, nor pillow but this stone, or grave but that sea! Toss my wretched body there, when angry God has done tormenting me; why a grave for me, more, when she has none?'

"Springing to his feet, scowling, he broke away, back to the mountains, shady with night: it seemed that terrible burst of agony, long-pent, was the last of that lingering doubt which agonised him, the death-struggle of hope—for from that night he became totally silent.

"He found despair at last (as the three revellers of Chaucer did death), 'under the green tree.'

"Beneath that ancient chesnut tree, which had been their favourite retreat, and which still stood, inscribed by her playful hand with her own death and burial, her dreadful green monument on the bank of the sea, he now sat in the sun, and in the storm, for ever silent, like some melancholy idiot; there he was to be found, his head hung down; his chin, with long beard, untimely gray, resting on his breast; his clasped hands and arms stretched in listless length before him in his lap; his clothes—his wedding dress, long worn to tatters, pinned about him with thorns, leaving his tanned skin visible through its rags moving in the wind.

"Standing high and lonely as it did, on a green promontory, that tree was a mark for thunder, and had been twice struck by lightning within the memory of man.

"After intense heat in the summer, a murky gloom gathering over sea and shore announced a coming thunderstorm, soon deepening to a sort of night at noon-day.

"As former storms, shivering that tree's top, had taught her the danger of standing beneath it, the tender Gwynneth, who loved her her brother in all his dumb strangeness as much as ever, hastened towards him, to try to bring him away, just as the thunder was beginning hollowly in the black sea-distance.

"As the first flash quivered blue around him, she saw a smile—the first for years—play on his sunken features; and when she took his hand, though he would not quit his place, he surprised her with a smile of gratitude, proving him fully conscious of her fond fears for him.

"'Ever my good sister, and my fond,' said he, and kissed her; but when she urged him to seek other shelter from the storm, 'Nay, Gwynneth, back,' he said, with a composure astonishing and delightful to her as his newly-returned speech and returning humanity, 'you think this is a storm to me, as it is to you:' he continued (the rain, and wind, and thunder, already raging around them), 'hurry home, home, dear wench, and leave me to my hurricane, for it's a peace to me, a very calm! There has been such an eternal storm here—such a thunder here, beat, beat, roaring, rolling!' pointing to his heart and to his head; 'save me, hide me, from the bright flowery earth and the summer-sky, that shut-up charnel-house door I've been knocking at for her so long, and not a ghost answered!—that vault up yonder that I've cried to for her, and it smiled me mad with its dumb blue! That was the dumb storm I could not bear. There was a flash! run, wench, run—its dangerous.'

"The shock of a lightning-stroke (if not that of his own heart's mad emotion within) that moment prostrated him at the foot of the tree: a dreadful rushing noise, as of splitting ice, astounded his sister; and opening her eyes again, after the flash, to see the cause, a sight struck her soul that made them close again in faintness.

"The trunk was rent from top to bottom, laying open the tree's inward hollowness, unknown before; and through the fissure appeared an upright skeleton, the grim skull-face greened by damps to the appearance of linched stone; the ribbed cage of what had been a snowy bosom, hung still with black shreds, the remains of dress, flesh, and sinews now undistinguishable from each other! the arm-bones, even still inextricably wedged in the cavity, told the tale of a frightful death.

"The unfortunate bride, as soon as she had surmounted that brow where her father had seen her for the last time, had climbed into that tree to hide herself, while her pursuers passed; and finding it hollow at top, had hastily slid down through the opening among the boughs, and became fixed in her efforts to reascend (though the height was not great), in the manner boys have frequently lost their lives in chimneys.

"Poor Gwynneth had the presence of mind to come between her brother, now struggling upon his feet, and that ghastly object.

"In vain! as if he had already caught a glimpse of it, he pushed her hastily aside, and the lost bride and bridegroom faced each other close again; the change and the ruin of the living face scarcely less great and horrible than that of the dead.

"With body shivering, teeth chattering, eyes dilating with horror, the thunder-stricken man only pointed ghost-like, and smiled on his sister such an indescribable ghastly smile, as conveyed to her, more than words or shrieks, the strangely mixed horror and pleasure of meeting again—and meeting thus.

"The secret was revealed at last.

"What were his feelings?

"More of them than that shocking smile betrayed was never known, for, bending his face towards hers, who had been so long near to him yet so long parted, before his lips and the lipless half-circle of snowy teeth met, he sunk down, and never spoke again.

"The distortion of that hideous smile remained on his corpse face, frozen there by death, and there remained, even when one coffin received him and her, whose loss had made his youth age, and his very life a death.

"The fatal tree, as long as its shattered trunk remained standing, was known as the 'Ceubren yr Ellyll,' 'the spirit's hollow tree;' for there was often seen by fishermen, in a moonlight midnight, as they awaited morning in their boats, on a calm sea, an apparition of dry bones, frightfully mimicking the actions of life; the white skull rounded with the mockery of wild flowers, which had garlanded the hair of the lost bride that morning; and the bony arms raised often to the teeth rapidly; as if in rage of hunger.

"Such a figure, they said, magnified by mists, that passing, enveloped it as in a shroud, would stand for hours on the round brink of the promontery.

"Others had seen, in the last of twilight, two figures, hand in hand, the skeleton bride and the wild-man bridegroom, as they called the spectres; he, with his beard, long hair, and nails like talons, fixing his stony eyes, and she, her eyeless sockets, on the calm sky and silvered clouds, as if still scowling dumb complaint against the heavens, which had been to them so merciless.

"Nor would ever bird, excepting the owl and foul cormorant, it was believed, alight on the boughs, nor any animal rest under the shade of that black, thunder-stricken ruin of a tree—the grave of love —the ghastly Ceubren yr Ellyll."

CHAPTER CXLII.

THE PLOT TO POISON TOM DRAKE.

SUSAN BROCKTON and Sweetheart Loo watched hourly by Tom Drake's side, and bedewed his pillow with their tears.

Little did they think that while they were exerting their utmost to preserve the life of the gallant buccaneer, and using every means in their power to hasten his recovery, that others were forming a terrible plot to rob him of the little life that remained.

Yet such it was, for having of late lost so many of the gallant band, Ben Barnacle, who officiated as leader in the absence of their gallant chief, had recruited their strength by a number of fresh hands, several of whom were deserters from the King's navy; others seamen who, for various causes, chose the wild and daring life of a buccaneer, in preference to their own peaceful calling.

Among the number was Dick Traverse.

Of a roving and reckless disposition, and more foolhardy than wise, he thought he could accomplish miracles.

Therefore, for a stipulated sum, he offered to poison the daring buccaneer captain, and likewise to betray their secret, and let the enemy into the stronghold.

He thought if he could once get their daring chief out of the way, the rest could be easily accomplished.

One night, when the brave Susan Brockton, worn out with her weary watching, lay down to rest, the traitor thought it would be his best chance.

Sweetheart Loo had fallen into a momentary slumber, and the cowardly villain, seeing that both were asleep, resolved to carry out his villainous designs.

With stealthy tread he crept into the cavern where the wounded captain lay.

Cautiously he looked about to ascertain if any human eye was watching his movements, and having assured himself to the contrary, he crept, with a cat-like movement, to the table on which lay the medicine and stimulants to be administered to the wounded man.

With trembling hand he drew a paper from his breast, which contained a small portion of white powder, and, having first ascertained which was the bottle that contained the medicine, he carefully emptied the contents of the paper into it.

Then, having taken a glance round to see whether he had aroused either of the nurses, and assuring himself he had not, with a noiseless and cat-like movement, he strode out of the cavern, and hurried along the various passages that led from the stronghold, and, by way of a narrow and tortuous path, he gained the road.

Having proceeded some distance along the border of a dark, thick wood, he darted in amongst the thick foliage, and was quickly lost to view.

Now, for the first time, he ventured to draw breath, and cautiously glanced around him, for he fancied he heard a rustling in the bushes behind him.

He listened attentively, but not a sound was to be heard, and it was too dark to see anything distinctly.

"Fool that I am," he muttered, "to start at my own shadow; "it was only the bushes closing in my wake. They're too busy at the Black Rock to trouble about me."

Then, taking a silver whistle from beneath his clothes, he blew a low, shrill note.

In a very few minutes a rustling of the bushes told him that his signal had been heard, and two men, each well armed, quickly made their appearance.

One of the men was no other than Colonel Hawkins, the other his right hand supporter and confidential friend, Corporal Ramrod, who was as stiff in his ideas as he was in his manners.

"How have you succeeded?" inquired the colonel, eagerly.

"Well, you see, I've had rather a tough job, yer honour, for them cussed gals would not leave him a moment, but I managed it at last. I put it in his physic."

"Then there's no fear of him troubling us any more, although I would sooner have had the pleasure of putting a rope round his neck."

"I suppose you'll give us the yallar boys now, won't you?"

"Certainly not; you will not have them until we have completely rooted out this infernal nest, and as you say they have treasures untold concealed within their caves, of course you will receive your reward according to the booty captured."

Dick Traverse did not seem at all pleased with the fresh arrangement, and he appeared very uneasy.

"Ain't you going to give me a little for this new job?" he inquired.

"What job?"

"Oh, now you wants to act green. Don't you know I've done for the captain?"

"How can I know, unless I see him?" coolly rejoined the colonel.

"Why you've got my word for it, ain't you?"

"And that is all?" coolly replied the colonel.

"And ain't that enough—did you want me to holler out to the gals to be witnesses?" he cried, angrily.

"And you have my word for the money," answered the colonel.

It was evident Dick had promised to do more than he intended; he had managed to effect the poisoning, at least so far as he knew, and he had anticipated receiving the blood-money for doing so.

He had also promised to lead the soldiers into the stronghold, but well knowing the daring and resolute disposition of the smugglers and buccaneers, he feared they would have no easy task to rout them out.

But he hoped that if they would give him the money, he might be able to lead them as far as he considered prudent, and then, in the event of being repulsed, he might manage to effect his escape, and leave them to their fate.

But now he found out his mistake.

All the castles he had built had fallen to the ground, and he had fallen under their ruins.

"Then I suppose you mean to do me out of the money?" said Dick, who was greatly vexed.

"Not at all. You shall have it when you have earned it," was the cool reply.

"So you think I've not earned it; you don't believe that I've m—"

He stopped short, and looked around at the dark, overhanging branches as though he feared the trees should hear that dreadful word, and for the first time he became aware of the horrible crime he had committed.

A slight trembling seized his burly frame, but he was not one to allow such a terrible deed as that to trouble his mind for long.

"How am I to prove I've done it?"

"There is only one way," said the colonel, doggedly.

"Name it?"

"You must lead us into the stronghold, and then we shall find the dead body."

"Then it must be done to-night," said the trembling wretch, for he almost feared to enter the cavern again, and yet he had gone too far to retract.

"Yes, this very night, and with as little delay as possible. I have fifty of my best men concealed in this wood, and I have sent a body of the coast-guards to cut off the buccaneers who are engaged in landing the contraband. There is no fear but what we shall succeed, and, if you prove true, in less than an hour we shall be within those rocky walls."

The eyes of the traitor flashed with anger; twice had his word been doubted, and he scowled fiercely at the colonel.

"What!" he cried, in a husky voice, "do you doubt my honesty? Do you think I would deceive you? Do you think I am not a man of my word?"

"Ask your comrades that question," retorted the colonel, "we have not been long enough acquainted for me to judge."

The villain drew a pistol from his belt, and presented it at the head of the colonel.

The colonel, anticipating his intentions, seized his wrist, and held the point of his highly-polished sword against the villain's breast.

Instinctively he clutched the blade with his left hand, and tried to force the point from his breast.

His attempts were futile, for the sword being sharp cut his hand.

The colonel did not wish to put an end to his miserable existence, although he could have done so instantly, for even had he thrust the point of the sword aside, the corporal stood ready, sword in hand, to defend his superior officer.

The eyes of the trembling wretch glared furiously at his assailant.

"Fool!" cried the colonel, "do you think that I want to kill you? Do you think that I have met you here for that purpose?"

These words seemed to arouse the traitor from his state of apathy, and the colonel withdrew the point of his sword.

The buccaneer, being disengaged, folded his brawny arms across his chest, still holding the pistol in his hand, and surveyed the colonel in silence.

The colonel was the first to speak.

"Look here," he said, assuming a friendly tone, "we have met here for one object, and now it is within our grasp we must not disagree. You promised to lead us to the secret entrance of the cavern, and now we have got so far you may as well take us the rest, and earn your reward."

The buccaneer stood several seconds, evidently struggling to overcome the anger that had been aroused in his breast by those last few words.

At length he said, as he replaced his pistol—

"I agree to do so on one condition."

"Name it."

"That you never split on me, and never let 'em know who it was that led you there."

"Agreed, I swear."

"Then farewell for the present. In one half hour from this I will meet you at the green lane. I will sound a low whistle; then follow me."

Dick Traverse turned hurriedly from the spot, and made his way along the road, muttering curses on the colonel for not rewarding him for what he had done.

Scarcely had he gone, when the colonel and his worthy companion held a short consultation.

"I tell you what it is, colonel," said Corporal Ramrod, "that feller don't mean us any good. I think he's going to give us the slip. I'm a good mind to watch him, and see where he goes."

"Do so, if you like," answered the colonel, "but be careful, for if any of the buccaneers should see you, your life will pay for your rashness."

"Oh, never fear, colonel, I'll turn sideways to 'em, and then they won't see me, and it'll take a good marksman to hit me."

So saying, he darted through the bushes in the direction Dick had so recently gone, and so thin was he that he scarcely seemed to touch the branches, and the slightest rustling was all that marked his progress.

Previous to this a dark figure might have been seen issuing from the other side of the wood, with hurried steps.

In a few moments he climbed a jagged and dangerous rock, which, to all appearance, was no easy task, and suddenly disappeared in one of the dark fissures.

This was no other than Bob Hauler; he had noticed Dick Traverse leaving the stronghold; he also noticed that he was flurried in his manner.

Suspecting all was not right, he cautiously followed him, and had heard all the plot.

When he heard the villain own to the murder of their beloved captain, he felt for a moment as though a thunderbolt had struck him, and he could scarcely refrain from sending a bullet through the murderer's brain. But prudence overcame his intrepidity, and he listened in breathless astonishment to their daring plans.

Then, hurrying from the spot, he made his way to a secret passage, by which he could gain the stronghold long before the other should arrive.

He was hurrying through a dark crevice, formed by the rending of the rocks, when his progress was arrested by the form of a man coming in the opposite direction, instinctively each grappled the other, and fell heavily to the hard ground.

"Who are you?" cried Bob, who had managed to fall uppermost, and held his opponent by the throat.

"It's me," gasped the prostrate man, for Bob held him so firmly by the throat, that he could scarcely articulate a sound.

"And who's me?" interrogated Bob, fiercely.

"Why, me, you fool," answered the man, Bob having relaxed his grasp a little to allow the man to answer.

"Well, I don't unhook my graplins till I knows who you are."

"Let go, you fool!"

"No; I'm blest if I do!"

"Do you hear? Let me go!"

"I may, p'raps, when I know what ship, and where bound."

"Why, it's Jerry."

"Rather a queer hanimal. too, for a feller to meet with in the dark" cried Bob, indulging himself with a hearty laugh.

"Why, you old fool," cried Jerry, groping for his cap that had been knocked off in the scuffle, "do you mean to say you didn't know me? Why, you nearly strangled me."

"I would quite, if I'd a-known it was a Jerry," rejoined Bob, bursting into another fit of laughter.

"Well, what are you doing here. Bob? Why ain't you down on the beach?"

"I was just going to ask you the same question," rejoined Bob.

"Well, it's soon answered. There's about forty of them cussed rats tackled us, and I've just come to get more help, for they fight like devils."

"Oh, the coastguards has dropped on you, has they? Well, I expects about fifty of the redcoats here directly. There's a traitor in the camp. I hears he's poisoned poor Captain Tom."

"You don't say so!" exclaimed Jerry, starting back in dismay; "then death to the murderer!"

"Well, you just pull yourself together, and shake them 'ere covies off, and I'll manage the rest. It's that cussed Kernal Hawkins ag'in. I knows him."

"All right; then here goes. You've made me feel devilish queer about the gullet, though."

"And you'll feel a devilish sight queerer one o' these days, old chum."

Jerry did not appear to relish the joke, but hurried on his way.

Bob hurried to the inner cavern.

On his way he met two of the band, who were hurrying down to the beach, and having informed them in as few words as possible of the proposed invasion, he advised them to stay and look out for the traitor.

On arriving at the cavern, where the wounded chief lay, he was delighted to hear that for the present the assassin had been frustrated in his murderous design, and that the gallant captain had escaped from his villainous design.

For the faithful Susan, though worn out with watching, and although she had retired to her rude couch, could not go to sleep.

Sue was laying buried in gloomy thought, when the treacherous villain stole into the chamber.

She saw him examine the bottles, and take the paper from his breast and pour the contents into the bottle.

When he had gone, she examined the bottle he had tampered with, and discovered a thick sediment in it.

Bob Hauler, on hearing the welcome news, instantly left the cavern, and hurried to the spot where he had promised to meet the men.

Meanwhile, Dick Traverse had discovered that all was quiet in the cavern, and also that all, or nearly all, of the buccaneers were engaged in running the cargo, and he had again sallied forth to lead the soldiers to the stronghold.

On he came, with tottering step—for he well knew his doom were he to be discovered—the soldiers, who had dismounted and had left their horses concealed in the wood, following close behind him.

Scarcely had he turned a point of the rock which hid him from the view of the soldiers, than four sturdy fellows sprang upon him.

His first impulse was to clutch his pistol and fire at the foremost of his assailants, who fell wounded to the earth.

"Keep back!" Dick cried. "I'll sell my life dearly!"

"Don't make a fuss, my tulip," rejoined one of the men, stepping quickly behind him, and dealing him a blow with a formidable staff.

It fell with crushing force on the back of Dick's neck, and he dropped to the earth as if dead.

"He won't trouble us much, just yet," said the man who had struck the blow. "Give a hoist, pals, and we'll carry him to a quieter corner than this."

The sturdy fellows hoisted him on their shoulders, and bore him away.

"Have you got him safe, comrades?" said Bob Hauler, in an undertone, when the men returned.

"Safer than the bank," rejoined one of the men. "Fer there may be a slight chance of getting money out of the bank, but there's not the slightest chance of him getting out of here."

"Better stow our mate out of the way ti'" he comes to," suggested another.

As there was likely to be rather a warm encounter, the suggestion was carried into effect, and the wounded man borne to an inner cave.

The men were returning, when they heard a heavy step approaching, accompanied by the clank of spurs.

The men crouched down to await the coming of the stranger.

In another moment the colonel appeared in view.

Before he was aware of his danger, he was pounced upon, borne to the ground, gagged, without being able to offer any resistance, bound hand and foot, and carried away to keep the traitor Traverse company.

The corporal came next and was served like the colonel.

Then came the heavy tramp of soldiery, marching through a narrow pass.

As the foremost of the men was about to turn an angle of the rock, a rumbling noise was heard over their heads, and, in a moment, a mass of huge stones came crashing down, blocking up the narrow passage.

The soldiers seeing their danger, turned, and made a precipitate retreat.

CHAPTER CXLIII.

DARING EXPLOIT OF TOM DRAKE.

The authorities, exasperated at the audacious intrepidity of Captain Tom Drake, determined to rid the coast of so formidable an enemy.

They issued orders that no expense was to be spared, and that every means was to be resorted to, for the furtherance of the great object they had in view.

Several vessels of light draught and good sailing qualities were manned and armed for the occasion, and were ordered to cruise off that part of the coast where they were certain the stronghold of the daring buccaneers must be located, whilst several detachments of soldiers were posted at easy distances to cut off all retreat inland.

Thus arranged, it was thought impossible for the buccaneers to escape, and they felt assured that their efforts would be crowned by a speedy annihilation of the whole crew.

Meanwhile, the gallant Captain, having recovered, had not been idle.

Disguised as a farmer, he had frequented the various fishing towns and small villages inland, and had even conversed with the soldiers, and having sounded and gained information, he returned to the cavern.

Every precaution was taken to fortify the stronghold, and bridges were formed across the various chasms.

They were so constructed that the weight of two men coming upon them would cause the ledge of rock upon which they rested to give way, and they would, consequently, be precipitated into the dark abyss beneath.

Huge masses of stone were loosened on the summits of the lofty rocks that overhung the various passes that led to the secret entrances of the cavernous stronghold.

One man, by the aid of a lever, could hurl them from the lofty heights on to the besiegers, crushing them beneath at any moment.

Kegs of gunpowder were also inserted in the crevices of the rocks, over which the besiegers would have to pass, and long trains were formed, so that, in case of an emergency, access to the cavern would be completely cut off.

At least, to all appearance the buccaneers could still obtain supplies and provisions by means of a subterranean passage naturally formed in the rocks, that led to a cave in which the water flowed at high tide.

Having thus arranged matters, gallant Captain Tom, accompanied by Bob Hauler, sallied forth on a daring and dangerous expedition.

Next day, two sailors, poorly clad, and apparently the worse for liquor, were at an ale-house, and by their gestures, and the way in which they were moving their arms about, it was evident they were doing a strong argument.

The stoutest of the two appeared not to be very well pleased, and giving his quid a sharp twist, he seated himself upon the rude bench that served the place of a table, and folding his arms, pulled away rapidly at an inch-and-a-half of black clay.

His companion, in hitching up his canvas trousers, lost his balance, and thus causing him to give what he called a weather-roll, and, before he could recover himself, he came in violent contact with an officer who was passing, and who proved to be the lieutenant of one of the armed cruisers.

The lieutenant looked daggers at him.

The sailor, having once more attained the perpendicular, gazed in his face with a vacant stare.

"I axes yer honour's pardon," said the sailor, "but, you see, I happened to get too much grog aboard, and it's made me top-heavy."

"I've a good mind to send you on board my vessel, and order you to have three dozen over your bare back," said the lieutenant, angrily.

"I axes yer honour's pardon," rejoined the sailor, "But if I should happen to go aboard yer honour's craft, I should like the stripes on my arm instead of my back."

"You would have to alter greatly, my fine fellow, if you went there, I can assure you," said the lieutenant, sharply, "and take a little more water and less grog."

"Why, as to that, your honour, we have had water enough, for, you see, me and my shipmate here have been shipwrecked, and we are the only two saved out of all the crew."

"Oh, indeed!" said the lieutenant, eyeing them narrowly.

"Yes, yer honour, and I've lost every stick but what I've got on, but my chum's wuss nor me, for, you see, he's close reefed."

"So I see."

"Yes, yer honour, and as we happened to have a shot in the locker, we thought we might as well make a clean ship, and then start afresh."

"What do you intend doing?"

"Well, yer honour, we doesn't know exactly. Me and my shipmate was just agrufying the p'int when yer honour hove in sight."

"Should you like to join the navy?" inquired the lieutenant, in a careless tone.

"Oh! I shouldn't mind, but I leaves it all to my chum, 'cos we means to stick together like pitch."

"You could both join, you know, and as you appear to be in distress, it would be a fine thing for you; besides, you might get promoted. I dare say you are a thorough seaman?"

"Well, I can hand, reef, and steer with anyone that ever trod the deck, and as to knotting and splicing, I can do it in the dark, and on a pinch I could do a bit in this line," he said, pointing to the lieutenant's sword, "or lay a gun with any man in the fleet."

"Bravo!" said the lieutenant, patting him on the shoulder; "you are just the man I want. You had better come with me at once."

"Well, you see, yer honour, I'm jambed between two winds. There was one of the smuggling covies axed us to go and lend a hand to run a swingling cargo of stuff, and he told us we should be well paid, have oceans of grog and mountains of baccy, and all for nothing, d'ye see, but I can't tumble to it. I might cotch two ounces of lead through my upperworks, and that'd clap a stopper on my chewing, d'ye see, and p'rhaps they'd do me out o' my grog."

"Perhaps your companion will join us?" said the lieutenant.

"Here, Bill, just come here and overhaul yer log, old tar."

"Aye! aye!" was the reply, and Bill came rolling up to the lieutenant, and placing his hands in the waistband of his trousers, took several severe tugs at the short black pipe, and stared inquiringly in the face of the lieutenant.

"Well, my man, have you any objection to join the navy, or do you mean to go on this smuggling expedition? If you do, mind, you are sure to be either killed or taken prisoner, for the channel is full of cruisers."

"Well, your honour, it's a job I don't like to tackle, but the cove told me that a whole fleet couldn't take 'em. He said that Captain Tom Drake knowed the ropes too well, and that he could go and shave the lord high admiral's head while he was asleep, and he shouldn't know it."

"Did you say Captain Tom Drake?" inquired the lieutenant, eagerly.

"Yes, your honour. He said they expected two large luggers richly laden."

The lieutenant gave a low whistle.

"He shan't escape this time. Will you join our ship, lads? There's lots of prize money to be had now."

"If my mate does, I will. What do you say, Tom?"

"Well, I think I'll try a cruise in his honour's craft."

"Well done, my lads. We have no time to lose. Do you know the country about here?" he said, turning to Bill, who was no other than daring Captain Tom Drake.

"I knows enough, your honour, to find my way about. Besides, I can talk a little English."

The lieutenant could not repress a smile, and he walked into the inn, and called for pen and paper.

Meanwhile, the reckless captain employed his time in writing with a lead pencil on a leaf of his pocket-book

"Here you are, my man," cried the lieutenant, handing him a note. "Can you read?"

"A little," was the careless rejoinder.

"Take this note to Colonel Hawkins. If you forget the name, and cannot read it, show it to some one. and they will read it for you. Now go, and bear a hand back; you will find a boat waiting for you on your return."

"Aye, aye, your honour!" replied the daring captain, and placing the note in his hat, he hurried away.

The lieutenant and the other sailor, who was none other than Bob Hauler, jumped into a boat, and was soon alongside a smart little schooner that lay in the bay.

Captain Tom had not proceeded far along the road, when he struck into a small wood, and drawing the note from beneath the lining of his tarpaulin hat, he quickly perused it, and then, tearing it up into small pieces, he put it into his mouth and chewed it.

"Ha, ha, my boy!" he muttered half aloud. "You'll find I'm a match for you yet."

A few minutes brought him through the wood, and he hurried rapidly along a narrow ledge of rock. that led to one of the entrances to the cavern.

"Who goes there?" shouted a gruff voice, as he turned an an angle of the rock.

No one could be seen, but the barrel of a musket protruded from a crevice in the rock.

The pass-word was given, and the musket disappeared.

On arriving in the cabin, he was met by Ben Barnacle.

"Well, captain," inquired Ben Barnacle, "how have you succeeded?"

"Better than I expected; here are your instructions," said Tom Drake, tearing a leaf from his book.

"All right, captain," rejoined Ben. and having read the contents, he continued, "I'll get the boats ready at once," and hurried from the cavern.

Meanwhile, the captain had written another note, and placing it in the lining of his hat, muttered—

"I'll put the old boy on another scent; little does he expect another visit from his old friend Captain Drake. Ha! ha! ha! I'll drive him mad before I have done with him!"

The colonel was busy writing when his valet announced that a sailor, meanly clad, wished to see him on very important business.

'A sailor?' he said. musingly, "what can he want with me; important business you say? Well, really, I am tired of sailors and buccaneers for they have played me so many tricks—but never mind; bring me my pistols, then show him up.'

The pistols were accordingly brought, and in due time the sailor was ushered into the apartment

"What is your business?" inquired the colonel. eyeing him suspiciously, for he expected a pistol would shortly make its appearance from the hat in which he kept fumbling, and when the note made its appearance he seemed quite disappointed.

"Here's a note, your honour, from the lieutenant," said our hero, in an assumed tone of voice.

The colonel snatched the proffered note from the buccaneer's hand and hastily tore it open.

As he perused it, the stern expression of his features relaxed, and before he had finished it, a smile gradually illuminated his lineaments.

"Are you going back to the lieutenant?"

"Tell him I shall attend to it; there is no one wishing to see this scoundrel caged more than I do, and I shall do all that lays in my power towards effecting his capture."

On gaining the deck of the vessel, gallant Captain Tom was for a moment staggered.

She was just the very craft that would suit his purpose.

"With her," he thought to himself, "I could sail round the world in search of my darling little craft."

For a moment he appeared wrapped in deep thought, when the voice of the lieutenant awoke him from his reverie.

"Well, my lad, did you deliver the note?"

"Yes, your honour," answered Tom Drake, assuming a careless tone, "and the luftenant said he'd attend to it, and that right willingly."

"Quartermaster, tell the boatswain to pipe all hands to heave up the anchor," said the lieutenant descending the cabin ladder.

"Aye, aye, sir," was the rejoinder, as that worthy functionary hastened to obey the order.

In a very few moments the anchor was hove up, and the sails set, and the little schooner moved steadily through the slightly ruffled water before a gentle breeze, keeping well out in the offing.

Captain Tom having told the lieutenant that he had been mate on board the vessel that had been so recently lost, gave him the rate of quartermaster, and Bob Hauler, who knew everything pertaining to a gun, was elected gunner's mate, as a vacancy existed in that capacity, through the late gunner's mate having been accidentally drowned.

Towards evening a thick haze obscured the horizon, and gradually increased till it had assumed a thick fog.

When the lieutenant, thinking it unsafe to keep under weigh, for they were now tacking across the track in which the two luggers were expected to be seen, he gave orders to run in under the land, and bring to an anchor.

"Load the guns," cried the lieutenant, "and set a strict watch; let every man stand by for a call. You understand what I mean." he continued, "and a month's black list for the last man at his quarters."

Admirably arranged curtain masks were withdrawn from her bulwarks, revealing a bristling tier of guns, which were quickly loaded and run out.

An apparently inexhaustible array of small arms cutlasses, and boarding-pikes, with an ample service of ammunition, were brought on deck from the well-stored magazine below, and conveniently arranged in racks and lockers around the masts.

Port-hole slides were loosened.

Grapnels unlashed.

Boats made ready for lowering away.

All was effected with an unerring noiseless precision which utterly defied the slightest idea of hurry and confusion.

The crew, with the exception of those who had to keep watch, now went below, the gunner's mate, Bob Hauler, examined the guns and small arms to see that they were properly arranged and ready for an emergency.

"What cheer, old feller," said Bob, addressing the quartermaster of the watch; "what's the matter with you—got the tooth-ache I spose?"

"You're right, my hearty, and I've chewed about eight sticks of cavendish, this blessed night, and it ain't eased me a bit."

"Why don't you ax that new covey to take your watch for you, I don't suppose he'd mind; at least he won't if he's like me, for I can't go to sleep the first night on board a strange craft."

"I wish you wouldn't mind carrying this shooting stick for me, then, old feller," interposed the marine who was sentry for the watch, and whose duty it

528

... walk from one side of the vessel to the other, abaft the mainmast.

"Well, I doesn't mind," rejoined Bob, "that is, if you let me wear that ere nobby coat o' yourn."

"Oh, I don't mind doing that, old feller; I only wish I wasn't going to put it on any more," said the marine, as he handed his coat and cartouch box to Bob.

"Why, you makes a first-rate marine, old feller," said the marine, eyeing Bob Hauler, who, by this time had arrayed himself in the marine's coat and brought the musket to his shoulder. "I'll go below, and just turn in on top of your hammock."

So saying, he disappeared.

Meanwhile, Captain Tom, who had been actively engaged in preparing for the anticipated encounter with the buccaneers, made his appearance on the quarter-deck with a can of oil in his hand, and commenced trimming the binnacle lamp.

"I lay them coves don't think we're laying here so snug for 'em, shipmate," said Tom Drake, addressing the quartermaster. "I lay we'll give 'em such a warming as they arn't had for a long time. Hallo! what's the matter with you?" he inquired, in an assumed tone of surprise.

"Why, one o' these cussed grinders aches so tarnationally that it almost drives me mad," answered the quartermaster, replenishing his quid.

"Oh, you're in love, eh—you want a good strong dose of salts," was our hero's cool reply.

"A dose o' salts, and so does my old dad's wooden leg want a blister," growled the quartermaster. "I see you're one of Job's comforters. If you was any sort of a shipmate you'd keep a feller's watch for him, for it's this cussed fog that gets into this old hollow grinder and makes it ache so."

"Well I don't mind doing that," said Tom, "if you launches out that bottle I see you stowing away a few hours ago."

"Agreed," cried the quartermaster, as he dived down the hatchway.

"How are you getting on, captain?" asked Bob, approaching the gallant captain; "did you oil the muskets?"

"Yes, and I've taken the wicks out of the lamps, and—hark!" both listened attentively, and a slight splash could be heard in the water at no great distance.

"'Tis the boats," whispered Tom; "have you spiked the guns?"

Before he could answer, the quartermaster appeared, bearing the bottle of rum.

"Here you are, mates," he said, pouring out a stiff glass for each, and bestowing the same compliment on himself, "but what's that splashing in the water?"

"Why, it's only an old porpoise lost his way in the fog," said Captain Tom.

The fog was now so dense, that any object at a boat's length from the schooner could not be perceived, and as Captain Tom and his faithful follower had no doubt the splash was caused by the expected boats, their first object was to silence the quartermaster.

As quick as thought, the buccaneer captain slipped the handkerchief from his own neck, and forced it into the mouth of the unsuspecting quartermaster, who, at first, thought it was some new method of drawing teeth; but when Tom Drake placed his knee in his back, and knotted the handkerchief tightly behind his head, he began to smell a rat, as the saying is, and tried to grapple with his assailant.

Captain Tom drew him gently to the deck, and bound him, and then laid quietly down by the taffrail.

Meanwhile, Bob Hauler had gone forward and secured the sailor who was keeping watch on the forecastle.

Every moment the splash became more audible, and through the fog a large boat, or yawl, shot noiselessly alongside the ship, and a dozen men cautiously mounted the side.

Two more boats soon loomed in the haze, and came alongside, for the daring buccaneer had placed his signal, a red lamp, over the stern, and by that means the boats were directed to the spot.

About fifty seamen, well armed, soon took possession of the schooner's deck, and Captain Tom walked deliberately to the lieutenant's state-room, to inform him that the buccaneers had at length hove in sight, and at that moment were within pistol-range.

"Beat to quarters!" thundered the lieutenant, buckling on his sword-belt, and possessing himself of his pistols.

The roll of the drum was accompanied by the heavy tramp of eager feet, as each strove to gain the deck, fearing to be last at his gun.

Little did they know the fate that awaited them, or they would not have clamoured so violently.

At either hatchway there stood a body of the buccaneers, who, as each man appeared above the combings, seized him, and if armed, disarmed him, and passed him into one of the boats.

At length, by dint of great exertion, the lieutenant made his appearance, who, in his turn, was seized and handed aft.

"Where is that lubberly quartermaster?" he roared.

"Here, your honour," cried our hero, in a tone of cool indifference.

In a frenzy of rage, the lieutenant was about to draw his sword, but, to his great dismay, he found it had already been drawn by some person or persons unknown.

"A thousand curses!" he muttered. "This audacious scoundrel, Tom Drake, will yet escape me."

"I hope so, your honour," cried Tom, folding his arms, and gazing defiantly at the enraged lieutenant.

All the blue-jackets had, by this time, been ushered into the boats, and all attempts at resistance, it was evident, would be useless, for the buccaneers had formed in line along the bulwarks, and presented their pistols at the unarmed sailors, who appeared to sit very quiet, although much against their inclination.

The marines, who were the last, on hearing the loud altercation on deck, and seeing the commotion at the hatchway, drew back, and swore they would shoot down the first man that offered to molest them.

The gallant buccaneer captain, on hearing their determination, dashed down the ladder, closely followed by a party of his men.

The marines ordered them to advance no farther, or they would fire.

"Fire!" cried our hero.

After a short but severe encounter, the marines, finding themselves driven up into a corner, cried for quarter.

They were securely bound, and passed on deck, to be packed in the boats with the sailors.

Provisions were placed in each boat, and when all was ready for shoving off, the lieutenant was desired to take his seat in one of them, and the daring buccaneer, taking his hand, thanked him warmly for his kindness in assisting him to defy the authorities, and hoped he would remember him to them, and thank them, in his name, for the splendid vessel they had thus unconsciously placed at his disposal.

CLINGING TO CAPTAIN TOM THE FAIR GIRL WAVED THEM BACK.

by the time the boats had pushed off, the fog had greatly cleared away, and things could be distinguished at some distance.

Scarcely had the boats disappeared in the haze, when a bright flash appeared in an opposite direction, and the loud boom of a cannon burst upon their astonished ears.

The dim outlines of a frigate could now be seen through the mist, and at that instant Captain Tom disappeared from the deck.

The crew were busily engaged drawing the charges from the guns, for Bob Hauler had taken the precaution to thrust the priming wire down each touchhole, and insert a little water, for fear they might go off unawares.

Another gun now boomed from the frigate,

and, simultaneously, Captain Tom appeared upon deck.

Well knowing that the schooner was no match for the frigate, Captain Tom resolved to effect by stratagem that which it was certain he could not effect by force.

He now appeared dressed in the uniform of the lieutenant, and having ordered the stern boat to be lowered, he quickly sprang in, followed by five of his brave crew, who pulled vigorously towards the frigate, which had now hove to.

He was met at the gangway by the commander of the frigate, who grasped him warmly by the hand, and led the way to his cabin.

"Sit down," said the naval commander, familiarly, "Do you prefer wine, or spirits?"

"I am not particular."

"I presume you are on the same business as myself, if I may judge from the locality I find you in," said the commander.

"Well, I am after Tom Drake, and I almost captured him this very night."

"You don't say so?"

"I do, really, on my honour, Mr. —— I have not the pleasure of knowing your name."

"My name is Simmonds, sir," said the commander; "but I have not the pleasure of knowing yours," jocularly.

"First, answer me one question, Mr. Simmonds," said Captain Tom, in a tone of well-feigned surprise. "What frigate is this?"

"The 'Indefatigable.'"

Indeed! then it's very fortunate I fell in with you, for I have sealed orders for you. I only received them yesterday, and as I have been a long time on foreign stations, you may easily conceive I am not very well acquainted with the channel squadron."

"Certainly," said the commander; "it is, as you say, very fortunate. I have to proceed up channel, it appears, for it says not to be opened until abreast of Cherbourg. Something very important, I dare-say. Come, drink, friend; you have not yet honoured me with your name."

"Dauntless!" answered the buccaneer, looking him full in the face.

"And your vessel?" interrogated the commander.

"The 'Indefeasible,' manned by a fearless crew, and armed with twelve twenty-four brass howitzers," cried Tom Drake.

The commander stood for a moment astounded; at length he said—

"I suppose you keep a log of all that, or else you would surely forget it?"

"Oh, no, I have a very good memory."

"I think you said, Mr. Dauntless—I believe that's the name." Tom Drake nodded an assent, "that you gained some information of the whereabouts of this notorious buccaneer?"

"Why, I was as close to him as I am to you, and closer if anything."

"You don't say so?"

"I do."

"And why did you not capture him?"

"I did try to, but just as I went to grasp him, he vanished."

"Where to?"

"I cannot say, that is the mystery."

"And you really mean to say you saw him? I only wish I had been in your place, I would have given him a hard tussle for it."

Tom's daring recklessness nearly overcame his prudence, and he could scarce refrain from revealing himself, and testing the bravery of the opiniated commander.

Having finished his wine, he rose from his seat, and prepared to depart.

At the gangway, he thanked the commander for his kind attention, and shaking him heartily by the hand, said, jocularly—

"If you do not mind honouring me with a visit on board my little nut-shell, you will do me a great favour, and as you feel so interested in this Tom Drake, I will show you the spot on which he stood when I saw him aboard my vessel."

The commander's curiosity and excitement was now at its highest pitch; he felt as though he could give five years of his existence to gain one glance at the renowned buccaneer.

"I will accept your invitation, Mr. Dauntless," said the commander; "I would walk fifty miles to see anything pertaining to this mysterious being."

"Quartermaster," he said, turning to that individual, who had been eyeing the schooner through the glass, and had ventured his opinion on the merits and demerits of the noble-looking craft, "lower the galley, and pipe galley's crew away."

"Aye, aye, sir," answered the quartermaster, as he hurried towards the boatswain's mate, to give the orders.

The shrill whistle of the boatswain's pipe sounded on the deck of the frigate as our hero gave orders to push off and pull on board.

On gaining the deck of the schooner, Captain Tom gave a few hasty orders, and then descended below to prepare for the reception of his important visitor.

On arriving on board the schooner the commander was received with as much decorum and ceremony as though it were a man-of-war.

Captain Tom, who had by this time returned to the deck, ushered him below, and they were soon engaged in deep and earnest conversation.

"By-the-bye," said the commander, who, by this time, began to feel the effects of the wine, of which he had partaken rather freely, "you were going to show me where this fellow stood."

"I will before you leave," said Tom, with a smile.

"Well, I'm going now."

"The last place he stood was where I am now at this present moment, and he left this bottle of scent here." As Tom spoke he thrust a recently discharged pistol close to the commander's nose.

"That's rather peculiar scent, too," said the commander, trying to steady his gaze. "I suppose that is his favourite perfume."

"I believe he uses no other," said the daring captain, placing great emphasis on his words.

The commander, who could scarcely keep his feet, now staggered towards the door, and was assisted by Ben Barnacle to the deck above.

While the commander was making his way on deck, Tom Drake had donned his own distinguishing garb, which had been brought by one of the boats, and then followed him.

"Since you are so considerate, I will just indulge you in that little whim of yours," he said; "that is, I will let you have a glance at the buccaneer in person."

At these words the captain appeared sobered a little, and his eyes opened to their full extent.

Captain Tom stood before him in bold defiance, his arms folded across his breast, and a smile upon his handsome face.

For a moment the commander looked stupified, and when at length he found speech, he said, sternly—

"Do not try to play off any of your jokes on me, or perhaps you will find me a dangerous plaything."

"I fear you not," said Tom, defiantly. "I care no more for your threat than I do for your power."

The commander, sobered, gazed at him with a look of mingled doubt and surprise.

At length he spoke.

"If I were certain that the Tom Drake of which I have heard so much talk, and of whom I am now in search, stood before me, I would not leave this spot without trying my hand at him."

"Unless you doubt my word, you may be assured he is here. My name is Tom Drake."

"You said your name was Dauntless."

"So it is, and always will be by nature, yet still am I Tom Drake."

The commander was astounded, and could see that if he resorted to any violent measures, he would soon fall a victim to his own folly, so he turned on his heel, and made a retreat to the boat, with a laugh, to imply that he doubted the assertion, but, in reality, feeling afraid of the bold buccaneer.

Burning with rage, he ordered the bowman to shove off, firmly resolved to give the schooner a good peppering with his fourty-four thirty-two pounders, but on looking round for his vessel, he found she was more than a mile distant.

Tom Drake had ordered his crew to fill the yards, and the ship was sailing from the frigate.

"Give way, you lubbers!" roared the enraged commander. "A month's black list for the boat's crew, if you are not on board in five minutes."

His anger was in no way appeased by the defiant laugh that rose from the deck of the schooner.

The men bent lustily to their oars, but by the time they reached the frigate, she was nearly three miles astern of the schooner, whilst on the port bow was a vessel, with a long, low hull, coming down before the wind like a gull.

"See all clear for action," cried Tom Drake. "I can't make out this strange sail, yet she shows an ugly row of teeth."

Everything was quickly cleared away, and every one at their post ready for an encounter.

Whatever she might be, it was evident that the schooner must not lay her alongside, for the frigate was still in pursuit, with every stitch of canvas she could set to the breeze.

On approaching nearer, the strange sail proved to be a brig of considerable size, and was pierced for eight guns on each side, but only seven of them appeared to be mounted.

Her decks swarmed with men, with cutlasses slung to their waists, and pistols stuck in their girdles.

A shot from the brig crossed the schooner's bow. At the same instant the brig hauled to the wind, and ranged alongside.

"A French privateer. by all that's holy!" said Tom Drake, addressing Ben Barnacle, who stood at his elbow, as the tri-coloured flag was run up and fluttered in the breeze.

It was evident the Frenchman meant mischief, and the gallant buccaneer knew full well that his small complement would have to fight courageously to beat off their superior antagonist.

"Now, my brave comrades!" he cried, rushing into their midst, sword in hand, "you have got a desperate fellow to deal with, and it will require all our united exertions to beat off his attacks. We must fight hand to hand and shoulder to shoulder. Directly she fires give her a broadside!"

Scarcely had the words escaped his lips, when a shower of iron from the brig dashed over the schooner, doing but little damage. And ere the sound had died away, when, with a shout of defiance, the buccaneers returned the fire.

Broadside after broadside was exchanged in rapid succession, and both vessels were completely enveloped in smoke.

"Crack on, my gallant heroes!" cried Tom Drake. "Elevate one degree this round!"

"Bravo, my lads!" he cried, as the ponderous missiles flew on their errand of destruction, and went crashing through the bulwarks and port-holes of the enemy, sweeping the men from their guns.

But though the Frenchmen were falling like sheep before the withering fire of the gallant buccaneers, they were so numerous that the guns were quickly manned by others of the crew.

"Bravo, my gallant friends!" cried the undaunted Tom.

Many of Captain Tom's little band lay already weltering in their gore.

Still the survivors fought desperately to revenge the death of their fallen comrades.

The sweat rolled in heavy drops from their reeking brows, as they plied the guns with that sullen determination that told how deeply they felt the loss of their brave companions.

"Give them another broadside, my brave fellows!" cried Tom, as he dashed among the gallant crew, and aided them to run out the guns.

"Carry away the wounded, quick, my lads!" and the order was speedily obeyed by the seamen.

The Frenchmen had suffered severely.

Upon the deck lay heaps of slain and wounded, and at intervals parties were obliged to throw the dead overboard.

The bulwarks and spars were one mass of splinters, and the two foremost guns were unable to be worked any longer.

The French captain flew about the deck like a maniac, as he saw his noble vessel cut to pieces by the deadly fire of the buccaneers, who fired three broadsides to two of the Frenchman's.

The spars of both vessels were sadly shattered.

The sails riddled like a sieve, and the crews of both vessels were laying about in heaps, and the scuppers ran with the blood of the fallen.

Tom Drake gazed mournfully along the blood-stained deck, as he saw his beloved followers fall wounded by the Frenchman's heavy shot.

"Stand to your guns, my hearts of oak," he cried. "Give them another broadside."

Scarce had the death-dealing messengers left the mouth of the cannons, when the Frenchman's flag came down.

A loud shout of triumph arose from the schooner, and told that though they had suffered greatly they were unconquered.

The mainmast of the brig fell over the side with a crash, but the little schooner, still continuing her course, for it had been a running fight, and both vessels were fast sailors, soon left the brig behind.

The frigate, which had been crowding on all sail, in the hope of catching Tom Drake, while engaged with the brig, now pounced upon his helpless prey like a hungry shark, and made a great prize of the disabled and resistless Frenchman.

Over eighty of the Frenchman's crew had fallen in the fierce struggle.

Only twelve of the gallant buccaneers had been slain, but fifteen of their number lay badly wounded.

The sight of so many of his brave little band laying stretched upon the deck, bleeding from ghastly wounds, saddened the heart of gallant Tom Drake.

"Don't look so sad, captain," cried Bob Hauler, who stood by his side, "there is not a man on board but would willingly die to support our cause; for we are as one, and while we are fighting, we are fighting for ourselves as well as for our gallant captain."

As he spoke, he observed the features of his gallant captain suddenly assume an ashy paleness, and he staggered to one of the stanchions for support.

Bob Hauler flew to his assistance, and caught him in his grasp, as he was about to fall on the deck.

"Good Heavens! come here, doctor, quick!" he cried. "Our captain, I fear, has fought his last battle. Good heavens! He is fainting! Water, quick!"

Bob Hauler, on placing his arm round the body of his captain, to enable him to stand, discovered, for the first time, that he had been seriously wounded.

A splinter from one of the fallen spars had entered his shoulder below the blade bone, and it required the united efforts of Tom and the doctor to draw it from the wound, so deeply was it embedded in the flesh.

Not a groan or a sound did the gallant buccaneer allow to escape his lips, during the painful operation.

At length the wound was dressed, and the captain was placed in his cot by his mournful followers, who feared they were about to lose their beloved captain.

Silently and mournfully the brave fellows cleared away the sad emblems of the great devastation caused by the heavy metal of the Frenchmen, which had been poured from her ponderous guns in the terrible conflict.

Scarcely a sound was to be heard, as they trod softly on the deck, for fear of disturbing the last moments of their devoted captain.

Captain Tom was not so dangerously hurt as his anxious followers supposed.

He lay on a couch in his own cabin in a dreamy stupor, thinking of the eventful scenes he had passed through of late, and the cruel fate the smugglers had imposed upon him by extracting a promise from him to marry Susan Brocton, for though he admired her for her beauty, the whole affections of his heart was given to gentle Minnie Atherton, who, in the depth of her love, had forsaken all to be with him, and had followed and nursed him through most of his dangerous career.

Thinking thus, and wondering how he could avoid the union with Susan, which would wreck his life's happiness, and keep his troth with his own gentle bride, Minnie, he was aroused by a light footfall.

Starting up to meet the dear girl, Minnie, who had come to the ship in a boat with his devoted followers, he held out his arms to receive her, but overcome by weakness, he staggered, and almost fell.

Horrified by the pallor of his face, and the blood-stains on his clothes, the beautiful girl uttered a startled cry as she caught sight of Captain Tom.

It was the first time they had met for many days, but, for a moment, when she first came aboard.

They had lots to say to each other now, but the dear girl, seeing his weakened condition, would not allow him to talk, and with many a tender and loving caress, watched anxiously by his side while he slumbered.

She had heard rumours of his proposed marriage with the girl he had saved from the wreck, and although she could not doubt his love for her, and his own honour, she knew the power of the lawless band he had to control, and feared they might force him to do that which he would never do by his own free will.

With these painful thoughts troubling her, she watched and waited for the time when she could learn the truth from him.

CHAPTER CXLIV.

HOW CAPTAIN TOM FRUSTRATED THE PLANS OF HIS ENEMIES

WHEN our hero left Colonel Hawkins with the instructions from the lieutenant of the schooner, he was impatient for the time to arrive when he could reek his vengeance on Tom Drake.

But our hero, who had acted his part of the ignorant sailor so well as to deceive the hawk's eyes of the colonel, when he stood before him, had destroyed the original note of the lieutenant's, and substituted one of his own, which, if acted upon, would effectually frustrate the cunning plot of his enemies.

The purport of Tom Drake's note was, that the colonel, with a party of his men, was to lay concealed within a short distance from that which the lieutenant had named, and in the event of the buccaneers escaping, he was to cut off their retreat, among whom was supposed to be the redoubtable Tom Drake.

The colonel was in ecstacies as he read the contents of the note for the twentieth time.

"I'll make the villain suffer," he muttered through his clenched teeth. "Now shall I be able to have my revenge for the insults he has heaped upon my head! Capital plan!" he muttered. "Escape will be impossible. At nine o'clock! I'll be there at eight. I know the spot well. Twenty picked men. I'll take thirty! Oh, I fancy I have him now!" he cried, half aloud, as he clenched his hands, and went through the pantomimic exultations of twisting the neck of his imaginary victim.

So great was his excitement, and so little did he actually know what he was doing, that he hurriedly took up a large punch bowl, and placed it on his head, imagining it to be his smoking cap.

Nor did he discover his error until he felt the sensation caused by its cold contents trickling down his back.

"Curse the thing," he muttered, as he raised the bowl, and dashed it to the floor, "if Mrs. H. was to see me now she would certainly say I was the worse for liquor, and very likely have the audacity to say I was drunk."

Then he hurried out of the room, muttering something that would certainly have shocked the ears of Mrs. H., or any other lady, had they been present.

Some hours later, a party of mounted soldiers were proceeding down the road that led to the sea coast.

These were the thirty picked men which Colonel Hawkins had selected to accompany him on his nocturnal expedition.

They proceeded along the road carefully, for a thick fog that prevailed rendered the objects around indistinct, and as the saying is, they could scarcely believe their own eyes.

The colonel, who did not exactly lead his men, but rode alongside of them, was lost in deep thought, and already in his imagination had he captured the bare-faced villain, as he termed him.

When just as he was in the act of shaking the poor unlucky devil he imagined in his grasp, he slightly checked the near rein, and the horse, which was a thorough-bred one, instinctively obeyed the slight pressure, reared, and strode into a ditch.

The gallant colonel, still grappling fiercely with his imaginary foe, turned a somersault over the horse's head, and was landed, as a nautical acquaintance would have termed it, on his stern in the slush and mire.

Several of the soldiers instantly dismounted, and went to his assistance.

His indignity was at its height, whilst his dignity was at its lowest, and he bit his lips with rage as the suppressed laughter of the soldiers broke on his ear.

"I tell you what, my fine fellows," he said, passionately, "a little extra drill would not be thrown away on you, and perhaps it might teach you that which you never learnt at school—to treat your superiors with respect."

Having relieved his outraged feelings, he once more resumed his seat upon his horse's back, and for the present forgot the object of his expedition.

The tittering of the soldiers died away, for it was necessary that the utmost caution should be observed now they were nearing the haunt.

The fog was still very dense, and the colonel, fearing to be left behind, lest the smugg'——

fall upon him, ordered his men to quicken their pace, but at the same time to keep their horses well in hand, so that they could halt at any moment.

"Ah!" he muttered, half aloud, "'tis true these men loveth darkness better than light, because their deeds are evil."

It was not because the colonel was of a religious turn of mind that he quoted this line of Scripture, far from it, but the darkness of the night, added to the peculiar business which had brought him out on so dismal a night, had brought them to his mind.

Far better would it have been for him had he thought of the other few words, which were more appropriate to him in his present position.

"Take heed, lest ye stumble."

For, as they were cantering down the road, the head of the unfortunate colonel came in contact with an overhanging bough, which flung him violently to the ground.

And in his hurry to scramble to his feet, he stumbled, and rolled over and over, till at length he found himself scrambling in a ditch.

This time the soldiers could not restrain from a loud burst of laughter, and, as Dick Ramrod observed, if a park of artillery had suddenly appeared in their front, he could not for the moment have looked serious.

The colonel lay almost buried in the slimy water. He tried in vain to get a foothold, or dig his fingers in the muddy bank to assist him to extricate himself from his no enviable position.

It was some moments, and, indeed, not till the roars of laughter had a little subsided, that any of them could aid him to ascend the bank.

At length they arrived at the end of their journey without further mishap.

It was a thick copse, or small wood, bordering on the coast, and in here it was thought advisable to leave the horses and the body of the men, while the colonel proceeded further along the road, accompanied by several of the soldiers, whom he placed in various positions to listen for and give warning at the slightest sound of an approaching boat.

The place at which they arrived was well adapted for smuggling.

A line of lofty cliffs bounded the coast.

An opening was formed by a deep gully, and afforded space for a large-sized cart to pass between the lofty walls of chalk.

Sentries having been posted at several points to give the alarm, the remainder were permitted to assume whatever position of ease suited their different tastes, with strict orders to be in readiness at a moment's notice.

A select few chose a quiet spot under an overhanging chalk cliff, when, after some time had elapsed in almost perfect silence, one of the men suggested that Tom Webster, an old, bronzed warrior, should relate a story, to while the time away.

Having obtained silence, he commenced—

"For some considerable time, peace had existed between the Natchez nation (one of the aboriginal tribes of America) and those tribes nearest to their borders, strengthened by a league against the French for mutual protection, which led to much friendly intercourse and reciprocal offices of kindness.

"A casual interview between a young and gallant warrior of one of them, and a Natchez girl, produced impressions which, matured by time, ripened into mutual attachment.

"Overtures were made to the family of the maiden, and presents exchanged.

"The union was regarded by all as auspicious to the interests of both nations.

"The bright moons and beautiful skies of the south never smiled on a happier pair than the warlike Alama and the dark-eyed, youthful Xalissa.

"About this period the arts and gold of the French prevailed over the faith of some of the nations heretofore united with the Natchez in opposition to the intolerable oppressions heaped upon them by these adventurers.

"Falsehoods were invented, and treacherous designs attributed to all parties in the league through emissaries and spies secretly sent among them.

"Complaint and recrimination were followed by aggression and open hostility.

"The hatchet was unburied, and the runners bearing the red symbol of combat passed rapidly among the tribes.

"The first onset was between the Natchez and the native tribe of Alama, and so sudden, that the last interview between him and Xalissa was broken off by the terrific cry of their respective tribes, summoning the youthful warriors to the work of death.

"Alama, high in reputation and command, reluctantly obeyed the call.

"He panted not for the glories or dangers of war, but sighed for days of peace and happiness with his beautiful Fawn.

"This was the name of Xalissa, when translated into our tongue.

"With it well corresponded her starry eye, fringed with lashes as dark and silky as the raven plume that decked her hair.

"Her slender form was as graceful as the neck of the swan clearing the waters of her own blue lake, and her tiny foot and agile step elastic as the tread of the young panther upon the quicksands of her native stream.

"It is unnecessary to dwell on the bloody scenes which ensued, or to detail the various fortunes that attended these destructive wars, stirred up by the fatal policy of the French.

"So far as the present contest was involved, the Natchez were successful.

"They had routed their enemies, and taken many captives, who, according to the usages of savage warfare, were condemned to torture.

"Among them was Alama.

"All the friendly sentiments heretofore existing between the tribes, were superseded by that settled and deadly hate, characteristic of barbarians.

"Alama, after fighting with the desperation of a tiger, pierced like a target with a hundred arrows, fell into the power of the Natchez.

"His wounds, though dangerous and numerous, were not destined to prove mortal.

"His athletic form, in the vigour of youth and manly strength, had been trained and hardened amidst enterprise and danger; and his soul rose superior to misfortune and suffering.

"This heroic bearing only exasperated his enemies, and sealed his doom; but under present prostration, he was deemed an unfit object for the extremities of an Indian execution; it was therefore deferred.

"Xalissa, in the agony of her soul, had witnessed his sufferings, but dared not exhibit the sympathies she so deeply felt, or betray an emotion calculated to rouse suspicion, and thus precipitate his destiny.

"One thing she had resolved upon, notwithstanding the fearful obstructions opposed to her designs—to save or perish with him!

"Among the Natchez were certain superannuated women, generally blind or crippled, pretending to supernatural powers, and dealing in witchcraft.

"These beldames were held in undefined and superstitious awe by young and old.

"When captives were brought in by the warriors, their misfortunes were aggravated by every insult that the resources of savage ingenuity could suggest; and not the least were the revilings, taunts, and incantations of these hags, to whose power they were subjected preparatory to execution.

"They dressed themselves in strange and fantastic attire, and wore hideous masks, to heighten the effect of their uncouth and antic ceremonies.

"They were unquestioned in their proceedings, being avoided by all, through mingled emotions of fear and detestation.

"Xalissa availed herself of this superstition to effect her designs.

"Habited in the disguise of these pretended magicians, she came by night to the place where Alama was confined.

"It was an enclosure, strongly constructed of stakes sunk in the ground, and covered by like materials, firmly set on in the form of a roof.

"On the outside, a gallery, composed lightly of cane, and covered with branches, sheltered a numerous guard, and the entrance was constantly occupied by a powerful Indian.

"These precautions interposed difficulties of no ordinary kind; the approach of Xalissa was, however, unobstructed; the Indian reverently gave way, and she was soon at the side of the prisoner.

"He had been accustomed to such scenes, and marked the entrance of his supposed tormentor with perfect unconcern.

"She performed over him various unmeaning ceremonies; she heaped abuse and insult on the victim, cast opprobrium upon his name and tribe, and, kneeling over him, chaunted those low, sad tones, which warn the captive of doom and death.

"Then she recited the victories of the Natchez, their deeds of renown, and the glories of their ancestors, uttering new imprecations on their foes.

"At length, however, as the curiosity of the guard subsided, she gradually brought her face nearer to that of Alma, and, taking his hand, addressed him in a whisper—'Let your eyes be open, your tongue still, your face unchanged—I am here to save you! Fear not; I am Xalissa!'

"The warrior, overcome by love, gratitude, and joy, with a heart bursting to give expression to his emotions, exerted, nevertheless, the control over his feelings so remarkable in the Indian.

"'Your wounds,' resumed the beautiful girl, with her mouth close to his ear, while she was heaving her arms in all the frenzy and eccentricity of the character she had assumed, 'your wounds will not suffer you to fly—promise to obey me. To-morrow I will tell you all—promise!'

"Alama pressed her hand in token of assent, but whispered, as he did so, 'My foot is heavy, but my hand is not weak. Cut the thongs that bind me; give me my hatchet. I will yet open our path to the forest.'

"'No blood must be shed,' rejoined Xalissa. 'My brother guards you; he must not die by your hand. You have promised! Silence! The Natchez are wary. If I am suspected, we are lost! I will come again.'

"She now sprang suddenly to her feet, and, cking her body to and fro, often repeated the same lik mockeries, and then slowly left the prison.

"Here she wandered about among the guards, who were lying sluggishly around the fire, took their bows in her hands, and pronounced over them certain cabalistic words, at the same time dancing round them with grimaces and frantic gestures.

"Having thus familiarised herself with those whom she intended to deceive, she laid a plan for accomplishing a most important design in relation to their arms, and lulled suspicion, she retired.

"The following day the same mummery was repeated; and the guard, not only unsuspecting, but exhibiting some symptoms of disgust and weariness at the perseverance of the sorceress, lay indolently about the dungeon, thus enabling Xalissa briefly to unfold her plans.

"'To-morrow you are doomed to the stake. We must fly to-night. The warrior who guards the door, I have told you, is my brother; his life must be safe—at least till all else fails. We must exchange dresses. I know the passes to the river, which you do not; wounded, you could not escape, I will break the guard. When the Natchez pursue me, take your course to the Humachitto. I will meet you where it joins the Mississippi. Fear not for me—the bow-strings will be charmed. My foot is light. Be silent—obey, and we are safe.'

"Then, with a wild and unearthly shriek, she seized a firebrand, and, renewing her sybil-like denunciations and incoherent maledictions, her voice sank away, as if from the exhaustion of passion, into coarse and direful tones; the notes were taken up by the guard excited to fury, and the song of death rang fearfully among the surrounding echoes.

"Xalissa returned at night, prepared to accomplish her hazardous purpose.

"She had brought with her a vegetable acid, active and powerful in its effects; and with this, in the progress of her pretended witchcraft, she managed to touch all the bow-strings.

"The savages were passive and unsuspecting, for they regarded her as being supernaturally inspired, and excited to new raptures by the near prospect of vengeance and blood.

"So soon as all became silent, and the watch-fire sunk down upon the embers, she again seated herself by the side of Alama, and cautiously severed the cords which bound him.

"She took his bright head-piece, and clasped it on her own brow.

"She then put her mask upon him, and threw around him the party-coloured tunic she had worn, at the same time enveloping her little person in his hunting shirt, stiff with blood from numerous and ghastly wounds.

"She now took the position he occupied, while Alama, assuming hers, personated the character of the tormentress, while she appeared as the wounded and condemned captive.

"These changes were effected more silently and rapidly than can be explained by words.

"Fuel had been added to the fire by the Indians, and, by the time they were accomplished, the flame went up, bright and sparkling, in the midst of a savage but picturesque group, worthy the pencil of Salvator Rosa.

"Now was the moment for action.

"Xalissa sprang forward, and, by a blow dealt with all her force, threw her brother from his balance, and passed him.

"He, not doubting that the prisoner had escaped while the old woman slept, raised a whoop which alarmed all his companions.

"They seized their bows, and, before Xalissa had passed beyond the light of the fire, twenty arrows were drawn upon her, either of which must have proved mortal; but the charm she employed proved effectual, and the bow-strings snapped into a thousand pieces!

"They were, of course, relinquished, and the whole band, with a shout of vengeance, pressed hotly on the flying girl.

"We now return to Alama.

"The brief communications which necessarily passed between him and Xalissa, and the engrossing interest of the occasion, did not enable him properly to appreciate the motives of this generous girl.

"All now flashed upon his mind.

" After his fetters were removed he might have passed the guard, as she had done, and with no greater hazard; but she dreaded lest Alama, in the struggle for escape, would endanger the life of her brother; or, that stiff from wounds, he would be overtaken in flight.

" But, if these apprehensions had proved groundless, his ignorance of the passes might involve him in difficulty, or, at best, leave him to contend, at fearful odds, with those who could tread blindfold every bayou and deer-path of these intricate defiles.

" On the other hand, disguised as she was, she did not deem it possible that the Indians would suspect any stratagem, and, consequently, the pursuit being drawn upon her, Alama, though wounded, might, in a few hours, be beyond the fear of danger.

" So far all had succeeded; and the prisoner left the scene of his sufferings unmolested, and with new feelings of admiration and affection for the devoted maid.

" Divesting himself of his encumbrances, he was soon buried in the recesses of the forest, and turned his yet feeble steps to the point designated by her.

" In the meantime the lovely Fawn, impelled less by fear for herself than anxiety and affection for him, fled before her pursuers.

" Her light and symmetrical form, borne along as if by the breeze, seemed to flit onward like some bird of night on its noiseless wing.

" The Indians, in the outset, were in no doubt of overtaking the wounded prisoner, and laughed in scorn at the shallow attempt made to escape, where cunning had not been resorted to, and where physical power or personal bravery could not avail.

" They were, however, speedily undeceived, and derision turned into utter astonishment at the spectacle of a wounded and emaciated prisoner, with the speed of a deer, setting at defiance their fleetest runners.

" With every inducement, therefore, to urge them on, they encouraged one another to new efforts and redoubled exertion.

" They now rapidly approached the rugged and uneven ground which marks the line of the 'Ellis Cliffs.'

" The continual abrasion of the Mississippi undermines huge banks of earth, overhanging here the margin of the precipitous shore, leaving frightful chasms and deep bayous running on a level with the river, and at various angles to its course, far up into the heights.

" This, together with the springs, bursting out at various altitudes, and passing through sandy or decaying strata, produces, particularly in the rainy season, a melting and sinking of the soil, and a waving, uneven surface.

" On the return of the summer suns, the soil becomes baked, and is extremely rigid and disagreeable to the feet.

" It was here that Xalissa, struggling against difficulties and dangers, and beset by enemies active and persevering, found her strength beginning to yield.

" From the operation of causes just detailed, the pass to the river, formerly used by the Natchez, had been cut off, and another one was now resorted to, though farther and more circuitous.

" The former ran along a narrow ridge, between tow deep ravines.

" Across this a rain gutter had been formed, which, gradually widening, had become a deep and dangerous gulf, deemed impassable by the foot of man.

" The object of those in pursuit was, therefore, to cut off the retreat of Xalissa by the new route, should she attempt it, and drive her upon one of which they supposed her ignorant, being that

abandoned as impassable by reason of the ' break.' Xalissa, however, knew them both.

" She strained every nerve to reach the new and safe descent. It was in vain.

" The poor girl, nearly exhausted, found, as daylight approached, that her brother, the fleetest of the Indians, was gaining upon her, and that, in fact, escape by mortal means was almost hopeless.

" She, therefore, ceased her flight, and paused, as if collecting her powers for some desperate resource.

" Upon this the Indians, secure of their victim, sent forth a yell of triumph.

" Xalissa now turned suddenly, and went directly down the deserted pass.

" In this attempt no interference was offered by the Natchez.

" On the contrary, when they reached its entrance, and saw her pent up between the highlands and the chasm, without hope of escape either to the right or the left, their joy was uncontrolled, and a savage and exulting cry rang ominously among the cliffs.

" The enthusiastic girl felt that a moment had arrived, involving her own fate and that of her wounded lover; for her capture must expose the stratagem, and place his fate beyond the reach of hope.

" Between these probabilities and personal danger, there was in her mind no hesitation.

" She hastily threw off the hunting shirt taken from Alama, tightened the belt that clasped her person, and with a fearless bound, cleared the appalling gulf, now spreading forth its terrors between her and the astonished and baffled savages.

' Pausing for a moment, to recover from the stunning effect of the leap, she raised her beautiful eyes in adoration to her divinity, whose warm rays were just emerging from the east.

" To her his rising seemed invested with new glories; perhaps she believed that he contemplated her enterprise with favour, and thus benignly smiled on its success.

" Be it, however, as it may, she offered to Heaven the purest of all sacrifices—the tribute of an innocent and grateful heart; then, plunging forward into the forest, she sought the shores of the Mississippi.

" Every common emotion, which might be supposed to influence the pursuers on such an occasion, was merged in utter astonishment, and they stood lingering on the edge of the precipice, wrapt in silent admiration.

" They were unwilling, however, to follow the example of courage they had witnessed, and, turning their course to the adjoining pass, rushed tumultuously down.

" They repaired to the outlet, where Xalissa must gain the level, trusting that the intricacies of the path would impede her flight.

" But they were too late; a light impression on the waving sand, disappearing almost as soon as seen, was an unequivocal indication of her having passed there on her way to the river.

" Hopeless of success, but impelled by curiosi they followed to the margin, and there, on the pr trate body of a noble oak, whose gigantic limbs far out into the stream, they beheld her stand calm, secure, and unconcerned.

" Collecting herself for a last effort, she gave shout expressive of victory, waved her hand token of defiance, and plunged into the dark a angry stream.

" The waters closed over her, and they saw her no more.

" The Natchez returned disappointed and ashamed.

" Fortunately for themselves, as they seem

they brought with them the funeral shirt of Alama as evidence of their story.

"This circumstance, the situation of their bowstrings, discoloured, rotten, and useless, the sudden restoration of their prisoner, his great speed, and unaccountable knowledge of the defiles, and finally, his prodigious leap and sudden disappearance, afforded ample ground for attributing the whole to demoniacal interference and supernatural agency.

"This construction soothed their own vanity, and, for the moment, satisfied the nation; but so soon as it was discovered that Xalissa had disappeared, no doubt existed that she was privy to the escape.

"In that way, however, it remained for time to develope.

"Alama, in the meanwhile, unobstructed and unpursued, reached the mouth of the Humachitto; and there, upon the bank, trembling with anxiety for his safety, sat his beloved girl!

"She sprang forward, in her artlessness and affection, and clasped in the arms of the wounded chief, hid her face, radiant with joy, in his manly bosom.

"They speedily reached the native forests of Alama, where the exalted virtues of Xalissa received additional lustre from this distinguished act of heroism, and where she was amply rewarded, in the affections of her chosen warrior, and the gratitude of a nation.

"The hostile tribes again became friends, and Alama and Xalissa, with the aged warriors and the youth of both nations, would often assemble upon the heights which have been described, to amuse themselves in their plays and pastimes; and the scene of the adventure witnessed many a jest at the expense of the Natchez guard.

"Frequently, too, with wonder and admiration, did they measure the incredible vault that Xalissa had accomplished; and, in honour of her virtue, and in commemoration of the achievement, they called it The Fawn's Leap."

The conclusion of Tom Webster's story was received with such loud shouts of acclamation that the officer in command came hurrying up to ascertain the cause, and advised them to be a little quieter or they would frustrate all the proposed plans of capture.

After a short silence, Corporal Sims volunteered the next, and in a clear voice began—

"He who has been to Rotterdam will remember a house of two stories which stands in the suburbs, just adjoining the basin of the canal that runs between that city and the Hague, Leyden, and other places.

"I say he will remember it, for it must have been pointed out to him, as having been once inhabited by the most ingenious artist that Holland ever produced, to say nothing of his daughter, the prettiest maiden ever born within the hearing of the croaking of a frog.

"It is not with the fair Blanche, unfortunately, that I have at present anything to do; it is with the old gentleman, her father. His profession was that of a surgical instrument-maker, but his fame principally rested on the admirable skill with which he constructed wooden and cork legs.

"So great was his reputation in this department of human science, that they whom Nature or accident had curtailed, caricatured, and disappointed in so very necessary an appendage to the body, came limping to him in crowds, and however desperate their case might be, were very soon, as the saying is, set upon their legs again.

"Many a cripple who had looked upon his deformity as incurable, and whose only consolation rested in an occasional sly hit at Providence, for having entrusted his making to a journeyman, found himself so admirably fitted—so elegantly propped up by Mynheer Turningvort—that he almost began to doubt whether a timber or cork supporter was not, on the whole, superior to a more commonplace and troublesome one of flesh and blood.

"And, in good truth, if you had seen how very handsome and delicate were the understandings fashioned by the skilful artificer, you would have been puzzled to settle the question yourself, the more especially if, in your real toes, you were ever tormented with gout or corns.

"One morning, just as Master Turningvort was giving its final smoothness and polish to a calf and ankle, a messenger entered his studio (to speak classically) and requested that he would immediately accompany him to the mansion of Mynheer Von Wodenblock.

"It was the mansion of the richest merchant in Rotterdam; so the artist put on his best wig, and set forth with his three-cornered hat in one hand, and his silver-headed stick in the other.

"It so happened that Mynheer Von Wodenblock had been very laudably engaged, a few days before, in turning a poor relation out of doors, but, in endeavouring to hasten the odious wretch's progress downstairs, by a slight impulse à posteriore (for Mynheer seldom stood upon ceremony with poor relations) he had unfortunately lost his balance, and tumbling headlong from the top to the bottom, found, on recovering his senses, that he had broken his right leg, and that he had lost three teeth.

"He had at first some thoughts of having his poor relation tried for murder; but, being naturally of a merciful disposition, he only sent him to gaol on account of some unpaid debt, leaving him there to enjoy the comfortable reflection that his wife and children were starving at home.

"A dentist soon supplied the invalid with three teeth, which he had pulled out of an indigent poet's head at the rate of ten stivers a-piece, but for which he prudently charged the rich merchant one hundred dollars.

"The doctor, upon examining his leg, recollecting that he was at that moment rather in want of a subject, cut it carefully off, and took it away with him in his carriage to lecture upon it to his pupils.

"So Mynheer Wodenblock, considering that he had been hitherto accustomed to walk, and not to hop, and being, perhaps, somewhat prejudiced in favour of the former mode of locomotion, sent for our friend at the canal basin, in order that he might give him directions about the representative with which he wished to be supplied for his lost member.

"The artificer entered the wealthy burgher's apartment.

"He was reclining on a couch, with his left leg looking as respectable as ever, but with his unhappy right stump wrapped up in bandages, as if conscious and ashamed of its own littleness.

"'Turningvort, you have heard of my misfortune, It has thrown me into a fever, and all Rotterdam into confusion; but let that pass. You must make me a leg, and it must be the best leg, sir, you ever made in your life.'

"Turningvort bowed.

"'I do not care what it costs'—Turningvort bowed yet lower—'provided it outdoes everything you have yet made of a similar sort. I am for none of your wooden spindleshanks. Make it of cork: let it be light and elastic: and cram it as full of springs as a watch. I know nothing of the business, and cannot be more specific in my directions; but this I am determined upon, that I shall have a leg as good as the one I have lost. I know such a thing is to be had, and if I get it from you your reward is a thousand guineas.'

"The Dutch Prometheus declared that, to please Mynheer Von Wodenblock, he would do more than human ingenuity had ever done before, and undertook to bring him, within six days, a leg which would laugh to scorn the mere common legs possessed by common men.

"This assurance was not meant as an idle boast.

"Turningvort was a man of speculative as well as practical science, and there was a favourite discovery which he had long been endeavouring to make, and in accomplishing which, he imagined he had at last succeeded that very morning.

"Like all other manufacturers of terrestrial legs, he had ever found the chief difficulty, in his progress towards perfection, to consist in its being apparently impossible to introduce into them anything in the shape of joints, capable of being regulated by the will, and of performing those important functions achieved under the present system, by means of the admirable mechanism of the knee and ankle.

"Our philosopher had spent years in endeavouring to obviate this grand inconvenience; and though he had undoubtedly made greater progress than anybody else, it was not till now that he had believed himself completely master of the great secret.

"His first attempt to carry it into execution was to be in the leg he was about to make for Mynheer Von Wodenblock.

"It was on the evening of the sixth day from that to which I have already alluded that, with this magic leg, carefully packed up, the acute artisan again made his appearance before the expectant and impatient Wodenblock.

"There was a proud twinkle in Turningvort's grey eye, which seemed to indicate that he valued even the thousand guineas, which he intended for Blanche's marriage portion, less than the celebrity—the glory—the immortality, of which he was at length so sure.

"He untied his precious bundle, and spent some hours in displaying and explaining to the delighted burgher the number of additions he had made to the internal machinery, and the purpose which each was intended to serve.

"The evening wore away in these discussions concerning wheels within wheels, and springs acting upon springs.

"When it was time to retire to rest, both were equally satisfied of the perfection of the work; and, at his employer's earnest request, the artist consented to remain where he was for the night, in order that, early next morning, he might fit on the limb, and see how it performed its duty.

"Early next morning all the necessary arrangements were completed, and Mynheer Von Wodenblock walked forth to the street in ecstacy, blessing the inventive powers of one who was able to make so excellent a hand of his leg.

"It seemed, indeed, to act to admiration. In the merchant's mode of walking, there was no stiffness, no effort, no constraint.

"All the joints performed their office without the aid of either bone or muscle.

"Nobody, not even a connoisseur in lameness, would have suspected there was anything uncommon, any great collection of accurately-adjusted clock-work under the full, well-slashed pantaloons of the substantial-looking Dutchman.

"Had it not been for a slight tremulous motion occasioned by the rapid whirling of about twenty small wheels in the interior, and a constant clicking, like that of a watch, though somewhat louder, he would even himself have forgotten that he was not, in all respects, as he used to be, before he lifted his right foot to bestow a parting benediction on his poor relation.

"He walked along in the renovated buoyancy of his spirits, till he came in sight of the Stadt-house; and just at the foot of the flight of steps that lead up to the principal door, he saw his old friend Mynheer Vanoutern waiting to receive him.

"He quickened his pace, and both mutually held out their hands to each other by way of congratulation, before they were near enough to be clasped in a friendly embrace.

"At last the merchant reached the spot where Vanoutern stood; but what was that worthy man's astonishment to see him, though he still held out his hand, pass quickly by, without stopping, even for a moment, to say, 'How d'ye do?'

"But this seeming want of politeness arose from no fault of our hero.

"His own astonishment was a thousand times greater, when he found that he had no power whatever to determine either when, where, or how his leg was to move.

"So long as his own wishes happened to coincide with the manner in which the machinery seemed destined to operate, all had gone on smoothly; and he had mistaken his own tacit compliance with its independent and self-acting powers for a command over it, which he now found he did not possess.

"It had been his most anxious desire to stop to speak with Mynheer Vanoutern; but his leg moved on, and he found himself under the necessity of following it.

"Many an attempt did he make to slacken his pace, but every attempt was in vain.

"He caught hold of the rails, walls, and houses, but his leg tugged so violently, that he was afraid of dislocating his arms, and was obliged to go on.

"He began to get seriously uneasy as to the consequences of this most unexpected turn which matters had taken; and his only hope was, that the amazing and unknown powers which the complicated construction of his leg seemed to possess, would speedily exhaust themselves.

"Of this, however, he could as yet discover no symptoms.

"He happened to be going in the direction of the Leyden Canal; and when he arrived in sight of Mynheer Turningvort's house, he called loudly on the artificer to come to his assistance.

"The artificer looked out from his window with a face of wonder.

"'Villain!' cried Wodenblock, 'come out to me this instant!

"'You have made me a leg with a vengeance! It won't stand still for a moment! I have been walking straight forward ever since I left my own house, and, unless you stop me yourself, Heaven only knows how much farther I may walk. Don't stand gaping there, but come out and relieve me, or I shall be out of sight, and you will not be able to overtake me.'

"The mechanician grew very pale—he was evidently not prepared for this new difficulty.

"He lost not a moment, however, in following the merchant, to do what he could towards extricating him from so awkward a predicament.

"The merchant, or rather the merchant's leg, was walking very quick, and Turningvort, being an elderly man, found it no easy matter to make up to him.

"He did so at last, nevertheless, and, catching him in his arms, lifted him entirely from the ground.

"But the stratagem (if so it may be called) did not succeed, for the innate, propelling motion of the leg hurried him on along with his burden at the same rate as before.

"He set him, therefore, down again, and, stooping, pressed violently on one of the springs that protruded a little behind.

" In an instant the unhappy Mynheer Von Wodenblock was off like an arrow, calling out, in the most piteous accents—

" ' I am lost! I am lost! I am possessed by a devil in the shape of a cork leg! Stop me! for Heaven's sake, stop me! I am breathless—I am fainting! Will nobody shatter my leg to pieces? Turningvort! Turningvort! you have murdered me!'

" The artist, perplexed and confounded, was hardly in a situation more to be envied.

" Scarcely knowing what he did, he fell upon his knees, clasped his hands, and with strained and staring eyeball, looked after the richest merchant in Rotterdam. running with the speed of an enraged buffalo, away along the canal towards Leyden, and bellowing for help as loudly as his exhaustion would permit.

" Leyden is more than twenty miles from Rotterdam, but the sun had not yet set, when the Misses Backsneider, who were sitting at their parlour window, immediately opposite the Golden Lion, drinking tea, and nodding to their friends as they passed, saw some one coming at furious speed along the street.

" His face was pale as ashes, and he gasped fearfully for breath; but, without turning either to the right or left, he hurried by at the same rapid rate, and was out of sight almost before they had time to exclaim, ' Good gracious! was not that Mynheer von Wodenblock, the rich merchant of Rotterdam?'

" Next day was Sunday.

" The inhabitants of Haarlem were all going to church, in their best attire, to say their prayers, and hear their great organ, when a being rushed across the market-place, like an animated corpse— white, blue, cold, and speechless, his eyes fixed, his lips livid, his teeth set, and his hands clenched.

" Everyone cleared a way for it in silent horror; and there was not a person in Haarlem who did not believe it a dead body endowed with the power of motion.

" On it went through village and town towards the great wilds and forests of Germany.

" Weeks, months, years passed on, but at intervals the horrible shape was seen, and still continues to be seen, in various parts of the north of Europe.

" The clothes, however, which he who was once Mynheer Von Wodenblock used to wear have all mouldered away.

" The flesh, too, has fallen from his bones, and he is now a skeleton—a skeleton in all but the cork leg, which still, in its original rotundity and size, continues attached to the spectral form, a *perpetuum mobile*, dragging the wearied bones for ever and for ever over the earth.

" May all good saints protect us from broken legs, and may there never again appear a mechanician like Turningvort, to supply us with cork substitutes of so awful and mysterious a power!"

Corporal Sims's story received as hearty shouts of praise as did Webster's, although not in so loud a tone, and all relapsed into comparative silence again.

Hour after hour they waited in anxious expectation, but the sounds for which they so anxiously listened did not greet their ears.

The colonel began to despair.

The hopes he had so fondly cherished would not be realised.

He shivered in the cold night air, and almost wished he had never ventured from home.

" Oh, Lord! Oh, Lord!" he muttered, as his teeth chattered to the tune of the man that could not get warm. " I shall suffer for all this. I shall have my old friend the rheumatics visit me again."

In this mournful strain he continued, much to the amusement of the soldiers, until the fog gradually began to disperse, when one of the soldiers, who had been placed on the watch, announced that the splash of oars could be distinctly heard on the beach.

The soldiers were now ordered to be in readiness, and the colonel made his way to the beach.

The splash of oars was now audible to all, and at length the dim outlines of a boat appeared through the haze.

" Let them land!' cried the colonel, " before we attack them."

The men in the boat soon sprang to the beach and made their way towards the gully, and two other boats in rapid succession grounded on the beach.

The soldiers were ordered to prevent those who had first landed from leaving the gully, hoping that those who had arrived last were the boat or boats belonging to the schooner.

The soldiers marched forward, blocking up the passage, and called upon the men to surrender.

A burst of defiant laughter answered them, and they rushed upon the soldiers, who fired a volley amongst them, but only a few were wounded; for they were accustomed to this kind of work, and sank down on one knee, thus allowing the bullets to pass over their heads.

Before the soldiers could reload their carbines, they fell upon them, and attacked them furiously.

Owing to the narrowness of the place, the soldiers were unable to use their swords with the effect they could have done had they been mounted and had more room.

The sailors, who had closed with them, warded off their blows with the various weapons with which they had armed themselves.

Some had by this time taken possession of the soldiers' carbines, and were using them as clubs, dealing fearful blows on all sides.

Those who had first seized the oars were doing great execution among the soldiers by raising them in the air and allowing them to fall heavily upon their heads, knocking many of them down.

So fearful was the attack of the sailors, and so numerous were they, that the soldiers could not stand long against them, and gradually gave way.

Meanwhile, the colonel having caught sight of the lieutenant, and believing him to be no other than Tom Drake, made his way through the mass to where he was, laying about him in right good earnest with one of the carbines.

Before the lieutenant could defend himself the sword of the colonel had descended upon his skull, and he fell, badly wounded.

At the same instant one of the sailors, failing in warding off the blow from the head of his commander, aimed a tremendous blow at the head of the colonel, felling him to the ground.

Most of the soldiers, who were half numbed through having been exposed to the cold night air and the dampness of the fog, had fallen under the fierce and powerful blows of their sturdy foes.

Those who had as yet remained unhurt, or only slightly bruised, made for the thicket, and tried to mount their horses.

They were prevented by the sailors, who followed so closely upon them that they were instantly surrounded and overpowered.

" Just sheer on one side, Master Squeaker," said a tall, athletic seaman, to a middy, as he thrust him gently on one side, thereby causing him to fall over on his beam-ends, " this is my man, and now I want's to ax him what little game he calls this, and by whose 'thority he dare molist the crew of one of his Majesty's vessels o' war."

" Thank you for your kindness, Mr. Tarbucket,

said the middy, rather indignantly, as he once more assumed his perpendicular. "you must recollect, sir, that you are not training a gun; and I would also have you remember that I am one of the officers in his Majesty's navy."

"I'm glad to hear it, for if all was officers in his Majesty's navy, why we should soon feel the claws of the French eagle in our backs."

"Yes, and if you don't mind your eye," retorted the middy, "you will soon feel the claws of the British lion in your back."

"Oh, that's how the wind blows, is it Master Squeaker; well just don't let me catch you asleep again in your watch on deck, that's all, or else you'll find a change of wind in the morning."

"Now then," cried the sailor, turning to the soldier he had addressed before, "I've put a question to you, now I wants the answer; now then, out with it, none of your tack and half tack, and dodging Pompey round the long boat, let's have it, like Paddy's hurricane, upright and down-straight."

The soldier looked perplexed, and his eye wandered from that of the sailor to the cudgel he flourished so menacingly over his head.

But it puzzled him to tell which was the hardest, the stern features of the sailor or the stout piece of oak he held in his hand.

"Now, my hearty, pull yourself together, an' overhaul your log, 'cos if you don t I shall have to introduce my lawyer to you, and if he gives you one of his letters you'll find it devilish hard to read."

"Why," said the soldier, not wishing to put the sailor to further trouble, "ain't you buccaneers?"

"What buccaneers?" interrogated the sailor, rubbing his eyes as if it would assist his hearing.

"Tom Drake's crew."

"Oh! is that the cove you're arter?" cried the sailor. "Why, hang his ugly carcase, he's got aboard our snug little craft somehow, and sent all hands of us adrift in his own boats."

"You don't say so?" said the soldier, in surprise.

"I do, though," rejoined the sailor, "and if you don't believe me, call me a liar, and I'll knock them blessed daylights out for you."

Both parties soon found out, to their sorrow, that they had been too hasty, for if they had only held their temper a few moments at the onset, they might have saved many broken heads, and several lives; three of the soldiers had been killed in the melee, and four of the sailors.

Now, it was no use regretting.

The only thing they could do was to see to the wounded.

A couple of ambulance waggons had been sent for during the course of the night by the colonel, who had determined to send his share of the booty up to his own house for safety.

They now came in very handy to convey the wounded soldiers and sailors up to the quarters.

The colonel and the lieutenant, who had been singled out from the rest, were the first placed in the waggon.

Having placed the rest of the wounded in the waggon, those of the soldiers who had not been wounded mounted their horses.

The sailors made a rush to gain possession of the other horses.

And five or six mounted the horses, as though they were camels.

The colonel, who had only been stunned by the blow, now returned slowly to consciousness.

The first words he spoke he inquired if they had secured the buccaneer chief; the soldier, to pacify him, answered in the affirmative.

Next morning, the colonel was informed of the great error they had fallen into, and, likewise, that he had almost killed a lieutenant in the navy through his impetuosity.

Greatly was he mortified on learning the sad condition of the lieutenant, but greater was his mortification on finding that after he had been out all night in expectation of capturing the said Captain Tom Drake, he was as far off as ever.

When at length, after a lapse of time, the lieutenant was enabled to tell him how he had been served, the truth flashed across the colonel's mind.

"Confound the fellow!" he muttered between his clenched teeth, "it was no other than himself that brought me the note, and I gave him a guinea to drink my health."

The lieutenant, though still suffering great pain, could not help smiling, as the colonel recounted the daring exploits of the buccaneer.

"But there, the fellow can disguise himself so completely that the devil himself would not know him," said the colonel. "In fact, when I saw you I felt certain it was him, and that he had assumed that disguise to deceive me."

"Then I have to thank him for this ugly blow, for I have received it in his stead?"

"And I am very sorry for it. But never mind; I hope I shall meet him again face to face some day."

"I don't," said the lieutenant, smiling. "I'll take good care that I don't send him to you again; once is quite enough for me."

CHAPTER CXLV.

THE COASTGUARDSMEN MAKE AN ATTEMPT AT CAPTURE.

MEANWHILE the smugglers and buccaneers were engaged in deadly conflict with the coastguards.

Scarcely had the boats touched the beach, when a host of the land sharks poured down upon the sands.

Waving their cutlasses in one hand, and grasping a pistol in the other.

Then commenced a fearful and bloody onslaught.

The smugglers fighting for free trade and liberty.

The coastguardsmen for duty, honour, and prize money.

The buccaneers fought bravely against the overwhelming numbers of their enemies.

The coastguards dashed at them like hungry wolves, and threatened to crush them beneath their overwhelming force.

Now did the brave buccaneers miss their gallant captain.

Oftimes did they fancy they heard his manly voice urging them on above the din of strife.

Their implacable foes fought savagely to wrest the boats from them in the hope of sharing a glorious prize, for they were loaded with merchandise of the costliest description.

The gallant little band fought desperately hand to hand, determined to yield to none but death.

The clash of arms and report of the pistols, mingled with the cries and groans of the fallen, told how well they fought for their liberty.

It was evident the bold buccaneers must soon give way to their more formidable opponents.

Although there were already more of the coastguardsmen laying amongst the slain, yet still their numbers greatly exceeded that of the boats' crews.

Again the buccaneers rally, and, with a shout of victory or death, boldly dash on their foes.

Their bright blades glitter in the feeble rays of the moon, as they cut right and left among their foes, dealing death and destruction around.

Now they are surrounded by the coastguards, who are cutting them down with their blood-stained weapons, as though they were trimming a hedge.

Now, again, the little band appears to gather fresh strength, and carve their way through their desperate foes, who surround them on all sides like

Then the coastguardsmen beat them back, and drive them from the boats, and they are fast losing ground.

Still, unconquered and unsubdued, they fight gallantly, shoulder to shoulder.

But it is evident they cannot hold out much longer, for there is scarcely one of the brave and daring little band but what is bleeding from wounds.

Still their bold and resolute spirit will not allow them to yield.

They would sooner be hacked into a thousand pieces than be beaten.

Weaker and weaker their little force is growing, whilst the coastguardsmen almost number them three to one.

Just as they are about to fall beneath the remorseless fury of their opponents, a shout is heard.

It is Ben Barnacle leading a body of stout fellows to the assistance of the buccaneers.

"Lay on, my gallant sea dogs!" roared Ben. "Lay on, for the love of your gallant captain!"

"Follow them up!" he cried, as the coastguardsmen began to retreat.

"Show them no mercy, give them no quarter, let them have cause to remember this night's work!"

It was plainly seen that the coastguardsmen were fast giving way, whilst the buccaneers followed closely upon them; and soon the battle was decided in favour of the buccaneers, who, securing their prisoners, and attending their wounded, repaired to their stronghold.

CHAPTER CXLVI.

THE PIRATE BARQUE IN DANGER.

AFTER the battle between the "Will-o'-the-Wisp" and the pirate, Red Ralph discovered that the gallant ship had received more damage than was at first thought; he took command, and set the men to work.

On sounding the pumps it was found the vessel was making much water, and a party was told off to work the pumps, and drive plugs into the shot holes.

Emily and her mother had suffered unknown torments during the encounter, and as they sat trembling with fear, and startled at the loud roar of the cannons, they prayed that the battle would speedily terminate.

But when they saw the men enter the cabin with the almost lifeless body of Bentley, a feeling of pity crept over them, and for a moment they forgot the terrible agony they had endured, and the fearful position in which they were placed, and bound up his wounds with as much care and attention as though he were a protector instead of a destroyer of their happiness.

Long and anxiously did they watch for returning animation, and when he once more opened his bloodshot eyes, they could not suppress a shudder, although they knew they had little to hope for at his hands.

"Water! water!" gasped the wounded man.

Emily held a glass of water to his parched lips, which he emptied with avidity, and sank back exhausted on his pillow.

"Mother," said Emily, "I think he is better now. A little sleep will do you much good. You had better retire, and seek that repose which you so much need, whilst I watch his couch and administer to his wants."

"I am weary and wretched, dear child," said Mrs. Johnson, "yet I cannot leave your side. You will again be molested if I do."

"Fear not, mother," said Emily, drawing a dagger from her bosom; "I have this to protect me."

Then, in a firm tone, added, "I am not what I was. They have aroused a fierce spirit within me, and the once gentle girl has become a tigress."

"Do not rely too much on your strength, dear Emily; what would it be compared to that of one of these inhuman monsters? Would to Heaven we were once more freed from this horrid captivity."

"Do not weep, mother, a still small voice whispers sweetly in my ear that we shall once more see our native land, and gladden the hearts of our anxious friends who have watched so long for our return."

"Nay, daughter, do not buoy yourself up with false hopes, you know not the intentions of these barbarous wretches, or you would not dream of escape."

"I cannot help it, mother, but go, repose yourself; I have nothing to fear from the captain, he will be many days before he rises from his bed."

Mrs. Johnson at length yielded to the importunities of her daughter, and retired to the state-room, leaving Emily to watch John Bentley who was suffering greatly from his wounds.

Emily, left to herself, sat wrapped in the most gloomy thoughts until, worn out, she sank into a profound slumber.

Scarcely had she done so, when Bentley rose up in his bed, cold drops of perspiration stood out upon his brow, and he gazed vacantly around.

"Thank Heaven he has gone," he said, in a hoarse voice, "would it were for ever! The horrid vision will haunt me to the death."

Then, striking his heated brow, he fell back with a groan.

Meanwhile, Red Ralph used his utmost endeavours to render the ship seaworthy, but, in spite of all his skill, the water still gained on the pumps, and the men showed evident signs of dissatisfaction.

This did not escape Red Ralph's notice, and he gave orders to turn the ship's head in the direction of the nearest land, then descended to the cabin to attend to Bentley.

As he entered his eye wandered from the haggard features of Bentley, to the pale, and care-worn face of Emily, as she lay in a sleep.

A smile of satisfaction played on his lips, and taking the fair girl in his arms, raised her from the seat.

With a piercing scream Emily awoke, and tried to free herself from his embrace, but her efforts were too feeble, and the wrecker, with a grin, only tightened his grasp upon the struggling victim.

"Curse you," cried Bentley, hoarsely, as he rose in his bed, "release the girl, or I will fire!"

Red Ralph turned sharply and appeared astonished at beholding the captain sitting upright, grasping a pistol; then, holding the fair form of Emily before him, he said, tauntingly—

"Fire, if you have the courage!"

Scarcely had he uttered these words when he was seized from behind by the hair, and dragged to the floor.

It was Mrs. Johnson, who aroused by the cry of terror, had come to her daughter's assistance; thus aided, Emily tore herself from his arms, and drawing the dagger from her breast, held it menacingly over the prostrate wrecker.

"Hold your hand," cried the trembling wretch, "I did not mean to harm you!"

"Liar," Emily replied, "I am aware of your intentions; each word you utter is a lie, and you had best keep silent, or you may tempt me to bury this weapon in your blackened heart."

Red Ralph quailed beneath her steady gaze, and Emily and her mother retired to the state-room, carefully bolting the door after them.

"A thousand curses on you, Bentley," he said,

GUARDED BY HIS FAITHFUL FOLLOWERS, CAPTAIN TOM BORE THE SENSELESS GIRL UP THE STEPS.

bitterly; "why do you interfere between me and that gal?"

Bentley's eye flashed fiercely, then, in a hollow voice, he answered—

"I have again seen that terrible vision," Red Ralph.

"What vision do you mean? Surely your brain is wandering—you have taken leave of your senses —you are an idiot?"

"No, I have not; I saw him again for the second time, his mutilated arms outstretched towards me."

"Who do you mean?"

"Mr. Thompson, the captain of the 'Lovely Sue,' and he swears he will not leave me until I land the females in England."

"What nonsense you talk. Did you not settle him?"

"I did."

"Then how can he he harm you?"

"How does he harm me? Does he not haunt me, night and day? and even now I can feel his death grasp on my leg!"

"And you are foolish enough to think of taking these girls to England?"

"I am."

"Then allow me to tell you, that it never can be, not while Red Ralph, the Wrecker, lives."

Bentley's eye lit with a glow, and he gazed upon the Wrecker with a look of fiendish hatred, then, in a husky tone, said—

45

"Fool, dare you dispute my word? I say they must go to England, and what I say is law."

"Oh, very well then, you had better take them; but first you must get another ship, for this one won't float much longer."

"How's that?" inquired Bentley, alarmed.

"Why, she's riddled with shot, and I have turned her head to the African coast, but I fear we shall never reach it."

The gruff voice of the boatswain, "Land, oh!" down the companion, abruptly terminated their conversation.

Red Ralph hurried to the deck, and scanned the bold headland with his glass, then turning to the crew, he said—

"Keep the pumps going, lads; in a few hours, with this breeze, we shall be in smooth water."

"Aye, aye," replied the men, as they set to with fresh vigour, and struggled to keep the gallant barque afloat until she should reach the shore.

Red Ralph nervously paced the deck as they gradually neared the land, and towards the afternoon they entered a small cove that formed a natural harbour, whilst the lofty cliffs that reared their heads on either hand sheltered any vessel that might be laying there from the heavy gales that swept the coast at certain periods.

Having rounded a reef of rocks, they ran the vessel on the sandy beach, and secured her with an anchor, that she might not go off with the succeeding tide.

Then they set to work in good earnest, preparing for the coming night.

Several of the men were dispatched in search of wood and water, whilst others hastily rigged tents with the sails, and conveyed the females and the wounded pirates on shore.

Having gathered plenty of the wood, they lit a large fire around their encampment, to keep them from the attacks of the wild beasts, whose feet-marks they could see in the sand, and whose roars, as the shades of evening closed around, echoed through the forest.

It was no pleasing sound to those who had been told off to keep watch, and the roars of the fierce animals caused them to look strangely at each other.

"Hallo, shipmates," cried a tar, "are you afraid of these customers?"

"Not exactly, you know," answered one of the men, who at the same time could not keep from trembling, "but they're not very pleasant, 'specially in the dark."

A low growl, at no great distance, caused them to start, and on looking in the direction of the sound, they were dismayed at beholding a pair of fierce and glittering eyes glaring upon them.

Each moment they appeared nearer, and at length they could discern the shaggy mane of a large lion, who greeted them with a tremendous roar.

The tar eyed him narrowly, and, on seeing him approach a part where the fire burnt less fiercely, he advanced to meet him.

Whether it was his bravery, or whether it was because the fire was between them, I will not say, but certain it was, he went boldly up to where the lion stood, and faced him fearlessly.

Snatching a burning brand from the fire, he hurled it forcibly in the face of the monster who did not appear to think it a friendly act, and, shaking his head violently, to dislodge the glowing embers from his shaggy mane, gave a terrible roar, and was about to spring upon his adversary.

The tar, quick as thought, drew a pistol from his belt, and fired, but missed his mark, and the bullet passed over the head of the enraged beast.

For a moment the lion stood amazed, the force of the ball had partly stunned him, but quickly recovering, he prepared for another spring, and the daring tar, anticipating his intention, thrust another flaming brand in his face.

Howling with pain, the furious monster turned, and rushed madly from the spot, and was soon lost in the dark recesses of the forest.

"That's the way to settle them customers," said the bold tar, hitching up his trousers, and giving his quid an extra roll.

Then, turning to a shipmate, who was shivering and quivering as though about to fall into a thousand pieces, he said—

"What's the matter with you, you long streak of lightning? There's no fear of his tackling you; he wants summut more than skin and bones. If he has anyone it'll be old Jock. He's as fat as a porpoise, and if he get's hold of him, maybe he let us go a day or two longer."

The person to whom he alluded was a short, thick-set Scotchman, who did not seem to appreciate the flattery, and cast a look of envy on his long companion, and, by his gestures, implied he would willingly exchange his round, plump form, for the tall, thin, marrowless bones of the other.

The tar, by this action, had raised himself so high in the estimation of his shipmates, that he might now have told them the biggest lie with impunity, for they had sufficient proofs of his bravery and courage.

"That's the way to settle them covies," he said, with an air of importance. "I wish I had all the lions now that I have killed in my time."

"Have you ever killed any?" inquired Jock, in surprise.

"Ah, my boy, many a thousand!"

"What did you do with 'em?"

"Oh, only skinned 'em!"

"They'd pay well, then, if you came to kill many?"

"Yes; I made two or three fortins, but I spent the lot in rum. Now, I'll tell you how I tricked one of the old chiefs that belonged to the part where our ship at that time lay, taking in a cargo of furs."

Every eye was fixed intently upon him, as he seated himself upon the stump of an old tree, and commenced his yarn in an impressive tone.

"Well, the place was swarming with wild hanimals, and the only hanimals that was at all scarce was tigers; for they'd killed 'em all but two, that was one hemale and one shemale.

"Well, you must know that the chief wanted to get up a fresh stock, and had the only two that was left put ashore on a small island, to see if they would breed.

"So he gives strict orders that none of his tribe was to kill 'em, and if they did, they were to suffer a 'nominous death.

"Well, you see as how I was bent on having a lark, so I gets the darkie cook to go with me to this said island, and leaves him to mind the boat.

"Well, I hunts about a long time afore I drops across either of the tigers; but at last I twigs one on 'em, safely moored under a large tree, and fast asleep.

"Well, I walks rounds him two or three times to make sure he was asleep, and then I takes my handkerchief off my neck, and ties it over his head, so that, if he should happen to wake, he wouldn't know me.

"Well, shipmates, I takes out my knife, and begins to skin him."

"What, alive?" inquired several voices, in surprise.

"In course. I wasn't allowed to kill him, or else I should have been tortured to death.

"Well, as I was saying, I begins to skin him, an

had got about half way, when he gave a loud snore' and I was afraid I'd disturbed him, so I waits a few moments till he was sound ag'in.

"At last I got him all skinned but his head, and now I was tickled—how was I to manage?

"I was afraid to take the handkerchief off his head

"'But,' says I to myself, 'old boy, don't let this lick you; don't let this little job pawl your capstan.

"'This ain't half so bad as when you skinned the rattlesnake, and when he darted at you, you held the skin up afore him, and he went into it again the wrong way, and had the rattle at his head instead of his tail.'"

"Yer doesn't mean to say you did it, did yer?" inquired Jock, in alarm.

"Well, I did it, mates, or I'm a liar!

"He was so tarnation wild at having such a noise so close to his ears, and he got so tarnation savage that he went mad."

At this juncture, his listeners, who had been gazing in open-mouthed wonder at the serious face of the narrator who had never allowed a muscle of his features to move, showed evident signs of disbelief, and made gestures to each other, which implied that a choking sensation had crept over them.

The tar's words had stuck in their throats and they were unable to swallow them comfortably.

But he could allow them to express their opinions, and he continued—

"Well you see, shipmates, I was determined to have that 'ere hanimal's skin at all hazards.

"That is, providing I didn't have to kill him.

"So I takes the handkerchief off his head, and, in a very few seconds, I had pealed him like a horange, barring his nose.

"And just as I was finishing, although I took a great deal of care, somehow or other the knife slipped and just entered a little way into the flesh.

"With a growl he sprang to his feet and glared round furiously.

"His eyes flashed fire, the hot breath poured out of his distended nostrils, and he lashed his tail with fury.

"'It's up with you now,' Sam, thought I, 'you're safe to get collared.'

"But still, I couldn't help smiling, as I peeped out at him, for I had wrapped myself up in his skin, and laid down along side of him, and he thought, of course, that I was his mate.

"Well, he looks around three or four times, and then looks towards where I lay, and I began to fancy he smelt a rat somewhere; but I laid quiet.

"So he gives another orful growl, a cold shudder just as though he had turned out of a warm bed on a cold frosty morning.

"My heart began to beat like a dead lamb's tail, as the saying is, and I expected every minute to be skull-dragged out of my nest.

"He wagged his tail faster.

"And my heart beat faster.

"At last he gives a tarnation lash with his tail, for a fly had rested on his hinder part, and he turned his head to see where it had bit him, then he trembled violently, and I thought he was going to fall down.

"'You are in a nice fix, Sam,' thought I, for I could see by his looks that he'd found out someone had stole his clothes.

"But I never stirred a hinch.

"At last he turns agen to look at me, and I trembles all over like a leaf.

"At length he stops short, as though a thought had suddenly struck him, and he gives an ugly look at me, as much as to say—

"'I don't like to wake you up, old gal, till I find my clothes!'

"For he didn't like the thought of her seeing him naked.

"And with that he suddenly darts off into the bushes, and I made all sail for the boat."

"And what did you do with the skin?" inquired Jock.

"I takes it up to the chief, and offers to sell it to him."

"And didn't he find you out?"

"Yes; but don't you see, when we searched for the tigers, we found 'em both alive.

"My one was peeled, and I thought they would all have busted with larfing when they see him scudding under bare poles."

The yarn being finished they all indulged in hearty roars of laughter.

But a piercing scream, appalling in its effect, suddenly terminated their mirth.

For several seconds they stood as though rooted to the spot, when another scream of terror, more fearful than the first, burst on their terrified ears, and awoke them from the stupor that had momentarily fallen upon them.

Sam was the first to recover speech.

"What can it be, shipmates?" he inquired, in a tone of alarm. "Surely that cussed lion has not burst into the tents, and we have been yarning here taking no heed!"

"Quick, lads!" he cried, "see to your pistols!"

Before he could utter another word, the scream was repeated, although it was fainter this time, as though it were some one in their last moments, and about to resign their parting breath.

"By heavens! it's in the ladies tent. Oh, Heaven! we are too late! Ere this he has torn them limb from limb, and even now he is feasting on their flesh!

"Come on, lads!" he cried to the trembling men.

Then the men, collecting their scattered senses, rushed to the tent, fearing to gaze upon some horrible scene.

CHAPTER CXLVII.

THE LAST OF RED RALPH.

As the lovely Emily and her aged mother lay the tent, although greatly fatigued with the hardships they had endured, they could not sleep.

At length the aged dame dozed off into a troubled sleep, but the affrighted maiden never once closed her eyes.

As she lay, she heard the sailors conversing, and her young heart beat violently when she heard the report of the pistol Sam had fired at the enraged lion.

Trembling with fear she lay, starting at every sound, whilst her excited imagination pictured horrible scenes.

The blaze of the watch-fire reflected through that portion of the tent opposite to where she lay, whilst the other part of the tent was darkened, as it was composed of several thicknesses of canvas, alike to exclude the heavy night dews and for fear it might rain.

She tried vainly to close her weary eyes in sleep; horrible thoughts filled her mind, and still more horrible visions flitted before her eyes.

As she lay trembling with fear, she fancied she heard a slight rustling in the canvas, and rose up in bed and looked around, but nothing could she see; all was still as death.

Then again she lay down, but not to sleep.

A strange foreboding of some coming evil had taken possession of her mind, and she lay listening in breathless anxiety.

Again the same rustling sound caused her to rise in a sitting posture.

This time it was not fancy, for she saw, by the feeble light, the dark figure of a man creeping stealthily towards her.

Her first impulse was to awaken her mother, which she did, by shaking her violently; the next instant a rude hand grasped her slender wrist, and dragged her forcibly from the bed.

Her mother, who had awakened, flew to her assistance, and seized her assailant, but her futile efforts were of no avail.

With one blow the savage wretch felled her, and vainly strived to stifle the cries of his victim.

Emily struggled frantically to free herself from her brutal assailant, and uttered a piercing scream, which aroused the pirates.

When they entered the tent, hard-hearted and callous as they were, they could not suppress their indignation when they saw the brutal wretch struggling with the fair and helpless maiden.

The guilty wretch cowered beneath the stern gaze of the men, and relaxed his hold of the terrified girl, who flew to where her mother lay, stunned by the powerful blow of the wrecker.

"Fools!" cried Red Ralph, who was maddened at being interrupted; "what do you want? Who summoned you hither? Why have you thus intruded on the privacy of this tent?"

"Ask yourself that question," said Sam, indignantly, "and then tell me what business you have in here?"

Red Ralph glared furiously at the men, and bit his lips with rage, as he gazed upon their stern features and knitted brows, and said—

"Go to your duty, and for the future wait till you are called. Go! leave the tent," he thundered, as the men hesitated to obey.

"They can do as they like," said Sam. "But I don't leave you alone with that gal."

"Nor I," said Jock; "I arn't going to top my boom till you does, Master Ralph. You've no more right here than we has."

"Curse you for a set of fools! Go to your duty."

"I arn't going away till you does," said Jack.

"Then take that!" cried Red Ralph, savagely, as he drew a pistol from his belt, and presented it at the speaker.

He drew the trigger, and the ball entered the man's shoulder.

Being a powerful man, he soon recovered from the shock, and after the sharp pain had subsided a little, he flew at the wrecker with the fury of a tiger, and before he could defend himself, he grasped his throat in his sinewy hand, and buried his fingers in his flesh.

Jock's bloodshot eyes glared furiously at his assailant, who struggled fiercely to release himself from his convulsive grasp.

The face of the wrecker was black and swollen, and his eyes almost started from their sockets, whilst the veins of his forehead were swollen almost to bursting.

The blood flowed freely from the wound in Jock's shoulder, and it was apparent that he could not much longer keep up the fierce struggle.

Both men were rapidly growing weaker.

They staggered, and fell heavily to the ground.

Sam, who had stood anxiously watching the fierce struggle, flew to the assitance of the wounded man; aided by several of his mates—for, by this this time, they had all mustered upon the scene—and having, by dint of great exertion, unclasped the fingers of the wounded man from the throat of Red Ralph, they proceeded to bind up the wound, and staunch the blood that was gushing out.

"Dead!" muttered Jack, as he gazed upon the blackened features of the wrecker, not one line of the hard lineaments of which had relaxed in their severe expression. "He'll trouble no one anymore, the black-hearted villain."

"I hope he is dead, cuss him!" said Sam, who was binding up the wound. "He's given you a nasty pill. Lift up the gal," he said, addressing those around him. "Don't stand there like a lot of stuffed porpoises. I think she's fainted."

"All right, old fellow; don't lose your temper," said one of the men, as he raised the girl in his arms. "I'm darned if they aren't as dead as mutton, both on 'em."

"She ain't dead," replied Sam, angrily. "She's on'y in a faint. Get a bucket of water."

"The old 'un's got a nasty poke," said Skysail Jack, as he raised Mrs. Johnson from the ground. "I don't think she'll weather Cape Death this bout."

"Nor I, either, Jack; but she shan't ground on the Shoal of Despair for the want of water to float her over, if I knows on it."

So saying, he poured half the contents of the bucket over the head and shoulders of the insensible woman, and emptied the rest over her daughter.

"What the devil are you up to, you lubberly crew?" cried Sam. "Do you want to swamp 'em? Ain't you never seen a woman faint afore?"

"No. I aren't had much 'sperience in these matters; but, strike me lucky, the sight of that gal makes my mouth water!"

"It oughter make your eyes water," retorted Sam, "if you had any feelin'."

"I don't know what you call feelin'. Do you want me to shed a few crocodile tears? But see, here comes the cap'n, staggering along like a ship in a heavy sea way."

All eyes were now turned towards the opening in the tent, through which John Bentley had thrust his brawny shoulders.

"What's the meaning of all this?" he interrogated, fiercely, as his eye wandered from one to the other. "Where is Red Ralph?"

"There he lays, cap'n, as quiet as a lamb," said the man, holding the empty bucket in his hand.

"And he's nearly killed the women."

A sarcastic smile passed over the dark features of Bentley.

One glance was sufficient to convince him of the truth of the man's assertions.

"Curse the fellow!" he said, taking a step forward, and placing his hand upon the girl's breast.

"Has she slipped her wind, cap'n?" enquired Sam, eagerly.

"Not a bit of it; she has only fainted. Convey her to the bed gently," he said, as the rough sailors lifted her anything but tenderly. "Beware that you hurt her not, I would not have her harmed."

He watched the men eagerly as they conveyed their lovely burden to the bed, and then he turned his fierce eyes to where the wrecker lay.

A demoniac smile overspread his swarty visage, and his scornful lips quivered as he gazed upon the rigid features of his companion.

"Cuse the fellow!" he muttered, "how I hated him! Yet through his endeavours to satisfy his fierce passions he has rendered me good service. He has done that which I had not the courage to do. He has rid me of the old woman, and now I have the daughter to myself. I shall soon tame her, and bend her to my will."

He was aroused from his soliloquy by the voice of one of the men, inquiring what they had best do with the body of the wrecker.

"What shall you do with him?" cried Bentley

emphatically. "Throw his vile carcase into the wood! He has disobeyed my order; he has dared to mock the Tiger of the Sea, now let the tiger of the forest rend his false heart from his breast, and tear his flesh into a thousand pieces with its fangs!"

The men trembled as they listened to the fearful words of the pirate, and quailed beneath his withering glance.

"You have heard my orders," he said, with an impatient gesture. "Now obey them, and take this old withered hag with you."

"Are you sure she's dead, cap'n?" inquired one of the men, who, in spite of the rude and boisterous life he was leading, could not help shuddering as he raised the inanimate form of the old woman.

And a pang of remorse shot through his heart, for it reminded him that he once had a mother of his own.

"Dead, of course she's dead—have I not said so? Take her away directly, and remember I am captain, and as such will be obeyed. So be careful how you you play with the Tiger of the Sea."

He glared furiously at the man as he spoke, and grasped the butt of a pistol.

The movement was observed by the man, who well knew the vindictive spirit of the captain.

Raising the woman in his arms, he bore her from the tent without deigning to offer a reply.

The watch-fire burnt fiercely around their encampment, and the pirates, although fearing the threats of their captain, feared still more the fury of the raging elements.

It would be madness to attempt to pass the fiery barrier, and so intense was the heat that they could not with safety approach within two or three yards of the blazing circle within which they were enclosed.

"I arn't going to get roasted, Sam, if you are," said the man who held the woman in his brawny arms; "I can stand water, but I'm hanged if I can stand this blistering fire!"

"Same here, shipmate; I wouldn't go through that blaze for the best cap'n that trod a ship's plank. Let's lay our lump of salt junk down here, mate."

"Aye, aye, so say I," replied the man, as he dropped the legs of the wrecker on a mound behind one of the tents.

The other men soon followed their example, and laid the woman gently on the ground beside the wrecker, and covered them over with a piece of sail cloth.

Having rid themselves of their unpleasant burdens, they re-entered the tent where the captain stood, feasting his gloating eyes on the fair and lovely form of the unfortunate girl as she lay upon the rude couch.

The poor girl, whose senses had been shattered by the fearful excitement, now gave signs of recovery.

A deep sigh escaped her breast, and a shudder pervaded her frame.

"She's coming round, cap'n," said one of the men.

"So much the better," rejoined Bentley. "The sooner she gets over this the sooner she'll have expended all her grief, and be able to listen to reason."

"Reason!" muttered Sam, shrugging his shoulders.

"Or persuasion, or something else," said the pirate, turning fiercely towards Sam, who had spoken rather louder than he intended.

"What do you intend to do with her, cap'n?" inquired Sam, who appeared to possess the most feeling of any of the men assembled, for a look of pity stole over his features as he gazed upon the pale face of the poor young girl.

"Do with her?" iterated the captain, fiercely. "Who gave you leave to question me? Am I not allowed to do as I think proper with her? She is my lawful prize."

Sam fixed his steady eye upon the captain, and was about to reply, when, with another sigh, the suffering girl opened her eyes, and glanced upon the faces of those around in a bewildered manner.

Bentley advanced, and placed his brawny arm under her head.

For some moments the eyes of Emily remained fixed on his own; then, with a convulsive movement of the lips, she shrieked—

"Murderer! murderer!"

At the sound of those fearful words, as they echoed through the tent, the pirate's face paled.

But the momentary qualm passed away, and he was again the callous brutal captain of a horde of pirates.

A scornful smile curled his lip, and he gazed defiantly upon his helpless victim.

For a moment she met his gaze, and returned his scornful glance.

What a world of meaning did that single glance convey.

It was but for an instant only that she lay powerless as a child.

With the fury of a tigress she tore herself from his loathsome embrace, and, bounding up, stood before her cruel oppressor.

Her lustrous eyes flashed with an unearthly fire.

Her thin lips were compressed.

Her slender form drawn up to its full height.

For a few moments she gazed upon the swarthy visage of the pirate, who had leapt to his feet, then her lips parted, and she hissed rather than spoke the word—

"Murderer!"

Beneath the glance that accompanied the expression, the eye of Bentley dropped.

Raising her arm, and pointing her finger towards him, she exclaimed in a calm but subdued tone—

"Murderer, where is my mother?"

"Peace!" yelled the pirate, starting forward, and grasping the wrist of her extended arm. "Beware, or my dirk shall drink your heart's blood, and your fate shall be the same as that of him who defied me!"

"Assassin!" she replied, "think of the work of your bloody hands; what have you done? Did you not put the crew of the "Lady Sue" to a bloody and merciless death, and now you have slain my only friend, my mother?"

"Bah!" said the pirate tauntingly, "what harm have I done to you? I love you too well to harm you."

"Love me?" reiterated the girl, fiercely. "Love me—a ruffian, the murderer of my aged mother, the destroyer of my happiness—love me! Does not the word love stick in your throat? Does it not choke you?"

Bentley clenched his teeth firmly together, and seemed about to spring upon her, but the glance of that suffering, half-maddened girl held him rooted, as it were, to the spot.

"Fiend—"

"Silence!" he exclaimed, as he bit his lips with passion, and grasped the handle of his dirk. "Another word, and—"

"Strike, assassin, if you have the courage!" exclaimed the young girl, interrupting him, and at the same time presenting her snowy breast to his upraised arm.

"Another word, and I bury it in your heart!" he hissed, between his clenched teeth.

"Strike!" she answered, in desperate coolness, "and tarnish the bright blade with the blood of her whose mother you have murdered!"

Bentley's arm fell powerless by his side.

"Beware how you taunt one who never forgets nor forgives!" exclaimed the pirate, nervously clutching the handle of his dirk.

The woman's lips curled contemptuously.

"I scorn your threats and defy your power!"

"By heavens! this is too much!" he cried, hoarsely, as he rushed upon the defenceless girl, brandishing the glittering weapon.

Bentley thought better of his rashness, and hastily retired, leaving two of the crew to guard her tent, with strict orders not to allow her to leave, or any one to visit her.

Then the guilty wretch sought his own bed, but not to sleep.

His conscience would not let him, and he tossed restlessly on his pillow.

Strange figures seemed to flit about the room, which assumed the forms and features of his victims.

There was a mother with a baby at her breast, pointing her fingers menacingly at him.

By her side a hoary-headed old man, whose silver locks were dabbled with gore.

Then came the captain of the "Lady Sue," stretching his mangled arms towards him, the purple stream oozing from his maimed wrists, and he could see the pale lips move as though he were cursing his murderer.

Large drops of perspiration rolled from Bentley's brow, and his wild, glaring eyes, were fixed on the ghastly figure.

He tried to turn his head, but could not, and he could plainly feel the hands clutching his legs.

Suddenly the figure disappeared, and in its place he saw Emily and her mother.

From the brow of Mrs. Johnson the life stream was flowing, and raising her hand she pointed to the entrance to the tent.

Instinctively he turned his eyes in that direction, and there, to his horror, he beheld the wrecker, his features black and swollen, and his dilating eyes glaring furiously upon him.

For several moments the pirate lay transfixed with horror, then, springing from his bed, he rushed towards the wrecker.

But he was gone, and he was alone.

Nothing was to be seen, save the figures of the pirates, as their forms were reflected through the canvas by the glare of the watch-fire.

In a frenzy of rage he rushed to Emily's tent, and approaching the man who kept sentry on that side nearest his own, cried, furiously—

"What mean you by this? How dare you disobey my order? I told you not to allow that woman to leave the tent."

"She has not," replied the man, "neither has any one entered."

"Liar!" thundered Bently. "Will you tell me this to my teeth?"

Then, drawing his sword, he added—

"I will run you through, if you repeat that lie."

"'Tis no lie!" replied the man, boldly.

Bentley's eye flashed furiously, and he said, bitterly—

"'Tis the last lie you shall utter to me. I have seen her."

Then, grasping his sword more tightly, he thrust it through the man's body.

The man fell to the earth with a deep groan.

The group of pirates who had been disturbed by the voice of the captain, on seeing their comrade fall, uttered a cry of terror.

"What's the matter with you?" growled Bentley. "Do you wish to be served the same? For if you do, I can soon oblige you."

"Not so soon as you think," muttered Sam; then,

casting an inquiring glance at the terrified crew, said—

"Are you going to submit to this tyranny? If you are men, you will assist me to clap a stopper on this fellow's jaw."

"Right you are, Sam," answered one of the men, drawing his cutlass, "we must put a stop to this bloody work, or we shall be ground down like slaves."

Bentley's brow lowered as he gazed at his crew, for though he could not hear their conversation, he could see by their movements that they did not approve of his rash act.

Turning the body over with his foot to ascertain if it were dead, he drew his pistols, and, calling the men by name, ordered them to take away the body.

"Do it yourself," replied the foremost of the two. "Finish the work you have begun!"

"Do as I have ordered you!" cried the pirate, imperatively, "or dread the consequences."

"I will not."

"Take that, then," hissed Bentley, levelling his pistol. "I will be obeyed, if I have to shoot half of you."

Bentley fired the pistol, and the man fell, but scarcely had he done so when Sam, exasperated at the captain's cruelty, struck him on the head with a bough he held in his hand, and felled him senseless to the earth.

Then, turning to his comrades, he said—

"Now, lads, is our time for liberty. We can repair the brig and leave this coast, and rid ourselves of these tyrants, they are only fit company for the wild beasts of the forest."

"Bravo, Sam!" cried the pirates; "we will stick together, but first we will secure Bentley, and see after the girl."

"Very well, clap a rope round him," said Sam, then entering Emily's tent.

She was seated on the side of the bed, wringing her hands, and the tears coursed down her pale cheeks; but when Sam entered, she sprang to her feet, and said, in a tone of sadness—

"What brings you here? Am I to be insulted by all the crew?"

Sam's heart was softened by the tones in which she spoke these words, and smoothing the locks from his brow, said—

"I have not come to insult you, miss, I have come to see to your comfort. You are no longer a prisoner; you can walk where you please. In a few days, I hope, we shall be able to leave this place."

"If so, where is my poor mother?" said Emily, sobbing. "Tell me where they have lain her?"

Sam knew not how to answer this question, and Emily, seeing him hesitate, said—

"I am afraid you are playing me false. Tell me, where is my mother? You know, for you assisted to carry her out."

"I did," replied Sam, "and yet I cannot answer your question."

"Then you threw her out to be devoured by wild beasts?"

"No; she was laid behind the tent, but where she is now I cannot say, for she disappeared suddenly."

Emily buried her face in her hands, and wept bitterly.

"Mother, mother!" she sobbed. "I have lost my only friend."

"Cheer up, miss, you must not give way like that," said the rough sailor. "I will protect you from further insult, and restore you to your friends as soon as possible."

Emily could not speak, her heart was almost broken, she feared she would never more behold her

she loved so dear, and raising her lily hand, she made a sign that she wished to be alone.

Sam understood her meaning, and, with a sigh, he left the tent.

On reaching the beach, he found the crew already at work repairing the vessel, plugging the shot holes, and putting in new planks where required.

Day after day they continued their labour, until she was once more ready for sea, and the next morning they agreed to launch her.

This accomplished, they conveyed the stores on board, when the alarm was raised that Bentley, who had hitherto been bound hand and foot, was nowhere to be found.

This news caused great consternation amongst the pirates; they looked at each other distrustfully, and they thought it expedient to leave the island immediately.

The last boat-load had been pulled to the ship, and some of the crew were engaged in weighing the anchor, when the figure of a man crawled from beneath the canvas and sails that were in the boat, and, crawling through an open port, disappeared.

The sails were set, boats lashed, and the "Will-o'-the-Wisp" once more ploughed the blue waters.

How joyfully did the pirates watch the receding shore, and with a favouring wind, the noble vessel bore away to the northward.

But their joy was doomed to be of short duration, for as they were about to elect Sam captain, John Bentley suddenly appeared amongst them, and, with lowering brows, said fiercely—

"You might have consulted me first, do you not know that I am captain?"

So astonished were they at his mysterious appearance that they could not answer, and with an air of apparent coolness he drew a brace of pistols from the belt of one of the men, and placed them in his own, then possessing himself of another pair in the same way, and holding them in a threatening attitude, shouted—

"Who amongst you dare dispute my right?"

"I do," cried Sam.

Bentley glared furiously at the speaker, and was about to fire at him, but Sam, anticipating his design, seized the barrel of the pistol, and closing with his adversary, a fierce struggle ensued.

Bentley, though a powerful fellow, found it no easy task to overcome Sam, and, fearing he would get the better of him, drew a knife and plunged it in the breast of the honest tar.

Enraged at this, Sam's messmates fell upon the pirate, and would have slain him, had not some of the crew interceded for him, then, springing back, he cried—

"Stand off, you mutinising set, or I will run you up to the yardarm. Have you thus forgotten yourselves? I would have you know that I am still captain, and those who do not obey me shall die."

CHAPTER CXLVIII.

THE INTERESTS OF SCIENCE.—DOCTOR SHRIKE WANTS ANOTHER HEAD.

To explain more fully the thread of this story, we must convey the reader back to chapter cxix., on the eventful night of Tom Drake's glorious but terrible battle with Admiral Ellis's fleet.

The next morning dawned brightly over the waters.

A dazzling sun lit up the scene of the previous night's conflict, and the black and battered hulls of a few of Admiral Ellis's late fleet could be seen rising out of the placid ocean.

Some of the vessels had sunk, others had been burnt to the water's edge, telling of the terrible effects of Dutch Paul's mysterious fire.

As for the ship of the gallant Tom Drake, his crew had been at work all night. All night hammers rang and lights burned on the deck of the "Will-o'-the-Wisp," until morning saw it look quite taut and respectable, with few of the marks of the previous night's encounter.

Dutch Paul and Iron-Arm were not idle, either.

Their ships had been sadly damaged, and it would require at least a week to repair them.

Thus matters stood on the morning after the great battle.

The dead had been buried in the depths of the sea, and the wounded on Captain Tom's ship were left to the tender mercies of Doctor Shrike and his able assistant, Jacop.

Dr. Shrike, of course, was in his glory, as he had turned his attention, in a scientific point of view, to the collection of the gory trophies of the preceding night's battle.

Twenty-nine heads, dripping with gore, the faces of which bore the most unmistakable signs of a premature and horrible death, were piled one upon the other in the cockpit.

Twenty-nine heads!

The doctor thought the even number was there —just thirty.

Had he dreamt it, or had he been duped?

"That rascal, Jacop, is at the bottom of it all," he said, as he began surveying his ghastly treasures. "I'll teach him not to play any tricks upon me. Jacop—Jacop, I say. Come here, you ugly rascal!"

At first the vampire's assistant did not answer.

"Jacop, come here, I say!" bellowed Doctor Shrike, stamping his foot on the boards in fury.

A smothered sound came from the darkness.

It sounded as if some one was choking.

"By all that's blue," cried the doctor, "if the fellow is not eating again! I hope he may choke. He! he! Ho! ho! What a beautiful subject he would make!"

Jacop, coming forward, with his mouth crammed full of salt pork, and being somewhat frightened of his master, retreated again.

"Come back, you rascal, come back!" shrieked the vampire, "come back, this minute, or I'll kill you, you scoundrel!"

Jacop was terribly alarmed.

He saw that old Shrike carried one of his formidable surgical instruments in his hand, which he flourished in a manner that was enough to frighten any man with Jacop's nerves.

"Are you coming, you unhung villain?" cried Shrike, advancing a step or two with his dangerous weapon, and brandishing it above his head. "I'll soon let you know whether you are going to obey me or not, you rascal."

"I—I ain't a-disobeying you," stuttered Jacop, getting as far as he could out of the reach of his irate master.

"What do you mean?" thundered the vampire, still advancing, to the mortal terror of his subordinate. "Do you see this, Jacop?—ha! ha! ha! One cut, and your head will make the even number."

"Murder! murder!" shrieked Jacop. "You don't mean to assassinate me, doctor?"

"In the interests of science, you scoundrel—in the interests of science. Dare you have an objection to be one among the honoured thirty?"

Jacop had a decided objection.

He backed and backed until he fell over a bucket of water that was behind him.

"Help—murder!" roared Jacop.

"Shout away, you raw-boned effigy," grinned the doctor. "Ha! ha! ha! ha! You are not going to cheat me out of my head. Come, you idle villain, do you object to the operation? It can be done in a twinkling—he! he! he!"

The tortures that Jacop endured in those few short moments were enough to last a man of his stamp for a lifetime.

The vampire rushed forward and caught him by the leg.

Jacop yelled and struck out furiously.

"No good, Jacob; no good," said Doctor Shrike, exultantly. "It is useless for you to struggle. If you kick any more, I'll have to amputate a leg. Ho! ho! ho! Ha! ha! ha! Think what a splendid subject you'll make, Jacop! I'll bleach your skull nice and white, Jacop—nice and white, my man, so that you'll be a credit to your old master wherever you are seen."

But the vampire's assistant could not see the fun of it.

It harrowed his feelings to that degree that he kicked, lunged, and swore in a most terrific manner, until the doctor was obliged to let his leg go.

"So you object, do you, Jacop?" gasped Doctor Shrike, breathing very hard from his recent exertion. "Who ever heard of such ingratitude? He! he! he! You'll come to some bad end yet, Jacop. I know you'll be hanged, Jacop—I am sure of it!"

While this was going on, the irrepressible Jerry Mizzen, and his chum, Bob Hauler, were close observers.

Jerry had to stuff a handkerchief in his mouth to keep himself from laughing.

"I say, Bob!" said Jerry; "what do you think of that? A pretty go in, isn't it?"

"I should think it was," said Bob.

"I wonder does the varmint mean doing him any harm?" said Jerry.

"I don't know. It looks jolly like it. He's a head short, so he says, and he wants one more to make it up. Listen! there they go—at it again!"

"Jacop, you are a very ungrateful fellow, Jacop," said Doctor Shrike, "and I don't mind telling you so, Jacop. Here I come forward in the interests of science, and ask you politely for your head, and you have the audacity and ingratitude to refuse me. But I'll have your head yet, Jacop—I'll have your head yet, my man, and if I don't give it a bleaching, may I be—well, no matter. I'll remember you, Jacop—I'll remember your ingratitude yet, Jacop!"

Jacop kept very quiet, in fact, was too terrified to answer him.

"Why don't you speak, you long-legged anatomy?" shrieked the vampire. "Have you lost the use of your tongue, you scoundrel? Here, let me stick a few inches of this dissecting-knife into you. Perhaps that will wake you up! Ha! ha! ha! he! he! he! Only two inches—only two inches, Jacop!"

The doctor's laugh was truly awful.

Jacop now leaped to his feet, as if he had been charged by a legion of adders.

"You have a decided objection to the knife, have you, Jacop? Ha! ha! I thought I'd wake you up a little! Come, now, tell me where you have hidden that thirtieth head. If you don't, I'll take yours off to make up the number."

"You—you had only twenty-nine, Doctor Shrike," stammered Jacop.

"You lying rascal, you! Do you want me to give you a prod of this knife?"

And the doctor lunged out with his dissecting knife.

Jacop gave a terrified cry, and leaped back at least two paces.

"Oh, don't, don't! What have I done that you should treat me as if I was a dead 'un?" groaned Jacop.

"I'll treat you presently, you lying scoundrel?" cried the vampire, preparing to give another lunge.

"Oh, don't!" cried Jacop, seeing that his master was coming rather too close to him to be pleasant. "Keep that dreadful knife away from me."

"You are afraid of it, Jacop, my man. Ha! ha! ha! I see you are afraid of it!"

"Enough to make anyone afraid, I should think," said Jacop, ruefully. "I wish you would go away, Doctor Shrike. You'll make me so nervous just now that I'll be unfit for anything."

"Where's the other head, then, you rascal?" thundered Doctor Shrike, forcing his assistant into the corner.

"There was only twenty-nine, sir," trembled Jacop, retreating as the vampire advanced.

"Twenty-nine, you cold-blooded villain! Twenty-nine, did you say? Dare you tell me that again to my teeth? Ha! ha! he! he! I'll soon settle you, you scoundrel!"

And Doctor Shrike looked as if he meant it as he yelled out the words.

"Help! murder!" shrieked Jacop. "Put that knife away, or else I'll die of fright!"

"Where's the other head, then, you thief? Where is it? Tell me, or I'll bleed you to death!"

"Oh! oh!" moaned Jacop, "there was only twenty-nine. I am sure of it."

"Twenty-nine heads," muttered the vampire; "can it be possible that I have made a mistake? No, I'll not believe it. The villain is working against the interests of science. What a glorious opportunity there would be of study if the other head was there! Humph! I can see no other way out of my difficulty but by having his."

The vampire had some evil grudge against his assistant, so he spoke aloud, that he might frighten the poor fellow out of his wits.

Doctor Shrike tried the keen edge of his knife, and looked at Jacop with a satisfied grin.

"It will do nicely," he muttered, aloud. "One strong sweep, and his head will come off as cleverly as if he had been guillotined. Ha! ha! ha! he! he! he! What a nice bleached skull it will make!"

Jerry Mizzen and Bob Hauler were looking on, convulsed with laughter.

They were so placed above the doctor and his assistant that they could not very well be seen unless the vampire happened to look up, and scan before him very narrowly.

"They are a couple of curious 'uns, ain't they, Bob?"

"I should think so," said Bob, shaking his head.

"I should like Captain Tom to catch 'em as they stand now," said Jerry.

"What good would that do?" asked Bob.

"Why, he'd put 'em both in irons, and that would do both of 'em good, I reckon."

"I don't think it would make 'em a whit better," replied Bob; "besides, Captain Tom would only laugh at them."

"Don't you make a mistake in that," said Jerry, shaking his head. "Captain Tom wouldn't put up with that darned vampire having all them heads, I am sartin. I tell you what, Bob—if you like, we'll have a little fun."

Bob Hauler was always in for a spree of any kind, so he requested Jerry Mizzen to go on.

"There's young Martin," said Jerry, calling the attention of Bob at the same time to a middy who stood turning over the pages of a book some few paces away from them.

"Well, yes—I see him—what of him?" said Bob, eagerly.

"Well, then, I mean sending him arter Cap'n Tom," said Jerry, with a smile on his humorous face. "Have you a bucket of water close handy, Bob?"

"Shiver my timbers! I don't know what you

are driving at—don't speak in riddles, Jerry—come to the p'int at once."

Bob Hauler was sorely puzzled, and he looked like it.

"A bucket of water for the varmints down below," said Jerry in explanation; "they want a bath, Bob."

"Very likely," said Bob, grinning.

"And as for the vampire," went on Jerry, "he wants his head deweloping."

"In the worst possible way," seconded Bob.

"Well, I am going to dewelop it for him, and that will help science, too, as he calls it. Il'll put bumps on his head what was never on afore. Ain't they beauties, Bob?"

Jerry Mizzen held up four or five tremendously large potatoes.

"Is that the way you mean altering the shape of his head?" asked Bob, repressing a desire to laugh.

"Sart'inly it is—a very good way to do it, too, I can tell you. Ask to feel his head after it's done, Bob, and you'll agree with me."

"He! he! he!"

"Ho! ho! ho!"

"Well, I never heard of such a way of deweloping bumps afore, Jerry."

"I don't think you did," said Jerry, with a self-satisfied giggle; "I don't think you did, Bob. It's a new wrinkle in the science, it is."

"What about young Mister Martin?" asked Bob, recollecting that the middy had some errand to go on.

"Send him off at once for Cap'n Tom," said Jerry.

Bob Hauler walked over softly to the middy, and after a few whispered words, the young man disappeared in the direction of Captain Tom's cabin.

"That'll do, nicely," said Jerry, rubbing his hands in ecstacy. "What are the varmints doing now, Bob?"

"The vampire has Jacob by the nose."

"Werry good sitivation—splendid sitivation, Bob. I suppose he's laying down the law to him?"

"It looks like it. But you can't hear the varmint from here. He seems hissing his words out like some ugly sarpint or another."

"And Jacop?"

"Is a-trembling as if he had a touch of the quiversem-quaverems."

All this time Jerry Mizzen was getting his bucket of water ready to his hand, and selecting the biggest potatoes he could find from a little bag at his feet.

"Which do you intend giving them first?" asked Bob, "the water or the taters?"

"I think the water first," replied Jerry, "seeing as how they must be werry uncomfortably dry arter their warm discussion. You are the best shot, Bob—take the taters."

Bob Hauler took half a dozen of the potatoes, which he piled very artistically on his left arm, the said left arm being held close into his body.

"Any of these for Jacop?" asked Bob, laconically. "Does his bumps want deweloping?"

"I think they do," said Jerry, recollecting the service the vampire's assistant intended rendering him the night before. "I think they do, in the worst kind o' way."

"In the interests o' science?" said Bob.

"Jest so. Now let the ugly warmints have it. I think we have waited long enough for 'em!"

"Besides, Captain Tom'll be here in a minute."

A glance sufficed to show that Doctor Shrike still held his subordinate by the nose.

This was exactly what Bob and Jerry wanted.

It would give their aim greater accuracy.

"Now, Jerry, let 'em have it," whispered Bob Hauler.

Slosh! went the bucket of water right over the vampire and his assistant.

They were nearly smothered.

Not a cry could they utter for some moments.

"Now then for the taters, Bob," said Jerry, highly delighted at the drenching he had given them; "and mind that none of 'em misses their mark. Raise bumps on their heads as big as turnips. Go it, old son!"

Bob Hauler needed no such instructions.

He detested the vampire and hated his assistant.

The first potato he threw caught Doctor Shrike on that part of the cranium termed by phrenologists the bump of venerations from which it bounded like a cricket ball.

"Oh, murder!—thieves!—fire!" yelled the For the moment he must have imagined that he was on dry land.

The second potato caught Jacob on the nose and sent the blood flying in all directions.

But Bob Hauler was not done yet with them.

Every one of his potatoes told with effect.

And soon there was such a yelling below tha. was never heard before or after.

Captain Tom Drake arrived just in time to see his worthy doctor bellowing and dancing up and down the place like a madman.

And Jacob was even worse than his master.

CHAPTER CXLIX.

THE BRITISH CAPTAINS.—AN OFFICER OF LIBERTY. —"MAN OVERBOARD!"

LATER on in the day Captain Tom and some of his principal officers were on deck.

The "Will-o'-the-Wisp" looked nearly as taut and trim as ever.

Captain Tom's lieutenants' were discussing a very grave question indeed.

What to do with the officers they had captured in the last night's conflict was a puzzling question to them.

Many and diverse were the opinions of the officers for awhile.

"Run them into the first port," suggested Iron-Arm, after they had conversed on the subject for a long time.

"And release them on their parole," added Harry Vere.

"I, for one, wouldn't give much for their parole," grumbled Ben Barnacle.

"Especially if they are any way like the little admiral," echoed another.

"I hope Captain Tom doesn't intend releasing him."

The last officer who spoke was a fledgling—one of the late middies who called out for the execution of Admiral Ellis on a former occasion.

"If he does, we'll have a nice hornet's nest about our ears," said another. "That cursed admiral is a perfect demon, and he thirsts for our gallant leader's life still."

Such indeed was the case.

The ferocious little admiral was as unforgiving and as revengeful as ever.

Captain Tom Drake was in a dilemma.

He had promised not to stop the execution of Ellis if they caught him again.

How could he break his word—although he was still averse to shedding his blood?

Admiral Ellis was a very brave man, and for this Captain Tom could not help feeling some pity as well as admiration for him.

Besides for the commodore, his brother, he had the highest respect, and would, if he could, avoid giving him pain in any way.

"Come, come, gentlemen, let us not be ungenerous," said Captain Tom, after profoundly thinking the matter over. "We have gained the victory against terrible odds, therefore let us try and be magnanimous to a fallen enemy."

Our hero was always gallant and generous to a fault.

Many a time had he spared the man who had struck at his life.

And more than ever had he cause now to be thankful that he and his brave companions, had emerged from the frightful peril they had so lately been in.

"I know my brave comrades will not be so ungenerous," said Captain Tom Drake, "as to deprive these gallant men of their liberty. You must remember, gentlemen, that they were fighting under the King's commission—that they were in a manner forced, by their honour, to attack and seek our destruction."

As Captain Tom spoke, a murmur passed from lip to lip.

"What about that little serpent of an admiral?" cried one. "Did his honour force him to seek our destruction?"

"He alone excepted," rejoined Captain Tom, with difficulty repressing the inward rage that was boiling up in his breast.

He was not the man to be dictated to by anyone.

And his officers knew that well.

But they had not yet got over the effects of their previous night's engagement, nor the loss of the brave men who had fallen in that useless struggle.

For all this Admiral Ellis was to blame, and he was denounced by most of the officers in terms of bitterness and hate.

Captain Tom saw that he was standing on a mine, and very wisely closed the discussion by sending for the captive captains—Teddington, Hanwell, and Morris.

The British naval commanders were marched to the quarter-deck of the "Will-o'-the-Wisp" in charge of Captain Tom's middies.

Two were wounded—Hanwell and Morris.

The whole were uncovered.

Their position was very trying and humiliating, and they felt it most acutely.

With bowed heads and dejected looks, they stood before Captain Tom Drake.

Captain Tom advanced from the midst of his officers, and addressed them.

"Gentlemen, yesterday you came to seek my life, and those of my brave followers. Is it not so?"

"It is," they replied, straightening up, while some of the fire of the proverbial British lion blazed from their eyes.

"And to-day you are captives and helpless," said Captain Tom, with more sympathy than triumph in his tone.

"Such is the fortune of war," rejoined Hanwell, sadly.

"Gentlemen, believe me, that I don't gloat over your downfall," said Captain Tom, "and, to show you that I can be a generous enemy to a brave foe, I am willing to give you your liberty."

The word "liberty" seemed to astound them.

They looked up into Captain Tom's face almost doubtfully.

But in that honest, open countenance, they saw the word "deliverance" as plainly as if it had been written there.

For an instant a look of joy flushed the faces of the sturdy veterans.

Could they believe their ears? This noble boy, that Admiral Ellis taught them to believe a very fiend incarnate, and whom they had hunted for months and months, through mere wanton excitement, could they believe, indeed, that he was magnanimous enough to offer them life and liberty."

But the terms—the terms. Perhaps they could not accept the offer?

Once more the gallant captains bowed their heads.

Captain Tom, with a glance of his keen eye, read what was passing in their minds.

He smiled, and simply went on—

"You are told," said he, "that I am a pirate—that I have no regard for human life—that I have wantonly shed blood like water. To all these charges I give the most emphatic denial. I have been driven to the life that I lead—it was not at the time my own choosing—but now I would not give it up, nor surrender one right of it, for all the wealth of the Indies. Take this answer back to your master, King George—whom God bless and prosper—and make known to the world that Captain Tom Drake is not so bad as he's painted."

A ringing cheer followed these words, for many, of the men and mids of the "Will-o'-the-Wisp" had collected on the quarter-deck.

By the time the repeated cheering had subsided, Captain Tom Drake had arranged for the removal of the English captains to better quarters.

Meanwhile, he sent Ben Barnacle below to obtain their paroles, which, after a brief consultation with each other they reluctantly handed to him.

The specified terms of the paroles in question were that they should not engage in any expedition against Captain Tom Drake for one year.

This matter settled, Ben Barnacle ascended to the quarter-deck, and mingled with his brother officers.

This was fated to be a busy day for Captain Tom.

Iron-Arm had a great deal to communicate to him, and consult him about.

One of his vessels was rendered, by the late desperate engagement, useless.

In fact, it was rapidly sinking, and his crew had been all the day busily removing whatever was valuable from its hold.

"So it's Reuben Harpy's vessel," said Tom, a gleam of triumph lighting up his fine eyes. "So, so, my bitterest and most cowardly enemy is at last in my power!"

"And a most ruffianly crew the villain had."

"I cannot doubt it," replied Captain Tom, "and as cowardly as they were ruffianly, I'll be bound."

"You would say so, if you had only seen them fight," rejoined Iron-Arm.

"But you were speaking of Israel Shawm," interrupted our hero. "What of the treacherous hound?"

Captain Tom detested the very name of this miserable Jew ever since his base betrayal of him to the authorities.

"He is dead," repeated Iron-Arm.

"Dead!" exclaimed our hero, evidently taken by surprise. "You don't mean to say that the hoary villian Shawm is dead!"

"I do, indeed—he was murdered."

"By whom?"

"One of Reuben Harpy's men, an Englishman named Rufus; a stout villain, but as unscrupulous as he is daring. I dreamt the other night that the fellow was hanging from one of our yardarms, and I have no doubt he will be before long."

Captain Tom seemed to be buried in profound thought. Something had struck his mind, no doubt, and he appeared to be reflecting deeply.

Iron-Arm looked on without interrupting him.

He knew his youthful leader's moods too well, and waited in patience for him to speak again.

Captain Tom's next inquiry was for Hester Shawm, the beautiful Jewess.

He was glad to hear that she had been rescued from the brute force and hateful passions of Reuben Harpy.

While Iron-Arm was giving a rather graphic and, indeed, somewhat amusing account of his engagement with the Brazilian privateer, there was a commotion heard, and, simultaneously, a Babel of voices swept over the calm sea rung upon the ears of those standing upon the deck of the "Will-o'-the-Wisp."

"Man overboard!" came the cry, in loud, piercing accents.

Iron-Arm and Captain Tom rushed to the ship's side.

The cry—"Man overboard!" rang loudly over the rippleless waters.

"It comes from your craft!" cried Captain Tom.

Iron-Arm's vessel was a hundred and fifty yards at least from the "Will-o'-the-Wisp."

They bent their eyes searchingly in that direction, and saw the deck crowded with seamen, who were looking over the side and watching the water.

The pinnace was lowered from the ship's side with the rapidity of thought, and four men leaped into it.

Another moment they were pulling stoutly for an object which appeared above the surface of the water.

It was the head and face of a man, horribly distorted, and covered with brine.

A quick, sudden gleam of sunshine fell upon the face.

Captain Tom uttered a great cry as he recognised it.

"By Heaven, it is Reuben Harpy!" he exclaimed.

CHAPTER CXL.
REUBEN HARPY TURNS UP.

"Save him! save him!" roared Captain Tom. "Don't let the scoundrel drown at any risk!"

The men replied by a responsive shout, and pulled boldly towards the struggling man.

Before they reached the spot Reuben Harpy sank once more.

"He's gone, by Heaven, this time!" exclaimed Iron-Arm, excitedly.

Indeed he was intensely interested in the rescue of the villain Harpy, and watched every movement of the men in the pinnace with the greatest anxiety.

Captain Tom, at this moment, was in no enviable mood.

He thought that his wicked cousin had escaped him—indeed, escaped his vengeance.

"He is gone at last," said Tom.

But he was mistaken for once. Reuben Harpy came to the surface again, half-dead, and almost insensible.

The instant he appeared above the surface, one of the men in the pinnace caught him by the hair, and, with the assistance of a comrade, the rascal was hauled "high and dry," out of the water.

He was dripping like a drowned rat, and was as powerless as an infant.

Without any ceremony the men threw lines at the bottom of the boat, and began pulling leisurely back to the vessel.

About this time Doctor Shrike, and his vampire assistant appeared on the deck of the "Will-o'-the-Wisp."

Jacop's nose was swelled to twice its original size, and his master's bald pate had a marvellous development of various bumps from the size of a pigeon's egg upwards.

Jerry Mizzen and Bob Hauler were also on deck,

but they, for the best reasons in the world, kept at a respectable distance from Doctor Shrike, who had a strong suspicion that the aforesaid Jerry and Bob had some hand in the said development.

Bob and Jerry looked very grave—especially on the right side of their faces, which happened to be turned to the vampire and his subordinate.

"Jacop," said Doctor Shrike, "who is that subject that they have just pulled out of the water?"

Jacop, of course, did not know, and answered accordingly.

"I would give a good deal for that subject, Jacop," said Doctor Shrike again, in a most oily and smooth tone of voice. "Do you think he is dead, Jacop?"

Of course, as the doctor came on deck, the same time as Jacop, Jacop knew as little of the matter as the doctor.

But he answered in an haphazard sort of way, for he saw the vampire leering very slyly at him, and thinking that he might be meditating some such sport as the prod of a dissecting knife, or the the amputation of a leg, he considered that it might be just as well, under the peculiar circumstances, to be on good terms with him.

Besides the, doctor was rather short-sighted, and that was one in his favour.

"I think he is dead, sir," replied Jacop, retreating a little, thinking it best to be on the safe side, should the violence of Doctor Shrike's feelings overcome him.

"Do you think so truly, Jacop? Do you really think so?" said Shrike, with a chuckle, that sounded most marvellosly like that of an evil spirit. "I think so myself, Jacop. He! he! he! I really think so myself, Jacop."

"Yes, sir," stammered, Jacop, keeping a wary eye on the vampire's movements.

"You'll go over to the ship at once, Jacop, and bring that subject directly to me."

Jacop, taking a good start, mumbled, "He'd be blowed if he would!" and his kind, but eccentric master, ended by chasing him down the hatchway with a belaying-pin.

But Doctor Shrike was not to escape thus.

Jerry Mizzen lay in wait for him on one side, and Bob Hauler on the other.

Jerry had a swab behind his back.

Of course he wore a most innocent and harmless expression.

In fact he wasn't looking at the vampire at all.

Bob Hauler was gazing dreamily in another direction—also with a wet dishcloth behind his back, which, for the slight consideration of a "chaw" of tobacco, he borrowed from the cook.

Doctor Shrike saw the two men.

But he did not dream that they were lying in wait for him.

Jerry's face wore a look that would have beguiled a saint.

And, of course, Bob Hauler's mind was actuated by such noble sentiments, that practical joking was out of the question.

The vampire, with his belaying pin, passed down the hatch.

He had not got down many steps, when he suddenly felt something soft and moist come slap on his head—indeed, on the very tender place where Bob had inflicted sundry bumps some time before with the potatoes.

Of course, Doctor Shrike was surprised, as well he might be.

He was about to turn to ascertain the cause of this moist and peculiar substance, when the not over-clean swab, came flap in his face.

This completed his discomfiture.

He fell down the remainder of the steps, and began howling. "Murder!"

The men and officers, who were up to this moment looking over the ship, came hurrying to the spot.

Before they got there, however, Jerry Miszen and Bob Hauler stepped away, and, without a smile on their faces, began talking to some of their comrades.

Doctor Shrike did not appear any more that day, neither did his co-labourer, Jacop.

We are apt to think that they had enough for one day of practical joking.

Rueben Harpy, preserved from a watery grave by the men in the pinnace, was quickly carried on the deck of Iron-Arm's vessel.

The doctor was in immediate attendance upon him, and succeeded in pumping several quarts of water out of Reuben's stomach.

After this he began to come round very quickly, and soon was taken back to keep the company of his fellow-prisoner, the Rufus that we have introduced to the reader, in connection with the murder of Israel Shawm.

Let us go a little way back, to explain how this catastrophe to the cunning Reuben occurred.

Reuben Harpy, ever since Iron-Arm defeated him and captured his vessel, was kept a close prisoner with the man Rufus.

There was a small room or cabin told off for them on the lower deck.

In front of this was placed a guard, with strict orders to shoot them down should they attempt to escape.

And no sentinel was allowed to remain on this post more than two hours at a time.

This precaution was taken to prevent the prisoners from bribing them, as there were a good many rather unreliable characters on the vessel, which Iron-Arm intended getting rid of the moment he reached port.

Reuben Harpy had tried this game of bribing two or three times, but found that it failed, as the men who were guarding him up to the present were proof against being bought.

But Reuben did not despair, although he showed his weakness in various ways, much to the disgust of his fellow prisoner, Rufus, who, whatever else he might be, was at least a brave and daring fellow.

Up to the night of the fearful naval engagement, Reuben bore up very well, considering the coward heart that he possessed.

But the booming of the heavy cannon, and the lurching and bounding of the vessel whenever a broadside was fired, sent his heart quaking into his boots.

He moaned and groaned all night, to the intense disgust of his companion.

Reuben never for an instant thought that this battle was advantageous to him.

He might have taken hope from even the sentinel's words, who said that the opposing ships were part of Admiral Ellis's fleet.

But this had no consideration whatever for him.

He was thinking of his miserable life—thinking that any stray cannon ball might come crashing through the timbers of the ship, and so kill him.

How Reuben felt during the engagement is beyond pen to describe.

But when he heard, early next morning, from the sentry at the door of the cabin, that Captain Tom Drake had taken part in the great sea fight, and that he had likewise come off victorious, he was ready to drop with fear.

Anything but meet his injured cousin.

He would throw himself into the sea without a murmur if he could only escape that just vengeance which he knew would be inflicted on him.

Rufus, as we have said before, watched all these various emotions with disgust.

"Why can't ye keep a stiff upper lip?" he would say. "Shiver my timbers! if I ever saw a greater coward in my life!"

CHAPTER CLI.
THE COWARD.

"You may call me a coward," said Reuben Harpy, with a shudder, "but you don't know what this terrible Captain Tom is—he has been my curse ever since childhood—I know him too well not to fear him."

"A cousin of yours I have heard you say," returned Rufus, sneeringly. "Why, you ought to be as loving as kittens, instead of turning on each other like two poisonous serpents. I know what I should do—I should forgive. Ha! ha! ha! Forgive, until a good opportunity offered, then I should give him a dose of—no matter what. Ha! ha! ha!"

Again the English pirate's demon-like laugh rung horribly through their prison-room.

"Don't laugh again like that, Rufus," implored Reuben. "It makes me so terribly nervous. I always think when you give way to such sort of mirth that—"

"A certain place below is yawning for you," said Rufus, chuckling with fiendish delight. "I know that'll be my fate! And yours? Oh, you'll go to Heaven. Ho! ho! ho! I was always considered a prophet from the time I left the cradle."

Reuben walked up and down the narrow limits of the little cabin distractedly.

Bitterly did he regret his companionship with Rufus, the pirate.

This man seemed to mock all his woes, and rejoice in all his misfortunes.

Sometimes Reuben Harpy thought that his companion was mad.

The singularity of his conduct, especially when the hour of midnight approached, frightened him out of his wits.

The agony to be shut in with such a man was punishment enough.

So thought the cowardly captain of the privateer.

Rufus would walk up and down frequently during the night, lunging out with his clenched fists, and swearing in the most frightful manner.

This, if nothing else, was enough to drive Captain Harpy mad.

And it nearly did so.

"I had a horrible dream last night, Captain Harpy," said Rufus, with another of his horrible laughs. "I dreamt that that unbelieving dog of a Jew, Israel Shawn, came to me. Curse him! it would have been better if he had stayed away, for it shook my nerves awfully. And what do you think he came for, Captain Harpy? Guess now. Ha! ha! ha! I knew you couldn't! Well, I shall tell you. The unbelieving dog actually wanted me to put his head on again for him, and try my good cutlass once more. But I wasn't such a fool. Ho! ho! ho! Rufus knew a thing worth two of that. I told him to go about his business, and not to bother me. But the obstinate bloodsucker wouldn't move a peg, so I let out with my fist, thinking to give him one, but my hand only cleft the air. When I looked up again, Israel Shawn was gone. Curse me! Ho! ho! ho! Even the dead are afraid of Black Rufus! I wonder did the old thief come for his darling gold? You have that, captain—you have it, I say, and if he wants it, let him call on you for it!"

Another devilish laugh, that made Reuben Harpy's blood freeze in his veins.

There was a stealthy noise outside the door of the cabin.

The ex-privateer captain listened.

AND FALLING ON HER KNEES, THE YOUNG GIRL APPEALED TO HIM FOR MERCY.

"Hist!" he whispered, warningly, "some one comes!"

Rufus grew as quiet as a child, while Reuben Harpy listened with the most painful intensity.

It was only the relief of the sentinel, and all grew still again.

Reuben was glad that the other sentinel was gone —perhaps he could work his way into the good graces of the present one.

He had notes and gold concealed on him to the amount of thousands.

Surely they would not all resist a bribe?

There must be some one amongst them who prized gold higher than ————.

Such a thought entered Reuben's heart like a ray of hope.

Before, his soul had been black with despair.

He would wait and try.

He had not long to wait. however, nor had he to make the advances himself.

There came a gentle tap at the door.

The guilty Reuben's heart almost ceased to beat.

The few moments which intervened since the change of the guard seemed like so many weeks to him.

The first knock at the door of the cabin remained unanswered.

The ex-privateer felt his legs trembling under him, and all the breath in his body seemed to have left him.

He as soon recovered himself, however, and crept on tip-toe to the door.

"What do you want?" he asked, in a hoarse whisper.

"Captain Harpy," came the soft reply.

Reuben Harpy could scarcely restrain his joy.

Had this man come to effect his deliverance?

He felt that it was so.

That little ray of hope that at times lights up the most gloomy and wretched existence bounded into Reuben's heart, and gave him renewed courage, and renewed hope.

"I am Captain Harpy," replied the ex-privateer, scarcely concealing his joy. "You have come to—"

"Effect your deliverance, if possible," was the reply.

"Oh, joy!—joy!" exclaimed the cowardly wretch. "You have come to save me—thank God!"

Reuben seldom used the name of his Creator with any degree of gratefulness—only when he was in the direst trouble.

But now the exclamation came with deep gratitude from his heart.

"Sh! you mustn't speak so loud," cautioned the sentinel, "or else we'll be heard, and our plans defeated. Be cautious, and all will be well."

"Oh, thanks!—thanks!" trembled Reuben.

"Listen to me for a moment," said the guard, in a very low tone; "bend your head as near to the door as you can, so that you may hear every word. I have a good deal to tell you, but I mustn't allow any of those swabs of buccaneers to catch me, or I am afraid the negotiation would end in a short shrift and a long rope. Captain Tom's men—curse them!—are not very particular."

"No! no!" said Reuben, "they are not."

"Listen, then. I got down here by the merest accident. I made the fellow who was to take the sentinel's place drunk, and now he is in his hammock, where I expect he'll sleep for the next twelve hours, at least. As they have all been very busy on deck, no notice was taken of the change, so I passed muster and came down here."

"Who's that?" said Rufus, at this moment starting up; "you, Israel Shawm? Curse you! Why do you torment me? Captain Harpy, where are you, and who are you speaking to?"

If Black Rufus, who was now stretched on a pile of hammocks in the cabin, had taken the trouble to open his eyes, he would have seen Reuben Harpy's head leaning rather mysteriously against the door.

But as he did not take the trouble to open his eyes, Reuben answered him that he was only speaking to himself for company's sake.

This reply of Reuben's seemed perfectly satisfactory.

The burly ruffian rolled over on his right side, and seemed, as if by magic, to go off into a profound slumber.

All was still in the cabin once more.

"Whom have you there?" asked the false sentinel, in a whisper.

"Black Rufus," replied Reuben.

"Your second officer?"

"The same."

"That's awkward," said the sentinel. "There will be much more trouble to get two out than one."

"Let him stay here," rejoined Reuben, with the innate selfishness of his nature. "If we take him out it will ruin all—he's mad!"

"Mad?" exclaimed the sentinel. "Good heavens! you don't mean that?"

"He is, indeed," said Reuben. "You may take my word on it."

"I am sorry for that," said the sentinel; "he was as brave a fellow as ever trod the quarter-deck. But it can't be helped, I suppose. Besides, they'll not hang him, as they know little or nothing of him."

Reuben Harpy shuddered, and trembled like an aspen leaf.

"But I," thought the coward; "if I don't escape, they'll either hang me, or do something worse. Tom Drake will have no mercy on me. I have done him too much injury already. I wish I could strike him dead at my feet, curse him! I'll never be happy until he's dead—never!"

"Captain Harpy," whispered the sentinel, from without, "while I have yet time, I may as well give you a few items of news. You know, I suppose, that Admiral Ellis's fleet has been whipped most shamefully by Captain Tom's few paltry vessels?"

"I have heard it," groaned Reuben. "Nothing seems to withstand that terrible fellow, Captain Tom Drake."

"He seems to have both the powers of earth and heaven at his disposal. Old Ellis was terribly whipped—terribly whipped, indeed; and all his captains, but one or two, are prisoners—even to the commodore, his brother, and the admiral himself. They say that the commodore is a splendid fellow, but that the little admiral is a mean, surly hound, though as brave as death and the grave itself."

"I have no doubt," whispered Reuben, a little impatiently; "but tell me something else, and clear this terrible suspense from my mind. Is Captain Tom's fleet much damaged?"

"Not so much as was at first supposed," replied the man. "They have been very busy all the morning on the 'Will-o'-the-Wisp,' clearing away all signs of last night's fight. They must have had a great many killed and wounded on board."

"And Captain Tom himself?" asked Reuben Harpy, with a wild throbbing of the heart.

"Oh! he has escaped from the encounter as usual," replied the man, "with hardly a scratch."

"Curses—a thousand curses!" muttered Reuben. "Why was he not shot down? Will the fates be for ever on his side?"

"Were you speaking, Captain Harpy?"

"No; I was merely thinking how strange it is that that man always escapes. He seems to bear a charmed life."

Although Reuben Harpy called Captain Tom a man, in the true sense of the word he was yet a boy—a boy at least in years, with the courage of ten men in his heart, and the ability of as many more in his brain.

No man had ever done what Captain Tom had—he was truly invincible, and successful in everything.

Oh, how this dastardly cousin hated and feared him, and now more than he had ever done!

The very name of Captain Tom Drake made Reuben Harpy quake and tremble in his boots.

If he were a thousand miles away at this moment he would give away all the wealth that the world could bestow on him.

Thoughts such as these ran through Reuben Harpy's mind as he listened to the account given by the false sentinel.

"Well," he went on, "so Captain Tom has escaped without a scratch, and will be coming over to see me. I wish to avoid that meeting if possible."

He tried to speak as cool and collected as he could.

"That's what I thought," replied the sentinel; "and not only that, but I heard from the men that it was his purpose to come and visit you as soon as he gets his ship in order."

"Did you hear nothing more?" whispered Reuben, with the clammy beads of perspiration breaking out on his forehead, for he was now in a terrible fright.

"A good deal more," replied the man, "and not very favourable to you either, Captain Harpy. To tell you the plain honest truth, I shouldn't like to be in your place."

Reuben Harpy groaned.

"But never despair," said the sentinel, "there's a possibility of your getting away yet."

"How—how?" asked Reuben, eagerly, for he felt like a drowning man grasping at a straw when all other hope had gone.

"Listen to me," said the man. "You were kind once to me when I was set upon by some of the officers of your ship, and I have never forgotten that act since. I can rescue you; but you must follow my instructions implicitly."

"Yes, yes. But who are you? Your voice sounds familiar to me now. Come, tell me, that I may know my preserver," said Reuben, eagerly.

"Not yet," replied the sentinel; "it will be time enough to tell you that when I've got you out of the scrape."

"True. Now your instructions; and I will follow them to the letter?"

"The shore is not such a great distance from here."

"Say you so," rejoined the prisoner, joyfully. "Oh, for a breath of the free pure air!" he added, "to fan my fevered brain. God in Heaven, I never knew what liberty meant until now."

"You are not the only one that has experienced that feeling," returned the guard. "But hark! I hear a footstep. I fear we have been speaking too loud. Away from the door, sir, as quick as you can."

Reuben stepped back as lightly as he could from the door, and simultaneously a heavy footstep resounded outside.

CHAPTER CLII.

A NARROW ESCAPE.

REUBEN HARPY, the instant he stepped back from the door of his prison-room, listened intently.

With a wildly-beating heart and bated breath, he heard the heavy step come tramp! tramp! in the direction of the sham sentinel.

What if all should be discovered?

The mere thought sent a chill of ice through his blood, and he staggered helplessly against the side of the vessel.

Fortunately for him, Black Rufus was in a deep slumber.

At last the heavy step resounding outside came to a sudden pause—the new-comer, whoever he was, stopped short in front of the little cabin.

Reuben Harpy, recovering himself by a mighty effort, crept as near to the door as he could, prepared to drink in every word that passed between the two men.

He heard the following—

"Has any one been here with you lately?"

It was the voice of the new arrival, delivered in a tone imperious and at the same time suspicious.

"Not a soul," returned the sentinel, promptly.

"Are you sure?"

"Positive."

"Then I must have been mistaken," replied the other, "yet I could have sworn I heard two voices speaking somewhere about here. When did you relieve the other sentry?"

"Twenty minuits ago?"

"And your prisoners?"

"Are quiet enough. I believe they are both asleep."

"Are you in the habit of talking to yourself while on guard?"

"Sometimes."

"Humph!" muttered the man, "it must be the fool himself, then. Look here, my good fellow, you have got into a very bad practice, and the sooner you get out of it the better. Take my advice, and keep your tongue from wagging, or you may get something that you don't bargain for."

"I'll take your advice," was the short answer.

"And mind that your prisoners don't escape."

"I'll take good care of that."

The new-comer, after a few more more words of a precautionary kind, got into an excellent communicative humour.

"You'll soon be relieved, at least of one of your prisoners," he said.

"Oh, indeed. I'll not be sorry for that."

"I thought you wouldn't. Ha! ha! ha! The less trouble you fellows have the better. Captain Tom Drake will be over here presently."

"Captain Tom Drake!" exclaimed the sentinel, as if surprised at the information.

"Aye, Captain Tom Drake. It seems to astonish you, friend," said the man, evidently scanning the other narrowly.

"In truth it does," replied the sentinel, who saw the benefit now of getting some news of Captain Tom's movements. "What can he want over here, I wonder? He must have some very good reason for coming."

"He has. I suppose you don't know that th' Reuben Harpy is one of his bitterest enemies."

"One of the prisoners inside there?"

"Yes."

"I heard something of the kind," said the sentinel, carelessly. "But one mustn't give heed to every idle rumour, or he'll have enough of work on his hands. So this Captain Harpy is his most bitter enemy, is he?"

"He is, and his cousin to boot. But the story is too long to tell you now, and it won't much matter, for in a few hours—ha! ha! ha!—he'll be swung up to one of our yard-arms like a scarecrow."

Reuben Harpy, on hearing this, could have fallen on the spot.

With a smothered groan he sank on his knees, and the noise, though slight, seemed to have reached the ears of those on the outside.

"Hilloa! what's that?"

"I really don't know," replied the sentinel; "one of the prisoners, I suppose."

"I thought you told me they were both asleep?" said the new-comer, a little suspiciously.

"I believed so; but perhaps they have a habit of talking in their sleep," replied the sentinel.

But this answer scarcely satisfied the man whom he was addressing.

"It may be so," he rejoined, after a pause, "but it's better to make sure."

The words came as a warning to Reuben Harpy.

He instantly slunk away to the other side of the cabin, and stretching himself on some hammocks, began to breathe in a manner that indicated that he was asleep.

The sham sentinel was greatly alarmed to think that the ex-privateer would be caught listening at the door.

There was a small grating in the cabin door.

But this was closed.

It took a little time to open it, and by the time that the guard's companion exposed a view of the cabin, he caught, through the semi-darkness, the strong outlines of two sleeping figures stretched upon the ground.

He listened.

He could hear the deep breathing of Reuben Harpy, and the more sonorous snoring of the pirate, Rufus.

This seemed to satisfy him, and much to the sentinel's gratification.

"Look!" he cried. "They are both asleep."

The guard bent a glance through the grating and saw the forms of the two persons stretched as in slumber.

He emitted a low chuckle, and came to the conclusion that Reuben was more cunning than he took him to be.

Slight as the sound was, the other turned on him suspiciously.

"You are laughing," he said. "What have you been laughing at?"

The sentinel burst out into another chuckle.

He thought this the best way to act, to prevent his questioner from harbouring any suspicions of his conduct.

"Ha! ha! ha!" he laughed; "Captain Harpy little knows what's in store for him. Swung up like a strangled dog at the yard-arm. Ho! ho! ho! won't it be glorious? Do you know why I laugh so much?"

"No, I don't," said the other.

"Because he murdered my second cousin. Ho! ho! ho!—won't it be grand sport?"

The sentinel's caclinatory performance was catching, for the other laughed as long and as loudly as he did himself.

Reuben Harpy could have hugged his unknown friend in his arms for playing his part so well, but his cowardly heart, notwithstanding all this, trembled at the prospect of meeting his much-injured cousin.

He would sooner throw himself into the sea fifty times over than be hung up like a dog, with his enemy gloating over his agonies.

The very thought was a living hell to him.

In agony and suspense, he waited for the man to leave, so that he could urge upon his unknown friend to release an assist in his escape.

Soon the buccaneer retired, apparently well satisfied that the prisoner would be guarded strictly, and when his footsteps died in the distance, Reuben Harpy arose from the pile of hammocks on which he had thrown himself, and again made his way to the door.

The slide of the grating had been sent to.

This was done by the sentinel, to more effectually prevent the other from having any suspicions.

Reuben now heard the guard calling him—

"Captain Harpy— Captain Harpy!"

The man's voice was no louder than a whisper.

Reuben, responding, bent his head close to the door, so that his ear got in line with a crack that enabled the sounds to come through.

"I am here," said Reuben.

"A narrow escape," replied the sentinel.

"Yes, my good friend, thanks to you. I can never forget your brave conduct."

"Oh! don't mention that, sir," interrupted the sentinel. "I am very glad, however, that we escaped that prying rascal's lynx-eyes, for sharper eyes I never saw in man's head."

"Who was he?"

"A lieutenant, I should judge—a stranger on the vessel, or else I shouldn't have got off so easily. We have a lack of officers on board after last night's work, so they sent this one on from Dutch Paul's ship. I am glad they did so, for if one of our own officers came down I don't know what the consequences would have been. However, suspicious as the rascal was at first, he's gone away now with the assurance that I am one of the most loyal men on the vessel. You heard what he said?"

"Yes, yes," moaned Reuben.

"And that there's no mercy to be expected from the buccaneer captain."

"I heard all," said Reuben, trembling excessively.

"Then there's nothing now to be done but to get away as soon as you can."

"True—true. I would give twenty years of my life to be out of this cursed vessel. Oh, Heaven! what a fool I was not to give up that miserable Jew's daughter!"

"If you had done so," said the sentinel, "you might have saved your ship and your men, too. But it's no use sighing over spilt milk now, captain. This is not the moment for groans or moans, it's the time for action."

The man had spoken the truth.

In about an hour or two, Captain Tom Drake would be on the deck of Iron-Arm's ship, adjudging the sentence of death on his wicked but cowardly cousin.

"I can well understand that there is nothing to hope from Captain Tom," said Reuben, in a voice trembling with fear; "and the longer I stay here the less chance I will have of escape."

"So long as you remain on this ship, the more aggravative will be your danger," replied his guard. "So now let us be brief and understand each other. You know that I run a great risk in serving you."

"Yes, my brave, good, noble fellow; but I'll reward you for it," said Reuben, trembling. "I would not have you do all this for me for nothing."

Reuben at first surmised that the proffered services of the sentinel were of the most unselfish nature.

But he speedily found out that he was slightly mistaken in his estimate, and that it was with his guard as it is with many other people, "no money, no work;" or, in other words, "if you don't pay me down an equivalent sum for the danger I run, I'll leave you to your fate."

The ex-privateer after this, had not so much confidence in his would-be liberator.

But what could he do now but follow his instructions?

And pay the sum demanded for his liberty.

"Now, my kind deliverer," said Reuben, in a tone of the deepest gratitude, "let us look at the matter in a purely business point of view. What can I give to remunerate you for the danger that you run? Let us hasten, or presently it will be too late. Don't be afraid of naming a sum, and if you accompany me in my flight I will reward you with five times as much."

The sentinel did not answer Reuben for a moment.

He seemed deeply reflecting upon the risk of going away with the ex-privateer.

"I can hardly go with you," he said, at last, "for many reasons. Besides, one man can escape far better than two. If you reach the rocks unnoticed, you can easily conceal yourself among them until these fellows are away; then you'll have no difficulty after in hailing some passing vessel, especially as some of the fleet will sure to be around here in chase of the pirates. Don't imagine these Britishers will bear tamely with their defeat."

"Oh! I would they would crush this terrible curse of my life!" groaned Reuben Harpy.

"And so they will—depend upon it, they will. You don't imagine for a moment that a few miserable pirates will put down such a navy as Britain has? No! no! Before six months there'll not be a buccaneer of the Drake order on the seas."

Did this man speak in earnest when he prophesied the destruction of the gallant Captain Tom and his men?

Many of our readers may imagine that he did.

But such was not the case.

The sentinel only said this to please Captain Harpy.

"Now," went on the sentinel, "as there is little or no time to discuss this question any further, and as every moment is of the utmost importance to us, I'll be brief with my terms as well as my instructions. You don't care to take Lieutenant Rufus with you?"

"N-no," stammered Reuben. "It would ruin everything."

"I think so myself," rejoined the sentinel; "and now tell me the sum you will pay me for my services. You know, captain, I run a great risk in helping you to escape."

"I know that, my friend," replied Reuben, "and don't imagine for a moment that I'll be a niggard in remunerating you. Will five hundred guineas be enough?"

The man gave a cry of joy, but instantly checking himself, he answered—

"It will do, captain—splendid remuneration for all the danger I run. I'll stake my life now that you'll have no difficulty to escape. But you must change your clothes, captain."

"How—how?" whispered the excited man.

"Oh, I have a suit of clothes here—I took good care of that, and whiskers, too, if you like to wear them. When you are togged up in these, captain, your own mother wouldn't know."

Reuben Harpy muttered something like a curse.

Whether against his mother or not, we are not at liberty to say.

But his excitement by this time was at its highest, and he waited impatiently for the door of the cabin to open.

"Softly, captain—softly," said the sentinel, in a precautionary tone. "You are not free yet, you know—take everything quietly, and all will be well."

It was useless to give a man of Reuben Harpy's nature this advice—it only tended to make him more excited than before.

However, the door of the cabin was opened, and the sentinel's face was exposed to Reuben's view.

He rather liked that face—perhaps because its owner promised him the liberty he was enduring a living death for.

The face, however, was anything but an honest one.

And the man himself, with his cunning leer, looked as big a rogue as you could any day pick out of a ship's crew.

Moreover, there was a treacherous lurk in his twinkling, black eyes, and the hard lines about his mouth gave you to understand that he was a man of considerable personal courage and firmness—a man who generally had his wits about him.

But Reuben Harpy was too much occupied by his thoughts to go to the trouble of scanning his deliverer's face.

Indeed, it is not likely that he took cognisance of his features at all.

The sentinel had a bundle in his hand.

"There are the clothes," he said. "Be as quick as you can, sir, and dress yourself. But be careful that you don't wake the lieutenant, or else there will be some trouble, and the devil to play generally. You'll find the whiskers at the bottom of the bundle. Now let me close the door, and dress yourself as quickly and as quietly as you can."

Saying this, the guard drew the door to.

Trembling with a dread that Black Rufus should wake up during the operation, Reuben Harpy quickly changed his clothes, and, fixing on his false whiskers, signified, by a whisper, his readiness to leave the cabin.

The sentinel once more opened the door, but, before Reuben could step forward, Black Rufus leaped to his feet with an oath.

The door was slammed to instantly, and all light from the outside excluded.

Reuben Harpy cowered against the side of the ship, his legs quaking under him with fear.

It was, perhaps, very fortunate for him that the place where he stood was quite dark, so that Black Rufus could hardly see the change effected.

The clothes he wore a few minutes before he adroitly slid to one side out of the way of the pirate should he come stumbling up to him.

"What's this?" cried Black Rufus, with an oath. "Are you going to leave me, Captain Harpy?"

Reuben summoned up all his courage.

"No. Why should you think so? You must have been dreaming," he replied. "How could you imagine that I would do such a thing?"

The pirate, looking dubiously before him, rubbed his drowsy, blood-shot eyes.

"How is it, then, that that door slammed?" he asked, with some degree of suspicion.

"A door slammed!" exclaimed Reuben, surprisedly.

"Yes, the door of the cabin—you don't mean to tell me that you know nothing of that. It went to with a bang not a minute since."

Reuben saw the utter uselessness of prevaricating any longer, so he simply acknowledged that the guard was at the door.

Then he began pacing up and down the darkest side of the cabin, as if nothing had happened.

It was a great effort for Reuben to do all this.

Every moment he dreaded that Black Rufus would be at his throat and tear off his disguise. But there was something worse than even this—his terror that the pirate, in his mad rage, would prevent him from leaving the cabin.

"You are not deceiving me, are you, Captain Harpy?" said Black Rufus, coming slowly and deliberately towards him.

Reuben Harpy trembled in every limb as he caught the demoniac glitter of the pirate's eye.

Fortunately, Black Rufus stopped ere he got two paces—hesitated—then turned on his heel and faced the door of the cabin.

Now was the time for Reuben Harpy to make a good impression on the mind of the pirate.

"Deceiving you!" he cried, forcing a laugh, and calling all his courage to his aid. "My dear Rufus, you must have been dreaming—when I leave here you leave also."

"Ha! ha! ha!" laughed the pirate, madly, "we'll leave together, will we? Won't it be jolly fun to be swung up to a yard-arm—swung up like dogs high and dry to fester in the sun. Ha! ha! ha!"

Again that horrible, mad chuckle ringing like the voice of an evil spirit through the cabin.

Reuben Harpy shuddered in every vein.

His blood turned to ice, and, with a low gasp of horror, he would have fallen but for the grateful aid of an iron stanchion close to him.

As it was, he was as helpless as a child.

The mere mention of hanging like a dog at the yard-arm of one of Captain Tom's ships was enough to drive him mad.

But Black Rufus, like a very fiend of malignity, went on as glibly as ever—knowing, with a madman's cunning, that he was inflicting the tortures of the damned on his companion.

A new terror seized upon the heart of Reuben Harpy.

He was afraid that the pirate, sooner or later, would attack him.

He saw a warning gleam of danger in his eyes, and his features, distorted with some hidden passion, were almost too awful to look at.

Reuben, by this time, was almost as much in dread of Black Rufus as he was of Captain Tom Drake.

Still he cowered in the darkest part of the cabin, keeping his eyes warily fixed on the movements of his companion, and preparing to call in the assistance of the guard, should the occasion demand it.

Thus stood Reuben Harpy, with the clammy perspiration bursting out on his forehead in heavy drops.

"If you'll say that you are not afraid of me," went on Black Rufus, with another mad laugh, "I'll tell you what I dreamt last night. Oh! it was a glorious dream! Are you listening? Come nearer, and I'll whisper it in your ear. Look at those hands, Captain Harpy. They are dyed crimson with gore—red! Ha! ha! ha! with the blood of the innocent. And there is Israel Shawn—curse him!—come to torment me. Off with his head again! Ho! ho! ho! what glorious sport! I should like to be cutting off heads every day, if I got such emeralds as that one hanging to their necks!"

Reuben, in spite of his terror of Black Rufus, pricked up his ears at these words.

He heard the pirate once or twice before mention this wonderful emerald.

Rufus paused in his speech, to give vent to a low, malicious chuckle.

Having had his laugh out, he proceeded.

"Yes," said the pirate, with a brutal oath; "I'd cut them off every day in the week, and as many more as you could bring me. But there is some cursed fatality attending this emerald. I dreamt last night that I took it from around my neck, and on looking at it, the light seemed to fade away. All at once it turned as crimson as blood; but glancing up, I thought it a gleam of sunshine for the moment that came glinting in through one of the open port-holes. But there was no sun, and the sky was as dark as pitch. 'Perhaps I am mistaken,' said I. Taking it in my hand, I looked again at it, and found it dark and sullen-looking, then suddenly it changed crimson, bespeaking blood. When I looked a third time its marvellously beautiful colour returned; but a shudder of horror, all the same, stole over me—an indefinable fear which I was unable to understand. I knew from that moment that I was doomed to die. But how?—how? You shall learn. The instant I was returning it to its hiding-place, a peal of horrible laughter smote upon my ear. I turned, but could see no one. The cold, clammy perspiration burst out upon my forehead, and rolled down my face. I can say that I never knew fear in its full meaning till then. I closed my eyes and ears to shut out both sight and hearing; but everything failed. The horrid laughter would still ring out, and then, in a moment of desperation, I leaped to my feet, and called upon spirit or devil to come forward, and let me know my fate; and, would you believe it, Captain Harpy, a little old man—a Mussulman—attired in the garb of a Grand Vizier, stepped out of the darkness and stood before me. Ha! ha! ha! I could hardly help laughing when I beheld this ugly specimen of humanity, with his small decrepit form and little weazened face. But there was something else that made me pause. His eyes shot forth flames of hell, which burned into my very soul. I could laugh no longer. I knew this little man, dressed as a Grand Vizier, was the arch-fiend himself. I mustered up courage, however, to speak to him.

'Why do you come here to trouble—to torture me?' I asked. 'I come to warn you of death,' was his reply. 'When the Emerald of the Sea turns to a crimson hue, you have not many hours to live.' This information rather startled me. The emerald, as I before told you, had turned to a hue as red as blood. I trembled, because I knew that a horrible death was awaiting me, and that no earthly power could save me. When I looked up again, the little old man was gone, and a horrible burst of laughter followed his disappearance."

Black Rufus, as he ceased speaking, plucked the emerald from his bosom, then turned it to the faint streak of light that came into the cabin from the open air.

Reuben watched the movement shudderingly.

In spite of all his danger, this magnificent gem seemed to charm him to a sense of perfect security, and he would almost risk anything, even life itself, at that moment, to possess it.

"Look! look!" cried Black Rufus, hoarsely. "The green has turned to crimson! Ha! ha! ha! I told you so! I told you it would be my death warrant!"

And, with a frightful yell, the pirate fell prostrate on the floor of the cabin.

The sentinel, fearing that something terrible had occurred, knocked at the door, but, as Reuben's desire at that moment was to possess himself of the fatal emerald, he responded by a double tap, whispering through the crack, that it was only the pirate Rufus in one of his mad fits.

This explanation seemed to satisfy his guard amply.

Then Reuben, by an irresistible impulse, made a step forward to secure his prize; but as he did so the faint streak of light falling on the emerald made him pause, completely overawed.

The ex-privateer was not a man of courage at any time, and never was he so completely cowed as now.

The blood-red hue of the great sea jem summoned up all the latent superstition in his nature, and he slunk back, trembling like a child.

"I wouldn't touch it for twenty thousand guineas," he hoarsely muttered. "I can almost fancy I see it dripping with gore. Black Rufus's dream was not a myth after all. Strange that premonitions of this kind should come to warn one of approaching death. Ugh! I could never touch it, were it valued at all the riches in the world."

The sea-green emerald had a strange fascination. Reuben could not take his eyes off, do what he would.

In horror he retreated step by step, until his back came with a sounding crash against the door, which alarmed the sentinel very much.

"Captain Harpy, don't make so much noise," he whispered. "They are pretty lively on deck just now, and might hear you."

Reuben knew this, from the noise of clanking chains and heavy footsteps above his head.

"I'll be with you in a minute or so," he said. "I am almost ready."

All this time, his eyes were greedily rivetted on the fatal gem.

What a strange fascination it possessed!

Yet he felt that if he touched it it would be certain death to him.

"I—I will think no more of the accursed thing!" he stammered, huskily. "And yet, such a feeling comes over me that I could hug it to my heart."

It was as much as the ex-privateer could do to withdraw his gaze from the mystic emerald, and signify to the guard outside that he was ready.

The door of the cabin opened noiselessly, and the sentinel looked in.

His eye caught the insensible form of the pirate stretched upon the ground.

"He's in rather a strong fit, sir. He doesn't seem to move a bit," said the sentinel.

"Quite insensible," replied the ex-privateer.

"So much the better, captain. I hope he'll remain so—at least, until I get you clear of the vessel. I must compliment you on your new rig—it is capital, sir. I am sure your dearest friend wouldn't know you."

The sentinel was not overdrawing the picture when he said that the disguise was good. It was simply excellent, and the buccaneer's clothes fitted Reuben Harpy as if they had been made for him.

The whiskers alone changed the whole contour of his face.

Even his most intimate friend would not know him as he stood attired in a sea-rover's picturesque garb, with a beard reaching down almost to his breast.

Reuben Harpy looked now like a man over thirty.

"I have to thank you for this," was his reply, "and I'll know how to reward you."

Without delay, the ex-privateer payed over the sum of five hundred guineas to his guard for his deliverance.

"And now you may follow me," said the sentinel, chuckling at the success of his bargain. "I must tell you this much, however, that it won't do for me to be too long away from my post, or they may smell a rat. There's another man in this business besides me, and when you get on deck you'll find, by looking over to the larboard side, a boat awaiting you. I can lead you up as far as the quarter-deck, and then I must hasten back. Once in the boat, make for the rocks, and you are safe."

Reuben Harpy's heart trembled with a fever of apprehension.

Was this man trustworthy?

Would he betray him the moment he got into the boat?

The sentinel gave him no time to think, but hurried him on deck.

The moment the sentinel and Reuben Harpy left, a female figure emerged from the darkness—a beautiful girl attired in the sombre habiliments of mourning.

It was the beautiful Jewess, Hester Shawm, who had been a silent listener to all that had taken place between the two men.

After looking for a moment after the disappearing figures of the sentinel and his late prisoner, she noiselessly opened the cabin door, and saw the burly form of Black Rufus—the murderer of her father—stretched upon the floor.

She knew the ruffian at once.

Her first intention was to avenge her father's death, by stabbing his murderer to the heart.

While in this state of mind, Hester drew a long, glittering dagger from a portion of her dress.

But her heart failed her.

She could not do this murder, after giving herself an instant's reflection.

She would leave him in the hands of Captain Tom, who, she knew, would mete out to her the justice she demanded.

Besides, could she not prevent the escape of the villain Harpy, which would be a double incentive for the gallant captain to grant her request.

These thoughts flashed like lightning through the brain of Hester Shawm.

She was about closing the door of the cabin, to hasten on deck and give the alarm of the prisoner's escape, when her eyes fell on the mystic emerald.

For a moment Hester Shawm was rivetted to the spot—it was the emerald she saw her father wear around his neck, which the brutal pirate must have appropriated to himself when he cut off his head.

Hester's first thought was to enter the cabin and pick it up, but at that instant she heard a noise of approaching steps.

It was the sham sentinel on his return to his post.

There was not a moment to be lost.

The beautiful Jewess closed the door of the cabin softly, and hurried from the spot, determined to give the alarm of the ex-privateer captain's escape the moment she reached the deck.

The guard drew up at the cabin door.

There was an expression of surprise and bewilderment on his face.

"I could have sworn," he said, trying to penetrate the darkness with his eyes, "that I heard footsteps. Is it possible that we have been watched? If so, this fool's escape will be discovered, and I shall be placed in a position of great peril. But the emerald—it must be seen to."

He softly opened the door of the cabin and stole in.

Black Rufus was still in the same position—stretched at full length, without a sign of life in his burly carcase.

Not waiting to see whether the pirate was actually dead or not, he picked up the great sea gem.

The brilliant light that shone from it dazzled his eyes.

It seemed to emit sparks of green fire.

"Bah!" muttered the sham sentinel. "That dream of Black Rufus was all humbug. The rascal has a disordered imagination. Besides, he's mad, and mad people come out with strange crotchets. As for the crimson hue, I can see nothing of it. Bah! It's a wonder that fool of a captain didn't take the trouble to pick it up, superstitious fool and worse folly! He has left a mine of wealth behind. Ah! What's that noise?"

There was a commotion on deck of hurrying steps and loud, angry voices.

He heard a heavy splash in the water, and hastily concealing the priceless gem, he hurried quickly from the cabin.

This explains Reuben Harpy's attempt at escape, and how it miscarried through the interference of Hester Shawm, the beautiful Jewess.

CHAPTER CLIII.

TREACHERY.

TEN minutes after Reuben Harpy had been rescued from a watery grave, a boat was lowered from the davits of the "Will-o'-the-Wisp."

Captain Tom Drake, descending the ship's side, got into it, and was followed by two or three of his favourite officers.

The boat was pulled rapidly in the direction of Iron-Arm's vessel, and, in a few minutes, Captain Tom and his officers mounted the deck, and were cheered lustily by the crowd of buccaneers and middies who surrounded them.

Everyone was ready to tell his story of the attempted escape; but Iron-Arm, not wishing Captain Tom's ears to be dinned by so many accounts, summoned the lieutenant he left in charge into the captain's presence.

That worthy was below, making the proper investigations to explain the mystery, but hearing his chief's order, he hurried at once to the quarter-deck.

Saluting his chief and Captain Tom with the respect due to their superior ranks, he awaited in silence for them to speak.

Our hero contented himself by leaving the matter entirely in the hands of his trusted friend, Iron-Arm, as the latter was now on his own ship; and it would be out of good-taste, on his part, to interfere.

Nor could he have left it in better hands.

"Will you give me an account of this remissness of duty on your part, Lieutenant Harbison?" said Iron-Arm, somewhat coldly. "I thought the discipline on this vessel was such that a prisoner could not get away so easily from under the very nose of the man who guarded him?"

Harbison winced under the stern look of his leader, but, recovering himself, he replied—

"I should have thought so myself, captain, but for the one fact that we have several hands aboard from the Brazilian privateer."

Iron-Arm, for the first time, thought it was a great mistake to have given these men their liberty; but as they were strong fellows and good sailors, he permitted as many of them as liked to join him.

The lieutenant was not so much to blame for his apparent dereliction of duty, after all.

Yet, at the same time, Iron-Arm had given strict orders that none of these men should be permitted to guard the prisoners, as he found out that many of them were in favour of their late captain, and might take the first chance to liberate him.

"I think I instructed you," said Iron-Arm, at last, "that none of the privateers were on any account to be told off as sentinels."

"Such were your orders, captain," replied the lieutenant.

"Then, why were they not obeyed?"

"To the best of my belief they were."

"Good heavens! have we traitors among our own men?"

"I think not, sir."

"Then how do you account for this fellow's attempted escape?"

"Here is one who can account for it," said a young midshipman, coming forward with Hester Shawm.

The instant the beautiful Jewess cast her eyes on Captain Tom, a rich blush suffused her cheeks, and her eyes dropped.

Tom appeared not to observe this embarrassment. He looked on as coldly and quietly as ever.

Recovering herself, Hester gave an account of all she had heard pass between the two men, and the bribe paid to the sham sentinel by Reuben Harpy for his liberty.

"You are sure, Miss Shawm, that it wasn't one of our men?" said Iron-Arm, addressing himself to the Jewess.

"I am certain, sir, that the man belonged to Captain Harpy's privateer," she replied, "for I have seen him often before on that vessel, while I was a prisoner on it."

The answer was enough.

Strict search was immediately made among the crew to find the man.

But in vain.

Below decks was searched.

With the same result.

The steward of the late privateer had disappeared as mysteriously as if he had been swallowed up in the depths of the ocean.

But what was more mysterious still, Reuben Harpy had gone, too.

Captain Tom, when he heard the results of the search, was terribly annoyed to find that his arch-enemy, Reuben Harpy, had escaped him.

He had not even seen him!

He puzzled his brain to think how the rascal could have got away.

This time the prisoner had been, through the great confusion that prevailed on the vessel, thrown into the cabin without even a sentinel to guard him.

Captain Tom cursed the privateer's men in silent, but bitter oaths, for he was almost sure that they had some hand in the conspiracy, as the steward had in the first attempt at Reuben Harpy's escape.

Our hero paced up and down the quarter-deck, with the bitterest of bitter thoughts agitating his mind, wondering whether he should ever again meet his guilty cousin face to face.

While employed in such meditations as these, the man in the maintop signalled a sail.

"Where away?" cried Iron-Arm, coming forward with his glass.

"Straight on our weather-beam," replied the look-out.

Iron-Arm affixed his glass, and scanned the horizon.

But he failed to see the slightest symptoms of the approaching sail.

"Do you try, Captain Tom," he said, handing the glass to our hero. "Ever since last night's engagement, I am positively blind."

Captain Tom, forgetting for a moment his annoyance, quietly took the glass and adjusted it to his eye.

"Well, can you see anything?" asked Iron-Arm, who was impatient to know the result.

"Yes," replied Tom. "There's a vessel approaching us sure enough. It may be a friend or it may be an enemy. If an enemy, she'll have to show a pair of light heels to get away."

"Ha! ha! ha!—you are right, captain; although some of our craft, after last night's fight, is not what they should be."

"No, but that will matter little. Take the glass and see if you can see her now."

Iron-Arm complied, and again scanned the horizon.

He gave an exclamation of delight, for he could now see that he had not altogether lost his eyesight.

"I can see the tops of her masts well enough," he replied, "and the longer I took the more distinctly I make them out. You have a sharp eye, Captain Tom."

Our hero laughed.

"And you have not, I suppose, friend Iron-Arm?"

"Ho! ho! ho!" laughed the giant, "I used to fancy I had one time."

Iron-Arm had lowered the glass, and was taking a view of the rippleless water three or four miles off.

With a sudden exclamation, down came the giant's heavy hand on his hip.

"What's the matter?" asked Captain Tom.

"By Heaven, there's something else besides yonder ship coming towards us!"

Captain Tom looked in the direction indicated, and saw a something on the waste of waters which looked very much like a boat.

"The glass! the glass!" he cried, excitedly.

Iron-Arm, still scanning the water with his eyes, handed the glass to him.

One look was enough.

Captain Tom saw that it was a boat, and, moreover, that there was some one in the bottom of that boat.

It struck our hero's mind as suddenly that that some one was his hateful and cowardly cousin, Reuben Harpy.

At first sight, the little craft seemed as if it were coming towards the vessel, but a second look, however, convinced our hero that such was not the case.

Had Captain Tom reflected, he might have seen that a slight breeze had sprung up since he first caught sight of the approaching vessel; which certainly influenced the little craft in going the direction it did.

"Let the pinnace be lowered and manned!" shouted Captain Tom.

This order was instantly obeyed.

Four brawny buccaneers leaped in and caught the oars in their hands, followed by Captain Tom, Iron-Arm, and three or four middies.

"Now, lads, pull!" cried our hero.

There was a spurt, and the boat flew like a feather through the water.

Captain Tom kept his glass on the fugitive craft from time to time. But to his astonishment it seemed to make very little progress.

"This is strange," he muttered; "yet it has a sail hoisted."

Yes, it had a sail hoisted, or rather the apology for one, and a very dirty and discoloured affair it was.

It looked at first sight like a worn-out piece of tarpaulin which came in handy when nothing else could be found, and which rather impeded than increased the speed of the little vessel it was attached to.

"I wonder can the rascal be playing us any trick?" thought Captain Tom, who, when he started, was almost as certain as he was of his life that the figure at the bottom of the boat was no other than Reuben Harpy.

After an half hour's hard pulling, they dashed past the pursued craft, but instead of discovering Reuben Harpy, Captain Tom found one of his own midshipmen.

It was a youth whom we introduced to the reader on a few occasions before.

He was lying at the bottom of the boat on his face—apparently dead.

They gently turned the poor fellow over, and discovered an ugly gash on his forehead, which had not been inflicted by cutlass or sabre, and which must either have been the result of a pistol bullet or a gunshot.

They soon found out that he was not dead.

Captain Tom had a flask of water with him, with which he bathed the wound in the poor lad's forehead, and, after removing the congealed blood as well as he could from the wound, he bound up his head very carefully, and helped the men with him into the boat.

This done, they pulled back to Iron-Arm's ship, and were soon on the deck with their wounded charge.

Captain Tom now gave orders for the middy to be carried below, and sent a messenger at once to the "Will-o'-the-Wisp" for Doctor Shrike.

For, whatever peculiarities the old vampire had, no one doubted his ability as a doctor.

All this being done, Captain Tom directed his attention once more to the approaching ship.

Of course the distance between the vessels had visibly decreased.

And yet they were a great distance from each other notwithstanding.

Our hero made very little progress with his glass, for up to this time he was unable to tell anything of the strange vessel that was bearing down on him.

It might be a pirate, for all he knew to the contrary, or a British war-ship, both of which were, in a manner of speaking, equally his enemies.

While Captain Tom was thus engaged, Doctor Shrike despatched a messenger to him.

It was our old acquaintance, Jacop, who looked terribly red, and swollen about the nose.

"Well, Jacop," said Captain Tom, cheerfully, "what does your master require of me?"

"It's the young middy, captain," replied Jacop. "He's recovering."

"Oh, indeed. I am glad to hear it."

"Yes, sir, as he's not a bad sort. He's not like Bob Hauler or Jerry Mizzen, I assure you."

"Very likely not," said Captain Tom, laughing. "They have been playing you some practical joke, I suppose, Jacop?"

"Look here, Captain Tom, that will tell you what they have been doing."

And the vampire's assistant pointed to his discoloured nose.

"Why, I declare, Jacop, your nose is swollen."

"I should think it was, sir," said Jacop, ruefully.

"How did they do that?"

"With potatoes," blubbered Jacop.

"Are you quite sure they did it? Did you see them do it?"

"No, sir," stammered Jacop. "They took good care—the villains!—to get out of the way before I could catch them."

"Never mind, Jacop; it's all a bit of fun after all. But I promise you," said Captain Tom, "that you shall serve them out in a far worse manner yourself some day."

Jacop seemed satisfied with this assurance, and led his young leader to the cabin where the wounded midshipman lay.

The middy, under the fostering care of Doctor Shrike, was getting around rapidly.

He was sitting up when Captain Tom entered the cabin, chatting glibly with Doctor Shrike.

"How are you now, my poor fellow?" said our hero, advancing, and taking the wounded boy's hand. "Are you any better?"

"Oh! much better, thank you, Captain Tom. The good doctor here and his medicines have relieved me wonderfully."

In fact, the middy and Doctor Shrike were on the best of terms; and among all the midshipmen on board the "Will-o'-the-Wisp" he was the erratic old doctor's favourite.

They got on very well together, as the vampire was pleased to express it.

"I have sent for you, Captain Tom," said the middy, a tear glistening in his eye, "to convey the last words to you of my poor murdered shipmate."

Captain Tom was surprised.

"Ned Maynard murdered!" he exclaimed, scarcely believing that he had heard aright. "Be calm, boy, and tell me by whom."

"I was going to tell you, captain, and God knows how it bleeds my heart to bring you such mournful tidings. But—but he died, Captain Tom, as you would expect—brave to the last, with his noble chief's name on his dying lips."

"Go on, boy—go on!" cried Captain Tom, deeply affected. "Don't keep me in suspense. How did this happen? Woe to his murderers, for I shall have blood for blood!"

There was a painful pause in the little cabin.

Doctor Shrike and even his assistant, Jacop, were affected.

The middy, as soon as he could recover, proceeded with his account, but in a very tremulous voice, scarcely audible to his hearers.

"During last night's fight," said the middy, repressing a great sob that was rising in his throat, "both me and Ned Maynard were captured by a boat's crew of the enemy.

"Threatened with all kinds of vengeance, we were dragged aboard their ship.

"I had given up all as lost—thought my gallant captain and his noble vessel destroyed.

"'What is there to live for?' I whispered to Ned. 'Let us end our miseries by throwing ourselves into the sea.'

"'Softly,' said Ned. 'There may be a chance yet of escape, and I am sure our brave Captain Tom and his daring crew will beat these dogs off. Put your trust in God, but never think of taking your own life. What would you advise me to do? I'd sooner suffer a thousand deaths first.'

"Ned was much calmer than I am now, and there was a heavenly light in his eyes which I could not help comparing to that of an angel.

"'You have never seen me flinch from death yet, Tom,' said the brave boy, 'but I should consider it not only cowardly, but sinful, to take my own life. Trust in God, Tom—trust in God—He will see us through. And as for our good, brave captain—hark! to those distant hurrahs! Victory! victory!' he shouted, above the battle-cry of the enemy. 'Captain Tom is victorious! Thank God—thank God!'

"Amid the flame, and smoke, and shouts, I was conscious that you, noble captain, was the victor!"

The noble boy paused to wipe the tears of gratitude and joy from his eyes.

Then, when sufficiently composed, he proceeded—

"We were now set upon by several ruffians, who bore us to the deck, uttering the most frightful curses on our heads.

"And before we could speak or protest against their savage violence, we were carried below, and loaded with irons.

"My thoughts were so bitter at this moment, that I could have killed myself if I had the power.

"But I looked at my noble companion, and there grew a great strength in my heart to bear my misfortunes with patience.

"Soon all sounds of the terrible battle died away, and shortly after I was conscious, by the lurching and heaving of the ship, that we were going out to sea.

"That terrible night I passed in the most awful agony, and my life through that whole night was as a living hell.

"Tired out and wearied almost to death, I fell into a restless slumber, and only awoke when I felt myself roughly handled by some of the ship's crew, who, taking our irons off, hurried us on deck.

"The deck was crowded with soldiers and officers, whose stern, unrelenting faces told us our fate.

"'You are the young villain who shouted victory last night,' said he who appeared to be the captain, addressing Ned Maynard; 'and you meant it for Captain Tom, I suppose?' he added, with a malignant sneer wreaking his thin, hard lips.

"Poor Ned was very pale, but he was not the lad to lie, even to save his life.

"He replied that he was.

"'You'll not retract?' said the savage captain.

"'No, not to save my life,' replied Ned, with heroic fortitude.

"'Ha! ha! ha! Then we'll give you a taste of British lead. Forward, my men, with your matchlocks!'

"A dozen soldiers stepped up with their guns, and poor Ned was ordered to stand upon the bulwarks.

"'Retract!' thundered the captain, 'or you die!'

"'Never!' replied the undaunted youth. 'Hurrah for Captain Tom, and God bless him!'

"The word of command was given, the soldiers advanced, and fired a deadly volley into the body of the hapless youth.

"I closed my eyes, and heard the dying voice of my brave comrade blessing his gallant leader, Captain Tom Drake."

CHAPTER CLIV.
THE OATH OF VENGEANCE.

CAPTAIN TOM DRAKE felt a thrill of horror pervade his frame as he listened to the repetition of the dying words of poor Ned Maynard.

"What a fate—what a cruel, cruel fate!" he muttered. "Oh, the coward—the coward! But blood cries for blood, and I swear he shall die!"

No one heard his words.

They were spoken to himself rather than to those in the cabin.

While the account was being given of the murder of poor Ned Maynard, one might have heard a pin drop.

But at the end of it, the brutal assassination of the noble middy wrung from the hearers cries of rage and indignation.

"It was a base murder!" cried Doctor Shrike, carried away by his feelings.

"A cowardly, brutal murder!" echoed the middy, the tears rolling down his pale cheeks.

"As base, infamous, and cruel a murder as I ever heard of," repeated Doctor Shrike. "Hum! I wish I had that captain here—perhaps he wouldn't feel the point of my dissecting-knife as I ran it into his ugly, cowardly carcase. I wish I had the scoundrel's head," muttered the doctor, as an after thought. "It would help science materially—ahem!"

"I know what I'd do to him," said Jacop, almost blubbering; "I'd flay him alive first and burn him after, I would—that's what I'd do for him!"

"Shut up!" said the vampire. "What do you understand of the matter? You don't know what you are talking about, Jacop."

It was a favourite practice of Dr. Shrike when in any state of great mental excitement to endeavour to fasten a quarrel upon his assistant.

And now there seemed a good opportunity for doing so.

"Y-yes I do, Doctor Shrike," stammered Jacop.

But before he even ventured on such a contradiction, he put at least a couple of paces between himself and his master, so that if the vampire meditated an assault he would first have to pass Captain Tom.

"Will you tell me you do when I say you don't, you rascal?" cried Doctor Shrike, in a voice that made poor Jacop tremble, even to the very tips of his fingers. "Besides, you long, lean, hungry vagabond you, you haven't the courage to skin a flea, let alone a human being. Now say you do again, you villain! and I'll let a little of the bad blood out of you."

Captain Tom and the middy, notwithstanding the painfulness of the subject, were nearly bursting their sides from suppressed laughter.

It was capital sport to see Jacop and his master in one of their tantrums.

As Jacop did not venture to contradict the vampire a second time, the opportunity of a good row was lost to them.

And, of course, the worthy doctor, in the presence of his captain, could not force the quarrel, more especially now as his assistant became very mute, and had retreated to the farther end of the cabin.

When all was restored to order once more, Tom Drake asked the middy to explain how he escaped the clutches of the captain of the British war vessel.

"I will tell you, sir," replied the brave midshipman, continuing his narrative.

"The moment they shot poor Ned Maynard, I expected my turn would come next.

"When I opened my eyes, and looked where my poor friend stood, to receive that terrible volley, I could see nothing but the blood-bespattered bulwarks.

"Ned was gone!

"The bullets of the soldiers had done their murderous work, and the poor fellow had fallen into the sea.

"Instinctively I crept forward, to look over the side of the ship.

"No one prevented me.

"There was a silence as of death among the soldiers.

"Even the officers seemed inoculated by the same feeling—a burning shame at the part they had taken in the murder.

"Of course, there was one exception—that one was the cruel and bloodthirsty captain.

"He alone seemed to rejoice in his foul and unjustifiable deed.

"Approaching the bulwarks, I looked into the ocean, but the darkness still held sway over the waters, and I could discern nothing.

"Poor Ned Maysard must have been killed before even he sank.

"With a heavy heart, I stepped back, caring little whether my life was spared or not, now—I could die as my brave comrade died, with the name of my noble captain on my lips.

"I even wished for death at that moment, for a more miserable being didn't exist on the face of the earth.

"I was not left long to my gloomy reflections, however, before the captain came forward.

"'Do you see,' he cried, savagely, 'how I treat the myrmidons of Captain Tom Drake. Ha! ha! ha! I wish the noble captain was here himself, and I would serve him in like manner.'

"'Murderer!' I cried, 'pollute not the name of my noble chief by mentioning it. If you desire to glut your vengeance further, I am still left. Do your worst. I defy you!'

"'Oh, I see!' said the captain, chuckling maliciously, 'you want to follow your companion, do you? Perhaps it would be a pleasure for you to die like him. No, no, my fine fellow. Your fate shall be worse—far worse than his. I'll give you one chance for your life. Ha! ha! ha! your death shall be a lingering one.'

"I felt so disgusted and horrified by the presence of this cruel murderer that I did not deign to answer him.

"He was not going to shoot me, I knew that.

"But that he had devised some terrible scheme for my destruction I was equally aware.

"I was not left long in doubt.

"The villain gave orders for one of the boats to be lowered.

"I could see now what he meant.

"They were going to abandon me on the open sea, where scarcely a ship passed once in a month.

"'Oh, God!' I thought, 'this fate is horrible.'

"I had read of the terrible sufferings of shipwrecked mariners, and shuddered involuntarily at the bare idea of what my own sufferings would be, abandoned in a strange sea, without provisions and without water.

"I knew that this was the captain's object, and that, moreover, not a morsel of food or a drop of water would be put into the boat with me.

"Days might elapse before I should see even a passing sail, and then too far to attract the slightest attention.

"The agony I endured in those few brief moments was indescribable, a hundred deaths seemed to come upon me all at the same time, and then I reflected what a happy release had been my poor comrade's.

"The boat was soon lowered, and the captain ordered me to be thrown in, laughing maliciously at the fate that awaited me.

"'Ha! ha!' he cried, 'you will defy me, will you? Better a thousand times that you had been shot than abandoned as you are. A pleasant voyage to you, my fine fellow, and if you should ever meet your noble captain in the other world, give him my compliments. 'Ha! ha! ha!'

"I felt now that the boat had been shoved off from the ship's side.

"'A word more!' shouted the captain. 'They say that I am the best shot in the navy.'

"'In mercy take my life!' I cried, thinking that his hard, cruel heart had somewhat relented, 'for any fate would be preferable to being left to perish thus.'

"'Take your life!' he cried, mockingly, back. 'Oh, no! my fine fellow. Such is not my intention. Don't flatter yourself that my disposition is so merciful. But I mean leaving you a mark, nevertheless. A trial of skill,' he went on, laughing devilishly. 'They say I am the best shot in the navy, and I am going to make the trial. Besides, a little lead will accelerate your sufferings. Look out!'

"I exposed my body that I might receive his murderous bullet, hoping that it might either pierce my heart or go crashing into my brain.

"He fired—I fell, and from that moment until the time I found myself on board this noble vessel I remained insensible."

"The coward!" exclaimed Captain Tom—"the base, cowardly murderer! Did you discover his name?"

"No, captain; it seemed to be kept a profound secret."

"Nor the name of his ship?"

"Of that I am equally in the dark."

"But you would know the villain again if you saw him?"

"Most assuredly, sir. His face was one that I can never forget. A more ugly and savage-looking wretch I never saw in the whole course of my life."

"It is very strange," said Tom Drake, musingly, "that a captain in his Majesty's navy should be guilty of such a base, murderous, and cowardly act. Whatever their other faults—and they are many—I could hardly believe one of their number capable of so brutal and ruffianly an outrage. By the Heaven above me!" added our boy hero, "I'll find out the villain wherever he is, and he shall suffer tortures and such a death as he never dreamt of!"

"So he shall, so he shall, captain," said Dr. Shrike, a gleam of satisfaction lighting up his old eyes. "Leave him to me and Jacop, Captain Tom, we'll settle him—won't we, Jacop? Ha! ha! ha! He'll have the wrong people to deal with when he'll have me and Jacop!"

"Surely, master, surely," said the vampire's assistant.

"Who told you to speak, you rascal, you?" cried Doctor Shrike, threatening Jacop with his fist. "Keep quiet, you villain, until you are spoken to!"

"B-but I was spoken to, doctor," stuttered Jacop.

"You lie, you wretch! And even if you were, you should not have answered back!"

"Very well, doctor, I am agreeable," said Jacop; "but you ain't satisfied when I don't speak, and you are ready to jump down my throat when I do."

This was a wonderful effort of Jacop's to pluck up so much courage as to beard his master to his teeth.

But it must be remembered that Captain Tom was in the cabin, and that Jacop took heart of grace in consequence.

The vampire's assistant almost trembled now at his boldness.

He had been standing on a mine, and up to that moment he had not realised his danger.

The doctor's look was terrible.

Jacop shrunk up like a ball, expecting that the doctor would attack him even in spite of Captain Tom's presence.

"You ungrateful hound you!" roared Doctor Shrike, "you have the impertinence and audacity to say that you are agreeable! Ha! ha! agreeable indeed! Perhaps you don't know who you are talking to, my friend Jacop? Perhaps you are not aware that there is a dissecting knife near your vile carcase ready to let a little of the evil blood out of your dirty skin?"

"Oh, don't—don't doctor!" cried Jacop, apprehensive that the violence of the vampire's passions might take a more tragic form; "if I have offended you, I humbly beg your pardon, sir!"

"Offended me!" exclaimed Doctor Shrike, indignant that a gentleman of his high scientific attainments should for a moment be offended by such a worm as his assistant. "Offended me!" "Ha! ha! I should like to be offended by a lying, ugly, skulking piece of humanity such as you. You long-legged villain, I think you want me to lose that calm placidity befitting a philosopher and a gentleman. But you shan't, you ungrateful wretch. I'll not dirty my hands or my knife by touching you."

Jacop was very glad that his irate master had come to that heroic and gentleman-like conclusion.

It eased his mind very much indeed.

As he had an especial horror of dissecting knives, as well as the other instruments his master used.

Captain Tom just waited long enough to be highly amused, and seeing that the worthy doctor had toned down a little, and that there was no further likelihood of a renewal of hostilities, he bid the middy "good-bye," expressing a hope for his speedy recovery, after which he hastened on deck.

On the quarter-deck he found Iron-Arm and his lieutenant.

The giant was taking the bearings of the strange craft that was approaching them.

It was still many leagues off.

But that could be easily accounted for, as there was an almost entire absence of breeze, and what there was of a most unfavourable nature, so that the vessel was compelled to tack repeatedly.

The buccaneers watched her movements with intense interest.

Captain Tom took the glass from the hands of his lieutenant, and bent one keen, searching glance over the sea.

For once in his life he was puzzled.

Puzzled, because everything about her looked so quiet and peaceful.

"A singular craft, captain," said Iron-Arm, when Captain Tom withdrew the glass from his eye.

"Singular enough," replied Tom, carelessly.

"I can't make her out at all. I fancy, however, that there is something not quite right about her."

"Quite likely," said our hero, apparently abstracted.

His answers were like those of a man deeply absorbed in his own reflections.

"The most innocent-looking three-decker I ever saw for seas so strange as well as so dangerous," pursued Iron-Arm, never tired of forcing the matter on the consideration of his superior.

"An East Indiaman in disguise," ventured one of the younger officers, turning to Iron-Arm, laughingly.

"With a rich cargo aboard," said another.

"In the shape of arms and munitions of war," ended the young officer before alluded to.

"By Heaven! you are right, sir!" cried Captain Tom. "More likely a pirate, or a British man-of-war. I'll vouch my existence she is no Indiaman."

"The rascals know their book, though," rejoined Iron-Arm. "They have rigged her out so that even Lucifer himself couldn't tell what manner of craft she is."

Iron-Arm was right.

If a British war vessel, she did not bear the slightest resemblance to one.

If a pirate, she had the most un-cutthroat-like appearance imaginable.

"What's to be done?" asked Iron-Arm.

"Why, go out and meet her!" replied the gallant buccaneer.

"Will she wait for you to come up to her, think you?"

"That depends. She is big enough, and ugly enough, too, to hold her own against a little craft like the 'Will-o'-the-Wisp.'"

"The 'Will-o'-the-Wisp' has taken the shine out of many a better ship," said Iron-Arm. "But the beggar doesn't seem a bit afraid. See! she comes on in all the consciousness of her own strength and audacity!"

"We'll see how long her strength and audacity will last her," replied Tom. "Lower the pinnace!"

The deck of Iron-Arm's vessel was crowded with seamen and middies.

When they heard what Captain Tom said, they gave a hearty shout, which, if the approaching vessel had only heard it, would have made her pause in her onward course, before she came any further.

"Hurrah for Captain Tom! Long live our buccaneer king!" they all shouted.

Our hero bowed, in graceful acknowledgment.

The cheer was repeated with such hearty goodwill as to draw all the crews of the various craft to their decks.

A responsive shout rolled over the sea the moment they saw what was going to happen.

The pinnace was lowered.

Captain Tom and his officers leaped in.

Stout, strong arms now pulled for the "Will-o'-the-Wisp," and the light boat cleft through the water like an arrow, while the graceful curves of her dropping oars flashed out in the afternoon sun like so many brilliant gems.

Captain Tom and his followers were soon aboard their gallant craft.

Meanwhile, a pretty strong breeze sprung up, and the "Will-o'-the-Wisp," having weighed anchor, spread all sail, and started out to meet the pretended East Indiaman.

Captain Tom was ever on deck, watching the movements of the strange ship.

With Iron-Arm continually by his side, either taking observations with the glass, or consulting him on the probabilities of battle.

The breeze was now more than ever against the stranger.

Her progress was even slower.

Every quarter of an hour or twenty minutes she tacked about, and the distance between them visibly decreased each minute.

But on she came, heedless, and apparently fearless.

"Well, what do you think of her now?" asked Tom, addressing Iron-Arm, who had for the twentieth time, at least, raised and lowered his glass in a survey of the peaceful-looking craft bearing down on them.

"Hang it all, if I can make her out!" said Iron-Arm.

"No!"

"She'd puzzle the arch-fiend himself, I know. I know she wishes us to believe she is a trader. But that's all moonshine. She's too quiet even for one of those craft."

"Especially for an East Indiaman," said Captain Tom, laughing. "I'll bet my life we'll see a bristling array of cannon presently, or I'm a Dutch-

WITH A HOARSE CRY, THE SMUGGLER SPRANG UPON HIM

man. How many men can you count on her decks?"

"Not more than a dozen."

"Very peaceful-looking lubbers, ain't they?"

"Very. A little too peaceful to my liking. I'll tell you what, captain, it's all humbug about her ports."

"Masked, I should imagine," said our hero.

"I'm certain of it."

"How many guns do you think she carries?"

"Forty, at least"

"Then it will be a tough fight."

"And a long one."

"What matters it?" said Captain Tom, gaily. "It will only be another victory added to the long list on the records of our noble vessel."

"And another capture, I hope."

"I'll endeavour to make it so. Let this pretended Indiaman but come on as she does at present, and we'll board her before the darkness sets in."

This was no idle boast.

Captain Tom and his gallant buccaneers had taken even larger ships than the one approaching them.

On sped the " Will-o'-the-Wisp."

Cleaving the waters like a thing of life.

No bird could be more graceful on its onward progress than the gallant little craft speeding on its way to meet the three-decker.

And up to this time the pretended East Indiaman preserved a death-like silence.

47

It came on as if in utter unconsciousness of the " Will-o'-the-Wisp's " approach.

The death-like stillness was enough to awe the stout-hearted crew of our gallant little vessel, who brave though they were, had much of the credulity and superstition of men who pass their lives at sea.

Everyone now seemed to be inoculated by a secret fear.

There were, of course, a few exceptions to this on board.

Among these were Captain Tom and Iron-Arm, and a few others, who had long since divested their minds of these latent superstitions.

Men who knew the world too, and who did not believe in spectre ships, or barques, or anything of the kind. For they attributed the reason of the intense silence on board the strange ship to its proper cause.

Captain Tom saw the looks of fear that pervaded the countenances of his gallant buccaneers, and he thought it high time to put a stop to it.

' Double shot the guns!" he cried.

This order was promptly obeyed.

Jerry Mizzen and Bob Hauler, who were aboard the " Will-o'-the-Wisp," were in their glory.

The two gallant " salts " were inseparable, and attended as usual to the one gun, which they secretly loaded to the very muzzle, intending to give the stranger a little more than was bargained for.

" I think that will do, Bob."

" I think it will, Jerry."

" Capital medicine for lubbers o' that kind."

" Jest so, Jerry. I hope the gun mayn't burst, though."

" Oh, no fear o' that. We've bunged it up to the muzzle more'n once."

" But we may do it once too often, mind. I shouldn't like as how Cap'n Tom comes to hear of it, though."

" Nor should I."

" There would be the very devil to pay if he did, But I say, Jerry, old boy, a new idea strikes me."

" What is it?" asked Jerry.

" How would you like to have the varmint stride o' this here bull-dog when we fires it off?"

" What a joke!" said Jerry. " Wouldn't it be splendid!"

" I don't think it would, at least for him," said Bob; " but I fancy the lubber would jump higher than he ever did afore—eh, Jerry?"

" Jest so," said Jerry. " But wouldn't it be better to have him in front while we fires it off, ten to one he'd get the full benefit of it then."

" Oh, what a cold-blooded villain you are!" exclaimed Bob. " I didn't know as how you was sich an unmitigated assassin, Jerry."

" Assassin be blowed!" exclaimed the irrepressible Jerry.

Whatever else he might have said was broken by a sudden roar.

Jerry and Bob were nearly thrown off their feet.

There was a violent concussion and a cloud of sulphurous smoke.

" Blow me! but that was awfully suddint like," said Jerry, regaining his equilibrium. " It nearly took my sea legs from under me. Where are you, Bob?"

" Here," replied his comrade.

" Don't you think Cap'n Tom took advantage of us that time?"

" I think he did; but it's all your fault."

" How is that?" asked Jerry.

" You was a-jabbering there so much that we couldn't hear the word o' command."

" It wasn't me; it was you," replied Jerry, unblushingly.

" Oh! don't tell such a lie, Jerry. I'm ashamed

of you," said Bob. " But let us not be late. Take sight at once, and give it to the beggar the moment you hear the word."

While Jerry was sighting the piece, Bob was watching the effect of the shot on the pretended East Indiaman.

She was not more than three-quarters of a mile off.

The shot fired from the " Will-o'-the-Wisp " had perforated her bows.

Let us hasten on deck for a moment and see why these guns had been fired.

Captain Tom, Iron-Arm, and most of his officers were on the quarter-deck.

And not more than a mile from the " Will-o'-the-Wisp " was the pretended East Indiaman.

The buccaneers were, however, suddenly made aware that that soi-disant trader was giving them the " slip."

She had veered round with the rapidity of thought, and was now flying before the wind at a pretty good speed.

For a moment, Captain Tom and his officers were thunderstruck.

What did the stranger mean by this manœuvre?

This was just what Captain Tom and his officers wished to know.

But, stranger still, there seemed no more bustle aboard the East Indiaman than formerly.

Her decks were denuded of seamen, if we except five or six on the quarter-deck, and these stood more like stone statues than human beings.

For they never made even a single movement.

By some mysterious means or other the stranger succeeded in crowding on all sail.

How it was done Heaven alone knows.

Neither Captain Tom, nor a solitary soul on board the " Will-o'-the-Wisp " could account for it.

" They have some secret machinery at work," said Iron-Arm. " All this is done by human agency."

' Of course," said Tom. " But they have given our chaps a deuced fright, for all that."

Such was indeed the fact.

The buccaneers of the " Will-o'-the-Wisp " were indeed frightened.

The latent superstition that had been lying dormant within them was thoroughly aroused now, and they regarded the strange vessel, and its apparently scanty crew, as belonging not to this world.

Captain Tom did not relish the idea of his brave crew being terrified.

He would very soon prove to them that the strange vessel was worked by human agency.

" The noble fellows have been deceived by all this jugglery," said Iron-Arm. ' And it's about time to put a stop to it. What do you think, Mr. Vere?"

Harry was near Iron-Arm, looking at the strange craft through his glass.

" I really don't know what to think," he replied, thoughtfully. " There is something mysteriously strange about her."

' Do you mean to say that you are inoculated by her trickery, lieutenant? I thought better of your judgment," said Iron-Arm.

" Don't be so hasty in your conclusions, sir," replied Harry. " I do not for a moment desire you to think that I am inoculated by her trickery, though I don't mind saying she is the strangest and the most mysterious vessel I ever clapped eyes on."

' That is no answer to my question, lieutenant," went on Iron-Arm, laughing. " Are you superstitious?"

" A strange question to ask, truly."

" But a proper one—pardon me, if I say so."

" But to what does the question tend?" asked Lieutenant Vere.

"Do you observe those men?"

Harry looked at the point indicated, and beheld the awe-stricken glances of the buccaneers, who regarded the pretended Indiaman with looks of horror.

"There you see the results of superstition," said Iron-Arm, pointedly, when the young lieutenant had done looking.

"So I observe. Perhaps you see the same look of horror on my face?"

"Oh, no. You have not got to that stage yet."

"I am glad you think so," was the sarcastic response.

All further conversation was interrupted by Captain Tom.

The boy chief came forward with his speaking-trumpet.

He was now within hailing distance.

"Ship ahoy!" cried Captain Tom.

His voice rolled over the deep like the notes of a silver clarion.

No response.

"Ship ahoy!" again hailed the young chieftain.

The strange vessel continued in her course without even taking the trouble to respond.

The captain of the buccaneers thought that possibly his voice did not reach the East Indiaman, so he cried out louder and more prolonged, until his very words rang again over that great waste of waters.

"Ship ahoy! Heave-to, or else I'll fire into you!"

The echo of his own voice only came back.

The few men on the quarter-deck of the East Indiaman could be seen new with great distinctness.

But it was observed that they had not moved a step from where they stood before.

Captain Tom saw the evil effects this would have on his crew, so he resolved to come to some instant and decisive action.

"I'll make the lubbers move," he muttered.

At that moment the East Indiaman veered round until her bows were almost facing the "Will-o'-the-Wisp."

"Run out the two carronades!" cried Tom.

The members of the crew told of this work obeyed his order in silence.

It was easily seen that they did not relish the job.

"Fire!" cried the young chief.

A roar like thunder followed the command.

The buccaneers stood aghast.

The heavy round shot sped over the sea with a rushing sound, and, almost simultaneously with the combined reports of the carronades, sent splinters flying from the bows of the Indiaman.

"Well aimed!" cried Captain Tom. "Now we'll see whether the lubbers will reply to us."

These were the combined reports which nearly threw Jerry Mizzen and Bob Hauler off their feet.

All signs of fear now vanished from the buccaneers.

For they knew that they had to deal henceforth with mortals like themselves.

Even the fellows on the quarter-deck of the Indiaman disappeared as if by magic.

They were no longer, as it were, carved in stone, but hastened away to get some shelter, fearing that another shot from the "Will-o'-the-Wisp" might prove more disastrous to them.

The Indiaman—for such we will persist in calling it—veered round, and sped before the wind like a frightened bird.

Her bows, though somewhat shattered, had not deteriorated much from her speed.

It was nearing sunset now, and the breeze was springing up stronger and stronger.

On sped the two vessels.

The "Will-o'-the-Wisp" was gaining rapidly on the Indiaman.

And this the latter seemed to realise.

For she seemed to pause for an instant in her flight to return the salute of the "Will-o'-the-Wisp."

Like a flash of light, all her ports were bristling with cannon.

Her decks were crowded with men.

The scarlet uniforms of marines could be discerned among the crew.

Their bayonets glistened in the descending sun, and altogether the before-pretended Indiaman looked a very formidable enemy.

With the same celerity, a Union Jack was run up to the mizzen, and she appeared what she really was—a British man-of-war.

"Hallo!" cried Captain Tom, "our mysterious friend shows her colours."

"And her teeth," said Iron-Arm.

"Which we'll have to draw," rejoined the young chief of the buccaneers.

Far from being dismayed by the formidable armament of their enemy, the gallant crew of the "Will-o'-the-Wisp" broke out into a loud cheer.

"Hurrah for gallant Captain Tom!" they cried. "Long live our buccaneer king!"

A shout of defiance was hurled back from the war-vessel.

The decks were cleared for the fight, which they knew would be a hard and stubborn one.

Zelie, coming on deck, was ordered below, by Captain Tom, who had no desire to imperil that brave girl's life.

The man-of-war now prepared to pour a broadside into the "Will-o'-the-Wisp."

She shot round like lightning for that purpose.

Captain Tom was equally prepared.

One single order to his brave buccaneers.

A terrible roar from the war-vessel followed almost simultaneously, and her rain of murderous shot whistled by the stern of the "Will-o'-the-Wisp," ploughing up the sea, at least a hundred yards off.

The buccaneer's broadside was more effective, and did considerable damage to her opponent's hull, and mizzen mast besides.

The ships were now so near each other, that Tom commanded his men to stand-by with the grapnels.

All his orders were never better executed.

The buccaneers were as cool as cucumbers.

And only too glad to pay the British man-of-war off for the little deception she practised on them.

The "Will-o'-the-Wisp" was splendidly handled.

Not a single shot of the war vessel had told upon her as yet.

Night, however, was drawing in fast.

The sun had gone down with a glitter as red as blood, and a darkness was spreading rapidly over the sea.

All traces of Captain Tom's fleet was now shut out, so, if the worst came to the worst, he had to rely entirely on the endurance of his brave buccaneers, and the sailing qualities of his tight little brig.

It was a gigantic undertaking—boarding a "three-decker" of his Majesty's navy.

But Captain Tom's heart never failed him.

He was equal to any emergency, and had proved it before that day in many a hard-fought battle.

Nearer came the ships.

And then was felt a resounding crash that made the "Will-o'-the-Wisp" tremble in every beam.

"Pikes and cutlasses to the front!" cried Tom Drake.

The grapnels were thrown out, and the "three-decker," in an instant, was made fast to the "Will-o'-the-Wisp."

Now was the time.

The buccaneers and middies rushed forward like an avalanche, and with loud shouts boarded the man-of-war.

Here a terrific hand-to-hand encounter took place.

Twice the middies and buccaneers were repulsed, and as many times they bounded forward again, headed by their gallant young leader.

Captain Tom fought like a lion.

Iron-Arm struck out with his huge iron mace right and left, and many a red-coated marine and blue-jacket fell bleeding and senseless on his own deck.

Nor was Ben Barnacle behind.

Wielding a huge cutlass, he hewed a way for himself through the man-of-war's crew until his keen sword ran red with blood.

The carnage was terrible.

Pistol shot succeeded pistol shot.

Sword clashed against sword amidst the wildest confusion, and hoarse, angry shouts of the combatants.

The cries and groans of the wounded and dying, and the furious curses of the struggling men, was a din in itself of the most frightful character.

But above all these evidences of the terrific hand-to-hand battle, was heard the manly, clear tones of Captain Tom.

"One more charge like that, my brave buccaneers and the ship is ours!"

"Not yet!" roared a voice.

Tom Drake noted from where the voice came.

He saw a party of half a dozen officers near the binnacle, and in their centre the tall form of one whose head towered above the rest.

"Not yet!" roared this man.

Tom knew that this was the captain of the man-of-war.

The constant flashes of the small arms lit up his swarthy features.

He was an ugly-looking wretch.

Such features might have done credit to the most bloodthirsty pirate on the seas.

This man Captain Tom singled out.

He had a vague idea that this was the scoundrel who shot poor Ned Maynard, and he was resolved, at all risk, to get him into his power.

"On, on, my brave lads!" shouted the boy captain. "Make way there, you lubber!"

And Captain Tom, with one sweep of his trusty blade, brought his nearest opponent to the deck.

But another leaped to confront him in an instant

Their steels clashed, and the man fell with a bitter oath.

The gallant buccaneer had lopped his arm off.

So great was the prowess of Captain Tom's arm, that his enemies, though thickly outnumbering the few faithful followers who fought by his side, gave way, and fell back in the wildest confusion.

Nothing could exceed the rage of the British captain when he saw his men giving way.

He rushed forward himself, yelling—

"Curse your cowardly hearts! are you afraid of a few paltry cut-throats, headed by a boy?"

"You lie!" cried Tom Drake. "If any one on this vessel is a cut-throat, you are the man!"

"Ha! ha! my rascally buccaneer, your insulting words will not save you. I suppose you are that boy pirate and murderer, Captain Tom Drake! Your days are numbered, cursed stripling, and your vessel will soon become the property of the King."

There was a sudden cessation of hostilities when the two leaders spoke.

The boarders and boarded looked on, as it were, to gain breathing time.

They could not help contrasting the two captains.

The one so brave, noble, and handsome.

The other the personification of ugliness and cruelty.

It must in justice be said that the crew and marines of the "three-decker" disliked the arbitrary tyrant who lorded it over them.

They fairly hated him.

And small wonder, too.

For many a brave fellow's back smarted even now from the effects of the cruel "cat."

It had been set to work for the most trivial offences.

Perhaps they had not fought so well as they might have done.

And because of this very fact.

How now could they help comparing the two leaders and passing favourable opinions in their own minds on our noble hero—the brave and dashing captain of the buccaneers.

With such a leader, they might scour the world.

More than half of them at that moment would have gone over to Captain Tom's side had they dared.

But discipline prevailed, and they were bound, as in bands of iron, to the fortunes of a man whom they detested.

We have said that all hostilities for the moment had ceased.

The two leaders stood glaring at each other like tigers.

Captain Tom was now more than ever assured that this fiend in human form was the deliberate and merciless murderer of the poor midshipman.

"You say my days are numbered," replied Tom, in answer to the British captain's exultant taunts; "and that my noble vessel will become the property of the King. Let me tell you, murderer as I know you to be, that your own days are numbered, and that your ship will, instead, become the property of Captain Tom Drake, and his crew of buccaneers! I accuse you of the murder of as noble-hearted a boy as ever stepped, and I have sworn to have your life!"

"These are brave words, young springald," replied the captain; "brave, boastful words! But on what grounds do you accuse me of murder? Be more explicit, young sir," he said, ironically.

"Did you not shoot down a young midshipman of the 'Will-o'-the-Wisp,' without even giving him the benefit of one of your mock courts-martial? Answer me that!"

"If you refer to the young rascal I had shot from the bulwarks of my ship, early this morning, I say yes."

"By saying so, you have signed your death-warrant!" cried Captain Tom Drake, furiously.

His opponent laughed derisively.

"And I'll do the same to you, if I catch you!" he said.

"Murderer—thrice accursed murderer!—you have spoken your doom!" said Tom.

And with that he made a bound forward, bearing down all opposition.

The buccaneers fought like tigers, mowing down the enemy on every side until the very decks ran red with their blood.

Nothing could withstand the ferocity of their attack.

In the heat of the battle, Captain Tom got separated from his few faithful followers.

Hewing a way for himself over the bodies of those who were so daring or so wilful as to oppose him, he made his way direct for their captain.

His tall form he could see towering above the others by every vivid flash of the fire-arms.

At last he reached him, in spite of the tyrant's angry shouts to hew him down.

"Now, defend yourself, murderer!" he cried, "for I swear to you that I shall dye my blade red in your heart's blood!"

This was no idle threat.

The brutal captain turned as pale as death.

Notwithstanding his shouts of "Down with him!" Captain Tom stood before him, with his ensanguine blade lit up by every lurid flash that illuminated the deck—stood like an angel of revenge, from whom there was no escape.

Their blades crossed.

The cruel captain fought with the desperation of despair.

But it availed him not.

Ere a dozen passes were made, his sword was shivered like a piece of glass.

And with the word "mercy" upon his cruel lips, Tom's blade pierced his heart.

He fell like a log.

Without even a groan!

And thus was avenged the murder of poor Ned Maynard.

Those who witnessed the combat never stirred.

Twenty times they could have shot Captain Tom down, but he seemed to bear a charmed life, and the only pistol-bullet that was fired at him passed harmlessly by—not harmlessly, either, for it struck a marine who was going to run him through the back, and the fellow fell down, howling out his death agony.

But while this was going on, Captain Tom exposed his brave crew to serious danger.

More serious, indeed, than he thought.

The blue-jackets and marines had retreated before the victorious onslaught of Captain Tom's buccaneers.

They left a portion of the deck to the dead and dying.

Now came a grand opportunity for the first lieutenant, who, since his leader's death, was virtually captain.

This man, as quick as thought, ran out a couple of carronades, and before the buccaneers were aware of the fact, opened a terrible fire on them.

The fore part of the deck was literally swept by a murderous hail of grape and canister, and the buccaneers were mowed down like sheep in the shambles.

Then, with loud shouts, the blue-jackets and marines, headed by their officers, rushed forward.

The fight which ensued was of a brief but terrific description, finally ending in the defeat of Captain Tom's crew, who were driven in the wildest confusion over the side.

It was with the greatest difficulty that they reached the deck of the "Will-o'-the-Wisp," conscious that they had lost many a brave comrade without gaining any decided advantage themselves.

The ships swung apart.

And each party seemed to have had enough of the fight.

But had the brave buccaneers dreamed for an instant that their gallant young chief was still aboard of the man-of-war, they would have forced their way back at every risk, and rescued him or perished.

But such was the case.

Captain Tom, by order of the first lieutenant, was surrounded and disarmed.

Though not before his sword was broken in his grasp.

"Captain Tom Drake, we have you at last," said the lieutenant, a sardonic smile illuminating his features.

At his side stood the second and third lieutenants.

and behind these again the marines and blue-jackets, armed to the teeth.

Captain Tom with a look of despair saw it was a little vessel unless its grapnels and towing lad.

Any other man placed in the same position would have given up all hope.

But not so Tom.

The look of despair faded instantly from his handsome features, and he faced his captors boldly, and with scorn, still retaining his broken sword.

"Yes, my bold buccaneer, you are in our power at last," said the lieutenant, "and your fate shall be a warning to others."

"Indeed," said Tom, with a sneer on his proud lip. "I have been in worse situations than this before, my good friend, and have escaped them."

"You shall not escape this time," replied the lieutenant, "I give you my word for it."

"I have done you a service," rejoined Tom, laughing.

"How so?"

"By killing that miserable captain of yours."

"Murdering him, you mean," said the other.

"You are mistaken," replied Tom, dauntlessly. "I slew him in fair and honourable fight, much more than he deserved, I assure you."

"Well, how can this affect your position?" asked the lieutenant, who, if truth must be told, was not over sorry for his leader's death.

"Inasmuch as this," replied Tom, with the most perfect coolness, "by killing him I have gained you a captaincy."

"Splendid reasoning, certainly, but I cannot see how this affects your position."

"If you only liberate me, it will, most certainly," replied Tom.

"Curse your coolness, sir! I think you are the most audacious fellow that ever breathed."

"I am glad you think so. But you must, nevertheless, acknowledge that I have done you a service."

"And I'll do you one before you are many minutes older, by swinging you up at the yard-arm."

"That's what I call the basest ingratitude," said Tom, whose only object was to gain time for he knew the moment that they discovered his absence on the "Will-o'-the-Wisp," that they would return and at every hazard rescue him.

"Base ingratitude, you scoundrel!" yelled the first lieutenant. "Dare you speak to me thus? It would be base ingratitude to his Majesty King George to let you live another hour."

"Why return evil for good, my friend?" said Tom, chaffingly.

"Curse the fellow's coolness and impudence both!" muttered the lieutenant. "Hang me! he beats all the buccaneers and pirates I ever saw in my life. It's a confounded pity, though, that I should hang such a brave fellow like a common malefactor at the yard-arm. But it must be done, and done quickly, if done at all. Seize and bind him!" he cried, aloud, to some of the marines and blue-jackets who were near him.

But none of them stirred.

"Do you not hear me, fellows!" he roared. "Seize and bind that villainous buccaneer, I say!"

The men stepped forward to obey him.

Before they could lay a hand on Captain Tom, however, a piercing shriek rung out upon the night.

"What the devil is that?" asked the lieutenant, turning round.

The men stood transfixed.

The rustle of a woman's dress was heard, and before the marines or blue-jackets could stop her, a female broke through their ranks, and threw her arms around Captain Tom's neck.

"A woman!" exclaimed the astonished lieutenant, who would as equally expected a thunderbolt to fall into their midst. "Where the deuce did she drop from?"

Captain Tom looked up reproachfully.

It was Zelie, who came in his hour of danger, like a beautiful apparition, to comfort him.

"Oh, Zelie! Why have you done this?" he asked, sadly.

Tom was not the man to flinch from danger, but this unexpected incident unnerved him.

He blamed the brave, devoted girl for disobeying his order.

Indeed he had strictly enjoined her to remain in the cabin of the "Will-o'-the-Wisp" until after the engagement.

But in her desire to be near him, she had broken that injunction.

"Do not blame me, dear Tom," she said, in a tender tone that went straight to the brave boy-captain's heart. "I could not bear to think that you were in danger, and I away from you."

"Hallo!" roared the lieutenant. "What the devil does all this mean? Tear them apart, I say, or we'll never get through this cursed job!"

The marines and blue-jackets again advanced.

"Come, madam," said the lieutenant, trying to be a little polite, "release the young man, or I'll not answer for the consequences."

"What, to die a shameful death?" she cried, bitterly. "Never!"

"Then the fault lies at your own door, madam," replied the lieutenant. 'Quick, men! Don't hesitate an instant! Tear them asunder!'

Captain Tom tried to disengage himself from her loving arms.

The marines and blue-jackets rushed forward.

Much against their will, though.

But they had to obey, nevertheless, for disobedience to their lieutenant's command was mutiny, and mutiny meant death.

They rushed forward, we say; but, clinging to Captain Tom, the fair girl waved them back.

"Advance another step!" she cried, with the fire of a tigress flashing from her eyes, "harm but one hair of his head, and the man who does it dies!"

And she looked as if she was capable of keeping her word.

Zelie had drawn two beautiful pistols from a concealed portion of her attire, and levelled them point-blank at the first and second lieutenants' heads.

"Order your men off," she added, addressing the senior lieutenant.

The old officer quailed beneath her fierce glances.

He saw that he had awakened a devil in her, and that one word from his lips, other than she dictated, would seal his own death warrant.

Brave as he was, he was not prepared to die just yet, so he gave the order for the men to retire.

This they did, glad of the chance.

Next moment came a sudden crash, which nearly threw them off their feet.

"What the devil is that?" asked the lieutenant

The reply came in loud shouts, and a simultaneous discharge of firearms.

"Repel boarders!" he shouted. "It's that cursed buccaneer vessel down on us again!"

He was right.

The "Will-o'-the-Wisp" came in search of Captain Tom Drake.

And her brave crew of buccaneers and middies beat down all opposition to get at their beloved leader.

Tom Drake and Zelie, in the confusion that ensued, reached that part of the deck where the buccaneers were.

Their arrival was hailed with loud shouts and glad cries of welcome, and before those on the man-of-war could recover from their surprise, brave Tom Drake, Zelie, and his gallant crew, had regained the deck of their own vessel.

CHAPTER CLV.

TOM DRAKE MEETS WITH FURTHER ADVENTURES.

CAPTAIN TOM, in the weakened state of his crew, thought it little use to have another bout with the man-of-war.

He accomplished all he wished for in the death of its cruel captain.

Besides, he taught the crew and officers a lesson they wouldn't likely forget for some time.

And having done this he was satisfied.

"I'll give them a parting piece of advice, nevertheless," said Tom to Iron-Arm.

Taking up the speaking trumpet, he cried—

"Lieutenant ahoy!"

"It's that cussed Captain Tom Drake again," said the lieutenant of the man-of-war. "Confound his impudence! I wonder what does he want now?"

"Pour a broadside into him," suggested the second lieutenant.

"Confound me! how can we? We are thoroughly used up. I never got such a licking before in my life. Broadside indeed! The fellow would riddle us like a sieve if we attempted such a thing. Oh, no! I'm too old a dog for that. We must be as civil as we can without exactly compromising our dignity. We'll meet him again, depend upon it, and then we can serve him out. There's his bellow again through that confounded speaking trumpet."

"Lieutenant, ahoy!" cried Captain Tom.

"Ahoy! What do you want?" roared the officer, back.

"To give you a little good advice, lieutenant; and this is it. Whenever you have Captain Tom Drake in your power again, keep a sure grip on him, will you?"

"You may depend upon that, my gallant young fledgling. He'll not get away so readily as he got away to-night."

"Good-bye!"

"Good-bye, till we meet again, then look out for squalls and roaring catamounts!" added the lieutenant, in a lower tone.

Of course Captain Tom did not hear the latter part of the sentence, for the very good reason that the lieutenant had withdrawn the speaking-trumpet from his lips.

The "Will-o'-the-Wisp" now sailed on her way back to rejoin the rest of the fleet.

But she was doomed not to go far without meeting another adventure.

Which, if not so prolific of a certain purpose as the first, was, at least, equally dangerous.

As if by magic, the darkness rolled up like some huge curtain from the ocean.

The stars and moon shone forth, and lit up the sea for miles.

"Sail-oh!" cried the look-out.

It was not necessary to ask where.

A vessel was unconsciously bearing down on them.

The instant it caught sight of the "Will-o'-the-Wisp" it veered round, and pursued a different course.

At this time it was not more than half a mile off.

Captain Tom fancied more than once that he heard screams issuing from the vessel.

This awoke our gallant hero's suspicions.

Tom took up his glass, and, with one of his eagle glances, saw his suspicions more than confirmed.

He now resolved to give chase, and, giving the

word, the " Will-o'-the-Wisp " was hastening in the track of the strange brig, with all her sails spread out to the breeze.

It was an exciting chase.

The vessels were very evenly matched.

Of the two, the " Will-o'-the-Wisp " had the odds.

She was a swifter sailer, perhaps.

When Captain Tom fancied that he was near enough, he took up his speaking trumpet, and hailed the pursued craft.

" Brig ahoy!"

" Ahoy!" came a ringing voice from the brig.

" Heave to!" cried Captain Tom.

" What if we won't?" came the answer.

" Then you'll compel me to fire into you," said Tom.

" Fire, and be hanged!" was the reply.

" A nice. civil fellow that, isn't he?" said Captain Tom. " He deserves some consideration at my hands, in the shape of an iron pill."

One of the carronades was run out, being double-shotted, and the aim taken.

" Fire!" cried Captain Tom.

The answer was a loud roar—a flash of dusky flame, and a peculiar rushing sound, followed by a cloud of sulphurous vapour.

Captain Tom, as far away as he was from the brig, could hear one of his iron messengers go crashing through her timbers.

" Well aimed!" cried the buccaneer. " If that doesn't bring her to her senses, we'll try what virtue there is in another."

The dense cloud of smoke cleared away.

Tom saw the damage done.

The cannon ball had ploughed right through her stern.

Besides this, the force of the shot created some momentary panic on deck, which didn't last long, for the brig, without heaving-to, sent back her return compliment.

The heavy weight of iron whistled through the " Will-o'-the-Wisp's " shrouds, but did no further damage.

" A clean shot, but too high," said Captain Tom, looking up at the shrouds, and the great rent the cannon-ball made in them. " Now, lads, don't let her recover herself. Give her a broadside this time, and if that don't make her heave-to, I don't know what will."

By very little skilful manipulation, the "Will-o'-the-Wisp" was brought round on her side.

The guns were run out in a trice, followed by a mighty roar, that made every timber in the gallant vessel tremble again.

Then the iron hail of the " Will-o'-the-Wisp " sped on its message of death and destruction.

" I thought that would do it," said Captain Tom, as the smoke cleared away. " See! she is utterly helpless, and in our power!"

So it seemed.

The brig hove to with very little of the smart look she wore ten minutes before.

Her bulwarks were shattered frightfully.

She appeared, at first sight, nothing more than a complete wreck.

None of her masts were gone, though some of her yards were splintered, and her sails perforated by the heavy shot.

Soon the " Will-o'-the-Wisp " hove alongside.

Grapnels were thrown out.

But boarding the strange brig was not so easy a task as might be imagined.

The torn decks swarmed with fierce, ruthless-looking corsairs, armed with pikes cutlasses, and pistols.

" Follow me, my brave lads!" cried Captain Tom, leaping fearlessly over the shattered bulwarks, into the very midst of this swarm of armed ruffians, who, with loud, savage oaths, threw themselves upon him.

The gallant Tom might have paid dearly for his heroic bravery at that moment had it not been for such excellent supporters as Iron-Arm, Ben Barnacle, and other brave fellows.

These fought like lions through the throng of assassins, warding off every blow from their beloved leader's head.

" The cabin! the cabin!" cried Captain Tom, who heard loud and piercing screams proceeding from that direction. " Hew them down, my brave buccaneers, and follow me!"

A score of the middies followed in their brave leader's track, while Ben Barnacle and his gallant comrades kept the piratical horde at bay.

Iron-Arm, notwithstanding the terrible strain of his previous fight with the man-of-war's men, was never in better form in his life.

Wherever he struck, down went a pirate—sometimes two—either senseless or dead.

His heavy mace became a terrible weapon when wielded by one of his endurance and strength, and so the fierce pirates thought, for the most powerful of them tried to get out of his way whenever they saw him coming near them.

But we must not leave Captain Tom.

Followed by his brave middies, the gallant leader of the buccaneers made his way, after receiving two slight wounds, to the cabin.

He was just in time to see a burly ruffian snatching up the shrinking form of one of the fairest young creatures he had ever looked upon.

She was the very personification of all that was lovely and beautiful in a woman.

" Help! help!" cried the affrighted girl, struggling to free herself from the ruffian's rude embrace. " Oh, sir, for the love of Heaven, help me!"

It was to Tom Drake she appealed.

Her bright eyes fell upon his noble form and handsome features as the first who entered.

And from that moment she instinctively felt that she would be delivered by no one but him.

" Don't be alarmed, my dear," said Captain Tom, coming up to the pirate, and dealing him such a terrific blow that he was compelled to release his hold of the girl. " Now, you ruffianly skunk!" added Tom, " come forward, and I'll give you a repetition of thedose."

The pirate glared at him like a tiger, and drew his long, gleaming cutlass from its sheath.

" That's your play, is it?" said Tom. " Take charge of the young lady, one of you. I'll soon polish the ruffian off."

One of the middies took charge of the girl, who had become insensible.

Tom drew his sword.

The pirate, with a furious oath, made a savage lunge at him.

Tom very skilfully parried it.

" Now," said the gallant captain of the buccaneers, " it is my turn. Look out for your nose, for I mean slicing a bit of it off for you. It will add materially to the picturesqueness of your appearance."

Captain Tom was as good as his word.

After the first four or five passes, he, with a downward cut, sliced the fellow's nose in such a manner that the pirate disappeared from the cabin, yelling with pain.

" I don't think that that ruffian will trouble us any more," said Tom, quite coolly. " I've left a mark on him by which I shall know him again, should I ever meet him."

" Captain Tom Captain Tom!" cried a voice from above, at this moment. " Hurry up, for Heaven's sake, if you don't wish to be surrounded!"

It was one of his brave middies, beating back the attack of a horde of ruffianly pirates, who were trying to force their way into the cabin.

Captain Tom, obeying the warning voice, without a moment's hesitation, caught the insensible girl in his arms, and rushed up the companion-way, preceded by some of his middies, and followed by the others.

Guarded by his faithful followers, Captain Tom bore the poor girl up the steps.

The middies had to fight desperately hard to force a passage through the armed ruffians, who tried to surround them.

Captain Tom had his hands full, and could consequently do nothing but urge his brave fellows on.

One of the ruffianly pirates threw a grenade into their midst.

But this, fortunately, did not go off.

The brave midshipmen fired their pistols right and left, and had the satisfaction of seeing more than one of their enemies fall.

At last Captain Tom cleared the threatened danger, and was once more among his gallant buccaneers with his fair charge.

The pirates, meanwhile, fled in all directions, and as nothing more was to be done aboard the pirate brig—they having collected all the treasures they could find—the captain and his brave crew found themselves once again on their own tight little vessel, which now, under a full press of canvas, and having a strong breeze in its favour, sped over the sea like a graceful bird.

CHAPTER CLVI.

REUBEN HARPY.

With the permission of the reader, we will now retrace our steps a little way.

Very few of our readers, we think, will have an idea what became of Reuben Harpy and the sham sentinel.

The vessel was searched fore and aft, without any success.

The various cabins, and down deep into the holds, but in vain.

All signs of Reuben Harpy and his pretended guard had disappeared, as if the two men had been swallowed deep into the ocean.

No boats had left the brig's side, except it was Captain Tom's, so that even this means of escape had been denied them.

Let us, therefore, investigate the mystery of their strange and, at that time, unexplainable disappearance.

When the ex-privateer captain was fished out of the sea in his attempt to escape, a great deal of confusion prevailed on the brig.

Hauled on deck like a drowned rat, more dead than alive, and trembling in every limb, his future safe-keeping was consigned into the hands of anyone who liked to take him.

Most of the crew didn't care about the job, and as they were all employed, more or less, in looking over at the "Will-o'-the-Wisp," to catch a glimpse of Captain Tom, the lot of taking him below fell to the confederate of the sham sentinel.

Half dragging Reuben Harpy after him, he hurried him down the companion-way.

Our sentinel was at his post, guarding most zealously the pirate Rufus, who had either lapsed into insensibility, or was in a very profound sleep.

To be sure, the sham sentinel expressed the greatest astonishment to see his friend, the ex-captain, returning—especially returning drenched from head to foot.

A few words from his confederate, however, served to explain all; and now the guard had to set his wits to work the best way he could to remedy the evil.

That someone had been listening to his conversation with Rufus he had not the slightest doubt, and that that someone would be able to point him out to Iron-Arm, or any of his officers, he was equally positive.

In a manner of speaking, he was in as dangerous a fix as was the ex-captain himself.

If caught, and the guilt fastened on him, as he had no doubt it would be, he would be strung up, without a hope of mercy, at the yard-arm.

Brave and daring a man as he was, he shuddered involuntarily at the mere thought of meeting such a fate.

In fact, he had no relish for hanging.

Possessing the great sea-emerald had something to do with this fact, perhaps, as he naturally rejoiced in such a treasure, by which he hoped, should he ever escape from the brig, to realise a fortune—and a large one.

Now, the sham sentinel was by no means a bad fellow.

But he was very avaricious, notwithstanding.

Not, however, as some people understand avarice, but rather with a desire, perhaps, of accumulating wealth for spending it, rather than for retaining it.

He could never exactly be a miser, yet he could gloat over any coveted treasure with a miser's sordid love, and spend it in luxurious and riotous living next day.

This man was full of schemes.

His brain was ever at work—planning, planning, from morning till night.

Furthermore, as is usual with such men, he was a man of considerable ingenuity.

True, his life had been almost a failure up to this time, but he had the deplorable habit of going just a little too far, and this "little too far" was the cause of most of his failures.

But all such a man wanted was a little wealth, and he would turn the world with it.

He had that coveted wealth now next to his heart, stolen from another who had likewise stolen it in his turn from the reeking and gory throat of Israel Scawm, whom he butchered, not to obtain the fatal gem, for he knew not of its existence, but through the sheer wanton cruelty of his nature.

Such a man as the sham sentinel was sure to plan and scheme hard for his life.

And he did so.

He was thinking now how to slip through the fingers of the crew of the brig.

It was no easy matter.

Next to impossible now to get away in an open boat in broad daylight.

And if they caught him on board, his life would pay the penalty.

What was to be done then?

He thought, and thought, and thought.

At last a sudden, bright idea struck him.

He had been down in the hold where the powder was stored.

The barrels were all supposed to be full, but he knew that two or three of them were empty.

In fact, he had emptied one of the barrels himself, not with any deliberate design of blowing up the ship, but the idea then, as now, struck him that he might require one.

The powder he stored in some empty kegs, so that it was equally safe there as in the barrel.

There was not a moment to be lost, and the sham sentinel was as rapid in execution as he was in thought.

He could depend upon his confederate for a supply of food when he needed it, yet with his assistance he hoped to leave the vessel that night.

There were always boats lowered, and it was an easy matter to get into one of them, and pull away in the darkness.

The crew of Iron-Arm's brig were not very vigilant, and less so than ever since the engagement with Admiral Ellis's fleet.

Reuben Harpy was trembling from the wet and the cold, combined with his fears.

The sham sentinel pitied him, he looked such a wretched, miserable object.

He called his confederate aside a moment, and whispered to him.

The man shook his head, and, with a gleam of intelligence flashing from his eyes, he went up on deck.

Did he know about the empty powder-barrels?

Evidently he did, for there was a tacit understanding between them that he was to steal down the hold with the news, and with food to strengthen them for the journey that the sham sentinel had designed they should take together.

"Come, Captain Harpy," said the sentinel, taking his dripping arm within his own, "this place is getting a little too dangerous. We must go somewhere else."

Reuben Harpy made no reply, but followed him like a frightened cur.

He would go anywhere rather than fall into the hands of Captain Tom—into the very sea itself.

They proceeded on until they got to the hold.

Reuben paused when he gazed down into those dark depths.

He began to grow afraid and suspicious.

"Where are you taking me to?" he asked, in a trembling voice.

"Where those on board the brig will not find you," was the reply. "Fear not. Trust to me, and you'll yet escape to snap your fingers at that dreaded buccaneer."

Reuben, by this answer, seemed more satisfied that his companion would act with perfect good faith towards him.

But he shivered and shook as if the very marrow in his bones was freezing.

His late guard quickly noticed his condition.

"This will never do," he said. "At all risks, you must get your dry clothes."

"They are in the cabin," answered Reuben. "I think I can get on well enough in the ones I have on."

"Nonsense! you'll take your death," said the other. "At all risks you must get your dry clothes. Stay here. I'll go for them myself, as I know the way better than you."

Reuben was very glad that he did "know the way," for nothing short of being forced, physically, would entice him to enter the cabin where the mad pirate was.

The cowardly wretch almost dreaded his own shadow.

Even being left alone for a few minutes nearly frightened him out of his wits.

The sham sentinel, with a noiseless step, hurried from the spot.

He was not long gone before he returned with a bundle of Reuben Harpy's clothes.

"Now, captain, I think you'll be comfortable," said the man. "But don't change them yet—not till we get below. Hark! what noise is that? By Heaven! they are searching the ship for you."

The search we have before described had really commenced.

Loud, angry voices were heard, and the tramp of heavy footsteps rung out upon the close, dank air.

"Come, follow me, quickly," said the sentinel, "and, as we have no light to guide us, mind how you tread. It is lucky the fellows left this place open, or we might have had some little difficulty in getting down."

They now descended some dozen steps to the brig's powder magazine.

All was intense darkness—a darkness as pitchy as Erebus itself, where one couldn't see a step before him.

"Take my hand," said the sentinel, preserving the same very low and cautious tone. "I know the place so well that it's impossible for me to stumble over anything."

Nor did he overrate his powers in that direction—he walked in and out among the barrels of powder with startling accuracy.

"Now we'll come to a halt and look about us," said the sham sentinel.

Reuben certainly did look about him, but could see nothing only the darkness.

The angry voices of the searchers died away.

Their heavy steps were heard no more, and the solemn stillness that reigned in the hold was only broken by the scampering of numerous rats who were dislodged from their retreats by the intruders.

"Now, Captain Harpy, I think you may change your clothes here," said his companion. "I don't imagine these lubbers will trouble us any more, at least for some time to come—they must be searching some other part of the brig."

Reuben Harpy wished the "lubbers" to the devil, and in their company Captain Tom Drake, for to our gallant boy hero he attributed most of the misfortunes that had befallen him.

He did not think that he himself was the source of those mishaps.

Oh, no.

That would be entirely out of the question.

Cursing his unlucky stars, Reuben Harpy threw off his wet clothes and attired himself in his dry ones.

When he got these on, he felt a little more comfortable and composed.

"Where can I put this bundle of wet things?" he asked.

"Give them to me, captain—I'll put them away. It wouldn't do to have these knocking about, if the rascals should take it into their heads to come down."

"No," replied Reuben, with a shiver; "they'd soon overhaul us pretty quick. Throw them anywhere you like, my good fellow, so that you put them out of sight."

"Depend on me for doing that, sir. I'll put them where no one will find them, you may take your oath."

The sentinel took up the bundle of dripping clothes, and stowed them away in a twinkling.

"I'll give them all the money I have on me if they find them now, Captain Harpy," he said.

"What have you done with them?"

"Thrown them into a well."

"Thrown them into a well!" exclaimed the astonished privateer. "You don't mean to say that there is a well down here?"

"I do; and from that well your common sailor's rig will go into the sea."

"What if a man could escape that way?" said Reuben.

"He'd get drowned to a dead certainty," replied the other. "He'd be sucked in under the brig in the twinkling of an eye, and there he'd remain until all the breath was out of his body. After that he'd become food for the fishes."

Reuben Harpy could not help an involuntary shudder passing through him.

"Such a fate!" he muttered.

"Would not be quite so bad as hanging at a yard-arm," replied the other, carelessly. "Pardon me! I overheard your remark, and it struck me that that would be the right answer for it. If the worst came to the worst, I'd sooner leap down that well than take my chances of life at the hands of the buccaneers."

"But you have nothing to fear from them," said Reuben, forgetting for the moment the part his companion took in liberating him.

"Haven't I, sir? I tell you I have everything to fear. For example, you must not forget the part I took in releasing you. That alone would be punishable by death if they caught me. But there are other things that have come to their knowledge that would even give me a less chance."

"Then you are not down here by choice?" said Reuben.

"Not I. There is no choice in the matter. By this time I'd be kicking my heels up in the air, no doubt, if I had only gone on deck, or remained at my post. They have found out all, and their punishment would be swift and terrible. But, thank Heaven! I have my wits about me, and that is the reason that I am here. No man fears death less than I, but I should like to be spared a few years more before I bid my final adieu to the world."

"You are a strange fellow," said Reuben, not particularly desiring to enter into a discussion that related to hanging, or to any other unnatural mode of leaving the world.

"Many, very many, think that," replied the sentinel; "but I take a philosophic view of matters, and I find it to be the best plan after all. Besides, it keeps the mind in proper order. Many people go and meet trouble half-way. I never do so, but wait until it comes up and clutches me, then I grapple with it. And after that I know who gets the best at the battle."

"Well, I must say one thing, you are not only a true philosopher, but a very brave fellow."

"Thank you, captain. You have told me what I knew a long time ago. However, let me tell you where you are."

"Where are we?" asked Reuben.

"In the enemy's powder magazine," was the reply.

"Good God!" cried the ex-captain, leaping up.

"Oh, don't alarm yourself, sir. There is nothing really very serious in being in a powder magazine. I'd just as soon be here as on deck, only for the confounded rats and the bad smell—two inconveniences I really object to, but which I cannot help all the same."

Reuben Harpy was astounded.

This man had nerve enough for a hundred such as he.

"He talks about a powder-magazine as if it were a drawing-room," said Reuben, in breathless amazement. "Well, for my part, I have a thorough and decided objection to powder magazines."

His companion laughed quietly.

"I knew you have," he said.

"How did you know that?"

"Because I read it in your nature the first time I ever saw you," replied the man, bluntly. "But the subject is unpleasant, therefore let us go to something else."

The ex-privateer was glad, indeed, that he did go to something else.

This faint intimation of his cowardice stung him to the quick.

"I know," said the sham sentinel, "that you would like to see what your surroundings look like. It is not likely that these fellows will trouble us immediately, and as I have a little lantern here, I may as well light it."

"Light a lantern in a powder magazine!" cried Reuben, starting back in horror. "Good God! if you attempt such a thing here, you'll blow both us and the brig into the elements!"

"You needn't alarm yourself a bit, captain. There is no danger."

"What! No danger where there is tons of gunpowder stored over the hold? I entreat you, my good fellow, not to risk your life and mine, too, in this mad attempt."

The sentinel only laughed in his sleeve.

"You are giving way to useless fears," he said, putting on air of great gravity. "I'll prove to you that your terrors are groundless."

Reuben Harpy begged of him to do nothing of the kind.

But the sentinel persisted.

Instead, however, of taking a flint and steel from his pocket, he produced a little lamp already lit.

"So you see there is nothing dangerous in it after all," he said, laughing.

Reuben was very much surprised.

He had backed, in his terror, to the steps.

Now he returned, very much ashamed of his cowardice.

The hold was nearly full of barrels.

All these contained, or were supposed to contain, gunpowder.

It was a dangerous cargo for any vessel to carry.

Reuben Harpy stared aghast at such a sight.

It almost made his hair stand on end.

"Do all these contain powder?" he asked, scarcely believing his eyes.

"Yes, with a few exceptions. There are two or three barrels that have nothing at all in them. Wouldn't it be glorious sport to blow the cursed vessel, crew, and all up in the air!"

"What do you mean?" cried the ex-privateer, aghast.

"Only this. Should those rascally buccaneers come down here and discover us now, while we are in the act of talking, how easy it would be to knock the head off one of these barrels here, and make terms to them, which they would not dare to refuse."

"This man is getting as mad as Black Rufus," said Reuben, his legs quaking under him. "By getting out of Captain Tom's clutches, I have got into the hands of a madman. I thought he was a philosopher; but philosophers, they say, are sometimes mad. I almost wish Satan flew away with me before I came here."

The sentinel could see what was passing in Reuben's mind, and slightly smiled at his foolish fears.

He had frightened him enough, and now he thought it high time to leave off.

"Come, come, Captain Harpy," he said, "what is the matter with you? Are you frightened?"

"Enough to make anyone frightened, I should think," almost blubbered the privateer.

"You don't think for an instant that I meant what I said?"

"Yes, I do."

"Nonsense."

"It is no very great nonsense to frighten one's life out."

"Do you imagine I meant what I said about the buccaneers?"

"I really can't tell; but you looked very serious when you said it."

"You told me I was a philosopher."

"I think I made a mistake, unless philosophers are mad."

"Do you think, then, that I am mad?"

Reuben was familiarising himself with the fellow's humour by this time.

"Well, I have had no ground lately to think otherwise," he answered.

"Well, you said I was brave?"

"I said so, truly."

"I suppose you have changed your opinion?"

"Oh, not at all!"

"Do you think a madman can be brave?"

"Most assuredly I think."

"Well, do you know what, Captain Harpy," went on the sentinel, "I never thought you had so much humour in you before. I think a good position and favourable circumstances might make you a very great wag."

Reuben Harpy laughed.

He had a far better opinion of the sentinel now than he had a few minutes ago.

The man had only been jesting with him, and, perceiving that this was the case, he returned the compliment by doing a bit of joking himself in return.

"I am rather sorry now that we made all this noise, Mr. Harpy," said the sentinel.

"Why?"

"The discussion was a very useless, I may say, reckless one. But even philosophers will have their sport at times. Don't you think that the case?"

"I should be very sorry to disagree with you," said Reuben, "perhaps they do. But it strikes me that this is a most curious and strange place to make sport in."

"I am forced to agree with you in that respect, Captain Harpy; and I think we have made a little more noise than we ought to have done. It is a melancholy fact that, when exposed to the greatest amount of danger, at times, to treat our positions with levity. I will admit to you that either of our voices might have been heard from above, and if such had been the case, nothing would have saved us from a violent death."

"What would you have done with the powder?" asked he who was now gaining courage.

"Well, that would have been our only and last chance. It is likely it would have had the effect of frightening the buccaneers in such a manner, that we might bring them to our terms. But before we attempted any hand on their cursed crew, they could have to send their leader to me—Captain Tom Drake. I could rely on that man's word sooner than I could on any other, Iron-Arm, of course, excepted."

"A curse upon Tom Drake!" said Reuben, under his breath. "He's the author of all my misfortunes and the bane of my life—curse him!"

The sentinel, however, heard him not.

He was too absorbed in reflections of his own.

Reuben looked upon him as an after-thought to all his goings-on.

Whatever his reflections were, they were broken by the sudden sounds of voices, and the heavy tramp of footsteps.

They were a long distance off yet, but evidently approaching the hold in which the powder was stored.

The sentinel was quickly on the alert.

He set the glare of a barrel, throwing the glare of his little lantern unconsciously on the pale, agitated features of Reuben Harpy.

Hearing the approaching sounds, he leaped instantly down.

"Here they come at last," he whispered. "Now to test the safety of the empty powder barrels."

By the bright glare of the lantern, the empty barrels were instantly picked out from among many of the others.

"Come this way, Captain Harpy," whispered the sentinel, "and be cautious that you don't stir or breathe above your breath."

He pointed to one of the empty barrels.

It was just large enough for Reuben to squeeze himself into it.

The sentinel was pale as death, and he swore softly against his rival.

It did not take an instant for the sentinel to conceal himself.

The moment he did so, he congratulated himself, and got into another barrel, but taking care beforehand to send to the side of his little lantern.

The sentinel was not a second too soon.

Footsteps were heard descending the steps which led to the magazine.

Hardly had the sham sentinel concealed himself in the empty powder barrel when the persons who were descending the steps to the hold paused suddenly.

"Jacob! Jacob, I say! Where are you taking me to?" roared a voice.

The voice, as the reader is aware, was Doctor Shrike's.

That great luminary of learning and medicine, whether he had mistaken his way or not, was naturally enough very anxious to know where he was.

And neither he nor his assistant had a light.

Which, of course, made matters much worse.

"Come here, you scoundrel! I'll wring your neck, you villain! Only let me get at you, that's all!"

"What have I done, sir?" blubbered Jacob.

"What have you done? Why, you have lost us, you scoundrel, that's what you have done! Where the devil are we, I'd like to know?"

"You are descending to the cabin, sir."

"You lie, you long-legged wretch! Do you dare to tell me such a base falsehood to my very teeth? Only for the reason I hold your head in, I'd kick you like a football, you blustering scoundrel!"

"My head again," thought Jacob. "Poor head! he's all the time thinking of it. I am sure he never goes to bed of a night without fancying that he has it under his pillow. Oh, my poor cranium!—what a world of trouble you cause some people! But I suppose he must have it, and all because he's made up his mind to study something wonderful in phrenology. Well, if he is disposed to get a better skull to it than I have, I suppose he must have it. Oh, why did I ever become acquainted with a doctor! He's been the ruin of my young life!"

The last words Jacob unluckily uttered aloud.

And the vampire, as a matter of course, heard them.

Doctor Shrike was greatly enraged thereat, because he thought they had some reference to himself, which they indubitably had.

"Curse you, take that!" he yelled, lunging out his huge foot.

The sharp point of his boot caught poor Jacob in a sore spot behind, and the force of the kick sent him head over heels down the remaining steps, yelling—

"Murder!"

It's a great wonder that Jacob's neck was not broken by the fall.

And it might have been, but that he came against one of the powder barrels, and partly saved himself.

Besides, Jacob's continued bawling was sufficient to attest that he was not quite killed.

"A ruined life, eh?" cried the doctor, chuckling with savage glee; "how did you like that, Jacob, my son? I'll tame you presently, my dear boy. Ha! ha! ha! Only let me come down to you, and I'll cut you into mincemeat!"

Jacob now actually thought his last hour was come, and so began roaring lustily for mercy.

"Oh, Doctor Shrike, don't kill me!—in mercy

ake, don't kill me! I am not fit to die yet! I am not, indeed!"

"So much the better," replied the fiendish doctor. "So much the better, you gormandising villain! It will make you all the fitter to go to—to the devil. Ahem!"

And to Jacop's great horror, Doctor Shrike deliberately descended the steps, and felt around for him in the darkness.

In the meantime, the assistant managed to squeeze himself in between two powder barrels.

Here he kept perfectly still.

Not daring even to breathe.

"Come out, you rascal! Where are you, you rat!" roared the irate doctor, groping through the darkness, but in vain.

Jacop, in the very terror of his life, still did not dare to breathe.

His terrified imagination painted the enraged vampire with a large dissecting knife in his hand.

"Won't you come out, you scoundrel?" cried Doctor Shrike, still making an unavailing search for his assistant. "Am I to be looking about here and breaking my shins in the darkness for you, you villain! Oh, you rogue, only let me lay hands on you once, and I'll—I'll take the skin off your body! Curse me, if I won't!"

Doctor Shrike swore.

This fact, if anything, was enough to show the violence of his passions.

Jacop always dreaded his master the more in such crises of his rage.

So he took particular care to keep quiet, and remain where he was, in spite of the doctor's aspirations to come out.

Doctor Shrike, in his search for his incorrigible co-labourer, had the misfortune to come very near the barrel in which the sham sentinel was hidden.

In fact, in his eagerness to find Jacop, he knocked up against that barrel, and would have overturned it but for the fact that there was someone in it to prevent him.

The sham sentinel was in the best of possible humours.

And his very soul leaped with joy when he knew that the doctor was near him.

Of course Doctor Shrike could not always be groping about in the darkness, even though he had the laudable purpose in his mind of pummelling the recreant Jacop the instant he caught sight of him.

So he paused at this identical barrel to recover his breath a little.

A splendid opportunity presented itself.

Doctor Shrike was leaning against the barrel profoundly contemplating the darkness, and vowing bitter vengeance against Jacop.

Very close, indeed, to the aforesaid barrel were a few empty powder kegs with the tops knocked out.

They were within easy reach of the sham sentinel's hand.

Without disturbing the doctor's reverie in the least, the man straightened up—he had some time before quietly removed the top of his barrel—and sending over his hand, clutched one of the kegs.

Another moment, and he had it poised in both hands.

Meanwhile, the doctor's meditations were as follows—

"I wonder where that scamp, Jacop's, gone? I should like to have him under my thumb just for five minutes; if I wouldn't polish him off, may I never cut another leg off. Can it be possible the rascal's got away and given me the slip? Yet if he had I should have heard him go up the steps. He's still down here, I'm sure, hiding among these cursed barrels. I wonder what they contain? Pork? No! For if they contained pork I should

have smelt it. There's a deuce of a lot of them though. Shouldn't be surprised if it's the powder magazine. Oh, Lord! if it went off, what would become of us—I mean me, myself individually? Selfish reptile that I am! Upon my honour, I begin to feel afraid. I, who have lopped off heads—I mean arms and legs innumerable—begin positively, to feel afraid; and if some evil spirit, for instance should clutch me, I should—

"Murder!"

Doctor Shrike's reflections came to a very sudden and unexpected close.

"Murder!"

The only word the learned doctor was able to get out, for the sham sentinel, with a sudden downward force, brought the empty keg over the doctor's head, and, by so doing, nearly smothered him.

Doctor Shrike, certain now that he had been attacked by an evil spirit, rushed frantically for the steps.

But he made a miscalculation.

He took the wrong way, although he was far from being aware of it, and by doing so, came crash up against Jacop.

That amiable individual had, in the lull that succeeded the storm, crept out from his lair, with the laudable intention of sneaking up the steps.

But by his attempt he came to grief.

Poor Jacop got such a smash on the nose from the keg, that he fell as if shot, and rolled over and over on the floor of the hold, yelling and screaming—

"Murder!"

Though the collision was disastrous to the assistant, it had quite a different effect on the master.

It freed him from the miserable keg, and his unfettered reason once more returning, he very naturally imagined that his assailant was no other than his faithful Jacop.

Faithful no longer, however.

For the servitor who had the audacity to put his hands on the sacred person of his master must needs suffer for it.

Reasoning thus analogically, Doctor Shrike followed up his momentary advantage by making a furious attack on his assistant, whose cries guided him to the spot where he lay very accurately.

Doctor Shrike first caught Jacop by the leg and pulled him all over the hold.

Jacop's head—by accident or intention, it matters little—came against sundry barrels.

The staves of the barrels proved considerably harder than Jacop's head, and as the doctor still continued in his even course, and as he was, furthermore, not likely to desist from it, Jacop roared and bellowed lustily for assistance.

"Help! help! Murder!" cried the awfully-terrified assistant.

But, notwithstanding these cries, the doctor pursued the even tenour of his way, bumping Jacop's head, whenever he got the chance, against the staves of every powder-barrel he came to.

"Help! help!" roared Jacop, nearly half dead with pain and fright.

"Shout, you villain—shout!" cried Doctor Shrike, in great glee. "I'll learn you, you villain, to put any of your infernal machinery on my head—ha! ha! ha!"

From bellowing for assistance, Jacop took to imploring.

But no use.

Dr. Shrike was in the most execrable humour just then, firmly believing as he did that Jacop was the sole and only cause of his present difficulties.

"Who put that infernal keg on my head? Ha! ha! Didn't I catch you at it? Shout, you ruffian

"EXECUTIONER, DO YOUR DUTY!" CRIED THE DEATH PIRATE

—shout! Beg for mercy as long as you will, from me you shall receive none."

Jacop, seeing that he did himself no good by imploring, took at once to cursing.

With the same beneficial results—a bump every now and again against some powder barrel.

Jacop was soon made aware that cursing only made the doctor more furious, and, as a consequence, materially increased his sufferings.

Exerting all the power of his lungs, he again roared for help, fondly believing that his cries would be heard either in the cabin or on deck.

This time he was not disappointed.

There came distant sounds, as of approaching footsteps.

These sounds grew louder.

Jacop, deriving new hope, struggled furiously to get his leg from the clutches of his master.

Lunging out with his remaining foot, he caught the vampire such a kick that he sent him sprawling among the barrels.

"Murder! murder!" bellowed Jacop, expecting that the doctor would come rushing again at him.

But he was deceived.

Doctor Shrike was firmly wedged in between two barrels.

The sounds of the footsteps grew louder.

Voices were heard.

Jacop took heart, and arose to his feet.

He painfully rubbed his battered head, and stretched his bruised limbs.

He found no bones broken, however, but sundry bumps as big as pigeons' eggs over portions of his body, and more especially on his head.

Jacop, when he found that he had yet a little life left in him, began blubbering like a child.

By this time the advancing party reached the top of the hold, and hearing the loud blubbering below, held down the lanterns they carried to see who it was.

"Who are you, and what are you doing there?' a loud voice cried.

CHAPTER CLVII.

THE ESCAPE.

"Oh, thank Heaven!" blubbered Jacop, "there's some help come at last."

"Did you hear my question?" cried the speaker, in a passion. "Who are you, and what do you want down in the hold?"

Doctor Shrike, at this juncture, made a movement to extricate himself from the barrels; and failing so to do, uttered a most sepulchral groan.

"What the deuce is that?" asked the speaker. "Did you hear it, Jinks?"

Jinks, as might naturally be supposed, was not deaf, and heard it distinctly.

"Yes, sir; but I'll swear it didn't come from that lubber in the magazine."

"The magazine!" yelled Jacop, leaping at least two feet from the ground. 'Oh, murder! We are in a powder magazine!"

"The fellow is not alone, I see," said the first speaker. "Close up, men, and on your lives permit no one to pass."

Jacop heard a shuffling of feet.

The doctor, in his ineffectual attempts to extricate himself, groaned even more hollowly.

His assistant was ready to faint with terror.

Jacop hadn't the power of speech even to answer the simple question put to him.

"What the deuce are they up to now?" asked the man who was in command of the party.

"I can only see one, and his legs are shaking under him like aspens."

"We'll make him shake to a better tune before we are done with him, Jinks."

"I believe you, sir. A couple o' dozen strapped to one of the guns will bring him to his senses, I'll bet."

This was adding new terrors to the already-afflicted Jacop's imagination, who certainly was doomed by relentless fate to meet fresh misfortunes and perils every minute and hour of his existence.

"Oh! oh! oh!" he groaned, fancying already that his poor back was being scored with a stout rope's-end.

"You may groan as long as you like, you rascal!" cried the officer; "but we'll teach you whether you have a tongue in your head or not. Steady with your lanterns, men! Follow me, and capture the villain! I shouldn't wonder but he has that fellow Harpy there with him."

Reuben, from his place of concealment, heard the officer's words, and trembled.

Down the men came, and pounced instantly upon Jacop.

Their lanterns flashed in ruddy gleams through the thick atmosphere of the hold.

Jacop was "landed" before he could utter a word, and borne to the ground.

Without waiting to pay attention to his cries for mercy, they bound him hand and foot, and leaving him cursing his hard fate, went in search of the other party.

After some hunting about the hold, they found Shrike firmly imbedded between two barrels.

It was very easy to explain why the doctor didn't speak.

Jacop's terrific kick stunned him so completely that he was not even aware of what was taking place around him.

The buccaneers were, also, comparatively speaking, new hands and strangers.

And not being acquainted with the imposing and intellectual appearance of Shrike, they bounded upon him like vultures, and tore him with unnecessary violence from between the barrels.

"Come out, you scoundrel, come out! So you were stowing yourself away, were you?" chuckled the officer. "A good case for the yard-arm, and you'll get it, too, you lubber!"

To be called a lubber under such circumstances was a thing that no man in his proper senses could put up with.

Up to this time Doctor Shrike had been almost unconscious of his surroundings.

But that low term "lubber," applied to a gentleman of his ability and accomplishments, had a very material effect.

Indeed, a very beneficial effect.

For it brought him to his senses.

"A lubber!" he cried. "A lubber! Who calls me a lubber?"

"I do," replied the officer, shoving his fist in his face.

"Then you shall pay for it, sir—you shall pay dearly for that word, sir," said the vampire, furiously. "Jacop! Jacop, I say! Where are you, you scoundrel? Come here, directly, or I'll be the death of you, you villain!"

The buccaneers were very much surprised at all this.

For an instant they thought they had a madman to deal with.

The new-fledged lieutenant came to the conclusion that by some means or other he had made a blunder.

Doctor Shrike looked sane enough.

He was a little furious, no doubt.

There was a savage light in his eyes, too.

But any man under great mental excitement, or even under ordinary excitement, might look the same.

And this the lieutenant very naturally thought.

As for his men, when they took a second view of the cadaverous specimen of humanity before them, they did not know what to think of him.

He was tall, gaunt, and bony.

His skin was the colour of wrinkled parchment or dirty mahogany.

He had not an ounce of spare flesh on his whole body, but in his long bony fingers he had a grip of iron.

One of the men felt this, while he was gazing rudely into the doctor's face.

"You'll know me again won't you?" said Shrike, grinning. "Ha! ha!—he! he! Perhaps you didn't feel my finger nails go into you?"

The man winced with pain, and took good care to keep his distance from the doctor, in future.

"May I demand an explanation for this uncalled-for violence?" cried Shrike, turning upon the lieutenant.

"I think there's some unfortunate mistake here," said that officer.

"A mistake! I should think there was a mistake, sir!" cried Shrike. "And a very great mistake, too, sir! permit me to say. If this is the way you treat Captain Tom Drake's head surgeon, you'll find yourself in the wrong box—in the wrong box, sir, depend upon it. Ha! ha!—he! he! Perhaps you don't know who I am?"

The lieutenant stood aghast.

He had heard of the celebrated Doctor Shrike.

But the misfortune was he had never met that gentleman.

This tall, thin, skinny-looking individual with the parchment face, but high forehead, must be the doctor. Must be, indeed! He was sure of it!

"I beg to apologise, sir," said the lieutenant. "Have I the honour of addressing Doctor Shrike?"

"You have, sir," said the doctor, with a savage frown.

"I am very sorry—"

"You needn't be sorry, sir, not at all," said the vampire, furiously, "I don't want any one to be sorry, sir."

"But, my dear sir—"

"Don't but me, sir—don't but me! I was never the butt for any man's practical jokes in my life, and I am not going to be now, sir. Do you hear that, sir?"

"How the deuce am I to remedy my folly?" thought the lieutenant. "The old fool is dead set against an apology. What am I to do? I'll try him once more. May I speak, my dear doctor?" this in a very humble tone.

"You may, sir—you may."

"Well, I was going to observe—"

"Observe as much as you like, sir. Do you see, sir, how patiently I listen to you?"

"Very patiently, indeed," thought the lieutenant.

"Go on, sir! Why do you hesitate? Ha! ha! ha! Are you afraid of Doctor Shrike, the only scientific man among you?"

The lieutenant was beginning to lose his temper.

"Dr. Shrike, it is no use wasting words any longer. If you like to accept my apology, you may. If not, you can do the other thing. I can only say that this has been an unfortunate mistake all round, and that I am truly sorry that you have been subjected to any violence. If you had not been down here, it would not have occurred. Therefore, you must blame yourself for what has taken place. You are a stranger on the brig, and as a stranger, you should not be where we found you."

A new light dawned on the vampire's dazed intellect.

"Where he found me?" he muttered. "Where the deuce am I, then?"

The question, though propounded to himself, was heard by the lieutenant.

"You are in the magazine of the brig," he replied.

"The deuce I am! And these barrels?"

"Are chock full of gunpowder."

Dr. Shrike turned as pale as a sheet.

"I thought of striking a light here one time," he said.

"If you had you would have blown us all into eternity, yourself and that blubbering fellow yonder included."

The "blubbering fellow" groaned aloud, and struggled furiously with his bonds.

"What a narrow escape!" cried the doctor. "I was not aware I was so near death's door. But how did you come here, lieutenant?"

"I'll explain to you, doctor, in a few words. While I was on the quarter-deck one of the men came running to me with the intelligence that some person was being murdered in the hold."

"The bellowing of that fellow, Jacop—curse him! But go on—go on, lieutenant. Don't let me interrupt you."

"Well, sir, I collected a few of the buccaneers together, thinking it was that rascally privateer, Harpy, strangling some one."

"Harpy—Harpy, who is Harpy?" asked the doctor, interruptingly. "I think I have heard that name before."

"Of course you have. A short time ago he commanded a Brazilian privateer, and latterly he has been a prisoner on board the brig. This morning he tried to escape, and got soused in the brine for his pains. They should have let the cowardly villain sink, and then we'd have heard no more of him. As it was, he was saved, and directly after he escaped through the connivance of another scoundrel, not a whit better than himself."

"This fellow Harpy is Captain Tom Drake's cousin."

"And his most bitter enemy," rejoined the lieutenant. "If I had had my will, he should have been hanged like a dog at the yard-arm the first day he came here. But now the deuce knows where the fellow is. We have searched every place in the vessel in vain for him. I'd like to catch the cowardly lubber, and hang him! if I wouldn't string him up on my own responsibility. Now you know why we came down, sir."

"Ha! ha! Perfectly—perfectly."

"Have you been in the hold long?" asked the lieutenant.

"A considerable time. And by Esculapius, sir, the sooner I get out of it the better."

"It's no very pleasant place, doctor, to be among all those barrels of powder. The very thought of your going to strike a light is enough to make one's flesh creep. But how did you get here?"

Doctor Shrike pointed to Jacop.

That ill-used individual was on his back, looking the very picture of woe-begone misery.

"Your servant, I suppose?" said the lieutenant.

"My assistant, you mean! He holds the legs and arms sometimes, while I saw them off. A very useful fellow in his way, especially when I have a fit of kicking or pummeling come suddenly on me."

"Stands it like a martyr, I should judge by his present appearance."

"There you are wrong, lieutenant. The scoundrel actually objects to it."

"Objects to it? Then he must be an ill-organised wretch!"

Jacop groaned—groaned in the bitterness of his spirit.

"Do you hear that, sir?" cried Doctor Shrike; "do you hear it, sir? Does that show tractibility? He is even in open rebellion now, bound as he is! What do you think of the scoundrel, sir, whose conduct is so disgraceful?"

"He must be an irreclaimable villain."

"Villain is no name for him, sir. He's worse—far worse! But I can be charitable, lieutenant, in spite of his base ingratitude—in spite of his many failings. The milk of human kindness, sir, permeates my veins when I see a human creature suffering—even such a human creature as that reptile, Jacop!"

The men tittered.

But Doctor Shrike was not the man, however, to quench any ebullition of suppressed mirth.

As long as the buccaneers kept within the strict bounds of propriety, he would be the last one in the world to lay an embargo upon their feelings.

"What are we to do with this ungrateful villain, sir?" asked the lieutenant, casting a ferocious glance at poor Jacop, but in reality bursting with hidden mirth.

"Release him, lieutenant, by all means. Release him to be a better man, and let us hope he may."

Jacop was soon freed of his bonds, and assisted to his feet.

After a kick or two, delivered to him by his beloved master, the whole party mounted the steps, and made the best of their way on deck.

When they were gone, the sham sentinel leaped out of his barrel, and burst into a hearty laugh.

"Come on, captain, there's no more danger," he said, tapping the barrel of the ex-privateer.

Reuben Harpy crawled out more dead than alive.

Every bone in his body ached.

He had never been in such a dreadful cramped position in his life before.

And so long.

It was enough to murder him by inches; for, being a much bigger man than the sham sentinel, he felt the narrowness of space which the dimensions of the barrel allowed him most acutely.

"How do you feel now?" asked the sentinel.

"Half dead."

"I laughed myself sick."

"I didn't hear you."

"Not likely, captain. I wasn't such a fool as to laugh loud; but I was bursting with inward mirth, nevertheless."

"I wish I could say the same." said Reuben Harpy, ruefully. "I was never in such a cramped-up situation in my life."

And, he might have added, in so much fear.

"I am glad, however, that those fellows didn't knock about the barrels much. There was every chance of discovery."

"Nonsense."

"But I thought so."

"Not in the least. The danger was nothing."

The coward, Harpy, thought otherwise.

His grovelling fears made his limited hiding-place a living hell to him.

But he said nothing about that.

"What a jolly row there was!" said the sham sentinel.

"I didn't think it very jolly," replied Reuben.

"What, not that doctor chap and his assistant?"

"They made an awful clatter, if that's what you mean. But as for anything jolly, I couldn't see anything jolly in them. I must confess I wished them both to the deuce. They, at least, were a devilish nuisance."

"Gracious heavens, captain! where's your taste? They were the very life and soul of the place. Oh! what pummelling, bumping, and shouting! I never heard the like in my life. Doctor Shrike is a host in himself; and as for Jacop, I think it would make any man's fortune to go and exhibit him at a penny a head."

"I think him a confounded fool," interrupted Reuben Harpy, grumblingly.

"Now, I think him, on the other hand, a capital fellow. Old Shrike couldn't live without him no more than he could fly. The doctor is a bit of a philosopher evidently, but philosophers must have their sport as well as other people. I think I gave Shrike a terrible fright that last rally. What do you think I did?"

"I don't know," said Reuben, indifferently.

"Well, I'll tell you what I did. Shrike, after tiring himself out looking for Jacop, came and leant up against my barrel. I think he was in a meditative mood, for he was considering a long time. 'Well,' said I to myself, 'I'll give you a fright, old boy.' I remembered that there were some empty kegs near me with the tops knocked out. Stretching my hand out carefully, I seized one which I thought large enough to go over his head. While he was so profoundly reflecting, I got my keg in both hands, elevated it with the utmost caution above his head, and just waiting a good chance, brought it down with all my force. It must have come with considerable weight on his shoulders, for it staggered him. He managed to get out the one word 'Murder!' and then bounded away as if the arch-fiend was pursuing him. Ha! ha! ha! The fun after that was something marvellous. I wouldn't have missed it for a good deal."

"I wish you wouldn't talk so loud," said Reuben, fearfully. "You don't know who may be listening to us up above there."

"Bah! Your imagination is too excited, captain."

"Is it?" cried Reuben, in a kind of hoarse whisper. "Hark to that!"

"You are right, by George!" replied the sentinel, in a lower tone. "There's some one coming, sure enough. Get into your barrel, captain—quick!"

And after he saw Reuben safe, the sham sentinel got into his own, and let the top down carefully.

No one for an instant could imagine that there was any one in the hold now.

The quiet and intensity of death prevailed there.

Not even a breath disturbed the dark and fetid atmosphere.

The footsteps of the person approaching were those of a man.

Easily told by the awkward way the foot came down; not with that light, agile, springy elasticity which always, or nearly always, characterises the step of a woman.

On he came.

Not pausing for an instant, he descended the steps.

With every step Reuben Harpy's heart gave a great thump against his ribs.

And a person placing his ear against the barrel must have heard the thumps very distinctly.

But there was no cause for alarm.

The man spoke when he got to the bottom of the steps, and, in an instant, the sham sentinel leaped out of his barrel, and greeted his confederate.

For he it was.

"Come out, Captain Harpy!" cried the sentinel. "It's all right."

On this assurance, Reuben came forth, glad once more to be liberated from the circumscribed and disagreeable limits of his hiding-place.

The man brought some food with him, which the two semi-prisoners wolfed up without ceremony.

"How is the world up above?" asked the sham sentinel, when he had done munching.

"I have a great deal to tell you," replied the man, "and good news, too."

"Bravo!"

"In the first place, the buccaneers have given up the search."

"Did they search much?"

"Considerably."

"So they have given it up, have they? I feel truly grateful to them. They are very considerate indeed."

But recollecting himself, he added—

"Where do they think we are, then?"

"They don't know. They swear you are not on the vessel, so that's good enough isn't it?"

"You are a trump, old fellow! That's splendid news indeed!"

"But you have not heard all yet."

"The deuce I haven't!"

"Oh, no. There's some more to come yet."

"You are worth your weight in gold. Why, you are even making Captain Harpy smile."

"As if you could see his face in the darkness. Well, no matter whether you can or not."

"Go on. Don't mind me. Let us hear all the news. It's transcendant, every word of it."

"Captain Tom Drake has left with the 'Will-o'-the-Wisp.'"

"Come now," said the sentinel, "don't be piling up the agony. That's a deuced sight too good to be true. Do you hear that, Captain Harpy?"

"Yes," replied Reuben. "I would to Heaven it were true."

"It is true, I assure you," said the man.

"Then may Heaven's curse light upon him, and clear him from my path!" cried Reuben, fiercely.

"Hush! not so loud! We may be heard even here."

"Pardon me. I was carried away by the intensity of my feelings. You don't know how I hate that man."

And fear him, too, he ought to have said, if his cowardly and craven heart permitted him.

Reuben Harpy was a great hypocrite and a greater coward.

It was as music to his soul to hear that the "Will-o'-the-Wisp" and her gallant commander had sailed.

But where was that noble vessel gone?

This he was to hear presently.

"Yes," said the man, "it's away, as sure as a gun. I'll tell you how it happened, too. Some hours ago a strange sail was seen approaching—a suspicious-looking craft she was, too—thought to be an East Indiaman, but having more or less the cut of a pirate or man-of-war, in spite of her peaceful looks. Captain Tom was continually watching her movements."

"Tom Drake on board here!" murmured Reuben Harpy, with an internal shudder.

"Oh, yes, and watching this strange ship all the time through his glass.

"But as none could make her out, he finally had the boat lowered, and leaping in with his officers, was pulled to the 'Will-o'-the-Wisp.'

"Twenty minutes later, the brig swung round to the breeze, and with a full press of canvas on, glided out like a graceful swan to meet the stranger; and there you have my story in a nutshell, just as I have seen it."

"A most daring act to do," said the sham sentinel. "What kind was the vessel, though?"

"A three-decker."

"Then Captain Tom Drake's fate is sealed!" cried Reuben, in a hoarse, exultant whisper.

"What do you think of that?"

"Because the three-decker is a British man-of-war, carrying an armament sufficient to blow the 'Will-o'-the Wisp' out of the water at the first broadside. Mark my words! Tom Drake has played his last card."

"Perhaps you have the spirit of prophecy on you," said the sentinel, jocosely.

"It matters not. I believe that the end is near. Was that a gun I heard, or only the wind? Hark!"

They all listened.

A hoarse roar fell upon their ears.

It might be the voice of the rising breeze lashing over the sea, or the report of a single gun at a very great distance.

"I thought it was the firing of cannon," said Reuben, listlessly. "Perhaps I am mistaken."

He was not mistaken.

It was one of the carronades of the "Will-o'-the-Wisp" discharged at the British war vessel.

The opening of the ball of carnage and death had begun.

The men in the hold remained silent for a long time, each absorbed in his reflections.

The sham sentinel was the first to break the silence.

"We must leave here to-night,' he said, "the whole three of us—that is, if you have no objection to go," he added, appealingly, to his confederate. "You and I have known each other for a long time now, and I don't see why we should part."

"Nor do I," said the other. "I agree to go with you."

"Bravo! Give me your hand."

It was arranged now that the sham sentinel's friends should go on deck, and ascertain how matters stood there, and, if possible, have a boat lowered so that they could get in from one of the portholes, and glide away without being observed.

If possible, he was also to muffle the oars.

In the event of failing in this, they were to pull softly until such time as they got clear of the brig.

With these instructions, the man left them, and went on deck.

He was not away more than three-quarters of an hour when he returned loaded with two bundles.

"Here is something I have brought you," he said, "that may be necessary. Now, Captain Harpy, you can be a common buccaneer for once, while my friend here transforms himself into a lieutenant."

"Where the deuce did you get these?" asked the sentinel, opening the bundle.

"Well, I'll tell you the truth — our good friend the luff is asleep, and I borrowed his clothes. You are nearly about a size, and I thought they might fit you. Try them on, and let's see how you look in them."

"Well, upon my sacred word, you are almost as clever as I am myself. Won't the luff, when he gets up, do some tall swearing—I rayther guess he will. You'll see how I'll act the lieutenant should we be over-hauled."

"They fit you to a T. Turn round and let me have a look at your back."

The lantern was held by Reuben, while the sham sentinel's friend surveyed him both back and front.

"Capital!—capital! There's not a buccaneer in Captain Tom's service will stop you. Now, when you are both dressed, I'll request you to come in with me."

"How is the night?"

"Dark—dark as pitch. Splendid night for running away. Boat down, and oars muffled. We'll not have the slightest difficulty. Are you both ready?"

"Yes," was the reply.

"Then follow, and don't forget your identity."

The sham sentinel was supposed to personate Lieutenant Harbison—a gentleman whom he could mimic pretty well.

Having disposed of the bundles of left-off clothes in the empty powder barrels, they mounted the steps, and made their way to that part of the vessel by which they intended to leave.

They were subjected to no interruption until they got near their journey's end.

A dark figure stepped out suddenly into the semi-light of a lamp.

The dull flicker flashed on his cutlass.

Reuben Harpy stepped back dismayed.

"By Heaven, sir!" hissed his companion, "if you hesitate now, all is lost. March boldly forward, and leave the rest to the man who has risked so much for you."

Reuben felt ashamed of his cowardice.

Bracing himself up, he resolved to pass the guard, with as bold and defiant an air as he could.

"Who goes there?" challenged the sentinel.

The supposed Lieutenant Harbison stepped into the light, and, after answering the usual formula, the three passed on.

It was the work of almost an instant to pass through one of the port-holes into the boat.

The night was still as dark as pitch, and when the frail craft sped gently over the dark sea, there was not a soul on board the brig to observe it.

"I say, Bob!"

"Hallo!"

"Come this way a minute!"

It was Jerry Mizzen hailing Bob Hauler, his boon companion and chum.

Not a quarter of an hour had elapsed since their last fight with the pirate.

"Well, old sore-head, what do ye want now?"

grumbled Bob, coming up. "Can't yer let a fellow snooze for ten minutes, curse yer, without making all that confounded row? Come to the p'int at once. What is it?"

"Bob, what the deuce is the matter? Yer ain't got into one o' yer grumbling fits ag'in, have ye? Shiver my timbers, pal! yer a curious-looking cove anyhow, an' never satisfied."

"What do ye mean, Jerry?"

"I mean what I say, Bob. Yer always grumblin,' and yer never contented."

"That means a fight, I suppose?" said Bob.

"Tread on the tail o' my coat if yer like. I'm not in the habit o' mincing my words," replied Jerry.

"Do ye want a punch in the head?"

"If yer not quiet, I'll give you one."

"Hum! Come on then, and look out for yer nozzle. I'll draw claret this time."

And Bob, rubbing his eyes to bring his vision up to the fighting point, squared out.

Jerry, not dismayed, rolled up his shirt sleeves.

"Is it going to be a friendly smack in the eye?" asked Jerry, complacently.

"Curse ye, yes!" replied Bob.

"And no ill-feeling arter?" said Jerry.

"Sart'inly not. Do ye want me to kiss and blubber over ye afore ye've commenced. Stand out like a man, and arter thrashing ye, I'll go back and take my forty winks."

"Agreed!" said Jerry. "Come on, Bob. Look out for yer tater-trap!"

"Look out for your own, ye lubber. Take that!"

Bob, by a beautifully scientific "move," just skinned Jerry's nose.

First blood for Bob.

Jerry's proboscis was slightly grazed—in fact, slightly discoloured.

But the indomitable Mizzen was not a bit frightened, although he saw, for an instant or two, a thousand stars floating before his eyes.

No; he was anything but scared.

He came up smiling.

"First knock on the conk!" exclaimed Bob.

"First blood!" responded Jerry. "Look out, Bob!"

By a dexterous movement, the irrepressible Mizzen "landed" Bob one in the stomach.

Bob, through some peculiar means caused by the pain, assumed the letter V directly.

"One for me!" exclaimed Jerry.

"One for you!" groaned Bob.

"Time!" cried Jerry.

"Not yet," said Bob. "I'll be better, presently. You've upset my vittles, you have."

Jerry regarded his old friend with a look of pity —indeed, of deep commiseration.

But, determined to let him have his revenge, he quietly folded his arms across his breast, and, like a gladiator of old, magnanimously waited for Bob to come round a little.

Bob, after pressing his stomach for the twentieth time, came up to the scratch.

"Ready?"

"Yes."

"Then here goes!"

A little sparring, and Bob "landed" Jerry one between the eyes, which sent him sprawling.

"Two to me!" exclaimed Bob.

"Y-y-es!" groaned Jerry.

"Shall I pick you up?"

"No, let me lie here for a few minutes; I'll revive soon. Oh! oh! oh! That was something awful!" groaned Jerry.

"What was something awful?" asked Bob.

"Did you hear me?" asked Jerry, in a tone of deep sorrow.

"In course I did," replied Bob. "Wasn't you a-saying that something was something awful?"

"Oh! oh! oh!" groaned Jerry.

"What's the matter with ye? Why don't ye stand on yer feet?"

"Oh! oh! oh!" continued Jerry, groaning deeply.

"There's something wrong with him, I really believe," said Bob to himself. "I wouldn't have anything happen my old pal for the world. He's got the stomach-ache, else he's grieving arter that Injun girl. I wish I'd a drop o' good grog, and it would revive him in a minute."

Bob approached the prostrate Jerry, with a look of deep sympathy in his honest face.

Strange to say, it did not occur to him, for even an instant, that the force of his blow was the prime and only cause of all poor Jerry's groaning.

"Are you better, old pal?"

"Oh! oh! oh!" groaned Jerry. "Bear with me a little, Bob. I'll be all right in a minute or two."

"Where do ye feel the pain?" asked his sympathetic friend.

"In—in the eyes, Bob, in the eyes!" stammered Jerry, sadly.

"Queer," said Bob, reflectively. "I never knew afore that a stomach-ache went into the eyes. It must be a new sort o' complaint. I wonder whether it's Yaller Jack as is attacking Jerry. But we ain't in the right part o' the world for Yaller Jack, so it can't be Yaller Jack neither. Now, old Shrike would be able to tell us, if he hadn't so much to do. No, bother Shrike! He's a grudge ag'in poor Jerry, an' might p'ison him. How are ye now, Jerry?"

"Better, Bob—a little better."

"Are we going to finish that fight out or not?" asked the honest fellow. "I don't want ye to go without yer revenge, Jerry. I think it would be a cruel, heartless thing for me to do that. So come, old pal, let me help ye to yer feet, and we'll try and finish it off, so as there'll be no ill-feeling in the matter."

Jerry, by way of answer, pointed, with a sepulchral groan, to Bob's handiwork.

His eyes were already swollen, and becoming discoloured.

Bob shrank back aghast.

"Did I do that?" he asked.

"Yes, you did," groaned Jerry.

"Why didn't you tell me of it afore?"

"What good would that do?" said Jerry.

"Because then I'd have punched my own head."

"No, Bob; don't do anything so rash."

"I'll do it, if ye only tell me. Shiver my timbers! I'll put mourning afore my eyes for a month! Curse me! I thought as how it was the stomach-ache ye had!"

And Bob, throwing his arms around his beloved Jerry's neck, began to sob most piteously.

"Oh, no, no, no!" cried Jerry, "don't go on that way, Bob, or ye'll have me doing the briny business myself. I'm all right, old pal—I'm all right. A smack between the peepers isn't a-going to kill Jerry. Oh, no."

"Shut up, ye lubber, how can I help crying?" blubbered Bob.

"Now, that'll do," said Jerry, "that'll do. I can well understand yer feelings, old feller. Here, take a swig out o' this, and it'll set yer to-rights."

From that moment Bob's grief subsided.

A "swig" meant something comforting to the inside, and Bob held out his hand to receive the proffered flask, which Jerry passed into it.

The flask went up, and Bob's mouth opened.

A deep draught, a smack of the lips, and the worthy mariner's grief passed away like a cloud from before the face of the sun.

"Darn capital stuff! Where did yer get it?" he asked.

"Got it aboard that 'ere pirate. But here's Captain Tom. It won't do for him to catch us at this kind of game."

"Slope then, and I'll follow you."

And without another word the worthy mariners disappeared down the companion-way.

Captain Tom smiled as he saw the two old comrades sneaking away.

He had been all the time a silent witness to their little fistic dispute, and was highly delighted to find that it ended so amicably.

"Capital, though very eccentric fellows," soliloquised Tom.

"Very!" rejoined a deep voice at his elbow.

Looking round, he saw the towering form of Ben Barnacle.

"I didn't know that you were here," said Tom.

"Hum!" replied Ben. "I have been watching the sport, like yourself."

For a moment our hero was annoyed.

Annoyed to think, or, rather, to have others think, that there was the slightest lack of discipline on board his vessel.

But this feeling, in presence of a devoted and faithful follower, was unworthy of him.

And so it passed with almost the same rapidity as it came.

"They are two of the strangest fellows I ever came across," said Ben. "One moment on the best of terms, the next at loggerheads. But they generally end up their differences pretty decently."

"By embracing and sobbing over each other," replied Captain Tom, laughing. "But no matter; they are good, honest fellows, and so long as I am captain of the 'Will-o'-the-Wisp,' I'll hold them privileged."

"It wouldn't be wise to tell them so," said Ben.

"Perhaps not. But the rascals may have heard it already. I think, however, that I can depend on them not abusing my desire to be kind to them."

Just then, Ben Barnacle made a sign to his young commander.

Captain Tom comprehended it in a moment.

"There's some one listening," he said, in a whisper.

"Yes."

"Who is it?"

"One of the very rascals we were speaking about."

"Bob Hauler?"

"No, Jerry, the redoubtable and irrepressible Jerry. And something must be done to cure him of his mania. I find it a common practice with him. He has got into a bad habit, and we must break him off it."

"How?" asked Tom Drake, very much amused.

"By the cold water cure."

"Drenching him?"

"Precisely. But go on with the conversation, Captain Tom, for if he suspects anything, the rascal is as cunning as a waggon load of monkeys, and will run for cover before we can get at him."

Captain Tom went on, and the unconscious Jerry, hearing repeated references made to himself and Bob, strained his ears to listen, and drank in every word.

To do so he left himself an open mark for the enemy.

For he had already ascended one or two of the steps of the companion-way.

Without flagging, the conversation proceeded with all due decorum and gravity.

The services of Bob and Jerry were discussed at full length.

Ben Barnacle, rather carelessly, looked over his shoulder two or three times, and each time he did,

his sharp eyes caught the open mouth and inquisitive features of Jerry Mizzen.

Close to Ben Barnacle's hand was a bucket brimming over with water—icy cold—which Jerry had been so kindly considerate as to place there.

"Yes," said Ben, edging nearer and nearer to the bucket, "I think you should lay restrictions to a certain extent on Mizzen's privileges."

"Curse him!" muttered Jerry, "what does he mean by laying instructions on my privileges. Ain't I to have my grog when I want it? Is that what he's arter? I could never believe as how Mr. Barnacle would turn on a poor cove like that. Hum! he shan't have it all his own way neither. I ain't a-going to be done out o' my privileges if I can help it. Come, Jerry, ye lubber, move up another step, so as you can hear what's coming next. 'Forewarned, forearmed' that's what they used to put down in my copy-books when I was a kid."

Jerry, suiting the action to the word, moved up another step.

"Yes," said Ben Barnacle, with a sly wink at Tom. "Jerry Mizzen takes too much grog. More's the pity."

"That's good on him, anyway," muttered Jerry. "I thanks him in the name of my grog. I am obleeged to him for his good opinion. Go on, my hearty, go on. I'm a-listenin' to yer all the time. Perhaps I'll turn te'totaler arter yer werry capital conversation. Perhaps I will."

"Do you really think he takes too much grog?" said Tom.

"I am sure of it, captain. He certainly doesn't get top-heavy more than five times a week. But that is a little too much for any man."

"And twice on a Sunday," put in Jerry, grinding his teeth. "If that's not defermation of chericter, I want to know what is. I d'n't object to a lie sometimes; but a lie as ruins a feller critter's reportation is as bad as a-murderin' of him in the dark. Move up another step, Jerry, my boy, or yer'll just miss some o' this werry delightful talk about yer."

Jerry moved up accordingly.

Ben Barnacle made a move also.

It was in the direction of the bucket of water.

Still continuing the conversation, he got his hand on the handle.

Did the irrepressible and now enraged Jerry observe that movement?

Not he.

Jerry's auricular faculties were strained to the utmost tension—indeed, too much so for his own good.

"Yes," went on Lieutenant Barnacle; "and I have another objection to his privileges. He takes his grog too strong."

"Too strong!" exclaimed Captain Tom.

"Too strong!" muttered the enraged Jerry.

"Yes, sir; I say too strong."

"Well, that can be easily remedied by putting plenty of water into it," said Captain Tom.

"Do you order him water?"

"I do, unhesita'ingly."

"Then he shall have water."

With the rapidity of thought, Ben Barnacle wheeled round, bucket in hand, and before even the irrepressible Jerry was aware of the movement, the lieutenant sent the whole contents down the companion-way.

"Swash!" went the water.

The unfortunate Jerry was in a very favourable situation to get the full contents in his face, and it came with such force as to, for an instant or so, completely take away his breath.

Jerry Mizzen rolled down the steps as if he had been shot, and when he regained his breathing power, began to bellow murder.

"What's the matter?" cried Ben Barnacle, rou-

thing to the companion-way. "Did you hear the cry of murder, captain?"

"Yes, surely," replied Tom, exerting a great effort to keep down his mirth. "What can it be?"

"Murder, no doubt. I'm sure there's a murder going on below. Bob Hauler is perhaps cutting Jerry Mizzen's throat. This must be seen to, captain. It will never do to have cold-blooded murders like this done aboard of the 'Will-o'-the-Wisp.' It must be seen to at once."

CHAPTER CLVIII

CAPTAIN ANGEL AGAIN.

JERRY MIZZEN heard this dialogue between Captain Tom Drake and his lieutenant.

But it did not serve to increase the placidity of his temper, or generate one magnanimous thought in his bosom.

No, gentle reader, quite the contrary.

Brushing the water from his face, and interlarding certain remarks of his with some very tall swearing, he slunk away in the darkness, bitterly regretting that he had not gone away long before that.

When they knew that he was fully out of hearing, Captain Tom and Ben Barnacle indulged their up-to-this suppressed mirth by laughing heartily.

"I think we have cured Jerry of eavesdropping at last," said Ben.

"It's most likely that he will meet me to-morrow with a scowl on his face as ferocious as a wild beast."

"And you?"

"Oh, I will salute him as usual, with the most smiling and cheerful 'Good morning, Jerry,' imaginable. He'll not know how to take it at first; but seeing the tables so completely turned on him, he will laugh over his own misfortunes, and be apt to treat the bucket of water as a very light matter indeed. What a beautiful night it is, Captain Tom!"

"Charming. The moon never shone brighter, nor the stars clearer. We are fortunate, indeed, in having such weather. Look at that glorious expanse of ocean, silvered like some gigantic mirror by the moonbeams. Pray hand me the glass, lieutenant."

Ben Barnacle handed the instrument to his commander, who, adjusting it, carried it to his eye.

"By Heaven, lieutenant!" he cried, suddenly, "it seems our night's work is not done yet. Take the glass, and tell me what you see to leeward of us."

Ben Barnacle took the instrument in his hand, and, adjusting it to his eye, swept the point indicated.

A sudden change came over his face.

He was powerfully agitated.

"It is as you say, captain," he cried. "There's been some foul work going on."

"You are right. Foul and brutal work, too."

"There are two. I can see no more, and one is helpless, and at the mercy of the other."

"And that other is a pirate," said Captain Tom, emphatically.

"Assuredly, sir. And I think there is little time to be lost either, if you wish to be of any service to the weaker vessel."

Ben Barnacle paused, lowered his glass, and paced the deck with excited steps.

Nothing angered him so much as the thought of any unfortunate craft falling into the hands of these terrible pirates.

He knew that their practices were cruel and at all times barbarous, and that few of the unfortunates who fell into their clutches ever escaped with life

The women, if there were any, these terrible cor

sairs sold into slavery, while the men they must barbarously and ruthlessly murdered.

It was no wonder then that Ben, with his great and whole-souled sympathy, shuddered through every fibre of his iron body at the mere thought of the fate of the wretched crew who were unfortunate enough to encounter the pirates.

Captain Tom knew Ben's nature almost as well as his own.

But, without speaking, he took the glass from the excited man's hand and bent another searching glance over the moonlit sea.

"By heavens!" he cried, "the pirate has hauled off, and its victim seems a total wreck. There is no time to be lost, Mr. Barnacle."

"Aye, aye, sir," answered the lieutenant.

"Alter the course of the brig at once, and crowd on all the sail you can."

"Aye, aye, sir."

Ben set about his work now with great earnestness.

A shrill whistle brought the boatswain to his side.

"Boatswain!"

"Aye, aye, sir"

"Pipe all hands on deck."

"Aye, aye, sir."

In another instant the boatswain's piercing whistle split the night air, echoing and re-echoing through the brig.

Most of the buccaneers, aroused so suddenly from their slumbers, rushed upon deck half-dressed.

But that did not prevent the work from being done.

Every stitch of canvas that the "Will-o'-the-Wisp" could carry was unfurled to the breeze, her course was changed as instantaneously, and she ploughed the flashing waters like a race horse in the wake of the disabled and plundered vessel.

For the time being we leave Captain Tom, his gallant little brig and dashing crew, bearing down where their assistance was perhaps needed.

It is day.

A brilliant, glorious day, redolent in sunshine, and with a clear bracing sea-air rippling the ocean.

A hundred miles more or less from where Captain Tom's little fleet lay at anchor a large-sized schooner under a heavy press of canvas, and cleaving through the sea as swift as a bird of prey, held her course in that direction.

Had she continued her speed at the same rate as she was now going she must of necessity sight the buccaneers some time before sundown.

The schooner, with her snowy sails, long tapering masts, and general rakish appearance, was not at all the kind of craft to gain the confidence of any strange vessel that might happen to be passing.

Her appearance was, without doubt, smart and trim, and she was, moreover, a good sailer.

But, on the other hand, she was a pirate.

Which made all the difference.

As she skims the blue and gleaming waters of the sea under this snowy mass of canvas, without, we may say, either rock or motion to denote that she was moving, we will invite the reader on deck.

Perhaps we might as well enter the cabin.

The captain of this schooner is an old friend of ours.

He has been a slaver and smuggler in his time, and now he has turned his talents to a new branch of ruffianly industry, that of plundering vessels on the high seas.

But he is not the man to content himself with plunder alone.

He must also have blood.

And heaven help the unfortunate crew who f

into his clutches, for they may expect no mercy at his hands.

Pacing up and down his cabin is this restless leader of ruthless murderers.

His hands in a manner tied.

For the last four or five days he has not sighted even a passing vessel, and his active mind requires renewed action, and his sanguinary hand itches to imbrue itself once more in the blood of his fellow man.

Five days now—what a long, wearisome time—and no vessel This inactivity is the ruin of men of action. Even had I that devil of a Yates here to quarrel with, it might serve to pass the time away. But curse the fellow!—he's dead. I saw the shark bite him through until his red blood spurted out and dyed the white seething waters around me. With all his faults, Yates was a man after my own heart, a dare-devil fellow who had no more compunction for shedding his brother worm's blood than drinking a glass of water. Ha! ha! ha!"

At that moment the door of the cabin opened.

A boy entered.

A pale-faced lad of about twelve or thirteen.

The captain turning round saw him.

"Well, young whipper-snapper, what the devil do you want now? But, first, tell me why you didn't knock before you came in here?"

"I did, sir."

"You did?"

"Yes, sir."

"Then I must have been confoundedly deaf. Do you mean to tell me that you knocked at that door, and that I didn't hear you?"

"You might have heard me, sir; but as you were talking to yourself—"

"Talking to myself; a likely story. If you come in again without knocking, I'll have your back well tanned. And now, your errand? Be quick, or I may take it into my head to order you a dozen right off."

"A strange sail, sir," replied the lad, without showing the slightest sign of fear. "The first officer wants you on deck."

"Here, you young rascal, you. Here's a shilling for you. Mind that you knock the next time, or I'll have the flesh flayed off your bones. Do you hear me?"

"Yes, sir."

The boy took the shilling and went away laughing.

The captain, soon following, hastened on deck.

Here he found his first lieutenant watching the movements of a distant sail with considerable interest.

"Well, lieutenant, in luck at last," said Captain Angel, for he it was.

The first lieutenant was a smart enough fellow in his way, but he had a brutal and villainous face, on which "gallows" was as plainly written as if it had been indelibly stamped there.

He was forty, perhaps more.

Broad, muscular, and as strong as a Hercules, but without that sharpness and decision of character which characterised Captain Angel.

His features were broad.

And so was his body.

Intellectuality was his failing.

Simply because he was not the possessor of it.

For all that, his features bespoke any amount of low cunning.

And as to physical courage, he was surfeited with it.

For this and his low cunning and various other reasons, Captain Angel had selected him for his first lieutenant.

"Well, lieutenant, we are in luck at last, although five or six days is a long time to wait for it."

"Truly, Captain Angel. I think this time that we can secure a prize that will be worth taking."

"Do you think so?"

"I am sure. Take the glass and satisfy yourself."

Captain Angel took the glass and adjusted it.

He swept a keen glance over the bright and slightly rippled sea.

After continuing his gaze for a few moments, he gave vent to a cry of intense satisfaction.

"Good!" he exclaimed. "We have a prize this time worth the taking."

"She looks to me like an East Indiaman. If that be the case," said the lieutenant, "she'll be laden down with treasure."

"I suppose you have run across many of these in your time?"

"Oh very many. And all rich prizes. But sometimes they fight like the very deuce."

"So much the better," said Angel, rubbing his hands in glee. "I always like an enemy to fight; for, don't you see, that gives you an excuse to settle his hash for him."

"I should never wait for any excuse at all, captain," said the lieutenant, shrugging his shoulders.

"You don't exactly understand me yet, my dear lieutenant. Do you not know that it's so much off your conscience if you can taunt an enemy to come out and do battle with you, especially if that enemy is weaker than yourself But if there's no resistance it takes away all the honour that one man has in killing another, that's what I am driving at. You comprehend me now?"

"Quite."

"I see our prize is coming on unconscious, little thinking what's in store for her."

"I am afraid she won't continue in the same course long, captain," said the lieutenant, who was watching her every movement through his glass.

"Nonsense! Why should you think so?"

"Because even now I fear she begins to smell a rat."

"Humph! we'll see very soon. But have you ordered the men below?"

"Yes; shortly after the look-out signalled the sail."

"And the ports?"

"Are all as right as can be. Even if she came within a half a mile of us, she wouldn't know that we had a gun on board. There is nothing suspicious, save the raking-masts and general build of the boat."

"That will be no obstacle. She'll come on, depend upon it."

The lieutenant shook his head.

"It's a strange sea, Captain Angel, and strangers fight shy of each other."

"Have you ever been here before?"

"Twice; and would sooner go anywhere else."

The captain gave the order now to have some of the pirates up, supposing, and very justly, too, that if the stranger saw none of the crew on her decks, she would get suspicious, and suddenly veering round, go off in another direction.

Nearly a dozen of the pirates came on deck now, attired as British merchant seamen.

By such means Captain Angel fondly hoped to lure the large and supposed richly-laden vessel to her destruction.

We shall see how he succeeded in his wicked and murderous design.

Notwithstanding that these men were dressed as honest British sailors, there was something in their appearance of so savage and ruffianly a character that it would be hard to mistake them for anything but what they were—a set of pirates and cut-throats.

The ship came on nearer each minute.

Indeed, never dreaming of danger, but rushing evidently into the pirate's clutches.

Captain Angel paced the quarter-deck, rubbing his hands with guilty joy, and chuckling with great satisfaction, at the prospect of so much treasure coming into his coffers and so many human lives sacrificed.

The doomed ship is now within a mile of the schooner.

Is there no earthly power to warn her?

Ah! she is no longer blind, but veers round quick as the lightning's flash.

The pirate captain gives vent to an exclamation of rage, and stamps the deck furiously.

The first lieutenant hastens up.

"I told you so, sir," he said. "The jade's just come far enough to take the measurement of our rig, and not being satisfied with this noble schooner, takes to her heels."

"We'll soon put a stop to her gallop," said Captain Angel, swearing out a frightful oath. "Double shot and run out the carronades. All hands on deck."

Both orders were promptly executed.

In less than a minute the deck was swarming with ruffians of almost every nation, armed to the teeth with cutlasses, pistols, and pikes.

"Now, to give her a couple of our indigestible pills," said Angel, smiling with malicious glee. "If she doesn't heave-to then, we'll pour a broadside in and sink her. Rather would I do it than give her a single chance of escape."

Captain Angel was soon aware that the sailing qualities of the vessel he was pursuing were equal to his own, and might in the end prove superior.

When all was ready, the order was given to fire.

The double report of the carronades went thundering over the sea, but the iron messengers, falling short of their mark, expended their fury on nothing but sea-water.

Captain Angel, furious at being thus baffled, resolved to get a little nearer, if possible, before he fired any more shots.

All the canvas they could get on the schooner was crowded up.

The chase now became one of the most exciting and lively character.

In the interim, the breeze greatly increased, and the two vessels sped on late into the afternoon, neither gaining upon the other.

It became apparent, as far as speed was concerned, that they were equally matched.

The sun went down and still the schooner kept in the wake of the runaway, determined to bring her to before the darkness set in.

The pirate captain hailed with joy an accident that occurred to the pursued about this time.

The ship, it was evident, in the hope of escaping her pursuer, was carrying more sail than she was capable of bearing

The breeze was strong, and the machinery of one of her yards getting displaced, the great rounded mass came to the deck with a thunderous crash, bearing down cordage, canvas, and all before them.

The shock was so great that before the noble vessel could recover herself the pirates had got within half-a-mile of her, and poured in a deadly broadside.

The merchantman replied feebly with her two or three guns, but these were instantly silenced, and soon the pirate schooner bore down on her, and, coming alongside, threw out her grapnels, and a torrent of fierce, savage men, with cutlass, pike, and pistol, bounded over her shattered bulwarks, striking right and left at the handful of brave men who opposed them.

The fight was brief, but as long as it went on the decks ran red with the blood of both pirate and merchantman.

An old man with long white hair, who was evidently the captain of the doomed ship, led his handful of brave English sailors on and on again.

But the gallant fellows were cut down as fast as they came up, till not one of them remained.

The old man alone seemed to bear a charmed life.

His cutlass was red with the blood of his enemies.

Up to this the pirate captain had paid little attention to him.

Seeing him stand alone over the bodies of those who were dead or dying, and with a cutlass red to the hilt with blood in his hands, he uttered a frightful oath and bounded towards him.

But he stepped back the moment he caught that noble face and unquailing eye.

With a startled cry he had recognised the features.

"So is is you, John Gregory—you again who have crossed my path. Lucky for you, old man, that my sword was not sheathed in your heart. Had I known it was your ship, I should have avoided it. But the harm that's done cannot now be remedied. All I can say is that I am sorry for this slaughter, and not for any one's sake but your own."

"Captain Angel!" murmured the old man, dropping his gory sword from between his nerveless fingers, and turning as pale as death.

The pirate captain motioned to two of his men who came forward, and taking each an arm forced old John Gregory gently away over the shattered bulwarks of his doomed ship to the deck of the schooner.

Captain Angel free from the presence of old Gregory, set about plundering his ship.

While he was thus engaged, several of the pirates rushed on deck, dragging with them three very pretty-looking girls, whom they found secreted in the cabin.

The scene of so much bloodshed on deck was too much for the poor girls, who, expecting to meet the same fate, shrieked and begged for mercy piteously.

Captain Angel was attracted to the spot by the noise.

He came forward with his drawn sword in his hand, red with the blood of more than one of the poor fellows, who defended their ship with their lives

Seeing him with the still reeking blade in his hand, a savage scowl on his fierce features, and fearing that he was going to take her life, one of the maidens, impelled by an unhappy sense of her danger rushed forward.

And falling on her knees, the young girl appealed to the pirate captain for mercy.

CHAPTER CLIX.
THE LAST OF BENTLEY.

IN order to clear up one point in our story, we must take the liberty of going back to chapter cxlvii, where we left Bentley threatening with death any of the pirates who disputed his authority as captain of the "Will-'o-the-Wisp."

Knowing the desperate and hardy character of this man, the pirates hung back, and by that moment of indecision the captain was saved.

"Back—back every one of you!" cried Bentley, fiercely. "Remember the first who resists me suffers death. I am captain here, and let he who disputes my right step out if he dare!"

None moved.

The pirates were completely subdued.

The bravest of them all—poor Sam—lay stark and dead in their midst.

Bentley's quick eye saw that the game was in his own hands.

A scornful smile curled his lips.

With nerves of iron he stoood confronting these desperate men, a pistol in each hand, deliberately levelled at the heads of the nearest.

It was a picture for an artist at this moment, these cowed pirates and their daring, desperate leader.

"Come," he said, at last. "Let us put an end to this farce; it has been played long enough. Go back to your duty every one you, and I'll forgive you. But beware! The man who is guilty of insubordination hereafter shall swing at the yard-arm."

There was no mistaking Bentley's terrible look.

That he meant what he said was too plainly palpable.

The pirates now sullenly gave in, and poor Sam's body was hoisted up in strong arms, elevated above the bulwarks, and thrown into the sea.

After this, the authority of Bentley was never disputed.

But the pirate leader, to be more secure, took care to surround himself by those in whom he could repose most trust.

Three of his favourites were installed first, second, and third officers without delay, and on the others he was continually showering favours.

So that, in a comparatively short time, the unfortunate Sam's death was forgotten, and the men began to view their captain in the light of an hero, or something better still—a very good fellow, who, in reality, was not so black as he was painted.

But the devil put on the skin of a lamb, and thereby deceived them for the time.

A week on the open ocean!

The weather gloriously fine, and the winds all that the heart could desire.

Every day's sail of the "Will-o'-the-Wisp" brought John Bentley nearer the snowy cliffs of old England.

The man's superstitious nature could not resist the appeals of the imagined vision that said in the dark hours of night when Bentley tossed restlessly and fearfully on his pillow—

"Return to England with my wife and daughter. Beware how you disobey me!"

Scarcely had the vessel been four days on her homeward journey when Emily's mother very singularly turned up.

She had not been killed, as was supposed, by the blow of Red Ralph.

The ruffian's merciless fist stunned her, but no more, and some of the crew taking compassion on the poor woman concealed her in the hold of the brig until such time as Bentley could be disposed of.

Happy was the meeting between mother and daughter after those days of agony and suspense.

The weeping Emily could hardly realise the fact, and embraced her mother over and over again.

But what was the effect on Captain Bentley?

Strange as it may appear, it removed a great load from his mind.

For did not the vision say—"Return to England with my wife and daughter," and now he could perform his dreaded visitant's behest to the very letter.

From that time forth Bentley harboured no evil design on Emily, nor in any way annoyed her with his presence.

Too much afraid of provoking the wrath of the vision, he did his best to get to England with all possible speed.

But now we draw to a climax in this part of our story.

Captain Bentley was not long in reaching that part of the coast from where he started out, his intention being to land Emily and her mother somewhere on the shore, and then put to sea again and become a pirate in reality, capturing and plundering every merchant ship he came across.

We will see how far his plans succeeded.

One dark night the "Will-o'-the-Wisp" anchored not a mile from the shore, and a small boat put off and was rowed rapidly through the darkness.

In this boat was Captain Bentley, four brawny seamen, Emily, and her mother.

Not a solitary word passed between them.

The men had instructions before they started where to land, and they pulled for a point well known to them.

It was a place they had used many a time when smuggling to land the contraband articles of their calling.

Here they thought they would be safe and not likely to be interrupted.

How far they were correct in their surmise, the reader will presently learn.

The peculiar grating of the keel of the boat told the pirates now that they had reached their destination.

The oars were shipped, and the boat secured.

Just as the pirates were landing the women, the pitchy dark heavens were suddenly illumined by a bright flash of lightning, the thunder began to roll, and the night to betray every evidence of the raging of a violent storm.

In that brief but brilliant interlude of light, Bentley bent a searching glance on his surroundings.

The coast was clear as they all thought, and Emily and her mother were assisted out of the boat.

So far Bentley's mission had been performed without a word passing between them.

Was it his intention now to abandon them among those gloomy rocks alone and unprotected from the fierce violence of the storm that threatened?

We shall see.

Bentley, approaching the shivering women, spoke for the first time.

"I have so far obeyed the behest of your dead father," he said, addressing Emily. "I have landed you on English ground as he directed, and having fulfilled my mission, I leave you. Don't imagine that this act of mine has been dictated by any feeling of pity or commiseration for you. If you do, you mistake the nature of the man who has dared so much to get you into his power. With these words I leave you. Shift for yourself as well as you can. Farewell! I return now to the deck of the 'Will-o'-the-Wisp.'"

"Not yet, base pirate!" thundered a voice, and ere Bentley or his men could make one movement to get to the boat, a dozen black forms came rushing out of the darkness.

Emily and her mother found themselves lifted off their feet, and borne they knew not where.

Bentley, with his eyes flashing fire, seeing no possibility of escape, turned to confront the new-comers.

"Not yet, John Bentley," said the voice. "I have a little matter to settle with you before you go."

"Who are you that dare dispute my path?" cried Bentley, drawing a loaded pistol from his belt, and cocking it.

"One you ought to know," was the reply. "One

who, by your internal machinations, you thought to lure to his death."

"It is false!" cried Bentley, with a fierce oath.

"It is true, base pirate and would-be murderer! Behold!"

A forked flash of lightning broke through the sombre clouds overhead, and, as if by magic, lit up the landing-place.

"Lieutenant Rayner!" exclaimed the pirate, starting back with an involuntary shudder.

The hand which held the pistol shook like an aspen, and so great was his terror at this unexpected apparition, that he would have fled, but that retreat was simply put out of his power.

He was surrounded by smugglers.

A few of Captain Tom's middies were also on the ground.

Each and all were armed to the teeth.

"And know, likewise," went on Lieutenant Rayner, "that I am aware of your base plot to fasten the onus of your crime on Captain Tom Drake. Throw down your pistol, villain, for escape is impossible. Before another hour, the 'Will-o'-the-Wisp' will be in the hands of her gallant commander."

"Never!" cried Bentley, uttering a frightful oath.

"We'll see that," said Lieutenant Rayner, quietly. "Upon him, men, and disarm him!"

There was a sudden rush, the flash and sharp, ringing report of a fire-arm, followed by a yell of agony.

Instantaneously, a brilliant flash of lightning broke from the murky clouds, and lit up the scene.

John Bentley uttered a loud cry of triumph, for he thought he had shot the lieutenant.

But how speedily was he deceived when his fierce eye caught the still form of one of the poor middies, stretched in death, not five paces from him.

With a horrible yell of disappointment, the infuriated pirate threw his pistol at the head of the nearest of his enemies, and was making for the boat.

"Don't let him escape, on your lives!" thundered Rayner, rushing forward.

Bentley paused for a moment in his furious course, drew a knife, and was about to plunge it into the lieutenant's heart, when one of the smugglers, with a hoarse cry, sprang upon him.

The struggle which ensued was terrific.

Bentley's foot slipped, and the smuggler succeeded in wresting the knife from him, and, in the excitement of the moment, sheathing it in his heart.

A horrible howl of agony, and the pirate captain, with a dying oath on his lips, fell over the landing-place into the sea, and the waters closing over him, he was seen no more; the other pirates were easily disarmed, and made prisoners.

But hardly was the brief fight at an end when a new arrival appeared on the scene.

It was Captain Tom.

A few hurried words sufficed to explain to our hero all that had taken place, and nothing could exceed his joy than when he was informed that his own gallant 'Will-o'-the-Wisp' was anchored out in the bay not more than a mile from the landing place.

The captured pirates were now brought before Captain Tom, and answered all his questions readily.

He discovered from them that the ruffian, Bentley, had somewhat ingratiated himself into the good graces of his men more through the force of his own daring and iron will than through any respect or love they bore for him.

After gaining this information, Captain Tom re-solved to lose no time before he put out for his gallant brig and discover himself to the men, feeling assured that it would be better to take it by peaceable means than to use force.

In this resolve Lieutenant Rayner, who had become his friend since he discovered that he was not the murderer of his brother, sided with him.

"Yes, my dear captain, that will be your best plan," said Rayner, shaking his hand warmly. "Return to your noble vessel, and be assured that Gus Rayner will always remain your friend."

"It would hardly do for the authorities to hear you say that," replied Captain Tom, laughing, "especially that amiable soldier and good friend of mine, Colonel Hawkins."

"A snap of my finger for the old fool. He has already left the service."

"And Sir Henry Wharncliffe?"

"By a strange transition of character thinks very highly of you, and would now as eagerly shield you from the authorities as he would some time since hunt you down or deliver you into their hands."

"I could hardly imagine all that," said Captain Tom, surprised at this information. "However, I am very grateful to Sir Henry for his good opinion. The only man I have now to dread is Admiral Ellis."

"The little viper has put out to sea," replied the lieutenant.

"I am aware of it. Everything at present seems to be in my favour. Farewell, lieutenant, and God bless you!"

So saying the two young men shook hands and parted, perhaps to never meet again.

Captain Tom, leaping into the boat, was accompanied by four of the smugglers.

They were volunteers, the pirates being left prisoners in charge of their comrades.

Up to the time that our hero and the four smugglers got into the boat the storm was only threatening.

Many a clap of thunder crashed over the seething waters, and many a flash of lightning illuminated their crested waves.

But the oars bent to the efforts of four strong men, and the boat flew on in the direction of the "Will-o'-the-Wisp."

Captain Tom knew that he might have some trouble in gaining the deck of his well-beloved vessel, but once on that deck with the news of Bentley's death, and his slightest command would be obeyed.

He was certain that this would be the case.

The pirates on board the brig caught sight of the returning boat by the frequent flashes of lightning which broke from time to time across the murky heavens.

But they never dreamt for an instant that it was Tom Drake who was in the stern sheets.

Bentley had gone away with the women, and Bentley and their four comrades they expected would return with the boat.

Let us see in what light they took their disappointment.

A few more strokes of the oars and Captain Tom and his four smugglers shot alongside the brig.

In a very short time they were on its deck.

Every nerve in our gallant hero's body thrilled with a strange emotion, and a power came into his heart that he had never before experienced.

He felt the strength of a dozen men in his single arm.

Who now dared resist his authority?

The answer soon came.

The second officer was the first to discover the deception.

CAPTAIN TOM, WITH A SIGNIFICANT GESTURE, APPROACHED DUTCH PAUL.

"Treachery—treachery!" he cried at the top of his voice. "Below there! We are betrayed!"

The pirates, alarmed by these cries, came rushing up the companion-way, some with pistols in their hands, others with cutlasses, and not a few with pikes.

The situation was revealed to them in an instant.

They could see five black forms standing together on the quarter deck.

A sudden flash of lightning which shot through the murk lit these forms to their view.

One and all knew Captain Tom, and they hesitated before rushing upon him.

"Down with him!" cried the first officer, bounding forward with his naked cutlass.

He was followed by the second and the third.

But a shot from Captain Tom's pistol stretched the first lifeless on the deck, and the other two hesitated.

This was Captain Tom's only chance.

"Men," spoke our young hero, in a voice that rung like a clarion through the night. "I know that you will not follow the example of these foolish, misguided fellows who have dared to thus attack me. I am your captain, the true and lawful owner of this noble vessel, and the man who usurped that right has met this very night the death his crimes so richly deserved—I mean John Bentley, the would-be murderer of Lieutenant Rayner."

Had a thunderbolt fallen into their midst, it

would not have surprised the pirates more than this news.

John Bentley dead!

A thrill of joy ran through their hearts, for after all his pretended kindnesses, they now found out that they had been deceiving themselves—that they never had any real affection for the man who had so lately commanded them, rather, indeed, the opposite.

Captain Tom, with his eagle eye and keen intuition, saw, in an instant, the point gained.

"Bentley is dead," he said, "and met the death he, by virtue of his cruelty and crimes, deserved. Am I right, men?"

Without hesitating, they shouted, as in one voice, "You are, Captain Tom!"

"I thank you from my heart," replied our noble hero, knowing that it was necessary to use a little cajolery to gain them over to his side. "And now men, am I captain of the 'Will-o'-the-Wisp' or not?"

The answer, without the slightest hesitation, was given in the affirmative.

"You are—you are—you are!" repeated several voices.

"Then I order these two men, who would dare dispute my authority, to be instantly disarmed and arrested."

With a loud shout, half-a-dozen of the pirates sprang on the second and third officers, who, before they could make any resistance, were disarmed and hurried below, where they were left heavily ironed.

Thus Captain Tom gained the mastery of his gallant craft in the space of a very few minutes, and with the sacrifice of only one life.

It may be here necessary to state that the "Thunderer," which our gallant hero so cleverly ran out from under the very noses of Admiral Ellis and Captain Hall, was blown up by an explosion originating in her magazine.

During the absence of the "Will-o'-the-Wisp," Susan Brocton rejoined her father.

This, too, at the urgent request of Captain Tom, who had no desire to deceive the poor girl who was devotedly attached to him.

With her went Sweetheart Loo, loving our hero in the secret depths of her heart, and fondly looking forward to the time when she might meet him again.

Of course Captain Hall got another ship, though he was severely reprimanded for the loss of the "Thunderer."

And now turn we to pretty Mrs. Hawkins, who also cherished a secret affection for Tom, and her jealous husband often asserted that she was more attached to our gallant hero than to himself, which, if the truth must be told, was, in the main, correct.

Having given these various explanations necessary, and, as a consequence, most essential to the reader, we once more take up the thread of the story where we left off.

———

CHAPTER CLVIII.

A SCENE OF HORROR.

WE once more return to Captain Tom, who, as the reader will remember, was hastily pursuing his course to the plundered and nearly dismantled vessel.

The breeze was strong, and the "Will-o'-the-Wisp" flew rapidly on her way, but too late, however, to be of any material service to the vessel she was hastening to succour.

From time to time Captain Tom's glass was pointed in the direction of the rapidly receding pirate.

This vessel, in point of speed, was nearly equal to his own, and he knew that it would be only sheer folly on his part to give her chase.

Presently the "Will-o'-the-Wisp" hove to alongside the ship which had been attacked.

Not a sign of life—not a sound came from the doomed vessel.

Captain Tom hastily made his way over her shattered bulwarks, followed by his band of gallant buccaneers and middies.

What a sight!

The deck ploughed up here and there by the iron missiles of the pirate, the blood-bedabbled planks bearing their accumulations of mutilated, shattered human flesh, some with arms cut off, some legs, and, at intervals, a headless body, told how fierce had been the fight.

Not an inch of the deck but had been disputed to the bitter end.

Gallant and brave men were lying in heaps where they had fallen!

The ruthless pirates had only too surely, too fatally done their savage and merciless work.

Not a wounded man, or a dying one either, could be seen from one end of the deck to the other.

As Captain Tom gazed on this terrible sight, he could not repress a feeling of horror involuntarily stealing over him.

He turned away heartsick, feeling the thickened human gore almost running beneath his feet!

"This is frightful!" said Captain Tom, in a hoarse, almost inaudible voice. "Let us hasten below; there may be someone who has escaped their merciless and barbarous hands."

Glad of the order—for the men and officers were as heartsick of the sight as their leader—they rushed down the companion-ladder, and searched the various cabins.

Not a human being met their eyes, either killed, wounded, or living.

Trunks and cases were broken open, and the contents which were of the least value were scattered around in the direst confusion.

All spoke of wreck and ruin!

There had been females also on board, as could be told by the various articles of feminine apparel scattered over the place.

What had become of those unfortunate creatures, Captain Tom could only surmise.

Their bodies were not anywhere to be seen among the slain, and the only conclusion that he could arrive at was, that they had been taken on board the pirate before the latter shoved off.

He now ordered one of the buccaneers to go on deck and see if he could recognise the body of the captain among the heaps of slain.

The man went, but soon returned with the information that anybody answering that description was not to be found.

"Strange!" muttered Captain Tom. "One would naturally have thought he suffered the same fate as his brave followers. For it was no laggard defence. And the man who could organise it must have been one who feared death but little."

However this may be, the skipper had disappeared.

Captain Tom, in searching the captain's cabin, by accident came across a few hurried notes.

A strange feeling came over him.

Prompted by curiosity, he held them up to the light of the lamp.

An involuntary exclamation burst from him.

He knew the writing at once.

"Gracious Heaven!" he cried. "How came this here?"

The explanation was at hand, for the captain's signature was at the bottom, and that signature *John Gregory.*

This discovery for an instant confounded the cool and otherwise iron-nerved Tom.

His Uncle Gregory commander of that doomed ship!

A mistake.

Oh! this was madness.

Might there not be another John Gregory?

The world was wide, and there were people to be met with every day of the same name.

False, delusive hope!

So there was.

But the writing; the writing was in his own uncle's hand—the protector and fosterer of his childhood.

Tom felt one or two scalding tears roll down his cheeks.

A long vista of years rolled away, and discovered him once more the happy schoolboy fondly loved by the most devoted of mothers.

But Tom's iron nature would not allow him to dwell on such a subject long.

Besides, there were others in the cabin besides himself who looked upon him for his heroism and gallant acts with an adoration and worship almost irreverent.

His slightest act was observed, and some marked significance attached to it.

In this presence he, therefore, could not give way to his feelings.

By an iron effort he mastered his emotion, and began to read by the aid of the lighted lamp the few hurried—we may say agitated—notes of his uncle.

The mind that dictated them was evidently much excited at the time, and the hand that traced them trembled, as could be seen at a glance from the writing.

"As this may be my last day in life," so went the notes, "I can only say that I have made every effort that was in my power, or the power of man, to find my lost sister."

Here the name of Tom's mother was written in full.

"But my every effort has been crowned with a complete and miserable failure.

"I have penetrated the heart of every country, but in vain. All traces have been lost, though I am sure that she still lives.

"Having thus failed in the object that was nearest my heart, I care no longer to live.

"I am a burden to every one round me, and a misery to myself.

"For a third time my vessel has been chased and sacked by pirates, and now I know the end is drawing near, and that they will sacrifice me to their vengeance.

"A few hours at most, and all that remains of John Gregory will be a piece of lifeless clay.

"But if this should fall into the hands of any human being who has a spark of humanity left he will forward, or try to have it forwarded, to Captain Tom Drake, commonly known to the world as the Boy Buccaneer.

"By obliging me in this last request—the request of a man whose life may not be prolonged more than a few hours—he will be rewarded by the sum of two hundred guineas, which he will find in the cabin (mentioning the particular spot).

"Tell him also that his uncle's property has got, through wicked fraud and violence, into the hands of a man named Sanderson, late a lieutenant in his Majesty's navy.

"Let him beware of this man who has been the main cause of his poor mother's disappearance, and of my troubles."

The whole wound up with the writer's signature.

Captain Tom, in his agony, crushed the note in his clenched hand.

But he gave no further expression to his agitation, as that was not the place or time for it.

Forgetting, or not desiring to take the money from where it was concealed, he was on the point of hurrying on deck when a very black-skinned sausage-lipped negro was brought into him.

This man was evidently one of the crew, and the only one apparently saved.

He was brought in trembling from excessive fright.

Tom looked at him, and could hardly repress a smile when he observed his terror, which assumed such a comical character that most of the middies, in spite of their chief's presence, burst out laughing.

"Well, Sambo, where do you come from?" asked Tom.

"Me don't know whar me come from, massa, me in such a state ob fright."

"Don't you? Well, look around. Do you see anything the matter with us? Do we look like honest sailors or bloodthirsty pirates?"

Sambo was not at all reassured by his inspection, for some of the buccaneers had very curious dresses on, which in a manner resembled those of the pirates who had some time since taken their departure.

"Well, have you looked?"

"Yes, massa."

"Well, what do you think of us now?"

"I think you am all genelmen, massa—ebery one ob you."

But, notwithstanding this assurance, the negro's looks belied his words, for he glanced with the greatest possible terror all round him.

"Eh, Sambo? That's a lie, isn't it?" said Tom.

"Y-yes, massa," answered the poor negro, not well knowing what he was saying.

"That we are not gentlemen?"

"Oh, no, massa. I say you am all genelmen—ebery one ob you."

"You don't look frightened do you?"

"Oh, no, Massa Captain. I am berry happy."

"Don't tell lies, Sambo. You know you are not."

"Berry well, Massa Captain. If you say I isn't, I isn't."

"That's coming nearer the mark. Now tell me. Are you the only survivor on this vessel?"

"I am de cook, massa."

"I mean are you the only survivor?"

"Surbibor—surbibor," muttered the black, looking very perplexed. But a happy thought seeming to strike him, his eyes brightened up, and he answered readily. "Oh, yes, massa, I is de only surbibor. No oder cook on dis yare vessel—yah! yah! I do de bottle-washing, tater-peeling, an' cookin' de j'ints all myself."

The negro thought this a good answer.

And so it was a very comical one.

"He doesn't understand you aright," said Ben Barnacle, laughing in spite of himself.

"Come, then, Sambo," said Tom, "are you the only man that these pirate devils have spared?"

The negro's face lit up with a gleam of intelligence.

"Oh, Massa Captain! Now me know what you say. Yes, sah; me am de only person they am spared."

"How did they come to spare you, then?" asked Tom.

"Me go down de hold, you see, massa, and me then git into an ole box, an' when de pirate debils come dey no find me. Yah!—yah!—yah!"

"Oh, that was the way, was it? You are a lucky fellow, Sambo, to escape as you did. You need not be afraid of us though. We are not pirates; only came to save your vessel, and arrived here late."

"T'ank God!—t'ank God, massa, dat you say you no pirates," exclaimed the negro, with clasped hands. "Me only afraid you was; dat's all."

"Well, now you see that we are not?"

"Me see, massa."

"What was your captain's name?"

"John Gregory, massa. Massa John Gregory."

"Was he good to you?"

"Good!" exclaimed the negro, raising his streaming eyes. "good, sah? Massa Captain Gregory was a perfect angel ob light. He was good to eberybody, and too good to dis yar poor nigger by far."

"Do you know the name of the pirate captain, Sambo?"

"Yah! yah! Dat I do, Massa Captain."

"Well, and what what was his name?"

"Angel. But it ought to be debil, massa—debil it ought to be."

"You are right; I'll not forget that name," said Captain Tom, with closely-compressed lips. "I suppose you have no desire to stay any longer on board this wreck, Sambo?"

"No, massa—no, sah. Dis ole nig don't want to stay here any longer. Massa Captain Gregory am gone, an' dis ole nig want to go alse."

"Well said, Sambo. But answer me one thing. Do you know where Captain Gregory is?"

The negro scratched his woolly pate for a moment or two, then he answered quite readily—

"Yes, Massa Captain. When de pirate debils come down de hold, dis nig hear dem—yah! yah! Spoke 'bout Massa Gregory."

"What did they say of him?" asked Captain Tom.

"Dey say him gone on board de pirate. Dat Angel or debil, tels de pirates to treat him well. Dat's all, Massa Captain."

"That's enough, Sambo. You will now come on board the 'Will-o'-the-Wisp,' and we'll treat you well as long as you like to stay with us."

"T'anks, Massa Captain, t'anks! You am berry good—berry good indeed, Massa Captain."

After a most diligent search in the holds, to see if any others of the crew had escaped the general slaughter, the buccaneers, Captain Tom, and the black cook made their way on deck.

The silver moon shone down on a scene of blood that baffles our pen to describe, and which made the hearts of the brave crew of the "Will-o'-the-Wisp" tremble to contemplate.

They were glad enough when they got on the deck of their own brig—glad enough indeed, to escape this awful scene of general carnage and desolation.

It would be many a year—at least, they hoped so—ere they would again see such a sight.

The "Will-o'-the-Wisp" swept past the doomed ship five minutes later on her homeward track.

Tom expected, before the dawn, to rejoin the vessels of his fleet.

Most of the officers were now assembled on the quarter-deck, glancing back, with looks of horror, at what had been, but a few hours since, a noble vessel, manned by a brave and gallant crew.

But now a perfect wreck, riddled with murderous shot, and reeking with human gore.

"It seems a pity," said Ben Barnacle, sighing deeply, "that such a ghastly sight should be left above the sea."

"What would you do?" asked Tom.

"Sink it," replied Ben, quickly; "a single broadside would send it to the bottom without the waste of another shot. It strikes me as cruel to let it stay where it is. The bodies of the poor murdered crew will be far better in the sea than festering in the sun."

"Truly said," echoed Lieutenant Vere. "Let us, in the name of common decency, sink her."

"Aye, aye! Sink her!" cried several voices.

All took the same view as Ben Barnacle and Lieutenant Vere.

As Captain Tom was also in favour of that measure, the "Will-o'-the-Wisp" paused in her course, and her broadside was instantly brought to bear on the unfortunate ship.

Every gun was double-shotted.

At the word "Fire!" there came a terrible roar as of thunder. The little brig rebounded from the shock. A long, brightly lurid sheet of flame shot from her, and the messengers of destruction sped with loud and rushing sounds on their errand.

The decks of the "Will-o'-the-Wisp" became enveloped in a thick, stifling cloud of smoke.

Nothing could be observed for nearly half a minute.

A terrible crash was of course heard—a crash as of some great thunderbolt undermining the foundation of a mighty edifice.

Then when the sulphur-laden vapour rolled away, it could be seen how terrible had been the effect of the "Will-o'-the-Wisp's" broadside, every shot of which had crashed through the timbers of the doomed vessel, many even striking below her water-mark.

"She is sinking!" cried Ben Barnacle.

Looking in that direction, they saw the ship settling down very rapidly.

Having accomplished an act of humanity, the little brig veered round, and pursued her course as before.

The breeze was not so strong as it had been.

But it served to fill the sails of the "Will-o'-the-Wisp" very well.

And the moon shone brightly down, and the stars glinted prettily overhead, while the slightly-rippled ocean looked out for miles like one immense sheet of silver.

Below deck were our irrepressible and good friends Bob Hauler and Jerry Mizzen.

As much awake as ever, two old sea-dogs like them could be.

"I say, Bob."

"Well, Jerry?"

"What do yer think o' that 'ere ship that we just settled?"

"Think! Why, that it was the horriblest sight I ever clapped lights on. I wish as how yer wouldn't mention it again, Jerry. The mere thought of it is enough to make one as sick as a dog."

"So I say, Bob, so I say."

"Then why can't ye hold yer darned jaw, then?"

"Because I have something to tell you, Bob."

"Hang the feller! What has he got to tell me?" thought Bob. "He ain't been a-killing anybody, I hope. He's so orfully mysterious that a person would think he had been a-doing of some great offence. Well, Jerry, go on, and cut yer yarn short, for I know how long yer generally takes to tell a story when yer once begins."

Jerry Mizzen looked at his old messmate reproachfully.

"Well, why don't yer go on, curse yer?" cried his comrade.

"All right, Bob. Don't be in such a funk It's something worth hearing, this is."

"Nothing as they can scrag yer for?"

"What!"

"You must be deaf, Jerry. I'll say it over again, seeing as how yer an old pal o' mine. Ye have done nothing as how they can scrag ye for, have ye? Yer haven't been gone and committed yerself, I hope."

Jerry burst out into a loud laugh.

"Hallo! hallo!" cried a gruff, half-sleepy voice from the darkness.

"Hallo!" bawled Jerry. "Anyone a-disturbing of yer?"

"Is that you, Jerry Mizzen?"

"Yes, it is. What does yer honour want, if it ain't axin' too much?"

"I want you to go to sleep, you lubber, and not be making such a row."

"Who's making a row?"

"Why, you are."

"Then I'm able to make one. So go to sleep, yerself, old son. There's no one a-disturbin' of you, I reckon. You must have been a-dreaming it."

"I'll let Captain Tom know of this in the morning," threatened the voice.

"Let him know, and be banged! If yer gives me any of yer jawing tackle, I'll come over and punch yer head for ye."

"And if he doesn't, darn me! I will," sang out Bob.

This was a little too much for the "disturbed" one.

He then and there collapsed.

And they heard no more of him.

Bob having so effectually silenced the buccaneer now objected to Jerry's noise, found himself in honour bound to begin on his old comrade.

"Can't yer splice that cussed jaw o' yours?" he cried, "and not be a-making that confounded disturbance. I never heard sich a cove. Wag, wag, wag. His tongue is never still."

"Yer d n't mean that 'ere base hinsinuation for me, do you?" said Jerry.

"Yes, I do."

"Then I hopes as how you'll keep yer tongue to yerself in future."

"All right, old son."

"And that ye'll not speak to me."

"Werry good."

"So that ends it."

"So say I."

"Well?"

"Well?"

"Ain't yer done yet?"

"Yes, I am; but you ain't it seems."

"Bother! You will have the last word, Bob, say what I will."

"And so will you, Jerry."

"Come, old friend, let us not quarrel."

"Agreed."

"Now, will you listen quietly without any of them 'ere interruptions?"

"Go on."

Jerry, assured that Bob would remain perfectly still while he spoke, cleared his throat, and proceeded—

"Well, yer must know, old pal, when Captain Tom went below on that 'ere ship, I was not very far behind him."

"I am sure of that," said Bob, pointedly.

He was, no doubt, thinking of the grog Jerry might have had.

"Shut up!" cried Jerry. "I thought as you was going to keep quiet while I spoke."

"So I am old pal. Proceed."

"Well, then, when Captain Tom went into the skipper's cabin I was close at his heels."

"So you told me afore," cried Bob. "Go on, old son."

"Can't yer screw that jaw o' yours down a little, and stop interrupting of a feller when he's telling you a yarn? If yer don't, by Jupiter, ye'll have to tell it yerself."

"Go on, Jerry. I'll not speak another word."

"All right, Bob. Let me see that you'll keep yer word this time, for I hates interruptions as I hates the —"

"Devil," put in Bob.

"You've taken the very word out of my mouth," said Jerry. "Well, to make a long story short—"

"And a short one long," added Bob.

"Shut up, you lubber! How can I get on if you are always interrupting me? Well, as I was saying, I followed Captain Tom into the skipper's cabin, and before I had been a few minutes there, I saw him pick up a bit o' paper."

"Werry surprising, that," said Bob.

"Werry," said Jerry. "Well, as I was a-saying, when your confounded tongue interrupted me, Captain Tom picked up this paper, and on this paper was a lot o' writing."

"Well, did you read it?"

"That's what I just did."

"It's well for you that Captain Tom didn't catch you. How did yer manage it?"

"Well, I'll tell yer, Bob. When Captain Tom was a-reading, I was a-looking over his shoulder."

"You are a fine skunk, you are," said Bob, with a shrug of disgust, "to go an' pry into a genelman's private affairs."

"It wasn't exactly a private affair, Bob, because, yer sees, he picked it up."

"And you read it?"

"Of course."

"Well, what was it all about? It must a-been very interesting, that you are taking such a long time to tell it. Hum! Go on, Jerry. I told you as how it would be a yarn as long as to-day and to-morrow."

"But this isn't," said Jerry, quickly. "And if you'll only listen a little, and in patience, you'll come to the same conclusion."

"Well, you read the note," said Bob. "What the dooce was in it to make it so jolly interesting?"

"A good deal more'n you dream of. The moment I looked at it, I could tell who it came from."

"Oh, indeed!"

"Yes, Bob. Now, who do ye think it came from?"

"The Death Pirate?"

"No. Guess again."

"His Satanic Majesty?"

"No."

"Well, if it's something worse—Admiral Ellis, then," cried Bob, triumphantly.

"Nonsense! Admiral Ellis is a prisoner."

"Oh, so he is. I forgot all about that," said Bob.

"Do you give in then?"

"Stow that, Jerry, if yer don't want a smash on yer conk. I never gave in in my life."

"Well, I suppose I'll have to tell yer," said Jerry, in a tone of disappointment. "Though I'd rayther ye'd a guessed it yerself. It came from John Gregory."

"What, John Gregory—Captain Tom's uncle," cried Bob.

"Yes, Bob, Captain Tom's uncle, surely."

"How the deuce did it come there?"

"Easy enough. John Gregory was the captain."

"What, of the vessel we've just sunk?"

"Yes."

"Humbug!"

"He was, though."

"Nonsense!"

"Well, I could never ha' believed it, seeing as how the old genelman was gouty when we knew him, Bob."

"But, you dunderhead, you, they cured him o' that in the loonatic asylum."

"So they did, Bob. But the note was from him, at any rate. You know I'm a pretty good reader, though a cussedly bad speller, so it ended up by my reading every word of it."

Jerry now entered, as well as he was able, into the gist of John Gregory's few notes, and Bob listened spell-bound until his comrade had done

"Well, did Captain Tom take the two hundred guineas?"

"Not he?"

"How werry foolish of him!"

"Werry. But as he had forgotten 'em, like, I took good care to take 'em for him."

"Oh, you willain! You are the biggest willain unhung, Jerry."

"Why should you think so?" asked Jerry, taken suddenly aback by this information.

"Why do I think so? Well, now, you'll have to give me a little time to answer that 'ere question. But you've got the yaller boys about you, haven't you, Jerry?"

"Yes, my hearty."

"Splendid spree when you go ashore, Jerry."

"Glorious! Grog to any extent. Listen to this, Bob. Did you ever hear sich sweet music in yer life?"

Jerry thrust both his hands into his pockets, and tinkled the guineas together so as to make Bob's very mouth water.

"Do you think they are snoozing, Bob."

"Y-yes, I think they are," stammered Bob. "Why do you ask?"

"Simply because I wants a light, old pal."

"For what?"

"To show you all this gold, and to count it, too. I means counting every one of 'em. I think there's the two hundred fully here. But I'm not sartin. Get a light, Bob, and I'll let you go shares with me."

Bob, after some hesitation, procured a little lamp, which he immediately lit.

The two comrades were sitting on a large case.

The lamp was placed between them.

Jerry emptied his pockets of the shining metal until a large glittering heap flashed out.

Bob was delighted.

Jerry rubbed his hands gleefully, and chuckled with inward pleasure.

"Now, who's a-going to count these yaller boys?" asked Jerry.

"I will," replied Bob, readily.

"No, you won't. I think I'll count 'em myself."

"Oh, you suspicious young varmint! I had a better opinion of you than that, Jerry."

"So you might. But, yer sees, if I counts 'em myself there'll be no mistakes. I don't think for a moment as how you'd pocket any of 'em. Mind that, Bob."

"Then what objection have you to me counting 'em?"

"Because yer not as good a counter as me, Bob."

"Oh, very well! go on."

"Now I means putting each in a little pile o' twenty guineas. One! two! three! four!—"

"That's not right!" exclaimed Bob. "You have put one too many there."

"So I did, Bob. You are quite correct. I put five and counted four. But you know, old pal, mistakes occur in the best o' regulated families. Five! six! seven! eight! nine! ten!—"

"Hold on!" yelled Bob. "That's eleven."

Bob Hauler was not aware that he had shouted at the top of his voice.

His mind was so intent on the gold.

"What's yer shouting hold on for?" cried Jerry. "Do yer mean to say I put more'n ten there?"

"Yes, I do. I was watchin' o' you, and saw you put eleven."

"So I did—so I did," said Jerry, now discovering his mistake. "I'll get my hand in in a few

moments, and then I'll go on all right. Eleven! twelve! thirteen! fourteen! sixteen!—"

"What deuced nonsense!" cried Bob. "Now you put one too little."

"Did I, by gum?"

"Yes, you did. You said sixteen instead of fifteen."

"Well, we'll just go over 'em again."

And Jerry did go over them again, but making the same mistake as before, until Bob lost all patience with him.

Jerry, being rather a sensitive man, asked Bob if he could do any better.

Bob, being a very modest one, said he would try.

And the counting was resumed, and seemed to prosper under Bob's great talent for calculation.

Bob went on very rapidly.

But by so doing he lost all caution, and shouted out the numbers almost at the top of his voice.

As to Jerry, he was so much engrossed in the various little piles that were growing up under Bob's fostering supervision, that he also lost all the little prudence he had, by expatiating on the size and weight of every guinea.

This was rather unfortunate for Bob and Jerry, seeing that there were vultures in the shape of a dozen buccaneers, whose argus-eyes were watching their movement through the darkness.

No doubt these merciless cormorants had the evil design in their hearts of rushing forward and seizing the spoils.

At least their actions denoted that this was their intention.

"One! two! three! four! five!" exclaimed Bob.

A sudden sound caught the ears of the irrepressible Jerry.

"What the deuce is that?" cried Bob, pausing in his work. "Was that you, Jerry?"

"No, it wasn't me," replied Jerry,

"I could have sworn that I heard a noise."

"So could I."

"Look!"

Jerry did look.

But just in time to be too late.

The buccaneers were well hidden behind huge bales and cases.

"Go on again, Bob. It's only someone on deck."

Bob again pursued the even tenour of his way.

But he had not proceeded far when there was a sudden rush.

The lamp was extinguished.

The gold was scattered all over the place.

Bob Hauler and Jerry Mizzen were knocked over like nine pins.

There was now a general scramble for the guineas, and when the buccaneers had satisfied their cupidity by taking all they could get, they as quickly decamped, without leaving a trace that they had been there, if we except the struggling figures of Bob Hauler and Jerry Mizzen, who had, by some unexplainable means, got locked in each other's arms, and fancying that each had an enemy, were pummelling away in the most unmerciful fashion.

No sooner had they spoken, than they discovered their mistake.

And such vituperative abuse never came from any two tongues as was heaped on the heads of the merciless villains, who took them at such disadvantage.

Bob swore a good round oath that he would be revenged.

But Jerry, after a while, very humbly contented himself by picking up all the gold he could find.

And the reader may be sure, after this general onslaught, that there was very little left to pick up.

Bob and Jerry, now seeing that nothing further could be done at present, very wisely groped their way towards their hammocks, crept in, and were soon in a profound sleep.

The dawn had crept up in the eastern horizon ere the "Will-o'-the-Wisp" sighted the other vessels of her little fleet.

And it was an hour after sunrise before she swept past them.

The "Will-o'-the-Wisp's" appearance was hailed by loud cries of welcome from the crews of the different craft that lay at anchor.

When she hove to, Dutch Paul and the other captains came on board to congratulate the gallant Tom Drake on his safe return.

The "Will-o'-the-Wisp" showed very few signs of her previous night's adventures, and the captains, when they were informed of all she had gone through, were surprised and in ecstacies at the excellent manner in which she was handled.

Tom now informed them of his intention to follow up the pirate Captain Angel.

And they all promised to do their best in assisting him to run the atrocious pirate down and punish him for the inhuman crimes of which he had been guilty.

"When do you start?" asked Dutch Paul.

"To-morrow morning by sunrise," replied our hero.

"So soon?"

"If possible, yes. But I have a great deal of work to get through before then."

"I know you have. There is Admiral Ellis, for instance, and his brother, the commodore. As much as I like the commodore—who is a noble old fellow—I detest his miserable brother."

"I hear your men—especially the middies—are thirsting for his life."

"I am afraid they are," replied Tom.

"Then satisfy the rascals—satisfy them!" cried Dutch Paul. "The world will never miss such a viper as Ellis, and you will have one powerful enemy the less to deal with."

"The most powerful and the most wicked," said our hero, thoughtfully. "And, as for gratitude, Admiral Ellis has not the slightest grain of it in his composition."

"Now, what if you were to let him escape to-day?" said the smuggler.

"He would seek my life to-morrow," replied Tom.

"Then such a man ought to die, captain; and if you spare him, you are a fool."

After very little more conversation, Captain Tom's interview with the captains was at an end, and they left the "Will-o'-the-Wisp" for their own vessels.

Captain Tom had very often thought of Minnie Atherton during the brief time that he was separated from her, and he resolved that night to go over to the island for both her and her companion.

While he was reflecting on all the work he had cut out for himself, a message came from Iron-Arm's brig, with the strong intimation that he was wanted immediately there.

A boat was manned at Captain Tom's order, and in less than five minutes he was on board of the brig.

CHAPTER CLIX.

BLACK RUFUS AT THE YARD-ARM.

When Captain Tom mounted the deck of the brig, he found Iron-Arm and several of his officers awaiting him there.

The deck was crowded with middies and buccaneers, and Tom could see at a glance that there was considerable excitement among them.

What was the cause of it?

Another glance explained all.

Black Rufus, bound, and with fiercely-glaring eyes, was held by two stout fellows of the crew.

The pirate was foaming at the mouth.

His great rough hands were empurpled with blood, and not five paces from him was stretched the beautiful Jewess, Hester Shawn, still and cold in death.

The body had been found below and brought on deck.

And Black Rufus was the murderer.

The fellow had escaped from the cabin in which he was confined by some unaccountable means, and in his mad fury had attacked the girl, whom he found following him.

He recognised her at once, and one stroke of a keen knife that he had rid her of a life that had become a burden and a misery to her.

Thus the poor Jewess died at last.

Black Rufus, in trying to escape, was secured, and now stood awaiting the just doom passed on him, only to be ratified by Captain Tom's presence.

The wretch seemed fully conscious of his fate, and glanced around like a tiger.

But he was too well secured, however, to break away from the two men who held him.

"Ha! ha!" he cried, on beholding Captain Tom, "you have come to see me die, have you?"

Captain Tom turned away from the wretch, and, after regarding poor Hester Shawn's beautiful features—more beautiful still, in death—he approached the group of officers who stood on the quarter-deck.

"So the wretch has killed the poor girl?" he said, addressing himself to Iron-Arm.

"Yes, Captain Tom; ruthlessly murdered her."

In the conversation that ensued, Iron-Arm's lieutenant gave a brief account of how the murder took place, and where the body of poor Hester was found.

"And now nothing remains," said Captain Tom, "but to carry out the sentence. Let it be done quickly, for I sicken looking at the fellow. A more cowardly and wretched murder could not be committed."

As Iron-Arm was not on his vessel at the time, he had to take the account of the murder from his first officer.

Iron-Arm, it will be remembered, was with Captain Tom, and took part in all his adventures from the time he attacked the man-of-war up to the boarding of poor John Gregory's ship.

He, therefore, only reached his brig some few minutes before our hero, and was as much surprised and horrified as Tom at the fate of the unfortunate but beautiful Jewess.

The officers all left the quarter-deck now, to witness the execution of Black Rufus.

The wretch, when he saw them approaching, laughed with devilish malignity.

"Ha! ha!" he cried. "You have come to see a man die, have you? And you shall see one—curse you!—you shall see one! Aye, aye! look as long as you like on that gory form. Black Rufus's was the hand that struck the blow. Do you think, dogs —ha! ha!—that he is afraid to own it? The father fell beneath his good cutlass, and now the daughter lies in death from as worthy a stroke."

"The wretch!" cried Captain Tom. "He glories in the deed."

"I imagine he must be mad," said Iron-Arm.

"It will not save him, nevertheless," replied Captain Tom, "for swing he shall. Give the cold-blooded murderer time to say one prayer, then fasten the noose round his neck, and hoist him up to the yard-arm."

All the necessary preparations had been made

Not very far from the wretched murderer's head dangled the fatal rope, which was soon to be called into use.

Black Rufus, of all the others, seemed the most unconcerned as to the manner of his death.

He viewed the dangling instrument of death with a look of supreme scorn, and tried to imitate its pendulous motion, as it swayed to and fro in the breeze, by moving his head from side to side.

One of the officers now drew near him.

"Say a prayer," he said, "for you have not many minutes to live."

"A prayer!" exclaimed the pirate, scornfully—"a prayer from the man who knows scarcely the meaning of the word! Begone, dog! If you think it worth your own paltry salvation, mumble a prayer for yourself. Look at my hands, I say! Do such men as Black Rufus pray? Behold those blood-empurpled hands, and then tell me is there any hope here or hereafter for the pirate and the murderer?"

"There is hope, wretched man," replied the young officer, in a voice that trembled with emotion. "Ask God in one single prayer to pardon you for this great crime."

"Come not to me to preach!" cried Black Rufus, furiously. "I tell you, young man, your words are thrown away. I was conscious of this some time ago—conscious that I should meet this ignominious end. It came in a dream, and I knew that it was nigh."

Iron-Arm nudged Captain Tom to call his attention.

"How very singular," he whispered.

"What?" asked Tom.

"That this wretched murderer's dream should be so nearly coincident with my own."

"Ah! I remember now. But listen."

"Yes," continued Black Rufus, hoarsely. "I dreamt it—dreamt that my fate would be an ignominious one. And only last night a vision came to warn me that I must die. 'Ha! ha! ha!—die at the yard-arm like a strangled cur. Where is Reuben Harpy?—where is he, the dog, to desert me at this hour of my extremity? Base, cowardly dog! He promised never to leave me. Bring him forward some of you! Away, I say! and if I am to die let him not escape. Ha! ha! ha!'

Black Rufus chuckled horribly, anticipating in his madness that Reuben Harpy would instantly be brought on deck.

But no one moved.

And the pirate's swarthy face grew purple with rage.

The veins in his forehead swelling to bursting.

"What! Is my order not to be obeyed?" he yelled.

"Dare you refuse the last request of a dying man? Ah! Now I see!" he shrieked. "You have let the villain escape! Curses—a thousand curses on you all!"

His tall, powerful form struggled in the grip of the two strong men who held him, swaying them from side to side, like so many children.

At that moment he seemed possessed of a strength almost superhuman.

Tugging with the ferocity of a tiger at his bonds, he, with one Samsonic effort of strength, burst them, dashing his guards to the deck.

What the pirate would have done now, there was no telling.

The consequences might have been fearful had not the gigantic Iron-Arm sprung upon him, and after a terrific struggle bore him to the deck, after which others came up with strong cords and secured him.

"Hang the wretch up!" cried Captain Tom. "It is useless wasting any more time on him!"

Black Rufus, without further delay, was dragged beneath the yard-arm, and the noose quickly adjusted to his neck.

The wretched pirate struggled furiously, and made superhuman efforts to release himself.

But in vain.

The cords which bound him now were more than human strength could sunder.

Cursing and blaspheming in the most awful manner, the pirate was hoisted to his doom.

The spasmodic writhings of his body and features for the first few minutes were terrible.

But they grew less and less.

And at the end of ten Black Rufus's lifeless body swung to and fro in the breeze.

"The end!" muttered Captain Tom, looking with a shudder of horror on the pirate's burly form.

Without loss of time, Black Rufus's body was cut down, and with a chain shot secured to his legs, was thrown over the bulwarks into the sea.

A loud splash, some foam and bubbles on the water.

Nothing more.

And the murderer sunk for ever from human sight.

CHAPTER CLX.

THE DEATH PIRATE MAKES AN IMPORTANT CAPTURE.

An act of retributive justice had been done.

The mystic power of the great Sea Emerald once more was shown.

There was nothing left now for Tom but to consign the poor Jewess to the waves.

He gave orders to that effect.

And after the burial service had been read, all that remained of the unfortunate Hester was lowered into the sea.

The waves parted to receive her gory and lifeless body, and Tom, with a strange feeling of sadness creeping over his heart, hurried from the deck, leaped into his boat, and was pulled rapidly for the "Will-o'-the-Wisp."

Here he was received by Lieutenant Vere.

Harry was just the man he wanted to see, considering that he had made up his mind to send him over to the island, for Minnie Atherton and Jennie.

He thought the poor girls had been long enough there, and that they would be wondering how the battle ended; and, indeed, alarmed for both his and the lieutenant's safety.

No sooner did Captain Tom communicate his wish, than Harry gladly accepted the responsibility, declaring that he would set off at once.

While he is preparing for his trip to the island we will go a little way back, and trace the fortunes of Reuben Harpy and his two companions.

The reader is aware that we left them in the brig's boat, making their way to the dark pile of rocks which loomed up from the island.

Their movements were characterised by the greatest caution as they went.

Every dip of the oar was watched with the most painful and anxious suspense.

More especially on the part of Reuben, who fancied at least a hundred times that there were some boats pursuing them.

At last they passed all the vessels.

They grew less careful now, and struck out vigorously for the shore.

The only fear they entertained was that the moon might burst through the clouds.

Or that the clouds might roll away and leave them exposed to the gaze of the buccaneers.

These and kindred fears made Reuben's moments miserable.

But as the moon did not break out, or the clouds roll away, the ex-privateers had some hopes that they might yet escape.

Hopes that never for an instant deserted the minds of the sham sentinel or his companion.

For if the worst came to the worst, the late sentinel could personate Lieutenant Harbison, and capture would be impossible.

Besides, his two companions were dressed as buccaneers.

When they got about a mile from the last vessel, they took off the pieces of canvas they had on the oars, and bent themselves with a will to their work.

The boat almost flew through the water.

The oars bent and curved as if they were every instant going to snap in two.

Another five or ten minutes, and they would be among the rocks.

Reuben steered as well as the darkness would allow him.

The point they make for is at length reached—the boat grates on the pebbles and sand, and securing it to a jutting point of rock, they leap ashore.

What was now to be done?

To look about the island and ascertain its length and breadth, and every matter connected with it.

This plan was a good one.

Perhaps they might conceal themselves for a few days until the buccaneers were gone.

Surely this must be an island where vessels were passing every few days.

The mere thought gave them a desire to pursue their investigations at once.

But it never struck them, though, that some of the buccaneers might be there.

They would have to act very prudently in their search.

This they knew.

"Well, Captain Harpy," said the sham sentinel, after allowing himself a little breathing time, "do you feel any better after your trip?"

Reuben replied in the affirmative, but qualified his answer by saying that he thought they were still in great peril.

"Nonsense. You have escaped their hands this time, captain, and if you take my advice, it's unlikely that you'll ever get into 'em again."

The ex-privateer was all curiosity to know what that advice might tend to.

"I will tell you," said his late guard. "Give up the sea, and enter into some respectable business. Believe me, captain, you were never cut out for a sailor, and dry land is the best place, after all, for you."

Reuben might have been offended by the man's strange familiarity if he had been in any other situation.

But placed as he was he had to put up with it the best way he could.

"I'll tell you what I was thinking of, as we were coming along, captain," said the man. "I was thinking what an advantage it would be to have such a fellow as me in business with you."

"Were you, indeed," said Reuben, scornfully.

"I was indeed, captain."

"What makes you think that?" asked Reuben.

"Well, I don't exactly know. But I thought you were cut for that sort of thing, I am sure you wouldn't cheat a fellow. That is the reason I'd like to have such a gentleman as you in with me."

"We'll talk of that another time," said Harpy. "But, for Heaven's sake, drop the subject at present."

"As you like, but I thought I would just mention it," said the sentinel.

"Certainly. I quite understand the favour you would confer on me. But we'll talk the matter over at some more fitting moment."

"Bravo, captain! I see you are dropping in with my views. Peter, here, would give his head, the rascal, if he had such a chance as I offer to you. Wouldn't you, Peter?"

Peter was conscious of a nudge in his side.

And Peter answered "Yes."

A thing which might be expected of him.

One thing was apparent, however, in all this.

The sham sentinel was playing a part, and if he played it well, he expected that he would be a gainer by it by some thousands.

But for all his discrimination, discernment, and knowledge of the human character, Reuben Harpy deceived him.

Reuben was by no means such a fool as he looked.

The conversation on business matters consequently dropped, and the men made their way, as well as they could, across the island.

Their local knowledge of the place was limited indeed, very limited, from the fact that they knew hardly anything about it.

An exception may be made, however, in the case of Peter, the sham sentinel's accomplice.

This gentleman had a talent for listening.

And he listened, too, to some advantage.

The buccaneers often spoke of the island.

But even their knowledge was not great.

However, Peter picked up some little information from their conversation about the peculiarities of the rocks, and other things connected with it.

And everything he heard he made the greatest possible use of.

The island, they soon discovered, was not of very great extent.

It might have been a mile and a half across it, or perhaps more.

Its length was not much greater.

So they soon traversed the greater part of it.

One might have the idea, looking from the sea, that its principal features were gigantic, lichencovered rocks.

But once on the island, they would be agreeably disappointed.

As most of these stupendous, basaltic masses faced the water.

Some towering up to the height of a hundred and twenty feet, and even more, and looking as if they would, when night approached, touch the very clouds.

The island was a marvellous piece of deception.

Apple, pear, and plum trees grew there in abundance.

The three men set to, and filled their pockets with the various fruit so temptingly within their reach.

Having ate their fill, they now took the longitudinal bearings of the island, with the hope of reaching some sheltered spot where they could repose for a few hours.

All of a sudden, the thick darkness was dissipated.

The moon shone out.

And the stars gleamed like diamonds overhead.

The whole island was lit up by a light marvellously clear and brilliant.

What a glorious panorama of beautiful scenery opened to them!

Reuben could never have believed that such a circumscribed little piece of land, surrounded by rude rocks, could possess so many beauties.

But there they were, lit up by the clear, silvery light of the moon.

Beyond, and at some distance, rolled the limitless ocean, from which a gauze-like vapour arose.

But not a vessel could be seen.

Reuben Harpy was struck dumb.

His first thought was that the buccaneers had gone.

But how could they go in so short a time?

This was what puzzled him.

If he had only for a moment reflected, he might have known that they stood now almost on the other side of the island.

This was explained by Peter, and Reuben, thereat, was very much disappointed.

They came now suddenly upon a hut, built of the rude material that walled in the island.

Had they got there a little sooner they would in all probability have seen a light issuing from the hut.

However, thinking that there might be a possibility that it was occupied, they very cautiously approached the door and listened.

Their suspicions were confirmed.

They heard voices.

Two evidently belonged to females.

The other to a very aged man, for the tones were both feeble and tremulous.

"By Heaven!" whispered the sham sentinel, "we have trapped in for something at last."

"What is the matter?" asked Harpy, alarmed at the thought that they might be courting danger by staying there.

"Nothing very much. But there are two girls here."

"Two girls!"

"Yes, and a very old man, as far as I can make out."

"Is that all?"

"Yes. But, by Jove! there may be some one else there, too."

"Then come away," whispered Reuben, fearfully. "We'll seek shelter somewhere else."

"There is nothing to alarm you, captain. Stay where you are, and I'll listen to what they are saying. If there is any danger, I'll soon let you know."

Reuben and Peter squatted down on a huge boulder, while the sham sentinel bent his ear to the door.

He heard the following—

"Oh, why don't they come?" said a sweet girlish voice. "Perhaps they will never come," it added, in a sad tone.

"Oh, don't—don't fear for them, miss," replied the aged and tremulous tones of a very old man. "Nothing has happened to Cap'n Tom, depend on it."

"Alas! I wish I could think so. If he escaped that frightful battle, I am sure he would have been here long since."

"But he may have a lot to do, miss," said the second voice, encouragingly. "After a battle, a cap'n has all he can attend to to get his craft in order. Old Joe Bunting wasn't in the navy forty year without knowin' that much. And if it warn't for my old rheumatic limbs, miss, I'd a bin down to the beach long afore this to see how matters stood. Though I feel purty sartin that it's all right."

"Oh, bless you, old man, bless you, for those kind words."

"Thankey, miss—thankey. I feel purty sartin that is, I'm sure, the cap'n has thrashed old Ellis. Beg yer pardon, Mrs. Vere—beg yer pardon, ma'am. I forgot as how he was yer father. Come, there's a dear, don't cry, don't cry! I hates to see a purty critter like you a-cryin'. Old Joe Bunting, ma'am, sarved with your father as many as thirty years ago, and he was a bad—no, ma'am, I don't mean bad—he was as good a commander as I ever sarved under."

"You are only saying that to please me, Joe," said Jenny, through her tears.

"No I aren't, ma'am—I am sure I arn't. I sarved under him and fought and bled under him, too. Ah! those were good times—good times," mumbled old Joe, regretfully. "I'll never see their like again, ma'am. I was a youngster then, compared to what I am now, and could run and jump and swim with any of 'em. Ah!" exclaimed the old man, rising feebly to his feet, "I thought I heard a noise! Did you hear it, ma'am? Did you, miss?"

"No," said Minnie.

"No," repeated Mrs. Vere.

"Well, then, my old ears must have deceived me," rejoined the aged sailor, and down he sat again. "I used to have sharp ears though, ma'am—very sharp ears, one time. I was noted through the whole fleet for my quick hearing then. But now, as I'm growing older, everything seems to leave me."

But Joe Bunting's ears had not quite deceived him.

There was a sudden, almost noiseless sound.

And he heard it.

It was caused by the sham sentinel stooping down to peer through a crack in the door.

For tired of listening, he wanted to get a view of the parties within, and, in so doing, saw old Bunting rise to his feet, and heard him utter the exclamation.

One glance was enough to assure him that from that quarter there was at least no danger to apprehend.

Leaving the door of the hut, he walked now on tip-toe to where Reuben sat.

"There is something that concerns you in there, Captain Harpy," he whispered.

"Concerns me! What do you mean?"

"I suppose you know a young lady by name Minnie Atherton?"

The question made Reuben leap from the boulder.

"Good heavens! Is she there?" he whispered, hoarsely.

"Softly, captain, softly. Don't spoil all. She is there, and in your power! Now you have the means to avenge yourself. Go and peep through that small knot-hole in the crack there, and you will see for yourself."

Reuben crept softly to the spot indicated, and peeped through the knot-hole.

It was Minnie Atherton, standing there in all her glorious womanhood.

Those proud but gentle features were unmistakable.

Reuben came back with an exultant glow at his heart, his hands clenched, and his whole manner excited.

"It is she!" he hoarsely whispered.

"Did I not tell you so?"

"Yes."

"And the other is the wife of his lieutenant—a fellow, I believe, calling himself Vere."

"Yes."

"A glorious opportunity of running away with both of them, captain."

"This Minnie Atherton is my cousin."

"So much the better. Besides, is she not Captain Tom's betrothed? Likewise, I tell you, Captain Harpy, you'll never have another chance like this."

The ex-privateer felt that it was so.

"What are we to do?" he asked.

"Why, get them into our power. Demand them to open the door, and if they don't, find a means of getting in without their consent."

"How?"

"By breaking it open."

"And the old man?"

"Knock him on the head. It is easy enough to settle him. Yet I shouldn't like to hurt the poor old fellow, for all that."

"I'll tell you what," said Reuben. "We'll try and mimic Captain Tom's voice."

"That won't do. If we waste any more time, we'll be late."

"True. Ah! What is that?" muttered Reuben, turning suddenly round. "Cast your eyes for a moment in yonder direction. Is that one of the buccaneer vessels?"

The night was so clear and bright that they could see to an immense distance over the sea.

The sham sentinel looked in the direction pointed out by Reuben.

A noble vessel lay at anchor about a quarter of a mile from the shore.

Indeed, it seemed to hug the very rocks, so close did it appear to them.

"It's not a buccaneer," replied the sham sentinel after a brief inspection.

"Well, what is it then?"

"More like a pirate," was the reply.

"I wish it was," said Reuben, speaking aloud.

"Then have your wish!" thundered a voice almost at his elbow, and before he could make the slightest resistance, he was seized in powerful arms, and swung completely round.

His comrades were also seized.

Hardly had they time to look who their assailants were, when they were thrown to the ground, and bound in a twinkling.

"Ha! ha! ha! You didn't think the devil was so near you," laughed a harsh, grating voice at this moment.

Reuben looked up, and beheld a face that for an instant inspired him with a nameless terror.

"The Death Pirate!" he involuntarily exclaimed.

"The Death Pirate!" cried the sham sentinel, looking up almost simultaneously. "Then we are lost."

"Lost!" echoed Peter. "I should say we were."

"Not so," said Reuben Harpy. "Say rather that we are saved."

Surrounding them stood a dozen fierce, savage-looking men armed to the teeth.

And one stood above them all, taller by six inches than any one of them, this was the Death Pirate, with his hideous and ghastly mask of death.

Reuben Harpy was right, for the moment he discovered himself to this awful-looking personage, both he and his comrades were released from their bonds.

The sham sentinel was thunderstruck to find himself once more on his feet, and with his head on his shoulders.

It was a pleasure that he had not anticipated.

As for Peter, he was agreeably disappointed.

The Death Pirate now called Reuben Harpy aside, and Reuben, having a wholesome terror of the monster, followed him like a dog.

Their interview lasted about a quarter of an hour.

When the pirate came back, he ordered his men to break down the door of the hut, a task which they very soon accomplished.

Poor old Joe Banting, in disputing their passage, had his skull smashed in, and the terrified girls, in spite of their cries and screams for mercy, were bound and gagged, after which they were conveyed on board the pirate ship.

But the end was not yet.

The pirates came back to the hut in force, expecting to lay hands on Captain Tom next day, should he return safe from his expedition.

Their chief did not forget, nor had he forgiven him, and he would have given a mine of wealth that moment to have him in his power.

Next day, about noon, Harry Vere came to the island.

He was accompanied by the third officer and four or five of the buccaneers.

Among the latter were our old friends Bob Hauler and Jerry Mizzen.

They had no sooner got on shore and secured the boat, than they made for the hut.

It was situated in the most out-of-the-way part of the island.

What was their alarm upon reaching it to find the door broken down, marks of a recent conflict, and the lifeless and gory body of poor old Joe Banting stretched across the threshold.

But Jenny and Minnie were gone.

Harry Vere rushed about the place, frantically calling them by name.

But no answer.

There is no knowing what the young lieutenant would have done to himself at this time, but that his attention was called by one of the buccaneers to a vessel that lay hugging the shore.

He had not looked at it more than half a minute, when he suddenly cried—

"Good God! it is the Death Pirate!"

"So it is, sir," said Jerry Mizzen. "I knows the cut of her jib well."

"Then my poor wife and Miss Atherton are aboard of her!"

"Right you are, sir!"

"What's to be done?" asked the junior lieutenant.

"What's to be done? Can you ask, sir?" cried Harry. "Let us away instantly to Captain Tom, and, once in the 'Will-o'-the-Wisp,' we'll soon overhaul yon villainous pirate."

"Not yet!" thundered a voice. "Not yet, my fine fellow!"

There was a great clatter and rush of feet, and, in an instant, a score of men, armed to the teeth, bounded from behind the rocks, and surrounded Lieutenant Vere and his party.

So sudden had been the attack, that they had not even the shade of a chance of defending themselves.

Harry Vere struck one pirate bleeding to the earth.

But he was in an instant after disarmed and bound along with his followers.

"This is a rum go, Bob!" cried Jerry Mizzen, ruefully.

"Hold yer row, ye lubber—hold yer row!" growled Bob.

Having a wholesome fear of the gallant Tom Drake's prowess, the Death Pirate contented himself now by taking his prisoners on board, weighing anchor, and putting out to sea.

For a long time he hugged close into the shore, to escape the sharp eyes of the buccaneers.

It was his intention to order Harry Vere for immediate execution.

He had him in his power once before, but the young lieutenant had escaped him—escaped, too, in an almost miraculous manner.

But this time the Death Pirate resolved that there should be no miscarriage of his plans, and with a cruelty worthy of his merciless nature, he had poor Jenny conveyed on deck, not to witness her husband's execution, but to behold instantly after his headless remains.

The junior lieutenant was also on deck, with his arms bound behind him.

Harry, seeing no means of escape, prepared himself, by a brief prayer, to meet his doom.

At a word from the terrible Death Pirate, who stood close by, encased in his heavy armour, a hideous-looking black advanced with his gleaming yataghan.

This was the executioner of the pirate ship.

Harry gazed on him with tightly-compressed lips, and with a pale, determined face.

The word rung out from behind the Death Pirate's ghastly mask.

The executioner, baring his arm, advanced.

The young lieutenant stood up bravely to meet his fate.

"Executioner, do your duty!" thundered the Death Pirate, who fancied that he saw the hideous-looking black hesitate.

But scarcely had the last word of the command rung out, when a terrible shriek awoke a hundred echoes on the deck, and Jenny Vere, breaking frantically from the pirates who held her, rushed forward, and threw herself at the feet of their terrible chief.

While this terrible scene was taking place, Dutch Paul, who had seen the pirate vessel from the shore take his departure, hastened back to a little hut known only to himself and followers, and which was concealed from prying curiosity by shelving rocks and huge crags.

This was a spot the smuggler prince very often visited—that is, whenever he was near the island.

As he entered, a great noise and shouting of many voices rang upon his ears.

A clinking of glasses, and clouds of tobacco smoke wafted in his face.

A dozen of the buccaneers were drinking, smoking, and enjoying themselves to the full bent of their inclinations.

But seeing their chief enter with a look of profound thought and annoyance on his massive face, they desisted from their merriment, and in a moment there was a silence as of the grave in their midst.

The buccaneer prince had no time to lose.

He called one of the men to him.

"Conduct Captain Tom Drake here at once," he said, in a voice in which there was extreme agitation. "Away with you! You will find him at the western extremity of the island."

The buccaneer, without replying, left the hut, and in less than a half an hour Captain Tom was in his presence.

Paul was seated at a rude table with a bottle in his hand when Captain Tom entered.

Our hero seemed aware of what he had been sent for, and with a significant gesture approached him.

"I know what you would say," he interrupted. "But I have already seen him."

"Seen whom?" was the interrogation.

"The Death Pirate."

This was startling intelligence indeed.

How could Captain Tom have seen this dreaded chieftain and he at the other end of the island.

This Dutch Paul would like to know very much.

The smuggler had not even seen the pirate, although he was nearly a mile and a half nearer the vessel than Captain Tom was.

The answer of the boy captain was puzzling.

"You surprise me very much," said Paul.

"Pray how?" asked Tom.

"You say you saw this merciless fiend in person."

"You misunderstood me."

"I am sure your words were to that effect."

"Oh, no! You are mistaken. I meant his ship."

"That's another thing. I could not imagine how you, a mile and a half off, could be more favoured than myself. I also saw his vessel, and am very glad he has taken his departure."

"I am not," replied Tom. "A brush with the sea wolf would do me good."

Dutch Paul shuddered involuntarily on hearing his words.

Why he did so, Captain Tom was at loss to make out, knowing well that the smuggler prince was as brave and daring a man as ever trod a quarter-deck.

"He must have some secret dread of this merciless fiend," he thought.

It now struck Captain Tom that the Death Pirate had been on the island.

A shiver ran through his frame as he thought of the two helpless girls protected only by an old and feeble man.

If Harry Vere had been too late, the girls were now in the power of the pirate.

This reflection almost drove him frantic.

But whatever agonies he endured, he carefully hid from the lynx-eyes of the smuggler.

"This rascally pirate will be far enough off by this time," he said, addressing Paul.

"The farther, the better," was that gentleman's reply. "I was just thinking that he might possibly have been on the island," said Tom.

"I am almost certain of it."

"Then it's time for me to be going."

"Why away in such a hurry?" cried Dutch Paul. "Come, captain, join us in a horn of good liquor. I'll vouch for its purity."

"Not now—not now!" replied Tom. "Let me have four of your men instead."

"Have them all, captain—have them all, if they be of any use to you. All the good I can see in the lubbers is a continual drinking, smoking, and shouting."

Tom half smiled.

But his thoughts were far away, and his great desire was to hurry from the hut immediately.

Matters might not be quite so bad as he thought.

However, it was necessary to use despatch, so the men were selected, and as he and they were passing out, Dutch Paul hailed them.

"Hold on, Captain Tom; I'll go with you," he cried. "And, by-the-way, I forgot one thing—about the young ladies you sent over to the island, prior to the engagement with Ellis's fleet."

"Indeed!" said Tom, annoyed that he treated the matter so lightly.

The four smugglers, Captain Tom, and Dutch Paul, without wasting any more time, left the hut.

They were all well armed.

Each man had a cutlass at his side, and two good navy pistols in his belt.

Not that they anticipated any fighting.

But this was a precaution they always took on any expedition.

Hurrying over the broken ground as well as they could, they soon came in sight of the hut.

There was a silence as of death over the rude building.

No one appeared to be moving.

But they were too far away yet to discern anything unusual about the place.

Still, a strange fear smote Tom Drake's heart.

The quiet of the surroundings was somewhat too intense, and a small voice whispered within him that all was not quite right.

At our hero's command, the little party broke into a run, and were soon at the hut.

An explanation came at last!

There were signs of a recent conflict in and around the rude hovel.

The door was splintered to pieces, and what was left of it hung only on one hinge.

Across the threshold lay poor old Joe Bunting's dead body, as before described, his white locks dabbled in thick black blood.

The hut consisted of two rooms.

WITH A WILD CRY, SHE SANK UPON HER KNEE.

These rooms were searched in vain—their two occupants were gone.

While Captain Tom was immersed in his most bitter thoughts, a smuggler came running into the room.

He had a pistol in his hand, and one which evidently was not his own.

It was Harry's, and had been dropped in the scuffle with the pirates.

"This belongs to my lieutenant," said Captain Tom. "I see it all. The ruffians have attacked and captured them. Follow me! It may not be too late yet."

They rushed from the hut into the open air, and cast their eyes seaward.

But the pirate ship was some distance off

Though still hugging into the shore.

Which was done, of course, to escape observation.

The sea was almost without a ripple.

And the swelling sails of the pirate gleamed out like sheets of snow in the sun.

Captain Tom cast his eyes with a sad, longing look in the wake of the vessel.

Then those eyes grew fierce and bright, for he had made up his mind to start off in instant pursuit.

All his motions were watched by Dutch Paul with a painful anxiety.

"I am sorry," said the smuggler, "that I can be of no assistance to you. And it will be almost madness to follow in the track of the pirate alone."

50

"The 'Will-'o-the-Wisp' is equal to the task," replied Tom briefly. "Farewell, captain! When you next hear of me, rest assured the mission of Tom Drake will have been accomplished."

"And you have no fear of the result?"

"Not the slightest. If life and strength be left, I'll overhaul the pirate in twenty-four hours. Good-bye!"

"Good-bye! And carry with you my best and most earnest wishes for your success."

Captain Tom shook hands with the smuggler, and, bounding amongst the rocks, almost instantly disappeared, watched by Paul with unmistakable looks of wonder and admiration.

"Brave, noble, and chivalrous to the last!" muttered the smuggler.

Dutch Paul and his four men now set about disposing of the body of poor old Joe, which work having been completed to their satisfaction, they made the best of their way back to the hut where they left their companions.

Meanwhile, we follow the steps of our gallant buccaneer.

Captain Tom did not abate his speed until he reached his boat.

He found his men in the same position as when he had left them, with the one difference, that they were now indulging in a quiet smoke together.

So accustomed were they to Captain Tom's ways, that they knew the moment they caught sight of him that there was something very unusual up.

So, without waiting for his order, they emptied the ashes out of their pipes, leaped into the boat, and took up the oars.

Our hero was in the stern-sheets in an instant.

"Now, my brave lads," he cried. "Pull for the 'Will-o'-the-Wisp,' and the sooner you get there the better."

The boat, with one stroke, shot into deep water.

Four oars bent with a will, soon increased the distance between them and the land.

The brig was exactly a mile and a half from the shore, and, as the tide was running in, it took them a little longer than it would otherwise to reach it.

Captain Tom, once on board his brig, was surprised at the confusion that prevailed there.

He soon made himself master of the cause, however.

Admiral Ellis had escaped.

"But how?"

The question was one that no one aboard the "Will-o'-the-Wisp" could answer.

When had he been missed?

Even that no one could tell.

Whatever occurred to Admiral Ellis, or however he got away from the brig, was buried in the profoundest mystery.

Captain Tom, though he did not shew it, was rather pleased than otherwise, that the cruel and stern little Admiral had escaped.

It took a great load off his mind.

For he had no wish to have Ellis's blood on his hands, even though he was his bitter enemy.

Our hero, when the excitement caused by the little English Admiral's escape had somewhat subsided, called his officers and middies together, and quietly informed them of what had taken place on the island, and his intention to start forthwith in the track of the pirate.

This was hailed by loud cries of satisfaction, as all prepared to lend a hand to getting the brig put off.

Meanwhile, Captain Tom sent for Iron-Arm.

And not ten minutes elapsed before that redoubtable individual was on the deck of the "Will-o'-the-Wisp."

"I must leave you for a time," said Tom.

Then our hero briefly recapitulated all that had taken place.

"I would much rather you would take me with you," said Iron-Arm. "Your danger in facing that scoundrel alone, troubles me."

"Fear not," replied Captain Tom, "so long as the 'Will-o'-the-Wisp' is under my feet, and my brave crew at my back, I have no fear of the results. Besides, I want you to take charge in my absence of Commodore Ellis and the rest of the prisoners."

Iron-Arm knew his chief too well to argue the point any further with him.

So he consented to remain behind, and at once took charge of the prisoners.

Commodore Ellis and the three commanders were now hurried on deck, and after a few words from Captain Tom, were conducted, under a guard, to the small boat, and, with Iron-Arm in the stern-sheets, rowed to the latter's vessel.

The anchor of the "Will-o'-the-Wisp" was soon weighed, the sails unfurled, and veering round to the wind, she started off in the track of the pirate.

Of course, as they were on the opposite side of the island, they could not catch a glimpse of the pirate ship.

But, rounding a point in the towering cliffs two miles off, they came in sight of her.

She was a great distance off.

Many leagues, in fact.

But Captain Tom, not despairing, kept the "Will-o'-the-Wisp" well in her course, under a perfect cloud of sail.

The pirates had evidently observed their presence before they moved far round the point of rocks, and, as a consequence, clapped on all the canvas their vessel could carry.

Now began what might be called a long chase, and a stern one.

The "Will-o'-the-Wisp's" superior sailing qualities, however, appeared to tell with good effect.

She was, though it might not have been at first observed, unconsciously gaining on the pursued minute after minute.

The buccaneers and middies were in the highest possible spirits.

And counted upon a rich harvest from the accumulated hoards of the pirates.

It did not strike them that they would be unsuccessful.

They made up their minds to conquer.

And conquer they would.

Besides, they held this death pirate in great horror, as well as detestation, and, having had an encounter with him before, though an unsuccessful one, they resolved to make up for it this time, by defeating him, and capturing his vessel.

Besides this, he was a most cruel and rapacious tyrant.

A more merciless ruffian could not be found in any part of the globe.

The terror of the seas, and the ruthless butcher of hundreds, nay, thousands of brave English sailors.

And the crew of the "Will-o'-the-Wisp," having all this in their minds, resolved that he had been so long enough, and that it was time now to put a stop to it by aiming a crushing blow at his dreaded power.

Never were men more eager for battle than the buccaneers.

Captain Tom, who was no mean physiognomist, beheld all the fierce determination in the faces of his men with exultation.

Seconded by such a crew, he had no fear of the

fiendish pirate nor of his nearly equally fiendish companions.

The afternoon was beautiful.

Warm and generous—the rays of the sun transforming the ocean into one mass of gold.

And the blue sky, spanning the golden waters, almost cloudless, while a fragrant and balmy air fanned the expectant faces of the buccaneers.

The officers of the "Will-o'-the-Wisp" were not idle while their noble brig was speeding after the enemy.

Their glasses were constantly in their hands or adjusted to their eyes.

Captain Tom, the centre spirit of all, watched the pursued even more narrowly than any of the others, perhaps.

And he had very good reason so to do, seeing that the woman he loved most on earth was in the power of this dreaded and merciless fiend who commanded the "San Josef."

While Tom was watching the pirate ship narrowly through his instrument, he observed a sudden commotion on its decks.

A swarm of armed men instantly sprang into sight.

But they crowded so one upon the other that he could not, even by the aid of his powerful glass, observe what was taking place there.

Ben Barnacle, though sharp of eye and keen of perception, used his instrument to little better purpose.

He could see nothing but a swaying, excited mass of men, hustling and elbowing each other.

"Can you tell me what's wrong with that rascally pirate, lieutenant?" asked Captain Tom, lowering his glass.

"No. I regret to say I can't. I have tried my instrument several times, but in vain. It seems that there are several hundred men huddled up in a heap together. But anything further goes beyond the power of my glass."

"And mine, too," added Tom. "Heaven grant there is nothing wrong about to happen, Harry!"

"I hope not. But stay. I'll try my instrument again."

He did so, and swept the pirate's deck with one keen, searching look.

"Ah!" was his sudden exclamation. "I now see what's the matter."

"What?" asked Captain Tom, eagerly.

"The miscreants have Lieutenant Vere bound. And there's a hideous black among them."

"A black!" exclaimed Captain Tom. "Then, by Heaven! that's the Death Pirate's executioner. Look again, lieutenant, for God's sake!"

The gallant buccaneer chief turned perceptibly pale at the thought that the brave Harry Vere was in danger.

"In the midst of the swaying, excited throng, I discern the figure of a lady. Ah! God's mercy! It is Mrs. Vere, for she now turns her face this way, as if appealing to us for aid."

"And she shall not appeal in vain!" cried Tom, excitedly. "But go on, lieutenant—go on! What else do you see?"

"One burly form stretched out on the deck, encased in gleaming armour."

"The Death Pirate!" cried our hero exultingly. "Slain, perhaps. God grant it is so!"

"He is wounded, at any rate," replied Ben.

"Hurrah!" cried Tom.

"Hurrah!" cried all the officers, in one loud, prolonged cheer, for they listened with the intensest interest to every word which fell from Ben's lips.

"It seems strange," muttered Tom, "that the pirate should be down, and wounded, too."

"No wonder his myrmidons are so excited," cried another.

But Ben Barnacle, still watching the "San Josef," went on—

"Ah! I now see," he cried, "who's been the cause of this arch-miscreant's fall!"

"Who? Who?" asked several voices

"Why," replied the lieutenant, with a flashing eye, "none other than our eccentric comrades, Jerry Mizzen and Bob Hauler. Poor fellows! They stand in great danger now. The pirates rush at them as if they were going to sacrifice them on the spot."

"And how do they face the enemy?" asked Captain Tom, eagerly.

"With two good cutlasses in their hands," was the reply, "and stern determination in their hard-bronzed faces. Bravo, Bob! bravo, Jerry! That was a good parry—a noble thrust!"

"The miscreant horde have buccaneers now to deal with, and not merchantmen."

"Aye! aye! They give thrust for thrust, and parry for parry."

"Brave, noble fellows!" cried Captain Tom. "I fear, though, we shall never see them again on the 'Will-o'-the-Wisp.'"

"I am afraid not," replied Ben, sadly. "They have saved Lieutenant Vere at the hazard of their own lives. The conflict grows fiercer, and the pirates cut and slash at our brave lads in the most terrific manner. It's impossible for them to save themselves, brave as they are. Force of numbers at last prevail, but not until many of their blood-thirsty assailants strew the deck. They are driven to the bulwarks, inch by inch. Their only chance of safety now is in the sea."

"A sad chance truly," said one of the officers.

"You may well say that," replied Ben, who still kept his eye rivetted on the decks of the pirate. "But far better that they perish in the ocean than fall beneath the cowardly blades of these murderous pirates."

"They have reached the bulwarks at last," cried Ben. "Why don't the fools leap into the sea? Ah! I see why, there are two or three hungry sharks in the water."

Bob Hauler catches sight of their merciless maws, and, as he does so, his good cutlass trembles in his hand.

A huge pirate, knowing his weakness, rushes upon him, and, with a blow, fells him to the deck.

"I can't look no longer," added the lieutenant, with a shudder. "The brave boys are gone, and nothing remains now but to avenge them."

"Aye! aye!" responded his hearers.

"For every life these accursed pirates take we shall have twenty."

A scene of the greatest confusion and excitement prevailed now on board of the "Will-o'-the-Wisp."

The news that Bob Hauler and his comrade, Jerry, were murdered by the pirates ran through the brig like wild fire.

And, as Bob and Jerry were great favourites with all, the buccaneers swore to tread ankle-deep in the pirates' blood.

Nothing now could equal the stern and fixed determination in the faces of these hardy adventurers, whose feelings had been so grossly outraged by the supposed murder of two of their comrades.

Leaving the "Will-o'-the-Wisp" in this state, we will return for a little while to the "San Josef."

Prior, even, to the situation in which we left Lieutenant Vere, which was one, as the reader will allow, of the greatest possible danger.

Bob Hauler and Jerry Mizzen had been taken on board of the pirate ship securely bound—in fact, with their hands pinioned behind them.

Of course they were, in this condition, as helpless as children.

Unable, even, to be of the slightest assistance to themselves.

If Bob had the use of his hands, notwithstanding his danger, it is more than likely he would have exerted his fists to some effect on more than one or two grinning, malicious faces.

The pirates, by their jeers, taunted the old comrades almost beyond endurance.

And Bob Hauler only prayed to have the use of his hands for five minutes or less, so that he could show them what mettle there was in a pair of British fists.

"If I wouldn't pay the rascally lubbers off," said Bob, "my name ain't Hauler. See that grinning monkey, Jerry?"

"Yes," replied Jerry. "He's a nice, perlite type o' the genelman, ain't he? I'd like to screw his darned neck off!"

"So would I, Jerry. It's unfortunate, ain't it?"

"What?"

"To be tied up like a mangy cur, without the means o' defendin' yourself."

"You are right, Bob. Such fellows as these allays takes a mean advantage of one."

"They are heathens, Jerry. They don't know any better."

"Then they ought to be taught better, that's all," said Jerry.

"I would make a werry good schoolmaster, in their case," said Bob. "They'd grin on the other side o' their faces if I had a half an hour at 'em. Blood, skin, an' hair, would be flying all over the shop."

"Or the deck," put in Jerry.

"Well, yer needn't take a fellow up for a little bit of a mistake like that," said Bob. "The meaning is all the same—shop or deck is all as one."

"Do you think so, old pal?"

"Sartinly."

"Wery well, then, I suppose it must be all right," said Jerry. "Only I was jist thinkin' as how shop was a wery unnautical name."

"Unnatural name?"

"No, no; unnautical, Bob—unnautical. Its a word as scholars uses."

"Then scholars ought to be ashamed o' themselves," said Bob. "And if I was a craktic, and a a judge, I should try them for murdering the King's English."

"Yes, old feller; they hadn't ought to use sich wulgar words. They are reg'lar crack-jaws."

"So they are, Jerry. But what do yer think o' the sitivation we've got ourselves into, old pal."

"Very bad, indeed," said Jerry.

"Couldn't be worse, could it?"

"No, not a bit."

"I wish I had a mill-stone round my neck, and I'd go and drown myself."

"What, commit suencide?" cried Jerry, aghast.

"Aye, commit suencide! Why not? Here I am as helpless as a kitten, already."

"Ditto," cried Jerry.

"And my arms are as tight to my body as if they was fixed there. I hope as how some charitable Christian would come forward an' give a feller a hand.

"Charitable Christians," replied Jerry, with a rueful visage. "You'll find a great many of 'em here, I don't think. Look at that 'ere feller, grinning at us like a Cheshire cat. That'll tell yer how charitable he feels!"

Jerry called the attention of Bob to a savage-looking pirate, who was regarding the two comrades with a sort of ferocious joy.

The fellow was well-armed, having in his hand a yataghan, and a brace of pistols in his belt.

"I only wish I had a chaw of backey," said Bob, with a significant look at Jerry, "I'd larn that fellar to look the other way."

"But yer hands?" said Jerry.

"Bother the hands! Don't you think Bob Hauler can use his mouth as well as his hands? I'd show you how I'd sarve that ugly-looking varmint if I had the backey."

"One in the eye," said Jerry, meditatively. "A handsome shot, Bob."

"I am aware of it, old pal. But I'll bet you an even guinea, to a farthing rushlight, I'd make a proper bull's-eye of his figure head. It would be a jolly lark, too, to douse one of his top-lights."

Jerry thought the same.

But whether the pirate came to that unique conclusion or not was another thing.

He, however, advanced towards them with anything but a smile on his face.

Even the grin had faded from his saturnine-looking countenance, much to Jerry's alarm, who expected now that it was all up with both of them.

"I say, Bob," said Jerry, in a lower voice. "The pirate's advancing on us"

"Let him come," said Bob. "Be ready to receive wisitors, Jerry. You've got the use of yer feet, old chum."

Jerry certainly had.

But he had no very great desire to call them into action.

"What if he should understand English, Bob?"

"What if he should?"

"He'll spiflicate us for what we've been saying about him. He's a werry savage-looking, ferocious brute. Look at his eyes, Bob."

"Are you afeard, Jerry?"

"Oh, no. But I'm just a little cautious, yer see."

"That's just another name for being very much frightened. However, old pal, I'll stick to you, let the worst come to the worst. Give him a thirty-two pounder when he comes up."

The "thirty-two pounder" was one of Jerry's enormous feet.

On came the pirate, slowly, and very deliberately, pausing every now and then to regard our two friends with a look that he intended should terrify them.

Bob winked his eye at him, and puckered up his mouth, hinting, at the same time, that he thought the pirate "a werry nice gentlemen indeed," especially in the "walking line."

Jerry said nothing but eyed him very anxiously. He paused.

Bob nodded for him to come on, as both of them he said, would be "werry glad to make his acquaintance."

"Won't we, Jerry?" said Bob.

Jerry, as he did not wish to commit himself by making a false statement, simply nodded.

"Noticed you afore," said Bob. "And thought you a werry handsome man. Didn't we, Jerry."

"Yes," faintly articulated Jerry, "and we thought him a werry nice genelman indeed—ever so much nicer nor any of the others."

Jerry's serious aspect now would have deceived a saint.

The pirate, who evidently had a knowledge of English, came up smiling.

"Don't forget the thirty-two pounder, Jerry," muttered Bob.

"All right, old pal," whispered Jerry.

"And send him this way if ye can, so as I may have a chance to land him one myself."

"Arter this yer 'll see no more of them pirate fellars 'll trouble us."

"Good-day," said Jerry, "I'm werry glad you've come. Expected a wisit from you ever since we came ab'ard. I wish I had the power to shake hands with you. But as they're in bondage we must consider that 'ere honour as good as done. I know my old pal here is a-dying to make your acquaintance. Ain't ye, Bob?'

"Decidedly," said Bob. "A nicer or a more politer genelman I never seen in the whole course of my life."

"He's werry handsome," said Jerry. "Don't you think so, Bob?"

"Werry. Han'some is no name for him. Shiver my timbers! he's angelic! Now, Jerry, the thirty-two pounder. Werry delightful weather, ain't it, sir?' this with a friendly nod at his visitor.

Whatever reply that amiable individual was going to make was closed very abruptly by Jerry's "thirty-two pounder."

The pirate, deceived by the apparent friendliness of the two comrades' manner, came up smiling.

When he was within two feet of Jerry Mizzen he paused.

Jerry measured his distance very artistically, and, with one kick sent him flying against Bob Hauler.

Bob, prepared, lunged out with terrific force, and caught the pirate a kick in the stomach, which sent him rolling over the deck.

"I think that 'll suit his turn very nicely, Jerry."

"I think it will," said Jerry, quite innocently.

"He musn't blame me for it, though. For, if he hadn't a-come so near me, I shouldn't have let out as I did."

"I know you wouldn't Jerry. But self-preservation, they say, is the first law of Nature."

"And so a feller must defend himself."

"Sartinly."

"Besides he had no right to come a wisiting us without proper letters of introduction."

"Sartinly not."

By this sort of reasoning the two comrades thought themselves perfectly justified in acting as they did.

The pirate was still rolling about the deck, evidently suffering considerable agony.

For the reader must know that the kick Bob Hauler gave him was no very light one.

How the matter was going to end there was no telling.

Jerry Mizzen feared that they had been too precipitate in their action.

As to the cool, calculating Bob, he was unmoved, and viewed the antics of the pirate, as he rolled from side to side, with a quiet enjoyment that was really delightful.

"A splendid acrobat, Jerry," said Bob.

"Werry good, but werry painful. Poor fellow! I'm werry sorry for him."

"So am I," said Bob, "werry. But there, he's rising to his feet now. Look out for him, Jerry."

"Oh, Lor'! You don't mean to say as how he's on his feet again?"

"Yes, I do. And here he comes with that 'ere blessed yataghan in his hand. It looks as sharp as a razor, and shines like silver."

"Oh! oh! oh!" groaned Jerry.

"What are ye 'oh-ing!' about?" asked Bob. "There's nothing to be afeard on. He's only a rascally pirate, and one good buccaneer is worth twenty of 'em. Give him a taste of yer thirty-two pounder, and that'll settle him."

The pirate now staggered to his feet, and came up, swearing and groaning in a terrific manner.

Jerry looked awfully alarmed, in spite of the advice his friend Bob gave him.

A gleaming yataghan in the hands of a ferocious enemy was a little more than he could view with unconcern.

So he watched the approach of the grim pirate with anything but that placidity which Bob exhibited.

Besides, Jerry was a couple of steps nearer the pirate than Bob.

And this, as the reader must acknowledge, made a great difference to him.

Jerry endeavoured to close his eyes and put on a look of deep resignation.

But in vain.

The effort was a lamentable failure.

He could not meet his fate thus.

The "thirty-two pounder" must be called again into requisition, and if he lost his life in the effort, why there was no help for it.

So the heroic Jerry prepared to resist to the last, the infuriated pirate, together with his gleaming yataghan.

"Land him one, Jerry;" was Bob's placid advice.

"I wish you'd keep your jawing tackle quiet," said Jerry. "How am I to do it if yer shouting out like that? The fellow hears you already."

"But what does that matter when he doesn't understand me," said Bob.

"Doesn't he? Don't make a mistake, murder!" yelled Jerry, suddenly, as the pirate came near to him. "Keep back, I say! or it will be the worse for you."

But the pirate was not the man to give way because Jerry asked him.

He drew nearer and nearer, flourishing his weapon and uttering ferocious threats.

The latter in broken English, which Bob and Jerry understood very well.

He intimated something about slicing Jerry's throat, and tearing out his heart, and all that sort of thing.

Could any mortal man endure this and be resigned?"

Certainly not.

And that was the case with Jerry, who now used his voice to some advantage, with various cries, such as "Murder!" and "Help!"

Now such cries as these were of frequent occurrence on board the "San Josef."

But only at certain times, however.

For instance, when the ruffianly crew were butchering unarmed and defenceless merchantmen who fell in their power.

As this was not at present the case, a great many of the pirates rushed aft to ascertain the cause of the disturbance.

The Death Pirate was among the number.

Jerry grew suddenly very courageous, and, sending out his "thirty-two pounder" with the full force of his body, let the man with the yataghan have it in such a manner as to send him like a shot at least six yards off

This last stroke rendered the pirate insensible.

His comrades, seemingly rejoicing in his downfall, laughed immoderately.

Bob Hauler was convulsed.

The irrepressible Jerry was even himself greatly affected.

Tears ran down his cheeks.

Not tears of joy or grief, but genuine ones of hearty laughter.

As the Death Pirate's hideous mask was on his face, no one could see how he felt.

Or whether he viewed poor Jerry's creditable performance in a favourable light or not.

It turned out after a little that the Death Pirate was very angry.

With whom?

Jerry?

Not at all.

Jerry, in a few brief moments, was looked upon as a hero, who deserved that his name should be inscribed on the ship's books for a noble and chivalrous act.

"Take that caitiff away!" thundered the dreaded chieftain, pointing with his finger to the insensible body of the pirate.

"Aye! aye! sir!" responded three or four of the men, separating from the rest, and bearing down in the direction of Jerry's late assailant.

These men Bob took to be English, for they spoke the English language with a good English accent.

"And when you get him down in the hold," went on the Pirate, "put him in irons."

"Aye! aye! sir!" was the response.

They clutched the unfortunate man, and was bearing him from the deck, when they paused to listen to a further command.

"When he comes to his senses," cried the grim chief, "touch the soles of his feet up with bamboos! I'll learn the caitiff to disobey orders!"

The insensible pirate was now carried below by the men who had charge of him.

The Death Pirate now called one of his lieutenants aside, and after whispering to him for some time, left the deck, and disappeared below.

As soon as he was gone, the lieutenant came up to Jerry.

His face wore a very bland and amiable expression.

Both Jerry and Bob thought the omen a very good one.

Perhaps he was going to offer them their liberty.

As gallantry such as Jerry's was prized more or or less all over the civilised world.

Bob thought it best to wear the most serious expression he could put on.

Not so Jerry.

His scowl was positively ferocious.

This our irrepressible friend considered to accord well with his gallant action of kicking the wretched pirate over the deck.

Besides, brave and daring spirits always looked ferocious at certain times.

And this was Jerry's cue.

So he acted up to it to the letter.

The pirate lieutenant was impressed visibly by Jerry's ferocious looks.

CHAPTER CLXI.

BOB HAULER AND JERRY MIZZEN'S ADVENTURES ON THE PIRATE SHIP.

YES, we reiterate that the pirate lieutenant was undoubtedly impressed.

But though impressed he was not much affected.

He came up with the same placid and amiable smile lingering on his lips.

And Jerry, it must be confessed, was rather surprised.

"By gum," said Jerry, to himself. "I thought I'd make him afraid. But he doesn't seem terrified a little bit!"

Jerry was right.

Ferocious as he looked, this man viewed him with the most perfect equanimity.

Retaining his self-possession in the most wonderful manner.

"I wonder what he's up to," thought Jerry. "Come to offer me liberty, no doubt. But, blow me, if I'll accept of it, unless they let Bob off as well."

The lieutenant now stopped in front of him.

His first words assured Jerry that his thoughts were correct.

"I am instructed by my noble chief to offer you liberty," said the man. "You have prepossessed him in your favour by hurling that recreant to the deck."

"You mean, of course, that 'ere kick I gave him," interrupted Jerry, loftily.

"Why can't yer let the gentleman go on," reproved Bob. "How can he tell you what the cap'n said if you keep putting your lingo in?"

"Purceed," said Jerry, pacifically. "Purceed, noble lieutenant—I am all ears and attention."

"In offering you your freedom," continued the lieutenant of the "San Josef," "you must know the captain confers a great boon on you."

"A benefit on mankind," suggested Jerry, loftily.

"Shut up!" cried Bob. "How can the genelman speak when you all the time a-interrupting ef him? Go on, worthy lieutenant—go on!"

"Aye, do," said Jerry. "There's nothing as 'll give me greater pleasure than to hear the noble captain's commands—unless I heard of his death, darn him!" added Jerry in a lower tone.

"Did you speak?" inquired the lieutenant, fancying that he heard some of the muttered words.

"Not a word, yer honour," replied Jerry, "I was just a-thinking though, what a favour the Death ——, I mean the noble and generous Captain was confering on me."

"Jest so," added Bob.

"Well, then, you are to have your liberty on one condition."

"Did you say unconditional?"

"No! I said on one condition."

"On one condition. Wery good. Let us hear the condition?"

"It is that you join our ship as one of the crew."

"I'll be hanged and chained up if —"

"Sh!" whispered Bob. "If you talk like that you'll ruin everything."

"What was that you said?" asked the lieutenant, that placid and benevolent smile almost fading from his face.

Jerry might have irretrievably committed himself if Bob permitted him to answer the pirate's question.

So he took good care to answer that question himself.

"My noble comrade here is very deeply affected by your captain's kindness," said Bob, "and he hails his offer with the very greatest delight."

"But he said something about 'hanged' and 'chawed,'" said the lieutenant.

"So he did. But he's always werry deeply affected when he uses them 'ere expressions. I wonder as he's not weeping tears of joy afore this at sich an offer. I thinks as how yer werry ungrateful, Jerry."

"No I arn't," responded Jerry, forcing a tear into his eye.

"Yes, you are," persisted Bob. "Or else you'd be shedding tears as big as peas. Go down on yer knees Jerry, and thank the noble lieutenant for his werry accommodating kindness."

"Oh, no. He need not do that. Does he accept the offer? That's all I want to know."

"In course he does, yer honour."

"Stop, my friend. Let him speak for himself."

"Say yes—swear to anything," whispered Bob, emphatically.

"But what are they going to do with you?" asked Jerry, in a whisper.

"Oh, never mind me," replied Bob.

"But I do mind you," replied Jerry. ' Aren't we been chums for years?"

"Yes, yes! anything you like. But don't keep this feller a-waiting a minute more, or we are both lost. Once you are free, you can easily give me a little assistance, and then, if we don't do something between us to liberate the officers, my name isn't Hauler. Agree to whatever he says. That is your only chance."

"Come, now, what is it to be?" cried the lieutenant. "It's no use whispering all day to decide so simple a question."

"So I say," cried Bob. "I wish I was only offered it, that's all!"

"That will depend on your comrade," replied the lieutenant. "Should he unhesitatingly accept my noble captain's proposal, you may consider yourself as good as free. But on the same conditions."

"To join the crew of the 'San Josef'?"

"Just so."

"I'd be only too glad of the chance, sir."

"Then you may consider it as good as done."

"I agree to it," said Jerry.

"To fulfil all the conditions imposed on you?"

"Every one of 'em."

"I have no doubt you'll make two slashing pirates."

"We'll stake our lives on that," said Bob. "Won't we, Jerry?"

"Aye, aye, Bob."

"I leave you now," said the lieutenant, "to communicate both your intentions to the captain."

The pirate turned on his heel, and was about hurrying away, when Jerry hailed him.

"Look here, yer honour, this is not fulfilling the first part of the engagement, is it?"

The lieutenant stopped.

"How so?"

"You haven't taken the cords off my hands yet, yer honour."

"Oh, I forgot all about them. I'll very soon clear you of them."

He called a pirate forward, who was lounging about the deck.

"Release this brave fellow from his bonds," he said.

"I hope yer honour arent a-going to forget me," cried Bob.

"I must first speak to the captain about you," replied the lieutenant.

So saying, he hurriedly left the deck and walked below.

The pirate who was told off to sever Jerry's bonds, had a good sharp knife, and soon cut them through.

Jerry saw with horror that there were two or three spots of blood on the knife, and he had no doubt, from that moment, but it had been used a short time back for a far different purpose—to wit, cutting some unfortunate wretch's throat.

The instant Jerry was liberated, the pirate tried to wheedle himself into his good graces.

But Jerry determined to cut the man.

This was harder work than he expected, however, for the fellow clung very tenaciously to him.

His flattering eulogiums on Jerry's bravery were numerous.

He admired his pluck and the cut of his jib.

His figure was handsome, and his clothes admirable.

But there was one drawback to all these perfections.

Jerry had been on the "Will-o'-the-Wisp."

"And you consider that 'ere a fault, do you?" said Jerry.

"I do," replied the pirate.

"Then, take that, and go to the devil!" roared Jerry.

And down the pirate rolled from a blow of Jerry's fist.

He might have got up, and made a rush at him with his cutlass, but he had the fate of his comrade before his eyes, so, instead, he picked himself up from the deck, and quietly slunk away.

"That feller's landed, at any-rate," said Jerry.

"You are right," replied Bob. "It's not likely as he'll try and make your acquaintance again. But I say, old pal, it's rayther dangerous to be doin' that sort of thing on such a craft as this. You'll be getting every one of the blessed pirates down on you if you don't mind."

"I wish Cap'n Tom would only show up," said Jerry. "I wonder if he has missed Lieutenant Vere, yet?"

"Depend upon it he has."

"Then he's sure to give instant chase," said Jerry.

"Aye, sure to. But I fear as it 'll be too late to save the lieutenant, unless we gives a hand in."

"That's what we must do. We are not a-goin' to let Mr. Vere swing like a mad dog, or a common murderer, not we."

"But there's his wife," said Jerry. "I almost forgot all about her."

"Poor critter! so did I."

"And worser than all, Captain Tom's young lady's aboard. It's a mighty unfortunate business, all through. For no one knows where it 'll end or how it 'll end."

The pirate lieutenant now appearing put an end to further conversation.

He walked up to them.

There was a gratified smile on his face.

Bob considered this in itself an omen of good luck, so he looked forward to a speedy deliverance from his bonds.

For no man ever failed in what he undertook, and came up smiling as the pirate did.

"Well, my lads," cried the luff. "I have settled that matter with the captain."

"Bravo!" cried Bob, in pretended delight. "I haven't heard better news for a twelve-month."

"And your names are to be entered in the ship's books."

"Sartainly, yer honour. I expected as much. You almost makes me shed tears of joy, you do."

"I am glad you take the matter so to heart," said the lieutenant. "And I hope you'll forget your old commander in the new life that you are about to lead."

"May I be cursed if I do!" muttered Bob.

The same thoughts permeated the noble Jerry's mind.

But they took good care to answer in a manner that was pleasing to their patron.

"Forget him!" said Bob.

"Forget him!" echoed Jerry.

"Forget him! I should think we would forget him!" they shouted simultaneously.

"What is Captain Tom to us, or we to Captain Tom?"

"Nothing," said the lieutenant. "Certainly not. I am very much gratified indeed, that the captain has not misplaced his confidence in you."

"So are we," thought Bob and Jerry. "And we'll presently show you, old feller, how far you can depend upon us."

"You may now release your comrade," said the lieutenant, addressing Jerry. "And when you go below, you will be furnished with a couple of cutlasses and a brace of pistols each."

The lieutenant said no more, but turned on his heel and walked off.

Jerry cut the bonds of his comrade in a twinkling.

Bob held out his arms and looked at the marks the cords made in his flesh.

But they didn't trouble him much, now that he was free.

After stretching himself once or twice with an air of great comfort, he hurried down the companion-way with Jerry, to get their arms.

The executioner, a hideous, burly-looking black, was also the armourer of the "San Josef."

They found him employed in sharpening a gleaming yataghan, which he took care to inform them, was one that he was speedily going to use.

As the man spoke good English, the following conversation ensued:

"So you are going to use that 'ere yataghan on some one's neck, are you?" said Jerry.

"Yes, master, I am."

"A sharp kind o' medicine for any one who doubts the power of the captain of this ship," said Jerry.

The black grinned hideously.

"You would say that if you saw me give the stroke," he rejoined.

"We are inclined to think so," replied the two comrades, without at all desiring to see that extraordinary feat performed.

"I have cut off the heads of a good many in my time" said the executioner.

"You have?" cried Jerry, aghast.

"More than six hundred," replied the black.

Bob and Jerry shuddered.

"This pirate ship must be a very hell!" thought the honest sailors. "They can have no respect for human life."

"Yes; six hundred and fifty at the least," repeated the black.

"All executions?"

"Every one of them."

"It's no wonder, then, that you have got yer hand in," cried Jerry, trying to regard the fellow's preparations calmly. "I suppose now you bring your victim's head off with one stroke?"

"Generally. That is if he doesn't stir from his position."

"And if he does?"

"Then he gets mangled, and I have often to use four or five cuts to put him out of his misery."

"That's horrible!"

"Bah! It's only child's play, when once you're used to it," said the black.

"Sanguinary wretch!" muttered Bob. "He seems like all the rest on this 'ere ship to delight in the sheddin' of human blood."

Jerry, for his part, was as much disgusted as Bob.

But he continued his inquiries, hoping, nevertheless, to elicit something that would, in the end, be of advantage to both of them.

"So you say you are sharpening that 'ere sword for immediate use?" went on Jerry, addressing the black.

"You are right, master."

"Going to take place to-day?" asked our irrepressible friend, carelessly.

"Aye, soon enough," was the reply.

"When?"

"In less than a half an hour."

"I wonder who the deuce they're going to execute?" asked Jerry of himself. "Perhaps that feller as I gave the kick to. I shouldn't wonder but it is, seeing that the captain isn't over and above pleased with him. First, I give him the thirty-two pounder. Second, he's shoved down the hold, and heavily ironed. Third, the pirate captain orders the bastinado. Fourth, they are going to

behead him! If that ain't punishment, tell me what is. But I better ask, to make sure. I say, Mister Executioner! Who are ye going to use that 'ere weapon on?"

"One of Captain Drake's lieutenants," replied the executioner.

"What! One of Captain Tom's lieutenants," cried Jerry, startled at the information.

Whatever danger he thought the young officer in, he did not anticipate that it would come so soon.

"There must be some mistake," said Bob.

"No mistake at all," replied the executioner. "His name, I believe, is Vere, and he once served in King George's navy. Both of you know him well, as he formerly belonged to the same ship."

While they were still talking, one of the pirates came down with the information that there was a vessel sighted rounding the tall cliffs of the island, and that the said vessel was no other than the "Will-o'-the-Wisp."

As the pirate volunteered this information he watched both Tom and Jerry narrowly, expecting, no doubt, to find a look of exultation on each of their faces.

But as these gentlemen were aware of his anxiety in that respect, they put on a perfectly stolid look, such as a marble statue might wear, or an image carved in wood.

The pirate was disappointed, and showed his disappointment very palpably.

Inwardly our two honest buccaneers trembled with excitement.

This was news indeed!

The gallant "Will-o'-the-Wisp" bearing down on the "San-Josef."

They heard a noise above deck.

Sounds of clapping on sail, and slightly changing the course of the vessel.

"They'll want me on deck, I suppose, soon," said the executioner.

"That is just one of the reasons why I came down here," replied the pirate. "And now, having delivered my message, I must leave you with your two excellent companions."

So saying, he favoured Bob and Jerry with a malicious glare, and backed out of the place up the companion-ladder.

Our buccaneers did not even look at the ruffian. Their minds were otherwise engaged.

The executioner, having got through with the sharpening and burnishing of his yataghan, thought it but fair to devote a little of his spare time to his visitors.

He had an order from the luff to give them a bran-new cutlass each.

And he handed them over, expatiating on the flexibility and temper of the blades.

Then came a brace of pistols for Jerry, and another for Bob.

Armed with these, the buccaneers were a host in themselves.

"Now, you can both follow me," said the executioner, "that is, if you have any wish to be present at the execution."

"Certainly we have," said Jerry and Bob in a breath. And they all went on deck together.

Here the burly black left them to attend to the horrid duties of his office.

Jerry and Bob took a good look around them.

They could see that the deck was swarming with pirates who had collected together to be present at the execution.

They never saw so many savage, hideous-looking monsters in their lives before, and they could hardly imagine where they all came from.

"There's a good many of these animals aboard the 'San Josef,'" said Jerry, with considerab.

dismay in his voice. "I didn't think as how they could muster in such a force as this, Bob."

"Didn't you?"

"No, that I didn't. Why there must be at least three hundred of 'em on deck."

"And another two or three hundred below, perhaps," said Bob. "The 'San Josef' is a confoundedly disagreeable customer to deal with, I should think."

"Don't speak so loud, Bob. Look at that 'ere yaller-faced wretch! He's all the time a-watching of us."

"So he is. I'd like to give him an old chaw in his toplights."

"It would make him looked crooked for some time, I reckon," observed Jerry.

"Hold on! I'll settle him in a minute," said Bob.

Bob had been chewing for some time.

There was nearly half an ounce of tobacco in his mouth.

He put his finger in carelessly and took it out, and, without appearing to pay the slightest attention to the pirate, rolled it up in a large-sized ball.

Having completed this, and not being in any particularly hurry, he turned slightly round.

He saw the pirate wasting considerable time and attention on him.

In fact, looking with a suspicious eye on the brannew cutlasses they both had, and dividing his attention between them and the pistols in their belts.

Bob thought it high time to put a stop to this kind of espionage, so, without apparently noticing the man, he took his measure instantly.

His height, his breadth, and the distance between his eyes.

He could see that the pirate was a formidable-looking customer enough.

Bob took this fact into consideration in the event that the ruffian might object to his mode of treating him.

And, if angry, how far he might possibly go.

Hauler, however, had very little fear of the consequences of his act.

He generally depended on his own strength and daring to get him out of any scrape he might get into.

Then, again, our buccaneer was a very good boxer, as the irrepressible Jerry many times discovered, to his cost.

So Bob, measuring his distance well, and having made himself thoroughly cognizant of the powers and endurance of his man, took aim, appearing to do so quite carelessly, and sent the immense chew of tobacco, with all his force, through the intermediate space that separated him from the pirate.

It did not seem to cost Jerry a solitary thought, as he was engaged, most innocently, contemplating the heavens.

And, as for Bob, when he had thrown his chew, he thrust his hands into his pockets with all the coolness imaginable.

Would anyone think for an instant that he was wrong, or that it was his intention to inflict one moment's suffering on any human creature.

Surely not.

That face, with all its broad and manly lineaments, spoke of nought but cheerfulness, contentment, and goodwill towards his fellow man.

No one could think for a moment, after a survey of those placid features, that Bob Hauler could find it in his heart to tread on a worm, let alone throw a large chew of tobacco into the eye of a fellow creature.

Bob's aim, however, was simply splendid.

Which was attested by the pirate's furious oaths and curses.

The fellow received the whole chew of tobacco in his right eye, much to his pain and disgust, and greatly to the amusement of our friends, Bob and Jerry.

Hearing his cries, as he tried to dislodge the tobacco from his eye, the two comrades turned round and appeared very much surprised at what had occurred.

"Well, I be blowed!" said Jerry. "If you haven't gone and thrown yer chaw into that poor critter's eye."

"What a shame!" said Bob.

"Shame arn't no name for it," cried Jerry. "How will it be if he loses one of his orptics?"

"Oh, I don't think as it'll be so bad as that. I'll go and see how the poor feller's a-feeling, and, if possible help him to get that nasty backey out."

But the pirate had passed that stage of sympathy.

He didn't wait for Bob's kind offices, but rushed down the hatchway, swearing furiously and uttering threats that were only equalled by their ferocious significance.

"Pirate number three," cried Bob. "We shortly have 'em all landed at this rate. And we'll make the 'Josef,' at the same time, too jolly hot to hold us."

Jerry thought the same.

Many of the crew of the pirate ship had observed Jerry's act, and laughed until the tears actually rolled down their cheeks.

To all this, however, Bob and Jerry paid not the slightest attention.

They rather looked painfully impressed than otherwise at what had been done.

The first, second, and third officers were now on the quarter-deck of the "San-Josef," taking the bearings of their pursuer every little while.

They kept a keen watch upon her.

Jerry and Bob had their eyes turned in the direction of the pursuing craft.

And they had no doubt that it was their own beloved brig, the "Will-o'-the-Wisp," although the distance between them was too great for them to be sure of it.

But one thing after a while was very observable to our bucaneers.

And it was this.

That the brig was gaining on the "San Josef."

And the longer they looked the more apparent became the fact.

The "San Josef" was, certainly, a vessel of excellent sailing qualities.

But, when compared with the "Will-o'-the-Wisp," the difference was immediately observable.

The pirate ship made every effort to get away.

But the tight little brig came gallantly on, and it seemed that Captain Tom's words would be verified within the twenty-four hours named, to the smuggler on the island.

But twenty-four hours was a long, long waiting.

"Well, Jerry," said Bob, rubbing his hands with great satisfaction, "the craft as is a-following us must be no other than our 'Will-o'-the Wisp.'"

"Do you really think so?"

"Think so! I am certain of it, man. Ther not another vessel on the high seas as would com on so graceful."

"So you are sure that it is the 'Will-o'-the Wisp,' Bob?"

"Sure! Why, yes. Where's yer eyesight, ye lubber? Can't yer tell your gallant little craft from anything o' the kind on the ocean? What ship sails so taut and trim as the 'Will-o'-the-Wisp?'"

"Hold yer row, Bob. You are speaking too loud, them pirates have ears like adders."

"So they have, I must, therefore, be more care

l, old chum. But may Heaven grant that Captain Tom will be here in time to save the women!"

"Heaven grant he may, Bob, for I feels werry anxious about 'em.

"More so than for yourself?"

"In course. Men can rough it out, but women sinks under a little trifle."

"You are right. I wonder where our other comrades are?"

"They have clapped 'em in irons, in the hold!"

"Then we must release them."

"I am with you, old pal. It would be a cursed shame to let the brave lads lie down there, and we up here."

"They are men and brothers, Jerry. Though I don't mind telling you, that I thinks as how they had a hand in taking our gold last night."

"Oh, the villains! They desarve ten thousand deaths, if they had, Bob."

"Nonsense, Jerry! It was only done for a lark! We have ourselves very much to blame for what took place. But, even if they did it wilfully, it would be werry cruel to let 'em remain prisoners, and we having our liberty."

"So it would. Let us go down at once, and release 'em."

"Agreed. But I say, Jerry. I have a plan in my mind, a wery good one, too. You see that 'ere ugly black feller?"

"The executioner?"

"Yes."

"Well?"

"He'll soon be engaged in his diabolical calling."

"Yes—curse him!"

"Well, I mean purwenting the consummation of that 'ere crime."

"Bravo! But how?"

"Come down below, and you'll soon see. Don't appear to be in a hurry, or else them 'ere prying pirates will smell a rat."

"Go on, Bob. I understand you. Down ye go! I'll not be in any particular hurry."

Bob and Jerry now, as if going about their legitimate business, made for the companion-ladder.

No one noticed them.

All eyes were centred on one point—the point of the anticipated execution.

No sooner were they below than the two old shipmates made for the armoury of the vessel.

Having entered it they paused.

"What's to be done now?" asked Jerry.

"Take them 'ere two files."

"All right, Bob. I have 'em."

"Werry good. Let me see—now a half a dozen cutlasses. I wonder is any of these loaded?"

Bob referred to the numerous firearms that were in the racks, of which there were two or three tiers.

"I think so."

"Let us try one."

They did so, and found it loaded.

They tried another, and found it the same.

"Every one of 'em," said Jerry; "and some almost to the muzzle."

"Did you understand me when you were on deck that the pirates had only their cutlasses and yataghans by their sides?"

"Sartinly. I never thought of that, Bob."

"You can see the very drift now, can't you, old pal?"

"What a splendid idea!' cried Jerry. "I am very glad that we haven't to go far, as there's a couple o' gallons of water left here, werry kindly, by our noble friend and wirtuous acquaintance, the executioner."

"Then help me to do it, and we'll soon make them 'ere matchlocks and pistols worthless, at least, for the time."

The two buccaneers set to work immediately, and before a few minutes had elapsed, every firearm in the racks, except those they had took for their and comrades' use, were well saturated with water, and thereby rendered perfectly harmless.

This done, they started for the hold, in which they knew their comrades were confined, carrying as many pistols and cutlasses with them as they could.

Fortunately, they met no one on the way, and soon had the satisfaction of releasing their companions, who were, instead of being ironed, only bound in cords.

To take the buccaneers on deck at present would be madness.

So they all agreed upon a signal.

At the firing of two pistol shots, they were to rush up from the hold, and render all the assistance they could to effect the liberation of Harry Vere.

The Death Pirate, if he was on deck at the time, was to be struck down.

But this was a task not so easy to perform as might be imagined, seeing that the miscreant was encased from head to foot in a complete suit of glittering armour.

"Don't despair," said Bob. "Armour or not, we'll be sure to find some place where we can stick the pointed cutlass into him."

"Aye, aye," responded Jerry. "But I'd like to tear that horrible mask off his face, though. I wonder what he'd look like with that off."

"Not very presentable, you may depend," replied Bob.

"I'd swear he wouldn't," said Jerry.

"Well, all is settled now," went on Bob, after a little further conversation. "Mind, comrades, you are to come up when you hear the two pistol-shots."

"All right, shipmate," replied the buccaneers. "We knows the signal, and you may rely on us."

Bob and Jerry were about to leave the hold, when they heard a sudden noise from above.

Some one was evidently creeping with stealthy steps towards the opening.

"Hark! What's that? Didn't you hear a noise, Bob?"

"Hold your row, you lubber! Do you want every one in the ship to hear us?"

"Some skulking pirate, I'll be bound," whispered Jerry, more cautiously.

"Aye," said Bob. "But if I don't manage to outwit him, may I be chawed up into a hundred pieces."

Then, he added, aloud, for the benefit of the prying, eaves-dropping person above—

"Werry good, messmates—werry good! you will stick to that Captain Tom—darn him!—and you'll hang up to the yard-arm, too, as sure as eggs is eggs! Now take my advice, and when the luff of the 'San Josef' comes down here a wisiting of you, tell him as how you'll join him; and when yer says it, mean it, too, d'ye hear! for he's a right down good gentleman, he is. And if he sees yer honest and straightforrard-like, he won't be a bit hard on yer. Dam Captain Tom! and darn anyone as sticks to him, say I! If that doesn't suit that sneaking, listening pirate above," added Bob, in a whisper, "I don't know what will. And look ye here, messmates," continued Bob, at the top of his voice, "once fer all, I must tell ye, if I didn't know that he had grievances on board that 'ere 'Will-o'-the-Wisp,' and you was a-going to desert the first chance you got, I'll be hanged and chawed up into little pieces if I wouldn't have left ye to yer fate. Say you join at once, and don't be a-hesertating about it, or darn me I'll go up and tell the luff, and he'll sling ye up to the yardarm like dogs or herrings afore ye've time to say amen."

"Bravo!" cried a voice at this moment, from the top. "That's the way to talk to them."

Bob seemed thoroughly confounded that anybody should, all this time, have been listening to his discourse.

So he uttered an exclamation.

"Oh, Lord! I've got myself into a fine scrape now, haven't I?" said Bob.

"Don't be afraid, my good fellow," said the voice. "Your zeal will be fittingly rewarded, depend upon it."

Bob knew now that the owner of the voice was no other than the luff.

And having a partiality for that kind gentleman, he came to the conscientious conclusion of securing him to keep him out of harm's way, if for no other purpose.

Here then was offered a good chance.

A chance that Bob intended speedily to avail himself of.

So solicitous was he indeed for the luff's welfare that he intended making him a prisoner forthwith, and keeping him down in the hold until such time as the "fortune of war," or something else, might permit them to dispose of the "Death Pirate."

Thoughts like these coursed through the mind of our amiable and placid friend.

And he resolved, moreover, not to be baulked in any design he undertook.

But how was he to get the luff into his power?

This was the question.

He hit upon an expedient in a moment.

"I beg yer honour's pardon," said Bob, very humbly. "But ye almost made me leap out o' my boots. Fancy yer honour a-catching me in sich a predicament as this."

"Don't mention it, my noble fellow—don't mention it," said the luff. "It is all done for a good purpose, no doubt."

"I hope yer'll continue to think so, at least, for a few more minutes," thought Bob.

Then he replied, aloud—

"Aye, aye, yer honour—all done for for a very good purpose, I assure you. But I didn't imagine for a moment as how anyone was a listening to me."

"Think no more of it," replied the luff. "I know you are a very good fellow."

"I am werry glad yer thinks so," thought Bob. "Maybe you'll have reasons to alter your opinion in a minute or two, my noble Salamander. If you don't it'll not be the fault of Bob Hauler, I'm sartin."

"Have you anyone down there besides the prisoners?" asked the luff.

"Not a soul," replied Bob, nudging Jerry.

"Where's your comrade?"

"On deck, sir."

"He's bound to see that execution take place, then, I suppose."

"I should think as how he was, seeing as Lieutenant Vere—who is as big a hupstart as ever stepped—is a-going to be swung off."

"They are not going to hang him, you know."

"No, in course not, yer honour."

"We do all our executions aboard the 'San Josef' by cutting off the heads of the culprits," volunteered the luff, condescendingly.

"And a werry good way to sarve the varmints, sir," replied Bob. "I wish they'd only make me executioner, and I'd show them some clean cutting, I assure you."

"I have no doubt," said the luff. "But as we have an executioner at present, it's not likely we'll need another for some years to come."

"That's werry unfortunit," said Bob, sighing deeply. "It's a good berth, amply provisioned, and I'm afeared the only one I'm a-fitted for.'

"Nonsense! Don't say that," said the luff.

"Well, yer honour, perhaps I'm werry wrong like. It's not for an ignorant fellow like me, to know what he's best suited for. But there's my comrade Jerry, yer honour—a better fellow never broke bread nor Jerry—well, yer honour, he's a little touched on that 'ere execution, werry much indeed."

"Ho! Ho! How so?"

"Well, I hope, sir, as how you won't be vexed." Bob paused.

"Oh, not at all. But, go on. What is he annoyed about?"

"Well, Jerry, yer honour, takes it werry much to heart ye see."

Here a pause, as if Bob was choking dome rapidly-rising sobs.

"What does he take to heart? Speak up, man!"

"The execution of Lieutenant Vere, yer honour," replied Bob.

"What! doesn't he want him to be executed."

"Oh, yes, yer honour. That's just what he does want."

"What is it, then?"

"He takes it to heart 'cause—'cause he'd like to strike the the blow himself."

Jerry shuddered. He was going to give the lie at once to this, but Bob clapped his hand over his mouth.

"That's a curious idea of your friend's," said the lieutenant, musingly.

"Yes, very curious, sir. That's what I was just a-thinkin' of myself. But then, Jerry is a curious feller altogether, yer honour, and sometimes as windictive as a mad bull in a chayney shop."

"Ho! ho! Now I see how the wind blows. He has a grudge against this Lieutenant Vere?"

"Lor' bless yer honour's soul!" replied Bob, "he avoids him as he would a nest o' rattlesnakes. Jerry's like a lamb sometimes, yer honour. But when he's roused up a little, he becomes a roaring lion."

Jerry had the greatest difficulty now to keep himself from indulging in a fit of roaring laughter.

Our impressible friend was not aware, in all his dealings with Bob Hauler, that that innocent individual could spin so many falsehoods, and in so brief a time.

"I am sorry that we can't oblige your friend," said the lieutenant. "There's no doubt that this Vere—this rascally lieutenant of buccaneers—has outraged his feelings very much; and the only consolation we can give him, I regret to say, is to be present at his execution. Now, tell me, my friend, how have you succeeded with these fellows below? At present, the 'San Josef' is rather short of hands, and a few good seamen, more or less, who would be true to our noble chief's interests, would be received with open arms, and treated well. Plenty of prize-money, oceans of grog, and the fat and pick of every ship that comes in our way."

"The offer would be enough to tempt Satarn himself, yer honour," said Bob, enthusiastically.

"What?"

"I say the offer would be enough to tempt the Devil, sir. And they must be werry hard-hearted wretches, indeed, as would refuse it."

"I should think so," repeated the luff. "However, I'll not forget your zeal, my good fellow. I shall report all this to the captain, and as you are a good sailor, and know something of navigation, I have no doubt the first chance he gets he'll make an officer of you."

"Thankey—thankey, sir. You makes my werry heart melt with over-brimming gratitude. What do ye think of that you parcil o' warmints?" cried Bob, turning to the buccaneers, with sudden ferocity. "Don't yer feel ashamed o' yourselves for yer ingratitude? Aye, you may well sob—you may well cry, you set of ungrateful reptiles, you. Yer 'll come to yer senses werry soon, when it 'll be too late—when every mother's son o' you is a-swinging on the yardarm."

Could the lieutenant of the "San Josef" believe his own ears?

He heard sobbing, and moaning, and deep sepulchral groans coming up from the hold.

Such sobs and groans as would melt a heart of granite.

His heart softened.

He was but a man.

And an Englishman.

"Come, come, my brave fellows," he cried. "Don't give way like that."

He tried to peer deep into the hold, from whence these signs of contrition and penitence issued.

Now, had he been Argus-eyed, he might have been able to penetrate the darkness, and, by so doing, detect the irrepressible Jerry doing his "level best" at the groaning and weeping dodge.

But, not being Argus-eyed, and having no power of vision but a pair of limited and rather weak eyes, he was forced to the conclusion that the grief was very intense indeed, and of a nature the most painful and heartrending.

The weeping and groaning continued.

Chief performer, Jerry Mizzen.

The lieutenant could stand it no longer.

At the invitation of Bob, he came down to assuage those indications of deep grief, if possible, and to promise them his protection and favour in future.

Very much surprised was this generous and beneficent man when he found himself suddenly seized, thrown violently to the floor, and, before he could call for assistance, bound and gagged beyond a possibility of escape or outcry.

Much more surprised was he to hear the voice of the amiable Hauler thundering in his ear that if he made one movement to effect his escape, it would be at the risk of his worthless life.

Jerry Mizzen, to frighten him, clapped the cold muzzle of a pistol to his head, threatening to blow his brains out if he even stirred.

"That's the way we sarve out sich varmints as you," said Jerry, very maliciously. "Stir an inch, and I'll send an ounce or two of lead through your napper!"

The luff, being a sensible, though not a very sharp man, thought, in his present helpless condition, the less he stirred the better.

He was very angry with himself, however, for being duped so easily.

But he reflected that a few buccaneers had little chance with the crew of the "San Josef," so, notwithstanding his present unpleasant plight, he laughed quietly in his sleeve, resolving to have his revenge on his captors before the day was out, yet.

Bob and Jerry could not waste any more time in the hold, so, giving the lieutenant in charge of their comrades, with repeated instructions how to act when they heard the firing of the shots, they at once hurried up the steps, and made the best of their way on deck.

CHAPTER CLXII.

BOB AND JERRY DICTATE TERMS TO THE PIRATES.

WHEN Bob Hauler and Jerry Mizzen once more found themselves on the deck of the "San Josef," they beheld a scene that rivetted their attention, besides greatly perplexing them as to their future action.

Harry Vere was in the centre of a throng of ferocious ruffians.

There were at least a hundred more now on deck than there were before.

And all had their side-arms—yataghans and cutlasses—hanging at their belts.

But not one had a matchlock, or even a pistol.

So Bob and Jerry thought they had done a very wise and creditable act, after all, by rendering all the pistols and matchlocks in the armoury useless.

What a plight the pirates would be in when they discovered that their fire-arms wouldn't go off!

And then, should Captain Tom's vessel bear down on the "San Josef," how easy would be the capture!

But a great—a very great—distance intervened still between the two ships.

However, our two buccaneer friends were sure now that the gracefully and strongly-built little craft astern of them was the "Will-o'-the-Wisp."

But little satisfaction would this be to them if the gallant Harry Vere suffered an ignominious death.

In that case their own fate would be the more sure, swift, and terrible.

Thoughts like these made Bob and his comrade tremble, brave men as they were.

The miscarriage of a single plan they knew would end in the destruction of them all.

But the two buccaneers, with all their eccentricities and jollity, were men who too often faced death to be afraid of it now.

Casting their eyes round them, they saw, as we before stated, that the decks were literally swarming with armed pirates.

And in the centre of this horde of ruffians and cut-throats, one single figure was the observed of all observers.

It was Harry Vere, his arms pinioned to his sides, his tall form drawn up to its full height, and his face wearing a pale, but determined expression.

With an unquailing and fearless eye, he viewed all around him, prepared, indeed, to meet the horrible fate that awaited him like a man.

Whatever emotions swayed him internally, they were not to be seen in those closely-compressed lips, or in those stern, flashing eyes.

Hard-hearted and stony as were their natures, a murmur of admiration fell from the lips of the pirates who assembled to see him die.

They were forced to confess that they had never yet seen a man come forth to meet his death so bravely, and, indeed, so firmly.

He had everything on his side to rivet him to life.

A profession which he loved, a beautiful young wife, to whom he was, by every fond tie of affection, devotedly attached, a vigorous youth, health, and strength of body and mind.

How very hard was it then to die!

Perhaps no one felt it more acutely, more bitterly, than poor Harry himself.

But he despised exhibiting the real nature of his feelings to an enemy so cruel and so merciless as the Death Pirate.

One thing, however, nerved him more than anything else to meet the terrors of death.

And that was the absence of Jenny.

As the two buccaneers beheld the noble form and pale face of the young lieutenant, they could not resist the tears starting to their eyes.

But as these evidences of emotion would ill suit the company they were in, they instantly controlled them, and looked on as the others did, without

WITH DRAWN SWORDS THE TWO MIDDIES RUSHED TO THE RESCUE.

betraying any other feeling than an interest in the execution.

There were other parties, however, who attracted the attention of the buccaneers besides Harry Vere.

One, the black executioner, who now looked more hideous than ever.

The other, the Death Pirate, who stood leaning up against the bulwarks, with a tall spear in his hand, encased in shining armour, his features hidden behind that horrible death mask with which our readers have already some acquaintance.

The eyes of this latter personage seemed to gleam like living coals upon his gallant young prisoner.

The Death Pirate was a powerful monster, and stood at least six inches above any of the pirates present.

No one knew who he was, and evidently no one had ever seen his face.

From this hideous-looking wretch, Bob and Jerry's eyes were turned to a little group of three persons who stood by themselves.

Bob had not looked long, when he uttered a smothered exclamation.

One of the party he recognised.

And that one was Reuben Harpy, who had, among the rest, come up to see the execution, and who took a ferocious delight in witnessing the death of a brave man, not because he had ever injured him, but because he was Captain Tom's lieutenant.

Perhaps it would be as well to inform the reader at this point that when Lieutenant Vere and his comrades were captured on the island, Reuben Harpy and his two companions were on the " San Josef."

This was precisely the reason why Bob had not seen him before, and the sole cause of his sudden stifled exclamation.

" Jerry !" whispered Bob, " look afore you, and see if you can recognise any one."

Jerry had been looking in the direction indicated, and had seen the little group of three men.

But as Reuben Harpy's face was then turned a little away from him, he withdrew his gaze, not dreaming for an instant that Captain Tom's base cousin stood only a few paces from him.

But this time he did recognise him.

And gave an involuntary start.

" Good Heavens !" he muttered, " if it aren't Reuben Harpy !"

" The same. But be werry quiet, and don't speak above yer breath, or ye'll attract the attention of them rascally pirates."

" Well, who'd a-thought it," whispered Jerry, " to have seen Reuben Harpy here !"

" I'll bet you what you like," rejoined Bob, " that he's been the sole and only cause of all our trouble."

" Think so ?"

" I'm sart'in of it. You know what a rumpus they kicked up about him on Iron-Arm's brig. When he escaped from there, he must have got to the island."

" And then ?"

" Sold us to this cussed Death Pirate. It's all his doing, Jerry. I am as sure and sart'in of it as I'm now standing on the ' San Josef.' "

" It looks a mighty clear case of treachery against him."

" Oh! what can you expect from a sneaking, cowardly lubber like that? But, darn me, if I don't wentilate a hole through his cussed carcase when the time comes, my name's not Hauler !"

" I'd at least put him from doing any more harm to Captain Tom," said Jerry, with a whispered imprecation.

" Or harm to anyone else, either," said Bob. " You leave the matter in my hands, old pal, and see if I don't settle his goose for him."

" And the other two fellers, I suppose, is proud of him ?

" Them's the chaps as helped him to escape, I've no doubt."

" And our other officer?" said Jerry. " I wonder does the warmints intend putting him to death, too ?"

CHAPTER CLXIII.
MRS. DRAKE TURNS UP.

must now return for a brief time to trace the gress of Captain Angel.

The reader will remember the position in which we left the captain, with the young girl on her knees appealing for mercy to him.

But, as it subsequently came to pass, her fears were ill-grounded.

It was not the intention of Captain Angel to take her life, or that of either of her companions.

Blood enough had been spilt already that night.

And the merciless pirate thought so too.

" Take them away !" he cried, angrily. " Do the silly fools think I mean murdering them ?"

Three or four of the pirates obeying his comm went forward, and carried them aboard schooner.

All the pirates had by this time returned from the lower part of the vessel.

Many of them laden down with treasure.

Angel's eyes sparkled with avaricious greed as he beheld so much wealth in the possession of his myrmidons and giving them the order to carry it aboard the schooner, he was about to follow himself, when his lieutenant came up and warned him of of the approach of a strange craft.

This, as the reader is aware, was no other than the " Will-o'-the-Wisp."

" Where away ?" asked Angel.

The lieutenant pointed in a line almost direct with the ship's bows.

It was a bright, moonlight night, and the hull, spars, and sails of the " Will-o'-the-Wisp " were clearly visible.

Angel took up his glass, and bent one long look at the approaching brig."

" A smart craft," he muttered, " and, if I make no mistake, one, too, that will show her teeth, if she comes up."

His second in command overheard the remark.

" You are right," he replied ; " a dangerous beggar and it strikes me a craft I have seen in other waters, too, before to-night."

" You have."

" Aye, indeed, have I. Doubtless, sir, you've heard of the celebrated boy buccaneer, Tom Drake ?"

Angel started at the name, and turned a shade paler.

" Tom Drake !" he exclaimed. " Can it be possible that this is the ' Will-o'-the-Wisp.' "

" I am almost sure of it. Permit me to take the glass for an instant."

The lieutenant adjusted the instrument to his eye, and bent one sharp glance at the stranger.

It was quite enough.

If he had a doubt before on his mind, he had none now.

So he lowered the instrument as one might expect a man to do who was convinced that he was right.

" Well ?" asked Captain Angel, watching the movements of the brig, breathlessly.

" Just as I thought," replied the lieutenant. " It's Captain Tom Drake's brig—the ' Will-o'-the-Wisp !' "

" Then it will be dangerous to loiter here any longer ?"

" I should think so, unless you wish to come in collision with her."

" I am not so ambitious," replied Angel. " Besides, this boy-devil I do not wish to meet."

The lieutenant laughed, and followed Angel on board his schooner.

They now released their grapnels, and swung clear of the ship they had plundered.

With every stitch of canvas spread, the pirate took a directly opposite course to the buccaneer.

And by the time the " Will-o'-the-Wisp " came up to the ill-fated vessel, the schooner was almost beyond the reach of pursuit.

The night that followed was spent aboard the pirate ship amid drinking, shouting, and blaspheming.

It was an awful night for the few wretched captives, who, crouching together in fear, thought that at any moment the fierce pirates might rush in and murder them.

Captain Angel alone withstood the temptation of these orgies.

He was a man whose mind was too much under control to take part in them.

Towards early dawn the pirates grew more boisterous and infuriated, maddened by the liquor they found on poor Gregory's vessel, most of which they purloined for their own use, and this unknown to their captain.

Though the first lieutenant had not gone quite so far as the rest, he was, nevertheless, in a beastly state of drunkenness, and as unable to quiet the men as he was to issue any rational order.

All these shouts, songs, and blasphemous oaths had little effect on the imperturable Angel.

He was as hardened to them as he was to the sufferings of others.

"Shout, sing, and blaspheme your fill," he muttered, as he strode the deck; "ha! ha! There is at least one who has strength of mind enough to resist your infernal orgies, and who uses you just as long as it suits his purpose, and no longer."

As the second officer was on deck and sober, the captain, giving him a few instructions, descended to his cabin to snatch a few hours repose.

He was not long there before he was in a profound sleep, from which he was awakened, however, by loud shrieks.

"What the deuce is that?" he cried, leaping up.

He listened for a moment.

The shrieks were repeated even in an intenser key.

They rung in shrilly echoes into the cabin.

The captain waited no longer, but hurried up on deck.

He saw a sight now that made his eyes flash with anger.

About a dozen of the drunken ruffians were on the point of bearing the girls below.

"Hold!" thundered Captain Angel. "Is this the way you obey orders? Release the girls, you drunken villains! Release them, or take the consequences!"

The men were for a moment astounded to hear his voice.

They little dreamt that their captain would interfere with them, knowing his merciless and sanguinary nature as they did.

In their sober senses, they would certainly have obeyed his commands without questioning it.

But now that they were drunk and maddened with liquor, they only paused a moment, and that moment to defy him.

"Attend to matters that concern yourself, Captain Angel!" cried one drunken, burly-looking fellow.

"This to me!" cried Angel, in a perfect fury.

"Aye, even to you, captain, if you like to take it as such. You leave men here free to act and think as they like."

"You have spoken your doom!" thundered Captain Angel, snatching a pistol from his belt.

A sharp, clear report rang through the night, and the pirate, with a yell of agony, fell forward on his face.

A few convulsive twitchings of his limbs, and his burly body was still and motionless in death.

This seemed to sober the rest of the party.

They released their hold of the girls, and shrank back to look at each other in dismay.

And the poor captives, taking advantage of their momentary hesitation, fled like frightened fawns down the companion-ladder.

But Captain Angel had more work to do yet.

There was more blood to be shed ere he gained the mastery over those those ruthless spirits, who had long looked upon his encroachments as a commander with a jealous eye.

From their dismay they grew to uttering loud clamours.

Angel could see that there was a storm brewing, and that, if he did not instantly quell it, it would be all the worse for himself.

He was a man, as the reader already knows, of a very firm and decisive mind.

Quick to think, and, indeed, as rapid to execute.

The men, from low, angry clamourings, broke forth into fierce shouts.

The gory body of their murdered comrade before their eyes goaded them almost to desperation.

Some drew their weapons, as if meditating a rush on their captain.

And those who did not, spoke their intentions pretty plainly.

Now was the time for Captain Angel to show that spirit of command which always characterised and never fairly deserted him, even in the greatest of dangers.

Throwing his recently discharged pistol aside, he drew from his belt another.

"What, you mutinous hounds!" he cried; "would you threaten me? Down with your weapons, I say! The first man who disobeys me, dies!"

The pirates, still undecided, did not know whether to rush upon him or not.

The clear moonlight fell upon his hard, stern features, and lit them to their view.

And they saw such a steady, unswerving determination in their look, that it made them pause.

"Not obeyed yet?" cried Angel, in a voice of thunder. "Then die!"

The pistol was discharged at the nearest of the pirates, who, with a yell of agony, fell on the deck and rolled over motionless.

Captain Angel, with a sardonic grin on his face, threw his emptied weapon among the dumbfounded pirates, and coolly drew another.

The ruffians, as well as sobered, were completely cowed.

Those who had drawn their arms let them fall from their hands, and were moving away.

"Come back!" cried the captain. "Heave yonder carrion overboard!"

Tremblingly and reluctantly, they took up the bodies of their slain comrades, and tossed them into the sea.

"Now away, all of you!" cried Angel; "and let the lesson I've taught you be one that will sink deep into your memories."

The pirates, without answering, like well-whipped curs, slunk off, and disappeared below.

"I have taught the scoundrels a lesson this time," said Captain Angel, chuckling. "In future they'll know that I am master here."

Scarcely an hour elapsed, following this incident, when a strong breeze blew up.

And the moon going down it became quite dark.

Long before this the "Will-o'-the-Wisp" entirely disappeared, and the pirate captain had no fear of pursuit.

The early morning was now coming on, and the captain, no longer feeling a sense of drowsiness, remained on deck, buried in his reflections, which were many and varied enough.

While he was deeply pondering and looking over the weather-side into the water, he felt some one gently touch his elbow.

He turned round sharply and met the eyes of the second officer rivetted on him.

"What is it?" he asked quickly.

"I saw you buried in your reflections, sir, and I didn't wish to disturb you."

"Well, is that all you have to say?"

"Oh, dear, no! I have just been watching an object for the last ten minutes on our weather-beam, but it's so deuced dark I can't make it out. It looked to me something like a boat, or a raft."

"Some shipwrecked mariners," rejoined the captain. "Hand me the glass."

The night glass was handed to him.

But at that moment a shout came up from the ocean—a scream of such marked agony that it could not be mistaken.

The darkness grew thick and dense.

But the captain with his glass had better success than his mate.

The object he saw was enough to excite him to take immediate steps for its rescue.

The schooner's course was slightly changed, and in less than five more minutes a boat was lowered and the second officer and four men got in and pulled towards the dark object that was tossed about at the mercy of the rapidly rising waves.

When they drew near enough they could discern that it was a raft.

Its two sole occupants being a tall and somewhat majestic woman, and a youth—a young sailor—little more in years than a boy.

The latter was stretched insensible on the raft, to which he was, in fact, lashed.

While the former, with her long hair streaming in the wind, held in her hands a rope, by which she seemed to be directing the motions of the frail craft.

When she caught sight of the approaching boat she gave a wild cry and sunk upon her knee, holding the rope as it were even more firmly in her grasp.

"Another spurt, my men!" cried the second officer.

The spurt was given, and the boat flew alongside the raft.

In an instant the pirate leaped on the lashed and broken spars, and releasing the young sailor from the cords that secured him, carried his insensible form on board the boat.

The woman followed them in silence.

The men now took up their oars and pulled for the schooner, and in less than ten minutes they were on its deck.

While the boy was carried below, the woman was brought before Captain Angel, evidently to be questioned how she and her companion came on the raft.

For a moment they were face to face, and but for a moment.

The next the woman started back in fear and trembling, uttering the name of Captain Angel in a voice little better than a shriek.

"Aye, aye, Mrs. Drake; we have met once more!" cried the pirate. "I have long looked for this moment to come."

We once more return to Bob Hauler and Jerry, as they witnessed the preparations for the execution.

Their attention was attracted to the junior lieutenant.

He was near the mainmast, and his arms bound to his sides.

He was as helpless as a child, and looked upon the preparations that were being made for the execution of Harry Vere with looks that boded little good to those who took part in them.

Everything was now ready.

And the Death Pirate had already given the word.

But, as we have passingly alluded to this before—especially to the interruption where Jenny rushes forward between the executioner and his victim—we will, as a matter of course, make no further reference to it, but come to a point that put to the test all the energies and bravery of our two buccaneer friends.

They, seeing a momentary advantage gained by this sudden and unexpected interruption of the execution, hastened to put their plans into force.

The two men, drawing their cutlasses, bounded with such fury against the pirates, that they gave way both right and left, so that Bob and Jerry, in an incredibly brief time, found themselves face to face with the Death Pirate.

This was the object they had been working for, and, having attained it, they now made the best use of their time by an instant onslaught on the captain of the "San Josef."

Their onset had been so furious and unexpected, that the pirates were transfixed to the spot, and were unable to move hand or foot to their chief's assistance.

Everyone was, for the time, thrown into sudden consternation.

Even the Death Pirate himself had not the slightest chance to defend himself.

Before he could turn round and confront the two buccaneers, they dealt him, with their sharp and heavy cutlasses, a shower of heavy blows that brought him to the deck.

All this occurred in less than an instant.

And Bob and Jerry, seeing the formidable pirate go down, determined to put an end to his life then and there.

Before any of his men could rush to his assistance, the pirate chief was wounded in a half-dozen places, and, through the great weight of his armour, he was unable to move from where he was lying.

Now, we come to a point we must pass over, for if the reader remembers, it is described by Ben Barnacle, who witnessed the combat from the quarter-deck of the "Will-o'-the-Wisp."

And here the gallant Ben gives the buccaneers up as lost, at that state of the combat where poor Jerry is hurled to the deck by one of the pirates.

But Jerry, when all hope and success seems to have deserted him, is saved by the superior skill and coolness of Bob, who, warding off the terrible blow of the huge pirate, lunges out with his already dripping cutlass, and runs him through the body.

This feat saved Jerry's life, and gave him a chance to resume his feet and his cutlass at the same time, which he now, for a moment or so, used to greater advantage than ever.

The two comrades had received several wounds in defending themselves.

But, notwithstanding this, both fought like lions, hewing down every pirate that came in their way.

They seemed to bear a charmed life.

But the fight could not last much longer.

Mere force of numbers would, in a very few seconds, decide it in favour of the pirates.

A most daring idea now occurred to Bob.

It was to take possession of the pirate ship, and make terms to his enemies.

Not delaying an instant, he proceeded to put it into execution.

Taking the brace of pistols from his belt, he, with the rapidity of thought, fired them.

Not into space.

But at the heads of two of his foremost assailants.

The shots told with effect, and the men rolled over in their death agony.

This was a signal for the buccaneers below.

Besides, the object of creating a momentary panic among the pirates was the result.

Before the smoke rolled away, Jerry followed up the advantage by firing two more.

The sudden and rather unexpected discharges of the fire-arms had the effect now of bringing many of the pirates from the other end of the ship, where Harry's Vere's execution was to take place, and where the pirate chief lay badly wounded and bleeding.

Bob and Jerry, profiting by this advantage, cleared all obstacles, and joined now by those buccaneers from below, very soon liberated the two lieutenants from their bonds, and put a cutlass and a brace of pistols into each of their hands.

This was done, as it were, all in a moment, and before the pirates could well recover themselves, the seven buccaneers created still further confusion and panic amongst them by firing their pistols into their midst with deadly precision.

Nearly a dozen of the "San Josef" men fell in the discharge, and when the smoke cleared away, the buccaneers were nowhere to be seen.

Even Jenny and Minnie had disappeared.

Many of the pirates rushed frantically to the bulwarks, and looked over into the sea, expecting, perhaps, to find a boat there.

But neither boat nor anything else met their view.

So they concluded that they had not escaped that way.

They must be in the vessel still.

But where?

Below, no doubt.

Leaving some of their number to attend the wounded, and a few others to see to their captain, they hastened below, under the leadership of the black executioner, and their second and third officers.

If they caught the buccaneers just then, they would have sacrificed them instantly to their fury.

With angry and vengeful shouts, they made their way to the armoury.

The arms were, however, seemingly as they had been left.

The matchlocks in their places, too, tier over tier, and evidently untouched.

Of course the muzzles of some of the matchlocks were a little damp.

But might not that be expected from the thick, damp fog that rolled up from the sea the night before.

The black executioner was very much gratified that his armoury was in such good condition.

"If those villains of buccaneers only had the gumption," he said, "they might have rendered every fire-arm here useless."

"How?" asked the third officer.

"By pouring water into the muzzles of the match-locks," replied the executioner. "Ha! ha! by so doing they'd have put the crew of the 'San Josef' to serious inconvenience. Humph! I see they have taken a few cutlasses, and a few braces of pistols with them. But out of so many we can well spare them.

"You are right," said the second officer, who now ordea his men to take each a matchlock from the rack.

This they did.

There was a search made now for the first lieutenant.

But nowhere could that gentleman be found.

His name was called out at the top of the voices of the searchers.

But no response came back in answer.

The pirates were very much puzzled, and wondered where the first officer could have gone, for now that the Death Pirate was so badly wounded he was virtually commander of the "San Josef."

Of course, as he could not be found, the command devolved on the second officer, who at once set to work to hunt up the buccaneers.

While he is searching the various holds of the "San Josef," we will go back a little.

To where we left the buccaneers.

During the smoke occasioned by the rapid discharges of the pistols, Bob Hauler and Jerry took care to have Minnie and Jenny in their midst.

And before the smoke cleared away the eccentric Bob led them down the companion-ladder much to the surprise of Lieutenant Vere, and the other officer, who could see not the least benefit accrue from such a step.

But as Bob reassured them to have no fear, and that he knew what he was about, they followed him without a murmur.

Even Jerry, who had the greatest faith in Bob's powers, was as much struck with astonishment as was the others.

He could not imagine what good his comrade could do by going below at such a moment.

It was, in his opinion, simply imperilling their lives.

CHAPTER CLXIV.
THE BUCCANEERS AT BAY.

WHAT did Bob Hauler mean by such conduct?

It was really shameful!

Jerry protested mentally against it.

But, as that had no effect on Bob, he uttered loud and bitter complaints, in which the words "madness," "base ingratitude," "villainous deception," came in indiscriminately.

Was Bob enraged at this ferocious side attack of Jerry's?

Not at all.

He rather enjoyed it.

Took the matter as cool as a cucumber.

For he was as sure as of his own existence that his plan to escape from the pirates' power would be successful.

He had not roamed about the "San Josef" for nothing, not he, during the brief time he had been at liberty.

And he had made a rather important discovery.

Where the magazine of the enemy was situated.

To this he was now leading them.

He nearly forgot one thing, however.

The first lieutenant was still in the hold.

He knew the advantage of retaining his prisoner, so, with Lieutenant Vere's consent, he despatched two of the buccaneers down to bring him up.

And he was brought up accordingly.

Bob now explained in very few words where he was taking them to, and they all agreed, even to the irrepressible Jerry, when they heard the buccaneer's plans, that he was doing the best thing under the circumstance.

They had no time to lose now, so they pushed forward with the first lieutenant of the "San Josef" in their midst, for the powder magazine.

Guide and leadership was all left to Bob, who showed himself thoroughly capable of the charge.

In a very few minutes, and without the aid of a light of any kind, they found themselves in the magazine.

Where powder in immense quantities was stowed.

Their position in this very dark place was rather awkward at first.

Bob, however, soon obviated the difficulty by leaving the hold for a few minutes, then returning with a small dark lantern, no doubt the property of some of the pirates.

This lit up their position.

Revealing barrels and kegs piled the length and breadth of the magazine.

"Take up yer positions, genelmen and ladies," said Bob. "This'll be the last place the pirates'll search."

"Do you think they'll come here at all?" asked Harry, who now left everything in the buccaneers' hands.

"Sartain of it," was the reply.

"Then we may as well prepare for them at once."

"That's what I'm just going to do. Here, you Jerry!" cried Bob, at the top of his voice.

Jerry was deeply offended to be hailed in such a disgraceful manner.

The irrepressible one did not even stir from where he was.

"Come here, I tell you!" cried Bob. "Is yer deaf?"

"P'raps I am," replied Jerry, loftily. "What if I am?"

"Waxed again, you lubber?"

"Enough to make anyone waxed, I should say. I'd just like to know who you're a-talking to, Bob Hauler?"

"Perhaps yer a lord in disguise," said Bob, innocently. "If so, I begs ten thousand pardons, and, what's more, promise never to offend again. My dear Jerry, yer not angry with me, are yer?" said Bob, insinuatingly.

The soft, insinuating tones and imploring look of Hauler were more than Jerry could stand.

One bound forward, and he had Bob's hand in his own, shaking it convulsively.

"Do you feel better now?" asked Bob.

"Werry much better," answered Jerry, with something like a sob rising in his throat.

"What was wrong with you, old pal?"

"I am werry sensitive, Bob.

"Sensitive?"

"Werry much so, indeed. Look ye here, Bob, don't go playin' any of yer pranks on me when all these ladies and genelmen is present."

"What pranks? I ain't played yer any pranks, Jerry. Explain yerself, so as I may know what yer a-driving at."

Jerry did so.

Told him, in fact, how he had insulted his dignity.

Bob giggled, and finally wound up by begging Jerry's parden, and promising never to do it again.

Mizzen, on the strength of that promise, embraced the delinquent.

And after that they were the best of friends once more.

If Lieutenant Vere had not been aware of the peculiar eccentricities of Bob and Jerry, he would have been very angry indeed with them, and no doubt alarmed at the delay which took place to settle a dispute so trivial in its nature.

Bob now gave Jerry the lamp, and set about searching for some weapon to knock the head of one of the barrels in.

He found a hatchet among some kegs.

Just the very thing he needed.

He might have used his cutlass.

But the cutlass snapping would have deprived him of a good weapon—a weapon which had shown its qualities in the late desperate encounter.

A few strokes of the hatchet knocked the head of the powder-barrel in, and revealed to them sufficient powder to blow the "San Josef" out of the water.

They shuddered as they looked.

"How easy," they thought, "to fire the whole magazine."

One little spark flying into the barrel would be sufficient to explode all.

Heavens, what a fate!

Certainly there would not be a moment's pain, as they would all be blown to pieces in a second.

We again say they shuddered as they thought of the destruction which a single spark might work in the magazine.

Yet far better be blown to pieces than fall again into the hands of the pirates.

They knew that nothing would save them, if this took place, from the most horrible of deaths.

"I think that'll frighten the wretches if anything will," said Bob, complacently viewing the now opened barrel. "I've not the least doubt but my plan 'll succeed. If they don't agree to the terms, they are more than mortal men, that's my opinion."

Bob now caught the lieutenant of the "San Josef's" eyes fastened on him.

The man, bound and gagged as he was, was evidently trying to read his most inmost thoughts.

"And that's yer little game, is it?" said Bob, to himself. "You think I won't blow yer all to kingdom come, do yer? Wait a minute, ye white-livered varmint, and if I don't put a sudden fear of death into yer heart, my name's not Hauler."

He walked over to Lieutenant Vere.

They both went aside a little, so that their words might not be heard.

"What is it, Hauler?" asked Harry.

"Yer honour sees that 'ere first lieutenant yonder?" said Bob.

"Yes, yes."

"He's been a-watching of all our movements like a weasel. He's inclined to think that we aren't a-going to blow this 'ere ship up."

"Indeed!" said Harry.

"I'm sart'in of it," replied Bob.

"Then the best thing you can do is to make him think otherwise," said the lieutenant.

"Sart'inly. Weasel or no weasel, he's not a-going to catch Bob Hauler asleep. If he thinks that, he'll find himself in the wrong shop."

"This lieutenant is a power in himself now aboard the 'San Josef,' Hauler," observed Vere.

"I know it, yer honour," said Bob, "cause he's wirtually the commander since the Death Pirate's wounded. I hope the scoundrel doesn't recover."

"I hope not."

"I never worked a thing so well in my life. Me and Jerry was down on him like an avalanche; and before he knew where he was, he had the points of our good cutlasses into him."

"I'll not forget to inform Captain Tom of your gallant conduct, if we ever get aboard the 'Will-o'-the-Wisp' again."

"Thankee, sir. But don't put yerself out a bit about that. I'm as sart'in as that I am in the 'San Josef's' magazine that we'll be aboard our little brig afore to-morrow morning."

"Good. You give me heart, my brave fellow. Then you are sure that this plan of yours will be successful?"

"Never more sartin of anything, sir. What better position could we be in? We have the enemy's magazine, and her wirtual commander in our possession, and we'll blow her to pieces if he doesn't agree to everything we say. He'll have plenty of influence with his men, depend upon it, sir."

"But you are not going to rely on those piratical hounds now, are you?"

"How, sir?"

"You are not going to believe them if they say that we can leave the ship unmolested?"

Bob smiled.

The lieutenant did not yet comprehend the spirit of his expedient.

"No, yer honour," he replied. "I, for one, couldn't believe a word as came from their lying throats."

"No, I should think not. We know what a revengeful set they are, and the moment we left the magazine they would rush upon us, and soon disarm us."

"Aye, aye, sir; and if they succeeded in that our lives wouldn't be worth twopence. They're a wery sanguinary and rewengeful lot, yer honour."

"Very," said the lieutenant.

"And I mean putting it out of their power to do us harm. I say again, yer honour, that before to-morrow morning we'll once more be aboard of the 'Will-o'-the-Wisp.'"

"Well, on my word, Hauler, you are a very wonderful fellow. Now away, and work your will on this lieutenant. Do anything you like. But don't frighten the ladies."

"That was just the werry point I was coming at"

said Bob. "I thought you might prepare Mrs. Vere and Miss Atherton for some o' the orful threats I was going to make use of to that ere scrumptious pirate. I know he's a werry sensible man, and may not believe a word of what I'm a-going to tell him. But if force of character, expression, and general ferocity of manner 'll do anything, Bob Hauler is the man. And now I thank yer honour for listening to me so long and so patiently, and I mean giving yer ample time to conwey that ere piece of intelligence to them as it most consarns."

"The pirates are very long in coming this way, are they not?" said Harry.

"Don't be in a hurry, sir," said Bob. "They'll be here soon enough, depend upon it."

Hauler now made his way to the open powder barrel, where stood his friend, Jerry, with his ample face well puckered over with thought.

The wounds the two comrades had received in their late encounter, were of so indifferent character, that we may say they suffered little or no inconvenience from them.

So this, at least, had nothing to do with Jerry's reflections.

"A penny for yer thoughts," said Bob, coming up. "I'll be hanged, old feller, yer looks as solemn as a country churchyard. What's the matter with yer? Are yer meditating on sudden death?"

"No," replied Jerry, looking up. "I was jist a thinking of that 'ere Crucla, and wondering whether I should see her again."

"Take a chaw of backey, and shut up!" said Bob. "You're always talking nonsense. I suppose yer a-goin' to blubber ag'in. If yer dees, I must tell you once for all, as how there's no grog to be had for love er money."

"Splendiferous thought!" cried Jerry, as a sudden gleam of intelligence lit up his broad, honest face.

"What's in the wind, now?"

"You said there was no grog?"

"No more there aren't."

"You are mistaken."

"You don't say so."

"Yes I do."

"Then produce the sparkling beverage," cried Bob, who either thought that Jerry was working upon his imagination, or telling a wilful and deliberate lie.

"That will I, and in an hinstant," replied Jerry.

"Hold! Where are you going to?" cried Bob.

"To the pirate lieutenant," replied Jerry, hastening away.

Jerry put on such a ferocious look as he approached the poor luff, that that humble individual thought his last hour had come.

Jerry, with resounding steps, came on.

The luff was sure now that all was up with him.

He closed his eyes, as if to shut out the murderous blow.

While he was in in this condition, half-somnolent, half-quiescent, he felt a hand thrust into one of his pockets.

He thought, secondly, that the vile and murderous Jerry was about to rob him.

In this he was right.

But not of money, er valuables.

Oh, no!

Jerry despised such dross.

He very dexterously fished out a flask, and shook it, to ascertain if its contents were of proper depth or not.

The pirate believing himself out of danger, opened his eyes and caught Jerry in the act.

But that dignified individual giving him another withering and ferocious glare, turned on his heel and walked back to Bob.

Bob was overjoyed to see a flask of such dimensions.

It must hold at least a pint.

"What did I tell you," said Jerry, triumphantly.

"I knew as how you was speaking the truth," returned Bob, trying to fasten a grip on the flask.

"That be blowed! Ha! ha! Bob, you don't come over me in that way. There's nothing like being honest, old pal."

"So I say," returned Bob. "Did you ever see me do a dishonest action in your life?"

This very loftily.

"Yes," unhesitatingly replied Jerry, "many a one."

No doubt Bob would have knocked Jerry down for such an aspersion, if the time, place, and grog permitted him.

But by such a proceeding there was something to lose.

And nothing to gain.

So Bob pocketted the insult for the present, resolving, however, to have his revenge out on Jerry at some more fitting time.

Jerry seemed to know the power he possessed, and actually had the temerity to laugh, as if casting a doubt on Bob's honesty was quite a joke.

Off, at last, came the head of the flask, up went the mouth to Jerry's lips, and that gentleman promised by the deep draught he was imbibing, to leave very little, if any, of its contents when he withdrew it again.

"Hold on!" cried Bob, not relishing Jerry's method of imbibation.

"What'll I hold on for?" asked Jerry, gently removing the flask from his lips, and looking very innocently at his "chum" and brother.

"What'll you hold on for? That's a purty question," said Bob. "If you don't come to an anchor, don't ye see, there'll not be a drop left in the flask."

"I don't see," said Jerry, coolly, returning the mouth of the vessel to his lips.

"Obstinate warmint!" hissed Bob, and with one bound he caught hold of the flask, and with one wrench, twisted it out of Jerry's hand.

Jerry, as a matter of course, was preparing to recover it, when Bob, landing out his fist, sent Jerry sprawling on the floor.

"Take that, you greedy lubber," cried Bob, between gulps. "Would yer rob a feller critter of his grog? You ought to be hanged, Jerry."

"So ought you," almost blubbered Jerry. "If you call that 'ere a decent way to treat a chum and a brother, I don't."

"No, more do I. Ha! ha! Jerry, you got the worst of it that time—eh, old boy?"

"You is a most unmitigated villain, Bob," groaned Jerry.

"The pot calling kettle black," retorted Bob, gulping down the last drop in the vessel. "But come, old pal, let us not be enemies. Here's your flask safe and sound as when I got it."

"And empty," groaned Jerry, looking the very picture of woe and misery. "You're a most desperate willain, Bob."

"Ditto, Jerry. But come let us be friends, as I don't think either of us can afford to quarrel just now."

"No, we can't Bob. There's them cursed pirates."

"Where?"

"I didn't mean here. I say that we'll have to settle them presently."

"True, Jerry. Embrace me!"

The two old comrades were locked in each other's arms, not a little to the amusement of the onlookers who, in spite of their danger, could not help being inoculated by the humour of Jerry and Bob's performances.

Jerry and Bob having settled their dispute thus amicably, and cast the bone of the late contention from them (i e., the flask), prepared for the arduous labours of their various tasks.

While Jerry was engaged among the powder, Bob strolled over to the lieutenant of the "San-Josef" for the purpose of giving him a little wholesome advice.

That gentleman, as the reader is already aware, was bound and gagged.

But otherwise he had all his senses about him.

"This, then, is the villain I gave liberty to," he thought bitterly.

Bob came up looking very grave and determined.

The lieutenant imagined he could see his death-warrant already in his face.

Bob when he came within two paces of the frightened luff, paused.

Solemn, and grave-looking as a parson, was our faithful buccaneer.

"Well, miserable man," said Bob, "your fate is sealed. Perhaps you have some prayers to say, so I'll give you the advantage of saying them. But mind, one cry for help and I'll put you to horriblest torture as was ever inflicted."

Bob recorded this assertion with one of his most ferocious looks.

And after terrifying the prostrate lieutenant as he thought sufficiently, he untied the strings of the gag, and withdrew it from his mouth.

"I suppose you understand me now," said Bob, retaining all the ferocity of his appearance. "The first word you utter that's not an answer to my question, I'll put the gag in your mouth ag'in, and bore little holes in you with the point of this cutlass."

The lieutenant nodded without speaking a word.

As much as to say he knew what his fate would be if he disobeyed the order.

"Now," said Bob, "I'll let yer into a bit of a secret. The Death Pirate, I've no doubt, by this time is off the hooks—I mean dead."

Dead!

The luff was going to utter an involuntary exclamation.

But Bob's finger was up again, and he knew what that meant.

So he controlled his feelings as well as he could.

"Yes, that ere savage miscreant is dead, no doubt," said Bob, "and that makes you captain o' this 'ere vessel. You understand?"

"Yes," replied the morose captive. "You want me to—to promise—."

"I wants yer to do nothing o' the kind," said Bob. "Keep yer cussed tongue still, and only answer to the questions as put to yer, or you'll get the point of my cutlass atween yer ribs. Do ye hear that?"

The pirate groaned.

His position was unbearable.

He, a captain of the "San Josef," and not daring to use his tongue.

The very thought was incredible, even monstrous.

But the wretched luff, anticipating what he might get by disobedience, controlled his feelings.

So he groaned and groaned.

But that was all he could do.

"You are virtually, captain now," said Bob.; "and, if yer only acts decently, perhaps, yer life may be spared. As for our own lives, we don't care a button for 'em, and would just as soon die now as at any other time."

Of course, Bob told a very deliberate lie.

But the luff in his fears thought of nothing but his life and the command of the "San Josef."

The former had, indeed, now become doubly

precious to him, for it had always been his greatest ambition to command the pirate ship.

So he was willing to agree to any terms that Bob might see fit to impose on him.

Now this was very condescending on the part of the luff, seeing that he could not act very well otherwise.

"Now," said Bob, "You see that 'ere powder?"

The luff answered—

"Yes."

Very hesitatingly though, indeed.

"You are sure there's no mistake in the vane o' your wision?"

The luff was positive that he saw a barrel at the place indicated, and that that barrel was open.

"I suppose you must be aware in yer duties in this 'ere ship that that 'ere barrel contains powder," said Bob.

The pirate tremblingly replied that he was conscious of it.

"So much disposed of," said Bob. "Now for the next point. It would be very easy to blow that barrel up, wouldn't it?" said Bob.

"Very," was the lieutenant's trembling answer.

"Good God!" he shuddered.

He thought that he had to deal with a lunatic.

Could any man in his right senses be so cool and systematic?

"And when the barrel would blow up," continued Bob, "I suppose as how there would be a general explosion, for all them 'ere other barrels would go off as well. Then I'd like to know where you and your gang o' pirates would be?—blown into the elements, in as many pieces as there are sands in the ocean. I told you afore, I reckon as we'd rather prefer that 'ere kind o' death to any other."

The pirate lieutenant, trembled violently.

What was he to do?

What did this inveterate and savage enemy of his, require of him?

Bob, having now thoroughly terrified the luff, and having, at the same time, greatly amused those who were listening to him, thought it high time now to state the terms by which the "San Josef," the pirates, and the first lieutenant might be saved.

"Yer see how completely I have you in my power?" said Bob.

"Yes," groaned the luff.

"And that I can blow you into a thousand pieces in a second?"

"I am sure you can," said the luff.

"Very well," said Bob. "Nothing more remains now, but to tell you how you may be saved."

The lieutenant pricked up his ears, eagerly.

Anything to avoid such a death.

"Well, you must do and speak as I wish you," said Bob. "The pirates 'll be here presently, and as you are wirtual captain now, it's left to you whether you save yourself or not. All I can say is, yer 'll have to be very careful, and the more good you get of 'em the better. Now, them's yer instructions," said Bob, "and if yer fails—"

"If I fail?" trembled the luff.

"It will be yer own fault, and ye'll have tc suffer for it."

"They may not obey me," observed the luff, confusedly.

"That be blowed!" cried Bob. "Obey you or not, you know what's to follow. Liberty by making 'em tractable—death if they gets anyway insolent. My comrade, Jerry there, will hold a pistol ready to fire in that barrel, while I remain with you to dictate terms to yer comrades."

"I'll do my best," said the luff, trembling from head to foot.

"No man can do more," sang Bob.

The luff, no doubt, thought this a concession.

But if he did, he was doomed to be mistaken.

Bob meant it for nothing of the kind.

As he soon found out.

"As I was jist observing," resumed the buccaneer, "no man in the world can do more than his best."

"No, certainly not," replied the luff, gaining considerable courage by this acknowledgment.

"But that won't protect you in the least from the results of failure," rejoined Bob. "So I hopes as how you'll understand that."

Again the unfortunate luff collapsed.

His fears now grew only too palpable.

"Coward!" muttered Bob, in disgust. "He's almost afraid of his own shadder. But it won't do to frighten him, neither. I say, luff, when them 'are pirates come here, you just speak according to my dictation. Roll out yer words like an organ, and give 'em plenty o' sound. We don't wish to take yer ship, but we desire to leave it quiet and unmolested. Remember, a captaincy and life depends on yer efforts. Keep a stiff upper lip, and swear as how yer'll hang the first varmint as is refractory."

The luff promised all this faithfully.

But groaned and sighed in a manner quite awful.

At this juncture there was heard a noise of approaching steps.

At first faint and indistinct.

But louder and clearer they rung each moment.

"Here they come!" cried Bob. "Now, do what I tell yer, or take the consequences."

"Yes," tremblingly answered the luff.

"Jerry!" cried Bob.

"All right, old pal. What's wrong?"

"Here comes them willains o' pirates. Prepare for 'em."

"Right you are, old son."

"Take yer stand at the barrel."

"That's done," cried Jerry.

"Have ye got yer pistols in order?"

"Put a brace of bullets into 'em, if that's right."

"Good! When I tell yer to fire, let drive."

"Where?" asked Jerry.

"Into the powder, ye dunderhead."

"Oh, Lor'!" exclaimed Jerry, pretending to be very much frightened.

"What's yer saying 'Oh, Lor,' for?"

"Nothing, Bob."

"One would think as how yer was a-frightened."

"Not a bit."

"But I say they would."

"I was never more plucky in my life. Fire into this barrel, yer says?"

"Yes, and if one shot isn't enough, send in two."

"Right ye are. Yer commands shall be obeyed to the letter. As good to die one way as the other."

Jerry thereupon pretended to be very busily engaged with the priming of his pistols.

"Yer sees," said Bob, addressing his prisoners, "I have only to give the word, and up goes the 'San Josef' with every soul aboard."

It was not necessary to suggest such a horrible fate to that gentleman's horrified imagination.

He made up his mind some time since, to do everything that Bob asked of him.

And despair lent him power, also, to use the most terrific threats, should the pirates dare to disobey even a single order he gave.

Loud and angry voices were now heard.

Among them, only angrier and louder than any of the rest, the black executioner's.

"I'd like to have the varmint by the throat for ten seconds," muttered Bob. "I'd still his tongue for ever for him, I would."

The same intention very strangely permeated Jerry's noble heart.

For the executioner was giving vent to the most horrible oaths and threats of vengeance against the buccaneers.

"I only want to catch a sight of them!" cried this sable ruffian, ending up with the various cruelties he intended inflicting in case they were recaptured.

"He only wants to catch a sight of us, does he?" thought Jerry. "The black varmint won't be long a-having that pleasure. But he'll be erfully disappointed when he does."

Bob was right.

The executioner of the "San Josef" hardly expected that they were in the magazine.

By a pre-concerted arrangement, Bob, before they came up, sent the slide of his lamp to, and in a moment all was pitchy darkness.

The pirates paused in their search.

They had evidently not seen the reflection of Bob's light.

"I wonder where they are?" said one of the men. "We have searched every hold in the vessel, and are as far off now catching them as ever."

"How strangely the luff has gone, too," observed another.

"And at a time when his services were most needed. For with all his faults, he's a good sailor, and has a more thorough knowledge of navigation than even the captain."

The last speaker was the third officer.

"Mind what you are saying," said the second. "Such language on board the 'San Josef' will not be tolerated."

"But it's the truth," replied the other.

Here there was a gibberish of many tongues, which had the effect of silencing both speakers.

"They're in the magazine, I'll stake my head," said the executioner, who had bent over and heard some whispering going on in the hold.

"Do you think they would dare—"

"Dare! They would dare Satan himself. Those two ruffians—Bob and Jerry, as they are called—are the most daring dare-devils I ever met."

"What a splendid character they're a-giving of us," thought Bob.

"Our names 'll go up at a premium," muttered Jerry.

"Go it, old sons," said Bob. "You don't know how much good you're a doing of us."

"Desperate ruffians we know," said one of the pirates.

"I suppose you haven't yet got over that blow the rascal gave you?"

"That's me," said Bob, chuckling.

"No, I have not; and, what's more, I mean to have revenge for it."

"Ha! ha! ha! Wait till you catch him first."

"Let the magazine be searched," said the second officer.

"Remember," cautioned the third, "I'll not accept the responsibility of going down there."

"Why not?"

"Simply because, if any firing takes place we'll be blown into atoms."

"Bah! Where are your pistols?"

"We haven't any."

"Then what are you afraid of?"

"Those of the buccaneers."

"They have, at least, a brace of pistols each," said the executioner; "that I know. And they are not particular in using them either."

"Then, what do you propose?"

"Harangue them from above here."

"And if we get no answer?"

"We'll conclude they're not there."

At this moment a bright streak of light flashed up from the magazine.

The pirates fell amazed, if not alarmed.

As they did not know at that moment but that the light might be an exposed one.

"What's that?" cried the second officer.

"A light in the magazine. Can't you see?" said the executioner. "They are below, depend upon it."

"You are right, your Sartanic Majesty," cried Bob, stepping forward. "Down here, we are among the enemy's powder."

"And we mean blowing ye into smithereens, if yer not very partic'larly polite and civil," bellowed Jerry.

The pirates—bloodthirsty wretches though they were—were horrified.

They had had more than enough of Bob and Jerry already.

And their good opinion of these gentlemen had considerably decreased.

Indeed, they thought them quite capable of anything.

"What cold-blooded villains," cried the executioner, whose demoniac nature viewed almost everything in the light of a joke. "I wonder how many seconds, on a rough calculation, it would take to blow the San Josef out of the water?"

"Perhaps you'd like them to try the experiment," said the second officer, viciously.

"I? Not at all, I have no desire just yet to be blown into atoms, I assure you."

"Then keep your cursed tongue still," said the lieutenant. "Now to come to some arrangement with the fellows below."

"They have greatly the advantage of us," observed the third officer. "We are in a perfect fix now if ever we were."

"That's the size of it," said one of the men, "so the sooner we get away the better."

Many of the pirates thought exactly the same.

But the second officer would not agree to such a proceeding.

"We may as well surrender the ship at once," he said, "if we do that—besides the 'Will-o'-the-Wisp' is bearing down on us rapidly."

The reader will understand that there were plenty of pirates on board to work the vessel.

And that those over the hold numbered not more than thirty or forty at the most.

Bob's dark lantern threw a pretty strong glare over the magazine.

The pirates looking down took matters in at a glance—beheld Jerry Mizzen with a loaded pistol standing sentry over an empty powder barrel.

If they were horrified before they were ten times more so now.

Many of them stepped back, shuddering violently.

If they had dared, more than half of them would have left the spot at once, and would have been only too glad to get away.

But the pirates discipline was such that they must remain even if they were to die the next minute.

The second officer, who was a brave man, came now a little to the front, and actually descended down one of the steps.

Bob observed the action, and advised him if he had any respect for his life to keep back, and at the same time turning to Jerry said, with great firmness—

"If you catch any o' these fellers coming down more than two steps fire your pistol."

Jerry ferociously nodded, and kept his eyes fixed on the steps.

"Werry good," said our irrepressible friend.

"Two steps, and I'll blow them into the middle of next week."

The second officer, brave as he was, stepped back.

"There's one here as would wish to speak to you," said Bob, coming forward with his lamp.

Again the second officer made an advance.

"Keep where you are," cried Bob, "or I'll not answer for the consequences."

"Don't be in a hurry," bawled Jerry. "We don't want you down here yet a bit."

"Now," said Bob, stepping back. "Permit me to hassist you."

This to the luff, whom he without much difficulty helped to his feet.

"Now, mind how yer speaks," said Bob.

The prisoner tremblingly nodded.

"Well, first of all, let them know you are down here."

The luff, in as firm a voice as he could, hailed the second officer.

"What! you there, sir?" cried the latter, very much surprised.

"Tell him you are a prisoner," said Bob.

"Yes, my good friend, I am here, and, unfortunately, a prisoner."

"Just as I expected," said the executioner. "It's a great wonder we are not all prisoners."

"Hold your row!" cried the second officer. "What right have you to be putting your tongue in."

"As much right as anybody else."

"If you answer me in that way again, I'll have you put in irons."

"You can do as you please," was the cool reply.

"Away with him! Clap him in irons!" cried his superior.

Two or three of the pirates immediately pounced on the executioner, and bore him from the spot glad only of the opportunity.

"Now, I imagine there'll be no more interruptions," said the lieutenant, grinding his teeth.

Nearly half of the pirates present no doubt would like to have been hauled off the same way.

For though a cruel and bloodthirsty lot, they were at heart more or less cowardly.

The second officer of the "San Josef," having succeeded in restoring order, addressed himself once more to the imprisoned luff.

"I am very sorry to see you in such a position. Can anything be done for your liberation?"

"Tell him there can," prompted Bob.

"There can," repeated the luff.

"Pray let me know what can be done for you? We can't very well rush down the steps of the magazine and rescue you."

"For God's sake don't attempt it," prompted Bob.

"For God's sake don't attempt it," said the luff.

"For if you do, we'll be all blown into pieces," urged Bob.

"For if you do, we'll all be blown into pieces," repeated the luff.

"Humph! Then there's no way whatever of rescuing you," said the second officer.

"None by using violence," prompted Bob.

"None by using violence," said the poor luff.

And he gave a deep groan, meanwhile, as the words left his lips.

"I don't really see what can be done," said his subordinate. "If we attempt a rescue, these fellows will blow up the ship."

"You are right, and they won't think long about it," prompted Bob.

"You are right, and they won't think long about it," said the luff.

"They set no value on their lives," urged Bob

"They set no value on their lives," repeated the luff.

"And if they are not away from this 'ere ship in half an hour, they'll explode the powder," said Bob.

"And if they are not away from this ship in half an hour, they say that they'll ex-explode the powder," repeated the luff.

This was an agony unendurable.

But how could he avoid it?

"Do you honestly think, sir, that they mean to go as far as that?" inquired the second officer.

"There's not a doubt of it," prompted Bob.

"There's not a doubt of it," said his prisoner.

The luff found his position so degrading now, that he was almost sinking with shame.

But his life was too precious to trifle with his tormenter. Besides, he felt sure that if he did not speak as Bob wished him, he would never have the chance of leaving the magazine alive.

"I am so very puzzled," mused the second officer, "that I hardly know what to do, or what to say."

"Where's the captain?" inquired the luff, at the instigation of Bob.

"Wounded," was the reply.

"Wounded! you don't mean that?"

"Yes; and very dangerously, too."

"And the 'Will-o'-the-Wisp?'"

"Is bearing rapidly down on us. Something must be done. And as you are virtually in command now, tell me what to do. Our position is dangerous in the extreme."

"Tell him this," said Bob, "that if the pirates, each and all of them, will lower their arms into the magazine, they will escape the terrible consequence of having the 'San Josef' blown into the elements."

"God in Heaven! you don't expect they will surrender up their arms?"

"Shut up!" hissed Bob, fiercely. "And pay attention to my instructions, or else I'll set fire to the powder before you can say Jack Robinson. You've a desperate man to deal with, when you've Bob Hauler, I can tell yer.

What could the poor luff do?

He was afraid of his life to make even one objection after such a threat.

So, under the fluent tongue of Bob, he revealed the situation in nearly the same language.

The second officer was astounded.

Surrender up their arms!

The idea was preposterous—absurd.

Might as well have asked them to be prisoners at once.

The rapid utterances of the indignant second officer were interrupted by the buccaneer.

"Look ye here," said Bob, stepping a little from his prisoner. "Them's our tarms, and them's what we mean to stick by. If, in less than a half an hour, we're not off the 'San Josef,' we'll blow her up with every soul on her! There's no mistaking our intention, old feller, so we give you fair warning."

And Jerry, having made this speech, stepped back.

The crisis had arrived

What was to be done?

Surrender their arms?

If they did, they would be entirely at the mercy of the buccaneers.

For even seven brave, resolute men with pistols and cutlasses were worth hundreds without them.

Besides, the buccaneers had already shown them that, inferior in numbers as they were, they were not to be despised.

"What's the answer?" cried Bob.

"We'll want time to consider that," came the reply.

"Then, be at your own peril," said the buccaneer. "We don't want to take prisoners, but we must either leave the 'San Josef,' or blow her up. There's no choice in the matter."

"Can we depend on your word?"

"In what way?"

"That you'll put out from the vessel the moment you are at liberty?"

"That's our intention. I believe Lieutenant Vere, who is an honourable gentleman, will tell you the same. Am I right, yer honour."

"Perfectly," replied Harry. "Our only desire is to leave the 'San Josef' unmolested."

"Will you take this responsibility on yourself lieutenant."

The second officer appealed to the luff.

"He can't help himself," said Bob. "No more can you."

"I desire to know whether he takes the responsibility on himself of surrendering up his arms?"

"Answer," whispered Bob.

"Certainly," replied the luff. "I hold you blameless."

"Very good. The arms shall be brought here at once."

The second officer now gave some instructions to one of his men, who went away forthwith.

"Hold on a moment," cried Hauler. "I forgot one thing. You must surrender into our hands Reuben Harpy and the two men that came aboard with him."

"By all means let those men be given up," said the luff, "they are not of our crew, and have nothing in common with us."

"But they are under the captain's protection," said the second officer.

"Deliver them up at my risk," said the luff.

"And take care how you bind 'em," put in Bob.

"Be it so. I'll see that they're secured at once."

Another messenger was despatched.

The pirates were only too glad that they got off so cheaply.

In five or ten minutes there was heard the tramp of many feet.

Bob threw the light of his lamp on Jerry and the barrel to give a most significant effect.

But these were the men who had ransacked the armoury for guns, pistols, yataghans, and cutlasses.

Down were lowered a dozen of the weapons at the time.

And as fast as they came they were carried away by the three buccaneers and the two lieutenants, and piled at the other end of the magazine.

Hundreds of them were so piled until Bob fancied that every gun, cutlass, and pistol in the ship must be there.

"You have them all now," said the second officer, as the last matchlocks, pistols, cutlasses, and yataghans were lowered, "and we are entirely at your mercy."

"Which we don't mean to take advantage of," said Bob. "But Reuben Harpy and his two companions aren't here."

"The 'San Josef' has been searched, and they are not to be found. I hope you'll not hold us responsible for their absence. You ought to have instructed us before, and we should then have taken means to prevent their escape."

"It's all gammon about their escape," said Bob.

"I assure you it's not."

"Take his word, Hauler," whispered Harry. "The rascals would only be an encumberance to us."

"Very good, yer honour. But, first of all, I

means going on deck, and taking a squint round, like. Who knows but some of the villains may be ready the moment we leave here to make a rush upon us, and make us prisoners again?"

"They wouldn't dare, without arms."

"I know that, yer honour. That's just the the thing I'm arter. I'll just see if they have any in their possession, Jerry!"

"Yes, old pal."

"I'm going to air myself a little; and, if I don't get back under ten minutes, be sure you fire into the barrel."

"Werry good," said Jerry.

Bob, having given this command with a countenance replete with ferocity, made his way up the steps, and passed through the thirty or forty pirates with the greatest composure in the world.

No one offered to molest him.

All drew aside respectfully to let him pass.

He anticipated this, or he would never have undertaken to trust himself with them alone.

Having reached the deck, he saw the pirates here and there discussing the probable issue of the surrender of their arms.

But not a yataghan, or a cutlass or a matchlock was there among them.

The "Will-o'-the-Wisp" was at least seven miles off yet, and the pirates cast many a gloomy look in its direction.

Now Bob, that he had thus far succeeded, ordered the pirates to slacken sail.

They looked at each other for a moment in indecision.

But they knew that they dare not disobey him.

So they set about their work, though very reluctantly.

Next Bob ordered them to be in readiness to lower a boat.

They were very glad of this.

Their swarthy faces instantly brightened.

And Bob, having completed all the necessary arrangements now to leave the "San Joseph," hurried below.

But it struck him that he had something more to do yet.

To batten the pirates down.

CHAPTER CLXV.
THE STRANGE LUGGER.

THE instant that Ben Barnacle withdrew the glass from his eye, a scene of the greatest excitement prevailed on board the brig.

To think that two of their comrades were murdered almost before their eyes, was too much for the buccaneers.

They were literally frantic.

They vowed to retaliate in the most dreadful manner the moment they overhauled the pirate.

Every inch of canvas that the brig could possibly carry was clapped on.

And it was then the "Will-o'-the-Wisp" showed the effects of her sailing qualities.

Notwithstanding all the pirates could do, she was rapidly gaining on them.

And Captain Tom thought that he might yet catch up to them before the night was out.

Twenty-four hours he had given himself.

But it seemed quite likely that he would accomplish it in half the time.

All of a sudden, a peculiar haze came over the sea, and suddenly hid the "San Josef" from them.

Some time before that, they discerned a strange sail almost in line with their bows.

She was then coming towards them.

But this miserable haze shut everything out.

Not a quarter of a mile could they see in front of

he brig's bows, and so thick was the haze that it more resembled a fog than anything else.

Half an hour passed, and by that time, fortunately the haze rolled up from the sea like a huge curtain, and mixing itself with the clouds or vapours above, disappeared entirely.

They could now see the pirate pretty distinctly.

She had changed her course somewhat.

But they had imperceptibly altered their own, so in reality the same distance was kept up between them.

The brig, perhaps, gaining a little on the "San Josef."

But about the strange sail.

She was still coming on.

Making, as it appeared, direct for the "Will-o'-the-Wisp's" bows.

She had not changed her course a particle.

There was something mysterious about the strange vessel.

Not a man appeared on her decks.

And not half her sails were set.

She was moving exactly like a log through the trough of the sea.

Seeming, as it were, at the moment guided by no human hand.

An awful and impressive silence seemed to surround her.

She was now only two miles off.

Her rig was that of a lugger.

But certainly a very large one.

The officers of the "Will-o'-the-Wisp" had been up to this so deeply interested in the chase of the pirate, that they had scarcely taken any notice of her.

And only now their attention was more thoroughly called by Ben Barnacle.

The strange pilot who had performed such wonders prior to the terrific engagement between Ellis and Tom Drake, seemed to be watching her with great attention.

A look of uneasiness would sometimes steal over his face, and then the average gloom that nearly always enclouded his features would again settle there.

More than once Captain Tom bent a peculiar look on the man, trying, as it were, to read his thoughts.

But the moment he caught Tom's eyes fixed on him he would turn away, and appear to be regarding the sea in a mysteriously-absent manner.

"Strange man," muttered Tom. "No one seems to know what he is. He baffles even the ingenuity of Ben Barnacle, who reads the human countenance like an open newspaper or a book. But whatever or whoever you are, mysterious man, you have done us a service that can never be forgotten. Will it always be so, I wonder? Will he always act the part of a trusty friend and adviser?"

Captain Tom's reflections were answered by the simple monosyllable—

"Yes."

He started.

The colour rushed to his face, for he found the pilot regarding him with a peculiar—nay, with even a look of marked significance.

"Did you speak?" said Tom.

"Yes," was the marked reply. "I spoke in answer to your thoughts."

"Perhaps you heard them," said our hero, not knowing now but that he might have spoken them aloud.

"In spoken language, no," replied the strange pilot. "I read them in the varied expressions of your face."

"You must be a subtle physiognomist," said Tom.

The pilot merely smiled, but returned no answer.

THE SMUGGLER, WITH A DEEP GROAN, FELL FORWARD ON HIS FACE.

"I thought I might have spoken what I was thinking," went on Tom. "However, you guessed my thoughts whether I spoke them or not, and you answer 'Yes.' The omen is good. But what make you of yonder vessel we see approaching?"

The pilot sighed.

"A strange way to answer a question," thought Tom.

"She looks to me very strange from here," continued our hero. "There doesn't seem to be a soul aboard of her, and the very spirit of death and the grave seems to reign around her."

Again the strange pilot sighed.

He turned from Tom, and muttering that the end is come, walked, like one in a dream, to the wheel.

"He's a strange fellow," muttered Tom. "I wonder what does he mean by using that expression? Upon my life, I have sometimes doubts as to his sanity! But the question is, can it be possible that a man who exercises such will and force of character, such extraordinary genius in cases of extreme emergency, and, withal, such coolness under fire—can it be possible, I repeat, that this wonderful and mysterious being, whose very presence strikes me at time with such unexplainable awe—can it be possible that he is mad?"

Tom, thus musing, took the glass once more, and bent it on the lugger.

But nothing yet could he see.

The mysterious craft still ploughed on.

But, as it seemed to many, by no human agency

Captain Tom hailed it through his speaking trumpet, but only his own voice came back in echo—

"Ship ahoy!"

Ten minutes more the "Will-o'-the-Wisp" veered round, to prevent being run into by the strange lugger.

And the moment she got clear of it, they heard one of the most fearful, horrifying shrieks it was ever their lot to hear.

"Good God!" cried Captain Tom. "Did you hear that, Barnacle?"

"Yes," replied Ben. "I wonder what it all means? I see no one as yet on the deck."

"Now, if I were superstitious at all," said the gallant buccaneer chief, "I would say that it was something supernatural."

"And so would I. But we'll soon find out."

"Lower a boat!" cried Captain Tom, seeing that the lugger was in a fair way to leave them.

The crew looked from one to the other in surprise.

But the order was promptly obeyed, for all that.

The boat was lowered over the side in an instant.

Captain Tom, Ben Barnacle, and even the strange pilot leaped in.

The "Will-o'-the-Wisp," by a second manœuvre, stood almost still.

The long boat was crowded with middies and buccaneers.

The latter took up the oars, and pulled with all their might for the lugger.

The boat flew through the water, and was soon alongside.

Securing it to the stern of the lugger, they climbed on board.

But as this was not a very easy task while the vessel was in motion, they met with some difficulty.

A loud cry arose from the decks of the "Will-o'-the-Wisp," and, at the same time, a second terrible shriek rang out from the lugger.

Two of the middies, who were as active and as lithe as cats, were in another instant on her deck.

What a sight met their eyes!

A savage-looking ruffian in the act of burying a keen, glittering knife in the breast of a young girl, whose age could not at most be more than eighteen or nineteen, and who seemed to be so paralysed with the terror of her awful situation, that she could no longer even scream or cry for assistance.

With a simultaneous shout, the two middies bounded forward with their swords.

All this occurred in much less time than we take to write it.

The loss of another few moments might have proved fatal to the girl.

But the loud cries of the midshipmen made the ruffian pause in his murderous work.

And that instant she wrenched her hands from him, and flew behind her protectors.

Seeing only a couple of mere lads on the deck, the would-be murderer rushed forward with a terrific imprecation, the fires of fury flashing from his eyes, and his whole frame trembling with rage.

But he had others now to confront besides the middies.

Captain Tom, Ben Barnacle, and the strange pilot appeared on the deck of the lugger, followed by several of the buccaneers.

No sooner had the ruffian caught sight of the pale and deadly stern face of the pilot, than he uttered a yell of disappointment and rage.

"You here!" he cries in a voice of intense fury. May the curses of heaven light upon you!"

"At last—at last!" thundered the other, in an exultant voice. "We have met at last, Jonas Redfern! I have been all these long, weary years seeking you, but now, murderous and accursed villain, you are in my power."

"Not yet!" cried the other in a voice trembling between fear and passion; "thus do I foil you!'

He would have leaped into the sea.

But ere he could do so, the pilot was upon him.

Captain Tom and the others, now thought it high time to interfere, and were rushing forward with cutlass and pistol, when the strange pilot waved them back.

"Back all of you!" he thundered, "this miscreant belongs to me. To me alone must he answer for his crimes. Behold! Thus do I let out the life that has caused so much cruel suffering and misery!"

They were both armed with long knives.

Their only weapons.

And both, too, were of the same stature, and apparently of the same strength.

Captain Tom and the buccaneers, not wishing to anger the mysterious pilot, held back.

And now began a struggle that, for its ferocity, was unparalleled.

Up and down the deck they went, battling with all the energy of rage and despair.

Sparks of fire flew from the blades of their weapons as they clashed, bent, and rang against each other.

Sometimes the fight seemed all in favour of the pilot.

At other times his enemy had the advantage.

Wounded and bleeding, they still fought round and round each other, until the deck of the lugger echoed and re-echoed with the clash of their weapons.

Both were silent and stern as death, their eyes fixed relentlessly and in hatred upon each other.

It now grew evident that the end was at hand.

Not much longer could either man last, for the red blood was spurting out from a dozen wounds in various parts of their bodies.

Captain Tom now thought it high time to interfere, if alone, for the purpose of saving the mysterious man who had been of so much assistance to him.

He was on the point of bounding forward to put an end to the fight, when a loud and agonised cry came from Redfern.

The first human sound indeed that he had uttered since the beginning of the conflict.

What had caused it?

It was soon evident to all.

There was an opening in the bulwarks of three or four feet, and to this the pilot had forced back the would-be assassin, with the intention, no doubt, of ending the battle by hurling him into the sea.

The wretch seemed to be conscious of the fate that awaited him, for a loud and agonised cry burst from his throat.

"Ha! ha!" shrieked the strange pilot. "The time has come! Villain! Redfern! I have you at last!"

He threw the ensanguined knife on the deck, and with a loud, triumphant cry, sprang upon him.

A mortal terror seized the ruffian.

He stepped back, and the pilot losing his footing, they both fell with a loud splash into the sea.

Captain Tom and the buccaneers bounded forward at the same moment.

But they were too late to be of any assistance to the pilot.

They heard the splash, and looking over the side, beheld the two men under the waves.

"The end has indeed come," observed Tom, sadly.

"The pilot's words, though uttered perhaps unconsciously at the time, have come to pass."

And so saying he cast his eyes on the seething surging element beneath.

"Come," he said. "Let us away."

"Hold for a moment!" cried Ben. "For if I mistake not they'll come again to the surface, although they were locked fast enough in each other's arms when they went down."

For an instant longer they looked over the side.

The water was suddenly agitated.

The heads of the two men appeared above the surface.

Next came their shoulders, and then half their bodies.

The deep green of the sea was ensanguined with blood.

And the two enemies came up as they went down, locked in a death grip.

Their faces pallid, their eyes flashing fire, and every look fixed in deadly hatred.

The only perceptible difference between them was that one had a weapon and the other had not.

Now began one of the most furious struggles of all in the water.

Redfern shot out with a madman's strength to release himself from the clutches of his antagonist.

His object was only too apparent.

The other held his hands in such a manner that he could not use his knife, which, if he could, if only for an instant, would release him for ever from his enemy, the pilot.

He struggled and squirmed so that the water flew into white specks of foam.

Tom Drake saw the advantage this murderous wretch had, and was determined to put it out of his power.

And, for this purpose, he drew a pistol from his belt, and only awaited the moment that he could fire without incurring the risk of cutting the pilot.

For almost a minute it was dangerous; for good a shot as Tom was, he might have struck the wrong man.

At last the opportunity came.

He cocked his pistol, and taking aim, was going to fire, when the sea was furiously agitated, and a new enemy appeared on the scene.

A cry of horror went up from the onlookers, for the seething waters parted, and there appeared instantly after the head of a monstrous and ferocious-looking shark.

His double row of teeth snapping viciously, he made direct for his victims.

The nearest to him was the pilot, who, as his back was turned, had not yet caught sight of him.

But Jonas Redfern was not so fortunate.

Perceiving the dreadful monster approaching, he uttered a frightful shriek, and putting forth an almost superhuman effort of strength, he wrenched himself free from the other's grip.

But in so doing he more effectually put himself in the power of the shark.

For the effort caused him to swing round to the very position the pilot occupied a moment before.

The pilot now for the first time seemed conscious of the shark's presence.

A low cry of horror burst from him.

But he never stirred from where he was.

He seemed fascinated to the spot.

The maws of the savage-looking monster opened.

For an instant there was a display of its two rows of gleaming teeth.

Redfern was within its reach.

A frightful and heart-rending cry of horror that made every man's blood turn to ice.

There was heard a loud crunching of bones, and, in another second, Redfern's body was snapped in two, and his blood dyed the waters around.

It was horrible for those on the deck of the lugger to witness such a scene.

It would have been more horrible still, if it had been the pilot's body, which had been thus swooped.

But so great was the sensation caused by this unexpected and horrible incident, that neither Captain Tom nor one of his men could do anything else but look on.

For several moments were they transfixed where they stood.

And only when a new danger presented itself did they awake from their lethargy.

Again the shark appeared, having almost. incredible to relate, in so brief a time disposed of his victim.

The monster's teeth gleamed as white as ever.

On he came, evidently determined to make another meal.

The pilot, had he not been a most powerfully constitutioned man, must long since have sunk from loss of blood.

But now he struck out with the energy of despair to escape those terrible maws which were hungrily opening for him.

There seemed very little chance of this, however good and powerful a swimmer as he was.

The shark made after him, his eyes flashing, and his two rows of glittering teeth snapping viciously.

Captain Tom, thoroughly aroused from his stupor now, on seeing the danger of the wounded man, brought his pistol up and fired.

The bullet took effect in the monster's back, but only increased its fury.

Several shots were now fired.

All of which took more or less effect on the shark.

But none of which, however, appeared to be fatal, for the monster put after his victim with greater fury than ever, and seemed in a likely way to come up with him.

The chase was now so exciting and unusual, that all were thrilled with horror.

Captain Tom saw that there was not a moment to be lost, if he would save the pilot.

His resolve was formed in an instant.

It was a desperate undertaking, but he remembered the great service this man had been to him in one of his most trying difficulties, so he prepared to face danger, even death itself, to effect his rescue.

No one imagined what was passing in our gallant hero's mind, and every eye was strained in the utmost horror on the movements of the shark.

The wretched pilot's efforts to elude his ferocious enemy, were now almost superhuman.

He struck out with a power incredible for one who had been, as he was, covered with wounds.

But this last effort of a strong man's strength would avail him little.

Another moment, and he would be crunching between those horrible jaws.

The burst of horror that came from the throats of the buccaneers was thrilling; and, indeed, the general terror was more increased by the brave heroic action of Captain Tom.

Our hero snatched a short sword from one of the middies, and rushing towards the bows of the lugger, before a hand could be stretched forth to prevent him, he dived into the sea.

The shark was evidently for a moment confused.

He heard the loud splash close by, and wondering very probably what had caused it, paused in the chase

Captain Tom arose on the surface at the expiration of a couple of seconds, with his gleaming weapon in his hand.

He was fully two yards from the shark, and awaiting with firmly-compressed lips, and flashing eyes, its attack.

For an instant it seemed that the monster, was

confounded by his audacity, and held back to get a better view of him.

Meanwhile our hero hailed those on board the lugger.

"Never mind me!" he cried. "Go to the assistance of the pilot, or the brave fellow will sink."

They saw that such indeed was the case.

The wounded man from the immensity of his efforts had become thoroughly exhausted, and now that the chase of himself was at an end was rapidly sinking.

A ringing cheer burst from the throats of the buccaneers.

Not a few leaped into the boat and pulled with all their might for the sinking pilot.

Ben Barnacle, with a long, sharp knife between his teeth, leaped into the sea, resolving that Tom should not fight the shark alone

The gallant fellow sank from view for a moment, but soon came to the surface with his good blade in his hand ready to divert the attention of the monster from Tom.

He had come up a little in rear of the shark, as this he intended should be his mode of attack, while Tom attacked him in front.

The monster, through his wounds, had now become thoroughly infuriated, and lashed the water with his tail into huge-crested waves.

Ben was nearly blinded by the spray.

But advancing boldly nevertheless he gave the shark a keen cut with his cutlass, which made him snort with pain.

Tom was nearly smothered with the water that the monster threw up, but brushing it hastily from his eyes he tempted the huge shark to come on by thrusting his short sword at him.

But this manœuvre failed.

The monster turned round with the suddenness of thought on Ben Barnacle, whom he no doubt intended making a meal of forthwith.

Ben, as cool as a cucumber, was prepared to receive him.

Captain Tom, taking advantage of the shark's rear, now struck out in good earnest.

A few strokes brought him within arm's-length.

Taking what he considered a vital part of the monster's huge carcase, he lunged out with his weapon, and had the satisfaction of burying it several inches in the shark's body.

Another thunderous snort and a fierce lashing of the tail, and the shark turned from Ben Barnacle to pursue Tom.

The sea in the vicinity of the encounter by this time had turned a deep crimson colour.

Streams of blood spurted from the shark's body, and even covered the two gallant fellows in the water.

Meanwhile, and while all this was occurring, the pilot was picked up.

But the instant they got him into the boat he fainted.

The boat, as might be expected, was now propelled to the assistance of the two brave buccaneers, who were battling with the huge shark.

But Tom, seeing it approach too near, told his men to keep back for a little while longer.

Which they did.

But not without feeling that our gallant hero and his brave lieutenant's lives were in danger.

On came the shark again, lashing up the water in great fury, and resolved not to be foiled this time in getting a grip of Tom.

But in this he miscalculated his chances somewhat.

He seemed to forget the presence of the indefatigable Ben behind him, who, with his good cutlass, pierced his huge carcase a second time.

Ben, after performing this feat, dived down to get within prodding distance of the shark's belly.

The acts of both Ben and Tom on this occasion were almost simultaneous.

The captain, forcing the fighting, pressed upon the shark, and when that monster, opening his tremendous maws, anticipating a good bite, he found the short sword firmly embedded in the roof of his mouth.

So firmly embedded, indeed, that our gallant hero could not withdraw it.

This, as might be expected, put an end to the shark's biting.

At almost the same instant he received Ben Barnacle's cutlass to the hilt in a more vital part.

In fact, in his intestines.

As Ben thought it too much trouble to withdraw his weapon, he came to the surface deluged with blood.

And the shark, after a few more feeble lashes with his tail, rolled over on his back perfectly motionless.

A ringing cheer now burst from the throats of the buccaneers, and Tom and Ben were handed into the boat, looking little if any the worse for their encounter.

By this time the "Will-o'-the-Wisp" was close alongside, and they were all taken on board.

The question now came up, what was to be done with the shark and the lugger.

The lugger had evidently been abandoned by its crew, and when it was searched by the buccaneers, not even a paper or anything else of value could be found on board it.

So they thought that they might as well abandon it.

The shark they left where it lay, having an unpleasant idea of finding the mangled body of Redfern in its belly.

Besides, they had lost too much time already, so, spreading all sail, the "Will-o'-the Wisp" once more pursued its course after the pirate.

CHAPTER CLXVI.

CAPSISED BY A WHALE.

"Yes, I think that will be a good plan," said Bob Hauler, reflectively. "We'll batten these pirates down by all means."

Bob, with this amiable intention in his mind, left the deck of the "San Josef," and returned to the magazine.

The pirates scowled darkly at him as he passed through their ranks, and Bob, catching one scowling blacker than the rest, removed a goodsized chew of tobacco from his mouth, and coolly rolling it up, took aim and threw it in his eye.

The fellow gave a yell of agony, and would no doubt have annihilated our worthy friend on the spot, but Bob coolly cocked a pistol and ran it against his nose.

The pirate, still rubbing his eye, leaped back as if he had been shot.

"That's the way to sarve such varmints as you," said Bob, coolly, going down the steps.

As no one made any further indications of hostility, Bob walked quietly into the magazine.

There he found Jerry and the others in exactly the same positions as he left them.

Our irrepressible friend, with leaded pistol in hand, was looking into the powder barrel, every now and then giving vent to a broad grin on the right side of his face, and a serious, even anxious expression on his left.

For be it known that Jerry had the rare faculty of manipulating his features as he liked.

Sometimes it would appear that he was crying on

one side of his face, while if you went round to the other it was actually bursting with mirth.

It was the firm belief of our friend Jerry that they were proceeding in the most admirable way to hocus the pirates.

The rest of the company looked very grave indeed, as if everything depended on Bob Hauler's plans.

The luff of the "San Josef" wore a most pitiable look.

Because he thought, and very rightly too, that there were other conditions to be made yet, which the pirates no doubt would have some objection to.

Bob now went to the two lieutenants, and told them of his intention to batten down the pirates in one of the holds of their vessel.

"Do you think they'll agree to that?" asked Harry.

"Sartinly, yer honour. They can't do anything else."

"Oh, yes, they can; they can refuse, you know."

"We'll soon see," said Bob. "Now, Jerry," yelled Bob, "keep a strict eye on that 'ere powder-barrel, and if I gives you the word don't hesitate, but fire into it."

"All right, old pal. You needn't be afeared on that point. Only raise yer little finger, and, blow me, I'll send them up like a rocket!"

Jerry gave an ominous click to the trigger of his pistol, which sent a shudder of horror to the heart of every pirate within hearing of it.

Especially the luff, who was under the charge of one of the buccaneers.

Bob Hauler now advanced to the steps of the magazine.

With the evident intention of haranguing the pirates above him.

Every one listened; every head was bent forward to catch his slightest word.

"Look ye here!" cried Bob. "I have something more to say to yer yet afore I'm done with you, and while sayin' it, I'll be as brief as I can."

Bob felt like a great commander haranguing his troops.

His form was stretched to its fullest height and proportions, and his eyes flashed both a conscious superiority to the crew of murderers and cut-throats above him.

"Well, then," went on Bob, "all I'm going to say is that I mean battening yer down—"

A few hoarse cries from the pirates interrupted him.

"Can't yer keep quiet for a minute?" said Bob, with rising indignation. "How are you to know what I'm going to say unless you listens to me? I am a man of few words, I am, so keep quiet until I have spoken."

The pirates seeming now to pay the greatest attention, Bob went on—

"For the safety of me and my companions here, I am going to batten you down. Now, don't give way to them 'ere rising fits of indignation, or you'll get the worst of it. You can remain in one of the holds for half an hour or so, and after that time you can do as you like. It's not too much to ask of you, and as I can waste no more time, will you go peaceably, or are we to use force? You're aware, I suppose, by this time, that we are well armed. Besides this, I've only to give the word to my friend Jerry there, and he'll blow the 'San Josef' up lock, stock, and barrel."

"Only put yer little finger up," cried Jerry, quietly, "and I'll blow 'em all to perdition! I don't care a straw what it's to be."

As for Jerry's ferocious utterance, the pirates stood it no longer.

One of the crew came forward and whispered in his leiutenant's ear.

What the nature of his communication was was only known to the lieutenant and himself.

After a pause, as if deliberating the matter over, the second officer coincided with the first, and agreed to the battening down process.

Leaving Jerry still in the hold with the loaded pistol in dangerous proximity to the barrel, they all ascended to the deck, and collecting the other pirates together they descended into one of the holds, and were securely battened down.

The Death Pirate, being wounded, was, of course, forgotten.

Having completed every arrangement for leaving the "San Josef," Jerry was called up.

Without further delay they all got in the boat, and were soon leaving the vessel behind them.

They could see the "Will-o'-the-Wisp" in the distance, and their hearts bounded with delight at their marvellous escape.

But a little incident here occurred that is worthy of note, and which seemed to make their attempted escape a futile one.

They had not thought for some time of what had become of Reuben Harpy and his two colleagues.

But they were now very soon made aware of the fact that the scoundrels were still on board the pirate ship.

Scarcely had they cleared the stern of the "San Josef" by twenty or thirty yards, when they were suddenly made aware of a sudden commotion on the deck of that they had just left.

"What the deuce is that?" cried Bob.

The answer came back in a malicious laugh.

And from the deck of the pirate ship they had just quitted.

The laugh was followed by something much worse.

The sharp crack of a pistol shot rang over the waters.

And the aim was not so badly taken either, for it cut off one of Jerry Mizzen's locks in its course, and doing no further harm, went buzzing into the sea some yards beyond.

"A close shave," observed Jerry, picking up his severed lock, and regarding it rather mournfully. "Some of them darned pirates have escaped our attention, Bob. Do you see anyone?"

"No. Do you?"

Jerry let his oar glide lazily in the water, and stood up in the boat to take a clearer view of the deck of the pirate.

By so doing, our friend unconsciously made himself a very good mark for the enemy.

The sharp report of another pistol rang out, and Jerry's buccaneer head-dress was shot from his head.

"I can see no one," said Jerry, gazing rather ruefully into the water after his perforated cap. "I wish I could, and I would give him one as he wouldn't care to forget."

"Sit down or you'll make a target of yourself," said Lieutenant Vere, whose almost exclusive attention was now devoted to the two ladies.

He made them lay at the bottom of the boat out of harm's way.

Jerry, after making an unavailing effort to regain his cap, let it glide with the waves, not, however, without uttering silent curses on the head of the miscreant who fired the shot.

They now pulled lustily at the oars to get as far away as they could from the boat before the next shot was fired.

A third shot rung out.

But this time it fell astern of them.

"I am determined to find out who this coward is!" cried Harry Vere, leaping up in the boat.

He cocked a pistol, and held it in his hand in readiness.

He saw a malicious face appear some six or seven inches above the bulwarks.

He appeared to take no notice of it.

But, notwithstanding all this, his eyes were in reality watching every movement that the owner of the face might think fit to adopt.

At last he caught the fellow rising up.

Cautiously at first.

But soon half of his body was exposed to view.

Lieutenant Vere could also see that there was a pistol in his hand, with which the villain was carefully taking aim.

Now was his time.

With the rapidity of thought, Harry brought his pistol up and fired.

There was a loud cry of agony.

The man straightened up for a moment, fired his pistol at random, and staggered over the deck, yelling with pain.

They all saw him quite distinctly, except Jenny Vere and Minnie Atherton, who lay at the bottom of the boat to be out of danger of the shots.

Bob Hauler knew him directly.

And so did Jerry Mizzen.

It was the cowardly Reuben Harpy, who, out of danger himself, took this method of gratifying his miserable hankering after revenge.

It was his intention, no doubt, to hit the girls.

But Jerry Mizzen was the only sufferer.

Minus a lock of hair, and a nearly new head-dress.

Lieutenant Vere thought now, as he had wounded this cowardly ruffian, that they could go on without further molestation.

But in this he was doomed to disappointment.

Reuben Harpy's two companions had not been idle.

While the former was firing at those in the boat, the latter were liberating the pirates.

This was altogether unexpected, and notwithstanding the trouble Bob Hauler took to batten down these blood-thirsty wretches they, were soon enabled by the aid of the sham sentinel and his colleague to emerge from their place of imprisonment, and rush upon deck.

But prior to this they made pell-mell for the magazine and collected whatever available arms they could lay hands on.

Of course the matchlocks and pistols were not of the slightest use.

The charges in them being dampened by the ingenious and timely method of the two buccaneers.

Nothing could exceed the fury of the luff, who desired nothing better now than to get Bob Hauler and Jerry Mizzen into his power.

If he succeeded in effecting their capture, he resolved to make a most terrible example of them.

Were it not for this reason, he would, no doubt, have fired one of the carronades at the boat, and sunk her.

The pirates lowered a couple of long-boats over the side of the "San Josef," and gave instant chase.

Harry Vere and his companions observed this movement, and for a moment lost all heart, as the pirates in the boats were six times their number.

But it struck him as suddenly that he and the buccaneers had fire-arms, a great advantage which they possessed over the enemy, so he once more took heart to make a vigorous defence, and give the crew of the "San Josef" a little more than they bargained for.

"Here they come!" cried Bob Hauler, as he saw the boats put after them.

"We're in a fix now, if ever we were," cried Jerry. "But no matter, we'll give 'em a desperate struggle for it. Oh, that 'Will-o'-the-Wisp!' It seems to be such a long distance off!"

"And I declare," said Bob, "it doesn't seem to be moving a bit."

And Bob's remark at that moment was true to the letter.

As the gallant little brig had paused to take u those on board the lugger—Captain Tom, Bo Barnacle, and the other buccaners and middies.

All eyes were now directed anxiously in th course of the "Will-o'-the-Wisp," and it gave them considerable encouragement a few minutes after to see that she was again rapidly bearing down on them.

Lieutenant Vere took care before he left the deck of the "San Josef" to procure himself a glass, with which he cast many an anxious glance in the direction of the approaching brig which was even a great distance off yet.

His attention was soon attracted in another direction.

A hoarse cheer arose from the pirate boats as they flew in pursuit of the buccaneers, propelled by vigorous hands.

How long the pursuit might last there was no telling, as the buccaneers took good care to select the best boat they could find on the "San Josef," and which, plied by equally strong arms, flew like an arrow through the water.

Of course the pirates had the advantage in numbers, for they could relieve each other when the one set of oarsmen were tired, and so keep up the same speed all along.

Bob Hauler and Jerry Mizzen perceived all this with dismay, and, although they bent with a will to their work, they soon became conscious that their enemies were gaining on them.

"And do yer see that 'ere luff?" cried Bob. "I know what he'll do, if he once gets me into his power. It will be a short shrift and a long rope."

"Or something worse," put in Jerry. "Do you see the varmint, how he stands in the bows, Bob? It is he that is inciting them on to chase us. I can see him looking thunder and lightnin' at us."

"You have werry good eyesight, Jerry," laughed Bob, "so that we must take all as you says for granted."

But our irrepressible friend thought it was no laughing matter, while there were so many savage fellows in the rear thirsting for their blood.

He viewed the matter in a very grave light indeed.

There was no laughing on one side of his face now.

He looked, in truth, more like crying on both sides.

For these accursed pirates were coming on at a most extraordinary speed, and lessening the distance between them each moment, in spite of the buccaneers' most mighty efforts.

Harry, now having a great responsibility on his shoulders, consulted the junior lieutenant as to what was best to be done.

It was the opinion of that officer, as they had ammunition, a few matchlocks, and plenty of pistols, to check the speed of their pursuers by firing occasionally into them.

The benefits that would result from such a line of conduct might, in the end, save them.

So the buccaneers, bending to their work, took hope again.

Those who had not oars in their hands made themselves otherwise useful by loading the firearms that had been discharged.

Meanwhile, the pursuing boats gained fast on them.

As might well be expected, considering their relative positions.

The pirates saw something unusual going on in the buccaneers' boat.

But they did not know very well what it was.

Of course they never expected that the buccaneers would be such unmerciful heathens as to fire upon them.

They, however, through force of vigorous pulling, got within range.

The moment they did so, they were considerably taken aback to hear the loud cry of "Fire!"

Surely not on board the "San Josef?"

Oh, dear, no!

They next, while they were looking about them, heard a ringing discharge of several shots.

What did it mean?

The answer presently came, for two or three of their number threw down their oars, and with shrieks and yells of pain, rolled over into the bottom of the boat.

These were at least done for, as far as rowing was concerned.

But as there were a great number in the boat, there were others to take their places.

A ringing cheer broke from the buccaneers at the success of their first volley.

Answered by one of rage and loud defiance from the pirates, who, since the firing, were now more than ever determined to come up with them.

Jerry Mizzen and Bob Hauler witnessing the results of the shots fired, were in their glory.

"I see we'll give the varmints a little trouble yet," said Jerry.

"Right you are, old son," cried Bob. "That volley knocked three of them off the hooks, at any-rate. Now spurt out, Jerry, and mind as how you put all yer strength into yer oar. Because I know you're a lazy dog when yer likes."

"And you are not, Bob. So that's one consolation."

By this time Lieutenant Vere and the others were prepared to deliver another volley.

But this time they selected pirate boat number two.

Which the luff commanded.

This man was by far too busy to warrant a continuance of his task.

So Lieutenant Vere thought.

And so thought all the buccaneers.

The luff was evidently in a great rage, for he was urging and threatening his men in the same breath.

Besides, he was gesticulating with the utmost ferocity.

A stop must be put to this.

The second volley was, consequently, directed on the second boat.

Lieutenant Vere now paid his attentions solely to the luff, whom he began to look upon as a very dangerous enemy.

"Fire!" came the startling command.

This was followed immediately by the simultaneous reports of three or four fire-arms.

The damage done this time was not so great—at least, not so damaging to human life.

The luff of the "San Josef" staggered from the bows of the boat, and would have fallen over the side, but that he was caught in the stalwart arms of one of the pirates.

At first it seemed that he was shot through the head.

But, on a nearer inspection, it was discovered that the bullet had only glanced along his forehead.

The luff thought he was killed, no doubt.

But he did not like the idea of being cut off so suddenly.

Especially now that he was in virtual command of the "San Josef."

When he was told that it was only a flesh wound, great was his rejoicing.

But he felt very giddy and ill all the same.

The only other shot that told out of the volley was one that inflicted a slight wound on the left wrist of one of the oarsmen.

But he merely took the time to ascertain whether there was any bone broken or not, and finding that there was not, he went on with his work as coolly and as calmly as ever.

"That 'ere volley was not so good as the first," said Jerry. "I'm glad, however, that that cowardly skunk of a luff got the full benefits of the lieutenant's shot."

"I am sorry to say that I see little difference in him," said Lieutenant Vere, who overheard the remark. "The bullet must only have glanced across his forehead. I meant that it should have passed through his brain."

"Better luck next time, yer honour," said Bob.

"No, my good fellow," rejoined the lieutenant. "I am afraid that I have given him something that he'll profit by. Depend upon it, in future he'll keep out of harm's way.

Harry was right.

The luff of the "San Josef" stood no longer in the bows, but got well into the stern-sheets.

He had too much respect for his head to risk it again by making himself a target for the enemy to fire at.

He cursed himself again and again that he had not got his pistols with him.

It was a piece of the most foolish oversight that he had left his fire-arms in the care of the executioner, who was so great a dolt as not to secure the armoury on his leaving it.

He was resolved, however, that the executioner should suffer for this lack of duty the moment he returned to the "San Josef."

Every now and then a shout of triumph would go up from the pirates as they saw that they were gaining on the buccaneer boat.

But soon this shout would change to yells of pain, curses, and blasphemy, as some one of their number would get hit by the unerring shot of a buccaneer.

But the issue promised to be speedy.

And all, indeed, in favour of the pirates, for what resistance could the few buccaneers, encumbered as they were with two girls, make to so many strong men, armed with yataghans and cutlasses as they were?

There seemed no hope.

The "Will-o'-the-Wisp" was bearing down upon them very quickly it is true.

But they could be all murdered a very long time before the brig came up.

Lieutenant Vere viewed all now with a keen despair.

His anxiety was not for himself or the buccaneers, but for his pretty gentle wife and Minnie Atherton.

What would become of them?

Better indeed to kill them with his own hand than that they should fall into the clutches of the pirates.

He knew their merciless natures only too well.

He knew that they were the veriest cowards living one moment, and the next the most brutal and cruel butchers.

What was to be done?

They had expended most of their ammunition in firing, and latterly, indeed, with little effect, as the pirates in each boat kept a look-out now, who warned them when the buccaneers were going to fire.

So the pirates at last were always prepared,

and threw themselves at the bottom of the boat until the storm of shot passed over.

Which, in consequence, inflicted very little injury.

The buccaneers soon saw how utterly helpless they were.

The pirates each moment increased their speed whilst they were compelled to slacken theirs. For what can a few brave men do against so many?

The climax was approaching.

The struggle was nearly at its end, and the buccaneers were thoroughly exhausted and worn out by their long and fatiguing exertions.

And it seemed to all in the boat that they could not hold out much longer.

Then why waste their strength, but prepare to meet their pursuers with their good cutlasses and other arms in their hands?

If it had to be a struggle, they would take good care to make it a fearful one, and one, indeed, that would thin the numbers of the pirates materially.

Better to die fighting with arms in their hands than to agree to a base surrender, which they knew would only bring them the most violent of deaths, to say nothing of tortures which these wretches the pirates, were well known to inflict on their enemies.

Death before surrender!

This, then, was their battle-cry.

"I say, Bob," whispered Jerry, "this seems to be a gone case, doesn't it? There seems to be no chance of escaping them 'ere pirates, does there?"

Bob shook his head ruefully.

"I think not, Jerry. I fears as how there is no more chance fer us, lad."

"That's my opinion, Bob. I don't care so much for myself, though."

"Nor do I."

"It's the poor wimmen as I looks to."

"Same here."

"Do you think there's no way o' savin' them, Bob?"

"There may be; but, upon my word, I can't see it."

"Think again," said Jerry. "Is there nothink in yer proolific brain, Bob, as 'll get 'em out of a difficulty?"

"I can't see it," repeated Bob, again.

"Nonsense! I know yer can if yer only likes. Think, Bob, think."

Bob did think, and hit upon a very novel plan.

"Well?" said Jerry.

"I've got it," said Bob.

"Hurrah!" burst forth Jerry.

"Hold hard, Jerry. Don't make such a row," said Bob. "It's only an experiment."

"I knows all about that."

"And if it fails?"

"It'll not fail, Bob."

"How do you know, you lubber, you?"

"I'm sure it'll not. What is the plan, Bob?"

"I thought you knew all about it," said Bob.

"Now, yer asking just proves to me that you don't."

"Who said that I did, you lubber?"

"You are a donkey, Jerry."

"And you are an ass, Bob."

"Well, a donkey and an ass, you fool, is all the same. But no matter. I'll tell you my plan."

"Do so, Bob."

Bob began scratching his head, as if to collect his scattered ideas.

While his companion put on a look of the most profound attention.

But Bob evidently took a different view of the case after a moment's reflection.

Whereat Jerry was much disappointed.

Bob, to mollify his rising wrath a little, hinted

that time did not admit of him explaining his plans.

Of course, with this explanation Jerry had to be satisfied.

"Jerry!"

"Yes, Bob."

"I think I saw you with a piece of old tarpaulin."

"Well?"

"I wants that 'ere tarpaulin. I'll have some very good use to make of it presently."

Jerry dived his hand into his pocket, and handed over the tarpaulin forthwith.

Whereupon Bob took one of the loaded pistols from his belt, and wrapped it up very carefully in it.

"What's the meaning of this?" cried Jerry.

"You'll see presently," was the answer. "Now, all I wants is for 'em to fire one more volley, and then I'm off."

Jerry Mizzen was puzzled.

Where was the noble Bob off to?

But as Bob would not volunteer any more explanations, Jerry muttered—

"Off, indeed! I think the poor feller is going off his nut, that's sartin."

The pirates had pulled so rapidly, that they were not many boats lengths off now.

A shout of triumph burst from their throats.

In another few moments they would have the unfortunate buccaneers in their power.

"Lieutenant Vere," whispered Bob, going over to him. "Give the devils a volley, as I means putting a stop to their gallop."

Harry was beginning to have an excellent idea of Bob Hauler's powers of strategy.

A glance full of intelligence passed between the buccaneer and his officer.

The lieutenant gave the order, and four pistols and one matchlock belched forth their contents of death.

The boat was enveloped in a thick cloud of smoke.

The aims had been very true.

Hoarse cries of pain went up from the pirates in the first boat, and their progress was delayed for a moment.

Bob Hauler, in the confusion and smoke that ensued, swung himself over the side of the boat, and diving into the sea, made direct for the pirates.

So quickly and cleverly was this done, that no one missed him.

Bob was one of the best swimmers on the "Will-o'-the-Wisp," and by far the best diver.

He could keep under water a very long time, so that his present feat did not come amiss to him.

Before the pirates could recover from their dismay, and pick up their wounded, our brave buccaneer came up alongside of them.

While he was under water a very bright idea came into his mind.

It was, if possible, to capsize the pirates' boat.

First of all he would try the pistol shot, the report of which he knew would go a great way to frighten and increase their confusion.

The reason that he dived into the sea may now be palpable enough to our readers.

First, it was his intention to fire a bullet through the pirates' boat below the water-mark.

This was the reason that he was so careful about his pistol.

And to guard against any miscarraige of his plans, he took the precaution to wrap the pistol in the old piece of tarpaulin which Jarry gave him.

Which had the effect he anticipated.

As it keep the pistol nice and dry.

But to return to Bob.

When his head appeared above the water, along-side the first of the pursuing boats he was made aware of the great confusion in the midst of the pirates, who were doing all in their power to alleviate the sufferings of their wounded comrades.

Bob instantly saw that the time for action had come, and that if he remained there much longer he must be discovered.

Our buccaneer was as quick to act as he was to think.

Lightly gripping a hold of the boat with one hand, he very quickly and dexterously removed the covering of tarpaulin from his pistol.

He found the arm perfectly dry, and ready for use.

So, cocking it, he took aim and fired.

The report of a pistol so close to them threw the pirates into great consternation, more especially as one of their comrades uttered a piercing yell of agony.

Bob Hauler's shot had pierced the boat as if it was pasteboard, and passed through one of the ruffian's legs.

Now was the time for capsizing the boat.

The smoke from the pistol completely hid him from view.

And as most of the pirates rushed for the other side, not knowing well where the shot had come from, it was a very easy matter even without Bob's great strength to capsize them.

A sudden exertion of his arms and shoulders together, with all the strength of his body combined, sent the boat over on its side, and the remaining pirates losing their seats, and rolling also in that direction, overturned the craft completely.

The next moment, at least, between twenty and thirty men were struggling helplessly in the water.

And what was fortunate at the time for the buccaneers, there seemed no chance of saving them.

The pirates in the other boat now with cries of alarm put out to their assistance.

It would evidently take a long time to pick them all up.

And it was more than likely that many of them —especially the wounded — would find watery graves.

Bob Hauler, seeing that nothing further could be done at present to increase the confusion of the enemy, struck out for the boat of his friends, which had now paused in its course, wondering very much for a moment how the boat of their enemies had been capsized.

Jerry was the first to miss his old comrade, and wondered very much where he had gone.

It did not strike him for an instant that Bob meditated anything so dangerous as the errand he went on.

Lieutenant Vere was also puzzled for a minute.

He soon, however, guessed the real state of affairs when he heard the report of the pistol, and saw the gallant Bob making his way through the water back to the boat.

"Gallant fellow!" thought Harry. "He's worth his weight in gold."

They now pulled a little way back to take Bob in.

And a few instants later the brave fellow was, as calmly as if nothing had occurred, sitting in the stern-sheets, where both lieutenants shook him by the hand, and complimented him on his brave and gallant act.

If Jerry had not been a sincere friend of Bob Hauler's, it is very likely that he would now have been jealous of him.

But, like the others, he rejoiced in his old comrade's success, and was very proud to hear the words of praise that were lavished on him.

The pirates, however, were not so long as might have been expected in picking their comrades up.

There were some of them sank before they got assistance.

But these were principally the wounded.

The capsized boat was at last righted and manned by those that remained of its former crew.

When all was righted, the word was given again to start, and the pirates, with hoarse yells of rage, were once more in the wake of the buccaneer boat, which, by this time, had got a good distance ahead of them.

Each minute, however, decreased that distance, and the crews of the pirate boats promised once more to come up with the buccaneers.

But the most energetic of all intentions will sometimes fail, and this our friends of the "San Josef" soon discovered to their cost.

When within about eight or nine boat-lengths of the little craft ahead of them, they became conscious of a strange upheaving of the sea.

What could it portend?

Surely not an earthquake or an eruption beneath the ocean?

They glanced at the rolling of the sudden, tremendous billows, and wondered—nay, were terrified.

The billows grew larger.

The foam bubbled and boiled in their wake.

Paralysed, they threw down their oars, and with horror in their hard bronzed faces looked from one to the other for an explanation.

All that they could see was that the waves grew larger and larger, and that the sea boiled like some huge, gigantic cauldron.

But, to their greater horror, the solution to all these strange and terrific evidences came soon enough.

There was one last terrific upheaving of the sea, and the boat was tossed up high in the air with its living freight.

Amid shrieks and yells of agony and horror, a terrible monster appeared above the deep.

It might vie in size with the "San Josef," so gigantic was it.

The boat that was sent up into the air came down smashed to atoms, and the struggling forms of its crew struggled for dear life among the immense billows.

For a moment the great fiery eyes of this extraordinary sea monster rolled furiously, and with a tremendous snort that nearly capsized the other boat it sank from view.

The pirates in the second boat, having succeeded in righting their little craft, looked now around them with pale and horror-stricken faces—faces ghastly with terror and dismay.

They were even too helpless to go to the assistance of their drowning comrades, most of whom sank before any aid could be given them.

At last, not seeing the monster appear, they took courage to save the remaining few who were still struggling in this agitated sea.

Now, all this was observed with the most profound astonishment and horror by the crew of the buccaneer boat.

First, the sudden and unexplainable lashing of the ocean.

Then the rolling of huge billows, almost mountainous in height.

Again, the mysterious propelling of the pirate boat into the air.

And, lastly, the appearance of this monstrous sea denizen, that had caused all this disturbance and loss of life.

All that the buccaneers were afraid of was that this huge monster, after paying his respects to the pirates, might pay them a visit.

Every cheek paled at the mere thought.

Even the irrepressible Jerry Mizzen and Bob Hauler were thus affected.

They waited in fear and trembling for the monster's approach.

But after seeing it disappear in the depths of the sea, they calmed down a little, and rather rejoiced than otherwise that he had made his appearance so unexpectedly and in so summary a fashion.

It was fortunate, indeed, for them that this unexpected yet horrible incident came about, for they were, using an oft-quoted expression, on their last legs.

They were so thoroughly exhausted from their efforts to get away, that they found it next to impossible to continue them much longer.

So they presently began to look upon this terrible monster's interference as a most wonderful dispensation of Providence.

They now beheld, to their great joy, that the pirates had had enough of the chase, and that after they saved as many as they could of their comrades, they were putting slowly and discontentedly back in the direction of the " San Josef."

Indeed, the " San Josef" remained almost stationary where the boats had left it.

The buccaneers rolled after them a derisive cheer, to which they responded with one of intense fury.

But they kept on their course, and nothing, it was very evident, would induce them to take up the chase again.

In time the pirates got back on board their ship, and when they did they tried the effect of a few cannon balls on the little boat, which, however, ploughed up the sea a long way astern of it.

They were out of distance, and the buccaneers could snap their fingers at them, and make all the derisive motions they liked, which could easily be seen with the glass.

It must not be imagined for an instant that Mrs. Vere and Minnie Atherton had nothing to say during all this time.

By their encouraging words they helped to keep up the drooping spirits of the crew, and force them to greater and more lively exertion.

They had a great objection at first to remain at the bottom of the boat.

But when Harry explained to them that this was necessary to the buccaneers' well-being, they quietly acquiesced to it.

Let us new pass over the brief time that elapsed before they were taken on board the " Will-o'-the-Wisp."

Need we say that the rejoicings were very great, indeed, on their recovery, and Bob Hauler and Jerry Mizzen were congratulated and praised to their hearts' content, especially when the whole of their peculiar adventures were related.

Captain Tom was now more than ever determined to catch up to the pirate ship.

The sun went down, and darkness came on, and the " Will-o'-the-Wisp " ploughed swiftly through the waters in a direct course for the " San Josef."

The night proved one of storm, however, and when the morning broke the horizon was scanned in vain.

The " San Josef " had wholly disappeared.

CHAPTER CLXVII.

THE " BLUE LOBSTER " AGAIN.

"WELL, shiver my timbers, Bob, here we are at last, and the place doesn't seem a bit altered since we left it."

" Doesn't it ?"

" Not a bit."

" What about Simon Nagg, Jerry, and the ' Blue Lobster ' ?"

" Well, he's gone, to be sure; but the ' Blue Lobster ' is owned by someone else—a darned sight a better feller than ever Simon Nagg was. I just heard so in the village."

" Fie, Jerry !" cried Bob. " One would think yer knowed better."

" Eh ?"

" I say one would think yer knowed better than to be speaking sich nonsense," repeated Bob. " To go and believe what idle villagers says is monstrous."

" I didn't know that," said Jerry, innocently. " Ain't the villagers as good as anybody else, Bob ?"

The buccaneer shrugged his shoulders in disgust.

" Not a bit of it," he replied.

" How does yer come to that conclusion ?"

" Because they're an idle, back-biting lot, as knows everybody's business but their own."

This was, indeed, information for Jerry Mizzen, who, having been a villager once himself, was going to reply rather hotly to it.

But his intention was interrupted by the appearance of a third party on the scene.

A tall, sinister-looking man, dressed in black, with a broad-brimmed hat slouched well over his brows.

" Hallo, Bob ! Who the deuce is this ?"

" The devil, I suppose," replied Bob, carelessly. " He's got a villainous-looking face, whoever he is."

" And there's a sea-going cut about him," said Jerry. " But I'll swear not an honest one."

" Put him down for a pirate," quoth Bob. " Give me a chaw of baccy, Jerry. I left mine at the last tavern."

" I'd like to give him a chew in the eye," said Jerry, meditatively, as he watched the stranger coming up. " I don't at all like the cut of his jib, Bob."

" Nor I. But where's that chaw of baccy ?"

" I forgot that, Bob. Here you are."

Jerry, in the meantime, pulled about an ounce of " twist " out of his pocket, which he handed over to his comrade.

" Thankee !" said Bob. " Now we are straight again."

Our buccaneer took out his knife, and cut the long piece of twist in two even parts.

One part he rolled up and shoved into his mouth, and by direct manipulation, got between his gums and his teeth.

The other part he put in his pocket.

By this time the man in the black suit had come up.

It was growing dusk, so that they could not very readily discern his features, concealed as they were by the slouched hat.

" Good afternoon," said the suspicious-looking stranger.

" Same to you, old feller," said Bob. " But I think as how it's getting like evening now."

" So it is," replied the stranger.

" Thank you," said Bob.

" What do you thank me for ? " asked the stranger.

" Nothing at all," replied Bob. " It's just a habit I have vich I contracted in my infancy. No offence, I hope ?"

" Oh, no ! Not the slightest," replied the stranger. " I suppose you know pretty well all of the country around here ?"

" Pretty much every inch of it," said Bob.

" Seafaring man ?"

" Something of that 'ere kind," said Bob.

" You are a rum fellow," said the stranger.

" So they tells me," said Bob.

" And your comrade ?"

"Is the same. The rummer he is, the better I like him."

"No, no!" cried the stranger, "I don't mean that. His profession you say is—"

"Between a brigand and a man-o'-war's man," replied Bob, without a smile on his face.

"Equivalent to a pirate, I suppose?" said the stranger, with a grating laugh.

"You've just hit it; you couldn't have done it better," rejoined Bob, with imperturbable gravity.

But the man in the ebony clothes and slouched hat was just as imperturbable.

Jerry Mizzen's curiosity was awakened as to how all this would end.

He tried to derive some intelligence from Bob's face, but failed.

"Any more questions to ask?" said Bob.

"Only a few more, and then I'll be done."

"Curse his infernal impudence!" muttered Jerry. "I never heerd the like It's a great wonder to me that Bob hasn't given him one on the conk afore this."

It was indeed surprising that such an irascible fellow as Bob had not done so sooner.

But there was something in the stranger's manner that prevented him.

"You know the 'Blue Lobster?'" said the sinister-looking gentleman.

"Perfectly."

"It was kept by one Simon Nagg?"

"To be sure."

"Not the same proprietor now, I hear?"

"No."

"Simon Nagg went away. Did you ever hear where he went to?"

"No."

"Ner his wife?"

"Neither of 'em. I don't poke my nose into other people's affairs as much as that."

"No, I suppose not. You don't look like it—ha! ha! ha! Come, answer me one thing, my good fellow."

"I am not yer good feller," said Bob, "and never means to be either."

"Now it's coming!" thought Jerry.

But Jerry was wrong.

Bob was as cold as a piece of ice.

And it takes warm blood, as everybody knows, to fire one up to the pitch of an assault.

"No offence, I hope?" said the stranger, apologetically.

"None at all," said Bob. "Purceed with yer werry mild questioning, old feller."

"He rather likes it," thought Jerry. "But how long he'll continue to do so is a hoss of another colour."

"Well, then, I suppose you knew an old gentleman named Gregory. John, I believe, is his name. He had property about here."

"I knew him very well," replied Bob. "He was a very great friend of mine."

"Oh, indeed! And is he living round here now?" asked the stranger.

"No," replied Bob, "fer one day he werry mysteriously disappeared, and another feller, as had no right at all there, came into the property. Perhaps you have heard of him?"

"I can't say that I have," returned the stranger.

"His name's Sanderson, and he was a lieutenant once in his Majesty's navy," said Bob.

"A relative, I suppose?"

"Nothing o' the kind, ole feller."

"Well, how, in the name of goodness, could he come into the property when he was no relation?"

"By fraud and violence," replied Bob.

"Well, you say the old gentleman has disappeared. Has anything ever been heard of him since?"

"Twice," replied Bob.

"Dear me! You surprise me. Twice say you?"

"Twice," repeated Bob. "Once in a loonatic asylum, and another time—"

But our buccaneer stopped.

He thought he was going a little too far

"And the other time?" prompted the stranger

"I think I've told yer just about enough," said Bob; "so yer gets no more out of me—not if I knows it."

"Come, come, there's a good fellow."

"You can 'good feller' me as long as yer likes; but I thinks as how I've told yer a little too much already."

"Will nothing tempt you to go any farther?"

"Nothing as you can bring to bear on me," replied Bob.

"Don't be obstinate."

"Curse his impudence!" thought Jerry. "What a darned impertinent fellow he must be! I wonder why Bob puts up with him. I'd have knocked the piratical-looking lubber in the eye long since."

But Bob was as cool as a cucumber.

He was not a bit put out.

Now, all this was surpassingly strange to Jerry.

But if he knew what Bob had in his mind he would not think so.

"Don't be obstinate," said the stranger. "What do you say to a couple of guineas?"

"I says nothing to 'em."

"I mean giving them to you."

"What odds?"

"Well, you are a strange fellow."

"Have you only found that out now? First you waste yer precious breath in calling me a rum feller, and now because I can't see my way clear to two guineas, I'm a cussedly strange feller. Although you didn't say cussedly, I'll admit."

"Two guineas are not to be earned, then?"

"I didn't say anything about two guineas being earned. I only says as how yer wasting yer precious breath all to no purpose."

Bob had his suspicions.

And Bob acted in this perfectly stolid and puzzling manner to find out whether he was right or wrong.

The man with the sinister-looking face could, to use a well-worn expression, make neither head nor tail of him.

What object had he to ask all these questions?

Who was he?

Where did he come from?

And what benefit would he derive if he got them all answered?

These were the questions that Bob Hauler asked of himself.

He had come on shore from the "Will-o'-the-Wisp" for a certain object.

In the furtherance of this object he had been accompanied by Jerry Mizzen.

The two old comrades were as one—inseparable.

Wherever one went the other was also sure to follow.

And though their quarrels were frequent, and often came to blows, they were always the best of friends ten minutes after.

Captain Tom and Ben Barnacle were also away from the brig.

They had a great object to accomplish.

And this they hoped to accomplish successfully before they returned to the "Will-o'-the-Wisp."

But as, at any moment, the authorities might get wind that the quiet little vessel lying out in the Sound was the buccaneer brig, they could not act too cautiously.

Moreover, those who had left the "Will-o'-the-Wisp" were all in the same neighbourhood, though separated perhaps a few miles from each other.

Strange to say, that Bob, though he viewed the sinister-looking gentleman suspiciously, he had no wish to avoid him.

He now rather fancied that he had seen him before.

Where he could not tell.

But that he had seen him he was certain.

"Now," thought Bob, "I wouldn't mind betting my head to a farthing that 'ere piratical-looking gent knows a little more'n he pretends. Besides all this, I'm as sartin as of my life that he come from that 'ere Angel or devil as they call him—the captain of the pirate schooner. I don't know whether it would exactly do to tell him the second place we heard from the old genelman. The varmint might get suspicious. No, I'll not tell him. But I see he's anxious to find out something. Very good, my hearty. But it's not yer guineas as'll find out anything, I can tell yer. It takes a curious coon to come over Bob Hauler. He's not so green as he's cabbage-looking."

"As you seem to be so determined, my friend, to withhold what you were going to communicate—"

"I beg yer pardon, old feller," said Bob, quickly interrupting him; "I thinks as how you're perverting the truth. I wasn't a-going to make any communication."

"No!"

"Certainly not. What do yer take me for? A fool?"

"On the contrary, I think you a very sharp fellow, and as you will not tell me, I will not force you. But I'll tell you what you can do."

"What?"

"Do you know the Blue Lobster?"

"Certainly. You know that as well as I do."

"Well, will you meet me there at ten to-night? It will be to your advantage if you do."

"Well, I never refuses a good chance," said Bob. "But what is the object? All talk and no cider? Eh?"

"Not so. I think you'll leave pretty well satisfied, with a purse of gold more in your pocket than when you came in."

"Good!"

"You'll be there, then?"

"Of course, I will."

"Precisely at ten?"

"Just to the minute! When the clock strikes the last stroke of ten, you'll see me. And perhaps before," added Bob to himself. "There's something there as I wants to find out werry badly. Black Bill, as they calls him, 'll be meditating some treachery."

With that, the sinister-looking stranger bidding the two inseparable comrades good-bye, sauntered along the country lane, and soon disappeared from sight.

"A strange coon that," said Jerry, looking after his disappearing figure with a curious eye. "I wonder, Bob, that you took half of his impudence from him."

"Do you?" rejoined Bob. "It's a good thing, Jerry, as you wonder at something, anyhow. As for me, I never wonders at anything. I am so used to the ways of the world now, that if you told me that the moon was made of green cheese I wouldn't doubt yer word."

"I say, Bob, what the deuce was he a-driving at all the time?"

"Now, Jerry, will yer take my adwice?"

"Sartinly, Bob."

"Then don't ask too many questions, and people won't tell you too many lies."

"Humph! You are mighty independent, Bob. I never asks you a question but you gives an evasive answer."

"Well, then, that ought to teach you to be werry careful," replied Bob. "And now don't be sticking yer nose into affairs as doesn't consarn you."

Jerry, seeing how futile his efforts were to get anything out of Bob, collapsed and said no more.

The "Blue Lobster," the country tavern introduced to the reader at an earlier stage in our story —had not very much changed since we were there last.

The proprietorship, of course, had passed into the hands of another.

Our readers may ask was it for the better?

Our reply is decidedly in the negative.

The same disreputable characters met there as when Simon Nagg had it.

Smugglers, tramps, and vagabonds of all descriptions.

Besides, in the bar-room of the "Blue Lobster" all the gossip of the surrounding country was freely discussed and adjudicated upon.

Whether it was a death, or a marriage, or a capture of poachers, or a piece of unusual scandal, and sometimes to a piece of very common scandal, indeed, such as one man running away with another man's wife, and leaving a family of six or seven small children to subsist on nothing, or if not able so to do, to fall into the clutches of the parish authorities—the beadle and men of that ilk, to wit.

Nor had the "Blue Lobster" changed in its exterior appointments a bit.

The same old sign swung there as usual, and creaked and screeched in every gust of wind as it had always done.

As for the walls, they had never been whitewashed since Simon Nagg left it, and if the ghost of that respectable and amiable gentleman could visit the sphere of his former labours, he would have been highly delighted to find that not a single alteration had been made in it.

To the "Blue Lobster" Jerry and Bob then made their way as the darkness came on.

When they passed under the rude porch, their ears were saluted by some snatches of an old song —a song, indeed, well remembered by them, as they had heard it often before.

As they passed in, a dense cloud of tobacco-smoke met them in the face.

Their nostrils were also affected more or less by the fumes of the various liquors that were then and there being consumed.

But such trivial matters as these had only a passing interest for our worthy buccaneers, who, without pausing to listen to the snatches of the song, or to inhale the pleasant odours of the liquors, passed into the bar-room.

Here they found over a dozen men seated at a substantial table, each having his grog or his ale before him.

They were for the most part a rough-looking lot, with faces bronzed and as hard as iron.

These fellows, when Bob and Jerry entered, turned their attention from the singer, a dark, villainous-looking man, to the new-comers.

Keen and even suspicious glances were bent on them.

But our buccaneers, before leaving the "Will-'o-the-Wisp," took the precaution to come thoroughly disguised.

So the looks were bent in vain.

For not one in the room knew them.

The vocalist, perceiving that the attention was diverted from himself, paused in his song, and also threw a curious glance at our friends, as much as to say—

"Who the deuce are you, that my singing is to be stopped in this manner?"

Bob, catching this man's ferret-like eyes fixed inquiringly upon him, winked, and then slapped his

THE YOUNG LADY CONTINUED READING, UNCONSCIOUS OF THE PRESENCE OF HER ENEMY.

forefinger to the side of his nose to give a more graceful emphasis to the action.

Whether the man was offended by this mode of Bob's or not, it is hard to say.

He did not speak not even wink.

But frowned as black as a thunder cloud, much to Hauler's gratification and amusement.

The man appeared to measure him from head to foot, as if to find whether it was of any use to quarrel with him.

But the inspection, brief as it was, assured him that it was not.

And that if he attempted such a thing, he might very likely get the worst of it.

Having satisfied his conscience on this point, he once more resumed his song, amid a noisy clanging of pewter pots and a clinking of glasses, which using an expression of a once amiable friend of ours, was a caution to deaf adders.

The song finally came to a conclusion.

So did the man's liquor.

He called for more, and was served.

Meanwhile, Bob Hauler and Jerry Mizzen were enjoying themselves over two glasses of steaming grog punch, and a couple of long pipes.

The comrades, without appearing to take any notice of the rest of the company, were conversing in low tones.

"Yes, Jerry," said Bob, "I shouldn't wonder but as how Black Bill would like to make our acquaintance. I observed him taking stock of me—curse him! But I think he thought better of it, and left well enough alone."

"He's a black, treacherous thief enough!" said Jerry, puffing away at his pipe.

"You are right, old pal. A more treacherous scoundrel doesn't exist."

"I believe as how he must fancy he has a good voice," said Jerry. "I'm sure he thinks as how he can beat a nightingale to pieces."

'Why do you think that?" asked Bob.

'Because he's always a-singing, I'm sure," said Jerry. "He must have fallen in love with his own voice, or he wouldn't continue to go on in that way."

"Oh, indeed!" said Bob, laughing. "I think it's hypocrisy, Jerry—downright hypocrisy!"

"What's hypocrisy?"

"That man's singing."

"Don't yer think he means it?"

"Not a bit of it."

"Then he must be an outrageous villain."

"A wolf in lamb's clothing, Jerry. For them as sings and whistles have generally their hearts in the right places."

"You are right, Bob. I do a good deal of whistling and singing myself."

"Werry complimentary, and werry proper," said Bob. "You always affects me werry much, Jerry, when I hears yer praising yerself. It's delightful exercise, Jerry, especially for one's wanity. But, hallo! Pay attention to this, the newest piece of scandal on the board."

Bob and Jerry's undivided attention was now attracted to a little man who sat at the extreme end of the bar-room smoking a pipe half as long as himself, and taking an occasional draught out of a pewter tankard which stood close to his hand.

This insignificant little individual was regaling the company with the latest piece of scandal.

"Yes," he said, "it is true, gentlemen. Wilkinson did run away with Groggins's wife, and left eight of a family behind him.

'Some said it was through one thing.

"Some said another.

"But none of them knew as much as I did of the matter.

"For fourteen years, gentlemen, I made and mended boots for the Grogginses, and found them always good payers and very desirable customers.

"That 'ere Wilkinson was always a scamp.

"For look you, gentlemen, didn't he kill his first wife?"

A profound sensation in the bar-room, followed by an elevation of pewter pots and steaming grog glasses!

"What did he do with her?

"And what did he do with his second?

"Poor thing! he drove her into a madhouse!"

This announcement created a perfect storm of hisses.

The little shoemaker's importance was swelling visibly, for between the pipe and glass and his story he pitched his voice into a very high key indeed.

Not only did he do this, but he arose to his feet that he could roll his words out with greater effect.

"I always said that Wilkinson was a scamp," thundered the little shoemaker, "and now I am more than ever convinced of it.

"What do you think he did to me last year?"

"What? What?" cried several voices.

"Well, I'll tell you, gentlemen," said the little man, lowering his voice impressively. "He had the infernal impudence, and confounded audaciousness, to come to my place a twelvemonth last Michaelmas and order a pair of boots."

'There's a man with a grievance!" whispered Jerry.

"I thought as much," said Bob. "But don't let 'em catch us talking, or the little fire-eater will shut up."

"Yes, gentlemen, he had the confounded impudence and owdaciousness—and I say this advisedly—to come over to my place and order a pair of boots.

"I was struck at first with the coolness of the thing.

"Then I viewed the action in as grave a light as possible.

"But I never lost my temper, never, gentlemen, for an instant."

"What a pity!" whispered Bob.

"A downright shame!" responded Jerry.

"No, gentlemen, I never lost my temper for an instant, I say, and if anything, I was even calmer than I am at this moment.

"I thought to myself, 'so you come to order a pair of boots, do you?'

"'You haven't paid me for the heels of them 'ere other ones I fixed up for you.'

"'You are a precious scoundrel, you are!'

"However, gentlemen, I kept my temper.

"'Grubbins,' said he, 'you know how I like my boots?'

"'Pretty reasonable, sir,' said I.

"'I don't mean that,' said he. 'You can charge what you like for 'em, so as you make 'em good.'

"'Very good, sir,' said I, for I was determined to act respectful like to the very last. 'Perhaps you'll now pay me for the heels of them other ones,' said I.

"'What other ones?' said he.

"'Why, them as I heeled for you last Christmas,' said I.

"'Goodness gracious me, Grubbins,' said he, 'they quite escaped my memory.'

"I had no doubt of that, gentlemen.

"But to make a long story short, his blarney got the better of me, and I made him the boots, and to sarve him out as I thought, put two or three shillings more on to them."

"Which he didn't dispute, of course?" said some of the company.

"I must own, gentlemen, that he didn't dispute the price at all.

"But the thing is he took the boots, wore them several months, forgot all about your humble servant, and when I sent in my bill, what do you think he did?"

"Perhaps paid you for them," said one.

"No he didn't—guess again."

"Sent you the price of the heels, then?"

"He didn't even do that," said the little shoemaker. "Perhaps some of you other gentlemen will guess."

The index finger of his right hand was very emphatically pointed to Bob Hauler and Jerry Mizzen.

"Perhaps some of you gentlemen will guess," he repeated.

"Told you to go home and bag your head," replied Bob.

"Or tallow yer nose," said Jerry.

The little shoemaker turned away from the foregoing gentlemen with a look of deep contempt.

Intellectually, he thought they were decidedly beneath him.

Decidedly beneath his notice.

Some of the company scowled at Bob and Jerry.

And our two friends, not much put out, returned the compliment with interest.

"As no one can guess," said the little shoemaker, "and as moreover two gents in the company have been decidedly insulting, I'll tell you what he did.

"He sent the shoes back after having worn them for six months, with his compliments.

"The man who will do that, gents, is no gentleman—a bad man, and will come to a bad end.

"I even go so far as to prophesy that he will die a dog's death!"

"What, for not paying for a pair of boots, mate?" cried Jerry.

"I am not addressing myself to you, sir," replied the little man, "I have noticed your insulting conduct before, sir, and I speak advisedly, sir. So now, if you please, sir, you will keep quiet and not be a bone of contention, or an eyesore to the company."

"Say no more, Jerry," whispered Bob. "The little man is vain. Let him go on."

After this advice from Bob, Jerry Mizzen collapsed, and the little shoemaker, highly gratified that his words had taken so much effect on the enemy, sat down, took up his tankard, and drunk success to the company all round, but parenthetically leaving out the two strangers from any such consideration.

He now resumed his pipe, and puffed quietly for a few seconds.

And, as if the company expected that he was not done yet, they kept very quiet.

After having collected his thoughts a little, and puffed away at his "long clay" for a moment or two, the little man began again.

"There's an old saying, gentlemen," said he, "that it's an ill wind that blows no one good.

"The Grogginses, since Mrs. Groggins left 'em, are much better off now than they were ever before.

"Everything seems to prosper with 'em.

"Two or three—I don't mean to say, gentlemen, that I know the exact number—but either two or three of the cows calved yesterday.

"Besides, one mare had the pleasure to-day, at twelve o'clock and thirty minutes precisely, of foaling.

"This all seems most extraordinary, gentlemen.

"But I'll venture to say that if Mrs. G. had not run away with that rascal and lying thief, Wilkinson, the cows and mare would have gone all the other way."

"They would have gone back on their breeding, perhaps," said Jerry.

Whereupon the company viewed Jerry with much favour, and even laughed heartily at his witticism.

The only man who seemed to look at our buccaneer's interruption in the light of a grievance was the little shoemaker.

The audacity of Jerry was unparalleled in his eyes.

To him, at least, the witticism was intolerable.

In the excitement of the moment, he dropped his pipe.

It smashed into a dozen pieces.

But even here his troubles did not end.

As he was speaking a few minutes later, and to add greater force to his words, he brought his hand down, as he supposed, on the table.

But he seemed to forget the exact spot where stood his tankard of beer, for not a moment before had he it replenished.

Down came his hand.

It did not meet the table.

The tankard received a blow that sent it right into another man's face, who bent forward to catch the full effects of the little shoemaker's words, was deluged over with beer, and not only deluged with over beer, but received a stunning crack from the pewter measure.

"That's the effects of virtuous indignation," observed Bob, placidly; "and who's to blame for it but you, Jerry?"

Though Bob Hauler was placid, the recipient of this unexpected favour was not.

Nearly smothered with beer, and howling from the force of the blow, he made directly for the man of leather, and not waiting to ask whether the offence was intended or not, slipped into him without a moment's delay or hesitation.

Being a larger and brawnier man than the shoemaker, the shoemaker, of course, had no chance.

Before he could even get out of danger, a well-directed blow sent him clear over the table, where he had the misfortune to land into the arms of Black Bill.

Black Bill had his head severely bumped against the panelling.

Now, as the smuggler was at that moment in a very profound meditation, and as a lump on the side of his head as big as a pigeon's egg was the result of the unfortunate Grubbins' coming up against him, he did not, as might well be expected, relish it.

Uttering a hoarse curse, he rubbed the side of his head, arose to his feet, caught the little shoemaker in his brawny arms, and forthwith threw him back again over the table.

This time Grubbins alighted on the corn of a gentleman who had been listening very eagerly to the earlier part of his discourse.

But whatever respect the said gent had for his powers as a scandal-monger, was lost sight of the moment the poor shoemaker alighted on his corn.

No longer was he bound to respect him.

Physical pain borne must be met by physical pain inflicted.

Without much reasoning, and only giving vent to certain oaths, caused by the pain of his torturing corn, he seized the little shoemaker, and began striking him right and left with his fists, interlarding his exercise with an occasional—

"Take that, you scoundrel! Perhaps it will learn you next time who you tread on."

How long this irate individual would have continued thrashing the poor little shoemaker there is no telling.

The company, instead of interfering with the man's diversion, were highly amused, and all agreed that Grubbins rightly deserved what he got.

But there were, however, two more sympathetic individuals in the company.

These were Bob and Jerry.

They thought the poor little man got much more than he deserved, and as he was in a fair way of being thrashed within an inch of his life, they thought it high time to interfere.

Bob leaped up.

Jerry was also on his feet.

They both rushed forward simultaneously, and, after some expostulation with the man of the corn, succeeded in rescuing the unfortunate Grubbins, who, with tears in his eyes, thanked his preservers, and thinking it is the wisest plan to get away, walked out of the Blue Lobster with all the speed in his power.

CHAPTER CLXVIII.
BOB AND JERRY'S ADVENTURE.

WHEN Bob Hauler and Jerry Mizzen had succeeded in rescuing the little shoemaker from the virtuous rage of the man with the corn, and after seeing Grubbins take his departure from the door, they quietly returned to their seats.

As their glasses were empty, they had them refilled, and, taking up their pipes, went on smoking in silence.

The instant that the shoemaker was gone, order was quickly restored to the somewhat turbulent element of the Blue Lobster.

The man with the corn recovered his usual placidity.

He even expressed his regret for the violent manner of his attack.

It was his opinion that Grubbins wasn't a bad fellow after all, and even if he did at times poke his nose into other people's affairs, he had many qualities that effectually counterbalanced that evil.

He was, on the whole, very sorry indeed for what he had done, and thanked the two strangers collectively and individually for their good services.

And as Grubbins was not present, whom he knew very well to be a highly-respectable and pleasant gentleman, and to show them that there was no ill-feeling in the matter, he would drink that gentleman's good health.

Which he did amidst the applause of certain of Grubbins' supporters.

He had one thing more to say, however.

And that was this—

That it was a matter of very great regret to him that Black Bill should have lost his usual placidity, which he knew was very becoming in a gentleman of his pursuits and profession.

But he knew the noble gent was as sorry for what took place as he was, and that a bump on the side of a gentleman's head, the size of a pigeon's egg, was no joke, delivered intentionally or otherwise.

Having had his say, the man with the corn sat down.

And Black Bill responded.

His speech was very brief indeed.

Black Bill simply said, "Thank you!" and, having gulped down his glass, resumed his seat.

"I think this is what they calls promoting the harmony of the meeting," said Jerry.

"Werry likely," said Bob, "it's now a quarter to ten. I wonder how they'll feel by twelve?"

"Purty lively, I imagine," said Jerry. "They've given us evidence of what they can do already."

"The frequenters o' the Blue Lobster are quite capable of anything—from murder down to manslaughter."

"I see that that 'ere Black Bill is in no werry pleasant humour."

"He's still rubbing his head."

"Must have got a good crack against that panelling."

"I believe you, Bob."

"I wish it had broken his darned neck, for he's a reg'lar viper."

"And as treacherous as Satan."

"What! Satan is an angel compared to him. But hark, Jerry! What are they up to now? I declare speaking of Captain Tom."

"We'll listen, Bob."

"That we will, old son."

"I am very glad that our disguises are so perfect."

"Same here. Otherwise that 'ere cussed Bill would have the coastguards after us by this time. Listen, Jerry, and don't speak a word, for at this point we may be of some service to Captain Tom. If there's any interruption to be made, let it come from me."

The conversation of the habitues of the Blue Lobster bar-room had indeed turned on the affairs of our gallant hero.

"Speaking of Captain Tom Drake," said Black Bill, "I could tell you a queer tale consarning him if I liked."

"I suppose you knew him when he was a lad about here?" said a second speaker, inquiringly.

"Didn't I though, that's all? Why, I knew the whole root and branch of 'em, from John Gregory down," replied the smuggler.

"And that precious Reuben Harpy as well, I'll be bound to say?"

"Yes, and him as well, for he was one of the family, and a nasty sneak he was, too, and as big a coward as ever walked. If you like I'll tell you a story of some of this young gentleman's capers, and perhaps then you'll agree with me."

"Go ahead, by all means!" cried the company.

"Well, then, it was when I was in a more comfortabler situation than I am now, and when I had plenty o' money and plenty o' men, too, to back me.

"One day this young devil comes to the cave, and says he—

"'I suppose your name is Black Bill?'

"'That's my cognomen,' says I. 'What's in the wind?'

"'It's a little sarvice I want you to do for me,' says he.

"'A sarvice?' said I, in my own mind, thinking by the lad's appearance that he couldn't be more that ten or twelve at most, 'I wonder what blessed sarvice a jigger like him wants me to do?'

"'Well,' said I, 'spit it out! Anything gone wrong with yer?'

"'Yes,' he said, 'a good deal. But no matter what's gone wrong. I wants to know whether yer willing to earn a purse o' gold.'

"'A purse o' gold!' cries I, opening my eyes very wide and regarding the little fiend with astonishment. 'Of course I am willing to earn it. Only tell me how it's to be done, and I am yer man.'

"'Listen,' said he. 'I have an enemy up at the Hall, and I wants him removing in the worst possible way.'

"'An enemy!' says I.

"'Yes,' says he. 'An enemy, and I wants you to remove him. He's been in my way a long time,' says he, 'and if you do the thing quickly and well, you shall have the purse of gold.'

"Well, as you may well imagine, I didn't know what to think of this little varmint.

"He was as cool as a cucumber.

"And as innocent-looking as a lamb.

"He meant murder, I knew that very well.

"But as I didn't care murdering any one, and as I didn't know which way else to get the money, I was in a reg'lar quandary, and began a-reflecting like how to get out of it.

"'How old are you?' said I, to gain time.

"'Eleven next birthday,' said he.

"'You are a werry fine lad for that age,' said I.

"'Do you think so?' said he.

"'Yes I do,' said I. 'Perhaps now you'll be a little more explicit like?' said I. 'Who is it that yer wants removing?'

"'First of all promise me that you'll do it,' said the little varmint. 'I am not going to tell you afore you promises me.'

"What could I do but promise?

"'You'll never tell any one?' said he.

"'Certainly not,' said I.

"'Then here goes,' said he, as cool as a piece of ice. 'Perhaps you may know or have seen a boy called Tom Drake?'

"'Bless yer little soul!' said I, 'I know him as well almost as my own mother. He's down here every day a-fishing, and a daring little rascal he is.'

"'That's him,' said he. 'Curse him!' said he. 'He's always been the plague of my life, and my mother hates and detests him,' said he.

"'What is that for?' asked I.

"'Because he's a favourite of my Uncle Gregory's,' said he. 'That's what it's for.'

"Now, what I was to do with this young cuss I didn't know.

"So I reflected.

" The little viper was calmly a-watching of me.

"I could see him eyeing me rather suspiciously.

"'Well,' said I, to myself, 'it's not very often, Black Bill, as you gets the offer of a purse of gold. But as for committing murder—that's against yer nature. Hum! is there no other way o' earning that purse o' gold,' said I, 'without cutting young Tom Drake's throat?'

"I never did such a thing afore, and I made up my mind I wasn't a-going to do it now.

"After a moment or two's thought, I began to see my way clear o' the difficulty.

"' 'Why not kidnap Tom Drake?' said I, in my mind.

"The thing could be done easily enough.

"Get him aboard some outgoing ship as cabin-boy, or something o' that sort, and there was the money at once.

"But would the little varmint be satisfied with the yarn I'd spin him?

"I could say that I enticed him into a boat, and threw him into the sea.

"That was just my plan, and would answer admirably.

"Having come to this conclusion I looked up.

"'Well,' said the little reptile. 'What's yer answer? Are you going to do it or not? For if you don't I must get somebody as will.'

"'I'll do it,' said I. 'You can depend, young master, that Tom Drake 'll not trouble you much longer. He'll make capital food for the fishes,' said I.

"'Do yo mean that, Black Bill?' said he.

"'In course I do,' replied I. 'Yer ain't a-going to imagine that I'd lose a purse of gold for such a young varmint as that?'

"'No, I should think not,' said he. 'And now when can you do it?' said he.

"'This very night,' I replied. 'You can remove all doubts off yer mind, for he's as good as booked.'

"You should see how the little varmint's eyes sparkled as I told him this.

"He was a merciless little fiend, I can tell you.

"And as I afterwards found out, as great a coward as he was even merciless.

"Well, gents, the little villain, however, had not finished yet.

"He was for prying into the ins and outs of everything

"'How are you going to kill him?" asked he.

"'I ain't a going to kill him,' replied I.

"'No! What then?' said he.

"'I am going to drown him,' replied I.

"'That'll do as well,' said the little varmint. 'Do anything so as you get him out of the way—for ever. Mind, it must be for ever,' said he, putting plenty of stress on the word.

"'Rest yerself content, young master,' I replied. 'The moment Tom Drake gets into my clutches he's a gone coon.'

"'Now listen,' said I, 'and I'll tell you what I mean doing'

"The little reptile cocked up his ear, and drank in every word.

"'Yes, yes—go on,' said he, appearing very anxious to hear how Tom Drake was to be disposed of. 'Go on,' said he, 'I'm all attention.'

"Well, gents, you may imagine I spun him a very good yarn.

"Which was this—

"That as his cousin came down a-fishing every day in the vicinity of my place, that I, on the pretence of showing him a better fishing-place, would entice him into my boat, and when we got out far enough, topple him over into the sea, which, even if he could swim, would be so far out that he couldn't save himself.

"Now this plan seemed to meet the young varmint's approval very much.

"But the part of my bargain was to receive the purse of gold at once.

"'I should like to see the work done first,' said the shrewd little rascal.

"'You would?' said I; 'very well. Come and see it done, then, and bring the gold with you.'

"But do you think he would do this?

"Not he!

"He was too much of a coward to risk his own precious skin.

"Besides, he had too great a dread of his cousin.

"I was very glad, you may be sure, gents, at the time, that the proposal came so readily to my lips.

"'Well, as you won't come,' said I, 'to see the thing done, I'll not move hand or foot in the matter until I get the money.'

"This answer for a moment seemed to confound the little reptile.

"At last he hauled out the gold, saying, as he did so—

"'Here's the money. Now let me see that you won't play me false.'

"'Play you false!' cried I, very angry like. 'Do you doubt my word, then? Ain't I a honourable genelman, as does everything I says? It's a good job you are not a man,' said I.

"'Oh! don't get angry,' rejoined he, for he really believed I was in a temper, and got away as far as he could out of my reach. 'Don't be angry, Black Bill,' said he. 'I didn't mean to doubt yer honesty for a minute, only if you do the thing well there'll be another purse of gold to follow that.'

"With that, this precious Reuben walked off, and I saw no more of him until a couple of days after.

"But I'm going ahead of my story.

"When he was gone, I set about counting the gold, and found fifty-three guineas in the purse.

"'Not bad pay for one day's work,' thinks I. 'I suppose they're all right; they seem to be proper weight, and have the right ring about them.'

"Now, at that time there was a cove as I knew a long while coming backwards and forwards.

"He was the captain of a little schooner, and a bigger devil never walked a quarter-deck.

"You mustn't imagine as how he was a jolly fellow, or anything like that.

"I mean as how he was a devil incarnate, and sart'inly one o' the most unconscionable scoundrels I ever met.

"Now, this was just the very fellow I wanted, and, as we had transacted a few business matters afore together, I thought I'd have have no difficulty in winning him over to take the boy away, and leave him in some foreign land, or some deserted island, where we'd never hear any more of him.

"Now, this fellow's vessel, as it happened, had just come in that day, and was lying in the offing to take in fresh water, and waiting for a bit of a breeze to blow up.

"I got a couple of my fellows together, and we went out there.

"I soon found that he was going to the Indies.

"Also that he wanted a cabin boy.

"But as he was a sly old fox, I kept everything about as dark as I could from him.

"'You wants a cabin boy, I hear,' said I.

"'That's just the very thing I do want,' said he.

"'Well,' said I, 'if you'd like a good one,' said I, 'I think I can get one for you. But it must be on this consideration, that you don't bring him back again.'

"Well, would you believe it, gents, the sly old fox had his suspicions aroused instantly.

"'Ho! ho! Why not bring him back again?'

"'That's my business,' said I. 'However, if you like to take him, you are welcome to him.'

"'Is there no premium?' he asked.

"'Not a penny piece,' said I. 'Take him or leave him, just as you please. If you don't, I'll get some other one as will, and I'll be glad to get him, too,' said I.

"'Stop a minute,' said he. 'You want to get this boy out o' the way?'

"'That's just what I do want,' replied I.

"'And not a penny premium?'

"'Not a farthing nor the fraction of a farthing. But if you like, we'll crack a couple a bottles o' wine over the business, and if that won't do, I must go to some other market.'

"'I calculate I'll take him,' said he. 'So let us have the bottles of wine and seal the agreement.'

"So down we went to the cabin.

"The bottles were opened, and we were soon making ourselves jolly comfortable.

"The captain of the schooner was a shrewd sarpint of a Yankee, named Yates.

"I suppose many among you gentlemen must have known him?

"Very well, then, he shoved the wine into me as fast as he could.

"And all to pick my secret out of me.

"But as I was as shrewd as he was, he made nothing by the operation.

"Now the question was, when was I to bring the boy?

"That night, or the next day?

"'That night,' I replied.

"As the time was fixed on, I shook hands with my shrewd Yankee sarpint, and leaping into my boat, was pulled to the cave.

"Now, the next thing on the board was to get young Tom Drake into my power.

"Mind you, gents, at that time I rather liked the lad, but money was everything, and a purse of gold was not to be picked up every day. Besides, I considered that I was doing him a service, and that going to a foreign land would enable him to see plenty of life, which was just the very thing for him.

"Late that afternoon young Tom came, as was his custom, to do a little fishing.

"I was there all snug enough waiting for him.

"While he was getting his gear into order I came up.

"'Hallo, Master Tom!' said I, seeming surprised to see him. 'You here?'

"'Yes, my hearty,' replied Tom, 'I am here to the good as you see. I should have been away though to-day, but I couldn't resist the temptation of coming down to have a fish.'

"'I am very glad you have come, Master Tom,' said I. 'I was jist a-looking for you, but some one told me that you had gone away.'

"'So I was expecting, Bill,' said he. 'But you see I am here to the good yet. Now, to come to the point,' said he, 'what were you looking for me for?'

"'Just this, Master Tom,' said I, 'I knows of one o' the best fishing places in E gland, and knowing how you delight in good fishing, I thought I'd jist tell you.'

"'Thank you, Bill,' said young Tom, 'I am much obliged to you,' said he. 'But I think as how I know the best fishing places myself.'

"'You do!' cried I. 'You are surely joking, Master Tom,' said I.

"'No I aren't,' said he. 'I've knocked about here long enough to know what is what, and which is which,' said he.

"'The knowing young varmint,' thought I. 'I'll have some trouble with him yet.'

"And so it afterwards proved.

"Tom Drake was a sharp 'un, I can tell you, even in those days.

"I tried all my arts of persuasion to get Tom into the boat.

"But do you think he would go?

"Not he.

"Where young Tom didn't want to go no one could drive him.

"That's a fact.

"However, as I saw that Master Tom wouldn't come to terms nohow, I was determined to use force.

"'Look here, Master Tom,' said I, 'you must get into that boat.'

"'Get into what boat?' said Tom.

"'That boat,' said I.

"'I'll see you blowed first!' said Tom, 'and then I won't.'

"'You won't?' said I.

"'I won't,' said he.

"'Then I'll be under the disagreeable necessity of making you,' said I. 'Come, get into that boat at once, or—'

"'Or what?' said Tom, stepping back, and looking as bold as brass.

"'Or I'll—'

"'You'll what?' said Tom, interrupting of me. 'Do you think, villain, as I'm afeared of you?' cried he.

"And at the same time he broke his fishing-rod in two halves, and gripping the bigger portion in both hands, he made a step or two forward.

"You should see that little devil's eyes, gents.

"Talking about flashing fire—flashing fire was no name for 'em at that moment.

"One would have thought that he would be afeard of such a big fellow as me.

"But not a bit of it.

"He held his ground like a lion.

"I tried to scare him by a look.

"But there was no quailing in Tom's eyes, for he looked straight and unflinchingly into my own.

"'I must confess, gentlemen,' said Black Bill, 'that I was almost ashamed at that moment that I had taken the fifty-three guineas.

"He looked so brave and noble, like.

"But what was done now couldn't be undone.

"And I knew that if I didn't do it somebody else would.

"Now it occurred to me that if I dallied with Master Tom much longer that some one would be coming that way and get him out of my clutches, and then the other fifty-three guineas, which I had set my heart on, would be as good as lost.

"'See here, Master Tom,' said I, 'I don't wish to harm you, and if you get into that boat you'll see everything'll be all right.'

"'And if I don't get into the boat I suppose everything'll be all wrong,' said Tom, provokingly.

"'Yes, and you'll find it so,' replied I. 'Will you listen a moment, Master Tom?' said I.

"'Go ahead. I'm not above listening,' said he.

"'Well, you look here,' said I. 'Me and some of my pals have made a wager.'

"'Indeed,' said he. 'But tell me, how does the wager affect me, my tulip?' said he.

"'Well, in just this way, young master,' returned I. 'We have made a wager that I can't get you to go to the new fishing-grounds with me. They said as how you was so fond of the old ones that you wouldn't move a peg from 'em. I said as how I could make you. You know what I mean, Master Tom; that's not the exact or proper word, perhaps; but I said it at any rate, and they took it up, and in the end we put a stake of five guineas on the result. Now, Master Tom,' said I, 'would you have a poor cove lose all that 'ere money?'

"'Who did you bet with?' asked he.

"'Jerry Mizzen and Bob Hauler,' replied I.

Jerry at this stage of the story nudged Bob with his elbow, and Bob winked his eye in return, as much as to say, "Don't be alarmed, I'm taking everything in."

"'Jerry Mizzen and Bob Hauler,' said Master Tom. 'I thought they had more sense,' said the little varmint.

"'Look here, Black Bill. Your villainous game won't work,' said he. 'And now once for all, if you have pranks to play, play 'em on somebody else.'

"With that, the young cub was walking away.

"Any of you gents may have asked, why hadn't I rushed upon him afore, and taken him by force into the boat?

"That wasn't my object.

"My object was to get him away without making any outcry.

"So I planned and schemed, but all my planning and scheming failed, and I was forced to adopt other measures.

"'Stop, my tulip!' cried I, seeing him shoulder his broken fishing-rod, as if with the intention of giving me the slip; 'stop a minute. We're not going to part company in that way.'

"'Indeed!' said Tom, with a sneer on his lips. 'If I mean going, you are not the one to prevent me, Black Bill. So good-day, and when you are foolish enough again to make wagers, see as how it aren't Tom Drake you make 'em on. Good-day, Black Bill—good-day.'

"'Come, my kiddy!' cried I, in a rage, 'this game has gone far enough.'

"'Too far?' replied he. 'You can, however, give my compliments to Jerry Mizzen and Bob Hauler, and hand them over the money you've lost. But to make sure that you do so,' added he, 'the next time I see Bob and Jerry I'll tell 'em all about it. Good-day again, old rooster.'

"It was no use bandying further words with the cub, so with one bound I gripped him by the shoulder.

"'There's the boat, Master Tom,' said I, 'and that's just the place you'll have to go in, too.'

"'Have to!' cried Tom, getting into a desperate rage. 'I'll show you whether I'll have to or not.'

"He squirmed round about a half-dozen times, and I lost my grip of him.

"'Now!' cried he, 'if you don't want braining, you had better step out of my path.'

"I was on the point of rushing upon him again when he gave me rather a hard one on the side of the head, which, though not quite stunning me, raised a bump as big as a pigeon's egg.

"My blood was up at this, and I was not wanting for a good cudgel in my hand, I went forward again, with the intention of beating his guard down, and in this manner obtaining the mastery over him.

"The task was not so easy, however, as I expected.

"Tom was a very strong lad, besides that, he had the courage of a lion, so when I came up to him, instead of running away, he stood his ground unflinchingly.

"You should see at that moment, gents, how he handled that broken fishing-rod.

"He was a perfect little master of fence, and every blow I aimed at him he parried with the ease of an accomplished swordsman.

"I soon found that Master Tom was giving it to me pretty hot.

"His broken fishing-rod played about my legs in a werry extraordinary manner.

"But it was gall and wormwood to my heart, to be bested by a little scorpion like this, so furiously rushing forward, I broke through his guard, but not without getting a blow that made the blood spout from my head.

"This was a little more than my nature could bear.

"I caught the little varmint in my arms, and would have no doubt strangled him on the spot, but who should come rushing up to his assistance but Jerry Mizzen and Bob Hauler.

"Whether they had been listening to what I was saying or not, I couldn't tell.

"But up they came and threw themselves on me and hurled me back against the rocks.

"'Curses!' cried I, 'what do you mean?'

"'I'll soon show you!' roared Bob, 'if you don't let that 'ere lad alone. You are a coward,' said he, 'to go and attack a mere boy like that.'

"'You think so,' said I, wiping the blood from my face. 'Perhaps I'll give you a chance o' testing that directly.'

"'You can give me a chance now, if you like,' said Bob. 'Don't think I'm afeard of you, Black Bill.'

"'Nor he mustn't think as I am,' said Jerry Mizzen.

"'And as for me, I'll thrash him within an inch of his life,' put in Master Tom. 'All I want is fair play.'

"'Bravo, youngster! We think you've given him enough already,' cried the other two.

"How I cursed the lubbers.

"But all to no use.

"They only laughed at me, and said I richly got what I deserved.

"Seeing that I had no chance now, I hurried from the spot, determined, at least, to have revenge on Bob Hauler and Jerry Mizzen.

"Young Tom's blows left an indelible mark on my mind, and, what was still worse, a deep scar on the side of my head.

"From that moment I never forgave the youngster, and whenever I had a chance, tried to do him all the injury I could.

"But I never succeeded in getting him away for all that, and the end was that Yates had to leave without his cabin boy, and Reuben Harpy had to do without his gold."

"Do you mean to tell me that he didn't ask it back?" said one of the company.

"Of course he did. But what was the use? I considered myself fully entitled to it. My head was battered enough, and I had taken trouble enough, too, to earn the money, and if young Tom didn't suddenly disappear from the hall, it was not my fault."

"You are right," replied the company.

"I did my best," said Black Bill, "and got a broken head, and fifty-three guineas for my pains. And that, gentlemen, is my story."

The motley company once more replenished their glasses, and smoked their long pipes.

All this time, Jerry and Bob had listened with the greatest attention to the somewhat long yarn of Black Bill, and when it was done, they enjoyed a little quiet talk to themselves.

"Well, Bob, what do you think of that 'ere story?" said Jerry.

"What do I think of it?" said Bob. "Why, that we know more now of that affair than we did afore. Who'd ever think that the little varmint, Reuben Harpy, would have given Black Bill fifty-three guineas to put Captain Tom out o' the way?"

"There's a little reptile for you!"

"I believe you," said Bob. "A worser reptile

never crawled the earth than Reuben Harpy. I wonder what put it into Black Bill's head to tell this story to-night? Now we know why he is Captain Tom's enemy."

"And why he wanted him to go into the boat," said Jerry. "Who'd ever have believed that that viper, Reuben, would have gone and done such a thing at such an age as that?"

"I see you don't see the thing clear yet," said Bob.

"Indeed!" said Jerry.

"I am sure and sart'in you don't. Do you think that Reuben done all this himself?"

"Why, yes. Who else could a-done it?"

"Oh! what a dunderhead you are, Jerry! Your intellects is so blunted that you can't see a hole through a ladder."

"You are werry complimentary, Bob."

"I'm telling the truth, Jerry. Did it never strike you, while Black Bill was telling his story, that Reuben Harpy's mother was at the top and bottom of the young villain's infernal plan?"

"No, by Neptune, it didn't!"

"I told you as how you was dull, Jerry. Now, that's just the very thing as struck me most of all. Reuben Harpy's mother, of course, hated Tom Drake, and she drilled this hopeful young varmint up to what he did. So there's the whole thing in a nut shell for you."

"And now we know more than ever we knew, Bob."

"Just so. But there, it's gone ten, and that black-looking fellow hasn't come yet. Black Bill and him would make a very good team, wouldn't they Jerry?"

"A splendid team," replied Jerry. "But stop a minute, there's something more on the boards yet. Listen."

"Yes," said Black Bill, "that family's a ruined one to a dead sartinty. First of all, off goes that 'ere Tom Drake. Reuben Harpy follows, then Mrs. Drake disappears, and then old John Gregory and Mrs. Harpy follow the remainder. I say that 'ere family is ruined—gone and bust up."

And with this remarkable assertion, the smuggler took another drink, and an extra puff at his pipe.

"Well, upon my word it's strange," observed one of the company. "I wonder where they can all have gone to?"

"You are right; it is strange," replied Bill. "But perhaps I could let a little light on the mystery if I only chose."

"You could?" said a tall, bronzed-faced man, sitting in one corner of the room.

"Aye, that I could," rejoined the smuggler.

"Why don't you then?" asked the individual in question.

"Because I don't chose—that's why I don't," replied Bill.

"A very good reason," said the bronzed-faced man, thoughtfully; "a very good and proper reason too—because you don't chose—ahem! Sich an answer ought to be printed in letters of gold. But how is it that this Lieutenant Sanderson came in for the property?"

"That's another bit o' mystery that Black Bill, perhaps, doesn't chose to explain," put in another of the company.

"But it does seem strange, too, that a man, who is no earthly relation of the Gregories, should come into the estates of old John."

"That's the p'int at issue," said the bronze-faced man. "He seems to lord it up there as if the estates came to him through a direct line of ancestry. Some say that they put old John in a madhouse. I don't know how true that is, however. But others said

he went out to the Indies and died there. A werry likely story, and good enough for anyone as believes it; but I for one don't believe it."

"But why don't you?" inquired another speaker, bending a look on him as if he would have read him through and through.

"Because I believe he's as living," was the reply.

"But no one has ever heard that."

"That's all you know," said he of the bronzed face "I'll stake a bowl of punch for the company round that our good friend, Bill, here has heard of him."

"But if he doesn't chose to tell us, how are we to know?"

"There you are again. That's where the difficulty lies."

"Jest so."

"But I know one man as could tell you if he was here."

"Who is that?"

"I don't think you'd know him if I was to tell you."

"His name?" cried several voices at once.

"Well, as the genelmen present is so werry anxious to know, his name is, or rather was, Angel. You see, genelmen, I am precise, for he may be dead long since. He was a seafaring man and a captain, and a devil of a fellow he was, too, by all accounts. The servants up at the hall can tell you a little more than that about him, I reckon."

"Captain Angel!" repeated more than one of the company. "Why, that was the long, stern gentleman—a visitor of Lieutenant Sanderson's."

"Not only a visitor," said the bronzed-faced man, impressively; "but his master, too. This may seem a strange thing to you, genelmen, but believe me it is true."

"I agree with you there," said Bill. "Captain Angel was Lieutenant Sanderson's master, if there ever was a master."

"Was this Captain Angel ever in His Majesty's navy?" asked another.

"It was rumoured so," replied the smuggler. "And now coming to think of it, I am sure that he was. But I fancy, at present, that he is in some other service."

"The service of the devil," said one.

"Well, not very far from it," replied Black Bill. "He's either a pirate or a slaver, and that's as bad."

"Well, in that case he's not much worse than Tom Drake," said another; "for Tom is the captain of a buccaneer brig."

"And there's a price on his head, too," added Black Bill. "I'm bound to get the reward some day, depend upon it."

"I'd like to give him a reward with my fist," whispered Jerry.

"Don't be in a hurry," said Bob, "that'll come soon enough. Only wait and listen."

"Yes," resumed Black Bill, "I'm bound to get that reward. I tried it on afore, but failed. But the next time I'm a-going to make sure work of it. You'll hear something afore long as'll surprise you, I'm pretty sartin."

Bob and Jerry pricked up their ears.

What did the smuggler mean?

Did he see through their disguises?

Bob and Jerry moved very uneasily in their chairs.

But as Black Bill did not look their way, they began to be more easy in their minds.

"Yes," went on Black Bill, "I'am not going to tell any of you what I do know. But you'll hear the tune of two thousand guineas chinking in my pockets afore long."

"Which I suppose you are going to get by the capture of Captain Tom?" said one.

"Exactly."

"Then you'll find him a tough customer to deal with."

"I've dealt with him before," replied the smuggler, laughing, "and I know what he's made of."

"Tell me why so large a reward as two thousand pounds is offered?" asked another inquisitive individual.

"Why? Well, that's a good one, to be sure. I thought you knew. Why, for murder and piracy on the high seas to be sure."

Such an announcement in the bar-room seemed to cause a sensation.

"Oh, then, he has gone as far as murder, has he?" said one.

"A fine beginning," added another. "But who's to prove that he's either a pirate or a murderer?"

"There's plenty to prove it," replied Black Bill. "Scores, nay, hundreds."

"Perhaps our friend Bill is one of the number," said the bronze-faced man, with a slight touch of sarcasm in his tone, "perhaps he can prove it in the same way as he proves everything else."

"Well, if it comes to the test, I can do that too," said the smuggler. "I accuse him of one o' the worst murders as ever was perpetrated."

Bob and Jerry were on their feet in an instant.

Their beloved chief accused of murder by a ruffian like Black Bill.

This was surely too much.

They would hurl the foul charge in the teeth of the scoundrel who uttered it.

"Who accuses Tom Drake of murder?" thundered Bob, with flashing eyes; "is it you, Black Bill? If it is, say so, and I'll give you such a thrashing as you never had before!"

Of course, Bob knew very well that it was Black Bill who had spoken.

But if the man withdrew the charge, he wished to give him the benefit of it.

Now, the leaping of the supposed strange sailors to their feet had considerable effect on the sage frequenters of the "Blue Lobster."

Their jabberings ceased at once.

And they looked with some astonishment on our two buccaneers, not dreaming for an instant that Captain Tom would have found defenders so near them.

Most of these rough, bronze-visaged men were well on in liquor.

Three sheets in the wind, using a nautical expression, and ready for a fight or any other thing that came in their way.

As for Black Bill, he had lost all control.

Instead of taking little or no notice of the two comrades, he was on his feet in an instant, looking savage and furious.

"I am the man who accuses Captain Tom Drake of murder," he cried. "But I'd like to know who you are that defend him."

"It matters little who we are," replied Jerry. "But we means forcing the dirty lie down your throat, at any rate."

"Curse you! We'll soon see that!" cried Black Bill.

With one bound he was over the table, and in the middle of the bar-room, confronting the two buccaneers.

"I'm the man as accuses Captain Tom Drake of murder," he said, "and if you want to know more, I am Black Bill, the smuggler, who never put himself out of the way for man or mortal. But there is one thing I would like to know—who you are—and what's more, you don't leave this 'ere bar-room afore I do?"

"Indeed!" sneered Bob.

"Hear our dunghill rooster!" echoed Jerry.

"I more than fancies," said Black Bill, "that you are the identical men we want. There's something in the cut of your jibs that I have seen before."

"Well, look out for yours, at any rate," said Bob, "as I mean planting one on that 'ere conk of yours, as'll make you see a thousand stars in less than a minute. Sit down, old pal. It won't take me long to polish this rascal off. And after I've done it, I'll make him eat his words."

Bob removed nothing, but stood as he got up.

Jerry sat down watching the movements of his comrade with interest, and resolved that if any of the rest should interfere, to join in.

Black Bill—the bullying, swaggering, treacherous smuggler—threw his cap off, rolled up his sleeves, tied a handkerchief around his waist, prepared to give Bob Hauler, as he firmly believed, a tremendous thrashing.

Nor was he the only one in the company who was convinced of it.

They were all.

Of course, we except Jerry Mizzen, who had no doubt at all in his own mind of the result.

But for all that, Black Bill was a powerful ruffian, and known to be a good boxer.

In fact, he was the bully of the Blue Lobster.

"Come on, now," said the smuggler, "and we'll very soon decide this little matter, after which, I mean writing your words down on a piece of paper, and making you eat 'em."

"You have just reminded me," said Bob, very calmly, "that writing is a very good idea, and, depend upon it, I'll profit by it. Now, you black swab, I'm ready for you!"

Bob Hauler took his position up so carelessly, that Black Bill anticipated an easy victory.

"He's no boxer," thought the ruffian, "and one or two rounds will be enough for him. Then I'll show the company a bit of fun. Fancy eating his own words! Ha! ha! ha!"

Black Bill, squaring out in true gladiatorial style, advanced on his antagonist.

Bob stood almost with folded arms awaiting him.

Some thought that he looked dangerous.

But that was, perhaps, a mistake.

However, on came Black Bill, conscious in his own mind of victory.

Making a feint, he aimed a terrific blow at Bob's head.

Our buccaneer countered it nicely, and being the soberer man of the two, he succeeded, before the smuggler could get away, in "landing" him one on the side of the nose, which made the blood spurt from his nostrils in streams.

"How do you like that?" cried Bob. "Come on, and get another at the other side!"

"Claret's werry cheap," said Jerry. "Tapped it nicely that time, comrade"

Bob knew now that his man was getting dangerous.

The blow had more than sobered him.

The company, too, looked on the fight with evident relish, for they saw that Black Bill's temper was up, and they consequently anticipated what the stranger would catch.

Black Bill, not heeding the blood that was spurting from his nose, advanced furiously, but at the same time observed considerable caution in coming up.

He sparred for a few moments, and took Bob on the left ear, from which some blood came, but only from a slight scratch, of which our buccaneer took not the slightest notice.

Bob sparred around Black Bill for a short time without putting a single blow in.

The smuggler, knowing his man now, had become thoroughly cautious, and moved his position from one place to another, so as not to give Bob a chance

Our buccaneer, equally cautious, followed him, and, after making two or three feints, succeeded in planting a terrific blow under the smuggler's right ear, which knocked that gentleman clean off his legs.

"First knock down for our side!" echoed Jerry, who was getting now to view his comrade's performance in a very interesting light.

The last blow that Bob had given Black Bill was a tremendous one.

The smuggler was picked up bleeding, and almost senseless from a cut in his left temple.

No longer were the frequenters of the Blue Lobster calm and quiet observers.

They could see that their bully and champion was beaten, and they leaped to their feet to make a fierce onslaught on the victor.

With hoarse cries, they bounded forward with the intention of giving him a rough handling, when the door of the bar-room was suddenly opened, and the sinister-looking man in black, whom Bob and Jerry met in the lane, walked into the room.

CHAPTER CLXIX.

THE STRANGE SCHOONER.

THE "Will-o'-the-Wisp" lay at anchor at least six miles from the shore.

There was nothing in her appearance that would arouse the remotest suspicion.

No more peaceful brig, as far as looks were concerned, sailed the sea.

For a few days before Captain Tom and his gallant crew had effected so complete a change in her that the most lynx-eyed coastguard on the station would have passed her by without entertaining the slightest suspicion as to the real nature of her calling, and if asked would, no doubt, have answered that she had the cut and build of a respectable trader.

Ports she seemed to have none, and the few of her crew that appeared occasionally on deck were soberly dressed, and had the gravity of British merchantmen.

So much for the "Will-o'-the-Wisp" in her new disguise.

But the brig was not the only vessel that lay at anchor there.

Not more than a quarter of a mile distant a schooner was at anchor—a strange-looking craft of singular build, and long raking masts.

But otherwise there was not anything more strange or striking in her appearance to attract attention.

She was evidently waiting to get a supply of water and provisions on board before setting out on her voyage.

Captain Tom had his eye fixed on this craft very often during the day, having a strange suspicion in his mind that he had seen it before.

But where?

The question puzzled him.

He determined as long as they were together, however, to keep a good watch on the schooner's movements.

Our hero had been ashore twice since the "Will-o'-the-Wisp" lay at anchor, and both he and some of his crew walked where they liked with impunity.

How long this fancied security was to last there was no telling.

At last the night of the third day set in as dark as an absence of moon and stars could make it.

The night was unutterably calm.

All on board the schooner seemed to be either dead or asleep, for not a sound came from her decks, and all that could be discerned of her was a bluish light burning at her masthead.

That very afternoon Captain Tom got a note from Lady Arbuthnot.

Of course our hero had made his arrival known to her ladyship, and the day before had consigned Minnie Atherton to her care.

Now, Lady Arbuthnot's note was very brief.

It was to this effect—that she wanted to see Captain Tom at his earliest convenience.

"His earliest convenience" meant any time that he could come with safety there.

So our hero, during the later part of the afternoon, busied himself in preparing for the journey.

Nothing could be so favourable to it as this night, so pitchy dark, and so unutterably calm.

While he was on the quarter-deck for the last time that evening to give his instructions, he fancied that he heard a smothered shriek issuing from the black depth of the waters beyond.

He tried to pierce the almost impenetrable darkness, but without much effect.

Yet he thought that he detected a something moving noiselessly on the calm, unrippled surface of the sea.

The cry again came.

But in lower cadence.

As if the party who gave vent to it was being smothered.

"By heavens! there is something wrong in that direction!" cried Tom. "I must see to it."

At a call from him, one of the middies brought his glass forward.

Ben Barnacle came on deck at the same time all ready for the journey.

He had also heard the muffled cry.

And his suspicions were consequently aroused, as well as Tom's.

Our hero, by the aid of his instrument, detected a boat moving noiselessly through the water.

He made out also that there were four or five persons in it, and that an object apparently bound lay at the bottom of it.

Whether that object was a man or a woman, he could not for the life of him tell.

But he was decided on one step, however.

And that was to go after the boat, which was making in a direct line for the schooner.

Ben Barnacle coincided instantly with this step.

Oars were muffled, and a boat lowered instantly from the side of the "Will-o'-the-Wisp."

Half a dozen men got in.

Among the number, Captain Tom and Ben Barnacle.

The men, with muffled oars in their hands, shot noiselessly from the side of the brig in the wake of the strange boat.

They moved like spectres over the smooth, dark sea, and approached the schooner with that caution deemed advisable and necessary to the occasion.

Steadily the buccaneers bent to their work, and on flew the boat without even the sound of a dipping oar.

They were soon made aware of one fact, however.

That it would be impossible for them to reach the boat before its occupants were aboard the schooner.

But our hero intended to board the schooner himself, let the danger be what it would.

If there was any foul play going on, which he

was more than sure of, he was determined to prevent it.

"I have looked on that craft for the last day or two with the gravest suspicions," he whispered to Ben. "Besides, it strikes me very forcibly that I have seen it somewhere before, although I cannot clearly make out where."

"She's a suspicious customer, to say the least," replied Ben, "and wants looking after in the worst way."

"You are right," rejoined Tom, "and I am determined to find out what she is before another half hour passes over my head. It wouldn't surprise me much if we discovered one of our old enemies in her."

"Not the Death Pirate?"

"Strange that you should have suggested the Death Pirate. That thought has been uppermost in my mind all day."

"Besides, he escaped the wounds that Bob Hauler and Jerry Mizzen inflicted on him."

"True," replied Tom.

"Yet I am inclined to think," said Ben, "that he would scarcely have the audacity to anchor so near a British port."

"Why, Ben?"

"In the first place, it is so very much out of his usual latitude."

"He would have the daring and audacity to anchor anywhere, my dear fellow," replied Tom. "You quite mistake him altogether if you think he wouldn't. But I want to ask you one question, lieutenant."

"Well, captain?"

"Did it ever strike you who this Death Pirate was? He's undoubtedly an Englishman."

He felt Ben Barnacle's arm, as he put the question, trembling.

It became evident that his faithful follower was very much excited.

Tom, however, appeared to take no notice of this, and put the question again.

"I have my suspicions," Ben replied, evasively. "I may be right, or I may be wrong."

"Who, then, do you think he is?" asked Captain Tom.

"Ah, captain! you must pardon me for not giving you an answer to that question. The time has not come to—"

Ben Barnacle, as if afraid he had said too much, suddenly broke off, and was silent.

Tom, not desiring to awake bitter recollections in his faithful follower's breast, contented himself with his unfinished answer, hoping soon himself to unmask and find out who this Death Pirate was.

They could now see the strange schooner looming up like some hideous monster from the deep.

They were within a hundred yards or so of her, and it behoved them to move with greater caution than ever.

Not that they could be observed from the deck of the schooner, for that was almost impossible on such a night.

But the slightest sound, or the dipping of an oar, might give the alarm to those on board.

On a nearer approach they were made aware of some commotion on board.

It was evident that some of the crew of the schooner were drunk, for they grew all of a sudden very noisy.

This was rather favourable to Captain Tom and his party, who could now approach the schooner without exciting any alarm.

Less than a minute elapsed, and they were alongside.

The drunken part of the crew were evidently below deck, as could be seen from the few tiny streaks of light that flashed out on the waters.

But, at the same time, there were voices heard from above, and Captain Tom and Ben Barnacle prepared to listen.

One of the parties who spoke was evidently under the influence of liquor.

His voice was harsh and brutal.

"So I've got you in my power at last," said this person, "and I mean paying you, too, for the trouble you have given me.

"I'll tame your fiery spirit, you minx. You talk about loving that other fellow, do you. I wish I could only catch him, and I'd show you then the tortures I'd inflict.

"Ha! ha! I never forgot that blow he gave me yet. He thought I forgot it, did he! But he was mistaken. I am a man who never forgives nor forgets an injury!"

"Oh, God! will no one save me from this monster?" cried a female voice, in trembling accents.

"Monster you call me, do you?" repeated the harsh tones of the man. "Very good, my lady. I am a monster, am I? Ha! ha! Perhaps you'll say that before I am done with you. As for calling on any one to help you, you had better be careful. There's the gag, you minx, the gag. That I guess, will effectually silence your cries. You little thought to-night, when that polite little love-letter was sent to you, that you'd now be in the hands of one you have caused so much suffering and misery."

"Oh, brutal man! what injury have I ever done you that you should thus seek my ruin?"

"What have you done to me?" laughed the ruffian, coarsely. "What use is it answering such a question? You know what you have done to me. Who, first, was the cause of my imprisonment? Who drove me to sea? Who made me the villain I am? Who but you, you, you?"

And the man, as he hissed out the words, actually ground his teeth with rage.

"Could I help that?" moaned the other. "If you were sent to prison, I didn't put you there; neither did I drive you to sea; and as you are a villain by your own owning, God knows it was not of my making."

"You lie! It was!" hissed the partly-intoxicated ruffian. "If you had given me your love—"

"Oh, be reasonable, and take pity on me!" implored the maiden. "How could I give you what I never felt!"

"You gave it to another! Curse him!" cried the man, furiously. "Didn't you do that?"

"Alas! how can I answer you?"

"Answer me? Give him up, and I'll forgive you."

"Never!"

"Then I'll have his heart's blood!"

"Monster!"

"Aye, aye! you can 'monster' me as long as you like. But he shall not escape my vengeance. To-morrow night he dies."

The lady gave a faint scream, and then all became as still as death.

Captain Tom and Ben Barnacle waited to hear no more, and climbed with some difficulty to the deck of the schooner.

At that moment, as if by magic, the moon burst forth, the black clouds rolled away, and the stars came glinting from the skies.

This sudden manœuvre of Lady Moon was so unexpected that it staggered both Tom and Ben, who, crouching behind a gun carriage, took a good view in front of them.

The light of the moon lit up the deck as plain as day.

A novel sight opened to their eyes.

A young girl of between twenty-two or twenty-three years was bound by her arms and body to the mizzen-mast.

Her face was deathly pale, and there were tears coursing down her cheeks.

Not many paces from her stood the half-drunken ruffian before alluded to.

His dress was that of a smuggler.

He had a crimson sash round his waist, which, with the fur cap on his head, and the pair of thick, heavy sea-boots on his feet, heightened his ruffianly appearance very much.

A burly-looking fellow he was, too, whose age looked to be every year of forty.

But being of a dark sallow complexion, perhaps this added somewhat to his elderly looks.

On this ruffian's drunken visage was a gleam of deadly hatred, a look that a fiend might wear in the pursuit of a lost soul.

There was a flash so diabolical in his eyes, that the young girl closed hers, shudderingly, to avoid their horrible fascination.

It was evident that she had not seen his face so fully before; and, perhaps, would not have done so, but for this unexpected bursting out of the moon.

The ruffian seemed to guess all the horror and loathing she felt for him, and his evil-looking eyes filled up with fury.

His frame grew convulsed with passion.

"You abhor and hate me," he almost screamed. "What loathing you had for me before has been thrice intensified by this cursed moonlight. But close your eyes as you will, your are mine—mine," he hissed, "and you go forth from here dishonoured and ruined, to be pointed at with the finger of scorn, for I'll take good care to let the world know you were the mistress of—"

"Monster!" she shrieked, interrupting him. "Your vile words do not affect me! Rather would I suffer a thousand deaths than to be the victim of your unholy passions."

"Say you so, my ladybird? Ha! ha! Who's to help you?"

"God," she replied, solemnly. "That God who watches your evil acts, and condemns them, and to whom you will have to answer one day for your many crimes."

The poor girl's words only seemed to infuriate the ruffian.

"Do you think so?" he cried, mockingly. "We'll see now whether your God will help you or not. You call on him, minx, in vain! You are wholly and utterly in my power. And now for the test."

With a furious imprecation on his lips, he rushed forward.

What his intention was Captain Tom did not wait to ask himself.

Signing to Ben Barnacle to remain where he was Tom Drake bounded from his place of concealment.

He fancied for a moment that he saw the glittering blade of a knife in his hand.

And imagining so, he thought he would be too late to rescue the unhappy girl from a horrible death at his hands.

Tom made up his mind what to do in a second.

Snatching a pistol from his belt, and not taking into account the consequences that might result from the act, he cocked it, and fired into the face of the advancing ruffian.

The quick, whip-like crack of the pistol awoke a hundred echoes through the quiet night, and the man, with a deep groan, fell forward on his face.

CHAPTER CLXX.

THE PLOT TO ENTRAP CAPTAIN T

OUR next scene!

A country lane, four or five miles from mouth, the hour verging late into the afternoon, sky unclouded, and the sun shining down with bright brilliant effect over all.

Trees and hedges never looked more beautiful or picturesque in their variegated bloom, and the songs of a thousand birds fell with wondrous melody on the ear.

But to complete the picture, three travel-stained, bronzed-faced men strode along the lane, directing their course towards the well-known seaport before named.

To sum the whole briefly up, these three dusty and wayworn figures were our old acquaintances.

Reuben Harpy, the sham-sentinel, and the prying, inquisitive Peter.

Three companions in roguery, who, having stuck to each other so long, were likely to remain together some time longer.

Reuben had thoroughly recovered from the wound which he received at the hands of Harry Vere, and only a livid scar remained to show were the bullet had glanced.

As for the sham-sentinel, he was in the best of possible spirits, and regaled his companions with numerous and "interesting" anecdotes, to which our friend Reuben listened for the most part with either a lazy apathy or a grumbling impatience.

Of course the quiet, eaves-dropping Peter took in everything as usual, chuckling sometimes at his companion's droll humour, or putting in an occasional word himself.

But presently anecdotes grew stale and uninteresting, and a conversational strain took its place.

The sham sentinel beginning with the affairs of Admiral Ellis, who, from his words, was evidently saved from some very great danger.

For the reader has not forgotten, of course, that the little admiral had disappeared by some unexplainable means some time before, from our hero's brig, the "Will-o'-the-Wisp."

However, the conversation begun as follows—

"A lucky thing," said the sham sentinel, addressing Reuben Hary, "that we saved little Ellis from the raft. I wonder how he got there? A curious place I should imagine for one of his Majesty's admirals."

"Not so very curious," replied Reuben, "considering he was a prisoner on board that rascal Tom Drake's ship. The little admiral, when he told me all about it, was fuming with rage, and there's no doubt he'll have the villain, Drake, yet."

"A very difficult matter to speculate on, Captain Harpy, seeing that the buccaneer has eluded him so many times."

"What does that matter?" cried Reuben, with an impatient gesture. "You may run a man into a corner a great number of times, and at last catch him."

"Even so," replied the other.

"But you must acknowledge that, so far, he has failed most disgracefully."

"Why disgracefully?" questioned the ex-privateer.

"Well, in the first place, he has pursued him with a fleet of war ships, each and every one double the tonnage of the 'Will-o'-the Wisp,' and then, instead of taking this scourge of the seas, blundered into one of the most inglorious defeats on record, where a few smugglers and buccaneers not only defeated his fleet, but for the most part destroyed it. If that is not failing disgracefully, captain, tell me what is."

THE FIGHT ON THE SMUGGLER SCHOONER.

"Humph!" rejoined Reuben, logically, "that's all you know about it. I tell you Admiral Ellis has been the right man in the right place, and he will have that cursed Tom Drake yet. And not only that, but I shall have the pleasure of seeing him hang like a dog."

"Well, for my part, I hope you will. Such an invincible and daring customer as Captain Tom has lived a little too long. He has thrown every one else in the shade, so that it's about time he was cut off and hung up to dry like many a better man. But we must give the devil his due, all the same."

"Indeed!" sneered Harpy.

"In the first place he has been very magnanimous." went on the other.

"Magnanimous. Pray tell me how he has been magnanimous?"

"By releasing the three captains and the commodore."

"He could not do anything else, my good fellow."

"He might have hanged them."

"And would have done so, too, no doubt, only that his own interests were at stake."

Reuben was always ready to put a bad construction on everything magnanimous or noble.

"That is what you think, captain?"

"Most certainly."

"Well, now, I'll tell you why I have a different opinion. In the first place, his interests could not possibly be at stake. For why? They would hang him if they caught him, whether he did it or not.

And no one knew this better than Captain Tom Drake himself; therefore, so far as that was concerned it did not matter a straw to him whether he strung them up or didn't string them up. Reason number one. Reason number two, it put him to some inconvenience in landing his prisoners."

"In what manner?" demanded Reuben.

"Well, the manner was this. He went very much out of his way to put them into a suitable port."

"Nonsense! Any port would have done as well."

"Now there you are wrong, captain. For the commodore and his three comrades were thoroughly broken down in health."

"You seem to have gleaned considerable information while you were in Southampton," said Reuben, sarcastically.

"Perhaps. But that is not here nor there, and I feel so tired that I wish we were at our journey's end. How far are we from Portsmouth?"

"Five miles, I should judge. It may be more."

"An hour and a half's walk," said the sham sentinel.

"Say two hours," put in Peter. "Snail pace at that."

"None of your snail pace for me," said Reuben. "Come, strike out. I am as fatigued myself as any of you."

"And I as hungry as if I had not eaten a bit for twenty-four hours. How I long to reach the first eating-house! Even philosophers must eat. Ha! ha! ha!"

"It's no joke to laugh at," said Peter, ruefully. "I can feel my backbone making a perpetual attack on my stomach."

"Poor fellow! I wonder how you can survive it all," sneered the sham sentinel. "You are a sorry dog, Peter. Nothing seems to trouble you but your belly."

"If I didn't trouble about my belly, no one else would for me," retorted Peter. "But for goodness sake let us push forward if we are going to, and get in before the night comes on"

"An hour or so before sunset would be better, Peter. Never mind, my inquisitive one. You need not be afraid that you are going without your supper."

"Don't talk about supper yet," growled Peter. "Let us have tea afore you talk of supper."

"Exactly, my noble comrade. You don't think I would deprive you of a meal, do you?"

Peter muttered that he would take good care he shouldn't.

"I tell you what," said Peter. "This last month or so I've been literally starved."

"Too much salt junk doesn't agree with you, Peter?"

"No; nor salt pork, either," replied Peter. "And as for them hard biscuits, they go against my grain altogether."

"Very true. Your teeth are not on edge sufficient. Peter."

"A very good reason," replied Peter, "seeing that I have nearly lost the whole of them, and all through perpetually munching salt junk, pork, and biscuits as hard as the devil himself."

"Never mind, old boy, there's a little change in store for you."

"About time there was."

The fluency of the "silent one" on this occasion was remarkable.

Even the sham sentinel had never heard him speak so much.

And he had been acquainted with him for many years.

No doubt the influence of hunger had this extraordinary effect on him.

The trio now having got through with all they had to say, pursued their way in silence.

Many schemes ran through Reuben's mind.

And all regarding his cousin, Tom Drake, whom he determined yet to avenge himself upon.

He had always shown a bitter, unrelenting spirit ever since he was a boy.

And as he grew up to manhood, his merciless and unforgiving disposition grew stronger than ever.

A coward he was always.

But now his cowardice had become intensified—indeed, intolerable.

Perhaps through associations.

Or to the dangers to which he had for some time back been exposed.

Tom Drake must fall into his power sooner or later.

He was as assured of this as he was of his own existence.

Fortunately, or, rather, unfortunately, he had the notorious little admiral for an ally.

With his assistance, he could work wonders.

Such were the thoughts that coursed through the mind of the ex-privateer captain.

And with a prospect—and a very good one, he thought—of their success, he trudged along the road rejoicing.

Reuben was, indeed, in very good humour with himself.

Consequently, he forgot all the fatigues of his journey.

"My first object will be," he thought, "to seek out the little admiral. He told me, on his leaving Southampton, that it would be more than likely I should see him in Portsmouth. How the admiral will take his defeat at the hands of Tom Drake I can't tell. Some say that he has blundered. I have no doubt of it. Then comes the trouble. The onus of his failure may be of serious disadvantage to him. But the Admiralty will never permit the stigma of that defeat to rest on the admiral's shoulders, without trying in some way to rectify it. They will, no doubt, put at his disposal another fleet, which, if they do, the career of Mr. Tom Drake will come to a speedy end. Another advantage will be mine if they give him the command. I can follow in the tracks of my rascally cousin, and be present when they capture him."

Our worthy friend, Harpy, was so sure of success now, that he could not for an instant think of such a word as "failure."

Nor did he for a moment imagine the dangers in the way.

Or that his vile, cowardly nature would soon be put to the test in his present schemes.

Until then, he might plan and scheme as much as he liked.

Two-thirds of the five miles had been already accomplished before a word passed between them.

Each had been too much busied with his own thoughts.

The sham sentinel had a goodly treasure that he wished to dispose of.

It was getting rather unpleasant to carry about with him.

This wonderful sea emerald became a great weight on his mind.

He had not forgotten the terrible remarks of Black Rufus.

And, brave as he was, he often shuddered, as he thought of them.

Every morning he quietly withdrew from his companions, to take a peep at his treasure.

But still the colour remained unchanged.

And so long as it did so he had no fear.

But might not the deep sea-green turn to a crimson hue at any moment?

This question always arose in his mind.

Thereby causing him considerable uneasiness.

While on board the pirate vessel, he was in constant dread of his life.

The crew of the "San Josef" were a desperate set, and the slightest provocation given by him might be the means of depriving him of his life, and, consequently, of the gem, that he almost valued in an equivalent degree.

But up to the present all had gone well.

And neither of his companions ever dreamt of his having the emerald.

It was his intention, after landing at Southampton, to get a purchaser.

But on making a few inquiries, which did not at all satisfy him with the jewellers there, he resolved upon carrying it with him to Portsmouth.

In this he no doubt acted wisely.

We shall soon see, however, whether he did or not.

The inquisitive Peter's mind was occupied by far different thoughts.

He had neither the great sea emerald nor Captain Tom to think of.

Nor was he bent on any extraordinary gastronomic feat.

Not at all.

Reuben Harpy and the sham sentinel came in for a considerable share of his reflections.

How long were they going to remain together?

How could he induce the ex-privateer captain to hand him oversome of his money?

For he was not without knowing that he possessed a large amount.

Had they been on that lonely highway together, he did not scruple to think that the worthy Reuben would take very little of his property away with him.

Money he wanted, and money he must have.

But how?

That was the question.

He weighed it over in his mind, but still he could see no prospect of getting any.

Certainly Harpy, in his munificence, might give him a few pounds.

But a few pounds was not enough.

A hundred pounds would be of some consideration.

Anything less of little or no consequence.

Reuben Harpy, if he did not come down like a generous paymaster, must suffer for it.

Again his thoughts reverted to the sham sentinel.

A man whom he had known for years, and yet knew comparatively little of.

He seemed very jubilant.

Why was he so jubilant?

He was a man who generally took life as it came.

He was never low spirited, nor yet had he ever known him to be in very high spirits.

There was some secret in all this that he should like to make himself master of.

He would do so, too, before he was much older.

Was it possible that anything of any value had come into his possession?

The time would shortly arrive to solve that question.

In the meantime, Reuben Harpy was an object of his greatest solicitude.

Thus the time passed away, and before they were scarcely aware of the fact, they were entering the strongly-fortified town of Portsmouth.

They passed through one of the gates guarded by red-coated soldiery, and then directed their steps into the very heart of the old seaport.

The sham sentinel and his companion had never been there before.

Reuben, however, had, and knew every hole and corner in it.

He took them down narrow, dark streets, and led them into broad thoroughfares, where hundreds of people were passing and repassing.

The sun was on the decline, and the streets were lined with all kinds of wayfarers, who often favoured Reuben and his two companions with curious looks, not knowing well what to make of them.

Indeed, the trio were covered with dust from head to foot, and had all the appearance of footsore tramps, who had travelled a long distance.

But Reuben, the sham sentinel, and Peter, were not at all disconcerted by the frequent and inquisitive glances of the numerous passengers.

They pursued their way with the same indifference as if they had not been gazed at at all.

Presently they came to a turning that led into a narrow lane, which was not very remarkable for either its cleanliness or style of architecture.

Down this Reuben plunged, followed, as before, by the sentinel and Peter.

The narrow street reeked with filth, and our travellers had to lay violent hands on their noses to prevent the disagreeable odours from having effect on them.

Here they saw frowsy women seated at every doorstep, and frowsier men reeling from one side to the other of the street, in a state of beastly intoxication.

The windows of the houses were in most cases in a frightfully dilapidated condition.

Whole panes were out, and found substitutes in bundles of greasy rags or filthy discoloured paper.

On the whole, this neighbourhood was the reverse of charming, or even cleanly.

More than a half dozen times our travellers were hailed, and not deigning to answer these oft-repeated calls, were soundly and vituperatively abused for their lack of civility and politeness.

Once they made their way out of this street, they breathed more freely, and bent their steps with greater composure.

"Thank goodness we are out of that place!" said Reuben, when they had emerged into another street. "The villainous smells nearly gave me an headache."

"And me, too," said Peter. "I have got worse than a headache. Such odours on an empty stomach are far from agreeable."

"Still thinking of your stomach, Peter," laughed his colleague. "Upon my conscience, I never saw such a fellow."

"Didn't you, indeed? Well, I did. My stomach seems to trouble you a great deal."

"It does so. And to prove that it does, here's an eating-house."

"The one I intended taking you to," put in Reuben. "It's thoroughly respectable."

"Don't mention it, sir," said Peter. "Anything will do on a pinch like the present."

"You had better go back, then, and regale yourself with those delightful odours," laughed the sham sentinel.

"To oblige you, I have a good mind so to do."

"No, my dear Peter, you need not take that trouble. Follow Captain Harpy, and your immediate wants will be attended to."

The place they now stopped before had, for a Portsmouth restaurant, an appearance of grave respectability, and was generally patronised by young midshipmen whose vessels lay out in the Sound or in the docks.

And there was a goodly few of these young gentlemen there when they entered.

Reuben Harpy had often patronised this place himself when he was in a like position, and so, using a slang expression, "knew the ropes" pretty well.

Calling on the waiter, they were soon accommodated with a box, which the three entered.

In a very few minutes they were served with what they required, and being very hungry from their long travel, they set to on the viands with a zest that told well for their appetites.

Neither spoke a word while they were undergoing this operation.

And, as a consequence, Reuben was fated to hear something from the occupants of the box next to them.

By this time most of the midshipmen, having disposed of their meals, had gone, leaving Reuben, his two companions, and the persons in the other box, almost the sole occupants of the eating-house.

Of course we except the waiters and the proprietor, who were lounging about the restaurant waiting for more people to come in.

The sham sentinel was going to speak, but Harpy nudged him to be quiet.

Then Reuben listened to the following dialogue, which, though conducted in very low tones, fell distinctly on his ear—

"There's a good many as would like to know what we know, Bill."

"You are right, Dan; but they shan't, for all that."

"No, I believe you. We ain't such fools as to give our secrets over in that way. And yet sometimes I wonder which would be the best plan."

"What do you mean, Dan?"

"Why, just this. Whether it would be better to give Captain Tom the tip, or sell him to the little admiral. I know Ellis would give a good price for him."

"You are right."

"Yet we might get a better one from Captain Tom."

"Don't believe it. He would only laugh at you."

"Well, you know him best then."

"I ought to, seeing as I knew him from his childhood up. I haven't forgot one thing, Dan."

"What's that?"

"He gave me an ugly cut once."

"That is, he cut your acquaintance?"

"No, you fool. Look here! What do you call that?"

"A scar, I reckon."

"And a rather deep one."

"Just so. But what has that to do with it?"

"Everything, you lubber. Do you think I'm going to forgive a man as puts such an ugly scratch on my face as that?"

"Was it in fair and honest fight?"

"Well, I suppose you may call it so. But that makes no difference. It is there, and there it will remain."

"Werry likely. But I say, old fellow, don't you think that 'ere wrong to keep in a grudge for a cove 'cause he gives you a broken pate?"

"The object is money."

"Decidedly."

"Very well, then. That settles the matter."

"In course."

"Do you think for an instant that Tom Drake will give you any?"

"Eh?"

"I say, do you think that Tom Drake will give you any?"

"Why not?"

"I have explained that to you afore. I'm actually getting out o' patience with you, Dan. You seem so bull-headed."

"Bull-headed!"

"Yes, bull-headed. That's the expression. No offence, of course Dan."

"Sart'inly not. But go on, Bill. Let me see what you are a-driving at."

"Well, I'm driving at this, and if you be the sensible feller I've always took you to be, you'll agree with me."

"Of course I will."

"Then listen, and don't interrupt me. Now, for argument's sake, let us say as how you called on Captain Tom. You found him on board his ship. You was shown into his cabin. A bottle of wine was opened. You was told to sit down, and lush at his expense, or, rather, at the expense of them unfortunate crafts he's robbed time after time. Well, supposing as how you was treated in this kindly way—which I know you wouldn't be—supposing, I say, as you was treated in that 'ere fashion, next yer business would be inquired into. What are you to say?"

"I would say—"

"Don't interrupt me, Dan."

"Well, go ahead. I thought as how you was asking me a question."

"You have no right to think, Dan. Now, there you go again. 'A still tongue makes a wise head,' but you are not the man as has it, that's evident. Well, as I was saying, supposing he asked you yer business. What are you to say?"

"I—"

"Hold on a minute, and don't be so cussedly impatient. Well, then, supposing he was to ask you that? You would say then—"

"I would say—"

"Stop a minute, you varmint! You would say, then, 'Captain Tom, I've come to tell you of something that consarns you very much.'

"'Indeed!' he would say. 'Consarns me? In what way?'

"''There's a conspiracy formed ag'in you,' you would reply.

"''What conspiracy?' he would ask.

"''I am not at liberty to tell you,' you would say, 'only on sartin conditions.'

"''Well, what are the conditions?' he would ask.

"''Money,' you would reply.

"Well, then, you'd both get a-puzzling of each other faster than I am a-talking.

"But he'd find you out afore you got a red penny from him.

"And then do you know what he'd do to you?"

"What?"

"He'd tell some of them to give you an elevation at the yard-arm."

"No!"

"Yes, but he would; and if he didn't do that he'd have you thrown overboard, and let you sink or swim just as you pleased."

"I can never believe it, Bill."

"But it's a fact, Dan; I know Captain Tom Drake of old.

"Now, on the other hand, let us see what sort o' treatment Admiral Ellis would give you.

"You go Ellis's house, and you asks—

"'Is the admiral in?'

"The footman looks at you for a moment with an eye o' suspicion."

"Why should he look at me with an eye o' suspicion, Bill?"

"Well, I tell you why.

"In the first place, you are not werry handsome."

"Ditto."

"In the next place, 'willain' is painted all over yer mug. You needn't get angry. It's only a compliment I am a-paying of you."

"A deuced fine compliment, too."

"Well, never mind about that. It's how a man takes it, you see. If you said it to me, I should think as how you was speaking the truth, and doing me a kindness, to boot."

"Humph!"

"I assure you I would.

"But that's not here nor there. Well, then, in the third place, he'd know you was no honest sailor by the cut o' yer toggery.

"But that would make no difference.

"He'd say—

"'What do you want of Admiral Ellis?'

"'I wants to see him,' you'd reply, and then you'd add—

"'On werry important business.'

"That would be enough for the lacquey.

"He'd look at you with less and less suspicion, and put you down perhaps as a commodore or something of that kind in disguise. You needn't laugh, Dan. There's nothing like making yerself important, whether you feels that way or not. However, the lacquey runs off and tells the admiral, and the admiral puts his finger on the side of his nose, and looks werry wise like for a minute or two.

"Then all of a sudden he's bursting with impatience to see you.

"Finally you are shown up to him, and he looks at you for a minute, from head to foot, not knowing well what to say.

"At last you opens the ball by coming to the p'int at once.

"All of a sudden, little Ellis is werry glad to see you, and asks you to be seated.

"But let us see for a minute the difference in the treatment of Admiral Ellis and Captain Tom.

"The little admiral doesn't threaten to hang you, nor does he threaten to souse you into the sea.

"No, quite the reverse.

"He compliments you, and says as how you are a clever fellow.

"Then he promises you the reward, all to yourself, and gives as an earnest of what he's a-going to do himself a hundred guineas out of his own pocket.

"There you are, Dan. Now, there's a vast difference atween Captain Tom and the admiral. Isn't there?"

"Werry much so, indeed."

"Well, now, who are you going to sarve? Captain Tom or the admiral? Don't be afeared o' speaking out, Dan. I've a great deal o' respect for your opinion."

"The admiral of course."

"That's the ticket. The thing then, is as good as done, and we'll share the reward atween us."

"Agreed! But ain't you a-coming up with me to Admiral Ellis's?"

"Sartinly not. Too many spoons spoil the broth, Dan."

"Werry good. And you expect half the reward, Bill?"

"Exactly."

"And you won't come?"

"How can I?"

"Why can't you?"

"Well, it's werry easy answering that question, Dan. Well, you know old Ellis has a grudge ag'in me."

"Well?"

"And he'd hang me as sure as eggs is eggs."

"Do you think that he would?"

"I'm sartin that he would."

"Then I won't ask you to come. But I say, Bill. Where am I to say he is?"

"Tell him as he's at anchor in the Sound."

"So I will."

"When will you go up?"

"As soon as it's dark."

"Werry good. But be careful how you act in this matter. And, above all, don't be a fool, Dan."

"I'll not, Bill, depend upon it."

"Where can I meet you later on?"

"At the Yellow Alligator."

"Werry good. I'll be there."

At this point the conversation dropped, and the two men, taking up their hats, left the eating-house.

CHAPTER CLXXI.

THE GREAT SEA EMERALD.

REUBEN HARPY listened intently to the foregoing conversation, and was immensely elated at what he had heard.

Once or twice he made up his mind to reveal himself to the two men, one of whom he knew as the bitter enemy of Captain Tom Drake.

But, after a moment's reflection, he thought better of it.

The man Dan was to call on Admiral Ellis when it grew dusk.

It would be a very easy matter for Reuben to get there an hour or two before him, and take all the credit to himself of bringing the first news.

Reuben, consequently, made up his mind to start at once.

Bidding his two companions for the present good-bye, and appointing a place to meet them in three or four hours from then, he left the restaurant.

The first barber's he came to he went in and got shaved.

At another place, well known to him, he tidied himself up a little, and when he again sauntered into the street, he looked quite a different man.

The change in his appearance was considerably for the better.

He could appear now before the old admiral quite respectable, and not be looked upon with an eye of suspicion by the footman.

We leave Reuben Harpy for the present, hastening his steps in the direction of Admiral Ellis's residence, and return to his companions, the sham sentinel and Peter.

These two worthies were not deaf to the "confab" between Bill and Dan.

They overheard nearly every word of it.

Their eyes were also open, as well as their ears, as they afterwards proved after Reuben had gone out.

Peter winked his eye very knowingly, and clapped his finger expressively on his nose.

The sham sentinel went through another pantomimic effort that was equally ingenious.

"A nice go that, isn't it?" said Peter.

"Very much interested, I should imagine, Peter."

"Very."

"But it can scarcely be wondered at. As a friend of Captain Tom's one might expect it," said the sentinel.

"I agree with you there," replied Peter. "But what's your opinion?"

"Regarding what?" asked his colleague.

"Regarding Captain Harpy, and the other two gentlemen."

"Oh, he means blocking their game."

"That's evident."

"And he will do it, too."

"Wouldn't it be a lark if we blocked his, though! What is the reward?"

"Two thousand pounds."

"And a hundred down on the nail from the admiral."

"That's only a supposition."

"Supposition or not, it's worth trying."

"You are too late."

"Not a bit of it. Captain Harpy is not going up that way before the admiral. Let me see. He'll have a shave first."

"Yes."

"How long will that occupy?"

"Ten minutes."

"Very good. Ten minutes. Ten minutes is a long time."

"Yes, if you were hanging that length it would be, Peter."

"Surely. But then after a shave comes fixing up a little. That will take a half an hour, at least."

"A half an hour and ten minutes. How much does that make?"

"Forty minutes. A good long start," said Peter, musingly.

Peter rose to his feet.

"Where are you going?" demanded the sham sentinel.

"I'll meet you in one hour and ten minutes," replied Peter. "It just strikes me that I have a little business to attend to."

His colleague smiled.

"I'll meet you just as the clock strikes eight," resumed Peter. "Let me see, it is now ten minutes to seven. I suppose you don't know where the Yellow Alligator is?"

"No."

"I'm in the same fix myself. But that difficulty can be soon remedied. Waiter!"

The waiter came running up at once.

"Where is the Yellow Alligator?" inquired Peter.

"Two miles from here, sir. When you go out, turn to your left, and keep on straight, until you get on to the Portsmouth road. It's about two miles good from here."

"Thank you," said Peter, and without another word he took up his hat and hurried out.

The sham sentinel had a very hearty laugh when he was gone.

"A shrewd rogue that Peter is!" he mentally ejaculated. "I am very glad, however, that he has gone, as I have a little errand of my own to perform. Let me see. The Yellow Alligator, at ten minutes past eight. I'll be there if I can, and punctually to time. If I can't, he'll have to wait."

As everything was paid for, he was on the point of leaving the restaurant.

But it struck him at the moment that he might inquire the nearest direction to the largest jeweller's shop in the town.

The waiter having obliged him with the information, he slipped a piece of silver into his hand, and hurried off to dispose of the mystic emerald, which had, of late, become so heavy a burden unto him.

It struck him, as he was going along the street, however, that it would not hurt his good looks to have a shave, and a general tidying up.

He sauntered into a place, and was not more than a quarter of an hour there, when he came out a new man — with a clean shave, brushed clothes, polished boots, and hair done to the nicety of perfection.

He very shortly after reached a large jeweller's shop.

The largest, indeed, in Portsmouth, and a minute's looking in at the windows convinced him that he had come to the right place, and where he was sure that he could dispose of his jewel to some advantage.

Without an instant's hesitation, he passed into the shop.

There were several ladies there, making small purchases.

Such as diamond rings, bracelets, ear-rings, and necklaces.

The sham sentinel paid no attention to this fact, however, but sought out the proprietor.

A bald-headed man, with a keen, sharp face, and small, penetrating eyes, came forward.

The sham sentinel, the moment he looked at him, knew that this was his man.

So he at once, and without any circumlocution, told him his business.

"Come this way," said the proprietor, briefly. "Let me see your emerald."

The jeweller conducted him into a small, private room at the end of the shop, where they would not likely be disturbed.

The first look that the old jeweller had at the magnificent sea emerald almost took away his breath.

He never saw such a gem in his life before.

How it sparkled and radiated in the light!

Even his finest diamonds, as far as brilliancy was concerned, were nothing to compare with it.

All the avarice of the man's nature was aroused.

He would give the world to call it his own.

"A magnificent emerald," he murmured.

"There's not another in the world to be compared with it," was the reply.

"It is, in truth, magnificent! What do you ask for it, my friend?"

The old jeweller's hands locked together in ecstacy.

"Seven thousand guineas," replied the sham sentinel.

"Pshaw! you ask too much!"

"Well, then," coolly rejoined the other, "I must be off elsewhere, where I may get a purchaser who knows the real value of it."

And he wrapped it up again with the same coolness as he had exposed it.

Taking the brilliant effect of the great sea emerald from before his eyes was like depriving the old jeweller of life.

He wrung his hands in agony.

Already was the powerful influence of this extraordinary gem at work on him.

Was he doomed to be another victim?

We shall soon see.

"Stop, young man!" he cried, in vain trying to control himself. "Give me a glance of the gem for a second."

"What's the use?"

"I'll be a purchaser."

"It is not likely."

"Why do you say not likely?"

"Because you seem to think the price I ask an extraordinary one. Now, I believe the reverse."

Slowly he unrolled the wrappings from the emerald.

"Five thousand five hundred!" cried the excited jeweller.

"No."

"Well, then, say six thousand, and then, so help me heaven, I lose by it."

"No."

"Six thousand five hundred."

"No. Not a fraction less than the seven thousand."

"Oh! how can I part with so much?" groaned the avaricious diamond merchant.

"Very well. The bargain is at an end," rejoined the sham sentinel.

"Stop! I'll give you the seven thousand."

"In that case the emerald is yours. Give me your cheque for the amount, and the jewel is yours."

The jeweller, with trembling fingers, wrote out the cheque, and the great sea emerald passed into his possession.

How long it was to remain in it was another thing.

Had he but seen the pair of fierce eyes rivetted on him from the exterior of the little window of the private room, he must have shuddered.

They remained there a minute, and then disappeared.

"A beautiful, beautiful stone!" murmured the old jeweller, communing with himself. "There's not another in the world of the same kind, I'll be bound. Ah! those changing colours! It must be the light of the setting sun falling on it. Yet no sun can penetrate here. It is very, very strange!"

It was, indeed, strange.

The green of the emerald had turned to a beautiful crimson!

The old jeweller glanced up to see where the light could come from.

When he looked down again, the gem had resumed its deep brilliant green.

A peculiar expression came into the eyes of the sham sentinel as he hurried from the place.

The next day the jeweller was found murdered in his bed, his throat cut from ear to ear, and several thousand pounds' worth of jewellery missing from his shop.

As for the sea-green emerald, it was not to be found.

In the interval, however, the sentinel had managed to cash his cheque.

CHAPTER CLXXII.

THE HUNDRED-POUND NOTE.

WE now return to Harpy.

Reuben got to Admiral Ellis's house in time to find that there had been somebody else there before him, who gave the admiral precisely the same information.

While he was going on, the admiral interrupted him.

"Hold, Mr. Harpy!" he cried. "I have heard all that before."

"You surprise me, admiral. Then I must be late."

"Why, yes, as far as that is concerned. There was a fellow here a short time ago, whose face I've seen before, though I can't say where. He ran exactly over the same thing, and by way of payment, before he started, demanded a cool hundred, which I gave him. I regret now that he anticipated you. But the moment he left I put a spy on his steps."

"What kind of man was he, admiral?"

"A rough-looking fellow, strongly-built, with a rather serious face, and in height about five feet eight inches."

"The same!" exclaimed Reuben Harpy. "I thought so."

"The same what?" quickly inquired Ellis.

"The same man, admiral."

"I do not even comprehend you now."

"Well, I'll be more explicit, Admiral Ellis."

Whereupon Reuben entered into a rather long account of his connection with the sham sentinel and Peter.

How they first got acquainted.

How they escaped from Iron-Arm's brig, and their final capture on the island, by the Death Pirate's crew.

Admiral Ellis listened with some interest to this account, and after it was done he said—

"I was sure that I had seen the man before. It is the man Peter, no doubt. However, I am sorry that you didn't come sooner, and that would have prevented the fellow from walking away with my hundred pounds. The next thing to inquire into is whether the fellow will play us false, and seek to warn that accursed buccaneer, Captain Tom."

"The best thing is to prevent him, admiral."

"How?" asked Ellis.

"Arrest him."

"But we can prove that he has done nothing, yet. Let us first prove that he is going to play the traitor, and then we may secure him as we like."

"Then we may be too late," urged Reuben, who desired nothing better now than to see his late fellow traveller in prison.

He was very angry with Peter, as he considered

that that individual had played him a very scurvy trick, indeed.

He had taken a decided and mean advantage of him.

He never stopped to consider how mean he was himself.

Oh, no! this was out of the question.

While he was urging Admiral Ellis to give an order for the arrest of Peter, the spy came back and after being announced, entered the room.

Reuben was going to withdraw.

But upon a sign from the admiral he remained.

The man who came in was admirably adapted by nature for his calling.

He had an ugly, skulking, hang-dog look about him.

His eyes were keen and penetrating.

His nose pointed.

In fact, all his features wedged out like a hatchet, the predominant traits of which were low cunning, a little tact, and much shrewdness.

This was the man that had been sent to watch the generally quiet and inquisitive Peter's movements.

"Well, Bromley," said the admiral, "what news have you? Did you track your man?"

"Yes, yer honour," replied Bromley.

"Good! He didn't see you?"

"Nor he, sir; I took good care of that."

"Well, which direction did he take?"

"He called in at the Yellow Alligator, sir; but mayhap yer honour doesn't know where that is?"

"Yes, I do, Bromley. Go on."

"Well I followed him in there."

"Well?"

"And then I saw him calling for a pint, and I did the same, keeping my eyes all the time, of course, fixed on his movements."

"Did anyone join him there?"

"Not a soul. After watching him for some time, I thought it only right to get back to you."

"Ah, Bromley, you made a mistake."

"How so, sir?"

"You shouldn't have left the Yellow Alligator. Your man will give you the slip."

"I took good care of that, sir. Guessing the slippery nature of the fellow, I left another cove to watch him."

"Good! You acted wisely."

"I think so, sir."

"The same as you always do."

"Oh, sir! you overwhelm me."

"But there's another thing to look to yet," said the admiral. "I hope you have not lost sight of that, Bromley."

"What is it, sir?"

"For instance, the fellow might leave."

"I have already arranged all that, yer honour. The moment he leaves the Yellow Alligator, my man follows him."

"And then?"

"He sends a messenger direct to me, so that, act as he will, he cannot possibly escape."

"You may go now, Bromley," said the admiral, "and rest assured that I'll not forget the service you have done me. Stop a moment, though. Do you require any money?"

"Not any at present, sir."

"Very well. When you do, say so."

"I'll be sure to do that, sir."

Saying which, the spy bowed himself out of the room.

Once the door was closed, Admiral Ellis had a quiet chuckle to himself.

And, of course, Reuben, following his example, joined in.

"What do you think of him?" asked little Ellis when his chuckling had subsided.

"A very clever fellow, indeed," rejoined Reuben. "My good friend, Peter, will find it a rather hard matter to get out of his clutches."

"There's not the slightest danger of that," said the admiral.

"I should think not," replied Reuben.

"But who the devil have we here?" cried the admiral, as he heard a knock at the door of the apartment. "Come in!"

The door opened, and in walked the footman.

"What is it?" demanded Ellis.

"A man on important business, sir."

"Important business again! Show him in."

Reuben Harpy could guess who the visitor was.

He had, all along, expected him.

And now that it was dark, he was sure that he was not mistaken.

Not a minute passed when a square, squat-looking man entered.

There was something rakish about his looks.

Indeed, it would have been very hard to tell whether he was a man-of-war's man, a pirate, or a smuggler.

His dress partook of the three characters, and the combination was striking.

Harpy had not seen the man's countenance before, but he knew his voice instantly.

The new-comer's face was as ugly as his figure.

It was deeply scarred, and marked over with small-pox.

Admiral Ellis was able to tell what this man was at a glance.

He surveyed him from head to foot before he spoke.

"Well, my man, your business?" said the admiral, rather testily.

"Werry good, yer honour. But don't yer think we had better be alone?"

"Alone! What for?"

"Because the business I come upon is so werry important, yer honour. In any other event I shouldn't have the least objection to this 'ere other genelman being in the room."

"Indeed!" sneered the admiral. "Very kind of you to say so, to be sure."

"I meant no offence, sir."

"Doubtless not. But as this gentleman is a friend of mine, I wish him to remain. Take a seat Mr. H. until I hear what this fellow has to say. Now go on, and mind that you are not trifling with me."

Still the man hesitated, and cast uneasy looks towards Reuben.

"Why don't you go on, sir?" thundered the little admiral.

"Beg pardon, sir. I hope you won't be offended, sir; but—but, I think I had better call to-morrow."

"I warned you not to trifle with me, you rascal!"

"Lord bless yer honour, I'm not a trifling with you! It would be last thing that would come into Dan Seadrift's mind. But, yer honour—"

"Never mind your buts!" roared the admiral. "What I want you to do is to come to the point. You need not be afraid of this gentleman."

Dan thought to himself that his friend Bill had greatly overdrawn the splendid reception he was to meet with.

And had he known that this was to be his treatment, it is more than probable that he would have kept at a safe distance from Ellis's presence.

Ellis was well-known to be a little fiend in human form, who would just as soon order him the "cat" as not, or perhaps press him on one of his war vessels.

These facts were not very much relished by our friend Dan.

And in his heart he cursed Bill for being the means of urging him to this interview.

Now, as he expected better treatment from Captain Tom, he was sorry that he did not go at once in search of him.

But what was done could not now be undone.

It, however, struck him very suddenly that he might play a double game, and derive some benefit from both parties.

It would only be right to at least revenge himself on Admiral Ellis.

"Well, yer honour," said Dan, "as you say as how this gentleman'll not be in the way, I'll go on to state why I came here."

"Do so, and don't be too circumlocutory."

"Sarcum what, yer honour?"

"I say circumlocutory, you muddle-head. Perhaps you don't know what that is. I didn't expect you would. Well, it means this, in plainer phraseology, tell your story, stick to the point, and don't go beating too much about the bush."

"I understand, yer honour, now," said Dan; "and if you catch me at that kind o' work, I'll give you leave to kick me downstairs."

"I might do something worse, you rascal!"

"Very well, yer honour, whatever you do I'll not take it amiss if you find me spinning a yarn as has nothing in it. But in the first place, and I hope yer honour will excuse me, there's to be a little money down."

"A little what?" thundered Ellis.

"A little money down, yer honour."

"Curse your impudence, sir! What do you mean?"

"Well, I means just this, yer honour. I comes here with very valuable information, and I expects to get paid for it."

"Those are the very words of that other rascal," muttered Ellis. "Do you understand this fellow, Mr. H? I can't make head nor tail of him."

"Perhaps it's some information regarding Captain Tom Drake," replied Reuben, who, of course, knew very well that it was.

"Another of the same crew, I suppose," growled Ellis. "A man must needs be made of hundred-pound notes."

Dan Seadrift's lower jaw fell.

Hundred-pound notes!

That was just the very thing he came for.

Could it be possible that someone had been there before him?

His worthy pal, Bill, for instance?

Bill deceive him in that shameful way!

If so, he would make a vigorous attempt to break his head the first time he caught sight of him.

"So you have come here prepared to give me information, and you want money for it?" said the admiral.

"That's about it, yer honour."

"Is my friend right? Does this in any way refer to Captain Tom Drake?"

"Lord, sir! who'd think as how the genelman would a-guessed it in that 'ere way? It is perfectly astonishing."

"I'll make something else astonishing for you presently," muttered Admiral Ellis. Then, speaking aloud, "Where is this rascally buccaneer? Do you know?"

"That's what I've come to tell you, sir," replied Seadrift. "But the terms is cash down."

"I'll give you cash down directly, you rascal!" muttered the little admiral.

But he, nevertheless, concealed his rising indignation as well as he was able.

"Cash down, you say?"

"Them's the terms, sir."

"How much do you want?"

"A hundred pound down."

"A mere trifle!"

"Thankee, sir."

"I suppose you have no objection to waiting, my good fellow?"

"Not in the least, admiral."

Dan Seadrift's expectations rose.

His friend Bill had not been far out after all.

He would be treated like a prince, no doubt, presently.

"You are sure you will send no one else here for money?" said the admiral.

"Lord bless your honour, how could I?" replied the ingenious Seadrift. "I couldn't think o' such a thing."

"Oh, I suppose not. In the meantime, I will see about getting the hundred-pound note. Ahem! You had better sit down and have a glass of wine, while I am away."

Such condescension, and from an admiral of his Majesty's navy, was overwhelming.

It affected our friend, Dan Seadrift, so much that tears started into his eyes.

However, he sat down, and on a motion from the little admiral, helped himself to a glass of wine from a decanter that stood on the table before him.

And all this to Reuben Harpy's unutterable horror, who thought Admiral Ellis had taken leave of his senses.

For what else could he think?

The admiral, with a wicked grin on his face, implored Dan Seadrift to make himself at home, and not, on any account, to spare the wine, but to drink as much as he liked of it.

The illustrious Bill's friend promised implicit obedience to this, and the admiral, bidding Reuben Harpy to wait, left the room.

The noble Dan, if he knew what was in store for him, would not have gone on drinking the wine so contentedly.

But not knowing that, he managed to gulp down several glasses in a very happy frame of mind.

While Admiral Ellis was away for the "hundred-pound note," Dan Seadrift was building impossible castles in the air.

And thus he communed with himself—

"A hundred-pound note? Good. I'm werry sorry as how I can't share it with Bill, for Bill has been a werry good friend o' mine, and I've known him a werry great number of years.

"But what's the use o' making two halves of it? That would spoil it; and again, what's the use o' making three parts? That would be worse, and as for making four parts, that would be worser still.

"Even if I said I got fifty pounds, there would be five-and-twenty for Bill.

"I think as how I had better say that I got nothing.

"Will he believe me, though?

"Let me see—he owes me two and sixpence, and if I borrow a half-a-crown of him, that'll make it right.

"Fellers as have money never borrows, which, as scollard is say, is an understood fact.

"Now, if I borrows money, how can I have any myself?

"But I'll treat Bill out o' the half-crown, so as he'll be satisfied.

"I hates to see a feller-critter hocussed in any way, darne, if I don't.

"But I thinks now as that 'ere is arranged all up to the knocker.

"Then the reward—that'll come in good time.

"But Captain Tom? What about him?

"Money is the object, Dan, and money you must get."

"In course I'll go and see Tom Drake. Why not?

"Did he ever do me any injer? I should say not.

"And, again, isn't his money as good as any other man's? Of course it is."

After these profound cogitations, Dan Seadrift thought he could see his way clear.

And furthermore determined to follow his course of reasoning to the letter.

But, alas! the most mighty schemes fall to the ground like the baseless fabrics of a vision.

Dan Seadrift had simply over-reached himself.

Let us see what followed.

Twenty minutes passed by, and footsteps were heard on the stairs.

Could it be the little admiral returning?

It seemed strange!

There were so many of them!

Perhaps Ellis had brought his friends to see a good honest fellow like Dan Seadrift.

Dan, at the thought, put on a look of comparative dignity, which suited his great squat features admirably.

The light of conscious honesty flashed from his eyes.

In his own estimation he was a perfect hero.

The steps approached nearer.

This was to be the consummation of his triumph, then?

Evidently so, indeed.

For the parties outside paused in front of Ellis's drawing-room.

The reader must not mistake us, and fancy that it was his library.

Yes, there they stopped, and soon the door flew open, and the admiral himself appeared, a look of demoniac glee on his pale, withered lips.

"Forward! March!" he cried.

In walked about a dozen brawny-looking men-o'-war's men into the room.

"Halt!" cried Ellis.

The dignified expression, and that look of conscious virtue and honesty, instantly left Dan Seadrift's face.

His jaw fell at the same time.

What was the meaning of all this?

The answer soon came.

"Forward! March! Seize him!" cried Admiral Ellis.

Poor Dan Seadrift was at once secured, beyond a possibility of escape.

He was kicked, and cuffed, and finally bound.

He roared for mercy.

But it availed him not.

"Now take him down!" thundered the malicious little admiral, "and give him that hundred-pound note!"

He was taken down accordingly.

What befell him there the reader is at liberty to imagine.

CHAPTER CLXXIII.
THE PLOTTERS.

AFTER Dan Seadrift was dragged from the room, Reuben Harpy was forced to laugh in spite of himself.

The little admiral's mirth was immoderate.

"A hundred pounds, the rascal wanted, did he?" he chuckled. "Well, all I can say is that he'll get his hundred pounds with compound interest."

Reuben Harpy, having arranged a plan with Admiral Ellis for the capture of Captain Tom Drake, soon after left.

He bent his steps in the direction of that place of popular resort for sailors and smugglers, the Yellow Alligator.

This was the place where he had appointed to meet his two companions.

Would he say anything to Peter regarding his call on Ellis?

Should he condemn his meanness and treachery?

Should he make reference to the hundred-pound note that Peter had so cleverly extracted from the little admiral?

At first he thought he would.

But on more mature reflection he deemed it advisable not to do so.

He, however, made his way with all speed to the Yellow Alligator, where he arrived in good time to see the place pretty well crowded.

Old Zachariah was up to his eyes in business.

There was not much difference in the old gentleman's looks now than when we last saw him.

His one eye shone out as bright as ever.

Mrs. Magpie was still the same.

The company at the Yellow Alligator were principally composed of sailors, smugglers, pirates, and highwaymen, as well as numerous footpads.

They were all very jolly when Reuben entered.

He soon recognised his two companions, who were seated away from the rest of the party, indulging in a quiet smoke, and speaking in very low tones.

Both seemed surprised that Reuben should come in so soon.

Peter looked as innocent as if nothing had ever happened.

One might have imagined that he would have looked quite pleased after his success.

But such was not the case.

The man was as grave and as serious as ever.

"You have both been here a long time I suppose?" said Reuben, pointedly.

"Oh, yes, a very long time," said Peter, unabashed. "We were expecting you in here every minute. Couldn't have imagined where you had gone to, captain."

"Oh, indeed!" ejaculated Reuben. "Wondered what kept me, of course?"

"Precisely."

"I was away attending to a little business."

"Thought you were. Might have taken me with you, captain, as I was very desirous of seeing what kind of a place Portsmouth is."

"You would, no doubt, have no objection to walk up to the admiral's with me to-morrow?"

"What admiral's?"

"Ellis's."

"Don't like him. In fact, shouldn't care to see him," said Peter.

"Had you ever any business transactions with him?"

Peter looked up with a wonderfully innocent expression.

"Why, bless you, no, captain," he replied. "Why should you think that?"

"It just struck me that you might have had, that's all."

"Why, bless you, no. I never do business with admirals."

"Liar!" muttered Reuben.

"What did you say, captain?"

"Oh, nothing. I was merely remarking what an agreeable day it has been."

"Fiddledee and Betty Martin," said Peter, in an under tone. "He knows who called on the admiral—that's certain. However, I don't care a straw whether he does or not. I was thinking of making a raid on his money. But now that I have a hundred-pound Bank of England note in my possession I can afford to be charitable. An honest and virtuous career opens before me. Ahem! after fleecing the little admiral, I think I may retire on my laurels."

Peter was actually giving fluent expression to his thoughts in words.

Words, however, uttered to himself.

Never had Peter spoken so glibly before as he did that day.

It puzzled Reuben Harpy.

And it puzzled the sham sentinel more.

Reuben Harpy, after passing a few words with Peter's colleague, busied himself with looking around the room.

To be less noticed, he smoked a long clay pipe, as did most of the others in the bar-room.

Besides, he had a glass of steaming grog before him.

Very soon he detected the keen-visaged, ferret-eyed Bromley.

Also another with him, keen and sharp like himself.

This latter gentleman Reuben had no doubt was the man Bromley had left to watch Peter's movements when he came to the admiral's.

The keen-visaged Bromley noticed Reuben long ago; in fact, on his first entrance to the tavern, but not a sign, or even a motion, of the simultaneous recognition passed between them.

They were as perfect strangers to each other, as if they had never met.

Harpy, in many respects, was a very cunning fellow.

Besides, he had considerable penetration, and intuition of character.

This man might yet be of service to him.

He put that down in his own mind.

For he did not know what moment he might need his assistance.

Reuben now turned his eyes away from the two spies, and bent them on another object that attracted his attention.

A man seated all alone at the extreme end of the table.

Who was he?

The reader will soon learn.

The party favoured by his glances now we have met before.

He was a strong, burly, ferocious-looking man, with matted black hair, and a beard and whiskers as dark as ebony.

His eyebrows were shaggy, and his eyes deep-set in his head.

But what was strangest of all for so savage-looking a fellow, he seemed to be possessed of considerable dry humour, unmistakably shown in those deep, dark, and flashing eyes.

This man was well known to Reuben Harpy.

He knew him when he was a boy, and had cause to remember him by a loss of fifty-three guineas.

In truth, the party to whom we refer was no other than Black Bill, who was impatiently awaiting the return of his comrade, Dan Seadrift.

The minutes passed into an hour.

But no Dan came.

This was indeed strange.

Perhaps Dan had come to grief.

Or, having succeeded in getting the money from Admiral Ellis, he had given his comrade and sworn brother, Black Bill, the slip.

However, one thing was very evident in all this, that the suspicions of Black Bill increased as the time sped.

Reuben Harpy was conscious of every thought that passed through his mind, and as he was so intently regarding him, Black Bill met his eyes with a savage frown.

But Reuben, nothing abashed, soon attracted his attention in a different light.

Why not make himself known to Black Bill?

He knew him to be Captain Tom's deadly enemy,

and, with his assistance both he and Admiral Ellis would get on all the better.

He made a motion to him.

It escaped the eyes of everyone in the company except Black Bill, who by that motion knew that Reuben wished to communicate with him.

We are wrong if we say that it escaped the eyes of the whole of the company.

Old Zack caught the movement, and judging that there was something wrong, determined to watch them.

He did, and presently saw Reuben Harpy walk out of the bar-room.

Reuben was not gone more than a minute when Black Bill arose from the table, and also left the room.

Old Zack, when he thought a proper interval of time had elapsed, left the bar-room also, and was soon out in the open air.

The night was rather dark.

There was no moon, and only a few stars glinted overhead.

But it was light enough for the host of the Yellow Alligator to distinguish the forms of Reuben Harpy and Black Bill.

The latter was known very well to Old Zack, but the former he had never seen before that night.

Old Zack was naturally of an inquisitive turn, and from the moment he caught the almost imperceptible signals between the two men, he resolved to fathom their mysterious proceedings, cost what it might.

He, moreover, knew that Black Bill was a thoroughly unscrupulous villain, and had no doubt, as far as that gentleman was concerned, that there was mischief hatching.

It behoved Zachariah, now that he was out in the open air, to act with caution.

To approach these two men, and hear their conversation, was no easy matter.

To do it he must run some risk, for even in the imperfect light he might, at any moment, be discovered, and thus defeat his intention of playing the eavesdropper.

Fortunately, the road was not a very open one.

On either side ran a line of elm trees, which pretty well shaded the road.

Besides this, the hedges were tall and the ditches deep, which gave the landlord of the Yellow Alligator every chance to conceal himself.

Old Zack at once got into the ditch on the right, which, as the season had been unusually fine, was perfectly dry.

Along this he crept with the stealth of a panther after the two men.

He was not long in coming up to them, and though their tones were not loud, he could hear every word that they spoke with the utmost distinctness.

The conversation went on as follows—

"It's some time since we met before," said Reuben, "and I scarcely wondered at your not knowing me."

"Scarcely, indeed, Mr. Harpy. Whoever thought of seeing you again?"

"I suspect no one. I suppose they all about our place thought me dead?"

"That was the general opinion," replied Bill. "But here we see you again as large as life and twice as handsome. Well, I'm jiggered, this is a meeting."

"Unexpected."

"You may well say that, Mr. Harpy. It was only the other night I was speaking about you."

Reuben pricked up his ears.

"Speaking about me, were you?" he said.

"You can't have forgotten that 'ere fifty-three guinea business, Mr. Harpy."

"No, my good fellow."

"Well, that was the subject of conversation. However, let us say no more about that, for what was done then could not be helped, and you may believe me or not, sir, it was not my intention to cheat you out of the money."

"Well no matter about that now, Bill. Let bygones be bygones," said Reuben.

"Agreed, master. I always had a high regard for you," said the smuggler, "and never forgave myself for not being of service to you Well, lord, sir, I am very glad that I have met you. Especially it was good for sore eyes to see you in such a place. Been long in Portsmouth, Mr. Harpy?"

"To-day I came in," replied Reuben, "and am quite tired from the journey."

"You have had a journey, then?"

"Oh, yes, and a long one. I started from Southampton this morning early, and got in Portsmouth some time before sundown. The old place doesn't seem very much changed, Bill."

"No," replied Bill; "not very much. Especially the Yellow Alligator, is just as it always was —neither better nor worse."

"I must admit I know very little of it."

"It could not be expected, sir. Your walk in life was werry different from mine. Expected by this time, if you was alive, to see you admiral."

"I am grateful to you for thinking so," replied Reuben. "But tell me this. What kind of a person is the landlord of the Yellow Alligator? He seems to have some queer-looking fish about him."

"Well, that was just what I was remarking in my own mind to-night. But old Zack is one o' the right sort although he does sometimes poke his nose into affairs that don't concern him."

Old Zack, who was well hidden in the ditch, emitted a low chuckle, which, however, did not reach the ears of Reuben or the smuggler.

He took good care of that.

"He's as queer a-looking fish as any of the rest," observed Reuben. "An old sailor, I suppose?"

"Not exactly," replied Bill. "He was a sodger, though, and lost his eye in the American war—I mean the war for independence. He's what they call a Kentuckian. I suppose by that they means a full-blown Yankee. However, let that be what it may, Old Zack can generally see more with his one eye than other people with their two. He's as sharp as a nest o' rattlesnakes and adders put together, and as shrewd as any cove I ever met with. You should see him out-wit the officers when they come here. It's very laughable at times to see how he tricks 'em. They hates him as they hates the devil."

"The officers," observed Reuben. "What officers?"

"Why, police officers, sir."

"Oh, indeed! What the deuce do police officers want there? Perhaps after smugglers or pirates?"

"Not that, Mr. Harpy."

"What then?"

"Smugglers and pirates ain't the only people who come here. There's plenty of highwaymen and footpads as well. When there's a robbery anywhere done in the neighbourhood they first of all searches the Yellow Alligator, and if they can pounce upon their man they do so. But bless you, sir, they have to be pretty sharp when they get over old Zack. He's a caution, he is."

"Do you mean to say, then," said Reuben, "that he shields highwaymen and footpads?"

"Why, bless you, yes."

"It's a wonder they don't bring it home to him."

"That's just the very thing they can't They are always a-trying of it, but, somehow or other, fails. The Yellow Alligator is a marvellous old place, full of nooks and crannies that no one would ever dream of. When the officers goes a-searhing these, they generally comes to grief, and invariably goes away without the prizes they expects to take. He an amazing old fellow, is that landlord, I can tell you."

Old Zack chuckled quietly to himself.

He thought that both Reuben and the smuggler would find him a little more amazing than they anticipated.

"But they are surely not come out here to talk all that rot?" said old Zachariah, to himself; "no, there's an undercurrent somewhere, and that undercurrent I guess I must find out. I wonder do they think now that anyone is listening to them, and they keep up this conversation for the purpose of throwing them off the scent?

"I don't think they could have seen me going into the ditch. However, a minute or two longer'll let me know. Go ahead, my tulips! Old Zack has only one eye, but he has two good ears, and furthermore he knows that there's some hidden villainy in all this clap-trap. Go ahead, my tulips! Zachariah Ma gie has a good memory, and a wonderful deal o' patience."

CHAPTER CLXXIV.

THE LANDLORD OF THE YELLOW ALLIGATOR HEARS SOMETHING THAT INTERESTS HIM.

REUBEN HARPY and the smuggler at last came to the point.

"Your visits to the Yellow Alligator are very frequent, I suppose?" said Reuben.

"Not so werry much as that," replied the smuggler. "To tell you the truth, I wouldn't a-been here to-night, only just waiting for a pal o' mine. He went on a bit of an errand, and I expected him back an hour or so ago."

"Oh, indeed! Perhaps it's not likely that he will come back now. An hour or more waiting for a man to keep his appointment is a very long time."

"A long time truly, sir; but as my pal Dan is werry long-winded it may be that he'll not get back for another hour yet."

"Oh, I see. Did he go anywhere in particular?"

"Well, if I must tell you, he went a-wisiting one o' the admirals."

"A friend of his?"

"Oh, not in the least. It was a matter of business. Whether he succeeds or not in his undertaking I can't tell. There's money attached to it, which it's most likely as he will get."

"Much?"

"Oh, a hundred pound or so."

"Which you expect him to share with you?"

"Just so, sir."

"It's rather awkward that it should be a money matter," said Reuben.

"How so, sir?"

"Well, you see he might not come back."

"That's just the werry thing that struck me, Mr. Harpy. I must tell you, sir, that I am getting decidedly suspicious."

"And no wonder," said Reuben. "Waiting for a man who has all the money in his possession is not a sure thing."

"I'm begin to think. But hang it all, sir, he wouldn't go and turn on old pal like that. I should think Dan Seadrift is more of a man."

"Dan Seadrift?"

"That's his name, Mr. Harpy and we have known each other for many years."

"Just so," said Reuben. "But that fact won't prevent him from deceiving you, if he feels so inclined. Now, tell me the name of the admiral that your friend has gone to see."

Reuben knew, of course.

But he had an object in putting the question.

What that object was will be presently apparent.

"Well, I don't know that I am at liberty to tell you, sir."

"Very well, then. Keep it to yourself," said Reuben, pretending to be annoyed in this want of confidence evidenced by his companion.

"No offence, I hope, Mr Harpy," replied Black Bill. "I don't mean as how you couldn't be trusted; don't believe it for a moment. And as for telling you, I suppose I may as well. It was Admiral Ellis that he visited, and whether the admiral sees his way clear to give him a hundred pound note or not is more than I can tell."

"Of course, a hundred pound note is something," observed Reuben, reflectively.

"A very great deal," rejoined Black Bill. "Sich a sum is not to be picked up every day. But what he gives in exchange is worth every penny of the money."

"Now we're coming at it," thought Zack. "There's a great deal o' beating about the bush; but I reckon the secret'll come out yet. A great waste o' words, but something under the surface, nevertheless, that'll be of profit to the mind as well as the purse. Humph! it strikes me as that Harpy knows more of the matter than he pretends. We'll, however, soon see."

"Worth every penny of the money?" said Reuben. "You speak in riddles, Bill. What is worth every penny of the money?"

"The information that Dan's prepared to give Admiral Ellis."

"Oh! ah! Now I begin to understand you. Your friend, Dan, is gone up to Ellis's to dispose of some important matter that he has heard."

"And something, too, that is very true, Mr. Harpy," replied Black Bill. "If Dan only makes Ellis view the matter in a proper light he'll not grudge five times the amount. A hundred pounds is nothing for such news as Dan Seadrift can give him. I should be sorry to think that Dan sloped with the money. I've always found him honest, and a thoroughly dependable man. Perhaps he might be led into temptation, and go the wrong way; but I can hardly think so."

"The fact is," said Reuben, "it's about time now that we should understand each other better. Now listen, Bill. We know each other a long time, don't we?"

"A long time, indeed, Mr. Harpy; that is, if a 'long time' means knowing you from your infancy up."

"True," said Reuben. "And now, as we know each other so long, heaven knows we ought to at least trust each other."

"So I say."

"Perhaps, Bill, you are not aware that I know Admiral Ellis."

"I wasn't quite aware of the fact, sir."

"Well, you may know it now. Besides that, we are very good friends I am not jesting. We are in truth the best of friends."

"Then you might have been of very great assistance to us, sir, more especially as the information that Dan Seadrift took to the admiral consarned an old and esteemed friend of yours."

"Indeed."

"It does so, sir. A man for whose friendship you have the werry highest possible respect."

"You stagger me," said Reuben.

"I knew as how I should, sir. Captain Tom Drake, sir, is, I believe, a werry great friend of yours?"

"Oh, very."

"And a cousin, to boot?"

"And a cousin, to boot."

THE ESCAPE.

"A werry nice gentleman is Captain Tom for them as can see it."

"I understand you."

"I speak pretty plainly, and to the point."

"You do. There's an undercurrent of sarcasm though in all you say. In the first place," said Reuben, "Captain Tom is no friend of mine, but my most bitter, unrelenting enemy."

"That's understood."

"Well?"

"We are both equal, Mr. Harpy, in that respect."

"So I see. You love him —"

"As the devil loves holy water, and you may be sure that isn't much."

"I see what they are driving at now," said Zack to himself. "So this precious Harpy is Captain Tom's cousin? Very good, Mr. Harpy, very good. We'll see whether your little game'll be blocked or whether it won't. These amiable gentlemen have a very curious roundabout way of talking, going on the principle, of course, that the longest way round is the nearest way home."

Reuben Harpy, in all his pretended ignorance of the matter, was very desirous to find out how far Black Bill could be trusted, and whether he had now the same hatred of Tom Drake as he had formerly.

This was, perhaps, the reason that he pretended to be entirely ignorant of the whole thing.

Reuben Harpy having ascertained after a few more interrogatories that the smuggler could be depended upon, gave a brief account now of all that had taken place, ending up with poor Dan Seadrift's ultimate plight at the hands of the malicious little admiral.

Black Bill, though annoyed very much that Dan Seadrift's plan miscarried, had to laugh very heartily at the manner in which his old comrade had been pounced upon.

"You may rely on one thing, however," said Reuben. "If Dan got the hundred pound note, you would never have received a penny of it."

"Do you mean to say as how he'd go back on an old pal like that?" cried the smuggler.

"I not only say it, but I am sure of it," rejoined Reuben. "While the admiral was away for the men-of-war's men, I watched Seadrift's countenance narrowly and read it like an open book. His intention was not to give you a penny."

"Then he deserved what he got," replied Bill, indignantly. "If you are right in what you say, Mr. Harpy, I'll never trust to the friendship of a pal again."

"At least, not too much," replied Reuben. "Friendship is all very well as far as it goes, but when hundred pound notes are in the way, friendship goes a begging."

"I am afeared it does, Mr. Harpy. But I think you mentioned that the fellow who has the note is now in the bar-room of the Yellow Alligator."

"Yes."

"Then I have only to say that he's in a very dangerous place, and that if he doesn't lose the note afore the morning, he may consider himself lucky."

"That rogue of a landlord may perhaps manage to get it from him."

"I beg yer pardon, I think the landlord, considering everything, a very honest man."

"Indeed!"

"Yes. He has a queer lot of characters coming to his place from time to time certainly, but I'll be bound to say that he wouldn't cheat a man out of a farthing."

"You have a very high opinion of him?"

"The best."

"I thank him for his good opinion," thought Zachariah, "but it makes him none the less a villain in my eyes."

"If you were deceived," said Reuben.

"I'd be very much surprised."

"No doubt. But tell me how is Peter to lose the hundred-pound note?"

"How is he to lose it? In a great many ways. I don't mind telling you, as you are a man as knows something, and an old acquaintance of mine, that that note would be of the greatest possible service to me at the present moment."

"What am I to infer from that?"

"Just one thing. I have made up my mind that I have more right to it than he has."

"And that you mean robbing him?"

"Don't say robbing, Mr. Harpy. That's an ugly word. I mean borrowing it."

"Without the intention of paying it back."

"Exactly. I makes it a rule never to pay borrowed money."

"Ha! ha! ha!" chuckled Reuben. "I hope you'll succeed that's all."

"You can leave that to me, sir. If I don't succeed, there'll be no one to blame but myself."

"That is understood," said Reuben. "Now come to another point not exactly touched upon yet."

"That is just the point I want to hear," thought Zachariah. "Some reference to Captain Tom, no doubt."

Zachariah was right, as it soon after appeared.

"You must know, then," said Reuben, "that while you were conversing with Seadrift in the eating-house I was almost at your elbow."

"No."

"I say yes; and, what is more, heard every word you said."

"I must have been a dolt to speak so loud," said the smuggler.

"You didn't speak loud," said Reuben. "But you must remember that I was in the next box."

"And your companions were there also?"

"There also might have been a chance that some of Tom Drake's buccaneers were knocking about."

"Motto in future—avoid eating-houses for private conversation. I don't know that I should have taken the trouble to hear what you were saying, but Captain Tom Drake's name incidentally cropped up, so I took care that not a word after that should escape me."

"And your companions?"

"I have no doubt heard all as well."

"That was the worst."

"I should think so, considering that fellow Peter took such advantage of it."

"But you left the eating-house before they did, Mr. Harpy."

"That is true. But you must remember I wished to present myself before the admiral in a little decent trim, and it would scarcely do to have gone there as I was then—unshaven and covered over with dust."

"I can well understand that; and yet, if you had not been so particular, that prying Peter would not have been there before you."

"Very true. But what's done now," said Reuben Harpy, "cannot be undone; and I don't know that it makes much difference in any way."

"I am glad to hear you say that, sir. But the business that brought you to the Yellow Alligator to-night?"

"I came to see you," replied the ex-privateer, unblushingly.

Such, of course, as the reader is aware, was not the case.

It was only while he was there that it struck his mind that the smuggler could be of great assistance to him.

Captain Tom's brig was in the 'Sound,' and it would be a very easy matter, indeed, for Black Bill to go out in his lugger, or the lugger's boat, and discover something regarding the "Will-o'-the-Wisp" that would be of very material advantage to them.

The best plan for Admiral Ellis and Reuben would be to take the gallant buccaneer without any great show of force.

The capture would be easier, and the chances less against it.

For this purpose was it then that he thought of engaging the services of the smuggler, Bill.

"You came to see me, sir?" said the smuggler, taken very much aback. "How did you know that I was here?"

"Well, you mustn't forget that I heard your conversation."

"True, I had forgot that."

"You made the appointment with Seadrift of meeting him here."

"In course I did. What a queer jigger I am. I am losing all my memory. Well, you came here to see me, Mr. Harpy?"

"To be sure I did. It just struck me after I had left the restaurant that you would be just the man for this kind of work."

"What kind of work?"

"The one we were just referring to. pardon. I rather thought my plan the a. In the first place, you are a friend of Captain Tom's."

"No, curse him, I am not! He

thing over that fifty-three guinea business that I haven't forgotten yet."

"The scar."

"That is just what I mean."

"Well, friend Bill," laughed Reuben, "it hasn't improved your looks much."

"No, curse it; no."

"Well?"

"I'd do anything to get that upstart strung up. Of course, the reward offered for him is another inducement."

"Certainly."

"And if I moved a hand in the matter, and he was taken, I must have every penny of it."

"You need not be afraid of that," said Reuben. "If we succeed in capturing him, and through your efforts, every penny of the two thousand pounds shall be yours."

Black Bill emitted a satisfied chuckle.

"Them's to be the terms of agreement?"

"Decidedly."

"Then I'm with you in every case."

"Would you like to call with me on Admiral Ellis to-morrow?"

"No, sir. I have certain reasons for keeping away from that gentleman. The same atmosphere would not be healthy for us. Besides, promise me one thing, Mr. Harpy—that you won't mention my name to the admiral?"

"Well, if that's in the way, I'll do so."

"Thank you. And now what is the programme? It is better to understand what one is going to do than to be running bull-headed at the matter."

"Of course it is. Well, Tom Drake must be taken."

"That's settled."

"It will be a hard task, I've no doubt."

"You may be assured of that, Mr. Harpy—a mighty hard task indeed, for the fellow is a devil and not a man at all."

"Well, then, we must succeed in chaining the devil," chuckled Reuben. "You understand?"

"Perfectly."

"And it must be done quickly."

"Or not at all. Well, you may depend on me, Mr. Harpy. If I don't take Captain Tom Drake this time, I'm a Dutchman. But every penny, mind, of the two thousand pounds must be mine."

"That's already understood. Now for the best manner of proceeding in the matter. It's not likely that the 'Will-o'-the-Wisp' will remain long at anchor."

"Not in the Sound, at any rate, sir."

"Very well then, the thing must be done at once."

"That I already understand."

"Good."

"Well?"

"To-morrow night, if possible."

"I could reconnoitre the place to-morrow night; but as for taking Captain Tom, that's a different thing."

"Well we must do our best."

"We will so, sir. And if Tom Drake isn't by the heels i prison afore three days are over his head, you m y call me a fool."

"You are confident."

"I'll make sure of him this time, you can depend your life on it, sir. Two thousand pounds is something. Besides, he is a man I have never forgiven since the time I took your fifty-three guineas."

"I can well understand that. The mark of his stroke is indelible."

"It will never wear out, Mr. Harpy."

"No, I expect not. However, we must act in the matter with the greatest prudence, for the fellow

has many ears, and gets information in the most startling manner."

"I know that, sir. Well, what do you deem it most advisable to do?"

"Let me think. How far is his vessel out in the Sound?"

"About four or five miles."

"How did you come to discover that it was the 'Will-o'-the-Wisp?' asked Reuben, curiously. "It is not possible that she has come into the Sound without assuming a disguise?"

"Oh, no," replied the smuggler. "The devil himself would hardly know her now—in fact, she is not like the 'Will-o'-the-Wisp' at all. Anyone, to look at her, would think that she was a peaceable trader, for no one would ever take her for the buccaneer brig It is marvellous, Mr. Harpy, what a change has been made in her."

"Ah!"

"In fact, extraordinary. Well, ye see, sir, I was cruising the day before yesterday about the Sound, and thinking of having a look at the smart trader, as I thought her. I made a reg'lar circuit round and round, and managed to come quite near her. While I was looking, something very much like a port opened, and I was sure I caught sight of the muzzle of a gun. 'This is something unexpected,' said I to myself. 'Port holes and guns aboard. This must be seen to,' said I. But as I had no wish for 'em to notice me just yet, I went on another tack, and came round to the starboard side. While I was there, paying attention to nothing particular, I saw a boat lowered, and four or five men get into her. I looked at 'em from the corners of my eyes. 'Well,' said I, 'my kiddies, if you are honest traders, Black Bill never smuggled a bale o' goods er a cask o' brandy in his life.'"

"Were they not dressed as merchant seamen, then?"

"Why, bless you, yes! You could scarcely tell the difference atween them and any honest sailors. But seeing the port-hole, and the cannon, and what not, made me decidedly suspicious, and I was forced to conclude that there was something more in the matter than I could yet make out. At last the fellows, not seeming to observe me, put away from the brig, and made for the shore. Taking another good look at my honest trader, and surer every moment that all was not right, I put out after 'em, but in such a way that they could not suspect that I was following them. So well so good. As my little craft was a swift sailer, I was nearly in shore as soon as they were. But before I could speak to any of them they leaped out of the boat, and walking quickly away, disappeared. Having secured my own craft, I thought I might just as well take the bearings of the one they left. On I went for that purpose. I passed the boat leisurely enough, and repassed it, without appearing to take the slightest notice, as I more than half fancied that there might be eyes bent on me from my honest trader. At last I ventured to look in, and saw a piece of paper lying in the stern sheets. 'Perhaps this will give some clue,' said I, to myself, 'as there appears to be writing on it.' I found afterwards that it was a piece of a torn letter, and whose name do you think was on it, sir?"

"I really can't guess," said Reuben.

"Well, Captain Tom's. I tried to make more out, but couldn't do it. I knew one thing, however, now, that my honest trader was no other than the 'Will-o'-the-Wisp,' and with that I quietly slunk away, resolved to profit by it."

"And you did?"

"So far I may safely say so. If things go right, it will be a matter of two thousand pounds in my pocket."

"I am sure of it."

"But if it should not be Captain Tom Drake after all?" said Reuben.

"There's no fear of that, sir. A little thing cropped up that night that more than proved it.

"I was in the Blue Lobster. You know where the Blue Lobster is, of course, Mr. Harpy?"

"Simon Gagg's old place. I should think I did. Well?"

"Two queer-looking customers came in there that same night. I had my suspicions, and resolved to watch them. The matter ended in a fight, and I got a knock on the nose, that nearly struck me senseless, but not before I had discovered that these two fellows were buccaneers. They were evidently disguised. But yet there was something in their faces that I thought I knew. I had been speaking of Jerry Mizzen and Bob Hauler a little before, and I more than half suspect that these two gentlemen were my old acquaintances—curse them!"

"You have great love for Jerry Mizzen and Bob Hauler."

"Werry much so, indeed. I could kneel down and kiss the ground they walked on, I'm so fond of 'em."

"No doubt. But these fellows you think were Jerry Mizzen and Bob Hauler?"

"Yes. I am sure of it. Because Bob was, and always had been, a good boxer in his way. And he gave a few harder ones than I expected, I can tell you."

"No matter, you'll be able to return the compliment soon, perhaps."

"I hope to. The compliment I'd like to return, is to swing 'em up."

"You need have no fear. That will come all in good time."

"I hope so."

"Well, now, listen to me. If we are too long from the Alligator, there are certain prying fellows there who will grow suspicious. If possible, we must avoid all that kind of thing."

"You are right."

"Besides, it would be very easy for a person to listen to all we are saying. You see, in the first place, there are two deep ditches, the night is confoundedly dark, if we except the few stars, and there is plenty of copse-wood and trees about."

"That's just where the trouble is."

"It would be no joke if that confounded landlord, with his one eye, followed us out."

"You are right. I wouldn't put it past him at all."

"It would be almost a good idea to look into those ditches."

Zack, hearing this intention, crept from the spot with the stealth of a cat.

He heard enough, and as Captain Tom was a friend of his, he thought it might be just as well to hurry back to the Yellow Alligator and despatch a messenger to warn him.

"I'll soon block the varmint's game," said old Zack, to himself. "They think they have Captain Tom between their fingers, do they? I'll very soon show them whether they have or not. What a scoundrel that precious cousin of his must be! Black Bill, bad as he is, would hardly sell one of his own blood. But I'll be even with them both. As for pilfering that hundred-pound note from innocent-looking Peter, I'll take jolly good care that he doesn't, for I mean putting him on his guard at once. Look out for yourselves, my kiddies!" muttered Zack, "or you'll be apt to fall into the same trap as you are laying for others."

Zachariah shook his clenched fist in the direction of Reuben Harpy, and soon after disappeared.

After the plotters satisfied themselves that there was no one listening to them, they returned into the road and resumed the conversation where they had left off.

"There was no one in the ditches, after all."

"No. But it's always best to make sure."

"Decidedly. And now for Captain Tom."

"I think you had better start off."

"What! and leave my hundred-pound note in the possession of that sneaking varmint, Peter?"

"I gladly do anything for you, Mr. Harpy, but you know that is expecting a little too much. I'll tell you what might be done, however."

"What?" said Reuben.

"Couldn't you get that Peter out?"

"Well?"

"And I could manage the rest."

"What! Do you want me to take part in robbing the fellow?"

"Don't call it that, Mr. Harpy. I have a decided objection to the word robbing, for in this case the hundred-pound note is either mine or Dan Seadrift's. Do you understand, sir?"

"I certainly think you are better entitled to it, than Peter," replied Reuben. "But remember, by delaying, you are risking the two thousand."

"No, I am not, and I'll tell you why I am not. After getting this precious fellow to disgorge, I'll hurry off at once. Do you see?"

"No, I can't say that I do. Peter may most likely object to disgorging."

"Compulsory force, Mr. Harpy. If that doesn't bring the varmint to terms, I don't know what will."

"You'll find him a rough fellow."

"That says nothing. I've handled rough fellows before, and I've generally come out first best."

Now, Reuben had no earthly objection to the course Black Bill intended pursuing.

This, of course, providing that he was not dragged into it.

But being on the ground while he robbed the man was another thing.

Black Bill could deal with him as he thought fit—that was, if he took the whole matter in his own hands.

But the ex-privateer was too cunning, as well as too prudent, to expose himself to what he considered an unnecessary danger.

He, therefore, point-blank refused to have anything to do with the matter.

"If you can lure him out yourself, you may," he said; "but, otherwise, I can have nothing to do or say in the matter."

"Well, that settles it, then," said the smuggler, in a tone of deep disappointment.

"As far as I am concerned, it does," replied Reuben. "But you shan't lose by it, I promise you."

"But I do lose by it," grumbled the smuggler. "A hundred-pound note remaining in that fellow's possession is just a hundred-pound lost to both me and Dan Seadrift."

"Don't annoy yourself," said Reuben. "I have just thought of making that amount over to you myself."

"Now?" cried Bill, his eyes flashing in the expectation of getting the money from his companion.

"Not exactly now. But the minute Tom Drake is secured, I'll hand you over one hundred pounds."

This information was rather a disappointment to our friend Bill.

But he was, for all that, forced to put up with it, and take the disappointment in the most patient humour he could.

"Therefore, in the event of my securing Captain Tom—"

"The hundred pounds are yours."

"Not to come out of the reward?"

"Certainly not. On that head you can rest yourself easy."

"Well, there's one thing, Mr. Harpy," said the smuggler, "if Captain Tom gets away from me, he'll only have to get away from one other."

"Who is that?" inquired Reuben, curiously.

"The devil!" was the reply. "And now you can leave the matter entirely in my hands."

Reuben Harpy promised to do that.

"I can get a score of desperate fellows about me at a moment's notice, and if we don't succeed in bagging the buccaneer before he's much older, my name's not Bill Evans."

"Well, and now you'll start?"

"Yes."

"And when may I expect to hear from you?" asked Reuben.

"It'll not be long, you may depend."

"To-morrow?"

"Some time then. It may be late in the evening, or it may not be until the next day, and then you can safely conclude that Captain Tom's buccaneering days are over."

"Good! You speak very hopefully."

"I speak of a sartinty. And now good night, Mr. Harpy, and don't forget as every penny of the reward is to be my own."

"I'll not forget that," said Reuben. "But stop a minute; another word before you go. Where am I to hear from you?"

"Call at the Yellow Alligator, and there'll be a note left for you. But what is still better, I'll send a man, and he'll be on the look-out for you."

"Thanks! And now good night, and every success attend your efforts. I know I may depend on your prudence."

But before Reuben could get his last words out, the smuggler was gone.

The ex-privateer having nothing more to do, made his way back to the bar-room of mine host Zachariah.

CHAPTER CLXXV.

THE ESCAPE OF CAPTAIN TOM FROM THE SCHOONER

We may now return to the tap-room of the Blue Lobster, where we left its frequenters in the greatest excitement and commotion.

For the moment, they intended rushing upon Bob Hauler and Jerry Mizzen, when the sinister-looking stranger appeared.

There was something extraordinarily striking in in this man's appearance.

Something to strike the half-drunken crew of the Blue Lobster with awe.

They therefore paused in their furious onset.

The loud, angry voices ceased as if by magic.

And the stranger, after glancing at all for a moment, with a look of scorn and contempt, strode into the room.

"What!" he cried, in a harsh, grating voice. "Would you all rush upon two men? Is this what you call English fair play? Back every one of you to your seats, and don't make fools of yourselves!"

The half-drunken ruffians shrunk back like well-whipped hounds.

The metallic glare of the stranger was more than they could stand.

He seemed to hold a power in his hands that was truly marvellous.

Perhaps the only two in the room that were not so much affected by his entrance, were our two buccaneer friends, Bob and Jerry.

Bob, rather flurried from his late exertions, was puffing away like a huge porpoise.

He now staunched the blood that was flowing from his ear, but all the time bending a strange look on the new-comer.

In the lane he had not seen him to so good a advantage.

It was dark, and the sinister-looking strange slouched hat was drawn well over his brows.

But now, in the light of the bar-room, obtained a good view of him.

Bob Hauler was never so much struck with man before in his life.

The stranger's height seemed at least to be feet four or five.

He was as straight as a dart.

His shoulders broad and square, with a frame decidedly osseous—all muscle and bone—and a face that might have done credit to the arch-fiend himself.

It is no wonder that Bob, after a few cursory glances, was visibly impressed with the appearance of this Mephistophilean gentleman.

And less wonder that Jerry was even more so.

"Well, my friends," said the sinister-looking stranger, coming forward, "I have managed to get here, as you see; but, I believe, quite a quarter of an hour later than I appointed. In the meantime, you have been indulging in a little fistic display. But I perceive," addressing Bob, "that you are not much the worse for it. I see you have placed your antagonist *hors de combat* I expected as much. And now be good enough, some of you, to carry him outside. The night air will revive him."

The men, however, never moved from their seats.

The stranger bent a glance on them that was perfectly appalling.

"Did you not hear what I said?" he thundered. "Four of you take that hound out!"

The rough, bronze-faced men, perceptibly shuddering, arose from their seats.

"I don't want all of you," he cried. "Four will be enough. The four men nearest to me"

The four men indicated stepped forward, scarcely knowing, indeed, why they did so.

Black Bill had been stunned, and was breathing heavily.

They caught him up in their arms, and carried him out.

"A good riddance to bad rubbish," observed the stranger. "And now, my good fellows, what will you drink?"

Bob Hauler and Jerry Mizzen, viewing the stranger now with a little less repugnance, thought they would replenish their glasses with the same liquor as they had been drinking before.

The order was given, and the glasses brought in.

But the sinister-looking man never called for anything for himself.

Neither did he smoke the pipe that was kindly offered to him by our friend Bob.

There was something very strange in all this.

But our two friends did not think it worth while to make it a special object of comment.

Perhaps the sinister-looking man might be a teetotaller.

"More likely," thought Jerry, "he's the devil in disguise."

Whether our friend Jerry was right or not we shall not take the liberty to judge.

Everyone in the room was inoculated with a strange silence.

Not a word was spoken, only what the stranger and our two buccaneers thought proper to say, and they spoke in such low tones that no one else could hear them.

At last Jerry and Bob emptied their glasses, and at a sign from the sinister-looking man, walked out with him.

The moment they left the bar-room the Babel of tongues were let loose, and the situation canvassed in more ways than one.

As it is not our intention at present to follow Jerry and Bob in the company of their extraordinary-looking companion, we may return at once to where we left Captain Tom on the deck of the schooner.

The firing of our hero's pistol had rather at the time an unlooked-for effect.

It alarmed the men who were drinking below.

That there were not many on the schooner was evident.

But the few that were, came rushing up the companion way to ascertain the cause of the shot.

Of course this they did the moment they reached the deck.

The moon shone down on a scene that rather startled them.

The man who had been shot lay a few paces from Captain Tom, weltering in his blood.

He was apparently lifeless.

Ben Barnacle had also come out from behind the gun, and he was now in the act of severing the young lady's bonds.

But what was still more surprising for the men who came rushing upon deck they caught sight of others clambering up the side of the schooner.

These were the few buccaneers who, hearing the sharp report of the pistol, and fancying that Captain Tom was in danger, were hastening to his assistance.

All this had for a few moments a curious effect on the half-drunken crew who rushed up the companion-ladder.

They stood actually dazed and bewildered.

Not knowing which way to turn.

For they imagined at the time that their danger was indeed great, and their enemy numerous.

Now, if Captain Tom and Ben Barnacle had only acted wisely at this stage, they might, if they so felt inclined, have captured the schooner and taken the few of its crew prisoners.

The men who rushed up the companion-ladder numbered in all only fourteen.

And these were bewildered and partly drunk, so that if Captain Tom had used a little strategy at the time he might have made them an easy prey.

But instead, his only object seemed to be the rescue of the girl, and that of getting away from the schooner as quick as he could.

This indecision was nearly fatal to both him and his men.

For, as the crew of the schooner discovered no more men coming up the sides, and that they had only had to cope with a few buccaneers not half their number, they instantly realised the position, took courage, and prepared to either kill or drive their enemies into the sea.

Our hero, when too late, saw the almost fatal mistake he had made.

He should have rushed upon them the moment they came on deck, and then, he had no doubt, but the good cutlasses and pistols of his men would do the rest.

But the opportunity, it seemed, was lost.

The crew of the schooner, perceiving that there were so few to oppose them, recovered themselves in a moment.

And being well armed, they, with loud shouts, advanced on Captain Tom and his men.

The buccaneers, though greatly inferior in point of numbers, were not a bit dismayed, but prepared to meet them.

Several pistol shots were fired.

One of Captain Tom's men fell with a bullet through his head, which so enraged his companions that, rushing forward with drawn cutlasses, they were soon warmly engaged with their enemies.

The din of the fight became deafening!

The hoarse, angry shouts of the schooner's crew awoke numberless echoes over the quiet sea.

And were responded to by the lusty cries of the buccaneers, who laid about them in good style, and for some time it seemed a problem as to which side would be the victorious one.

The ringing clash of blades, the firing of an occasional pistol shot, together with the angry shouts and imprecations of the combatants, made a scene of extraordinary and terrific uproar almost impossible to describe.

Especially as the night had been so remarkably calm previously.

But Captain Tom's clear, clarion-like notes were heard above all this confusion.

"Follow me, my brave lads!" he cried. "We'll soon put this rascally horde to flight."

And well did the gallant buccaneer acquit himself.

Whenever he struck a blow, down went an enemy.

Ben Barnacle also acquitted himself bravely, and fought by the side of his young chief with the strength of a lion.

But as their adversaries were far more numerous, and being also brave, daring men, they found it most difficult to withstand their furious onslaught.

For the first few minutes the victory would seem to decide itself in favour of the buccaneers, who, with this consciousness, became more impetuous in their attacks.

But how long did this last?

Not long, unfortunately.

Two of the buccaneers had already fallen, and, although five of the schooner's men had shared the same fate, still there were so many of them left that all hope seemed finally to have left Captain Tom and Ben Barnacle.

As for those left of the buccaneers, both our hero and his lieutenant knew that they would fight to the last man.

The brave fellows had at last to give way step by step, much to the chagrin of their leader, who, as the reader may judge, could not expect them to do impossibilities.

The men they were opposed to were, perhaps, the fiercest assailants they had ever met.

Besides, perceiving that there were so few of them, had the effect of making their attack more furious.

At this stage, it seemed all up with the brave buccaneers.

The intention of the schooner's crew was apparent.

Their object was to force the buccaneers over the bulwarks into the sea.

And it seemed quite likely that they would accomplish that result.

But at this moment an unexpected occurrence took place.

An occurrence, indeed, that was favourable to Captain Tom and his few men.

The moon that had been shining out so brightly before became suddenly overclouded, and in an instant all on the deck of the schooner was shrouded in intense darkness.

If Captain Tom was to save the remnant of his little force, now was his time.

For an instant there was a pause in the conflict.

The overclouding of the moon had a peculiar effect.

Bewildering, indeed, the senses of the half-intoxicated crew of the schooner.

For we may say that they had not yet thoroughly recovered from the effects of all the grog they had consumed.

Captain Tom immediately took advantage of their hesitation by making for that side of the schooner which his boat was on.

A few whispered words to his men, and they stole stealthily through the darkness.

By taking their two dead comrades with them, they judged that it would only imperil their safety, so they therefore left them where they lay.

We must here state that while the fight was going on between the buccaneers and the schooner's crew that the young girl Captain Tom had succeeded in rescuing had fainted.

Our gallant hero's intention was not to leave her, so he picked her up from the deck in his arms and noiselessly followed his men.

As the night had grown all of a sudden as dark as pitch, his action was not discovered until he reached the bulwarks.

Then the schooner's crew seemed to awaken from their half-drunken lethargy, and with loud shouts made for the side of the vessel.

But ere this the buccaneers began their descent into the boat. The girl was lowered, and all seemed in a fair way of making good their escape.

Captain Tom and Ben Barnacle, however, would not move from the deck until they saw all their men safely in the boat.

As they were on the point of following themselves, up rushed their assailants, who just barely managed to distinguish their forms in the darkness.

Ben, seeing now that there was no time to get into the boat without endangering his own or Captain Tom's life, turned, and with his cutlass faced the enemy undauntedly.

The first that came up fell from a terrific cut of his good blade.

Ben now fought with the fury of a lion at bay, at the same time calling on his young leader to escape.

"Never!" cried Captain Tom, turning on the schooner's men and fighting right and left.

His blows flew about with the rapidity of lightning.

And, indeed, for a moment the two noble fellows beat the enemy back.

But two men opposing so many could not long be successful.

And what now was far worse, Captain Tom and Ben Barnacle heard the few buccaneers who had escaped into the boat clambering again up the netting of the schooner.

Their intention, of course, being to assist their captain and his lieutenant.

Pressed on all sides, Ben Barnacle and his noble young chief still kept the horde of ruffians at bay.

But it seemed now as if all would be lost, and Ben cried again for Captain Tom to escape.

"For heaven's sake, Captain Tom," he cried, "get into the boat! Another moment of indecision, and all is lost"

"I cannot desert you, Ben," said Captain Tom, striking down a huge opponent who was vigorously opposing him.

"But the men, captain!" cried Ben, breathlessly. "Save them, if you will not save yourself. See! they come!"

Our hero saw that his lieutenant's words were only too true, for the first buccaneer's head had already appeared above the bulwarks.

"Back!" cried Captain Tom, in a voice of thunder. "Into the boat, on your lives."

But the first buccaneer, not heeding him, leaped on deck, and advanced with his drawn cutlass in his hand.

"Do, for heaven's sake, captain," cried Ben, "get into the boat, or we shall never leave this accursed schooner alive!"

"And you?"

"Never mind me," replied Ben. "Once you show these men the example, I will follow you."

Ben, at the same time, struck another of his assailants down, and fought with greater fury than ever to give Captain Tom a chance to get away.

Our hero, well knowing Ben Barnacle's firm and determined spirit, fought for a few moments desperately to create a diversion in his favour, and having succeeded in doing so, he made the best of his way over the bulwarks into the boat, whither he was followed by the buccaneers who had clambered up the netting to his assistance.

Ben, seeing the deck now clear of his comrades, made a vigorous defence for a few moments, then backed to get away from them.

The instant he neared that part of the bulwarks over which the buccaneers disappeared, he made two or three slashing cuts that completely staggered his assailants.

Now was the time to take advantage of the suddenness of the attack.

While the crew of the schooner paused, as it seemed, in bewilderment and doubt, Ben Barnacle bounded over the bulwarks.

He, however, missed his grip of the netting, and down he went with a heavy splash into the sea.

For a time the dark waters closed over him.

But he soon re-appeared on the surface, and struck out for the boat, which lay only eight or nine yards from where he had fallen.

It was the work of a moment to get him into the boat, and before the schooner's men could realise what had taken place, the little party of buccaneers were several boats' lengths ahead.

The darkness was so great, however, that they could not see it.

Although they could hear the dipping of oars and the low exultant laughs of their late adversaries.

All the men of the schooner could do now was to give vent to loud, angry cries, and fire a few pistols off in the direction they thought the boat was taking.

But the shots were only answered by a few derisive cheers from the buccaneers as they pursued their way through the darkness.

It may be asked why a boat's crew from the "Will-o'-the-Wisp" had not put out when they heard the sounds of the conflict ring out from the deck of the schooner?

To this question we reply that Captain Tom had given strict orders that whatever the crew of the "Will-o'-the-Wisp" should hear they were on no account to leave the brig.

This order they obeyed to the letter, not imagining at the moment, though, the great danger through which the mere handful of buccaneers were passing.

Our hero, in giving his order, had acted with considerable prudence, as there were always lynx-eyed coastguards prying around, who would only be too delighted to have made the acquaintance of the "Will-o'-the-Wisp," or to even get an inkling of who her gallant commander was.

Two thousand pounds on a man's head was unpleasant enough, to say the least.

And as Captain Tom had no desire to get into the clutches of the coastguards or any of their crew, he resolved to keep himself as quiet as possible.

But the good work he did on the schooner was only the beginning of his adventures that night.

And he moreover soon found himself beset by more dangers than he expected.

There were others besides the crew of the " Will-o'-the-Wisp " who had heard the firing on board the schooner.

The sounds of the conflict were heard to an almost incredible distance.

For the night was very calm and still, and the firing of a pistol, or the clashing of a sword, could be heard, perhaps, a few miles off.

There was a lugger at anchor some two miles from the schooner, with thirty or forty coastguards aboard.

The firing of pistol-shots, and the clashing of swords breaking on the still night air, was heard quite distinctly by these gentlemen.

They were a wakeful, as well as a shrewd set, and so concluded instantly that there was something wrong going on.

And, thus concluding, determined to discover what it was.

For this purpose, a boat was manned by between fifteen or twenty coastguards, and pulled rapidly in the direction from whence the sounds came.

Had Captain Tom been aware that these fellows were coming towards him, he would instantly have changed his course, and given them a wide berth.

But not being so aware, he came within hailing distance before he hardly knew it.

" I wonder who the deuce is coming now ? " said Ben, who, without seeing the boat of the coastguards, could hear the dip of the oars distinctly, and also the murmur of voices in conversation.

" Heaven knows," replied Tom. " I shouldn't be surprised a bit, though, but it's some of those absent schooner's men, returning to their vessel."

" Or a party of coastguards attracted by the firing."

" Do you think there's a possibility of eluding them ? " asked Tom.

" There may be."

" The night is so dark."

" True."

" We might change our course."

" A good idea, captain."

" Let it, then, be done at once."

" Hold hard, the fellows have already heard us."

This was true.

Captain Tom's boat now stopped, and for a moment or two all was as still as death.

" Boat ahoy ! " came a voice through the darkness.

" Will it do to answer them ? " asked Ben.

" I think so," replied Tom.

" It will at least show that we are not afraid," said Ben.

" Boat ahoy ! " came the voice again.

" Ahoy yourself ! " cried Tom, " what's gone wrong ? "

" Heave-to ! "

" We have already done that. What do you want ? "

" A look at you."

" Then look ! "

" It's so confoundedly dark. Come nearer."

" Who and what are you ? " cried Tom.

" What a question ! You are not afraid of us, I hope."

" That depends," said Tom. " If you are honest sailors, certainly not."

" We are fishermen," came the response.

" Oh, indeed ! "

Captain Tom knew very well that this was a lie and so put them down immediately as coastguards.

Now, of all others, these he wished to avoid.

" What's to be done, Ben ? " asked Tom. " These fellows, I am sure, are coastguards."

" To be sure they are. How can we give them the slip ? "

" I am thinking."

" If we make off, they will be after us."

" And ten to one catch up," said Tom.

" Fortunately we are favoured by the darkness."

" True. But I am afraid it won't be for long. Look, Ben ! "

Ben did look, and saw the sky clearing rapidly.

In a few minutes more the moon would be shining out as brilliantly as ever.

CHAPTER CLXXVI.

THE ESCAPE

Now, Captain Tom and his lieutenant concluded that they were in a bad fix.

To cope with the coastguards successfully in their present state, they knew, would be next to impossible.

But how were they to avoid them?

What could they do, under the circumstances?

The question puzzled them.

" Ahoy there ! Why don't you come forward ? " cried the voice from the darkness.

" We were just thinking," replied Captain Tom.

" Thinking ! Thinking of what ? "

" Whether we should trust ourselves with you, or not."

" Ha ! ha ! that's a good one, at any rate."

" Glad you think so."

" What are you afraid of ? "

" Nothing, particularly."

" Then why not come on ? "

" Why don't you come on yourself ? Who are you, that we should obey your orders ? "

" You'll find out very soon. Ha ! ha ! ha ! "

" Ha ! ha ! ha ! " laughed Captain Tom, in response.

" What are you laughing at, fellow ? "

" What are you laughing at, fellow ? "

Captain Tom's daring nature could not resist giving them as good as they gave.

" You abominable scoundrel ! " cried the voice from the darkness. " What do you mean by poking fun at us in that way ? "

" I might term you a worthless scoundrel," retorted Captain Tom, " but I have better manners."

" Give way, men, let us dally no longer with them ! " cried the voice, this time in fury.

" Hold on a minute," said our hero, " you might run into us."

" If you don't make a move, we will very soon do that."

" I am sorry that you are losing your temper," said Captain Tom. " But perhaps, before you run us down, you'll give your act a little reflection. Remember that you are endangering several lives, as no one in this boat can swim a stroke."

This information seemed to cause some little hesitation on the part of the coastguard leader, who called to his men to stop a little.

" I have no desire to run into you," said the man who had spoken before, " and, as the sky is clearing, we can afford to wait a minute. We'll soon have moon enough to show us who you are. You are a cursed insolent fellow, to say the least."

" Thank you, very much," said Captain Tom. " I might say ditto, but I'll treat you with more civility."

There was a pause for a moment or two after this, when the leader of the coastguard again spoke.

" Ahoy there ! "

" What is the matter now ? " asked Tom.

" I want to ask you a question."

" Go ahead then."

"Did you hear anything unusual a short time ago?"

"Yes, I did."

"Oh, you did? Ahem! We'll come at something presently."

"I should hope so," replied Tom. "We have been coming at something for some time, and seem as far away from it as ever."

"What do you mean, you rascal?"

"You are rather prolific in names. 'Scoundrel,' 'rascal,' and the next, I suppose, will be 'villain.' Eh, my friend?"

"You think I am jesting," retorted the other; "but you'll presently find out your mistake, unless you quickly answer me."

"I have no objection. I told you to go ahead."

"Well, then, did you hear any firing a short while ago?"

"Yes, I did. I heard a little of your firing," was the reply. "And you were not sparing in your volleys, either."

"Insolent scoundrel!" cried the coastguard. "I will no longer waste time with him."

"I shouldn't, if I were you," replied Tom, laughingly. "Now, lads, give way!"

The buccaneers shot out as the moon came flooding over the sea.

"There they go, by heavens!" cried the coastguard leader.

"Yes, old fellow!" roared Captain Tom; "and now catch us, if you can!"

The boat of the buccaneers was bearing down rapidly on the shore.

For our gallant hero took good care to divert suspicion from the "Will-o'-the-Wisp," by taking an altogether opposite direction.

Indeed, the suspicions, if any, would be attracted to the schooner.

"Heave-to!" cried the leader of the coastguard; "or I'll fire into you!"

"Fire, and be hanged!" cried Tom, and urging his men on, the boat almost flew through the water.

There was a simultaneous discharge of fire-arms from the coastguard.

Our hero felt a sudden sharp pain in his shoulder.

The shots rattled about the boat.

But otherwise did no harm.

"You are hit, captain!" said Ben, with an expression of deep solicitude for his young leader.

"Only a mere scratch," replied Tom. "Pull hard, lads, and we'll soon be out of their range."

The coastguards, by firing their volley, lost a little time, which gave the buccaneers the advantage of increasing their distance from them.

And perceiving the useless effects of their volley, the moment the smoke cleared away, they gave vent to loud cries of rage and disappointment.

They decided now to waste no more ammunition until they came nearer.

Of course the coastguards had considerable advantage in their favour.

They were nearly three to one, and every stroke of their oars lessened the distance between them.

"Heave to, there!" bellowed the leader.

"Go and hang yourself!" cried Ben.

"If I mistake not, we'll hang you presently, my fine fellow," shouted the infuriated coastguard. "Give way, men—give way! We'll soon come up to the scoundrels!"

The men of the pursuing boat bent to their work with a will.

And it presently became evident that the buccaneers would soon be at their mercy.

It seemed a bad look-out for Captain Tom and his men.

And nothing seemed more certain than their capture.

If the darkness had continued, they might have had a chance of escape.

But that opportunity was now lost, and each moment the coastguard boat gained on them.

A daring plan now came into Captain Tom's brain.

He would go back and meet his pursuers.

No sooner thought of than acted upon.

The coastguards, perceiving that they were now nearly up to the buccaneers' boat, made the quiet sea ring with their cheers.

On they came, not abating their speed one jot.

Captain Tom thought it high time to stop them.

But how was he to do it?

The reader will soon learn.

Giving the order, the buccaneer's boat suddenly veered round, and the men having implicit confidence in the tactics of their leader, pulled with all their might towards the pursuing craft.

This was coming along with lightning-like impetuosity!

"Stop!" cried the coastguard chief, in evident alarm, "where are you running to?"

But before they could port their helm, the boat of the buccaneers struck them direct on their gunwale, and passed clean over them.

When Captain Tom looked round, he could see the struggling forms of the coastguards battling with the waves, and the boat, with its dripping keel, shining out in the moonbeams.

In fact, the force of the other boat running into it had capsized it.

Captain Tom would hardly, enemies as they were, have left these men to drown.

But a look was sufficient to convince him that they could swim, and, furthermore, he saw some of them already trying to right the boat, in which they finally succeeded.

He did not wait any longer than to see two or three of them get into it, and then, giving the word, he put as fast as he could for the shore.

He had no fear now that the coastguard boat would trouble them any more that night, for it would at least take them twenty minutes to pick all their comrades up, and, perhaps, another twenty to bale their craft, and pick up the oars.

What was also very much against the coastguards, the night grew suddenly dark.

The moon disappeared under a great panoply of dense black clouds.

Indeed, everything now seemed to favour Captain Tom's escape.

As no cries of distress broke upon their ears, from where the coastguards' boat had been capsized, they continued in their course, materially increasing their speed.

In less than an hour from the time of this last incident, our hero's boat grated on the shore.

During the run to shore, the girl had recovered, and gave an account of her capture by the ruffian whom Captain Tom had shot.

It appeared that they were both of the same village, and that the fellow was an irreclaimably bad character, who persisted in annoying her with his addresses.

Loving another, and having only contempt and hatred for the man who was so continually annoying her, she scornfully rejected his advances, which so incensed him, that he swore he would some day carry her off.

For the time being, the poor girl was in dread of her very life, not knowing but that the villain might some day accomplish what he had sworn.

But after serving a certain time in prison for poaching and other misdemeanours, he strangely enough disappeared from the village for a long time.

Indeed, for nearly two years nothing was heard

of him, when he suddenly turned up as second officer of the smuggler schooner, for he had been to sea before, and was considered an accomplished seaman.

The schooner having cast anchor in the Sound, he, with some of his comrades, made their way to the shore.

They now proceeded to the village.

It was night.

The cottage was reached.

But they found her absent.

Now came the difficulty of discovering where she was.

As they had disguised their unlawful calling under the garb of honest sailors, they apprehended no danger from the authorities, and on making inquiries from the unsuspecting villagers, soon found out where she was.

And when they arrived at the lady's house, to which they were directed, the smuggler lieutenant, forcing an entrance, proceeded alone to the apartment, and found his victim seated.

A book was in her hand, which she read, unconscious of the presence of her enemy.

And that very night he succeeded in accomplishing what he had sworn over two years before.

This was the account given by the fair girl that Tom had rescued, and the gallant buccaneer was glad that he had been there in time to save her.

Nothing remained now but to see her safely to the village.

This task Tom entrusted to one of the buccaneers.

And thanking our hero for his gallant conduct, she was soon on her way home—the home which at one time she thought she would never see any more

Captain Tom had a great deal more to do that night before he could set foot on the "Will-o'-the-Wisp."

He had his summons from Lady Arbuthnot to attend to.

Leaving the boat in charge of the few buccaneers, he set out with Ben Barnacle.

To reach her ladyship's meeting place they had to pass through a dense wood.

And this was some few miles in extent.

Captain Tom and his lieutenant, being well armed, did not take the trouble to scan their surroundings much.

If they had, they would have observed that they were closely watched.

Indeed, keenly watched by two sharp, ferret-like eyes, which, the moment they entered the wood were conspicuous in a burly form and a most villainous-looking face.

A man darted from behind some thick copsewood, and followed noiselessly in their tracks.

It would perhaps be hard to tell the nature of this fellow's usual occupation.

His attire had the three distinctive characteristics of pirate, sailor, and smuggler.

However, whether he was one more than the other it matters little.

Suffice it to say that he followed like a shadow after the captain and his lieutenant.

Who were easy in their minds, and thoroughly unconscious that they had this villainous-looking spy behind them.

As the moon had once more broke forth, the grim darkness of the wood was to a great extent dissipated, which made their walk through the wood more pleasant, and removed many obstacles that would otherwise be in the way.

Many old recollections came back to Captain Tom's mind, as he had very often, when a boy, passed through this piece of woodland, and that, too, when it bore a bad name, through the numerous robberies and murders which had been perpetrated in it

One incident in particular came up in his mind, which related to his father, and which he had heard more than once from his mother.

It was at a time when his father had first come to that part of the country when he was a very young man, and some year or two before he had entered the navy.

"This is a gloomy place," said Ben Barnacle, opening the conversation by looking around him.

"You are right," replied Tom. "But it's not nearly so bad as it was years ago. Robberies and murders were very numerous here one time."

"So I have heard," said Ben, carrying his hand to his cutlass, for strangely enough, at that moment, he fancied he could see two or three dark figures huddled together, as if only waiting to pounce on them.

On a nearer approach, however, he discovered his mistake.

For the two or three dark figures turned out to be no more nor less than a couple of stunted trees that had long since withered.

Indeed, in the distance, and uncertain light of the wood, they would have deceived any one's eyes.

"Well, I must say that was I greatly deceived that time," said Ben, releasing the grip that he had taken from the hilt of his cutlass.

"Deceived! In what respect?" asked Tom.

"I could almost have sworn that those stunted trees," replied Ben, "were men lying in wait for us."

"It wouldn't be a bad place for an ambuscade," rejoined Captain Tom, thoughtfully.

"You are right, it wouldn't."

"So let us keep a sharp look-out, and take care that we are not pounced upon."

"It might be as well to do even that," said Ben, "for one doesn't know sometimes from where the danger will come."

"True, and here we would be placed at disadvantage by any sudden attack. However, as we have a brace of pistols and two good cutlasses each, I don't much fear an attack. But we were talking, I believe, of the dangers of passing through this wood many years ago."

"Yes," replied Ben; "that was where you left off. I have heard some strange stories relating to it myself. Perhaps you could oblige me with one that I have not heard, captain."

"Well, to while away the time, and make the journey less tedious, I suppose I might do worse," said Tom. "Besides, the account I am going to give you relates directly to my own father."

"To your father?" interrupted Ben.

A spasm of agony seemed to shoot through his frame.

But Tom, busy collecting his thoughts to give some interest to his narrative, passed it by unnoticed.

"My father was then a very young man," began the captain, "and had newly come to the county.

"One evening, as he had occasion to ride a distance of twenty miles to meet his father, he started through this wood, deeming that by so doing he would save four or five miles, besides having the advantage of passing through so solitary and quiet a place.

"Being only a stranger, he had, of course, not heard any of the current stories regarding the wood, and if he had, I believe it would not have deterred him from thus making the journey.

"For in respect of danger he was as brave as death itself.

"Well, he took the best path he could through the wood.

"It was moonlight when he started.

"But he had not proceeded more than three-quarters of a mile by the bridle-path when everything became suddenly as dark as pitch.

"It soon became evident that there was a storm hovering in the air.

"But my father pushed on, regardless of all these evidences, and had the hope, in spite of the darkness, of passing through the wood in safety.

"His progress, however, was very slow.

"He could no longer see even a half-dozen yards before him, and instead of leaving matters to the judgment of his horse, as he should have done, he urged the poor animal forward in a direction he anticipated was the right one.

"But here he made a mistake.

"The horse wanted to go one way.

"He another.

"And so perverse and determined had he become that he soon got into a wrong path that led him deeper into the heart of the forest.

"Conscious, when too late, of his folly, he tried to rectify his mistake.

"But he discovered presently that he had gone a great deal too far, and that it was almost impossible to get out of the inextricable labyrinth that he was now in as to pass through the eye of a needle.

"One appeared as hopeless as the other.

"The silence of the wood grew awful and impressive.

"Yet there were ghostly sounds every now and then, that made my father, brave a man as he was, shudder to his very heart's core.

"He could not understand them.

"And for the first time he grew sorry that he had taken the journey.

"Again he attempted to get into the right path, and again he failed.

"He at last dismounted.

"As he saw there was no hope for him but to remain there until the morning.

"While he was giving way to the most bitter reflections, he heard a sudden rustle among the bushes.

"The rustle grew louder and louder.

"A gust of wind swept through the trees, and the moaning blast swept by, with many a ghostly groan.

"My father tried to pierce the darkness, which was deep and profound.

"But not a soul met his eye, although the strange rustle among the bushes continued and grew louder.

"For a moment his brave heart beat tumultuously.

"A strange suspicion of impending danger flashed through his mind.

"What could it be?

"He had never been superstitious.

"But now he was forced to confess that he was so for the first time.

"As the rustle among the bushes continued, my father, recovering himself by a great effort, resolved to fathom the mystery.

"As he had dismounted, he took the bridle-rein of his horse on his arm, and was proceeding for the bushes, when a very black form emerged therefrom.

"There seemed to my father at first sight to be an immense something on its back.

"The horse backed in terror.

"And its master for a moment was not in a much better frame of mind.

"'Be you devil or human being,' cried my father, at last, 'you don't pass unchallenged!'

"A low laugh greeted his words.

"'Come,' said my father, regaining courage, 'who are you, and what is your business?'

"Another laugh.

"'If you don't answer, and that quickly,' cried my father, drawing a pistol from his pocket, 'by heavens I'll make you!'

"And he would have been as good as his word, too, if the strange being had not stopped.

"The ominous click of the pistol had more effect than his words.

"The strange-looking figure threw the bundle down, and came more out from the bushes.

"'You ask me who I am,' it said. 'If the information be of any benefit to you, I am a human being like yourself, journeying through this forest, I believe, with an equal right to protect myself.'

"Though the tones of this fellow's voice were very surly, you may be sure that they had a very pleasant effect on my father, who, before that, viewed him in a comparatively supernatural light.

"'But you have no right to frighten people in that manner,' replied my father, laughing. 'I suppose you are lost in this strange wood the same as myself?'

"'There you are wrong,' replied the unknown. 'I was merely making my way home. But I suppose the storm will catch me before I get there.'

"'That is disagreeable enough,' said my father. 'But I think my case, of the two, is the worst one.'

"'How so?'

"'Because I have lost my way, and the confounded place is so intricate and dark, that I have grave doubts of finding it again.'

"'That is certainly bad for you,' replied the unknown, chuckling at the same time to himself at the difficulty my father had got himself into.

"'Now, I'd be willing to give a guinea to any one that would put me on the right road,' said my father, hoping that would tempt the unknown to offer his services.

"But in such a thought, however, he was disappointed.

"For the man neither answered yes or no.

"'Yes,' my father continued. 'I shouldn't mind giving two guineas.'

"'I have no doubt,' replied the unknown, drily. 'You have got yourself into a mess, and I'm afraid you'll have to get yourself out of it the best way you can.'

"'Come, now, my friend, you are acquainted with the intricacies of this wood, I've no doubt,' said my father.

"'I have passed through it often enough for that,' replied the man; 'but I am sorry that I can't be of any service to you.'

"'Would not two guineas tempt you?'

"'No, nor five, to-night.'

"'Well, then, I suppose I must remain here and take my chances of the storm.'

"'That, I am afraid, you will have to do. But let us not be too fast,' said the unknown. 'I knew an old wood-cutter a half a mile from here. Perhaps he, for a slight consideration, would give you shelter and then in the morning you could resume your journey without fear of again being lost. Besides, he has ample stabling for your horse.'

"My father, thinking that this was preferable to being out all night, thought the idea excellent.

"But if his strange companion would not guide him there, how could he find his way?

"'All this is very well,' said my father; 'but, pray, how am I to get there?'

"'As I am going in that direction, I'll point it out,' replied the unknown. 'By the way, I have a big bundle here, and as a half a mile is a half a mile, perhaps you would have no objection to me putting it on the back of your horse?'

"'Not in the least,' said my father. 'Bring forward your bundle.'

"The bundle—a peddler's one, apparently—was carried between them, and fastened securely to the horse's back.

"This being done, my father followed close at the heels of the peddler, who seemed to know every turning in the wood, although the darkness was as dense and profound as the night could make it.

"At last his conductor pointed out a wretched-looking hovel that loomed up from an open space in the wood.

"They now stopped, and the peddler, with the assistance of my father, got his pack down.

"'There's the wood-cutter's,' said the man resuming his load, 'and now I must bid you good-night!'

"'Good-night!' said my father.

"He slipped a piece of money into his hand, and before he could ask him a single question, his unknown conductor was gone.

"'A strange character, that,' said my father, when the peddler was gone. 'Now, I can't understand why he should be so averse to earning a few honest guineas. His calling is humble enough, and there's no doubt his pack would never bring him that amount, even in a week.'

"My father saw a light burning in the wood-cutter's window, and thought it high time to seek shelter there, as the storm was coming on.

"No longer hesitating, he went towards the hut, and knocked loudly for admittance.

"He could hear footsteps inside, and shortly after the withdrawal of bolts and bars.

"The door was swung partly open.

"A face appeared.

"The face of a man deeply wrinkled and scarred.

"'Who are you, and what do you want?' he demanded, on seeing my father.

"'I am a traveller, and have lost my way in the forest,' was the reply. 'I have been directed here as the only place in which I could put up my horse and find shelter.'

"Now, to tell you the truth, my father did not like the appearance of this fellow at all.

"But what could he do?

"He must get shelter somewhere, and villainous-looking as the wood-cutter was, he was very glad of the chance of putting up with him.

"The fellow could see at once that his visitor was a gentleman, and agreed to give him a place for the night.

"'It may not be very suitable,' said the wood-cutter, 'for my home is very humble, as you see. But whatever we have you are welcome to.'

"'You do not dwell alone, then?' said my father, thinking that, as he had used the pronoun in the plural sense, that others must be living with him.

"'Oh! yes, I am quite alone,' was the reply 'I have lived in this retired spot quite thirty years now, without a soul to bother me, if I except visitors like yourself, who sometimes crave the shelter of my humble hut for the night. But come in and rest yourself, for you must be fatigued, and perhaps hungry.'

"They both now entered the hut together, and my father was struck with the spaciousness of the apartment, besides the ample furniture contained therein.

"It was more than he could have expected in a poor wood-cutter's humble abode.

"But his host did not give him long to reflect, for he at once opened a conversation.

"'You have come a long distance?' said he

"'Not very,' replied my father. 'A half-dozen miles would cover the whole journey that I have so far taken.'

"'You surprise me!' exclaimed the wood-cutter.

'Do you mean to tell me that you have only come six miles?'

"'That is certainly the distance travelled, as far as I can judge. It may have been more, it may have been less.'

"'Then you are a resident about here?'

"'Only lately. I started out to meet my father, and taking what I considered a short cut, lost my way in the wood.'

"'That is very unfortunate,' replied the wood-cutter. 'I suppose he will be very anxiously awaiting you?'

"'You may say that,' returned my father. 'Indeed, as I shall not get there to my appointment, he'll not know what has become of me.'

"'Had you far to go?'

"'Twenty miles.'

"'A considerable distance.'

"'Not so much with such a horse as mine is.'

"'It looks like a valuable animal.'

"'It is.'

"One thing struck my father in this man's conversation.

"He spoke like a gentleman.

"What was he?

"A recluse, who, tired of the world and its vanities, had thus removed himself for ever from it?

"It was hard to say.

"The wood-cutter's face was a perfect study.

"Lines, seared and scarred, and at times positively repulsive, and even ferocious, were traced there everywhere.

"Yet the tones of his voice did not at all partake of his character.

"For they were soft and modulous.

"What could have induced the wood-cutter, then, to take to this life?

"My father in vain sought for a reason, and tired of thinking the matter over, was about to divert his mind with something else, when his host again addressed him.

"'Who directed you here?' he asked.

"'One who seemed to know you well,' my father replied 'A peddler—'

"'A peddler!' interrupted the wood-cutter.

"'So at least I should judge by his appearance, as he carried a large pack, and was evidently in a great hurry to get home.'

"'He seemed to know me?'

"'Quite well; and besides, knew how to get here through the darkness. I offered him two guineas to get me clear of the wood—'

"'And he—'

"'Refused it—was quite independent of so paltry a sum, although I am sure he couldn't make the same amount in a week.'

"'Possibly not. But now I think I know who you refer to. He didn't tell you his name?'

"'No.'

"'It must be Peter—honest Peter Gray, who occasionally pays a visit to my humble abode to see if he can dispose of a few of his wares. Quite an independent fellow is Peter. But a very honest peddler he is, nevertheless, and that is more than you can say for most of his craft.'

"'A very eccentric fellow, I should judge?'

"'Very. I could tell you a great many curious stories about him if I only chose But I forget—you must be hungry, and I have indeed very little to offer you. But what there is you are welcome to, as I before said.'

"There is, perhaps, one thing I forgot to tell you, lieutenant," said Captain Tom.

"What is that?" asked Ben.

"That my father asked the wood-cutter, prior to putting up the horse, to guide him through the wood,

THE FIGHT WITH THE PIRATES.

and he would be agreeable to pay him anything he asked for his services.

"But the man refused, and that led my father to stay in his place all night.

"Well, to go on with my story. The fellow left the apartment to procure something to satisfy the cravings of his guest's appetite.

"And while he was gone my father had a good look at the room.

"He found out now that there were many more things than he had seen at first there.

"In one corner—the darkest corner—there was a bed.

"In another a half-a-dozen heavy cutlasses.

"In still another, pistols and ma'chlocks in any number.

"Over the fireplace daggers of every conceivable shape, some in sheaths and others shining out bright and unspotted.

"Now this, as you may judge, awakened sundry suspicions in his mind.

"What were all these for?

"Surely not fit ornaments for such a place.

"Then, again, all appeared to be in perfect condition, without a spot of rust on any of the cutlasses, the matchlocks well oiled and apparently having seen recent service.

"My father thought it would be just as well to take a nearer inspection of these implements of warfare.

"He took up the lamp for that purpose, and was

approaching them, when in walked his host, with a look of anger on his face.

"'Is this the way you treat my hospitality?' he cried, 'prying around the moment I have my back turned!'

"'I was merely glancing at the strange collection of swords and pistols you have,' my father replied, 'and did not imagine that there was any harm in so doing.'

"'Perhaps not,' grumbled his host; 'but I hardly care to see people prying into things that don't concern them. These matchlocks, pistols, swords, and daggers that you see belong not to me. I have already informed you that I occasionally have visitors.'

"'You have,' my father answered.

"'Well, then, these belong to them—hunters and others, who very often come here for a day's sport. I hope that will satisfy you that they are not mine.'

"'Oh, yes!' replied my father. 'I'd be very sorry to be guilty of doubting your word. But how comes it that hunters use cutlasses?'

"'You are very inquisitive, young man,' replied his host. 'I suppose I'll have to tell you the cutlasses are not the property of the hunters.'

"'Whose, then?' asked my father, determined to have a fair and honest answer to his question.

"'You must first promise me that you'll say nothing of what I am going to tell you to anybody,' said the other.

"'First tell me,' said my father, 'if I do so, will it be to the injury of others?'

"'Not in the least; the only sufferer will be the revenue of the country. You may now, no doubt, understand me.'

"'These arms belong to smugglers,' said my father. 'You need say no more. I will keep the secret.'

"There were many things, however, connected with the wood-cutter's residence anything but satisfactory.

"But my father, after this, concealed his real feelings as well as he could.

"Although a feeling of impending evil hung heavy on his heart.

"He had only one pistol, and that he left in the holster of his saddle.

"To go back now for it would only serve to arouse the suspicions of his host.

"What was he to do?

"It soon became apparent that he had fallen into a den of murderers, from whom, doubtless, there was no escape.

"One thing he very readily recalled to his mind.

"On his first entrance into the hut, he exposed a very valuable gold watch, and looking up saw the greedy avaricious eyes of the old wood-cutter rivetted on him.

"This was a matter for his consideration, and of very grave consideration indeed.

"Besides, he had a considerable sum of money about him in Bank of England notes, which he was to have given to his father on their meeting.

"The wood-cutter soon set the table, and the meal was soon placed, which my father did not do much justice.

"All [the] time sleep was approaching, and only [...]

[several illegible lines]

"He [was] ... the time had to escape ... himself.

"The only conclusion he could come to was to leave the hut.

"But if he left it, he would then be exposed to the uncertainties of the wood.

"The storm, too, was coming on, as he could hear by the fierce moans of the wind and the solitary clap of thunder that broke for the first time overhead.

"The wood-cutter seemed to be as much engaged with his own thoughts as my father was with his.

"At last he arose to his feet, and my father also got up.

"'Why don't you sit down and rest yourself?' said his host, as if surprised at his action.

"'I was thinking of going,' returned his visitor.

"'What! start out on such a night as this?'

"'Why not?'

"'You must be mad to think of such a thing. Ah! and here comes the storm in good earnest. Hark!'

"A thunder clap at this moment broke deafeningly through the heavens, a flash of lightning of intense brilliancy followed it, then a gust of wind shrieking among the trees burst open the door with a crash and extinguished the lamp.

"The wood-cutter uttered an oath and banged the door, to which had only been on the latch, and which he bolted for better security.

"The darkness, however, was only momentary.

"The owner of the hut re-lit the lamp, and once more its flickering light illuminated the spacious apartment.

"'What do you think of that?' cried the wood-cutter—in, as it seemed to my father, low, exultant tones. 'Would you face such a night and a good shelter offered to you? If so, you may depart,; but, I, for one, will not answer for your life.'

"My father, of course, asked what dangers.

"'Such as these,' replied the wood-cutter, 'the lightning and thunder, together with those frightful blasts. Hark to them! Did you ever hear their like? Many a mighty tree is uprooted such a night, and many a valuable life has been lost by foolish daring. Go, if you like—but beware of the storm!'

"Of the two evils, my father chose the one of greater comfort, which he of course expected to find in the hut.

"Having settled the matter by re-seating himself, his host again left the apartment to regale his visitor with some good old English ale, as he expressed it.

"While he was gone, my father very adroitly secured two of the pistols, which he quickly ascertained were loaded and in good condition.

"These he concealed about his person, thinking that he would, no doubt, have use for them before long.

"Scarcely had he concealed the firearms, when the wood-cutter re-entered the apartment with a stone jug in one hand, and two bottles in the other.

"The jug was overflowing with ale, the white foam running down its sides.

"The bottles, however, as was evident at a glance, contained wine.

"'Now,' said the wood-cutter, 'I will tell you a story.'

"'Perhaps you would rather hear one of my last,' said his [...]

"'I don't care [...]

[illegible lines]

"'It is not a long [...]' said the wood-cutter, and may give you some little light into human character.

"'Well, in the first place, you must know that I was not always in this position.

"'I occupied a far different situation to being a wood-cutter in such an outlandish place as this.

"'I must tell you that I am a gentleman by birth.'

"My father, of course, had taken this for granted.

"For although the man's face was villainous, he had the appearance of a gentleman—at least, in manners and conversation.

"And sometimes there was a certain stateliness about him that could not be mistaken.

"My father was obliged to acknowledge that he was very much surprised to see him occupy the humble position of a wood-cutter.

"'It may, or may not surprise you, but what I am going to tell you is nevertheless a fact,' replied his singular host.

"'In the first place, I have a university education.'

"'And so are a gentleman,' said my father.

"'That may, or may not be,' replied his strange host.

"'But permit me to go on with my story, without interruptions.'

"My father, perceiving the peculiarities of the wood-cutter, remained silent.

"While he continued.

"'After spending a certain time at Sandhurst, I was commissioned as midshipman on his Majesty's ship, "Serapis."

"'There I got on very well, and after a few years, was made a lieutenant in the lower grade.

"'When I say a lower grade, I mean a third lieutenant.

"'Such were the ranks in those days. First, second, and third.

"'However, I was fortunate enough to become the third lieutenant of his Majesty's ship, "Serapis."

"'So well so good.

"'Everything went on as well as could be expected.

"'I must tell you, at this time, that we lay at Portsmouth Sound.

"'There were many vessels there—a squadron, in fact, of our fleet, under the command of a rear-admiral.

"'The admiral's daughter I was very much attached to.

"'We were introduced to each other nearly a twelvemonth before I obtained my lieutenancy.

"'And from that moment, I may say, our acquaintance ripened into love.

"'But she had a tyrant of a father, who, hearing that we came together a little too often, put his veto on our meetings.

"'He also treated her very harshly, and although I was not on his vessel, I was made to feel the bitterness of his resentment.

"'I was resolved, however, to be even with him, and for this purpose had a note conveyed to his daughter.

"'Having a trusty agent in a brother officer, I found no difficulty in communicating with her.

"'I urged, with all the passion of my nature, that she should leave the ship.

"'After a little urging, she gave her consent.

"'And in the night time I attired myself as a common sailor, and repaired on board the ship, on which she was, unfortunately for herself, confined, as it gave her the determination to resist such tyranny.

"'The night was dark.

"'And I must tell you that my effort ended in success.

"'The sentinels were bribed.

"'My friend had taken all this trouble beforehand.

"'So that our escape was an easy matter enough.

"'Would to heaven it were not so!'

"'Why?' asked my father, somewhat surprised that the wood-cutter should express himself in this manner.

"'Why!' exclaimed the other. 'For simply this reason.

"'I lost my bride and my commission at the same time.

"'For as I was lowering myself, with her in my arms, down the anchor chain, a volley was fired upon us, and she was pierced to the heart by over a dozen bullets, whilst such a miserable villain as you see before you escaped—escaped to taste the bitterness of the most miserable lot that ever fell to a human being.

"'Since then my life has been a total wreck.'

"The wretched wood-cutter covered his face with his hands, and for several moments seemed to be absorbed with deep grief, which I, you may be sure, was loth to interrupt.

"'Let the storm rage as it will!

"'So long as there's good liquor flying about, there's no fear of having the blues.'

"His host quickly produced from a cupboard two drinking cups, each of which he filled with the contents of the jug.

"My father, perceiving that he drank himself, also drank, and was somewhat surprised to find that the ale was in every way superior to what was generally to be had.

"The draught refreshed him very much, and had on him a slightly invigorating influence.

"But my father did not permit himself to be deceived by this effect.

"Indeed, he strangely enough anticipated what was coming.

"'Now,' said the wood-cutter. 'as you have tried my ale, what do you think of it?'

"'Never drank better.'

"'Which proves that you are not a bad judge,' returned his host; 'for people who favour me by visiting me acknowledge it to be the best they ever drank in their lives. It may be so; but to my palate it is more than delicious. It is very seldom that I take it, though, only when I have company.'

"'I may consider you abstemious, then?' said my father, forcing a laugh.

"'Consider me nothing of the kind, stranger. I prefer the stronger drink.'

"'Wine?'

"'No, you are wrong. Whisky is my favourite drink. And now, coming to think of it, I forgot to bring the bottle. First of all, however, you will try this wine, which is of excellent brand, and the most mellow you could get if you were to search the country through. It comes from that country of glorious vintage—France. Ha! ha! You can guess at whose hands? My good friends the smugglers never use my poor hut without in some way remunerating me, and in a very handsome manner, too. This bottle, as you perceive, has been opened before."

"'I see it has,' replied my father, who by this fact had his suspicions more and more aroused.

"And he furthermore resolved, that if he drank the wine, the wood-cutter should also drink it.'

"His host now produced a wine-glass, and filled it with the wine.

"'Are you not going to drink?' asked my father, quite innocently.

"'No,' was the answer. 'I never indulge in other than beer or whisky. They are quite good enough for me.'

"'................ for me,' replied my father, ... the preferred glass.

"'.... you are used to wine?' remonstrated his host.

"'Oh, yes. But I never drink wine at another man's table unless he partakes of it himself.'

"The wood-cutter eyed my father with a keen, penetrating look.

"But there was nothing in his guest's face to lead him for a moment to imagine that he suspected anything.

"He had composed his features admirably.

"He wore a look of calm good-nature, and his eyes were bright and pleasant-looking from the effects of the ale.

"Failing to detect anything like a suspicion, the wood-cutter turned away with a look of disappointment, which he found it impossible to conceal.

"'Well, perhaps you will take a little whisky?' he said.

"'No, thank you,' replied my father. 'I never drink whisky.'

"'Well, then, if you won't, you won't,' returned his host, with an angry growl.

"Whereupon, he got up from the table, and left the room.

"My father knew that he was gone for his whisky.

"'Perhaps it would be better, after all,' he thought, 'to pretend to take the wine.'

"But how could he manage without drinking it?

"My father reflected for a moment, and soon hit upon a plan.

"Whether it was to succeed or not was another thing.

"When the wood-cutter came back with his bottle of whisky, he said—

"'You seem to be very angry with me, my friend?'

"'Enough to make one,' growled the other, 'when you refuse .... good wine. If you call that appreciating hospitality, I don't.'

"'Well, come now,' said my father, 'don't be cross any longer; as it is your desire, and as it seems to please you, I don't care if I do have a little of your wine. Fill up, my friend, fill up.'

"He could see the wood-cutter's eyes sparkle with satisfaction as he poured the wine again into the glass, which he had previously returned to the bottle.

"His guest took the glass from his hand, with a smile that would have deceived a saint, and said at the same time, raising it to his lips—

"'I drink to you, sir!'

"And here a very fortunate occurrence came to my father's aid, a peal of thunder, that seemed to rock the hut to its very foundation, and a flash of lightning that nearly blinded them.

"The uproar was terrible!

"Several branches fell to the ground, occasioning a groan ..... and when the wood-cutter could recover his ..... vision he saw my father with the empty glass in his hand.

"A ..... of triumph shot from his eyes as he thought that his guest had only too surely drank of its drugged contents.

"My father observed all this, but said nothing.

"The storm had now set in in earnest.

"Furious gusts of wind shrieked around the wood-cutter's hut.

"Tremendous rain beat in at the window, threatening to .... very panes of glass, and the light .... combined to make the night a very dreadful one.

"My father now pretended to a drowsiness, to the intense satisfaction of his treacherous host.

"First he closed one eye, and then the two, and

would open them drowsily and look half-unconsciously around him.

"At such times he could see how pleased the wood-cutter looked.

"His ugly face being occasionally puckered over with smiles.

"'You seem drowsy, my friend,' said his host, addressing my father.

"'I am, indeed,' he replied with a great yawn. 'I would give anything this moment to be in bed, as I was up the greater part of last night enjoying the society of a few friends.'

"'I can well understand how fatiguing that must be,' rejoined the wood-cutter, 'and as you so badly need rest, it might be just as well, perhaps, to show you to your chamber.'

"My father nodded drowsily, and was shown up some wooden steps to his room.

"For it appeared that the wood-cutter's hut was in reality no hut at all, but contained four or five good-sized apartments.

"Once there, his host left him with the lamp in his possession, which he of course thought his guest would not very long need.

"In this, however, he was doomed to be mistaken.

"My father now staggered over the floor, and put the lamp on the table, prudently judging that the wood-cutter would be watching him through the keyhole.

"Such, indeed, was the fact.

"But the moment my father heard his retreating steps in descent of the stairs, all his drowsiness left him, and he looked much brighter than he did all the evening.

"The truth was, he had emptied the contents of the drugged wine-glass under the table during the sudden hubbub of the storm.

"My father thought now that he would examine the room.

"He took the lamp from the table, and turning down the clothes, looked at the bed.

"He saw there were spots of blood on the white sheets.

"On these he gazed with a look of horror.

"'The result of some cold-blooded murder,' he thought, 'and in this way they would dispose of me!'

"He turned his attention now from the bed to other portions of the room.

"To his dismay, he saw the apartment contained no window.

"It had had a window one time, but it had been built in with brick.

"My father was not without seeing, after he had examined it a little, that many a death struggle had taken place in this room, and it might possibly witness also his own death.

"His reflections, as you may very well believe, were of no quiet nature.

"He put the lamp on the table, and sat down beside it to think.

"To think, indeed, how he could best escape from this den of murderers and thieves.

"As he was more certain than ever, now, that they were no better.

"He took out his pistols and examined them again, to make sure that they were all right.

"A few moments convinced him that they were.

"'So well, so good,' said my father, 'and if the worst comes to the worst, I have at least a few of their lives in my hands. I would give all the money I have about me now to be once more on my horse, even though it were only in that miserable wood. I see always inclined to curse myself to think that I was such a fool as to choose a forest path, and if fortune should favour my escape, I'll see that I never get into such a fix again.'

"These were my father's thoughts as he dwelt on his unfortunate situation.

"He now judged it best to put out the light, as it would no doubt greatly facilitate his escape.

"Not long, indeed, had he extinguished the lamp, when he heard voices below.

"Voices in low-whispered conversation.

"He approached the door as if to open it, but discovered to his horror that it was locked.

"'They have indeed trapped me,' thought my father, viewing his unlucky position in the most critical light.

"He next bent his ear to a crack in the door to listen.

"By so doing he could hear the voices distinctly.

"What surprised him most was, that among the four or five speakers he could distinguish the tones of the peddler.

"'So the peddler is the ruffian who decoyed me to this place,' he murmured. 'Scoundrel! His life shall pay the penalty of his treachery!'

"He had hardly time to move back from the door when he heard footsteps on the stairs, and a voice, which he knew to be his treacherous host's, say—

"'He's sound asleep enough by this time, and one cut of your knife will place him beyond a possibility of waking.'

"'Possibly it may,' thought my father, 'but not before I have tried the effect of these two pistol-shots. So come on, you rascally murderers—you'll find there is one, at least, prepared for you.'

"The ruffians, jabbering together, came up the stairs.

"My father got behind the door, and just waited for them to open it.

"A catch was sprung, and the door opened slightly.

"Of course the room was all in darkness.

"'As dark as pitch,' said the wood-cutter. 'He must have extinguished his lamp before getting into bed. But before proceeding further, I must tell you that that gold watch of his is for me.'

"'We have agreed already on that,' grumbled one of the ruffians. 'But whatever money he has on him, together with his horse, is for me and my pals. Open the door.'

"The door was now opened wide.

"But just as the murderers were stalking into the room, my father appeared before their astonished eyes, and fired two shots in succession.

"Two of the men fell with awful cries of agony down the stairs, and my father, with the force of a battering-ram, propelled himself on the others, striking right and left with his discharged pistols.

"The wood-cutter's hut became instantly dark, and my father, over the bodies of the struggling and wounded ruffians, made for the door, opened it, and was out in an instant in the air.

"The storm had altogether ceased, and what was more fortunate still, a force of some dozen cavalrymen came up who had lost their way in the wood, and were attracted to the wood-cutter's hut by the firing.

"A few moments sufficed to explain how matters stood, and the soldiers entered the hut.

"A light was procured, by the aid of which they found two of the ruffians dead—strangely enough the wood-cutter and the peddler, who had each received a bullet through his head.

"Two others were stunned by the blows of the discharged pistols, and the two who remained uninjured were instantly secured and bound.

"I won't enter into particulars what became of these fellows, but my father, together with his money and horse, were saved, and thanking the little force of cavalrymen for their assistance, he resumed his journey."

Now, Ben Barnacle was deeply affected by this account.

But passing that over, we once more resume our narrative proper.

CHAPTER CLXXVII.

THE MYSTERIOUS SPY STILL ON THE WATCH.

CAPTAIN TOM and his lieutenant had now emerged from the wood.

Ben was conscious for some time that they were followed.

He saw a dark figure tracking them like a shadow.

But fearing, by interrupting Captain Tom's story, that the fellow might take to his heels, he wisely refrained from mentioning the circumstance until such time as they got some distance along the high-way.

Even the highway was far from being light.

The hedges were tall, and the trees over-arching the road.

"Captain," whispered Ben, "don't look round. But it's just as well to tell you we are watched!"

"Watched!" echoed Tom.

"Yes, and have been so for some time," replied Ben; "before even we left the wood."

"The deuce we have! What is to be done, then?"

"Nothing, now. Let us push on as if we didn't know he was following us. I'll keep a sharp eye on his movements, you may depend. But we must continue the conversation, or he'll have an idea that he's seen."

"Better begin another story," suggested Captain Tom.

"Capital! One just comes to my mind, which I reckon will end rather curiously for our friend behind us. Pay attention, captain, but at the same time take an occasional peep over your shoulder."

"All right. Go on," said Tom.

"Well, as I was saying," continued the lieutenant, speaking loud enough for the spy to hear him. "As I was saying, the wood has changed very much since your father's adventure there. But I can tell you a story which, if not as interesting, will be at least quite as true as the one you just related.

"'Once upon a time,' so the story goes, a strange-looking vessel came into the Sound, and lay at anchor for several days there.

"She was the wonder of all who beheld her.

"A neater or more graceful little craft could not be seen anywhere.

"Some thought she was a trader.

"Others had altogether a different opinion to that, and put her down in their own minds as a contrabandist.

"But there were also a few who believed her to be a pirate.

"One thing was certainly against the stranger, however.

"The inquisitive ones could not believe in a vessel whose crew were so reticent.

"For whatever questions were put by them, the answers given were invariably more or less unsatisfactory.

"This could not be borne for an instant by these sensible and intelligent villagers, so they hit upon a plan to find out.

"For this purpose they all met in the bar-room of the Blue Lobster.

"This was their usual meeting place, where, over long pipes and steaming glasses of grog, they began the discussion.

"'I should like to find out,' said Bill Jones, 'what these fellows mean by keeping so much to themselves.'

"'Yes, and so should I,' said Nat Simon. 'Is there no way of doing it?'

"'That's just the very point,' said another gentleman. 'The purpose, indeed, for which we have met here. The question is whether she is an honest trader, or not?'

"'And the thing is,' put in another, 'whether she is not in reality a smuggler.'

"'I'll be hanged if I don't think she's a pirate!' said still another.

"'A pirate? Ha! ha!' cried Bill Jones. 'A pirate, indeed! You must have taken leave of your senses, good neighbour. If you had but hinted that she was a smuggler, I'd have believed you.

"'But to call such a craft a pirate, goes a little beyond the bounds of both common sense or even probability.'

"'It is just as likely that we are all wrong,' said Nat Simon. 'I believe we met here for one certain and particular purpose.'

"'Yes, neighbour,' said one.

"'Not to waste time in foolish—I may say useless—argument,' went on Simon. 'But to adopt measures at once, to—'

"'Yes, to—' cried they all.

"'Let me finish my sentence,' cried Nat Simon, very much annoyed at this interruption. 'And please don't anticipate my meaning.'

"'Go on, Simon—go on!' cried his hearers.

"'Well, gentlemen, I am in the hands of the company. And if I am told to go on, I suppose I must go on.'

"'Certainly. Now let us have something good. Your venerable tongue has never said anything that hasn't had point in it yet.'

"'Thank you, gentlemen,' returned Nat. 'I am very proud of your appreciation, I assure you. But I was going to observe, when I was somewhat rudely interrupted, that any discussion on the subject in hand would be highly reprehensible unless we arrive at some given point.

"'It is all very well for a certain gentleman here to-night to say that the strange craft lying out in the Sound at present is a smuggler.

"'Where's his proof, gentlemen?

"'That is the question.

"'Another goes farther than that again, and says she's a pirate.'

"'But he doesn't tell us, gentlemen, why she is a pirate, or how she is a pirate.

"'Can the gentleman give me the distinguishing marks of a pirate?

"'I'll venture to say that he cannot, and I speak advisedly, too, for my grandfather was a sea-captain thirty-one years, six months, three weeks and four days.

"'And I'll go farther, gents, by venturing on a statement which you may think very close calculation, indeed, but which I don't; which is to this effect, that I can even tell you the minute my lamented grandfather left his ship, aye, indeed, even to the exact time he took to shake hands with each and every one of his crew.

"'I can tell you—give you an accurate approximate, gentlemen, of all this, were I to be put to it.

"'But I know, neighbours, you are by far too wise and sensible to press me on that point, being, as you must be already aware, a very painful one.

"'But to return to where I left off when I incidentally introduced my late lamented grandfather.

"'I again say, gentlemen, that certain members of the company, who, as far as I am myself concerned, shall be nameless, brought very peculiar and grave charges forward.

"'One gentleman persists in saying that a certain craft lying now at anchor in the Sound is what?'

"'Nothing more nor less than a smuggler.'

"'The charge, after all, is not so grave, gentlemen, but that there might be a worse one.

"'But mark you, the person who so kindly volunteers this information does not or cannot tell you why she is a smuggler.

"'Still another goes farther, and without a moment's sound or honest reflection, styles her a pirate right off.

"'Now, gentlemen, I leave it to you to say whether this last charge is nothing more nor less than a lamentable one.

"'In my eyes, it is very much so.

"'However, all I can say is, that if you wish to probe the matter thoroughly, you must arrive at some well-defined point of action.'

"Now, as you may well be sure," said Ben, "when this gentleman sat down, a great many angry ones rose up and pitched into him in a manner that was peculiarly astounding.

"Some said that Nat was nothing better nor worse than a tissue of deceit and falsehood combined.

"Others, that he was a villain from his birth.

"However as soon as the hubbub settled a little, Bill Jones said that he would wager anyone in the company five guineas that he would find out that very evening what the strange craft was.

"Of course, a great many there were willing to take it up.

"So far the matter was settled, and towards evening Bill sauntered down to the sea-side, knowing full well that the crew were always coming and going from the vessel.

"He waited perhaps an hour, when he saw a boat lowered from the craft's davits, and several men get into it.

"When he perceived that they got half the distance to the shore, he concealed himself behind a huge boulder.

"And in another minute he had the satisfaction to hear their boat's keel grate on the beach.

"'Ha! ha!' said Bill to himself, 'it is most likely I'll hear something now that may be of advantage to me.'

"But he listened for a word from the silent crew in vain.

"Not a solitary sentence came from them.

"They secured their boat, and walked off in silence.

"But Bill Jones was not the man to be duped like this.

"He determined to follow them.

"And follow them he did.

"Of course, always keeping at a safe distance.

"For they were a cunning lot of fellows, the crew of the strange vessel, and could smell danger a great way off.

"When they came to the skirts of the wood we have just passed through, the five men—for there were only five of them—separated.

"Two went one way.

"Three the other.

"The two that Bill Jones thought of following were those he supposed had some command.

"These bent their steps through the wood.

"Bill Jones—cunning dog as he was—followed close at their heels.

"The night was something like the present—clear, moonlight, and calm.

"Perhaps you may ask me," said Ben, "why the two men of the strange craft did not detect their follower.

"I will soon tell you that.

"In fact, the principal of the two was telling a story, just as I am now.

"And, consequently, did not take notice that there was a spy on his track.

"The other was not so, for hardly had he got half way through the wood when, looking over his shoulder, he observed a black figure stealing along the bushes.

"Now, without mentioning this circumstance to his companion, he let him proceed with his story.

"So well so good.

"But, nevertheless, he kept a watchful eye on the motions of the gentleman behind him.

"And, in fact, did it in such a way that Bill Jones did not for a moment suspect that he was seen.

"Bill was, I must tell you, in the most glorious of spirits.

"He was chuckling at the success of his plan.

"For every step of the road he was finding out more and more concerning the mysterious vessel that lay so quietly in the Sound.

"'Ah! my friends,' thought Bill, to himself, 'five guineas are five guineas, and easily earned, to say the least.

"'How I will surprise some of them!' thought Bill, 'when they find out how easily I have discovered the mystery over which they have been muddling their brains.

"'Ahem! I'm not such a fool as I look,' chuckled this cunning fellow. 'And so they will think before I have done with them.

"'Let me see what time I can be back.

"'It is now ten.

"'Well, say half-past eleven.

"'That will do very well.'

"But, somehow, the best of cunning fellows sometimes overreach themselves.

"Bill Jones—cunning dog as he was, was not an exception to the rule.

"He did overreach himself.

"And I'll tell you how.

"The second of the two began a story, just as I am now.

"Of course, it was not the same kind of story by any means.

"But I say he began one.

"And when he got to a certain point in it, he lowered his voice.

"As there was something very mysterious he had to recount.

"Something, indeed, of the most extraordinary import.

"Well, of course, just as I lower my voice now, he lowered his.

"Well, cunning Bill Jones did not exactly see the fun of being left out in the cold.

"So he closed up a little.

"Indeed, he came several paces nearer, resolved, not to let even a word escape him."

At this point in his narration, Ben Barnacle sunk his voice very low.

He had, as the reader may well imagine, a purpose in it.

Which purpose was to discover how far in advance they were of their follower.

"He has come much nearer," whispered Captain Tom.

"Good! There is no possible escape now for the scoundrel. I have a few words of my story yet to tell, and then I will pounce on him like a catamount on a hare."

This being settled, Ben afterwards resumed his story.

"Well, as I was saying, Bill Jones, resolving to master every detail of the trip, was not going to be cheated out of any choice bit of news.

"He did not like these low tones at all.

"So he crept nearer.

"Expecting, as you may well imagine, to hear something astounding, and by which he could surprise the respectable frequenters of the Blue Lobster.

"'Deuce take the fellows!' cried Bill. 'Why don't they speak out, so as one can hear them? I'll go a little nearer. Never mind; the greater the danger, the more the glory, they say.'

"Whereupon, the cunning varmint came considerably nearer.

"So near, indeed, that he could almost hear every word they whispered.

"Well, now, what do you think these men did?"

"I can't say," said Tom.

"Well, one of them did just as I am doing now. Wheeled suddenly round, and before my brave Bill Jones could get away, pounced upon him!"

Ben Barnacle's movement was very rapid.

He had turned like lightning, and before the surprised spy could run a hundred yards, he had him by the nape of the neck.

Now began a furious struggle.

The man was no child, and was bent on escaping.

And Ben Barnacle found, as powerful as he was, that he had almost his match in strength of muscle and agility.

Captain Tom would now have interfered to secure the ruffian, but Ben waved him back.

"Leave him to me! I can manage him!" cried Ben.

"Curse you! Let go of me!" screamed the man.

"Not before I have you bound and gagged, you skulking scoundrel! How do you like the story of Bill Jones, eh, you unmitigated scamp!"

The spy now squirmed and twisted in an awful way.

But it was no use.

He blasphemed and swore terribly.

But one had as much effect as the other.

Ben stuck to him like a vice.

And there was no getting away, either.

But there was one thing that nearly came fatal to our lieutenant.

The fellow ceased his struggles for a moment all of a sudden, and remained perfectly limp in the hands of his captor.

But only for a moment, though.

The next he gave a sudden wrench.

For this Ben was prepared.

But he did not expect, however, that the ruffian meditated shooting him.

In fact, he had never considered whether the man had a pistol or not.

He was soon made aware of that fact, however, by the spy suddenly drawing from his belt the weapon in question, and with another movement, quite as sudden, he placed it against his temples.

His finger on the trigger would have served to discharge it.

And the buccaneer officer would have paid the penalty with his life.

But the sharp eyes of Captain Tom detected the movement.

In an instant he bounded over the intervening space, and the next struck the pistol up.

The same moment it went off with a loud bang.

The spy, seeing that he had failed, gave vent to a frightful oath, and struggled furiously once more to free himself.

But Ben's wrath was aroused at this dastardly attempt to take his life.

So, exerting all his strength, he hurled the villain to the ground, and fell upon him, doing this by design, and knocking nearly all the breath out of his body.

It was the work of a moment now for Captain Tom and Ben Barnacle to bind him.

"That was a narrow escape," said the lieutenant, "and I am thankful to you, Captain Tom, for saving my life."

"Don't mention it," replied Tom. "It was only by the merest accident I caught the ruffian's movement and saved you. Now, what is the best to be done with the fellow?"

"The rascal rightly deserves death, if for nothing else but attempting to spy on our actions."

"And for being an assassin in intention," added Tom. "But no matter, we may as well spare the wretch's life, and content ourselves by putting him where he cannot harm us."

"Agreed," said Ben. "But where?"

"What kind of a place is that on the other side of the hedge?"

"A meadow," replied the lieutenant, who had gone and looked.

"Used or disused?"

"Evidently disused."

"We can leave him there until we send some of our men for him."

"Certainly."

"Ah! here's a rent in the hedge. That will do very well to get him through into the meadow. Besides, I hear that there are wild animals in the forest, which, during our absence, may very likely be on visiting terms with him."

"That is true."

"And I know that they will enjoy each other's company. I'll give you a hand with him, lieutenant. It will be little matter how we force him through the hedge."

"Not much," rejoined Ben. "Especially if the hedge is a prickly one."

"Besides, his body is rather bulky," added Tom.

The ruffian had up to this time been glaring at them with bitter hate in his eyes.

But, not heeding the deadly expression in his villainous face, they took him up from the road, and carried him to the rent mentioned before in the hedge.

It seemed almost impossible to get his burly form through, at first.

The rent was none of the largest, as Ben observed.

"Of the two, it would be easier to throw him over," said Captain Tom.

The bound spy, on hearing this, tried to struggle. But in vain.

His bonds were too well secured, and only cut into his flesh.

"What do you think?" said Tom.

"The hedge is too high," remonstrated Ben.

"In that case, the greater will be his fall," added Tom.

"With what result?"

"A broken back, or his head knocked into his shoulders," rejoined Tom.

Now, the idea of throwing this burly ruffian over the hedge was never for a moment intended, as the reader may well anticipate.

But it was done, nevertheless, to increase his fears.

Which it did materially.

Great beads of perspiration burst from his forehead and rolled down his face.

His massive frame shook with the horror that he experienced.

And his eyes rolled in agony.

For the next instant his face grew death-like and haggard.

When they perceived that they had sufficiently terrified him, they bore the rent in the hedge again, and after much trouble and labour, they succeeded in pushing him through.

Now as there was a slight fall on the other side, over he went, and in spite of his gag, a hollow groan escaped him.

"So far we have put the rascal out of harm's way," said Captain Tom. "But we must not leave him in the meadow like that."

"What are we to do?"

"Bind him to a tree, as I see there are a pretty thick clump of them in the field."

"You are right; that will certainly be a good plan."

"Get through, then!"

"I shall find it difficult, I imagine. You get through first, captain."

Tom, after some little difficulty, found himself on the other side.

But being aware how the spy fell down, he saved himself by leaping into the field.

By doing this, he nearly came plump on the ruffian, who lay grovelling beneath.

Ben Barnacle, after much forcing, and after enduring several scratches, followed, and in a few seconds they carried the spy between them to the thick clump of trees before spoken of.

In the most retired spot they could find they bound their prisoner.

Hoping that the buccaneers would find him there when they came in search of him.

"Now, rascal," said Ben, "the less you attempt to struggle the better; and the first attempt to groan—but I think the gag will deter you from that—and you'll have a bullet sent through your brain. For we'll have a man here to watch you in less than half an hour. So mind how you act if you place any value on your worthless life."

As far as the most deadly hatred went, the man's eyes pronounced it readily enough.

If a look could have annihilated them, they would have met their fate then and there.

But they only laughed, and got once more into the highway.

Though taking good care not through the rent in the hedge by which they came.

They went a little higher up, where they were fortunate enough to find a gate, and over this they got and resumed their journey.

They kept up a running conversation on the way.

But this we need not enter into.

At last they drew up at the place of appointment —the ruins of a little roadside church.

Here Lady Arbuthnot was to meet Captain Tom.

In the moonlight they saw a female figure issuing from the ruins.

The figure was closely veiled.

But Captain Tom had a suspicion that this was not Lady Arbuthnot.

And he was right.

In fact, this woman had not the majestic figure of her ladyship, and was rather short for even one of her sex.

But he concluded, nevertheless, that she came from Lady Arbuthnot, and so he approached to meet her.

"Captain Tom Drake?" said the female figure, stopping.

"Yes, madam, at your service," replied our hero, removing his hat, and bowing. "You come from her ladyship, perhaps?"

"Yes," replied the woman. "And with a message for Captain Tom Drake."

Our hero smiled.

"Could she not come herself?" he asked.

Then, checking himself—

"Perhaps that would be expecting too much?"

"Not in the least," replied the woman; "and her ladyship told me to be sure to tell you this. I am Lady Arbuthnot's maid, and know but too well the unfortunate cause that has detained her."

"A jealous husband," thought Tom; "no matter. We'll have to see her ladyship some other time, when circumstances will be more auspicious."

[...illegible lines...]

[...] could see [...] she uncovered her face, and displayed a rather pretty one, full of dimples and smiles.

There was a rich flush on her cheek, and a gleam [...] shot from her eyes as she for a moment [...] the graceful proportions and handsome face of our hero.

Had it been any other man than Tom, he would [...] been flattered by all this attention bestowed on him by so pretty a girl.

But our hero, with a smile on his face, only repeated his question, and was handed a letter addressed to him, in her ladyship's own handwriting.

Tom could not account for it.

But the very look of it fired his heart.

He tore it open.

The contents ran as follows—

"DEAR CAPTAIN TOM,—

" I was unable to come myself, so was obliged to send the note by my maid. Minnie and Jenny are both well. They do not know that I am writing. But for God's sake, if you value your liberty, get back to the 'Will-o'-the-Wisp' at once, and weigh anchor at your best possible speed, as the authorities are apprised of your being in England. Admiral Ellis is more than ever determined to capture you, and has made a boast, so far as I can understand, to have you in his power within twenty-four hours. You may rely on this information, as it comes from one who has a desire to serve you. Farewell, and God bless you!"

Here Lady Arbuthnot's name followed in full.

"I suspected as much," said Tom, handing her ladyship's note to the lieutenant. "What do you think of it, Ben?"

Barnacle read it through.

"I think our danger is not diminished by remaining here," he said.

"You are right," replied Tom. "A note to her ladyship, and I am off."

He hastily scribbled a few lines on some paper and folded it up.

This he handed to the maid, requesting her to hand it over to her mistress on her return.

Then thanking her, both he and the lieutenant moved away.

"I thought as much," said Tom, as they hastened their return journey. "This fellow was sent to dog our steps."

"Fortunately, we settled him. And now we'll have to act with greater caution than ever. Once on board the 'Will-o'-the-Wisp,' we may defy them."

"What a bitter little villain!" muttered Tom.

"To whom do you refer?" said Ben.

"Admiral Ellis. It is hard to think that I have saved his life so many times, and he pursuing me with this remorseless hate."

"He is determined on your capture, it seems," said Ben. "But we'll foil him yet."

"I hope so," said Tom. "However, the sooner we get to our boat the better."

They soon got to the skirts of the wood, and [...] on among the trees, where the moon was still shining down, and lighting up their path.

The walk was pleasant.

And they moved with speed, observing, however, the greatest caution, and looking very often on either side of them, so as not to be led into any ambush, or surprised by hidden enemies, who might, perchance, be behind any bush or tree.

However, they passed through the wood in safety, and, we may say, in silence.

For hardly a word passed between them.

[...illegible lines...]

[...] so very light that you could almost see to pick a pin up.

For about an hour and a half now it had been as fine as any one could wish.

But, suddenly, the moon became obscured by great, rolling, black clouds, and even its [...] shut out by wreaths of heavy vapour.

And the moment they emerged from the forest they found that the night had grown as dark as a funeral pall, so black, indeed, they could scarcely see a dozen yards before them.

The remainder of their journey was short.

Less than a quarter of an hour would bring them to their boat.

Indeed, all danger seemed over, and Captain Tom and his lieutenant moved in high spirits towards that part of the shore where their little boat was secured.

A bright gleam of moonlight broke out from the great, black clouds.

They could see their boat secure enough where they had left it, and the buccaneers, as they thought, seated in the stern-sheets.

At that point of the shore were some high, rugged rocks.

An army could almost hide itself behind them.

But these loomed out unsuspiciously, and the particles of which they were formed gleamed and sparkled like diamonds in the sudden light of the moon.

The peeping out of the orb of night was only momentary, however, and a darkness, as black and dense as ever, succeeded its disappearance.

But on trudged Captain Tom and his lieutenant, with hopeful hearts.

Not anticipating for an instant that anyone was behind the rocks, and only thinking that they had escaped the trap that was being laid for them.

Ben was the first to show any signs of suspicion.

He thought he detected the hand and face of a man looking out from behind one of the huge boulders.

And he was not far wrong, for the instant he caught Captain Tom's arm to pull him back, a dozen black forms leapt out from behind the rocks, and with loud shouts, followed by the discharge of a few pistol-shots, rushed upon them.

"Betrayed!" exclaimed Ben Barnacle, flung one of his pistols at the nearest of his assailants.

CHAPTER CLXXVIII.

BOB AND JERRY IN DIFFICULTIES.

WE must return now, for a brief time, to our two buccaneers, Bob Hanker and Jerry Mizer, who, having left the Blue Lobster with their stranger companion, bent their steps in the direction of John Gregory's old property, now in the possession of Lieutenant Sanderson.

The night was a little different to the time they entered the once respectable tavern of our old friend Simon Gagg.

It was no longer quite so dark.

A few stars peeped out from beneath the wreaths of rolling clouds that obscured the heavens.

And a delightful breeze had blown up, sighing plaintively through the roadside trees and hedges.

The night was, in truth, all that Bob and Jerry could desire, as they did not wish it to be over light, through a fear of discovery.

Though the sinister-faced man had become less obnoxious in their eyes, they could not yet even comprehend him.

Who was he, and where did he come from?

These were questions our two buccaneers asked themselves repeatedly.

Without, however, getting any satisfactory solution to their questions.

The enigma was too hard to solve.

Another thing that came into their minds.

How did this strange being exercise so all-powerful an influence over the actions of the rough, bronze-visaged frequenters of the bar-room at the Blue Lobster?

Did they know him?

Had they ever seen him before?

It did not seem from their behaviour that they had—one way or the other.

Puzzling and mystifying was all this to our two old buccaneers, Jerry Mizzen and Bob Hauler.

They cudgelled their brains in vain for answers to these remarkable questions.

The only conclusion that they could come to was the power of will over will.

Which the sinister-faced man evidently possessed in an extraordinary degree.

Bob had already found one thing out, however.

And that was whenever by chance or design he bent his keen eyes on the well-marked countenance of the stranger, he always felt something marvellously like an electric shock passing through his entire frame.

Now it so happened that our good friend Jerry was in this respect equally impressed.

The buccaneers were also philosophers in their way.

But all their philosophy, backed, as it was, by a somewhat extraordinary perception of character, availed them nothing.

They could no more penetrate the stranger's designs than if he had been carved in wood or cut out of stone.

His hard, strong, sinister-like face was like iron, and reflected no single thought or feeling.

All very strange—even startling—was this to Bob and Jerry, who gave up their task of prying into his motives as a foolish and even fruitless one.

They had gone some distance up the road before any of them spoke.

The sinister-visaged man was, however, the first to break the silence.

"I am glad," he said, "that I came to your rescue in time. The villains, if I hadn't, would certainly have eaten you up."

"Do you think so?" cried Bob.

"I am sure of it. What are two men against nearly a score?"

"True," replied Bob. "But yet I have known one single man to quell twenty afore now."

"And to make 'em cower like hounds at that," put in Jerry.

"For instance, yourself," ventured Bob. "They 'peared to have more fear of you than if you had a hundred men at your back."

The stranger permitted a curious kind of smile to come into his face, which, however, was unnoticed by both Bob and Jerry.

"Well, it's very wonderful how one man, at certain times, can wield so much power," he said, meditatively. "It surprised me as much as it did you, I assure you. It was only the result of an experiment, which, perhaps, by the merest accident, turned out successful."

"You don't force that 'ere down my throat," thought Bob. "Accident, indeed! I should just like to see where the accident comes in."

Jerry, on the other hand, was inclined to believe that it was a sudden bold stroke of the stranger's.

Which even he himself might succeed in if he only thought it worth while trying.

Now, it must be remembered that our good buccaneer friend was very vain.

And thought himself capable of anything in cases of emergency.

"Yes, now that you have mentioned it," resumed the sinister-faced man, "I have seen instances myself where men with a little reckless daring may overawe a hundred—nay, even more."

"You have?" cried Bob.

"That have I."

"I'd like to possess that faculty," said Bob, musingly, "and then I'd know what I'd do."

"Ahem! you would set the world on fire, perhaps?"

"Well, not exactly make such a big conflag—conflag—— Let me see, what is that 'ere word?"

"Conflagration you perhaps mean?" said the sinister-visaged man.

"That's it! that's it!" cried Bob. "Conflaggerashun, sure enough. What a thing it is to be a scholard, eh, Jerry?"

"You are right, old pal. That's what my late lamented dad used to tell me—no, not me—I mean my mother.

"He used to say—'Well, Missis Mizzen, what do you think of our Jerry? Don't you think he'll make a fine scholard afore we're done with him? Isn't he got the head of a great man on his two shoulders? Look at that head!' he'd cry. 'That's the kind o' head I likes to see on a boy's shoulders. I'll wager my life,' says he, 'if he goes on in that 'ere way o' learnin' that alphabet, we'll see him yet a "ral" of some kind.'

"'A "ral!"' says my mother, with a swelling of her bosom to show the delight she felt. 'A "ral!" Then let him be an admiral, and fight the battles of his country.'

"'There might jest be many a worse,' said my father, who always took the greatest pleasure in me. 'He shall be an admiral, Sal,' said he. 'I myself have fought the battles of my country long enough, with the loss of a few of my old limbs, and it'll soon be about time that he'll peg in and show what stuff he's made of.'

"'Bravo, Ben!' said my mother. 'I knew you was always a good sort, and a true hero to the backbone. And, as for Jerry, he shall fight 'em. But is there a chance of him getting to be an admiral the first going off?'

"'Now, Sal,' said my father, a-interrupting of her, 'you are talking silly. How can he be an admiral at first without sarving his apprenticeship? Come down a peg or two, Sal—come down a peg or two.'

"'Well, a midshipman, then?'

"'That's nearer the mark.'

"So you see," added Jerry, "I was to be made a midshipman at the first going off.

"Nothing less would suit my ambitious parient, as she was werry ambitious.

"First of all, however, they was to make a scholard of me, and, after that, all was easy walking.

"So they thought, and so I thought.

"But, bless you, after going into book-larning over head and ears, and through the multiplication tables as if they was nothing, my father and mother both died very suddenly, and left me little else than a few books, a poor, lone orphan in the world.

"I was put out by this unfortunate sarcumstance, you may be sure.

"But, after a little reflection, I said to myself—

"'What's the good a-crying over spilt milk?

"'They are gone, and I'm sorry for it.

"'But all the weeps in the world 'll not bring 'em back ag'in.

"'So here goes to make myself contented and happy.'

" ' First, now,' said I to myself, ' I am a scholard.

" ' So well, so good.

" ' What is to be done next ?'

" Then the old conversations of my father and mother used to come up in my mind.

" They were both ambitious that I should lose a limb or two, fighting for my country.

" I can't say exactly that my own ambition went so far.

" ' A leg is a leg, and an arm is an arm,' said I to myself.

" ' Oh, no! that won't do, Jerry, my boy!' said I, ' to give way to that 'ere uncontrolled spirit of ambition o' yours.

" ' It's all werry well to lose a father's limbs.

" ' But as they are the only limbs he has, he should be careful of 'em.'

" That was just the identical thought that struck my mind.

" ' Werry good,' said I. ' Jerry, my boy, if you have nare a leg, it will be harder work to mount the ladder o' fame, unless you're carried up neck and crop, which is a most unlikely thing that you will be.

" ' Take your old dad's advice, as far as one thing is consarned, Jerry,' said I ; ' if you can be an admiral be one. But an admiral with two good legs and two good arms is better than an admiral without them.'

" Any one, if he likes to look into it, can see the force o' that.

" Well, then, making up my mind to keep out of danger as well as I could, in the event of my getting into any, I offered my sarvices to a navy lieutenant, who, like my poor dad, thought he saw the makings of a great man in me.

" ' An admiral!' said he, when he heerd me speaking about being an admiral.

" ' I am sure you'll be an admiral in a year or two,' said he, ' and, perhaps, in less than a half a dozen, commander of the whole fleet.'

" ' But, first of all,' said he, ' you must agree to sarve his Majesty faithfully.'

" ' I have already made up my mind to do that,' said I.

" ' I am very proud to hear you say that,' he replied. ' Come along,' said he, ' we'll werry soon have you in the service.'

" And he had very soon, indeed—a little sooner than I cared for.

" I expected to be a midshipman straight off.

" But I presently found out that I'd been building all my castles in nothing but air, and that the slightest shifting o' the wind tumbled 'em over as fast as I built 'em up.

" Now this was, as you may naturally expect, a sort of disappointment.

" All my ideas of admirals and midshipmen came to nothing, and I found that the lieutenant had just been a-drawing the long bow a little, and that all I got for my ambition was a sharp rope's-ending a heard and more times a week.

" I soon got tired of the navy, as you may well think.

" Aboard ship was rocking, and as the rope's-ending were very severe at times, and anything to ..... about high time as I ..... in other words, taking my .....

..... got all my effects together ..... the sea, gave ..... th .....

..... ambition to be an admiral ..... feeling less.

..... likes to lose a leg or arm for the ..... glory of their country; but Jerry Mizzen is one as has a very decided objection to all that

'ere sort of thing, and prefers a-having all of his limbs at his command. "

" What a selfish wretch you are, Jerry," said Bob, who had listened with remarkable composure to his old comrade's account of his naval experiences.

" A selfish wretch! What for ?" cried Jerry.

" The way you are speaking."

" Because I don't want to lose an arm or leg for my unfortunate country," said Jerry. " I'll see my country blowed first, and then I won't. You leave Jerry Mizzen alone, Bob Hauler. He knows what he's a talking about."

" Our good friend's account of his experiences has amused me very much," said the stranger, " and as he himself says that he has only two legs and an equivalent number of arms, it would be very hard indeed for him to spare even one of them. And as for the country being an ungrateful one, I'll perfectly agree with him in that."

" Thank you, sir," said Jerry. " I am very glad to hear you say that. It removes a great load off my mind."

" No doubt of that," said Bob. " You are a very great coward, Jerry, and a most unmitigated villain."

" Why, Bob ?"

" Because you are not a hero."

" I don't want to be a hero."

" Nor a patriot ?"

" No, nor a patriot, even. I only wants to be what I am. Bridle your young ambition, Bob, or else it will some time or other bring you to grief."

" You think so ?"

" I am sartin of it."

Jerry thus far having related his experiences, the conversation once more reverted to the scene in the bar-room of the Blue Lobster.

" Yes," said Bob, " even if the whole twenty of them did come on, they might have found it rather hot for them."

" Indeed ?"

" Yes, you may be sure of it. For, in the first place," added the buccaneer, " we had a brace of good pistols each."

" True," replied the sinister-faced man. " But that might not avail you much."

" Make no mistake," said Bob. " It would avail us a good deal, I should think."

" In the second place, they never misses fire," put in Jerry ; " and we had the lives of four of the villains at least in our hands."

" But if you had succeeded in using them you might then expose yourself to a more serious danger," said the sinister-visaged stranger. " Do you follow me ?"

" Not exactly," replied Bob.

" I wonder what he means ?" thought Jerry. " Expose ourselves to a more serious danger ? How ?"

The question propounded in Jerry's mind was answered as quickly by the stranger.

" You would both expose yourselves to the risk of discovery," he said.

Bob pretended a woeful ignorance.

" The risk o' what ?" he asked.

" The risk of discovery," was the marked reply ; " which, besides doing harm to both of you, would, in all probability, injure others as well."

" Oh, that's a good 'un," muttered Bob, loud enough for the sinister-visaged stranger to hear him. " Wonder what he means ? Who here be fears no foe—identies, I suppose, in disguise ?"

" No such thing,' said the stranger. " Because you both there. Your comrades are Sam Drake, and the name of your skiff is the " Will-o'-the-Wisp. ".

The stupid announcement came like a thunderbolt on Bob Hauler.

All found out!

Good heavens! who was this man, then?

Bob, in the height of his surprise and bewilderment, leaped back.

In doing so, he came heavily on Jerry's corn, making that gentleman howl with pain.

"Hallo!" cried Bob, turning on his old comrade with sudden ferocity, "what do you mean by trying to trip a feller up in that 'ere fashion?"

Jerry might well have asked Bob—and, indeed, with some reason, too—what he meant by inflicting such sudden and unprovoked chastisement on him.

This he might have done if the excruciating torment of his corn permitted him.

But anything like reasonable inquiry at such a moment was out of the question.

So Bob, failing to get an answer from Jerry, if we except an occasional howl, began to do some tall swearing, in which the "irrepressible one" came in for a very fair share of abuse, interlarded with sundry heavy adjectives as qualifiers.

Bob, having thus worked off the steam of his wrath to his own satisfaction, next turned his attention to the sinister-faced man.

"Buccaneers do you call us, eh?" said the rather irate Hauler. "Well, that's information any way."

The strange gentleman smiled.

A very knowing smile, indeed, lingered around his lips.

"If there were proofs needed, I could give them to you," he said.

"You could?" echoed Bob.

"I could, indeed."

"What do you think o' that, Jerry?"

As Jerry had by this time recovered himself, he asked his old comrade what he referred to.

"Didn't you hear what our friend here says?"

"No."

"He calls us buccaneers, and that we are the crew of Captain Tom Drake's brig the 'Will-o'-the-Wisp.'"

"Indeed! Well that is sartinly information," said Jerry.

"The 'Will-o'-the-Wisp' musn't be a werry big vessel to be manned by only two men," said Bob, winking at his comrade. "Perhaps you are captain and I am the first lieutenant."

"Well, what about the other members of the crew?"

"Well, supposing you are the buccaneers, and I am the midshipmen."

"Well, who is going to be the pilot?"

"We'll take that in turns, so as there'll be no mutiny on board."

"Agreed, old pal. Shiver my timbers! I always took you to be a genius."

"Don't flatter my wanity too much, Jerry. But how is the toes?"

"Cussedly bad, Bob. Corn's coming up, too, instead of going down."

"That's very bad indeed. Bread'll be werry dear presently."

"I don't mean corn—wheat—you fool!"

"Don't call yer brother a fool, Jerry. It's werry bad manners."

"Is it," said Jerry.

"Yes it is, and if you say it again I'll have to knock you on the conk to teach you different. But, pray, Jerry, what do you think of us being buccaneers?"

"Never."

"Yes; that's what he said."

"Well, I must only think as how its werry surprising," said Jerry.

"More nor surprising," added Bob. "It's been a thunderbolt and streaked lightning put together. It's knocked me all of a lump. I wonder what the gentlemen'll make us out next?"

"Perhaps post-captains," ventured Jerry.

"Or admirals," added Bob.

"Which would be a werry great piece o' politeness on his part. However, yer not a-going to be put out at that."

"Oh, not at all."

"A libel will never have any effect on yer."

"I should think not."

"Then pluck up yer spirits, old pal, and thank the strange gentlemen for the discovery he has made."

"You do it, Jerry, I am so deeply affected. Do you see them 'ere tears a-running down my cheeks?"

"Oh, werry distinctly. I can see 'em coming along like a reg'lar torrent."

Now the amount of feeling shown by the two comrades affected our sinister friend very little.

He beheld all that was passing with a serious and composed countenance.

"I do not desire to prevent you from having your joke out," said he of the sinister face, "but in order to prove to you that I know who you are, I will relate a little encounter that took place between Captain Tom Drake, his lieutenant, Iron-Arm, and two ruffianly Spanish pirates, who had followed them one night to assassinate them."

Bob nudged Jerry, to call his attention to the communication that the sinister-faced man made.

"Iron-Arm," whispered Bob; "I think we ought to know that gentleman."

"I should really think we ought," returned Jerry; "but a still tongue, they say, makes a wise head."

"Oh, Jerry, it's a pity as how you wasn't a philosopher."

"Never mind yer chaff now, Bob; the gentleman is going to tell a story."

"Well, let him go a-head, then; I don't wish to interrupt him."

The stranger looked at the two old comrades for a moment meaningly, then proceeded—

"I may recall this to your memory,' he said, merely for the purpose of convincing you that I know a great more of you than you imagine, or, rather than you would have me believe.

"I can tell you of many a heroic achievement performed by the gallant Tom, and his no less gallant and powerful lieutenant.

"The incident I refer to happened about two summers back.

"Captain Tom had been on the Spanish main for some time, much to the discomfort of certain pirates there.

"These were all Spaniards.

"A revengeful set, who had taken a great dislike to Captain Tom for various reasons.

"In fact, he was too honest for them.

"Too noble in disposition, and would not let them have too much of their own way so far as plundering and murdering went.

"One pirate schooner he attacked with the 'Will-o'-the-Wisp,' and made such examples of its crew and commander, that many of the others grew afraid to arouse his ire, and so were more careful in all their subsequent attacks.

"Of course, merchantmen were, in a manner speaking, no more safe then, than they were before.

"As they were still plundered whenever the pirates got a chance of coming down on them.

"But the hideous butchery was spared these unfortunate sailors.

"There was no more walking the plank.

"No more cutting of throats, or clapping boiling hot pitch caps on the heads of their victims.

"That was all done away with.

THE NIGHT ATTACK

"And all, as I have said before, through Captain Tom.

"But he came nearly being the victim to his notions of humanity.

"One night, after it had been ascertained that Tom Drake and his lieutenant, Iron-Arm, would leave their vessel to visit a friend of theirs some distance from the shore, two of the most desperate of the Spanish pirates were told off to follow and murder them.

"This being the only way they could get rid of their dreaded enemy.

"The night was nearly like the present, with hardly a star in the heavens.

"The country was lovely

"Not a house for miles.

"A strong breeze was blowing, so that Captain Tom and his companion could not hear the steps of those behind them.

"It was a night that one might have selected for the consummation of desperate and wicked crimes.

"For robbery, in fact, and assassination.

"On Captain Tom and his companion went, not dreaming for an instant that there were persons behind following them with a murderous intent.

"They were in the highest possible spirits, and conversing gaily on some little matter that had occurred to them during the day.

"They were now in one of the most silent and quiet parts of the road.

"The intended murderers took advantage of its intense loneliness.

"Rushed forward with cutlasses and pikes.

"Another instant, and Captain Tom and his companion would have been stricken down, but that a hare, disturbed by their sudden rush, sped past, uttering frightened cries.

"Iron-Arm had just time to turn round with his mace, when the two murderous ruffians were on the spot.

"The struggle for a time was terrific.

"But Iron-Arm, with his mace, succeeded in felling one of his assailants, and Captain Tom managed to serve his man in like manner.

"At the expiration of a couple of minutes, both the pirates were dead, and Captain Tom and his lieutenant proceeded on their journey.

"But their escape had been very providential.

"Their lives had been saved by a hare.

And thus the sinister-faced man ended his story.

By-and-bye the road began to grow even lighter.

Had Bob and Jerry turned their heads at the right moment, they might have caught a glimpse of three or four dark figures behind them.

These stole along the road in the deeper shadow of the trees and hedges.

Every now and then they came into view.

Then, after taking a cautious look at the three men, would again disappear like spirits in the darkness.

We assert if Bob and Jerry had seen these strange watchers, they would not have given way so much to that spirit of badinage, and would have been apt to look upon their surroundings with alarm.

But as they had not caught sight of the figures, their danger was undreamt of.

"Well, my friends, as you have had your fun out by this time," said the sinister-faced man, "perhaps you will agree with me to enter upon some other subject which will be more pleasant to your feelings."

"Nothing can be so pleasant to our feelings than to put us down as buccaneers," said Bob.

"It's quite delightful, I can tell you," added Jerry. "All I want now is for some genelman to tell me that I'm King o' the Cannibal Islands."

"You would make a werry good King o' the Cannibal Islands, you would," said Bob.

"I would make as good a king of 'em as you any day," retorted Jerry.

"I am sure you wouldn't."

"I am sure I would. I knows my book about kingcraft better than you."

"Self praise is no recommendation, Jerry."

"That's all you know about it, Bob. If I don't give praise where it's desarving, no one else will."

"Ha! ha! ha!" laughed Bob. "That is sart'inly a good one. Go ahead, Jerry, old son. Don't forget to blow that 'ere trumpet o' yours."

"If I don't blow it, no one else 'll take the trouble," replied Jerry. "As for them old copy-book sentences, we've got ahead of 'em. They was all a mistake, and civilisation proves that what I am saying is correct. I say, Bob."

"Yes."

"Take my advice, and if there's any praise to have for a reg'lar good action, have it. I've done a good deal o' that 'ere work in my life, and I've never burst up yet. It's only either rogues, fools, or jackasses as won't say a little something for themselves, at times, if they are conscious of deserving of it. Take the tip, old feller, a man with a good heart, ambition, talent, and unselfishness is sure to know whether he s got anything in him or not, and, on the same principle, when a little excited, is sure to speak about it, too. The silent coves put him down as a fool. Why? Because they are

themselves too cunning, as well as cautious, to give expression to their real feelings. If they did so, there'd be nothing but a continual blowing of trumpets. These covies allus puts me in mind of a cat watching a mouse. A wink is as good as a nod to a blind hoss, Bob. I suppose you com—comp—comp—aye, that's it—comprehend me?"

"What elorquence!" cried Bob, casting an eye of favour on Jerry. "I didn't think as how there was that much in you, old pal."

"That's because you were taken up so much with your own abilities, Bob. You know the fable o' the cat watching the mouse?"

"Don't mention it. I'm beginning to think that you are about right."

"Do you?"

"Certainly I do."

"Then I'm very glad as how you have come down to that. It's allus a pleasure, Bob, for me to hear words o' wisdom come from your lips."

"None o' that, old pal."

"But I say it is."

"You are a-flattering of me."

"No, I'm not, Bob. I'm willing to give you due credit o' being a clever feller."

"Well, that, at least, is a concession," said the sinister-visaged man. "But don't you think—both of you—that you have proceeded in that strain long enough?"

"Perhaps we have," replied Bob. "So I wote that we go on another tack."

"Hear, hear!" cried Jerry. "That's what I call speaking sensible-like."

"Whatever Jerry says, after this, I'm a-going to stand to it," said Bob.

"Bravo, Bob! We're as good pals as ever we were."

"Well, now to resume our little chat," said the sinister-faced man. "Neither of you, I believe, forget what we were talking of in the earlier part of the evening."

"You mean in the lane?" inquired Bob.

"Yes, in the lane. We spoke of John Gregory."

"And Simon Gagg," put in Bob.

"Also a great many others, too numerous to mention," ventured Jerry, "especially one or two individuals who would be no credit to any one."

"Reuben Harpy, and noble and sincere men of that sort," said Bob, "who are worth in the current coin of the world, a farthing a dozen."

"Bravo, Bob! You have just about hit it. They are worthless scum of the earth."

"The drippings of humanity."

"Just so. But now to turn our attention to the inquiries of our friend here."

"I was going to remark," said the sinister-visaged man, "that old John Gregory disappeared in a very mysterious way."

"Very," said Bob and Jerry, both in a breath.

"And Mrs. Drake."

"And Mrs. Drake, too. In fact it was a general weeding out by which that disgraceful and owdacious rascal, Lieutenant Saunderson, got into the property."

"I don't think he got in by any honest means," said Jerry, pointedly. "At least that letter—"

"Shut up, you varmint!" cried Bob, who thought his old comrade was going to commit himself by telling all he knew in reference to the one found in the cabin of the doomed merchantman, and put there by the hands of Captain John Gregory.

"Bob—Bob! this isn't parliamentary language," said Jerry. "You have made friends with your old pal, and now you are going to abuse him."

"What about that letter?" asked the stranger.

A cautious wink from Bob, put Jerry on his guard.

"What letter, sir?" said Jerry.

"You were speaking about a letter, were you not?" replied the other.

"Oh, yes!" returned Jerry, with great alacrity. "I was a-thinking o' the letter I got from my dear old dad, bless his old soul!"

"Why, I thought you said a short time back that your father was dead?"

"Jerry's got his foot in it at last," thought Bob.

"Liars should have good memories," muttered Jerry. "I'm afraid I've busted myself completely up. It was a mistake to have mentioned that 'ere letter. And the second mistake was, if possible, worse than the first. Now, I wonder how I am to get out of it? Let me see, is my grandfather living? No. Nor my great grandfather? No; he's as dead as mutton, long since. Never mind; I'll shoulder the lie on to him. Well, I did say that," added Jerry, aloud. "And, what is more, I mean a-sticking to my words, too. My father is dead, and I'm a poor, homeless orphan."

"I can't make that out," said the stranger. "If he's dead, how can you have received a letter from him?"

"I didn't exactly say from him," cried Jerry, pretending to be very deeply affected by the circumstance.

"Then from whom?"

"I have other fathers, besides one," said Jerry.

"Indeed!" said the stranger.

"That's somewhat surprising," thought Bob. "He's getting himself into a worse fix every minute. If I was Jerry, I wouldn't open my mouth at all."

"Yes," replied Jerry. "I have a *grandfather!*"

"Wonderful coincidence!" echoed the sinister-faced man. "I have a grandfather, also."

"The devil is his grandfather, no doubt," thought Bob.

"You have a grandfather?" cried Jerry. "Then he must be a very old one."

"He is. And yours?"

"Is old likewise. One hundred and ten years, six months, thirteen days, and forty-five minutes. Werry close calculation that!"

"Werry," said Bob, who was only too glad to see that his old friend Jerry was re-asserting himself.

"Devil or not, Jerry will get the best of him yet," said Bob.

And in this opinion Bob was not far from being right.

Jerry was thoroughly prepared now to meet the stranger on his own point of vantage.

"Perhaps it'll be as well to explain to you," he said, "that my grandfather, although having lived to reach that age, is as hale and hearty as if he wasn't fifty; and what is more, he's got the use of every faculty, and his eyesight's so good that he can almost thread a needle in the dark. Besides, he can write and dictate a letter like a brick, and that is one of the many reasons that I call him my dear old dad."

"Indeed," said the stranger, but in such a tone of voice that made it quite apparent that he cast a doubt on Bob's veracity. "But that doesn't explain the letter yet."

"And that's all the explanation I can give you, at any rate," replied Jerry, quite firmly. "Let us turn the conversation on something else."

The sinister-visaged man tried in various ways after this to draw both Bob and Jerry out.

But the buccaneers were too cunning.

Therefore, he had to give up his task as a bad one.

Now, up to this, everything had gone on quite admirably.

Bob and Jerry succeeded in holding their own, despite the keen penetration of their companion who now betokened a look of annoyance on his face.

The black figures who were following Bob, Jerry, and their companion up, drew nearer.

Was it their intention to make a sudden attack on the three men?

If not, why should they be dogging their steps in this way?

The question was soon answered.

Bob was aware of the fact that a peculiar rustling noise rung out behind him!

Had it discontinued, he would have thought it was the wind brushing through the foliage.

As it did not the circumstance made some impression on him, and he clapped his hands on his pistols.

"Be on your guard," he whispered to Jerry.

"What's the matter?"

"Don't ask now. Look to your firearms."

As Jerry knew that there were some circumstances under which Bob played no jokes, he took his advice, and in an instant was prepared for the worst.

The rustling continued.

And grew louder.

At last a stealthy step could be heard.

Suddenly the sinister-faced man clapped his hands.

And from that instant, Bob knew how to act.

"Traitor!" cried Bob, drawing his pistols, and facing their strange companion.

But ere he could utter another word, there was a sudden rush of feet from behind, and the two comrades found themselves surrounded by nearly a dozen men.

But, Bob and Jerry were anything but frightened.

They went to work like the stout-hearted buccaneers they were, and blazed away at the enemy.

The sinister-faced man had strangely enough disappeared.

For when Bob looked round to give him a shot for his treachery, he was gone.

Bob Hauler and Jerry Mizzen fought like lions.

But, having fired their pistols, were finally disarmed, thrown into the middle of the road and securely bound.

They had the satisfaction, however, of shooting three of their assailants.

"We are in a purty fine fix now, if ever we were," said Bob.

The next thing they knew, they were gagged, and taken hastily from the spot.

CHAPTER CLXXIX.
CAPTAIN ANGEL AGAIN.

FOR a brief time, we change our scene.

Once more are we in the mansion of poor old John Gregory.

The time is night.

Dark and cloudy as ever night set in.

But the house is ablaze with light, and the library especially is illuminated brilliantly.

Lieutenant Sanderson has had visitors there that night.

But the hour is waxing late, and the visitors are gone, and Sanderson alone paces the rich, soft carpets of his library.

His footsteps give no sound, and, with arms folded across his breast, he is buried in profound and gloomy thought.

At times he pauses to bend one glance out on the night.

But everything beyond is buried in pitchy, impenetrable darkness.

Not even the glimmer of a star can be seen through the black, murky clouds.

The sighing of the rising breeze through the rich foliage of the trees in front awakes a thousand ghostly echoes, until Sanderson has to close the window, and resume his walking up and down the room.

This man's mind is never happy.

Sleeping or waking, his guilty conscience is filled with hideous visions.

In vain he tries to dissipate them.

But no!

Wine is as weak as water, and the strongest brandy is little better.

His ill-gotten wealth sits heavily on him.

Indeed, he would almost wish now that he could get rid of it.

But never!

It hangs to him like a frightful nightmare.

The only moments of repose he ever finds is when his house is filled with guests, who pour their adulations into his ear, neglecting not to make him think he is all-powerful, and one of the happiest beings in existence.

For a moment he forgets himself.

No, we are wrong.

Not entirely forgets himself, for that he can never do.

But he tries to drink in their flattering eulogiums—endeavours, indeed, to think that he, of all his surrounding companions, is the happiest.

Under the influence of strong wines and bright, sparkling conversation, he is not quite so miserable.

But the instant his crowd of servile adulators take their departure, the same old frightful phantasia follows him from room to room, giving him no peace, and making him wish that he was dead.

Thus passes the life, day in and day out, of this miscreant's career.

Not a moment's happiness.

Always in guilty terror!

Fearing every instant that his crimes will be discovered, and that a death of ignominy will be the result.

Captain Angel he has given up thinking of altogether.

He fancies that that once hated enemy is dead.

Indeed, one dark, stormy night, a few months before, a villainous-looking man came to his place, and, after obtaining an interview, informed him that his arch-enemy had fallen into the hands of Barbary pirates, and was, after a short shrift, made to walk the plank, and heaved over into the sea.

He sunk from view, and was never seen afterwards.

This fellow told his story with such an earnest face that Sanderson believed him, and sent him away with a well-filled purse for his information.

The guilty lieutenant now that he had got rid of a most dangerous enemy, for some time felt easier in his mind, and even flattered himself that the time would come when he would be happy.

But vain hope!

Three or four weeks after he was just as miserable as ever, and hoped that his hated rival was alive to relieve him of a burthen that sat like lead at his soul.

He would only be too glad now if he could restore Angel to life, and hand him over every fraction of the property.

But we are describing this night.

The man Sanderson is oppressed with strange fears.

His face is haggard, his eyes bloodshot, and his once stalwart frame, a feeble picture of what he once was.

The library looks very comfortable.

A brilliant fire burns in the well-polished grate, and wafts an air of comfort through the apartment.

There is everything in that room that can conduce to the comfort, and even luxury, of its one solitary occupant.

The ivory-inlaid table groans beneath a profusion of wines and brandies of the costliest description.

But these serve not to cool the man's parched lips or fevered brow.

They rather increase his sufferings, for their contents only burn his blood, without giving him that coveted moment of forgetfulness.

"My God, what a life is a life of guilt!" murmured the wretched man, as he paced the library. "If these frightful thoughts continue they must end in sending me to the madhouse. But, God knows, I deserve nothing better. The torments of hell consume me, body and soul! Never a moment's peace! Oh! if I could only have foreseen this, what agony—what sufferings I might have spared myself. But for that wretched woman I should never have gone so far, and even she, in the bitterness of her hate, and fiendish malignity, haunts me, and serves with the other horrible visions to make my life intolerable."

Sanderson paused to give utterance to his thoughts—had paused with hands clenched convulsively, and starting eyeballs and chattering teeth.

Notwithstanding the warm healthful glow that the fire threw out he shook like an aspen.

Shook, indeed, as if exposed to the most bitter of bitter cold nights.

Sounds of approaching steps came ringing into the library.

Perhaps some of the guests of the evening returning.

The sounds cheered him.

Anything now but to be by himself.

Indeed, any companionship was better than being alone.

A "rat-tat!" rung into the room, and on an invitation to enter, the door opened, and an head was thrust in.

The powdered head of one of Sanderson's footmen.

The ghastly face and wild eyes of the lieutenant made the man draw back quicker than he had thrust his head in.

Indeed, the great change in his master's features startled him very much.

"Fool! What are you staring at me in that way for?" cried Sanderson, furiously. "Come forward, or by heavens, I'll kick you downstairs!"

As the man well knew what Sanderson was capable of doing under paroxysms of violent rage he came in tremblingly.

Indeed, if the lieutenant felt inclined, he would have found no difficulty in putting his threat of kicking this man downstairs into execution.

For the fellow was weak and thin, and, no doubt, consumptive.

"Now what is your errand?" cried Sanderson, somewhat appeased at the cringing, servile manner of his attendant. "Have any of those gentlemen come back who were here this evening?"

"No, sir."

"Well, who then?"

"A person who wishes to see your honour?"

"I know that, you fool! But who is this person? Did he give you his name? What is he like?"

To all these rapid inquiries the attendant returned answers in a stammering, confused sort of way.

"I—I don't know who he is, sir? He—he didn't give me his name. He—he—he looks—"

"Like what, you scoundrel? Answer me at once, or I'll give you what you deserve!"

What he "deserved" was, no doubt, a summary

ejectment from the library, and the following up of the other part of his kind threat.

Now, as this was not at all agreeable to the man with the powdered locks, he answered his master with less hesitation.

"He appeared like one of those smugglers we occasionally see in the village, your honour. He may be a seaman, and, again, he may not."

"What a doltish ass! What do you mean by saying that he may be a seaman and he may not be a seaman?"

"I mean this, sir—that he has a seafaring cut about him. But he doesn't look like an honest man. He is tall and thin; his face is one I can never forget—a most villainous-looking physog., sir."

"Indeed!"

"I assure you of it, sir."

"Well, what does he want?"

"To see you."

"And wouldn't send his name up?"

"He objected to that, yer honour."

"Who the fiend can he be?" thought Sanderson. "Tall, thin, with a villainous-looking look about him. A great many might answer that description. Tell this villainous-looking fellow that if he don't send up his name that he cannot see me," added the lieutenant, aloud.

"Your visitor is here to answer for himself!" cried a harsh, grating voice from the door at this moment.

The tones were familiar.

They sent a chill of ice to Sanderson's heart.

Could the ocean throw up its dead?

The answer came by the tall, thin, villainous-looking gentleman walking past the astonished footman, and announcing himself.

Before he passed the threshold, however, he caught the footman by the nape of the neck, and ejecting him from the room, closed the door.

Sanderson gaped with horror.

His eyes seemed to start from their sockets.

A livid terror overspread his face.

There stood before him, indeed, the very man whom he had an instant before been thinking of.

His arch-enemy.

Captain Angel!

This was the individual whom he thought had been dead.

And still thought was dead.

The superstitious element of his whole nature was thoroughly roused.

"Back—back!" he cried, in a stifled voice, and the next moment he fell senseless at the pirate's feet.

With a glare of hatred, Angel leant over him.

A malignant fire shot from his eyes.

What his intention was at that instant is hard to say.

Sounds of hurried steps were heard on the stairs.

No doubt the footmen returning with assistance.

Angel straightened up, and faced the door.

A smile of contempt lit up his face.

The door was flung open.

A dozen servants appeared, armed with every available weapon they could find.

"That's him—that's him!" cried the attendant, "that's the villain who forced his way into Mr. Sanderson's presence. I told him to stop below. But he would come up, and this is the result!" pointing to the prostrate body of his master.

"The lieutenant is dead, no doubt!" said he, who appeared to have the lead.

"And murdered by this villainous fellow!" said another.

"Let us rush upon him!" cried a third.

"Aye, aye; that's the way to secure him. Besides, we can keep him here till the police comes."

Their intentions were good.

But their courage was not.

So, instead of rushing forward, they held back.

There was something stern and deadly in the glitter of Captain Angel's eye, which was quite enough to warrant them keeping at a safe distance from him.

Besides, the pirate had deliberately exposed two heavy navy pistols, which he as deliberately cocked.

Indeed, whatever brave act they meditated at the outset, vanished now like a fleeting cloud from the sun's surface.

Not one out of the dozen dared advance over the threshold.

But rather stood there trembling or retreating into the passage.

"Well, why don't you come on?" cried Angel, decisively. "Fools! do you think for a moment I came here to slay your master?"

The pirate captain's voice terrified them almost more than his pistols.

"Come," cried Angel, "give me proper treatment, and proper treatment shall you receive. In the first place, permit me to tell you I am an old friend of your master's, and believing me dead, he has fainted. Begone, you lazy rascals! " he added, "or I'll take the liberty presently of putting it out of your power. Begone!"

The servants were moving away thoroughly frightened, when Angel called out for two of them to stay.

"You two nearest the door will do," he cried. "The rest may go."

But, contrary to his order, they were all moving off, when the pirate, stepping forward, caught one by the shoulder, and pulled him forcibly into the library.

"Now, be off!" he cried, to the others. "If I see any of you again to-night, woe beside you."

The ominous click of one of his pistols was enough.

The well-fed, lazy servants, waiting to hear no more, ran down the stairs as fast as they could, until even the sounds of their steps were lost.

The man he hauled so unceremoniously into the room he treated a little better after that.

Especially that the others were gone.

Angel seemed to possess a wonderful power—indeed, if we may be allowed to use the expression, a true magnetic power—which he exercised with excellent effect on the terrified domestics.

"You see, your master has only fainted," said Angel, addressing the person he forced into the room.

"Yes, sir, I see that," replied the man.

But his words came tremblingly.

It could be seen that he was still very much frightened of the pirate.

"We must revive him," said Angel.

"I think we must, sir."

"Have you any water here?"

"I should judge that there must be some, sir."

"Then go and get it, and we'll try what effect it will have."

"Might I suggest one thing, sir?"

"A hundred, if you like, if you don't take too long."

"A little brandy, sir."

"What about the brandy?"

Angel could see the servant's eyes cast lovingly on the various bottles that lined the ivory-inlaid table.

"It's a good reviver, sir. I may say, a splendid reviver."

"For whom? For you, or your master?"

"Oh, sir! Could you for a moment imagine that I would think of myself?"

"I am sure I don't know. But from the sparkle in your eyes, one would think that you did want it for yourself. But as for that, my good fellow, a bottle will never be missed. so take one. Should it be found out, rely upon it, that I will screen you."

If the footman's eyes sparkled before, they sparkled ten times as much now.

A bottle of brandy for himself!

The thought was overpowering!

Yes, he would take it at once.

Considering the old adage that a bird in the hand is worth two in the bush.

Of course bottles of Cognac did not apply to either birds or bushes.

But it would no doubt have the effect of making him as merry as the former, and as luxuriant and, perhaps, thorny in his feelings as the latter.

As who, having a drop in, was not either apt to be uproariously merry, or cantankerously quarrelsome.

Such were the thoughts of our friend the footman, who began to look on Captain Angel as a very condescending gentleman indeed.

The footman walked over to the table to possess one of those pint bottles which he coveted.

But Angel's grating voice brought him to a sudden pause.

"Where are you going, my friend?"

"For one of those bottles of brandy, yer honour."

"For a bottle of brandy?"

"Yes, yer honour. Didn't yer honour tell me to get one?"

"Stop a minute!" cried Angel. "Don't be in a hurry. There is something else to do yet."

"Well, yer honour?"

"Where's that water?"

"Oh, to be sure, sir; I forgot all about it. I'll be back in a minute."

"You are not going to leave the room?" said Angel.

"There's none here, sir."

"No?"

"No, sir."

"Come, now! How do you know?"

"I don't think there is."

"Have you tried?"

"Only by looking around me."

"You haven't used your eyes to good purpose, my friend," said Angel. "I can see plenty of it—decanters, in fact, full."

"In that case, there's no need of going from the room."

"I should think not," replied the pirate. "But I see water is not needed now. He is coming to."

Such, indeed, was the case.

Lieutenant Sanderson was slowly but surely recovering.

"Take your bottle, and be off," said Captain Angel. "And remember, should I catch you any more in this room to-night, I'll break every bone in your body!"

"There's no fear of my coming here again to-night, sir. And if you catch me, I'll give you leave not only to break my bones, but also to break my neck in the bargain."

The footman was only too glad to thus easily escape the presence of this ferocious-looking pirate.

For pirate or smuggler he had no doubt now but he was.

He rushed forward, took a bottle of the precious liquor from the table, and quickly decamped from the room, closing the door after him.

Meanwhile, the master of the mansion opened his bloodshot eyes.

For an instant or two he was unconscious of where he was.

Or, indeed, of who he was with.

But only for an instant.

He soon caught the cold, merciless face of Angel.

Whose flashing eyes were bent in deadly hatred on him.

He was so frightened that he could not for some time even utter a syllable.

He had not got over the notion yet but that it was the pirate captain's disembodied spirit that appeared to him.

And when he did manage to find utterance, he began to shriek loudly for help.

"Help! Help!" rang in startling cadences through the library, awaking a hundred ghostly echoes through the old house.

But Angel, giving vent to an oath, soon silenced him by clapping his hand over his mouth.

"Curse you! Can't you keep still?" cried the fierce pirate.

These words, indubitably human, had some effect.

They had the effect of making him believe that Angel was living instead of dead.

Angel living?

This thought terrified him almost more than the other.

Perhaps the pirate captain had come to demand satisfaction for the attempt that had been made to murder him.

Sanderson knew only too well the desperate and revengeful character of his colleague!

He now expected nothing less than death at his hands.

And, for a moment, closed his eyes in despair.

Indeed, his terror of Angel had always been great.

"Open your eyes, fool!" cried the pirate, in his harsh, grating tones, "or perhaps I shall be forced to open them for you."

Sanderson, without complying, gave vent to a deep groan.

"Do you still think that I am dead?" cried Angel, with a malicious laugh. "The account I sent you worked well. Ha! ha! ha! Fell into the hands of Barbary pirates, and then made to walk the plank, and hurled into the sea! So you thought your dear friend Argal would never more trouble you? Eh, Sanderson? Is that what you thought? Conscience in the strength of your honesty and virtue, after that you became happy—grew indeed very happy. How has all this ill-gotten wealth got on with you—eh, Sanderson? You don't seem to thrive on it—ha! ha! ha!"

The captain's merciless laugh sent a chill of ice through the blood of Lieutenant Sanderson.

He unclosed his bloodshot eyes slowly.

Looked upon his persecutor in a half-imploring manner.

But no mercy—not even the remotest spark—could he discern in those deep, sinister eyes.

They were hard as steel.

Cold and pitiless.

"It is no use, Sanderson," went on his tormentor. "You have made your bed, and there you must lie. Now, permit me, first of all, to help you to your feet. I don't do this, mind, out of any feeling of sympathy for your condition, but rather that you can hear what I have to say in a position not quite so grovelly. By heavens, man! you have wasted to almost nothing. Sanderson, a shadow of his former self.

"Ha! ha! ha! I know parties to whom this, no doubt, would be very capital news. But why should I speak of them? You shall see them yourself before long, and the interview, no doubt, will delight you."

Angel now picked up his former colleague as if he had been a child, and having so done, carried him quite as easily to a chair.

Of course Sanderson made a very great struggle to get away.

This indignity was a little too much for him.

And it lent him courage to make a vigorous effort for his release.

But all this did not avail him a bit, as Captain Angel held him in his arms as if he had been in a vice.

"Come, my infant, what is the good of struggling?" cried Angel, jeeringly. "You are by no means as strong as you have been, Sanderson. Your ill-gotten gains have weighed so heavily on your soul that they have not only reduced you in bulk, but weakened you materially. Who could ever think that sudden great wealth would have such influence?"

"Leave me, monster!" cried Sanderson, no longer able to control his rapidly-rising indignation, in which even his dread of the merciless pirate sank for the time into utter insignificance.

"Leave you!" cried Angel, banteringly. "Ah, my dear Sanderson, you ask too much. We cannot part like this. Besides, there is some little reckoning between us—the discharge of a little debt, for instance. You cannot have so treacherous a memory as to forget that there is a nice little settlement between us. It is not much, my dear Sanderson—not very much, indeed. But as I am the creditor, &c., &c., you must permit me to tell you we cannot part thus. Ha! what a liver you are, my dear friend. Brandy, wines, &c. Why, it's enough to make one's mouth water. Perhaps a stimulant may have some good effect upon you. Allow me to help you to one."

Captain Angel strode over to the ivory-inlaid table, and poured out a glass of the brandy.

This he drank himself.

And, indeed, seemed to relish it very much.

While he was thus engaged, Lieutenant Sanderson was stealing a march on him, or was rather making for the door to call in the assistance of his menials.

He wondered how it was that they had let this man pass them.

There were plenty in the house, and by their aid he hoped to secure Angel, or if not, to eject him from the place.

But the pirate's sharp eyes observed the movement.

He drew forth a pistol.

A certain death-like click broke upon the silence of the room.

Sanderson turned, and saw the dangerous gleam of the polished fire-arm.

"Come back!" cried Angel, in his cold, grating tones. "Come back, Sanderson, or I'll put a bullet through your head!"

And the lieutenant well knew that his enemy was quite capable of doing that.

He paused.

Paused to consider whether he would go on or come back.

But the deadly barrel of the pistol pointed in line with his head was a little too much for him.

He walked slowly back.

His face deadly pale, his teeth chattering with rage and fear.

"Ha! ha! my dear Sanderson, I knew that you would obey me!" laughed the pirate. "Besides," he added, "if you did call your powdered lacqueys, they would not have answered you."

"What! Have you made them all prisoners, then?" cried the lieutenant, in sudden fear.

"Well, not exactly, my noble comrade, not exactly."

"What then?" demanded the terrified, yet brutal Sanderson, with grinding teeth.

Oh! if he had only the power at this moment, he would have taken this man's life a hundred times over.

But he was powerless.

The trump card was in the hands of his enemy.

CHAPTER CLXXX.

SANDERSON FACE TO FACE WITH JOHN GREGORY AND MRS. DRAKE.

"You ask me, 'what then?'" said Angel, forcing a glass of brandy into Sanderson's hand. "I'll tell you 'what then.' Your lazy, overfed lacqueys came up here with the intention to overpower me, believing I had killed you. It did not take me long to send them back again in a different way to what they came. And now, let me inform you, that if you were to shout murder at the top of your voice, you need expect no assistance at their hands."

"Cursed cowards!" groaned Sanderson.

"That is really a fact," replied Angel. "Cowards they, indeed, are."

Angel's deep malignity could not be hidden under the rather affable exterior he assumed.

He resembled, at that moment, a cat on the point of pouncing upon a mouse.

Nor was Sanderson deceived by his manner.

He knew that something terrible was to occur yet.

What that something was he would like to find out.

"I suppose you feel a little better now?" said Captain Angel. "Your brandy is excellent, and will, no doubt, have a good effect. Compose yourself. Sorry to see you look so haggard. But that —ha! ha! ha!—is perfectly understood. The ways of the transgressor, my dear Sanderson— The rest, you know, is not worth repeating."

The lieutenant looked up in despair.

Then spoke slowly, so slowly, that every word seemed to tremble on his lips.

"Oh! Why do you inflict further torture on me?" he asked.

The tones were imploring.

Angel laughed spitefully.

"Why do I torture you?" he repeated. "For the very good and sufficient reason that I like to."

"Is it money you require?"

"Why do you ask?"

"Because I can pay you nobly—"

"To keep away," interrupted the other. "Ha! ha! ha! Money we all need."

"Name your sum," cried the other, eagerly.

He half fancied that Angel was in need of gold.

Now, if he handed him over a large sum, he might, quite possibly, get rid of him.

No sooner did this idea strike the lieutenant than he brightened up.

"Don't be afraid that I cannot give you the amount you require," he said.

"How very generous you are! Really, my dear Sanderson, your kindness is overwhelming."

"You have only to state the amount."

"Only to state the amount?"

"I said only, because I can give you whatever you ask."

"And pay me for all the trouble you have given me?"

"Even to that."

"And the agony you have caused me?"

"My dear Angel!"

"And the misery, and even poverty, you have inflicted on me?"

"That's too bad."

"Let bygones be bygones—eh?"

"Do so, I implore you!"

"What an angel of forgiveness you are, Sanderson. I suppose, now, that you forgive me?"

"Oh, yes. Need you ask?"

"And that I, of course, forgive you."

"I hope so, indeed, from the bottom of my heart."

"So do I. It is a great pity that this Christian quality should not be more exercised. Oh, Sanderson, why are we not all better men."

"Why, indeed!" rejoined Saunders, sighing.

"The world is a very depraved one, old boy."

"So it is."

"And I am conscious we have both been bad men."

"I am afraid we have."

"Then let us go in for reform. What say you, Sanderson?"

Sanderson, as the reader may expect, could see all this levelled at him.

But thinking it best to agree with everything the other said, he entered with some spirit into it.

"I think that would be a very good plan, captain. Indeed, I have no longer any ill-feeling for you, and I am sure that you harbour none for me."

"Then, why can't we be friends?"

"Aye, indeed, why can't we?"

"Very well then. Now for the amount?"

"Name it."

"A hundred thousand pounds, then."

"A hundred thousand!" exclaimed Saunderson, aghast. "You are surely jesting?"

"Not I. I never jest on money matters."

"No."

"You may take my word for it. A hundred thousand pounds, not a fraction less."

"Do you really think I could realise that sum?"

"I have not given it one thought."

"Then you must not be unreasonable."

"Of course not."

"A hundred thousand pounds," repeated the lieutenant, musingly.

"That is the amount to a farthing."

"It seems incredible."

"What?"

"That you should think for an instant of such a thing."

"Indeed."

"It would be impossible!"

"Nothing is impossible to men of your kind, lieutenant."

"You are mistaken."

"Nonsense!"

"But I say you are."

"Then if I am, I am."

"I am glad you concede that point."

"But I concede no point. It is a matter of business—a matter, indeed, of pounds, shillings and pence, waiving friendship a-oneside."

A hundred thousand pounds!

Sanderson was staggered at the demand.

Where could he get such a sum?

Would the property realise it?

It might.

But he doubted it very much.

Had he even twenty thousand at his bankers?

No!

Emphatically no!

Ever since he came in for poor old Gregory's property, he led a very dissipated life.

The agonies he endured at first found some balm in squandering a great portion of the ready money that fell into his hands.

His balls and levees cost something.

Fabulous amounts were lost on races.

Besides, he had now the name of being the most hospitable gentleman in the county.

People did not, when they found him so generous, take the trouble to enquire how and by what means he came into John Gregory's estates.

They knew he spent his money with all the munificence of a prince.

And so they did not take the trouble to inquire further.

What was it to them how he came in for his money if he only regaled them with superb suppers, fine wines, and equally fine cigars.

He might, indeed, have been one of the most infamous wretches on the face of the earth, for all they cared.

And thus stood Lieutenant Sanderson with the county gentlemen.

But now about the hundred thousand pounds.

Seriously thinking, Captain Angel could not be in earnest.

He began in a bantering strain, and, no doubt, ended in one by making this exorbitant demand.

The very thought was absurd on the face of it.

Even twenty thousand would be very unreasonable, seeing how Sanderson had gone on while the property had been in his possession.

He could not give even that sum.

And that was one-fifth of what was asked.

Yes; Angel must surely be jesting.

Or, perhaps, working on his fears.

The lieutenant hoped that it might be the former.

"Well, putting friendship a-oneside," said Sanderson, "you a k too much."

"Do you really think so?"

"Most certainly, captain."

"Then you'll not agree to those terms?"

"I can't."

"Very well, then, that ends it."

"Oh, my dear captain, consider!"

"I have, within the last minute."

"And do you still stick to your orignal demand?"

"Emphatically, yes."

"Good heavens!"

"What means the exclamation?"

"Are you in your right senses, my dear Angel?"

"I should hope so, my dear Sanderson. Do I look like a man insane?"

"Well, no," stammered the lieutenant, who did not yet know what to make of Angel's demand.

It was more puzzling and perplexing to him than ever.

Seeing that the pirate captain persisted in it.

"I don't look as one insane, then? Very good. A hundred thousand pounds is my demand. You know, my dear Sanderson, that I have you in my power, and a word from me would put an halter round your neck. I should, however, be very loth to go such extremes, unless," he added, very markedly, "you compelled me!"

Sanderson shuddered.

He knew the devilish nature of his enemy only too well.

It was the cat and mouse business over again.

He was too helpless, in fact, to help himself.

And Angel, he was only too surely aware, would show him no mercy.

This merciless ruffian he thought was dead.

Indeed at times he wished that he was living.

The agonies he endured were horrible.

Perhaps an hour ago he would have only been too glad if Angel were living, so that he could hand him over that which made his life a burthen to him.

But now that he appeared in life, and in the flesh, there was a sudden revulsion of feeling.

A sudden desire, if possible, to stick to all he had.

He found happiness now in thinking of that which had one short hour ago given him so much pain and misery.

"Do you, without jest, really mean what you

y ?" said he, addressing Angel.

"Certainly," replied the fiendish pirate. "Why should you think that I meant anything else ?"

"The demand seems so preposterous."

"Indeed !"

"And, besides, could never be met."

"That is worse. However, it will have to be met."

"You have stated the result of non-compliance."

"I have."

"Then, monster, do your worst !"

"Monster to me ? I am really surprised at you, Sanderson. For a moment, I never expected such treatment. I was your dear friend, Angel, not many moments ago, and now I am a *monster*. Could you not pile the abuse up a little higher ? It would be very delightful, indeed. We were going to reform, and all that sort of thing, a little while since. But there goes reformation to the winds. Not only that, but you acknowledge that you were a very bad man, and that—not exactly as I state it—you were my enemy. We had assumed that great Christian quality of forgiving each other. And now, after all this, you actually turn on me and call me monster !—and all because my present necessities demand a hundred thousand pounds."

"But remember, sir, that you threatened to hang me !"

"And, my dear Sanderson, you can depend on my doing it, too, if you don't concede to my demands."

"But I can't."

"You can't ?"

"I tell you no, no, no, a thousand times."

"Now, to come to the point, Sanderson—why can't you ?"

"Because it would be impossible for me to get one-fifth of the sum."

"Impossible ?"

"I say impossible. There's scarcely twenty thousand pounds at the bankers'."

Captain Angel chuckled like a fiend.

"Oh, my dear Sanderson," he said, "you have been playing a nice game, haven't you ? Twenty thousand pounds at the bankers'. Two hundred thousand originally. Been making money, Sanderson, fast—very fast, my good friend."

"You mean spending it, and losing it."

"I see you understand the irony. Had the property mortgaged, I suppose ?"

"Not come to that yet."

"You are a really wonderful fellow, upon my soul, Sanderson. When you are swung off, we'll never meet your like again, I am sure. I wonder what would old John Gregory say if he turned up ?"

"John Gregory !" exclaimed the now terrified lieutenant.

"Yes, John Gregory ! He would think you a precious scamp, wouldn't he ?"

"But he is dead."

"Where's your proof ?"

"Oh, I've had sufficient proof."

"The old doctor, for instance ?"

Sanderson turned from pale to livid.

The old doctor !

His secret was in the doctor's hands, and he paid him well for it.

Could the old rascal have betrayed him, then ?

No !

It would not have been to his interest.

How came Angel to mention the doctor, then, with such marked significance ?

There was some under-current, of whose existence he knew nothing, and could only slightly guess at.

John Gregory was surely dead.

He was positive of that.

For had he not seen the old man lying in death with his own eyes ?

In his coffin, in fact.

And was not that coffin sealed up, taken away, and lowered into the grave ?

All this he had seen likewise.

"The old doctor, for instance," repeated Angel. "A very nice, unassuming old gentleman he is, too, Sanderson."

But the lieutenant did not say anything.

He was thunderstruck.

The reference to the doctor of the asylum was enough to arouse all his suspicions.

What could he do ?

Or say ?

Would it be wise to question Angel ?

And if he did, would Angel answer him ?

It seemed very unlikely that he could get much out of a man like his late colleague.

So he gave up the thought almost as soon as it came into his head

What could he do now ?

Angel was far more bitter and relentless than before.

Hidden as it was under a passibly quiet exterior. Should he defy him ?

And if he did, what would be the result ?

Denounced !

Brought to trial !

Executed !

Meeting a most ignominious end.

And all because he still held property that would only bring ruin with it.

Property that was not his own, and defrauded from another.

Estates for the possession of which we may say he had waded through human gore.

No, he would not die such a death.

It might just be possible that he could find time to draw some of the money, or perhaps the whole of it out of the bank, and leave for some out-of-the-way place, where this awful Angel could not find him.

This he thought might be possible.

But he must work his cards well to do even that.

Above all, it would behove him to act with great caution, as the pirate captain was a man of great cunning and unlimited resource.

In Captain Angel he had an enemy of no mean capacity, indeed.

"Now, captain," said Sanderson, "it is hardly worth while wasting any more time. I have just been reflecting for the last few seconds, and can't see my way clear out of the difficulty. I have come to this conclusion, however, to pass into your hands the property."

"And everything else with it ?" added Angel.

"To be sure. That was my intention."

"Indeed !" sneered Angel. "You are very generous, brother Sanderson."

"Do you doubt my word, sir ?"

"Not for a moment."

"Well ?"

"I say you are generous. What more can I say ?"

"And you accept—"

"The twenty thousand pounds also in the bank."

"I meant to have made especial mention of that."

"Indeed ! I thank you," said Angel.

"How kindly considerate you are !"

Sanderson found that he had more than his match in Angel.

And he bit his lips to conceal the rage he felt.

The crafty captain would dupe him yet.

And he knew it.

Twenty thousand pounds in the bank.

That twenty thousand would pass into the coffers of Angel.

He was sure of it.

Oh! how he hated this man!

And every moment intensified that hate.

"Yes," resumed Angel, "that bank money must be delivered to me by to-morrow afternoon."

Was this a loop-hole of escape?

For a moment it seemed that it was.

But only for a moment.

As the pirate captain soon enlightened him.

"One hour after noon to-morrow the money will be placed in your hands."

"By whom?" asked Angel, insinuatingly.

"By me."

"It is very kind of you," said the pirate, "but I really don't see how you can manage it."

"Why?" asked Sanderson.

"Because I am afraid I'll be unable to let you out of my sight."

"I can go to the bank with you."

"Oh, no, that will never do."

Something like a curse came from Sanderson's lips.

"Very well, then," he said, "if you are going to treat me so scurvily, you may do what the devil you like. But remember that neither a fraction of the property nor the twenty thousand pounds shall be yours."

"A warm night, Sanderson. Your blood, no doubt, wants cooling a little. A blow on the water, for instance, would benefit you very much. Ah! I see the reason all your windows are closed."

Angel, keeping a sidelong look on Sanderson, walked over to one of the windows, and threw it wide open.

"Ah, my comrade; that is much better," he said.

Captain Angel, remaining at the open window, fumbled for a moment in his pocket.

He presently drew something out.

This something he placed to his lips.

And in an instant a shrill whistle cleft the night air.

Sanderson sprang to his feet, alarmed.

The shrill whistle was answered by someone from the outside.

Lieutenant Sanderson, anticipating danger, would have bounded out of the library, but he was detained in the strong grip of the pirate captain.

"Not so fast, my dear Sanderson," said this polite gentleman. "You will keep me company for some time, as I expect visitors."

The lieutenant struggled with the desperation of a madman to free himself.

But all to no purpose.

He was held in a grip of iron.

Perceiving the uselessness of his struggles, he began crying at the top of his voice for help, until the walls of the old mansion seemed alive with echoes.

Captain Angel shook him like a huge rat.

"Keep quiet, fool, or I'll shake your life out!" he cried.

Sanderson, however, continued bellowing out for his assistance.

Footsteps were heard in ascent of the stairs.

Not of the servants.

For they were too heavy.

The sounds, indeed, were those of heavy sea-boots.

Sanderson gave himself up for lost.

He ceased his cries for assistance, and lay perfectly motionless in the arms of his persecutor.

Suddenly the door of the library was burst open.

A dozen rough, heavy-bearded men entered, armed to the teeth.

A half a glance would pronounce their calling.

They were Captain Angel's men, and belonged to the pirate schooner.

Without speaking, Angel pointed to the trembling Sanderson.

Three or four of the men advanced from the rest.

caught hold of the lieutenant, threw him to the floor, and bound and gagged him instantly.

Very few words, indeed, passed between the pirate captain and his crew.

A minute later, and Sanderson found himself carried down the staircase, through one of the passages, out into the night.

His brain was on fire!

It was a relief, indeed, to feel the fresh night breeze fanning his fevered brow.

But then he was a prisoner.

Perhaps going to meet a cruel death.

Angel, his arch-enemy, was at last triumphant.

The lieutenant, when they got into the road, was bundled into a light waggon drawn by two strong horses.

The smugglers all got in, except Captain Angel.

He remained behind.

He gave no reason for so doing.

But no doubt his intention was to return to the house.

Angel, before he left, saw the vehicle move along the road at a tremendous speed.

Bumping over stones.

Sometimes rolling from one side to the other.

How long it would remain in the road was another question.

Sanderson felt every moment was going to be his last.

The mad speed of the horses frightened him.

Miles and miles did the light waggon roll on in this way, until the lieutenant felt his body all over bruises and sores.

Lying at the bottom of the vehicle, he was bumped from one side to the other.

And glad indeed was he when his journey came to an end.

When the waggon stopped, Sanderson was hauled somewhat roughly out.

He could hear the ripple of water, and feel a fine cooling breeze pass over his parched lips, bearing on their breath a refreshing spray.

He knew that he was by the seaside.

Although the night was dark, and objects quite indistinguishable.

Not even a star glimmered in the whole firmament.

But this fact seemed to make no difference to the pirates, who, after hauling Sanderson out of the waggon, hurried him rudely along, and finally ended by throwing him into the bottom of a boat.

Several of the pirates got in and pulled with all speed from the shore.

Those that were left returned to the waggon, and the wheels could soon be heard going as formerly.

Sanderson might have been about three-quarters of an hour on the water.

He could not have been more, when the boat stopped.

Stopped alongside of a large schooner.

And even here the men's voices were not heard much above a whisper.

The lieutenant, without much ceremony, was hauled upon deck, and conducted below.

The gag was taken from his mouth, and he was relieved of his bonds.

"You'll have company here," said one of the men who conducted him down, "a gentleman and lady, that perhaps you have some acquaintance with."

A sudden light flooded the cabin.

Lieutenant Sanderson observed that there were two other persons there besides himself and his two pirate conductors.

These persons turned suddenly.

A great flash of light lit up their faces.

Sanderson looked at them with horror, for there

a few paces from him, stood, as he had seen them in life, but haggard and aged—John Gregory and Mrs. Drake!

The lieutenant, on seeing those whom he thought dead, threw up his arms wildly, staggered forward, and fell senseless!

CHAPTER XX.

BOB HAULER AND JERRY MIZZEN FIND THEM-SELVES IN VERY UNPLEASANT QUARTERS.—THE CAVE.

"Well, Bob, we've got ourselves into a fine mess now!"

"You are right, Jerry. I imagine we are tightly fixed for some time to come."

"That's not a werry good consolation."

"No, old fellow. I should think as how it wasn't."

"Better be in Black Bill's clutches, even."

"Far better, Jerry."

"Who would think that that 'ere sinister-looking cove would have acted so shabby."

"I warn't so much surprised at it, Jerry."

"No!"

"Not a bit."

"Well, you are a rum cove, Bob. If you had only said it afore, we would have been prepared for him."

"What's done, cannot be undone, Jerry."

"I'm afeared it can't, Bob. I wish as how yer proolific brain would devise some plan for our release."

"I wish it would. But it's not in acting order, old pal. I feels my head swelled as big as a pumpkin. Old Shrike would be right glad to have it now, Jerry. He might find the dewelopment in one certain part very great."

"Much greater than Jacop's when we deweloped his with the taters."

"Much. I feel a bump the size of a turnip on my head, Jerry."

"What! so big as that, Bob?"

"Every bit, old pal. The feller must have hit me with a marling spike, or summat o' that sort. But I think I caught his phiz, and will know him again. However, that won't take the dewelopment off my head, Jerry."

"I am sure it won't, Bob. But then, yer see, there's the satisfaction o' meeting him again."

"Decidedly."

"You say you have spotted him."

"That I have, and I mean settling accounts with him afore I leave the place."

"That's werry thoughtful of you, Bob."

"Do you think so."

"I am sure it is. No matter, Bob, our turn comes next."

"A sudden idea strikes me," cried Bob. "Let me alone until I pon-ponder over it."

Jerry, according to Bob's request, instantly held his tongue.

But where were our friends Bob and Jerry?

We know that they fell into the hands of Philistines.

Whether they were smugglers or pirates is another thing.

The foregoing dialogue took place in a cave by the sea-side.

Indeed, a cave well-known to our two buccaneer friends, who often patronised it, when they led the career of smugglers.

They were still bound hand and foot.

But their considerate captors had taken the gags from their mouths, on condition, however, that they did not attempt to give an alarm to any person who might be passing outside.

They were now alone in the cave, and had been so for nearly twelve hours.

But there was no prospect of escape, even had they got rid of their bonds, as they were considerately informed by their captors that two of their number, with a brace of pistols each, guarded the entrance to the cave, and had strict orders to shoot them down like dogs if they made any such attempt.

So that our two friends, Bob and Jerry, were tightly fixed indeed.

And completely in the power of the pirates.

As the two buccaneers had no doubt now but that the men who kept strict watch over them belonged to that profession.

"I can see it all," said Bob, after the lapse of a few moments. "This is a trap to catch Captain Tom. I shouldn't wonder a bit but that long, lean, hungry, sinister-looking fellow is in the pay of that malicious little reptile, Admiral Ellis."

"I was almost going to say," put in Jerry, "that it serves the captain right for not shooting him, when he had him in his power."

"Don't be uttering such treason, Jerry."

"I can't help a-thinking of it, Bob."

"Very well; but you know, old pal, you have no right to think. Captain Tom does that 'ere sort o' thing, and men of ability."

"Bob Hauler among the number, of course?"

"I hope as how you won't be throwing out such insinuations, Jerry; for blow me if I like 'em!"

"But you are a-throwing 'em out yerself. You know the old saying, Bob: people as lives in glass houses mustn't throw stones."

"Blow yer old sayings!" growled Bob.

"Blow yours, too!" muttered Jerry.

"What did yer say?"

"Nothing."

"Then mind as how yer says nothing. I've had a little too much already of your jaw, Jerry."

"Ditto, Bob."

"Yer knows as how yer safe, I reckon."

"So do you."

"And now yer imposing on good nature."

"Ho! ho!"

"I'll 'ho! ho!' you on the other side of your face presently."

"You be hanged, Bob! Who's a-speaking to you?"

"You are, aren't you?"

"Not I! I wouldn't be seen a-speaking to you for an iron guinea, I wouldn't. You calls yerself a man o' genius, and here you are a-cornered in like a rat."

A sudden noise outside the cave now put them on their guard.

They thought for a moment that some of their captors had returned.

But in this they were, however, mistaken.

As such was not the case.

"Did you hear that noise, Bob?"

"Yes," replied the buccaneer. "I wonder what it is? Some dog scampering over the beach."

"More likely one of them rascally pirates," returned Jerry. "Shouldn't wonder but they're a-listening to us."

"Well, they'll not gain much information by that operation," said Bob.

"Let us speak lower, then."

"Agreed."

"How long do you think we've been here?"

"Lord knows!"

"Nearly twenty hours, I should judge."

"Not so much."

"Well, fifteen?"

"About that. But I say, Jerry, do you feel hungry?"

"Don't I though, that's all!"

"A piece o' salt junk and a hard biscuit would be very pleasant now."

"Jolly!"

"One meal and a half in sixteen hours is not quite enough for fellows o' our stripe. What do you say, Jerry?"

"I should say as how it wasn't, old pal."

"And no means a-getting more—that's the devil of it."

"I wish them villains o' pirates would come back and give us something as we could put our teeth through—eh, Bob?"

"I wish they would, Jerry. I also wish another thing."

"What is that?" asked Jerry.

"That they'd cut these infarnal bonds of mine!"

"Would you leave a chum and brother in the lurch, you lubber?"

"Sartinly not. For if they released me don't you see it wouldn't take me long to do a like operation for you. Then two good cutlasses in our hands, and we'd show 'em the stuff we are made of."

"Right you are, Bob. But has no expedient—as Captain Tom calls it—come into yer noble brain yet?"

"That's the werry thing, Jerry. Something has just struck me."

"Bravo! I knew as how it would."

"Shut up, you cantankerous varmint! Do you want all the world to know what I'm a-going to do? You ought to be ashamed o' yerself, Jerry, and ought to know better. Why don't you be calm and cool like me, and not let that hot-blooded spirit o' yours prewail over yer prudence and common sense?"

"What do you mean, Bob? You are werry insulting, allow me to say."

"I haven't patience with you, Jerry. You see that I've hit upon a plan, and you go and make that confounded noise to let everybody know it Why don't yer speak in whispers, like me? You are not a baby now, Jerry."

"No more aren't you, to be giving way to that 'ere uncompromising spirit o' yours."

"Well, no matter. There's a little settlement to come off a-tween us."

"Then the sooner it's settled the better," said Jerry, indignantly. "Upon my word, Bob, you are the most insulting warmint I ever met. Shiver my beam! I'd like to have a couple o' rounds with you. Perhaps that would bring you to your senses, and make you speak a little civiler to a feller."

"You go to——"

"The devil, you would say. Never mind; the devil is a far better feller than you, Bob, or any o' your breed."

"Well, I might say the same o' you if I was any way unpolite," returned Bob. "But hark, Jerry. What have we here? There's some one on the outside now, sure enough."

"By Neptune! you are right, Bob. Listen!"

They now heard sounds distinctly proceeding from the exterior of the cave.

Both buccaneers strained their hearing faculties to the utmost.

They heard the tramp of feet on the beach.

The tramp of many men

And besides these sounds, a confused murmur of voices.

The two comrades had no doubt now but that these were their captors returning.

These evidences gained weight by the footsteps coming more distinctly to their ears, and by the fact that they were evidently approaching the cave.

"Here they are back again!" said Bob.

"Well, I'm not werry sorry for that," replied

Jerry; "especially if they bring anything with them in the eating line."

"And the drinking line, too. Besides, I'm nearly perishing for a chew of tobacco."

"So am I."

"Be quiet. Here they come."

Bob was right.

They could now hear the tramp of the men as they came into the cave.

There must be a dozen or over a dozen of them at least.

"Well," said one, who appeared to have some command, "how have these fellows conducted themselves? Have they given you any trouble—called for assistance, or anything of that kind?"

"We'll see if our guards give us a good charicter," whispered Bob.

"No," replied the man. "As far as we know, they have kept very quiet."

"What am I to understand by such an answer?" said the other. "You have not been away from your post, surely?"

"Not ten yards at any time."

"And you have not heard them? There may just be a possibility that the rascals have got away."

"Or asleep," ventured another.

"That is quite likely. However, it will not take us a moment to see. They don't seem to be the kind of men likely to be disheartened, considering they are in such good hands."

Tramp! tramp! came the pirates.

Bob and Jerry closed their eyes, pretending to be locked in the arms of peaceful slumber.

"Babes in the wood," muttered Bob, snoring heavily.

"What the deuce is that?" cried the leader of the pirates, alarmed by these sonorous sounds, which proceeded from our two friends' capacious gullets.

The mystery was soon explained, as they caught the burly forms of the two buccaneers stretched out upon some straw, in an apparently deep sleep.

"They don't seem to feel their situation much," said the leader, flashing the light of a lantern into Bob's face.

"They take it very easy, at all events," said another. "considering that they've only had one meal and a half since they've been here. Ah! there! that one is talking. Let us hear what he has to say."

Bob Hauler gave over snoring, and began to speak in a way men usually speak when they are in a disturbed sleep.

"I shouldn't mind if I did join you," said Bob, getting out his words very slowly and stammeringly. "But—but shiver my timbers! this 'ere aren't ex-exactly fair.

"Be—be a pirate, did yer say? A-avast heaving there! Is this here a right—right and proper way to treat a man as is a-going to—to join yer? No junk, no biscuits, no baccy, no nothing.

"I'd sooner be—be hacked down like a—a dog than starved to death. Give—give me plenty o' grog, baccy, and vittles, and I'll follow yer to the devil if yer wants me.

"But—but don't starve me, or—or I'll knock some o' yer bulkheads in, damme if I don't! Hurrah! hurrah! For the life of a pirate on the rolling sea! Hurrah! hur—"

Bob broke off at this interesting point, and began snoring louder than ever.

The pirates listened with amazement to all the supposed sleeper said.

During Bob's dodge to hoodwink his captors, Jerry went on with his snoring, though he, too, muttered some words about an "empty belly" and about "grub."

"The poor fellows are actually starving," said

CAPTAIN TOM WARNED BY THE WIZARD OF THE CLIFFS.

the leader, compassionately. "I think we might as well wake them up, and give them something to eat. What brawny, lusty chaps they are! By all accounts they are the best men Captain Tom has.

"He has evidently not treated them well, and now they want to change masters. They'd make a splendid addition to our gallant crew, for, in my eyes, they look a host in themselves. I already begin to like them. If pirates they want to be, pirates they shall be."

The others nodded in appreciation of their leader's words.

But a sudden thought struck the speaker.

Perhaps Bob and Jerry were not asleep, after all.

He would try.

The glare of the lamp was strong.

If they could bear that across their eyes, they were asleep.

If not, they were playing a nice ruse on him.

Now, as it happened, our friend Bob's eyes were not altogether shut.

Nor, indeed, were Jerry's.

They detected what was passing through the pirate leader's mind, and prepared themselves accordingly for the test.

The man with the lantern threw the full glare of its light on Bob's eyes first.

Passed it, and repassed it.

Bob stood the test well, and snored as loudly as ever.

Test one was thoroughly satisfactory.

Test two, after a few moments, was equally so.

And then the pirate leader concluded that they were both in a very deep sleep, indeed.

Having tested the two men thoroughly, he in command, followed by his men, penetrated deeper into the cavern.

Bob and Jerry meanwhile laughing in their sleeves at the easy and perfectly simple way in which they had outwitted their enemies.

But enemies no longer.

The cavern was rather an extensive one.

The pirates when they were about twenty yards from our two buccaneer friends set about making a fire.

They had plenty of fuel in the place to keep burning for a month.

So they soon had a blazing fire.

The heat of which was very comforting to Bob Hauler and Jerry Mizzen.

Especially that they had a knowledge that they would shortly be served with food, perhaps grog, and no doubt, likewise, tobacco as well.

Now, all this was very cheering to reflect on.

Men who had vigorous stomachs, and who could digest almost anything, were not likely to be in the best of tempers after so long a fast.

Bob and Jerry were now in such a mood that they would snap at anyone or anything.

Even at each other.

As the reader had already seen.

But as the fire blazed brightly, our buccaneers got into better spirits.

They could also see, through their partly-opened eyes, the number of men that were there.

Fourteen, all told.

The leader to wit.

But Bob and Jerry, though conscious of all this, continued their snoring.

Listening, at the same time, to every word that fell from the pirates' lips.

And they heard the following story, relating to their own little brig, the "Will-o'-the-Wisp," and her gallant commander, Captain Tom.

"It is some years ago now," said the pirate who volunteered the account.

"We were cruising in the Bay of Naples—or, I should say, to be more correct, that we put in there for water and provisions.

"This was an easy task enough in those days, as we had no coastguards to deal with, and, as for the men-o'-war cutters, I really believe that they had as much to do with piracy on the high seas as we.

"However, we were not long at anchor in the bay, when we received a visit from a Roman nobleman who was residing at the time in Naples.

"How he came to discover that we were free rovers, I cannot tell.

"But this he did.

"And one night, when it was dark enough, his boat shot alongside of our schooner, and he asked to be taken on board.

"'What is your errand?' asked our lieutenant.

"'Are you the captain?' he demanded.

"'I am not,' replied the luff. 'But you can tell me your business, I suppose, as well as if I were?'

"The fact is, you see, the lieutenant was rather afraid that their being there had somehow or other got to the ears of the authorities.

"So, in consequence, he had to exercise a little discretion.

"'I suppose you have some command here?' said the visitor.

"'Yes, I have. I am the first officer,' replied the luff.

"'That alters the case materially,' returned the man in the boat. 'Perhaps you would have no objection to let me aboard now, as I have something very particular to communicate?'

"'Better communicate it from where you are,' said the luff. 'We have no secrets aboard this vessel. Besides, I see that you have three or four men with you.'

"'What does that matter?' said his visitor. 'If I have a dozen, I mean no harm to you. You had better let me come aboard to see your captain. I have business that'll put a good round sum in his pocket.'

"While they were talking in this way who should come on deck but the skipper.

"'What's all this row about?' he cried, for he was not the man to stand on much ceremony with anyone.

"'Who are you, and what do you want?' he bellowed over the side.

"He could distinguish the boat, of course, and the black figures of the men.

"But the night was dark, and, as he could not see their faces or their dresses, he grew suspicious that all was not right.

"He now gave a whisper for some of the crew to be ready with cold shot to sink the boat if all was not right.

"'You are the captain, I presume?' said the voice from the boat in very good English; 'and if you are, I am going to put something into your hands that you will thank me for. It is only an hour's work, and it will be as good as four thousand pounds in your pocket.'

"Now this, to say the least, was a tempting offer.

"Four thousand pounds was worth risking.

"'Your promise is very fair,' said the skipper. 'But, to be brief, what do you require doing?'

"'Allow me to come on deck, and I will tell you,' said the unknown.

"'Very well, then,' replied the captain. 'But I warn you any tricks will be severely punished.'

"The man laughed as he answered, 'You need not fear, captain; I come as a friend, and to engage your services.'

"Now you may be sure that we were all a little surprised at this talk that was going on.

"But at last up came the man from the boat, assisted by some of our chaps, and the moment that he was on deck we could see that he was a gentleman.

"There was something in his manner that awed rough fellows like us.

"However, the captain took him below, and there he remained for about a half an hour.

"They had, no doubt, been talking and arranging some place to act on the following night, as was afterwards found out, as I was one of the men told off for the duty.

"This foreign gentleman, when he got through his business with our skipper, got back again into his boat and pushed off, and presently disappeared in the darkness.

"No more was said about the matter until the next night.

"The following morning, however, a strange kind of a brig came into the bay and anchored about a quarter of a mile from us.

"We all looked upon her with a strange kind of suspicion.

"For we knew very well that she was not what she pretended to be, so we resolved to have our eyes on her, thinking that she was there in reality to watch our movements.

"All that day some of her crew were hovering about our schooner, and although they were dressed as ordinary merchant seamen, we could tell at a glance they were not such.

"We could not quarrel with them very well, so

we let them go about as they liked, with the intention, if they came too near, to drop a few cold shots by accident into their boat, which might be the means, perhaps, of teaching them better manners.

"However, the lubbers were too cunning to give us that chance.

"In this way the night came on.

"A vastly different one to the night before, for there was a bright moon shining, and the waters of the bay gleamed out for miles.

"At about nine o'clock the skipper came on deck.

"'Now, boys,' said he, 'how many of you will volunteer to go on a little expedition with me?'

"Fifty men at once stepped to the front.

"'Avast there!' said he, 'I don't want so many of you. A dozen will do.'

"The dozen were soon selected.

"I among the number.

"Each man armed himself with a good cutlass and a brace of pistols.

"Next a boat was lowered, and we got in, and were soon scudding over the bay for the shore.

"The captain now explained the mission we were bound on.

"The Roman gentleman, or nobleman, who came on board the night before agreed to pay our captain four thousand pounds to abduct a Spanish lady, whom he had fallen in love with.

"He had tried to do the business by fair means, but failing so to do, resolved that she should be his at any risk.

"Now, this young lady's father, as it happened, was a Spanish nobleman, who was altogether against the union, as were also her two brothers, and, strange to say, the young lady herself had a decided objection.

"She, in fact, stung the Roman to madness by her treatment.

"And he resolved to have revenge for the slight offered him.

"This is why he paid a visit to our schooner, and offered the captain so large a sum to take the matter in hand for him.

"Now, there was something in the affair of an abduction that just suited us.

"Besides, we were to be well paid for it, which was better.

"The keel of our boat at last grounded on the shore, and we leaped out.

"Some time before that, we had observed a craft following in our wake.

"But we took no notice of the fact, as there were plenty of fisher boats plying about, and it was not unlikely that it might be one of them.

"Strange to say, we forgot all about the brig in the prospect of being successful and handling the coin.

"Which was a matter of very great consideration, I can tell you.

"However, we found out the house where these Spanish Dons lived; and as our visit was quite unexpected, we beat down all opposition in a very short time, killing two of the servants, and pistoling one of the brothers.

"The rest we gagged, the young lady herself undergoing that operation.

"Having done all we wanted, we next retraced our steps as quick as we could to where we left our boat, carrying our fair prisoner with us.

"But here we were doomed to encounter something that we didn't bargain for.

"As we were passing the pillared ruins of what was once a fine old Neapolitan residence, out rushed about two dozen men, armed to the teeth.

"The moon lit their stalwart forms distinctly to our view, and I was not a minute in recognising some of them as the crew of the strange brig.

"A desperate battle now ensued.

"Our captain fought like a lion.

"But what was the use?

"Those who attacked us were two to one.

"Besides, they fought as well as we did, if not better.

"In less than ten minutes most of our men lay bleeding on the ground.

"In another ten we were all disarmed, and at the mercy of our assailants, and the girl, whom we carried off, taken from us.

"But here comes the strange part of the story.

"Our captain was taken up before a young man who seemed little better than a boy, but who, in the melee, fought like a devil incarnate.

"'Now,' he said, 'as you are beaten, I will give you two choices—either to accompany us as a prisoner on board the "Will-o'-the-Wisp," or ransom yourself in one thousand pounds. I am Captain Tom Drake, and I believe you have heard of me before.'

"I must tell you that our captain had, and cursed the day he ever met him.

"However, to end my story, the one thousand pounds were paid, and the girl returned to her father."

And this story ended, they had very little else to learn from the pirates' conversation.

The men all seemed intent upon preparing a meal, for, in a manner speaking, they were about as hungry as our two friends.

This was certainly the most interesting part of the arrangement.

At least, so thought the two buccaneers, who were already greedily devouring, in their own minds, the preparing meal.

Tobacco and grog, of course, came in for an ample share in their consideration.

To be without these articles of consumption was, as far as they were concerned, to be without everything else.

So it cheered their hearts amazingly to hear the pirates speak so glibly of the good things in store for the night.

That they anticipated spending a jolly one was evident from their conversation and preparations.

To prepare the supper—for supper we may take the liberty to call it—did not take very much time.

A half an hour at most.

And when this was done, the pirate leader left his companions, and went forward to our two buccaneers.

Of course, seeing that talented individual approaching, their snoring grew thoroughly deafening.

The pirate was astounded that his prisoners possessed such breathing powers.

But the reader must not for a moment imagine that he was in the least degree frightened.

On he came with a steady step, and as Bob Hauler was a little nearer than Jerry, he bent down, gripped that gentleman by the shoulder, and began shaking and calling him at the same time.

"Now, then!" he cried, "don't sleep your blessed senses away, but wake up and have something to eat."

Bob pretended to be very angry, and asked him what the devil he meant by disturbing him in that way.

"What do I mean, you lubber? Come, wake up, and you'll soon see."

Bob, with a great yawn, opened his eyes, and looked at the pirate leader with a bewildered expression.

"Who the deuce are you?" he said. "I've never seen you afore."

"Very likely not," replied the pirate. "But that doesn't say that we may not be friends yet. I should judge now, that you and your comrade are pretty hungry after your long fast."

"Hungry is no name for it," grumbled Bob. "I was never sarved so shabbily in my life, and as for my poor comrade there, I believe he must be on the very verge of starvation."

"I'll wake him up then. How he snores!"

"He always does that sort o' thing," said Bob. "Always a-disturbing of some one, he is. I wish I had only my hands free, and I'd give him a reviver as he wouldn't forget for some time."

"You would?"

"Wouldn't I though! Sledge-hammers would be nothing to it."

"You are a rum fellow, and I rather like you."

"Thank you werry much," said Bob. "Your noble sentiments bring tears into my eyes. Oblige me by giving that 'ere snoring comrade o' mine a good kick, as it's almost impossible to wake him up by any other means."

"Oh, no, I'll not do that. Better try the more gentle method of shaking him."

Which the pirate leader did, and had the satisfaction soon of seeing the irrepressible one open his eyes.

Jerry, giving vent to a terrific yawn, shook himself like a huge mastiff, and demanded what the row was.

"Rouse him with a kick," bawled his sympathising comrade, "and that'll soon tell him what it is."

"You be blowed!" cried Jerry, ferociously.

"Come, now, my good fellows, we'll have no quarrelling here," said the pirate leader, interfering "If you want to spend a good and pleasant night with us, you had both better conduct yourselves civilly. I must tell you that the men are taken up very much with you, and, knowing that you care little for the 'Will-o'-the-Wisp,' or her commander, would be glad for you to join them."

"How?" asked Bob.

"In eating or the drinking line?" put in Jerry.

"In both, my friends."

"But how can we when we are bound down like this?" said Bob, innocently.

"You'll not long be so, if you'll agree to one thing."

"We'll agree to anything."

"Bravo! You are the right sort of fellows. But you may slightly misunderstand me."

"I don't think we do," said Bob. "You means to give us a good blow out. That's what you means, isn't it?"

"I mean more than that, my friend."

"Well, what do you mean, then? Speak out?"

"In the first place, we are pirates."

"Pirates!" exclaimed Bob.

"Pirates!" echoed Jerry.

"How surprising!" said Bob.

"Werry," added Jerry.

"Yes, we are pirates. How would you like to join us?"

"Not at all, if you treat us in the way we was treated in that 'ere 'Will-o'-the-Wisp.'"

"Then you acknowledge that you were badly treated on the 'Will-o'-the-Wisp?'"

"Bad treatment is no name for it," said Bob.

"Worser treatment I never experienced," added Jerry.

"I hope as how I never sees the 'Will-o'-the-Wisp' again," said Bob.

"Hell upon earth," echoed Jerry.

"I see, my friends, that we'll find no difficulty in coming to some arrangement. Will you join our schooner or not?"

"Providing good treatment is guaranteed—yes."

"Then it's all settled."

"Not exactly," said the cautious Bob. "There's something more to be said afore that takes place. Plenty of provisions?'

"More than you can eat."

"Grog?"

"Quantity unlimited."

"Backey?"

"More than you can chew."

"Bravo!" cried Bob and Jerry in a breath. "That's the place for us!"

"Then you agree?" cried the leader of the pirates, ecstatically.

"Agree!" said Bob.

"Agree!" cried Jerry. "I should think as how we was fools if we didn't. What say you, Bob?"

"The werry same, old pal. Agree to anything—to sinking vessels right and left."

"Then you'll be pirates?"

"In course we will."

"Bravo, lads! I can see you are the right sort."

"Now about the bonds?" said Bob.

"You shall be released at once from them. Ho! there, one of you!"

A pirate came forward from among his comrades.

"Good news, lad!" cried his leader. "These two noble fellows here agree to join us."

The man was perfectly astounded at Bob and Jerry's extraordinary condescension.

He made the roof of the cavern ring with his loud huzzas.

The other pirates did not know what to make of it.

They came rushing forward in a body, and when told of what occurred, split the dome of the cavern with their cheers.

But this was rather too dangerous an exercise to last.

As it might reach other ears than friendly ones.

Besides, the sentinel at the entrance came in to warn them not to make too much noise.

A half a minute after that Bob and Jerry were free of their bonds.

There now set in a general rejoicing.

Supper was served up on a rude table hastily extemporised.

And need we say that Bob and Jerry did ample justice to the meal, as both were as hungry as wolves, or hunters.

Steaming hot grog came next.

Tobacco went round the table in great quantities.

Songs were sung.

Bob and Jerry took an active part in everything.

Even condescended to dance a sailor's hornpipe in conjunction, on the massive table.

Such a night of jollity the pirates had seldom seen.

Besides, they could hardly before bring themselves to believe that Bob and Jerry were such good fellows.

But they had the proof now, and they fairly idolized them.

Bob and Jerry's minds, however, were filled with far different thoughts

Thoughts, indeed, that would materially decrease the pirates' high respect for them.

The faithful fellows took the situation in at a glance.

They saw now that all was plain sailing, and that whatever they meditated against their new acquaintances, the pirates, would in the end be very successful.

What they did, and how they succeeded, will be left to another chapter.

CHAPTER CLXXXII.

WONDERFUL EXPLOITS OF BOB AND JERRY.

WE promised, in the last chapter, to give the reader an account of Bob and Jerry's performances among the pirates in the cavern.

And now we mean performing that promise as well as we can.

The reader will acknowledge that their position there at first was anything but enviable.

Who but men of Bob and Jerry's eccentric abilities would have succeeded so peculiarly to outwit these detestable sea robbers.

Who but a man of Bob's unique genius would have thought of the snoring dodge, and speaking under the deepest of somnolent influences?

Men do sometimes speak in their sleep.

Now, as all our readers are aware, this fact is nothing extraordinary.

It is done every night in the year.

But Bob's performance was a matter of pure genius.

Bob, indeed, was a born actor.

Nor was Jerry a bad one in his line, and we must all own that he did his part to perfection.

Now, the pirates, under the exhilirating effects of good grog and excellent tobacco, together with their invaluable adjuncts, dance and song, were beginning to lose all the little prudence they ever had.

They would, at last, have trusted Bob and Jerry anywhere.

Even out of the cavern if they desired it.

As some new additions came in in the shape of four or five stray smugglers, the general rejoicing increased.

Bob and Jerry were at once introduced to these with half-intoxicated ceremony.

Besides, they were pledged over and over again in steaming hot glasses of grog, and even raw liquor was drunk with more or less gusto.

Our buccaneers' glasses were filled every five minutes, and oftener if they could only dispose of their contents.

But let us for a moment see what our two cunning friends did.

Did they take glass for glass with the pirates?

Not they.

They knew better.

Out of every five glasses of hot grog four of them went under the table.

Where they ought to go.

Bob and Jerry intended to keep their wits about them.

And they did so.

It was with the greatest delight that Captain Tom's men saw the effects of the pirates' frequent imbibations.

A half-dozen of them were already under the table, snoring in drunken stupor, and deluged over with the grog that Bob and Jerry should have taken, and which they didn't take.

Four or five more would shortly go the same way, as could be seen plainly by the way they reeled about the cavern, in their vain attempts to shake each other's hands.

Our delightful friends imitated them so well that a sober onlooker would have put them down as drunk as any of the others.

But this was Bob and Jerry's game, especially as they found that they were keenly watched by one keen-eyed smuggler, who took good care to drink little of any of the contents of the grog glasses.

Why this gentleman should be so suspicious, Bob and Jerry were at a loss to conceive.

But they, nevertheless, watched him as keenly as he watched them.

Bob, moreover, resolved to play him a trick which he would not be likely to forget.

How was he to do it?

The man up to this, had not drunk more than one glass of grog.

Nor could he be prevailed upon to take a second.

Bob, however, determined he should take a second.

And that that second would be sufficient to answer all purposes.

Not more than ten minutes elapsed when five more of the pirates went under the table, and out of the smugglers three met a similar fate.

So in this manner, numbers had visibly decreased, much to the gratification of Bob and Jerry, who would shortly only have the sentinels outside the cavern to deal with.

Our buccaneers, with two good cutlasses in their hands, would soon manage these.

Now, Bob's plan was this, regarding the wide-awake smuggler.

It just struck his memory that he had an opiate in his pocket of great power, and speedy effect.

He had tried it once before, and knew its value.

He would try it again, and see its results on the smuggler.

There was a somewhat lengthy history connected with this opiate.

Which, however, we will not pretend to enter into.

Suffice it to say that it came into the possession of our friend Bob, and that that gentleman intended making very good use of it.

Now, how was he to get this lynx-eyed smuggler to take it?

The task was puzzling.

As the fellow could not even be persuaded to drink.

Bob thought the matter over while he was reeling and staggering across the cavern floor in the attempt to grip some imaginary person's hand.

Bob hit upon a plan with the suddenness of thought, and prepared to put it into execution.

Ladling out a glass of grog, he staggered over to the wide-awake smuggler in such a manner that that individual must have thought him very drunk indeed.

Bob slipped his opiate into the glass beforehand taking good care not to let his vigilant observer see him.

So naturally, indeed, did our buccaneer stagger over to the smuggler, that that gentleman came to the firm conviction that he had been deceived, and that Bob was in reality as drunk as any of the rest.

With no doubt a stronger stomach and brain to guard against its effects.

Thus reasoned the lynx-eyed gent as he saw our friend stagger over to him.

"Hic! old feller," said Bob, making believe that he found it difficult to get out a word without stumbling over it—"hic! You—hic!—don't drink. Pledge me—hic!—in this!"

"In what?"

"In—hic!—this glass. We are all brothers—hic!—ain't we? Hic!—I should—hic!—think we were! Hic!—hic!—hic!"

The three "hics!" settled the business.

The wide-awake smuggler wasn't proof against so many.

So with a smile and a civil "thank-you," he took the glass out of Bob's hand.

And, furthermore, as apparently drunk as he was, our worthy friend saw that he didn't throw it under the table.

When the smuggler got the glass to his lips, Bob, by the purest accident, reeled against him, and sent every drop of its contents down his throat.

The man was nearly choked.

Tears came into his eyes.

But how could Bob help that?

The buccaneer, seeming to be conscious that he had done wrong, "hicked" away as hard as ever, and begged between every "hic" ten thousand pardons for knocking against him.

On the score that Bob was drunk, the smuggler accepted the apology.

But not long after he had drunk the glass of grog was he in a state of blissful wakefulness.

He staggered twice.

Grasped the table bewilderedly.

And, finally, lost his senses by rolling head-first under the table.

The last of the smugglers also followed him.

Now, no sooner did this delightful pair—Bob and Jerry—discover that they were alone, than they instantly straightened up, and gave vent to a prolonged chuckle.

All these proceedings had been most extraordinary, and revived their spirits very much.

"Fine bit o' play-acting, Bob."

"Splendid, Jerry."

"That wide-awake cove tumbled over very sudden, it seems to me," said Jerry, displaying unusual thought.

"Grog doesn't agree with him," said Bob.

"Should say not after that 'ere display of his conwivial faculties."

"Grog's not in his line, Jerry. The stronger the liquor the better for that varmint."

"I can't understand though, yet, how water could have such an effect on him. It's werry surprising! I never knew that water had that power afore."

"Well, it do seem extraordinary," said Bob. "It's not to be accounted for, that's the truth, Jerry. But I fancy we've got rid of 'em all now!"

"But the fellers outside?"

"Oh! we'll settle them soon enough. But wait a minute."

"What are ye going to do?"

"Furnish myself with a good cutlass and a brace of pistols, to be sure. You do the same," said Bob.

The old comrades set to work now to select the best cutlasses they could find, and also the best pistols.

The pirates were all turned over, and the said weapons taken possession of.

"Now," said Bob, "it won't do to put these on just yet."

"Why?" said Jerry.

"Simply 'cause we've a little more work to do."

"Work to do!" exclaimed Jerry. "What work have we to do but to get out o' this place as quick as we can?"

"You can't see a hole through a ladder, Jerry. You are so drunk."

"That be blowed for a tale, Bob!"

"Well, look here, now. Didn't you think of one thing?"

"What thing?"

"That the pirates and smugglers have a great deal too much whiskers on one side o' their faces?"

"I didn't notice that."

"Well, you'll see it in a minute, only keep your weather eye open."

Jerry was amazed.

Bob's language was full of mystery.

His eyes were as wide open as any one's.

But what could he see if he exhibited twice as much wakefulness?

Jerry not only saw Bob take a pair of scissors from his pocket, but likewise saw that eccentric individual calmly and deliberately at work on one of the pirate's bushy whiskers, which he sheared off with wonderful facility.

Only from one side of his face, however.

The other was left unshorn.

"Now you see what I mean, Jerry," said Bob, shearing away at another fellow's whiskers as hard as he could.

Jerry was lost in astonishment.

What put that idea into Bob's head?

He should like to find out.

But there was no time now to inquire.

Bob's shearing progressed very rapidly until he was aroused by the sounds of approaching steps.

"Take the scissors, Jerry," said Bob, "for I hear some one a-coming."

"What'll I take the scissors for?"

"You see what I've been doing?"

"Yes."

"Well, go you and do the same, until I see what this 'ere feller wants. On, I know what he's coming for now. He thinks I've forgot him. The grog—the grog, Jerry."

"In a minute, Bob."

"No, go on with your shearing. I don't want you to get it."

Jerry proceeded exactly as he had seen Bob proceed, and promised to do good work in a very brief time.

Bob, on the other hand, took out a little—very little indeed—of his opiate, and dropped it in a glass of grog.

With this he sallied forth to meet the approaching sentinel.

He staggered and reeled as any drunken man naturally would.

"Hilloa! old feller! Hic!—was—hic!—almost forgetting you. Take this—hic!—it will warm the cockles—hic!—of your good old—hic!—heart."

The sentinel, harbouring no suspicions of a drunken fellow like Bob, took the glass and drained it at a gulp.

He thought it rather strong.

Bob swore between a dozen "hics" that it wasn't, and that it was only imagination.

"Imagination or—or not," said the fellow, "I am —am a-going."

"Go, then," said Bob.

And he went accordingly.

But in a manner that he did not expect.

For he went head first between Bob's legs.

And that gentleman, giving him a gentle kick, left him there, and made his way back to Jerry.

Now Jerry being a capital hand at the scissors, progressed rapidly while Bob was away.

He had sheared away in the most artistic fashion.

Well, this was not saying much for our buccaneer friend, seeing that he was the brig's barber on more than one, or even two occasions.

Out of all the pirates and smugglers, there were now only four left.

And these Bob took the pleasure of operating on.

All the pirates and smugglers looked a most comical sight when the job was finished.

Bob and Jerry could not help giving vent to a low chuckle of satisfaction.

Indeed, their feelings after this auspicious performance can be better imagined than described.

But what would the feelings of these misguided men be, who had been shorn, when they returned to consciousness?

Ah, reader, we leave that for you to imagine!

Now, Bob and Jerry, having completed this task to their satisfaction, buckled on the cutlasses which they had appropriated, and, thrusting the pistols into their belts, prepared to leave the cavern.

A sudden thought, and Bob paused.

"What's wrong with you new?" asked Jerry.

"Have a little more work to do, old pal?"

"Work to do, eh?"

"Yes, Jerry; our task's uncomplete."

"You mean incomplete?" said Jerry, loftily.

"Well, uncomplete or incomplete; I suppose it's all the same. One word's as good as another."

"And sometimes a jolly sight better, Bob."

"Stow yer jawing-tackle, Jerry. Yer always going on with some tomfoolery or the other."

"Well, what does yer mean doing, then?"

"You'll see in a minute," returned Bob, who forthwith, by the aid of charcoal and that delightful colour, "red-raddle," began a new feature in the artistic art.

Before ten minutes the pirates and smugglers—if they then and there had the power of looking into a looking-glass—would not have known themselves, so creditably, and, in fact, wonderful, was our friend Bob's performance.

"That, I think, will do now," said Bob. "The pirate leader is sarved out every bit as bad as the rest."

"I should say worse," put in Jerry. "You have cut all one side of his hair off his head. You must be a werry hard-hearted feller, Bob."

"I know I am. I glory in being hard-hearted," said Bob. "There is only one more man I should like to have in my clutches now."

"Who is that?"

"That long, lean, hungry varmint with the sinister face. I'd shave him, and paint him off to perfection, I would."

"That 'ere is understood," said Jerry. "But mind as how he don't get you into his clutches first."

"What do you mean?"

"I means this—if we don't get away from here it may happen to turn out that we won't get away at all. And, after the performance as has been going on here, they'd show us little mercy if they once caught us."

"That is right, Jerry, Come along. We'll get out of this as soon as possible."

The two old comrades now walked in the direction of the outlet from the cave.

They had to be very cautious when they got a little distance, as they could hear the steps of the other sentinel on the outside.

"What does this mean?" asked Jerry, pointing to the second sentinel, who lay stretched out as if he were dead.

"I suppose he's been taking too much grog," said Bob.

"Like the rest," added Jerry. "Sad cases of depravity, Bob."

"Werry."

"Men of that kind should be temperate in all things."

"So they should, Jerry. And if I had my will, I'd send you to convert 'em."

"Come now, old pal; you don't mean that?"

"Yes, I do; but stop yer jaw. There's that 'ere sentinel a-listening."

"How are we going to sarve him?"

"Leave him to me. Let me go on first."

Bob went on first.

And Jerry followed close behind.

The sentinel who had stopped, now resumed his walking.

Everything outside the cave was as dark as pitch.

Everything inside was little better.

At least, such was the case where Bob and Jerry picked their steps.

"I forgot one thing," said Bob.

"What is that?" asked his comrade.

"I forgot them cords as they tied us with."

"Shall I go back and fetch them?"

"Sartinly."

"Werry good."

And Jerry at once departed.

Our buccaneer was not long away when he came back with the cords.

These were exactly what they wanted to bind the fellow outside.

They could soon improvise gags.

And the rest was easy work enough.

On again they crept to the mouth of the cavern.

They very soon got there, and cowered close against the jagged wall.

In so doing a piece of detached rock rolled at their feet.

The sudden noise, breaking on the stillness of the night, alarmed the sentinel.

He paused in his walk.

Came back to the mouth of the cave.

"Is that you, Bill?" he cried.

Another word had scarcely time to pass his lips when Bob bounded upon him like a tiger.

"No, it's not Bill, it is me," he replied; "and if you make a particle o' noise, I'll blow your brains out!"

The sentinel was taken so thoroughly aback, that the buccaneer found it child's play to throw him on the ground.

Jerry next rushed out, and placing the cold muzzle of the pistol at the pirate's head, swore that if he made one articulate sound, he would scatter his brains all over the beach.

There was nothing left for the sentinel but to submit quietly, and allow himself to be bound and gagged, which he soon was.

Next, Bob and Jerry dragged him into the cave and left him there.

Having thus rid themselves of the sentinel, they now bent their course along the beach, hoping that either moon or stars would come out shortly, to show them where they were.

A slight breeze, as it happened, was blowing against them.

It was, indeed, well for them that it was not blowing the other way, or they would, without doubt, have walked into a very nice trap—not exactly laid for them.

But for their captain and some others

What we refer to was a murmur of voices that fell rather indistinctly at first on their ears.

But which grew more distinctly as they proceeded.

The buccaneers paused to confer with each other.

"What do you make that out, Jerry?"

"Those voices?"

"Yes."

"They might be coastguards."

"And again they mightn't."

"Pirates, perhaps?"

"Or smugglers!"

"Well, one's almost as bad as the other."

"We was walking into a nice trap, only for this 'ere breeze."

"You are right. Had we better go back?"

"No, I think not. Let us push forward."

"Do you think it would be advisable?"

"I can't say yet. Only we might fall into a worse trap, that's all, by going back."

"Worse, 'cause it would be unexpected."

"Precisely so."

"Well, the order is to push on?"

"It is."

"Very good. Then we'll have to do it with some caution."

The buccaneers went on again.

But their progress was very slow.

As they could no longer hear the voices.

Which made them doubly cautious.

Besides, the night was as black as it could be

Not a star was to be seen from one end of the firmament to the other.

But, all of a sudden, the huge black clouds that curtained the heavens seemed to roll away, and a few bright stars peeped out.

This, to a certain extent, dissipated the darkness.

So much so, indeed, that our buccaneer friends could see where they were going.

Some hundreds of yards in front of them loomed out tall frowning rocks.

But, besides, there they could detect nothing.

One thing, however, they heard footsteps approaching the rocks.

Who, even the advancing parties where they were on the other side of these tall basaltic masses.

An instant later the moon suddenly burst from behind a cloud, and lit up the night with almost the brilliancy of daylight.

Bob and Jerry not wishing to expose themselves unnecessarily, got behind a huge rocky boulder.

Hardly had they thus concealed themselves, when they heard the hoarse shouts and imprecations of men, followed by the sharp whip-like cracks of several pistol shots.

CHAPTER CLXXXIII.

TERRIFIC STRUGGLE WITH THE SMUGGLERS.

"ANY letter for me, here?"

"Let me see. You are the gent as was here last night?"

"Yes."

"Well, then there's no letter."

"Not even a messenger?"

"Not a messenger even. But, hold! Where did you expect him from?"

"From— No matter where. I'll wait until he comes."

This brief dialogue took place at that notable resort, the Yellow Alligator, and the two persons who took part in it were our well-known acquaintances, Reuben Harpy and Old Zack Magpie.

No doubt, Reuben would have been more communicative, but Old Zack's one eye had a most peculiar effect on him.

That one eye he had taken a most inveterate dislike to.

In the first place, it was too bold.

In the second, too keen.

In the third, too trying.

Now for each and all of these qualities Reuben had the most repugnant abhorrence.

Old Jack was an enemy in his eyes at once, so, without wasting further words or time on him, he sauntered into the bar-room.

As the sun had only a short time before set, the bar-room was not so crowded.

He, however, noticed his two old comrades there.

Peter and the sham sentinel.

These two were enjoying themselves over a game of cards, which they wanted Reuben to take part in, and which Reuben, for various reasons, refused.

"Now, Peter, I caught you cheating that time," said the sham sentinel.

"Really, now, you wrong me most grievously," replied Peter, with a look of innocence that might have put a cherub to the blush.

"I caught you at it."

"Really—really—really now—this is too bad."

"Bad or not, let me not catch you at it again."

As the game was resumed, Reuben took no more notice of them.

Although he put Peter down, in his own mind, as a very great rogue.

The ex-privateer captain went to the extra-vagance of having a bottle of mine host's best wine before him.

And thus, and with the aid of a few choice cigars, he regaled himself for more than an hour.

But no letter came.

Neither did there a messenger.

Reuben was growing impatient, and began by cursing Black Bill under his breath.

"Shouldn't wonder but the rascal has sold me," he said. "If so, I'll put Admiral Ellis on his track, who will settle matters more effectively than pleasant with him. Curse him! What does he mean by having me wait here, borne down as I am by anxiety?"

And the ex-privateer, after swearing some silent but bitter oaths, went on drinking his wine and smoking his cigar.

Meanwhile the bar-room was filling with its usual frequenters.

Smugglers, pirates, highway robbers, and footpads.

Besides several "runners," who intermingled with them, drank with them, and even, over "friendly" games, quarrelled with them.

Old Zack had all he could do at times to keep them in order.

While Reuben Harpy was bitterly engaged in his thoughts, a man hastily entered the bar-room very travel-stained, and, apparently, greatly fatigued.

This man looked all about him as if searching for some one.

His eye at last caught the solitary figure of Reuben Harpy, for Reuben was seated alone, thinking whether it would, or not, be worth his while to remain in the bar-room any longer.

The ex-privateer captain seemed to answer the description of man the travel-stained person was seeking.

So, without more ado, he went forward to him.

At that moment Reuben looked up.

The man's travel-stained garments attracted his attention.

This, indeed, must be the messenger he was so anxiously expecting.

"I believe you are Mr. Harpy?" said the man, in a whisper.

"Well, what if I am?" said Reuben, pretending to be very busily engaged with his thoughts.

"If you are, I have a message for you," was the reply.

"Yes. From whom?"

"You may happen to know a gent called Black Bill?"

"Yes, I do happen to know him."

"Well, he sent me then," added the man.

"Enough," said Reuben Harpy. "You are the man Bill Evans sent."

"I have given you proof of that already," was the reply.

"You have, truly."

"And now—"

"We start."

"Very well, then. But, stay! You must be fatigued after your tiresome journey, and a little refreshment may be desirable."

"Just as you please," replied the messenger. "I can either do with, or without it."

The man's manner was rather independent, which fact somewhat gave offence to the immaculate Reuben, who held in utter detestation such a quality, unless manifested in the upper classes.

In these he did not care how far their spirit of independence went.

But for a mere smuggler, or something worse, he didn't know which, to show such a trait, was hardly to be expected.

Reuben, therefore, bit his lips, but manifested no other outward sign of his displeasure.

The ex-captain of the Brazilian privateer called for another bottle now of wine, and a few choice cigars.

The former he placed at the disposal of his travel-stained companion.

The latter he took good care to appropriate to his own use.

"The prospect then is good," began Reuben, after lighting another cigar, and filling out a glass of the wine for the messenger.

"The prospect of what?" asked the messenger.

Reuben cast a rapid glance around him to see that no one was within hearing, before he answered.

Then he replied—

"The capture of Captain Tom."

"Oh," replied the man, "you may rest yourself contented on that point. If the prospect was not good I shouldn't be here."

Reuben's eyes sparkled with the fierce joy he felt.

Captain Tom captured!

What a moment of inexplicable bliss would this be to him!

How savage and even unrelenting was his hate for the cousin to whom he attributed all his misfortunes!

For it never occurred at all to our worthy acquaintance that he was in reality the author of his own misfortunes.

Oh, no!

Every accident he met with was laid at the door of Captain Tom, who had, according to his opinion, been the scourge and bane of his whole life from boyhood up.

He could not yet get it out of his mind how he lost his vessel, the Brazilian privateer.

All through that frightful fellow, Iron-Arm, one of Captain Tom's lieutenants, and so, one of his bitter enemies, whom he hoped yet, by treachery and other influences, to crush.

Reuben Harpy favoured the man with the travel-stained raiment by drinking a glass of the wine and for several minutes after he was completely enwrapped in his own thoughts.

In imagination he could already see his hated cousin adorning the yard-arm of one of Admiral Ellis's vessels.

He could see the spasmodic and agonized workings of that noble form, as he met this ignominious end.

But why should he not see his face?

That was covered up.

They would scarcely hang men like brutes.

Even in civilized England at the time we write.

Heaven knows how cruel were the naval regulations at that time.

When they would flog an unfortunate fellow-creature for a mere nothing.

And very often hang him for little more.

This was a disgrace—an everlasting disgrace—on the escutcheon of that boasted English civilisation which paraded before the world its vaunted superiority in all things that were noble and humane.

But they are now matters of the past, only to be re-called with the deepest abhorrence and disgust.

The accursed "cat" has left both our army and navy, for ever.

"And a good job, too!" we fancy we can hear some of our readers exclaim.

"And a good job, too!" we repeat from the bottom of our hearts.

As death, to being tied up and flogged like a dog, is preferable any time.

But a truce to moralising.

Let us rather keep within the bounds of the Yellow Alligator, and so follow in the steps of Reuben Harpy and the travel-stained messenger.

We say Reuben smoked sometimes in silence, conjuring up the most delightful visions (delightful to him, but with a corresponding horror to our readers) regarding the manner of Captain Tom's speedy exit from this world of trouble and cares.

You ask, had Reuben any doubt of the results?

We answer, not the slightest.

He was sure that our hero's lease of life had nearly run out.

As sure, indeed, as he was, that he was sitting in the bar-room of the Yellow Alligator, sipping his glass of wine, and smoking his fine Havanah cigar.

So far, indeed, had Reuben's thoughts carried him.

There was no such word as failure now.

He knew the nature of Black Bill too well.

And also that the smuggler was almost as bitter in his hatred of Captain Tom as he was himself.

Now Reuben Harpy was not aware of it.

But his every motion was watched by Old Zack, whose suspicions only grew by the arrival of the messenger.

Old Zack had only one eye.

But that eye was a sharp one, penetrating at times into the most hidden thoughts of others.

Aye, and at a time, too, when others dreamt that they were in the most perfect security.

Now, the landlord of the Yellow Alligator knew very well that the sham sentinel and Peter, were two of Reuben's connections.

Not only by the dialogue that he had listened to the previous night, but by numerous signs and occasional little passages of a friendly conversational nature that took place between them.

No one in the world would ever have dreamt that our good friend Zack was so attentive an observer of the actions of his guests.

But such a fact did not alter the case a particle.

Old Zack's eye in truth was far better than most people's two.

Which was, perhaps, the principle cause of his outwitting the officers of justice so many times.

All these gentlemen knew Zack well, and gave him credit for being a sharp, shrewd fellow.

But they did not know the half of it, for all their cunning and penetration.

Oh, no!

Old Zack was the most innocent-looking individual imaginable at time.

That is when he desired to be so.

"So they think that they are going to trap Captain Tom," said the old landlord. "Well, let 'em try it, that's all. That 'ere Reuben is a gone coon if Captain Tom only sets a-hold on him; and, if I don't put him on his track, blow me sky high!"

This was an expression that Zack very often used, following it up by a chuckle that nobody enjoyed but himself.

From the fact, perhaps, that no other one heard it.

"They'll be leaving presently," mused Jack, taking an extra puff at his long pipe, "and I don't see no earthly objection to their being followed. Now, that I think, there's that Ostler Jem—a cunning varmint, is Jem—he has nothing to do to-night. Why not send Jem after them? Why not? It will serve to keep the outrageous skunks out o' too much mischief. Now, Jem can handle a bludgeon with anybody. That 'ere Captain Harpy—as he's called—is only a coward. It will be easy disposing of him. But the other chap, I see, is a little tougher. Let me see—how is the affair to be managed?"

Zack, with a few extra puffs at his long clay, thought the matter over.

Zack was not the man to think long before he came to some mode of action.

He removed the pipe from his mouth.

Tapped his forehead twice.

Put his index finger gracefully along the side of his nose.

And so concluded to leave the matter entirely in the hands of Jem, the ostler.

Who, being on the ground, had a better chance of knowing what to do.

"Jem never disgraced me yet," said the landlord, "and I'm sure he's not going to do so now. Besides, Jem, when he's put to it, is as cunning and quick as a rattlesnake. I have a great liking for Jem—he never fails in what he undertakes, so I'll leave the matter entirely in his hands. The note I sent I am sure has reached its destination, so that'll put Captain Tom on his guard. So much done in the matter. Good! And now for Jem."

Old Zack, the very picture of innocence and abstraction, walked carelessly out of the bar-room.

No one noticed him.

We are wrong.

Reuben Harpy had his eye occasionally bent on him.

But yet he never dreamt that old Zack was meditating mischief.

So he smoked his cigar contentedly enough, resolved to make himself comfortable up to the time they were setting out.

Now, let us hasten for a few moments in the steps of the one-eyed landlord of the Yellow Alligator.

That gentleman sauntered out of the bar-room into the passage.

His walk was slow—even abstracted—at first.

But the moment he was sure that there were no eyes bent on him, the abstraction fled, and the pace quickened.

In an instant he was out into the night.

Making his way for the stables.

Where he was sure to find Jem, the ostler, occupied *ad libitum* in his usual doze.

Now, Jem, though a very good servant, was not the man to kill himself by overwork.

Whenever he could, he took to his sleep as readily as an infant to its mother's milk.

Sometimes it took Old Zack all his time to wake Jem.

Sundry kicks often brought him to, of course.

But Jem, on the whole, thought this a very great liberty, and, as the reader may well suppose, strongly objected to it.

Jem, when he was aroused in this peculiar way out of his somnolent state, generally gave the reasons why and wherefore he did not answer his master at first.

Some of these reasons were rather peculiar.

The ostler always swore that he was not asleep.

His master that he was.

Then would come on a contradictory cross-fire, which usually threatened to end in a fight.

But which, for certain reasons best known to Jem and his master, generally terminated in the most loving assurances of their high esteem and regard for each other.

Old Zack had a thorough objection to burning a lamp whilst Jem slept.

"It was an owdacious waste of valuable light," he said.

Jem, however, thought otherwise, and as he never admitted to being asleep, the matter became very difficult indeed, for our friend Zack's legislation.

Many a time he had a good mind to thrash Jem, and would have done so, too, only for the good and sufficient reason that he feared that Jem would thrash him.

Jem was a powerful fellow, and possessed indomitable will.

Besides, he had youth on his side.

And Zack was old.

Jem's eyes were singularly good.

He had two.

Zack had only one, so that a quick, athletic fellow like Jem, if he so desired, could come the "blind side" of Zack in a very few minutes.

Zack, however, made his way for the stables, confidently anticipating that his friend Jem was enjoying his usual placid doze with swinging lamp to keep away his enemies the rats.

So sure was the one-eyed landlord of the Yellow Alligator to find him in this situation, that he began to call—

"Now, then!" almost before he got to the door.

His "now, then," however, had no effect.

Zack passed through the door into the stables.

A loud and angry snore saluted his ears.

But, nothing daunted, he went forward.

The swinging lighted lamp was in its usual place. Dissipating the darkness of the stables.

Jem, stretched out on a bundle of straw, face upturned, mouth wide open, eyes closed, snores like the distant roars of the ocean.

If all these evidences did not indicate sleep, we should like to know what did.

"He says he never sleeps," said Zack, surveying the burly figure of his ostler. "Oh, of course he doesn't. Perhaps he might hear a whisper or the report of a cannon about two yards off. How he enjoys it!" said Zack, tickling his mouth with a straw that he appropriated from the bundle on which the watchful Jem was sleeping.

Jem took no notice of this treatment, however.

No doubt, thinking it beneath him to be annoyed by such trifles.

If anything he snored the louder.

"No, he doesn't sleep," said the landlord, "he only slumbers. And what snores! He beats the venerable Mrs. Magpie all to fits, and she can keep a whole regiment awake any night. I wonder the horses ain't a-frightened. But, gentle creatures, I suppose they've got used to it, in the same manner as one might possibly get used to hanging—possibly, indeed!"

Old Zack was, for a moment, lost in contemplation.

Thought how savage his ostler would be to be disturbed.

Especially when he knew the errand he was to go on.

"Never mind," said Zack, "people can't always indulge in snores. Sleep was invented for a good purpose—this ain't one of 'em I'm pretty well sartin. Here goes, whether he takes it in good part or not."

"Jem! Jem! Rouse up, I say! What! are ye going to sleep all yer brains away in that 'ere manner! You'll have none left at all just now. Rouse up, I tell you!"

Whether Jem had a proper respect for his master or not we cannot say.

But we do know this—that Jem, though the summons for him to arise was a very loud one, took not the slightest notice.

"Squalling bears and roaring catamounts!" exclaimed Old Zack; "what's the meaning o' this? Don't you hear your master calling on you, you infernal villain? Am I going to burst my wind-bags for nothing? Jem, Jem, I say! Get up, you lazy thief! Here's a pot of home-brewed I've brought you."

But neither the home-brewed nor Old Zack's voice were sufficient incentives to rouse Jem out of his present lethargy.

He went on snoring as regularly as ever.

The face was still upturned.

The eyes shut, and the mouth open.

Zack, seeing how ineffective all his efforts had been so far, hit upon a new expedient.

Jem, he well knew, was decidedly averse to kicking.

He, in fact, had an utter disrelish for that mode of operating, and threatened, should it be persisted in, that he would retaliate.

Now, Zack also saw the utter uselessness of this mode of procedure, especially as it might, perchance, be inflicted on himself; so he hit upon a new plan.

Jem's mouth was wide open.

Straws had no effect.

Tickling with straws had about as much effect on the ostler's mouth as it would have had on a piece of stone, or a piece of iron.

As Jem, whenever they were offered him, freely imbibed the ales and good liquors of the Yellow Alligator, Zack could see no harm in testing his ostler's powers in a new line.

Jem had an utter abhorrence of water "pure and undefiled."

Zack knew it.

And, as a consequence, Zack took pity on his weakness.

As stable water—we mean the water the horses drank, and which they had been for some time dipping their noses in—was not "pure and undefiled," Zack thought that this came within the nature of his ostler's wants.

And, so thinking, procured about a quart of it in a half-gallon tankard.

"Now, if this dose doesn't bring him to his senses," said Zack, "I don't know what will. That he is thirsty is an evident fact, or why should he keep his mouth so wide open? Here goes," added the amiable landlord of the Yellow Alligator, approaching his sleeping ostler, and bending down over him, "here goes. If this doesn't bring him up quicker than a flash of light, I don't know what will!"

Though his intention, in his own mind, was amost laudable one, it had a very decided effect on the sleeping ostler, who, not being in so deep a slumber as Zack anticipated, heard his cruel intention with a feeling akin to horror.

He mastered his emotions, however, and allowed the landlord to bend down with the tankard.

Just as Zack was going to pour it into his gaping mouth, Jem opened his eyes.

"Hallo! What is this?" cried the ostler, pretending to be very much surprised. "Wanting to make me drunk, eh?"

Zack started back aghast.

"Good liquor—eh?" snarled Jem. "Brown October, or homebrewed, Mr. Magpie—which?"

Jem rose up from his recumbent position.

"Going to make me drunk afore I was awake, eh?" snarled Jem. "Do you call that 'ere the action of a gentleman? If you do, I don't. I calls it darned mean to intoxicate a feller in his sleep."

Zack was so dumbfounded that he could not speak a word.

So, as a matter of course, Jem had it all his own way.

"Thank you, master, I see your good intentions," continued Jem, keeping up the same, bantering tone. "But now as you have brought the Brown October, or homebrewed, perhaps yer'll oblige me by leaving it and the stables at the same time."

"Not good for you, Jem—not good for you," said Zack, now managing to speak.

"Anything wrong with the home-brewed, or the brown October, eh?"

"Nothing very much," answered Zack.

"Perhaps a little too old, eh?"

"That's about it."

"And somewhat musty?"

"Ay, a little too much so, Jem. Forgot and brought the wrong beer."

"Exactly. Open barrel, I suppose?"

"Something like that."

"Fashioned after the shape of a horse-trough, eh?"

Zack was beginning to smell a rat, and so wished himself out of the stable.

"Small beer, with a slight touch of slime in it?" went on Jem. "Werry good stuff for them as likes it; but I don't."

"Didn't think you would, Jem."

"Give it to one of them animiles," said Jem, pathetically. "Make him sick and vomit all under a quarter of an hour."

"Treacherous varmint!" muttered the irrepressible ostler.

"What's that?" cried Zack, who could scarcely believe his ears.

"Just made observation to myself how kind it was for you to come to see me. You must feel a werry great interest in my welfare, Mr. Magpie?"

"Yes, confound you, too great an interest for my own pocket."

"Come now," said Jem, "don't spill the brown October or home-brewed, for that costs something. Werry much obliged to you, I am sure, for bringing it here. Might oblige you by drinking, but can't as I'm teetotaller."

"Teetotaller!"

"Yes, that's about it. So take a good swig out o' the tankard, and what you can't drink give to that 'ere animile over there. He wants purging or poisoning; it doesn't matter which."

Zack had no doubt now but that his plan was discovered.

CHAPTER CLXXXIV.
THE OSTLER'S MISSION.

It just struck Zack that his good ostler, Jem, was not asleep after all, as he fondly imagined.

Those snores.

Did they betoken sleep?

That ponderous form.

The open mouth, and those well-closed eyes.

Did they not betoken sleep?

Had Jem, the ostler, been deceiving him all this time?

Did his loud and peculiar snorings indicate only his strange manner of reflecting on a new way of cleaning and rubbing down the next horse that came under his fostering care.

Those well-shut eyes, too!

There was matter for deep contemplation.

Jem, the ostler, was either a very great fool, or, indeed, a greater philosopher.

Old Zack didn't know which.

He only knew that his "little game," beyond a possibility of doubt, was discovered.

And that an explanation must take place, and that quickly.

"See here! You weren't asleep?" said Zack, emptying out the contents of the tankard in a pail that stood near him.

"No, I wasn't no more than you are. And you seem to be wide-awake enough, master."

"Well, what caused you to snore so loud?" said Zack.

"Simply because it's my style," replied the worthy ostler. "I suppose now, you'd be werry much surprised if anybody was to ask you why you didn't wear two eyes instead of one?"

"I should be, indeed," answered Zack "Because I don't wear any."

"Nature has given you one."

"No, Nature gave me two, Jem."

"Well, you haven't two now, at any rate," said Jem.

"That's because I lost one in defence of my country," rejoined Zack. "It'll be a long time, Jem, afore you lose one in defence o' yourn."

"You don't know that," said Jem. "I'm as capable o' losing one in defence o' my country as you are in defence o' yourn. But that is not the argument," said the ostler.

"What is not the argument?"

"What you are a-talking of now."

"Well, go on."

"In the first place," continued Jem, "you said as how you didn't wear eyes. Admitted that you don't wear two, still you wear one. At least your face wears it, and that is just the same thing. Do you see the logic o' that 'ere argument Mr. Magpie?"

"No, I don't," answered Mr. Magpie.

"Then you are as blind as I took you for. In course yer face is ornamented with one eye. Now if you had a drapery o' black round it, every one as has any sense would know that you were in mourning. Come, now, I have you there, Mr. Magpie. Don't young widders wear mourning?"

"And old ones, too, for the matter of that," said Zack.

"Not so much as the young ones," was the sage rejoinder.

"Why not?"

"Because they don't."

"Give me a reason."

"I'll give you twenty if you want them. In the first place, why do young widders wear mourning more than old ones?"

"Yes, that's the question."

"Well, then, I am going to tell you why. Young widders, Mr. Magpie, allays look like young widders. Why? For the simple reason that they ain't got enough o' married life yet, and detests that state o' single blessedness, and so wishes to set their caps for some other one."

"Yes, a great many of them do that sort of thing," said Zack, thoughtfully.

"Besides," resumed Jem, "young widders are more or less attractive, and so long as they wears the widder's weeds they have everyone a-running after them, either for their supposed money or their good looks."

"That's a fact," said Zack, who began to look upon Jem in the light of a very oracle.

"Then you admit it," said Jem.

"Yes," replied Zack.

"Then how does the one eye business affect you now?" said Jem.

"About the same as before. My vision is as strong as ever."

"I don't mean that," said Jem. "Will you own or not that you wear your eye the same same as any other ornament?"

"Certainly not," replied Zack.

"Then the argument's ended," said Jem. "You know the old saying—'Convince a fool against his will, and he'll hold the same opinion still.'"

"Confound yer impudence!" cried Zack. "Do you put me down for a fool, then?"

"It's how yer takes it," said Jem. "I well remember an old saying as we had in school."

"If the cap fits, wear it?" interrupted Zack.

"Precisely so. We, therefore, now stands on the same footing. How about the home-brewed, or the brown October?"

"I thought that 'ere affair settled!"

"Oh, no," replied Jem. "It can only be settled by giving me a quart of the real October."

"Confound you, then, come on! I know you'll have your way, right or wrong," cried Zack.

"However, the terms of agreement is, that you mustn't get drunk."

"What! drunk on a pot of prime October!" cried Jem, in amazement; "drunk on a pot of prime October! What are ye thinking of, master?"

"So you believe you can hold yerself straight if I give you the treat?"

"Do I believe it? Why, in course I do. A pot of ale will have no more effect on me than a pint of gruel in an elephant's belly."

"Very well, then, come on. But mind, I have some heavy business for you to-night."

Whereupon Zack entered into an explanation of all he desired him to do.

"That's all very well, master," said Jem, "but you must take into account the night's rest."

"The night's rest? Yes; I have taken that into account. You'll certainly have to lose your night's rest, Jem."

"What is a night's rest worth, master?"

"What is it worth?"

Zack couldn't very well see what Jem was driving at.

And, if he could, we must say that he closed his eyes to the fact.

"Yes, master, what is the loss of a night's rest worth?"

"It's worth pulling up the next night," said Zack, innocently.

"No doubt, master—no doubt. But it's worth something more to one as can't pull it up. A night's rest lost is jist a night's rest unredeemed."

"Why, you infernal villain, you, you are always sleeping!" cried Zack.

"Don't go and commit yerself, master; that is deformation of character."

"And so amenable to the laws o' the land," added Zack. "You are a precious scoundrel, you are, Jem, to go and speak about prosecuting one as has been so good to you, and has tended you like a blessed infant since you have been here."

"All that is werry good, master," said Jem, "but it doesn't alter the point a bit. A night's rest is a night's rest, you know."

"Hang your night's rest, Jem! Don't be harping on that 'ere subject all night. What are yer terms?"

"Two days' wages—double extra work," replied Jem.

"Well, come on, then, and don't waste any more time, and you shall have all you ask," said Zack. "Get your best cudgel, Jem."

"I have it, master. Which of them fellers do you want knocking down?"

"Both of 'em, Jem—both of them, if you see it in any way necessary."

"Very good. You may consider it done, then."

Master and man now walked out of the stable and entered the tavern.

Old Zack gave a peep into the bar-room, and saw Reuben Harpy on the point of leaving with his companion.

The landlord in an instant apprised Jem of this fact, and urged him to dispose of the contents of his tankard with all the speed he could, so by the time that Reuben and the messenger left, Jem was ready to follow them.

The night was the kind he wanted.

It was as dark as pitch.

And with a slight breeze blowing.

Jem kept as near as possible to them, and walked with great stealth and caution.

While the irrepressible ostler is observing all this necessary caution, we may as well follow in the company of Reuben and the messenger.

"Now," said Reuben, "we can speak here without a fear of being overheard. Tell me the ins and outs of the whole thing."

THE MIDNIGHT ASSASSINS.

"It won't take me long to do that," replied the messenger. "In the first place, Captain Tom has left the brig."

"Left the brig? On some kind of errand, I suppose."

'No doubt. But he has left it at anyrate.

"As there were only two of our men on the beach at the time, they could do nothing.

"Captain Tom had four or five men with him.

"Besides a man named Barnacle."

"Oh! yes, one of his lieutenants," interrupted Reuben. "Pray, go on."

"Perhaps it was. Our men at that moment were not in a position to tell.

"However, Captain Tom and his followers started for the wood. Of course, you know the wood?"

"Yes."

"Well, they started there, and, on reaching it, the buccaneers separated.

"Two went one way, and three the other.

"Captain Tom and this Barnacle went by a bridle-path through the wood.

"One of our men followed them.

"The other made for the cave as fast as his legs could carry him.

"Fortunately, Bill Evans, and nearly a score of men were there.

"These set out to go after the captain and his lieutenant.

"But Bill, knowing how well they would be

watched by the man who was tracking them, thought better of it, and made instead, for the rocks, near which the buccaneers' boat was moored.

"They found the boat there all right, and being aware that Tom would have to come back to it to get to his brig, they took up a position behind some great boulders."

"Captain Tom will then be captured by this," observed Reuben, with fierce joy.

"He may, and he may not."

"What do you mean by 'he may, and he may not'?" cried Reuben, rather angrily.

For whether the messenger spoke honestly or not, he would have preferred words of encouragement coming from his lips to ones of indifference.

"Well, simply this," answered the man. "Captain Tom may not have returned, and that would certainly be enough to prevent the very thing that you expect, and the thing that we hope for."

"I am very glad to hear you speak so," said Reuben. "I was beginning to think that you were indifferent to the matter, whether it went one way or the other."

"I cannot be indifferent to any thing that will bring money," was the reply.

"No. I see. That would be rather unnatural. Money is the grand aim of life."

"And revenge," put in the other.

But not with any marked utterance.

However, it struck home.

Reuben felt a strange thrill run through him.

"Aye, revenge!" muttered Reuben. "That, in reality, is the main object of my life!"

It was, indeed, the main object of his life.

Revenge!

Jem heard the most of this conversation.

Besides, he knew something of the generous, noble nature of Captain Tom as well.

He gripped his cudgel, as if he would make short work on the spot of the two men he was following.

Although it was far from his honest disposition to fall on men from behind.

But these fellows deserved it.

Yet even did he strike down the messenger and Reuben, what would be the results to Captain Tom?

Good ones?

He could not see that they would.

Captain Drake would be captured in any event.

No; for once he would disregard the advice of Old Zack, and follow the bent of his own prudence.

Another thing came into his mind.

What service would he be to Captain Tom and his brave lieutenant were he fortunate enough to get there before they emerged from the wood?

The game was hazardous

He could, no doubt, by observing a little caution, conceal himself near the wood to warn the youthful chief of the trap that was laid for him.

That, in his mind, would certainly be the best plan thought of yet.

He only wished one thing in his power, however, and that was, that he could get together a dozen stout fellows like himself, and then they would give the smugglers more than they bargained for.

Of such men he knew plenty.

But the question was, could he spare the time to get them?

There were several fishermen—old acquaintances of his—who would only too gladly assist; but then they lived at such distances from each other, that it would take considerable time and trouble to call them together.

The idea was abandoned as impracticable.

While his mind was influenced by these various thoughts, he forgot to observe that caution with which he had set out, and so came very nearly being discovered.

In going too near the ditch he partly stumbled.

The noise attracted the attention of those in front.

He had only just time to hide himself in the roadside coppice, when the two men came up.

They began searching up and down both sides of the road.

"I am almost certain that I heard a footfall," said Reuben. "We had better look, as there may be some one following us."

"There may be," replied the messenger. "But it won't be well for them if there is," he added, with a deep oath. "I am not the man to be trifled with, I assure you."

Jem, the ostler, heard very distinctly the ominous click of a pistol, so held his breath, until by the exertion all the blood in his body rushed up to his head.

"I heard the noise myself," observed the messenger. "Yet it is just possible that we are mistaken regarding the footstep.

"However, a few minutes more or less, will soon let us know. Go on the other side, and beat about that copsewood, while I do the same on this!"

Reuben, on any other occasion, would have strongly objected to such an arrangement.

The mere thought of being exposed in such darkness to an unknown danger, terrified him.

But plucking up all his courage, and that was not very much, he tremblingly obeyed.

He went on the other side.

The side, indeed, on which Jem, the ostler, was hidden.

Reuben's search, as the reader may anticipate, was not a very minute one.

Indeed, he hardly touched the coppice at all.

And even if Jem was not so well concealed as he was, he would as undoubtedly have escaped.

The ex-privateer contented himself by merely making a little rustle among the bushes, and looking about him.

As to his companion.

He made a most thorough investigation, and was soon convinced that their fears were groundless.

So he came back into the road, and was rejoined there by Reuben.

"We were deceived that time," he said.

"It looks like it," replied Harpy. "But it would be as well, perhaps, to keep a good look-out."

"Yes. No harm can be done by that."

And so they trudged on again.

Jem, when they were a safe distance away, got out of the coppice, and followed them.

But there is hardly any need of entering into a description of the whole journey.

Reuben and the messenger's conversation chiefly turned on Captain Tom.

At this point the information was gleaned that Black Bill wished to have the honour and glory of Captain Tom's capture all to himself.

And that he desired no interference of the little admiral.

If Ellis wished it, he could see to the taking of the brig.

And that was all the honour that Bill Evans intended he should have.

Now, Reuben Harpy was not averse to this arrangement.

Admiral Ellis had always failed in effecting the capture of Captain Tom, and he might do so again.

Fate was against him

It was yet to be proved whether it was against Black Bill or not.

At last they got on the sea-beach.

Reuben, without inquiring, knew well where the rocks referred to were.

He had often played among them when he was a child.

So that he could find his way to them even in the dark, and without a guide.

The moon burst out now, and Jem, the ostler, perceiving the rocks in the distance, found it necessary to take another road.

This for prudence sake.

Besides, it would carry him nearer to the wood from which Captain Tom and Ben Barnacle would emerge.

In his present locality, Jem was by no means a stranger.

He had fished there very often before he became an ostler.

In fact, followed that profession.

The road he now took diverged quite away from the sea-side, and was a very roundabout one.

But he hoped yet to be in time to warn Captain Tom and his brave comrade of the ambush of the smuggler horde.

He was not very far on his way, when the moon appeared behind a cloud.

Everything in a moment was as black as pitch.

Not much longer was he when he heard pistol-shots fired from among the rocks.

"I am too late to save Captain Tom!" he exclaimed; "but I'll strike a blow, any way, for his sake."

And saying this, he hurried through the darkness in the direction of the rocks, as fast as his legs could carry him.

CHAPTER CLXXXV.

BOB AND JERRY PLAN THE RESCUE OF CAPTAIN TOM.

A COUNTRY lane not many miles from Portsmouth Sound.

The time nearing dusk.

The sun gone down about a half an hour—perhaps a little over that.

On the road are three figures.

Two look like sailors.

Their hard, bronzed visages have a dash of the salt spray about them.

The third is a person of a different cast.

His appearance is decidedly "horsey."

If this fact were wanting, there's the ostler's garb to guide you to a more exact and emphatic certainty of his calling.

All three, however, are as stout, stalwart fellows as you would wish to meet.

Who, then, were they?

Can't the reader guess?

We believe we hear some one exclaiming, "Bob and Jerry!"

Right, reader!

But the third?

"The ostler of the Yellow Alligator."

Right, again!

Who could mistake the man in his peculiar outfit?

It must be confessed that Jem was half asleep, as he plodded along that quiet road.

And no wonder either, when we take into account the absence of the proverbial "forty winks."

Forty winks, did we say?

Forty winks was a mere fleabite to our worthy friend, Jem the ostler.

He who, by his own account, never slept.

And who, by Old Zack's, did little else than thus fritter away his time.

But we are not going to be as uncharitable as Old Zack, who, if the truth was known, slept more than Jem and Mrs. Magpie put together, and snored

louder than either of them individually or collectively.

"Feel tired, Bob?" inquired Jerry.

"Cussedly so," replied Bob.

"And our friend Jem here?"

"Could sleep for six months," replied Jem. "Worse luck! I can get nowhere to lay my head."

"How many miles are we from the Yellow Alligator?"

"Nine," replied Jem, "and nine too many; at that I'll be asleep afore I gets half-way."

"You ain't half a chap."

"No, I don't think I am," replied Jem, ruefully. "It would be a great pleasure to get back to my stable once more, I can tell you."

"To have your sleep out?"

"Exactly."

"Old Zack will be rayther alarmed at your absence, won't he?"

"I guess he will."

"And he'll have heard that Captain Tom is taken long afore this."

"Now, there comes the difficulty," cried Jem. "The blessed old Kentuckian will lay all the blame on to me."

"Lay the blame of what?" asked Jerry, who desired to be enlightened on this point.

"Why, the capture of Captain Tom. He'll say it was my fault. Zack Magpie is one of the most suspicious varmints living. Coming to think, there'll be no sleep for me for the next week."

"Oh, nonsense!"

"You may call it so, if you will. But it's the downright truth for all that."

"Eh?"

"I say he'll firmly believe I've been the cause of all Captain Tom's misfortunes."

"How can he?" asked Jerry.

"Oh, easy enough."

"But tell him from us—"

"Tell him from you? What good will that do? Once he takes a notion in his head, there's no getting it out again. Farewell, then, to sleep or any sort o' enjoyment for the next six days at least," said Jem, pathetically.

And the poor ostler, as he spoke, looked the very picture of misery and combined drowsiness.

"Do you mean to say the old fellow's so bad as all that?" inquired Bob.

"He's worse—far worse, Mr. Hauler," replied Jem.

"Come, come—don't be giving your master so bad a character. Every one knows old Zack too well, I reckon, to take all that in."

"The libel is infamous," said Jerry.

"Infamous," corrected Bob.

"That's what I was a-going to say, when you interrupted of me," said Jerry, with a gesture which partook slightly of the indignant.

"What a thing it is to be a scholard," said Bob, jeeringly. "I thought scholards never made sich mistakes."

"There you are wrong, Bob. A slip o' the tongue is no poison to the mind."

"Come, Jerry, you have misquoted that 'ere passage. Listen to one as knows it."

"You be blowed! Are you putting yourself up as a scholard? What impudence! A person as heard you would surely think you were fresh from colledge."

"There's where they'd show their good sense," rejoined Bob. "It's more than they'd think of you, at all events, Jerry. But stop a moment I'm blessed if our friend Jem the ostler isn't a-going to sleep!"

"Needles, they say, is a werry good thing."

"Or pins."

"Or penknives."

"Have you got one?"

"No. Have you?"

"No. But I've got my nose slitter and tater-chopper."

"Werry good weapon in its way, but Jem might have an objection to it."

"I have, and a werry decided objection," said Jem, waking up. "None o' yer nose-slitters or tater-choppers for me, old fellers."

"What! We thought you war' dead asleep, Jem."

"No, I was only reflecting. I never sleeps," said Jem.

"That's a fibber!" cried Jerry. "I wonder you aren't ashamed o' yerself."

"Or afeared of himself," put in Bob.

"Of what should I be ashamed or afeared?" cried Jem.

"In the first place, you oughtn't to tell a lie."

"In the next, you ought to be afeared the first critter you rubbed down would kick your brains out."

"Well, that's a good 'un! One would think that neither of you moralists never told a lie in your lives; and I am quite as certain that you tell a hundred of 'em daily."

"Where's your proof?" cried Bob and Jerry, in a breath.

"In your wisages," replied Jem. "Never mind, old fellers, a joke's a joke, and it's no use getting riled over it. Besides, here I must leave you."

The country lane along which they trudged debouched at this point into a broad and even highway.

From this road no fewer than three or four lanes branched off, leading in different directions.

"I take this one," said Jem, "as it will spare me at least a mile and a half's walking. Shall I have the pleasure of seeing you at the Yellow Alligator, or not?"

"That will depend very much on the state of affairs with Captain Tom," replied Bob; "and now good-bye, and remember me to old Zack."

"And don't forget *me!*" cried Jerry; "besides, we both thank you for your werry able support."

"Only for which," added Bob, "we'd both a-been in the stone-jug as well as the captain. Shake hands, Jem, and let there be no ill-feeling atween us."

The trio now shook hands, and Jem, without more ado, started forward on his journey.

Whether the ostler would be able to keep awake until he reached old Zack's was another question.

Bob and Jerry, after watching him until he was out of sight, sat down on the side of the road, and taking out their pipes and lighting them, gave way to their reflections.

These were none of the brightest.

The comrades smoked in silence until the darkness set in.

Then Bob was the first to speak.

"A good fellow, that 'ere ostler," said Bob. "Knew him when he was much younger than he is now."

"A boy?"

"Nearly about that. A good job he came up last night, else we'd a-been in a fine pickle."

"You are right, Bob. It's enough to break one's heart to think that Captain Tom's in chokey!"

"In what?"

"In gaol."

"Why couldn't you say that a-fore?" grumbled Bob. "You are always a-bringing that 'ere foreign lingo o' your'n in."

"Come, come, that be blowed for a tale!"

"What be blowed for a tale?"

"What you call foreign lingo is good, respectable English."

"I don't want to argue the point with you, Jerry, for I knows you'll have your own way, so let us come to business at once."

"I wish we would come to business, for I'm sick o' talking nonsense."

"Well, in the first place, the 'Will-o'-the-Wisp' is off to Purfleet."

"And before she gets there she'll put the beggars off the scent."

"If skill and prudence 'll do it, she is sure to succeed," replied Bob. "But that's no benefit to Captain Tom, for all that. We must get the captain out o' prison, Jerry."

"To be sure we must, Bob. Just the thing I was a-thinking of. Too early to meet Lieutenant Vere yet, though."

"Yes. It was half-past nine, he said."

"Between that and ten. It's nine o'clock, now."

"Not so much as that."

"Well, a quarter to nine, then."

"That's nearer. Ah! I have it, Jerry!"

"Ah!" thought Jerry, "here comes something now. Bob's always a-getting some new idea into his head. You have what, Bob?" said Jerry, aloud.

"I've struck upon a plan that may help Captain Tom to escape."

"Bravo!" cried Jerry. "The plan is sure to be a good one, Bob."

"It is. Listen, and I think you'll agree with me."

"Go on," said Jerry, who thought Bob was the most wonderful fellow he ever met. "Purceed, Bob—purceed!"

"Well, it is this, then. I mean a-visiting him in this 'ere prison."

"Well?"

"And once I'm in there, I'll take good care as Captain Tom gets out."

"How?"

"By hocussing the jailers, of course. But, first of all, how can you get in; and if you get in, how can you get out?"

"You leave that to me," said Bob. "I believe I knew generally what I'm a-doing."

"You do, Bob—you do. Poor Captain Tom, Bob! How glad he'll be to see you! And you."

"What, Bob? You don't mean to take me too?"

"Yes, I do."

"Bravo! that's better news than I have heard for a long time. Yet I fails to see still how you can release Captain Tom, without having a pitched battle with every one in the prison."

"Strategy—strategy!" cried Bob. "All's fair in love and war, Jerry."

"That's the old maxim, Bob. But how do you mean purceeding?"

Bob clapped his finger to the side of his nose, and looked very wise.

"Do you think you could do the minister, Jerry?"

"Do I think I could do what?"

"The minister, you lubber! Isn't that plain enough?"

"No, it isn't," said Jerry. "The minister! What kind of a minister?"

"One o' those parson chaps."

"Well, perhaps I could."

"You are scholard enough."

"Well?"

"And you can patter dog-Latin, and all that sort of thing?"

"I can give them some sort o' foreign lingo, and, as they are only jailers, they'll not know the difference."

"Not they," said Bob. "You can give them hog Greek, if you like. But you'll want to dress up in a clerical habit, Jerry, and you aren't exactly slim enough."

"What!" cried the irrepressible one. "Do you mean to say all parsons are slim, then?"

"Most parsons ought to be, if they aren't. I know some of 'em live well, and grow fat and rosy; but I know the good 'uns give away, and grow lean and pale. Now, I want a good one, or none at all. You don't answer that description, Jerry. Your face wou'd be all against you."

"But I could say that I had seen twenty years' of foreign service, and had only just come home from the East Indies."

"Your breath smells o' baccy, Jerry."

"What o' that? I could say that I had the toothache, and every one knows as how baccy is good for the toothache."

"Then, again, you have, by no manner o' means, a good set o' teeth."

"You had better try 'em," said Jerry, opening his mouth wide, and snapping his grinders maliciously.

"I don't say as they are not good," went on Bob; "but they are mahogany-painted, and copper-plated. That's all against you, Jerry."

"They are no worse than yours, Bob, and I'll try them on a piece of salt junk, or a beef-steak, with you, anyday."

"No, you don't; not at my expense, Jerry. I know your disposition for beef-steaks well—alas! too well," said Bob, sighing lugubriously. "But I'll tell you what we can do, Jerry."

"What?"

"We can both go there in company."

"But who is going to play the parson? What good is it going there without the parson?"

"I have hit upon a plan, Jerry. Now, how would Mr. Vere look as a parson?"

"He's slim," said Jerry.

"And pale," added Bob.

"He can speak Latin."

"And Greek."

"And French, too, if they want it. Besides—"

"Besides?"

"He's a gentleman."

"That's where the point comes in, Jerry. Your true genelman will never disgrace himself."

"You are right, Bob. And as Mr. Vere is a true genelman, it's werry likely that he'll play the parson to perfection."

Bob took several puffs at his pipe.

Jerry followed suite.

And for a few minutes not a word was spoken.

"Of course it's their intention not to let Captain Tom live long," said Bob, at last.

"They generally gives 'em a few days to prepare for death," added Jerry.

"Then there's a wisiting order."

"Of course."

"Where is that to come from?"

"Couldn't Mr. Vere get one?"

"I think not, Jerry—I think not. He's down in the black books It wouldn't do for the lubbers to catch him. But an idea strikes me, Jerry."

"Well?"

"Well, what do you think of Lady Arbuthnot? She is werry fond of Captain Tom, Jerry."

"Werry, Bob."

"And she's acquainted with all the big 'uns."

"Admirals, and such like."

"Yes."

"Lord Kilcrew is a friend of hers—a curious gent, Bob; but a werry kind-hearted man. He's no enemy of Captain Tom's, I'm sure."

"No, that he's not. Besides, he's one o' the principal admirals. Lord Kilcrew will do well enough, Jerry."

"Lady Arbuthnot is beautiful."

"Enchanting."

"Handsome from the head to the heels!"

"A curious way of expressing it, Jerry; but no matter so as her ladyship's not present to hear you. Who'll take a note to her ladyship?"

"I will, if you like," said Jerry.

"I see what you are arter, Jerry," said Bob. "You want to flirt a little with that 'ere servant gal."

"Don't call her a sarvant gal, Bob, 'cause she aren't."

"Well, a lady's-maid, then."

"That's something better. But to come to the point, Bob. How are we to go? As sailors, or not?"

"No, not as sailors," replied Bob. "Lackeys would be better. Footmen of his Reverence's. We played footmen before, Jerry, if you remember?"

"Not exactly footmen—waiters, Bob."

"It's all the same—waiters or footmen. They are chips off the one block."

"Well, say we go as footmen."

"Of course."

"Then what's to be done?"

"The parson'll go and administer consolation to the unfortunate prisoner, Captain Tom."

"Yes, yes."

"Then you and me—the lackeys—'ll go in and amuse the warders. They are a jolly set o' fellers, and'll not have any objection to a little good liquor. It must be werry strong, though, as they've mighty tough stomachs, and heads on 'em as hard as bulls."

"They are bull-headed, then?"

"Yes; the same as you, Jerry."

"Now, I considers that an unprovoked insult. Bob, do you think that 'ere a fair way to treat a feller comrade? Because, if you do, I don't. And that's about the truth of it."

"You may consider what you like, Jerry. But shut up for the present, and give me time to arrange all I have to do, afore Lieutenant Vere comes up."

After the knuckle "rapping" administered by Bob, Jerry sank into silence.

Fairly collapsed.

And considerably affected.

What the irrepressible one did on this occasion was to smoke his pipe.

Which he puffed very vigorously until the tobacco in the bowl looked red-hot in the darkness.

And Bob also smoked.

Puff! puff! puff!

It seemed for some minutes that the two old comrades were smoking for a wager, so fiercely did they pull at their pipes.

Under aggravated causes, either smoking or chewing was always a panacea for all the human ills which Bob and Jerry were heirs to.

Tobacco, then, was the prime invigorator and regenerator on which Bob and Jerry thrived admirably.

Indeed, they grew fat on it.

Talk of laugh and grow fat!

Both Bob and Jerry could grow fat without laughing, and tobacco was the real secret of their success in this direction.

Let us pass over the three-quarters of an hour that elapsed before Harry Vere got on the ground by giving an account of how Captain Tom and his lieutenant were captured.

The instant that our hero and Ben Barnacle discharged their pistols, they knocked two of the smugglers over.

They now fought like lions.

But being surrounded by over a score of well-armed, desperate men, they fought in vain.

They were just on the point of being overpowered, when our two old friends Bob and Jerry came up.

Whatever they could do was done.

Their cutlasses, however, were met by a dozen blades, so that they had more than they could do to defend themselves.

Wherever they struck, down went an enemy.

But as other enemies popped up at every step, Bob and Jerry gave up all hope of either escaping themselves, or of being of any service to their leaders.

Indeed, their hearts grew black with despair.

For they saw that they could not continue the fight.

Several of the smugglers had already fallen.

Black Bill went down under a blow from Captain Tom.

Whether he was wounded seriously or not, Bob and Jerry were unable to tell.

But they could hear the ruffian groaning with pain.

By this time two others came up.

The two others were Reuben Harpy and the smuggler.

Reuben, too great a coward to take part in the fight, slunk back behind the rocks.

And from there repeatedly urged the men to capture Captain Tom.

Of course Reuben, as well as he was able, changed his voice for the occasion.

He feared his injured cousin so much that he dared not trust himself to speak in his own tones.

Now, besides Reuben Harpy and the messenger, a reinforcement came up to the number of a half-dozen men.

What they were no one tried to find out.

Every one was too much engaged with his own affairs to pay attention to the affairs of others.

So the fight progressed.

The buccaneers who had returned to the boat were captured, and Captain Tom and his friends were very likely soon to be placed in a similar situation.

Everything now looked very gloomy indeed for the buccaneers.

There was no prospect of escape.

And scarcely a prospect to defend themselves.

Captain Tom's sword snapped, as, with a mighty stroke, it came clang on the cutlass of an enemy.

The fine blade had been tried too much that night, and the consequence was that our hero was left to the mercy of his opponent.

A half dozen of the smugglers, seeing him thus helpless, threw themselves upon him, and bore him to the ground.

Ben Barnacle made a desperate attempt with his mighty strength and good cutlass to release his chief.

But he, in turn, got disarmed.

Nor were the smugglers a moment in binding them.

About this time, another came upon the spot.

This was our good friend Jem, the ostler.

All he had was his stout cudgel.

He saw how matters stood in a moment.

Captain Tom and his lieutenant were prisoners.

Bob and Jerry were old acquaintances of his.

He saw that they were hard pressed, and that in a few moments more they would be in the power of their enemies.

A smuggler had fallen where he stood.

He bent down and picked the man's pistol up.

Without hesitating an instant, he broke like an avalanche through the ranks of the smugglers, and with his heavy cudgel struck about him right and left.

So terrific, indeed, was the stout ostler's onslaught that, for the moment, the smuggler horde gave way, and fell back astonished and bewildered.

This was what Jem, the ostler, wanted.

He knew that there was no possibility of rescuing Captain Tom or Ben Barnacle, so he devoted all his good services to Bob and Jerry.

Bob and Jerry might get away.

Bob and Jerry, he was determined, should get away.

But how?

His quick mind had formed a plan for this object some time before.

The boat now was the only means of escape.

The few smugglers who had charge of it before were nowhere to be seen.

In the excitement and clash of the fight, they had deserted their charge, with the intention of taking part in the capture of Captain Tom.

Now came the opportunity.

Whispering a word in Bob's ear, he fired the pistol he had taken from the dead smuggler.

Bob and Jerry followed his example.

There was a perfect din from the reports of the fire-arms.

Three of the smugglers fell.

A great cloud of smoke enveloped all.

And attendant on the confusion produced by this unexpected salute both the ostler and the two buccaneers, brushing past their enemies, got into the boat.

Nor were the smugglers aware of the fact when the boat shot out into deep water.

Bob and Jerry were splendid oarsmen, and pulled with all their might.

Fortunately for them, the whole sea was again draped in darkness.

The moon going out with the suddenness of thought, and the black surging clouds rolling with the same unexpected rapidity over the stars.

All the smugglers could hear was the derisive laughter of the two buccaneers, as they shot through the darkness.

If their enemies had been ever so inclined, they could not have followed them.

At this point they had neglected the precaution of having a boat, holding a notion in their minds that the one owned by the buccaneers was all sufficient for the occasion.

How villainously they were deceived the reader may imagine.

The smugglers were in such humour now that they listened for an instant to the soft, deep dip of the oars.

As the darkness was so intense, this was all they could be guided by.

Fancying that they might hit Bob and Jerry, and, possibly, their accomplice, the ostler, they fired several pistol-shots, judging, as well as they could, the direction by the sound of the oars.

But only a peal of derisive laughter came back.

After that the buccaneers continued to row unmolested, while the ostler sat in the stern-sheets.

Let us pass, however, over this, by briefly informing the reader that our two old friends had, within the hour, returned with a boat load of mids and buccaneers, to rescue their gallant chief and his lieutenant.

These were under the command of Harry Vere.

When they reached the beach, all they could see of the signs of the recent conflict were pools of blood, a few broken cutlasses, one sword, and several discharged pistols.

As for other evidences, there were none.

Captain Tom and Ben Barnacle were gone, and so were the smugglers.

All that the boat's crew could do now was to return to the " Will-o'-the-Wisp," and, by a pre-arrangement between Tom and Harry, to put out for Purfleet.

This was agreed on several days before, in the event of anything befalling Captain Tom.

Perhaps it was a wise measure.

We shall see.

There were three men who did not accompany the " Will-o'-the-Wisp."

These were Bob, Jerry, and Lieutenant Vere.

Of course there was a fourth.

Our philosophic friend, Jem, the ostler.

He, too, came away from the brig, with the intention of starting at once for Old Zack's place.

Old Zack, he imagined, would be very much alarmed by his absence, and would, no doubt, think that his ostler was either dead or enjoying himself to the exclusion of his rightful duties as ostler to that famous resort of multitudinous frequenters, the Yellow Alligator.

Now, as we have got thus far in explanation of what befell Captain Tom, his lieutenant, and the sailing of the " Will-o'-the-Wisp " for Purfleet, we will resume by opening another chapter.

CHAPTER CLXXXVI.

WHAT BOB AND JERRY, ASSISTED BY LIEUTENANT VERE, DO IN THE PRISON.

OUR old friends, Bob and Jerry, were on the most amicable and affectionate terms when Lieutenant Vere came up.

He found the two comrades engaged in animated conversation on the results of Bob's plan.

Jerry was sure that it would succeed, and that they would have their darling Captain Tom out in less than twenty-four hours.

And Bob, though not so sanguine, was nearly quite as confident as his comrade.

" I don't think it'll be quite so hard, sir, arter all," said Bob, after he had explained his schemes to the lieutenant. " Only you do the parson, and we'll have Captain Tom and Mr. Barnacle out o' that 'ere prison-hole within two days."

" You seem very hopeful, my good fellow," said Harry. " Heaven grant that it may be so. I, at least, will do all in my power to forward that object."

" Then it's as good as done, yer honour," said Jerry. " As nothing comes amiss to my noble comrade here."

" Avast there, Jerry! None o' yer flattery," cried Bob. " You ought to be ashamed o' yerself, a-putting vanity into my mind."

" I am not a-doing anything o' the sort," remonstrated Jerry. " Catch me putting wanity in any one's mind; least of all in Bob Hauler's."

" Oh, you are a sad case of depravity, Jerry."

" I'm sorry to hear you say so. I thought I was a werry saint on earth."

" Without wings."

" Saints don't wear wings."

" Cherubims, then ?"

" No, nor cherubims neither.   That 'ere quality 'blongs to angels."

" Oh, what a donkey you are, Jerry !"

" A donkey !" cried Jerry.

" A complete jackass," added Bob.

" Now you are only trying my temper."

" No, I'm not. You said cherubims hadn't wings."

" No more they haven't."

" That shows what colledge you've been into. You are a fine scholard, you are, Jerry, and don't know that much. Cherubims, you goose, is angels."

" No !"

" But they are."

" Then it's my mistake.   I didn't mean to say as how they warn't angels."

" Oh, what a lie !"

" You might have said fib, Bob, considering Lieutenant Vere is present."

" Well, to flatter yer vanity, I will say fib, Jerry. Now, if that doesn't satisfy you, I have no other apology to make."

Jerry was absolutely crushed.

He wouldn't venture on another word.

To be used in such a shameful manner before his superior was too bad.

But even grief must drown itself.

Jerry turned away from his companions, as it were, to wipe away a tear.

But did he wipe away that tear ?

Nothing of the kind.

By an adroit movement of his right hand, he took something from his pocket.

That something turned out to be a flask.

And that flask contained nearly a half-a-pint of the best brandy.

Jerry, by another adroit movement, carried the said flask to his mouth.

He thought that the darkness would conceal that movement from the lynx-eyes of Bob.

Did it do so ?

Not quite.

Bob immediately detected that there was something wrong, and was just as eager to ascertain what.

Not for worlds would he have poor Jerry shed unavailing tears—tears of deep, profound grief and remorse—which he knew that Jerry very often shed, especially when in his cups, and grieving over his lost Cruela.

Bob's tender heart was always touched by these deep evidences of Jerry's sorrow.

Could nothing in the world assuage it ?

Bob's great remedy was gone !

The panacea for Jerry's ailments was drunk up hours ago, so nothing new remained but words of sympathy.

But such sympathy, as the reader knows, is preferable to no sympathy at all.

And that was exactly how Bob felt on the point.

Our buccaneer had only one object in his mind now, and that object a desire to relieve Jerry's overburdened mind.

Why could he not bear a portion of his grief ?

He would try.

He stepped forward with the stealthy tread of a cat, looked over his " chum " and brother's shoulder, and caught him in the act of gulping down the contents of the flask.

Bob's indignation was too great to give utterance to words.

It would, indeed, be a mere waste of time.

Instead, he gripped the flask, and before Jerry was aware of it, wrenched it out of his hand.

Sympathy for the irrepressible one at such a juncture would only be so much waste of time.

Did Bob take that course ?

Certainly not.

Bob only hungered for the contents of the flask.

Jerry had already paid his devoirs to it.

And Jerry had enough, and more than enough.

It is evident that Bob took this view of the matter, for he quickly and quietly gulped what was left in the flask down his throat.

In the meantime, keeping an eye on his comrade to see that he did not come too near during that operation.

When he was done, he placidly handed Jerry the empty flask.

" Werry good liquor that, Jerry," said Bob.

"Comforting to the stomach and soothing to the palate."

Jerry hadn't the heart to say anything, but pocketed the empty flask sorrowfully, and indeed for the rest of the journey walked on moodily enough.

Now, Bob, on the other hand, was in the best of spirits, and kept up a running conversation with Lieutenant Vere as they jogged smartly over the road.

"Then it's all arranged for to-morrow night, yer honour?" said Bob.

"All. I don't see what we can do sooner. You are sure that Lady Arbuthnot will procure the order to see him?"

"As sartin as I am of my own existence, yer honour. It is a well-known fact that her ladyship's very fond of Captain Tom. Then there's Lord Admiral Kilcrew—that 'ere Irish nobleman—he's as fond of Lady Arbuthnot."

"So that there will really be no difficulty in the way?"

"Not the slightest, sir. Then there's Jerry! One of the best critters in Christendom for delivering messages. I'll back him against anyone for drinking grog and delivering messages."

Jerry uttered a hoarse growl.

"You can see he's vexed just at present, yer honour. But Jerry will come round to his usual temper just now. What about that sarvant gal, Jerry?"

"You be blowed!" grumbled Jerry.

"Come, now, don't be cross, my worthy brother. You ain't a-going to kick up shines about that 'ere drop of brandy, are you? Besides, you war playing a werry mean part, and you know you were."

Jerry never answered.

But looked ferociously at Bob.

Bob pretended not to notice this circumstance, but went on talking with Lieutenant Vere.

However, it was arranged that the following night was the one for Captain Tom's escape.

Jerry, in the meantime, was to call on Lady Arbuthnot, and get the order at once, if possible.

While Bob undertook to purchase three suits, by which they could disguise themselves.

He knew that there were plenty of places in Portsmouth where clothes of the description he wanted, could be bought.

In another half an hour, Bob, Jerry, and the lieutenant got into Portsmouth, where, after arranging for a meeting next night, they separated.

The young lieutenant had a suit of civilian's clothes on, so that nobody could recognise him as one of those connected with the "Will-o'-the-Wisp."

And it would be equally hard to take Bob and Jerry for buccaneers.

As they were also more or less disguised.

But we may now pass over the intervening twenty-four hours.

The order for the admittance of a clergyman into the prison was secured, as Captain Tom had little more than forty hours longer to live.

Bob purchased the suits.

The lieutenant attired himself in his.

And Bob and Jerry in theirs.

All seemed going on very smoothly indeed.

The night, as it happened, turned out a very stormy one.

The rain came down in torrents.

Loud claps of thunder rumbled hoarsely through the heavens, and vivid flashes of lightning lit up the dense darkness.

Now, this was the night of all nights that would facilitate Captain Tom's escape.

The wind moaned through the streets, and, as it grew later, not a passenger was to be seen.

It was too uncomfortable, by far, to be exposed to the rude violence of the storm, so the various wayfarers had hurried home to enjoy the warmth of their fire-sides, and to dream of the speedy execution of our gallant young buccaneer.

Besides, the fierce gusts of wind, the lightning, thunder, and rain, the night was bitter cold.

Bob, Jerry, and the lieutenant took care before starting out to prepare themselves for any emergency, so they concealed about their persons a brace of pistols each, to have them at hand in case of need.

Besides these, Bob and Jerry had supplied themselves with "pocket pistols," in the shape of well-filled flasks of the strongest brandy that they could get.

At ten o'clock precisely a covered carriage might be seen stopping at a certain house.

At a signal, the door opened, and a footman and clergyman came out.

The clergyman got into the carriage.

The footman on the box with the driver.

The footman and driver were well-known to each other.

In fact, they were our old friends, Bob and Jerry, each disguised so as to baffle the most lynx-eyed jailer in existence.

"It's a werry disagreeable night," said Bob, as they got on a little.

"Cold, too," said Jerry.

"Lightning, and thunder, and rain," added Bob. "Warders not so watchful to-night."

"Would prefer, no doubt, a good fire and plenty o' grog."

"Got yer pocket pistol?"

"Yes. Have you yours?"

"Yes; carefully buttoned up in this 'ere full-braided coat. How do you like it, Jerry? Does it look well?"

"Very well, indeed. One would think as how it was made for you."

"Is the wig all right?"

"The wig! It couldn't be better. It's quite delightfully powdered."

"Hope the rain doesn't wash it off."

"No fear o' that, if yer keep yer cape over your hat."

"A good thought, Jerry. I am much obliged to you. How far are we from this 'ere prison?"

"About half a mile."

"Well, we'll be there in a jiffey. But mind as how ye play yer part well. No sailor's lingo, mind that. 'Shiver my timbers,' and all that sort o' thing, you must keep out. It's not in the vocab—What do you call it?"

"Vocabulary," corrected Jerry.

"Well, it's not in the wocabulairy."

"That's not it, Bob. Vocabulary."

"Well, no matter whether it's vocabulairy or wocabulery—it's all as one. Can you tell a story, Jerry?"

"Can I tell twenty of 'em?" ejaculated the irrepressible one.

"There's no need o' your telling twenty. Tell one, and tell it good."

"All right, Bob."

"Can you sing a song?"

"Well, some says as how I can."

"I like yer modesty much, Jerry. It's werry charming. Well, you'll sing a song and tell a story."

"What! in a prison?"

"Why not in a prison? And mind, if yer tell 'em any lies, tell 'em good ones."

Jerry promised to do all this.

And Bob added that he would, also, if he found it necessary.

"For a while them varmints o' warders may be cantankerous," said Bob. "But we must soften them down a little while the lieutenant is a-doing the amiable for Captain Tom. There's nothing like good strong brandy for warders, Jerry. The stronger you give it them the better. Then a song, followed by a story, will put 'em in ecstacies with themselves. They will take everything in like lambs, while we manage to take Captain Tom out and ourselves, too."

This arrangement met Jerry's direct approval.

"And," added Bob, "don't forget I may have occasion to run out to see if his Reverence wants any help for that 'ere unfortunate prisoner. I may have to settle accounts with one o' the jailers—the feller as is guarding Captain Tom. In so doing, mind, whatever you do, to sing 'em a rattling stave while I'm away."

"How will Tom Bowling do, eh, Bob?"

"A werry good song. Has it a long chorus, Jerry?"

"I'll sing it now if you like, and then you'll see whether it has or not," said Jerry.

But Bob objected decidedly to this course, as it might attract too much attention.

"Sing any song you know," cried the buccaneer, "any song that has a long tail at the end of every verse."

"A long tail," echoed Jerry. "What do you mean by a long tail, Bob?"

"Well, a long chorus, then; it's all the same," replied Bob. "One, for instance, as has plenty a-jingling of glasses and rattle of cans, stamping of feet and clapping of hands. Them's the songs for a stormy night, and the escape of a prisoner. Spend a guinea on 'em—spend two—spend five—spend anything so as you make 'em jolly. But hold, that won't do," added the cautious Bob—"that might make the varmints suspicious. You have got silver on you?"

"Yes."

"Then don't expose the gold. The golden key is everything, Jerry; but the silver one'll have to do this time."

"Right you are, Bob. We can't be very far from the prison now. How it rains, and that thunder and lightning is enough to scare anyone. Lash up the horses, Bob; they are about the laziest animiles I ever saw."

"There's no need, Jerry, for here we are at the prison."

"A beautiful residence for our gallant captain, Bob."

"Silence, you fool! Keep that tongue o' yours quiet! Do you want 'em all to know who we are?"

"Well, supposin' I get down," said Jerry, "and wake 'em up a bit."

"Well, do so; but mind what you are about."

The carriage stopped befort a dark, ominous-looking building, and Jerry got down from the box and rang a rather loud peal at the bell.

Nor was this long in being answered.

A small grating was drawn back, and a grumbling face demanded what they wanted.

"The Reverend Ebenezer Catchem," replied Jerry, "comes with an order to see the prisoner Tom Drake, to give that unhappy individual the last consolations o' religion."

"Hypocrite!" muttered Bob. "He's capable of anything. Unhappy individual, indeed!—ahem!"

"Come to see a prisoner, you say?" grumbled the voice.

"That's it, old fellar; and if you don't mind opening that 'ere gate, his reverence 'll come in."

"Wait a minute, then."

The grating went to with a bang.

The warder was away perhaps five minutes when he came back.

Jerry now heard a clanking of chains and a withdrawal of bolts.

The next minute a small wicket in the gate swung open, and a light flashed through into the rain and darkness of the night.

"The Reverend Ebenezer's order," said the man, testily.

"You'll have to wait a minute," replied the irrepressible one, "the reverend gentleman isn't come out, yet."

"Oh, I see, you have a carriage with you."

"Do you think we would come here without one?" said Jerry. "I am drenched as it is," replied Jerry, almost savagely.

Mizzen row returned to the carriage, opened the door, and handed the Reverend Ebenezer out with all due ceremony.

Next the order was produced.

The warder held it up to the light of his lamp for a moment to see that it was duly authenticated, and perceiving that such was the case, and that it was signed by a very high official indeed, became more respectful, and said that he would only be too happy to send the Reverend Ebenezer to Captain Tom's cell.

"You see, your Reverence," said the man, "the poor wretch hasn't long to live, and a little religious comfort will serve to prepare him for the journey he's going to take."

"You think so?" said Jerry.

"Yes. Don't you?" said the warder.

"Well, they say he'll be hanged, as sure as eggs is eggs. But you know the old saying, there's many a slip atwixt the cup and the lip."

"Ha! ha!" laughed the jailer. "In this case it will be a short shrift and a dance at the yard-arm."

"Cease this sinful levity," cried the Reverend Ebenezer Catchem, reprovingly.

"Yes, yer reverence, it's werry sinful," observed Jerry. "These 'ere jailers don't seem to have more hearts in their bodies than stones. The way they view the shuffling off of a feller critter is truly horrible!"

The Reverend Ebenezer seemed to be very solemnly impressed, and waved the man with the lamp to go forward.

"Your reverence isn't a-going to leave me here," cried Bob, at this moment. "I'm as wet as a drownded rat, and when you come back, if I have to stay here I'm afraid there'll be nothing left of me."

Bob thought it better to make this appeal to get into the prison, where his services would shortly be required.

"No, my poor man. We can't leave you out there," replied the Rev. Ebenezer. "I remember me that you were up all last night and a part of the night before. Besides, you got wet twice already this week."

"That is true, your reverence."

"But who will take care of the carriage and horse while he's away?" ventured the warder.

"They usually takes care of themselves," replied Bob. "The horse is one of the most perfect pieces of intelligence I ever saw."

"Very well, then; if you can venture on leaving him, do so. But, remember, you mustn't hold the prison authorities accountable if you find both absent when you come back."

"That's our look-out, old fellar," said Jerry.

"Very good. Now, reverend sir, if you come this way you will soon be shown into the prisoner's cell."

The Reverend Ebenezer did follow, and behind him came Bob and Jerry, going through a very pantomime of grimaces.

The wicket closed behind them, and they heard

the harsh grating of bolts and bars as their conductor shot them into their places.

Now, it so happened that Bob and Jerry were about right when they anticipated that the warders of the prison would be enjoying themselves.

They were enjoying themselves.

The apartment where nearly a dozen of these men sat was comfortable with the glow and warmth of a bright fire.

The Reverend Ebenezer Catchem—*alias* Lieutenant Vere, was not delayed long when one of the warders was despatched with him to Captain Tom's cell.

The reverend gentleman saw with some surprise, and not a little joy, that discipline was rather lax in that prison.

The warders trusted too much to locks, bolts, and bars, and on this night—especially while the storm of wind and rain raged without—they were enjoying themselves over long pipes and foaming tankards of strong ale.

As Bob and Jerry entered the warders' room, one of the number, who looked as if he had seen much service by sea, was relating to his fellow warders one of Captain Tom Drake's exploits.

The buccaneers pricked up their ears and listened.

The warder went on as follows—

"Three years ago this month," said the man, "I happened to be cruising about in the north.

"At that time, as you all know, I was in his Majesty's navy, and a very good berth I had of it, too.

"But no matter, those days are gone by, and as a man must be content with his present lot, it's no use to sigh for them to come back to him.

"It was while I was there that the following story happened.

"Which will prove to you the daring and reckless nature of this Captain Tom.

"Captain Parker—he was my captain at the time—got the news that this desperate buccaneer was seen on several occasions in one of the villages, and he thereupon resolved on his capture.

"As Parker was Tom Drake's old commander, and as Tom had served him a rather sharp trick by stealing a war vessel from under his nose, Parker thought he was in duty bound to take him at all risks.

"So one dark night a couple o' dozen men were told off to go to the village.

"I among the number.

"Before starting, we were ordered to disguise ourselves as merchant seamen, and as there was plenty o' togs on board we were not long before we came out in as complete a rig as you ever saw.

"No one would for a moment imagine that we were men-o'-war's men.

"A brace of pistols each were then given to us, and, instead of cutlasses, we armed ourselves with heavy bludgeons.

"The captain, after inspecting us, was so well pleased with our looks, that he ordered a couple of extra glasses of grog to be given to each man.

"'Now, lads,' said Captain Parker, 'you know your mission. Remember, if you succeed in capturing this dare-devil, Tom Drake, the reward of two thousand guineas 'll be divided amongst you.'

"This was certainly a good inducement, so we gave the captain a hearty cheer, got into our boat, and pulled away from the ship.

"The boat's crew, as it so happened, were under the command of a lieutenant named Gaston.

"He owed Tom Drake a grudge for a wound he got from him one night in Admiral Ellis's gardens.

"So we knew what would be the consequences if they met.

"Our lieutenant never spoke a word as we pulled to the shore, but we could see, by his fixed features and flashing eyes, that there was some hot work for us should we happen to lay eyes on this buccaneer or any of his gang.

"Our boat at last grated on the beach, and we leaped out.

"The village was, perhaps, a mile, or a mile and a half from where we landed.

"And the road one of the lowliest ones you can imagine, as it led between two great walls of rock, that towered for hundreds of feet above our heads.

"There was something awfully gloomy about this place, more especially as the night was so dark that you could scarcely see your hand before you.

"But on we went, thinking of nothing but Captain Tom and the two thousand guineas.

"Our men chatted a little as we proceeded.

"But the lieutenant still remained silent, seeming, as it were, to be too far above the men who were under him to speak to them.

"This rather nettled our chaps, as you may well believe, for we were all going on the same dangerous errand—for dangerous we knew it would be to attempt the capture of so bold and brave a buccaneer.

"Whatever Lieutenant Gaston's thoughts were no one could tell.

"He was dark and sullen, and when one of our men ventured to address a remark to him, he silenced him with a low growl, which was anything but gentlemanly or even civil.

"But something occurred before we got to the end of our journey that made him speak, silent and sullen as he was.

"All of a sudden a storm set in from the sea.

"We had been expecting it all along that night, but now it burst overhead through the thick, black clouds in thunder and lightning and heavy torrents of rain.

"Besides, for a few minutes a wind set in that would have almost blown you off your feet.

"We drew our sou'-westers well over our necks to prevent the heavy drops of rain from pouring down our backs, and buttoned our great pea-jackets to the throat, to save our fire-arms from the drenching shower.

"But, singular to state, the storm which came on so suddenly abated as if by magic, and the wind died out in a faint moan, resembling the cry almost of a human being.

"We thought now we should have no more bother, but to get to our journey's end, which could not, at this time, be more than a quarter of a mile at most.

"But all of a sudden the tall, jagged masses of rock on our right were lit up by a bright glare that made the narrow road look as light as day.

"We thought for a moment that it was a flash of lightning, but as it continued burning, and grew brighter and brighter, we looked up to the side of the jagged masses to discover the cause of it.

"We almost leaped back in horror at the sight that met our eyes.

"What do you think we saw?

"I'll tell you what we saw.

"One of the most unearthly-looking beings that ever greeted mortal sight, standing on a shelving rock at least eighty feet above our heads, and surrounded on every side by bright, lurid flames.

"The sight was one that made us leap back for a moment in terror.

"This creature had long white hair, and was dressed in every respect like a Druid.

"If one of those ancient gentlemen could come back to earth again, he would have found in this strange being a distinct likeness to himself, excepting, perhaps, that his face was like that of a corpse, or that his eyes shot a fire that was anything but earthly.

"However, we were all pretty well terrified, I can tell you, when we saw this strange creature, and the way he seemed to be surrounded by those bright lurid flames.

"He held out his hand threateningly.

"'You go in quest of Captain Tom, he cried, in unearthly accents; 'but beware.—beware!'

"'Beware of what?' replied Lieutenant Gaston, calling up all the courage he could to his aid, for he at first had been as much terrified as we were. 'Speak, strange being!' cried the luff 'Tell us of what we are to beware?'

"'Ha! ha! ha! Have I not spoken?' laughed the unearthly figure. 'Return to your ship, and you will bless the hour that you saw the Wizard of the Cliffs—dare disobey him, and you will curse the minute you were born! You seek Captain Tom Drake? I have warned him, and—ha! ha! ha! he's prepared—prepared! Go to the village, and you go to your death! Take timely heed, and now away!'

"He waved his long bony hand warningly in the light of the flames, the burning masses that lit the rock were scattered through the air, and fell swirling down into the road. The next moment he was gone.

"'A trick of the enemy!' cried Gaston. 'Push on, men! Push on!'

"But we looked at the matter in a graver light, and, to tell you the truth, were inclined to disobey him.

"But we knew what the consequences would be if we did, so we resumed our march sullenly, and without a word.

"I may tell you, comrades," said the warder, "that it was no very comfortable thing walking that solitary road after the warning given us by the Wizard of the Cliffs; and, as it was a splendid place for an ambuscade, we didn't know the moment that we might be pounced upon.

"And we were pounced upon before we got four hundred yards further; and, before we could well defend ourselves, half our number were slain, and many of the other twelve disarmed and taken prisoners.

"Out of the whole twenty-four, only me and the lieutenant got back to the ship; and all through not obeying the warning of that strange being, the Wizard of the Cliffs."

Jerry and Bob heard the last of this story, and enjoyed it amazingly, as they now knew that many of the difficulties which they had anticipated at first were removed.

Singing songs and telling stories!

"Good!" thought Jerry. "That'll give me a chance to throw a stave in."

"Most part o' these 'ere fellows have been in the navy," said Bob, to himself, "and if me and Jerry don't settle 'em, my name ain't Hauler."

So assured were Bob and Jerry now of their success, that they could almost have danced with joy.

Bob, whose "locality" had a greater development than Jerry's, resolved to accompany the Reverend Ebenezer to Captain Tom's cell.

As the warders were agreeable to this arrangement, Bob followed his clerical master.

They went down some long rambling passages which would have puzzled a less-observant eye than our old buccaneer.

But he took note of everything as he went along, so that he could be able, in case of need, to go back there again without experiencing difficulty.

They at last stopped before Captain Tom's cell.

There was a warder walking up and down in front of it.

The only one, indeed, in the whole range of passages.

Bob looked upon this as a good omen.

The difficulties in Captain Tom's way were growing agreeably less.

This, at least, in Bob Hauler's opinion.

The man challenged them as they came up.

Only a mere matter of form, however, as there was light enough in the passage to see everything that was going on.

No one could approach without the warder recognising whether he was a prison official or not.

However, the Reverend Ebenezer's conductor replied, "A friend!"

And that was all sufficient, for the warder lowered the point of his cutlass at once, and permitted them to come up.

"An order to see Captain Tom Drake," said the man who came with them. "The Reverend Ebenezer Catchem, Jerry, to console the wretched prisoner, afore he's strung up."

"Another, Jerry," thought Bob. "I hope he's not sich a knowing cove as Jerry Mizzen, or it's all up with us."

Had Jerry heard this from the lips of his "chum" and "brother," he would have been highly gratified.

His vanity would have been puffed out amazingly.

However, this Jerry, the warder, seemed to be a man of somewhat taciturn disposition.

He merely nodded.

Next rattled some huge keys in his belt.

Afterwards proceeded to unlock and unbolt the massive door of Captain Tom's cell.

All this scarcely took a minute.

We should have said at this stage, however, that our gallant hero and Ben Barnacle were confined here together.

Will the reader permit us to go a little way back and see how Captain Tom and his brave lieutenant took their imprisonment?

Did they dream in their lonely prison hours that they were deserted by their friends?

Not they.

They knew the crew of the "Will-o'-the-Wisp" too well for that.

And they harboured no fear but that their escape was being planned while they lay there.

Let us now see what took place during the earlier part of that day.

A little after midday a visitor was announced.

And a lady at that.

Who could this lady be?

Minnie or Jenny?

No!

Captain Tom hoped not, as the scene between them would have been a very painful one indeed.

Our hero desired to spare the only woman he loved on earth the pain of such a meeting.

Ah! there was Zelie!

The corsair maiden would be heartbroken to think that her beau ideal was in prison.

He had pity for the poor girl who loved him so tenderly.

And whose love he could never possibly return.

No!

In his present unfortunate plight he had no desire to see her.

It however turned out neither of those, but a woman of a far bolder cast of mind, and who loved Tom almost as passionately as any.

But who never showed any other affection but that of a sister for a brother.

In fact, it was Lady Arbuthnot!

The jailers were astounded.

They could hardly believe their eyes.

Her ladyship visit one who was shortly to die the death of a felon—to meet an ignominious death at the yard-arm?

All this went beyond their comprehension.

They could not understand the great love Lady Arbuthnot bore for our brave hero.

Besides, she was married.

So it became the talk of the place for many hours afterwards.

However, her ladyship did come, presented her order, and was admitted.

But let us enter upon a little dialogue that took place between Captain Tom and his lieutenant some hours prior to her ladyship's visit.

"This is a gloomy place, Captain Tom," said Ben.

"I would rather be out of it," said Tom, quietly; "but at present there seems to be little prospect of it."

"I am afraid not," said Ben. "That fellow outside can't be bribed."

"No."

"And if he could, there would be a hundred other obstacles in the way."

"All of which I am sure we would overcome if we were only on the outside of this cell with two good swords in our hands and a brace of pistols each. We have been in worse scrapes than this before, Ben."

"And have got out of them, captain."

"True. Therefore let us not despair."

"I know not the meaning of the word," replied the lieutenant.

"That I know by experience," said Tom. "But hark! That rascal outside is listening, so let us be prudent of what we say."

They could hear a stealthy footstep.

And they knew it be their guard's.

They could also see that the grating was darkened, for in every cell door there was a litte iron grating, which served two purposes—as ventilation and also as a point from which the warder could watch his prisoners.

Being fully by this time aware of the eavesdropping proclivities of their friend in the corridor, they resolved to throw him off the scent, so Tom proceeded.

"I am afraid it's all up with us, Ben," he said.

"I regret to say that I think the same."

"No chance of getting out of such a strong place as this is."

"None."

"A short shrift and a long rope, lieutenant."

"That will be the end of it, captain."

"I have given up all hope."

"And so have I."

"But I'll show the rascals that Captain Tom Drake can die like a man."

"And I'll take good care that they shan't see me show the white feather."

"Bravo, Ben! I knew that would be your answer. We have faced death too many times together to fear it now."

"So we have, captain. Then let it come, and we'll show the villains how two brave men can die."

This was enough for the man outside the cell door.

He had no desire to listen any longer.

He felt sure in his own mind of the safe-keeping of Captain Tom and his companion, more so now, indeed, as they now appeared so resigned in their anticipation of an ignominous death.

Could the warder have heard the low chuckle that followed his departure, he would have been, indeed, inclined to alter his opinion materially.

But, not hearing that low chuckle, he went away with secret satisfaction.

Indeed, he did not see why he should not leave his post for a few seconds.

There was strong ale and good grog in the warders' room, and up to this the forgetful fellows had only brought him one glass, and that glass what he considered very weak grog indeed.

Being a landsman, he was not satisfied with grog alone, so he stole away with the laudable object of mixing it with the aforesaid ale.

Captain Tom and Ben Barnacle were conscious of his departure.

The passage was always well lighted both by day and night.

So the lieutenant trod quickly and noiselessly to the grating just in time to see his fleeting shadow on the corridor wall.

"He's gone," said Ben, returning, "and the devil go with him, for he's a scurvy fellow, to say the least."

Now, Captain Tom and Ben Barnacle knew that they would be left to themselves for a little while, so they decided to talk unreservedly on all matters.

"I hope Bob Hauler and Jerry Mizzen got to the 'Will-o'-the-Wisp,'" said Captain Tom.

"Oh! there is little fear of that," replied Ben. "By this time the ' Will-o'-the-Wisp ' is far enough away."

"I believe the little admiral set his heart upon her capture."

"You may be sure he did."

"It would break my heart to think for an instant that our dear little brig fell into his clutches."

"And mine, Captain Tom, and mine," said Ben. "But you may depend she is not in his power yet, nor is she likely to be."

"I hope everything will turn out as you anticipate. But this is what I am most afraid of," added Tom, "that some of our gallant crew, in their desire to rescue us, may be led into some imprudent act."

"I don't think so," replied Ben. "That they will attempt to be of some assistance to us there can be no doubt; but, at the same time, they will not neglect your instructions, depend upon it. The whole thing seems to me pretty clear. The ' Will-o'-the-Wisp ' will weigh anchor, and sail from the Sound at once—perhaps put in at Purfleet or some other place in a new disguise. Then— But here comes this fellow the warder back again."

"Not another word," said Tom.

They both kept very quiet now, as they could hear the warder's return steps quite distinctly.

The fellow, they knew, had been imbibing, for they were conscious that he staggered from one side of the corridor to the other as he came up.

"Getting drunk," thought Tom. "About time he was, that's all I can say."

The man, forgetting his former caution, came up and looked in at the grating as he did before.

But this time without any desire to conceal the fact.

CHAPTER CLXXXVII.

LADY ARBUTHNOT VISITS CAPTAIN TOM'S CELL.

One hour later Captain Tom was made aware that a lady came to visit him.

"Captain Tom Drake!" cried a rather unsteady voice through the grating. "A lady come to see you."

The door of the cell was unlocked, and the bolts shot back, and the heavy iron bar removed.

The door swung open, and in walked the lady who had come to see our gallant buccaneer chief.

WITH A JOYOUS SHOUT CAPTAIN TOM APPEARED AT THE OPENING.

The visitor was Lady Arbuthnot, as we have said before.

But Captain Tom heard other steps.

Not those of a lady, because they were too heavy.

Her ladyship brought one of the shrewdest of her household with her—a young footman—a confidential servant, in fact, who remained outside the cell, to keep the gaoler from peeping and listening.

This footman had not yet reached his twentieth year, but he was overflowing with humour and wit, and had a great fund of anecdote as well at his disposal.

Now, the warder relished all this, especially from the fact that the aforesaid footman had brought a flask of the best liquor with him.

While these two worthies were conversing on the outside of the cell, Lady Arbuthnot conveyed the intelligence to Captain Tom and his lieutenant that measures were being taken to facilitate their escape.

Besides giving them to understand what was to take place that night.

Our gallant hero was about to speak to return his thanks when her ladyship, with a gesture of her hand, waved him to silence.

"Say nothing now," she said, "lest you may be heard. I can depend on my man outside, therefore the more prudence we exercise at present the better."

Captain Tom agreed with Lady Arbuthnot in this, but as their eyes met he could not help taking her hand and holding it in his for a few moments.

And he felt that hand tremble within his own.

And he encountered those eyes humid in tears.

What did all this denote?

That Lady Arbuthnot loved our gallant buccaneer tenderly and devotedly.

Even so.

Though she had never mentioned her great love in words, these were indications that could never be mistaken.

Captain Tom felt it, and a deep sorrow came over his heart for this noble woman who was little less than his guardian angel.

Her ladyship, not trusting herself to a further display of feeling, withdrew her hand from the youthful chief, and walking to the grating in the cell door, called the attention of the warder.

The interview was at an end.

The cell door opened, and Lady Arbuthnot, gently pressing Captain Tom's hand, passed out, and was joined by the young footman.

The warder relocked and rebolted the cell door, and conducted them to the end of the corridor, where another warder was waiting for them, and thus they were soon outside the prison walls.

Who can tell the different feelings that swayed the mind of Lady Arbuthnot after her interview with Captain Tom?

Very few, indeed, could guess the tumultuous feelings of her ladyship's heart, as she stood for a moment after leaving the prison to contemplate its gloomy walls.

Leaving Lady Arbuthnot, we once more return to Captain Tom's cell.

They were prepared for the visit that night of Bob, Jerry, and the *soi disant* parson.

Besides, they thought it an excellent plan.

At first, they doubted of its success, but reflecting on the versatility and genius of the indomitable Hauler, and the bravery and prudence of Harry, seconded by the ability of Jerry, they began to view the scheme in a more hopeful light.

Finding that their guard, whose faculties were well steeped in liquor, was not so wideawake as one in his positoin should be, they began, without much fear of being overheard, to talk the matter over.

"I think that Hauler is a perfect genius," said Captain Tom.

"You may well say that," replied Ben. "I never saw a man in his position so full of plans and schemes in my life."

"If he doesn't succeed, it will be a wonder to me."

"And to me, too."

"The parson is to be played by Harry. A rather new rôle for him; but his ability will stand him in good stead, and I have no fears for his success."

"Oh, depend upon it, captain, that he knows what he is about."

"I am not afraid of that," said Captain Tom; "and once we are outside these prison walls, it will take them all their time to catch us again."

"There will be one difficulty in the way, however."

"And what is that?" asked Tom.

"To pass the warders' room."

"True, that will certainly be difficult. But Bob Hauler will overcome that difficulty I am sure."

"Then, again, how can they bring the cutlasses and pistols in?"

"The pistols quite easy. As for the cutlasses, there will be little chance of that."

"Unless our friend the parson smuggles them in under his gown."

"A good idea!" said Tom. "I wish they'll only think of that. Five well-armed desperate men can do a great deal when they are put to it."

"I can quite agree with you there, captain. Let us hope for the best. A good cutlass in my hand, and I should be unwilling to turn my back to four such fellows as those warders. There is one thing, however, that has given me some pleasure."

"What is that?" asked Tom Drake.

"To know that our gallant little brig is out of danger. Ellis will bite his finger nails off when he hears of it."

"Oh! the malicious, nasty little viper!" exclaimed Captain Tom.

"Not so loud, captain," said Ben. "The fellow outside is not so drunk but that he may hear something we say. Stop a minute; I'll go and see where he now is."

Ben Barnacle, suiting the action to the word, trod quietly to the cell door, and looking through the open grating, took a peep out into the passage.

What he saw made him laugh almost outright.

The warder, who was beginning now to experience the full effects of the liquor he imbibed, was going through a series of drunken pantomimic gestures, much to the amusement of our friend Barnacle.

The fellow presented a picture of drunken imbecility, and was squaring out at his shadow that he saw moving on the wall.

On one occasion, thinking that he had his shadow —or, rather, what he considered his tormentor— where he wanted it, he lunged out a tremendous blow, and his hand, of course, meeting the wall of the corridor, made him, drunk as he was, actually bellow with pain.

By this means, he became aware of the disagreeable fact that the prison walls were considerably harder than his knuckles, which were hacked and bleeding from the force of his own blow.

The pain of his wounded hand did more to sober him and bring him to his senses than anything else could possibly have done.

And our friend Ben Barnacle, seeing him thus recovering, left the grating and returned to the side of Captain Tom, who, hearing the bellowing of the unfortunate warder, wondered very much what could be the matter.

And his lieutenant was not long in telling him.

Now several hours slipped away.

The warder was relieved, and another put in his place.

At last night came on.

It proved a very stormy one, as the reader has already been told.

It rained and thundered incessantly, much to the delight of our hero and his lieutenant, who looked upon the storm as an omen of good.

Nine o'clock came, and then ten.

But, no Bob and Jerry, nor the *soi disant* parson.

Could anything have taken place to prevent them?

This question came into Captain Tom's mind at least a score of times.

At last they thought they heard, through the angry roar of the storm, a roll of carriage wheels.

Hope again grew in their hearts.

They heard the roll of the carriage wheels suddenly stop.

Now, they knew that the occupants of that carriage could be no other than Bob, Jerry, and Harry Vere.

They were not long left in doubt.

They heard steps in the passage.

The door of the cell was thrown open, and in

walked the clerical gentleman, the Rev. Ebenezer Catchem.

"The Rev. Ebenezer Catchem to see Captain Tom Drake!" said the jailer.

CHAPTER CLXXXVIII.

JERRY MIZZEN HOODWINKS THE WARDERS OF THE PORTSMOUTH PRISON

"YES, gents! Don't think for a moment that I am telling you a lie. My master, the Reverend Ebenezer, is one o' the most extraordinary men living.

"Perhaps it would be werry interesting at this point to tell you a little o' what he has gone through.

"But first of all let us fill up and drink to his Reverence's werry good health, as he's a man and a gentleman he is, and I've no doubt 'll give you a couple of guineas each on his second visit.

"Never saw a more generous genelman in my life than the Reverend Ebenezer.

"He's worth a million to-day if he's worth a penny.

"Now this is a flask o' liquor that came all the way from the West Indies.

"That's where my master was afore he came here; and I can tell you this, gents, the contents is a hundred years old if it's a day.

"Come, then, let us have yer horns—I mean your glasses, and if you don't say it's the best liquor ever you drank, may I be strung up as high as Captain Tom Drake."

"Hear! hear!"

"That's it, gents! Don't be afeared of yer voices. Dewelope 'em, and show as how yer dignity is not at wariance with yer stomachs. Now, gents, to the health o' my werry good master, the Reverend Ebenezer Catchem. Every man up with his glass. It's a fortune to every one of yer.

"Now, three times three for the Reverend Ebenezer!

"Hurrah! hurrah! hurrah!"

"Hurrah! hurrah! hurrah!" cried all the warders, who were fairly inoculated by Bob Hauler's eloquence, combined with the liquor "all the way from the West Indies."

Besides, his promises had a most wonderful effect, too.

Two guineas each, with an earnest promise of more from the Reverend Ebenezer, was worth considering.

"Now," said Bob, when the cheers for the reverend gentleman had subsided, "now for a song. Let me see, I've a bag-load, if I could only think of them. 'Tom Bowling' is a grand old song, but I haven't the woice to sing it. Will that 'ere genelman oblige with the patch over his left eye? I know he can give us a good one, and arter that I'll just tell you one o' the wonderful adventures of the Reverend Ebenezer."

"Hear! hear! A song! a song!"

"Will the genelman with the patch over his eye oblige?"

"Yes."

The gentleman with the patch over his left eye was willing to oblige, only the present honourable company must not expect too much, as he—the gentleman with the patch—was there and then suffering from a very bad cold.

"Never mind the cold!" shouted Bob. "We'll excuse you, old fellow, for that. Give us one with a chorus."

"What do you say to a drinking song?"

"Hear! hear! A drinking song!"

"Mind you all join in the chorus."

"Go ahead, old feller! You needn't be afeard o' that."

"Very good. Then here goes!"

And the man with the patch sung the following, and was joined by the rest of the warders at the top of their voices—

"Come, landlord, fill the flowing bowl,
   Until it does run over,
Come, landlord, fill the flowing bowl,
   Until it does run over.

For to-night we'll merry be,
For to-night we'll merry be,
For to-night we'll merry, merry be,
   In the morning we'll get sober."

"In the morning we'll get sober," ended Bob.

The man with the patch sung this chorus over twice.

But as his memory failed him, he could go no further.

The company jogged his memory repeatedly, but with no better success.

All he knew was the chorus.

While they were debating whether he should attempt another song or not, Bob Hauler went out and Jerry Mizzen stepped in.

"Where's the parson's servant?" asked one of the warders, observing that Bob was absent.

"Here I am, old feller," replied Jerry.

"No, not you; the other one."

"Oh! he's with the Reverend Ebenezer," returned Jerry. "I see as how you are enjoying yourselves, gentlemen."

"To be sure," replied one. "But there, that comrade of yours is gone and cheated us out of our story."

"You don't say so!" cried Jerry, incredulously.

"Yes, I do."

"Then he must be an unmitigated villain!"

"Come, now, old fellow, you are going a little too far," said one of the warders. "Perhaps he wouldn't be well pleased with you if he heard you call him that."

"Why, bless you, he is one o' the best-tempered fellers in the world. He'd only take it as a compliment. But stay, comrades! How goes the liquor?"

"Very little of it left, I reckon. That your comrade brought was a drop of the right sort."

"You mean the West Indie stuff?"

"That's it, mate."

"Fortunately," said Jerry, "it's not all gone yet, and to prove to you that it isn't, I have a flask still left."

At this announcement of the "irrepressible one," the eyes of the warders brightened and their mouths watered.

"Here you are," said Jerry. "Nothing like it in Portsmouth."

"No."

"I'll bet any genelman in the company a guinea that there isn't. Pass round your glasses this way, gents."

The glasses were passed, and after being partly refilled, were handed back to their respective owners.

"Now for a toast!" said Jerry.

"A toast! A toast! Hear, hear!" cried the warders, showing pretty well the effects of the previous liquors they had been drinking.

"Here's that we may have cause to remember each other in the time to come!" said Jerry.

For a moment they looked into Jerry's face in doubt, not knowing well what to make of his words.

But the rough, honest lineaments of our bold buccaneer defied suspicion.

So they drank the toast with loud acclamations,

and even went so far as to say that our friend Jerry was the best fellow they had ever met.

Jerry appeared to be highly flattered at the encomiums that were lavished on him.

"Thank each and everyone of you, genelmen," he replied. "You have touched my heart in its most tenderest spot. I believe I am right in saying this, genelmen; and, believe me, gents, it's with some difficulty that I keep the tears from forcing themselves into my eyes. The Reverend Ebenezer shall know all about this; and if there is one man as ll reward you more than another, it is he. Accept my thanks again, genelmen, and I hope as how our acquaintance will be carried on on the same friendly terms."

"Hurrah! hurrah!" shouted the warders. "Very neat and graceful, isn't it, comrades?"

"Now, gents," continued Jerry, "as my friend promised you a story, and has been called away suddenly, I don't see why I shouldn't take up the cudgels for him."

"Hear! hear!"

"Mind, genelmen," said Jerry, "it would be werry vain for me to go and say that I can tell a story as well as my comrade, 'cause I can do nothing of the kind, but I'll do the best I can, and no man can do more than that."

"Hear! hear!"

"Tell us something about the Rev. Ebenezer!" cried the warders.

For since they had been informed that he was so immensely rich, they took very great interest in him.

"That's just what I was going to tell you," replied Jerry. "One of his adventures in the West Indies."

"Hear! hear! Couldn't be better!" cried the warders. "Tell us about the West Indies!"

"Well, you must know, once upon a time," said Jerry, "they were going to hang a sartin individual, a pirate, whose name for the moment has slipped my memory, for piracy on the high seas.

"Now, it so happened that this man had made a great deal of noise in the world, so the parties in power made up their minds to put a stop to his career at once.

"No one dreamt for a moment that there was a chance of his escaping.

"In fact, the prison where he was confined was just as strong as this, and, as near as I can remember now, built on the same plan.

"Indeed, every one was against this gallant pirate except the ladies o' the place, who all loved him because he was young, and not only young, but handsome.

"However, the last two or three days he had to live the prison was alive with visitors.

"Every beautiful gal in the place came to see him, and to grieve with him over his sad fate.

"But there was one in particular—a fine, handsome young lady of about nineteen—who made up her mind, come what might, to assist in his escape.

"And this was one who had fallen dead in love with him at first sight.

"But who was she to get to help her?

"That was a question she asked herself over and over again, more than a hundred times.

"Who was bold enough to go into the prison and change places with him?

"Now, it so happened about that time that this dear little gal was puzzling her brain over the matter, my master, the Reverend Ebenezer, came into the town.

"He was well-known there before in connection of wisiting prisons.

"Besides, he had the reputation o' being a werry kind-hearted man.

"However, the young lady who fell so desperately in love with the handsome pirate heard of his arrival as well as the rest, and determined to go and look him up.

"'If any one is able to assist me, he is the man,' she said.

"But when she asked herself whether so pious a genelman would help in the escape of a prisoner, and that prisoner a pirate, a weight as heavy as lead came on her heart, and for a moment she gave the undertaking up in despair.

"It was only for a moment, though.

"She knew the prevailing weakness of the Reverend Ebenezer too well.

"I don't mean any harm by this, gents, for my master was above committing himself in that sort o' way, and indeed above suspicion.

"He is none o' yer hypocrites, he isn't, although he loved to look on a pretty face as well as anyone."

"And would have no objection, perhaps, to kiss a pretty pair of lips," ventured one of the warders, roguishly.

"Well, perhaps not, gents. However, to make a long story short, she came to this conclusion.

"Said she to herself—

"'I'm a nice-looking gal, and with a little persuasion I may prevail on the Reverend Ebenezer to help me. He'd spare human suffering, I know, if he could; besides that, he has great influence, and is werry rich.

"'But bein' a minister o' the Church, he might refuse doing what I want of him.

"'Very well, then, all I can do is to go prepared.'

"What do you think she meant by that, gents?

"A few words will serve to explain to you.

"She jest meant to go armed to the teeth.

"And if kind words wouldn't prevail, to try what virtue there was in a brace o' pistols with a couple o' bullets in each of 'em.

"Indeed, she meant shooting his Reverence first, providing he refused to grant her prayer, and herself after.

"Having come to this resolution, nothing could move her from it.

"However, she waited until the next day, and then called on the Reverend Ebenezer.

"His Reverence was at home, as it so happened, and the fair visitor, after sending up her card, was admitted to his library.

"When she removed her veil, my master thought he never in all his life looked upon so handsome a face.

"It was as radiant as the sun.

"Her eyes were bluer than the bluest sky, and as for a well-turned arm and graceful figger, there was nothing to be compared with her.

"For several minutes the Reverend Ebenezer looked upon her, speechless with surprise.

"What had she wisited him for?

"He couldn't tell no more'n the dead.

"Nor did he dream that there was such a gal before in all the West India Islands.

"His heart beat twice as fast as the tick of a watch as he took in all her charms.

"I am sure he must have blushed.

"However, whether he blushed or not, she got the upper hand of him, and when he led her to a seat he was as dead in love with her as she was with Cap—I mean the bold, handsome pirate.

"She saw her advantage, o' course, and made the most of it.

"She wasn't long in telling him what she called for, only, not knowing the Reverend Ebenezer so well as she might, she took care not to let him know of her love for the young fellow in prison.

"Now, my master listened patiently to all she had to say.

"And she pleaded so well that he was spell-bound.

"He could do anything for so lovely a critter.

"But this he believed was entirely out of his power.

"Then, as a clergyman, he could not very well move in the matter.

"But to everything he said she was always ready with a plausible argument against it.

"And then her eyes!

"They had the power o' working wonders.

"Three-quarters of an hour did they talk the matter over, and my master, notwithstanding her charms, still held out.

"In fact, couldn't see his way clear.

"'Who is this young man?' said the Reverend Ebenezer, 'that he finds one so eloquent and beautiful to plead for him as you?'

"Of course her answer was a falsehood.

"But what could she say?

"She told my master that the young pirate was a very near and dear relative of hers

"'A lover, perhaps,' said the Reverend Ebenezer, slyly.

"'Oh, no,' she replied; 'nothing at all in that line.'

"You are surely not married?' said my master, wondering, indeed, at the time why he had asked that question.

"Of course her answer was that she was not.

"'Well, upon my word, I don't see what I can do,' said the Reverend Ebenezer. 'I am against capital punishment, and I am sorry for you and all that, yet I don't see how I can assist you.'

"'Perhaps you don't want,' she said, a little angrily.

"'Oh, no, you mustn't think that, my dear,' said the Reverend Ebenezer, taking her hand in his own, and pressing it, without knowing well what he was about. 'You mustn't say that. If I could only see of what assistance I would be to you, I'd only too willingly undertake to do my best.'

"'Now you speak like a Christian and a genelman,' she said; 'and as you don't know what's to be done, I'll tell you.'

"So she ups and tells him a plan that he would never have dreamt of.

"And what do you think it was?"

"What?" "What?" cried several of the warders, who by this time were getting pretty well under the influence of the liquor that was passed round.

"Well, I'll tell you, gents.

"But mind, it must be a secret, or it may come against the Reverend Ebenezer at some other time.

"You needn't be afeared of us," cried the warders. "Anything you tell us here'll go no further."

"I think, genelmen, as how I can trust you," said Jerry, "so here goes, and as you are all sober, I hope it'll be a lesson to each of you."

"What do you mean?" cried several of the warders, in a breath.

"Nothing insulting, gents; a bit o' friendly advice I was going to give you that was all, as who knows but the same affair may occur in this prison as well as in any other?'

"Oh," said two or three of his hearers, "if that's all, you may rest your mind easy. We have not had an escape of a prisoner for twelve years."

"Jest so, genelmen—jest so," said Jerry. "I think as how there's werry good smart discipline observed here, and allow me to say I never met a finer lot o' fellers in my life."

All this little flattery of the "irrepressible one" went down amazingly.

"Yes," resumed Jerry, "she hit upon a plan that surprised the Reverend Ebenezer with all his knowledge.

"And it was this—

"That she would first get an order to visit the prisoner the following day, to prepare him for an escape the same night."

The warders, drunk as they were getting, pricked up their ears, and looked at Jerry rather suspiciously.

But as the "irrepressible one's" face wore the most innocent look in the world, he was allowed to continue.

And yet they could not help thinking that the West Indie case was in a great measure very much like their own, regarding Captain Tom.

Had they been sober they would have taken the account in its literal sense, and Jerry would have ruined matters by his seeming imprudence.

But they were rather too drunk to take cognisance of this fact.

So Jerry proceeded.

"'But how are you going to succeed, my dear?' said the Reverend Ebenezer, lost in astonishment.

"'Oh, easy enough,' she replied. 'You jest listen to me a moment.'

"'After preparing this unhappy young man for what he may expect to take place during the night, I will purchase some files to saw away his fetters.'

"'But how can that be done?' asked my master, more and more puzzled. 'My dear young lady, you are not taking into account the warders—the prison is full of warders.'

"'I know that,' she replied, 'and I've hit upon a plan for settling 'em.'

"With that she up and told him everything.

"What she was going to do, and how she was going to succeed, and all to that, until the Reverend Ebenezer was forced to take the same opinion as she did of the matter.

"There was no such word as failure in the whole thing."

"But you have no told us the whole of her plan," said one of them.

"Time enough, my son, for that," said Jerry. "I'll be coming to the main point directly, and then you'll agree with me that strong walls, iron doors, and bolts and bars, is no proof against wiolent love such as this was.

"Very well, at last the lady left, and I showed her out into the street.

"I saw her ankle just as she was going down the steps, and I was obliged to take another look or two afore I closed the door.

"'I wonder what you've been up to?' said I to myself.

"'The Reverend Ebenezer is caught and trapped, I suppose' said I. 'And I'm sartin he is if he caught a glimpse of that ere ankle.'

"I wasn't left long in the dark, however.

"Master sent for me during the next day, and told me all from beginning to end.

"I was delighted, I can tell you, and so was my comrade when he came to hear of it, too.

"What do you think it was?

"Well, I'll tell you.

"To go to the prison, both of us, my noble comrade to drive a close carriage that we engaged, and me to act as footman.

"You may well look astonished, gents.

'The case was something like the present one; indeed, werry like the present one, if I may use the expression.

"However, as this I am talking about was done in the West Indies, there the resemblance ends.

"Well, gents, night came on at last, and it was a night, too, I can tell you.

"It rained and thundered as if the Heavens were coming down.

"But go we must; there was no choice left, one way or the other.

"The Reverend Ebenezer was never known to break his word, nor was he going to do it then.

"So a little after nine up drives a carriage and pulls up before my master's house.

"My comrade was the coachman, as I told you afore, and he was for all the world like a drownded rat—just the same as he was to-night, gents, only perhaps a little worse.

"However, to make a long story short, the young lady had been there before us to warn this gallant young pirate—for, mind you, there was only one in the cell—to warn him, I say, to get ready to break the prison that night.

"So well, so good.

"He was prepared, at all events.

"At last the reverend genelman came out o' the house and got into the carriage.

"Me and my comrade were on the box at once, as innocent as two lambs, each fortified with a flask o' good liquor to keep the cold and wet out.

"I must tell you it was cold and wet enough that night, even in that warm climate.

"However, off the carriage drove through the pelting rain, and twenty minutes' good driving brought us afore the prison gate.

"We soon got admittance when the order was shown, and in a few moments we were in the warders' room, where a rousing fire was burning, and everything looking very comfortable like.

"Now, all this was werry nice, considering that we were both wet through.

"And jest as you are to-night, genelman, they were drinking and enjoying themselves.

"Well, yesee, as they were jolly chaps, we thought we'd jest join 'em for a time while the Reverend Ebenezer was doing the amiable for the dashing young pirate in the cell.

"There was no objection to this, so we joined in and had a nice time of it, telling stories and singing songs just as we've been to-night.

"One of the flasks was nearly empty, when out I hauls the other just as I'm doing now, and passes it round with the greatest civility and politeness."

Jerry, suiting the action to the word, took out his flask, appeared to take a good swig himself, and passed it to the warder nearest to him, who, too drunk to have any suspicion, took it, drank from it, and handed it to the next.

And so the flask passed all round, until there was not a drop left of its contents.

"My story is nearly at an end," said Jerry.

After drinking from this flask, they began to feel a strange sense of drowsiness come over them.

One by one they rolled over and under the table.

"Ha! but here comes my noble comrade. Perhaps he will finish the story for me."

At that instant Bob walked into the warders' room.

He had been listening to a great deal of Jerry's story, and felt personally delighted with it.

He had even seen the drugged flask passed round—for drugged it was—and looked upon the villain Jerry's deceit with considerable favour.

"He's done it better than I expected,' he muttered. "We'll only have two or three to master, and then the prison is ours. We can do what we like then."

"Hallo, gents!" cried Bob. "It gives me werry great pleasure to see you enjoying yourselves so well.

"I knew my comrade here was just the man to suit yer. And as for the Reverend Ebenezer, he's doing as well as can be expected.

"That 'ere Captain Tom has a heart o' stone and it takes a good deal o' preaching and sermonising to take any great effect on him.

"Ha! hold up, small beer! Where is yer a-falling to?"

The drugged liquor had taken effect.

One of the warders, with a drowsy yawn, rolled under the table.

Another followed him.

And still another, until a half-dozen, at least, lay side by side.

This was a good beginning.

But there were several yet left.

Even these were thoroughly helpless.

But one of them seemed to have an indistinct sense that they were betrayed, and so tried to give the alarm.

But his words died away in his throat, and he, too, rolled over senseless.

In less than a quarter of an hour there was not a man left in the warders' room who was not lying without sense or motion on the floor.

Bob and Jerry, the moment they saw the last man fall, hurried out into the passage to meet Captain Tom and Ben Barnacle, who were still in their cell, enjoying the companionship of the Reverend Ebenezer Catchem.

The Reverend Ebenezer, Captain Tom, and Ben Barnacle got on very well, and were only awaiting the return of the said Bob and Jerry.

Now, as these gentlemen had one or two more to cope with before they could altogether consider themselves masters of the situation, they set about their work at once.

The guard at Captain Tom's cell was to be disposed of.

As that gentleman had not partaken of any of the drugged liquor, he was pretty wide awake.

A fact not at all relished by our two friendly buccaneers.

"Now," said Bob, "as you have done very well to-night, old pal, perhaps you'd advise the werry best and easiest way o' silencing that other feller."

"I thought as how there was two of 'em?" said Jerry.

"So there is. But one at a time, you know, old pal."

"Very well, the feller over Captain Tom's cell."

"Decidedly. What's to be done with him?"

"Why, put him in Captain Tom's cell, gag and bind him."

"A werry good plan. I'll tell you what I was thinking of, Jerry."

"What, Bob?"

"Well, jest this, old pal. Why not put 'em all in Captain Tom's cell, and turn the lock on 'em. But stay, who'd know that they were there. I don't like to go to extremes with the lubbers, Jerry, seeing that they were only doing their duty."

"Ha! ha! ha!" chuckled the "irrepressible one."

"So they were—so they were, Bob. Doing their duty, and guarding their prisoners well."

"Let me see," said Bob. "How many prisoners are there in this establishment altogether?"

"More than you'll take out!" cried a voice that rung loudly through the passage, and in a moment they found themselves fiercely attacked by two of the warders.

CHAPTER CLXXXIX.

REUBEN HARPY AND BLACK BILL.—DAN SEA-DRIFT FALLS INTO THE HANDS OF THE COAST-GUARDS

"Yes, you can depend he gave us a tough struggle, captain. I got a blow on the sconce that nearly knocked the life out of me. Besides, there's a piece of my left ear gone. I tell you what. Mr.

Harpy, the reward was earned hard enough, and your fifty pounds to the back of it, too."

"I am sorry, Bill, that you got such rough handling," said Reuben.

"So you may, but that won't mend matters a bit."

"But there's the reward."

"I don't believe I should have risked Captain Tom's capture but for that," replied the smuggler.

"And the fifty pounds as you just mentioned?"

"I meant that to be paid down on the nail, of course."

"On the what?" asked Reuben, who did not quite understand the smuggler's peculiar phraseology.

"Well, ye see, Mr. Harpy, ' On the nail ' means money down," said Bill, bluntly; "that is, the money paid the moment that cousin o' yours was taken. He's taken and lodged safe enough now. And it is only right that I should be paid at once for my work."

"Of course, Bill; who denies your right?" said Reuben.

At the same moment he took a pocket-book from his pocket and handed a crisp new note to the smuggler.

Bill was stretched out on an old iron bedstead, and covered over with some torn sails.

His face was pale, even haggard.

His ear bound up where it had been mutilated by a bullet from Captain Tom's pistol.

His head also bandaged where he had received a blow from the ostler's bludgeon.

Altogether, the rough, burly smuggler presented a pitiable sight as he lay stretched out on the old rickety bedstead, and even Reuben Harpy thought that he deserved the paltry fifty pounds he promised him.

Black Bill, unwell as he was, snatched the bank-note greedily from the hand of his employer, and held it up to the light to see that it was genuine.

Finding it so, after a brief examination, he put it away.

"And now," said he, "I hope they won't cheat me out of that 'ere reward."

"Certainly not. I'll make known the case to Admiral Ellis at once," replied Reuben.

"Thank you. But when am I to get it? That is the question that troubles me most now."

"Very soon after this Captain Tom's execution."

"That's rather unfortunate."

"Why so?" asked Reuben.

"Because Captain Tom is one of the most slippery coves I know of."

"Slippery or not, he'll not get out of this scrape, I can tell you."

"Do you think so?" asked Bill, his eyes brightening.

"Oh, never more certain of anything in my life. There's not the slightest shade of a chance for him. He's in a prison now where there has been only one escape in a dozen years."

"But he might make the second," suggested the smuggler, doubtfully.

"I hope you won't trouble your mind any more about the matter," said Reuben. "You must get well now, and if you keep an uneasy mind it will take you some time before you are on your feet again."

"I know that, captain; but the sooner that 'ere reward is paid over the sooner I'll be better. Look at me, captain, and tell me that you don't mean to let anyone cheat me, and that you'll not handle a penny yourself."

Reuben would rather not have turned his face for the smuggler's inspection.

But what could he do?

Black Bill would grow only the more suspicious if he did not.

Reuben, therefore, slowly turned.

But at first with averted eyes, which, however, by a mighty effort, he brought fully to bear on the smuggler's keen black ones.

Bill, after scanning him narrowly, appeared satisfied, and again lowered himself on his wretched couch, from which he had partly arisen to look at the other.

"Are you satisfied?" asked Reuben, managing still to look the smuggler straight in the face.

"Yes, perfectly. I know as how you wouldn't cheat a poor fellow, whatever the others did."

A grim smile broke over Reuben's face.

For that was just what he intended doing.

He did not give Black Bill fifty pounds for nothing.

He had not lost sixty-three guineas before through him without making up his mind to pay himself back.

As for honour, he possessed none.

So it would trouble him very little indeed to take the credit of our hero's capture on himself.

All the foregoing occurred in Black Bill's cave— a cave which Jerry Mizzen and Bob Hauler were well acquainted with, as they had been guilty of many a smuggling transaction together there.

The burly Bill in the action with Captain Tom and Ben Barnacle, had lost seven or eight men.

He did not come off quite so well as he expected.

It had been his intention to surprise the two leaders before they could turn to defend themselves.

But the treacherous moon coming out, revealed his plan too soon.

Yet even then his chance might have been a better one only for the unexpected reinforcement of Bob and Jerry, seconded by the strong arm of the stout ostler, who that night showed the true stuff he was made of ; and who gave Black Bill the blow that stretched him senseless on the beach.

That old Zack's man was engaged in the late encounter by some means or other came to the smuggler's ears, and he vowed to be even the moment he could move, with both him and his master.

"They couldn't have made a worse enemy," said Bill to himself. "Besides, the ostler was the feller as gave me the blow. No other one had a bludgeon in that crowd but him, I'll swear. So let that cursed one-eyed landlord and his miserable servant look out, for they've made a deadly enemy of a man as never forgives nor forgets an injury."

Indeed, the smuggler's mind was agitated by the most bitter and deadly thoughts whenever he reflected on that blow from the ostler's stick.

So he determined to have a revenge that was deadly in its nature.

He could afford to wait for that, too; for one of Black Bill's cardinal virtues was patience.

The time Reuben Harpy was with him he was alone in the cave.

Therefore, the conversation they had was undisturbed.

"The fact is," said Reuben, resuming their talk after a minute or two's pause, "the fact is, Bill, only for those cursed buccaneers, Bob Hauler and Jerry Mizzen, we could have taken the ' Will-o'-the-Wisp ' nicely."

"You are right. They spoiled that little game to a dead sartinty. Curse 'em! there's bad blood atween us, and it must be drawn sooner or later. I owe that villain Bob one for the thrashing he gave me in the Blue Lobster. And I'm not the cove to forget such things in a hurry."

"Certainly not. I don't blame you a bit, Bill. But that accursed vessel disappeared very soon after they escaped in the boat."

"Admiral Ellis made a mull o' the whole thing,' said Bill. "He waited a little too long, and the brig, of course, got away, as one might naturallye x- pect it to. I wonder old Ellis ain't a little sharper arter all the experience he's had. I know if I was commander, the whole lot would be bagged by this. But curse these delays! they never comes to no good," added the smuggler, with a bitter oath.

"That is true," replied Reuben. "But Ellis will take the 'Will-o'-the-Wisp' yet. He has cruisers by this time all round the coast."

"What good is that?" grumbled Bill. "The brig is far enough away from any point on the coast by this time."

"Perhaps I know a little more of the movements of the brig than you do."

"Perhaps so," replied the smuggler. "But it is not likely that it will risk capture. But hark! some one comes! I hope it ain't any of them 'ere revenue chaps."

"Don't forget Admiral Ellis," rejoined Reuben. "You have nothing to fear now, whatever you had done before in the shape of smuggling."

The cause of the interruption soon presented him- self.

Dan Seadrift, and a pitiable sight he looked.

He was almost as pale and haggard as the wounded smuggler.

His clothes were torn, and his face covered over with scratches.

"What, Dan Seadrift!" cried Bill, his face light- ing up with some animation.

"Yes, Bill, Dan Seadrift; and a nice-looking picture he looks, too. But what is the matter with you? It seems as how you've fared a deuced sight worse than even I."

"I might as well ask you the same question, Dan, as you yourself looks a pretty-looking sight. I thought we sent you after that 'ere Captain Tom and his lieutenant, and it appears to me as how you've been enjoying yourself in getting drunk, and having yer face scratched by some o' them 'ere Portsmouth gals."

"Well, it does look something like it," replied Dan, ruefully. "But beg yer pardon, sir," turning to Reuben. "I think I've seen your phizog some- where before."

"That's very likely," replied Tom's villainous cousin. "Admiral Ellis's, perhaps?"

There was a quiet sneer on Reuben's lips.

"That hundred-pound note business," said Sea- drift; "I remember it well. Ha! ha! ha! That little rascal of an admiral had me there. I don't blame him much, for all that, as he himself was sold. I should like to catch that feller as sold him. It would be a great pleasure, that meeting, I can tell you."

Reuben trembled as he saw the devilish look that came into Dan Seadrift's face.

He thought, indeed, that that gentleman looked at him more or less suspiciously.

"Do you think I had any hand in the affair?" he asked.

"The affair of the hundred-pound note?"

"Yes."

"Well, I shouldn't like to say as you had."

"Well, I must tell you that I had not, so don't blame me for what took place there."

"Of course not," said Bill. "Dan has too much sense for that, I should think. Mr Harpy is a gen- tleman, Dan, and I've known him since he was a little boy, and I've never known anything wrong of him," this only with a too perceptible sneer. "So mind you, comrade, there must be no ill feeling in the matter."

"Decidedly not. But I'd like to know who got that hundred-pound note."

"Well, if yer werry particular in knowing, I'll tell yer."

And with that the smuggler entered into an account, as far as he was able, of the neat way in which sly Peter managed the whole thing.

"A nice genelman is that 'ere Peter," said Dan, when he had done. "Would like to make his acquaintance very much. Where does he put up at?"

"It is not unlikely but you'll find him at the Yellow Alligator to-night, if you go there," said Reuben.

"But, mind, he's a rough customer," put in Bill. "Manage to fleece him of the fifty pounds, and we'll divide."

"We'll speak of that when I get the note," said Dan, slyly. "I'll be off to the Yellow Alligator to-night, and I'll not leave it empty-handed, depend upon it. What kind of a-looking chap is he?"

A description was given at this point of Peter's looks.

"That will do," said Dan. "I'll know the cove the minute I see him."

No allusion was made to Peter after this.

That Dan Seadrift was to become the possessor of that gentleman's fifty-pound note was finally settled; at least, in Dan's own mind.

"Now, Dan," said Black Bill, "how is it that you didn't follow that 'ere Tom Drake and his lieutenant up?"

"I did follow 'em up."

"You look as if you had been on a jolly good spree instead."

"Do I? Well, I have not. I followed the two coves through the wood. But that 'ere cursed moon would come out, and they discovered me, and this is the result," said Dan, pointing ruefully to his face. "That was done by forcing me through a hole in the hedge, as you could hardly put an infant through. But not content with this, what else do you think they did?"

"Tell us, Dan—tell us, and don't be asking us to guess," cried Bill.

"Well, they just tied me up to a tree until they could send some o' their cursed buccaneers to fetch me. I thought they'd have done what they said. But they never did so. And there I remained until within three hours since."

"You don't really mean to pitch that yarn?" cried Black Bill, hardly believing him.

"Well, here I am to prove it. Do I look like a man as had a morsel of anything in him for a week? Look at my jaws! They were full and round when I left. They are holler enough now, aren't they?"

"And you were tied all that time up to the tree?" said Reuben with a slight shudder.

"Yes, I was; but here I am, with a little life left in me yet. I had a little o' bread and cheese, and that is all ever since. You see, they had me in a disused meadow, gagged as well as bound, so that there was no chance o' getting away, or crying out, either. Only for a countryman happening by accident to come into the field, I'd have starved and perished outright, and none would be the wiser until they picked up my skeleton. Curse Tom Drake, and curse his lieutenant! I have suffered enough through 'em, at all events."

"Never mind," said Bill, "I have had reason enough to curse 'em, too. You see how Tom Drake and his pals have laid me up, but now they are in limbo, and a few days will see the last of both of 'em."

"What! do you mean to say they are collared?" cried Dan, leaping up.

"That's just what I do mean," said Bill.

"Hurrah!"

"Don't make a row, Dan! I say they are in

limbo—in a strong prison in Portsmouth, just waiting the day of execution."

Dan Seadrift's ugly face beamed with fierce pleasure, for the sufferings he endured in the disused meadow were not to be soon forgotten.

"I have as much hatred for Ben Barnacle if not more than for Captain Tom," said Black Bill. "I should like to do one thing, however."

"What is that?" asked Reuben.

"I should like to have the executing of that cursed Ben in my own hands."

"No!"

"I would, though. I'd give fifty pounds out of the reward to string him up myself."

"Very well, then," said Reuben. "It is most likely Admiral Ellis will give you that pleasure. However, I'll speak the matter over to him."

"Do so, Mr. Harpy, and see if I don't torture him at the last moment. I have just a little account of years' standing to settle with him. He hasn't forgot that account, I don't believe. If he has, I haven't, that's all."

The smuggler's haggard face, as he spoke, lit up with a great deal of malignance and wickedness combined.

As there was an ample supply of provisions in the cave, Dan Seadrift, at the instigation of Black Bill, set about preparing a meal, which he soon got ready, and almost as quickly disposed of.

After a little more conversation, Reuben left the cave, and as the smuggler had his suspicions, he sent Dan Seadrift to dog his steps and report progress.

That gentleman was not at all averse to following the ex-privateer.

And he moreover determined not to be caught napping this time, as in the case of Captain Tom and his lieutenant.

But notwithstanding all his caution, Dan Seadrift came to grief.

In fact, fell into the hands of a party of coastguards, who recognised him as a man they had been on the search of for some time.

Dan struggled hard.

But his struggles availed him little.

He was finally bound, gagged, and was soon aboard a coastguard lugger, where he was as quickly put in irons.

CHAPTER CXC.

ADMIRAL ELLIS INFORMED OF CAPTAIN TOM'S ATTEMPTED ESCAPE.

REUBEN HARPY'S course after that was uninterrupted, as there was no Dan Seadrift to follow him.

He reached Admiral Ellis's in good time, was admitted, and found the little admiral in very high spirits indeed.

Reuben, after partaking of a glass of wine with the malicious little fellow, opened the conversation at once with his late gallant exploit of capturing Captain Tom.

The admiral was not at first inclined to believe him.

At least, he looked upon his valorous account with some doubt.

But as Reuben protested with considerable energy, Ellis partly changed his opinion, and gave him credit for some of the results of the encounter.

"It was a hard fight, I can tell you, admiral," said Reuben. "We had from twenty to thirty buccaneers to deal with, if we had one, and only for a dozen or so of them escaping in a boat when a reinforcement came up, we should have had the 'Will-o'-the-Wisp,' too, by this time."

"Who composed the reinforcement?" asked Ellis, doubtingly.

"Well, we can hardly tell—the night, you see, admiral, was dark, some say fishermen, others a boat's crew of the 'Will-o'-the-Wisp's' men. However, we had little time to find out, as we had enough to do to look after our prisoners."

"Truly. But who lays claim to the reward of this capture?" asked Ellis.

"Well, I can see no more fitting person than your humble servant. I care very little for the money," added Reuben, averting his eyes; "but he who claims the honour of the capture must also claim the money, I suppose. Whatever he does afterwards with it is another matter."

The little admiral was not to be deceived.

He saw through Reuben at a glance, and from that moment resolved to sift the matter thoroughly, as he had still some doubts that Harpy was entitled to the reward.

After a few more words, they parted.

As the reader might anticipate, Reuben took good care to keep the name of Black Bill out of the conversation.

For a very good reason, indeed, he never alluded to him at all.

Next night was the night on which Captain Tom and his lieutenant was to escape.

Reuben had dropped into the admiral's rath, early in the evening, and through the frightful storm that was raging, he had to stay there until it was over.

Nine o'clock, and then ten passed, and the tempest raged as furiously as ever.

Admiral Ellis was very silent.

Even thoughtful.

The roll of the thunder, the intense flashes of lightning, the hoarse moans of the wind, and the patter of the rain had no interest whatever for him, nor did they even call one remark from his lips.

But there was something, however, that had a different effect.

The noise of hurrying steps as they came quickly up the stairs.

The admiral leaped to his feet, and just at the same moment there came a double tap at the door.

"Come in!" cried Ellis.

The door opened, and Bromley entered.

Bromley, with a cat-like stealth, closed the door behind him.

"What now, Bromley?" asked the admiral.

The spy looked for a moment at Reuben.

"You need not hesitate," said the admiral, who understood that look.

"Very well, yer honour," replied Bromley. "Some information regarding Tom Drake."

"Anything of importance?"

"Of great importance yer honour."

"What is it, then? Be quick!"

"It has just come to my knowledge, admiral, that there is an attempt being made to get Captain Tom Drake out of prison to-night."

"What!" reared Ellis. "An attempt to get Tom Drake out of prison? By Heaven, Bromley, perhaps he's already out!"

"No fear of that, sir."

"Why do you say 'no fear?'"

"Because they've not had the time to do it, yer honour."

"Are there many of them, then?" asked Ellis.

"Only a few. But they are cunning knaves, and think they are doing a big thing. They'll, however, find themselves mistaken, for I've—"

"What, Bromley?"

"Set a couple of fellers on their track, yer honour, who'll stick to them like wax. I'll tell you how I got the information, if you like, admiral."

"No time for that now, Bromley," cried Ellis, impatiently. "While you are telling your story these fellows may be escaping. Let me see, what's to be done?"

The little admiral paused, and reflected.

"I have it!" he cried. "Be off at once, Bromley, and get a couple of dozen marines and blue-jackets together. Here is my written order to that effect."

The admiral scribbled a few lines on some paper, and handed it to the spy.

Bromley, without a word, was going to leave the room, when Ellis called him back.

"Take a glass of brandy before you go. The night is cold and wet."

Bromley took the glass of brandy, and then left the apartment.

"That man is worth his weight in gold," observed Ellis, admiringly. "He has very little to say, and what he takes in hand he always goes through with it. He never fails in anything he undertakes."

"It would be a very lamentable thing, indeed," rejoined Reuben, "if Tom Drake gets away after all our trouble to take him."

"Very," replied the admiral. "But I think there's not much fear of that. But what a night is is!" added Ellis, for the first time going to one of the windows, and drawing the blinds aside. "A fine night for an escape, truly."

"Especially an escape from prison," said Reuben. "To tell you the truth, I have a strange presentiment that this daring buccaneer will get away."

"To-night?"

"It might be to-night."

"Well, presentiments can't altogether be disregarded. Come, sir, will you start with me for the prison at once, and see that the fellow *doesn't* escape?"

Reuben would certainly prefer staying where he was.

But what would the little martinet think of him if he objected?

Put him down as a paltry coward, as a man of no energy, or something worse.

Reuben, therefore, had no choice left him in the matter but to agree to follow the admiral out into the storm.

With seeming alacrity he leaped to his feet, and said he was ready to go at once.

"Very well, Mr. Harpy," replied Ellis; "and now for the marines and blue-jackets. Follow me."

Ellis hastily left the apartment, followed by Reuben.

They soon passed out the front door of the little admiral's residence, and thus into the street.

The storm still raged violently.

The rain came down in torrents.

The thunder screeched hoarsely above them, and every now and then a great flash of lightning, lighting up the murk of the night, dazed them almost to blindness.

Reuben shivered from top to toe, and drew his cloak closer round him, while the admiral, as if he had been used to such storms all his life, went on through the torrents of rain, the lightning and thunder, without a shiver or even a remark.

He walked so quickly, that Reuben found it difficult to keep pace with him.

At length they arrived at the barracks, just in time to catch Bromley passing through the gate with his two dozen men.

The light of the two large lamps lit up the huge drops of rain that fell and reflected on the tarnished matchlocks of the marines as they passed beneath them.

The blue-jackets had their cutlasses in their sheaths, but the butts of their huge navy pistols peeped out from beneath their jackets.

"Halt!" cried Ellis.

They knew the old admiral's voice, and came to a standstill.

"Bromley!"

Bromley stepped forward.

"You know the nearest route to the prison?"

"Yes, yer honour."

"Back to your place, then. You lead the detachment!"

The spy stepped back.

"Forward! march!" cried the admiral.

And the men were again in motion.

On through the pelting rain and hoarse gusts of wind.

The regular tramp of drilled men broke on the storm-tossed night air, and the sounds were borne away and lost in the distance.

Many a solitary watchman peeped out half-drowsily from his box to see them go by, wondering where in the world they could be going at such an hour, and on such a night.

They puzzled their brains in vain.

The marines and blue-jackets passed by, and were swallowed in the darkness.

But Admiral Ellis was doomed to meet an adventure before he got to the prison.

Passing down one of the narrow lanes a quarter of a mile from the gaol, the admiral's ears were saluted by deep groans that proceeded from one side of the street.

The men heard them likewise, but without pausing, were passing on.

Ellis's curiosity was, however, aroused.

Perhaps it was some poor creature wounded, and dying in the storm.

Whatever little humanity the admiral had was shown on this occasion.

He called for the marines and blue-jackets to halt.

They did so.

The groans rung out louder.

Every part of the lane was pitchy-dark.

At that moment, however, a brilliant flash of lightning lit up the murk and revealed to the admiral's eyes, and those of his men, a huddled human form lying on one side of the road.

The figure of a man, seeming to be enduring all the agonies of dissolution.

The flash was only momentary, and passing away left the street as dark as before.

"Some unfortunate creature dying, perhaps," said Ellis. "It's our duty to see who it is, and do what we can for him."

It fortunately happened that there were two or three dark lanterns in the company.

These were called into use at once.

A great glare of light soon streamed across the street as the admiral, Reuben, and a subaltern of the marines approached the spot where the man lay.

A glance sufficed to prove that he belonged to the better classes of society.

Another look showed he was wounded in the left breast, as he lay partly on his right side, groaning with pain, and almost huddled up like a hedgehog.

The poor wounded wretch was conscious of the presence of those who came up, however.

The light of one of the lamps lit up his livid features.

Such a look of agony Reuben had never before seen.

The face was that of a young man not yet twenty-four, and his hair, drenched by the rain as it was, was fine and as black as jet.

The gory stream of life was ebbing rapidly from his wound. It was only too evident that he had very little longer to live.

"He's past our aid, sir," said the subaltern,

saluting Ellis. "We can do nothing for him, so, in my humble opinion, the best thing is to push on."

"Silence, sir!" cried the admiral.

The marine officer felt the reproof, and drawing back abashed, said no more.

Ellis bent down, and examined the man's wound.

The poor wretch turned his dying eyes upon him with a most pitiful, imploring expression.

"He is past all hope," murmured the admiral "The wound is mortal."

"Shot down by some robber or assassin," said Reuben, shudderingly. "The streets of Portsmouth are not very safe, even on such a night as this."

The wounded man endeavoured to speak.

But the words at first died away in his throat.

"He wishes to speak," said Reuben. "If he only could we might, perhaps, find out something about him."

"True," said Ellis. "We'll see what effect this will have."

And he produced a flask from one of his pockets It was three parts full of brandy.

Screwing the top off, he forced a little of the liquor between the dying man's parched lips.

There was a strange gurgle in his throat.

They all thought it was his last.

But they were mistaken.

The brandy revived him.

Enabled him, indeed, to speak, but in so low a tone at first that his words were scarcely audible, even to the admiral, who was bent over him.

At last the words grew more distinct, the voice stronger.

"Is—is there no hope?" he asked of Ellis. "Am—am I really dying?"

"I am sorry to say you have very few moments more to live," replied the admiral. "Therefore if you have anything to say I'd advise you to do so while you yet have the use of your speech."

"Oh, God!" groaned the wounded man. "More! more, for God's sake!"

He pointed with a look of dying despair at Ellis's flask.

The admiral held the vessel to his lips, and he drank greedily of its contents.

But he went beyond his strength.

His eyes glazed.

An unnatural gurgle in his throat announced that he was a corpse.

The lamp was held closer to his face.

But the features were rigid, the eyes glazed, and then they knew in reality that he was dead.

"The brandy has killed him," said the admiral. "He swallowed too much, and we can do no more for him."

"Is there no possibility of discovering who he is?" ventured Reuben.

"I forgot that," said Ellis. "Bromley! Come this way a minute!"

Bromley, who had been grumbling heartily at the delay, left the ranks, and stepped forward.

"Yer honour?"

"Did you ever see this poor fellow's face before?" asked the admiral.

The spy looked narrowly at the rigid features by the aid of the lamp.

"I think I have, admiral," he replied, after a few moments' scrutiny; "but where I can't just now say. However, it will not take me a minute to find out."

Saying so, Bromley bent over the corpse, and began turning out his pockets in so professional a manner, that one would think that he had been used all his life to robbing the dead.

Those who followed his movements drew back in disgust.

Bromley at last turned out a heavy pocket-book. "Ha! ha! Here's a clue at last!" cried he.

Exhibiting the contents of the pocket-book was the work of a moment.

These were varied.

Two ten-pound Bank of England notes.

Four or five guineas in gold.

Some silver.

A half-dozen letters, the envelopes of which were addressed to the great Portsmouth diamond merchant and jeweller who was murdered a few days before, together with a little well-padded case, containing some jewellery, perhaps.

Here was a discovery, indeed!

The astute Bromley rubbed his hands in glee.

They had all heard of the murder of the wealthy old jeweller.

Indeed, it still caused the greatest excitement in Portsmouth.

Detectives had been sent out to get a clue of the murderer, but in vain.

Here, however, was a clue at last.

It was no wonder, then, that the spy rubbed his hands so ecstatically.

That the young man who lay a corpse at his feet had something to do with the said murder, he was convinced.

Slowly he opened the case.

What a dazzling radius of light flashed out in the glare of the lamps!

The brilliancy nearly blinded them.

It was a very unexpected sight to Bromley, and self-possessed as he was, he let the case and its contents fall in his excitement.

The lamps were lowered.

What met their astonished eyes?

The great Sea Emerald, that had been sold to the old jeweller a few days before, and for which he was murdered!

· · · · ·

We may now return for a brief time to Peter and the sham sentinel, whom we left at the Yellow Alligator, engaged over their game of cards.

Several times had the sham sentinel caught Peter in the act of cheating, and the reader may be sure that this sort of work did not improve his temper.

In fact, from discussing the merits and demerits of the game, they were nearly coming to blows, and would have done so, too, when their attention—fortunately, perhaps, for themselves—was attracted in another direction.

They heard the name of Captain Tom mentioned, and, looking round, saw a little dark man, of a decidedly seafaring look, haranguing six or seven others who surrounded him.

In truth, as he had mentioned our hero's name, they had a great desire to know what this was all about.

Nor were they long in discovering.

The little man was recounting to his companions one of Captain Tom's adventures, and as this was the case it made it all the more interesting to their ears.

And so they listened to the following:—

"Yes, gents, it was one of the most remarkable perils that ever this extraordinary young man ever passed through.

"The account will be very brief, but none the less interesting.

"I was a smuggler at the time, as many of you here already know.

"And one of my pals took a violent dislike to the captain.

"I can't tell you what it was for, but he determined to have his revenge on him; and knowing where Tom put up at the time, he got a young ballet girl into his confidence, to act in concert with him.

"Now, you must know that this young woman was as beautiful as a wax figure, but had the heart of a very demon, for all that.

"In fact, she had been married before she was fifteen, but taking a dislike to her husband, one night coolly and deliberately poisoned him.

"All this my pal knew, and being, though a big fellow, a little bit of a coward, he thought he could not do better than to get this female fiend to act as his accomplice.

"At first, she objected rather strongly.

"But as he threatened to disclose what he knew about her to the police in case she held out, she finally consented, and so one night away both of them went, effected an entrance into the house where Captain Tom was staying, and each armed with a dagger, they proceeded to the chamber where he slept.

"Pushing back some tapestry, they entered his bed-room, and would, in all likelihood, have despatched him there and then only for a singular occurrence that took place.

' It was this, gents.

"It so happened that a fine Newfoundland dog that Captain Tom had petted very much got, by some means or other, into his room that night, and being, like all such animals, very watchful, he heard the woman's footstep, light though it was, and leaped up instantly, and pinned my pal, the smuggler, before he could make even one movement to get away from him.

"Seeing the dog at the throat of her accomplice, the woman screamed at the top of her voice, and so awoke the captain, who, at the best of times, was only a light sleeper.

"Of course he leaped out of his bed at once, and confronted his would-be murderers.

"Nor was he a little surprised to see her companion in the Newfoundland's clutches.

"I must only tell you this, that the buccaneer was too bold and brave a man to make war on a woman, even though she came for such a purpose; but he was determined not to call the dog off until he throttled—perhaps I may use that expression, gents—her accomplice.

"My pal had no chance with the dog, and the more he cried out the faster it held on to him, until there was not a breath left in his body.

"And when Tom called the dog off he was dead.

"After showing the woman quietly to the door, and removing the dead body into the passage, he went back to his bed again, and slept as quietly as if nothing had happened.

"And so ends my story, genelmen."

CHAPTER CXCI.

HOW BOB AND JERRY SERVE THE TWO SPIES AND THE WARDER —THE SUMMONS AT THE GATE OF THE PRISON.

We now return to Bob and Jerry.

We must admit that our gallant friends, the buccaneers, were somewhat surprised by this sudden and unexpected onslaught made upon them at the ending of a prior chapter.

But they had no time to think.

They were assailed with such vigour that, for a time, it seemed very likely that one of the men's words would come literally true, and that it would be entirely beyond their or their leader's power to leave the prison.

What a fix!

But our buccaneers were not disheartened for all that.

There was more, much more, depending on them than their own liberty.

The liberty of Captain Tom and his brave lieutenant and Harry Vere.

So, when they were attacked, they turned round on their assailants and defended themselves as well as they could in the darkness of the passage.

They could not even distinguish the faces of the men who attacked them.

But they were quite sure that their assailants we none of the men whom they had left to all all intents and purposes senseless and speechless in the warders' room.

They were sure that they had disposed of these in such a way that they would not recover for some hours.

Bob, still defending himself, tried a ruse.

"Treachery—treachery!" he cried, in an assumed voice. "The villains mean surprising the prison. Draw yer cutlass, comrade, and we'll soon make short work of them."

Of course, as Jerry had no cutlass, he could not draw one.

Bob was in the same plight.

But strange to say, Bob's ruse had some effect.

Their assailants, thinking that they might be mistaken after all in their men, paused in their furious attack.

As they both had stout bludgeons, and knew well how to wield them, Bob and Jerry were not sorry that they did so.

"Who are you, then?" said one of the men.

"Who are we?" cried Bob. "Dare you ask, you brace of cowardly murderers? Who are we? That's a fine question! Come, comrade, stand on no ceremony. Draw your cutlass, and hack the villains down!"

"Hold!" cried one of the men. "There's a mistake somewhere."

"I should think there was," said Jerry.

"The mistake is on their side," added Bob. "We'll learn 'em not to assault warders in the execution o' their duty afore they leave this prison! Come, surrender, or else we'll cut you down!"

"Come, come," said the man. "You are mistaken in us entirely. We took you for the buccaneers who came to help Captain Tom to escape."

"What!" roared Bob. "Captain Tom escape! Do you hear that, comrade? Where's that parson chap?"

"He's giving consolation to the unhappy prisoner," replied Jerry; "and a werry nice sort o' gentleman he seems to be, too "

"You are mistaken; he's not a parson at all," said the man.

"What!" cried Jerry. "You don't mean that?"

"Yes, I do; he's a buccaneer!"

"A buccaneer!" cried Bob and Jerry, in a breath.

"I thought there was something willainous about him," said Bob. "But who, then, are the other coves?"

"They are also buccaneers. They have been playing a fine game in the prison while you have been talking here. Every man in the warders' room is either asleep or dead drunk. But there may be time yet to secure the villains. Lead the way to the cell, and if four of us can't master them, I'm a Dutchman, that's all."

Bob and Jerry, all this time, had been edging nearer and nearer to them.

The place was quite dark, or nearly so.

Which fact was of considerable advantage to our buccaneers, who approached them without the others being at all suspicious of their movements.

"Let us on," said the man. "Admiral Ellis will be here soon with a force, no doubt, of marines and blue-jackets."

This was certainly information for our two friends.

THE MASSIVE BARS SHIVERED LIKE GLASS UNDER THE BUCCANEER'S BLOWS.

What they had to do now must be done quickly.

The old comrades had signalled to each other, in spite of the darkness of the passage.

When they thought they got near enough, with a bound they were on their two late assailants, and pinned them before they could utter a word.

The heavy bludgeons were wrenched from their hands, and in an instant their late owners were felled insensible.

"That's the way to sarve the varmints!" said Bob. "Now, Jerry, old pal, you take one, and I'll take the other. And we'll drag them in the direction of Captain Tom's cell. We haven't much time to spare. Werry glad we got the news of little Ellis's movements."

"When he comes to the prison he'll find the birds have flown," said Jerry. "Won't that be grand sport! Heave away, Bob! Off with your man, and I'll follow ye."

The two buccaneers now put out some of their great strength and carried the insensible men down the passage to the cell in which Captain Tom and Ben Barnacle were incarcerated.

But there was another obstacle to be surmounted.

The half-drunken warder who kept watch in the corridor.

Bob and Jerry, when they got to the end of the dark passage, put down their loads, laying their men up against the wall while they attended to the wants of the other gentleman.

" Now," said Bob. " I suppose these 'ere fellers 'll stay quiet until we settle the warder ?"

Jerry had no doubt but they would.

So the two buccaneers crept on until they got to the corridor.

A peep round the corner satisfied them that the warder was on the alert.

Whether this individual was suspicious or not there was no telling.

But Bob and Jerry caught him listening at the door of Captain Tom's cell.

" He's an honourable cove, he is," said Bob, " listening to other's people's talk. What's best to be done, old pal ?"

" Done !" cried Jerry. " Why, rush upon him at once, to be sure."

" He has a cutlass."

" I see he has. Take it from him."

" We have neither cutlass nor pistol."

" Well, if we take his, we'll have one between us."

" You're a wise man, Jerry. It's easy to say take it from him ; but it's another thing to do it. No, I've a better idea."

" Do you think he suspects anything ?"

" I don't know, but here goes !" said Bob. " Be as drunk as you can, Jerry."

" We ought to be, arter all that liquor we took."

" Sartinly."

" Well, come on, then !"

" I am with you. Lead the way. You are supposed to be the drunkest, and I only two sheets in the wind !"

The old comrades now staggered into the corridor.

Jerry appeared very drunk.

Bob was little better.

Their unsteady gait alarmed the warder.

And he straightened up from his listening attitude instantly.

Bob saw at a glance that he suspected nothing.

" Keep up, comrade," hiccoughed Bob, " it'll never do for the Reverend Ebenezer to catch you like that."

" All right, comrade," replied Jerry, " a-attend b yer own business—hic ! I don't want any o' your interference."

" Hallo ! What's this ?" cried the warder, who was rather under the influence himself. " Been taking a little too much grog, old fellows ?"

" Yes, old feller," replied Bob.

" Who dares say I'm drunk," cried Jerry. " I am—hic !—as sober as a judge. I'll bring you— hic !—all up for defermation o' charicter."

" Come, come, draw it mild, comrade," replied Bob. " No one's a-insulting of yer. I appeals to the warder if anyone's a-insulting of yer ?"

" No, no, my good friend," cried the warder, staggering forward. " No one says as yer drunk."

" They—hic !—had better not," said Jerry, fiercely.

" Sh !" cried the warder, putting up his hand. " His Reverence is in there, and it won't do for him to hear you, you know."

" Who cares for his Reverence !" hiccoughed Jerry, with pot-valiant ferocity. " Let them as cares for him hold their tongues—not me."

" You ought to be proud of such a good master," remonstrated the warder, still drawing nearer.

" Let them as cares for him be proud of him—I ain't," said Jerry, noisily.

The warder thought this a very good opportunity of further remonstrating with the " irrepressible one," and telling him of the wickedness of his ways.

Who knows but he might step into Jerry's shoes by the manœuvre ?

The situation would be far preferable to the one he held at present.

No doubt the Reverend Ebenezer had already heard the blustering voice of his drunken servant, and was by this time probably disgusted with him.

Now was the time if ever to get into the reverend gentleman's favour.

So forcing his cutlass into its sheath, he walked straight up to Jerry and Bob.

This was what the " irrepressible one " and his comrade most desired.

On he came.

Bob staggered from side to side.

While Jerry grew very noisy, and began to roll out the first notes of one of the Reverend Ebenezer's hymns.

The warder held up his hand two or three times to enforce silence.

But Jerry couldn't see it, and continued singing.

At last the warder came up and laid his hand on his shoulder, in a kind, brotherly sort of way, preparatory to delivering him the lecture on the " wickedness of his ways."

The warder was hardly aware of it when he found himself suddenly thrown to the ground, his cutlass taken from him, his hands bound, and an ugly sort of gag forced into his mouth.

It was all done in a minute.

Indeed, before he had time to cry out.

That warder, we will venture to say, was never so much deceived in his life when he saw the two comrades straighten up after their labours perfectly rational and sober.

Jerry now possessed himself of the key of Captain Tom's cell, and unlocked and unbolted the door, and finally threw it open.

Our hero, Ben Barnacle, and Harry Vere, emerged therefrom, an d seemed very much gratified at what they saw.

Bob, as spokesman, now briefly recounted all that occurred.

" So Ellis has got wind of the affair," said Tom; " then it's time to be moving, for he'll be here soon enough."

Bob and Jerry, assisted by Ben Barnacle, did not take more than a few minutes to remove the three men so lately captured.

The two that Bob and Jerry knocked down were still insensible.

And they were carried to Captain Tom's place of late confinement, and shoved in with the warder.

Then the door was relocked, bolted, and the iron bar put up, and thus were they left to reflect on how basely they had been duped.

A few moments after, Captain Tom and his buccaneers were in the warders' room.

Our hero could not help but smile on the joint performance of the comrades.

Every warder in the place lay stretched under the massive table, insensible.

Having had a good laugh at the way in which they had been duped, they were about to leave the prison, when a loud summons at the gate rung into the warders' room.

<hr>

CHAPTER CXCII.

THE ESCAPE.

LOUDLY rang the summons on the prison gate.

Bang ! bang ! bang !

For a moment the buccaneers were astounded.

They knew well what that summons meant, and by whom delivered.

Bang ! bang ! bang !

" Those cursed marines !" cried Jerry. " I am afraid we are too late, Bob."

" I am afraid so, too," said Bob.

Bang! bang! bang!

"They're a devilish impatient lot, to say the least of them," grumbled Bob. "I wish they'd give us just a few minutes to think."

A dark cloud passed over Captain Tom's face.

They all saw it, and, seeing it, gave up every hope.

"There's nothing now to be done but fight for it," said Ben, sadly.

He knew, indeed, that they would never have such an opportunity to escape again.

Each of the buccaneers now armed himself with a cutlass to defend himself to the last.

The summons again rang loudly on the gate.

"What a clatter!" said Bob. "They'll break the gate down if we don't go and answer them."

"Stay!" cried Captain Tom, a sudden thought striking him. "There's a means of escape yet left us."

They saw their chief's face brighten.

And from that they knew that there was some chance still open to them.

Captain Tom's quick eye took in everything in the apartment.

He saw that there was a smaller room—a closet, seemingly—leading from the one occupied by the warders.

The key was in the lock.

He strode over to the door and opened it.

It was not a closet.

It was nearly as large a room as the other—in fact, a store-room, where the employés of the prison stowed away any useless lumber they found about the place.

Captain Tom had his plan formed in a moment.

Giving the buccaneers instructions to carry the insensible warders into the other room, and to clear the tables of cans, bottles, pewter-pots, and glasses, he hurried away to answer the repeated summonses.

One would think that they were going to break the gate down, so loudly did they hammer at it.

Captain Tom drew back the small grating noiselessly, and peeped through.

He could see the glare of two or three lamps flashing about through the darkness and rain, and by their aid he detected the forms of about, as nearly as he could guess, two dozen marines and blue-jackets.

He could see also that the banging noise on the gate was produced by the butts of the marines' matchlocks.

Besides all this, he could see two dark figures standing back from the rest.

A sudden glare from one of the lamps lit up their faces.

They were those of little Ellis and his cowardly and malignant cousin, Reuben Harpy.

"So, so," he thought to himself, "you have come, have you? Very good, my fine cousin; I'll make you suffer for this yet."

Captain Tom now made a noise at the little grating purposely to attract attention.

The loud banging at the gate ceased.

"Who are you?" cried Tom, in a harsh, grating voice, which he assumed for the occasion, "and what do you want?"

"It's about time that you heard us, you rascal!" cried the little admiral, with an angry growl. "You have kept us long enough in the storm here."

"And likely to keep you longer," said Tom, "unless you tell me who you are. We are not to be humbugged in this establishment, I can tell you. Fair words and more civility, master, would suit you a great deal better, believe me."

"Insolent scoundrel!" muttered the admiral. "But it is no use to be annoyed with him. He knows his duty, it is evident. Bromley, I want you!"

The hatchet-faced spy came quickly to the side of his master.

"Tell that saucy rascal what we want, and be as civil as you can in doing so, or else we'll not get in there to-night."

Bromley hurried off, and explained the whole thing to the supposed warder.

"Ah! so it's Admiral Ellis, is it?" said Tom, somewhat mollified. "We expected him a long time ago, and were very much disappointed at his not coming. Two chaps got here some time since with a story about Captain Tom Drake's escape. Glad they did, or else we'd have been placed in a fine fix."

"A hard struggle with the villains, I suppose?"

"You may say that, comrade. It took all the warders, and they have not done yet. I have only just left them, and it's as much as my place is worth to be away from the gate."

"And that is perhaps the reason that you did not hear us," said Bromley. "We have been hammering at the gate these last ten minutes."

"Sorry for you, but can't help that," said Tom. "I suppose it's still raining very hard?"

"Look for yourself," replied the spy.

Captain Tom made all this delay purposely, to give his companions inside a chance to remove the insensible warders and other things that might arouse the suspicions of the little admiral and his party.

It being his intention to admit them.

Indeed, his fertile brain was not at loss to form a bold plan to outwit his malicious little enemy.

Bromley, while Captain Tom was surveying them through the small grating in the gate, had hurried back to Ellis.

He now returned.

"The admiral must be admitted," he said.

"Our rules are strict here. The admiral must wait until I hunt up the governor," replied Tom, "and inform him of his arrival."

Bromley muttered a savage oath.

But he knew that swearing at the supposed gatekeeper would avail him nothing.

So he asked rather civilly how long that gentleman would be before he could come back with an answer.

"Under ten minutes," replied Tom; then, closing the grating, he returned to the buccaneers.

The warders by this were all carried into the other room, and all the drinking utensils on the table were cleared away.

The fire burned as brightly as ever, and the apartment presented a very orderly appearance indeed.

No one in the world would suspect what had been done there that night.

"We have very little time to spare now," said Captain Tom. "Admiral Ellis and about two dozen men are waiting outside to be let in. I told one fellow I'd be back in less than ten minutes, and it won't do to be over that time. Now, listen to my plan."

They all drew round him.

"I mean that they shall come in. Give me that wig and pair of false whiskers, lieutenant."

Harry Vere had brought with him a wig and pair of whiskers to facilitate Captain Tom's escape.

These he handed over to his leader.

Tom passed quickly into the other room and took the clothes off one of the insensible warders.

It was the work of very few moments to attire himself in them.

As there was a looking-glass in the apartment,

he adjusted the wig and whiskers; and there was a complete metamorphosis at once.

And when he buckled on a cutlass to his side, and attached a large bunch of keys to his belt, even his own men would not have known him were they not aware of the fact.

Jerry Mizzen and Bob Hauler were in ecstacies.

They never saw so peculiar a change in any man in the whole course of their lives.

Tom had given his nose a dab of rouge, and he then looked to perfection a swaggering, grog-drinking warder.

"How do I look?" asked the captain, when he had completed his disguise.

"Yer own blessed mother wouldn't know you, yer honour," said Bob. "I never saw sich a complete change in any one in my life."

They all agreed that this was so

"Now listen," said our hero, "to a few instructions that I'm about to give you. Remember, you must lock yourselves in that room. Let me see how the key works."

Tom walked over to the door, locked, and unlocked it.

The key turned in the wards of the lock without giving out the faintest sound.

"That will do," said Captain Tom, returning.

"It may be possible," he went on, "that the little admiral will leave some of his marines and blue-jackets here while he goes to search up the governor and the other warders. In that case, as they are very wet and miserable, I'll get them to put their arms in the rack and draw round the fire. At the words 'Make yourselves comfortable, comrades,' turn the key in the lock, open the door, rush out, and then it will be a matter of no very great difficulty to overpower them. But above all things, be careful how you open the door."

They promised implicit obedience to his instructions.

But Bob, as an after-thought, suggested the drugged liquor that still remained in one of the flasks.

"As they are all sober, it will have an immediate effect on them," said Bob.

As Bob's plan was seconded by the two lieutenants and Jerry Mizzen, Captain Tom adopted it.

The buccaneers now got into the room and locked themselves in, while Tom went back to the gate.

"Hallo!" he called out through the small grating.

"Hallo!" was the response. "Are we to wait here much longer?"

"Admiral Ellis I want, not you," said Tom.

"I am Admiral Ellis," was the reply.

"Oh, yer honour! Beg yer pardon!" said Tom. "I wasn't aware I was addressing you. But the governor—"

"What the deuce does the governor say? Does he mean keeping us here any longer? Perhaps he'll explain his conduct!" cried the irate little admiral.

"That's his business, not mine, yer honour," replied Tom, gruffly. "You see, I'm forced to go by the rules."

"Hang the rules!" cried Ellis. "Are you going to let us in or not?"

"Well, if you only listen, I'll tell you what his honour says. Don't fly into a passion with me. I've nothing to do with it. I'm paid for doing my duty, and if all the admirals in England came here, I couldn't let them in without doing that."

"A deuced impudent fellow!" muttered Ellis, "but a man that will not be swerved from his duty one inch. Hang it! as insolent as he is, I can't help admiring his straightforward, blunt honesty

Well, now, be quick and tell me what your governor said," he added, aloud.

"Well, he says this," replied Tom, "to tell you that he is very sorry to cause you any inconvenience, but that he is at present engaged in seeing to his prisoners, therefore that he cannot come to let you in himself."

"A deuced polite sort of a governor he is," said Ellis.

"You are right, admiral," replied Tom; "very much so, indeed. His politeness 'll never kill him; that's one thing certain."

Tom, without any more delay, opened the gates, and let the whole party in.

The blue-jackets and marines were in very bad humour, and Admiral Ellis, Reuben Harpy, and Bromley were in little better.

They were all drenched to the skin.

Captain Tom kept his eye on Reuben Harpy, anticipating a chance now of paying him in full for all he had done.

Following at the heels of our hero, they all walked into the warders' room, where their eyes were gladdened by a big, roaring fire.

But Admiral Ellis was too much of a martinet to take more than a passing glance at it.

He demanded at once where the governor was.

Tom told him that he had strict orders from his honour not to leave the vicinity of the gate any more that night.

Ellis looked narrowly at him.

Tom bore the scrutiny well.

There was such a look of conscious integrity and independence in his face that the admiral was satisfied that he had a man of more than ordinary will, power, and honesty to deal with.

Tom's disguise was admirable.

And his voice suited his disguise.

"I'll direct yer honour," said Tom, "and that's all I can do."

And our hero with that sent him by the longest route to the cell he so lately occupied himself.

Down a lot of puzzling passages.

Some dark, some light, but the whole forming a labyrinthian maze that would puzzle a dozen admirals all done up in one.

Ellis listened, and was going to expostulate.

But what was the use of expostulating?

It would, he knew, be lost on such a man as the supposed warder.

So he gave up the task in despair.

Not wishing to waste more time, he left four of the marines in the warders' room (as Tom anticipated) to keep watch there, while he pushed on with the rest to assist the governor, if he found that necessary, or to taunt Captain Tom with the force he had at his command.

Our hero led him to believe that quite likely his assistance would be needed.

To Tom's regret, Reuben Harpy accompanied the admiral, so that put it out of his power to retaliate on Reuben for his treachery.

Now, as Captain Tom knew that he had very little time to spare, he set about his work at once.

He got the four marines to put their match-locks in the arm-rack.

They were not proof against a good fire, nor were they proof against the flask of drugged liquor.

They swallowed every drop, and would have swallowed more, no doubt, had there been any left.

Tom, in a few moments, saw that the brandy—for brandy it was—was beginning to take effect.

The marines showed every symptom of drowsiness, and, of course, ascribed it to the heat of the fire.

Captain Tom, however, ascribed it to another thing—the drugged contents of the flask.

But he could not afford to wait too long for even that to take effect.

So he uttered the magical words—

"Make yourselves comfortable, comrades!"

In an instant the door of the other room was noiselessly opened, and the four marines, before they knew it, were pounced upon and hurled to the floor.

Their resistance, if they had been allowed to make any, would, in any event, have been a very feeble one, as the drugged liquor had already taken great effect on them.

"Now, bind and bundle them into the other room," said Tom.

They were bound accordingly.

That part of the business, however, was scarcely necessary, for by the time the buccaneers lifted them from the floor they were thoroughly insensible.

They were thrown into the inner apartment, notwithstanding this fact.

But as the buccaneers were about leaving the warders' room, a face looked in at the door, a smile full of triumph in it.

That face was Bromley's!

CHAPTER CXCIII.

THE PURSUIT.

"It's no use!" cried Bromley. "It's all up with you, my lads! You may as well give in quietly, and—"

Whatever else he might have said was rudely interrupted by a blow from Bob Hauler's fist.

"Take that, you varmint!" cried Bob.

If the blow had taken proper effect, our five friends could have walked out of the prison there and then, and Admiral Ellis and his party would have been none the wiser of it.

But, as it happened, the spy was expecting something of the kind, and, by adroitly stepping back, he, in a measure, saved himself.

The buccaneer's brawny fist, nevertheless, staggered him.

"Help! help! Murder!" cried Bromley.

"Silence the infernal whelp!" hissed Jerry, rushing forward, and aiming another blow at the spy.

Bromley, however, saved himself by retreating into the passage, and bellowing at the top of his voice for assistance.

"Help! help!" he cried. "The prisoners are escaping!"

Bob Hauler was going to fire his pistol at the fellow when Captain Tom stopped him.

The ring of hurrying footsteps was heard echoing along the passage.

It was Admiral Ellis and his party, alarmed by the cries of the spy, returning to see what was the matter.

Captain Tom and his few buccaneers had no time to lose, if they wanted to escape, so, at a word from Tom, they were out of the warders' room in a moment.

Fortunately, our hero had the ponderous key of the gate on him.

With a bound forward, he was not a moment in opening it, and all would have gone well had not a little incident occurred as they were passing out of the gate, which, for the time being, put Captain Tom and his little party in great jeopardy.

There were two or three blue-jackets left secretly to guard the outside, and this was unknown to Tom Drake or any of his men; and these, hearing the cries that still rung out, ran forward to intercept the buccaneers.

Not only that, but Bromley, taking courage from this fact, actually clutched Jerry Mizzen from behind, and fastened a grip on him that our friend couldn't very well shake off.

"Let go, curse you!" cried Jerry, trying a manner of dodges to release himself.

But all to no purpose.

For if he turned to the right, Bromley also turned to the right.

If he turned to the left it was just the same.

The tramp of the approaching marines and blue-jackets rang out more distinctly, and Jerry, finding himself unable to get away from the clutches of the spy, ground his teeth in despair.

And still Bromley continued to cry out—

"Help! help! The prisoners are escaping!"

"Cursed whelp!" cried Jerry, "you won't release me, won't you! Bob! Bob! I say!"

Bob heard the cries of his old comrade, and wondered what was wrong with him, for they were all out of the prison gate some time before, while Captain Tom and Ben Barnacle were hotly engaged with the two blue-jackets.

These were stout, stalwart men, and as brave as they were powerful, so that our hero and his lieutenant had as much as they could do for a time to defend themselves from their furious attacks.

Bob turned back on hearing his old comrade calling him, and was rather surprised, it must be confessed, to see his helpless situation.

"All right, Jerry," cried Bob. "Don't put yourself out, my lad, I'll soon settle the varmint!"

And thereupon, Bromley soon found himself in a tight fix from which he could not escape, before Bob's ponderous fist made itself acquainted with one side of his face.

Bromley reeled for a moment like a drunken man, and releasing his hold of the irrepressible Jerry, fell in a huddled heap on the hard pavement of the passage.

Jerry was hardly released when two or three of the marines, with fixed bayonets, made their appearance.

"Here they come!" cried Bob. "Now, Jerry, there's no time to be lost!"

The two old comrades, without waiting to see any more of them, bounded for the gate.

The marines halted, levelled their pieces, and fired.

One of the bullets took Jerry Mizzen's hat off.

But in other respects, both the old comrades escaped unhurt.

"Stop, on your lives!" cried a voice (it was Admiral Ellis's) "Stop, or you are dead men!"

"You be blowed!" cried Bob and Jerry, as they leaped through the open gate.

"Forward, men!" cried Ellis. "Remember the reward!"

It now seemed all up with our friends.

But no; there was the key!

"Captain Tom! Captain Tom!" cried Bob, "the key! quick, or the varmints will be through the gate!"

Our hero had only at that instant disposed of his man, and knowing that there was not a moment to be lost, ran forward with the key.

But at the same instant the marines and blue-jackets, under the command of the little admiral, rushed up, and before Bob could pull the gate to, so that Captain Tom could lock it, one of the men inserted his matchlock in the jam of the door, thereby effectually preventing what they most desired.

Nothing more could be done under these unfortunate circumstances, so our hero gave the word for every man to look after himself.

Captain Tom was the last to leave the gate, not, however, before he had fired both his pistols, with what effect in such a hubbub it was impossible for him to discover.

Even the carriage was gone.

So that even this means of escape was cut off from them.

Ben Barnacle, after a tough struggle, had also settled his man, and now he came up to beg of Tom to leave the gate, and let him take his place.

But our hero's instructions in this respect were peremptory, and Ben had to leave him with a sad heart.

Even Bob and Jerry hesitated.

They, however, knew their gallant young chief too well to go against his wishes, so they, as well as the others, appeared to take to their heels, and make the best of their way from the prison walls.

But we shall learn hereafter whether they did so or not.

Now, all this passed in less than a minute.

All evidences of the storm had cleared away, and a few stars were beginning to peep out from the heavens.

Captain Tom now thought it high time for him to make his escape, so, releasing his hold of the gate, he bounded along the road with the speed of the whirlwind.

Some of the marines, who were exerting their strength to pull it open, fell suddenly back among their comrades, and for a time created great confusion.

Admiral Ellis swore himself hoarse, and threatened the men under him with all sorts of vengeance in the event of Captain Tom or any of his buccaneers getting away.

When the bold marines and blue-jackets had sufficiently recovered to rush through the gate, they were greatly surprised to see no one there but the two blue-jackets who had fallen beneath the cutlasses of Captain Tom and Ben Barnacle.

They certainly heard a distant scampering of feet.

And that was all.

"Where's that rascal, Bromley?" cried the little admiral, in great wrath.

He was quickly informed that that "rascal, Bromley," was lying insensible in the passage.

Admiral Ellis stamped on the sodden ground furiously.

The men had never seen him in a greater passion, and this, with his previous threats, was enough to terrify the wits out of them.

While Admiral Ellis was working himself into a fury, our hero and his party had got well under weigh, with little prospect of being retaken.

But the malicious little fellow was not going to let them escape if he could help it, so he ordered his men to run off in different directions, and at all hazards to recapture the fugitives.

He saw the utter uselessness of using threats, so he offered heavy rewards to all who returned successful.

But where had Bob and Jerry gone, meanwhile?

They were not very far away, the reader may be sure.

They heard every word the little admiral uttered, and now was their time to act.

They were resolved to save Captain Tom, and that was principally the reason that they had gone no farther than the prison walls.

"Now, Jerry," said Bob, ' if you only act up to yer old reputation, we'll lead these 'ere marines and blue-jackets a nice little run."

"In other words, a wild-goose chase," replied the irrepressible one. "Do we run together?"

"No, you take one way and I'll take the other, and make as much noise as you can, so as they'll be sure to follow us. Some one took that 'ere blessed carriage, or Captain Tom might have got in it."

"You are right. But about making a noise, Bob?"

"Well, let me see. You have a pistol charged?"

"Yes."

"And I have another. Now, here they come! They bear the distant scampering of steps, so let us lead them off the scent. Fire your pistol, Jerry, when I tell you."

Jerry agreed to do so.

Bob signified that he thought it would be better after all that they should keep together.

Meanwhile, the blue-jackets and marines were told off in fives and sixes.

When they were ready to start, Jerry Mizzen, at the command of his old and trusty comrade, fired his pistol.

The bullet struck the barrel of a matchlock, and sent that arm whizzing out of its owner's hand.

The flash partly lit up Jerry's figure, but so indistinctly that the little admiral, who happened at the moment to be looking that way, could not tell whether it was Captain Tom or his lieutenant.

But he was sure it was one or the other of them.

To heighten the deception, Bob tried to imitate Captain Tom's voice, and did it so well that the little admiral was sure that it was no other than the gallant buccaneer himself.

"After him, men!" thundered Ellis. "It is no other than that rascally buccaneer, Captain Tom. Fifty pounds down to the party who takes him, dead or alive!"

At the word "Forward!" six or seven men dashed out, and Bob and Jerry, as might have been expected, took to their heels.

Several shots were fired after them, all of which, fortunately, in consequence of the darkness, missed their mark.

But this was not the only party which started out in pursuit.

The remaining marines and blue-jackets took other directions, headed by the little admiral, his subaltern, and Reuben Harpy.

Admiral Ellis had, indeed, now no time to look to those of his men who were either killed or insensible, for in his own mind he had more important work on hand, and that the re-capture of our gallant hero, and likewise those who assisted in his escape.

But for the time being we cannot do better than to follow Bob and Jerry, who appeared to be making the most extraordinary efforts to escape the six or seven marines and blue-jackets pursuing them.

But in reality our two good friends were taking the matter very easy, indeed, and laughing in their sleeves at the efforts of their pursuers to come up to them.

As the reader may guess, among their other qualifications, Bob and Jerry were both excellent runners, and the longer the distance the better they ran

The only thing they had to fear now was that they might be intercepted by others, who, alarmed by the shots from matchlocks and pistols, might appear on the scene at any moment.

More especially the old seaport's night watch might be on the alert, and any meeting with them would, no doubt, prove fatal.

Indeed, preclude all possibility of escape.

"I reckon we must bring this kind of work to an end," said Bob. "We have led 'em far enough from Captain Tom and the others by this time, and there is no fear of their recapturing 'em."

"Do you think they're all after us, then?" asked Jerry.

"No doubt of it."

"Now, there's wher' I think you make a mistake."

"Why do you think that?"

THE PURSUIT.

79

"For this reason. In my opinion, Admiral Ellis is not such a fool as to send every available man he has after Captain Tom, even though he should suppose one of us to be him. Don't you see that?"

"I think you are right, Jerry," replied Bob. "There are others to be taken besides our gallant leader."

"Bob Hauler and Jerry Mizzen, for instance."

"Precisely. But Bob Hauler and Jerry Mizzen are not the principal individuals—there's the two lieutenants."

"True, Jerry; I was almost forgetting that. Then we must give these fellows the go-by, I suppose?"

"Yes."

"How many do you think there are of 'em?"

"Not more'n six or seven. Listen! See if you can tell by the tramp of their feet."

The two buccaneers paused a moment.

But only a moment.

The next they were satisfied that the pursuing party did not exceed that number.

"Stop 'em! Stop 'em!" yelled the voices behind.

A couple of match-locks were fired.

The din was terrific, for they were now running along a very narrow street.

The bullets, as usual, however, missed our two friends, but the reports had, nevertheless, the effect of bringing several night-capped heads to their bed-room windows, to find out the cause of the disturbance.

"This won't do," thought Bob. "We'll be in the clutches of some of the night watch afore long, if all this firing and shouting is allowed to continue."

"Stop! Stop the rascals!" yelled the voices of the marines and blue-jackets, who came along the street panting from their exertions.

Now, it so happened that an old night watchman who, being awake at the time, and hoping to distinguish himself, rushed out of his box, in order to bar the progress of our two friends.

He might, possibly, have succeeded in doing some mischief had he been less demonstrative.

But as he rushed out of his box, shouting at the top of his voice, and flourishing his stave, Bob had ample time to give him a blow that sent him rolling over and over in the mud.

"Murder!" bellowed the watchman, who was far from expecting this treatment. "Murder! Help! Thieves!"

Jerry stopped for a moment to have a laugh at him.

But at a word from Bob, they turned a corner of the street, and as quick as thought darted down a dark court.

This they did to avoid their pursuers, for they thought it was about time now that they got rid of them.

But it did not strike our good friends at the time that it might just be possible that they had got themselves into a trap.

Down they crept on tip-toe along the dark court, and they could hear their pursuers coming up, panting and blowing like porpoises.

As they could not see those they were pursuing, they paused at the top of the court, not knowing evidently what to do.

They were, indeed, afraid that their men had given them the slip, as they could not see a trace of them, nor even hear the sounds of their footsteps.

It now struck Bob, for the first time, that there might be no outlet or inlet to the court but the one.

In that case they were trapped nicely.

They pushed on, however, as noiselessly as they could, hoping that the marines and blue-jackets would pass the court.

But in this they were disappointed.

The men were still undecided in their movements.

As they could not hear the echo of any footsteps in the street, they had to conclude that those they were pursuing were hidden somewhere in the vicinity.

Bob and Jerry had to move now very cautiously indeed, as it seemed to them that their pursuers had strong suspicions that they were in the court.

"Stop a minute," whispered Bob; "these fellows are talking. Let us hear what they have to say."

"I propose to move on," said Jerry. "How do we know if there's another opening to this place? We are nicely fixed, now, if there isn't."

"Hold yer noise, you fool!" hissed Bob. "What right have you to suggest sich a thing? I know how it'll be; you'll bring all these blessed jollies and salts down on us afore we know where we are. 'Sh! They are speaking."

The marines and blue-jackets, tired of looking around them, now began to speak in low tones.

But low as they were, every word came distinctly to our two friends' ears.

"I shouldn't wonder if they give us the slip yet," said one.

"Where do you think they have gone?" asked another.

"Perhaps down this court," suggested a third.

"Nonsense!" said the first. "There is no outlet to the court but this one, so we have them if they are."

This was information to our two buccaneers, but they had more than suspected that before.

No outlet to the court!

Then there were no means of getting away save by keeping perfectly quiet.

It was just possible that their enemies would pass on.

This was providing they made no noise.

Besides, the court was intensely dark, and they knew their pursuers had no lanterns or even any means of procuring a light.

"We must squat down here for a little while," whispered Bob. "We have one advantage over those fellows, which is that we can see them and they can't see us."

This was very true.

They could see the figures of the marines and blue-jackets distinctly without being themselves seen.

"I'll tell you what," said one of the men-of-war's men. "These cussed buccaneers are as cunning as rattlesnakes. I somehow think that we are not after the right man after all."

"Just the very thing I was going to remark," said another. "Between you and me, I think we are jolly well sold."

"What will Admiral Ellis think of the business?" said another.

"He need never know anything about it."

"Bosh! Just the very thing he'll find out afore twenty-four hours have passed."

"I agree with Jack in that. Old Ellis has ears as long as to-day and to-morrow put together. Shiver my timbers! we are in a nice pickle now, if ever we were in one. This cussed darkness and other matters combined have played the very devil with us. I am sorry now that we were told off for the duty. The scoundrels have led us a fine dance, and what is worse, we'll gain nothing by it."

"Only a good drenching," put in another, "and the loss of a night's rest."

"I only hope you may escape with that loss," said still another. "The old admiral is as venomous as a serpent, and he'll put us down in his black books as sure as fate if we return unsuccessful. Something must be done."

Bob and Jerry, from this conversation, began at first to feel hopeful, but now it seemed every moment that their chances of escape grew less and less.

That their pursuers would search the court was more than evident.

This was just the thing they wished to avoid.

Besides, our two buccaneers, as the reader will remember, had fired off their pistols.

Which were, consequently, now of no use to them.

But they had their cutlasses still left.

"We are trapped at last, Jerry," said Bob. "I don't see any way of getting out o' this mess, for as sure as we stand here, the cusses 'll end up by giving this 'ere place a thorough inwestigation."

"Investigation," corrected the irrepressible Jerry.

"Jerry," reproved Bob, in a whisper, "this ain't the time for corrections, schollard as you think yourself. What's to be done now?—that is the question."

"Well, old pal, I don't know what can be done. Suppose we make a sudden rush for it?"

"No use, Jerry, no use. Where's our pistols?"

"Why, here they are, aren't they?"

"But they are empty, you dunderhead. What good is empty pistols?"

"Not much," replied Jerry, ruefully. "But we have cutlasses, and good ones."

"True. But two cutlasses against seven men armed to the teeth isn't worth mentioning."

"What if we try 'em?"

"No, I tell you, no! It will never do, Jerry. Besides, we ain't a-fighting pirates now. A blue-jacket is worth two pirates any day."

"Perhaps you are right," said the irrepressible one.

"I know I am. But be more cautious, old pal. If you elewate yer voice, we'll be in for it as sure as eggs is eggs."

"All right, Bob! I'll take care not to speak too loud. But we can, all the same, move to the further end of the court."

"Perhaps that will be the best thing we can do, under the sarcumstances. But, stop a minute, let us see what these fellers intend doing!"

"If only a few of them would just oblige us by going away, we could settle the others in a very short time."

"But don't you see the lubbers won't move a peg from the top of the court. I should like myself very much to see three or four of 'em leave. I am not at all afraid but we could manage the rest."

They were now aware that the marines and blue-jackets had made up their minds to march in a body down the court.

"Follow me!" whispered Bob. "If anything's to be done, we must do it immediately."

Bob and Jerry made their way to the other end of the court, and were soon aware of the unpleasant fact that they could move in that direction no farther.

Their progress was intercepted by a dead wall.

"I wish we had a light," observed Jerry, forgetting for a moment that their enemies were at the other end of the court.

"A light!" almost hissed Bob. "Do you want to ruin us, you fool?"

"Oh, I forgot! A light would certainly do that sort o' thing. But, I say, Bob!"

"Speak lower, you lubber, you!"

"They'll not hear me, I am sure!"

"Won't they, though! I shouldn't like to trust them too much," said Bob. "What a fool you must be, Jerry, to make sich an ignorant observa-tion. Why, you donkey, don't you know that as we are now situated, the slightest sound will reach their ears. So be careful, or you'll find it out to yer cost."

Indeed, if we may use the expression, our friends were at this stage in a fine fix.

They could go no farther.

And if they went back, there would be a very good prospect of their being riddled by the bullets of the enemy.

Whatever move they made now was apparently hopeless to them.

Indeed, there seemed no possibility at all of their getting away.

What was to be done?

Bob wracked his brains in vain, and was forced to acknowledge at last that he was never in such a plight before in his life.

What ill-fortune induced him in the first instance to go down that miserable court?

He cursed his unlucky stars for doing it.

And if he by some miraculous means or other got out of this scrape, he vowed internally never to be caught in another.

"Bob," whispered Jerry, suddenly, "a thought strikes me."

"Indeed!" whispered Bob, back.

Bob was at that time growling under his breath like a bear with a sore head, so the reader may think it a great want of civility and brotherly feeling on his part to address Jerry as he did.

"Well," said the old buccaneer, "if a thought's struck you, tell me what it is."

Jerry went on to explain that there might possibly be a door in some portion of the wall of the court, either on one side or the other.

"For instance," said Jerry, "the side entrance to one of the houses."

"By Neptune! that never struck me!" said Bob. "So there might, Jerry."

"What say if we search?"

"Very good, old pal; only be careful, as I said before."

"No fear, Bob; we'll not make quite so much noise as to disturb any of those watchful genelmen at the ether end of the court."

"Well, if we are going to do it, we have no time to lose."

While the marines and blue-jackets were discussing whether they should make a thorough search of the court or not, Bob and Jerry were feeling all over the walls to find whether a door existed there or not.

Imagine their surprise, then, when the earth suddenly opened beneath their feet, and the pair disappeared down a dark abyss.

CHAPTER CXCIV.

BOB AND JERRY HAVE ANOTHER MYSTERIOUS ADVENTURE.—THEY MEET WITH AN OLD ACQUAINTANCE.

As our two friends so mysteriously disappeared, an old man rushed from a neighbouring house with a flaming torch, which lit up the whole of the court.

"Hallo, what's the row?" he growled savagely, glaring at the panting man-of-war's men.

"Looking for two fellows we are bound to nab," replied one; "they've sheered off, but damme, we'll over-haul 'em yet!"

"Well, every success to you. But don't turn respectable folk out of their beds. Good night."

The discomforted host, seeing they were baffled, muttered a few oaths, and then retraced their steps.

Meanwhile, Bob and Jerry had found a foothold, and were rubbing their bruised limbs.

They had not fallen far, but the place was so

total darkness, and when they groped about, they found it strewed with empty casks and cases.

"Brandy, by Jove!" whispered Jerry. "I can smell it. But every blessed one is empty."

"Never mind, let us find a way out of this. That's a trap of some kind we've fallen down. There's no chance of going back that way. There's another opening somewhere."

"Here it is, mate—hold on to me. I'll lead the way, no matter wher' to. This has been a smuggler's crib, I'll be bound, at one time."

"But the captain? I wonder how he is getting on?"

"All right by this time, I should say. Come along, we can do no good here."

Jerry Mizzen stretched his long brawny arms about the arched passage he had discovered, and led the way, using both feet and hands as a guide.

The passage was dry for some distance, when it grew tortuous, the floor rugged, and the walls exceedingly damp.

Suddenly they came to an abrupt turn, then they descended a steep flight of steps, and eventually made their way to the end of a long, low passage, against the roof of which they continually bumped their heads.

"Hush! listen! voices ahead! Bob, do you hear them?"

"I do," replied Jerry, "and, by Jove. Here's a light, too. Go ahead steady.

It was only at that moment that the pair bethought themselves that they had dropped their weapons in their fall, and had not stopped to recover them.

Time was too precious, however, for them to go back.

They crept on very cautiously.

Presently, as if by magic, they came upon a small opening on their left, and through it some distance they discovered the open sea.

As the moon broke occasionally through the clouds, they could see a man reclining against a projecting piece of rock, with a musket resting in the hollow of his left arm.

The aperture, however, was too small for them to creep through.

They were bound to enter a large cavern, if they meant to go on.

In that cavern they saw three men seated on what appeared to be spirit kegs, before them was a large flask, and a dricking horn.

The whole was lit up by a wood fire, and our adventurous pair paused for a moment to contemplate the group.

One was a muscular fellow, with swarthy features, and a heavy black moustache.

The second was of slighter build, but very similar in complexion and features.

The third was much fairer, and there was something more superior about his manner and build, as he rose and strode to the fire to light a cigar.

They were all well armed, and a sort of Corsair dress, with a hat jauntily slouched on one side.

His figure partly shielded our adventurers from the light, and taking advantage of his shadow, they glided behind a huge cask.

"Captain," said one of the trio, when the one with the cigar was re-seated. "I should like to hear you repeat the story of your first voyage, and how you became a prisoner in the hands of the Algerines."

"I should very much like to hear it," chimed in the other. "We all know how you escaped, but how did you get there?"

Bob and Jerry nudged each other, and then strained their ears to listen.

This what they heard, though they little dreamt at the commencement how nearly it concerned themselves.

"I was a boy when I took my first trip to sea—a careless, giddy, thoughtless boy, you'll say, when I tell you that I left a good home to travel on the pathless deep.

"I was bent on going, however.

"I had a strong desire to see the wonders I had read of in foreign lands; so I contrived to stow myself in the dark hold of the 'Arethusa' on special service.

"It's years ago now, but the incidents attending that voyage were so fully impressed on my youthful mind that I remember them quite well to this day. I can still see the fierce look of Ben Barnacle as he hauled me out from between the bags of biscuits, where I had been jammed by the rolling of the ship for three long days and dreary nights, the most pitiable object that ever was seen.

"Ben, however, was not a bad fellow. After giving me a 'stern chaser' as he termed it, with a rope's end, he took me under his care, and promised to make a smart sailor of me if I would only listen to his instructions.

"I thanked him, promised to do anything he might wish, and, as a commencement, he initiated me into the mystery of mixing his grog, a commodity of which he was extremely fond.

"This was Ben's greatest weakness.

"He would do nothing without grog, and he was never so happy as when he had a bucketful before him, so that he could bale it out at his pleasure.

"We had a stormy passage; head winds and beating rains sorely tried the patience of the crew, and seriously affected the temper of Ben, whose insatiable thirst was at its height, and his rum beaker at its lowest ebb.

"Our captain's orders, however, compelled him to put into Gibraltar Bay, and, yielding to the persuasion of the lieutenant, he decided upon letting the boys have a run ashore, Ben's watch (the star-bowlines) being the first in turn.

"'Three days' leave, yeo ho! There's luck, boys!' said the old boatswain, smacking his thigh, and giving his tarpaulin hat a knowing rake. 'Won't we make the gold shake as we foot it round the town?'

"So saying, the old seaman tumbled over the bulwarks and dropped into the boat, to the no small merriment of the liberty men, and the total destruction of the purser's new hat.

"One long, ringing cheer, a hearty 'give way, boys,' and the boat, plied by a dozen oars, left the side, and headed for the pier.

"Ben was the first to land.

"Springing on to the wet, slippery steps, he turned to the sailors, who were to return with the boat, and said—

"'Bear a hand, my hearties, we shall have a regular snorter directly. Don't you see it coming? It'll be a stiff 'un, and no gammon!'

"Every eye was turned in the direction of a black cloud, now evaporating into a cold, chilling mist, which fell in the town like small rain.

"Other eyes had already espied this strange precursor of the storm, and the fishermen were hauling up their boats, and the seamen belonging to the coasting vessels in the bay were looking out for the safest anchorage for their tiny crafts.

"The 'Arethusa's' boat had barely reached the ship when the storm came on with such sudden fury that it was found necessary to hoist the boat on board, and send down the topgallant masts, and by midnight the brig was riding out the gale with both anchors down.

"For three days the storm raged incessantly;

top-masts had to be housed, the cables paid out to the bitter end, and the jibboom shortened in.

"All communication was then cut off between the shipping and the shore; no boat could live in the furious sea, no boat could be launched through the heavy surf, so that the captain as well as the liberty men, whose leave had now expired, were compelled to remain on shore.

"This was hard lines for those on board, who were waiting to be relieved.

"Many were the angry expletives vented on their ill-luck.

"To add to this, when the weather moderated sufficiently, the captain came off in a shore boat, and swore with a terrible oath that not another man should have liberty till the ship was paid off.

"This, of course, was terrible news.

"What could be the meaning of this strange conduct?

"Had the watch on leave caused a disturbance in the town?

"Such were the questions asked by one of the other, and various were the surmises, but nothing further could be gleaned until the return of the liberty men.

"Their story was the old one, of course.

"Ben had got foul of an old Jew, who tried to cheat him; and Ben, in a drunken frolic, had capsized the old man's shanty, and half-killed two sentries for taking the part of the Jew.

"The crew, exasperated at having their rum stopped, vowed vengeance on old Ben. They'd salt him, that they would, and that with a vengeance!

"'Wait till the old grampus comes alongside,' said one, 'we'll pickle and salt him too! He's sure to be three sheets in the wind; aye, and —'

"'Ahoy, there! Throw us a rope!' shouted a gruff voice, interrupting him.

"Like magic a score of heads were thrust through the ports and lined the bulwarks, and the word was passed from mouth to mouth—'It's Ben, and he's groggy.'

"The boatswain strode leisurely to the gangway, and hailing one of his cubs (as he termed the ordinary seamen) he ordered him to overhaul the stay and yard tackle, so as to hoist the boatswain on board.

"He had a presentiment that the tackle would be needed, therefore he had kept it handy.

'One glance at the object lying at full length in the boat's bottom was enough to confirm Bill's suspicion. Old Ben was reclining gracefully at ease looking something like a stuffed porpoise.

"'How shall we sling him?' asked the boatman in the stern, glancing wistfully at the inanimate form. "He's as full as a butt. We've had a tough job with him. He smells like a rum cask just broached.'

"'Sling him bung up,' growled Bill. 'Bring a lantern, boy, and throw a light on the subject.'

"'The devil a bit of light must go near him, shure!' cried the other boatman, in dismay. 'He'll blow up, and send us all to glory, faith, and ——Och! whirra! what the devil are you after?'

"Bill had dropped a huge 'strop' on the fellow's head, almost dislocating his neck, and causing him to roar out most lustily.

"'Sling away!' roared the boatswain's mate. 'Bear a hand there, you lubbers! Do you want any help?'

"'Faix! we've a boat full already,' growled the irate Hibernian. 'I've a mind, shure, to sling the baste by the neck!'

"In the meantime there was a great confusion on deck.

"Since the arrival of the boat, it had become quite dark, and lanterns were flashing about in different parts of the ship.

"The hands had been turned up to man the yard and stay tackle, and the falls were rove through leading blocks on deck and stretched away forward.

"There was a suppressed giggle amongst the seamen as they grasped the rope and steadied it hand taut, ready to run away with it.

"'All ready, all clear?' shouted Bill Bowers.

"'Aye, aye! all clear!' was the response.

"Then sounded the shrill whistle, 'walk away,' and Ben's corpulent form was swaying in mid air a few feet below the yard-arm.

"Dick Dawson (the sailor who had suggested the salting and pickling of Ben) held the stopper on the rope, and at the word 'belay,' he gripped it tight, so that the quarter-master might take a turn with the fall round the cleat, so as to lower the boatswain steadily to the strain of the stay tackle which was to swing him on board.

"At this juncture a sad calamity occurred.

"The rope stopper suddenly gave way, the stay tackle was let go, and down dropped Ben like a flash of lightning.

"Fortunately, the boatmen had taken the precaution to haul the boat ahead, or the weight, assisted by the velocity of his fall, would have shivered her planks to atoms.

"As it was, his collision with the water was something fearful.

"The spray flew in cascades over the boatmen, nearly drowning them, and then the body floated on the surface of the water like the carcase of a dead whale.

"There were strong indications of merriment amongst the ship's crew as they rushed to the bulwarks, and gazed at the strange sight through the gloom, but it was soon suppressed.

"'Confound you all for a lubberly set of swabs!' roared Bill Bowers, taking one bound from the hammock netting to the deck.

"'Hoist away handsomely, you thick-headed idiots!' he yelled, almost bursting with rage. 'You shall sweat for this, every one of you, before the night's out.'

"Almost choking with suppressed laughter, the sailors obeyed.

"Bill, speedily as possible, hurried Ben Barnacle to his berth, and then he desired to be left alone.

"The captain and lieutenant were in the cabin, discussing events over a bottle of port, little dreaming what was passing so near them.

"It was Christmas time, and the captain resolved that the sailors should enjoy themselves, and the noise on deck, he thought, was occasioned by the hoisting on board the provisions he had ordered from the shore.

"The boatswain's mate, for reasons of his own, did not acquaint them with the true state of affairs just then.

"When left alone, he busied himself in stripping the wet clothes off the inebriated seaman, and disencumbering him of the serpent-like folds of some mysterious article that was wound tightly round his body beneath his shirt.

"This mysterious and ghostly-looking article the boatswain's mate coiled away carefully in the corner of a sea-chest, and then assiduously set to work in restoring to consciousness poor Ben.

"Having divested him of all his wet clothing, and replaced them with a dry shirt and a pair of flannel drawers, Bill with some difficulty lifted the limp form into the bunk, and then sought the assistance of the doctor.

"'Wh-what the furies is all this about, eh?' queried the little man, as, with an awful cadaverous-looking face, he staggered into the berth

'Drunk, as usual, I suppose? Does he want bleeding?'

"The Vampyre, as he was termed, was a long way on the road to intemperance himself, and the cold glitter of his malicious grey eyes seemed reflected on the bright blade of the lancet he held in his thin bony hand.

"'He wants something, and quickly, too,' answered Bill, ill-humouredly. 'The lubbers have drowned him, I believe—they doused him overboard.'

"'Ah!' ejaculated the doctor, with an air of profound gravity, as, with one hand, he held on to the side of the bunk to steady himself, and with the other grasped his instrument, 'I'll get the pump to work on him immediately. 'Are there any b-bones broken think you?'

"'Not a timber started; but I can tell you he has swallowed enough salt water to drown Old Nick. So get your pump-gear shipped as soon as possible, or I won't give a fig for his life!'

"'Not dead y-yet,' said the doctor, with all the seriousness due to his profession. 'I must bleed him. y-you know. Just open a vein a little, a—a—and—'

"'There is more water in him than blood,' interposed Bill, 'rig the pump tackle, I'll get a bucket.'

"The Vampyre rewarded Bill with one of his vicious glances.

"Returning the knife to its case, he reluctantly prepared the stomach-pump and thrust the flexible tube between Ben's teeth.

"At that moment the brig gave a sudden roll, throwing the doctor, whose spider-like legs seemed incapable of bearing him, half-way into the bunk on top of his patient.

"'O-o-oh!' yelled the doctor, to the full pitch of his attenuated lungs. 'Oh, murder, murder!'

"'What the deuce is the matter?' queried Bill Bowers, with difficulty suppressing a grin.

"'Oh, murder, it's off, right through the bone. Oh, Jerusalem! make him let go!'

"'Let go what—are you jammed?' asked Bill, with aggravating coolness. 'You seem to have learnt to dance a very neat hornpipe, and—'

"'The deuce take your jaw, do for Heaven's sake open. O-o-oh, there goes the flesh '—and with one bound he leapt almost to the cabin ceiling,

"The boatswain's mate could no longer control his mirth.

'He burst into a loud fit of laughter, whilst the doctor went through all the writhings and contortions of a newly-skinned eel.

"'What a fool you were to put it between his biscuit-crackers,' growled Bill, as with the smallest possible amount of tenderness he thrust the point of a marlinspike between the boatswain's teeth. 'There—pull away, now's the time!'

"'And quite time, too,' vociferated the doctor, viewing compassionately the injured member, which was deeply indented with the compression of the boatswain's teeth. 'I'll bleed him, that I will, and give him an emetic.'

"There was a savage glitter in the doctor's cold grey eye, and his thin lips pursed into a malicious grin as he finished speaking, and with great care he selected from his case a formidable-looking instrument, which he strictly reserved for such like operations.

"Sobered with the pain, he set systematically to work, and having drawn as much blood as was sufficient in his estimation, he bandaged up the arm, felt his pulse, and then administered a strong emetic, which acted upon the boatswain at once.

"'There, that's saved his life—the rascal!—and in return for my pains I shall probably lose a finger,' said the doctor, maliciously. 'But he is

not out of my hands yet. I'll physic him for this before I've done with him.'

"'That won't be long first. I believe you've killed him," replied Bill Bowers, looking him seriously in the face. 'Look at him now. Why, shiver me, if he ain't turning all the colours of a dying dolphin!'

"'A dying duck, more likely. Why, he is as strong as a horse. I'll bleed him again in the morning,' said the doctor; and then, chuckling to himself at the prospect of again using his favourite weapon, he shuffled away to his berth.

"'Bleed him again, will he?" muttered the boatswain's mate, shaking his fist at the retreating form. 'Well, we'll see. But there is many a slip between the cup and the lip, and so he'll find out before morning.'

"While this scene was being enacted in the steerage berth of the 'Arethusa,' a scene of a different nature was being enacted on the lower deck forward.

"All was jollity and fun.

"Some were footing it to the merry strings of the fiddle, others were engaged in spinning yarns, whilst the elder hands had retired to the quietude of the forecastle to laugh and chat over the joke they had played upon old Ben.

"This state of affairs, however, was not permitted to last very long.

"An order was passed forward for the noise to cease, as Ben Barnacle was not expected to live.

"This, of course, put a damper on the merriment at once.

"Those who had gloried the most in the joke were the first to see their folly, and to sink at once into the depths of sorrow and contrition.

"'Poor old Barnacle! He's gone, then,' sighed an old Jack Tar, whose sides were still aching from the effects of an immoderate fit of laughter. 'Poor Ben! With all his faults he was a jolly good shipmate, and I'm sorry that I had a hand in the affair.'

"'Bah! Do you think he'll haunt yer?' growled a bull-headed foretopman. 'If his time's come, how can we help it? Why, he was always the first in a bit of fun and mischief. You should have seen him capsize the old Jew's shanty. Old Beelzebub could not have done it cleaner.'

"But this argument failed in dispelling the sadness that pervaded the ship. Ben Barnacle, with all his faults, was a general favourite with the crew, and the prospect of losing him, especially under such circumstances, made him appear doubly dear to them.

"Every half-hour, as the ship's bell was struck, some one glided aft to inquire how he got on, and the answer was each time less satisfactory, until the mournful news was announced that he was dead.

"'Dead!' No one had the courage to repeat the word 'dead!' and the sting of conscience made every man look upon himself as a murderer.

"Very few cared to turn into their hammocks; they could not sleep; their guilty consciences pricked them and made them restless.

"What was passing aft no one dared to inquire. Everything seemed hushed in death-like silence; only the lights streaming from the cabin windows and skylight bore token of one moving about in the after-cabin of the vessel.

"The suspense was awful.

"How had the boatswain slipped his cable?

"Who had he blamed as the cause of his death? Had he spoken at all, or had he drifted out of the world, unconscious, and without squaring up his log, before entering that unknown port?

"Such were the reflections of the most serious minds as they conversed in low and mysterious

CAPTAIN TOM DRAKE.

whispers, whilst the most superstitious crouched in their hammocks in silent fear and trembling.

"From an awe-inspired state they were suddenly aroused by the ship's bell striking the midnight hour, chorused by the cheery voice of the sentry—'All's well!'

"'Eight bells,' said an old tar, who was entertaining a group of open-mouthed listeners with the superstitious yarn of the Flying Dutchman. 'Eight bells, my hearties; this is the time when spirits walk about, you know.'

"'Fiddlesticks!' interposed the bull-headed foretopman. 'I never saw anything uglier than myself (which was a positive fact), and I have sailed in all sorts of craft, boarded pirates, captured slavers, and—'

"He paused suddenly, and turned his eyes to the ladder, on which the hurried footsteps of some one leaving the deck was suddenly heard.

"The ladder, by this time, was the central attraction of all eyes; in fact, their gaze was actually rivetted, especially when the sentry, white as a sheet, and trembling in every limb, made his appearance.

"One glance at him was sufficient to strike the little group of story-tellers with terror, and set their knees in motion, whilst their tongues seemed glued, as it were, to the roofs of their mouths.

"The new-comer was the first to break the spell.

"'Oh, Lord, boys!' he gasped, 'I've seen it!'

"'Seen what?' queried the bully, in a softer tone than he had hitherto adopted.

"'Oh, Lord, the ghost! Boo-o-o! Didn't it frighten me!'

"'I should think so, you great calf,' growled the bully, mustering all his courage to look bold. 'What was it like?'

"Every neck was craned forward at this.

"Dilated eyes were seen peering from beneath the blankets in the hammocks, and every ear was strained to its utmost tension to catch the least sound.

"The sentry was some moments mustering sufficient courage to speak.

"'It was Ben!' he gasped, at length.

"'What, Barnacle!' echoed the foretopman. 'Then it was a real ghost, I suppose?'

"'Real, of course, or how did I see it?'

"A shudder went through the whole of his listeners, not excepting the bullying foretopman.

"'Hang me for a swab if I don't lay him, then!' he said, braggingly, bringing his right fist into the palm of his left hand with a smack. 'I'll lay the ghost, boys; where did you see him?'

"'Just abaft the mainmast,' was the reply, in a softened whisper. 'I saw him as plain as I see you. He walked across the deck, right through the bulwarks, and up to the yard-arm, just where he hung by the tackle before we let him go.'

"'The dev—dickens he did!' said the topman, with an incredulous wink. 'I'd like to see him. By Jove, I'd a shortened his cable. Stand clear there; let me go up and have a look.'

"'He's gone now,' interposed an old tar, persuasively, 'don't be rash. If you offend the ghost, remember'—

"'Stuff and oakum! clear a gangway!' growled the bully, elbowing his way through the crowd.

"There was a dead silence; everyone looked at the topman's retreating form as though they were gazing upon it for the last time.

"Not a word was spoken by the rest. They exchanged glances with each other in silence, until the topman's footsteps were heard walking rapidly aft.

"When the bully returned he was not the same man that left the lower deck a few minutes before.

"He was pale and ghastly, speechless, as it were, for he uttered not a word, but crept in silence to his hammock.

"'What could he have seen?'

"'Had he laid the ghost as he promised?'

"'Had the ghost spoken to him?'

"Such were the whisperings of the crew, but the only man that could answer them was dumb, and so they all dispersed, not to sleep, but to pray for the morning light to dispel their fears.

"There was a motley group when the hands were turned up next morning to wash decks.

"Eyes bleared and bloodshot, cheeks pale with fear and want of rest, whilst the furtive glances cast at the steerage hatchway spoke more than their tongues dared to utter.

"The boatswain, of course, was soon edified with the story, and the quiet smirk of his features showed that it was not the first he had heard of it.

"He listened, however, in well-feigned astonishment, combed his beard with his fingers, and chewed away at his quid as though in deep meditation.

"'You did not see it yourself, Ned?' he asked when the old quartermaster had finished.

"'I didn't; shiver me if I wanted to.'

"'How do you know it was true, then?'

"'Ah!' ejaculated the old tar; 'how do I? Do you think I'm a fool? Don't you think I know when a fellow's seen something supernatural? He wouldn't believe it at first; but, depend upon it, he saw more than he cared to tell.'

"'Who!'

"'You think he believed it, then?'

"'Sartin of it. You should have seen his figurehead when he slunk away to his hammock.'

"'It's plain, then, that the ship is haunted, and we must get rid of the corpse somehow. By-the-bye, have you seen it yet?'

"'No, I—I wouldn't for the world. Poor Ben, he's gone, and I hope the cap'n will give him decent burial, for all our sakes.'

"When the boat was called away to put the captain on shore, there were many anxious faces visible from the ports.

"It was reported that he had gone to make arrangements for the funeral.

"However, he did not put in an appearance again that day, and, as darkness set in, a sadness overspread the ship's company again.

"The sailor whose duty it was to keep the midnight watch on deck was in a terrible funk.

"He had no heart to join in the making of the huge Christmas pudding, but he drank a good share of the extra grog, which was served out for them to cheer themselves on the Christmas Eve.

"The youngsters, however, enjoyed themselves pretty cheerily.

"The fiddle played on the lower deck, and many a good old sea song was sung on the forecastle head.

"As eight bells drew nigh, these sounds gradually began to cease.

"One by one the stragglers on the upper deck slunk below, leaving the sentry to pace his post alone, and the cook to make preparations for the Christmas dinner.

"The cook was too busily occupied with his duties to think of ghosts and such like, but the sentry, in spite of his efforts to the contrary, could not keep his eyes off the steerage hatchway.

"He did not, however, notice a figure glide into the shadow of the galley, and creep under the quarter of the longboat.

"But he heard the officer of the watch call out eight bells, and as he turned after striking it, he

CAPTAIN TOM DRAKE BAFFLES THE FRENCH GENERAL.

saw a sort of shadowy figure ascend the hatchway and walk to the larboard bulwarks.

"Just then the figure turned and faced him, and the sailor set up a shriek that rang through the ship like a death-knell.

"Those who heard it started in horror at the sound.

"Strong men trembled, and their bronzed cheeks paled.

"For my own part I shivered and shook like a billy-boy in stays.

"Since the announcement of Ben's death I was the only boy on board that had dared to venture so far aft as the taffrail, and then I was kindly invited with a rope's end.

"Boy-like, I had taken advantage to peep down the companion hatchway, when I saw and heard the Vampyre and Bill Bowers in deep altercation.

"'I tell you he's my lawful subject,' said the Vampyre, warmly, at the ꞏꞏꞏꞏ ꞏꞏꞏꞏ watching the

opportunity to squeeze his spare form past the herculean figure of the boatswain.

"'It is expressly stated on the articles that I should make a post-mortem examination of any one dying aboard,' he added, fiercely, 'and this is a fit case for my inspection.'

"'I don't care, he's my chum, though he's slipped his wind, and you're not going to cut him up like salt junk.'

"'How can I register his death?'

"'Put it down as dropsy—say he was waterlogged, and that you, you ring-tailed swab, was too lazy to rig the pump. I'll put my blessed signature to that, and no gammon!'

"'And I'll put my signature to you if we get into action, such a mark as you won't rub out. This shall be my pen. Its writing is indelible when dipped in red ink.'

"As the Vampyre uttered this threat, he flourished a long, keen, glittering lance above his head, and eyed the boatswain's mate with such a demoniacal look that made the very marrow in my bones to curdle, and me to slink away with every hair bristling on my head.

"No wonder, then, that I had an hour's whispered conversation with my shipmates before I curled myself up in my hammock to sleep.

"It is not at all surprising that, when that horrid sound awoke the silent echoes of the lower deck, we sprang up in bed, our teeth chattering like the cuddy door in a hurricane.

"The hammock of the bullying foretopman was slung to the bulkhead, not many feet from me, and I could hear him groan with terror.

"But he never moved, only to draw his blanket closer round him.

"There was not a man on the lower deck with a nerve strong enough to go above and ascertain the cause of that soul-piercing shriek; they would rather endure the terrible agony of suspense.

"No one envied Dick Trimmer the sight he saw; his description of it the next morning was enough.

"'Shiver me if ever I saw such a figure-head afore,' he said, filling the gaping mouths and extended ears of his listeners. 'It was like Ben's, and yet it warn't, you know. It had a some sort of a cut about it like the Flying Dutchman's, only it was green and ghastly, smoke coming from its eyes and nose, and. oh, lor—'

"'What's the matter?' queried one.

"'There was a hawful smell o' brimstone, Sam, just like the devil I once saw on the stage.'

"'But it didn't hurt yer?'

"'Not at all.'

"'Did it speak?'

"'Not a word, but—

"'Well?'

"'Why, it did worse.'

"'That's coming to the point; pay out the slack, Dick.'

"'Well, as I said afore, he faced me, trimmed his lamps right fair for my cutwater; then, raising his weather flipper, till it was on even keel with my figure-head, he pointed with his other fin to the yard-arm.'

"'Was that all?'

"'No, it wasn't. Just as I was trying to heave myself together, and 'bout ship, the spectre, for it was a real spectre, winks his codfishy eyes at me, and then sails right through the bulwark and up to the very yard-arm we used in hoisting the boatswain aboard.'

"'The dev— the deuce he did.'

"'It's a fact. May I never salute my Polly again on Common Hard if I'm not uncoiling the right hawser.'

"'Did he have nothing to hold by?' asked an incredulous listener in the group.

"'Not a rope yarn, I'll swear to that.'

"'Did he walk on nothing?'

"'Never a blessed thing, but I didn't see him come down, boys. I took to scudding, and fell over the cook, who was crawling on his hands and knees from the galley.'

"'Then it warn't the Flying Dutchman?' said one of the anxious listeners, drawing a deep breath. 'I've seen him scores of times, and therefore I knows a bit about it.'

"'Ah, he wears a wooden leg,' said the foretopman, before mentioned.

"'Ay, he does now—at least, ever since he tried to board a whaler I was in, but I took off one of his legs with a tomahawk, as he would not go away when spoken to civilly.'

"This piece of braggadocia met with the general disapprobation of the crew, who soon found out what occurred upon deck.

"It came out that the sailor on watch no sooner saw the horrible vision than a sickening sensation came over him, and he fell down in a swoon.

"How long he remained unconscious no one knew, not even himself, for as I said before, there was no one bold enough to go to his assistance; but when he slowly and fearfully opened his eyes, he saw lying beside him the cook in the same blissful state of unconsciousness, and Bill Bowers bending over the pair of them.

"'Come, rouse up, my hearties, what is the meaning of all this?' said the boatswain's mate, gruffly. 'This is a pretty state of things, to find the sentry asleep on his post, and the cook in a state of glorious blissfulness.'

"'Asleep!' gasped the seaman, opening his eyes in alarm. 'Asleep! did you not see it then?'

"'See what? Why, are you drunk, too? What is there to see but a pair of stupid fools? Come, pull yourselves together, or I'll set the hose at work upon you; and you, young fellow, if I report you, you will be flogged for sleeping in your watch.'

"Thus admonished, the sentry rose to his feet, and assisted Bowers in putting fresh life into the cook, which was a task of no little difficulty, as the poor fellow had been frightened nearly out of his wits.

"Sadly crestfallen, and mystified with the past events, the discomfited pair returned to their duty, looking as sheepish as it was possible for them to look, yet with a promise that Bowers would not report them.

"But the cook's disaster did not end here.

"On returning to the galley, he found that the plum-pudding (a very monster it was, too) was gone, and a goose he had finished plucking had vanished—spirited away in some mysterious manner—and, of course, this was all blamed to old Ben's ghost.

"The tale of horror told on that eventful morn needs no repeating.

"What food there was for the sailors' superstition!

"There was no doubting about the ghost now: the ship was most assuredly haunted.

"It was the bo'sun's ghost.

"This led to a general meeting of the whole ship's crew, to discuss the best means of ridding the vessel of such a pest; and it was decided that no one should answer the call on deck, nor do duty of any description, until the body was removed from the ship, either by burial ashore or overboard.

"Thus resolved, the men in a body went aft, and demanded to see the first lieutenant, but he had secretly left the ship to do honour at a party on shore; so that all depended on the second luff.

"He was a jolly fellow, light-hearted and full of fun, ever ready for a joke, and as fond of mischief as a monkey.

"As the men demanded the removal of the body from the ship, he consented, though it was against the laws of the authorities on shore, that the boatswain should be buried overboard, just as though the ship was at sea.

"This gave general satisfaction, and the sailmaker was ordered to bring his things aft, and sew the body in a hammock.

"Bill superintended the doing of all this. He prepared the shot, and the body, which was of enormous rotundity, was, after some difficulty, encased in its canvas coffin.

"At length the hour (12 at noon) arrived, when the burial was to take place, and a mournful sight it was for a dull Christmas morning.

"The ship's bell tolled the mournful dirge, the grating was placed ready at the gangway, and the body, borne by four sturdy seamen, was placed in position ready to take its final leave.

"The crew, with bared heads, stood in silence on the deck, the Union Jack, half masted, floating lazily over their heads, and the tolling of the muffled bell striking its death notes into their very hearts.

"The second laff read the service for the burial of the dead at sea, and finally the body was launched overboard, followed by the dull, sullen splash which so truly represents the dull thud of the clods as they fall on the coffin during a burial on shore.

"All else was hushed into silence, every one present was fully impressed with the solemnity of the occasion, and not one weather-beaten cheek but was moistened by the dew of a salt tear.

"All at once the boatswain's mate's stentorian voice broke the silence with—

"'It floats! it floats! By Jove, we shall all get hung.'

"Quick as lightning the cutter was lowered, and the floating coffin was seized by a stout tar who was rather bolder than the rest, for it was now an undoubted fact that the devil had something to do with the body of the unfortunate Ben.

"'By jingo! this is a queer start,' said the second luff, with a mischievous glitter in the corner of his left eye; 'if old Beelzebub has nothing to do with this I'm a Dutchman, that's all. But there,' he added, 'I always said that water would never drown old Ben, he was too fond of his grog for that.'

"There was not a grin, not a smile, on the elongated visages of the sailors, who on any other occasion would have retorted with some crack joke. They all looked as serious as could be, and shrank in horror from the body as it was hoisted on board.

"A low, fiendish chuckle was at that moment heard proceeding from the companion hatchway, then the pale, cadaverous face of the doctor was thrust forth.

"'Ah! the devil will have his due,' he hissed, savagely, 'you cannot cheat him so easily as you did the poor doctor! No, no, Mr. Bowers, he will have his rights in spite of your cunning trickery!'

"Bill Bowers turned and faced the Vampyre with a withering look that seemed almost to make him writhe beneath it.

"'You alligator,' said Bill, 'if anyone has occasion to fear old Firespit's graplins, it's yourself; by jingo, there is more sin in your little finger than in all Ben's carcase.'

"'Aha! so you say, but no matter—you may rob the poor doctor, but the devil will not be robbed. He! he! he! Mr. Bowers, your friend Ben is only going a little before to look out a warm corner for yourself.'

"There was an awe-inspiring silence as the doctor disappeared, and the faces of the sailors lengthened to an alarming extent.

"They all wore such a terrifying expression, in fact, that I scarcely knew of which to be most afraid—them, or the haunted corpse.

"'Sailmaker,' demanded the second luff, 'did you properly shot this hammock, sir?'

"'Indeed, I did; there was weight enough to sink a jolly-boat.'

"'But not enough to sink a jolly dog, it seems. Old Ben was a jolly dog, and no gammon; but I think you have been gammoning us, Master Hatchet.'

"'Not at all, sir; I well ballasted him head and stern, so that he might choose which end first he would like to go down.'

"'Then you have, doubtless, made some mistake; rip up the hammock and see.'

"'Not I, sir; Tom Hatchet is no coward, but he don't care about meddling with supernat'ral beings. For my part, I'd as soon ship as sailmaker aboard the "Flying Dutchman," as stitch another man up

in his hammock while I'm aboard of the Arethusa!"'

"Bill Bowers was the only one on board who possessed pluck enough to defy the Evil One.

"To the utter amazement of the shivering and shaking group, he cut open the hammock to see whether the shots were still inside.

"They were; but to the astonishment of all present, during their submersion they had been suddenly transformed into wood, and Bill now drew them forth in the shape of the bow-chaser's tompions.

"This was, indeed, a miracle.

"The seamen, ever prone to superstition, stood dumb-stricken.

"Boylike, I was half inclined to sneak away below; but, like the rest, a strange fascination seemed to root me to the spot.

"At length Bill spoke again, and his words set all the teeth in our head chattering—

"'Hang me if Old Nick hasn't kidnapped the body of Ben Barnacle!'

"'Oh Lord!' moaned one of his listeners, sanctimoniously.

"'Heaven preserve us!' echoed another, touching his forelock with reverence.

"'It serves him right,' chimed in the Vampyre, thrusting his head a little way up the hatchway.

"'And that serves you right!' thundered the boatswain's mate, snatching from the hammock a pair of sea-boots and hurling them at the doctor's head.

"There was a suppressed howl, and then Bill proceeded to investigate still further the contents of the hammock.

"'Look here, mates,' he said, holding up something tied very neatly in canvas, 'this is the missing plum-pudding, and this,' he added, thrusting his hand in again, 'is the lost goose. There are six *dead marines* (empty bottles), which, when in life and full of *spirits*, were the pride of our doctor the Vampyre, and this—'

"The elongated visages began to soften at this, one old sailor even ventured a smile as Bill drew forth a long string of bladders, now filled with air, but formerly used by the boatswain for smuggling his grog aboard.

"'Who owns it?' queried Bill Bowers, after a pause.

"'The ghost,' answered a voice somewhere up aloft.

"'Take it then,' replied Bill Bowers.

"'Ay, ay,' responded the voice, and then the form of Ben slid swiftly down one of the backstays into the midst of the astonished group.

"A cry of horror burst simultaneously from the lips of the terrified seamen, but the boatswain's voice soon dispelled all our fears.

"The sailors eyed each other sheepishly at first, when they found they had been the victims of a well-contrived joke, but after a while, when matters were explained, those who had been the most afraid were the first to join in the hearty laugh that followed, and most willingly did they respond to the toast that was then drunk to 'BEN BARNACLE and his GHOST.'"

Jerry Mizzen and his friend listened with open mouth and 'bated breath to the recital of this yarn, and communicated their feelings and approval to each other, by sundry pinches and digs in the ribs as the speaker proceeded. More than once their excitement had nearly brought them to grief, but with wonderful stoicism they restrained the desire to give vent to their thoughts in speech.

They both knew that what the stranger had stated was correct, with the exception that the captain was no other than Admiral Ellis, and that certain other personages had not received their right appellations.

But this they accredited to the speaker's youth at the time.

He was but a boy, unacquainted with ship life, and moreover, by his own confession, a stowaway at a time when the terrors of the press-gang were in full swing.

Our friends, however, did not let this trouble them much.

They did certainly wonder what this had to do with the speaker being taken prisoner.

Had their patience lasted longer, they might have heard, but the irrepressible Jerry was born a child of misfortune, and therefore his path in this life was not allowed to run too smooth.

Jerry loved to hear a good ghost story, as dearly as he dreaded to encounter a real ghost, and in his eagerness to catch every word, he craned his neck so far forward that he overbalanced himself, and sent the cask with a hollow bumping sound rolling into the centre of the large cavern.

Thus startled, the trio sprang to their feet, and faced round just as Bob and Jerry, like two beaten curs, were making for the passage they had entered by.

"Betrayed!" thundered the man who had been speaking. "Cut them down if they offer to stir."

In an instant one of the men leapt into the opening they were making for, and the next our bewildered adventurers felt the keen point of a sword touching the throat of each.

CHAPTER CXCV.

THE SCOUT BRINGS STRANGE NEWS ABOUT CAPTAIN TOM DRAKE—BOB AND JERRY HAVE A PLEASANT TIME FOR REFLECTION—THE PORT ADMIRAL STARTS ON A PORTENTOUS JOURNEY.

BOB HAULER was the first to recover his self-possession, and he would have given some explanation, or rather have invented some excuse, had they given him time. As it was, the hollow thumping of the cask, accompanied by the man's voice, brought several others armed with cutlasses and pistols rushing from another chamber of the cavern.

"What ho, captain," queried the foremost of the men, gazing in astonishment at the strange spectacle before them, "zounds! you have caught a pretty fine pair of rascals. How came they here, your honour?"

"That we must find out," said the leader, lowering his voice, "we are discovered, comrades, but we will fight to the death."

"Who has betrayed us?" asked several in a voice.

"I know not; a more lubberly brace of swabs I never before met with; take them away, Stephen, and by the sanctity of the oath which binds us all, secure them so that they may not escape."

"I will see to that, captain," answered the man addressed as Stephen.

"A brace of handspikes and a few fathoms of rope will moor them as securely as any ship in the harbour of Portsmouth."

Placing his pistols in his belt, and returning his cutlass to its leathern sheath, he motioned one of the others to follow him, and disappeared.

Bob made another effort to speak, but was kept in silence by the sword point being pressed harder to his throat.

Jerry saw the folly of this unnecessary torture, and very wisely held his peace.

Unarmed as they were, it was but folly to make any open resistance.

Besides, there were four if not more to keep each of them in subjection.

They had no doubt that they looked a pretty pair, and that the captain was perfectly justified in believing them to be a brace of hulking vagabonds.

Their faces and hands were grimed with dust and dirt, and their wet garments bore evidence of their recent encounter and flight.

Jerry looked woefully crestfallen as Stephen and his companion appeared again.

They each carried a brace of handspikes and a coil of stout rope.

"This will settle them, comrades," remarked Stephen as he threw his burthen on the stone floor.

"Enough to hold a seventy-four," replied his comrade, following suit.

"Trussing is the order, I presume, captain?"

The leader merely nodded an assent.

Bob and Jerry were quickly seized by willing hands.

A handspike was thrust between the hollow of their arms and across their backs, where it was held by a few sharp turns of the rope and a sailor's hitch.

They were then forced down into a sitting posture, another handspike was thrust between the bends of their knees, and, in less time than we can record it, they were so bound that they could move neither hands nor feet.

"Bravo! Steve," echoed those who had been earnestly watching these manœuvres.

"I was not on the Barbary Coast for nothing, you see," Stephen coolly remarked, eyeing the dejected pair complacently.

The man's cool effrontery made Bob and Jerry wince more than the cruel biting of the hitches.

They were neither of them afraid of a little pain, as we have already seen, but to be tortured and jeered at as well was more than their patience could withstand.

"You'd find me a Barbary Tartar," said Jerry, savagely, "if I once had you in my grip."

"But you'll never have that pleasure, my hearty, so take it comfortable. I have let you down pretty easy, so be quiet."

Bob and Jerry gave another wince.

They began to feel that their position was not to be a very comfortable one.

It was no use complaining, however; all they could do was to grin and bear it with patience.

They cut a most ludicrous figure, as at a sign from the leader four stout fellows advanced and carried them between them to the farther end of the cave, and seated them very carefully against the stone wall.

"It's all up with us this time," said Jerry, dejectedly, when they were alone. "A pretty pickle we've got into."

"It's all through you, you clumsy crocodile!" growled Bob. "I should like very much to punch your head."

"You'll never have that pleasure," replied Jerry, sarcastically mimicking Stephen. "Yours 'all be off afore then."

"And so will yours, you scarecrow, it's half off when you open that blessed biscuit locker of yourn."

At the word biscuit, Jerry's stomach began to growl.

"A biscuit and a toothful of rum wouldn't be very acceptable now, would it, Bob?" he queried, eyeing his companion ruefully.

"I shouldn't care about it," replied Bob, assuming a bold tone.

They were both of them far from being jolly.

What kind of company they had fallen into was to them a puzzler.

They had hoped that by listening to the yarn

they might have learnt something, and broken in upon it at the proper time and place.

Their position was anything but enviable.

They were both hungry and thirsty from their late exertions, and the ropes were beginning to give them excruciating pain.

In the meantime the other occupants of the cave were not idle.

The leader and his two principal colleagues held a consultation between themselves.

They, too, were very much puzzled as to what they should do or what they might expect.

Some of the band had been dispatched to search the inmost recesses of the cave, and others had been sent to scour the rocks, but all parties returned with the news that no further explanation of the mystery was to be found.

Towards morning, however, a man with a stout pea-jacket and sou'-wester, and a thick comforter round his throat, strode into the cavern.

He brought with him a deal of news.

Evidently he had been walking or running pretty sharp, for he seemed out of breath.

In a very few words he informed them that the whole town was in commotion, that a rascally pirate named Captain Drake had been captured and thrown into prison, that Admiral Ellis, who had hitherto been held in the highest esteem by the Government, had by his foolhardiness allowed the daring pirate to escape, and that the port admiral had ordered Admiral Ellis's arrest and suspension until they could try him according to the articles of war.

In continuance he said that it was reported that a French frigate had, under cover of the darkness, run into a neighbouring bay and cut out a couple of Indiamen that had been convoyed there by a British man-of-war, to take shelter from the storm during the night, and was towing them rapidly towards the coast of France.

"And they've slipped clean away," queried the leader, as the man paused for a moment to get breath.

"Clean gone, your honour; they've sent the best ship they had in harbour to overhaul them, but all their swift sailors, excepting this Admiral Ellis's, are out looking for Captain Drake's cruiser. She's a perfect demon at sailing, and all they can do they can't catch her."

"Captain Tom Drake," said the leader, thoughtfully, "did you hear the name of his wonderful ship?"

"The 'Will-of-the-Wisp,' your honour."

"Then it is the same. There cannot be two Tom Drakes."

"Very likely not, captain; but he may have twenty names, as they say his ship has; why, he runs under their very noses; his very guns have touched muzzles with theirs, and yet he has slipped away from them, laughing."

"Incredulous! I should like to see this miracle of the age. There was one Captain Tom Drake, but he was not exactly a pirate. Why, I was on board the same ship with him."

"You, captain?" exclaimed several voices together.

"Ay; I was."

"Well, that's a caulker!" exclaimed the newcomer. "I thought you'd been a prisoner in Algeria as far back as you could remember?"

"Perhaps so," answered the captain, gloomily. "I was knocked overboard in action, and afterwards picked up by those Algerian devils, and I might have been there now had they not trusted so many of us aboard the galley, which we took the first opportunity of running away with."

A quiet smile flitted across the noble features of the speaker as he remembered the mutiny, and how

nicely they had conquered the corsair crew, and run away with the vessel and its rich freight

"But of this Captain Tom Drake," he said, changing the subject; "I have met with those during my captivity who have described him as a bold buccaneer, no pirate, but a thorough heart of oak, a gallant seaman; why, even those barbarians have spoken of his glorious deeds, and how he cut through their fleet with a single ship, as no two other ships in that engagement would have dared to have done."

"Well, they call him a pirate here, anyhow, captain; there's a thousand pounds reward offered for him alive or dead. I wonder they let him go when once they had him."

"Ha! ha! ha! if he's the slippery eel you describe him they could not hold him, you may depend. I should like to see him very much."

The leader gave a sort of hysterical laugh, and then dropped into the same moody strain again.

He had scarcely done speaking when they were startled by the boom of a heavy cannon.

It sounded strangely in that hollow cavity in the steep cliffs, and gave one the impression of a volcano bursting above their heads.

It was the alarm gun from the fortress.

All who heard it knew that something very uncommon had happened.

The inhabitants of Portsmouth and its vicinity were at that time pretty well used to being woke up by the firing of artillery, but the alarm gun was only used on special occasions.

It was not yet daylight.

The gray precursor of dawn had not yet broken through the leaden clouds even.

The wind had lulled a little and the rain had ceased, but that was all.

Many a weary eye had not closed in sleep that night—many a head had been tossing restlessly on its pillows.

Even the old port admiral had not retired as he was wont.

He was on a visit with his daughter to a relative who was dying, but as soon as he heard that the renowned Captain Tom Drake was captured and in prison, and that a portion of the French fleet had been seen hovering about the Channel, he ordered his carriage and prepared for home at once.

The road he had to travel was not a pleasant one.

It was full of deep ruts and other dangers that a man of his years might well have shunned on such a night.

But no expostulations, no entreaties could turn him from his purpose.

His daughter knew too well how useless it would be to remonstrate with him.

The storm, the lightning, the thunder, not even the goat had terrors for him when he heard that the French flag was flaunting in British waters.

He did not know, when he called for his cocked hat and gold-headed stick, that Admiral Ellis was ashore and on his way to the prison; he had left him as a sort of safeguard to the port during his absence.

He had great confidence in the little admiral.

When the carriage lamps were lit and all ready, he seated himself on the soft cushions, saw that the doors were all securely closed, and then folded his big cloak around him.

His daughter, a sweet girl of seventeen, took her seat opposite him. From the first, when her father spoke of going, she was determined to accompany him.

She to some extent inherited the old admiral's inexorable nature, and besides she always deemed it her duty to be by his side when travelling.

The coachman and one solitary footman were the

only ones that complained of the journey on such a night, and they gave a cold shiver and an inward blessing when the great gates of the mansion closed behind them.

CHAPTER CXCVI.

THE PURSUIT OF CAPTAIN TOM DRAKE—TOM'S LIFE IS IN DANGER—THE PORT ADMIRAL IN TROUBLE—CAPTAIN TOM TO THE RESCUE.

On, on, like an arrow shot from a bow flew our gallant hero, Captain Tom, his pursuers following on his track like a pack of wolves.

Among the foremost runners, and there were some swift ones among them, one or two threw away their heavy muskets, leaving those in the rear to pick them up or stumble over them, just as it might chance to be, and trusted to their cutlasses and pistols.

Thus lightened, they quickened their speed, and got over the rough ground more easily.

Captain Tom, however, would not part with his sword.

It got between his legs, and more than once nearly threw him down.

Still, on he went, not knowing where the road he had chosen might lead him to.

In fact, he never let the thought trouble him.

He felt so confident of outdistancing his pursuers that he only thought of drawing them off the track of his buccaneers, and then, by strategem, throwing them off his own scent, and by making a circuit round a wood he could just discern at no great distance, make his way to the place where he and his followers had appointed to meet.

This arrangement, however, was more easily settled than carried out.

Before he had gone a mile he found that the big navy cutlass dangling at his heels was a sore drag upon his movements.

And yet he kept on, his proud spirit could not allow him to give in.

At times as the wind changed he fancied he could hear the hard breathing of those behind him.

He could not tell whether they had him in sight or not, and he dared not look back to ascertain, for reasons of the most obvious nature.

He would have liked very much to have known how many were actually following on his track.

Had there been any number within reason he would have turned and faced them—met them hand-to-hand.

It would be madness almost to have done so without knowing whom he had to encounter.

Fate however, stepped in and decided the question.

On one side the road—that opposite to where the wood lay, there grew a sprinkling of bushes here and there, not thick nor close enough to have concealed any one by day, but enough to render any one good assistance by night.

Under the shadow of these he glided swiftly along, and if the moon had chanced to have come out it would not have revealed him, so that he had no cause to fear on that point.

But in this very security lay his danger.

As he bounded along, his cutlass rattling a clump, clump, on the heels of his high knee boots, he came in contact with a low stone wall, and over he went into a deep gully or ditch.

In falling, his head struck against a stone, that stunned him, and he rolled over a huddled heap, the water like a torrent sweeping over his body and legs.

His pursuers, in the excitement of the chase, nearly shared his fate.

A long legged marine, who had been very offi-

cious in guiding the others, did go over, but not near where our hero fell.

His cry gave the rest warning barely in time to check their impetuous course.

"Have you—you got him?" cried the fat old corporal of marines, gasping for breath, as he came up in the rear of all.

"We've lost old Ramrod," was the terse reply; "he's gone down here, and if he ain't in Fiddler's-green by this time, it's a caution."

"Humph! — Fiddler's-green," came from the porpoise-like figure. "It is a good job he had somewhere to go to. If you ever reach there I shall consider you fortunate. It's easier for a ramrod to—whew——"

A gust of wind swept up the deep gully at that moment and stopped his breath.

"I suggest that we make for some port of safety till daylight," he grunted, as soon as he could make himself heard. "I don't suppose we should get any of the reward if we'd nabbed him," he added to himself.

He was about right there.

The blue-jackets quickly settled the matter so far as they were concerned.

One of their number happened to know of a grog-store not far from there.

He offered to lead them to it, and they all followed him at a pretty brisk pace.

They had been gone some time when our hero came to himself again.

He was drenched to the skin, but fortunately no bones were broken.

As he dragged himself from his watery couch a sound caught his ear.

He paused and listened.

It was repeated.

His quick instinct told him that it was the cry of a female.

"Some one in distress," he muttered; "by Jove, I must move more sharply."

Dazed and bewildered as he was he soon recovered his feet.

He had unconsciously ascended the opposite side of the gully.

He paused one moment to consider in which direction the sound proceeded; the next moment he was guided by the shrill cry of—

"Help, murder, help!"

It was not quite so dark now as it had hitherto been.

He could discern through the gloom that a bridge crossed the chasm not many yards away.

That that was the main road he had not the slightest doubt; but a thickly-wooded copse divided him from it. Pressing the foliage aside, he swiftly but silently made his way through it to the other side of the copse and listened.

"My daughter, my daughter! You have killed her, you scoundrels!" he could hear someone say.

"We shall not stand nice about killing you, if you don't hand over," someone else replied.

"Robbers, footpads!" Captain Tom muttered, grinding his teeth. "I must be cautious, or I may spoil all."

He felt for his cutlass as he muttered this, for he feared that in his fall he might have lost it.

It was all right, and so he just loosened it a little, so that it might be handy.

"There is more than one," thought Tom, as he prepared to rush forward. "The lady has fainted, I have not the least doubt of that."

Tom strained his eyes in the hope of seeing something to guide his movements, but a row of tall trees made the road at that part impenetrably dark.

He was surprised at not seeing a light, for all respectable vehicles in these days carried lamps or a lantern to lead them clear of the ruts and fallen trees that usually lined the roads.

Availing himself of the darkness, he crept stealthily forward, and presently he could discern the dim outlines of horses and a carriage partly overturned.

Then a light from one of the carriage lamps suddenly flashed forth; it had been purposely covered with something by the footpads, or whatever they were.

Tom's quick eye took in all it revealed at a glance.

Four ruffianly-looking fellows, armed with bludgeons and great horse pistols, were busily at their work.

Two of them were securing the coachman and footman, a third was holding on to the horses' heads, whilst a fourth was busy opening the carriage door.

"Capitally arranged," thought our hero, as he stood ready for a bound; "now, who shall be first? I can't settle you all at once."

There was no time to consider.

The huge ruffian at the carriage-door had thrust his burly head in, and, with a pistol in one hand and a dark lantern in the other, once more demanded the occupants to "hand out."

The ruffian this time added a deep oath and a threat to his imperative command.

"I tell you I have no valuables about me, you piratical rascal," a voice from within replied; "and if I had I would shoot you down first, you scoundrel!"

"Sharp words, capting, considering you have no shooter," said the ruffian, with a grin. "Now, you are only aggravating the case, as the judge says, by keeping this lady here in a faint. You'd better hand out respectably, you know like a good, brave capting as you are."

Captain Tom could not see the face of the person addressed as captain.

He could make out by the voice that it was an old man.

And, when he spoke again, he was evidently choking with rage.

"Confound you! do you know I am the port admiral?" he burst out. "I could have you hung, shot, anything I liked, you audacious villain!"

Our hero pricked up his ears at this speech.

"That's all very well for your pirate fellows," said the robber, with a grin, "but we don't happen to be them sort of coves; no port admirals frightens us, we're genelmen all of us bred and born. Come, tip up, or else I'll make yer. We're no Tom Drakes as you put in limbo so nicely."

The robber gave a coarse laugh, which was echoed by his accomplices.

Captain Tom Drake could not help smiling in spite of the chagrin he felt at his name being so loosely handled, and he was half inclined to spring at the villain's throat there and then.

Prudence for once checked him.

He did not care a pin how many times they robbed the port admiral, providing they did him no harm, for Tom in his heart bore the old admiral no ill will. His thoughts were centered in the fate of the lady.

He was wondering whether she was young and handsome.

In spite of all he had passed through he was still a great admirer of the fair sex, and especially of beauty.

"I should like to see her face," he thought.

A sudden movement on the part of the robber just enabled him at that moment to catch a cursory view of a pale upturned face, and the old admiral trying to support a figure with his right arm.

Tom's cheeks glowed when he saw this, slight as the view was.

There was a deadly meaning in his look, as he saw the coarse robber turn his brutal gaze upon her.

"For her sake," said the robber, hissing the words, as it were, between his teeth. "I command you, old man, to give us all you possess, before I brain you."

"Settle him at once, Dick!" cried the ruffian, who held the horses; "while you're playing with that old fool, we're wasting time, and werry likely to get nabbed."

"All in good time, pal," rejoined Dick, savagely. "I'm down on him presently if 'e don't shell all out and promise us a hundred pounds into the bargain for all the trouble he's put us to."

"Do you dare persist in this infamy after I have told you who I am?" yelled the admiral, red with passion. "Mind you, I am not like one of the common seamen, whom you waylay and plunder of their prize money at will. I am admiral of the port, admiral of Portsmouth, admiral of Spithead, where I could swing you at the yardarm if I had you there."

The robber burst into a hoarse laugh at this.

The idea of his going to Spithead to be strung up, when the Governor of Newgate, or of any of his Majesty's gaols, were quite willing to do him the same favour!

Dick's comrades were getting tired of all this.

Daylight would soon break upon them, and even the slight soughing of the wind through the almost leafless branches made them fancy they could hear some one on the road.

Our hero was also losing his patience.

He saw the ruffian, urged by the voices of his companions, make a movement as though about to use further violence.

He heard the click of the hammer of the heavy horse-pistol.

It was pointed at the old admiral's head.

Then he heard the faint voice of the lady as she slowly came to and uttered the one word:

"Murder!"

Faint as the cry was, Captain Tom could not resist that pathetic appeal.

His young blood was up in a moment.

His heart seemed to leap as it were into his throat.

His dark eyes flashed and lit with a deadly fire.

"Murder! help—help! Is there no one——"

The gallant Captain Tom waited to hear no more.

Four to one, but had there been forty instead, the sinewy arm of the bold buccaneer would have cut its way amongst them.

"Yes, I am here," he cried fiercely, as with the bound of a young tiger, he sprang across the sloughy road, and with his cutlass, cut down the robber to the earth.

Bang! and then a loud shriek, as the old admiral fell from his seat to the floor of his carriage.

"Good God! is he hit, and all through my folly?" cried Tom, in a breath of wild despair.

"Ay, and so are you," howled the fellow, who had let go the horses' heads, and fired his pistol point blank at our young hero, as he rushed to the carriage door.

Bang! bang! two more discharges, and the bullets whizzed close to Tom Drake's ear.

"Not hit yet," he thundered as he turned upon his assailants, who, bludgeons in hand, rushed furiously at him.

All was the direst confusion in a moment.

The horses reared, plunged, and kicked like furies.

The coachman yelled to the top of his voice with fear.

Into the ditch rolled the footman, adding to the

din by uttering hideous howls such as might come from the lips of a roasted monkey.

Meanwhile Tom fought desperately with his assailants; they had closed with him in spite of all his efforts to the contrary, and a blow from one of their bludgeons had almost deprived him of the use of his sword-arm.

It was well for him that they were not rich enough to possess more than one pistol each, his own was useless, owing to his falling into the water, but his lithe, supple form was equal to all their brute strength, for he flung them from him as though by some supernatural power.

Once at arm's length he could bring his cutlass into full play in earnest.

It was getting daylight now, and as he faced round to defend himself from a treacherous blow behind he beheld the fair occupant of the carriage gazing on him in silent admiration.

This gave him fresh courage, renewed his youthful vigour, and added fresh strength to his sinewy arm.

He needed it at this moment too, for the ruffian he had first cut down was recovering fast; he was only stunned by the blow, for his brutal skull was sufficiently thick to resist the blunt blade of the cutlass, but he had an ugly gash across his brow.

Tom took in his position at a glance.

His case was growing more desperate than ever.

One swift point, parry and thrust, and a bludgeon flew into the air, and its owner staggered away wounded.

Another sharp turn of the wrist and another ruffian fell back with his left leg severely mangled, and then our gallant hero with his remaining strength used the flat of his cutlass so dexterously upon the sides, ribs, and shoulders of the remaining one until he backed into the hedge, and then took to his legs and ran.

This had all transpired so suddenly, and the robbers had made so dexterous a retreat, that Tom, though he had often been placed at a much greater disadvantage, could scarcely believe his own senses.

He stood for a moment dazed as it were in bewilderment, until the voice of the admiral's beauteous daughter recalled him to his senses.

Beauteous she really was, and Tom forgot for the time the vow he had pledged and the duty he owed to his own peerless Minnie.

But his love was pure, and though he stood for an instant gazing upon the fair girl before him in admiration, as she smiled her gratitude through her tears, his breast was unsullied by one guilty thought.

"Thanks, thanks, noble stranger," she said, in a tone of softened sweetness; "a thousand thanks; to whom, pray, do we owe our great and merciful deliverance?"

"Fair lady, name it not," our hero replied, with an assuring smile; "I am not hurt, not even scratched; therefore, as I have not lost one drop of blood in your cause and that of your father, I do not deserve your praise."

"Still we do owe you something," she said in the same sweet tone. "My father might have been slain, and I might have been subjected to more brutal violence. Is there no small boon we might confer upon you? My father is rich and I—"

She drooped her silken eyelids as she spoke, for our gallant buccaneer had taken her soft white hand in his, and raised it unconsciously to his lips.

The sudden hush of her silvery voice aroused him from his blissful lethargy, and to relieve her maiden modesty he said:

"Good lady, I hope your father is not hurt?"

"Not much; merely a little frightened for my sake," she replied, as she smoothed back his silvered

locks and revealed his brow, which was merely blackened by the powder from the ruffian's pistol.

"And who said I was?" growled out the old admiral, suddenly. "Ah! what is all this about? Have I been asleep—dreaming—or what the dev— Why, I—I thought," he added, confusedly, "that I'd just run that confounded Ellis up to his own yard-arm, and shipped that rascal of a Captain Tom Drake off to Tower-hill to be beheaded."

"Both of which merciless deeds I hope you will never be guilty of, dear pa," answered the fair girl, as she drew his warm cloak and rugs about him, and seated him as comfortably as she had done on their leaving the mansion.

She was not aware that the old port-admiral had sent a swift messenger on horseback before they started on their homeward journey.

He doated on his daughter, and confided in her to some extent, but he did not tell her all his secrets.

Sometimes, in an unguarded moment, she could glean more from him than she could by all her coaxing and endearments, and they were not a few.

Captain Tom, during their short acquaintance, had learnt enough of the character of the man he had to deal with to know that he had no child to play with.

He could not help smiling at the complimentary manner in which the old admiral spoke of him.

But the old veteran began to grow uneasy.

He longed to know how his dispatches had been carried out, and what steps had been taken to recover what they had lost.

What he would have thought had he known how near he was to the dreaded pirate we must leave our readers to guess.

But, with all his faults, the old veteran had some good qualities.

He was not slow in ordering the offender to be punished; yet he was as ready to reward anyone who merited it.

As an instance, as soon as he heard how cowardly his men had behaved during the late encounter, and how gallantly our hero had fought, he felt he could give him anything.

"Young man," he said, eyeing our hero narrowly; "I thank you for saving our lives, and if a hundred pounds or so can do you any service you may have it by merely presenting this card to my secretary."

Few could have faced his steady glance without flinching, as our hero did, when he took the card and read the address, and then turned it to read what the port admiral had written on it with pencil.

Tom was astounded even at his own audacity.

He was astonished, too, at what he read.

The missive ran thus:—

"Give the bearer, on demand, one hundred, or five hundred pounds if he should need it, to be debited to my private account."

Tom could not help laughing at the joke. A thought of devilment at that moment passed through his mind; as the old admiral thrust his head out of the opposite window to see what progress his men were making with the horses, Tom took a card similar to the admiral's from his pocket, and wrote on it:

"Give the Buccaneer Captain Tom Drake, on demand, one hundred, or five hundred lashes if he needs them, and debit it to my private account."

"Pardon me, but you have omitted to sign it," said our hero, with a polite bow, handing his own card to the admiral.

"So I have! What a lubber I must be; confound it all! But wh-what's this?"

Our hero's face moved not a muscle.

His wonderful self-control was never more developed than at that moment.

The old admiral could not believe his own eyes, as the saying is, so he put on his gold spectacles.

When he had read it and re-read it three or four times, he laid back in his seat and glared at our hero in wonderment.

Tom would have given him anything he possessed for his thoughts at that moment.

Truth to tell, the old sea-dog did not know his own thoughts at that moment.

He did not know whether to be angry or pleased at the boy's audacity.

He scanned him from top to toe, and was much struck with our hero's figure, which he had not troubled himself to notice until now.

"Captain Tom Drake," the admiral muttered unconsciously, loud enough, however, for our hero to hear.

"That's me," Tom answered with perfect nonchalance.

"Then the devil take you!" blurted the port admiral.

"No, no; I mean, surrender in the name of the king."

"To you, sir?" queried Tom.

"To me, sir; you are my prisoner, return the card I gave you, you scoundrel."

"So that you may get the reward offered for my capture, and cheat me out of my five hundred pounds," said Tom, coolly.

The old admiral began to splutter tremendously. He was so choked with rage that he could not articulate clearly one word.

He regretted having so carelessly left his sword and pistols behind him, but regret was useless now

As soon as he could loosen his tongue he called on his lacqueys to arrest Captain Tom; but they did not, or pretended not to hear him; besides, they were both of them wet and shivering with cold, and longed to get home to their comfortable quarters.

"You idiots!" yelled their incensed master; "you shall suffer for this! Go on—no; get down. Seize him, you blockheads, seize him!"

Tom Drake kept a wary eye on their movements; he had not the least doubt that they were both armed or had firearms under the seat, and that they had not time, being so suddenly surprised, to use them upon the robber.

They might muster courage enough to pop a pistol at him on the sly and give him a nasty knock, but that was the only fear he had of them.

Even the horses were impatient at the delay; they pawed the ground and snorted, for the keen morning air was not very agreeable to their stiffened flanks.

Just as the old admiral was blustering and even beginning to swear, the loud boom of a cannon startled them, and off they went at a furious pace, and the turn of the road hid them from our hero's view.

Tom was sorry in one way that the parting between the old admiral and himself should have been so sudden, for his devil-may-care nature gloried in the fun of teazing the old gentleman, whose life he had risked his own to save only a few minutes before.

He was half inclined as it was to run to the bend of the road, and see if the carriage was travelling in safety; but, on second thought, he considered it most prudent to see to his own safety.

It would have been better for him had he decided on this before, for a pair of eyes at that moment glared at him from an opening in the bush, and then a head protruded, and two stout seamen crept from the foliage and stepped softly up behind him.

One of them carried a sort of hand-net, with a long haft to it, and this he adroitly swung into the air and brought down over our hero's head.

Tom was for the moment staggered.

He was netted safe, the iron ring pinned his arms tightly to his side, and rendered him powerless in that quarter.

It was not in his nature, however, to yield meekly and without a struggle, but all his efforts to free himself were useless; some half-dozen blue-jackets pounced upon him, and others, seizing upon the long handles of the net, dragged him along, and bore him away in triumph.

---o---

CHAPTER CXCVII.
CAPTAIN TOM DRAKE RECAPTURED.

BOLD CAPTAIN TOM cut a perfect figure in his new character, and his proud spirit galled as he was compelled to listen to the rude ribaldry and coarse jokes of his captors.

"A capital haul this time, Ned," said one of the blue-jackets, as he turned his quid in his cheek, and tugged away at the long pole; "better than fighting the Frenchies, eh, mate?"

"Well, rather, it's a out-an-out invention; there some good fish been caught in that net, I'll wager."

"But not so valuable; only fancy, when we get the shiners, won't we foot it out on Plymouth Hard, eh, mate?"

"Do you think they'll let us?"

"In course they will; aint we 'titled to the reward; and aint we caught the pirate that's cost the guv'ment more'n a score o' millions hard cash down?"

"That's true, at all events, shipmate; but what a fool that lubber of a land swab was not to try and fish him himself; he'd a ugly crack across the figure'd, though, he won't forget it for a month or two."

"And I'm sartin he didn't need it to make his ugly bows more han'sum, Ned. I wonder how he came to run athwart the hawse of this buccaneer fellow?"

"Well, he didn't seem to care about telling us that, and it warn't our place to ax too many questions. I wonder what's up at the fort, Ned?"

Ned pointed his thumb significantly over his shoulder.

"That was a livener, just to let 'em know this joker had escaped. What a fool he must 'a been not to sheer out when he'd slipped us so nicely. I'm sorry for the young chap, though; he's not a bad looking fellow, and never did us harm."

"He would if he'd got away, and he would if he was to slip us now. All the 'scuses in the world wouldn't a saved our backs. I shall be glad when we get them stone walls round him agen."

"I hope we don't meet those cursed jollies, Ned," added the other, softly; "it'll be the toss up of a biscuit that we lose the prize-money if we do; Hullo! dam-me, if that aint the corporal of marines yonder."

From what he could glean from their conversation, and sundry hints dropped from the other party, our hero concluded he owed his capture to the ruffian he had belaboured with his cutlass.

It seems he made his way to the very house Jerry Mizzen and Bob's pursuers had adjourned to after their fruitless search in the court.

He had gone there, no doubt, to seek among its lawless frequenters some one who could attend to the wounds of his companions, and shelter them until they were able to return to their old haunts.

Tom's heart sank a little as he saw about twenty marines follow their corporal round a rocky point in the path his captors were leading him.

The iron ring of the net, too, added to his discomfiture.

... pressed so tightly down to his hips that it ... his arms and stopped the blood from circu-...

Had it not been for this, the bold buccaneer would have made another struggle for liberty, for the meeting between the bluejackets and marines was not by any means friendly.

They held a short consultation, and with many oaths and sundry invectives, both parties claimed the possession of their illustrious prisoner.

Cutlasses were drawn and muskets brought to the shoulder, and a regular melée was carried on for some time.

Although annoyed, Tom could not help being a little amused at the jealousy his capture had occasioned.

To be bartered for, for what to him was such a paltry sum, was enough to gall the spirit of our gallant hero.

Had he been taken in a fair fight he would not have felt it so keenly.

As it was he was not sorry when a body of troopers dashed down the road and demanded he should be given up to them

The officer who led them was a fine, handsome young fellow, and strode his horse with such ease and grace that our gallant captain could not help admiring him.

Saluting the corporal of the marines, he demanded who it was they were dragging, as it were, like a lion going to be slaughtered; and when he learnt that it was Captain Tom Drake he commanded his immediate release.

Somehow, soldier though he was, his heart seemed to yearn towards the daring boy leader. As he scanned his bold figure he thought it a pity that one who could have done justice to king and country should have broken its laws and placed himself in such a position.

Captain Tom bowed his thanks to the young officer, when the cruel iron was removed from his cramped limbs.

The young officer courteously returned his salute.

He had not expected to find such refinement in the daring Buccaneer he had been sent in search of.

"Captain Tom Drake," he said, bowing with some stiffness; "I hold a warrant here to capture you, and alive or dead to take you to the fortress. I had no wish to convey you there in the disgraceful manner in which I found you, therefore, I will take your word as an officer and a gentleman that you will accompany us without resistance."

"As an officer that was once in the service of your king, and a gentleman, as I can prove by my birth, I promise you," replied our hero, with an almost imperceptible bow; "but when I cease to be your prisoner I shall avail myself of any opportunity to escape, and once more on the deck of my gallant 'Sea Bird' I will defy the world to capture me."

"That is agreed, then. I like your noble spirit and would assist you," he added, lowering his voice, "but I must fulfil a soldier's duty."

Ordering one of his troopers to dismount, he motioned our hero to take his place, and the horses' heads were turned in the direction of the fortress.

The governor of the fortress was surprised to see our hero led in without bond or shackle.

Not many hours before he had been ordered to prepare the strongest dungeon for our hero's reception as soon as he should be captured, or for any of his crew.

Captain Tom could not help smiling at the ludicrous and crest-fallen look of the governor as he saw Tom so tamely led in.

In the stern lines on his brow Tom could read that he had a martinet to deal with, and that he expect no pity from him.

Indeed, he never for a moment dreamt of such thing as pity.

Had the governor mentioned such a thing and offered to let him roam about the fortress on his parole of honour, he would not have accepted it. He was determined to stay there no longer than he possibly could help.

He longed to join his crew once more, but that at present was out of the question.

Had he been at all of a desponding nature, the strong walls and stout iron bars that guarded the casements would have made him give up all hope of liberty for the future.

As it was, his quick discerning eye took in everything as he passed along, even the dress and armament of the soldiers, who guarded him so closely to his cell, that cell which was to be his abode until he was led forth to hear his sentence

And that sentence was to be DEATH.

CHAPTER CXCVIII.

A PRISONER IN THE FORTRESS—CAPTAIN WOUNDS THE GOVERNOR—IN THE DUNGEONS OF THE BLACK TOWER.

OUR hero could imagine that he was being led to a part of the fortress whence escape would be impossible.

Along damp stone passages, with groined roofs and massive stone walls, that were built to resist the heaviest artillery that could be brought to bear upon them.

In some places the moisture was dropping from the walls and roof, and the damp atmosphere made our bold captain even shiver.

They were nearly half an hour traversing the tortuous passages.

Some of them were utterly dark, so that one of the gaunt soldiers had to carry a lighted torch.

The governor led the way in silence.

He seemed well acquainted with every turn and cranny.

He had been in charge of the stronghold for many years.

The medals that adorned his breast and an ugly scar across his cheek showed that he had been an old veteran.

Having ascended and descended steep flights of steps slimy with moisture, and passed under, as Captain Tom Drake imagined, a moat, they entered a long, low corridor, studded with doors on each side.

Tom, bold as he was, could not repress a shudder as the lurid glare of the torch fell on the rusty iron work and bars and bolts.

"They intend burying me alive," he thought to himself; "in some dark, noisome dungeon, where the rats will feed upon my carcase, where my remains will lay hidden until my name is forgotten, and my fate will never be known."

Thus he soliloquised as they still marched on, startling the rats, and crushing the slimy reptiles that strewed the floor beneath their feet.

Tom was just wondering how much farther they intended taking him, when they came to a massive oak door, sheathed with iron, and secured with massive, broad bars, of more than an inch in thickness.

The governor stepped on one side to allow the head warder and his assistants to pass him.

The bold buccaneer chief winced a little, as the key was placed in the lock, and the heavy bolt shot back.

It required the whole strength of the three men

to undo the fastenings, they were so corroded from disuse.

The ponderous door resisted their combined efforts all together.

The halberds of the soldiers had to be used upon it before it would give way.

And when it did go, it was very slowly, and emitted a horrible screeching sound that set all their teeth, even to the governor's, grating and on an edge.

Captain Tom thought this was the door of his cell, but he was mistaken.

A flight of stone steps was before them, the top of which was not even reached by the glare of the torch.

Our hero paused a moment to look upward before crossing the threshold of that ponderous door.

He took a survey, too, of the rusty hinges and the massive lock.

He was calculating what chance there was of breaking through such a mass of bolted wood and iron.

The governor read his thoughts in an instant.

He gave Tom a look that our hero did not much relish.

There was more meaning in that look than a volume of words would have expressed.

Captain Tom gave an involuntary sigh; then he drew himself to his full height and braced himself firmly for the occasion.

The passing of that gate would have made the heart of the stoutest man quail, especially if placed in our hero's position.

The governor motioned him to proceed, but our hero heeded him not for the moment.

"Lead on, march!" said the governor to the man-at-arms who held the torch. "To the Black Tower with the pirate rebel!"

"No pirate, and no rebel!" thundered Tom, glancing fiercely at the governor. "I am still captain of the 'Will o' the Wisp.'"

"You are my prisoner," answered the veteran, sternly. "I will take all care that you do not escape"

"Am I so dangerous, then?" asked our hero, fixing his eye firmly on him. "Does it take a score of you to lead a boy through these hideous passages?"

"I would have fifty if I needed them," replied the governor, sternly. "I have two hundred men at my immediate command."

He paused to observe what effect his words had upon our hero.

Our noble captain met his gaze without flinching.

The governor's boast had driven the cold chill from his heart, and warmed him, as it were, into new life.

"Had you twenty thousand men at your back, I would not fear you," he said: "I have faced the cannon's mouth, and surely I would not flinch from you. 'Tis cowards who fear, and I am no coward."

The governor bit his lip, and made a sign for the torch-bearer to proceed.

Two of the soldiers caught hold of our hero and forced him a step forward.

"Unhand me, minions," he cried, as he shook them from him. "I take no insults from you, if I do from your dog of a master here. Lead on!"

The governor's eyes fired up fiercely.

His stern lips puckered up and his brow darkened like thunder.

Slowly, and with ominous tread, the cavalcade ascended the stone steps, and then they were in the lower chamber of the Black Tower.

It was not ill-named.

Everything about the place was black.

The walls seemed to be hewn out of solid black granite.

They were in a large circular chamber, and our hero counted six doors in that horrible looking place, which he had no doubt had not been opened for many years.

The governor pointed with his drawn sword to one of them, and the head gaoler, who seemed to be well acquainted with his signs and significant gestures, opened one of them, and disclosed to our hero's gaze a sight that made our bold hero recoil for a moment in disgust.

This cell, like the chamber, was of the same dark hue, and, with the exception of a stone pitcher, was void and empty of every appurtenance that a dungeon even in those days was supposed to contain.

There was a small opening just large enough to admit a small streak of light, and through it a faint glint of sunshine managed to peep as though by stealth.

The soldier with the torch bent forward so that our hero might get a good view of the interior. What horrible vision was it that so entranced him? What hideous object was it that made his youthful frame quiver so fearfully for a moment?

In a sitting posture against the dark wall was a human skeleton, the remains of one who had died in that horrible dungeon; some one of noble blood, no doubt; some one who had been taken prisoner in the turbulent times when kings themselves fought, and so many heads were brought to the scaffold.

Captain Tom averted his gaze with a shudder.

"This," said the governor, "is your abode for the nonce, my gallant captain, and there," pointing with his sword to the skeleton, "will be your companion until I can find you one less cheerful."

Tom Drake could stand to hear no more.

The governor had touched upon a chord that was at its utmost tension.

"Fiend!" he cried, drawing his form up to its full height; "fiend! I will stand your devilish taunts no longer. Lend me a sword, one of you," he added, turning to the soldiery; "if there is a man—a soldier—among you, let me measure blades with this fiend in mortal shape."

The governor turned ashy pale.

He saw that our hero was really in earnest.

The soldiers drew back as though worked by machinery.

In their hearts, for they were no cowards, they would have liked to have seen fair play.

"What, ho! is it treason, then?" thundered the governor, as he read the men's thoughts in their looks. "Have you forgotten your oath of allegiance to your King? Seize the rebel, or——"

Before he could utter another word Tom sprang forward, and, snatching a sword from the sheath of one of the men, he aimed a blow at the governor that made him stagger against the wall.

Fortunately for him, he was able to guard the blow quickly, or it would have laid him open to the waist.

But the old man was strong, and, even at his age, he was considered one of the best of swordsmen.

Tom followed up the attack with considerable activity, and the governor soon found that in the youth before him there was enough true mettle to have carried him on the battle-field.

Strange to say, not one of the men stepped forward to the governor's assistance.

Not one of them even ventured to speak a word.

They stood speechless, spell-bound, as it were.

In the excitement of the moment they quite forgot the punishment attending their neglect of duty.

Meanwhile the pair had fought their way, foot by foot, into the very centre of the outer chamber where they slashed away at each other as only two good swordsmen could do.

Once or twice our hero's sword was within an inch or so of the old governor's heart, and if Tom Drake had only forced the blade home he would have slain him outright; but somehow the brave boy seemed to check his arm purposely.

Truth was, Captain Tom did not want to take his life.

What pleasure would it have been to him to have slain him on the spot?

If he could only wound him so that he might give him as much pain as possible, it would be more gratifying.

The governor, on the other hand, was not so considerate. Blinded with passion, he cut and thrust with all his fury.

He would have slain our young hero without the slightest compunction, and have gloried in the act.

Captain Tom was simply getting warm now, for it must be remembered that his clothes were still muddy and wet.

The damp chill air of the dank passages had numbed his limbs and chilled his young blood.

The heat of his passion had somewhat cooled too.

But this sort of work could not last long.

The combatants having drawn back for a moment to grip their swords more firmly and to straighten the muscles of their arms, again stood foot to foot, and their blades once more crossed.

The man-at-arms' blunt, heavy sword would have been no match against the keen, steel, supple blade of the governor, had it been in a less skilful hand than that of Captain Tom Drake.

Tom saw many opportunities when he could have whipped it through him without using any extra exertion.

After a few more strokes, which made the vaulted roof ring again and the sparks fly about as though from a blacksmith's anvil, the governor's arm fell by his side, and his sword dropped from his hand.

The governor gave him a look of deadly hatred as he placed his left hand on the wounded limb.

"You have wounded me," he hissed. "But it is not the first blow I have received from a rebel."

"Miserable cur, I could have taken your life," said Captain Tom. "I spare it now," he added; "it is worthless; and if any of your myrmidons' here need a trial of my skill I am willing to oblige them."

The soldier whose sword it was stepped forward to snatch it from his hand, but our hero's quick eye detected his movement.

"Not yet," he said; "not yet.'"

He stepped back from the soldier, and fixed a look upon him that made him cower and quail.

"Surrender it to me," said the captain of the guard. "I command you."

"Take it if you can," was Tom's only reply.

The man saw that he was in earnest, and the rest, fearing the consequences, closed in our hero, who was again ready to renew the fray.

What might have been the consequences it is hard to say, had not the warder, a strong, brutal-looking fellow, stepped up behind Tom Drake.

He held a heavy bunch of keys in his hand, which was capable of felling an ox.

These he wielded suddenly in the air, and bringing them down on the head of our gallant youth, stretched him senseless and bleeding on the stone floor.

With a coarse laugh the warder's two assistants raised the boy's prone form, and threw him into one corner of the cell, leaving him lifeless, for all they knew or cared, in a huddled heap.

Then the heavy door was closed, the rusty bolts adjusted, the key grated in the lock, and the glare of the torch, and the hurried footsteps of the party died away, and all was gloom in the Black Tower.

CHAPTER CXCIX.

THE MEETING OF THE ADMIRALS.—THE ARREST OF ADMIRAL ELLIS.—A STRANGE CRAFT.

WHEN the testy old admiral arrived at his mansion he found a number of petty officers and seamen clustered around the gates, awaiting his arrival, which was announced by three ringing British cheers, such as sailors alone know how to give with perfection.

His carriage and its equipments were in a most shocking plight, and the coachman and footmen were not much better; but these were soon taken charge of by the bluejackets, who shouldered the carriage and carried it bodily into the coach-house.

The horses, too, were soon safely housed in the stable amid much fun, for the sailors enjoyed the sport, as they termed it, and all signs of the wrecked carriage were soon relieved from the gaze of the idle spectators who were lounging about in groups, discussing the various topics of the day.

In the meantime a party of officers—admirals, captains, and lieutenants, had descended the steps and conveyed the old port admiral and his daughter into the mansion.

"The blue chamber. Usher them into the blue chamber you thick-skulled lubber," growled out the testy admiral to his powdered attendant. "Don't stand there like a seventy-four at anchor; let them have wine, anything so long as they don't get—there, away with you. I will join them as soon as I have made myself a little bit ship-shape."

It took him only a few minutes to wash and brush up, and then he joined the party, who were lively and convivial; and then he commenced business in earnest.

There was a large pile of despatches, some from the Admiralty, others from abroad, and a few from the ships then in harbour.

Some of the senior officers were assisting his secretary to open them, and the latter having read them handed those of most importance over to the admiral.

"No news of the 'Will o' the Wisp,' he grumbled to himself; "where the deuce—ah! what is this?"

The face of the bluff old seaman changed to every hue of the rainbow, and then settled down to a crimson blush as he scanned the last document.

"Hang it, look at that, Jarvis," he grunted, as he handed it to a gray-haired old veteran. "That Ellis—I always thought he would. Let him be placed under arrest immediately," he added to his secretary.

The secretary wrote out the order as desired, the admiral signed it, and Jarvis was intrusted with its fulfilment.

"Gentlemen," he said, addressing the other officers, "that Captain Tom Drake is again at large. I have seen him my own self, with my own eyes, not very long since. I was in hopes that he was an impostor, but this dispatch confirms the fact."

"Very awkward indeed," ventured one of the admirals; "just at this moment we have our hands full with the enemy. Old Bony intends giving us a real rub up this time."

"Are they at sea again, think you?"

"Nine sail of the line were reported off Cape St. Vincent by a schooner that arrived this morning."

"Only nine."

"You must remember we have no ships in port

CAPTAIN TOM THRUSTS HIS SWORD THROUGH THE BODY OF THE PIRATE.

ready for actual service; all our swift sailers are scattered about looking for the 'Will-o'-the-Wisp.'"

"I wish she was blown up," grunted the old port-admiral; "I'd give a thousand guineas out of my own purse this moment if I could see her fragments in the air. Her boy crew—for they are but boys—are a perfect set of devil's imps!"

He wound up with something like an oath.

None of the other officers dared to break in upon the conversation.

They wisely held their tongues, and listened with intense interest.

We should be wrong in saying they listened with patience, for there were some fiery spirits among them who longed to be afloat again, tussling with their old enemy.

Some of them did not even care whether the boy buccaneers were captured or not.

In fact, some of them gloried in our hero's pluck.

One old commodore went even so far as almost to say so, adding that he would rather have one slap at the French than capture a hundred "Will-o'-the-Wisps."

The old admiral knew not whether to smile or frown at him.

At that moment a messenger arrived, bringing fresh news.

It was the recapture of our gallant hero, Tom Drake.

This news somewhat appeased the old admiral's wrath.

"In the fortress, eh? Well, he won't slip his cable from there. I know old Fitzgerald too well. I am sorry the military have the praise of his capture though. What a lubberly set we shall appear in the eyes of the public."

All the officers present coincided with this.

The governor of the fortress had artfully omitted to state how shamefully he had been be ten by his heroic ptive and the heartless manner in which he had been thrown into the dungeon.

One hour later all the officers had left.

They were each armed with a commission, and all of them were ordered to get their ships manned and victualled, and ready for sea at once.

At Chatham and Sheerness all the Government works were in full swing.

On the Thames all the old hulks were being bought up, or pressed into the storing and victualling department.

There was a report spread, which caused some commotion in the metropolis, that one little vessel, a brig, had actually resisted a Government cutter that had tried to board her, and had even fired upon the cutter under the very muzzles of the guns of the forts of Tilbury and Gravesend.

This vessel was no other than the saucy little "Will o' the Wisp;" she had anchored there, the wind and tide being against her, on her way to Pu fleet.

Her middy crew had shot away the cutter's mast, and sailed down to the Nore before those on shore were aware that anything so serious had happened.

They had even landed at Sheerness and bought up a ton of gunpowder that had been smuggled to a rendezvous they well knew without exciting any suspicion, though the guard boats were continually rowing up and down, and round the fleet, to prevent their crews deserting.

Portsmouth and Plymouth, as we are aware, was all life and bustle.

The flag ship and the Government station were continually signalling each other, whilst the long pendants fluttered in the breeze from the tall masts of the various men-of-war.

One unpretentious little craft was lying at anchor in the Sound doing nothing in particular, so far as outward appearances went.

A few of her hands, in tarry jackets and trousers, were employed in the rigging or slung over the side with a paint pot and brush, giving her sides a dab here and there where it needed it.

No one would have thought how actively engaged were those on board of her.

Little did the flag-ship admiral dream that the eyes of one, who was leisurely polishing the brass-york round the companion-way, were watching his signals and reporting them to another who stood on the companion-ladder with a book in his hand.

The coast guard signalman at the flag-staff had certainly noticed her neat build and tall rakishness of her masts, but her clumsily rolled-up sails deceived even his practical eye.

However, it was not until she was suddenly missed the next morning that any one took any interest in her, and then the lieutenant of a sloop-of-war, that was engaged in pressing seamen from the different vessels entering or anchored about the port, was summoned to show cause why the "Flying Squirrel" and the "Will o' the Wisp" should not be one and the same vessel.

Certainly, no one thought of this before, but now every one thought it possible.

Admiral Ellis, who might be classed as no one at the present moment, was the only one who doubted her peaceful calling.

From his place of durance vile he had spied her with his glass, and was almost certain of his recognition.

But the cantankerous little admiral was so disgusted with his treatment that he would not even hint his suspicion.

"They may find it out," he mumbled to himself as he paced up and down his room, fretting and fuming like a caged eagle. "Let them glory in their wisdom. I am but a fool. Bah! they shall not clip the wings of this bird for nothing."

He told all this to Reuben Harpy afterwards, but it was too late then, she had slipped off, and no one knew in what direction.

---o---

CHAPTER CC.

WHAT BEFEL JERRY MIZZEN IN HIS CAPTIVITY—BOB HAULER HAS A MISFORTUNE—THE CAROUSAL IS SUDDENLY INTERRUPTED.

THE mysterious occupants of the cavern had quite forgotten their prisoners in the excitement caused by the various reports that were continually being brought in, whilst Bob and Jerry were chattering away like two monkeys.

They were both as hungry as hunters, and as dry as two such thirsty souls could be, and were dying, as they described it, for a chew of tobacco or a puff of the pipe.

Jerry was the worst of the two.

His sufferings were very acute.

He had such a powerful sense of smell that a breaker of rum at the opposite end of the cavern seemed to him right under his nose.

"I wish they'd have a little compassion on us, Bob," he said, looking at his companion very dejectedly; "I wish they'd take it right away or move it a little bit closer."

"Move what?" said Bob, who had fallen into a momentary abstraction.

"Why, that horrid stuff over there. It gives me a pain in my vitals to smell the effluvia of it all this way off."

"What would be the use of their taking it away?" queried Bob, sarcastically.

"Well, out of sight out of mind, you know."

"And if they brought it closer?"

"Why, we might dip our noses in the bung-hole."

"So might a pig fly. Why don't you walk over to it and dip your nose in if you are so fond of it?"

There was a wicked twinkle in Bob's eye as he said this.

He would have given anything himself for a toothful at that moment.

As the possibility of getting any was out of the question, he found some relief in teasing Jerry.

"I wish I could," returned the irrepressible one.

"It's no use wishing if you don't follow it up, Jerry."

"I'd follow it up, and swallow it down, too, if I could," said Jerry, "and think it no trouble. Why can't you?"

"Because I don't like it, Jerry."

"Oh, you fibber!"

"How am I a fibber, Jerry? I'm not obliged to like it if I don't like it, am I?"

"You might step and fetch it just for me, Bob."

"Hold on your jawing tackle, some one's coming. By Jove! it's a female, too. What's she got there; can you see?" said Bob, in a whisper.

"Grog, I think. No it aint; it's baccy, Bob."

It was a woman.

They could see that she was very young, and beautiful, too, as she bent over the fire and raked the embers together.

She was dressed very much like Zelie.

Her bright eyes and smiling face led them to suppose that she was not a captive.

Bob's mouth fairly watered as he saw by the firelight that she carried a huge roll of tobacco leaves that had been soaked in rum and bound tightly together.

"I'd like a chew, Jerry," whispered Bob.

"I'd like a smoke," Jerry answered.

"I wonder what lingo she speaks?"

"Furren, no doubt, Bob. What's she up to, I wonder?"

They were not kept long in suspense.

There was a pile of cutlasses laying in one corner of the cave, and having run her thumb along the edges of one or two of them, in a thorough systematical way, she selected one.

With it she knelt down by a block of wood, and commenced chopping up the tobacco with wonderful dexterity.

This done, she rolled it several times through her hands, and placed it on the head of an upturned cask.

Bob and Jerry stared in wonderment.

"Speak to her, Bob," said Jerry.

"Not likely."

"I'm here to help you if anything happens."

"Very likely; but nothing won't happen. Don't you take me for a fool. If you weren't so fast in making a noise we wouldn't be trussed up here like a couple of turkeys."

"I'll speak to her, Bob, by jingo I will. I want a smoke, that baccy's making my belly growl awfully. If I can only get a smoke it will be as good as a feed to me."

"Ahem!" Jerry muttered, just loud enough to attract her notice as she was going away.

She turned round and looked towards them, but could see no one, as they were in the shade.

"Ahem!" Jerry repeated.

Bob was afraid to breathe.

"Hold your jaw," he muttered.

"You're not frightened, are you, Bob?"

"Not I, Jerry; keep still, you may frighten her, and that may get us into more trouble. Here she comes."

With cautious step the female walked towards them, and observing their peculiar predicament, she bestowed upon them a look of pity and wonderment, as might be expected.

Seeing that they were strangers, she was about to leave them without any comment, when Jerry's voice arrested her

"Water, water," he muttered, just sufficiently loud for her to hear. "I'm dying."

"Dying?" said the female, approaching them without fear, seeing they were so helplessly bound.

"Yes, I'm dying of thirst and hunger."

"I cannot give you any food without the captain's orders," she replied. "What are you? How came you here?" she added.

"Two poor sailors, as has lost themselves, and they've put us here," Jerry answered, piteously.

"You have been taken for spies, I suppose?"

"They've mistaken us for something of that sort, but we're not. I can swear we're not. Can't you give us a bit of baccy and a drop of—of—water?"

"I could do so, but I dare not. If you are spies the captain will know how to deal with you; no one dare do it without his consent."

"But he wont know it," suggested Jerry.

"Well, perhaps there will be no harm," she replied, partly to herself and partly to Jerry. "Mind the captain must not know it, though."

"Never fear, I hope he will soon come and release us," said Jerry, growing bolder.

She stepped lightly away without making him any reply, and from a cavity in the wall of the cavern produced a pitcher, and then stood to listen.

A footstep had startled her, but it soon died away again, and then she went up to the block of wood before mentioned, and from the floor around it she collected a few loose leaves of the tobacco which had fallen, and very shortly her dexterous fingers had converted them into two very neat cigars.

Having lighted both at the fire, which was now burning up brightly, she took up the pitcher, and, having taken another cautious glance around, stepped on tiptoe up to our two unfortunates, and

having given them both a good drink, she placed in each of their mouths one of the lighted cigars.

Neither of them could thank her for this charitable act, as they had to clutch the ends of their cigars with their teeth.

Smiling quietly to herself, as well she might, at the two comical figures they cut, their benefactress then tripped lightly away, and having replaced the pitcher in the niche, left the cavern.

Bob, to the no small wonderment of Jerry Mizzen, chawed up his cigar and bit off the lighted end without any ceremony, considering the trouble their benefactress had taken in administering to their wants.

Then he emptied his mouth of a quantity of juice, and thus addressed his companion in misfortune:—

"Well, Jerry, now are you happy? Is your unreasonable concience satisfied?"

"Just a little," mumbled Jerry, almost losing his weed in the effort. "I wanted a pipe, not this unshipshapeable swab of a thing; its nearly choking me."

Bob Hauler gave an inward chuckle; the smoke got up poor Jerry's nose and filled his eyes, besides nearly choking him.

"What are you grinning at, you—you baboon?" grunted Jerry, emptying his mouth of a cloud that would have filled any ordinary apartment. "Aint it bad enough without you making game of a fellow?"

"I did'nt make the cigar, Jerry, my dear fellow."

"But you are poking fun at a cove. Whew! this is enough to stifle Old Nick."

"Lay it down for a moment, then," said Bob Hauler, chewing his cud very leisurely.

Jerry was making all kinds of grimaces, and Bob was obliged to indulge in a fit of laughter.

Jerry glared at him savagely through the gauze-like mist. Jerry had got his wish, but it was one of the most uncomfortable smokes he had ever experienced.

The tobacco being dry and loosely rolled had become as it were one heated mass, and was burning so rapidly that his nose was each moment in imminent danger of being scorched if not roasted.

Jerry still held on to it, though, and puffed away at it with the determination of a desperate man. He knew not when he would get another such indulgence, bad even though it might be.

He wished in his own mind that he had followed Bob Hauley's example.

But it was too late now.

There was only about an inch left, and that was merely a glow very much resembling the form of a burning cauliflower, if our readers can imagine such a facsimile.

Bob was still twisting his jaws about and making all the show he could of his enjoyment, when suddenly he let out a suppressed, "Oa!"

Jerry turned to learn the cause of this, and to his glee he beheld the seat of Bob Hauler's trousers on fire.

A draught would have set him in a blaze all over; at present they were only smouldering, as it were, but sufficiently to give Bob a good scorching.

The end he had bitten off the cigar was the cause of this.

It was Jerry's turn to laugh now.

This merriment, however, was not destined to be of long duration.

In an incautious moment he let his own stump fall into the hollow just below where his waistcoat should have reached, if he had worn any.

They were a pair of most disconsolate mortals now.

They were both being roasted alive, only in directly opposite directions.

Both were totally helpless; they could not move hand or foot to help themselves or assist each other.

What was worse, Jerry's promise forbade them crying out, or calling upon any one to aid them.

Bob Hauler was the best off.

By wriggling and wriggling he could manage to keep his fire under, but he could not prevent a certain portion we shall not name being severely blistered.

But Jerry was most singularly placed.

He heaped a thousand blessings on the devoted head of their kind benefactress, and wished the confounded swab of a cigar—as he nautically termed it—was in a place that is described as being much warmer than the position either of them then held.

Jerry Mizzen was more nimble, even on ordinary occasions, than his companion, and now his superiority was about to be severely tested; by every possible manœuvre he tried to dislodge the ignited stump, but to no avail; he might wriggle and twist to his heart's content, but it still stuck there.

There was but one way of doing it, and that was by turning his body clean over.

He could not roll over sideways, the ends of the handspikes prevented that; he must go head under heels or no way at all—backwards or forwards, it mattered not which.

He decided upon the latter; it was the easiest, and, in fact, the most practicable. The wall was behind him, whilst the floor before him went down at a gentle slope.

Jerry had turned "head over heels," as he expressed it, hundreds of times when a boy, and had acquired the art of "tucking in his tuppenny," but he had never tried it in the "turn-turtle" sort of fashion he must now adopt.

But there was no time now allowed for thinking. Jerry found that his pinions had got slackened by his exertions, which allowed his muscles more play and his body a little more spring.

The fire, too, was spreading, and he was beginning to blister, as Doctor Shrike would have said, most beautiful. In about twenty seconds he had performed the act of the famous jumping frog, and in about half as many more his head went under him, and off he started, rolling like a ball, down the sloping floor to the other side of the cavern.

This was done so suddenly that Bob Hauler forgot his own pain, and gazed after him in open-mouthed dismay.

But he burst out in a fit of laughter when he saw Jerry strike the opposite wall, and remain, heels upwards, on his back, fixed between a cask of rum and a bag of sea biscuits.

"Bravo, Jerry!" he shouted at the top of his voice, forgetful of his peril in doing so. "Bravo Jerry, well done, my hearty! That's capitally good!"

Jerry didn't think so; his rapid journey had nearly knocked the wind out of him.

He had certainly got rid of the remaining portion of the cigar, but his clothes were still ignited, and as soon as his lungs were inflated again he set up a most discordant howl.

This brought the very men who had assisted at their lashing-up into the cavern, and they set up a regular roar of laughter as they seized hold of our unfortunate friend and conveyed him back to his former position again.

They never troubled to ask him how he got into such a fix, and took it for granted that he had only endeavoured to get rid of his smouldering garment, and as they put him down in his old spot, as a piece of joke they covered him up with some other articles of the cargo.

As to Bob, not a groan escaped his lips in consequence. [...illegible...]

Our two friends did not speak to one another for sometime after this. Truth to tell, Bob was suffering so much that he was not in a talking humour, and he knew that Jerry was sure to have a good laugh at him.

In the meantime about a dozen of the band had entered the cavern, and producing various articles from sundry mysterious nooks and crevices, of which there seemed to be no lack, they rigged up a couple of benches, and, by the aid of barrels and planks, made seats sufficient to accommodate about a score or so.

These impromptu benches, or tables, were quickly spread with steaming hot viands, such as joints of meat, heaps of vegetables, sea biscuits, cans of soup, and bottles of grog.

Then the woman before mentioned brought in a pile of wooden platters and wooden spoons that had at some time been brought over from Holland by a smuggling lugger, or some such craft.

When all was satisfactorily arranged, another group of the smugglers or freebooters, or whatever they might be, for neither Bob nor Jerry could make out their calling, straggled in and took their places.

Then they all fell to with a will, but in a most orderly manner, considering the roughness of their external appearances.

Bob and Jerry eyed them eagerly.

They had fasted so long that they were nearly famished, but their eyes glistened when two of the band, loaded with the good things, approached them and loosened their bonds, so as to allow them the free use of their hands.

When the tables were cleared, long Dutch pipes, bottles of schiedam, and smuggled brandy, together with the tobacco the woman had chopped up, were strewn about the tables, and other preparations made for a jovial carousal.

The men, whatever their vocation might be, seemed to know how to enjoy themselves.

They had been on some secret expedition, and had evidently been successful, for from their conversation they were pretty well satisfied with themselves.

Whilst Bob and Jerry were refreshing the inner man, the party began to grow very convivial, the long pipes were brought into requisition, glasses and drinking horns were filled with the liquors, and sundry voices called on Jack Spritsail for a song.

"Bravo!" shouted a dozen voices at once. "Go it, Jack; pipe up. Give us one of your old sea-ditties," was the cry.

And so great was the majority for Jack Spritsail to sing that he was compelled, though rather reluctantly, to comply with their request.

"Before I set sail," he said, standing up to address them, "let me tell you there's a jolly long chorus to every verse; so I expects you one and all to give us a lift."

This was unanimously agreed upon, and then he commenced:—

Hurrah! hurrah! for the deep blue sea,
Hurrah for the sparkling foam!
Let us give a cheer for the rattling breeze,
That rocks the sailor's home.

The firm white sail with the flowing sheet,
That bend too to cling it [...illegible...]
And one more cheer for the [...] jolly crew
That is [...illegible...]

CHORUS.

Then hurrah! hurrah! hurrah!
[...illegible...]
[...illegible...] hurrah?
[...illegible...]

"For the wind that whistles through the shrouds,
That tosses the sparkling spray,
As we laugh at the storm, as the ship glides on,
Let us merrily shout, hurrah—
Hurrah, hurrah, hurrah!"

This chorus was given with hearty good will, and repeated several times, amid the clattering of glasses, and the rattling of drinking horns on the rude benches and seats.

The cavern rang again with the din and clatter.

"Go ahead, old Spritsail," was the general outcry.

"Spit it out into my old tarpaulin hat if it sticks in your hawse pipe," cried the seaman who was serving out the grog.

Thus pressed, the old tar struck up again in the same stentorian voice—

"Then about hooray, as the anchor we weigh,
From its watery, silvery bed,
And three good cheers, as our flag appears
Run up to the mainmast head.
For the guns that protrude, from our vessel's sides
With their muzzles dazzling bright,
And the ship that bears us through the storm,
Or carries us through the fight.
Then hurrah, hurrah, hurrah!"

Here the chorus was struck up again, and repeated over and over as before.

It was just the very song that suited the occasion.

The grog was handed round, and the singer was called upon to pay out another cable's length of slack:—

"As our good ship glides with lightning speed
Through the storm-lashed, crested wave,
And shakes the spray from her sharpened prow
As it points to the prize we'll have.
And the man at the wheel, as true as steel,
That guides the vessel aright,
And the moon then lends us her murky rays
To keep the foe in sight.
Then hurrah, hurrah, hurrah!"

This verse called forth the same hearty cheers, and was applauded in the same manner as the preceding ones, but the old salt's voice was growing husky.

"That's all of it, my hearties," he said, as he took up his pipe to light it.

"No—no; you don't gammon us in that way; there's another stave," shouted several of the band. "Pipe up; we aint going to let you shirk off in that ugly fashion."

The old sailor remonstrated in his rude way, but it was of no use.

They thumped, and hammered, and shouted, and kicked up such a bobloo that he was obliged to "pipe up" again.

"Now, mind, only one more verse," he said, bringing his hard fist down on the head of the cask before him to enjoin silence.

"All right, we won't be too hard upon you, but we must have the lot."

"Then a hearty cheer for the lasses sweet
Who greet us wherever we land,
Let us always fight in their defence,
And take in ours their hand;
And a hip hurrah shout out, my boys,
For our captain, so noble and bold.
So let us be jolly and drown melancholy,
For there's lots of good grog in the hold.
Then hurrah, hurrah, hurrah!"

Jack Spritsail had barely finished his song and the chorus had not died away, when one of the two that occupied the cave when Bob and Jerry first entered

it rushed in, and by a wave of his hand demanded silence.

There was a general hush and a clear-out; the tables and planks mysteriously vanished, and no one would have thought such a thing had ever happened.

Bob and Jerry were astounded at the sudden metamorphosis.

While they were staring about they saw two seamen-like looking men pass the entrance, bearing a burden—a man—between them; the face pale and bedaubed in blood, was towards them, and they immediately recognised it.

That face was no other than Ben Barnacle's.

_____

CHAPTER CCI.

CAPTAIN TOM DRAKE PLANS HIS ESCAPE FROM THE FORTRESS—THE MERRY MIDS HAVE A SHARP SEA-FIGHT

CAPTAIN TOM DRAKE was some hours before he returned to anything like consciousness after the severe and cruel handling he had received from the warder and his assistants.

The place seemed wrapped in darkness, and he remained some time in a sort of dazy stupor, but as time wore on his eyes became more accustomed to the gloom, and a gradual sense of his horrible position dawned upon him.

He tried to raise himself from the damp floor, but his limbs were too stiff and bruised, but he managed after a while to rest himself on his elbow, and then the terrible truth flashed to his heated mind

We have before observed that there was a sort of loop-hole or embrasure high up in the wall, and that this admitted a little light, but it was very little indeed, simply a gloom, that rendered what objects there were about him visible.

That he had been visited by some one there was a proof, for a jug of water was near to his hand, and a handful of coarse straw had been placed beneath his head, and that was all he could see, excepting the grim and ghastly object that was seated opposite to him and rested against the blackened wall.

Tom shuddered at the horrible sight.

His brain reeled again as he thought of this devilish refinement of cruelty.

A thousand other thoughts flew in rapid succession through his mind.

He did not fear death in a general sense of the word; he had faced it boldly in a hundred different shapes, but it had never appeared to him in so terrible a form as it did now.

There sat his deathly companion before him, its fleshless cheek resting in its fleshless hand, and the elbow resting on its knee, glaring at him, as it seemed; and his heated imagination pictured it glaring at him with glassy, deep-set eyes, and grinning at him as in very mockery of his woe

It was enough to turn the brain of one much older and more experienced in the world's sinful ways than was our hero.

Turn which way he would, those eyes seemed to follow him and pierce into his inmost soul.

When he closed his eyes the vision was still there, and made him wish that he had never again seen the light, and that his young life had passed away never to return, during the time of his unconsciousness.

In his misery he even wished for darkness, in the hope that it would make him sleep, and place him again in a dreamy state of forgetfulness.

But the more he wished for this the more wakeful he seemed to be, and his eyelids refused to perform their office; he could not keep them closed they seemed drawn and puckered up, and a strange fascination se med to hold him in that position that brought his eyes in proximity with those of his grim companion.

The faint glimmer of light would not grant him even the pleasure of judging whether it was the morning or evening of the day; it simply informed him that it was day, and that was all.

After laying thus for what appeared to him an age of unutterable misery, he managed to shift himself into a more comfortable posture; his pain grew less, but he could not feel that it was only a numbness that was deceiving him.

He was painfully aware that his proud spirit and vigorous constitution were sadly broken down, but he suddenly remembered the pitcher and that there was water in it, and he stretched forth his hand to get a drink, in the hope that it might refresh him.

In doing so his hand came in contact with some hard substance; it was a loaf of the coarsest texture possible, but he managed to force down a mouthful or two of it, and then he felt stronger.

Another draught from the pitcher, and then his memory strengthened.

"No, I must not die," he muttered, half aloud. "I will bear up until the axe is above my head, or the halter is round my throat. Tom Drake must not lay here and die; I can see it graven on the wall, on the very forehead even of that mass of bleaching bones which recalls to memory Reuben Harpy, my false cousin, and the villain Sanderson."

In this strain he went on until he fell asleep, and when he awoke he knew that it was day again, for a thin, yellow streak fell on the dingy wall of the dungeon.

"Ah, now, I remember," he exclaimed, as he threw off the lethargy that hitherto bound him, and sprang to his feet. "They said this was the Black Tower. I know that one side of it overlooks the coast, but how am I to reach that loophole?"

He forced down a morsel of the bread, and gulped down a small drop of water, and then set his wits to considering.

He spied above him, almost in the centre of the roof, a kind of hook, that at one time had been used to suspend some instrument of torture, and from that he formed his first idea.

He longed to see the sky once more, and to feel the warm beams of the sun, and though the very idea seemed madness in itself, he did not despair.

The plan he had formed was a horrible one, but he was fully resolved to try it, and the assistant he was going to use was his fleshless companion— the skeleton.

First of all he took off his belt and cut it into strips, then his outer garment he tore into long thin shreds, and placing hem on the floor of the dungeon, he seized the bony form and began dismembering it.

This done, he lashed the bones firmly together, as a boy would make an impromptu fishing-rod, until he had made a long pole, as it were, which nearly, with his outstretched arm, reached the ceiling, and on the top of all he secured the ghastly skull.

"Thus far, so good," he said, as he measured certain distances with his eye. "Ah, I have it, there's the pitcher."

The loophole was nearly eight feet in height from the floor; added to which there was the thickness of the wall, some few feet sloping inwards, the smooth stonework of which was greasy with slime, so that the bars that guarded it on the outer side could not have been reached even with a ladder from within.

Captain Tom, however, had formed his plans.

First he placed the pitcher directly under the hook in the ceiling, then he reared up his pole, and steadying it and himself on the pitcher, managed by sheer strength and a deal of ingenuity to sus-

pend his mechanical contrivance to the hook by one of the holes in the skull.

When properly fixed, this novel apparatus was equal to a knotted rope to climb, and Tom skimmed up it like a shot, in true sailor fashion.

Tom, from his elevation, was not long in taking the survey that was necessary to his next movement.

He was down like a shot on the mouth of the pitcher, and seizing the lowermost bone, with a firm grip, in both hands, he swung himself backwards and forwards, and then took a flying leap into the loop-hole and clutched the iron bars in safety.

It was a dangerous leap; he might have broken his neck, but his success fully made up for the danger.

Once firmly perched there, he could command a good view of the coast, and the open sea stretching far away, its broad bosom dotted here and there with vessels of every size and calling, from the humble fishing boat to the big three-decker far away, looking out for the foe, the Frenchmen.

To a lover of the sea the ocean is at all times and seasons a lovely sight, but on this particular morning it possessed additional charms, at least so our hero thought, as he took in the whole survey at a glance.

In the foreground, and just beneath him, the yellow water plainly marked out the bed of the deadly quicksand.

Then, the hue of dark green farther away, where the water was deeper, and, lastly, the dark blue of the horizon, showed to perfection the bright clouds as they rose to catch the glorious reflection of the sun.

Captain Tom Drake's heart seemed to bound with the waves as they rolled onward, borne by a steady breeze which set the vessels all in motion.

He could feel the soft breeze on his cheek, and smell the salt sea-weed on the rocks beneath him; but presently he beheld a sight that sent the blood coursing through his veins, and set his cheeks aglow.

It was a little vessel, with every sail set, neat, and taut, her tacks bowsed down, and her sheets trimmed with the greatest nicety.

She was steering for a narrow neck of land, where the rocks were thickly studded, and to what would have appeared to an inexperienced eye an impenetrable barrier.

Tom was watching her very narrowly, and wondering what could have possessed her daring captain to seek such danger, when a gun startled him, and, on turning his head, he beheld a man-of-war following closely on her heels.

It was from this vessel the gun was fired.

She was evidently giving chase to the little brig, who still kept on her course heedless of the summons to heave to.

Tom, from his first sighting of the brig, had fallen desperately in love with her.

Her clean cut and neat trim was just such as a sailor could have wished for, and Tom longed to be upon her snowy deck, of which he now and again caught a glimpse between the sails

"A smart craft," he muttered, as the little brig shot into a dangerous channel between the rocks. "She's well handled, too. I've gone through it a hundred times myself; but, with the exception of my own sweet little 'Will o' the Wisp,' I never saw another vessel take the Devil's Gulf so easily."

Just where the little craft had disappeared the sea was breaking in huge waves, which sent the foam hissing over the black heads of the dangerous rocks, and the gallant ship staggered a little as she went through.

Those on board the man-of-war seemed for the moment astounded at the captain's audacity.

They fired their bow guns at her, but still she kept on.

Tom from his high perch could see over the tall rocks and watch the movements of the little vessel.

He could see her crew on the deck, some at the guns, others at the braces ready to trim the yards, and one at the helm with a cocked hat on, similar to the one he wore himself.

Whether she was a pirate or a smuggler he could not form the least idea.

That she was something of the sort he felt certain, or why was she daring such danger?

But the figure with cocked hat engrossed his thoughts the most; he handled the wheel with such seamanlike grace and ease.

Tom could hear the shrill whistle of the boatswain on board the frigate, and even at that height hear the man in the chains giving the soundings of the lead line.

"By the deep six."

"By the mark five."

Then the boatswain piped again, and the voice of the commander shouted through his speaking trumpet:—

"All hands 'bout ship."

This order was soon executed.

The frigate swung round with her head from the land, and stood into deep water again.

As she came up to the wind she fired the whole of her larboard broadside at the little craft, but did no apparent damage; her crew only returned the compliment with a defiant cheer.

"Bravo!" Tom cried in his excitement, "well done; that's no ordinary coaster to manœuvre in that fashion; they can laugh at the frigate if they don't let her guns reach them."

His eye followed the little vessel as she wound in and out the tortuous channel, her sides almost touching the rocks, which at times were hidden by the foam.

Under any circumstances, and with the brightest look out and the smartest pilot, the navigation near shore amongst those reefs and rocks was most dangerous.

By this time the frigate had got into good soundings.

Again her head swung round, and her sails were trimmed on the same tack as before.

But she steered her course outside the dangerous shoals, and this gave the little vessel the advantage of half a mile or so.

The latter did not appear to make any attempt nor any signs of entering into action with her superior antagonist.

Her sole bent seemed to be running away.

The frigate, on the other hand, seemed fully determined on hunting her down. She spread additional sails, and the ship was trimmed to her very best sailing point.

There was a nice top-gallant breeze, just enough to draw out the good qualities of both vessels.

As they heeled over to the pressure, Tom could see all that passed on their upper decks.

He could even see the men at the guns on the frigate's main deck through her open port-holes.

They were loading and ramming home another charge to send a message to the runaway.

This time the little brig did not take it so coolly; they trained their midship gun and sent a shot whistling through the frigate's shrouds.

This caused some commotion on board the man-of-war.

The Union Jack was run up, and her officers and crew were giving and executing orders with that alacrity for which the British seaman is so proverbial.

Meanwhile the brig was making the best possible use of her heels, but she was drawing near to the most difficult part of all.

It was a dangerous passage between two rocks where the tide was hissing, and foaming, and rushing like a race-horse, dead against her.

This was known by the name of the Dead Man's Race, and was only used as a last and most desperate resource by the smugglers when hotly pressed by the Revenue cutters.

He was a bold man, however, who would make the attempt.

It was the fear of the halter alone that could nerve him to do it.

But the crew of the brig seemed to take to it quite coolly; every brace was steadied taut, and the sails trimmed to the greatest nicety as her head was pointed to the broken water, that sent its spray flying into the air to the height of a hundred feet.

Tom held his breath as he saw the gallant little bark stagger with the shock at their first meeting.

His heart stood still for a while as she lifted on a big wave and then disappeared beneath a huge breaker.

Then, as she rose once more, and her canvas belled to the increasing breeze, he gave a loud shout of joy.

At that moment he felt as much interest in the fate of the little craft as though it were his own, and his fingers itched to be clutching the wheel spokes that guided her so bravely on.

Presently the dangerous passage was made, and the gallant brig was in smoother water, in a sort of lake or basin formed by its formidable surroundings, that shut it in from the open sea.

Tom would have been at home in that wild spot.

As he observed, he had passed through that dangerous channel a hundred times or more.

He knew every twist and turn, every rock and sunken reef, the soundings of the lake-like basin, and the compass bearings of each inlet and outlet.

The frigate was still bowling on; her heavy pressure of sail, and the advantage of open sea room was enabling her to gain upon her little prey.

But the fearless crew of the gallant brig was in no way daunted until a shot was heard in a totally opposite direction, and a sloop of war shot out from a huge jutting point and made for the opening by which the brig was about to escape into the open sea.

By this unforeseen circumstance, the passage of the brig was effectually cut off.

She was hemmed in, and all escape seemed to be hopeless.

Captain Tom watched in breathless suspense the effect of this new coincidence.

Would the brig surrender, and the crew give themselves up, or would they hold out, and stand the risk of being battered to pieces by the cross fire of the frigate and the sloop?

A shot from the frigate's bow-chaser warned them that the time allowed for the decision was very brief.

Even the sloop showed the impatience of the commander by firing a shot between the two masts of the brig.

That she must yield, or be disabled seemed but too plain.

Attempting to escape seemed simply madness.

She was just in nice range of both vessels, ponderous missiles and a splinter falling from the fore-top-mast showed that she had skilful gunners to deal with.

However, the little brig did not care to yield so easily.

Having braved so much, and faced such dangers, her crew were not likely to give in without a struggle.

They intimated as much, by suddenly veering

round, and putting the little brig right before the wind.

Those on board the frigate and the sloop of war were astounded at this decision, so hastily formed.

Even Tom felt a little surprised.

"True pluck there! I should like to be with you, my brave lads," he shouted, forgetful that from his lofty elevation they could not hear him.

He even forgot, in the excitement, his own helpless captivity, and the horrors he had so recently passed through.

"Curse them!" yelled the commander of the sloop of war, as he sent a shot bowling after them, and shouted for his lieutenant to "clap on all sail."

He hesitated a moment what course to pursue, and signalled to the frigate, whether it was worth his risking his ship to follow the audacious little brig by venturing into the channel by which the brig had intended to escape.

The reply was a premonitory "No!" or the commander must take all risk upon himself, and be responsible for his own action.

To relieve the reader of all further suspense, we may explain that the frigate was commanded by none other than our miserable little Admiral Ellis, who, aided by a good lie and the intercession of his friends supported by the interest of Captain Angel, Lieutenant Sanderson, and Reuben Harpy, had regained his commission.

From what Reuben told him he had no doubt that the careless little trader lying so snugly in Portsmouth Harbour was the "Will-o'-the-Wisp."

At all events, after his disgrace, he was determined to make up for it by boarding every vessel bearing two masts that came in his way.

Now the supposed trader happened to be the "Will-o'-the-Wisp," and chance brought the frigate down upon her when she was hovering on the coast, watching an opportunity to land and effect the release of Captain Tom Drake.

The middies, by watching the signals between the flag-ship and the look-out on shore, learned that their beloved leader was in some fortress on the coast, and from what they gleaned and what they imagined, they were soon on their way to release him.

A thick fog had enabled Admiral Ellis to surprise them on their way, and send a boat's crew to overhaul their papers.

When the boat pulled alongside, however, the man-of-war crew found they had a set of tartars to deal with, and on the lieutenant in charge ordering a rope to be thrown over for him to ascend by, he was answered by a dozen youthful faces grinning through a port-hole at him.

This made his blood boil.

"Board her at once!" he shouted to his boat's crew, who, being fully armed, and quite certain that Captain Tom was on shore, and, in fact, in limbo, anticipated an easy capture.

But they were quickly undeceived.

Captain Tom Drake was not on board, neither was Ben Barnacle, and his lieutenant, Harry Vere, was also safely incarcerated; but his middies were, and they were, heart and soul, bound in the little brig.

So as soon as the boat's crew mounted the side, they tumbled them overboard like so many rats, and sent them, some into the sea, and others sprawling into the bottom of the boat.

Then, firing a shot or two from the brass guns, as a farewell salute, the brig made all sail and ran for it.

The middies did not intend to show fight unless compelled to do so.

They wanted to get all their hands aboard again first.

But Admiral Ellis was not to be so easily shaken off.

In the vindictiveness of his nature, he meant to hunt them down at all hazards.

And this little brig that Captain Tom had been admiring so much was no other than his own darling "Will o' the Wisp."

So neatly had she been disguised that his discerning eye had for a time, as it were, been blinded.

It was not at all surprising then, that though from his peculiar position he failed to recognise her at once, that his heart should yearn towards her, and that he should unconsciously take so much interest in her welfare and that of her crew.

At that very moment, when she was just beneath his nose, he thought her snugly anchored at Purfleet, which the reader remembers was to be their place of rendezvous; and where she would likely have been, and her boy crew anxiously awaiting their leader's return, had it not been for the officiousness of the captain of the coastguard cutter.

When Admiral Ellis saw the prize, that was almost in his grasp, making sail away again, he fairly foamed with rage. To sink the gallant little brig and annihilate her crew, was now his full intention.

As she made for the Dead Man's Race again, he fired a heavy broadside from his lower and main deck guns point blank at her, which, if it had taken good effect, must have settled her at once.

As it was, the tide and wind being in her favour, the trim little craft shot like an arrow through the race, and once more threaded the windings and turnings of the narrow and dangerous channel.

By this time the frigate was full before the wind.

She had even her studding sails set to aid her speed, and the sloop-of-war was fast following in her wake.

Both vessels had their guns trained to the very extreme, and laid as accurate as could be to hit the little brig and stop her progress, either by disabling her or sinking her outright.

Captain Tom's heart almost bled for the little vessel as he saw this cruel preparation.

Had it not been for the stout bars that held him captive, in the impetuosity of his nature, he would have leaped from that giddy height, in the hope of rendering her some assistance.

As it was, he cheered the little brig on, and hissed at the men-of-war, just as though they could hear him, and he clutched at the iron bars as he would have grasped his good steel sword.

Imagine his indignation, then, when he saw the great sheets of lurid flame and the blinding clouds of smoke dart from the muzzles of the war ship's sides.

Then heard the roar that vibrated like a thousand thunders along the steep cliff, and went in rolling echoes for miles along the coast, startling the seabirds and making the very air resound again.

Then, before the air could recover its former stillness and the smoke clear away, and the gallant little barque, whose annihilation seemed so certain, could be visible, there was another shot fired, and a shout that hurled defiance back into the very teeth of the crews of the men-of-war arose from the brig.

Captain Tom, in the heat of the moment, and in his excitement to get a better view of what was going on, had thrust his head and the upper part of his body through the narrow opening between the massive bars.

In doing so, his cocked hat, which he had flattened and placed in his bosom during his flight from the prison walls, became disengaged, and went fluttering downwards over the edge of the steep cliff, and he lost sight of it, perhaps, for ever.

In fact, he scarcely noticed its descent; other objects engrossing his whole attention.

The sails of the little brig were riddled in holes and some of her cordage had been cut away, but otherwise she had received no material damage, at least, so far as he could discern, her hull did not appear to be much damaged.

Then what was it that made his cheek for a moment blanch and then change to a fiery glow?

What made his hands clench, and his bosom heave so tumultuously?

Why did he shout till he was hoarse and then utter a silent thanksgiving for the safety of the little craft that had passed through that terrible ordeal as it were, unscathed?

It was a flag.

A flag that he remembered well.

One that he could never forget, never desert, and loved as dearly as his own life.

It was a piece of black bunting, with a narrow streak of crimson run through it horizontally.

That very flag Ben Barnacle had so hastily put together when under the heavy firing and blazing of the Algerine forts, and when our hero was elected and christened Captain Tom Drake.

He hallowed and revered that simple, but significant emblem, and so did every one of his crew.

It was only brought to light on certain occasions, but the middies in revenge had kept it ready, and hoisted it when the moment came that they could engage the vindictive little admiral.

When Admiral Ellis saw this there was no bound to his rage.

He cursed and foamed and stamped his foot on the quarter-deck, but he could do no more, for the little brig, aided by a strong breeze that sprang up and the swift course of the current, sped along so swiftly, that his guns, even with a double charge of powder, could not reach her, and then, as his rage was nearly choking him, and his voice became inarticulate, the little "Will o' the Wisp" swept round a sharp curve, shot through a narrow passage that seemed to be merely a mass of foam, and disappeared behind a line of towering rocks.

This happened so quickly that our hero could scarcely believe it real.

He pinched and punched himself to ascertain whether he was really still in the flesh or in the other world, or, what was more possible, in a dream.

Admiral Ellis gave such vent to his passion that he fell down in a fit, and was conveyed below.

Then his officers, after a long consultation, wore the frigate round, and bore away, giving up the task as hopeless.

As to the sloop of war, she hovered about in the hope of seeing the brig appear again from some mysterious opening, until she was obliged to sheer off and seek for safety, as a shot had knocked a great hole in her hull, just below the water-line.

Captain Tom Drake was so overpowered by the sight, and so exhausted from weakness and the imaginary share he had taken in the fight, that he swooned, and slipped from the loop-hole back into his dungeon.

The fall stunned him.

He might have been killed outright, and his rebellious career and glorious achievements ended, had it not been for the careful of some straw that prevented his brains being dashed out on the spot.

He must have lain there a very long time, when he moved faintly, came to, and found some one bathing his brow and chafing his bruised temple.

A faint light rendered visible the spot, but it was so ... that he could be ... hour of ... that was ...

"... Well, my Captain Tom ... ... as the ... of ... ... as the quicken he had ... ..."

am glad you've come to. Look up, it is your old friend, Ben."

"Ben—Ben!" he uttered feebly.

His brain was too much bewildered to understand the full import of the words.

"Yes, your old friend, Ben."

"What Ben?"

"Why, Ben Barnacle, to be sure."

"Ben Barnacle?"

"Aye, don't you know me?"

"Impossible."

"But it's true."

"Ben Barnacle, our Ben?" he queried.

"Just so, as true as you are our Captain Tom."

"I can't believe it."

"You may then. I'm not a ghost, depend upon that."

"But here; where am I?"

Captain Tom was still in doubt.

The more he came to the greater his bewilderment.

"In the devil's own den—but cheer up."

"But you are not Ben, you cannot be," said our hero.

"I am, and I always mean to be while I've a flipper to handle a pistol, or wield a cutlass. Come, rouse up, captain, old boy."

"Are you a prisoner, then?"

"I hope not, but I may be if I stay here too long."

Tom wiped the clammy moisture from his brow.

"Ben, tell me how you got here," said Tom Drake.

"Plenty of time, captain. You get round first," Ben replied.

"This is a mystery," Tom murmured, as he again relapsed.

"Now, now, none of this, captain; it won't do," Ben said.

He was anxious about the captain's safety.

Captain Tom was still incomprehensive.

Ben chafed his hands, and poured the remaining drops of water over him.

This revived him a little.

"Rouse up—rouse up," Ben uttered hoarsely, listening at the same time for any sound.

"But how came you here?" Tom queried, still in doubt.

"I walked here, and I am going to walk back, and you must accompany me," was Ben's curt answer.

"Where to?"

"Freedom."

"Impossible."

"I say it's not, it's a fact. You can see me, feel me, I am all alive, Captain Tom."

Still Tom maintained the same obstinacy.

Had he not had the blow occasioned by his fall his conduct would even have been excusable; as it was, his incredulity was but natural.

If Ben were not a captive, and incarcerated with him, how came he there, he thought.

Tom was about to question him again, but Ben raised him to his feet.

"Come on," he said, huskily, "or we may delay too long. If you don't come quickly, I must carry you."

"What, have you really penetrated into this dungeon—made my concealment through these thick stone walls?"

"Had you been at the devil I'd have sought you," answered Ben. "Come, get on my back, captain, I'd carry you out of this like a tired away," he added, resolutely.

The idea of being compared to a tired child served to wake up a bit.

He smiled a ... of ... ... and Ben, ... a ... ... in the ...

supported him with his brawny arm, and led him to the stone staircase.

Ben kicked aside the prone form of a stalwart man-at-arms that lay at the head of the steps, and descended as rapidly as our hero's weak state would admit of; then, seizing the captain's lithe form in his giant arms, strode rapidly along several dank, noisome, passages. such as our hero did not remember passing through before.

Ben staggered with his burden up a steep of slimy steps, and then paused to rest himself.

"Can you walk now?" he whispered in Tom's ear.

"Yes; I shall be all right, when I can breathe a bit."

"There's a loop-hole just here, and a big hole not far away. Bear up if you can for a moment."

"Listen! what is that?" said Tom Drake, in an undertone.

"Footsteps! Tom, by Jove! they are coming this way too; they have discovered something. Go on, push a-head in front of me."

"And leave you? Not if I die for it."

"Yes, you must or we shall be lost. I left a musket just here, you take it. It's loaded."

"And you?"

"Never fear, don't trouble about me."

"What, leave you alone, and unarmed?"

"Not alone, Tom, I've got this."

Ben unslung from his waist a huge bludgeon, studded with spikes.

It was his favourite weapon.

"This never missed fire, and it won't now," he muttered, hoarsely.

Tom felt more at ease then.

The footsteps, however, were growing more distinct, and so they agreed to put out the torch.

Ben trod all the sparks out with his foot after dashing the torch against the wall of the passage.

"They've seen us, go on," Ben cried, impatiently. "Grope along the wall; you'll smell freedom presently."

As he uttered this a light shone from the far end of the passage, and the tramp of a dozen mailed feet awoke the echoes.

In the fortress they still preserved a good many of the old customs, among others a body of halbardiers clad in half mail.

It was to this that Tom and Ben owed their providential escape so far.

As it was Ben feared they would be overtaken, as Tom could not run very fast.

The soldiers were coming at the top of their speed, which was not very considerable.

The slime on the floor retarded them a good deal.

Even Tom and Ben found it difficult to keep their feet.

However, Tom did not want to come to blows in his present weak state.

He had had enough fighting for the present, he needed a little rest.

Presently they saw daylight on ahead.

Tom made for this in double quick time.

It was awfully slow work groping along in the dark, as the juttings and abutments along the walls caused them to traverse about double the distance.

This was how the soldiers gained upon them so.

Guided by the daylight in front the buccaneers made rapid progress, and a loud shout arose from a dozen throats as Captain Tom, musket in hand, appeared at the opening in the wall.

"Hurrah—hurrah! for Captain Tom Drake!" shouted a motley group—a mixture of smugglers and buccaneers.

Jerry Mizzen, and Bob Hauler assisted our hero through the hole, while the others lent Ben a hand

At that moment the foremost soldier, who had outrun his companions, thrust out his halberd, and then poked his head through the wall.

This was a very unwise and unfortunate proceeding on his part, for at that very moment one of the motley group stepped to one side of the gap, and with one blow buried the sharp point of his pickaxe in his skill.

The soldier fell with a groan, never to rise again by his own exertions, and blocked up the opening with his burly corpse.

His comrades drew back, horrified and in dismay, and in that moment our gallant captain and his rescuers disappeared.

CHAPTER CCII.

THE BUCCANEERS GO TO THE RESCUE OF HARRY VERE.

ABOUT one hour later the buccaneers, the rescued, and the rescuers were seated in a cave, discussing a good meal and talking over various matters.

"I know where he is," said Ben; "and if you will allow me, captain, I'll undertake that bit of business for you."

"No, no; you want all the glory, Ben."

"It's only for glory I live, captain. If Harry Vere, our bold lieutenant, is in those walls, why, out he must come, that's all."

"But you are not captain yet, Ben; you must obey for a little while longer—at least till I——"

"That won't be yet awhile, captain. Shiver me! I hope you'll live to order many a reef to be shaken out; but if Harry, as I say, is in there, I must be the one to get him out."

"You must not go alone, Ben, I won't trust you." Captain Tom smiled, as he spoke.

Ben Barnacle indulged in one of his stern frowns.

"Can't trust me, eh, Captain Tom?" he said.

"I said I won't, and I don't mean to; either of you may accompany me, but there must not be too many of us. I may add the fewer the better."

"Well it would excite suspicion if we were to let them see us, but we must be cautious. For my part I would rather live down the lower hold among the rats, than in that dungeon where I found you; by Jove, what a time it seemed before I overtook that fellow with the torch He took as much felling as a bullock, too, but he dropped like a deep-sea lead when I did land him one properly."

"I should say there was not much chance for him after you measured with him; but time, Ben, time is fleeting—look at the sun yonder.

Ben cast his eyes towards the opening of the cave, and saw that the sun was rapidly declining.

Captain Tom got up, and armed himself.

He buckled on a stout sword, and thrust a pistol in the scarf round his waist, then he put on his cocked hat.

It was rather wet, but he did not mind that.

He never so much as dreamed of seeing it again.

He was very pleased he had recovered it again, as it was a mark of distinction, and added to his dignity.

The scarf he had borrowed from one of the men, and the sword belt too, for his own he had cut up in the dungeon.

He selected two stout fellows to accompany him, and each one, in addition to being well armed, took with him a coil of rope.

Bob and Jerry were very much dejected at not being allowed to accompany the expedition.

They sauntered down to the beach, as they were desired, to keep a look-out for the "Will o' the Wisp," as Captain Tom supposed she would not be very far from the coast.

The rest of the band were allowed to sit and smoke, and spin their yarns in the cave during their absence.

Captain Tom and Ben then sauntered forth, followed by the two smugglers, who were to assist them in releasing Harry Vere.

They travelled along pretty sharply, keeping under the shadow of the brushwood and scrubs that lined the summit of the rocks for fear of being seen, and avoided every part that was likely to be a beaten track.

It was fortunate they took this precaution.

They had not travelled more than a mile when a circumstance happened that might have proved serious, but as it was, it rendered them very great service.

In a shallow part of the rocks two men had ensconced themselves to smoke a pipe, and avoid a sharp shower of rain that had overtaken them very suddenly.

Captain Tom halted his party and followed the two men's example.

It was always his plan never to throw away an opportunity of gaining information, especially if it was at all likely to prove serviceable to any member of his crew.

He had heard sufficient to guarantee his listening, and so he thought he would do so.

Creeping as close as prudence would allow him, he heard the following colloquy:—

"Well, Janson, what is your particular opinion of these smugglers. Dont you think they are growing immensely thick at the present day?"

"I've no particular opinion of them at all, Jack. I only know this, they give us plenty of work, and if I had my will, I'd hang and quarter them as they used to do in former times. Lor bless me, they lets them off as easy now as winking. I would'nt stand palavering with them as they do up yonder. Depend upon it, they carries all the news over to the Frechies."

"I don't think that there will be much chance of that one carrying any more news, Janson; the Governor is regular out of sorts at losing that Tom Drake. By all accounts, he was a desperate sort of character. How the deuce did they manage to find out his cage, I wonder?"

"Wonder! why these fellows could fly if need be. But we must see after him, and find him. It might be something in our way, you know."

"Yes, a topper over the skull—the same as Peter got. By St. George, that was cleverly done; but, as I said before, the other one will have no such chance. He will be watched like a mouse."

"I heard he was placed in the inner fort; is that true?"

"As true as you're there. The smugglers can climb about the rocks like cats, you know, so they've given them a moat to cross this time. They'll never think of crossing that, and if they attempt to they're sure to be shot down."

"True, comrade; but let us be going; the rain ceases, and we must be at the roll call, whether we catch this fellow, or no."

"There, that is the top of the inner fortress, you can see it nicely from here; you see they must cross the moat, scale the wall, and then there is the corridor through the tower where Jemmy keeps guard."

"Ay, and that's pretty strong; the casemates are all heavily barred, and the gate that leads to the inner courtyard is about the strongest we have."

"Yes, it's all up with the young fellow. I wonder he was ever led away by such a gang, he looks fit for something better."

"Well, we none of us know what we may come to in time, but there's little chance, at all events, that he'll escape the rope. His comrades, now they've got the captain out, will think no more about him. He may stick in his cell and rot for what they'll care."

So saying, the two soldiers, for such they were, left their shelter.

It was a formidable structure that the buccaneers had to enter, and it took them a few moments to consult and consider after they had taken a hasty, but minute, survey of its strong walls and the slimy moat.

The moat had to be crossed and the walls to be scaled.

But how?

At first sight it seemed an impossibility.

Armed sentinels were pacing the embattlements of the adjoining towers, from which they could command a view of all that part of the stronghold.

Leaving the two buccaneers, however, Captain Tom and his faithful adherent, Ben Barnacle, crept from their concealment and made for the grassy slope that faced the low parapet that guarded the edge of the moat.

Ben had his huge, club-like weapon slung handily from his waist, and a coil of small heaving-line, with a grappling hook attached, in his left hand.

A sturdy elder tree yielded them shelter until the two sentinels on the towers that flanked either end of the walls reached the limits, and having exchanged mutual glances, as much as to say all was right, turned and strode leisurely away to the far end of the battlements.

This was the chance Tom had waited for.

"Now, Ben," he whispered, "forward!"

Ben took the small line in his left hand, and, having ascertained that it was all clear for running, he seized the grappling hook in his right hand, and descended the grassy slope at a smart trot.

Quick as thought he rested his left foot on the edge of the parapet wall, and, swinging the grappling in the form of a sounding-lead, let it go with such force that it spun through the air like a rocket, and dropped the other side of the conical-shaped stonework that crowned the summit of the wall, and became securely fast.

Captain Tom waited not to utter a word.

Success depended solely on their promptitude. As Ben tightened the line and held on to his end securely, Tom threw himself over the parapet and began the ascent, hand over hand, in true seaman fashion, his legs dangling over the moat.

To peep over the wall and see all clear was but the work of a moment to Tom.

Then he drew himself up and sat astride upon it, and commenced hauling up the small line, to the end of which one of the buccaneers had bent on a stout rope, and this he also hauled up and paid down into the courtyard of the fortress.

He then lowered the grappling-hook and the small line after it, and then he descended himself.

This was easily effected, and with little danger. There were plenty of broad crevices in the massive stonework, and a huge buttress afforded him concealment.

No sooner did his feet touch the ground than our hero gave the rope two or three strong jerks, and then held on to it while Ben made the ascent.

Ben was neither so light nor so nimble as Captain Tom Drake, but he made small bones of this little job, and very soon joined our hero.

There was a deal to do yet before they reached the cell of the lieutenant, Harry Vere.

One false step, or a movement executed too soon would spoil all they had done.

In the event of a surprise, the two buccaneers outside had their instructions how to act.

But Tom and Ben both felt confident of their success.

The courtyard they were in bore the appearance

of not being very much frequented, the stone paving being covered with green moss, and the dank grass where our buccaneers stood reaching to the top of their knee boots.

Across this yard was another stone building, flanked by a drawbridge and a moat, the former leading to the inner towers of the fortress.

"That is our way," Tom pointed out to Ben; "let us cross and try yonder portal."

The portal was a massive oaken door that would have taken some battering down, and appeared to be locked. Imagine their surprise then to find it yield to their touch.

It surprised them still more to find another door in front of them ajar, and hear what sounded like voices proceeding from it.

Tom cautiously opened the door, and descended a flight of stone steps, when he found himself in a sort of vault surrounded by huge casks, which emitted the odour of home-brewed October.

The personages whose voices Tom had heard were seated at the farther end in front of a lamp, discussing the merits of the last brewing, and both of them—for there were only two—seemed to have been sampling it pretty freely.

These two worthies were the under-butler and the under-warder, two devout worshippers at the shrine of St. Al(e)phage, and the mulberry tint of their jolly noses gave proof of their regular attendance.

"Confound the fellow," broke out the warder suddenly, as a thought seemed to strike him; "if he had'nt got away, Jones, I could have given you another hour of my company."

"And I could have emptied a bottle of good schiedam with you," said the under-butler. "I've got one stowed away, boy, and yet I aint no smuggler."

"Smuggler, Jones, I should say not indeed; it's hard enough for us to get along smoothly in our humble capacities, but to be smugglers, oh! lord, no; a rope always dangling over one's head, and a bullet or a yard of cold steel ever ready to find its way to your heart, besides a chance of being drowned!"

"Quite right, but then they always seem happy over it. Now there was that young chap—Captain, what's-his-name?—as you spoke of just now, see how he took it. Why you said yourself he'd never live till the morning, after the doing you'd given him, when he'd winged the guvner."

"So I thought, Jones, and this young officer we've got now, as belongs to them buccaneer fellows, or pirates, as my mate calls 'em, is just such another one. He doesn't care a rap; he calls himself a liftenant and one of England's hearts of oak, and all such garbage, but it don't go down here, you know."

"Not like this stuff. Come, time was short with you just now, tip up another measure. You'll be thirsty enough, pulling them old rusty bolts and bars about. You must go and visit him, of course."

The butler merely threw out this hint as a feeler. He knew very well that the under-warder was bound to visit his prisoner, but he wanted his society; he was bent on a fuddle that day, and he needed a companion.

The under-warder, however, was inexorable.

There were punishments within the fortress to keep the inmates within bounds.

"Of course I must," replied the warder, dangling his bunch of keys, "or," he added, with a knowing nod, "I wouldn't."

With this he emptied the brown jug he held in his hand, and sluggishly departed.

Tom followed him, and in passing Ben's place of concealment, he communicated to him in a few words all that had passed.

Our two buccaneers seemed to hit upon one another's plans mutually.

They both crept softly after the warder, Ben keeping in the rear.

The unmistakable tramp of armed men startled them as they were about to enter a dimly-lighted passage.

And, following the warder's example, they hid themselves in one of the many dark nooks until they passed by.

"The guard!" muttered Tom; "this is another spoke in our wheel of fortune. Yonder fellow is half seas over, and he did not care about meeting them."

"Shall I knock him clean over?" asked Ben in a whisper.

"Not yet; he must show us the way first."

The warder, having listened till the footsteps died away, and having examined his keys to see if they were all there, then gave a quiet "whew."

He was about to retrace his steps when a thought occurred to him.

"What an old fool I am!" he ejaculated, "I have the key here. Didn't Bill hand it to me with instructions to take the greatest possible care of it? Well, he need'nt have troubled himself about that; he knows I am very careful—very, very careful."

With this soliloquy he reached the other end of the passage, and taking a key from his breast-pocket opened a low door, and emerged into the open air.

To our friends the rush of pure air was quite a relief, and the sight of the key in the lock left by the warder was indeed quite refreshing.

They quickly slipped out after him, locked the door on the outside, and followed him at a distance across a drawbridge that was lowered, and had evidently not been used for some time.

The warder then paused for a moment to select a key from his own bunch to undo another door, and then Tom dropped on all fours, and approached as near him as prudence would allow him, with the agility of a monkey.

The warder evidently had not missed the key he had left behind, but at the same time he was most cautious in taking his own keys with him.

When he had unlocked this door, he took the key out and inserted it into the lock on the other side, with the object, no doubt, of locking the door behind him. Tom had suspected this.

He could almost read the warder's intentions in the cunning twinkle of his eye.

"All right, old boy," he thought to himself.

Then, as the warder stepped inside, and was closing the door after him, Tom thrust the door open and sprang in upon him.

There was a sharp tussle for a few moments, for the warder was a big, powerful fellow, and had he not been taken so by surprise, our buccaneer captain would most likely have found his match.

As it was, the warder was quickly overpowered, and he trembled and turned of a ghastly pallor as the light from a loophole revealed our hero's features.

He might well have taken our hero for a ghost, had it not been for the firm and unmistakeable flesh-like grip that he held him with.

He was about to cry out, when our hero gripped him by the throat and almost choked him.

"That's it, captain; settle him," said Ben, as he joined his youthful commander. "Just allow me to give him one."

"No, no, Ben; shed no blood unnecessarily; besides," he added in Bob's ear, "we have not yet discovered Harry's cell."

"Right, captain; and the key?" Ben whispered.

"It's one of these," replied Tom; "and this accommodating fellow must go with us."

Ben waited to hear no more.

Time was flying very rapidly.

THE TRAITOR'S GRAVE.

The clock of an old tower had struck the hour just previously.

With Tom's assistance Ben Barnacle whipped the warder upon his back and carried him away from the door, which Tom carefully locked and barred after him, to a spot where it was less likely they might be overheard.

The warder was coming to now.

He was astounded, if not horrified, on finding he had two assailants instead of one.

He was utterly awed, and did not hesitate a moment in answering the questions Tom put to him.

In fact, he pointed out the key of Harry Vere's cell with the greatest civility and alacrity.

"Now, I suppose I may go?" he said, with the air of one who had bought his liberty. "I can render you no further assistance."

"You can point out the cell."

As Tom spoke he eyed the fellow keenly.

He fancied he could read treachery in the fellow's sunken eye.

Ben's fingers were itching to give the warder a "topper."

He did not like the fellow's look at all, but a gesture from Tom restrained him.

The warder, on the other hand, was racking his brain to devise some means of raising an alarm.

To cope with the two buccaneers was hopeless, and he also remembered now that in his hurry to visit the battery he had left his pistols behind him.

Putting a very fair face on the matter, he pretended to yield readily to our hero's commands.

But our buccaneers were too well acquainted with the ways of the world to be thrown off their guard thus easily.

It was a matter of life or death with them, and a third party also.

At a nod from Tom, Ben took a piece of rope from his pocket, and, pinning the warder's elbows tight behind him, bound them fast.

A small piece of line with a running noose was then placed round the warder's neck, the end brought down his back, passed through the lashing at his elbows, and steadied just taut enough to make its wearer feel uncomfortable.

"Now, lead on," commanded Tom Drake; "and if you give the least sign of treachery we shall brain you without mercy."

The warder led the way in silence.

It was a difficult read, and without his aid they would never have been able to find the way.

The passages had been built in an intricate style, so that a prisoner or anyone led or guided to any part of the stronghold might not find their way out again without a guide.

A great many of the passages were so much alike that out heroes might have been deceived into the belief that the warder was taking them through the same passages twice, or even thrice, only for Ben making his private mark upon the wall at every turn with the stem of his clay pipe.

Although they moved along at a brisk pace their journey seemed to be endless, and as they were all silent the time appeared doubly long.

At length, however, their silence was about to be broken.

As they were traversing a passage fitted with arm-racks for about fifty stand of musketry and various appliances for the working of heavy guns, Tom noticed that the warder's step became less regular.

He was perfectly sober now.

The fumes of the October had worked quite off of him by this.

His step was like that of one undecided whether to go forward or to hang back.

This prepared Tom Drake for something, and that something he discovered a moment afterwards.

That passage led into a large semi-circular chamber, with deep embrasures for guns should necessity need them, but at the present time the openings were guarded by tremendous iron bars.

This did not at all surprise our hero. The old fortress, from what he had seen of it, and that was quite sufficient to warrant his opinion, had been built solely for defence and strength.

But what did astonish him was the sight of three armed men grouped together, and leaning on their firelocks, in deep consultation.

They were arguing some point, and raised their voices from a whisper to loud imprecations, as one or the other differed in his opinion.

Tom Drake drew the cord round the warder's neck tighter on beholding this.

"Villain," he hissed, "this is the trap you thought to lead us into." Now, the cell, or by heaven you stir not another inch alive."

The guilty wretch trembled as Captain Tom Drake took from his bosom a gleaming poignard and held it over his heart.

There was a diamond on the top of the hilt that took the warder's eyesight away for the moment.

He trembled like an aspen with fear, and his limbs shook beneath him.

In the blindness of his cupidity he had never so much as dreamt of failure.

He could do nothing now, however, but to submit to everything, and to trust to providence.

Concealing his chagrin as well as he could, he led the way to a strong door, which Tom Drake soon unlocked and then threw open.

The door was in one of the passages they had already passed through, therefore they had left behind the chamber the soldiers were on guard in, so that their actions were not observed by them.

"Harry Vere!"

"Captain Tom!"

Such were the first words that broke the silence of the dreary tomb, for a tomb certainly could not have been more cold and cheerless than the dungeon in which Tom Drake found his young lieutenant.

Not a ray of light ever penetrated that dismal den, only the faint glimmer that stole in when the door was opened, and that very seldom occurred after a prisoner was once incarcerated, until he was taken out to be executed, or was lucky enough to get a reprieve.

There was no visible place even for admittance of air, although it must have been ventilated in some way; nor was there any sign of a seat—not even of a handful of straw.

Harry Vere quickly explained this.

By some fiendish contrivance, a strong current of cold air—cold as the atmosphere in the icy regions—continually swept the floor of the cell, thus compelling the weary prisoner to keep on his feet, and to pace back and forth the dark chamber until human nature gave way, and he sank down exhausted and perished with the cold.

This was the fate of many a one whose death by violence would have raised the voice of the nation. It left behind it no marks, and death was therefore attributed to natural causes.

It took Vere only a moment to explain this, but that moment's delay was dangerous.

In the meantime, the under-warder's long absence had been noticed, and his mate Bill had been sent to seek for him.

Failing in his search, he repaired to the guard-room to make inquiries, but he could gain no information.

The captain of the guard happened at that moment to enter, and, having learnt from the sergeant-at-arms the cause of the warder's complaint, he suddenly remembered that he had forgotten to execute a fresh order he had received from the governor.

It was to this effect—he was to take the prisoner, Harry Vere, entirely under his charge, and the sergeant-at-arms was to keep the key of his cell in his possession, and to deliver it to no one, unless by the captain's order.

As soon as he heard that the under warder was missing, he immediately sent a guard of four men to search for him; and they, meeting the head warder, induced him to accompany them.

The head warder had keys of every part of the fortress; for, by a skilful manipulation of his own which had cost him many years of hard study, he managed to make a few keys open a certain number of locks, which lightened his burden considerably.

With the natural instinct associated with his capacity he made straight for Harry Vere's cell, never doubting for one moment that on his way he would fall in with his subordinate coiled up in some corner, fast asleep.

We must explain that the under warder's visit to the cellarman, or under butler, was not entirely unknown to him, and he was not averse to a good tankard of ale on the sly himself.

"Now, what shall we do with this reptile?" said said Tom Drake, looking round at his followers. "You, Mr. Vere, have the right to name his punishment."

"Leave him in here," said the lieutenant; "they only open a little slide to put the food in, so they are sure not to discover him till they come to take me out."

This was no sooner suggested than acted upon.

The poor terror-stricken wretch gave an owl-like screech as they gagged him and threw him in.

Captain Tom Drake little imagined that this very man had assisted in throwing him into his dungeon, in the Black Tower, but yet he did not feel any pity for him.

He would have done anything sooner than kill him unless it was necessary.

They locked the cell door, however, and, taking the bunch of keys with them, they departed rapidly and as silently as possible, leaving the soldiers in the chamber in total ignorance of their visit.

Ben Barnacle piloted them through the intricate windings, and they would soon have crossed the drawbridge; but just as Ben put the key in the lock to open the door, the head warder inserted his key on the outer side.

This of course caused confusion in both parties; but Ben still kept his key in the lock.

This gave the buccaneers a few moments to find out how the wind blew.

Captain Tom aided by Harry Vere, who had refreshed himself from a flask Ben carried with him, climbed up to a loop-hole and saw the soldiers upon the drawbridge.

This was very awkward.

With the key in the lock it was no use trying concealment.

Tom recognised the voice of the head warder, as with sundry invectives, he ordered his subordinate to open the door.

"You blundering knave," he shouted, "do you think this will gain you anything? To-morrow morning I will have you scourged if you don't open to me immediately!"

"This is awkward," said Tom, turning to his followers; "but it will not do for us to remain here; come this way, quick lads."

Tom on his way had taken an architectural survey of the fortress, and he had noticed one barred casemate near the drawbridge, and this had particularly taken his attention.

Tom and his followers soon reached it, but just at that moment the door was burst open, and the head warder saw their shadows on the opposite wall.

Little dreaming of the danger he was rushing into, he flew head long down the passage, and Ben with one stroke laid him lifeless on the stone floor.

"Guard the passage," cried Ben, ' I'll soon clear a gangway. And you, Captain Tom, just keep an eye on the fellows outside."

As he spoke he handed Vere his pistols and commenced operations on the iron work.

The soldiers were quite unprepared for all this, and therefore they showed some confusion. A couple of them had followed the warder in, and wondered where he could have disappeared so suddenly.

Those on the outside were surprised to see Ben wielding his heavy bludgeon with such effect, and wondered within themselves as the iron bars gave way under his ponderous blows.

They were startled from their reverie by the voice of their comrades calling them to their aid.

This was a critical moment for our buccaneers.

They were in total ignorance of the numbers they had to contend with.

The halloaing and shouting, and hasty treading of feet, made it appear as though a whole host had come down upon them.

But there was no time to waste.

Quick as thought, Tom led the way through the opening, followed by his trusty friends, and the trio prepared for a rush all together across the bridge.

"Fire, fire, shoot them down!" thundered the sergeant to his men, and a shower of bullets whistled very close to the heads of our gallant buccaneers, but not one of them was hit.

Tom led the way to the door of which he held the key, and having passed his followers through it he closed and locked it after them.

In a few minutes more the whole party stood ath the wall.

Vere needed no incentive to urge him to k; he was up the rope, and across the
a id say knife.

Ben ascended next, and Tom stayed behind, pistol in hand, to keep the soldiers at bay.

By this time the whole fortress was in arms.

The firing of the soldiers' muskets had alarmed the whole garrison; the reports had even reached the ears of the buccaneers on watch for their comrades, and they began to fear for their safety.

When the soldiers caught sight of Captain Tom Drake they raised a loud shout, and, battering down every obstacle with the butt-ends of their muskets made towards him.

Captain Tom was up the rope like a cat.

The sentinels on the battlements fired several shots at him, but without avail.

Even the Governor had been alarmed, and had joined in the chase.

He just arrived in time to see Tom stride the top of the wall, fire one shot at his pursuers, and disappear.

Ben hauled on the rope, and let it drop into the moat, and then the buccaneers thought fit to beat a retreat.

It was entirely owing to the confusion of the soldiers, and the way in which they lumbered in each other's road, that our gallant captain and his faithful few escaped so far without being killed.

The soldiers on the battlements poured a deadly volley after them from their long matchlocks and arquebusses.

Our heroes, however, had nearly gained a place of safety, when another unforeseen accident occurred.

A party of coastguardsmen that had been prowling about the rocks came upon them full butt.

They, too, had been alarmed by the report of firearms.

As soon as Tom's little party saw them, they prepared for a fight.

The officer in charge of the coastguard party was not justified in commencing hostilities at once.

They were to look after the interests of the revenue department, and to seize upon contraband goods, but upon this occasion they seemed bent upon doing anything.

They drew their cutlasses and levelled their pistols, and advanced upon Tom's little party at once.

'Surrender!" cried the coastguard officer, "or we will riddle you with shot! The more trouble you give us the worse for yourselves!"

This arrogant speech aroused Tom's ire.

"Surrender we never will!" he answered; " and as to riddling us with shot, why we laugh at your threat. We usually make scarecrows and shark's meat of such carrion as you. I should like to know by what and whose authority you molest us. At all events, we shall not give in so easily as you imagine."

The coastguard officer was taken aback by Captain Tom's bold answer.

More than one noticed how his eye quailed beneath the boy leader's stern gaze.

He halted his men, and seemed for a moment undecided how to act.

Tom's fantastic dress puzzled him a little, and as to Ben, with his big sea boots, and his huge club in his brawny hand, he was a perfect myth.

"Better to settle them quietly than to bring the garrison down upon us," whispered Vere to Captain Tom.

"But the fellow's insolence! I cannot stand that," answered our hero, tartly.

The coastguard officer whispered a few words to one of his own men, and he in turn slunk back amongst the others, and communicated something to them.

The buccaneers could only surmise the p the whispering.

They saw that the coastguardsmen meant coming down upon them with a rush, and they prepared for them.

It was a rocky pass, leading down to the beach, where they met, so that our buccaneers held the higher ground, and this, no doubt, caused the leader of the coastguardsmen to hesitate as he did.

Captain Tom Drake was not the one to waste his time in useless palaver. The events of the past week seemed to him to have occupied an age, and without any beneficial results.

He looked round at his little party, that numbered five, including himself, and weighed their chances with the twelve burly coastguardsmen and their leader, in a hand-to-hand mêlée.

If they dallied much longer there was a possibility of their being hemmed in by the soldiers, who were sure to follow in pursuit, and this rendered the case of the buccaneers doubly desperate.

Captain Tom turned to the leader of the coastguards, and, eyeing him fiercely, cried—

"Order your men to face about and retire, or take the consequences on your own head. I am Captain Tom Drake, and these are my buccaneers."

The effect of these words were electrical.

The coastguard party stood for a moment astounded.

Captain Tom Drake, and a thousand pounds reward, almost at the point of their cutlasses!

It seemed incredible.

The officer was so paralysed that he could neither move nor speak; in fact, he was more powerless than his men.

Often in his dreams he had been so placed, face to face, with the daring buccaneer, but he little thought that dream would ever be realised.

Whilst they were all staring aghast, afraid to move, yet eager to seize so rich a prize, Ben Barnacle rushed forward into their midst, and, wielding his massive club right and left, made a pathway for his young chief through the formidable group.

Lieutenant Vere and the two buccaneers followed closely upon them, striking out as they went with whatever weapons they chanced to be armed.

The coastguardsmen, if astounded before, were still more so by Ben's fierce and sudden attack.

They gave way on all sides, and their weapons flew in every direction.

Broken heads, arms, and bruises were for the time at a discount, while the oaths and denunciations heaped on Ben's head were anything but flattering.

His face wore a quiet smile as he turned and kept the enemy at bay, and he only retreated when he saw a party of armed soldiers enter the other end of the pass.

The pursuit was getting too hot now for the buccaneers to stand at trifles, but they were not far off from the cave they were making for.

The coastguardsmen, smarting with pain, and mad and with anger, followed them up closely, shouting to each other as they went to keep close together, and not to be satisfied until they revenged the injuries their comrades had sustained.

At certain intervals the buccaneers faced round and gave their pursuers a few bullets, just to check them, then on they would go, again loading their pistols as they ran.

At the entrance of the secret way that led to the cavern they made a last stand, and fired a terrible galling volley at the coastguardsmen, and then suddenly disappeared.

A loud shout greeted our hero as he made his appearance in the cave, and a dozen voices or so took up the shout of—

"Hip, hip, hurrah! for our Captain Tom Drake!"

Captain Tom, weary and worn out as he was for want of sleep, could not help smiling at this simple but true-hearted demonstration of the loyalty of the gruff and grimy-looking little group around him.

Bob and Jerry had not been idle all this time.

They had certainly kept a good look out for the "Will-o'-the-Wisp," but at the same time they had provided a good repast for the comfort of the inner man.

There was not one among the group that was not ready to welcome this

And as a huge stone had been rolled into the cavity by which they had entered, they all sat down to discuss the welcome meal.

CHAPTER CCIII.

CAPTAIN TOM BOARDS THE 'WILL-O'-THE-WISP."—OUR HERO GETS A LETTER OF MARQUE, AND DECEIVES THE PORT ADMIRAL

'OH, oh! here they come, Captain Tom; such a host of em, by jove, skyblue jackets and horse marines are fools to em. Capsize the soup, boys—don't let the beggars have any of it, they look hungry enough to eat a grindstone."

Such was Jerry Mizzen's harangue as he rushed into the cave from seaward, where he had been keeping watch, and his words needed no interpreting.

By stopping up the entrance by which Tom and his party had entered, they had forced their pursuers to take a wide circuit round the rocky fastnesses, and now they were coming in numbers.

There was no doubt that every pass and every cranny of the rocks were well guarded, but the buccaneers could laugh at their enemies so long as they were only on land.

There was a yawl concealed in a little nook hard by and once on board of this the buccaneers were safe.

Tom gave the order at once to embark.

There was just time, and no more, for them to pull out of reach of the soldiers' long firelocks, and so he considered it wise to be moving.

Every one heartily acquiesced in this, and they set up a galling shout of defiance as they shot round a point and disappeared from the view of the soldiers, who were left in terrible disappointment on the beach.

*   *   *   *   *   *   *

It was a glorious morning when Captain Tom Drake found himself on board his little craft.

All hands were as busy and as light-hearted as bees, and even the guns seemed to shine more brightly than they had done for some weeks.

Captain Tom was dressed in a brand new suit from top to toe, and his gold epaulettes and diamond hilted sword set off his princely form to great advantage.

He glanced proudly up at the neatly stowed canvas, the evenly trimmed yards, and the ropes, that were each so prepared as to be ready for running at a moment's notice.

On the deck, too, the guns and everything were ordered with the same precision, and a hand was here and there employed in remedying any defect in the newly-coiled ropes, and touching up the brasswork.

From this Tom's attention was directed to the shore. He expected visitors, and the sight of a boat leaving a small creek, gave him evident satisfaction.

He paced the quarter-deck till the boat came alongside, and three persons boarded the vessel from it.

They were the three mysterious men Bob and Jerry had seen in the cave.

Captain Tom shook hands with all three of them

"Welcome to the 'Will-o'-the-Wisp,'" he said, raising his cocked hat. "Shall we go below, gentlemen, or do you prefer staying on deck?"

"Perhaps it would be better to go below, if it puts you to no inconvenience," said the one we have before introduced as the leader, and who now appeared to act as spokesman. "There is no necessity for a dozen listeners."

Several of the elder buccaneers had already stole aft as far as the limits, and several of the young middies, to catch a view of the strangely-attired visitors.

The state cabin was very neatly fitted up.

Tom had had all the velvet cushions restuffed, and recovered, and the splendid fixtures cleaned up or replaced by new ones.

The visitors seemed very well pleased with the handsome mirrors and gorgeous arras that adorned the sides of the cabin, and also the splendid collection of side-arms and pistols, neatly arranged between the after-cabin windows, that were trophies Tom had taken in his various engagements.

But they had business of importance on hand, and time was too precious to waste it idly.

"And so I hear," Tom commenced when they were seated, "that you have been in my company before; that you were taken prisoner by the Barbary pirates, and after a long and wearisome captivity escaped in one of the pirate vessels."

"Just so; and proud we are to have met you here, though we were rather astonished when your two clumsy but faithful adherents came blundering into our place of concealment."

"And annoyed you, no doubt?" said our hero.

"Well, yes, a little," replied his guest, "but that's all over. We have come now to offer you any assistance you may think worthy to accept."

"I am very much indebted to you already. Had it not been for your boat I might not be here now," said Captain Tom. "Ben Barnacle would not have seen my hat fall over the cliff, and he might have hunted a month before he found out in what part of the fortress I was confined."

"Don't mention it. Ben's version of your career was sufficient to guarantee our actions. Say, will you accept our offer, and as many of my men as are willing to join your flag?"

"I must first know to whom I am about to be indebted for all this," said Tom, thoughtfully. "I have not yet learnt your name."

The spokesman of the party glanced round the cabin to see that no intruder was listening, but not being satisfied with this he leant forward and whispered in Tom's ear.

What he communicated to him in those few moments no one knew; certain it was that it produced a magical effect upon Tom Drake.

He turned pale at first, but he soon regained his composure.

"Then you knew my uncle?" he said.

"Well; very well indeed," was the laconic reply.

"And Minnie Atherton?"

"Slightly."

"Enough to remember her, I suppose?"

"Just so; but you must consider I was but a boy."

Tom saw that this questioning was irksome to his visitor, so he changed the subject.

"How many of your men will join me?" Tom asked.

"About six, no more; the others prefer staying where they are."

"For some reason of their own, I suppose."

"Yes, and a good reason, too."

"Private?" queried Tom.

"Well, so far as this, I may tell you—not many fathoms down amongst those rocks lay the remains of the good ship we were wrecked in, and in her hold there is a chest of Spanish doubloons, as heavy as four men could lift."

This was a piece of intelligence Tom was not prepared for.

He had divers among his crew who would soon fish this up, but then what might be the consequence?

It took him but a few moments to weigh this through his mind.

He was not afraid that a share of this would tempt any of his brave crew to leave him, but it might cause a jealousy between the two parties, and a fight, perhaps, and besides, it would compel him to remain on the coast some time longer.

He did not want to stay any longer inactive, and as for the treasure, he could get plenty of that for the seeking.

"And you leave them with that, I suppose?" Tom said.

"Yes," was the reply, "we have plenty in the cave for our wants; the barque was crammed with costly merchandize, plundered when we mutinied and took possession of her. They had forgotten that Englishmen were not born to be slaves, and so they trusted us a little too far, as they found to their cost."

"And sorrow, no doubt, for they are very feeling-hearted," added Tom.

"Well, we didn't stay to ask. Some of the fleet gave us chase, but we outstripped them, and shipwrecked we landed on our native shore."

"And now come here to offer your services to one whose calling is the most hazardous?"

"It will be pleasure; it will serve to drive away gloomy thoughts that have been engendered by news I have heard since our arrival. Say, what is your candid opinion of our offer?"

"That it is most generous and self sacrificing, and if you do not wish to retract it I will and do accept it."

"Well done. What say you, comrades?" ejaculated the speaker, rising.

"Agreed, agreed!" cried the others, rising also.

"Then let every one drink to each other's success," said Tom Drake, filling the glasses with sparkling wine, "and let us each swear to be true to each other, and never to raise a weapon in anger or jealousy against each other's lives."

"'Tis well; we swear it!"

They chinked their glasses together, and emptied them, which Tom replenished again and again until their hearts warmed to each other, and they became knitted in the bonds of brotherhood.

* * * * *

A little later in the day our hero, Captain Tom, ascended the broad steps leading to the entrance of the port-admiral's mansion.

He was met in the hall by a powdered flunkey, who inquired his pleasure, and held his thumb and finger ready for his card.

"The port-admiral," said our hero, in a voice and manner that made the fellow start.

"Your name; your card," suggested the flunkey, trembling.

"Captain White! Be sharp, fool! The way."

Tom's sharp tone and quick tap on the hilt of his sword had the desired effect.

The man of peace was not accustomed to such peremptory orders.

With a puzzled look and a slight start, he drew back a pace, and then started at full speed up one of the staircases.

Tom followed close on his heels, and arrived at the door just as he had given it a tap.

As the door opened, Tom saw that the old veteran was alone, and, without waiting for any ceremony, he stepped in.

T e old admiral looked up at him in amazement.

He was about to reprimand hi n for the intrusion, but, seeing the visitor was a stranger, he was astounded.

Tom, s eing hi momentary embarrassment and that he was at a loss to express him elf, relieved him by at once entering into business, for he did not know how soon they might be disturbed.

Besides, it was an opportunity he very lit le expected, and it was not likely he was going to throw it away.

"Captain White," said our hero, in anticipation of the question the admiral was about to ask. "I wish to speak to you privately; no one will in'rude b re, I presume."

"Captain White!" stammered the admiral; "a d pray who the devil are you that you dare intrude on my privacy? Hi! ho! there, you confounded flour pate; what the dev——"

"Hush! don't be rash; keep seated. I hear you have offered a reward for the cap ure of Tom D ake?"

Tom ut ered these wo ds so quick and mechanically that the old admiral was thrown completely off his guard.

It was like pouring oil on the troubled waters.

"Well, well," ejaculated the admiral.

"I mean to catch him."

"You—you? The dev——"

"I do; and, what's more, I don't mean to let him go again."

"We'll, well; but how do you mean to ——"

"Do it? Why, by your assistance."

The port-admiral was wound up to a perfect pitch of excitement by this t m .

"What assistance?—what assistance? Go on."

"Well, I want you to give me a letter of marque."

"You do? Dash my toplights! Are you joking?"

"Not a bit of it; I'm in earnest," said T m with emphasis. "Tom Drake, and a thousand pounds," he added, not waiting for the admiral to reply; "that's not joking, is it? I know his movements; I can track him. With a letter of marque, I can give him battle, hammer his ship to pieces, take him prisoner, bring him here, and claim the reward."

This was all spoken, as it were, in a breath. By following him up sharply, Tom had not given him time to think or consider the feasibility of this rash assertion.

"Is that all you require?' asked the admiral, who began already to see a great hero in the youthful figure before him.

"An order on any of his majesty's vessels to supply me with ammunition, or render me any assistance I may require," returned Tom.

"Oh, yes—yes; but you have a ship and crew fit to carry out your ideas, I mean?"

"Decidedly; or why should I be here? But I have no time to lose; he is widening the distance every moment I waste here."

"Very true; I thought not of that." And the old veteran, scarcely aware of what he was doing, wrote out the order immediately.

"Whi e, Captain White, you say? John, Thomas, or wh t?" he asked, in the same excited manner, as he took a parchment roll from a heap before him, and b gan filling it in.

"Tom—Thomas," said our hero, forgetting himself for a moment.

"Where do you hail from?"

"London, Liverpool, anywhere," replied our hero, becoming in his turn a little bit confuse .

"Tut, tut. No, no; anywhere won't do. What po t did you clear from last?'

"Liverpool. I have the papers here, somewhere; confound it, I've left them aboard. Al through

hurrying; time flies quicker than one can call it. Hang it! Dang it! Tom Drake, you shall pay for all this when I catch you."

Tom saw that the old admiral was becoming more reflective, and that he must renew the excitement if he wished to succeed.

"Ship's name?" asked the old veteran.

"The 'R cer,' six hundred tons, eleven guns, two hundred and twenty men; draws seven een feet of water; barque rigged, clinker built, copper bottomed, lower masts i on b und, store room well found, pumps duly clamped, and——"

"There, there, Be ay, belay! That will do. Here you are, Captain White, and the devil blacken you if you don't soon bring back that confounded rebel—Tom D ake."

"That's settled. Now for a fair wind, a d may the devil blacken and bruise me, to , if you don't see Captain Tom Drake when I return."

So saying, Tom placed the packages in his breast, buttoned up his coat, and, taking up his cocked hat, bowed himself out of the room.

As he left he did not observe another party enter the apartment by an opposite door.

Chuckling within himself at his success, he was about to descend the stairs when the rustling of silk startled him, and on turning his head he beheld the lovely creature he had seen in the carriage on the night he fought with the robbers.

Taking off his hat, he bowed gracefully to her and took one step nearer towards her.

The young lady did not recognise him until then. On that adventurous night Tom's face was grimed and his clothes soiled with mud, but the lady's quick eye soon recognised his features.

"Is it you, sir, and he e?" she said, half tremblingly. "Are you not afraid?"

"Afraid of what?" Tom asked in his most winning tone. "I have been to see your father, and he would not harm me, surely?"

"He would have you arrested, cast into prison again," she answered sorrowfully. "Do not trust him too far, dear Tom, for—for—"

"For what, pretty one?" Tom asked, clasping her s ft hand gently in his.

"For my sake," was her blushing reply.

"Why, you do not care so much for me?" he cried, drawing her gently to him.

"I care for your safety as you once cared for mine," she answered. "My father, as I tell you, would like to see you in prison again. You have many enemies. I often hear your name mentioned."

As the lady finished speaking, a loud shouting was heard in the room Tom had just left.

"Captain Tom Drake! Seize him. Captain Tom Drake! Hold him, some of you, hold him."

"Fly, fly! You are discovered," said the terrified girl; and Tom could feel her heart panting as he pressed her to him.

"Farewell; it must be so," Tom said, imprinting a fervent kiss on her soft lips. "Farewell, we shall yet meet again."

He pressed his lips to hers once more, and as he did so the door of the room opened, and the parchment visage of the little Admiral Ell s appeared, as he shouted at the top of his voice for assistance.

Tom gave him one withering, defiant look, then, gently untwining his arm from the waist of the fair girl, he bowed gallantly to her, and, replacing his cocked hat, took only two leaps down the stairs.

The shouts of the admiral were by this time echoed all over the mansion, and a hue-and-cry was raised. The guard was turned out, and a hundred persons at the very least were in pursuit of our gallant hero.

But he did not falter. He walked steadily away

at first, so as not to cause excitement, and as soon as he got out of sight he ran with all his might towards the coast.

"Pull! Pull like demons," he said to his own trusty crew, as he leaped into the gig which he had left waiting for him. "They pursue us. Pull! pull away, lads. We must not be taken."

The bold mids gave way with a will.

Their ashen blades bent at each stroke like a lancewood bow.

The sharp prow of the gig cut through the water without a ripple, and in less than half-an-hour they were all on board the "Will-o'-the-Wisp," and the gig hoisted up to the quarter davits.

CHAPTER CCIV.

CAPTAIN TOM DRAKE GOES ON PARTICULAR SERVICE.—CHASED BY A MAN-O'-WAR.—CAPTAIN TOM VISITS THE MYSTERIOUS HAUNT.

"ALL hands ahoy!"

Such was the cry raised by a stentorian voice on board of the "Will-o'-the-Wisp," as the sky, that had a short time previously been brightened by the sun, became suddenly darkened.

The crew tumbled up from both fore and after-hatches, and took a cursory view of the horizon to windward, where heavy, sombre clouds were rapidly rising.

Captain Tom stood on the quarter-deck, glass in hand.

He was looking very serious and thoughtful, and the buccaneers watched in anxious suspense their young leader's face.

There was a cold, chilling air, and, as some of the crew had turned hastily out of their hammocks and rushed on deck with only their trousers and shirts on, they felt rather shivery.

One or two slipped down below to put on a guernsey or a pea jacket, but they were not absent a minute.

Harry Vere and Ben Barnacle stood together near the break of the poop, looking in the same direction as the captain.

"We shall have a snorter directly, Mr. Vere," said Ben. "It'll be down on us in a crack when it does come."

"Let it come, then," said Harry. "It will be a treat to feel the old ship roll again, after the miserable life we've had on shore."

"Well, a good stout plank and a stiff breeze is at any time more preferable than being crowded up like rats in those stone walls; and a good sniff of powder would be a treat after the foul stench of these musty dungeons."

Captain Tom's voice interrupted their conversation.

"Barnacle," he said, "let the hands have a glass of grog. Be handy! There's not much time! We shall soon know what we are to have."

Even as he spoke the wind began to freshen, and the air to grow colder, and a damp sort of mist pervaded the atmosphere.

Ben went to the hatchway to pass the word to the steward, when, to his surprise, he saw the grim visage of Dr. Shrike, and just below him his assistant, Jacop, with a case of surgical instruments under his arm.

"Hallo! what are you doing here," Ben said to the doctor, after he had passed the word below. "You've got your ammunition with you, I see."

Ben glanced significantly at the case that held the doctor's instruments of torture, as he spoke, and the doctor returned him one of his most ghastly and horrible grins.

"Ah, let them have grog. give them plenty; they'll fight all the better," said the doctor, showing

his yellow, fang like teeth. "When will they begin, Mr. Barnacle, when will they begin?"

"Before another bell strikes," answered Ben, humouring him; "they'll have a tough job too, or I'm a Dutchman! Go below, doctor—go below; if you're wanted I'll call you, and any particular cases I'll send down below to you."

"Thank you, Mr. Barnacle, thank you. Don't let me miss one," said the doctor, rubbing the palms of his bony hands together. "It's a long time since I had a good subject, and —"

Ben turned away to issue some order, and then the parchment-visaged old vampyre began counting on his fingers.

"Yes; they are all gone—every one of them!" he cogitated, presently. "As fine a set of heads as any one could have wished, and you, Jacop," he added, glancing down at his assistant, "threw them every one overboard!"

"I was ordered to," replied Jacop in a whining tone, but at the same time grinning in his sleeve at the doctor's discomfiture. "I didn't want to throw them overboard you know that Mr Shrike."

"Don't mister me, you rascal. Call me doctor, if you please, or I'll skin you alive," said the doctor, savagely. "You're lazy, Jacop, and that will be your ruin."

"I'm not lazy," whimpered Jacop. "Didn't I pick all the flesh off five of the skulls, until they were as clean as an elephant's tooth?"

"But you threw them overboard, you scoundrel, and wasted all your labour. Why didn't you boil them as I desired you, and then you might have polished the whole five-and-twenty, and I might have had them now."

"But we're going into action," he added, "and bear this in mind—put every limb and bone out of the captain's sight. Don't let him know anything, for if you do, I'll settle you; I'll put you away as quiet as a mouse, and I'll put your skeleton in the museum."

Jacop winced fearfully at this.

He had dreamt, on more than one occasion, that the doctor was going to secretly poison him.

It made his flesh fairly creep when the doctor spoke of sending his skeleton to the museum.

By this time the sky had considerably darkened, and the wind had freshened into a stiff breeze, whilst the sea began to ripple and dash with violence against the ship's side.

"Take in the topgallant-sails," Captain Tom said to his lieutenant. "Be quick, Harry; we shall want to reef presently. What this black bank is coming down upon us I cannot yet tell. I shall be glad when this suspense is over."

Those whose duty it was soon sprang aloft to furl the topgallant-sails, and the rest of the buccaneers took their respective stations in various parts of the ship, every ear strained to catch each sound, and every hand ready to grasp a rope.

The three strange beings who had volunteered their services were also on the poop ready to render assistance.

They had brought their chests and such valuables aboard as they needed during Captain Tom's temporary absence, and had secreted the bulk of their costly treasures in one of the deep recesses of the cave where it was not likely to be discovered by prying eyes until they returned to reclaim it.

All this passed in much less time than it has taken us to record it.

The black clouds were rapidly advancing, forcing a cold, biting blast before it.

Presently it struck the gallant "Will-o'-the-Wisp" on the starboard beam, causing her to heel over considerably with the shock, and hail-stones as big as peas showered down upon the deck.

"Reef topsails, up foresail, and in jib!" shouted

Captain Tom, through the speaking-trumpet he had taken from its brackets, near the binnacle.

The order was obeyed with alacrity.

The sails mentioned were as neatly stowed as hands could stow them, and the gallant ship sped on like an arrow through the icy shower of hail-stones.

Captain Tom was in his glory now.

It was quite refreshing to hear the noble vessel dash against the huge waves, and to see the spray flying from the bows nearly to the foretop.

But it was a perilous task for the sailors, the buccaneers aloft, for their hands and limbs were so numbed with cold that they could scarcely handle the stout canvas, or hold on to the yards, to prevent falling into the surging sea.

Tom stood by the binnacle, smiling as each fresh wave, tipped with foam, dashed against the "Will-o'-the-Wisp," sending her into the air, and filling her upper deck with water.

None but Captain Tom knew their destination; they could only know that the wind was fair, by the yards being a little squared, and the ship going a point or two free.

As soon as the sails were trimmed and all made snug aloft, the hands who had been turned up from their sleep were sent down again, and a double look-out was set ahead.

"Send a couple of good hands to the wheel," said Tom Drake to Harry Vere, whose watch it was on deck. "I am going below for a few minutes. I won't be long."

So saying, the youthful leader stepped below, and Jerry Mizzen and Bob, muffled up to the eyes and a plug of tobacco in the cheek of the latter, very reluctantly took their places at the wheel.

The hail peppered down most fearfully, rendering the deck unsafe to walk upon, and the wind was so piercing cold that any part of the flesh exposed to 't was rendered so numb and feelingless, that those on deck longed for the hour that would bring them relief.

In the meantime Drake was in his cabin with the three strangers, overhauling his chart.

"There, that is our course," he said, drawing his finger across the paper, "with this wind we shall not be long in running across, but let me," he added, impressively, "again warn you of the risk you run in linking your fate with mine."

"I am fully prepared," said he, who had acted all along as spokesman, "and as for my companions here, I think they will not flinch from any danger Will Gordon dares to face."

"What say you, Longton?" he added, addressing the tallest of the other two.

"I am ready for anything," was the answer.

"And you, Harvey?"

"I have none but myself to care about."

"That is settled, then," said Captain Tom, rolling up the chart, and returning it to the locker he had taken it from.

Captain Drake struck a silver gong and, to the surprise of his newly-made allies, Zelie answered the summons.

They stared almost with rudeness at the beautiful corsair maiden in her picturesque dress.

At a sign from our hero Zelie drew aside a silken screen, and from a swinging sideboard produced decanters and glasses, which she placed in the rack fitted to the table.

She then replenished the fire that was burning in a bronze stove with solid silver bars, and then withdrew from the cabin.

Tom was prepared for his guests' surprise.

In fact, it was a good opportunity for him to break the ice to them, and to prevent any unpleasantness hereafter.

In a few words he briefly explained to them how she first came on board, and informed them that she undertook the duties of page to him of her own free will and that she was entered in the ship's book as one of the crew.

This was true.

But Zelie had a more selfish motive for occupying so menial a position.

She loved the young chief, and she acted as page simply to enable her to share as much of his company as possible, and to remain near him whenever he was on board and free from duty.

Zelie had suffered greatly, both bodily and mentally, during the last few months.

She had worked as one of the crew, in various disguises.

Sometimes dressed as a smuggler, at others as a buccaneer, and had passed as one of the mids on several occasions.

Her jealous eye had watched the young chieftain with anxious care, and followed him through danger when it was practicable, and she would have willingly shared his danger and captivity could she have done so.

This done, Captain Tom let the subject drop.

"Now, friends," he said, "I will disclose to you some of my intentions, but I beg you will not pry into, nor meddle with any of my affairs that I may think proper to keep secret."

To this they all consented.

"Well," he continued, "it is my ambition to carve out for myself and my followers a name, which already is world wide, that may be handed down to posterity, and that will be cherished, equally, by those who respect me."

"Hear, hear," answered his companions.

"First of all then, I am going to France to visit one who can aid me materially; at the sametime I have other business to transact, which for the present, I wish to keep to my own self. Will that satisfy you."

"Hear, hear," was the response. We are content to be guided by you," said Will Gordon.

"Aye, and to die for you if necessary," said Longton.

"And I, too," chimed in Harvey.

The voice of Ben Barnacle put an end to their farther conversation on the subject, and all four of them went on deck.

"What's up now?" said Tom Drake, buttoning his sea jacket over his uniform. "Any danger to the vessel, Ben?"

"No, captain, but there's a vessel sighted from the yard-arm."

Tom strode forward.

The vessel was leaping over the waves in such a manner that he was obliged to steady himself by the fore bitts.

"Mast head," he shouted.

"Ay, ay."

"You sight a ship—where away?"

He was almost obliged to screech—the wind was so terrific

"On our lee bow."

"Can you make her out?"

"No."

"Can you see her rig?"

"That of a frigate."

"Is she going our way?"

"Yes, we're overhauling her."

Tom waited to hear no more.

He sprang into the rigging agile as a cat, and ascended to the yard.

"A man-o'-war, sure enough," he said, to the buccaneer on the look-out, "she's labouring heavily too she must carry a double tier of guns; she looks like a forty four, we must give her a wide berth."

In a few minutes he was down on deck and beside the wheel.

"Keep her away a couple of points, Bob; square the yards a little," he said to Ben.

This was done.

The "Will-o'-the-Wisp" rode more easy now.

Almost before the wind she skimmed along with increased speed.

Tom, in the meantime, watched the strange sail with his glass. She could be seen from the deck now.

Tom's keen eye soon made her out to be a huge man-o'-war, but whether French or English he could not tell, as the hail was still pelting down like peas shot from a sack, and the stranger showed no colours.

Whatever she was, Tom did not consider it prudent to run too near her, under existing circumstances.

As eight bells struck, the weather began to break a little, however, and the hail-storm had nearly passed over.

Tom paced the quarter-deck with rapid, uneven strides. He did not wish to meet with an enemy just on the present occasion. He wanted to complete the object he had in hand, and then he did not mind meeting with a foe.

In the first dog-watch the weather so far moderated and cleared up, that both vessels could see each other distinctly, although they were several miles apart.

"That's a Frenchman I'll swear by the rig," he said, addressing Harry Vere.

"And she's waiting for us, too," said the lieutenant.

"All the better for us," said Tom. "I want to draw her away from the port I wish to enter."

"Let the watch stand by to shake out or reef," he added, presently.

The buccaneers were at their stations in a moment.

Captain Tom and Harry Vere still kept watching the man-o'-war's movements.

She was evidently trying to overhaul them, for she spread her lighter canvas, which had hitherto been furled.

Captain Tom also gave orders to make sail.

"It will be dark soon," he muttered to himself; "I can slip out of her way then, if the moon does not show too much light."

Darkness was creeping on apace, and there was every appearance of fine weather; and so Tom gave word to set all sail, even to the royals and top-gallant stun-sails.

Tom Drake watched with anxious eye every movement of the man-of-war.

Streak after streak of snowy canvas he saw shoot up from her dark hull, and then belly out to the evening breeze.

But, by Tom's careful management, he had placed her a long way astern of the "Will-o'-the-Wisp," and both vessels were going at about an equal speed.

This would not do for our hero, however.

To win the race, he must make his ship go the speedier of the two, and this he did by having the bow chasers run aft and shifting some of the heavy shot.

This gave them the advantage of a knot and a half per hour—a great consideration, as they had about six or eight good hours' run before them.

Before eight bells at midnight this advantage began to show itself, for the man-o'-war was hull down.

But Tom was not yet satisfied; so, when the watch was called, he made all hands bowse on the sheets and halyards, and had the studding-sail sheets and tacks hauled taut.

It must have been very galling to the man-o'-war to see him walk away from him, hand over hand, as Tom did now.

"I'll just take an hour's nap," Tom said to Harry, whose watch was then on deck. "We shall make our port," he added, laughing, "before that bird wakes in the morning!"

Even then Harry Vere did not know what his young commander was making such speed to the French coast for, and as Tom had not offered to explain to him, he wisely refrained from asking him.

It was nearly four o'clock when our hero was awakened.

He heard a voice in French hailing them, and he was on deck like a shot.

"Hallo! what are you?" queried Tom, in the same language.

"A fishing lugger," was the reply. "We've lost a mast—can you give us an old spar? What are you?"

"A trader in ballast. We're running for port, having sprung a leak," answered Tom.

"Do you want a pilot?"

"No; it will be daylight soon."

"There's a heavy sea on the bar, mind!"

"I know it. Stand clear of us, if you don't want to be run down! I'm not going to carry away my spars to please you!"

Tom could hear the Frenchman rap out a good round oath at the intelligence.

"Won't you heave to?" was asked, almost in the same breath.

"Can't stop, we're sinking."

"The devil swamp you, then," was the kind rejoinder; "you won't heave to, you won't take a pilot, and you won't give us a spar."

"I'll give you a round shot if you don't sheer off, you frog-eating puppy," Tom answered.

As they swept past the lugger the buccaneers, who were looking over the side, saw how wisely Tom had acted.

The lugger, one of the largest build, was crammed with men, and under the sails that were laid ready for hoisting, they could just see the muzzles of two long swivel guns.

"A trap," said Tom, as Harry Vere approached him. "A Government vessel looking out for smugglers, I should say there was over a hundred men packed there, in her bottom, herded together like so many swine."

As the lugger dropped away astern, those on board the "Will-o'-the-Wisp" could hear the Frenchmen chattering and swearing at each other like so many monkeys. They were taken in that time, and they did not seem to relish it.

The man-of-war by this time was quite out of sight.

Captain Tom, therefore, needing no further disguise, shaped his course direct for his destination.

It was barely daylight when the "Will-o'-the-Wisp" ran into the port and dropped her anchor, and then Captain Tom had the signal chest overhauled, and the flags of several nations were placed ready for hoisting.

There were a great number of vessels anchored off and moored in shore, so that Tom's little brig excited no particular notice.

Besides, in order to avoid suspicion, our hero had run in close under the guns of a battery, quite in an opposite direction to that in which the smuggling vessels sneaked in, and embarked or landed their cargo.

The crews of the various vessels and the shore folks were just on the stir, when Tom, after partaking of a good breakfast and a stiff tumbler of brandy, disguised himself, and ordered his cutter to be lowered.

He had on a pair of soft deck boots, blue tight-fitting breeches, a short jacket, such as was worn by the superior officers in those days, and a round sealskin cap.

Under his jacket he placed a pair of neat pistols, and buckled a short sword round his waist.

Thus equipped, he stepped into his boat, having previously given his lieutenant, Harry Vere, instructions how to act during his absence, which he calculated might be some hours.

He took Ben Barnacle, Bob and Jerry, and a couple of middies with him in the boat, and then proceeded ashore.

They landed at a remote part of the harbour, and Tom having given Bob Hauler a handful of money, started on foot into the interior, as it were.

But this was only a ruse.

The French authorities were, at that period, very jealous, and watched everyone with a suspicious eye.

Almost at every step a gendarme would stop you and demand your passport, which, if you did not happen to possess, and there was the slightest look of a foreigner about you, would render you liable to a visit to a French prison, and that one visit was a sure guarantee that you would never wish for a second.

Captain Tom Drake stepped off with a light foot, keeping a wary eye that he was not watched, and gradually edging away to the left, for he wanted to gain a promontory some distance along the rockbound coast.

As he had purposely chosen a circuitous route, it was hours before he arrived at his destination, which was a wild and dreary spot, and seemed utterly deserted by every human being.

The ruins of an old monastery, and a few ragged tumble-down huts that at one time had been inhabited by some of the poorer peasantry, were the only signs of any living creature ever visiting the spot.

A few old crab trees, and a tuft of dingy grass was the only verdure about there, so that the place was as wretched and miserable as it well could be.

Tom hesitated for a time as though he were lost, but after a moment's reflection, and a careful scrutiny he appeared to be all right.

On the one side, the side he selected, there were innumerable heaps of dingy, gray, basaltic rocks, piled carelessly as it were one upon another, and after some difficulty he found an opening between these scarcely large enough for a man's body to squeeze through.

This led, however, to a natural staircase, which after innumerable twistings and windings in and out led him down to a sort of platform not quite on a level with the beach.

This was studded here and there with lumps of coarse brambly weeds, and Tom, having drawn one aside at the risk of tearing all the flesh from his hands, disclosed another small opening, which like the first, led to a narrow flight of stone stairs, and at the bottom he found himself in a cave into which the tide apparently flowed at high water.

Here, again, our hero seemed at a loss.

The small gleam of light that streamed in from seaward was sufficient to show that there was no visible opening, but Tom began groping about the wall, and tapping here and there with the butt of a pistol.

At length one portion gave forth a sound more hollow than the rest, but so slightly perceptible that none but the keenest ear could have detected it, and to this he devoted all his future energies.

It was a long and weary task, however; there seemed to be no difference in that part of the wall to any of the rest, but he ran his hand over it, and groped carefully about the surface for nearly a quarter of an hour.

At length a cry of joy escaped him; his finger had found a part that yielded.

It was a secret spring, and as he pressed it with his thumb a portion of the wall about four feet square slowly ascended, and disclosed a large opening.

Tom stepped hastily through and took a step forward, and as he did so there was an ominous click, as of a heavy windlass pawl, and then the stone descended as noiseless and more rapid than ascended into its place.

Captain Tom was in a fix then.

The place into which he had entered, now the stone was closed, was as dark as pitch.

He seemed afraid to step forward, and to go back was impossible.

At length a thought struck him.

Knocking the charge out of one of his pistols, he gave it an extra priming, and, tearing a piece off his neckerchief, he snapped the lock and lit the rag with the flash from the priming of the pistol.

By this means, simple as it was, he was enabled to get a dim view of the place he was in, and to discover a small outlet on the opposite side to that where he stood.

This narrow opening was the way to another long, narrow, winding passage that led to a cave, which was known to the smuggling fraternity as the Devil's Well.

Tom could get no further than this by his own exertions, but he took a small silver whistle from his pocket and blew three shrill notes.

Then, in answer to this, a portion of the roof moved aside, and a head and shoulders leaning over the gap was just visible in the gloom.

"Who's there?" asked the owner of the head and shoulders, peering down on our hero.

"C. T. D," was the simple and short rejoinder. "Come, bear a hand; I have waited the best part of a day in getting here."

Without any further parleying, the man up aloft lowered a small ladder, and, springing lightly up it, Captain Tom found himself in a large, dry, vaulted chamber.

Seated in one corner were a number of men—a score, perhaps—dressed in the garb of the smuggling faternity, some of them with short duck petticoats reaching to the knee, and some with heavy sea boots, and others without.

Among the group that was seated round the crackling embers of a wood fire, for it was exceedingly cold, Tom did not observe a pair of sinister eyes watching him, nor two of the party withdraw from the group and exchange a few whispered words together.

Had he done so, and have had an inkling of their thoughts, there would have been bloodshed then and there upon the spot.

As it was the buccaneer chief was too engaged with the business that brought him there, and so the pair slipped out from the cave and were no more seen there during Tom's stay.

The party to whom Tom addressed himself was a tall, handsome fellow about thirty years of age, with a pale, thoughtful face, and a small jet moustache on the upper lip. The rest of his face was smooth and appeared to be newly shaven.

The dress, though soiled, was one of the most costly kind; it was made of the finest cloth, of an azure blue, and fitted him neatly, whilst the buttons of fine gold and the trimmings showed that he was something more than the leader of a common horde of ruffians.

He led our hero to the far end of the cave, and, drawing aside a screen formed of a roll of silk, ushered him into a small chamber, comfortably furnished, and they seated themselves at a table that was well supplied with the requirements for the nourishment of the inner man.

Here the two held a long and earnest consultation, exchanging sundry papers, and each one making notes at certain points of the conversation until our hero intimated his intention to leave.

It was noticeable that neither of them during the whole interview used a word of English or French, but carried on their dialogue in Spanish, probably that no inquisitive ear might listen to them.

Tom Drake was about to take his departure by the way he came, but the tall man, whoever he was, would not allow him, telling him that if he would conform to the rules of being blindfolded he would lead him to a spot in a very few minutes not far from the port.

Captain Tom yielded to this, and, after threading a number of labyrinthian passages, his conductor desired him to halt.

Tom suddenly found the fresh air fanning his cheek, and when his conductor took leave of him with a hearty grip of the hand Tom found he was in one of the principal streets leading to the quay.

CHAPTER CCV.

BLACK BILL'S TREACHERY—THE HORRORS OF A FRENCH PRISON—CAPTAIN TOM DEFEATS THE FRENCH GENERAL.

CAPTAIN TOM hurried on with a quick step, for he wanted to get on board again, and so deeply engrossed was he with his own thoughts that he failed to notice that he was being followed.

A party of gendarmes were, however, on his track, and a sinister, black-visaged ruffian was following in their rear.

The gendarmes marched at a sharp double, but they did not overtake our hero until he nearly arrived at the port, and then two of the party pounced upon him, two of them seizing upon his arms from behind, while the other two, with fixed bayonets, barred his way in front.

By a dexterous manipulation the black-browed ruffian following behind removed our hero's sword, and, drawing his hairy cap over his sinister visage, slunk away.

Captain Tom Drake, as soon as he could recover himself, demanded by what right or by whose order he was arrested, but he could get no satisfaction. He was roughly seized, his elbows fastened behind him, and marched off at once, to the only momentary astonishment of the onlookers, who were accustomed to such sights every day.

With the same roughness and as little ceremony, our hero was marched from place to place, until he finally tired of expostulating, and at length he was taken to the fortress attached to the battery, beneath the guns of which his ship was then lying snugly at anchor.

Captain Tom had hitherto escaped the humiliation of a French prison; he had heard of such, but now he was doomed to experience one in all its horrors.

He was not placed in a dungeon by himself, for the French at that time had more prisoners than they had cells to put them in, so that he was only one out of about thirty, huddled and squeezed as it were, into a den in which there was scarcely room to breathe.

Each one was chained to the wall, from which he was never released for any purpose until death, from the cruelty, and not unfrequently the prisoner's own hand put an end to his suffering.

Tom's heart was almost broken by the sight.

How long was he to languish in that pestilental

e knew that some languished for years, and then knew what charge was to be brought against

then, hope to ever see liberty again?

There was no means even of letting his brave followers know his whereabouts, or they would not let him remain there without making a desperate effort to rescue him.

In this manner he passed the time, his young breath almost stifled within him with the foul stench that arose from the accumulations on the foid floor, until the governor, with his guard, passed round to remove the dead that had succumbed since the morning, and to see that the number was correct.

There was a bitter smile of sarcasm on the general's lips as his eye rested on our hero.

His nationality was enough, without committing any crime to warrant the general hating him.

Every taunt, every jeer possible, he heaped upon him.

Tom bit his lips till his teeth almost met as he endeavoured to conceal the passion that was working in his breast.

The general had aroused a foul fiend within him, such as Tom, perhaps, had never before known.

"I shall yet be even with you," he said bitterly; "and then, mind you, I will not leave one sou in your debt."

The general gave a hoarse brutal laugh, which was echoed by his followers, as they left the pestilental den of death.

Time wore on, and though the cold air came through the narrow grating overhead, the heat and the fumes became more almost than mortal could bear.

Tom had witnessed the horrors of a slave hold, but this sight was worse—to see white men, presumably Christians, huddled together, and crouching in the filth, worse than cattle during transit.

Tom's blood was at boiling heat.

The muscles of his body seemed to crack again.

The veins of his forehead were swollen and corded up almost to bursting.

It was horrible, ten thousand times too horrible to bear.

As Tom was thus fuming and galling, his brain bordering on the very verge of madness, he pulled and tugged involuntarily at his chain, as though he would snap every link.

Presently a cry of mingled astonishment and joy escaped him.

The chains that held him by the wrists to the wall came from their time-corroded fastenings, and he was free.

Free at least so far that he could pace up and down the small allotment of space.

Free so far that he could stretch and use his limbs, but yet he was a prisoner.

There was the iron-bound door, with the sentinels facing the stone gallery outside.

How was he to escape them?

There was the grated window.

Was it secure, or was it, too, corroded?

He would try; perhaps no one had ever had the courage or the opportunity to test it before.

Nerved by desperation, and with a young heart full of hope, he made the attempt to reach the bars, and succeeded.

The chains dangling at his wrist retarded his progress a deal, but still he worked on.

He did not give himself time even to catch his breath.

Once on the narrow ledge he worked and tugged at the bars like a tiger, when it vents its pent up fury on the bars of its cage.

At length one yielded.

His sinewy muscles caused the iron bars to bend, and the lead that held it secure into the socket, in the masonry soon gave way.

Then another started.

This achievement brought the feeble cheers from

the pale, parched lips of the miserable denizens around him, and shouts of encouragement, though it could bring them no hope, came from the poor half-starved wretches, who, in their excitement, forgot for one happy moment the horrors to which they were doomed.

Thus number two was removed, and Tom could wait to do no more.

Thrusting himself feet first through the opening thus made, he forced himself clear by sheer strength and frenzied desperation; and with a jerk that nearly dislocated his neck he dropped into the courtyard.

Gathering up his chains so as to prevent them chinking he hastened from the spot, not knowing whether he went, but in a kind of wild delirium.

Presently the sound of voices around him to a sense of his danger.

Voices as of men in angry dispute.

One voice above the rest startled our hero.

He had heard it before, but where?

It was quite familiar to him; but, as is often the case, the nearer we are to an object the farther we seem away.

Try all he knew he could not recall to mind whose voice it could be

The dispute became louder and waxed warmer; in the patois of the country he fancied he could hear himself talked about.

It was a horrible jargon, dished up with a mixture of slang, and so the meaning of many words were completely lost to him.

The sounds came from a side chamber or some sort of receptacle at the end of the long line of buildings, and there was an opening or window just within his reach, similar to the grated aperture by which he had just made his escape. To clutch the narrow sill, and to draw himself up noiselessly, until he could get a view of the interior of the room, was but the work of a moment, and then he saw all he required.

This was the guardroom, and one of the gendarmes that had seized our hero was standing with his back to the fire, playing with the blade of a sword, which Tom Drake instantly recognised as the one he brought with him on shore.

And who was the other man—for there were two—the man with his back towards our hero?

Who was he?

Tom asked himself this question a dozen times, but the man, as though in bitter mockery of him, still continued to face the other way.

Tom felt half-inclined to throw something at the fellow, or to make some noise to attract his attention and cause him to turn.

Tom was consulting with himself the advisability of doing this, when the gendarme in his ignorance of handling a piece of true steel, bent the blade and allowed it to spring from his hand.

It its fall it must have landed edge down on the man's toes, and this proximate danger, making him start back, gave our hero a view of his face.

Tom could almost have fallen.

The face he saw was that of a man he supposed was on the other side of the Channel.

Captain Tom could scarcely believe his own eyes, or credit even his own senses.

It was Black Bill.

Yes, Black Bill, whom he thought was in England, working out the vile machinations of the deadly enemies of our gallant buccaneer chief.

The pair having come to no settled arrangement about the sword, now walked out in the courtyard, and Tom, owing to the darkness, experienced no difficulty in concealing himself behind the massive brickwork abutments.

When the pair were gone Tom stole silently into the guard-room, and there, to his joy, was his sword lying on a bench.

To secure this was but the work of an instant, but Tom wanted something to free himself of the manacles.

There was a cupboard, and Tom, in a state of feverish excitement, opened the door, when, to his unspeakable joy, he beheld, not only a file, but the very pair of pistols he had hidden under his jacket on coming on shore.

This was joy—joy unspeakable—to him.

To secure them, to free himself of the chains, was not a task of much labour to him, and soon he was free—free as the air.

Tom, in the ecstacy of his glee, could scarcely restrain shouting a loud hurrah.

However, prudence preponderated, and Tom, seeing his things all secure, and, having brushed his clothes with his hand, went in search of another outlet.

At the main entrance he remembered seeing, as he came in, a strong body of a score or more soldiers, besides a number of field-pieces, loaded with canister and grape, ready to mow down any of the prisoners who might dare venture to escape.

What other place of egress there was he knew not.

The moon was now up and riding in the cloudy sky, but she could not render him much assistance if he did not know which way to turn.

Presently however, fortune seemed to decide his fate.

A gendarme with a lighted flambeau was coming along the courtyard.

Tom was compelled to keep ahead of this man to prevent his being seen, for if he stayed where he was no mortal possibility could prevent his discovery.

Therefore, with stealthy, cat-like tread, he glided on until a circumstance occurred, unprecedented in the history of naval heroes. He met with another misfortune, that rendered him good for evil.

He was hurrying along, looking at the moon, above all things, and thinking; perhaps, in the order of moody, moon-struck lovers, he was wondering to himself whether she was at that same moment watching the lovely Phœbe, and admiring her pure and silvery glory.

And yet such is life in every clime, but we must not for a moment dig ess from our story.

Tom was hurrying on, we'll say dreaming of nothing, utterly unconscious of all around him, when he suddenly came against something that sent him reeling backwards.

It was not a hard body or substance; it was something soft and yielding, yet sufficiently solid to give resistance.

Captain Tom was utterly astounded, and the drum of his ear seemed almost to be broken, when the general's harsh, discordant voice sounded a round oath.

Yes, Tom had actually run full-butt against the rotund form of General Flameeater.

The general was no less astounded than our hero, and when he recovered his eyes flashed with a deadly fire.

"Cursed fiend," he hissed, "do you haunt me, or am I doomed to a phantasy of the brain? This is madness! Surely I am going mad."

Tom Drake drew back in awe for a moment, utterly powerless to speak.

His tongue was as it were glued to the roof of his mouth, and his whole frame seemed paralyzed.

Presently two private soldiers approached that part of the battery.

The mellow moon and the silver-spangled waters no doubt had tempted them there to smoke a cigar and to promenade

BLACKBEARD WAS FOILED IN HIS FOUL INTENTION.

As soon as they saw our hero hatless, and in a dress so directly in opposition to any worn by the members of the fort, they, too, began to stare, and a dozen questions were asked all in a breath.

"The rascal, the rogue," gasped out the general, almost choking with passion; "seize him, seize him. In the name of the king, seize him!"

The soldiers had their fire-arms with them, and in an instant the two locks clicked ominously together, but before the pieces could be levelled or the general draw his sword, Tom sprang on to one of the heavy guns, and, firing the only pistol he had loaded, shot the general in the shoulder.

This drew a horrible oath from the general and a shout of execration from the soldiers, who fired

point blank at our hero, expecting to bring him down.

But the gallant captain waved his hand high in the air, and, with a loud shout of defiance, leapt from the battery wall into the water beneath.

There were a dozen shots fired in rapid succession. Then all was still, and the black, murky clouds obscuring the face of the moon, left all in sombre, darkness, and the fate of Captain Tom Drake, as it were, wrapped in a sable pall.

CHAPTER CCVI.

THE BATTLE WITH THE FRENCH FRIGATES—DUTCH PAUL TO THE RESCUE—THE PIRATE'S FATE.

"HALLO, what's that, Bob?" exclaimed Jerry

Mizzen, as, starting up from the bottom of the boat where he had been sleeping, he rubbed his eyes and looked towards the battery.

"Don't know, Jerry, something up, I suppose; some poor devil of a prisoner, perhaps, been trying to make his escape."

"Not much fear of that, Bob," said Jerry, scratching his head.

"Why Jerry?"

"The Frenchers don't let you go so easily."

"But if you did slip off, Jerry, how could they stop you?"

"Well they couldn't waste all that powder over one poor devil, would they?"

"It might have been some one of importance, you know."

Jerry rubbed his eyes and scratched his head again.

"It might be our Captain Tom, Bob," Jerry suggested.

"So it might; but I don't think he's such a fool as to get into their clutches."

"There's no telling. Here comes Barnacle. Ben's sure to know all about it."

Barnacle at that moment came down the quay.

There was a terrible frown on his brow, and a fierce glitter in his eye as he neared the boat.

"Has the captain turned up?" was the first question he asked.

Bob and Jerry were afraid almost to speak.

There was something so ominous in Ben's voice.

He repeated the question before either of them had the courage to answer.

Bob Hauler was the first to break the spell.

"We wondered," he said, "where you both had got to."

Ben shaded his eyes with his hands and peered across the dark waters of the harbour.

"What are those devils blazing away at, from the fort?" he mentally ejaculated.

"I can see some one overboard," he added, as a bright flash from one of the guns lit up the lurid waters for a moment.

"By Jove, it's Tom Drake," exclaimed Jerry Mizzen.

"Do you think so?" queried Bob.

"I'm sartin of it."

"Then, by jingo, we'll soon be alongside of him," said Hauler.

The buccaneer rolled up his sleeves, and gave one or two revengeful nips at his quid.

Ben Barnacle waited to hear no more.

He gave one spring into the boat, and, rousing up the middies in the bows with his stentorian voice, gave the order to push off.

In one moment more the boat propelled by the long ashen oars and the strong sinewy arms of her gallant crew, sped from the quay, and made for the spot where a dark object was dimly visible in the water.

The gunners were still at work at the battery.

Flash after flash told of the deadly aim they were taking.

The buccaneers' boat had a narrow escape from being hit by them.

Ben Barnacle had his right hand on the tiller, and his left hand steadying his yet all the time.

"Pull, pull, boys; pull swiftly a few strokes as hard as you can," Ben suddenly exclaimed. "There there, steady, steady, pull starboard," he cried, as the boat sped with lightning swiftness on its errand of mercy.

In the hurry of pushing off Ben had not paused to consider the possibility of the dark object he saw in the water being the head and shoulders of an escaped convict.

His heated imagination could picture no other than that of his dearly-beloved chief.

What was his joy then when he heard his name pronounced in a well known voice:—

"Ahoy, Ben, is that you?"

"By Neptune it is no one else," Barnacle replied. "Look out, Captain Tom, we'll have you aboard in a jiffy."

At that moment Ben's brawny arm was stretched forth, and his hand clutched the collar of our hero's buccaneer jacket.

A hearty ringing cheer broke the stillness of the night as our hero was hauled into the boat.

The firing from the battery had now ceased.

"Well done, boys, well done," said Captain Tom, as with a hearty grip he shook his followers in turn by the hand; "give way aboard, lads; we must get out of this before morning."

The buccaneers needed no other incentive than their young chieftain's voice to urge them to fresh action, and in less than five minutes they were once more on board the "Will-o'-the-Wisp," and Tom Drake was changing his dripping garments.

"Hallo! what's this?" said Harry Vere, as he held up the jacket to the light and disclosed a shot hole in the shoulder. "By old Beelzebub, you've had a very narrow escape, captain."

"Rather tight work, Harry," was Tom's rejoinder.

"Not winged, I hope? Ah, blood on your shirt, eh?"

There was an ugly graze on Tom's shoulder, and Doctor Shrike was called at once to give it his attention.

The Vampyre, followed by his imp Jacop, was down in the state cabin like a shot.

"The captain wound d; perhaps his arm to be amputated," were his thoughts as he descended the cabin ladder.

He loved the young chief; but, at the same time, he was rather disappointed that his wound only needed a little dressing with lint and diachylon plaister.

Tom could not repress a smile as he read in the doctor's cadaverous visage the working of his mind.

In fact he could hardly refrain from laughing right out as he saw the vengeful look he gave poor Jacop.

"Put them away, you imp of satan," he said to Jacop, as that worthy knelt down to gather up the saws and dissecting knives that, according to custom he had strewn on the cabin floor. "I'll have your head off some day, you ape-like effigy."

Jacop did not venture a reply.

The dark cloud on his master's brow boded Jacop no good.

"An ape's effigy eh, you old bag's face," he muttered savagely to himself. "I'll be even with you some day, for all this master shark's tooth."

It was well for Jacop that he did not utter this above his breath.

On the way back to his cabin, the doctor picked his teeth with one of his favourite probes.

Bob and Jerry were seated on the hatchway coamings enjoying a passing of hot coffee and rum and a biscuit when the doctor passed by.

Jerry playfully made a joke as the doctor went below, and the latter, not approving of it gave Jerry such a playful prod behind from below, that made him spring at least six feet, and drew from him a most unearthly howl of pain.

Bob could not help improving this favourable opportunity.

He burst out into a roaring fit of laughter.

His sides fairly shook with mirth as he beheld Jerry's woeful visage.

But his countenance also quickly changed for the doctor, thinking he was laughing at him, and in fact he did not care to hear anyone but himself laugh, crept softly up the ladder and gave Bob a good dose.

"Oh! oh!" yelled Bob, as he sprang to his feet also and spilt the hot coffee down his chest. "Oh! oh! murder, I'm killed; Jerry you blackguard, this is all through you."

Jerry's howling had brought the middies and the chief part of the crew on deck, and when they saw the pair capering about the deck like two dancing dervishes, it set them all in a roar.

Captain Tom and even Harry Vere came on deck to see what was the matter.

Ben Barnacle at that moment dropped from the after shrouds.

"Hist, hist, close your ports, you cheerful babbies," he said, closing his spy glass with a snap to enjoin silence. "There's a dozen boats at least fully armed coming off from shore."

"What?" inquired Captain Tom.

"A fleet of boats are pulling this way," was the answer.

"They have discovered my destination, then?" said the captain.

"Aye, and all through that cowardly villain. Black Bill. sir."

"Black Bill!"

There was a touch of incredulity in Tom's tone.

"Yes, Black Bill; he betrayed you. At least I heard as much as I sauntered about the town."

"Then it is to him I am indebted for my temporary lodging, my narrow escape, a wet skin, and this scratch upon my shoulder. Well, well, Black Bill, I will be even with you for this."

As may be expected, Will Gordon, Longton, and Harvey had come upon deck before this.

Will Gordon at the mention of the boats had sprang up the main-rigging with his glass.

By the aid of the moon he could discern that what Ben said was perfectly true.

A flotilla of boats, filled with armed men, was heading towards the "Will-o'-the-Wisp."

The Frenchmen had evidently been put upon the track of the gallant Tom, and were now intent upon boarding and seizing his vessel.

"We'll fight for it first," said the young chief, as his quick eye took in everything at a glance; "but we'll be moving nevertheless. Did you see that?"

As he spoke a blue light flashed from one of the loop-holes of the watch tower of the fortress, and was answered by a red light from one of the men-of-war that lay anchored at the entrance of the harbour.

The signal was momentary, and showed that the guard ship had been put on the alert by the bustle at the fortress.

Captain Tom Drake gave the order at once to get the "Will-o'-the-Wisp" under weigh.

And this order was not given one moment too soon.

Through the sea mist they could see that the French war ship had dropped her sails.

She was probably getting up her anchor to come to the assistance of the boats that were still sweeping onward with muffled oars.

The bold buccaneers were not long in completing their warlike arrangements.

Everything was done so swift and silently that it appeared to be the work of a magician.

The anchor was hove up, the sails set, and the gallant little ship was skimming through the water like a duck.

But their enemies were watching their movements very narrowly.

Signals flashed and rockets darted up in various directions.

Even the big watch fire on the beacon was lit up, and sent up its ruddy glare for miles out into the bay.

This gave the buccaneers a better view of their perilous position.

In the evening and during the night several men-of-war had dropped anchor, either to receive orders or in the anticipation of a storm, and now our hero found himself neatly hemmed in, and in a regular wasps' nest.

Captain Tom Drake bit his lips, and seemed rather perplexed at the powerful array set against him.

But his was not the heart to despair.

He had faced danger equal, if not superior to the present.

All the war ships expecting a big three-decker were now in motion, and now nothing was left to our gallant little band but to surrender or boldly run the gauntlet.

A shot from the bow gun of one of the frigates gave the signal for the action to commence, but Captain Tom did not deign to answer it.

Then the boats, armed with light four-pounders, began to throw in their shot.

But Tom still maintained a galling silence.

The sails of the "Will-o'-the-Wisp" were nicely trimmed for handling, and every man was at his post and ready for any emergency.

On the poop, near the wheel, our hero, trumpet in hand, stood giving his orders in a firm, but subdued tone.

Tom's coolness was most galling to the Frenchman.

In the impetuosity of their natures they would have blazed away at each other rather than to have borne the suspense.

At length the time came, however.

One of the frigates that was to windward ran down, and gave our buccaneers the whole of their broadside.

"That's hot, captain," said Ben, his cheek flushing with indignation; "shall I give them one from our long Tom?"

"Not yet, Ben, not yet."

"Not yet, why you're not going to let them smash us up, are you?"

Tom gave a quiet smile.

"Be calm Ben, mind your wheel," he said. "Be steady, listen to me."

The frigate's fire would have done great damage had her commander been less hasty, as it was she swept past, and not one shot took effect on the "Will-o'-the-Wisp."

Tom kept his ship's head steadily on for the mouth of the harbour, where two frigates were manœuvring ready to give him a warm reception, but our buccaneer did not affect to notice them; in fact, he seemed totally blind to their presence.

It was now getting light, and the watch fire was dying out, whilst the chilly mist of a November morning rendered the position of the men at the guns rather unpleasant.

Here and there the glow from the matches in the fire buckets could be seen through the open ports, but on board Tom's ship all was as quiet and immoveable as though they were going to make no resistance.

Tom now beckoned to Lieutenant Vere.

"See every gun well laid," he said, in an undertone. "Your broadside batteries lay point blank for their hulls. Your bow guns and waisters point for their rigging. When I give the word, let every man be ready to fire."

Harry Vere glided rapidly along the deck, giving each middy his orders, and then he returned to the poop.

The "Will-o'-the-Wisp" was now in fair range of the two frigates, and the boats were coming down hand over hand.

One of the frigates wore round to give Tom the full benefit of his broadside, but our hero handled his ship so deftly, that the French captain was foiled in his design.

At length Tom had brought his ship almost between the two.

"Now, stand ready," he said, in a voice just sufficiently loud to be heard fore and aft.—

Then presently his clear voice rang out—

"Fire!"

This was done so momentarily and unexpected that the Frenchmen were fairly staggered.

One frigate's deck was completely swept, and her main-top mast came tumbling down.

The other frigate, being of taller build, received the iron shower just below her ports, but her fore-rigging was terribly cut about, and daylight could be seen through many of her sails, whilst the splinters flew in a shower in all directions.

This check was a sad blow for the Frenchman, and Tom followed it up with such promptitude and decision that the French sailors even had to desert their guns, being unable to stand against Tom's withering fire.

The "Will-o'-the-Wisp" had good weigh on her by this time, and the boats appeared to be dropping astern, when the admiral's flag was run up for the other ships to rally and bear down to the support of the two frigates.

Tom had not sought such a battle as this.

He wanted all his ammunition for another purpose.

However, he was determined not to waste one pound of gunpowder if he could prevent it.

The sailors in the boats were now pulling with all their might, and Tom could see that in a short time they would lessen the distance between them considerably.

He ordered the stern chasers to be pointed, and with his own hand he fired the first shot amongst them.

Tom had taken his aim well.

The shot went through the foremost boat, sinking her, and ricochetting, killed three of the marines seated in the stern sheets of one of the hinder ones.

This act of Tom's staggered the rowers in the boats for a time, but the comrades of the marines killed set up a howl of execrating rage that it aroused the others to fresh action.

With redoubled exertion they plied their oars, and made them creak again, which set the boats spinning, as it were, through the water.

Captain Tom Drake, quick as he was at forming a project, seemed lost for a moment in the present emergency.

His vessel, in fact, was not in the fighting trim she had been formerly.

The chain armour was stowed in the lower ho'd and buried beneath the stores, and even had it been otherwise it had lain so long in disuse that it needed a deal of repairing.

The crew, too, stood in need of a good drilling.

The only things he could rely on in battling against such great odds were the true British pluck of his gallant tars, the capital condition of his guns and other armaments, and the taut firmness of everything aloft.

As yet no shot had done him serious harm.

There was a long rent in one of the topsails, but the sailmakers had managed to patch it up for the present.

In the meantime the French captains were obeying as far as possible the order of the admiral.

Crowding every available sail they steered for the "Will-o'-the-Wisp," their heads so pointing that they must all meet and hem in the little brig in their very centre.

Tom's ship was going at a very fair speed, for the wind had freshened considerably since they got under weigh, and though the royals were set it was evident they would soon have to be taken in.

The masts and yards bowed a good deal and the cordage cracked and creaked as the little ship keeled over, when Tom hauled her to about a point so as to make a clear run for it.

But an unforeseen accident occurred.

A piece of old wreck laid on a sand bank near the harbour mouth, and the tide being high, hid it from view, so that Tom was not aware of this new danger until he heard the keel grating against it.

This shock gave the brig a sudden check, and while Tom and his officers were paying attention to this, a strange sail popped round the headland.

The bucaneers were apprised of this by the voice of a middy aloft.

All eyes were at once turned on the stranger.

There was something very peculiar about that vessel.

Her rig, build, and trim were rather fascinating to one in the nautical profession.

Tom was quite charmed with her, and for a moment forgot his own peril. She seemed, in fact, a second "Will-o'-the-Wisp."

She carried a curious little flag at her mast head.

There was a strange device on it too, but the wind blew it in such a way that it could not be made out from the brig.

Captain Tom and Lieutenant Vere both tried to make it out with their spy-glasses.

All this had transpired in a very few moments, but nevertheless it had given the Frenchman a no slight advantage.

A smart thirty-six led the van, and he measured distance with a round shot.

'Well aimed, but wasted," remarked Ben, drily, as it sped under the mainsail and dropped into the sea.

"They have gained on us," replied Tom, maintaining his usual calmness; "give them a word from our stern bully, Mr. Barnacle."

The junior lieutenant was already for action; his brawny arms were bared to the shoulder, his shirt was thrown open exposing his broad chest, and his duck trousers rolled up to the knee, gave his muscles full play.

Motioning to the two middies, who stood near the after capstan, he sprang on the taffrail and took a good survey of the pursuing vessels.

The smoke from the bow chaser of the smart thirty-six was clearing away, so that he could see the sailor who had just fired, and, leaping down to deck again, Ben muttered something between his teeth, and took his station at the rear of his favourite gun.

There was no occasion for him to speak.

Serving the vent with his left thumb, he seized a match from the fire bucket with his right hand, and blew away the smouldering ash.

At the word "ready" his quick eye glanced along the deadly tube, then, seeing all clear, he applied the match to the touch hole, and the terrible missile sped on its way.

The effect of that shot was soon known by the horrible shrieks that rent the air.

About twenty Frenchmen were collected on the forecastle, and of these about sixteen, including the sailor before named, were scattered about in mangled heaps.

The bucaneers set up a deafening cheer, to which the French seamen responded with terrible oaths and curses.

All discipline seemed to be lost for the time on board the pursuers.

The men flew in confusion to their guns, smashing each other's toes with the rammers and handspikes, while the various captains shouted their orders without studying even the ordinary rules.

Broadsides were fired at the "Will-o'-the-Wisp" in rapid succession, but without attention being paid to the requisite seamanship; so that powder was wasted and shots thrown away to the unmistakable disgust of the buccaneers.

In the midst of this Ben gave them several unerring shots, and added to the general dismay and confusion.

This, no doubt, as Captain Tom afterwards remarked, saved the gallant little brig.

Had the whole force surrounded her as they at first intended, it must have gone very hard with the buccaneers.

The partly dismantled frigate turned back at this, and went straight away to her anchorage to repair damages.

It was a critical time for the French fleet to have a vessel rendered unseaworthy.

They did not know one moment from another when the English squadron might make its appearance on the coast.

More than one Government was at that time dreading a war with England, and preparing against an invasion.

The French admiral, surrounded by his officers, witnessed from the deck of the guardship the confusion of the frigates.

"Le diable!" he muttered, meaning the devil in English. "The saucy sprat is giving us a licking."

He ordered his own private signal to be made, censuring the captains and desiring them to show more energy and courage.

Even at that distance Tom could faintly hear the dissatisfied shouts of the people on shore, who lined every point to watch the progress of the fight.

Upon the ramparts there was a great gathering of the military, and the very flag hoisted at gun fire on the fortress seemed to hang in shame its diminished head.

Tom in his heart pitied the Frenchmen, though he felt that in a fair engagement he would like to meet them on the open sea at the rate of twenty of their men to his one.

As matters had so far gone, Tom and his tight little crew would most certainly have come off the victors.

But the "Will-o'-the-Wisp" was not yet out of danger.

There was the strange craft, under a heavy press of sail, bearing down like a racehorse, evidently intent upon cutting off our hero's retreat.

Added to this, the French captain's crew, burning with shame and smarting under the indignity, were rallying and taking up the chase in right earnest.

As the stranger approached Tom prepared to give her a broadside, when a voice through a speaking trumpet hailed him.

"Ahoy, there, Tom Drake, put your ship about!"

"Not for you," shouted Tom Drake, placing his hands both sides his mouth.

"Then go to the deuce and be grinned at," was the rejoinder.

"By whose order?"

"Mine, have you forgotten me?"

Tom snatched up his glass hastily, and scanned the vessel's deck.

"What! are you Dutch Paul?" he shouted, at the top of his voice.

"It is me. Where the deuce have you been stowed away? I have hunted all over the seas for you."

Tom gave the order to tack about.

When the vessels were both abreast, he held a short parley with the commander of the "Yellow Vulture."

The French captains were surprised at this extraordinary manœuvre. They thought that the "Will-o'-the-Wisp" had surrendered, and that they had thus been robbed of the capture of Captain Tom Drake.

They were quickly undeceived when the flags of both vessels were hoisted simultaneously.

The younger captains shuddered when they saw the dread emblems floating side by side in the morning air.

Accounts of the terrible liquid fire of Dutch Paul had already reached their ears.

They would have run in under the guns of the battery had it not been for a dread of the consequences.

Dutch Paul smiled as he saw the leewardmost ship edge away, so that they would have to tack about and stand in.

"I'll just singe that fellow's wings," he said to Tom Drake. "You keep on, and let that frigate on the starboard feel your metal."

This was agreed on without any demur.

The French captains were not at all pleased with this arrangement, but they could not very well help themselves.

They were bound to put up with the severe chastisement in store for them.

With grape and shell and double-shotted guns Tom gave the foremost frigate a severe hauling.

The boy buccaneers seemed to breathe new life as they found themselves in company with their old ally.

Tom seemed doubly pleased.

As for Ben Barnacle, he danced about and rubbed his hands with joy.

"Come on, Bob and Jerry," he shouted to those two worthies, who leaped out of the galley with a couple of red-hot shots slung in an iron bucket.

All was bustle and activity now aboard of Tom's ship.

There was equal confusion and heaps of swearing aboard the men-of-war.

They had calculated upon such a sudden change in affairs.

Dutch Paul had by this time overhauled his man, and given him a terrible warning.

He did not trouble about the liquid fire at present; he poured in a shower of red-hot grape that seemed to be produced from some infernal agency.

This soon cleared the crowded deck of the frigate, and the ship, thus left to her own management, quickly drifted ashore.

The frigate Tom engaged was rendered by this time unmanageable.

The spars and sails were in many parts set on fire.

As to her crew, they were fearfully burnt and cut up.

Tom's blood was warming to the fray now.

He was wreaking terrible vengeance for the insults he had been subjected to in the prison.

Having rendered the frigate incapable of doing him further harm, except by her blowing up, he chased the others who had turned back and run for shelter under the guns of the fort, and then left them.

Tom then signalled to Dutch Paul to follow him out to sea, and when they were well clear of the land, Dutch Paul lowered his boat, and went on board the "Will-o'-the-Wisp."

Both commanders warmly pressed each other's hand as they met on the quarter deck.

"I owe you a thousand thanks," said Tom, gratefully, "for this timely aid."

"Don't name it, Captain Tom," said Paul, handing our hero a cigar.

"You know I don't smoke," laughed our hero, as he took the choice weed, which was about the size of a marlinspike.

"But on this occasion you must—just to please me."

"To please you I will, then. Just to show no ill-feeling;" and with this the pair descended to the state-cabin.

"Come, light up," said Paul; "let us enjoy a few moments together. I must leave you soon. How have you been going along? How did you get in amongst those French devils? And, above all, what do you mean doing with yourself now?"

Dutch Paul asked all these questions in a breath.

Tom gave him a brief account of his career, and Dutch Paul, after he had finished his third bottle of wine, told his own story.

"And now," said he, "I want you to do me a favour. In the first place, there is a terrible scourge upon the seas. The Black Pirate, you have heard of him, of course?"

"We once met, and I vowed we should only meet once again," answered Tom.

"Good! Then let me inform you that he is on the coast. A few days' run, with a fair wind, will bring you in his track. Show him no mercy, and bring his flag to me, and I will then be your friend. Aye, your slave, Captain Tom, even to the death."

"That will be a dearly bought favour, Paul, will it not?" asked Tom.

"Not at all. I hate him; he hates me; and I would kill him for the injury he has wrought me; but you shall know all in time. Against all I do he seems to bear a charmed life; but he must die; his terrible career must be shortened, and you, Captain Tom, can do it."

"And I will, fear not for that."

"I doubt not your word; I feel certain you will earn the reward I offer."

"Or die in the attempt," added Tom.

Dutch Paul took our hero's hand and pressed it fervently.

"Now I have had your promise fear not to demand of me any favour," he said.

"And," he added, "take this packet, do not break the seal till you wish to see me, and then you will know where I am to be found."

Dutch Paul returned to his ship soon after this; the sky bore tokens of a storm.

Then, waving each other adieu, and dipping their flags three times to each other in token of respect and good faith, they parted.

Captain Tom Drake went on his way, fully intent on scouring the seas and keeping his promise with Dutch Paul.

It was a week or more, however, before Tom could gain any intelligence of his whereabouts.

He had run into a little bay for fuel and water when he saw a small wreath of smoke curling up from a dense clump of trees, and thither he bent his way, whilst Bob and Jerry, with four of the buccaneer crew, went in search of their wants.

Ben Barnacle accompanied our hero.

They looked at their pistols, and loosened their cutlasses before entering into the dense undergrowth, and after a search of an hour or more their toil was rewarded.

It was a sort of hut, formed of leaves and twigs, with one side open, so that they could see within.

And there they discovered a woman bending over the form of a sick man, who was evidently wounded.

Tom approached cautiously, but the cracking of the dry twigs betrayed his presence.

The female rose and turned, and, seeing a human face, she gave a startled scream.

"What again! No, spare him, spare him; kill me, or both of us if you will," she uttered, in piercing accents.

"Fear not, fair one," said Tom, giving her an assuring smile. "I have come to succour, not to slay. There, be calm, and tell me how you came here."

"Are you not a pirate, then?" she asked, glancing timidly at his weapons.

"I am not, but I am in search of one, the Black Pirate," answered Tom, scarce knowing what he said.

The girl shuddered.

Tom could not help admiring her beauty.

She stood like a statue before him, trembling like a young fawn.

Tom had seen the face before, but could not tell where.

"What makes you tremble so?" he asked, sinking his voice to a whisper at a sign from her; "and how came you here?"

"This is my father, sir," she said. "Two days ago the vessel in which we were passengers was boarded by the dreadful pirate you name, and most of the crew were murdered. My father was wounded, and I and he, only yesterday, were landed on this island to starve and die in any form, which was considered an act of mercy."

"Very merciful, indeed," said Tom, biting his lips. "Only yesterday, you say?" he added, thoughtfully.

"Yes; and I strayed hither with my father, built this hut, and, finding plenty of water and a pistol and some ammunition, which the pirate accidentally or unintentionally left behind, I have been able to minister food to my wounded patient."

Tom's cheek glowed with admiration at the courage of the brave girl, who could not have seen more than twenty summers.

"But you will leave this place now, and come with me?" he said.

"No, sir, I dare not. I will not leave my father. He sleeps now, and he may never more awaken in this world: but then I can bury him, and mourn over the grave of one I hold so dear."

Tom was astounded at the girl's bravery and devotion.

He knew human nature, however, too well to trust to all he heard.

"You had much better accompany me," he said. "My men are within hail, my ship lays in the bay. I have every comfort on board you can desire, and——"

The weeping maid checked him.

"I have said," she answered, "unless you force me. Go, sir, and leave us. I have trusted too much to the frailty of man already. My mind is made up, my purpose fixed, and nothing on earth can shake it."

Tom saw by her resolute eye that persuasion was useless, so, bidding her farewell, he returned to Ben, who was about to seek for him, thinking he had fallen into some snare.

The boat was already half loaded, and as Tom was anxious to overtake the pirate he went aboard and weighed anchor at once.

Every bay and inlet he searched, but could find no further trace of the fiend he searched for until the third day, when a sail was reported on the lee.

Captain Tom took his glass and ascended to the main top, and after a careful scrutiny, he became certain from the suspicious movements of the strange vessel that it was the one he sought.

Disguising his ship as a merchantman, he made all sail towards her, and hailed her when within easy speaking distance.

There was a cold, sharp air for the climate, so that both captains could wear a thick watch coat without giving rise to any suspicion.

As satisfactory answers were given on both sides too, the pirate, for Tom's quick perception told him

It was he, considered that his secret was safe, and now that he had nothing to do but to board and seize his prize.

Tom was determined to be first, as the pirate was about to run up his terrible flag, Tom threw off his watch coat and at the same moment the buccaneers that lay in readiness sprang up from between the guns and fired a deafening broadside into the pirate ship.

Blackbeard was never more astounded than at this moment.

The very deceit he had so often practised had now been practised on himself.

He cursed and foamed for a short space and then he prepared for the worst.

Strange to say, he had had a terrible foreboding of late that his time had nearly come, and this had made him more laxative than usual.

Still he did not totally despair of meeting with success; he was a daring man and had passed through many ordeals.

To slay and to plunder was his motto, and to fight to the death was his terrible resolve.

He was only staggered by the first shots as they hurtled about his head, and sent the spars tumbling about his ears, for Tom did not want to damage the hull.

With a hoarse, almost choking, voice he gave the orders to his hideous followers; but Tom had completely forestalled him. He dashed the "Will-o'-the-Wisp" alongside, and before the smoke from the cannon rolled away, Captain Tom Drake, followed by a faithful few, leapt on board the pirate ship.

Then a terrible conflict ensued.

The pirates surrounding their chief boldly held the poop, but the buccaneers, well led as they were, drove them back foot by foot.

Tom Drake soon sought out his man.

With his sword-blade crimsoned to the hilt, he fought his way to where the Black Pirate stood.

Then their eyes met, and a recognition that brought to memory some deadly feud lit up the orbs of both with deadly anger.

More than once our hero nearly paid the penalty for his rashness, and had it not been for Ben's strong arm, the deadly knife or the reeking cutlass, wielded by a treacherous hand, would have let out his young life's blood.

While the fierce havoc was waging on the quarter-deck, a war as fierce was being carried on on the forecastle and in the waist.

But despite their desperate efforts, the pirates gave way before the fine onslaught of the buccaneers, and foot up foot they gained possession of the deck.

Meanwhile the two chieftains fought as only two men could fight under such circumstances; throwing their pistols aside, they strode over the bleeding bodies of the slain, and a desperate struggle for the possession of the pirate's flag ensued.

The black emblem, embrued with the blood of the slain, was half resting on the deck, and as the jewelled hand of the fiend relaxed its hold of the hilt of the broken weapon, Captain Tom thrust his sword through the body of the pirate chief.

CHAPTER CCVI.

BLACK BILL'S TREACHERY IS DISCOVERED—CONDEMNED TO DEATH—A TRAITOR'S DOOM.

THE escape of a prisoner from that cell in which our gallant buccaneer had been lodged and chained was so rare an occurrence that it caused quite a commotion.

The rattle of musketry, the beating of drums, and the sharp ping of the small cannon that were fired at the fugitive, brought hundreds of people flocking to the port, in the midst of which confusion the buccaneers' boat slipped away, and was not observed.

In the meantime the treachery of Black Bill reached the ears of those in the mystic cave of which we gave an account in a previous chapter.

Had the treacherous villain kept his own counsel it would not have been so easy to bring the guilt home to him, and he might by this delay have watched an opportunity to slip away in some smuggling craft, and have got back to England.

As it was, he was quickly tracked and brought to summary justice, and the very next day he was brought to trial.

François Goupille was the chief of this daring band of smugglers who inhabited this nefarious haunt, and Black Bill became acquainted with them through sharing at times their dangerous enterprises.

They were most of them Englishmen, outlawed for various crimes, and their leader, too, had been banished through some political squabble between himself and the English Government.

There was also among them a fair-haired, blue-eyed girl of eighteen, whose father had belonged to the band, but was mortally wounded in a brush with a government cruiser.

She lived among them, tended their wounds, and did them good service in time of need.

She was, in fact, a general favourite with the smugglers.

Black Bill had rendered her a service once; he had saved her life when she was almost drowned by the capsizing of a boat.

She was the only one among them that cared a straw, or felt any compunction at Black Bill being placed on his trial.

She pleaded very earnestly for him, and used all her interest with Francois when it was announced that Black Bill had been found guilty, and that he was to pay the penalty of his crime by the forfeit of his life.

A smuggler that Bill had taken into his confidence was the chief witness against him, and his evidence was so clear and palpable that it was useless for Black Bill to deny it.

His crime was looked upon as an offence the most heinous by the smuggling community, and all but the fair girl, Gemfrede, were loud in clamouring for his death.

There was only one thing to settle now, and that was the mode of putting him to death, and who should be the executioner, for not one of the smugglers, although revolting at his crime, liked the idea of taking his life in cold blood.

Had it been in the excitement of the fight there was not one would have hesitated a moment to put a bullet or a cutlass through the body of an enemy. But this job looked too much like murder, and they all shrank from it.

But François the Smuggler Chief was a man of the most indomitable will.

He liked justice, and was merciful when it was merited, but as he had passed the sentence he was determined it should be carried out.

His plan, therefore, was that Black Bill should run the gauntlet of the whole of the smuggler crew.

Black Bill forthwith, in accordance with this plan, was ushered through a subterranean passage that led into the very heart of a wood, and it was from this point he was to start on his race for life or death.

The smugglers had not yet heard of this plan.

They had been preparing for an expedition, and they were only awaiting for the settlement of a few preliminaries before they started.

It was during one of their carousals that they discussed the matter pretty freely, and expressed their opinions more openly than they would have dared at any other time.

They one and all declared that one man's life was too petty a thing to bar their sailing for a while yet.

Francois overheard their grumblings.

"Empty cups, and fill no more," cried he, in a thundering voice, "Dash them down, I say."

The smugglers grumblingly drained their drinking vessels.

"Now, get sober as much as you can. Baptist, cut loose this man, and watch him well."

They severed the cords, and let Black Bill recover from the cramps and stoppage of the circulation.

Genifrede dared not rejoice at this seeming lenience, for the savage smile of Francois portended nothing very merciful.

"Hark ye, prisoner, traitor and spy, you merit browning over a slow fire," began Francois, "but my friend here has interceded, and I'm going to behave like a lamb to you."

The smugglers showed their teeth in broad grins at the notion.

"You're a strong man, but a bit benumbed by being tied up. Now my pets here aint on an even keel, seeing how they've been at liquor. That makes the game even."

Francois pointed to the forest, whose edge was a score of yards away.

"You shall have so much start. Make for the salt water. My men shall use nothing but steel upon you. If they overtake you before you dip foot in the brine, why—why—there's an end of you and good riddance!"

"But if you so much as damp a finger tip in a shallow on the beach, the raven of my flock that fleshes his beak on you shall taste the red pepper lanted with a score of gashes in his hide!"

"You all hear that?"

"Ay, that we do!"

The smugglers all nodded assent, and showed their impatience to begin the hunt for the human prey.

They put aside their firearms.

They lightened their dress to run better, and drew their belts tighter.

Bill made his preparations too.

"It will only be anguish to her, if I die here under her eyes,' thought he. 'It will be best for me to fall in the dark thicket, in the death-grapple of some of these scoundrels!"

He could not believe he, so weak, could reach the haven through the mass of briars.

As no opposition was made to his doing what he could to aid himself in the flight for his life he had hastily bound up his feet in rude sandals of strips of canvas that was tough enough to keep out the thorns.

He had little to carry, as all his apparel was his shirt and trowsers.

There was no use in delay.

So he drew himself up boldly, and confronted the smuggler chief.

"I am ready," said he.

"Stop!" said Francis.

The Frenchman took up a horn from the ground, and only filled it with spirits.

"No, no!" shouted the smugglers. "As he is, let him run!"

"Peace, you young hounds," cried Goupille haughtily, 'If you clamor again I'll lend him sword and dagger—by this hand, I will!"

He turned to the prisoner.

"Take this stuff," said he, "when you get to the woods, toss it off and fly!"

Bill clutched the vessel.

"Good-bye,' said he to Genifrede, who was held back by the smuggler chief.

One look he gave upwards, to see by what star he should be guided, and he began the task.

On reaching the forest trees he lifted up the horn to his lips.

"Long life to true hearts, and eternal death to the black-souled servants of the fiend!"

So he shouted, and poured the liquid fire into him.

Hurling the horn far from him towards the bloodhounds, he whirled round on his heels and plunged into the gloomy tangle.

With a loud whoop at his defiance, the hunters darted over the sand to pursue him.

The drink did wonders.

In an instant it had coursed to Black Bill's heart, and then was dispersed over all his exhausted system.

Every nerve burning, every vein leaping, he seemed to be lifted up on wings.

He was well nigh driven mad, that was the truth.

Straight on he went, only swerving for trees and rocks.

He never felt it at all as he crashed through the undergrowth where the twigs and thorns lashed and pierced him.

The smugglers had spread out, so as to be sure not to let him escape, one side of them.

Black Bill could hear their calls to one another, and the screams of the birds fluttering up into the nightwind at such a noise as they made.

He had tried to keep straight on his way, but a small brook that ran down to the seaside compelled him to take a turn.

That brought him back for some yards, and he ran nearly into the arms of a foe.

Both came together so roughly that they were naturally stunned and surprised.

Black Bill recovered himself first.

Springing forward from the tree against which he had been dashed, he fell upon the still staggering ruffian.

Bringing him to the ground, the two, interlocked in deadliest grapple, rolled over and over.

Bill saw, even in the shadow, that the fellow was opening his saucer mouth to call for help, and he summarily prevented that.

He had got hold of the smuggler's pistol, and he jammed its butt right into the man's jaws.

The next instant Bill had the mastery.

In only a minute more, he left the man senseless, and was flying away.

He had the smuggler's cutlass in his hand.

It afforded him means to sell his life for a higher price.

Meanwhile, it came in handy for cutting away among the brush.

The pursuers were collecting together, and, from stray words that came from them to the fugitive's ear, he believed they were in fear that they had overshot him.

As they "tried back," Bill was worming on through a very thick clump of prickly thorns.

He did not dare endeavour to go around it, as on both sides of him he heard the trampling of feet and the clatter of weapons.

At last, bleeding by a hundred gashes, he scrambled out of the thorns.

The aroma of the seaweed told him that he was near his goal.

He paused to take breath and listen.

He heard, not twenty yards from him, some three or four men who were stealing ahead of the line he was on.

There was no resource except to bear away a little to the right hand and plunge into the briars.

Unluckily, he had hardly thrust himself into the brambles a few steps than one of the twigs hooked on the hammer of the pistol that he had taken from the smuggler, pulled it back, and let it fall.

The explosion scorched his side a little, but the bullet went down into the dead leaves on the ground.

"Here he is! there goes the swab!" shouted a dozen voices.

All were turned to that quarter instantly.

Bill uttered a yell of defiance, tossed the smoking pistol from him, and, steel in hand, struck away at the bushes.

The men after him, clothed thickly, or wearing leather breeches, could stamp through the prickles better than he.

They gained on him.

Five or six shots resounded, and the flash lit up the forest.

"Stop firing!" roared Francois all at once. "He'll have a chance the more under cover of the smoke."

That was true enough.

Still Bill crashed on.

Better a lacerated skin than the torments the sea-demons might devise.

The pursuers and the chased man were so close now that he heard their every motion.

The noise they made drowned his steps.

Finding some easy way, three of the pirates had darted on, and were now in advance of Black Bill.

The sea-shore was within a biscuit toss.

But this trio were between the strand and the young lieutenant.

"It's a scrimmage alone can clear the way," muttered the traitor, grasping the cutlass convulsively; "somebody's got to be beaten, and it shan't be me."

So saying, he jumped out of cover.

He found himself on the grass of a small glade.

The three men were so surprised by his bold and unexpected appearance that only one of them had his hanger drawn.

Bill cut down one of the others at the very instant that he laid a hand on the weapon in his belt.

The birds overhead shrieked dismally as the man howled forth his last breath in agony.

Black Bill did not look to see the effects of that stroke.

Whirling his sword upward again, he let it fall a second time, and it only ceased to cut after having cleft another of the smugglers clean through the collar-bone.

He missed his footing, and fell to the sod, his neck and breast being instantly deluged with blood.

His sudden fall nearly wrenched the entangled blade out of the traitor's hand.

The latter held firm nevertheless, but the metal being poor stuff, the cutlass broke a few inches from the loosened hilt.

The last of the three, who had his sword out, had been too much astonished and horrified to intervene yet.

It was not until Bill lifted the fragment of blood-dripping iron upon him that he remembered himself.

The traitor, full of desperation at being so near the promised safety and yet in danger of failing to attain it, did not see with his passion filled eyes that so little of a weapon had been left to him.

So, when he delivered a cut, he struck much too short.

That helped him.

For the force of his attack threw him forward under the arm of the pirate.

Up came the whole mass of pursuers.

It was "do or die" now.

Their hands were already extended, armed with firearms or pointed steel.

"Take him alive—take him alive! or I'll be the

death of some of you!' cried Francois, tramping over some cactus plants.

But did not wait for their attack.

Taking advantage of the smugglers changing their pikes and hangers from right to left hand to grasp him, he wrenched himself from the embrace of the one who had clutched him.

Fierce as a hungry tiger, he struck out right and left, and cleared a space around him.

They formed a ring enclosing him.

He flung himself at the weakest point, but two men were there.

They might as well have tried to stop a shark in its career as to check Black Bill, who heard the wash of the sea just before him.

Bruised and maimed he left them both, as he flew between them.

"Hurrah!" shouted he.

Recovering from the defeat, all followed.

But a smuggler, knee deep in the water, stood breathless but undaunted, bleeding but defiant, on the promised place of salvation.

He in the water stood calmly awaiting Black Bill's approach.

The hunted wretch, seeing that his hopes were cut off in that quarter, turned like a stag at bay, and darted off like a roe towards a narrow neck of the beach.

Part of it was sand and part of it was shingle, and at high tide it was always covered.

Inspired with a sudden desire for the existence that he had been ready to lay down, the lieutenant bounded away, splashed through the few inches of water, and ran out along the edge of the sand.

The smugglers turned, and proceeded on his track.

They had to go in single file.

That was one thing in favour of the fugitive.

If he could reach the end of the point, the high rocks there would shield him from pistol shots.

He strained every nerve to do so, giving all his energies to that, and not glancing behind.

He had all but attained the rocks when he heard a strange series of cries behind him.

So singular were they that he could not help looking back.

To his amazement, the most of his hunters, still moving, seemed out in halves!

Only their bodies were above the level of the moist path.

Then only their waists, and, still sinking, they bid fair to go down to their armpits.

The ground had been shaky to Bill's light tread; the heavy boots of the smugglers had churned the sand into motion, and mixed up the water with it.

There was a circling movement in the quicksand, and the whirl so increased in force that the engulphed men were spun round faster and faster, proclaiming that they had fallen into the power of a land-eddy.

The ones thus entrapped dropped their weapons and tried to scramble out.

But there was no foothold in the yielding stuff, and nothing to grasp to pull themselves out with.

The more they sought to tread water or wade out of the snare the deeper and faster they settled in the slough.

It was folly to seize hold of a neighbour, for if they lifted themselves an inch by that means, it was at the cost of burying themselves deeper in the next moment.

This grappling one another caused angry words, and blows very quickly after them.

So the smugglers were to be seen perishing in the quicksand, their hands on one another's throats.

Three out of ten escaped.

Two were near enough in shore to get upon less shifting ground, and then on dry sand.

The other had been the foremost, and had been so close upon Black Bell's heels as to have passed over the danger almost as happy as he.

Only hindered by the edge of the eddy catching him, this fellow would have been able to have arrested Bill, but that the scene behind him had enchained his steps.

There was indeed an awful fascination in seeing those companions in crime dragged under, as though by some unseen but irresistible hand.

They had disappeared to their necks, but their arms waved desperately for a time.

But the sunset force never ceased its work.

They had to descend, slowly but surely.

At length only the heads, with swollen eyeballs and mouths blue with discolouration, and open from the effects of strangulation, remained above the mire of sand and brine, broken with bubbles that contained the last grasps of the wretched smugglers.

A pause, but not a silence, for sobs and smothered groans formed a last appeal to the inevitable.

The next instant all that was human was vanished.

Not a lock of hair floated on the whirl, while the sweeping motion ceased, and the disturbed grain-floated back to form again that straight and narrow way which had been a path of death to so many.

Francois had viewed the absorption of his crew with affright.

When his amazed eyes could see no more of the strugglers, he uttered a howl of rage.

"Seize that scoundrel, Baptist!" screamed he to the smuggler, who had reached the rocks, and stood beside Black Bill. "Cut him to pieces for being the bait to the desert's trap!"

That shout startled the man to whom it was addressed.

No matter what his feelings were towards the hounded wretch, he must obey.

Black Bill was too much spent now to offer much resistance, and that would have been less than nothing towards Baptist, who was comparatively fresh, and had his cutlass poised over him.

Shapeless he gathered himself together to finish this too long and too unequal a contest.

At that juncture, during the silence that fell around, a shot resounded.

And all beheld the would-be executioner forget his intended stroke as the bullet overtook him.

It needed but a slight push from Bill for him to hurl the wounded Baptist back into the quicksand.

The eddy was no more loth to swallow the corpse than it had been to gulp down the animated.

"Who fired that shot?" cried Francois Goupille, looking around.

"I!"

So replied a voice, soft and feeble, but steady of tone.

And Genifrede stepped out of the brake, the smoking pistol in her slight hand.

She was breathless with running through the mazes of the wood, and pale with the exertion, but not a jot abashed by the fierceness of the pirate chieftain's gaze.

"I did it!" repeated she, firmly. "And that is but little to what I would do for the man that does me service."

Fierce and bitter were the execrations of the smugglers that followed Genifrede's words; by the very act that she had perpetrated to save the traitor's life she had not only sealed his fate but her own too.

"Death, death!" was the shout of the few surviving smugglers, and had it not been for the voice of the smuggler chief, Black Bill and Genifrede would shortly have wound up their account in this world.

Black Bill, overpowered by his exertions, was soon seized upon and dragged half bleeding to one of the smuggler's haunts, of which there were many about the rocks, while the captain strode up to Genifrede.

"Well, minx," he said after a pause; "so you love this black visaged ruffian, do you? It is as well to know such secrets as it often saves a deal of unpleasantness. Now I have preserved your life I desire you to leave our company at once. If you are seen here again, depend upon it all I can say or do will not save you from your justly merited punishment."

"All you can say or do!" sneered the indignant girl; "How many lives do you owe me? Could I not have betrayed you hundreds of times if I so wished? Base fool, idiot, I scorn your threat. You cast me off now just because I repay a bounden duty. You seek the life of Black Bill for betraying Tom Drake; and what is this Tom Drake to us that he should be so carefully preserved and looked after?"

"Hark you, girl," replied the smuggler, "I seek no quarrel with you. I merely bid you to leave us and return no more. Black Bill, when the rest of our band returns, will be tried again according to our laws, and he will be acquitted or condemned to death again. For my own part I would lynch the able villain at once."

"I believe you. You are a fiend in human form," hissed the fair taunter.

"So fiendish that he has pitied you," hissed the other in return.

"Then show not your pity to another. Death and pity such as yours are both on an equal par."

The smuggler bit his lips.

The girl had an answer for his every word.

He had once loved her, and now even would have loved her had she not aroused his jealousy.

As he was not in a humour to parley with her further, he strode away from her in the direction of the cave.

*　　*　　*　　*　　*　　*

It was night, a storm was raging without, heavy seas thundered upon the beach, and the wild sea-gull gave its own peculiar screech as it disported itself about the head of the lofty cliffs.

But in the deep recesses of the Smuggler's Stronghold no sound could be heard, not even the rumble of the sea.

All was silent as the grave.

A court martial was being held.

One solitary lamp hung in the centre of the cave, and lit up the solemn scene.

Its rays fell upon the grim visages of the assembly that had met to try Black Bill, the traitor, a second time for his life.

The wretched culprit stood in the centre of the group, grim and ghastly looking, his pale face contrasting strangely with those who were about to pronounce his sentence.

It was a horrible one.

The decision arrived at was that the traitor should be buried alive in the sands, his head just appearing above the surface, for the wild vultures to pick at, and there to remain until the salt waves flowed and ended his wretched existence.

Black Bill spoke not; but the muscles of his face quivered and his flesh seemed to creep, as the horrible doom was pronounced in solemn and stentorian tones.

The storm had ceased when the culprit was led to his doom. The tide was just ebbing, and the fierce rays of the sun were just beginning to blaze out.

It was not till the hole had been dug, and the miserable wretch thrust into it, feet downwards, that he opened his mouth to his executioners.

But they were deaf to his appeal for mercy.

They gloated over his misery as the sand was filled in and trodden down hard by the heavy sea boots of the smuggler executioner.

He might as well have appealed to the rocks for mercy.

Even to the ravenous birds that were already swooping about his head in readiness to begin their horrible meal.

But Black Bill's villainous heart failed him most when he found himself alone.

When the salt-laden air fanned his fevered brow, and left its deposit on his parched lips.

"Help, help! Water!" he shrieked.

The screech of the wild sea bird alone answered to his call.

The only aid he received was from them as they swooped down and dug their sharp beaks into the flesh of his quivering brow, and allowed the warm blood to trickle down his face and moisten his parched tongue.

And there he was for many hours listening to the sullen roar of the crested swell.

He was to endure this agony for a whole day, until the sun went down, and the rising tide washed out the life of the betrayer of Captain Tom Drake.

CHAPTER CCVIII.

A FRIEND IN NEED—THE PIRATE AND THE MERCHANTMAN.

For many long hours Black Bill endured his excruciating torture, the rising waves howling their dirge in agonised ears, and threatening shortly to put an end to his misery.

But Ralph was not doomed to die yet.

He still had a friend in Genifrede, and her friendship, fanned into a flame by revenge, had ripened into a feeling almost akin to love.

There was a sort of destiny that seemed to link her fate with his.

To have been revenged on Francois the proud girl would have braved almost any hardship or danger.

And yet she had no real feeling in her heart for Black Bill; she, in fact, loathed the very name of a traitor or a spy.

Yet, with a woman's nature, and, smarting under the slights and insults of the smuggler chief, she felt bound to suffer anything for the very man her soul in reality detested.

Hers were the ears that alone heard the cries of the doomed wretch.

Her heart alone softened to his supplication.

Just when all hope was gone, and the guilty wretch fancied he had seen the sun set for the last time, the bold girl crept from a secret crevice in the rocks and with her own hands released him from his horrible position.

Furthermore, she procured him a disguise, so that he might fly out of reach of his enemies, whose oath bound them to follow him to the furthermost end of the earth.

But what good she did by thus commiserating the ex-smuggler, and how he rewarded her, we must leave to times—the developer of all mysteries.

* * * * *

The Spanish coaster "Antonio," had cleared from Cadiz as with a light but fair wind for her northern course.

She had about thirty men aboard her, some of these being English seamen who were going to the American colonies.

Soon after they had bowled out of the port, they saw that a small foreign craft, a two-masted schooner, came along the coast.

Instead of entering the harbour this new vessel fell off before the wind, and shifting her sails wing and wing, she took the same line that the Spanish coaster had sailed over.

All day long the two vessels were in sight of one another.

There could hardly be a doubt of the real character of the schooner. For, trimming her sails just as her leader did, all her efforts seemed to be directed to keeping in view.

Probably, seeing the proximity of the port, she did not care to enter in an engagement during which some man-of-war might appear.

Towards dark, at the time when the land wind dies away and the sea breeze flies into shore, the air softened into a calm.

At intervals a cat's-paw ruffled the glassy undulations.

Otherwise, they might have taken in the sails at once.

The schooner got her long oars out and began to loom up large.

"Their sweeps are out, Ralph," said one of the English sailors to a neighbour leaning over the bulwarks.

"Ay, and she's coming up hand over fist," answered the sailor, who was no other than Black Bill. "A bad egg she, or she wouldn't be so strong manned for a little 'un of her tonnage."

"Right there, mate. Ah! there's the Spaniard a distributing arms."

The captain of the "Antonio," sure that the dogger of his vessel was bent on making fight, was indeed giving out the weapons.

There was a cutlass or pistol for every man.

Ralph and his friend chose axes as the handiest thing for them.

The ex-smuggler was in fact more acquainted with this sort of weapon.

The two bow chasers were old three-pounders, but were serviceable at short range.

There was a gun on board, an article of cargo, a six-pounder.

The captain did not hesitate about breaking bulk for it.

They opened the main hatch, upset the packages that were in the way, and soon unearthed the desired box.

A blow or two of Ralph's axe knocked the board asunder.

The ex-smuggler was resolved to sell his life dearly.

As many hands as could lay hold did, and in half an hour the piece was mounted on a carriage.

They chopped the starboard gunnel through to widen a port, and ran the new gun out at this embrasure.

By this time the stranger had come up under the impulse of the sweeps.

They could guess how numerous a crew the schooner contained, as they had four men to each sweep, rowing three aside.

Besides there were more crowding the decks.

The Spaniards expected as the schooner forged ahead, her sails laying flat as a board, that they would receive a broadside first thing.

But hauling in the sweeps, and passing within easy hail, the crew of the stranger remained at their stations.

But the chief man on the quarter-deck, putting his hand to his mouth, and smoothing away his heavy black moustache and beard, halloa'd—

"Schooner ahoy! Name and master?"

"I'll answer him fair," said the Spaniard.

He lifted his voice.

"The 'Antonio!' I'm Anibal Gogliso. What are you?"

"Blackbeard's longboat! old Goodeyes! Depress that gun, or you'll have something hot heaved on to some of you!"

"You be hanged, we are not to be bullied!" Ralph shouted.

He cared nothing for arguing when he had his shirt sleeves rolled up.

As he spoke, he and his three friends working the six-pounder did depress it a little.

But not so much as Black Beard had desired.

Only so much as to bring it to bear on the pirate.

The gun exploded with a deafening discharge and recoiled with such force as to upset it from the carriage, which it had been too weakly attached to.

"If that bit of good advice don't suit it's a pity, but we can't sarve 'em out more!" said Ralph, looking down ruefully at the dismounted cannon.

The shot had lodged in the hull of the pirate ship shaking it tremendously.

The Spaniards and English raised a cheer, but the more numerous marauders drowned it with a yell of rage and menace.

"Isn't that a puff of wind, there aloft?" cried the Spanish captain, holding up his moistened hand.

"On'y a breath! died away. But the sea-breeze is a coming!" cried a man on the maintop, who was reloading the musket that he had fired.

"My men," said Captain Gogliso, "it'll be hot work, but if we can keep it up, we can run before them when the breeze comes."

"There's nothing like trying," returned Ralph for the crew.

With all his faults, the disguised ruffian, as the reader is aware, could be plucky at times, the more especially when his own life was concerned in the result of the action.

Now Blackbeard had only pursued the Spaniard because he wanted to perform the neat little transaction of changing ships.

He had found his little vessel very inconvenient for so large and noisy a flock of villains.

Hence he did not reply to the shot with so murderous a volley as was in his power to do.

The two were in a current, and if that impulse continued they might be drifted unpleasantly close to shore.

The set of the current had swept the light schooner round to the stern of the heavier laden schooner.

The small arms were re-echoing in the tops and below.

The coaster's defenders were greatly protected by their smallness of numbers, as they fired into a mass and had to be aimed at separately.

Only sheering off a point as her jibbom grazed the schooner's stern, the pirate came forcibly against the after windows.

Through them and over the taffrail, the marauders entered the prize, every one armed.

The pirate chief fired his long pistol at the ex-muggler.

The shot missed him and killed the Spanish captain.

The defenders of the coaster fell back.

More of the robbers were swarming up.

"Holy Virgin!" said the first mate; "shall we give in, Senor Englishman?"

"Give up, and be tied back to back and rolled like pudding balls into the sea?" sneered Ralph. "Not me! I'm for holding out as long as there's a flash of powder in a pistol pan!"

"We'd sooner die, eh?" said the Spaniard.

"By a long shot."

Spaniards and English, they determined not to let the notorious miscreant have them to torment.

They had beaten a retreat down into the waist.

They would have been slaughtered there as in a pen.

But Blackbeard was too eager to finish.

"Fight close!" cried he, drawing his cutlass after having emptied his pistols.

There was a horrible flash of fury in his eye.

He drove his own men before him.

There were half a dozen of the Spaniards who were cut off from their comrades.

They took to the main shrouds.

One or two were run through with boarding-pikes.

The rest offered targets to the marksmen below.

It was pitiful to behold them, dropping blood at every rattling that they drew themselves up.

Growing weaker each minute, their climbing was slower and slower, until they scarcely moved, but remained flattened in against the cordage.

One or two stiffened there in death.

The others were too heavy to be upheld by their bloodless hands, and soon pitched over into the greedy waves.

The pirates began to mount the rigging to get at the fellows in the tops, who were galling their companions with shots, blocks, and cannon balls.

"Don't let one give you the go-by!" cried the pirate chief. "Run down after that fellow in the forecastle. Don't you see him there? Look sharp, ye are not one, or I'll make some of your peepers as big as a bunghole!"

The scoundrels had swept forward to the windlass, bearing a red carpet covered with a score of dead and dying under foot.

Blackbeard stood by the starboard cat-head, leaning on his cutlass.

"Ha, ha!" laughed he, "It's as lively an hour as ever I saw."

One of the men fallen, covered with wounds, on the forecastle, had got upon his feet.

It was Ralph.

One glance showed him that, during his being struck down, every one of his friends and allies had been cast into everlasting sleep.

With all the power of which he was capable, he struck at the rover chief with the first thing that met his hand.

It was half a rammer, one of the bow-chaser's set.

Under such a stroke, Blackbeard fell, like the oak upon which a thunderbolt had spent its force.

The pirates, who had been unable to prevent so unexpected a reprisal, now awoke to revenge.

But Ralph, hurling the club fall in their faces, threw himself over the bows of the pirate ship.

As he did so, a stray shot glanced off the forebits and entered his shoulder.

At the same moment there was a call from the hardful left on the pirate schooner.

"There's the breeze rising!" said they.

There was a fresh ruffle on the surface, and the sails began to wrinkle.

Both vessels began to move. The lesser one worked free of the coaster's stern, and fell off.

"Don't let that scoundrel die!" screamed the pirate chief.

A flask of brandy had been applied to his lips and some of it getting spilt, he had been returned to consciousness by the smarting.

"Don't let him die, the villain! I want to torture him, to cut his heart out; a thousand flames seize him!"

"He's over the bow, sir, on an end of the flying-jib down haul."

"Have him up!"

Here lay the puzzle.

It was all very well to say "have him up!" but a greater man than the gentle-hearted Blackbeard could not compel a man to cling to a rope.

The schooner was going through the water at a very slight pace.

Ralph could keep his grip, nevertheless, if that had been all.

"Here's a rope's end, old fellow," said one pirate. "Shall I heave the slack to you?"

THE COMBAT IN THE FOREST.

"Thank you! I'm considering. I'm ready to die!"

"Die? Wa ain't thinking of a chap that fought so stout. Come up, and sign the articles for a jolly cruise."

"Oh, don't you wish you could tempt me! No such boat for me!"

"He's let go the line, sir!" said they all.

Ralph had let himself float free.

The ship slowly passed him.

At the stern he caught the end of another rope cut in the action, and trailing.

"Make it fast round you!" said one of the rovers again.

"You needn't be afeard, you didn't kill the cap'en!"

"Didn't i? Wore luck! Wish I'd stayed abroad and below, and given him a wrapper of flame for a watch coat!"

"There's another for that!" cried a voice.

The speaker popped his head out of one of the cabin windows.

"What you, Steve?" said Ralph, hardly believing his eyes.

Their heads were not ten feet from one another, but then Steve was high up from the surface.

"What cheer?"

"My life line's veered out," answered Ralph "All above slain by the picaroon's mate."

"I've pinned two that come below after me. There's the table and a locker agin the door, and I can hold out till I lay the train," said Pete.

"Lay the train!" echoed Ralph, in the same low voice that the other used.

"Ay. I've a bag of powder here, and mean to have one flare-up afore the rascals all sail her!"

"Good!"

It was impossible for the swimmer to get into the

window even had he been stronger, unless with some assistance.

The reason of Pete being left to himself so long was obvious enough.

The pirates had cleared away a boat over the side, unseen by him, and now it appeared close to him.

"Luck to you, Steve! Remember, duty's duty! and there's a way aloft for even us rough souls!"

The boat rounded the stern and was nearly upon him.

The stroke oar and the second seat man rose, shipping their oars, and held themselves in readiness at the bow to lift the sailor in.

But, even as their eager hands were outstretched, the stout old tar let go the rope, threw up his arms straight over his head, and sank.

They touched his very hair, but already the water had closed over him with an ominous sound.

When he came up he was twenty feet off.

Before the boat could overtake him he had gone under again.

He rose again and was made prisoner.

Then the boat made for the pirate schooner, which lay nearer them than the vessel they had quitted.

In the meantime, the pirate chief had been filled with vexation at the resolute way in which the brave salt who had left him with a bleeding head had gone to his death.

He turned his attention now to the interior of his prize.

Since the seaman in the cabin had killed the couple of pirates who had gone below after him, and blocked up the door, there were but two ways of getting at him.

One was to lower one's self to the cabin windows, and break through them.

But it was rather risky to travel by that route.

The fellows held back.

While one watched to hinder any escape by that way, there was a party set hammering at the door.

Only a few at most could be supposed to have taken refuge under hatches, so that Blackbeard was easy as regarded that.

Had he been aware that these were only the last of the thirty left, he would have been still more delighted at his conquest.

Of his better-armed men the defenders of the Spaniard had only slain eight, but three more were so badly wounded, that in the hot weather they were not likely to recover.

The pirates were handling the sails, and the little pink had been hailed to follow in the wake.

Midnight was near at hand, and still the door had resisted the axes.

It bid fair to be down presently, if only in chips.

By lantern light the hold and forecastle had been searched and the goods were brought up on deck.

To the music of that fierce pounding on the cabin-door, for the dozen ruffians to be in at the death of the one survivor, the plunderers overhauled the booty.

"I'll have to jump down in among ye, and flatten in your jib," cried Blackbeard, angrily.

He was standing at the doorway of the cabin entrance looking down on his men.

"What are you at, you lubber?" he shouted.

"What have you found?" thundered Blackbeard.

To his surprise, he saw they were hauling a female out of an empty case.

There was a law among the pirates that no female should live aboard their ship.

In their brutal fierceness they would have torn her to pieces there and then had not Blackbeard burst down among them.

A glance of recognition passed between him and the fair captive.

"What, Genifrede!" he cried, forgetting his late fury in the moment of his astonishment. "What brings you here, girl?"

The nature of the pirate seemed to be changed from that moment.

In the meantime others of the crew had battered down the cabin door and poor Pete into pieces, and pitched his remains overboard.

The battle now being ended, it only remained to clear away the relics of the bloody strife, and to sluice down the decks that were streaming with gore.

Then the guns, ammunition, and other valuables were transferred to the Spanish prize, and the pirate schooner sunk, taking with her the record of the horrible crimes that had been perpetrated on her decks.

Genifrede had a cabin fitted up to herself, for the pirate captain was determined that no harm should come to her.

He had a strong guard placed at her door, for he was afraid that his crew would still persist in taking her life.

Blackbeard then had the prisoner Ralph brought before him, and judge of his surprise when he beheld in the ex-smuggler's repulsive visage the face of an old acquaintance.

Black Bill cowered beneath the pirate chief's deadly frown; the ex-smuggler had not recognized him before.

There was evidently an old grudge between them; Black Bill had once played him false in some dark business.

Whatever it was, the pirate chief's anger boded him no good.

"Take him away," he said, fiercely; "place him in irons, and chain him in the lower hold."

The order was obeyed and then the pirate captain returned to Genifrede.

"You must leave this ship," he said; "I will have you placed comfortably on one of the islands; for the injury I once did your uncle, Dutch Paul, I will make this atonement."

He then questioned her concerning her being found in the same ship as Black Bill, to which she did not return him the most truthful answer, simply informing him that she had taken passage unwittingly in the schooner in which Black Bill had previously shipped as a seaman.

That evening the pirate sighted land, and the vessel was anchored, and then Genifrede was handed upon deck.

The pirate captain's boat was at the starboard gangway, ready manned.

On seeing no signs of Black Bill, Genifrede looked around searchingly, and then turned her large eyes on the captain, appealingly.

He diverted his gaze, and only motioned for her to descend the ladder slung over the side.

In another moment she was safely caught in a pirate's stalwart arms and handed along to the stern sheets.

Blackbeard was presently by her side.

He flung a boat cloak over her knees, and took the tiller ropes.

"Shove off," said he.

The boat was pushed away and, the men bending to their oars, she was soon out of the dark shade that the vessel cast around her.

The shore, a small island, half of sand and rock, and then of a swampy and thickly wooded nature, was reached in a few minutes.

"Light the lantern," said Blackbeard; "one man can be boat-keeper. Follow me, you others."

With Genifrede in their midst, the party went

over the beach o the first rise of ground, where a hut rose amid tangled grass.

The light of the lanterns showed the cabin, pretty strongly built, had been put up by some turtle-catchers, who had slept there and cooked at the door.

"It will do," said Blackbeard. "Tom, get you down to the boat again and bring up the biscuits and the hammock."

The articles of housekeeping were soon laid out in the hut, and the hanging bed rigged up.

The young girl had sat down on a stone mantled with weeds, and let her gaze wander from the barque, gently riding at her mooring, to the several men who were obeying orders in the mild lamplight.

Thanks to their skill and activity, the hut was made habitable.

Upon that Blackbeard came to her.

The sailors withdrew a few yards, to light a pipe or two, or to scan the weather sky with a critical glance.

"My poor girl," said the youth, standing before her, "I am sorry to have you brought into contact with this moment. You know that your uncle, whom I dislike, murdered several of my men."

"Stay, I do not blame him for harm done me in fair fight. I could almost pardon him," said the crafty pirate; "but I could not let him go, and yet retain the respect of my followers.

"They would obey me to more than that extent, but I do not want to play the tyrant over such brave and faithful hearts. I have done much for you. I would not have a hand even in trying the smuggler. I have left all that to the crew.

"Fear not, they will be just, even in their revenge."

The girl had bowed her head, as if she could not find words to utter.

"Stand apart, you with the lights," said the pirate captain, then, "and swing the lanterns half a dozen times."

That was the signal that the officers and company were to loose the sails and prepare to heave up the anchor.

Presently a bright flame shot up, and a cry of alarm came across the still waters of the bay. It was taken up wildly by the pirates on shore, and echoed by the pirate captain.

"Hands aboard!" shouted he, running down the beach. "All in! shove off! sharp's the word! pull away, pull!"

Genifrede was left alone on the strand.

Instinctively she kept her eyes on the vessel, so prominent now that the red and golden streamers floated over her.

A current that had set in after the slack water had fallen, and the tide had began to run out, carried the cutter out of the direct line, notwithstanding the vigorous rowing.

In spite of all, it was evident that they could not reach the barque in a very short time.

Genifrede gazed from the sands.

She saw the flames leap up or fall low, now changing the circle of water into a ring of crimson or letting the darkness fall all around again.

At last the ship seemed surely doomed by the conflagration.

The blaze reached the mainyard, and the canvas, had it been drier, would have been kindled; it was not furled, but only caught up loosely.

Every line of the upper works stood out clearly in the light.

Genifrede could see the men, like black ants seeming to be running in and out amid the lurid glare.

A hoarse murmur had come already to her ears, but now the sea breeze bore a fierce shout to the

his figures appeared to her letting the fire do its worst, while all dropped down from aloft, and gathered from other quarters to collect amidships.

Even at that distance, the brightness was such and her vision so strained, that the ropes were distinct from the starboard mainbrace, swinging slack.

One end was on board, the other, after running through a block, dangled at the earing-post, in a noose.

The shouting was renewed more fiercely than before, and louder.

The slack of the line was payed away, and a man jumping up into the main shrouds, caught the lowered loop and pulled it on deck.

Genifrede could not prevent her attention being fixed on that cord.

Amid a continuance of the clamour, the figures were seen all in motion.

The line was tautened.

The loudest, most savage, most joyous of cheers, resounded.

Genifrede closed her eyes, or rather tried to shut them.

A mist crept over them.

Then she swooned, and when she recovered she saw that the fire on board the pirate ship had been extinguished.

There was some object, too, in the water alongside the vessel.

It was a small boat.

It tended shoreward.

Of the three men in it, two rowed single and the other pulled a pair.

What could these men, come from the cruiser, be sent for?

Only one mission could be theirs.

She was filled with terror.

At first she could hardly muster enough strength to rise.

But the boat had passed over the current sweeping around the island, and was rapidly nearing the beach.

There could be no doubt that where she had remained was their destination.

She rose to her feet and looked wildly about her.

Before her the open sea and the oncoming boat.

Behind her the thicket of beech, plums, burton trees, and others.

She turned to fly.

The men were just shipping oars and crowding into the stern so that their conveyance might run the farther upon shore.

They saw that she was taking to flight, and they shouted to her.

Her ears translated their words into such as spurred her on.

With all her might she ran into the woods.

The three men left the boat beached.

The tide was going out now.

Genifrede heard a crashing, mingled with oaths.

There was a vigorous pursuit of her.

They called out after her all the time, but she was too frightened to catch more than the mere sound.

She did not know where she was going.

It was by a miracle only that her slight form was not torn to pieces by the interwoven boughs.

As it was her dress was tattered by a hundred prickly palms or thorn bushes.

The hunters seemed to have missed her track.

It was in time none too soon.

She was all but entirely exhausted.

At last, being caught by the brambles that ran on the ground, she missed her footing and fell

Her head came in contact with a stone, and she sank into unconsciousness.

The last dread of being caught remained with still great terrors in her senselessness.

Such was the torment of her mind that she awoke.

How long she must have been in the swoon she did not know.

She was in the same place.

It was colder, and she judged morning to be near at hand.

There was no sound except the rustle of leaves, and the distant wash of the sea upon the strand.

The stars were sparkling brightly and that was the light.

But then starlight in the tropics is very different to a night time elsewhere.

She could not remain there, and yet she was equally afraid to stir.

The men might be on the watch close to her, waiting for a misstep to point her out.

Still she could no bear inaction in her nervous state.

The darkness of the forest had shadows that made her shudder.

The creeping plants and Spanish moss that festooned from the boughs took the shape of that tangled man which was ever present to her eyes.

Groping her way till her eyes were accustomed to the gloom under the trees, she went from the heart of the wood.

She had not chosen her path, but her wandering led her to the sea-shore.

It grew lighter and lighter at every step, and ere long she was on the open sands.

Their glistening made each pebble lying on them plain to the view.

Genifrede, just stepping out of the covert, suddenly recoiled.

There was a man on the sand, high and dry.

But even her timid glance told her that she need fear nothing from him.

Such complete quiescence argued helplessness in the subject.

For some minutes she remained crouching close to the bushes.

But there was nothing like life around her, only the receding waters casting a ripple ashore regularly and mournfully.

Her fears had lessened.

Compassion sprang up in its place, and she blamed herself for having hesitated so long.

Cautiously leaving the shade, she went down the sands.

Two or three times she started, and prepared to turn back.

The pirate ship had gone now, but the prone form still lay stretched upon the sands.

Even to one of her inexperience, when she stooped over the form, the closeness of death to so cold and pale a face and limp a figure was clear.

That sensation was sharpened to accurate pain by the feeling that followed.

The icy white face and shoulders were scratched and cut by floating stuff that it had been dashed against.

The seaweed was tangled with the hair.

But the glimmer above was sufficient for her to recognise Black Bill.

From him she had parted at one awful time when, seeming to be in safety herself, he was surely doomed.

Now they came together.

He bloodless as a corpse, and she with a great fright hovering over her.

She found that a little warmth yet lingered in his breast.

Knowing that the spot was too exposed for her safe for him, both for fear of the sea returning and of being seen by the three sailors from the cruiser, she seized the body by the shoulders and dragged it away.

Even after she had drawn it into the thicket she took it still farther.

There was some distance between them and the hut.

It was hard for her to convey him there, but Heaven gave her strength.

Perhaps the being pulled over the more or less rough ground did the half-drowned man no harm.

At least she found that his breathing was audible as she pulled him into the hut.

Her alarm had greatly subsided since she was no longer alone, and had something to engage her mind with.

She exerted herself to the utmost in bringing him to.

After a long, long while, full of many hopes suddenly quenched, the girl felt her heart leap.

Her companion, his eyes still closed, made a babbling with his pale lips, which seemed to mean:—

' Drink! drink!'

Tossed on the wave, scorched by the sun, smarting at every pore with the brine; thirst had been the fiend that had most tormented the castaway.

Genifrede started up.

The scarf about her neck would hold enough water to give a drink.

But where was fresh water to be obtained on that sea-girt isle?

Could she dig deep in the sand she might find some strained sufficiently.

But that side of the island happened to be either stony or sandy, and shells were not to be seen, or were too small or too shattered to do for digging.

To look for a piece of a tree limb, or to collect the heavy dew from leaf and leaf, were both mere loss of precious time.

Again the sufferer murmured his want, louder than before, although his eyes continued closed.

Above the low syllable he repeated, the girl fancied she caught another sound.

When she had stepped out of the cave, she heard it more clearly.

It was running water.

Not the wash of the thrown up ripple returning to the wave, but the gentle, uninterrupted music of a tiny waterfall.

Half her scarf she hung up on a bush to guide her back, and she ran towards that point.

In another instant she found herself on the brink of a pool.

Its colour and its stillness proved its depth.

It was like a beautiful sheet of jet marble.

Every now and then a line of bubbles would run along the level and break sluggishly; it was some tenant of the pond.

At one end a little brooklet rolled down a pile of stones and scarcely disturbed the mass it added to.

Dark as it looked, it was doubtless fresh and drinkable.

As she dabbled the scarf in it she was alarmed by it being pulled from her hand.

Something very strong had darted under water at the light hued web and carried it away.

As she caught her breath after the sudden start that this had given her, she was aware that she was no longer alone.

It could not be Bill recovered magically that was beside her.

That red shirt, the belt garnished with weapons, the rough face—she had seen many such on board.

The man gazed at her, at first with surprise and then altogether with rapture.

"Well, my charmer!" said he, in a husky voice balancing himself on both legs wide apart, as if he were on deck in a cross sea. "Well, little love, here you are! I've only been half-an-hour sarchin' th' islet for you and didn't 'spect to find you afore mornin'. Hows'ever, since you are so soon within hail, let's have a buss, lassie, to open the action like?"

On one side the thicket of prickly pear, on the other and at her back the pond; before her the drunken sailor blocked up the way.

She tried to run by him as he leaned one side unsteadily, but he was too quick for her.

In the very act her wrist was seized in the powerful hand and she was swung back roughly on the grass.

On her knees she remained, and clasped her hands.

"Oh, kill me!" moaned she, "kill me at once as you were sent to do!"

"Who was? Kill you? Ha, ha! Me and my mates were sent by the capt'n to look arter you till we bears in three days from him——"

"No!"

"Don't lay hands on me, then!" she shudderingly said.

"Pooh! But I likes the gals what fires up! I do, by Jove!"

"If you touch me he shall know, and he is prompt to avenge."

"Ha, ha! Hold your noise! Come, stow it, or I'll knife you! Avast heaving! By thunder, you're a fool! My mates are t'other side, to leeward, of the island! There's no one to hear."

"Help, help!"

Yet she could not hope that Bill, so feeble, so far from ability to help, would be raised by a miracle to her assistance.

Fruitless her struggle in such powerful hands.

Each time that she sought to run she was dragged back.

Twice beat down to her knee, she rose as many times and fluttered in the brutal embrace like a petrel in a seagull's claws.

All at once, as she, breathless with striking the hard headed ruffian, feared she was about to swoon in the wretch's grasp, both of them started.

Both glanced into the thicket.

They saw the shadow, catching a little glimmer of the starlight, defined upon the mass of thorny ea, parels.

But at a second glance her lightened heart was loaded down again.

The seaman laughed gladly, relieved from dread of an interference.

The new-comer wore the red shirt that was the principal item of the uniform of the pirates

"Aint it you Pete?" cried the pirate, holding the girl down. "Thought so, bo'l" added he, as the stranger advanced, apparently in pain. "You al'ays was a most for'ad man, and you've parted cable too soon, Arter me is manners!"

He stooped over the trembling, shrinking girl.

"Come, that kiss, my light-of-love!"

"Oh, no, no, no! Oh, help! help!" shrieked the terrified girl.

The rascal clapped one broad hand over her mouth.

With the other he made a threatening gesture.

The stranger had not spoken yet.

He moved, dragging himself along like one paralysed, but forcing himself onward by energy of mind.

Had his face been turned upward, its deathly pallor would have been plain.

But the sailor who had overpowered the poor girl did not notice him.

Content in the belief that his threat would leave the field to himself, he took away his palm from Genifrede's face and pressed his foul mouth to her very.

At this sight, the stranger uttered a hoarse cry of frenzy.

One could see the blood rushed into every vein so that his white face was instantly suffused with vermilion.

Getting the better hand of his lassitude, he reached the brink of the pool in three long leaps.

More like a rock hurled from a hill-top than a man, he fell upon the seaman.

He himself was so stunned by the shock that he fell back senseless.

The other, dashing forward, went rolling into the pond.

It was about mid-deep where he fell.

On finding bottom, he turned furious and began to wade to shore.

Genifrede could have fled now, exhausted as she was, but she had not the heart to leave him who had saved her, to the ruffian's revenge

Catching up a fragment of wood that had been broken under their feet in the assault, she prepared to combat him.

If she could keep him from climbing the bank, her superior station might gain her the victory.

But, as she nerved herself for the encounter, she beheld the seaman stop.

The next instant he gave a howl of pain, and seemed to miss his footing.

Dancing wildly in the water, now throwing up his arms in agony, now plunging them frantically beneath the surface, he seemed to have gone mad.

His struggles grew weaker and weaker.

He sought to reach the bank, but still the invisible power drew him back.

Plunging from side to side, rocking to and fro, up to his neck one moment and then again half out of water, the man changed his position every moment.

In one of his wild leaps, Genifrede thought she saw something with the quickness of lightning at the wretch's limbs.

But the bubbles and splashing covered all that immediately.

With a horrid oath, screamed out in his torment, the man's arms and body rose upward from one deep plunge, in which he had almost gone under.

The trunk and arms were all that were there.

Now, as Bill and his companion gave a cry of deep horror, the black form of an alligator glided away across the dark but ensanguined pool.

CHAPTER CCIX.

THE FRIGATE IN A STORM.

It was a dark, tempestuous night, and the gallant ship laboured heavily in the storm-lashed sea that hissed and foamed around her, in huge black waves crested with snowy foam.

Fierce, heavy gusts that threatened to rend the sails from their fastenings and tear away the masts, swept through the rigging as the vessel heeled over at an angle of forty-five degrees, for the squall had suddenly taken her.

The boatswain's pipe had summoned all hands, and the sailors, with bare feet, scrambled up the hatchways and clung to various parts of the ship to prevent themselves being washed away by the huge waves that continually swept the deck of the gallant frigate.

A noble vessel the "Ajax."

She carried thirty-six guns and a crew of over four hundred men and boys, all told, and as the blue lightning vividly flashed and the thunder heavily rolled, she rose on the boiling surge, and seemed, like her namesake, to bid a very defiance to the storm.

Captain Bluster stood on the poop when the squall burst upon them; he had his glass in his hand, and had evidently been watching for some ship, which, owing to the blackness of the night, was a task of no little difficulty.

"In top-gallant sails, clew down topsails, and haul the courses snug up," thundered the captain at the pitch of his voice.

"Luff, luff," he added, to the man at the wheel, "hold on, lads, in the rigging or——"

He could not finish; an enormous wave rose like a mountain as high as the mizzen-top, broke on the poop and swept the deck fore and aft, carrying everything loose before it.

Captain Bluster clung to the companion until the immense body of water had passed, and then he sprang to the wheel, which was flying round unrestrained, the helmsman having been hurled from his post with a broken arm, and left in the lee scuppers.

"Help here, or she'll broach to; the masts will snap like reeds," shouted the captain above the howling of the blast.

Dick was clinging to the lee mizzen shrouds, where he stood dripping with wet, briny ooze, his hair hanging about his face like a wet mop, but no sooner did he hear the captain's voice than he flew to his side.

"It is well she answers her helm, captain," he said, as he assisted to heave the wheel hard up, and the ship payed off; "had that wave stove in our quarter, we should have had a long swim for it, sir."

"The rocks would have been the first land we made," replied the captain. "This is pirate-hunting with a vengeance; I detest it, hugging a lee shore in Trafalgar Bay on such a night as this; damme, give me sea-room and a fair fight."

"Aye, your honour," replied the young sailor; "had we good sea room and a Frenchman clapt alongside, we could wish for no better sport. The French are noted for their dancing and music, but there's nothing I know of makes them hop on the light fantastic or try the power of their lungs like the music of a British broadside."

"What is up with the main topsail?" asked the captain of the quartermaster of the watch, as he delivered the wheel into his care and told him to keep the ship full and by. "Go forward, Dick, and see the other topsails are ready for hoisting, and yet the maintop men have now laid out."

It was impenetrably dark, and, as Dick walked forward with his eye aloft, he stumbled against some one crouched under the lee of the boats lashed amidships.

A blow, followed by an oath, was Dick's reward, and without waiting to ascertain whose hand had struck him in the mouth, he lunged out and felled his assailant by a blow under the ear.

A flash of lightning at that moment lit the deck, and by its momentary flash Dick discovered the first lieutenant sprawling at full length, his pale, cadaverous face distorted with rage.

A kind of awe crept over the sailor on finding he had struck his superior, which might end in his disgrace, although the blow was given in just resentment.

There was a malicious gleam in the lieutenant's eye as he rose to his feet, and hissed:

"Scoundrel! dearly shall you repent this blow. 'Tis well I warded off the knife."

"Liar!" thundered Dick "I had no knife, and I have a mind to wring your neck for this assertion; we have long been ill friends, ay, from the time we met in the house of Colonel Dartmoor, and now you can work out your revenge; but first you will have to prove that I struck you at all!—at least, in the cowardly manner you assert."

"A witness is not hard to get; some one must have seen the blow," replied the lieutenant, with a sneer.

A face somewhat similar to the lieutenant's at that moment rose from one of the boats amidships, and a voice drawled out in a sneaking tone:—

"I seed him strike yer, yer honour."

"And who are you?" asked the lieutenant, pretending not to recognise the voice.

"Tom Plug, one of the carpenter's crew. I've been seeing to the boats for fear they might be wanted, Mr Pembroke."

Percy Pembroke, the officer's name, understood the invented excuse of the carpenter's mate of seeing to the safety of the boats; he knew from former experience that he had been studying his own safety and comfort; he, the carpenter's mate, being renowned for his skill in "dodging Pompey," or in other words, eluding work.

"And you saw him with the knife, did you not?" asked Percy, giving the man the suggestion.

"As plain as if it was daylight," was the cool reply.

"'Tis false," cried Dick, his cheek flushed with indignation; "no one can say Richard Dawson ever disobeyed his officers or broke the discipline of his ship. 'Tis false, I say, that I raised a knife against you or even struck you, knowing who you were. I did but return the blow dealt me by some coward hand."

"That we must leave to the decision of your superiors. Go aloft and see what ails those fellows; the sail will not be reefed to night."

Dick glanced aloft where some twenty men were trying to lay out on the weather yardarm, in obedience to the squeaking voice of a middy who was endeavouring to make himself heard, but whose orders it was impossible for the men to fulfil, as the sail had got somehow entangled with the foot-rope, and flapped about in such a manner as to threaten instant death to any that might venture upon the yard.

"Do you hear me, Dawson," asked the lieutenant, as the sailor paused to look aloft, "or am I to report you for refusal of duty?"

Dick was too choked to answer, but he leapt silently into the rigging and mounted the shrouds.

"Stand aside, Mr. Jones," he said to the middy, detecting at a glance the cause of the middy's perplexity. "Lie down into the top, sir," he added, as he passed him in the topmast rigging and mounted to the crosstrees; the next moment he had slidden down the topsail lift and was seated astride the weather topsail yard-arm.

Dick had given himself a task, none of the easiest, to clear the sail, for it flapped furiously against the yard, and the reef tackles threatened to give way, whilst the canvas grew harder and stiffer as the cold sleet began to fall and saturate it.

The first lieutenant had an object in sending Dick aloft instead of having him placed under immediate arrest; a motive that corresponded well with his own black treacherous heart.

"Tom Plug," he said, when the two were alone, "you will have to swear to what you have seen, and mind and mention the knife; it had a black horn handle, you remember."

"Aye, aye, your honour, there was light enough for me to see all that. I suppose it will be a job for court-martial."

"Very probable; but do you think anyone else witnessed it? You might inquire, you know, of your friends; you can earn a five-pound note between you."

This latter part of the speech not only caused Tom to open his ears, but also open his eyes, and with a cunning leer he replied—

"I'll see, I'll see, sir; trust Tom Plug for finding a wedge."

With this he slunk away, and the lieutenant went aft, muttering,

"Thus will I rid me of the only stumbling-block in my way, remove the one dark spot on the horizon of my life, the only man that shares my hope of happiness."

"Ah, ah, how long have I wished for an opportunity like this! He has placed a chance in my way that I would not miss for the prize money of a whole cruise; now what will the proud minx say, the haughty jade that preferred the suit of the buccaneer, Tom Drake, to that of an officer of wealth and title? Pooh, she must yield."

The captain, mounted on a gun-carriage, was trying to pierce the blackness to leeward, and he was about to give orders for the leadsman going into the chains, when, on stepping down, he found himself face to face with Percy Pembroke.

"Well, sir," he said, "you have taken your time in reefing the topsail; are you aware that we are driving fast towards the shore? If not, it is time you became cognisant of the fact. Who is that out on the yard-arm?"

"I know not, Captain Bluster, but I have a charge to prefer against the boatswain's mate, Richard Dawson. He has attempted my life."

"Richard Dawson—impossible!"

"True, sir, he drew his knife, and, failing in his intent, he leapt into the rigging. I have one or more witnesses to prove it."

It was too dark for the captain to notice the malicious smile that accompanied this speech, but the tone of the speaker's voice was anything but in his favour.

In the meantime Dick was doing his utmost endeavours aloft, and the middy, dreading a severe reprimand for the delay, tried to force his way out on top of the yard to Dick's assistance, in utter disregard of the sailors in the top warning him of his danger.

Presently a startling cry assailed Dick's ears—a cry that was never to be forgotten by those who heard it, and he just caught sight of a falling body in the darkness

The gallant fellow did not wait to hear that cry repeated; he guessed from whom it came, and, grasping the topsail lift with one hand, he bounded on to the yard, and leapt overboard from the giddy height after him.

Fortunately for the boy, he fell close to the ship's side, and grasping a rope, he managed by dint of great exertion to crawl into one of the ports, where exhausted he fell down and remained hidden from all observation.

With Dick Dawson it was otherwise.

Being a good swimmer he rose like a cork to the surface, and as he rose and fell on the turbulent waves, he looked about for the least sign of the middy, and listened for the feeblest cry.

Nought but the white crest of the billowing waves met his gaze through the inky darkness, and no sound but the roaring of the wind and the surging waves met his ear; yet, heedless of his own safety, he continued his painful watch and buffeted the waves that seemed eager to clasp him in their last and cold embrace.

On board the frigate all was bustle and confusion.

The cry of "man overboard" sent the sailors, who were not at the time aloft, rushing on to the poop, where the stern voice of the captain restored them to order, and dispersed them in various parts of the ship.

"Hard down with the wheel, haul in the weather braces," shouted the captain through his speaking trumpet, "cutter's crew man the first cutter."

With an alacrity, such as only British seamen can display, the order was obeyed, but the cutter's

after tackle had only lowered the boat a few feet when it was discovered to be foul.

"Belay," piped the boatswain, whose quick eye detected the fault just in time to prevent the utter destruction of the whole of the boat's crew; but scarcely had he given a man orders to clear away when the stern of the boat dropped into the sea, swamped, and left the men clinging to the thwarts.

"What lubber has done that?" roared the boatswain, as he seized a rope and threw it over to the men's assistance; "the swab ought to be seized up and flogged to within an inch of his life."

He cast a glance full of meaning at the first luff, who stood near the after davit, for he fancied he had seen the blade of a knife glitter in his hand.

The lieutenant returned his look with a malignant scowl, the purport of which was not difficult for the boatswain to discern.

"What is the cause of this, Mr. Pipes?" asked the captain angrily of the boatswain. "Lower the second cutter if this one is swamped"

Pipes made no reply, but walked to the other quarter boat, whither a number of men had flown, and were already casting off the grips and lashings.

The first lieutenant was also there shouting to the men, who were thrown into great confusion by his various orders.

"I would thank you to leave this duty to me," said Pipes, giving the lieutenant an angry glance; "the life of a better man than yourself is being jeopardised by your foolery."

He muttered this last part of his speech; but whether the lieutenant heard it or not it is difficult to say; certain it was he turned away heaping a bitter invective on the head of Pipes.

These incidents had passed more rapidly than we have been able to describe them, so that in less than five minutes from the time of the outcry the second cutter, with her fearless crew, was lowered safely in the water, and the men bent gallantly to the oars.

The coxswain, standing in the stern sheets, swept his keen eye over the troubled waters, in what was evidently the vain hope of seeing the pale face of either our hero or the middy, for as yet the boy's shivering form had not been discovered lying between the guns.

After half-an-hour's useless search, a light from the frigate's gaff recalled the boat and the men with saddened hearts and drenched garments returned on board.

The main-top rail being by this time reefed, was hoisted, the yards braced round, and the frigate once more put on her proper course.

With nervous and anxious stride the captain paced the deck, dissatisfied in mind at the conduct of his first officer.

He knew that some jealousy, though concerning what he could not imagine, existed between the boatswain's mate and Percy Pembroke.

It was a relief, in some measure, to him when it was announced that the middy, Edward Jones, was safe, though the loss of the gallant seaman, Dick Dawson, grieved him more than, perhaps, would the loss of any other of his crew.

"Well Percy, what do you think of this night's work?" he asked of that individual as he joined him on the quarter deck.

"Think," replied the other evasively, "that if he had been born to be hanged he would not have been drowned!"

"You think, then, if this had not occurred, he would have been——"

"Hanged, sure enough. It is as well perhaps as it is, for he has saved me from an unpleasant duty. He raised a knife to me, as I previously informed you, and nothing could have saved him from his doom. I have two witnesses, if not more, who saw him strike the blow."

"This affair is truly unfortunate, though from a previous knowledge of the man, his loyalty and strict attention to duty, I could not have believed this of him had it come from any other lip."

The captain turned his head, and seemed to be trying to pierce the sombre gloom that enshrouded the weather horizon.

"It grieves me no less deeply than yourself, that one so brave and daring in other respects should so far degrade himself as to become an assassin," said the first luff, in well-feigned sympathy. "I sadly deplore his fate, though in duty to the service, and in honour to myself, I can do no other than report this to the admiral on our arrival in port."

Their conversation was, at this moment, broken by a cry from the masthead.

"Sail, oh!"

"Where away?"

"On the lee beam."

Captain Baster seized his night-glass, and sprang into the rigging to get a view of the stranger.

"The Death Pirate, I'll swear!" he exclaimed on returning to the deck. "Mr. Pembroke, the pirate must not escape me. He is safely embedded in the bay, and we must crawl down upon him unawares."

The storm was still raging fiercely, and the wind keep veering and hauling several points.

This kept the crew of the frigate at work, and for the time drove from their memory the terrible fate of the gallant seaman, Dick Dawson, whose fearful doom had sadly depressed the spirits of all on board —not excepting Percy, whose guilty conscience scretly smote him

CHAPTER CCX.

A VOICE FROM THE DEEP.

"Hard-up, you lubber," shouted the Death Pirate, as the squall caught the sails of the brigantine, and threw her over on her beam.

"By the fiends, you'll send us all to glory before our time."

"Ay, what with wind and rocks, we shall have enough to do this night to keep ourselves afloat," answered the lieutenant, springing to the wheel. "Ah, me, we just caught her in the nick of time."

The wheel ropes creaked, the masts bent, and the sails flapped with a violence that shook the vessel from stem to stern.

Then, with a sudden effort, the gallant sea-boat mounted a huge billow, and the pirates, who had been watching her movements with the anxiety of men whose very existence depended upon her exertions, drew a deep breath of relief.

"'Tis well, I thought we should have foundered," said the pirate captain; as Benito stepped to his side."

"The clouds still look wild and lowering."

"I shall be glad when the morning breaks; but what is the look-out about? Do you not see something to windward there?"

"Nothing, Benito."

"Not a black speck rising now and then upon the foam?"

"Well, I do see something but it must be fancy."

"Can you hear anything?"

Benito drew the captain to the ship's side, and listened.

"I can hear something—a sea-mew I should say."

"A human voice more likely; no one else seems to have seen or heard it."

"It is only our imagination; the wind howling through the cordage," said the captain, in the hope of turning the lieutenant's attention from it; "by Jupiter! how it blows. Confound it, we are getting drenched here with the spray."

Benito was not so easily persuaded; he grasped one of the shrouds and leant over the bulwarks, heedless of the waves that threatened at times to wash him away.

"It is a voice and a human form, I dare wager," said Benito, as he shielded his eyes with his hand, and tried to pierce the gloom; "look there, Benito, it's drifting fast this way."

"What can it be? Where can it come from?" said the pirate captain, with a tone of uneasiness in his voice.

"We have not sighted a vessel all the night, and there is no land to windward of us for hundreds of miles."

"Still there may have been a wreck; the waves may have robbed us of a golden treasure. There! Now do you believe me?" he exclaimed.

A voice hoarse and faint was borne towards them on the wind.

Several of the pirates now had their attention drawn towards it, and with eager glances they crowded to the bulwarks

Jason, a square-built, bullet-headed Dutchman, crawled up into the fore-rigging, and made his way into the fore-top, where the look-out was stationed.

From this elevation they had a more indistinct view of the strange object than on deck, but the pair soon had their attention directed to the weather horizon, viewing something that appeared like a sail.

In the meantime those below were gazing overboard in breathless silence; each succeeding wave swept the mystic object nearer towards them.

The voice, however, grew fainter and fainter, and at last it ceased altogether.

There was a strange commotion amongst that motley crew, a superstitious whispering, as one huge roller, tipped with foam, raised the strange object aloft on its crested head.

"A man!" echoed several voices.

"A man!" chimed in the lieutenant; and then Benito, clutching a rope, stood ready to lower himself down over the vessel's side.

"Now, now!" was the general exclamation, and Benito had flung himself over into the sea, and stretched forth his arm towards what appeared the upturned face of a drowned man.

In an instant his sinewy arm encircled the inanimate form, and detaching it from a pair of oars that kept it afloat, he shouted to the pirates to haul in the rope. A minute or two passed, and then Benito and his prize were landed on the deck, and a light was flashed upon the pale and livid features.

"A youth!" exclaimed the Death Pirate, "and," he added, starting, "he wears the rig of a man of war's man. By Heavens, this is a night of mystery, Benito!"

"A strange mystery, too," replied Benito, with a shrug. "Where the devil he has sprung from I cannot imagine."

"You may depend upon it there is a man-of-war somewhere about here," answered the captain; "below with him, lad, there may be a chance of his recovery, and then——"

"He will most likely betray us for our kindness."

A sinister smile wreathed the lips of the captain as he followed the body into the cabin, and then his brow became thoughtful.

Benito motioned the pirate on deck, and then entered the state-room, from which he returned almost immediately with a small mahogany case.

From it he took a small vial, and pouring a few drops of its contents into a tumbler of brandy, he placed it to the lips of the youth, who began at once to show signs of recovery.

"Well done, Benito; well done," muttered the pirate, hoarsely, in an undertone. "The scorpion lives, as you observed; for our trouble we may be rewarded with its sting."

"We may chance it. I am burning to know how he came here."

"So am I—but see, he moves—his eyes are open —more grog, Benito—more grog. Ah, ah! his chest heaves freely. The danger is past."

The eyes of the youth slowly opened, and the filmed orbs rolled as it were around, and then settled on the features of the pirate captain.

He seemed like one charmed by a serpent.

Those eyes, basilisk like, seemed to hold him in a spell, which he had not the power to shake off.

Benito eyed his commander with wonderment and alarm.

"Captain!" he said, endeavouring to rouse him from his lethargy, "what, in the name of the furies, ails you?"

"Ah!" gasped the captain, as he turned his head towards his lieutenant, and drew in a deep breath. "Ah! Benito—brandy—brandy——"

Benito filled a tumbler with the fiery spirit, and the captain gulped it down at a draught. "There! I am better now," he exclaimed.

"What ailed you?" inquired Benito, eyeing his altered countenance. "In storm or fight I have never seen your cheek blanch so before; nay, not when you tore the wife from the arms of her bleeding husband, and threw the weeping babe into the sea."

The Death Pirate gave him a meaning glance.

"It was a qualm passed over me," he said; "it is passed—say no more about it."

Benito did as he was desired, though he could not drive the circumstance wholly from his mind, and then he raised the youth and placed him on a couch.

The vessel was pitching very heavily, so Benito placed a velvet cushion in such a manner as to prevent him from falling off, and then after administering a little more brandy, he left him to recover.

The heavens were still cloudy; the dark leaden masses still continued to rise up from the horizon, and the pirates, grouped about the deck in whispered conversation, kept their eyes steadily fixed on the entrance to the cabin.

Benito paced the deck in moody thought, his eyes continually reverting to the weather horizon, then to the sails aloft, until he settled down in deep abstraction.

He was so busy with his thoughts that Jason, after several endeavours to make himself seen, approached him and tapped him on the shoulder.

"Well," ejaculated Benito, in a tone that augured no good to the intruder—"well, why do you take this liberty?"

"Beg pardon, sir, but there's a suspicious-looking craft away to wind'ard there; I fancy they've seen us, too, for she's bearing down like a race-horse."

"A ship?" cried Benito, who seemed both annoyed and bewildered. "Could you make out her rig and build?"

"Devil a bit of it; it's as black as thunder over yonder; I caught sight of her just now when the sky cleared a bit."

"This must be the man-of-war," muttered the pirate lieutenant. "No matter, we are well disguised, and the sea is too rough for them to board us. How was she heading, Jason?" he asked.

"About sou-sou-west, sir; she's coming slap down upon us from that quarter," he added, pointing.

"Then it's time to be moving. Keep the hands on the alert, bo'sun, I'll speak to the captain."

So saying, he strode towards the cabin and disappeared.

CHAPTER CCXI.

THE PIRATE'S THREAT—DOWN IN THE LOWER HOLD.

BENITO, on entering the cabin, was surprised to find the captain and the stranger seated at the table, eyeing each other with that strange glassy stare which he had observed before.

Neither of them observed his entry; they both sat as immovable as statues, and so Benito drew back in the shade determined to watch them.

The pirate was the first to break the silence, and when he spoke his voice was hollow and husky.

"Young man," he said, "what brought you on this ship? I can see that you belong to a vessel of war?"

"A frigate—the 'Ajax.'"

"Ah!"

"Why do you start? Do you know that ship?"

"No, no," replied the pirate, confusedly; "but it is a strange thing that you should come here."

"Not at all," replied the stranger, rising; "we have been beating about here in search of a pirate, one Fernando Dominique, and I firmly suspect that you know him."

"Me!" thundered the pirate, rising and drawing a pistol from his belt; "boy, be careful how you speak; a stray word might be rewarded with a stray bullet, and look here, I don't want to kill you yet."

"Do you know me, then?"

"Know you? Aha, we know each other too well to part company yet. You have come from the 'Ajax,' you say, perhaps you can tell me what they think of the pirate, and, to be candid with you, I will inform you first of all that you are on board the Death Pirate's ship."

"There is many a worse place," replied the youth, with affected carelessness, "and her captain must be greatly respected by his Majesty when he sends a ship with three or four hundred men to invite him to his domains."

"In irons, I suppose," sneered the pirate, sarcastically.

"You are aware that there is a heavy price upon his head, and that if we were standing on board the 'Ajax,' as we stand here now, it would give the captain great pleasure, and add to the prize money of the crew."

The pirate smiled and fixed his eye on the features of the youth, and then ironically said—

"Then gain is the object for which you came here. Placed at the head of a boat's crew, I suppose you thought of boarding me by surprise? Well, such is the impetuosity of youth. But how you dared to venture on such a night is more than I can imagine."

The young sailor, in spite of the dangerous position in which he was placed was rather amused at the joke he was playing upon the captain, and to carry it still further he replied—

"Such a risk, if we had succeeded, would have well rewarded the adventurers."

"It would; but you must have been mad to attempt it. Now listen to me. You are here——"

"Not of my own free will," interrupted the youth, "but fate has so ordained it; of course it is but reasonable that I should wish to get back to my ship again."

The pirate captain laughed.

"Do you think such a thing will ever happen? Never! It will be reported that you were lost with the rest of the boat's crew, and nothing more will be thought of you. I can kill you if I like, pitch you overboard again to take your chance with the waves, and who is to know that you were picked up by, or even saw the Death Pirate?"

CHAPTER CCXII.

WILL GORDON TAKES COMMAND OF THE PIRATE SHIP.

CAPTAIN TOM DRAKE withdrew his reeking weapon from the body of the pirate captain, and motioned to Ben Barnacle to secure the sombre flag.

Then another fierce struggle ensued.

It was not for long, however.

The pirates, now their chief was slain, lost all heart, and fell into confused disarray.

Captain Tom's crew drove them back foot by foot, and followed them up with furious slaughter.

At length they crowded in a huddled mass on the forcastle, and the marines, resting their muskets on the hammock-nettings of the "Will-o'-the-Wisp," poured into the pirates such a volley that completely cowered them.

Some leapt overboard in their dismay.

Others took to the rigging.

The remainder sought shelter down below.

"No quarter!" shouted Tom Drake. "No quarter; kill every one who carries arms!"

And his orders would have been promptly carried out had it not been for Harry Vere.

"Stay," he cried to a party of mids who were about to leap down the hatchway; "who will surrender."

About a dozen of the marines threw down their arms instantly.

"We yield, we yield," was their frantic cry.

And that cry alone saved them.

There was a fierce, vengeful fire in Tom's eye.

His sword dripping red, and his pistol ready cocked smote terror to the pirates' cowardly hearts.

"Why do you pause?" he asked fiercely, of his lieutenant.

"Why do you countermand my orders?"

"Mercy," was Harry's reply; "they are beaten; they cower like so many cowardly dogs. When you are calm, captain, you will acknowledge we have shed enough blood."

Tom paused for a moment.

His features began to relax.

He began to look his former self again.

"I will spare them," he said huskily, "but only on one condition."

"What is that?" asked Harry.

"They must lay down their arms, and muster on the quarter deck."

Tom then strode away, and Harry Vere repeated the captain's stern mandate.

Without a moment's hesitation the pirates in the rigging and on the forecastle delivered up their arms to Bob and Jerry.

They then filed aft, bareheaded, on to the quarter-deck.

The marines on board of the "Will-o'-the-Wisp" covered them with their muskets, and the middies, with drawn cutlasses and loaded pistols, lined the quarter-deck.

It was quite a sight to see the fierce, grim visages, grimed with powder and smeared with blood, looking crestfallen and meek, like so many lambs.

Then another party of Tom's crew brought up those from the forecastle.

Captain Tom then came up from below.

He had been down in the cabin and perused the document that Dutch Paul had given him.

Tom Drake was calm now.

At least one would have judged him to be so from external appearances.

Whatever were his thoughts he did not betray them.

Striding on to the poop, sword in hand, he eyed the pirates narrowly.

"Stand out those," he said, "who prefer liberty to being swung up to the yard-arm."

Nearly all of the pirates stood forward.

A few hung back and demanded what conditions he was about to make.

"I will give you liberty, but you must either leave this ship or serve under my flag."

One or two began growling at this.

Some thought that it was arbitrary on his part, others that he was hasty in asking their decision without reflection.

Captain Tom, however, was in no humour for arguing points.

"Yes or no," he said, "must be your answer."

Tom drew a pistol from his sash, and cocked it as he spoke.

He was evidently fixed upon some purpose, and that purpose was not likely to be shaken.

Seeing how matters stood, the pirates soon gave way.

Only four out of the whole number were averse to the decision.

These were quickly seized, and actually hung at once by the hands of their own comrades.

This was a terrible test.

Captain Tom had done this to see how far they were in league with each other.

Then, as the bodies swung in mid air, he read the oath of allegiance, and made each man swear on the hilt of Tom's own diamond-hilted sword.

Captain Tom smiled when this was done.

Turning to Harry, he said:

"This is another commencement of our immortal reign. Overhaul the ship, and see what damage is done to her."

"But these men?"

"Let them assist in clearing away."

"Will it be safe?" asked Harry.

"Do you think we cannot trust them?"

"There is not much faith to be placed in such fellows, captain."

"And there are exceptions," replied Tom; "you begged their lives, and you must answer for their conduct."

Harry Vere shrugged his shoulders.

He did not care to take the responsibility of the behaviour of such a lawless set on himself.

"I will see to them," he said; "but if they play me false, look out."

Captain Tom had descended to the cabin again; this time accompanied by Will Norton.

"Now, sir," began our hero; "if you wish to do me a service, and would like our desperate profession, I give you an opportunity to show your zeal, and to win a name for yourself."

"I should be most happy," returned Will.

His answer was short, for he was thinking.

Wondering what it could be Tom Drake was going to communicate to him.

"I will give you command of this ship," said Tom, "and you shall have sufficient men to work her until you can run into some port and ship fresh ones."

Norton was staggered.

For the moment he thought he was dreaming.

The offering was too magnificent.

"And what do you need in return?"

"Simply what I have before asked you—to carry my flag."

Will Norton clasped his hand.

"There is nothing on earth I could wish for better."

"Then take her and do your best with her. Longton and Harvey can act as your lieutenants, and everything must go well."

One hour later the "Will-o'-the-Wisp" left the prize, and her crew with the newly elected captain gave three cheers for Captain Tom Drake as they parted company.

Our hero paced the quarter-deck for some time afterwards, buried in deep thought.

Now and again he would pause and direct his gaze athwart the horizon.

Then he would resume his nervous stride and go on muttering to himself.

At length he went below, and sent a middy to summon Harry Vere.

Zélie was busied in preparing some hot brandy when Harry went into the cabin.

Captain Tom motioned her to begone.

Then he said to his lieutenant:—

"Harry, my friend, there is a deal of work for us to do."

Vere saw that his face was pale and anxious, so he replied:

"Well, captain, only say the word, I am with you."

"I am aware of that; but I want advice most."

"Has anything happened, then?"

"Yes, the Death Pirate is at work."

"Ah!" ejaculated Harry.

"It's true; listen to this."

Tom took from his bosom the packet given to him by Dutch Paul.

It ran thus:

"That accursed fiend, the Death Pirate, is again at his old work. He has been seen hovering about the Thames, and I have every reason to fear he has abducted your darling Minnie! If so, the villain has taken her to his old haunt, and by this time, after being baffled so often before, may have forced her by threats or some horrible torture to submit to his horrid proposals.

"If so, let your vengeance be sure and swift.

"Submit him to the terrible torture of the Three Crosses and the Bloody Hand.

"My information is the more reliable as I have seen one of his crew—a deserter—and his words go greatly towards confirming my suspicions. Enclosed you will find a true map with the bearings, distances, &c. that lead to his horrid den; also a chart of the Spanish Main, and all the islands infested by those fiendish marauders of the sea."

When Tom had finished this astounding epistle Harry Vere struck the table with the hilt of his dirk.

Then he exclaimed, in a tone of bitterness—

"I would this were as near to his black heart as it is to my hand, Tom."

"You would strike home?"

"That would I."

Then he added, after a moment's deep silence on the part of both—

"Dutch Paul, I believe, was on some important mission of his own. I, too, have heard a strange story from one of Blackbeard's crew."

"Indeed!"

"I have."

"Does it concern us?"

Tom took a deep draught of the steaming liquid, and Harry followed his example.

Harry then went on.

"His version is this:—

"Not many days since Blackbeard boarded a Spanish merchantman, and discovered on board of her two persons well known to him. The one answers exactly to the description of Black Bill, and the other was a female whom no one could make out."

Tom listened in feverish excitement, and then interrupted him.

"It could not be Jenny or Minnie?"

"No; but he left her on the island we visited, and I have no doubt by that that Blackbeard meant her some mischief."

"This is strange news, Harry — very, very strange."

"But it explains in some way the mystery of the you discovered in the hut."

"And the wounded man?"

"It might, as she said, have been her father."

"Or ——'

"Black Bill you would suggest, Tom; no, no; that Bill, so the man avers, was lynched for setting fire to the pirate ship, and his body was thrown overboard."

"Then the mystery grows with the recital, Harry? How did Black Bill get on board the Spaniard?"

"He was one of the crew; the man knows no more than this."

"Then we will steer back to the island again at once, and ascertain for ourselves the truth; let the sails be trimmed and the ship's course altered."

Harry Vere acquiesced in this.

Finishing his liquor, he tripped lightly on deck.

Then there was a rattling of cordage and blocks; the sails flickered, and the "Will-o'-the-Wisp" fell over on the other tack, heading for the island they had last left.

There was a stiff breeze, and nothing of importance occurred until the island was sighted, and the "Will-o'-the-Wisp" entered the bay. Captain Tom took his own boat's crew, and landed on a different part of the island to the former occasion.

The coast at this point was bold and rocky, which Tom calculated would allow him to land without discovery by those on shore.

Tom, all the better to effect his purpose, took with him only a herculean black, and one that Tom intended to send forward as a spy, so that he himself might not be seen.

The Black Sancho, as he was named, was a fellow Tom had liberated from the hold of a slaver, and was frightfully devoted to our hero, so that he had no fear of treachery from him.

As they walked along the beach, however, and were seeking a pathway through the cliff, Sancho gave a startled cry, and Tom heard his pistol click.

"Stand back, captain. Look out!" cried Sancho.

Tom raised his eyes, and immediately sprang back.

He was barely in time.

A stone of prodigious weight was dislodged from the rock above him, and fell crashing on the sands close to our hero's feet.

Sancho's cry had saved his life.

The stone by its dislodgment revealed the sinister features of Black Bill.

Our hero was astonished, but only momentarily.

"Seize the scoundrel!" he cried, as Sancho's pistol bullet struck harmless on the rock.

Tom, followed closely by Sancho, sprang up the jagged projection, but too late to seize the villain, who, with a cry of horror, effected his escape.

The pair nevertheless followed in pursuit.

But Blackbeard evaded their vigilance for some time, until he was at length hauled out by the hair of the head from a hole into which he had squeezed his burly form.

"You shall die for this," said Tom, his bright eyes flashing with indignation at the thought of the cowardly deed.

Then he sounded a signal, which was quick answered by his boat's crew, and the ex-smugg gagged and bound, was taken down to the beach

Then Captain Tom headed a party to seek for girl, but after an hour's fruitless search, and be overtaken by night, they returned to the "Will-the-Wisp."

Black Bill stubbornly refused to give any account of himself or the girl; in fact as he had let his thick, stubby beard grow, which had been for some months shaved off, he hoped to avoid recognition.

But Captain Tom was not likely to be so easily deceived.

There was no mistaking the villainous visage in any country or clime, after it had once been seen.

Tom's only perplexity now was how to punish the bloodthirsty ruffian adequately to his crime.

The black-muzzled villain cowered and scowled under the gaze of our gallant hero.

There seemed now no chance of the ex-smuggler and traitor evading his just doom.

Black Bill did not entirely give way to despair.

If they would give him time he doubted not that the arch fiend that had hitherto watched over him and spared him to wreak fresh villainy, would spare him a little longer.

"And," he muttered to himself with a curse, "if it be true that the devil takes care of his own, he will surely not desert me now."

"At least," he thought, "I will place confidence in him, for as surely as he has aided me so far, and that he will claim me for his own some day, so surely will he assist me in the present."

With this consolation, poor as it was, and faint as it might seem to many, the guilty wretch was heavily ironed and placed in the lowermost hold with the rats.

There were plenty of them, too.

The hold was literally swarming.

This was considered a good sign, and possibly accounted in a great measure for Tom not losing any of his crew by desertion.

At all events, Black Bill found it anything but a comfortable abode.

He could see the eyes come up and glare at him through the darkness.

Occasionally, one more daring than the rest, would pounce on him and make its sharp teeth penetrate Bill's garments and flesh.

Truth to tell, these said rats were the scavengers of Dr. Shrike.

The lower hold was just beneath the cock pit, and down a small opening that admitted air Jacob often got rid of the pieces of flesh that came from the doctor's private dissecting room.

Before Bill had long been there he had many such relics showered down upon him.

Often would he be awakened from his transitory dreams by the cold, clammy pieces, the doctor's trophies of the late engagement, dropping upon his upturned face.

This was the greatest torture perhaps that the villain could endure.

Though ever ready to take life, yet he shuddered at anything pertaining to a corpse.

A dead man's shroud would have terrified him into fits.

The fighting of the rats as they disputed with each other; even the most putrid morsel struck a chill to the ex smuggler's stony heart, and made the cold beads of sweat ooze from his icy brow.

Never, perhaps, in the course of his miserable life had Black Bill endured so much agony of mind.

He could sleep but seldom.

In fact, only when nature was thoroughly exhausted.

But we must leave him for awhile.

Leave him to reconcile himself to the horrible revels of his still more horrible companions, and to the dull splash of the sea as it smote suddenly the stout oaken sides of the vessel.

Captain Tom Drake shaped his course according to that indicated by the chart; but in mid ocean his ship struck upon a sunken reef, which compelled him to bear down on an island, just visible on his lee, to repair.

The leak was so great that all pumps had to be worked, and all hands had to use their utmost endeavours to keep the ship from sinking.

But the bold buccaneers put forth their strength, and united all their efforts, to keep the "Will-o'-the-Wisp" free from water.

In this predicament none thought of the prisoner until Jerry, who was sent down to ascertain the locality of the leak, came rushing on deck with his hair standing on end.

"What's the matter?" exclaimed Bob Hauler, who was nearly knocked over by Jerry in his impetuous flight up the hatchway. "Do you mean to capsize a fellow, you lubberly swab?"

"Capsize the de-devil!" gasped Jerry Mizzen, almost petrified with terror; "and he's down below, or my name's not Jerry."

"The deuce he is," echoed Bob, sharing his comrade's alarm; "did you see him?"

"I did, and no gammon, Bob; give me a toothful of rum, or I shall faint."

Bob began to suspect something now.

Bob had a bottle of the favourite beverage stowed in the breast of his shirt.

"No—no, Jerry," he said, winking slyly; "you don't catch me so easy as that. If you want extra rum get it by fair, honest means the same as I do."

"No matter how you get it," replied Jerry, "I know you have some about you. I can smell it. S'welp my Blue Peter, what a fright the old gentleman gave me."

"It's a pity he didn't nab you right out," retorted Bob, who now firmly believed that Jerry had witnessed his purloining of the rum. "You'd do well together; the pair of you would always be dry."

"Not if we had a bottle between us, mate," said Jerry, coaxingly.

"It would always be empty," sneered Bob.

"That would be our misfortune and no crime, Bob —you know," urged Jerry.

"It is your misfortune now," Bob retorted, "and you would like to be criminally guilty of emptying mine. There is no fear of you ever requiring to be pumped out."

"I might some day, Bob; and you wouldn't like to see a chum go down with his pumps choked."

Bob could not resist this appealing thrust.

"Here you are," he said, handing Jerry the precious treasure. "Now, then, steady, don't pump it too dry."

Jerry was too much engaged to answer him.

He glued his lips to the neck of the bottle, and would have drained it dry at once.

Bob snatched it from him, however, just in time to rescue about half of its contents.

"You thirsty swab," growled Hauler. "You'd have mopped it all up at once, bad luck to you; but what about the devil?"

"He's down below, Bob, as safe as needles; but I'm not going to swear to please you. Go down and see, if you're not frightened."

"It 'ud take a dozen such sights to frighten me," answered Bob, as he swallowed the rum and tossed the empty bottle into the sea.

"Then down you go," blustered Jerry; "you know the old gentleman better than I do; you've seen him oftener."

Bob and Jerry were now getting excited.

They might have got to blows had not their loud talking attracted the notice of Ben Barnacle.

"What's the row about now, between you two mummies' in ps?" he asked, in a stentorian voice. "Is this a time to be quarrelling, and the ship sinking all the while?"

"It's all through him," Jerry answered, mimicing a tone of meekness which he was far from feeling.

"All through whom?" queried Ben. "You, Hauler," he added, turning fierce on that personage.

"No, it's old Nick, he means; he's seen him, so he sez."

TOM DRAKE KNELT BY THE BLOCK.

"An I maintain it. I saw him with ny own eyes and nobody else's "

"Avast, there! Belay your slack line at that; you have p yed out enough to suit me."

"But not enough to suit me." was Jerry's answer. "I wish you had hold of him, or he had hold of you. Feeling, they say, is the real truth, and perhaps you'd believe me then."

"What do you mean? Where's the lantern?" queried Ben.

"Down below; he pulled it out of my hand," Jerry said.

Ben could not endure any more of this.

"Stand aside!" he bellowed, and in an instant, rushed below, where to his astonishment, he heard the hideous noise of the prisoner, who was up to his neck, almost, in water in the lower hold.

The Vampyre was the only one that his cries had reached, as all the rest of the crew were engaged on deck, but he would not give h ms cxxur nor raise an alarm, as he thought, if he kept quiet, Bill's body would supply him with a very good subject

And he was partly right.

In fact, one might say he was not at all wrong. For what with the rolling of the ship, the stench of the bilge-water, and the horror of the rats swimming about, Bill was almost as good as dead.

When he was rescued, it took them some time to bring him to.

Doctor Shrike had to resort to bleeding and a

87

variety of other different operations, in which he prided himself as well-skilled.

Ben Barnacle had quite a trouble to prevent the old Vampyre from going too far.

He would have settled Bill, to a certainty, had he been allowed his own way.

At all events, thanks to an iron constitution, and perhaps a little assistance from the genius that had always aided him in his hour of danger, Black Bill, once more saw the light and began to breathe more freely.

Still the leak could not be found and the noble vessel had to be oerched on the softest bed of sand Tom could select when they reached the island.

This island, like the one they had previously visited, bore no outward or visible sign of being inhabited.

Flocks of birds of various coloured plumage, took to flight as the sails flapped and clattered against the masts.

Shoals of fish of different hues, even to the hungry ground shark, darted away from the vessel's keel as it clove its way through the shallow water.

But Captain Tom did not take so much heed of all this.

There was one little object that seemed solely to engross his interest.

It was a strange object to be there, too.

A boat half-full of water jammed between two rocks of coral.

It was of English build, too.

Perhaps from some wreck.

Or how could it have come there?

As soon as Tom had seen to the necessary arrangements for rendering his ship safe, he sprang ashore to examine it.

There was no name upon it, but a strange device carved upon the stern.

From this little episode alone Tom could guess that that boat once belonged to the famous Blackbeard.

But how came it there?

Why had it been left?

A boat, and of English build more especially, was in those parts, a treasure not to be overlooked or scouted at.

Tom thought of all this, and it set his brain a wondering.

There was only one answer he could give to the query.

It was that some of Blackbeard's men had deserted and stolen the boat, which, being of no further use to them, they had deserted.

But if this were the case, the men must still be on the island; and so he was determined to explore it on the first opportunity.

He deferred the exploration only till the next day.

Captain Tom took with him four or five hands, as he did not know what might occur, and what danger was to be met with in this strange, weird place.

The island was thickly wooded, and was plentifully supplied with fruit of various kinds, but there was no signs of any town, village, or even a settlement.

After travelling about for a long while and having their clothes torn almost to shreds, they were about to give up in despair, when the report of a gun and the clamouring of angry voices startled them.

The noise seemed to come from a deep wood, studded so thickly with briars and prickly pears, that they could scarcely force a way through.

The controversy seemed to be kept up in a sort of jargon, a mixture of broken English and bad Spanish.

Tom Drake, however, could glean enough from the mixture of the two languages to learn that a female was the cause of the contention.

This he at once surmise proceeded from the runaways of Blackbeard's crew.

They pushed gently forward, making as little noise as possible.

However, they were doomed to disappointment and surprise.

Through an opening in the brushwood, and in a small clearing in the forest, they saw a female with her arms behind her, apparently bound to a tree, and two individuals quarrelling for her possession.

The one was a tall, powerful Indian, attired in the scanty raiment most suited to the climate, and the other was a European or American, dressed somewhat similar to a backwoodsman or a trapper.

The former was standing with his back to the girl, wielding a huge tomahawk, and the latter was defending himself with the butt end of his clubbed rifle.

Such were their respective positions when Tom's party discovered them.

From what cause or from whom the quarrel first proceeded Tom was left to his own conjecture, but a closer scrutiny of the girl assured him that it was the female he had seen on the other island.

This perhaps partly accounted for the boat.

Blackbeard had left three of the pirates on the island to look after his fair charge during his absence but of them no trace had been visible after the first day of their landing.

Of course Captain Tom did not know of all this; he did not know of the man being hurled into the pool by Black Bill, but we may venture to suggest that the ex-smuggler had some knowledge of the whereabouts of the other two had he chosen to disclose it.

The truth was that Black Bill one morning having come upon them in a state of drunkenness, having emptied a small keg of raw rum during their short stay on shore, the ex-smuggler, for reasons that need no explaining, thrust his knife into the heart of each of them, and thus rid himself of two neighbours that might have proved very troublesome.

Thus left alone with the lady on the island, of which he was the sole possessor, he looked upon her as his property by right, and, having forgotten the girl's kindness to him in the hour of his peril, began to tyrannise over her, so that she escaped from him in the boat by which the pirates had reached the shore.

The boat, then at the mercy of the wind and current, drifted to where our hero had found it, and this, though our hero was as yet ignorant of the fact, was the cause of its being found in its present disabled and deserted state.

But this is getting ahead of our story.

Captain Tom Drake was at his wit's end to account for the presence of the two men of opposite colour and nationality, though he partially surmised how the girl had got there.

He was still pressing his way gently forward through the brushwood, making but slow headway, owing to the enlargement of the briars, when the conflict between the two men grew more desperate.

The Indian wielded his huge weapon with terrible force and precision, giving the white man no chance of a blow, and keeping him in full and desperate play to guard himself from his opponent's terrible onslaught.

The blade of the tomahawk fell with a loud clatter on the barrel of the trapper's rifle, and the forest rang again with the clang of their angry voices and the clash of the steel.

Once the trapper broke in through the wary Indian's blows and nearly dealt him a blow which must have smashed his skull, even had it been of the more than ordinary thickness, for which the Indian race is renowned.

But the Indian came up quickly to the attack again.

There was a wound upon his shoulder, as though caused by the rifle bullet of his opponent, and this perhaps was the cause of the Indian not settling the difference between them sooner.

The trapper, though a much smaller man, seemed, too to possess a wonderful sinewy strength.

He was well skilled, too, in his own particular mode of warfare, for he made the Indian wince, and brought the big beads of sweat out of the Indian's copper skin.

As for himself, he was reeking with moisture, showing that his efforts, almost superhuman, were telling upon him fast.

Tom and his companions had they chosen might have dashed forward and ended the terrible fray, but they seemed as it were fascinated with the grand display of courage and skill, and in fact a spell seemed to hold them back and prevent them using that little extra exertion it needed.

But this kind of warfare could not last long.

Both men were growing weaker and weaker.

The Indian's blows were aimed more irregular and with less force.

The trapper's guard was becoming less steady, and was more easily broken down.

At length the tall Indian, as if by a powerful effort of nature, drew his form erect.

His broad chest expanded and took in a full breath.

Then his sinewy muscles seemed girded together with iron bands, and he made a terrific lunge.

The trapper saw what was coming, but, either from a laxity of strength or a lack of energy, probably, owing to the lightning rapidity by which it was done, could not prepare his guard in time, and the tomahawk descended, splitting him from head to chine.

There was but one appalling shriek as the skull crashed and with that shriek the spirit of the trapper was borne away from the body for ever.

Even the Indian seemed paralyzed with horror at the terrible deed he had committed, as he gazed in silent awe upon the mutilation and devastation his hand had caused.

"Peace be to his soul," Tom heard him mutter as he bowed his head in solemn reverence and dropped the gory weapon to the ground.

Then sank down on the earth himself, utterly exhausted.

Up to this time the terrified girl had remained mute and motionless.

Scarcely a muscle of her features had moved.

She was rooted in absolute horror at the fierce battle she had witnessed.

Her lips bloodless.

Her eyes dilated.

Her form statuesque and marble-like.

Even her hair did not appear to wave in the least in the chilling evening air.

But when the fatal deed was done.

When the dull crash had smitten upon her ear.

And when the trapper fell with that unearthly and despairing cry, the blood seemed to once more course through her veins.

She seemed as though suddenly changed from marble into life.

It was a terrible moment to all who witnessed that sight.

It was enough to have appalled the stoutest heart.

And when the young girl's lips parted and sent forth a cry that seemed to rend the very heavens, Tom Drake and his party broke away from the spell, and cleft their way through the thorny brambles with their cutlasses.

They were but two minutes in reaching the spot.

And then Captain Tom, severed the girl's bonds and caught her in his arms just as she was about to fall swooning to the ground.

CHAPTER CCXIII.

THE DEATH PIRATE'S THREAT—THE ABDUCTION OF MINNIE ATHERTON.

DICK DAWSON was astounded at the Death Pirate's decision.

He had threatened to murder him in cold blood.

He knew that there was some reason for the pirate wishing to get rid of him, but there was a pall that hung over that mystery that had never been removed.

That he belonged to the "Ajax," a frigate purposely fitted out for pirate hunting and scouring the seas, could not be the only cause of the Death Pirate's vindictiveness.

There was something more than that.

True her commander, Captain Bluster, was armed with fifty warrants of arrest

Conspicuous amongst them was the name of Captain Tom Drake's vessel, and any known ship that had served or still served under his flag.

The English Government had not forgotten the great battle.

They had not wiped from their memory the great loss they sustained on that occasion.

They were determined as soon as the opportunity offered to be revenged for the humiliation of their ships, though it was brought on them by themselves and the few meddling myrmidons around them.

But the Death Pirate hated the 'Will-o'-the-Wisp" and its commander, as deadly as he did any government cruiser.

He was an enemy to all and everyone, and every man's hand was raised in anger against him.

All this Dick knew, but there was one thing, and it was a most unpleasant fact—his arm was not powerful enough to cope with the Death Pirate single-handed.

It would be simply throwing away his young life in a forlorn hope, so he mustered courage and strength and prepared for the very worst.

There was but one alternative to save his life, and that was to feign obedience to the Death Pirate.

To pretend to yield and lie with his hideous views.

And so by dissembling he hoped to live on until an opportunity offered for his escaping.

It was not a cheerful prospect for a brave heart such as Dick's.

However, he was resolved to bear it for the present.

To take the oath of allegiance to a man he thoroughly abhorred.

To enter upon a life at which his young heart recoiled.

In a word, to do that which would make him look with hatred even upon himself.

And so he consented.

He took the oath that made him a pirate of the sea

He vowed the vow that bound him to take the life of even his own parent and dearest of kin.

To spare no one.

Old and young.

Ugly and beautiful.

All were to share the same fate alike.

He looked a bold and handsome fellow enough in the costly uniform the pirate supplied him with.

But then he feared to look into his own heart.

He shuddered to think how he would look in their gaudy attire hanging at the yard-arm.

Then he would endeavour for a time to banish

these horrible thoughts from his mind but then they recurred to him again and again, and he would pray secretly for Heaven to lend him strength to bear up against the terrible ordeal.

And so a week passed.

A week of the most horrible suspense.

For he knew not at what moment some ill-fated ship might have in sight, and he would be compelled to take the life of his fellow-creatures in cold blood.

And so the pirate ship sailed on, her captain evidently bent on no settled purpose.

Strange to say, he did not even sail in the track which the laden merchantmen were supposed to take.

He steered wide, as it were, evading not only the men-of-war, but also the ships that he might have taken and made an easy prey.

And so it was, until one dark night, when Dick was summoned to the captain's presence.

"Well, Dick," said he, still assuming the terrible mask, which he never suffered to reveal his features in the presence of any one; "I am glad to see you have so far obeyed my commands, and reverenced the laws of my ship. I have now to command you on a different kind of business to that you have hitherto been used to."

Dick felt terribly uneasy.

He had no doubt that the Death Pirate was about to exact something from him, the very refusal of which would call upon him his displeasure, and perhaps give him a pretext for putting him to death.

The pirate, through the eyes of his terrible mask, eyed him narrowly, and seemed to read in those youthful features what was passing in the boy's mind.

"Listen," he said, in a voice that was meant to be suave and encouraging, but sounded through the mask harsh, grating, and unearthly. "I wish you to put on the uniform you wore when you came on board; I want you to go ashore on particular duty."

The pirate chief placed great emphasis on the words.

He seemed to want to fully impress upon the boy that he would win his favour by complying readily, and that if he refused his doom would be sealed.

"You will have to land blindfolded," he went on. "You will then be led to a mansion, a certain window of which will then be pointed out to you, and a balcony by which you can effect an entrance into the chamber.

"A password that will gain you admittance to that chamber will be given you at a proper moment, and the occupant of that room, a young lady, must by you be led to the foot of the garden at the back of the mansion, where you will find some one awaiting her."

Dick trembled slightly, and a blush for a moment suffused his cheek.

With a powerful effort, however, Dick pressed back the feeling, and endeavoured to listen calmly to the voice of his commander.

Dick saw at once through the foul plot, and his imagination was racked to think who that victim was to be.

Dick, however, still maintaining his composure, was resolved to carry out the deceit.

He was determined when the time came to betray the would-be abductor.

The pirate continued—

"Do not think to deceive me or hang back, but remember that every bush, every tree nook, or cranny will contain one of my spies, and at the least sign of you swerving or playing me false, or even failing to succeed where success is so certain I will have you put to a death more horrible than you can conceive, and more torturing than even the power of darkness could inflict upon you."

The Death Pirate's threat had a wonderful effect on young Dick.

At one time he felt he would openly refuse the pirate's power, and spurn his cruel mandate.

But then he would not serve the fair victim nor render any service to himself by so doing; his better plan would be to encourage the deceit and leave the rest to providence.

At the midnight hour the vessel was hove silently to.

A boat was noiselessly lowered from the davits.

And all that the pirate had planned was carried out, even to the pointing of the balcony and the manner in which it was to be ascended.

This was all accomplished in darkness and silence.

All that broke the stillness was now and then an ominous click of the pistol carried by his conductor.

At length the guide halted and whispered, "Now away."

And then Dick fancied he could hear somewhere in the vicinity the tramp of military footsteps.

Yet he knew not where he was.

With a heavy heart, however, he obeyed mechanically his mysterious guide.

He sprang up the creeping ivy, and gained the balcony.

Then, repeating the mysterious password given by his guide, he waited until a milk-white hand, within the window, made a sign that he was heard.

Then presently the casement was opened, and Dick was held for a moment in the warm and loving embrace of a girl who no doubt mistook him for one who had been absent some time.

Then with an adroit ease that very much astonished Dick the fair form, whose face he could not recognise in the thick gloom, glided as it were from the balcony to the ground, and Dick swiftly followed.

Dick glanced timidly around.

He knew that the dark shadows that seemed to form a portion of the shrubbery around were the forms of the spies placed so as to watch his actions, and so he glided almost in a state of unconsciousness in the direction indicated by the Death Pirate.

As they reached the end of the garden the dark forms that had followed and closed in upon them, aided by the shrubbery, seized both Dick and the fair girl, and as she gave a sort of half smothered cry, Dick recognised the voice of Minnie Altherton.

Dick trembled for the poor girl's fate as he thought of the horrors she would endure, now fairly in the power of the dreaded Death Pirate.

CHAPTER CCXIV.

THE DEATH PIRATE SAILS FOR HIS RENDEZVOUS— DICK IN THE PIRATE'S HOLD—CHASED BY A MAN-OF-WAR.

THERE was great consternation in the mansion at Purfleet when the abduction of Minnie was discovered.

An alarm was instantly given to the garrison stationed at the picturesque little village hard by.

A search was quickly instituted, but, though traces of many footmarks were found in the extensive grounds and shrubs, and flowers were trampled down, yet the Death Pirate had effected his purpose so well that there was no fear of his being overtaken.

His swift vessel was well out to sea before a cruiser could be sent in chase of her, though a smart Government cutter was sent on to the Nore with a dispatch to the admiral of the fleet then lying there ready for a cruise.

With considerable forethought the brave Dick Dawson had scribbled a few hasty lines on the ivory handle of a broken dirk and left it on the balcony.

This was all he could do, and it served the purpose of informing Mrs Drake and Jenny Vere that the Death Pirate was the abductor of Minnie.

And so the dread pirate sailed on, chuckling in fiendish triumph to himself as he crowded on all sail night and day, and sailed for the West Indian Isles.

With considerable tact the foul fiend evaded, as before, the many vessels that were scouring the seas in search of him, and put to the best use every slant of wind that favoured him.

A Dutch sloop-of-war and a Spanish galleon, however, that fell by accident in his way he plundered and burnt, having first mutilated and murdered the crews for the edification of his own bloodthirsty followers, and especially the black executioner.

During the performance of the terrible orgie, Dick by some means assisted four of the galleon's crew to escape in a boat, and this brought down on him the pirate's vengeful ire.

He would have slain him there and then, only that the Death Pirate reserved him for a worse fate; he considered that his crime was befitting a more lingering death.

Dick, bold as he was, could not help shuddering at the fierce pirate's oaths, as the boat with the fugitives grew smaller and smaller, and eventually disappeared in the darkness of night.

The plucky youth was stripped to his trousers and shirt and thrust into the lazarette, a narrow hold in the after run of the ship, under the after cabin

He was loaded with a heavy chain, which added considerably to the fiendish torture of his imprisonment, which was in itself enough to break down the proudest spirit and make the prisoner long for death in any form.

Owing to the narrow build of the vessel Dick's prison in the after run was such that he could neither lay down nor stand in it; borne down by the weight of the chain, he was crouched in a huddled heap, rolling from side to side with the motion of the ship.

There he was left groaning, his skin bruised and grazed as it ground against the hard, damp planking that lined the stifling hold.

To Minnie Atherton, however, the pirate was extremely kind in his way.

The best of everything on board—and the Death Pirate was an epicure for one of his horrible calling —she could have; her cabin was most sumptuously and fastidiously arranged and furnished, and a small slave page boy was always ready at her slightest call.

There was fruit, too, in plenty, for the Spanish galleon was not long from port, and costly jewels and fabrics, of which the proud Spaniards, in those days, boasted themselves the master.

* * *

It was at early dawn that the blue outlines of the islands to which they were bound were sighted by the pirate.

Almost at the same moment, too, as he finished dressing, and was adjusting his terrible mask, the lieutenant shouted down a pipe, communicating from the cabin to the deck, that a vessel, a strange sort of sail, was bearing towards them.

"It's a man-of-war, too," said the officer, as the Pirate captain came up the companion-hatch.

"Is it? Then curse her," was the Death Pirate's fierce reply.

He had not been on deck many moments, when his stern voice set his motley crew all in motion.

The drowsy watch was turned up, and all was activity and bustle in an instant.

This was just the time when he most wished to be unmolested, for he was close to his rendezvous, and he had anticipated landing without molestation.

He shouted out wildly for more sail to be made— darting hither and thither, cursing cuffing, and imparting to the pirates some of his own energy.

Next he seized a spy-glass and ran up to the mast-head, and took a long look at the strange ship now fast approaching.

What he saw was by no means re-assuring.

The breeze had caught the vessel now, and drifted away all the haze, so that there was a clear view of the sea right to horizon.

About twelve miles off on his port-beam, he saw a large square-rigged vessel coming right down on him.

She was under full sail, and her appearance and size proclaimed her a man-of-war—a large frigate.

Sailing as she was, right before the wind, and heading direct for the pirate, in an hour or so at the outside she would be within easy range, unless he could by altering his course escape her.

But the pirate was beating nearly due east, parallel to the land and lines of rocks and reefs, distant only a little more than a quarter of a knot.

The land itself was scarcely more than a mile distant, so close had he kept in.

Under the circumstances, it would seem that the Death Pirate was caught in a trap.

He could not put her helm up and try her speed at a stern chase, for there was the land close on her lee.

It was useless to turn back, for the frigate would by altering her course slightly, so as to steer across her bows, get within range in less than an hour.

To keep on ahead seemed open to the same objection; but nevertheless it was ahead the pirate looked, scanning minutely and carefully the distant landmarks, and looking eagerly among the rocks and reefs for openings and channels.

After five minutes thus spent he came down.

All possible sail had been made on the vessel.

Meanwhile, the strange vessel, steering a course direct for the pirate, bore down at the rate of at least eight miles an hour.

" I should have thought that the cursed Britishers would have had enough to do in chasing the French cruisers that are playing such havoc with their commerce to interfere with us. Confound them!" the Death Pirate muttered.

"That's just it," growled he. "They take us for a rebel privateer, trying to make into Havannah."

"But by law they've no right to attack us within three miles of the shore."

"Bah! what do they care for law? It's our own courage and good fortune we must depend on. If I can only get her inside the reef, I'll land the girls, though I lose the ship."

"How?" asked his lieutenant, who had listened to his soliloquy.

"I'll run her full butt ashore. They can't follow us with the frigate, for she draws too much water."

"But they may follow with the boats?"

"They can't get alongside with the boats before I've got the girls out. If it comes to a finish, I'll stop them with our long friend here."

As he spoke he pointed to the pivot gun, still covered up with tarpaulin.

The breeze freshened considerably; and now the fast clipper ship glided along at the rate of some eleven knots.

Her great speed did not seem to have been sufficiently allowed for by the pursuing frigate, for whereas she was at one time broad abeam and steering right across the bows, she had dropped back on the quarter, and was forced to haul her to wind, and steer a course more nearly parallel to that of the chase.

This was an advantage for the latter, but not so great a one as it might have been had there been more sea-room.

It was certain that, keeping on their respective courses at the same rate of speed, in the course of half-an-hour at latest the frigate would be within easy range.

Minutes slipped on, and the pirate gliding through the water like a witch, might have distanced her pursuer with ease could she have made more of a stern chase of it by keeping away.

But the dangerous rocks on her lee, quite close, sometimes so near that a biscuit might have been tossed into the breakers, prevented that; it was even necessary to haul her wind a little so as to get a better offing.

All this while the Death Pirate was in the foretop, anxiously scrutinising the rocks and reefs ahead, which at a little distance seemed to form a complete line of barrier, but on getting up to them resolved themselves into isolated rocks and patches, the sea breaking furiously over all.

Between these various rocks and clusters of rocks, which now made a belt nearly a quarter of a mile wide, running parallel with the shore, there were channels and patches of deep water.

But for a vessel to seek a passage through these thickly-strewn dangers would be a work of desperate peril.

It would have been a delicate operation even for a boat.

Nevertheless, having made up his mind that this was his only chance of saving his cargo of slaves, the Death Pirate determined to risk it.

On sped the two vessels—partner and pursued—the frigate momentarily drawing nearer to the pirate.

"By the sandals of San Antonio!" cried he, shutting up the glass with a bang, "I see the crab passage."

"The crab passage!" exclaimed the luff; "you would never mean to take her through that, under sail, and chased!"

"By all the saints, I do, though; I can do it, and she shall do it, or leave her ribs on the rocks."

"Bang."

A puff of white smoke from the bow of the chase told whence the report had come.

At the same moment the British flag was run up to the breeze.

"Show our ensign—the Spanish flag," said the Death Pirate giving his lieutenant a meaning glance. "In a quarter-hour more we ought to be nearly safe."

The Spanish flag was hoisted in reply, but beyond this no notice was taken of the gun, which from a man-of-war always means "heave-to."

After an interval of a couple of minutes another puff of white smoke belched forth from the bows of the frigate.

This time it was followed by the roar of a round shot as well as the report, which was much sharper and harder.

The cannon ball pitched into the water right astern of the pirate, and so close as actually to throw the spray over the taffrail.

"That's a pretty strong hint," said the pirate, coolly. "I suppose for politeness' sake we must at all events pretend to take notice of it."

"If we don't, they'll plump the next one into us, I reckon," the lieutenant said.

"All hands shorten sail," said the captain, "clew up the topsails take in the square foresail, mizen

gaff topsail, and flying jib. Bear a hand, lads," he hoarsely thundered.

This was to the crew, and the Death Pirate of course spoke in Spanish, or rather a bastard tongue between Mexican, Indian, and Spanish.

"Run you forward and get the light sails in," he said to an officer, "I'll take the helm a bit. Bear a hand."

The frigate seemed for a time astonished at seeing the chase take in sail, and that rapidly.

Of course she could have no idea of the manœuvre the Death Pirate contemplated, and her lighter sails were also taken in, as it seemed quite certain that in a very few minutes she would be close up with the slaver.

The instant the light sails were taken in and secured, the Death Pirate placed the mate at the wheel, and, seizing the speaking trumpet, prepared to carry out his desperate attempt.

"All hands wear ship, stand by the jib, the mainsail, and foresail. Hard down with the helm."

Answering to her helm, the head of the pirate ship came sweeping round to the north, and in half a minute her prow was pointed right to the rocks, and the wind right aft.

"Starboard! starboard!" cried the captain, his eyes firmly fixed on a large rock with a conical peak, against the base of which the sea beat furiously, sending the spray yards off.

"Steady! So."

The vessel's head was now all but pointed direct for this rock.

On her present course, she must shave it with her larboard bow, if she did not absolutely strike on it.

The relative positions of the frigate and the pirate were now entirely changed.

The latter was at this time heading shoreward, and the frigate, in place of being a little abaft her larboard beam, was now on her starboard quarter.

The pirate ship was under full sail again, and each moment now took her further from her pursuer.

As for the frigate, she backed her main-yard, and lay as though her commander was mystified by this sudden and strange manœuvre on the part of the pirates.

It seemed as though the latter were about to rush headlong on to the rocks, for at a little distance off no channel could be seen, nothing but a belt of broken and stormy white water.

Every moment, every fathom gained, was of vital importance to the pirate, and under full sail she dashed amidst the dangerous rocks and reefs.

"Ain't I steering too close to that big rock, captain?" asked the helmsman.

"That big rock's our safety. There's deep water within ten feet of it" replied the Death Pirate, emphatically. "Steady! So. That will do."

The next minute the vessel actually plunged amongst the broken water, so close to the rock, that it seemed a man might have jumped on to it.

"Port your helm a little. So. That will do. Steady!"

A minute or two she went ahead, and then the Death Pirate shouted:—

"Hard-a-port!"

As the vessel answered to her helm, her starboard bow absolutely scraped against a half-sunken reef.

The pirates held their breath, half fearing to hear and feel the fatal bump which should tell that the ship had struck.

But she escaped with a graze only, and slid along into smooth water to meet another and larger rock right ahead.

This was avoided by bringing her right up in the wind on the port tack, when once more she was kept away, and stood direct for the shore again.

The slaver had by this time pass.d safely through more than half the breadth of the dangerous belt of rocks and sunken reefs.

It was now the frigate began to understand the daring manœuvre.

Now when it was almost too late, and her prize was about to escape from her grasp—for, of course, it was out of the question for so large a vessel to venture on so dangerous an example.

Bang—bang—bang—went her guns—the whole of her starboard broadside—and in an instant the roar of the round shot was heard in the air all around.

It hurtled and whistled and shrieked in a terrible manner, and the mate declared that he actually felt the wind of some of the cannon balls.

Nevertheless, not one shot of the whole broadside crashed either hull or rigging, and the pirate sped swiftly on, and was close to the open water.

The frigate was in fact astern now, and every fathom she went took her of course further away.

Before the frigate could reload or tack to present the other broadside, the chase would certainly have passed through all the dangerous rocks, and be in a fair way of escape.

True, she would be within range for a minute or so, perhaps, but it was hardly likely she would receive more than a chance shot or two, and the pirate was prepared to take the risk of that.

"Santissima Trinidada!" he cried with blasphemous glee, as the swift cutter shot into the clear water between the rocks and the land, "we have escaped—the saints and angels have befriended us."

The Death Pirate through his ghastly mask grinned at the idea of himself and the crew having been befriended by saints and angels.

"I was thinking whether it might not have been the foul fiend who has done us a good turn," his lieutenant remarked, with grim humour; "then no longer will we insult him by calling him the foul fiend. Steward, bring up a bottle of Malaga and glasses."

They were brought, and the Death Pirate, filling his own glass and that of his mate, shouted with a defiant laugh—

"Here's health and success to the Prince of the Infernal Regions—our good friend henceforth will we call him, not the foul but the fair fiend!"

And with that remark the pirate ship glided into smooth water, leaving all rocks and reefs behind her.

Scarcely had this defiant toast been drank than again was heard the dull boom of cannon, and a few seconds afterwards great splashes and jets of water, shot aloft a few fathoms from the vessel, told that the British had not yet finished with their amiable attentions.

"Blaze away, my boys," cried the pirate captain, triumphantly; "you may take a spar, knock a hole in a sail or two, or even hull me, but in five minutes, please my patron saint, San Diavolo, we shall be out of range."

The ship was not hit in any part by shot, and kept on her course, her head was directed for a point bearing about south-east.

Distant, perhaps, seven miles from the other side of this point was the creek which the pirate wished to fetch, and to reach which he had been compelled to take such an unusual and dangerous course.

As soon as the manœuvre could possibly be executed, the frigate was brought round on the other tack, and another broadside discharged.

This time some damage was done.

The foretopmast was shot away, and several round shot tore holes in the sails.

One cannon ball struck the taffrail, and a splinter therefrom dangerously wounded the man at the wheel.

It was not possible for the frigate to bring her other broadside to bear before the chase could be virtually out of range. The Death Pirate, well knowing this, was in high glee, and felt absolutely confident of safely running the vessel in.

The frigate, after delivering the last broadside tacked and stood off from the rocks as too dangerous neighbours.

The pirate, seeing this, shouted triumphantly:

"Bravo! All hail to our patron saint.

"Now, let us drink to St. Diavolo."

Bang! Bang!

Bang! Crash!

Three loud reports, and the smashing of timber.

The Death Pirate was reclining lazily on a battle axe, looking out seawards at the frigate, when this fresh alarm came.

Instantly he leaped to his feet, ran over to the starboard side, leaned on the rail, and, holding on to the mizen-rigging, looked out in the direction where the cannonade came

He saw three large man-of-war boats, each with a gun mounted at the bow.

From the flag-staff at the stern of each there floated a flag—the British ensign.

"My glass!" roared he, still standing on the rail, and holding on to the rigging. "Quick, d——n you."

In a moment or two the telescope was brought.

The pirate captain snatched it, placed it to his eye, and had a look.

He could read the name on the hatband of the sailors of the English boats.

"Ten thousand devils!" he roared; "it's the boats of the 'Ajax,' that chased us on the Gold Coast. She's come in first, and laid in wait for us. We have been betrayed."

Scarcely were the words out of his mouth when Bang! bang! bang!

But the shots took no effect.

The pirate ship, caught in an eddy, was whirled mysteriously out of sight of the frigate.

CHAPTER CCXV.

THE "WILL-O'-THE-WISP" UNDERGOES REPAIRS—ZELIE'S PLOT SUCCEEDS—HORRIBLE CRUELTIES OF THE DEATH PIRATE.

CAPTAIN TOM DRAKE found to his sorrow that the gallant little "Will-o'-the-Wisp" had sustained more damage than he had at first anticipated.

The copper sheathing was in places ripped from her bottom, and the hole made by the rocks was so jagged that it compelled the removal of several of the planks.

So, beside living on board, they rigged a tent with the sails and awnings on shore.

The adding to their number of the fair girl Tom had brought with him from the forest and the wounded Indian necessitated this.

Then there was the prisoner, Black Bill.

Captain Tom had elicited enough from the girl whom he had placed under the temporary care of Zelie that she was no other than Genifrede, the female he remembered seeing in the smuggler's cave on the coast of France.

He also learnt that in order to escape the importunities and the tyranny exercised over her by Black Bill she had taken the pirates' boat and drifted to the island where Captain Tom discovered her.

She had no knowledge of the two men who were fighting for her possession.

In her wanderings she had come upon them suddenly.

It was arranged between the two rivals that

they should bind the fair girl to the tree while they fought out their supposed grievance.

Dr. Shrike and his faithful Jacop took charge of the Indian.

Under their careful and tender services the hardy Islander soon recovered.

He could, as we have before observed, talk sufficient English and Spanish jargon to make himself understood.

From him Captain Tom Drake gained a deal of information.

To his surprise, he learnt that the Indian had resided for many years on the island he was in search of, and had actually at one time seen the Death Pirate, and knew the haunt to which the notorious pirate resorted in his hours of leisure.

This Indian's name was Manello.

He was, as we before observed, of tall, Herculean frame; not very handsome to look upon, but very fantastically dressed.

Like the generality of his race, he was very sagacious, and greatly given to superstition.

It appeared from his version that the tribe had been located on the island, when a band of monks, accompanied by a number of Spanish soldiers, drove them from their village into the interior, and set themselves up a citadel and built a fortress.

He told the Captain various anecdotes of the superstitious rites of these monks, the cruel warfare they waged against the Indians, and also the lessons of terror that they had impressed upon the Indian settlers.

Tom Drake was all anxiety to get his ship afloat again.

This delay was giving the Death Pirate time to perpetrate his villainy.

Besides, there was another important circumstance.

Zelie, though crafty enough to try concealment, was growing jealous of her charge.

She, on her part, was not blind to the favourable glances with which Captain Tom viewed the clear blue eyes, sunny hair, and still fairer skin of the daughter of France.

The proud Corsair maiden had, from her first presence on board the buccaneer rover, made up her mind to entertain no rival.

No matter at what cost, she was determined to get rid of Genifrede.

She soon found one to assist her in this.

It was Bill, the ex-smuggler.

He was still kept in irons on board, but owing to carrying out the repairs he was confined in a different part of the vessel.

As soon as possible, and when a high tide was expected, the buccaneers dug away the sand from around the vessel, and laid out a kedge in deep water.

With this, when the tide rose, the gallant brig was hove off the sand, and once more ploughed her way across the seas, under a stiff press of sail.

Cloud upon cloud was packed the white canvas, from the stout canvas courses to the light duck royals and skysails, which, towering high, seemed almost to scrape the firmament; and the studding sails below and aloft, extended by the booms run out from either yardarm, kissed the favouring breeze, and seemed almost to bury the symmetrical hull of the "Will-o'-the-Wisp."

On—on—over the sparkling sea, cleaving the dark-green waves and disturbing the flying fish which rose in ai very shoals, the brave ship bore on, bearing the bold buccaneers to the goal for which they were bound.

Zelie in the meantime was not idle.

She had contrived to hold communication with Black Bill.

The exultant villain, in his turn, gave her his crafty advice

Aided by this the corsair maiden managed to effect a reconciliation between Genifrede and Black Bill.

It was then arranged that some night when the wind fell light a boat should be silently lowered, and the pair should leave the ship.

This required the constant vigilance of Zelie.

But the opportunity came at last.

It was carried out, too, with much more success than might have been anticipated, from the fact that a strict watch was kept on board the "Will-o'-the-Wisp" night and day.

Captain Tom Drake devoted a great part of his time to the studying of the chart with which Dutch Paul had furnished him.

While Harry Vere was navigating the course of the ship, Tom Drake was closeted in his cabin making acquaintance with the intricate passages and shoals that abounded on the Spanish main.

During this busy time the escape was effected, and was not discovered until too late.

Captain Tom Drake was angered beyond bounds when he heard of this.

The sentries who had been on guard during the night he severely punished.

His thoughts were so engrossed with the probable fate of his darling Minnie, however, that he gave most of his time to that particular object, and he would spend hours in questioning and cross-questioning the Indian.

Then he would pace the deck, fuming like a caged eagle

His brow would darken ominously, and as he muttered vengefully to himself, his hand would clutch involuntarily the hilt of his short dress sword.

How great was the relief, then, when the Indian, pointing to a thick cluster of trees, informed him that there lay hidden the mouth of a secret passage that led up to the fortress, which the Death Pirate had chosen for his stronghold.

"There, too," said the islander, "lie hidden treasures, so rare and costly, that they would make the eyes of an Emperor glisten."

Bob and Jerry happened to overhear this.

"By Jove!" Jerry Mizzen exclaimed, rubbing the palms of his horny hands together.

"It's all a fakement," Bob returned drily.

"Do you think so?" asked Jerry.

"Am I a fool, you swab?"

"Yes, if I'm a swab," retorted Jerry.

"Then go and see for yourself."

"I would if I'd half a chance. I should like to go in for a lump while I'm about it; there's heaps of riches, piles of stuff to be had here, if we only knew where to look for it."

Harry Vere failed not to gain all the information he could from the islander about the secret passage, but the Indian was reticent on many points.

Whenever he was questioned his answer was given with a shudder.

This evasion, of course, only heightened the curiosity of his questioners.

Ben Barnacle also caught the mania

They were all at fever heat to get on shore.

It was Captain Tom Drake's intention, however, to go point blank to the fortress.

His impatience would not allow of him going on a wild goose chase.

The Indian's knowledge was very vague on this point.

He knew that the fortress existed, that some one of importance resided there, to see after it in the Death Pirate's absence, and that he had a guard of soldiers, or mercenary band, to quell the risings of the settlers and resist the raids made upon the stronghold by the Indian tribes.

The vague information and the chart supplied by Dutch Paul were all Captain Tom had to work upon.

As the "Will-o'-the-Wisp" neared the island, Tom could see that it was surrounded by a belt of rocks.

When near enough, he sent Harry, Ben, and a party of mids ashore, in a boat, on an exploring expedition.

In the meantime Tom stood off and on, making observations and preparing for his own exploration.

While so engaged an English frigate suddenly made its appearance, and Tom made up his mind at once to board her.

He ran up the Brazilian flag to his main-mast head, hoisted the Union Jack at the fore, and displayed the English ensign from his after peak.

This achievement rather nonplussed Captain Bluster.

He put his ship before the wind and ran down on the buccaneer's ship, intending to board her.

But Tom frustrated his friendly design by lowering his own gig and going to meet the frigate.

Captain Bluster was more perplexed than ever when he saw a figure in the boat's stern with a cocked hat and epaulets on.

He met our hero, however, at the gangway, with all due honours.

A guard of marines were drawn up, and presented arms as our hero stepped on board.

Nevertheless, Captain Bluster assumed all his proper dignity.

"I have the pleasure of addressing—" he began, as they both bared their heads to each other.

"Captain White, of the Brazilian navy," answered Tom Drake.

"You have a smart ship, Captain White," said the English Captain, eyeing Tom's ship with unfeigned admiration.

"And a staunch crew," Tom responded.

"Cruising, I suppose, Captain White?"

"Pirate hunting," answered Tom.

"There is a very devil of a fellow about here then for you to catch; your ship is of lighter draught than mine, so you will have a better chance than I."

Tom plucked up his ears.

"This may be the Death Pirate," he thought.

From further information he gained, he felt certain his surmise was right.

He was determined, too, to profit by the occasion.

He produced the document given him by the port admiral, and desired to be furnished with ammunition, as his own was getting short.

This the captain of the frigate reluctantly acceded to.

Tom then, having obtained all he wanted and listened to Captain Bluster's account of his chase of the pirate and her mysterious disappearance, took a glass of grog with the captain, and proceeded on board again.

Captain Tom was very pleased when the frigate was hull down again, for he did not want the captain to interfere with his present arrangement.

In the mean time Harry had been on shore and discovered they were on the back of the Island, and so he pulled along the coast about a mile or so, to reconnoitre and to find a fitting inlet from the sea to admit of Tom Drake landing with his expedition.

As they rowed along Ben suddenly gave an outcry.

"Something straight ahead, Mr. Vere!" said he; "can't see for the sun."

Harry shielded his eyes from the rays of the rising orb.

"A stray spar," said he. "It lies in our way; we'll see. Pull away, lads, pull!"

In half an hour they had come up with the object.

Around it the waves were lashed to foam by the furious and ravenous movements of a dozen sharks, snapping at one another, and at the tit-bit just beyond their teeth.

It was a large flag-buoy.

To it was tied a living man.

Around his neck was wound the bight of the flag cord, so that, if the fastenings to his hands should break or come undone, he would hang himself by pitching forward.

But, to prevent him killing himself, when the pangs of exposure and the reflected glare to famine and thirst should drive him mad, his legs were secured, so that he should not slip down, and so strangle himself.

At every dip of the buoy the sharks swarmed forward to receive the prey, but ere they could turn to open their maws the float would right itself, and snatch the victim from their ravenous jaws.

Above the buoy was a cloud of birds, screaming, fluttering, making swoops now and then

But ever scared by the flaunting of a flag on the pole.

The boat drew near, and the men lay on their oars.

A puff of wind straightened the streamer, till it lay flat as a board.

On a jet black field, in red letters, was the word—
"TRAITOR!"

"He's dead," said one.

But at the sound of the human voice, the bonded figure shuddered, and the breath came hoarsely in a sob between the lips, bleeding and crusted with the salt, dried from the spray.

"Cut him down," said Harry. "No one can tell what a waif may be worth."

At that moment the buoy dipped.

A young shark, as if knowing that the newcomers were rescuers, launched himself upwards to seize the prey.

"Stand aside!" cried Ben.

He rushed to the prow, from seat to seat, and caught up the boat-hook.

An instant he poised it over the white belly of the fish.

"There!" cried he, darting it, harpoonwise, "there's something sweet for your gullets."

The sharks, as the blood spouted out and flavoured the brine, followed the victim, and soon tore him to pieces.

Meanwhile, the suspended man was taken down.

Harry wiped the face of the senseless form with his sleeve.

"By Saint Denis!" cried he, "it's my friend Dick Dawson! Who could have done this?"

One of the mids turned his blanched face towards him, and mutely levelled a trembling finger at the buoy.

They all looked.

They had not before noticed that on its side was a name—

The "Death Pirate."

Harry scanned the horizon eagerly at this.

The ocean was vacant.

Except straight ahead, where a dark cloud steadily hovered.

"Pull away, lads," said he, on seeing this. "The men have kindled a fire to signal us. Lay down to it with a will! Spring, while you're about it!"

While the oarsmen rowed on lustily, Harry Vere devoted himself to reviving his friend.

Dick, his brain almost turned by the frightful fate that he had been consigned to, remained long in that state of unconsciousness.

Suddenly an exclamation broke from the bow-oar.

"Better look yonder, Mr. Vere."

Harry started up from bathing Dick's face.

The pillar of smoke, which he had long before descried, indeed came from a fire.

But it was a fire that made him shudder with pain.

'Pull away, men,' cried he, letting Dick come to life himself, while he grasped the tiller-rope 's more seamanly.

In ten minutes, the long boat had come within easy sight of the shore of a long promontory of azure limestone, called the Blue Key.

The sunbeams fell in a bright orange glare all around on shore and wave.

On the water its light was outvied by the ruddy blaze of a large brig on fire from stem to stern, from royal mast to water's edge.

The hull was a mass of conflagration, the yards and masts and booms rained down the incandescent rage of the fresh-bent sails, unfurling luridly of themselves.

On the sands and rocks, the sun's rays glinted on broken weapons that were still gripped in stiffened hands, lopped off from perforated bodies.

Still again, half floating, half held by their weight on the shingle, rocked other corpses, around which the beautiful angel-fish were in schools like a flock of flies about carrion.

When any of these bodies were caught by the reflux and came out into deep water, the sharks speedily rent them into ensanguined tatters.

The boat pushed on.

The canopy of smoke, sparks, and tongues of fire overhead, the road obstructed by charred timber and streaks of burning tar.

The boat was run upon the beach.

The middies ran to each man, one after another, but life had been let out of all by pistol, cutlass, or pike.

"Who has done this ruin?" cried the lieutenant, in rage. "Will no one speak?"

"Look!" cried Dick Dawson, who had been dragged out of the boat and dropped on the sand.

He was pointing in the direction of the sun.

All eyes were bent thitherward, like his own.

On the broad face of the orb was defined the full sail of a vessel.

She seemed to be on a holiday, streamer at the fore and main and peak.

But above all, on the main, a large banner spread out, broad as a top-sail, in silken glory.

This blotting out the disc of fire, the strange craft had a wierd and ghastly look.

She seemed not to cleave the blue of the sea with keel, or the azure of the sky with spars, but to float in that crimson radiance.

Harry Vere knew her.

"The Death Pirate!" cried he. "Pull aboard, boys, pull away for dear life!"

And the sailors with him and Dick, glanced on the pall of vapour shrouding the consumed hull, and on the corpses reddening the shore, and shuddered.

CHAPTER CCXVI.

TOM DRAKE'S ANGER—HARRY VERE AND HIS PARTY EXPLORE THE SUBTERRANEOUS PASSAGE.

THE buccaneers were some hours reaching the "Will-o'-the-Wisp."

When they did so, and Captain Tom heard their recital, Tom's blood perfectly boiled with anger.

But when he saw Dick Dawson, and learnt from him how he had been compelled by the merciless pirate to assist in the abduction of Minnie, and that she had been landed on the island, our hero fairly groaned, and beads of sweat poured down his agonised features.

"Vengeance!" he muttered, hoarsely. "Vengeance! I will be dearly avenged for this."

This was all he spoke at that time.

He motioned Harry Vere to follow him to his cabin.

Then he summoned Zelie by the gong, and made her a sign.

Presently the Corsair girl appeared with two bottles of the strongest brandy, and Captain Tom, in his momentary frenzy, knocked off the neck of and emptied one bottle into a silver goblet, and drained off the contents at a draught.

The other bottle he divided between himself and the young lieutenant.

"Harry," he said, "this is a severe trial for us both. Thank Heaven that Minnie is safe, but she may not be so for long. I must discover the nest where that fiend in human shape hides his quarry. I will not rest till I discover and rescue her."

"And I?"

"You must take such hands as you need and seek the mysterious entrance, so that by that outlet none of his myrmidons may escape."

*   *   *   *   *

One hour later Harry Vere, Ben Barnacle, Bob Hauler, and Jerry, with the Indian for a guide, left the "Will-o'-the-Wisp," and proceeded to the shore.

Marnello led them by secret paths to a cave in the hill side.

The trees growing thickly all around kept them from fear of discovery from the palace distant, beside, as it was.

"Now," said Harry to the guide, "you assure me that this gap, here, leads to an underground passage by which the governor's mansion may be reached?"

"Yes. You are sailors, and have a pocket compass. You take your bearings, and there you are."

"And you do not know more about this passage?"

"I don't know anything, sir. Nor anybody else. There's no native of Antigua would go down into the subterraneans."

"Why not? Let's have the whole story, while my men get all their equipment ready."

The buccaneers were all armed well, and had lengths of rope, &c., so as to be ready for any emergency.

"It's a short tale," replied Marnelo. "Yonder big building was built by the Indians, over whom were the monks, who converted them and civilised them."

"Aha! taught 'em how to hew stones, to build houses for the priests? Go ahead," said Jerry.

"Well, this was long ago, at the early settlement. The savages got savage one day——"

"Wanted to build houses for themselves and family?" suggested the young lieutenant.

"I don't know, sir. However, these Indians attacked the monastery, beat back the monks, and chased them through all the chambers."

"And slaughtered them all?" said Ben Barnacle.

"Not exactly. They did butcher some. But here's the mystery. They drove the priests from hall to room, from room to the last of them. They burst the door in and rushed in, but the holy fathers had vanished!"

"A miracle!" cried Jerry with a grin.

"Well," said Marnelo, doubtfully, "everybody did say so for about two hundred years. But another tale sprang up then."

"Oh, indeed?"

"Yes. Two Spanish pirates were shooting on the hills here, when a wounded bird fluttered away into this cave. One of the pirates followed it. He came out of the cavern, told his comrade that he had found a long passage built up——"

"And that's it?" said Harry Vere, pointing to the black tunnel before them.

"That's it. As I was saying, the two pirates went into the hole, and penetrated to a considerable depth. They managed to get out all right, but dreadfully frightened."

"Well, how?"

"They found the interior of that great hill like a buried house. The monks had built it up in halls, cells, and kitchens, and everything."

"Whew! You don't mean to say that the hunters found the monks fat and lively after two hundred years?" laughed Ben.

Mannelo shook his head.

"No, but the pirates found a great chamber with a floor of skeletons! and, what was more horrible, there wasn't one bone left to another!"

"How was that? Did the Indians get down there?"

"Oh no. That's the enigma. The pirates told their story. No one would believe them. They got tired of being called liars, and offered to go down again with any party."

"A pleasant invitation, truly," remarked Harry, "and the pirates, no doubt, concocted it for their own purpose."

"Senor Terribio, nephew of the governor of that day, and half-a-dozen more young gallants, agreed to make the exploration. They came here, followed by half the city. They went down, with plenty of blessed candles and a long rope, that they uncoiled as they went in."

'Stay a minute, my men,' called out the lieutenant. "Go on, Mannelo."

"Very little more, sir.

"In about a quarter of an hour the rope was shaken. The party were coming back. Suddenly the people standing here, just like you or I, heard a roar or a yell, or some terrible sound that they had never known before.

"There were brave men there, senor, but the whole crowd shook like so many leaves.

"They hastened to pull in the rope, and half climbing, half dragged, Senor Terribio was got out of the cave.

"He fell down senseless among them all.

"When he came to life, he wouldn't speak a word till he was in the high cathedral. Then, pale and trembling he solemnly, in the presence of the altar, declared that he and his companions, while looking at the hall strewn with dust and bones of men, had beheld, rising out of the ground, the Devil!"

"What?" cried Harry, taken aback.

"The Devil! Maldita, the Prince of Evil himself!" replied Mannelo, crossing himself. "The apparition had wings, claws, and teeth! and such teeth and claws! Senor Don Terribio saw his five or six comrades struck down and bitten through like a squirrel champing nuts.

"He had his sword out and made a lunge, but the blade was knocked out of his hand in a minute. He fled to the hole, grasped the rope, and could not tell even how he had been saved. He had heard a direful flutter of monstrous wings behind him, and the last sound in his ears was that inexpressibly appalling shriek of rage, which the people without had also heard."

"Whew!" whistled the young captain, again.

"Laugh away," said Mannelo; "I only know that nobody ever went down that gully hole since."

"But Don Terribio, the coward who deserted his friends?"

"No coward, senor. He was a famous soldier in European wars. He never was himself after that day. He had used to be the very devil himself among the gay of the South Quarter, but he shunned the world, and, for all the interest he took in anything but pious acts, he might as well have been a priest out and out."

"And the friends of his?"

"Never heard of."

"Will you come along?" inquired Harry of the Indian.

"No," replied Mannelo. "I don't suppose there's another man on the island who would have come so near as this."

"Well, take care of yourself, then. Good-bye!"

"The saints have you in keeping!"

The buccaneers of the "Cruiser" were left to themselves.

"If you like," Ben answered.

So saying, the buccaneer scrambled into the cave.

Soon he entered a narrow tunnel, built up strongly, and of a circular shape.

The buccaneer had to crawl through it.

This narrowness had evidently been designed for the better defence of the entrance.

After a gentle descent of some thirty feet, Harry found himself in twilight, and in a large cave.

Stones were built up on the sides, but the earth had fallen in here and there.

In a few moments the buccaneers were all together.

"Strike a light," said Harry.

Ben produced some dry rope-ravel, and lit it by flashing some powder in a pistol pan.

The candles they had brought were then lit.

But scarcely had they crossed the first cave and entered a very long corridor, than Harry said—

'Halt! This won't do. Though every one of us carry a candle, there is not light enough with this subterranean passage so lofty.'

He unhooked the flask at his belt, and poured the brandy into a hollow of a flagstone under foot.

"Do the same," said he to the others.

They passed him their gourds or bottles cheerfully.

"We'll have lots to drink," said he, "before long, if this road's right."

He poured out all the liquor.

While so doing, he looked around.

"Ah," said Jerry, "I know what you are after."

He produced from his capacious pocket a length of rope, from which he cut three yards or so.

This, doubled up and twisted, formed a piece of a couple of feet long and several inches thick, while being almost as stiff as a solid body.

The cut ends and bight of this Harry also sopped in the brandy.

Then he bound that extremity all round with some sailcloth.

"That will burn for some time," said Ben, approvingly.

"Shall we light it now?" asked Bob, about to apply the candle to it.

"No. Not till we actually need it," answered the lieutenant.

That moment seemed near at hand, for even while the words dropped from his lips, a sound, not made by them, echoed ominously in the corridor.

"Hark! hark!" cried they all.

"The wind," said Ben Barnacle.

"More like the whizz of wings," replied Harry.

And he was right.

The same thought presented itself to each of the four friends.

The sound was, in truth, precisely like that drumming a pheasant will often make, only inconceivably louder, and hence more frightful.

"Be it what it may," said Harry Vere, at once, "this is no place so slippery and contracted in room, for us to meet it."

With that, lighting the spirituous torch, he strode forward.

His naked sword was in his other hand.

Bob came next, holding ready the pistols.

Then Ben with the candle.

And Jerry in the rear.

The buccaneers kept their weapons ready, for fear of an attack.

Against their expectation, not a thing was visible or audible in the corridor, up or down.

"Shall we go back?" asked one.

"Put it to the vote. I'm for going on."

"And I—and I!" said the others in a breath.

"So am I," said old Ben, "if it comes to that. Only I likes to be prudent when one don't know what thing of the earth above or depths here below, one may have to face."

To the end of the corridor they went.

To their right was a turning.

They went into it.

After some twenty feet, a little down-sloping, they came to another turn, in the direction of the long corridor which they had so long been traversing.

This new tunnel stretched along for a good distance, as well as the absence of any other light than their own permitted them to judge.

There was a circular box of masonry in an ample recess.

Harry went over to it with Ben.

"It's a well," said the young lieutenant.

Boyishly, he dislodged one of the stones of the curb.

The mortar was good, though, and he had to apply force.

The square, heavy piece of stone, toppled inwards, fell into the black mouth.

Rumble, rumble was the sound, now and anon, as it bounded from side to side.

Fainter and fainter faded away the entombed echoes.

"Deep, I tell you," said Harry Vere.

After a space, which seemed incredibly long to the listeners, a complete cessation of even the most feeble noise told that the stone had reached the end of the lengthy shaft.

"I would not like to have to wait for a drink till the water was hauled up out of there," laughed the youth.

Ben approached the candle to the pit's mouth.

"They once did use it," said he. "You can see marks of a framework at the top here. Ah!"

A rush of air up the orifice had blown out the light.

"Yes," said Ben, suddenly, "the lieutenant seems to have woke up the air."

"Something more, too."

As Harry spoke he pushed with all his might at the stone coping.

"Bear a hand, quick!" cried he.

Jerry up with his foot, armed with its heavy boot, and dealt the already shaken stone such a kick that a huge mass tumbled off its setting into the hole.

It thundered down.

It had reached perhaps, half-way, when it seemed to encounter something.

The collision caused quite an audible shock.

Then a piercing and terrifying shriek of something in agony rang up the mine to chill the listeners to the marrow.

"Mercy! What in the name of Heaven's that?" exclaimed they, starting back.

The like of it had never startled any of them before.

The echoes died suddenly away of that horrid scream, being drowned by the louder ones of the fallen stones pounding on the bottom.

Once again that outcry resounded from the core of the gulf, but weaker—much weaker—than before.

There was a silence below and above.

Ben mechanically, with a shaking hand, lit his taper at his comrade's flaming link.

A third time the inarticulate accents of the unknown in torment reached the sailor's ears.

It would seem, too, that the torture-wrung cry was heard elsewhere.

For a sort of answering call quite forcibly responded.

Very faintly, but, nevertheless, perceptibly, the whirring sound which had first alarmed the companions uprose.

It ceased; to be followed by a whimper of pleasure, which equally changed into a murmur, that to a growl, and ended with a positively astounding wail.

"It must have been Old Scratch that was hit by the stones when coming up," said Bob, "and that's young Nick grieving for him."

"It's no jest, sir. I'm older than you, my lad, but I never heard the like of that."

"Nor I neither, Ben."

"Nor I. Nor do I ever want to do so again," said Jerry, griping his cutlass-hilt convulsively.

However, the cause of their uneasiness was hushed.

All was still down the bowels of the earth.

Jerry pushed over some more stones at a nod from the lieutenant.

They all stood ready, but there was merely the rattle of the missiles.

Nothing more.

"Come on," said Harry, more lightly.

They followed him with readiness.

But hardly had they gone up the turn of the lobby than Jerry, who brought up the rear with Bob Hauler, turned around, pressed his shoulder, and pointed.

Bob saw what a fear-stricken countenance his mate wore, and rightly concluded that the matter row was no laughing one.

The others turned the same.

Supported by two paws, garnished with talons like a bear's or a tiger's, a head the size of a wolf, or a very large fox, rested on the broken edge of the deep well.

The glare from the flambeau was reflected by its blazing eyes and grinding teeth.

More than its head, it's neck and shoulders rose into view.

The buccaneers were appalled already by what they had seen of it.

The hideousness of the monster, so little unveiled yet, was increased, impossible as that may seem, by another head, the eyes of which were shut, and the ears limp and drooping, that was over its shoulder.

"Good God!" ejaculated Vere.

Except that exclamation, they were all too fascinated to move or speak.

They forgot they had weapons in their hands.

They gazed, that was all they could think of doing.

Up rose the object, black as sin.

The eyes, ferocious beyond expression, yet swam in grief—a grief so evident and so poignant, that the fiendish visage almost grew human.

Folded up and ribbed, netted and hairy, the unused wings that were attached to the brawny arms or forelegs, and to the other limbs, as they were presently to behold, now appeared.

With an effort the mammoth bat clambered over the circular wall down upon the slabs.

It shook off its load.

For the head, which had increased its aspect by having the appearance of belonging to it, really appertained to another form of the same species, but smaller.

A PERILOUS MOMENT.

This second one, borne on the back by the other, had been hooked on to its shoulder by its claws.

When shaken off upon the stones, it half spread itself out, ere settling down at full length, an inert mass.

Its body, on the back, which was uppermost, and its head, had the fur scraped off here and there, and were all powdered with lime and stone dust.

Blood speckled its dark skin, and even streaked it in one or two places.

The live animal surveyed the dead one almost tearfully, and then turned its ferocious orbs on the enemy.

It would actually appear as though the being, divining that the death-givers to its mate would be found above, had carried, with infinite trouble, that carcase to confront them.

For a second the single avenger eyed its little band of foes.

Then, standing up on its hind legs, set far apart, the talons scratching the stony floor, it opened widely the arms.

From wrist to wrist the wings unfolded, and from ankle to ankle.

But by some unaccountable provision of nature, the line of the outer edge did not extend either curved inward, or straight from member to member.

In the middle, that is at its breast-height, a splint of bone so projected that it widered the web.

The whole sweep of the flying membrane from tip to tip could not have been less than five yards.

The figure stood, though its legs were wide apart, perhaps as many feet high.

It gnashed its teeth.

It saw the buccaneers range themselves, with flashing lights and sword-blades, in the entrance of the passage.

Of flight, not one of them dreamed.

Three or four times the monster flapped its wings, taking a step between a double hop and a stride at each time.

Its claws rattled as an accompaniment to the champing of its jaws.

As this beginning of an approach was so slow, the buccaneers fancied that they would have plenty of time to prepare for it, brief as was the space between.

But, most unexpectedly, uttering an angry scream, surpassing in thrilling and terror-striking intensity any that it had ever split that awful cavernous air with, it flew like lightning forward.

Not expecting this, the four buccaneers were overwhelmed by the gigantic sweeping pinions.

Jerry groaned with terror.

Harry alone had escaped, thanks to the torch which he had happened to hold at that terrible moment.

His sword, thrust at random into the wings of the bat, had fallen from it harmlessly, dashed from his hand.

As he started back, unwounded, but a little bruised, he could see, by the uncertain flickering of his fanned torch, that the beast had enfolded the three of his companions in the compass of that inky mantle.

Horrified, he could not move.

But the hideous jaws, open to let out an awfully fiendish growl, opened still wider to snap at the victims just under them.

Another moment, and the already half-suffocated men would have surely been bitten to death.

The lieutenant of the "Will-o'-the Wisp" blamed himself, for his really pardonable pause.

Then he leaped at the animal as fearlessly as if it had been not near so unearthly and horrid.

Dauntlessly he began, vigorously he continued, his efforts to set his friends at liberty.

A dagger in his left hand, the flaming torch in his right hand, he stabbed and banged away at the head of the monstrous pteredactyl.

It at least could not bite his comrades.

The flambeau, put out by such a series of sounding blows, fell from his hand.

All was darkness—blackness—in the cavern.

All was gloom, but far from silence.

Indescribable was the devilish clamour of the wild beast's growls, spittings, and howls, both of rage and pain, for its head was all scorched.

Forgetting its three captives almost, it clawed at the young champion.

It could see in the dark.

His dagger-strokes at random missed even so great a target, at times.

It fell upon the youth.

All rolled upon the stones.

"Blung bung!" went hollowly two pistol shots.

Ben, pressed against the breast of the monster and squeezed up with his two fellows, had overcome the first confusion, and, excited by the pain of suffocation, had pulled the triggers of his brace of fire-arms, even at the risk of killing his friends.

The swords of the others, half strangled as they were, were useless all this time.

Amazed at the explosion, though the two-fold wounds it received only inflamed its rage, the beast, choking, too, with the sulphurous vapour that began to steal up out of its bosom, unfolded its wings.

The three mariners drank greedily of the free air.

For the exuding perspiration of the animal was not excessively fragrant.

The struggle was not concluded.

The monster yelled, snapped at Harry, who parried its bite with a slash of his sword, opened its pinions with a force that rolled Ben off one side and Bob the other, and fell bodily on the lieutenant and Jerry.

It bore them to the ground.

Its furious onset would have easily pulled down a horse or a lion.

Ben, while still rolling, encountered something sharp, which scratched his hand.

It was a sword.

He scrambled to his feet.

The eyes of the creature, gloating over the bodies of his fallen friends, shone in the obscurity, perfect beacons.

The bold buccaneer marched quickly to it, and with all the force he could put into his arm he delivered a lunge.

"We must kill or be killed!" cried he.

The well-thrust steel ran along under the lower jaw, pierced the throat, escaped the main vein and the vertebræ behind by a miracle, and bore back the beast to the wall.

Ben pressed on.

The blade entered to the very hilt.

The point met an interstice between two stones of the wall, penetrated the mortar deeply, and there remained.

The creature flapped its wings, torn and broken in places, clawed at the air, howled and battled.

All in vain.

It was pinned to the wall by the blade, no less effectually than a moth is attached to cardboard.

A fragment of the spirit-soaked rags that had helped to form the improvised link still sparkled in a corner.

Ben ran to it, picked it up, swung it in the air till it flamed, found the candle by its means, and lit it.

What he beheld was certainly not cheering.

The young lieutenant lay across Bob's body, both senseless.

Jerry Mizzen was rising, looking ruefully at the arm of his jacket, torn into strips by the bat's claws, and stained with its blood.

He picked up his knife.

"There's your sword, mate," said Ben, laughingly now.

He pointed to the transfixed thing, which had both ceased making motion and complaint.

"Let it stay," said Jerry. "I'd rather it were through him than he loose and tearing about. Ah!"

And he drew a long breath of relief.

When a few drops of brandy, luckily left, were sprinkled on the faces, and a few more drops put upon the tongues of the two insensible men, they showed signs of life.

In ten minutes all were ready to move on again, or as they might decide.

"Is it quite dead?" asked Harry Vere.

He was examining the apparent corpse.

"Quite, I should say," replied Ben Barnacle; "I have been watching it."

"It is easy to make sure," remarked Bob.

He had recharged his pistols.

"I'll blow his ugly head into a thousand bits," said he, stepping forward.

Harry pulled him back.

"No, no. It is useless to waste powder and ball. He's welcome to the sword if that's way you would shatter it. Let us be off from here. I never felt such a pang in all my born days as that monster gave me when I beheld him enclose you all—I mean when you three were all buried under his horrible wings."

"A wrap-rascal I don't fancy," laughed Bob Hauler, hoarsely.

"I couldn't use my sword, and how Ben managed to pull a trigger I don't see."

"I don't know myself," said Barnacle, "and if our black friend on the wall knows, he don't look as if he could impart much information, now."

"Thanks to you!" said the other three.

They all pressed Ben's hand.

A last look was given to the fiend-like form.

otionless as if carved of the stone it was hanging against.

Turning their backs on their conquered antagonist, which they would not have done while he lived, the four, recovered now from any petty injuries they had received, proceeded along the vaulted road.

After a while, it sloped a little, rising a foot in fifty or so.

Then a short turn, a level passage, another turn, and a passage ending in a door.

It was decayed, but still held together.

It could have been beaten down easily.

But the bar and a bolt were inside, on their side, and the key was in the lock.

The latter was of no use, for rust had prevented it from turning.

Bob battered at the iron plate.

He had it off in a few seconds.

"I don't think much of locks," said Harry, abruptly, as they were passing through.

"No," returned Ben, "a hand requires practice more than strength, and, aided by a clever head, I don't think but that a man could enter a king's palace easily."

"Or get out of a king's prison," said Jerry.

They all laughed, but it was a hoarse and hollow laugh.

They were mounting a flight of stone steps.

At the top, Harry Vere turned:

"Friends, we are approaching the level of the ground. Let nobody speak. Am I to be leader still?"

They all nodded assent.

At the end of the still vaulted path from the head of the stairs was another flight.

They ascended it.

On the landing, Harry beckoned to Bob.

There was a door.

Bob went to work on it, with less noise than before.

"Jerry," whispered Vere, "run back to the last door, and report how it looks on this side."

The lieutenant nodded to imply that he comprehended, and retraced his steps.

Enough light came down to him.

He returned.

"There are marks all over it, around the lock and about where the bar-pivot is. They couldn't get through, though," concluded he.

"As I thought," observed Harry. "This door has a lock more than a hundred and fifty years newer than those we have been pushing through. Somebody has tried to come down exploring, but has been stopped by that door."

"It wouldn't check me long," remarked Bob Hauler chuckling.

"Ah, but it is old now."

Meanwhile, Bob had picked the lock with a dagger point.

He tried the door.

"No bolt," said he, "but a bar."

Harry turned round.

"You see, somebody, long after the monks, buried themselves alive far beneath the sunbeams, found out his way."

Bob had tapped the upper part of the door all over.

At last he smiled.

He fitted a tool, taken from his pockets together, selected a spot in the panel, and went to work drilling a hole.

The others watched his actions tranquilly.

One hole bored, Bob made another a couple of inches above it, on the same line.

He replaced his bit by a fine saw, by the aid of which he cut down from one hole to the other.

That saw he laid aside for one still finer.

When that was in play, the sound was not of ed wood, but of metal biting away metal.

Presently he stopped.

Out of his pocket he drew a fine, but extremely strong, horse-hair line.

He formed a large loop, and introduced it through the slit with a delicate pair of plyers.

He drew it tight, and went on filing again.

At last, he pulled out his saw, put away all his instruments, and pushed the door with all confidence of its opening.

In fact it gave way, a little rustily, but with no other resistance.

They looked at the other side.

Half of the sundered bar was hanging by the horse-hair line.

"Pretty," said Jerry, as Bob laid down the piece of iron, and pocketed the twine that had prevented its falling and making a noise.

"Oh, that's nothing," said Bob. "But no more talk, I propose."

After half-a-dozen steps, the road seemed to end.

There was only a slit in the side wall of about the width of a man at the shoulders.

"Steps!" said Harry. "The light!"

He advanced upwards.

The narrow flights, very irregular, with frequent turns, apparently without cause, continued almost endlessly.

Not a window, loophole, or slit, let in light.

There were one or two air-holes though.

The termination was an iron plate.

The lieutenant examined it by the help of the candle.

The knob in its centre yielded when pressed.

The plate moved on one side.

Harry pushed it as far as it would go.

An opening, square, about five feet high by three wide, was before them. It gave a view, only arm's reach from it, of a stone wall.

The youth looked down.

"Oh!" said he.

He saw a large slab of stone beneath him, and two dogs of ornamental brass.

"It's a fire-place," said he. "We're in a chimney!"

Cautiously, by means of the jutting stones, he descended.

"Come down. No fear of spoiling your clothes, for there hasn't been a fire lit here since we were little boys."

"Sweep ho!" said Jerry, following him.

Jerry was inclined to be funny just then.

The four stood in a high and wide apartment, as rich, as grand, but as deserted and dusty as anything else.

"Take a chair, one and all," said Harry Vere, sitting down himself, after dusting a chair. "This is all too lonely for us to fear intrusion. Empty your pockets of the provisions," added he to Jerry. "Let's have our snack. Our late adventure with that child of Davy Jones, who would have eaten us, ought to have sharpened our appetites."

CHAPTER CCXVII.

THE ROOMS WITH THEIR SHADOWY TENANTS—THE PHANTOM'S TRAGEDY—THE PALE TERROR.

THE wing of the palace, completely abandoned, was not likely to be suspected as the refuge of the buccaneer explorers.

The only portion in use was where the Dark Pirate had lodged his captive, Minnie Atherton.

The sailors waited till the rest of the day and night should pass.

They kept quiet, and took by turns the slumber they were all so much in need of, till morning.

At early dawn, Harry, whose youth made uncommonly active, made two discoveries.

He was peeping out through a hole in the ruined blind, and through the encrusted pane of the glazed window, which he had to clean, upon the kind of enclosed court or garden that it commanded.

Whom should he see in the dawn's grey streakings, attended by a stern duenna, but Minnie!

If she had looked entrancing in the light of the cabin of the Death Pirate, much more beautiful was she in the clear pure air.

Graceful as the flowers she bent to pluck, fresh as the dew that glistened on their blossoms, lovely as those buds themselves, Harry, with that transcient, far off glimpse, felt his heart leap to be thus blessed with another view of her.

He watched her enter the house.

He saw that the duenna, who appeared to be a mere attendant, was really a guardian, and that Minnie was evidently a prisoner under her.

Harry Vere had not yet fairly made up his mind what he should do.

He discovered so far that Minnie was alive, though a prisoner.

At noon he determined that he would try and see her.

' Let us go and find the treasure," said he, then.

The floor they were on was the second over the ground floor.

The one above had no outlet.

There was no egress to this, except the chimney place, and its secret door connecting with the staircase in the wall; the regular stairs to above and below excepted.

They descended.

The rays of the sun, filtering through the coated panes of the blinded casements above, had let some light illumine the place.

Here there was none at all.

They had to ignite the wick of what was left of the extremely useful coil of waxed string.

Its glimmer fell upon the interior of a room, very magnificently gilded, and enriched with carvings, on the ceiling, the walls, the cornices, and round the doors. It had one window. The curtain was torn down from it, and smooth boards replaced it,

They entered the apartment, to which the one they had just left served as an ante-chamber.

Its windows were also boarded up, but the heavy curtains, fleecy with woolly dust, still hung by their brazen but tarnished rings on a rod of the same spoilt metal.

There was a tall cabinet, a writing stand, a praying-desk, a dressing-table, a closet in one corner, and in another a large bed, over which, to match its ponderous frame, was the framework of a canopy.

But the curtains, the valance, all the decorations and appendages of the couch, had been removed.

This stripping of the place impressed the scene with a still more lonely air.

Why some things were taken, and others, of equal value, left, was unaccountable.

It would seem as if the workmen had been interrupted while half through their labours.

"Come on," said Harry.

Wondering, they passed into the next of the series.

A very grand hall rather than a room.

At one end, to the seamen's right as they entered by the side, was the chief object between the four walls.

Besides it were a long table and many chairs.

Flanked on either side by a window, boarded up, and the curtains half disengaged, was a low dais or staging, approached by three broad steps.

Four iron posts, thin, gilded, rose each at a corner and ended in the ceiling.

Arranged so as to slide on them, but now wrenched out of place, and within a few feet of the stage, resting on the remains of a crushed chair, was a square, befringed, laced, embroidered top.

Its face, or lower part, was of satin and velvet, gold and silver, exquisitely worked. This showed that it must have been up against the ceiling, a canopy to the kind of throne.

But its body and top was one extremely weighty mass of metal, heavy enough to crush an ox, bone, and body.

No marvel that the chair underneath it was all ruined, stout as it was.

The buccaneers approached it with awe.

"Stay," said Ben, who bore the light.

He pulled back Harry, who preceded him.

He indicated what caused his act.

At their feet, on the carpet, between the head of the long table and the dais, was a great patch or dark stain.

On looking closer, it was found to be surrounded by other spots, which continued and led to the dais.

Its upper flooring was stained still more plentifully than the carpet.

"Some bloody deed," said Harry Vere. "By the style of the chairs I should say whatever did happen was years ago."

So saying, he went round the head of the long table and crossed the room

His friends walked close to him.

Ben Barnacle was last.

As the three before him were stepping through on that side which offered no resistance, the faithful rearward cast a glance, more from habit than aught else, over his shoulder.

Whatever he saw, it rooted him to the spot, except that it made him wheel quite around to see it better.

Too much affected to speak, he grasped the arm of Harry convulsively.

The latter, pained as well as startled by the grip, uttered an exclamation.

He very naturally looked around.

"What now, Ben?" queried he.

The words were frozen on his suddenly-chilled lips.

He could look on aghast; that was his utmost power.

On hearing Harry's low cry of surprise, the other two imitated his action.

The magical influence did not spare them.

All four bewitched eyes glared at the room on the threshold of which they were immovably planted.

It was the same, yet different.

The duskiness that had previously been alone lessened by the adventurers' little light, was gone.

Nothing was there to furnish a single gleam, and for all that, a vague and shifting pallid lustre floated all around.

It was of the nature of the will-o'-the-wisp, (pardon the allusion) or like the moonlight one sees in a dream.

Unnatural was it; unnatural were the new objects it hovered around.

The whole table, each side and the end, was surrounded by seated persons, men and women.

Richly dressed, their faces not unhandsome in shape, yet so unearthly glittered their gold and tinsel, so corpse-like was the violent tint of their countenances, that only their being immaterial and shadowy made a view of them possible.

Granting them more substantial, no one human could have let his eyes linger for the sixtieth of a second on them, and not go mad.

There were dishes on the board, but the smoke that rose slowly from the uncovered meats was like exhalations from a fat churchyard on a hot summer's day.

There was a peacock, cooked in its plumage, and a boar's head garnished and glazed, but the eyes in the long feathers were eyes shining like phosphorescent eye-balls of fish; and the teeth of the boar were grinning while it rolled its half-baked, discoloured orbs on the guests.

None of them had eyes for the detestable regales.

They were all staring—staring with a force and fixedness hard to conceive, at the end of the hall where rose the platform.

To that turned the attention of the living witnesses as well.

They could hardly believe what they beheld.

The fallen canopy was down, and yet its likeness was up, up against the ceiling.

The crushed chair was yet dismembered, and nevertheless there stood, as if unharmed, the very semblance of itself.

And more; a man sat in the counterfeit.

His face and hands were very white, perhaps because his attire was a suit of rich black velvet. His hair and beard were light, but seemed to be of a yellower hue from a species of fire they caught from the reflection of his eyes.

Like lightnings issuing upwards from a tomb—lightnings of hell, not heaven—shone they upon the figures confronting him.

This stood upon that stain of the carpet on which Ben Barnacle had prevented his friend from stepping.

It was a female shape.

In a golden-coloured robe trimmed with red, her olive complexion glowed like burnished copper, her jet eyes sparkled like black diamonds, and her raven hair gleamed like a dark blush on Satan's face.

Another visage still, only the head not the body, was visible.

The curtains veiled the rest.

For behind their folds, deep in the cloudy embrasure of one window, appeared to be hidden a man.

That countenance of his, dark like the woman's, and possessing a rude likeness to hers, covered with crisp, black locks, and marked with a ferocious moustache, owned eyes which flared with the changeable brightness of white hot coals.

He watched the woman bow to the man on the seat.

He watched the latter rise, and extend her hand to accept his.

A dagger gleamed in the grasp of the spy.

There was a shudder of the canopy, on high.

Without a sound, which made the ghastly act all the more appalling, down came that loaded mass with the swiftness and the deadliness of a thunderbolt.

The rising man was forced back into his just-quitted seat, and that and him were both together brought to earth, crushed, crushed, crushed—one into splinters of wood, the other into a pulp of flesh.

As this occurred, the man, who had doubtless cut the cord that had upheld the destroying canopy, darted out, and plunged the dagger again and again, quicker than eye could wink, into the bosom of the woman.

The guests at table started up.

A blueish, flickering light streamed on their suddenly bared blades

This was the picture :—

The fallen square upon what had been a human shape. A woman with a dozen gashes in her bosom, sinking to the floor. Her triumphant murderer hastily dyeing his guard, dripping with her heart's blood, in the ruddy current running down the platform steps. The spectral guests in all the attitudes of surprise, horror, and amazement.

But, lifelike as was the play, still there was a mocking air in all the actors, and an unreal veil over all that prevented the living gazers from throwing off their enchantment, and punishing the double

assassin as their hearts would have otherwise prompted them to do.

The murderer, dropping his instrument of crime, slowly moved towards them.

Harry, unable to cry out, to lay hand on a weapon, drew back one step on Ben Barnacle.

He against Bob, Bob against Jerry Mizzen.

They were outside of the room.

The phantom still came on.

They still drew back.

They saw that the hall was empty and dark again.

Were all that train of grisly figures to follow this single one yet visible?

It alone continued to follow them, or rather chase them.

They recoiled up the room.

It crossed it altogether.

A door opened at a wave of its hand.

With its other it beckoned them.

They could not resist.

They saw only it, not one another.

Turning their face to that awful guide's, one by one they followed.

Harry seemed to have been singled out, for by some mysterious impulse, he could not help taking the lead of the adventure

How far they went, what they passed through, they did not think of noticing.

All they were aware of was that through darkness they went, only seeing that supernatural avant courier before, always the same in pace, always the same command in his air.

At length he stopping, they halted.

They were in another room, small, and only containing a table, a chair, and a bed.

On the table was a coffer.

It was a metal box, banded with enamelled strips of ornamental gilt.

The key was in the lock.

With a wave of the hand that answered all the ends of speech, the spectre pointed to that box.

Then he called off their attention to himself again.

The murderous light in his repulsive eyes had died away, and altogether the spirit that clothed him was less substantial than before.

As the moon fades before the sun's coming, he—villanous reflex of vengeful assassination—appeared to wane before the approach of something brighter and better.

He crossed the room and displayed to them the secret spring of an unsuspected door.

He was gone.

Bob lit the candle on the table.

It shot up a merry flash, and even sparkled cheerily.

Harry flung up the unfastened lid of the coffer and discovered—We must leave that to another chapter.

CHAPTER CCXVIII.

TOM DRAKE LANDS ON THE ISLAND—TAKEN PRISONER—CONDEMNED TO DEATH.

CAPTAIN TOM DRAKE did not follow in the wake of the pirate ship "San Josef," but after making a circuitous sweep of a mile or two along the coast he entered the intricate winding and channels that surrounded the island, and disappeared just as mysteriously as did the Death Pirate from the eyes of those aboard the frigate.

Tom guided the little brig with his own hand through the dangerous pass.

Then he found how true was the chart given to him by Dutch Paul.

Once through the narrow channel he found himself in a basin large enough to contain a formidable fleet, and walled in by tremendous high barriers of rocks.

"There's no doubt many a pirate fleet has lain hidden whilst the men-of-war have been seeking them," said Captain Tom to one of his chief middies.

"Aye, captain, and I wonder you have not smelt it out before this; but I suppose we are not too late yet?"

"I mean to have a try," was Tom's answer.

He appeared very thoughtful.

His keen eye was all the time scanning the high cliffs to shoreward.

"I wonder how Harry Vere and his party are getting on?" he said presently.

The middy did not reply.

He shrugged his shoulders ominously.

He was not pleased with the idea of Harry trusting to the Indian.

If the Islander had proved false, how were they to render him assistance?

There was no fear, however, of him being left to an unknown fate whilst any of the buccaneers remained to search for him.

Besides there were four of them, and they were the right sort to make a pretty good resistance in the case of an ambuscade.

Such were the middy's thoughts when Tom's voice aroused him.

"Heave the lead," he commanded.

This was done.

"Seven fathoms," sang out the middy.

"Bright yellow sand," was his next announcement as he examined the armour.

Tom then ordered the light sails to be taken in, and the 'Will-o'-the-Wisp" just forged slowly ahead.

At each call the helmsman announced the shallowing of the water, until the cry was:—

"Five fathoms."

Tom then clewed up his sails and dropped his anchor.

Then a couple of boats were cleared away, and Tom Drake called his crew aft.

When the buccaneers were all mustered on the quarter-deck, our hero thus addressed them.

"Now, lads, one and all, you are doubtless aware of the mission that called us here; and I have no doubt that it is a mission as dangerous as any we could have chosen; but I have faith enough in you to believe that not one of you will flinch from it."

"Hear, hear," shouted the buccaneer crew.

"I have many a time seen your mettle tried, and in the direst danger or the fiercest fight I have never known you to quail or to shrink from my side."

"Hear, hear."

"Hurrah for Captain Tom!"

Tom Drake held up his hand and made a sign to them not to be too incautious, as the very rocks by which they were surrounded might have ears.

"In facing these Spaniards," he added, "if the Indian's story be true, we shall have devils to beard, demons whose tortures of the Inquisition are not unknown to you; so that if any of us are taken prisoners we may prepare for the worst."

"We are prepared."

Tom read the truth of this reply in their features.

He could see that it needed no words of his to strengthen their determination.

They knew that they were bound to the rescue of Minnie, and every one was ready to die in her cause.

Tom saw there was no necessity to speak further.

He simply grasped the hand of each, and then commenced to give orders.

Their form of landing took him but a few moments to settle.

He did not intend to take with him any formidable force.

Himself, four middies, and two marines were all he needed.

These he took with him in his own boat.

The other boat, fully manned, and armed, was to follow, and wait at the place of landing their return.

Captain Tom had already espied a narrow gorge between two rocks, with a sort of shelf, where the boats could safely land, and to this he steered.

"Now, lads," he said, as he sprang from the stern sheets of the boat; "see to your arms. Let there be no misfiring; no stroke of a cutlass even thrown away."

He said no more.

Slowly they defiled up the narrow gorge, where the grass and brushwood bore token of the pass being used as a landing-place very recently, and they kept on in silence until they came to the narrow entrance of a dark tunnel.

Although bearing signs of ancient date, Tom's quick eye detected that it was not only the work of Nature but was also indebted to the handiwork of man.

Tom made a torch of a dry branch before entering it, yet he was loth to do so, but it was fortunate for them all that he did so, as it quickly proved.

Having penetrated about twenty feet, the passage widened, and in the centre of what might be termed a cavern there was a deep opening or well.

Tom held down the impromptu torch, and tried to penetrate the chasm to its depth.

He could not do so. But a stone thrown by one of the middies showed that it was of considerable depth.

Into this they would certainly have fallen and been lost for ever if Tom had not procured the torch.

But around this well or basin on either side there was a narrow ledge, just sufficiently wide for one to pass at a time, and then even the least slip or false step would have proved fatal.

Tom and his followers gave a shudder as they peered down into the inky darkness.

They had little doubt that if they could have penetrated to the bottom it would have revealed some horrible disclosures.

The bones of many of the victims of the Spanish governor and the monks of old.

This was a place well suited to the Death Pirate.

The sight of it the more fully confirmed our hero that he was on the right track to that horrible miscreant's haunt.

But there was no time for meditation.

Tom boldly led the way, and he and his six gallant followers disappeared again in another dark, cavernous opening on the opposite side.

This was as narrow as the first, but a trifle higher, so that they were relieved from the pain of stooping and the risk of dashing their heads against the rugged projections of the roof.

And so they kept on.

Tom sounding the walls and flooring with his sword.

His followers, trusting to his guidance, and listening with strained ears to every rustle or clink caused by their dress or weapons.

Tom had warned them to do this, for he had a sort of misgiving as to the success of their enterprise.

He had experienced such a feeling as now only once before in his hazardous life.

The night previous he had dreamed of his mother

and he had done so on the occasion before, and this preyed on his mind.

Her image haunted him even now.

He feared that this portended no good to Minnie.

Should he be too late to rescue her?

Should he find her a mangled corpse?

Had she been subjected to the gross insults of the pirate?

And worse, had she been victimised and tortured by the monks?

These thoughts harrowed his very soul as they wended their course along, what appeared to Tom in his present mood, the Valley of Death.

In the midst of these thoughts Tom Drake, with all his prudence and caution, stumbled.

His foot had caught against something that escaped his notice.

His torch too, fell from his hand, and suddenly extinguished.

But he soon sprang to his feet again.

In doing so, he trod upon that something that had caused his fall.

He stooped down and felt about.

His hand came in contact with an iron ring.

Then presently he felt a sort of ridge of about two feet square.

"A trap-door," he muttered; "perhaps our passage lay that way. However, we will try for another light."

They had provided themselves with wood for fresh torches, but Tom discovered that in his fall he had lost his tinder box.

By rubbing two pieces of stick, cut into a peculiar form, together, they succeeded in procuring another light.

Aided by this, they made a careful examination of the trap, but found it too heavy for them to raise.

A few feet from it, and just where our hero's head must have fallen, they discovered another deep chasm.

This too, was in an enlargement of the passage, and had a ridge only on one side, and at a glance the buccaneers saw that the pit was bricked and filled with machinery.

This then, no doubt, was another horrible place of torture.

Tom proceeded more cautiously after this.

His brain was more cloudy than ever.

Like a lump of lead his heart seemed to weigh down in his breast.

Presently they came to a flight of rough-hewn steps—and they ascended.

Two hundred and fifty, one of the middies counted.

At the top they found an old postal-door; it was open, and bore marks of having been severely battered.

The buccaneers now began to think that their journey must now nearly be ended.

Once they fancied that a gush of fresh air streamed in upon them.

Still they kept on.

Silent and cautious as before.

Fearing to speak, and listening to each sound.

But their suspense was not yet come to an end.

The passage they were now in was certainly broader and flagged with stones, but it seemed that it was never to end.

Its termination was in another flight of steps, a huge barred door with a small grating above, which admitted the fresh air the buccaneers had felt.

Handing one of his middies the torch, Captain Tom immediately proceeded to force the door, which was of some strength, but yielded to his exertions eventually.

Passing through, our heroes found themselves in a casemated chamber, the guns overthrown and shots lying about, bearing evidence of the place having stood a siege at some time.

This Tom conjectured was a sort of tower or outer bastion of some large and formidable fortress, so he proceeded with more caution, noting carefully each object they passed in their way.

Tom crept into one of the casemates and peered out.

There he saw a courtyard walled in and flanked about with many towers.

Then he ascended a flight of stone steps and took a survey from one of the many loop-holes.

He thus discovered that the island was well vegetated; that there was a river winding, perhaps, to its very centre, and that the taller towers commanded a view of the sea.

More than that Tom Drake could not discover.

He was in search of Minnie, and it now laid with his own judgment to learn the whereabouts of her prison home.

Some parts of the fortress were so dilapidated that it seemed it had not been used for many years, whilst others of more modern date bore traces of a warlike band.

At times the buccaneers fancied they could hear the clanking of armour or the footfall of an armed sentinel on the surrounding battlements.

"And you are not wholly wrong," said Captain Tom Drake, straining his accurate ear. "Stay you here and watch, while I go forward and reconnoitre."

With this he climbed into one of the casemates, and, squeezing himself through the aperture, disappeared.

The middies waited for him, and watched until their patience was exhausted.

Then the sun set, and it gradually grew darker

At length the shades of night fairly darkened all.

It was not a pleasant situation for the middies and the marines to be placed in.

To go back to the boat they had to meet over again all the dangers they had encountered, but they did not so much fear them as the thought of leaving their chief.

They consoled themselves with the suggestion that the brave buccaneer captain had made some important discovery, and concealed himself until the darkness rendered it safe for him to return to them.

There was a moon, however, and one of the buccaneers had thoughtfully provided himself with a flask of brandy, and with these they managed to wile their anxious watch away.

In the meantime how fared our gallant Captain Tom. On landing in the courtyard, his quick eye eagerly scanned the lofty towers, and believing no eye was watching him, he glided round the courtyard, and after a deal of difficulty, gained the habitable part of the stronghold.

Then, to his surprise, he beheld a more modern building, a mansion, from which the sounds of music streamed.

Instinct seemed to lead him to this particular spot.

A simple voice seemed to say that his Minnie was imprisoned there.

And so he gained more courage.

His natural prudence, in a measure, relaxed.

He committed the very fault, that at any other time, and under other circumstances, he would have shunned.

He stood in the very centre of the open courtyard, and gazed up at the palatial windows with the setting sun glaring full upon him.

He was observed, as might be supposed, by one of the sentries on the battlements, and while he was standing fascinated and rooted to the spot a voice of armed men surrounded him and made him prisoner.

The Spaniards handled our hero just as if he were an ox instead of a human being, but he felt not their harsh treatment.

He was most astounded at the wary manner in which he had been entrapped.

One desperate struggle for liberty he gave, but it was hopeless and futile.

As he succumbed he gave one more glance at the window which had so chained him to the spot, and again he saw a face that he could not be mistaken in recognising.

"Minnie, Minnie!" he exclaimed, as beads of sweat oozed from his brow. "Oh! my darling, shall I ever see you again?"

His guards seemed astounded at this display of weakness in one so brave and noble looking

They looked at each other, the captain gave an order in Spanish, and our hero was hurried quickly away.

At the first onset they took the precaution to disarm and pinion him, for they could see that a proud spirit, then lying dormant, might be easily aroused at any moment.

As they placed his cocked hat on his head and led him away Minnie Atherton gave a loud shriek.

This reached our hero's ears even through the glass of the casement.

It appalled him for an instant, but he recovered himself momentarily, and walked on with a firm step in the midst of his guards.

The dungeon to which he was consigned was not one of the description he had anticipated.

Chains there were, and strong iron rings set in the wall, but otherwise everything was as comfortable as he could have wished.

The walls were hung about with rich damask and a costly carpet covered the paved floor, and a handsome ottoman served as a seat or couch.

The mahogany table was a fixture, and this even had a damask cloth folded upon it.

In fact, the only features that reminded our hero that he was in prison were the chains, to the end of one of which his left ancle was manacled and the absence of any window or aperture to admit the daylight.

From the lofty groined ceiling however, suspended a silver lamp, which cast a dim, flickering light around the apartment.

Captain Tom Drake surveyed the apartment with mingled astonishment and doubt.

There was too much of an air of civility about it to suit him.

He had no doubt that this room was set apart for illustrious prisoners and that the captain of the guard, believing him to be some one of note, had acted on his own responsibility in placing him there.

In confirmation of this a soldier in superior costume and bareheaded visited him shortly and spread the cloth, that was soon after covered by other bareheaded servitors, with costly viands and various delicate fruits in which the island abounded.

There were cigars too, and a small oil lamp was left just to show that the prisoner was well guarded, and could be prevented at any moment from doing mischief.

Captain Tom Drake ate very sparingly.

He quaffed nearly a bottle of the best wine at a draught, and then lit a cigar.

Then he threw himself back on the soft velvet cushions of the ottoman, and endeavoured to compose his thoughts.

But he could not do this.

A thousand thoughts chased each other through his whirling brain, and a hundred visions fluttered across his closed eyes.

Thoughts of his Minnie, of Harry Vere, and of companions, of the brave hearts he had left in the tower, and lastly, but not least, of the "Will-o'-the-Wisp," and the remnants of his devoted buccaneer crew.

Divided as they were, it was no wonder he should feel uneasy.

Besides his bold, restless spirit could not brook long to be inactive.

And so he went on quaffing the wine, he knew not why, and smoked the cigars simply for companionship.

Alas! how changeable are the habits of man.

How truthful the axiom that "circumstances alter cases."

But time wore on as it always will, and morning came, though with our hero it was still night, and then the door of his prison chamber was thrown open.

Captain Tom was wide awake; in fact he had not slept, but he was not prepared for the sight that greeted him.

First came the soldier servitors that had attended him the previous night, and as they departed with the viands that were left, a priest bearing a crucifix, closely followed by the guard, entered.

Tom eyed the priest or monk with an air of diffidence, and, seeing the order to which he belonged, inquired with a glance the business that brought him there.

One can imagine that this inquiry was not necessary, but formal as it was, the priest made answer:

"To prepare you, my son, for your trial."

Captain Tom rose to his feet, and, with a scowl of disdain, said—

"Of what am I accused?"

"Being a spy, my son," was the priest's cool answer.

The gallant boy drew his proud form still more erect.

"Who dare be my accuser?' he asked.

"Signor Gonzalvo, the governor of this island," the priest replied.

"Let him dare accuse me, then, and by all above——"

Our hero stopped short in his speech.

He made the motion of clutching his sword, forgetting, in the moment of his excitement, that it was gone, and that he was a prisoner, with his leg manacled.

"My son," broke in the priest, seeing the brave boy's excitement; "invoke not the heavens to pour their wrath upon you. If you are found guilty, die not with a lie upon thy youthful lips."

Captain Tom eyed him with the same proud scorn.

"Lead me hence," he said; "but taunt me not with thy presence."

The priest bowed his head; then, devoutly lifting his eyes, raised the cross and kissed it.

The captain of the guard then motioned his men, who cast off the manacles, and led our hero from the chamber in the same form they had entered it, the priest leading the way, muttering prayers as he went.

The scene was solemn and impressive enough, and no doubt, had our hero been differently placed, he would have thought so.

As it was, he looked upon it as a mummery, and he longed for the journey to be at an end.

At times, with his head bowed, his left arm folded across his chest, and his chin leaning on the bent fingers of his right hand; at others, his eyes raised to the lofty ceiling that, even now in its crumbling state, still bore traces of the mighty powers of once-proud Spain.

He walked—amongst it seemed—along the corridors, here and there lit up by the glorious morning sun.

At length the judgment-hall was reached.

Its walls draped in black gave it a sombre hue.

Already the judgment-seat, on a raised dais, approached by a few steps, at one end of the hall, and a party of Spanish soldiers, mailed and armed, were drawn up in two lines on either side.

Tom, whether from the drowsy effects of the wine or the impressive aspect of the scene, seemed suddenly to lose all his wonted nerve and courage.

He listened with perfect indifference and meekness to the accusations brought against him.

Even when the sentence of death was pronounced against him he spoke not a word.

And so he was led away to the scaffold in the grand courtyard, and the headsman appeared with his axe.

Tom's frame never for a moment quivered even.

He suffered himself to be bound with the same meekness, and when desired by the executioner, Tom Drake knelt down by the block.

When the clattering caused by the mustering of the armed men who surrounded the scaffolding had ceased, and the voice of the priest became more audible in the stillness, our hero's calmness never forsook him.

Even when his neck was placed on the block, and the gleaming axe was poised above his head, the same calm smile rested on his handsome features.

But from that instant, and just as the headsman had taken true measurement of the mark.

When he was taking the necessary precautions to ensure his aim, a loud British cheer rang out, and Tom sprang to his feet.

Fortunately the headsman's axe had descended with such force as to bury its blade in the wood, and Tom, taking advantage of the moment, leaped from the scaffold into the midst of his gallant band of buccaneers.

Snatching a halberd from one of the astounded soldiery, Tom cleared off a crescent of heads at one sweep.

And then the gallant little band, back to back, kept their astounded foes at bay.

How this mysterious change was effected we must now explain.

CHAPTER CCXIX.

THE CONTENTS OF THE MYSTIC CASKET—A STRANGE WARNING—THE FIGHT.

HARRY VERE and his handful of buccaneers closed round the mystic casket as the young lieutenant opened the lid.

Then they all peered in before Harry drew forth its contents.

The sight they saw for a moment dazed their bewildered eyes.

There were hundreds of jewels, not large, but of the greatest rarity, and almost of every hue they could mention, and when Harry allowed them to feast their eyes to his satisfaction, he swept the precious stones aside to see what else it might contain.

What they then saw set them all shuddering.

There was a dagger crimsoned with gore, and a human skull, bleached so white, that it contrasted horribly with the ensanguined blade.

There was also a long epistle, too long for them to read then, and which Harry put back as Bob and Jerry's teeth, probably owing, as Ben charitably suggested, to the cold damp air of the apartment, were all of a chatter

There was only a parchment beside these—that is so far as their examination went.

It was hard to read, but by doing so slowly, Harry contrived to give himself and his three hearers an idea of it

'I, Cosmo di Porali, am a free citizen of the great and grand Republic of Venice. A Spanish ambassador had in his suite a noble secretary, who wronged my daughter and stole her away. I found her and him. I heard he was to occupy this palace, as he was governor. I disguised myself. I offered myself to his steward as decorator with rare, novel, and pleasing devices. I had my own way in the mansion. What I did you have seen. Scorn ever to wrong a woman. Seek ever to avenge her wrongs and maintain your honour!'

That was the whole.

They were about to comment on it, but their speech was enchained yet.

But not by the same influence of incomparable terror, but by another power, gentler yet as binding.

They looked up.

Between them and that wall through which the spectre of the vindictive Italian had disappeared, was another visitant, not of this world.

All in white, with a face flooded with a radiance like the placid reflection of a sleeping moonbeam on an unruffled lake, as swiftly graceful as the lilies that unfold their petals on the same smooth brim, this phantom relieved their hearts.

Another fright, and their agony would have been past bearing.

Lovely as was the vision, it revealed another charm by smiling encouragingly on them.

Then she summoned all their attention.

She pointed to the wall beside her.

"Listen!"

She scarcely seemed to have uttered the word, so faintly was it breathed.

She faded away into nothing.

As she vanished, another word had flown from her lips.

"Act!"

For a minute, each as he had been, not a stir did the buccaneers make.

Then, drawing a breath of relief together, they looked at one another.

"Listen and act," repeated Ben, breaking the silence.

"Ah!" said Harry. "And here are some things that will be very useful in the acting part."

He went to the wainscoting, to the part which had attracted his attention.

A trophy of horse-pistols, daggers long and short, and, best of all, four swords hung there.

All of the blades he took down.

Feeling the weight of each, bending them, trying a cut and a thrust, he selected two.

A long and truly formidable rapier he took for himself.

"Giachimo dele' Arti, Milagno."

That was the inscription accompanied with a significant, transfixed heart, graven on the blade.

"Milan make," said the young buccaneer. "I could not have guessed better."

And he handed the other weapon to Bob, who was unarmed.

It was a light and thin cut-and-thrust sword, elegant, the handle of ivory and gold, and little steel chains here and there in extremely good taste.

Harry read off the motto it bore.

"'In love and war, push forward'; or, go in and win," added he; "that is better English of it."

"Hark!" said Ben Barnacle. "Here's scaldrags."

Lieutenant Vere motioned all to be hushed.

A sound of steps was audible, cautiously marching in the next room.

They all approached the wall.

"We are to 'listen,' remember," said Harry as he saw Jerry flourishing his cutlass.

"And to 'act' too," said the latter.

But he did as he was advised.

CAPTAIN TOM DRAKE.

When the footsteps halted the altercation was at its height, and from what they could hear there were two female captives in the governor's palace, and one of them, whose name appeared to be Florida, had been the subject of a gambling transaction between the Spanish governor and number of his favourite courtiers, who had been specially invited to take part in it.

They had all been drinking pretty freely, but amongst the rest the buccaneers could hear the names of Uedro, Gargaison, and Duro the most used.

The governor's name they easily learnt was Gonsalvo, and he was evidently disputing with some one whose name did not transpire, but who it would seem was an English officer, as to the justice of releasing an English captive that had been left on the island a day or two previously.

This captive Harry felt certain was no other than Minnie Atherton.

As he listened he found that the quarrel was growing hotter every moment.

The Spaniard's fierce blood was rising, and so was the English officer's metal.

The latter it would appear had some friends on his side, but they appeared to be quarrelling with some of the Spaniards in a room farther back, or on the stairs.

Harry Vere at this juncture made a hole in the panel of the door with his dirk and peeped through.

The Englishman was at that moment taking an oath to see justice done to the English girl, who was clinging to his arm for protection.

The Spaniards were jeering him, and avowedly declared that his friendship for the girl was all a boast, and that he desired her freedom to accomplish his own evil intentions.

The Englishman, fired at this, drew his sword and made a mark on the floor with its point.

He then stepped back and eyed the Spaniards so fiercely that the foremost hesitated to cross the mark.

"I'll kill the first of you who steps foot across that line!" cried the officer.

"Then I'm the first man!" cried the governor. "Let's see you kill! Come on, you fellows!"

"There's more not far below," continued the governor; "and if you don't deliver your sword immediately, I'll save the gallows the task, and chop your head and arm off!"

"The gallows!" repeated the Englishman, puzzled, still on guard.

"The gallows, of course!" said the Spaniard, in answer, as he led on his dissipated courtiers another step. "We knew you for all your innocent air."

"We know you!" chorussed the gang.

"You're crazy, knaves," retorted the officer, lowering the point of his sword. "My intentions are honourable."

"So you say!" sneered one.

"Very fine, my prince of pirates, but you are as crafty as Satan."

"Sirrah, you lie!"

"You lie, dog!"

The Englishman turned.

The same glance that told him that Minnie had suddenly been spirited away from the corner where he had placed her for safety, showed him four men behind him, mysteriously come through the wall.

Had he turned more quickly, he would have seen the secret door gape and emit the four buccaneers.

He only saw them in the room, as it was.

Against them, too, he hurriedly put himself on guard.

But the first words of their young leader set his fears in that quarter at rest.

"We are friends," said that leader, sword in hand.

"English, by all the devils!" exclaimed the Spaniard, recoiling.

Still the governor had numbers on his side, and determined to try an attack, in which he had so much to gain.

There was the guard's help coming soon.

Clash! went his rapier on the fine sword of Harry Vere.

He was cunning enough to avoid meddling with the elder seamen, whose metal he guessed.

The combat was commenced instantly.

All were mingled together.

Here Bob's long Italian rapier described a sweep which defended the breast from three simultaneous thrusts.

There Ben Barnacle felt his blade encounter that peculiar yielding resistance that flesh of a living being offers to a piercing instrument.

In this corner Jerry, his back against the wall, his foot on a dying wretch, whom a slash over the head and ear had so soon brought to the ground, traced zigzags with his trenchant steel.

Gonsalvo and Vedro had driven Harry into another corner.

The room was empty of furniture, save two chairs and an old cabinet, over to which the young lieutenant retreated.

With a kick, dealt during a breathing spell, Harry flung over the cabinet on its face.

It formed a barrier, and at the same time a pedestal to him.

By mounting that, he became superior in height to his two antagonists.

He could reach their breasts and their heads.

His two adversaries could only make points at his chest.

Domineering over the whole chamber of battle, drunk with the sparks that flew from the reddened swords, filled with an energy that came from the view of such a scene, the youth felt himself fired with that heroic feeling best expressed in our manly tongue by "to do, or to die!"

"Give in, you young knave!" shouted a new comer.

It was a very tall man, Gargaison by name.

A moment disengaged from Ben by a swaying of the ring around him, he thought he would put the valuable governor under an obligation to him, if he should take the noble youth in the flank.

"Give in, or I'll gut you like a lark."

So tall was he, towering over Gonsalvo, that he was almost as high as the youth on the elevated stand.

Harry's flaming eyes glowed bright with indignation at the coward making the party three to one.

"Dastard! take care!"

He warded off an upward thrust from Gonsalvo, a side cut from Gargaison, and retaliated by drawing an inch or so of his weapon over Vedro's fingers.

"Ow!" howled the latter, dropping his cutlass.

"Take care?" sneered Gargaison, covering his head to receive a downward sweep before he returned it. "Of what?"

"You are not long for this earth, master six feet of uselessness!" retorted the young buccaneer.

He had risen on tiptoe and moved forward, so reckless that Gonsalvo, seizing the chance, prepared to push in at the opening.

With all the strength of which he was capable, Harry swung his sword up, around, and down on the tall man's head.

The latter had his hanger up on guard.

The meeting of the metal made a myriad of sparks fly off.

The undermost blade beaten down, lowered its end.

The other following it, drew its point from the temple transversely over the nose and cheek to the jaw.

The big bully dropped his weapon from his disabled hand, and covered his slashed and blood-running features with his ten fingers.

Like a thought, Harry was quick.

As he recovered his sword, he made a little turn that saved his heart from the governor's lunge, and pushed his blade at the tall ruffian's body.

It found its way between two ribs, and buried itself therein.

The man fell back.

So suddenly, that the dealer of his death, unable to keep his balance, fell forward, sword's hilt still in his hand, its other end half buried in the dying man.

So was he pinned to the floor helpless.

Harry Vere fell on top of his body, half kneeling.

At the same time Vedro and the governor were moved by a similar thought.

The former picked up his cutlass with his bleeding hand, the other lifted his.

Both of their weapons impended over the prostrate youth.

His foot slipped in the blood of the dying man.

Past ability to rise, or even throw up his unarmed hand to protect himself, Harry believed that his next breath would be the last he was ever to draw.

Ben saw the lieutenant's danger.

Ben had run the man opposed to him through the shoulder, and almost severed his sword arm with a swift cut.

Douro, the other opponent of his, fought with a loaded bludgeon in lieu of the steel, for in the first encounter with Bob Hauler he had been disarmed.

He was swinging it about his head and aiming at Ben.

The latter felt but too certain that if ever that club dashed against his blade, it would hardly be useful after such a weighty shock.

Hence he avoided any clashing with the cudgel, while he kept the man in play.

Douro was certain to be tired out first, having the heavier instrument to wield.

Thus was the seaman engaged at the important moment when the two swords of Damocles hung over Harry's bent form.

Ben gave an exclamation of pain.

With the sudden and sure spring of a serpent stretching out his coils, his lithe steel glided along the bravo's club, and slid still further through his left arm into his side.

Douro yelled with agony.

Red bubbles broke on his lips, as he half wheeled round, grasped at the air, and fell on the floor.

Five minutes after he was dead.

Ben whipped out the fatal instrument from the sufficient orifice, and leaped to the spot where his presence was so much required.

Such was the fury in the upward sweep which he gave Vedro's down-coming blow, that the latter's cutlass remained stationary, but quivering all over from tip to haft in his palsied hand.

The next instant an extension of Ben's left arm and clenched fist sent him rolling clean through the threshold of the door.

In vain did Gonsalvo, just warned in time, seek to change his attack on Vere, into a defence of self.

Back over his head Ben Barnacle forced his arm, twisting his wrist till the pain was beyond endurance.

As Gonsalvo swung himself half round to ease the turn of his hand, the buccaneer flung him from him.

"Think yourself lucky you are let wear out your shoes," said he.

Now, as that shove was applied to the uppermost portion of the Spaniard's body, sending him along, he would have speedily reached the ground head foremost.

But Ben, with a kind of justice, lifted his foot instantly, and applied, lower down on the governor's back, one of those kicks which till then Gonsalvo was not utterly ignorant of.

The consequence was that, perfectly upright, but not raising his feet, he skimmed along the floor without power to check his flight, met Vedro just rising in the doorway, knocked him down again, and after executing an admirable summersault, stood on his head for a space in an angle of the next room.

Harry Vere then rose.

"Thanks," said he, giving his hand to Ben.

The latter shook it heartily, motioned him to arm himself, and plunged into the still continuing fray.

For all was not over so soon.

The young lieutenant had ranked himself side by side with Bob, and they rivalled one another in defending themselves against double their number.

They were not wounded, though their clothes were ruffled and ripped in places.

But they had killed their man a-piece.

As for Jerry, he had pierced the thigh of one of his brace of opponents, and made him rest himself, half-sitting, against the wall, making him look a subject for Doctor Shrike.

As Ben prepared to help whoever should most need him, he saw Bob's cutlass flash out, and one of the pair before him leap in the air to fall immediately.

Ben then rid him of the third, by attacking that individual himself.

Freshened by his short respite, the buccaneer bid fair to make short work of him.

Each had his man now.

Harry was watching Vedro and Gonsalvo outside the door.

As the first-named, the breath knocked out of his body, was too weak to rise, he was not very formidable.

The governor, with his position changed from the topsy-turvy to a more natural one, was diving his hand into his bosom, no doubt to staunch some painful wound.

Hence Harry could not take his attention off them.

Well that he did not so!

For what should he see but one of the supposed corpses, his face bathed in blood from his split skull, rising on his shattered leg and one hand.

With the other he held a pistol.

His own hate foiled his bloody intent.

For he had ample time to kill the nearest foeman to him, if he had quickly pulled the trigger.

Harry, if winged even, could not have reached him in time.

Almost glued to the spot by horror at such devilish coolness, the youth beheld that dying man, who sought to give death to others, deliberately wait till a pause in the changes of the fighting men should answer his purpose.

It was the hand of Bob that had stretched him there.

It was Bob, too, at whom he steadily aimed.

Bob neither saw him nor suspected his wicked purpose.

In two long leaps Harry was over by the man

with one cut he severed the hand, just pressing the trigger, from the extended arm.

It fell, detached in tender sinew and flesh, bone, and skin, from the member, which spouted out blood.

With the life in death that has been known to make a stricken-off head blush at an insult, the hand, still grasping the fire-arm, moved, as if some unknown monstrosity crawling on the carpet with three of its stiffening fingers.

It was but a spasm.

But the convulsive pressure sufficed.

The trigger was pulled, the hammer, faced with flint, dropped in the pan, and found enough powder unshaken out to spread its sparks.

A ringing report filled the chamber with its sound.

The harmless load, the bullet bounding along the floor, filled it with smoke and a flash of flame.

As the scream of pain still hung upon the lips of the would-be assassin, foiled and punished, the young lieutenant's streaming sword found the way to his black heart.

The smoke circled all through the place, all the more thickly from being so confined.

Still the fight went on.

The four seamen and the man they had befriended, confronted the four surviving men, and drove them back.

At the sound of the pistol shot within, a cry, peculiar, and of the nature of a signal, echoed outside and below.

"Hilli-i-ahoy!" cried Vedro, in reply.

The rush of many feet on the hollow stairs was heard.

Then Gonsalvo, who had not been searching in his bosom for a wound, as Harry had imagined, hurriedly and with joy tried to scramble upon his feet.

With all the breath he could command he raised an appealing call.

An answer came.

The sound of heavy feet drew nearer.

"This way, captain! Help, Senor Goupille, help!" bellowed he.

He and Vedro scrambled to their feet.

The approaching succour inspired the rascals with fresh power.

But it was also a spur to their enemies.

With a fury that their opponents could not begin to meet, the five allies beat down all guards, turned the edges and points from them, and bundled their antagonists out of the door to stumble over Gonsalvo and the other, busy in halloaing the reinforcements on.

"Who burnt powder?" roared the captain's hoarse voice.

He glared around, in the smoke, wrathfully.

"Who burnt powder, I say? Do you want all the servants up? The palace is roused now—and a curse on ye! Where's senor governor? Well, Senor Gonsalvo, what's all this over one man?"

"One man!" groaned the Spaniard.

He hastened to explain to Goupille all that had occurred.

The latter started in amazement.

'Men of the 'Will-o'-the-Wisp' here, and their young lieutenant? Plague on it, if I had only known! Where?"

"In there!"

The captain lifted up his voice, while he pounded on the stone floor with the hilt of his sword.

"Tumble up here, quick, all hands!" cried he.

Besides the three or four sailors who had come up stairs with him, more rushed from the dining-hall, and began to swarm up the stairs.

"There's the lopers inside," continued the Frenchman, "that wrecked the craft we were going to have merry cruises on! D'ye hear, fore and aft?"

"Aye, aye, sir!"

"No clapping in bilboes for them, but death!"

"Death!" chorussed all.

The door through which the surviving combatants had been shoved had been slammed very rudely on them.

In fact, Ben, Bob, and Jerry had instantly dragged the bureau on which Harry had been mounted, to the door, and propped it against the panels.

Quick as they, Harry flung the now broken pair of chairs against that.

The bodies, not one of which had life, were piled on top of that barricade.

"Heavy, if nothing more," said old Ben. "That will give us a bit of respite."

They heard Goupille growling as he listened to the governor's quick recital.

'Now," said the captain, "don't stand there gaping at the shut door, you set of curs!"

The fact was that the story Gonsalvo had to tell, supported by the bloody and battle-stained look of the remaining sufferers, had prevented the company expressing eagerness to open the entrance.

"Shall I wake you up?" snarled the captain, swinging his sword menacingly.

Still motionless stood the soldiers.

"Scampia!" cried the captain of the guard, to one of them, "as the door wont open, try your halbards."

As really the lower part of the door was immovable from the weights placed against its base the smashing in of the upper was the feasible plan.

In a trice Scampia's weapon had ripped out the oaken plank.

All of the soldiers drew back their heads from the opening, in full expectation of their curiosity being saluted by a volley of bullets, or a few inches of steel.

"Now, then, what do you see?" cried the captain, advancing.

As the chamber was very quiet, that—to those men who had been told that the fighters were within—was only the more sinister.

The captain of the guard boldly thrust his head in the burst-through gap.

"You awkward, scared crows!' said he, "there's nobody there."

"Nobody!" echoed the Spanish soldiery.

How that assurance relieved them all.

Busy as bees, they hammered on the door; and had its fragments down on the pile in a minute or two.

The captain took hold of Scampia by the waist, and rolled him clean over the heap of bodies, right into the chamber.

"Empty," said he.

But the corpses and the blood stains, the severed hand and the weapons, assured him that the governor's story had been only too full of truth.

And it was to this very circumstance that Captain Tom's trial and intended execution had been pushed on so hastily.

CHAPTER CCXX.

THE BATTLE WITH THE SPANISH SOLDIERY—RETREAT TO THE CAVE—HORRIBLE CRUELTY OF THE SPANIARDS.

THE lieutenant of the "Will-o'-the-Wisp" and his little party, on finding that the Spanish governor had called the guards, made their retreat as quickly as possible; but as their way lay not backward but forward, they did not go back by the subterranean passage; but, finding a casement that led into a courtyard, they dropped lightly from it, closing the casement after them.

A DOZEN INDIANS SUDDENLY APPEARED.

Ben Barnacle was the one to whom this latter task was assigned.

And as he turned to j in his companions, he was somewhat startled to find a bevy of middies grinning at him from a loop-hole in one of the adjacent towers.

In an instant he was by the side of Harry Vere.

"Look—look," he said, pointing.

"Ah, by Jove, the mids of the ' Will-o'-the-Wisp!'" Harry exclaimed. "Come on, lads, let us join them at once."

This was no sooner said than put into execution.

There were two walls to scale and as many court-yards to cross; but, aided by the rope which Ben always took care to provide on such occasions, the task was of no great difficulty.

Harry's first act was to enquire for Captain Tom; but, the answer not being satisfactory, Harry Vere was determined to go in search of him, leaving the nine buccaneers to talk over their adventures.

The lieutenant was not long absent, though it seemed to his companions that he had been away an hour.

They all eyed him in fact as a pack of hungry wolves might have been expected to have done on seeing their prey.

He looked very pale, did Harry.

There was a mystified air about him that they thought boded no good.

"What's up, Mr. Vere?" said Ben Barnacle, breaking the silence. "Nothing happened to the captain, I hope."

Harry whispered in his ear.

Ben started back with a cry of alarm.

"Buckle to, lads,' he said hoarsely. "See to your barkers. Our brave captain is in danger."

"No!" exclaimed the buccaneers in a voice, and as with one motion their cutlasses leapt from their scabbards.

"Yes, he is to die a traitor, a spy, a felon's death on the scaffold—he is to be—"

69

Ben's speech was interrupted.

"No, by heavens, not while we have weapons and arms to wie'd them."

"Away then, let us to the rescue; every moment shortens his existence" cried Ben.

The buccaneers were soon in readiness.

Harry Vere led the way from the ruined fortress, and the marines brought up the rear.

Stealing along under shadow of the walls, creeping on hands and knees through the dank grass, they approached the place assigned for the execution.

The scaffold was a fixture, for in those days it was considered an ornament rather than a disgrace to any military stronghold.

The sight of their gallant captain bareheaded and pinioned on the scaffold gave the buccaneers the pluck and spirit of double their number.

They were only in time to save him.

There was not a moment to lose.

"Quick, lads," cried Harry, "cheer and board."

No sooner had he spoken than the ringing cheer Tom had heard awoke the echoes of the grand court-yard, and like a host of furies the bold buccaneers fell upon the men-at-arms.

Cutlass and pistol were both used with good effect, and, as Captain Tom leapt from the fatal spot, old Ben severed the rope that bound our hero's arms with his sheath knife.

This was only the commencement of a fierce and bloody strife.

There were only eleven in all of the buccaneer crew, while the Spaniards, independent of the slain and wounded lying around, even now more than doubly outnumbered them

But the buccaneers had the advantage of them in weapons.

The men-at-arms, never for a moment dreaming of an attack, had only their long pikes and halberds, and these in close quarters were in no way equal to the cutlasses and pistols of the buccaneers.

Captain Tom at the first opportunity possessed himself of a sword, and he made good use of it when he found one.

He clove the head pieces of the soldiery, and thrust his sword point in the interstices of the mail of his opponents, so that the courtyard soon streamed in gore, and the iron shod feet of the men-at-arms found difficult foothold on the slippery pavement.

Captain Tom rallied his little band with continual cheers.

"Hurrah for the 'Will-o'-the-Wisp.' Think of poor Minnie" shouted he.

But at every word the buccaneers laid their strokes on harder, and made their steel clash and emit sparks as it came in contact with the iron mail of the soldiery.

Harry Vere Ben Barnacle, and Jerry fought side by side most of the time, Bob being somewhat in the rear, and doing a little in the way of carving on the unarmoured backs of the Spanish guardsmen.

Bob was a little out of place here, but he had been cut off from the rest, and he was not the one to waste a good opportunity.

As to the marines, with their muskets and bayonets, they did good service in picking off the matchlock-men, who had taken their stand on the scaffold, and were very choice in the selection of their mark.

Every shot they fired seemed to be aimed at the young buccaneer chief, who was rendered the more conspicuous by his snow-white shirt and bared head.

Thus the fight waged on, the combatants surging and swaying to and fro.

Oaths, curses, and the cries of mental agony or victory being mingled together.

At length Tom, seeing his little band being

broken up, and hearing the Spanish trumpeter announce that reinforcements were coming, thought it prudent to withdraw from the scene.

At length an opportunity offered itself.

The drawbridge was down and the portal open, and the brave little band, mustering as well as they could, gave the enemy one parting volley and fled to a cave hard by.

From thence they anticipated an easy retreat to some place where they might reach the ship; but, alas! their troubles were not yet ended.

On calling a muster, which only took a few minutes, several of the little band were missing

Harry Vere for one, and this grieved Captain Tom very sore.

"What think you of the scoundrels?" he queried of old Ben; "why have they not followed us? Perhaps they have beat a retreat in order to lure us from our stronghold."

"It is hard to say," rejoined Old Ben, "but I do not like their protracted silence; it bodes no good to us for you may rest assured that they are plotting mischief."

As if to confirm his words, a rush of approaching footsteps was heard from without, followed by a loud and ferocious cheer.

"Surrender!" exclaimed a loud, stern voice which our hero at once recognized as belonging to the Spanish governor. "We will smoke these hornets out of their nests. Bring higher the rushes."

"Mother of heaven! what is their purpose?" gasped a marine, falling upon his knees and clasping his hands.

"You have his purpose from his own lips," returned Captain Tom. "He means to stifle us with smoke."

A babel of oaths and laughter now rang from outside the cavern, while the inmates uttered cries of derision.

Thin jets of blue curling smoke now began to ooze through the crevices of the huge masses of rock by which the entrance of the cavern had been blocked up.

A hot and suffocating vapour permeated the place, accompanied by a horrible stench of burning.

The agony endured by the victims of this diabolic act of atrocity were appalling; they appeared to be inhaling the searing blast from a seven-times heated furnace, which seemed to scorch and wither up their very entrails

Their eyes started from their sockets, they madly clutched the idle air with their distorted fingers in all the fearful agonies of strangulation.

In vain they attempted to cry out—their parched lips and tongues could utter no sound; their lungs were filled with the suffocating fumes, and they were fain to writhe upon the ground in mortal horror and agony.

Still the Spanish demons without gave vent to their devilish glee and triumph in shouts of triumphant laughter. Even in this extreme moment, though wounded, Captain Tom's courage and presence of mind did not desert him.

Failing in his efforts to utter an intelligible sound, he made signs to his buccaneers, who, immediately comprehending his intention, hastened to second his efforts.

Quick as thought, he selected the strongest of the band, and, he, setting the example, they applied their brawny shoulders and sinewy arms to the topmost boulder of the rocky barricade, and heaved with might and main till the perspiration, induced by heat and exertion, streamed from their over-strained limbs.

A sudden jolt, and they blunder forwards.

They have succeeded in dislodging the rock; it thunders down with a booming crash, twisting through the pyre of burning rushes, and filling the air with a shower of sparks and flame'ets.

Then the smoke soared up to the roof of the cave, eddying hither and thither in currents, and the blessed sea-breeze wafted in, and once more the wrecked prisoners drew the breath of life.

"Look to your weapons, comrades!" cried Tom Drake, in a loud husky whisper, the blood foaming from his lips, " better a quick death than this foretaste of purgatory. We will make a sally for life and freedom."

The buccaneers answered with a faint, but passionate cry, intended for a cheer.

Captain Drake tightened his belt, drew his glittering sword from its sheath, and, dashing through the opening in the rocks, flung himself upon the Spaniards with indomitable valour.

Enraged at the defeat of their ruthless stratagem, the soldiers fought with the utmost fury.

Their leader, a fine looking, black-bearded fellow, at once attacked our hero.

Their swords clashed, and they contended with all the hardihood that desperation and personal hatred could inspire.

Cap'ain Tom's sword clove the helmet of the Spaniard, inflicting a frightful gash in his head, but in the instant of victory the brave buccaneer chief was borne down by a charge of the enemy, and his body pierced with lance-points.

Still the fight went on with undiminished vigour.

Tumult and confusion, wild shouts and cries of pain or triumph, and the rush of the contending parties was kept up without interruption.

The buccaneers fought as only men who have nought to gain and all to lose, can fight. Old Ben took the lead in every desperate charge, his hair "all dabbled in blood," but his arm smiting with the strength of an invincible lion.

At length came a delicious shout from the buccaneers.

"Hurrah! hurrah! We are saved!"

It was true, though late ; the middies on board hearing the sounds of strife had effected a landing, and, with yells of mingled wrath and exultation, threw themselves upon the foe with reckless ardour.

———

CHAPTER CCXXI.

HARRY VERE'S DISCOVERY — THE STORY OF THE DYING SAILOR.

LEAVING Cap'ain Tom and his reinforcement of middies to settle matters with the Spaniards, let us follow the fortunes of the brave Harry Vere.

Having seen Minnie, and now certain that she was a prisoner in the Spaniard's palatial residence, he was determined at all hazards, if he could not rescue her, to at least have an interview with her.

This was a daring resolve, especially as he knew the desperate and fiendish character of the governor.

However, Harry was not to be daunted.

Taking advantage of a moment when the fight was at its height, he slipped away unobserved, and took up a position where he could view the numerous towers of the fortress.

There was one tower in particular that attracted his notice more than the rest.

It was of a most peculiar structure.

About twelve feet from the summit, and just below the battlements, there was a projection of stone work, which would allow of a rope pending from it to drop outside the bastion wall.

It was a structure something like a granary, and no doubt at one time the fortress was previsioned by its aid, when the Spaniards were afraid to lower the drawbridge or open the portal gates.

While Harry was looking upward at this, he fancied he saw something white flutter from one of the casements, and as his eye got more accustomed to the distance he made it out to be a handkerchief held in a lily-white hand.

Presently he saw a face, and the blood seemed to come through him afresh as he gazed and recognised the features of Minnie.

Harry in his excitement was about to rush from his concealment, to signal to her, when she, doubtless guessing his intention, warned him by a gesture to remain where he was.

Harry saw the prudence of this instantly.

There was a head and face, probably of her jailor, at the loophole just beneath.

But Harry had risked the chance of being called a coward by stealing away from the fight, and especially by those who might have forgotten that the rescue of Minnie was the sole cause of the buccaneers visiting the island.

Harry was on the alert for the least chance o entering the tower.

It came at last.

At the very moment when Captain Tom and hi followers beat their retreat.

The loud shouts and the pistol volley caused the jailor to turn his head.

Then Harry bounded across to a portal door that had been left negligently ajar, and leaped up the stone stairs with the agility of a roe.

He counted the different flights as he went.

By this he knew when he reached the landing, from the loophole of which he had seen the face of the jailor.

He passed the dark visaged jailor very cautiously.

In fact, Harry crept on almost with catlike stealth.

The black bearded Spaniard had his head thrust out as far as possible to obtain a view of the fight, or probably Harry would have dropped him one on his cranium.

Harry quickly reached the next landing.

Panting from his exertion he paused at the first door he came to.

He examined the lock.

It was very old indeed.

With the point of his dirk he picked the lock easily.

Then he entered the narrow cell.

"Minnie," he said, for the gloom almost blinded him.

There was only a moan.

What could it mean ?

He never thought for a moment that he might have entered the wrong cell.

The moan was repeated.

"Minnie," he again whispered.

Then he tried to pierce the gloom.

He also took a pace forward.

But still no answer came.

He was so puzzled that he seemed rooted to the spot.

He uttered the name for the third time.

Then he was about to turn away, when he fancied he saw something move.

It looked very much like a handful of rags.

Still it must be living.

The moans had proceeded from it.

What could it be?

All these questions flitted like wildfire through his brain.

For the moment he forgot all about Minnie.

He stooped down to view the strange object closely.

As he did so, another moan ca
torious heap.

Then a bony hand was stretched forth, and the almost fleshless fingers clutched Harry by the leg.

Harry Vere chilled with horror at this.

It seemed so death-like, that grip.

But the voice of a man, or rather what should have been a man, aroused him to his senses.

"Ah! I see you are a friend," said the object, in a voice almost inarticulate. "You have come to see me die, to hear my last words on this earth."

"Poor mortal! who art thou?" said Harry, sadly.

"One who has known sorrow. One who has felt pain. One who has endured that which I hope you never will, young man."

Harry was so impressed with the poor fellow's speech that he forgot altogether the object that brought him to the tower.

He listened, as it were, entranced and in silent pity.

"Will you," continued the strange being, "listen to the recital of a dying wretch, whose days, whose very hours are numbered? For I learnt from your first entry that you were in search of a female, even as I was in search of a daughter, and it has brought me to the misery in which you now behold me."

Harry became more interested as the man proceeded.

"What was her name?" he asked, almost unconsciously.

"Florida, she was my only child, sir; should you ever meet her in your wanderings will you tell her the fate of her sire, and tell her that his last breath was a blessing upon her head."

The young buccaneer was anxious to hear the man's story, the more so, as he had heard the name mentioned by the Spaniards in their quarrel.

But time was speeding swiftly.

He, therefore, impressed upon the man the necessity of beginning his story, which he did in the following simple manner:—

I will not weary you with a long recital (said the dying man) suffice it, that our vessel was bound to the West Indies, where the Yellow Jack seized upon our crew and carried them off one by one.

The captain, mate, and the majority of the crew dead, what was to be done? Natives were employed by the agent to get on loading the ship, and in time we were ready for sea, with a full cargo of cocoa-nut oil and log-wood.

But how to get the ship home would have puzzled anybody but the rascally agent who was employed by our owner, for, in addition to the want of captain and mate, the former, during the delirium attendant upon the fever, had thrown overboard all the nautical instruments and charts.

The agent was good at expedients.

Not far from us there was another vessel belonging to different owners. Her mate was a notorious ruffian in the African trade, and our agent promised him if he would on his own responsibility and risk, get our ship to England, he should, over and above his just pay, receive a share of the cargo.

Meanwhile, one or two seamen and seven natives were shipped for the passage home.

One evening late the new captain joined; he had stolen some instruments from his former ship, and, at day dawn, we weighed and put to sea, having at that time on board only six casks of provisions; and the greediness of the agent to fill us with oil had barely left in the brig twelve days' water.

This, indeed, was a sorry look-out for us. All the crew grumbled terribly, and the new captain became greatly frightened when he was informed how little there was in the vessel.

Going ashore to the agent, the captain begged for more water and provisions; but the rascally agent, knowing that the still more rascally captain dared not remain, now answered—

"Never mind your shortness of provisions, you will soon be in the track of homeward-bound ships."

And with this answer our roguish commander was obliged to be content.

So we got under weigh, every man with a growl upon his lips and discontent at his heart. Scarcely, however, had we reached the mouth of the river, when we found a boat with six armed men running nearly under our bows.

"Be the holy poker," exclaimed Pat, an Irish seaman, "that looks like business. The fellows are all armed; what can they be after?"

"No good, I'll warrant," cried a sailor near us; "they are pirates and intend boarding us."

"Pirates!" said Pat. "Not a bit of it; it's the skipper of the 'Mary Jane' come after his"——

But Pat did not finish his sentence, which would have run, "instruments of which our new skipper has robbed him," for our captain at the same moment came up to where we were standing.

"You rascally thief," cried aloud the commander of the boat; "throw over my quadrant, sextant, and charts, or by Neptune we'll board you."

At this our noble chief only laughed, which annoyed the boat's crew, and they commenced to put their skipper's threats into execution.

Seeing which our hero seized a large axe and, standing at the gangway, swore a dreadful oath that he would cash out the brains of the first man who tried to come on board.

"Bedad, he don't mane it; he dare not," whispered Tom.

But, alas! the next instant one of the boat's crew, who had clambered up the chains, fell backwards, with his skull split in two by the axe.

"It's murder," exclaimed several of our men; and, bad as most of them were, I believe a cold shudder ran through every one of them.

But no one attempted to seize him, as a better ordered crew would certainly have done.

No, they let him pass into his cabin, with his bloodless face and his heart quivering at, perhaps, the ultimate consequences of his crime; while the rest of the boat's party, either in fear, or, perhaps, with a faint hope that surgical aid might even yet avail their stricken comrade, fired a single volley of musketry, and then pulled towards the shore.

Would that it were the only murderous deed performed by that cruel wretch.

By pressing all sail we soon got out to sea and out of all danger of being boarded by anything the then very feeble European authorities had it in their power to send in chase of us.

Soon—very soon, commenced our miseries—aye, miseries most dire.

The very next day after we left the river we were put upon an allowance of water; and almost as soon we found, at least Pat and I, that, compared with our new captain, the one who had brought the ship from England was an angel.

The possibility of running short of water at sea was terrible to contemplate, the reality horrible.

For three weeks we had a foul wind, and at the end of that time we had but a few gallons of water left; a dreadful death threatened us.

In this juncture the captain now kept the ship away for some island; but he ought to have done so sooner.

When he came to announce the scarcity of water he brought with him a small pot full of the fluid, now to us of a thousand times the value of gold, and, calling all hands aft, he served it out among us to the last drop, by a spoonful at a time.

Fearful was the week that followed; the wind was scant, and our deeply-laden leaky craft did not move through the water; we ceased to speak to each other; we seemed like so many deaf and dumb creatures, and sometimes ruffians who had long been strangers to tears would be seen weeping like so many children, and praying to God for mercy.

Then it became dead calm, with a scorching sun, and the clouds, which sometimes mustered on the horizon, brought neither rain nor wind.

Here we would sit and watch the setting sun, and darkness closing in upon us; for then the dew would fall, and all night long we wretched, most wretched creatures would crawl about, licking the moisture from the spars, decks, and paintwork of the ship's side.

We all became wickedly selfish. I remember that Jim and I had, by good chance, a strong tin kettle. I set to work to boil sea-water, and condense the vapour; but, alas, I hardly made a pint of fresh water in twenty four hours.

However, we succeeded in supporting ourselves without having recourse, as the majority of the crew had, to drinking salt water, and thus avoided being attacked with dysentery, as those poor creatures were.

My friend the Irishman, who had persuaded me to join the cruise. one morning burst out—

"Oh, my friend, it's meself that should be beat black and blue, for why did I ever persuade you to take to such a divil's own life? It's dying by inches that you are, me poor frind."

"Nonsense, Pat, we are all taking the same chance on the same planks, with the same God above us. Repining is useless," said I.

"Ah, me frind, it isn't for meself that I repine"

"Hilloa," I exclaimed, as I heard the report of a pistol, "what's the meaning of that?"

"Look; take care of yourself, the skipper's gone clane mad," replied Pat.

And sure enough the captain, with a loaded pistol in his hand, was running round the ship, chasing one of the crew, a Frenchman we had shipped in the coast.

Fortunately, although the skipper fired the second pistol, the Frenchman remained unhurt.

Such fracas had now become common. The cause of that, however, was as follows:—

The Frenchman had discovered that the captain had secreted several bottles of rum for his own especial consumption, and, as discipline was now totally at an end, he purloined some of the bottles, and ran forward with them, chased by the captain.

When the Frenchman, however, descended into the forecastle among the other men, the captain did not dare follow or call him to account, for to the crew those bottles of rum were a prize of hundreds of times more value than if they had been filled with diamond dust.

The skipper, at all times of unreasonable temperament, after this fracas, seemed to have lost all restraint over his passions, and seldom did a day pass without some act of wanton cruelty.

Our first watch, the Frenchman happened to be licking the dew off the capstan on the quarter-deck.

This the skipper usually appropriated as his perquisite, and, in a fury at what he considered the Frenchman's insolence, he took up a piece of heavy wood which happened to be at hand, and, as the sailor leaned over the capstan, struck him with full force on the back of his head.

The Frenchman's cap saved his life, but his lips were cut through and his front teeth loosened. He gave a yell of rage, and rushed into the cook's caboose for a knife.

The captain, at the same time, got a pistol out of the cabin; a scuffle ensued, in which the pistol was fired without effect, but the Frenchman gave the captain an ugly cut across the ear with his knife, when fortunately at this juncture the crew inter-

fered, and the maddened belligerents were separated.

But alas! that I should have to record, that sad even as was the scene, it was but the forerunner of tragedies to come.

It was the day after—our miseries had become by so many hours the greater—when Pat, coming into the captain's cabin where I was engaged, cried joyfully as he caught up two of the rum bottles:—

"Bedad, Tim, here's something that'll keep the life in us a day or two longer. Let us drain all the empty bottles."

"It is a glorious notion," I exclaimed.

"What's a glorious notion, you skulking lubber?" cried the savage skipper, as he entered the cabin with a cudgel in his hand.

We told him.

And, half mad already, and making ludicrous grimaces, he swore at Pat and I by turns.

"We'll go to the store-room. Come, my lads, come," he said, "and drain the bottles. But," he added, his countenance, as he spoke, changing to one of savage ferocity, "not a word of this, or by——," a fearful oath, "I'l murder the pair of you."

"The Irish fiend!" we both murmured to ourselves.

Stealthily we proceeded to the store-room, and bottle by bottle we drained till we had succeeded in obtaining in all about two quarts of the most villainous of compounds, but which to us at that time was as nectar—the drink of the gods.

For some reason or other not known to us, perhaps policy, the skipper changed his mind about keeping our discovery a secret from the crew. Then coming on deck, with his own hands he gave one spoonful to each man.

The remainder he took to his own cabin.

Then came the chief act of the tragedy.

Unfortunately a young man who was at the helm half-delirious with fever and thirst had kept his eye upon the skipper's movements—nay, through the cabin light he had seen where he had placed the precious liquid.

Thus an hour afterwards, fancying no one would see him, he watched an opportunity. left the helm, ran down below, and before Pat or I could stay him had drunk every drop of what was left.

"Madman!" I exclaimed, "your life is not worth an hour's purchase."

"Let them take it," exclaimed the poor wretch; "I would long since have saved them the trouble, but I am too great a coward."

Now the captain must have been on the watch also, for as the poor fellow spoke he entered the cabin and knocked him down with a boat-hook. Then, before Pat or I could interfere as we intended, he called for the native Africans and ordered him to be stripped and lashed to the rigging for a flogging.

Never shall I forget that sight. It was fearful. The captain first beat him unmercifully with a rope's-end, and then made the Africans in turn do the same; the rest of the crew, Pat and I included, were far too weak to interfere, although I believe, bad as they were, there was not one among them who did not long to make the brute change places with the poor wretch on the rigging.

Pat and I went to him after he was cut down; he was almost flayed on the back, and of course insensible.

We dashed sea water over him, and after a time he came too, but he was dying.

"For the love of Heaven," he cried, turning his glazed eyes in our faces, "for the love of Heaven when you get to England, tell how cruelly I have been murdered."

These were his last words, for that same day he died.

The brutal captain was frightened at this death,

SUPPORTING HIS INSENSIBLE BURDEN HE SEIZED THE ROPE.

the more so, however, that the crew was so greatly excited, and the Frenchman as a ringleader called him to his face a murderer, at the same time vowing that he should be hung, if God spared them to reach home.

The skipper's fears, however, did but seem to render him the more insensible to humanity; for on the morrow he insisted upon the drunken creature, who called himself a doctor, dissecting the corpse and holding a post-mortem examination.

Anything more horribly revolting than the whole scene I defy the world to produce; the instruments used were the knives and saws in daily use on board the ship, for the doctor had none of his own.

All his hands were sent for, much nonsense was spoken by the captain and doctor to prove the man died from natural causes, after which the body, just as it was, was thrown overboard for the sharks that were cruising about to fight and gorge upon.

It was enough to make one go mad to see such horrors perpetrated, and the feeling of the misery was something impossible to describe.

During the ensuing week several men died; the poor Frenchman was of the number. He never lived to carry out his threat of vengeance; and we were in the last stage of exhaustion when God, taking mercy on us, sent us assistance in the shape of a foreign vessel, that very humanely gave us a quantity of water and a little biscuit.

Had she been a countryman we should one and all have abandoned the brig, but we could not explain to them what we wanted; indeed, they did not appear to wish to have us as shipmates, which was not to be wondered at considering what a cutthroat set of villains all the crew looked.

After utter want we had now, with care, sufficient water and food to reach some place, where a man-of-war could be found to help us if the winds were foul.

I must do our villainous skipper the justice to say that he pointed this out to the crew and begged them to refrain from taking more than a certain small allowance.

But no—our sufferings were not to end so soon.

Men who have been so long starving go suddenly mad.

So it seemed with our crew. They had been starving.

Now we had a fair breeze and provisions, and they determined to feast; the consequence was as had been foretold, we met foul winds after passing these Islands, which through bad navigation could not be sighted, and again did we run short of water; and although in a higher latitude and cooler climate still we suffered fearfully.

Nearly all the English seamen died, and the cooper became dangerously ill, while Pat and I were so weak as to be hardly able to walk. As for the skipper, although at times he looked distressed, he had become if possible more brutal than ever.

A fresh wind sprung up, we squared yards to it, but could not make much sail, for who were to reduce it if a gale came on?

Ships seemed to avoid us, for we wore all the signs of a ship with the plague. Our yards and sails looked what sailors call "no how," and the vessel wallowed in rather than sailed over the sea.

We had even ceased to go aloft to look for vessels in sight, and our crew, now reduced to six men, were just keeping body and soul together by means of condensed steam caught in a cloth, that we sucked in turn.

Scurvy, fever, and thirst had reduced us to perfect scarecrows; we no longer heeded the cruelties or curses of our skipper, and had only sense enough left to go to the helm in turn and keep the brig's head upon her course.

No help came.

No, not until we were in soundings, and then merely through getting so close to a ship in the night she could not in common humanity run away from us, when at day-light we hoisted the colours union downwards.

"Bedad, the bastes won't see us!" cried Pat, staring all eyes in the direction of the stranger.

"You are wrong, she bears down upon us," I cried exultingly, as I ran to the fore-top.

The vessel that bore down on us proved to be a pirate, her captain one of the most merciless wretches ever known; and when he got us on board and heard our different stories, some he deliberately shot, one had to walk the plank, but I was brought here a prisoner, for what purpose, I do not know.

"But it matters not," said the prisoner, his voice growing feebler. "I am going fast; would that I had died long ago."

Harry, seeing that the man was sinking fast, and that he could render him no aid, bade him good-bye.

Then he gently closed the door of the cell, and listened.

Footsteps were moving below.

This aroused him to action.

There were more doors on the landing, but there was only one he cared about trying.

It had a new lock, and this attracted his notice.

But even that did not resist his efforts long.

His dirk, by the peculiar formation of its point, was as good as any skeleton key.

The door yielded to his manipulation, and as he opened it slowly he beheld, midway between him and a stream of light, that peeped in at the loophole, Minnie Atherton.

She turned at the moment, and seeing him, sprang forward.

"Hush," he said. "For heaven's sake, be silent."

Minnie obeyed, though very reluctantly. She had a thousand questions to ask; a thousand things to tell him; but he bade her be silent, for he could hear the heavy footsteps of the jailor moving restlessly about.

In the first flush of joy at their meeting, however, their lips for a moment were glued in a fervent kiss.

Having discovered that all was quiet below, and that there was no sign of an alarm, Harry fastened the door and blocked it up with a huge table.

"Now," said he, "let us think of some plan of escape. The fellow below seems very watchful, and were he not, and I could get you into the court yard, how could I take you farther?"

"I have braved many dangers, you know, Harry, and I have suffered many insults since I came here," she answered, looking tearfully into his eyes "But first of all, how is my darling, Tom?"

"You saw him, did you not?" replied Harry, evasively.

"Yes, yes; but——"

"And he was quite well, then?"

"But, but——"

"No doubt he is all right now."

"You think so?" she asked, appealingly.

"I have no reason to believe otherwise."

Harry tried to escape her gaze.

He did not want to lie.

He was not so sure that his captain had not been smitten down.

His endeavour was to ease her fears without criminating himself.

It was a hard task to deceive a fond, devoted girl like Minnie.

She had seen a deal of the world's deceit for one so young.

She had also learnt that to dissemble at times was necessary.

And so she appeared outwardly to believe Harry

Vere, though at the same time her heart was filled with the worst of fears.

"Well," said he, "in order to change the unpleasant subject, let us look to ourselves."

"And," added he, affecting a laugh; "we will then talk of dear Tom and my darling, Jenny."

Minnie was quite subdued by this.

She could feel how very selfish she had been.

In her own misfortune she had quite forgotten that of others.

Besides Harry and Jenny were man and wife, while Tom and Minnie were as yet but lovers, and this she could acknowledge, made a wide difference.

But for all that Minnie had a touch of human nature about her.

Her own troubles was her first consideration.

She loved Tom almost to devotion, and her heart would have broken had she seen him lying a corpse.

But this is a sentiment that all woman are prone to, especially in her first love, and so Harry Vere forgave her.

The day was far advanced now, and as Harry had fasted for many hours, he gladly accepted her offer to share with her the food she had been provided with when she was made an occupant of the cell.

It consisted of cold fowls, wine, and various fruits, which at that moment were quite a luxury to the buccaneer.

He made her eat hearty too, and when they had finished he gathered up the fragments and thoughtfully placed them in his pocket.

Then he left her for a while, and ascended to the next landing of the tower to reconnoitre.

There he discovered not only what he had anticipated, but more.

That chamber or landing had been used for provisioning the fortress in time of siege, and a coil of rope there when lowered would clear the outworks and the outer edge of the moat.

All this Harry quickly perceived with nautical instinct.

He measured the distance with his eye, and took in all at a glance.

Then as delicately as possible he communicated to her his plans.

She agreed without any useless demur, and so he led her at once to the floor above.

He then uncoiled the rope and lowered it gently till it reached the ground.

With the handkerchief from his neck he bound her to his waist.

And then grasping the rope in true sailor fashion, he committed himself to the care of one more powerful than all, and began the perilous descent.

Minnie was a little terrified at first at their horrible danger, and when she found herself swinging in mid air with nought but the buccaneer's clutch to prevent their being dashed to pieces, a quiver of fear shook her delicate frame, and she became dizzy.

Still in the momentary convulsion she clutched firmly the form of the noble youth, and so they gradually descended.

But alas! troubles seldom come singly.

As she came to with a start she gave an involuntary cry, and this awoke the fierce janitor from his evening's snooze, and he sprang to the loophole in dismay.

What he saw made him draw back and stare in bewilderment.

He stared for a moment in abject terror.

In the uncertain light he imagined at first that it was a spiritual vision, and he uttered an Ave Maria.

But he soon recovered himself, and, seeing it was no vision but real flesh and blood, his prayers were succeeded by a fierce string of oaths.

Then he drew a pistol, and with an invective that made even the heart of the brave Harry Vere chill with horror, he levelled it point blank at the pair.

Harry had the presence of mind to swing the rope, and this made the grim ruffian miss his mark.

Nevertheless, the bullet whizzed close to Minnie's cheek, cut away one silken lock of her hair, and severed a strand of the rope.

Harry Vere uttered a silent prayer.

Then he lowered himself, hand under hand, with increased rapidity, until his feet touched terra firma.

With a fervent ejaculation he caught up Minnie in his arms, and sought shelter in the thickly surrounding shrubs.

He tore his hands and clothes with the prickly pears and cactuses, but he cared not, for the report of the pistol had set the alarm bell ringing, and the clank of armed men hurrying to the courtyards, and ramparts sounded discordantly on the still air.

The young buccaneer did not stop until sheer exhaustion compelled him, and to his joy and surprise as he sank down he heard the murmur of a rippling stream.

He was so overjoyed that he knelt down and uttered a prayer of thankfulness.

Making a drinking cup of a cocoa-nut shell, he moistened Minnie's lips and bathed her forehead, which soon revived her, and then he took a deep draught of the grateful beverage himself.

Have made a bed of dried grass for Minnie, and a shelter of boughs and leaves to shield her from the dew, he strayed to a grove hard by, where he sank down to seek that repose he so much needed.

CHAPTER CCXXII.

DOCTOR SHRIKE—HUGH BALDRICK APPEARS.

CAPTAIN TOM DRAKE, wounded as he was, still took his place at the head of his gallant crew, but the reinforcement, though fresh, was not strong enough to follow up the retreating Spaniards, so that Tom decided upon returning on board.

Our hero was greatly mortified at the enterprise being a failure.

He was grieved, too, at the loss of several of his beloved crew.

Harry Vere, Bob Hauler and Jerry Mizzen were reported as missing at the muster in the cave, and now one of the marines, named Michael Meekly, was added to that number.

Ben Barnacle tore and raved like one mad.

He swore by all the martyrs of the inquisition that he would find the missing buccaneers or deeply revenge them.

Dr. Shrike had plenty of work to do

Jacob and he were up to their armpits in work for the best part of a day.

Jacob led a most unpleasant life.

When there was no bandaging or splintering to do, the doctor and his assistant were busily preparing various mysterious nostrums for a purpose which he wisely kept a secret.

Truth to tell, though the doctor affected great grief at the disappearance of the four buccaneers, he inwardly wished that they might return no more alive.

The idea was that he could persuade Captain Tom to allow him to embalm them.

This notion was so fixed in his mind, that he even let out the secret to the carpenter, and bribed him to make four cases ready to place the embalmed bodies in.

It was a serious joke, but the carpenter pretended

to accept the bribe, and to carry out his orders to the very letter.

The carpenter still had faith that they would turn up all right again, for with out Bob and Jerry, whose eccentricities were the life and soul of the crew, the "Will-o'-the-Wisp" would not have been half the ship she was.

Captain Tom, in the meantime, had determined to take a short trip to revive the spirits and health of his crew.

He had consulted Ben about this, and they had both come to the conclusion that it would be madness to attempt to rescue Minnie at present, for if they should attempt a siege on the fortress, and it should prove a failure, it would bring certain destruction on Minnie's devoted head.

As they were cruising a few miles off the island a sail was suddenly descried.

"Hugh Baldrick, by Jove!" exclaimed Tom, after viewing the ship some moments.

'Baldrick!' ejaculated Ben, who was at the wheel. "What wind brings him in this quarter, captain?"

"Rambling, as usual, I suppose; we shall all meet together again some day I hope, Ben."

"I hope so too," replied the bluff junior lieutenant; "but it's an ill wind blows nobody good. Ah! he sees us, and is bearing down."

Hugh Baldrick was soon alongside the "Will-o'-the-Wisp," and a very few words served to explain how matters stood between the two commanders.

It was very soon arranged that both vessels should run in and settle the matter with the Spaniards.

Hugh Baldrick, though not well acquainted with the coast, had been there before.

His plan was that they should run in boldly to the shore, and, having all things in readiness, land all the force they could, and attack, if possible, the fortress in front and rear.

This plan seemed feasible enough.

But there was one other consideration.

How would Minnie fare in the meantime?

"Let us hold a parley with the governor," said Hugh; "and if he offers to refuse to deliver her to us three en to blow his old tumble-down shanty into the air."

"Very well," said Captain Tom; "but I am leaving much of this to you, mind."

"Ha—ha!" laughed Hugh. "Leave it to me, indeed. It is not much you leave to any one; but there, you are quite right, trust to no one, that is my motto."

And so they drew into the shore, and a formidable armament they presented when all the boats were lowered and fully manned.

They took with them a couple of small four-pounders, thinking they might be useful, and then they prepared to land.

But all these preparations had not been going on unobserved.

From the look-out tower of the fortress the governor and a few of his most faithful adherents had watched the manning and arming of the boats.

They, therefore, as soon as the boats were in range, let loose their dogs of war, and the iron missiles fell around in showers, ploughing up the water, and sending cascades flying in the air.

Captain Tom commanded the right wing of the flotilla, which advanced in the form of a crescent, and Hugh Baldrick commanded the left wing—keeping the two launches with the four pounders in them in the centre.

They encouraged the efforts of the buccaneers, and with a will the brave fellows pulled on, cheering at intervals and making their ashen blades bend at every stroke.

Meanwhile the cannon balls fell thickly around them.

One of those heavy missiles would be quite sufficient to sink a boat.

But they all escaped, and at length reached the shore in safety.

Here they were drawn up, and left in charge of a slender guard.

The main body then pushed on towards the rear of the fort.

Captain Tom and Hugh Baldrick marched at their head.

They hoped to find the rear of the fort indifferently guarded.

Surely it had never been built to stand a siege shorewards.

And yet when they came near unto it, it looked so.

The walls were of immense height and thickness.

True no guns frowned forth from them in this direction.

But then, how were the walls themselves to be scaled?

And no doubt when the top was won then their difficulties would only just have begun.

Doubtless the Spaniards still alive in the fort outnumbered them considerably.

But that was the contingency that least alarmed them.

At last they came to the very wall itself.

Steel caps and halberds were now seen to glitter on the summit.

They had no scaling ladders.

To reach the top seemed an impossible feat.

But Tom Drake, with all the assurance possible, made his trumpeter sound a parley, and then hailing the commandant of the fortress, who approached and looked over the battlement, he ordered him to surrender, or threatened that he and every soldier under his command should be put to the sword.

Scarcely, however, had the words escaped from the buccaneer's lips than the clatter of hoof strokes was clearly audible, and a party of cavalry the next instant debouched from the shelter of a grove of trees close by, and made a furious attack on his band of warriors.

So sudden was it, that the buccaneers recoiled before them, and fell into considerable disorder; but the stentorian voice of our hero quickly rallied them, and a most desperate conflict ensued.

The Spanish horsemen outnumbered the buccaneers, but the latter fought with such desperate energy that they beat them off again and again, though some of their party would sometimes get cut off and surrounded.

It was upon one of these occasions that Captain Tom suddenly missed Baldrick; but he had seen him but a moment before in a particular direction, so he started in search.

He was not long in finding him.

He was not a moment too soon.

The redoubtable freebooter was down on his back, his broken sword lying under him, and three Spanish soldiers had their sword-points at his throat.

"Hold!" shouted Captain Tom; "the first man who strikes dies. What, three to one? and he disarmed and prostrate! Shame on ye, for Spanish paltroons."

The three Spaniards were for a moment cowed by his resolute bearing, and in the interval Baldrick recovered his feet, and had picked up his own broken weapon.

This he hurled in the face of one Spaniard, and so heavily that the fellow fell insensible to the ground, whilst at the same instant Tom Drake slew another

The third turned to flee, but ere he could escape, Tom's sword was plunged into his back up to the very hilt, and he fell dead over the bodies of his companions.

"You arrived just in time, my friend," said Hugh Baldrick.

"A minute later, and I should have forfeited my pledged word," replied Tom Drake.

"I will not thank you, because I can only do so in the same strain."

"It matters not; one day you will requite me for all," answered Tom.

"Ay, with a dukedom, if I ever live to be a reigning sovereign."

Our hero smiled—a smile of strange portent —but said:—

"Come, Hugh, my friend, pick up one of the dead Spaniard's swords in lieu of thine own broken weapon, and return to the glorious fight, for our friends may have need of us. Yet, what do I see? By every saint in Heaven, the Spaniards are flying!"

'Twas indeed the case; they were, and in a wild stampede too

The horsemen striking home with their spurs far more zealously than a few minutes before they had done with their swords, and those who had been dismounted, and they were many, relying on their heels.

The buccaneers did not trouble to pursue them, they had a more pressing matter on hand.

The subjugation of a fort.

But suddenly a terrible explosion filled the air.

CHAPTER CCXXIII.

THE STRANGE SAIL—HORRIBLE DOINGS OF THE PIRATE CHIEF—HARRY VERE'S DESPAIR

SEAMEN, like Harry Vere, although worn with fatigue, could not rest more than a few hours at a time.

The moon was riding splendidly in the heavens when he awoke, and having refreshed himself with a sluice in the stream, he felt greatly revived.

One thing though rather annoyed him.

In his hasty descent from the tower he had left his sword behind him.

He still had his pistols though, and there he primed, and then he went to see that his charge was all safe.

Minnie was soundly sleeping still.

He did not like to wake her.

And so he sauntered a little way through the bush to reconnoitre his position.

How far he had gone, buried in deep thought, he knew not, when on suddenly arriving at a steep mound he ascended it.

From its summit he caught a glimpse of the sea, and with a natural impulse he made his way down towards the shore.

It was his intention to look around for any sign of the "Will-o'-the-Wisp" or any of her crew, for he felt certain that Tom Drake, if he had himself escaped from the Spaniards, would not leave the coast without first endeavouring to find him.

Then there was Minnie, and this made his surmise doubly certain.

Somehow or other he never for a moment entertained the idea that Tom Drake would be recaptured.

Besides if he was the rest of the crew would be sure to search the island for their missing companions.

The indomitable nature of the buccaneer crew was such, in fact, that they never for a moment allowed the thought to cross them of being worsted, even when the chances against them were almost certain.

Thus Harry stood gazing on the placid waters, thinking over the strange events of the last two days.

Wondering when he should return to old England again, and whether he should find his own darling Jenny safe and in health as when he had last left her.

It was just such an hour as would tempt one to reflection.

The air balmy and cool, the sandflies playing in the distance, and the still air broken only by the murmuring swell and the busy hum of a thousand insects.

Suddenly, awakening from his musing, which had made him quite forgot his search, he looked up

The sea was an uneven mirror of silver far and near.

He was about to move away when he descried a speck in the distance.

It was not the "Will-o'-the-Wisp."

The moon lit on the new-comer's canvas, but they glinted the rays back with a white surface.

The stranger was a large brigantine, Harry saw, as the space between her and the islet diminished.

She seemed headed towards that very group, and presently towards that very island.

Her destination was reached at last.

On her decks, white with the moonbeams, men began to run.

Her studding sails and stay-sails, for she had had the light wind on her quarter, had been taken in before.

Now her fore and mainsail were let fall, and the square topsails brailed up.

The anchor was let go, for the look-out saw her stem swing round as the currents fought with the hull, still steadied by the jibs.

But they, too, were let down by the run, and the strange brigantine rode at anchor, still as if cast of metal and embedded on a face of melted silver.

Harry was puzzled.

She was too far off land to have come only to be moored there, and yet too near the islets to have chosen the spot for a roadstead of any permanency.

A glance of his expert eye told him that the sails were in readiness for a speedy departure.

Even as he saw that, he observed a small skiff launched overboard, and then pushed by the man who had jumped into it, towards the gangway aft.

After some minutes, this boat was shoved off from the two-master.

Four men were in it.

Two at the stern.

Two pulling the oars.

The small boat came straight for the islet, the steersman heading, without regard for the many eddies and whirls over and around the coral reefs.

As soon as Harry made sure that their destination was his own refuge, he returned to the thicket to watch.

Having arrived there on all fours, and gradually steadied himself erect, Harry found that he had a good place of observation.

Only one man was in the little skiff.

He was bailing it out, and singing in a low voice to himself a verse of that rude rhyme which meant much in those days, when its subject was chief of cut-throats on the Spanish main.

Harry examined the fellow more closely.

He had a villainous phiz, and his seaman's dress was more remarkable for an ugly but fearful predominance of black than anything else.

His belt, as broad as a horse's girth, was full of long pistols and a knife or two.

As the youth scanned him, unsuspected himself, the sailor finished casting the water from the boat bottom, and lying down in the sternsheets, appeared to study the sky, his face up, and his body at full length.

Harry heard him vent half-a-score of oaths in connection with a remark that he felt sleepy, but dared not shut his eyes.

In revenge, he began to sing again.

Harry glanced from the melodious rascal to the brigantine.

He shook his head.

"They're no good, ship or bands," muttered he. "Let me see what these fellows are come for."

He could have slain the sailor as he lay on his back, but the death would have been useless.

Harry Vere had to mount the first eminence to see what had become of the three other strangers.

After a while, and after changing his place of observation, he not only descried them, but approached them as nearly as he could.

Unfortunately for the eavesdropper, the three were on a level space, upon which the moon's rays poured.

He had to remain out of earshot, for they were the only bushes to cover him.

Under a clump of sand-plum trees, as they are called, but mere shrubs as they are, the youth ensconced himself to look, if he could not overhear.

One of the three men, a sailor like the boatman, was a powerful fellow.

He was applying all his strength to digging a large hole in the soft earth.

The second, sitting on a rather large box, was smoking a cigar.

He was also a large man.

His dress, as well as his easy attitude while the other worked, bespoke an officer, perhaps the captain.

In his cap was a black gull's feather.

But all the watcher's attention was centred on one characteristic of his.

He wore his beard so long and large that it seemed to cover his chest from shoulder to shoulder, and down to his belt, where it flowed over silver-hilted dagger and gold damascened pistol-butt.

It was of a glossy black.

Its deep blackness added to the effect of its profusion and the man being so tall and large boned, Harry himself felt a sensation of the nearest approach to fear that he had ever known.

And he dreaded to whisper the thought that came to him.

There could be no doubt now what manner of ship that anchored vessel was.

She was a pirate

That hole that was being dug under the pirate's terrible eyes, ah! what was it to hold?

That third man was, where?

Bound hand and foot, prostrate on the sand, gagged as well.

Vere felt his hand stealing to his pistols, and a wild desire seized him to rush out, and prove to the pirate that there was one man at least who feared not to tell him that the sea was angry, the land sick, for his fiendish crimes.

But a horrible fascination weighed on him, and compelled the youth to continue to gaze.

His hand on his weapon still, he looked on, prompted a good deal by his own curiosity.

The voices, only a murmur to Harry, were important to him.

The pirate captain flung aside the end of his cigar.

"Nearly through, Buxton?" queried he.

The spademan rested a moment.

"Pretty near, cap'ain. Only I wish one of the men were doing it instead of me, your first mate," returned he, bluntly.

"Pooh! I can trust you, Philip, but none of the rascals. A little more of this pleasant work,

eh? and we can dig up the buried soil here and elsewhere, and live like princes in any land, even in England."

"I was steward to a rich man once myself captain," said Buxton.

"And you cheated him till you were worth more than he himself, and could hire better lawyers to get you off?"

"Not much, captain. I never have to do with land sharks or any of the same fry. The nobleman said I shared his income, I said he lied, locked the room door, and when I left the chamber, a dying man, very much like my lord, breathed his last, pinned to the wainscot!"

"Ah! Philip! It was lucky I fell in with you my boy," said the chief, playing with his beard.

"It didn't matter! If I hadn't met with you at Panama, and become your first mate, I'd have scared up a ship of my own somewhere. They're easy got."

"Too easy," said the pirate captain, with an oath. "What's this Governor Gonsalvo was telling me? That the seas hereabouts were being swept by a buccaneer—a child, 'sdeath?"

"A child, captain, that fought like a devil, like a man of the right sort. I like the way in which he christened his ship, I do!"

While he spoke, Buxton never ceased to thrown up the earth in great masses.

He seemed to have reasoned that the sooner he got through the disagreeable task the better for him.

He was knee-deep in the trench already.

"Peace, Philip!" growled the other. "I can't bear any one, boy or greybeard, to rove over these waters besides me. Didn't I blow Captain Kidd's first schooner to smithereens because he came down into the Cuban seas?"

"You did, captain; there's no gainsaying that."

"I'll have no second desperado of the Deep to dispute my sway of terror. Curse me! it would ruin the trade. Merchants shudder now to send a keel to the Indies—what would it be if they hear half-a-dozen sea-wipers are lurking for prey? With but one they have a chance"

"Not when the 'Death Pirate' is afloat."

The pirate smiled grimly.

"Likely! I say, old partner of mine, there is little sight for a lumbering old gold galloon when the Death Pirate shoots over the brine with sail out below and aloft, and the brass rings circling inside the portholes! Ha, ha!"

"The shot! and they won't bring to! The half-a-dozen balls, or the whole broadside! The boarding in the smoke! The flash and the slash! The groaning, screaming men!" said Philip, enthusiastically, brandishing his spade.

"And the weeping women!" added the captain, showing his teeth amid the black hair of moustache and beard.

Both laughed, as they exchanged a look.

Fiends would have envied such a glance.

The young captain heard that peal of demoniacal mirth, and so hateful was its accent, that again he felt the impulse to spring forth.

He even stirred to return to his comrades, and gain the assistance requisite to overpower such evidently formidable men.

But he paused anew, for Buxton had leaped up out of the pit.

"There, captain." said he, "is it deep enough?"

The other looked into the hole, and then let his eyes wander to the small box and the pinioned man.

"It'll serve," rejoined he.

Thereupon the first mate of the "Death Pirate" took up a piece of sailcloth and spread it, doubled up, at the bottom of the excavation.

This done, the pirate opened the small chest.

Philip stood in the gap, while his superior handed him in piece meal, the contents of that box.

here were riches incalculable, and in all shapes.

First, a silver dish made trebly precious by its embossery by some great master; then a cup of rock crystal, with a stem of cornelian, and a stand of solid gold.

Here half-a-dozen jewelled dagger-hilts were wrapped up in a cloth of gold.

Next, the pirate tossed to his mate, a bunch of necklaces of all the precious stones

A roll of lace let gems glint through its priceless meshes.

In a word there were ornaments of every kind among the plunder.

At the end of the mass, came the more solid ware.

Three or four little cases of silver coin, and some ingots, the gold of which had been rudely run into the bars.

' That's all?" inquired Philip, tucking the tarpaulin around the layer of riches.

"That's all."

Philip scrambled out of the pit.

"Now then for the coverlet," said he, laughing grossly.

The pirate rolled the bound man to the brink of the chasm.

Vere instantly cocked his pistol.

"Death or not to me!" muttered he; "they shan't bury the poor wretch under my eyes without my lifting a hand."

But the prisoner was let lay there.

The change of position allowed the moonbeams to fall on the captive's face.

Harry strained his eyes.

"Where have I seen that face before?" thought he. "Oh! I recall it. It is Mannelo—the fellow who showed us how to enter the governor's palace. How can he have come here?"

Simply enough, as Blackbeard could have told him.

That marauder of the main had returned freshly to that part of the ocean.

He went to visit his old friend the governor.

Gonsalvo eagerly welcomed him.

Moreover, he found Captain King quite ready to fall foul of the young commander of the "Will-o'-the-Wisp," which bid fair to eclipse the fame of his vessel.

In the meantime, Captain King, who happened to be in a talkative humour, discovered that an Indian had rendered Tom Drake great assistance in discovering the island, and so mentioned that he "wanted a man."

Gonsalvo smiled, fully understanding the villain's drift, and said that he, the governor, could no doubt spare the traitor who had been of such service to our hero. The pirate captain assented.

Gonsalvo willingly released Mannelo from his dungeon (for he had been seized in the town by spies), and turned him over to the freebooters.

These explanations over, let us return to the moonlit strand.

To the victim, the grave-diggers, and the lonely witness.

The pirate had stooped till his lips were close to the captive's ear.

"Never strain and try to speak, fool," said he. "The blood-vessels are ready to burst on your forehead, in your fear. Fear not this! that you are to be buried alive!"

What could the demi-demon mean, by hinting that the wretch's fate was to be worse than an entombment of the living!

The pirate chief stooped on the opposite side of the gap, to that on which Philip had also bent.

Then the pirate captain waved his arms as if he were beckoning invisibles to him, from all quarters of the atmosphere, where the silvery notes glittered softly in the moonbeams.

After that he bowed his head for a space.

Next, he saluted the four points of the compass.

In a deep, low tone he began—

"So let the band of thy fell chosen watch over the ghostly banner that I plant upon the guard of my treasure!"

Then he rose.

Philip continued stooping, but he bent over the form beside him, and clapping a long pistol, that he had already bended and primed, to the ear of Mannelo, he let the heavy hammer descend.

Harry, spell-bound during the impious ceremony that he had witnessed, but hardly understood, heard the loud report, and started.

Then the smoke that enveloped the trench for a moment, was lightly swept towards him.

When it was totally dispersed, he saw the chief and Philip vigorously shovelling the ear h into the pit.

Mannelo's bleeding corpse was gone.

Soon the mound that heaved up above the level of the ground betrayed that it had gone to overspread the ingots and the jewels.

And the pirate, stamping on the last spade-full of clay, ended the invocation.

"Lay the flesh brands the mark of the beast upon this spot for six whole months, oh, Satan! In half-a-year I swear to come, and soul in body or stripped of flesh, I will relieve this guard!"

Even as he spoke, a cloud, the only one upon the sky, stole darkling over the moon.

And that sound of the water that is styled the "calling of the sea" echoed forth all around the edge of the shore, as if the whole island was encompassed by flying things, whose wings were fluttering.

In the darkness that the cloud sent down, the pirate chief and his comrade went away.

Furious at himself for having been held back by the horror what he had beheld had given, Harry sprang from his covert, and dashed to the spot.

But the cloud broke into rifts, and by the spars of light that gladly lanced downwards, Harry saw the fresh earth, a pool of blood, and a stray jewel, half trampled into the sandy soil.

He wavered one moment.

His frantic impulse was to tear up the clods again with his fingers, but cooler reasoning told him that such a patch of blood, mixed with the hair, could only be from a man dead already.

He turned to the thicket, and pushed on towards the pirate's boat

Luckily for him, the thorns and matted undergrowth prevented him falling directly into the hands of the buccaneers.

Besides his haste misled him.

Suddenly he found himself floundering up to his knees in water.

Another fragment of the cloud was obscuring the disc.

Harry had blundered into a little creek that ran into the land between rows of rushes.

But he did not turn back, and, still eager to avenge the heartless assassination, he flung himself forward, and waded collar-bone deep to the other side.

As he reached the bank, caught at the reeds and held on, before scrambling out to recover breath, the moon once more appeared.

The moonlight showed him a form close to his own.

A rough hand was extended, and grasped his collar.

THE CORSAIR MAIDEN'S STRATAGEM.

"By all the devils, what fellow have we here?" growled a deep voice, as its owner dragged Harry upon the shore.

It was Philip Buxton.

He had heard the noise of the young officer's falling into the creek, and had gone thither to see what it was.

Harry Vere had recovered breath.

He was in no mood for parley or delay.

Before Philip could utter a second speech, the youth had slipped his knife in hand, up under the other's arm.

With all the vigour of indignation at the fresh remembrance of the cold-blooded murder, he thrust the blade home.

Not once, but thrice, and even when Buxton's huge body dragged him into the water as it fell, the young commander repeated the stroke.

But Buxton had time to cry out:—

"Hallo! Captain! oh! death!"

Harry heard a trampling of feet bearing down the sand-plumes and the cat-tail reeds.

Instinctively he dashed off the stiffening fingers on his arms and neckcloth, and leaped into the shadowy side.

Under the mass of rushes he buried himself.

At the next instant the pirate captain, his cutlass drawn, appeared on the other side.

The second seaman followed him.

Buxton's body, face down in the stream, was sluggishly floating in the shadow, not ten feet from Harry's hiding-place.

'Fury and flames!" vociferated the pirate; "is that Phil's body? Death of a dozen lives. How came he dead?"

Then he turned wrathfully to his companion.

'You poor wretch; why stand you here staring, Bowser? Get you in, and haul him ashore, till we see if he lives!"

And not to let the fellow mistake the order, he

70

caught hold of him by the neck and seat of his duck trousers, and heaved him towards the floating corpse.

As soon as Bowser had recovered from the souse, which made him drop the cutlass that he had held in his fist, he waded down the stream after the body.

The pirate followed him along the bank.

The current had seized upon the body now, and Bowser had to quicken his pace to overreach it.

At almost the very minute that he prepared to dart upon it, Captain King saw the sailor stop, stagger, and fall forward.

"Help! Murder!" howled he.

The pirate chief saw his man, with a black mass seeming to strike against his breast.

Then a short but pointed snout, with beads of glittering eyes set on either side, sparkled like a snake's at the end of the shield.

At the other extremity, a long lash, swishing the ripple for a second, whirled in the air like a waggoner's whip.

In vain the sailor sought to push it off.

The lash whistled in the air and over his arms; the point struck sharply into the wretch's eye.

Bowser gave an awful yell.

He battled with the devil-fish, half-serpent, as it was in all the agonies of coming death.

Again the fish repeated its blow.

This time Bowser fought weaker.

He missed his footing and fell heavily upon the water.

The poisoned tail whisked above him as in triumph.

The pirate chief recoiled in affright.

"The sting-ray! He's past help!" cried he.

The tumult in the water had stirred up the red mud and sand.

And the waves had turned over Buxton's body.

So the pirate gazed upon the water seemingly changed to blood, the only relief to the dyed surface being the ghastly, swollen face of Bowser, and the whiter, and as appalling one of Philp.

The pirate dared not utter the blasphemy on his lips.

He turned on his heel, and crashed into the thicket like a wild bull.

Harry had levelled his pistol at him, and, as he fled, pulled the trigger.

But he had not thought of the immersion.

The barrel was half filled with water, and every grain of powder was washed out of the pan.

He waded once more across the water, heedless if it contained more of such fatal denizens.

But he missed the track that the captain of the brigantine had made, and went wrong at every step.

When he did reach the shore he saw that his pursuit was fruitless.

Captain King had long since jumped into his boat, and now, sculling like a madman, he was a quarter of the way to the "Death Pirate" in the offing.

Harry could do but one thing more.

That was to look for the cutlass dropped by the pirate, which he did, and very soon he found it.

This was a great boon to him.

His pistols were still wet from the immersion, and would be of no use to him in a sudden emergency.

It was now quite time, he thought, for returning to his sleeping charge.

And so he cast about him for the track he had made for the beach, but he would not have found it without great difficulty had it not been for the mound, with a clump of trees on its summit, from whence he had first gained a view of the ocean.

Harry hurried forward with all the speed the thickly-grown bushes would allow him, but on arriving at the place where he had left Minnie in sweet repose, his young heart was thrilled with horror.

There was the bed of grass, and the sheltering leaves; but Minnie was gone.

"Fool—fool that I was," he cried, in his agony, "to leave her here without first speaking."

"Where can she have wandered?" he went on; and then, as the terrible thought occurred to him, he added: "The Indians—perhaps they have discovered her."

Harry Vere now reproached himself very severely for his careless neglect.

He had rescued Minnie from one horrible position, only to doom her to another doubly terrible.

But as fretting and pining, without any decided action, was worse than useless, he quickly strung his nerves, and prepared to make atonement for his error.

But which direction should he take?

Which way had the savages led their captive, if Minnie was their captive?

And then what could his single arm avail against a tribe of warlike Indians?

These were questions that would scarcely bear thinking upon, and were much more difficult to answer.

But Harry was not so easily cast down.

He had experienced a little of Indian life.

It was morning now, and though the sun shone brightly the dew still hung in glassy beads upon the foliage and the fruit that weighed the branches down on either side of him.

A thought struck him as he looked around almost in dismay.

Could he discover any traces of the trail?

He went back and examined the grassy couch.

It was not disturbed as though there had been any struggling.

The grass about too seemed undisturbed.

There was not even a trace of his own footsteps, and this puzzled him.

But the grass here was dry and springy, and the leaves grew so thickly overhead that there was scarcely a chance of any dew penetrating to this particular spot.

And so he walked on a few paces and, using an old expedient often practised by the hunters in the backwoods, he looked towards the sun and then threw his dirk into the air.

When it descended its point rested almost in the same direction he had taken in the morning.

This decided him.

He pursued his way thoughtfully, his eyes still bent on the ground, until at length a glad cry escaped his lips.

He had approached a patch of soft sandy soil, and upon this he saw the impression of a very small foot.

The footprints, light as they were, continued, and it gave him some relief to find that there were no marks of a mocassin, as he had expected to find.

This raised his hopes.

He pursued his way now with a lighter heart.

The trail, too, when once struck, was not very difficult to follow.

Still it required a very keen eye to detect it, for the step seemed as light as the trip of a fairy.

Harry Vere, however, followed it up for about two or three hundred yards without experiencing any difficulty until he came to a shallow brooklet, and then it ceased.

Harry's heart sank for a moment.

Crossing the stream he wandered frantically up and down either bank, but he could get no further clue to the trail.

Presently he raised his eyes.

What was that fluttering in the distance?

It was a piece of cotton-like substance, caught on the thorns of a cactus tree.

Harry beat his steps thither with all speed.

"Joy! joy!" he exclaimed, "it is a portion of her dress;" and then he stood for a moment to contemplate it.

Then he lowered his gaze to the dewy sward where a carpet of flowers of various hues were just opening their tiny petals, and the joy on his lips was quickly replaced by a cry of horror.

His eye rested on the broad mark left by the tread of an Indian's mocassin.

This was supplemented by another, then another, and following up the trail he discovered the remains of a fire and signs of a party of Indian's having encamped there for the night.

It was no wonder that the brave youth was horrified.

In his dilemma he scarcely knew what to do, or how to act.

Farther on, too, he saw a scalp fresh and gory, which had been dropped by one of the tribe, perhaps in his struggle in bearing Minnie away.

Harry turned from the sight in loathing and disgust.

Then, scarcely knowing what he was about, he dashed on through the valley that led between two steep hills.

How far he travelled he knew not; he seemed to have flown on the wings of the wind.

The Indians so far had not taken any particular pains to conceal their trail, but on arriving at a narrow river, where there were signs of their having once more encamped, Harry found the trail cut off.

Harry Vere, however, still kept on his untiring perseverance.

He examined the grass all around, carefully viewed the sand on the river brink, and rigorously searched the bushes around.

It were better in one way that he had not been so particular.

It would have spared him a deal of pain.

As it was his anxiety was greater than ever.

In one of the bushes he discovered the trace of a canoe having rested there, added to which there was a broken tomahawk and some human bones, which immediately filled him with the idea that those he had been following were cannibals.

This was not at all cheering.

Should he hit the right track and come up with the Indians, there was little chance of his coming off the victor, and to be eaten by the savages, perhaps roasted alive, was not very pleasant to contemplate.

But he had gone so far, and he was not the one to give up his purpose so readily.

He had got two good pistols; they were dry now, and these he well loaded and primed from a little water-proof case that he wore slung across his shoulders and under his jacket.

He woke up the edge of the rusty cutlass too on a stone hard by, and stuck the broken tomahawk in his belt opposite his dirk.

By this it may be seen that the young buccaneer was well armed.

His only scarcity was food and water, for the river on the bank of which he stood was quite brakish, and for all he knew ran right through the island from sea to sea.

But there were plenty of bananas, pine apples, cocoa-nuts and peaches, so that there was no fear of his being starved.

Had our hero been gifted with a sweet tooth, he might have lived a long time in luxury; as it was, accustomed to the sea biscuits and salt meat of the vessel, he grew tired of these sweet sickly fruits at the first outset.

He therefore ate very sparingly of these delicacies.

He took only just sufficient to sustain him for the present, and then he went about in the vain hope of discovering by which way of the stream the canoe had departed.

This enigma would have puzzled a wiser head than Harry's.

The subtle Indians had even obliterated all signs of their embarking.

Harry Vere had recourse again to his dirk, and when it fell it pointed across the stream.

He was not surprised at this; indeed, he had suspected as much.

And so he prepared to cross the river which was running with the force of a mountain torrent.

Harry would have given much to have had a companion with him at this time.

Being on shore and off his element made him feel the more lonely.

Had he been adrift in a boat at sea he would have had less difficulty to choose his course.

Now he was only guided by circumstances or destiny, and that had appointed his path across the river.

Harry Vere was a good swimmer, and though the swiftness of the current warned him not to face it, he would have ventured in rather than have turned tail, but there were other matters to consider.

His pistols and his ammunition.

"Worse difficulties than this at sea," thought Harry, as his keen eye searched around, "and I have overcome many a one in our gallant 'Will-o'-the-Wisp.'"

He gave a start as he half muttered the name of his brave little vessel.

There was a charm in that very name that bound her buccaneer crew to her, and at its sound it awoke the same old fire that had aided her gallant captain to gain so many achievements.

Even in that solitary spot Harry felt this mystic power.

In the rushing of the stream as it dashed from boulder to boulder he fancied he could hear the huge wave clashing against the bow of his own sturdy ship. And the soft balmy air, as it shook the 'topmost leaves, seemed to be playing with the cordage. And for a moment he fancied the salt-laden air of the boundless ocean was fanning playfully his sun-tanned cheeks.

But he was made too painfully aware that this was only a delusion, by the rapidly-sinking sun, and a dismal rattling of——what——

He looked about him, but could see nothing to cause this strange noise.

It sounded like a number of hard hollow substances rattling together.

Harry's curiosity was aroused.

It seemed to him that the island abounded in wonders and mystifications.

He followed the sound.

It seemed to proceed from a lime grove close by.

Thither he repaired.

Cautiously he looked about.

It was not exactly without a certain mixture of fear, as he afterwards confessed.

At length his curiosity was rewarded by a sight that made his very blood curdle.

Suspended from two of the tallest trees were two half skeletons.

Such was the manner at least in which Harry spoke of them; and he was never known to tell that story more than once, it had filled his mind so full of horror.

The victims apparently had been bound together by the right and left wrists, and then hoisted up by the remaining wrists to two opposite trees.

This of itself must have been horrible torture, as

The fiendish perpetrators had evidently forced the trees together and then let them go, so as to fasten the arms of their victims as tight as a clothes line.

Then they lighted a fire under their victims, and gradually roasted their lower extremities, until they were sufficiently cooked for their palates; then the limbs were dismembered, and the cannibalistic crew regaled thereon.

This latter part Harry surmised from the relics lying around.

However, that decided him not to rest in that quarter any longer.

He at once, therefore, selected a tall tree with a bark as tough and supple as a hemp line, and the bark he commenced tearing off in long, narrow strips.

Then he found a huge log, or tree trunk, and this he rolled to the river's edge; and then he knotted all his strips of bark together.

When knotted, the rope of bark, he calculated, would reach about two-thirds or more across the stream, and Harry could measure pretty accurately with the naked eye.

This done Harry took his coil of bark in his hand, and made one end fast to a tree a little way up the stream; and then, placing the bight of his rope round the stump of a branch about two feet from the end that was to be the prow of his little bark, he launched the log and jumped on to it just as it began to feel the force of the stream.

By this means Harry hoped to steer his raft across the river, and the only serious difficulty he experienced was to keep his footing on the awkwardly-shaped mass when it rolled and twitched as the current caught it in different parts.

By veering out and holding on Harry quickly effected his purpose.

The log shot in an oblique direction across the stream; and, when Harry had veered out his line to the extreme end, he held on to it for a second, and then let go.

His raft then shot like an arrow to the opposite bank, and Harry leapt on shore.

He was pleased to think he had placed the river between himself and the hideous sight he had just beheld, but he little thought what still greater horrors were in store for him.

It was rapidly darkening now.

Although he had performed everything with extreme expedition, yet it took up a deal of time.

Once across, however, he was in a still greater difficulty than ever; there might be wild beasts or some sort of carnivorous animals that he had not found on the other side of the river.

He had not thought of this before, but it now occurred to him.

To travel in the darkness would be useless, and to camp out openly in the forest alone, and in a place to which he was an entire stranger, was at least one of the most uncomfortable reflections.

He decided, however, to make his bed in a tree for that night, and so he set about selecting one.

The one he chose was a very tall one; it had a profusion of boughs all growing near the top; and so, with sailor-like celerity, he "skimmed up" the trunk, and stretched himself at full length on one of its stoutest members.

The darkness closed in so rapidly that he had only time to get comfortably ensconced before it was night.

Harry was fearfully stiff, and his hands felt terribly sore as he lay pondering over the events of the past day, and wondering what would turn up on the morrow, and being worn out he very soon fell asleep.

The young lieutenant had not chosen the most comfortable couch; his hands placed one on the other pillowed his cheek, and the hard bark of the limb made several indentures in his flesh, which was only protected by a pair of thin duck trousers.

But Harry had chosen this perch in case he might be visited by any of the midnight prowlers, for he was aware that if there were any such about they would soon scent him and make small bones of his carcase.

Yet for all this Harry slept sounder than he did on the previous night.

The sun had risen long before he awoke.

He was about to stretch himself and go through the various performances of one suddenly awaking from a sound sleep, when the strange feeling came over him that some one was watching him.

It was a strange fancy, but for all that he could not shake it off, and as he lay on his cheek his eyes glanced upwards, and there, horrors of horrors, was a pair of eyes staring him through.

They were eyes of no ordinary nature.

Eyes that once seen could never be forgotten.

Eyes that possessed that magnetic power that those who once gazed on them could scarcely tear his visage away.

It was the eyes and head of a huge boa constrictor.

It was pending from a branch above him, and was preparing to dart upon his prey.

Harry saw the horrible vision, as it were, through a mist.

The bright sun was shining resplendently, and the silver grey and green of the huge monster's skin, lit by it, seemed like the scaled armour of some demon of the pit.

The snake was slowly working its body and measuring the distance of its prey with as much care and more cunning than an architect measures his lines.

Harry had great difficulty in repressing a cry.

Had he done so it would perhaps have cost him his life.

As it was, he gradually slipped his hand down to his waist and secured the tomahawk, and then as the hideous fangs and open jaws came closer to our buccaneer's face and the hot fetid breath poured, as it were, upon his cheek, one swift, sharp stroke of the tomahawk, and the head was severed from the trunk.

Harry gave the blow such impetus, however, that the jerk threw him from the bough, and down he fell with a dull thud.

Vere thought for a moment that he must be smashed, but a yielding substance beneath him broke his fall, and on recovering his feet he discovered that his preserver was a wild hog, who had been patiently watching for hours for the buccaneer to come down and supply him with his breakfast.

"Thank you, my kind friend," said Harry, picking up his cutlass that had fallen from its sheath; "thank you. I pray for seeing your backbone broken to treat of feeing my own."

"Dead as a nail," added Harry as he eyed the plump carcase of his deliverer. "What a joke this will be if ever I return on board alive again. To think that in the midst of this wilderness I should be befriended by a pig."

"This proves that we none of us know what is in store for us, but for a pig to give up the ghost in that undignified manner, without its proverbial grunt, is something comical."

Harry was so amused with this idea that he laughed aloud, and then he became thoughtful as the echoes died away and left him again in silence.

"Well," he said to himself, after he had indulged in a little reverie. "Poor Mr. Pig, as I have deprived you of a meal, you must afford me one;" and so saying he cut a good steak from the choicest part of the hog, and lit a fire and cooked it

Harry ate prodigiously at this meal, for he knew

not whence the next might come, and then he started again on his journey.

* * * * * * * *

Three days had elapsed since the death of the hog, and Harry was tired and footsore and weary of his search, when suddenly as he rose from the ground on the top of a hill where he had slept, he was surprised to behold the sea not more than half a mile distant.

There was a marked difference in the aspect of this part of the coast and the other part Harry had seen.

He concluded from this that he had wandered right across the island.

But this was of very small importance; he might only have crossed a neck of land.

Whilst he was pondering and viewing the wild scenery that stretched far away upon his right and on his left, he was startled by a loud "halloo."

It was such a shout as he had never heard from an Indian.

His heart began to palpitate.

It was the voice of a human being, he felt certain. Was it friend or foe?

"No matter," he muttered to himself, "I care not which it be, so long as I have the consolation of hearing a human voice."

He had scarcely given utterance to the words when two figures came into view in a ravine just beneath him.

They were dressed as seamen too.

"Hillio-o-o o-o!" Harry shouted at the pitch of his voice.

"Hillio-o-o-o-o!" was the reply.

He saw the men turn about and look around in amazement.

Presently one of the men saw him, and waved his hand for him to descend.

This was the most easy way of coming together.

Harry had simply to sit down on the loose fine sand and slide down from one shrub to another, and it took but a few minutes to join the strange men.

Being well armed Harry had no fear of joining them thus abruptly

The others appeared more scrupulous, and eyed him very carefully as he came down.

They seemed all the while to be talking to each other.

When they got near enough to discover each other's features the strange men set up another shout as before.

"What, Harry!" they exclaimed, running towards him. "Is it possible, are you alive, Mr. Vere?"

"Alive in every sense of the word, Bob, but how the deuce did you and Jerry get here?"

"Walked it," said Jerry Mizzen; "we've been walking for a whole week or more. It's the devil's own place, sure enough. I wish we was aboard our own snug craft again, I do."

"And so do I, my lads. Have you anything to eat?"

"The devil a bit, nor a drop to drink," answered Bob Hauler. "I wish we had. It's famishing we've been, haven't we, Jerry?"

"Worse Bob, fair starving; fruit, fruit, fruit every day, and just about here even that is getting scarcer."

"Eaten it all?" said Harry, affecting to laugh.

"I suppose so," Jerry grumbled. "I know it's made my stomach sore, and I'd give the world for a jolly good solid meal."

"But how did you get here?" queried Harry.

"Got cut off somehow during the fight with the Spaniards; lost ourselves in seeking for the ship and we've been wandering about ever since."

Harry Vere could not help smiling.

It seemed so strange that the three should meet in that outlandish spot

But he gave them a few cheering words, and they all agreed to make for the coast, and see what they could pick up.

They were all as hungry as hunters and gasping for a drink.

Owing to the soreness of their feet, for their boots that were not made for shore travelling, had fairly caved in, the trio were some hours reaching the coast, when, to their joy, the first sight they saw was a quantity of wreckage strewed about the sands.

"Bravo! Corn in Egypt!" said Bob kicking in the head of a biscuit barrel and handing round to his companions several of the contents that had escaped damage from the salt water.

Bob and Jerry sat to work ravenously on these, but Harry ate only a mouthful or two.

The consequence was, that when the two buccaneers had eaten their fill, they were so parched, and their spittle so dried up, that they were almost mad.

For nearly two days Harry had not touched any moisture, save the milk of a cocoa-nut, and that was curdled.

But he did not repine.

He hoped they would soon sight a vessel.

In fact they all expected that the "Will-o'-the-Wisp" would discover them before long.

The portions of wreckage occupied nearly a quarter of a mile of the coast.

It was strewn here and there, just as though it had been cast ashore in a storm.

Harry could find no trace of the ill-fated vessel's name.

They found several bodies of her unfortunate crew.

These they carried up clear of the next tide, and laid in a row together.

This was solemn work.

In the meantime their own cravings for water was growing more intense.

Bob could stand it no longer, so he stole away.

Jerry did not notice his going or he would have followed.

The faithful fellow became very uneasy, when Bob was missed.

"By Davy! he gone too," he ejaculated; "he'll get lost, and then how shall we find him?"

"Fear not, he is not very far away" answered Harry. "I should think he's been taught a good lesson not to wander about after all this."

"Shiver me here he comes!" cried Jerry, exultingly. "What the Dickens has he got there though, stowed away under his wing?"

Bob happened to overhear Jerry's last remark.

"Mother's milk you booby," he replied, "some of the right sort, too, no gammon; taste it, Mr. Vere."

As the buccaneer spoke, he drew forth a keg which was slung by a strap over his shoulder, and having removed the bung, held it towards the young lieutenant.

Any one who has known what it is to have suffered greatly from the agonising torments of thirst, will understand the eagerness with which Harry Vere glued his lips to the bunghole and drank ravenously until he could drink no longer.

The welcome draught gave him new life.

"Dear, precious water," he cried, in an ecstasy; "what are all the rich wines in the world to a thirsty man compared to thee? Where did you discover it?" he asked, eagerly.

"There's a spring up in the wood yonder, not far from here," replied Bob Hauler, pointing towards the dark forest.

"Thank heaven for such a treasure," fervently exclaimed Harry. "What should we have done without it?"

Jerry and Bob had both a weakness for "old

Jamaica," but they yielded to the lieutenant's argument with reference to the spring.

' I dessay we shall find it come in werry 'andy," said the former; "a chap can't 'xac'ly wash 'isself in rum."

Feeling much refreshed by the cool draught he had drank, the thoughts of the young man reverted to the unburied bodies of the shipwrecked sailors.

"We must not leave these poor unfortunates to be washed away by the waves or devoured by the fishes," he said.

"Certainly not," returned Bob Hauler; "we'll give 'em Christian burial, but as the tide'll be out for some time, I thought I'd look round first. 'Cos you see we was rather dry, and wanted a drink."

"As I did myself," Harry interposed.

"But now we're ready, an' we'll soon put our poor fellow-creatures under ground," said Jerry. " Heaven rest 'em."

A couple of spades were soon discovered amongst the ship's chattels, and with these a sufficient number of graves were dug.

In these were reverently laid the bodies of the dead seaman, after which the graves were filled up and the sand tightly pressed down upon them.

Then the three buccaneers stood over the dead, and each one murmured a brief but silent prayer according to his own feeling at the moment, and the ceremony was at an end.

Having thus performed the duties of respect to the departed, it now became imperative that the living should provide for themselves.

There was a large quantity of useful articles scattered upon the sand, and these they went to work carefully to collect, or rather to drag out of reach of the returning tide, until they could convey them to the spot in which they determined to locate themselves for the time being.

By common consent, this was arranged, to be on the borders of the forest facing the sea.

They would thus be able to attract the attention of any vessel that came sufficiently near, whilst the thicket behind would shelter them from the sun, and the eyes of savages, if there were any.

Having plenty of sail-cloth, a temporary tent was soon erected by Bob and Jerry, and before evening they were all comfortably lodged in their new habitation.

They had a good stock of the necessaries of life, amongst which were furniture, weapons, firearms, shot and bullets.

And besides these, they had discovered a quantity of rum, brandy, whisky and wine, together with tea, coffee, and cocoa, that would last them with care for a week or more.

There was also plenty of tools and iron-work, including nails, screws, locks and bars.

Much of the ship's dry stores had come to land injured.

Of these, flour, rice, and biscuits were not the least valuable.

Amongst the chests collected from the wreck was one, rather larger than the rest and particularly heavy.

Before they had time to open this, they were enlightened as to its contents in the following manner:—

As they sat in the opening of the tent towards the close of the afternoon, smoking their pipes, their eyes naturally roamed over the mingled mass of property by which they were surrounded, and Jerry, being gifted with a lively imagination, remarked:—

"If there was any natives in the vicinity, it wouldn't be a bad idea to open a marine store shop, would it?"

Harry laughed, as he replied,—

"The prospect does certainly seem to suggest something of that kind. But I fancy we shall find our stores more valuable for home consumption than as articles of merchandise."

"P'raps so," admitted Jerry; "if we've got to stay 'ere for the rest of our natural lives, I don't suppose we shall have more than enough for ourselves. An' o' course it's our bounden dooty to look out for number one."

"That old oak chest," said Bob, pointing with professional admiration to a large, massive-looking box amongst the lumber, "is a fine specimen of carpentering. I should say it were not only watertight but air-tight."

"I wonder what it contains," said Harry Vere, a little curiously.

"Well," returned Jerry Mizzen, shutting one eye and contemplating the wooden machine, "that's not werry easy to say. It might be linin, it might be wearin' apparel, or it might be old boots and shoes."

"Or carpenter's tools," suggested Hauler.

"Or it might be empty," added Harry; "but the shortest way of deciding would be to open it."

"Well, p'raps it would," said the luff.

Harry rose, and followed by his companions approached the chest.

He applied his hand to the lid. It was not locked, and he raised it.

A general exclamation of surprise burst from all present.

It certainly contained wearing apparel, and a pair of old shoes, but in these articles there was a human body—the body of a marine, who lay curled up nose and knees together, with his eyes shut, and perfectly still.

"Lor bless me, it's a soldier!" ejaculated Jerry; "is he alive or dead?"

In order to arrive at a proper conclusion, Bob dived down to the bottom of the chest, and, seizing the marine by the collar of his jacket, bawled—

"Ahoy! if ye're alive, tumble out."

Suiting the action to the word, he gave the marine a jerk and lifted him out of the chest.

' Oh, murder!" shrieked the unfortunate, waking from his sleep, and trying to fall on his knees. "Don't kill me; I'm dead as it is! Oh, mother! Peter!

"'Old yer row, yer lubber," cried the good-natured Hauler. "What's the good of calling for them here? They aint tropercal wegitables."

The marine, in spite of his bewilderment, recognising the voice, opened his eyes and looked eagerly around him.

"What, Jerry! Bob Barnacle! Mr. Vere!" he exclaimed, incredulously; "is it really you, and not yer ghosteses?"

"Of course it's us," returned the two former.

"Oh, wot a blessing," fervently ejaculated the marine.

"I got into this 'ere chest when I thought the ship was a goin' to bits, and I went to sleep and dreamt as I was down at the bottom of the briny deep. Just as you lifted me out of the box, I thought a tremendous crab had collared me; instead of wich I finds myself on dry land, surrounded by old pals."

These expressions of exultation came faintly from the lips of the speaker, who, having uttered them, quietly fainted away.

"Poor fellow," said Harry, "he's exhausted. Give him some water."

"With a dash of rum in it," suggested Jerry.

"No, without the rum," countermanded the lieutenant.

Some water, fresh from the spring, was fetched by Bob, and placed to the marine's lips, who, having swallowed about half a gallon, came immediately to his senses, and expressed himself ready for something more solid.

Some food from the ship's stores was quickly placed before him, after having devoured which he declared he was " as right as a trivet."

As soon as the marine was in good talking trim the buccaneers naturally inquired how he came there, and this he explained in a very few words.

It appeared that when the Spaniards smoked the cavern the marine fell a victim to its dire effects, and laid on the ground gasping and choking for air until he became insensible.

But fortunately for him he had fallen face downwards, and when the fresh air poured in it inflated his lungs afresh, and he came to only to find himself deserted and the sole occupant of the cave.

Every trace too of the ' Will-o'-the-Wisp " was gone, so, not caring to fall into the hands of the Spaniards, whom he had every reason to believe would show him no mercy, he ran away with a boat he found on the beach and stood out to sea

He was picked up by a small man-of-war, who in turn fell in with the Death Pirate, and after an hour or so fighting the man-of-war was boarded, her crew some of them murdered, the vessel set fire to, and abandoned to her fate.

More than this, the marine did not know; he, frankly acknowledged that he was down below during the greater part of the action, and that when the ship was reported to be in danger he hid himself in the empty chest, and no more was seen of him till the present discovery.

The sun had now set, and it grew rapidly dark A lamp was kindled in the tent, and a fire lighted, and a steaming kettle of coffee made.

This, with the addition of biscuits, formed the evening meal, and having finished it, our buccaneers thoroughly tired with their day's exertions, stretched themselves on the ground and were in a few minutes in profound repose.

*   *   *   *   *

The whole party woke the next morning much refreshed with their night's rest.

Breakfast over, Harry said—

" I think it would be as well to reconnoitre the country on which we are thrown together."

" So do I," acquiesced the marine, eagerly ; " let's go in search of 'ventures. This is a queer country, sir, and there's lots to see."

" You go in search !" exc'aimed Jerry, laughing. "Why yer'd faint away at the werry fust appearance of anything wentursome."

"I begs yer parding, Mr. Mizzen, but I shouldn't do anything of the sort,"returned the marine, indignantly. " I aint afeard of anything on land. Its only the water as I've a horror of."

This statement was to some extent true, but it caused Harry to inquire—

" If so, what could have induced you to adopt a sailor's life ?"

" Well, sir, the reason's jest this : I've got a brother as is of a regler roving disposition. Well, sir, he goes abroad, and no one never hears no more of him. Well, sir, mother took to frettin', cos Peter was a sort of a pet of her's, and she says to me—

"' Jack,' says she, ' I know I shall worrit myself into an early grave if I don't see my Peter agen.'

"' Don't do that, mother,' says I ; ' I'll go and look after him.

"' Do,' says mother, ' and thankee for yer dootiful considerations of my feelin'.'

" And so you see, Mr. Vere, that's how I came to take to the ocean."

<hr />

CHAPTER CCXXIV.

ZELIE'S SOLILOQUY—THE FIGHT WAXES FIERCER —CAPTAIN TOM DRAKE GAINS A VICTORY.

LET us step on board the '' Will-o'-the-Wisp," as she rides at anchor about two cables' length from the stately vessel of Hugh Baldrick.

Upon the quarter-deck of the "Will-o'-the-Wisp," reclining under an awning that shielded her from the rays of the golden noonday sun, was Zelie, the corsair maiden.

Her eyes were bent shoreward, which at intervals she swept with a spyglass, as she watched the dark figures of the besiegers, enveloped at times in the quick puffs of smoke from the pistols and muskets of the buccaneers.

Her quick eye took in all their movements.

She could see the glittering headpieces, and the gleaming arms of the Spanish men-at-arms as they crowded on the battlements, and hurled great stones and other missiles on to those below.

Few would imagine the thoughts that were passing in that beautiful girl's mind at that moment.

How vividly her dark eye wandered from point to point.

Then as her hopes and fears were alternately raised her fair bosom rose and fell, and her hands clenched until the pink nails dented into the flesh.

But Zelie was not watching the course of the battle so intently.

There was one form on whom her gaze was alone centered.

Through the white puffs of smoke, the fiery form from point to point dashing here and there, that form was ever before her eyes.

It was Captain Tom Drake who formed the subject of her vigil.

She could see his handsome form and his cocked hat glittering with gold and jewels as he leapt from one point of danger to another, and led his gallant tars against the Spanish soldiery.

On a cushion at her feet sat a girl, her attendant, her slave forsooth, and as she cast up her plaintive eyes from time to time to inquire her mistresse's wish, she seemed to share the anxiety of her lovely mistress.

Since their departure from the French coast, Sybil had noticed a marked change in the Arabian girl, Zelie.

She had noticed that her lips were feverish, and that when sitting alone a hectic flush would suffuse her delicate cheeks.

The slightest footsteps of the young chieftain would cause her to start, and even in her sleep her bosom would heave tumultuously, and she would sob and moan and utter strange words, and at times even spring from her couch and gaze vacantly around her.

At such times the slave girl would become alarmed.

On more than one occasion she made a movement to summon our hero, but her mistress guessing her intent would motion her to be silent, and wave her back to her place.

Sybil was quite old enough to know the feeling that existed between our hero and the corsair maiden.

She had seen and heard enough to learn that Zelie was desperately jealous of him.

She had seen her mistress listening for hours at the arras that separated her cabin from that of Captain Tom.

It was at such times that she had heard that Minnie was a captive, that her life as well as her liberty was in jeopardy, and, in fact, that Captain Tom's mission to the strange coast was to rescue her, and to revenge every insult offered her, even at the risk of his own life.

Zelie virtually bore Minnie no ill-will ; she would have loved her, had circumstances permitted her to do so, as a sister ; but she was her rival, she stood between her and the object she idolised, and while Minnie lived, Zelie could only look up to our hero as her protector.

This was the cause of Zelie's anxiety.

It was this that banished sleep from her eyes, and stole away her peace of mind.

Night after night this had been the subject of her dreams.

Horrible thoughts had at times occurred to her.

She had felt the sensation as of hideous snakes crawling about her bosom, and gnawing their way into her heart.

Once the fiendish idea occurred to her of ending her misery by poisoning herself and our hero, and she had even prepared the poison and the wine ready for mixing when the sound of Captain Tom's voice aroused her and even caused her to abandon her purpose.

It was only the night previous to the battle that Zelie had one of these horrible visitations.

She had heard Ben Barnacle's story, which was the sure confirmation of Minnie being a captive in the Spaniard's stronghold.

True Ben had not seen her; but then Harry Vere had.

Having overheard this, it set her mind thinking and wondering more than ever.

Even now, as she sat between hope and fear, watching the daring achievements and hair-breadth escapes of Captain Tom, she was racking her brain for some plan of her future movements.

For some days she had been studiously reading one of the books in her native tongue, many of which Tom had allowed to remain in her own private library, as he could not read Arabic, and had not sufficient time at his disposal to study it.

This particular book, with its mystic cabalistics, was the comfort and companion of her solitary hours.

Sometimes she would feign indisposition, and then she would call in the aid of Doctor Shrike.

With a bow and a scrape that worthy would soon be in attendance.

And then they would sit for an hour.

He watching her lovely form, and picturing to himself the ornament she would be to his collection if he could only embalm her, and she questioning him as to the nature of different drugs and chemicals, and writing down their Latin names and their properties.

Sometimes she would persuade him to bring her a sample of each, always impressing upon his mind that it was to be kept entirely secret from all on board, and more especially from Captain Tom.

Doctor Shrike gave his word of honour without the least hesitation.

He did not even venture to inquire for what purpose she wanted them.

"Some experiment" he thought. "Ah! well, there may be an accident, and I may have the job of amputating one of those beautiful limbs. Well, it all assists the advancement of science. Oh that we could only embalm them alive as when dead! What an improvement it would be!"

And so, rubbing his hands at his own horrible thought, he would dive down below, and bury himself in the seclusion of his own cabin.

The doctor, though simple in his way, was not so easily hoodwinked as might be supposed, although he so readily consented to keep the secret, yet he was determined in his own mind to watch Zelie's movements on every possible occasion.

To do this he knew he must assume the most perfect indifference, and so he patiently waited and watched.

In the meantime Zelie was as astute and cunning as the doctor; she had got hold of Jacop, who for sundry little luxuries which he was not supposed to know even the existence of, much less to indulge in, supplied her with such little articles as she stood in need of.

Sybil was entrusted with the management of this.

She was affable and winning in her ways, and if the doctor was enraptured with Zelie, Jacop was completely overpowered with one glance at her attendant.

Captain Tom Drake had taken nearly all the available hands on shore with him, leaving only a few, such as the carpenter and his crew, the cook and his mates, Shrike and his attendant, and a couple of seamen to look after the ship.

By these, as may be surmised, the operations on shore were eagerly watched, and when the fort blew up the hands on both ships raised as vociferous a cheer as they possibly could.

Zelie uttered a cry and rushed to the vessel's side.

Her dark eyes dilated wildly as she tried to pierce the thick clouds of smoke and debris that for a time filled the air and hid the combatants from her view.

"Safe, safe, thank God, he is safe!" she cried aloud, clasping her hands; "but she, what of her?"

As she uttered these last words her whole demeanour suddenly changed.

That beautiful girl, who seemed only born to be loved and admired, was turned, as it were, into a demon; her large eyes darted forth fierce fire from under the finely pencilled brows that contracted over them, and hung like a cloud of thunder above them.

Firm, erect, rigid in every limb, her arms stretched down by her side, her hands clenched, and her teeth and lips hard-set; she looked truly fit to hurl the thunderbolts of Jove.

Sybil drew back from her in alarm.

She had never seen her mistress look so terrible.

Statuesque as marble, and firm as a deeply rooted oak, she stood, her delicately moulded form and rounded limbs being shown to their fullest advantage.

*   *   *   *   *

As the fort blew up, Captain Tom and Hugh Baldrick called off their men, and warned them to take heed of the falling debris that would have descended in a shower upon their devoted heads.

"Stand aside!" cried our hero. "Hurrah, lads. Look out, we have sprung a mine. The demons have fallen into their own snare"

"Oh, you are safe, then?" exclaimed Hugh Baldrick, rushing up to our hero, and clasping him by the hand. "By Jove! I thought it was all up with you just now. When I saw that mine explode almost beneath your feet, I thought you had taken a passport for a journey through the air."

"Not yet, Baldrick," said our hero, smiling and returning the smuggler's grasp; "I prefer better companionship than those scurvy Spaniards. Their own craftiness and deceit has proved their ruin."

"So long as you are safe, never mind them, Tom," returned Hugh. "They have spared us the trouble of killing them. Now, what shall we decide on as our next point of attack?"

By this time the attacking parties were drawn up, and formed into two compact squares, a short distance from the scene.

The light wind sluggishly rolled the clouds of smoke and dust away, and cleared the air, so that the two commanders could see the extent of damage done.

Of the fort nothing now remained but a heap of ruins, but beyond it was a strong wall about thirty feet high and apparently of immense thickness.

"A tough job, comrade," said our hero, eyeing the huge barrier.

"Yes," replied Hugh thoughtfully, "this tower was only a sort of breastwork. I can see the drift of the rascally Spaniards now."

"It's pretty plain; seeing they could not hold the breastwork long, they laid a train to the magazine so that when we got nicely into the fort they could send us to glory. But through their negligence or one of our stray shots, the explosion took place before all was ready."

'Just so—ha, ha," laughed the gentleman smuggler.

"I wonder whose powder it was they made so free with? By St. George and the big dragon we had a narrow escape that time!"

Tom laughed and nodded.

His quick eye was eagerly scanning the scene.

He could see that a number of soldiers were crowding to the battlements of the towers and other fortifications around.

It puzzled him somewhat to see so many soldiers, and he wondered where they all sprang from, as, according to the Indian's statement, the force did not exceed two hundred men.

Tom could count nearly that number now, and then there must be many others at their respective posts.

It took but a few moments for Tom to make these hasty calculations.

The men on the battlements were preparing to salute them with their artillery, and so the leaders once more prepared for action.

Tom and Hugh held a short consultation, then Hugh and a party of his men disappeared, and the buccaneers were left to carry out the orders of their daring chief by themselves.

"You see," Tom said, addressing his small but formidable little party, "they are loading their old tin pots and carronades. One-half of them will not go off, but the rest may thin our numbers considerably, so throw up a battery, and from its shelter we may pick off a few of those iron-capped heads, and afterwards board them in the smoke."

The buccaneers greeted his words with a cheer, and slinging their muskets across their shoulders, they soon formed a pretty strong barricade with the stout beams and other parts of the ruined fort.

It was formed into three breastworks, one behind the other, and behind these the buccaneers crouched down, and prepared to receive the fire of the enemy.

They were not a moment too soon.

Tom had barely time to see his men properly placed and throw himself down behind a huge block of masonry, when the guns from the battlements belched forth.

The report was not simultaneous, but sounded like a peal of crackling thunder; and, as Tom predicted, several of the guns exploded with their charge and carried off the heads of two of the gunners.

The carronades did their work more effectually, and very few of Tom's party would have been left had it not been for the shelter they had thrown up in front.

No sooner had the shots done hurtling than Tom gave the order "fire."

The buccaneers retaliated with a sharp volley which drove the gunners from the embrasures, and gave Hugh Baldrick time to come up with his party with a couple of rude scaling ladders.

The buccaneers kept the Spaniards at bay while the scaling ladders were raised, and then with a true British cheer Hugh Baldrick and his smugglers swarmed up them.

Gonsalvo himself was on the battlements and with his long rapier he tried to rally his men to their guns, but the fire of Tom's party was so fierce that not one of them dared to show his head above the stone work.

The governor, enraged at this, rushed from the battlements, and, collecting several of his chevaliers and friends about him, with a few trusty pike-men and musqueteers, made a sally forth from a port hard-by with the intent of silencing the deadly fire of the buccaneers.

Tom's eye glistened as he saw the governor advance.

He longed to cross swords with that worthy, and measure steel with some one whose blood it was not unworthy of him to spill.

Gonsalvo also selected his man, and in his own mind had made short work of "the stripling."

The meeting between the buccaneers and the soldiery was like the meeting of two mimic armies.

The chevaliers hung back at the first onset; they did not like the cut-and-slash style of the mids; their rapiers were made for finer work.

While Tom and Gonsalvo were engaged the middies played sad havoc with their opponents.

They cut about them without discrimination, crashing a helmet here, piercing a corset there, and laying four or five of the stalwart soldiers on the sword dead or seriously wounded.

The Spanish chevaliers did their best in defending themselves from their hardy opponents.

They stood their ground well for a time, but at length gave way, and eventually turned tail and ran back to the postern, which they entered and closed with a bang, and bolted and secured behind them.

Hugh Baldrick and his party had a desperate struggle to gain the battlements, but the smugglers battled with them so bravely that they gained a footing before the soldiers were hardly aware of their presence.

A fierce hand-to-hand conflict then ensued, and blood began to flow freely, and the smugglers would have gained an easy victory had it not been for one of the gunners.

He slipped away unseen and loaded a small cannon in one of the embrasures, and turned its muzzle towards that part of the battlement where the smugglers were thickest in numbers.

Seeing what their comrade had done, the Spaniards gathered new courage, but their long pikes and halberds would have stood them poor service had it not been for their straight swords, with which fortunately for them they chanced to be armed.

Hugh Baldrick's powerful arm was well tried on this occasion. His deadly cut and thrust put several of the soldiers *hors de combat* and sent several of the gunners to their last account.

The chief officer had selected the captain of the artillery, and they, being pretty fair swordsmen, and being by chance in a spot where the fight raged less fierce, had a chance of testing each other's skill.

But this sort of warfare could not last long.

Steel blades began to quiver and strong arms began to waver, and many of the soldiers cried for quarter when the cutlass was at their throat.

At length a loud huzzah came up from below, and soon after Captain Tom, with a score of his brave followers at his heels, leaped through an embrasure.

Hugh Baldrick had winged his adversary at that moment, and only spared his life as an act of mercy, but on condition that the wounded man should lead them, if his services were required, to the governor's palatial mansion.

"We have settled our batch; we have taken twelve prisoners, but the governor has escaped," cried Tom, breathless.

"Then we shall have little to do in silencing these," said the smuggler; "we have been three to one, but with your reinforcement we shall soon put the weight on our own side."

Hugh had just time to look round at the dead and dying as they lay heaped together or singly some between the overturned guns and others stretched on the gory flag-stones.

He sighed in silence as he gazed on the still, prone forms of his followers, several of them stiff in death.

But his mind was quickly diverted from this to matters of more pressing moment.

The fresh onslaught of the buccaneers filled the Spaniards with dismay; they turned and fled precipitately, tumbling over each other down the stone staircase, and those behind trampling over the fallen without mercy.

The smugglers and buccaneers could not follow them as closely as they wished, owing to the darkness of the narrow staircase, but they kept a pretty smart pace behind them, and caught up with the hindermost ones in the courtyard.

Captain Tom then gave orders for the wounded to be conveyed to the boats.

Then the dead were lowered down and conveyed to the beach.

"Now," said Hugh Baldrick to the man he had wounded, "it is time for you to fulfil your contract. Are you ready—yea or nay?"

"Ready," spoke the wounded man in a hollow voice. "I will keep my word though it break my heart."

"Bravely spoken," cried the smuggler. "Tom, heave round here; here is one who needs your attention."

"In what way?"

"He will show you to the inner courtyard, to the governor's mansion, in fact to the place where all the fine ladies are kept."

"All," exclaimed Tom; "it is but one I seek."

"And that one you will see also," said the smuggler.

"Let him lead the way, then."

The wounded pikeman seemed half to regret his promise; but a look from Hugh banished all his scruples.

In their descent to the courtyard they had to grope their way over the trampled bodies of the dead that here and there lay on the narrow steps.

Captain Tom and the Prince of Smugglers shrugged their shoulders as they had to pass through this ordeal.

The wounded man gave a groan, but whether from pain or sympathy none but himself knew.

Fighting was still going on in the courtyard.

A desperate few had made a last stand there.

Alas! for them. It gave their comrades a chance of escape, but to them it was certain death.

Tom and Hugh followed their guide, to alleviate whose suffering Hugh had torn off the shirt of one of the dead and bound up his arm.

The man winced, and a peculiar smirk curled his lip; but Hugh took no notice of this during the operation. He never for a moment thought that the soldier, having given his word, would prove treacherous.

Tom motioned to several middies as he passed along, and they followed closely behind through the paved galleries and gloomy passages through which the guide led them.

"We are nearly there," said the pikeman. "You have but to reach the bottom of this aisle, and your desire is fulfilled. I can accompany you no further, I feel faint."

Neither Tom nor Hugh pressed the man further.

Tom simply thrust open a door indicated, and passed through.

It was a long vaulted passage they were in, and when they had traversed about half of it, Tom gave a cry that warned his companions.

Captain Tom felt the floor give beneath his feet, and he gave a sort of spring forward, and, on look-ing back, he beheld a deep chasm from which he had so narrowly escaped.

The hole was of such dimensions that Tom and Hugh must both of them gone down had not Tom been quick.

A huge slab, about eight feet long, was worked by some hidden mechanism; the weight set it in motion, and when relieved, it returned again to its former situation with a dull thud.

Tom looked at Baldrick significantly.

"Well," said the latter, "what do you think of the rogue?"

"Think," said Tom, almost slipping an oath; "well, I could cut such a villain's throat without mercy; he is not fit to live, if such is his word of honour."

"So say I; but how are we to stop this trap?"

"By the aid of this."

As Tom spoke, he took from the wall a ladder; it had ten spokes.

"Ah, about ten feet," he added, "that will reach; try it, it will bear more than your weight."

Tom laid it down and measured, and finding it was secure, they passed over it.

When they arrived at the end of the passage, which was lit by a glimmer through slits in the wall, they came to a curiously shaped chamber from which several passages led, but they were so dark that the explorers dared not venture into one of them.

"Sold, to a certainty," exclaimed Hugh; "this comes of being merciful to a Spaniard; by heaven, I will not spare another's life; I will be revenged, ay, doubly for this!"

"You will not," said Tom Drake; "you will as freely forget and forgive."

"No! Captain Tom!" exclaimed Hugh, vehemently. "I swear I will not." And he kissed the handle of his jewelled dirk, and snapped it as he replaced it in its sheath.

Captain Tom Drake beckoned to one of his middies.

"Walters, go back and try that door."

The middy tripped lightly off, and returned in a few minutes.

"Well," said Tom, "it is closed and fast with a spring; the inner side is covered with sheet iron."

"Then we are entombed," said Hugh Baldrick.

His voice sounded hollow, but as they all looked around them, they felt how truthful were his words.

To add to their dismay, the day was fast drawing to a close, and deepening shadows above began to pour their fitful glimmer through the slits in the massive walls.

CHAPTER CCXXV.

THE DEATH'S HEAD INDIANS—MINNIE DISCOVERED

HARRY VERE and his companions were greatly refreshed after a night's sleep in the hut.

They breakfasted early, and recruited their strength with hot coffee and such provisions as had washed from the wreck.

"Now," said Harry, "it is my intention to explore the island more thoroughly. Minnie, I have reason to fear, is in the hands of the Indians. I must discover their village, and though she should be in the wigwam of the chief, I will rescue her, or——"

"Lose your top knot," broke in Jerry, with a shudder.

The marine gave a short whistle and shrugged his shoulders.

"A fine speculation," he whispered in Bob's ear, as that worthy ceased masticating a hard biscuit.

"Are you going alone?" Bob queried, after a pause.

"If no one will accompany me."

"If," said Jerry, emphasising the word. "Who has refused?"

"None."

"Whom did you ask?"

"No one."

"Then don't put any if's in the way, Master Harry. I for one will fight forty Injuns and as many chiefs for Minnie—Miss Atherton, I mean."

"Ay! she a neat little craft," broke in Bob; "as neat and as trim as our 'Will-o'-the-Wisp.' Why, lord love her! it won'd break my heart if any harm came to her, and all through a lubberly swab of an Injun."

Bob's speech brought a soft tear to Jerry's eye.

"Why, we all loves her, Bob," he said, in a sort of melodramatic voice. "Aint she our captain's, and aint she part of the ship's crew, aint she—aint she lovely, too, and aint we come all this way to fetch her home, ay, Bob?"

"That's plain sailing enough, Jerry, but don't go blubbering like a sperm whale over it; if we mean finding her let's do it. I hate people as goes and spouts like a blubber fish. I like action. Perhaps while we're moored here tightening our skins, the Injins are eating her for breakfast."

"Bob," he said "did you mean it?"

"Mean what, you watery-headed porpoise?"

"That I was a blubber fish."

"In course I did."

"Then you're a shark, Bob," retorted Jerry.

"Who said I wasn't?" said Bob, coolly.

"I said you was."

"Then take that for your cheek," said Bob, drily, and he smacked a lump of soaked biscuit in Jerry's watery eye.

Jerry's blood was up.

"You alligator," he exclaimed, "I'll have blood for this, and may the Injins eat me if I don't be revenged."

And so saying Jerry caught Bob fair on the point of the snout with a hard biscuit with such force as to break that edible in two, and draw a crimson stream from Bob's nasal organ.

"Oh, Moses!" jerked out Bob, as he sprang to his feet and clapped his hand upon the wounded member. "Sky scrapers and tweezers, that's worse than an insult!"

"You deserved it," said Jerry, wiping his blinded eye.

"Did I?" exclaimed Bob, still smarting from the tingling of the blow. "Well, take that, you lubber, and that, you cod-fish-headed swab!"

Bob gave the irrepressible a couple of such digs in the ribs as made him sound like a drum, and then the pair closed and pummelled into each other for the space of about three minutes in such a manner that Harry was obliged to interfere.

"Come, now, no fighting," he said, raising his voice. "There now, be friends. Aint you ashamed to fall out at such a time and in such a place as this? Is this how you show your respect for Miss Minnie?"

"I'd die for her, I would," said Jerry. "But that Bob, the sneak, he don't care no more about her than Jacop cares for his master."

Harry Vere, with a few more words, assuaged their anger, and made them shake hands and be friends.

The lieutenant then filled a flask with water, and putting some biscuits and cold salt pork in a bag, girded his sword about his waist, stuck his pistol in his belt, and prepared to leave the hut.

"Where are you going?" said Bob and Jerry, simultaneously.

"Many miles, perhaps, before I return," was Harry's answer.

"And leave us here?" Jerry queried again.

"Decidedly! you can then fight to your hearts content, and if one gets killed there will be two left to bury him."

This was a sad rebuke.

The combatants felt it acutely, and hung their heads abashed.

Jerry pretended to be wiping his eye with the sleeve of his shirt, and Bob kept rubbing his nose as gently as he could with a piece of old canvas.

"Well, master Harry," Bob said after a while, "it's cowardly to see you go away alone, and it's hard for us to be left here; but look you, we are not going to be the skunks you take us for; we're bound to be in the same boat and row along with you."

"I'm pleased to hear you say so," said Harry, gaily; "bear a hand, boys, and rig; look sharp, for you see the day is crawling on our heels."

Bob, Jerry, and the marine were very soon equipped.

They took plenty of provender with them, and, placing a few planks across the opening of the hut, they started off through the thickly wooded country.

For two whole days and nights they wandered on without success, not even seeing so much as the trail of an Indian, nor, in fact, the signs of any human being save themselves.

But Harry found the journey not so monotonous as when alone, and he certainly would have enjoyed himself had it not taken to raining at night.

At length, one morning, having ascended a steep hill, they were rejoiced to see the wigwams of the Indians far down in a plain below them.

This was the settlement no doubt to which Minnie had been taken.

Harry was filled with joy and excitement, and he walked on with hasty step, at times outstripping his companions.

The Indian village was a long way off, in fact, farther than they had anticipated, and Harry informed them that if they wished to reach the wigwams by nightfall they must keep pace with him, or otherwise he should have to press forward and leave them.

The marine was half inclined to hang back, but for shame's sake he was induced to keep on, in fact he was sorry that he came at all.

Yet he was afraid to be left alone in that wild desert.

Bob and Jerry walked along in moody silence.

They were picturing to themselves gory scalps and gleaming tomahawks.

This shore work was quite out of their latitude.

But still they stuck to Harry, and kept their stations about a yard in his rear, so that the whole four formed a gloomy, meditating, and straggling company.

Bob at length broke the dreary silence.

"You've fought with Injuns, haven't you, Jerry?"

"Rather. I guess you know that, Bob?"

"Who licked?"

"I did, of course. Who else do you think did? Why do you ask?"

"Oh! don't get angry—don't get vicious."

"I aint going to do neither."

"Then answer a perlite question."

Jerry was not in a mood for joking.

"Go on, then, ax away, and I'll answer," he said, petulantly.

"Did they scalp you?"

"Do I look like it?"

"Well, what's that bald patch on your head?"

Jerry turned his glistening eyes viciously on his interrogator.

"That bald patch, as you call it, is honourable, Mr. Hauler; it's the care and worrit a looking after you as caused that wool to comb off."

" Wool, Jerry; why what's left looks like oakum; you don't mean to say you ever had wool on that timber head?'

Jerry gave him another reproving look.

"Handle your words more carefully, Mr. Hauler, or I shall have to haul you over the coals, mind; I don't like this joking, let me tell you, and especially at such serious times."

" Then don't shiver your mizzen at me, Mr. Jerry; you aint aboard a billy-boy, you know."

" But I'm very close to a-a-a——"

" What the deuce is up?'

Jerry was too flabbergasted to speak.

The little hair on his head stood up and raised his hat quite an inch from its usual place of adjustment.

"Are you mad?" queried Bob, turning round sharply and facing him.

Harry Vere, hearing a sharp altercation, turned back.

' Quarrelling again?" he said.

"No, Jerry's gone mad; a sunstroke, perhaps."

" What, beneath these trees, in this cool shade?"

'' He's gone off then."

Jerry by this time had recovered a little.

''Look there," he said to Harry, pointing with his finger.

Harry looked in the direction indicated.

It was his turn to be a little alarmed now.

Bob and the marine, who had just come up, looked also, and they gave an inward shudder.

To their sight in an opening between the trees, they could see a dozen or more Indians naked as they were born, saving a white streak down each arm and leg, and the same mark along each rib, and the head and face painted to represent a skull.

"The Death's Head Indians," said Harry Vere, scarcely drawing his breath "It is well they have not seen us; they are performing a war dance."

" Death's Head devils!" cried Jerry, between his chattering teeth. " Oh, Lord! what horrid monsters they do look."

Our adventurers stood for some moments rooted to the spot; they could not muster courage even to draw back into concealment.

Meanwhile the group of horribly fantastic figures danced wildly about, and went through their superstitions rite.

Mocky the Marine was totally conflabbergasted.

He could neither speak, shriek, cry out, nor utter a word.

He was too far gone for anything, in fact, and Harry, seeing how his companions were affected by the sudden sight, and well knowing that a great deal depended on himself, suddenly roused and led them into a thick grove for shelter.

Bidding them partake of their evening meal, Harry then took a good draught of water and crept forth to watch the antics of the terrible Death's Head Indians.

Harry saw them disperse, and then, creeping back to the trio, he bade them remain in their concealment till his return, and then he glided swiftly down the slope, under shelter of the trees and shrubs, in the direction of the Indian village.

Harry Vere was as nimble as a cat, and his sharp, lynx-like eyes looked about him in every direction, and examined carefully each object within their reach.

And so he went on, until he could hear distinctly the voices of the Indians in and about the wigwams, and at length he found himself within half a pistol shot of one of the pickets who were already placed for the night.

As darkness set in, Harry could see a number of dusky figures moving about before the wigwams in the gloom, and so he laid still and quiet, breathing no harder than was positively necessary, and his quick ear strained to catch each sound.

He had already recognised the wigwam of the chief; he could pick it easily by the innumerable strings of human teeth and the extraordinary quantity of scalps that adorned the entrance.

He fancied even that he could hear Minnie's voice sounding from that wigwam, but it might be fancy; yet it gave him hope, and bade him not despair.

Harry could make out, however, that something extraordinary was going on, if only from the number of scouts that kept continually arriving, and the busy hum that came from one large wigwam, where he supposed a council was being held, for he could see, as the folds of the opening were thrown aside, that a great number of white-headed warriors were squatted in a circle around a large wood fire, smoking their calumets and gesticulating violently.

Harry thought this a very good opportunity for satisfying his curiosity.

And so he crawled silently on his belly to the back of the old chief's wigwam, taking care to lie flat whenever the sentry's face was towards him, until he gained the shelter of the wigwam.

At that moment the sentry stooped down, and after a short space a faint light glimmered, and then a bright flame burst up from a wood fire that had previously been laid.

Harry was exceedingly annoyed at this; but he afterwards found that it was to his advantage.

It gave him the opportunity of watching the sentry, or any one who passed to and fro, whilst he, so long as he kept in the shade, was free from all observation.

The young buccaneer was now close to the wigwam, and he could distinctly hear the voices of two persons talking.

They were the voices of females, and one he could easily recognise was that of Minnie.

The other he could not hear so plainly, nor could he recognise it as at all familiar.

Harry tried to draw attention by scratching at the buffalo hide, but it was to no purpose, and so he took his dirk and cut a slit about a foot long.

Then extending the opening he peered through and saw two females seated on a pile of furs.

" Hist—hist!"

He made a low sound with a movement of his lips, and this caused the females to turn and recoil with horror from the back of the wigwam.

' Lost, lost," thought Harry, and he seriously thought of escaping to the wood, for he was afraid the females in their terror would cry out and raise an alarm, and that all would be discovered.

Minnie, however, possessed a wonderful power of mind.

She certainly glanced timidly around her as any one would in a strange place, but seeing no danger and nothing to be afraid of she went on with her conversation as before.

When all was composed Harry again ventured.

" Minnie, Minnie Atherton," he whispered.

The captives started as though they had been shot.

To hear that name pronounced distinctly and in a tongue evidently English was certainly mysterious, especially as they could see no one from whom it might proceed.

Harry, however, slit the hole still deeper, and thrusting his head through made himself known.

Minnie's astonishment now was, if anything, greater than ever.

It was Harry Vere's voice and his face to a certainty, but how did he get there?

How did he discover her in that secluded spot, where it had taken the Indians, who knew the path and had their own canoes, nearly a week to travel?

TOM DRAKE DISCOVERS IRON ARM.

These thoughts passed vividly through Minnie's mind, but Harry gave her no time for reflection.

"This way," he whispered. 'Come hither, I would speak."

Minnie was by his side in an instant.

"Are you ready," he said, "to accompany me from this, or ——"

"Ready! Indeed I am at any moment, and my friend here, if you would allow her to accompany us."

"But," she added, sinking her voice to a whisper, "we must be cautious, for the chief and the warriors are in council. They fear the treachery of the whites, and they would not mind putting you to the torture to make you confess you know something about it."

Harry motioned her to be silent; and, making sure that the sentry had his eyes averted from them, he took his dirk, and with it extended the rent unto the ground, and Minnie and her companion passed through.

Harry saw the sentry at that moment turn.

Vere's heart almost ceased to palpitate.

The Indian had evidently heard a sound.

His quick ear must have heard the rustling of a dress.

Harry watched his opportunity, and as soon as the Indian altered his gaze Harry led the two females to the dark forest, and they were quickly hidden from view in its deep recesses.

It was Vere's intent to work his way round to where he had left his companions, but in the darkness they wandered on, without even a star to guide them.

The last few nights had been exceedingly wet, and the present bid fair to be the same.

The atmosphere was heavy and cloudy; dark leaden masses rolled across the horizon, blotting out the stars, and obscuring the moon.

Harry prayed that the night might be fair; that the Indians might not so easily strike on their trail, for he had not the least doubt, that if caught, the savages would put them to some horrible torture.

And so they wandered on through the gloom

night, praying for morning, yet fearing that it might come too soon.

Harry would have made double the headway, had it not been attended by the females, for though they drew their dresses closely around them, yet they were continually catching in the brambles and thorn bushes, which impeded their progress considerably.

It must have been, so far as Harry could calculate, fully an hour past midnight, when the females complained of fatigue.

Up to this time, they had borne up bravely, and battled with the thick undergrowth which had rendered their journey both arduous and perilous.

As to Harry, his task had been one of excessive labour; he had to clear the way in front and drop behind occasionally, and place his ear to the ground and listen for any footsteps that might be following them.

He was fully aware that, as soon as the girls were missed, swift-footed scouts would be sent in pursuit.

It was therefore more advantageous to them to make a detour from the beaten track, and though it would prolong their journey yet would it make it more safe.

The lieutenant had heard and read more of Indian manners than he had actually learnt by experience; but for all this he was well up in Indian tactics, in fact his assiduity and cunning would have put many an old trapper to the blush.

It was on a green sloping bank, near to a spring that bubbled from a rock, that he first allowed his fair companions to rest, and then when they had sufficiently refreshed themselves he again urged them on their journey.

Harry Vere knew full well that he had lost his way, but he kept it a secret from the girls, as he did not wish to alarm them unnecessarily.

When daylight dawned they had placed some miles between them and the Indian encampment, but for all this they were not yet safe, and Harry then began to wonder how it had fared with Bob, Jerry, and the marine.

The morning was simply one of splendour.

Birds of various hues were singing, and hopped from tree to tree, whilst myriads of insects filled the air with their busy humming.

It was not till after the first day that Harry found out the inconvenience of travelling, and that was when he had to supply food for the three of them.

The first day they lived as it were on their fears, but now their appetites began to be sharpened, and they felt that they could eat enormously.

Harry could have provided plenty of animal food, had he dared to fire his pistol or light a fire, but these two things were the very ones that he was compelled to abstain from, as it would have brought any enemy in the vicinity immediately into their presence.

True it might have brought his shipmates to them, but the chance was not worth the risk, and so they satisfied their cravings with fruit and lost not a moment in speeding on their journey.

All this time Harry had simply been guided by the sun, but on the third day found themselves on the banks of the river, which Harry had crossed on the log.

Harry did not, however, wish to cross that river again, as that way led to the fortress and the town, but he kept along its banks until he could find some sign by which he might shape his course to the hut.

It was not until then that Harry found out the truly awkwardness of his position.

His keen eye detected that his fair companions were breaking down under the fatigue and sinking for the want of proper nourishment, and though

they made no complaint he could see that they were footsore, and that their delicate frames could not stand much more of this rude mode of travelling.

Even tough and hardy as he was owing to a seaman's life he could not shake off a feeling of fatigue at times, and so this began to worry him, and his once lightsome spirit began to fail him.

But for all that Harry was not the one to "down topsails," at troubles in the distance; there was some true British pluck in him yet.

He was one of "England's hearts of oak" and he meant to prove himself as such.

"The back is made to the burden," he would mutter to himself, and then he would cheer up his companions with some simple anecdote, and so they would trudge along braving dangers and difficulties, the very recital of which at other times would have made them recoil and tremble.

"What would Jenny think if she saw us now?" he said, smiling, as he hoisted Minnie on to his shoulder, and waded through a stream up to his waist in water with her.

"Well, she would think we were the naughty children that stayed from school to go blackberrying in the woods," Minnie replied.

"Look at my tattered garments, why they are nothing but a bunch of ribbons.'

"And you, Florida," she added, turning to her fair companion, "are worse, if possible, than I."

As they were journeying on in this way, joking and laughing, a cracking of dry twigs and the rustling of bushes startled, and put a sudden stop to their merriment.

"Hold!" said Harry, drawing his sword. "Let me see what is that."

Harry placed himself in front of the two girls, and assuming an attitude of defence prepared to meet whatever was in store for them.

He had scarcely done so when, to the astonishment and horror of all, the foliage parted and a dozen Indians, armed with their war clubs and tomahawks, stepped into the path before them.

Harry was for the moment astounded.

A deathly pallor overspread his cheek.

But he quickly recovered himself, and, clutching his sword more firmly, he drew a pistol from beneath his jacket.

The Indians drew back at this.

They did not like the look of the little weapon, the terrible power of which the Spaniards had taught them in many a severe lesson.

"Fear not, stand fast," whispered Harry, encouragingly to his fair companions, as he backed himself against them, and forced them gently into a bush.

Harry could tell that they were trembling violently, and this gave him renewed pluck.

"Waugh!" granted a fierce Indian, a warrior who appeared to act as leader of the dusky gang, "Where is the pale face conducting the prairie flowers?"

Harry saw by the bullying tone of the Indian, which he had doubtless acquired through the brutal treatment and oppression of the Spaniards, that he must be firm with him, and, well knowing that no persuasion or gentle treatment of any kind would preserve his scalp whole, then replied:—

"To their homes with the pale faced braves. Where else does the warrior think?"

"Waugh, let the pale face stand aside, Oolozu, the Death's Head chief, has chosen them for his daughters.'

Harry cocked his pistol with his thumb, and, scorning the figurative language of the true Indian tribes, made answer—

"Let the chief hide his ugly head, and you, you copper skinned snake, clear my path, or by the father of the great waters I'll swamp you."

The Indian uttered a fierce growl very much resembling a bear, and motioned his followers to keep close to him.

Harry quickly divined his object, and was determined to strike the first blow.

"God strengthen my arm," he muttered fervently, in which short prayer he was joined by his fair companions.

"Ugh!" grunted the Indian again. "The spirit of the great waters is angry with the pale face for the lie he has uttered, and Ouluzu sends his warriors and braves to follow him with the war hatchet. Let the pale flowers come forth; Lanarka will shed the blood of the pale face and take his scalp."

"Waugh! I defy you," thundered Harry Vere. "Do you take the pale face for a child? Let the white brave pass, and you and your dusky swabs, sheer off."

Lanarka, not knowing the full import of the words, but judging that they conveyed an insult, knitted his dark brow in anger.

His eyes dilated wildly and gave forth a dusky glow, and the bands of his muscles swelled up as he clutched the heavy tomahawk.

Harry saw he was about to attack him, and he was prepared.

He saw the dark lips curl in scornful hate and the wavering glance that boded treachery.

And then, when the Indian thought his foe was off his guard, he hurled a treacherous blow at Vere, who instantly fired his pistol and shot the Indian dead.

The bullet enter Lanarka's left breast, passed out obliquely near the spine, and lodged in the jaw of one of the Indians behind him.

The wounded Indian gave a howl of pain and, staggering forward, fell across Lanarka's body; his tomahawk, still clasped in his hand, descending with full force on the toes of one of his companions, severing the five members from the foot.

This decisive action cowed the rest of the Indians, and for a time they stood paralysed.

Harry in the meantime put his sword between his teeth, reloaded the emptied barrel, and stood ready for the next one to step forward.

He anticipated a general rush, and it required all his energy to steady his nerve.

It was all in his favour that Minnie and Florida were not of the ordinary squeamish disposition. Their courage had been tried, and their vicissitudes had to some extent prepared them for such scenes.

Harry Vere, even while loading his pistol, had scarcely dared to take his eyes off his enemies for one moment. He knew their subtle nature, and that they would not hesitate to use any treacherous means to compass his death.

Independent of the one killed and two wounded, there were still nine Indians left, and it rather puzzled him to get rid of all them.

Three or four in the background had clustered together, and were holding a whispered consultation.

Presently two of them slipped away, and were lost sight of in the bushes.

Harry became uneasy at this.

The dusky crew had commenced their tactics, and now was his time to circumvent them.

Passing his dirk to Minnie, he gave her a meaning look, which she seemed perfectly to understand.

Then he addressed himself to his foes:—

"Braves of Oeluzu," he said, "the spirit of the great waters is angry; let the pale faces depart in peace, or prepare yourselves for the happy hunting grounds."

"Waugh!" growled the Indian, whose toes were cut off. "Waugh! The pale face is a liar; Lanarka only sleeps. Lenona will hold the pale face brave a prisoner till Lanarka wakes."

"You red-skinned Indians," Harry replied, boiling with impatience, "stand aside, or I will cut you down."

At that moment the girls gave a slight scream, and Harry half turned his head.

He saw the bare arm of a savage through the bush behind the girls.

Minnie's dirk flashed for a second, and then there was a sharp cry. She had buried the blade in that naked arm.

Then there was another cry, fainter than any that had been uttered yet, and the bushes became suddenly agitated.

Some one was chopping away at them with all his fury.

This was the other Indian that had slunk away, and Harry, seeing that he was also attacked in the rear, fired at random through the thick of the bush.

A hideous howl proclaimed the effect of his aim.

This stirred the others into action.

They could have hurled their tomahawks at Harry Vere, and have thus maimed him, but the proximity of the females prevented them, and so they determined to attack him in a body.

Harry had his other pistol ready for them.

Lenona advanced waving his hatchet, and uttering fierce vows of vengeance, but at that moment three shots were simultaneously fired, and three of the Indians rolled over.

Then came a shout.

The bushes were violently agitated, and the dry branches crackled as though some one was breaking a way through.

"Hallo! just in time," shouted a well-known voice. "Come on, Jerry. Hurrah! here's fun for us now."

The buccaneers came upon the scene with a dash, flourishing their cutlasses and waving their pistols, much to the astonishment and chagrin of the dusky myrmidons.

Harry Vere hailed their presence with a shout of joy.

"One a piece, lads. Hurrah! select your men! Down with the red devil's! Give it to them hot!"

Harry set the example.

With one bound, he sprang over the dead body of Lanarka, and hurled a deadly blow at Lenona.

That gentleman, taken suddenly aback, had scarcely time to defend himself, for Harry followed up the attack with more than ordinary vigour.

"Give in, you caitiffs!" Harry shouted. "I want not to take your lives. I have shed enough blood already. Yield, I say, or, by the spirit of the white man, we will slay you!"

The buccaneers each held a loaded pistol in their hand, and they could have settled accounts at once, but they were chary with their powder, for they knew not what enemies they might yet have to contend with.

The Indians were big, powerful fellows, and their clothing, simply a girdle of feathers, allowed the free use of their brawny limbs.

But the gallant "Will-o'-the-Wisps" were too much for them.

Their sharp eyes and rapid movements kept the Indians dancing round.

Micky had the smallest Indian of the lot, but he was a crafty devil.

He kept Micky hard at work until the sweat oozed from him; and, in spite of Harry's mandate to save the powder, the marine felt greatly inclined to use his pistol.

There was quite a little war now waging in the dell.

Sparks were flying in all directions, and the birds on the trees immediately took wing, as the clash of steel broke the stillness of the air.

At length Lenona slipped and fell, and Harry stepped on his throat; then, stooping, snatched the tomahawk from his hand, and with it smashed in the Indian's skull.

Harry stepped aside from the spluttering of blood and brains, when he heard a deep groan.

He turned sharply, and beheld Minnie with her dirk buried in the back, just between the shoulders, of the Indian who had lost his toes.

While Harry was engaged, he had crept from his hiding-place, and, stealing behind the lieutenant, would have settled him, had not Minnie given him his *coup de grace*.

"Well done, Minnie!" said Harry Vere, smiling his thanks. "We shall make a veteran of you before this work is done. Keep your eye on the bush yonder. Our work is not finished yet."

Minnie withdrew the reeking blade with a shudder.

She almost recoiled at the deed she had done.

"I was forced to it," she murmured to herself. "God forgive me; it is the first time I took a human life."

Harry by this time had left her side and joined the fray.

The three remaining Indians were fighting desperately with the buccaneers.

The fate of their companions fired them so with madness that they fought more like demons.

Bob and Jerry were sorely put to it.

Jerry's sword had snapped off half way, and he was only fighting with the stump.

Harry went to his assistance at once.

With one well-directed blow Harry nearly severed the Indian's right arm, and the tomahawk dropped from the disabled member as the Indian gave a fiendish yell.

Micky and Bob were still hard at work.

Micky had torn the kerchief from his neck and was using his cutlass as a two-handed sword, while the Indian he was opposed to was using his tomahawk as a club.

Bob Hawker had an awful tough customer to handle.

His dusky foe was evidently a warrior of some standing, for his cheeks and the upper part of his body were almost covered with scars.

The Indian was fighting like one mad.

Yells, execrations, and fearful oaths he uttered at every stroke he gave, and his trenchant weapon cut into Bob's cutlass until the blade was like a saw.

Bob had managed to slip off his jacket and roll his shirtsleeves up to the shoulder, and yet he could not settle his man.

Both himself and the Indian were bleeding from several wounds.

But one or both would soon have to give in.

They were both winded, and the exertion was beginning to tell on them.

"Leave him alone, Harry; don't touch him," Bob gasped. "I shall scuttle him presently."

The Indian half turned to see whom he addressed when Bob was just lunging out, and that movement cost him his life.

The buccaneer was thrusting heavily home at that moment.

He felt the guard yield as the Indian partly turned, and Bob, stumbling as it were forward, buried his cutlass to the hilt in the savage's chest.

Micky at that moment settled his man also.

By some lucky chance as he swung his sword round he whirled the tomahawk from the Indian's grasp, and recovering himself quick, the marine thrust his blade through the neck of his bitter foe.

This was done so quick that Micky could scarcely believe it, but he drew the ensanguined blade from the throat of the dying savage, and wiped it on the grass.

"Thus endeth the fray," he said to Bob, who was ruefully eying the deep notches in his cutlass;

"I'm glad it's over. I don't want any more fighting for some time."

"The more the merrier," replied Bob, drily; "it keeps one's hand in. It was a tough job, but it's over now."

He had scarcely spoken when a tomahawk whizzed past them, and buried itself in the earth two yards away.

"Hullo! more yet," exclaimed Jerry.

"Yes; there he is," cried Harry, whose attention was drawn by the sound.

He pointed with his finger, and they all looked in the direction indicated.

Leaning against a tree, faint and weak from the loss of blood that was streaming from the muscles of his arm, stood an Indian, the pallor of death on his face, and a gleam of deadly hatred in his partly glazed eye.

This was the Indian Minnie had stabbed at in the bush.

She had severed the muscles of his arm with the dirk, but in the very moment of death, as it were, the feeling of revenge was so strong upon him that he mustered all the power he was master of, and hurled the deadly weapon with full force.

Then he sank against the tree overpowered, and finally sank exhausted to the earth.

This ended the sanguinary fray, and twelve lifeless objects lay around on the blood-soaked grass.

When the sounds of strife ceased, both Minnie and Florida fainted.

Harry caught Minnie as she was about to fall, and Bob lent his assistance to Florida.

Bob knew about as much of this sort of work as he did of handling a new-born babe.

"Hi, Jerry, come here, you hedgehog! Give us some water, quick!"

"Hedgehog, eh!" groaned Jerry; "well, I ain't a baboon. Why, shiver me, if you don't handle the lady as gently as a monkey would a cocoa-nut."

"I'll handle you like a marlinspike!" cried Bob, "if you're not handy. Don't you see the lady's going off to glory?"

"She looks more as if she was becalmed," said Jerry; "loosen her throat gear a bit; as my Poll says, she's bowsed up a little too tant."

"Now then, steady, don't waste the precious stuff, and clap a stopper on your jaw. There now, you son of a shrimp catcher, do you see how you're spilling it?"

"Not me, Bob, it's my hand's nervous a bit. Would the lady like a drop of rum?"

"Would you?"

"I wouldn't mind; here comes Micky."

"Hallo! in a faint," said the marine, walking up.

"Yes, you walking sentry-box. Can you fetch her out of it?"

"I might by kissing her," replied Micky, rapturously eying the girl's fair features. "Lor, she's a plump'un, Jerry, aint she?"

"I don't know," said Jerry. "I'm no advocate for what you call the opposite sex. I like a good man, and a toothful of jolly good rum; bust the women, hang me if I ever did like 'em."

"How's that?"

"I don't know. I suppose it's my nature."

"And werry unnatural, too, Jerry. Why, I admires 'em."

"You'd better tell the lady so, and then she'll come too, perhaps."

"If I thought she would, I'd tell her heaps of things."

"I daresay you would, you're a lady-killer, maybe?"

"No, I loves 'em too much. What colour's her eyes—have you seen 'em, Bob?"

"No more than you see of 'em now. They're booiful though, I've no doubt."

"Cuddiebyfied," broke in Jerry.

Bob gave him a dig in the ribs that doubled him up for the space of five seconds.

"Go steady, Hauler," Jerry cried, as soon as he could get breath. "Silence! she's coming round now."

"Good luck!" cried Meeky, rubbing his hands in glee.

"Now you'll see her eyes," said Jerry, mischievously.

"Codfishy, I'll wager," he added.

Bob gave him a look that made Jerry sheer off a yard or so.

Florida started when she opened her eyes and found herself in the arms of the rough sailor.

She uttered a faint cry, and then swooned again.

It was no wonder, for Bob certainly did look like some wild man; his beard and whiskers almost hid his face and eyes; they had not been shaved or trimmed for nearly a month.

"Oh, you image! your beauty's gone and killed the lady," said Jerry, grinning. "You shall go to the Emperor of Turkey to see after his wives."

Bob caught up the first thing to hand, and flung it at Jerry's head.

It missed.

Jerry chuckled.

It chanced to be a small leathern flask that held the rum.

Jerry caught it up, and went through two or three steps of a hornpipe.

"Jolly, by Jove!" he exclaimed.

Bob looked at him in utter dismay.

He looked all about for a place where he could rest his charge, but he could see none.

"Come here, you glutton; bring that back," he bellowed.

"Fetch it."

Bob could not.

"Bring it here."

"I can't, I'm busy."

"Bring it here, I say."

Bob raised his voice pretty high this time.

"I can't; it's too heavy."

"Can't you try, Jerry?"

"I am trying, Bob."

Bob was beginning to lose his temper.

Jerry, by this time, had had sundry good sips.

"Try a little harder, Jerry," said Bob coaxingly.

"I'm trying my hardest, Bob 'pon my soul."

"Come here, then; confound you!"

"What, for you to punch me, eh?"

"No, on my word."

"You mean in my ribs."

"I'd bast you," muttered Bob to himself, "if I had hold of you."

Then he called out in the same persuasive tone:—

"Jerry, old fellow."

"Yes, Bob, my hearty."

"Just look here."

"What's to be seen?"

"Come and look."

"All right."

"Come along."

"Don't hurry a fellow."

"What are you doing?"

"I'm—I'm do-doing nothing."

Jerry had slunk behind a huge cactus, and was mugging himself with the rum.

Bob knew this, to his sorrow.

Jerry, however, had not stolen the rum; Bob had thrown it at him.

"The spiteful brute," Jerry muttered; "he might have split my head, and cracked the bottle."

"O-o-o-oh!"

Jerry could hardly give vent to this exclamation.

He felt as though an enormous crab had caught him by the nape of the neck.

"I'll O you, and R you, too," exclaimed a gruff voice.

"Is that you, Bob, old chum?"

"Not so much of your old chum; I'm Hauler."

"Well Bob, old pal."

"None of your old pals. Where's the bottle."

"Here, chum."

Bob clutched it.

He shook it.

Then he turned it upside down.

"Why, it's empty!"

"Is it, Bob?"

"In course it is."

"Just as you threw it, then!"

"What do you mean?"

"Just as you flung it away."

"Flung it away!"

"Yes, just as you emptied it you flung it away!"

Bob just then began to see the drift of Jerry.

"I suppose it was empty, then?" he drawled.

"No doubt about it, but then you should mind where you throw things when you've done with them, you know!"

"Did it hit any one, then?" queried Bob.

"No; but it might, you know, and it might 'a killed somebody; I believe you've cracked it."

Jerry could not turn his head to look at Bob; that worthy held him by the nape of the neck with a grip of iron.

He could tell that Bob was pretty well nettled, though, and the convulsive grip of his fingers told Jerry when a shot hit him home.

Jerry had the laugh all on his side this time; but he was afraid to indulge in it in his present awkward position.

Bob saw at once how he had sold himself.

He could have turned round and punched his own head for his foolishness.

He had guarded that drop of rum very carefully.

It was all they had.

He had kept it to serve a nip round when it was cold at night.

There was more than a quart.

It was all gone now, though.

There was no way of replenishing it either.

This was worse than all.

"Jerry," at length he said, "you're a rogue."

"And you're a wagabond for saying it," retorted Jerry.

"You're worse—you're a thief."

"And you're a fibber."

"Didn't you steal the rum?"

"What?"

"Didn't you steal the rum? Now, confess."

"I won't criminate myself for no one. I picked up the empty bottle, that was all."

"And it was empty, you say?"

"Why, you know it was, Bob."

Bob was getting awfully wild.

"You fibber," he bawled out, "you emptied it."

"Well, say I did, just to please you. You know I can't abear rum."

This was the last straw on the camel's back.

Bob gave Jerry such a hoist behind with his knees that it sent him flying.

He leapt quite a couple of yards.

"Oo!" was all he could utter as he went flying.

Bob had a touch of what is termed the needle.

"You shark-jawed, hungry-bellied swab!" he vociferated, "I'd like to eat you raw. I'd——"

"Like to have the rum over again, wouldn't you?"

"I'd like to knock it out of you, you grampus!"

Jerry laughed, and looked round for a clear place

to run, just as the voice of Harry was heard calling them.

Bob was vexed enough already; but he almost boiled within himself when he saw Micky with his arm round Florida's waist, seated on a mound, chatting.

"Another demon. Well, I be danged, they have it all their own way, and Bob's left in the cold."

Thus he vented his good-humoured spleen as he walked up to Vere and Minnie.

Jerry took up the empty flask, and followed him at a distance.

"There's a toothful left in it yet," he muttered, as he shook it near his ear.

Then he slunk behind a bush, and let the last drop gurgle down his throat.

CHAPTER CCXXVI.

GONSALVO VISITS THE PIRATES' CAVE.—THE DIS-
COVERY OF IRON ARM.—CAPTAIN TOM HAS A
STRANGE ADVENTURE.

WHILST Captain Tom Drake and his handful of buccaneers were fighting the chevaliers and silencing a gun on a fort that had newly opened fire, Gonsalvo, as we before observed, slipped away in the confusion, leaving his followers to fight the battle by themselves.

Taking to his heels, he ran, with all the speed his heavy accoutrements would allow him, in the direction of the town, which was in a hollow adjoining the eminence on which the fortress was built.

Suddenly he paused, as though a thought had crossed him.

Then he looked back to see whether he was followed.

Being satisfied with his scrutiny, he wiped the perspiration from his brow with the back of his hand, and then walked off sharply, in the direction of the cliffs.

"Where is the Death Pirate now?" he muttered, striking the hilt of his sword in passion. "Can he have deserted me in this, my hour of danger?"

"No," he added, after a painful pause. "He cannot know of this. He does not dream even that my fortress is being pillaged, and my men mown down by that infidel of a boy buccaneer."

"Infidel! Aye, he is an infidel, he scorned even the prayers of the priest. He looked upon death as though he had faced it a hundred times before. Then his escape from the scaffold was a miracle; and lastly this attack. Bah, I will not stand it."

He folded his arms and faced towards the forts, from the embrasures of which a shot or two was at intervals sluggishly fired.

"Ah, we are almost beaten! I will seek Lodac, and hear from him the news."

He stamped his foot on the hard earth, then, casting a wistful glance to seaward, he gave a deep sigh and moved away.

The sounds of strife had now in some measure abated. His friends, he supposed, if beaten had retired before the foe, and sought safety either by clambering up to the most inaccessible points of the rocks, or in the numerous sea-caves along the beach.

Gonsalvo did not return by the same route that he came, but proceeded in an opposite direction till he reached a wide gap or ravine on the inland side of the cliff

Without a moment's hesitation, he crept over the verge of the abyss, and at the imminent risk of breaking his neck, commenced climbing down, until he got his foot upon a narrow ledge or parapet midway between the summit of the cliff and the brawling stream that rushed over its rocky channel at the base of the precipice.

His position at this moment was perilous in the extreme,—on either hand the frowning rock, above the dark blue sky, below impenetrable darkness and the sullen plash of the current.

Step by step Gonsalvo moved along the narrow verge until he reached an aperture in the rocks, scarcely large enough to admit the passage of his body; into this hole he thrust his head and shoulders.

Wriggling like a serpent, he entered a dark, low, and narrow vaulted passage that seemed to go down, with a steep and rugged incline into the very bowels of the earth.

Searching in a cranny he found a torch and lit it.

Disturbed by his intrusion, a whole colony of bats flew out from the crannies in the rocks, and, uttering shrill squeaks of alarm, blundered out on their leathern wings and wheeled off into the open air.

Gonsalvo soon lost his clutch upon the torch, which was struck from his hand by one of these imp-like hybrids, and at once extinguished, so he was forced to grope his way as well as he could in the darkness.

This he did with much trouble and some danger, scratching and bruising himself by contact with the razor like angles of the rock. At length he found himself standing up to his knees in the water of a subterranean pool.

Gonsalvo rested for awhile, supporting his half-exhausted frame by leaning heavily against the rocky walls.

Looking before him, he descried a pale glimmer of light.

It was hard to tell the extent of this cavernous passage, but two hundred or two hundred and fifty feet was not far from the truth.

The floor was quite level, being covered with fine sand mingled with pebbles and shallow ponds.

After going a certain way, the cave became tortuous, the light vanished, and Gonsalvo missed his torch.

At length he reached the end of the passage, to find himself in a vault about a hundred feet in height, and of a conical shape.

On one side of it was a small opening similar to that by which he had entered, and through it there struck in a stream of ruddy light

Clambering through this aperture, Gonsalvo, after proceeding a little way, came to a high yawning opening, through which he passed, and entered a large cavern.

Here the scene was changed, as if by the power of enchantment, for, instead of the dark and lonely labyrinths he had been threading, behold a spacious chamber, brightly illumined by torches, stuck in sconces around the walls, and crowded by a throng of men, women, and children, who greeted his sudden and unlooked-for entrance with shouts and screams of consternation.

A score of muskets were levelled at him, while the women and their little ones fled before him, or huddled together like a flock of frightened sheep.

Then came a shout.

"It is Gonsalvo!"

The band then gathered eagerly around him, and questioned him as to the way by which he had reached them, and whether it would not be possible for them to escape by that way.

"You are safer where you are," returned Gonsalvo. "The entrance by which I reached this cave was as dark and difficult as the entrance to the unknown regions.

"I never tried it but once before, and after that attempt should have been content to leave it to the foxes and the bats, had I not been compelled once more to traverse it. It may afford an outlet for

ALMOST SUFFOCATED, HE REACHED THE HATCHWAY.

some of the strongest and boldest of men, but impracticable for the women and children."

At this there was a general murmur of discontent.

"Thank heaven," he said, cheerfully, and glancing his black eyes round, "that so many of you are for the present safe; and it will take some considable time before the buccaneers can reach you here."

The women, who were the wives and mistresses of the Death Pirate and his desperate crew, crowded round him in fear.

"Is there any danger, think you?" asked one of the women, "who seemed to take the lead.

"For the present no, but where is Ludoc. Has he not returned?'

" He has not, unless he is in the outer cavern," replied the woman.

"Let him be sought for, then. Where are the men at such a time?"

"In the outer cave; they heard the firing at the fortress, and sent us here."

"It is well, but they should have come to my assistance."

"Ah! who is this?"

At that moment the tramp of feet sounded on the rude steps at the other end of the cave, and a figure clad in the dress of an eastern fisherman staggered into the cave.

"Ludoc, by the saints and wounded!" exclaimed the governor. "How comes this—speak."

The man reeled and, placing his hand to his brow, fell on a wooden bench.

Two of the women rushed to his assistance immediately.

"Where are you hurt?" they exclaimed in terror.

Then the wounded man unclosed his lips, and gasped:

"Rum—rum! I am parching! I am dying."

Gonsalvo rushed forward.

There was blood running down the man's sleeve.

Gonsalvo seized a long Spanish knife and ripped off his jacket and shirt, so as to expose his shoulder.

There was a ghastly wound, and blood was trickling from it freely.

"The rum," cried Gonsalvo. "Here, quick, bathe the wound, some of you; he must not die, his message is important to us all."

The governor seized the keg, and without any ceremony he took a hatchet and dashed in the head, and filled a huge goblet with the liquor.

Taking a deep draught himself, he then handed the rest to the wounded man, who drained the goblet to the dregs.

This revived Ludoc for a moment, but did not satisfy him, for he gasped for more.

He was supplied, and in a few minutes more his wound was dressed.

It was simply a flesh wound, not near so bad as they had anticipated, but the man seemed to be suffering much pain.

"Well, Ludoc, what news bring you?" inquired Gonsalvo eagerly.

"None," was the reply.

"None; have you been to the island?"

"Aye, I have not long left there."

"And the Death Pirate?"

"He has not been seen."

"And no other vessel, not even the——"

"None; an English man-of-war, though, has been seen somewhere on the coast."

' English—curse the English, they are our bane.'

"They are in search of some vessel; several wrecks are reported on the coast," said Ludoc.

"Confound it, this is how we lose our spoil. Did you pass the fortress on your way hither?"

"I did—worse luck—and that is how I got this ugly scratch. There was a party of devils swarming up the ladders, and one fellow fired a pistol at me and nearly brought me down. I had to run for it, but luckily I escaped."

"It was fortunate, but you bear no good news. Ah, here comes Sancho."

A huge black descended the steps and strode into the cavern.

On seeing Gonsalvo he doffed his broad-brimmed sombero, and made a polite bow.

The governor eyed him as though he would read his thoughts.

"You are from the town," Gonsalvo suggested.

"I left there an hour since; all is confusion, the fishermen have hauled up their boats, and every house is barricaded, they fear the English will come down upon them."

"The cowards," hissed Gonsalvo.

"Not quite so, they expect the spitfire English will be down upon them. It is rumoured that the fortress has given in, and Captain Tom Drake, the daring boy buccaneer, is in the fortress searching for his——"

"Say no more, Sancho Captain Tom Drake, a mere boy, do you think he has beaten us? I wish the Death Pirate were here, he would soon settle this bit of a squall.'

"But there are two ships in the bay."

"Two toys; a dozen of his crew would wipe out the lot, but we must hold out till one of our ships return. We must not give in without a struggle."

He paused a moment, and stood in deep thought. Then suddenly he burst out,

"Let all the men be gathered, they shall go with me to the fortress; these English must be driven aboard their ships, or cut down, else we all will perish, and the treasures we have amassed will be taken away.

"The treasure is well guarded, and scouts are placed about the rocks, the beacon I have also prepared for lighting."

"That may bring us aid, but not till night. I must have some men to man the guns. They must be sharp fellows, too. Do you mind me, Sancho? We have no child's play before us now."

"You shall have good men, and true, cap'ain. I know the men I shall choose; these are the mutineers of the Spanish galleon, they are well up in war."

"Better than my soldiery; they are an idle set. They have had no fighting so long that they know not a cannon from a matchlock."

"Where shall I lead them?"

"To the fortress at once."

"Farewell, then I will do your bidding; fifty good strong men shall be at your service in less than one hour."

"I must have a hundred more than that. I shall need them."

"It shall be so. I will away at once."

"Stay, have we no galleons in the port fit for service?"

"I will see."

"Quick, then, away. I place implicit faith in you. Ludoc, are you better?"

"Yes, but I'm confoundedly stiff."

"You can see to the women being armed; there are plenty of muskets, cutlasses, and pistols. They must fight, Ludoc, and so must every man of us."

"We will," cried the women in a voice, and they hugged their little ones passionately to their breasts and kissed them.

While Gonsalvo was speaking and attending further arrangements in the cave, another man sprang down the steps and leapt into their midst.

He gave a start on seeing Gonsalvo.

The governor eyed him fiercely.

His hair was dishevelled, his face flushed, and the perspiration fairly oozed from him.

Gonsalvo desired an explanation of this strange conduct

"Another vessel has arrived in the bay," he gasped, scarcely able to draw his breath.

"Friendly?"

"The reverse; they are preparing to land."

"Is it another buccaneer cruiser, then?" queried the governor, turning ashy pale.

"Dutch Paul," answered the man.

Gonsalvo started.

"By all the fiends, then, we are lost!"

The women gave a shriek and clustered together.

"Fools!" thundered Gonsalvo, darting an angry flush from his dark eyes. "Would you bring the very vultures down upon us? Idiots, you know not what you do."

The women grew silent, and drew the young ones closer to them.

For a few moments their grief overpowered them, and then they became calm and silent.

Ludoc had moved from the couch, and presently appeared with a pile of arms, which he threw down in the centre of the cavern.

"Zingara," he said, addressing the olive-complexioned woman who had taken the lead in speaking. "Serve out the weapons. You must defend your offspring."

One would scarcely have thought to find so much affection in that rude assembly.

There were many handsome women and young girls amongst them, but now, as they drew the terrified children into their midst, and seized upon the heavy matchlocks and pistols, they each looked as fierce as a tigress.

Gonsalvo smiled.

It was a cruel bitter smile though.

He was thinking if he had an army of such women, nerved by the same incentive, what execution he could do to the invaders.

Gonsalvo thoroughly hated the English and everything pertaining to them.

Indeed, he had cause for it.

Their pirate vessels, from a large fleet, had been reduced to a small squadron by the English cruisers.

But this visitation of Tom Drake's was the worst blow of all.

They had never found anyone bold enough to attack their strongholds, nor to dispute their rights on shore, except the Indians, and they gave them some trouble at times

"Pedro," said Gonsalvo, turning to the last comer, "how learnt you this?"

"With my own eyes I saw the ship sail in, toss up her sails, drop her anchor, and hoist out the boats. Dutch Paul's flag was flying at the main."

"You knew it, then?"

"In a moment. Many a brush I have had with his crew. This mark," showing his cheek, "was done by one of his sea devils."

"Then you should know it," remarked the governor, grimly.

"I shall never forget it," hissed the pirate, clenching his teeth. "I have lived since only to avenge it, and now that time is come."

"And while you were on the look-out did you see any of our fleet?"

"Nine; but I heard some of our friends were about the coast; the masked chief was cruising off here yesterday."

"The Death Pirate?"

"Yes; he was chasing a vessel."

"Then I must away; the beacon must be lit. We must use every energy in this struggle, and depend only on our own resources till aid arrives."

"But the fortress is carried, I am told!"

"Who told you? What idiot spread this wildfire in our midst?"

"A soldier, one of your men-at-arms; he is now in the town bearing the news like a fireship in a fleet."

"Or a fiery brand in the jungle? Away, Pedro; collect all the men you can, and set the guns of the masked battery in a position for use."

Pedro snatched up a cutlass, and, having thrust two huge pistols in his belt and a few cartridge in the bosom of his shirt, left the cavern as speedily as he had entered it.

"A brave fellow," muttered Gonsalvo, as he followed the pirate with his fierce eyes. "If I had had a hundred such as he at the first onset, I should not be as I am now."

"Zingara," he added aloud, turning to the group of fierce women, "do your best in my absence. I may return ere long."

So saying, he turned away, and disappeared as mysteriously as he came.

*   *   *   *   *

In the meantime Tom Drake and his party were prisoners in the fortress, and, owing to the darkness of the passages, they found no way of extricating themselves.

Captain Tom held a consultation with Hugh Baldrick, and, after racking and puzzling their brains, a decision was reached at last.

It was this—there were several passages leading from the half-circular chamber, and Tom took upon himself to explore them until he could find one with an outlet.

He ordered every middy to take off his shirt and tear it into long, narrow slips, and by twisting and knotting these together he made a long string, which he coiled in his hand, and gave to Hugh Baldrick.

Then he whispered a few words to the gentleman smuggler and, taking one end of the string, disappeared in one of the dark labyrinths, Hugh Baldrick allowing the string to slip gently through his hand.

Tom Drake, fearless of danger, but still using caution, made his way to the end of the passage, when he found his road barred by a door, and in searching for some spring or fastening he discovered a light through a small hole.

This was enough.

There was a road to liberty.

He immediately made a signal for Hugh to join him.

"What have you found?" asked the smuggler.

Tom directed his eye to the hole in the door.

"Right you are, Tom. This barrier must give way."

That was the proper and best mode of expressing it.

They both used their combined efforts, and after a stout resistance the door yielded, and they found themselves in the chapel.

Candles were burning on the altar, and this was the light they saw.

Captain Tom and Hugh Baldrick gave a chuckle.

"We are in now," said the smuggler; "let us make the best use of our time."

Tom stepped up to the altar and took one of the lighted candles, and gave another to his companion; a third he blew out and thrust in his breast, and the fourth he left burning to keep the devil away.

"Bravo!" said Hugh Baldrick, "you are a capital economist."

"Always be provident with the works of Providence," said Tom, drily. "Now for an exploration."

There were two doors leading to the chapel besides the one they had entered by, and one of these they found gave way with an easy pressure.

Tom signalled to the mids.

"Find a way out of this place, lads. Try that

door, but tread everywhere as though a chasm yawned beneath your feet."

The middies needed no warning

They approached the door carefully, but they gave it such a one, two, three with their broad backs that it flew open, tearing away some portion of the decayed woodwork.

One of the middies snatched the remaining candle from the altar to show them a light and they found they had entered a narrow passage wide enough only for one abreast, and the walls on each side they found were studded with little doors.

A middy opened one of the doors and discovered a small cell in which a bald-headed monk was kneeling down before a crucifix counting his beads.

The middy closed the door gently again, and shuddered; they were the cells of the monks, and the buccaneers did not want to disturb them in their devotions.

Had it been a different place the mids would have been ripe for any mischief.

The door Tom had opened led to a dark groined passage.

This was most likely the way to liberty.

They would try it.

There was a flight of stone steps, too, in one corner of the chapel. Tom thought he would examine that first. Candle in hand he ascended them, and reached nearly to the top when his head struck the stone ceiling.

"A trap by Jove!" he muttered, and then he carefully examined the stonework.

This bore his thoughts for a moment miles away, and reminded him of the little chapel over the cliff.

'Strange coincidence," he thought and he searched about the stonework for a secret spring.

He discovered it at last, and, with only a gentle pressure, he found that one end of the square stone began to rise.

He pressed it harder, and gradually, not with a jerk, the stone rose of itself on end, and Tom saw a square opening, through which he poked his head, and rose a step higher.

He took another step, and by the light of the candle, which he had stuck in a crevice of the stonework below him, he saw that he was entering a chamber.

All was silent, so he ascended, impelled by curiosity, as much as anything; for from the first he had no hope of finding any means of egress that way, but as he raised himself he was surprised to find himself in a small dungeon, and that a figure, monstrous in proportions, was seated on a stone, between himself and the grated window.

He was about to dive down below again, and close the trap—he was so startled—when a voice in English arrested him.

"Good God!—who's that?" exclaimed the weird looking figure.

"Do you wish to know?" asked Tom, plucking up courage

"I do, if you are mortal; speak again—answer me."

"I am alive, can't you see I am?"

"I can see something, but my eyes are weakened by this cursed glimmer."

'That's a voice I know somewhere," muttered Tom; "but it's deuced hollow."

There was a light rattle of a chain as the figure moved a little.

"Who are you? what are you? and how came you here?" queried Tom, in a breath: "answer me quickly, I have no time to waste."

"Good heaven! it must be! Are you not Tom Drake?"

"That's no answer to my question."

"It must be Captain Tom. Do you not know me—Iron Arm?"

Tom felt as though a shot had hit him.

Surely he could not be in his senses.

This was the last place he would have expected to find his gallant follower.

As soon as he could recover himself, he called to Hugh Baldrick.

The smuggler captain ascended and took with him the light, and they both entered the cell.

It was Iron Arm sure enough.

He was fearfully emaciated and hollow cheeked.

Both Tom and Hugh were shocked to see him in such a state; but while they were asking him questions they managed to relieve him of his irons.

Tom questioned the buccaneer, but he had a very short story to tell.

It was simply this:—

As he was cruising about in the Caribbean sea one evening, they sighted a sail, and clapped on canvas to give her chase, as it was supposed she was a pirate.

The chase sailed like a fury; in fact, Iron Arm had seen no vessel that could beat her, except the "Will-o'-the-Wisp."

Iron Arm used all his seamanship in trying to overhaul her, but it was useless; so, giving the helm into the hands of his first lieutenant, whom the day previously he had had cause to quarrel with, he went below to catch an hour's sleep.

What further transpired, or what happened during his sleep, he knew not.

His first awakening was in the cell where they found him.

"What?" cried his listeners in a breath.

'I awoke and found myself here."

"You must have slept," ejaculated Tom.

"I did. I suppose I was drugged."

'Quite likely, and by the lieutenant."

"No one else I should think, unless some one helped him."

"Do you suspect any one?"

"No."

"No other one on board you had words with?"

'Well, I corrected the cook, a black fellow, for poisoning a dog against my wish."

"And he made your coffee?"

"He did."

"Then he drugged you, perhaps intended to poison you, but didn't give you enough."

"That's quite likely. I never thought of that."

"You make a poor commander then, Iron Arm, you want your eye on every little incident; but come, let us move out of this," said Tom; "we have a heap of work before us."

There was a door in the cell studded with big nails and sheeted with iron, but it was bolted and barred on the outside in addition to being locked.

They tried to force it, but they could not.

Iron Arm was only a child to what he once was.

Tom had a drop of brandy in his pocket, which he had forgotten, and he gave it to him, and that revived him.

They all three then descended to the chapel, where the middies were anxiously awaiting them.

They had found a passage leading into a court-yard.

They left the chapel, all of them glad to breathe the fresh air again.

There was scarcely a sound stirring in that quarter, if there was any fighting going on it must be far away.

They all listened and strained their ears, and they fancied they could hear a faint sound of musketry.

Tom's men were under orders not to waste powder where steel would do equally as well.

It was growing dark.

Tom fancied he saw a light.

His followers missed him in a moment, and could

not tell which way he had gone, he darted off so suddenly.

He had turned an angle of the wall, and taken a dozen or more strides, when he found himself gazing at the very window and on the very spot where the guard arrested him.

He was staggered for the moment to find himself there.

It was the same room he was gazing up at; but it was only dimly lighted.

He fancied he could see shadows moving about.

There was a creeper growing up the wall, so he clutched this and climbed up to the window like a monkey and peered in.

There he saw a dozen females, all beautiful as houris. Some wringing their hands, others on their knees, as if in prayer.

There were a number of gallants too, in their court dresses, each one doing his best to console the weeping ladies.

Amongst the gallants, Tom recognised several of the courtiers who had rushed upon him, with the governor, from the sallyport.

Tom gazed wildly and vacantly about, in the hope of recognising a face amongst the ladies; he thought of seeing Minnie, but he was disappointed.

His heart sank like lead.

Where could she be?

Had his rashness in attacking the fortress caused her to be confined in some foul dungeon?

The thought seared his brain.

It drove him almost to madness.

Such a feeling came over him that he was almost filled with the fury of a demon.

Scarce knowing what he did, he dashed in the casement with his sword, and leapt into the room to the terror and confusion of the inmates.

The ladies shrieked, but Tom heeded them not, and the gallants swore as they recognised him, but he faced them like a fiend.

'Where is my Minnie? Dastards, answer me," he cried. "I will have the blood of every one of you, if you do not satisfy my question."

The chevaliers gazed on him in silent awe and dread.

His bronzed cheek was crimsoned, and the fire of a furnace seemed to blaze in his fierce dark eyes, which made the gallants recoil, though all of them drew their rapiers.

"Dogs—hounds!" he shouted till the walls of the lofty hall rang again; "why do you stare? why do you gaze? why do you not answer?"

And with this he sprang fiercely upon the one nearest him and seized him by the throat.

Then with a muttered curse, and a very demon in his look, he placed the cold keen point of his sword against the cringing Spaniard's throat, and pressed firmly but gently against the skin until it made the smallest incision possible in the flesh.

The Spaniard quivered for an instant with the sharp pain, then became immovable, not daring to move, afraid to cry out, and scarcely able to breathe.

It was a sight such as a sculptor would have envied.

To see that group chained to the spot and turned, as it were, all into statues of living marble.

Tom's cheeks were the only ones that bore any resemblance to flesh or life.

They were glowing with a heat like red-hot coals.

His brain was burning as though it had been seared, and as the warm blood coursed rapidly through his veins he felt his arm begin to tremble.

This caused the Spaniard he had seized to recoil and utter a cry of horror.

This also startled our hero, and caused his heart that for a time had ceased to beat, to resume its

functions again, and his parched tongue to separate from the roof of his mouth.

"Fiend," he hissed, rather than spoke, "where is my Minnie? Why do you torture me thus? Speak, accursed one, or I will slay you at my feet."

One or two of the others, aroused at this, were about to rush to their friend's assistance, but Tom awed them with a look, and kept each one in his place immovable.

There was a terrible moment of suspense.

A suspense truly awful so long as it lasted.

But one of the ladies, unable longer to bear the mental strain, sprang up from her kneeling posture, and, with a shriek that seemed almost to rend the roof, fell forward in a fit upon the floor.

Several of the boldest of the ladies flew to her assistance, and with eyes not tear-dimmed now, but dried gazed reproachfully at our hero, as though accusing him of being the author of the sufferings of their companions.

One of the ladies, a beautiful brunette, more courageous than the rest, even dared to address our hero.

'Senor," she said, curling scornfully her proud lip, "is this how you show your English breeding? Is this the act or conduct of a gentleman, to enter thus abruptly into the presence of ladies with a bared rapier, and to threaten to commit murder in their presence without the slightest provocation?"

Tom Drake was completely quelled.

He released his intended victim, and drew back completely abashed.

His sensitive pride was touched, the words of rebuke had entered his very soul, he knew that he was in fault, and he stood confessed.

Tom was passive now.

It was as though a storm in its height had ceased, and been succeeded by a calm.

Turning to the ladies, he took off his seal-skin cap for his own cocked hat he had lost in the fight, and then he spoke:—

'I crave your pardon, senoritas, a thousand pardons; if you wish me I acknowledge that my conduct was not correct; but when you learn the feelings that actuated me to this, and the cause that prompted me to commit so great a fault, I am sure you will forgive me. It is not in my nature to offend any of you, and Captain Tom Drake would scorn the act, the very thought that would pain the feelings and shock the delicacy of a lady if uttered in her presence."

Captain Tom here bowed respectfully, and the ladies, gazing from behind their fans at him, graciously curtseyed, and then he went on:—

"If you will accept this explanation, and graciously forgive me, I will never so offend again, and this I swear on the hilt of my sword, and will never break my promise."

This simple and unpretending speech did more for Tom than a thousand saintly prayers amongst the fair courtezans.

They thought him an angel, a paragon of virtue, the very model of beauty and purity.

They clustered round him, placed their soft arms round his neck, and kissed and hugged him so that he was put to the blush.

The chevaliers gazed at him in silent wonderment and horror.

They looked at each other, and twisted their moustachios until they were at their fiercest possible point.

They glared at him in envy, and felt they could have rushed upon him like so many hungry dogs, but the fear of humiliation kept them back, and they had to repress the fiery indignation of their Spanish blood, and chew the bitter cud that stuck in their throats like gall.

Tom comforted them with quiet, assuring smiles, which was ten times more galling than all.

They felt it in its full intensity.

They winced under it, they quailed, and at length, after making the most horrible grimaces imaginable, they fairly stamped upon the floor in passion.

Tom was in ecstacies.

He smiled the more, he bowed to the ladies and returned their kisses and caresses with that graceful ease which had always won him the affection of the fair sex.

The gentler sex were now growing jealous of each other, and Tom, seeing that matters were about to take another change, deemed it prudent to carry the farce no further.

"Now. ladies and gentlemen all," he said, as he gently withdrew himself from the last fair one's embrace, "I have one more favour to ask of you."

He bowed so gracefully to the chevaliers, and smiled so winningly on the ladies, that his prayer was already, in imagination, answered.

"You have a lady here, a captive," he went on, "Minnie by name, who was torn from her English home by the fiendish contrivance of the Death Pirate. Can you tell me, can you guide me to the place of her present captivity?"

"She's gone, escaped," said several in a breath.

"Gone!" echoed our hero.

"Yes, she was rescued from the tower by a sailor."

Tom clutched at the arras for support.

The news fairly astounded and overwhelmed him

The lovely brunette stepped forward and handed him a brimming glass of sparkling wine, and this revived him.

The boom of distant cannon and the sounds of fierce strife came sailing on the breeze at that moment, and aroused him to action; then, waving an adieu to the ladies and casting a glance at the chevaliers, which implied they might meet again, he sprang from the window into the court-yard, and disappeared in the gathering gloom.

CHAPTER CCXXVII.

CAPTAIN TOM ARRANGES HIS FORCES—A STRUGGLE FOR VICTORY — DEATH OF THE SPANISH GOVERNOR—AND DEFEAT OF THE PIRATE HORDE

WHEN Gonsalvo left the cavern of the pirates, he made his way, by paths only known to himself, to the head quarters of the town.

There he found many of the gossips and old veterans assembled, discussing the events of the day, and listening to the prophecies of an old crone, who had gained the reputation of a witch.

Some of her listeners were deeply impressed with her words.

"Avert the omen!" they murmured, "it is bad, indeed."

Gonsalvo, however, a thorough sceptic as he was a thorough rascal, laughed scornfully.

"Are you not, who should be men and soldiers, ashamed to be disheartened by such morbid nonsense?" he said. "We have but our own credulity to blame for what has happened, and I can but wonder that a shrewd man like yourself, Pedro, could have been so easily taken in. It is that traitor, the Englishman, who has betrayed us!"

"That is not my opinion," rejoined the other, a scarred and grisly veteran; "the Englishman plainly hates the buccaneers as much as we do, and Pedro, he is too good a judge of human character to be deceived."

The governor looked round upon the speaker and frowned; but the veteran's face was impassable, and, in truth, he did not look like a man that could be easily brow-beaten.

He had an exceeding ashy and olive complexion, his brow was wrinkled and furrowed, his hair and beard abundant though grisly grey; but undimmed by time, his eyes were large, brilliant and intensely black.

"If the Englishman be not a traitor, where is he now?" asked Gonsalvo.

"I will tell you," replied the old man with perfect composure; "I saw him fight his way out of the cave, using his thin and rapid blade, as fatal as it was wonderful,—the buccaneers gave way before them; their escape was miraculous; even so was Florida's!"

"Florida!" exclaimed Gonsalvo, with a violent start, "Is she not here?"

"No," replied the Spaniard; "she is with the English noble, for noble he is, I'll dare be sworn. It matters not; she is safest in his protection, for he bear a charmed life, and, like Achilles, appears to be invulnerable."

"It may be her life will be spared on account of her beauty," said Gonsalvo; "there seems to have been two parties of the buccaneers—one that invaded us by sea, and the other by land."

"It was so," returned the veteran; "the flotilla was commanded by the boy captain himself."

"Then if he captures Florida, he will have his revenge on us," returned Gonsalvo.

He spoke almost as if "the wish were father to the thought," for Florida had shown such a decided preference for his rival, that he felt so enraged against her, as to concern himself little for her fate.

"What course did the Englishman take; I mean our pretended friend, who dared, even before my courtiers, to insult me? If he has taken Florida, where has he gone?"

"To the hills, no doubt; but I saw a band of Indians about that time hovering around the walls."

"Then by this time they are either slain or captured," said Gonsalvo, maliciously. "Yet, where is the other girl, Minnie, that was rescued by the sailor?"

"Oh, my head is not a riddler of riddles. Hark, what is that firing of guns? and the sound comes this way."

"It does," cried Gonsalvo, turning sharply, and hurrying rapidly away.

Gonsalvo made his way through a ravine, at the head of which Pedro had marshalled about four hundred mercenaries of the most fierce and abominable type.

They were clad in all sorts of parti-coloured garb, a mixture of pirate, fisherman, and brigand, and their arms varied from the old arquebuss to the more modern musket. They all had swords of some kind, and a pair of pistols stuck in their belt or sash.

The governor, with drawn sword, selected the leaders, and, having divided the men into companies, gave them each their post.

He himself strode on to watch the tide of battle unencumbered.

It was near to a large cavern that Dutch Paul's men had landed, and there the fight was waging fast and fierce.

The buccaneers, though seemingly scattered, were falling more in order now that they were joined by Captain Tom.

One party was working round to the rear of the fortress, whilst the rest gradually pushed on to the town.

One of the buccaneers, on seeing Gonsalvo leading a party of Spanish cut-throats to shelter in the cave, fired a shot at him.

His escape was almost miraculous; the bullet whizzed close to his ear, and lodged in the vaulted roof of the cavern.

IN HIS FURY HE RAISED THE AXE TO STRIKE.

Gonsalvo instantly took his revenge by a furious lunge, which stretched the buccaneer at his feet.

The fighting now grew most desperate, for the Spaniards, though surprised, were by no means overpowered.

In this emergency Gonsalvo gave every proof of courage and sagacity, for though a great rascal he was a good soldier and a man of great determination and ability.

His first care was to secure the women and children who inhabited huts on the cliffs in a place of at least temporary safety. In order to do this he put himself at the head of a small party of picked men, and, surrounding the women, this devoted little band fought their way through the opposing horde till they reached the mouth of the cave, into which the women and children were hurried.

Now there was an old brass carronnade—the spoil from some Turkish vessel captured by the Death

Pirate—which had been mounted on a rock just above the entrance of this cave.

Gonsalvo instantly manned this gun, and opened fire upon the buccaneers, and for some considerable time kept them off, whilst under cover of this fire another party of pirates made frequent sallies from the cave, each time repulsing their foes with heavy loss.

Still the pirates were so vastly outnumbered that the result of the conflict was only a matter of time. Gonsalvo perceived this, and, though almost driven to despair, bethought him of a desperate scheme which, if successfully carried out, might preserve at least a remnant of the band until the Death Pirate should return to bring relief.

"Pedro," said the Governor, addressing that sturdy corsair, "do you and your men work the gun, while Sancho and the rest loosen those masses of rock and hurl them down upon the heads of these infidels. My desire is to block up the entrance to the cavern, in which we may stand siege until the chief's return."

"It is all very well to talk of working the gun," grumbled Pedro; "but the fact is, that I have but four more rounds of ammunition."

"It is to be regretted," said Gonsalvo. "But complaining will do no good. Reserve your fire till I give the signal. Tom Drake's lesson should teach us economy."

He then stalked away with perfect coolness, and called to Sancho and such of the men as he had picked out for the duty, to hurl down the pieces of rock into the narrow defile that led to the cavern mouth.

Baffled and infuriated by the desperate and unexpected resistance they encountered, the buccaneers charged again and again, to force an entrance into the cave, nearly paying the penalty of their rashness, and perishing in the attempt in falling crushed beneath the huge stones hurled down on their heads.

Louder and louder pealed the Spaniards' war-cry above the din of the battle, and fainter and fainter resounded the counter-cheers of the buccaneers, who, though ever fighting with the most dogged resolution, never began to lose heart.

Meanwhile Gonsalvo exerted himself with the utmost energy, regardless of bullets that whistled about him like a shower of hailstones.

He was here, there, and everywhere—commanding, cheering, or reproving, as the case demanded and exposing himself in the most reckless manner to the deadly firing of his antagonists.

"Come hither, Pedro," he said, beckoning one, who, with an iron crow-bar, was working to unloosen one of the masses of rock.

The smart half-naked fellow came to the side of the leader.

"I am here, Gonsalvo," he said. "What do you want with me?"

"Look up comrade," said the governor, laying his hand on the man's naked shoulder. "The face of this cliff is rugged and steep, and would try the muscles of the most experienced mountaineer at the best of times. Do you think you can scale the height?"

The man gave an upward glance.

"But under such a fire!" he remonstrated.

"I know it is a dangerous feat," said Gonsalvo; "but the more danger the more honour, you know. Will you do it?"

"I will try," said the pirate.

"'Tis bravely spoken; you are a noble fellow," said Gonsalvo.

"But when I reach the top, what am I to do?"

"First, cast your eyes to seaward and ascertain whether the 'Death Ship's' sails are heave in sight, —judging from the message brought me, the captain cannot be far off now."

"Good! And is that all?"

"No," returned Gonsalvo. "Whether or not you sight the vessel, at once fire the beacon as a signal for aid."

"It shall be done, or at least attempted," was the reply. "But should I fall forget not to tell Father Thomaso to pray for my soul."

"I will not fail to do so," said the Spanish Governor. "But take courage, man; as soon as you have started I will open fire upon Tom Drake, and before he has time to rally, you can place yourself out of range."

"I go," said Pedro.

"Take yonder torch with you," said Gonsalvo.

Pedro picked up a smouldering piece of resinous wood, and, glancing heedfully up the face of the cliff, commenced his hazardous ascent.

The cliff was terribly steep, and almost as smooth as an ordinary stone wall, but by sticking his dagger between cracks and crevices, the daring pirate contrived, though not without the greatest difficulty, to raise himself a few feet up the ascent.

Gonsalvo watched him in breathless anxiety as slowly and painfully he crept higher and higher, clinging for dear life to every little projection; the governor then turned to the men who were serving the gun.—"Now, comrades," he said, "attend! One, two, three! Fire!"

The match was applied to the vent of the gun, there was a flash, a dense cloud of smoke issued from the mouth of the carronade, and a loud report bellowed among the echoing rocks and hills like a clap of thunder.

The buccaneers gave a yell of defiance and as the shot tore through their closely serried lines, they broke, then closed, and fired a deadly volley of musketry.

"Bravely done!" said Gonsalvo. He then turned to watch the progress of the climber.

Pedro had nearly reached the summit of the cliff, but appeared to have reached a point of the greatest difficulty. This was a sharp and and narrow ledge at a dizzy height. Here he stood, his bare feet and hands cut and bleeding, his limbs quivering, not with fear, but from the effects of violent exertion.

The governor set up a shout of encouragement "On, my brave lad!" he cried, "another effort, and you will succeed."

Pedro could make no reply, for he had enough to do to maintain his critical position.

Slowly and cautiously he lifted his foot, and succeeded in planting it upon a jutting boulder of the rock, but his foot slipped—he uttered a wild cry, he came sliding down the cliff.

Just, however, as Gonsalvo watched him, his blood curdling with awe and apprehension, he once more caught a hold upon the ledge which he had secured before, and was for the moment safe.

Gonsalvo, still keeping his eyes fastened upon the gallant fellow, stood almost unconscious of the noise of the fight that raged around,—the shouts, the shrieks, the clashing of swords, and the rattle of musketry.

Pedro then got his foot on the ledge, and once more began his ascent, this time making better progress than before; he had already got his hand on the verge of the cliff, when a sharp report resounded from the rock opposite.

The pirate gave a yell of despair and agony; immediately afterwards the point on which he had been standing was void, and his body came whistling down and, falling into the abyss below, was dashed to pieces.

Gonsalvo drew a deep breath, but he was not the man to be baffled by one failure; his resolution was at once taken and was worthy of that excelling courage which was the redeeming point in his character.

Snatching up the torch, which fell at his feet he sprang across the chasm and began to scale the rocks with the agility of a squirrel.

Bullets "pinged" into the cliff close to his head, one even grazing his cheek, but still he struggled bravely on, and in less time than is occupied in the narrative, triumphantly reached the summit. Here he paused for a moment, tossed his cap in the air with a shout of exultation, and immediately hurried away to fire the beacon.

The three ships' crews were hard at it all this while.

A heavy shower of shot and bullets were pouring from the battlements of the principal tower.

Captain Tom, sword in hand, was flying hither and thither, encouraging his men, directing their movements, and now and again denting the head-piece of some of the soldiery.

Hugh Baldrick and his followers were endeavouring to dislodge a fierce band of desperadoes, lodged in an old castle, which the smugglers were demolishing piecemeal with the fire of one of their big guns.

Dutch Paul was nearest to the town, and his men, being fresh, and being more exposed, were the greatest sufferers; and Iron Arm, with the aid of the boat's guard and a party of marines, was removing the dead and wounded.

But the buccaneers had but yet begun their dreadful labours.

They marched at once towards the town, and reached it by the morning.

The ships remained opposite the ruined fortress, in the charge of only a few men.

Directly the town was reached, a strong party was detached to the monasteries and nunneries, who seized all the priests and nuns, and forced them to reveal where they had concealed their altar-plate and other treasure.

The governor was not only a man of courage, but one also of talent; and after some effectual endeavours to rally the townsmen to defend the town, he retired with the bravest of the inhabitants and all the military into the strongest of the remaining castles, and from thence opened an incessant and destructive fire upon the invader.

But this fire did not in the least intimidate the buccaneers; drawing as near to the embrasures as possible, every gun that the Spaniards fired upon their foes below cost them two or three men—so excellent were the buccaneers as marksmen.

This sanguinary battle raged till noon, the various towers thundering forth their artillery, shaking the houses and tearing up the streets with their heavy ordnance, which was unceasingly replied to by the rattling of the musketry and the wild shouts of the buccaneers.

Captain Tom Drake, always under cover, yet seeming to be present everywhere, attended by a chosen body of guards, calmly directed the whole of the operations, attending to the various details with the collectedness of one to be an admiral.

It was now full noon, and no apparent impression had been made upon the towers, and that one defended by the governor was doing slight execution upon the assaulters.

It was in vain that the buccaneers endeavoured to burn the doors of the fortress with combustibles, for the Spaniards showered upon their heads all manner of engines of destruction.

Even Tom and his captains began to waver, and deem their position no longer tenable.

Longer to fight seemed but to be a more speedy means for the fatal destruction of all his force; to fly would be equally disastrous, and to remain where they were impossible but as dead bodies.

He got his men under cover, however, and the firing ceased for awhile.

But the buccaneers were by no means idle.

They employed their time in constructing several rude scaling ladders.

The governor, before the assault commenced, was again summoned, but he replied that "whilst he lived there should be no surrender."

Up the scaling ladders the pirates then rushed with ruthless fury, bearing with them fire pots and hand grenades, which, so soon as they had attained the top of the wall, they fired and flung down among the Spaniards below, and then immediately followed the slaughter and confusion that they had occasioned.

The resistance after this was but feeble.

First the Spaniards threw down their arms by twos and threes, and then they all submitted, with the exception of the brave governor.

He was determined to die then and there, and slew some of the buccaneers when they were in the act of offering him quarter, and some of his own soldiers for advising him to take it.

To all applications and entreaties he replied that he preferred dying with arms in his hands, like a soldier, to being hung as a traitor and a coward.

Whilst thus he raved and fought, a piercing cry was heard, and his wife and daughter, with streaming hair and bitter sobs, flung themselves on their knees before him, to spare their lives and his own.

At length, a shot from the pistol of our hero pierced his breast, and he fell, mortally wounded, with the hurrahs of the buccaneers filling his ears, as he closed his eyes for ever in the sleep of death.

CHAPTER CCXXVIII.

BOB HAULER AND HIS COMPANIONS BUILD A BOAT— THE WRECK OF THE SHALLOP—A LUCKY WIND-FALL.

WHEN Harry and his party arrived at the hut, Bob and Jerry fitted up a temporary cabin for the ladies, and Harry, assisted by Micky, overhauled the stores and clothing.

They were all in a very shaky state after the expedition.

Minnie and Florida were in fact almost naked.

Fortunately they found a bale of stuffs and calico among the wreckage, and these the women quickly converted into raiment.

That evening as they partook of their meal before retiring Florida related how it was she came in the company of Minnie, and they both recounted the treatment they received at the hands of the savages.

That evening, as the buccaneers sat at the cabin door smoking their pipes, and the women were preparing the evening meal, the four men talked over their future arrangements.

They had enough food to last them several days, but when that was gone, where were they to get more?

With careful husbanding, and a few fish and birds they might catch, they could manage for a fortnight, but after that, even on the most scanty allowance, they would have no bread.

In the meantime, however, they would do all in their power to find the "Will-o'-the-Wisp," but in doing so they had two very unpleasant enemies to avoid; they were the Indians on the one hand, who, from what they had seen were frequently making journeys to the coast, and on the other, the Spaniards, who would capture and imprison, if not put them to death.

So make matters worse, Harry, who had to take everything entirely upon himself, was not certain of the distance he was from either of them.

At any moment they might drop down upon them, and massacre them for all they knew; therefore their position was not the most enviable.

Nevertheless, they cheered each other up, as much as possible, and the girls did all in their power to conduce to their comfort.

Little did they know what fresh dangers were in store for them, and it was as well that they were kept in ignorance of it, or it would have changed their few comfortable hours into those of misery.

Bob was sitting on a box, which he had converted into a tool-chest, and as he blew out the thick clouds of smoke, his eyes just came in a line with a stack of timber, which they had saved from the wreck.

Bob was a bit of a carpenter, in his way.

He could patch a hole, caulk a seam, or put in a stanchion if required, but he was no hand at fancy work.

Bob was therefore a very useful man on board a ship.

As he sat now pondering over different things

and turning and twisting matters over in every way, the thought occurred to him that there was another mode of travelling except by land—if they had a boat they might coast along.

This was a capital idea, and he hinted it to Harry.

"I like the idea very much," said Harry; "but do you think if we assisted you that you could put a boat together and make it water-tight?"

"We might try."

"So we might."

"We could do a deal in a week," broke in Jerry, who was quite delighted with the idea.

"We don't want one of particular beauty, you know," said Harry. "It might be square for that matter—a sort of ship would do for us."

"But you have no nails," said Micky, who had hitherto been a silent listener.

"Wooden pegs," said Bob; "tree nails, you know, will do."

"And pitch?"

"We may find some kind of resin that will do."

"Then you have all you require," said Harry, who had began to take the matter into serious consideration.

"Yes; and to-morrow morning I mean to make a start."

They turned in that night with a lighter heart than they had possessed for many a day.

Bob lay the greater part of the night planning and measuring and fixing his pieces of timber, in his imagination.

It was in this way that he designed the shape and build of the boat, and took an account of his stores.

In the morning they were all on the move at daylight; and Bob, in the first place, began to overhaul his stores.

The wood, being ready-dressed, was a great assistance to him.

If he had had to cut down the trees and to dub and trim them, it would have taken a deal longer.

As it was, he had got his keel already planned and laid by breakfast time.

The meal over, they were at it again in earnest; and, as every one assisted with a will, the work went on very rapidly.

When the heaviest of the work was done, and the boat or shallop—for such was about the shape of it—was nearly ready for the finishing stroke and the fittings, Harry looked up his old canvas and cordage, and prepared to make the sails.

This occupied some time; but at length came the finish, and then the launch.

This was a glorious day, and the wind and the weather could not have been more favourable.

The little bark rode capitally on the water.

She was tight, too, at least making only just enough water to amuse one hand now and then at bailing.

Bob had drawn a sort of resinous gum or varnish from a particular tree he found in the woods, and this served him for pitch.

They were very cosy when they were once afloat and everything was on board.

It was proposed that they should run in shore every night, haul the boat up and fix a tent with the sail and some spare canvas, and thus crawl along.

This they did for the first and second day, but on the third the wind fell and a swift current catching the boat swept it near to a cluster of coral rocks, which almost proved the destruction of the little craft.

By skilful seamanship and careful management, however, they avoided this danger, and were able to steer the boat into safety; but towards noon the sea rose and lashed the sea into foam, and in spite of all seamanship or practical skill the boat was hurled against a reef of coral and was dashed to pieces.

The sea was now running tremendously high, and the huge waves broke in angry breakers on the coral reefs, against which the occupants of the boat were fiercely dashed.

The increasing gale now raged with prodigious fury, and the wind howled with a peculiar weird-like sound that seemed like the death knell of our unfortunate adventurers.

One tremendous wave, mountainous in size, and giant-like in power, concentrating its force, hurled its fury against the coral reef, and all felt that the terrible moment was come that was to decide their fate.

Down, down, beneath the mountainous torrent the little party disappeared, then rose like so many dark specks in the seething foam.

Harry Vere, half stunned, managed to clutch Minnie by the arm, and another wave drove them over the inner reef, and swept them shorewards.

Harry was completely exhausted by this time.

The fierce battle with the furious element had deprived him of all power; still he clung to Minnie until there came a roaring and humming in his ears, a great and painful pressure on his head; then all was darkness, and his senses left him.

Bob, Jerry, and the Marine were swept in a different direction, and were borne by a strong current towards a huge rock, covered with slimy weeds, and so slippery that it seemed impossible for a human being to gain a foothold thereon.

Both of our old friends were strong and powerful swimmers, and being unencumbered, they clung to the vegetation, and drew themselves up clear of the surf.

Then they took breath and looked around for their companions.

They were nowhere to be seen.

Nothing but the dark green waves and the feathery foam.

It was now getting dark, and the prospect was anything but cheerful.

The slimy rock, it was plainly evident, could not be their resting place for long.

Already the tide had risen so that the waves washed up to their knees, and their fingers were getting cramped with clutching the slimy seaweed.

A reef of rocks, many of them above water, over which the breakers still raged, lay between them and the shore, and the certainty of being dashed to pieces precluded all attempts at reaching it, till the weather became more moderate and the sea less agitated.

But when might that be? And how long were they to resist the united attacks of the hunger and fatigue?

Both felt that death was at hand, but they were determined to die together; and although speaking was out of the question, a grip of reassurance was exchanged between them, and both being good swimmers, they struck out in the darkness, without knowing where they were going, but resolved not to die without a struggle.

At length the dreaded moment came; a huge wave mounting higher than the rest swept them from the rock, and hurled them again into the frothing sea.

Jerry would have sunk then, but Bob held him up, and struck out boldly until Jerry recovered a little and resumed his efforts to save his own life.

In such a sea swimming soon became fatiguing, and the many hours' watching also began to tell upon them.

As they grew weaker their hands clung together with a last fond grip.

All hope departed now; and although they still swam on, it was the feeble exertion of despair.

The touch of their hands said "Farewell," and with a last look upon the darkness of the heavens Bob was about to sink, when something touched his foot; then he was lifted up and dashed most cruelly upon a hard rock.

Wounded and bleeding as he was, he clung to it with one hand in desperation holding fast with the other to Jerry, who appeared to be insensible.

For a moment the waters receded from them, then with a rush and a roar another wave came on and lifted them again only to dash them down as before.

Bob now rapidly shifted his arm and got it round Jerry's waist; alive or dead he was resolved to cling to his friend to the last.

As the water receded he arose to his feet and made a rush forward.

The rocks were rough, and he stumbled twice before the returned wave reached him; it caught him up as before, and striking out he was thrown down apparently with less violence, and lay exhausted unable to move.

With his friend close to his side, he awaited the renewed attack of the waters, but the next wave only just covered his body, and once raised him.

The next only flowed around his body, and that was the last.

The tide was going out, the wind was falling, and he was saved.

But how about poor Jerry?

He lay like a log, cold and still, while Bob with a foreboding heart chafed his hands.

This failing, Bob raised him up, and worked his arm-like wings to expand his chest, but for a long time without success.

The wind died quickly away, and although the ocean still dashed violently to and fro, the noise of waters was not so deafening, and the grey light of early dawn was rising in the east.

Forgetful of his own sorrow and suffering, Bob knelt beside his friend, hoping, fearing, waiting and praying for his restoration.

At length his efforts brought forth fruit, and the hapless Jerry opened his eyes.

Bob clasped his hands in thankfulness, but Jerry's first words were not of a very devotional character.

"Oh! for a toothful of rum," he gasped. ' My lips are parched and my throat is burning"

' Look up,' cried Hauler; "and be grateful that we're so far safe. Look around; we're not on board of our gallant ship.'

Dazed and bewildered, Jerry did so; and then, with his horny palm, dashed the salt ooze from his brow.

Then, feebly, he asked of his chum—

"Where are we?"

"At present on a solitary piece of rock, apparently; but the light is so dim that I cannot see if we are in the vicinity of a coast or not. Judging by the foam, we are upon a rock in the midst of a heap of them."

Jerry was silent for a moment, then he said—

"Where are our companions? Where is Minnie? Where is Harry, and—'

"Gone—all gone, I am afraid," answered Bob, interrupting him.

"Are we really alone?"

"As far as I can see; when the planks of our boat parted and went down—what an awful crash it was—I heard our comrades shrieking and crying in the sea."

"So did I."

"But all is still now."

"Yet some of them may be saved."

"Let us hope so; but all danger for us is not over. The rock we are upon is not five hundred yards long, and the tide is going out; and tides return, Jerry."

"So they do, but before that daylight will be here, and we will have a swim for it again."

Jerry was still very faint and weak, and he vomited a deal of salt water, after which he felt better and sat up beside Bob to talk over their prospects.

It was not a cheerful subject, but it was the most vital to them, and they discussed it without any irreverence to any of their late comrades, who were buried, as they supposed, beneath the deep.

Slowly the light in the east brightened, the first ray of the sun darted through the fast breaking clouds, and both the buccaneers, obeying an impulse, started to their feet to view the scene around them.

The scene though grand was not promising.

Ahead lay the sea still turbulent, and far away in the offing.

The view behind was even less inviting.

A shoal of rocks of every variety of shape and form showed their dangerous heads above the deep, and beyond a long line of land lay like a fog dimly visible in the early light of morning.

' Very cheering " said Jerry, sighing.

"There is our island, Jerry," returned Bob; " as soon as you feel strong enough we must make an effort to reach it."

"I'm ready now, the sooner the better; but first have a look about for sharks.'

"There are none here."

"You can't tell, and those fellows have a leg off in a twinkling. I could not return to my native land," he added, with a slight return to his old drollery, "with a wooden leg."

"There seems but little fear of that,' rejoined Bob; "at present the only thing that ever had life which I now see around me is yonder poor fellow."

He pointed to a dead sailor, who was lying at the foot of the rock upon which they rested; his attitude and look showing that he was without doubt as dead as a stone.

The buccaneers eyed the sad relic in silent fear, and shuddered.

Some other vessel beside their own frail craft must have suffered in the gale; and yet, the thought struck them simultaneously, they had seen that upturned face before.

' Ugh! this is a sad beginning," said Jerry, as he turned his head with a shrug.

"And it may be the end," returned Bob; "but it is no use thinking of it now, Jerry; a swim for life we must have, or share the same cruel fate."

They stepped to the edge of the water, and launched themselves in.

The wind had now entirely subsided, and the waves had sunk into an easy swelling motion, which did not impede their progress; but the fatigue of the night told upon them, and they were glad to rest upon another rock about a hundred yards towards the shore.

It was a curious mass of stone rising from the sea, sloping up evenly on one side and hanging over like a projecting cliff upon the other, but miniature in form, rising at the most not more than twelve feet from the sea.

Bob was the first up, and Jerry followed, panting and blowing like a grampus.

As he sat down by Bob's side a very distinct groan sounded in their ears.

While they stared at each other it was repeated.

' Who's that?' said Bob Hauler, in a whisper.

' Some poor fellow."

"Can you see him?"

"No."

"Give a shout."

"Hallo! Who is it?"

"Oh! help," was the almost immediate reply.

It came from the foot of the rock under the overhanging part, and Bob lying flat down beheld a form, which he immediately recognised as Micky, clinging to it like a limpet.

" Swim round," said Bob, overjoyed to find another saved. " we can't help you there."

" I dare not leave go," replied the marine, despairingly, " if I did I am sure I should sink."

" Nonsense; if you swam so far, you can swim round here."

" But I didn't swim," replied Micky. " I came on a piece of the boat."

" Here, catch hold of my hand," cried Bob, kneeling down; " now then, hold on Give a hand, Jerry, here we are," and the marine was hauled up beside them, looking very much indeed like a limp rag.

" Three still missing from the mess," mused Bob, sadly; " but how did you escape being dashed to pieces?"

' When the boat struck," explained the marine, with a shiver, " my arm got entangled with the main sheet. Then I went down in the boiling foam; how far I don't know, I was insensible. Then a fearful shock brought me to. I saw the wreck swept away in a whirling eddy. There was a rock almost within my reach. I struck out and clung to it where you found me, and—and——"

" You are here, and the rest are gone," said Bob, mournfully.

" There's the boat," said Jerry, " lying in yonder shoal with the bottom stove in."

' Yes, that's her remains, and nobody near her. Poor hope is there that any of the others are saved!"

" Poor Harry, and the poor girls!" murmured the rest.

" Sitting here, however," said Jerry, " won't get us ashore; the tide will soon turn. Can you swim, Micky?"

" Not far," replied the marine, miserably.

" Well, will you promise to go quietly?"

" Do you think it is safe?" asked Micky nervously.

" It is unsafe to stop here," returned Bob, quietly.

" Not safe?"

" No; think of the tides. Place your hand upon my shoulder, and off we go."

Micky promised to obey, and the trio, stepping from the rock, committed themselves to the deep.

But they did so with a certain amount of misgiving, natural to those who have been compelled to swim for life in strange waters.

The first idea which passed through their minds was the probability of any sharks cruising thereabouts.

But only Micky gave vent to his thoughts in words.

" Oh, dear! oh, dear!" he moaned; " if there should be any sharks about."

" Do you think they would touch you?" asked Jerry, angrily.

" I don't know, I'm sure."

" I do," replied Jerry. " Sharks are much daintier than people give them credit for. If they go in for anything this morning they will go in for something plump and good-looking, like Bob or me."

" Speak for yourself," said Bob, with a laugh; " I am in no hurry to become food for such ravenous sea wolves."

" I am sure we shall never get ashore," groaned Micky, as they struggled on.

' You won't," growled Jerry, " unless you keep quiet; I, for one shall turn you up in another minute. I'm dying for a toothful of rum."

Awed by this threat Micky subsided into silence, and Bob and Jerry gallantly breasted the waters with their charge between them.

Fortunately for them, the ocean was almost a dead calm, and the water, hitherto so turbid, was now a beautiful smooth blue, and as transparent as glass.

The rocks for which they were making, as a sort of half-way house between them and the shore, were perfectly reflecting, and every passing cloud, lazily floating o'er the sky, found its image in the placid sea.

At any other time the buccaneers would have enjoyed a dip in such a place—a perfect fairy land for bathers—but their apparent isolation from all human kind, their anxiety respecting the fate of the crew, the uncertainty of their future life ashore, all cast a chill upon them, a natural dread which they could not shake off, and they pushed their way through the sea with a haste and energy they would not have pursued under ordinary circumstances.

" Oh! there's the fin of a shark," suddenly yelled Micky.

And Jerry, startled, left hold of him.

But fortunately for him, Bob held him fast.

This fin proved to be nothing more than a piece of rock, which had hitherto escaped their observation; and the marine having been duly admonished for his hasty alarm, they reached the resting-place chosen, and, climbing the rock, lay down with thankful hearts for a few moments' rest.

Bob lay stretched out with his eyes fixed upon the sea; there was not less than eight fathoms of water, but he could see the bottom distinctly, with its coral reefs in process of formation, and huge masses of seaweed clinging thereto.

There were no signs of life; but several dark objects, which Bob thought were oblong rocks smoothed by the action of the sea, attracted his attention, and he was about to call Jerry's attention to them as remarkable objects of the stone creation, when one of them slightly shifted its position.

Had it really moved, or was it only the movement of the water?

He lay still watching for a few moments, and then another shifted.

This time there was no mistake, for its position was almost reversed, and it turned lazily over, revealing a white surface underneath and the unmistakable fearful jaws of the voracious ground shark.

There was no doubt of it.

These apparently inanimate objects were sharks, and Bob's bosom was chilled as he thought of the probable fate of himself or his companions, or all of them.

But he neither uttered a cry nor suffered his face to betray him.

For all safety rested upon coolness and resolution.

The tide he knew was rising fast, and setting in steadily for the shore, for many little fragments of wreck went slowly by them, and floating seaweeds were steadily approaching.

In half an hour the rock would be covered, and then they must swim perforce; and by that time those lazy objects below might be aroused from their torpor and rushing about eagerly in search of prey.

Better risk the swim now—it was their only chance of safety.

" Are you ready now?" he asked Jerry, in a low tone.

" Quite," answered Jerry.

" I think we had better wait another minute or two," said Micky.

" Certainly you can if you wish it," returned Jerry. " Come on, Bob."

But as Micky had no wish to be left behind he

WITH A GALLANT DASH, THEY ATTEMPTED TO BOARD.

dropped into the water with a moan, and as discretion, put a hand upon each of his friends' shoulders.

As Bob dropped into the sea, he cast a shuddering look below.

The whole of the sharks—a dozen in number—turned slowly over, and he expected to feel their deadly grip, but not one rose to the surface.

The shore was not more than a hundred yards away, and they reached it without molestation.

As soon as they were fairly resting on the shingle, Bob told them the danger they had escaped.

Jerry said nothing, but he felt his limbs with an air of satisfaction, as if mentally congratulating himself upon being still in a sound condition.

Micky turned pale, and registered a vow not to bathe while he remained on the island.

Having rested awhile, they resolved upon going on a tour of inspection on the island, as Jerry remarked, "to find out what there was eatable.

It was an island, one of those gems set in the sea, upon which Nature has lavished everything beautiful in the most prodigal style.

Verdure ran down to the edge of the waves, and often the salt water washed both fruit and flowers, growing in ripe but apparently unappropriated luxuriance.

On one side of the island huge cliffs turned towards the sky.

Verdure of every description covered their surface; creepers hung in festoons, flowers blossomed in every crevice, upon the very sands below beautiful plants reposed in security.

The sea, now quiescent, lay some distance out, but the tide had turned, and it was slowly and lazily returning.

Watching it stood half a dozen men, in sailor costume, castaways evidently like themselves.

The buccaneers eyed them carefully, and then approached them with some caution.

"Yea-ho, mates, what cheer?' cried Bob Hauler, so as to warn them of their proximity.

The six men faced about, and stared in wonderment.

"Who the devil are you, and where do you hail from?" said one, gruffly, eyeing the trio from truck to keel.

"Don't be angry, lad," remonstrated Bob, stepping forward of the rest; "we're deuced hungry, but we won't eat you."

"You'll find us tough 'uns, if you attempt it," said another.

"Well we won't, but who are you?"

'Poor devils out of work," was the reply.

Jerry ran his forefinger across his teeth.

"There's more about," he said, jocularly.

"Then stand off!" said the first speaker sullenly.

As the fellow spoke, he touched the hilt of his cutlass, that was stuck naked in his belt.

Bob and Jerry nudged each other, and Micky drew back a step—he was more than a little afraid.

'What are you—pirates?" queried Bob.

"Not exactly, but we're not frightened; you're not the most honest, if I may go by the cut of your jib."

'There's not much to plunder here," retorted Jerry, looking around.

"No, and that's what keeps rogues honest,' sneered the other. "I don't suppose you'd be too particular, if you had the chance."

One of the party, a Dutchman, was about to chime in, but the speaker checked him with——

"Delay there, you Dutch bottomed galliot, don't break our ear-drums with your confounded lingo, let one bird pipe at a time."

The Dutchman, thus rebuked, gave a fierce scowl.

"You shall have your way dis time, Master Gunnel," he growled. "John Smith will have his some day."

"To the devil with you, you old schnapps keg," said the other; 's op your confounded jaw tackle. It's all through your lubberly steering we're here, and the bones of the good 'Spitfire's' bumping on the rocks"

"Oh—Ah! Got for dam Master Gunnell. Where vos de first luff, and who put de captain in de hands of de pirate?"

"Silence fool—you have said enough," spoke Gunnell. "I'll put a hole in your gullet if you speak again."

The sailor held his weapon threateningly, and Bob fearing that it might end in a serious quarrel endeavoured to reconcile them.

"Avast, mates," he said, "I see we are brothers in distress, we are castaways like yourselves, let us be friendly."

"There are few friends on this island," replied the sailor, in doubt. "If your intentions are honest why did you not answer the questions I first put to you? Dick Gunnell is not afraid to speak his mind, but he won't be bullied."

Bob Hauler swallowed this bragadocia with very ill-grace.

Both he and Jerry felt inclined to land the fellow a "hot un."

But prudence, however, restrained them and perhaps it was all for the better, for there was no doubt that blood would have been shed.

After a little parlying, our buccaneer learnt that their vessel, the "Spitfire," had been blown on to the rocks, and was now stuck fast on a jagged point that had gone through her planking.

Bob then explained that they belonged to the "Will-o'-the-Wisp;" and, at the mention of Captain Tom Drake's ship, the whole six of the sailors held out their rough hands, and wanted to shake flippers with our buccaneers at once.

"Captain Tom Drake!" exclaimed the man who had acted as spokesman. "Then you knew our late captain—Iron Arm, as he was called?'

"Shiver my timbers if I don't!' said Bob, puzzled.

"Well, he's gone now; and a wonder it is that we're here. The Death Pirate, when he took Iron Arm away and scuttled our ship, thought we would all go to the bottom ere this; but we've hung out, and had it not been for that lubberly Dutchman, we should be all afloat and atanto now."

Jerry Mizzen was too hungry to listen any longer to explanations; so he broadly hinted that it was time to be moving.

Micky coincided with him in this, and Bob quickly followed suit; and so the party marched along the beach, and climbed over the scattered boulders, in the direction of the stranded ship.

But what had become of Harry and his two fair charges in the meantime? Let us see.

CHAPTER CCXXIX.

IMPRISONED IN THE MYSTERIOUS CAVE—DESPAIR OF MINNIE AND HARRY VERE.

WHEN Harry Vere returned to consciousness he found himself lying on the sandy shore of what seemed to be a vast grotto or cave.

Minnie still clung to him, and to her he directed his first care.

Dragging her inanimate body on to the shore, he soon perceived that she was not dead but only in a deep swoon.

After a time she showed signs of reviving, and he set about reconnoitring the place in which he found himself.

A faint greenish light pervaded it, the source of which he could not divine.

Look as closely as he would, he could see no aperture at the top—no opening out into the open sea from from the water, which here was tolerably calm.

A vast dome-shaped grotto, or cave, lined with furze rugged boulders, and with many little caves or recesses at the back.

There was a strip of sandy shore, on to which they had been washed, and behind that rugged rocks, large and small.

But what puzzled and dismayed him a good deal was the fact that he could discover no means of egress or ingress whatever.

A curved wall of rock came from the dome-shaped roof down to and below the surface of the water.

It was plain that they must have been sucked far beneath the surface by the current or whirlpool —have been drifted within the barrier, and then risen again.

Harry now perceived many pieces of wreck—barrels and casks—floating about within this cave without entrance or exit, and knew that they must have been drifted in the same manner.

And presently he perceived that the greenish light proceeded from the sea itself, and was brightest all along the rocky barrier.

From this he judged the latter only went a little way below the surface, and the light proceeded from the outer world, from which they to all appearance were entirely excluded.

Harry was determined to conceal from his companion the horrible thought that racked his brain at that moment.

From the back of the cavern he gathered a heap of dried sea-weed, and spreading it out he made a comfortable couch on which he gently laid the form of the fair girl, and then he sat himself down, a prey to the most bitter reflections.

From what he could see they were prisoners in the cell, or dome-shaped cavern.

It was not any way consoling either to think they had no food, but there was fresh water, and that bubbled from several fissures in the rocks.

Harry Vere sat for some time buried in reflection, and then exhausted nature claimed that repose it needed, and he too fell asleep.

How long he slept he had no chance of knowing, but when he awoke it was totally dark, and, save for a slight rumbling, not a sound was heard.

Then for hours he lay waiting for the dawn, hours that seemed to him an age.

At length it came, and then Harry felt relief.

Minnie still slept on.

She seemed to be in a trance as it were.

There was a peculiar odour in the cavern.

A stifling smell that seemed to press like a weight upon the brain and to cause an oppression of the chest.

Harry concluded that this was the cause of Minnie's deep slumber.

Her delicate constitution was not adapted to so close an atmosphere.

Once Harry thought he would awaken her, but then she looked peaceful and happy while she slept, and he did not wish to awaken her to a sense of their misery.

Harry then rose from his seat, and, as the light increased, he took a more careful survey of the cavern, and in its mysterious recesses endeavoured to find an opening.

But his search was in vain.

Some of the fissures would extend twenty or thirty feet into the solid rock, and then terminate in a pool of water or a bubbling spring.

After this Harry began to lose heart.

He was sick and faint for want of food, and the stifling heat that increased as the sun rose and the day advanced.

With a sigh, he cast himself on the sand and gave way to despair.

Harry Vere now thought that their last hour must soon surely come.

They could not long subsist on water alone, and there was but slight hope of escaping, only by the way they had entered, and that seemed a sheer impossibility.

Harry, by shading his eyes, could see some fathoms down, still there was no bottom, and no termination to the wall of rock that went deep into the crystal water.

He dived down, but yet he could not discover the termination, the water under the surface being strangely agitated, and preventing his body from sinking very deep.

He made several attempts, however, determined not to be beaten if he could possibly avoid it, and as he rose to the surface for the third time, a dark object struck the water with a heavy splash, and swept past him quick as lightning.

What it was Harry could not see for the moment.

It must have been something very heavy, for it set the water in a state of agitation for some time.

He waited for some moments thinking if it was buoyant it might again rise to the surface.

But it did not, and this set him thinking what it could be.

The noise startled Minnie, and aroused her from her slumber, and springing from her rude couch she directed Harry's attention to the roof of the cavern.

Harry looked up and gave a start.

A portion of the roof had fallen, and through the opening thus made, he saw the faces of Bob Hauler, and Jerry Mizzen.

Consternation was strongly marked in the features of the buccaneers.

They were puzzled at finding Harry and Minnie in that strange place.

In the mellow green light cast from the water, the captives certainly looked very weird and ghastly.

Both Bob and Jerry rubbed their eyes, for they could scarcely believe that they were not the victims of some optical delusion.

Harry was the first to break the painful silence.

"Hallo, Bob!" he shouted, "what are you doing there?"

"Is it you, Harry?" returned Hauler, scarcely knowing whether to be pleased or otherwise.

"It is, Bob. Can you see any way of assisting us out of this?"

"Not at present," replied Bob, in perplexity.

"Have you a rope at hand?"

"No; we've nothing but what we stand upright in."

"We might get something that'll serve as well," suggested Jerry, scratching his bare head.

"Hallo! what's up? Made some discovery?" asked a strange voice.

Then the rough bearded face of the new-comer was thrust over the opening, and Harry in his turn was filled with wonderment.

He was at a loss to conjecture who the new-comer could be.

Presently he heard several other voices, and the faces of the six sailors were in turn presented to Harry's view.

"By jingo! you've got into a strange crib," said the last comer, almost doubting the truth of what he saw. "Have you no way of getting out below there?"

"None."

"How did you get there, then?" queried the man, in astonishment.

"By accident. And that, I presume, was the means that led to our discovery," answered Harry, equally perplexed.

Harry could hear those above conversing in a loud tone.

They were holding an argument, and using strong language.

Harry Vere could make out that they were discussing various means of effecting his deliverance.

Suddenly Jerry put his head over the opening and shouted down —

"Hold on, Mr Vere; we'll have you out of that shelt in the turning of a handspike. Keep your heart up, Miss Atherton. I s'pose you have'nt come across Miss Florida."

"We have not," replied Harry sadly; "if she is not with you I fear she has met her fate."

"I hope not," said Bob, joining in; "there's a hope you know, if it's ever so faint."

"Where is Micky?"

"Oh, he's down below scrambling among the rocks, it's rough sailing about this quarter. There's a ship ashore about a quarter of a mile away, some of her crew that we've just dropped on have gone on in search of a rope."

Harry's heart leapt with joy at this cheering news Minnie was delighted.

Until now she was not aware of the danger they had been placed in.

Seeing how matters stood she clasped her hands in gratitude, and breathed a fervent prayer to heaven for their deliverance.

But the danger was not yet over.

Bob and Jerry warned them to keep from under whilst they removed several loose pieces of rock and made all safe for the ascent.

It seemed a long time before the relief came, and in the interval the buccaneers recounted the strange adventures that led to their meeting.

A loud shout greeted the return of the sailors with a coil of rope, which was lowered down the opening and held securely by strong hands.

Harry Vere quickly secured Minnie to the end of the rope, and then gave the signal for those above to haul away.

This delicate operation was soon performed and Harry was not long in following, and grateful were they to breath the fresh air once more.

It was a joyous meeting. Bob and Jerry shook the hands of the young lieutenant until he felt as though his arms would drop off, and his shoulders were in danger of dislocation.

Even Minnie had to undergo the same operation, only in a milder form.

The survivors of the "Spitfire's" crew stood watching them not only with interest but in silent awe; they thought of their own comrades, and how happy they would have been could they have only given them the warm grip of friendship once more.

Harry Vere, however, felt it his duty to obliterate all signs of sorrow, not only in himself, but his companions, if only for the sake of Minnie, who was suffering both bodily and mentally from the vicissitudes and hardships fate had crowded upon her.

He sighed inwardly, and a tear moistened his eye as he observed the great change the last few hours had wrought in the brave-hearted girl.

Then he turned his attention to the ship.

She was lying almost dry, perched as it were, on a pinnacle of rock, and he mentally began to calculate on the chances of getting her afloat. It was a rough road they had to travel.

Great bounders and massive rocks lay in their way, and over these they would have to climb and scramble as best they could.

They now stood on a huge boulder of peculiar shape, and Harry, had he been differently circumstanced, would have stayed to examine it and discover if possible the mysterious means by which they had become incarcerated.

But time was winging fast, and Minnie showed evident signs of great distress, so that Harry saw that what was to be done must be done quickly.

Fortunately, the sailors who brought the rope had the forethought to bring a couple of broken oars and pieces of spars with them, which they picked up on their way, and with these they soon lashed together a sort of litter, by which means they conveyed Minnie over the rugged rocks.

Bob and Jerry, with Micky for an assistant, were deputed to the task.

Harry and the rest then pressed forward until they reached the bay, which bore evidence of more than one wreck having taken place there.

"So that is your ship?" said Harry to Dick Gunnell, who, by the way, was an old experienced seaman. "We must examine her and get her afloat, if possible."

"Ay!" replied the old tar; "and that quickly. You see here, sir, that this place has been tumbled about by an earthquake. Look yonder how the water whirls and hisses. There's hidden rocks and hidden caves all about this part of the coast, and who knows but we may have another storm down upon us in a crack?"

"You're about right," said Harry, taking a quick survey around; "here they come with their precious burden. Tumble to," he added to those around him, "and make some sort of an arbour for the lady."

The men obeyed while Harry Vere and Dick walked along the beach to examine a black object half buried in the sand.

"A boat," cried Harry, as they reared it. "Truly, fortune is about to turn her wheel in our favour. Yeo, ho! come here, a couple of you!" he shouted.

Willing hands soon cleared away the sand, and strong arms set the boat upon her keel and launched her.

Under the thwarts there were a couple of oars, and Dick, having cut a couple of thowl pins out of a piece of drift wood the four jumped in and pulled off to the stranded ship.

The 'Spitfire' was a stout-built craft, fortunately, or she would never have held together as she had done in such a predicament; a sharp-pointed rock had penetrated her tough oaken planking, but otherwise she was not materially injured.

Harry took a survey of her position at once.

The tide being down he could walk around her, and on climbing to her deck and examining her cabin they found everything comparatively dry.

Harry was quite pleased.

Even in the lower hold they found that the water had left, and the ropes, stores, and such like, were none the worse for their immersion.

Harry sent the two sailors ashore at once with the boat for Bob, and a small store of provisions, and such refreshments as the cabin readily afforded.

Harry, Bob, and Dick now laid their heads together, as to how they were to get themselves afloat.

It was a task requiring some skill.

The huge breakers that had swept the deck and washed the crew from the vessel had fixed her so firmly on the rock that, independent of her own weight, she stood as immoveable as the rock itself.

Bob dived down below and was absent for a few minutes.

"All right," he said, as he rejoined his companions; "the magazine is not much damaged, we can get enough dry powder to blow away this rock; and if you don't mind, Master Harry, and will leave it to me, I will do it to your satisfaction."

Harry yielded to this.

He had seen enough of Bob's handywork to know what he was capable of

Bob during his smuggership had discovered and practised many mysterious arts.

It was to his sole management, then, that the work was confided, and in less than two days the rock had been blown away piece by piece, and the vessel at high water was floated into a sandy part of the beach, and the rock extracted from her planking.

In the meantime Minnie was attended with all possible care.

The worry and overstrain had brought upon her a fever, and almost turned her brain.

The buccaneers Jerry and Micky, were one or the other constantly in attendance upon her, and they watched and administered to her with all a brother's care.

Harry Vere's attention was almost wholly devoted to the repairing of the ship.

Each day he saw some fresh confirmation that the place was subject to volcanic eruptions. Distant rumblings and strong agitations of the sea were observed each day.

Rocks, too, suddenly disappeared, and fresh ones appeared in other places.

This was a warning that they must not dally too long.

Therefore, he pushed the work on with all speed, and their toil was at length rewarded by seeing the "Spitfire" afloat.

On the fourth day a strange incident occurred.

They were all seated round the wood fire partaking of their last meal ashore, and watching the noble vessel as she lay like a model in an inland lake, so motionless and still, and the flag at the mainmasthead barely fluttering in the light, gentle air, when the sound of human voices startled them.

Like lightning the buccaneers sprang to their feet, and, seizing any weapon at hand, faced about to meet the danger and to battle hand to hand with the intruders.

It was a fierce-looking group they saw.

About a score of bearded fellows, neither copper-coloured nor black; half naked, and looking fierce as wolves.

On seeing the ship they let out a yell, and, observing the food which was steaming hot and arranged on wooden platters, or kids, they set up a shout that would have eclipsed a host of cannibals for fierceness.

"Back, back!" thundered Harry Vere, baring his weapon and springing to the front of his little band. "Keep off! Beware! A bullet for the first who dares advance."

"Fool!—babbler!" cried one of the on-comers, checked but only for a moment. "Death is but death. We crave for life!"

There was a terrible meaning in his sunken eyes, hollow cheeks, and the hard-set jaws, that showed he was full of determination, and Harry could not but reflect how hunger and privation had changed the nature of a man to that of a beast of prey

Harry paused involuntary as the man drew back, and the point of his cutlass for a moment lowered, but he immediately recovered himself and was on guard.

With fierce oaths and horrible menaces the rest pressed on, forcing the leader of the horde in front of them, until they were not many yards apart from the buccaneers, who, shoulder to shoulder stood ready to resist their attack and to defend their property.

It was apparent that a desperate and bloody fight must now ensue.

Only a couple of the buccaneers were armed with pistols and cutlasses.

The attacking party, on the contrary, had several pistols and rusty weapons; but it was quite probable they had no ammunition.

But there was no time to calculate chances.

It was a moment of peril and necessitated sharp action.

"Come on; hang not back," thundered one of the half-famished wretches. "Blood or food! Come on, give way."

As he spoke he waved his rusty sword to his companions, and then, addressing the last words to Harry, he made a spring at the young lieutenant like a fierce tiger cat.

As he did so Gunnell leaped to Harry's assistance, and cut the fellow down with one fell swoop.

"Blood—blood!" cried the others, pressing on. "Blood—blood! Down with them! Cut out their hearts, and pluck their livers from them!"

This was clamoured as it were in a breath.

In a voice of one man they all uttered it.

"Blood—blood!"

This was the cry as panting they bore down like a host of fiends.

Dick Gunnell then raised his crimsoned weapon, and upheld it reeking as it was, between himself and the clamouring crowd.

"Fools!" he yelled—almost hissed; "do you know me not? have you become blind? I am Dick Gunnell You are my late shipmates, but how changed"

"We want food, Dick," cried one, venturing another step, but keeping his eye on Dick's pistol; "we are starving."

"Whence come you?" asked Dick.

"Only from the other side of this rocky cliff," answered the seaman, pointing to a huge barrier of rock-work; "we have been there since the night of the wreck, hoping to sight some vessel."

"Why did you not discover us before?" asked Harry Vere.

"We were afraid, all the country inland of us seemed to be deep fissures and barren rocks. Danger menaced us at every step; not a tree nor a blade of grass was to be seen. Rendered desperate, and about to cast lots, we chose the only alternative, to endeavour to break from our prison and bear the agony one more day."

"And so you ventured the passage of that dark rift that seems more like the entrance to the region of Hades?"

"Ay, did we; at the risk of life But let us not partly; it is well perhaps that we have met Yonder you have a ship; you need a crew; and with her we can seek the shores where plenty can be found."

Harry Vere was fully aware of this fact.

He ordered more provisions to be prepared, and distributed. After which all hands were to embark.

A cabin had been prepared for Minnie's reception, and her removal was Harry's first care.

Jerry and Micky assisted him; Bob Hauler still following up the repairs of the ship

Minnie was so weak, though slowly recovering from the fever, that she fainted away during her passage in the boat, and so Harry had some difficulty in getting her up the ship's side.

Bob and Micky, however, got on board, and threw over a rope. Then Harry Vere, clasping the insensible form of his fair companion round the waist, seized the rope firmly, and held on to it whilst the two buccaneers hauled up the pair.

It was a great relief to Harry, and a weight off his mind, when Minnie Atherton was once more placed in comfortable quarters.

He had everything arranged for her as neatly as circumstances would permit, and then he got the crew on board, and set sail from that ill-starred coast, that had threatened to be their last resting-place.

But the beam of happiness that flit d over the young lieu'enant's features as he saw Minnie Atherton's gradual approach to health would have b en sadly clouded had he seen the dark, sinister visage, and the fierce scowling eyes that watched him each time he entered and left the cabin.

But the ship sailed on, and all, to outward appearance, was happiness, and so he remained undisturbed.

* * * * * * *

Bob Hauler and Jack Smith, the Dutchman, were up aloft repairing the rigging, when Bob, suddenly looking round, and taking a survey of the watery expanse, beheld what at first appeared to be the carcase of a dead whale, rolling about in the short chopping sea.

He watched it for some time, and at length made it out to be the wreck of a vessel water logged, at least, so it appeared to him.

Having satisfied himself on this point, he turned to his companion, who was staring at the strange object in open mouthed wonderment.

"Now, Jack, you're got lungs like a bull! Just let 'em know below that I spy a hulk—a wreck on the sea to wind'ard."

"Een wrak op zee," said the Hollander, speaking in his own sweet language.

"Yaw," replied Bob, laughing; "only say it in better English."

The other laughed with a sound like a rumble in a schnapps keg, and, laying down the end of the rope that he was splicing the lift with, he hung over the deck.

"Wreck ho! drifting down on us hand over fist!"

"What's she like?" was the reply from the deck.

"Two stumps standing!" rejoined Bob, singing out himself in a style to alarm the sleepers. "If you sight the line about two points our side of the sun's glare, you'll see her, sir."

The officer brought his spy-glass to bear on the object.

He passed the word to Harry, and he came up on deck.

"Certainly, Mr. Gunnell," said he to the officer's remark, "we will see her nearer. My glass is better than yours, and I fancy there's a man or woman tied to the foremast heel."

"Yes, sir, it does look like something now."

"Will we fetch her in two tacks, think you?'

"Oh yes, sir, just about. Bo's'n, all hands to wear ship."

Ph—it—whit—tie—whit! went the whistle.

"Tumble up here half a hundred of you! All hands to the braces! Slack away there, lee! Haul taut that foresheet! Edge away, wheelsman! Wide awake, you thick-fingers on the middle jib—jam it tight, man, till the foretay sail fills! Up helm now! and let her lay along a point more, con closer—closer! Steady, steady!"

There was a creaking of the yards and boom, a jumping of the ropes in the blocks, and a thumping of the rudder, but immediately the "Spitfire" sheered away from the frothing spot, where she had half turned as on a pivot.

"The beauty!" said Harry, looking up to see every stitch draw. "You on the foretop, shake out the royal again, and you may show the edge of the sky sail, if it feels soft enough aloft."

"Aye, aye, sir!" said the two men up there, a couple of light lads who feared not to climb to the dizzy altitude where the fifth sail looked like a napkin from the gunnel line.

"The beauty!" said Harry again, as the rushing of the barque came to his ears like melody.

"Ah, sir, where's the lovely woman," said Bob, that could go about, in or out of stays, like this little 'un, eh, sir?"

To any green-hand, it would have seemed a puzzle that the vessel was to reach the neighbourhood of the dismantled hulk, by speeding away from it.

But the wind compelled that, to arrive at the destination directly, the barque would have had to sail into the wind's eye.

After taking a long stride, she fell off again, executed a second half-turn, and lay over, so as to cut between the water whence rose the breeze, and the object of her course.

As they drew nearer the latter, the colour of the sea lightening betrayed a bright bottom and a certain shallowne s.

"We must deaden headway," said Harry Vere; "ugly to run on a shoal for curiosity's sake."

He passed an order quickly, and the carpenter brought a new deep-sea line.

"Arm the lead," said the boatswain.

They rubbed the plummet with fat out of the cook's kettle.

Bob Hauler took up the coil of stout line and the weight, and got over the bulwark into the fore-chains.

"Lay hold there. Stand by to haul in. Hup, hup, hup!" cried Bob, swirging the lead.

It hurtled forward, flying before the ship.

But she soon glided up to the spot where it had sunk, and presently the men manning the line had their faces sternward as they pulled on the dipping cord, tight as wire.

The lead brought up sand.

Another cast, as well as the colour of the water, proved that they were near a sand bank, and perhaps a coral reef.

"Ready a-lee!' cried the officer Gunnell.

"Aloft there, clue up sky-sails! In, r'yals! Let the t'-gallants rest. Now then down flying jib! Let it drag in the spray. Haul up foresail, and get the f'cast e clear. Bo's'n, rouse some of those lazy tars."

This stripping of sail sensibly diminished the speed.

"Mainto'-bowl're, there, slack away! Let go main-brace! Jerry, does she mind the mizzen well?"

Jerry at the helm, revolving the wheel, responded that she'd do.

"Have the port chain clear," said Harry. "You may have to anchor."

"Shall I go aboard, sir, or Hauler?" inquired the first mate.

"I will."

"Captain's cutter crew, in with the oars, clear away! Lower a bit now; steady, that will do."

The barque was under sufficient sail to bring her speedily as near the wreck as it was prudent to venture.

They brought her aback, and, seizing that instant, Vere leapt down into his boat.

Bob was coxswain, and Jack was stroke oar.

Jerry and three more filled up the complement.

It was a short pull to the wreck.

She presented a most lamentable sight.

Not only had she been the sport of the weather, but her ruin had mainly been caused by her having been a-fire.

The flames had despoiled her of most of the upper work and burnt away the decks.

She had been a dainty little boat in her day, it was evident.

As the cutter passed around her stern to accost her on the lee in the smooth water, Vere uttered an exclamation.

Her cabin windows were encircled by a mass of once gilt carving, with the royal arms of Great Britain shining out, and her name was, though obscured by smoke, discernible.

CAPTAIN TOM WATCHED THE STRANDED VESSEL.

"The White Swan."

With much emotion, Vere bade the men make haste.

Jerry shipped his oar, as did the rest, and took up the boat-hook.

Bob ported the tiller, and the cutter ran against the charred and rotten side.

Jerry drove the pike-head deep into the worm-eaten timber, and laughed at the splinters he struck off.

"You can't damage a wrecked ship," said he.

They held the yawl close to the vessel's side, and Harry sprang up on deck.

The fire had burnt the inside almost completely out.

The hold was full of water, on which floated boxes, splinters, and casks.

Amid them, wrecks of mortality, were sundry bodies, but so swollen, so eaten by the fish that had thriven from minnows to large ones on that horrid food, that one could hardly credit that they had ever represented men.

The deck and the ragged bulwark was carpeted and tapestried with seaweed, green or black

In and amid its tangles, clung, crawled, and crept, snails, sea spiders, crabs, and some young eels.

The foremast, where most of the planks had been consumed, stood shattered some eight feet from the floor level.

To it, attached by ropes, still remained a man— the bleached, withered, shadow of a man.

One arm was free.

It was clear that he had lashed himself there, not to be swept away by the seas, that no doubt had so often washed over the drifted schooner from side to side, and from fore to aft.

In some places the flesh had dropped away from the bones.

But the brine that had encrusted it had preserved it from corruption.

Pale as a spectre, enveloped in a glaze of salt, it was sad to look upon ; its one arm waving, held by the clothing, as if in mockery of life.

"Beg pardon, cap'en," said Bob, as his superior was gazing on this mute witness of the devastation. " Seems to me here's something !"

The captain looked down on the deck to which the old sailor pointed.

A sword, its gilt handle and steel blade tarnished with the sea air, was driven upright in the deck, as if to point out what was beneath it.

Vere saw that he should require time now.

So he bade Ben make the signal agreed on to the "Spitfire."

Ben ran forward on the heel of the bowsprit, and fired a pistol in the air.

The "Spitfire," in premonition at the ready about, wore round, stood for the wreck again, kept the lead going till she found a proper berth, and then let go her port anchor with some seventy fathoms of chain, a pretty good scope of cable in ten fathoms water.

After the iron had taken ground, they began to clew up sails, and make the ship comparatively snug, while hauling her up to anchor.

In the meantime, Harry had examined the planks in between which the sword had been stuck.

A hand, vigorous at first, but growing weaker, had cut, more or less deeply, many letters into the wood.

There was a date, and then followed some indistinct lines, referring to certain members of the crew.

The rest said that the carver of the letters was the captain.

He had been left for dead, and when he recovered, found the schooner on fire.

But it had burnt itself out, and then he escaped.

Escaped only to linger out his life.

With the mariner's habit, he had cut each day, the points that the winds prevailed from, and once or twice the sight of a sail.

At length a tempest compelled him to lash himself to the mast, and there he had been stifled or perished by famine.

By the young captain's orders, they cut the cords.

A scrap of sail was fished up out of the hold.

The body was wrapped up in it, with some bars and bolts of iron at the feet, and plunged over the side.

There was but one clue to the whereabouts of the destroyer.

The carved plank recorded

The "Death Pirate" steered north-west on parting company.

But the pirate had no certain destination like an honest ship.

Nevertheless, Vere deemed that sufficient thread to be followed.

No doubt he would come across some fresher finger-post on the pirate's track.

So the "Spitfire" was headed towards the American coast.

As she ran out of the Gulf of Mexico three days after none would have recognised her.

False strips of canvas were nailed to her sides, from stem to stern, and made her upper works seem high.

Her rig was that of a barque still, but her light sky-sail masts had been taken down.

Indeed the change in the weather kept the canvas well under hand.

There were unsteady north-easterly blows now and then, and fogs had several times imparted an ugly hue to the sunlight.

They had made the under circuit of Cuba, and

had heard from a "molasses drogher," or treacle-carrying tub of a boat, that a disabled vessel had put into Havana some weeks before, having narrowly escaped being captured.

The Death Pirate was reported in the Gulf stream.

They were doubtless on the right track.

On this afternoon, as they felt they were leaving the warmer latitudes, it came on to blow pretty fresh, with rain, from the north-east with a rising sea.

There was a warning that squalls were coming, one after another, by the flaws that made the reefed topsails quiver.

While the rattling of the wet and slackened ropes in the blocks, the creaking at the slings of the yards, and the junction of the topmasts and masts, were sufficiently ominous.

The young captain, pacing the quarter-deck, wrapped up in oilskin from head to foot, put his trumpet now and then to his lips.

Now the "Spitfire" was eased a trifle by the head ; then a reef was shaken out of the topsails as the wind lulled.

As night drew on the whole sky above was thick with black clouds.

They were in several layers, some massed and scarcely moving, the outer ones skurrying over the heavens like race-horses.

The young commander shook his head as he looked to the weather. After a short time, " send down top-gallant and royal yards !" ordered he.

By nightfall the barque was plunging over a white cap sea, with fore-staysail, main storm-staysail, main and foresail and mizzen, alone shown, and they were dreadfully curtailed of their fair proportions.

Two men were put to the wheel, for the rollers so severely smote the rudder, that one would have been flung off at the critical moment.

The first watch was strengthened too.

" Rough night ahead, bo'," growled Bob, buttoning up his monkey-jacket to the throat.

" I don't care while the rain keeps off,' returned Jerry. " A dry blow's nothing."

Jerry had ensconced himself forward under the bow-chaser, pulling the gun's tarpaulin over him.

He laughed as the bow would be poised a moment in the air, and then dart forward and downward, smashing the waves like a mighty hammer.

Jerry only grinned when the spray of a green sea came inboard, and drained off his tarpaulin.

" What a jolly old piece of oak he is," said Dick, walking up and down with Smith, as they heard Jerry singing,

The sky all around was very black ; the sea was dark blue except the white of the crests.

A lurid tinge was on the glistening ship.

There was no sound of man's walking, except the tramp, tramp, of the half-dozen on the watch, as they moved up and down the restless floor.

The wind whistled above and around, the seas bumped against the rudder and stern, or bounded along the sides.

There was the heavy splash as the rollers were overtaken by the barque and cleft in two, and the shower of spray deluging the prow.

It was pleasant, amid all this tumult to hear the watch in a low, but cherry voice, singing to the time of their own foot-falls as they took the main sheet to the capstan and hove it taut :—

> Oh, jolly to be a sailor boy,
>   The sea with plummet to sound ;
> And find how many fathoms length
>   The barque is from the ground.

When the first watch prepared to turn in there was rain falling, and so, as is traditional, the relieved gnard invited their replacers to hurry up, as there was a fine shower-bath waiting for them.

Contrary to expectation, the first part of the night passed thus smoothly.

But at the hour when it should have been dawn, yet no light revealed itself on the waste, there was a peculiar feeling in the tendency to a calm, that alarmed the old sailors.

They took unusual precautions against the enemy so awfully threatening.

The "Spitfire" seemed hardly to be a ship at all, so far as any spread of canvass went.

She rolled along now rather than sailed.

But where another might have run away, the young captain kept on his course, almost in the teeth of the storm.

Finally the foreshadowed terror came.

The far-off line seemed to lift one moment, while a streak of lightning played on the edges of the dense masses of vapour.

Soon after, a rumble of thunder ran all round the vastness.

That was the signal for the unchaining of the cyclone.

There was seen a wall coming on, a wall of wave and spray, of rain-laden air and cloud-drifts

One could not tell where the air joined the ocean.

"It's a rouser," said Bob Hauler, shaking his head, " but we've made all snug, and we'll do it."

"Yaw," said Smith, "but I don't know Hooge boomen vangen veel wind."

"What does that lingo mean to say?" queried Bob.

Jerry laughed.

"The Dutchman says big booms catch much wind. True enough, and we are heavily sparred."

They found presently that the Hollander was right.

That mountainous roller had already approached the vessel.

Harry sprang himself to the wheel.

"Meet her, meet her!" roared he, laying hold of the spokes with the three men. "It may stave her bow in, but passion of me! we shall go down facing it!"

"Hold on by your teeth!" yelled Bob, banging the forehatch down.

All seized some firm rope.

There was one terrifying space.

The ship, in a dead calm, rose on a wave and rested in the air.

It seemed that her head would never come around

But it did just in time.

The mountain towered, as high as her fore cross-trees, lifted as she was herself.

Then, head and ears into it, the "Spitfire" boldly plunged.

A mass of water, snapping the jib-boom, tumbled on to the fore-deck, and rushed all the way along to the quarter-deck.

The barque heeled over till she shipped water at the lee gunnel.

On her side thus she continued, until the first blast had spent its force.

By a miracle the shock had not shifted her ballast.

Two of the side guns were lifted from the runners by the wash, their cable-lashings was severed, and away to leeward they spun over into the waves.

The violence of the gale prevented the weight sinking them, and they seemed but as footballs as they flew.

The "Spitfire" slowly was regaing the upright.

The men below bumped against the bulkhead and stanchions at the lurch given the hammocks, tumbled out half dressed, and hastened to go on deck.

All thought that their last hour was now come.

Knee-deep in the water circling on the deck, unable to find room enough to leap out of the scuppers, Gunnel, clinging to the weather bulwarks amidships, was giving out the orders to the men.

The broken jib-boom, pulled back to the ship on the sheltered side, by its tangle of stays and the flying jib, was thumping at the forechain, and threatening to drive the larboard bower through the planks.

That done, the surge would have found the entrance that it coveted, and woe to each living soul then.

One of the watch slid down the incline, leant over the bulwark, and sawed at the nearest rope.

But ere his knife could sever half the strands of that one line, a blast made the barque dip again.

A torrent of foam and spray blinded all eyes, and when they could see again, they peered in vain for the seaman who had been hurled into eternity.

"It's dragging her head round!" cried Harry, in a lull of the wind. "She's falling off fast. Must I go to cut it away myself?"

"No, no, sir!" cried all those forward.

"Keep cool," said Bob, taking an axe from a neighbour's hand. "If I go where Tom's gone, it'll be soon enough for the next man to have a turn."

He let go his hold of a spike, and glided over the slippery boards into the suds on the depressed lee side.

Dauntlessly he slung himself over the side, and vigorously they saw his axe plied.

Now in, now partly out of the breaking masses, in a cloud of spray all the while, the tar kept chopping at the tangled cordage.

The boom was less nearly chained to the bow now, and it yielded to the eddies whirling at the edge of the slack water.

Presently Bob gave a shout.

Bill slid down the incline, and helped him to climb in again.

He had dropped the hatchet in making a last cut. It sufficed.

The spar gave in to the pressure, and, no longer towed, was speedily bobbing up and down in the trough of the sea abaft.

As if to stifle the joy that all felt as the "Spitfire" obeyed the helm, and pointed her cutwater nearer the tempest, a new terror alighted on the barque.

"Fire! fire! fire!"

It was the Dutchman who shouted.

Bob pushed him down off-handed.

But the alarm had been heard below.

The men under hatches, whom the captain would not let come up, as there was hardly room for the handful on the exposed upper-works, burst up the hatches, and swarmed on deck

Fortunately, the fury of the elements had abated

The ship rode steadily, though far from on an even keel.

"Fire! fire!" resounded over the ship.

The hardy faces grew ashy pale.

A zigzag of lightning had fallen on the billows, and seemed to kindle them into tossing lanterns far and near.

The gale bore flames upon its wings, and as it sang through the rattlins, left fragments of the phosphorescence on the ropes and ratlines.

The thunder still rumbled in the distance, and many of the sailors, guilt-stricken with the lives they had previously led, gazed on each other in terror.

Harry Vere was on the poop.

"Go forward, Bob, for heaven's sake," he said to Hauler, who was standing near; "close those bawblers' mouths, or they'll frighten Minnie to death."

Bob obeyed.

He leaped along the deck, and dealt blows about him with his fist, which served for the time to silence the most uproarious.

"Stand by the wheel here," cried Harry, to Jerry Mizzen, who was belaying the maintopsail brace; "I'll go below and see what all this means."

And so saying he sprang down the companion-ladder, and entered the after cabin.

A strong smell of sulphur pervaded the place, and smoke was here and there issuing from the crevices in the bulkhead.

Presently a bright flash through one of the chinks told him that there was fire in the lower hold.

Quick as thought, he descended to ascertain where this new danger lay, and to his horror he discovered that which he had no doubt was a dastardly attempt to blow up the ship.

A keg of gunpowder had been strewed about, and a train laid to the magazine, but, fortunately, a sea that had broken aboard had gone down the main hatch, and thus frustrated the attempt.

A streak of lightning, however, had stricken the mast and passed through the deck by the mast-hole, and set fire to the crest of the powder, which not only fizzed, but set alight a bucket of raw tar which had been placed handy for the purpose.

This, however, would soon communicate itself with the bulkhead, and the coils of tarred rope stowed away there, and in time if the ravage was not checked the magazine would in turn be visited.

Harry caught up a piece of damp canvas, and with it stifled the fire in the blazing tar bucket, then half-blinded and stifled with the thick black vapour he returned to the after cabin.

When he reached Minnie he found her in a state of unconsciousness.

Petrified with fear by the shouting of the men on deck, and fearing she was left there alone to die, together with the smoke, she had swooned.

Harry Vere raised her in his arms, and almost suffocated with the smoke reached the hatchway.

Having reached the deck plenty of willing hands were in attendance.

Micky the Marine was among them, and to his care Harry for the time confided his tender charge.

A dry lower studding sail was hauled out of the boatswain's store cabin and spread under the weather bulwark of the quarter-deck, and Minnie was gently placed on this and restoratives applied.

Harry Vere and a couple of stout seamen then went down below.

"Curse the varmint, may I clap my claws on his throat brails," cried Dick Gunnel, who happened to be one of the party; "I'll throttle him without mercy, or my name's not Dick."

It was plainly to be seen that a dark deed had been premeditated by some one.

The barrel of gunpowder had been taken from the magazine for use in emergency, and to make or answer signals with, and had been placed where no light, excepting the electric fluid could reach it.

The scorched and blackened flooring planks of the lower hold showed where the powder had been strewn, and other signs bore token of the culprit having been disturbed.

A few buckets of salt water prevented all danger for the present, and Harry, having satisfied himself that the lock of the magazine had not been tampered with, and that it was still secure, returned to the deck.

His next act was to relieve Micky of his charge, and, ordering Bob Hauler to supply him with a musket and ten rounds of ball cartridge, he set him sentry over the hatchway, and then addressed a few soothing words to the weeping girl.

"Fear not, Minnie," he said, "this storm will soon be over, and then we shall have the blessed sunshine once more; cheer up, let us hope for the best, and look forward to brighter and better days."

Minnie sighed, and raised her drooping eyelids.

"Alas, for me," she sighed, "there is no hope, no more bright days, no more sunshine."

"Say not so," replied Harry, smiling. "Your lips shall again ring with cheerful laughter, your eyes glisten with their wonted mirth, and—"

"Never," she sighed, interrupting him; "Never till I meet my dear Thomas again; his bright welcome smile can alone gladden my heart, his soothing voice can alone raise my drooping spirits. And the soft pressure of his hand can only remove the dull weight that is fast sinking me into the grave."

Harry Vere gazed in pity upon her pale, wan face.

Her eyes were dim and sunken.

Her cheeks hollow, worn and careworn.

Lips, once ruby, were now pallid and parched, and the dimple had disappeared from her chin.

Harry Vere's thoughts soared far away as he watched her silken hair play with the gentle breeze.

He thought of his own darling wife.

Would they meet again.

Dare he hope, dare he even dream of such a joy.

Alas! who could say, whose penetration could dive into the future?

Still there was hope, and Harry availed himself of that comfort.

The gale by this time had so far subsided that the light upper sails could be trusted to kiss the soft breeze and as the sharp prow of the gallant barque dipped in the sparkling brine the dolphins sported in playfulness under the bows.

An ottoman was brought from below and placed on the quarter-deck for Minnie, and the soft sea breeze seemed to revive her and restore the carmine to her cheeks.

The watch was then set, and those below piped to breakfast, and Harry, Jerry, and Bob, went below to consult, leaving Dick Gunnell in charge of the deck, and Jack Smith, the Dutchman, to look after the wheel.

————

CHAPTER CCXXX.

THE NEGRO'S TREACHERY—DESTRUCTION OF THE PIRATES' STRONGHOLD—CAPTAIN TOM DRAKE IN NEW DANGER.

THE desperate onslaught of Tom Drake's party, though it had proved successful, had not yet quelled the fiery spirits of the fierce Spaniards.

Though they, to outward appearance, had thrown down all their weapons, yet some of them still had long knives and stilettos concealed about them.

With these deadly weapons they made many cowardly assaults, so that the buccaneers were compelled to bind some of them with strong cords, or anything they could lay their hands upon.

Ben Barnacle was the most prominent in this work.

Whilst Captain Tom, Iron Arm, and Hugh Baldrick were engaged in various parts of the battered fortress, Ben, with only a few buccaneers, seized upon the most villainous of the band and thrust them, bound by the wrists, into a strong-vaulted chamber in the lower portion of one of the towers that remained standing.

Ben's task was not easy, nor unattended with great danger. A chance shot from a stray pistol more than once nearly ended his career.

But the old seaman, fearless of danger, paused not in his work, and he cheered on his followers, who were bleeding from many treacherous wounds.

When engaged with one portion of the refractory band of desperadoes, a powerful black, armed with a heavy axe, appeared suddenly on the scene and, felling one of the buccaneers, who endeavoured to seize him, he caught Ben Barnacle by the neck in his powerful grasp.

Then in his fury he raised the axe to strike Ben down, but the buccaneer quick as thought, with his left hand, which was all he had at liberty, drew his cutlass and thrust it into the left breast of the infuriated black.

The sharp pain caused the powerful black fellow to wince, and his upraised arm to quiver and fall to his side; then Ben, shaking himself free from the hands of one of the pirates, that had seized him from behind, finished off the black, and then settled accounts with the ruffian who had seized him.

In the meantime Captain Tom Drake had issued such orders to his colleagues as would render the siege of the fortress complete, whilst Dutch Paul, with a party of smugglers, demolished the town and set fire to the principal houses.

The shrieks of the women and the shouts and oaths of the men, half fishermen, half pirates or wreckers, as the chance might be, were truly appalling, as the lambent flames rose in the air and the dense smoke curled up in dark volumes to the sky.

These, added to the cracking of timber and falling of huge beams and rafters as the stronger built houses yielded to the fierce element and sent the live sparks into the adjoining smaller tenements, made the scene truly awful, and reminded one of a war on a much larger scale.

Captain Tom had ample opportunities to exhibit his good generalship.

Like a will-o'-the-wisp he flitted about, now here, now there, followed only by a few middies, who dived fearlessly with him into the dark caves and recesses in which the place abounded.

In some of these they found the lame, the maimed, and the blind huddled in terrified heaps, with the craven-hearted who had sought shelter there, and at length they discovered the subterranean cavern in which the pirates' wives and children were assembled.

The entrance was guarded by a score or more of the mercenary crew of a lugger that had been out cruising for fresh prey, and had returned, recalled by the firing of the cannons and the alarm beacons that were blazing on the headlands to attract any of the piratical fleet that might be cruising about the island.

Captain Tom Drake cut his way through this desperate band, but finding that only women, though they were armed, occupied the cavern, he pursued the survivors of the defenders of the cavern, who had taken the wise precaution to place as much distance as possible between themselves and our hero and his companions.

Darkness was setting in now.

The bloody fight was also drawing to a close.

Still the fell work of destruction and pillage was vigorously going on.

Guns were dismounted and their carriages tumbled over, whilst such shot and powder as could be saved from the magazine was carried down to the boats ready for conveyance on board.

Heaps of treasures also were piled up on the beach, together with such arms as were considered useful, and tobacco and rum and such stores as could be found were added to the incongruous mass.

"Come on, lads," cried Tom Drake, as the young urchins who accompanied him paused to view the strange occupants of the cavern. "Have you never before seen a woman?"

Tom was obliged to say this, and assume an air that was quite foreign to his nature.

He saw that the young urchins were inclined to show clemency to the, truly speaking, handsome women who clustered in the centre of that subterraneous abode.

To give them their due, it might be said that many of them, even in that day, could not have

found their superiors in the proud court of Spain, but Tom was obliged to close his eyes to beauty just then, for he felt inwardly as much inclined to linger and gaze upon the picturesque spectacle as the young midr.

The night was not particularly dark; there was no moon, but the halo cast from the galaxy of stars overhead, shed a soft light on the scene.

Aided by this, Tom and his companions had no trouble in following the flying fugitives.

Tom thought they would have made for the burning town, and have lent what assistance they could to their comrades there, instead of which they edged away under the cliff, and made along the coast.

Tom and the mids kept sharply on their heels, but they gave them some trouble to overhaul them.

Captain Tom, nimble as a deer, soon outstripped his companions.

In fact he was gaining on the mercenaries fast.

They, too, appeared to be aware of this.

Their shouting was plainly audible as they urged each other to renewed exertions.

Tom Drake fired a pistol at them, thinking to bring them to, but as the bullet whizzed harmlessly past them, they only laughed at his labour.

Tom was so excited that he did not observe that the numerous turnings and twistings of the outjutting crags had hidden him entirely from the view of the buccaneers.

It was only when Captain Tom discovered that the pirates had eluded him that he began to think of the danger he might be rushing into.

As the party disappeared amid the rude crags he paused for a moment to look around him.

It was a wild spot.

Huge cliffs reared their heads above him.

Innumerable crags, rugged and uneven, lay on one side and before him.

Behind him, in the gloaming, he could just define the narrow pathway he had travelled, and it made him shudder.

He was alone.

Not one of the middies who had started with him in the chase was to be seen.

"How had they chanced to miss him?" was the question he asked himself.

Why had they not kept pace with him?

He quite forgot his own extraordinary powers and speed.

As he was looking and listening, he fancied he heard the splash of oars.

Then he stooped down, and, looking over the rocks to seaward, he saw a large yawl being pulled swiftly from the land.

Its occupants, he had no doubt, were the piratical miscreants that had escaped from him.

Who or whatever they might be, they were pulling for bare life, and this made him uneasy.

His thoughts had hitherto been so bent ahead that he feared he would not be able to retrace his way back.

"Fool that I was," he muttered, "not to take more heed, and bestow more attention on the objects I passed; but, there, it is done. I am here, and I must make the best of it."

As he muttered this and stood gazing behind him, a huge black object bounded along the narrow ledge, and came panting to his side.

As it drew nearer, he saw to his astonishment that it was a big black dog.

The creature whined piteously as it sprang up to him and licked his hand, which was holding a pistol.

Tom was thinking at the time which it was better for him to do.

Try a shot at the boat, or save his powder in case he needed it.

The boat might be too far away, and then there was a likelihood of his missing her in the uncertain light.

He meditated for some moments.

Then he replaced the pistol in his belt as though he had decided.

The dog, seeing this, pawed his hand, and began whining piteously as before.

Tom turned and stooped to caress the animal, and as he did so his foot caught in a crevice, and, stumbling forward, he fell heavily and sprained his ankle.

As he fell, the pain caused Tom to groan audibly, and the dog, fearing he was about to strike him, darted away a few yards, and then turned to look at him.

Tom was now in an awkward predicament.

On rising, he found he could not walk, in fact he could scarcely stand.

He looked about for a place where he might seat himself, but the only place suitable to that purpose was some distance from where he stood.

Using his sword as a staff he tried to reach the spot, but he soon found that he could not do so, only by crawling on all fours.

It was a painful task even in that way.

By dint of exertion, however, he gained his object, and he was thankful on reaching the rocky shelf to find it covered with thick moss.

Vexed at his carelessness, and bemoaning his fate, Tom sat, unconscious of the day's presence, gazing on the sea which stretched far away in the shadowy mist before him, when he fancied he heard a sound, which to him at that moment was most welcome.

It was the sound of water.

He listened.

It was not far away.

This was cheering, but he could not move about to look for it.

In the meantime, finding his ankle beginning to swell, and the hard sea boot pressing painfully upon it, he removed the boot and allowed the joint the benefit of the cool air.

This eased it so much that after a short rest he was enabled to crawl about, and eventually discovered a thin streak of water dribbling from rock to rock.

There were several hollows that received it in its way, holding about a gallon or so each, and into one of these he thrust the aching limb, and refreshed himself with a drink from another hollow just by.

Wetting his handkerchief, he wiped the dust and sweat from his brow, and lighting a cigar, which he chanced to have in his pocket, he leant back and unconsciously suffered himself to sleep.

Captain Tom was not much of a smoker.

He sometimes indulged in a cigar just to keep others company.

Until now he had failed to discover the soothing properties of the narcotic weed.

He had often laughed at Bob and Jerry, when they growled at their supply running short.

When he awoke he was greatly refreshed.

He took a long deep draught of the cool liquid, and just moistened his lips with the contents of his brandy-flask, which unluckily was nearly empty.

Tom had quite forgotten the dog, and he was startled when his hand came in contact with a furry coat.

The faithful creature had nestled down by the side of the rock on which our hero was resting.

It was perfectly at home, and seemed pleased to have found a companion.

The captain, however, felt annoyed.

He conjectured the poor animal was hungry, and having no food for himself, Tom could not share a meal with him.

While Tom was pondering, and gazing at nothing

in particular, his eyes wandered to seaward, and far away in the offing he saw a big ship sailing round and round, as though caught in the outer circle of a whirlpool, and then suddenly shoot ahead.

Then it as suddenly stopped, and commenced rolling, as a vessel does when she is hard and fast ashore.

Presently the masts began to totter and fall, and the huge mass of sails, spars, cordage, and so forth, thundered heavily on the deck, or fell into the sea.

As the ship struck, a huge wave arose, and followed the ill fated vessel.

Then, changing its dark green head to a snowy whiteness, it dashed over the bulwarks and decks of the stranded ship.

Captain Tom listened, and borne towards him on the breeze came the cry of the ill-fated crew as they were swept away and sank in the boiling sea.

"Gone, all gone!" exclaimed Tom, startled, and forgetting his injury in his excitement, he drew on his boot and sprang up.

"And yet there may be some left," he added, thoughtfully, and he unslung his spy-glass from his neck, and scanned the turbulent waters.

He could discern nothing but a few black specks between the wreck and the land, yet he did not despair, for he gathered an armful of dry wood and weeds, and kindled a fire.

"This will guide them to a landing-place," he thought; "Heaven grant that some, if only a few, may be saved."

With these muttered words still on his lips, he turned to climb higher up the cliff, but he had forgotten his hurt, and he fell down a gully some thirty or forty feet deep.

When Tom's body struck the first object in his descent, he fancied that all the wind was crushed out of his body; then he gave a loud gasp, and rolled further down the deep opening.

The dog gave a loud bay as the form of the young chieftain disappeared, and then stood baying as though calling for assistance.

Then presently the moon shone forth and, penetrating the dark crevice, revealed a dark form, and a pale upturned face, half buried in a clump of mossy leaves.

CHAPTER CCXXXI.

BOB HAULER AND JERRY MIZZEN FORM A PLOT TO DISCOVER A CULPRIT—A HANDFUL OF TOUGH YARNS

THERE was a steady breeze, and the "Spitfire" sailed along merrily, when Bob and Jerry with several others of the crew mustered on the forecastle to smoke their evening pipe, and enjoy the customary can of grog during the dog watch.

It was not many evenings after the conclave had met in the cabin to discuss the best means of discovering the villain who had tried to blow up the ship.

Bob and Jerry, with their customary love of fun, pushed the can about, sang several jolly sea songs, and tripped a few steps to the merry tune of a hornpipe, until they got most of the crew about them and the can being emptied was filled and refilled again.

By this time all hands began to grow jolly, but the singing and dancing grew wearisome, and so Bob and his chum—who were always the leaders—proposed that each one should spin a yarn, no matter how tough.

It was further mooted that if possible the yarn should be about something concerning their own voyages in life, and as sailors are not particular in "laying it on pretty thick," the proposal was readily agreed to by all.

The liquor was again passed round, pipes were lit, old chaws renewed, and every one who preferred sitting to standing brought his "starn" to an anchor on any available spot he could find.

Gentleman Jack, or Johnny the Bo'd, a bright eyed jolly-looking tar, who feared neither fire or water, gunpowder or steel, was the first volunteer.

He was an Irishman, and according to his own account was of very good birth, but he was renowned as the biggest fibber on board, and perhaps for this reason he always obtained the most listeners, and received, as his reward, a jolly good share of chaff.

In telling some stories he would imitate his natural brogue, but the one he prized himself on the most he always spoke in the plainest of English, and this won him the name he now bore.

"Hurrah, Gentleman Jack!"

"Bravo, Johnny the Bold!"

"Pipe up, Sir John!"

These and other expressions were shouted by the merry group; but Gentleman Jack did not care, he only laughed as heartily as the rest.

Jerry, having restored silence by beating a phillibiloo on the bottom of an empty rum beaker with a pair of belaying pins, the sailor began:—

' The house of Sir John Purcell, situated in Ireland, was attacked by a desperate gang of robbers, who forced the windows of the parlour adjoining to the room in which he had just retired to rest.

"They appeared to him to be many in number, and, his first determination being to make resistance, it was with no small mortification that he reflected upon his unarmed condition.

"He was positively destitute of a single weapon of the ordinary sort.

"It happily occurred to him that, having supped in the bed-chamber that night, a knife had been left behind by accident.

"In the dark he proceeded to grope for it, and fortunately found his only available means of defence before the door leading into his apartment had been broken open.

"While he stood in calm but resolute expectation that the progress of the robbers would soon lead them to his presence, he heard the furniture which had been placed against a nailed-up door expeditiously removed, and immediately afterwards the entrance was forced.

The moon shone with great brightness, and, when the door was thrown open, the light streaming in through three large parlour windows afforded bold Sir John a view that might have made an intrepid spirit not a little apprehensive.

"His bed-chamber was darkened to excess in consequence of the shutters of the windows, as well as the curtains, being closed.

"While enveloped in gloom, he saw standing before him, by the brightness of the moonlight, a body of men, all armed, and, of those who were in the van, he observed a few blackened.

"Aided only by the knife he so fortunately found and a dauntless heart, Sir John Purcell took his station by the side-door.

"There was a moment of silence, and one of the villains entered from the parlour into the dark room occupied by Sir John.

"Instantly, as he advanced, the knife was plunged into his body.

"The robber reeled back, crying out, with a blasphemous oath, that he was killed.

"A second advanced, and was received in a similar manner.

"A voice from without then gave orders to fire into the dark room.

"As the ruffian who had received them stood in the act of firing, Sir John, with superhuman coolness, looked at his intended assassin, and, without

betraying any audible emotion to point out the exact spot upon which he was standing, calmly calculated his own safety from the shot which was preparing for him.

"He saw the contents of the piece must pass within an inch of his body, but he stood firmly without flinching, and the deadly leaden messengers harmlessly lodged in the wall.

"As soon as the robber fired, Sir John Purcell made a pass at him with his knife and wounded him mortally.

"His dying shriek summoned his followers, who immediately rushed forward from the parlour into the dark room.

"It was now that the baronet recognised the deepest sense of danger, but, unoppressed, he determined to surmount it.

"He thought all chance of preserving his own life was over, and he resolved to sell that life still dearer to his intended murderers than even what they had already paid for the attempt to deprive him of it.

"He did not lose a moment after the ruffians had entered the room to act with the same resolution he had hitherto pursued.

"A fourth opponent was wounded, but as Sir John gave his last blow he also received one on the head and found himself grappled with.

"Shortening his hold he stabbed at the man with whom he was engaged.

"The floor was slippery and the adversaries fell.

"On the ground Sir John Purcell made a thrust with his knife.

"This, though made with all his force, did not seem to produce the decided effect which similar thrusts had in the beginning of the conflict.

"The baronet examined the point of his weapon with his finger, and found that the blade of it had been bent near the point.

"As he lay struggling on the ground, he tried but unsuccessfully, to straighten the curvature of the knife; but while one hand was employed in this attempt he fancied that the grasp of his antagonist was losing its pressure, and in a moment or two afterwards he was wholly released from it.

"The limbs of the robber were unnerved by death.

"Sir John found that the vanquished foe had a sword in his hand.

"This he immediately seized, and gave several blows with it.

"The combat was not of long duration, for the robbers, finding so many of their party had been either killed or wounded, employed their hands in removing the bodies

"Sir John Purcell took this opportunity of retiring into a refuge a little apart from the house, and in it remained for a short time.

"The robbers dragged their wounded companions into the parlour, and, having lifted their bodies out of the windows in the end, took them away.

"When they retired, their intended victim returned to the house.

"His man servant, who had not put in an appearance during the unequal and murderous contest, was called up, and received the warm upbraidings his cowardice deserved.

' Sir John Purcell next aroused his wife and grandchild, who were the only inmates, and, putting them in places of safety till daylight, took other precautions such as circumstances pointed out.

"Some few years after the grandchild of Sir Purcell's, then a boy of about nine, was out shooting, and by accident, wounded the serving man, who was then steward of the estate, and all hope of his recovery was given up.

"But just before his death he confessed that he was the instigator of the robbery.

"He had cunningly given the ruffians all information, and had even promised to let them in, only that Sir John, sitting up rather late that night, frustrated his design.

"In fact it was owing to his grandchild, a shabby, surly-headed little rascal being troublesome, and, taking it into his head to cut one of his wisdom teeth that particular night; and that particular grandson—was this particular child, and that's a particular fact, so help my Bob, Jones, and St. Pattrick, and if yez don't belave me, ax me grandpa."

This salubrious wind-up brought roars of laughter from the sailors.

Tears started and rolled from their eyes; chaws of tobacco made their exit the wrong way; the grog went round and all were as merry as grigs.

"Bravo! Paddy Purcell, long life to yer honour," shouted Jerry, whirling a belaying pin in the form of a shillalah. "Call upon the next wun, me hearty, and don't be after tazing us wid a delay."

"Belay, you lubber!" cried Bob, correcting him; at the same time giving him a playful smack on the nose, which sent Jerry reeling from the deck bucket, on which he was perched, and made him discover a thousand stars that would have puzzled even Herschel to have given a name to.

Jerry gave Bob a vicious look, as he regained his dignified perch, and then another can of the best old Jamaica was handed round.

The next one called upon was a pale-faced melancholy personage, who acted as surgeon or in any capacity where his services were needed.

He began his story thus:—

"The night was dark with the gathering storm; the wind sighed mournfully among the trees, and wailed in every key of anguish through the rocky defiles and along the surface of the deep, roaring river that lay soughing at my feet.

"The red glare of the lightning, at short intervals, set forth in all their savage grandeur the wild, uncultured beauties of the scene.

"The loud thunder rolled with many a booming echo through the sulphur-laden air.

"All nature groaned in that hard travail with which alone a fierce western storm may be launched upon the world, and yet I did not tremble, nor seek the shelter of my rustic cabin, for 'twas to behold such scenes as this—to feel the wild, exultant joy which now coursed madly through my veins—that I had fled from my study away on the Atlantic shore.

"Here, some seventy miles from any other human habitation, I had built me a little hut; and, for the last month, had lived and enjoyed the first real freedom and happiness it had ever been my lot to know.

"The fierce elemental war that was raging around me had inflated my bosom with a strange, unreasonable joy, when suddenly another sound broke upon my ear.

"Surely it was the splash of oars

"Holding on by the shrubbery, I bent forward and peered down into the black abyss.

"But, between the flashes of lightning, the darkness was rendered even more dense, and I could see nothing.

"At length, however, a flash, more prolonged and vivid, broke through the inky blackness of the sky, and clearly revealed to me a boat containing two persons—the one a man of middle age, bearded and harsh-looking, the other a girl, young, beautiful, and seemingly in the deepest distress.

"A moment after, the man's voice reached me through the fierce mutterings of the storm.

"'Mary,' he said, 'here, surrounded by these terrors, you shall swear that you will marry me, and maintain eternal silence regarding the past, or here you shall die. Choose!'

"'Death, to one as young as me, is almost always terrible,' replied, with melancholy calmness, the sweetest voice I had ever heard; 'but, unwelcome though it be, it is a thousand times preferable to a union with such as you.'

"'The water is deep between these high rocks,' responded the man, with fiendish significance; 'and you do not, surely, forget the heavy weight which I have taken the precaution to fasten to your neck.'

"'With the cord eating into my flesh, I am not likely to forget your brutality. But God is more merciful than man, and I would go to Him; therefore be quick, and end my misery at once.'

"'Curse you then, go!'

"And in the next instant there was the sound of a heavy plunge, a sound that fell upon my ears like the knell of doom.

"Then the strange power that had hitherto held my faculties in its iron grasp suddenly released them, and, uttering, a wild, unearthly cry, I leaped from the rock on which I had been standing, into the black vortex below!

"Down, down, with seemingly unchecked swiftness through the seething waters, till at last I reached the granite bottom.

"Mechanically I seized with one hand a rude fragment of rock, its weight, I designed, should hold me down till the mission on which I had come should be accomplished.

"With my feet and remaining hand I groped about the rocky bed of the river in quick, nervous quest of the body, dead or living, of the unknown being for whom I had perilled so much.

"My bosom heaved as though it would burst.

"My eyes seemed about to start from their sockets.

"My strength was rapidly leaving me.

"My hold upon the fragment of rock was becoming less tenacious; and yet I struggled on, till at last—glorious reward of all my suffering—my hand came in contact with the object of my search.

"Instantly releasing the stone which I had hitherto carried, I eagerly clutched the inanimate body, and strove to rise with it through the black waters; but my effort was vain till the memory of the death-insuring weight of which I had heard the murderer speak, flashed across my mind.

"Then, drawing my bowie-knife, I quickly found the cord that bound the weight to her person, and severing it, ascended with my precious burden—I knew not then how precious—to the foam-covered surface of the river.

"I was a strong swimmer, and a few moments before could have sustained, with perfect ease, the weight which now, exhausted as I was, seemed dragging me down, in spite of my most determined efforts.

"Must I, then, after all my maddening toil, abandon the hope that till now had cheered me on, and sink with her I had sought to save, to the death that lay hungering for us on the river's bed?

"No!

"Heaven would surely not desert me now.

"This thought gave fresh impetus to my flagging energy, and a moment later my hand struck against a spur of the rocks which formed the river-bank.

"Then sustaining myself by the rugged inequalities in the face of the cliff, I moved rapidly downward with the tide, and soon my feet finding bottom, I gained the hard, shingly beach.

"Mentally thanking Heaven for scarcely-expected preservation, I paused a few seconds, to gather breath and strength, and then, resuming my load, climbed the steep hill, through the down-pouring rain that was now deluging the earth, to my little cabin among the trees near the summit.

"In the darkness I partially disrobed the inanimate body of her whom in life I had heard called Mary; then, after wrapping her in my warm woollen blankets, and lighting my lamp, I procured my brandy flask, and poured a little of its contents down her throat.

"The cord to which the weight had been attached, and which had been fastened in a running noose around her neck, had apparently so tightened when she was thrown from the boat, that she had been able to swallow but little water; therefore the necessity of subjecting her to the hard treatment by which alone, in the circumstances then surrounding me, water could have been made to leave the stomach, was unfortunately obviated, and I at once gave all my energy to the work of restoring circulation about the heart.

"At last, after what seemed an age of increasing effort, her heart began to pulsate.

"Again I applied my brandy-flask to her lips, and after forcing a few drops of the revivifying liquid down her throat, renewed my exertions to restore animation to her yet almost death-cold body.

"Finally, a faint sigh escaping her lips, she opened large, dark eyes, raised them for a moment, in a dreamy kind of intelligence, to my face, and then, with a smile of ineffable sweetness, settled back into a quiet slumber.

"Shading the lamp, I sat down by the rude couch and listened to the faint, regular breathing of my patient till morning dawned.

"Then I silently withdrew, and set about making such addition to my cabin as her presence had rendered necessary.

"The storm had passed, leaving scarcely a trace of itself behind, and I found it difficult to realise that the occurrences of the preceding night were not unnatural creations of the overstrained imagination.

"In this frame of mind I at length returned to my patient, partly to see if she had yet awakened, and partly to ascertain if she was not a myth.

"If the latter had proved to be the case, though I should have regretted it deeply, I hardly think I would have been much surprised; but, on entering, all my doubts, fears, and speculations were laid at rest, for my lovely visitor was not only there in proper person, but was also wide awake, and gazing in strange bewilderment about my modest mansion.

"'Pardon me, Miss——,' I stammered, blushing like a schoolboy. 'I would not intrude; but you have been very ill—you must yet be weak. Permit me to get some food for you.'

"'Thanks, sir,' she replied, smiling sweetly. 'I feel that you have been very kind to me. But how came I here? Memory recalls to me a scene,' and she shuddered visibly—'a last, horrid scene, which should have rendered this impossible.'

"'Pardon me,' I returned; 'but for the present I must positively forbid you to speak, or even think of the past. Let it suffice that you are now absolutely free from all danger, save that which your late illness may entail.'

"The beautiful unknown, possessing a naturally good constitution, rapidly recovered her health and strength, and on the second morning after her strange arrival at my hermitage, took upon herself the duty of cooking our frugal meal.

"'Stay,' she said, when, after breakfast, I was about to take down my rifle and go in search of the means of replenishing our larder; 'I am now strong, and would know what length of time I have been here.'

"'This is Wednesday,' I answered, resuming my seat; 'and it was at about one o'clock on Monday morning that you came.'

"'You rescued me from death. Pray tell me all.'

"Had there been a possible excuse for doing so I would have avoided recounting to her the events of that horrible night; but there was not, and so, after deliberating for a minute, I told her the whole story.

"'Ah! how much I owe you!' she exclaimed, when I had reached the end. 'I can never remove the deep obligation under which your noble act has placed me.'

"'You can only do so, by striving to forget it,' I responded, again rising to take down my gun.

"'Your extreme delicacy,' she said, regarding my movement with a faint smile, 'compels you to forego the pause which might be thought a tacit inquiry regarding the cause that produced the very peculiar circumstances in which you found me.'

"'That you have a most unscrupulous enemy, I am aware,' I responded, almost vehemently; 'that he was frightened hence by my unearthly shout and his own superstitious fears, and that therefore you are now perfectly safe from him, I honestly believe; and that you are eminently worthy, I feel with all the strength which only divine inspiration could bestow. This is all I care to know until such time as the wounds which may be in your past shall have been healed; then, if it be your will, you shall find in me an attentive listener.'

"Eight days after I stood with her, gazing out upon the setting sun from one of the parlour windows of a first-class hotel in New York.

"'To-day,' she was saying, 'I complete my twenty-first year; to-morrow you shall learn my history.'

"'If it please you to give me your confidence,' I replied, 'it will be happiness for me to receive it; but do not, I pray, let a mistaken sense of gratitude prompt you to this.'

"''Tis my pleasure, that you hear my story,' she responded, with one of her infinitely sweet smiles.

"'Then it will be joy for me to listen,' I exclaimed.

"And no longer able to restrain the passion with which she had inspired me, I seized her hands in both of mine, and poured out, in a torrent of such eloquence as only the deepest feeling can give us the power to utter, a declaration of my fond, devoted, enduring love.

"The blushes that at first suffused her lovely face were, a moment after, softly deepened by the flood of happy tears that covered them, and, casting herself upon my bosom, she murmured, in low tremulous accents,—

"'Yes, yes, your love is returned; but you do not know me yet. Till to-morrow we must part.'

"And quickly disengaging herself from my embrace, she quitted the apartment, leaving me to grope about helplessly in the darkness.

"From that time I never saw her more.

"She had fallen a victim I feared to the foul fiend who had made the two attempts on her life, and this drove me to madness.

"I was now desperate, helpless, despoiled of the treasure I loved. I cared not what became of me, and that was the cause of my going to sea, and why I am here."

"It's your story now, Ebony," said Jerry to the black cook, who had been listening in the background, and "dodging pompey" between the long boat's bow and the cook's galley. "I should think you could spin a good twister, by the look of your flying-jib."

"Me! I no sabbe anytink," said the creole, grinning till his white teeth glistened again. "Me poor black man; you call me Ebony. I know notink—yah, yah, yah!"

Bob had crept round the long boat, and at that moment, just as the repulsive-looking rascal was about to slink away, Hauler's huge hand caught him by the nape and thrust him forward.

"There you are, Ebony, safe aboard and snugly moored," said Bob, forcing the cook down into his own seat—a coil of rope. "Now, pay out slack as hard as you can. Time's skimming along like a flying-fish after a shoal of squid."

"Let him wet his beak," said Jerry, grimly. "It's too bad to hand him so roughly; you'll rub the paint off his figur-'ead, if you go on like that. Pull away at the can, old boy, and then reel off your log-line at the rate of knots."

"Aye, aye, let's have it, Ebony," shouted a dozen voices at once.

"I lay it's a stiff un afore he begins," said old Ben, who at that moment came forward from coming from the wheel.

"I can see it booming in the chops of his channel."

"Order, belay all," shouted Jerry, beating a tum-tum.

"Order yourself," said Micky, poking his nose in with a grin, "Order him to begin; you're a reg'lar Mizzen all abaft, and no go ahead in you at all."

Jerry landed the Marine one with his drumstick just below the short tails of his coat, which made the white duck of his pantaloons crack again, and brought the Marine to "attention" like a shot.

"You swab!" said Micky, "do you think every one's like you, got a halligator shell to cover him, you old salt water, rum-guzzling, sea horse, of a shellback?"

The tars burst into loud merriment, as they witnessed the contortions of Micky, and the fearful grimaces he made, and then Ebony commenced his yarn:—

"Bill was not a slave, and never had been.

"He was born on the island of Cuba, of very humble but poor parentage, and early in life he had learned the lessons of revenge.

"His father was a native-born Spaniard, but, early emigrating to Mexico, he married an Indian woman. From thence he removed to the island where Bill was born.

"Bill inherited all the fiery passion of his father and the cunning of his mother, and these qualities were fully cultivated and developed by the life he led, the dangers he encountered, and the teachings of his sire.

"He early instilled into his young mind the idea that he was born to prey upon mankind in general —that he had no friends save among those of his own class—that the wealthy were his natural foes, and that as enemies he should deal with all such.

"His father lived in an obscure spot on the coast, and his life was given up to depredations, in which the son joined at a very early age.

"They became a terror to the country for many miles around their abode; and well might they have been so, for many were the planters' mansions which had been consumed by fire, themselves kindling the flames, and more than one had been stricken down dead, either by the deadly stiletto or the unerring rifle.

"But the country was at length thoroughly aroused, and his father was hunted like a wild beast.

"For some time he succeeded in eluding the vigilance of his pursuers, but he was penned up at last, surrounded in a deep gorge, from which there was no escape.

"From his place of concealment Bill saw the avengers closing in upon them.

"The father, finding that he must be discovered, came boldly forth, and challenged his enemies to mortal conflict.

"He had a motive in doing so.

"He knew that he would be found, and that his life would pay the forfeit of his crimes, and so he resolved, if possible, to save his son by attracting attention all to himself.

"This was not from any especial affection he bore his boy, for his love for him, if he had any, was of a tigerish sort, but it afforded him satisfaction to think that if Bill escaped alive he would have an avenger of his death.

"Fifty armed men were closing in upon the outlaw Spaniard, and still he stood facing them, immovable.

"He was called upon to throw down his weapons and surrender, but he replied with a mocking laugh, raised his rifle and fired, and had the grim satisfaction of seeing one of his foes fall dead.

"Instantly after he received a dozen bullets in his body, and fell to the earth bleeding and dying; but yet he seemed to retain the strength of a lion, for as the avengers closed in upon him, he fought desperately with his knife, even until he had been literally hacked into pieces.

"It was at the instant of his death that his Indian wife rushed to his side, seized his bloody weapon, and renewed the combat.

"But as she was known to be almost as desperate and bloodthirsty as himself, little mercy could be accorded her, and in a moment after she was stretched lifeless upon the dead and mangled remains of her husband.

"The avengers would not probably have given Bill a thought, unless they should chance to see him, now that both father and mother had been killed.

"But for all this he could not resist the inclination to avenge his mother's death as far as possible.

"So he approached the mouth of the cave where he had been concealed, raised his rifle, took careful aim, and fired.

"The leader of the avengers uttered a shriek and fell forward upon his face.

"At the same time Bill gave back an answering shout, and then darted off among the rocks.

"Fifty bullets rattled around him, but the obstructions were such that no one had been able to take accurate aim, and he remained unharmed.

"He knew the pathway he intended to travel well, and in this he had the advantage of those who at once commenced the pursuit.

"But still he heard their shouts behind him, and knew that every effort would be made to secure his capture.

"It was not long before he reached the water, and drawing forth a small boat from its concealment in an undergrowth, he launched it, sprang in, and shot out into the deep.

"And he was not a moment too soon, for the avengers came up, fired a volley after him, and he found that he was only a few feet beyond the range of their rifles.

"But they could not follow him, for there were no other boats at hand.

"Bill knew very well now that it would not be safe for him to return to the island, as he was marked, and his capture would be almost certain, and his life sacrificed.

"He did feel a longing for revenge upon those who had killed his father and mother, but in securing that revenge he had to risk too much.

"He, therefore, resolved to leave the island for ever.

"Whither he should go he cared not, and for several hours he had pulled on, far out into the gulf, before he stopped to ask himself the question as to where he should bring up, or to think of the danger he was encountering.

"But with regard to the danger his position was soon brought home to him.

"For some time a storm had been gathering, and

from the appearance of the sky it would be such a one as the frail craft he occupied would scarcely be able to weather.

"He scanned the vast expanse of water far as the eye could reach, but not a sail was to be seen.

"The clouds were gathering thicker in the heavens; the moaning of the sea and distant tempest became louder and louder, and seemed to approach nearer and nearer.

"He could see afar off the white-capped waves rolling higher and higher, and the spray was even flying about him.

"On came the roaring tempest, but Bill sat firmly in his boat to receive the blast. It struck him

"His little craft leaped into the air, and then plunged down into the trough of the sea again, groaning and cracking at every bound; but still Bill clung to his oars, and kept her headed with the wind, hoping, and almost believing, that he could outride the fearful storm.

"For two hours he thus battled with the waves, but he felt that his strength was fast failing him, for his efforts had been almost superhuman.

"Darkness was coming on.

"He felt sick and faint; he tried to make a last effort—it was a feeble one, and he fell exhausted upon the bottom of his craft, and unconscious.

"After a time he revived.

"He saw dark faces around him, and he heard voices.

"The storm had died out, and the moon shone brilliantly above his head.

"Affairs were quickly explained.

"Bill had been rescued from his perilous situation by a party of wreckers, whose headquarters were on one of the Bahama Islands, known as Big Belial.

"To say that the young villain was delighted with the prospect before him would be but feebly to express his joy.

"Not only had he escaped death, but he had fallen into just such hands as, above all others, he would have chosen.

"The wreckers were pleased with the idea of his joining them, and the boy felt that he could now have a large field for the exercise of his daring qualities.

"The dying groans and shrieks of those wrecked upon the Bahama banks would be sweet music to his ears, and he longed to be at work in his new calling, which he at once resolved should be a bloody one.

"For the next five years Bill remained with the wreckers, and he soon became one of the leading spirits, for the daring he exhibited at once won for him distinction.

"During that term of years he had been so merciless that even many of the most hardened around him shuddered at his crimes, and some of them remonstrated with him, for the distant authorities had become aroused by the numerous atrocities which had been committed, and the wreckers began to fear that he would bring trouble upon them.

"From this fact his popularity began to decrease, and with it his influence.

"Bill was not slow to discover this fact, and he became uneasy.

"Those for whom he had felt a sort of brutal affection had crossed his path, and hatred for them now took possession of his heart.

"For the past five years, so intent had he been on slaughter only, that he had never thought of accumulating gold, but now he resolved to enrich himself, and then leave the island for ever. He watched for the opportunity, and it was not long before that opportunity occurred.

"The alarm had been sounded; a vessel had been driven upon a rocky reef, in a furious tempest, and it was reported that both passengers and crew had perished.

"At once a dozen boats put off, Bill and three others occupying one of them.

"The craft proved to be a rich prize, for she was laden with merchandise, and, what was still better, in her cabin was found a large quantity of gold.

"The precious metal was transferred to Bill's boat, and while the others were busily engaged in sorting out the most valuable goods, he and his three companions pushed off and rowed towards the shore.

"Now was the time for the villain to act. An oar was lying by his side, and with a sudden and desperate movement, he brained his three companions, and then threw their bloody and lifeless forms overboard.

"No one had observed the deed committed, and, seizing the oars, he struck out towards the Gulf Stream, intending to reach the Florida coast.

"All day and all night he kept on his way, and when daylight dawned the smoky shore could be seen in the distance.

"But another storm had arisen, and it promised to be a furious one.

"The villain struggled hard, but it was of no avail, for, when only half a mile from the shore, his craft struck a reef, and was badly shattered, splitting in the centre.

"He saw his gold sink, but he had no time for cursing at his disappointment, for he was compelled to put forth desperate efforts to save his own life.

"More bent upon revenging himself upon mankind than ever, he soon found himself ashore, and penniless.

"The first position offered was that of a deckhand on a steamer, which was plying to Mobile. But even here his desperate character soon manifested itself, and he was arrested and placed in irons for attempting to kill the captain of the craft.

"At Mobile he was lodged in prison; and, after his release, he made his way back on board the boat.

"He managed to conceal himself among the cotton bales and his devilish plans were soon formed.

"At the stern of the steamer he had placed a small boat in tow, with which to make his own escape, and then he waited the hour for the consummation of his plans.

"At night the alarm of fire was given, and there was the usual panic.

"But Bill had not calculated his position well, for the steamer was just passing the narrow strip of water connecting the two lakes, and to strike the shore, and land the passengers in safety, was but the work of a few moments. And then the fire was extinguished.

"The villain resolved that he would not be foiled thus, but would still burn her before she reached the end of her voyage, and once more he secreted himself on board the craft.

"Once more he attempted to light the incendiary fire, but sharp eyes were upon him, and he was seized in the very act.

"For him there was now no mercy, and when the steamer reached her berth, there was one dead man on board, and this was not Ebony Bill, but the man who had been clever to betray him.'

"And that was—" said Jerry, winking slyly at Bob."

"Nobody here," echoed Ebony, his voice hollow and his eyes flashing fiercely. "He was found in his bunk with a knife through his throat that pinned him to the woodwork."

"Whose knife?" queried Bob.

"No matter; owner was ever found for it."

"And what became of Ebony?"

"He went to sea and was never more heard of."

"Drowned, I s'pose?"

"I s'pect so."

Ebony gave a sullen glare at the listeners, and then made a movement to go, as though he thought he had said enough.

"Do you think he's dead?" asked Ben Barnacle, epping purposely in his way.

"Dead as a dolphin striker; p'raps eaten by a ark, p'raps swallowed by a whale, or travelling about in the hold of a crocodile on the banks of the Nile."

"And maybe he's alive," suggested Micky. "He might a been chucked up agin like Jonah."

"He might," returned the cook in the same hollow voice, "but there's never a fisherman as have caught him, and if there was he'd never land him ashore."

So saying, the cook slunk away to his caboose, scowling horribly, and muttering some mysterious jargon to himself.

"Queer fish that, Jerry," said Bob, when all the sailors dispersed and formed themselves into different knots.

"Aye, Bob, you're right, and if we fish him we're bound to land him."

"So say I," chimed in Micky, who had overheard their conversation.

"Did you notice his lock, and how he fingered his knife as he finished the yarn?" said Ben Barnacle.

"I did," Jerry answered, "and you're no barnacle if you don't stick to him after that; he is the villain without a doubt. I'd just like to hand him over to the tender mercy of old Strike; the vampyre would analyse his blood free of all charge."

"I'm of the same opinion," said Bob.

"And I, too," said Micky; "yours was an artful dodge to bowl him out."

CHAPTER CCXXXII.

CAPTAIN TOM A CAPTIVE—THE INDIANS' CAMP—A STRANGE DISCOVERY—CAPTAIN TOM ON THE TRAIL

CAPTAIN TOM DRAKE slowly and painfully awoke from the death-like slumber in which we left him when he fell from the cliff.

As he became more conscious so the pain increased, until it became agony almost unendurable.

"What could it be that was torturing so?" he thought, for he could not open his heavy eyelids.

What was it burning his wrists and ankles like red-hot wires?

He tried to collect his thoughts.

Gradually reason dawned upon him.

He began to remember, though but faintly, his journey along the cliffs, the shipwreck, the beacon-fire, and lastly, but faintest of all, his precipitation from the crag.

"But how came I here?" he muttered, as he languidly unclosed his eyes. "What foul fiend has treated me thus?" he added, as he found he was unable to move.

Then he raised his head and glanced towards his feet, and discovered that his limbs were fettered with strips of green hide, and so firmly bound as to cause him the pain he was suffering.

It was a long time before he became fully aware of the utmost extent of his danger.

He could see a log fire blazing not many yards away from him, and signs of an Indian having camped and cooked there.

He could see a stream of water, too, and he would have given the world, as the saying goes, for a drink at the moment.

"And was it an Indian that treated him so?" he thought. "Was it a redskin, or one of Manillo's tribe?"

This was a question he asked himself, but no voice within him answered; he was obliged to lay and groan; for groan he did, in his agony, and without the least sign or chance of any succour.

Presently he heard a step.

So light, so stealthily, that he knew it at once to be that of an Indian.

It was approaching.

His ear was so acute, that he could almost hear the soft grass crunch even under that light tread.

Still he listened, fearful to draw his breath.

He closed his eyes himself, too, only allowing himself to peep through the lashes, and then he saw what he dreaded in his position—an Indian, armed with tomahawk and scalping-knife, and a pipe or calumet stuck in his belt of wampum.

Tom gave an imperceptible shudder.

The scalp on his head began to move, and his flesh began to crawl.

And yet he was a stranger to fear.

He had never in his life flinched from death.

What was it then made his blood course so irregularly through his veins, and made the beads of sweat ooze from his racking brow?

It was the fear of that horrible knife.

It was the thought that the horrid demon would whip off his scalp, and after otherwise torturing him, depart in fiendish triumph with his gory trophy.

He would have faced the wild beast of the forest, or a score of such demons as the one now approaching, had he but his arms and fair play.

But to lay there bound, suffering agony enough already, and to be tortured without being able to raise hand or foot in his defence, it was too horrible.

The savage approached him.

With fierce glittering eyeballs, he stooped down over him.

Tom could fancy his were piercing into his very soul.

He could feel in fancy his hot breath on his cheeks.

He could imagine that the Indian's one hand was about to seize his hair, and that the other was already upon the haft of the scalping-knife, ready to perform the ghastly operation.

This was agony that few of the strongest men could endure.

It required all Tom's courage and strength of nerve to repress a cry, and to restrain the impulse to open his eyes and face his persecutor.

But Tom's wisdom luckily prevailed, and his nerves stood him good in that time of awful need.

"Waugh!" he heard the savage grunt. "The pale-faces trespass on the red man's hunting-ground; but the pale-face sleeps; I will not awake him; the red deer will not take his tuft until he wakes, and sees his enemy's face and feels his torture."

Then he heard the Indian rise and depart as stealthily as he came.

As Tom lay shuddering, filled with horrible thoughts, other voices approached.

They were the voices of white men.

THE MYSTERIOUS MISSIVE.

Were they friends or foes?

Should he hail their presence with joy or sorrow?

They approached with less caution than the Indian.

Presently one spoke.

"Hallo! mates; who the devil have we here—some sea robber come to share with us the spoil of which we can never get enough?"

"Think you so, Cap'n?"

"Do I think so, Malatesto Diavalo! I cannot think otherwise. Look at his trim; does he look more honest than any one of us, and yet they call us robbers?"

"Certainly not; but——"

"Away with your bats, Pedro; he can do us no harm lying here; we can return at any time and let light into him if we choose."

"I should like his boots," said another voice, gruffer than the rest, and more calculating in its speech; "they're worth—how many dollars do you think, Ned?"

"A score in this part."

"I'd have 'em, were it not for the trouble of taking them off."

Tom wished in one sense that he would take them off, as it would free his legs; especially if he would leave him his old ones.

He would have liked the ruffian to stay behind alone to effect his purpose. Tom felt certain he could manage one, whereas he was sure that with the four he would stand no chance at all

"Come along," said the one addressed as captain, on seeing the other hesitate. "I must have that gal; the redskin has got her hidden away somewhere."

"But you're not positive of that."

"I am quite; you skunk, look here, do you see this?"

Tom just opened his eyes the least bit, so as to get a glimpse of the group.

But our hero had no cause to fear, the four ruffian

were too much engrossed with something they had found in or near the encampment.

It was a portion of a lady's dress, and of the finest texture. Tom recognised it at once, by the pattern, as a portion of dress Milly wore the last time they parted.

It made his pulse throb wildly, and set his brain as it were on fire.

Had it not been for his bonds he would have sprung up at all hazards, and snatched it from the ruffian's grasp.

While he was gazing at it with wildly dilated eyes the ruffian placed it in his breast, and having hit upon the Indian's trail the others followed him in single file.

When they were gone, Captain Tom was resolved to free himself, and to follow on their track at all risks.

He soon hit upon a scheme to get loose.

He rolled to the side of the log, worked till his back was towards it, and then reached back his hands till the thongs were above the fire.

It was terrible, that fire eating into the flesh, but he bore it.

The chords of his wrist in front would be the last to suffer, and though the flesh on his arms went, he might yet be strong enough to aid her; for, all this time, he had but one thought—to get free, and help poor Minnie.

He could hear the wet hide "sizzle"—but, though he suffered such agony that the sweat rolled down from his brows, yet he uttered no groan.

Firmly he held his pinioned wrist to the fire, straining all the time to part the burning bonds.

At last they parted, and with hands, wrists, and arms red and raw, his hands were free.

He loosened the thongs which bound his legs and ankles, and threw himself upon the log which had served in its fiery heat to free him.

Then he staggered down to the brook and bowed his head to the cold, rushing waters, and drank freely.

The water seemed to give him new life.

He placed his hot, suffering hands and arms in it for a moment, then rose and looked around for some cooling leaves to bind around them.

There was an aloe close by, and squeezing the juice from its pungent leaves he dressed his wounds with it, and that eased the pain.

Joy filled his heart when he saw, where the Indians had cut their fish-spears on the day before, a small, sharp hatchet, such as many hunters who camp out carry in their belts.

Grasping it in his right hand, he sprang forward into the forest, taking the trail made by the robber captain and his men, without the least trouble or hesitation.

He was at least free and, though poorly armed, ready to die for or with the object of his heart's adoration.

Glancing from time to time only on the plain trail of men who had no thought of pursuit, Tom rushed on, forgetful of pain, his will giving him strength and activity which was wonderful when we consider his sufferings.

His eyes, piercing the gloom of the forest, reaching from tree to tree and rock to rock, swift to catch the sight of bird or beast, were also intent in watching for those whom he pursued.

On, on he rushed, until the red woods were left behind—on, until in a wild and savage region of rocks, thorny chapparal, and stunted shrubbery, where he could hear the roar of the distant sea, he lost the trail.

It ended abruptly in a small stream which coursed from the mountain towards the ocean.

Whether those who entered it went up or down he could not tell, but he knew that thus far they had followed the Indian, and here were most likely put at fault by his cunning.

Tom went first a little way up, and then he saw their tracks again.

The four men with boots on had left the water, and had hunted right and left, where a rocky ridge spread out, for signs of the Indian.

The rocks were yet wet with drippings from their feet, but they had evidently come back to the water disappointed.

Of course they would now go down the stream.

Swiftly he went a little way, and then, close to a clump of thick furzy bushes, he halted, for he heard voices close at hand.

He had bent an instant to think, and in that instant with a mighty leap he bounded clear over the bushes and landed out of sight of the stream, without having left a mark of his exit from it.

Not a second too soon either.

In less than a minute he heard the voice of the captain talking to his men.

He could hear all they said, as they approached wearily and slowly.

That had been down the stream to the seaside, and had found no trace of the Dacotah—seen no sign of Anita.

From the moment the track reached the water they had lost it.

They were now undecided what to do.

They halted so near to where Tom lay hidden, that but for the screen of bushes he could have looked right into their eyes.

"Cap'n," said one, "why should we waste time in the search? It is most likely the senorita is dead before this. Why not go back and hang or burn that cursed hunter, and then go to look for the new rendezvous of the band? We have lost the trail, and can't find it."

"You speak truth," said the captain, gloomily. "I can't stand much more of this kind of travel. With a horse under me I never tire. But this tramping wears one's soul out with vexation."

"And one's boots as well," growled the other; "I'm getting foot-sore, and all through you, cap'ain."

"You shall have the boots Tim; only wait till we find the gal. The boots can't walk alone, and the feet in them cannot move them."

Tom heard the robbers move on, talking as they went.

He remained in his hiding place until he knew they had plenty of time to reach their old trail, and then he began slowly to creep out towards the stream.

It was well he went slowly, for before he was out of the water he heard the sound of something in the water down the stream.

The noise in the water increased, but it was not loud.

Whatever it was it moved with great caution, whether man or animal.

Breathlessly he lay and watched; and to his joy he saw, with form bent, his eyes evidently following those who had given up the pursuit, the Indian.

He was alone, and his crafty face fairly danced with fiendish glee as he saw his pursuers take their back trail.

That he saw it Tom knew, because the Indian halted, and stood while he peered away towards the south.

Tom saw his own rapier in the hands of the Indian, his belt, with knife and revolver in it, about the Indian's body, and could he but get where the Indian must pass in reach, he would spring out in a death grapple and get his arms.

No—that would not do.

Minnie was hidden somewhere, Tom thought, with such cunning that, except the Indian was trac to the place of her concealment, it would never be found.

He must be followed to find her.

Most likely gagged and bound, she lay helpless somewhere near by.

Tom held his breath when the Indian, with a satisfied look, retraced his way down the stream.

He saw him pass within a spear's length, and he made no sound as the red fiend went by.

Oh, had that weapon been in his own hands, how quickly Tom would have stayed his steps.

But the Indian went on, and at last his steps told that he was down the stream so far that Tom might creep out to try and follow him.

Heedless of pain, Tom forced the bushes aside and crept into the water.

Without rising, for he knew that a glimpse of his form would cause a loss of all hope of seeing her alive, if at all, Tom crept on in the water.

On, just as fast as he could, without making much noise.

The Indian was out of sight when he got into the stream, but soon Captain Tom saw him again.

He was moving on in a much more careless way, apparently satisfied that he would be pursued no further.

Tom Drake hurried on, and as he went further down and nearer the sea he was less cautious, for he thought the sound of the ocean waves in the Indian's ears would lessen the danger of sounds reaching him from the stream.

Suddenly—where a tree overhung the creek, jutting out from a rocky ledge above—the Indian disappeared.

Tom could not tell how—he saw that its branches nearly reached the water, yet he could see below them, and the Indian was not in the water.

"He has drawn himself up into that tree, and thus reached the shore," thought Tom. "Now if I follow the stream he will see or hear me. I must gain that bank by another route."

Tom at once crept ashore.

Then creeping, without a thought of the pain of his scorched arms, over rocks and through bushes, noiseless, and oh! how slow to one so anxious, he pressed towards the point where the Indian was last seen.

He found that he was approaching a rocky ravine —great ledges on either hand of flinty rock, and more free-sheltering bushes in his route than he desired.

Suddenly he came to a dead stop.

He heard a low, plaintive voice.

It was hers—it was she.

He crept on, careless almost if he did make a noise, so that he could get quickly to her side.

All too careless, indeed, for approaching a steep part of the ledge, he crept upon a shelving rock, and as he did so, it gave way and he rolled with it down a declivity into a gully amid a cloud of dust.

The clattering stones made a noise which could not but be heard by her, and, of course, by the Indian, if he was there.

Tom, terribly bruised, groaned, not with his pain, but the thought that he must be discovered before he could be in a position to have anything like an equal chance with the Indian.

As he struggled to rise as quickly as he might, to lessen the distance between him and his enemy before the discovery, now inevitable, was made.

CHAPTER CCXXXIII.

MRS. DRAKE AND JENNY VERE ENTERTAIN FEARS FOR THE SAFETY OF THE "WILL-O'-THE-WISP"— A STRANGE VISITOR—THE MOORISH CORSAIRS.

THE mysterious disappearance of Minnie Atherton weighed sorely on the mind of Mrs. Drake.

Fears for the safety of her boy had long ago wrought lines in her pale, wan cheeks, and her hair sprinkled by the hand of time, had become of a silvery whiteness.

Jenny Vere was continually by her side endeavouring to comfort her.

Like a brave little heroine she strove to hide her own sorrows by the aid of a cheerful smile, which, however, was only assumed to raise Tom's mother from the utter despondency into which she was sinking deeper and deeper each dreary day.

Jenny, poor girl, had sorrow enough of her own.

Her fears for her own husband's safety preyed heavily upon her.

Harry had never been so long absent at one time without writing a line or letting her know by some means how he was, and so she began to fear that some ill had befallen him.

A friend of Harry's in the Government service had hitherto kept her well informed of the movements of the "Will-o'-the-Wisp," but this friend had failed to bring her any tidings of late.

No wonder, then, that the young bride wept in the solitude of her chamber.

No wonder then that Mrs. Drake's matronly eye detected the secret grief that was undermining the young girl's constitution, and eating like a canker worm into her very vitals.

Jenny was only deceiving herself when she thought she was deceiving Mrs. Drake, but the widow encouraged her in her belief, and professed even at times to be comforted by her words.

And so the weary time dragged on, until Jennie's pale face told its own tale of the suffering she endured, and she was compelled to throw off the mask, and mingle her tears with those of Captain Tom's mother.

The widowed mother and the young wife had retired to a remote part of the mansion, far away from the apartments used by the domestics, so that they might not disturb the equanimity of those who had to pursue their daily avocations, or create in their minds an alarm which their haggard faces could not fail to do if they had mingled amongst them.

One solitary, faithful attendant waited upon them, and strove by her careful and strict attention to their wants to comfort them, but she, alas! wore but a false smile, and her step, though light and nimble when about her duties, grew silent and mournful whenever she entered the chamber of the sorrowing ones.

Peggy was a girl of wonderful energy and, under ordinary circumstances, of a cheerful disposition, but the present state of affairs made her sad and thoughtful, and set her wondering what could have become of her young mistress, Minnie Atherton.

One morning, as she stood in one of the lower offices, her fingers playing nervously with the hem of her natty apron, she was startled by the casement being hastily thrown open, and the sudden appearance of a strange man as he stepped over the sill into the room, and thrust a letter into her trembling hand.

The visitor was to all appearance a seafaring man, and though there was nothing about him to cause her apprehension yet she shuddered at the sight of the man and the mystery that enshrouded his movements.

"Hush," he whispered hoarsely, as he placed his lips close to her ear, so close indeed that his thick, stubbly beard touched her cheek. "If you have any regard for your young mistress, or love for your young master, Captain Tom, utter not a word, not a syllable of the means I have used to convey this to you."

Peggy took hold of the mysterious missive, and

yed the s ranger with a look of mingled astonishment and alarm.

S e could not speak.

Her lips seemed glued.

Her tongue was parched and powerless.

The man's searching glance seemed to pierce her through.

After a moment's pause, he again addressed her.

" Look here," he said, in the same harsh tone, " this letter is of serious importance; take heed that it falls into no one's hands but those of Mrs. Drake. I have braved many dangers to bring it here, and one word from you to any one will place us all in danger; you, of course, will be hung or transported, so breathe not a word to any one, not even to your sweetheart; for I doubt not that a plump, buxom lass like you have one, if not many of them."

Peggy blushed.

Even in her fear she felt the effects of the sailor's flattery.

The crafty villain saw this in an instant, and he smiled inwardly; his treacherous scheme was working well.

The girl began already to banish her reserve.

The wedge once inserted, he began at once to drive it firmly home.

" I have often heard our brave captain speak of you," he added, craftily; " he spoke very highly in your favour. Lord bless those pretty black eyes of yours; I wish I'd been the captain, I'd have married you long ago; how would you like to be the captain's wife, eh, lass? How would you like to travel on the sparkling sea to foreign parts, to see the Emperor of China; eh, girl? Lord love you, if you were aboard our craft for a month, you'd never want to leave it again."

" Is my mistress there—Minnie Atherton?" she eagerly inquired.

" Ay, is she, bless her darling heart; she's the pride of our crew. I don't wonder at the captain falling over head and ears in love with her; and he's a smart, handsome chap, too; everybody goes through fire and water for him; but her eyes don't sparkle like yours. Lord love you, I wish you were aboard with us."

Peggy blushed still deeper.

Her round cheeks glowed with youthful ardour, and she even allowed the crafty seaman to touch her under the chin.

In her confusion she did not observe the man quietly bolt the door to prevent interruption from that quarter.

She was scarcely conscious of what he did, when he seated himself in a chair, and drew her closely to him.

In that secluded spot she scarcely ever saw a fresh face, therefore her conduct was excusable.

At that moment a footstep was heard on the gravel path without.

The villain started, and looked around for some place of concealment.

There was a large closet in the corner, and into this he squeezed his burly form, giving the confused girl a glance so full of deadly import as to make her fully understand his meaning.

He had scarcely done so when a face appeared at the open casement.

" Well, Peggy, my lass, you don't look very smiling this morning. Down in the mouth again. Anything fresh happened?"

It was the head gardener who thus spoke.

" No, nothing fresh, only I don't feel well," was her evasive answer.

She cast a side glance towards the closet, the door of which creaked slightly.

" Oh well, lassie, keep up thy heart, girl, I'll get thee a lover some day; he'll cheer thee up, some day, girl."

And so saying the man walked away, much to the relief of the trembling girl.

" I must away now," said the strange visitor, as he made his appearance and listened to the receding footsteps. " Don't forget the letter, and for your own sake think of what I have told you."

Then, stealing a kiss from the cherry lips of the trembling girl, he sprang through the casement and disappeared in the shrubbery.

Mrs. Drake was astounded when Peggy handed her the letter.

" From my son—my own darling Tom!" she exclaimed, excitedly, as with trembling hand she broke the seal and tore open the letter. " Thank God—thank God! now my prayer is answered."

She glanced her eye hurriedly over it, and then handed it to Jenny Vere, who stood looking upon her in feverish excitement.

" Read it—read it, Jenny! I cannot," she muttered; " my eyes are dim; a thousand sparks dance before my vision; my brain whirls. I—I feel I shall faint."

Peggy, who had stood spell-bound, as it were, all this time, flew to her assistance, and caught her in her arms just as she swooned and was about to fall.

Jenny Vere caught up the letter and hastily read it. It ran thus :—

" MY DEAR MOTHER,—Take passage for Gibraltar as soon as you can; I will meet you there. Keep this secret. Bring Jenny with you, don't forget; and, dear mother, as you love me, do not breathe a word of my whereabouts to anyone not concerned. I have entrusted Bob Hauler to deliver this; he is a staunch friend. Tell Jenny that Harry is quite jolly, and in high hopes of seeing her soon. All is going on well. Minnie is in good health and spirits, and in hopes of seeing you soon.—Yours very affectionately,   " TOM."

" P.S.—Do not forget to keep this secret."

Jenny felt as light as a young fawn when she had done reading this.

She carefully folded up the missive, and then assisted Peggy to restore Mrs. Drake to consciousness.

*   *   *   *   *   *   *

It was a glorious morning, the golden sun glinted the waves, and a light breeze whistled through the cordage of the gallant ship as she ploughed her way across the Bay of Biscay, in the direction of the Gibraltar Gut.

It was the season when seamen most dread the passage of the dangerous Gut, and when the big waves of the Bay of Biscay tore about the good ship as though it were a cockle-shell; but those on board the " Clara Jane " bore stout hearts, and had no fear of danger from the treacherous elements.

On board the ship were two passengers, females, and they were Mrs. Drake and Jenny Vere.

Jenny Vere was not a stranger to the locality.

Often had she travelled that road, even when a child, with her father, and in her numerous voyages she had picked up no small knowledge of seamanship and navigation.

She could box the compass with many a good seaman; understood the soundings by the lead line; had studied the theory of handling the sails and yards; and could even take a trick at the wheel.

But since she had been married to Harry Vere she had made the various charts her sole companions, and many and many a lonesome hour had she passed away in pricking off the supposed course of her husband upon the chart, and calculated the different currents that might bear him onward in his course, or bear him away in an entirely opposite direction.

So that theoretically, if not practically, Jenny was as good as many of our seamen of the present day.

So far the voyage had been prosperous, but at length a storm arose, and the turbulent waves began tossing the vessel about in their rude playfulness.

The lightning flashed, the thunder rolled, and the rain poured down in one incessant shower, threatening to deluge all beneath it.

The "Clara Jane" was a stout-built craft.

Her sails were all brand new, and she seemed capable of weathering even the fiercest gale.

But, alas! human nature is but frail.

Two of her crew were blown from the topsail yard while reefing, and four poor fellows were swept from the jibboom when taking in a sail by a huge wave that towered like a mountain, and then broke over the gallant ship.

Captain Jordan, on finding his crew thus unhappily reduced, ordered his vessel to be hove to, and she lay like a log rolling in the trough of the sea.

So violent was the tempest that all on board expected she would go down at any moment.

Jenny Vere, perhaps, was about the stoutest-hearted on board at that time.

She had braved many a storm in the company of her father, and with his stout arm to protect her in his younger days, she had been taught to know no fear.

But the storm lulled as the morning dawned.

The wind fell light, the sails were set, and the gallant ship was again headed on her course, and the gloom cast over the ship by the loss of the six brave men that were drowned.

The captain was not in the best of spirits.

He had spoken a vessel, the captain of which informed him that a fleet of Moorish corsairs were hovering about the mouth of the Gut.

He commanded his own crew to keep a strict look out, and divided his few remaining hands in the best manner possible.

They were standing along at the rate of five or six knots when suddenly the voice of one of the men was heard ringing through the ship:

"Sail O!"

"Where away?' inquired the captain, as he darted aloft, glass in hand.

"Two points off the lee bow," was the answer.

The mate was soon aloft.

Directing his glass in the indicated direction, he soon made out the stranger to be one of the corsair fleet, heading directly towards him under a press of canvas.

This was discouraging.

Mrs. Drake, when she heard the news, wrung her hands, while Jenny showed more emotion than usual.

"And are they really corsairs?" she asked.

"Ay," said she; ' they have a number of vessels, and doubtless there have been five or six in chase of us."

"It is unfortunate," remarked the captain "Shorthanded as we are, and with only one gun aboard, we cannot hope to do much against such an enemy."

"We cannot escape them either," said the mate. "At the rate that fellow is sailing he must soon overtake us."

' Alas! fortune indeed seems against us," said Mrs. Drake. "I had thought our troubles were all at an end."

Meanwhile the corsairs were coming up fast.

The ship was brought round and headed away from the pursuer, although it was plain that this was of little use, as she kept gaining, cleaving the water with her sharp bow like a knife.

The gun forward was charged with slugs and old iron, and wheeled aft and pointed at their pursuer.

At length, when the latter was in range a shot was fired from a smaller piece, which had been found in the hold and brought up.

The shot was well aimed.

It struck the corsair's main-topmast, and his mainsail was seen to go down by the run.

"A good shot!" said the mate, rubbing his hands; "a few more like that would disable the fellow so that he could do us no damage."

A new mainsail, however, soon was rigged, and, in spite of his utmost efforts, the mate could not hit that, although he fired six shots at it in succession.

Among the men there was an old grizzly fellow, named Ben Bunt.

This sailor had, for some time, been critically watching the movements of the young man.

Now he came aft, and touched his cap.

"If you will give me a chance at that gun," said he, "I think I can do a little at such target practice; seeing as I've been a gunner aboard a sloop-of-war."

"Ay, ay," answered the captain; "I have never seen such service, my man, and am therefore willing to give you a trial."

The eyes of the old man lighted up with grim satisfaction.

"If I do say it myself," said he, "I was reckoned one of the best gunners aboard the sloop, and I hope I haven't forgotten my hand."

So saying, the speaker took his place at the gun, and having carefully pointed it, he applied the match.

Watching the Moorish craft, the spectators were surprised to see her mainmast go to splinters.

"Well done!" cried the captain; "a few more shots like that, and away goes the fellow's headgear!"

Again the old tar, after the gun had been loaded, placed himself at the piece and fired.

Unfortunately, the piece being an old one, it now exploded, and the sailors narrowly escaped injury, some of the iron fragments flying within an inch of them, and others passing to leeward, and falling, with a hissing noise, into the sea.

"There is the other gun left to us, at all events," said the mate.

The old sailor, Ben Bunt, inspected the piece narrowly.

"It has a large crack in it," said he; "it may or may not explode at the first fire."

"You think, then, we could fire one shot?" inquired the captain.

"I'm not sure of it," answered Ben Bunt; "it has a bad look, and aboard a war craft would have been condemned long since."

The captain gazed wistfully towards the Moorish vessel.

"I wish we could fire her one more shot," said he.

"I'll try it," answered Ben, resolutely; "it is worth risking, especially with the seaboard;" glancing at the two women.

"If it should burst, you will probably perish," cried Jenny. "No, no—I would not advise you to risk firing that shot."

"I'm an old hulk," answered Ben, "and my life is worth nothing in comparison to yours and t'others. Stand clear, all of you, and I'll fire that shot!"

"No," exclaimed the captain. "You shall point the gun; then stand out of harm's way, while I fire."

The old sailor shook his head.

"If anybody fires the piece, it must be me, sir. It may not explode, after all; so stand clear, I say, all hands."

The captain, however, would not consent to this.

He waited until the old sailor had pointed the gun.

Then, in an authorative voice, he bade him stand aside.

The old sailor obeyed reluctantly.

"Nay," exclaimed the mate, "you must not run this risk. The gun will explode—I am sure of it and——"

A shot came bowling along from the corsair, and striking the ship's fore-yard, this was seen to fly to splinters

Mrs. Drake, who stood near Jenny, instinctively clasping her round the waist, drew her away.

At the same moment the captain, who, although the splinters were flying around him in all directions, stood cool and unmoved, applied the match to the gun.

The piece thundered, and, as had been expected, exploded, but fortunately for him who had fired the shot, in only three pieces, which flew whistling over his head, and fell into the sea.

Nevertheless, the shot was not without its effect.

It struck the corsair's foremast, and sent it crushing by the board.

"Good!" exclaimed the captain, grasping the old tar by the hand. "This is your work."

"And mighty glad I am, sir," answered the veteran, "that the gun didn't do you any mischief when it cracked."

The mate came up and looked closely at the young man as if to make sure he was not hurt.

"Not a scratch," said he. "Heaven be praised!"

"Nor I." said the second officer, who was near.

"What do you think now?" inquired Mrs. Drake. "Can they overtake us?"

"I am afraid they can," said the captain. "They are even now repairing damages, which would not hinder their overtaking us, as they carry more canvas than we do."

The man at the helm was ordered to do his best; but, although a good steersman, Jenny could perceive that in this respect he was far inferior to herself.

Accordingly she took the helm, when every sailor aboard was astonished.

By this time, however, the corsairs had rigged another mast and set more canvas, so that their vessel gained rapidly on the other craft.

The captain, meanwhile, was issuing orders to the men under his command.

Some canvas and spare spars having been brought up from the hold, a jury-mast was rigged forward and furnished with a foretopsail, which drew well, sending the vessel along with accelerated speed.

In fact the merchantman now almost "held her own," and strong hopes that she would be able to escape were entertained.

All aboard now watched the corsair intently as she came on, with all her canvas set, flinging the water away from her bows.

The merchantman, meanwhile, made good progress, and her crew felt hopeful.

Suddenly a heavy puff of wind came from the north-west, and away went the jury-mast.

"She gains too fast for us now!" cried the mate, "she is crawling upon us."

Even as he made this remark, the corsair's speed slackening, showed that the wind had died away in her vicinity.

"That is good for us," exclaimed the captain, "I'm afraid the lull will be of short duration."

"Yes, there is a puff of wind wrinkling the water in her vicinity, already," said the mate.

When half an hour had passed, the corsair was again within easy range, and fired several shots, which flew whistling about the spars and rigging of the merchantman, though fortunately, without doing any damage.

The captain headed up for the Gut, which was now but a mile ahead.

Could he once reach that, he felt that their escape was sure.

But he had doubts that he would be able to do so, as the shots from the pursuing craft were now falling thick and fast.

On came the pursuer, and now one of her shots, striking the maintopmast of the other craft, sent it flying into splinters.

The merchantman could not be well steered with a portion of the wreck hanging over her side, and it seemed as if she must soon fall into the power of her enemy who was now scarcely half a mile from her, her decks and rigging alive with the dusky crew, who split the air with their yells.

One tall fellow was seen at the topmast waving his fez cap wildly about his head.

"That is Hassam!" exclaimed the captain, "unless I am much mistaken. Heaven help us if we fall into the hands of that fellow."

On came the corsair, while the other craft made scarcely any headway.

"I am almost sorry we hove to now," said the mate.

"We must do the best we can," said the captain, firmly. "Few as we are, we can at least fight to the last."

The corsair soon was within speaking distance.

"Ha!" screamed the corsair, from the masthead, "we have you now."

"And we show no quarter," screamed a stout Moor, waving his sword above his head. "We cut into many pieces! Ha, ha!"

Mrs. Drake stood white and trembling by the rail.

"We are lost, lost!" she moaned, wringing her hands.

"Do not despair," cried Jenny; "I have thought of a stratagem which may succeed."

"And what is that?" inquired the captain.

"The rocky passage is but a quarter of a mile distant," answered the young woman, "and the current is rapidly carrying us towards it. If we can only put these fellows off a short time, we may yet succeed in getting the ship through."

"Ay, but how is that to be done?" queried the captain.

"Leave that to me," answered Jenny.

So saying, she mounted the poop, trumpet in hand, fully disclosing herself to the enemy.

Jenny understood the Moorish tongue, and hastily uttered a speech.

Then, to the astonishment of all, she paused for a reply.

"Speak, speak!" cried the corsair, eagerly, his bloodshot eyes turned wistfully upon the speaker. "What you want to say? You consent to be my wife?"

"There is no help for it," she answered. "Yes, if you will agree to spare the people aboard here, and not molest them further, I will consent to go aboard your craft."

"Me get you whether you come or not," cried the giant, exultingly. "You in my power."

"No, for I will put an end to my life before you come aboard, unless you promise to let this ship and her people go free."

Hassam shrugged his shoulders

"And if me consent, you will come aboard?"

"Yes."

"It is well, me give my word."

"Then have your craft up into the wind that I may come aboard in the boat."

"It is well," answered Hassam.

So saying he gave orders to his dusky crew, who soon backed the foreyard.

"Faith, what means that? Do you really intend

"WHERE IS THE TRAITRESS?" THEY SHOUTED IN A BREATH.

to go ?" inquired the captain, as the girl motioned to lower the boat.

"No," she replied; "but I intend to have the boat lowered that he may suspect nothing."

"And what do you really intend to do ?"

"You will see," she answered.

No sooner was the boat lowered than the young woman, suddenly seizing the helm, which she had relinquished to one of the men, directed the ship into a strong current, which drew her rapidly towards the passage of the Gut.

"There, keep her as she is," whispered she to the same man who had previously held the wheel.

Then she walked to the gangway and descended into the boat, having previously instructed the men to follow her.

They did so, and Jenny now bade them seize their oars and pull ahead.

This was done, the captain, however, taking care that the warp should not be cast off the pin.

"There, that will do!" exclaimed the young girl; "now we can go aboard again."

The boat was pulled alongside, and its occupants taken aboard amid the yells of the corsairs, who now understood the deception which had been practised on them.

To seize the helm, and guide the rapidly drifting ship straight for the passage now, was with Jenny the work of a moment.

The corsairs pursued as far as they dared, but would not trust themselves to the current which the young girl had so fearlessly entered.

On went the ship, while shot after shot from the corsairs came howling through the rigging.

Meanwhile Jerry, standing calm and fearless at the helm, guided the ship on her perilous way, and eventually, though with greater difficulty than before, succeeded in passing through the channel.

"We are safe now!" she cried, as the mate came admiringly to her side.

"I never saw anything like it," said he. "No person but yourself could guide the craft safely through such a place."

The men applauded her skill with cheers, directing many an admiring glance upon the fair pilot.

"The first thing to do now is to repair damages," said she, looking up at the stump of the mainmasts.

"Ay, that's true," said the captain; "and we will go about it at once."

He did so, and the ship soon was running along under jury masts, dead before the wind, fast leaving astern the corsairs, who, by backing and filling, was making vain endeavours to weather the dangerous line of rocks.

* * * * * * *

By the morning of the next day, the ship had made good progress to the south, and was standing along under all the canvas she could bear.

Dark clouds, however, had now gathered, and the wind was hauling ahead so that she soon was obliged to tack.

Thus the vessel now stood along nearer to the Barbary coast than was at all relished.

"I am afraid this wind is going to hold," said the captain to his mate.

"So am I," he answered; "but if we can continue to bear up well towards the west, I have hopes that we may yet succeed in keeping clear."

The wind, however, kept hauling more ahead, knocking the craft off at an alarming rate.

By noon the men were sent aloft to watch for suspicious sails.

Not long were they there when their voices were simultaneously heard.

"Sail O!"

"Where away?" queried the captain.

"Two sails—one to windward and the other to leeward," was the response.

"What do they look like?"

"Can't make out very well, sir, but think one of them is a corsair."

The captain mounted the rigging, and with his glass he narrowly inspected the two sails.

One of them, as he had feared, was a corsair, and the other looked like one, although being so far away to leeward, and half concealed by the mist in that quarter, he could not ascertain to a certainty.

"If they are both enemies," muttered the captain, "we cannot hope to escape."

He remained aloft watching the two vessels until at last a thick mist hid them from sight.

"Well?" inquired the mate, when at length the captain descended from aloft.

"We had better keep off," said the young man. "One vessel evidently is a corsair, and in search of us. The other I know nothing about. We had better make towards the one about which we know nothing."

"Yes; it may prove a friend," said his companion.

Accordingly they stood towards the stranger and were making good headway, when suddenly the wind showed signs of hauling round.

This knocked the vessel off several points, giving the corsair, with her good supply of canvas, an advantage.

On she came like a sea gull scooping up the waves and gaining fast.

The men looked despondent, and even the captain turned slightly pale.

"That vessel," said he, after surveying it a moment through the spy-glass, "belongs to one not less cruel than Hassam. Heaven help us if we fall into his power."

"We must hope for the best," said the mate; "we have escaped so far, and I do not think we will be so unfortunate as to be caught at last."

"Meanwhile," said Jenny, "the other vessel, having the wind in her favour, may come up in time to save us, provided she prove a friend."

All aboard kept their gaze upon the other craft, and as she drew nearer, they were convinced by her appearance that she was either an English or an American vessel.

But while they were watching her a thick fog, which had gradually been gathering, settled on the water and veiled her from sight.

They kept on as they had been doing, directing the vessel as close to the wind as possible, while look-outs were posted in various parts of the ship.

Meanwhile the wind hauling still more ahead, the merchantman, with her scant supply of canvas, made little progress.

Suddenly one of the look-outs ran to the captain, saying he heard the noises of ropes and yards in the mist.

"Where away?" he inquired.

"About two points off the weather-bow," was the response.

"It is the corsair," said he, as he sprung on the knightheads and peered through the mist.

"Can you see her?" queried Jenny.

"No, but I hear her," answered he.

In fact, the noise of blocks and yards was now plainly distinguished.

The captain went to the helm, and there, with his usual composure always shown in emergencies, he stood and directed the craft upon her course.

Steadily, with her canvas just lifted, the vessel glided on her way, making as much progress as was possible under the circumstances.

Meanwhile the noise made by the rushing of the corsair's bows through the water now could be heard, and the spectators looked anxiously, expecting every moment to get sight of her masts and yards.

At last these were visible, looming up through the fog.

Nearer drew the enemy every moment, her crew, with their tiger yellow faces, thronging about the rail and gazing towards the merchantman.

The sight seemed to inspire them with demoniacal exultation.

Their wild yells were splitting the air.

Then the report of a gun was heard, followed by the crashing of a heavy shot.

It struck the merchant ship under the counter.

The water, with ominous, gushing sound, was heard pouring into the hold.

She was sinking!

"Heaven help us!" cried the passengers, gathered on the poop.

"Ay, we are lost, sure enough!" exclaimed the mate; "no hope for us now. Had we not better take to the boat?" he added, addressing the captain.

Ere the latter could answer, another shot came howling along, striking the boat, and shivering it to splinters.

It passed so near Jenny that one of the locks of her fair hair was severed and blown into the sea.

"You had better leave that place," said the captain; "it is the most perilous part of the ship."

"No," answered the fair girl; "I will not desert my post until I am forced to do it."

Meanwhile the ship was fast settling.

Her bulwarks were already nearly on a level with the water, and she lay over almost on her beam-ends.

The corsairs hailed the situation of their prey with exultant yells.

"Oh, what can we do now?" exclaimed Mrs. Drake. "All is lost!"

"They shall not take us without a struggle!" cried the captain.

As he spoke he procured several cutlasses and some loaded muskets, which he had noticed hanging up in the cabin.

These he distributed among the crew.

"Little use they will do us,' said the first mate.

"On the contrary, they will enable us to die like men," said the captain, in a calm, stern voice.

He then pointed to some spare spars and ropes which were on deck.

"Rig a raft at once, my men," said he. "We will not go down while there is a plank left."

With his own hands he assisted to make the raft, giving his directions with perfect coolness, in spite of the peril of their situation.

The raft was soon prepared.

It was dropped on the side opposite to that which the corsairs were approaching.

"Now," said the captain, "we must get these on it for a barricade," pointing to some large bales of silk which had previously been brought up from the hold.

He was promptly obeyed, for all his companions seemed to feel the cheering magnetism emanating from this brave man.

When the preparations were completed, the captain first assisted Mrs. Drake and then Jenny Vere to the raft.

The captain's wife was pale and trembling, but, although serious and sad, had not lost her resolution.

Soon all were on the raft, the captain being the last to descend.

It was high time he did so, as the ship already gave signs of soon making her last plunge.

"Now then," said the young man, as he cut the rope holding the raft to the ship, "we are adrift, and may contrive to keep our assailants at bay for awhile at least. They shall not have the satisfaction of capturing us without a hard struggle."

"No," said the first mate; "we are cornered, and as no quarter will be shown us, we had better die struggling than give ourselves up without a blow."

The raft, loosened from the ship, was caught by a slight current, which carried it several fathoms from the vessel.

The latter now lay with her stern under water and her bows up, surging from side to side, while the rumbling of the water as it poured into her hold was distinctly heard.

"She will soon go down," said the captain.

All watched the ship, and at length beheld her make the final plunge.

First her bows, with a sudden jerk, went under, then she made a sidelong sheer to starboard; then down she went, diving out of sight for evermore.

This brought into full view the corsair craft on the other side.

As soon as they saw the people on the raft, the dusky horde set up a loud shout, while the captain aboard was heard issuing some hasty order.

"They are going to run us down," said Jenny.

"They cannot do it without tacking," said the captain, "by which time we may get out of their way and compel them to tack again."

In fact, the captain had made a mistake.

His vessel, as she came down, passed within speaking distance of the raft.

Then again the captain was heard giving an order.

Instantly half-a-dozen dusky fellows leaped, pistol in hand, on the rail of the passing craft.

The others, meanwhile, stood watching them, with exultation plainly depicted on their swarthy faces.

"Now, men," said the captain, quickly, "we must turn this bale of canvas, so that it will cover us."

He pointed, as he spoke, to the roll nearest the edge of the cliff.

This the men seized, and in a moment they had it between them and the levelled pistols of the corsairs.

The latter fired just as the others had succeeded in accomplishing this manœuvre, and their shots, as a consequence, were warded off by the bales of silk.

The next moment the corsairs were beyond pistol-shot.

"They are bringing one of their larger guns to bear upon us!" cried the captain.

"That may do some damage," said the mate; "but I am in hopes they will miss their aim."

A moment later a flash of fire leaped out from the pirate's stern, and the shot came humming on.

It passed over the top of one of the bales, just grazing it.

"Good!" cried the mate; "but now they are coming round, and may make a better shot next time."

In fact the corsair craft was now veered round, heading this time a little to leeward of the raft.

Another gun was fired, as she passed within half a mile of the raft; but as this was somewhat hidden by the fog, the aim had not been very true, and the second shot passed over the heads of the little party.

"They are tired of such work," said the mate, noticing that no other gun was brought to bear.

"Yes, and they are now going to lower and attack us by boat," said Jenny, who had been intently listening to every word spoken by the captain of the pirate ship.

"Ay, sure enough," cried the captain, as the corsair came up into the wind, with everything rattling. "They think to make short work of us, but they may find it harder than they expected."

A moment after the pirate had come up into the wind, a boat was seen lowered alongside.

Into it sprang a crew of several dozens of men, armed to the teeth, and commanded by a sturdy looking fellow stripped to the waist, his white duck trousers confined with a blue sash, in which were thrust several dirks and a pistol.

"Here they come!" screamed one of the ladies, as she cowered behind the bales. "Nothing can help us now."

Then, noticing the firm aspect of Jenny Vere, who in spite of her peril, wore a look of calm resolution, she endeavoured to nerve herself to the same degree of courage.

It was, however, in vain, although it was evident that even in that dreadful hour she thought of her companion before herself.

"Heaven grant us thy succour in our need," she muttered.

Then she clasped her hands, and, with face upturned and her lips half parted, she offered up a prayer.

Meanwhile the others, peering over the canvas bales, watched the boat as she came on.

"We have a floating fortress here," said the captain; "and now, men look will to your guns, and don't fire until I give the order."

"Ay, ay, sir," was the low but firm response.

"And when you do fire, be sure that you aim well," continued the mate; "let every one pick out his man."

"Ay, ay, sir."

The boat was dashing on, pulled by vigorous arms, towards the raft.

Soon it was within speaking distance, where the one who headed it made signs to his crew to stop pulling.

"It is useless to try to fight me and my men," he shouted, in broken English; "we got more guns, more men than you, and quick kill."

"That remains to be proved," returned the captain. "True you have the advantage of numbers, but some of them must fall before you take us."

"We quick see about it," retorted the corsair; "pull ahead!" he added to his men.

The rowers bent to their work, and the boat came on, cleaving the waters like a knife.

"Had we not better fire now?" whispered the first mate, when the boat was within twenty yards or so of the raft.

"No, not yet. We have no ammunition to waste," was the response. "Wait a few minutes longer, and you will hear the order."

"But see!" continued the mate; "they have stopped pulling, and are all standing up, ready to fire upon us."

"Let them fire!" answered the captain; "it will be so much the better, as they will only waste powder and shot."

Just as he spoke the corsair commander gave the order, and the crack of the pistols was heard.

Then whizzed the bullets, some of them lodging in the bales, and others passing over them.

"Had we not better fire?" inquired the mate, somewhat impatiently, while every man grasped his musket firmly.

The corsairs having reloaded again betook themselves to their oars, and the boat continued to advance.

"They will try to take us by assault," said the helmsman.

"Yes," answered the captain; "they will not attempt to fire until they board us."

On came the boat, but the captain said not a word more until the craft was within about two fathoms of his "floating fortress."

"Now, men!" he whispered; "take good aim, and let each one kill his man, when I give the order."

Instantly the barrels of the muskets were pointed across the bales of silk.

"Fire!" shouted the captain.

The muskets were simultaneously discharged, and every shot took effect, stretching six of the enemy dead and wounded in the boat.

"Pull! pull on!" screamed the corsair leader, stamping up and down, either with anger, or from the pain caused by a shot, which had taken off one of the fingers of his left hand.

The corsairs who had fallen incommoded the others, so that some time passed ere they were able to use their oars.

They pulled vigorously, the boat shooting straight for the raft.

"Load!" ordered the captain; "lively, men, lively, and there may be a chance of another shot."

The men, encouraged by their first success, had soon re-loaded.

"Now, then, ready!" added the captain.

Again the boat was scarcely a fathom distant—those deadly musket barrels were pointed towards the foe.

"Fire!" was the order.

And another half-dozen of the enemy fell.

Again were the oarsmen incommoded, but the boat, having already received sufficient impetus, dashed on, and a minute later struck the raft.

With yells, pistols and cutlasses drawn, the corsairs now sprang on the raft.

But there were the bales in their way, and to get at the assailants they must climb over them.

"Back!" ordered the corsair leader; we board 'em behind—on other side of raft!"

The boat was again manned and directed to the other side of the raft.

The captain had drawn his little force to that quarter, and now a desperate hand-to-hand conflict took place.

The pirates were two to one of their opponents, but the latter fought with such desperation as may only be shown by those in a similar situation.

As fast as a pirate put his foot on the raft, he was either run through with a cutlass or knocked senseless with a clubbed musket.

This state of affairs, however, could not of course last long.

The corsairs using their pistols, shot down all the men except the captain and the chief mate.

Upon the former several dark fellows pouncing, were about running him through with their cutlasses, when Jenny flung herself between them and the mate.

"Hold!" she screamed in the Spanish dialect, "Hassam does not want this man to be killed!"

The one who headed the boat had already slain the mate with his cutlass, and now he rushed toward the spot where Jenny was pleading for the young man's life.

"What's that?" he exclaimed.

She repeated what she had said.

"It is false!" he exclaimed. "I do not believe Hassam gave any such order."

"You will be sorry if you do not obey him," said the young girl. "We spoke his craft yesterday, when he agreed, on condition of my becoming his wife, to let this man go free."

The corsair stood irresolute.

To disobey an order from Hassam must, he knew, be attended with speedy and sure death.

Nevertheless, he doubted the truth of Jenny Vere's assertion, believing it was merely a ruse to save the man's life.

"Shall we kill?" inquired one of the corsair crew, neither of whom had yet lowered his cutlass.

"Wait!" said the other.

He reflected several minutes, scowling meanwhile, and moving about, restless with the pain of his severed finger.

Meanwhile the Moors, still with their blood-stained weapons raised, stood impatiently awaiting orders.

"Yes," continued Jenny Vere; "this man and woman were not to be harmed."

"How happens it, then, that you are not with him, if you consented to be his wife?" inquired the corsair leader, still speaking in his native tongue, so that the mate could not determine what was said, although he, of course, knew by the manner of Jenny that she was pleading for his life.

"Our vessels were separated by the gale," responded the young girl.

"Well," said the corsair chief, "this matter must be looked into. We must take you aboard our craft, and keep you there until we can speak Hassam's vessel."

The men returned their cutlasses to their sheaths, and the mate, with Jenny and Mrs. Drake, was made to enter the boat.

This soon was pulled alongside the corsair craft, the captain of which scowled on seeing the three white prisoners.

"What means this?" he inquired. "Why did you not kill all—cut them into a thousand pieces?"

The man explained, when the captain shrugged his shoulders, remarking that he did not believe the girl's story.

"However," he added, "take them below, and we will perhaps soon fall in with Hassam, when we can satisfy ourselves."

The three prisoners were conducted into the hold, a low, cramped place, smelling strong of bilge-water and deficient in air.

"What will they do with us?" inquired Mrs. Drake, when the hatches had been fastened over them.

The conversation between Jenny and the Moors having been carried on in the native tongue, she, like the captain, was ignorant of most all that had been said.

The young girl soon explained.

"Then," said Mrs. Drake, "our fate is uncertain. They may fall in with Hassan at any moment, when your deception will be discovered."

"Yes; but let us hope that they will not find us until some man-of-war comes to our aid."

CHAPTER CCXXXIV.

CAPTAIN TOM DRAKE GETS AN UGLY SCRATCH—THE DEATH INDIAN'S MYSTIC WARNING—THE OLD SCOUT'S DISCOVERY.

CAPTAIN TOM was not quite crafty enough for the red-skinned savage.

He had disappeared in the foliage, and baffled all Tom's skill and ingenuity to discover him.

However, our hero was determined not to give up the search until he had exhausted every means in his power of discovering the redskin who had stolen from him his intended bride.

Captain Tom's only weapon was the hatchet, and with this he had but a poor chance against his own long-ranged weapons which the Indian now possessed.

The thought of Minnie, however, troubled our hero the most.

He trembled for her safety, and shuddered as he thought of the horrible tortures to which she might be subjected.

Even by this time, for all he knew, she might be made the sport of the red-skinned fiends, whose horrible propensities had induced them to choose the dread appellation of the Death Indians.

Captain Tom had heard of them, but he had never witnessed their horrible rites.

He knew that they were a tribe of the most bloodthirsty wretches imaginable.

This was in itself sufficient to make him uncomfortable.

Armed with this knowledge, we need not wonder that Tom did all that human nature could do to find the hiding-place or the trail of the savage who had so easily baffled him.

In this manner he found himself a long way down the creek—in fact, in what might be called a river, for it gradually widened, and continued to do so the more, the farther he advanced.

Presently he suddenly came upon a party of flat boatmen, who, in the season, made a good harvest by gathering wild honey.

Tom soon made himself at home with these men, who, having finished loading their cargo, were about to take their leave, and they offered our hero any assistance they could render him in the way of boating.

There were twelve men in all, for the flat boat was a large one, carrying two masts, and decked over fore and aft.

These men were under the leadership of an old scout, who had been born, as it were, on the border with a rifle in his hand.

In fact, he had earned the reputation of being a dead shot.

He was a fine, jolly sort of fellow.

His height was considerably over six feet, and his frame was equally broad and muscular.

He reminded our hero of Iron Arm, only that his visage was more sinister, and his hair of a brighter red.

For assistants he had two men.

One the skipper and steerer, and the other his mate.

Old Dan was the name by which the former was addressed, and the other, a much younger man, was named Harry Hardy.

They would have been away before this only that there had been some dispute about leaving some skins behind, for the old scout had been indulging in his favourite habit of potting a few wild animals such as chanced to fall in his way.

They had just decided upon taking them on board and passing the night on a small island that until now had escaped our hero's notice.

Being weary and hungry our hero accepted their invitation to dine and sup with them.

"The more the merrier," said Harry, slapping his thigh. "There's plenty to grub us all, and there's a good soft bed large enough on the island yonder."

As he spoke a well-known sound startled them.

"Injins about," said the old scout, placing his forefinger beside his nose.

His quick eye instantly detected a party of redskins filing along on the edge of a high cliff; but they disappeared as suddenly, and before a rifle or musket could be brought to the shoulder.

A puff of smoke and a sharp crack, however, pointed out where they had disappeared.

Captain Tom Drake dropped to the earth.

"Snakes and thunder, he's hit!" cried the scout, swinging round.

Tom was bleeding a little from a wound on his head.

A bullet had grazed his ear, and caused a nasty abrasion on the side of his head.

All the men were on the alert instantly at this.

"Curse them!" cried Harry Hardy, half cocking the lock of his rifle; "I should just like to catch a glimpse of one of their hideous portraits."

"And I," cried several in a breath; "it would be a warm reception for them."

The scout was the only one who did not express his opinion.

He stood silent and thoughtful.

It was evident something was working in his mind.

What it was he left the others to judge.

Never for a moment did he take his eye off the spot where the white smoke puffed out.

Presently his mind became settled, and he lowered the hammer of his rifle, and slung the weapon over his shoulder.

He did not stop to make any inquiries, but at once lent his assistance in bringing the captain to.

By a free use of cold water upon the face and head this was soon effected, and as soon as Captain Tom had recovered sufficiently to sit up, his head was carefully bandaged.

The scout now asked:—

"Did you see the redskin that fired the shot, Harry?"

"No; he was concealed in a clump of bushes," returned Harry. "I saw the puff of smoke, and that was all. It is curious that Paul did not discover the red assassin."

"It's purty hard to see a snake in the grass, sumtimes, lad; but when I fust hearn the r'port of the gun, I'd a sworn it war the identical crack of Scalping Jack's rifle; and if it wern't for the welt on the captain's head, I'd go a land title in Jerusalem that it war the crack of Dan's gun."

"But where can Dan be?" asked Harry in a suspicious tone.

"Thunder and cats, captain!" exc'aimed the scout, "hope ye don't think Dan done it—bet he'll give a good account of himself when he turns up—aha! what did I tell ye?"

At this juncture Dan appeared on the river bank, waving a glossy scalp above his head, and shouting triumphantly.

"Ho, ho, ho!" roared the giant scout, as he tossed his hat into the air with joy; "you've got an eye fur bisness, and a finger fur skulps, Dan."

"Thank you for the compliment, old boy," Dan shouted back from the shore, "but it was a snug little foot-race I had for the varmint's topknot; did he do any damage to the crew?"

"Scratched the captain's head a leetle, that's all," returned the scout; "but do ye want to come aboard the boat?"

"As it's not far to the Banks, s'pect I'd better keep the shore," replied Dan.

"D'ye think thar's more reds about?" asked the scout.

"Not in this immediate vicinity; I think the lad that used to sport this 'ere scalp was a scout, and all alone; and he's still all alone, if the wolves havn't got to his carcass yit."

Dan turned into the forest and proceeded rapidly down the stream, keeping a little in advance of the boat.

Half-an-hour, and the Banks were reached.

They consisted of a dozen or more islands of white sand without the least sign of vegetation upon them; in fact, they were nothing more than sandbars, most of the year under water.

The island upon which our friends landed was the largest of the group, and covered around the upper edge with a lot of old logs and decaying vegetation that at some previous time had drifted there.

"Tarnal furies!" were the first words of the old scout as he leaped from the boat on to the island, and pointed down at the innumerable moccasin tracks in the sand; "thar's been a hull tribe of them rovers of Satan on this 'ere island, and if I mistake not, they've been here within the last hour."

Captain Tom and his new-made friends could not help smiling at the blunt, earnest assertion of the scout; still its import made a deep impression upon them.

He was seldom at fault in such matters.

By this time the shadows of evening were

gathering fast, and so dispositions were at once made for passing the night.

By the united strength of the party the flatboat was drawn partly upon the beach, and then, mounting its deck, the crew produced their supply of provisions, and partook of a hearty supper.

Supper over, pipes and "yarns," as was usual on such occasions, were indulged in for a while by all, except the scout, who, with his heavy rifle resting in the hollow of his left arm, kept a ceaseless watch upon all sides.

The scout would not allow a fire to be lighted, for fear that it would show a lurking enemy where to aim, as they were not beyond rifle range of either shore.

So, after their pipes and yarns had been exhausted, each of the party rolled himself in a blanket and lay down upon the dry sand to rest, with his rifle, primed for instant use, at his side.

Soon they were all asleep.

Besides the breathing of his friends, the scout could hear the mournful chirping of a cricket in the driftwood, and the harsh croaking of a solitary bull-frog far down the river.

He listened for other sounds, but heard nothing. To him so much silence boded evil.

When he could hear the hoot of the owl, the scream of the night-hawk, the cry of the whip-po-will—in fact, a general song of all animated nature —he knew that no lurking enemy was near.

The moments dragged wearily on—all the while the darkness seemed deepening.

Still the scout was in a manner accustomed to such nights of darkness, and he never for an instant ceased his vigilance until induced to do so by sight of a very strange phenomenon.

In the middle of the river, about two hundred yards above them, he saw a dull red light swinging to and fro like a pendulum.

But he was unable to tell by what power it was produced, and how it came there, or really what it was.

So intently did the scout fix his gaze, in fact his whole attention, upon the strange object, that he failed to see and hear a shadowy figure moving among the sleepers behind him, stopping by each one, and, taking up his rifle, remove the priming, then move on to the next.

We say he failed to hear this mysterious prowler, for he moved like a serpent, and the sand muffled every sound of his tampering with the guns.

The scout kept his eyes upon the bar of light.

Presently its oscillations began to grow shorter and shorter—finally it came to a rest.

The scout started, and his fingers tightened upon the barrel of his rifle.

The object had changed its form.

Instead of the dull bar of light he beheld five letters of fire gleaming through the darkness like the red eye of doom, throwing their long and skeleton-like rays far out into the gloom and fog

When his eyes had become accustomed to the dazzling glare of the light he started with a feeling of mysterious awe, for he saw that those five glowing letters formed the word—

"DEATH!"

"Death! death!" repeated the scout; "is't a warnin' of a comin' fate? Ah, yes, yes! I told 'em thar war death in the air. But by what power is sich a warnin' given? Surely thar's some human agency 'bout it."

"There must be."

Captain Tom stood before him.

But another—a shadow—form was there also, and, as the coldly-whispered werd DEATH came from the blue lips of the Phantom figure,

Captain Tom Drake fell to the earth.

[THE END]

www.ingramcontent.com/pod-product-compliance
Lightning Source LLC
Chambersburg PA
CBHW081136020726
47504CB00009B/1884